Dan Cassidy's
WORLDWIDE GRADUATE SCHOLARSHIP DIRECTORY

5th Edition

By
Dan Cassidy

CAREER
PRESS
Franklin Lakes, NJ

DAN CASSIDY'S WORLDWIDE GRADUATE SCHOLARSHIP DIRECTORY, 5TH EDITION
Cover design by Design Solutions
Printed in the U.S.A. by Book-mart Press

To order this title, please call toll-free 1-800-CAREER-1 (NJ and Canada: 201-848-0310) to order using VISA or MasterCard, or for further information on books from Career Press.

The Career Press, Inc., 3 Tice Road, PO Box 687, Franklin Lakes, NJ 07417
www.careerpress.com

Library of Congress Cataloging-in-Publication Data is available upon request.

I wish to thank all of those who have made this 5th edition of *DAN CASSIDY'S WORLDWIDE GRADUATE SCHOLARSHIP DIRECTORY* the best ever! My sincere thanks and gratitude go to:

The staff at NSRS, especially:

> Tammy M. Parnell and Richard E. Merwin,
> Research and Computer Engineering heads, and

> Jean E. Van Dyke and Joseph D. Gargiulo,
> Administration and Public Relations heads.

A very special thank you to Jim Eason at ABC's KGO & KSFO Radio, San Francisco—
the man who made NSRS possible!

Larry King, for taking NSRS national!

Darcy Mortenson, typesetter.

And Career Press, et al., especially Ron Fry, President.

Contents

Introduction v

How To Use This Book xxxiv

Quick Find Index 1

Field of Study Index 23

Scholarship and Awards Listings 45

Helpful Publications 539

Career Information 553

Alphabetical Index 561

Introduction

The information in *DAN CASSIDY'S WORLDWIDE GRADUATE SCHOLARSHIP DIRECTORY* was compiled from the database of the largest private sector financial aid research service in the world. Located in Santa Rosa, California, NATIONAL SCHOLARSHIP RESEARCH SERVICE (NSRS) began tracking private sector scholarships in the late 1970s using a specialized computer system. As awards increased and research uncovered new sources for today's students, the addition of the INTERNATIONAL SCHOLARSHIP RESEARCH SERVICE (ISRS) doubled the size of this independently developed database. Prospective college students and present undergraduates will find the information in this book valuable in directing their applications and broadening their prospects for scholarship selection.

THE FACTS

According to the Association of Fund Raising Counsel, more than 80 percent of the grant applications that went to more than 44,000 foundations in the United States were either misdirected or filled out improperly. Many scholarships, fellowships, grants, loans, and internships go unclaimed each year—not because students do not qualify, but because they don't know that the money is available. In 1997, NSRS surveyed the private sector scholarship sources and the results found that 3.5 percent, or almost $1 billion, of these private sector monies went undistributed. There is a great need to organize this "paper chase" of information into a workable source for today's student. Utilizing the data collected in this book, students will have a broad base of information to convert to their advantage. The monies are there. Apply for them!

PRIVATE SECTOR FUNDS

Philanthropy in the United States is alive and well. Charitable donations, which totaled $58.67 billion in 1982, grew to a whopping 329.91 billion in 1997. Of that amount, nearly 15 percent (or $49.49 billion) goes into the United States educational system. The private sector funds 53.65 percent of the available scholarships, fellowships, grants, and loans domestically. An additional $30-plus billion is dispersed by other countries worldwide.

And that amount increases daily. The interest alone on a properly invested $2 million is easily $100,000 annually. Private sector resources for higher education are as varied as the awards themselves.

Many scholarships are renewable. You simply sign for them year after year. Most allow you to "piggy-back" several individual scholarships. The average undergraduate scholarship is $5,000 per year, ranging from a low of $100 to a high of $25,000. Graduate level fellowships range from $10,000 to $60,000-plus. If you are an undergraduate student or planning to on to undergraduate school for an associate's or a bachelor's degree, be sure to get a copy of *Dan Cassidy's Worldwide College Scholarship Directory*, 5th Ed. Order from NSRS at (800) HEADSTART or from Career Press at (800) CAREER-1. Some graduate and postgraduate research projects can yield a quarter of a million dollars or more in funding. As inflation spirals, so does the cost of education and the need for financial assistance.

INVESTIGATE THE POSSIBILITIES

Don't think you can't apply because you earn too much money; 80 percent of the private sector does not require a financial statement or proof of need. Don't think that application deadlines occur only in the fall; private sector deadlines are passing daily because often they are set to coincide with the tax year or organizational meeting dates. Don't believe that grades are the only consideration for an award; many application questions deal with your personal, occupational, and educational background; organizational affiliation; talent; or ethnicity. Ninety percent are not concerned with grades. Don't be concerned with age; many organizations are interested in returning and mid-career students. In fact, age is not a restriction, especially since half of all students are now over the age of 25. This is a big jump from 3 years ago when only 1 in 4 was over 25. This is because many students are going back to school after starting families or changing careers as we shift from the industrial wave to the high-tech wave. The Business and Professional Women's Foundation awards hundreds of scholarships to applicants who must be older than 25 or even 35. There is a scholarship at the California state colleges for students over the age of 60 for lifelong learning.

PLAN TO COMPETE AND QUALIFY

The plan is simple—use this book and every other resource you can find. Inquire at your institution's financial aid office about government assistance and private endowments at the school. If you are a high school student—in any year—begin by writing to 10 or more schools. Select a range of institutions that interest you, both large and small, public and private. Request the application materials and school catalogs; many privately endowed scholarships and fellowships are listed in the school catalog under financial aid. A significant number of these go unclaimed because qualified students do not know they exist! The information is available, but the commitment and determination to find it must come from the individual student.

The private sector is easily accessed with this book by using the tables provided to cross-reference applicable scholarships. Choose as many as you qualify for, and request application forms and any pertinent materials. Some have specific requirements for applicants, such as a personal interview, the submission of an essay or related work, or a promise to work for the company on completion of study and/or the earning of a degree. Others may have paid internships or work advancement programs. Still others may simply require that you fill out an application form.

The money is there, and much of it goes unclaimed. Even the most common scholarship sources—Rotary, Lions, Elks, Zonta, and so forth—are complaining that students are not applying. Students who do not take the time to inquire lose every advantage. Earning your degree will widen many avenues for your future, and the rewards are incalculable. The resources to achieve your goals are available to you; you need only pursue them.

> "The resources of the scholar are proportioned to his
> confidence in the attributes of the intellect."
> —Emerson

Good luck! And remember: There's nothing to it but to do it!

Sincerely,
Daniel J. Cassidy, President and Founder, NSRS

JUST FOR FUN: A POTPOURRI OF SCHOLARSHIPS by NSRS

(Note: The following sources are identified in this book by their record numbers. For those few sources that are not listed in this book because they apply to one particular school, the numbers in parentheses identify the source reference in our database. To find out more about the sources not detailed in this book, call NSRS at (707) 546-6777.)

1. The **Countess of Munster Musical Trust** has scholarships in varying amounts for British and Commonwealth citizens studying music. Record 1254.

2. The **International Society of Arboriculture** invites horticulturists, plant pathologists, and entomologists to pluck a grant for the study of shade trees. Records 1460 & 1922.

3. Your tuition troubles could be gone with the wind if you are a lineal descendant of a worthy Confederate soldier. Contact the **United Daughters of the Confederacy** about their $400 to $1,500 scholarships. Record 3889.

4. If you or your parents are actively involved in Harness Racing, you might be eligible for one of the **Harness Tracks of America** scholarships, worth $2,500 to $3,000. Record 3584.

5. If you are a dependent child of a worker in the footwear industry, you could be eligible for a scholarship of up to $2,000. It's a patent idea from **Two/Ten International Footwear Foundation**. (T13/R294)

6. A **Hilgenfeld Foundation for Mortuary Education** scholarship is available to qualified individuals interested in the funeral service or funeral education fields. Record 3301.

7. *Jen unu mil pundo—nun ek*! (Here's a thousand pounds—now go!) If you understood that, you might be eligible for a **Norwich Jubilee Esperanto Foundation** scholarship of $500 to study Esperanto in the United Kingdom. Record 1216.

8. For a left-handed freshman enrolled at Juniata College and who needs the money, **Beckley Scholarship Foundation** offers $700. (T13/R265)

9. **Descendants of the Signers of the Declaration of Independence** offers scholarships worth $1,200 to $2,000 to students whose ancestors signed the Declaration of Independence. Record 3521.

10. The **Association of Former Agents of the U.S. Secret Service** offers scholarships of $500 to $1,500 to undergraduate law enforcement and police administration students. You do have to give your real name, but fingerprints won't be necessary. (T95/R33)

THE TOP 10 INTERNATIONAL SCHOLARSHIPS FOR INTERNATIONAL STUDENTS

1. The **Association of International Education** in Japan sponsors programs of six months to one year for international undergraduate and graduate students to pursue studies in Japan. Records 3392-3394.

2. Female graduate students from any country may contact the **British Federation of Women Graduates** if they wish to pursue study and/or research in Great Britain. Record 293.

3. Graduate students under age 31 can receive a stipend to spend one academic year in South Africa through the **South African Department of Arts, Culture, Science, and Technology**. Stipends are available to those who wish to gather information for a thesis or study project that they are working on at their home universities. Record 3823.

4. The **American Association of University Women Educational Foundation** offers non-U.S. citizens the opportunity to pursue full-time study or research in the United States. Applicants must be female graduate or postgraduate students. Record 25. (T13/R569)

5. Do you speak German? If so, and you are between 20 and 35, you could be eligible for the **Austrian Cultural Institute**'s awards to doctoral and advanced graduate students to pursue study and research in Austria. Record 3417.

6. If you have ever written a letter to a friend about your experience in a foreign country, then you are ready to enter the **World of Knowledge**'s scholarship contest, which is open to foreign graduate students who will be attending college in the United States. An essay, "Letter to a Friend," about adjusting to life in America, is required. Record 3983.

7. Danish citizens wishing to study in the U.K. should contact the **Anglo-Danish Society**. Awards of up to £175 each month are given for up to six months of study. Record 3846.

8. Students in various European countries can apply to the **Netherlands Organization for International Cooperation in Higher Education**. Grants are given for study in the Netherlands. Records 3738-3740.

9. The **International Council for Canadian Studies** offers many opportunities for Canadian citizens to pursue study or research at the graduate or postgraduate level in various countries. Applicants must have a working knowledge of the relevant language of instruction. Record 313. (T13/R783)

10. Students of Mongolian heritage who are citizens of Mongolia, the People's Republic of China, and the former Soviet Union can receive a scholarship from the **Mongolia Society** to pursue studies in the United States. Records 3705-3706.

THE TOP 10 INTERNATIONAL SCHOLARSHIPS FOR U.S. STUDENTS

1. College students may apply to the **Rotary Foundation of Rotary International** for the opportunity to study in a foreign country. Both the student's home country and the country of intended study must have Rotary Clubs. Record 3801. (T13/R134)

2. High school sophomores or juniors with a minimum 3.0 GPA can join **Youth For Understanding International Exchange** to Germany. Students live with a host family in Germany. There is no language requirement. (T13/R1200)

3. Undergraduate and graduate students of Italian ancestry can receive $2,000 from the **National Italian American Foundation** to pursue studies in Italy. Academic merit, community service, and financial need are considered. Record 13. (T13/R984)

4. **Zeta Phi Beta Sorority Educational Foundation** provides $500-$1,000 to U.S. undergraduate and graduate students planning to study abroad. Awards are also given to foreign students wishing to study in the United States. Record 273. (T13/R1037).

5. High school students wishing to attend secondary school in another country should contact **AFS Intercultural Programs**. Students from fifty different countries live with host families in this international exchange. (T13/R89)

6. Bundle up and head to Scandinavia with the **Centre for International Mobility**. CIMO and The Fulbright Center offer graduate scholarships to U.S. citizens under the age of 35 to study and carry out research in Finland. Record 3465.

7. U.S. citizens accepted to or enrolled full time at the **Institute for American Universities** in Cedex, France may receive $500 to aid with tuition. (T14/R245)

8. The **Cyprus Children's Fund** awards scholarships to U.S. citizens and residents of Greek or Greek Cypriot heritage who wish to pursue studies in Greece or Cyprus. Greek and Cyprus citizens may receive awards to study in the U.S. Record 3856.

9. The **Youth Foundation, Inc**. offers scholarships for a U.S. undergraduate's junior year abroad. Selection is based on character, need, scholastic achievement, objective, motivation, potential for leadership, and good citizenship. (T13/R1430)

10. The **Institute for the International Education of Students** gives scholarships for study in many countries. The organization supports students with a wide variety of interests and abilities and who represent a wide range of social and economic backgrounds. Record 3609.

THE TOP 10 CELEBRITY SCHOLARSHIPS

1. **Bill Cosby** and his wife, Camille, have been called the "First Family of Philanthropy" for their generous donations to various colleges, which exceed $28 million dollars. Contact Spellman College for further information.

2. The **Eddie Murphy/Paramount Pictures** $25,000 Writing Fellowship is a postgraduate film and television writing internship at Paramount Pictures presented to eligible graduates of Hampton University and Howard University who are tuned into television and screen writing. Check with these colleges.

3. **The Scripps Howard Foundation** offers the Charles M. Schulz Award of $2,500 to an outstanding college cartoonist working at a college newspaper or magazine. Record 2874. (T71/R17).

4. "Average yet creative," is the punch line for junior telecommunications majors at Ball State University. The **David Letterman Telecommunications Scholarship Program** could pay your way to graduation if you are an average student with a very creative mind. (T93/R19).

5. **Spike Lee** and **Columbia Pictures** offer production fellowships to students in their second or third year of graduate study at the New York University Tisch School of the Arts. Two $5,000 fellowships are awarded per year to graduates in production, filmmaking, and acting. Contact Tisch School of the Arts. (T71/R24)

6. Morehouse College received $1 million from Oprah Winfrey to establish the **Oprah Winfrey Endowed Scholarship Fund**. Contact Morehouse College. (T14/R122)

7. **Debbie Allen** and **Phylicia Rashad** created the Dr. Andrew Allen Creative Arts Scholarship of $15,000 on behalf of their father. A command performance is requested from undergraduate juniors and seniors at Howard University who display excellence in drama, song, and dance. (T74/R33)

8. Are you between the ages of 17 and 22 and living in the Golden State or the Lone Star State? If you are a Mexican-American resident of California or Texas and enrolled in an undergraduate program, can apply for the Vikki Carr Scholarship of up to $3,000. (T13/R502)

9.   **Lionel Richie** has made a $500,000 donation for an endowment in the business school at Tuskegee University. Contact Tuskegee University.

10.   **Miniere's Network** offers Minnie Pearl Scholarships to financially needy high school seniors who have a significant bilateral hearing loss and good grades, and who have been accepted for enrollment by an accredited university, college, or technical school. (T13/R293)

THE TOP 10 CORPORATE SCHOLARSHIPS

1.   Employees of the **Sara Lee Corporation** (and their children) can apply for a student loan of up to $2,500 for study at an accredited institution. (T13/R708)

2.   Calling all high school seniors! **GTE** offers scholarships to dependents of full-time employees who are planning to begin full-time study at an accredited undergraduate college or university. (T13/R140)

3.   **McDonald's Golden Arches** scholarships are available to New York Tri-State-area residents planning to attend their first year of college full-time. Applicants must be U.S. citizens or permanent residents and show evidence of either community service or employment. (T13/R58)

4.   High school seniors can get financial assistance from the **American National Can Company** scholarship program. These scholarships are available for undergraduate study to dependents of company employees. (T13/R405)

5.   **Capital Cities/ABC, Inc.** Merit Scholarship Programs offers awards to dependent children of Capital Cities/ABC employees. (T13/R451)

6.   The **Midas International Corporation** offers scholarships to dependents of current Midas employees. (T13/R477)

7.   If you are a high school senior and a dependent of a **Citibank** employee, you can receive a scholarship of up to $5,000 for undergraduate study. (T13/R489)

8.   **Philip Morris** offers a scholarship program "to-bacc-you" in your scholarship quest. Open to children of full-time employees. (T13/579)

9.   The **Union Pacific Railroad** offers an employee dependent scholarship program to high school seniors in the top quarter of their class. (T13/R684)

10.   Dependents of **Levi Strauss & Company** employees can apply for scholarships of up to $1,000 for full-time undergraduate study. (T13/R561)

THE TOP 10 SCHOLARSHIPS FOR WOMEN

1.   The **California Junior Miss Program**'s scholarship competition is open to girls in their junior year of high school who are U.S. citizens and California residents. The winner receives $15,000 for books, fees, and tuition at any college in the world. (T13/R763)

2. The **Women's Western Golf Foundation** has $2,000/year awaiting female high school seniors who are U.S. citizens and who have high academic standing, financial need, and an involvement with golf. Skill is *not* a criterion! (T13/347)

3. The **National Federation of the Blind** offers the $3,000 Hermione Grant Calhoun Scholarship to legally blind women who are undergraduate or graduate students studying in any field. Record 240. Record 238. (T13/R786)

4. For female returning students, the **Jeanette Rankin Foundation** awards $1,000 to a woman aged 35 or older who is a U.S. citizen enrolled in vo-tech training or an undergraduate program. (T13/R18)

5. Are you a female undergraduate in the natural or social sciences? If so, you can apply to the **Association For Women In Science Educational Foundation**'s Dr. Vicki L. Schechtman Scholarship. The award, for U.S. citizens with a minimum 3.0 GPA, may be used for tuition, books, housing, research, and/or equipment. Record 41. (T14/R54)

6. The **Landscape Architecture Foundation** offers $1,000 Harriett Barnhart Wimmer Scholarships to women who have demonstrated excellent design ability in landscape architecture, have sensitivity to the environment, and who are entering their final year of undergraduate study. Record 444. (T63/2)

7. For modern-day Rosie the Riveters, the **Society of Women Engineers'** General Electric Foundation Scholarship offers $1,000 to women who are U.S. citizens studying engineering or computer science. Applicants must be high school seniors entering an accredited school as freshmen. Record 348. (T61/R7)

8. The **Astrae National Lesbian Action Foundation**'s Margot Karle Scholarship gives $500 to female students whose career path or extracurricular activities demonstrate political or social commitment to fighting for the civil rights of gays and lesbians. (T13/R1012)

9. **Mervyn's California/Women's Sports Foundation Scholarship Fund** has $1,000 for college-bound high school senior girls involved in athletics. The program is *not* limited to California residents. Record 3981.

10. The **International Society of Women Airline Pilots** offers $500 to $1,500 ISA International Career Scholarships to women throughout the world who are pursuing careers as airline pilots and have at least 750 hours of flight experience. Records 389-393.

THE TOP 10 SCHOLARSHIPS FOR MEN

1. Have you earned your merit badge? The **Fred A. Bryan Collegiate Students Fund** offers trust-fund scholarships to male graduates of South Bend High School in Indiana, with preference given to those who have been Boy Scouts. Recipients receive between $1,400 and $1,600 for undergraduate study at an accredited college or university. (T13/R47)

2. The **Phi Kappa Theta National Foundation** scholarship program offers undergraduate scholarships to members of the Phi Kappa Theta fraternity. Five scholarships are awarded based on financial need. (T13/R472)

3. Australian male opera singers may apply for the Sir Robert Askin Operatic Travelling Scholarship offered by **Arts Management P/L**. Australian citizenship is required, and applicants must be between the ages of 18 and 30. Record 1237.

4. The **NAACP National Office** offers the Willems Scholarship for male members of the NAACP studying engineering, chemistry, physics, or mathematics. Undergraduates receive $2,000; the graduate award is $3,000. Records 318, 2017, and 2106.

5.   American males of Anglo-Saxon or German descent should contact the **Maud Glover Folsom Foundation, Inc.**, which offers $2,500 to those under age 35 for use in prep school, high school, college, and advanced education. (T13/R1150)

6.   The **Boys & Girls Clubs of San Diego** offer scholarships to male high school students planning a career in medicine, law, engineering, or political science from the Spence Reese Scholarship Fund. Preference is given to students who live within a 250 mile radius of San Diego. Boys Club affiliation is not required. (T14/R286)

7.   The **Elmer O. & Ida Preston Educational Trust** offers a half-grant and half-loan award to male residents of Iowa who are pursuing a collegiate or professional study at an Iowa college or university. Applicants must be planning for a career in Christian ministry and must provide a recommendation from a minister commenting on the student's potential. Record 3536.

8.   The **Young American Bowling Alliance** offers the Chuck Hall Star of Tomorrow Scholarship of $4,000 to male students up to age 21 who are amateur bowlers and members of ABC or YABA. Applicants must be high school seniors or undergraduates attending college. (T13/R872)

9.   The **Raymond J. Harris Education Trust** offers scholarships of various amounts to Christian males for use at nine Philadelphia area colleges. Students must be studying medicine, law, engineering, dentistry, or agriculture. Record 343.

10. The **American Dental Hygienists Association** has several scholarships designated for under-represented groups in that field, specifically minorities and men. Records 2559-2564.

THE TOP 10 SCHOLARSHIPS FOR MINORITIES

1.   The **Council on International Educational Exchange** offers Bailey Minority Scholarships of $500 for minority students who are studying in any field. The scholarships are for study, work, volunteer, and home-stay programs almost anywhere in the world. (T13/R1096)

2.   Ethnic minority students enrolled at accredited colleges or universities who demonstrate financial need and academic excellence may qualify for $2,500 Lena Chang Scholarship awards from the **Nuclear Age Peace Foundation**. Two letters of recommendation and an essay on ways to achieve peace in the Nuclear Age and how one hopes to contribute to that end are required. Record 3760.

3.   Minority undergraduates with a 3.0 minimum GPA desiring to spend a semester or summer studying in a participating foreign university and who demonstrate leadership potential and extracurricular involvement in multicultural or international issues may qualify for International Scholarships for Minorities from the **American Institute for Foreign Study**. There is one scholarship that consists of full program fees and transportation, and there are five semester scholarships of $1,000. (T13/R1269).

4.   The **Jackie Robinson Foundation** offers scholarships of $5,000 per year for four years to minority college-bound high school seniors. The program includes counseling and assistance in obtaining summer jobs and permanent employment after graduation. (T13/R1354)

5.   Ethnic minorities with disabilities who are gifted and talented may meet the criteria for Stanley E. Jackson Scholarship Awards of $500 from the **Foundation for Exceptional Children**. (T13/R70)

6.   The **Aviation Scholarship Foundation** offers opportunities for minority or low-income students in the Chicago area to take a one year-long program of weekend flight training. (T14/R713)

7. Women of color who are interested in sports, physical education, and other sports-related careers have the opportunity to receive Jackie Joyner-Kersee/Ray Ban Minority Scholarships of $4,000-$5,000 from the **Women's Sports Foundation**. Record 166.

8. Faculty may nominate African American, Native American, Hispanic, and Asian American high school seniors planning to enter college for the **Gates Millenium Scholars Program**. Awards are based on academic performance in math and science, school activities, leadership potential, and need. Applicants must be U.S. citizens. Record 174.

9. Disadvantaged and/or minority students entering a program leading to a B.A. or an M.A. in architecture may have the ability to receive scholarships from the Minority/Disadvantaged Scholarship Program, which is from the **American Institute of Architects/American Architectural Foundation**. Record 417.

10. The **American Association of Law Libraries** offers a George A. Straight Minority Stipend Grant of $3,500 to a minority group member who is a college graduate with library experience and who is working toward an advanced degree to further his or her law library career. Record 1078.

THE TOP 10 RELIGIOUS SCHOLARSHIPS

1. The **David and Dovetta Wilson Scholarship Fund** offers scholarships of $1,000 to college-bound high school seniors who are U.S. citizens and who are selected for their academic achievement and involvement in the community, and involvement in religious activities. (T13/R834)

2. The **Memorial Foundation for Jewish Culture** offers an International Scholarship Program for Community Service, which is open to any individual, regardless of country of origin, for undergraduate study that leads to careers in the Rabbinate, Jewish education, social work, or religious functionaries outside the United States, Israel, and Canada. Recipients must commit to serve in a community of need for three years. Records 917-920.

3. Scholarships are being offered to high school graduates who are from the southeastern United States and who wish to study ministry, missionary work, or social work by **The Heath Education Fund**. Records 1389 and 3277.

4. The **American Foundation for the Blind** offers a Gladys C. Anderson Memorial Scholarship of $1,000 to a woman who is legally blind and studying religious or classical music at the college level. A sample performance tape of voice or instrumental selection is required. Record 184. (T74/R75)

5. Various scholarships for students in the field of pastoral (religious) music are available from the **National Association of Pastoral Musicians**. Applicants must be members of this organization in order to receive a scholarship. (T74/R30)

6. **Women of the Evangelical Lutheran Church in America** offer Belmer-Flora Prince Scholarships for women who are ELCA members planning on studying for ELCA service abroad that does not lead to a church-certified profession. Women must be U.S. citizens, over the age of 21, and have experienced an interruption in schooling for at least two years since high school. Record 1396.

7. The $2,500 Leonard M. Perryman Communications Scholarship for Ethnic Minority Students is offered by the **United Methodist Church** to an ethnic minority undergraduate junior or senior who is enrolled in an accredited school of communications or journalism. The student must have a Christian faith and be pursuing a career in religious communications. Record 3891. (T93/R2)

8. Ministerial students who are enrolled in a master's program in theology that may be leading to ordination in a main-line Christian denomination could possibly qualify for **Harding Foundation** grants of $2,400/year. Record 1366.

9. The **Presbyterian Church (U.S.A.)** offers its members scholarships if they are high school seniors planning to pursue full-time studies at participating colleges. Applicants must be U.S. citizens/permanent residents and demonstrate financial need. Record 3784. (T13/R280)

10. The **Earnest and Eurice Miller Bass Scholarship Fund** offers scholarships to undergraduate student members of the United Methodist Church and who are planning careers in the ministry or other religious careers. Record 3891. (T75/R47)

THE TOP 10 KINDERGARTEN-GRADE 12 SCHOLARSHIPS

1. Students in grades 7-12 have the opportunity to win up to $5,000 from the **Alliance for Young Artists and Writers, Inc**. Applicants must demonstrate a talent in art, photography, writing, or interdisciplines. Cash grants are awarded and can be used for any field of study. (T14/R254)

2. Have you ever had the desire to fly? The **Stephen M. Price Foundation** is giving economically disadvantaged boys and girls between the ages 14 and 16 who reside in the Jacksonville, Florida area the opportunity to earn a private pilot's license. (T13/R1252)

3. The **Veterans of Foreign Wars of the United States** have an annual Voice of Democracy Audio-Essay Scholarship contest. The contest is open to students in grades 10, 11, and 12 who attend public, private, and parochial high schools. Awards range from $1,000 to $20,000. (T13/R179)

4. It has become easier for needy students in Washington to attend private schools. The **Washington Scholarship Fund** is offering up to $1,700 per year to students in kindergarten through grade 12. (T13/R1346)

5. **AFS Intercultural Programs** has created the International Exchange Student Program to give high school students the opportunity to study abroad for a semester or a year with financial assistance. Students live with host families and attend local secondary schools. (T13/R89)

6. Students between the ages of six and 21 and who have moderate to profound hearing loss are being given the opportunity to win scholarships by the **Alexander Graham Bell Association for the Deaf**. In order to qualify, students must use speech and residual hearing and/or speechreading as a primary form of communication. Records 3333-3334 and 4285.

7. The **John Edgar Thomson Foundation** is offering financial assistance to the daughters of deceased railroad workers between infancy and age 22, depending on whether or not a higher education is sought. (T13/R1263)

8. Financially needy Hawaiian residents who are orphans, half-orphans, social orphans (neglected or abused), or children born out-of-wedlock are being offered scholarships for preschool, summer programs, private schools, and college by the **Teresa F. Hughes Trust**. Record 3839.

9. Scholarships and awards can be earned by students who participate in a sewing, knitting, or crocheting competition. The **National Make it Yourself With Wool Competition** involves creating a wool garment from a current pattern. The fabric must contain at least 60% wool. (T13/R1189)

10. The **U.S. Space Camp Foundation** created an essay competition to award partial to full tuition to Space Camp. The competition is open to students in grades 4 through 12. (T13/R1241)

THE TOP 10 TRAVEL SCHOLARSHIPS

1. Have you completed two years of university coursework or the equivalent in professional experience? If so, the **Rotary Foundation of Rotary International** is offering to pay up to $23,000/year for you to travel and study internationally. Record 3801. (T13/R134)

2. If you are a female athlete and you enjoy to travel, then here is the perfect opportunity for you. The **Women's Sports Foundation** is giving up to $1,500 to individual athletes and up to $3,000 to teams. These grants are available for training, coaching, equipment, and travel. Record 3981.

3. The **International Astronomical Union** is offering to pay for the travel expenses of graduate students, postdoctoral fellows, or faculty-staff members at any recognized educational research institution or observatory to visit institutions abroad for at least three months. Record 1549.

4. **Woods Hole Oceanographic Institute** is awarding a $3,900 stipend and a possible travel allowance to students who have completed their junior year of college or are beginning graduate school. They must be studying in any field of science with an interest in oceanography. The students will travel to Woods Hole, MA, and study there for twelve weeks during the summer. Record 167.

5. The **Archaeological Institute of America** is offering $3,000 to a college graduate who is interested in working on a scholarly project relating to Aegean Bronze Age archaeology. Preference will be given to the projects that require travel to the Mediterranean. Record 423.

6. Are you interested in studying leprosy or tuberculosis? The **Heiser Program for Research in Leprosy and/or Tuberculosis** is offering up to $28,000 plus a travel allowance in postdoctoral fellowships and research grants. Record 2472.

7. If you can speak and read French, German, or Dutch, then you could qualify for a graduate fellowship in Belgium. The **Belgian American Educational Foundation** is offering 10 awards per year to applicants who have a master's degree or who are working toward a Ph.D. The award includes round-trip travel to Belgium, living expenses, tuition, and fees. Record 3427.

8. If you are a minority student with a 2.0 GPA or higher, you might qualify to spend the summer abroad. **Youth for Understanding International Exchange** chooses 40 students every year to spend a summer in select countries where they will live with host families. (T13/R721).

9. Have you ever wondered what it would be like to live in a castle? The **Giacomo Leopardi Center** is offering to pay the tuition and travel expenses for the first 300 students who apply. The school is located in Italy and it teaches the Italian language and culture. Records 889 and 1209.

10. High school sophomores, juniors, and seniors are being given the opportunity to spend two or three weeks at sites in North or Central America by the **Earthwatch Student Challenge Awards**. This gives them the opportunity to have an intimate look at the world of science and state-of-the-art technology. (T13/R1212)

THE TOP 10 ARTS SCHOLARSHIPS

1. **The Christophers** offers a film and video contest for college students to create an image expressing an annual topic. Awards are based on the ability to capture theme, artistic/professional proficiency, and adherence to rules. Record 1065.

2.   The **Ladies Auxiliary to the Veterans of Fo=reign Wars of the United States** gives high school students an opportunity to express their patriotism through art. Annual awards are given for works on paper or canvas in a variety of styles. (T71/R4)

3.   U.S. citizens of Japanese ancestry may wish to join the **Japanese American Citizens League** to be eligible for their creative arts award. Undergraduate and graduate students should create projects that reflect the Japanese-American experience and culture. Record 103. (T71/R15)

4.   The **Princess Grace Foundation** offers scholarships for students under age 25 in acting, directing, and design at U.S. schools. Record 1168. (T74/R78)

5.   Aspiring Austrian artists and architects who wish to apply their trade in the U.S. should contact the **Austrian Cultural Institute**. Grants are available to spend time at the Mak Center in Los Angeles, which has a year-round schedule of exhibitions, symposia, lectures, performances, workshops, and publications. Records 997 and 1196.

6.   Want to see how Buzz and Woody came to life? **Pixar Animation Studios** offers summer internships for college and university students to obtain hands-on experience in animation. Record 1046.

7.   Playwrights and composers should submit an original full-length play or musical to the **Stanley Drama Award Competition.** The work must not have been professionally produced or received tradebook publication. Record 1174.

8.   The **Canada Council for the Arts** offers grants to young and established professional Canadian artists. The program is designed to give artists the free time necessary for personal creative activity and to help them improve their skills in performing arts, visual/media arts, or creative writing. (T14/R217)

9.   High school seniors and 17-18 year olds in the creative and performing arts should contact **The National Foundation for Advancement in the Arts** to enter their talent contest. Areas include dance, jazz, music, photography, theatre, visual arts, voice, and writing. (T14/R314)

10.   The **National Scholarship Trust Fund of the Graphic Arts** provides high school seniors, undergraduates, and graduate students with scholarships and fellowships in printing, publishing, and graphic technology. A minimum 3.0 GPA is required. (T71/R28)

THE TOP 10 ATHLETIC SCHOLARSHIPS

1.   The **Western Golf Association** offers scholarships to U.S. high school seniors who have served as caddies at WGA member clubs. Applicants must be in the top 25% of their class, have outstanding personal character, and demonstrate financial need. (T13/R80)

2.   The **Francis Ouimet Scholarship Fund** offers scholarships to Massachusetts residents who have worked as golf caddies, in pro shops, or as superintendents of operations at a Massachusetts golf course. (T13/R109)

3.   NCAA student-athletes can receive scholarships from the **National Collegiate Athletic Association** for graduate or undergraduate study, depending on GPA and financial need. Applicants must be nominated by a faculty athletics representative at their school. Records 3715-3716.

4.   Do you want to be the next Picaboo Street? The **Women's Sports Foundation** provides financial assistance to female athletes and women pursuing sports-related careers. Record 3981.

5. Kansas students who have participated in high school athletics may apply to the **American Legion of Kansas** for a scholarship to be used at any Kansas college, university, or trade school. (T13/R776)

6. The **National Horseshoe Pitchers Association** gives awards to students under age 18 who compete in a horseshoe pitching league. (T13/R884)

7. The **Community Foundation of Western Massachusetts** offers scholarships to graduating seniors of Gateway Regional High School in Huntington, MA, and Longmeadow High School in Longmeadow, MA. Applicants must have a strong interest in and have excelled in athletics. Record 3491. (T14/R77 and T13/R908)

8. Caddies at New Jersey golf clubs can receive undergraduate scholarships from the **New Jersey State Golf Association**. Awards are based on scholastic achievement, financial need, and length of service as a caddie. (T13/R498)

9. High school seniors who are involved in some type of athletics can apply to **Footaction USA** if they have a minimum 2.0 GPA and are U.S. citizens. (T13/R1018)

10. The **Aromando Family Educational Foundation** offers scholarships to aspiring teachers and theologians. Applicants must have at least two varsity letters in one or more high school-sanctioned athletic or extracurricular programs, be of Italian ancestry, be practicing Roman Catholics, and have a minimum 3.0 GPA. (T14/R409)

THE TOP 10 AVIATION SCHOLARSHIPS

1. Scholarships are being made available for students studying in the fields of aviation and aerospace by **Ninety-Nines, Inc. International**. Eligibility requirements vary. Records 403 and 3313.

2. Calling all Amelia Earharts! The **International Society of Women Airline Pilots** offers scholarships to women who are interested in pursuing careers in flying the world's airlines. Applicants must have a U.S. FAA Commercial Pilot Certificate with an Instrument Rating and a First Class medical certificate. They also must have 750 flight hours. Records 389-393.

3. Undergraduate juniors and seniors who have scholastic plans leading to future participation in the aerospace sciences and technologies have the ability to win the *Dr. Robert H. Goddard Space Science and Engineering Scholarship* from the **National Space Club**. Records 328-329.

4. Those who prefer the business end of aviation should contact the **Aviation Distributors and Manufacturers Association International**, which offers scholarships to students pursuing careers in aviation management or as professional pilots. (T14/R7)

5. The **Vertical Flight Foundation** gives scholarships of up to $2,000 to undergraduate and graduate students who have proven interests in pursuing careers in some aspect of helicopter or vertical flight. Record 411.

6. Minority graduate students who are studying science and engineering qualify for **National Aeronautics and Space Administration** scholarships if they are considering a career in space science and/or aerospace technology. Records 394-395.

7. Civil Air Patrol cadets pursuing studies in Ground and Air Training for FAA private pilot licenses qualify for a $2,100 Major Gen. Lucas V. Beau Flight Scholarship, which is being offered by the **Civil Air Patrol**. (T14/R66)

8. The **Aircraft Electronics Association Educational Foundation** offers scholarships to students studying avionics and/or aircraft repair and who are attending postsecondary institutions, including technical schools. Records 19, 371, and 3286.

9.   Students who have a GPA of at least a 3.0 and have completed half of their course of study may qualify for an Al and Art Mooney Scholarship of $1,000, which is offered by **Mooney Aircraft Pilots Association Safety Foundation**. Applicants must be members of MAPA and have a career objective that would promote flight safety. (T14/R301)

10. The **EAA Aviation Foundation** offers two Aviation Achievement Scholarships of $500 and up annually to individuals who are active in sport aviation. The scholarships are to be used in order to further the recipients aviation education training. (T14/R2)

THE TOP 10 LUCRATIVE SCHOLARSHIPS

1.   The **Science Service Intel Science Talent Search** is for high school seniors who submit a report of an independent research project in science, math, or engineering. Forty finalists are invited to Washington, D.C. to compete for the first-place prize of $100,000. (T14/R362)

2.   **AT&T Bell Laboratories** offers full tuition plus fees and a $13,200 yearly stipend to minority students enrolled in an accredited engineering, math, or computer science program at the doctoral level. Record 531.

3.   The **American Historical Association** offers fellowships in aerospace history to spaced-out Ph.D.'s and Ph.D. candidates. Ph.D.'s can get up to $25,000 and Ph.D. candidates up to $16,000 by spending six months to a year doing research in the NASA historical offices. Record 2900. (T94/R40)

4.   The **American Heart Association Division for Research** offers upwards of $45,000 to help promising physicians and scientists (with M.D. and Ph.D. degrees, respectively) develop independent research careers. Record 2150.

5.   Postgraduate students could get $12,500 for research in vacuum science from the **International Union for Vacuum Science**'s Welch Foundation Research Scholarship. Record 610.

6.   The **Semiconductor Research Corporation** offers fellowships to Ph.D. candidates in areas relevant to microelectronics. They provide $1,400 per month plus tuition. (T66/R6)

7.   **Chatham College** offers a Merit Scholarship Program of up to $10,000 per year to women entering the college for their first year. (T13/R37)

8.   The **Alcoholic Beverage Medical Research Foundation** offers grants to staff and faculty of public or private non-profit organizations in the U.S. or Canada. Up to $40,000 is to be used for research into the biomedical and psychosocial effects of alcoholic beverages. Record 2354.

9.   The **Harry Frank Guggenheim Foundation** offers up to $35,000 for postgraduate students in the behavioral sciences, social sciences, or humanities to help students find out why people act the way they do. Records 1918, 2751, and 3182.

10. **IBM** will provide $12,000 plus tuition for full-time graduate students pursuing their Ph.D. who engaged in research that is related to IBM. Records 544 and 604.

RECOMMENDATIONS BY DAN CASSIDY AND COLLEAGUES

After using this book to track down all your potential sources of funding, you may find that you still need additional help. Following are some excellent sources that NSRS recommends. (These are also listed in the "Helpful Publications" section.)

LAST MINUTE COLLEGE FINANCING, $20. Whether your child will start college in 15 years or next semester, this helpful guide answers such questions as "How do I get the money together in time?", "How do I locate quality low-cost colleges?", and "How do I find sources of financial aid that I may have overlooked?" Record 4030.

LAST MINUTE COLLEGE FINANCING (book), **SCHOLARSHIP RADIO SHOW** (audio cassette), **KIDS, COLLEGE, & CASH** (VHS tape), $35 for the kit. Resources to help students in their search for financial aid. Record 4030.

COLLEGE BOUND FAMILY LIBRARY, $142. A package of books, booklets, and audio and video tapes that should be in the library of every family with children. What colleges have the programs best suited for your child? What resources are available to you to help you pay for college? Contact NSRS for a complete list of this package. Record 4021.

GUIDE TO TRAVEL GRANTS, $20. An 80-page booklet containing hundreds of sources of funding for travel in various fields of study and professions. Record 4029.

FLY BUCKS, $20. A 30-page booklet containing more than 80 sources of funding for education in aeronautics, aviation, aviation electronics, aviation writing, space science, aviation maintenance technology, and vertical flight. Record 4055.

GUIDE TO PRIVATE SECTOR KINDERGARTEN-12TH GRADE SCHOLARSHIPS, $20. A 90-page booklet of scholarships for elementary and secondary private schools with introduction on how to apply. Record 4028.

For information about the above, write or call:
National Scholarship Research Service
Box 6694
Santa Rosa, CA 95406-0694
(707) 546-6777

■ ■ ■ ■ ■

THE MEMORY KEY, $12.99. Practical, easy-to-use handbook helps students with study skills and anyone dealing with information overload, shedding light on how memory works and what you need to do to achieve memory improvement. (T11/R196).

THE DEBT-FREE GRADUATE: HOW TO SURVIVE COLLEGE WITHOUT GOING BROKE, $13.99. Tells students how they can stay out of debt while taking simple and easy measures, while still having the time of their lives at college. (T11/R198).

HOW TO STUDY, $12.99. Includes how to create a work environment, excel in class, use the library, do research online, and more. (T11/R200).

THE GREAT BIG BOOK OF HOW TO STUDY, $15.95. More than 400 pages of useful information and advice, written in a direct, motivational style that will help students regain the confidence they need to succeed in school. (T11/R221).

ADVENTURE CAREERS, $11.99. Comprehensive source for information about completely different and decidedly non-routine career paths is packed with practical how-to's, lists of contacts, and first-hand experiences. (T11/R224).

THE CAREER ATLAS, $12.99. Details education and experience requirements for 400 career paths within 40 occupational areas. (T11/R226).

THE COLLEGE SURVIVAL INSTRUCTION BOOK, $6.99. Filled with tips, advice, suggestions, and secrets for making your college life more interesting and rewarding. (T11/R227).

101 GREAT ANSWERS TO THE TOUGHEST INTERVIEW QUESTIONS, $11.99. For part-time job seekers or those seeking permanent careers, this guide includes an overview of the interviewing process and a full range of possible interview topics. (T11/R56).

THE CREATIVE GUIDE TO RESEARCH, $16.99. Guide for students, professionals, and others pursuing research, describing how to find what you need, online or offline. (T11/R199).

"ACE" ANY TEST, $8.99. Walks test-takers through successful test preparation, including reading for maximum retention, researching the teacher's test-giving history, and "psyching up" for test day. (T11/R201).

For inforamtion about the above, write or call:
The Career Press, Inc.
3 Tice Rd., P.O. Box 687
Franklin Lakes, NJ 07417
(800) CAREER-1

■ ■ ■ ■ ■

ACADEMIC YEAR ABROAD, $44.95 plus $5 handling. The most complete guide to planning study abroad. Describes more than 1,900 post-secondary study programs outside the U.S. Concise descriptions provide the information you need on costs, academic programs and credits, dates for application, and more. Record 4000.

VACATION STUDY ABROAD, $39.95. Describes more than 1,800 summer or short-term study-abroad sponsored by United States colleges and universities and foreign institutions. Record 4128.

All orders must be prepaid. (IIE pays domestic postage.) If you have questions, write or call:
Institute of International Education (IIE)
Publications Service, IIE
809 United Nations Plaza
New York, NY 10017
(212) 984-5330

■ ■ ■ ■ ■

MAKING IT THROUGH COLLEGE, $1. Handy booklet describing how to make it through college. Includes information on coping with competition, getting organized, study techniques, solving work overloads, and much more. Record 4085.

For information, write to:
Professional Staff Congress
25 West 43rd Street, 5th Floor
New York, NY 10036

■ ■ ■ ■ ■

TEN STEPS IN WRITING THE RESEARCH PAPER, $9.95. Arranged to lead students through the writing of a research paper step-by-step, from finding a suitable subject to checking the final copy. Easy enough for the beginner, complete enough for the graduate student. 177 pages. Record 4119.

For information, write to:
Barron's Educational Series Inc.
250 Wireless Blvd.
Hauppauge, NY 11788

■ ■ ■ ■ ■

NEED A LIFT?, $3. Outstanding guide to education and employment opportunities. Contains complete information on the financial aid process (how, when, and where to start), scholarships, loans, and career information addresses. Record 4091.

For information, write to:
American Legion National Emblem Sales
P.O. Box 1055
Indianapolis, IN 46206

■ ■ ■ ■ ■

COLLEGE FINANCIAL AID EMERGENCY KIT, $6.95 (prepaid). Forty-page booklet filled with tips on how to meet the costs of tuition, room and board, and fees. Advice on what is available, who to ask, and how to ask! Record 4023.

For information, write to:
Sun Features Inc.
Box 368 (Kit)
Cardiff, CA 92007

■ ■ ■ ■ ■

COLLEGE FINANCIAL AID FOR DUMMIES, $19.99. Dr. Herm Davis and Joyce Lain Kennedy suggest "great ways to pay without going broke." For high school and college students and adults returning to school. Record 4024.

For information, see the Web site, call, or write:
IDG Books Worldwide, Inc.
919 E. Hillsdale Blvd., Ste. 400
Foster City, CA 94404
(800) 762-2974
www.dummies.com

■ ■ ■ ■ ■

THE CARE BOOK (College Aid Resources for Education), $29.95. This publication was developed by Dr. Herm Davis to be a hands-on daily reference for counselors as well as for families. It assists students in finding statistics on colleges and comparing college costs, enrollments, form requirements, and so on. Includes a CD-ROM money planner. Record 4121.

For more information, write or call:
National College Scholarship Foundation, Inc. (NCSF)
16728 Frontenac Terrace
Rockville, MD 20855
(301) 548-9423

■ ■ ■ ■ ■

FISKE GUIDE TO COLLEGES, $18. Describes the 265 top-rated four-year colleges in the U.S. and rates for academics, social life, and quality of life. Record 4053.

For information, write to:
Times Books
400 Hahn Road
Westminster, MD 21157

■ ■ ■ ■ ■

INDEX OF MAJORS AND GRADUATE DEGREES, $18.95. Add $4 postage and applicable tax. Describes more than 600 major programs of study at 3,200 undergraduate and graduate schools. Also lists schools with religious affiliations, special academic programs, and special admissions procedures. Record 4070.

For information, write to:
College Board Publications
Two College Way
Forrester Center, WV 25438

■ ■ ■ ■ ■

PETERSON'S GUIDE TO FOUR-YEAR COLLEGES, $24.95. Detailed profiles of more than 1,900 accredited four-year colleges in the U.S. and Canada. Also includes entrance difficulty directory, majors directory, and college cost directory. (T11/R87).

PETERSON'S GUIDE TO TWO-YEAR COLLEGES, $19.96. Includes information on 1,600 junior and community colleges in the U.S. and Canada. Lists programs offered, tuition costs, and available financial aid. (T11/R82).

For information about the above, see the Web site or write to:
Peterson's Inc.
P.O. Box 2123
Princeton, NJ 08543-2123
www.petersons.com

■ ■ ■ ■ ■

COLLEGE DEGREES BY MAIL AND MODEM, $12.95 plus $4.50 shipping and handling. John Bear, Ph.D. describes every approach known to earning a degree without ever taking a single traditional course! It lists 100 reputable colleges that offer bachelor's, master's, and law degrees, as well as doctorates, through home study. The book also lists colleges reputed to be diploma mills and cautions against them. Record 4022.

For information, write to:
Ten Speed Press
P.O. Box 7123
Berkeley, CA 94707

■ ■ ■ ■ ■

HOW TO WIN A SPORTS SCHOLARSHIP, $19.95 plus $3 shipping and handling. Easy-to-use workbook that teaches high school students and their families a step-by-step process for winning sports scholarships. You don't have to be a superstar! $100,000 scholarships are offered in 35 sports each year. More than $500 million is awarded annually. There is a special section for female athletes. 250 pages. (T11/R8).

For more information, write to:
Hastings Communications
P.O. Box 14927
Santa Rosa, CA 95402

■ ■ ■ ■ ■

OCCUPATIONAL OUTLOOK HANDBOOK, $16.95. Annual publication designed to assist individuals in selecting appropriate careers. Describes approximately 250 occupations and includes current and projected job prospects. Record 4093.

CFKR CAREER MATERIALS CATALOG, Free. Catalog of printed materials, software, and videotapes covering career planning, college financing, and college test preparation. For primary grades through graduate school. Record 4014.

For information about the above, see the Web site, call, or write:
CFKR Career Materials
11860 Kemper Rd., #7
Auburn, CA 95603
(800) 525-5626
www.cfkr.com

■ ■ ■ ■ ■

JOURNALIST'S ROAD TO SUCCESS, $3. Comprehensive source book for high school and college students who are interested in journalism careers. Helps choose colleges that offer the best combination of academic programs, practical experience, and scholarships. Record 4080.

NEWSPAPERS, DIVERSITY, AND YOU, Free. Information on grants, scholarships, and internships specifically for minority high school and college students, along with articles written by professional journalists of color. Record 4092.

For more information about these, see the Web site, call, or write:
Dow Jones Newspaper Fund
P.O. Box 300
Princeton, NJ 08543-0300
(800) DOW-FUND
www.dj.com/newsfund

■ ■ ■ ■ ■

HOW TO FIND OUT ABOUT FINANCIAL AID, $37.50. In addition to this guide, Gail Ann Schlachter has written several books on financial aid. Subjects include The Disabled & Their Families; Veterans, Military Personnel & Their Families; Women; and Minorities. Records 4068, 4047, 4048, 4033, and 4031.

For information, call or write:
Reference Service Press
5000 Windplay Dr., Ste. 4
El Dorado Hills, CA 95762
(916) 939-9620

■ ■ ■ ■ ■

SAMPLE TIME-SAVING FORM LETTER REQUESTING APPLICATION INFORMATION

Use this sample letter as a guide to create a general letter requesting information. Photocopy your letter and address the envelopes for mailing. Include the name of the scholarship you are applying for with the address on the envelope, so the scholarship/program staff will know which scholarship(s) you are requesting. Remember to apply well in advance of the deadlines. You should keep a calendar to keep track of them.

Date

Scholarship Program Office

Dear Scholarship Director:

Please send me application forms for any scholarships or fellowships that you might offer. I am enclosing a self-addressed,
stamped envelope for your convenience in replying.

Sincerely,

Mark Hoffman
5577 Skylane Blvd., Ste. 6A
Santa Rosa, California 95403
(707) 546-6777

THE PLAN

Once you have written to scholarship sources for complete information, you might consider starting three financial aid boxes to maintain your information. You might call them "Government Funding," "School Endowments," and "Private Sector."

The Government Funding Box

Put all information from state and federal programs in this box.
Remember:
Dept. of Education (800) 4FED-AID
　　　　　　　　　(800) 433-3243
The Coordinating Board for your state is in your phone book under "Government" or call your school.

The School Endowments Box

The college catalog's financial aid section will usually list the endowments and scholarships from alumni and local businesses.
Put the catalogs in this box.

The Private Sector Box

This box should contain materials you have gleaned from this book and/or from your NSRS personalized and expanded computer printout.
Call (707) 546-6777.

THE SEARCH

Believe it or not, just about everything about you will come into play in your search for scholarships. Your ancestry, religion, place of birth and residence, a parent's union or corporate affiliation, or your interest in a particular field can all be eligibility factors.

Using the tables in this book, the average student will find between 20 and 100 different private sector scholarship sources. Write to them and ask for their scholarship applications and requirements.

Write to each source as far in advance of their deadline as possible, and don't forget to send a self-addressed, stamped envelope—it not only expedites the reply, but it is polite and shows that you care about applying. Also, some organizations do require one.

Remember to list the name of the specific scholarship you are inquiring about on the outside of the envelope. That way the person opening the mail will know where to direct your inquiry. Replies to these letters should be sorted into the appropriate boxes.

THE GOVERNMENT BOX

Please, please fill out the Free Application for Federal Student Aid (FAFSA) from the federal government. You can get a FAFSA from any high school, junior college, college, or university, by phoning (800) 4FED-AID ((800) 433-3243), or by going online to www.fafsa.ed.gov. The nice thing about this phone number and Web site is that you can track your information—what schools it was sent to per your request and when. At the very least, these state and federal forms are the beginning of your scholarship profile at the financial aid office at a school. Most schools are now using these forms for their private endowment-based scholarship. So even if you do not receive government funding, you will be ready to apply for loans from various outside school sources, such as banks and school-based programs, such as school endowments, scholarships, fellowships, grants, loans, college work study, athletic, military ROTC, and so on. So the FAFSA is a must, no matter what!

On a quiet Saturday or whenever you have time, sit down and review the information. In the "Government" box, you will find that the state and federal forms are very similar, asking a multitude of questions regarding income, assets, and expenses. Don't automatically exclude yourself from state and federal funding thinking that you or your family make too much money. These programs vary tremendously from state to state and the federal programs have changed quite a bit. For example, there is no longer a $32,500 limit on the amount parents can earn in order to qualify for a student loan. But since that limit has been raised to $45,000, there will be less federal money to go around, so be sure to get in line quickly.

A bit of good news in the student loan arena is that the federal government will no longer consider the value of your house or farm to determine the amount of aid for which you qualify. I cannot stress enough the importance of filing the FAFSA; please do it no matter what!

THE SCHOOL ENDOWMENTS BOX

You will usually find a list of endowments from alumni listed in the financial aid section of the college catalog. Often endowments to schools are not advertised and may go unclaimed. For example, at a small school like the University of San Francisco, the total endowments average $20to $30 million per year. At Ivy League schools, endowments range from $100 to $200+ million each year. Of those endowments, 10-15 percent goes to the financial aid office in the form of scholarships, fellowships, grants, and loans.

You will discover that sources in the "School Endowments" box are really just other forms of private sector scholarships. The difference is that endowment money is given directly to the school and is administered exclusively by the school's financial aid office, so you must deal directly with the college. You'll find that the myths I talked about earlier also apply to these private endowments—again, don't exclude yourself because of those old clichés regarding your grades, financial status, deadlines, or age.

Source: American Association of University Women Educational Foundation.

Career Development Grants Dept. 60; 2201 N. Dodge St. Iowa City, IA 52243-4030	*Include scholarship name as well as organization name & address on envelope.*
Telephone: (319) 337-1716	*Call if you don't receive application by a month or so before deadline.*
Amount(s): $2,000 - $8,000	
Deadline(s): January 2nd	*Don't request info too late! Write at least a month before deadline for an application.*
Area(s): All fields of study	
Description: Open to women who currently hold a bachelor's degree and are preparing for career advancement, career change, or re-entry into the workforce. Special consideration given to women of color and women in non-traditional fields. Must be U.S. citizen or permanent resident.	*Different foundations have different definitions of "financial need," "academic achievement," etc. Don't rule yourself out until you have exact descriptions from the foundations themselves.*
Information: A total of 75 awards are available annually. Write to the Grant Coordinator at above address for an application.	*Don't forget to include contact name if given.*

THE PRIVATE SECTOR BOX

With your "Private Sector" box, you will find that once you have seen one or two forms, you have pretty much seen them all. Usually they are one or two pages asking where you are going to school, what you are going to major in, and why you think you deserve the scholarship. Some scholarship sources require that you join their organization. If the organization relates to your field of study, you should strongly consider joining because it will keep you informed (by way of newsletters, magazines, and so forth) about developments in that field.

Some scholarship organizations may want you to promise that you will work for them for a period of time. The Dow Jones Newspaper Fund offers up to $80,000 in scholarships annually for journalism and mass communications students. In addition, a two-week intensive course (equivalent to advanced editing courses in most journalism departments) is followed by summer employment at a newspaper, where interns receive a weekly salary. This could even yield a permanent job for the student.

THE ESSAY

Most organizations awarding scholarships require an essay as part of the application process. The essay is the most important part of the private sector scholarship search.

The following excerpt from the University of California at Los Angeles (UCLA) application material emphasizes the importance of the essay and contains good advice no matter where you are going to college:

The essay is an important part of your application for admission and for scholarships.

For these purposes, the University seeks information that will distinguish you from other applicants. You may wish, therefore, to write about your experiences, achievements, and goals. You might, for example, discuss an important life experience and what you learned from it. You might also describe unusual circumstances, challenges, or hardships you have faced. School activities and experiences are also topics to discuss in your essay, but they do not need to be the focus.

Rather than listing activities, describe your level of achievement in areas you have pursued—including employment or volunteer activities—and the personal qualities revealed by the time and effort you have devoted to them.

Also, discuss your interest in your intended field of study. If you have a disability, you may also include a description of its impact on your experiences, goals, and aspirations.

The University seeks information about any exceptional achievements, such as activities, honors, awards, employment, or volunteer work, that demonstrate your motivation, achievement, leadership, and commitment.

Make sure your essay is neatly typed, is well written, and does not contain grammatical errors or misspelled words.

THE APPLICATION

When filling out scholarship application forms, be complete, concise, and creative. People who read these applications want to know the real you, not just your name. Scholarship applications should clearly emphasize your ambitions, motivations, and what makes you different from everyone else. Be original!

Your application should be typed—neatness counts. (I had a complaint from one foundation about a student who had an excellent background and qualifications but used a crayon to fill out the application.)

Once your essay is finished, make a master file of it and other supporting items. Photocopy your essay and attach it to each application. If requested, also include: a resume or curriculum vitae, an extracurricular activities sheet (usually one page), transcripts, SAT or ACT scores, and/or letters of recommendation (usually one each from a teacher, employer, and friend) outlining your moral character. If you have any newspaper articles or other press clippings, you might include them as well.

APPLICATION CHECKLIST

The following supporting documents may be requested with your application. I suggest you make a master file for these documents and photocopy them. You can then just pull a copy from your file and attach it to each application upon request.

1. Your essay.
2. Your extracurricular activities sheet.
3. A curriculum vitae if in college, or a resume if you are in the job market.
4. Transcripts.
5. SAT or ACT scores.
6. Letters of recommendation.
7. Any newspaper articles or press clippings about yourself (if you have any).

Mail your applications early, at least a month before the deadline.

THE CALENDAR

I also find it helpful to keep a calendar with deadlines circled so you can stay organized. You can hang it above your three scholarship boxes so it is easily visible. Each application should have its own file within the boxes. On the outside of the file, you might rate your chances of getting the scholarship on a scale of 1 to 10.

If a scholarship application deadline has passed, save it for the next year. If you are turned down for a scholarship, don't worry. Some organizations want to see if you will apply a second time. The important point is to stay motivated and be persistent.

WHERE THE INFORMATION IN THIS BOOK CAME FROM

The information in this book was compiled from the database of the largest private sector college financial aid research service in the world: National Scholarship Research Service (NSRS), located in Santa Rosa, California.

Since the late 1970s, NSRS has been using computers to research and update information on potential sources of financial assistance for college students. Many thousands of students have used NSRS's services to locate sources offering financial aid.

NATIONAL SCHOLARSHIP RESEARCH SERVICE (NSRS)

NSRS computers store information about thousands of private sector aid programs worldwide for all levels of study: high school freshmen, high school students preparing to enter college, undergraduates, graduate students, doctoral students, and postdoctoral researchers. Note that there are even scholarships for junior high school students—usually contests from groups, such as Duracell, DuPont, General Learning Corporation, and many more.

NSRS is the only service since 1979 that serves high school freshmen through postdoctorates worldwide! It also is the only service with Dan Cassidy's Scholarship Alert, which automatically informs the scholarship sources for you of your eligibility. Scholarships will notify you directly of application deadlines and requirements and will mail you their application materials automatically.

Applicants for NSRS services first complete a biographical questionnaire, indicating their particular area(s) of interest. This information is entered into the computer, which searches NSRS files for the scholarships for which the applicant may qualify. Since each applicant has a different background and each of the thousands of aid programs have different requirements, this computer search can save valuable time and money and often provides students with potential sources of aid for which they might never have considered applying.

When you consider that all the financial aid programs listed in this book are constantly changing—with new application dates and qualifying requirements, for example, you may want to utilize these services.

Since NSRS is a division of *Cassidy Research Corporation*, a California Corporation since 1979, there is a modest fee for the services provided. For a product list, write or call:

National Scholarship Research Services
Box 6694
Santa Rosa, CA 95406-0694
24-Hour Phone: (707) 546-6777
24-Hour Fax: (707) 546-6785
E-mail: nsrs@msn.com
www.1800headstart.com

THE WORLD WIDE WEB

National Scholarship Research Service (NSRS) is traveling on the World Wide Web's super highway.

Throughout the world you can communicate with "Mr. Scholarship," Daniel J. Cassidy, president and founder of NSRS, by using the worldwide highway at the following NSRS addresses:

NSRS Web site

www.1800headstart.com

Cassidy Endowment for Education (CEE) Web site
(a non-profit public benefit corporation)

www.fastap.org

The Cassidy Endowment for Education (CEE), a public benefit non-profit organization, is pleased to announce this year that it will be providing scholarships for graduate studies.

Please call 707-546-6898 for an application, or visit the Web site at www.gradstudies.com.

If you need help in starting or managing a scholarship, or would just like to donate to the Cassidy Endowment for Education's scholarship program, please phone or write:

Cassidy Endowment for Education
5577 Skylane Blvd., Ste. 6A
Santa Rosa, CA 95403
Phone: (707) 546-6898
Fax: (707) 546-6897
E-mail: scholarshipmanager@hotmail.com

America Online e-mail address

nsrs@aol.com

MicroSoft Network e-mail address

nsrs@msn.com

IMPORTANT NOTE

This book is an abridged version of the NSRS worldwide database, serving high school freshmen through postdoctorates worldwide—and kindergarten through grade 12 at private schools. For a more comprehensive search for sources of educational financing, write to NSRS, now with Scholarship Alert auto-notification to the scholarship source, saving you time and money! You just wait for the scholarship applications to arrive in the mail at your doorstep.

Every effort has been made to supply you with the most accurate and up-to-date information possible, but—even as this book goes to print—awards are being added and application requirements are being changed by sponsoring organizations. Such circumstances are beyond our control.

Since the information we have supplied may not reflect the current status of any particular award program you are interested in, you should use this book only as a guide. Contact the source of the award for current application information.

If questions arise during your search for educational funding, you are welcome to call an NSRS counselor at (707) 546-6777.

SCHOLARSHIP SEARCH SCAMS

If they guarantee a scholarship or if the information is free, buyer beware! Think about it. The decision for scholarship selection is decided *only* by the scholarship organization itself, not by someone selling you the information. Most of these online organizations with free information on the Web are just selling your very personal information to mailing houses. It's like Grandma used to say: *"Nothing is free, and you get what you pay for!"*

A disturbing number of scholarship sponsoring organizations have reported in recent months that they are receiving a high volume of inquiries from students who are *not qualified* for the awards about which they are asking.

Because of the number of these types of reports, we are investigating the origins of the misguided inquiries. Most often we find that someone has taken *only* names and addresses from our scholarship books and is selling the information—a general listing of scholarships available in a particular field of study—to students without regard to the student's qualifications. Most of these operations make no effort to match the student's educational goals and personal background with the requirements of the scholarships.

The books that we publish contain 40 tables in the front of the book, along with the source description, providing accurate cross-matching of the student's characteristics to the requirements of scholarship sources. National Scholarship Research Service (NSRS) and the publishers of our books are doing all we can to stop any abuse of our copyright that might result in an inconvenience to our scholarship-sponsoring organizations. We've assisted the Federal Trade Commission in closing down some of these operations, and we are currently pursuing others.

Lastly, if any scholarship service is so-called free or guarantees a scholarship, savings bond, or even a fountain pen, beware! If it sounds too good to be true, then it probably is. Since it is solely at the discretion of the scholarship-sponsoring organizations to choose their scholarship recipients each year, these scholarship search scams cannot guarantee that users of their services will get a scholarship. Use this book to accurately cross-match scholarship sources for which you are eligible and avoid those scholarship search scams who merely copy information from our books.

Be sure to check out our Education Round Table to be safe in finding good, honest information from reliable sources at www.1800headstart.com or call us at (707) 546-6777.

How to Use This Book

Each award, book, and resource listed has a record number following it. All of our indexes are based on these record numbers. Here is a short guide to finding the information you need:

QUICK FIND INDEX

Most private-sector awards have certain eligibility qualifications. We have selected several of the most common requirements for this index. Here you can find awards targeted to people of a particular race, religion, or family ancestry, for people who will be studying in a particular state or community, for the physically handicapped, and much more. Simply go through each of the tables and write down the reference numbers that apply to you. Then proceed to those sources and read each one carefully to see if you qualify.

FIELD OF STUDY INDEX

Since the awards listed in this book are also based on your intended field of study, we have structured this index along the lines of a college catalog.

First, look under your particular field of study ("School of Business"). Then, look under your area of interest ("Accounting") and, finally, under your specific subject ("Banking"). In this section, you will find record numbers that reference both financial aid awards and other resources that can help you in your career. Again, since there might be several eligibility requirements you must meet in order to be able to qualify for any listed award, be sure you read each listing *carefully* and that you meet the requirements of the award before requesting an application.

SCHOLARSHIP AND AWARD LISTINGS

Each listing contains a very condensed description of the award, its eligibility requirements, deadline dates, and where to get more information or an application.

You will notice a large "General" section. These are awards that do not usually specify a particular field of study in their eligibility requirements. You need to use the indexes provided and read each listing carefully to see if you might qualify for one of these awards.

Use the information we have provided only as a guide. Write to the source for a complete description of qualifications.

HELPFUL PUBLICATIONS

This section contains a selection of books and pamphlets that we consider helpful to students. These publications are excellent sources of information on a wide variety of college and financial aid subjects.

If you discover a publication you find particularly helpful, let us know so we can share the information with others.

CAREER INFORMATION

This is a list of organizations that can help you decide where to study, give you information on job opportunities available in your field of study, and much more. We encourage you to write to these organizations for information.

ALPHABETICAL INDEX

This index lists the reference number of every award, book, and career organization included in this book.

LEGEND FOR QUICK FIND INDEX AND FIELD OF STUDY INDEX

D = Dependent

DIS = Disabled

DEC = Deceased

NOT D = Not Dependent

G = for Graduate Study only

For example:

Choose **Fireman** if you are a fireman.

Choose **Fireman-D-DIS** if you are a dependent of a disabled fireman.

Choose **Fireman-D-DEC** if you are a dependent of a deceased fireman.

Choose **Fireman-NOT D** if you are a dependent of a fireman but are not a fireman yourself.

Choose **Fireman-G** if you are a graduate student who is a fireman.

B = Booklet source in "Helpful Publications" section.

C = Career source in "Career Information" section.

Quick Find Index

ARMED FORCES

A Current Member, 4048
A Dependent-Current Member, 3378, 3489, 3553, 3794, 3827, 4048
A Dependent-Former Member, 3374, 3378, 3429, 3489, 3513, 3549, 3553, 3652, 3657, 3682, 3777, 3794, 3974, 4048
A Dependent-Retired Member, 3513, 3682, 3794
A Former Member, 3374, 3513, 3607, 3682, 3704, 3747, 3751, 3767, 3825, 3948, 3975, 4048
A Spouse-Current Member, 3378, 3736, 3794, 3827, 4048
A Spouse-Former Member, 3378, 3429, 3513, 3657. 3794, 4048
A Widow-Former Member, 3378, 3513, 3657, 3794, 3974, 4048
State National Guard, 3606
Stationed Overseas, 3736
US Air Force ROTC, 274, 1808, 2064
US Air Force-Reserve, 2188, 2669
US Army-1st Cavalry Div Assn, 3549
US Marines (any branch), 3736
US Marines-Corpsman (NOT D), 3682
US Marines-Marine Tanker, 3682
US Navy (any branch), 3736
US Navy-Corpsman (NOT D), 3682
US Navy-Reserve, 2169, 2648
Vet Deceased in Retir-D, 3553, 3657, 3794
Vet-Blind, 3429
Vet-Deceased, 3549, 3553, 3657, 3974
Vet-Deceased in Service-D, 3553, 3652, 3657, 3686, 3794, 3826
Vet-Desert Shield/Desert Storm, 3549, 3751, 3767, 3777, 3825
Vet-Disabled, 3489, 3549, 3553, 3657, 3777, 3825, 3948
Vet-Disabled in Service-D, 3553, 3657, 3686
Vet-Duty on Aircraft Carrier-D, 3836
Vet-KIA-D, 3378, 3489, 3553, 3652, 3777, 3794, 3985
Vet-MIA-D, 3378, 3489, 3553, 3652, 3657, 3794, 3827, 3985
Vet-POW-D, 3378, 3489, 3553, 3652, 3657, 3794, 3827, 3985
Vet-Vietnam, 3513, 3549, 3652, 3751, 3767, 3777, 3825
Vet-WWII or Korea, 3767, 3777, 3825

CITY/COUNTY INTENDED STUDY

Chicago IL/USA, 51, 200, 852, 997, 998, 1108, 1243, 2824
London UK, 1112, 1522, 1523, 2922, 2997, 2998, 2999, 3000, 3001
Los Angeles Metro CA/USA, 866, 972, 1115, 1188, 2849, 2850, 2851, 2852, 2925, 3006, 3370
New York City NY/USA, 125, 232, 450, 997, 1029, 1282, 2298, 2601, 2865, 3130, 3185, 3256, 3793
Orange CA/USA, 2849, 2850, 2851, 2852
Philadelphia Metro PA/USA, 1619, 1691, 1870
Rome IT, 826, 827, 978, 979, 1745, 1746
Ross OH/USA, 3778
San Diego Co./CA/USA, 2161, 2271, 2414, 2579, 2642
San Francisco CA/USA, 1318
Venice IT, 79, 440, 786, 890, 1011, 1133, 1265, 1364, 1777, 2749, 2941, 3032, 3109
Ventura CA/USA, 2849, 2850, 2851, 2852
Washington DC/USA, 124, 163, 179, 241, 1038, 1783, 2965, 3151

COMPANIES

Basin Electric Power Co.-D, 3424
Bedding Plants-D/S/P, 3425
Corporate employee-D, 3523
Deerfield Plastics-D, 3492
Dixie Yarns, 3523
Haggar-D, 3583
Mervyn's, 3693
Nat Arts Matrls Trd Assn-D/S/P, 3712
Nat Arts Matrls Trd Assn NAMTA, 3712
Tri-State Gen/Trans Assn-D, 3883
Wyoming Dept of Corrections, 3984
Wyoming Dept of Corrections-D, 3984

REGION OF INTENDED STUDY

Africa, 133, 275, 476, 514, 577, 629, 710, 765, 935, 936, 965, 1113, 1226, 1490, 1692, 1768, 1789, 1809, 1872, 1972, 2923, 3261, 3506, 3611
Antarctica, 3506
Asia, 77, 229, 991, 1238, 1327, 3506, 3636
Australia, 869, 1141, 1327, 3506
British Commonwealth, 1141, 1995, 3488, 3714, 3756, 4007
Caribbean, 965, 1226, 1649, 3506, 3611
Central America, 965, 1226, 1327, 1546, 3506, 3611
Europe, 10, 19, 76, 83, 98, 303, 316, 371, 542, 602, 666, 792, 795, 878, 902, 908, 965, 999, 1031, 1141, 1196, 1226, 1286, 1327, 1533, 1537, 1552, 1553, 1648, 1706, 1772, 1903, 2004, 2014, 2090, 2091, 2103, 2197, 2297, 2487, 2600, 2672, 2747, 2761, 2836, 2938, 3031, 3104, 3120, 3180, 3241, 3286, 3326, 3506, 3582, 3611, 3731, 3867, 4045
Far East, 965, 992, 1226, 1239, 3506, 3611
Greenland, 3506
Middle East, 77, 423, 815, 840, 945, 965, 988, 1093, 1226, 1759, 1760, 1761, 2789, 2909, 3506, 3611
North America, 66, 104, 230, 316, 353, 565, 620, 661, 662, 914, 983, 1141, 1327, 1424, 1553, 1856, 1884, 1885, 2014, 2103, 2186, 2197, 2297, 2431, 2459, 2487, 2600, 2672, 2706, 3249, 3291, 3851
Oceania/Pacific Rim, 965, 1226, 3506, 3611
South America, 965, 1226, 1327, 3506, 3611
South Asia, 965, 992, 1226, 1239, 3506, 3611
Southeast Asia, 965, 992, 1226, 1239, 3506, 3611

COUNTRY OF INTENDED STUDY

Albania, 829
Australia, 869, 1050, 1327, 1412, 1413, 1414, 1461, 1462, 1463, 1520, 1529, 1554, 1555, 1556, 1650, 1651, 1652, 1712, 1713, 1714, 1865, 1898, 2336, 2407, 2467, 2468, 2471, 2622, 2690, 2991, 2992, 3134, 3200, 3399, 3401, 3403, 3404, 3405, 3406, 3408, 3409, 3411, 3412, 3413, 3414, 3415, 3416, 3517, 3546, 3581, 3604, 3816, 3817, 3918, 3920, 3921, 3924, 3934, 3936, 3937, 3943, 4235
Austria, 850, 996, 1104, 1196, 1242, 1818, 1923, 2413, 3326, 3418, 3419, 3420
Belgium, 112, 299, 326, 332, 412, 798, 1032, 1290, 1405, 1418, 1823, 1836, 1841, 1845, 2201, 2301, 2766, 3049, 3128, 3427
Bulgaria, 829
Canada, 19, 20, 32, 141, 151, 216, 248, 250, 251, 252, 299, 322, 326, 332, 359, 371, 417, 467, 567, 584, 608, 640, 641, 653, 661, 662, 692, 817, 841, 861, 940, 947, 963, 968, 1043, 1058, 1081, 1083, 1085, 1086, 1087, 1295, 1390, 1405, 1415, 1418, 1437, 1440, 1441, 1475, 1481, 1508, 1509, 1526, 1546, 1551, 1568, 1595, 1628, 1629, 1673, 1683, 1718, 1800, 1823, 1841, 1845, 1884, 1929, 1933, 1950, 1951, 1962, 1981, 1982, 2024, 2052, 2135, 2149, 2154, 2191, 2196, 2220, 2247, 2268, 2283, 2294, 2333, 2353, 2421, 2422, 2435, 2461, 2463, 2464, 2485, 2486, 2500, 2502, 2529, 2531, 2598, 2619, 2620, 2621, 2633, 2644, 2645, 2646, 2670, 2712, 2791, 2827, 2861, 2862, 2875, 3014, 3026, 3027, 3198, 3199, 3264, 3286, 3316, 3325, 3395, 3425, 3454, 3457, 3506, 3510, 3548, 3611, 3713,

3714, 3771, 3845, 3895, 3896, 3897, 3898, 3901, 3914, 3917, 3922, 3940, 3944, 3958, 4036, 4058, 4087

China, 867, 921

Colombia, 3613, 3617, 3619

Costa Rica, 1428, 1487

Cyprus, 3856

Czech Republic, 829, 881, 1357

Denmark, 299, 326, 332, 999, 1405, 1418, 1823, 1841, 1845, 3372, 3511, 3759, 3846, 3847, 3872

Egypt, 192, 838, 1202, 1758, 3222

Finland, 999, 2532, 3324, 3372, 3465, 3616, 3617

France, 299, 313, 326, 332, 435, 805, 859, 874, 928, 1008, 1042, 1159, 1200, 1261, 1304, 1380, 1405, 1418, 1532, 1575, 1771, 1786, 1823, 1833, 1841, 1845, 2190, 2478, 2479, 2747, 2758, 2774, 2836, 2844, 2928, 2938, 2969, 3031, 3096, 3104, 3180, 3231, 3241, 3484, 3617

Gambia, 3487

Germany, 299, 326, 332, 805, 886, 928, 1042, 1089, 1132, 1159, 1207, 1208, 1304, 1363, 1380, 1405, 1418, 1575, 1786, 1823, 1841, 1845, 1923, 2774, 2940, 2950, 2969, 3001, 3108, 3337, 3562, 3617, 3618

Ghana, 3487

Greece, 299, 326, 332, 423, 836, 839, 840, 988, 1091, 1093, 1120, 1405, 1418, 1757, 1759, 1760, 1761, 1823, 1841, 1845, 2909, 3856

Guinea, 1649

Hungary, 829

Iceland, 299, 326, 332, 811, 922, 999, 1405, 1418, 1823, 1841, 1845, 3372

India, 768, 830, 1192, 2777, 3135, 3260, 3353, 3487, 3594, 3622

Iran, 10, 792, 908, 3120

Iraq, 423, 840, 988, 1093, 1759, 1760, 1761, 2909

Ireland, 303, 878, 938, 1533, 1537, 1706, 1903, 2004, 2090, 2091, 3426, 3789

Israel, 976, 1230, 2815, 3323, 3354, 3665, 3849

Italy, 52, 53, 73, 74, 79, 99, 100, 299, 326, 332, 414, 423, 440, 786, 796, 826, 827, 840, 853, 854, 882, 889, 890, 962, 977, 978, 979, 988, 1011, 1020, 1021, 1066, 1093, 1120, 1133, 1144, 1145, 1179, 1209, 1231, 1265, 1276, 1364, 1371, 1372, 1405, 1418, 1745, 1746, 1759, 1760, 1761, 1777, 1799, 1823, 1841, 1845, 1921, 2013, 2062, 2101, 2295, 2743, 2744, 2749, 2762, 2909, 2917, 2918, 2932, 2933, 2941, 2954, 2955, 3023, 3024, 3029, 3030, 3032, 3087, 3088, 3100, 3101, 3109, 3617,

3627, 3731

Jamaica, 3487

Japan, 229, 314, 797, 910, 911, 1211, 1212, 1327, 1410, 2192, 2482, 2763, 3138, 3336, 3392, 3393, 3394, 3396, 3538, 3617, 3635, 3636, 3690, 3881

Kenya, 133, 936, 1789, 3261

Liechtenstein, 1923

Luxemburg, 299, 326, 332, 1405, 1418, 1823, 1841, 1845, 1923

Malawi, 3487

Malaysia, 3487

Mexico, 152, 353, 565, 620, 640, 641, 661, 662, 1197, 1201, 1204, 1424, 1508, 1509, 1546, 1628, 1629, 1856, 1884, 1981, 1982, 2189, 2621, 3506, 3611, 3617, 3620, 3851

Mongolia, 10, 792, 793, 795, 906, 908, 2759, 2761, 3120

Namibia, 1315

Netherlands, 299, 326, 332, 1405, 1418, 1823, 1841, 1845, 3617, 3738, 3739, 3740, 4116

New Zealand, 91, 108, 1327, 1465, 1520, 1898, 2291, 2460, 3622, 3671, 3689, 3753, 3754, 3941, 3942

Nigeria, 3487

Norway, 137, 299, 326, 332, 356, 809, 819, 930, 999, 1405, 1418, 1427, 1480, 1590, 1667, 1823, 1841, 1845, 1853, 1859, 2222, 2331, 2530, 2780, 3372, 3803

Pakistan, 3487

Poland, 829, 916

Portugal, 298, 298, 299, 300, 326, 332, 1404, 1404, 1405, 1406, 1418, 1822, 1822, 1823, 1824, 1841, 1845

Romania, 829

Russia, 908

Samoa, 3487

Sierra Leone, 3487

Singapore, 2519, 3734

South Africa, 475, 576, 628, 709, 1520, 1871, 1898, 1958, 1971, 2063, 2337, 2498, 2652, 3426, 3822, 3823

Spain, 299, 326, 332, 1405, 1418, 1823, 1841, 1845, 3617, 3700, 3828

Sri Lanka, 3487, 3622

Sweden, 146, 147, 148, 256, 957, 999, 1681, 1797, 2802, 2803, 2804, 2878, 2993, 3143, 3144, 3276, 3372, 3835

Switzerland, 80, 160, 891, 969, 1923, 2942, 3004, 3033, 3068, 3110, 3148, 3612

Tanzania, 3487

Thailand, 2, 38, 282, 375, 425, 485, 520, 586, 642, 842, 1400, 1434, 1510, 1630, 1699, 2728, 2820, 3873

Trinidad & Tobago, 3487

Turkey, 10, 299, 326, 332, 421, 422, 423, 769, 770, 771, 792, 833, 834, 835, 840, 908, 984, 985, 986, 987, 988, 1090, 1093, 1405, 1418, 1521, 1753, 1754, 1755, 1756, 1759, 1760, 1761, 1769, 1823, 1841, 1845, 2725, 2726, 2904, 2905, 2906, 2909, 3120

Uganda, 3487, 3622

Ukraine, 3844

United Kingdom, 84, 105, 110, 139, 155, 156, 180, 263, 293, 294, 299, 303, 303, 312, 326, 332, 355, 360, 361, 364, 388, 409, 433, 434, 439, 442, 454, 465, 491, 492, 497, 510, 542, 548, 563, 566, 571, 594, 595, 602, 609, 617, 621, 649, 650, 664, 697, 702, 722, 723, 732, 734, 735, 736, 738, 759, 761, 785, 805, 928, 939, 941, 1042, 1071, 1072, 1109, 1112, 1159, 1177, 1184, 1216, 1304, 1314, 1335, 1373, 1380, 1393, 1394, 1405, 1418, 1426, 1450, 1468, 1478, 1486, 1522, 1523, 1537, 1537, 1547, 1548, 1575, 1588, 1605, 1682, 1706, 1706, 1735, 1786, 1798, 1801, 1823, 1831, 1832, 1841, 1845, 1847, 1858, 1860, 1864, 1868, 1903, 1903, 1938, 1960, 1961, 1995, 2004, 2004, 2028, 2050, 2051, 2057, 2059, 2091, 2091, 2130, 2131, 2132, 2133, 2138, 2213, 2231, 2273, 2318, 2329, 2334, 2335, 2342, 2410, 2476, 2499, 2520, 2533, 2534, 2535, 2536, 2545, 2615, 2627, 2658, 2764, 2765, 2774, 2807, 2845, 2885, 2922, 2953, 2969, 3002, 3045, 3046, 3058, 3059, 3064, 3065, 3066, 3127, 3317, 3348, 3390, 3391, 3426, 3433, 3434, 3435, 3436, 3437, 3438, 3439, 3441, 3443, 3477, 3478, 3485, 3505, 3582, 3601, 3603, 3622, 3735, 3756, 3789, 3848, 3852, 3853, 3865, 3874, 3875, 3876, 3877, 3894, 3899, 3900, 3903, 3904, 3905, 3906, 3907, 3908, 3909, 3910, 3911, 3913, 3915, 3916, 3923, 3925, 3926, 3927, 3928, 3929, 3930, 3931, 3932, 3933, 3935, 3959, 4117, 4241

United States, 4, 6, 7, 8, 9, 14, 15, 17, 18, 19, 20, 23, 26, 27, 31, 32, 34, 36, 40, 42, 44, 45, 50, 56, 60, 66, 68, 69, 81, 86, 87, 89, 90, 93, 94, 115, 119, 123, 130, 138, 139, 151, 152, 153, 154, 158, 167, 172, 181, 183, 186, 193, 197, 199, 202, 215, 216, 236, 238, 248, 250, 254, 268, 269, 270, 288, 290, 291, 292, 296, 299, 302, 304, 305, 306, 318, 320, 321, 332, 333, 337, 338, 339, 340, 341, 358, 362, 363, 366, 367, 371, 382, 385, 394, 407, 408, 417, 430, 438, 445, 447, 448, 455, 456, 457, 466, 472, 479, 480, 481, 482, 483, 484, 490, 495, 502, 503, 504, 505, 506, 507, 508, 509, 511, 519,

528, 530, 533, 535, 539, 543, 544, 549, 554, 556, 557, 558, 559, 560, 561, 563, 569, 572, 584, 585, 593, 600, 603, 604, 608, 615, 616, 617, 619, 624, 625, 635, 640, 641, 648, 658, 661, 662, 663, 672, 673, 679, 680, 684, 685, 686, 687, 688, 689, 691, 692, 694, 700, 705, 714, 721, 727, 729, 731, 740, 744, 748, 749, 750, 751, 752, 753, 755, 757, 760, 762, 774, 778, 779, 780, 783, 784, 789, 790, 791, 800, 801, 802, 803, 804, 805, 807, 816, 817, 821, 822, 823, 824, 831, 845, 847, 851, 856, 861, 871, 880, 883, 885, 898, 899, 900, 901, 915, 924, 925, 926, 927, 928, 940, 942, 943, 946, 947, 956, 960, 961, 964, 965, 973, 974, 975, 992, 997, 1010, 1014, 1015, 1027, 1028, 1030, 1034, 1035, 1036, 1040, 1041, 1042, 1045, 1046, 1051, 1056, 1057, 1058, 1074, 1075, 1077, 1081, 1083, 1085, 1086, 1087, 1099, 1101, 1111, 1125, 1131, 1135, 1140, 1141, 1150, 1151, 1153, 1156, 1157, 1158, 1159, 1163, 1168, 1183, 1190, 1198, 1205, 1214, 1215, 1225, 1226, 1239, 1285, 1288, 1292, 1295, 1302, 1303, 1304, 1329, 1342, 1344, 1358, 1359, 1367, 1368, 1375, 1376, 1377, 1378, 1379, 1380, 1381, 1382, 1386, 1392, 1397, 1401, 1402, 1405, 1418, 1419, 1420, 1421, 1422, 1423, 1429, 1430, 1437, 1439, 1440, 1441, 1443, 1446, 1448, 1453, 1456, 1457, 1464, 1466, 1474, 1475, 1477, 1481, 1489, 1503, 1508, 1509, 1512, 1514, 1517, 1518, 1519, 1538, 1540, 1542, 1544, 1546, 1562, 1563, 1565, 1566, 1573, 1574, 1575, 1576, 1581, 1582, 1583, 1584, 1585, 1587, 1591, 1592, 1593, 1594, 1595, 1599, 1600, 1601, 1602, 1603, 1608, 1610, 1611, 1614, 1615, 1616, 1617, 1618, 1619, 1628, 1629, 1631, 1640, 1641, 1642, 1645, 1646, 1654, 1655, 1656, 1660, 1661, 1662, 1663, 1664, 1666, 1668, 1669, 1670, 1671, 1672, 1673, 1675, 1676, 1677, 1691, 1701, 1708, 1710, 1716, 1717, 1721, 1726, 1727, 1728, 1729, 1731, 1734, 1739, 1743, 1744, 1763, 1765, 1766, 1774, 1775, 1782, 1784, 1785, 1786, 1787, 1794, 1795, 1807, 1819, 1820, 1823, 1835, 1838, 1845, 1851, 1866, 1867, 1869, 1870, 1884, 1893, 1895, 1897, 1901, 1906, 1907, 1910, 1912, 1920, 1924, 1929, 1931, 1932, 1939, 1944, 1945, 1948, 1950, 1951, 1953, 1954, 1959, 1968, 1970, 1981, 1982, 1988, 1990, 1996, 2005, 2007, 2012, 2017, 2018, 2020, 2021, 2023, 2032, 2033, 2034, 2035, 2036, 2037, 2040, 2048, 2049, 2060, 2061, 2072, 2078, 2080, 2085, 2088, 2093, 2094, 2100, 2106, 2107, 2112, 2116, 2117, 2118, 2119, 2120,

2121, 2124, 2128, 2129, 2137, 2140, 2141, 2142, 2144, 2145, 2146, 2147, 2149, 2154, 2156, 2158, 2160, 2163, 2164, 2165, 2166, 2177, 2178, 2179, 2180, 2191, 2195, 2204, 2205, 2207, 2210, 2220, 2229, 2230, 2232, 2247, 2257, 2265, 2267, 2268, 2270, 2272, 2274, 2278, 2285, 2292, 2293, 2294, 2304, 2305, 2307, 2309, 2310, 2314, 2320, 2321, 2323, 2325, 2326, 2333, 2340, 2341, 2344, 2349, 2372, 2382, 2384, 2386, 2387, 2388, 2389, 2390, 2391, 2392, 2393, 2400, 2412, 2416, 2426, 2428, 2435, 2442, 2443, 2445, 2446, 2447, 2448, 2449, 2458, 2474, 2475, 2494, 2495, 2501, 2504, 2508, 2509, 2510, 2511, 2512, 2513, 2515, 2518, 2523, 2525, 2526, 2529, 2540, 2544, 2547, 2551, 2559, 2560, 2561, 2562, 2563, 2564, 2566, 2570, 2578, 2580, 2590, 2598, 2605, 2607, 2608, 2611, 2619, 2620, 2621, 2625, 2626, 2633, 2634, 2639, 2641, 2643, 2656, 2659, 2660, 2661, 2662, 2670, 2679, 2680, 2681, 2683, 2691, 2692, 2699, 2703, 2705, 2710, 2711, 2712, 2719, 2722, 2730, 2732, 2734, 2737, 2739, 2741, 2742, 2745, 2748, 2755, 2756, 2757, 2769, 2770, 2771, 2772, 2773, 2774, 2781, 2782, 2783, 2784, 2790, 2791, 2808, 2809, 2811, 2812, 2813, 2816, 2817, 2819, 2830, 2831, 2832, 2833, 2834, 2842, 2847, 2848, 2854, 2855, 2856, 2857, 2860, 2861, 2862, 2872, 2875, 2885, 2898, 2911, 2913, 2920, 2926, 2934, 2935, 2936, 2939, 2943, 2945, 2946, 2947, 2949, 2957, 2958, 2959, 2960, 2961, 2962, 2963, 2966, 2967, 2968, 2969, 2972, 2980, 2981, 2982, 2983, 2984, 2989, 2995, 3007, 3009, 3010, 3014, 3016, 3017, 3018, 3019, 3025, 3037, 3038, 3040, 3041, 3043, 3044, 3051, 3052, 3054, 3058, 3069, 3072, 3077, 3079, 3081, 3086, 3089, 3093, 3095, 3097, 3099, 3114, 3115, 3116, 3117, 3118, 3119, 3122, 3123, 3124, 3125, 3132, 3138, 3149, 3150, 3153, 3155, 3156, 3161, 3163, 3173, 3174, 3175, 3176, 3178, 3198, 3202, 3215, 3216, 3220, 3224, 3226, 3230, 3236, 3253, 3255, 3258, 3278, 3279, 3283, 3286, 3290, 3296, 3316, 3319, 3328, 3329, 3339, 3349, 3351, 3355, 3357, 3371, 3373, 3375, 3380, 3381, 3425, 3440, 3442, 3452, 3472, 3480, 3481, 3483, 3492, 3508, 3513, 3514, 3516, 3520, 3521, 3533, 3548, 3555, 3557, 3583, 3586, 3587, 3609, 3611, 3629, 3637, 3648, 3656, 3659, 3663, 3664, 3672, 3679, 3681, 3705, 3706, 3710, 3713, 3715, 3719, 3720, 3721, 3722, 3723, 3724, 3737, 3744, 3756, 3757, 3759, 3762, 3769, 3770,

3771, 3776, 3780, 3786, 3793, 3795, 3796, 3810, 3812, 3813, 3814, 3825, 3836, 3837, 3841, 3856, 3865, 3866, 3871, 3880, 3882, 3884, 3892, 3912, 3914, 3938, 3939, 3945, 3949, 3953, 3976, 3979, 3982, 3982, 3983, 3989, 3990, 3997, 4000, 4009, 4027, 4032, 4036, 4038, 4043, 4056, 4058, 4067, 4087, 4088, 4098, 4099, 4114, 4126, 4128

Vietnam, 817, 817, 947, 947, 2791, 2791
Yugoslavia, 423, 829, 840, 988, 1093, 1759, 1760, 1761, 2909
Zambia, 3487

COUNTRY OF RESIDENCE

Antigua/Barbudau, 65, 537, 3297, 3621, 3770
Argentina, 3621, 3770
Australia, 111, 735, 772, 773, 848, 849, 990, 994, 995, 1094, 1102, 1103, 1194, 1195, 1240, 1241, 1345, 1346, 1515, 1516, 1547, 1992, 1993, 2082, 2083, 2406, 2407, 2465, 2469, 2735, 2736, 2822, 2823, 2914, 2915, 3021, 3022, 3059, 3084, 3085, 3164, 3165, 3227, 3228, 3399, 3400, 3402, 3407, 3409, 3411, 3937, 3949, 3973, 4235
Austria, 997
Bahamas, 3621, 3770
Barbados, 65, 537, 3297, 3621, 3646, 3770
Belarus, 3766
Belize, 2473, 3621, 3646, 3770
Bolivia, 3621, 3770
Brazil, 3621, 3770
Bulgaria, 770, 834, 986, 1755, 2726, 2905
Burma, 211, 1222, 2597, 2668, 3242, 3766, 3852
Cambodia, 211, 2597, 2668, 3242
Canada, 5, 20, 32, 57, 60, 61, 62, 131, 132, 141, 150, 224, 251, 252, 297, 324, 325, 398, 399, 421, 432, 551, 552, 611, 612, 637, 652, 663, 676, 677, 715, 731, 735, 769, 776, 833, 836, 839, 857, 860, 862, 886, 938, 984, 1084, 1085, 1091, 1147, 1148, 1162, 1207, 1295, 1308, 1416, 1417, 1437, 1505, 1525, 1547, 1570, 1571, 1625, 1700, 1704, 1719, 1720, 1753, 1757, 1759, 1767, 1772, 1821, 1839, 1840, 1884, 1920, 1935, 1936, 1947, 1978, 2000, 2012, 2026, 2027, 2039, 2069, 2100, 2123, 2196, 2215, 2306, 2353, 2354, 2355, 2420, 2421, 2473, 2484, 2485, 2486, 2531, 2582, 2645, 2708, 2725, 2738, 2844, 2845, 2862, 2863, 2864, 2904, 2921, 2924, 2973, 3028, 3091, 3158, 3199, 3264, 3330, 3331, 3395, 3453, 3454, 3455, 3456, 3457, 3458, 3459, 3460, 3499, 3502, 3621, 3622, 3646, 3680, 3701, 3765, 3834, 3843, 3844, 3897, 3898, 3902, 3958, 4203

Chile, 3621, 3770
China, 211, 2597, 2668, 3242, 3706, 3949
Colombia, 3621, 3770
Costa Rica, 2473, 3621, 3646, 3770
Cuba, 2473, 3646
Czech Republic, 770, 834, 986, 1755, 2726, 2905
Dominica, 65, 537, 3297, 3621, 3770
Dominican Rep., 2473, 3621, 3646, 3770
Ecuador, 3621, 3770
El Salvador, 2473, 3621, 3646, 3770
Finland, 3465
Germany, 3336
Grenada, 65, 537, 3297, 3621, 3770
Guatemala, 2473, 3621, 3646, 3770
Guyana, 3621, 3770
Haiti, 2473, 3621, 3646, 3770
Honduras, 2473, 3621, 3646, 3770
Hungary, 770, 834, 986, 1755, 2726, 2905
India, 3949
Indonesia, 3949
Ireland, 443, 1019, 1143, 1275, 1287, 2159, 2547, 3821
Israel, 1388
Jamaica, 65, 537, 2473, 3297, 3621, 3646, 3770
Japan, 3138, 3690, 3949
Korea (North), 211, 2597, 2668, 3242, 3949
Korea (South), 211, 2597, 2668, 3242, 3949
Laos, 211, 2597, 2668, 3242
Malaysia, 3949
Mexico, 8, 9, 93, 94, 637, 663, 715, 731, 790, 791, 900, 901, 1505, 1625, 1884, 1920, 1978, 2012, 2069, 2100, 2473, 2756, 2757, 3040, 3041, 3118, 3119, 3621, 3770
Mongolia, 3706, 3766
New Zealand, 111, 735, 1547, 1609, 3399, 3942
Nicaragua, 2473, 3621, 3646, 3770
Norway, 3803
Panama, 2473, 3621, 3646, 3770
Papua New Guinea, 3399
Paraguay, 3621, 3770
Peru, 3621, 3770
Philippines, 3949
Poland, 770, 834, 986, 1755, 2726, 2905, 3663
Romania, 770, 834, 986, 1755, 2726, 2905
Russia, 10, 792, 3120, 3766
Samoa, 175, 227, 909, 2956, 3121
Singapore, 3949
Slovakia, 770, 834, 986, 1755, 2726, 2905
South Africa, 735, 1547, 2497
St. Kitts/Nevis, 65, 537, 3297, 3621, 3646, 3770
St. Lucia, 65, 537, 3297, 3621, 3646, 3770
St. Vincent/Grenadines, 65, 537, 3297, 3621, 3646, 3770
Suriname, 3621, 3770

Taiwan, 3949
Thailand, 211, 2597, 2668, 3242, 3949
Trinidad & Tobago, 2473, 3621, 3646, 3770
Ukraine, 3766, 3845
United Kingdom, 12, 46, 109, 312, 355, 388, 409, 442, 465, 497, 510, 543, 548, 566, 603, 609, 621, 664, 697, 732, 735, 736, 759, 1109, 1177, 1213, 1262, 1267, 1268, 1287, 1315, 1320, 1385, 1426, 1486, 1547, 1548, 1605, 1682, 1735, 1770, 1798, 1858, 1960, 2050, 2130, 2159, 2436, 2499, 2534, 2535, 2547, 3317, 3463, 3560, 3656, 3817, 3821, 3853, 3865, 3916, 4241
United States, 1, 6, 13, 14, 20, 22, 23, 25, 31, 32, 45, 50, 53, 54, 60, 79, 113, 115, 121, 122, 126, 130, 132, 148, 171, 175, 199, 201, 207, 224, 227, 243, 249, 256, 261, 272, 274, 277, 280, 285, 286, 305, 311, 317, 326, 331, 333, 334, 335, 337, 338, 339, 340, 341, 342, 344, 362, 368, 369, 373, 374, 378, 379, 385, 405, 415, 421, 422, 423, 428, 429, 435, 440, 451, 452, 453, 469, 473, 474, 478, 479, 480, 481, 482, 483, 484, 488, 489, 495, 501, 502, 503, 504, 505, 506, 507, 508, 512, 513, 515, 518, 523, 524, 531, 539, 542, 554, 555, 556, 557, 558, 559, 560, 561, 570, 574, 575, 578, 582, 589, 590, 592, 600, 602, 614, 615, 616, 626, 627, 630, 633, 635, 637, 645, 646, 647, 658, 663, 667, 670, 673, 675, 680, 681, 682, 684, 685, 686, 687, 688, 689, 690, 691, 701, 707, 708, 711, 713, 714, 715, 718, 719, 720, 729, 731, 739, 744, 745, 746, 748, 749, 750, 751, 752, 753, 754, 755, 763, 764, 766, 768, 769, 786, 795, 807, 814, 825, 827, 829, 833, 836, 837, 839, 840, 850, 851, 854, 861, 874, 886, 887, 888, 890, 908, 909, 916, 923, 930, 938, 943, 944, 946, 957, 959, 964, 965, 966, 971, 979, 980, 984, 985, 988, 1004, 1011, 1016, 1049, 1057, 1063, 1068, 1069, 1070, 1080, 1084, 1085, 1089, 1091, 1092, 1093, 1104, 1119, 1133, 1136, 1147, 1148, 1161, 1168, 1175, 1180, 1182, 1187, 1191, 1198, 1201, 1202, 1207, 1218, 1223, 1224, 1225, 1226, 1227, 1258, 1265, 1269, 1271, 1295, 1296, 1308, 1323, 1325, 1326, 1328, 1330, 1333, 1334, 1340, 1364, 1384, 1386, 1389, 1419, 1429, 1431, 1437, 1471, 1473, 1474, 1502, 1503, 1505, 1532, 1540, 1559, 1576, 1577, 1578, 1579, 1581, 1582, 1583, 1584, 1585, 1586, 1587, 1600, 1607, 1625, 1656, 1657, 1658, 1660, 1661, 1662, 1663, 1664, 1665, 1666, 1676, 1681, 1686, 1697, 1700, 1708, 1721, 1722, 1723, 1724, 1726, 1727, 1728, 1729, 1730, 1731, 1746, 1748, 1753, 1754, 1757, 1759, 1760,

1771, 1772, 1777, 1787, 1788, 1795, 1808, 1813, 1816, 1817, 1841, 1848, 1849, 1851, 1852, 1861, 1862, 1863, 1866, 1874, 1883, 1884, 1890, 1891, 1910, 1920, 1926, 1927, 1932, 1939, 1940, 1941, 1942, 1944, 1945, 1946, 1948, 1949, 1954, 1965, 1966, 1974, 1977, 1978, 1985, 1986, 1991, 2011, 2012, 2016, 2023, 2029, 2030, 2032, 2033, 2034, 2035, 2036, 2037, 2038, 2040, 2041, 2055, 2056, 2064, 2066, 2068, 2069, 2070, 2075, 2076, 2081, 2093, 2100, 2105, 2112, 2113, 2114, 2116, 2117, 2118, 2119, 2120, 2121, 2122, 2124, 2134, 2136, 2143, 2148, 2150, 2167, 2175, 2185, 2187, 2194, 2207, 2208, 2212, 2216, 2217, 2223, 2236, 2241, 2242, 2249, 2255, 2276, 2278, 2288, 2290, 2296, 2309, 2310, 2316, 2317, 2321, 2322, 2324, 2326, 2332, 2351, 2354, 2355, 2358, 2359, 2361, 2362, 2373, 2386, 2387, 2388, 2389, 2390, 2391, 2392, 2393, 2456, 2473, 2474, 2492, 2493, 2504, 2515, 2518, 2521, 2542, 2543, 2548, 2566, 2567, 2589, 2590, 2590, 2596, 2599, 2607, 2613, 2614, 2656, 2656, 2667, 2671, 2686, 2696, 2701, 2718, 2719, 2723, 2725, 2727, 2749, 2761, 2776, 2787, 2806, 2808, 2826, 2830, 2848, 2862, 2872, 2878, 2881, 2890, 2892, 2899, 2904, 2907, 2909, 2918, 2928, 2941, 2956, 2971, 2982, 2994, 3005, 3011, 3013, 3019, 3024, 3032, 3034, 3050, 3053, 3054, 3061, 3062, 3069, 3086, 3088, 3095, 3096, 3106, 3107, 3109, 3121, 3129, 3132, 3138, 3144, 3145, 3149, 3150, 3157, 3158, 3158, 3172, 3189, 3190, 3231, 3235, 3240, 3250, 3257, 3258, 3277, 3287, 3288, 3289, 3304, 3315, 3318, 3328, 3332, 3339, 3340, 3341, 3342, 3343, 3344, 3346, 3348, 3349, 3353, 3370, 3372, 3385, 3421, 3423, 3444, 3447, 3451, 3464, 3466, 3468, 3470, 3479, 3482, 3489, 3494, 3511, 3512, 3518, 3520, 3531, 3532, 3535, 3537, 3547, 3549, 3551, 3552, 3559, 3569, 3570, 3571, 3577, 3582, 3585, 3588, 3590, 3591, 3597, 3608, 3609, 3611, 3621, 3625, 3631, 3637, 3638, 3640, 3641, 3642, 3643, 3646, 3650, 3652, 3658, 3659, 3661, 3664, 3668, 3669, 3670, 3672, 3681, 3683, 3684, 3685, 3688, 3692, 3694, 3695, 3696, 3699, 3703, 3704, 3709, 3726, 3727, 3728, 3729, 3730, 3731, 3732, 3742, 3744, 3746, 3747, 3750, 3752, 3757, 3758, 3762, 3767, 3768, 3769, 3770, 3781, 3782, 3783, 3784, 3793, 3794, 3796, 3796, 3802, 3809, 3811, 3813, 3819, 3820, 3821, 3824, 3825, 3826, 3827, 3831, 3832, 3833, 3838, 3841, 3842, 3855, 3856, 3864, 3880,

3888, 3889, 3891, 3893, 3947, 3953, 3957, 3971, 3974, 3975, 3976, 3979, 3982, 3983, 3989, 3990, 4000, 4009, 4045, 4065, 4073, 4091, 4128
Uruguay, 3621, 3770
Venezuela, 3621, 3770
Vietnam, 211, 2597, 2668, 3242
Yugoslavia, 3766
Zimbabwe, 3426

CURRENT GRADE POINT AVERAGE

Low (under 2.0), 4134
Average (2.0 - 3.0), 15, 32, 120, 211, 255, 260, 318, 381, 671, 1189, 1318, 1488, 1558, 1653, 1715, 1925, 2017, 2106, 2597, 2623, 2668, 2854, 2855, 2896, 3020, 3074, 3082, 3242, 3294, 3307, 3360, 3377, 3381, 3428, 3475, 3555, 3564, 3565, 3591, 3599, 3645, 3667, 3710, 3718, 3741, 3749, 3763, 3778, 3859, 3862, 3891, 3919, 3952, 3969, 4134
High (3.0 - 3.5), 6, 14, 15, 16, 18, 22, 23, 24, 30, 32, 58, 59, 62, 67, 82, 104, 116, 117, 120, 121, 123, 130, 131, 163, 164, 174, 192, 205, 207, 210, 211, 212, 230, 236, 238, 255, 260, 265, 293, 294, 309, 318, 320, 321, 344, 365, 368, 369, 373, 374, 381, 433, 434, 437, 446, 447, 448, 453, 473, 474, 491, 492, 499, 512, 513, 549, 550, 556, 567, 573, 574, 575, 594, 595, 626, 627, 634, 649, 650, 661, 662, 671, 674, 679, 707, 708, 722, 723, 741, 742, 763, 764, 800, 808, 838, 893, 894, 914, 916, 923, 943, 963, 1034, 1057, 1081, 1082, 1083, 1084, 1085, 1087, 1114, 1126, 1150, 1153, 1162, 1171, 1172, 1189, 1193, 1214, 1318, 1350, 1351, 1352, 1353, 1354, 1375, 1383, 1384, 1390, 1445, 1467, 1475, 1483, 1488, 1494, 1520, 1526, 1541, 1545, 1558, 1565, 1567, 1600, 1604, 1638, 1643, 1653, 1676, 1679, 1683, 1709, 1715, 1734, 1758, 1795, 1800, 1829, 1884, 1898, 1911, 1925, 1930, 1947, 1950, 1954, 1962, 2001, 2017, 2019, 2022, 2039, 2041, 2052, 2068, 2071, 2097, 2106, 2109, 2123, 2135, 2139, 2153, 2204, 2206, 2210, 2215, 2223, 2269, 2278, 2305, 2308, 2314, 2332, 2508, 2514, 2554, 2557, 2559, 2560, 2561, 2562, 2563, 2564, 2568, 2589, 2597, 2605, 2607, 2611, 2621, 2623, 2639, 2668, 2679, 2718, 2778, 2825, 2830, 2838, 2839, 2854, 2855, 2858, 2896, 2961, 2973, 2982, 3020, 3052, 3071, 3074, 3082, 3095, 3111, 3112, 3151, 3152, 3172, 3222, 3232, 3235, 3242, 3243, 3249, 3288, 3289, 3294, 3307, 3360, 3361, 3368, 3375, 3377, 3381, 3383, 3385, 3405, 3406, 3408, 3428, 3434, 3435, 3437, 3438,

3439, 3440, 3442, 3443, 3454, 3475, 3480, 3486, 3498, 3499, 3507, 3524, 3533, 3543, 3552, 3555, 3564, 3565, 3567, 3574, 3576, 3579, 3580, 3591, 3595, 3596, 3599, 3610, 3611, 3612, 3628, 3645, 3664, 3667, 3669, 3715, 3718, 3719, 3720, 3721, 3722, 3723, 3724, 3741, 3749, 3760, 3763, 3764, 3765, 3776, 3778, 3795, 3806, 3819, 3859, 3860, 3862, 3891, 3917, 3919, 3952, 3969
Excellent (above 3.5), 6, 7, 14, 15, 16, 18, 22, 23, 24, 30, 32, 36, 58, 59, 62, 67, 68, 82, 104, 116, 117, 120, 121, 123, 130, 131, 163, 164, 174, 192, 193, 205, 207, 210, 212, 230, 236, 238, 246, 247, 248, 255, 260, 265, 293, 294, 302, 305, 309, 316, 318, 320, 321, 344, 348, 349, 350, 351, 365, 368, 369, 373, 374, 381, 385, 433, 434, 437, 446, 447, 448, 453, 473, 474, 491, 492, 495, 499, 512, 513, 539, 549, 550, 556, 564, 567, 573, 574, 575, 594, 595, 600, 626, 627, 634, 639, 649, 650, 658, 661, 662, 665, 669, 671, 674, 679, 707, 708, 722, 723, 729, 741, 742, 763, 764, 800, 808, 838, 893, 894, 914, 916, 923, 943, 963, 1034, 1057, 1081, 1082, 1083, 1084, 1085, 1087, 1114, 1126, 1130, 1150, 1153, 1162, 1171, 1172, 1189, 1193, 1214, 1318, 1350, 1351, 1352, 1353, 1354, 1375, 1383, 1384, 1390, 1445, 1467, 1475, 1483, 1488, 1494, 1507, 1520, 1526, 1540, 1541, 1545, 1550, 1553, 1558, 1565, 1567, 1600, 1603, 1604, 1627, 1638, 1643, 1647, 1653, 1676, 1679, 1683, 1708, 1709, 1715, 1734, 1758, 1795, 1800, 1829, 1884, 1898, 1910, 1911, 1925, 1930, 1947, 1950, 1954, 1962, 1980, 2001, 2014, 2017, 2019, 2022, 2039, 2041, 2052, 2068, 2071, 2093, 2097, 2103, 2106, 2109, 2123, 2135, 2139, 2153, 2156, 2197, 2204, 2206, 2210, 2215, 2218, 2219, 2220, 2223, 2269, 2278, 2297, 2305, 2308, 2314, 2332, 2422, 2487, 2508, 2514, 2527, 2528, 2529, 2554, 2557, 2559, 2560, 2561, 2562, 2563, 2564, 2568, 2589, 2600, 2605, 2607, 2611, 2617, 2618, 2619, 2621, 2623, 2639, 2672, 2679, 2718, 2778, 2819, 2825, 2830, 2831, 2838, 2839, 2854, 2855, 2858, 2896, 2961, 2973, 2982, 3018, 3020, 3052, 3071, 3074, 3077, 3082, 3095, 3097, 3111, 3112, 3151, 3152, 3172, 3196, 3197, 3198, 3222, 3232, 3235, 3243, 3249, 3288, 3289, 3294, 3307, 3360, 3361, 3368, 3375, 3377, 3381, 3383, 3385, 3390, 3405, 3406, 3408, 3428, 3433, 3434, 3435, 3437, 3438, 3439, 3440, 3441, 3442, 3443, 3445, 3454, 3480, 3486, 3497, 3498, 3499, 3500, 3507, 3533, 3543, 3552, 3555, 3562, 3564, 3565, 3567,

3571, 3574, 3576, 3579, 3580, 3591, 3595, 3596, 3599, 3610, 3611, 3612, 3628, 3645, 3664, 3667, 3669, 3699, 3711, 3715, 3716, 3718, 3719, 3720, 3721, 3722, 3723, 3724, 3741, 3749, 3760, 3763, 3764, 3765, 3776, 3778, 3788, 3795, 3806, 3860, 3862, 3878, 3891, 3917, 3919, 3938, 3952, 3969, 3979

CURRENT SCHOOL PROGRAM

Non-Degree Course, 34, 114, 166, 267, 370, 396, 397, 1328, 2185, 2288, 2456, 2596, 2631, 2667, 2897, 3219, 3240, 3282, 3285, 3309, 3311, 3785, 3955, 3977, 3978, 3997
Part-Time, 2563
Transfer Student, 3480, 3482, 3808, 3841
Graduate, 1, 3, 5, 6, 7, 10, 11, 12, 15, 16, 18, 19, 21, 22, 23, 24, 25, 27, 29, 30, 31, 32, 33, 34, 35, 39, 45, 47, 48, 49, 50, 51, 52, 53, 57, 58, 59, 60, 63, 64, 66, 67, 68, 72, 74, 75, 76, 80, 83, 84, 85, 86, 87, 88, 95, 96, 97, 98, 99, 100, 101, 102, 103, 105, 106, 109, 110, 112, 113, 116, 117, 118, 119, 120, 121, 123, 124, 125, 126, 127, 128, 139, 144, 145, 147, 148, 149, 150, 151, 152, 153, 154, 155, 156, 158, 159, 164, 165, 166, 168, 169, 170, 171, 173, 174, 175, 176, 177, 179, 180, 182, 183, 184, 185, 186, 187, 189, 190, 191, 194, 195, 198, 199, 200, 203, 204, 206, 207, 208, 209, 210, 211, 213, 214, 215, 216, 226, 227, 228, 229, 232, 234, 236, 237, 238, 239, 240, 241, 242, 243, 245, 246, 247, 248, 250, 253, 255, 256, 257, 258, 260, 262, 263, 264, 265, 266, 267, 271, 272, 273, 274, 275, 277, 278, 279, 284, 292, 301, 302, 303, 305, 308, 309, 310, 311, 312, 315, 316, 317, 318, 319, 320, 321, 323, 324, 327, 328, 329, 330, 331, 332, 337, 338, 339, 340, 341, 344, 346, 347, 348, 349, 351, 352, 353, 354, 356, 357, 358, 360, 361, 364, 365, 368, 369, 370, 371, 372, 374, 377, 380, 381, 382, 383, 385, 387, 388, 394, 395, 397, 398, 400, 401, 402, 406, 411, 412, 413, 415, 416, 418, 419, 427, 430, 431, 432, 437, 438, 439, 442, 445, 446, 447, 448, 449, 450, 451, 453, 455, 458, 459, 460, 461, 462, 463, 464, 466, 467, 468, 469, 473, 474, 475, 476, 477, 480, 481, 482, 483, 484, 487, 490, 495, 497, 498, 499, 500, 502, 503, 504, 505, 506, 507, 508, 511, 512, 513, 514, 515, 516, 517, 522, 525, 532, 533, 536, 539, 541, 542, 543, 545, 546, 547, 548, 549, 550, 551, 553, 557, 558, 559, 560, 561, 563, 565, 569, 570, 572, 573, 574, 575, 576, 577, 578, 579, 580, 581, 583, 584, 588, 591, 593, 598, 600, 602, 603, 605, 606, 607, 609, 610, 611, 613, 615, 616, 617, 618, 620,

622, 624, 625, 626, 627, 628, 629, 630, 631, 632, 634, 635, 636, 644, 648, 654, 655, 656, 658, 660, 661, 662, 663, 664, 665, 666, 667, 668, 669, 670, 672, 674, 676, 678, 679, 684, 685, 686, 687, 688, 689, 691, 692, 695, 696, 698, 700, 701, 703, 704, 705, 706, 707, 708, 709, 710, 711, 712, 714, 715, 717, 721, 727, 729, 731, 732, 733, 734, 735, 736, 737, 739, 740, 741, 742, 743, 748, 749, 750, 751, 752, 753, 755, 758, 760, 762, 763, 764, 765, 767, 772, 773, 776, 777, 782, 785, 788, 789, 792, 796, 798, 800, 806, 807, 808, 814, 818, 819, 825, 836, 838, 839, 841, 843, 848, 849, 850, 851, 852, 853, 854, 856, 857, 859, 860, 862, 866, 869, 870, 872, 881, 886, 891, 895, 897, 902, 908, 909, 911, 912, 913, 916, 917, 919, 920, 921, 922, 923, 931, 933, 935, 940, 942, 943, 944, 949, 950, 951, 954, 957, 958, 959, 961, 962, 966, 967, 970, 971, 981, 983, 991, 993, 994, 995, 996, 997, 998, 999, 1000, 1002, 1006, 1008, 1009, 1013, 1014, 1020, 1021, 1022, 1023, 1024, 1025, 1028, 1029, 1030, 1031, 1032, 1033, 1034, 1038, 1039, 1043, 1046, 1047, 1048, 1050, 1051, 1052, 1053, 1054, 1055, 1056, 1057, 1059, 1060, 1061, 1062, 1064, 1065, 1066, 1069, 1070, 1071, 1072, 1077, 1078, 1079, 1091, 1102, 1103, 1104, 1105, 1106, 1107, 1108, 1109, 1111, 1112, 1113, 1115, 1117, 1120, 1123, 1124, 1126, 1127, 1131, 1132, 1138, 1140, 1141, 1144, 1145, 1146, 1148, 1149, 1150, 1153, 1155, 1161, 1169, 1173, 1176, 1177, 1178, 1179, 1181, 1182, 1183, 1184, 1187, 1191, 1192, 1193, 1194, 1195, 1196, 1197, 1198, 1200, 1202, 1204, 1207, 1208, 1210, 1212, 1213, 1214, 1216, 1218, 1219, 1221, 1222, 1223, 1227, 1228, 1229, 1233, 1238, 1240, 1241, 1242, 1243, 1252, 1254, 1255, 1259, 1261, 1264, 1268, 1276, 1278, 1282, 1283, 1286, 1289, 1290, 1291, 1293, 1296, 1300, 1301, 1307, 1309, 1313, 1318, 1319, 1321, 1322, 1324, 1329, 1333, 1334, 1335, 1336, 1337, 1338, 1345, 1346, 1347, 1348, 1349, 1351, 1352, 1353, 1354, 1356, 1357, 1360, 1362, 1363, 1365, 1367, 1370, 1371, 1372, 1373, 1374, 1375, 1381, 1383, 1384, 1387, 1389, 1391, 1392, 1393, 1394, 1395, 1396, 1398, 1399, 1402, 1403, 1408, 1411, 1416, 1418, 1419, 1422, 1424, 1425, 1427, 1428, 1431, 1432, 1433, 1435, 1436, 1437, 1438, 1439, 1440, 1442, 1443, 1444, 1445, 1448, 1449, 1450, 1451, 1453, 1454, 1455, 1458, 1459, 1460, 1464, 1466, 1467, 1469, 1470, 1474, 1475, 1476, 1477, 1478, 1481, 1482, 1483, 1484, 1485, 1487, 1488, 1490, 1493,

1494, 1495, 1497, 1498, 1503, 1504, 1515, 1516, 1518, 1519, 1521, 1526, 1526, 1527, 1528, 1529, 1530, 1534, 1535, 1536, 1537, 1538, 1540, 1541, 1544, 1545, 1546, 1547, 1548, 1549, 1550, 1552, 1553, 1558, 1559, 1561, 1562, 1565, 1567, 1569, 1570, 1572, 1581, 1582, 1583, 1584, 1585, 1587, 1593, 1595, 1599, 1600, 1603, 1604, 1607, 1608, 1609, 1611, 1612, 1613, 1614, 1616, 1620, 1621, 1622, 1631, 1632, 1634, 1635, 1636, 1637, 1638, 1640, 1641, 1642, 1644, 1647, 1648, 1653, 1654, 1660, 1661, 1662, 1663, 1664, 1666, 1670, 1673, 1674, 1675, 1676, 1677, 1678, 1679, 1680, 1681, 1684, 1686, 1687, 1688, 1689, 1690, 1692, 1694, 1695, 1696, 1698, 1700, 1701, 1706, 1708, 1709, 1715, 1719, 1726, 1727, 1728, 1729, 1731, 1732, 1734, 1736, 1738, 1740, 1741, 1742, 1749, 1750, 1757, 1758, 1759, 1766, 1767, 1768, 1769, 1770, 1773, 1779, 1783, 1791, 1792, 1793, 1794, 1795, 1796, 1799, 1801, 1808, 1809, 1811, 1812, 1815, 1819, 1827, 1828, 1829, 1830, 1831, 1834, 1836, 1837, 1839, 1842, 1843, 1844, 1845, 1846, 1851, 1855, 1856, 1857, 1859, 1864, 1865, 1868, 1871, 1872, 1875, 1876, 1877, 1881, 1882, 1884, 1885, 1886, 1887, 1889, 1896, 1897, 1902, 1903, 1905, 1906, 1910, 1911, 1914, 1919, 1920, 1921, 1922, 1925, 1926, 1928, 1930, 1934, 1935, 1937, 1944, 1945, 1948, 1950, 1951, 1953, 1954, 1955, 1957, 1959, 1963, 1967, 1971, 1972, 1975, 1976, 1984, 1992, 1993, 1996, 1999, 2000, 2003, 2004, 2009, 2011, 2012, 2013, 2014, 2015, 2016, 2017, 2018, 2019, 2022, 2025, 2026, 2032, 2033, 2034, 2035, 2036, 2037, 2040, 2041, 2042, 2043, 2045, 2053, 2059, 2062, 2063, 2064, 2066, 2067, 2068, 2071, 2074, 2082, 2083, 2084, 2085, 2091, 2093, 2096, 2097, 2099, 2100, 2101, 2102, 2103, 2104, 2105, 2106, 2107, 2108, 2109, 2110, 2111, 2116, 2117, 2118, 2119, 2120, 2121, 2124, 2132, 2133, 2138, 2139, 2143, 2148, 2151, 2156, 2157, 2161, 2162, 2163, 2167, 2168, 2170, 2171, 2172, 2176, 2177, 2179, 2181, 2183, 2184, 2185, 2187, 2191, 2193, 2197, 2199, 2200, 2201, 2202, 2203, 2204, 2205, 2206, 2207, 2209, 2210, 2211, 2212, 2218, 2219, 2220, 2223, 2225, 2228, 2229, 2230, 2232, 2234, 2237, 2238, 2239, 2240, 2241, 2242, 2243, 2244, 2245, 2246, 2248, 2250, 2251, 2254, 2255, 2256, 2257, 2258, 2260, 2261, 2262, 2263, 2268, 2271, 2272, 2273, 2275, 2276, 2277, 2278, 2279, 2280, 2283, 2284, 2287, 2288,

2290, 2294, 2295, 2297, 2298, 2299, 2300, 2301, 2302, 2303, 2304, 2305, 2306, 2308, 2309, 2311, 2312, 2313, 2314, 2315, 2316, 2317, 2327, 2329, 2332, 2333, 2335, 2338, 2340, 2341, 2343, 2344, 2345, 2346, 2347, 2348, 2350, 2357, 2358, 2359, 2360, 2372, 2383, 2398, 2399, 2400, 2401, 2403, 2404, 2409, 2410, 2414, 2415, 2416, 2422, 2424, 2427, 2431, 2441, 2442, 2444, 2445, 2446, 2453, 2454, 2456, 2485, 2487, 2492, 2494, 2495, 2499, 2501, 2508, 2514, 2515, 2527, 2528, 2529, 2539, 2540, 2544, 2546, 2549, 2552, 2553, 2554, 2555, 2556, 2557, 2558, 2561, 2562, 2563, 2565, 2567, 2568, 2569, 2570, 2571, 2573, 2574, 2575, 2576, 2577, 2579, 2580, 2581, 2583, 2584, 2585, 2586, 2589, 2590, 2591, 2592, 2593, 2594, 2595, 2596, 2597, 2598, 2600, 2601, 2602, 2603, 2604, 2605, 2606, 2607, 2608, 2609, 2610, 2611, 2612, 2613, 2614, 2617, 2618, 2619, 2620, 2623, 2624, 2625, 2626, 2628, 2629, 2630, 2631, 2632, 2634, 2635, 2636, 2637, 2638, 2640, 2642, 2643, 2644, 2646, 2647, 2649, 2650, 2651, 2652, 2653, 2656, 2657, 2659, 2661, 2663, 2664, 2665, 2666, 2667, 2668, 2670, 2672, 2675, 2676, 2677, 2678, 2679, 2680, 2681, 2682, 2683, 2684, 2685, 2686, 2691, 2692, 2694, 2697, 2698, 2700, 2701, 2702, 2703, 2704, 2706, 2708, 2709, 2712, 2713, 2714, 2716, 2717, 2719, 2720, 2721, 2722, 2735, 2736, 2738, 2740, 2741, 2744, 2754, 2755, 2762, 2764, 2765, 2766, 2775, 2778, 2779, 2783, 2787, 2792, 2794, 2796, 2797, 2801, 2804, 2805, 2807, 2814, 2816, 2818, 2821, 2822, 2823, 2824, 2825, 2827, 2829, 2830, 2831, 2832, 2833, 2834, 2835, 2837, 2840, 2841, 2842, 2847, 2849, 2850, 2851, 2852, 2853, 2854, 2855, 2856, 2857, 2858, 2860, 2861, 2862, 2863, 2865, 2866, 2867, 2868, 2871, 2872, 2873, 2874, 2876, 2877, 2878, 2879, 2891, 2892, 2893, 2894, 2897, 2898, 2900, 2903, 2914, 2915, 2916, 2917, 2918, 2920, 2921, 2922, 2923, 2924, 2925, 2930, 2933, 2940, 2942, 2945, 2948, 2954, 2955, 2956, 2958, 2959, 2960, 2961, 2964, 2965, 2976, 2977, 2981, 2982, 2987, 2989, 2990, 2991, 2992, 2994, 2996, 3002, 3005, 3008, 3011, 3012, 3013, 3015, 3018, 3019, 3020, 3021, 3022, 3023, 3024, 3028, 3030, 3033, 3034, 3036, 3037, 3038, 3042, 3043, 3044, 3045, 3046, 3047, 3048, 3049, 3050, 3051, 3052, 3053, 3055, 3058, 3059, 3060, 3061, 3062, 3063, 3065, 3066, 3067, 3069, 3070, 3071, 3073, 3074, 3075,

3082, 3083, 3084, 3085, 3086, 3087, 3088,
3089, 3091, 3092, 3094, 3095, 3097, 3101,
3102, 3105, 3108, 3110, 3113, 3114, 3115, 3120,
3121, 3122, 3123, 3124, 3125, 3126, 3127,
3128, 3129, 3130, 3131, 3133, 3134, 3137,
3140, 3142, 3144, 3145, 3147, 3149, 3152,
3154, 3157, 3158, 3164, 3165, 3166, 3167,
3169, 3170, 3171, 3172, 3173, 3175, 3177,
3184, 3185, 3188, 3189, 3192, 3194, 3196,
3197, 3198, 3203, 3206, 3207, 3211, 3212,
3215, 3216, 3218, 3219, 3221, 3222, 3227,
3228, 3229, 3232, 3233, 3234, 3235, 3237,
3238, 3240, 3242, 3245, 3246, 3247, 3248,
3252, 3253, 3254, 3256, 3257, 3258, 3259,
3266, 3268, 3270, 3271, 3275, 3277, 3278,
3279, 3281, 3282, 3284, 3285, 3286, 3287,
3289, 3291, 3293, 3294, 3298, 3299, 3300,
3301, 3302, 3303, 3304, 3305, 3306, 3308,
3310, 3311, 3312, 3317, 3320, 3321, 3322,
3323, 3325, 3326, 3327, 3328, 3329, 3330,
3331, 3332, 3333, 3338, 3342, 3344, 3345,
3346, 3347, 3348, 3350, 3351, 3354, 3355,
3356, 3358, 3359, 3360, 3361, 3362, 3363,
3364, 3365, 3366, 3367, 3368, 3369, 3370,
3371, 3372, 3373, 3374, 3375, 3376, 3377,
3378, 3379, 3380, 3381, 3382, 3383, 3388,
3389, 3390, 3392, 3393, 3394, 3395, 3397,
3399, 3400, 3401, 3402, 3403, 3404, 3407,
3408, 3409, 3410, 3411, 3412, 3415, 3419,
3420, 3421, 3422, 3423, 3424, 3425, 3426,
3429, 3430, 3431, 3433, 3436, 3440, 3441,
3442, 3443, 3444, 3445, 3446, 3447, 3449,
3450, 3451, 3452, 3453, 3455, 3456, 3457,
3458, 3461, 3462, 3463, 3466, 3467, 3468,
3469, 3470, 3471, 3472, 3473, 3474, 3475,
3476, 3479, 3480, 3481, 3482, 3483, 3484,
3485, 3487, 3488, 3489, 3490, 3492, 3493,
3494, 3495, 3496, 3501, 3502, 3503, 3504,
3505, 3507, 3508, 3509, 3511, 3512, 3513,
3514, 3515, 3516, 3517, 3518, 3519, 3520,
3521, 3524, 3525, 3528, 3529, 3530, 3531,
3533, 3534, 3535, 3536, 3537, 3538, 3539,
3540, 3541, 3543, 3544, 3545, 3546, 3547,
3548, 3550, 3551, 3552, 3554, 3555, 3556,
3557, 3559, 3560, 3561, 3563, 3564, 3565,
3566, 3567, 3568, 3569, 3570, 3571, 3572,
3574, 3575, 3576, 3577, 3578, 3580, 3581,
3582, 3583, 3584, 3589, 3590, 3591, 3595,
3597, 3598, 3599, 3601, 3602, 3604, 3605,
3606, 3607, 3608, 3609, 3610, 3611, 3612,
3613, 3614, 3616, 3617, 3618, 3620, 3621,
3622, 3623, 3624, 3625, 3626, 3627, 3628,
3630, 3631, 3632, 3633, 3634, 3635, 3636,
3637, 3638, 3639, 3641, 3642, 3643, 3644,

3645, 3647, 3648, 3649, 3651, 3653, 3654,
3655, 3656, 3658, 3659, 3660, 3661, 3662,
3664, 3666, 3668, 3669, 3671, 3672, 3673,
3674, 3675, 3676, 3680, 3681, 3682, 3683,
3684, 3685, 3686, 3688, 3691, 3692, 3694,
3696, 3699, 3700, 3701, 3702, 3703, 3705,
3707, 3708, 3710, 3711, 3712, 3715, 3716,
3717, 3718, 3719, 3720, 3721, 3722, 3723,
3724, 3725, 3726, 3727, 3728, 3729, 3730,
3731, 3732, 3733, 3734, 3735, 3736, 3737,
3738, 3739, 3740, 3741, 3742, 3743, 3745,
3746, 3747, 3748, 3749, 3750, 3751, 3752,
3755, 3756, 3757, 3760, 3761, 3762, 3763,
3765, 3766, 3768, 3769, 3770, 3771, 3772,
3773, 3774, 3775, 3776, 3779, 3780, 3782,
3783, 3784, 3785, 3786, 3787, 3788, 3789,
3792, 3794, 3795, 3796, 3798, 3799, 3800,
3802, 3805, 3806, 3807, 3808, 3809, 3810,
3811, 3812, 3813, 3814, 3815, 3816, 3817,
3818, 3820, 3823, 3824, 3825, 3826, 3827,
3829, 3830, 3831, 3833, 3835, 3836, 3837,
3839, 3840, 3841, 3842, 3843, 3844, 3845,
3846, 3847, 3848, 3850, 3851, 3852, 3854,
3855, 3857, 3858, 3859, 3860, 3861, 3862,
3863, 3864, 3865, 3866, 3867, 3868, 3870,
3871, 3872, 3873, 3874, 3875, 3876, 3877,
3879, 3880, 3881, 3882, 3883, 3884, 3885,
3886, 3887, 3888, 3889, 3890, 3891, 3893,
3894, 3896, 3899, 3900, 3902, 3903, 3908,
3909, 3910, 3911, 3912, 3913, 3914, 3915,
3916, 3917, 3920, 3921, 3922, 3923, 3925,
3926, 3927, 3929, 3930, 3931, 3932, 3933,
3935, 3936, 3938, 3939, 3940, 3943, 3944,
3946, 3947, 3950, 3951, 3952, 3953, 3957,
3958, 3959, 3960, 3961, 3962, 3964, 3965,
3966, 3968, 3969, 3970, 3971, 3973, 3976,
3977, 3978, 3979, 3982, 3983, 3984, 3985,
3986, 3987, 3988, 3989, 3990, 3991, 3992,
3997, 4000, 4004, 4006, 4009, 4014, 4015,
4016, 4017, 4018, 4019, 4022, 4027, 4035,
4038, 4041, 4044, 4045, 4052, 4056, 4058,
4061, 4062, 4063, 4064, 4065, 4067, 4068,
4069, 4070, 4072, 4073, 4080, 4083, 4086,
4087, 4092, 4093, 4104, 4112, 4115, 4117,
4118, 4122, 4130, 4177, 4178, 4179, 4183,
4215, 4254
Masters, 2, 4, 5, 9, 28, 30, 34, 36, 38, 46, 47, 52,
54, 56, 57, 61, 70, 83, 87, 90, 94, 97, 98, 104,
110, 113, 118, 139, 141, 144, 146, 148, 149,
157, 163, 168, 172, 175, 186, 187, 190, 191,
192, 193, 201, 202, 205, 215, 226, 227, 230,
231, 236, 240, 251, 252, 256, 262, 274, 282,
284, 296, 297, 312, 319, 324, 327, 330, 333,
334, 341, 342, 356, 357, 359, 368, 369, 375,

377, 384, 388, 395, 398, 400, 405, 417, 420,
425, 427, 432, 442, 449, 452, 458, 459, 463,
473, 474, 475, 485, 487, 497, 500, 501, 507,
508, 512, 513, 520, 522, 525, 532, 535, 538,
548, 551, 553, 554, 555, 563, 567, 574, 575,
576, 586, 588, 591, 597, 609, 611, 613, 614,
616, 617, 626, 627, 628, 634, 638, 639, 640,
641, 642, 644, 652, 655, 664, 666, 676, 678,
680, 681, 689, 690, 691, 704, 707, 708, 709,
717, 726, 732, 743, 744, 745, 753, 754, 755,
763, 764, 772, 773, 774, 789, 791, 806, 807,
818, 819, 828, 831, 842, 848, 849, 853, 857,
860, 864, 899, 901, 902, 909, 911, 914, 916,
916, 931, 938, 941, 948, 957, 961, 962, 963,
970, 994, 995, 1008, 1018, 1027, 1033, 1052,
1053, 1058, 1061, 1066, 1077, 1086, 1102, 1103,
1114, 1139, 1140, 1170, 1173, 1179, 1194, 1195,
1212, 1240, 1241, 1245, 1261, 1291, 1321,
1328, 1345, 1346, 1355, 1358, 1366, 1368,
1374, 1382, 1390, 1400, 1416, 1419, 1423,
1427, 1434, 1452, 1457, 1459, 1473, 1474,
1482, 1484, 1491, 1506, 1507, 1508, 1509,
1510, 1515, 1516, 1525, 1529, 1534, 1546,
1551, 1552, 1570, 1576, 1577, 1586, 1587,
1588, 1594, 1613, 1624, 1626, 1627, 1628,
1629, 1630, 1634, 1646, 1648, 1656, 1665,
1666, 1671, 1672, 1674, 1678, 1680, 1681,
1683, 1684, 1688, 1699, 1704, 1719, 1721,
1722, 1730, 1731, 1736, 1741, 1767, 1787,
1792, 1793, 1797, 1799, 1800, 1808, 1815,
1820, 1821, 1837, 1839, 1844, 1846, 1848,
1851, 1852, 1859, 1871, 1889, 1896, 1901,
1904, 1906, 1935, 1939, 1940, 1945, 1946,
1948, 1962, 1963, 1971, 1979, 1980, 1981,
1982, 1984, 1992, 1993, 2001, 2026, 2029,
2037, 2038, 2040, 2052, 2053, 2063, 2064,
2071, 2074, 2082, 2083, 2084, 2088, 2089,
2108, 2111, 2112, 2113, 2121, 2122, 2124, 2135,
2156, 2157, 2162, 2164, 2179, 2199, 2205,
2254, 2255, 2257, 2258, 2261, 2263, 2274,
2293, 2299, 2313, 2353, 2397, 2400, 2401,
2404, 2407, 2409, 2415, 2446, 2462, 2463,
2495, 2497, 2531, 2559, 2560, 2564, 2567,
2570, 2571, 2574, 2575, 2577, 2582, 2605,
2608, 2610, 2621, 2638, 2639, 2645, 2661,
2674, 2681, 2688, 2711, 2712, 2714, 2716,
2721, 2728, 2735, 2736, 2737, 2741, 2755,
2757, 2775, 2776, 2777, 2784, 2793, 2802,
2810, 2814, 2819, 2820, 2822, 2823, 2842,
2863, 2875, 2877, 2878, 2898, 2908, 2914,
2915, 2917, 2921, 2956, 2971, 2993, 3003,
3008, 3018, 3020, 3021, 3022, 3023, 3025,
3038, 3041, 3047, 3050, 3054, 3055, 3058,
3060, 3064, 3073, 3077, 3082, 3084, 3085,

3087, 3091, 3115, 3117, 3119, 3121, 3127, 3129, 3132, 3133, 3135, 3142, 3143, 3144, 3146, 3151, 3154, 3164, 3165, 3175, 3188, 3190, 3192, 3199, 3204, 3217, 3227, 3228, 3229, 3249, 3258, 3259, 3260, 3264, 3267, 3276, 3280, 3296, 3310, 3315, 3316, 3323, 3330, 3331, 3351, 3355, 3387, 3400, 3402, 3403, 3404, 3405, 3411, 3412, 3415, 3426, 3430, 3459, 3479, 3486, 3497, 3498, 3499, 3500, 3505, 3515, 3517, 3533, 3546, 3558, 3581, 3589, 3604, 3617, 3618, 3619, 3620, 3621, 3622, 3631, 3643, 3656, 3698, 3707, 3754, 3761, 3798, 3800, 3802, 3835, 3843, 3844, 3845, 3859, 3866, 3867, 3871, 3894, 3896, 3900, 3915, 3920, 3921, 3923, 3924, 3935, 3941, 3942, 3943, 3944, 3963, 3968, 3973, 3991, 4000, 4009, 4045, 4067, 4083

Masters 1st Year, 14, 111, 130, 136, 244, 295, 335, 336, 350, 479, 493, 534, 556, 564, 596, 608, 651, 682, 683, 725, 746, 747, 1081, 1082, 1083, 1084, 1085, 1087, 1185, 1350, 1471, 1472, 1524, 1579, 1580, 1658, 1659, 1703, 1724, 1725, 1849, 1850, 1900, 1942, 1943, 1998, 2030, 2031, 2087, 2114, 2115, 2214, 2319, 2522, 2616, 2687, 2716, 2870, 2975, 3229, 3595, 3764, 3949

Masters 2nd Year, 62, 136, 293, 294, 335, 373, 433, 434, 491, 492, 594, 595, 649, 650, 682, 722, 723, 746, 880, 1045, 1163, 1471, 1520, 1579, 1658, 1724, 1849, 1898, 1942, 1958, 2030, 2114, 2269, 2716, 2870, 3288, 3406, 3434, 3435, 3437, 3438, 3439, 3588, 3822, 3927

Masters 3rd Year, 62, 136, 293, 294, 373, 433, 434, 491, 492, 594, 595, 649, 650, 722, 723, 880, 1001, 1045, 1163, 1520, 1898, 1958, 2269, 2289, 2716, 2870, 3017, 3288, 3406, 3434, 3435, 3437, 3438, 3439, 3465, 3588, 3822

Post-Masters, 97, 118, 155, 189, 190, 274, 322, 818, 878, 903, 1061, 1149, 1307, 1321, 1415, 1533, 1568, 1674, 1718, 1808, 1854, 1933, 2024, 2064, 2090, 2260, 2403, 2573, 2574, 2624, 2688, 2707, 2714, 3065, 3134, 3188, 3324, 3403, 3404, 3426, 3505, 3511, 3604, 3613, 3620, 3663, 3690, 3761, 3907, 3934, 3973, 4045, 4073

Doctorate, 2, 5, 8, 20, 26, 28, 30, 37, 38, 40, 41, 42, 43, 47, 55, 57, 70, 78, 79, 87, 89, 90, 93, 97, 98, 108, 110, 115, 122, 134, 137, 138, 139, 140, 141, 142, 144, 148, 149, 160, 168, 181, 186, 187, 190, 191, 196, 197, 205, 215, 220, 221, 223, 226, 239, 240, 249, 250, 251, 252, 254, 256, 268, 270, 274, 281, 282, 284, 287,

288, 289, 298, 299, 307, 312, 313, 319, 324, 327, 330, 333, 334, 341, 342, 345, 356, 359, 362, 368, 369, 373, 375, 377, 384, 386, 388, 395, 398, 400, 405, 407, 419, 420, 421, 422, 423, 425, 427, 432, 436, 440, 442, 449, 452, 463, 473, 474, 475, 485, 487, 496, 497, 500, 501, 507, 512, 513, 519, 520, 522, 525, 526, 527, 528, 529, 532, 538, 540, 544, 548, 551, 553, 554, 555, 563, 567, 571, 574, 575, 576, 585, 586, 588, 591, 597, 601, 604, 609, 611, 613, 614, 615, 616, 617, 626, 627, 628, 634, 637, 638, 640, 641, 642, 644, 655, 659, 664, 666, 673, 675, 676, 678, 680, 681, 688, 689, 690, 692, 704, 707, 708, 709, 717, 726, 730, 732, 743, 744, 745, 752, 753, 754, 763, 764, 769, 772, 773, 781, 783, 784, 786, 789, 790, 793, 794, 804, 805, 806, 809, 813, 814, 816, 817, 818, 819, 823, 824, 826, 828, 829, 830, 831, 833, 840, 842, 844, 845, 846, 848, 849, 857, 858, 860, 861, 863, 873, 879, 884, 885, 887, 890, 892, 898, 899, 900, 902, 903, 906, 907, 910, 911, 915, 916, 916, 918, 924, 927, 928, 929, 931, 934, 937, 940, 942, 944, 946, 947, 948, 957, 960, 961, 962, 963, 964, 967, 969, 970, 973, 974, 978, 981, 984, 985, 988, 992, 994, 995, 1008, 1010, 1011, 1015, 1033, 1035, 1041, 1042, 1049, 1056, 1058, 1061, 1066, 1077, 1086, 1093, 1098, 1099, 1100, 1102, 1103, 1122, 1125, 1130, 1133, 1135, 1140, 1146, 1158, 1159, 1160, 1164, 1171, 1172, 1179, 1181, 1194, 1195, 1206, 1211, 1212, 1217, 1218, 1225, 1239, 1240, 1241, 1245, 1261, 1265, 1281, 1291, 1303, 1304, 1305, 1321, 1341, 1342, 1343, 1345, 1346, 1359, 1361, 1364, 1368, 1374, 1379, 1380, 1386, 1388, 1390, 1397, 1400, 1404, 1405, 1407, 1416, 1421, 1423, 1427, 1429, 1434, 1447, 1452, 1456, 1457, 1459, 1465, 1473, 1480, 1481, 1482, 1484, 1491, 1496, 1499, 1500, 1505, 1506, 1508, 1509, 1510, 1511, 1512, 1513, 1515, 1516, 1522, 1523, 1529, 1534, 1543, 1546, 1551, 1552, 1557, 1563, 1566, 1570, 1574, 1575, 1576, 1577, 1586, 1589, 1590, 1592, 1594, 1595, 1599, 1601, 1613, 1619, 1623, 1624, 1625, 1626, 1628, 1629, 1630, 1634, 1639, 1645, 1646, 1648, 1655, 1656, 1665, 1667, 1669, 1671, 1672, 1673, 1674, 1675, 1678, 1680, 1681, 1683, 1688, 1691, 1693, 1699, 1711, 1716, 1717, 1719, 1721, 1722, 1730, 1736, 1741, 1745, 1751, 1753, 1754, 1760, 1761, 1762, 1763, 1764, 1767, 1776, 1777, 1780, 1785, 1786, 1787, 1790, 1794, 1799, 1800, 1802, 1804, 1807, 1808, 1815, 1818, 1822, 1823, 1825, 1826, 1833,

1837, 1838, 1839, 1844, 1846, 1848, 1851, 1852, 1853, 1859, 1860, 1862, 1866, 1870, 1871, 1874, 1878, 1879, 1889, 1892, 1893, 1894, 1896, 1904, 1906, 1907, 1913, 1915, 1916, 1917, 1929, 1931, 1935, 1939, 1940, 1945, 1946, 1951, 1953, 1958, 1961, 1962, 1965, 1971, 1974, 1978, 1979, 1981, 1982, 1984, 1987, 1988, 1989, 1992, 1993, 1995, 2001, 2005, 2008, 2010, 2020, 2021, 2026, 2029, 2036, 2037, 2038, 2048, 2051, 2052, 2055, 2058, 2063, 2064, 2071, 2072, 2074, 2077, 2078, 2079, 2082, 2083, 2084, 2095, 2108, 2111, 2112, 2113, 2120, 2121, 2122, 2128, 2131, 2135, 2136, 2144, 2147, 2152, 2153, 2154, 2155, 2156, 2157, 2158, 2162, 2171, 2174, 2179, 2180, 2190, 2195, 2199, 2202, 2205, 2206, 2207, 2209, 2222, 2232, 2234, 2249, 2252, 2253, 2254, 2255, 2257, 2258, 2261, 2263, 2264, 2265, 2266, 2282, 2285, 2292, 2293, 2299, 2308, 2309, 2312, 2313, 2321, 2328, 2331, 2333, 2334, 2336, 2344, 2349, 2353, 2355, 2362, 2365, 2368, 2370, 2373, 2378, 2382, 2385, 2389, 2390, 2397, 2400, 2401, 2404, 2407, 2409, 2413, 2415, 2432, 2433, 2437, 2446, 2447, 2453, 2461, 2462, 2463, 2473, 2475, 2479, 2490, 2495, 2496, 2497, 2500, 2505, 2514, 2515, 2516, 2530, 2531, 2537, 2541, 2542, 2551, 2564, 2567, 2570, 2571, 2574, 2575, 2577, 2588, 2603, 2608, 2609, 2610, 2620, 2622, 2638, 2639, 2645, 2651, 2655, 2661, 2662, 2674, 2676, 2681, 2684, 2688, 2690, 2694, 2699, 2705, 2707, 2710, 2711, 2712, 2714, 2715, 2717, 2725, 2728, 2729, 2730, 2731, 2732, 2733, 2735, 2736, 2741, 2746, 2747, 2748, 2749, 2750, 2755, 2756, 2758, 2759, 2760, 2770, 2773, 2774, 2775, 2776, 2780, 2782, 2784, 2786, 2787, 2788, 2790, 2791, 2793, 2800, 2803, 2808, 2809, 2810, 2812, 2814, 2820, 2822, 2823, 2836, 2842, 2847, 2863, 2875, 2877, 2878, 2898, 2904, 2908, 2909, 2910, 2911, 2912, 2914, 2915, 2919, 2921, 2927, 2937, 2938, 2939, 2941, 2943, 2949, 2950, 2957, 2958, 2959, 2960, 2968, 2969, 2970, 2971, 2973, 2974, 2981, 2983, 2985, 3004, 3007, 3008, 3010, 3012, 3018, 3020, 3021, 3022, 3026, 3031, 3032, 3038, 3040, 3043, 3044, 3047, 3054, 3055, 3058, 3060, 3064, 3068, 3069, 3073, 3076, 3078, 3079, 3080, 3082, 3084, 3085, 3090, 3091, 3103, 3104, 3106, 3109, 3115, 3116, 3117, 3118, 3122, 3123, 3124, 3125, 3127, 3132, 3133, 3139, 3142, 3144, 3148, 3149, 3150, 3154, 3155, 3156, 3160, 3161, 3162, 3164, 3165, 3168,

3175, 3176, 3179, 3180, 3181, 3190, 3192, 3199, 3200, 3201, 3202, 3204, 3210, 3213, 3216, 3217, 3220, 3223, 3224, 3225, 3227, 3228, 3239, 3241, 3255, 3259, 3262, 3264, 3265, 3267, 3274, 3280, 3283, 3288, 3315, 3316, 3323, 3330, 3331, 3344, 3349, 3353, 3355, 3386, 3396, 3400, 3402, 3403, 3404, 3411, 3412, 3413, 3415, 3426, 3427, 3448, 3454, 3459, 3460, 3469, 3479, 3486, 3490, 3497, 3498, 3499, 3500, 3505, 3515, 3517, 3524, 3533, 3546, 3558, 3562, 3581, 3603, 3604, 3617, 3618, 3619, 3620, 3621, 3622, 3631, 3638, 3643, 3656, 3663, 3665, 3698, 3707, 3713, 3714, 3750, 3753, 3754, 3761, 3791, 3798, 3800, 3802, 3822, 3828, 3835, 3843, 3844, 3845, 3859, 3866, 3867, 3871, 3894, 3896, 3897, 3898, 3900, 3901, 3905, 3906, 3909, 3915, 3920, 3921, 3924, 3935, 3942, 3943, 3944, 3963, 3967, 3968, 3973, 3991, 4000, 4009, 4038, 4045, 4060, 4067, 4069, 4132

Doctorate 1st Year, 269, 295, 363, 479, 493, 531, 534, 592, 596, 647, 651, 720, 725, 822, 1524, 1610, 1703, 1739, 1867, 1900, 1932, 1968, 1991, 1998, 2023, 2060, 2081, 2087, 2137, 2310, 2518, 3229, 3595, 3764, 3878, 3949, 4071

Doctorate 2nd Year, 69, 143, 293, 294, 363, 433, 434, 435, 491, 492, 594, 595, 649, 650, 722, 723, 815, 874, 880, 945, 1520, 1532, 1610, 1739, 1771, 1772, 1867, 1898, 1968, 2060, 2137, 2269, 2789, 2928, 3027, 3096, 3229, 3231, 3406, 3434, 3435, 3437, 3438, 3439

Doctorate 3rd Year, 69, 92, 293, 294, 433, 434, 435, 491, 492, 594, 595, 649, 650, 722, 723, 815, 874, 880, 945, 1520, 1532, 1771, 1772, 1898, 1994, 2165, 2269, 2289, 2320, 2352, 2458, 2525, 2789, 2928, 2978, 2997, 2998, 2999, 3000, 3001, 3017, 3027, 3096, 3231, 3343, 3406, 3434, 3435, 3437, 3438, 3439, 3588, 3904

Doctorate 4th Year, 69, 92, 161, 293, 294, 433, 434, 491, 492, 594, 595, 649, 650, 722, 723, 815, 880, 945, 1520, 1898, 1994, 2165, 2269, 2289, 2320, 2352, 2458, 2525, 2789, 2978, 2997, 2998, 2999, 3000, 3001, 3343, 3406, 3434, 3435, 3437, 3438, 3439, 3588, 3904

Doctorate 5th Year, 69, 92, 161, 293, 294, 433, 434, 491, 492, 594, 595, 649, 650, 722, 723, 815, 880, 945, 1520, 1898, 1994, 2269, 2320, 2352, 2458, 2525, 2789, 2978, 2997, 2998, 2999, 3000, 3001, 3343, 3406, 3434, 3435, 3437, 3438, 3439, 3588, 3904

Post-Doctorate, 10, 71, 73, 79, 81, 97, 118, 131,

133, 134, 137, 140, 141, 155, 161, 178, 189, 190, 224, 235, 252, 274, 276, 280, 291, 293, 294, 298, 299, 300, 304, 314, 322, 325, 326, 332, 356, 362, 367, 395, 399, 407, 410, 421, 423, 433, 434, 436, 440, 475, 478, 491, 492, 494, 518, 545, 552, 562, 568, 576, 582, 594, 595, 599, 605, 612, 623, 628, 633, 649, 650, 657, 677, 693, 699, 709, 713, 722, 723, 724, 728, 756, 766, 768, 769, 770, 771, 772, 773, 775, 778, 779, 784, 786, 787, 792, 793, 795, 797, 799, 801, 802, 803, 804, 805, 809, 810, 812, 814, 817, 818, 819, 820, 821, 824, 827, 830, 831, 832, 833, 834, 835, 840, 848, 849, 858, 866, 868, 876, 877, 878, 879, 880, 882, 887, 888, 890, 896, 906, 908, 910, 915, 925, 926, 927, 928, 929, 934, 936, 937, 939, 942, 944, 946, 947, 961, 967, 968, 970, 972, 975, 979, 980, 984, 986, 987, 988, 992, 994, 995, 1010, 1011, 1015, 1017, 1036, 1040, 1041, 1042, 1049, 1056, 1061, 1075, 1080, 1089, 1090, 1093, 1102, 1103, 1115, 1116, 1133, 1135, 1137, 1149, 1151, 1156, 1157, 1158, 1159, 1160, 1162, 1164, 1181, 1188, 1190, 1194, 1195, 1203, 1211, 1215, 1217, 1218, 1239, 1240, 1241, 1265, 1270, 1302, 1303, 1304, 1305, 1307, 1321, 1340, 1345, 1346, 1364, 1368, 1369, 1376, 1377, 1378, 1379, 1380, 1386, 1388, 1401, 1404, 1405, 1406, 1409, 1410, 1415, 1417, 1418, 1420, 1427, 1429, 1480, 1492, 1501, 1502, 1515, 1517, 1520, 1522, 1523, 1531, 1533, 1539, 1549, 1568, 1571, 1573, 1574, 1575, 1578, 1589, 1590, 1591, 1596, 1597, 1599, 1601, 1606, 1616, 1617, 1619, 1633, 1649, 1657, 1667, 1668, 1674, 1675, 1685, 1691, 1696, 1697, 1702, 1705, 1707, 1718, 1720, 1723, 1733, 1737, 1743, 1746, 1747, 1748, 1750, 1752, 1753, 1755, 1756, 1760, 1774, 1777, 1778, 1780, 1781, 1782, 1784, 1785, 1786, 1788, 1789, 1790, 1794, 1802, 1805, 1808, 1810, 1813, 1822, 1823, 1824, 1825, 1840, 1841, 1845, 1847, 1853, 1854, 1859, 1860, 1863, 1866, 1870, 1871, 1873, 1877, 1880, 1883, 1898, 1899, 1908, 1909, 1915, 1918, 1923, 1924, 1927, 1933, 1936, 1938, 1941, 1947, 1949, 1952, 1953, 1961, 1964, 1966, 1970, 1971, 1973, 1977, 1992, 1994, 1995, 1997, 2002, 2006, 2024, 2027, 2028, 2039, 2046, 2048, 2051, 2054, 2056, 2057, 2061, 2063, 2064, 2065, 2069, 2070, 2082, 2086, 2090, 2092, 2098, 2108, 2123, 2125, 2126, 2128, 2131, 2141, 2145, 2146, 2147, 2159, 2160, 2166, 2178, 2186, 2189, 2192, 2196, 2202, 2208, 2213, 2215, 2216, 2217, 2222, 2224, 2260, 2270, 2291, 2306,

2307, 2318, 2322, 2323, 2324, 2325, 2326, 2328, 2331, 2334, 2337, 2339, 2351, 2356, 2358, 2359, 2360, 2363, 2364, 2366, 2367, 2369, 2371, 2384, 2386, 2387, 2388, 2392, 2394, 2395, 2396, 2403, 2405, 2406, 2408, 2411, 2412, 2417, 2418, 2419, 2420, 2423, 2425, 2426, 2432, 2434, 2435, 2436, 2438, 2439, 2440, 2443, 2448, 2449, 2450, 2451, 2452, 2455, 2457, 2458, 2459, 2460, 2464, 2468, 2472, 2473, 2474, 2476, 2477, 2478, 2480, 2481, 2482, 2483, 2484, 2486, 2489, 2491, 2493, 2496, 2498, 2502, 2503, 2504, 2505, 2506, 2507, 2509, 2510, 2511, 2512, 2513, 2519, 2520, 2521, 2523, 2524, 2526, 2530, 2531, 2532, 2537, 2541, 2543, 2547, 2548, 2566, 2573, 2574, 2578, 2603, 2615, 2624, 2641, 2660, 2676, 2707, 2714, 2723, 2724, 2725, 2726, 2735, 2736, 2743, 2748, 2749, 2751, 2752, 2753, 2759, 2761, 2763, 2767, 2769, 2771, 2772, 2773, 2774, 2780, 2781, 2785, 2787, 2791, 2792, 2795, 2808, 2809, 2810, 2811, 2822, 2823, 2864, 2899, 2901, 2904, 2905, 2906, 2909, 2914, 2915, 2925, 2931, 2932, 2934, 2935, 2941, 2945, 2946, 2947, 2949, 2950, 2951, 2952, 2957, 2962, 2963, 2966, 2967, 2968, 2969, 2970, 2972, 2979, 2980, 2981, 2983, 3006, 3009, 3016, 3021, 3022, 3026, 3029, 3032, 3035, 3065, 3084, 3085, 3099, 3100, 3106, 3107, 3109, 3120, 3134, 3138, 3141, 3150, 3159, 3164, 3165, 3168, 3174, 3182, 3183, 3187, 3188, 3199, 3202, 3203, 3205, 3213, 3217, 3227, 3228, 3236, 3244, 3261, 3262, 3264, 3266, 3269, 3280, 3323, 3324, 3335, 3336, 3337, 3340, 3349, 3383, 3391, 3400, 3402, 3403, 3404, 3414, 3416, 3417, 3418, 3426, 3434, 3435, 3437, 3438, 3439, 3505, 3506, 3510, 3511, 3526, 3527, 3546, 3558, 3594, 3604, 3613, 3617, 3619, 3620, 3621, 3622, 3646, 3663, 3665, 3670, 3689, 3690, 3697, 3737, 3750, 3761, 3790, 3804, 3866, 3867, 3895, 3904, 3907, 3913, 3934, 3973, 3991, 4004, 4044, 4045, 4060, 4061, 4067, 4068, 4073, 4118, 4122, 4132

Post-Graduate, 6, 11, 12, 32, 39, 40, 74, 84, 99, 100, 102, 108, 109, 112, 127, 145, 173, 189, 190, 196, 197, 204, 216, 229, 247, 248, 253, 275, 285, 312, 323, 329, 353, 354, 356, 361, 378, 383, 388, 395, 402, 406, 412, 428, 442, 454, 464, 472, 475, 476, 480, 483, 488, 497, 514, 523, 526, 548, 565, 576, 577, 589, 609, 610, 618, 620, 628, 629, 645, 653, 654, 664, 665, 668, 702, 709, 710, 718, 732, 734, 735, 736, 737, 761, 765, 777, 794, 796, 798, 819,

839, 850, 856, 858, 859, 865, 870, 903, 907,
910, 911, 935, 949, 950, 951, 952, 953, 954,
961, 965, 967, 999, 1000, 1020, 1021, 1022,
1028, 1030, 1032, 1044, 1050, 1060, 1064,
1074, 1077, 1104, 1111, 1112, 1113, 1127, 1144,
1145, 1176, 1181, 1196, 1200, 1211, 1212,
1213, 1219, 1222, 1226, 1254, 1268, 1276,
1286, 1290, 1319, 1349, 1367, 1371, 1372,
1385, 1387, 1393, 1403, 1412, 1413, 1414,
1424, 1425, 1427, 1428, 1433, 1441, 1444,
1454, 1458, 1459, 1460, 1461, 1462, 1463,
1469, 1470, 1485, 1487, 1490, 1519, 1528,
1544, 1547, 1548, 1550, 1554, 1555, 1556,
1569, 1598, 1632, 1635, 1640, 1647, 1649,
1650, 1651, 1652, 1654, 1689, 1692, 1712,
1713, 1714, 1759, 1768, 1773, 1791, 1801,
1809, 1816, 1832, 1836, 1843, 1847, 1856,
1857, 1859, 1860, 1871, 1872, 1881, 1882,
1890, 1902, 1921, 1922, 1934, 1937, 1938,
1957, 1961, 1971, 1972, 1985, 1999, 2013,
2025, 2028, 2042, 2043, 2045, 2047, 2051,
2059, 2062, 2063, 2075, 2101, 2108, 2110,
2127, 2131, 2132, 2149, 2182, 2201, 2202,
2213, 2219, 2220, 2243, 2247, 2260, 2273,
2278, 2279, 2283, 2286, 2295, 2301, 2304,
2311, 2318, 2335, 2357, 2397, 2398, 2403,
2406, 2410, 2424, 2444, 2465, 2466, 2467,
2469, 2470, 2471, 2485, 2494, 2499, 2501,
2520, 2528, 2529, 2533, 2534, 2535, 2536,
2550, 2573, 2574, 2586, 2603, 2615, 2618,
2619, 2633, 2640, 2652, 2676, 2682, 2720,
2729, 2730, 2744, 2760, 2762, 2766, 2794,
2796, 2797, 2798, 2799, 2801, 2805, 2830,
2837, 2866, 2879, 2898, 2900, 2903, 2908,
2916, 2920, 2922, 2923, 2933, 2934, 2935,
2948, 2954, 2955, 2964, 2987, 2989, 2991,
2992, 3002, 3014, 3030, 3049, 3089, 3095,
3101, 3128, 3131, 3140, 3158, 3170, 3191, 3195,
3197, 3198, 3206, 3207, 3208, 3209, 3211,
3234, 3254, 3268, 3270, 3271, 3272, 3273,
3275, 3298, 3312, 3323, 3324, 3342, 3371,
3372, 3403, 3404, 3408, 3409, 3413, 3414,
3415, 3416, 3419, 3428, 3436, 3440, 3442,
3443, 3463, 3477, 3478, 3485, 3487, 3488,
3508, 3509, 3516, 3538, 3546, 3560, 3592,
3593, 3596, 3601, 3623, 3635, 3636, 3644,
3671, 3739, 3740, 3745, 3755, 3766, 3774,
3799, 3812, 3816, 3851, 3852, 3866, 3867,
3873, 3874, 3875, 3876, 3877, 3881, 3894,
3899, 3900, 3907, 3911, 3918, 3925, 3936,
3937, 3959, 3982, 4007, 4035, 4038, 4062,
4065, 4067, 4072, 4104, 4117

DEGREES RECEIVED

Associates (AA/AS), 3687
Bachelors (BA/BS), 6, 66, 77, 82, 118, 158, 175,
212, 227, 244, 283, 285, 297, 316, 324, 335,
336, 341, 342, 373, 376, 378, 398, 414, 418,
426, 428, 431, 456, 469, 470, 475, 486, 488,
506, 507, 508, 521, 523, 551, 561, 572, 576,
587, 589, 608, 611, 615, 616, 619, 625, 628,
643, 645, 652, 676, 682, 683, 688, 689, 690,
691, 694, 703, 709, 716, 718, 746, 747, 752,
753, 754, 755, 757, 772, 773, 776, 807, 837,
848, 849, 862, 875, 893, 894, 904, 909, 931,
977, 994, 995, 1069, 1070, 1081, 1082, 1083,
1084, 1085, 1092, 1102, 1103, 1182, 1183, 1194,
1195, 1231, 1240, 1241, 1333, 1334, 1345,
1346, 1392, 1416, 1419, 1471, 1472, 1473,
1474, 1515, 1516, 1525, 1553, 1570, 1579,
1580, 1585, 1586, 1587, 1608, 1612, 1643,
1649, 1658, 1659, 1664, 1665, 1666, 1687,
1704, 1719, 1724, 1725, 1730, 1731, 1740,
1814, 1816, 1821, 1835, 1839, 1849, 1850,
1851, 1852, 1871, 1874, 1888, 1890, 1904,
1935, 1942, 1943, 1944, 1945, 1946, 1948,
1971, 1974, 1983, 1985, 1992, 1993, 2014,
2026, 2030, 2031, 2035, 2036, 2037, 2038,
2040, 2063, 2073, 2075, 2082, 2083, 2103,
2114, 2115, 2120, 2121, 2122, 2124, 2173, 2197,
2211, 2214, 2249, 2278, 2281, 2297, 2315,
2319, 2373, 2463, 2487, 2522, 2582, 2587,
2600, 2616, 2621, 2654, 2672, 2687, 2727,
2735, 2736, 2738, 2777, 2817, 2822, 2823,
2830, 2838, 2839, 2848, 2863, 2907, 2914,
2915, 2924, 2929, 2956, 3021, 3022, 3055,
3084, 3085, 3095, 3098, 3111, 3112, 3121,
3133, 3135, 3164, 3165, 3188, 3192, 3227,
3228, 3243, 3258, 3259, 3260, 3288, 3339,
3341, 3351, 3400, 3402, 3403, 3407, 3410,
3426, 3433, 3441, 3454, 3455, 3456, 3457,
3458, 3459, 3460, 3580, 3595, 3598, 3619,
3620, 3627, 3687, 3748, 3761, 3781, 3786,
3792, 3849, 3866, 3867, 3871, 3924, 3938,
3941, 3944, 3965, 3968, 4017
Bachelors of Science (BSc.), 1458, 1689
Registered Nurse (RN) 2169, 2173, 2188, 2233,
2235, 2281, 2390, 2462, 2480, 2587, 2645,
2648, 2654, 2666, 2669, 2677, 2682, 2688,
2689, 2693, 2695
Masters (MA/MS), 54, 188, 201, 276, 283, 285,
376, 378, 426, 428, 456, 457, 486, 488, 509,
521, 523, 587, 589, 619, 643, 645, 694, 716,
718, 757, 903, 932, 953, 1147, 1307, 1747,
1810, 1814, 1816, 1873, 1888, 1890, 1973,
1983, 1985, 2044, 2065, 2073, 2075, 2175,
2259, 2390, 2402, 2463, 2572, 2689, 2799,
2995, 3209, 3273, 3404, 3427, 3465, 3627,
3663, 3687, 3713, 3761
Master of Social Work (MSW), 3155, 3254
Master of Science (MSC), 1458
Doctor of Education (ED.D), 188, 1578, 1657,
1723, 1788, 1941, 2259, 2402, 2521, 2572,
3687
Juris Doctorate (JD), 167, 1430, 1618, 1744,
2142, 2813, 3016, 3072, 3153
Doctor of Philosophy (Ph.D), 26, 133, 167, 188,
276, 283, 285, 306, 376, 378, 426, 428, 457,
486, 488, 509, 521, 523, 587, 589, 643, 645,
655, 716, 718, 766, 770, 780, 801, 802, 803,
804, 821, 834, 868, 883, 925, 926, 927, 936,
953, 975, 980, 986, 1036, 1040, 1041, 1075,
1080, 1116, 1151, 1156, 1157, 1158, 1190, 1203,
1205, 1215, 1302, 1303, 1340, 1376, 1377,
1378, 1379, 1420, 1423, 1430, 1446, 1534,
1542, 1573, 1574, 1578, 1591, 1594, 1618,
1634, 1649, 1657, 1668, 1671, 1710, 1723,
1744, 1747, 1748, 1755, 1775, 1782, 1784,
1785, 1788, 1789, 1803, 1805, 1806, 1810,
1814, 1816, 1873, 1882, 1888, 1890, 1912,
1927, 1941, 1973, 1983, 1985, 2007, 2044,
2065, 2073, 2075, 2094, 2142, 2175, 2196,
2259, 2307, 2361, 2372, 2376, 2377, 2379,
2391, 2393, 2402, 2421, 2428, 2429, 2430,
2448, 2464, 2472, 2473, 2486, 2493, 2503,
2507, 2513, 2516, 2517, 2521, 2532, 2572,
2723, 2726, 2745, 2769, 2771, 2772, 2773,
2781, 2784, 2799, 2811, 2813, 2899, 2905,
2936, 2962, 2963, 2966, 2967, 2968, 2986,
2995, 3009, 3016, 3072, 3153, 3155, 3178,
3209, 3261, 3273, 3357, 3414, 3416, 3510,
3687, 3689
Doctor of Science (SC.D), 167, 276, 283, 285,
306, 376, 378, 426, 428, 486, 488, 521, 523,
587, 589, 643, 645, 655, 716, 718, 780, 821,
883, 1205, 1430, 1446, 1534, 1542, 1578,
1618, 1634, 1657, 1710, 1723, 1744, 1747,
1775, 1788, 1810, 1814, 1816, 1873, 1888,
1890, 1912, 1941, 1949, 1973, 1983, 1985,
2007, 2065, 2073, 2075, 2094, 2142, 2217,
2324, 2391, 2393, 2473, 2491, 2503, 2516,
2517, 2521, 2745, 2811, 2813, 2936, 3072,
3153, 3178
Doctor of Veterinary Med.(DVM), 1927, 1949,
2216, 2217, 2322, 2324, 2493
Doctor of Dental Science (DDS), 1949, 2216,
2217, 2322, 2324, 2356
Doctor of Osteopathy (DO), 1578, 1657, 1723,
1788, 1941, 1949, 2217, 2324, 2374, 2375,
2376, 2380, 2381, 2387, 2388, 2391, 2393,
2448, 2516, 2517, 2521, 2524

Doctor of Medicine (MD), 1578, 1657, 1723, 1788, 1927, 1941, 1949, 1956, 2145, 2146, 2169, 2173, 2175, 2186, 2188, 2196, 2216, 2217, 2224, 2226, 2233, 2281, 2322, 2324, 2361, 2372, 2374, 2375, 2376, 2380, 2381, 2386, 2387, 2387, 2388, 2391, 2392, 2393, 2398, 2420, 2421, 2428, 2429, 2430, 2448, 2449, 2450, 2459, 2464, 2472, 2473, 2480, 2486, 2491, 2493, 2503, 2507, 2516, 2517, 2521, 2524, 2532, 2566, 2587, 2648, 2654, 2669, 2693, 3155

ETHNIC BACKGROUND

Aboriginee/Indigenous, 3028, 3409, 3740

African American, 22, 23, 25, 28, 59, 90, 166, 174, 186, 191, 210, 249, 260, 267, 281, 306, 307, 309, 317, 319, 327, 330, 368, 369, 386, 394, 400, 420, 449, 473, 474, 496, 500, 512, 513, 540, 550, 553, 574, 575, 601, 613, 626, 627, 639, 659, 670, 672, 678, 707, 708, 730, 739, 740, 742, 743, 763, 764, 780, 781, 883, 884, 899, 1083, 1122, 1126, 1189, 1205, 1206, 1328, 1354, 1361, 1407, 1446, 1447, 1457, 1507, 1542, 1543, 1559, 1562, 1567, 1624, 1627, 1639, 1646, 1710, 1711, 1775, 1776, 1826, 1829, 1837, 1844, 1862, 1863, 1912, 1913, 1965, 1966, 1980, 2007, 2008, 2016, 2018, 2022, 2055, 2056, 2094, 2095, 2097, 2105, 2107, 2109, 2111, 2136, 2144, 2148, 2257, 2261, 2293, 2400, 2404, 2542, 2543, 2570, 2575, 2631, 2711, 2745, 2746, 2854, 2855, 2896, 2897, 2936, 2937, 3010, 3013, 3103, 3117, 3156, 3158, 3178, 3179, 3219, 3239, 3282, 3350, 3486, 3649, 3677, 3692, 3707, 3760, 3806, 3892, 3939, 3950, 3968, 3977, 4092

American Indian/Eskimo, 22, 23, 25, 28, 59, 90, 154, 174, 186, 191, 210, 249, 279, 306, 307, 309, 310, 317, 319, 330, 368, 369, 386, 394, 420, 473, 474, 496, 512, 513, 540, 550, 569, 574, 575, 601, 626, 627, 632, 639, 659, 670, 672, 707, 708, 730, 739, 740, 742, 763, 764, 780, 781, 871, 883, 884, 899, 1009, 1083, 1122, 1126, 1205, 1206, 1264, 1361, 1399, 1407, 1446, 1447, 1457, 1497, 1498, 1507, 1542, 1543, 1559, 1562, 1567, 1621, 1622, 1624, 1627, 1639, 1646, 1695, 1710, 1711, 1775, 1776, 1812, 1826, 1829, 1830, 1837, 1844, 1876, 1912, 1913, 1976, 1980, 2007, 2008, 2016, 2018, 2022, 2094, 2095, 2097, 2105, 2107, 2109, 2111, 2144, 2148, 2151, 2229, 2250, 2257, 2261, 2293, 2340, 2383, 2400, 2404, 2540, 2565, 2570, 2575, 2625, 2635, 2691, 2711, 2722, 2739, 2745, 2746, 2926,

2936, 2937, 3010, 3013, 3093, 3103, 3117, 3156, 3158, 3178, 3179, 3230, 3239, 3279, 3351, 3352, 3382, 3388, 3389, 3428, 3486, 3509, 3516, 3518, 3539, 3555, 3568, 3574, 3596, 3600, 3649, 3677, 3694, 3702, 3707, 3755, 3760, 3783, 3813, 3886, 3887, 3960, 4092

Arab, 1141

Asian, 22, 23, 25, 59, 174, 186, 191, 210, 211, 249, 306, 309, 317, 368, 369, 394, 473, 474, 512, 513, 574, 575, 626, 627, 639, 670, 672, 707, 708, 739, 740, 763, 764, 780, 883, 1126, 1205, 1446, 1507, 1542, 1559, 1562, 1627, 1710, 1775, 1829, 1912, 1980, 2007, 2016, 2018, 2094, 2097, 2105, 2107, 2144, 2148, 2257, 2261, 2400, 2404, 2570, 2575, 2597, 2668, 2745, 2936, 3010, 3013, 3156, 3158, 3178, 3242, 3649, 3677, 3707, 3760, 4092

Hispanic, 6, 22, 23, 24, 25, 59, 90, 174, 210, 249, 306, 307, 309, 317, 319, 330, 347, 368, 369, 386, 394, 473, 474, 496, 512, 513, 540, 550, 574, 575, 601, 626, 627, 639, 659, 670, 672, 707, 708, 730, 739, 740, 742, 763, 764, 780, 781, 883, 884, 899, 1083, 1122, 1126, 1205, 1206, 1361, 1368, 1407, 1446, 1447, 1457, 1507, 1542, 1543, 1559, 1562, 1567, 1627, 1639, 1646, 1710, 1711, 1775, 1776, 1826, 1829, 1837, 1844, 1855, 1912, 1913, 1980, 2007, 2008, 2016, 2018, 2022, 2094, 2095, 2097, 2105, 2107, 2109, 2111, 2148, 2161, 2271, 2278, 2293, 2414, 2579, 2642, 2711, 2745, 2746, 2830, 2936, 2937, 3010, 3013, 3095, 3103, 3117, 3158, 3178, 3179, 3239, 3421, 3552, 3591, 3649, 3675, 3677, 3707, 3760, 3952, 4092

Minority affiliation, 14, 17, 63, 117, 126, 130, 249, 330, 331, 451, 556, 662, 943, 1057, 1078, 1148, 1170, 1489, 1600, 1676, 1795, 1844, 1905, 1954, 2111, 2211, 2212, 2245, 2315, 2316, 2539, 2555, 2613, 2686, 2826, 2851, 2982, 3053, 3094, 3189, 3257, 3382, 3947, 4010, 4031, 4046, 4092, 4109

EXTRACURRICULAR ACTIVITIES

Athlete-College, 72, 2592, 2835, 3177, 3237, 3381, 3981, 4020

Athlete-High School, 3381, 3981, 4020

Athlete-NCAA, 3715, 3716, 3981, 4020

Aviation, 3853

Caddie or Golf, 3576, 4098

Community Service, 6, 67, 82, 101, 107, 135, 174, 210, 212, 233, 309, 875, 893, 894, 1126, 1643, 1829, 2097, 2198, 2278, 2488, 2673, 2830,

2838, 2839, 3056, 3095, 3111, 3112, 3136, 3186, 3232, 3243, 3247, 3251, 3263, 3381, 3677, 3717, 3776, 3809, 3956

Dog Shows, 3525

Harness Racing, 3584

Horsemanship, 3356, 3980

Inv.w/Asian/Pacif/Amer.comm'ty, 3385

Licensed Radio Amateur, 517, 580, 581, 2818, 3358, 3359, 3360, 3361, 3362, 3363, 3364, 3365, 3366, 3367, 3368, 3626

Licensed Radio Amateur-D-DEC, 517, 581, 2818

SCUBA Diving, 1732

School Clubs, 174, 210, 309, 350, 1126, 1829, 2097, 3381

Soccer, 3667

Student government, 82, 212, 350, 893, 894, 1643, 2838, 2839, 3111, 3112, 3243, 3381

FAMILY ANCESTRIES

African, 2855, 3950

American Indian, 3382, 3388, 3389, 3509, 3555, 3755, 3813

Arapaho Tribe (Northern), 3818

Arapaho Tribe of Oklah., 3471

Armenian, 36, 193, 2156, 2819, 3018, 3077, 3380, 3381, 3541, 3567, 3662, 4032

Cambodian, 3513

Canadian, 3556

Cheyenne Tribe of Oklah., 3471

Chinese, 211, 867, 2167, 2276, 2597, 2668, 3242, 3472

Choctaw Nation of Oklah., 3474

Cuban, 7, 68, 302, 2831, 3097

Cypriot, 3679, 3856

Danish, 3370, 3759

Finnish, 1220, 3370

French, 3556

Greek, 532, 1896, 2084, 2162, 2415, 3515, 3679, 3856

Hopi, 3428, 3596

Hualapai Tribe, 3600

Italian, 13, 121, 923, 1296, 2206, 2207, 2208, 2308, 2309, 2514, 2515, 2718, 3726, 3727, 3728, 3729, 3730, 3731, 3732, 3820, 3850, 3888

Japanese, 103, 176, 228, 912, 2193, 3042, 3248, 3396, 3632, 3633, 3634

Jewish, 875, 3545, 3643, 3863

Korean, 211, 2597, 2668, 3242, 3864

Laotian, 3513

Mexican/Hispanic, 24, 28, 186, 191, 307, 319, 347, 386, 420, 496, 540, 601, 659, 730, 781, 884, 1122, 1206, 1361, 1407, 1447, 1543, 1624, 1639, 1711, 1776, 1826, 1837, 1855,

1913, 2008, 2095, 2144, 2257, 2261, 2400, 2404, 2570, 2575, 2746, 2937, 3103, 3156, 3179, 3239, 3421, 3449, 3486, 3552, 3675, 3952

Miccosukee, 3554

Mongolian, 3705, 3706

Native Hawaiian, 25, 2148, 3013

Norwegian, 955, 3370

Oneida Tribe of Wisconsin, 3763

Pacific Islander, 59, 186, 191, 306, 307, 368, 369, 386, 473, 474, 496, 512, 513, 540, 574, 575, 601, 626, 627, 659, 707, 708, 730, 763, 764, 780, 781, 883, 884, 1083, 1122, 1205, 1206, 1361, 1407, 1446, 1447, 1542, 1543, 1639, 1710, 1711, 1775, 1776, 1826, 1912, 1913, 2007, 2008, 2094, 2095, 2144, 2257, 2261, 2400, 2404, 2570, 2575, 2745, 2746, 2936, 2937, 3103, 3156, 3158, 3178, 3179, 3239, 3649, 3760, 4092

Polish, 27, 2816, 3664, 3781, 3879

Puerto Rican, 25, 306, 307, 319, 386, 496, 540, 601, 659, 730, 780, 781, 883, 884, 1122, 1205, 1206, 1361, 1407, 1446, 1447, 1542, 1543, 1639, 1710, 1711, 1775, 1776, 1826, 1837, 1912, 1913, 2007, 2008, 2094, 2095, 2148, 2745, 2746, 2936, 2937, 3013, 3103, 3178, 3179, 3239, 3486

Scandinavian, 955, 3370

Seminole, 3554, 3813

Serbian, 3814, 3832

Shoshone Tribe (Wind River), 3815

Spanish (from Spain), 3552

Swedish, 3370

Vietnamese, 3513

Welsh, 1316, 3735, 3830

FOREIGN LANGUAGES SPOKEN

Bengali, 1192

Chinese, 921

Danish, 3511

Dutch, 3427

East Indian, 1192

English, 33, 52, 53, 77, 80, 98, 146, 160, 192, 224, 291, 407, 408, 436, 508, 666, 691, 755, 807, 853, 854, 879, 891, 902, 969, 1067, 1076, 1128, 1141, 1300, 1349, 1401, 1419, 1474, 1517, 1552, 1587, 1601, 1602, 1648, 1666, 1689, 1731, 1797, 1921, 1932, 1948, 2013, 2023, 2040, 2048, 2049, 2062, 2101, 2124, 2128, 2129, 2160, 2175, 2270, 2295, 2310, 2412, 2478, 2518, 2519, 2578, 2641, 2742, 2802, 2803, 2845, 2885, 2886, 2887, 2888, 2889, 2890, 2917, 2918, 2942, 2983, 2984, 2993, 3004, 3023, 3024, 3027, 3033, 3039,

3068, 3087, 3088, 3110, 3143, 3148, 3258, 3276, 3373, 3511, 3581, 3616, 3663, 3690, 3706

Finnish, 1220, 3616

French, 80, 145, 160, 313, 464, 891, 954, 969, 1060, 1141, 1219, 1319, 1485, 1833, 1957, 2190, 2478, 2479, 2720, 2758, 2827, 2844, 2885, 2942, 2987, 3004, 3027, 3033, 3039, 3068, 3110, 3148, 3373, 3427, 3457

German, 850, 886, 996, 1089, 1104, 1141, 1196, 1207, 1242, 2950, 3373, 3419, 3427, 3511, 3562, 3616, 3618

Hindi, 1192

Italian, 3627

Japanese, 910, 1211, 3373, 3690

Latin, 1089

Russian, 908, 3373

Spanish, 33, 1067, 2889, 3039, 3373, 3619, 3620, 3700, 3828

Swahili, 3373

Swedish, 3616

Tamil, 1192

Telugu, 1192

HONORS/AWARDS/CONTESTS

Giftd Vis/Performing Artist, 310, 996, 1009, 1025, 1055, 1242, 1247, 1249, 1250, 1264, 1273, 1283, 1294, 1310, 1312, 1317, 1830

Kansas Scholar, 3651

LEGAL CITY OF RESIDENCE

Atlanta GA, 3559

Aurora IL, 3397

Baltimore MD, 3464

Boston MA, 3534, 3579

Brooklyn NY, 295, 493, 534, 596, 651, 725, 1524, 1703, 1900, 1998, 2087

Chicago IL, 315, 1411, 1834, 2102

Chicopee MA, 3493

Detroit MI, 3541

Eliot ME, 2185, 2288, 2456, 2596, 2667, 3240

Enfield CT, 3494, 3631

Glendale CA, 3575

Greenland NH, 2185, 2288, 2456, 2596, 2667, 3240

Hudson MA, 3971

Jamestown NY, 3470

Kittery ME, 2185, 2288, 2456, 2596, 2667, 3240

La Canada/Flintridge CA, 3575

La Crescenta CA, 3575

Lodi CA, 3383

Long Island NY, 3692

Los Angeles CA, 129, 404, 3314

Lubbock TX, 3673

Montrose CA, 3575

N. Hampton NH, 2185, 2288, 2456, 2596, 2667, 3240

New Bedford MA, 3743

New Castle NH, 2185, 2288, 2456, 2596, 2667, 3240

New York NY, 3346, 3692

Newington NH, 2185, 2288, 2456, 2596, 2667, 3240

Parkersburg WV, 3870

Portsmouth NH, 2185, 2288, 2456, 2596, 2667, 3240

Rye NH, 2185, 2288, 2456, 2596, 2667, 3240

Springfield MA, 3491

St. Louis MO, 3709

Suffield CT, 3494, 3631

Verdugo City CA, 3575

Wakefield MA, 3476

Washington DC, 75, 1004, 1006, 1119, 1258, 3642

York ME, 2185, 2288, 2456, 2596, 2667, 3240

LEGAL REGION OF CITIZENSHIP

Africa, 250, 275, 476, 514, 577, 629, 692, 710, 765, 940, 1367, 1459, 1481, 1490, 1595, 1673, 1692, 1779, 1809, 1872, 1951, 1972, 2333, 2620, 2888, 3326, 3610, 3740, 3943

Asia, 211, 1367, 2597, 2668, 3242, 3393, 3874, 3881

British Commonwealth, 858, 1012, 1134, 1254, 1266, 1521, 1769, 1770, 2042, 2057, 2224, 2490, 2871, 3137, 3488, 3506, 3610, 3648, 3754, 3786

Caribbean, 8, 9, 93, 94, 790, 791, 900, 901, 2756, 2757, 2887, 3040, 3041, 3118, 3119, 3326, 3610, 3646, 3740, 3943

Central America, 8, 9, 93, 94, 790, 791, 900, 901, 1367, 2756, 2757, 2843, 3040, 3041, 3118, 3119, 3326, 3610, 3740, 3943

Europe, 66, 76, 292, 303, 382, 430, 490, 533, 543, 593, 603, 648, 721, 775, 1012, 1134, 1220, 1266, 1367, 1402, 1443, 1518, 1537, 1631, 1701, 1706, 1766, 1819, 1825, 1897, 1903, 1996, 2004, 2085, 2091, 2163, 2272, 2416, 2580, 2643, 2742, 2871, 2885, 2998, 3137, 3604, 3610, 3766, 3943

Far East, 2, 38, 282, 375, 425, 485, 520, 586, 642, 842, 991, 992, 1238, 1239, 1400, 1434, 1510, 1630, 1699, 2728, 2820, 3326, 3528, 3610, 3881, 3943

Middle East, 3326, 3610, 3943

North America, 104, 230, 345, 346, 914, 1884, 2069, 2843, 2871, 3137, 3249, 3943

Oceania/Pacific Rim, 3399, 3528, 3610, 3740,

3881

South America, 8, 9, 93, 94, 790, 791, 900, 901, 1367, 2756, 2757, 2843, 3040, 3041, 3118, 3119, 3326, 3610, 3740, 3943

South Asia, 2, 38, 282, 375, 425, 485, 520, 586, 642, 842, 991, 992, 1238, 1239, 1367, 1400, 1434, 1510, 1630, 1699, 2728, 2820, 3326, 3393, 3528, 3610, 3740, 3874, 3881, 3943

Southeast Asia, 2, 38, 282, 375, 425, 485, 520, 586, 642, 842, 991, 992, 1238, 1239, 1367, 1400, 1434, 1510, 1630, 1699, 1801, 2728, 2820, 3326, 3393, 3528, 3610, 3740, 3881, 3943

LEGAL COUNTRY OF CITIZENSHIP

Albania, 298, 300, 1404, 1406, 1822, 1824, 3739

Armenia, 298, 300, 1404, 1406, 1822, 1824

Australia, 111, 424, 773, 849, 989, 990, 995, 1094, 1095, 1103, 1195, 1235, 1236, 1237, 1241, 1254, 1346, 1412, 1413, 1414, 1461, 1462, 1463, 1516, 1529, 1554, 1555, 1556, 1650, 1651, 1652, 1712, 1713, 1714, 1825, 1993, 2083, 2336, 2406, 2407, 2622, 2690, 2736, 2823, 2915, 3022, 3059, 3085, 3134, 3165, 3200, 3228, 3292, 3399, 3402, 3409, 3411, 3415, 3739, 3936, 3937, 3943, 3949, 4235

Austria, 291, 996, 997, 1196, 1242, 1401, 1517, 1825, 2160, 2270, 2412, 2578, 2641, 3417, 3511, 3738

Azerbaijan, 298, 300, 1404, 1406, 1822, 1824

Bahamas, 1254, 1885, 2706, 3291

Bangladesh, 39, 1254

Barbados, 3646

Belarus, 298, 300, 1404, 1406, 1822, 1824, 3739, 3766

Belgium, 74, 298, 300, 332, 412, 818, 1061, 1321, 1404, 1406, 1418, 1822, 1824, 1825, 1845, 2744, 2933, 3030, 3101, 3511, 3738

Belize, 1428, 1487, 3646

Bosnia/Herzegovina, 3739

Brunei Darassulam, 1141, 3478

Bulgaria, 298, 300, 1404, 1406, 1822, 1824, 3511, 3739

Burma, 1222, 3766, 3852

Canada, 5, 32, 57, 61, 62, 96, 97, 123, 131, 132, 140, 141, 150, 151, 216, 224, 248, 251, 252, 260, 297, 298, 300, 313, 324, 325, 332, 345, 346, 398, 399, 412, 418, 432, 462, 551, 552, 611, 612, 637, 652, 676, 677, 715, 758, 812, 813, 839, 857, 860, 886, 938, 999, 1062, 1082, 1084, 1085, 1086, 1087, 1147, 1148, 1162, 1171, 1207, 1254, 1295, 1307, 1308, 1404, 1406, 1416, 1417, 1418, 1437, 1476, 1505,

1525, 1551, 1570, 1571, 1625, 1704, 1719, 1720, 1767, 1772, 1821, 1822, 1824, 1833, 1839, 1840, 1845, 1885, 1935, 1936, 1947, 1978, 2000, 2026, 2027, 2039, 2069, 2123, 2190, 2191, 2196, 2215, 2220, 2245, 2246, 2268, 2283, 2294, 2306, 2353, 2390, 2420, 2421, 2479, 2484, 2485, 2486, 2529, 2531, 2582, 2598, 2619, 2621, 2644, 2645, 2646, 2670, 2706, 2708, 2758, 2785, 2786, 2827, 2843, 2844, 2845, 2863, 2864, 2921, 2973, 3026, 3028, 3091, 3092, 3158, 3166, 3198, 3199, 3264, 3291, 3330, 3395, 3432, 3453, 3454, 3455, 3456, 3457, 3458, 3459, 3460, 3461, 3499, 3502, 3511, 3538, 3558, 3610, 3616, 3617, 3618, 3619, 3620, 3621, 3622, 3645, 3646, 3680, 3701, 3714, 3765, 3828, 3897, 3898, 3902

China, 39, 921, 3478, 3511, 3705, 3739, 3875, 3949

Colombia, 1428, 1487

Costa Rica, 1428, 1487, 3646

Croatia, 3739

Cuba, 3646

Cyprus, 3478, 3679, 3856

Czech Republic, 298, 300, 881, 1357, 1404, 1406, 1822, 1824, 3511, 3739

Denmark, 74, 298, 300, 332, 412, 818, 1061, 1321, 1404, 1406, 1418, 1822, 1824, 1845, 2744, 2933, 3030, 3101, 3371, 3738, 3835, 3848

Dominica, 1254

Dominican Rep., 1428, 1487, 3646

Egypt, 838, 1141, 1758, 3222, 3511, 3739

El Salvador, 1428, 1487, 3646

Estonia, 298, 300, 1404, 1406, 1822, 1824, 3739

Fiji, 39, 1254

Finland, 3371, 3511, 3604, 3738, 3835

France, 74, 298, 300, 332, 412, 818, 1061, 1321, 1404, 1406, 1418, 1822, 1824, 1825, 1845, 2744, 2933, 3030, 3101, 3483, 3604, 3738

Gabon, 39

Gambia, 1254, 1588, 3487

Georgia, 298, 300, 1404, 1406, 1822, 1824, 3739

Germany, 74, 298, 300, 332, 412, 818, 1061, 1321, 1404, 1406, 1418, 1822, 1824, 1825, 1845, 2744, 2933, 3030, 3101, 3335, 3336, 3337, 3511, 3604, 3738

Ghana, 1254, 1588, 3487

Greece, 74, 298, 300, 332, 412, 532, 1404, 1406, 1418, 1822, 1824, 1825, 1845, 1896, 2084, 2162, 2415, 2744, 2933, 3030, 3101, 3511, 3604, 3738, 3856

Grenada, 1254

Guatemala, 1428, 1487, 3646

Haiti, 3646

Honduras, 1428, 1487, 3646

Hungary, 298, 300, 1404, 1406, 1822, 1824, 3511, 3604, 3739

Iceland, 298, 300, 332, 412, 811, 1404, 1406, 1418, 1822, 1824, 1825, 1845, 3371, 3511, 3738, 3835

India, 39, 1254, 1588, 3478, 3487, 3594, 3739, 3837, 3949

Indonesia, 39, 3478, 3739, 3876, 3949

Iran, 39, 1141

Iraq, 1141

Ireland, 74, 443, 1012, 1019, 1134, 1143, 1266, 1275, 1280, 1825, 2547, 2744, 2933, 3030, 3101, 3604, 3738

Israel, 976, 1012, 1134, 1230, 1266, 2815, 3511, 3603, 3739

Italy, 74, 99, 100, 298, 300, 332, 412, 796, 818, 1020, 1021, 1061, 1144, 1145, 1276, 1321, 1371, 1372, 1404, 1406, 1418, 1822, 1824, 1825, 1845, 2744, 2762, 2933, 2954, 2955, 3030, 3101, 3511, 3604, 3738

Jamaica, 1254, 1588, 3487, 3646

Japan, 39, 314, 797, 1410, 2192, 2482, 2763, 3138, 3392, 3393, 3394, 3396, 3478, 3511, 3690, 3739, 3881, 3949

Jordan, 1141, 3739

Kazakhstan, 298, 300, 1404, 1406, 1822, 1824

Kenya, 1254

Korea (North), 3876, 3949

Korea (South), 39, 77, 3876, 3949

Kuwait, 1141

Kyrgyzstan, 298, 300, 1404, 1406, 1822, 1824

Latvia, 298, 300, 1404, 1406, 1822, 1824, 3739

Libya, 1141

Liechtenstein, 1825

Lithuania, 298, 300, 1404, 1406, 1822, 1824, 3739

Luxemburg, 74, 298, 300, 332, 412, 818, 1061, 1321, 1404, 1406, 1418, 1822, 1824, 1845, 2744, 2933, 3030, 3101, 3738

Macedonia, 298, 300, 1404, 1406, 1822, 1824, 3739

Malawi, 1254, 1588, 3487

Malaysia, 39, 1254, 1588, 3478, 3487, 3876, 3949

Malta, 1254, 1825

Mexico, 8, 9, 93, 94, 152, 345, 346, 354, 637, 715, 790, 791, 900, 901, 1425, 1428, 1487, 1505, 1625, 1857, 1885, 1978, 2069, 2189, 2621, 2706, 2756, 2757, 2805, 2843, 3040, 3041, 3118, 3119, 3291, 3610, 3739

Moldova, 298, 300, 1404, 1406, 1822, 1824

Mongolia, 39, 793, 793, 906, 906, 2759, 2759,

3705, 3766
Morocco, 3739
Mozambique, 1254
Nepal, 39
Netherlands, 74, 298, 300, 332, 412, 818, 1061,
1321, 1404, 1406, 1418, 1822, 1824, 1825,
1845, 2744, 2933, 3030, 3101, 3604
New Zealand, 111, 1254, 1609, 3134, 3399, 3415,
3932, 3936, 3942, 3943
Nicaragua, 1428, 1487, 3646
Nigeria, 1254, 1588, 3487
Norway, 11, 102, 298, 300, 332, 412, 668, 956,
1022, 1404, 1406, 1418, 1822, 1824, 1825,
1845, 3371, 3738, 3835, 3866
Pakistan, 39, 1254, 1588, 3478, 3487
Panama, 1428, 1487, 3646
Papua New Guinea, 1254, 3399
Philippines, 39, 3949
Poland, 292, 298, 300, 382, 430, 490, 533, 593,
648, 721, 1402, 1404, 1406, 1443, 1518, 1631,
1701, 1766, 1819, 1822, 1824, 1897, 1996,
2085, 2163, 2272, 2416, 2580, 2643, 3511,
3663, 3739
Portugal, 74, 298, 299, 300, 332, 412, 1404,
1405, 1406, 1418, 1822, 1823, 1824, 1825,
1845, 2744, 2933, 3030, 3101, 3511, 3738
Romania, 298, 300, 1404, 1406, 1822, 1824,
3739
Russia, 10, 298, 300, 792, 1404, 1406, 1822,
1824, 3120, 3528, 3739, 3766
Samoa, 1254, 1588, 3487
Saudi Arabia, 1141
Sierra Leone, 1588, 3487
Singapore, 39, 1254, 2519, 3478, 3949
Slovakia, 298, 300, 1404, 1406, 1822, 1824, 3739
Slovenia, 298, 300, 1404, 1406, 1822, 1824,
3739
South Africa, 323, 475, 576, 628, 709, 1254,
1469, 1569, 1871, 1934, 1971, 2025, 2063,
2110, 2311, 2337, 2496, 2497, 2498, 2652
Spain, 298, 300, 332, 412, 1404, 1406, 1418,
1453, 1822, 1824, 1825, 1845, 3511, 3738
Sri Lanka, 39, 1254, 1588, 3487
St. Kitts/Nevis, 3646
St. Lucia, 3646
St. Vincent/Grenadines, 3646
Swaziland, 1254
Sweden, 1825, 3371, 3738, 3835
Switzerland, 1825, 3604
Syria, 1141
Taiwan, 932, 3478, 3949
Tajikistan, 298, 300, 1404, 1406, 1822, 1824
Tanzania, 1254, 1588, 3487
Thailand, 39, 139, 563, 617, 3058, 3478, 3876,

3949
Tonga, 1254
Trinidad & Tobago, 1588, 3487, 3646
Turkey, 298, 300, 332, 412, 1404, 1406, 1418,
1822, 1824, 1825, 1845, 3478, 3511, 3739
Turkmenistan, 298, 300, 1404, 1406, 1822, 1824
Uganda, 1254, 1588, 3487
Ukraine, 298, 300, 1404, 1406, 1822, 1824,
3739, 3766, 3845
United Arab Emirates, 1141
United Kingdom, 12, 66, 74, 105, 109, 110, 293,
294, 298, 300, 332, 353, 355, 409, 412, 433,
434, 438, 465, 491, 492, 510, 565, 566, 594,
595, 620, 621, 649, 650, 697, 722, 723, 737,
759, 806, 818, 856, 858, 990, 1012, 1050, 1061,
1094, 1111, 1134, 1213, 1254, 1262, 1266,
1267, 1268, 1280, 1321, 1348, 1385, 1404,
1406, 1418, 1424, 1426, 1448, 1486, 1519,
1520, 1596, 1605, 1682, 1733, 1735, 1798,
1822, 1824, 1825, 1845, 1846, 1856, 1858,
1898, 1952, 1960, 2050, 2125, 2130, 2273,
2490, 2499, 2547, 2744, 2775, 2920, 2933,
3030, 3045, 3089, 3101, 3127, 3323, 3434,
3435, 3437, 3438, 3439, 3440, 3442, 3477,
3478, 3485, 3560, 3603, 3627, 3648, 3655,
3656, 3738, 3786, 3816, 3846, 3847, 3849,
3851, 3853, 3869, 3872, 3894, 3900, 3912,
3913, 3915, 3916, 3926, 4117, 4241
United States, 1, 4, 6, 8, 9, 14, 16, 22, 23, 24, 25,
27, 28, 32, 33, 40, 41, 42, 43, 44, 45, 50, 52,
53, 56, 70, 74, 79, 90, 93, 94, 96, 97, 103, 112,
115, 116, 122, 123, 125, 126, 127, 129, 130,
132, 135, 140, 148, 154, 160, 163, 164, 171,
172, 174, 175, 176, 184, 186, 191, 191, 197,
199, 202, 209, 210, 213, 214, 216, 224, 227,
228, 229, 236, 244, 248, 249, 255, 256, 260,
261, 272, 274, 276, 277, 278, 280, 285, 286,
287, 288, 289, 290, 296, 298, 300, 301, 305,
306, 307, 309, 311, 317, 318, 319, 326, 328,
329, 331, 332, 333, 334, 335, 336, 337, 338,
339, 340, 341, 342, 344, 345, 346, 356, 362,
363, 364, 365, 368, 369, 372, 373, 374, 378,
379, 381, 384, 385, 386, 394, 401, 402, 404,
405, 410, 412, 414, 415, 416, 418, 420, 422,
423, 428, 429, 431, 435, 439, 440, 446, 450,
451, 452, 453, 462, 471, 473, 474, 477, 478,
488, 489, 495, 496, 499, 501, 502, 503, 504,
505, 506, 507, 508, 512, 513, 515, 516, 518,
523, 524, 527, 528, 529, 530, 531, 535, 538,
539, 540, 550, 554, 555, 556, 557, 558, 559,
560, 561, 568, 569, 570, 573, 574, 575, 578,
579, 582, 589, 590, 592, 597, 600, 601, 614,
615, 616, 623, 626, 627, 630, 631, 633, 637,
639, 645, 646, 647, 658, 659, 670, 672, 673,

674, 675, 679, 680, 681, 682, 683, 684, 685,
686, 687, 688, 689, 690, 691, 699, 701, 707,
708, 711, 712, 713, 715, 718, 719, 720, 726,
729, 730, 739, 740, 741, 742, 744, 745, 746,
747, 748, 749, 750, 751, 752, 753, 754, 755,
758, 763, 764, 766, 767, 768, 774, 780, 781,
782, 786, 790, 791, 793, 795, 798, 807, 808,
814, 815, 819, 825, 826, 827, 829, 831, 837,
839, 840, 844, 845, 846, 847, 850, 851, 853,
854, 861, 874, 883, 884, 886, 887, 888, 890,
899, 900, 901, 906, 908, 909, 911, 912, 916,
930, 938, 944, 945, 946, 955, 957, 959, 960,
964, 965, 966, 969, 971, 977, 978, 979, 980,
985, 988, 992, 1007, 1008, 1011, 1032, 1035,
1049, 1068, 1069, 1073, 1080, 1082, 1084,
1085, 1086, 1087, 1089, 1092, 1093, 1098,
1099, 1100, 1101, 1104, 1121, 1122, 1124, 1126,
1132, 1133, 1147, 1148, 1168, 1171, 1180, 1182,
1186, 1187, 1191, 1192, 1193, 1198, 1201,
1202, 1205, 1206, 1207, 1208, 1212, 1218,
1223, 1224, 1225, 1226, 1227, 1231, 1239,
1260, 1261, 1265, 1271, 1290, 1295, 1308,
1325, 1326, 1328, 1330, 1333, 1339, 1340,
1341, 1342, 1343, 1344, 1361, 1362, 1363,
1364, 1367, 1383, 1384, 1386, 1396, 1398,
1404, 1406, 1407, 1408, 1418, 1419, 1427,
1429, 1432, 1437, 1446, 1447, 1450, 1457,
1467, 1468, 1471, 1472, 1473, 1474, 1476,
1495, 1500, 1502, 1505, 1507, 1511, 1512,
1513, 1514, 1530, 1532, 1540, 1542, 1543,
1559, 1562, 1567, 1576, 1577, 1578, 1579,
1580, 1581, 1582, 1583, 1584, 1585, 1586,
1587, 1606, 1607, 1610, 1620, 1623, 1624,
1625, 1627, 1639, 1646, 1656, 1657, 1658,
1659, 1660, 1661, 1662, 1663, 1664, 1665,
1666, 1681, 1685, 1686, 1694, 1697, 1708,
1710, 1711, 1721, 1722, 1723, 1724, 1725,
1726, 1727, 1728, 1729, 1730, 1731, 1737,
1739, 1745, 1746, 1747, 1748, 1749, 1754,
1760, 1762, 1763, 1764, 1765, 1771, 1772,
1775, 1776, 1777, 1787, 1788, 1808, 1810,
1811, 1813, 1816, 1817, 1820, 1822, 1824,
1826, 1828, 1829, 1836, 1837, 1841, 1842,
1843, 1845, 1848, 1849, 1850, 1851, 1852,
1859, 1861, 1862, 1863, 1866, 1867, 1868,
1873, 1874, 1875, 1879, 1883, 1885, 1890,
1891, 1892, 1893, 1894, 1895, 1901, 1910,
1912, 1913, 1924, 1926, 1927, 1930, 1932,
1939, 1940, 1941, 1942, 1943, 1944, 1945,
1946, 1948, 1949, 1964, 1965, 1966, 1968,
1973, 1974, 1975, 1977, 1978, 1980, 1985,
1986, 1987, 1988, 1989, 1990, 1991, 2007,
2008, 2011, 2016, 2017, 2018, 2019, 2022,
2023, 2029, 2030, 2031, 2032, 2033, 2034,

2035, 2036, 2037, 2038, 2040, 2041, 2054,
2055, 2056, 2060, 2064, 2065, 2066, 2067,
2068, 2069, 2070, 2075, 2076, 2077, 2078,
2079, 2080, 2081, 2088, 2093, 2094, 2095,
2097, 2105, 2106, 2107, 2109, 2112, 2113, 2114,
2115, 2116, 2117, 2118, 2119, 2120, 2121, 2122,
2124, 2134, 2136, 2137, 2138, 2139, 2143,
2144, 2148, 2154, 2164, 2172, 2173, 2175,
2182, 2185, 2187, 2191, 2193, 2201, 2205,
2210, 2212, 2214, 2216, 2217, 2220, 2223,
2229, 2230, 2232, 2239, 2242, 2245, 2246,
2249, 2255, 2257, 2261, 2261, 2264, 2265,
2266, 2267, 2268, 2274, 2278, 2280, 2281,
2286, 2288, 2290, 2293, 2294, 2301, 2310,
2314, 2316, 2319, 2321, 2322, 2324, 2326,
2332, 2339, 2340, 2341, 2344, 2347, 2351,
2358, 2359, 2361, 2362, 2373, 2386, 2387,
2388, 2389, 2390, 2391, 2392, 2393, 2400,
2404, 2404, 2456, 2474, 2492, 2493, 2518,
2521, 2522, 2529, 2539, 2540, 2542, 2543,
2544, 2549, 2566, 2567, 2570, 2575, 2575,
2587, 2590, 2590, 2596, 2598, 2605, 2607,
2608, 2611, 2613, 2616, 2619, 2621, 2623,
2625, 2626, 2629, 2653, 2654, 2656, 2656,
2667, 2670, 2681, 2686, 2687, 2691, 2692,
2698, 2703, 2706, 2711, 2719, 2722, 2723,
2727, 2730, 2731, 2732, 2733, 2734, 2737,
2744, 2745, 2746, 2749, 2756, 2757, 2759,
2761, 2766, 2776, 2778, 2787, 2789, 2806,
2808, 2816, 2830, 2843, 2858, 2866, 2872,
2878, 2881, 2883, 2890, 2892, 2899, 2907,
2909, 2910, 2911, 2912, 2913, 2917, 2918,
2928, 2933, 2936, 2937, 2940, 2941, 2956,
2964, 2971, 2994, 3004, 3005, 3011, 3013,
3016, 3019, 3023, 3024, 3025, 3030, 3032,
3034, 3040, 3041, 3042, 3049, 3053, 3054,
3056, 3061, 3062, 3068, 3069, 3071, 3076,
3078, 3079, 3080, 3081, 3086, 3087, 3088,
3095, 3096, 3101, 3103, 3106, 3107, 3108, 3109,
3117, 3118, 3119, 3121, 3128, 3130, 3131, 3132,
3136, 3138, 3144, 3145, 3148, 3149, 3150,
3151, 3152, 3156, 3157, 3158, 3158, 3160,
3161, 3162, 3163, 3171, 3178, 3179, 3189,
3190, 3198, 3216, 3223, 3224, 3225, 3226,
3229, 3231, 3239, 3240, 3248, 3256, 3257,
3258, 3263, 3279, 3287, 3288, 3289, 3291,
3294, 3296, 3312, 3314, 3315, 3318, 3327,
3339, 3340, 3341, 3342, 3343, 3344, 3347,
3348, 3349, 3351, 3352, 3354, 3366, 3367,
3369, 3372, 3373, 3374, 3385, 3390, 3391,
3421, 3427, 3429, 3430, 3433, 3437, 3441,
3443, 3446, 3451, 3465, 3472, 3482, 3484,
3486, 3489, 3492, 3494, 3506, 3511, 3516,
3521, 3528, 3531, 3533, 3535, 3539, 3552,

3557, 3559, 3561, 3563, 3565, 3567, 3569,
3588, 3591, 3600, 3605, 3606, 3607, 3608,
3609, 3625, 3628, 3632, 3633, 3634, 3636,
3639, 3642, 3643, 3645, 3646, 3650, 3652,
3658, 3660, 3664, 3667, 3669, 3670, 3681,
3686, 3692, 3695, 3699, 3703, 3704, 3706,
3709, 3710, 3711, 3735, 3737, 3745, 3752,
3758, 3767, 3768, 3776, 3777, 3778, 3781,
3782, 3783, 3784, 3792, 3793, 3794, 3796,
3802, 3806, 3809, 3813, 3819, 3820, 3821,
3824, 3831, 3836, 3838, 3841, 3856, 3860,
3864, 3867, 3878, 3879, 3880, 3885, 3886,
3887, 3888, 3889, 3891, 3893, 3928, 3939,
3946, 3947, 3948, 3951, 3953, 3960, 3964,
3967, 3976, 3977, 3978, 3979, 3982, 3983,
3989, 3990, 4027, 4065, 4091
Uzbekistan, 298, 300, 1404, 1406, 1822, 1824
Vanuatu, 1254
Venezuela, 1428, 1487
Vietnam, 3478
Yemen, 1141
Yugoslavia, 3511, 3766
Zambia, 1254, 1588, 3487
Zimbabwe, 3426

LEGAL COUNTY OF RESIDENCE

Alameda CA, 3862
Barnstable MA, 1023, 1278, 2176, 2284, 2441,
    2591, 2657, 3305
Bergen NJ, 3692
Berkshire MA, 3494, 3631
Big Horn MT, 3524
Brevard FL, 3667
Bucks PA, 2826
Burgundy Region FRANCE, 145, 464, 954, 1060,
    1219, 1319, 1485, 1957, 2720, 2987
Campbell WY, 3524
Clark NV, 3850
Columbiana OH, 2168, 2277, 2427, 2583, 2647
Contra Costa CA, 3858, 3862
Converse WY, 3503
Cook IL, 315, 1411, 1834, 2102, 2194, 2296,
    2599, 2671, 3250
Dupage IL, 2174, 2282, 2437, 2588, 2655
Dutchess NY, 3692
El Paso TX, 344, 453, 1384, 2041, 2223, 2332,
    3535
Escambia FL, 1360, 2181, 2593, 2594, 2663, 2664
Essex NJ, 3692
Fairfield CT, 3692
Franklin MA, 3494, 3495, 3631
Hampden MA, 3494, 3495, 3597, 3598, 3631
Hampshire MA, 3494, 3495, 3631
Hudson NJ, 3692

Humboldt CA, 3602
Hunterdon NJ, 3692
Johnson WY, 3524
Kendall IL, 3397
Kent MI, 3859, 3860
Kern CA, 3599
Lorain OH, 3490
Los Angeles CA, 129, 404, 2850, 2851, 2852,
    3314, 3643
Lubbock TX, 3673
Marin CA, 3444, 3638, 3639, 3640, 3641, 3681,
    3862
Middlesex NJ, 3692
Monmouth NJ, 3692
Morris NJ, 3692
Napa CA, 3858, 3862
Nassau NY, 295, 493, 534, 596, 651, 725, 1524,
    1703, 1900, 1998, 2087
Ocean NJ, 3692
Okalossa FL, 1360, 2181, 2593, 2594, 2663, 2664
Orange CA, 2850, 2851, 2852
Orange FL, 3667
Orange NY, 3692
Osceola FL, 3667
Passaic NJ, 3692
Powder River MT, 3524
Putnam NY, 3692
Queens NY, 295, 493, 534, 596, 651, 725, 1524,
    1703, 1900, 1998, 2087
Richmond NY, 3692
Rockland NY, 3692
Rosebud MT, 3524
Ross OH, 3778
Sacramento CA, 3858
San Diego CA, 2161, 2271, 2414, 2579, 2642
San Francisco CA, 3638, 3639, 3640, 3641, 3862
San Joaquin CA, 3858
San Mateo CA, 3638, 3639, 3640, 3641, 3776,
    3862
Santa Clara CA, 3638, 3639, 3640, 3641, 3776,
    3862
Santa Rosa FL, 1360, 2181, 2593, 2594, 2663,
    2664
Schuykill PA, 3585
Seminole FL, 3667
Shasta CA, 3569
Sheridan WY, 3524
Solano CA, 3858, 3862
Somerset NJ, 3692
Sonoma CA, 145, 464, 954, 1060, 1219, 1319,
    1485, 1957, 2720, 2987, 3638, 3639, 3640,
    3641, 3862
Spokane WA, 3964
St. Louis MO, 3709

Suffolk NY, 295, 493, 534, 596, 651, 725, 1524, 1703, 1900, 1998, 2087
Sullivan NY, 3692
Sussex NJ, 3692
Travis TX, 3398
Ulster NY, 3692
Union NJ, 3692
Ventura CA, 2850, 2851, 2852
Volusia FL, 3667
Walton FL, 1360, 2181, 2593, 2594, 2663, 2664
Warren NJ, 3692
Westchester NY, 3692
Wood WV, 3870
Yolo CA, 3858

LEGAL STATE/PROVINCE OF RESIDENCE

Alabama, 1389, 3277, 3321, 3360
Alaska, 1535, 1636, 3785, 4034
Alberta CANADA, 3331, 3843, 3844
American Samoa, 175, 227, 909, 2956, 3121, 3369
Arizona, 3422
Arkansas, 3361, 3378, 3379
Bermuda UK, 3756
British Columbia CANADA, 3166, 3432, 3461
California, 103, 2707, 3370, 3447, 3449, 3450, 3451, 3530, 3541, 3575, 3576, 3602, 3639, 3641, 3643, 3662, 3677, 3858, 3887, 4144
Colorado, 3468, 3654, 3806
Connecticut, 370, 1742, 3285, 3362, 3494, 3683, 3744
Delaware, 311, 1374, 2011, 2187, 2199, 2290, 2299, 3034, 3047
District of Columbia, 124, 179, 241, 1004, 1038, 1119, 1258, 1783, 2965, 3642
Florida, 437, 1007, 1121, 1260, 1389, 1445, 1541, 1638, 1709, 1911, 2593, 2663, 3277, 3551, 3552, 3554, 3667, 3813, 4054
Georgia, 1389, 2228, 2262, 2338, 2576, 2637, 3277, 3360, 3368, 3571, 3572, 3647, 3774, 3833, 3972
Hawaii, 828, 3475, 3589, 3839, 3881
Hong Kong UK, 3592, 3593
Idaho, 3361, 3785
Illinois, 213, 214, 315, 387, 1016, 1136, 1269, 1411, 1834, 2102, 2171, 2194, 2296, 2599, 2651, 2671, 3250, 3302, 3366, 3367, 3397, 3605, 3606, 3607, 3832
Indiana, 255, 2623, 3366, 3367, 3832
Iowa, 207, 517, 581, 2589, 2818, 3172, 3235, 3536, 3625, 3707, 3832, 3956
Kansas, 517, 581, 2157, 2263, 2409, 2577, 2638, 2818, 3126, 3649, 3650, 3651, 3652, 3698, 3878

Kentucky, 3657, 3658
Louisiana, 177, 234, 1389, 1558, 1653, 1715, 1925, 2015, 2104, 3277, 3423, 3773
Maine, 370, 2182, 2286, 3285, 3362, 3678, 3744
Manitoba CANADA, 3680
Maryland, 1389, 2200, 2300, 2675, 3048, 3252, 3277, 3685, 3686, 3687, 3688
Massachusetts, 370, 1277, 1356, 2585, 2650, 3105, 3233, 3285, 3362, 3493, 3494, 3495, 3534, 3566, 3743, 3744
Michigan, 13, 3422, 3694, 3695, 3696, 3698, 3832
Minnesota, 671, 2202, 2603, 2676, 3307, 3555, 3698, 3702, 3703, 3704, 3832, 3956
Mississippi, 113, 1389, 3050, 3129, 3277, 3462
Missouri, 517, 581, 2818, 3668, 3698, 3919
Montana, 1033, 1291, 3361, 3524, 3785, 3999
Nebraska, 517, 581, 2818, 3698, 3854
Nevada, 3742, 3887
New Brunswick CANADA, 3761
New Hampshire, 370, 1431, 2241, 2701, 2709, 3285, 3299, 3322, 3362, 3556, 3744, 3745
New Jersey, 116, 499, 674, 741, 1470, 1930, 1937, 2019, 2211, 2315, 2858, 3541, 3746, 3747, 3748, 3781, 3831, 3946
New Mexico, 3749
New York, 126, 127, 331, 451, 2212, 2316, 2612, 2613, 2685, 2686, 2866, 3053, 3131, 3189, 3257, 3446, 3541, 3750, 3751, 3752, 3793
North Carolina, 243, 1161, 1389, 2317, 2614, 3277, 3431, 3479, 3537, 3550, 3757, 3758
North Dakota, 3564, 3565, 3956
Ohio, 3762, 3772, 3857
Oklahoma, 3365, 3522, 3547, 3577, 3691
Ontario CANADA, 1307, 3701, 3764
Oregon, 3332, 3361, 3759, 3767, 3768, 3769, 3785
Pennsylvania, 380, 471, 1073, 1186, 1289, 1339, 2590, 2656, 2826, 3293, 3358, 3529, 3777, 3861
Puerto Rico, 3421
Quebec CANADA, 3558, 3764
Rhode Island, 370, 3285, 3362, 3567, 3684, 3744, 3775, 3796
Scotland UK, 775, 1385, 2419, 3448, 3463
South Carolina, 339, 504, 559, 686, 750, 1389, 1583, 1662, 1728, 2034, 2118, 3277, 3430, 3469, 3628, 3824
South Dakota, 3531, 3825, 3826, 3827, 3956
Tennessee, 340, 505, 560, 687, 751, 1063, 1175, 1323, 1389, 1584, 1663, 1729, 2119, 3277
Texas, 198, 1347, 1366, 2740, 2930, 3365, 3398, 3535, 3741, 3842, 4057
Utah, 3953

Vermont, 370, 3285, 3362, 3466, 3744, 3955
Virgin Islands, 175, 227, 909, 2236, 2696, 2956, 3121, 3421
Virginia, 1389, 3277, 3504, 3532, 3540, 3674, 3957
Washington, 2237, 2238, 2345, 2346, 2546, 2628, 2697, 3361, 3759, 3785, 3960, 3961, 3962, 3963, 3964
West Virginia, 1389, 3277, 3540, 3732
Wisconsin, 3366, 3367, 3832, 3956, 3974, 3975, 3976
Wyoming, 170, 265, 706, 1690, 3320, 3524, 3893, 3985, 4114
Yukon CANADA, 3461

MARITAL STATUS

Divorced, 934, 1164, 1217
Married Parent, 43, 44, 289, 290, 529, 530, 846, 847, 971, 982, 1088, 1100, 1101, 1187, 1234, 1343, 1344, 1513, 1514, 1764, 1765, 1894, 1895, 1989, 1990, 2079, 2080, 2266, 2267, 2733, 2734, 2912, 2913, 3005, 3080, 3081, 3162, 3163, 3225, 3226, 3573
Single, 934, 1008, 1164, 1217, 1261, 3352, 3373, 3648, 3912, 3974
Single parent/1 minor child, 3379
Unmarried Parent, 43, 44, 289, 290, 391, 529, 530, 846, 847, 971, 982, 1088, 1100, 1101, 1187, 1234, 1343, 1344, 1513, 1514, 1764, 1765, 1894, 1895, 1989, 1990, 2079, 2080, 2266, 2267, 2733, 2734, 2912, 2913, 3005, 3080, 3081, 3162, 3163, 3225, 3226, 3379, 3389, 3573
Widowed, 934, 1164, 1217, 3974

OCCUPATIONAL GOALS

Aeronautics/Astronautics, 19, 328, 329, 371, 397, 401, 402, 408, 1602, 1842, 1843, 2049, 2129, 2964, 2984, 3286, 3311, 3312, 3997, 4055, 4147, 4163
Armed Forces, 2230, 2341, 2544, 2626, 2692, 4286
Artist, 787, 896, 1005, 1012, 1017, 1025, 1033, 1134, 1137, 1266, 1270, 1283, 1291, 1369, 1778, 2753, 2952, 3035, 3183, 3244
Author/Writer, 408, 1012, 1128, 1134, 1266, 1602, 2049, 2129, 2984, 4186, 4292
Automotive Industry, 350, 671, 3307
Christian Service, 209, 211, 782, 1124, 1362, 1365, 1408, 1637, 1828, 2183, 2239, 2287, 2347, 2454, 2549, 2595, 2597, 2629, 2665, 2668, 2698, 3238, 3242, 4067
Curator, 124, 179, 241, 1029, 1030, 1031, 1038, 1059, 1783, 2965

Flight Engineer, 19, 371, 392, 397, 3286, 3311, 3997, 4147, 4163

Government Service, 3788

Historian, 124, 179, 241, 408, 1038, 1602, 1783, 2049, 2129, 2965, 2984, 4062

Journalism, 2832, 2833, 2834, 2849, 2851, 2852, 2854, 2855, 2856, 2857, 2894, 3449, 4080, 4092

Law Enforcement, 2994, 3010, 3061, 3070, 3074, 3145, 4200

Librarian/Archivist, 124, 179, 241, 1038, 1059, 1081, 1082, 1083, 1084, 1085, 1783, 2965

Ministry, 198, 209, 211, 782, 1124, 1347, 1350, 1351, 1352, 1353, 1354, 1358, 1359, 1362, 1365, 1366, 1382, 1385, 1389, 1391, 1408, 1637, 1828, 2183, 2193, 2287, 2454, 2595, 2597, 2665, 2668, 3238, 3242, 3277, 3977, 3978, 4067

Missionary, 198, 209, 782, 1124, 1347, 1362, 1389, 1396, 1408, 1828, 2239, 2347, 2549, 2629, 2698, 3277, 4067

Music, 51, 200, 787, 852, 896, 998, 1012, 1017, 1023, 1025, 1033, 1108, 1134, 1137, 1243, 1245, 1251, 1266, 1270, 1278, 1283, 1286, 1291, 1293, 1322, 1329, 1337, 1369, 1778, 2203, 2302, 2604, 2678, 2753, 2824, 2952, 3035, 3183, 3244, 3305, 3308, 3996, 4057, 4089

Newspaper Industry, 3449

Pilot, 19, 114, 371, 389, 390, 391, 393, 396, 403, 3286, 3309, 3313, 3997, 4055, 4126, 4127, 4147, 4151, 4163, 4291

Police Administration, 2994, 3061, 3145

Priest or Nun, 209, 782, 1124, 1362, 1408, 1828, 4067

Rabbi, 209, 782, 920, 1124, 1362, 1408, 1828, 4067

Radio/TV, 51, 200, 852, 998, 1108, 1243, 2824, 3792

Research Scientist, 244, 307, 336, 355, 386, 408, 409, 465, 496, 508, 510, 540, 566, 601, 621, 659, 683, 691, 697, 730, 747, 755, 759, 781, 807, 884, 931, 1012, 1122, 1134, 1206, 1266, 1361, 1407, 1419, 1426, 1447, 1472, 1474, 1486, 1543, 1580, 1587, 1602, 1605, 1639, 1659, 1666, 1682, 1711, 1725, 1731, 1735, 1776, 1798, 1826, 1850, 1858, 1913, 1943, 1948, 1960, 2008, 2031, 2040, 2049, 2050, 2095, 2115, 2124, 2129, 2130, 2214, 2227, 2319, 2391, 2393, 2464, 2475, 2522, 2616, 2687, 2742, 2746, 2937, 2984, 3055, 3103, 3133, 3179, 3192, 3239, 3258, 3259

Teacher, 37, 92, 175, 177, 192, 198, 211, 213, 214, 227, 234, 243, 249, 258, 260, 265, 269, 281, 306, 307, 345, 386, 496, 540, 601, 659, 730, 780, 781, 822, 883, 884, 909, 958, 964, 1122, 1149, 1161, 1205, 1206, 1221, 1225, 1300, 1322, 1347, 1361, 1407, 1446, 1447, 1542, 1543, 1637, 1639, 1710, 1711, 1775, 1776, 1826, 1912, 1913, 2007, 2008, 2015, 2089, 2094, 2095, 2104, 2183, 2186, 2287, 2317, 2391, 2393, 2454, 2459, 2561, 2595, 2597, 2614, 2665, 2668, 2745, 2746, 2936, 2937, 2956, 3103, 3121, 3178, 3179, 3238, 3239, 3242, 3323, 3373, 3851, 4194, 4237, 4279

Transportation/Traffic Man., 151, 152

Travel Industry, 32, 33

OCCUPATIONS

Accountant, 105, 3045

Adult Professional, 32, 50, 145, 148, 167, 199, 256, 329, 402, 464, 508, 691, 755, 779, 807, 851, 931, 954, 957, 1060, 1064, 1176, 1198, 1219, 1319, 1328, 1367, 1419, 1430, 1474, 1485, 1587, 1618, 1666, 1681, 1731, 1744, 1843, 1948, 1957, 2040, 2124, 2142, 2720, 2742, 2813, 2878, 2879, 2895, 2964, 2987, 3055, 3072, 3086, 3133, 3144, 3153, 3192, 3258, 3259, 3312, 3677, 3717, 3766, 3851, 3997, 4014, 4093, 4112

Air Traffic Controller-D, 3327, 3997, 4163

Architect, 418, 431, 441, 443, 454, 470, 1019, 1143, 1275

Artist, 443, 859, 997, 1003, 1004, 1005, 1007, 1012, 1016, 1019, 1033, 1055, 1063, 1118, 1119, 1121, 1134, 1136, 1143, 1175, 1200, 1253, 1258, 1260, 1266, 1269, 1275, 1291, 1323, 2895, 3469, 3663

Attorney, 105, 3045

Author/Writer, 162, 217, 218, 329, 402, 408, 443, 811, 859, 929, 949, 950, 952, 953, 967, 1003, 1004, 1007, 1012, 1016, 1019, 1063, 1064, 1064, 1094, 1096, 1118, 1119, 1121, 1123, 1129, 1134, 1136, 1143, 1154, 1160, 1175, 1176, 1176, 1181, 1200, 1253, 1258, 1260, 1266, 1269, 1275, 1305, 1323, 1349, 1387, 1602, 1843, 2049, 2129, 2794, 2796, 2798, 2799, 2840, 2879, 2879, 2903, 2929, 2944, 2964, 2970, 2984, 3098, 3140, 3193, 3206, 3208, 3209, 3268, 3270, 3272, 3273, 3312, 3469, 3663, 4059

Calif Youth Authority-D-DIS, 3451

Calif Youth Authority-D-DEC, 3451

Calif Youth Authority-S-DEC, 3451

Calif Youth Authority-S-DIS, 3451

Chiropractor, 2455

Cinematographer, 1003, 1007, 1012, 1016, 1118, 1121, 1134, 1136, 1253, 1260, 1266, 1269

Clinical Social Worker, 107, 233, 2198, 2488, 2673, 3186, 3251, 3254

Composer, 859, 1003, 1004, 1007, 1012, 1016, 1063, 1118, 1119, 1121, 1134, 1136, 1175, 1200, 1232, 1253, 1258, 1260, 1262, 1266, 1269, 1311, 1323, 3469

Conservatn of Natrl Resources, 508, 691, 755, 807, 1419, 1474, 1587, 1666, 1731, 1948, 2040, 2124, 3258

Dept Corrections-D-DEC, 3451, 3605

Dept Corrections-D-DIS, 3451, 3605

Dept Corrections-S-DEC, 3451

Dept Corrections-S-DIS, 3451

Engineer, 348, 355, 409, 465, 480, 484, 508, 510, 566, 621, 635, 691, 697, 714, 733, 755, 759, 807, 1419, 1426, 1474, 1486, 1503, 1587, 1605, 1666, 1682, 1731, 1735, 1798, 1858, 1948, 1960, 2040, 2050, 2124, 2130, 3258

Firefighter, 95, 2602, 3246, 3303, 3306, 3725

Firefighter-D-DEC, 3451, 3605, 3614, 3686, 3718, 3725

Firefighter-D-DIS, 3451, 3605, 3686, 3725

Firefighter-S-DEC, 3451, 3718, 3718

Firefighter-S-DIS, 3451

Foodservice/Hospitality, 4164

Government Official, 905

Harness Racing, 3584

Harness Racing-D, 3584

Health Care Administrator, 2566

Journalist, 60, 1033, 1064, 1064, 1067, 1176, 1176, 1286, 1291, 1835, 2817, 2828, 2840, 2843, 2844, 2845, 2846, 2848, 2869, 2871, 2872, 2876, 2879, 2879, 2880, 2882, 2883, 2884, 2885, 2887, 2889, 2895, 2929, 3098, 3137, 3586, 4059

LPN/LVN, 2644, 2674

Landscape Architect, 414, 977, 1231

Librarian, 225, 3012

MD/DO Family Medicine, 107, 233, 2198, 2202, 2488, 2603, 2673, 2676, 3186, 3251

MD/DO Gen. Internal Medicine, 2202, 2603, 2676

MD/DO General Pediatrics, 107, 233, 2198, 2202, 2488, 2603, 2673, 2676, 3186, 3251

MD/DO Obstetrics/Gynecology, 2202, 2603, 2676

Merchant Seafarer, 1742

Merchant Seafarer-D, 1742

Musician, 1251

Non-Profit Faculty/Staff, 2354, 2428, 2429, 2430

Nurse-Midwife (Certified), 2202, 2603, 2676

Performer, 443, 1003, 1004, 1007, 1012, 1016, 1019, 1063, 1118, 1119, 1121, 1134, 1136, 1143, 1175, 1253, 1258, 1260, 1266, 1269, 1275,

1298, 1299, 1309, 1320, 1323, 3469

Photographer, 859, 1003, 1004, 1007, 1016, 1026, 1064, 1064, 1118, 1119, 1121, 1136, 1176, 1176, 1200, 1253, 1258, 1260, 1269, 2879, 2879, 2884, 2888, 2890, 3469

Physician Assist-Primary Care, 2202, 2603, 2676

Pilot, 129, 403, 404, 3313, 3314

Pilot-Commerical, 114, 389, 390, 393, 396, 3309, 3319, 3997, 4055, 4163

Pilot-Helicopter, 114, 396, 3309, 3319, 3997, 4055, 4163

Police-D-DEC, 3451, 3605, 3686

Police-D-DIS, 3451, 3605

Police-S-DEC, 3451

Police-S-DIS, 3451

Rabbi, 919

Realtor, 3793

Realtor-D, 3793

Registered Nurse (RN), 2202, 2480, 2566, 2603, 2636, 2644, 2645, 2666, 2674, 2676, 2677, 2682, 2688, 2689

Rescue Squad Member, 2602, 3306

Research Scholar or Scientist, 32, 39, 40, 50, 97, 137, 148, 162, 167, 196, 197, 199, 217, 218, 219, 226, 244, 256, 286, 300, 304, 306, 314, 325, 329, 336, 355, 379, 399, 402, 409, 429, 465, 484, 489, 494, 510, 524, 526, 532, 552, 566, 590, 599, 612, 621, 635, 646, 657, 677, 683, 697, 714, 719, 728, 747, 759, 772, 773, 779, 780, 783, 797, 809, 811, 848, 849, 851, 858, 876, 877, 883, 885, 910, 915, 929, 935, 949, 950, 952, 953, 957, 967, 970, 975, 994, 995, 1012, 1028, 1030, 1055, 1075, 1102, 1103, 1112, 1125, 1134, 1146, 1149, 1160, 1181, 1190, 1194, 1195, 1198, 1205, 1211, 1240, 1241, 1266, 1305, 1345, 1346, 1349, 1367, 1387, 1406, 1410, 1417, 1426, 1430, 1446, 1460, 1472, 1480, 1486, 1503, 1515, 1516, 1531, 1539, 1542, 1549, 1571, 1580, 1590, 1605, 1618, 1633, 1635, 1659, 1667, 1681, 1682, 1705, 1707, 1710, 1720, 1725, 1735, 1744, 1773, 1775, 1780, 1781, 1798, 1817, 1824, 1840, 1843, 1850, 1853, 1854, 1858, 1860, 1891, 1896, 1902, 1908, 1912, 1922, 1936, 1943, 1949, 1955, 1960, 1961, 1986, 1992, 1993, 1994, 1999, 2002, 2006, 2007, 2027, 2031, 2042, 2043, 2045, 2050, 2051, 2076, 2082, 2083, 2084, 2092, 2094, 2115, 2130, 2131, 2142, 2162, 2192, 2214, 2217, 2222, 2225, 2319, 2323, 2324, 2331, 2386, 2388, 2392, 2415, 2452, 2465, 2469, 2471, 2480, 2482, 2483, 2491, 2522, 2526, 2530, 2532, 2547, 2550, 2616, 2687, 2729, 2730, 2735, 2736, 2742, 2745, 2763, 2780, 2794, 2796,

2798, 2799, 2810, 2813, 2822, 2823, 2847, 2864, 2878, 2914, 2915, 2922, 2929, 2934, 2936, 2939, 2945, 2957, 2958, 2959, 2960, 2964, 2970, 2989, 3009, 3021, 3022, 3043, 3044, 3072, 3084, 3085, 3086, 3098, 3122, 3123, 3124, 3125, 3140, 3144, 3153, 3164, 3165, 3178, 3195, 3206, 3208, 3209, 3217, 3227, 3228, 3268, 3270, 3272, 3273, 3280, 3312, 3323, 3336, 3357, 3400, 3402, 3469, 3483, 3484, 3506, 3511, 3526, 3527, 3663, 3665, 3766, 3835, 3851, 3866, 3867, 4035, 4044, 4060, 4061, 4072, 4118, 4122

Respiratory Care Practitioner, 2398, 2566

School Business Management, 3838, 4042

School Principal/Head, 3838, 4042

Sculptor, 1003, 1007, 1118, 1121, 1253, 1260, 3469

Teacher's Assistant, 107, 233, 2198, 2488, 2673, 3186, 3213, 3251

Teacher-College, 50, 92, 128, 199, 219, 222, 226, 229, 242, 249, 253, 281, 283, 306, 362, 376, 426, 484, 486, 521, 587, 635, 643, 714, 716, 736, 775, 779, 780, 850, 851, 855, 858, 859, 867, 883, 886, 910, 952, 953, 965, 975, 1039, 1075, 1104, 1110, 1155, 1190, 1198, 1199, 1200, 1201, 1205, 1207, 1211, 1226, 1301, 1322, 1368, 1429, 1446, 1503, 1531, 1542, 1548, 1549, 1564, 1598, 1633, 1705, 1710, 1775, 1814, 1866, 1888, 1912, 1924, 1949, 1983, 2002, 2007, 2047, 2073, 2094, 2127, 2175, 2196, 2217, 2323, 2324, 2326, 2358, 2359, 2360, 2386, 2387, 2388, 2392, 2419, 2435, 2444, 2485, 2486, 2491, 2506, 2511, 2526, 2745, 2768, 2798, 2799, 2808, 2810, 2867, 2936, 2980, 3009, 3086, 3150, 3178, 3208, 3209, 3213, 3217, 3272, 3273, 3280, 3323, 3345, 3483, 3484, 3488, 3506, 3526, 3527, 3663, 3665, 3801, 3851, 3998, 4112

Teacher-Non College, 50, 92, 107, 128, 175, 199, 206, 219, 222, 225, 226, 227, 229, 233, 242, 253, 257, 258, 261, 366, 837, 851, 859, 886, 909, 958, 1003, 1039, 1068, 1092, 1118, 1149, 1155, 1180, 1198, 1200, 1201, 1207, 1221, 1224, 1244, 1253, 1301, 1322, 1330, 1564, 1615, 1861, 1869, 2134, 2140, 2198, 2488, 2673, 2727, 2768, 2806, 2867, 2907, 2956, 3086, 3121, 3186, 3213, 3251, 3318, 3323, 3345, 3384, 3483, 3484, 3838, 3851, 3998, 4042, 4112

Translator, 50, 199, 811, 851, 1198, 3086

Travel Industry, 33

U.S. Federal Employee, 2428, 2429, 2430, 3543

U.S. Federal Employee-D, 3543

ORGANIZATIONS

4-H Club, 3503

Am Acad. of Fac. Pla & Rec Sur, 2438, 2439, 2440

Am Art Therapy Assn, 2556

Am Assn of Bioanalysts, 3338

Am Coll Nurse-Midwives Fdn, 2634

Am College Health Care Exec, 2245, 2246

Am Geophysical Union, 3349

Am Historical Assn, 2902

Am Optometric Assn, 2252

Am Radio Relay League, 3358

Amer Dietetic Assn, 2707

Animal Behavior Society, 1886

Appaloosa Horse Club, 3376

Appaloosa Horse Club-D, 3376

Appaloosa Youth Foundation, 3376

Arctic Slope Regional Corp., 3377

Arctic Slope Regional Corp.-D, 3377

Assn Engineering Geologists, 727, 1538

Assn Operating Room Nurses, 2639

Assn Women's Health AWHON, 2640

Aust. Fed University Women, 772, 773, 848, 849, 994, 995, 1102, 1103, 1194, 1195, 1240, 1241, 1345, 1346, 1515, 1516, 1992, 1993, 2082, 2083, 2735, 2736, 2822, 2823, 2914, 2915, 3021, 3022, 3084, 3085, 3164, 3165, 3227, 3228, 3399, 3400, 3402, 3407, 3410

Biochemical Society, 1994, 2042

Boys/Girls Clubs of Amer., 54, 201

Brit. Fed. of Womn Graduates, 3399, 3401, 3410, 3440

CA Assn Marrige Famly Thrpst, 3167

Canadian Nurses Foundation, 2646

Canadian Society for Chem.Eng., 653

Canadian Society for Chemistry, 1999

Chemical Inst-any Commonwealth, 2042

Chemical Society of Japan, 1999

Coast Guard Mutual Assistance, 3945

Cst Guard Mutual Assist-D, 3945

Danish Sisterhood of Amer., 3512

Daughters of Penelope, 3515

Daughters of Penelope-D, 3515

DeKalb Cnty(IL) Farm Bureau-D, 2171, 2651

Democratic Nursing Org SAfrica, 2652

First Cathlc Slvak Ladies Assn, 3548

First Untd Meth Ch St.Cloud MN, 1637, 2183, 2287, 2454, 2595, 2665, 3238

Fond du Lac Reservation, 3555

GCSAA-D (golf course group), 3578

Int'l Assn of Fire Fighters-D, 3614

Int'l Fed. University Women, 772, 773, 848, 849, 994, 995, 1102, 1103, 1194, 1195, 1240, 1241, 1345, 1346, 1515, 1516, 1992, 1993, 2082,

2083, 2735, 2736, 2822, 2823, 2914, 2915,
3021, 3022, 3084, 3085, 3164, 3165, 3227,
3228, 3399, 3400, 3402, 3410, 3623, 3635
Int'l Soc. Clinical Lab Tech-D, 3624
Int'l Soc. Clinical Lab Tech, 3624
Jap.Amer.Citizens Leag., 103, 176, 228, 912, 2193,
3042, 3248, 3632, 3633
Jap.Amer.Citizens Leag.-D, 103, 176, 228, 912,
2193, 3042, 3248, 3632, 3633
Knights of Columbus, 231
Knights of Columbus-D, 231
Laramie County WY Farm Bureu-D, 3666
Lutheran Brotherhood, 3676
Maids of Athena, 3515
Marine Corps Tanker Assn, 3682, 3682
Marine Corps Tanker Assn-D, 3682, 3682
Milit. Order Prpl Heart-DESC, 3699
Military Order Purple Heart-D, 3699
Minnesota United Methdst Conf, 1637, 2183,
2287, 2454, 2595, 2665, 3238
Mortar Board, 3708
Mycological Society of America, 1929
NAACP, 318, 2017, 2106, 3710
Nat Assn Exec Secs, 3310
Nat Assn Exec Secs-D, 3310
Nat Assn Retired Federal Emp-D, 3544
Nat Athletic Trainer Assn, 2607
Nat Councl of Teachers of Engl, 1149
Nat Custms Bkrs.& Fwkrs. Assn, 120
Nat Soc Accountants-D-any rel., 123
Nat Speleology Society, 1572
Nat Twenty & Four, 3733
Nat Twenty & Four-D, 3733
New Mexico Farm/Lvstk Bureau, 3749
New Mexico Farm/Lvstk Bureau-D, 3749
Order of Ahepa-D, 3515
Portuguese Continental Union, 3782
Professional Horsemens Assn, 3787
Professional Horsemens Assn-D, 3787
Red River Valley FP Assn-D, 3794
Reserve Officers Assn of US, 3795
Royal Col of Veterinary Surgns, 2335
Royal Neighbors America, 3802
Royal Society of Chemistry, 2042, 2043, 2044,
2045
Ruritan, 3805
So. Africa Assn Women Grads, 1958, 3822
Soc of Architect Historians, 461
Soc of Bio. Psychiatry, 2227
Soc of Vertebrate Paleontology, 1796
Soil Conservation Society, 1483, 1604, 1679
Special Libraries Assn, 1171, 1172
United Daughters Confederacy-D, 3889
Western Sunbathing Assn, 3969

Western Sunbathing Assn-D, 3969
World History Assn, 2977
Wyoming Farm Bureau, 3986
Wyoming Farm Bureau-D, 3986
Wyoming Fed Women's Clubs-D, 3987
YMCA Staff, 107, 171, 233, 272, 2198, 2488,
2673, 3186, 3251

PHYSICAL HANDICAPS
General, 187, 2258, 2401, 2571
Any Handicap, 187, 308, 541, 1827, 1905, 1914,
2009, 2096, 2184, 2258, 2401, 2571, 3166,
3914, 3954, 4036, 4047, 4108
Blind, 184, 194, 238, 278, 320, 321, 372, 416,
447, 448, 477, 516, 549, 579, 631, 712, 767,
800, 913, 1034, 1150, 1214, 1375, 1398, 1432,
1495, 1565, 1620, 1694, 1749, 1811, 1875,
1975, 2067, 2204, 2305, 2508, 2679, 2961,
3052, 3344, 3346, 3347, 3461, 3719, 3720,
3721, 3722, 3723, 3724, 3757, 3958, 3962,
4077
Cooley's Anemia, 3726
Deaf/Speech/Impaired, 65, 237, 537, 2303, 2606,
3297, 3333, 3334
Hemophilia/Bleeding Disorder, 3868
Learning Disability, 3468, 4125, 4231
Visually Impaired, 278, 372, 416, 477, 516, 579,
631, 712, 767, 1398, 1432, 1495, 1620, 1694,
1749, 1811, 1875, 1975, 2067, 3507

PREVIOUS/CURRENT/FUTURE SCHOOLS
Academy of Vocal Arts PA/USA, 1229
Amer Academy in Rome ITAL, 414, 826, 827, 977,
978, 979, 1231, 1745, 1746
Amer Film Institute USA, 1045, 1163
Amer Univ in Cairo EGYPT, 192, 838, 1758, 3222
Amer Univ of Rome ITAL, 3731
Amherst College MA/USA, 3496
Asian Inst Tech THAILAND, 2, 38, 282, 375, 425,
485, 520, 586, 642, 842, 1400, 1434, 1510,
1630, 1699, 2728, 2820
Aust. Nat'l Univ AUSTRALIA, 3412
Brandeis Univ MA/USA, 2919
Brown Inst MN/USA, 2881
Cal Poly-Pomona CA/USA, 445, 1464
Cal Poly-San Lus Obspo CA/USA, 445, 1464
Cal State-San Jose CA/USA, 3808
Catholic Univ of Amer DC/USA, 3660
Chateleck HS Sechelt/BC/CAN, 3834
Chinese Univ HONG KONG, 3473
Chinook HS MT/USA, 3672
City Univ of New York NY/USA, 1499, 1500,
1623, 1751, 1878, 1879, 3076
College of St Elizabeth NJ/USA, 3481

College of St. Francis IL/USA, 3482
Columbia Univ NY/USA, 60, 257, 1045, 1163,
1499, 1500, 1623, 1751, 1878, 1879, 3076
Concordia Univ CAN, 61, 62, 205, 872, 1001,
1117, 1245, 1355, 2001, 2089, 2170, 2584,
2649, 2829, 3169, 3497, 3498, 3499, 3500,
3501, 3502
Cornell Univ NY/USA, 1499, 1500, 1623, 1751,
1878, 1879, 3076
Dalhousie Univ CAN, 3510
Deakin Univ AUSTRALIA, 3517
Elphinstone HS Gibsona/BC/CAN, 3834
Emory Univ GA/USA, 779
European Univ Inst ITAL, 73, 74, 882, 2743,
2744, 2932, 2933, 3029, 3030, 3100, 3101
George Washington Univ DC/USA, 163, 1130,
3151
Georgetown Univ DC/USA, 2010, 3496
Griffith Univ AUSTRALIA, 3581
Harv Univ Business Sch MA/USA, 81, 2947
Harvard Univ MA/USA, 3560, 3587, 3655
Haystack Mountain ME/USA, 1013, 3300
Healdsburg HS CA/USA, 1293, 2203, 2302, 2604,
2678, 3308
Hebrew Univ ISRAEL, 3665
Holyoke Catholic HS MA/USA, 3496
Indiana Univ IN/USA, 3486
Inst Papr Sci & Tech GA/USA, 663, 731, 1920,
2012, 2100
Jacksonville St. Univ AL/USA, 3630
Jacksonville Univ FL/USA, 3629
John Cabot Univ Rome/ITAL, 13, 3731
King's College London/UK, 1373
Lincoln Univ NEW ZEALAND, 108, 1465
London School Econ/PolySci UK, 2764, 2765,
3046
Maryland Inst Coll Art MD/USA, 1027
Mass Inst of Tech MA/USA, 70, 384, 538, 597,
726, 3655
Mercyhurst College PA/USA, 1289
Michigan State Univ MI/USA, 3486
NY Univ NY/USA, 1045, 1163, 3727
No. Amer Bapt Seminary SD/USA, 1381
Northwestern Univ IL/USA, 3486
Nova Scotia Coll of Art CAN, 1043
Ohio State Univ OH/USA, 3486
Pender Harbour HS PH/BC/CAN, 3834
Penn State Univ PA/USA, 3486
Pine Bluffs HS WY/USA, 3780
Purdue Univ IN/USA, 3486
Queens Univ of Belfast UK, 938, 939, 1478,
2329, 3789, 3790, 3791
Ripon College WI/USA, 1048, 1169, 1313
Rockefeller Archive Ctr NY/USA, 3799

Sonoma State Univ CA/USA, 3819
Specs-Howard MI/USA, 2881
Technion Inst Tech ISRAEL, 3665
Texas A&M Univ TX/USA, 3840, 3841
Towson State Univ MD/USA, 3882
Trent Univ CAN, 567, 963, 1390, 1683, 1800, 1962, 2052, 2135
Tufts U-Fltcher Law Sch MA/USA, 3102
Tulane Univ LA/USA, 3884
Tuskegee Institute AL/USA, 262, 357, 1684, 1963, 2053, 2721
Union Theol. Seminary NY/USA, 1351
United Negro Colleges USA, 3692, 3892
Univ Acadia CAN, 3325
Univ Adelaide SO. AUSTRALIA, 2269
Univ Alberta CAN, 359, 968, 2058, 3895, 3896, 3897, 3898
Univ Birmngham UK, 3899
Univ Bologna ITAL, 2208
Univ Brunei DERUSSALEM, 1649
Univ CA-Davis CA/USA, 445, 1464, 1967
Univ CA-Irvine CA/USA, 445, 1464
Univ CA-Irvine Ext. CA/USA, 445, 1464
Univ CA-Los Ang. Ext. CA/USA, 445, 1464
Univ CA-Los Angeles CA/USA, 445, 825, 866, 972, 1045, 1115, 1163, 1188, 1191, 1464, 2925, 3006
Univ Calgary CAN, 467, 3901, 3902
Univ Cambridge UK, 364, 571, 1801, 1868, 2138, 3064, 3903, 3904, 3905, 3906, 3907, 3908, 3909
Univ Chicago IL/USA, 1351, 3486
Univ Colorado CO/USA, 1531, 1633, 1705, 2002
Univ Delaware DE/USA, 2996
Univ Exeter UK, 3910
Univ Glasgow UK, 155, 3065, 3911
Univ Hawaii HI/USA, 3528
Univ Hull UK, 3913
Univ Illinois IL/USA, 3486
Univ Iowa IA/USA, 3486, 3914
Univ Kansas KS/USA, 3878
Univ Leeds UK, 3916
Univ London UK, 2997, 2998, 2999, 3000, 3001
Univ Manchester UK, 156, 180, 263, 360, 702, 761, 1071, 1864, 2807, 3066
Univ Manitoba CAN, 157, 3003, 3146, 3917
Univ Massachusetts MA/USA, 3495
Univ Melbourne AUSTRALIA, 3918
Univ Michigan MI/USA, 3486, 3697
Univ Minnesota MN/USA, 3486
Univ Missouri-Rolla MO/USA, 3919
Univ Nevada-Reno NV/USA, 2874
Univ New Brunswick CAN, 3922
Univ New England AUSTRALIA, 3924

Univ New Mexico NM/USA, 1926, 1927, 2492, 2493, 2891
Univ Newcastle AUSTRALIA, 3920, 3921
Univ Oxford UK, 361, 1393, 1394, 1588, 2059, 3925, 3926, 3927, 3928, 3929, 3930, 3931, 3932
Univ PA-Wrtn Sch of Bus PA/USA, 140
Univ Penn PA/USA, 3912
Univ Queensland AUSTRALIA, 3934
Univ Rochester NY/USA, 1228, 2873
Univ S. California CA/USA, 820, 1045, 1163, 3385
Univ S. Dakota SD/USA, 3067, 3147
Univ Stockholm SWEDEN, 146, 1797, 2802, 2803, 2993, 3143, 3276
Univ Tasmania AUSTRALIA, 3937
Univ Tennessee TN/USA, 3938, 3939
Univ Texas-Arlington TX/USA, 1337, 2894, 3950, 3951, 3952
Univ Toronto CAN, 3940
Univ Utah UT/USA, 2343
Univ Virginia VA/USA, 1185
Univ W. Australia AUSTRALIA, 1865
Univ Waikato NEW ZEALAND, 1609, 3753
Univ Windsor CAN, 3944
Univ Wisconsin-Madison WI/USA, 3486
Vanderbilt Univ TN/USA, 1351, 1611
Von Karman Institute BELGIUM, 412
Washington Univ MO/USA, 3965
Wellesley Coll Alumni MA/USA, 3966
Wellesley College MA/USA, 3966
West Virginia Univ WV/USA, 3967, 3968
Wheatland HS WY/USA, 3970
Yale University CT/USA, 1351, 1499, 1500, 1623, 1751, 1878, 1879, 3076

RELIGIOUS AFFILIATION

Atheist/Agnostic, 209, 782, 1124, 1362, 1408, 1828
Baptist, 1348, 1381
Catholic, 3481, 3556, 3660
Christian, 211, 343, 808, 1263, 1349, 1360, 1365, 1383, 1479, 2181, 2221, 2330, 2594, 2597, 2664, 2668, 2778, 2893, 3057, 3242, 3321, 3530
Christian Science, 3329
Christn Chrch-Disc. of Chrst, 1350, 1351, 1352, 1353, 1354
Episcopal, 1359, 1360, 2181, 2594, 2664
Jewish, 67, 82, 104, 212, 230, 315, 893, 894, 913, 914, 919, 920, 1411, 1643, 1834, 2102, 2194, 2296, 2599, 2671, 2838, 2839, 3111, 3112, 3229, 3232, 3243, 3249, 3250, 3354, 3590, 3638, 3639, 3640, 3641, 3642, 3807, 3863

Lutheran, 198, 1347, 1358, 1396, 2239, 2347, 2549, 2629, 2698, 3676, 3977, 3978
Muslim, 316, 1553, 2014, 2103, 2197, 2297, 2487, 2600, 2672, 3855
Presbyterian, 249, 1382, 3783, 3784
Protestant, 3536
Unitarian, 1391, 3063
United Methodist Church, 1366, 1637, 2183, 2287, 2454, 2595, 2665, 3238, 3891

SEX

Female, 4, 16, 25, 34, 41, 42, 43, 44, 56, 61, 63, 106, 118, 164, 165, 166, 172, 202, 249, 266, 267, 277, 287, 288, 289, 290, 293, 294, 295, 296, 297, 317, 330, 348, 349, 350, 351, 365, 389, 390, 391, 392, 393, 403, 413, 415, 433, 434, 491, 492, 493, 515, 527, 528, 529, 530, 531, 534, 535, 550, 564, 573, 578, 592, 594, 595, 596, 630, 639, 647, 649, 650, 651, 652, 662, 669, 670, 711, 720, 722, 723, 725, 739, 742, 772, 773, 774, 776, 803, 828, 843, 844, 845, 846, 847, 848, 849, 862, 892, 926, 934, 970, 971, 982, 990, 994, 995, 1001, 1037, 1088, 1094, 1098, 1099, 1100, 1101, 1102, 1103, 1112, 1152, 1157, 1164, 1187, 1189, 1194, 1195, 1217, 1234, 1240, 1241, 1297, 1341, 1342, 1343, 1344, 1345, 1346, 1352, 1378, 1396, 1492, 1507, 1511, 1512, 1513, 1514, 1515, 1516, 1520, 1524, 1525, 1559, 1567, 1627, 1693, 1703, 1704, 1762, 1763, 1764, 1765, 1820, 1821, 1844, 1892, 1893, 1894, 1895, 1898, 1900, 1901, 1958, 1980, 1987, 1988, 1989, 1990, 1991, 1992, 1993, 1998, 2016, 2022, 2066, 2077, 2078, 2079, 2080, 2081, 2082, 2083, 2087, 2088, 2105, 2109, 2111, 2139, 2148, 2164, 2239, 2240, 2264, 2265, 2266, 2267, 2269, 2274, 2347, 2348, 2350, 2539, 2549, 2552, 2582, 2629, 2630, 2631, 2632, 2698, 2700, 2731, 2732, 2733, 2734, 2735, 2736, 2737, 2738, 2772, 2822, 2823, 2896, 2897, 2910, 2911, 2912, 2913, 2914, 2915, 2922, 2924, 2967, 2990, 3005, 3013, 3021, 3022, 3025, 3071, 3078, 3079, 3080, 3081, 3084, 3085, 3094, 3152, 3160, 3161, 3162, 3163, 3164, 3165, 3188, 3218, 3219, 3223, 3224, 3225, 3226, 3227, 3228, 3281, 3282, 3284, 3296, 3313, 3319, 3339, 3340, 3341, 3342, 3343, 3352, 3375, 3399, 3400, 3401, 3402, 3403, 3404, 3405, 3406, 3407, 3409, 3410, 3421, 3434, 3435, 3436, 3437, 3438, 3439, 3440, 3446, 3455, 3456, 3457, 3458, 3459, 3460, 3481, 3509, 3515, 3520, 3545, 3546, 3559, 3566, 3573, 3576, 3615, 3623, 3713, 3720, 3728, 3753, 3755, 3771,

3797, 3821, 3822, 3833, 3853, 3869, 3887, 3904, 3931, 3932, 3947, 3951, 3965, 3972, 3977, 3978, 3979, 3980, 3981, 3982, 3987, 3991, 3992, 3993, 3994, 4011, 4014, 4020, 4021, 4023, 4024, 4025, 4026, 4028, 4029, 4030, 4033, 4037, 4040, 4053, 4074, 4081, 4082, 4085, 4093, 4119, 4121, 4123, 4124, 4129, 4136, 4153, 4159, 4291

Male, 318, 343, 669, 970, 1237, 1389, 1479, 2017, 2106, 2221, 2330, 2539, 3057, 3277, 3536, 3573, 3615, 3797, 3887, 3964, 3993, 3994, 4014, 4021, 4023, 4024, 4025, 4026, 4028, 4029, 4030, 4037, 4040, 4053, 4074, 4081, 4082, 4085, 4093, 4119, 4121, 4123, 4124, 4129, 4136, 4294

SORORITY/FRATERNAL

Alpha Epsilon Rho, 2859
Beta Phi Mu, 1106
Delta Gamma, 3519
Delta Gamma-D, 3519
Delta Phi Epsilon, 3520
Eta Sigma Phi, 1120
Gamma Theta Upsilon, 1545
Kappa Omicron Nu, 2715, 2716, 2717
Kappa Omicron Phi, 2714
Phi Alpha Theta, 2974, 2975, 2976, 2977, 2978
Phi Delta Kappa, 245
Phi Eta Sigma, 3779
Phi Kappa Phi, 3595
Pi Gamma Mu, 2779
Tau Beta Pi, 352
Zeta Phi Beta Sorority, 3284, 3992

STATE/PROVINCE OF INTENDED STUDY

Alabama, 1470, 1937, 3328, 3360, 3630
Alaska, 1535, 1636, 4034
Alberta CANADA, 467, 2353, 3330, 3331
Arizona, 3422
Arkansas, 3378
British Columbia CANADA, 3166
California, 216, 445, 1464, 2707, 2821, 3383, 3385, 3449, 3450, 3637, 3677, 4144, 4177, 4178, 4179
Colorado, 58, 59, 1531, 1633, 1705, 2002, 3654
Connecticut, 370, 975, 1075, 1190, 1470, 1499, 1500, 1623, 1742, 1751, 1878, 1879, 1937, 2425, 3009, 3076, 3285, 3472, 3744
Delaware, 1470, 1937, 2996
District of Columbia, 75, 124, 179, 241, 911, 1006, 1038, 1212, 1470, 1783, 1937, 2853, 2965, 3386, 3387
England UK, 303, 1537, 1706, 1903, 2004, 2091, 3928

Florida, 437, 1007, 1121, 1260, 1445, 1470, 1541, 1638, 1709, 1911, 1937, 3552, 3553, 3554, 3667, 3813, 4054
Georgia, 1470, 1937, 3360, 3571, 3774, 3833
Hawaii, 3839
Hong Kong, 3473, 3592
Illinois, 213, 214, 387, 3302, 3482, 3605, 3606, 3607
Indiana, 255, 1338, 1470, 1937, 2623
Iowa, 1338, 2837, 2948, 3536, 3707, 3956
Kansas, 3649, 3650, 3651, 3653, 3698, 3878
Kentucky, 1470, 1937
Louisiana, 177, 234, 1470, 1558, 1653, 1715, 1925, 1937, 2015, 2104
Maine, 370, 1013, 1470, 1937, 2425, 3285, 3300, 3659, 3744
Manitoba CANADA, 1338
Maryland, 911, 1212, 1470, 1937, 2200, 2230, 2300, 2341, 2544, 2602, 2626, 2675, 2692, 3048, 3252, 3306, 3386, 3387, 3685, 3688
Massachusetts, 70, 370, 384, 538, 597, 726, 1277, 1470, 1937, 2425, 3285, 3560, 3744
Michigan, 3422, 3694, 3696, 3697, 3698, 3859, 3860
Minnesota, 101, 671, 1338, 2150, 2202, 2603, 2676, 3247, 3307, 3698, 3702, 3704, 3879, 3956
Mississippi, 113, 1470, 1937, 3050, 3129, 3462
Missouri, 1338, 3698
Montana, 3999
Nebraska, 1338, 3698
Nevada, 2821, 3742
New Hampshire, 370, 1470, 1937, 2425, 3285, 3744, 3745
New Jersey, 116, 301, 499, 674, 741, 1470, 1530, 1930, 1937, 2019, 2211, 2315, 2858, 3472, 3481, 3746, 3748, 3831, 3946
New Mexico, 1927, 2493
New York, 126, 127, 128, 242, 331, 451, 1039, 1155, 1301, 1470, 1499, 1500, 1623, 1635, 1751, 1773, 1878, 1879, 1902, 1937, 2212, 2316, 2613, 2686, 2853, 2866, 2867, 3053, 3076, 3131, 3189, 3257, 3446, 3472, 3751, 3752, 3829
North Carolina, 1470, 1937, 3479, 3757
North Dakota, 1338, 3956
Northern Ireland UK, 806, 938, 939, 1478, 1846, 2329, 2775, 3789, 3790, 3791
Nova Scotia CANADA, 3510
Ohio, 1470, 1937, 3762
Oklahoma, 3522, 3691
Ontario CANADA, 131, 1162, 1338, 1947, 2039, 2123, 2215, 2973, 2979, 3458, 3701, 3764, 3765, 3944

Oregon, 3767, 3768, 3769
Pennsylvania, 140, 343, 1289, 1470, 1479, 1937, 2221, 2330, 2590, 2656, 2826, 3057, 3480, 3529, 3777
Quebec CANADA, 61, 62, 205, 872, 1001, 1117, 1245, 1355, 2001, 2089, 2170, 2584, 2649, 2829, 3169, 3497, 3498, 3499, 3500, 3501, 3502, 3764
Rhode Island, 370, 1470, 1937, 2425, 3285, 3567, 3744, 3796
Scotland UK, 303, 562, 693, 756, 787, 896, 1017, 1137, 1270, 1369, 1385, 1395, 1468, 1537, 1597, 1706, 1778, 1903, 2004, 2046, 2091, 2126, 2418, 2753, 2952, 3035, 3183, 3244, 3448, 3463, 3804, 3911
South Carolina, 339, 504, 559, 686, 750, 1470, 1583, 1662, 1728, 1937, 2034, 2118, 3469
South Dakota, 1338, 3825, 3826, 3956
Tennessee, 340, 505, 560, 687, 751, 1470, 1584, 1663, 1729, 1937, 2119
Texas, 136, 159, 198, 264, 1336, 1347, 1366, 2740, 2870, 2930, 3452, 3561, 3840, 3841, 3842, 4057
Utah, 2343, 3953
Vermont, 370, 1470, 1937, 2425, 3285, 3744
Virginia, 216, 911, 1212, 1470, 1937, 3386, 3387, 3489, 3674, 3957
Washington, 2238, 2346, 3961, 3963
West Virginia, 911, 1212, 1470, 1937
Wisconsin, 1338, 3976
Wyoming, 170, 265, 706, 1690, 3074, 3320, 3815, 3818, 3986, 3987, 3988, 4114

UNIONS

AFL/CIO, 4001
AFL/CIO-D, 4001
Am.Fed. of Teachers, 3345
Screen Actors Guild, 3812
Screen Actors Guild-D, 3812
Unit.Food/Comml Wkrs-Loc.555-D, 3890
Unit.Food/Comml Wkrs-Loc.555-S, 3890
Unit.Food/Comml Wkrs-Loc.555, 3890
Wyoming Peace Off Assn-WPOA-D, 3074, 3074

UNUSUAL CHARACTERISTICS

1st Generation US Citizen, 3552, 3871
1st Generation US Citizen-D, 3552, 3871
Cancer Survivor, 3628
Child of Unmarried Parent, 3839
Descendant-Decl of Indep Signe, 3521
Descendants-Confederate Soldie, 3889
Descendants-Seafarer, 3743
Economic/Cultural Disadvantage, 65, 126, 317, 331, 451, 537, 670, 739, 1455, 1559, 1644,

1905, 1919, 2016, 2105, 2211, 2212, 2315, 2316, 2613, 2686, 3053, 3189, 3257, 3297, 3322, 3346, 3347, 3389, 3398, 3423, 3445, 3475, 3522, 3539, 3550, 3564, 3674, 3677, 3741, 3746, 3748, 3776, 3800, 3839, 3854, 3861, 3879, 3961

From Former Soviet Union, 920, 3511, 3705, 3706, 3766

GED, 3356, 3693

Gay or Lesbian, 397, 832, 2724, 3159, 3311, 3375, 3559, 3772, 3773, 3774, 3785

Gay or Lesbian-D, 3862

Greencard Holder, 3871

Male NonRegstrnt Selective Ser, 3563

Non-Drinker, 3467

Oklahoma City Bomb Victim-D, 3542

Orphan, 3839

Parent Deaf/H.Imp Chld undr 6, 3334, 3334

Re-Entry Student after 2yrs, 43, 44, 247, 289, 290, 295, 348, 349, 351, 355, 409, 465, 493, 510, 529, 530, 534, 566, 596, 621, 651, 697, 725, 759, 846, 847, 1100, 1101, 1343, 1344, 1396, 1426, 1486, 1513, 1514, 1524, 1605, 1682, 1703, 1735, 1764, 1765, 1798, 1858, 1894, 1895, 1900, 1960, 1989, 1990, 1998, 2050, 2079, 2080, 2087, 2130, 2219, 2266, 2267, 2528, 2618, 2733, 2734, 2912, 2913, 3080, 3081, 3162, 3163, 3197, 3225, 3226, 3456, 3977, 3978

Re-Entry Student after 5yrs, 43, 44, 247, 289, 290, 348, 349, 351, 529, 530, 846, 847, 1100, 1101, 1343, 1344, 1396, 1437, 1513, 1514, 1764, 1765, 1894, 1895, 1989, 1990, 2079, 2080, 2219, 2266, 2267, 2528, 2618, 2733, 2734, 2912, 2913, 3080, 3081, 3162, 3163, 3197, 3225, 3226, 3341, 3456, 3977, 3978

Re-Entry to Workforce 2+yrs, 348, 355, 409, 465, 510, 566, 621, 697, 759, 1426, 1486, 1605, 1682, 1735, 1798, 1858, 1960, 2050, 2130

Refugee/Asylee, 3513, 3590

Unadopted Orphan, 3839

Field of Study Index

SCHOOL OF BUSINESS

General, 1, 2, 3, 4, 5, 6, 7, 8, 9, 10, 11, 12, 13, 14, 16, 17, 38, 46, 49, 56, 57, 68, 93, 94, 102, 109, 130, 164, 172, 202, 282, 296, 302, 365, 375, 425, 485, 520, 535, 556, 573, 586, 642, 668, 774, 790, 791, 792, 842, 860, 900, 901, 1022, 1213, 1400, 1434, 1438, 1489, 1510, 1630, 1699, 1820, 1901, 2088, 2139, 2143, 2164, 2242, 2274, 2278, 2728, 2737, 2756, 2757, 2820, 2830, 2831, 3011, 3025, 3040, 3041, 3071, 3091, 3095, 3097, 3118, 3119, 3120, 3152, 3296, 4037

BUSINESS ADMINISTRATION

General, 2, 4, 5, 8, 9, 11, 12, 13, 14, 25, 38, 46, 47, 56, 57, 61, 62, 77, 81, 83, 89, 90, 93, 94, 95, 102, 103, 109, 111, 116, 130, 139, 148, 163, 168, 171, 172, 202, 256, 272, 282, 296, 375, 425, 485, 499, 520, 535, 556, 563, 586, 617, 642, 668, 674, 741, 774, 790, 791, 842, 860, 898, 899, 900, 901, 957, 1022, 1213, 1400, 1434, 1456, 1457, 1510, 1630, 1645, 1646, 1681, 1699, 1820, 1901, 1930, 2019, 2088, 2148, 2164, 2274, 2292, 2293, 2710, 2711, 2728, 2737, 2756, 2757, 2814, 2820, 2858, 2878, 2947, 3008, 3013, 3025, 3040, 3041, 3058, 3073, 3091, 3116, 3117, 3118, 3119, 3144, 3151, 3154, 3246, 3296, 3303, 4037

Accounting, 18, 20, 24, 34, 37, 45, 58, 59, 61, 62, 69, 85, 91, 92, 103, 105, 110, 123, 126, 149, 154, 158, 331, 451, 569, 572, 625, 1183, 1392, 1608, 2212, 2229, 2316, 2340, 2540, 2613, 2625, 2686, 2691, 2722, 3019, 3045, 3053, 3060, 3127, 3189, 3257, 3279, 4138, 4139, 4140, 4141

Actuarial Science, 78, 140, 4142, 4227

Advertising, 22, 23, 4145

Art Administration/Mngmnt, 51, 64, 128, 132, 200, 242, 852, 998, 1039, 1108, 1155, 1243, 1301, 1308, 2824, 2867

Auditing, 92

Aviation/Airport Management, 19, 114, 129, 371, 396, 404, 3286, 3309, 3314, 3997, 4163

Banking, 26

Business Ethics, 118, 3188

Club Management, 159

Data Processing, 65, 158, 537, 572, 625, 1183, 1392, 1608, 3297, 4187

Economics, 7, 13, 16, 26, 39, 40, 41, 42, 43, 44, 52, 53, 55, 68, 73, 74, 78, 79, 80, 81, 84, 86, 97, 98, 99, 100, 103, 106, 110, 112, 115, 119, 131, 133, 134, 138, 139, 142, 143, 146, 147, 156, 157, 160, 164, 167, 180, 197, 263, 287, 288, 289, 290, 302, 360, 365, 440, 527, 528, 529, 530, 563, 573, 617, 666, 673, 786, 796, 798, 844, 845, 846, 847, 853, 854, 882, 890, 891, 902, 936, 937, 968, 969, 1011, 1020, 1021, 1032, 1071, 1098, 1099, 1100, 1101, 1133, 1144, 1145, 1162, 1265, 1276, 1290, 1341, 1342, 1343, 1344, 1364, 1371, 1372, 1421, 1430, 1466, 1511, 1512, 1513, 1514, 1552, 1589, 1592, 1618, 1648, 1669, 1744, 1762, 1763, 1764, 1765, 1777, 1789, 1790, 1797, 1836, 1864, 1892, 1893, 1894, 1895, 1947, 1987, 1988, 1989, 1990, 2039, 2077, 2078, 2079, 2080, 2123, 2139, 2142, 2201, 2215, 2264, 2265, 2266, 2267, 2301, 2328, 2730, 2731, 2732, 2733, 2734, 2743, 2744, 2749, 2762, 2766, 2782, 2788, 2802, 2804, 2807, 2813, 2831, 2860, 2910, 2911, 2912, 2913, 2917, 2918, 2932, 2933, 2941, 2942, 2947, 2954, 2955, 2985, 2993, 3003, 3004, 3023, 3024, 3029, 3030, 3032, 3033, 3037, 3049, 3051, 3058, 3066, 3068, 3071, 3072, 3078, 3079, 3080, 3081, 3087, 3088, 3090, 3097, 3100, 3101, 3109, 3110, 3114, 3127, 3128, 3139, 3143, 3146, 3148, 3152, 3153, 3160, 3161, 3162, 3163, 3201, 3223, 3224, 3225, 3226, 3253, 3261, 3262, 3265, 3276

Economics/Business History, 71, 81, 100, 110, 146, 796, 1021, 1145, 1372, 1797, 2762, 2802, 2931, 2947, 2955, 2993, 3127, 3143, 3276

Finance, 13, 26, 40, 61, 62, 97, 106, 119, 139, 155, 197, 563, 617, 1466, 2730, 2860, 3051, 3058, 3065, 3253, 4155

Golf Course Management, 1451, 1452, 1453, 3578

Grocery Industry, 15

Hotel Administration, 32, 159, 4225

Industrial & Labor Relations, 97, 162

Industrial Distribution, 11, 102, 115, 668, 673, 1022

Information Systems, 61, 62

Insurance, 78, 140, 4227

Integrated Resource Mngmnt., 35, 122, 675

International Business, 7, 8, 9, 48, 50, 52, 53, 68, 80, 93, 94, 103, 110, 120, 121, 145, 160, 168, 199, 302, 464, 790, 791, 851, 853, 854, 891, 900, 901, 923, 954, 969, 1060, 1198, 1219, 1319, 1436, 1485, 1957, 2720, 2756, 2757, 2814, 2831, 2917, 2918, 2942, 2987, 3004, 3008, 3023, 3024, 3033, 3040, 3041, 3068, 3073, 3086, 3087, 3088, 3097, 3105, 3110, 3118, 3119, 3127, 3148, 3154

Labor Studies/Human Resources, 97, 161, 162

Management, 5, 30, 39, 57, 61, 62, 64, 66, 82, 88, 115, 117, 119, 158, 212, 547, 572, 607, 625, 634, 660, 673, 860, 893, 1183, 1392, 1466, 1608, 2071, 2099, 2838, 2860, 3051, 3091, 3111, 3253, 4232, 4254

Manufacturing, 30, 106, 115, 122, 137, 350, 634, 673, 675, 809, 1480, 1590, 1667, 1853, 2071, 2222, 2331, 2530, 2780

Marketing, 3, 22, 23, 49, 61, 62, 108, 128, 144, 159, 242, 463, 1039, 1155, 1301, 1438, 1484, 1680, 2867, 2877, 3142

Merchandising, 115, 673

Operations Research, 70, 88, 384, 538, 547, 597, 607, 660, 726, 2099, 4254

Organizational Behavior, 118, 3188

Production/Operations Mngmnt., 30, 35, 122, 634, 675, 2071

Public Administration, 28, 36, 63, 67, 87, 95, 113, 125, 135, 148, 163, 168, 193, 215, 256, 420, 450, 789, 957, 1140, 1624, 1681, 2755, 2814, 2819, 2842, 2878, 3008, 3038, 3050, 3056, 3073, 3077, 3094, 3115, 3129, 3130, 3136, 3144, 3151, 3154, 3232, 3246, 3256, 3263, 3303, 4063, 4169, 4272

Public Relations, 22, 23, 27, 124, 127, 128, 136, 144, 179, 241, 242, 463, 1038, 1039, 1155, 1301, 1484, 1680, 1783, 2816, 2866, 2867, 2870, 2877, 2965, 3131, 3142

Purchasing, 115, 673

Real Estate, 96, 4155

Real Estate Appraising, 4155

Recreation/Resource Managemnt, 21, 169, 182, 271, 1233, 2553

Restaurant Management, 15, 159, 2719, 4164, 4208

Retail Management, 75, 96, 115, 159, 673, 1006

Sports Management, 21, 72, 165, 166, 169, 182, 266, 267, 271, 1233, 2348, 2553, 2592, 2630, 2631, 2835, 2897, 3177, 3218, 3219, 3237, 3281, 3282

Traffic Management, 28, 29, 31, 151, 152, 153, 358, 420, 466, 481, 511, 624, 700, 760, 1624, 3215, 3278

Transportation, 28, 29, 31, 98, 150, 151, 152, 153, 170, 346, 358, 420, 466, 481, 511, 624, 666, 700, 706, 760, 902, 1552, 1624, 1648, 1690, 3215, 3278, 3320, 4151

Travel & Tourism, 32, 33, 76, 159

Youth/Human Svc Agcy Adm, 54, 101, 104, 107, 141, 201, 230, 233, 252, 914, 2198, 2488, 2531, 2673, 3186, 3199, 3247, 3249, 3251, 3264

SCHOOL OF EDUCATION

General, 4, 56, 124, 156, 172, 173, 174, 175, 176, 177, 178, 179, 180, 181, 202, 204, 210, 227, 228, 234, 235, 241, 245, 263, 265, 270, 281, 296, 309, 360, 383, 535, 654, 774, 777, 799, 823, 870, 909, 912, 1000, 1038, 1071, 1126, 1397, 1403, 1444, 1528, 1632, 1783, 1820, 1829, 1864, 1901, 2015, 2088, 2097, 2104, 2164, 2274, 2424, 2737, 2767, 2807, 2812, 2956, 2965, 3025, 3042, 3066, 3121, 3187, 3248, 3296, 3373

EDUCATION

General, 4, 40, 56, 82, 87, 92, 124, 128, 148, 156, 172, 173, 174, 175, 176, 177, 178, 179, 180, 181, 192, 196, 197, 202, 204, 205, 209, 210, 212, 213, 215, 227, 228, 229, 234, 235, 241, 242, 243, 245, 249, 250, 253, 254, 256, 262, 263, 265, 270, 281, 296, 309, 345, 357, 360, 383, 526, 535, 654, 692, 774, 777, 782, 789, 799, 823, 870, 893, 909, 912, 940, 957, 1000, 1038, 1039, 1071, 1124, 1126, 1140, 1155, 1161, 1301, 1362, 1397, 1403, 1408, 1444, 1481, 1528, 1595, 1632, 1673, 1681, 1684, 1783, 1820, 1828, 1829, 1864, 1901, 1951, 1963, 2015, 2053, 2088, 2089, 2097, 2104, 2164, 2274, 2317, 2333, 2424, 2614, 2620, 2721, 2729, 2730, 2737, 2755, 2767, 2807, 2812, 2838, 2842, 2867, 2878, 2956, 2965, 3025, 3038, 3042, 3066, 3111, 3115, 3121, 3144, 3187, 3248, 3296, 3373, 4194, 4279

Administration/Management, 36, 183, 193, 229, 249, 2819, 3077, 4278

Blnd/Visuly Impared Education, 184, 194, 195, 216, 246, 247, 248, 2218, 2219, 2220, 2527, 2528, 2529, 2617, 2618, 2619, 3196, 3197, 3198, 4084, 4192

Child Care, 107, 233, 2198, 2488, 2673, 3186, 3251

Christian Leadership Education, 198, 211, 1347, 2597, 2668, 3242

Deaf/Hearing Impaired Ed., 185, 186, 187, 188, 189, 191, 203, 216, 236, 237, 243, 246, 247, 248, 1161, 2218, 2219, 2220, 2256, 2257, 2258, 2259, 2260, 2261, 2275, 2303, 2317, 2399, 2400, 2401, 2402, 2403, 2404, 2527, 2528, 2529, 2569, 2570, 2571, 2572, 2573, 2575, 2581, 2605, 2606, 2614, 2617, 2618, 2619, 3196, 3197, 3198, 4084, 4192

Early Childhood Education, 104, 107, 190, 211, 230, 233, 243, 261, 264, 914, 1068, 1161, 1180, 1224, 1330, 1861, 2134, 2198, 2317, 2488, 2574, 2597, 2614, 2668, 2673, 2806, 3186, 3242, 3249, 3251, 3318

Elementary Education, 107, 211, 233, 238, 243, 257, 258, 261, 264, 273, 958, 1068, 1161, 1180, 1221, 1224, 1330, 1861, 2134, 2198, 2317, 2488, 2597, 2614, 2668, 2673, 2806, 3186, 3242, 3251, 3318

English as Second Language, 50, 192, 199, 218, 221, 225, 261, 851, 1068, 1180, 1198, 1224, 1330, 1861, 2134, 2806, 3086, 3318

Gifted/Talented Education, 226

Health Education, 21, 182, 232, 244, 261, 336, 683, 747, 1068, 1180, 1224, 1233, 1282, 1330, 1472, 1580, 1659, 1725, 1850, 1861, 1943, 2031, 2115, 2134, 2214, 2298, 2319, 2522, 2553, 2601, 2616, 2687, 2806, 3185, 3318

Journalism Education, 206

Language Development, 190, 2574

Learning Disabled Education, 141, 214, 216, 217,

218, 221, 225, 236, 243, 246, 247, 248, 251, 252, 259, 260, 1161, 2218, 2219, 2220, 2317, 2527, 2528, 2529, 2531, 2538, 2605, 2614, 2617, 2618, 2619, 3196, 3197, 3198, 3199, 3214, 3264, 4084, 4192

Music Education, 51, 128, 200, 208, 242, 852, 998, 1039, 1108, 1155, 1243, 1259, 1301, 1322, 2824, 2867, 3996

Orientation/Mobility, 184, 194

Physical Education, 21, 54, 104, 165, 166, 169, 182, 201, 230, 232, 239, 240, 243, 261, 266, 267, 271, 914, 1068, 1161, 1180, 1224, 1233, 1282, 1330, 1861, 2134, 2298, 2312, 2313, 2317, 2348, 2553, 2601, 2609, 2610, 2614, 2630, 2631, 2806, 2897, 3185, 3218, 3219, 3249, 3281, 3282, 3318

Post-Secondary Education, 20, 238, 249, 269, 281, 345, 822

Reading Education, 243, 264, 1161, 2317, 2614

Reading Education-G, 217, 218, 219, 220, 221, 222, 223, 224, 225, 264

Secondary Education, 211, 238, 243, 257, 258, 264, 273, 958, 1161, 1221, 2317, 2597, 2614, 2668, 3242

Sign Language, 237, 2303, 2606

Special Education, 141, 194, 207, 214, 216, 217, 231, 243, 246, 247, 248, 251, 252, 255, 259, 260, 1161, 2218, 2219, 2220, 2317, 2527, 2528, 2529, 2531, 2538, 2589, 2614, 2617, 2618, 2619, 2623, 3172, 3196, 3197, 3198, 3199, 3214, 3235, 3264, 4036, 4050, 4084, 4108, 4109, 4110, 4111, 4113, 4192, 4284

Technology Education, 261, 1068, 1180, 1224, 1330, 1861, 2134, 2806, 3318

Youth Leadership, 54, 104, 107, 171, 201, 211, 230, 233, 268, 272, 914, 973, 1807, 2198, 2349, 2488, 2551, 2597, 2668, 2673, 2699, 3007, 3186, 3220, 3242, 3249, 3251, 3283, 4293, 4294

SCHOOL OF ENGINEERING

General, 2, 4, 7, 16, 38, 41, 42, 43, 44, 56, 68, 126, 153, 156, 164, 172, 174, 180, 202, 210, 244, 262, 263, 274, 275, 276, 277, 278, 279, 280, 281, 282, 283, 284, 285, 286, 287, 288, 289, 290, 291, 292, 293, 294, 295, 296, 297, 298, 299, 300, 301, 302, 303, 304, 305, 306, 307, 308, 309, 310, 311, 312, 313, 314, 315, 316, 317, 318, 319, 320, 321, 322, 323, 324, 325, 326, 327, 328, 329, 330, 331, 332, 333, 334, 335, 336, 337, 338, 339, 340, 341, 342, 343, 344, 345, 346, 347, 348, 349, 351, 352, 353, 354, 355, 356, 357, 358, 360, 361, 362, 363, 364, 365, 366, 367, 368, 369, 372, 375, 376, 377, 378, 379, 382, 385, 386, 388, 398, 399, 400, 401, 402, 405, 409, 415, 416, 425, 426, 427, 428, 429, 430, 433, 434, 442, 447, 448, 449, 451, 452, 453,

465, 466, 473, 474, 476, 477, 478, 485, 486, 487, 488, 489, 490, 491, 492, 493, 495, 496, 497, 500, 501, 502, 503, 504, 505, 507, 510, 511, 512, 513, 514, 515, 516, 518, 520, 521, 522, 523, 524, 527, 528, 529, 530, 533, 534, 535, 539, 540, 541, 548, 551, 552, 553, 554, 555, 557, 558, 559, 560, 565, 566, 573, 574, 575, 577, 578, 579, 582, 586, 587, 588, 589, 590, 593, 594, 595, 596, 600, 601, 609, 611, 612, 613, 614, 616, 620, 621, 624, 626, 627, 629, 630, 631, 633, 642, 643, 644, 645, 646, 648, 649, 650, 651, 652, 658, 659, 664, 670, 676, 677, 678, 680, 681, 682, 683, 684, 685, 686, 687, 689, 690, 697, 700, 707, 708, 710, 711, 712, 713, 716, 717, 718, 719, 721, 722, 723, 725, 729, 730, 732, 739, 743, 744, 745, 746, 747, 748, 749, 750, 751, 753, 754, 759, 760, 763, 764, 765, 767, 774, 780, 781, 797, 819, 842, 844, 845, 846, 847, 883, 884, 1009, 1071, 1098, 1099, 1100, 1101, 1122, 1126, 1205, 1206, 1264, 1341, 1342, 1343, 1344, 1361, 1384, 1398, 1399, 1400, 1401, 1402, 1404, 1405, 1406, 1407, 1410, 1411, 1415, 1416, 1417, 1418, 1424, 1425, 1426, 1427, 1429, 1432, 1434, 1443, 1446, 1447, 1469, 1471, 1472, 1473, 1479, 1486, 1490, 1495, 1497, 1502, 1510, 1511, 1512, 1513, 1514, 1517, 1518, 1524, 1525, 1530, 1537, 1540, 1542, 1543, 1553, 1559, 1565, 1568, 1569, 1570, 1571, 1576, 1577, 1579, 1580, 1581, 1582, 1583, 1584, 1586, 1605, 1610, 1615, 1617, 1620, 1621, 1630, 1631, 1639, 1656, 1658, 1659, 1660, 1661, 1662, 1663, 1665, 1682, 1684, 1692, 1694, 1695, 1697, 1699, 1701, 1703, 1704, 1706, 1708, 1710, 1711, 1718, 1719, 1720, 1721, 1722, 1724, 1725, 1726, 1727, 1728, 1729, 1730, 1735, 1739, 1743, 1747, 1749, 1762, 1763, 1764, 1765, 1766, 1775, 1776, 1787, 1798, 1808, 1809, 1810, 1811, 1812, 1813, 1814, 1815, 1816, 1817, 1819, 1820, 1821, 1822, 1823, 1824, 1825, 1826, 1827, 1829, 1830, 1833, 1834, 1835, 1837, 1839, 1840, 1841, 1842, 1843, 1844, 1845, 1848, 1849, 1850, 1851, 1852, 1855, 1856, 1857, 1858, 1859, 1864, 1865, 1866, 1867, 1868, 1869, 1872, 1873, 1875, 1883, 1888, 1889, 1890, 1891, 1892, 1893, 1894, 1895, 1897, 1900, 1901, 1903, 1910, 1912, 1913, 1914, 1933, 1934, 1935, 1936, 1939, 1940, 1942, 1943, 1945, 1946, 1960, 1963, 1968, 1970, 1972, 1973, 1975, 1977, 1983, 1984, 1985, 1986, 1987, 1988, 1989, 1990, 1996, 1998, 2004, 2007, 2008, 2009, 2011, 2014, 2016, 2017, 2024, 2025, 2026, 2027, 2029, 2030, 2031, 2032, 2033, 2034, 2037, 2038, 2041, 2050, 2053, 2059, 2060, 2061, 2064, 2065, 2066, 2067, 2070, 2073, 2074, 2075, 2076, 2077, 2078, 2079, 2080, 2085, 2087, 2088, 2091, 2093, 2094,

2095, 2096, 2097, 2102, 2103, 2105, 2106, 2110, 2111, 2112, 2113, 2114, 2115, 2116, 2117, 2118, 2119, 2121, 2122, 2130, 2137, 2138, 2139, 2140, 2141, 2151, 2160, 2163, 2164, 2184, 2187, 2190, 2192, 2197, 2204, 2212, 2214, 2221, 2223, 2250, 2264, 2265, 2266, 2267, 2270, 2272, 2274, 2290, 2297, 2305, 2311, 2316, 2319, 2330, 2332, 2383, 2412, 2416, 2479, 2482, 2487, 2508, 2522, 2565, 2578, 2580, 2582, 2600, 2613, 2616, 2635, 2641, 2643, 2672, 2679, 2686, 2687, 2721, 2728, 2731, 2732, 2733, 2734, 2737, 2745, 2746, 2758, 2763, 2776, 2805, 2807, 2808, 2820, 2831, 2848, 2863, 2864, 2910, 2911, 2912, 2913, 2936, 2937, 2964, 2971, 3025, 3034, 3052, 3053, 3054, 3057, 3066, 3071, 3078, 3079, 3080, 3081, 3097, 3103, 3132, 3150, 3152, 3160, 3161, 3162, 3163, 3178, 3179, 3189, 3190, 3215, 3223, 3224, 3225, 3226, 3239, 3257, 3278, 3296, 3312, 3315, 3343, 3617, 3711, 4065, 4148, 4183, 4196, 4197

AERONAUTICS

General, 2, 19, 38, 70, 129, 173, 204, 278, 282, 283, 284, 285, 286, 292, 305, 307, 312, 327, 328, 329, 334, 355, 370, 371, 372, 373, 374, 375, 376, 377, 378, 379, 381, 382, 383, 384, 385, 386, 388, 394, 395, 397, 400, 401, 402, 404, 405, 407, 408, 409, 412, 413, 416, 425, 426, 427, 428, 429, 430, 442, 449, 452, 465, 477, 485, 486, 487, 488, 489, 490, 495, 496, 497, 500, 501, 510, 516, 520, 521, 522, 523, 524, 533, 538, 539, 540, 548, 553, 555, 566, 579, 586, 587, 588, 589, 590, 593, 597, 600, 601, 609, 613, 614, 621, 631, 642, 643, 644, 645, 646, 648, 654, 658, 659, 664, 672, 678, 681, 697, 712, 716, 717, 718, 719, 721, 726, 729, 730, 732, 740, 743, 745, 759, 767, 777, 781, 842, 870, 884, 1000, 1122, 1206, 1361, 1398, 1400, 1402, 1403, 1407, 1426, 1432, 1434, 1443, 1444, 1447, 1486, 1495, 1510, 1518, 1528, 1540, 1543, 1562, 1577, 1601, 1602, 1605, 1620, 1630, 1631, 1632, 1639, 1682, 1694, 1699, 1701, 1708, 1711, 1722, 1735, 1749, 1766, 1776, 1798, 1811, 1814, 1815, 1816, 1817, 1819, 1826, 1842, 1843, 1848, 1858, 1865, 1875, 1888, 1889, 1890, 1891, 1897, 1910, 1913, 1940, 1960, 1975, 1983, 1984, 1985, 1986, 1996, 2008, 2018, 2029, 2048, 2049, 2050, 2067, 2068, 2073, 2074, 2075, 2076, 2085, 2093, 2095, 2107, 2108, 2113, 2128, 2129, 2130, 2163, 2272, 2416, 2424, 2580, 2643, 2728, 2746, 2776, 2820, 2937, 2964, 2971, 2983, 2984, 3103, 3179, 3190, 3239, 3285, 3286, 3288, 3289, 3294, 3311, 3312, 3314, 3315, 3997, 4055, 4126, 4127, 4146, 4147, 4151, 4163

Aerodynamics, 412, 4055

Aeronautical Engineering, 129, 328, 329, 394, 401, 402, 404, 412, 413, 672, 740, 1562, 1842, 1843, 2018, 2107, 2964, 3312, 3314, 4055

Aerospace History, 329, 402, 407, 408, 1601, 1602, 1843, 2048, 2049, 2128, 2129, 2964, 2983, 2984, 3312, 4055

Aerospace Technology, 129, 324, 325, 328, 329, 394, 398, 399, 401, 402, 404, 413, 551, 552, 611, 612, 672, 676, 677, 740, 1416, 1417, 1562, 1570, 1571, 1719, 1720, 1839, 1840, 1842, 1843, 1935, 1936, 2018, 2026, 2027, 2107, 2863, 2864, 2964, 3312, 3314, 4055

Astronautics, 328, 329, 373, 374, 401, 402, 1546, 1842, 1843, 2068, 2964, 3288, 3289, 3312, 4055, 4146, 4215

Aviation, 19, 114, 129, 173, 204, 371, 373, 374, 380, 381, 383, 387, 389, 390, 391, 392, 393, 396, 403, 404, 406, 618, 654, 777, 870, 1000, 1403, 1444, 1528, 1632, 2068, 2424, 3286, 3288, 3289, 3293, 3294, 3302, 3309, 3313, 3314, 3853, 4055, 4126, 4127, 4151

Aviation Electronics, 19, 114, 129, 371, 373, 374, 380, 387, 396, 404, 406, 618, 2068, 3286, 3288, 3289, 3293, 3302, 3309, 3314, 4055, 4127, 4151

Aviation Writing, 329, 402, 1843, 2964, 3312, 4055, 4127

Aviation/Aerospace History, 407, 408, 1601, 1602, 2048, 2049, 2128, 2129, 2983, 2984

Space Science, 324, 325, 328, 329, 373, 374, 394, 395, 398, 399, 401, 402, 410, 412, 413, 551, 552, 568, 611, 612, 623, 672, 676, 677, 699, 740, 1416, 1417, 1562, 1570, 1571, 1606, 1685, 1719, 1720, 1737, 1839, 1840, 1842, 1843, 1935, 1936, 1964, 2018, 2026, 2027, 2054, 2068, 2107, 2108, 2339, 2863, 2864, 2964, 3288, 3289, 3312, 4055

Vertical Flight, 411

ARCHITECTURE

General, 2, 38, 79, 126, 145, 277, 278, 282, 283, 284, 285, 286, 292, 293, 294, 312, 320, 321, 327, 331, 334, 344, 355, 368, 369, 372, 375, 376, 377, 378, 379, 382, 388, 400, 405, 409, 414, 415, 416, 417, 419, 423, 424, 425, 426, 427, 428, 429, 430, 431, 432, 433, 434, 440, 441, 442, 443, 447, 448, 449, 451, 452, 453, 454, 455, 456, 458, 461, 464, 465, 469, 470, 471, 473, 474, 477, 485, 486, 487, 488, 489, 490, 491, 492, 497, 500, 501, 510, 512, 513, 515, 516, 520, 521, 522, 523, 524, 533, 548, 553, 555, 566, 574, 575, 578, 579, 586, 587, 588, 589, 590, 593, 594, 595, 609, 613, 614, 619, 621, 626, 627, 630, 631, 642, 643, 644, 645, 646, 648, 649, 650, 664, 678, 681, 694, 697, 707, 708, 711, 712, 716, 717, 718, 719, 721, 722, 723, 732, 743, 745, 757, 759, 763, 764, 767, 786, 840, 842, 857, 890, 954, 977, 981, 988, 989, 1011, 1019, 1051, 1052, 1060, 1070, 1073, 1093, 1095, 1133, 1143, 1186, 1219, 1231, 1236, 1265, 1275, 1319, 1334, 1339, 1364, 1384, 1398, 1400, 1402, 1426, 1432, 1434, 1443, 1485, 1486, 1495, 1510, 1518, 1565, 1577, 1605, 1620, 1630, 1631, 1682, 1694, 1699, 1701, 1722, 1735, 1749, 1760, 1766, 1767, 1777, 1792, 1798, 1811, 1814, 1815, 1816, 1817, 1819, 1848, 1858, 1865, 1875, 1888, 1889, 1890, 1891, 1897, 1940, 1957, 1960, 1975, 1983, 1984, 1985, 1986, 1996, 2029, 2041, 2050, 2066, 2067, 2073, 2074, 2075, 2076, 2085, 2113, 2130, 2163, 2204, 2212, 2223, 2272, 2305, 2316, 2332, 2416, 2508, 2580, 2613, 2643, 2679, 2686, 2720, 2728, 2749, 2776, 2820, 2909, 2921, 2941, 2971, 2987, 3032, 3052, 3053, 3109, 3189, 3190, 3257, 3292, 3315, 4002, 4158, 4226

Architectural Engineering, 153, 358, 368, 369, 455, 457, 466, 473, 474, 509, 511, 512, 513, 574, 575, 624, 626, 627, 700, 707, 708, 760, 763, 764, 1051, 3215, 3278

Architectural History, 419, 421, 422, 436, 454, 458, 459, 460, 472, 769, 833, 879, 981, 984, 985, 1052, 1053, 1054, 1074, 1753, 1754, 1792, 1793, 2725, 2904

Design Arts, 414, 419, 443, 455, 460, 977, 981, 1019, 1051, 1054, 1143, 1231, 1275

Environmental Design, 419, 437, 446, 455, 460, 467, 981, 1051, 1054, 1445, 1467, 1541, 1638, 1709, 1911

Health Facilities, 418

History Preserv & Conserv, 454, 1035

Landscape Architecture, 126, 144, 331, 414, 419, 436, 437, 438, 439, 444, 445, 446, 451, 463, 879, 977, 981, 1231, 1445, 1448, 1450, 1464, 1467, 1484, 1541, 1638, 1680, 1709, 1911, 2212, 2316, 2613, 2686, 2877, 3053, 3142, 3189, 3257

Naval Architecture, 462, 468, 758, 1738, 4248

Urban Planning, 28, 125, 153, 358, 419, 420, 435, 437, 446, 450, 455, 466, 511, 624, 700, 760, 874, 981, 1051, 1445, 1467, 1532, 1541, 1624, 1638, 1709, 1771, 1911, 2928, 3096, 3130, 3215, 3231, 3256, 3278, 4287

CIVIL ENGINEERING

General, 2, 38, 116, 153, 275, 278, 280, 281, 282, 283, 284, 285, 286, 292, 293, 294, 295, 305, 307, 312, 327, 334, 337, 338, 339, 340, 341, 345, 346, 348, 349, 351, 355, 358, 368, 369, 372, 375, 376, 377, 378, 379, 382, 385, 386, 388, 400, 405, 409, 416, 425, 426, 427, 428, 429, 430, 433, 434, 442, 449, 452, 457, 465, 466, 473, 474, 475, 476, 477, 478, 479, 484, 485, 486, 487, 488, 489, 490, 491, 492, 493, 494, 495, 496, 497, 499, 500, 501, 502, 503, 504, 505, 506, 507, 508, 509, 510, 511, 512, 513, 514, 516,

518, 520, 521, 522, 523, 524, 533, 534, 539, 540,
548, 553, 555, 557, 558, 559, 560, 561, 566,
574, 575, 576, 577, 579, 582, 586, 587, 588,
589, 590, 593, 594, 595, 596, 599, 600, 601,
609, 613, 614, 616, 621, 624, 626, 627, 628, 629,
631, 633, 635, 642, 643, 644, 645, 646, 648,
649, 650, 651, 657, 658, 659, 664, 674, 678, 681,
684, 685, 686, 687, 689, 691, 697, 700, 707, 708,
709, 710, 712, 713, 714, 716, 717, 718, 719, 721,
722, 723, 725, 728, 729, 730, 732, 741, 743,
745, 748, 749, 750, 751, 753, 755, 759, 760,
763, 764, 765, 767, 781, 807, 842, 884, 1122,
1206, 1361, 1398, 1400, 1402, 1407, 1419,
1426, 1432, 1434, 1443, 1447, 1474, 1486,
1490, 1495, 1502, 1503, 1510, 1518, 1524, 1539,
1540, 1543, 1577, 1581, 1582, 1583, 1584,
1585, 1587, 1605, 1620, 1630, 1631, 1639,
1660, 1661, 1662, 1663, 1664, 1666, 1682,
1692, 1694, 1697, 1699, 1701, 1703, 1707, 1708,
1711, 1722, 1726, 1727, 1728, 1729, 1731, 1735,
1749, 1766, 1776, 1798, 1809, 1811, 1813, 1814,
1815, 1816, 1817, 1819, 1826, 1848, 1851, 1858,
1865, 1871, 1872, 1875, 1883, 1888, 1889,
1890, 1891, 1897, 1900, 1908, 1910, 1913, 1930,
1940, 1944, 1945, 1948, 1960, 1971, 1972,
1975, 1977, 1983, 1984, 1985, 1986, 1996,
1998, 2006, 2008, 2019, 2029, 2032, 2033, 2034,
2035, 2037, 2040, 2050, 2063, 2067, 2070, 2073,
2074, 2075, 2076, 2085, 2087, 2092, 2093, 2095,
2113, 2116, 2117, 2118, 2119, 2121, 2124, 2130,
2163, 2272, 2416, 2580, 2643, 2728, 2746,
2776, 2820, 2858, 2937, 2971, 3103, 3179, 3190,
3215, 3239, 3258, 3278, 3315, 4175
Construction, 346, 483, 498, 4182
Hydraulics, 480, 482
Public Works Administration, 31, 153, 358, 466,
481, 511, 624, 700, 760, 3215, 3278
Structural Engineering, 457, 483, 509

COMPUTER SCIENCE

General, 2, 4, 14, 16, 38, 41, 42, 43, 44, 56, 65, 70,
88, 130, 139, 154, 158, 164, 172, 196, 202, 275,
277, 278, 280, 282, 283, 284, 285, 286, 287,
288, 289, 290, 292, 295, 296, 305, 307, 308, 312,
324, 325, 327, 333, 334, 337, 338, 339, 340,
348, 349, 351, 353, 355, 359, 365, 368, 369,
372, 375, 376, 377, 378, 379, 382, 384, 385,
386, 388, 398, 399, 400, 405, 409, 410, 415, 416,
425, 426, 427, 428, 429, 430, 442, 449, 452,
465, 473, 474, 476, 477, 478, 485, 486, 487,
488, 489, 490, 493, 495, 496, 497, 500, 501, 502,
503, 504, 505, 506, 510, 512, 513, 514, 515, 516,
517, 518, 519, 520, 521, 522, 523, 524, 525, 526,
527, 528, 529, 530, 531, 532, 533, 534, 535,
536, 537, 538, 539, 540, 541, 542, 543, 544,
546, 547, 548, 549, 550, 551, 552, 553, 554,
555, 556, 557, 558, 559, 560, 561, 562, 563,
564, 565, 566, 567, 568, 569, 570, 571, 572,
573, 574, 575, 577, 578, 579, 581, 582, 585,
586, 587, 588, 589, 590, 591, 592, 593, 596,
597, 600, 601, 602, 603, 604, 606, 607, 609, 611,
612, 613, 614, 617, 620, 621, 623, 625, 626, 627,
629, 630, 631, 633, 642, 643, 644, 645, 646,
647, 648, 651, 658, 659, 660, 664, 676, 677,
678, 680, 681, 684, 685, 686, 687, 693, 697,
699, 701, 707, 708, 710, 711, 712, 713, 716, 717,
718, 719, 720, 721, 725, 726, 729, 730, 732, 742,
743, 744, 745, 748, 749, 750, 751, 756, 759,
763, 764, 765, 767, 774, 781, 842, 844, 845,
846, 847, 884, 963, 1098, 1099, 1100, 1101, 1122,
1183, 1206, 1341, 1342, 1343, 1344, 1361, 1390,
1392, 1398, 1400, 1402, 1407, 1416, 1417,
1424, 1426, 1432, 1434, 1443, 1447, 1486,
1490, 1495, 1502, 1510, 1511, 1512, 1513, 1514,
1518, 1524, 1540, 1543, 1567, 1570, 1571, 1576,
1577, 1581, 1582, 1583, 1584, 1585, 1597,
1605, 1606, 1607, 1608, 1620, 1630, 1631,
1639, 1656, 1660, 1661, 1662, 1663, 1664,
1677, 1682, 1683, 1685, 1686, 1692, 1694,
1697, 1699, 1701, 1703, 1708, 1711, 1719, 1720,
1721, 1722, 1726, 1727, 1728, 1729, 1735,
1737, 1749, 1762, 1763, 1764, 1765, 1766,
1776, 1787, 1798, 1800, 1809, 1811, 1813, 1814,
1815, 1816, 1817, 1819, 1820, 1826, 1827, 1839,
1840, 1848, 1856, 1858, 1865, 1872, 1875,
1883, 1888, 1889, 1890, 1891, 1892, 1893,
1894, 1895, 1896, 1897, 1900, 1901, 1910, 1913,
1914, 1935, 1936, 1939, 1940, 1944, 1960,
1962, 1964, 1972, 1975, 1977, 1983, 1984,
1985, 1986, 1987, 1988, 1989, 1990, 1991,
1996, 1998, 2008, 2009, 2022, 2026, 2027,
2029, 2032, 2033, 2034, 2035, 2046, 2050, 2052,
2054, 2066, 2067, 2070, 2072, 2073, 2074, 2075,
2076, 2077, 2078, 2079, 2080, 2081, 2084, 2085,
2087, 2088, 2093, 2095, 2096, 2099, 2109, 2112,
2113, 2116, 2117, 2118, 2119, 2126, 2130, 2135,
2139, 2162, 2163, 2164, 2184, 2229, 2264, 2265,
2266, 2267, 2272, 2274, 2339, 2340, 2415,
2416, 2540, 2580, 2625, 2643, 2691, 2722,
2728, 2729, 2731, 2732, 2733, 2734, 2737,
2746, 2776, 2818, 2820, 2863, 2864, 2892, 2910,
2911, 2912, 2913, 2937, 2971, 3025, 3054, 3058,
3062, 3071, 3078, 3079, 3080, 3081, 3103, 3132,
3152, 3160, 3161, 3162, 3163, 3179, 3190, 3223,
3224, 3225, 3226, 3239, 3279, 3296, 3297,
3315, 4083, 4180, 4181, 4187, 4254
Artificial Intelligence, 410, 546, 568, 606, 623, 699,
1606, 1685, 1737, 1964, 2054, 2339
Computer Graphics, 542, 543, 602, 603, 4039
History of Computing, 536, 545, 605

ELECTRICAL ENGINEERING

General, 2, 38, 70, 153, 158, 275, 277, 278, 280,
281, 282, 283, 284, 285, 286, 292, 293, 294,
295, 305, 307, 312, 327, 334, 341, 345, 346, 348,
349, 350, 351, 353, 355, 358, 368, 369, 372,
375, 376, 377, 378, 379, 382, 384, 385, 386,
388, 400, 405, 409, 410, 415, 416, 425, 426, 427,
428, 429, 430, 433, 434, 442, 449, 452, 456,
465, 466, 473, 474, 475, 476, 477, 478, 485,
486, 487, 488, 489, 490, 491, 492, 493, 494,
495, 496, 497, 500, 501, 507, 510, 511, 512, 513,
514, 515, 516, 517, 518, 519, 520, 521, 522, 523,
524, 525, 531, 533, 534, 538, 539, 540, 542,
543, 544, 546, 548, 553, 555, 565, 566, 568,
572, 574, 575, 576, 577, 578, 579, 580, 581,
582, 585, 586, 587, 588, 589, 590, 591, 592,
593, 594, 595, 596, 597, 598, 599, 600, 601,
602, 603, 604, 606, 608, 609, 613, 614, 615, 616,
619, 620, 621, 622, 623, 624, 625, 626, 627, 628,
629, 630, 631, 633, 642, 643, 644, 645, 646,
647, 648, 649, 650, 651, 656, 657, 658, 659,
664, 678, 681, 688, 689, 694, 697, 699, 700, 707,
708, 709, 710, 711, 712, 713, 716, 717, 718, 719,
720, 721, 722, 723, 725, 726, 728, 729, 730,
732, 743, 745, 752, 753, 757, 759, 760, 763,
764, 765, 767, 781, 842, 884, 1122, 1183, 1206,
1361, 1392, 1398, 1400, 1402, 1407, 1424,
1426, 1432, 1434, 1443, 1447, 1486, 1490,
1495, 1502, 1510, 1518, 1524, 1536, 1539, 1540,
1543, 1577, 1605, 1606, 1608, 1620, 1630,
1631, 1639, 1682, 1685, 1692, 1694, 1697,
1699, 1701, 1703, 1707, 1708, 1711, 1722, 1735,
1737, 1749, 1766, 1776, 1798, 1809, 1811, 1813,
1814, 1815, 1816, 1817, 1819, 1826, 1848, 1851,
1856, 1858, 1865, 1871, 1872, 1875, 1883,
1888, 1889, 1890, 1891, 1897, 1900, 1908, 1910,
1913, 1940, 1945, 1960, 1964, 1971, 1972,
1975, 1977, 1983, 1984, 1985, 1986, 1991,
1996, 1998, 2003, 2006, 2008, 2029, 2036,
2037, 2050, 2054, 2063, 2066, 2067, 2070, 2072,
2073, 2074, 2075, 2076, 2081, 2085, 2087, 2092,
2093, 2095, 2113, 2120, 2121, 2130, 2163, 2272,
2339, 2416, 2580, 2643, 2728, 2746, 2776,
2818, 2820, 2937, 2971, 3103, 3179, 3190, 3215,
3239, 3278, 3315, 4083, 4181, 4195, 4226
Communications, 88, 139, 324, 325, 398, 399, 406,
547, 551, 552, 563, 580, 607, 611, 612, 617, 618,
622, 660, 676, 677, 1416, 1417, 1570, 1571,
1719, 1720, 1839, 1840, 1935, 1936, 2026,
2027, 2099, 2863, 2864, 3058, 4254
Electrical Sci & Tech Hist, 545, 605
Electronics, 517, 580, 581, 2818
Microeletronics, 622, 4083
Vacuum Science, 583, 584, 610, 622

ENGINEERING TECHNOLOGY

General, 2, 30, 38, 116, 173, 204, 244, 250, 275, 277, 278, 280, 281, 282, 283, 284, 285, 286, 292, 293, 294, 295, 297, 305, 307, 312, 327, 333, 334, 335, 336, 337, 338, 339, 340, 341, 342, 345, 346, 348, 349, 350, 351, 355, 372, 375, 376, 377, 378, 379, 382, 383, 385, 386, 388, 394, 400, 405, 409, 415, 416, 425, 426, 427, 428, 429, 430, 433, 434, 442, 449, 452, 465, 476, 477, 478, 485, 486, 487, 488, 489, 490, 491, 492, 493, 494, 495, 496, 497, 499, 500, 501, 502, 503, 504, 505, 507, 508, 510, 514, 515, 516, 518, 520, 521, 522, 523, 524, 533, 534, 539, 540, 548, 553, 554, 555, 557, 558, 559, 560, 566, 577, 578, 579, 582, 586, 587, 588, 589, 590, 593, 594, 595, 596, 599, 600, 601, 609, 613, 614, 616, 621, 629, 630, 631, 633, 634, 642, 643, 644, 645, 646, 648, 649, 650, 651, 652, 654, 657, 658, 659, 664, 672, 674, 678, 680, 681, 682, 683, 684, 685, 686, 687, 689, 690, 691, 692, 695, 696, 697, 702, 710, 711, 712, 713, 716, 717, 718, 719, 721, 722, 723, 725, 728, 729, 730, 732, 740, 741, 743, 744, 745, 746, 747, 748, 749, 750, 751, 753, 754, 755, 759, 761, 765, 767, 777, 781, 807, 842, 870, 884, 940, 1000, 1122, 1206, 1361, 1398, 1400, 1402, 1403, 1407, 1419, 1426, 1432, 1434, 1443, 1444, 1447, 1471, 1472, 1473, 1474, 1481, 1486, 1490, 1495, 1502, 1510, 1518, 1524, 1525, 1528, 1539, 1540, 1543, 1562, 1576, 1577, 1579, 1580, 1581, 1582, 1583, 1584, 1586, 1587, 1595, 1605, 1620, 1630, 1631, 1632, 1639, 1656, 1658, 1659, 1660, 1661, 1662, 1663, 1665, 1666, 1673, 1682, 1692, 1694, 1697, 1699, 1701, 1703, 1704, 1707, 1708, 1711, 1721, 1722, 1724, 1725, 1726, 1727, 1728, 1729, 1730, 1731, 1735, 1749, 1766, 1776, 1787, 1798, 1809, 1811, 1813, 1814, 1815, 1816, 1817, 1819, 1821, 1826, 1848, 1849, 1850, 1851, 1852, 1858, 1865, 1872, 1875, 1883, 1888, 1889, 1890, 1891, 1897, 1900, 1908, 1910, 1913, 1930, 1939, 1940, 1942, 1943, 1945, 1946, 1948, 1951, 1960, 1972, 1975, 1977, 1983, 1984, 1985, 1986, 1996, 1998, 2006, 2008, 2018, 2019, 2029, 2030, 2031, 2032, 2033, 2034, 2037, 2038, 2040, 2050, 2066, 2067, 2070, 2071, 2073, 2074, 2075, 2076, 2085, 2087, 2092, 2093, 2095, 2107, 2112, 2113, 2114, 2115, 2116, 2117, 2118, 2119, 2121, 2122, 2124, 2130, 2163, 2214, 2272, 2319, 2333, 2416, 2424, 2522, 2580, 2582, 2616, 2620, 2643, 2687, 2728, 2746, 2776, 2820, 2858, 2937, 2971, 3054, 3103, 3132, 3179, 3190, 3239, 3258, 3315, 4269

Acoustics, 410, 568, 623, 699, 1606, 1685, 1737, 1964, 2054, 2339

Arc Welding Technology, 667, 3304, 4290

Automotive Technology, 170, 345, 346, 350, 671, 706, 1690, 3307, 3320, 4162

Chemical Engineering, 317, 337, 338, 339, 340, 350, 368, 369, 473, 474, 475, 502, 503, 504, 505, 512, 513, 531, 557, 558, 559, 560, 562, 574, 575, 576, 592, 598, 615, 626, 627, 628, 632, 638, 640, 641, 647, 653, 655, 656, 663, 670, 684, 685, 686, 687, 688, 693, 702, 707, 708, 709, 720, 731, 739, 748, 749, 750, 751, 752, 756, 761, 763, 764, 1498, 1506, 1508, 1509, 1534, 1536, 1559, 1581, 1582, 1583, 1584, 1597, 1622, 1626, 1628, 1629, 1634, 1660, 1661, 1662, 1663, 1677, 1726, 1727, 1728, 1729, 1871, 1876, 1920, 1971, 1976, 1979, 1981, 1982, 1991, 2003, 2012, 2016, 2032, 2033, 2034, 2036, 2046, 2063, 2081, 2100, 2105, 2116, 2117, 2118, 2119, 2120, 2126, 4172

Environmental Engineering, 98, 173, 204, 337, 338, 339, 340, 346, 383, 484, 502, 503, 504, 505, 557, 558, 559, 560, 570, 632, 635, 636, 637, 638, 639, 640, 641, 654, 655, 665, 666, 684, 685, 686, 687, 701, 703, 704, 705, 714, 748, 749, 750, 751, 762, 777, 870, 902, 1000, 1403, 1444, 1498, 1503, 1504, 1505, 1506, 1507, 1508, 1509, 1528, 1534, 1550, 1552, 1581, 1582, 1583, 1584, 1607, 1612, 1613, 1614, 1622, 1625, 1626, 1627, 1628, 1629, 1632, 1634, 1647, 1648, 1660, 1661, 1662, 1663, 1677, 1686, 1687, 1688, 1698, 1726, 1727, 1728, 1729, 1740, 1741, 1876, 1976, 1978, 1979, 1980, 1981, 1982, 2032, 2033, 2034, 2116, 2117, 2118, 2119, 2424, 2892, 3062, 4150, 4277, 4289

Htg; Refrgeratn & Air-Cond, 456, 619, 694, 757, 4220

Industrial Engineering, 11, 88, 102, 115, 122, 244, 324, 325, 336, 350, 398, 399, 412, 475, 547, 551, 552, 576, 607, 611, 612, 628, 660, 661, 662, 668, 673, 675, 676, 677, 683, 696, 709, 747, 1022, 1416, 1417, 1472, 1570, 1571, 1580, 1659, 1719, 1720, 1725, 1839, 1840, 1850, 1871, 1935, 1936, 1943, 1971, 2026, 2027, 2031, 2063, 2099, 2115, 2214, 2319, 2522, 2616, 2687, 2863, 2864, 4254, 4277

Industrial Hygiene, 153, 244, 336, 358, 466, 511, 624, 679, 683, 700, 747, 760, 1472, 1580, 1659, 1725, 1850, 1943, 2031, 2115, 2210, 2214, 2314, 2319, 2522, 2611, 2616, 2687, 3215, 3278

Manufacturing Engineering, 122, 324, 325, 350, 398, 399, 551, 552, 611, 612, 675, 676, 677, 696, 1416, 1417, 1570, 1571, 1719, 1720, 1839, 1840, 1935, 1936, 2026, 2027, 2863, 2864

Nuclear Engineering, 341, 342, 410, 507, 568, 615, 616, 623, 669, 688, 689, 690, 699, 752, 753, 754, 1473, 1586, 1606, 1665, 1685, 1730, 1737, 1851, 1852, 1945, 1946, 1964, 2036, 2037, 2038, 2054, 2120, 2121, 2122, 2339

Optical Engineering, 368, 369, 410, 473, 474, 512, 513, 568, 574, 575, 623, 626, 627, 698, 699, 707, 708, 763, 764, 1606, 1685, 1737, 1964, 2054, 2339

Photographic/Imaging Sci., 695

Power Generation, 346

Radar, 410, 568, 623, 699, 1606, 1685, 1737, 1964, 2054, 2339

Robotics, 696

MECHANICAL ENGINEERING

General, 70, 116, 244, 275, 277, 278, 280, 281, 283, 284, 285, 286, 292, 293, 294, 295, 305, 307, 312, 327, 333, 334, 335, 336, 337, 338, 339, 340, 341, 342, 345, 346, 348, 349, 350, 351, 355, 372, 376, 377, 378, 379, 382, 384, 385, 386, 388, 394, 400, 405, 409, 415, 416, 426, 427, 428, 429, 430, 433, 434, 442, 449, 452, 456, 465, 475, 476, 477, 478, 486, 487, 488, 489, 490, 491, 492, 493, 494, 495, 496, 497, 499, 500, 501, 502, 503, 504, 505, 507, 508, 510, 514, 515, 516, 518, 521, 522, 523, 524, 531, 533, 534, 538, 539, 540, 548, 553, 554, 555, 557, 558, 559, 560, 562, 566, 576, 577, 578, 579, 582, 587, 588, 589, 590, 592, 593, 594, 595, 596, 597, 599, 600, 601, 609, 613, 614, 615, 616, 619, 621, 628, 629, 630, 631, 633, 643, 644, 645, 646, 647, 648, 649, 650, 651, 657, 658, 659, 663, 664, 672, 674, 678, 680, 681, 682, 683, 684, 685, 686, 687, 688, 689, 690, 691, 693, 694, 697, 709, 710, 711, 712, 713, 715, 716, 717, 718, 719, 720, 721, 722, 723, 725, 726, 728, 729, 730, 731, 732, 733, 740, 741, 743, 744, 745, 746, 747, 748, 749, 750, 751, 752, 753, 754, 755, 756, 757, 759, 765, 767, 781, 807, 884, 1122, 1206, 1361, 1398, 1402, 1407, 1419, 1426, 1432, 1443, 1447, 1471, 1472, 1473, 1474, 1486, 1490, 1495, 1502, 1518, 1524, 1539, 1540, 1543, 1562, 1576, 1577, 1579, 1580, 1581, 1582, 1583, 1584, 1586, 1587, 1597, 1605, 1620, 1631, 1639, 1656, 1658, 1659, 1660, 1661, 1662, 1663, 1665, 1666, 1682, 1692, 1694, 1697, 1701, 1703, 1707, 1708, 1711, 1721, 1722, 1724, 1725, 1726, 1727, 1728, 1729, 1730, 1731, 1735, 1749, 1766, 1776, 1787, 1798, 1809, 1811, 1813, 1814, 1815, 1816, 1817, 1819, 1826, 1848, 1849, 1850, 1851, 1852, 1858, 1865, 1871, 1872, 1875, 1883, 1888, 1889, 1890, 1891, 1897, 1900, 1908, 1910, 1913, 1920, 1930, 1939, 1940, 1942, 1943, 1945, 1946, 1948, 1960, 1971, 1972, 1975, 1977, 1983, 1984, 1985, 1986, 1991, 1996, 1998, 2006, 2008, 2012, 2018, 2019, 2029, 2030, 2031, 2032, 2033, 2034, 2036, 2037, 2038, 2040, 2046, 2050, 2063, 2066, 2067, 2070, 2073, 2074, 2075, 2076, 2081, 2085, 2087, 2092, 2093, 2095, 2100,

2107, 2112, 2113, 2114, 2115, 2116, 2117, 2118, 2119, 2120, 2121, 2122, 2124, 2126, 2130, 2163, 2214, 2272, 2319, 2416, 2522, 2580, 2616, 2643, 2687, 2746, 2776, 2858, 2937, 2971, 3054, 3103, 3132, 3179, 3190, 3239, 3258, 3315, 4238

Mat'ls Science/Metallurgy, 153, 317, 341, 350, 358, 368, 369, 466, 473, 474, 475, 507, 511, 512, 513, 550, 574, 575, 576, 615, 616, 624, 626, 627, 628, 670, 688, 689, 700, 702, 705, 707, 708, 709, 724, 734, 735, 736, 737, 738, 739, 742, 752, 753, 760, 761, 762, 763, 764, 1547, 1548, 1559, 1567, 1614, 1702, 1851, 1871, 1899, 1945, 1971, 1997, 2016, 2022, 2036, 2037, 2063, 2086, 2105, 2109, 2120, 2121, 2417, 3215, 3278, 4243

Mining Engineering, 484, 635, 705, 714, 727, 734, 735, 736, 737, 738, 762, 1503, 1538, 1546, 1547, 1548, 1614, 1865, 4215

Naval Science, 4286

Naval/Marine Engineering, 462, 758, 1546, 1734, 4215, 4249

Petroleum Engineering, 705, 727, 762, 1491, 1538, 1546, 1614, 4215, 4261

SCHOOL OF HUMANITIES

General, 4, 8, 9, 10, 56, 79, 87, 93, 94, 100, 112, 137, 172, 173, 178, 181, 202, 204, 209, 215, 235, 269, 270, 275, 278, 296, 306, 307, 314, 356, 372, 383, 386, 416, 421, 440, 476, 477, 496, 508, 514, 516, 535, 540, 577, 579, 601, 629, 631, 654, 659, 691, 710, 712, 730, 755, 765, 766, 767, 769, 770, 771, 772, 773, 774, 776, 777, 778, 779, 780, 781, 782, 783, 784, 785, 786, 787, 788, 789, 790, 791, 792, 793, 794, 795, 796, 797, 798, 799, 800, 801, 802, 803, 804, 805, 806, 807, 808, 809, 810, 811, 812, 813, 814, 815, 816, 817, 818, 819, 820, 821, 822, 823, 824, 833, 834, 835, 848, 849, 862, 870, 883, 884, 885, 890, 896, 897, 900, 901, 906, 907, 908, 925, 926, 927, 928, 944, 945, 947, 980, 984, 986, 987, 994, 995, 1000, 1010, 1011, 1017, 1021, 1032, 1034, 1036, 1040, 1041, 1042, 1061, 1080, 1090, 1102, 1103, 1109, 1122, 1124, 1125, 1133, 1137, 1138, 1140, 1145, 1150, 1151, 1156, 1157, 1158, 1159, 1194, 1195, 1205, 1206, 1214, 1215, 1218, 1240, 1241, 1265, 1270, 1290, 1302, 1303, 1304, 1321, 1340, 1345, 1346, 1361, 1362, 1364, 1369, 1370, 1372, 1375, 1376, 1377, 1378, 1379, 1380, 1383, 1397, 1398, 1403, 1407, 1408, 1410, 1419, 1427, 1432, 1444, 1446, 1447, 1474, 1480, 1490, 1495, 1528, 1542, 1543, 1573, 1574, 1575, 1587, 1590, 1620, 1632, 1639, 1666, 1667, 1692, 1694, 1710, 1711, 1731, 1748, 1749, 1753, 1755, 1756, 1775, 1776, 1777, 1778, 1784, 1785, 1786, 1809, 1811, 1820, 1826, 1828, 1831, 1836, 1846, 1853, 1859, 1872, 1875,

1901, 1912, 1913, 1948, 1972, 1975, 2007, 2008, 2040, 2067, 2088, 2094, 2095, 2124, 2164, 2192, 2201, 2222, 2274, 2301, 2331, 2424, 2482, 2530, 2723, 2725, 2726, 2735, 2736, 2737, 2738, 2745, 2746, 2748, 2749, 2753, 2754, 2755, 2756, 2757, 2759, 2760, 2761, 2762, 2763, 2766, 2767, 2769, 2771, 2772, 2773, 2774, 2775, 2778, 2780, 2785, 2786, 2787, 2789, 2790, 2791, 2811, 2812, 2822, 2823, 2841, 2842, 2899, 2904, 2905, 2906, 2914, 2915, 2924, 2936, 2937, 2939, 2941, 2952, 2955, 2961, 2963, 2966, 2967, 2968, 2969, 3021, 3022, 3025, 3032, 3035, 3036, 3038, 3040, 3041, 3049, 3084, 3085, 3103, 3109, 3113, 3115, 3118, 3119, 3120, 3128, 3164, 3165, 3178, 3179, 3183, 3184, 3187, 3227, 3228, 3239, 3244, 3245, 3258, 3296, 3617, 4045, 4060

AREA STUDIES

General, 2, 38, 104, 173, 175, 204, 227, 230, 282, 306, 307, 375, 383, 386, 425, 485, 496, 520, 540, 567, 586, 601, 642, 654, 659, 730, 768, 770, 771, 772, 773, 777, 780, 781, 787, 788, 802, 803, 804, 810, 830, 834, 835, 838, 842, 848, 849, 855, 870, 883, 884, 896, 897, 908, 909, 914, 924, 925, 926, 927, 949, 963, 964, 964, 965, 966, 968, 986, 987, 994, 995, 1000, 1017, 1040, 1041, 1090, 1102, 1103, 1110, 1122, 1137, 1138, 1156, 1157, 1158, 1194, 1195, 1199, 1205, 1206, 1225, 1225, 1226, 1227, 1240, 1241, 1270, 1302, 1303, 1345, 1346, 1361, 1369, 1370, 1377, 1378, 1379, 1390, 1400, 1403, 1407, 1434, 1444, 1446, 1447, 1510, 1528, 1542, 1543, 1566, 1573, 1574, 1630, 1632, 1639, 1655, 1683, 1699, 1710, 1711, 1717, 1755, 1756, 1775, 1776, 1778, 1784, 1785, 1800, 1826, 1838, 1912, 1913, 1931, 1962, 2007, 2008, 2021, 2052, 2094, 2095, 2135, 2424, 2726, 2728, 2735, 2736, 2745, 2746, 2753, 2754, 2770, 2771, 2772, 2773, 2794, 2820, 2822, 2823, 2841, 2905, 2906, 2914, 2915, 2936, 2937, 2952, 2956, 2966, 2967, 2968, 3021, 3022, 3035, 3036, 3084, 3085, 3103, 3113, 3121, 3140, 3164, 3165, 3178, 3179, 3183, 3184, 3227, 3228, 3239, 3244, 3245, 3249, 3255, 3268, 3373

African Studies, 825, 935, 941, 1191, 3823

Afro-American Studies, 51, 200, 852, 998, 1108, 1243, 2824

Albanian Studies-G, 829

American Indian Studies, 831, 871, 942, 943, 1056, 1057, 1599, 1600, 1675, 1676, 1794, 1795, 1953, 1954, 2739, 2926, 2981, 2982, 3093, 3230

Ancient Greece, 423, 836, 837, 840, 868, 988, 1091, 1092, 1093, 1116, 1203, 1757, 1760, 2727, 2907, 2909

Armenian Studies, 794, 907, 2760

Asian American Studies, 567, 963, 1390, 1683, 1800, 1962, 2052, 2135

Asian Pacific Studies, 828, 3134

Asian Studies, 50, 199, 768, 851, 941, 1044, 1198, 3086, 3580

Australian Studies, 1096, 3134

Austrian Studies, 850, 1104

Azerbaijan Studies-G, 794, 907, 2760

British Studies, 454, 866, 967, 972, 975, 1075, 1115, 1181, 1188, 1190, 2925, 2934, 2935, 3006, 3009

Bulgarian Studies-G, 829

Byzantine Studies, 421, 436, 769, 770, 771, 833, 834, 835, 879, 880, 984, 986, 987, 1090, 1753, 1755, 1756, 2725, 2726, 2904, 2905, 2906

Canadian Studies, 432, 567, 776, 841, 857, 861, 862, 963, 968, 1390, 1683, 1767, 1800, 1962, 2052, 2135, 2738, 2921, 2924

Celtic Studies, 878, 1533, 2090

Chinese Studies, 867, 921, 932, 941, 970

Civil Rights, 176, 228, 804, 869, 912, 927, 931, 948, 950, 951, 952, 953, 1041, 1158, 1303, 1379, 1387, 1574, 1785, 2773, 2793, 2796, 2797, 2798, 2799, 2968, 3042, 3055, 3133, 3192, 3204, 3206, 3207, 3208, 3209, 3248, 3259, 3267, 3270, 3271, 3272, 3273

Classical Liberalism, 869

Classical Studies, 258, 423, 826, 827, 837, 839, 840, 958, 978, 979, 988, 1092, 1093, 1120, 1221, 1745, 1746, 1760, 2727, 2907, 2909, 2997, 2998, 2999, 3000, 3001

Czech Studies, 829, 881, 1357

Demography, 41, 42, 43, 44, 89, 90, 98, 133, 134, 287, 288, 289, 290, 527, 528, 529, 530, 666, 844, 845, 846, 847, 898, 899, 902, 903, 904, 905, 936, 937, 1098, 1099, 1100, 1101, 1341, 1342, 1343, 1344, 1456, 1457, 1511, 1512, 1513, 1514, 1552, 1589, 1645, 1646, 1648, 1762, 1763, 1764, 1765, 1789, 1790, 1892, 1893, 1894, 1895, 1987, 1988, 1989, 1990, 2077, 2078, 2079, 2080, 2264, 2265, 2266, 2267, 2292, 2293, 2328, 2710, 2711, 2731, 2732, 2733, 2734, 2910, 2911, 2912, 2913, 3078, 3079, 3080, 3081, 3116, 3117, 3160, 3161, 3162, 3163, 3223, 3224, 3225, 3226, 3261, 3262

East European Studies, 829, 863, 864, 865

European Studies, 52, 53, 73, 783, 805, 853, 854, 882, 885, 887, 928, 929, 1042, 1125, 1159, 1160, 1304, 1305, 1380, 1575, 1786, 2743, 2774, 2917, 2918, 2932, 2934, 2935, 2939, 2969, 2970, 3023, 3024, 3029, 3087, 3088, 3100, 3106

Finnish Studies, 1220

French Studies, 145, 250, 435, 464, 692, 783, 805, 859, 874, 885, 895, 928, 929, 934, 940, 954, 960, 1042, 1060, 1125, 1159, 1160, 1164, 1200, 1210, 1217, 1219, 1304, 1305, 1319, 1380, 1481, 1485, 1532, 1575, 1595, 1673, 1771, 1786,

1951, 1957, 2333, 2620, 2720, 2774, 2928, 2939, 2969, 2970, 2987, 3096, 3231

Gay/Lesbian Issues, 832, 2724, 3159

Georgia(the country) Studies-G, 794, 907, 2760

German Studies, 783, 885, 886, 1125, 1207, 2939

Greek Studies, 934, 1120, 1164, 1217

Human Rights, 89, 90, 176, 228, 810, 832, 869, 898, 899, 912, 931, 949, 950, 951, 952, 953, 1387, 1456, 1457, 1645, 1646, 2292, 2293, 2710, 2711, 2724, 2794, 2796, 2797, 2798, 2799, 3042, 3055, 3116, 3117, 3133, 3140, 3159, 3192, 3206, 3207, 3208, 3209, 3248, 3259, 3268, 3270, 3271, 3272, 3273

Hungary Studies-G, 829

Icelandic Studies, 811, 922

Immigration-G, 946, 1386

India Studies, 768, 830

International Studies, 5, 57, 80, 89, 90, 160, 810, 838, 860, 891, 894, 898, 899, 931, 949, 969, 1456, 1457, 1643, 1645, 1646, 2292, 2293, 2710, 2711, 2794, 2839, 2942, 3004, 3033, 3055, 3068, 3091, 3110, 3112, 3116, 3117, 3133, 3140, 3148, 3192, 3243, 3259, 3268

Iraquii Studies, 1770

Irish Studies, 938, 939, 967, 1181

Israel Studies, 894, 1643, 2839, 3075, 3112, 3243

Italian Studies, 73, 805, 826, 827, 882, 888, 889, 928, 929, 962, 978, 979, 1042, 1066, 1159, 1160, 1179, 1209, 1304, 1305, 1380, 1575, 1745, 1746, 1786, 1799, 2743, 2774, 2932, 2969, 2970, 3029, 3100, 3107, 3627

Italian/American Studies, 121, 923

Japanese Studies, 910, 911, 941, 1211, 1212

Jewish Studies, 82, 104, 212, 230, 872, 875, 893, 894, 913, 914, 917, 918, 919, 920, 1643, 2838, 2839, 3111, 3112, 3243, 3249

Latin America Studies, 8, 9, 93, 94, 790, 791, 873, 900, 901, 2756, 2757, 2927, 3040, 3041, 3118, 3119

Mediterranean Studies, 876, 877, 2997, 2998, 2999, 3000

Middle East Studies, 815, 838, 945, 2789

Mongolian Studies, 793, 906, 2759

Mycenaean Studies, 3002

Near East Studies-G, 815, 945, 2789

Norwegian Studies, 783, 885, 930, 955, 1125, 2939

Pacific Island Studies, 828

Palestinian Studies, 933

Persia/Iran Studies, 858

Polish Studies, 829, 916, 961

Population Studies, 89, 90, 98, 133, 134, 173, 204, 383, 654, 666, 777, 870, 898, 899, 902, 903, 904, 905, 936, 937, 1000, 1403, 1444, 1456, 1457, 1528, 1552, 1589, 1632, 1645, 1646, 1648, 1789, 1790, 2292, 2293, 2328, 2424, 2710, 2711, 3116, 3117, 3261, 3262

Post-Classical Studies, 826, 827, 978, 979, 1745, 1746, 2997, 2998, 2999, 3000, 3001

Precolumbian Studies, 436, 879

Renaissance Studies, 802, 804, 805, 925, 927, 928, 929, 1040, 1041, 1042, 1156, 1158, 1159, 1160, 1302, 1303, 1304, 1305, 1377, 1379, 1380, 1573, 1574, 1575, 1784, 1785, 1786, 2771, 2773, 2774, 2934, 2935, 2966, 2968, 2969, 2970, 2997, 2999

Romanian Stuides-G, 829

Scandinavian Studies, 148, 256, 783, 885, 955, 957, 967, 999, 1125, 1181, 1681, 2878, 2939, 3144, 3370

Soviet Studies, 794, 814, 907, 908, 944, 1218, 2760, 2787

Spanish Studies, 959, 1223

Turkish Studies, 421, 769, 770, 833, 834, 984, 986, 1753, 1755, 2725, 2726, 2904, 2905

Ukrainian Studies, 794, 863, 864, 865, 907, 2760

United States Studies, 856, 915, 942, 943, 956, 971, 1056, 1057, 1111, 1187, 1519, 1599, 1600, 1675, 1676, 1794, 1795, 1953, 1954, 2920, 2957, 2972, 2981, 2982, 3005, 3089

Venetian Studies, 79, 440, 786, 890, 1011, 1133, 1265, 1364, 1777, 2749, 2941, 3032, 3109

Vietnam Studies-G, 817, 947, 2791

Welsh Studies, 3735, 3830

Women's Issues, 82, 212, 268, 803, 810, 843, 892, 893, 926, 948, 950, 951, 952, 953, 973, 974, 1157, 1378, 1387, 1807, 2349, 2551, 2699, 2772, 2793, 2796, 2797, 2798, 2799, 2838, 2967, 3007, 3111, 3204, 3206, 3207, 3208, 3209, 3220, 3267, 3270, 3271, 3272, 3273, 3283, 3339, 3979

Yugoslavian Studies-G, 829

ART

General, 79, 99, 100, 112, 145, 156, 173, 180, 204, 261, 263, 310, 360, 383, 440, 443, 464, 469, 654, 772, 773, 777, 784, 786, 787, 796, 798, 800, 801, 808, 818, 848, 849, 870, 890, 896, 942, 943, 954, 976, 982, 991, 994, 995, 996, 997, 1000, 1001, 1003, 1004, 1007, 1008, 1009, 1010, 1011, 1012, 1016, 1017, 1019, 1020, 1021, 1023, 1025, 1032, 1033, 1034, 1036, 1037, 1043, 1048, 1050, 1055, 1056, 1057, 1060, 1061, 1063, 1068, 1070, 1071, 1072, 1088, 1102, 1103, 1118, 1119, 1121, 1133, 1134, 1136, 1137, 1143, 1144, 1145, 1150, 1151, 1152, 1169, 1175, 1180, 1184, 1194, 1195, 1214, 1215, 1219, 1224, 1230, 1234, 1238, 1240, 1241, 1242, 1253, 1258, 1260, 1261, 1264, 1265, 1266, 1269, 1270, 1275, 1276, 1278, 1283, 1290, 1291, 1297, 1313, 1319, 1321, 1323, 1330, 1334, 1335, 1345, 1346, 1364, 1369, 1371, 1372, 1375, 1376, 1383, 1403, 1444, 1485, 1528, 1599, 1600, 1632, 1675, 1676, 1777, 1778, 1794, 1795, 1830, 1836, 1861,

1864, 1953, 1954, 1957, 2134, 2201, 2301, 2424, 2720, 2735, 2736, 2748, 2749, 2753, 2762, 2766, 2769, 2778, 2806, 2807, 2815, 2822, 2823, 2914, 2915, 2941, 2952, 2954, 2955, 2961, 2963, 2981, 2982, 2987, 3021, 3022, 3032, 3035, 3049, 3066, 3084, 3085, 3109, 3128, 3164, 3165, 3183, 3227, 3228, 3244, 3305, 3318, 3601, 3617, 3627, 3711, 4005

Animation, 993, 1046, 1047, 1062, 4003, 4153

Art Administration/Mngmnt, 51, 128, 200, 242, 459, 460, 852, 998, 1029, 1039, 1053, 1054, 1059, 1108, 1155, 1243, 1301, 1793, 2824, 2867

Art Conservation, 1028, 1029, 1030, 1031, 1049, 1059, 1791

Art History, 79, 99, 100, 124, 179, 241, 414, 419, 421, 422, 423, 440, 459, 460, 472, 766, 769, 770, 771, 784, 786, 787, 796, 826, 827, 833, 834, 835, 840, 880, 890, 896, 942, 943, 962, 975, 977, 978, 979, 980, 981, 984, 985, 986, 987, 988, 1010, 1011, 1015, 1017, 1020, 1021, 1028, 1029, 1031, 1035, 1038, 1044, 1049, 1053, 1054, 1055, 1056, 1057, 1059, 1066, 1074, 1075, 1080, 1090, 1093, 1133, 1135, 1137, 1144, 1145, 1179, 1190, 1231, 1265, 1270, 1276, 1340, 1364, 1369, 1371, 1372, 1599, 1600, 1675, 1676, 1745, 1746, 1748, 1753, 1754, 1755, 1756, 1760, 1777, 1778, 1783, 1793, 1794, 1795, 1799, 1953, 1954, 2723, 2725, 2726, 2748, 2749, 2753, 2762, 2899, 2904, 2905, 2906, 2909, 2941, 2949, 2952, 2954, 2955, 2965, 2981, 2982, 3009, 3032, 3035, 3109, 3183, 3244, 3627

Cartooning, 993, 4137, 4170, 4171

Ceramic Arts, 1001, 1013, 1044, 3300

Commercial Art, 4219

Crafts, 11, 102, 668, 942, 943, 1013, 1022, 1056, 1057, 1599, 1600, 1675, 1676, 1794, 1795, 1953, 1954, 2981, 2982, 3300, 4185

Design, 124, 179, 241, 414, 459, 977, 1038, 1043, 1053, 1055, 1231, 1783, 1793, 2965

Drawing, 1001, 1005, 1055

Fashion Design, 75, 128, 145, 242, 464, 954, 1002, 1006, 1039, 1060, 1155, 1219, 1252, 1301, 1319, 1485, 1957, 2703, 2720, 2867, 2987, 4202

Film & Video, 51, 128, 200, 242, 443, 852, 976, 998, 1001, 1018, 1019, 1039, 1045, 1065, 1069, 1108, 1139, 1143, 1155, 1163, 1182, 1230, 1243, 1275, 1301, 1333, 2815, 2824, 2867, 4203, 4245

Fine Arts, 471, 996, 997, 1001, 1027, 1028, 1043, 1073, 1186, 1242, 1339

Graphic Arts, 124, 179, 241, 460, 1013, 1038, 1047, 1054, 1058, 1067, 1783, 2875, 2889, 2965, 3300, 3316, 4039, 4218, 4219

Interior Design, 419, 455, 981, 1051

Multimedia, 1003, 1047, 1058, 1118, 1253, 2875, 3316

Museum Education, 458, 459, 460, 1029, 1052, 1053, 1054, 1792, 1793

Numismatics, 983

Painting, 414, 424, 471, 977, 989, 990, 1001, 1005, 1073, 1095, 1186, 1231, 1236, 1339, 3292

Photography, 471, 1001, 1026, 1064, 1073, 1176, 1186, 1339, 1732, 2862, 2879

Printing, 802, 804, 805, 925, 927, 928, 1001, 1040, 1041, 1042, 1055, 1156, 1158, 1159, 1302, 1303, 1304, 1377, 1379, 1380, 1573, 1574, 1575, 1784, 1785, 1786, 2771, 2773, 2774, 2966, 2968, 2969, 4039, 4219

Printmaking, 1001, 1005, 4039, 4219

Sculpture, 423, 424, 471, 840, 988, 989, 1001, 1005, 1043, 1073, 1093, 1095, 1186, 1236, 1339, 1760, 2909, 3292

Textile Design, 75, 1006, 1013, 1014, 1055, 2703, 3300

Visual Arts, 414, 443, 977, 992, 1003, 1019, 1023, 1024, 1025, 1050, 1118, 1143, 1231, 1239, 1253, 1275, 1278, 1283, 3305

ENGLISH LANGUAGE / LITERATURE

General, 87, 99, 209, 215, 261, 307, 386, 496, 540, 601, 659, 730, 766, 772, 773, 781, 782, 787, 788, 789, 800, 801, 802, 803, 804, 805, 848, 849, 884, 896, 897, 925, 926, 927, 928, 980, 994, 995, 1004, 1007, 1016, 1017, 1020, 1034, 1036, 1040, 1041, 1042, 1063, 1068, 1072, 1080, 1102, 1103, 1117, 1119, 1121, 1122, 1124, 1136, 1137, 1138, 1140, 1144, 1149, 1150, 1151, 1156, 1157, 1158, 1159, 1175, 1180, 1184, 1189, 1194, 1195, 1206, 1214, 1215, 1224, 1240, 1241, 1258, 1260, 1269, 1270, 1276, 1302, 1303, 1304, 1323, 1330, 1335, 1340, 1345, 1346, 1361, 1362, 1369, 1370, 1371, 1375, 1376, 1377, 1378, 1379, 1380, 1407, 1408, 1447, 1543, 1573, 1574, 1575, 1639, 1711, 1748, 1776, 1778, 1784, 1785, 1786, 1826, 1828, 1861, 1913, 2008, 2095, 2134, 2723, 2735, 2736, 2746, 2753, 2754, 2755, 2769, 2771, 2772, 2773, 2774, 2806, 2822, 2823, 2841, 2842, 2896, 2899, 2914, 2915, 2937, 2952, 2954, 2961, 2963, 2966, 2967, 2968, 2969, 3021, 3022, 3035, 3036, 3038, 3084, 3085, 3103, 3113, 3115, 3164, 3165, 3179, 3183, 3184, 3227, 3228, 3239, 3244, 3245, 3318, 3373, 4101

American Literature, 856, 971, 1015, 1077, 1111, 1130, 1135, 1146, 1187, 1519, 2898, 2920, 2949, 3005, 3089

Archival Administration, 805, 928, 1042, 1159, 1304, 1380, 1575, 1786, 2774, 2969

Bibliography, 79, 440, 786, 805, 890, 928, 1011, 1042, 1077, 1107, 1133, 1159, 1265, 1304, 1364, 1380, 1575, 1777, 1786, 2749, 2774, 2898, 2941, 2969, 3032, 3109

British Literature, 805, 866, 928, 929, 972, 975, 1015, 1042, 1075, 1112, 1115, 1135, 1159, 1160, 1188, 1190, 1304, 1305, 1380, 1575, 1786, 2774, 2922, 2925, 2934, 2935, 2949, 2969, 2970, 3006, 3009

Classics, 100, 423, 796, 836, 837, 840, 868, 988, 1021, 1091, 1092, 1093, 1107, 1116, 1145, 1203, 1372, 1757, 1760, 2727, 2762, 2907, 2909, 2934, 2935, 2955

Creative Writing, 424, 471, 967, 982, 989, 1003, 1012, 1018, 1037, 1064, 1073, 1088, 1095, 1096, 1117, 1118, 1128, 1134, 1139, 1142, 1152, 1176, 1181, 1185, 1186, 1189, 1234, 1236, 1253, 1266, 1297, 1339, 2868, 2879, 2896, 3292, 4186

Debate-Forensics, 1048, 1169, 1313

Folklore, 51, 200, 852, 998, 1108, 1243, 2824

French Literature-G, 934, 1164, 1217

General Semantics, 1127

Library Sci.-Law, 1078, 1079, 1114, 1177, 3317, 4230

Library Sci.-Medical-G, 1114, 1147, 1148, 1177, 3317

Library Science, 174, 210, 243, 309, 1081, 1082, 1083, 1084, 1085, 1086, 1087, 1097, 1105, 1106, 1114, 1126, 1131, 1141, 1161, 1170, 1171, 1172, 1173, 1177, 1829, 2097, 2317, 2614, 3317, 4051

Linguistics, 41, 42, 43, 44, 158, 287, 288, 289, 290, 527, 528, 529, 530, 572, 625, 771, 835, 844, 845, 846, 847, 987, 1090, 1098, 1099, 1100, 1101, 1113, 1183, 1341, 1342, 1343, 1344, 1392, 1511, 1512, 1513, 1514, 1608, 1756, 1762, 1763, 1764, 1765, 1768, 1892, 1893, 1894, 1895, 1987, 1988, 1989, 1990, 2077, 2078, 2079, 2080, 2264, 2265, 2266, 2267, 2731, 2732, 2733, 2734, 2906, 2910, 2911, 2912, 2913, 2923, 3078, 3079, 3080, 3081, 3160, 3161, 3162, 3163, 3223, 3224, 3225, 3226

Literature, 79, 99, 100, 131, 440, 443, 471, 771, 783, 786, 796, 835, 850, 855, 885, 890, 962, 967, 971, 987, 1011, 1019, 1020, 1021, 1066, 1073, 1090, 1104, 1107, 1110, 1125, 1132, 1133, 1143, 1144, 1145, 1146, 1162, 1179, 1181, 1186, 1187, 1199, 1208, 1265, 1275, 1276, 1339, 1363, 1364, 1371, 1372, 1756, 1777, 1799, 1947, 2039, 2123, 2215, 2749, 2762, 2906, 2939, 2940, 2941, 2954, 2955, 3005, 3032, 3108, 3109

Oratory, 1153

Philology, 880, 1089

Playwriting, 967, 1012, 1018, 1069, 1096, 1123, 1134, 1139, 1168, 1174, 1178, 1181, 1182, 1189, 1266, 1324, 1333, 2896, 4094

Poetry, 424, 471, 989, 1012, 1073, 1095, 1117, 1128, 1134, 1165, 1166, 1167, 1185, 1186, 1189, 1236, 1266, 1339, 2896, 3292

Reading/Literacy Research-G, 217, 218, 219, 220, 221, 222, 223, 224, 225

Screenwriting, 128, 242, 1012, 1018, 1039, 1045, 1069, 1076, 1134, 1139, 1155, 1163, 1182, 1189, 1266, 1301, 1333, 2867, 2896, 4094

FOREIGN LANGUAGE

General, 12, 109, 261, 306, 307, 386, 496, 540, 601, 659, 730, 772, 773, 780, 781, 800, 801, 848, 849, 855, 883, 884, 964, 964, 965, 966, 994, 995, 1034, 1036, 1068, 1102, 1103, 1110, 1122, 1132, 1150, 1151, 1180, 1194, 1195, 1199, 1205, 1206, 1208, 1213, 1214, 1215, 1224, 1225, 1225, 1226, 1227, 1228, 1240, 1241, 1330, 1345, 1346, 1361, 1363, 1375, 1376, 1407, 1446, 1447, 1542, 1543, 1639, 1710, 1711, 1775, 1776, 1826, 1861, 1912, 1913, 2007, 2008, 2094, 2095, 2134, 2735, 2736, 2745, 2746, 2769, 2806, 2822, 2823, 2914, 2915, 2936, 2937, 2940, 2961, 2963, 3021, 3022, 3084, 3085, 3103, 3108, 3164, 3165, 3178, 3179, 3227, 3228, 3239, 3318, 3373

African Languages, 825, 1191

Arabic, 1202

Asian Languages, 50, 199, 851, 1198, 3086

English, 1222

Esperanto, 1216

Finnish, 1220

French, 145, 145, 464, 464, 859, 895, 934, 954, 954, 1060, 1060, 1164, 1200, 1210, 1217, 1219, 1219, 1319, 1319, 1485, 1485, 1957, 1957, 2720, 2720, 2987, 2987

German, 886, 1196, 1207

Greek-G, 258, 868, 934, 958, 1116, 1120, 1164, 1203, 1217, 1221

India Languages, 1192, 1192

Italian, 889, 1209, 3627

Japanese, 910, 911, 1211, 1212

Latin, 258, 958, 1120, 1221

Russian, 814, 944, 1218, 2787

Spanish, 959, 1197, 1201, 1204, 1223, 4112

Turkish, 1193

PERFORMING ARTS

General, 51, 79, 99, 200, 261, 310, 440, 443, 772, 773, 786, 808, 818, 830, 848, 849, 852, 890, 976, 991, 992, 994, 995, 998, 1004, 1007, 1009, 1011, 1012, 1016, 1019, 1020, 1033, 1050, 1061, 1063, 1068, 1072, 1102, 1103, 1108, 1119, 1121, 1133, 1134, 1136, 1143, 1144, 1175, 1180, 1184, 1194, 1195, 1224, 1230, 1238, 1239, 1240, 1241, 1243, 1258, 1260, 1264, 1265, 1266, 1269, 1271, 1275, 1276, 1291, 1292, 1315, 1316, 1321, 1323, 1330, 1335, 1345, 1346, 1364, 1371, 1383, 1777, 1830, 1861, 2134, 2735, 2736, 2749, 2778, 2806, 2815, 2822, 2823, 2824, 2914, 2915, 2941, 2954, 3021, 3022, 3032, 3084, 3085, 3109, 3164, 3165, 3227, 3228, 3318, 3601, 3711, 4094, 4120

Accordion, 1232

Choral Conducting, 1307

Costume Design-G, 1002, 1030, 1252
Dance, 21, 182, 232, 424, 443, 471, 989, 1003, 1019, 1025, 1073, 1095, 1118, 1143, 1186, 1233, 1235, 1236, 1253, 1275, 1277, 1282, 1283, 1320, 1339, 2298, 2553, 2601, 3185, 3292
Drama, 79, 128, 242, 424, 440, 443, 471, 786, 890, 989, 996, 1003, 1011, 1019, 1023, 1025, 1039, 1048, 1069, 1073, 1095, 1118, 1133, 1143, 1155, 1169, 1178, 1182, 1186, 1236, 1242, 1253, 1265, 1275, 1278, 1283, 1301, 1313, 1320, 1324, 1333, 1339, 1364, 1777, 2749, 2867, 2941, 3032, 3109, 3292, 3305, 4094, 4193, 4203
Horn, 1273
Human Movement Studies-G, 232, 1282, 2298, 2601, 3185
Instrumental, 208, 424, 989, 1003, 1095, 1118, 1236, 1244, 1245, 1253, 1254, 1255, 1259, 1267, 1268, 1289, 1317, 1318, 1322, 1336, 1337, 3292
Jazz, 1314, 1331, 1332
Music Composition, 79, 112, 208, 414, 440, 469, 786, 798, 890, 977, 996, 1008, 1011, 1032, 1037, 1048, 1070, 1133, 1152, 1169, 1174, 1231, 1232, 1242, 1251, 1255, 1256, 1257, 1259, 1261, 1263, 1265, 1272, 1281, 1287, 1289, 1290, 1295, 1296, 1297, 1306, 1311, 1313, 1318, 1320, 1327, 1328, 1329, 1332, 1334, 1364, 1777, 1836, 2201, 2301, 2749, 2766, 2941, 3032, 3049, 3109, 3128, 3996, 4089, 4133
Music Performance, 51, 79, 112, 145, 200, 208, 424, 440, 443, 464, 469, 786, 787, 798, 852, 890, 896, 954, 989, 996, 998, 1008, 1011, 1017, 1019, 1023, 1025, 1032, 1048, 1060, 1070, 1095, 1108, 1133, 1137, 1143, 1169, 1219, 1236, 1242, 1243, 1244, 1245, 1254, 1255, 1259, 1261, 1265, 1270, 1275, 1278, 1281, 1283, 1289, 1290, 1293, 1296, 1313, 1318, 1319, 1320, 1327, 1329, 1334, 1336, 1337, 1364, 1369, 1485, 1777, 1778, 1836, 1957, 2201, 2203, 2301, 2302, 2604, 2678, 2720, 2749, 2753, 2766, 2824, 2941, 2952, 2987, 3032, 3035, 3049, 3109, 3128, 3183, 3244, 3292, 3305, 3308, 3996, 4089, 4133
Music Research, 802, 804, 805, 925, 927, 928, 929, 1030, 1040, 1041, 1042, 1156, 1158, 1159, 1160, 1281, 1302, 1303, 1304, 1305, 1329, 1377, 1379, 1380, 1573, 1574, 1575, 1784, 1785, 1786, 2771, 2773, 2774, 2966, 2968, 2969, 2970
Opera & Music Management, 132, 208, 443, 1019, 1143, 1229, 1255, 1259, 1275, 1281, 1285, 1308, 1320, 3996, 4089
Orchestra, 208, 1244, 1259, 1286, 1338, 3996, 4089
Organ, 1273, 1309
Piano, 208, 1248, 1249, 1250, 1256, 1259, 1273, 1288, 1296, 1300, 1317, 1325, 1327, 1338, 3996, 4089

Singing, 208, 424, 982, 989, 1088, 1095, 1229, 1234, 1236, 1237, 1254, 1255, 1259, 1280, 1284, 1285, 1288, 1294, 1298, 1299, 1310, 1312, 1317, 1320, 1326, 1327, 1328, 1336, 1337, 3292, 3996, 4013, 4089, 4095, 4096
String Instruments, 208, 1244, 1247, 1259, 1279, 1286, 1288, 1327, 3996, 4089
Trumpet, 1274, 1331
Violin, 1246, 1273

PHILOSOPHY

General, 41, 42, 43, 44, 99, 100, 158, 209, 287, 288, 289, 290, 307, 386, 496, 527, 528, 529, 530, 540, 567, 572, 601, 625, 659, 730, 766, 772, 773, 781, 782, 787, 788, 796, 800, 801, 802, 803, 804, 805, 808, 844, 845, 846, 847, 848, 849, 884, 896, 897, 925, 926, 927, 928, 950, 963, 980, 994, 995, 1017, 1020, 1021, 1034, 1036, 1040, 1041, 1042, 1080, 1098, 1099, 1100, 1101, 1102, 1103, 1122, 1124, 1132, 1137, 1138, 1144, 1145, 1150, 1151, 1156, 1157, 1158, 1159, 1183, 1194, 1195, 1206, 1208, 1214, 1215, 1240, 1241, 1270, 1276, 1302, 1303, 1304, 1340, 1341, 1342, 1343, 1344, 1345, 1346, 1355, 1361, 1362, 1363, 1369, 1370, 1371, 1372, 1375, 1376, 1377, 1378, 1379, 1380, 1383, 1387, 1390, 1392, 1407, 1408, 1447, 1511, 1512, 1513, 1514, 1543, 1573, 1574, 1575, 1608, 1639, 1683, 1711, 1748, 1762, 1763, 1764, 1765, 1776, 1778, 1784, 1785, 1786, 1800, 1826, 1828, 1892, 1893, 1894, 1895, 1913, 1962, 1987, 1988, 1989, 1990, 2008, 2052, 2077, 2078, 2079, 2080, 2095, 2135, 2264, 2265, 2266, 2267, 2723, 2731, 2732, 2733, 2734, 2735, 2736, 2746, 2753, 2754, 2762, 2769, 2771, 2772, 2773, 2774, 2778, 2796, 2822, 2823, 2841, 2899, 2910, 2911, 2912, 2913, 2914, 2915, 2937, 2940, 2952, 2954, 2955, 2961, 2963, 2966, 2967, 2968, 2969, 3021, 3022, 3035, 3036, 3078, 3079, 3080, 3081, 3084, 3085, 3103, 3108, 3113, 3160, 3161, 3162, 3163, 3164, 3165, 3179, 3183, 3184, 3206, 3223, 3224, 3225, 3226, 3227, 3228, 3239, 3244, 3245, 3270, 4104
Biomedical Ethics-G, 1367
Theology, 79, 181, 198, 249, 270, 344, 440, 453, 786, 787, 800, 801, 823, 880, 881, 890, 896, 946, 1011, 1017, 1034, 1036, 1133, 1137, 1150, 1151, 1214, 1215, 1265, 1270, 1347, 1348, 1356, 1357, 1360, 1364, 1366, 1368, 1369, 1373, 1374, 1375, 1376, 1381, 1384, 1385, 1386, 1388, 1389, 1391, 1393, 1394, 1395, 1397, 1777, 1778, 2041, 2181, 2199, 2223, 2299, 2332, 2585, 2594, 2650, 2664, 2749, 2753, 2769, 2812, 2941, 2952, 2961, 2963, 3032, 3035, 3047, 3109, 3183, 3233, 3244, 3277, 3722, 3957, 3972, 4067

SCHOOL OF NATURAL RESOURCES

General, 2, 38, 138, 167, 173, 204, 209, 278, 279, 282, 291, 292, 298, 299, 300, 307, 314, 315, 322, 324, 325, 332, 353, 354, 355, 356, 362, 372, 375, 382, 383, 386, 398, 399, 409, 416, 425, 430, 465, 477, 485, 490, 496, 508, 510, 516, 520, 533, 540, 551, 552, 565, 566, 579, 586, 593, 601, 611, 612, 620, 621, 631, 642, 648, 654, 659, 676, 677, 691, 697, 712, 721, 730, 755, 759, 767, 777, 781, 782, 797, 807, 819, 842, 870, 884, 1000, 1122, 1124, 1206, 1361, 1362, 1398, 1399, 1400, 1401, 1402, 1403, 1404, 1405, 1406, 1407, 1408, 1409, 1410, 1411, 1412, 1413, 1414, 1415, 1416, 1417, 1418, 1419, 1420, 1421, 1422, 1423, 1424, 1425, 1426, 1427, 1428, 1429, 1430, 1432, 1434, 1443, 1444, 1447, 1461, 1462, 1463, 1474, 1486, 1487, 1495, 1497, 1510, 1517, 1518, 1528, 1543, 1554, 1555, 1556, 1568, 1570, 1571, 1587, 1591, 1592, 1593, 1594, 1605, 1618, 1620, 1621, 1630, 1631, 1632, 1639, 1650, 1651, 1652, 1666, 1668, 1669, 1670, 1671, 1682, 1694, 1695, 1699, 1701, 1711, 1712, 1713, 1714, 1718, 1719, 1720, 1731, 1735, 1744, 1749, 1766, 1776, 1798, 1811, 1812, 1819, 1822, 1823, 1824, 1826, 1828, 1834, 1839, 1840, 1845, 1856, 1857, 1858, 1859, 1866, 1875, 1897, 1913, 1933, 1935, 1936, 1948, 1960, 1975, 1996, 2008, 2024, 2026, 2027, 2040, 2050, 2067, 2085, 2095, 2098, 2102, 2124, 2130, 2142, 2151, 2160, 2163, 2192, 2250, 2270, 2272, 2383, 2412, 2416, 2424, 2482, 2565, 2578, 2580, 2635, 2641, 2643, 2728, 2746, 2752, 2763, 2781, 2782, 2783, 2784, 2805, 2808, 2813, 2820, 2863, 2864, 2937, 2951, 3072, 3103, 3150, 3153, 3179, 3239, 3258, 4076, 4159, 4279

AGRICULTURE

General, 2, 17, 38, 89, 90, 119, 137, 173, 204, 244, 250, 278, 282, 292, 306, 307, 323, 335, 336, 342, 343, 355, 372, 375, 382, 383, 386, 409, 416, 425, 430, 437, 465, 477, 485, 490, 496, 508, 510, 516, 520, 533, 540, 566, 579, 586, 593, 601, 621, 631, 642, 648, 654, 659, 682, 683, 690, 691, 692, 697, 712, 721, 730, 746, 747, 754, 755, 759, 767, 777, 780, 781, 807, 809, 842, 870, 883, 884, 898, 899, 940, 1000, 1122, 1205, 1206, 1361, 1398, 1400, 1402, 1403, 1407, 1412, 1413, 1414, 1419, 1426, 1428, 1431, 1432, 1434, 1443, 1444, 1445, 1446, 1447, 1449, 1455, 1456, 1457, 1458, 1459, 1461, 1462, 1463, 1465, 1466, 1469, 1471, 1472, 1473, 1474, 1478, 1479, 1480, 1481, 1483, 1486, 1487, 1488, 1489, 1495, 1510, 1518, 1528, 1541, 1542, 1543, 1554, 1555, 1556, 1569, 1579, 1580, 1586,

1587, 1590, 1595, 1604, 1605, 1620, 1630, 1631, 1632, 1638, 1639, 1644, 1645, 1646, 1650, 1651, 1652, 1658, 1659, 1665, 1666, 1667, 1673, 1679, 1682, 1694, 1699, 1701, 1709, 1710, 1711, 1712, 1713, 1714, 1724, 1725, 1730, 1731, 1735, 1749, 1766, 1775, 1776, 1798, 1811, 1819, 1826, 1849, 1850, 1852, 1853, 1858, 1875, 1897, 1911, 1912, 1913, 1919, 1934, 1942, 1943, 1946, 1948, 1951, 1960, 1975, 1996, 2007, 2008, 2025, 2030, 2031, 2038, 2040, 2050, 2067, 2085, 2094, 2095, 2110, 2114, 2115, 2122, 2124, 2130, 2163, 2214, 2221, 2222, 2241, 2272, 2292, 2293, 2311, 2319, 2329, 2330, 2331, 2333, 2416, 2424, 2522, 2530, 2580, 2616, 2620, 2643, 2687, 2701, 2710, 2711, 2728, 2745, 2746, 2780, 2820, 2860, 2936, 2937, 3051, 3057, 3103, 3116, 3117, 3178, 3179, 3239, 3253, 3258, 4015, 4148, 4149

Agribusiness, 119, 1466, 1488, 2860, 3051, 3253

Agricultural Engineering/Mech., 346

Agricultural Marketing, 119, 1466, 2860, 3051, 3253

Agronomy/Crop Sciences, 1451, 4150

Animal Science, 1477, 1886, 4152

Dairy Science, 1477

Farm Management, 119, 1466, 2860, 3051, 3253

Floriculture, 437, 446, 1433, 1437, 1439, 1440, 1441, 1445, 1460, 1467, 1541, 1638, 1641, 1709, 1881, 1911, 1922, 4206

Golf Grounds Mngmnt, 1451, 1452, 1453, 3578

Herb Studies, 1454

Horticulture, 3, 48, 49, 437, 438, 439, 445, 446, 1433, 1435, 1436, 1437, 1438, 1439, 1440, 1441, 1442, 1445, 1448, 1449, 1450, 1460, 1464, 1465, 1467, 1468, 1470, 1541, 1638, 1709, 1881, 1911, 1922, 1937, 4206, 4223

Poultry Science, 1455, 1477, 1644, 1919

Soil Science, 144, 145, 463, 464, 954, 1060, 1219, 1319, 1412, 1413, 1414, 1460, 1461, 1462, 1463, 1475, 1482, 1484, 1485, 1546, 1554, 1555, 1556, 1650, 1651, 1652, 1678, 1680, 1712, 1713, 1714, 1922, 1950, 1957, 2720, 2877, 2987, 3142, 4150, 4215, 4283

Turf/Grounds/Range Management, 144, 446, 463, 1453, 1467, 1476, 1482, 1484, 1678, 1680, 2877, 3142, 4274

Turfgrass Science, 1451, 1453

EARTH SCIENCE

General, 2, 38, 41, 42, 43, 44, 244, 275, 278, 279, 280, 282, 287, 288, 289, 290, 291, 292, 295, 297, 303, 305, 306, 307, 321, 322, 323, 333, 334, 335, 336, 337, 338, 342, 355, 363, 366, 372, 375, 382, 385, 386, 405, 407, 408, 409, 416, 425, 430, 448, 452, 465, 476, 477, 478, 484, 485, 490, 493, 494, 495, 496, 501, 502, 503, 508, 510, 514, 516, 518, 520, 527, 528, 529, 530, 533, 534,

539, 540, 554, 555, 557, 558, 566, 577, 579, 582, 586, 593, 596, 599, 600, 601, 614, 621, 629, 631, 633, 635, 642, 648, 651, 652, 657, 658, 659, 680, 681, 682, 683, 684, 685, 690, 691, 697, 705, 710, 712, 713, 714, 721, 725, 728, 729, 730, 744, 745, 746, 747, 748, 749, 754, 755, 759, 762, 765, 767, 780, 781, 807, 842, 844, 845, 846, 847, 883, 884, 924, 942, 943, 1056, 1057, 1098, 1099, 1100, 1101, 1122, 1205, 1206, 1341, 1342, 1343, 1344, 1361, 1398, 1399, 1400, 1401, 1402, 1407, 1412, 1413, 1414, 1415, 1419, 1426, 1432, 1434, 1443, 1446, 1447, 1461, 1462, 1463, 1469, 1471, 1472, 1473, 1474, 1486, 1490, 1495, 1497, 1499, 1500, 1501, 1502, 1503, 1510, 1511, 1512, 1513, 1514, 1515, 1516, 1517, 1518, 1524, 1525, 1531, 1535, 1537, 1539, 1540, 1542, 1543, 1545, 1554, 1555, 1556, 1565, 1566, 1568, 1569, 1576, 1577, 1579, 1580, 1581, 1582, 1586, 1587, 1599, 1600, 1601, 1602, 1605, 1610, 1614, 1615, 1620, 1621, 1623, 1630, 1631, 1633, 1636, 1639, 1650, 1651, 1652, 1655, 1656, 1658, 1659, 1660, 1661, 1665, 1666, 1675, 1676, 1682, 1692, 1694, 1695, 1697, 1699, 1701, 1703, 1704, 1705, 1706, 1707, 1708, 1710, 1711, 1712, 1713, 1714, 1717, 1718, 1721, 1722, 1724, 1725, 1726, 1727, 1730, 1731, 1735, 1739, 1749, 1751, 1752, 1762, 1763, 1764, 1765, 1766, 1775, 1776, 1787, 1794, 1795, 1798, 1809, 1811, 1812, 1813, 1819, 1821, 1825, 1826, 1838, 1848, 1849, 1850, 1852, 1858, 1867, 1869, 1872, 1875, 1878, 1879, 1880, 1883, 1892, 1893, 1894, 1895, 1897, 1900, 1903, 1908, 1910, 1912, 1913, 1931, 1933, 1934, 1939, 1940, 1942, 1943, 1946, 1948, 1953, 1954, 1960, 1968, 1972, 1975, 1977, 1987, 1988, 1989, 1990, 1992, 1993, 1996, 1998, 2002, 2004, 2006, 2007, 2008, 2021, 2024, 2025, 2029, 2030, 2031, 2032, 2033, 2038, 2040, 2048, 2049, 2050, 2060, 2067, 2070, 2077, 2078, 2079, 2080, 2082, 2083, 2085, 2087, 2091, 2092, 2093, 2094, 2095, 2110, 2112, 2113, 2114, 2115, 2116, 2117, 2122, 2124, 2128, 2129, 2130, 2137, 2140, 2151, 2160, 2163, 2204, 2214, 2250, 2264, 2265, 2266, 2267, 2270, 2272, 2305, 2311, 2319, 2383, 2412, 2416, 2508, 2522, 2565, 2578, 2580, 2582, 2616, 2635, 2641, 2643, 2679, 2687, 2728, 2731, 2732, 2733, 2734, 2745, 2746, 2770, 2776, 2820, 2910, 2911, 2912, 2913, 2936, 2937, 2971, 2981, 2982, 2983, 2984, 3052, 3054, 3076, 3078, 3079, 3080, 3081, 3103, 3132, 3160, 3161, 3162, 3163, 3178, 3179, 3190, 3223, 3224, 3225, 3226, 3239, 3255, 3258, 3315, 3349, 4065, 4279

Astronomy, 41, 42, 43, 44, 287, 288, 289, 290, 305, 334, 385, 394, 405, 452, 495, 501, 527, 528, 529, 530, 539, 550, 555, 600, 614, 658, 672, 681,

729, 740, 742, 745, 844, 845, 846, 847, 878, 942, 943, 1056, 1057, 1098, 1099, 1100, 1101, 1341, 1342, 1343, 1344, 1492, 1499, 1501, 1511, 1512, 1513, 1514, 1515, 1516, 1533, 1540, 1546, 1549, 1562, 1567, 1577, 1598, 1599, 1600, 1611, 1675, 1676, 1708, 1722, 1751, 1752, 1762, 1763, 1764, 1765, 1794, 1795, 1848, 1878, 1880, 1892, 1893, 1894, 1895, 1910, 1940, 1953, 1954, 1987, 1988, 1989, 1990, 1992, 1993, 2018, 2022, 2029, 2047, 2077, 2078, 2079, 2080, 2082, 2083, 2090, 2093, 2107, 2109, 2113, 2127, 2264, 2265, 2266, 2267, 2731, 2732, 2733, 2734, 2776, 2910, 2911, 2912, 2913, 2971, 2981, 2982, 3078, 3079, 3080, 3081, 3160, 3161, 3162, 3163, 3190, 3223, 3224, 3225, 3226, 3315, 4159, 4160, 4215

Astrophysics, 305, 385, 394, 495, 539, 600, 658, 672, 729, 740, 1540, 1562, 1708, 1910, 2018, 2093, 2107, 4159, 4217

Cartography/Geodetic Surveying, 802, 804, 805, 925, 927, 928, 1040, 1041, 1042, 1156, 1158, 1159, 1302, 1303, 1304, 1377, 1379, 1380, 1493, 1494, 1522, 1523, 1546, 1573, 1574, 1575, 1784, 1785, 1786, 2771, 2773, 2774, 2966, 2968, 2969, 4215

Cave Research, 1527, 1546, 1572, 4215

Desalination-G, 637, 638, 639, 640, 641, 665, 1505, 1506, 1507, 1508, 1509, 1550, 1625, 1626, 1627, 1628, 1629, 1647, 1978, 1979, 1980, 1981, 1982

Energy, 98, 137, 138, 333, 346, 554, 598, 656, 666, 680, 744, 809, 902, 1420, 1421, 1422, 1423, 1480, 1536, 1552, 1557, 1576, 1578, 1590, 1591, 1592, 1593, 1594, 1648, 1656, 1657, 1667, 1668, 1669, 1670, 1671, 1721, 1723, 1787, 1788, 1853, 1939, 1941, 2003, 2112, 2222, 2331, 2521, 2530, 2780, 2781, 2782, 2783, 2784, 3054, 3132

Environmental Education, 98, 250, 484, 570, 635, 655, 666, 692, 701, 703, 704, 714, 902, 940, 1481, 1503, 1534, 1552, 1595, 1607, 1612, 1613, 1634, 1648, 1673, 1686, 1687, 1688, 1740, 1741, 1951, 2333, 2620, 2892, 3062, 4289

Fish/Game/Wildlife Management, 167, 924, 1430, 1566, 1618, 1655, 1717, 1744, 1838, 1931, 2021, 2142, 2770, 2813, 3072, 3153, 3255

Forestry/Forest Science, 98, 250, 323, 324, 325, 398, 399, 437, 506, 551, 552, 561, 611, 612, 666, 676, 677, 692, 902, 924, 940, 1412, 1413, 1414, 1416, 1417, 1445, 1461, 1462, 1463, 1469, 1481, 1483, 1529, 1541, 1544, 1551, 1552, 1554, 1555, 1556, 1558, 1566, 1569, 1570, 1571, 1585, 1588, 1595, 1604, 1638, 1640, 1648, 1650, 1651, 1652, 1653, 1655, 1664, 1673, 1679, 1709, 1712, 1713, 1714, 1715, 1717, 1719, 1720, 1838, 1839, 1840, 1911, 1925, 1931, 1934, 1935,

1936, 1944, 1951, 2021, 2025, 2026, 2027, 2035, 2110, 2311, 2333, 2620, 2770, 2863, 2864, 3255, 4076, 4210, 4211, 4274

Geography, 41, 42, 43, 44, 134, 158, 287, 288, 289, 290, 435, 506, 527, 528, 529, 530, 561, 572, 625, 844, 845, 846, 847, 856, 874, 937, 1098, 1099, 1100, 1101, 1111, 1183, 1341, 1342, 1343, 1344, 1392, 1511, 1512, 1513, 1514, 1519, 1521, 1522, 1523, 1532, 1545, 1546, 1564, 1585, 1589, 1608, 1664, 1762, 1763, 1764, 1765, 1769, 1771, 1790, 1892, 1893, 1894, 1895, 1944, 1987, 1988, 1989, 1990, 2035, 2077, 2078, 2079, 2080, 2264, 2265, 2266, 2267, 2328, 2539, 2731, 2732, 2733, 2734, 2768, 2910, 2911, 2912, 2913, 2920, 2928, 3078, 3079, 3080, 3081, 3089, 3096, 3160, 3161, 3162, 3163, 3223, 3224, 3225, 3226, 3231, 3262, 4214, 4215

Geology, 316, 337, 338, 339, 340, 367, 502, 503, 504, 505, 506, 550, 557, 558, 559, 560, 561, 562, 684, 685, 686, 687, 693, 705, 727, 735, 736, 742, 748, 749, 750, 751, 756, 762, 1491, 1515, 1516, 1520, 1538, 1546, 1547, 1548, 1553, 1560, 1561, 1567, 1581, 1582, 1583, 1584, 1585, 1596, 1597, 1603, 1614, 1616, 1617, 1660, 1661, 1662, 1663, 1664, 1726, 1727, 1728, 1729, 1733, 1743, 1898, 1944, 1952, 1970, 1992, 1993, 2014, 2022, 2032, 2033, 2034, 2035, 2046, 2061, 2082, 2083, 2103, 2109, 2116, 2117, 2118, 2119, 2125, 2126, 2141, 2197, 2297, 2487, 2539, 2600, 2672, 4215, 4216, 4217

Geophysics, 305, 367, 385, 484, 495, 539, 600, 635, 658, 714, 729, 1496, 1503, 1526, 1531, 1540, 1546, 1603, 1616, 1617, 1633, 1705, 1708, 1743, 1910, 1970, 2002, 2061, 2093, 2141, 2539, 3349, 4215, 4217

Geoscience, 41, 42, 43, 44, 287, 288, 289, 290, 337, 338, 410, 484, 502, 503, 527, 528, 529, 530, 557, 558, 568, 623, 635, 684, 685, 699, 714, 748, 749, 844, 845, 846, 847, 1098, 1099, 1100, 1101, 1341, 1342, 1343, 1344, 1412, 1413, 1414, 1461, 1462, 1463, 1503, 1511, 1512, 1513, 1514, 1546, 1554, 1555, 1556, 1560, 1561, 1581, 1582, 1606, 1650, 1651, 1652, 1660, 1661, 1685, 1712, 1713, 1714, 1726, 1727, 1737, 1762, 1763, 1764, 1765, 1892, 1893, 1894, 1895, 1964, 1987, 1988, 1989, 1990, 2032, 2033, 2054, 2077, 2078, 2079, 2080, 2116, 2117, 2264, 2265, 2266, 2267, 2339, 2731, 2732, 2733, 2734, 2910, 2911, 2912, 2913, 3078, 3079, 3080, 3081, 3160, 3161, 3162, 3163, 3223, 3224, 3225, 3226, 4215

Hydrology, 173, 204, 305, 337, 338, 383, 385, 410, 412, 495, 502, 503, 506, 539, 557, 558, 561, 568, 600, 623, 632, 636, 637, 638, 639, 640, 641, 654, 658, 665, 684, 685, 699, 703, 704, 729, 748, 749, 777, 870, 1000, 1403, 1412, 1413, 1414, 1444, 1461, 1462, 1463, 1483, 1496,

1498, 1504, 1505, 1506, 1507, 1508, 1509, 1528, 1540, 1546, 1550, 1554, 1555, 1556, 1581, 1582, 1585, 1604, 1606, 1612, 1613, 1616, 1622, 1625, 1626, 1627, 1628, 1629, 1632, 1647, 1650, 1651, 1652, 1660, 1661, 1664, 1679, 1685, 1687, 1688, 1689, 1698, 1708, 1712, 1713, 1714, 1726, 1727, 1737, 1740, 1741, 1876, 1910, 1944, 1964, 1976, 1978, 1979, 1980, 1981, 1982, 2032, 2033, 2035, 2054, 2093, 2116, 2117, 2339, 2424, 4215, 4217, 4289

Limnology, 636, 703, 704, 1412, 1413, 1414, 1461, 1462, 1463, 1504, 1554, 1555, 1556, 1596, 1609, 1612, 1613, 1650, 1651, 1652, 1687, 1688, 1698, 1712, 1713, 1714, 1733, 1740, 1741, 1952, 2125, 4289

Materials Sci. & Engineering, 305, 317, 385, 410, 495, 539, 568, 600, 623, 658, 670, 699, 729, 739, 1540, 1546, 1559, 1606, 1685, 1708, 1737, 1910, 1964, 2016, 2054, 2093, 2105, 2339, 4215

Meteorology, 367, 410, 568, 623, 699, 1520, 1531, 1546, 1563, 1606, 1617, 1633, 1685, 1705, 1716, 1737, 1743, 1898, 1964, 1970, 2002, 2020, 2054, 2061, 2141, 2339, 4215

Mineral Economics, 484, 635, 714, 1503

Mineral Engineering, 484, 635, 714, 1503, 1546, 1560, 1561, 4215

Radiology, 410, 568, 623, 699, 1520, 1606, 1685, 1737, 1898, 1964, 2054, 2339

Riparian Area Management, 636, 665, 703, 704, 1504, 1550, 1612, 1613, 1647, 1687, 1688, 1698, 1740, 1741, 4289

Surveying Technology, 301, 1530, 1546, 4215

Water Resources Policies, 98, 250, 636, 637, 638, 639, 640, 641, 665, 666, 692, 703, 704, 902, 940, 1412, 1413, 1414, 1461, 1462, 1463, 1481, 1496, 1504, 1505, 1506, 1507, 1508, 1509, 1546, 1550, 1552, 1554, 1555, 1556, 1595, 1612, 1613, 1625, 1626, 1627, 1628, 1629, 1647, 1648, 1650, 1651, 1652, 1673, 1687, 1688, 1689, 1698, 1712, 1713, 1714, 1740, 1741, 1951, 1978, 1979, 1980, 1981, 1982, 2333, 2620, 4215, 4289

ENVIRONMENTAL STUDIES

General, 2, 28, 38, 89, 90, 98, 137, 138, 144, 148, 173, 204, 244, 250, 256, 262, 278, 279, 282, 292, 307, 333, 335, 336, 337, 338, 339, 340, 342, 355, 357, 372, 375, 382, 383, 386, 409, 416, 420, 425, 430, 437, 463, 465, 477, 485, 490, 496, 502, 503, 504, 505, 508, 510, 516, 520, 533, 540, 554, 557, 558, 559, 560, 566, 567, 570, 579, 586, 593, 601, 621, 631, 632, 642, 648, 654, 655, 659, 665, 666, 680, 682, 683, 684, 685, 686, 687, 690, 691, 692, 697, 701, 703, 704, 712, 721, 730, 744, 746, 747, 748, 749, 750, 751, 754, 755, 759, 767, 777, 781, 807, 809, 842, 870,

884, 894, 898, 899, 902, 924, 940, 957, 963, 1000, 1122, 1206, 1361, 1390, 1398, 1399, 1400, 1402, 1403, 1407, 1419, 1420, 1421, 1422, 1423, 1426, 1432, 1434, 1443, 1444, 1445, 1447, 1455, 1456, 1457, 1471, 1472, 1473, 1474, 1480, 1481, 1482, 1483, 1484, 1486, 1495, 1497, 1498, 1500, 1510, 1518, 1528, 1531, 1534, 1535, 1541, 1543, 1550, 1552, 1566, 1576, 1578, 1579, 1580, 1581, 1582, 1583, 1584, 1586, 1587, 1590, 1591, 1592, 1593, 1594, 1595, 1604, 1605, 1607, 1612, 1613, 1619, 1620, 1621, 1622, 1623, 1624, 1630, 1631, 1632, 1633, 1634, 1636, 1637, 1638, 1639, 1643, 1644, 1645, 1646, 1647, 1648, 1655, 1656, 1657, 1658, 1659, 1660, 1661, 1662, 1663, 1665, 1666, 1667, 1668, 1669, 1670, 1671, 1673, 1677, 1678, 1679, 1680, 1681, 1682, 1683, 1684, 1686, 1687, 1688, 1689, 1691, 1694, 1695, 1699, 1701, 1705, 1709, 1711, 1717, 1721, 1723, 1724, 1725, 1726, 1727, 1728, 1729, 1730, 1731, 1735, 1740, 1741, 1749, 1766, 1776, 1787, 1788, 1798, 1800, 1811, 1812, 1819, 1826, 1838, 1849, 1850, 1852, 1853, 1858, 1870, 1875, 1876, 1879, 1897, 1911, 1913, 1919, 1931, 1939, 1941, 1942, 1943, 1946, 1948, 1951, 1960, 1962, 1963, 1975, 1976, 1996, 2002, 2008, 2021, 2030, 2031, 2032, 2033, 2034, 2038, 2040, 2050, 2052, 2053, 2067, 2085, 2095, 2112, 2114, 2115, 2116, 2117, 2118, 2119, 2122, 2124, 2130, 2135, 2151, 2163, 2183, 2214, 2222, 2250, 2272, 2287, 2292, 2293, 2319, 2331, 2333, 2383, 2416, 2424, 2454, 2521, 2522, 2530, 2565, 2580, 2595, 2616, 2620, 2635, 2643, 2665, 2687, 2710, 2711, 2721, 2728, 2746, 2770, 2780, 2781, 2782, 2783, 2784, 2820, 2839, 2877, 2878, 2892, 2937, 3054, 3062, 3076, 3103, 3112, 3116, 3117, 3132, 3142, 3144, 3179, 3238, 3239, 3243, 3255, 3258, 3450, 4150, 4199, 4283, 4289

Biodiversity-G, 98, 666, 902, 1500, 1552, 1623, 1648, 1649, 1879, 3076

Conservation, 144, 173, 204, 383, 437, 463, 654, 777, 870, 1000, 1403, 1412, 1413, 1414, 1444, 1445, 1461, 1462, 1463, 1482, 1484, 1500, 1528, 1541, 1544, 1554, 1555, 1556, 1623, 1632, 1638, 1640, 1641, 1650, 1651, 1652, 1678, 1680, 1709, 1712, 1713, 1714, 1879, 1911, 2424, 2877, 3076, 3142

Ecology, 98, 144, 437, 463, 666, 902, 942, 943, 1056, 1057, 1445, 1482, 1484, 1541, 1552, 1599, 1600, 1635, 1638, 1648, 1649, 1675, 1676, 1678, 1680, 1709, 1773, 1794, 1795, 1902, 1911, 1953, 1954, 2877, 2981, 2982, 3142

Environmental Economics, 98, 144, 463, 570, 632, 666, 701, 902, 1484, 1498, 1552, 1607, 1622, 1648, 1680, 1686, 1876, 1976, 2877, 2892,

3062, 3142

Environmental Health, 144, 173, 204, 244, 336, 383, 437, 463, 637, 638, 639, 640, 641, 654, 683, 703, 704, 747, 777, 870, 1000, 1403, 1444, 1445, 1472, 1484, 1505, 1506, 1507, 1508, 1509, 1528, 1541, 1580, 1612, 1613, 1625, 1626, 1627, 1628, 1629, 1632, 1638, 1654, 1659, 1680, 1687, 1688, 1709, 1725, 1740, 1741, 1850, 1911, 1943, 1978, 1979, 1980, 1981, 1982, 2031, 2115, 2214, 2304, 2319, 2424, 2522, 2616, 2687, 2877, 3142

Environmental Science, 98, 144, 170, 337, 338, 339, 340, 410, 437, 463, 502, 503, 504, 505, 506, 557, 558, 559, 560, 561, 568, 570, 623, 632, 637, 638, 639, 640, 641, 666, 684, 685, 686, 687, 699, 701, 703, 704, 706, 748, 749, 750, 751, 902, 942, 943, 1056, 1057, 1412, 1413, 1414, 1445, 1461, 1462, 1463, 1484, 1498, 1505, 1506, 1507, 1508, 1509, 1535, 1541, 1552, 1554, 1555, 1556, 1581, 1582, 1583, 1584, 1585, 1599, 1600, 1606, 1607, 1612, 1613, 1622, 1625, 1626, 1627, 1628, 1629, 1636, 1638, 1648, 1650, 1651, 1652, 1654, 1660, 1661, 1662, 1663, 1664, 1675, 1676, 1680, 1685, 1686, 1687, 1688, 1690, 1709, 1712, 1713, 1714, 1726, 1727, 1728, 1729, 1737, 1740, 1741, 1794, 1795, 1876, 1911, 1944, 1953, 1954, 1964, 1976, 1978, 1979, 1980, 1981, 1982, 2032, 2033, 2034, 2035, 2054, 2116, 2117, 2118, 2119, 2304, 2339, 2877, 2892, 2981, 2982, 3062, 3142, 3320

Limnology, 1609

Pollution, 98, 173, 204, 244, 336, 383, 654, 666, 683, 703, 704, 747, 777, 870, 902, 1000, 1403, 1444, 1472, 1528, 1546, 1552, 1580, 1612, 1613, 1632, 1648, 1659, 1687, 1688, 1725, 1740, 1741, 1850, 1943, 2031, 2115, 2214, 2319, 2424, 2522, 2616, 2687, 4215, 4289

Rain Forest Studies-G, 1649

Range Management, 437, 924, 1445, 1541, 1551, 1566, 1588, 1638, 1655, 1709, 1717, 1838, 1911, 1931, 2021, 2770, 3255, 4274

Waste Disposal/Mngmnt, 173, 204, 383, 654, 777, 870, 1000, 1403, 1444, 1528, 1632, 2424

Wildlife Studies, 173, 204, 383, 654, 777, 870, 942, 943, 1000, 1056, 1057, 1403, 1444, 1528, 1558, 1599, 1600, 1632, 1642, 1653, 1672, 1674, 1675, 1676, 1715, 1794, 1795, 1925, 1953, 1954, 2424, 2981, 2982

MARINE SCIENCE

General, 2, 38, 167, 244, 275, 278, 279, 280, 282, 292, 295, 297, 303, 305, 306, 307, 322, 333, 334, 335, 336, 337, 338, 339, 340, 342, 355, 367, 372, 375, 382, 385, 386, 405, 409, 410, 416, 425, 430, 437, 452, 465, 468, 476, 477, 478, 485, 490, 493, 494, 495, 496, 501, 502, 503, 504, 505, 508, 510, 514, 516, 518, 520, 533, 534, 539, 540, 554, 555, 557, 558, 559, 560, 566, 568, 577, 579, 582, 586, 593, 596, 599, 600, 601, 614, 621, 623, 629, 631, 633, 636, 642, 648, 651, 652, 657, 658, 659, 680, 681, 682, 683, 684, 685, 686, 687, 690, 691, 697, 699, 703, 704, 710, 712, 713, 721, 725, 728, 729, 730, 744, 745, 746, 747, 748, 749, 750, 751, 754, 755, 759, 765, 767, 780, 781, 807, 842, 883, 884, 924, 1122, 1205, 1206, 1361, 1398, 1399, 1400, 1402, 1407, 1412, 1413, 1414, 1415, 1419, 1426, 1430, 1432, 1434, 1443, 1445, 1446, 1447, 1461, 1462, 1463, 1471, 1472, 1473, 1474, 1486, 1490, 1495, 1497, 1502, 1504, 1510, 1518, 1524, 1525, 1537, 1539, 1540, 1541, 1542, 1543, 1554, 1555, 1556, 1558, 1566, 1568, 1576, 1577, 1578, 1579, 1580, 1581, 1582, 1583, 1584, 1586, 1587, 1605, 1606, 1612, 1613, 1617, 1618, 1619, 1620, 1621, 1630, 1631, 1638, 1639, 1650, 1651, 1652, 1653, 1655, 1656, 1657, 1658, 1659, 1660, 1661, 1662, 1663, 1665, 1666, 1677, 1682, 1685, 1687, 1688, 1691, 1692, 1694, 1695, 1696, 1697, 1698, 1699, 1701, 1703, 1704, 1706, 1707, 1708, 1709, 1710, 1711, 1712, 1713, 1714, 1715, 1717, 1718, 1721, 1722, 1723, 1724, 1725, 1726, 1727, 1728, 1729, 1730, 1731, 1732, 1734, 1735, 1736, 1737, 1738, 1740, 1741, 1742, 1743, 1744, 1749, 1750, 1766, 1775, 1776, 1787, 1788, 1798, 1809, 1811, 1812, 1813, 1819, 1821, 1826, 1838, 1848, 1849, 1850, 1852, 1858, 1870, 1872, 1875, 1877, 1883, 1897, 1900, 1903, 1908, 1910, 1911, 1912, 1913, 1925, 1931, 1933, 1939, 1940, 1941, 1942, 1943, 1946, 1948, 1960, 1964, 1970, 1972, 1975, 1977, 1996, 1998, 2004, 2006, 2007, 2008, 2021, 2024, 2029, 2030, 2031, 2032, 2033, 2034, 2038, 2040, 2050, 2054, 2061, 2067, 2070, 2085, 2087, 2091, 2092, 2093, 2094, 2095, 2112, 2113, 2114, 2115, 2116, 2117, 2118, 2119, 2122, 2124, 2130, 2141, 2142, 2151, 2163, 2214, 2250, 2272, 2319, 2339, 2383, 2416, 2521, 2522, 2565, 2580, 2582, 2616, 2635, 2643, 2687, 2728, 2745, 2746, 2770, 2776, 2813, 2820, 2936, 2937, 2971, 3054, 3072, 3103, 3132, 3153, 3178, 3179, 3190, 3239, 3255, 3258, 3315, 3743, 4065, 4289

Fisheries, 1693, 1700, 1732, 1734, 4041, 4205

Marine Biology-G, 437, 1445, 1541, 1638, 1700, 1709, 1734, 1736, 1911, 4041

Marine Technology, 410, 568, 623, 699, 1606, 1685, 1732, 1734, 1736, 1737, 1964, 2054, 2339, 4041, 4253

Oceanography, 305, 324, 325, 363, 367, 385, 398, 399, 410, 495, 539, 551, 552, 568, 600, 611, 612, 623, 658, 676, 677, 699, 724, 729, 1412, 1413,

1414, 1416, 1417, 1461, 1462, 1463, 1531, 1540, 1546, 1554, 1555, 1556, 1563, 1570, 1571, 1596, 1606, 1610, 1617, 1633, 1650, 1651, 1652, 1685, 1702, 1705, 1708, 1712, 1713, 1714, 1716, 1719, 1720, 1732, 1733, 1734, 1737, 1739, 1743, 1839, 1840, 1867, 1899, 1910, 1935, 1936, 1952, 1964, 1968, 1970, 1997, 2002, 2020, 2026, 2027, 2054, 2060, 2061, 2086, 2093, 2125, 2137, 2141, 2339, 2417, 2863, 2864, 4041, 4215, 4253

Rivers/Lakes, 1412, 1413, 1414, 1461, 1462, 1463, 1554, 1555, 1556, 1609, 1650, 1651, 1652, 1712, 1713, 1714

NATURAL HISTORY

General, 276, 278, 292, 306, 307, 333, 355, 372, 382, 386, 409, 416, 430, 465, 477, 490, 496, 510, 516, 533, 540, 554, 566, 579, 593, 601, 621, 631, 648, 659, 680, 697, 712, 721, 730, 744, 759, 767, 770, 780, 781, 834, 883, 884, 986, 1122, 1205, 1206, 1361, 1398, 1402, 1407, 1426, 1432, 1443, 1446, 1447, 1486, 1495, 1518, 1542, 1543, 1576, 1578, 1605, 1620, 1631, 1635, 1639, 1656, 1657, 1682, 1694, 1701, 1710, 1711, 1721, 1723, 1735, 1747, 1749, 1755, 1766, 1773, 1775, 1776, 1787, 1788, 1798, 1810, 1811, 1819, 1826, 1858, 1873, 1875, 1897, 1902, 1912, 1913, 1939, 1941, 1960, 1973, 1975, 1996, 2007, 2008, 2050, 2065, 2067, 2085, 2094, 2095, 2112, 2130, 2163, 2272, 2416, 2521, 2580, 2643, 2726, 2745, 2746, 2905, 2936, 2937, 3054, 3103, 3132, 3178, 3179, 3239

Anthropology, 41, 42, 43, 44, 133, 134, 146, 268, 287, 288, 289, 290, 435, 527, 528, 529, 530, 567, 766, 844, 845, 846, 847, 874, 935, 936, 937, 942, 943, 963, 973, 980, 1056, 1057, 1080, 1098, 1099, 1100, 1101, 1113, 1340, 1341, 1342, 1343, 1344, 1390, 1499, 1501, 1511, 1512, 1513, 1514, 1532, 1589, 1599, 1600, 1675, 1676, 1683, 1696, 1748, 1750, 1751, 1752, 1758, 1762, 1763, 1764, 1765, 1768, 1771, 1772, 1774, 1779, 1780, 1781, 1782, 1789, 1790, 1791, 1794, 1795, 1797, 1800, 1801, 1802, 1803, 1804, 1805, 1806, 1807, 1877, 1878, 1880, 1892, 1893, 1894, 1895, 1953, 1954, 1962, 1987, 1988, 1989, 1990, 2052, 2077, 2078, 2079, 2080, 2135, 2178, 2264, 2265, 2266, 2267, 2307, 2328, 2349, 2443, 2513, 2551, 2660, 2699, 2723, 2731, 2732, 2733, 2734, 2802, 2899, 2910, 2911, 2912, 2913, 2923, 2928, 2962, 2981, 2982, 2993, 3007, 3078, 3079, 3080, 3081, 3096, 3099, 3143, 3160, 3161, 3162, 3163, 3174, 3220, 3222, 3223, 3224, 3225, 3226, 3231, 3236, 3261, 3262, 3276, 3283, 4154

Archaeology, 41, 42, 43, 44, 79, 287, 288, 289, 290, 421, 422, 423, 432, 440, 527, 528, 529, 530,

567, 769, 770, 771, 786, 787, 826, 827, 831, 833, 834, 835, 836, 840, 844, 845, 846, 847, 857, 880, 890, 896, 935, 942, 943, 962, 963, 978, 979, 984, 985, 986, 987, 988, 1011, 1017, 1030, 1056, 1057, 1066, 1090, 1091, 1093, 1098, 1099, 1100, 1101, 1113, 1133, 1137, 1179, 1265, 1270, 1341, 1342, 1343, 1344, 1364, 1369, 1390, 1511, 1512, 1513, 1514, 1521, 1546, 1599, 1600, 1675, 1676, 1683, 1745, 1746, 1753, 1754, 1755, 1756, 1757, 1759, 1760, 1761, 1762, 1763, 1764, 1765, 1767, 1768, 1769, 1770, 1777, 1778, 1779, 1780, 1791, 1794, 1795, 1799, 1800, 1801, 1802, 1803, 1804, 1805, 1806, 1892, 1893, 1894, 1895, 1953, 1954, 1962, 1987, 1988, 1989, 1990, 2052, 2077, 2078, 2079, 2080, 2135, 2264, 2265, 2266, 2267, 2725, 2726, 2731, 2732, 2733, 2734, 2749, 2753, 2904, 2905, 2906, 2909, 2910, 2911, 2912, 2913, 2921, 2923, 2941, 2952, 2981, 2982, 3032, 3035, 3078, 3079, 3080, 3081, 3109, 3160, 3161, 3162, 3163, 3183, 3223, 3224, 3225, 3226, 3244, 4157, 4215

Genealogy, 802, 804, 805, 925, 927, 928, 1040, 1041, 1042, 1156, 1158, 1159, 1302, 1303, 1304, 1377, 1379, 1380, 1573, 1574, 1575, 1784, 1785, 1786, 2771, 2773, 2774, 2966, 2968, 2969

Museum Studies, 124, 179, 241, 458, 459, 942, 943, 1030, 1031, 1038, 1052, 1053, 1056, 1057, 1059, 1521, 1599, 1600, 1675, 1676, 1769, 1783, 1792, 1793, 1794, 1795, 1953, 1954, 2965, 2981, 2982

Paleontology, 942, 943, 1056, 1057, 1499, 1501, 1546, 1599, 1600, 1675, 1676, 1696, 1750, 1751, 1752, 1779, 1780, 1781, 1794, 1795, 1796, 1877, 1878, 1880, 1953, 1954, 2981, 2982, 4215, 4258

Primatology-G, 1779, 1780, 1781

SCHOOL OF SCIENCE

General, 4, 56, 112, 137, 156, 172, 174, 180, 202, 209, 210, 244, 261, 263, 274, 275, 276, 278, 279, 280, 283, 284, 285, 286, 292, 296, 297, 298, 299, 300, 307, 308, 309, 310, 313, 315, 319, 324, 325, 326, 328, 329, 330, 332, 334, 335, 336, 341, 342, 347, 353, 354, 355, 356, 360, 362, 363, 364, 366, 372, 376, 377, 378, 379, 382, 386, 398, 399, 401, 402, 405, 409, 416, 426, 427, 428, 429, 430, 452, 465, 476, 477, 478, 486, 487, 488, 489, 490, 496, 501, 507, 510, 514, 516, 518, 521, 522, 523, 524, 533, 535, 540, 541, 551, 552, 555, 565, 566, 577, 579, 582, 587, 588, 589, 590, 593, 601, 611, 612, 614, 616, 620, 621, 629, 631, 633, 643, 644, 645, 646, 648, 652, 659, 676, 677, 681, 682, 683, 689, 690, 697, 710, 712, 713, 716, 717, 718, 719, 721, 730, 745, 746,

747, 753, 754, 759, 765, 767, 774, 781, 782, 785, 798, 806, 808, 809, 819, 884, 924, 1009, 1032, 1068, 1071, 1122, 1124, 1126, 1180, 1206, 1224, 1264, 1290, 1330, 1361, 1362, 1383, 1398, 1399, 1402, 1404, 1405, 1406, 1407, 1408, 1411, 1416, 1417, 1418, 1424, 1425, 1426, 1427, 1429, 1432, 1443, 1447, 1471, 1472, 1473, 1480, 1486, 1490, 1495, 1497, 1502, 1518, 1525, 1543, 1566, 1570, 1571, 1577, 1579, 1580, 1586, 1590, 1605, 1610, 1615, 1620, 1621, 1631, 1639, 1655, 1658, 1659, 1665, 1667, 1682, 1692, 1694, 1695, 1697, 1701, 1704, 1711, 1717, 1719, 1720, 1722, 1724, 1725, 1730, 1735, 1739, 1747, 1749, 1766, 1776, 1798, 1808, 1809, 1810, 1811, 1812, 1813, 1814, 1815, 1816, 1817, 1818, 1819, 1820, 1821, 1822, 1823, 1824, 1825, 1826, 1827, 1828, 1829, 1830, 1831, 1832, 1833, 1834, 1835, 1836, 1837, 1838, 1839, 1840, 1841, 1842, 1843, 1844, 1845, 1846, 1847, 1848, 1849, 1850, 1851, 1852, 1853, 1854, 1855, 1856, 1857, 1858, 1859, 1860, 1861, 1862, 1863, 1864, 1866, 1867, 1868, 1869, 1872, 1873, 1875, 1883, 1888, 1889, 1890, 1891, 1897, 1901, 1913, 1914, 1931, 1935, 1936, 1938, 1940, 1942, 1943, 1945, 1946, 1960, 1961, 1965, 1966, 1968, 1972, 1973, 1975, 1977, 1983, 1984, 1985, 1986, 1996, 2008, 2009, 2021, 2026, 2027, 2028, 2029, 2030, 2031, 2037, 2038, 2050, 2051, 2055, 2056, 2060, 2064, 2065, 2067, 2070, 2073, 2074, 2075, 2076, 2085, 2088, 2095, 2096, 2097, 2102, 2111, 2113, 2114, 2115, 2121, 2122, 2130, 2131, 2134, 2136, 2137, 2138, 2140, 2151, 2163, 2164, 2184, 2190, 2201, 2213, 2214, 2222, 2250, 2272, 2274, 2301, 2318, 2319, 2331, 2383, 2416, 2479, 2520, 2522, 2530, 2542, 2543, 2565, 2580, 2582, 2615, 2616, 2635, 2643, 2687, 2737, 2746, 2758, 2766, 2770, 2775, 2776, 2778, 2780, 2805, 2806, 2807, 2808, 2848, 2863, 2864, 2937, 2964, 2971, 3025, 3049, 3066, 3103, 3128, 3150, 3179, 3190, 3239, 3255, 3296, 3312, 3315, 3318, 3617, 4065, 4103, 4159, 4279

BIOLOGY

General, 4, 41, 42, 43, 44, 56, 116, 172, 202, 244, 250, 262, 275, 276, 278, 280, 283, 284, 285, 286, 287, 288, 289, 290, 292, 295, 296, 303, 305, 306, 307, 308, 322, 323, 324, 325, 333, 334, 335, 336, 341, 342, 355, 357, 363, 367, 372, 376, 377, 378, 379, 382, 385, 386, 398, 399, 405, 409, 416, 426, 427, 428, 429, 430, 452, 465, 476, 477, 478, 486, 487, 488, 489, 490, 493, 494, 495, 496, 499, 501, 506, 507, 508, 510, 514, 516, 518, 521, 522, 523, 524, 527, 528, 529, 530, 532, 533, 534, 535, 539, 540, 541, 551, 552, 554, 555, 561, 566, 567, 577, 579, 582,

587, 588, 589, 590, 593, 596, 599, 600, 601, 611, 612, 614, 616, 621, 629, 631, 632, 633, 643, 644, 645, 646, 648, 651, 657, 658, 659, 663, 674, 676, 677, 680, 681, 682, 683, 689, 690, 691, 692, 697, 710, 712, 713, 716, 717, 718, 719, 721, 724, 725, 728, 729, 730, 731, 741, 744, 745, 746, 747, 753, 754, 755, 759, 765, 767, 774, 780, 781, 807, 844, 845, 846, 847, 883, 884, 924, 940, 942, 943, 963, 1056, 1057, 1098, 1099, 1100, 1101, 1122, 1205, 1206, 1341, 1342, 1343, 1344, 1361, 1390, 1398, 1402, 1407, 1415, 1416, 1417, 1419, 1426, 1432, 1443, 1446, 1447, 1455, 1469, 1471, 1472, 1473, 1474, 1481, 1486, 1490, 1495, 1498, 1499, 1500, 1502, 1511, 1512, 1513, 1514, 1518, 1520, 1524, 1537, 1539, 1540, 1542, 1543, 1566, 1568, 1569, 1570, 1571, 1576, 1577, 1578, 1579, 1580, 1585, 1586, 1587, 1595, 1599, 1600, 1605, 1610, 1617, 1619, 1620, 1622, 1623, 1631, 1639, 1644, 1655, 1656, 1657, 1658, 1659, 1664, 1665, 1666, 1673, 1675, 1676, 1682, 1683, 1684, 1691, 1692, 1694, 1697, 1701, 1702, 1703, 1706, 1707, 1708, 1710, 1711, 1717, 1718, 1719, 1720, 1721, 1722, 1723, 1724, 1725, 1730, 1731, 1735, 1739, 1743, 1747, 1749, 1751, 1762, 1763, 1764, 1765, 1766, 1775, 1776, 1787, 1788, 1794, 1795, 1798, 1800, 1809, 1810, 1811, 1813, 1814, 1815, 1816, 1817, 1819, 1820, 1826, 1827, 1838, 1839, 1840, 1847, 1848, 1849, 1850, 1851, 1852, 1858, 1860, 1862, 1863, 1867, 1870, 1872, 1873, 1875, 1876, 1878, 1879, 1883, 1887, 1888, 1889, 1890, 1891, 1892, 1893, 1894, 1895, 1896, 1897, 1898, 1899, 1900, 1901, 1903, 1906, 1908, 1910, 1912, 1913, 1914, 1917, 1918, 1919, 1920, 1921, 1924, 1930, 1931, 1932, 1933, 1934, 1935, 1936, 1938, 1939, 1940, 1941, 1942, 1943, 1944, 1945, 1946, 1948, 1949, 1951, 1953, 1954, 1960, 1961, 1962, 1963, 1965, 1966, 1968, 1970, 1972, 1973, 1975, 1976, 1977, 1983, 1984, 1985, 1986, 1987, 1988, 1989, 1990, 1996, 1997, 1998, 2004, 2006, 2007, 2008, 2009, 2012, 2013, 2019, 2021, 2023, 2024, 2025, 2026, 2027, 2028, 2029, 2030, 2031, 2035, 2037, 2038, 2040, 2050, 2051, 2052, 2053, 2055, 2056, 2060, 2061, 2065, 2067, 2070, 2073, 2074, 2075, 2076, 2077, 2078, 2079, 2080, 2084, 2085, 2086, 2087, 2088, 2091, 2092, 2093, 2094, 2095, 2096, 2100, 2101, 2110, 2112, 2113, 2114, 2115, 2121, 2122, 2124, 2130, 2131, 2135, 2136, 2137, 2141, 2162, 2163, 2164, 2179, 2184, 2213, 2214, 2217, 2264, 2265, 2266, 2267, 2272, 2274, 2295, 2310, 2311, 2318, 2319, 2324, 2333, 2415, 2416, 2417, 2446, 2518, 2520, 2521, 2522, 2542, 2543, 2580, 2615, 2616, 2620, 2643, 2661, 2687, 2721, 2731, 2732, 2733, 2734, 2737, 2741, 2745, 2746, 2750,

2751, 2770, 2776, 2858, 2863, 2864, 2910, 2911, 2912, 2913, 2936, 2937, 2971, 2981, 2982, 3025, 3054, 3076, 3078, 3079, 3080, 3081, 3103, 3132, 3160, 3161, 3162, 3163, 3175, 3178, 3179, 3181, 3182, 3190, 3223, 3224, 3225, 3226, 3239, 3255, 3258, 3296, 3315, 4065, 4148, 4165, 4166, 4279

Botany, 41, 42, 43, 44, 287, 288, 289, 290, 437, 527, 528, 529, 530, 844, 845, 846, 847, 1098, 1099, 1100, 1101, 1341, 1342, 1343, 1344, 1433, 1445, 1460, 1470, 1475, 1511, 1512, 1513, 1514, 1541, 1596, 1619, 1638, 1691, 1709, 1733, 1762, 1763, 1764, 1765, 1870, 1881, 1892, 1893, 1894, 1895, 1911, 1915, 1916, 1922, 1937, 1950, 1952, 1958, 1987, 1988, 1989, 1990, 2077, 2078, 2079, 2080, 2125, 2264, 2265, 2266, 2267, 2731, 2732, 2733, 2734, 2910, 2911, 2912, 2913, 3078, 3079, 3080, 3081, 3160, 3161, 3162, 3163, 3223, 3224, 3225, 3226

Enology/Viticulture, 145, 464, 954, 1060, 1219, 1319, 1485, 1884, 1885, 1957, 1967, 2706, 2720, 2987, 3291

Entomology, 632, 1460, 1498, 1499, 1500, 1622, 1623, 1751, 1876, 1878, 1879, 1904, 1905, 1922, 1976, 3076, 4198

Evolutionary Biology, 1499, 1500, 1623, 1635, 1751, 1773, 1878, 1879, 1902, 2413, 3076

Health Physics, 335, 342, 410, 568, 623, 682, 690, 699, 746, 754, 1471, 1473, 1579, 1586, 1606, 1658, 1665, 1685, 1724, 1730, 1737, 1849, 1852, 1921, 1932, 1942, 1946, 1964, 2013, 2023, 2030, 2038, 2054, 2101, 2114, 2122, 2295, 2310, 2339, 2518

Microbiology, 475, 576, 628, 709, 1871, 1874, 1909, 1921, 1932, 1971, 1974, 2013, 2023, 2063, 2101, 2249, 2295, 2310, 2373, 2413, 2518, 4244

Molecular Biology-G, 1909, 1932, 2023, 2310, 2518

Mycology-G, 1929

Neurobiology, 1907, 1932, 1955, 1956, 2005, 2023, 2180, 2225, 2226, 2285, 2310, 2444, 2447, 2450, 2502, 2518, 2548, 2662, 3176

Ornithology, 1501, 1642, 1677, 1696, 1750, 1752, 1877, 1880, 1882, 1928, 1969

Parasitology-G, 1923

Physiology, 131, 1162, 1907, 1926, 1927, 1932, 1947, 2005, 2023, 2039, 2123, 2180, 2215, 2285, 2310, 2447, 2492, 2493, 2518, 2662, 3176

Teratology, 1959

Virology-G, 1932, 2023, 2310, 2518

Zoology, 1501, 1558, 1596, 1653, 1696, 1715, 1733, 1750, 1752, 1877, 1880, 1886, 1925, 1952, 2125

CHEMISTRY

General, 41, 42, 43, 44, 116, 131, 177, 234, 244, 262, 275, 276, 278, 280, 283, 284, 285, 286, 287, 288, 289, 290, 292, 295, 303, 306, 307, 308, 311, 316, 317, 318, 322, 323, 324, 325, 334, 335, 336, 337, 338, 339, 341, 342, 344, 355, 357, 363, 367, 372, 376, 377, 378, 379, 382, 386, 398, 399, 405, 409, 410, 416, 426, 427, 428, 429, 430, 452, 453, 465, 475, 476, 477, 478, 486, 487, 488, 489, 490, 493, 494, 496, 499, 501, 502, 503, 504, 506, 507, 508, 510, 514, 516, 518, 521, 522, 523, 524, 527, 528, 529, 530, 531, 533, 534, 540, 541, 550, 551, 552, 555, 557, 558, 559, 561, 562, 566, 567, 568, 576, 577, 579, 582, 587, 588, 589, 590, 592, 593, 596, 598, 599, 601, 611, 612, 614, 615, 616, 621, 623, 628, 629, 631, 632, 633, 637, 638, 639, 640, 641, 643, 644, 645, 646, 647, 648, 651, 656, 657, 659, 663, 670, 674, 676, 677, 681, 682, 683, 684, 685, 686, 688, 689, 690, 691, 693, 697, 699, 709, 710, 712, 713, 716, 717, 718, 719, 720, 721, 724, 725, 728, 730, 731, 739, 741, 742, 745, 746, 747, 748, 749, 750, 752, 753, 754, 755, 756, 759, 765, 767, 780, 781, 807, 844, 845, 846, 847, 883, 884, 924, 963, 1098, 1099, 1100, 1101, 1122, 1162, 1205, 1206, 1341, 1342, 1343, 1344, 1361, 1384, 1390, 1398, 1402, 1407, 1415, 1416, 1417, 1419, 1426, 1432, 1443, 1446, 1447, 1469, 1471, 1472, 1473, 1474, 1486, 1490, 1495, 1498, 1502, 1505, 1506, 1507, 1508, 1509, 1511, 1512, 1513, 1514, 1515, 1516, 1518, 1524, 1536, 1537, 1539, 1542, 1543, 1553, 1559, 1566, 1567, 1568, 1569, 1570, 1571, 1577, 1579, 1580, 1581, 1582, 1583, 1585, 1586, 1587, 1597, 1598, 1605, 1606, 1610, 1617, 1620, 1622, 1625, 1626, 1627, 1628, 1629, 1631, 1639, 1655, 1658, 1659, 1660, 1661, 1662, 1664, 1665, 1666, 1677, 1682, 1683, 1684, 1685, 1692, 1694, 1697, 1701, 1702, 1703, 1706, 1707, 1710, 1711, 1717, 1718, 1719, 1720, 1722, 1724, 1725, 1726, 1727, 1728, 1730, 1731, 1735, 1737, 1739, 1743, 1747, 1749, 1762, 1763, 1764, 1765, 1766, 1775, 1776, 1798, 1800, 1809, 1810, 1811, 1813, 1814, 1815, 1816, 1817, 1819, 1826, 1827, 1838, 1839, 1840, 1847, 1848, 1849, 1850, 1851, 1852, 1858, 1860, 1862, 1863, 1867, 1871, 1872, 1873, 1874, 1875, 1876, 1883, 1888, 1889, 1890, 1891, 1892, 1893, 1894, 1895, 1897, 1899, 1900, 1903, 1908, 1912, 1913, 1914, 1920, 1921, 1930, 1931, 1933, 1934, 1935, 1936, 1938, 1940, 1942, 1943, 1944, 1945, 1946, 1947, 1948, 1960, 1961, 1962, 1963, 1964, 1965, 1966, 1968, 1970, 1971, 1972, 1973, 1974, 1975, 1976, 1977, 1978, 1979, 1980, 1981, 1982, 1983, 1984, 1985, 1986, 1987, 1988, 1989, 1990, 1991, 1992, 1993, 1996, 1997, 1998, 2001, 2003, 2004, 2006, 2007, 2008, 2009, 2010, 2011, 2012, 2013, 2014, 2015, 2016, 2017, 2019, 2021, 2022, 2024, 2025, 2026, 2027, 2028, 2029, 2030, 2031, 2032, 2033, 2034, 2035, 2036, 2037, 2038, 2039, 2040, 2041, 2046, 2047, 2050, 2051, 2052, 2053, 2054, 2055, 2056, 2057, 2060, 2061, 2063, 2065, 2067, 2070, 2073, 2074, 2075, 2076, 2077, 2078, 2079, 2080, 2081, 2082, 2083, 2085, 2086, 2087, 2091, 2092, 2094, 2095, 2096, 2100, 2101, 2103, 2104, 2105, 2106, 2109, 2110, 2113, 2114, 2115, 2116, 2117, 2118, 2120, 2121, 2122, 2123, 2124, 2126, 2127, 2130, 2131, 2135, 2136, 2137, 2141, 2163, 2184, 2187, 2197, 2213, 2214, 2215, 2223, 2249, 2264, 2265, 2266, 2267, 2272, 2290, 2295, 2297, 2311, 2318, 2319, 2332, 2339, 2373, 2416, 2417, 2487, 2520, 2522, 2542, 2543, 2580, 2600, 2615, 2616, 2643, 2672, 2687, 2721, 2731, 2732, 2733, 2734, 2745, 2746, 2770, 2776, 2858, 2863, 2864, 2910, 2911, 2912, 2913, 2936, 2937, 2971, 3034, 3078, 3079, 3080, 3081, 3103, 3160, 3161, 3162, 3163, 3178, 3179, 3190, 3223, 3224, 3225, 3226, 3239, 3255, 3258, 3315, 4065, 4176, 4279

Atmosphere Chemistry, 324, 325, 394, 398, 399, 407, 408, 410, 551, 552, 568, 611, 612, 623, 672, 676, 677, 699, 740, 1416, 1417, 1531, 1562, 1563, 1570, 1571, 1601, 1602, 1606, 1633, 1685, 1705, 1716, 1719, 1720, 1737, 1839, 1840, 1935, 1936, 1964, 2002, 2018, 2020, 2026, 2027, 2048, 2049, 2054, 2107, 2128, 2129, 2339, 2863, 2864, 2983, 2984, 4217

Biochemistry, 41, 42, 43, 44, 287, 288, 289, 290, 361, 475, 527, 528, 529, 530, 576, 628, 632, 653, 709, 844, 845, 846, 847, 1098, 1099, 1100, 1101, 1341, 1342, 1343, 1344, 1498, 1511, 1512, 1513, 1514, 1622, 1762, 1763, 1764, 1765, 1871, 1874, 1876, 1892, 1893, 1894, 1895, 1907, 1921, 1932, 1971, 1974, 1976, 1987, 1988, 1989, 1990, 1995, 1999, 2001, 2005, 2013, 2023, 2059, 2063, 2077, 2078, 2079, 2080, 2101, 2180, 2249, 2264, 2265, 2266, 2267, 2285, 2295, 2310, 2373, 2413, 2447, 2518, 2662, 2731, 2732, 2733, 2734, 2910, 2911, 2912, 2913, 3078, 3079, 3080, 3081, 3160, 3161, 3162, 3163, 3176, 3223, 3224, 3225, 3226

Carbohydrate Chemistry, 2058

Geochemistry, 1531, 1633, 1705, 2002, 4217

Organic Chemistry, 562, 693, 756, 1597, 1999, 2046, 2126

Pesticide/Contaminant Rsrch-G, 2000

MATHEMATICS

General, 4, 16, 41, 42, 43, 44, 56, 88, 164, 172, 174, 177, 202, 210, 234, 244, 261, 274, 276, 277, 278, 283, 284, 285, 286, 287, 288, 289, 290, 292,

295, 296, 303, 305, 306, 307, 308, 309, 315, 318,
323, 330, 333, 334, 335, 336, 340, 342, 355,
363, 364, 365, 366, 367, 372, 376, 377, 378,
379, 382, 385, 386, 405, 409, 415, 416, 426, 427,
428, 429, 430, 452, 465, 477, 486, 487, 488,
489, 490, 493, 494, 495, 496, 501, 505, 508, 510,
515, 516, 519, 521, 522, 523, 524, 527, 528, 529,
530, 531, 532, 533, 534, 535, 539, 540, 541, 547,
550, 554, 555, 560, 566, 567, 573, 578, 579,
585, 587, 588, 589, 590, 592, 593, 596, 599,
600, 601, 607, 614, 615, 621, 630, 631, 643, 644,
645, 646, 647, 648, 651, 657, 658, 659, 660,
680, 681, 682, 683, 687, 688, 690, 691, 697, 711,
712, 716, 717, 718, 719, 720, 721, 725, 728, 729,
730, 742, 744, 745, 746, 747, 751, 752, 754,
755, 759, 767, 774, 780, 781, 807, 844, 845,
846, 847, 883, 884, 963, 1068, 1098, 1099, 1100,
1101, 1122, 1126, 1180, 1205, 1206, 1224, 1330,
1341, 1342, 1343, 1344, 1361, 1390, 1398,
1402, 1407, 1409, 1411, 1419, 1426, 1432, 1443,
1446, 1447, 1469, 1471, 1472, 1473, 1474,
1486, 1495, 1511, 1512, 1513, 1514, 1515, 1516,
1518, 1524, 1537, 1539, 1540, 1542, 1543,
1567, 1569, 1576, 1577, 1579, 1580, 1584,
1586, 1587, 1596, 1605, 1610, 1615, 1617, 1620,
1631, 1639, 1656, 1658, 1659, 1663, 1665,
1666, 1677, 1682, 1683, 1694, 1701, 1703, 1706,
1707, 1708, 1710, 1711, 1721, 1722, 1724, 1725,
1729, 1730, 1731, 1733, 1735, 1739, 1743,
1747, 1749, 1762, 1763, 1764, 1765, 1766,
1775, 1776, 1787, 1798, 1800, 1808, 1810, 1811,
1814, 1815, 1816, 1817, 1819, 1820, 1826, 1827,
1829, 1834, 1844, 1848, 1849, 1850, 1852,
1858, 1860, 1861, 1867, 1868, 1869, 1873,
1875, 1888, 1889, 1890, 1891, 1892, 1893,
1894, 1895, 1896, 1897, 1900, 1901, 1903,
1908, 1910, 1912, 1913, 1914, 1934, 1939, 1940,
1942, 1943, 1946, 1948, 1952, 1960, 1961,
1962, 1968, 1970, 1973, 1975, 1983, 1984,
1985, 1986, 1987, 1988, 1989, 1990, 1991,
1992, 1993, 1996, 1998, 2004, 2006, 2007,
2008, 2009, 2015, 2017, 2022, 2025, 2029, 2030,
2031, 2036, 2038, 2040, 2050, 2051, 2052, 2060,
2061, 2062, 2064, 2065, 2066, 2067, 2069, 2072,
2073, 2074, 2075, 2076, 2077, 2078, 2079, 2080,
2081, 2082, 2083, 2084, 2085, 2087, 2088,
2089, 2091, 2092, 2093, 2094, 2095, 2096, 2097,
2098, 2099, 2102, 2104, 2106, 2109, 2110, 2111,
2112, 2113, 2114, 2115, 2119, 2120, 2122, 2124,
2125, 2130, 2131, 2134, 2135, 2137, 2138, 2139,
2140, 2141, 2162, 2163, 2164, 2184, 2214, 2264,
2265, 2266, 2267, 2272, 2274, 2311, 2319, 2415,
2416, 2522, 2580, 2616, 2643, 2687, 2731, 2732,
2733, 2734, 2737, 2745, 2746, 2752, 2776,
2806, 2910, 2911, 2912, 2913, 2936, 2937, 2951,
2971, 3025, 3054, 3071, 3078, 3079, 3080, 3081,

3103, 3132, 3152, 3160, 3161, 3162, 3163, 3178,
3179, 3190, 3223, 3224, 3225, 3226, 3239,
3258, 3296, 3315, 3318, 4006, 4065, 4100, 4236,
4237, 4254
Physics, 16, 41, 42, 43, 44, 131, 164, 274, 280, 287,
288, 289, 290, 305, 316, 317, 318, 323, 334, 337,
338, 339, 341, 363, 365, 367, 374, 385, 394,
395, 405, 407, 408, 412, 452, 475, 478, 495, 501,
502, 503, 504, 507, 518, 519, 527, 528, 529, 530,
539, 550, 555, 557, 558, 559, 562, 567, 573,
576, 582, 585, 600, 614, 615, 616, 628, 633, 658,
663, 670, 672, 681, 684, 685, 686, 688, 689,
693, 709, 713, 724, 729, 731, 739, 740, 742, 745,
748, 749, 750, 752, 753, 756, 844, 845, 846,
847, 878, 963, 1098, 1099, 1100, 1101, 1162,
1341, 1342, 1343, 1344, 1390, 1469, 1502, 1511,
1512, 1513, 1514, 1515, 1516, 1533, 1540, 1553,
1559, 1562, 1567, 1569, 1577, 1581, 1582,
1583, 1596, 1597, 1598, 1601, 1602, 1610, 1617,
1660, 1661, 1662, 1683, 1697, 1702, 1708,
1722, 1726, 1727, 1728, 1733, 1739, 1743,
1762, 1763, 1764, 1765, 1800, 1808, 1813,
1848, 1851, 1862, 1867, 1871, 1883, 1892,
1893, 1894, 1895, 1899, 1910, 1920, 1921, 1934,
1940, 1945, 1947, 1952, 1962, 1965, 1968,
1970, 1971, 1977, 1987, 1988, 1989, 1990,
1992, 1993, 1997, 2012, 2013, 2014, 2016, 2017,
2018, 2022, 2025, 2029, 2032, 2033, 2034, 2036,
2037, 2039, 2046, 2047, 2048, 2049, 2052,
2055, 2060, 2061, 2062, 2063, 2064, 2068, 2070,
2072, 2077, 2078, 2079, 2080, 2082, 2083, 2086,
2090, 2093, 2100, 2101, 2103, 2105, 2106, 2107,
2108, 2109, 2110, 2113, 2116, 2117, 2118, 2120,
2121, 2123, 2125, 2126, 2127, 2128, 2129, 2132,
2133, 2135, 2136, 2137, 2139, 2141, 2197, 2215,
2264, 2265, 2266, 2267, 2295, 2297, 2311, 2417,
2487, 2542, 2600, 2672, 2731, 2732, 2733,
2734, 2776, 2910, 2911, 2912, 2913, 2971, 2983,
2984, 3071, 3078, 3079, 3080, 3081, 3152, 3160,
3161, 3162, 3163, 3190, 3223, 3224, 3225, 3226,
3289, 3315, 4217, 4267
Statistics, 30, 167, 277, 338, 415, 503, 515, 558,
578, 630, 634, 685, 711, 749, 1430, 1582, 1618,
1661, 1727, 1744, 2033, 2066, 2071, 2117, 2142,
2813, 3072, 3153

MEDICAL DOCTOR

General, 1, 4, 25, 56, 112, 126, 131, 137, 154, 172,
202, 244, 279, 291, 292, 296, 308, 311, 313, 314,
316, 321, 331, 336, 343, 344, 382, 430, 448, 451,
453, 490, 533, 535, 541, 569, 593, 637, 639,
640, 641, 648, 679, 683, 721, 747, 774, 797, 798,
809, 1032, 1162, 1290, 1293, 1360, 1374, 1384,
1399, 1401, 1402, 1410, 1443, 1472, 1479, 1480,
1497, 1505, 1507, 1508, 1509, 1517, 1518, 1553,
1565, 1580, 1590, 1621, 1625, 1627, 1628,

1629, 1631, 1637, 1659, 1667, 1695, 1701,
1725, 1766, 1812, 1818, 1819, 1820, 1827, 1833,
1836, 1847, 1850, 1853, 1897, 1901, 1914,
1924, 1938, 1943, 1947, 1978, 1980, 1981,
1982, 1996, 2009, 2011, 2014, 2028, 2031, 2039,
2041, 2085, 2088, 2096, 2103, 2115, 2123, 2143,
2148, 2149, 2150, 2151, 2152, 2153, 2156, 2157,
2158, 2160, 2161, 2163, 2164, 2165, 2167, 2168,
2171, 2172, 2173, 2174, 2175, 2176, 2181, 2182,
2183, 2184, 2185, 2187, 2188, 2190, 2191, 2192,
2193, 2194, 2195, 2197, 2199, 2200, 2201, 2202,
2203, 2204, 2206, 2207, 2210, 2211, 2212, 2213,
2214, 2215, 2216, 2221, 2222, 2223, 2228, 2229,
2230, 2231, 2232, 2233, 2235, 2236, 2237,
2239, 2240, 2242, 2247, 2250, 2263, 2270,
2271, 2272, 2274, 2276, 2277, 2280, 2281,
2282, 2284, 2286, 2287, 2288, 2290, 2294,
2296, 2297, 2299, 2300, 2301, 2302, 2305,
2306, 2308, 2309, 2314, 2315, 2316, 2318, 2319,
2322, 2330, 2331, 2332, 2338, 2340, 2341,
2342, 2344, 2345, 2347, 2350, 2370, 2383,
2385, 2409, 2412, 2414, 2416, 2427, 2437, 2441,
2454, 2456, 2475, 2479, 2482, 2487, 2496,
2497, 2498, 2508, 2514, 2515, 2519, 2520, 2522,
2530, 2540, 2544, 2545, 2546, 2549, 2552,
2565, 2577, 2578, 2579, 2580, 2583, 2587,
2588, 2591, 2594, 2595, 2596, 2598, 2599,
2600, 2603, 2604, 2611, 2613, 2615, 2616, 2625,
2626, 2627, 2628, 2629, 2632, 2633, 2635,
2638, 2641, 2642, 2643, 2647, 2651, 2652,
2653, 2654, 2655, 2657, 2664, 2665, 2667,
2669, 2670, 2671, 2672, 2675, 2676, 2678,
2679, 2686, 2687, 2691, 2692, 2693, 2695,
2696, 2697, 2698, 2700, 2722, 2737, 2758,
2763, 2766, 2780, 3011, 3013, 3014, 3018, 3025,
3034, 3047, 3048, 3049, 3052, 3053, 3057, 3128,
3171, 3189, 3216, 3238, 3240, 3250, 3252, 3257,
3279, 3296, 3308, 3383, 3413, 3414, 3416, 3621,
3972, 3995, 4071, 4087, 4088, 4241, 4242
Anesthesiology-G, 2169, 2189, 2209, 2234, 2648,
2684, 2694
Cardiology-G, 532, 1896, 2084, 2162, 2189, 2415
Family Practice-G, 2173, 2188, 2202, 2205, 2235,
2281, 2587, 2603, 2608, 2654, 2669, 2676,
2681, 2695
Gynecology-G, 2202, 2205, 2224, 2603, 2608,
2676, 2681
Naturopathy, 1915, 4247
Nephrology-G, 2189, 2196, 2484, 2485, 2486
Neurology-G, 1907, 2005, 2180, 2186, 2188, 2195,
2235, 2285, 2444, 2447, 2450, 2459, 2502,
2548, 2662, 2669, 2695, 3176
Obstetrics-G, 2202, 2205, 2224, 2603, 2608, 2676,
2681
Ophthalmology-G, 2283
Orthopedics-G, 2173, 2188, 2208, 2235, 2281,

2587, 2654, 2669, 2695

Osteopathy, 25, 154, 569, 2148, 2172, 2195, 2205, 2211, 2229, 2238, 2280, 2315, 2340, 2346, 2540, 2608, 2625, 2653, 2681, 2691, 2722, 3013, 3171, 3279, 4257

Pathology, 1949, 2166, 2189, 2217, 2324, 2426, 4259

Pediatrics, 107, 233, 2147, 2198, 2202, 2205, 2425, 2488, 2603, 2608, 2673, 2676, 2681, 3186, 3251, 4260

Psychiatry, 246, 247, 248, 1774, 1906, 1955, 1956, 2144, 2145, 2146, 2154, 2155, 2170, 2173, 2177, 2178, 2179, 2195, 2205, 2218, 2219, 2220, 2225, 2226, 2281, 2442, 2443, 2446, 2527, 2528, 2529, 2584, 2587, 2608, 2617, 2618, 2619, 2649, 2654, 2659, 2660, 2661, 2681, 2741, 3099, 3156, 3169, 3173, 3174, 3175, 3196, 3197, 3198, 3236, 4270

Surgery-G, 2159, 2169, 2173, 2188, 2189, 2202, 2209, 2234, 2235, 2281, 2587, 2603, 2648, 2654, 2669, 2676, 2684, 2694, 2695

Urology-G, 2173, 2188, 2196, 2235, 2281, 2374, 2375, 2376, 2484, 2485, 2486, 2587, 2654, 2669, 2695

MEDICAL RELATED DISCIPLINES

General, 1, 112, 137, 154, 244, 279, 291, 292, 316, 321, 336, 343, 382, 430, 448, 490, 533, 569, 593, 648, 683, 721, 747, 798, 809, 1032, 1290, 1293, 1399, 1401, 1402, 1443, 1472, 1479, 1480, 1497, 1517, 1518, 1553, 1565, 1580, 1590, 1621, 1631, 1637, 1659, 1667, 1695, 1701, 1725, 1766, 1812, 1818, 1819, 1836, 1847, 1850, 1853, 1897, 1924, 1938, 1943, 1996, 2014, 2028, 2031, 2085, 2103, 2115, 2143, 2151, 2157, 2160, 2161, 2163, 2174, 2176, 2183, 2185, 2194, 2197, 2201, 2203, 2204, 2206, 2207, 2213, 2214, 2221, 2222, 2229, 2230, 2231, 2237, 2239, 2240, 2242, 2250, 2262, 2263, 2270, 2271, 2272, 2282, 2284, 2287, 2288, 2296, 2297, 2301, 2302, 2305, 2306, 2308, 2309, 2318, 2319, 2330, 2331, 2336, 2340, 2341, 2342, 2345, 2347, 2350, 2383, 2409, 2412, 2414, 2416, 2437, 2441, 2454, 2456, 2487, 2496, 2497, 2498, 2508, 2514, 2515, 2519, 2520, 2522, 2530, 2540, 2544, 2545, 2546, 2549, 2552, 2565, 2576, 2577, 2578, 2579, 2580, 2588, 2591, 2595, 2596, 2599, 2600, 2604, 2615, 2616, 2622, 2625, 2626, 2627, 2628, 2629, 2632, 2635, 2637, 2638, 2641, 2642, 2643, 2652, 2655, 2657, 2665, 2667, 2671, 2672, 2678, 2679, 2687, 2690, 2691, 2692, 2697, 2698, 2700, 2722, 2766, 2780, 3011, 3049, 3052, 3057, 3128, 3200, 3238, 3240, 3250, 3279, 3308, 3383, 3413, 3414, 3416, 3621, 3972, 3995

Acupuncture/Oriental Medicine, 4143, 4144

Allied Health-G, 2336, 2622, 2690, 3200

Chiropractics, 126, 331, 451, 2195, 2212, 2316, 2455, 2613, 2686, 3053, 3189, 3257, 4173, 4174

Dentistry, 1, 4, 56, 126, 172, 202, 296, 311, 331, 343, 451, 535, 679, 774, 1374, 1479, 1820, 1901, 2011, 2088, 2143, 2149, 2164, 2167, 2172, 2173, 2182, 2187, 2191, 2199, 2200, 2210, 2211, 2212, 2216, 2221, 2228, 2232, 2242, 2247, 2269, 2273, 2274, 2276, 2280, 2281, 2286, 2290, 2294, 2299, 2300, 2314, 2315, 2316, 2322, 2330, 2337, 2338, 2344, 2357, 2587, 2598, 2611, 2613, 2633, 2653, 2654, 2670, 2675, 2686, 2737, 3011, 3014, 3025, 3034, 3047, 3048, 3053, 3057, 3171, 3189, 3216, 3252, 3257, 3296, 3413, 3414, 3416, 4099, 4190

Dentistry-Prosthodontics-G, 2243

Health Care Administration, 6, 250, 679, 692, 940, 1481, 1595, 1673, 1951, 2149, 2185, 2210, 2245, 2246, 2247, 2248, 2278, 2288, 2314, 2333, 2352, 2389, 2456, 2596, 2611, 2620, 2633, 2667, 2830, 3014, 3095, 3240, 4224

Homeopathy, 1915, 4221, 4222

Lab/Clinical Science, 2255, 2262, 2389, 2567, 2576, 2637

Medical Anthropology-G, 1782, 2307, 2513, 2962

Optometry, 126, 331, 410, 451, 568, 623, 679, 699, 1606, 1685, 1737, 1964, 2054, 2172, 2182, 2210, 2212, 2238, 2244, 2252, 2253, 2280, 2286, 2314, 2316, 2339, 2346, 2611, 2613, 2653, 2686, 3053, 3171, 3189, 3257, 4255, 4256

Pharmacology, 41, 42, 43, 44, 287, 288, 289, 290, 323, 527, 528, 529, 530, 679, 844, 845, 846, 847, 1098, 1099, 1100, 1101, 1341, 1342, 1343, 1344, 1469, 1511, 1512, 1513, 1514, 1569, 1762, 1763, 1764, 1765, 1874, 1892, 1893, 1894, 1895, 1907, 1915, 1921, 1932, 1934, 1949, 1974, 1987, 1988, 1989, 1990, 2005, 2013, 2023, 2025, 2077, 2078, 2079, 2080, 2101, 2110, 2168, 2180, 2185, 2200, 2210, 2216, 2217, 2249, 2251, 2264, 2265, 2266, 2267, 2277, 2285, 2288, 2295, 2300, 2310, 2311, 2314, 2320, 2322, 2323, 2324, 2325, 2326, 2343, 2369, 2370, 2373, 2427, 2447, 2456, 2518, 2525, 2526, 2541, 2583, 2596, 2611, 2647, 2662, 2667, 2675, 2731, 2732, 2733, 2734, 2910, 2911, 2912, 2913, 3048, 3078, 3079, 3080, 3081, 3160, 3161, 3162, 3163, 3176, 3223, 3224, 3225, 3226, 3240, 3252, 4097, 4262, 4263, 4264, 4265

Pharmacy, 126, 323, 331, 451, 679, 1469, 1569, 1874, 1907, 1915, 1921, 1932, 1934, 1974, 2005, 2013, 2023, 2025, 2101, 2110, 2149, 2168, 2180, 2191, 2200, 2210, 2212, 2247, 2249, 2251, 2254, 2262, 2277, 2285, 2294, 2295, 2300, 2310, 2311, 2314, 2316, 2321, 2343, 2370, 2373, 2427, 2447, 2518, 2541, 2576, 2583, 2598, 2611, 2613, 2633, 2637, 2647, 2662, 2670, 2675, 2686, 3014,

3048, 3053, 3176, 3189, 3252, 3257, 4097, 4262, 4263, 4264, 4265

Podiatry, 126, 331, 451, 2149, 2195, 2212, 2247, 2289, 2316, 2613, 2633, 2686, 3014, 3053, 3189, 3257, 4268

Public Health-G, 6, 89, 90, 97, 134, 244, 244, 250, 268, 336, 336, 683, 683, 692, 747, 747, 898, 899, 937, 940, 973, 1456, 1457, 1472, 1472, 1481, 1580, 1580, 1589, 1595, 1645, 1646, 1654, 1659, 1659, 1673, 1725, 1725, 1790, 1807, 1850, 1850, 1943, 1943, 1951, 2031, 2031, 2115, 2115, 2185, 2214, 2214, 2278, 2288, 2291, 2292, 2293, 2304, 2306, 2319, 2319, 2328, 2333, 2349, 2389, 2456, 2460, 2522, 2522, 2551, 2596, 2616, 2616, 2620, 2667, 2687, 2687, 2699, 2710, 2711, 2830, 3007, 3095, 3116, 3117, 3220, 3240, 3262, 3283, 4132

Speech Pathology, 126, 185, 186, 187, 188, 189, 191, 203, 237, 243, 331, 451, 1161, 2212, 2256, 2257, 2258, 2259, 2260, 2261, 2275, 2303, 2316, 2317, 2399, 2400, 2401, 2402, 2403, 2404, 2569, 2570, 2571, 2572, 2573, 2575, 2581, 2606, 2613, 2614, 2686, 3053, 3189, 3257, 4161

Sports Medicine-G, 165, 232, 239, 240, 266, 1282, 2298, 2312, 2313, 2348, 2601, 2609, 2610, 2630, 3185, 3218, 3281

Veterinary Medicine, 126, 137, 323, 331, 344, 451, 453, 809, 1384, 1431, 1469, 1478, 1480, 1569, 1590, 1667, 1853, 1886, 1934, 2025, 2041, 2110, 2168, 2172, 2182, 2212, 2216, 2222, 2223, 2241, 2268, 2277, 2280, 2286, 2311, 2316, 2322, 2329, 2331, 2332, 2334, 2335, 2385, 2427, 2530, 2583, 2613, 2647, 2653, 2686, 2701, 2780, 3053, 3171, 3189, 3257, 4288

Veterinary Medicine-G, 137, 323, 809, 1469, 1480, 1569, 1590, 1667, 1853, 1934, 2025, 2110, 2168, 2172, 2182, 2222, 2277, 2279, 2280, 2286, 2311, 2331, 2427, 2530, 2583, 2586, 2647, 2653, 2780, 3170, 3171, 3234, 3298, 4288

MEDICAL RESEARCH

General, 137, 154, 173, 204, 244, 279, 291, 292, 313, 314, 316, 321, 336, 382, 383, 430, 448, 490, 533, 569, 593, 648, 654, 683, 721, 747, 777, 797, 809, 870, 1000, 1399, 1401, 1402, 1403, 1410, 1443, 1444, 1472, 1480, 1497, 1517, 1518, 1528, 1553, 1565, 1580, 1590, 1621, 1631, 1632, 1637, 1659, 1667, 1695, 1701, 1725, 1766, 1774, 1812, 1818, 1819, 1825, 1832, 1833, 1847, 1850, 1853, 1862, 1863, 1897, 1906, 1907, 1924, 1938, 1943, 1965, 1966, 1996, 2005, 2014, 2028, 2031, 2055, 2056, 2085, 2103, 2115, 2136, 2151, 2157, 2160, 2161, 2163, 2174, 2176, 2178, 2179, 2180, 2183, 2185, 2190, 2192, 2197, 2204, 2206, 2207, 2213, 2214, 2222, 2229, 2230, 2231, 2237, 2239, 2240, 2250, 2263,

2270, 2271, 2272, 2282, 2284, 2285, 2287, 2288, 2297, 2305, 2306, 2308, 2309, 2318, 2319, 2331, 2340, 2341, 2342, 2345, 2347, 2350, 2352, 2353, 2355, 2363, 2383, 2394, 2409, 2412, 2414, 2416, 2418, 2419, 2424, 2434, 2437, 2441, 2443, 2446, 2447, 2448, 2449, 2454, 2456, 2474, 2475, 2479, 2482, 2487, 2494, 2495, 2496, 2497, 2498, 2499, 2500, 2508, 2514, 2515, 2519, 2520, 2522, 2530, 2532, 2539, 2540, 2542, 2543, 2544, 2545, 2546, 2547, 2549, 2552, 2565, 2577, 2578, 2579, 2580, 2588, 2591, 2595, 2596, 2600, 2615, 2616, 2625, 2626, 2627, 2628, 2629, 2632, 2635, 2638, 2641, 2642, 2643, 2652, 2655, 2657, 2660, 2661, 2662, 2665, 2667, 2672, 2679, 2687, 2691, 2692, 2697, 2698, 2700, 2722, 2741, 2758, 2763, 2780, 3052, 3099, 3174, 3175, 3176, 3236, 3238, 3240, 3279, 3383, 3621, 3972

Alcohol/Drug Abuse-G, 2354, 2541
Allergy-G, 2355, 2411
Alzheimer's Disease-G, 141, 247, 248, 252, 2219, 2220, 2364, 2366, 2372, 2528, 2529, 2531, 2537, 2618, 2619, 3197, 3198, 3199, 3264
Amyotrophc Latral Sclerosis-G, 2405
Arthritis-G, 2406, 2407, 2408
Asthma-G, 2395, 2411
Audiology, 186, 187, 188, 189, 2257, 2258, 2259, 2260, 2400, 2401, 2402, 2403, 2570, 2571, 2572, 2573
Biological Psychiatry-G, 2227
Biomedical Sciences, 173, 204, 383, 654, 724, 777, 870, 1000, 1403, 1444, 1528, 1578, 1632, 1657, 1702, 1723, 1782, 1788, 1862, 1863, 1899, 1926, 1927, 1941, 1965, 1966, 1995, 1997, 2055, 2056, 2086, 2136, 2185, 2288, 2291, 2307, 2417, 2418, 2419, 2424, 2456, 2460, 2473, 2492, 2493, 2499, 2513, 2521, 2523, 2542, 2543, 2596, 2667, 2962, 3240
Birth Defects, 2425, 4084, 4192
Cancer, 2372, 2379, 2380, 2413, 2420, 2423, 2476, 2477, 2478, 2480, 2481, 2501
Child Health, 107, 233, 246, 268, 973, 1807, 2198, 2218, 2349, 2425, 2488, 2527, 2551, 2617, 2624, 2673, 2699, 3007, 3186, 3196, 3220, 3251, 3283
Chiropractics, 2455
Cystic Fibrosis, 2432, 2433
Dental-G, 2356, 2357, 2499
Dermatology-G, 2435, 2523
Diabetes-G, 2358, 2359, 2360, 2361, 2362, 2483
Digestive Disorders-G, 2436
Drug Standards/Info-G, 2541
Endocrinology-G, 2523
Epidemiology-G, 1932, 2023, 2310, 2477, 2478, 2518, 2523
Epidermolysis Bullosa-G, 2434
Epilepsy, 1774, 1906, 1907, 2005, 2177, 2178, 2179,

2180, 2285, 2442, 2443, 2444, 2445, 2446, 2447, 2448, 2449, 2450, 2457, 2659, 2660, 2661, 2662, 2741, 3099, 3173, 3174, 3175, 3176, 3236
Facial Plastic Surgery, 2438, 2439, 2440
Genetics, 1906, 1907, 1932, 2005, 2023, 2179, 2180, 2285, 2310, 2413, 2446, 2447, 2457, 2518, 2661, 2662, 2741, 3175, 3176
Gerontology/Aging, 2364, 2365, 2366, 2367, 2368, 2369, 2370, 2371, 2372, 2382, 2523, 2524
Girls/Women Sports/Fitness, 2550
HIV/AIDS-G, 2355
Headache & Pain-G, 2509, 2510
Heart/Cardiovascular, 532, 1896, 2084, 2162, 2351, 2415, 2461, 2462, 2463, 2464, 2465, 2466, 2467, 2468, 2469, 2470, 2471
Hemophilia-G, 2511, 2512, 2682
Immunology-G, 1926, 1927, 1932, 2023, 2310, 2355, 2372, 2411, 2492, 2493, 2518, 2523
Inflammatory Bowel Disease-G, 2428, 2429, 2430, 2431
Kidney/Nephrology-G, 2196, 2484, 2485, 2486
Leprosy-G, 2472, 2490
Liver, 2384, 2385, 2421, 2422, 2436
Lukemia-G, 2491
Lung Disease-G, 1926, 1927, 2386, 2387, 2388, 2389, 2390, 2392, 2393, 2472, 2492, 2493
Lupus Erythematosus, 2494, 2495
Medicinal Botany-G, 1915
Mental Health Services, 246, 247, 248, 2218, 2219, 2220, 2507, 2527, 2528, 2529, 2617, 2618, 2619, 3196, 3197, 3198, 4084, 4192
Mental Retardation, 246, 247, 248, 259, 2218, 2219, 2220, 2457, 2527, 2528, 2529, 2538, 2617, 2618, 2619, 3196, 3197, 3198, 3214
Multiple Sclerosis-G, 2516, 2517
Myasthenia Gravis-G, 2504, 2505, 2677
Neuromuscular Diseases-G, 2503, 2504, 2505, 2677
Neuroscience, 1907, 1932, 2005, 2023, 2180, 2186, 2285, 2310, 2364, 2366, 2372, 2444, 2447, 2448, 2450, 2457, 2458, 2459, 2502, 2518, 2548, 2662, 3176
Olfactory-G, 3191
Ophthalmology, 2283, 2451, 2452, 2453
Pediatric Lung Disease-G, 2386, 2389, 2391, 2393, 2425
Reproductive Physiology/Biolgy, 2489, 3168
Respiratory Disease-G, 1926, 1927, 2168, 2277, 2396, 2397, 2398, 2427, 2492, 2493, 2566, 2583, 2647
Schizophrenia/Depression-G, 2506
Speech-Language Pathology, 185, 186, 187, 188, 191, 2185, 2256, 2257, 2258, 2259, 2261, 2288, 2399, 2400, 2401, 2402, 2404, 2456, 2569, 2570, 2571, 2572, 2575, 2596, 2667, 3240
Spina Bifida/Hydrocephalus-G, 2410

Strokes-G, 247, 248, 2219, 2220, 2461, 2462, 2463, 2464, 2528, 2529, 2533, 2534, 2535, 2536, 2618, 2619, 3197, 3198
Sudden Infant Death Syndrome-G, 2425
Toxicology-G, 1874, 1974, 2166, 2249, 2320, 2323, 2373, 2426, 2525, 2526
Urology-G, 2196, 2374, 2375, 2376, 2377, 2378, 2379, 2380, 2381, 2484, 2485, 2486
Women's Health-G, 268, 973, 974, 1807, 2349, 2551, 2699, 3007, 3220, 3283

MEDICAL TECHNOLOGIES

General, 154, 211, 244, 279, 291, 292, 297, 316, 336, 382, 430, 490, 533, 569, 593, 648, 652, 683, 721, 747, 1293, 1356, 1360, 1399, 1401, 1402, 1443, 1472, 1497, 1517, 1518, 1525, 1553, 1580, 1621, 1631, 1637, 1659, 1695, 1701, 1704, 1725, 1766, 1812, 1818, 1819, 1821, 1847, 1850, 1897, 1924, 1938, 1943, 1996, 2014, 2028, 2031, 2085, 2103, 2115, 2151, 2157, 2160, 2161, 2163, 2168, 2174, 2176, 2181, 2183, 2191, 2194, 2197, 2203, 2213, 2214, 2229, 2230, 2231, 2237, 2239, 2240, 2250, 2262, 2263, 2270, 2271, 2272, 2277, 2282, 2284, 2287, 2294, 2296, 2297, 2302, 2306, 2318, 2319, 2340, 2341, 2342, 2345, 2347, 2350, 2383, 2409, 2412, 2414, 2416, 2427, 2437, 2441, 2454, 2487, 2496, 2497, 2498, 2519, 2520, 2522, 2540, 2544, 2545, 2546, 2549, 2552, 2565, 2576, 2577, 2578, 2579, 2580, 2582, 2583, 2585, 2588, 2590, 2591, 2593, 2594, 2595, 2597, 2598, 2599, 2600, 2604, 2615, 2616, 2625, 2626, 2627, 2628, 2629, 2632, 2635, 2637, 2638, 2641, 2642, 2643, 2647, 2650, 2652, 2655, 2656, 2657, 2663, 2664, 2665, 2668, 2670, 2671, 2672, 2678, 2687, 2691, 2692, 2697, 2698, 2700, 2722, 3233, 3238, 3242, 3250, 3279, 3308, 3383, 3972, 3995
Animal Assisted Therapy-G, 2279, 2586, 3170, 3234, 3298
Art Therapy, 2554, 2555, 2556, 2557, 2558
Athletic Trainer, 72, 165, 166, 232, 239, 240, 266, 267, 1282, 2298, 2312, 2313, 2348, 2592, 2601, 2607, 2609, 2610, 2630, 2631, 2835, 2897, 3177, 3185, 3218, 3219, 3237, 3281, 3282
Audiology, 126, 185, 186, 187, 188, 189, 191, 203, 236, 237, 243, 331, 451, 1161, 2212, 2256, 2257, 2258, 2259, 2260, 2261, 2275, 2303, 2316, 2317, 2399, 2400, 2401, 2402, 2403, 2404, 2569, 2570, 2571, 2572, 2573, 2575, 2581, 2605, 2606, 2613, 2614, 2621, 2686, 3053, 3189, 3257, 4161, 4285
Clinical Chemistry, 4176
Dental Assistant, 2161, 2271, 2414, 2579, 2642, 4188
Dental Hygiene, 126, 331, 451, 2168, 2212, 2277,

2316, 2427, 2559, 2560, 2561, 2562, 2563, 2564, 2583, 2613, 2647, 2686, 3053, 3189, 3257

Dental Hygiene Education, 2559, 2560, 2561

Dental Hygiene-G, 2559, 2560, 2561, 2562, 2563, 2564

Dental Lab Tech, 4189

Dietetic Technician, 4191

Emergncy Medical Tech. (EMT), 2602, 3306

Exercise Physiology, 21, 182, 232, 239, 240, 1233, 1282, 2170, 2298, 2312, 2313, 2553, 2584, 2601, 2609, 2610, 2649, 3169, 3185

Health Information Management, 250, 692, 940, 1481, 1595, 1673, 1951, 2333, 2389, 2620

Health Information Technology, 250, 692, 940, 1481, 1595, 1673, 1951, 2333, 2389, 2620

Kinesiotherapy, 239, 240, 2312, 2313, 2609, 2610

Massage Therapy, 4233, 4234, 4235

Medical Assistant, 2161, 2271, 2414, 2579, 2642

Medical Records, 4240

Medical Technology, 1360, 2168, 2181, 2185, 2255, 2277, 2288, 2427, 2456, 2567, 2583, 2594, 2596, 2647, 2664, 2667, 3240, 4239

Music Therapy, 236, 2605, 4246

Occupational Health, 244, 247, 248, 336, 683, 747, 1472, 1580, 1659, 1725, 1850, 1943, 2031, 2115, 2214, 2219, 2220, 2319, 2522, 2528, 2529, 2616, 2618, 2619, 2687, 3197, 3198

Occupational Therapy, 126, 236, 255, 331, 451, 2168, 2191, 2212, 2277, 2294, 2316, 2336, 2389, 2427, 2583, 2598, 2605, 2613, 2622, 2623, 2647, 2670, 2686, 2690, 3053, 3189, 3200, 3257, 4050, 4108, 4109, 4110, 4111, 4113

Physical Therapy, 126, 236, 239, 240, 255, 331, 451, 679, 1360, 2161, 2168, 2181, 2191, 2210, 2212, 2262, 2271, 2277, 2294, 2312, 2313, 2314, 2316, 2414, 2427, 2576, 2579, 2583, 2594, 2598, 2605, 2609, 2610, 2611, 2613, 2623, 2637, 2642, 2647, 2664, 2670, 2686, 3053, 3189, 3257, 4050, 4108, 4109, 4110, 4111, 4113, 4266

Physician Assistant, 126, 331, 451, 679, 1360, 2173, 2181, 2202, 2205, 2210, 2212, 2281, 2314, 2316, 2327, 2587, 2594, 2603, 2608, 2611, 2612, 2613, 2654, 2664, 2676, 2681, 2685, 2686, 3053, 3189, 3257, 4049, 4075, 4105

Physiotherapy-G, 2336, 2622, 2690, 3200

Radiology Tech., 1360, 2173, 2181, 2281, 2568, 2587, 2593, 2594, 2654, 2663, 2664, 4273

Recreation Therapy, 232, 236, 239, 240, 1282, 2170, 2298, 2312, 2313, 2584, 2601, 2605, 2609, 2610, 2649, 3169, 3185

Rehabilitation, 207, 236, 239, 240, 2312, 2313, 2589, 2605, 2609, 2610, 3172, 3235, 4036

Respiratory Therapy, 1360, 2168, 2181, 2277, 2389, 2396, 2397, 2398, 2427, 2566, 2583, 2594, 2645, 2647, 2664, 4276

Speech Therapy, 126, 185, 186, 187, 188, 189, 190, 191, 237, 246, 247, 248, 331, 451, 2212, 2218, 2219, 2220, 2256, 2257, 2258, 2259, 2260, 2261, 2303, 2316, 2399, 2400, 2401, 2402, 2403, 2404, 2527, 2528, 2529, 2569, 2570, 2571, 2572, 2573, 2574, 2575, 2606, 2613, 2617, 2618, 2619, 2686, 3053, 3189, 3196, 3197, 3198, 3257, 4036, 4285

Speech-Language Pathology, 186, 187, 188, 189, 190, 191, 236, 237, 246, 247, 248, 2185, 2218, 2219, 2220, 2257, 2258, 2259, 2260, 2261, 2288, 2303, 2336, 2400, 2401, 2402, 2403, 2404, 2456, 2527, 2528, 2529, 2570, 2571, 2572, 2573, 2574, 2575, 2596, 2605, 2606, 2617, 2618, 2619, 2621, 2622, 2667, 2690, 3196, 3197, 3198, 3200, 3240, 4050, 4108, 4109, 4110, 4111, 4113

NURSING

General, 126, 154, 211, 244, 268, 279, 291, 292, 316, 321, 331, 336, 382, 430, 448, 451, 490, 533, 569, 593, 648, 683, 721, 747, 973, 1293, 1356, 1360, 1399, 1401, 1402, 1443, 1472, 1497, 1517, 1518, 1553, 1565, 1580, 1621, 1631, 1637, 1659, 1695, 1701, 1725, 1766, 1774, 1807, 1812, 1818, 1819, 1850, 1897, 1907, 1924, 1943, 1996, 2005, 2014, 2031, 2085, 2103, 2115, 2149, 2151, 2157, 2160, 2161, 2163, 2168, 2171, 2173, 2174, 2176, 2178, 2180, 2181, 2183, 2185, 2191, 2194, 2197, 2200, 2200, 2202, 2203, 2204, 2209, 2212, 2214, 2229, 2230, 2233, 2234, 2236, 2237, 2239, 2240, 2247, 2250, 2262, 2263, 2270, 2271, 2272, 2277, 2281, 2282, 2284, 2285, 2287, 2288, 2294, 2296, 2297, 2300, 2300, 2302, 2305, 2306, 2316, 2319, 2336, 2340, 2341, 2345, 2347, 2349, 2350, 2383, 2389, 2409, 2412, 2414, 2416, 2427, 2437, 2441, 2443, 2447, 2454, 2456, 2487, 2508, 2522, 2540, 2544, 2546, 2549, 2551, 2552, 2565, 2576, 2577, 2578, 2579, 2580, 2583, 2585, 2587, 2588, 2590, 2591, 2593, 2594, 2595, 2596, 2597, 2598, 2599, 2600, 2603, 2604, 2613, 2616, 2622, 2625, 2626, 2628, 2629, 2632, 2633, 2635, 2637, 2638, 2639, 2640, 2641, 2642, 2643, 2644, 2646, 2647, 2650, 2651, 2652, 2654, 2655, 2656, 2657, 2658, 2660, 2662, 2663, 2664, 2665, 2667, 2668, 2670, 2671, 2672, 2675, 2675, 2676, 2677, 2678, 2679, 2683, 2684, 2686, 2687, 2690, 2691, 2692, 2693, 2694, 2696, 2697, 2698, 2699, 2700, 2722, 3007, 3014, 3048, 3048, 3052, 3053, 3099, 3174, 3176, 3189, 3200, 3220, 3233, 3236, 3238, 3240, 3242, 3250, 3252, 3252, 3257, 3279, 3283, 3308, 3383, 3995, 4107, 4252

Anesthetist, 2169, 2172, 2173, 2202, 2209, 2234, 2280, 2281, 2587, 2593, 2603, 2648, 2653, 2654, 2663, 2676, 2684, 2694, 3171, 4251

Behavioral Sciences-G, 1774, 1906, 2170, 2177, 2178, 2179, 2389, 2442, 2443, 2446, 2584, 2649, 2659, 2660, 2661, 2741, 3099, 3169, 3173, 3174, 3175, 3236

Cancer Nursing, 2480, 2688

Gynecology, 2205, 2608, 2640, 2674, 2681

Hemophilia/Bleeding Disrdrs-G, 2682

Licensed Practical Nurse (LPN), 211, 2202, 2597, 2603, 2668, 2676, 2680, 3242

Medical-Surgical Nursing, 2169, 2173, 2188, 2202, 2209, 2234, 2235, 2281, 2587, 2593, 2603, 2648, 2654, 2663, 2669, 2676, 2684, 2694, 2695

Neonatology, 2640, 2674

Nurse Practitioner, 2202, 2205, 2603, 2608, 2612, 2676, 2680, 2681, 2685

Nurse/Midwifery, 2202, 2205, 2603, 2608, 2612, 2634, 2640, 2674, 2676, 2681, 2685

Obstetrics, 2202, 2205, 2603, 2608, 2640, 2674, 2676, 2681

Operating Room Nursing, 211, 2169, 2173, 2188, 2202, 2209, 2234, 2235, 2281, 2587, 2597, 2603, 2648, 2654, 2668, 2669, 2676, 2684, 2694, 2695, 3242

Pediatric, 107, 233, 2198, 2205, 2488, 2608, 2673, 2674, 2681, 3186, 3251

Research, 2389, 2636, 2677, 2682, 2689

Respiratory Nursing-G, 2645

NUTRITION

General, 89, 90, 262, 357, 898, 899, 1456, 1457, 1645, 1646, 1684, 1963, 2053, 2292, 2293, 2469, 2703, 2705, 2710, 2711, 2715, 2716, 2717, 2721, 3116, 3117, 4207

Cereal Science/Technology, 2702

Culinary Arts, 145, 464, 954, 1060, 1219, 1319, 1485, 1885, 1957, 2702, 2704, 2706, 2709, 2713, 2718, 2719, 2720, 2987, 3291, 3299, 4208

Dietetics, 154, 569, 2229, 2340, 2540, 2625, 2691, 2702, 2707, 2722, 3279, 4191

Food Management/Science/Tech., 15, 145, 464, 954, 1060, 1219, 1319, 1485, 1957, 2702, 2703, 2708, 2709, 2712, 2719, 2720, 2987, 3299, 4208, 4209

Home Econ/Fam&Consumer Sci, 1431, 2241, 2701, 2703, 2708, 2714, 2715, 2716, 2717, 4201

SCHOOL OF SOCIAL SCIENCE

General, 2, 4, 8, 9, 38, 40, 41, 42, 43, 44, 56, 73, 74, 79, 87, 93, 94, 100, 112, 137, 138, 142, 146, 147, 156, 167, 168, 172, 178, 180, 181, 196, 197, 202, 215, 235, 261, 263, 270, 282, 287, 288, 289, 290, 296, 306, 307, 313, 314, 334, 354, 360, 362, 375, 386, 405, 421, 425, 440, 452, 485, 496, 501, 520, 526, 527, 528, 529, 530, 535, 540, 555,

586, 601, 614, 642, 659, 681, 730, 745, 766, 769, 770, 772, 773, 774, 776, 780, 781, 784, 786, 787, 788, 789, 790, 791, 793, 794, 795, 796, 797, 798, 799, 801, 802, 803, 804, 805, 806, 808, 809, 812, 813, 814, 815, 816, 817, 821, 823, 832, 833, 834, 837, 842, 844, 845, 846, 847, 848, 849, 862, 871, 882, 883, 884, 890, 896, 897, 900, 901, 906, 907, 924, 925, 926, 927, 928, 944, 945, 947, 948, 949, 950, 951, 952, 953, 968, 980, 984, 986, 994, 995, 1010, 1011, 1017, 1021, 1032, 1036, 1040, 1041, 1042, 1068, 1071, 1080, 1092, 1098, 1099, 1100, 1101, 1102, 1103, 1122, 1133, 1137, 1138, 1140, 1145, 1151, 1156, 1157, 1158, 1159, 1180, 1194, 1195, 1205, 1206, 1215, 1218, 1224, 1240, 1241, 1265, 1270, 1290, 1302, 1303, 1304, 1330, 1340, 1341, 1342, 1343, 1344, 1345, 1346, 1361, 1364, 1369, 1370, 1372, 1376, 1377, 1378, 1379, 1380, 1383, 1387, 1397, 1400, 1407, 1409, 1410, 1420, 1421, 1422, 1423, 1425, 1429, 1430, 1434, 1446, 1447, 1480, 1510, 1511, 1512, 1513, 1514, 1542, 1543, 1564, 1566, 1573, 1574, 1575, 1577, 1590, 1591, 1592, 1593, 1594, 1618, 1630, 1639, 1655, 1667, 1668, 1669, 1670, 1671, 1699, 1710, 1711, 1717, 1722, 1744, 1748, 1753, 1755, 1762, 1763, 1764, 1765, 1775, 1776, 1777, 1778, 1784, 1785, 1786, 1797, 1820, 1826, 1833, 1836, 1838, 1846, 1848, 1853, 1857, 1861, 1864, 1866, 1892, 1893, 1894, 1895, 1901, 1906, 1912, 1913, 1917, 1918, 1931, 1940, 1987, 1988, 1989, 1990, 2007, 2008, 2021, 2029, 2077, 2078, 2079, 2080, 2088, 2094, 2095, 2098, 2113, 2134, 2142, 2164, 2179, 2190, 2192, 2201, 2222, 2264, 2265, 2266, 2267, 2274, 2301, 2331, 2446, 2479, 2482, 2530, 2661, 2723, 2724, 2725, 2726, 2727, 2728, 2729, 2730, 2731, 2732, 2733, 2734, 2735, 2736, 2737, 2738, 2739, 2740, 2741, 2742, 2743, 2744, 2745, 2746, 2747, 2748, 2749, 2750, 2751, 2752, 2753, 2754, 2755, 2756, 2757, 2758, 2759, 2760, 2761, 2762, 2763, 2764, 2765, 2766, 2767, 2768, 2769, 2770, 2771, 2772, 2773, 2774, 2775, 2776, 2777, 2778, 2779, 2780, 2781, 2782, 2783, 2784, 2785, 2786, 2787, 2788, 2789, 2790, 2791, 2792, 2793, 2794, 2795, 2796, 2797, 2798, 2799, 2800, 2801, 2802, 2803, 2804, 2805, 2806, 2807, 2808, 2809, 2810, 2811, 2812, 2813, 2814, 2820, 2822, 2823, 2836, 2841, 2842, 2899, 2904, 2905, 2907, 2910, 2911, 2912, 2913, 2914, 2915, 2924, 2926, 2930, 2932, 2933, 2936, 2937, 2938, 2941, 2951, 2952, 2955, 2963, 2966, 2967, 2968, 2969, 2971, 2985, 2993, 3008, 3021, 3022, 3025, 3029, 3030, 3031, 3032, 3035, 3036, 3038, 3040, 3041, 3049, 3066, 3072, 3073, 3078, 3079, 3080, 3081, 3084, 3085, 3093,

3100, 3101, 3103, 3104, 3109, 3113, 3115, 3118, 3119, 3128, 3135, 3139, 3140, 3141, 3143, 3150, 3153, 3154, 3159, 3160, 3161, 3162, 3163, 3164, 3165, 3175, 3178, 3179, 3180, 3181, 3182, 3183, 3184, 3187, 3190, 3201, 3203, 3204, 3205, 3206, 3207, 3208, 3209, 3210, 3211, 3217, 3223, 3224, 3225, 3226, 3227, 3228, 3230, 3239, 3241, 3244, 3245, 3255, 3260, 3265, 3266, 3267, 3268, 3269, 3270, 3271, 3272, 3273, 3274, 3275, 3276, 3280, 3296, 3315, 3318, 3617, 4045, 4069

COMMUNICATIONS

General, 2, 7, 27, 36, 38, 68, 72, 82, 116, 148, 193, 212, 256, 282, 302, 375, 425, 485, 499, 520, 570, 586, 642, 674, 701, 741, 772, 773, 788, 842, 848, 849, 893, 897, 957, 994, 995, 1102, 1103, 1138, 1189, 1194, 1195, 1240, 1241, 1345, 1346, 1370, 1400, 1434, 1510, 1607, 1630, 1681, 1686, 1699, 1930, 2019, 2592, 2728, 2735, 2736, 2747, 2754, 2816, 2819, 2820, 2822, 2823, 2827, 2831, 2835, 2836, 2837, 2838, 2841, 2847, 2858, 2878, 2892, 2896, 2914, 2915, 2938, 2948, 3021, 3022, 3031, 3036, 3062, 3077, 3084, 3085, 3097, 3104, 3111, 3113, 3125, 3144, 3164, 3165, 3177, 3180, 3184, 3227, 3228, 3237, 3241, 3245, 4078, 4079

Broadcasting, 36, 51, 193, 200, 852, 976, 998, 1108, 1230, 1243, 2815, 2819, 2821, 2824, 2825, 2826, 2850, 2854, 2855, 2856, 2857, 2859, 2871, 2881, 2891, 3077, 3137, 3449, 3792, 4167, 4168, 4203

Electronic Media, 1058, 2825, 2875, 3316, 3792, 4167

Financial/Business Journalism, 119, 1466, 2834, 2854, 2855, 2860, 2865, 3051, 3253, 4228

Journalism, 7, 27, 36, 51, 68, 87, 127, 136, 144, 193, 200, 215, 302, 463, 517, 581, 788, 789, 852, 897, 998, 1064, 1108, 1138, 1140, 1176, 1189, 1243, 1370, 1484, 1680, 2153, 2754, 2755, 2816, 2818, 2819, 2824, 2826, 2829, 2831, 2837, 2840, 2841, 2842, 2847, 2849, 2851, 2852, 2853, 2854, 2855, 2856, 2857, 2866, 2868, 2870, 2874, 2877, 2879, 2891, 2896, 2948, 3036, 3038, 3077, 3097, 3113, 3115, 3125, 3131, 3142, 3184, 3245, 3449, 3792, 4080, 4092, 4228, 4250

Medical Journalism, 2153, 2886

News Graphics, 1067, 2889

Newspaper Business, 136, 1189, 2826, 2870, 2873, 2896, 3449

Photojournalism, 1064, 1176, 2854, 2855, 2856, 2857, 2861, 2862, 2871, 2879, 2888, 2890, 2895, 3137, 4228

Print Journalism/Print Media, 136, 1189, 2826, 2869, 2870, 2891, 2896, 3449

Public Relations, 22, 27, 72, 127, 128, 136, 242, 570, 701, 894, 1039, 1155, 1301, 1607, 1643, 1686, 2592, 2816, 2835, 2839, 2866, 2867, 2870, 2892, 3062, 3112, 3131, 3177, 3237, 3243

Public Sector Communications, 36, 87, 136, 193, 215, 789, 1140, 2755, 2819, 2842, 2847, 2870, 3038, 3077, 3115, 3125, 3979

Publishing, 1107, 2853, 4039, 4219, 4228

Religious Journalism, 2854, 2855, 2893

Sports Reporting, 72, 166, 267, 2592, 2631, 2835, 2897, 3177, 3219, 3237, 3282

Technical Communication, 6, 324, 325, 398, 399, 551, 552, 611, 612, 676, 677, 1058, 1416, 1417, 1570, 1571, 1719, 1720, 1839, 1840, 1935, 1936, 2026, 2027, 2278, 2830, 2863, 2864, 2875, 3095, 3316

Television Industry, 51, 72, 200, 852, 998, 1108, 1243, 2592, 2824, 2835, 2854, 2855, 3177, 3237, 3792, 4168

Video Journalism, 2861

HISTORY

General, 52, 53, 73, 74, 79, 81, 99, 100, 124, 142, 145, 146, 157, 168, 179, 241, 268, 306, 307, 386, 423, 435, 440, 464, 496, 540, 601, 659, 730, 766, 770, 771, 772, 773, 780, 781, 786, 787, 796, 800, 801, 802, 803, 804, 805, 834, 835, 840, 848, 849, 853, 854, 874, 880, 882, 883, 884, 890, 896, 925, 926, 927, 928, 954, 968, 971, 973, 980, 986, 987, 988, 994, 995, 1011, 1017, 1020, 1021, 1034, 1036, 1038, 1040, 1041, 1042, 1060, 1080, 1090, 1093, 1102, 1103, 1112, 1113, 1122, 1132, 1133, 1137, 1144, 1145, 1150, 1151, 1156, 1157, 1158, 1159, 1187, 1194, 1195, 1205, 1206, 1208, 1214, 1215, 1219, 1240, 1241, 1265, 1270, 1276, 1302, 1303, 1304, 1319, 1340, 1345, 1346, 1361, 1363, 1364, 1369, 1371, 1372, 1375, 1376, 1377, 1378, 1379, 1380, 1407, 1409, 1446, 1447, 1485, 1532, 1542, 1543, 1573, 1574, 1575, 1639, 1710, 1711, 1748, 1755, 1756, 1760, 1768, 1771, 1775, 1776, 1777, 1778, 1783, 1784, 1785, 1786, 1797, 1807, 1826, 1912, 1913, 1957, 2007, 2008, 2094, 2095, 2098, 2251, 2349, 2551, 2699, 2720, 2723, 2726, 2735, 2736, 2740, 2743, 2744, 2745, 2746, 2747, 2749, 2752, 2753, 2762, 2769, 2771, 2772, 2773, 2774, 2788, 2802, 2814, 2822, 2823, 2836, 2837, 2899, 2903, 2905, 2906, 2909, 2914, 2915, 2917, 2918, 2922, 2923, 2928, 2930, 2932, 2933, 2936, 2937, 2938, 2940, 2941, 2947, 2948, 2951, 2952, 2954, 2955, 2958, 2959, 2960, 2961, 2963, 2965, 2966, 2967, 2968, 2969, 2974, 2975, 2976, 2980, 2985, 2987, 2992, 2993, 2994, 3003, 3005, 3007, 3008, 3021, 3022, 3023, 3024, 3029, 3030, 3031, 3032, 3035, 3043, 3044, 3061, 3073,

3084, 3085, 3087, 3088, 3096, 3100, 3101, 3103, 3104, 3108, 3109, 3122, 3123, 3124, 3139, 3143, 3145, 3146, 3154, 3164, 3165, 3178, 3179, 3180, 3183, 3201, 3220, 3227, 3228, 3231, 3239, 3241, 3244, 3265, 3276, 3283, 4062

Amer. Fgn Relations History-G, 52, 53, 80, 160, 853, 854, 891, 915, 969, 2917, 2918, 2942, 2957, 3004, 3023, 3024, 3033, 3068, 3087, 3088, 3110, 3148

American Civilization, 915, 1077, 2898, 2957, 2972

American Colonial History, 915, 1077, 2898, 2902, 2957, 2972

American History, 175, 227, 856, 869, 909, 971, 1015, 1077, 1111, 1135, 1187, 1519, 2898, 2900, 2901, 2919, 2920, 2929, 2943, 2944, 2945, 2946, 2949, 2956, 2972, 2978, 2986, 2990, 2996, 3005, 3089, 3098, 3121

American Indian History-G, 831, 871, 2739, 2900, 2926, 3093, 3230

American Industrial History-G, 2996

American Legal History-G, 3016

Antique Arms & Armor-G, 1030, 2908

Australian History, 2916, 2991, 2992

Aviation/Aerospace History, 329, 402, 407, 408, 1601, 1602, 1843, 2048, 2049, 2128, 2129, 2964, 2983, 2984, 3312

Baptist History-G, 2989

British History, 866, 975, 1015, 1075, 1112, 1115, 1135, 1190, 2922, 2925, 2934, 2935, 2949, 3009

Canadian History, 432, 776, 857, 862, 1767, 2738, 2900, 2921, 2924, 2972, 2973

Economic History, 71, 2931

Electrical Sci & Tech Hist, 79, 440, 786, 890, 1011, 1133, 1265, 1364, 1777, 2749, 2941, 2996, 3032, 3109

European History-G, 52, 53, 73, 80, 160, 770, 783, 805, 834, 837, 853, 854, 882, 885, 891, 928, 929, 969, 972, 975, 986, 1042, 1075, 1092, 1125, 1132, 1159, 1160, 1188, 1190, 1208, 1304, 1305, 1363, 1380, 1575, 1755, 1786, 2726, 2727, 2743, 2774, 2905, 2907, 2917, 2918, 2932, 2934, 2935, 2939, 2940, 2942, 2950, 2969, 2970, 2972, 2997, 3001, 3004, 3006, 3009, 3023, 3024, 3029, 3033, 3068, 3087, 3088, 3100, 3108, 3110, 3148

Historic Preservation-G, 1030

Historical Editing, 804, 805, 927, 928, 1041, 1042, 1107, 1158, 1159, 1303, 1304, 1379, 1380, 1574, 1575, 1785, 1786, 2773, 2774, 2968, 2969

Historical Writing, 802, 803, 804, 805, 925, 926, 927, 928, 929, 1040, 1041, 1042, 1077, 1107, 1156, 1157, 1158, 1159, 1160, 1302, 1303, 1304, 1305, 1377, 1378, 1379, 1380, 1573, 1574, 1575, 1782, 1784, 1785, 1786, 2307, 2513, 2771, 2772, 2773, 2774, 2898, 2901, 2903, 2944, 2962, 2966, 2967, 2968, 2969, 2970

Latin American History-G, 873, 2900, 2927, 2972

Medieval History, 421, 769, 833, 984, 1753, 2725, 2904, 2953, 2979, 2997, 2999

Military Science, 2916, 2995

Near/Mdle E. Ancient History-G, 2997, 3000

Science/Medical History, 41, 42, 43, 44, 287, 288, 289, 290, 334, 405, 452, 501, 527, 528, 529, 530, 555, 614, 681, 745, 783, 844, 845, 846, 847, 885, 942, 943, 1015, 1056, 1057, 1098, 1099, 1100, 1101, 1125, 1135, 1341, 1342, 1343, 1344, 1511, 1512, 1513, 1514, 1577, 1599, 1600, 1675, 1676, 1722, 1762, 1763, 1764, 1765, 1782, 1794, 1795, 1848, 1892, 1893, 1894, 1895, 1940, 1953, 1954, 1987, 1988, 1989, 1990, 2029, 2077, 2078, 2079, 2080, 2113, 2264, 2265, 2266, 2267, 2307, 2513, 2731, 2732, 2733, 2734, 2776, 2910, 2911, 2912, 2913, 2939, 2949, 2962, 2971, 2981, 2982, 3078, 3079, 3080, 3081, 3160, 3161, 3162, 3163, 3190, 3223, 3224, 3225, 3226, 3315

Texas History, 2740, 2930, 2988

US Army History-G, 2995

US Military History, 124, 179, 241, 1038, 1783, 2965

US Naval History, 124, 179, 241, 1038, 1783, 2965

World History, 2977

LAW

General, 1, 4, 16, 25, 52, 53, 56, 73, 74, 79, 86, 87, 97, 105, 112, 126, 135, 139, 149, 155, 156, 164, 167, 168, 172, 176, 180, 202, 215, 228, 263, 296, 311, 321, 331, 343, 360, 365, 440, 448, 451, 535, 563, 573, 617, 772, 773, 774, 786, 787, 788, 789, 798, 808, 848, 849, 853, 854, 882, 890, 896, 897, 912, 931, 994, 995, 1011, 1017, 1032, 1071, 1102, 1103, 1133, 1137, 1138, 1140, 1194, 1195, 1240, 1241, 1265, 1270, 1290, 1345, 1346, 1364, 1369, 1370, 1374, 1383, 1430, 1479, 1565, 1618, 1744, 1777, 1778, 1820, 1836, 1864, 1901, 2011, 2088, 2139, 2142, 2143, 2148, 2149, 2156, 2164, 2187, 2199, 2200, 2201, 2204, 2212, 2221, 2242, 2247, 2274, 2290, 2299, 2300, 2301, 2305, 2316, 2330, 2508, 2613, 2633, 2675, 2679, 2686, 2735, 2736, 2737, 2743, 2744, 2747, 2749, 2753, 2754, 2755, 2766, 2778, 2807, 2813, 2814, 2822, 2823, 2836, 2841, 2842, 2914, 2915, 2917, 2918, 2932, 2933, 2938, 2941, 2952, 2958, 2960, 3008, 3011, 3012, 3013, 3014, 3016, 3017, 3018, 3020, 3021, 3022, 3023, 3024, 3025, 3026, 3027, 3028, 3029, 3030, 3031, 3032, 3034, 3035, 3036, 3037, 3038, 3039, 3042, 3043, 3044, 3045, 3046, 3047, 3048, 3049, 3052, 3053, 3055, 3056, 3057, 3058, 3059, 3060, 3063, 3064, 3065, 3066, 3071, 3072, 3073, 3082, 3084, 3085, 3087, 3088, 3100, 3101, 3104, 3109, 3113, 3114, 3115, 3122, 3124,

3128, 3133, 3136, 3152, 3153, 3154, 3164, 3165, 3180, 3183, 3184, 3189, 3192, 3227, 3228, 3241, 3244, 3245, 3248, 3252, 3257, 3259, 3263, 3296, 3972, 4008, 4135, 4229

American Legal History-G, 3015

Business Law, 119, 1466, 2860, 3051, 3253

Criminal Justice, 45, 3010, 3019, 3020, 3064, 3067, 3070, 3082, 3147

Environmental Law-G, 119, 333, 554, 570, 680, 701, 744, 1466, 1576, 1607, 1656, 1686, 1721, 1787, 1939, 2112, 2860, 2892, 3051, 3054, 3062, 3132, 3253

Food and Drug Laws-G, 2541

International Law, 8, 9, 80, 93, 94, 160, 790, 791, 891, 900, 901, 969, 2756, 2757, 2942, 3004, 3033, 3040, 3041, 3064, 3068, 3069, 3110, 3118, 3119, 3148, 3149

Law Enforcement, 45, 113, 2994, 3010, 3019, 3050, 3061, 3070, 3074, 3129, 3145, 4200

Legal Medicine, 2149, 2247, 2541, 2633, 3014

POLITICAL SCIENCE

General, 8, 9, 10, 16, 41, 42, 43, 44, 52, 53, 73, 74, 79, 80, 82, 86, 89, 90, 93, 94, 112, 127, 142, 146, 148, 157, 160, 163, 164, 212, 256, 287, 288, 289, 290, 307, 362, 365, 386, 435, 440, 496, 527, 528, 529, 530, 540, 573, 601, 659, 730, 772, 773, 781, 786, 788, 790, 791, 792, 798, 844, 845, 846, 847, 848, 849, 853, 854, 856, 874, 882, 884, 890, 891, 893, 897, 898, 899, 900, 901, 931, 957, 968, 969, 994, 995, 1011, 1032, 1098, 1099, 1100, 1101, 1102, 1103, 1111, 1122, 1132, 1133, 1138, 1194, 1195, 1206, 1208, 1240, 1241, 1265, 1290, 1341, 1342, 1343, 1344, 1345, 1346, 1361, 1363, 1364, 1370, 1407, 1429, 1447, 1456, 1457, 1511, 1512, 1513, 1514, 1519, 1532, 1543, 1639, 1645, 1646, 1681, 1711, 1762, 1763, 1764, 1765, 1771, 1774, 1776, 1777, 1797, 1826, 1836, 1866, 1892, 1893, 1894, 1895, 1913, 1987, 1988, 1989, 1990, 2008, 2077, 2078, 2079, 2080, 2095, 2139, 2178, 2201, 2264, 2265, 2266, 2267, 2292, 2293, 2301, 2443, 2660, 2710, 2711, 2731, 2732, 2733, 2734, 2735, 2736, 2743, 2744, 2746, 2747, 2749, 2754, 2756, 2757, 2766, 2777, 2788, 2795, 2802, 2808, 2822, 2823, 2836, 2838, 2841, 2866, 2871, 2878, 2910, 2911, 2912, 2913, 2914, 2915, 2917, 2918, 2920, 2928, 2929, 2932, 2933, 2937, 2938, 2940, 2941, 2942, 2958, 2959, 2960, 2985, 2993, 2994, 3003, 3004, 3020, 3021, 3022, 3023, 3024, 3029, 3030, 3031, 3032, 3033, 3036, 3037, 3040, 3041, 3043, 3044, 3049, 3055, 3061, 3067, 3068, 3071, 3078, 3079, 3080, 3081, 3082, 3083, 3084, 3085, 3087, 3088, 3089, 3096, 3098, 3099, 3100, 3101, 3103, 3104, 3108, 3109, 3110, 3111, 3113, 3114, 3116, 3117,

3118, 3119, 3120, 3122, 3123, 3124, 3128, 3131, 3133, 3134, 3135, 3137, 3139, 3141, 3143, 3144, 3145, 3146, 3147, 3148, 3150, 3151, 3152, 3160, 3161, 3162, 3163, 3164, 3165, 3174, 3179, 3180, 3184, 3192, 3201, 3205, 3223, 3224, 3225, 3226, 3227, 3228, 3231, 3236, 3239, 3241, 3245, 3259, 3260, 3265, 3269, 3276, 3450, 3637, 3885, 4058

Arms Control-G, 16, 89, 90, 164, 365, 573, 898, 899, 1456, 1457, 1645, 1646, 2139, 2292, 2293, 2710, 2711, 3069, 3071, 3116, 3117, 3149, 3152

Foreign Policy, 36, 52, 53, 55, 80, 89, 90, 160, 193, 853, 854, 891, 898, 899, 969, 1456, 1457, 1645, 1646, 2292, 2293, 2710, 2711, 2819, 2917, 2918, 2942, 3004, 3023, 3024, 3033, 3068, 3077, 3087, 3088, 3090, 3110, 3116, 3117, 3126, 3138, 3148, 3979

Government, 6, 10, 55, 86, 125, 127, 135, 163, 175, 227, 333, 450, 554, 680, 744, 792, 871, 909, 1576, 1656, 1721, 1787, 1939, 2112, 2278, 2739, 2830, 2847, 2866, 2926, 2956, 3020, 3037, 3054, 3056, 3082, 3090, 3093, 3095, 3114, 3120, 3121, 3125, 3130, 3131, 3132, 3136, 3151, 3230, 3256, 3263, 3979

International Relations, 5, 6, 7, 8, 9, 16, 36, 50, 52, 53, 57, 68, 80, 89, 90, 93, 94, 157, 160, 163, 164, 167, 168, 193, 199, 302, 365, 573, 790, 791, 838, 851, 853, 854, 860, 891, 898, 899, 900, 901, 949, 969, 1132, 1198, 1208, 1363, 1430, 1456, 1457, 1618, 1645, 1646, 1744, 2139, 2142, 2278, 2292, 2293, 2710, 2711, 2756, 2757, 2794, 2813, 2814, 2819, 2830, 2831, 2871, 2917, 2918, 2940, 2942, 3003, 3004, 3008, 3023, 3024, 3033, 3040, 3041, 3068, 3071, 3072, 3073, 3077, 3086, 3087, 3088, 3091, 3092, 3095, 3097, 3102, 3105, 3108, 3110, 3116, 3117, 3118, 3119, 3126, 3137, 3138, 3140, 3146, 3148, 3151, 3152, 3153, 3154, 3268, 3580

Intrnationl Peace & Securty-G, 16, 52, 53, 80, 110, 164, 365, 573, 853, 854, 891, 949, 2139, 2794, 2795, 2917, 2918, 2942, 3023, 3024, 3033, 3071, 3087, 3088, 3110, 3127, 3138, 3140, 3141, 3152, 3205, 3268, 3269, 3580

National Security/Defense, 16, 110, 164, 365, 573, 2139, 3071, 3127, 3152

Public Policy, 6, 10, 63, 82, 86, 144, 161, 162, 167, 212, 463, 792, 869, 893, 894, 1430, 1484, 1500, 1618, 1623, 1643, 1680, 1744, 1879, 2142, 2278, 2795, 2813, 2830, 2838, 2839, 2877, 3037, 3072, 3076, 3094, 3095, 3111, 3112, 3114, 3120, 3141, 3142, 3153, 3205, 3243, 3269, 4063, 4064, 4169

Public Service, 6, 63, 82, 87, 113, 125, 127, 135, 168, 212, 215, 450, 789, 871, 893, 894, 1132, 1140, 1208, 1363, 1643, 2278, 2739, 2755, 2814, 2830, 2838, 2839, 2842, 2866, 2926,

2940, 3008, 3038, 3050, 3056, 3067, 3073, 3093, 3094, 3095, 3108, 3111, 3112, 3115, 3129, 3130, 3131, 3136, 3147, 3154, 3230, 3243, 3256, 3263, 3979, 4063, 4169

U.S.-European Issues-G, 52, 53, 80, 110, 148, 160, 256, 853, 854, 887, 891, 957, 969, 1681, 2878, 2917, 2918, 2942, 3004, 3023, 3024, 3033, 3068, 3087, 3088, 3106, 3110, 3127, 3144, 3148

U.S.-Israel Issues, 3075

U.S.-Italian Issues-G, 888, 3107

PSYCHOLOGY

General, 41, 42, 43, 44, 126, 142, 268, 287, 288, 289, 290, 306, 307, 331, 334, 386, 405, 451, 452, 496, 501, 527, 528, 529, 530, 540, 555, 601, 614, 659, 681, 730, 745, 772, 773, 780, 781, 787, 788, 832, 843, 844, 845, 846, 847, 848, 849, 883, 884, 896, 897, 931, 948, 950, 951, 952, 953, 973, 994, 995, 1017, 1098, 1099, 1100, 1101, 1102, 1103, 1122, 1137, 1138, 1194, 1195, 1205, 1206, 1240, 1241, 1270, 1341, 1342, 1343, 1344, 1345, 1346, 1361, 1369, 1370, 1387, 1407, 1446, 1447, 1511, 1512, 1513, 1514, 1542, 1543, 1577, 1639, 1710, 1711, 1722, 1762, 1763, 1764, 1765, 1774, 1775, 1776, 1778, 1807, 1826, 1848, 1892, 1893, 1894, 1895, 1906, 1907, 1912, 1913, 1940, 1987, 1988, 1989, 1990, 2005, 2007, 2008, 2029, 2077, 2078, 2079, 2080, 2094, 2095, 2113, 2170, 2172, 2177, 2178, 2179, 2180, 2212, 2264, 2265, 2266, 2267, 2280, 2285, 2316, 2336, 2349, 2442, 2443, 2446, 2447, 2551, 2584, 2613, 2622, 2649, 2653, 2659, 2660, 2661, 2662, 2686, 2690, 2699, 2724, 2731, 2732, 2733, 2734, 2735, 2736, 2741, 2745, 2746, 2747, 2753, 2754, 2776, 2788, 2792, 2793, 2795, 2796, 2797, 2798, 2799, 2800, 2801, 2810, 2822, 2823, 2836, 2841, 2910, 2911, 2912, 2913, 2914, 2915, 2936, 2937, 2938, 2952, 2971, 2985, 3007, 3021, 3022, 3031, 3035, 3036, 3053, 3055, 3078, 3079, 3080, 3081, 3084, 3085, 3099, 3103, 3104, 3113, 3133, 3139, 3141, 3155, 3159, 3160, 3161, 3162, 3163, 3164, 3165, 3168, 3169, 3171, 3173, 3174, 3175, 3176, 3178, 3179, 3180, 3183, 3184, 3189, 3190, 3192, 3200, 3201, 3203, 3204, 3205, 3206, 3207, 3208, 3209, 3210, 3211, 3213, 3217, 3220, 3223, 3224, 3225, 3226, 3227, 3228, 3236, 3239, 3241, 3244, 3245, 3257, 3259, 3265, 3266, 3267, 3269, 3270, 3271, 3272, 3273, 3274, 3275, 3280, 3283, 3315, 4102, 4271

Aromachology/Olfactory-G, 3191

Behavioral Science-G, 118, 153, 178, 232, 235, 358, 466, 511, 624, 700, 760, 799, 832, 1282, 1906, 1917, 1918, 2170, 2177, 2179, 2298, 2389, 2442, 2446, 2584, 2601, 2649, 2659, 2661, 2724, 2741, 2750, 2751, 2767, 3159, 3168, 3169, 3173, 3175,

3181, 3182, 3185, 3187, 3188, 3215, 3278

Child Development-G, 107, 233, 246, 2144, 2145, 2146, 2198, 2218, 2488, 2527, 2617, 2673, 2810, 3156, 3186, 3196, 3217, 3251, 3280

Clinical Psychology, 246, 247, 248, 2218, 2219, 2220, 2232, 2336, 2344, 2527, 2528, 2529, 2617, 2618, 2619, 2622, 2690, 3196, 3197, 3198, 3200, 3216

Counseling, 2389, 3221

Counseling Psychology-G, 3221

Developmental Disabilities-G, 107, 141, 233, 246, 247, 248, 252, 259, 2198, 2218, 2219, 2220, 2444, 2450, 2488, 2527, 2528, 2529, 2531, 2538, 2617, 2618, 2619, 2673, 3186, 3196, 3197, 3198, 3199, 3214, 3251, 3264, 4084, 4192

Human Sexuality, 3168, 3202, 3212

Marriage & Family Therapy-G, 3157, 3158, 3167

Mental Health, 246, 247, 248, 2218, 2219, 2220, 2527, 2528, 2529, 2617, 2618, 2619, 2810, 3196, 3197, 3198, 3217, 3280

Parapsychology, 3193, 3194, 3195, 4066

Pet Loss-G, 2279, 2586, 3170, 3234, 3298

Rehabilitation Counseling, 194, 207, 247, 248, 1774, 2177, 2178, 2219, 2220, 2442, 2443, 2528, 2529, 2589, 2618, 2619, 2659, 2660, 3099, 3166, 3172, 3173, 3174, 3197, 3198, 3235, 3236, 4036, 4275

Sports Psychology, 72, 165, 166, 266, 267, 2348, 2592, 2630, 2631, 2835, 2897, 3177, 3218, 3219, 3237, 3281, 3282

Substance Abuse Counseling, 2144, 2389, 3156

SOCIOLOGY

General, 41, 42, 43, 44, 97, 104, 119, 133, 134, 142, 146, 176, 228, 230, 268, 287, 288, 289, 290, 307, 386, 435, 496, 508, 527, 528, 529, 530, 540, 601, 659, 691, 730, 755, 772, 773, 781, 787, 788, 807, 810, 844, 845, 846, 847, 848, 849, 874, 884, 896, 897, 912, 914, 924, 931, 936, 937, 948, 949, 950, 951, 952, 953, 973, 994, 995, 1017, 1098, 1099, 1100, 1101, 1102, 1103, 1122, 1137, 1138, 1194, 1195, 1206, 1240, 1241, 1270, 1341, 1342, 1343, 1344, 1345, 1346, 1361, 1369, 1370, 1387, 1407, 1419, 1466, 1474, 1511, 1512, 1513, 1514, 1532, 1543, 1566, 1587, 1589, 1639, 1655, 1666, 1711, 1717, 1731, 1758, 1762, 1763, 1764, 1765, 1771, 1774, 1776, 1778, 1789, 1790, 1797, 1807, 1826, 1838, 1892, 1893, 1894, 1895, 1913, 1931, 1948, 1987, 1988, 1989, 1990, 2008, 2021, 2040, 2077, 2078, 2079, 2080, 2095, 2124, 2178, 2264, 2265, 2266, 2267, 2328, 2349, 2443, 2551, 2660, 2699, 2731, 2732, 2733, 2734, 2735, 2736, 2746, 2747, 2753, 2754, 2770, 2777, 2788, 2792, 2793, 2794, 2795, 2796, 2797, 2798, 2799, 2800, 2801, 2802, 2810, 2822, 2823, 2836, 2841,

2860, 2910, 2911, 2912, 2913, 2914, 2915, 2928, 2937, 2938, 2952, 2985, 2993, 3007, 3021, 3022, 3031, 3035, 3036, 3042, 3051, 3055, 3078, 3079, 3080, 3081, 3084, 3085, 3096, 3099, 3103, 3104, 3113, 3133, 3135, 3139, 3140, 3141, 3143, 3160, 3161, 3162, 3163, 3164, 3165, 3174, 3179, 3180, 3183, 3184, 3192, 3201, 3203, 3204, 3205, 3206, 3207, 3208, 3209, 3210, 3211, 3217, 3220, 3222, 3223, 3224, 3225, 3226, 3227, 3228, 3231, 3236, 3239, 3241, 3244, 3245, 3248, 3249, 3253, 3255, 3258, 3259, 3260, 3261, 3262, 3265, 3266, 3267, 3268, 3269, 3270, 3271, 3272, 3273, 3274, 3275, 3276, 3280, 3283, 4102, 4282

Hemophilia/Bleeding Disrdrs-G, 3254

Human-Animal Interactions-G, 2279, 2586, 3170, 3234, 3298

Social Service, 101, 126, 211, 331, 451, 871, 894, 1637, 1643, 2183, 2212, 2287, 2316, 2454, 2595, 2597, 2613, 2665, 2668, 2686, 2739, 2839, 2926, 3053, 3093, 3112, 3189, 3230, 3238, 3242, 3243, 3247, 3257

Social Work, 67, 104, 107, 126, 141, 146, 154, 207, 211, 230, 233, 252, 268, 331, 451, 569, 871, 914, 973, 1356, 1389, 1637, 1774, 1797, 1807, 2178, 2183, 2185, 2194, 2198, 2200, 2212, 2229, 2287, 2288, 2296, 2300, 2316, 2340, 2349, 2443, 2454, 2456, 2488, 2531, 2540, 2551, 2585, 2589, 2595, 2596, 2597, 2599, 2613, 2625, 2650, 2660, 2665, 2667, 2668, 2671, 2673, 2675, 2686, 2691, 2699, 2722, 2739, 2802, 2926, 2993, 3007, 3048, 3053, 3093, 3099, 3143, 3172, 3174, 3186, 3189, 3199, 3220, 3229, 3230, 3232, 3233, 3235, 3236, 3238, 3240, 3242, 3249, 3250, 3251, 3252, 3257, 3264, 3276, 3277, 3279, 3283, 3284, 4281

Sports Sociology, 72, 165, 166, 266, 267, 2348, 2592, 2630, 2631, 2835, 2897, 3177, 3218, 3219, 3237, 3281, 3282

Urban Affairs, 95, 125, 135, 153, 358, 450, 466, 511, 624, 700, 760, 3056, 3130, 3136, 3215, 3246, 3256, 3263, 3278, 3303

SCHOOL OF VOCATIONAL ED

General, 261, 1068, 1177, 1180, 1224, 1293, 1330, 1861, 2134, 2203, 2302, 2604, 2678, 2806, 3308, 3317, 3318, 3479, 3890, 4156

Aerospace studies, 329, 373, 374, 397, 402, 1843, 2068, 2964, 3288, 3289, 3311, 3312, 3997, 4055, 4163

Auto Mechanics, 170, 706, 1690, 3320

Aviation Maintenance Technolog, 19, 114, 129, 370, 371, 380, 387, 396, 397, 404, 3285, 3286, 3293, 3295, 3302, 3309, 3311, 3314, 3997, 4055, 4127, 4163

Baking Science, 2702, 3290

Bartending, 4012, 4106, 4164

Blacksmithing, 1013, 3300

Computer Technology, 65, 334, 405, 452, 501, 537, 555, 571, 614, 681, 745, 1058, 1577, 1722, 1848, 1940, 2029, 2113, 2776, 2875, 2971, 3190, 3297, 3315, 3316, 4083, 4180

Cosmetology/Barber, 3287, 4184

Dog Training (Service Anmls)-G, 2279, 2586, 3170, 3234, 3298

Fire Service, 95, 2602, 3246, 3303, 3306, 4204

Food Service, 15, 1885, 2706, 2709, 2719, 3291, 3299, 4164, 4208

Funeral Service, 3301, 4212

Gemology, 1013, 3300, 4155, 4213

Maintenance Engineering, 3290

Musical Instruments, 424, 989, 1023, 1095, 1236, 1278, 1293, 1337, 2203, 2302, 2604, 2678, 3292, 3305, 3308

Paralegal, 4, 56, 172, 202, 296, 535, 774, 1820, 1901, 2088, 2164, 2274, 2737, 3025, 3296

Pilot Training, 19, 114, 129, 371, 380, 381, 387, 396, 397, 403, 404, 671, 3286, 3293, 3294, 3302, 3307, 3309, 3311, 3313, 3314, 3853, 3997, 4055, 4126, 4127, 4163

Secretarial School, 3310, 4280

Truckdriving, 170, 706, 1690, 3320

Vertical Flight, 114, 396, 397, 411, 3309, 3311, 3319, 4055

Welding, 667, 3304, 4290

Scholarship and Awards Listings

SCHOOL OF BUSINESS

1 — ACCESS GROUP (Loan Programs)

1411 Foulk Road
Box 7430
Wilmington DE 19803-0430
302/477-4190 or 800/282-1550
FAX: 302/477-4080
Internet: www.accessgroup.org

AMOUNT: Varies

DEADLINE(S): Varies (last day of current school term)

FIELD(S): Law, Business, Medical, Dental

Loans at competitive rates to graduate students attending law, business, medical, dental, and a variety of other graduate and professional schools.

Must be a US citizen or legal resident. No co-signer required for qualified applicants. No need to locate a lender, and no interview required. Visit website or contact Pat Curry at above address for complete information.

2 — ASIAN INSTITUTE OF TECHNOLOGY (AIT Scholarship Program)

Development Office
PO Box 4, Klongluang
Pathumthani 12120 THAILAND
(66)(2) 516-0110-44 or 524-5032
FAX: (66)(2) 516-2126
E-Mail: ascao@ait.ac.th
Internet: www.ait.ac.th

AMOUNT: US $12,600-$37,960

DEADLINE(S): FEB 15; JUN 15; OCT 15

FIELD(S): Advanced Technologies; Civil Engineering; Environment, Resources, & Development; Business Management

Scholarships and grants open to citizens of Asian countries who are accepted by the institute as a master's or doctotal candidate. Selection is based on academic criteria, practical experience, gender, and country of origin; priority to Mekong Region countries and Asian countries of the former USSR.

250 awards annually. Contact AIT for an application.

3 — BEDDING PLANTS FOUNDATION, INC. (Harold Bettinger Memorial Scholarship)

PO Box 280
East Lansing MI 48826-0280
517/333-4617
FAX: 517/333-4494
E-Mail: BPFI@aol.com
Internet: www.bpfi.org

AMOUNT: $1,000

DEADLINE(S): MAY 15

FIELD(S): Horticulture AND Business/Marketing

Open to graduate and undergraduate students already attending a four-year college/university who have either a horticulture major with business/marketing emphasis OR a business/marketing major with horticulture emphasis. Cash award, with checks issued jointly in name of recipient and college/institution he or she will attend for current year. Must submit references & transcripts.

1 award annually. See website or send printed self-addressed mailing label (or self-addressed, stamped envelope) to BPFI after January 1st for an application. Recipient will be notified.

4 — BUSINESS & PROFESSIONAL WOMEN'S FOUNDATION (BPW Career Advancement Scholarship Program)

2012 Massachusetts Ave., NW
Washington DC 20036-1070
202/293-1200, ext. 169
FAX: 202/861-0298
Internet: www.bpwusa.org

AMOUNT: $500-$1,000

DEADLINE(S): APR 15

FIELD(S): Biology, Science, Education, Engineering, Social Science, Paralegal, Humanities, Business, Math, Computers, Law, MD, DD

For women (US citizens) aged 25+ accepted into accredited program at US institution (+Puerto Rico & Virgin Islands). Must graduate within 12 to 24 months from the date of grant and demonstrate critical finanacial need. Must have a plan to upgrade skills, train for a new career field, or to enter/re-enter the job market.

Full- or part-time study. For info see website or send business-sized, self-addressed, double-stamped envelope.

5 — CANADIAN BUREAU FOR INTERNATIONAL EDUCATION (Canadian International Development Agency Awards Program for Canadians)

220 Laurier Ave., W., Ste. 1100
Ottawa Ontario K1P 5Z9 CANADA
613/237-4820
FAX: 613/237-1073
E-Mail: smelanson@cbie.ca
Internet: www.cbie.ca

AMOUNT: $10,000/yr. Canadian (max.)

DEADLINE(S): FEB 1

FIELD(S): International Relations/Development; Business

For Canadian citizens/permanent residents seeking to participate in international development through a volunteer project of their own initiative. The development activity may be the fieldwork component of a master's degree program or a professional work/research project. Ph.D. candidates are NOT eligible. Also offers internships to master's students in business, administration, and management programs. Awards tenable up to twelve months and are taxable.

50 awards annually. Contact CBIE for an application.

6 — CONGRESSIONAL HISPANIC CAUCUS INSTITUTE, INC. (CHCI Fellowship Program)

504 C St., NE
Washington DC 20002
800/EXCEL-DC or 202/543-1771
E-Mail: comments@chci.org
Internet: www.chci.org

AMOUNT: Monthly stipend, round-trip transportation, & health insurance

DEADLINE(S): MAR 1

FIELD(S): Public Policy; Public Health; Telecommunications; Business

Paid work experience is open to Hispanics who have graduated from a college/university (with BA/BS/graduate degree) within one year of application deadline, and to currently enrolled graduate students. Must have high academic achievement (minimum 3.0 GPA), superior analytical/communication skills, leadership potential, and consistent active participation in activities for the common good. Must be US citizen/permanent resident or have student work visa.

16 awards annually. See website or contact CHCI for an application.

7 — CUBAN AMERICAN NATIONAL FOUNDATION (The Mas Family Scholarships)

7300 NW 35 Terrace
Miami FL 33122
305/592-7768
FAX: 305/592-7889
E-Mail canfnet.org
Internet: www.canfnet.org

AMOUNT: Individually negotiated

DEADLINE(S): MAR 15

FIELD(S): Engineering, Business, International Relations, Economics, Communications, Journalism

For Cuban-Americans students, graduates and undergraduates, born in Cuba or direct descendants of those who left Cuba. Must be in top 10% of high school class or maintain a 3.5 GPA in college.

10,000 awards/year. Recipients may re-apply for subsequent years. Financial need considered along with academic success, SAT and GRE scores, and leadership potential. Essays and proof of Cuban descent required.

8 — INTER-AMERICAN FOUNDATION (Field Research Fellowship Programs for U.S. , Latin American, and Caribbean Citizens)

901 N. Stuart St., 10th Floor
Arlington VA 22203
703/841-3800
FAX: 703/527-3529
E-Mail: correo@aif.gov
Internet: www.iaf.gov

AMOUNT: Varies

DEADLINE(S): APR 28

FIELD(S): International Relations, Social Sciences, Humanities, Latin American Studies

Fellowships for Latin American, Carribean, and U.S. doctoral level students for field research in Latin America and the Caribbean. Must be enrolled in U.S. university.

Access website for deadline and application information. Organization does not mail information.

9 — INTER-AMERICAN FOUNDATION (Master's Research Fellowships)

901 N. Stuart St., 10th Floor
Arlington VA 22203
703/841-3800
FAX: 703/527-3529
E-Mail: correo@aif.gov
Internet: www.iaf.gov

AMOUNT: Varies

DEADLINE(S): APR

FIELD(S): Latin American & Caribbean Studies, Internations Relations, Social Sciences, Humanities, etc.

Open to masters students enrolled in U.S. universities for field research in Latin American or the Caribbean. For citizens of Caribbean and Latin American independent countries, and the U.S.

Access website for deadline and application information. Organization does not mail information.

10 — INTERNATIONAL RESEARCH AND EXCHANGES BOARD (Russian-US Young Leadership Fellows for Public Service Program for Russian Citizens)

1616 H St., NW
Washington DC 20006

202/628-8188
FAX: 202/628-8189
E-Mail: irex@info.irex.org
Internet: www.irex.org

AMOUNT: Stipend + tuition, travel, living & housing

DEADLINE(S): NOV 30

FIELD(S): Community, Governmental, & Corporate Affairs; Policy Research & Development; Humanities

Grants of two to twelve months are available to graduate students who are Russian citizens/ permanent residents for brief visits to pursue scholarly projects on Central & Eastern Europe, Eurasia, or Mongolia. Must have equivalent of bachelor's degree and be below the age of 30 at time of application. Postdoctoral humanities scholars may pursue research in Turkey or Iran. Financial need NOT a factor.

45 awards annually. Not renewable. Contact Jessica Jeffcoat, Senior Program Officer, for an application.

11 — JANSONS LEGAT (Scholarships)

Blommeseter, Norderhov
3512 Honefoss NORWAY
32 1354 65
FAX: 32 1356 26
E-Mail: janlegat@online.no

AMOUNT: NOK 75.000,-

DEADLINE(S): MAR 15

FIELD(S): Business; Industry; Handcraft

Scholarships for Norwegian citizens for career support and/or postgraduate study. Financial need is NOT a factor.

30 awards annually. Contact Reidun Haugen for an application.

12 — LONDON CHAMBER OF COMMERCE AND INDUSTRY EXAMINATIONS BOARD (Charles R. E. Bell Fund Scholarships)

Thena House
112 Station Rd.
Sidcup Kent DA15 7BJ ENGLAND UK
081/302-0261

AMOUNT: 1,500 pounds sterling

DEADLINE(S): DEC 31

FIELD(S): Business Administration; Languages

Open to students who are engaged in commerce/ business or are commercial education teachers. Scholarships support postgraduate study in the United Kingdom or abroad. Must be UK citizen or legal resident. Financial need is considered.

Contact London Chamber of Commerce for an application.

13 — NATIONAL ITALIAN AMERICAN FOUNDATION (Norman R. Peterson Scholarship)

1860 19th St. NW
Washington DC 20009
202/530-5315

AMOUNT: One is $5,000; one is $2,500

DEADLINE(S): MAY 31

FIELD(S): Business/finance/economics

For undergraduate American students from the mid-west (Michigan-based) of Italian ancestry for study at John Cabot University in Rome.

For info. contact: Francesca Gleason, Director of Admissions at 011-39-6-687-8881.

14 — OAK RIDGE INSTITUTE FOR SCIENCE AND EDUCATION (Minority Student Administrative Summer Internship Program)

P.O. Box 117
Oak Ridge TN 37831-0117
423/576-6051 or 423/576-3165

AMOUNT: $335 to $420/wk.+ travel reimbursement

DEADLINE(S): FEB (mid-month)

FIELD(S): Business administration, management, finance, accounting, human resources, training, economics, public administration, computer science, and instructional technology

For minority students who have completed their junior or senior year in college or their first year of graduate school. Must be majoring in one of the fields listed above. A summer program, ten to twelve weeks, located at Oak Ridge, TN.

Funded through U.S. Department of Energy or Oak Ridge Associated Universities

15 — WOMEN GROCERS OF AMERICA (Mary Macey Scholarships)

1825 Samuel Morse Drive
Reston VA 20190-5317
703/437-5300
FAX: 703/437-7768
E-Mail: wga@nationalgrocers.org
Internet: www.nationalgrocers.org

AMOUNT: $1,000 (minimum)

DEADLINE(S): JUN 1

FIELD(S): Food Marketing/Management; Food Service Technology; Business Administration as related to the Grocery Industry

For students with a minimum 2.0 GPA attending a US college/university. Must be entering sophomores or continuing students in good standing in a 2-year associate degree or 4-year degree granting institution or a graduate program, planning a career in the grocery industry. Financial need NOT considered.

2+ awards annually. Renewable. See website or contact Anne Wintersteen at above address for an application.

16 — WOMEN IN DEFENSE (HORIZONS Scholarship Foundation)

NDIA
2111 Wilson Blvd., Ste. 400
Arlington VA 22201-3061
703/247-2552
FAX: 703/522-1885
E-Mail: dnwlee@moon.jic.com
Internet: www.adpa.org/wid/horizon/Scholar.htm

AMOUNT: $500+

DEADLINE(S): NOV 1; JUL 1

FIELD(S): Engineering, Computer Science, Physics, Mathematics, Business, Law, International Relations, Political Science, Operations Research, Economics, and fields relevant to a career in the areas of national security and defense.

For women who are U.S. citizens, have minimum GPA of 3.25, demonstrate financial need, are currently enrolled at an accredited university/college (full- or part-time—both grads and undergrad juniors/seniors are eligible), and demonstrate interest in pursuing a career related to national security.

Application is online or send SASE, #10 envelope, to Woody Lee, HORIZONS Scholarship Director.

17 — WOODROW WILSON NATIONAL FELLOWSHIP FOUNDATION/U.S. DEPARTMENTS OF COMMERCE AND AGRICULTURE (Fellowships)

CN 5329
Princeton NJ 08543-5329
609/452-7007
FAX: 609/452-0066
E-Mail: richard@woodrow.org
Internet: www.woodrow.org

AMOUNT: Varies

DEADLINE(S): Varies

FIELD(S): Commerce; Agriculture

Open to minority students in the US who are interested in careers in commerce or agriculture.

See website or contact WWNFF for an application.

BUSINESS ADMINISTRATION

18 — ACCOUNTING/NET (Account For Your Future Scholarship Program)

600 Stewart St., Ste. 1101
Seattle WA 98101
206/441-8285

FAX: 206/441-8385
E-Mail: money@accountingstudents.com
Internet: www.accountingstudents.com

AMOUNT: $1,000

DEADLINE(S): JUN 1

FIELD(S): Accounting

Scholarships for outstanding accounting students, undergraduate and graduate, sponsored by AccountingNet, John Wiley & Sons, and KPMG. Applications are accepted ONLY online.

3 awards annually. See website for details.

19 — AIRCRAFT ELECTRONICS ASSOCIATION EDUCATIONAL FOUNDATION (Scholarships)

PO Box 1963
Independence MO 64055
816/373-6565
FAX: 816/478-3100
Internet: aeaavnews.org

AMOUNT: $1,000-$16,000

DEADLINE(S): Varies

FIELD(S): Avionics; Aircraft Repair

Various scholarships for high school and college students attending post-secondary institutions, including technical schools. Some are for study in Canada or Europe as well as the US.

25 programs. See website or contact AEA for specific details and applications.

20 — AMERICAN ACCOUNTING ASSOCIATION (Fellowships)

5717 Bessie Drive
Sarasota FL 34233-2399
941/921-7747
FAX: 941/923-4093

AMOUNT: $2,500

DEADLINE(S): JUN 1

FIELD(S): Accounting

For US and Canadian residents accepted in a doctoral program accredited by the AACSB. Student must be planning a career of teaching at a college or university in the US or Canada. Awards are based on merit; financial need is NOT considered.

5-6 awards annually. Contact Judy Cothern at above address for an application.

21 — AMERICAN ALLIANCE FOR HEALTH, PHYSICAL EDUCATION, RECREATION & DANCE

1900 Association Drive
Reston VA 20191
703/476-3400 or 800/213-7193
E-Mail: webmaster@aahperd.org
Internet: www.aahperd.org

AMOUNT: Varies

DEADLINE(S): Varies

FIELD(S): Health education, leisure and recreation, girls and women in sports, sport and physical education, dance

This organization has six national sub-organizations specializing in the above fields. Some have grants and fellowships for both individuals and group projects. The website has the details for each group.

Visit website for details or write to above address for details.

22 — AMERICAN ASSOCIATION OF ADVERTISING AGENCIES, INC. (Multicultural Advertising Internship Program)

405 Lexington Ave.
New York NY 10174-1801
212/682-2500 or 1-800/676-9333
FAX: 212/573-8968
E-Mail: rhonda@aaaa.org
Internet: www.commercepark.com/AAAA/maip/

AMOUNT: $350/wk. + partial exp. and travel

DEADLINE(S): JAN 30

FIELD(S): Advertising; Marketing; Public Relations

A ten-week summer internship for minorities (African-American, Native American, Hispanic, or Asian) working in the advertising business. Must be U.S. citizen or permanent resident.

Write, call, or access website for application and information.

23 — AMERICAN ASSOCIATION OF ADVERTISING AGENCIES, INC. (Multicultural Advertising Internship Program)

405 Lexington Ave.
18th Fl.
New York NY 10174-1801
212/682-2500 or 800/676-9333
FAX: 212/573-8968
E-Mail: tiffany@aaaa.org
Internet: www.aaaa.org

AMOUNT: $350/wk. + partial expenses & travel

DEADLINE(S): JAN 22

FIELD(S): Advertising; Marketing; Public Relations

Ten-week summer internship in the US is open to African-Americans, Native Americans, Hispanics, or Asians interested in a career in advertising. Must be US citizen/permanent resident, have a minimum 3.0 GPA, and be a college junior, senior, or graduate student. Internships help students gain practical work experience and prepare them for entry-level positions. Scholarship program is also available for selected creative finishing schools.

75-100 awards annually. See website or contact AAAA for an application.

24 — AMERICAN ASSOCIATION OF HISPANIC CERTIFIED PUBLIC ACCOUNTANTS (Scholarships)

> 100 N. Main St., Ste. 406
> San Antonio TX 78205
> 203/255-7003
> FAX: 203/259-2872
> E-Mail: AAHCPA@netscape.net
> Internet: www.aahcpa.org

AMOUNT: Varies

DEADLINE(S): SEP 15

FIELD(S): Accounting

Undergraduates must be of Hispanic descent and have completed or be enrolled in an intermediate level accounting course. Graduate students must be of Hispanic descent and be enrolled in a program with an accounting emphasis or be in the last year of a 5-year accounting program. All applicants must have a minimum overall 3.0 GPA and be US citizens. Must submit offical transcripts, a letter of recommendation, copy of class schedule, and an essay along with application.

10-40 awards annually. Contact the AAHCPA Scholarship Committee for an application packet.

25 — AMERICAN ASSOCIATION OF UNIVERSITY WOMEN EDUCATIONAL FOUNDATION (Selected Professions Fellowships for Women of Color)

> Dept. 60
> 2201 N. Dodge St.
> Iowa City IA 52243-4030
> 319/337-1716, ext. 60
> FAX: 319/337-1204
> Internet: www.aauw.org

AMOUNT: $5,000-$12,000

DEADLINE(S): JAN 2

FIELD(S): Business Administration; Law; Medicine

For women of color in their final year of graduate study to increase their participation in historically underrepresented fields. Must be US citizen or permanent resident. Special consideration is given to applicants who show professional promise in innovative or neglected areas of research and/or practice in areas of public interest.

Contact AAUW for an application between August 1st & December 20th.

26 — AMERICAN INSTITUTE FOR ECONOMIC RESEARCH (Visiting Research Fellowships at AIER)

> Division St.
> P.O. Box 1000
> Great Barrington MA 01230-1000

> 413/528-1216
> FAX: 413/528-0103
> E-Mail: info@aier.org
> Internet: www.aier.org

AMOUNT: Tuition, room & board, and a cash stipend

DEADLINE(S): MAR 31

FIELD(S): Economics

Summer fellowships in economic science at the institute. Preference to applicants who have a Ph.D. or have completed all but their dissertations. For research in such areas as money, banking and credit; public and personal finance; economic and monetary history; the role of government in society; the methodology of economics; and the role of individual freedom, private property, and free enterprise in economic progress.

Send a cover letter, a 500-word outline of proposed course of research, a resume, and a copy of a recent publication or unpublished manuscript. Visit website for more information.

27 — AMERICAN INSTITUTE OF POLISH CULTURE (Scholarships)

> 1440 79th St. Causeway, Ste. 117
> Miami FL 33141
> 305/864-2349
> FAX: 305/865-5150
> E-Mail: info@ampolinstitute.org
> Internet: www.ampolinstitute.org

AMOUNT: $1,000

DEADLINE(S): FEB 15

FIELD(S): Journalism; Public Relations; Communications

Awards are to encourage young Americans of Polish descent to pursue the above professions. Can be used for full-time study at any accredited American college. Criteria for selection include achievement, talent, and involvement in public life.

$25 processing fee. Renewable. Send self-addressed, stamped envelope to Mrs. Harriet Irsay for an application.

28 — AMERICAN PLANNING ASSOCIATION (Minority Scholarship and Fellowship Programs)

> 122 South Michigan Ave., Ste. 1600
> Chicago IL 60605
> 312/431-9100
> FAX: 312/431-9985

AMOUNT: $2,000-$5,000 (grads); $2,500 (undergrads)

DEADLINE(S): MAY 14

FIELD(S): Urban planning, community development, environmental sciences, public administration, transportation, or urban studies

Scholarships for African-Americans, Hispanics, or Native American students pursing undergraduate degrees in the U.S. in the above fields. Must have completed first year. Fellowships for graduate students. Programs must be approved by the Planning Accreditation Board. U.S. citizenship.

Call or write for complete information.

29 — AMERICAN PUBLIC TRANSIT ASSOCIATION (Transit Hall of Fame Scholarships)

> 1201 New York Ave.
> Washington DC 20005
> FAX: 202/898-4029
> E-Mail: dfoth@apta.com
> Internet: www.apta.com

AMOUNT: $2,500 or more

DEADLINE(S): None

FIELD(S): Transit-related fields of study

For college juniors, seniors, or graduate students enrolled in a degree program in a fully accredited institution who demonstrates an interest in entering the transit industry. Criteria include interest in the transit field, financial need, leadership characteristics, scholastic ashievement, citizenship, extracurricular activities, and essay, and a brief in-person or telephone interview. Must be nominated by an APTF representative who can oversee an internship program.

Write to above address to inquire about how to be nominated and other information.

30 — AMERICAN SOCIETY FOR QUALITY (Richard A. Freund International Scholarship)

> P.O. Box 3005
> Milwaukee WI 53201-3005
> 800/248-1946 or
> 814/272-8575 - ask for item B0499
> FAX: 414/272-1734
> E-Mail: cs@asq/org
> Internet: www.asq.org

AMOUNT: $5,000

DEADLINE(S): APR 1

FIELD(S): Quality control in engineering, statistics, management, etc.

Scholarship for members and nonmembers worldwide enrolled in a Master's degree or higher level program with a concentration in any of the above fields of study. 3.25+ GPA required in undergraduate studies in engineering, sciences, or business.

Two letters of recommendation from persons qualified to assess the candidate's scholarly experience and a formal written statement (all in English) of approximately 250 words addressing the applicant's educational and career goals are required.

31 — AMERICAN SOCIETY OF CIVIL ENGINEERS (Jack E. Leisch Memorial Scholarship)

1801 Alexander Bell Drive
Reston VA 20191-4400
800/548-ASCE or 703/295-6000
FAX: 703/295-6333
E-Mail: student@asce.org
Internet: www.asce.org

AMOUNT: $1,500

DEADLINE(S): FEB 20

FIELD(S): Transportation/Traffic Engineering

For ASCE members enrolled full-time in a graduate program at a ABET accredited university that is also a member of the Council of Univ. Trans. Centers. Thesis topic is considered in selection. Award is to be used towards tuition. Membership application may be submitted along with scholarship application.

1 award annually. See website or contact ASCE for an application between October and February.

32 — AMERICAN SOCIETY OF TRAVEL AGENTS (ASTA) FOUNDATION (Scholarships, Grants, & Internships)

1101 King Street
Alexandria VA 22314
703/739-2782
FAX: 703/684-8319
E-Mail: MyriamL@astahq.com
Internet: www.astanet.com

AMOUNT: $200-$3,000

DEADLINE(S): JUN; JUL; DEC

FIELD(S): Travel, Tourism, & Hospitality

Various scholarships, research grants, and internships which are open to students for undergraduate or graduate study or professional development at institutions in the US or Canada. Minimum 2.5 GPA & a major in one of the above fields are required. Must be US/Canadian citizen or permanent resident. Financial need usually NOT considered.

30-50 awards annually. Renewable. See website or contact Myriam Lechuga, Manager, at above address for an application.

33 — AMERICAN SOCIETY OF TRAVEL AGENTS (ASTA) FOUNDATION, INC. (Fernando R. Ayuso Award)

1101 King St.
Alexandria VA 22314
703/739-2782
Internet: www.astanet.com

AMOUNT: Transportation, registration, accommodation, and food

DEADLINE(S): JUL 28

FIELD(S): Travel & Tourism

An internship opportunity for persons who have worked the travel industry for at least two years or who are have been enrolled in a college/univerisyt pursuing the study of the travel industry. The award is co-sponsored by the Ministry of Tourism for Spain and involves paid-for attendance at the International Travel Fair in Madrid, Spain. U.S. citizenship required. Purpose is to further the positive relationship between the tourism industries of Spain and the U.S.

Write or visit website for complete information and applications.

34 — AMERICAN SOCIETY OF WOMEN ACCOUNTANTS (Scholarships)

60 Revere Drive, Suite 500
Northbrook IL 60062
800/326-2163 or 847/205-1029
FAX: 847/480-9282
Internet: www.aswa.org/scholarship.html

AMOUNT: $4,000 (1); $3,000 (2); $2,000 (4)

DEADLINE(S): Varies

FIELD(S): Accounting

Scholarships for female accounting majors who are either full- or part-time students. Must have completed a minimum of 60 semester hours or 90 quarter hours and be enrolled in an accredited college, university, or professional school of accounting (which is designated to award a post-baccalaureate Certificate of Accounting). Membership in ASWA not required.

Applications must be made through the local chapter. Call ASWA for the name of a local chapter.

35 — APICS EDUCATION AND RESEARCH FOUNDATION (Donald W. Fogarty International Student Paper Competition)

5301 Shawnee Road
Alexandria VA 22312
800/444-2742
FAX: 703/354-8794
E-Mail: h_kather@apics.org
Internet: www.apics.org

AMOUNT: $100-$1,700+

DEADLINE(S): MAY 15 (submit papers to a local APICS chapter)

FIELD(S): Production/Operations Management; Resource Management

Awards offered for winning papers on the subject of production and operations management or resource management, including inventory issues. Open to full-time or part-time undergraduate or graduate students; NOT for high school students. Financial need is NOT a factor.

Up to 180 awards annually. For complete information, please call APICS customer service at the above 800 number to request a D.W.F. International Student Paper Competition Manual (item #01002) and the name of a local APICS chapter.

36 — ARMENIAN GENERAL BENEVOLENT UNION (Educational Loan Program)

Education Dept., 31 W. 52nd St.
New York NY 10019-6118
212/765-8260
FAX: 212/765-8209
E-Mail: agbuny@aol.com

AMOUNT: $5,000 to $7,500/yr.

DEADLINE(S): APR 1

FIELD(S): Education Administration, International Relations/Foreign Affairs, Communication, Journalism, or Public Administration

Loans for full-time students of Armenian heritage pursuing master's degrees in one of the above fields. Must be attending highly competitive institutions in the U.S. GPA of 3.5 or more required.

Loan repayment period begins within 12 months of completion of full-time study and extends five to ten years, depending on the size of the loan. Interest is 3% Write for complete information.

37 — ARTHUR ANDERSEN & CO. SCHOLARSHIP FOUNDATION (Fellowships for Doctoral Candidates at the Dissertation Stage)

225 N. Michigan Ave.
Chicago IL 60601-7601
312/580-0069

AMOUNT: $18,000 stipend + tuition

DEADLINE(S): MAR 1; OCT 1

FIELD(S): Accounting, taxes, information sciences, and related areas

Doctoral dissertation fellowships to support the development of university professors in the fields above. Open to Ph.D candidates who agree to teach at the university level for 3 years.

Write for complete information.

38 — ASIAN INSTITUTE OF TECHNOLOGY (AIT Scholarship Program)

Development Office
PO Box 4, Klongluang
Pathumthani 12120 THAILAND
(66)(2) 516-0110-44 or 524-5032
FAX: (66)(2) 516-2126
E-Mail: ascao@ait.ac.th
Internet: www.ait.ac.th

AMOUNT: US $12,600-$37,960

DEADLINE(S): FEB 15; JUN 15; OCT 15

FIELD(S): Advanced Technologies; Civil Engineering; Environment, Resources, & Development; Business Management

Scholarships and grants open to citizens of Asian countries who are accepted by the institute as a master's or doctotal candidate. Selection is based on academic criteria, practical experience, gender, and country of origin; priority to Mekong Region countries and Asian countries of the former USSR.

250 awards annually. Contact AIT for an application.

39 — ASIAN PRODUCTIVITY ORGANIZATION (Productivity Fellowships)

8-4-14, Akasaka
Minato-ku
Tokyo 107-0052 Japan
03/3408-7227
FAX: 03/3408-7226
E-Mail: ind@apo-tokyo.com

AMOUNT: Living allowance (hotel accomodation + incidental expenses)

DEADLINE(S): APR 2

FIELD(S): Business Mangement; Economic Development

Open to senior consultants, trainers, or researchers in the above fields who are citizens of one of the Asian Productivity Organization countries. Must have at least three years of experience in promoting productivity movement.

Contact APO for details.

40 — ASSOCIATION FOR INSTITUTIONAL RESEARCH (Research Grant)

114 Stone Building, FSU
Tallahassee FL 32306-4462
850/644-4470
FAX: 850/644-8824
E-Mail: air@mailer.fsu.edu
Internet: http://airweb.org

AMOUNT: $30,000/yr.

DEADLINE(S): JAN 15

FIELD(S): Social sciences, education, finance, economics

The Association provides one-year grants for doctoral or post-doctoral research appropriate for its program "Improving Institutional Research in Postsecondary Educational Institutions."

Must submit proposal, including budget. Contact organization for details.

41 — ASSOCIATION FOR WOMEN IN SCIENCE EDUCATIONAL FOUNDATION (AWIS Predoctoral Awards)

1200 New York Ave. NW, Suite 650
Washington DC 20005
202/326-8940 or 800-886-AWIS
E-Mail: awis@awis.org
Internet: www.awis.org

AMOUNT: $1,000

DEADLINE(S): JAN 16

FIELD(S): Various Sciences and Social Sciences

Scholarships for female doctoral students. Summary page, description of research project, resume, references, transcripts, and biographical sketch required. US citizens may study at any graduate institution; non-citizens must study at US institutions.

5-10 awards annually. See website or write to above address for an application and complete information.

42 — ASSOCIATION FOR WOMEN IN SCIENCE EDUCATIONAL FOUNDATION (AWIS Pre-doctoral Awards)

1200 New York Ave. NW, Suite 650
Washington DC 20005
202/326-8940 or 800/886-AWIS
E-Mail: awis@awis.org
Internet: www.awis.org

AMOUNT: $1,000

DEADLINE(S): JAN 16

FIELD(S): Various Sciences and Social Sciences

Scholarships for female doctoral students. Summary page, description of research project, resume, references, transcripts, and biographical sketch required. US citizens may study at any graduate institution; non-citizens must be enrolled in US institutions.

5-10 awards annually. See website or write to above address for an application and more information.

43 — ASSOCIATION FOR WOMEN IN SCIENCE EDUCATIONAL FOUNDATION (Ruth Satter Memorial Award)

1200 New York Ave., NW, Suite 650
Washington DC 20005

202/326-8940 or 800/886-AWIS
E-Mail: awis@awis.org
Internet: www.awis.org

AMOUNT: $1,000

DEADLINE(S): JAN 16

FIELD(S): Various Sciences and Social Sciences

Scholarships for female doctoral students who have interrupted their education for at least three years to raise a family. Summary page, description of research project, resume, references, transcripts, biographical sketch, and letter from your department to confirm eligibility required. US citizens may study at any graduate institution; non-citizens must attend US institutions.

See website or write to above address for more information or an application.

44 — ASSOCIATION FOR WOMEN IN SCIENCE EDUCATIONAL FOUNDATION (Ruth Satter Memorial Award)

1200 New York Ave. NW, Suite 650
Washington DC 20005
202/326-8940 or 800/886-AWIS
E-Mail: awis@awis.org
Internet: www.awis.org

AMOUNT: $1,000

DEADLINE(S): JAN 16

FIELD(S): Various Sciences and Social Sciences

Scholarships for female doctoral students who have interupted their education three years or more to raise a family. Summary page, description of research project, resume, references, transcripts, biographical sketch, and proof of eligibility from department head required. US citizens may attend any graduate institution; non-citizens must be enrolled in US institutions.

See website or write to above address for more information or an application.

45 — ASSOCIATION OF CERTIFIED FRAUD EXAMINERS (Scholarships)

The Gregor Building, 716 West Ave
Austin TX 78701
800/245-3321 or 512/478-9070
FAX: 512/478-9297
E-Mail: acfe@tpoint.net
Internet: www.cfenet.com

AMOUNT: $500

DEADLINE(S): MAY 15

FIELD(S): Accounting and/or criminal justice

Scholarships for full time graduate or undergraduate students majoring in accounting or criminal justice degree programs. Awards are based on overall academic achievement, three letters of recommendation, and an original 250-workd essay explaining why the applicant deserves the award and how fraud awareness will afect his or her professional career development. Also required is a letter of recommendation from a Certified Fraud Examiner or a local CFE Chapter.

Contact organization for applications and further details.

46 — ASSOCIATION OF MBAS (Business School Loan Scheme)

15 Duncan Terrace
London ENGLAND N1 8BZ UK
0171 837 3375
FAX: 0171 278 3634
Internet: www.mba.org.uk

AMOUNT: Varies

DEADLINE(S): None

FIELD(S): Business

Must be a permanent UK resident attending an accredited MBA program and have at least two years relevant work experience. Financial need NOT considered.

700 awards annually. Renewable. Contact Peter Calladine at above address for an application.

47 — AYN RAND INSTITUTE (Atlas Shrugged Essay Contest for Graduate Business Students)

4640 Admiralty Way, Suite 406
Marina del Rey CA 90292
310/306-9232
FAX: 310/306-4925
E-Mail: essay@aynrand.org
Internet: www.aynrand.org/contests

AMOUNT: $7,000-1st prize; $5,000-2nd prize; $2,500-3rd prize

DEADLINE(S): FEB 15

FIELD(S): Business

Essay competition for students enrolled in a graduate business program. Essays are judged on both style and content. Winning essays must demonstrate an outstanding grasp of the philosophical meaning of Ayn Rand's novel, Atlas Shrugged. Length: 1,000 to 1,200 words.

For information, contact your Business Ethics professor or visit the website.

48 — BEDDING PLANTS FOUNDATION, INC. (Ed Markham International Scholarship)

PO Box 280
East Lansing MI 48826-0280
517/333-4617
FAX: 517/333-4494

E-Mail: BPFI@aol.com
Internet: www.bpfi.org

AMOUNT: $1,000

DEADLINE(S): MAY 15

FIELD(S): Horticulture AND International Business

Open to graduate and undergraduate students already attending a four-year college/university who are majoring in horticultre or related field. Should wish to further understanding of domestic & international marketing through international horticulturally related study, work, or travel. Cash award, with checks issued jointly in name of recipient and college/institution he or she will attend for current year. Must submit references & transcripts.

1 award annually. See website or send printed self-addressed mailing label (or self-addressed, stamped envelope) to BPFI after January 1st for an application. Recipient will be notified.

49 — BEDDING PLANTS FOUNDATION, INC. (Harold Bettinger Memorial Scholarship)

PO Box 280
East Lansing MI 48826-0280
517/333-4617
FAX: 517/333-4494
E-Mail: BPFI@aol.com
Internet: www.bpfi.org

AMOUNT: $1,000

DEADLINE(S): MAY 15

FIELD(S): Horticulture AND Business/Marketing

Open to graduate and undergraduate students already attending a four-year college/university who have either a horticulture major with business/marketing emphasis OR a business/marketing major with horticulture emphasis. Cash award, with checks issued jointly in name of recipient and college/institution he or she will attend for current year. Must submit references & transcripts.

1 award annually. See website or send printed self-addressed mailing label (or self-addressed, stamped envelope) to BPFI after January 1st for an application. Recipient will be notified.

50 — BLAKEMORE FOUNDATION (Asian Language Fellowship Grants)

1201 Third Ave., 40th Fl.
Seattle WA 98101-3099
206/583-8778
FAX: 206/583-8500
E-Mail: blakemore@perkinscoie.com

AMOUNT: Tuition, transportation, basic living costs

DEADLINE(S): JAN 15

FIELD(S): Asian languages

Fellowships for advanced language study in Asia. For use at an instition selected by the applicant and approved by the Foundation. Applicant must be a graduate or professional school student, a teacher, a professional, or a business person; be working towards a specific career objective involving the regular use of an Asian language; be near an advanced level in that language; be a U.S. citizen or permanent resident. For full-time study during the term of the grant.

12-18 annual awards. For one year of study.

51 — BLUES HEAVEN FOUNDATION, INC. (Muddy Waters Scholarship)

2120 S. Michigan Ave.
Chicago IL 60616
312/808-1286

AMOUNT: $2,000

DEADLINE(S): APR 30

FIELD(S): Music; Music Education; African-American Studies; Folklore; Performing Arts; Arts Management; Journalism; Radio/TV/Film

Scholarship is made on a competitive basis with consideration given to scholastic achievement, concentration of studies, and financial need. Applicant must have full-time enrollment status in a Chicago area college/university in at least their first year of undergraduate studies or a graduate program. Scholastic aptitude, extracurricular involvement, grade point average, and financial need are all considered.

Contact Blues Heaven Foundation, Inc. to receive an application between February and April.

52 — BOLOGNA CENTER OF THE JOHNS HOPKINS UNIVERSITY - PAUL H. NITZE SCHOOL OF ADVANCED INTERNATIONAL STUDIES (Fellowships for Non-Americans)

Admissions Office
Via Belmeloro 11
40126 Bologna ITALY
+39/51/232-185
FAX: +39/51/228-505
E-Mail: admission@jhubc.it
Internet: www.jhubc.it

AMOUNT: Partial to full tuition

DEADLINE(S): FEB 1

FIELD(S): European Studies; International Relations; International Economics

One year at SAIS Bologna Center is open to graduate students with some background in political science, economics, history, or law and who are interested in problems confronting Europe and/or international relations. Possibility to continue for the second year toward an M.A. at SAIS in Washington, DC. Program is conducted in English; therefore, English fluency is required. This program is for non-US citizens.

Contact Bologna Center for an application.

53 — BOLOGNA CENTER OF THE JOHNS HOPKINS UNIVERSITY - PAUL H. NITZE SCHOOL OF ADVANCED INTERNATIONAL STUDIES (Fellowships for Americans)

SAIS
1740 Massachusetts Ave., NW
Washington DC 20036
E-mail: admission@jhubc.it
Internet: www.jhubc.it

AMOUNT: Partial to full tuition

DEADLINE(S): JAN 15

FIELD(S): European Studies; International Relations; International Economics

One year at SAIS Bologna Center in Italy is open to graduate students with some background in political science, economics, history, or law and who are interested in problems confronting Europe and/or international relations. Must be US citizen/permanent resident. Courses are conducted in English.

Contact SAIS for an application.

54 — BOYS & GIRLS CLUBS OF AMERICA (Robert W. Woodruff Fellowships)

1230 W. Peachtree St. NW
Training & Prof. Devel.
Atlanta GA 30309-3494
404/815-5776
FAX: 404/815-5736

AMOUNT: Up to $15,000

DEADLINE(S): JUN 15 (applications available MAR 1)

FIELD(S): Youth Leadership

Internships for Boys/Girls Clubs of America professionals who are enrolled in an accredited M.A. program or who possess M.A. degrees in a related field. Recipients agree to commit to 2 years of full-time employment with Boys/Girls Clubs of America following completion of studies.

Write for complete information.

55 — BROOKING INSTITUTION (Research Fellowships)

1775 Massachusetts Ave., NW
Washington DC 20036-2188
202/797-6000

AMOUNT: $17,500 stipend

DEADLINE(S): DEC 15

FIELD(S): Foreign Policy; Government; Economics

Open to Ph.D candidates nominated by their graduate departments. Applications from individuals not nominated cannot be accepted. Awards support research by Ph.D candidates who have completed all coursework except for the dissertation.

9 awards annually. Nomination forms may be obtained by your department head or from the address above.

56 — BUSINESS & PROFESSIONAL WOMEN'S FOUNDATION (BPW Career Advancement Scholarship Program)

2012 Massachusetts Ave., NW
Washington DC 20036-1070
202/293-1200, ext. 169
FAX: 202/861-0298
Internet: www.bpwusa.org

AMOUNT: $500-$1,000

DEADLINE(S): APR 15

FIELD(S): Biology, Science, Education, Engineering, Social Science, Paralegal, Humanities, Business, Math, Computers, Law, MD, DD

For women (US citizens) aged 25+ accepted into accredited program at US institution (+Puerto Rico & Virgin Islands). Must graduate within 12 to 24 months from the date of grant and demonstrate critical finanacial need. Must have a plan to upgrade skills, train for a new career field, or to enter/re-enter the job market.

Full- or part-time study. For info see website or send business-sized, self-addressed, double-stamped envelope.

57 — CANADIAN BUREAU FOR INTERNATIONAL EDUCATION (Canadian International Development Agency Awards Program for Canadians)

220 Laurier Ave., W., Ste. 1100
Ottawa Ontario K1P 5Z9 CANADA
613/237-4820
FAX: 613/237-1073
E-Mail: smelanson@cbie.ca
Internet: www.cbie.ca

AMOUNT: $10,000/yr. Canadian (max.)

DEADLINE(S): FEB 1

FIELD(S): International Relations/Development; Business

For Canadian citizens/permanent residents seeking to participate in international development through a volunteer project of their own initiative. The development activity may be the fieldwork component of a master's degree program or a professional work/research project. Ph.D. candidates are NOT eligible. Also offers internships to master's students in business, administration, and

management programs. Awards tenable up to twelve months and are taxable.

50 awards annually. Contact CBIE for an application.

58 — COLORADO SOCIETY OF CPAs EDUCATIONAL FOUNDATION (Scholarships for Undergraduates and Graduates)

7979 E. Tufts Ave., #500
Denver CO 80237-2843
303/773-2877 or 800/523-9082
Internet: www.cocpa.org

AMOUNT: $1,000

DEADLINE(S): JUN 30; NOV 30

FIELD(S): Accounting

For undergraduates and graduates who have completed intermediate accounting, have a 3.0 or better GPA, and are majoring in accounting at a Colorado college/university offering accredited accounting majors. Financial need considered.

Scholarships are renewable with re-application. See website or contact Gena Mantz at above location for an application.

59 — COLORADO SOCIETY OF CPAs EDUCATIONAL FOUNDATION (Scholarships for Ethnically Diverse Undergraduates and Graduates)

7979 E. Tufts Ave., #500
Denver CO 80237-2843
303/773-2877 or 800/523-9082
Internet: www.cocpa.org

AMOUNT: $1,000

DEADLINE(S): JUN 30

FIELD(S): Accounting

For ethnically diverse undergraduates and graduates who have completed intermediate accounting, have 3.0 or better GPA, and are majoring in accounting at a Colorado college/university offering accredited accounting majors. Must be African American, Hispanic, Asian-American, American Indian, or Pacific Islander. Financial need considered.

Renewable with re-application. See website or contact Gena Mantz at above location for an application.

60 — COLUMBIA UNIVERSITY (Knight-Bagehot Fellowship Program in Economics and Business Journalism)

Graduate School of Journalism
New York NY 10027
212/854-2711

AMOUNT: Tuition + stipend to offset living expenses

DEADLINE(S): MAR 1

FIELD(S): Business Journalism; Economics; Finance & related fields

Graduate fellowships at Columbia University open to qualified journalists with at least 4 years of experience who wish to enhance their understanding and knowledge in the above fields. For U.S. or Canadian print or broadcast journalists.

Up to 10 fellowships per year. Write for complete information.

61 — CONCORDIA UNIVERSITY (Bank of Montreal Pauline Vanier MBA Fellowship)

Faculty Commerce & Admin
1455 de Maisonneuve Blvd. West
Montreal Quebec H3G 1M8 CANADA
514/848-3809
FAX: 514/848-2812
E-Mail: awardsgs@vax2.concordia.ca

AMOUNT: $10,000/yr.

DEADLINE(S): APR 30

FIELD(S): Accounting; Decision Science & Information Systems; Finance; Management; Marketing

This two-year fellowship is offered to a woman with at least two years cumulative business experience who is a Canadian citizen/permanent resident and who is entering the full-time MBA program in the September session.

1 award annually. Contact the Graduate Program Director, Faculty of Commerce and Administration, at Concordia University for an application.

62 — CONCORDIA UNIVERSITY (Bessie Schulich Fellowship for Entrepreneurship)

Faculty Commerce & Admin
1455 de Maisonneuve Blvd. West
Montreal Quebec H3G 1M8 CANADA
514/848-3809
FAX: 514/848-2812
E-Mail: awardsgs@vax2.concordia.ca

AMOUNT: $3,000

DEADLINE(S): MAR 30

FIELD(S): Accounting; Decision Science & Information Systems; Finance; Management; Marketing

Open to Canadian citizens/permanent residents who have a minimum 3.0 GPA and who have demonstrated entrepreneurial skills. Applicants must have completed their first year of full-time studies (30 credits) and have between 27 and 18 credits left to complete their program. Candidates must be

registered full-time in the M.B.A. program throughout the duration of their award.

1 award annually. Contact the Graduate Program Director, Faculty of Commerce and Administration, at Concordia University for an application.

63 — CONFERENCE OF MINORITY PUBLIC ADMINISTRATORS (Scholarships and Travel Grants)

P.O. Box 3010
Fort Worth TX 76113
817/871-8325
Internet: www.compa.org

AMOUNT: $400 (travel grants); up to $1,500 (academic year)

DEADLINE(S): Varies

FIELD(S): Public administration/public affairs

COMPA offers two academic scholarships, at least five travel grants, and a $1,000 gift to the college that has the largest number of stdent registrants at its annual conference. Travel grants are for attending the conference. For minorities and women pursuing full-time education in the above fields and committed to excellence in public service and administration in city, county, state, and federal governments.

Contact Edwin Cook at above location for details.

64 — CONTRACT MANAGEMENT INSTITUTE (Scholarships)

1912 Woodford Road
Vienna VA 22182
703/448-9231
E-Mail: info@ncmahq.org
Internet: www.ncmahq.org/cmi/scholar.html

AMOUNT: Varies

DEADLINE(S): Varies

FIELD(S): Business: Contract Management specialty

Scholarships for undergraduate and graduate students enrolled in a business-orinted curriculum who intend to enter into the Contract Management field. Available from each of the eight NMCA regions. One program, the Martin L. Kaufman Memorial Scholarship, is for business students who intend to enter the military service of the U.S. upon graduation.

Inquire of organization for details.

65 — COOPERATIVE ASSOCIATION OF STATES FOR SCHOLARSHIPS (CASS) (Scholarships)

c/o Commonwealth Liaison,
Unit 310 The Garrison
St. Michael BARBADOS
809/436-8754

AMOUNT: Varies

DEADLINE(S): None

FIELD(S): Business application/computer science

Scholarships for economically disadvantaged deaf youth, ages 17-25, with strong leadership potential and an interest in computer science/business applications. Must be from Barbados, St. Kitts/Nevis, Grenada, St. Vincent, Antigua/Barbuda, St. Lucia, Dominica, or Jamaica.

Write to E. Caribbean Reg. Coordinator (CASS) at above address.

66 — CORNELL UNIVERSITY, JOHNSON GRADUATE SCHOOL OF MANAGEMENT (Thomas Angear Scholarships)

Admissions, Johnson Grad. School of Management, 315 Malott Hall,
Cornell University
Ithaca NY 14853-6201
607/255-4526 or 800/847-2082

AMOUNT: $10,000

DEADLINE(S): Varies

FIELD(S): Business management

Scholarship for European Community nationals to study business management at the above institution. Must have a BA degree or equivalent.

Renewable for 2nd year. Contact school for application details.

67 — COUNCIL OF JEWISH FEDERATIONS (Federation Executive Recruitment & Education Program Scholarships)

111 8th Ave.
New York NY 10011
212/598-3583
FAX: 212/475-6571
E-Mail: susan_sherr@cjfny.org

AMOUNT: $7,500 and $20,000

DEADLINE(S): FEB 1

FIELD(S): Social Work; Public Administration

Two-year course of study leading to a master's degree in social work and/or Jewish communal service and public administration. Applicants must demonstrate strong commitment to Jewish community service and have at least a 3.0 GPA.

Recipients must agree to work for a North America Jewish Federation for at least 3 years after graduation. Write for complete information.

68 — CUBAN AMERICAN NATIONAL FOUNDATION (The Mas Family Scholarships)

7300 NW 35 Terrace
Miami FL 33122
305/592-7768
FAX: 305/592-7889

E-Mail canfnet.org

Internet: www.canfnet.org

AMOUNT: Individually negotiated

DEADLINE(S): MAR 15

FIELD(S): Engineering, Business, International Relations, Economics, Communications, Journalism

For Cuban-Americans students, graduates and undergraduates, born in Cuba or direct descendants of those who left Cuba. Must be in top 10% of high school class or maintain a 3.5 GPA in college.

10,000 awards/year. Recipients may re-apply for subsequent years. Financial need considered along with academic success, SAT and GRE scores, and leadership potential. Essays and proof of Cuban descent required.

69 — DELOITTE & TOUCHE FOUNDATION (Doctoral Fellowship Program)

Ten Westport Road

Wilton CT 06897

203/761-3248

FAX: 203/834-2294

AMOUNT: $20,000

DEADLINE(S): OCT 15

FIELD(S): Accounting

Any doctoral student enrolled in a US school having a doctoral program in accounting is eligible to apply for this fellowship program after completing two semesters (or equivalent) of the doctoral program.

Up to 10 grants per year. Contact address above for complete information.

70 — DRAPER LABORATORY (Research Assistantships)

555 Technology Square

Cambridge MA 02139

617/258-2393

FAX: 617/258-2333

E-Mail: ed@draper.com

AMOUNT: Tuition + stipend

DEADLINE(S): Varies (same as MIT deadline)

FIELD(S): Engineering: Mechanical, Aero-Astro, Electrical; Computer Science; Operations Research

Open to US citizens pursuing graduate study in M.S. or Ph.D. programs at MIT.

30 awards annually. Renewable. Contact Draper Lab for an application.

71 — ECONOMIC HISTORY ASSOCIATION (Arthur H. Cole Grants-in-Aid)

226A Summerfield Hall, University of Kansas, Dept. of Economics

Lawrence KS 66045

913/864-3501

FAX: 913/864-5270

E-Mail: eha@falcon.cc.ukans.edu

AMOUNT: $1,500

DEADLINE(S): APR 1

FIELD(S): Economic History

Open to recent Ph.D.s wanting to do research in the area of economic history. Supports research in the field regardless of time period or geographic area. Must be members of the Economic History Association. For membership information, contact above address.

Contact above location for details of grant.

72 — ESPN (Internship Programs)

Human Resources Dept.

ESPN, Inc.

ESPN Plaza

Bristol CT 06010

No phone calls. Internet: espnet.sportszone.com/editors/studios/97faq.html

AMOUNT: Paid Internships

DEADLINE(S): OCT 1; MAR 1; JUN 1

FIELD(S): Television Industry, Public Relations, Sports

12-week internships in the spring, summer, and fall for undergraduate juniors/seniors and graduate students. Some areas require weekend/evening hours and a strong knowledge of sports. Interns receive hourly wages and take part in many company-sponsored activities. ESPN does not provide housing for students, but we do try to assist in finding suitable living arrangements once selected.

To apply for internship programs, please send cover letter and resume to the above address. If applying to the Communications Dept., please also enclose writing samples and send attention to Diane Lamb.

73 — EUROPEAN UNIVERSITY INSTITUTE (Jean Monnet Fellowship)

Via Dei Roccettini 9

I-50016 San Domenico Di Fiesole (FL) Italy

0039-055-46851

FAX: 0039-055-4685444

E-Mail: applyjmf@datacomm.iue.it

Internet: www.iue.it/JMF/Welcome.html

AMOUNT: 2,000,000-3,500,000 Italian lire per month (i.e. 1,025-1,750 ECU) + medical & family allowances (depends on whether fellow is in receipt of payment from another source and on extent of duties carried out at the Institute)

DEADLINE(S): NOV 1

FIELD(S): Europe: History, Society, Politics, Economics, Law

Post-doctoral fellowships. Fellows are required to make scholarly contribution to research on Europe within one of EUI's research projects or on topic, falling within general interests of the Institute. Publication of research is expected.

25 fellowships annually. Financial need NOT considered. See website or contact Dr. Andreas Frijdal at above address for complete information.

74 — EUROPEAN UNIVERSITY INSTITUTE (National Postgraduate Scholarships)

Via De Roccettini 9

San Domenico Di Fiesole (FI 50016) ITALY

0039/055-46851

FAX: 0039/055-4685444

E-Mail: applyres@datacomm.iue.it

Internet: www.iue.it

AMOUNT: $1,000/month + travel & medical/family allowances

DEADLINE(S): JAN 31

FIELD(S): Political Science; Social Sciences; Law; Economics; History

Open to graduate & postgraduate students at the Institute who have good honors and a research project having European dimension. Awards are available only to nationals of the Institute's member states. US citizens must have sufficient personal funds or another grant to cover maintenance & tuition; may apply to Fulbright Commission which may award up to two grants per academic year to US citizens with tuition-fee waivers.

130 awards annually. Renewable. Contact Dr. Andreas Frijdal for an application.

75 — FASHION GROUP INTERNATIONAL OF GREATER WASHINGTON DC (Scholarships)

P.O. Box 71055

Chevy Chase MD 20813-1055

212/593-1715 (in New York)

Internet: fgi.org/washington.htm

AMOUNT: Up to $2,500

DEADLINE(S): APR 1

FIELD(S): Fashion-related areas

Scholarshps for students majoring in fashion-related fields. Must be permanent residents of the Greater Metropolitan Washington DC area. Must either graduate from high school in June and/or have been admitted to an accredited institution or be enrolled in a university or college as an undergraduate or graduate student.

Application form and details are available on website or contact organization for further information.

76 — FONDATION MARCEL HICTER - COUNCIL OF EUROPE (Travel Bursary System)

Rue Cornet de Grez 14
B-1210 Brussells BELGIUM
+32/2 219 9886
FAX: +32/2 217 3572
E-Mail: fond.hicter@glo.be

AMOUNT: 5,000 FRF (max.)

DEADLINE(S): None

FIELD(S): Cultural Management

Open to students of European nationality who wish to pursue undergraduate or graduate studies in a European country that signed the European cultural convention. Financial need NOT a factor.

100 awards annually. Contact Isabelle Piette for anapplication.

77 — GALILLEE COLLEGE (Tuition Scholarships in Israel for Koreans)

P.O. Box 1070
Kiryat Tivon, 36000, ISRAEL
FAX: 972-4-983 0227
E-Mail: galilcol@actcom.co.il

AMOUNT: Varies

DEADLINE(S): Varies

FIELD(S): Business Management in various specialties

A tuition scholarship program at Galillee College in Israel for citizens of South Korea who are college graduates. The three-week program in management includes Port Management, Small Businesses and Industries, Tourism Management and Development, Health Systems Management, Environmental Management, and Urban Economic Development. Proficiency in English required. Applicants must be working at a policy-making level in their respective fields of management.

Contact Sylvia Walters, Deputy Director, Internaitonal Programmes, at above address for application information, location, and fees.

78 — GENEVA ASSOCIATION (Ernst Meyer Prize & Research Grants)

General Secretariat
18, chemin Rieu
CH-1208 Geneva SWITZERLAND
+4122 347 09 38
FAX: +4122 347 20 78

AMOUNT: 5,000-10,000 Swiss Francs

DEADLINE(S): Varies

FIELD(S): Economics; Actuarial Science; Insurance

The Ernst Meyer Prize is for university research work which makes a significant & original contribution to the study of risk & insurance economics. Research grants, covering a period of ten months, are for research into risk & insurance economics. Grants are primarily intended for research for thesis leading to a doctor degree in economics. Applications must be accompanied by a personal history, a description of the research undertaken, & letters of recommendation.

Contact the General Secretariat at the Geneva Association for applications.

79 — GLADYS KRIEBLE DELMAS FOUNDATION (Predoctoral & Postdoctoral Grants in Venice & the Veneto)

521 5th Avenue, Suite 1612
New York NY 10175-1699
212/687-0011
FAX: 212/687-8877
E-Mail: DelmasFdtn@aol.com
Internet: www.delmas.org

AMOUNT: $500-$12,500

DEADLINE(S): DEC 15

FIELD(S): Research of Venice and the former Venetian empire and study of contemporary Venetian society and culture.

Pre- and postdoctoral grants for historical research on Venice. Humanities and social sciences are eligible areas of study, including archaeology, architecture, art, bibliography, economics, history, history of science, law, literature, music, political science, religion, and theater.

Applicants must have experience in advanced research and be U.S. citizens/residents; grad students must have fulfilled all doctoral requirements except dissertation by Dec. 15.

80 — GRADUATE INSTITUTE OF INTERNATIONAL STUDIES (Scholarships)

P.O. Box 36
132 Rue do Lausanne
CH-1211 Geneva 21 SWITZERLAND
(+41 22) 731 17 30
FAX: (+41-22) 731 27 77
E-Mail: info@hei.unige.ch
Internet: http://heiwww.unige.ch

AMOUNT: Varies

DEADLINE(S): None

FIELD(S): International history and politics, political science, international economics, international law

Scholarships to support graduate diploma and Ph.D students already registered at the Institute. Open to applicants with excellent, active knowledge of one of the institute's two working languages, French & English, and sufficient passive knowledge of the other.

Contact above sources for complete information.

81 — HARVARD BUSINESS SCHOOL (Newcomen Postdoctoral Fellowship in Business History)

Harvard Business School
Morgan 295, Soldiers Field
Boston MA 02163
617/495-6008
E-Mail: esampson@hbs.edu

AMOUNT: $46,000

DEADLINE(S): NOV 1

FIELD(S): Business & Economic History

Open to scholars who received the Ph.D in history, economics, or a related discipline within the past 10 years and wish to improve their skills as they relate to these fields and engage in research at the Harvard Business School.

For complete information write to Nancy F. Koehn, Associate, at the above address, or E-mail assistant, Elizabeth Sampson, at above address.

82 — HILLEL INTERNATIONAL CENTER (The Bittker Fellowship)

Eran Gasko
1640 Rhode Island Ave. NW
Washington DC 20036
202/857-6637
202/857-6560
FAX: 202/857-6693
E-Mail: smusher@hillel.org
Internet: www.hillel.org/careermoves/
bittker.htm

AMOUNT: Professional Experience

DEADLINE(S): None specified

FIELD(S): Student Leadership/Jewish Awareness

One-year professional experience for an oustanding recent graduate, who coordinates student leadership and Jewish awareness activities nationwide. The Fellow establishes the network of student leaders and enhances their communication through national publications, conference calls, and the Internet. Task forces include Jewish Awareness/ Identity, Women's Issues, Graduate Student Life, and Education.

Contact Eran Gasko, Human Resources, for an application.

83 — HOBSONS PUBLISHING (Scholarship)

159-173 St. John St.
London EC1V 4DR UK
0171 336 6633
FAX: 0171 608 1034
E-Mail: rachel.mcclure@hobsons.co.uk
Internet: www.hobsons.com/10kschol.htm

AMOUNT: 10,000 pounds

DEADLINE(S): None

FIELD(S): Master's of Business Administration

Scholarship for an MBA student applying to Association of MBA's (AMBA) accredited schools in Europe. Applicant must submit a short essay about why he/she wishes to study for an MBA qualification.

Check website for information about company. Write for application details.

84 — HOUBLON-NORMAN FUND (Fellowships)

Secretary's Dept HO-1
Bank of England
Threadneedle St.
London EC2R 8AH ENGLAND
44 171 601 4751
FAX: 44 171 601 3668
E-Mail: margot.wilson@bankofengland.co.uk

AMOUNT: Varies (based on current salary)

DEADLINE(S): NOV 30

FIELD(S): Economics

Post-graduate fellowships tenable at the Bank of England open to all nationalities. Financial need is NOT considered.

1-3 awards annually. Contact Miss Margot Wilson at above address for an application.

85 — INDEPENDENT ACCOUNTANTS INTERNATIONAL EDUCATIONAL FOUNDATION, INC. (Robert Kaufman Memorial Scholarship Award)

9200 S. Dadeland Blvd., Suite 510
Miami FL 33156
305/670-0580
Internet: www.accountants.org

AMOUNT: $250-$2,500

DEADLINE(S): FEB 28

FIELD(S): Accounting

Open to students who are pursuing or planning to pursue an education in accounting at recognized academic institutions throughout the world. Must demonstrate financial need for larger sums; not required for $250 honorary textbook award.

Up to 20 awards annually. See website ONLY for complete information.

86 — INSTITUTE FOR HUMANE STUDIES (Koch Summer Fellow Program)

4084 University Dr., Ste. 101
Fairfax VA 22030-6812
703/934-6920 or 800/697-8799
FAX: 703/352-7535
E-Mail: ihs@gmu.edu
Internet: www.theihs.org

AMOUNT: $1,500 + airfare & housing

DEADLINE(S): MAR 1

FIELD(S): Economics; Politics; Law; Government; Public Policy

For undergraduates and graduates to build skills and gain experience by participating in an 8-week summer internship program. Includes 2 week-long seminars, the internship, and research & writing projects with professionals. College transcripts, essays, and application required. Financial need NOT a factor.

32 awards annually. Not renewable. Apply online or contact IHS for an application.

87 — INSTITUTE FOR HUMANE STUDIES (Summer Residential Program)

4084 University Dr., Ste. 101
Fairfax VA 22030-6812
703/934-6920 or 800/697-8799
FAX: 703/352-7535
E-Mail: ihs@gmu.edu
Internet: www.theihs.org

AMOUNT: All seminar fees: program cost, room/board, materials, and books

DEADLINE(S): MAR 1

FIELD(S): Social Sciences; Humanities; Law; Journalism; Public Policy; Education; Writing

For college students, recent graduates, and graduate students who share an interest in learning and exchanging ideas about the scope of individual rights. One-week and weekend seminars at various campus locations across the U.S.

Apply online or contact IHS for an application.

88 — INSTITUTE FOR OPERATIONS RESEARCH AND THE MANAGEMENT SCIENCES (INFORMS Summer Internship Directory)

P.O. Box 64794
Baltimore MD 21264-4794
800/4INFORMS
FAX: 410/684-2963
E-Mail: jps@informs.org
Internet: www.informs.org/INTERN/

AMOUNT: Varies

DEADLINE(S): Varies

FIELD(S): Fields related to information management: business management, engineering, mathematics

A website listing of summer internships in the field of operations research and management sciences. Both applicants and employers can register online.

Access website for list.

89 — INSTITUTE FOR THE STUDY OF WORLD POLITICS (Dissertation Fellowships)

1755 Massachusetts Ave. NW
Washington DC 20036
202/588-9797
Internet: fundforpeace.org/iswp.htm

AMOUNT: Varies

DEADLINE(S): FEB 16

FIELD(S): International Relations; Environmental Issues; Population Studies (Social Science aspects); Human Rights; Arms Control; Third World Development; Agricultural Development; Public Health, etc.

For doctoral candidates conducting dissertation research in above areas to promote scholarly examination of political, economic, and social issues that affect the security, well-being, and dignity of the peoples of the world. Financial need is a consideration. For citizens of any country.

Write for complete information.

90 — INSTITUTE FOR THE STUDY OF WORLD POLITICS (Dorothy Danforth Compton Fellowships)

1755 Massachusetts Ave. NW
Washington DC 20036
202/588-9797
Internet: fundforpeace.org/iswp.htm

AMOUNT: Varies

DEADLINE(S): MAR 16

FIELD(S): International Relations; Environmental Issues; Population Studies (Social Science aspects); Human Rights; Arms Control; Third World Development; Agricultural Development; Public Health, etc.

For masters or doctoral candidates researching in the above areas to promote scholarly examination of political, economic, and social issues that affect the security, well-being, and dignity of the peoples of the world. Must be African American, Hispanic American, and Native American students who are U.S. citizens and studying in U.S. institutions. Financial need is a consideration.

Write for complete information.

91 — INSTITUTE OF CHARTERED ACCOUNTANTS OF NEW ZEALAND (Coopers & Lybrand Peter Barr Research Fellowship)

Cigna House, 40 Mercer St., P.O. Box 11 342
Wellington NEW ZEALAND

64-4-474 7840

FAX: 64-4-473 6303

AMOUNT: Up to $10,000

DEADLINE(S): SEP 30

FIELD(S): Accounting

Fellowship offers financial assistance for projects that will benefit the accountancy profession in New Zealand. Open primarily to members of the Institue (other memberships considered).

Write for complete information.

92 — INSTITUTE OF INTERNAL AUDITORS RESEARCH FOUNDATION (Michael J. Barrett Doctoral Dissertation Award)

249 Maitland Avenue

Altamonte Springs FL 32701-4201

407/830-7600, ext. 274

E-Mail: jthompson@theiia.org

AMOUNT: $1,000-$10,000

DEADLINE(S): MAY 15; OCT 31

FIELD(S): Internal Auditing

Any doctoral candidate pursuing an advanced postgraduate degree (such as Ph.D. or DBA) in auditing, accounting, or business from an accredited educational institution is eligible to apply. Must intend to teach in the field of auditing for at least two years. Cover letter, dissertation proposal, and letters of recommendation required.

Size of grant based on amount considered necessary to allow candidate to complete dissertation research within one year. Payment begins when research does. Contact IIA for an application/more information.

93 — INTER-AMERICAN FOUNDATION (Field Research Fellowship Programs for U.S., Latin American, and Caribbean Citizens)

901 N. Stuart St., 10th Floor

Arlington VA 22203

703/841-3800

FAX: 703/527-3529

E-Mail: correo@aif.gov

Internet: www.iaf.gov

AMOUNT: Varies

DEADLINE(S): APR 28

FIELD(S): International Relations, Social Sciences, Humanities, Latin American Studies

Fellowships for Latin American, Carribean, and U.S. doctoral level students for field research in Latin America and the Caribbean. Must be enrolled in U.S. university.

Access website for deadline and application information. Organization does not mail information.

94 — INTER-AMERICAN FOUNDATION (Master's Research Fellowships)

901 N. Stuart St., 10th Floor

Arlington VA 22203

703/841-3800

FAX: 703/527-3529

E-Mail: correo@aif.gov;Internet: www.iaf.gov

AMOUNT: Varies

DEADLINE(S): APR

FIELD(S): Latin American & Caribbean Studies, Internations Relations, Social Sciences, Humanities, etc.

Open to masters students enrolled in U.S. universities for field research in Latin American or the Caribbean. For citizens of Caribbean and Latin American independent countries, and the U.S.

Access website for deadline and application information. Organization does not mail information.

95 — INTERNATIONAL ASSOCIATION OF FIRE CHIEFS FOUNDATION (Scholarship Program)

1257 Wiltshire Rd.

York PA 17403

717/854-9083

AMOUNT: $250-$4,000

DEADLINE(S): AUG 15

FIELD(S): Business and Urban Administration, Fire Science

Open to members of a fire service of a state, county, provincial, municipal, community, industrial, or federal fire department.

Renewable. Write for complete information.

96 — INTERNATIONAL COUNCIL OF SHOPPING CENTERS EDUCATIONAL FOUNDATION (Graduate Student Scholarships)

665 Fifth Avenue

New York NY 10022-5370

212/421-8181, ext. 396

FAX: 212-486-0849

E-Mail: jfields@icsc.org

Internet: www.icsc.org

AMOUNT: $5,000

DEADLINE(S): JUN 10

FIELD(S): Retail; Real Estate

For US and Canadian citizens to pursue graduate study in above fields. Grade point average and financial need are considered.

3 awards annually. Not renewable. Send a self-addressed, stamped envelope to Jodi Fields at above address for an application.

97 — INTERNATIONAL FOUNDATION OF EMPLOYEE BENEFIT PLANS (Grants for Research Program)

18700 W. Bluemound Rd.

P.O. Box 69

Brookfield WI 53008-0069

414/786-6710 Ext.8440

FAX: 414/786-8670

E-Mail: research@ifelop.org

Internet: www.ifebp.org

AMOUNT: $5,000 (Grad); $10,000 (Post-Grad)

DEADLINE(S): None

FIELD(S): Business/Finance; Labor/Industrial Relations; Economics; Law; Social/Health Concerns

Open to U.S. or Canadian citizens pursuing a graduate or post-doctoral degree from an accredited institution who have a thesis or dissertation approved by advisor or have worked for a nonprofit or research institution and hold a degree.

Grants to support original research on employee benefit topics (health care, retirement, income security). Write or call for complete information.

98 — INTERNATIONAL INSTITUTE FOR APPLIED SYSTEMS ANALYSIS (Fellowships for Young Scientists' Summer Program at the IIASA in Vienna, Austria)

A-2361 Laxenburg

AUSTRIA

617/576-5019

FAX: 617/576-5050

E-Mail: mcollins@amacad.org

Internet: http://www.iiasa.ac.at

AMOUNT: Airfare and modest living expenses

DEADLINE(S): JAN 15

FIELD(S): Population, global change, economics, air pollution, transportation, forestry resorces, energy stratiegy, risk modeling, dynamic systems modeling

For advanced graduate and predoctoral candidates with research interests compatible with IIASA projects. Must have working level of written and spoken English and academic accomplishments and publications demonstrating superior qualifications.

4-7 annual awards. Contact Dr. Margaret Goud Collins (in U.S.) or Ms. Margaret Traber (in Austria).

99 — ISTITUTO ITALIANO PER GLI STUDI STORICI (Federico Chabod & Adolfo Omodeo Scholarships)

12 Via Benedetto Croce

80134 Naples ITALY

0039/81/551-7159

FAX: 0039/81/551-2390

E-Mail: iiss@iol.it

AMOUNT: 12 million lires

DEADLINE(S): SEP 30

FIELD(S): History; Philosophy; Literature; Arts; Economics

Open to non-Italian citizens who have completed a university degree in the humanities (history, philosophy, & arts) in a non-Italian university. Intended to allow young scholars to participate in the work of the Institute and to complete personal scholarly research with the help of teaching staff of the Institute. Must submit birth certificate, university diploma, scholarly work, program of studies with indication of language skills, research proposal, & reference.

Renewable. Contact Dott.ssa Marta Herling, Secretary, for an application.

100 — ISTITUTO ITALIANO PER GLI STUDI STORICI - ITALIAN INSTITUTE FOR HISTORICAL STUDIES (Federico Chabod & Adolfo Omodeo Scholarships)

Via Benedetto Croce, 12

80134 Napoli ITALY

0039/81-5517159

FAX: 0039/81-5512390

AMOUNT: 12,000,000 Lira

DEADLINE(S): SEP 30

FIELD(S): Humanities; Social Sciences; History; Philosophy; Arts; Economics; Literature

For non-Italian citizens who have completed a university degree in Humanities dept. of a non-Italian university. Intended to allow young scholars to participate in the work of the Institute and to complete personal scholarly research with the help of teaching staff of the Institute. Must include birth certificate, proof of citizenship, university diploma, scholarly work, curriculum of studies w/ indication of language skills, research proposal, & reference letter.

2 awards annually. Contact Marta Herling, Secretary, at above address for an application.

101 — JAMES FORD BELL FOUNDATION (Summer Internship Program)

2925 Dean Pkwy., Ste. 811

Minneapolis MN 55416

612/285-5435

FAX: 612/285-5435

E-Mail: famphiladv@uswest.net

AMOUNT: $4,000 for 3 months

DEADLINE(S): APR 30

FIELD(S): Nonprofit Management; Community Service

Paid summer internships for graduate students pursuing careers in such areas as health and human services, conservation biology, education, and philanthropy. Must have an interest in non-profit management and community service. Preference given to individuals planning to remain in Twin Cities after graduation.

Contact Foundation for a list of internship opportunities after January 1st; students must apply for specific positions at organizations, not through the program itself.

102 — JANSONS LEGAT (Scholarships)

Blommeseter, Norderhov

3512 Honefoss NORWAY

32 1354 65

FAX: 32 1356 26

E-Mail: janlegat@online.no

AMOUNT: NOK 75.000,-

DEADLINE(S): MAR 15

FIELD(S): Business; Industry; Handcraft

Scholarships for Norwegian citizens for career support and/or postgraduate study. Financial need is NOT a factor.

30 awards annually. Contact Reidun Haugen for an application.

103 — JAPANESE AMERICAN CITIZENS LEAGUE (Sumitomo Bank of California Scholarship and Union Bank Scholarship)

1765 Sutter St.

San Francisco CA 94115

415/921-5225

E-Mail: jacl@jacl.org

Internet: www.jacl.org

AMOUNT: Varies

DEADLINE(S): APR 1

FIELD(S): Business; Accounting; Economics; International Trade

Open to JACL members or their children only. For California residents studying at any institution of higher learning (for the Sumitomo Bank Scholarship, the school must be in California), and who are studying in the fields of business, accounting, economics, or international trade.

For membership information or an application, send a self-addressed, stamped envelope to the above address.

104 — JEWISH COMMUNITY CENTERS ASSOCIATION (JCCA Scholarship Program)

15 East 26th Street

New York NY 10010-1579

212/532-4958, ext. 246

FAX: 212/481-4174

E-Mail: Webmaster@jcca.org

Internet: www.jcca.org

AMOUNT: Up to $7,500

DEADLINE(S): FEB 15

FIELD(S): Social Work; Jewish Communal Studies; Physical Education; Early Childhood Education; Cultural Arts

Open to graduate students of the Jewish faith who are enrolled in a master's degree program and are committed to a career in the Jewish community center field in North America. Must have an undergraduate GPA of at least 3.0, leadership potential, and a strong Jewish background.

8 awards annually. Financial need NOT a factor. Contact Michelle Cohen at above address for an application.

105 — JOHN RANKIN FUND (Travel Scholarships in Accounting or Law)

Trustees of the John Rankin Fund,

c/o Jonathan Stone Esq., The Hall

East Ilsley, Newbury RG20 7LW

Written inquiry

AMOUNT: 5,000 pounds

DEADLINE(S): MAR 31

FIELD(S): Accounting, Law

A bi-annual award for either a law or accounting student, barrister, solicitor, or qualified accountant to study abroad. Applicant must be under 26 on Oct. 1 of the year of application. Next award in 2000.

Write to organization for information.

106 — KARLA SCHERER FOUNDATION (Scholarships)

737 N. Michigan Ave., Suite 2330

Chicago IL 60611

312/943-9191

AMOUNT: Varies

DEADLINE(S): MAR 1

FIELD(S): Finance; Economics

Open to women who plan to pursue careers in finance and/or economics in the private manufacturing-based sector. For undergraduate or graduate study at any accredited institution. Send letter stating what school you attend or plan to attend, the courses you plan to take, and how you will use your education in your chosen career.

Renewable. With application request, please include above information as well as a self-addressed, stamped envelope to assure a prompt response.

107 — LADY ALLEN OF HURTWOOD MEMORIAL TRUST (Travel Grants)

21 Aspull Common
Leigh Lancs WN7 3PB ENGLAND
01942-674895

AMOUNT: up to 1,000 pounds sterling

DEADLINE(S): JAN 15

FIELD(S): Welfare And Education Of Children

A travel grant to those whose proposed project will directly benefit their work with children. People working with children and young people may apply, particularly those working with disabled and disadvantaged children. Successful candidates must write up an account of the work which the scholarship has funded. GRANTS ARE NOT FOR ACADEMIC STUDY; ONLY QUALIFIED INDIVIDUALS MAY APPLY.

Contact Dorothy E. Whitaker, Trustee, for application forms—available between May and December each year.

108 — LINCOLN UNIVERSITY (Sir John Ormond Scholarships)

PO Box 94
Canterbury New Zealand
(64) (3) 325 2811
FAX: (64) (3) 325 3850

AMOUNT: NZ$3,000 (post-grad); NZ$11,000 (doctoral)

DEADLINE(S): NOV 1; MAR 31

FIELD(S): Marketing

Open to doctoral and postgraduate students who wish to undertake research at Lincoln University in New Zealand on some aspect of marketing.

2 awards annually. Contact the Scholarships Officer at Lincoln University for an application and information on other scholarship programs.

109 — LONDON CHAMBER OF COMMERCE AND INDUSTRY EXAMINATIONS BOARD (Charles R. E. Bell Fund Scholarships)

Thena House
112 Station Rd.
Sidcup Kent DA15 7BJ ENGLAND UK
081/302-0261

AMOUNT: 1,500 pounds sterling

DEADLINE(S): DEC 31

FIELD(S): Business Administration; Languages

Open to students who are engaged in commerce/business or are commercial education teachers. Scholarships support postgraduate study in the United Kingdom or abroad. Must be UK citizen or legal resident. Financial need is considered.

Contact London Chamber of Commerce for an application.

110 — LONDON SCHOOL OF ECONOMICS AND POLITICAL SCIENCE (Scholarships)

Scholarships Office
Houghton St.
London WC2A 2AE ENGLAND UK
+44 (0) 171 955 7162/7155
FAX: +44 (0) 171 831 1684
E-Mail: scholarships@lse.ac.uk
Internet: www.lse.ac.uk/index/EDUCATE/
CONTACTS.HTM or www.lse.ac.uk/index/
restore/GRADUATE/Financial/text/
funding.htm or www.britcoun.org/eis/
profiles/lse/lsechp.htm

AMOUNT: Varies with award

DEADLINE(S): Varies

FIELD(S): Economics; Accounting; Finance; Political Science; International Relations

Various scholarships, awards, and prizes are available to international students. Several are for students from specific countries, and some are limited to certain fields of study. Some include all expenses, and others pay partial expenses. For undergraduates and graduate students.

Accessing LSE's website and using their "search" option, write in "scholarships," and a vast array of programs will appear.

111 — MACQUARIE BANK (Graduate Management Scholarship)

Secretariat
PO Box H68
Australia Square
Sydney NSW 1210 AUSTRALIA
612/9237 3333
FAX: 612/9237 4544
E-Mail: MBAschol@macquarie.com.au
Internet: www.macquarie.com.au

AMOUNT: US$35,000

DEADLINE(S): OCT

FIELD(S): Business Administration

Must be a citizen or permanent resident of Australia or New Zealand studying for a master of business administration, with work experience reflecting management expertise or potential. Must also be a bone fide candidate for full-time MBA studies and must not have already commenced those studies, either on a part-time or full-time basis. Financial need NOT a factor.

1 award annually. Renewable. Contact Gina Sennitt at Macquarie Bank for an application.

112 — MINISTRY OF THE FLEMISH COMMUNITY (Fellowships)

Embassy of Belgium
3330 Garfield St., NW
Washington DC 20008
202/625-5850/51
FAX: 202/342-8346
E-Mail: flemishcomdc@wizard.net

AMOUNT: Monthly stipend, tuition, & health care coverage

DEADLINE(S): JAN 31

FIELD(S): Art; Music; Humanities; Social Science; Political Science; Law; Economics; Science; Medicine

Open to US citizens under age 35 who wish to pursue graduate or postgraduate studies in Flanders, Belgium.

Contact Flemish Community for registration forms.

113 — MISSISSIPPI OFFICE OF STATE STUDENT FINANCIAL AID (Public Management Graduate Internship Program)

3825 Ridgewood Road
Jackson MS 39211-6453
601/982-6663
1-800-327-2980

AMOUNT: $1,000/month (up to 8 months)

DEADLINE(S): Varies (Established by program coordinator)

FIELD(S): Criminal Justice; Public Administration; Public Policy

For students pursuing a graduate degree in criminal Justice, Public Administration, or Public Policy, this program provides the opportunity to have practical experience working for state or local agencies and offices, including the state legislature. The intern works a semester with the state or local agency. For U.S. residents or eligible non-citizens who possess an alien registration card and who are enrolled at certain universities in Mississippi.

Must have earned a "B" or higher grade in one Quantitative Research Methods course.

114 — NATIONAL AIR TRANSPORTATION ASSOCIATION FOUNDATION (John W. Godwin, Jr., Memorial Scholarship Fund)

4226 King Street
Alexandria VA 22302
808/808-NATA or 703/845-9000
FAX: 703/845-8176

AMOUNT: $2,500

DEADLINE(S): None

FIELD(S): Flight training

Scholarship for flight training for any certificate and/or flight rating issued by the FAA, at any NATA-Member company offering flight training. Must accumulate a minimum of 15 dual or solo flight hours each calendar month.

Contact organization for details.

115 — NATIONAL ASSOCIATION OF PURCHASING MANAGEMENT (Doctoral Dissertation Grant Program)

2055 E. Centennial Circle
PO Box 22160
Tempe AZ 85285-2160
800/888-6276 or 480/752-6276
FAX: 480/752-7890
E-Mail: hjohnson@napm.org
Internet: www.napm.org

AMOUNT: $10,000

DEADLINE(S): JAN 31

FIELD(S): Purchasing & Supply Management

Open to US citizens/permanent residents pursuing a Ph.D. or D.B.A. in purchasing, business, management, logistics, economics, industrial engineering, or related fields at an accredited US university. Must submit transcripts, proposal abstract, letters of recommendation, and curriculum vitae. Financial need NOT a factor.

4 awards annually. Not renewable. Contact Holly LaCroix Johnson, Senior Vice President, for an application.

116 — NATIONAL ASSOCIATION OF WATER COMPANIES—NEW JERSEY CHAPTER (Scholarship)

Elizabethtown Water Co.
600 South Ave.
Westfield NJ 07090
908/654-1234
FAX: 908/232-2719

AMOUNT: $2,500

DEADLINE(S): APR 1

FIELD(S): Business Administration; Biology; Chemistry; Engineering; Communications

For U.S. citizens who have lived in NJ at least 5 years and plan a career in the investor-owned water utility industry in disciplines such as those above. Must be undergrad or graduate student in a 2- or 4-year NJ college or university.

GPA of 3.0 or better required. Contact Gail P. Brady for complete information.

117 — NATIONAL BLACK MBA ASSOCIATION INC. (Annual Scholarship Program)

180 N. Michigan Ave., Suite 1515
Chicago IL 60601
312/236-2622

AMOUNT: Varies

DEADLINE(S): MAR

FIELD(S): Business Management

Open to ethnic minorities enrolled in a business administration or management program at the master's or doctoral level.

Renewable. Write for complete information.

118 — NATIONAL CHAMBER OF COMMERCE FOR WOMEN (Scholarships & Research Grants)

10 Waterside Plaza, Suite 6H
New York NY 10010
212/685-3454

AMOUNT: Varies

DEADLINE(S): None

FIELD(S): Behavioral Science

Scholarships and grants open to women who are post-graduates, graduate students, and professionals in the behavioral sciences. Awards support study and/or research projects. Preference (but not limited) to organizational behavior and business ethics.

Write for complete information.

119 — NATIONAL COUNCIL OF FARMER COOPERATIVES (Graduate Awards)

50 F St., NW, Ste. 900
Washington DC 20001
202/626-8700
FAX: 202/626-8722

AMOUNT: $1,000 (1st prize); $800 (2nd); $600 (3rd)

DEADLINE(S): APR 1

FIELD(S): American Cooperatives

Open to graduate students working on theses or dissertations dealing with some aspect of economics, finance, operation, law, or structure of American cooperatives. May be in such fields as economics, business communications, sociology, etc.

3 awards annually. Not renewable. Contact NCFC Education Foundation for registration form.

120 — NATIONAL CUSTOMS BROKERS & FORWARDERS ASSN OF AMERICA INC (NCBFAA Scholarship)

1200 18th St. NW, Suite 901
Washington DC 20036
202/466-0222

AMOUNT: $5,000

DEADLINE(S): FEB 1

FIELD(S): International Business - Customs Brokerage or Freight Forwarding

Open to family members and employees of regular NCBFAA members who are interested in a career in customs brokerage or freight forwarding. Applicants must have a 2.0 or better GPA and submit a 1,000 to 1,500 word essay.

Write for complete information.

121 — NATIONAL ITALIAN AMERICAN FOUNDATION (Bolla Wines Scholarship)

1860 19th St. NW
Washington DC 20009-5599
202/530-5315

AMOUNT: $1,000

DEADLINE(S): MAY 31

FIELD(S): International studies—emphasis on Italian business or Italian-American history.

For undergraduate or graduate students of Italian heritage with a GPA of 3.0+ and a background in international studies. Must write an essay on "The Importance of Italy in Today's Business World." (3-pages, double spaced, typed.)

Community service and financial need considered. Write for appliacation and details.

122 — NATIONAL RESEARCH COUNCIL (Integrated Manufacturing Predoctoral Fellowships)

2101 Constitution Ave., NW
Washington DC 20418
202/334-2872
E-Mail: infofell@nas.edu
Internet: http://www. nas.edu/fo/index,.html

AMOUNT: $20,000 stipend; up to $15,000 for cost of education

DEADLINE(S): DEC 5

FIELD(S): Any area related to integrated systems of manufacturing or processing—engineering fields and other applied science fields, for example

Predoctoral fellowships sponsored by U.S. Dept. of Energy and administered by the National Research Council. Program seeks to create a pool of Ph.D.s trained in the integrated approach to manufacturing or processing, leading to better utilization of scarce resources, to improved energy efficiency, and to lessened degradation of the environment. For full-time study for up to three years at an appropriate academic institution.

12 awards. Contact above address or website for details.

123 — NATIONAL SOCIETY OF ACCOUNTANTS SCHOLARSHIP FOUNDATION (Stanley H. Stearman Scholarship Award)

1010 North Fairfax Street
Alexandria VA 22314-1574

703/549-6400
FAX: 703/549-2984
E-Mail: snoell@mindspring.com
Internet: www.nsacct.o = AMOUNT: $2,000/yr.

DEADLINE(S): MAR 10

FIELD(S): Accounting

For US or Canadian citizens in undergraduate or graduate programs in the US who have a minimum 3.0 GPA. Must be the spouse, child, grandchild, neice, nephew, or son/daughter-in-law of an active or deceased NSA member who have held membership for at least one year. Must include letter of intent, outlining reasons for seeking award, intended career objective, and how this award would be used to accomplish that objective.

1 award annually. Renewable up to 3 years. See website or contact Susan Noell, Foundation Director, for an application.

124 — NAVAL HISTORICAL CENTER (Internship Program)

Washington Navy Yard
901 M St., SE
Washington DC 20374-5060
202/433-6901
FAX: 202/433-8200
E-Mail: efurgol@nhc.navy.mil
Internet: www.history.navy.mil

AMOUNT: $400 possible honoraria; otherwise, unpaid

DEADLINE(S): None

FIELD(S): Education; History; Public Relations; Design

Registered students of colleges/universities and graduates thereof are eligible for this program, which must be a minimum of 3 weeks, full or part-time. Four specialities available: Curator, Education, Public Relations, and Design. Interns receive orientation & assist in their departments, and must complete individual project which contributes to Center. Must submit a letter of recommendation, unofficial transcript, and writing sample of not less than 1,000 words.

Contact Dr. Edward M. Furgol, Curator, for an application.

125 — NEW YORK CITY DEPT. CITYWIDE ADMINISTRATIVE SERVICES (Urban Fellows Program)

1 Centre St., 24th Fl.
New York NY 10007

212/487-5600
FAX: 212/487-5720

AMOUNT: $18,000 stipend

DEADLINE(S): JAN 20

FIELD(S): Public Administration; Urban Planning; Government; Public Service; Urban Affairs

Fellowship program provides one academic year (9 months) of full-time work experience in urban government. Open to graduating college seniors and recent college graduates. U.S. citizenship required.

Write for complete information.

126 — NEW YORK STATE HIGHER EDUCATION SERVICES CORPORATION (N.Y. State Regents Professional/Health Care Opportunity Scholarships)

Cultural Education Center, Rm. 5C64
Albany NY 12230
518/486-1319
Internet: www.hesc.com

AMOUNT: $1,000-$10,000/yr.

DEADLINE(S): Varies

FIELD(S): Medicine and dentistry and related fields, architecture, nursing, psychology, audiology, landscape architecture, social work, chiropractic, law, pharmacy, accounting, speech language pathology

For NY state residents who are economically disadvantaged and members of a minority group underrepresented in the chosen profession and attending school in NY state. Some programs carry a service obligation in New York for each year of support. For U.S. citizens or qualifying noncitizens.

Medical/dental scholarships require one year of professional work in NY.

127 — NEW YORK STATE SENATE (Legislative Fellows Program; R. J. Roth Journalism Fellowship; R. A. Wiebe Public Service Fellowship)

NYS Senate Student Programs Office, 90 South Swan St., Rm. 401
Albany NY 12247
518/455-2611
FAX: 518/432-5470
E-Mail: students@senate.state.ny.us

AMOUNT: $25,000 stipend (not a scholarship)

DEADLINE(S): MAY (first Friday)

FIELD(S): Political Science; Government; Public Service; Journalism; Public Relations

One year programs for U.S. citizens who are grad students and residents of New York state or enrolled in accredited programs in New York state. Fellows work as regular legislative staff members of the office to which they are assigned. The Roth Fellowship is for communications/journalism majors, and undergrads may be considered for this program.

14 fellowships per year. Fellowships take place at the New York State Legislative Office. Write for complete information.

128 — NEW YORK STATE THEATRE INSTITUTE (Internships in Theatrical Production)

155 River St.
Troy NY 12180
518/274-3573
nysti@crisny.org
Internet: www.crisny.org/not-for-profit/nysti/int.htm

AMOUNT: None

DEADLINE(S): None

FIELD(S): Fields of study related to theatrical production, including box office and PR

Internships for college students, high school seniors, and educators-in-residence interested in developing skills in above fields. Unpaid, but college credit is earned. Located at Russell Sage College in Troy, NY. Gain experience in box office, costumes, education, electrics, music, stage management, scenery, properties, performance, and public relations. Interns come from all over the world.

Must be associated with an accredited institution. See website for more information. Call Ms. Arlene Leff, Intern Director at above location. Include your postal mailing address.

129 — NINETY-NINES, SAN FERNANDO VALLEY CHAPTER/VAN NUYS AIRPORT (Aviation Career Scholarships)

PO Box 8160
Van Nuys CA 91409
818/989-0081

AMOUNT: $3,000

DEADLINE(S): MAY 1

FIELD(S): Aviation Careers

For men and women of the greater Los Angeles area pursuing careers as professional pilots, flight instructors, mechanics, or other aviation career specialists. Applicants must be at least 21 years of age and US citizens.

3 awards annually. Send self-addressed, stamped, business-sized envelope to above address for application.

130 — OAK RIDGE INSTITUTE FOR SCIENCE AND EDUCATION (Minority Student Administrative Summer Internship Program)

P.O. Box 117
Oak Ridge TN 37831-0117
423/576-6051 or 423/576-3165

AMOUNT: $335 to $420/wk.+ travel reimbursement

DEADLINE(S): FEB (mid-month)

FIELD(S): Business administration, management, finance, accounting, human resources, training, economics, public administration, computer science, and instructional technology

For minority students who have completed their junior or senior year in college or their first year of graduate school. Must be majoring in one of the fields listed above. A summer program, ten to twelve weeks, located at Oak Ridge, TN.

Funded through U.S. Department of Energy or Oak Ridge Associated Universities

131 — ONTARIO MINISTRY OF EDUCATION AND TRAINING (John Charles Polanyi Prizes)

189 Red River Rd.,
4th Floor
Box 4500
Thunder Bay Ontario P7B 6G9 CANADA
800/465-3957
TDD: 800/465-3958
Internet: osap.gov.on.ca

AMOUNT: $15,000

DEADLINE(S): Varies

FIELD(S): Physics; Chemistry; Physiology; Medicine; Literature; Economics

Monetary prizes are awarded to Canadian citizens/permanent residents who are continuing postdoctoral studies at an Ontario university. Awards are designed to encourage and reward academic excellence.

5 awards annually. Contact your university or the Ontario Council of Graduate Studies for an application.

132 — OPERA AMERICA (Fellowship Program)

1156 15th St. NW, Suite 810
Washington DC 20005
202/293-4466
FAX: 202/393-0735

AMOUNT: $1,200/month + transportation & housing

DEADLINE(S): MAY 7

FIELD(S): General or Artistic Administration, Technical Direction, or Production Management

Open to opera personnel, individuals entering opera administration from other disciplines, and graduates of arts administration or technical/production training programs who are committed to a career in opera in North America.

Must be U.S. or Canadian citizen or legal resident lawfully eligible to receive stipend.

133 — POPULATION COUNCIL (Fellowships in Population Sciences)

One Dag Hammarskjold Plaza
New York NY 10017
212/339-0636
FAX: 212/755-6052
E-Mail: rmohanam@popcouncil.org
Internet: www.popcouncil.org

AMOUNT: $25,000/yr. for 2 years

DEADLINE(S): OCT 31

FIELD(S): Population Sciences

Postdoctoral fellowships for study in population sciences in Nairobi, Kenya, Africa. Open to citizens of any country.

Two awards per year. Selection criteria will stress academic excellence and prospective contribution to the population field. For information and applications contact Raji Mohanam at above address. In Kenya, contact: Carol Libamira, APPRC Coordinator, Population Council, Mutichoice Towers, Upper Hill, P.O. Box 17643, Nairobi, Kenya. 254/2.713.480/1-3.

134 — POPULATION COUNCIL (Fellowships in Social Sciences)

Policy Research Division
One Dag Hammarskjold Plaza
New York NY 10017
212/339-0671
FAX: 212/755-6052
E-Mail: ssfellowship@popcouncil.org
Internet: www.popcouncil.org

AMOUNT: Monthly stipend, partial tuition/fees, transportation, book/supply allowance, & health insurance

DEADLINE(S): DEC 15

FIELD(S): Population Studies; Demography; Sociology; Anthropology; Economics; Public Health; Geography

Twelve-month award is open to doctoral & postdoctoral scholars for advanced training in above fields that deal with developing world. Doctoral students may request support for dissertation fieldwork/writing. Postdoctorates may pursue research, midcareer training, or resident training. Based on academic excellence, prospective contribution, & well-conceived research proposal. Preference given to those from developing countries.

See website or contact Fellowship Coordinator for an application.

135 — PRESIDENT'S COMMISSION ON WHITE HOUSE FELLOWSHIPS

712 Jackson Place NW
Washington DC 20503
202/395-4522
FAX: 202/395-6179
E-Mail: almanac@ace.esusda.gov

AMOUNT: Wage (up to GS-14 Step 3; approximately $65,000 in 1995)

DEADLINE(S): DEC 1

FIELD(S): Public Service; Government; Community Involvement; Leadership

Mid-career professionals spend one year as special assistants to senior executive branch officials in Washington. Highly competitive. Non-partisan; no age or educational requirements. Fellowship year runs September 1 through August 31.

1,200 candidates applying for 11 to 19 fellowships each year. Write for complete information.

136 — PRESS CLUB OF DALLAS FOUNDATION (Scholarship)

400 N. Olive
Dallas TX 75201
214/740-9988

AMOUNT: $1,000-$3,000

DEADLINE(S): APR 15

FIELD(S): Journalism and Public Relations

Open to students who are at least sophmore level in undergraduate studies or working towards a masters degree in the above fields in a Texas college or university. This scholarship is renewable by re-application.

Write to Carol Wortham at the above address for complete information.

137 — RESEARCH COUNCIL OF NORWAY (Senior Scientist Visiting Fellowship)

P.O. Box 2700 St. Hanshaugen
N-0131 Oslo NORWAY
+47 22 03 70 00
FAX: +47 22 03 70 01
E-Mail: intstip@nfr.no
Internet: www.forskningsradet.no

AMOUNT: NOK 25,000-1st 2 months; NOK 10,000-succeeding months

DEADLINE(S): Varies

FIELD(S): Bioproduction & Processing (including agriculture and veterinary science); Industry & Energy; Culture & Society (including social sciences and the humanities); Medicine & Health; Environment & Development; Science & Technology

Fellowships for scientists to work at Norwegian research institutes. Project funding does not include salary; expenses connected with the stay in Norway are covered.

For a list of institutions, contact the Research Council at above location. Then apply to institution, which then will submit fellowship application.

138 — RESOURCES FOR THE FUTURE (Joseph L. Fisher Dissertation Fellowships)

1616 P Street NW
Washington DC 20036-1400
202/328-5000
Internet: www.rff.org

AMOUNT: $12,000/yr

DEADLINE(S): FEB 26

FIELD(S): Economics and other Social Sciences related to environment, natural resources, or energy

Fellowship to graduate students in the final year of their dissertatio research in the above fields.

All information is on website. NO fax submissions.

139 — ROYAL THAI EMBASSY, OFFICE OF EDUCATIONAL AFFAIRS (Revenue Dept. Scholarships for Thai Students)

1906 23rd St. NW
Washington DC 20008
202/667-9111 or 202/667-8010
FAX: 202/265-7239

AMOUNT: Varies

DEADLINE(S): APR

FIELD(S): Computer science (telecommunications), law, economics, finanace, business administration

Scholarships for students under age 35 from Thailand who have been accepted to study in the U.S or U.K. for the needs of the Revenue Dept., Ministry of Finance. Must pursue any level degree in one of the above fields.

Selections are based on academic records, employment history, and advisor recommendations.

140 — S.S. HUEBNER FOUNDATION FOR INSURANCE EDUCATION (Fellowships)

Univ. Pennsylvania
430 Vance Hall
3733 Spruce St.
Philadelphia PA 19104-6301
215/898-9631

AMOUNT: Tuition & fees + $14,000 stipend

DEADLINE(S): FEB 1

FIELD(S): Insurance; Risk; Actuarial Science

Doctoral and postdoctoral fellowships tenable at the University of Pennsylvania's Wharton School of Business. US or Canadian citizenship required.

3 new awards annually. Write for complete information.

141 — SCOTTISH RITE CHARITABLE FOUNDATION (Research Grants)

Roeher Institute, Kinsmen Bldg.
4700 Keele St.
North York Ontario M3J 1P3 CANADA
416/661-9611
TDD: 416/661-2023
FAX: 416/661-5701
E-Mail: mail@aacl.org
Internet: www.aacl.org

AMOUNT: $10,000 (max. grads); $35,000 (max. postdocs)

DEADLINE(S): APR 30

FIELD(S): Human Services; Intellectual Disability

Open to Canadian citizens/landed immigrants enrolled in masters or doctoral programs at Canadian universities. Must state intent to pursue career in Canada and have definite research projects supported by an academic advisor or a Roeher Institute associate/consultant. Also available to postdoctoral researchers.

Renewable. Contact the Secretary, Awards Adjudicating Committee, at the Scottish Rite for an application and details on preferred research topics.

142 — SOCIAL SCIENCE RESEARCH COUNCIL (International Predissertation Fellowship Program)

810 Seventh Ave.
New York NY 10019
212/277-2700

AMOUNT: Varies

DEADLINE(S): Varies (TBA by participating universities)

FIELD(S): Economics; Political Science; Psychology; Sociology; other Social Science disciplines

Open to Ph.D. candidates enrolled in social science programs at 23 select universities and interested in supplementing disciplinary skills with area and language studies or acquiring advanced disciplinary training. Study program is preparation for research on Africa, Central Asia & the Caucasus, China, Latin America, the Caribbean, Near & Middle East, and South or Southeast Asia.

Contact Ellen Perecman for an application.

143 — SOCIAL SCIENCE RESEARCH COUNCIL (Program in Applied Economics)

810 Seventh Ave., 31st Fl.
New York NY 10019
212/377-2700

FAX: 212/377-2727
E-Mail: pae@ssrc.org
Internet: www.ssrc.org

AMOUNT: Varies

DEADLINE(S): MAR 5

FIELD(S): Economics

Open to students who have completed their first year of graduate studies in an economics (or related) Ph.D. program. Must show keen analytical aptitude and a solid grasp of the theories and methods taught in the core courses. Must also demonstrate genuine interest in analyzing substantive problems and an openness to new approaches in economics and other related disciplines.

See website or contact SSRC for an application after November 1st. Announcement of awards in early May.

144 — SOIL AND WATER CONSERVATION SOCIETY (SWCS Internships)

7515 N.E. Ankeny Road
Ankeny IA 50021-9764
515/289-2331 or 1-800/THE-SOIL
FAX: 515/289-1227
E-Mail: charliep@swcs.org
Internet: www.swcs.org

AMOUNT: Varies—most are uncompensated

DEADLINE(S): Varies

FIELD(S): Journalism, marketing, database management, meeting planning, public policy research, environmental education, landscape architecture

Internships for undergraduates and graduates to gain experience in the above fields as they relate to soil and water conservation issues. Intership openings vary through the year in duration, compensation, and objective. SWCS will coordinate particulars with your academic advisor.

Contact SWCS for internship availability at any timne during the year or see website for jobs page.

145 — SONOMA CHAMBOLLE-MUSIGNY SISTER CITIES, INC. (Henri Cardinaux Memorial Scholarship)

Chamson Scholarship Committee
PO Box 1633
Sonoma CA 95476-1633
707/939-1344
FAX: 707/939-1344
E-Mail: Baileysci@vom.com

AMOUNT: up to $1,500 (travel + expenses)

DEADLINE(S): JUL 15

FIELD(S): Culinary Arts; Wine Industry; Art; Architecture; Music; History; Fashion

Hands-on experience working in above or similiar fields & living with a family in small French village in Burgundy or other French city. Must be Sonoma County, CA, resident at least 18 years of age & be able to communicate in French. Transcripts, employer recommendation, photograph, & essay (stating why, where, & when) required.

1 award. Non-renewable. Also offers opportunity for candidate in Chambolle-Musigny to obtain work experience & cultural exposure in Sonoma, CA.

146 — STOCKHOLM UNIVERSITY - INTERNATIONAL GRADUATE PROGRAMME (Master's Programme in Swedish Social Studies)

Universitetsvagen 10F
Frescati
S-106 91 Stockholm SWEDEN
+46 8 163466
FAX: +46 8 155508
E-Mail: igp@statsvet.su.se
Internet: www.statsvet.su.se/IGP/home.html

AMOUNT: Tuition

DEADLINE(S): MAR 1

FIELD(S): Social Sciences; Economics; History; Anthropology; Sociology; Social Work; Political Science

Open to students who have completed a university degree in the social sciences with one of the above majors and who wish to study at Stockholm University in Sweden. Language of instruction is English.

Contact Stockholm University for an application.

147 — SVENSKA HANDELSBANKEN FOUNDATIONS FOR SOCIAL SCIENCE RESEARCH (Research Grants)

Secretary of the board
S-10670 Stockholm SWEDEN
Written Inquiry

AMOUNT: Stipend + expenses

DEADLINE(S): FEB 28

FIELD(S): Economics/Social Sciences

Graduate research grants in economics and social science. Area of interest must concern international payments and capital movement, the domestic payments, markets, and economic planning.

Grants are tenable in Sweden for up to one year. Renewable depending upon progress. Non-Swedish graduate students are requested to work in Sweden under supervision of a Swedish research institution. Write for complete information.

148 — SWEDISH INFORMATION SERVICE (Bicentennial Swedish-American Exchange Fund)

Bicentennial Fund,
One Dag Hammarskjold Plaza, 45th Floor
New York NY 10017-2201
212/483-2550
FAX: 212/752-4789
E-Mail: swedinfor@ix.netcom.com

AMOUNT: 20,000 Swedish crowns (for three- to six-week intensive study visits in Sweden)

DEADLINE(S): FEB (Friday of the first week)

FIELD(S): Politics, public administration, working life, human environment, mass media, business and industry, education and culture

Program is to provide opportunity for those in a positio to influence public opinion and contribute to the development of their society. Must be U.S. citizen or permanent resident. Must have necessary experience and education for fulfilling his/her project.

Send SASE to above address for details.

149 — THE AMERICAN ASSOCIATION OF ATTORNEY-CERTIFIED PUBLIC ACCOUNTANTS FOUNDATION (Student Writing Competition)

24196 Alicia Parkway, Suite K
Mission Viejo CA 92691
800/CPA-ATTY
FAX: 714/768-7062

AMOUNT: $250-$1,500

DEADLINE(S): APR 1

FIELD(S): Accounting; Law

Essay contest for accounting and/or law students.

Contact organization for current topics and rules.

150 — TRANSPORTATION ASSOCIATION OF CANADA (TAC Scholarships)

2323 St. Laurent Blvd.
Ottawa Ontario K1G 458 CANADA
613/736-1350
E-Mail: mcomeau@tac-atc.ca
Internet: www.tac-atc.ca

AMOUNT: $3,000; $3,250; $4,000, $5,000, and $6,000

DEADLINE(S): MAR 1

FIELD(S): Transportation

Scholarships to financially assist graduate students displaying high promise of future achievement in transportation. Award can be used worldwide. For Canadian citizens or legal residents.

5 awards per year. 1 award is renewable. Write for complete information.

151 — TRANSPORTATION CLUBS INTERNATIONAL (Ginger & Fred Deines Canada Scholarships)

P.O. Box 1072
Glen Alpine NC 28628
206/549-2251

AMOUNT: $500 and/or $1,000

DEADLINE(S): MAY 31

FIELD(S): Transportation Logistics; Traffic Management

For a student of Canadian naitonality and enrolled in a school in Canada or U.S. in a degree or vocational program in the above or related areas.

Type an essay of not more than 200 words on why you have chosen transportation or an allied field as a career path. Include your objectives. Send an SASE for further details.

152 — TRANSPORTATION CLUBS INTERNATIONAL (Ginger & Fred Deines Mexico Scholarships)

P.O. Box 1072
Glen Alpine NC 28688
206/549-2251

AMOUNT: $500 and/or $1,000

DEADLINE(S): May 31

FIELD(S): Transportation; Traffic Management

Open to students of Mexican nationality who are enrolled in a Mexican or U.S. institution of higher learning in a degree or vocational program in the above or related areas.

Type an essay of not more than 200 words on why you have chosen transportation or an allied field as a career path. Include your objectives. Send SASE for complete information.

153 — U.S. DEPARTMENT OF TRANSPORTATION (Dwight D. Eisenhower Transportation Fellowships)

U.S. Dept. of Transportation, Fed. Hwy. Admin., 6300 Georgetown Pike, HHI-20
McLean VA 22101-2296
703/235-0538

AMOUNT: Varies

DEADLINE(S): FEB

FIELD(S): Transportation—such majors as chemistry; materials science; corrosion; civil, chemical, & electronics engineering; structures; human factors; computer science; psychology.

Research fellowships for undergrads and grad students at any Dept. of Transportation facility or selected IHE. For three to twelve months. Research must focus on transportation-related research and development in the above fields.

Contact Ilene Payne, Director, Universities and grants Programs at above location for details.

154 — U.S. DEPT. OF HEALTH & HUMAN SERVICES (Indian Health Service Health Professions Scholarship Program)

Twinbrook Metro Plaza, Suite 100
12300 Twinbrook Pkwy.
Rockville MD 20852
301/443-0234
FAX: 301/443-4815
Internet: www.ihs.gov/Recruitment/DHPS/SP/SBTOC3.asp

AMOUNT: Tuition + fees & monthly stipend of $938.

DEADLINE(S): APR 1

FIELD(S): Health professions, accounting, social work

Open to Native Americans or Alaska natives who are graduate students or college juniors or seniors in a program leading to a career in a fields listed above. U.S. citizenship required. Renewable annually with reapplication.

Scholarship recipients must intend to serve the Indian people. They incur a one-year service obligation to the IHS for each year of support for a minimum of two years. Write for complete information.

155 — UNIVERSITY OF GLASGOW (Post-graduate Awards in Law & Financial Studies)

University of Glasgow
Glasgow G12 8QQ SCOTLAND UK
041/330-4551

AMOUNT: Research council maintenance equivalent

DEADLINE(S): FEB 28

FIELD(S): Financial Studies/Law

Research in topic specified by applicant approved by school of law. For study at the university of Glasgow. Must have good honours degree.

Awarded annually. Renewable. Contact Mrs. A.E. Wilson Clerk of the faculty for complete information.

156 — UNIVERSITY OF MANCHESTER (Awards for Research)

Secretary, Research and Graduate Support Unit
Manchester M13 9PL England
0161 275 2035
FAX: 0161 275 2445/7216

AMOUNT: Maintenance grant (approx) 5000 pounds p.a. plus payment of UK tuition fees.

DEADLINE(S): MAY 1

FIELD(S): Arts, Economics, Social Studies, Education, Science, Engineering, Biological Sciences, Law

The university offers research studentships for doctoral research in all disciplines. These awards are highly competitive. Applicants should hold at least a 2:1 degree or equivalent. Awards are renewable for up to 2 years.

Approx 50 awards per year. Please contact address above for complete information.

157 — UNIVERSITY OF MANITOBA (J.W. Dafoe Graduate Fellowship)

Faculty of Grad Studies
500 University Ctr.
Winnipeg Manitoba R3T 2N2 CANADA
204/474-9836
Internet: www.umanitoba.ca/faculties/graduate_studies/forms

AMOUNT: $15,000/yr.

DEADLINE(S): FEB 15

FIELD(S): Political Studies; Economics; History; International Relations

Open to entering M.A. students at the University of Manitoba in one of the above departments; area of study must focus on international relations.

1 award award annually. Renewable an additional year. Contact Faculty of Graduate Studies for an application.

158 — UNIVERSITY OF MARYLAND INSTITUTE FOR ADVANCED COMPUTER STUDIES (Graduate Fellowships)

University of Maryland, UMIACS
College Park MD 20742
301/405-6722
E-Mail: fellows@umiacs.umd.edu
Internet: www.umiacs.umd.edu/fellow.html

AMOUNT: $18,000/yr. + tuition, health benefits, office space, etc.

DEADLINE(S): JAN 15

FIELD(S): Computer science, electrical engineering, geography, philosophy, linguistics, business, and management

Two-year graduate fellowships in the above fields for full-time students interested in interdisciplinary applications of computing at the Univ. of Maryland. After the first two years, external research funds may be provided to continue support for the fellow, depending upon satisfactory progress and the availability of funds.

Three new awards each year. Selection will be based on academic excellence and compatibility between students' research interest and those of UMIACS faculty.

159 — UNIVERSITY OF NORTH TEXAS (Merchandising and Hospitality Scholarships)

Dean, School of Merchandising/Hospitality Management, P.O. Box 311100
Denton TX 76203-1100
817/565-2436
Internet: www.unt.edu/scholarships/smhm.htm

AMOUNT: Varies

DEADLINE(S): Varies

FIELD(S): Business: Merchandising and Hospitality Management

Several scholarships for students in the above fields are offered at the University of North Texas. Specialties and eligibility requirements vary.

See website for more information. Contact school for details.

160 — UNIVERSITY OF VIRGINIA (Albert Gallatin Fellowship in International Affairs)

International Studies Office
208 Minor Hall
Charlottesville VA 22903
804/982-3010
FAX: 804/982-3011
E-Mail: rgd@virginia.edu
Internet: www.virginia.edu/~intstu

AMOUNT: $11,250 and round trip travel from New York to Geneva

DEADLINE(S): MAR 2

FIELD(S): International studies

Nine-month fellowships for American doctoral candidates in international studies for study at the Graduate Institute for International Studies, Geneva; Switzerland. Must have a fairly functional ability in French as well as English proficiency.

Term is October through June. Write for complete information.

161 — W.E. UPJOHN INSTITUTE FOR EMPLOYMENT RESEARCH (Dissertation Award)

300 S. Westnedge Avenue
Kalamazoo MI 49007-4686
616/343-5541
FAX: 616/343-7310
E-Mail: webmaster@we.upjohninst.org
Internet: www.upjohninst.org

AMOUNT: $2,000 (1st prize); up to 2 $500 honorable mentions may also be given

DEADLINE(S): JUL 7

FIELD(S): Employment & Unemployment related issues

Dissertations are evaluated on policy relevance, technical quality of the research, potential impact on real-world problems, & presentation. Any person whose dissertation has been accepted from July 1st of the previous year to June 30th of the current year is eligible. Applicants must send a 10-page summary of the dissertation and a letter of endorsement from their dissertation advisor.

1 award annually. See website or write to above address for details.

162 — W.E. UPJOHN INSTITUTE FOR EMPLOYMENT RESEARCH (Grant)

300 South Westnedge Avenue
Kalamazoo MI 49007-4686
616/343-5541
FAX: 616/343-7310
E-Mail: webmaster@we.upjohninst.org
Internet: www.upjohninst.org

AMOUNT: up to $45,000 + $25,000 to conduct surveys/assemble data

DEADLINE(S): JAN 26

FIELD(S): Employment Relationships, Low Wages/ Public Policy, Social Insurance

Grants are for proposals that will lead to a book that contributes to the Institute's research program. Proposals evaluated on contribution to important policy issues/professional literature, technical merit, professional qualifications, likelihood of timely completion of project, cost effectiveness, & consistency with Institute's interests. Must submit 8 copies of both a 3-page summary & curriculum vitae. Subset of applicants will then submit 15-page proposal.

Fax and e-mail submissions will not be accepted. See website for details or write to above address.

163 — WOLCOTT FOUNDATION (Fellowships)

402 Beasley St.
Monroe LA 71203-4006
318/343-1602

AMOUNT: Tuition, books, & fees + $1,800 relocation allowance loan

DEADLINE(S): JAN 15

FIELD(S): Business Administration; Public Service; International Relations; Government; Public Admnistration

Open to students enrolled in accredited programs leading to a master's degree. Must be US citizen and have a minimum 3.0 GPA. Preference given to applicants with Masonic background. Fellowships are for a maximum of 36 semester hours and are tenable at George Washington University in Washington, DC.

Contact Dr. Beryl C. Franklin for an application.

164 — WOMEN IN DEFENSE (HORIZONS Scholarship Foundation)

NDIA
2111 Wilson Blvd., Ste. 400
Arlington VA 22201-3061
703/247-2552
FAX: 703/522-1885
E-Mail: dnwlee@moon.jic.com
Internet: www.adpa.org/wid/horizon/ Scholar.htm

AMOUNT: $500+

DEADLINE(S): NOV 1; JUL 1

FIELD(S): Engineering, Computer Science, Physics, Mathematics, Business, Law, International Relations, Political Science, Operations Research, Economics, and fields relevant to a career in the areas of national security and defense.

For women who are U.S. citizens, have minimum GPA of 3.25, demonstrate financial need, are currently enrolled at an accredited university/college (full- or part-time—both grads and undergrad juniors/seniors are eligible), and demonstrate interest in pursuing a career related to national security.

Application is online or send SASE, #10 envelope, to Woody Lee, HORIZONS Scholarship Director.

165 — WOMEN'S SPORTS FOUNDATION (Dorothy Harris Endowed Scholarship)

Eisenhower Park
East Meadow NY 11554
800/227-3988
FAX: 516/542-4716
E-Mail: WoSport@aol.com
Internet: www.lifetimetv.com/WoSport

AMOUNT: $1,500

DEADLINE(S): DEC 11

FIELD(S): Physical Education; Sports Management; Sports Psychology; Sports Sociology

For female graduate students who will pursue a full-time course of study in one of the above fields at an accredited graduate school in the Fall.

1-2 awards annually. Awarded in March. See website or write to above address for details.

166 — WOMEN'S SPORTS FOUNDATION (Jackie Joyner-Kersee & Zina Garrison Minority Internships)

Eisenhower Park
East Meadow NY 11554
800/227-3988
FAX: 516/542-4716
E-Mail: WoSport@aol.com
Internet: www.lifetimetv.com/WoSport

AMOUNT: $4,000-$5,000

DEADLINE(S): Ongoing

FIELD(S): Sports-related fields

Provides women of color an opportunity to gain experience in a sports-related career and interact in the sports community. May be undergraduates, college graduates, graduate students, or women in a career change. Internships are located at the Women's Sports Foundation in East Meadow, New York.

4-6 awards annually. See website or write to above address for details.

167 — WOODS HOLE OCEANOGRAPHIC INSTITUTION (Research Fellowships in Marine Policy and Ocean Management)

360 Woods Hole Road
Woods Hole MA 02543-1541
508/289-2219
FAX: 508/457-2188
E-Mail: mgately@whoi.edu
Internet: www.whoi.edu

AMOUNT: Varies

DEADLINE(S): FEB 16

FIELD(S): Social Sciences, Law, Natural Sciences

For professionals in the above fields who wish to apply their training to investigations of problems involving the use of the oceans. WHOI's objective is to provide a year-long advanced learning experience in ocean policy problems involving the interdisciplinary application of social science and natural science to marine policy problems. Fields currently emphasized: economics, statistics, public policy, natural resource management, and international relations.

For an application/more information, contact the Education Office, Clark Laboratory 223, MS #31, at above address.

168 — WORLD BANK (Graduate Scholarship Program)

1818 H St., NW, Rm. M-4035
Washington DC 20433
Written inquiry

AMOUNT: Tuition + fees, allowance, travel, etc.

DEADLINE(S): FEB 1

FIELD(S): Social sciences, law, business, public administration

For nationals of World Bank member countries under the age of 40. Must have a superior academic record, at least two years' experience in public service engaged in development-related activities, and have gained admittance to a university to pursue a post-graduate degree. Must return to hom country after degree.

For two years.

169 — WORLD LEISURE AND RECREATION ASSOCIATION (Scholarships)

WLRA Secretariat, 3 Canyon Court West
Lethbridge AB T1K 6V1 CANADA
403/381-6144
FAX: 403/381-6144
E-Mail: wlra@hg.uleth.ca
Internet: www.worldleisure.org

AMOUNT: Varies

DEADLINE(S): FEB 1

FIELD(S): Recreation & Leisure Studies

Scholarships intended to allow college seniors or graduate students in recreation or leisure services programs to attend international meetings/conferences or conventions, thereby gaining a broader perspective of world leisure and recreation.

See website or contact WLRA for an application.

170 — WYOMING TRUCKING ASSOCIATION (Scholarships)

PO Box 1909
Casper WY 82602
Written Inquiry

AMOUNT: $250-$300

DEADLINE(S): MAR 1

FIELD(S): Transportation Industry

For Wyoming high school graduates enrolled in a Wyoming college, approved trade school, or the University of Wyoming. Must be pursuing a course of study which will result in a career in the transportation industry in Wyoming, including but not limited to: safety, environmental science, diesel mechanics, truck driving, vocational trades, business management, sales management, computer skills, accounting, office procedures, and management.

1-10 awards annually. Write to WYTA for an application.

171 — Y'S MEN INTERNATIONAL - US AREA (Alexander Scholarship Loan Fund)

12405 W. Lewis Ave.
Avondale AZ 85323-6518
Written Inquiry

AMOUNT: $1,000-$1,500/yr.

DEADLINE(S): MAY 30; OCT 30

FIELD(S): Business Administration; Youth Leadership

Open to US citizens/permanent residents with a strong desire to pursue professional YMCA service. Must be YMCA staff pursuing undergraduate or graduate study and demonstrate financial need. Repayment of loan is waived if recipient enters YMCA employment after graduation.

Send self-addressed, business-sized envelope plus $1 for postage & handling to above address for an application.

SCHOOL OF EDUCATION

172 — BUSINESS & PROFESSIONAL WOMEN'S FOUNDATION (BPW Career Advancement Scholarship Program)

2012 Massachusetts Ave., NW
Washington DC 20036-1070
202/293-1200, ext. 169
FAX: 202/861-0298
Internet: www.bpwusa.org

AMOUNT: $500-$1,000

DEADLINE(S): APR 15

FIELD(S): Biology, Science, Education, Engineering, Social Science, Paralegal, Humanities, Business, Math, Computers, Law, MD, DD

For women (US citizens) aged 25+ accepted into accredited program at US institution (+Puerto Rico & Virgin Islands). Must graduate within 12 to 24 months from the date of grant and demonstrate critical finanacial need. Must have a plan to upgrade skills, train for a new career field, or to enter/re-enter the job market.

Full- or part-time study. For info see website or send business-sized, self-addressed, double-stamped envelope.

173 — CHARLES A. AND ANNE MORROW LINDBERGH FOUNDATION (Grants for Research Projects)

2150 Third Ave., N, Ste. 310
Anoka MN 55303-2200
612/576-1596
FAX: 612/576-1664
E-Mail: lindbergh@isd.net
Internet: www.isd.net/lindbergh

AMOUNT: $10,580 (max.)

DEADLINE(S): JUN 15

FIELD(S): Aviation; Aerospace; Agriculture; Education; Arts; Humanities; Biomedical Research; Exploration; Health & Population Sciences; Intercultural Communication; Waste Disposal Minimization & Management.; Adaptive Technology; Conservation

Open to individuals whose proposed projects represent a significant contribution toward the achievement of balance between the advance of technology and preservation of the natural environment. Financial need NOT a factor. Funding is NOT for tuition.

10 awards annually. See website for application.

174 — GATES MILLENIUM SCHOLARS PROGRAM (Scholarships for Graduate Students)

8260 Willow Oaks Corporate Dr.
Fairfax VA 22031-4511
877/690-4677
Internet: www.gmsp.org

AMOUNT: Varies

DEADLINE(S): FEB 1

FIELD(S): Engineering; Mathematics; Science; Education; Library Science

College presidents, professors, & deans may nominate graduate students who are African-Americans, Native Americans, Hispanic Americans, or Asian Americans in above fields. Based on academic performance, commitment to academic study, involvement in community service & school activities, potential for leadership, career goals, and financial need. Must submit transcripts and letters of recommendation. Must be US citizen with a minimum 3.3 GPA

Application materials available November 1st; scholars will be notified in May. Funded by the Bill & Melinda Gates Foundation, and administered by the United Negro College Fund.

175 — JAMES MADISON MEMORIAL FELLOWSHIP (Fellowship for Teachers)

2000 K St. NW
Washington DC 20006
202/653-8700 or 1-800/525-6928
FAX: 202/653-6045
Internet: www.jamesmadison.com

AMOUNT: $24,000 prorated over study period

DEADLINE(S): MAR 1

FIELD(S): Teaching American History/government, or social studies—concentration on the U.S. Constitution

Fellowships for teachers (senior fellows) in grades 7-12 in the above fields to pursue an MA degree. Also for full-time college seniors and grad students (junior fellows). U.S. citizens or U.S. nationals. Fellows are selected from each state and from D.C., Puerto Rico, Guam, Virgin Islands, American Samoa, Northern Mariana Islands, and Palau. Program designed to enhance teaching about the U.S. Constitution.

Application is on website or contact: American College Testing, P.O. Box 4030, Iowa City, IA 52243-4030; 800/525-6928; E-Mail: Recogprog@ACT-ACT4-PO.act.org

176 — JAPANESE AMERICAN CITIZENS LEAGUE (Minoru Yasui Memorial Scholarship)

1765 Sutter St.
San Francisco CA 94115
415/921-5225

FAX: 415/931-4671
E-Mail: jacl@jacl.org
Internet: www.jacl.org

AMOUNT: Varies

DEADLINE(S): APR 1

FIELD(S): Human & Civil Rights; Sociology; Law; Education

Open to JACL members or their children only. For graduate students with a strong interest in human and civil rights. Student must be currently enrolled in, or planning to enroll in, an accredited graduate school. Financial need NOT a factor.

40 awards annually. For membership information or an application, send a self-addressed, stamped envelope to above address.

177 — LOUISIANA OFFICE OF STUDENT FINANCIAL ASSISTANCE (Tuition Opportunity Program for Students-Teachers Award)

PO Box 91202
Baton Rouge LA 70821-9202
800/259-5626, ext. 1012
FAX: 504/922-0790
Internet: www.osfa.state.la.us

AMOUNT: $4,000/yr. (education majors); $6,000/yr. (math/chemistry majors)

DEADLINE(S): JUN 1

FIELD(S): Education; Math; Chemistry

Open to Louisiana residents pursuing undergraduate or graduate study at Louisiana colleges/universities and majoring in one of the above fields leading to teacher certification. Loans are forgiven by working as a certified teacher in Louisiana one year for each year loan is received.

Apply by completing the Free Application for Federal Student Aid (FAFSA). See your school's financial aid office or contact LOSFA for FAFSA form.

178 — NATIONAL ACADEMY OF EDUCATION (Spencer Postdoctoral Fellowship Program)

NY Univ, School of Education
726 Broadway, Rm. 509
New York NY 10003-9580
212/998-9035
FAX: 212/995-4435
E-Mail: nae.info@nyu.edu
Internet: www.nae.nyu.edu

AMOUNT: $45,000

DEADLINE(S): DEC 1

FIELD(S): Education; Humanities; Social Sciences

Fellowships of one or two years are open to individual researchers in education, humanities, or social and behavioral sciences. Research must have apparent relevance to education. Doctoral degree must have been received within the last five years. Based on past research record and quality of proposed project. Must submit project description, career history, referee form, curriculum vitae/resume, and example of past research relevant to education.

30 awards annually. Not renewable. Contact NAE for an application. Recipients notified in May.

179 — NAVAL HISTORICAL CENTER (Internship Program)

Washington Navy Yard
901 M St., SE
Washington DC 20374-5060
202/433-6901
FAX: 202/433-8200
E-Mail: efurgol@nhc.navy.mil
Internet: www.history.navy.mil

AMOUNT: $400 possible honoraria; otherwise, unpaid

DEADLINE(S): None

FIELD(S): Education; History; Public Relations; Design

Registered students of colleges/universities and graduates thereof are eligible for this program, which must be a minimum of 3 weeks, full or part-time. Four specialities available: Curator, Education, Public Relations, and Design. Interns receive orientation & assist in their departments, and must complete individual project which contributes to Center. Must submit a letter of recommendation, unofficial transcript, and writing sample of not less than 1,000 words.

Contact Dr. Edward M. Furgol, Curator, for an application.

180 — UNIVERSITY OF MANCHESTER (Awards for Research)

Secretary, Research and Graduate Support Unit
Manchester M13 9PL England
0161 275 2035
FAX: 0161 275 2445/7216

AMOUNT: Maintenance grant (approx) 5000 pounds p.a. plus payment of UK tuition fees.

DEADLINE(S): MAY 1

FIELD(S): Arts, Economics, Social Studies, Education, Science, Engineering, Biological Sciences, Law

The university offers research studentships for doctoral research in all disciplines. These awards are highly competitive. Applicants should hold at least a 2:1 degree or equivalent. Awards are renewable for up to 2 years.

Approx 50 awards per year. Please contact address above for complete information.

181 — WOODROW WILSON NATIONAL FELLOWSHIP FOUNDATION (Charlotte W. Newcombe Dissertation Fellowships)

CN 5281
Princeton NJ 08543-5281
609/452-7007
FAX: 609/452-0066
E-Mail: charoltte@woodrow.org
Internet: www.woodrow.org

AMOUNT: $15,500

DEADLINE(S): DEC 6

FIELD(S): Theology; Social Sciences; Humanities; Education

Open to Ph.D. candidates writing on topics of religious and ethical values. Must be pursuing full-time dissertation writing at graduate schools in the US, having completed all pre-dissertation requirements.

35 awards annually. Not renewable. See website or contact WWNFF for an application. Notification made in April.

EDUCATION

182 — AMERICAN ALLIANCE FOR HEALTH, PHYSICAL EDUCATION, RECREATION & DANCE

1900 Association Drive
Reston VA 20191
703/476-3400 or 800/213-7193
E-Mail: webmaster@aahperd.org
Internet: www.aahperd.org

AMOUNT: Varies

DEADLINE(S): Varies

FIELD(S): Health education, leisure and recreation, girls and women in sports, sport and physical education, dance

This organization has six national sub-organizations specializing in the above fields. Some have grants and fellowships for both individuals and group projects. The website has the details for each group.

Visit website for details or write to above address for details.

183 — AMERICAN ASSOCIATION OF SCHOOL ADMINISTRATORS (Educational Administration Scholarships)

1801 North Moore Street
Arlington VA 22209-1813
703/528-0700
FAX 703/528-2146
E-Mail: dpierce@aasa.org
Internet: www.aasa.org

AMOUNT: $2,000

DEADLINE(S): SEP 1

FIELD(S): School Administration

Open to graduate students currently enrolled in a school administration program who intend to make the public school superintendency a life career. Candidates must be nominated by the dean of the department of education at their university. Only one candidate may be submitted by each university.

6 awards annually. Not renewable. For more information, contact Darlene Pierce at the above address. Applications are available May 1st from chairs of educational administration departments that have "The I Can Make a Difference" Program—applications not available from AASA.

184 — AMERICAN FOUNDATION FOR THE BLIND (Delta Gamma Foundation Memorial Scholarship)

11 Penn Plaza, Ste. 300
New York NY 10001
212/502-7661 or TDD: 212/502-7662
FAX: 212/502-7771
E-Mail: juliet@afb.org
Internet: www.afb.org

AMOUNT: $1,000

DEADLINE(S): APR 30

FIELD(S): Rehabilitation and/or education of the visually impaired or blind

Open to legally blind undergraduate and graduate college students of good character who have exhibited academic excellence and are studying in the field of education and/or rehabilitation of the visually impaired and blind.

Must be U.S. citizen. Write or access website for further information. E-mail and fax inquiries must include a complete U.S. postal service mailing address.

185 — AMERICAN SPEECH-LANGUAGE-HEARING FOUNDATION (Graduate Student Scholarships)

10801 Rockville Pike
Rockville MD 20852
301/897-5700
FAX 301/571-0457

AMOUNT: $4,000

DEADLINE(S): JUN 6

FIELD(S): Communication sciences/disorders; speech pathology;speech therapy

Open to full-time graduate students in communication sciences and disorders programs and demonstrating outstanding academic achievement.

Applications available in February.

186 — AMERICAN SPEECH-LANGUAGE-HEARING FOUNDATION (Kala Singh Memorial Fund-International/Minority Student Scholarship)

10801 Rockville Pike
Rockville Pike, Rockville, MD 20852
301/897-5700
FAX: 301/571-0457

AMOUNT: $2,000

DEADLINE(S): JUN 6

FIELD(S): Communication sciences and disorders, speech/language pathology, audiology

Applicants must be international/ethnic minority graduate student studying communication sciences and disorders in the U.S. and demonstrating outstanding academic achievement.

Applications available in February.

187 — AMERICAN SPEECH-LANGUAGE-HEARING FOUNDATION (Leslie Isenberg Fund for Student With Disability)

10801 Rockville Pike
Rockville Pike, Rockville MD 20852
301/897-5700
FAX: 301/571-0457

AMOUNT: $2,000

DEADLINE(S): JUN 6

FIELD(S): Communication sciences & disorders

Open to full-time graduate student with disability enrolled in a communication sciences and disorders program and demonstrating outstanding academic achievement.

Applications available in February.

188 — AMERICAN SPEECH-LANGUAGE-HEARING FOUNDATION (New Investigator Research Grant)

10801 Rockville Pike
Rockville MD 20852
301/897-5700
FAX 301/571-0457

AMOUNT: $5,000

DEADLINE(S): JUL 20

FIELD(S): Speech/Language Pathology; Audiology

Research grant for new investigators to support clinical research in the above areas. Grants are designed to encourage research activities by new scientists who have earned their M.A. or Ph.D. within the last 5 years. Students enrolled in degree programs are ineligible.

Seven awards. Applications available in February.

189 — AMERICAN SPEECH-LANGUAGE-HEARING FOUNDATION (Student Research Grant in Clinical or Rehabilitative Audiology)

10801 Rockville Pike
Rockville MD 20852
301/897-5700
FAX 301/571-0457

AMOUNT: $2,000

DEADLINE(S): JUN 13

FIELD(S): Audiology

Student research grants available to graduate or post-graduate students in communication sciences and disorders desiring to conduct research in audiology.

Applications available in February.

190 — AMERICAN SPEECH-LANGUAGE-HEARING FOUNDATION (Student Research in Early Childhood Language Development)

10801 Rockville Pike
Rockville MD 20852
301/897-5700
FAX 301/571-0457

AMOUNT: $2,000

DEADLINE(S): JUN

FIELD(S): Research in early childhood language development

Research grant for graduate or post-graduate students in communication sciences and disorders desiring to conduct research in early childhood language development.

Applications available in February.

191 — AMERICAN SPEECH-LANGUAGE-HEARING FOUNDATION (Young Scholars Award for Minority Student)

10801 Rockville Pike
Rockville MD 20852
301/897-5700
FAX 301/571-0457

AMOUNT: $2,000

DEADLINE(S): JUN 6

FIELD(S): Speech/Language Pathology; Audiology

Open to ethnic minorities who are full-time college seniors accepted for graduate study in speech-language pathology or audiology. Applicants must be US citizens.

Applications available in February.

192 — AMERICAN UNIVERSITY IN CAIRO (Teaching English as a Foreign Language Fellowship)

420 Fifth Ave., 3rd Floor
New York NY 10017-2729
212/730-8800
FAX: 212/730-1600

E-Mail: aucegypt@aucnyo.edu

Internet: www.aucegypt.edu

AMOUNT: Tuition + stipend paid in Egyptian pounds

DEADLINE(S): JAN 15

FIELD(S): Teaching English as a Foreign Language at AUC

Open to students who enroll in the MA program at the American University in Cairo, Egypt, and whose native (or near-native) language is English. Preference to those with experience in the Middle East and teaching. GPA of at least 3.0 required.

Renewable for an additional year and intervening summer if work is acceptable. Contact Mary Davidson at above address for complete information.

193 — ARMENIAN GENERAL BENEVOLENT UNION (Educational Loan Program)

Education Dept., 31 W. 52nd St.

New York NY 10019-6118

212/765-8260

FAX: 212/765-8209

E-Mail: agbuny@aol.com

AMOUNT: $5,000 to $7,500/yr.

DEADLINE(S): APR 1

FIELD(S): Education Administration, International Relations/Foreign Affairs, Communication, Journalism, or Public Administration

Loans for full-time students of Armenian heritage pursuing master's degrees in one of the above fields. Must be attending highly competitive institutions in the U.S. GPA of 3.5 or more required.

Loan repayment period begins within 12 months of completion of full-time study and extends five to ten years, depending on the size of the loan. Interest is 3% Write for complete information.

194 — ASSOCIATION FOR EDUCATION AND REHABILITATION OF THE BLIND AND VISUALLY IMPAIRED (William and Dorothy Ferrell Scholarship)

4600 Duke Street, #430

PO Box 22397

Alexandria VA 22304

703/823-9690

FAX: 703/823-9695

E-Mail: aer@aerbvi.org

Internet: www.aerbvi.org

AMOUNT: $500

DEADLINE(S): APR 15 (of even-numbered years)

FIELD(S): Fields of study related to the blind/visually impaired

Scholarships for students who are legally blind, pursuing postsecondary education in a field related to services for the blind or visually impaired. Financial need NOT a factor.

2 awards annually. See website or contact Carolyn Sharp at above address for details.

195 — ASSOCIATION FOR EDUCATION AND REHABILITATION OF THE BLIND AND VISUALLY IMPAIRED (Telesensory Scholarship)

4600 Duke Street, #430

PO Box 22397

Alexandria VA 22304

703/823-9690

FAX: 703/823-9695

E-Mail: aer@aerbvi.org

Internet: www.aerbvi.org

AMOUNT: $1,000

DEADLINE(S): APR 15 (of even-numbered years)

FIELD(S): Fields of study related to the blind/visually impaired

Scholarships for students who are members of AER pursuing postsecondary education in a field related to services for the blind or visually impaired. Must become an AER member before applying. Financial need NOT a factor.

1 award annually. For membership information or an application, see website or contact Carolyn Sharp at above address.

196 — ASSOCIATION FOR INSTITUTIONAL RESEARCH (Fellowship to Summer Institute)

114 Stone Building, FSU

Tallahassee FL 32306-4462

850/644-4470

FAX: 850/644-8824

E-Mail: air@mailer.fsu.edu

Internet: http://airweb.org

AMOUNT: Varies

DEADLINE(S): JAN 15

FIELD(S): Social sciences, education

The Association provides fellowships to doctoral and postdoctoral researchers for its summer institute on "Improving Institutional Research in Postsecondary Educational Institutions."

Contact organization for details.

197 — ASSOCIATION FOR INSTITUTIONAL RESEARCH (Research Grant)

114 Stone Building, FSU

Tallahassee FL 32306-4462

850/644-4470

FAX: 850/644-8824

E-Mail: air@mailer.fsu.edu

Internet: http://airweb.org

AMOUNT: $30,000/yr.

DEADLINE(S): JAN 15

FIELD(S): Social sciences, education, finance, economics

The Association provides one-year grants for doctoral or post-doctoral research appropriate for its program "Improving Institutional Research in Postsecondary Educational Institutions."

Must submit proposal, including budget. Contact organization for details.

198 — B.M. WOLTMAN FOUNDATION (Lutheran Scholarships for Students of the Ministry and Teaching)

7900 U.S. 290 E.

Austin TX 78724

512/926-4272

AMOUNT: $500-$2,500

DEADLINE(S): Varies

FIELD(S): Theology (Lutheran Ministry); Teacher Education (Lutheran Schools)

Scholarships for undergrads and graduate students studying for careers in the Lutheran ministry or for teaching in a Lutheran school. For Texas residents attending, or planning to attend, any college in Texas.

45 awards. Renewable. Send for details.

199 — BLAKEMORE FOUNDATION (Asian Language Fellowship Grants)

1201 Third Ave., 40th Fl.

Seattle WA 98101-3099

206/583-8778

FAX: 206/583-8500

E-Mail: blakemore@perkinscoie.com

AMOUNT: Tuition, transportation, basic living costs

DEADLINE(S): JAN 15

FIELD(S): Asian languages

Fellowships for advanced language study in Asia. For use at an instition selected by the applicant and approved by the Foundation. Applicant must be a graduate or professional school student, a teacher, a professional, or a business person; be working towards a specific career objective involving the regular use of an Asian language; be near an advanced level in that language; be a U.S. citizen or permanent resident. For full-time study during the term of the grant.

12-18 annual awards. For one year of study.

200 — BLUES HEAVEN FOUNDATION, INC. (Muddy Waters Scholarship)

2120 S. Michigan Ave.

Chicago IL 60616

312/808-1286

AMOUNT: $2,000

DEADLINE(S): APR 30

FIELD(S): Music; Music Education; African-American Studies; Folklore; Performing Arts; Arts Management; Journalism; Radio/TV/Film

Scholarship is made on a competitive basis with consideration given to scholastic achievement, concentration of studies, and financial need. Applicant must have full-time enrollment status in a Chicago area college/university in at least their first year of undergraduate studies or a graduate program. Scholastic aptitude, extracurricular involvement, grade point average, and financial need are all considered.

Contact Blues Heaven Foundation, Inc. to receive an application between February and April.

201 — BOYS & GIRLS CLUBS OF AMERICA (Robert W. Woodruff Fellowships)

1230 W. Peachtree St. NW
Training & Prof. Devel.
Atlanta GA 30309-3494
404/815-5776
FAX: 404/815-5736

AMOUNT: Up to $15,000

DEADLINE(S): JUN 15 (applications available MAR 1)

FIELD(S): Youth Leadership

Internships for Boys/Girls Clubs of America professionals who are enrolled in an accredited M.A. program or who possess M.A. degrees in a related field. Recipients agree to commit to 2 years of full-time employment with Boys/Girls Clubs of America following completion of studies.

Write for complete information.

202 — BUSINESS & PROFESSIONAL WOMEN'S FOUNDATION (BPW Career Advancement Scholarship Program)

2012 Massachusetts Ave., NW
Washington DC 20036-1070
202/293-1200, ext. 169
FAX: 202/861-0298
Internet: www.bpwusa.org

AMOUNT: $500-$1,000

DEADLINE(S): APR 15

FIELD(S): Biology, Science, Education, Engineering, Social Science, Paralegal, Humanities, Business, Math, Computers, Law, MD, DD

For women (US citizens) aged 25+ accepted into accredited program at US institution (+Puerto Rico & Virgin Islands). Must graduate within 12 to 24 months from the date of grant and demonstrate critical finanacial need. Must have a plan to upgrade skills, train for a new career field, or to enter/re-enter the job market.

Full- or part-time study. For info see website or send business-sized, self-addressed, double-stamped envelope.

203 — CALIFORNIA GRANGE FOUNDATION (Deaf Activities Scholarships)

Pat Avila, 2101 Stockton Blvd.
Sacramento CA 95817
Written inquiry

AMOUNT: Varies

DEADLINE(S): APR 1

FIELD(S): Course work which will be of benefit to the deaf community

Scholarships students entering, continuing, or returning to college to pursue studies that will benefit the deaf community.

Write for information after Feb. 1 of each year.

204 — CHARLES A. AND ANNE MORROW LINDBERGH FOUNDATION (Grants for Research Projects)

2150 Third Ave., N, Ste. 310
Anoka MN 55303-2200
612/576-1596
FAX: 612/576-1664
E-Mail: lindbergh@isd.net
Internet: www.isd.net/lindbergh

AMOUNT: $10,580 (max.)

DEADLINE(S): JUN 15

FIELD(S): Aviation; Aerospace; Agriculture; Education; Arts; Humanities; Biomedical Research; Exploration; Health & Population Sciences; Intercultural Communication; Waste Disposal Minimization & Management.; Adaptive Technology; Conservation

Open to individuals whose proposed projects represent a significant contribution toward the achievement of balance between the advance of technology and preservation of the natural environment. Financial need NOT a factor. Funding is NOT for tuition.

10 awards annually. See website for application.

205 — CONCORDIA UNIVERSITY (Administration Management Society John Crawford Award)

Dept. Education
1455 de Maisonneuve Blvd. West
LB 501
Montreal Quebec H3G 1M8 CANADA
514/848-3809
FAX: 514/848-2812
E-Mail: awardsgs@vax2.concordia.ca

AMOUNT: $500

DEADLINE(S): SEP 20

FIELD(S): Education

Awarded to a full-time graduate master's or doctoral student. The selection of the winner will be made by the Department of Education based on academic excellence.

1 award annually. Not renewable. Contact the Chair of the Department of Education at Concordia University for an application.

206 — DOW JONES NEWSPAPER FUND (High School Journalism Teacher Fellowship Program)

PO Box 300
Princeton NJ 08543-0300
609/452-2820 or 800/DOWFUND
Internet: www.dj.com/newsfun/hsteach.html

AMOUNT: Tuition, room & board + travel expenses

DEADLINE(S): Varies (April-July)

FIELD(S): Journalism Education

Summer fellowships for high school journalism teachers and advisers to enhance their skills and receive graduate credit. Contact organization for workshop directory or access website for sites, dates, and subjects of various courses throughout the US.

Contact Dow Jones for details.

207 — EASTER SEAL SOCIETY OF IOWA, INC. (Scholarships & Awards)

P.O. Box 4002
Des Moines IA 50333-4002
515/289-1933

AMOUNT: $400-$600

DEADLINE(S): APR 15

FIELD(S): Physical Rehabilitation, Mental Rehabilitation, and related areas

Open ONLY to Iowa residents who are full-time undergraduate sophomores, juniors, seniors, or graduate students at accredited institutions planning a career in the broad field of rehabilitation. Must indicate financial need and be in top 40% of their class.

6 scholarships per year. Must re-apply each year.

208 — F.J. CONNELL MUSIC SCHOLARSHIP TRUST

1187 Simcoe St.
Moose Jaw Saskatchewan S6H 3J5 CANADA
306/694-2045

AMOUNT: $750 (Canadian)

DEADLINE(S): OCT 1

FIELD(S): Music

For students studying any aspect of music, such as education, performance, composition, history, etc. Must have completed the equivalent of one year of full-time music studies and be planning a professional career in music. No citizenship or residency requirements, but recipients will usually be Canadians.

Contact above location for details.

209 — FREEDOM FROM RELIGION FOUNDATION (Student Essay Contest)

PO Box 750
Madison WI 53701
608/256-5800
Internet: www.infidels.org/org/ffrf

AMOUNT: $1,000; $500; $250

DEADLINE(S): JUL 15

FIELD(S): Humanities; English; Education; Philosophy; Science

Essay contest on topics related to church-state entanglement in public schools or growing up a "freethinker" in religious-oriented society. Topics change yearly, but all are on general theme of maintaining separation of church and state. New topics available in February. For high school seniors & currently enrolled college/technical students. Must be US citizen.

Send SASE to address above for complete information. Please indicate whether wanting information for college competition or high school. Information will be sent when new topics are announced each February. See website for details.

210 — GATES MILLENIUM SCHOLARS PROGRAM (Scholarships for Graduate Students)

8260 Willow Oaks Corporate Dr.
Fairfax VA 22031-4511
877/690-4677
Internet: www.gmsp.org

AMOUNT: Varies

DEADLINE(S): FEB 1

FIELD(S): Engineering; Mathematics; Science; Education; Library Science

College presidents, professors, & deans may nominate graduate students who are African-Americans, Native Americans, Hispanic Americans, or Asian Americans in above fields. Based on academic performance, commitment to academic study, involvement in community service & school activities, potential for leadership, career goals, and financial need. Must submit transcripts and letters of recommendation. Must be US citizen with a minimum 3.3 GPA

Application materials available November 1st; scholars will be notified in May. Funded by the Bill & Melinda Gates Foundation, and administered by the United Negro College Fund.

211 — GRACE FOUNDATION SCHOLARSHIP TRUST FUND

P.O. Box 924
Menlo Park CA 94026-0924
Written inquiry

AMOUNT: $1,000 to $4,000

DEADLINE(S): JAN 31

FIELD(S): Christian

One-year scholarships for full or partial tuition payment for full-time study at an accredited college or university. For training future Christian ministers and professional workers in developing countries in Asia/Southeast Asia. Candidates must have completed one or more years of college in or near their native country, be a strong Christian, have a 3.0 or higher GPA, and be pursuing a career in either the ministry, medicine, teaching, or social service.

Renewable up to graduation—four years maximum—pending maintenance of 3.0 GPA. Applications available between Sept. 1 and Oct. 31. Must demonstrate financial need.

212 — HILLEL INTERNATIONAL CENTER (The Bittker Fellowship)

Eran Gasko
1640 Rhode Island Ave. NW
Washington DC 20036
202/857-6637
202/857-6560
FAX: 202/857-6693
E-Mail: smusher@hillel.org
Internet: www.hillel.org/careermoves/bittker.htm

AMOUNT: Professional Experience

DEADLINE(S): None specified

FIELD(S): Student Leadership/Jewish Awareness

One-year professional experience for an oustanding recent graduate, who coordinates student leadership and Jewish awareness activities nationwide. The Fellow establishes the network of student leaders and enhances their communication through national publications, conference calls, and the Internet. Task forces include Jewish Awareness/Identity, Women's Issues, Graduate Student Life, and Education.

Contact Eran Gasko, Human Resources, for an application.

213 — ILLINOIS STUDENT ASSISTANCE COMMISSION (David A. DeBolt Teacher Shortage Scholarship Program)

1755 Lake Cook Rd.
Deerfield IL 60015-5209
800/899-ISAC
Internet: www.isac1.org

AMOUNT: Tuition, fees, room/board or $5,000

DEADLINE(S): MAY 1

FIELD(S): Education—Teacher training

Scholarships and loans for Illinois students planning to teach at approved Illinois preschools, elementary schools, or secondary schools in a designated teacher shortage discipline.

300 annual awards. Illinois residency and U.S. citizenship required. Access website or write for complete information.

214 — ILLINOIS STUDENT ASSISTANCE COMMISSION (Special Education Teacher Tuition Waiver Program)

1755 Lake Cook Rd.
Deerfield IL 60015-5209
800/899-ISAC
Internet: www.isac1.org

AMOUNT: Tuition and fees

DEADLINE(S): FEB 15

FIELD(S): Special Education Teacher Training

Waiver of tuition and fees for Illinois students seeking initial certification in special education and who attend Illinois public universities.

300 annual awards. Illinois residency and U.S. citizenship required. Access website or write for complete information.

215 — INSTITUTE FOR HUMANE STUDIES (Summer Residential Program)

4084 University Dr., Ste. 101
Fairfax VA 22030-6812
703/934-6920 or 800/697-8799
FAX: 703/352-7535
E-Mail: ihs@gmu.edu
Internet: www.theihs.org

AMOUNT: All seminar fees: program cost, room/board, materials, and books

DEADLINE(S): MAR 1

FIELD(S): Social Sciences; Humanities; Law; Journalism; Public Policy; Education; Writing

For college students, recent graduates, and graduate students who share an interest in learning and exchanging ideas about the scope of individual rights. One-week and weekend seminars at various campus locations across the U.S.

Apply online or contact IHS for an application.

216 — INTERNATIONAL ORDER OF THE ALHAMBRA (Graduate/Postgraduate Scholarship Grants)

4200 Leeds Ave.
Baltimore MD 21229-5496
410/242-0660
FAX: 410/536-5729

AMOUNT: $400

DEADLINE(S): JAN 1; JUL 1

FIELD(S): Special Education

Open to graduate/postgraduate students enrolled in an accredited program for teaching the mentally challenged and the handicapped. For use in Canada and the states of California and Virginia and for members of the clergy in any state.

U.S. or Canadian citizenship required. Write for complete information.

217 — INTERNATIONAL READING ASSOCIATION (Albert J. Harris Award)

800 Barksdale Road
PO Box 8139
Newark DE 19714-8139
302/731-1600, ext. 226
FAX: 302/731-1057
E-Mail: gkeating@reading.org

AMOUNT: $500

DEADLINE(S): SEP 15

FIELD(S): Reading Disabilities

This prize recognizes outstanding published works (single- or joint-authored research-based articles) on the topics of reading disabilities and the prevention, assessment, or instruction of learners experiencing difficulty learning to read. Publications that have appeared in a refereed professional journal or monograph from June of the previous year to June of the current year are eligible, and may be submitted by the author or anyone else. IRA membership NOT required.

1 award annually. Contact Gail Keating, Projects Manager, Division of Research and Policy, at above address for guidelines.

218 — INTERNATIONAL READING ASSOCIATION (Dina Feitelson Research Award)

800 Barksdale Road
PO Box 8139
Newark DE 19714-8139
302/731-1600, ext. 226
FAX: 302/731-1057
E-Mail: gkeating@reading.org

AMOUNT: $500

DEADLINE(S): SEP 15

FIELD(S): Beginning Reading

This prize is to recognize an outstanding empirical study, or a literacy or reading related topic published in a refereed journal. Article must have been published between June of the previous year and June of the current year, and may be submitted by the author or anyone else. IRA membership is NOT required.

1 award annually. Contact Gail Keating, Projects Manager, Division of Research and Policy, at above address for guidelines.

219 — INTERNATIONAL READING ASSOCIATION (Elva Knight Research Grant)

800 Barksdale Road
PO Box 8139
Newark DE 19714-8139
302/731-1600, ext. 226
FAX: 302/731-1057
E-Mail: gkeating@reading.org

AMOUNT: $5,000 max.

DEADLINE(S): OCT 15

FIELD(S): Reading/Literacy Research

Grant is to assist researcher in a reading and literacy project. Research is defined as inquiry that addresses significant questions about literacy instruction and practice. Open to IRA members worldwide. Projects should be completed within two years.

1 award annually to researcher outside the US/Canada, 1 to a teacher-initiated research project, & up to 5 additional grants. For membership information, use extension 267. For guidelines, contact Gail Keating, Projects Manager, Division of Research and Policy, at above address.

220 — INTERNATIONAL READING ASSOCIATION (Helen M. Robinson Award)

800 Barksdale Road
PO Box 8139
Newark DE 19714-8139
302/731-1600, ext. 226
FAX: 302/731-1057
E-Mail: gkeating@reading.org

AMOUNT: $500

DEADLINE(S): JUN 15

FIELD(S): Reading/Literacy Research

Grant is to support doctoral students at the early stages of their dissertation research in the field of reading and literacy. Open to all doctoral students worldwide who are members of IRA.

1 award annually. For membership information, use extension 267. For guidelines, contact Gail Keating, Projects Manager, Division of Research and Policy, at above address.

221 — INTERNATIONAL READING ASSOCIATION (Jeanne S. Chall Research Fellowship)

800 Barksdale Road
PO Box 8139
Newark DE 19714-8139
302/731-1600, ext. 226
FAX: 302/731-1057
E-Mail: gkeating@reading.org

AMOUNT: $6,000 max.

DEADLINE(S): OCT 15

FIELD(S): Reading development/difficulty

This fellowship is to encourage and support doctoral research investigating issues in beginning research, readability, reading difficulty, and stages of reading development. Must be IRA member planning or beginning dissertation.

1 award annually. For membership information, use extension 267. For guidelines, contact Gail Keating, Projects Manager, Division of Research and Policy, at above address.

222 — INTERNATIONAL READING ASSOCIATION (Nila Banton Smith Research Dissemination Support Grant)

800 Barksdale Road
PO Box 8139
Newark DE 19714-8139
302/731-1600, ext. 226
FAX: 302/731-1057
E-Mail: gkeating@reading.org

AMOUNT: $5,000

DEADLINE(S): OCT 15

FIELD(S): Reading/Literacy Research

Purpose of this award is to facilitate the dissemination of literacy research to the educational community. Open to all IRA members worldwide.

1 award annually. For membership information, use extension 267. For guidelines, contact Gail Keating, Projects Manager, Division of Research and Policy, at above address.

223 — INTERNATIONAL READING ASSOCIATION (Outstanding Dissertation of the Year Award)

800 Barksdale Road
PO Box 8139
Newark DE 19714-8139
302/731-1600, ext. 226
FAX: 302/731-1057
E-Mail: gkeating@reading.org

AMOUNT: $1,000

DEADLINE(S): OCT 1

FIELD(S): Reading/Literacy

This award recognizes dissertations in the field of reading and literacy completed between September of the previous year and August of the current year. Open to all doctoral students worldwide who are IRA members.

1 award annually, & up to 9 finalists. For membership information, use extension 267. For guidelines, contact Gail Keating, Projects Manager, Division of Research and Policy, at above address.

224 — INTERNATIONAL READING ASSOCIATION (Reading/Literacy Research Fellowship)

800 Barksdale Road
PO Box 8139
Newark DE 19714-8139
302/731-1600, ext. 226
FAX: 302/731-1057
E-Mail: gkeating@reading.org

AMOUNT: $1,000

DEADLINE(S): OCT 15

FIELD(S): Reading/Literacy Research

Provides support during the first five years after completing doctoral study to a researcher outside the US and/or Canada who has shown exceptional promise in reading/literacy research. Must become member of IRA before applying.

1 award annually. For membership information, use extension 267. For guidelines, contact Gail Keating, Projects Manager, Division of Research and Policy, at above address.

225 — INTERNATIONAL READING ASSOCIATION (Teacher as Researcher Grant)

800 Barksdale Road
PO Box 8139
Newark DE 19714-8139
302/731-1600, ext. 226
FAX: 302/731-1057
E-Mail: gkeating@reading.org

AMOUNT: $1,000-$5,000

DEADLINE(S): OCT 15

FIELD(S): Reading/Literacy Instruction

Award is to support teachers in their inquiries about literacy learning and instruction. IRA members who are practicing K-12 teachers with full-time teaching responsibilities (includes librarians, Title 1 teachers, classroom, and resource teachers) may apply.

Several awards annually. For membership information, use extension 267. For guidelines, contact Gail Keating, Projects Manager, Division of Research and Policy, at above address.

226 — INTERTEL FOUNDATION, INC. (Hollingworth Award Competition)

4300 Sideburn Road
Fairfax VA 22030
703/591-1958

AMOUNT: $2,000

DEADLINE(S): JAN 15

FIELD(S): Education: gifted and/or talentd youth

An international competition for proposals of publishable research projects concerning gifted and/or talented young people. Projects may be sponsored by universities, school stystems, individual schools, public agencies, or private nonprofit organizations. Indivuals may apply, such as grad students, teachers, professors, educationl administrators, psychologists, etc.

Send SASE to Dr. Roxanne Herrick Cramer, Chair, Hollingworth Award Committee, at above address.

227 — JAMES MADISON MEMORIAL FELLOWSHIP (Fellowship for Teachers)

2000 K St. NW
Washington DC 20006
202/653-8700 or 1-800/525-6928
FAX: 202/653-6045
Internet: www.jamesmadison.com

AMOUNT: $24,000 prorated over study period

DEADLINE(S): MAR 1

FIELD(S): Teaching American History/government, or social studies—concentration on the U.S. Constitution

Fellowships for teachers (senior fellows) in grades 7-12 in the above fields to pursue an MA degree. Also for full-time college seniors and grad students (junior fellows). U.S. citizens or U.S. nationals. Fellows are selected from each state and from D.C., Puerto Rico, Guam, Virgin Islands, American Samoa, Northern Mariana Islands, and Palau. Program designed to enhance teaching about the U.S. Constitution.

Application is on website or contact: American College Testing, P.O. Box 4030, Iowa City, IA 52243-4030;   800/525-6928
E-Mail: Recogprog@ACT-ACT4-PO.act.org

228 — JAPANESE AMERICAN CITIZENS LEAGUE (Minoru Yasui Memorial Scholarship)

1765 Sutter St.
San Francisco CA 94115
415/921-5225
FAX: 415/931-4671
E-Mail: jacl@jacl.org
Internet: www.jacl.org

AMOUNT: Varies

DEADLINE(S): APR 1

FIELD(S): Human & Civil Rights; Sociology; Law; Education

Open to JACL members or their children only. For graduate students with a strong interest in human and civil rights. Student must be currently enrolled in, or planning to enroll in, an accredited graduate school. Financial need NOT a factor.

40 awards annually. For membership information or an application, send a self-addressed, stamped envelope to above address.

229 — JAPANESE GOVERNMENT (Monbusho In-Service Training For Teachers Scholarships)

350 S. Grand Ave., Suite 1700
Los Angeles CA 90071
213/617-6700, ext. 338
FAX: 213/617-6728
Internet: embjapan.org/la

AMOUNT: Tuition + $1,400-$1,800/month

DEADLINE(S): AUG

FIELD(S): Education/Educational Management

For study in Japan. Must be university graduate under 35 years of age in active service of primary or secondary schools or on staff at teacher training institutions and have at least five years of experience. Scholarship is for one-and-a-half years and includes Japanese language training, round-trip airfare, one-time arrival allowance, partly subsidized housing expenses, and partly subsidized medical expenses.

For more information or an application contact Mr. Cory Crocker, Japan Information and Culture Center, Consulate General of Japan, at above address.

230 — JEWISH COMMUNITY CENTERS ASSOCIATION (JCCA Scholarship Program)

15 East 26th Street
New York NY 10010-1579
212/532-4958, ext. 246
FAX: 212/481-4174
E-Mail: Webmaster@jcca.org
Internet: www.jcca.org

AMOUNT: Up to $7,500

DEADLINE(S): FEB 15

FIELD(S): Social Work; Jewish Communal Studies; Physical Education; Early Childhood Education; Cultural Arts

Open to graduate students of the Jewish faith who are enrolled in a master's degree program and are committed to a career in the Jewish community center field in North America. Must have an undergraduate GPA of at least 3.0, leadership potential, and a strong Jewish background.

8 awards annually. Financial need NOT a factor. Contact Michelle Cohen at above address for an application.

231 — KNIGHTS OF COLUMBUS (Bishop Greco Graduate Fellowship Program)

PO Box 1670
New Haven CT 06507-0901
203/772-2130

AMOUNT: $500/semester (up to 4 semesters)

DEADLINE(S): MAY 1

FIELD(S): Special Education

Open to full-time graduate students seeking a master's degree in a program designed for the preparation of classroom teachers of mentally retarded children. Applicants must be members in good standing of the Knights of Columbus, or the wife, son, or daughter of such a member or deceased member.

Contact the Committee of Fellowships at above address for an application.

232 — LABAN/BARTENIEFF INSTITUTE OF MOVEMENT STUDIES (Work-Study Programs)

234 Fifth Ave., Rm. 203
New York NY 10001
212/477-4299
FAX: 212/477-3702
E-Mail: limsinfo@erols.com

AMOUNT: $500-$1,500

DEADLINE(S): MAY 1

FIELD(S): Human Movement Studies

Open to graduate students and professionals in dance, education, health fields, behavioral sciences, fitness, athletic training, etc. Tenable for work-study ONLY at the Laban/Bartenieff Institute in New York.

Contact LIMS for an application.

233 — LADY ALLEN OF HURTWOOD MEMORIAL TRUST (Travel Grants)

21 Aspull Common
Leigh Lancs WN7 3PB ENGLAND
01942-674895

AMOUNT: up to 1,000 pounds sterling

DEADLINE(S): JAN 15

FIELD(S): Welfare And Education Of Children

A travel grant to those whose proposed project will directly benefit their work with children. People working with children and young people may apply, particularly those working with disabled and disadvantaged children. Successful candidates must write up an account of the work which the scholarship has funded. GRANTS ARE NOT FOR ACADEMIC STUDY; ONLY QUALIFIED INDIVIDUALS MAY APPLY.

Contact Dorothy E. Whitaker, Trustee, for application forms—available between May and December each year.

234 — LOUISIANA OFFICE OF STUDENT FINANCIAL ASSISTANCE (Tuition Opportunity Program for Students-Teachers Award)

PO Box 91202
Baton Rouge LA 70821-9202
800/259-5626, ext. 1012
FAX: 504/922-0790
Internet: www.osfa.state.la.us

AMOUNT: $4,000/yr. (education majors); $6,000/yr. (math/chemistry majors)

DEADLINE(S): JUN 1

FIELD(S): Education; Math; Chemistry

Open to Louisiana residents pursuing undergraduate or graduate study at Louisiana colleges/universities and majoring in one of the above fields leading to teacher certification. Loans are forgiven by working as a certified teacher in Louisiana one year for each year loan is received.

Apply by completing the Free Application for Federal Student Aid (FAFSA). See your school's financial aid office or contact LOSFA for FAFSA form.

235 — NATIONAL ACADEMY OF EDUCATION (Spencer Postdoctoral Fellowship Program)

NY Univ, School of Education
726 Broadway, Rm. 509
New York NY 10003-9580
212/998-9035
FAX: 212/995-4435
E-Mail: nae.info@nyu.edu
Internet: www.nae.nyu.edu

AMOUNT: $45,000

DEADLINE(S): DEC 1

FIELD(S): Education; Humanities; Social Sciences

Fellowships of one or two years are open to individual researchers in education, humanities, or social and behavioral sciences. Research must have apparent relevance to education. Doctoral degree must have been received within the last five years. Based on past research record and quality of proposed project. Must submit project description, career history, referee form, curriculum vitae/resume, and example of past research relevant to education.

30 awards annually. Not renewable. Contact NAE for an application. Recipients notified in May.

236 — NATIONAL ASSOCIATION OF AMERICAN BUSINESS CLUBS (AMBUCS Scholarships for Therapists)

P.O. Box 5127
High Point NC 27262
910/869-2166
FAX: 910/887-8451
E-Mail: ambucs@ambucs.com
Internet: www.ambucs.com

AMOUNT: $500-$6,000

DEADLINE(S): APR 15

FIELD(S): Physical Therapy, Music Therapy, Occupational Therapy, Speech-Language Pathology, Audiology, Rehabilitation, Recreation Therapy, and related areas.

Open to undergraduate juniors and seniors or graduate students who have good scholastic standing and plan to enter the fields listed above. GPA of 3.0 or better (4.0 scale) and US citizenship required. Must demonstrate financial need.

Renewable. Please include a self-addressed stamped envelope (SASE); applications are mailed in December; incomplete applications will not be considered.

237 — NATIONAL ASSOCIATION OF THE DEAF (Stokoe Scholarship)

814 Thayer Ave.
Silver Spring MD 20910-4500
301/587-1788
TTY: 301/587-1789
FAX: 301/587-1791
E-Mail: NADinfo@nad.org
Internet: www.nad.org

AMOUNT: $2,000

DEADLINE(S): MAR 15

FIELD(S): Sign Language; Deaf Community

Open to deaf students who have graduated from a four-year college program and are pursuing part-time or full-time graduate studies in a field related to sign language or the deaf community, or a deaf graduate student who is developing a special project on one of these topics.

Send a self-addressed, stamped, business-sized envelope to NAD for an application.

238 — NATIONAL FEDERATION OF THE BLIND (Educator of Tomorrow Award)

805 Fifth Avenue
Grinnell IA 50112
515/236-3366

AMOUNT: $3,000

DEADLINE(S): MAR 31

FIELD(S): Education: Elementary, Secondary, & Postsecondary

For legally blind students pursuing or planning to pursue a full-time postsecondary course of study in the US. Based on academic excellence, service to the community, and financial need. Membership NOT required.

1 award annually. Renewable. Contact Mrs. Peggy Elliot, Scholarship Committee Chairman, for an application.

239 — NATIONAL STRENGTH & CONDITIONING ASSN. (Challenge Scholarships)

P.O. Box 38909
Colorado Springs CO 80937-8909
719/632-6722
FAX: 719/632-6722
E-Mail: nsca@usa.net
Internet: www.colosoft.com/nsca

AMOUNT: $1,000

DEADLINE(S): MAR 1

FIELD(S): Fields related to body strength & conditioning

Open to National Strength & Conditioning Association members. Awards are for undergraduate or graduate study.

For membership information or an application, write to the above address.

240 — NATIONAL STRENGTH & CONDITIONING ASSN. (Student Research Grant Program)

P.O. Box 38909
Colorado Springs CO 80937-8909
719/632-6722
FAX: 719/632-6367
E-Mail: nsca@usa.net
Internet: www.colosoft.com/nsca

AMOUNT: $1,500

DEADLINE(S): FEB 3 (letter of intent); MAR 17 (submission)

FIELD(S): Fields related to body strength & conditioning

Research grants for graduate students who are members of National Strength & Conditioning Association. A graduate faculty member is required to serve as a co-investigator in the study.

Two annual awards. For membership information or an application, write to the above address.

241 — NAVAL HISTORICAL CENTER (Internship Program)

Washington Navy Yard
901 M St., SE
Washington DC 20374-5060
202/433-6901
FAX: 202/433-8200
E-Mail: efurgol@nhc.navy.mil
Internet: www.history.navy.mil

AMOUNT: $400 possible honoraria; otherwise, unpaid

DEADLINE(S): None

FIELD(S): Education; History; Public Relations; Design

Registered students of colleges/universities and graduates thereof are eligible for this program, which must be a minimum of 3 weeks, full or part-time. Four specialities available: Curator, Education, Public Relations, and Design. Interns receive orientation & assist in their departments, and must complete individual project which contributes to Center. Must submit a letter of recommendation, unofficial transcript, and writing sample of not less than 1,000 words.

Contact Dr. Edward M. Furgol, Curator, for an application.

242 — NEW YORK STATE THEATRE INSTITUTE (Internships in Theatrical Production)

155 River St.
Troy NY 12180
518/274-3573
nysti@crisny.org
Internet: www.crisny.org/not-for-profit/nysti/int.htm

AMOUNT: None

DEADLINE(S): None

FIELD(S): Fields of study related to theatrical production, including box office and PR

Internships for college students, high school seniors, and educators-in-residence interested in developing skills in above fields. Unpaid, but college credit is earned. Located at Russell Sage College in Troy, NY. Gain experience in box office, costumes, education, electrics, music, stage management, scenery, properties, performance, and public relations. Interns come from all over the world.

Must be associated with an accredited institution. See website for more information. Call Ms. Arlene Leff, Intern Director at above location. Include your postal mailing address.

243 — NORTH CAROLINA DEPARTMENT OF PUBLIC INSTRUCTION (Scholarship Loan Program for Prospective Teachers)

301 N. Wilmington St.
Raleigh NC 27601-2825
919/715-1120

AMOUNT: Up to $2,500/yr.

DEADLINE(S): FEB

FIELD(S): Education: Teaching, school psychology and counseling, speech/language impaired, audiology, library/media services

For NC residents planning to teach in NC public schools. At least 3.0 high school GPA required; must maintain 2.5 GPA during freshman year and 3.0 cumulative thereafter. Recipients are obligated to teach one year in an NC public school for each year

of assistance. Those who do not fulfill their teaching obligation are required to repay the loan plus interest.

200 awards per year. For full-time students. Applications available in Dec. from high school counselors and college and univerwity departments of education.

244 — OAK RIDGE INSTITUTE FOR SCIENCE AND EDUCATION (Industrial Hygiene Graduate Fellowship Program)

P.O. Box 117
Oak Ridge TN 37831-0117
423-576-9655
FAX: 423/576-8293
E-Mail: kinneym@orau.gov

AMOUNT:

DEADLINE(S): JAN 26

FIELD(S): Industrial Hygiene

A fellowship for first-year master's candidates who have undergraduate degrees in physical, life, environmental, or health sciences or enginering and who wish to pursue studies in industrial hygiene.

For details and application, contact above location.

245 — PHI DELTA KAPPA, INC. (Graduate Fellowships in Educational Leadership)

408 N. Union St.
PO Box 789
Bloomington IN 47401
812/339-1156
FAX: 812/339-0018
E-Mail: headquarters@pdkimtl.org
Internet: www.pdkimtl.org

AMOUNT: $1,500 (2); $750 (1); $500 (2)

DEADLINE(S): MAY 1

FIELD(S): Education

Open to Phi Delta Kappa members in good standing for completion of master's, specialist, or doctoral degrees which will enhance the member's leadership skills in the education profession.

See website or contact Shari Bradley at above address for an application.

246 — PILOT INTERNATIONAL FOUNDATION (Marie Newton Sepia Memorial Scholarship)

P.O. Box 5600
Macon GA 31208-5600
Written inquiries

AMOUNT: Varies

DEADLINE(S): MAR 1

FIELD(S): Disabilities/Brain-related Disorders in Children

This program assists graduate students preparing for careers working with children having disabilities/ brain disorders. Must have GPA of 3.5 or greater.

Applicants must be sponsored by a Pilot Club in their home town or in the city in which their college or university is located. Send a self-addressed, stamped envelope for complete information.

247 — PILOT INTERNATIONAL FOUNDATION (PIF/Lifeline Scholarship)

P.O. Box 5600
Macon GA 31208-5600
Written inquiries

AMOUNT: Varies

DEADLINE(S): MAR 1

FIELD(S): Disabilities/Brain-related Disorders

This program assists ADULT students re-entering the job market, preparing for a second career, or improving their professional skills for an established career. Applicants must be preparing for, or already involved in, careers working with people with disabilities/brain-related disorders. GPA of 3.5 or more is required.

Must be sponsored by a Pilot Club in your home town, or in the city in which your college or university is located. Send a self-addressed, stamped envelope for complete information.

248 — PILOT INTERNATIONAL FOUNDATION (Ruby Newhall Memorial Scholarship)

P.O. Box 5600
Macon, GA 31208-5600
Written Inquiries

AMOUNT: Varies

DEADLINE(S): MAR 15

FIELD(S): Disabilities/Brain-related disorders

For international students who have studied in the US for at least one year, and who intend to return to their home country six months after graduation. Applicants must be full-time students majoring in a field related to human health and welfare, and have a GPA of 3.5 or more.

Applicants must be sponsored by a Pilot Club in their home town, or in the city in which their college or university is located. Send a self-addressed, stamped envelope for complete information.

249 — PRESBYTERIAN CHURCH (U.S.A.) (Fund For Graduate Education)

100 Witherspoon Street
Louisville KY 40202-1396
502/567-5745
E-Mail: KSmith@ctr.pcusa.org
Internet: www.pcusa.org/highered

AMOUNT: Varies

DEADLINE(S): APR 30

FIELD(S): Education/Administration at Theological School

Provides scholarships for women and racial ethnic persons in doctoral studies. Applicants must be enrolled in a Ph.D/St.D/Th.D/Ed.D program in an accredited graduate institution, be preparing for or already engaged in teaching/ administrative positions in a college or theological school of the Presbyterian Church (U.S.A.), be members of the PC(USA), and demonstrate financial need.

Renewable. Contact Kathy Smith at above address for more information.

250 — ROCKEFELLER FOUNDATION (African Dissertation Internship Awards)

420 Fifth Ave.
New York NY 10018-2702
212/869-8500
212/764-3468
Internet: www.rockfound.org

AMOUNT: Cost of project

DEADLINE(S): None given

FIELD(S): Agriculture, environment, health, life sciences, population, and schooling

For African graduate students in U.S. and Canadian universities (but not to permanent residents) to return to Africa to carry out dissertation research at a local university or research institution. Priority given to above topics.

Students are strongly urged to be in the field for at least 12 months. Contact above location for details.

251 — ROEHER INSTITUTE (Graduate Research Grants)

Kinsmen Bldg.
York University
4700 Keele St.
North York Ontario M3J 1P3 Canada
416/661-9611

AMOUNT: up to $10,000

DEADLINE(S): APR 30

FIELD(S): Intellectual Disability

Research grants open to master's & doctoral candidates at Canadian universities who intend to pursue a career in Canada. Must be Canadian citizen or legal resident.

8 to 10 awards annually. Renewable if research projects show results and can be published in related journals. Write for complete information.

252 — SCOTTISH RITE CHARITABLE FOUNDATION (Research Grants)

Roeher Institute, Kinsmen Bldg.
4700 Keele St.
North York Ontario M3J 1P3 CANADA
416/661-9611
TDD: 416/661-2023
FAX: 416/661-5701
E-Mail: mail@aacl.org
Internet: www.aacl.org

AMOUNT: $10,000 (max. grads); $35,000 (max. postdocs)

DEADLINE(S): APR 30

FIELD(S): Human Services; Intellectual Disability

Open to Canadian citizens/landed immigrants enrolled in masters or doctoral programs at Canadian universities. Must state intent to pursue career in Canada and have definite research projects supported by an academic advisor or a Roeher Institute associate/consultant. Also available to postdoctoral researchers.

Renewable. Contact the Secretary, Awards Adjudicating Committee, at the Scottish Rite for an application and details on preferred research topics.

253 — SOCIETY FOR THE PSYCHOLOGICAL STUDY OF SOCIAL ISSUES (Teaching Materials Development Program)

PO Box 1248
Ann Arbor MI 48106-1248
909/607-0002
FAX: 313/662-5607
E-Mail: amarcusn@scrippscol.edu
Internet: www.spssi.org

AMOUNT: up to $5,000

DEADLINE(S): FEB 1

FIELD(S): Development of Teaching Materials

For the development of innovative teaching materials (e.g. videos, 35mm slide or computerized presentations, computer programs, game simulations, interactive websites, classroom demonstrations or exercises, etc.) that focus on social issues and that could be introduced into classrooms at any level. SPSSI will own copyright. Budgetary items could include equipment, supplies, salary for assistants, and travel. Salary for recipient NOT covered.

Contact Dr. Amy Marcus-Newhall at SPSSI for details. NO SCHOLARSHIPS AVAILABLE— REQUESTS FOR FINANCIAL AID WILL NOT BE ANSWERED.

254 — SPENCER FOUNDATION (Dissertation Fellowships for Research Related to Education)

900 N. Michigan Ave., Suite 2800
Chicago IL 60611-1542
312/337-7000
FAX: 312/337-0282
E-Mail: fellows@spencer.org
Internet: www.spencer.org

AMOUNT: $17,000 stipend

DEADLINE(S): OCT 10 (Request applications by then. Deadline is OCT 22.)

FIELD(S): Education

For Ph.D or Ed.D candidates who will soon complete all doctoral requirements except dissertation. Awards are not designed to finance data collection or completion of course work but to support final analysis and writing of dissertation.

Must be candidate for the doctoral degree at a graduate school in the U.S. Approximately 30 non-renewable fellowships per year. Write for complete information.

255 — STATE STUDENT ASSISTANCE COMMISSION OF INDIANA (Scholarships for Special Education Teachers & Physical/Occupational Therapists)

150 W. Market St., 5th Fl.
Indianapolis IN 46204
317/232-2350
FAX: 317/232-3260
E-Mail: grants@ssaci.in.us
Internet: www.ai.org/ssaci/

AMOUNT: $1,000

DEADLINE(S): Varies (with college)

FIELD(S): Special Education; Physical & Occupational Therapy

Open to Indiana residents pursuing full-time undergraduate or graduate study in special education or physical or occupational therapy at an Indiana college/university. Must be US citizen, have a minimum 2.0 GPA, and demonstrate financial need.

See website or contact SSACI for an application.

256 — SWEDISH INFORMATION SERVICE (Bicentennial Swedish-American Exchange Fund)

Bicentennial Fund,
One Dag Hammarskjold Plaza, 45th Floor
New York NY 10017-2201
212/483-2550
FAX: 212/752-4789
E-Mail: swedinfor@ix.netcom.com

AMOUNT: 20,000 Swedish crowns (for three- to six-week intensive study visits in Sweden)

DEADLINE(S): FEB (Friday of the first week)

FIELD(S): Politics, public administration, working life, human environment, mass media, business and industry, education and culture

Program is to provide opportunity for those in a positio to influence public opinion and contribute to the development of their society. Must be U.S. citizen or permanent resident. Must have necessary experience and education for fulfilling his/her project.

Send SASE to above address for details.

257 — TEACHERS COLLEGE AT COLUMBIA UNIVERSITY (Joseph Klingenstein Fellows Program & The Summer Institute)

Box 125
New York NY 10027-6696
212/678-3156
FAX: 212/678-3254
E-Mail: cjl35@columbia.edu
Internet: www.klingenstein.org

AMOUNT: $14,000 tuition allowance + $24,000 stipend

DEADLINE(S): JAN 15

FIELD(S): Education

Klingenstein graduate fellowships at the university are open to teachers from around the world currently working in independent schools, grades 5-12, who have more than five years of teaching experience. The Klingenstein Summer Institute is for secondary school teachers in the beginning of their careers, who have two to five years of teaching experience. Schools must have nondiscriminatory admissions policies.

12 one-year fellowships & 50 summer institute spots available annually. See website or contact Chris Lauricella at the Klingenstein Center for an application.

258 — THE AMERICAN CLASSICAL LEAGUE (Ed Phinney Commemorative Scholarship)

Miami University
Oxford OH 45056
513/529-7741
FAX: 513/529-7742
E-Mail: AmericanClassicalLeague@muohio.edu or a.c.l@mich.edu
Internet: www.umich.edu/~acleague/phinney.html

AMOUNT: Up to $500

DEADLINE(S): JAN 15

FIELD(S): Teachers or teacher candidates in the classics (Latin and/or Greek)

Scholarships of up to $500 to apply to first-time attendance at the League's institute OR up to $500 to cover cost of other activities that serve to enhance a teacher's skills in the classroom in the classics OR up to $150 for purchase of materials from the ACL Teaching and Materials Resource Center. Memberships required except for first-time attendance at institute.

Send request for information to above address.

259 — THE ARC (Research Grants Program in Mental Retardation)

500 E. Border St., Suite 300
Arlington, TX 76010
817/261-6003
FAX: 817/277-3491
E-Mail: thearc@metronet.com
Internet: http://www.theArc.org/welcome.html

AMOUNT: Up to $25,000

DEADLINE(S): APR 1

FIELD(S): Prevention, amelioration, or cure of mental retardation

The Arc invites applications from researchers from diverse sources—individuals and universities, hospitals, and professional organizations with research interests.

Contact Dr. Michael Wehmeyer, Assistant Director, Department of Research and Program Services, The Arc, at above address, or Ann Balson.

260 — THE COUNCIL FOR EXCEPTIONAL CHILDREN (Black Caucus Scholarship)

1920 Association Drive
Reston VA 20191-1589
Internet: www.cec.sped.org

AMOUNT: $500

DEADLINE(S): DEC 2

FIELD(S): Special education

Scholarship for a student pursuing a degree in Special Education and who is of African American background. Must be U.S. or Canadian citizen. Must be a student member of the Council for Exceptional Children. Min. GPA of 2.5 required.

Write to Coordinator of Student Activities at above address or visit website for further information. Application is on website.

261 — THE WALT DISNEY COMPANY (American Teacher Awards)

P.O. Box 9805
Calabasas CA 91372

AMOUNT: $2,500 (36 awards); $25,000 (Outstanding Teacher of the Year)

DEADLINE(S): FEB 15

FIELD(S): Teachers: athletic coach, early childhood, English, foreign language/ESL, general elementary, mathematics, performing arts, physical education/health, science, social studies, visual arts, voc/tech education

Awards for K-12 teachers in the above fields.

Teachers, or anyone who knows a great teacher, can write for applications at the above address.

262 — TUSKEGEE UNIVERSITY (Graduate Research Fellowships and Assistantships)

Admissions Office
Tuskegee University
1506 Franklin Rd., AL 36088
334/727/8500

AMOUNT: Tuition

DEADLINE(S): MAR 15

FIELD(S): Chemistry; Engineering; Environmental Science; Life Sciences; Nutrition; Education

Graduate research fellowships and graduate assistantships are available to qualified individuals who wish to enter Tuskegee University's graduate program in pursuit of a master's degree.

Write for complete information.

263 — UNIVERSITY OF MANCHESTER (Awards for Research)

Secretary, Research and Graduate Support Unit
Manchester M13 9PL England
0161 275 2035
FAX: 0161 275 2445/7216

AMOUNT: Maintenance grant (approx) 5000 pounds p.a. plus payment of UK tuition fees.

DEADLINE(S): MAY 1

FIELD(S): Arts, Economics, Social Studies, Education, Science, Engineering, Biological Sciences, Law

The university offers research studentships for doctoral research in all disciplines. These awards are highly competitive. Applicants should hold at least a 2:1 degree or equivalent. Awards are renewable for up to 2 years.

Approx 50 awards per year. Please contact address above for complete information.

264 — UNIVERSITY OF NORTH TEXAS (Scholarships for Elementary and Secondary Education Majors)

P.O. Box 311337
Denton TX 76203-1337
940/565-2992 (Elem.) or 940/565-2826 (Secondary)
Internet: www.unt.edu/scholarships/gelem.htm AND www.unt.edu/scholarships/teacher.htm

AMOUNT: Varies

DEADLINE(S): Varies

FIELD(S): Education: Elementary and Secondary Teaching

Several scholarships for students in the teacher education departments at the University of North Texas. Eligibility requirements vary.

See website for more information. Write to either Dept. of Elementary, Early Childhood, and Reading Education OR Dept. of Teacher Education and Administration/Secondary Education for details.

265 — UNIVERSITY OF WYOMING (Superior Students in Education Scholarship)

College of Education Undergraduate Studies Office
Room 100, McWhinnie Hall
PO Box 3374
Laramie WY 82071-3374
307/766-2533

AMOUNT: Varies

DEADLINE(S): OCT

FIELD(S): Education

For Wyoming high school graduates who have demonstrated high scholastic achievement and qualities of leadership and who plan to teach in Wyoming public schools. May attend the University of Wyoming or any community college in the state and major in education. Based on residency, ACT scores, grades, courses taken, school activities, letters of recommendation, and student responses to prepared questions. Must maintain a 2.5 GPA to remain in program.

16 awards annually. Renewable up to ten semesters (no more than five may be at a community college). Contact the University of Wyoming's College of Education Undergraduate Studies Office for an application.

266 — WOMEN'S SPORTS FOUNDATION (Dorothy Harris Endowed Scholarship)

Eisenhower Park
East Meadow NY 11554
800/227-3988
FAX: 516/542-4716
E-Mail: WoSport@aol.com
Internet: www.lifetimetv.com/WoSport

AMOUNT: $1,500

DEADLINE(S): DEC 11

FIELD(S): Physical Education; Sports Management; Sports Psychology; Sports Sociology

For female graduate students who will pursue a full-time course of study in one of the above fields at an accredited graduate school in the Fall.

1-2 awards annually. Awarded in March. See website or write to above address for details.

267 — WOMEN'S SPORTS FOUNDATION (Jackie Joyner-Kersee & Zina Garrison Minority Internships)

Eisenhower Park
East Meadow NY 11554
800/227-3988
FAX: 516/542-4716
E-Mail: WoSport@aol.com
Internet: www.lifetimetv.com/WoSport

AMOUNT: $4,000-$5,000

DEADLINE(S): Ongoing

FIELD(S): Sports-related fields

Provides women of color an opportunity to gain experience in a sports-related career and interact in the sports community. May be undergraduates, college graduates, graduate students, or women in a career change. Internships are located at the Women's Sports Foundation in East Meadow, New York.

4-6 awards annually. See website or write to above address for details.

268 — WOODROW WILSON NATIONAL FELLOWSHIP FOUNDATION/JOHNSON & JOHNSON (Dissertation Grants in Women's & Children's Health)

CN 5281
Princeton NJ 08543-5281
609/452-7007
FAX: 609/452-0066
E-Mail: charoltte@woodrow.org
Internet: www.woodrow.org

AMOUNT: $2,000 (for travel, books, microfilming, taping, computer services, etc.)

DEADLINE(S): NOV 8

FIELD(S): Women's & Children's Health

Open to doctoral students in nursing, public health, anthropology, history, sociology, psychology, or social work, who have completed all predissertation requirements at US graduate schools. Must have at least six months left to complete dissertation, which should include significant research on issues related to women's & children's health. Must submit transcripts, proposal, bibliography, & interest. Based on originality & scholarly validity.

15 awards annually. See website or contact WWNFF for an application. Winners announced in February.

269 — WOODROW WILSON NATIONAL FELLOWSHIP FOUNDATION (Andrew W. Mellon Fellowships in Humanistic Studies)

CN 5329
Princeton NJ 08543-5329
609/452-7007
FAX: 609/452-0066
E-Mail: mellon@woodrow.org
Internet: www.woodrow.org

AMOUNT: Tuition, fees, & stipend

DEADLINE(S): NOV 17

FIELD(S): Humanities AND Education

Open to students entering the first year of a Ph.D. program in the US. Must be pursuing humanistic studies and planning careers in college teaching.

80 awards annually. See website or contact WWNFF for an application.

270 — WOODROW WILSON NATIONAL FELLOWSHIP FOUNDATION (Charlotte W. Newcombe Dissertation Fellowships)

CN 5281
Princeton NJ 08543-5281
609/452-7007
FAX: 609/452-0066
E-Mail: charoltte@woodrow.org
Internet: www.woodrow.org

AMOUNT: $15,500

DEADLINE(S): DEC 6

FIELD(S): Theology; Social Sciences; Humanities; Education

Open to Ph.D. candidates writing on topics of religious and ethical values. Must be pursuing full-time dissertation writing at graduate schools in the US, having completed all pre-dissertation requirements.

35 awards annually. Not renewable. See website or contact WWNFF for an application. Notification made in April.

271 — WORLD LEISURE AND RECREATION ASSOCIATION (Scholarships)

WLRA Secretariat, 3 Canyon Court West
Lethbridge AB T1K 6V1 CANADA
403/381-6144
FAX: 403/381-6144
E-Mail: wlra@hg.uleth.ca
Internet: www.worldleisure.org

AMOUNT: Varies

DEADLINE(S): FEB 1

FIELD(S): Recreation & Leisure Studies

Scholarships intended to allow college seniors or graduate students in recreation or leisure services programs to attend international meetings/conferences or conventions, thereby gaining a broader perspective of world leisure and recreation.

See website or contact WLRA for an application.

272 — Y'S MEN INTERNATIONAL - US AREA (Alexander Scholarship Loan Fund)

12405 W. Lewis Ave.
Avondale AZ 85323-6518
Written Inquiry

AMOUNT: $1,000-$1,500/yr.

DEADLINE(S): MAY 30; OCT 30

FIELD(S): Business Administration; Youth Leadership

Open to US citizens/permanent residents with a strong desire to pursue professional YMCA service. Must be YMCA staff pursuing undergraduate or graduate study and demonstrate financial need. Repayment of loan is waived if recipient enters YMCA employment after graduation.

Send self-addressed, business-sized envelope plus $1 for postage & handling to above address for an application.

273 — ZETA PHI BETA SORORITY EDUCATIONAL FOUNDATION (Isabel M. Herson Scholarship in Education)

1734 New Hampshire Ave., NW
Washington DC 20009
Internet: www.zpb1920.org/nefforms.htm

AMOUNT: $500-$1,000

DEADLINE(S): FEB 1

FIELD(S): Elementary & Secondary Education

Open to graduate and undergraduate level students enrolled in a degree program in either elementary or secondary education. Award is for full-time study for one academic year (Fall-Spring). Must submit proof of enrollment.

Send self-addressed, stamped envelope to above address between September 1st and December 15th for an application.

SCHOOL OF ENGINEERING

274 — AEROSPACE EDUCATION FOUNDATION (Theodore Von Karman Graduate Scholarship Program)

1501 Lee Highway
Arlington VA 22209
703/247-5839

AMOUNT: $5,000

DEADLINE(S): JAN

FIELD(S): Science, Mathematics, Engineering

Open to Air Force ROTC graduate students who will pursue advanced degrees in the fields of science, mathematics, physics, or engineering. U.S. citizen or legal resident.

5 awards per year based on aptitude, attitude, and career plans. Write for complete information.

275 — AFRICAN NETWORK OF SCIENTIFIC AND TECHNOLOGICAL INSTITUTIONS - ANSTI (Postgraduate Fellowships)

PO Box 30592
Nairobi Kenya AFRICA
254-2-621234 or 254-2-622619/20
FAX: 254-2-215991
E-Mail: j.massaquoi@unesco.org OR
ANSTI@Net2000ke.com

AMOUNT: Fees, subsistence, & international travel

DEADLINE(S): JUN

FIELD(S): Basic & Engineering Sciences

Scholarships for postgraduate studies outside of applicant's home country. Must be African nationals not older than 36 years of age and hold a good bachelor's degree (at least 2nd class upper division). Applicants should apply for admission to host university as soon as possible. Fellowships tenable only in African universities.

10 awards annually. Renewable up to 2 years. Contact Professor J.G.M. Massaquoi for an application.

276 — AMERICAN ASSOCIATION FOR THE ADVANCEMENT OF SCIENCE (Science & Engineering Fellowships)

1200 New York Ave., NW
Washington DC 20005
202/326-6700
FAX: 202/289-4950
E-Mail: science_policy@aaas.org
Internet: www.aas.org

AMOUNT: $40,000+

DEADLINE(S): JAN 15

FIELD(S): Science; Engineering

Post-doctoral fellowships open to AAAS members or applicants concurrently applying for membership. Prospective fellows must demonstrate exceptional competence in an area of science or have a broad scientific or technical background. Those with MA degrees and at least three years of poast-degree professional experience may also apply.

U.S. citizenship required. For complete information on these one-year fellowships write to Director, Science Fellows Program at address above.

277 — AMERICAN ASSOCIATION OF UNIVERSITY WOMEN EDUCATIONAL FOUNDATION (Selected Professions Fellowships)

Dept. 60
2201 N. Dodge St.
Iowa City IA 52243-4030
319/337-1716, ext. 60
FAX 319/337-1204
Internet: www.aauw.org

AMOUNT: $5,000-$15,000

DEADLINE(S): JAN 2 (most); NOV 15 (engineering dissertation only)

FIELD(S): Architecture; Computer/Information Sciences; Engineering; Mathematics/Statistics

For women in final year of graduate study in fields where women's participation has been low. Must be US citizen or permanent resident. Special consideration given to applicants who show professional promise in innovative or neglected areas of research and/or practice in areas of public interest. Women in engineering master's programs are eligible to apply for either first or final year of study; special award for engineering doctoral students writing dissertation.

Applications available August-December.

278 — AMERICAN FOUNDATION FOR THE BLIND (Paul W. Ruckes Scholarship)

11 Penn Plaza, Ste. 300
New York NY 10001
212/502-7661 or TDD 212/502-7771
E-Mail: juliet@afb.org
Internet: www.afb.org

AMOUNT: $1,000

DEADLINE(S): APR 30

FIELD(S): Engineering, computer, physical, or life sciences

Open to blind or visually impaired undergraduate or graduate students pursuing degrees in the above fields. U.S. citizenship required.

Write to the above address or visit website for complete information.

279 — AMERICAN INDIAN SCIENCE AND ENGINEERING SOCIETY (A.T. Anderson Memorial Scholarship)

PO Box 9828
Albuquerque NM 87119-9828
505/765-1052
FAX: 505/765-5608
E-Mail: scholarships@aises.org
Internet: www.aises.org/scholarships

AMOUNT: $1,000-$2,000

DEADLINE(S): JUN 15

FIELD(S): Medicine; Natural Resources; Science; Engineering

Open to undergraduate and graduate students who are at least 1/4 American Indian or recognized as member of a tribe. Must be member of AISES ($10 fee), enrolled full-time at an accredited institution, and demonstrate financial need.

Renewable. See website or contact Patricia Browne for an application and/or membership information.

280 — AMERICAN SOCIETY FOR ENGINEERING EDUCATION (Army Research Laboritory Postdoctoral Fellowships)

1818 N St., NW, Ste. 600
Washington DC 20036
202/331-3525
FAX: 202/265-8504
E-Mail: projects@asee.org
Internet: www.asee.org/fellowship/

AMOUNT: $45,000-$55,000 + travel/relocation allowance

DEADLINE(S): Varies

FIELD(S): Engineering; Physical Sciences

Postdoctoral fellowships for US citizens/permanent residents to do research at Army Research Laboratories. Candidates must have completed their Ph.D. prior to appointment. Program is designed to increase involvement of creative and highly trained scientists and engineers from academia and industry in scientific and technical areas of interest and relevance to the Army. Research proposal should include clear objective and defined outcome. Financial need NOT a factor.

15 awards annually. Renewable. Contact Sandi Crawford at ASEE for an application packet.

281 — AMERICAN SOCIETY FOR ENGINEERING EDUCATION (Helen T. Carr Fellowship Program)

1818 N St., NW, Ste. 600
Washington DC 20036
202/331-3525
FAX: 202/265-8504
E-Mail: projects@asee.org
Internet: www.asee.org/fellowship/

AMOUNT: $10,000 (max.)

DEADLINE(S): JAN 15; MAY 15

FIELD(S): Engineering

Graduate fellowships are only available to African-American students who are currently engaged in planning to enter a career in higher education at a Historically Black Engineering College (HBEC). May be faculty or pusuing a doctoral degree. Financial need NOT a factor.

5 awards annually. Renewable. Contact Tim Turner at ASEE for an application.

282 — ASIAN INSTITUTE OF TECHNOLOGY (AIT Scholarship Program)

Development Office
PO Box 4, Klongluang
Pathumthani 12120 THAILAND
(66)(2) 516-0110-44 or 524-5032
FAX: (66)(2) 516-2126
E-Mail: ascao@ait.ac.th
Internet: www.ait.ac.th

AMOUNT: US $12,600-$37,960

DEADLINE(S): FEB 15; JUN 15; OCT 15

FIELD(S): Advanced Technologies; Civil Engineering; Environment, Resources, & Development; Business Management

Scholarships and grants open to citizens of Asian countries who are accepted by the institute as a master's or doctotal candidate. Selection is based on academic criteria, practical experience, gender, and country of origin; priority to Mekong Region countries and Asian countries of the former USSR.

250 awards annually. Contact AIT for an application.

283 — ASSOCIATED WESTERN UNIVERSITIES, INC. (AWU Faculty Fellowships)

4190 South Highland Dr., Suite 211
Salt Lake City UT 84124-2600
801-273-8900

AMOUNT: Varies.

DEADLINE(S): FEB 15

FIELD(S): Engineering, Mathematics, Science, Technology

Research fellowships for qualified college and university faculty members to encourage participation and contribution to research at one of 62 cooperating facilities. It is not necessary to be enrolled at an AWU member institution. Collaborations that include graduate and/or undergraduate students are encouraged.

For detailed information and list of cooperating facilities, contact above location.

284 — ASSOCIATED WESTERN UNIVERSITIES, INC. (AWU Graduate Fellowship Program)

4190 South Highland Dr. Suite 211
Salt Lake City, UT 84124-2600
801/273-8900

AMOUNT: Stipend ($1,300 per month & up) + tuition assistance and travel allowance

DEADLINE(S): FEB 15

FIELD(S): Engineering, Mathematics, Science, Technology

Open to master's and doctoral degree candidates to conduct research toward a thesis or dissertation at one of more than 62 cooperating facilities. Institutional affiliation and citizenship restrictions may apply for some awards or facilities. It is not necessary to be enrolled at an AWU member institution to apply for a fellowship.

Write to the above address for complete information.

285 — ASSOCIATED WESTERN UNIVERSITIES, INC. (AWU Postgraduate Fellowship)

4190 South Highland Dr. Suite 211
Salt Lake City UT 84124-2600
801/273-8900

AMOUNT: Stipend established by the host facility and varies by experience and discipline.

DEADLINE(S): Varies (Two to three months before the starting date)

FIELD(S): Engineering, Mathematics, Science, Technology

For college and university graduates who have completed all institutional requirements for an advanced degree from an accredited college or university in the U.S. A commitment to a professional career in science or engineering research is expected. U.S. citizenship or permanent resident status is required. Research is to be done at one of the 62 cooperating universities.

For detailed information and a list of cooperating facilities contact above address.

286 — ASSOCIATED WESTERN UNIVERSITIES, INC. (AWU Visiting Scientist Fellowships)

4190 South Highland Dr., Suite 211
Salt Lake City UT 84124-2600
801/273-8900

AMOUNT: Varies

DEADLINE(S): Varies (Two months prior to starting date)

FIELD(S): Engineering, Science, Mathematics, and Technology

Research fellowships for professionals with continued commitment to science and engineering. For use at one of 62 participating universities. US citizenship or permanent residency required.

For detailed information and list of cooperating facitilies contact above location.

287 — ASSOCIATION FOR WOMEN IN SCIENCE EDUCATIONAL FOUNDATION (AWIS Predoctoral Awards)

1200 New York Ave. NW, Suite 650
Washington DC 20005
202/326-8940 or 800-886-AWIS
E-Mail: awis@awis.org
Internet: www.awis.org

AMOUNT: $1,000

DEADLINE(S): JAN 16

FIELD(S): Various Sciences and Social Sciences

Scholarships for female doctoral students. Summary page, description of research project, resume, references, transcripts, and biographical sketch required. US citizens may study at any graduate institution; non-citizens must study at US institutions.

5-10 awards annually. See website or write to above address for an application and complete information.

288 — ASSOCIATION FOR WOMEN IN SCIENCE EDUCATIONAL FOUNDATION (AWIS Pre-doctoral Awards)

1200 New York Ave. NW, Suite 650
Washington DC 20005
202/326-8940 or 800/886-AWIS
E-Mail: awis@awis.org
Internet: www.awis.org

AMOUNT: $1,000

DEADLINE(S): JAN 16

FIELD(S): Various Sciences and Social Sciences

Scholarships for female doctoral students. Summary page, description of research project, resume, references, transcripts, and biographical sketch required. US citizens may study at any graduate institution; non-citizens must be enrolled in US institutions.

5-10 awards annually. See website or write to above address for an application and more information.

289 — ASSOCIATION FOR WOMEN IN SCIENCE EDUCATIONAL FOUNDATION (Ruth Satter Memorial Award)

1200 New York Ave., NW, Suite 650
Washington DC 20005
202/326-8940 or 800/886-AWIS
E-Mail: awis@awis.org
Internet: www.awis.org

AMOUNT: $1,000

DEADLINE(S): JAN 16

FIELD(S): Various Sciences and Social Sciences

Scholarships for female doctoral students who have interrupted their education for at least three years to raise a family. Summary page, description of research project, resume, references, transcripts, biographical sketch, and letter from your department to confirm eligibility required. US citizens may study at any graduate institution; non-citizens must attend US institutions.

See website or write to above address for more information or an application.

290 — ASSOCIATION FOR WOMEN IN SCIENCE EDUCATIONAL FOUNDATION (Ruth Satter Memorial Award)

1200 New York Ave. NW, Suite 650
Washington DC 20005
202/326-8940 or 800/886-AWIS
E-Mail: awis@awis.org
Internet: www.awis.org

AMOUNT: $1,000

DEADLINE(S): JAN 16

FIELD(S): Various Sciences and Social Sciences

Scholarships for female doctoral students who have interupted their education three years or more to raise a family. Summary page, description of research project, resume, references, transcripts, biographical sketch, and proof of eligibility from department head required. US citizens may attend any graduate institution; non-citizens must be enrolled in US institutions.

See website or write to above address for more information or an application.

291 — AUSTRIAN CULTURAL INSTITUTE (Max Kade Foundation Grants)

950 Third Ave., 20th Fl.
New York NY 10022
212/759-5165 or +43/1/51581-253
FAX: 212/319-9636
E-Mail: desk@aci.org
Internet: www.austriaculture.net

AMOUNT: Varies

DEADLINE(S): Varies

FIELD(S): Medicine; Natural Sciences; Engineering

Open to young Austrian scientists with several years of experience at universities or institutions. Must demonstrate capacity to pursue independent teaching or research activities in the US. Proficiency in English required.

See website or contact ACI for an application kit, or write to Osterreichische Akademie der Wissenschaften, Kommission fur Max Kade Stipendien, Dr. Ignaz Seipel-Platz 2, A-1010 Vienna, Austria.

292 — BOEING (Polish Graduate Student Scholarship Program)

Phone for details
314/234-2149

AMOUNT: Tuition, books, and fees for three years

DEADLINE(S): Varies

FIELD(S): Scientific and technical fields

Scholarships for students from Poland to pursue graduate studies in scientific and technical areas at American colleges or universities.

Call Jim Schlueter at above telephone number.

293 — BRITISH FEDERATION OF WOMEN GRADUATES (M.H. Joseph Prize for Non-UK Citizens)

4 Mandeville Courtyard
142 Battersea Park Rd.
London SW11 4NB ENGLAND UK
PHONE/FAX: 0171/498 8037

AMOUNT: 500+ pounds sterling

DEADLINE(S): SEP 10

FIELD(S): Architecture; Engineering

For female graduate students of any nationality (except UK) who will pursue studies in Great Britain. Must have completed at least four academic terms or three semesters; award is not made for first year of research. Chief criteria is academic excellence and proven ability to carry out independent research. Postdoctoral studies also eligible.

1 award annually. Application fee of 12 pounds sterling required. Send a self-addressed, stamped envelope (or self-addressed envelope with international reply coupons) for an application. Results announced by end of October.

294 — BRITISH FEDERATION OF WOMEN GRADUATES (M.H. Joseph Prize for UK Citizens)

4 Mandeville Courtyard
142 Battersea Park Rd.
London SW11 4NB ENGLAND UK
PHONE/FAX: 0171/498 8037

AMOUNT: 500+ pounds sterling

DEADLINE(S): SEP 10

FIELD(S): Architecture; Engineering

For female UK citizens who plan to pursue graduate studies overseas. Must have completed at least four academic terms or three semesters; award is not made for first year of research. Chief criteria is academic excellence and proven ability to carry out independent research. Postdoctoral studies also eligible.

1 award annually. Application fee of 12 pounds sterling required. Send a self-addressed, stamped envelope (or self-addressed envelope with international reply coupons) for an application. Award announced at end of October.

295 — BROOKHAVEN WOMEN IN SCIENCE (Renate W. Chasman Scholarship)

PO Box 183
Upton NY 11973-5000
E-mail: pam@bnl.gov

AMOUNT: $2,000

DEADLINE(S): APR 1

FIELD(S): Natural Sciences; Engineering; Mathematics

Open ONLY to women who are residents of the boroughs of Brooklyn or Queens or the counties of Nassau or Suffolk in New York who are re-entering school after a period of study. For juniors, seniors, or first-year graduate students.

1 award annually. Not renewable. Contact Pam Mansfield at above location for an application. Phone calls are NOT accepted.

296 — BUSINESS & PROFESSIONAL WOMEN'S FOUNDATION (BPW Career Advancement Scholarship Program)

2012 Massachusetts Ave., NW
Washington DC 20036-1070
202/293-1200, ext. 169
FAX: 202/861-0298
Internet: www.bpwusa.org

AMOUNT: $500-$1,000

DEADLINE(S): APR 15

FIELD(S): Biology, Science, Education, Engineering, Social Science, Paralegal, Humanities, Business, Math, Computers, Law, MD, DD

For women (US citizens) aged 25+ accepted into accredited program at US institution (+Puerto Rico & Virgin Islands). Must graduate within 12 to 24 months from the date of grant and demonstrate critical finanacial need. Must have a plan to upgrade skills, train for a new career field, or to enter/re-enter the job market.

Full- or part-time study. For info see website or send business-sized, self-addressed, double-stamped envelope.

297 — CANADIAN FEDERATION OF UNIVERSITY WOMEN (CFUW Memorial/ Professional Fellowship)

251 Bank St., Ste. 600
Ottawa Ontario K2P 1X3 CANADA
613/234-2732
Internet: www.cfuw.ca

AMOUNT: $5,000

DEADLINE(S): NOV 15

FIELD(S): Science & Technology

Open to women who are Canadian citizens/ permanent residents enrolled in a master's degree program in science and technology. Must hold at least a bachelor's degree or equivalent from a recognized university and have been accepted into, or be currently enrolled in the proposed program and place of study. May be studying abroad.

$25 filing fee. Contact CFUW for an application after August 1st. Candidates will be notified by May 31st.

298 — COMMISSAO INVOTAN/ICCTI (NATO Science Fellowships Program)

Av. D. Carlos I
126-6 o
1200 Lisbon PORTUGAL
+351.1.396 0313 (dir)
FAX: +351.1.397 5144

AMOUNT: Varies

DEADLINE(S): JAN 1; MAR 1

FIELD(S): Sciences and engineering

Doctoral and postdoctoral fellowships in almost all scientific areas, including interdisciplinary areas. For citizens of NATO countries and NATO's Cooperation Partner countries who wish to study or do research in Portugal.

May be renewable under certain terms. Approximately 40 new fellowships each year. Write for complete information.

299 — COMMISSAO INVOTAN/ICCTI (NATO Science Fellowships-Advanced and Senior Programs)

Av. D. Carlos I
126 o
1200 Lisbon PORTUGAL
+351.1.396 0313 (DIR)
FAX: +351.1.397 5144

AMOUNT: Varies

DEADLINE(S): APR 1; OCT 1

FIELD(S): Natural and social sciences and engineering

Doctoral and postdoctoral fellowships in almost all scientific areas, social sciences, and engineering. For citizens of Portugal who wish to study and/or do research in another NATO member country.

May be renewable under certain terms. Approximately 50 new fellowships each year. Write for complete information.

300 — COMMISSAO INVOTAN/ICCTI (NATO Senior Guest Fellowship)

Av. D. Carlos I
126 o
1200 Lisbon PORTUGAL
+351.1.396 0313 (dir)
FAX: +351.1.397 5144

AMOUNT: Varies

DEADLINE(S): APR 1; OCT 1

FIELD(S): Sciences and engineering

Postdoctoral fellowships open to senior scientists from other NATO countries and from countries of central & eastern Europe, NATO's Cooperation Partners. Must have high professional standing and wish to spend three weeks to a year in Portugal.

20 annual awards. Write for complete information.

301 — CONSULTING ENGINEERS COUNCIL OF NEW JERSEY (Louis Goldberg Scholarship Fund)

66 Morris Ave.
Springfield NJ 07081
973/564-5848
FAX: 973/564-7480

AMOUNT: $1,000

DEADLINE(S): JAN 1

FIELD(S): Engineering or Land Surveying

Open to undergraduate students who have completed at least two years of study (or fifth year in a five-year program) at an ABET-accredited college or university in New Jersey, are in top half of their class, and are considering a career as a consulting engineer or land surveyor. Must be U.S. citizen.

Recipients will be eligible for American Consulting Engineers Council national scholarships of $2,000 to $5,000. Write for complete information.

302 — CUBAN AMERICAN NATIONAL FOUNDATION (The Mas Family Scholarships)

7300 NW 35 Terrace
Miami FL 33122
305/592-7768
FAX: 305/592-7889
E-Mail canfnet.org
Internet: www.canfnet.org

AMOUNT: Individually negotiated

DEADLINE(S): MAR 15

FIELD(S): Engineering, Business, International Relations, Economics, Communications, Journalism

For Cuban-Americans students, graduates and undergraduates, born in Cuba or direct descendants of those who left Cuba. Must be in top 10% of high school class or maintain a 3.5 GPA in college.

10,000 awards/year. Recipients may re-apply for subsequent years. Financial need considered along with academic success, SAT and GRE scores, and leadership potential. Essays and proof of Cuban descent required.

303 — ENGINEERING & PHYSICAL SCIENCES RESEARCH COUNCIL (Studentships)

North Star Ave
Polaris House
Swindon SN2 1ET England
01 793-444000

AMOUNT: Maintenance & approved fees

DEADLINE(S): JUL 31

FIELD(S): Engineering & Physical Science

Research studentships for up to 3 years for Ph.D students, 1 year advanced course studentships for master's students. Tenable at U.K. institutions. Must be UK resident with relevant connection to UK for full award or with European Union member state with relevant connection to UK for fees-only award. Must have appropriate academic qualifications.

Approx 3,800 awards per year. Applications must be made through heads of departments. EPSRC does not accept applications direct from students. Write for complete information.

304 — ENGINEERING FOUNDATION (Grants for Exploratory Research)

345 E. 47th St., Suite 303
New York NY 10017
212/705-7835

AMOUNT: $25,000 maximum

DEADLINE(S): OCT 1

FIELD(S): Engineering

Seed funding for unique approaches in significant areas of engineering research. Project should be outside the scope of conventional funding sources. These grants are NOT intended for students— undergraduate or graduate.

Write for complete information.

305 — FANNIE AND JOHN HERTZ FOUNDATION (Fellowship)

Box 5032
Livermore CA 94551-5032
925/373-1642
Internet: www.hertzfoundation.org

AMOUNT: $25,000 stipend/yr. + $15,000 (max.) tuition allowance/yr.

DEADLINE(S): NOV 5

FIELD(S): Applied Physical Sciences

Open to graduate students with a minimum 3.75 GPA for studies in applied physical sciences, including math, engineering, computer science, biology, oceanography, aeronautics, astronomy, physics, and earth science. Must be US citizen/ permanent resident. Does not support study in pursuit of M.D. degree, although will support Ph.D. portion of a joint M.D./Ph.D. study program.

Renewable up to 5 years. Only 36 US schools are currently considered tenable. See website for an application and list of specific fields of study that are acceptable.

306 — FORD FOUNDATION/NATIONAL RESEARCH COUNCIL (Postdoctoral Fellowship for Minorities)

National Research Council
2101 Constitution Ave.
Washington DC 20418
202/334-2860
E-Mail: infofell@nas.edu
Internet: http//www.nas.edu/fo/index.html

AMOUNT: $25,000 + relocation and research allowance

DEADLINE(S): JAN 3

FIELD(S): Life and physical sciences, mathematics, engineering sciences, behavioral and social sciences, and the humanities

For U.S. citizens who received a Ph.D or Sc.D in the last 7 years and who are Native Amer. Indian or Alaskan, Black/African American, Mexican American, Native Pacific Islander, or Puerto Rican and who are or plan to be in a teaching or research career.

Contact above website or address for complete information.

307 — FORD FOUNDATION/NATIONAL RESEARCH COUNCIL (Predoctoral/ Dissertation Fellowships for Minorities)

2101 Constitution Ave.
Washington DC 20418
202/334-2872
E-Mail: infofell@nas.edu
Internet: http//www.nas.edu/fo/index.html

AMOUNT: $14,000 annual stipend + $6,000 grant to institution; $18,000 for dissertation fellowship

DEADLINE(S): NOV 3

FIELD(S): Most fields of study: sciences, humanities, engineering, behavioral science, social sciences, and computer science

Predoctoral and dissertation fellowships for students whose ethnicity is Alaskan Native, Black/ African American, Mexican American/Chicano, Native American Indian, Native Pacific Islander, or Puerto Rican. For research-based programs leading to careers in college teaching and research.

Contact above address or website.

308 — FOUNDATION FOR SCIENCE AND DISABILITY, INC. (FSD Science Student Grant Fund)

503 NW 89th Street
Gainesville FL 32607-1400

352/374-5774
FAX: 352/374-5781
E-Mail: rmankin@gainesville.usda.ufl.edu

AMOUNT: $1,000

DEADLINE(S): DEC 1

FIELD(S): Mathematics; Science; Medicine; Engineering; Computer Science

Open to graduate students with disabilities. May also apply as a fourth-year undergraduate accepted into a graduate or professional program. Awards are for some special purpose in connection with a science project or thesis in any of above fields. Student is required to write a 250-word essay which includes a description of professional goals/objectives, as well as purpose of grant. Transcripts and two letters of recommendation from faculty members are also required.

Contact Dr. Richard Mankin at above address for an application.

309 — GATES MILLENIUM SCHOLARS PROGRAM (Scholarships for Graduate Students)

8260 Willow Oaks Corporate Dr.
Fairfax VA 22031-4511
877/690-4677
Internet: www.gmsp.org

AMOUNT: Varies

DEADLINE(S): FEB 1

FIELD(S): Engineering; Mathematics; Science; Education; Library Science

College presidents, professors, & deans may nominate graduate students who are African-Americans, Native Americans, Hispanic Americans, or Asian Americans in above fields. Based on academic performance, commitment to academic study, involvement in community service & school activities, potential for leadership, career goals, and financial need. Must submit transcripts and letters of recommendation. Must be US citizen with a minimum 3.3 GPA

Application materials available November 1st; scholars will be notified in May. Funded by the Bill & Melinda Gates Foundation, and administered by the United Negro College Fund.

310 — GEORGE BIRD GRINNELL AMERICAN INDIAN CHILDREN'S FUND (Al Qoyawayma Award)

11602 Montague Ct.
Potomac MD 20854
301/424-2440
FAX: 301/424-8281
E-Mail: Grinnell_Fund@MSN.com

AMOUNT: $1,000

DEADLINE(S): JUN 1

FIELD(S): Science; Engineering

Open to Native American undergraduate and graduate students majoring in science or engineering and who have demonstrated an outstanding interest and skill in any one of the arts. Must be American Indian/Alaska Native (documented with Certified Degree of Indian Blood), be enrolled in college/university, be able to demonstrate commitment to serving community or other tribal nations, and document financial need.

Contact Dr. Paula M. Mintzies, President, for an application after January 1st.

311 — H. FLETCHER BROWN FUND (Scholarships)

c/o PNC Bank, Trust Dept.
P.O. Box 791
Wilmington DE 19899
302/429-1186

AMOUNT: Varies

DEADLINE(S): APR 15

FIELD(S): Medicine; Dentistry; Law; Engineering; Chemistry

Open to U.S. citizens born in Delaware and still residing in Delaware. For 4 years of study (undergrad or grad) leading to a degree that enables applicant to practice in chosen field.

Scholarships are based on need, scholastic achievement, and good moral character. Applications available in February. Write for complete information.

312 — INSTITUTION OF ELECTRICAL ENGINEERS (Postgraduate Awards)

Savoy Place
London WC2R 0BL ENGLAND
0171 240 1871 Ext. 2211/2235
FAX: 0171 497 3609
E-Mail: scholarships@iee.org.uk
Internet: www.iee.org.uk/Awards/pgsum.htm

AMOUNT: 1,000-6,000 pounds/yr.

DEADLINE(S): SEP 1; SEP 30

FIELD(S): Engineering

Scholarships for postgraduate students pursuing degrees in engineering who are residents of the United Kingdom.

Check website or contact organization for application details.

313 — INTERNATIONAL COUNCIL FOR CANADIAN STUDIES (Government of France Graduate Awards)

325 Dalhousie, S-800
Ottawa Ontario CANADA K1N 7G2
613/789-7828

FAX: 613/789-7830
E-Mail: general@iccs-ciec.ca
Internet: www.iccs-ciec.ca

AMOUNT: Tuition, travel, and living allowance

DEADLINE(S): OCT 31

FIELD(S): Pure and Applied Sciences, Social Sciences, Engineering, Medicine

One-year graduate scholarships open to Canadian citizens for study and research at the doctoral level. Sound knowledge of the French language is required.

Must hold masters degree. Cannot be held concurrently with other scholarships or remuneration. Write or access website for complete information.

314 — JAPAN SOCIETY FOR THE PROMOTION OF SCIENCE (Post-doctoral Fellowships for Foreign Researchers)

Jochi-Kioizaka Bldg.
6-26-3 Kioi-cho
Chiyoda-Ku
Tokyo 102 JAPAN
+81-3-3263-1721
Telex: J32281
FAX: +81-3-3263-1854

AMOUNT: 270,000 yen per month

DEADLINE(S): SEP 25; MAY 23

FIELD(S): Humanities; Social Sciences; Natural Sciences; Engineering; Medicine

Post-doctoral fellowships for advanced study & research in Japan.

Write for complete information

315 — JEWISH FEDERATION OF METROPOLITAN CHICAGO (Academic Scholarship Program for Studies in the Sciences)

One South Franklin St.
Chicago IL 60606
Written inquiry

AMOUNT: Varies

DEADLINE(S): MAR 1

FIELD(S): Mathematics, engineering, or science

Scholarships for college juniors, seniors, and graduate students who are Jewish and are residents of Chicago, IL and Cook County.

Academic achievement and financial need are considered. Applications accepted after Dec. 1.

316 — KING FAISAL FOUNDATION (Graduate Scholarship Program)

PO Box 352
Riyadh 11411 SAUDI ARABIA
966/1 465-2255
FAX: 966/1 465-6524

E-Mail: info@kff.com OR mprd@kff.com
Internet: www.kff.com OR
www.kingfaisalfoundation.org

AMOUNT: $400/mo. US allowance + tuition/fees paid directly to university + health insurance & travel

DEADLINE(S): None

FIELD(S): Medicine; Engineering; Physics; Chemistry; Geology

Open to graduate students who are Muslims under the age of 40. Must have BS degree, GPA of 86% or higher, and be accepted unconditionally by a university either in Europe or North America. Must be fluent in the language of area providing the studies. Selection based on academic performance.

Contact King Faisal Foundation for an application.

317 — MATHESON GAS PRODUCTS FOUNDATION (Scholarships)

PO Box 624
959 Rte. 46 E.
Parsippany NJ 07054-0624
Internet: www.mathesongas.com

AMOUNT: $5,000

DEADLINE(S): None

FIELD(S): Chemistry; Physics; Chemical Engineering; Material Science; Semiconductor Engineering

Open to financially needy graduate students who are African American, Latino, Asian, Native American, or female. Must be US citizens/permanent residents studying in above fields or related area.

Send self-addressed, stamped envelope to Jerry Cantrella, Director of Personnel, for an application.

318 — NAACP NATIONAL OFFICE (NAACP Willems Scholarship)

4805 Mount Hope Drive
Baltimore MD 21215
401/358-8900

AMOUNT: $2,000 undergrads; $3,000 grads

DEADLINE(S): APR 30

FIELD(S): Engineering; Chemistry; Physics; Mathematics

Open to NAACP male members majoring in one of the above areas. Undergrads must have GPA of 2.5+; graduates' GPAs must be 3.0+. Renewable if the required GPA is maintained.

Financial need must be established. Two letters of recommendation typed on letterhead from teachers or professors in the major field of specialization. Write for complete information. Include a legal size, self-addressed, stamped envelope.

319 — NAT'L CONSORTIUM FOR GRADUATE DEGREES FOR MINORITIES IN ENGINEERING & SCIENCE, INC. (GEM Fellowship Programs)

P.O. Box 537
Notre Dame IN 46556
219/631-7771
FAX: 219/287-1486
E-Mail: gem.1@nd.edu
Internet: www.nd.edu/~gem

AMOUNT: Full tuition & fees + annual stipend $20,000-$40,000 (M.S.) & $60,000-$100,000 (Ph.D.)

DEADLINE(S): DEC 1

FIELD(S): Engineering, Science

Master's & doctoral fellowships for underrepresented minorities (African American, Native American, Mexican American, Puerto Rican, & other Hispanic Americans). Must be US citizen. University must be a member of the Consortium (over 80 are).

200 M.S. & 25 Ph.D. fellowships annually. Financial need is NOT a factor. Contact G. George Simms, Executive Director, for an application.

320 — NATIONAL FEDERATION OF THE BLIND (Frank Walton Horn Memorial Scholarship)

805 Fifth Avenue
Grinnell IA 50112
515/236-3366

AMOUNT: $3,000

DEADLINE(S): MAR 31

FIELD(S): Architecture; Engineering

Open to legally blind students pursuing or planning to pursue a full-time postsecondary course of study in the US. Based on academic excellence, service to the community, and financial need. Membership NOT required.

1 award annually. Renewable. Contact Mrs. Peggy Elliot, Scholarship Committee Chairman, for an application.

321 — NATIONAL FEDERATION OF THE BLIND (Howard Brown Rickard Scholarship)

805 Fifth Avenue
Grinnell IA 50112
515/236-3366

AMOUNT: $3,000

DEADLINE(S): MAR 31

FIELD(S): Law; Medicine; Engineering; Architecture; Natural Sciences

For legally blind students pursuing or planning to pursue a full-time postsecondary course of study in the US. Based on academic excellence, service to the community, and financial need. Membership NOT required.

1 award annually. Renewable. Contact Mrs. Peggy Elliot, Scholarship Committee Chairman, for an application.

322 — NATIONAL RESEARCH COUNCIL OF CANADA (Research Associateships)

Research Associates Office
Ottawa Ontario K1A 0R6 CANADA
613/993-9150
FAX: 613/990-7669
Internet: www.nrc.ca/careers

AMOUNT: $39,366 Canadian

DEADLINE(S): None

FIELD(S): Natural Sciences; Engineering

Two-year research associateships are tenable at NRCC labs throughout Canada. Open to recent Ph.D.s in natural sciences or recent master's or Ph.D.s in engineering. Degrees should have been received within the last five years. Preference given to Canadians.

Renewable. See website or contact NRCC for an application.

323 — NATIONAL RESEARCH FOUNDATION (NRF Honors & Postgraduate Bursaries)

PO Box 2600
Pretoria 0001 SOUTH AFRICA
+27 012/481-4000
FAX: +27 012/349-1179
E-Mail: info@nrf.ac.za
Internet: www.nrf.ac.za

AMOUNT: Varies

DEADLINE(S): Varies

FIELD(S): Agriculture; Chemistry; Earth Sciences; Engineering; Biology; Mathematics; Physics; Forestry; Veterinary Science; Pharmaceutics

Open to South African citizens pursuing graduate/postgraduate studies in above fields.

500 awards annually. Contact NRF for an application.

324 — NATIONAL SCIENCES AND ENGINEERING RESEARCH COUNCIL OF CANADA (Graduate Scholarships)

Scholarships/Fellowships Division
350 Albert Street
Ottawa Ontario K1A 1H5 CANADA
613/996-3769
FAX: 613/996-2589
E-Mail: schol@nserc.ca
Internet: http://www.nserc.ca

AMOUNT: $15,700/year for 1st & 2nd years at masters or Ph.D level; $17,400/year (Ph.D level ONLY) 3rd & 4th years

DEADLINE(S): NOV 24

FIELD(S): Natural Sciences, Engineering, Biology, or Chemistry

Open to Canadian citizens or permanent residents who have earned or will soon earn a bachelors or masters degree in science or engineering. Academic excellence and research aptitude are considerations.

Write for complete information.

325 — NATIONAL SCIENCES AND ENGINEERING RESEARCH COUNCIL OF CANADA (Postdoctoral Fellowships)

Scholarships/Fellowships Division
350 Albert Street
Ottawa Ontario K1A 1H5 CANADA
613/996-3762
FAX: 613/996-2589
E-Mail: schol@nserc.ca
Internet: http://www.nserc.ca

AMOUNT: Individually negotiated

DEADLINE(S): Varies—average: $43,000

FIELD(S): Natural Sciences, Engineering, Biology, or Chemistry

Open to Canadian citizens or permanent residents who hold doctoral degrees in science or engineering. Academic excellence and research aptitude are considerations.

Write for complete information.

326 — NATIONAL SCIENCE FOUNDATION (NATO Postdoctoral Science Fellowship Program)

4201 Wilson Blvd.
Rm. 907
Arlington VA 22230
703/306-1630
FAX: 703/306-0468
E-Mail: porter@nsf.gov
Internet: www.ehr.nsf.gov/

AMOUNT: $2,750/month stipend + travel allowance

DEADLINE(S): NOV 1

FIELD(S): Science & Engineering

Postdoctoral fellowships in almost all scientific areas, including interdisciplinary areas. For US citizens who wish to study and/or do research in another NATO member country.

35 awards annually. See website or contact the National Administrator at above address.

327 — NATIONAL SOCIETY OF BLACK ENGINEERS (Scholarships)

1454 Duke St.
Alexandria VA 22314
703/549-2207
FAX: 703/683-5312
E-Mail: nsbehq@nsbe.org
Internet: www.nsbe.org

AMOUNT: Varies

DEADLINE(S): Varies

FIELD(S): Engineering and engineering technologies

Programs for black and other ethnic minorities in the fields of engineering and the engineering technologies. Organization offers pre-college programs, scholarships, career fairs, a journal, a newsletter, etc.

Contact organization for details.

328 — NATIONAL SPACE CLUB (Dr. Robert H. Goddard Scholarship)

2000 L Street, NW, Suite 710
Washington DC 20036-4907
202/973-8661

AMOUNT: $10,000

DEADLINE(S): JAN 8

FIELD(S): Science & Engineering

Open to undergraduate juniors and seniors and graduate students who have scholastic plans leading to future participation in the aerospace sciences and technology. Must be US citizen. Award based on transcript, letters of recommendation, accomplishments, scholastic plans, and proven past research and participation in space related science and engineering. Personal need is considered, but is not controlling.

Renewable. Send a self-addressed, stamped envelope for more information.

329 — NATIONAL SPACE CLUB (Dr. Robert H. Goddard Historical Essay Award)

2000 L Street, NW, Suite 710
Washington DC 20036-4907
202/973-8661

AMOUNT: $1,000 + plaque

DEADLINE(S): DEC 4

FIELD(S): Aerospace History

Essay competition open to any US citizen on a topic dealing with any significant aspect of the historical development of rocketry and astronautics. Essays should not exceed 5,000 words and should be fully documented. Will be judged on originality and scholarship.

Previous winners not eligible. Send self-addressed, stamped envelope for complete information.

330 — NATIONAL TECHNICAL ASSOCIATION, INC. (Scholarship Competitions for Minorities and Women in Science and Engineering)

6919 North 19th St.
Philadelphia PA 19126-1506
215/549-5743
FAX: 215/549-6509
E-Mail: ntamfj1@aol.com
Internet: www.huenet.com/nta

AMOUNT: $500-$5,000

DEADLINE(S): Varies

FIELD(S): Science, mathematics, engineering, and applied technology

Scholarships competitions for minorities and women pursuing degrees in the above fields. Additional scholarships are available through local chapters of NTA.

Check website or write to above address for details and for locations of local chapters.

331 — NEW YORK STATE HIGHER EDUCATION SERVICES CORPORATION (N.Y. State Regents Professional/Health Care Opportunity Scholarships)

Cultural Education Center, Rm. 5C64
Albany NY 12230
518/486-1319
Internet: www.hesc.com

AMOUNT: $1,000-$10,000/yr.

DEADLINE(S): Varies

FIELD(S): Medicine and dentistry and related fields, architecture, nursing, psychology, audiology, landscape architecture, social work, chiropractic, law, pharmacy, accounting, speech language pathology

For NY state residents who are economically disadvantaged and members of a minority group underrepresented in the chosen profession and attending school in NY state. Some programs carry a service obligation in New York for each year of support. For U.S. citizens or qualifying noncitizens.

Medical/dental scholarships require one year of professional work in NY.

332 — NORTH ATLANTIC TREATY ORGANIZATION (NATO Science Fellowships for Non-U.S. Citizens)

Boulevard Leopold III
Brussels BELGIUM
2/707-4231
E-Mail: science.fell@hq.nato.int
Internet: www.nato.int/science

AMOUNT: Varies (with country)

DEADLINE(S): Varies (with country)

FIELD(S): Most fields of Scientific study

Graduate and postdoctoral fellowships are available in almost all scientific fields, including interdisciplinary areas. Open to citizens of NATO member countries and NATO partner countries who wish to study and/or do research in another NATO member country or NATO partner country.

Program administered in each NATO country by a National Administrator. Write address above for address of your country's administrator.

333 — OAK RIDGE ASSOCIATED UNIVERSITIES (Laboratory Graduate Research Participation Program)

P.O. Box 117
Oak Ridge TN 37831-0117
423/576-4813

AMOUNT: $1,000-$1,200/mo. + allowance for dependents + tuition and fees reimbursement to a max. of $3,500/yr.

DEADLINE(S): Ongoing

FIELD(S): Life sciences, physical, and social sciences, mathematics, and engineering

For graduate students in one of the fields listed above who have completed all degree requirements except thesis or dissertation research. For full-time research under the joint direction of the major professor and a DOE staff member at one of various locations, primarily in the South. For six to twelve months.

Funded through U.S. Dept. of Energy, Office of Energy Reseach, and Office of Fossil Energy. Write for complete information.

334 — OAK RIDGE ASSOCIATED UNIVERSITIES (National Science Foundation Graduate Research Fellowships)

PO Box 3010
Oak Ridge TN 37831-3010
423/241-4300
FAX: 423/241-4513
E-Mail: nsfgrfp@orau.gov
Internet: www.orau.gov/nsf/nsffel.htm

AMOUNT: $15,000 stipend + $10,500 tuition allowance

DEADLINE(S): NOV 4

FIELD(S): Science; Math; Engineering; Computer Science

Three-year fellowships for graduate study leading to research-based master's or doctoral degrees in the above fields. Must be US citizens, nationals, or permanent residents at the time of application. Fellowships are awarded on the basis of ability. Women, minorities, and those with disabilities are

strongly encouraged to apply. One-time International Research Travel Allowance available.

1,000 awards annually. Contact Jeannette Bouchard for an application/more information.

335 — OAK RIDGE INSTITUTE FOR SCIENCE AND EDUCATION (Applied Health Physics Fellowship Program)

P.O. Box 117
Oak Ridge TN 37831-0117
423/576-2194 or 423/576-9279
E-Mail: COXRE@ORAU.GOV or
GRADFELL@ORAU.GOV

AMOUNT: $14,400 stipend + tuition and fees up to $9,000/yr paid to university + transportation costs up to $300/month

DEADLINE(S): JAN 26

FIELD(S): Engineering, mathematics, physical and life sciences

Fellowship in applied health physics to implement DOE's nuclear energy-related mission. Candidates must have B.A. degree in life or physical sciences, engineering, or mathematics. Recipients are subject to a service obligation of one year of full-time employment in a DOE facility for each academic year of fellowhip award.

For details and application, contact above location.

336 — OAK RIDGE INSTITUTE FOR SCIENCE AND EDUCATION (Industrial Hygiene Graduate Fellowship Program)

P.O. Box 117
Oak Ridge TN 37831-0117
423-576-9655
FAX: 423/576-8293
E-Mail: kinneym@orau.gov

AMOUNT:

DEADLINE(S): JAN 26

FIELD(S): Industrial Hygiene

A fellowship for first-year master's candidates who have undergraduate degrees in physical, life, environmental, or health sciences or enginering and who wish to pursue studies in industrial hygiene.

For details and application, contact above location.

337 — OAK RIDGE INSTITUTE FOR SCIENCE AND EDUCATION (Professional Internship Program/Oak Ridge National Laboratory)

P.O. Box 117
Oak Ridge TN 37831-0117
423/576-3426
423/576-3427

AMOUNT: $210 to $300/week + travel, tuition, and fees

DEADLINE(S): FEB 5; JUN 1; OCT 1

FIELD(S): Chemistry, environmental science, geology, hydrogeology, hydrology, chemical engineering, civil engineering, environmental engineering, mechanical engineering, computer science (technical database development)

Opportunities for graduates and undergraduates to participate in energy-related research projects that correlate with their academic and career goals. For 3 to 12 consecutive months.

Funded through Oak Ridge National Laboratory.

338 — OAK RIDGE INSTITUTE FOR SCIENCE AND EDUCATION (Professional Internship Program/Pittsburgh Energy Technology Center)

P.O. Box 117
Oak Ridge TN 37831-0117
423/576-3426
423/576-3427

AMOUNT: $235 to $325/week + travel, tuition, and fees

DEADLINE(S): FEB 5; JUN 1; OCT 1

FIELD(S): Chemistry, physics, environmental science, geology, chemical or environmental engineering, computer science, or statistics.

Opportunities for graduates and undergraduates to participate in fossil energy-related research projects that correlate with their academic and career goals. For 3 to 12 consecutive months.

Funded through U.S. Dept. of Energy, Office of Fossil Energy, and Pittsburgh Energy Technology Center.

339 — OAK RIDGE INSTITUTE FOR SCIENCE AND EDUCATION (Professional Internship Program/Savannah River Site)

P.O. Box 117
Oak Ridge TN 37831-0117
423/576-3426
423/576-3427

AMOUNT: $260 to $340/week + travel

DEADLINE(S): FEB 5; JUN 1; SEP 1

FIELD(S): Chemistry, computer science, environmental science, geology, engineering, or physics

Opportunities for high school junior and seniors, undergraduates, and graduates to participate in research projects that correlate with their academic majors and career goals. For 3 to 12 consecutive months at the Savannah River Site, SC.

Funded through the Savannah River Site, SC.

340 — OAK RIDGE INSTITUTE FOR SCIENCE AND EDUCATION (Science and Engineering Research Semester)

P.O. Box 117
Oak Ridge TN 37831-0117
423/576-2358
423/576-2310

AMOUNT: $225/week + travel + housing

DEADLINE(S): OCT; MAR

FIELD(S): Computer science, physical sciences, environmental and life sciences, and mathematics

Opportunities for high school junior and seniors and a few slots for graduates to participate in energy-related with laboratory scientists at Oak Ridge National Laboratory, TN. One semester with possibility of summer extension. Available two times a year.

Funded through the U.S. Dept. of Energy, Office of Energy Research.

341 — OAK RIDGE INSTITUTE FOR SCIENCE AND EDUCATION/U.S. DEPT. OF ENERGY (Office of Civilian Radioactive Waste Management Fellowship)

P.O. Box 117
Oak Ridge TN 37831-0117
423/576-0128
FAX: 423/576-8293
E-Mail: drostp@orau.gov

AMOUNT: $14,000/yr.

DEADLINE(S): JAN 16 (Received, not postmarked)

FIELD(S): Physical or life sciences, math, or engineering

Fellowships for graduate students at various participating universities to conduct research in the management of spent nuclear fuel and high-level raqdioactive waste. For M.A. and Ph.D. candidates. For up to 48 months. Must be U.S. citizen or permanent resident.

Funded through U.S. Department of Energy, Office of Civilian Radioactive Waste Management. Contact or call Ms. Portia Drost, MS-16, at above address for details.

342 — OAK RIDGE INSTITUTE FOR SCIENCE AND EDUCATION (Nuclear Engineering & Health Physics Fellowship Program)

105 Mitchell Rd. MS-16
Oak Ridge TN 37831-0117
423/576-2600 or 423/241-2890
E-Mail: johnsons@orau.gov or
daltonj@arou.gov

AMOUNT: $14,400/yr.

DEADLINE(S): JAN 26

FIELD(S): Engineering, physical and life sciences

Fellowships in nuclear engineering or applied health physics to implement DOE's nuclear energy-related mission. Candidates must have B.A. degree in life or physical sciences or engineering.

For details and application, contact Sandra Johnson or Jennifer Dalton at above location.

343 — RAYMOND J. HARRIS EDUCATION TRUST

P.O. Box 7899
Philadelphia PA 19101-7899
Written inquiry

AMOUNT: Varies

DEADLINE(S): FEB 1

FIELD(S): Medicine, law, engineering, dentistry, or agriculture

Scholarships for Christian men to obtain a professional education in medicine, law, engineering, dentistry, or agriculture at nine Philadelphia area colleges.

Contact Mellon Bank, N.A. at above location for details and the names of the nine colleges.

344 — ROBERT SCHRECK MEMORIAL FUND (Grants)

C/O Texas Commerce Bank-Trust Dept
PO Drawer 140
El Paso TX 79980
915/546-6515

AMOUNT: $500 - $1500

DEADLINE(S): JUL 15; NOV 15

FIELD(S): Medicine; Veterinary Medicine; Physics; Chemistry; Architecture; Engineering; Episcopal Clergy

Grants to undergraduate juniors or seniors or graduate students who have been residents of El Paso County for at least two years. Must be U.S. citizen or legal resident and have a high grade point average. Financial need is a consideration.

Write for complete information.

345 — SOCIETY OF AUTOMOTIVE ENGINEERS (SAE Doctoral Scholars Program)

400 Commonwealth Drive
Warrendale PA 15096-0001
724/772-4047
E-Mail: connie@sae.org
Internet: www.sae.org/students/schlrshp.htm

AMOUNT: up to $5,000/year

DEADLINE(S): APR 1

FIELD(S): Engineering Education

Forgiveable loan to assist & encourage promising doctoral students to pursue careers teaching engineering at college level. Must be citizen of North America (US/Canada/Mexico), holding degree from accredited undergraduate institution, & accepted into acredited doctoral program. For each year of eligible teaching upon graduation, one year's loan will be forgiven. Based on scholastic achievement, desire to teach, interest in mobility technology, & SAE advisor support.

3-4 awards annually. Renewable up to 3 years. See website or contact Connie Harnish, SAE Educational Relations Division, for an application. Notification is in June.

346 — SOCIETY OF AUTOMOTIVE ENGINEERS (Yanmar/SAE Scholarship)

400 Commonwealth Drive
Warrendale PA 15096-0001
724/772-4047
E-Mail: connie@sae.org
Internet: www.sae.org/students/schlrshp.htm

AMOUNT: $2,000 ($1,000/year)

DEADLINE(S): APR 1

FIELD(S): Engineering, as related to the Conservation of Energy in Transportation, Agriculture & Construction, and Power Generation

For graduate students and undergraduates in their senior year who are citizens of North America (US/Canada/Mexico). Based on previous scholastic performance with additional consideration given for special study or honors in the field of award, and for leadership achievement related to engineering or science. Emphasis will be placed on research or study related to the internal combustion engine.

1 award annually. See website or contact Connie Harnish, SAE Educational Relations Division, for an application. Notification is in June.

347 — SOCIETY OF HISPANIC PROFESSIONAL ENGINEERS FOUNDATION (SHPE Scholarships)

5400 E. Olympic Blvd., Ste. 210
Los Angeles CA 90022
323/888-2080

AMOUNT: $500-$3,000

DEADLINE(S): APR 15

FIELD(S): Engineering; Science

Open to deserving students of Hispanic descent who are seeking careers in engineering or science. For full-time undergraduate or graduate study at a college or university. Based on academic achievement and financial need.

Send self-addressed, stamped envelope to above address for an application.

348 — SOCIETY OF WOMEN ENGINEERS (B.K. Krenzer Memorial Re-entry Scholarship)

120 Wall St., 11th Floor
New York NY 10005-3902
800/666-ISWE or 212/509-9577
FAX 212/509-0224
E-Mail: hq@swe.org
Internet: www.swe.org

AMOUNT: $1,000

DEADLINE(S): MAY 15

FIELD(S): Engineering; Computer Science

For women who have been out of the engineering job market as well as out of school for a minimum of two years. For any year undergraduate or graduate study, full- or part-time, at a college/university with an ABET-accredited program or in a SWE-approved school. Must have a minimum 3.5 GPA. Preference is given to degreed engineers desiring to return to the workforce following a period of temporary retirement.

1 award annually. Send a self-addressed, stamped envelope to SWE for an application. Recipient is notified in September.

349 — SOCIETY OF WOMEN ENGINEERS (Chrysler Corporation Re-entry Scholarship)

120 Wall St., 11th Floor
New York NY 10005-3902
800/666-ISWE or 212/509-9577
FAX: 212/509-0224
E-Mail: hq@swe.org
Internet: www.swe.org

AMOUNT: $2,000

DEADLINE(S): MAY 15

FIELD(S): Engineering; Computer Science

For women who have been out of the engineering job market as well as out of school for a minimum of two years. For any level of study at a college/university with an ABET-accredited program or in a SWE-approved school. Must have a minimum 3.5 GPA.

1 award annually. Send a self-addressed, stamped envelope to SWE for an application. Recipient is notified in September.

350 — SOCIETY OF WOMEN ENGINEERS (General Motors Foundation Graduate Scholarship)

120 Wall St., 11th Floor
New York NY 10005-3902
212/509-9577
FAX 212/509-0224
E-Mail: hq@swe.org
Internet: www.swe.org

AMOUNT: $1,500 + $500 travel grant

DEADLINE(S): FEB 1

FIELD(S): Engineering: Mechanical, Electrical, Chemical, Industrial, Materials, Automotive, Manufacturing, Technology

For women entering 1st year of master's program at a college/university w/ ABET-accredited program or SWE-approved school. Must exhibit career interest in automotive industry or manufacturing environment. Must have minimum 3.5 GPA & demonstrate leadership by holding position of responsibility in student organization. Travel grant is to attend SWE National Convention & Student Conference.

1 award annually. Send self-addressed, stamped envelope to SWE for application. Recipient notified in May.

351 — SOCIETY OF WOMEN ENGINEERS (Olive Lynn Salembier Scholarship)

120 Wall St., 11th Floor
New York NY 10005-3902
800/666-ISWE or 212/509-9577
FAX 212/509-0224
E-Mail: hq@swe.org
Internet: www.swe.org

AMOUNT: $2,000

DEADLINE(S): MAY 15

FIELD(S): Engineering; Computer Science

For women who have been out of the engineering job market as well as out of school for a minimum of two years. For any year undergraduate or graduate study, full- or part-time, at a college/university with an ABET-accredited program or in a SWE-approved school. Must have a minimum 3.5 GPA.

1 award annually. Send a self-addressed, stamped envelope to SWE for an application. Recipient is notified in September.

352 — TAU BETA PI ASSOCIATION, INC. (Graduate Fellowships)

PO Box 2697
Knoxville TN 37901-2697
423/546-4578

AMOUNT: $10,000

DEADLINE(S): JAN 15

FIELD(S): Engineering

Graduate stipends for members of Tau Beta Pi who hold a bachelor's degree. Membership is not by application—only by collegiate chapter invitation and initiation.

22 awards annually. Write for complete information.

353 — THE BRITISH COUNCIL (Postgraduate Scholarships to Mexico)

10 Spring Gardens
London SW1A 2BN ENGLAND UK
+44 (0) 171 930 8466
FAX: +44 (0) 161 957 7188
E-Mail: education.enquiries@britcoun.org
Internet: www.britcoun.org/mexico/mexschol.htm

AMOUNT: Varies

DEADLINE(S): Varies

FIELD(S): Science and technology

The British Council in Mexico offers the opportunity, funded by the Mexican Council for Science and Technology (CONACYT), to British citizens to study in Mexico. Another way to receive information is to contact: CONACYT, Av. Constituyentes No. 1046, Col. Lomas Altas, C.P. 11950, Mexico, D.F. or E-mail to informa@mailer.main.conacyt.mx.

Contact with the source of information in London or in Mexico for details. In Mexico, the British Council Information Centre E-mails are: carmina.ramon@bc-mexico.sprint.com (Mexico City) or teresa riggen@bc-mexico.sprint.com (Guadalajara).

354 — THE BRITISH COUNCIL (Scholarships for Citizens of Mexico)

10 Spring Gardens
London SW1A 2BN ENGLAND UK
+44 (0) 171 930 8466
FAX: +44 (0) 161 957 7188
E-Mail: education.enquiries@britcoun.org
Internet: www.britcoun.org/mexico/mexschol.htm

AMOUNT: Varies

DEADLINE(S): Varies

FIELD(S): Social sciences, applied sciences, technology

The British Council in Mexico offers approximately 100 scholarshps per year in the above fields for undergraduates and graduates to study in the United Kingdon. Good level of English language retired.

The website listed here gives more details. For more information, contact: leticia.magana@bc-mexico.sprint.com. or contact organization in London.

355 — THE DAPHNE JACKSON MEMORIAL FELLOWSHIPS TRUST (Fellowships in Science/ Engineering)

School of Physical Sciences, Dept. of Physics, University of Surrey
Guildford, Surrey GU2 5XH ENGLAND UK

01483 259166
FAX: 01483 259501
E-Mail: J.Woolley@surrey.ac.uk
Internet: www.sst.ph.ic.ac.uk/trust/

AMOUNT: Varies

DEADLINE(S): Varies

FIELD(S): Science or engineering, including information sciences

Fellowships to enable well-qualified and highly motivated scientists and engineers to return to appropriate careers following a career break due to family comitments. May be used on a flexible, part-time basis. Tenable at various U.K. universities.

See website and/or contact organization for details.

356 — THE NORWAY-AMERICA ASSOCIATION (The Norwegian Marshall Fund)

Drammensveien 20C
N-0255 Oslo 2 NORWAY
011 47-22-44-76-83

AMOUNT: Up to $5,000

DEADLINE(S): Varies

FIELD(S): All fields of study

The Marshall Fund was established in 1977 as a token of Norway's gratitude to the U.S. for support after WWII. Objective is to promote research in Norway by Americans in science and humanities. For U.S. citizens.

Contact above location for further information.

357 — TUSKEGEE UNIVERSITY (Graduate Research Fellowships and Assistantships)

Admissions Office
Tuskegee University, 1506 Franklin Rd., AL 36088
334/727/8500

AMOUNT: Tuition

DEADLINE(S): MAR 15

FIELD(S): Chemistry; Engineering; Environmental Science; Life Sciences; Nutrition; Education

Graduate research fellowships and graduate assistantships are available to qualified individuals who wish to enter Tuskegee University's graduate program in pursuit of a master's degree.

Write for complete information.

358 — U.S. DEPARTMENT OF TRANSPORTATION (Dwight D. Eisenhower Transportation Fellowships)

U.S. Dept. of Transportation, Fed. Hwy. Admin., 6300 Georgetown Pike, HHI-20 McLean VA 22101-2296

703/235-0538

AMOUNT: Varies

DEADLINE(S): FEB

FIELD(S): Transportation—such majors as chemistry; materials science; corrosion; civil, chemical, & electronics engineering; structures; human factors; computer science; psychology.

Research fellowships for undergrads and grad students at any Dept. of Transportation facility or selected IHE. For three to twelve months. Research must focus on transportation-related research and development in the above fields.

Contact Ilene Payne, Director, Universities and grants Programs at above location for details.

359 — UNIVERSITY OF ALBERTA (Alberta Research Council Karl A. Clark Memorial Scholarship)

Graduate Studies & Research
105 Administration Bldg.
Edmonton Alberta T6G 2M7 Canada
708/492-3499
FAX 708/492-0692
Internet: www.ualberta.ca/gradstudies

AMOUNT: $20,000 Canadian

DEADLINE(S): MAR 1 (for nomination by department—check w/ dept. head for internal deadline)

FIELD(S): Computer Engineering; Computer Science

For a student in a MSc or Ph.D. degree program engaged in thesis research in the above areas and concerned with software and information technologies. Students may apply, in open competition, to hold the award for an additional year at the MSc level, and for an additional two years at the Ph.D. level.

1 award annually. Renewable (see above). Contact your Department Chair for complete information.

360 — UNIVERSITY OF MANCHESTER (Awards for Research)

Secretary, Research and Graduate Support Unit
Manchester M13 9PL England
0161 275 2035
FAX: 0161 275 2445/7216

AMOUNT: Maintenance grant (approx) 5000 pounds p.a. plus payment of UK tuition fees.

DEADLINE(S): MAY 1

FIELD(S): Arts, Economics, Social Studies, Education, Science, Engineering, Biological Sciences, Law

The university offers research studentships for doctoral research in all disciplines. These awards are highly competitive. Applicants should hold at least a 2:1 degree or equivalent. Awards are renewable for up to 2 years.

Approx 50 awards per year. Please contact address above for complete information.

361 — UNIVERSITY OF OXFORD (Graduate Unilever Scholarship)

St. Cross College
Oxford OX1 3LZ ENGLAND UK
+44 01865-278492

AMOUNT: 1,774 pounds sterling

DEADLINE(S): MAR 15

FIELD(S): Biochemistry; Engineering

Supplementary award is open to students undertaking graduate/postgraduate research at Oxford University.

Renewable up to 3 years. Contact Tutor for Admissions for an application.

362 — US ARMS CONTROL AND DISARMAMENT AGENCY (William C. Foster Visiting Scholars Program)

320 21st St. NW
Room 5726
Washington DC 20451
703/647-8090

AMOUNT: Salary + per diem

DEADLINE(S): JAN 31

FIELD(S): Arms Control; Nonproliferation; Disarmament

Program open to faculty of recognized institutions of higher learning who wish to lend their expertise in areas relevant to the ACDA for a period of one year. U.S. citizenship or permanent residency required.

Write for complete information.

363 — US DEPARTMENT OF DEFENSE (National Defense Science & Engineering Graduate Fellowship Programs)

200 Park Drive, Suite 211, P.O. Box 13444
Research Triangle Park, NC 27709-3444
919/549-8505
Internet: www.acq.osd.mil/ddre/edugate/s-aindx.html

AMOUNT: Full tuition and fees (tenure of 36 months)

DEADLINE(S): JAN

FIELD(S): Mathematical, physical, biological, ocean, and engineering sciences

Must be US citizens or nationals at or near the beginning of their graduate study in science or engineering, leading to a doctoral degree. NDSEG Fellowships are awarded for study and research in these disciplines of military importance.

Approximately 90 new three-year graduate fellowships each April. Fellows may choose appropriate US institutions of higher education, offering degrees in science and engineering. Contact the Program Administrator for more information.

364 — WINSTON CHURCHILL FOUNDATION (Scholarships)

PO Box 1240
Gracie Station
New York NY 10028-0048
212/879-3480
FAX: 212/897-3480
E-Mail: churchillf@aol.com

AMOUNT: $27,000 (includes tuition, fees, travel, & living/spousal allowances)

DEADLINE(S): NOV 15

FIELD(S): Engineering; Mathematics; Science

Open to US citizens enrolled in one of 55 participating US colleges and universities to pursue graduate study at Churchill College at Cambridge University in England. Must be between the ages of 19 and 26. Financial need NOT a factor.

11 awards annually. Not renewable. Must apply through home institution.

365 — WOMEN IN DEFENSE (HORIZONS Scholarship Foundation)

NDIA
2111 Wilson Blvd., Ste. 400
Arlington VA 22201-3061
703/247-2552
FAX: 703/522-1885
E-Mail: dnwlee@moon.jic.com
Internet: www.adpa.org/wid/horizon/Scholar.htm

AMOUNT: $500+

DEADLINE(S): NOV 1; JUL 1

FIELD(S): Engineering, Computer Science, Physics, Mathematics, Business, Law, International Relations, Political Science, Operations Research, Economics, and fields relevant to a career in the areas of national security and defense.

For women who are U.S. citizens, have minimum GPA of 3.25, demonstrate financial need, are currently enrolled at an accredited university/college (full- or part-time—both grads and undergrad juniors/seniors are eligible), and demonstrate interest in pursuing a career related to national security.

Application is online or send SASE, #10 envelope, to Woody Lee, HORIZONS Scholarship Director.

366 — WOODROW WILSON NATIONAL FELLOWSHIP FOUNDATION (Leadership Program for Teachers)

CN 5281
Princeton NJ 08543-5281
609/452-7007
FAX: 609/452-0066
E-Mail: marchioni@woodrow.org OR irish@woodrow.org
Internet: www.woodrow.org

AMOUNT: Varies

DEADLINE(S): Varies

FIELD(S): Science; Mathematics

WWLPT offers summer institutes for middle and high school teachers in science and mathematics. One- and two-week teacher outreach, TORCH Institutes, are held in the summer throughout the US.

See website or contact WWNFF for an application.

367 — WOODS HOLE OCEANOGRAPHIC INSTITUTION (Postdoctoral Awards in Ocean Science and Engineering)

360 Woods Hole Road
Woods Hole MA 02543-1541
508/289-2219
FAX: 508/457-2188
E-Mail: mgately@whoi.edu
Internet: www.whoi.edu

AMOUNT: Varies

DEADLINE(S): FEB 16

FIELD(S): Chemistry, Engineering, Geology, Geophysics, Mathematics, Meteorology, Physics, Biology, Oceanography

Eighteen-month postdoctoral scholar awards are offered to recipients of new or recent doctorates in the above fields. The awards are designed to further the education and training of the applicant with primary emphasis placed on the individual's research promise.

For an application/more information, contact the Education Office, Clark Laboratory 223, MS #31, at above address.

368 — XEROX TECHNICAL MINORITY SCHOLARSHIP (School-Year Tuition)

907 Culver Road
Rochester NY 14609
www.xerox.com/employment

AMOUNT: Up to $5,000 (varies according to tuition and academic excellence)

DEADLINE(S): SEP 15

FIELD(S): Various engineering and science disciplines

Scholarships for minorities enrolled full-time in a technical degree program at the bachelor level or above. Must be African-American, Native American, Hispanic, or Asian. Recipient may not have tuition or related expenses covered by other scholarships or grants.

If above requirements are met, obtain application from website or address above. Your financial aid office must fill out the bottom half of the form. Send completed application, your resume and a cover letter to Xerox Technical Minority Scholarship Program at above address.

369 — XEROX TECHNICAL MINORITY SCHOLARSHIP (Summer Employment Program)

Xerox Square
Rochester NY 14644
Written inquiry

AMOUNT: Up to $5,000 (varies according to tuition and academic excellence)

DEADLINE(S): SEP 15

FIELD(S): Various engineering and science disciplines

Scholarships for minorities enrolled in a technical degree program at the bachelor level or above. Must be African-American, Native American, Hispanic, or Asian. Xerox will match your skills with a sponsoring organization that will offer a meaningful summer work experience complimenting your academic learning.

If above requirements are met, send your resume and a cover letter to Xerox Corporation Corporate Employment and College Relations Technical Mfinority Scholarship Program to above address.

AERONAUTICS

370 — AERO CLUB OF NEW ENGLAND (Aviation Scholarships)

4 Emerson Drive
Acton MA 01720
978/263-7793
E-Mail: pattis22@aol.com
Internet: www.acone.org

AMOUNT: $500-$2,000

DEADLINE(S): MAR 31

FIELD(S): Aviation and related fields

Several scholarships with varying specifications for eligibility for New England residents to be used at FAA-approved flight schools in New England states.

Information and applications are on website above.

371 — AIRCRAFT ELECTRONICS ASSOCIATION EDUCATIONAL FOUNDATION (Scholarships)

PO Box 1963
Independence MO 64055
816/373-6565
FAX: 816/478-3100
Internet: aeaavnews.org

AMOUNT: $1,000-$16,000

DEADLINE(S): Varies

FIELD(S): Avionics; Aircraft Repair

Various scholarships for high school and college students attending post-secondary institutions, including technical schools. Some are for study in Canada or Europe as well as the US.

25 programs. See website or contact AEA for specific details and applications.

372 — AMERICAN FOUNDATION FOR THE BLIND (Paul W. Ruckes Scholarship)

11 Penn Plaza, Ste. 300
New York NY 10001
212/502-7661 or TDD 212/502-7771
E-Mail: juliet@afb.org
Internet: www.afb.org

AMOUNT: $1,000

DEADLINE(S): APR 30

FIELD(S): Engineering, computer, physical, or life sciences

Open to blind or visually impaired undergraduate or graduate students pursuing degrees in the above fields. U.S. citizenship required.

Write to the above address or visit website for complete information.

373 — AMERICAN INSTITUTE OF AERONAUTICS AND ASTRONAUTICS (Technical Committee Graduate Awards)

1801 Alexander Bell Drive, Suite 500
Reston VA 20191-4344
800/NEW-AIAA or 703/264-7500
FAX: 703/264-7551
E-Mail: custserv@aiaa.org
Internet: www.aiaa.org

AMOUNT: $1,000

DEADLINE(S): JAN 31

FIELD(S): Science, Engineering, Astronautics, Aeronautics

Open to graduate students who have completed at least one year of full-time graduate study. Must have in place or underway a university approved thesis or research project specializing in one of the listed technical areas. GPA of 3.0 or higher. Graduate study program must be in support of field of science and engineering encompassed by a specialized area. Must be endorsed by graduate advisor and appropriate university department head.

Write to the above address for complete information.

374 — AMERICAN INSTITUTE OF AERONAUTICS AND ASTRONAUTICS (Graduate Student Awards)

1801 Alexander Bell Drive, Suite 500
Reston VA 20191-4344
800/639-AIAA or 703/264-7500
FAX: 703/264-7551
Internet: www.aiaa.org

AMOUNT: $5,000

DEADLINE(S): None specified

FIELD(S): Astronautics; Aeronautics; Aeronautical Engineering

For graduate student research in the aerospace field.

Eight awards. Contact above address for complete information.

375 — ASIAN INSTITUTE OF TECHNOLOGY (AIT Scholarship Program)

Development Office
PO Box 4, Klongluang
Pathumthani 12120 THAILAND
(66)(2) 516-0110-44 or 524-5032
FAX: (66)(2) 516-2126
E-Mail: ascao@ait.ac.th
Internet: www.ait.ac.th

AMOUNT: US $12,600-$37,960

DEADLINE(S): FEB 15; JUN 15; OCT 15

FIELD(S): Advanced Technologies; Civil Engineering; Environment, Resources, & Development; Business Management

Scholarships and grants open to citizens of Asian countries who are accepted by the institute as a master's or doctotal candidate. Selection is based on academic criteria, practical experience, gender, and country of origin; priority to Mekong Region countries and Asian countries of the former USSR.

250 awards annually. Contact AIT for an application.

376 — ASSOCIATED WESTERN UNIVERSITIES, INC. (AWU Faculty Fellowships)

4190 South Highland Dr., Suite 211
Salt Lake City UT 84124-2600
801-273-8900

AMOUNT: Varies.

DEADLINE(S): FEB 15

FIELD(S): Engineering, Mathematics, Science, Technology

Research fellowships for qualified college and university faculty members to encourage participation and contribution to research at one of 62 cooperating facilities. It is not necessary to be enrolled at an AWU member institution. Collaborations that include graduate and/or undergraduate students are encouraged.

For detailed information and list of cooperating facilities, contact above location.

377 — ASSOCIATED WESTERN UNIVERSITIES, INC. (AWU Graduate Fellowship Program)

4190 South Highland Dr. Suite 211
Salt Lake City, UT 84124-2600
801/273-8900

AMOUNT: Stipend ($1,300 per month & up) + tuition assistance and travel allowance

DEADLINE(S): FEB 15

FIELD(S): Engineering, Mathematics, Science, Technology

Open to master's and doctoral degree candidates to conduct research toward a thesis or dissertation at one of more than 62 cooperating facilities. Institutional affiliation and citizenship restrictions may apply for some awards or facilities. It is not necessary to be enrolled at an AWU member institution to apply for a fellowship.

Write to the above address for complete information.

378 — ASSOCIATED WESTERN UNIVERSITIES, INC. (AWU Postgraduate Fellowship)

4190 South Highland Dr. Suite 211
Salt Lake City UT 84124-2600
801/273-8900

AMOUNT: Stipend established by the host facility and varies by experience and discipline.

DEADLINE(S): Varies (Two to three months before the starting date)

FIELD(S): Engineering, Mathematics, Science, Technology

For college and university graduates who have completed all institutional requirements for an advanced degree from an accredited college or university in the U.S. A commitment to a professional career in science or engineering research is expected. U.S. citizenship or permanent resident status is required. Research is to be done at one of the 62 cooperating universities.

For detailed information and a list of cooperating facilities contact above address.

379 — ASSOCIATED WESTERN UNIVERSITIES, INC. (AWU Visiting Scientist Fellowships)

4190 South Highland Dr., Suite 211
Salt Lake City UT 84124-2600
801/273-8900

AMOUNT: Varies

DEADLINE(S): Varies (Two months prior to starting date)

FIELD(S): Engineering, Science, Mathematics, and Technology

Research fellowships for professionals with continued commitment to science and engineering. For use at one of 62 participating universities. US citizenship or permanent residency required.

For detailed information and list of cooperating facitilies contact above location.

380 — AVIATION COUNCIL OF PENNSYLVANIA (Scholarships)

3111 Arcadia Ave.
Allentown PA 18103
215/797-1133

AMOUNT: $1,000

DEADLINE(S): JUL 31

FIELD(S): Aviation maintenance, aviaiton management, or pilot training

Scholarships for individuals in the above fields who are residents of Pennsylvania but can attend school outside Pennsylvania.

Three awards yearly.

381 — AVIATION INSURANCE ASSOCIATION (Scholarship)

Aviation Technology Department
1 Purdue Airport
West Lafayette, IN 47906-3398
954/986-8080

AMOUNT: $1,000

DEADLINE(S): FEB

FIELD(S): Aviation

Scholarships for aviation students who have completed at least 30 college credits, 15 of which are in aviation. Must have GPA of at least 2.5 and be a U.S. citizen.

Write to Professor Bernard Wuile at Purdue University at above address for application and details.

382 — BOEING (Polish Graduate Student Scholarship Program)

Phone for details
314/234-2149

AMOUNT: Tuition, books, and fees for three years

DEADLINE(S): Varies

FIELD(S): Scientific and technical fields

Scholarships for students from Poland to pursue graduate studies in scientific and technical areas at American colleges or universities.

Call Jim Schlueter at above telephone number.

383 — CHARLES A. AND ANNE MORROW LINDBERGH FOUNDATION (Grants for Research Projects)

2150 Third Ave., N, Ste. 310
Anoka MN 55303-2200
612/576-1596
FAX: 612/576-1664
E-Mail: lindbergh@isd.net
Internet: www.isd.net/lindbergh

AMOUNT: $10,580 (max.)

DEADLINE(S): JUN 15

FIELD(S): Aviation; Aerospace; Agriculture; Education; Arts; Humanities; Biomedical Research; Exploration; Health & Population Sciences; Intercultural Communication; Waste Disposal Minimization & Management.; Adaptive Technology; Conservation

Open to individuals whose proposed projects represent a significant contribution toward the achievement of balance between the advance of technology and preservation of the natural environment. Financial need NOT a factor. Funding is NOT for tuition.

10 awards annually. See website for application.

384 — DRAPER LABORATORY (Research Assistantships)

555 Technology Square
Cambridge MA 02139
617/258-2393
FAX: 617/258-2333
E-Mail: ed@draper.com

AMOUNT: Tuition + stipend

DEADLINE(S): Varies (same as MIT deadline)

FIELD(S): Engineering: Mechanical, Aero-Astro, Electrical; Computer Science; Operations Research

Open to US citizens pursuing graduate study in M.S. or Ph.D. programs at MIT.

30 awards annually. Renewable. Contact Draper Lab for an application.

385 — FANNIE AND JOHN HERTZ FOUNDATION (Fellowship)

Box 5032
Livermore CA 94551-5032
925/373-1642
Internet: www.hertzfoundation.org

AMOUNT: $25,000 stipend/yr. + $15,000 (max.) tuition allowance/yr.

DEADLINE(S): NOV 5

FIELD(S): Applied Physical Sciences

Open to graduate students with a minimum 3.75 GPA for studies in applied physical sciences, including math, engineering, computer science, biology, oceanography, aeronautics, astronomy, physics, and earth science. Must be US citizen/permanent resident. Does not support study in pursuit of M.D. degree, although will support Ph.D. portion of a joint M.D./Ph.D. study program.

Renewable up to 5 years. Only 36 US schools are currently considered tenable. See website for an application and list of specific fields of study that are acceptable.

386 — FORD FOUNDATION/NATIONAL RESEARCH COUNCIL (Predoctoral/Dissertation Fellowships for Minorities)

2101 Constitution Ave.
Washington DC 20418
202/334-2872
E-Mail: infofell@nas.edu
Internet: http//www.nas.edu/fo/index.html

AMOUNT: $14,000 annual stipend + $6,000 grant to institution; $18,000 for dissertation fellowship

DEADLINE(S): NOV 3

FIELD(S): Most fields of study: sciences, humanities, engineering, behavioral science, social sciences, and computer science

Predoctoral and dissertation fellowships for students whose ethnicity is Alaskan Native, Black/African American, Mexican American/Chicano, Native American Indian, Native Pacific Islander, or Puerto Rican. For research-based programs leading to careers in college teaching and research.

Contact above address or website.

387 — ILLINOIS PILOTS ASSOCIATION (Scholarships)

46 Apache Lane
Huntley IL 60142
Written request

AMOUNT: $500

DEADLINE(S): APR 1

FIELD(S): Aviation

Scholarships for individuals in aviation who are residents of Illinois and attending a college or university in Illinois.

Write for details.

388 — INSTITUTION OF ELECTRICAL ENGINEERS (Postgraduate Awards)

Savoy Place
London WC2R 0BL ENGLAND
0171 240 1871 Ext. 2211/2235
FAX: 0171 497 3609
E-Mail: scholarships@iee.org.uk
Internet: www.iee.org.uk/Awards/pgsum.htm

AMOUNT: 1,000-6,000 pounds/yr.

DEADLINE(S): SEP 1; SEP 30

FIELD(S): Engineering

Scholarships for postgraduate students pursuing degrees in engineering who are residents of the United Kingdom.

Check website or contact organization for application details.

389 — INTERNATIONAL SOCIETY OF WOMEN AIRLINE PILOTS (ISA International Career Scholarship)

2250 E. Tropicana Ave., Suite 19-395
Las Vegas NV 89119-6594
Written inquiry

AMOUNT: Varies

DEADLINE(S): None specified

FIELD(S): Airline Pilot Advanced Ratings

Open to women whose goals are to fly the world's airlines. For advanced pilot ratings, such as the U.S. FAA ATP certificate or equivalent.

Applicants must have a U.S. FAA Commercial Pilot Certificate with an Instrument Rating and a First Class medical (or equivalent). Also must have a minimum of 750 flight hours. Personal interview is required. Write for complete information.

390 — INTERNATIONAL SOCIETY OF WOMEN AIRLINE PILOTS (Fiorenze De Bernardi Merit Award.)

2250 E. Tropicana Ave., Suite 19-395
Las Vegas NV 89119-6541
Internet: www.aswap.org

AMOUNT: Varies

DEADLINE(S): Varies

FIELD(S): Airline Pilot Training

A merit scholarship for women throughout the world who are pursuing airline pilot careers. Selection based on need, demonstrated dedication to career goal, work history, experience, and recommendations.

To aid pilots with CFI, CFII, MEI, or any equivalents. Must have a US FAA Commercial Pilot Certificate with an Instrument Rating and a First Class medical (or equivalent). Candidates must have a minimum of 350 flight hours. Personal interview required. Contact Gail Redden-Jones at above address.

391 — INTERNATIONAL SOCIETY OF WOMEN AIRLINE PILOTS (Holly Mullins Memorial Scholarship)

2250 E. Tropicana Ave., Suite 19-395
Las Vegas NV 89119-6594
Internet: www.aswap.org

AMOUNT: Varies

DEADLINE(S): Varies

FIELD(S): Airline Pilot Training

A merit scholarship for women who are single mothers and pursuing airline pilot careers. Selection is based on need, demonstrated dedication to career goal, work history experience, and recommendations.

To aid pilots with CFI, CRII, MEI, or any equivalents. Must have a US FAA Commercial Pilot Certificate with an Instrument Rating and a First Class medical (or equivalent). Additionally, candidates must have a minimum of 750 flight hours.

392 — INTERNATIONAL SOCIETY OF WOMEN AIRLINE PILOTS (The International Airline Scholarship)

2250 E. Tropicana Ave., Suite 19-395
Las Vegas NV 89119-6594
Internet: www.aswap.org

AMOUNT: Varies

DEADLINE(S): None given

FIELD(S): Flight Engineering and Type Ratings

For women seeking careers in aviation and need Flight Engineer Certificates and Type Ratings on 727, 737, 747, 757, and DC-10 aircraft. For Flight Engineers, 1,000 hours flight time and a current FE written required. For Type Rating scholarship, an ATP Certificate and a current FE written.

Contact Gail Redden-Jones at above address.

393 — INTERNATIONAL SOCIETY OF WOMEN AIRLINE PILOTS-ISA+21 (ISA Scholarship Fund)

2250 E. Tropicana Ave., Suite 19-395
Las Vegas NV 89118-6594
847/599-9886
Internet: www.iswap.org

AMOUNT: Varies-$1,000-$3,000

DEADLINE(S): APR 1

FIELD(S): Aviation

For women pilots needing advanced ratings and certificates.

Must have a minimum of 750 flight hours and a Commercial Pilot's License.

394 — NATIONAL AERONAUTICS AND SPACE ADMINISTRATION (Graduate Student Researcher's Program-Underrepresented Minority Focus)

Mail Code FEH
NASA Headquarters
Washington, DC 20546
202/453-8344

AMOUNT: $22,000 1st year, renewable up to 3 years

DEADLINE(S): FEB 1

FIELD(S): Science, Engineering, Mathematics

For underrepresented minority groups in the fields of science and engineering (including African-Americans, American Indians, Hispanics, and Pacific Islanders), who may end up with a career in space science and/or aerospace technology. Must be US citizen and enrolled or accepted as a full-time graduate student at an accredited US college or university.

Write for complete information.

395 — NATIONAL AERONAUTICS AND SPACE ADMINISTRATION (NASA Training Grants)

NASA Headquarters, Code FE
Washington DC 20548
202/358-1517

AMOUNT: $22,000

DEADLINE(S): Varies

FIELD(S): Space Science/Physics

Grants for research in various specified topics in the fields listed above.

Contact Ahmad Nurriddin at above location for details.

396 — NATIONAL AIR TRANSPORTATION ASSOCIATION FOUNDATION (John W. Godwin, Jr., Memorial Scholarship Fund)

4226 King Street
Alexandria VA 22302
808/808-NATA or 703/845-9000
FAX: 703/845-8176

AMOUNT: $2,500

DEADLINE(S): None

FIELD(S): Flight training

Scholarship for flight training for any certificate and/or flight rating issued by the FAA, at any NATA-Member company offering flight training. Must accumulate a minimum of 15 dual or solo flight hours each calendar month.

Contact organization for details.

397 — NATIONAL GAY PILOTS ASSOCIATION (Pilot Scholarships)

NGPA-EF, P.O. Box 2010-324
South Burlington VT 05407-2010
703/660-3852 or
24-hr. voice mail: 703/660-3852
Internet: www.ngpa.org

AMOUNT: $1,500

DEADLINE(S): JUL 31

FIELD(S): Pilot training and related fields in aerospace, aerodynamics, engineering, airport management, etc.

Scholarships for tuition or flight training costs for student pilots enrolled at a college or university offering an accredited aviation curriculum in the above fields. Also for flight training costs in a professional pilot training program at any training facility certified by the FAA. Not for training for a Private Pilot license. Send SASE for application or visit website for further instructions.

For gay/lesbian applicants or others who can provide evidence of volunteering in an AIDS organization or in any group that supports the gay/lesbian community and their rights.

398 — NATIONAL SCIENCES AND ENGINEERING RESEARCH COUNCIL OF CANADA (Graduate Scholarships)

Scholarships/Fellowships Division
350 Albert Street
Ottawa Ontario K1A 1H5 CANADA
613/996-3769
FAX: 613/996-2589
E-Mail: schol@nserc.ca
Internet: http://www.nserc.ca

AMOUNT: $15,700/year for 1st & 2nd years at masters or Ph.D level; $17,400/year (Ph.D level ONLY) 3rd & 4th years

DEADLINE(S): NOV 24

FIELD(S): Natural Sciences, Engineering, Biology, or Chemistry

Open to Canadian citizens or permanent residents who have earned or will soon earn a bachelors or masters degree in science or engineering. Academic excellence and research aptitude are considerations.

Write for complete information.

399 — NATIONAL SCIENCES AND ENGINEERING RESEARCH COUNCIL OF CANADA (Postdoctoral Fellowships)

Scholarships/Fellowships Division
350 Albert Street
Ottawa Ontario K1A 1H5 CANADA
613/996-3762
FAX: 613/996-2589
E-Mail: schol@nserc.ca
Internet: http://www.nserc.ca

AMOUNT: Individually negotiated

DEADLINE(S): Varies—average: $43,000

FIELD(S): Natural Sciences, Engineering, Biology, or Chemistry

Open to Canadian citizens or permanent residents who hold doctoral degrees in science or engineering. Academic excellence and research aptitude are considerations.

Write for complete information.

400 — NATIONAL SOCIETY OF BLACK ENGINEERS (Scholarships)

1454 Duke St.
Alexandria VA 22314
703/549-2207
FAX: 703/683-5312
E-Mail: nsbehq@nsbe.org
Internet: www.nsbe.org

AMOUNT: Varies

DEADLINE(S): Varies

FIELD(S): Engineering and engineering technologies

Programs for black and other ethnic minorities in the fields of engineering and the engineering technologies. Organization offers pre-college programs, scholarships, career fairs, a journal, a newsletter, etc.

Contact organization for details.

401 — NATIONAL SPACE CLUB (Dr. Robert H. Goddard Scholarship)

2000 L Street, NW, Suite 710
Washington DC 20036-4907
202/973-8661

AMOUNT: $10,000

DEADLINE(S): JAN 8

FIELD(S): Science & Engineering

Open to undergraduate juniors and seniors and graduate students who have scholastic plans leading to future participation in the aerospace sciences and technology. Must be US citizen. Award based on transcript, letters of recommendation, accomplishments, scholastic plans, and proven past research and participation in space related science and engineering. Personal need is considered, but is not controlling.

Renewable. Send a self-addressed, stamped envelope for more information.

402 — NATIONAL SPACE CLUB (Dr. Robert H. Goddard Historical Essay Award)

2000 L Street, NW, Suite 710
Washington DC 20036-4907
202/973-8661

AMOUNT: $1,000 + plaque

DEADLINE(S): DEC 4

FIELD(S): Aerospace History

Essay competition open to any US citizen on a topic dealing with any significant aspect of the historical development of rocketry and astronautics. Essays should not exceed 5,000 words and should be fully documented. Will be judged on originality and scholarship.

Previous winners not eligible. Send self-addressed, stamped envelope for complete information.

403 — NINETY-NINES, INC. (Amelia Earhart Memorial Scholarships)

Box 965, 7100 Terminal Drive
Oklahoma City OK 73159-0965
800/994-1929 or 405/685-7969
FAX: 405/685-7985
E-Mail: 10476.406@compuserve.com
Internet: ninety-nines.org

AMOUNT: Varies

DEADLINE(S): Varies

FIELD(S): Advanced Aviation Ratings

Scholarships for female licensed pilots who are members of the 99s, Inc.

15-20 awards annually. Financial need considered. Contact Lu Hollander at above address for application and/or membership information.

404 — NINETY-NINES, SAN FERNANDO VALLEY CHAPTER/VAN NUYS AIRPORT (Aviation Career Scholarships)

PO Box 8160
Van Nuys CA 91409
818/989-0081

AMOUNT: $3,000

DEADLINE(S): MAY 1

FIELD(S): Aviation Careers

For men and women of the greater Los Angeles area pursuing careers as professional pilots, flight instructors, mechanics, or other aviation career specialists. Applicants must be at least 21 years of age and US citizens.

3 awards annually. Send self-addressed, stamped, business-sized envelope to above address for application.

405 — OAK RIDGE ASSOCIATED UNIVERSITIES (National Science Foundation Graduate Research Fellowships)

PO Box 3010
Oak Ridge TN 37831-3010
423/241-4300
FAX: 423/241-4513
E-Mail: nsfgrfp@orau.gov
Internet: www.orau.gov/nsf/nsffel.htm

AMOUNT: $15,000 stipend + $10,500 tuition allowance

DEADLINE(S): NOV 4

FIELD(S): Science; Math; Engineering; Computer Science

Three-year fellowships for graduate study leading to research-based master's or doctoral degrees in the above fields. Must be US citizens, nationals, or permanent residents at the time of application.

Fellowships are awarded on the basis of ability. Women, minorities, and those with disabilities are strongly encouraged to apply. One-time International Research Travel Allowance available.

1,000 awards annually. Contact Jeannette Bouchard for an application/more information.

406 — RTCA, INC. (William E. Jackson Award)

1140 Connecticut Ave. NW #1020
Washington DC 20036-4001
202/833-9339
FAX: 202/833-9434
E-Mail: hmoses@rtca.org
Internet: www.rtca.org

AMOUNT: $2,000 + plaque

DEADLINE(S): JUN 30

FIELD(S): Aviation Electronics; Aviation; Telecommunications

Open to graduate and postgraduate students studying in the above fields who submit a thesis, project report, or technical journal paper within 3 years of entry for the honorarium.

One award per year, NOT renewable. Contact Harold Moses at above address for an application.

407 — SMITHSONIAN INSTITUTION (National Air & Space Museum Guggenheim Fellowship)

National Air and Space Museum, MRC 312
Washington DC 20560
Written inquiry

AMOUNT: $14,000 (predoctoral); $25,000 (postdoctoral)

DEADLINE(S): JAN 15

FIELD(S): Historical research related to aviation and space

Predoctoral applicants should have completed preliminary course work and exams and be engaged in dissertation research. Postdoctoral applicants should have received their Ph.D within the past seven years. Contact Fellowship Coordinator at above location.

Open to all nationalities. Fluency in English required. Duration is 6-12 months.

408 — SMITHSONIAN INSTITUTION (National Air & Space Museum Verville Fellowship)

National Air and Space Museum, MRC 312
Washington DC 20560
Written inquiry

AMOUNT: $30,000 stipend for 12 months + travel and misc. expenses

DEADLINE(S): JAN 15

FIELD(S): Analysis of major trends, developments, and accomplishments in the history of aviation or space studies

A competitive nine- to twelve-month in-residence fellowship in the above field of study. Advanced degree is NOT a requirement. Contact Fellowship Coordinator at above location.

Open to all nationalities. Fluency in English required.

409 — THE DAPHNE JACKSON MEMORIAL FELLOWSHIPS TRUST (Fellowships in Science/ Engineering)

School of Physical Sciences, Dept. of Physics, University of Surrey
Guildford, Surrey GU2 5XH ENGLAND UK
01483 259166
FAX: 01483 259501
E-Mail: J.Woolley@surrey.ac.uk
Internet: www.sst.ph.ic.ac.uk/trust/

AMOUNT: Varies

DEADLINE(S): Varies

FIELD(S): Science or engineering, including information sciences

Fellowships to enable well-qualified and highly motivated scientists and engineers to return to appropriate careers following a career break due to family comitments. May be used on a flexible, part-time basis. Tenable at various U.K. universities.

See website and/or contact organization for details.

410 — U.S. DEPARTMENT OF DEFENSE (GLSIP- General Laboratory Scientific Interchange Program: NRC-NRL Post-Doctoral Program)

Naval Research Laboratory
Office of Program Admin. & Dev. Code 1006.17
Washington, D.C. 20375-5321
202/767-3865
DSN: 297-3865
FAX: 202/404-8110
Internet: www.acq.osd.mil/ddre/edugate/s-aindx.html

AMOUNT: Research Program

DEADLINE(S): None specified

FIELD(S): Computer science, artificial intelligence, plasma physics, acoustics, radar, fluid dynamics, chemistry, materials sci, optical sci, condensed matter and radiation, electronic sci, environmental sci, marine geosciences, remote sensing, oceanography, marine meteorology, space technology/sciences.

U.S. citizens who are recent postdoctoral graduates are selected on the basis of overall qualifications and techincal proposals.

Contact Jessica Hileman for more information.

411 — VERTICAL FLIGHT FOUNDATION (Scholarships)

217 N. Washington St.
Alexandria VA 22314-2538
703/684-6777
FAX: 703/739-9279
E-Mail: ahs703@aol.com
Internet: www.vtol.org

AMOUNT: $2,000-$4,000

DEADLINE(S): FEB 1

FIELD(S): Vertical Flight

These merit-based awards are open to undergraduate juniors and seniors and graduate students pursuing full-time studies in vertical flight at accredited schools of engineering. Must submit transcripts and references. Scholarships awarded to student once as an undergraduate senior, once as a master's student, and once as a Ph.D. student. Financial need NOT a factor.

See website or contact VFF for an application. Recipients notified by April 15th.

412 — VON KARMAN INSTITUTE FOR FLUID DYNAMICS (Diploma Course Scholarship)

72 Chaussee de Waterloo
1640 Rhode-St-Genese Belgium
32-2-359.96.11
FAX: 32-2-359.96.00
E-Mail: secretariat@vki.ac.be
Internet: www.vki.ac.be

AMOUNT: US $950/month

DEADLINE(S): MAR 1

FIELD(S): Aeronautics, Aerospace, Environmental Fluid Dynamics, Industrial Processes, Turbomachinery

For postgraduate study at the Von Karmen Institute in Belgium. Must be citizen of a NATO country. Financial need NOT considered.

25-30 awards annually. Contact J. F. Wendt, Director, at above address for complete information.

413 — ZONTA INTERNATIONAL FOUNDATION (Amelia Earhart Fellowship Awards)

557 West Randolph St.
Chicago IL 60661-2206
312/930-5848
FAX: 312/930-0951

AMOUNT: $6,000

DEADLINE(S): NOV 1

FIELD(S): Aerospace Sciences & Engineering

For female graduate students with a bachelor's degree in aerospace-related science and engineering. Must have superior credentials and have completed one year of graduate school or have completed a well-defined research and development program evidenced by a publication or senior research project.

35-40 awards annually. Renewable. Contact the Foundation Assistant at Zonta for an application.

ARCHITECTURE

414 — AMERICAN ACADEMY IN ROME (Rome Prize Fellowships in the School of Fine Arts)

7 East 60th Street
New York NY 10022-1001
212/751-7200
FAX: 212/751-7220
E-Mail: aainfo@aol.com
Internet: www.aarome.org

AMOUNT: $9,000-$15,000

DEADLINE(S): NOV 15

FIELD(S): Landscape Architecture; Architecture; Musical Composition; Visual Arts; Design Arts

For US citizens with a major and/or career interest in above fields for advanced study in Rome to pursue independent projects, which vary in content & scope. Applicants for six-month and one-year fellowships must hold a degree in the field of application. Six-month applicants must also have at least seven years professional experience and be practicing in the applied field. Interview, portfolio, recommendations, curriculum vitae, and research proposal required.

14 awards annually. Contact the Programs Department at the American Academy in Rome for an application.

415 — AMERICAN ASSOCIATION OF UNIVERSITY WOMEN EDUCATIONAL FOUNDATION (Selected Professions Fellowships)

Dept. 60
2201 N. Dodge St.
Iowa City IA 52243-4030
319/337-1716, ext. 60
FAX 319/337-1204
Internet: www.aauw.org

AMOUNT: $5,000-$15,000

DEADLINE(S): JAN 2 (most); NOV 15 (engineering dissertation only)

FIELD(S): Architecture; Computer/Information Sciences; Engineering; Mathematics/Statistics

For women in final year of graduate study in fields where women's participation has been low. Must be US citizen or permanent resident. Special consideration given to applicants who show professional promise in innovative or neglected areas of research and/or practice in areas of public interest. Women in engineering

master's programs are eligible to apply for either first or final year of study; special award for engineering doctoral students writing dissertation.

Applications available August-December.

416 — AMERICAN FOUNDATION FOR THE BLIND (Paul W. Ruckes Scholarship)

11 Penn Plaza, Ste. 300
New York NY 10001
212/502-7661 or TDD 212/502-7771
E-Mail: juliet@afb.org
Internet: www.afb.org

AMOUNT: $1,000

DEADLINE(S): APR 30

FIELD(S): Engineering, computer, physical, or life sciences

Open to blind or visually impaired undergraduate or graduate students pursuing degrees in the above fields. U.S. citizenship required.

Write to the above address or visit website for complete information.

417 — AMERICAN INSTITUTE OF ARCHITECTS/ AMERICAN ARCHITECTURAL FOUNDATION (Scholarship Program)

1735 New York Ave., NW
Washington DC 20006-5292
202/626-7511
FAX: 202/626-7420
E-Mail: felberm@aiamail.aia.org

AMOUNT: $500-$2,500

DEADLINE(S): JAN 31

FIELD(S): Architecture

Open to undergraduate students in their final two years or graduate students pursuing their master's degree in architecture. Awards tenable at accredited institutions in the US and Canada.

Applications available ONLY through the office of the dean or department head at an NAAB or RAIC school of architecture. Contact Mary Felber at AIA/ AAF for more information.

418 — AMERICAN INSTITUTE OF ARCHITECTS/ AMERICAN HOSPITAL ASSOCIATION (AIA/ AHA Fellowships in Health Facilities Planning and Design)

1735 New York Ave. NW
Washington DC 20006
202/626-7511
FAX: 202/626-7420
E-Mail: felberm@aiamail.aia.org

AMOUNT: $22,000

DEADLINE(S): JAN 15

FIELD(S): Architecture—Health Facilities

For architects, graduate students, and those in last year of undergraduate work in architecture who are U.S. or Canadian citizens for coursework or independent study. Funds provided by The American Sterilizer Company.

For one year. Write for complete information.

419 — AMERICAN INSTITUTE OF ARCHITECTS, NEW YORK CHAPTER (Haskell Awards for Student Architectural Journalism)

200 Lexington Ave., 6th floor
New York NY 10016
212/683-0023 Ext. 14

AMOUNT: Varies

DEADLINE(S): FEB 13

FIELD(S): Architectural Writing

Awards to encourage fine writing on architecture and related design subjects and to foster regard for intelligent criticism among future professionals. For students enrolled in a professional architecture or related program, such as art history, interior design, urban studies, and landscape architecture. Submit a news story, an essay or feature article, book review, or journal accompanied by a 100-word statement describing the purpose of the piece.

Write to above location for complete information.

420 — AMERICAN PLANNING ASSOCIATION (Minority Scholarship and Fellowship Programs)

122 South Michigan Ave., Ste. 1600
Chicago IL 60605
312/431-9100
FAX: 312/431-9985

AMOUNT: $2,000-$5,000 (grads); $2,500 (undergrads)

DEADLINE(S): MAY 14

FIELD(S): Urban planning, community development, environmental sciences, public administration, transportation, or urban studies

Scholarships for African-Americans, Hispanics, or Native American students pursing undergraduate degrees in the U.S. in the above fields. Must have completed first year. Fellowships for graduate students. Programs must be approved by the Planning Accreditation Board. U.S. citizenship.

Call or write for complete information.

421 — AMERICAN RESEARCH INSTITUTE IN TURKEY (ARIT Fellowship Program)

Univ Penn Museum
33rd & Spruce Streets
Philadelphia PA 19104-6324
215/898-3474
FAX: 215/898-0657

E-Mail: leinwand@sas.upenn.edu

Internet: mec.sas.upenn.edu/ARIT

AMOUNT: Varies

DEADLINE(S): NOV 15

FIELD(S): Humanities; Social Sciences; Turkish Studies

Two-month to one-year fellowships are for postdoctoral scholars & advanced graduate students engaged in research on ancient, medieval, or modern times in Turkey, in any field of the humanities & social sciences. Predoctoral students must have fulfilled all preliminary requirements for doctorate except dissertation. Applicants must maintain an affiliation with an educational institution in the US or Canada. Must submit curriculum vitae, research proposal, & referees.

Contact ARIT for an application.

422 — AMERICAN RESEARCH INSTITUTE IN TURKEY (KRESS/ARIT Predoctoral Fellowship in the History of Art & Archaeology)

Univ Penn Museum

33rd & Spruce Streets

Philadelphia PA 19104-6324

215/898-3474

FAX: 215/898-0657

E-Mail: leinwand@sas.upenn.edu

Internet: mec.sas.upenn.edu/ARIT

AMOUNT: $15,000 (max.)

DEADLINE(S): NOV 15

FIELD(S): Archaeology; Architectural History; Art History

Fellowships of up to one year are for students engaged in advanced dissertation research in above fields that necessitates a period of study in Turkey. Must be US citizen or matriculating at a US university. Must submit curriculum vitae, research proposal, and referees.

Contact ARIT for an application.

423 — ARCHAEOLOGICAL INSTITUTE OF AMERICA (Olivia James Traveling Fellowship)

Boston Univ

656 Beacon St.

Boston MA 02215-2006

617/353-9361

FAX: 617/353-6550

E-Mail: aia@bu.edu

Internet: www.archeological.org

AMOUNT: $22,000

DEADLINE(S): NOV 1

FIELD(S): Classics; Sculpture; Architecture; Archaeology; History

Fellowships for US citizens/permanent residents to be used for travel and study in Greece, the Aegean Islands, Sicily, Southern Italy, Asia Minor, or Mesopotamia. Preference given to individuals engaged in dissertation research or to recent recipients of the Ph.D. (within 5 years). Award is not intended to support field excavation projects, and recipients may not hold other major fellowships during tenure. At conclusion, recipient must submit report on use of stipend.

Contact AIA for an application. Awards announced by February 1st.

424 — ARTS MANAGEMENT P/L (Marten Bequest Travelling Scholarships)

Station House, Rawson Place

790 George St.

Sydney NSW 2000 Australia

(612)9212 5066

FAX: (612)9211 7762

E-Mail: vbraden@ozemail.com.au

AMOUNT: Aus. $18,000

DEADLINE(S): OCT 30

FIELD(S): Art; Performing Arts; Creative Writing

Open to native-born Australians aged 21-35 (17-35 ballet) who are of outstanding ability and promise in one or more categories of the Arts. The scholarships are intended to augment a scholar's own resources towards a cultural education, and it may be used for study, maintenance, and travel either in Australia or overseas. Categories are: instrumental music, painting, singing, sculpture, architecture, ballet, prose, poetry, and acting.

1 scholarship granted in each of 9 categories which rotate in 2 groups on an annual basis. Contact Claudia Crosariol, Projects Administrator, for more information/entry form.

425 — ASIAN INSTITUTE OF TECHNOLOGY (AIT Scholarship Program)

Development Office

PO Box 4, Klongluang

Pathumthani 12120 THAILAND

(66)(2) 516-0110-44 or 524-5032

FAX: (66)(2) 516-2126

E-Mail: ascao@ait.ac.th

Internet: www.ait.ac.th

AMOUNT: US $12,600-$37,960

DEADLINE(S): FEB 15; JUN 15; OCT 15

FIELD(S): Advanced Technologies; Civil Engineering; Environment, Resources, & Development; Business Management

Scholarships and grants open to citizens of Asian countries who are accepted by the institute as a master's or doctoral candidate. Selection is based on academic criteria, practical experience, gender, and country of origin; priority to Mekong Region countries and Asian countries of the former USSR.

250 awards annually. Contact AIT for an application.

426 — ASSOCIATED WESTERN UNIVERSITIES, INC. (AWU Faculty Fellowships)

4190 South Highland Dr., Suite 211

Salt Lake City UT 84124-2600

801-273-8900

AMOUNT: Varies.

DEADLINE(S): FEB 15

FIELD(S): Engineering, Mathematics, Science, Technology

Research fellowships for qualified college and university faculty members to encourage participation and contribution to research at one of 62 cooperating facilities. It is not necessary to be enrolled at an AWU member institution. Collaborations that include graduate and/or undergraduate students are encouraged.

For detailed information and list of cooperating facilities, contact above location.

427 — ASSOCIATED WESTERN UNIVERSITIES, INC. (AWU Graduate Fellowship Program)

4190 South Highland Dr. Suite 211

Salt Lake City, UT 84124-2600

801/273-8900

AMOUNT: Stipend ($1,300 per month & up) + tuition assistance and travel allowance

DEADLINE(S): FEB 15

FIELD(S): Engineering, Mathematics, Science, Technology

Open to master's and doctoral degree candidates to conduct research toward a thesis or dissertation at one of more than 62 cooperating facilities. Institutional affiliation and citizenship restrictions may apply for some awards or facilities. It is not necessary to be enrolled at an AWU member institution to apply for a fellowship.

Write to the above address for complete information.

428 — ASSOCIATED WESTERN UNIVERSITIES, INC. (AWU Postgraduate Fellowship)

4190 South Highland Dr. Suite 211

Salt Lake City UT 84124-2600

801/273-8900

AMOUNT: Stipend established by the host facility and varies by experience and discipline.

DEADLINE(S): Varies (Two to three months before the starting date)

FIELD(S): Engineering, Mathematics, Science, Technology

For college and university graduates who have completed all institutional requirements for an advanced degree from an accredited college or university in the U.S. A commitment to a professional career in science or engineering research is expected. U.S. citizenship or permanent resident status is required. Research is to be done at one of the 62 cooperating universities.

For detailed information and a list of cooperating facilities contact above address.

429 — ASSOCIATED WESTERN UNIVERSITIES, INC. (AWU Visiting Scientist Fellowships)

4190 South Highland Dr., Suite 211
Salt Lake City UT 84124-2600
801/273-8900

AMOUNT: Varies

DEADLINE(S): Varies (Two months prior to starting date)

FIELD(S): Engineering, Science, Mathematics, and Technology

Research fellowships for professionals with continued commitment to science and engineering. For use at one of 62 participating universities. US citizenship or permanent residency required.

For detailed information and list of cooperating facilities contact above location.

430 — BOEING (Polish Graduate Student Scholarship Program)

Phone
Phone for details
314/234-2149

AMOUNT: Tuition, books, and fees for three years

DEADLINE(S): Varies

FIELD(S): Scientific and technical fields

Scholarships for students from Poland to pursue graduate studies in scientific and technical areas at American colleges or universities.

Call Jim Schlueter at above telephone number.

431 — BOSTON SOCIETY OF ARCHITECTS (Rotch Travelling Scholarship)

52 Broad Street
Boston MA 02109-4301
617/951-1433, ext. 225

AMOUNT: $30,000 stipend

DEADLINE(S): JAN

FIELD(S): Architecture

Two-stage design competition for 8 months of travel throughout the world. Open to US citizens aged 35 or less who meet eligibility reqirements. Must hold degree from accredited school of architecture + 1 year in MA architectural firm OR degree from accredited MA school of architecture + 1 year in any US architectural firm.

Write to above address for an application.

432 — BRITISH COLUMBIA HERITAGE TRUST (Scholarships)

PO Box 9818 Stn Prov Govt.
Victoria BC V8W 9W3 CANADA
250/356-1433

AMOUNT: $5,000

DEADLINE(S): FEB 15

FIELD(S): British Columbia History; Architecture; Archaeology; Archival Management

Open to graduate students who are Canadian citizens or permanent residents. Criteria are scholarly record and academic performance, educational and career objectives, and proposed program of study.

Write for complete information.

433 — BRITISH FEDERATION OF WOMEN GRADUATES (M.H. Joseph Prize for Non-UK Citizens)

4 Mandeville Courtyard
142 Battersea Park Rd.
London SW11 4NB ENGLAND UK
PHONE/FAX: 0171/498 8037

AMOUNT: 500+ pounds sterling

DEADLINE(S): SEP 10

FIELD(S): Architecture; Engineering

For female graduate students of any nationality (except UK) who will pursue studies in Great Britain. Must have completed at least four academic terms or three semesters; award is not made for first year of research. Chief criteria is academic excellence and proven ability to carry out independent research. Postdoctoral studies also eligible.

1 award annually. Application fee of 12 pounds sterling required. Send a self-addressed, stamped envelope (or self-addressed envelope with international reply coupons) for an application. Results announced by end of October.

434 — BRITISH FEDERATION OF WOMEN GRADUATES (M.H. Joseph Prize for UK Citizens)

4 Mandeville Courtyard
142 Battersea Park Rd.
London SW11 4NB ENGLAND UK
PHONE/FAX: 0171/498 8037

AMOUNT: 500+ pounds sterling

DEADLINE(S): SEP 10

FIELD(S): Architecture; Engineering

For female UK citizens who plan to pursue graduate studies overseas. Must have completed at least four academic terms or three semesters; award is not made for first year of research. Chief criteria is academic excellence and proven ability to carry out independent research. Postdoctoral studies also eligible.

1 award annually. Application fee of 12 pounds sterling required. Send a self-addressed, stamped envelope (or self-addressed envelope with international reply coupons) for an application. Award announced at end of October.

435 — COUNCIL FOR EUROPEAN STUDIES (Predissertation Fellowships)

Columbia Univ
807-807A International Affairs Bldg.
New York NY 10027
212/854-4172
FAX: 212/854-8808
E-Mail: ces@columbia.edu
Internet: www.europanet.org

AMOUNT: $4,000 stipend (max.)

DEADLINE(S): FEB 1

FIELD(S): Cultural Anthropology; History (post 1750); Political Science; Sociology; Geography; Urban & Regional Planning

Awards are for research in France to determine viability of projected doctoral dissertation in modern history and social sciences. Recipients test research design of dissertation, determine availability of archival materials, and contact French scholars. Must be US citizen or permanent resident at a US institution and have completed at least two but no more than three years of full-time doctoral study by end of year. Institutional membership in Council is required.

6 awards annually. See website or contact Council for an application.

436 — DUMBARTON OAKS (Awards in Byzantine Studies, Pre-Columbian Studies, & History of Landscape Architecture)

1703 32nd St., NW
Washington DC 20007
202/339-6410

AMOUNT: $37,700/yr. (max.)

DEADLINE(S): NOV 1

FIELD(S): Byzantine Studies; Pre-Columbian Studies; History of Landscape Architecture

Residential doctoral & postdoctoral fellowships, and junior & summer fellowships for undergraduates are to support study and/or research in the above areas. All fellows are expected to be able to communicate satisfactorily in English.

Contact Dumbarton Oaks for an application.

437 — FLORIDA FEDERATION OF GARDEN CLUBS, INC. (FFGC Scholarships for College Students)

6065 21st St., SW
Vero Beach FL 32968-9427
561/778-1023
Internet: www.ffgc.org

AMOUNT: $1,500-$3,500

DEADLINE(S): MAY 1

FIELD(S): Ecology; Environmental Issues; Land Management; City Planning; Environmental Control; Horticulture; Landscape Design; Conservation; Botany; Forestry; Marine Biology; Floriculture; Agriculture

Various scholarships for Florida residents with a "B" average or better enrolled full-time as a junior, senior, or graduate student at a Florida college or university.

See website or contact Melba Campbell at FFGC for an application.

438 — GARDEN CLUB OF AMERICA (GCA Interchange Fellowship)

14 East 60th Street
New York NY 10022-1046
212/753-8287
FAX: 212/753-0134
Internet: www.gcamerica.org

AMOUNT: Varies (tuition, housing + allowance)

DEADLINE(S): NOV 15

FIELD(S): Horticulture and Landscape Architecture

Funds one graduate academic year for a British student wishing to study in the US. The purpose of this program is to foster British-American relations through the interchange of scholars in horticulture, landscape architecture, and related fields.

1 award annually. Send a self-addressed, stamped envelope to Ms. Shelley Burch at above address for complete information/an application.

439 — GARDEN CLUB OF AMERICA (Martin McLaren Scholarship)

14 East 60th Street
New York NY 10022-1046
212/753-8287
FAX: 212/753-0134
Internet: www.gcamerica.org

AMOUNT: Varies (tuition, housing + allowance)

DEADLINE(S): NOV 15

FIELD(S): Horticulture and Landscape Architecture

A work-study program for an American graduate student to study at universities and botanical gardens in the UK. The purpose of this program is to foster British-American relations through the interchange of scholars in horticulture, landscape architecture, and related fields.

1 award annually. Send a self-addressed, stamped envelope to Ms. Shelley Burch at above address for complete information/an application.

440 — GLADYS KRIEBLE DELMAS FOUNDATION (Predoctoral & Postdoctoral Grants in Venice & the Veneto)

521 5th Avenue, Suite 1612
New York NY 10175-1699
212/687-0011
FAX: 212/687-8877
E-Mail: DelmasFdtn@aol.com
Internet: www.delmas.org

AMOUNT: $500-$12,500

DEADLINE(S): DEC 15

FIELD(S): Research of Venice and the former Venetian empire and study of contemporary Venetian society and culture.

Pre- and postdoctoral grants for historical research on Venice. Humanities and social sciences are eligible areas of study, including archaeology, architecture, art, bibliography, economics, history, history of science, law, literature, music, political science, religion, and theater.

Applicants must have experience in advanced research and be U.S. citizens/residents; grad students must have fulfilled all doctoral requirements except dissertation by Dec. 15.

441 — GRAHAM FOUNDATION FOR ADVANCED STUDIES IN THE FINE ARTS (Research Grants)

Four West Burton Place
Chicago IL 60610
312/787-4071
Internet: www.grahamfoundation.org

AMOUNT: Up to $10,000

DEADLINE(S): JAN 15; JUL 15

FIELD(S): Architecture

Research grants open to individuals & institutions for specific projects relating to contemporary architecture planning. Grants do not support study or research in pursuit of an academic degree no scholarships available.

100+ awards per year. Write for more information.

442 — INSTITUTION OF ELECTRICAL ENGINEERS (Postgraduate Awards)

Savoy Place
London WC2R 0BL ENGLAND
0171 240 1871 Ext. 2211/2235
FAX: 0171 497 3609
E-Mail: scholarships@iee.org.uk
Internet: www.iee.org.uk/Awards/pgsum.htm

AMOUNT: 1,000-6,000 pounds/yr.

DEADLINE(S): SEP 1; SEP 30

FIELD(S): Engineering

Scholarships for postgraduate students pursuing degrees in engineering who are residents of the United Kingdom.

Check website or contact organization for application details.

443 — IRISH ARTS COUNCIL (Awards and Opportunities)

70 Merrion Square
Dublin 2 Ireland
Tel+353 1 618 0200
FAX:+353 1 661 0349/676 1302
E-Mail: info@artscouncil.ie
Internet: www.artscouncil.ie

AMOUNT: 500-1,500 pounds sterling

DEADLINE(S): Varies (with program)

FIELD(S): Creative Arts; Visual Arts; Performing Arts

Numerous programs open to young & established artists who are Irish citizens or legal residents. Purpose is to assist in pursuit of talents & recognize achievements.

Contact above address for an application.

444 — LANDSCAPE ARCHITECTURE FOUNDATION (Edith H. Henderson Scholarship)

636 Eye St., NW
Washington DC 20001-3736
202/898-2444
FAX: 202/898-1185
E-Mail: tpadian@asla.org
Internet: www.asla.org

AMOUNT: $1,000

DEADLINE(S): MAR 31

FIELD(S): Landscape Architecture

Scholarship available to any landscape architecture student who has in the past or is participating in a class in public speaking or creative writing. Must write a 200- to 400-word typed review of Edith H. Henderson's book "Edith Henderson's Home Landscape Companion."

Locate the book in a library or call 1-800-787-2665 or 1-800-241-0113 to order. Be sure and state that you are a landscape architect student applying for the Henderson scholarship.

445 — LANDSCAPE ARCHITECTURE FOUNDATION (LAF/CLASS Fund Scholarships)

Use website below
202/216-2356
E-Mail: tpadian@asla.org
Internet: www.asla.org

AMOUNT: $500-$2,000

DEADLINE(S): MAR 31

FIELD(S): Landscape Architecture or Ornamental Horticulture

Scholarships and internships for students enrolled in certain California colleges: California Polytechnic Institute (Pomona or San Luis Obispo), UCLA, UC-Irvine, and UC-Davis who show promise and a commitment to landscape architecture as a profession.

Access website for complete information.

446 — NATIONAL COUNCIL OF STATE GARDEN CLUBS, INC. (Scholarships)

4401 Magnolia Ave.
St. Louis MO 63110-3492
314/776-7574
FAX: 314/776-5108
E-Mail: scsgc.franm@worldnet.att.net
Internet: www.gardenclub.org

AMOUNT: $3,500

DEADLINE(S): MAR 1

FIELD(S): Horticulture, Floriculture, Landscape Design, City Planning, Land Management, and allied subjects.

Open to junior, seniors and graduate students who are U.S. citizens and are studying any of the above or related subjects. Student must have the endorsement of the state in which he/she resides permanently. Applications will be forwarded to the National State Chairman and judged on a national level.

32 scholarships are awarded. Write to the above address for complete information.

447 — NATIONAL FEDERATION OF THE BLIND (Frank Walton Horn Memorial Scholarship)

805 Fifth Avenue
Grinnell IA 50112
515/236-3366

AMOUNT: $3,000

DEADLINE(S): MAR 31

FIELD(S): Architecture; Engineering

Open to legally blind students pursuing or planning to pursue a full-time postsecondary course of study in the US. Based on academic excellence, service to the community, and financial need. Membership NOT required.

1 award annually. Renewable. Contact Mrs. Peggy Elliot, Scholarship Committee Chairman, for an application.

448 — NATIONAL FEDERATION OF THE BLIND (Howard Brown Rickard Scholarship)

805 Fifth Avenue
Grinnell IA 50112
515/236-3366

AMOUNT: $3,000

DEADLINE(S): MAR 31

FIELD(S): Law; Medicine; Engineering; Architecture; Natural Sciences

For legally blind students pursuing or planning to pursue a full-time postsecondary course of study in the US. Based on academic excellence, service to the community, and financial need. Membership NOT required.

1 award annually. Renewable. Contact Mrs. Peggy Elliot, Scholarship Committee Chairman, for an application.

449 — NATIONAL SOCIETY OF BLACK ENGINEERS (Scholarships)

1454 Duke St.
Alexandria VA 22314
703/549-2207
FAX: 703/683-5312
E-Mail: nsbehq@nsbe.org
Internet: www.nsbe.org

AMOUNT: Varies

DEADLINE(S): Varies

FIELD(S): Engineering and engineering technologies

Programs for black and other ethnic minorities in the fields of engineering and the engineering technologies. Organization offers pre-college programs, scholarships, career fairs, a journal, a newsletter, etc.

Contact organization for details.

450 — NEW YORK CITY DEPT. CITYWIDE ADMINISTRATIVE SERVICES (Urban Fellows Program)

1 Centre St., 24th Fl.
New York NY 10007
212/487-5600
FAX: 212/487-5720

AMOUNT: $18,000 stipend

DEADLINE(S): JAN 20

FIELD(S): Public Administration; Urban Planning; Government; Public Service; Urban Affairs

Fellowship program provides one academic year (9 months) of full-time work experience in urban government. Open to graduating college seniors and recent college graduates. U.S. citizenship required.

Write for complete information.

451 — NEW YORK STATE HIGHER EDUCATION SERVICES CORPORATION (N.Y. State Regents Professional/Health Care Opportunity Scholarships)

Cultural Education Center, Rm. 5C64
Albany NY 12230
518/486-1319
Internet: www.hesc.com

AMOUNT: $1,000-$10,000/yr.

DEADLINE(S): Varies

FIELD(S): Medicine and dentistry and related fields, architecture, nursing, psychology, audiology, landscape architecture, social work, chiropractic, law, pharmacy, accounting, speech language pathology

For NY state residents who are economically disadvantaged and members of a minority group underrepresented in the chosen profession and attending school in NY state. Some programs carry a service obligation in New York for each year of support. For U.S. citizens or qualifying noncitizens.

Medical/dental scholarships require one year of professional work in NY.

452 — OAK RIDGE ASSOCIATED UNIVERSITIES (National Science Foundation Graduate Research Fellowships)

PO Box 3010
Oak Ridge TN 37831-3010
423/241-4300
FAX: 423/241-4513
E-Mail: nsfgrfp@orau.gov
Internet: www.orau.gov/nsf/nsffel.htm

AMOUNT: $15,000 stipend + $10,500 tuition allowance

DEADLINE(S): NOV 4

FIELD(S): Science; Math; Engineering; Computer Science

Three-year fellowships for graduate study leading to research-based master's or doctoral degrees in the above fields. Must be US citizens, nationals, or permanent residents at the time of application. Fellowships are awarded on the basis of ability. Women, minorities, and those with disabilities are strongly encouraged to apply. One-time International Research Travel Allowance available.

1,000 awards annually. Contact Jeannette Bouchard for an application/more information.

453 — ROBERT SCHRECK MEMORIAL FUND (Grants)

C/O Texas Commerce Bank-Trust Dept
PO Drawer 140
El Paso TX 79980
915/546-6515

AMOUNT: $500 - $1500

DEADLINE(S): JUL 15; NOV 15

FIELD(S): Medicine; Veterinary Medicine; Physics; Chemistry; Architecture; Engineering; Episcopal Clergy

Grants to undergraduate juniors or seniors or graduate students who have been residents of El Paso County for at least two years. Must be U.S. citizen or legal resident and have a high grade point average. Financial need is a consideration.

Write for complete information.

454 — ROYAL INSTITUTE OF BRITISH ARCHITECTS (RIBA Research Awards)

66 Portland Place
London W1N 4AD England
0171 307 3616
FAX: 0171 307 3754
E-Mail: sue.mcgowan@inst.riba.org

AMOUNT: Up to 5,000 pounds sterling

DEADLINE(S): MAR 23

FIELD(S): Architecture

Awards are made to individuals for postgraduate research in fields relevant to the contemporary or historical study of architecture. Subject to be UK relevant. United Kingdom supervisor required.

Approximately 10 awards per year. Contact Leonie Milliner, Director, Centre for Architectural Education, at address above for complete information.

455 — SKIDMORE, OWINGS & MERRILL FOUNDATION (Interior Architecture Traveling Fellowship Program)

224 S. Michigan Ave., Suite 1000
Chicago IL 60604
312/554-9090
FAX 312/360-4545

AMOUNT: $7,500

DEADLINE(S): Varies (consult with school)

FIELD(S): Architecture or Interior Design

For a student graduating with a B.A. or M.A. degree from and accredited U.S. architectural or FIDER school. It will allow the Fellow to visit buildings and settings that are central to his or her area of interest and study.

Must submit portfolio and a proposed travel itinerary, etc. Write for complete information.

456 — SKIDMORE, OWINGS & MERRILL FOUNDATION (Mechanical/Electrical Traveling Fellowship Program)

224 S. Michigan Ave., Suite 1000
Chicago IL 60604
312/554-9090
FAX: 312/360-4545

AMOUNT: $7,500

DEADLINE(S): Varies (consult with school)

FIELD(S): Architectural Engineering, Electrical Engineering, or Mechanical

Candidates must have received a B.A. or M.A. degree in one of the above fields. It enables the Fellow to travel

in order to observe and analyze innovative building systems and technologies anywhere in the world.

Write for complete information.

457 — SKIDMORE, OWINGS & MERRILL FOUNDATION (Structural Engineering Traveling Fellowship Program)

224 S. Michigan Ave., Suite 1000
Chicago IL 60604
312/554-9090
FAX: 312/360-4545

AMOUNT: $7,500

DEADLINE(S): Varies (consult with school)

FIELD(S): Architectural Engineering, Structural Engineering, or Civil Engineering

Candidates must have received an M.A. or Ph.D. degree in one of the above fields. It enables the Fellow to travel in order to strengthen the connection between aesthetics and efficiency.

Write for complete information.

458 — SMITHSONIAN INSTITUTION (Cooper-Hewitt, National Design Museum-Mark Kaminski Summer Internship)

2 East 91st Street
New York NY 10128
212/860-6868
FAX: 212/860-6909

AMOUNT: $2,500 for 10-week period

DEADLINE(S): MAR 31

FIELD(S): Architecture, Architectural History, Design and Criticism, Museum Education, Museum Studies

These internships are open to college students considering a career in one of the above areas of study. Also open to graduate students who have not yet completed their M.A. degree. This ten-week program is designed to acquaint participants with the programs, policies, procedures, and operations of Cooper-Hewitt Museum and of museums in general.

One award each summer. Internship commences in June and ends in August. Housing is not provided. Write to Linda Herd at the above address for complete information.

459 — SMITHSONIAN INSTITUTION (Cooper-Hewitt, National Design Museum-Peter Krueger Summer Internship Program)

Cooper-Hewitt National Design Museum
2 East 91st St.
New York NY 10128
212/860-6868
FAX: 212/860-6909

AMOUNT: $2,500

DEADLINE(S): MAR 31

FIELD(S): Art History, Design, Museum Studies, and Museum Education, or Architectural History

Ten-week summer internships open to graduate and undergraduate students considering a career in the museum profession. Interns will assist on special research or exhibition projects and participate in daily museum activities.

Six awards each summer. Internship commences in June and ends in August. Housing is not provided. Write for complete information.

460 — SMITHSONIAN INSTITUTION (Cooper-Hewitt, National Design Museum-The Lippincott & Margulies Summer Internship)

Cooper-Hewitt National Design Museum
2 East 91st St.
New York NY 10128
212/860-6868
FAX 212/860-6909

AMOUNT: $2,500

DEADLINE(S): MAR 31

FIELD(S): Graphic, environmental, and industrial design

Ten-week summer internships open to graduate and undergraduate students considering a career in the fields listed above.

One award each summer. Internship commences in June and ends in August. Housing is not provided. Write for complete information.

461 — SOCIETY OF ARCHITECTURAL HISTORIANS (Rosann S. Berry Annual Meeting Fellowship; Keepers Preservation Education Fund Fellowship; Architectural Study Tour Scholarship)

1365 North Astor St.
Chicago Il 60610-2144
312/573-1365
FAX: 312/573-1144

AMOUNT: Varies

DEADLINE(S): Varies

FIELD(S): Architectural History and Preservation

Graduate student members of the society may apply to participate in an architectural study tour led by expert(s) of the region. Competition to award two student scholarships for attendence at annual meeting.

Three awards per year. Address inquiries to executive director Pauline Saliga.

462 — SOCIETY OF NAVAL ARCHITECTS AND MARINE ENGINEERS (SNAME Graduate Scholarships)

601 Pavonia Ave., Ste. 400
Jersey City NJ 07306
201/798-4800

FAX: 201/798-4975

Internet: www.sname.org

AMOUNT: Varies

DEADLINE(S): FEB 1

FIELD(S): Naval Architecture; Naval/Marine Engineering

Open to graduate students studying naval architechture, naval/marine engineering, or related fields at accredited institutions. Preference given to applicants who plan a career in the marine field. Must be US or Canadian citizen. One award is reserved for older, re-entry applicants who have five or more years of marine work experience after receiving bachelor's degree.

Contact Barbara Trentham at SNAME for an application.

463 — SOIL AND WATER CONSERVATION SOCIETY (SWCS Internships)

7515 N.E. Ankeny Road

Ankeny IA 50021-9764

515/289-2331 or 1-800/THE-SOIL

FAX: 515/289-1227

E-Mail: charliep@swcs.org

Internet: www.swcs.org

AMOUNT: Varies—most are uncompensated

DEADLINE(S): Varies

FIELD(S): Journalism, marketing, database management, meeting planning, public policy research, environmental education, landscape architecture

Internships for undergraduates and graduates to gain experience in the above fields as they relate to soil and water conservation issues. Intership openings vary through the year in duration, compensation, and objective. SWCS will coordinate particulars with your academic advisor.

Contact SWCS for internship availability at any timne during the year or see website for jobs page.

464 — SONOMA CHAMBOLLE-MUSIGNY SISTER CITIES, INC. (Henri Cardinaux Memorial Scholarship)

Chamson Scholarship Committee

PO Box 1633

Sonoma CA 95476-1633

707/939-1344

FAX: 707/939-1344

E-Mail: Baileysci@vom.com

AMOUNT: up to $1,500 (travel + expenses)

DEADLINE(S): JUL 15

FIELD(S): Culinary Arts; Wine Industry; Art; Architecture; Music; History; Fashion

Hands-on experience working in above or similiar fields & living with a family in small French village in Burgundy or other French city. Must be Sonoma County, CA, resident at least 18 years of age & be able to communicate in French. Transcripts, employer recommendation, photograph, & essay (stating why, where, & when) required.

1 award. Non-renewable. Also offers opportunity for candidate in Chambolle-Musigny to obtain work experience & cultural exposure in Sonoma, CA.

465 — THE DAPHNE JACKSON MEMORIAL FELLOWSHIPS TRUST (Fellowships in Science/ Engineering)

School of Physical Sciences

Dept. of Physics, University of Surrey

Guildford, Surrey GU2 5XH ENGLAND UK

01483 259166

FAX: 01483 259501

E-Mail: J.Woolley@surrey.ac.uk

Internet: www.sst.ph.ic.ac.uk/trust/

AMOUNT: Varies

DEADLINE(S): Varies

FIELD(S): Science or engineering, including information sciences

Fellowships to enable well-qualified and highly motivated scientists and engineers to return to appropriate careers following a career break due to family comitments. May be used on a flexible, part-time basis. Tenable at various U.K. universities.

See website and/or contact organization for details.

466 — U.S. DEPARTMENT OF TRANSPORTATION (Dwight D. Eisenhower Transportation Fellowships)

U.S. Dept. of Transportation

Fed. Hwy. Admin.

6300 Georgetown Pike, HHI-20

McLean VA 22101-2296

703/235-0538

AMOUNT: Varies

DEADLINE(S): FEB

FIELD(S): Transportation—such majors as chemistry; materials science; corrosion; civil, chemical, & electronics engineering; structures; human factors; computer science; psychology.

Research fellowships for undergrads and grad students at any Dept. of Transportation facility or selected IHE. For three to twelve months. Research must focus on transportation-related research and development in the above fields.

Contact Ilene Payne, Director, Universities and grants Programs at above location for details.

467 — UNIVERSITY OF CALGARY (Environmental Design Scholarships; Graduate Research Scholarships)

2500 Univ. Dr. NW, Rm 2180

Professional Faculties Bldg.

Calgary Alberta T2N 1N4 CANADA

403/220-6601

AMOUNT: $2,500; $3,920

DEADLINE(S): None specified

FIELD(S): Environmental Design

Open to graduate students who are or will be registered with the faculty of environmental design at the University of Calgary. Scholarships are awarded on the basis of merit.

Graduate research scholarships are renewable session by session. Scholarships have a duration of eight months. 10-12 scholarships and 25 research scholarships per year. Write for complete information.

468 — UNIVERSITY OF GLASGOW (Scholarships in Naval Architecture and Ocean Engineering)

Glasgow G12 8QQ

Scotland UNITED KINGDOM

0141 330 4322

FAX: 0141 330 5917

E-Mail: naval@eng.gla.ac.uk

Internet: www.eng.gla.ac.uk/Naval/questions/ scholar.htm

AMOUNT: 250 pounds per annum and more

DEADLINE(S): APR 30

FIELD(S): Naval Architecture; Ocean Engineering

Scholarships for undergraduate and graduate students in the above fields. Several awards are available, varying in amount and in year in school of recipients. First-year students can also apply to The Royal Institution of Naval Architects, 10 Upper Belgrave St., London, SW1X 8BQ, England (e-mail: hq@rina.org.uk).

See website for further information. Write for application forms.

469 — UNIVERSITY OF ILLINOIS COLLEGE OF FINE & APPLIED ARTS (Kate Neal Kinley Fellowship)

College of Fine and Applied Arts

608 E. Lorado Taft Dr., #117

Champaign IL 61820

217/333-1661

AMOUNT: $7,000 (3); $1,000 (3)

DEADLINE(S): FEB 1

FIELD(S): Art, Music, Architecture

Graduate fellowship for advanced study in the U.S. or abroad. Open to applicants with a bachelor's degree in the above areas. Preference given (but not limited) to applicants under 25 years of age and to graduates of the College of Fine and Applied Arts of the University of Illinois at Urbana-Champaign. Others are considered.

Write to Dr. Kathleen F. Conlin, Chair, Kinley Memorial Fellowship Committee, at above address. for complete information. Recipients may not participate in regular remunerative employment while engaged upon the Fellowship.

470 — WASHINGTON UNIVERSITY IN ST. LOUIS (James Harrison Steedman Memorial Traveling Fellowship in Architecture—Design Competition)

School of Architecture
One Brookings Drive
St. Louis MO 63130-4899
314/935-6293
FAX: 314/935-8520
E-Mail: steedman@arch.wustl.edu
Internet: www.arch.wustl.edu/steedman/

AMOUNT: $20,000

DEADLINE(S): DEC 12 (to request registration forms)

FIELD(S): Architecture

Award is for nine months of architectural study and travel abroad. Applicants should have received a professional degree in architecture from an accredited school within the last 8 years and have at least a year of experience in an architect's office. Send for registration forms or register on the website.

Awarded in even-numbered years. There is a $50 application fee. Write to Steddman Governing Committee, Marianne Pepper, Executive Director, at above address.

471 — WAVERLY COMMUNITY HOUSE INC. (F. Lammot Belin Arts Scholarships)

Scholarships Selection Committee
P.O. Box 142
Waverly PA 18471
717/586-8191

AMOUNT: $10,000

DEADLINE(S): DEC 15

FIELD(S): Painting; Sculpture; Music; Drama; Dance; Literature; Architecture; Photography

Applicants must have resided in the Abington or Pocono regions of Northeastern Pennsylvania. They must furnish proof of exceptional ability in their chosen field but no formal training in any academic or professional program.

U.S. citizenship required. Finalists must appear in person before the selection committee. Write for complete information.

472 — WOLFSONIAN-FLORIDA INTERNATIONAL UNIVERSITY (Fellowship Program)

1001 Washington Ave.
Miami Beach FL 33139
305/535-2632
FAX: 305/531-2133
E-Mail: wharton@fiu.edu

AMOUNT: Stipend, housing, travel, & research allowance

DEADLINE(S): MAY 31

FIELD(S): Art History; Architectural History

Postgraduate fellowships at the Wolfsonian to do scholarly research in the decorative arts, design, and architecture of the late-nineteenth to the mid-twentieth centuries. Offers full-time, in-residence research for a period of three to six weeks within the academic term, which runs from January to July each year. Also hosts Visiting Scholars in conjunction with institutional appointments. Honorary Associate Appointments also available. Financial need NOT a factor.

Contact the Research & Programs Officer for an application. Awards announced October 31st.

473 — XEROX TECHNICAL MINORITY SCHOLARSHIP (School-Year Tuition)

907 Culver Road
Rochester NY 14609
www.xerox.com/employment

AMOUNT: Up to $5,000 (varies according to tuition and academic excellence)

DEADLINE(S): SEP 15

FIELD(S): Various engineering and science disciplines

Scholarships for minorities enrolled full-time in a technical degree program at the bachelor level or above. Must be African-American, Native American, Hispanic, or Asian. Recipient may not have tuition or related expenses covered by other scholarships or grants.

If above requirements are met, obtain application from website or address above. Your financial aid office must fill out the bottom half of the form. Send completed application, your resume and a cover letter to Xerox Technical Minority Scholarship Program at above address.

474 — XEROX TECHNICAL MINORITY SCHOLARSHIP (Summer Employment Program)

Xerox Square
Rochester NY 14644
Written inquiry

AMOUNT: Up to $5,000 (varies according to tuition and academic excellence)

DEADLINE(S): SEP 15

FIELD(S): Various engineering and science disclpines

Scholarships for minorities enrolled in a technical degree program at the bachelor level or above. Must be African-American, Native American, Hispanic, or Asian. Xerox will match your skills with a sponsoring organization that will offer a meaningful summer work experience complimenting your academic learning.

If above requirements are met, send your resume and a cover letter to Xerox Corporation Corporate Employment and College Relations Technical Mfinority Scholarship Program to above address.

CIVIL ENGINEERING

475 — AECI LIMITED (AECI Post Graduate Research Fellowship)

Private Bag X2
Modderfontein SOUTH AFRICA 1645
011/605-3100

AMOUNT: Varies (South African Rands 3600)

DEADLINE(S): SEP 30

FIELD(S): Chemistry, Physics, Metallurgy, Biochemistry, Microbiology, Chemical Engineering, Civil Engineering, Industrial Engineering, Electrical Engineering, Mechanical Engineering, Instrument Engineering

Open to South African citizens who are graduate students who want to do research in one of the above areas. This fellowship is offered to strengthen post-graduate study and research in South Africa, particularly in the fields above.

Write to the above address for complete information.

476 — AFRICAN NETWORK OF SCIENTIFIC AND TECHNOLOGICAL INSTITUTIONS - ANSTI (Postgraduate Fellowships)

PO Box 30592
Nairobi Kenya AFRICA
254-2-621234 or 254-2-622619/20
FAX: 254-2-215991
E-Mail: j.massaquoi@unesco.org OR
ANSTI@Net2000ke.com

AMOUNT: Fees, subsistence, & international travel

DEADLINE(S): JUN

FIELD(S): Basic & Engineering Sciences

Scholarships for postgraduate studies outside of applicant's home country. Must be African nationals not older than 36 years of age and hold a good bachelor's degree (at least 2nd class upper division). Applicants should apply for admission to host university as soon as possible. Fellowships tenable only in African universities.

10 awards annually. Renewable up to 2 years. Contact Professor J.G.M. Massaquoi for an application.

477 — AMERICAN FOUNDATION FOR THE BLIND (Paul W. Ruckes Scholarship)

11 Penn Plaza, Ste. 300
New York NY 10001
212/502-7661 or TDD 212/502-7771
E-Mail: juliet@afb.org
Internet: www.afb.org
AMOUNT: $1,000
DEADLINE(S): APR 30
FIELD(S): Engineering, computer, physical, or life sciences

Open to blind or visually impaired undergraduate or graduate students pursuing degrees in the above fields. U.S. citizenship required.

Write to the above address or visit website for complete information.

478 — AMERICAN SOCIETY FOR ENGINEERING EDUCATION (Army Research Laboratory Postdoctoral Fellowships)

1818 N St., NW, Ste. 600
Washington DC 20036
202/331-3525
FAX: 202/265-8504
E-Mail: projects@asee.org
Internet: www.asee.org/fellowship/
AMOUNT: $45,000-$55,000 + travel/relocation allowance
DEADLINE(S): Varies
FIELD(S): Engineering; Physical Sciences

Postdoctoral fellowships for US citizens/permanent residents to do research at Army Research Laboratories. Candidates must have completed their Ph.D. prior to appointment. Program is designed to increase involvement of creative and highly trained scientists and engineers from academia and industry in scientific and technical areas of interest and relevance to the Army. Research proposal should include clear objective and defined outcome. Financial need NOT a factor.

15 awards annually. Renewable. Contact Sandi Crawford at ASEE for an application packet.

479 — AMERICAN SOCIETY OF CIVIL ENGINEERS (Arthur S. Tuttle Memorial Scholarship)

1801 Alexander Bell Drive
Reston VA 20191-4400
800/548-ASCE or 703/295-6000
FAX: 703/295-6333

E-Mail: student@asce.org
Internet: www.asce.org
AMOUNT: $3,000-$5,000
DEADLINE(S): FEB 20
FIELD(S): Civil Engineering

Award is for the first year of formal graduate tuition; undergraduates should apply during their senior year. Must a member of ASCE (Membership applications may be submitted along with scholarship applications).

See website or contact ASCE for an application between October and February.

480 — AMERICAN SOCIETY OF CIVIL ENGINEERS (Freeman Fellowship)

1801 Alexander Bell Drive
Reston VA 20191-4400
800/548-ASCE or 703/295-6000
FAX: 703/295-6333
E-Mail: student@asce.org
Internet: www.asce.org
AMOUNT: $3,000-$5,000
DEADLINE(S): FEB 20
FIELD(S): Hydraulics

Any member of ASCE may apply for this grant towards tuition, research, and living expenses that may be used towards expenses for experiments, observations, and compilations relating to hydraulics. May submit membership application along with fellowship application.

See website or contact ASCE for an application between October and February.

481 — AMERICAN SOCIETY OF CIVIL ENGINEERS (Jack E. Leisch Memorial Scholarship)

1801 Alexander Bell Drive
Reston VA 20191-4400
800/548-ASCE or 703/295-6000
FAX: 703/295-6333
E-Mail: student@asce.org
Internet: www.asce.org
AMOUNT: $1,500
DEADLINE(S): FEB 20
FIELD(S): Transportation/Traffic Engineering

For ASCE members enrolled full-time in a graduate program at a ABET accredited university that is also a member of the Council of Univ. Trans. Centers. Thesis topic is considered in selection. Award is to be used towards tuition. Membership application may be submitted along with scholarship application.

1 award annually. See website or contact ASCE for an application between October and February.

482 — AMERICAN SOCIETY OF CIVIL ENGINEERS (J. Waldo Smith Hydraulic Fellowship)

1801 Alexander Bell Drive
Reston VA 20191-4400
800/548-ASCE or 703/295-6000
FAX: 703/295-6333
E-Mail: student@asce.org
Internet: www.asce.org
AMOUNT: $4,000 + up to $1,000 (for physical equipment)
DEADLINE(S): FEB 20
FIELD(S): Hydraulics

For graduate students, preferably Associate Members of ASCE, to conduct research in the field of experimental hydraulics. Award is for tuition, research, and living expenses.

Offered every third year (2000, 2003, etc.). See website or contact ASCE for an application between October and February.

483 — AMERICAN SOCIETY OF CIVIL ENGINEERS (O.H. Ammann Research Fellowship in Structural Engineering)

1801 Alexander Bell Drive
Reston VA 20191-4400
800/548-ASCE or 703/295-6000
FAX: 703/295-6333
E-Mail: student@asce.org
Internet: www.asce.org
AMOUNT: $5,000
DEADLINE(S): FEB 20
FIELD(S): Structural Engineering

For ASCE members in any grade to create new knowledge in the field of structural design and construction. Membership application may be submitted along with fellowship application.

1 award annually. See website or contact ASCE for an application between October and February.

484 — AMERICAN SOCIETY OF CIVIL ENGINEERS (Trent R. Dames and William W. Moore Fellowship)

1801 Alexander Bell Drive
Reston VA 20191-4400
800/548-ASCE or 703/295-6000
FAX: 703/295-6333
E-Mail: student@asce.org
Internet: www.asce.org
AMOUNT: $5,000-$10,000
DEADLINE(S): FEB 20
FIELD(S): Geotechnical Engineering; Earth Sciences

For practicing engineers, earth scientists, professors, or graduate students to explore new applications of geotechnical engineering or the earth sciences to social, economic, environmental, and political issues. ASCE membership is not required.

Offered every two years (2000, 20002, etc.). See website or contact ASCE for an application between October and February.

485 — ASIAN INSTITUTE OF TECHNOLOGY (AIT Scholarship Program)

Development Office
PO Box 4, Klongluang
Pathumthani 12120 THAILAND
(66)(2) 516-0110-44 or 524-5032
FAX: (66)(2) 516-2126
E-Mail: ascao@ait.ac.th
Internet: www.ait.ac.th

AMOUNT: US $12,600-$37,960

DEADLINE(S): FEB 15; JUN 15; OCT 15

FIELD(S): Advanced Technologies; Civil Engineering; Environment, Resources, & Development; Business Management

Scholarships and grants open to citizens of Asian countries who are accepted by the institute as a master's or doctotal candidate. Selection is based on academic criteria, practical experience, gender, and country of origin; priority to Mekong Region countries and Asian countries of the former USSR.

250 awards annually. Contact AIT for an application.

486 — ASSOCIATED WESTERN UNIVERSITIES, INC. (AWU Faculty Fellowships)

4190 South Highland Dr., Suite 211
Salt Lake City UT 84124-2600
801-273-8900

AMOUNT: Varies.

DEADLINE(S): FEB 15

FIELD(S): Engineering, Mathematics, Science, Technology

Research fellowships for qualified college and university faculty members to encourage participation and contribution to research at one of 62 cooperating facilities. It is not necessary to be enrolled at an AWU member institution. Collaborations that include graduate and/or undergraduate students are encouraged.

For detailed information and list of cooperating facilities, contact above location.

487 — ASSOCIATED WESTERN UNIVERSITIES, INC. (AWU Graduate Fellowship Program)

4190 South Highland Dr. Suite 211
Salt Lake City, UT 84124-2600
801/273-8900

AMOUNT: Stipend ($1,300 per month & up) + tuition assistance and travel allowance

DEADLINE(S): FEB 15

FIELD(S): Engineering, Mathematics, Science, Technology

Open to master's and doctoral degree candidates to conduct research toward a thesis or dissertation at one of more than 62 cooperating facilities. Institutional affiliation and citizenship restrictions may apply for some awards or facilities. It is not necessary to be enrolled at an AWU member institution to apply for a fellowship.

Write to the above address for complete information.

488 — ASSOCIATED WESTERN UNIVERSITIES, INC. (AWU Postgraduate Fellowship)

4190 South Highland Dr. Suite 211
Salt Lake City UT 84124-2600
801/273-8900

AMOUNT: Stipend established by the host facility and varies by experience and discipline.

DEADLINE(S): Varies (Two to three months before the starting date)

FIELD(S): Engineering, Mathematics, Science, Technology

For college and university graduates who have completed all institutional requirements for an advanced degree from an accredited college or university in the U.S. A commitment to a professional career in science or engineering research is expected. U.S. citizenship or permanent resident status is required. Research is to be done at one of the 62 cooperating universities.

For detailed information and a list of cooperating facilities contact above address.

489 — ASSOCIATED WESTERN UNIVERSITIES, INC. (AWU Visiting Scientist Fellowships)

4190 South Highland Dr., Suite 211
Salt Lake City UT 84124-2600
801/273-8900

AMOUNT: Varies

DEADLINE(S): Varies (Two months prior to starting date)

FIELD(S): Engineering, Science, Mathematics, and Technology

Research fellowships for professionals with continued commitment to science and engineering. For use at one of 62 participating universities. US citizenship or permanent residency required.

For detailed information and list of cooperating facitilies contact above location.

490 — BOEING (Polish Graduate Student Scholarship Program)

Phone for details
314/234-2149

AMOUNT: Tuition, books, and fees for three years

DEADLINE(S): Varies

FIELD(S): Scientific and technical fields

Scholarships for students from Poland to pursue graduate studies in scientific and technical areas at American colleges or universities.

Call Jim Schlueter at above telephone number.

491 — BRITISH FEDERATION OF WOMEN GRADUATES (M.H. Joseph Prize for Non-UK Citizens)

4 Mandeville Courtyard
142 Battersea Park Rd.
London SW11 4NB ENGLAND UK
PHONE/FAX: 0171/498 8037

AMOUNT: 500+ pounds sterling

DEADLINE(S): SEP 10

FIELD(S): Architecture; Engineering

For female graduate students of any nationality (except UK) who will pursue studies in Great Britain. Must have completed at least four academic terms or three semesters; award is not made for first year of research. Chief criteria is academic excellence and proven ability to carry out independent research. Postdoctoral studies also eligible.

1 award annually. Application fee of 12 pounds sterling required. Send a self-addressed, stamped envelope (or self-addressed envelope with international reply coupons) for an application. Results announced by end of October.

492 — BRITISH FEDERATION OF WOMEN GRADUATES (M.H. Joseph Prize for UK Citizens)

4 Mandeville Courtyard
142 Battersea Park Rd.
London SW11 4NB ENGLAND UK
PHONE/FAX: 0171/498 8037

AMOUNT: 500+ pounds sterling

DEADLINE(S): SEP 10

FIELD(S): Architecture; Engineering

For female UK citizens who plan to pursue graduate studies overseas. Must have completed at least four academic terms or three semesters; award is not made for first year of research. Chief criteria is academic excellence and proven ability to carry out independent research. Postdoctoral studies also eligible.

1 award annually. Application fee of 12 pounds sterling required. Send a self-addressed, stamped envelope (or self-addressed envelope with international

reply coupons) for an application. Award announced at end of October.

493 — BROOKHAVEN WOMEN IN SCIENCE (Renate W. Chasman Scholarship)

PO Box 183
Upton NY 11973-5000
E-mail: pam@bnl.gov

AMOUNT: $2,000

DEADLINE(S): APR 1

FIELD(S): Natural Sciences; Engineering; Mathematics

Open ONLY to women who are residents of the boroughs of Brooklyn or Queens or the counties of Nassau or Suffolk in New York who are re-entering school after a period of study. For juniors, seniors, or first-year graduate students.

1 award annually. Not renewable. Contact Pam Mansfield at above location for an application. Phone calls are NOT accepted.

494 — EPPLEY FOUNDATION FOR RESEARCH (Postdoctoral Research Grants)

245 Park Avenue, 40th Floor
New York NY 10167
Written inquiry

AMOUNT: Up to $25,000

DEADLINE(S): FEB 1; MAY 1; AUG 1; NOV 1

FIELD(S): Physical Sciences; Biological Sciences

Postdoctoral grants for original advanced research in any of the physical or biological sciences. Open to established research scientists who are attached to a recognized institution.

Write for complete information.

495 — FANNIE AND JOHN HERTZ FOUNDATION (Fellowship)

Box 5032
Livermore CA 94551-5032
925/373-1642
Internet: www.hertzfoundation.org

AMOUNT: $25,000 stipend/yr. + $15,000 (max.) tuition allowance/yr.

DEADLINE(S): NOV 5

FIELD(S): Applied Physical Sciences

Open to graduate students with a minimum 3.75 GPA for studies in applied physical sciences, including math, engineering, computer science, biology, oceanography, aeronautics, astronomy, physics, and earth science. Must be US citizen/permanent resident. Does not support study in pursuit of M.D. degree, although will support Ph.D. portion of a joint M.D./Ph.D. study program.

Renewable up to 5 years. Only 36 US schools are currently considered tenable. See website for an application and list of specific fields of study that are acceptable.

496 — FORD FOUNDATION/NATIONAL RESEARCH COUNCIL (Predoctoral/Dissertation Fellowships for Minorities)

2101 Constitution Ave.
Washington DC 20418
202/334-2872
E-Mail: infofell@nas.edu
Internet: http//www.nas.edu/fo/index.html

AMOUNT: $14,000 annual stipend + $6,000 grant to institution; $18,000 for dissertation fellowship

DEADLINE(S): NOV 3

FIELD(S): Most fields of study: sciences, humanities, engineering, behavioral science, social sciences, and computer science

Predoctoral and dissertation fellowships for students whose ethnicity is Alaskan Native, Black/African American, Mexican American/Chicano, Native American Indian, Native Pacific Islander, or Puerto Rican. For research-based programs leading to careers in college teaching and research.

Contact above address or website.

497 — INSTITUTION OF ELECTRICAL ENGINEERS (Postgraduate Awards)

Savoy Place
London WC2R 0BL ENGLAND
0171 240 1871 Ext. 2211/2235
FAX: 0171 497 3609
E-Mail: scholarships@iee.org.uk
Internet: www.iee.org.uk/Awards/pgsum.htm

AMOUNT: 1,000-6,000 pounds/yr.

DEADLINE(S): SEP 1; SEP 30

FIELD(S): Engineering

Scholarships for postgraduate students pursuing degrees in engineering who are residents of the United Kingdom.

Check website or contact organization for application details.

498 — MIDWEST ROOFING CONTRACTORS ASSOCIATION (Construction Industry Scholarships)

4840 West 15th St., Ste. 1000
Lawrence KS 66049-3876
800/497-6722
E-Mail: mrca@mrca.org
Internet: www.mrca.org

AMOUNT: Varies

DEADLINE(S): JUN 20

FIELD(S): Construction

Applicants must be pursuing or planning to pursue a curriculum at an accredited university, college, community college, vocational, or trade school that will lead to a career in the construction industry. Three letters of recommendation required.

Contact MRCA for an application. Award is presented at Annual Convention and Trade Show.

499 — NATIONAL ASSOCIATION OF WATER COMPANIES—NEW JERSEY CHAPTER (Scholarship)

Elizabethtown Water Co.
600 South Ave.
Westfield NJ 07090
908/654-1234
FAX: 908/232-2719

AMOUNT: $2,500

DEADLINE(S): APR 1

FIELD(S): Business Administration; Biology; Chemistry; Engineering; Communications

For U.S. citizens who have lived in NJ at least 5 years and plan a career in the investor-owned water utility industry in disciplines such as those above. Must be undergrad or graduate student in a 2- or 4-year NJ college or university.

GPA of 3.0 or better required. Contact Gail P. Brady for complete information.

500 — NATIONAL SOCIETY OF BLACK ENGINEERS (Scholarships)

1454 Duke St.
Alexandria VA 22314
703/549-2207
FAX: 703/683-5312
E-Mail: nsbehq@nsbe.org
Internet: www.nsbe.org

AMOUNT: Varies

DEADLINE(S): Varies

FIELD(S): Engineering and engineering technologies

Programs for black and other ethnic minorities in the fields of engineering and the engineering technologies. Organization offers pre-college programs, scholarships, career fairs, a journal, a newsletter, etc.

Contact organization for details.

501 — OAK RIDGE ASSOCIATED UNIVERSITIES (National Science Foundation Graduate Research Fellowships)

PO Box 3010
Oak Ridge TN 37831-3010
423/241-4300
FAX: 423/241-4513
E-Mail: nsfgrfp@orau.gov
Internet: www.orau.gov/nsf/nsffel.htm

AMOUNT: $15,000 stipend + $10,500 tuition allowance

DEADLINE(S): NOV 4

FIELD(S): Science; Math; Engineering; Computer Science

Three-year fellowships for graduate study leading to research-based master's or doctoral degrees in the above fields. Must be US citizens, nationals, or permanent residents at the time of application. Fellowships are awarded on the basis of ability. Women, minorities, and those with disabilities are strongly encouraged to apply. One-time International Research Travel Allowance available.

1,000 awards annually. Contact Jeannette Bouchard for an application/more information.

502 — OAK RIDGE INSTITUTE FOR SCIENCE AND EDUCATION (Professional Internship Program/Oak Ridge National Laboratory)

P.O. Box 117
Oak Ridge TN 37831-0117
423/576-3426
423/576-3427

AMOUNT: $210 to $300/week + travel, tuition, and fees

DEADLINE(S): FEB 5; JUN 1; OCT 1

FIELD(S): Chemistry, environmental science, geology, hydrogeology, hydrology, chemical engineering, civil engineering, environmental engineering, mechanical engineering, computer science (technical database development)

Opportunities for graduates and undergraduates to participate in energy-related research projects that correlate with their academic and career goals. For 3 to 12 consecutive months.

Funded through Oak Ridge National Laboratory.

503 — OAK RIDGE INSTITUTE FOR SCIENCE AND EDUCATION (Professional Internship Program/Pittsburgh Energy Technology Center)

P.O. Box 117
Oak Ridge TN 37831-0117
423/576-3426
423/576-3427

AMOUNT: $235 to $325/week + travel, tuition, and fees

DEADLINE(S): FEB 5; JUN 1; OCT 1

FIELD(S): Chemistry, physics, environmental science, geology, chemical or environmental engineering, computer science, or statistics.

Opportunities for graduates and undergraduates to participate in fossil energy-related research projects that correlate with their academic and career goals. For 3 to 12 consecutive months.

Funded through U.S. Dept. of Energy, Office of Fossil Energy, and Pittsburgh Energy Technology Center.

504 — OAK RIDGE INSTITUTE FOR SCIENCE AND EDUCATION (Professional Internship Program/Savannah River Site)

P.O. Box 117
Oak Ridge TN 37831-0117
423/576-3426
423/576-3427

AMOUNT: $260 to $340/week + travel

DEADLINE(S): FEB 5; JUN 1; SEP 1

FIELD(S): Chemistry, computer science, environmental science, geology, engineering, or physics

Opportunities for high school junior and seniors, undergraduates, and graduates to participate in research projects that correlate with their academic majors and career goals. For 3 to 12 consecutive months at the Savannah River Site, SC.

Funded through the Savannah River Site, SC.

505 — OAK RIDGE INSTITUTE FOR SCIENCE AND EDUCATION (Science and Engineering Research Semester)

P.O. Box 117
Oak Ridge TN 37831-0117
423/576-2358
423/576-2310

AMOUNT: $225/week + travel + housing

DEADLINE(S): OCT; MAR

FIELD(S): Computer science, physical sciences, environmental and life sciences, and mathematics

Opportunities for high school junior and seniors and a few slots for graduates to participate in energy-related with laboratory scientists at Oak Ridge National Laboratory, TN. One semester with possibility of summer extension. Available two times a year.

Funded through the U.S. Dept. of Energy, Office of Energy Research.

506 — OAK RIDGE INSTITUTE FOR SCIENCE AND EDUCATION (U.S. Geological Survey Earth Sciences Internship Program)

P.O. Box 117
Oak Ridge TN 37831-0117
423/576-2358
423/576-4813

AMOUNT: $19,000 to $38,000, dependent on level

DEADLINE(S): Ongoing

FIELD(S): Geology, geography, biology, chemistry, environmental sciences, hydrology, forestry, civil engineering, computer sciences

Internships for undergrads, grads, or recent grads (within one year) students studying in the above fields to conduct projects to prepare for careers in earth sciences for up to two years. Location: USGS sites across the U.S.

Funded through the U.S. Dept. of the Interior, U.S.G.S.

507 — OAK RIDGE INSTITUTE FOR SCIENCE AND EDUCATION/U.S. DEPT. OF ENERGY (Office of Civilian Radioactive Waste Management Fellowship)

P.O. Box 117
Oak Ridge TN 37831-0117
423/576-0128
FAX: 423/576-8293
E-Mail: drostp@orau.gov

AMOUNT: $14,000/yr.

DEADLINE(S): JAN 16 (Received, not postmarked)

FIELD(S): Physical or life sciences, math, or engineering

Fellowships for graduate students at various participating universities to conduct research in the management of spent nuclear fuel and high-level raqdioactive waste. For M.A. and Ph.D. candidates. For up to 48 months. Must be U.S. citizen or permanent resident.

Funded through U.S. Department of Energy, Office of Civilian Radioactive Waste Management. Contact or call Ms. Portia Drost, MS-16, at above address for details.

508 — OPEN SOCIETY INSTITUTE (Environmental Management Fellowships)

400 West 59th St.
New York NY 10019
212/548-0600 or 212/757-2323
FAX: 212/548-4679 or 212/548-4600
Internet: www.soros.org/efp.html

AMOUNT: Fees, room, board, living stipend, textbooks, international transportation, health insurance

DEADLINE(S): NOV 15

FIELD(S): Earth sciences, natural sciences, humanities (exc. language), anthropology, sociology, mathematics, or engineering

Two-year fellowships for use in selected universities in the U.S. for international students. For students/professionals in fields related to environmental policy, legislation, and remediation techniques applicable to their home countries.

To apply, contact your local Soros Foundation or Open Society Institute. Further details on website.

509 — SKIDMORE, OWINGS & MERRILL FOUNDATION (Structural Engineering Traveling Fellowship Program)

224 S. Michigan Ave., Suite 1000
Chicago IL 60604
312/554-9090
FAX: 312/360-4545

AMOUNT: $7,500

DEADLINE(S): Varies (consult with school)

FIELD(S): Architectural Engineering, Structural Engineering, or Civil Engineering

Candidates must have received an M.A. or Ph.D. degree in one of the above fields. It enables the Fellow to travel in order to strengthen the connection between aesthetics and efficiency.

Write for complete information.

510 — THE DAPHNE JACKSON MEMORIAL FELLOWSHIPS TRUST (Fellowships in Science/ Engineering)

School of Physical Sciences
Dept. of Physics
University of Surrey
Guildford, Surrey
GU2 5XH ENGLAND UK
01483 259166
FAX: 01483 259501
E-Mail: J.Woolley@surrey.ac.uk
Internet: www.sst.ph.ic.ac.uk/trust/

AMOUNT: Varies

DEADLINE(S): Varies

FIELD(S): Science or engineering, including information sciences

Fellowships to enable well-qualified and highly motivated scientists and engineers to return to appropriate careers following a career break due to family comitments. May be used on a flexible, part-time basis. Tenable at various U.K. universities.

See website and/or contact organization for details.

511 — U.S. DEPARTMENT OF TRANSPORTATION (Dwight D. Eisenhower Transportation Fellowships)

U.S. Dept. of Transportation
Fed. Hwy. Admin.
6300 Georgetown Pike, HHI-20
McLean VA 22101-2296
703/235-0538

AMOUNT: Varies

DEADLINE(S): FEB

FIELD(S): Transportation—such majors as chemistry; materials science; corrosion; civil, chemical, & electronics engineering; structures; human factors; computer science; psychology.

Research fellowships for undergrads and grad students at any Dept. of Transportation facility or selected IHE. For three to twelve months. Research must focus on transportation-related research and development in the above fields.

Contact Ilene Payne, Director, Universities and grants Programs at above location for details.

512 — XEROX TECHNICAL MINORITY SCHOLARSHIP (School-Year Tuition)

907 Culver Road
Rochester NY 14609
www.xerox.com/employment

AMOUNT: Up to $5,000 (varies according to tuition and academic excellence)

DEADLINE(S): SEP 15

FIELD(S): Various engineering and science disclipines

Scholarships for minorities enrolled full-time in a technical degree program at the bachelor level or above. Must be African-American, Native American, Hispanic, or Asian. Recipient may not have tuition or related expenses covered by other scholarships or grants.

If above requirements are met, obtain application from website or address above. Your financial aid office must fill out the bottom half of the form. Send completed application, your resume and a cover letter to Xerox Technical Minority Scholarship Program at above address.

513 — XEROX TECHNICAL MINORITY SCHOLARSHIP (Summer Employment Program)

Xerox Square
Rochester NY 14644
Written inquiry

AMOUNT: Up to $5,000 (varies according to tuition and academic excellence)

DEADLINE(S): SEP 15

FIELD(S): Various engineering and science disclipines

Scholarships for minorities enrolled in a technical degree program at the bachelor level or above. Must be African-American, Native American, Hispanic, or Asian. Xerox will match your skills with a sponsoring organization that will offer a meaningful summer work experience complimenting your academic learning.

If above requirements are met, send your resume and a cover letter to Xerox Corporation Corporate Employment and College Relations Technical Mfinority Scholarship Program to above address.

COMPUTER SCIENCE

514 — AFRICAN NETWORK OF SCIENTIFIC AND TECHNOLOGICAL INSTITUTIONS - ANSTI (Postgraduate Fellowships)

PO Box 30592
Nairobi Kenya AFRICA
254-2-621234 or 254-2-622619/20
FAX: 254-2-215991
E-Mail: j.massaquoi@unesco.org OR
ANSTI@Net2000ke.com

AMOUNT: Fees, subsistence, & international travel

DEADLINE(S): JUN

FIELD(S): Basic & Engineering Sciences

Scholarships for postgraduate studies outside of applicant's home country. Must be African nationals not older than 36 years of age and hold a good bachelor's degree (at least 2nd class upper division). Applicants should apply for admission to host university as soon as possible. Fellowships tenable only in African universities.

10 awards annually. Renewable up to 2 years. Contact Professor J.G.M. Massaquoi for an application.

515 — AMERICAN ASSOCIATION OF UNIVERSITY WOMEN EDUCATIONAL FOUNDATION (Selected Professions Fellowships)

Dept. 60
2201 N. Dodge St.
Iowa City IA 52243-4030
319/337-1716, ext. 60
FAX 319/337-1204
Internet: www.aauw.org

AMOUNT: $5,000-$15,000

DEADLINE(S): JAN 2 (most); NOV 15 (engineering dissertation only)

FIELD(S): Architecture; Computer/Information Sciences; Engineering; Mathematics/Statistics

For women in final year of graduate study in fields where women's participation has been low. Must be US citizen or permanent resident. Special consideration given to applicants who show professional promise in innovative or neglected areas of research and/or practice in areas of public interest. Women in engineering master's programs are eligible to apply for either first or final year of study; special award for engineering doctoral students writing dissertation.

Applications available August-December.

516 — AMERICAN FOUNDATION FOR THE BLIND (Paul W. Ruckes Scholarship)

11 Penn Plaza, Ste. 300
New York NY 10001
212/502-7661 or TDD 212/502-7771

E-Mail: juliet@afb.org

Internet: www.afb.org

AMOUNT: $1,000

DEADLINE(S): APR 30

FIELD(S): Engineering, computer, physical, or life sciences

Open to blind or visually impaired undergraduate or graduate students pursuing degrees in the above fields. U.S. citizenship required.

Write to the above address or visit website for complete information.

517 — AMERICAN RADIO RELAY LEAGUE FOUNDATION (The PHD ARA Scholarship)

225 Main Street
Newington CT 06111
860/594-0200
FAX: 860/594-0259
Internet: www.arrl.org/

AMOUNT: $1,000

DEADLINE(S): FEB 1

FIELD(S): Journalism; Computer Science; Electronic Engineering

For undergraduate or graduate students who are residents of the ARRL Midwest Division (IA, KS, MO, NE) who hold any class of radio amateur license—or student may be the child of a deceased radio amateur.

1 award annually. Contact ARRL for an application.

518 — AMERICAN SOCIETY FOR ENGINEERING EDUCATION (Army Research Laboritory Postdoctoral Fellowships)

1818 N St., NW, Ste. 600
Washington DC 20036
202/331-3525
FAX: 202/265-8504
E-Mail: projects@asee.org
Internet: www.asee.org/fellowship/

AMOUNT: $45,000-$55,000 + travel/relocation allowance

DEADLINE(S): Varies

FIELD(S): Engineering; Physical Sciences

Postdoctoral fellowships for US citizens/permanent residents to do research at Army Research Laboratories. Candidates must have completed their Ph.D. prior to appointment. Program is designed to increase involvement of creative and highly trained scientists and engineers from academia and industry in scientific and technical areas of interest and relevance to the Army. Research proposal should include clear objective and defined outcome. Financial need NOT a factor.

15 awards annually. Renewable. Contact Sandi Crawford at ASEE for an application packet.

519 — ARMED FORCES COMMUNICATIONS AND ELECTRONICS ASSOCIATION (AFCEA Fellowshps)

4400 Fair Lakes Court
Fairfax VA 22033-3899
800/336-4583 Ext. 6149 or 703/631-6149
Internet: www.afcea.org/awards/scholarships.htm

AMOUNT: $25,000

DEADLINE(S): FEB 1

FIELD(S): Electrical engineering, electronics, computer science, computer engineering, physics, mathematics

Fellowships in the above fields for students working on doctoral degrees in accredited universities in the U.S.

Send a self-addressed, stamped envelope with information on the name of your school, field of study, GPA, and year in school to AFCEA Educational Foundation at above address. Applications available November through Jan 1.

520 — ASIAN INSTITUTE OF TECHNOLOGY (AIT Scholarship Program)

Development Office
PO Box 4, Klongluang
Pathumthani 12120 THAILAND
(66)(2) 516-0110-44 or 524-5032
FAX: (66)(2) 516-2126
E-Mail: ascao@ait.ac.th
Internet: www.ait.ac.th

AMOUNT: US $12,600-$37,960

DEADLINE(S): FEB 15; JUN 15; OCT 15

FIELD(S): Advanced Technologies; Civil Engineering; Environment, Resources, & Development; Business Management

Scholarships and grants open to citizens of Asian countries who are accepted by the institute as a master's or doctotal candidate. Selection is based on academic criteria, practical experience, gender, and country of origin; priority to Mekong Region countries and Asian countries of the former USSR.

250 awards annually. Contact AIT for an application.

521 — ASSOCIATED WESTERN UNIVERSITIES, INC. (AWU Faculty Fellowships)

4190 South Highland Dr., Suite 211
Salt Lake City UT 84124-2600
801-273-8900

AMOUNT: Varies.

DEADLINE(S): FEB 15

FIELD(S): Engineering, Mathematics, Science, Technology

Research fellowships for qualified college and university faculty members to encourage participation

and contribution to research at one of 62 cooperating facilities. It is not necessary to be enrolled at an AWU member institution. Collaborations that include graduate and/or undergraduate students are encouraged.

For detailed information and list of cooperating facilities, contact above location.

522 — ASSOCIATED WESTERN UNIVERSITIES, INC. (AWU Graduate Fellowship Program)

4190 South Highland Dr. Suite 211
Salt Lake City, UT 84124-2600
801/273-8900

AMOUNT: Stipend ($1,300 per month & up) + tuition assistance and travel allowance

DEADLINE(S): FEB 15

FIELD(S): Engineering, Mathematics, Science, Technology

Open to master's and doctoral degree candidates to conduct research toward a thesis or dissertation at one of more than 62 cooperating facilities. Institutional affiliation and citizenship restrictions may apply for some awards or facilities. It is not necessary to be enrolled at an AWU member institution to apply for a fellowship.

Write to the above address for complete information.

523 — ASSOCIATED WESTERN UNIVERSITIES, INC. (AWU Postgraduate Fellowship)

4190 South Highland Dr. Suite 211
Salt Lake City UT 84124-2600
801/273-8900

AMOUNT: Stipend established by the host facility and varies by experience and discipline.

DEADLINE(S): Varies (Two to three months before the starting date)

FIELD(S): Engineering, Mathematics, Science, Technology

For college and university graduates who have completed all institutional requirements for an advanced degree from an accredited college or university in the U.S. A commitment to a professional career in science or engineering research is expected. U.S. citizenship or permanent resident status is required. Research is to be done at one of the 62 cooperating universities.

For detailed information and a list of cooperating facilities contact above address.

524 — ASSOCIATED WESTERN UNIVERSITIES, INC. (AWU Visiting Scientist Fellowships)

4190 South Highland Dr., Suite 211
Salt Lake City UT 84124-2600
801/273-8900

AMOUNT: Varies

DEADLINE(S): Varies (Two months prior to starting date)

FIELD(S): Engineering, Science, Mathematics, and Technology

Research fellowships for professionals with continued commitment to science and engineering. For use at one of 62 participating universities. US citizenship or permanent residency required.

For detailed information and list of cooperating facitlies contact above location.

525 — ASSOCIATION FOR COMPUTING MACHINERY (Listing of Internships & Summer Jobs)

1515 Broadway, 17th Floor
New York NY 10036
1-800/342-6626 or +1-212/626-0500 (global)
FAX: +1-212/944-1318
Internet: www.acm.org/student/
internships.html

AMOUNT: Varies

DEADLINE(S): Varies

FIELD(S): Computer science

A listing on the Internet of several internships and summer employment in the field of computer science at various companies and colleges in the U.S., Canada, and elsewhere. Each one has its own requirements.

Access website for details.

526 — ASSOCIATION FOR INSTITUTIONAL RESEARCH (Fellowship to Summer Institute)

114 Stone Building, FSU
Tallahassee FL 32306-4462
850/644-4470
FAX: 850/644-8824
E-Mail: air@mailer.fsu.edu
Internet: http://airweb.org

AMOUNT: Varies

DEADLINE(S): JAN 15

FIELD(S): Social sciences, education

The Association provides fellowships to doctoral and postdoctoral researchers for its summer institute on "Improving Institutional Research in Postsecondary Educational Institutions."

Contact organization for details.

527 — ASSOCIATION FOR WOMEN IN SCIENCE EDUCATIONAL FOUNDATION (AWIS Predoctoral Awards)

1200 New York Ave. NW, Suite 650
Washington DC 20005
202/326-8940 or 800-886-AWIS
E-Mail: awis@awis.org
Internet: www.awis.org

AMOUNT: $1,000

DEADLINE(S): JAN 16

FIELD(S): Various Sciences and Social Sciences

Scholarships for female doctoral students. Summary page, description of research project, resume, references, transcripts, and biographical sketch required. US citizens may study at any graduate institution; non-citizens must study at US institutions.

5-10 awards annually. See website or write to above address for an application and complete information.

528 — ASSOCIATION FOR WOMEN IN SCIENCE EDUCATIONAL FOUNDATION (AWIS Pre-doctoral Awards)

1200 New York Ave. NW, Suite 650
Washington DC 20005
202/326-8940 or 800/886-AWIS
E-Mail: awis@awis.org
Internet: www.awis.org

AMOUNT: $1,000

DEADLINE(S): JAN 16

FIELD(S): Various Sciences and Social Sciences

Scholarships for female doctoral students. Summary page, description of research project, resume, references, transcripts, and biographical sketch required. US citizens may study at any graduate institution; non-citizens must be enrolled in US institutions.

5-10 awards annually. See website or write to above address for an application and more information.

529 — ASSOCIATION FOR WOMEN IN SCIENCE EDUCATIONAL FOUNDATION (Ruth Satter Memorial Award)

1200 New York Ave., NW, Suite 650
Washington DC 20005
202/326-8940 or 800/886-AWIS
E-Mail: awis@awis.org
Internet: www.awis.org

AMOUNT: $1,000

DEADLINE(S): JAN 16

FIELD(S): Various Sciences and Social Sciences

Scholarships for female doctoral students who have interrupted their education for at least three years to raise a family. Summary page, description of research project, resume, references, transcripts, biographical sketch, and letter from your department to confirm eligibility required. US citizens may study at any graduate institution; non-citizens must attend US institutions.

See website or write to above address for more information or an application.

530 — ASSOCIATION FOR WOMEN IN SCIENCE EDUCATIONAL FOUNDATION (Ruth Satter Memorial Award)

1200 New York Ave. NW, Suite 650
Washington DC 20005
202/326-8940 or 800/886-AWIS
E-Mail: awis@awis.org
Internet: www.awis.org

AMOUNT: $1,000

DEADLINE(S): JAN 16

FIELD(S): Various Sciences and Social Sciences

Scholarships for female doctoral students who have interupted their education three years or more to raise a family. Summary page, description of research project, resume, references, transcripts, biographical sketch, and proof of eligibility from department head required. US citizens may attend any graduate institution; non-citizens must be enrolled in US institutions.

See website or write to above address for more information or an application.

531 — AT&T BELL LABORATORIES (Graduate Research Program For Women)

101 Crawfords Corner Road
Holmdel NJ 07733-3030
Written inquiry

AMOUNT: Full tuition & fees + $13,200 stipend per year

DEADLINE(S): JAN 15

FIELD(S): Engineering; Math; Sciences; Computer Science

For women students who have been accepted into an accredited doctoral program for the following fall. U.S. citizen or permanent resident.

Fellowships are renewable for up to 5 years of graduate study. Write to special programs manager-GRPW for complete information.

532 — BODOSSAKI FOUNDATION (Academic Prizes)

20 Amalias Ave.
GR-105 57 Athens GREECE
3220 962
FAX: 3237 976

AMOUNT: Drs. 7,000,000

DEADLINE(S): DEC 31

FIELD(S): Pure mathematics, theoretical and applied computer science, operations research, cardiovascular diseases, developmental biology

Awards to support the creative work of young Greek academics and scientists and reward their endeavor in the advancement of learning and the creation of sound values. Must be of Greek nationality, parentage, or descent under age 40.

Contact above address for details.

533 — BOEING (Polish Graduate Student Scholarship Program)

Phone for details
314/234-2149

AMOUNT: Tuition, books, and fees for three years

DEADLINE(S): Varies

FIELD(S): Scientific and technical fields

Scholarships for students from Poland to pursue graduate studies in scientific and technical areas at American colleges or universities.

Call Jim Schlueter at above telephone number.

534 — BROOKHAVEN WOMEN IN SCIENCE (Renate W. Chasman Scholarship)

PO Box 183
Upton NY 11973-5000
E-mail: pam@bnl.gov

AMOUNT: $2,000

DEADLINE(S): APR 1

FIELD(S): Natural Sciences; Engineering; Mathematics

Open ONLY to women who are residents of the boroughs of Brooklyn or Queens or the counties of Nassau or Suffolk in New York who are re-entering school after a period of study. For juniors, seniors, or first-year graduate students.

1 award annually. Not renewable. Contact Pam Mansfield at above location for an application. Phone calls are NOT accepted.

535 — BUSINESS & PROFESSIONAL WOMEN'S FOUNDATION (BPW Career Advancement Scholarship Program)

2012 Massachusetts Ave., NW
Washington DC 20036-1070
202/293-1200, ext. 169
FAX: 202/861-0298
Internet: www.bpwusa.org

AMOUNT: $500-$1,000

DEADLINE(S): APR 15

FIELD(S): Biology, Science, Education, Engineering, Social Science, Paralegal, Humanities, Business, Math, Computers, Law, MD, DD

For women (US citizens) aged 25+ accepted into accredited program at US institution (+Puerto Rico & Virgin Islands). Must graduate within 12 to 24 months from the date of grant and demonstrate critical finanacial need. Must have a plan to upgrade skills, train for a new career field, or to enter/re-enter the job market.

Full- or part-time study. For info see website or send business-sized, self-addressed, double-stamped envelope.

536 — CHARLES BABBAGE INSTITUTE (Adelle & Erwin Tomash Fellowship)

103 Walter Library
117 Pleasant St., SE
Minneapolis MN 55455
612/624-5050
FAX: 612/625-8054

AMOUNT: $10,000 stipend + $2,000 approved expenses

DEADLINE(S): JAN 15

FIELD(S): History of Computing and Information Processing

Dissertation must address a topic in the history of computers and information processing. Applicants should submit biographical data and research plan. Transcripts and three letters of recommendation are required. There is no application form.

Write for complete information.

537 — COOPERATIVE ASSOCIATION OF STATES FOR SCHOLARSHIPS (CASS) (Scholarships)

c/o Commonwealth Liaison
Unit 310 The Garrison
St. Michael BARBADOS
809/436-8754

AMOUNT: Varies

DEADLINE(S): None

FIELD(S): Business application/computer science

Scholarships for economically disadvanted deaf youth, ages 17-25, with strong leadership potential and an interest in computer science/business applications. Must be from Barbados, St. Kitts/Nevis, Grenada, St. Vincent, Antigua/Barbuda, St. Lucia, Dominica, or Jamaica.

Write to E. Caribbean Reg. Coordinator (CASS) at above address.

538 — DRAPER LABORATORY (Research Assistantships)

555 Technology Square
Cambridge MA 02139
617/258-2393
FAX: 617/258-2333
E-Mail: ed@draper.com

AMOUNT: Tuition + stipend

DEADLINE(S): Varies (same as MIT deadline)

FIELD(S): Engineering: Mechanical, Aero-Astro, Electrical; Computer Science; Operations Research

Open to US citizens pursuing graduate study in M.S. or Ph.D. programs at MIT.

30 awards annually. Renewable. Contact Draper Lab for an application.

539 — FANNIE AND JOHN HERTZ FOUNDATION (Fellowship)

Box 5032
Livermore CA 94551-5032
925/373-1642
Internet: www.hertzfoundation.org

AMOUNT: $25,000 stipend/yr. + $15,000 (max.) tuition allowance/yr.

DEADLINE(S): NOV 5

FIELD(S): Applied Physical Sciences

Open to graduate students with a minimum 3.75 GPA for studies in applied physical sciences, including math, engineering, computer science, biology, oceanography, aeronautics, astronomy, physics, and earth science. Must be US citizen/permanent resident. Does not support study in pursuit of M.D. degree, although will support Ph.D. portion of a joint M.D./Ph.D. study program.

Renewable up to 5 years. Only 36 US schools are currently considered tenable. See website for an application and list of specific fields of study that are acceptable.

540 — FORD FOUNDATION/NATIONAL RESEARCH COUNCIL (Predoctoral/ Dissertation Fellowships for Minorities)

2101 Constitution Ave.
Washington DC 20418
202/334-2872
E-Mail: infofell@nas.edu
Internet: http//www.nas.edu/fo/index.html

AMOUNT: $14,000 annual stipend + $6,000 grant to institution; $18,000 for dissertation fellowship

DEADLINE(S): NOV 3

FIELD(S): Most fields of study: sciences, humanities, engineering, behavioral science, social sciences, and computer science

Predoctoral and dissertation fellowships for students whose ethnicity is Alaskan Native, Black/ African American, Mexican American/Chicano, Native American Indian, Native Pacific Islander, or Puerto Rican. For research-based programs leading to careers in college teaching and research.

Contact above address or website.

541 — FOUNDATION FOR SCIENCE AND DISABILITY, INC. (FSD Science Student Grant Fund)

503 NW 89th Street
Gainesville FL 32607-1400
352/374-5774
FAX: 352/374-5781
E-Mail: rmankin@gainesville.usda.ufl.edu

AMOUNT: $1,000

DEADLINE(S): DEC 1

FIELD(S): Mathematics; Science; Medicine; Engineering; Computer Science

Open to graduate students with disabilities. May also apply as a fourth-year undergraduate accepted into a graduate or professional program. Awards are for some special purpose in connection with a science project or thesis in any of above fields. Student is required to write a 250-word essay which includes a description of professional goals/objectives, as well as purpose of grant. Transcripts and two letters of recommendation from faculty members are also required.

Contact Dr. Richard Mankin at above address for an application.

542 — FRAUNHOFER CENTER FOR RESEARCH IN COMPUTER GRAPHICS (Student & Scholar Exchange Programs)

321 S. Main St.
Providence RI 02903
401/453-6363
FAX: 401/453-0444
E-Mail: info@crcg.edu
Internet: www.crcg.edu/Education/exchange.html

AMOUNT: Stipend for living expenses; transportation costs reimbursed

DEADLINE(S): None

FIELD(S): Computer graphics

Educational exchanges between U.S. and Europe for participants to become involved in the new information society. In the U.S., sites are in Rhode Island. In Europe, the Technical University of Darmstadt in Germany is the main site. Students conducting thesis research or practicums can stay for up to six months. Summer students normally stay for ten to twelve weeks.

Europeans apply to Dr. Joachim Rix, Dept. of Industrial Applications at above company, Rundeturmstr. 6, D-64283 Darmstadt, Germany. Phone: (+49) 6151 155 220; FAX: (+49) 6151 155 299. U.S. students apply to Bert Scholz at above address.

543 — FRAUNHOFER CENTER FOR RESEARCH IN COMPUTER GRAPHICS (Student & Scholar Exchange Programs)

321 S. Main St.
Providence RI 02903
401/453-6363
FAX: 401/453-0444
E-Mail: info@crcg.edu
Internet: www.crcg.edu/Education/exchange.html

AMOUNT: Stipend for living expenses; transportation costs reimbursed

DEADLINE(S): None

FIELD(S): Computer graphics

Educational exchanges between U.S. and Europe for participants to become involved in the new information society. In the U.S., sites are in Rhode Island. In Europe, the Technical University of Darmstadt in Germany is the main site. Students conducting thesis research or practicums can stay for up to six months. Summer students normally stay for ten to twelve weeks.

Europeans apply to Dr. Joachim Rix, Dept. of Industrial Applications at above company, Rundeturmstr. 6, D-64283 Darmstadt, Germany. Phone: (+49) 6151 155 220; FAX: (+49) 6151 155 299. U.S. students apply to Bert Scholz at above address.

544 — IBM TJ WATSON RESEARCH CENTER (IBM Cooperative Fellowship Award)

P.O. Box 218
Yorktown Heights NY 10598
914/945-3543
E-Mail: UnivRel@US.IBM.com

AMOUNT: $12,000 stipend + tuition

DEADLINE(S): FEB

FIELD(S): Research related to IBM's interests

Open to full-time graduate students pursuing their Ph.D at an accredited U.S. university. Must be engaged in research related to IBM. Must be nominated by the university department, chairman, or division head of the institute. Renewable.

Must participate in work-study/joint-study project. Write or telephone for complete information.

545 — IEEE (Fellowship in Electrical History)

IEEE History Center, Rutgers Univ
39 Union St.
New Brunswick NJ 08901-8538
732/932-1066
Internet: www.ieee.org/history_center/

AMOUNT: $15,000

DEADLINE(S): FEB 1

FIELD(S): Electrical & Computer History

Supports one year of graduate work in the history of electrical and computer science and technology at a college of recognized standing or up to one year of postdoctoral research.

Contact Robert Colburn for an application.

546 — IEEE COMPUTER SOCIETY (Richard Merwin Student Scholarship)

1730 Massachusetts Ave. NW
Washington DC 20036-1992
202/371-1013
FAX: 202/778-0884
Internet: www.computer.org

AMOUNT: $3,000

DEADLINE(S): MAY 31

FIELD(S): Computer science, computer engineering, or electrical engineering

Scholarships for active leaders in student branch chapters of the IEEE Computer Society who show promise in their academic and professional efforts.

Four awards. Contact above address or website for details.

547 — INSTITUTE FOR OPERATIONS RESEARCH AND THE MANAGEMENT SCIENCES (INFORMS Summer Internship Directory)

P.O. Box 64794
Baltimore MD 21264-4794
800/4INFORMS
FAX: 410/684-2963
E-Mail: jps@informs.org
Internet: www.informs.org/INTERN/

AMOUNT: Varies

DEADLINE(S): Varies

FIELD(S): Fields related to information management: business management, engineering, mathematics

A website listing of summer internships in the field of operations research and management sciences. Both applicants and employers can register online.

Access website for list.

548 — INSTITUTION OF ELECTRICAL ENGINEERS (Postgraduate Awards)

Savoy Place
London WC2R 0BL ENGLAND
0171 240 1871 Ext. 2211/2235
FAX: 0171 497 3609
E-Mail: scholarships@iee.org.uk
Internet: www.iee.org.uk/Awards/pgsum.htm

AMOUNT: 1,000-6,000 pounds/yr.

DEADLINE(S): SEP 1; SEP 30

FIELD(S): Engineering

Scholarships for postgraduate students pursuing degrees in engineering who are residents of the United Kingdom.

Check website or contact organization for application details.

549 — NATIONAL FEDERATION OF THE BLIND (Computer Science Scholarship)

805 Fifth Avenue
Grinnell IA 50112
515/236-3366

AMOUNT: $3,000

DEADLINE(S): MAR 31

FIELD(S): Computer Science

For legally blind students pursuing or planning to pursue a full-time postsecondary course of study in the US. Based on academic excellence, service to the community, and financial need. Membership NOT required.

1 award annually. Renewable. Contact Mrs. Peggy Elliot, Scholarship Committee Chairman, for an application.

550 — NATIONAL PHYSICAL SCIENCE CONSORTIUM (Graduate Fellowships for Minorities & Women in the Physical Sciences)

MSC 3NPS
Box 30001
Las Cruces NM 88003-8001
800/952-4118 or 505/646-6038
FAX: 505/646-6097
E-Mail: npse@nmsu.edu
Internet: www.npsc.org

AMOUNT: $12,500 (years 1-4); $15,000 (years 5-6)

DEADLINE(S): NOV 5

FIELD(S): Astronomy; Chemistry; Computer Science; Geology; Materials Science; Mathematics; Physics

Open to "all US citizens" with an emphasis on Black, Hispanic, Native American, and female students. Must be pursuing graduate studies and have a minimum 3.0 GPA.

Renewable up to 6 years. See website or contact NPSC for an application.

551 — NATIONAL SCIENCES AND ENGINEERING RESEARCH COUNCIL OF CANADA (Graduate Scholarships)

Scholarships/Fellowships Division
350 Albert Street
Ottawa Ontario K1A 1H5 CANADA
613/996-3769
FAX: 613/996-2589
E-Mail: schol@nserc.ca
Internet: http://www.nserc.ca

AMOUNT: $15,700/year for 1st & 2nd years at masters or Ph.D level; $17,400/year (Ph.D level ONLY) 3rd & 4th years

DEADLINE(S): NOV 24

FIELD(S): Natural Sciences, Engineering, Biology, or Chemistry

Open to Canadian citizens or permanent residents who have earned or will soon earn a bachelors or masters degree in science or engineering. Academic excellence and research aptitude are considerations.

Write for complete information.

552 — NATIONAL SCIENCES AND ENGINEERING RESEARCH COUNCIL OF CANADA (Postdoctoral Fellowships)

Scholarships/Fellowships Division
350 Albert Street
Ottawa Ontario K1A 1H5 CANADA
613/996-3762
FAX: 613/996-2589
E-Mail: schol@nserc.ca
Internet: http://www.nserc.ca

AMOUNT: Individually negotiated

DEADLINE(S): Varies—average: $43,000

FIELD(S): Natural Sciences, Engineering, Biology, or Chemistry

Open to Canadian citizens or permanent residents who hold doctoral degrees in science or engineering. Academic excellence and research aptitude are considerations.

Write for complete information.

553 — NATIONAL SOCIETY OF BLACK ENGINEERS (Scholarships)

1454 Duke St.
Alexandria VA 22314
703/549-2207
FAX: 703/683-5312
E-Mail: nsbehq@nsbe.org
Internet: www.nsbe.org

AMOUNT: Varies

DEADLINE(S): Varies

FIELD(S): Engineering and engineering technologies

Programs for black and other ethnic minorities in the fields of engineering and the engineering technologies. Organization offers pre-college programs, scholarships, career fairs, a journal, a newsletter, etc.

Contact organization for details.

554 — OAK RIDGE ASSOCIATED UNIVERSITIES (Laboratory Graduate Research Participation Program)

P.O. Box 117
Oak Ridge TN 37831-0117
423/576-4813

AMOUNT: $1,000-$1,200/mo. + allowance for dependents + tuition and fees reimbursement to a max. of $3,500/yr.

DEADLINE(S): Ongoing

FIELD(S): Life sciences, physical, and social sciences, mathematics, and engineering

For graduate students in one of the fields listed above who have completed all degree requirements except thesis or dissertation research. For full time research under the joint direction of the major professor and a DOE staff member at one of various locations, primarily in the South. For six to twelve months.

Funded through U.S. Dept. of Energy, Office of Energy Reseach, and Office of Fossil Energy. Write for complete information.

555 — OAK RIDGE ASSOCIATED UNIVERSITIES (National Science Foundation Graduate Research Fellowships)

PO Box 3010
Oak Ridge TN 37831-3010
423/241-4300
FAX: 423/241-4513
E-Mail: nsfgrfp@orau.gov
Internet: www.orau.gov/nsf/nsffel.htm

AMOUNT: $15,000 stipend + $10,500 tuition allowance

DEADLINE(S): NOV 4

FIELD(S): Science; Math; Engineering; Computer Science

Three-year fellowships for graduate study leading to research-based master's or doctoral degrees in the above fields. Must be US citizens, nationals, or permanent residents at the time of application. Fellowships are awarded on the basis of ability. Women, minorities, and those with disabilities are strongly encouraged to apply. One-time International Research Travel Allowance available.

1,000 awards annually. Contact Jeannette Bouchard for an application/more information.

556 — OAK RIDGE INSTITUTE FOR SCIENCE AND EDUCATION (Minority Student Administrative Summer Internship Program)

P.O. Box 117
Oak Ridge TN 37831-0117
423/576-6051 or 423/576-3165

AMOUNT: $335 to $420/wk.+ travel reimbursement

DEADLINE(S): FEB (mid-month)

FIELD(S): Business administration, management, finance, accounting, human resources, training, economics, public administration, computer science, and instructional technology

For minority students who have completed their junior or senior year in college or their first year of graduate school. Must be majoring in one of the fields listed above. A summer program, ten to twelve weeks, located at Oak Ridge, TN.

Funded through U.S. Department of Energy or Oak Ridge Associated Universities

557 — OAK RIDGE INSTITUTE FOR SCIENCE AND EDUCATION (Professional Internship Program/Oak Ridge National Laboratory)

P.O. Box 117
Oak Ridge TN 37831-0117
423/576-3426
423/576-3427

AMOUNT: $210 to $300/week + travel, tuition, and fees

DEADLINE(S): FEB 5; JUN 1; OCT 1

FIELD(S): Chemistry, environmental science, geology, hydrogeology, hydrology, chemical engineering, civil engineering, environmental engineering, mechanical engineering, computer science (technical database development)

Opportunities for graduates and undergraduates to participate in energy-related research projects that correlate with their academic and career goals. For 3 to 12 consecutive months.

Funded through Oak Ridge National Laboratory.

558 — OAK RIDGE INSTITUTE FOR SCIENCE AND EDUCATION (Professional Internship Program/Pittsburgh Energy Technology Center)

P.O. Box 117
Oak Ridge TN 37831-0117
423/576-3426
423/576-3427

AMOUNT: $235 to $325/week + travel, tuition, and fees

DEADLINE(S): FEB 5; JUN 1; OCT 1

FIELD(S): Chemistry, physics, environmental science, geology, chemical or environmental engineering, computer science, or statistics.

Opportunities for graduates and undergraduates to participate in fossil energy-related research projects that correlate with their academic and career goals. For 3 to 12 consecutive months.

Funded through U.S. Dept. of Energy, Office of Fossil Energy, and Pittsburgh Energy Technology Center.

559 — OAK RIDGE INSTITUTE FOR SCIENCE AND EDUCATION (Professional Internship Program/Savannah River Site)

P.O. Box 117
Oak Ridge TN 37831-0117
423/576-3426
423/576-3427

AMOUNT: $260 to $340/week + travel

DEADLINE(S): FEB 5; JUN 1; SEP 1

FIELD(S): Chemistry, computer science, environmental science, geology, engineering, or physics

Opportunities for high school junior and seniors, undergraduates, and graduates to participate in research projects that correlate with their academic majors and career goals. For 3 to 12 consecutive months at the Savannah River Site, SC.

Funded through the Savannah River Site, SC.

560 — OAK RIDGE INSTITUTE FOR SCIENCE AND EDUCATION (Science and Engineering Research Semester)

P.O. Box 117
Oak Ridge TN 37831-0117
423/576-2358
423/576-2310

AMOUNT: $225/week + travel + housing

DEADLINE(S): OCT; MAR

FIELD(S): Computer science, physical sciences, environmental and life sciences, and mathematics

Opportunities for high school junior and seniors and a few slots for graduates to participate in energy-related with laboratory scientists at Oak Ridge National Laboratory, TN. One semester with possibility of summer extension. Available two times a year.

Funded through the U.S. Dept. of Energy, Office of Energy Research.

561 — OAK RIDGE INSTITUTE FOR SCIENCE AND EDUCATION (U.S. Geological Survey Earth Sciences Internship Program)

P.O. Box 117
Oak Ridge TN 37831-0117
423/576-2358
423/576-4813

AMOUNT: $19,000 to $38,000, dependent on level

DEADLINE(S): Ongoing

FIELD(S): Geology, geography, biology, chemistry, environmental sciences, hydrology, forestry, civil engineering, computer sciences

Internships for undergrads, grads, or recent grads (within one year) students studying in the above fields to conduct projects to prepare for careers in earth sciences for up to two years. Location: USGS sites across the U.S.

Funded through the U.S. Dept. of the Interior, U.S.G.S.

562 — ROYAL SOCIETY OF EDINBURGH (BP Research Fellowships)

22/24 George St.
Edinburgh EH2 2PQ SCOTLAND
0131 225 6057
FAX: 0131 220 6889
E-Mail: rse@rse.org.uk

AMOUNT: 17,606 to 26,508 pounds sterling

DEADLINE(S): MAR 10

FIELD(S): Mechanical, Chemical, or Control Engineering; Organic Chemistry; Solid State Physics; Information Technology; Geologic Sciences

Research fellowships to Scotland higher education institutions. For post-doctoral researchers age 35 or under on the date of appointment (usually Oct. 1). For research in above disciplines.

Write for complete information.

563 — ROYAL THAI EMBASSY, OFFICE OF EDUCATIONAL AFFAIRS (Revenue Dept. Scholarships for Thai Students)

1906 23rd St. NW
Washington DC 20008
202/667-9111 or 202/667-8010
FAX: 202/265-7239

AMOUNT: Varies

DEADLINE(S): APR

FIELD(S): Computer science (telecommunications), law, economics, finanace, business administration

Scholarships for students under age 35 from Thailand who have been accepted to study in the U.S or U.K. for the needs of the Revenue Dept., Ministry of Finance. Must pursue any level degree in one of the above fields.

Selections are based on academic records, employment history, and advisor recommendations.

564 — SOCIETY OF WOMEN ENGINEERS (Microsoft Corporation Graduate Scholarships)

120 Wall St, 11th Floor
New York NY 10005-3902
800/666-ISWE or 212/509-9577
FAX 212/509-0224
E-Mail: hq@swe.org
Internet: www.swe.org

AMOUNT: $1,000

DEADLINE(S): FEB 1

FIELD(S): Computer Science; Computer Engineering

Open to women entering 1st year of master's program at a college/university with an ABET-accredited program or in a SWE-approved school. Must have a minimum 3.5 GPA.

10 awards annually. Send a self-addressed, stamped envelope to SWE for an application. Recipients are notified in May.

565 — THE BRITISH COUNCIL (Postgraduate Scholarships to Mexico)

10 Spring Gardens
London SW1A 2BN ENGLAND UK
+44 (0) 171 930 8466

FAX: +44 (0) 161 957 7188
E-Mail: education.enquiries@britcoun.org
Internet: www.britcoun.org/mexico/
mexschol.htm

AMOUNT: Varies

DEADLINE(S): Varies

FIELD(S): Science and technology

The British Council in Mexico offers the opportunity, funded by the Mexican Council for Science and Technology (CONACYT), to British citizens to study in Mexico. Another way to receive information is to contact: CONACYT, Av. Constituyentes No. 1046, Col. Lomas Altas, C.P. 11950, Mexico, D.F. or E-mail to informa@mailer.main.conacyt.mx.

Contact with the source of information in London or in Mexico for details. In Mexico, the British Council Information Centre E-mails are: carmina.ramon@bc-mexico.sprint.com (Mexico City) or teresa.riggen@bc-mexico.sprint.com (Guadalajara).

566 — THE DAPHNE JACKSON MEMORIAL FELLOWSHIPS TRUST (Fellowships in Science/Engineering)

School of Physical Sciences, Dept. of Physics, University of Surrey
Guildford, Surrey GU2 5XH ENGLAND UK
01483 259166
FAX: 01483 259501
E-Mail: J.Woolley@surrey.ac.uk
Internet: www.sst.ph.ic.ac.uk/trust/

AMOUNT: Varies

DEADLINE(S): Varies

FIELD(S): Science or engineering, including information sciences

Fellowships to enable well-qualified and highly motivated scientists and engineers to return to appropriate careers following a career break due to family comitments. May be used on a flexible, part-time basis. Tenable at various U.K. universities.

See website and/or contact organization for details.

567 — TRENT UNIVERSITY (Graduate Teaching/Research Assistantships)

P.O. Box 4800
Graduate Studies Officer
Peterborough Ontario CANADA K9J 7B8
705/748-1245

AMOUNT: $3,500 per term

DEADLINE(S): FEB 15

FIELD(S): Anthropology, Geography, Archaeology, Biology, Canadian Studies, Philosophy, Cultural Studies, Computer Science, Mathematics, Physics, Chemistry, Environmental Science/Studies

Teaching/research assistantships at Trent University in the above fields. Open to masters and doctoral candidates. Tenable for up to 4 terms spanning 2-3 years of study.

80 awards per year. Write for complete information.

568 — U.S. DEPARTMENT OF DEFENSE (GLSIP-General Laboratory Scientific Interchange Program: NRC-NRL Post-Doctoral Program)

Naval Research Laboratory
Office of Program Admin. & Dev. Code 1006.17
Washington, D.C. 20375-5321
202/767-3865
DSN: 297-3865
FAX: 202/404-8110
Internet: www.acq.osd.mil/ddre/edugate/s-aindx.html

AMOUNT: Research Program

DEADLINE(S): None specified

FIELD(S): Computer science, artificial intelligence, plasma physics, acoustics, radar, fluid dynamics, chemistry, materials sci, optical sci, condensed matter and radiation, electronic sci, environmental sci, marine geosciences, remote sensing, oceanography, marine meteorology, space technology/sciences.

U.S. citizens who are recent postdoctoral graduates are selected on the basis of overall qualifications and techincal proposals.

Contact Jessica Hileman for more information.

569 — U.S. DEPT. OF HEALTH & HUMAN SERVICES (Indian Health Service Health Professions Scholarship Program)

Twinbrook Metro Plaza, Suite 100
12300 Twinbrook Pkwy.
Rockville MD 20852
301/443-0234
FAX: 301/443-4815
Internet: www.ihs.gov/Recruitment/DHPS/SP/SBTOC3.asp

AMOUNT: Tuition + fees & monthly stipend of $938.

DEADLINE(S): APR 1

FIELD(S): Health professions, accounting, social work

Open to Native Americans or Alaska natives who are graduate students or college juniors or seniors in a program leading to a career in a fields listed above. U.S. citizenship required. Renewable annually with reapplication.

Scholarship recipients must intend to serve the Indian people. They incur a one-year service obligation to the IHS for each year of support for a minimum of two years. Write for complete information.

570 — U.S. ENVIRONMENTAL PROTECTION AGENCY—NATIONAL NETWORK FOR ENVIRONMENTAL MANAGEMENT STUDIES (Fellowships)

401 M St., SW
Mailcode 1704
Washington DC 20460
202/260-5283
FAX: 202/260-4095
E-Mail: jojokian.sheri@epa.gov
Internet: www.epa.gov/enviroed/students.html

AMOUNT: Varies

DEADLINE(S): DEC

FIELD(S): Environmental Policies, Regulations, & Law; Environmental Management & Administration; Environmental Science; Public Relations & Communications; Computer Programming & Development

Fellowships are open to undergraduate and graduate students working on research projects in the above fields, either full-time during the summer or part-time during the school year. Must be US citizen or legal resident. Financial need NOT a factor.

85-95 awards annually. Not renewable. See website or contact the Career Service Center of participating universities for an application.

571 — UNIVERSITY OF CAMBRIDGE (ICL Research Studentship in Automatic Computing)

New Museums Site
Pembroke Street
Cambridge CB2 3QG ENGLAND UK
01223 334603
FAX: 01223 334611
E-Mail: mal10@cl.cam.ac.uk

AMOUNT: Equivalent to UK Government Studentships

DEADLINE(S): None

FIELD(S): Computer Science

Award given every three years to support a Ph.D. student in the area of automatic computing. For use at the Computer Laboratory, University of Cambridge, England.

Tenable for not more than three years in the first instance, but a student may be re-elected for a fourth year. Contact Mrs. M.A. Levitt, Departmental Secretary, for complete information.

572 — UNIVERSITY OF MARYLAND INSTITUTE FOR ADVANCED COMPUTER STUDIES (Graduate Fellowships)

University of Maryland, UMIACS
College Park MD 20742
301/405-6722

E-Mail: fellows@umiacs.umd.edu

Internet: www.umiacs.umd.edu/fellow.html

AMOUNT: $18,000/yr. + tuition, health benefits, office space, etc.

DEADLINE(S): JAN 15

FIELD(S): Computer science, electrical engineering, geography, philosophy, linguistics, business, and management

Two-year graduate fellowships in the above fields for full-time students interested in interdisciplinary applications of computing at the Univ. of Maryland. After the first two years, external research funds may be provided to continue support for the fellow, depending upon satisfactory progress and the availability of funds.

Three new awards each year. Selection will be based on academic excellence and compatibility between students' research interest and those of UMIACS faculty.

573 — WOMEN IN DEFENSE (HORIZONS Scholarship Foundation)

NDIA

2111 Wilson Blvd., Ste. 400

Arlington VA 22201-3061

703/247-2552

FAX: 703/522-1885

E-Mail: dnwlee@moon.jic.com

Internet: www.adpa.org/wid/horizon/Scholar.htm

AMOUNT: $500+

DEADLINE(S): NOV 1; JUL 1

FIELD(S): Engineering, Computer Science, Physics, Mathematics, Business, Law, International Relations, Political Science, Operations Research, Economics, and fields relevant to a career in the areas of national security and defense.

For women who are U.S. citizens, have minimum GPA of 3.25, demonstrate financial need, are currently enrolled at an accredited university/college (full- or part-time—both grads and undergrad juniors/seniors are eligible), and demonstrate interest in pursuing a career related to national security.

Application is online or send SASE, #10 envelope, to Woody Lee, HORIZONS Scholarship Director.

574 — XEROX TECHNICAL MINORITY SCHOLARSHIP (School-Year Tuition)

907 Culver Road

Rochester NY 14609

www.xerox.com/employment

AMOUNT: Up to $5,000 (varies according to tuition and academic excellence)

DEADLINE(S): SEP 15

FIELD(S): Various engineering and science disciplines

Scholarships for minorities enrolled full-time in a technical degree program at the bachelor level or above. Must be African-American, Native American, Hispanic, or Asian. Recipient may not have tuition or related expenses covered by other scholarships or grants.

If above requirements are met, obtain application from website or address above. Your financial aid office must fill out the bottom half of the form. Send completed application, your resume and a cover letter to Xerox Technical Minority Scholarship Program at above address.

575 — XEROX TECHNICAL MINORITY SCHOLARSHIP (Summer Employment Program)

Xerox Square

Rochester NY 14644

Written inquiry

AMOUNT: Up to $5,000 (varies according to tuition and academic excellence)

DEADLINE(S): SEP 15

FIELD(S): Various engineering and science disciplines

Scholarships for minorities enrolled in a technical degree program at the bachelor level or above. Must be African-American, Native American, Hispanic, or Asian. Xerox will match your skills with a sponsoring organization that will offer a meaningful summer work experience complimenting your academic learning.

If above requirements are met, send your resume and a cover letter to Xerox Corporation Corporate Employment and College Relations Technical Mfinority Scholarship Program to above address.

ELECTRICAL ENGINEERING

576 — AECI LIMITED (AECI Post Graduate Research Fellowship)

Private Bag X2

Modderfontein SOUTH AFRICA 1645

011/605-3100

AMOUNT: Varies (South African Rands 3600)

DEADLINE(S): SEP 30

FIELD(S): Chemistry, Physics, Metallurgy, Biochemistry, Microbiology, Chemical Engineering, Civil Engineering, Industrial Engineering, Electrical Engineering, Mechanical Engineering, Instrument Engineering

Open to South African citizens who are graduate students who want to do research in one of the above areas. This fellowship is offered to strengthen post-graduate study and research in South Africa, particularly in the fields above.

Write to the above address for complete information.

577 — AFRICAN NETWORK OF SCIENTIFIC AND TECHNOLOGICAL INSTITUTIONS - ANSTI (Postgraduate Fellowships)

PO Box 30592

Nairobi Kenya AFRICA

254-2-621234 or 254-2-622619/20

FAX: 254-2-215991

E-Mail: j.massaquoi@unesco.org OR ANSTI@Net2000ke.com

AMOUNT: Fees, subsistence, & international travel

DEADLINE(S): JUN

FIELD(S): Basic & Engineering Sciences

Scholarships for postgraduate studies outside of applicant's home country. Must be African nationals not older than 36 years of age and hold a good bachelor's degree (at least 2nd class upper division). Applicants should apply for admission to host university as soon as possible. Fellowships tenable only in African universities.

10 awards annually. Renewable up to 2 years. Contact Professor J.G.M. Massaquoi for an application.

578 — AMERICAN ASSOCIATION OF UNIVERSITY WOMEN EDUCATIONAL FOUNDATION (Selected Professions Fellowships)

Dept. 60

2201 N. Dodge St.

Iowa City IA 52243-4030

319/337-1716, ext. 60

FAX 319/337-1204

Internet: www.aauw.org

AMOUNT: $5,000-$15,000

DEADLINE(S): JAN 2 (most); NOV 15 (engineering dissertation only)

FIELD(S): Architecture; Computer/Information Sciences; Engineering; Mathematics/Statistics

For women in final year of graduate study in fields where women's participation has been low. Must be US citizen or permanent resident. Special consideration given to applicants who show professional promise in innovative or neglected areas of research and/or practice in areas of public interest. Women in engineering master's programs are eligible to apply for either first or final year of study; special award for engineering doctoral students writing dissertation.

Applications available August-December.

579 — AMERICAN FOUNDATION FOR THE BLIND (Paul W. Ruckes Scholarship)

11 Penn Plaza, Ste. 300
New York NY 10001
212/502 7661 or TDD 212/502-7771
E-Mail: juliet@afb.org
Internet: www.afb.org

AMOUNT: $1,000

DEADLINE(S): APR 30

FIELD(S): Engineering, computer, physical, or life sciences

Open to blind or visually impaired undergraduate or graduate students pursuing degrees in the above fields. U.S. citizenship required.

Write to the above address or visit website for complete information.

580 — AMERICAN RADIO RELAY LEAGUE FOUNDATION (F. Charles Ruling, N6FR Memorial Scholarship)

225 Main Street
Newington CT 06111
860/594-0200
FAX: 860/594-0259
Internet: www.arrl.org/

AMOUNT: $1,000

DEADLINE(S): FEB 1

FIELD(S): Electronics, Communications, & related fields

For undergraduate or graduate students who hold a general class amateur radio license.

1 award annually. Contact ARRL for an application.

581 — AMERICAN RADIO RELAY LEAGUE FOUNDATION (The PHD ARA Scholarship)

225 Main Street
Newington CT 06111
860/594-0200
FAX: 860/594-0259
Internet: www.arrl.org/

AMOUNT: $1,000

DEADLINE(S): FEB 1

FIELD(S): Journalism; Computer Science; Electronic Engineering

For undergraduate or graduate students who are residents of the ARRL Midwest Division (IA, KS, MO, NE) who hold any class of radio amateur license—or student may be the child of a deceased radio amateur.

1 award annually. Contact ARRL for an application.

582 — AMERICAN SOCIETY FOR ENGINEERING EDUCATION (Army Research Laboritory Postdoctoral Fellowships)

1818 N St., NW, Ste. 600
Washington DC 20036
202/331-3525
FAX: 202/265-8504.
E-Mail: projects@asee.org
Internet: www.asee.org/fellowship/

AMOUNT: $45,000-$55,000 + travel/relocation allowance

DEADLINE(S): Varies

FIELD(S): Engineering; Physical Sciences

Postdoctoral fellowships for US citizens/permanent residents to do research at Army Research Laboritories. Candidates must have completed their Ph.D. prior to appointment. Program is designed to increase involvement of creative and highly trained scientists and engineers from academia and industry in scientific and technical areas of interest and relevance to the Army. Research proposal should include clear objective and defined outcome. Financial need NOT a factor.

15 awards annually. Renewable. Contact Sandi Crawford at ASEE for an application packet.

583 — AMERICAN VACUUM SOCIETY (Graduate Research Award)

120 Wall Street, 32nd Floor
New York, NY 10005
212/248-0200
FAX: 212/248-0245
Internet: www.vacuum.org/

AMOUNT: $1,000

DEADLINE(S): MAY 3

FIELD(S): Vacuum Science

Prizes awarded for graduate work in sciences and technologies of interest to the society. Nominees must be graduate students in accredited North American institutions. Awards are based on research excellence and student's academic record.

Approximately 10 prizes given annually. Winners also receive reasonable travel expences to attend the national symposium. Write for complete information.

584 — AMERICAN VACUUM SOCIETY (Russell and Sigurd Varian Fellow Award)

120 Wall Street, 32nd Floor
New York NY 10005
212/248-0200

AMOUNT: $1500

DEADLINE(S): MAR 31

FIELD(S): Electrial Engineering-Vacuum Science

Open to full time graduate students in accredited academic institutions in North America. For

experimental or theoretical research in any of the technical and scientific areas of interest to the society.

Numerous awards. Applicants are normally expected to graduate after September 30 of the year following the award. Write for complete information.

585 — ARMED FORCES COMMUNICATIONS AND ELECTRONICS ASSOCIATION (AFCEA Fellowshps)

4400 Fair Lakes Court
Fairfax VA 22033-3899
800/336-4583 Ext. 6149 or 703/631-6149
Internet: www.afcea.org/awards/scholarships.htm

AMOUNT: $25,000

DEADLINE(S): FEB 1

FIELD(S): Electrical engineering, electronics, computer science, computer engineering, physics, mathematics

Fellowships in the above fields for students working on doctoral degrees in accredited universities in the U.S.

Send a self-addressed, stamped envelope with information on the name of your school, field of study, GPA, and year in school to AFCEA Educational Foundation at above address. Applications available November through Jan 1.

586 — ASIAN INSTITUTE OF TECHNOLOGY (AIT Scholarship Program)

Development Office
PO Box 4, Klongluang
Pathumthani 12120 THAILAND
(66)(2) 516-0110-44 or 524-5032
FAX: (66)(2) 516-2126
E-Mail: ascao@ait.ac.th
Internet: www.ait.ac.th

AMOUNT: US $12,600-$37,960

DEADLINE(S): FEB 15; JUN 15; OCT 15

FIELD(S): Advanced Technologies; Civil Engineering; Environment, Resources, & Development; Business Management

Scholarships and grants open to citizens of Asian countries who are accepted by the institute as a master's or doctotal candidate. Selection is based on academic criteria, practical experience, gender, and country of origin; priority to Mekong Region countries and Asian countries of the former USSR.

250 awards annually. Contact AIT for an application.

587 — ASSOCIATED WESTERN UNIVERSITIES, INC. (AWU Faculty Fellowships)

4190 South Highland Dr., Suite 211
Salt Lake City UT 84124-2600
801-273-8900

AMOUNT: Varies.

DEADLINE(S): FEB 15

FIELD(S): Engineering, Mathematics, Science, Technology

Research fellowships for qualified college and university faculty members to encourage participation and contribution to research at one of 62 cooperating facilities. It is not necessary to be enrolled at an AWU member institution. Collaborations that include graduate and/or undergraduate students are encouraged.

For detailed information and list of cooperating facilities, contact above location.

588 — ASSOCIATED WESTERN UNIVERSITIES, INC. (AWU Graduate Fellowship Program)

4190 South Highland Dr. Suite 211
Salt Lake City, UT 84124-2600
801/273-8900

AMOUNT: Stipend ($1,300 per month & up) + tuition assistance and travel allowance

DEADLINE(S): FEB 15

FIELD(S): Engineering, Mathematics, Science, Technology

Open to master's and doctoral degree candidates to conduct research toward a thesis or dissertation at one of more than 62 cooperating facilities. Institutional affiliation and citizenship restrictions may apply for some awards or facilities. It is not necessary to be enrolled at an AWU member institution to apply for a fellowship.

Write to the above address for complete information.

589 — ASSOCIATED WESTERN UNIVERSITIES, INC. (AWU Postgraduate Fellowship)

4190 South Highland Dr. Suite 211
Salt Lake City UT 84124-2600
801/273-8900

AMOUNT: Stipend established by the host facility and varies by experience and discipline.

DEADLINE(S): Varies (Two to three months before the starting date)

FIELD(S): Engineering, Mathematics, Science, Technology

For college and university graduates who have completed all institutional requirements for an advanced degree from an accredited college or university in the U.S. A commitment to a professional career in science or engineering research is expected. U.S. citizenship or permanent resident status is required. Research is to be done at one of the 62 cooperating universities.

For detailed information and a list of cooperating facilities contact above address.

590 — ASSOCIATED WESTERN UNIVERSITIES, INC. (AWU Visiting Scientist Fellowships)

4190 South Highland Dr., Suite 211
Salt Lake City UT 84124-2600
801/273-8900

AMOUNT: Varies

DEADLINE(S): Varies (Two months prior to starting date)

FIELD(S): Engineering, Science, Mathematics, and Technology

Research fellowships for professionals with continued commitment to science and engineering. For use at one of 62 participating universities. US citizenship or permanent residency required.

For detailed information and list of cooperating facitilies contact above location.

591 — ASSOCIATION FOR COMPUTING MACHINERY (Listing of Internships & Summer Jobs)

1515 Broadway, 17th Floor
New York NY 10036
1-800/342-6626 or +1-212/626-0500 (global)
FAX: +1-212/944-1318
Internet: www.acm.org/student/internships.html

AMOUNT: Varies

DEADLINE(S): Varies

FIELD(S): Computer science

A listing on the Internet of several internships and summer employment in the field of computer science at various companies and colleges in the U.S., Canada, and elsewhere. Each one has its own requirements.

Access website for details.

592 — AT&T BELL LABORATORIES (Graduate Research Program For Women)

101 Crawfords Corner Road
Holmdel NJ 07733-3030
Written inquiry

AMOUNT: Full tuition & fees + $13,200 stipend per year

DEADLINE(S): JAN 15

FIELD(S): Engineering; Math; Sciences; Computer Science

For women students who have been accepted into an accredited doctoral program for the following fall. U.S. citizen or permanent resident.

Fellowships are renewable for up to 5 years of graduate study. Write to special programs manager-GRPW for complete information.

593 — BOEING (Polish Graduate Student Scholarship Program)

Phone for details
314/234-2149

AMOUNT: Tuition, books, and fees for three years

DEADLINE(S): Varies

FIELD(S): Scientific and technical fields

Scholarships for students from Poland to pursue graduate studies in scientific and technical areas at American colleges or universities.

Call Jim Schlueter at above telephone number.

594 — BRITISH FEDERATION OF WOMEN GRADUATES (M.H. Joseph Prize for Non-UK Citizens)

4 Mandeville Courtyard
142 Battersea Park Rd.
London SW11 4NB ENGLAND UK
PHONE/FAX: 0171/498 8037

AMOUNT: 500+ pounds sterling

DEADLINE(S): SEP 10

FIELD(S): Architecture; Engineering

For female graduate students of any nationality (except UK) who will pursue studies in Great Britain. Must have completed at least four academic terms or three semesters; award is not made for first year of research. Chief criteria is academic excellence and proven ability to carry out independent research. Postdoctoral studies also eligible.

1 award annually. Application fee of 12 pounds sterling required. Send a self-addressed, stamped envelope (or self-addressed envelope with international reply coupons) for an application. Results announced by end of October.

595 — BRITISH FEDERATION OF WOMEN GRADUATES (M.H. Joseph Prize for UK Citizens)

4 Mandeville Courtyard
142 Battersea Park Rd.
London SW11 4NB ENGLAND UK
PHONE/FAX: 0171/498 8037

AMOUNT: 500+ pounds sterling

DEADLINE(S): SEP 10

FIELD(S): Architecture; Engineering

For female UK citizens who plan to pursue graduate studies overseas. Must have completed at least four academic terms or three semesters; award is not made for first year of research. Chief criteria is academic excellence and proven ability to carry out independent research. Postdoctoral studies also eligible.

1 award annually. Application fee of 12 pounds sterling required. Send a self-addressed, stamped envelope (or self-addressed envelope with international reply coupons) for an application. Award announced at end of October.

596 — BROOKHAVEN WOMEN IN SCIENCE (Renate W. Chasman Scholarship)

PO Box 183
Upton NY 11973-5000
E-mail: pam@bnl.gov

AMOUNT: $2,000

DEADLINE(S): APR 1

FIELD(S): Natural Sciences; Engineering; Mathematics

Open ONLY to women who are residents of the boroughs of Brooklyn or Queens or the counties of Nassau or Suffolk in New York who are re-entering school after a period of study. For juniors, seniors, or first-year graduate students.

1 award annually. Not renewable. Contact Pam Mansfield at above location for an application. Phone calls are NOT accepted.

597 — DRAPER LABORATORY (Research Assistantships)

555 Technology Square
Cambridge MA 02139
617/258-2393
FAX: 617/258-2333
E-Mail: ed@draper.com

AMOUNT: Tuition + stipend

DEADLINE(S): Varies (same as MIT deadline)

FIELD(S): Engineering: Mechanical, Aero-Astro, Electrical; Computer Science; Operations Research

Open to US citizens pursuing graduate study in M.S. or Ph.D. programs at MIT.

30 awards annually. Renewable. Contact Draper Lab for an application.

598 — ELECTROCHEMICAL SOCIETY (Summer Research Fellowships)

10 S. Main St.
Pennington NJ 08534
609/737-1902
FAX: 609/737-2745
E-Mail: ecs@electrtochem
Internet: www.electrochem.org

AMOUNT: $4,000 (ECS); $3,000 (DOE)

DEADLINE(S): JAN 1

FIELD(S): Energy; Chemical Engineering; Chemistry; Electrical Engineering

Summer fellowships are open to graduate students at accredited colleges and universities in any country.

Purpose is to support research of interest to ECS, such as research aimed at reducing energy consumption.

8 awards annually (3 ECS, 5 Department of Energy). Contact ECS for an application.

599 — EPPLEY FOUNDATION FOR RESEARCH (Postdoctoral Research Grants)

245 Park Avenue, 40th Floor
New York NY 10167
Written inquiry

AMOUNT: Up to $25,000

DEADLINE(S): FEB 1; MAY 1; AUG 1; NOV 1

FIELD(S): Physical Sciences; Biological Sciences

Postdoctoral grants for original advanced research in any of the physical or biological sciences. Open to established research scientists who are attached to a recognized institution.

Write for complete information.

600 — FANNIE AND JOHN HERTZ FOUNDATION (Fellowship)

Box 5032
Livermore CA 94551-5032
925/373-1642
Internet: www.hertzfoundation.org

AMOUNT: $25,000 stipend/yr. + $15,000 (max.) tuition allowance/yr.

DEADLINE(S): NOV 5

FIELD(S): Applied Physical Sciences

Open to graduate students with a minimum 3.75 GPA for studies in applied physical sciences, including math, engineering, computer science, biology, oceanography, aeronautics, astronomy, physics, and earth science. Must be US citizen/permanent resident. Does not support study in pursuit of M.D. degree, although will support Ph.D. portion of a joint M.D./Ph.D. study program.

Renewable up to 5 years. Only 36 US schools are currently considered tenable. See website for an application and list of specific fields of study that are acceptable.

601 — FORD FOUNDATION/NATIONAL RESEARCH COUNCIL (Predoctoral/Dissertation Fellowships for Minorities)

2101 Constitution Ave.
Washington DC 20418
202/334-2872
E-Mail: infofell@nas.edu
Internet: http//www.nas.edu/fo/index.html

AMOUNT: $14,000 annual stipend + $6,000 grant to institution; $18,000 for dissertation fellowship

DEADLINE(S): NOV 3

FIELD(S): Most fields of study: sciences, humanities, engineering, behavioral science, social sciences, and computer science

Predoctoral and dissertation fellowships for students whose ethnicity is Alaskan Native, Black/African American, Mexican American/Chicano, Native American Indian, Native Pacific Islander, or Puerto Rican. For research-based programs leading to careers in college teaching and research.

Contact above address or website.

602 — FRAUNHOFER CENTER FOR RESEARCH IN COMPUTER GRAPHICS (Student & Scholar Exchange Programs)

321 S. Main St.
Providence RI 02903
401/453-6363
FAX: 401/453-0444
E-Mail: info@crcg.edu
Internet: www.crcg.edu/Education/exchange.html

AMOUNT: Stipend for living expenses; transportation costs reimbursed

DEADLINE(S): None

FIELD(S): Computer graphics

Educational exchanges between U.S. and Europe for participants to become involved in the new information society. In the U.S., sites are in Rhode Island. In Europe, the Technical University of Darmstadt in Germany is the main site. Students conducting thesis research or practicums can stay for up to six months. Summer students normally stay for ten to twelve weeks.

Europeans apply to Dr. Joachim Rix, Dept. of Industrial Applications at above company, Rundeturmstr. 6, D-64283 Darmstadt, Germany. Phone: (+49) 6151 155 220, FAX: (+49) 6151 155 299. U.S. students apply to Bert Scholz at above address.

603 — FRAUNHOFER CENTER FOR RESEARCH IN COMPUTER GRAPHICS (Student & Scholar Exchange Programs)

321 S. Main St.
Providence RI 02903
401/453-6363
FAX: 401/453-0444
E-Mail: info@crcg.edu
Internet: www.crcg.edu/Education/exchange.html

AMOUNT: Stipend for living expenses; transportation costs reimbursed

DEADLINE(S): None

FIELD(S): Computer graphics

Educational exchanges between U.S. and Europe for participants to become involved in the new information society. In the U.S., sites are in Rhode Island. In Europe, the Technical University of Darmstadt in Germany is the main site. Students conducting thesis research or practicums can stay for up to six months. Summer students normally stay for ten to twelve weeks.

Europeans apply to Dr. Joachim Rix, Dept. of Industrial Applications at above company, Rundeturmstr. 6, D-64283 Darmstadt, Germany. Phone: (+49) 6151 155 220, FAX: (+49) 6151 155 299. U.S. students apply to Bert Scholz at above address.

604 — IBM TJ WATSON RESEARCH CENTER (IBM Cooperative Fellowship Award)

P.O. Box 218
Yorktown Heights NY 10598
914/945-3543
E-Mail: UnivRel@US.IBM.com

AMOUNT: $12,000 stipend + tuition

DEADLINE(S): FEB

FIELD(S): Research related to IBM's interests

Open to full-time graduate students pursuing their Ph.D at an accredited U.S. university. Must be engaged in research related to IBM. Must be nominated by the university department, chairman, or division head of the institute. Renewable.

Must participate in work-study/joint-study project. Write or telephone for complete information.

605 — IEEE (Fellowship in Electrical History)

IEEE History Center, Rutgers Univ
39 Union St.
New Brunswick NJ 08901-8538
732/932-1066
Internet: www.ieee.org/history_center/

AMOUNT: $15,000

DEADLINE(S): FEB 1

FIELD(S): Electrical & Computer History

Supports one year of graduate work in the history of electrical and computer science and technology at a college of recognized standing or up to one year of postdoctoral research.

Contact Robert Colburn for an application.

606 — IEEE COMPUTER SOCIETY (Richard Merwin Student Scholarship)

1730 Massachusetts Ave. NW
Washington DC 20036-1992
202/371-1013
FAX: 202/778-0884
Internet: www.computer.org

AMOUNT: $3,000

DEADLINE(S): MAY 31

FIELD(S): Computer science, computer engineering, or electrical engineering

Scholarships for active leaders in student branch chapters of the IEEE Computer Society who show promise in their academic and professional efforts.

Four awards. Contact above address or website for details.

607 — INSTITUTE FOR OPERATIONS RESEARCH AND THE MANAGEMENT SCIENCES (INFORMS Summer Internship Directory)

P.O. Box 64794
Baltimore MD 21264-4794
800/4INFORMS
FAX: 410/684-2963
E-Mail: jps@informs.org
Internet: www.informs.org/INTERN/

AMOUNT: Varies

DEADLINE(S): Varies

FIELD(S): Fields related to information management: business management, engineering, mathematics

A website listing of summer internships in the field of operations research and management sciences. Both applicants and employers can register online.

Access website for list.

608 — INSTITUTE OF ELECTRICAL & ELECTRONICS ENGINEERS (Charles Le Geyt Fortescue Fellowship)

445 Hoes Ln.
Piscataway NJ 08855-1331
908/562-3840

AMOUNT: $24,000

DEADLINE(S): JAN 15 (of odd-numbered years)

FIELD(S): Electrical Engineering

Fellowship is open to first-year graduate students at recognized engineering schools in the U.S. or Canada. Awards support full-time study for one academic year.

Awards granted every other year. Contact above location for details.

609 — INSTITUTION OF ELECTRICAL ENGINEERS (Postgraduate Awards)

Savoy Place
London WC2R 0BL ENGLAND
0171 240 1871 Ext. 2211/2235
FAX: 0171 497 3609
E-Mail: scholarships@iee.org.uk
Internet: www.iee.org.uk/Awards/pgsum.htm

AMOUNT: 1,000-6,000 pounds/yr.

DEADLINE(S): SEP 1; SEP 30

FIELD(S): Engineering

Scholarships for postgraduate students pursuing degrees in engineering who are residents of the United Kingdom.

Check website or contact organization for application details.

610 — INTERNATIONAL UNION FOR VACUUM SCIENCE (Welch Foundation Scholarships)

Nortel Networks
043/11/K14, 3500 Carling Ave.
Nepean Ontario K2H 8E9 CANADA
613/763-3285
FAX: 613/763-4147
E-Mail: frsims@nortelnetworks.com
Internet: www.vacuum.org/iuvsta/welchapp.html

AMOUNT: $15,000 US

DEADLINE(S): APR 15

FIELD(S): Vacuum Science

One-year scholarship for promising young scholar who wishes to study vacuum science, techniques, or application in any field. Award is to encourage international cooperation, and winner spends a year in a research lab in another country. Candidates should have at least bachelor's degree; doctorate degree preferred. Applicants must make arrangements with lab of their choice outside of their native country. Must submit curriculum vitae, references, and proposal.

1 award annually. Not renewable. See website or contact the Administrator for an application.

611 — NATIONAL SCIENCES AND ENGINEERING RESEARCH COUNCIL OF CANADA (Graduate Scholarships)

Scholarships/Fellowships Division
350 Albert Street
Ottawa Ontario K1A 1H5 CANADA
613/996-3769
FAX: 613/996-2589
E-Mail: schol@nserc.ca
Internet: http://www.nserc.ca

AMOUNT: $15,700/year for 1st & 2nd years at masters or Ph.D level; $17,400/year (Ph.D level ONLY) 3rd & 4th years

DEADLINE(S): NOV 24

FIELD(S): Natural Sciences, Engineering, Biology, or Chemistry

Open to Canadian citizens or permanent residents who have earned or will soon earn a bachelors or masters degree in science or engineering. Academic excellence and research aptitude are considerations.

Write for complete information.

612 — NATIONAL SCIENCES AND ENGINEERING RESEARCH COUNCIL OF CANADA (Postdoctoral Fellowships)

Scholarships/Fellowships Division
350 Albert Street
Ottawa Ontario K1A 1H5 CANADA
613/996-3762
FAX: 613/996-2589
E-Mail: schol@nserc.ca
Internet: http://www.nserc.ca

AMOUNT: Individually negotiated

DEADLINE(S): Varies—average: $43,000

FIELD(S): Natural Sciences, Engineering, Biology, or Chemistry

Open to Canadian citizens or permanent residents who hold doctoral degrees in science or engineering. Academic excellence and research aptitude are considerations.

Write for complete information.

613 — NATIONAL SOCIETY OF BLACK ENGINEERS (Scholarships)

1454 Duke St.
Alexandria VA 22314
703/549-2207
FAX: 703/683-5312
E-Mail: nsbehq@nsbe.org
Internet: www.nsbe.org

AMOUNT: Varies

DEADLINE(S): Varies

FIELD(S): Engineering and engineering technologies

Programs for black and other ethnic minorities in the fields of engineering and the engineering technologies. Organization offers pre-college programs, scholarships, career fairs, a journal, a newsletter, etc.

Contact organization for details.

614 — OAK RIDGE ASSOCIATED UNIVERSITIES (National Science Foundation Graduate Research Fellowships)

PO Box 3010
Oak Ridge TN 37831-3010
423/241-4300
FAX: 423/241-4513
E-Mail: nsfgrfp@orau.gov
Internet: www.orau.gov/nsf/nsffel.htm

AMOUNT: $15,000 stipend + $10,500 tuition allowance

DEADLINE(S): NOV 4

FIELD(S): Science; Math; Engineering; Computer Science

Three-year fellowships for graduate study leading to research-based master's or doctoral degrees in the above fields. Must be US citizens, nationals, or permanent residents at the time of application. Fellowships are awarded on the basis of ability. Women, minorities, and those with disabilities are strongly encouraged to apply. One-time International Research Travel Allowance available.

1,000 awards annually. Contact Jeannette Bouchard for an application/more information.

615 — OAK RIDGE INSTITUTE FOR SCIENCE AND EDUCATION, U.S. DEPARTMENT OF ENERGY (Fusion Energy Sciences Fellowship Program)

105 Mitchell Road, MS-16
Oak Ridge TN 37831
423/576-2600
FAX: 423/576-8293
E-Mail: johnsons@orau.giv

AMOUNT: $1,300/mo. + $200/mo.

DEADLINE(S): JAN 26 (Received, not postmarked)

FIELD(S): Fusion energy sciences

Fellowships for Ph.D. candidates to pursue a degree in the fusion energy sciences at one of several participating universities throughout the U.S. Must be U.S. citizens or permanent residents. For students entering first or second year of graduate study. Must have B.A. degree in related field, such as applied mathematics or physics; chemical, electrical, mechanical, metallurgical, or nuclear engineering; or materials science.

Contact Sandra Johnson at above location for details and list of participating institutions.

616 — OAK RIDGE INSTITUTE FOR SCIENCE AND EDUCATION/U.S. DEPT. OF ENERGY (Office of Civilian Radioactive Waste Management Fellowship)

P.O. Box 117
Oak Ridge TN 37831-0117
423/576-0128
FAX: 423/576-8293
E-Mail: drostp@orau.gov

AMOUNT: $14,000/yr.

DEADLINE(S): JAN 16 (Received, not postmarked)

FIELD(S): Physical or life sciences, math, or engineering

Fellowships for graduate students at various participating universities to conduct research in the management of spent nuclear fuel and high-level raqdioactive waste. For M.A. and Ph.D. candidates. For up to 48 months. Must be U.S. citizen or permanent resident.

Funded through U.S. Department of Energy, Office of Civilian Radioactive Waste Management. Contact or call Ms. Portia Drost, MS-16, at above address for details.

617 — ROYAL THAI EMBASSY, OFFICE OF EDUCATIONAL AFFAIRS (Revenue Dept. Scholarships for Thai Students)

1906 23rd St. NW
Washington DC 20008
202/667-9111 or 202/667-8010
FAX: 202/265-7239

AMOUNT: Varies

DEADLINE(S): APR

FIELD(S): Computer science (telecommunications), law, economics, finanace, business administration

Scholarships for students under age 35 from Thailand who have been accepted to study in the U.S or U.K. for the needs of the Revenue Dept., Ministry of Finance. Must pursue any level degree in one of the above fields.

Selections are based on academic records, employment history, and advisor recommendations.

618 — RTCA, INC. (William E. Jackson Award)

1140 Connecticut Ave. NW #1020
Washington DC 20036-4001
202/833-9339
FAX: 202/833-9434
E-Mail: hmoses@rtca.org
Internet: www.rtca.org

AMOUNT: $2,000 + plaque

DEADLINE(S): JUN 30

FIELD(S): Aviation Electronics; Aviation; Telecommunications

Open to graduate and postgraduate students studying in the above fields who submit a thesis, project report, or technical journal paper within 3 years of entry for the honorarium.

One award per year, NOT renewable. Contact Harold Moses at above address for an application.

619 — SKIDMORE, OWINGS & MERRILL FOUNDATION (Mechanical/Electrical Traveling Fellowship Program)

224 S. Michigan Ave., Suite 1000
Chicago IL 60604
312/554-9090
FAX: 312/360-4545

AMOUNT: $7,500

DEADLINE(S): Varies (consult with school)

FIELD(S): Architectural Engineering, Electrical Engineering, or Mechanical

Candidates must have received a B.A. or M.A. degree in one of the above fields. It enables the Fellow to travel in order to observe and analyze innovative building systems and technologies anywhere in the world.

Write for complete information.

620 — THE BRITISH COUNCIL (Postgraduate Scholarships to Mexico)

10 Spring Gardens
London SW1A 2BN ENGLAND UK
+44 (0) 171 930 8466
FAX: +44 (0) 161 957 7188
E-Mail: education.enquiries@britcoun.org
Internet: www.britcoun.org/mexico/
mexschol.htm

AMOUNT: Varies

DEADLINE(S): Varies

FIELD(S): Science and technology

The British Council in Mexico offers the opportunity, funded by the Mexican Council for Science and Technology (CONACYT), to British citizens to study in Mexico. Another way to receive information is to contact: CONACYT, Av. Constituyentes No. 1046, Col. Lomas Altas, C.P. 11950, Mexico, D.F. or E-mail to informa@mailer.main.conacyt.mx.

Contact with the source of information in London or in Mexico for details. In Mexico, the British Council Information Centre E-mails are: carmina.ramon@bc-mexico.sprint.com (Mexico City) or teresa riggen@bc-mexico.sprint.com (Guadalajara).

621 — THE DAPHNE JACKSON MEMORIAL FELLOWSHIPS TRUST (Fellowships in Science/Engineering)

School of Physical Sciences
Dept. of Physics
University of Surrey
Guildford, Surrey
GU2 5XH ENGLAND UK
01483 259166
FAX: 01483 259501
E-Mail: J.Woolley@surrey.ac.uk
Internet: www.sst.ph.ic.ac.uk/trust/

AMOUNT: Varies

DEADLINE(S): Varies

FIELD(S): Science or engineering, including information sciences

Fellowships to enable well-qualified and highly motivated scientists and engineers to return to appropriate careers following a career break due to family comitments. May be used on a flexible, part-time basis. Tenable at various U.K. universities.

See website and/or contact organization for details.

622 — THE ELECTRICAL WOMEN'S ROUND TABLE INC. (Julia Kiene & Lyle Mamer Fellowships)

P.O. Box 335
White's Creek TN 37189
615/876-5444

AMOUNT: $1,000 to $2,000

DEADLINE(S): MAR 1

FIELD(S): Electrical energy and related fields listed below

Open to graduate students (or graduating seniors) pursuing an advanced degree in any phase of electrical energy, incl. communications, education, elec. util., elec. eng., elec. home appliances/equip. mfg., marketing research, etc.

The college or university selected by applicant must be accredited and approved by the EWRT Fellowship Committee. Send SASE to above location for complete information.

623 — U.S. DEPARTMENT OF DEFENSE (GLSIP-General Laboratory Scientific Interchange Program: NRC-NRL Post-Doctoral Program)

Naval Research Laboratory
Office of Program Admin. & Dev. Code 1006.17
Washington, D.C. 20375-5321
202/767-3865
DSN: 297-3865
FAX: 202/404-8110
Internet: www.acq.osd.mil/ddre/edugate/s-aindx.html

AMOUNT: Research Program

DEADLINE(S): None specified

FIELD(S): Computer science, artificial intelligence, plasma physics, acoustics, radar, fluid dynamics, chemistry, materials sci, optical sci, condensed matter and radiation, electronic sci, environmental sci, marine geosciences, remote sensing, oceanography, marine meteorology, space technology/sciences.

U.S. citizens who are recent postdoctoral graduates are selected on the basis of overall qualifications and techincal proposals.

Contact Jessica Hileman for more information.

624 — U.S. DEPARTMENT OF TRANSPORTATION (Dwight D. Eisenhower Transportation Fellowships)

U.S. Dept. of Transportation
Fed. Hwy. Admin.
6300 Georgetown Pike, HHI-20
McLean VA 22101-2296
703/235-0538

AMOUNT: Varies

DEADLINE(S): FEB

FIELD(S): Transportation—such majors as chemistry; materials science; corrosion; civil, chemical, & electronics engineering; structures; human factors; computer science; psychology.

Research fellowships for undergrads and grad students at any Dept. of Transportation facility or selected IHE. For three to twelve months. Research must focus on transportation-related research and development in the above fields.

Contact Ilene Payne, Director, Universities and grants Programs at above location for details.

625 — UNIVERSITY OF MARYLAND INSTITUTE FOR ADVANCED COMPUTER STUDIES (Graduate Fellowships)

University of Maryland
UMIACS
College Park MD 20742
301/405-6722
E-Mail: fellows@umiacs.umd.edu
Internet: www.umiacs.umd.edu/fellow.html

AMOUNT: $18,000/yr. + tuition, health benefits, office space, etc.

DEADLINE(S): JAN 15

FIELD(S): Computer science, electrical engineering, geography, philosophy, linguistics, business, and management

Two-year graduate fellowships in the above fields for full-time students interested in interdisciplinary applications of computing at the Univ. of Maryland. After the first two years, external research funds may be provided to continue support for the fellow, depending upon satisfactory progress and the availability of funds.

Three new awards each year. Selection will be based on academic excellence and compatibility between students' research interest and those of UMIACS faculty.

626 — XEROX TECHNICAL MINORITY SCHOLARSHIP (School-Year Tuition)

907 Culver Road
Rochester NY 14609
www.xerox.com/employment

AMOUNT: Up to $5,000 (varies according to tuition and academic excellence)

DEADLINE(S): SEP 15

FIELD(S): Various engineering and science disciplines

Scholarships for minorities enrolled full-time in a technical degree program at the bachelor level or above. Must be African-American, Native American, Hispanic, or Asian. Recipient may not have tuition or related expenses covered by other scholarships or grants.

If above requirements are met, obtain application from website or address above. Your financial aid office must fill out the bottom half of the form. Send completed application, your resume and a cover letter to Xerox Technical Minority Scholarship Program at above address.

627 — XEROX TECHNICAL MINORITY SCHOLARSHIP (Summer Employment Program)

Xerox Square
Rochester NY 14644
Written inquiry

AMOUNT: Up to $5,000 (varies according to tuition and academic excellence)

DEADLINE(S): SEP 15

FIELD(S): Various engineering and science disciplines

Scholarships for minorities enrolled in a technical degree program at the bachelor level or above. Must be African-American, Native American, Hispanic, or Asian. Xerox will match your skills with a sponsoring organization that will offer a meaningful summer work experience complimenting your academic learning.

If above requirements are met, send your resume and a cover letter to Xerox Corporation Corporate Employment and College Relations Technical Mfinority Scholarship Program to above address.

ENGINEERING TECHNOLOGY

628 — AECI LIMITED (AECI Post Graduate Research Fellowship)

Private Bag X2
Modderfontein SOUTH AFRICA 1645
011/605-3100

AMOUNT: Varies (South African Rands 3600)

DEADLINE(S): SEP 30

FIELD(S): Chemistry, Physics, Metallurgy, Biochemistry, Microbiology, Chemical Engineering, Civil Engineering, Industrial Engineering, Electrical Engineering, Mechanical Engineering, Instrument Engineering

Open to South African citizens who are graduate students who want to do research in one of the above areas. This fellowship is offered to strengthen post-graduate study and research in South Africa, particularly in the fields above.

Write to the above address for complete information.

629 — AFRICAN NETWORK OF SCIENTIFIC AND TECHNOLOGICAL INSTITUTIONS - ANSTI (Postgraduate Fellowships)

PO Box 30592
Nairobi Kenya AFRICA
254-2-621234 or 254-2-622619/20
FAX: 254-2-215991
E-Mail: j.massaquoi@unesco.org OR
ANSTI@Net2000ke.com

AMOUNT: Fees, subsistence, & international travel

DEADLINE(S): JUN

FIELD(S): Basic & Engineering Sciences

Scholarships for postgraduate studies outside of applicant's home country. Must be African nationals not older than 36 years of age and hold a good bachelor's degree (at least 2nd class upper division). Applicants should apply for admission to host university as soon as possible. Fellowships tenable only in African universities.

10 awards annually. Renewable up to 2 years. Contact Professor J.G.M. Massaquoi for an application.

630 — AMERICAN ASSOCIATION OF UNIVERSITY WOMEN EDUCATIONAL FOUNDATION (Selected Professions Fellowships)

Dept. 60
2201 N. Dodge St.
Iowa City IA 52243-4030
319/337-1716, ext. 60
FAX 319/337-1204
Internet: www.aauw.org

AMOUNT: $5,000-$15,000

DEADLINE(S): JAN 2 (most); NOV 15 (engineering dissertation only)

FIELD(S): Architecture; Computer/Information Sciences; Engineering; Mathematics/Statistics

For women in final year of graduate study in fields where women's participation has been low. Must be US citizen or permanent resident. Special consideration given to applicants who show professional promise in innovative or neglected areas of research and/or practice in areas of public interest. Women in engineering master's programs are eligible to apply for either first or final year of study; special award for engineering doctoral students writing dissertation.

Applications available August-December.

631 — AMERICAN FOUNDATION FOR THE BLIND (Paul W. Ruckes Scholarship)

11 Penn Plaza, Ste. 300
New York NY 10001
212/502-7661 or TDD 212/502-7771
E-Mail: juliet@afb.org
Internet: www.afb.org

AMOUNT: $1,000

DEADLINE(S): APR 30

FIELD(S): Engineering, computer, physical, or life sciences

Open to blind or visually impaired undergraduate or graduate students pursuing degrees in the above fields. U.S. citizenship required.

Write to the above address or visit website for complete information.

632 — AMERICAN INDIAN SCIENCE AND ENGINEERING SOCIETY (EPA Tribal Lands Environmental Science Scholarship)

PO Box 9828
Albuquerque NM 87119-9828
505/765-1052
FAX: 505/765-5608
E-Mail: scholarships@aises.org
Internet: www.aises.org/scholarships

AMOUNT: $4,000

DEADLINE(S): JUN 15

FIELD(S): Biochemistry; Biology; Chemical Engineering; Chemistry; Entomology; Environmental Economics/Science; Hydrology; Environmental Studies

Open to American Indian college juniors, seniors, and graduate students enrolled full-time at an accredited institution. Must demonstrate financial need. Certificate of Indian blood NOT required.

Renewable. See website or contact Patricia Browne for an application.

633 — AMERICAN SOCIETY FOR ENGINEERING EDUCATION (Army Research Laboratory Postdoctoral Fellowships)

1818 N St., NW, Ste. 600
Washington DC 20036
202/331-3525
FAX: 202/265-8504
E-Mail: projects@asee.org
Internet: www.asee.org/fellowship/

AMOUNT: $45,000-$55,000 + travel/relocation allowance

DEADLINE(S): Varies

FIELD(S): Engineering; Physical Sciences

Postdoctoral fellowships for US citizens/permanent residents to do research at Army Research Laboratories. Candidates must have completed their Ph.D. prior to appointment. Program is designed to increase involvement of creative and highly trained scientists and engineers from academia and industry in scientific and technical areas of interest and relevance to the Army. Research proposal should include clear objective and defined outcome. Financial need NOT a factor.

15 awards annually. Renewable. Contact Sandi Crawford at ASEE for an application packet.

634 — AMERICAN SOCIETY FOR QUALITY (Richard A. Freund International Scholarship)

P.O. Box 3005
Milwaukee WI 53201-3005
800/248-1946 or
814/272-8575 - ask for item B0499
FAX: 414/272-1734

E-Mail: cs@asq/org

Internet: www.asq.org

AMOUNT: $5,000

DEADLINE(S): APR 1

FIELD(S): Quality control in engineering, statistics, management, etc.

Scholarship for members and nonmembers worldwide enrolled in a Master's degree or higher level program with a concentration in any of the above fields of study. 3.25+ GPA required in undergraduate studies in engineering, sciences, or business.

Two letters of recommendation from persons qualified to assess the candidate's scholarly experience and a formal written statement (all in English) of approximately 250 words addressing the applicant's educational and career goals are required.

635 — AMERICAN SOCIETY OF CIVIL ENGINEERS (Trent R. Dames and William W. Moore Fellowship)

1801 Alexander Bell Drive

Reston VA 20191-4400

800/548-ASCE or 703/295-6000

FAX: 703/295-6333

E-Mail: student@asce.org

Internet: www.asce.org

AMOUNT: $5,000-$10,000

DEADLINE(S): FEB 20

FIELD(S): Geotechnical Engineering; Earth Sciences

For practicing engineers, earth scientists, professors, or graduate students to explore new applications of geotechnical engineering or the earth sciences to social, economic, environmental, and political issues. ASCE membership is not required.

Offered every two years (2000, 20002, etc.). See website or contact ASCE for an application between October and February.

636 — AMERICAN WATER RESOURCES ASSOCIATION (Richard A. Herbert Memorial Scholarships)

AWRRI

101 Comer Hall

Auburn Univ AL 36849-5431

715/355-3684

FAX: 715/355-3648

E-Mail: stdi@ltus.com

Internet: www.uwin.siu.ed/~awra

AMOUNT: $1,000 + complimentary AWRA membership

DEADLINE(S): APR 30

FIELD(S): Water Resources & related fields

For full-time undergraduates working towards 1st degree and for graduates. Based on academic performance, including cumulative GPA, relevance of curriculum to water resources, & leadership in extracurricular activities related to water resources. Quality & relevance of research is also considered from graduate students. Transcripts, letters of reference, & summary of academic interests/achievements, extracurricular interests, & career goals required (2 page limit).

2 awards annually: 1 undergrad & 1 graduate. Recipients announced in the summer. Contact Stephen Dickman, AWRA Student Activities Committee, for an application.

637 — AMERICAN WATER WORKS ASSOCIATION (Abel Wolman Fellowship)

6666 W. Quincy Ave.

Denver CO 80235

303/347-6206

FAX: 303/794-8915

E-Mail: vbaca@awwa.org

Internet: www.org/tande/eduframe.htm

AMOUNT: $15,000 stipend +$1,000 for supplies +up to $4,000 for tuition, etc.

DEADLINE(S): JAN 15

FIELD(S): Research in water supply and treatment

For students who show potential for leadership and anticipate completion of the requirments for a Ph.D. within two years of the award. Applicants will be evaluated on the quality of academic record, the significance of the proposed research to water supply and treatment, and the potential to do high quality research. Must be citizen or permanent resident of the U.S., Canada, or Mexico.

Renewable for a second year. Write for complete information.

638 — AMERICAN WATER WORKS ASSOCIATION (Academic Achievement Award)

6666 West Quincy Ave.

Denver CO 80235

303/347-6206

FAX: 303/794-8915

E-Mail: vbaca@awwa.org

Internet: www.org/tande/eduframe.htm

AMOUNT: 1st place: $1,000; 2nd place: $500

DEADLINE(S): OCT 1

FIELD(S): Subject related to drinking water supply industry

Award for a master's thesis or doctoral dissertation that has potential value to the water supply industry. This is not a scholarship but a cash award for outstanding work that has been completed.

Write for complete information.

639 — AMERICAN WATER WORKS ASSOCIATION (Holly A. Cornell Scholarship)

6666 W. Quincy Ave.

Denver CO 80235

303/347-6206

FAX: 303/794-8915

E-Mail: vbaca@awwa.org

Internet: www.org/tande/eduframe.htm

AMOUNT: $5,000

DEADLINE(S): JAN 15

FIELD(S): Engineering (Water Supply and Treatment)

Open to females and minorities (as defined by the U.S. Equal Opportunity Commission) who anticipate completion of a master's degree in engineering no sooner than December of the following year. Program was created by CH2M Hill, Inc. in honor of one of the firm's founders.

Contact organization for complete information.

640 — AMERICAN WATER WORKS ASSOCIATION (Lars Scholarship)

6666 W. Quincy Ave.

Denver CO 80235

303/347-6206

FAX: 303/794-8915

E-Mail: vbaca@awwa.org

Internet: awwa.org/tande/eduframe.htm

AMOUNT: $5,000 (Masters); $7,000 (Ph.D.)

DEADLINE(S): JAN 15

FIELD(S): Science and Engineering in the field of Water Supply and/or Treatment

For M.A. and Ph.D. level students at an institution of higher learning in Canada, Guam, Puerto Rico, Mexico, or the United States. For research into water supply and/or treatment.

Write for complete information.

641 — AMERICAN WATER WORKS ASSOCIATION (Thomas R. Camp Scholarship)

6666 W. Quincy Ave.

Denver CO 80235

303/347-6206

FAX: 303/794-8915

E-Mail: vbaca@awwa.org

Internet: www.org/tande/eduframe.htm

AMOUNT: $5,000

DEADLINE(S): JAN 15

FIELD(S): Research in the drinking water field

For students pursuing an M.A. or Ph.D. in the field of drinking water. This award is granted to Doctoral students in even years and Master's students in odd years. Can be used at an institution of higher education in Canada, Guam, Puerto rico, Mexico, or the U.S.

One award each year. Contact above location for details.

642 — ASIAN INSTITUTE OF TECHNOLOGY (AIT Scholarship Program)

Development Office
PO Box 4, Klongluang
Pathumthani 12120 THAILAND
(66)(2) 516-0110-44 or 524-5032
FAX: (66)(2) 516-2126
E-Mail: ascao@ait.ac.th
Internet: www.ait.ac.th

AMOUNT: US $12,600-$37,960

DEADLINE(S): FEB 15; JUN 15; OCT 15

FIELD(S): Advanced Technologies; Civil Engineering; Environment, Resources, & Development; Business Management

Scholarships and grants open to citizens of Asian countries who are accepted by the institute as a master's or doctotal candidate. Selection is based on academic criteria, practical experience, gender, and country of origin; priority to Mekong Region countries and Asian countries of the former USSR.

250 awards annually. Contact AIT for an application.

643 — ASSOCIATED WESTERN UNIVERSITIES, INC. (AWU Faculty Fellowships)

4190 South Highland Dr., Suite 211
Salt Lake City UT 84124-2600
801-273-8900

AMOUNT: Varies.

DEADLINE(S): FEB 15

FIELD(S): Engineering, Mathematics, Science, Technology

Research fellowships for qualified college and university faculty members to encourage participation and contribution to research at one of 62 cooperating facilities. It is not necessary to be enrolled at an AWU member institution. Collaborations that include graduate and/or undergraduate students are encouraged.

For detailed information and list of cooperating facilities, contact above location.

644 — ASSOCIATED WESTERN UNIVERSITIES, INC. (AWU Graduate Fellowship Program)

4190 South Highland Dr. Suite 211
Salt Lake City, UT 84124-2600
801/273-8900

AMOUNT: Stipend ($1,300 per month & up) + tuition assistance and travel allowance

DEADLINE(S): FEB 15

FIELD(S): Engineering, Mathematics, Science, Technology

Open to master's and doctoral degree candidates to conduct research toward a thesis or dissertation at one of more than 62 cooperating facilities.

Institutional affiliation and citizenship restrictions may apply for some awards or facilities. It is not necessary to be enrolled at an AWU member institution to apply for a fellowship.

Write to the above address for complete information.

645 — ASSOCIATED WESTERN UNIVERSITIES, INC. (AWU Postgraduate Fellowship)

4190 South Highland Dr. Suite 211
Salt Lake City UT 84124-2600
801/273-8900

AMOUNT: Stipend established by the host facility and varies by experience and discipline.

DEADLINE(S): Varies (Two to three months before the starting date)

FIELD(S): Engineering, Mathematics, Science, Technology

For college and university graduates who have completed all institutional requirements for an advanced degree from an accredited college or university in the U.S. A commitment to a professional career in science or engineering research is expected. U.S. citizenship or permanent resident status is required. Research is to be done at one of the 62 cooperating universities.

For detailed information and a list of cooperating facilities contact above address.

646 — ASSOCIATED WESTERN UNIVERSITIES, INC. (AWU Visiting Scientist Fellowships)

4190 South Highland Dr., Suite 211
Salt Lake City UT 84124-2600
801/273-8900

AMOUNT: Varies

DEADLINE(S): Varies (Two months prior to starting date)

FIELD(S): Engineering, Science, Mathematics, and Technology

Research fellowships for professionals with continued commitment to science and engineering. For use at one of 62 participating universities. US citizenship or permanent residency required.

For detailed information and list of cooperating facitilies contact above location.

647 — AT&T BELL LABORATORIES (Graduate Research Program For Women)

101 Crawfords Corner Road
Holmdel NJ 07733-3030
Written inquiry

AMOUNT: Full tuition & fees + $13,200 stipend per year

DEADLINE(S): JAN 15

FIELD(S): Engineering; Math; Sciences; Computer Science

For women students who have been accepted into an accredited doctoral program for the following fall. U.S. citizen or permanent resident.

Fellowships are renewable for up to 5 years of graduate study. Write to special programs manager-GRPW for complete information.

648 — BOEING (Polish Graduate Student Scholarship Program)

Phone for details
314/234-2149

AMOUNT: Tuition, books, and fees for three years

DEADLINE(S): Varies

FIELD(S): Scientific and technical fields

Scholarships for students from Poland to pursue graduate studies in scientific and technical areas at American colleges or universities.

Call Jim Schlueter at above telephone number.

649 — BRITISH FEDERATION OF WOMEN GRADUATES (M.H. Joseph Prize for Non-UK Citizens)

4 Mandeville Courtyard
142 Battersea Park Rd.
London SW11 4NB ENGLAND UK
PHONE/FAX: 0171/498 8037

AMOUNT: 500+ pounds sterling

DEADLINE(S): SEP 10

FIELD(S): Architecture; Engineering

For female graduate students of any nationality (except UK) who will pursue studies in Great Britain. Must have completed at least four academic terms or three semesters; award is not made for first year of research. Chief criteria is academic excellence and proven ability to carry out independent research. Postdoctoral studies also eligible.

1 award annually. Application fee of 12 pounds sterling required. Send a self-addressed, stamped envelope (or self-addressed envelope with international reply coupons) for an application. Results announced by end of October.

650 — BRITISH FEDERATION OF WOMEN GRADUATES (M.H. Joseph Prize for UK Citizens)

4 Mandeville Courtyard
142 Battersea Park Rd.
London SW11 4NB ENGLAND UK
PHONE/FAX: 0171/498 8037

AMOUNT: 500+ pounds sterling

DEADLINE(S): SEP 10

FIELD(S): Architecture; Engineering

For female UK citizens who plan to pursue graduate studies overseas. Must have completed at least four academic terms or three semesters; award is not made for first year of research. Chief criteria is academic excellence and proven ability to carry out independent research. Postdoctoral studies also eligible.

1 award annually. Application fee of 12 pounds sterling required. Send a self-addressed, stamped envelope (or self-addressed envelope with international reply coupons) for an application. Award announced at end of October.

651 — BROOKHAVEN WOMEN IN SCIENCE (Renate W. Chasman Scholarship)

PO Box 183
Upton NY 11973-5000
E-mail: pam@bnl.gov

AMOUNT: $2,000

DEADLINE(S): APR 1

FIELD(S): Natural Sciences; Engineering; Mathematics

Open ONLY to women who are residents of the boroughs of Brooklyn or Queens or the counties of Nassau or Suffolk in New York who are re-entering school after a period of study. For juniors, seniors, or first-year graduate students.

1 award annually. Not renewable. Contact Pam Mansfield at above location for an application. Phone calls are NOT accepted.

652 — CANADIAN FEDERATION OF UNIVERSITY WOMEN (CFUW Memorial/ Professional Fellowship)

251 Bank St., Ste. 600
Ottawa Ontario K2P 1X3 CANADA
613/234-2732
Internet: www.cfuw.ca

AMOUNT: $5,000

DEADLINE(S): NOV 15

FIELD(S): Science & Technology

Open to women who are Canadian citizens/ permanent residents enrolled in a master's degree program in science and technology. Must hold at least a bachelor's degree or equivalent from a recognized university and have been accepted into, or be currently enrolled in the proposed program and place of study. May be studying abroad.

$25 filing fee. Contact CFUW for an application after August 1st. Candidates will be notified by May 31st.

653 — CANADIAN SOCIETY FOR CHEMICAL ENGINEERING (J.E. Zajic Postgraduate Scholarship in Biochemical Engineering)

130 Slater St., Ste. 550
Ottawa Ontario KIP 6E2 CANADA
613/232-6252
FAX: 613/232-5862

E-Mail: cic_prog@fox.nstn.ca
Internet: www.chem-inst-can.org

AMOUNT: $1,000/yr.

DEADLINE(S): DEC 1

FIELD(S): (Bio)Chemical Engineering

This two-year award is open to postgraduate students enrolled in chemical engineering at a Canadian University. Applicants shall have engaged in research of a biochemical nature and shall have commenced such a program prior to application. Must be members of CSChE. Along with six copies of the application, must submit academic transcript, brief description of work undertaken, and two or three letters of support.

1 award annually. Contact the Program Manager, Awards, for an application. Award is given only in even-numbered years.

654 — CHARLES A. AND ANNE MORROW LINDBERGH FOUNDATION (Grants for Research Projects)

2150 Third Ave., N, Ste. 310
Anoka MN 55303-2200
612/576-1596
FAX: 612/576-1664
E-Mail: lindbergh@isd.net
Internet: www.isd.net/lindbergh

AMOUNT: $10,580 (max.)

DEADLINE(S): JUN 15

FIELD(S): Aviation; Aerospace; Agriculture; Education; Arts; Humanities; Biomedical Research; Exploration; Health & Population Sciences; Intercultural Communication; Waste Disposal Minimization & Management.; Adaptive Technology; Conservation

Open to individuals whose proposed projects represent a significant contribution toward the achievement of balance between the advance of technology and preservation of the natural environment. Financial need NOT a factor. Funding is NOT for tuition.

10 awards annually. See website for application.

655 — ECOLOGICAL SOCIETY OF AMERICA (Murray F. Buell and E. Lucy Braun Awards)

Ariz. State Univ. West, P.O. Box 37100
Phoenix AZ 85069
602/543-6934
FAX: 602/543-6073
E-Mail: sam.scheiner@asu.edu
Internet: www.sdsc.edu./ESA/student.htm

AMOUNT: $400

DEADLINE(S): JAN 31

FIELD(S): Ecology

A contest for the outstanding oral paper and/or outstanding poster presentation at the ESA Annual Meeting. For grads, undergrads, or recent doctorate (not more than 9 months past graduation).

Request info. from Dr. Samuel Scheiner, Dept. of Life Sciences, at above location for details.

656 — ELECTROCHEMICAL SOCIETY (Summer Research Fellowships)

10 S. Main St.
Pennington NJ 08534
609/737-1902
FAX: 609/737-2745
E-Mail: ecs@electrtochem
Internet: www.electrochem.org

AMOUNT: $4,000 (ECS); $3,000 (DOE)

DEADLINE(S): JAN 1

FIELD(S): Energy; Chemical Engineering; Chemistry; Electrical Engineering

Summer fellowships are open to graduate students at accredited colleges and universities in any country. Purpose is to support research of interest to ECS, such as research aimed at reducing energy consumption.

8 awards annually (3 ECS, 5 Department of Energy). Contact ECS for an application.

657 — EPPLEY FOUNDATION FOR RESEARCH (Postdoctoral Research Grants)

245 Park Avenue, 40th Floor
New York NY 10167
Written inquiry

AMOUNT: Up to $25,000

DEADLINE(S): FEB 1; MAY 1; AUG 1; NOV 1

FIELD(S): Physical Sciences; Biological Sciences

Postdoctoral grants for original advanced research in any of the physical or biological sciences. Open to established research scientists who are attached to a recognized institution.

Write for complete information.

658 — FANNIE AND JOHN HERTZ FOUNDATION (Fellowship)

Box 5032
Livermore CA 94551-5032
925/373-1642
Internet: www.hertzfoundation.org

AMOUNT: $25,000 stipend/yr. + $15,000 (max.) tuition allowance/yr.

DEADLINE(S): NOV 5

FIELD(S): Applied Physical Sciences

Open to graduate students with a minimum 3.75 GPA for studies in applied physical sciences, including math, engineering, computer science, biology, oceanography, aeronautics, astronomy, physics, and earth science. Must be US citizen/permanent resident. Does not support study in pursuit of M.D. degree, although will support Ph.D. portion of a joint M.D./Ph.D. study program.

Renewable up to 5 years. Only 36 US schools are currently considered tenable. See website for an application and list of specific fields of study that are acceptable.

659 — FORD FOUNDATION/NATIONAL RESEARCH COUNCIL (Predoctoral/ Dissertation Fellowships for Minorities)

2101 Constitution Ave.
Washington DC 20418
202/334-2872
E-Mail: infofell@nas.edu
Internet: http//www.nas.edu/fo/index.html

AMOUNT: $14,000 annual stipend + $6,000 grant to institution; $18,000 for dissertation fellowship

DEADLINE(S): NOV 3

FIELD(S): Most fields of study: sciences, humanities, engineering, behavioral science, social sciences, and computer science

Predoctoral and dissertation fellowships for students whose ethnicity is Alaskan Native, Black/African American, Mexican American/Chicano, Native American Indian, Native Pacific Islander, or Puerto Rican. For research-based programs leading to careers in college teaching and research.

Contact above address or website.

660 — INSTITUTE FOR OPERATIONS RESEARCH AND THE MANAGEMENT SCIENCES (INFORMS Summer Internship Directory)

P.O. Box 64794
Baltimore MD 21264-4794
800/4INFORMS
FAX: 410/684-2963
E-Mail: jps@informs.org
Internet: www.informs.org/INTERN/

AMOUNT: Varies

DEADLINE(S): Varies

FIELD(S): Fields related to information management: business management, engineering, mathematics

A website listing of summer internships in the field of operations research and management sciences. Both applicants and employers can register online.

Access website for list.

661 — INSTITUTE OF INDUSTRIAL ENGINEERS (Gilbreth Memorial Fellowship and E.J. Sierleja Memorial Fellowship)

25 Technology Park/Atlanta
Norcross GA 30092-2988
770/449-0461 or 800/263-8532
FAX: 770/441-3295
Internet: www.iienet.org

AMOUNT: $2,000 (Gilbreth); $500 (Sierleja)

DEADLINE(S): NOV 15

FIELD(S): Industrial Engineering

Graduate scholarships for active IIE members with at least three semester (5 quarters) of study remaining at an accredited college or university in the U.S. and its territories, Canada, or Mexico. A GPA of 3.4 or better is required. The Sierleja Fellowship is for students pursuing advanced studies in the area of transportation, preferably rail transportation.

Do not apply directly for these scholarships. Student must be nominated by their department head or faculty advisor. Nomination forms are sent to each school at the beginning of the fall term.

662 — INSTITUTE OF INDUSTRIAL ENGINEERS (United Parcel Service Scholarships for Female and Minority Students.)

25 Technology Park/Atlanta
Norcross GA 30092-2988
770/449-0461 or 800/263-8532
FAX: 770/441-3295
Internet: www.iienet.org

AMOUNT: $4,000

DEADLINE(S): NOV 15

FIELD(S): Industrial Engineering

Graduate and undergraduate scholarships for active IIE members with at least three semester (5 quarters) of study remaining at an accredited college or university in the U.S. and its territories, Canada, or Mexico. A GPA of 3.4 or better is required. One for a minority student, and one is for a female.

Do not apply directly for these scholarships. Student must be nominated by their department head or faculty advisor. Nomination forms are sent to each school at the beginning of the fall term.

663 — INSTITUTE OF PAPER SCIENCE AND TECHNOLOGY (Fellowship Program)

500 10th St. NW
Atlanta GA 30318
404/853-9500

AMOUNT: Full tuition plus $11,250 stipend

DEADLINE(S): MAR 15

FIELD(S): Chemistry; Chemical Engineering; Physics; Biology; Mechanical Engineering; Pulp and Paper Technology

Open to graduate students who are U.S., Mexican, or Canadian citizens or legal residents who hold a BS degree in the above fields. For a pursuit of a master of Science or Ph.D degree at the institute.

35 fellowships annually. Address inquiries to director of admissions.

664 — INSTITUTION OF ELECTRICAL ENGINEERS (Postgraduate Awards)

Savoy Place
London WC2R 0BL ENGLAND
0171 240 1871 Ext. 2211/2235
FAX: 0171 497 3609
E-Mail: scholarships@iee.org.uk
Internet: www.iee.org.uk/Awards/pgsum.htm

AMOUNT: 1,000-6,000 pounds/yr.

DEADLINE(S): SEP 1; SEP 30

FIELD(S): Engineering

Scholarships for postgraduate students pursuing degrees in engineering who are residents of the United Kingdom.

Check website or contact organization for application details.

665 — INTERNATIONAL DESALINATION ASSOCIATION (Channabasappa Memorial Scholarship Fund)

P.O. Box 387
Topsfield MA 01983
978/887-0410
FAX: 978/887-0411
E-Mail: idalpab@ix.netcom.com
Internet: www.ida.bm

AMOUNT: Up to $6,000

DEADLINE(S): Varies

FIELD(S): Desalination or water technologies

Open to applicants who have their bachelor's degree from a recognized university & graduated in top 10% of their class. Scholarships support graduate study & research in desalination & water re-use.

For complete information write to Patricia Burke or Nancy Fitzgerald at above address.

666 — INTERNATIONAL INSTITUTE FOR APPLIED SYSTEMS ANALYSIS (Fellowships for Young Scientists' Summer Program at the IIASA in Vienna, Austria)

A-2361 Laxenburg
AUSTRIA
617/576-5019
FAX: 617/576-5050
E-Mail: mcollins@amacad.org
Internet: http://www.iiasa.ac.at

AMOUNT: Airfare and modest living expenses

DEADLINE(S): JAN 15

FIELD(S): Population, global change, economics, air pollution, transportation, forestry resorces, energy stratiegy, risk modeling, dynamic systems modeling

For advanced graduate and predoctoral candidates with research interests compatible with

IIASA projects. Must have working level of written and spoken English and academic accomplishments and publications demonstrating superior qualifications.

4-7 annual awards. Contact Dr. Margaret Goud Collins (in U.S.) or Ms. Margaret Traber (in Austria).

667 — JAMES F. LINCOLN ARC WELDING FOUNDATION (Scholarships)

22801 Clair Ave.
Cleveland OH 44117-1199
216/481-4300

AMOUNT: Varies

DEADLINE(S): MAY 1 (through JUN 15, depending on program)

FIELD(S): Arc welding and engineering design

Open to high school students, college undergraduates, and graduate students, and to professionals working in the fields of arc welding and engineering design. Various programs are available.

Send self-addressed, stamped envelope to Richard S. Sabo, Executive Director, at above address.

668 — JANSONS LEGAT (Scholarships)

Blommeseter, Norderhov
3512 Honefoss NORWAY
32 1354 65
FAX: 32 1356 26
E-Mail: janlegat@online.no

AMOUNT: NOK 75.000,-

DEADLINE(S): MAR 15

FIELD(S): Business; Industry; Handcraft

Scholarships for Norwegian citizens for career support and/or postgraduate study. Financial need is NOT a factor.

30 awards annually. Contact Reidun Haugen for an application.

669 — LADIES OF NORTHANTS (Scholarship)

P.O. Box 6694
Coddingtown, CA 95406-0694
Written inquiry

AMOUNT: $250

DEADLINE(S): FEB 8

FIELD(S): Nuclear Engineering

The Ladies of Northants offers a scholarship to a woman over 40 who migrates to the United States from Northamptonshire England and is committed to a career in nuclear engineering. For undergraduate or graduate study.

Preference to natives of the village of Podington who have a 3.75 or better grade point average (4.0 scale) and can demonstrate financial need. Write for complete information.

670 — MATHESON GAS PRODUCTS FOUNDATION (Scholarships)

PO Box 624
959 Rte. 46 E.
Parsippany NJ 07054-0624
Internet: www.mathesongas.com

AMOUNT: $5,000

DEADLINE(S): None

FIELD(S): Chemistry; Physics; Chemical Engineering; Material Science; Semiconductor Engineering

Open to financially needy graduate students who are African American, Latino, Asian, Native American, or female. Must be US citizens/permanent residents studying in above fields or related area.

Send self-addressed, stamped envelope to Jerry Cantrella, Director of Personnel, for an application.

671 — MINNESOTA AUTOMOBILE DEALERS ASSOCIATION (MADA Scholarships)

277 University Ave. W.
St. Paul MN 55103-2085
612/291-2400
Internet: www.mada.org

AMOUNT: Tuition for one quarter at an accredited Minnesota technical institution

DEADLINE(S): Varies

FIELD(S): Automotive mechanics, automotive body repair, parts and service management, automotive machinist, automotive diagnostic technician

Tuition reimbursement in the above fields of study for students currently enrolled in a Minnesota technical school. Must have completed two quarters of study in the field, be planning to enroll in further study, have maintained an above average GPA, and be nominated by an instructor or class advisor at a Minnesota technical institution.

Contact instructor, guidance counselor, or check website above for more information.

672 — NATIONAL AERONAUTICS AND SPACE ADMINISTRATION (Graduate Student Researcher's Program-Underrepresented Minority Focus)

Mail Code FEH
NASA Headquarters
Washington, DC 20546
202/453-8344

AMOUNT: $22,000 1st year, renewable up to 3 years

DEADLINE(S): FEB 1

FIELD(S): Science, Engineering, Mathematics

For underrepresented minority groups in the fields of science and engineering (including African-Americans, American Indians, Hispanics, and Pacific Islanders), who may end up with a career in space science and/or aerospace technology. Must be US citizen and enrolled or accepted as a full-time graduate student at an accredited US college or university.

Write for complete information.

673 — NATIONAL ASSOCIATION OF PURCHASING MANAGEMENT (Doctoral Dissertation Grant Program)

2055 E Centennial Circle
PO Box 22160
Tempe AZ 85285-2160
800/888-6276 or 480/752-6276
FAX: 480/752-7890
E-Mail: hjohnson@napm.org
Internet: www.napm.org

AMOUNT: $10,000

DEADLINE(S): JAN 31

FIELD(S): Purchasing & Supply Management

Open to US citizens/permanent residents pursuing a Ph.D. or D.B.A. in purchasing, business, management, logistics, economics, industrial engineering, or related fields at an accredited US university. Must submit transcripts, proposal abstract, letters of recommendation, and curriculum vitae. Financial need NOT a factor.

4 awards annually. Not renewable. Contact Holly LaCroix Johnson, Senior Vice President, for an application.

674 — NATIONAL ASSOCIATION OF WATER COMPANIES—NEW JERSEY CHAPTER (Scholarship)

Elizabethtown Water Co.
600 South Ave.
Westfield NJ 07090
908/654-1234
FAX: 908/232-2719

AMOUNT: $2,500

DEADLINE(S): APR 1

FIELD(S): Business Administration; Biology; Chemistry; Engineering; Communications

For U.S. citizens who have lived in NJ at least 5 years and plan a career in the investor-owned water utility industry in disciplines such as those above. Must be undergrad or graduate student in a 2- or 4-year NJ college or university.

GPA of 3.0 or better required. Contact Gail P. Brady for complete information.

675 — NATIONAL RESEARCH COUNCIL (Integrated Manufacturing Predoctoral Fellowships)

2101 Constitution Ave., NW
Washington DC 20418
202/334-2872
E-Mail: infofell@nas.edu
Internet: http://www. nas.edu/fo/index,.html

AMOUNT: $20,000 stipend; up to $15,000 for cost of education

DEADLINE(S): DEC 5

FIELD(S): Any area related to integrated systems of manufacturing or processing—engineering fields and other applied science fields, for example

Predoctoral fellowships sponsored by U.S. Dept. of Energy and administered by the National Research Council. Program seeks to create a pool of Ph.D.s trained in the integrated approach to manufacturing or processing, leading to better utilization of scarce resources, to improved energy efficiency, and to lessened degradation of the environment. For full-time study for up to three years at an appropriate academic institution.

12 awards. Contact above address or website for details.

676 — NATIONAL SCIENCES AND ENGINEERING RESEARCH COUNCIL OF CANADA (Graduate Scholarships)

Scholarships/Fellowships Division
350 Albert Street
Ottawa Ontario K1A 1H5 CANADA
613/996-3769
FAX: 613/996-2589
E-Mail: schol@nserc.ca
Internet: http://www.nserc.ca

AMOUNT: $15,700/year for 1st & 2nd years at masters or Ph.D level; $17,400/year (Ph.D level ONLY) 3rd & 4th years

DEADLINE(S): NOV 24

FIELD(S): Natural Sciences, Engineering, Biology, or Chemistry

Open to Canadian citizens or permanent residents who have earned or will soon earn a bachelors or masters degree in science or engineering. Academic excellence and research aptitude are considerations.

Write for complete information.

677 — NATIONAL SCIENCES AND ENGINEERING RESEARCH COUNCIL OF CANADA (Postdoctoral Fellowships)

Scholarships/Fellowships Division
350 Albert Street
Ottawa Ontario K1A 1H5 CANADA

613/996-3762
FAX: 613/996-2589
E-Mail: schol@nserc.ca
Internet: http://www.nserc.ca

AMOUNT: Individually negotiated

DEADLINE(S): Varies—average: $43,000

FIELD(S): Natural Sciences, Engineering, Biology, or Chemistry

Open to Canadian citizens or permanent residents who hold doctoral degrees in science or engineering. Academic excellence and research aptitude are considerations.

Write for complete information.

678 — NATIONAL SOCIETY OF BLACK ENGINEERS (Scholarships)

1454 Duke St.
Alexandria VA 22314
703/549-2207
FAX: 703/683-5312
E-Mail: nsbehq@nsbe.org
Internet: www.nsbe.org

AMOUNT: Varies

DEADLINE(S): Varies

FIELD(S): Engineering and engineering technologies

Programs for black and other ethnic minorities in the fields of engineering and the engineering technologies. Organization offers pre-college programs, scholarships, career fairs, a journal, a newsletter, etc.

Contact organization for details.

679 — NAVY RECRUITING COMMAND (Armed Forces Health Professions Scholarships)

Commander
801 N. Randolph St.
Code 325
Arlington VA 22203-1991
800/USA-NAVY or 703/696-4926
E-Mail: omegahouse@erols.com
Internet: www.navyjobs.com

AMOUNT: $938/month stipend + tuition, fees, books, lab fees, etc.

DEADLINE(S): APR 28

FIELD(S): Medicine, Dentistry, Optometry, Physical Therapy, Pharmacology, Health Care Administration, Industrial Hygiene, etc.

Open to US citizens enrolled or accepted for enrollment in any of the above fields at an accredited institution in the US or Puerto Rico. Must qualify for appointment as a Navy officer and sign a

contractual agreement. Must be between the ages of 18 & 36 and have a GPA of at least 3.0.

See website, contact local Navy Recruiting Office, or contact Lieutenant Roger A. House, MPA, CAAMA, Medical Service Corps at above address.

680 — OAK RIDGE ASSOCIATED UNIVERSITIES (Laboratory Graduate Research Participation Program)

P.O. Box 117
Oak Ridge TN 37831-0117
423/576-4813

AMOUNT: $1,000-$1,200/mo. + allowance for dependents + tuition and fees reimbursement to a max. of $3,500/yr.

DEADLINE(S): Ongoing

FIELD(S): Life sciences, physical, and social sciences, mathematics, and engineering

For graduate students in one of the fields listed above who have completed all degree requirements except thesis or dissertation research. For full-time research under the joint direction of the major professor and a DOE staff member at one of various locations, primarily in the South. For six to twelve months.

Funded through U.S. Dept. of Energy, Office of Energy Reseach, and Office of Fossil Energy. Write for complete information.

681 — OAK RIDGE ASSOCIATED UNIVERSITIES (National Science Foundation Graduate Research Fellowships)

PO Box 3010
Oak Ridge TN 37831-3010
423/241-4300
FAX: 423/241-4513
E-Mail: nsfgrfp@orau.gov
Internet: www.orau.gov/nsf/nsffel.htm

AMOUNT: $15,000 stipend + $10,500 tuition allowance

DEADLINE(S): NOV 4

FIELD(S): Science; Math; Engineering; Computer Science

Three-year fellowships for graduate study leading to research-based master's or doctoral degrees in the above fields. Must be US citizens, nationals, or permanent residents at the time of application. Fellowships are awarded on the basis of ability. Women, minorities, and those with disabilities are strongly encouraged to apply. One-time International Research Travel Allowance available.

1,000 awards annually. Contact Jeannette Bouchard for an application/more information.

682 — OAK RIDGE INSTITUTE FOR SCIENCE AND EDUCATION (Applied Health Physics Fellowship Program)

P.O. Box 117
Oak Ridge TN 37831-0117
423/576-2194 or 423/576-9279
E-Mail: COXRE@ORAU.GOV or
GRADFELL@ORAU.GOV

AMOUNT: $14,400 stipend + tuition and fees up to $9,000/yr paid to university + transportation costs up to $300/month

DEADLINE(S): JAN 26

FIELD(S): Engineering, mathematics, physical and life sciences

Fellowship in applied health physics to implement DOE's nuclear energy-related mission. Candidates must have B.A. degree in life or physical sciences, engineering, or mathematics. Recipients are subject to a service obligation of one year of full-time employment in a DOE facility for each academic year of fellowhip award.

For details and application, contact above location.

683 — OAK RIDGE INSTITUTE FOR SCIENCE AND EDUCATION (Industrial Hygiene Graduate Fellowship Program)

P.O. Box 117
Oak Ridge TN 37831-0117
423-576-9655
FAX: 423/576-8293
E-Mail: kinneym@orau.gov

AMOUNT:

DEADLINE(S): JAN 26

FIELD(S): Industrial Hygiene

A fellowship for first-year master's candidates who have undergraduate degrees in physical, life, environmental, or health sciences or enginering and who wish to pursue studies in industrial hygiene.

For details and application, contact above location.

684 — OAK RIDGE INSTITUTE FOR SCIENCE AND EDUCATION (Professional Internship Program/Oak Ridge National Laboratory)

P.O. Box 117
Oak Ridge TN 37831-0117
423/576-3426
423/576-3427

AMOUNT: $210 to $300/week + travel, tuition, and fees

DEADLINE(S): FEB 5; JUN 1; OCT 1

FIELD(S): Chemistry, environmental science, geology, hydrogeology, hydrology, chemical engineering, civil engineering, environmental engineering, mechanical engineering, computer science (technical database development)

Opportunities for graduates and undergraduates to participate in energy-related research projects that correlate with their academic and career goals. For 3 to 12 consecutive months.

Funded through Oak Ridge National Laboratory.

685 — OAK RIDGE INSTITUTE FOR SCIENCE AND EDUCATION (Professional Internship Program/Pittsburgh Energy Technology Center)

P.O. Box 117
Oak Ridge TN 37831-0117
423/576-3426
423/576-3427

AMOUNT: $235 to $325/week + travel, tuition, and fees

DEADLINE(S): FEB 5; JUN 1; OCT 1

FIELD(S): Chemistry, physics, environmental science, geology, chemical or environmental engineering, computer science, or statistics.

Opportunities for graduates and undergraduates to participate in fossil energy-related research projects that correlate with their academic and career goals. For 3 to 12 consecutive months.

Funded through U.S. Dept. of Energy, Office of Fossil Energy, and Pittsburgh Energy Technology Center.

686 — OAK RIDGE INSTITUTE FOR SCIENCE AND EDUCATION (Professional Internship Program/Savannah River Site)

P.O. Box 117
Oak Ridge TN 37831-0117
423/576-3426
423/576-3427

AMOUNT: $260 to $340/week + travel

DEADLINE(S): FEB 5; JUN 1; SEP 1

FIELD(S): Chemistry, computer science, environmental science, geology, engineering, or physics

Opportunities for high school junior and seniors, undergraduates, and graduates to participate in research projects that correlate with their academic majors and career goals. For 3 to 12 consecutive months at the Savannah River Site, SC.

Funded through the Savannah River Site, SC.

687 — OAK RIDGE INSTITUTE FOR SCIENCE AND EDUCATION (Science and Engineering Research Semester)

P.O. Box 117
Oak Ridge TN 37831-0117
423/576-2358
423/576-2310

AMOUNT: $225/week + travel + housing

DEADLINE(S): OCT; MAR

FIELD(S): Computer science, physical sciences, environmental and life sciences, and mathematics

Opportunities for high school junior and seniors and a few slots for graduates to participate in energy-related with laboratory scientists at Oak Ridge National Laboratory, TN. One semester with possibility of summer extension. Available two times a year.

Funded through the U.S. Dept. of Energy, Office of Energy Research.

688 — OAK RIDGE INSTITUTE FOR SCIENCE AND EDUCATION, U.S. DEPARTMENT OF ENERGY (Fusion Energy Sciences Fellowship Program)

105 Mitchell Road, MS-16
Oak Ridge TN 37831
423/576-2600
FAX: 423/576-8293
E-Mail: johnsons@orau.giv

AMOUNT: $1,300/mo. + $200/mo.

DEADLINE(S): JAN 26 (Received, not postmarked)

FIELD(S): Fusion energy sciences

Fellowships for Ph.D. candidates to pursue a degree in the fusion energy sciences at one of several participating universities throughout the U.S. Must be U.S. citizens or permanent residents. For students entering first or second year of graduate study. Must have B.A. degree in related field, such as applied mathematics or physics; chemical, electrical, mechanical, metallurgical, or nuclear engineering; or materials science.

Contact Sandra Johnson at above location for details and list of participating institutions.

689 — OAK RIDGE INSTITUTE FOR SCIENCE AND EDUCATION/U.S. DEPT. OF ENERGY (Office of Civilian Radioactive Waste Management Fellowship)

P.O. Box 117
Oak Ridge TN 37831-0117
423/576-0128
FAX: 423/576-8293
E-Mail: drostp@orau.gov

AMOUNT: $14,000/yr.

DEADLINE(S): JAN 16 (Received, not postmarked)

FIELD(S): Physical or life sciences, math, or engineering

Fellowships for graduate students at various participating universities to conduct research in the management of spent nuclear fuel and high-level raqdioactive waste. For M.A. and Ph.D. candidates. For up to 48 months. Must be U.S. citizen or permanent resident.

Funded through U.S. Department of Energy, Office of Civilian Radioactive Waste Management. Contact or call Ms. Portia Drost, MS-16, at above address for details.

690 — OAK RIDGE INSTITUTE FOR SCIENCE AND EDUCATION (Nuclear Engineering & Health Physics Fellowship Program)

105 Mitchell Rd. MS-16
Oak Ridge TN 37831-0117
423/576-2600 or 423/241-2890
E-Mail: johnsons@orau.gov or
daltonj@arou.gov

AMOUNT: $14,400/yr.

DEADLINE(S): JAN 26

FIELD(S): Engineering, physical and life sciences

Fellowships in nuclear engineering or applied health physics to implement DOE's nuclear energy-related mission. Candidates must have B.A. degree in life or physical sciences or engineering.

For details and application, contact Sandra Johnson or Jennifer Dalton at above location.

691 — OPEN SOCIETY INSTITUTE (Environmental Management Fellowships)

400 West 59th St.
New York NY 10019
212/548-0600 or 212/757-2323
FAX: 212/548-4679 or 212/548-4600
Internet: www.soros.org/efp.html

AMOUNT: Fees, room, board, living stipend, textbooks, international transportation, health insurance

DEADLINE(S): NOV 15

FIELD(S): Earth sciences, natural sciences, humanities (exc. language), anthropology, sociology, mathematics, or engineering

Two-year fellowships for use in selected universities in the U.S. for international students. For students/professionals in fields related to environmental policy, legislation, and remediation techniques applicable to their home countries.

To apply, contact your local Soros Foundation or Open Society Institute. Further details on website.

692 — ROCKEFELLER FOUNDATION (African Dissertation Internship Awards)

420 Fifth Ave.
New York NY 10018-2702
212/869-8500
212/764-3468
Internet: www.rockfound.org

AMOUNT: Cost of project

DEADLINE(S): None given

FIELD(S): Agriculture, environment, health, life sciences, population, and schooling

For African graduate students in U.S. and Canadian universities (but not to permanent residents) to return to Africa to carry out dissertation research at a local university or research institution. Priority given to above topics.

Students are strongly urged to be in the field for at least 12 months. Contact above location for details.

693 — ROYAL SOCIETY OF EDINBURGH (BP Research Fellowships)

22/24 George St.
Edinburgh EH2 2PQ SCOTLAND
0131 225 6057
FAX: 0131 220 6889
E-Mail: rse@rse.org.uk

AMOUNT: 17,606 to 26,508 pounds sterling

DEADLINE(S): MAR 10

FIELD(S): Mechanical, Chemical, or Control Engineering; Organic Chemistry; Solid State Physics; Information Technology; Geologic Sciences

Research fellowships to Scotland higher education institutions. For post-doctoral researchers age 35 or under on the date of appointment (usually Oct. 1). For research in above disciplines.

Write for complete information.

694 — SKIDMORE, OWINGS & MERRILL FOUNDATION (Mechanical/Electrical Traveling Fellowship Program)

224 S. Michigan Ave., Suite 1000
Chicago IL 60604
312/554-9090
FAX: 312/360-4545

AMOUNT: $7,500

DEADLINE(S): Varies (consult with school)

FIELD(S): Architectural Engineering, Electrical Engineering, or Mechanical

Candidates must have received a B.A. or M.A. degree in one of the above fields. It enables the Fellow to travel in order to observe and analyze innovative building systems and technologies anywhere in the world.

Write for complete information.

695 — SOCIETY FOR IMAGING SCIENCE AND TECHNOLOGY (Raymond Davis Scholarship)

7003 Kilworth Lane
Springfield VA 22151
703/642-9090
FAX: 703/642-9094
E-Mail: info@imaging.org
Internet: www.imaging.org

AMOUNT: $1,000

DEADLINE(S): DEC 15

FIELD(S): Photographic/Imaging Science or Engineering

Scholarships for undergraduate juniors or seniors or graduate students for full-time continuing studies in the theory or practice of photographic or imaging science or engineering, including research in the theory or practice of image formation by radiant energy.

Write for complete information.

696 — SOCIETY OF MANUFACTURING ENGINEERING EDUCATION FOUNDATION (Scholarships& Fellowship)

One SME Drive
PO Box 930
Dearborn MI 48121-0930
313/271-1500
FAX: 313/240-6095
E-Mail: murrdor@sme.org
Internet: www.sme.org/foundation

AMOUNT: $500-$5,000

DEADLINE(S): FEB 1

FIELD(S): Manufacturing Engineering/Technology; Industrial Engineering; Robotics

Twelve scholarship programs and one fellowship are available annually to high school, undergraduate, and graduate students. Minimum GPA varies with each scholarship. Financial need NOT a factor.

61 awards annually. Renewable. Contact Dora Murray at SME for an application.

697 — THE DAPHNE JACKSON MEMORIAL FELLOWSHIPS TRUST (Fellowships in Science/Engineering)

School of Physical Sciences, Dept. of Physics, University of Surrey
Guildford, Surrey GU2 5XH ENGLAND UK
01483 259166
FAX: 01483 259501
E-Mail: J.Woolley@surrey.ac.uk
Internet: www.sst.ph.ic.ac.uk/trust/

AMOUNT: Varies

DEADLINE(S): Varies

FIELD(S): Science or engineering, including information sciences

Fellowships to enable well-qualified and highly motivated scientists and engineers to return to appropriate careers following a career break due to family comitments. May be used on a flexible, part-time basis. Tenable at various U.K. universities.

See website and/or contact organization for details.

698 — THE INTERNATIONAL SOCIETY FOR OPTICAL ENGINEERING (Scholarships and Grants)

P.O. Box 10
Bellingham WA 98225
360/676-3290
FAX: 360/647-1445
E-Mail: spie@spie.org
Internet: http://www.spie.org

AMOUNT: $500-$7,000

DEADLINE(S): APR 6

FIELD(S): Optics and optical engineering

Open to college students at all levels for study of optical or optoelectronic applied science and engineering. May be awarded to students in community colleges or technical institutes and to undergraduate and graduate students at colleges and universities.

Write to the SPIE Scholarship Committee Chair or visit website (address above) for complete information.

699 — U.S. DEPARTMENT OF DEFENSE (GLSIP-General Laboratory Scientific Interchange Program: NRC-NRL Post-Doctoral Program)

Naval Research Laboratory
Office of Program Admin. & Dev. Code 1006.17
Washington, D.C. 20375-5321
202/767-3865
DSN: 297-3865
FAX: 202/404-8110
Internet: www.acq.osd.mil/ddre/edugate/s-aindx.html

AMOUNT: Research Program

DEADLINE(S): None specified

FIELD(S): Computer science, artificial intelligence, plasma physics, acoustics, radar, fluid dynamics, chemistry, materials sci, optical sci, condensed matter and radiation, electronic sci, environmental sci, marine geosciences, remote sensing, oceanography, marine meteorology, space technology/sciences.

U.S. citizens who are recent postdoctoral graduates are selected on the basis of overall qualifications and techincal proposals.

Contact Jessica Hileman for more information.

700 — U.S. DEPARTMENT OF TRANSPORTATION (Dwight D. Eisenhower Transportation Fellowships)

U.S. Dept. of Transportation, Fed. Hwy. Admin., 6300 Georgetown Pike, HHI-20
McLean VA 22101-2296
703/235-0538

AMOUNT: Varies

DEADLINE(S): FEB

FIELD(S): Transportation—such majors as chemistry; materials science; corrosion; civil, chemical, & electronics engineering; structures; human factors; computer science; psychology.

Research fellowships for undergrads and grad students at any Dept. of Transportation facility or selected IHE. For three to twelve months. Research must focus on transportation-related research and development in the above fields.

Contact Ilene Payne, Director, Universities and grants Programs at above location for details.

701 — U.S. ENVIRONMENTAL PROTECTION AGENCY—NATIONAL NETWORK FOR ENVIRONMENTAL MANAGEMENT STUDIES (Fellowships)

401 M St., SW
Mailcode 1704
Washington DC 20460
202/260-5283
FAX: 202/260-4095
E-Mail: jojokian.sheri@epa.gov
Internet: www.epa.gov/enviroed/students.html

AMOUNT: Varies

DEADLINE(S): DEC

FIELD(S): Environmental Policies, Regulations, & Law; Environmental Management & Administration; Environmental Science; Public Relations & Communications; Computer Programming & Development

Fellowships are open to undergraduate and graduate students working on research projects in the above fields, either full-time during the summer or part-time during the school year. Must be US citizen or legal resident. Financial need NOT a factor.

85-95 awards annually. Not renewable. See website or contact the Career Service Center of participating universities for an application.

702 — UNIVERSITY OF MANCHESTER INSTITUTE OF SCIENCE & TECHNOLOGY (Mohn Research Fellowship)

PO Box 88
Manchester M60 1QD England
0161-236-3311
FAX: 0161-200-3635

AMOUNT: Approx. 4,000 pounds sterling

DEADLINE(S): APR 30

FIELD(S): Metallurgy/Materials Science; Chemical Engineering

Post-graduate fellowships for research in engineering technology (at UMIST). Preference will be given to those studying in the areas listed above.

For more information, contact the registrar at UMIST.

703 — WATER ENVIRONMENT FEDERATION (Robert A. Canham Scholarship)

Access website
Internet: www.wef.org

AMOUNT: $2,500

DEADLINE(S): MAR 1

FIELD(S): Water environment areas

Open to post-baccalaureate students in the environmental engineering or sciences field who agree to work in the environmental field for at least two years after completion of the degree. Must be a member of the Water Environment Federation.

A detailed statement of career goals and aspirations and three letters of recommendation are required. Write for complete information. Access website for details and application—go to "Member Programs," then to "Canham Scholarship." Organization will not mail this information!

704 — WATER ENVIRONMENT FEDERATION (Student Paper Competition)

Access website
Internet: www.wef.org

AMOUNT: $1,000 (1st prize); $500 (2nd); $250 (3rd)

DEADLINE(S): FEB 1

FIELD(S): Water pollution control and related fields

Awards for 500- 1,000-word abstracts dealing with water pollution control, water quality problems, water-related concerns, or hazardous wastes. Open to undergrad (A.A. and B.A.) and grad students.

Also open to recently graduated students (within 1 calendar year of Feb. 1 deadline). See website for details—go to "Member Programs" then to "Student Paper Competition." Organization will not mail this information.

705 — WOMEN'S AUXILIARY TO THE AMERICAN INSTITUTE OF MINING METALLURGICAL & PETROLEUM ENGINEERS (WAAIME Scholarship Loan Fund)

345 E. 47th St., 14th Floor
New York NY 10017-2304
212/705-7692

AMOUNT: Varies

DEADLINE(S): MAR 15

FIELD(S): Earth Sciences, as related to the Minerals Industry

Open to undergraduate juniors and seniors and grad students, whose majors relate to an interest in the minerals industry. Eligible applicants receive a scholarship loan for all or part of their education. Recipients repay only 50%, with no interest charges.

Repayment to begin by 6 months after graduation and be completed within 6 years. Write to WAAIME

Scholarship Loan Fund (address above) for complete information.

706 — WYOMING TRUCKING ASSOCIATION (Scholarships)

PO Box 1909
Casper WY 82602
Written Inquiry

AMOUNT: $250-$300

DEADLINE(S): MAR 1

FIELD(S): Transportation Industry

For Wyoming high school graduates enrolled in a Wyoming college, approved trade school, or the University of Wyoming. Must be pursuing a course of study which will result in a career in the transportation industry in Wyoming, including but not limited to: safety, environmental science, diesel mechanics, truck driving, vocational trades, business management, sales management, computer skills, accounting, office procedures, and management.

1-10 awards annually. Write to WYTA for an application.

707 — XEROX TECHNICAL MINORITY SCHOLARSHIP (School-Year Tuition)

907 Culver Road
Rochester NY 14609
www.xerox.com/employment

AMOUNT: Up to $5,000 (varies according to tuition and academic excellence)

DEADLINE(S): SEP 15

FIELD(S): Various engineering and science disclpines

Scholarships for minorities enrolled full-time in a technical degree program at the bachelor level or above. Must be African-American, Native American, Hispanic, or Asian. Recipient may not have tuition or related expenses covered by other scholarships or grants.

If above requirements are met, obtain application from website or address above. Your financial aid office must fill out the bottom half of the form. Send completed application, your resume and a cover letter to Xerox Technical Minority Scholarship Program at above address.

708 — XEROX TECHNICAL MINORITY SCHOLARSHIP (Summer Employment Program)

Xerox Square
Rochester NY 14644
Written inquiry

AMOUNT: Up to $5,000 (varies according to tuition and academic excellence)

DEADLINE(S): SEP 15

FIELD(S): Various engineering and science disclpines

Scholarships for minorities enrolled in a technical degree program at the bachelor level or above. Must be African-American, Native American, Hispanic, or Asian. Xerox will match your skills with a sponsoring organization that will offer a meaningful summer work experience complimenting your academic learning.

If above requirements are met, send your resume and a cover letter to Xerox Corporation Corporate Employment and College Relations Technical Mfinority Scholarship Program to above address.

MECHANICAL ENGINEERING

709 — AECI LIMITED (AECI Post Graduate Research Fellowship)

Private Bag X2
Modderfontein SOUTH AFRICA 1645
011/605-3100

AMOUNT: Varies (South African Rands 3600)

DEADLINE(S): SEP 30

FIELD(S): Chemistry, Physics, Metallurgy, Biochemistry, Microbiology, Chemical Engineering, Civil Engineering, Industrial Engineering, Electrical Engineering, Mechanical Engineering, Instrument Engineering

Open to South African citizens who are graduate students who want to do research in one of the above areas. This fellowship is offered to strengthen post-graduate study and research in South Africa, particularly in the fields above.

Write to the above address for complete information.

710 — AFRICAN NETWORK OF SCIENTIFIC AND TECHNOLOGICAL INSTITUTIONS - ANSTI (Postgraduate Fellowships)

PO Box 30592
Nairobi Kenya AFRICA
254-2-621234 or 254-2-622619/20
FAX: 254-2-215991
E-Mail: j.massaquoi@unesco.org OR
ANSTI@Net2000ke.com

AMOUNT: Fees, subsistence, & international travel

DEADLINE(S): JUN

FIELD(S): Basic & Engineering Sciences

Scholarships for postgraduate studies outside of applicant's home country. Must be African nationals not older than 36 years of age and hold a good bachelor's degree (at least 2nd class upper division). Applicants should apply for admission to host university as soon as possible. Fellowships tenable only in African universities.

10 awards annually. Renewable up to 2 years. Contact Professor J.G.M. Massaquoi for an application.

711 — AMERICAN ASSOCIATION OF UNIVERSITY WOMEN EDUCATIONAL FOUNDATION (Selected Professions Fellowships)

Dept. 60, 2201 N. Dodge St.
Iowa City IA 52243-4030
319/337-1716, ext. 60
FAX 319/337-1204
Internet: www.aauw.org

AMOUNT: $5,000-$15,000

DEADLINE(S): JAN 2 (most); NOV 15 (engineering dissertation only)

FIELD(S): Architecture; Computer/Information Sciences; Engineering; Mathematics/Statistics

For women in final year of graduate study in fields where women's participation has been low. Must be US citizen or permanent resident. Special consideration given to applicants who show professional promise in innovative or neglected areas of research and/or practice in areas of public interest. Women in engineering master's programs are eligible to apply for either first or final year of study; special award for engineering doctoral students writing dissertation.

Applications available August-December.

712 — AMERICAN FOUNDATION FOR THE BLIND (Paul W. Ruckes Scholarship)

11 Penn Plaza, Ste. 300
New York NY 10001
212/502-7661 or TDD 212/502-7771
E-Mail: juliet@afb.org
Internet: www.afb.org

AMOUNT: $1,000

DEADLINE(S): APR 30

FIELD(S): Engineering, computer, physical, or life sciences

Open to blind or visually impaired undergraduate or graduate students pursuing degrees in the above fields. U.S. citizenship required.

Write to the above address or visit website for complete information.

713 — AMERICAN SOCIETY FOR ENGINEERING EDUCATION (Army Research Laboratory Postdoctoral Fellowships)

1818 N St., NW, Ste. 600
Washington DC 20036
202/331-3525
FAX: 202/265-8504
E-Mail: projects@asee.org
Internet: www.asee.org/fellowship/

AMOUNT: $45,000-$55,000 + travel/relocation allowance

DEADLINE(S): Varies

FIELD(S): Engineering; Physical Sciences

Postdoctoral fellowships for US citizens/permanent residents to do research at Army Research Laboratories. Candidates must have completed their Ph.D. prior to appointment. Program is designed to increase involvement of creative and highly trained scientists and engineers from academia and industry in scientific and technical areas of interest and relevance to the Army. Research proposal should include clear objective and defined outcome. Financial need NOT a factor.

15 awards annually. Renewable. Contact Sandi Crawford at ASEE for an application packet.

714 — AMERICAN SOCIETY OF CIVIL ENGINEERS (Trent R. Dames and William W. Moore Fellowship)

1801 Alexander Bell Drive
Reston VA 20191-4400
800/548-ASCE or 703/295-6000
FAX: 703/295-6333
E-Mail: student@asce.org
Internet: www.asce.org

AMOUNT: $5,000-$10,000

DEADLINE(S): FEB 20

FIELD(S): Geotechnical Engineering; Earth Sciences

For practicing engineers, earth scientists, professors, or graduate students to explore new applications of geotechnical engineering or the earth sciences to social, economic, environmental, and political issues. ASCE membership is not required.

Offered every two years (2000, 20002, etc.). See website or contact ASCE for an application between October and February.

715 — AMERICAN SOCIETY OF MECHANICAL ENGINEERS (ASME Student Loans)

Three Park Avenue
New York NY 10016-5990
212/591-8131
FAX: 212/591-7143
E-Mail: malaven@asme.org
Internet: www.asme.org

AMOUNT: $3,000

DEADLINE(S): APR 15; OCT 15

FIELD(S): Mechanical Engineering

Loans for ASME student members who are undergraduate or graduate students in a mechanical engineering or related program. Must be citizens or residents of the US, Canada, or Mexico. Loans are 1% below the Stafford loan rate. Financial need is considered.

100 awards annually. Not renewable. Contact Nellie Malave at above address for an application or membership information.

716 — ASSOCIATED WESTERN UNIVERSITIES, INC. (AWU Faculty Fellowships)

4190 South Highland Dr., Suite 211
Salt Lake City UT 84124-2600
801-273-8900

AMOUNT: Varies.

DEADLINE(S): FEB 15

FIELD(S): Engineering, Mathematics, Science, Technology

Research fellowships for qualified college and university faculty members to encourage participation and contribution to research at one of 62 cooperating facilities. It is not necessary to be enrolled at an AWU member institution. Collaborations that include graduate and/or undergraduate students are encouraged.

For detailed information and list of cooperating facilities, contact above location.

717 — ASSOCIATED WESTERN UNIVERSITIES, INC. (AWU Graduate Fellowship Program)

4190 South Highland Dr., Suite 211
Salt Lake City, UT 84124-2600
801/273-8900

AMOUNT: Stipend ($1,300 per month & up) + tuition assistance and travel allowance

DEADLINE(S): FEB 15

FIELD(S): Engineering, Mathematics, Science, Technology

Open to master's and doctoral degree candidates to conduct research toward a thesis or dissertation at one of more than 62 cooperating facilities. Institutional affiliation and citizenship restrictions may apply for some awards or facilities. It is not necessary to be enrolled at an AWU member institution to apply for a fellowship.

Write to the above address for complete information.

718 — ASSOCIATED WESTERN UNIVERSITIES, INC. (AWU Postgraduate Fellowship)

4190 South Highland Dr., Suite 211
Salt Lake City UT 84124-2600
801/273-8900

AMOUNT: Stipend established by the host facility and varies by experience and discipline.

DEADLINE(S): Varies (Two to three months before the starting date)

FIELD(S): Engineering, Mathematics, Science, Technology

For college and university graduates who have completed all institutional requirements for an advanced degree from an accredited college or university in the U.S. A commitment to a professional career in science or engineering research is expected.

U.S. citizenship or permanent resident status is required. Research is to be done at one of the 62 cooperating universities.

For detailed information and a list of cooperating facilities contact above address.

719 — ASSOCIATED WESTERN UNIVERSITIES, INC. (AWU Visiting Scientist Fellowships)

4190 South Highland Dr., Suite 211
Salt Lake City UT 84124-2600
801/273-8900

AMOUNT: Varies

DEADLINE(S): Varies (Two months prior to starting date)

FIELD(S): Engineering, Science, Mathematics, and Technology

Research fellowships for professionals with continued commitment to science and engineering. For use at one of 62 participating universities. US citizenship or permanent residency required.

For detailed information and list of cooperating facitilies contact above location.

720 — AT&T BELL LABORATORIES (Graduate Research Program For Women)

101 Crawfords Corner Road
Holmdel NJ 07733-3030
Written inquiry

AMOUNT: Full tuition & fees + $13,200 stipend per year

DEADLINE(S): JAN 15

FIELD(S): Engineering; Math; Sciences; Computer Science

For women students who have been accepted into an accredited doctoral program for the following fall. U.S. citizen or permanent resident.

Fellowships are renewable for up to 5 years of graduate study. Write to special programs manager-GRPW for complete information.

721 — BOEING (Polish Graduate Student Scholarship Program)

Phone for details
314/234-2149

AMOUNT: Tuition, books, and fees for three years

DEADLINE(S): Varies

FIELD(S): Scientific and technical fields

Scholarships for students from Poland to pursue graduate studies in scientific and technical areas at American colleges or universities.

Call Jim Schlueter at above telephone number.

722 — BRITISH FEDERATION OF WOMEN GRADUATES (M.H. Joseph Prize for Non-UK Citizens)

4 Mandeville Courtyard
142 Battersea Park Rd.
London SW11 4NB ENGLAND UK
PHONE/FAX: 0171/498 8037

AMOUNT: 500+ pounds sterling

DEADLINE(S): SEP 10

FIELD(S): Architecture; Engineering

For female graduate students of any nationality (except UK) who will pursue studies in Great Britain. Must have completed at least four academic terms or three semesters; award is not made for first year of research. Chief criteria is academic excellence and proven ability to carry out independent research. Postdoctoral studies also eligible.

1 award annually. Application fee of 12 pounds sterling required. Send a self-addressed, stamped envelope (or self-addressed envelope with international reply coupons) for an application. Results announced by end of October.

723 — BRITISH FEDERATION OF WOMEN GRADUATES (M.H. Joseph Prize for UK Citizens)

4 Mandeville Courtyard
142 Battersea Park Rd.
London SW11 4NB ENGLAND UK
PHONE/FAX: 0171/498 8037

AMOUNT: 500+ pounds sterling

DEADLINE(S): SEP 10

FIELD(S): Architecture; Engineering

For female UK citizens who plan to pursue graduate studies overseas. Must have completed at least four academic terms or three semesters; award is not made for first year of research. Chief criteria is academic excellence and proven ability to carry out independent research. Postdoctoral studies also eligible.

1 award annually. Application fee of 12 pounds sterling required. Send a self-addressed, stamped envelope (or self-addressed envelope with international reply coupons) for an application. Award announced at end of October.

724 — BROOKHAVEN NATIONAL LABORATORY (Post-doctoral Research Associateships)

Brookhaven National Laboratory
Upton L.I. NY 11973-5000
516/344-3336

AMOUNT: $29,000 minimum

DEADLINE(S): Varies

FIELD(S): Chemistry, Physics, Materials Science, Biology, Oceanography, and Biomedical Sciences.

Post-doctoral research associateships tenable at Brookhaven National Laboratory for research to promote fundamental and applied research in the above fields. A recent doctoral degree is required.

25 associateships per year. Renewable for two additional years.

725 — BROOKHAVEN WOMEN IN SCIENCE (Renate W. Chasman Scholarship)

PO Box 183
Upton NY 11973-5000
E-mail: pam@bnl.gov

AMOUNT: $2,000

DEADLINE(S): APR 1

FIELD(S): Natural Sciences; Engineering; Mathematics

Open ONLY to women who are residents of the boroughs of Brooklyn or Queens or the counties of Nassau or Suffolk in New York who are re-entering school after a period of study. For juniors, seniors, or first-year graduate students.

1 award annually. Not renewable. Contact Pam Mansfield at above location for an application. Phone calls are NOT accepted.

726 — DRAPER LABORATORY (Research Assistantships)

555 Technology Square
Cambridge MA 02139
617/258-2393
FAX: 617/258-2333
E-Mail: ed@draper.com

AMOUNT: Tuition + stipend

DEADLINE(S): Varies (same as MIT deadline)

FIELD(S): Engineering: Mechanical, Aero-Astro, Electrical; Computer Science; Operations Research

Open to US citizens pursuing graduate study in M.S. or Ph.D. programs at MIT.

30 awards annually. Renewable. Contact Draper Lab for an application.

727 — ENGINEERING GEOLOGY FOUNDATION

c/o John W. Williams, Dept. of Geology
San Jose State Univ., San Jose CA 95192-0102
408/924-5050

AMOUNT: Up to $1,000

DEADLINE(S): FEB 1

FIELD(S): Engineering Geology

Graduate scholarships for AEG members. Awards based on ability, scholarship, character, extracurricular activities, and potential for contributions to the profession.

Write for complete information.

728 — EPPLEY FOUNDATION FOR RESEARCH (Postdoctoral Research Grants)

245 Park Avenue, 40th Floor
New York NY 10167
Written inquiry

AMOUNT: Up to $25,000

DEADLINE(S): FEB 1; MAY 1; AUG 1; NOV 1

FIELD(S): Physical Sciences; Biological Sciences

Postdoctoral grants for original advanced research in any of the physical or biological sciences. Open to established research scientists who are attached to a recognized institution.

Write for complete information.

729 — FANNIE AND JOHN HERTZ FOUNDATION (Fellowship)

Box 5032
Livermore CA 94551-5032
925/373-1642
Internet: www.hertzfoundation.org

AMOUNT: $25,000 stipend/yr. + $15,000 (max.) tuition allowance/yr.

DEADLINE(S): NOV 5

FIELD(S): Applied Physical Sciences

Open to graduate students with a minimum 3.75 GPA for studies in applied physical sciences, including math, engineering, computer science, biology, oceanography, aeronautics, astronomy, physics, and earth science. Must be US citizen/permanent resident. Does not support study in pursuit of M.D. degree, although will support Ph.D. portion of a joint M.D./Ph.D. study program.

Renewable up to 5 years. Only 36 US schools are currently considered tenable. See website for an application and list of specific fields of study that are acceptable.

730 — FORD FOUNDATION/NATIONAL RESEARCH COUNCIL (Predoctoral/Dissertation Fellowships for Minorities)

2101 Constitution Ave.
Washington DC 20418
202/334-2872
E-Mail: infofell@nas.edu
Internet: http//www.nas.edu/fo/index.html

AMOUNT: $14,000 annual stipend + $6,000 grant to institution; $18,000 for dissertation fellowship

DEADLINE(S): NOV 3

FIELD(S): Most fields of study: sciences, humanities, engineering, behavioral science, social sciences, and computer science

Predoctoral and dissertation fellowships for students whose ethnicity is Alaskan Native, Black/African American, Mexican American/Chicano,

Native American Indian, Native Pacific Islander, or Puerto Rican. For research-based programs leading to careers in college teaching and research.

Contact above address or website.

731 — INSTITUTE OF PAPER SCIENCE AND TECHNOLOGY (Fellowship Program)

500 10th St. NW
Atlanta GA 30318
404/853-9500

AMOUNT: Full tuition plus $11,250 stipend

DEADLINE(S): MAR 15

FIELD(S): Chemistry; Chemical Engineering; Physics; Biology; Mechanical Engineering; Pulp and Paper Technology

Open to graduate students who are U.S., Mexican, or Canadian citizens or legal residents who hold a BS degree in the above fields. For a pursuit of a master of Science or Ph.D degree at the institute.

35 fellowships annually. Address inquiries to director of admissions.

732 — INSTITUTION OF ELECTRICAL ENGINEERS (Postgraduate Awards)

Savoy Place
London WC2R 0BL ENGLAND
0171 240 1871 Ext. 2211/2235
FAX: 0171 497 3609
E-Mail: scholarships@iee.org.uk
Internet: www.iee.org.uk/Awards/pgsum.htm

AMOUNT: 1,000-6,000 pounds/yr.

DEADLINE(S): SEP 1; SEP 30

FIELD(S): Engineering

Scholarships for postgraduate students pursuing degrees in engineering who are residents of the United Kingdom.

Check website or contact organization for application details.

733 — INSTITUTION OF MECHANICAL ENGINEERS (Various Grants and Scholarships)

Educational Svs.
Northgate Ave.
Bury St. Edmunds
Suffolk IP32 6BN ENGLAND UK
(01284) 763277
FAX: (01284) 704006
E-Mail: k_frost@imeche.org.uk
Internet: www.imeche.org.uk

AMOUNT: Varies

DEADLINE(S): None

FIELD(S): Mechanical Engineering

Grants for study or research in mechanical engineering or a related science. Some require membership or student membership in the Institution of Mechanical Engineers. Some require U.K. residency. Grants are normally for periods of less than one year.

See website or contact IMechE for details.

734 — INSTITUTION OF MINING AND METALLURGY (Bosworth Smith Trust Fund)

Hallam Court
77 Hallam St.
London W1N 6BR ENGLAND
0171 580 3802
FAX: 0171 436 5388

AMOUNT: 3,000 pounds sterling

DEADLINE(S): MAR 15

FIELD(S): Mining/Metallurgy

Grants available for the assistance of postgraduate research in metal mining, non-ferrous extraction metallurgy, or mineral dressing. Applications will be considered for grants toward working expenses, cost of visits to mines/plants, and purchase of apparatus. Awards judged on academic excellence and scholarship, NOT financial need. Preference is given to IMM members.

Contact P.J. Martindale at above address for an application.

735 — INSTITUTION OF MINING AND METALLURGY (Edgar Pam Fellowship)

Hallam Court
77 Hallam St.
London W1N 4BR ENGLAND
071 580 3802
FAX: 0171 436 5388

AMOUNT: 2,250 pounds sterling (max.)

DEADLINE(S): MAR 15

FIELD(S): Exploration Geology; Extractive Metallurgy

For postgraduate study in subjects related to above fields. Open to young graduates domiciled in Australia, Canada, New Zealand, South Africa, or the United Kingdom who wish to undertake advanced study or research in the U.K. Based on academic excellence and scholarship, NOT financial need. Preference will be given to IMM members.

Contact P.J. Martindale for an application.

736 — INSTITUTION OF MINING AND METALLURGY (G. Vernon Hobson Bequest)

Hallam Court
77 Hallam St.
London W1N 6BR ENGLAND
0171 580 3802
FAX: 0171 436 5388

AMOUNT: 2,000 pounds sterling

DEADLINE(S): MAR 15

FIELD(S): Teaching of Geology as applied to Mining

Awards for the advancement of teaching and practice of geology as applied to mining. Awards may be used for travel, research, or other appropriate endeavor. Based on academic excellence and scholarship. Preference given to IMM members.

Contact P.J. Martindale at above address for an application.

737 — INSTITUTION OF MINING AND METALLURGY (Mining Club Award)

Hallam Court
77 Hallam St.
London W1N 6BR ENGLAND
0171 580 3802
FAX: 0171 436 5388

AMOUNT: 1,000 pounds sterling

DEADLINE(S): MAR 15

FIELD(S): Minerals Industry

Open to British subjects between the ages of 21 and 35 who are actively engaged (postgraduate study or in employment) in the minerals industry. Award is for travel to study mineral industry operations in UK or overseas. Based on academic excellence and scholarship, NOT financial need. Preference given to IMM members.

Contact P.J. Martindale at above address for an application.

738 — INSTITUTION OF MINING AND METALLURGY (Stanley Elmore Fellowship Fund)

Hallam Court
77 Hallam St.
London W1N 6BR ENGLAND
0171 580 3802
FAX 0171 436 5388

AMOUNT: 12,000-16,000 pounds sterling

DEADLINE(S): MAR 15

FIELD(S): Mining; Metallurgy

Fellowships tenable at a United Kingdom university for research into all branches of extractive metallurgy and mineral processing, and in special cases, for expenditure related to such research. Based on academic excellence and scholarship, NOT financial need. Preference given to IMM members.

Contact P.J. Martindale at above address for an application.

739 — MATHESON GAS PRODUCTS FOUNDATION (Scholarships)

PO Box 624
959 Rte. 46 E.
Parsippany NJ 07054-0624
Internet: www.mathesongas.com

AMOUNT: $5,000

DEADLINE(S): None

FIELD(S): Chemistry; Physics; Chemical Engineering; Material Science; Semiconductor Engineering

Open to financially needy graduate students who are African American, Latino, Asian, Native American, or female. Must be US citizens/permanent residents studying in above fields or related area.

Send self-addressed, stamped envelope to Jerry Cantrella, Director of Personnel, for an application.

740 — NATIONAL AERONAUTICS AND SPACE ADMINISTRATION (Graduate Student Researcher's Program-Underrepresented Minority Focus)

Mail Code FEH
NASA Headquarters
Washington, DC 20546
202/453-8344

AMOUNT: $22,000 1st year, renewable up to 3 years

DEADLINE(S): FEB 1

FIELD(S): Science, Engineering, Mathematics

For underrepresented minority groups in the fields of science and engineering (including African-Americans, American Indians, Hispanics, and Pacific Islanders), who may end up with a career in space science and/or aerospace technology. Must be US citizen and enrolled or accepted as a full-time graduate student at an accredited US college or university.

Write for complete information.

741 — NATIONAL ASSOCIATION OF WATER COMPANIES—NEW JERSEY CHAPTER (Scholarship)

Elizabethtown Water Co.
600 South Ave.
Westfield NJ 07090
908/654-1234
FAX: 908/232-2719

AMOUNT: $2,500

DEADLINE(S): APR 1

FIELD(S): Business Administration; Biology; Chemistry; Engineering; Communications

For U.S. citizens who have lived in NJ at least 5 years and plan a career in the investor-owned water utility industry in disciplines such as those above. Must be undergrad or graduate student in a 2- or 4-year NJ college or university.

GPA of 3.0 or better required. Contact Gail P. Brady for complete information.

742 — NATIONAL PHYSICAL SCIENCE CONSORTIUM (Graduate Fellowships for Minorities & Women in the Physical Sciences)

MSC 3NPS
Box 30001
Las Cruces NM 88003-8001
800/952-4118 or 505/646-6038
FAX: 505/646-6097
E-Mail: npse@nmsu.edu
Internet: www.npsc.org

AMOUNT: $12,500 (years 1-4); $15,000 (years 5-6)

DEADLINE(S): NOV 5

FIELD(S): Astronomy; Chemistry; Computer Science; Geology; Materials Science; Mathematics; Physics

Open to "all US citizens" with an emphasis on Black, Hispanic, Native American, and female students. Must be pursuing graduate studies and have a minimum 3.0 GPA.

Renewable up to 6 years. See website or contact NPSC for an application.

743 — NATIONAL SOCIETY OF BLACK ENGINEERS (Scholarships)

1454 Duke St.
Alexandria VA 22314
703/549-2207
FAX: 703/683-5312
E-Mail: nsbehq@nsbe.org
Internet: www.nsbe.org

AMOUNT: Varies

DEADLINE(S): Varies

FIELD(S): Engineering and engineering technologies

Programs for black and other ethnic minorities in the fields of engineering and the engineering technologies. Organization offers pre-college programs, scholarships, career fairs, a journal, a newsletter, etc.

Contact organization for details.

744 — OAK RIDGE ASSOCIATED UNIVERSITIES (Laboratory Graduate Research Participation Program)

P.O. Box 117
Oak Ridge TN 37831-0117
423/576-4813

AMOUNT: $1,000-$1,200/mo. + allowance for dependents + tuition and fees reimbursement to a max. of $3,500/yr.

DEADLINE(S): Ongoing

FIELD(S): Life sciences, physical, and social sciences, mathematics, and engineering

For graduate students in one of the fields listed above who have completed all degree requirements except thesis or dissertation research. For full-time research under the joint direction of the major professor and a DOE staff member at one of various locations, primarily in the South. For six to twelve months.

Funded through U.S. Dept. of Energy, Office of Energy Reseach, and Office of Fossil Energy. Write for complete information.

745 — OAK RIDGE ASSOCIATED UNIVERSITIES (National Science Foundation Graduate Research Fellowships)

PO Box 3010
Oak Ridge TN 37831-3010
423/241-4300
FAX: 423/241-4513
E-Mail: nsfgrfp@orau.gov
Internet: www.orau.gov/nsf/nsffel.htm

AMOUNT: $15,000 stipend + $10,500 tuition allowance

DEADLINE(S): NOV 4

FIELD(S): Science; Math; Engineering; Computer Science

Three-year fellowships for graduate study leading to research-based master's or doctoral degrees in the above fields. Must be US citizens, nationals, or permanent residents at the time of application. Fellowships are awarded on the basis of ability. Women, minorities, and those with disabilities are strongly encouraged to apply. One-time International Research Travel Allowance available.

1,000 awards annually. Contact Jeannette Bouchard for an application/more information.

746 — OAK RIDGE INSTITUTE FOR SCIENCE AND EDUCATION (Applied Health Physics Fellowship Program)

P.O. Box 117
Oak Ridge TN 37831-0117
423/576-2194 or 423/576-9279
E-Mail: COXRE@ORAU.GOV or GRADFELL@ORAU.GOV

AMOUNT: $14,400 stipend + tuition and fees up to $9,000/yr paid to university + transportation costs up to $300/month

DEADLINE(S): JAN 26

FIELD(S): Engineering, mathematics, physical and life sciences

Fellowship in applied health physics to implement DOE's nuclear energy-related mission. Candidates must have B.A. degree in life or physical sciences, engineering, or mathematics. Recipients are subject to a service obligation of one year of full-time employment in a DOE facility for each academic year of fellowhip award.

For details and application, contact above location.

747 — OAK RIDGE INSTITUTE FOR SCIENCE AND EDUCATION (Industrial Hygiene Graduate Fellowship Program)

P.O. Box 117
Oak Ridge TN 37831-0117
423-576-9655
FAX: 423/576-8293
E-Mail: kinneym@orau.gov
AMOUNT:
DEADLINE(S): JAN 26
FIELD(S): Industrial Hygiene

A fellowship for first-year master's candidates who have undergraduate degrees in physical, life, environmental, or health sciences or enginering and who wish to pursue studies in industrial hygiene.

For details and application, contact above location.

748 — OAK RIDGE INSTITUTE FOR SCIENCE AND EDUCATION (Professional Internship Program/Oak Ridge National Laboratory)

P.O. Box 117
Oak Ridge TN 37831-0117
423/576-3426
423/576-3427
AMOUNT: $210 to $300/week + travel, tuition, and fees
DEADLINE(S): FEB 5; JUN 1; OCT 1
FIELD(S): Chemistry, environmental science, geology, hydrogeology, hydrology, chemical engineering, civil engineering, environmental engineering, mechanical engineering, computer science (technical database development)

Opportunities for graduates and undergraduates to participate in energy-related research projects that correlate with their academic and career goals. For 3 to 12 consecutive months.

Funded through Oak Ridge National Laboratory.

749 — OAK RIDGE INSTITUTE FOR SCIENCE AND EDUCATION (Professional Internship Program/Pittsburgh Energy Technology Center)

P.O. Box 117
Oak Ridge TN 37831-0117
423/576-3426
423/576-3427
AMOUNT: $235 to $325/week + travel, tuition, and fees
DEADLINE(S): FEB 5; JUN 1; OCT 1

FIELD(S): Chemistry, physics, environmental science, geology, chemical or environmental engineering, computer science, or statistics.

Opportunities for graduates and undergraduates to participate in fossil energy-related research projects that correlate with their academic and career goals. For 3 to 12 consecutive months.

Funded through U.S. Dept. of Energy, Office of Fossil Energy, and Pittsburgh Energy Technology Center.

750 — OAK RIDGE INSTITUTE FOR SCIENCE AND EDUCATION (Professional Internship Program/Savannah River Site)

P.O. Box 117
Oak Ridge TN 37831-0117
423/576-3426
423/576-3427
AMOUNT: $260 to $340/week + travel
DEADLINE(S): FEB 5; JUN 1; SEP 1
FIELD(S): Chemistry, computer science, environmental science, geology, engineering, or physics

Opportunities for high school junior and seniors, undergraduates, and graduates to participate in research projects that correlate with their academic majors and career goals. For 3 to 12 consecutive months at the Savannah River Site, SC.

Funded through the Savannah River Site, SC.

751 — OAK RIDGE INSTITUTE FOR SCIENCE AND EDUCATION (Science and Engineering Research Semester)

P.O. Box 117
Oak Ridge TN 37831-0117
423/576-2358
423/576-2310
AMOUNT: $225/week + travel + housing
DEADLINE(S): OCT; MAR
FIELD(S): Computer science, physical sciences, environmental and life sciences, and mathematics

Opportunities for high school junior and seniors and a few slots for graduates to participate in energy-related with laboratory scientists at Oak Ridge National Laboratory, TN. One semester with possibility of summer extension. Available two times a year.

Funded through the U.S. Dept. of Energy, Office of Energy Research.

752 — OAK RIDGE INSTITUTE FOR SCIENCE AND EDUCATION, U.S. DEPARTMENT OF ENERGY (Fusion Energy Sciences Fellowship Program)

105 Mitchell Road, MS-16
Oak Ridge TN 37831
423/576-2600

FAX: 423/576-8293
E-Mail: johnsons@orau.giv
AMOUNT: $1,300/mo. + $200/mo.
DEADLINE(S): JAN 26 (Received, not postmarked)
FIELD(S): Fusion energy sciences

Fellowships for Ph.D. candidates to pursue a degree in the fusion energy sciences at one of several participating universities throughout the U.S. Must be U.S. citizens or permanent residents. For students entering first or second year of graduate study. Must have B.A. degree in related field, such as applied mathematics or physics; chemical, electrical, mechanical, metallurgical, or nuclear engineering; or materials science.

Contact Sandra Johnson at above location for details and list of participating institutions.

753 — OAK RIDGE INSTITUTE FOR SCIENCE AND EDUCATION/U.S. DEPT. OF ENERGY (Office of Civilian Radioactive Waste Management Fellowship)

P.O. Box 117
Oak Ridge TN 37831-0117
423/576-0128
FAX: 423/576-8293
E-Mail: drostp@orau.gov
AMOUNT: $14,000/yr.
DEADLINE(S): JAN 16 (Received, not postmarked)
FIELD(S): Physical or life sciences, math, or engineering

Fellowships for graduate students at various participating universities to conduct research in the management of spent nuclear fuel and high-level raqdioactive waste. For M.A. and Ph.D. candidates. For up to 48 months. Must be U.S. citizen or permanent resident.

Funded through U.S. Department of Energy, Office of Civilian Radioactive Waste Management. Contact or call Ms. Portia Drost, MS-16, at above address for details.

754 — OAK RIDGE INSTITUTE FOR SCIENCE AND EDUCATION (Nuclear Engineering & Health Physics Fellowship Program)

105 Mitchell Rd. MS-16
Oak Ridge TN 37831-0117
423/576-2600 or 423/241-2890
E-Mail: johnsons@orau.gov or daltonj@arou.gov
AMOUNT: $14,400/yr.
DEADLINE(S): JAN 26
FIELD(S): Engineering, physical and life sciences

Fellowships in nuclear engineering or applied health physics to implement DOE's nuclear energy-related mission. Candidates must have B.A. degree in life or physical sciences or engineering.

For details and application, contact Sandra Johnson or Jennifer Dalton at above location.

755 — OPEN SOCIETY INSTITUTE (Environmental Management Fellowships)

400 West 59th St.
New York NY 10019
212/548-0600 or 212/757-2323
FAX: 212/548-4679 or 212/548-4600
Internet: www.soros.org/efp.html

AMOUNT: Fees, room, board, living stipend, textbooks, international transportation, health insurance

DEADLINE(S): NOV 15

FIELD(S): Earth sciences, natural sciences, humanities (exc. language), anthropology, sociology, mathematics, or engineering

Two-year fellowships for use in selected universities in the U.S. for international students. For students/professionals in fields related to environmental policy, legislation, and remediation techniques applicable to their home countries.

To apply, contact your local Soros Foundation or Open Society Institute. Further details on website.

756 — ROYAL SOCIETY OF EDINBURGH (BP Research Fellowships)

22/24 George St.
Edinburgh EH2 2PQ SCOTLAND
0131 225 6057
FAX: 0131 220 6889
E-Mail: rse@rse.org.uk

AMOUNT: 17,606 to 26,508 pounds sterling

DEADLINE(S): MAR 10

FIELD(S): Mechanical, Chemical, or Control Engineering; Organic Chemistry; Solid State Physics; Information Technology; Geologic Sciences

Research fellowships to Scotland higher education institutions. For post-doctoral researchers age 35 or under on the date of appointment (usually Oct. 1). For research in above disciplines.

Write for complete information.

757 — SKIDMORE, OWINGS & MERRILL FOUNDATION (Mechanical/Electrical Traveling Fellowship Program)

224 S. Michigan Ave., Suite 1000
Chicago IL 60604
312/554-9090
FAX: 312/360-4545

AMOUNT: $7,500

DEADLINE(S): Varies (consult with school)

FIELD(S): Architectural Engineering, Electrical Engineering, or Mechanical

Candidates must have received a B.A. or M.A. degree in one of the above fields. It enables the Fellow to travel in order to observe and analyze innovative building systems and technologies anywhere in the world.

Write for complete information.

758 — SOCIETY OF NAVAL ARCHITECTS AND MARINE ENGINEERS (SNAME Graduate Scholarships)

601 Pavonia Ave., Ste. 400
Jersey City NJ 07306
201/798-4800
FAX: 201/798-4975
Internet: www.sname.org

AMOUNT: Varies

DEADLINE(S): FEB 1

FIELD(S): Naval Architecture; Naval/Marine Engineering

Open to graduate students studying naval architechture, naval/marine engineering, or related fields at accredited institutions. Preference given to applicants who plan a career in the marine field. Must be US or Canadian citizen. One award is reserved for older, re-entry applicants who have five or more years of marine work experience after receiving bachelor's degree.

Contact Barbara Trentham at SNAME for an application.

759 — THE DAPHNE JACKSON MEMORIAL FELLOWSHIPS TRUST (Fellowships in Science/ Engineering)

School of Physical Sciences
Dept. of Physics
University of Surrey
Guildford, Surrey
GU2 5XH ENGLAND UK
01483 259166
FAX: 01483 259501
E-Mail: J.Woolley@surrey.ac.uk
Internet: www.sst.ph.ic.ac.uk/trust/

AMOUNT: Varies

DEADLINE(S): Varies

FIELD(S): Science or engineering, including information sciences

Fellowships to enable well-qualified and highly motivated scientists and engineers to return to appropriate careers following a career break due to family comitments. May be used on a flexible, part-time basis. Tenable at various U.K. universities.

See website and/or contact organization for details.

760 — U.S. DEPARTMENT OF TRANSPORTATION (Dwight D. Eisenhower Transportation Fellowships)

U.S. Dept. of Transportation
Fed. Hwy. Admin.
6300 Georgetown Pike, HHI-20
McLean VA 22101-2296
703/235-0538

AMOUNT: Varies

DEADLINE(S): FEB

FIELD(S): Transportation—such majors as chemistry; materials science; corrosion; civil, chemical, & electronics engineering; structures; human factors; computer science; psychology.

Research fellowships for undergrads and grad students at any Dept. of Transportation facility or selected IHE. For three to twelve months. Research must focus on transportation-related research and development in the above fields.

Contact Ilene Payne, Director, Universities and grants Programs at above location for details.

761 — UNIVERSITY OF MANCHESTER INSTITUTE OF SCIENCE & TECHNOLOGY (Mohn Research Fellowship)

PO Box 88
Manchester M60 1QD England
0161-236-3311
FAX: 0161-200-3635

AMOUNT: Approx. 4,000 pounds sterling

DEADLINE(S): APR 30

FIELD(S): Metallurgy/Materials Science; Chemical Engineering

Post-graduate fellowships for research in engineering technology (at UMIST). Preference will be given to those studying in the areas listed above.

For more information, contact the registrar at UMIST.

762 — WOMEN'S AUXILIARY TO THE AMERICAN INSTITUTE OF MINING METALLURGICAL & PETROLEUM ENGINEERS (WAAIME Scholarship Loan Fund)

345 E. 47th St., 14th Floor
New York NY 10017-2304
212/705-7692

AMOUNT: Varies

DEADLINE(S): MAR 15

FIELD(S): Earth Sciences, as related to the Minerals Industry

Open to undergraduate juniors and seniors and grad students, whose majors relate to an interest in the minerals industry. Eligible applicants receive a scholarship loan for all or part of their education. Recipients repay only 50%, with no interest charges.

Repayment to begin by 6 months after graduation and be completed within 6 years. Write to WAAIME Scholarship Loan Fund (address above) for complete information.

763 — XEROX TECHNICAL MINORITY SCHOLARSHIP (School-Year Tuition)

907 Culver Road
Rochester NY 14609
www.xerox.com/employment

AMOUNT: Up to $5,000 (varies according to tuition and academic excellence)
DEADLINE(S): SEP 15
FIELD(S): Various engineering and science disclipines

Scholarships for minorities enrolled full-time in a technical degree program at the bachelor level or above. Must be African-American, Native American, Hispanic, or Asian. Recipient may not have tuition or related expenses covered by other scholarships or grants.

If above requirements are met, obtain application from website or address above. Your financial aid office must fill out the bottom half of the form. Send completed application, your resume and a cover letter to Xerox Technical Minority Scholarship Program at above address.

764 — XEROX TECHNICAL MINORITY SCHOLARSHIP (Summer Employment Program)

Xerox Square
Rochester NY 14644
Written inquiry

AMOUNT: Up to $5,000 (varies according to tuition and academic excellence)
DEADLINE(S): SEP 15
FIELD(S): Various engineering and science disclipines

Scholarships for minorities enrolled in a technical degree program at the bachelor level or above. Must be African-American, Native American, Hispanic, or Asian. Xerox will match your skills with a sponsoring organization that will offer a meaningful summer work experience complimenting your academic learning.

If above requirements are met, send your resume and a cover letter to Xerox Corporation Corporate Employment and College Relations Technical Mfinority Scholarship Program to above address.

SCHOOL OF HUMANITIES

765 — AFRICAN NETWORK OF SCIENTIFIC AND TECHNOLOGICAL INSTITUTIONS - ANSTI (Postgraduate Fellowships)

PO Box 30592
Nairobi Kenya AFRICA
254-2-621234 or 254-2-622619/20
FAX: 254-2-215991
E-Mail: j.massaquoi@unesco.org OR ANSTI@Net2000ke.com
AMOUNT: Fees, subsistence, & international travel
DEADLINE(S): JUN
FIELD(S): Basic & Engineering Sciences

Scholarships for postgraduate studies outside of applicant's home country. Must be African nationals not older than 36 years of age and hold a good bachelor's degree (at least 2nd class upper division). Applicants should apply for admission to host university as soon as possible. Fellowships tenable only in African universities.

10 awards annually. Renewable up to 2 years. Contact Professor J.G.M. Massaquoi for an application.

766 — AMERICAN COUNCIL OF LEARNED SOCIETIES (ACLS Fellowships)

Office of Fellowshops & Grants
228 E. 45th St.
New York NY 10017
Written Inquiry
AMOUNT: Up to $20,000
DEADLINE(S): SEP 30
FIELD(S): Humanities, Social Sciences, and other areas having predominately humanistic emphasis

Open to U.S. citizens or legal residents who hold the Ph.D or its equivalent. Fellowships are designed to help scholars devote 6 to 12 continuous months to full-time research.

Write for complete information.

767 — AMERICAN FOUNDATION FOR THE BLIND (Paul W. Ruckes Scholarship)

11 Penn Plaza, Ste. 300
New York NY 10001
212/502-7661 or TDD 212/502-7771
E-Mail: juliet@afb.org
Internet: www.afb.org
AMOUNT: $1,000
DEADLINE(S): APR 30
FIELD(S): Engineering, computer, physical, or life sciences

Open to blind or visually impaired undergraduate or graduate students pursuing degrees in the above fields. U.S. citizenship required.

Write to the above address or visit website for complete information.

768 — AMERICAN INSTITUTE OF INDIAN STUDIES (Senior Research Fellowships)

1130 E. 59th St.
Chicago IL 60637
773/702-8638
E-Mail: aiis@uchicago.edu
Internet: kaladarshan.arts.ohio-state.edu/aiis/aiishomepahge.htm
AMOUNT: $6,000-$14,000 + travel
DEADLINE(S): JUL 1
FIELD(S): Humanities

Postdoctoral fellowships open to US citizens or foreign nationals in residence at American colleges and universities. For specialists in Asian/Indian studies. Fellows must have Ph.D. and must agree to be formally affiliated with an Indian university while in India.

20-25 awards annually. Contact AIIS for an application.

769 — AMERICAN RESEARCH INSTITUTE IN TURKEY (ARIT Fellowship Program)

Univ Penn Museum
33rd & Spruce Streets
Philadelphia PA 19104-6324
215/898-3474
FAX: 215/898-0657
E-Mail: leinwand@sas.upenn.edu
Internet: mec.sas.upenn.edu/ARIT
AMOUNT: Varies
DEADLINE(S): NOV 15
FIELD(S): Humanities; Social Sciences; Turkish Studies

Two-month to one-year fellowships are for postdoctoral scholars & advanced graduate students engaged in research on ancient, medieval, or modern times in Turkey, in any field of the humanities & social sciences. Predoctoral students must have fulfilled all preliminary requirements for doctorate except dissertation. Applicants must maintain an affiliation with an educational institution in the US or Canada. Must submit curriculum vitae, research proposal, & referees.

Contact ARIT for an application.

770 — AMERICAN RESEARCH INSTITUTE IN TURKEY (Mellon Research Fellowships for Central and Eastern European Scholars in Turkey)

Univ Penn Museum
33rd & Spruce Streets
Philadelphia PA 19104-6324
215/898-3474
FAX: 215/898-0657
E-Mail: leinwand@sas.upenn.edu
Internet: mec.sas.upenn.edu/ARIT
AMOUNT: Stipend up to $10,500 for 2-3 month project (includes travel, living expenses, work-related costs)
DEADLINE(S): MAR 5
FIELD(S): Humanities; Social Sciences

For Czech, Hungarian, Polish, Slovakian, Bulgarian, and Romanian scholars holding a Ph.D. or equivalent who are engaged in advanced research in any field of the social sciences or the humanities involving Turkey. Must be permanent residents of these countries and must obtain formal permission for any research to be carried out.

3 awards annually. Previous fellows not eligible. See website or write to above address for details.

771 — AMERICAN RESEARCH INSTITUTE IN TURKEY (National Endowment for the Humanities Fellowships for Research in Turkey)

Univ Penn Museum
33rd & Spruce Streets
Philadelphia PA 19104-6324
215/898-3474
FAX: 215/898-0657
E-Mail: leinwand@sas.upenn.edu
Internet: mec.sas.upenn.edu/ARIT

AMOUNT: $10,000-$30,000

DEADLINE(S): NOV 15

FIELD(S): Humanities

Postdoctoral fellowships are to conduct research in Turkey for four to twelve months. Fields of study cover all periods in the general range of the humanities, including humanistically oriented aspects of the social sciences, prehistory, history, art, archaeology, literature, linguistics, and cultural history. There are two institutes, one in Istanbul and one in Ankara. Both have residential facilities for fellows and provide general assistance.

2-3 awards annually. Contact ARIT for an application. Notification by January 25th.

772 — AUSTRALIAN FEDERATION OF UNIVERSITY WOMEN - WESTERN AUSTRALIA (Joyce Riley Bursary)

Bursary Liaison Officer
PO Box 48
Nedlands WA 6909 AUSTRALIA
Written Inquiry

AMOUNT: Aus$1,700 - Aus$2,750

DEADLINE(S): JUL 31

FIELD(S): Humanities; Social Sciences

To support women graduates of a Western Australian university to complete a higher degree or post-doctoral research in Humanities or Social Sciences at a recognized university in any country.

Membership in AFUW or in IFUW is required. Contact above location for further information.

773 — AUSTRALIAN FEDERATION OF UNIVERSITY WOMEN - WESTERN AUSTRALIA (Joyce Riley Bursary)

Bursary Liaison Officer
PO Box 48
Nedlands WA 6009 AUSTRALIA
Written Inquiry

AMOUNT: Aus$1,700 - Aus$2,750

DEADLINE(S): JUL 31

FIELD(S): Humanities; Social Sciences

To support women graduates of a recognized university to complete a higher degree or post-doctoral research at a university in Western Australia.

Membership in AFUW or in IFUW is required. Write to above address for complete information.

774 — BUSINESS & PROFESSIONAL WOMEN'S FOUNDATION (BPW Career Advancement Scholarship Program)

2012 Massachusetts Ave., NW
Washington DC 20036-1070
202/293-1200, ext. 169
FAX: 202/861-0298
Internet: www.bpwusa.org

AMOUNT: $500-$1,000

DEADLINE(S): APR 15

FIELD(S): Biology, Science, Education, Engineering, Social Science, Paralegal, Humanities, Business, Math, Computers, Law, MD, DD

For women (US citizens) aged 25+ accepted into accredited program at US institution (+Puerto Rico & Virgin Islands). Must graduate within 12 to 24 months from the date of grant and demonstrate critical finanacial need. Must have a plan to upgrade skills, train for a new career field, or to enter/re-enter the job market.

Full- or part-time study. For info see website or send business-sized, self-addressed, double-stamped envelope.

775 — CALEDONIAN RESEARCH FOUNDATION (European Visiting Fellowships in the Humanities)

39 Castle St.
Edinburgh EH2 3BH SCOTLAND UK
0131 225 1200
FAX: 0131 225 4412
E-Mail: crf@murraybeith.co.uk

AMOUNT: Varies

DEADLINE(S): MAR 10

FIELD(S): Humanities

Awards provide funding to postdoctoral scholars in the Arts & Letters to spend up to six months doing research and participating in the academic life of host

institutions. Must be academic staff under age 60 who are either working in Scotland or are from continental European countries.

8 awards annually. Contact CRF for an application.

776 — CANADIAN FEDERATION OF UNIVERSITY WOMEN (Margaret Dale Philp Award)

251 Bank St., Ste. 600
Ottawa Ontario K2P 1X3 CANADA
613/234-2732
Internet: www.cfuw.ca

AMOUNT: $1,000

DEADLINE(S): NOV 15

FIELD(S): Humanities; Social Sciences

For women who reside in Canada and are pursuing graduate studies in the humanities or social sciences, with special consideration given to study in Canadian history. Must hold at least a bachelor's degree or equivalent from a recognized university and have been accepted into, or be currently enrolled in the proposed program and place of study.

$20 filing fee. Contact CFUW for an application after August 1st. Candidates will be notified by May 31st. Funded by CFUW/Kitchener-Waterloo.

777 — CHARLES A. AND ANNE MORROW LINDBERGH FOUNDATION (Grants for Research Projects)

2150 Third Ave., N, Ste. 310
Anoka MN 55303-2200
612/576-1596
FAX: 612/576-1664
E-Mail: lindbergh@isd.net
Internet: www.isd.net/lindbergh

AMOUNT: $10,580 (max.)

DEADLINE(S): JUN 15

FIELD(S): Aviation; Aerospace; Agriculture; Education; Arts; Humanities; Biomedical Research; Exploration; Health & Population Sciences; Intercultural Communication; Waste Disposal Minimization & Management.; Adaptive Technology; Conservation

Open to individuals whose proposed projects represent a significant contribution toward the achievement of balance between the advance of technology and preservation of the natural environment. Financial need NOT a factor. Funding is NOT for tuition.

10 awards annually. See website for application.

778 — CORNELL UNIVERSITY (Postdoctoral Fellowships)

c/o Society for the Humanities
A.D. White House
27 East Ave.
Ithaca NY 14853-1101

607/255-9274
FAX: 607/255-1422
E-Mail: humctr-mailbox@cornell.edu
Internet: www.arts.cornell.edu/sochum

AMOUNT: $32,000/yr.

DEADLINE(S): OCT 21

FIELD(S): Humanities

Annual postdoctoral fellowships at Cornell University. Each year there is a focal theme with fellows working on topics related to that theme. Their approach to the humanities should be broad enough to appeal to students and scholars alike. Applicant must have received Ph.D. degree at time of application. Financial need NOT a factor.

8 awards annually. Not renewable. Contact the Program Administrator for an application.

779 — EMORY COLLEGE (Andrew W. Mellon Post-doctoral Fellowships in the Humanities)

Dean Irwin T. Hyatt
Emory University
300 White Hall
Atlanta GA 30322-2110
404/727-6059

AMOUNT: Varies

DEADLINE(S): Varies

FIELD(S): Humanities

Fellowships at Emory are open to non-tenured junior scholars who have had their Ph.Ds for less than three years. Limited teaching and departmental duties. Opportunity to develop scholarly research. Duration is one year and renewable for another year.

Write for complete information.

780 — FORD FOUNDATION/NATIONAL RESEARCH COUNCIL (Postdoctoral Fellowship for Minorities)

National Research Council
2101 Constitution Ave.
Washington DC 20418
202/334-2860
E-Mail: infofell@nas.edu
Internet: http//www.nas.edu/fo/index.html

AMOUNT: $25,000 + relocation and research allowance

DEADLINE(S): JAN 3

FIELD(S): Life and physical sciences, mathematics, engineering sciences, behavioral and social sciences, and the humanities

For U.S. citizens who received a Ph.D or Sc.D in the last 7 years and who are Native Amer. Indian or Alaskan, Black/African American, Mexican American, Native Pacific Islander, or Puerto Rican and who are or plan to be in a teaching or research career.

Contact above website or address for complete information.

781 — FORD FOUNDATION/NATIONAL RESEARCH COUNCIL (Predoctoral/ Dissertation Fellowships for Minorities)

2101 Constitution Ave.
Washington DC 20418
202/334-2872
E-Mail: infofell@nas.edu
Internet: http//www.nas.edu/fo/index.html

AMOUNT: $14,000 annual stipend + $6,000 grant to institution; $18,000 for dissertation fellowship

DEADLINE(S): NOV 3

FIELD(S): Most fields of study: sciences, humanities, engineering, behavioral science, social sciences, and computer science

Predoctoral and dissertation fellowships for students whose ethnicity is Alaskan Native, Black/African American, Mexican American/Chicano, Native American Indian, Native Pacific Islander, or Puerto Rican. For research-based programs leading to careers in college teaching and research.

Contact above address or website.

782 — FREEDOM FROM RELIGION FOUNDATION (Student Essay Contest)

PO Box 750
Madison WI 53701
608/256-5800
Internet: www.infidels.org/org/ffrf

AMOUNT: $1,000; $500; $250

DEADLINE(S): JUL 15

FIELD(S): Humanities; English; Education; Philosophy; Science

Essay contest on topics related to church-state entanglement in public schools or growing up a "freethinker" in religious-oriented society. Topics change yearly, but all are on general theme of maintaining separation of church and state. New topics available in February. For high school seniors & currently enrolled college/technical students. Must be US citizen.

Send SASE to address above for complete information. Please indicate whether wanting information for college competition or high school. Information will be sent when new topics are announced each February. See website for details.

783 — FRIENDS OF THE UNIVERSITY OF WISCONSIN (Madison Libraries Humanities Grants-in-Aid)

728 State St.
Madison WI 53706
608/262-3243 or 608/265-2750 (ans. mach.)

AMOUNT: $1,000/mo.

DEADLINE(S): APR 1; OCT 1

FIELD(S): Research in the humanities appropriate to the collections

Two grants-in-aid annually for one-month's study in such areas as the history of science from the Middle Ages through the Enlightenment, a collection of avant-garde AMerican "little magazines," a American women writers to 1920, Scandinavian and Germanic literature, Dutch post-Reformation theology and church history, French political pamphlets of the 16th & 17th centuries, and many other fields.

Must be in Ph.D. program or be able to deomonstrate a recored of solid intellectual accomplishment. Must live outside a 75-mile radius of Madison, Wisconsin, U.S. Call/write for details.

784 — GETTY RESEARCH INSTITUTE FOR THE HISTORY OF ART AND THE HUMANITIES (Fellowships)

1200 Getty Center Dr., Ste. 1100
Los Angeles CA 90049-1688
310/440-7392
FAX: 310/440-7782
E-Mail: residentialgrants@getty.edu
Internet: www.getty.edu/gri/scholars

AMOUNT: $18,000 (doctoral); $22,000 (postdoctoral)

DEADLINE(S): NOV 1

FIELD(S): Arts; Humanities; Social Sciences

Open to doctoral and postdoctoral scholars whose areas of research fall within the year's chosen theme. Predoctoral candidates should expect to complete dissertations during the fellowship year. Postdoctorates should have received doctorate in humanities or social sciences within the last three years and be rewriting dissertations for publication. Tenable at the Getty Research Institute in Los Angeles, CA.

Contact Getty Institute for an application and current theme.

785 — GIRTON COLLEGE (Fellowships)

Secretary to the Electors
Cambridge CB3 OJG ENGLAND UK
338 999

AMOUNT: 9,000 pounds sterling (pre-Ph.D.) 11,100-11,700 pounds sterling (post-Ph.D.)

DEADLINE(S): Varies (usually around Oct. 4)

FIELD(S): Humanities or Science

Applications are invited for research fellowships at Girton College, Cambridge, Great Britain. Tenable for three years beginning Oct 1. The fellowships are open to men and women graduates of any university.

A statement of 1,000 words maximum outlining the research to be undertaken must be submitted. Write for form and complete information.

786 — GLADYS KRIEBLE DELMAS FOUNDATION (Predoctoral & Postdoctoral Grants in Venice & the Veneto)

521 5th Avenue, Suite 1612
New York NY 10175-1699
212/687-0011
FAX: 212/687-8877
E-Mail: DelmasFdtn@aol.com
Internet: www.delmas.org

AMOUNT: $500-$12,500

DEADLINE(S): DEC 15

FIELD(S): Research of Venice and the former Venetian empire and study of contemporary Venetian society and culture.

Pre- and postdoctoral grants for historical research on Venice. Humanities and social sciences are eligible areas of study, including archaeology, architecture, art, bibliography, economics, history, history of science, law, literature, music, political science, religion, and theater.

Applicants must have experience in advanced research and be U.S. citizens/residents; grad students must have fulfilled all doctoral requirements except dissertation by Dec. 15.

787 — INSTITUTE FOR ADVANCED STUDIES IN THE HUMANITIES (Visiting Research Fellowships)

Univ Edinburgh
Hope Park Square
Edinburgh EH8 9NW SCOTLAND UK
0131 650 4671
FAX: 0131 668 2252
E-Mail: iash@ed.ac.uk
Internet: www.ed.ac.uk/iash/homepage.html

AMOUNT: Non-stipendiary*

DEADLINE(S): DEC 1

FIELD(S): Arts; Social Sciences; Law; Music; Divinity

Postdoctoral research fellowships of between two and six months are tenable at the Institute for Advanced Studies in the Humanities. Based on academic record and publications. *Most fellowships are honorary, but limited support towards expenses is available to a small number of candidates. Fellows are allocated a study room within the Institute and hold one or two seminars during their tenure. Must submit research report at end of fellowship. No teaching required.

15 awards annually. Not renewable. Contact Mrs. Anthea Taylor for an application.

788 — INSTITUTE FOR HUMANE STUDIES (Humane Studies Fellowship)

4084 University Dr., Ste. 101
Fairfax VA 22030-6812
703/934-6920 or 800/697-8799
FAX: 703/352-7535
E-Mail: ihs@gmu.edu
Internet: www.theihs.org

AMOUNT: up to $12,000

DEADLINE(S): DEC 31

FIELD(S): Social Sciences; Law; Humanities; Jurisprudence; Journalism

Awards are for graduate and advanced undergraduate students pursuing degrees at any accredited domestic or foreign school. Based on academic performance, demonstrated interest in classical liberal ideas, and potential to contribute to the advancement of a free society.

90 awards annually. Apply online or contact IHS for an application.

789 — INSTITUTE FOR HUMANE STUDIES (Summer Residential Program)

4084 University Dr., Ste. 101
Fairfax VA 22030-6812
703/934-6920 or 800/697-8799
FAX: 703/352-7535
E-Mail: ihs@gmu.edu
Internet: www.theihs.org

AMOUNT: All seminar fees: program cost, room/board, materials, and books

DEADLINE(S): MAR 1

FIELD(S): Social Sciences; Humanities; Law; Journalism; Public Policy; Education; Writing

For college students, recent graduates, and graduate students who share an interest in learning and exchanging ideas about the scope of individual rights. One-week and weekend seminars at various campus locations across the U.S.

Apply online or contact IHS for an application.

790 — INTER-AMERICAN FOUNDATION (Field Research Fellowship Programs for U.S. , Latin American, and Caribbean Citizens)

901 N. Stuart St., 10th Floor
Arlington VA 22203
703/841-3800
FAX: 703/527-3529
E-Mail: correo@aif.gov
Internet: www.iaf.gov

AMOUNT: Varies

DEADLINE(S): APR 28

FIELD(S): International Relations, Social Sciences, Humanities, Latin American Studies

Fellowships for Latin American, Carribean, and U.S. doctoral level students for field research in Latin America and the Caribbean. Must be enrolled in U.S. university.

Access website for deadline and application information. Organization does not mail information.

791 — INTER-AMERICAN FOUNDATION (Master's Research Fellowships)

901 N. Stuart St., 10th Floor
Arlington VA 22203
703/841-3800
FAX: 703/527-3529
E-Mail: correo@aif.gov
Internet: www.iaf.gov

AMOUNT: Varies

DEADLINE(S): APR

FIELD(S): Latin American & Caribbean Studies, Internations Relations, Social Sciences, Humanities, etc.

Open to masters students enrolled in U.S. universities for field research in Latin American or the Caribbean. For citizens of Caribbean and Latin American independent countries, and the U.S.

Access website for deadline and application information. Organization does not mail information.

792 — INTERNATIONAL RESEARCH AND EXCHANGES BOARD (Russian-US Young Leadership Fellows for Public Service Program for Russian Citizens)

1616 H St., NW
Washington DC 20006
202/628-8188
FAX: 202/628-8189
E-Mail: irex@info.irex.org
Internet: www.irex.org

AMOUNT: Stipend + tuition, travel, living & housing

DEADLINE(S): NOV 30

FIELD(S): Community, Governmental, & Corporate Affairs; Policy Research & Development; Humanities

Grants of two to twelve months are available to graduate students who are Russian citizens/permanent residents for brief visits to pursue scholarly projects on Central & Eastern Europe, Eurasia, or Mongolia. Must have equivalent of bachelor's degree and be below the age of 30 at time of application. Postdoctoral humanities scholars may pursue research in Turkey or Iran. Financial need NOT a factor.

45 awards annually. Not renewable. Contact Jessica Jeffcoat, Senior Program Officer, for an application.

793 — INTERNATIONAL RESEARCH AND EXCHANGES BOARD (Mongolia Research Fellowship Program)

1616 H St., NW
Washington DC 20006
202/628-8188
FAX: 202/628-8189
E-Mail: edickson@irex.org
Internet: www.irex.org

AMOUNT: $7,000

DEADLINE(S): DEC 15

FIELD(S): Humanities; Social Sciences

Open to US and Mongolian citizens pursuing predoctoral or postdoctoral studies/research in the humanities and social sciences as related to Mongolia. Financial need NOT a factor.

4-5 awards annually. Not renewable. See website or contact Emilie Dickson for an application.

794 — INTERNATIONAL RESEARCH AND EXCHANGES BOARD (Consortium for the Humanities & Social Sciences)

1616 H St., NW
Washington DC 20006
202/628-8188
FAX: 202/628-8189
E-Mail: edickson@irex.org
Internet: www.irex.org

AMOUNT: $10,000 (max.)

DEADLINE(S): JAN 14

FIELD(S): Humanities; Social Sciences

Grant is open to students of any nationality who are pursuing a doctoral, postgraduate, or professional degree in the humanities or social sciences. Award must benefit a university in Armenia, Azerbaijan, Georgia, Russia, and/or Ukraine. Financial need NOT a factor.

20 awards annually. Not renewable. See website or contact Emilie Dickson for an application.

795 — INTERNATIONAL RESEARCH AND EXCHANGES BOARD (Short-Term Travel Grants)

1616 H St., NW
Washington DC 20006
202/628-8188
FAX: 202/628-8189
E-Mail: irex@info.irex.org
Internet: www.irex.org

AMOUNT: $3,000 (max.)

DEADLINE(S): FEB 1; JUN 1

FIELD(S): Humanities; Social Sciences

Open to US citizens/permanent residents who wish to pursue postdoctoral research in Central/Eastern Europe or Mongolia. Must have Ph.D. or equivalent professional degree. Financial need NOT a factor.

Not renewable. See website or contact Denise Cormaney, Senior Program Officer, for an application.

796 — ISTITUTO ITALIANO PER GLI STUDI STORICI - ITALIAN INSTITUTE FOR HISTORICAL STUDIES (Federico Chabod & Adolfo Omodeo Scholarships)

Via Benedetto Croce, 12
80134 Napoli ITALY
0039/81-5517159
FAX: 0039/81-5512390

AMOUNT: 12,000,000 Lira

DEADLINE(S): SEP 30

FIELD(S): Humanities; Social Sciences; History; Philosophy; Arts; Economics; Literature

For non-Italian citizens who have completed a university degree in Humanities dept. of a non-Italian university. Intended to allow young scholars to participate in the work of the Institute and to complete personal scholarly research with the help of teaching staff of the Institute. Must include birth certificate, proof of citizenship, university diploma, scholarly work, curriculum of studies w/ indication of language skills, research proposal, & reference letter.

2 awards annually. Contact Marta Herling, Secretary, at above address for an application.

797 — JAPAN SOCIETY FOR THE PROMOTION OF SCIENCE (Post-doctoral Fellowships for Foreign Researchers)

Jochi-Kioizaka Bldg., 6-26-3 Kioi-cho
Chiyoda-Ku
Tokyo 102 JAPAN
+81-3-3263-1721
Telex: J32281
FAX: +81-3-3263-1854

AMOUNT: 270,000 yen per month

DEADLINE(S): SEP 25; MAY 23

FIELD(S): Humanities; Social Sciences; Natural Sciences; Engineering; Medicine

Post-doctoral fellowships for advanced study & research in Japan.

Write for complete information

798 — MINISTRY OF THE FLEMISH COMMUNITY (Fellowships)

Embassy of Belgium
3330 Garfield St., NW
Washington DC 20008
202/625-5850/51
FAX: 202/342-8346
E-Mail: flemishcomdc@wizard.net

AMOUNT: Monthly stipend, tuition, & health care coverage

DEADLINE(S): JAN 31

FIELD(S): Art; Music; Humanities; Social Science; Political Science; Law; Economics; Science; Medicine

Open to US citizens under age 35 who wish to pursue graduate or postgraduate studies in Flanders, Belgium.

Contact Flemish Community for registration forms.

799 — NATIONAL ACADEMY OF EDUCATION (Spencer Postdoctoral Fellowship Program)

NY Univ, School of Education
726 Broadway, Rm. 509
New York NY 10003-9580
212/998-9035
FAX: 212/995-4435
E-Mail: nae.info@nyu.edu
Internet: www.nae.nyu.edu

AMOUNT: $45,000

DEADLINE(S): DEC 1

FIELD(S): Education; Humanities; Social Sciences

Fellowships of one or two years are open to individual researchers in education, humanities, or social and behavioral sciences. Research must have apparent relevance to education. Doctoral degree must have been received within the last five years. Based on past research record and quality of proposed project. Must submit project description, career history, referee form, curriculum vitae/resume, and example of past research relevant to education.

30 awards annually. Not renewable. Contact NAE for an application. Recipients notified in May.

800 — NATIONAL FEDERATION OF THE BLIND (Humanities Scholarship)

805 5th Avenue
Grinnell IA 50112
515/236-3366

AMOUNT: $3,000

DEADLINE(S): MAR 31

FIELD(S): Humanities (Art, English, Foreign Languages, History, Philosophy, Religion)

Open to legally blind students pursuing or planning to pursue a full-time postsecondary education in the US. Scholarships are awarded on basis of academic excellence, service to the community, and financial need. Must include transcripts and two letters of recommendation. Membership NOT required.

1 award annually. Renewable. Contact Mrs. Peggy Elliot, Scholarship Committee Chairman, for an application.

801 — NATIONAL HUMANITIES CENTER (Lilly Fellowships in Religion and the Humanities)

PO Box 12256
Research Triangle Park NC 27709-2256
919/549-0661
FAX: 919/990-8535
E-Mail: nhc@ga.unc.edu
Internet: www.nhc.rtp.nc.us:8080

AMOUNT: Stipend ($35,000-$50,000) + Travel Expenses (for fellow & dependents)

DEADLINE(S): OCT 15

FIELD(S): Religion & the Humanities

Postdoctoral fellowships for the study of religion by humanistic scholars from fields other than religion and theology. Fellows will form the core of a monthly seminar on religion and the humanities. Curriculum vitae, 1,000-word proposal, and three letters of recommendation are required.

3-4 awards annually. Contact NHC for application materials.

802 — NEWBERRY LIBRARY (Long-Term Fellowships)

60 West Walton Street
Chicago IL 60610-3380
312/943-9090
E-Mail: research@newberry.org
Internet: www.newberry.org

AMOUNT: Up to $30,000

DEADLINE(S): JAN 20

FIELD(S): Humanities, History, & related fields

Six postdoctoral fellowship programs are available for scholars wishing to use the Library's collection for writing or research. Fellowships last six to eleven months, and each have slightly different requirements.

See website for details and an application or write to above address.

803 — NEWBERRY LIBRARY (Monticello College Foundation Fellowship For Women)

60 West Walton Street
Chicago IL 60610-3380
312/255-3660
E-Mail: research@newberry.org
Internet: www.newberry.org

AMOUNT: $12,500

DEADLINE(S): JAN 20

FIELD(S): Humanities, History, Study of Women

Six-month post-doctoral fellowships for women in the early stages of their academic careers. For research, writing, and participation in the intellectual life of the Library. Applicant's topic must be related to Newberry's collections; preference given to proposals concerned with the study of women.

See website for application or write to above address.

804 — NEWBERRY LIBRARY (Short-Term Fellowships)

60 West Walton Street
Chicago IL 60610-3380
312/943-9090
E-Mail: research@newberry.org
Internet: www.newberry.org

AMOUNT: $800-$1,500/month

DEADLINE(S): MAR 1

FIELD(S): Humanities, History, & related fields

Nine programs for postdoctoral scholars or doctoral students at the dissertation stage. Study varies from two weeks to three months and is for those making use of Newberry's collections. Each program has slightly different requirements.

See website for details and applications or write to above address.

805 — NEWBERRY LIBRARY (Special Fellowships)

60 West Walton Street
Chicago IL 60610-3380
312/255-3666
E-Mail: research@newberry.org
Internet: www.newberry.org

AMOUNT: Varies

DEADLINE(S): DEC 15

FIELD(S): Humanities, History, & related fields

Fellowships for three months to one year for doctoral or postdoctoral students to study in Germany, France, or Great Britain in fields related to Newberry's collections. Some deadlines JAN 20th. Specific locations are: Wolfenbüttel, Germany; Ecole Nationale des Chartes, Paris, France; and the British Academy, Great Britain.

See website for more details and applications or write to above address.

806 — NORTHERN IRELAND DEPT. OF EDUCATION (Post-graduate Studentships)

Rathgael House
Balloo Road
Bangor Co. Down BT19 7PR N.IRELAND
01247-279279

AMOUNT: 5,295 pounds sterling + fees

DEADLINE(S): Varies (Check with Northern Ireland universities)

FIELD(S): Humanities; Science; Social Science

Research (Ph.D) and advanced courses (MA/MS) awards available for study in Northern Ireland. Must have been a resident of the United Kingdom for at least three years.

Research studentships renewable if work is satisfactory. Write for complete information.

807 — OPEN SOCIETY INSTITUTE (Environmental Management Fellowships)

400 West 59th St.
New York NY 10019
212/548-0600 or 212/757-2323
FAX: 212/548-4679 or 212/548-4600
Internet: www.soros.org/efp.html

AMOUNT: Fees, room, board, living stipend, textbooks, international transportation, health insurance

DEADLINE(S): NOV 15

FIELD(S): Earth sciences, natural sciences, humanities (exc. language), anthropology, sociology, mathematics, or engineering

Two-year fellowships for use in selected universities in the U.S. for international students. For students/professionals in fields related to environmental policy, legislation, and remediation techniques applicable to their home countries.

To apply, contact your local Soros Foundation or Open Society Institute. Further details on website.

808 — PEW YOUNGER SCHOLARS PROGRAM (Graduate Fellowships)

G-123 Hesburgh Library, University of Notre Dame
Notre Dame IN 46556
219/631-4531
FAX: 219/631-8721
E-Mail: Karen.M.Heinig.2@nd.edu
Internet: www.nd.edu/~pesp/pew/PYSPHistory.html

AMOUNT: $13,000

DEADLINE(S): NOV 30

FIELD(S): Social Sciences, Humanities, Theology

Program is for use at any Christian undergraduate school and most seminaries. Check with organization to see if your school qualifies. Apply during senior year. Recipients may enter a competition in which ten students will be awarded a $39,000 ($13,000/yr.) fellowship for three years of dissertation study. For use at top-ranked Ph.D. programs at outstanding universities.

NOT for study in medicine, law business, performing arts, fine arts, or the pastorate. Check website and/or organization for details.

809 — RESEARCH COUNCIL OF NORWAY (Senior Scientist Visiting Fellowship)

P.O. Box 2700 St. Hanshaugen
N-0131 Oslo NORWAY
+47 22 03 70 00
FAX: +47 22 03 70 01
E-Mail: intstip@nfr.no
Internet: www.forskningsradet.no

AMOUNT: NOK 25,000-1st 2 months; NOK 10,000-succeeding months

DEADLINE(S): Varies

FIELD(S): Bioproduction & Processing (including agriculture and veterinary science); Industry & Energy; Culture & Society (including social sciences and the humanities); Medicine & Health; Environment & Development; Science & Technology

Fellowships for scientists to work at Norwegian research institutes. Project funding does not include salary; expenses connected with the stay in Norway are covered.

For a list of institutions, contact the Research Council at above location. Then apply to institution, which then will submit fellowship application.

810 — ROCKEFELLER FOUNDATION (Postdoctoral Residency Program in the Humanities)

420 Fifth Avenue
New York NY 10018-2702
212/852-8286

AMOUNT: Varies (with institution)

DEADLINE(S): Varies (with institution)

FIELD(S): Humanities

Postdoctoral fellowships offered for 6 months to 1 year. For the support of scholars and writers whose research aids in understanding contemporary and cultural issues and extends international or intercultural scholarship.

Write to the address above for a list of host institutions offering fellowships.

811 — SIGUROUR NORDAL INSTITUTE (Snorri Sturluson Icelandic Fellowships)

PO Box 1220
121 Reykjavik ICELAND
354/562-6050
FAX: 354/562-6263
E-Mail: postur@mrn.stjr.is
Internet: www.mrn.stjr.is

AMOUNT: Varies (based on travel & living expenses)

DEADLINE(S): OCT 31

FIELD(S): Humanities

Open to writers, translators, and scholars (not to university students) in the field of humanities from outside Iceland, to enable them to stay in Iceland for a period of at least three months, in order to improve their knowledge of the Icelandic language, culture, and society. Preference given to candidate from Eastern or Southern Europe, Asia, Africa, Latin America, or Oceania. At conclusion, fellows must submit report on how grant was spent.

1 award annually. To apply, submit account of purpose & period of stay in Iceland, as well as details of education & publications. Snorri Sturluson was a famous Icelandic author.

812 — SOCIAL SCIENCES AND HUMANITIES RESEARCH COUNCIL OF CANADA (Postdoctoral Fellowships)

350 Albert St.
PO Box 1610
Ottawa Ontario K1P 6G4 CANADA
613/992-0691
FAX: 613/992-2803
E-Mail: z-info@sshrc.ca
Internet: www.sshrc.ca

AMOUNT: $28,428 Canadian

DEADLINE(S): OCT

FIELD(S): Social Sciences; Humanities

For Canadian citizens to do postdoctoral research in the humanities and social sciences. Financial need NOT a factor.

Renewable for one year. Consult website for complete program information or contact Jayne Holowachuk at SSHRC for an application.

813 — SOCIAL SCIENCES AND HUMANITIES RESEARCH COUNCIL OF CANADA (Doctoral Fellowships)

350 Alberta St.
PO Box 1610
Ottawa Ontario K1P 6G4 CANADA
613/992-0691
FAX: 613/992-2803
E-Mail: z-info@sshrc.ca
Internet: www.sshrc.ca

AMOUNT: $16,620 Canadian

DEADLINE(S): SEP

FIELD(S): Social Sciences; Humanities

Doctoral fellowships in the humanities and social sciences for Canadian citizens. Financial need NOT a factor.

Renewable for three years. Consult website for complete program information or contact Jayne Holowachuk at SSHRC for an application.

814 — SOCIAL SCIENCE RESEARCH COUNCIL (Eurasia Fellowship Program)

810 Seventh Ave., 31st Fl.
New York NY 10019
212/377-2700
FAX: 212/377-2727
E-Mail: eurasia@ssrc.org
Internet: www.ssrc.org

AMOUNT: $10,000 (graduate); $15,000 (dissertation); $24,000 (postdoctoral)

DEADLINE(S): NOV 1

FIELD(S): Soviet Studies

Open to US citizens/permanent residents enrolled in accredited graduate, dissertation, or postdoctoral programs in any discipline of the social sciences or humanities. Purpose is to enhance their disciplinary, methodological, or language training in relation to research on the Soviet Union and its successor states. Grants for summer language institutes also available.

See website or contact SSRC for an application.

815 — SOCIAL SCIENCE RESEARCH COUNCIL (Near & Middle East Fellowship Program)

810 Seventh Ave., 31st Fl.
New York NY 10019
212/377-2700
FAX: 212/377-2727
E-Mail: szanton@ssrc.org
Internet: www.ssrc.org

AMOUNT: Varies

DEADLINE(S): NOV 1

FIELD(S): Near & Middle East Studies

Open to US citizens currently enrolled in Ph.D. program in social sciences or humanities and will have completed two academic years of work toward the doctorate by June of following year. Graduates spend four to nine months preparing for dissertation research through training and study in the Middle East. Also open to US citizens to pursue dissertation research requiring field work in the Middle East. Research must be concerned with period since beginning of Islam.

See website or contact SSRC for an application.

816 — SOCIAL SCIENCE RESEARCH COUNCIL (Program on Philanthropy & the Non-Profit Sector)

810 Seventh Ave.
31st Fl.
New York NY 10019
212/377-2700
FAX: 212/377-2727
E-Mail: phil-np@ssrc.org
Internet: www.ssrc.org

AMOUNT: $18,000 research support + $5,000 write-up support

DEADLINE(S): DEC 8

FIELD(S): Humanities; Social Sciences

Open to full-time graduate students in the social sciences and humanities enrolled in doctoral programs in the US to support research on this country. Must have completed all requirements for Ph.D. except research component. Fellowship supports nine to twelve months of research and related expenses. Based on strong record of achievement. Research must contribute to knowledge in disciplines of philanthropy and nonprofit studies. Financial need NOT a factor.

7 awards annually. Contact Nazli Parvizi for an application.

817 — SOCIAL SCIENCE RESEARCH COUNCIL (Southeast Asia Fellowship Program)

810 Seventh Ave.
31st Fl.
New York NY 10019
212/377-2700
FAX: 212/377-2727
E-Mail: Lam@ssrc.org
Internet: www.ssrc.org

AMOUNT: $15,000 (dissertation); $30,000 (postdoctoral)
DEADLINE(S): DEC 15
FIELD(S): Vietnam Studies

Provides 12- to 24-month dissertation and postdoctoral support for research on Vietnam across the disciplines of the social sciences and humanities. Must be enrolled full-time in Ph.D. programs in any of the social sciences or humanities at accredited universities in the US or Canada and establish an affiliation with a Vietnamese institution. Postdoctoral fellows should already have sufficient command of the Vietnamese language to conduct research in Vietnam.

See website or contact SSRC for an application after September 30th. Awards announced by June.

818 — STUDENT AWARDS AGENCY FOR SCOTLAND (Scottish Studentships for Advanced Postgraduate Study)

Gyleview House
3 Redheughs Rigg
South Gyle
Edinburgh EH12 9HH SCOTLAND UK
Written inquiry or 0131 244 5847

AMOUNT: Varies
DEADLINE(S): MAY 1
FIELD(S): Arts; Humanities

Studentships for full-time research for graduate and advanced post-graduate study. Candidates must have been ordinarily residents in the British Isles for at least three years immediately preceding the start of postgraduate study and ordinarily residents of Scotland at the time of application. They should not have been resident during the three years period wholly for the purpose of receiving full-time education.

Must apply through university. Citizenship restrictions for EU applicants may apply. Further particulars & application forms are available from the post-graduate section at the above address.

819 — THE NORWAY-AMERICA ASSOCIATION (The Norwegian Marshall Fund)

Drammensveien 20C
N-0255 Oslo 2 NORWAY
011 47-22-44-76-83

AMOUNT: Up to $5,000
DEADLINE(S): Varies
FIELD(S): All fields of study

The Marshall Fund was established in 1977 as a token of Norway's gratitude to the U.S. for support after WWII. Objective is to promote research in Norway by Americans in science and humanities. For U.S. citizens.

Contact above location for further information.

820 — UNIVERSITY OF SOUTHERN CALIFORNIA (Mellon Postdoctoral Fellowship)

Office of Dean of Faculty
College of Letters Arts & Sciences
University Park
Mail Code 4012
Los Angeles CA 90089-4012
213/740-5294
Internet: www.usc.edu/dept/LAS/Faculty/mellon.htm

AMOUNT: $32,000 (approx.) + benefits
DEADLINE(S): Varies
FIELD(S): Humanities

Nine-month postdoctoral fellowships (September-May) at USC for junior scholars with concurrent one-year appointment as lecturer, carrying a reduced teaching load of one course per semester. Applicants should have received their Ph.D. within last seven years from date of appointment.

See website or contact USC for complete information.

821 — WOODROW WILSON INTERNATIONAL CENTER FOR SCHOLARS (Fellowships in the Humanities and Social Sciences)

1000 Jefferson Dr. SW
SRI MRC 02
Washington DC 20560
202/357-2841
FAX: 202/633-9043
E-Mail: wcfellow@sivm.si.edu
Internet: www.wwics.si.ed

AMOUNT: Up to $62,000
DEADLINE(S): OCT 1
FIELD(S): Humanities; Social Sciences

Open to individuals from any country who have outstanding capabilities and experience from a wide variety of backgrounds. Academic participants limited to post-doctoral level and should have published a major work beyond Ph.D dissertation.

Approximately 35 fellowships annually to scholars with outstanding project proposals, especially those transcending narrow specialties. Write for complete information.

822 — WOODROW WILSON NATIONAL FELLOWSHIP FOUNDATION (Andrew W. Mellon Fellowships in Humanistic Studies)

CN 5329
Princeton NJ 08543-5329
609/452-7007
FAX: 609/452-0066
E-Mail: mellon@woodrow.org
Internet: www.woodrow.org

AMOUNT: Tuition, fees, & stipend
DEADLINE(S): NOV 17
FIELD(S): Humanities AND Education

Open to students entering the first year of a Ph.D. program in the US. Must be pursuing humanistic studies and planning careers in college teaching.

80 awards annually. See website or contact WWNFF for an application.

823 — WOODROW WILSON NATIONAL FELLOWSHIP FOUNDATION (Charlotte W. Newcombe Dissertation Fellowships)

CN 5281
Princeton NJ 08543-5281
609/452-7007
FAX: 609/452-0066
E-Mail: charoltte@woodrow.org
Internet: www.woodrow.org

AMOUNT: $15,500
DEADLINE(S): DEC 6
FIELD(S): Theology; Social Sciences; Humanities; Education

Open to Ph.D. candidates writing on topics of religious and ethical values. Must be pursuing full-time dissertation writing at graduate schools in the US, having completed all pre-dissertation requirements.

35 awards annually. Not renewable. See website or contact WWNFF for an application. Notification made in April.

824 — WOODROW WILSON NATIONAL FELLOWSHIP FOUNDATION (Humanities at Work)

CN 5329
Princeton NJ 08543-5329
609/452-7007

FAX: 609/452-0066
E-Mail: robles@woodrow.org
Internet: www.woodrow.org

AMOUNT: Varies

DEADLINE(S): Varies

FIELD(S): Humanities

Offers programs to expand career opportunities for humanities Ph.D.s in the US. Programs include Innovation Awards for university-based initiatives, Practicum Grants for current students, and Career Postdocs at companies/organizations outside academia.

See website or contact WWNFF for an application.

AREA STUDIES

825 — AFRICAN STUDIES CENTER (African Language Scholarships—Title VI)

c/o UCLA
10244 Bunche Hall
Los Angeles CA 90002
213/825-3686/2877/2944

AMOUNT: $10,000 + tuition & fees

DEADLINE(S): JAN 8

FIELD(S): African Studies

For students in graduate programs studying an African Language at UCLA. U.S. citizen or permanent resident.

5-10 Awards per year. Awards can be renewed once. Write for complete information.

826 — AMERICAN ACADEMY IN ROME (Rome Prize Predoctoral Fellowships)

7 East 60th Street
New York, NY 10022-1001
212/751-7200
FAX: 212/751-7220
Internet: www.aarome.org

AMOUNT: $15,000-$17,800

DEADLINE(S): NOV 15

FIELD(S): Archaeology; Art History; Modern Italian Studies; Post-Classical Humanistic Studies

For doctoral study in Rome, Italy. Applicant must be US citizen with a major and/or career interest in above fields. Recommendations, proof of eligibility, and research proposal required.

$40 application fee. Contact the Programs Department at the American Academy in Rome for an application.

827 — AMERICAN ACADEMY IN ROME (Rome Prize Postdoctoral Fellowships)

7 East 60th Street
New York NY 10022-1001
212/751-7200

FAX: 212/751-7220
Internet: www.aarome.org

AMOUNT: $15,000-$17,800

DEADLINE(S): NOV 15

FIELD(S): Archaeology; Art History; Modern Italian Studies; Post-classical Humanistic Studies

For postgraduate study in Rome, Italy. Applicant must be US citizen or permanent resident with a major and/or career interest in above fields. Recommendations, proof of eligibility, and research proposal required.

Contact the Programs Department at the American Academy in Rome for an application.

828 — AMERICAN ASSOCIATION OF UNIVERSITY WOMEN - HONOLULU BRANCH (Pacific Fellowships)

1802 Keeaumoku St.
Honolulu HI 96822
808/537-4702

AMOUNT: $1,000-$5,000

DEADLINE(S): MAR 1

FIELD(S): Studies of Pacific Rim Countries & Islands

Open to female residents of Hawaii for graduate study or research in/on the Pacific Rim area which includes islands in the Pacific Ocean and lands bordering it (except mainland US). Must have been Hawaii resident for at least three years, be working towards a master's or doctorate degree, and demonstrate financial need.

5-8 awards annually. Contact the Pacific Fellowship Committee Chair for an application.

829 — AMERICAN COUNCIL OF LEARNED SOCIETIES (Dissertation Grants in East European Studies)

Office of Fellowships & Grants
228 E. 45th St.
New York NY 10017-3398
E-mail: grants@acls.org
Internet: www.acls.org

AMOUNT: up to $15,000 + expenses

DEADLINE(S): NOV 1

FIELD(S): East European Studies

Open to doctoral candidates for support of dissertation research or writing to be undertaken at any university or institution OUTSIDE of East Europe. US citizenship/legal residency required.

Contact ACLS for an application.

830 — AMERICAN INSTITUTE OF INDIAN STUDIES (Fellowship Programs)

1130 E. 59th St.
Chicago IL 60637
773/702-8638
E-Mail: aiis@uchicago.edu
Internet: kaladarshan.arts.ohio-state.edu/aiis/aiishomepage.htm

AMOUNT: Varies

DEADLINE(S): JUL 1

FIELD(S): India Studies; Performing Arts

Fellowships for post and predoctoral work in India studies at an Indian university (requires formal affiliation). Also some fellowships for artists who are accomplished in the performing arts of India.

These fellowships have varied requirements. Contact AIIS for complete information.

831 — AMERICAN PHILOSOPHICAL SOCIETY (Phillips Fund Grants for North Native American Research)

104 South 5th Street
Philadelphia PA 19106-3387
E-mail: eroach@amphilsoc.org
Internet: www.amphilsoc.org

AMOUNT: $1,500 (max.)

DEADLINE(S): MAR 1

FIELD(S): American Indian Ethnohistory or Linguistics

For graduate or postdoctorate research in North Native American linguistics and ethnohistory, i.e. continental US & Canada. Given for one year. Covers travel, tapes, and informants' fees; not for general maintenance or purchase of permanent equipment. Not for work in archaeology, ethnography, psycholinguistics, or pedagogy.

See website for details. For written requests, include self-addressed mailing label, indication of eligibility, nature of research, and proposed use of grant funds. Foreign students must state why study in US is necessary.

832 — AMERICAN PSYCHOLOGICAL FOUNDATION (Wayne F. Placek Awards for Scientific Research on Lesbian and Gay Issues)

750 First St., NE
Washington DC 20002-4242
202/336-5814
E-Mail: foundation@apa.org
Internet: psychology.ucdavis.edu/rainbow/html/apfawards.html

AMOUNT: up to $30,000

DEADLINE(S): MAR 15

FIELD(S): Behavioral/Social Science

To increase public's understanding of homosexuality & to alleviate stress that gays/lesbians experience in this & future civilizations. Proposals invited for empirical research from all fields of behavioral/social sciences. Proposals encouraged that deal with attitudes, prejudice, workplace issues, and subgroups historically underrepresented in scientific research. Must have doctoral degree/equivalent & be associated w/ college/university or research institute.

2 awards annually. Small grants (up to $5,000) also available for pilot studies/exploratory research in gay/lesbian issues. Contact above address for details.

833 — AMERICAN RESEARCH INSTITUTE IN TURKEY (ARIT Fellowship Program)

Univ Penn Museum
33rd & Spruce Streets
Philadelphia PA 19104-6324
215/898-3474
FAX: 215/898-0657
E-Mail: leinwand@sas.upenn.edu
Internet: mec.sas.upenn.edu/ARIT

AMOUNT: Varies

DEADLINE(S): NOV 15

FIELD(S): Humanities; Social Sciences; Turkish Studies

Two-month to one-year fellowships are for postdoctoral scholars & advanced graduate students engaged in research on ancient, medieval, or modern times in Turkey, in any field of the humanities & social sciences. Predoctoral students must have fulfilled all preliminary requirements for doctorate except dissertation. Applicants must maintain an affiliation with an educational institution in the US or Canada. Must submit curriculum vitae, research proposal, & referees.

Contact ARIT for an application.

834 — AMERICAN RESEARCH INSTITUTE IN TURKEY (Mellon Research Fellowships for Central and Eastern European Scholars in Turkey)

Univ Penn Museum
33rd & Spruce Streets
Philadelphia PA 19104-6324
215/898-3474
FAX: 215/898-0657
E-Mail: leinwand@sas.upenn.edu
Internet: mec.sas.upenn.edu/ARIT

AMOUNT: Stipend up to $10,500 for 2-3 month project (includes travel, living expenses, work-related costs)

DEADLINE(S): MAR 5

FIELD(S): Humanities; Social Sciences

For Czech, Hungarian, Polish, Slovakian, Bulgarian, and Romanian scholars holding a Ph.D. or equivalent who are engaged in advanced research in any field of the social sciences or the humanities involving Turkey. Must be permanent residents of these countries and must obtain formal permission for any research to be carried out.

3 awards annually. Previous fellows not eligible. See website or write to above address for details.

835 — AMERICAN RESEARCH INSTITUTE IN TURKEY (National Endowment for the Humanities Fellowships for Research in Turkey)

Univ Penn Museum
33rd & Spruce Streets
Philadelphia PA 19104-6324
215/898-3474
FAX: 215/898-0657
E-Mail: leinwand@sas.upenn.edu
Internet: mec.sas.upenn.edu/ARIT

AMOUNT: $10,000-$30,000

DEADLINE(S): NOV 15

FIELD(S): Humanities

Postdoctoral fellowships are to conduct research in Turkey for four to twelve months. Fields of study cover all periods in the general range of the humanities, including humanistically oriented aspects of the social sciences, prehistory, history, art, archaeology, literature, linguistics, and cultural history. There are two institutes, one in Istanbul and one in Ankara. Both have residential facilities for fellows and provide general assistance.

2-3 awards annually. Contact ARIT for an application. Notification by January 25th.

836 — AMERICAN SCHOOL OF CLASSICAL STUDIES AT ATHENS (Fellowships)

6-8 Charlton St.
Princeton NJ 08540-5232
609/683-0800
FAX: 609/924-0578
E-Mail: ascsa@axcsa.org
Internet: www.ats.edu/spons

AMOUNT: Up to $7,840 + room, partial board, and fee waiver

DEADLINE(S): JAN 5

FIELD(S): Classical Studies; Archaeology; Ancient Greece

Fellowships for study at ASCSA in Greece. Open to graduate students at American & Canadian colleges & universities. Recent graduates also are eligible. Residency in Greece required.

Access website for complete information and application or write for details.

837 — AMERICAN SCHOOL OF CLASSICAL STUDIES AT ATHENS (Katherine Keene Summer Session Scholarship for Teachers)

993 Lenox Drive, Suite 101
Lawrence NJ 08648
609/844-7577
E-Mail: ascsa@ascsa.org
Internet: www.asca.org

AMOUNT: $2,500

DEADLINE(S): FEB 15

FIELD(S): Classical Studies; Ancient Greece

Scholarships for American public secondary school teachers to attend summer sessions in the above program in Greece. Must include these topics in his/her course material.

Access website for complete information and application or write to Committee on Summer Sessions at above address for details.

838 — AMERICAN UNIVERSITY IN CAIRO (International Graduate Fellowships in Middle East Studies)

420 Fifth Ave.
3rd Floor
New York NY 10017-2729
212/730-8800
FAX: 212/730-1600
E-Mail: aucegypt@aucnyo.edu
Internet: www.aucegypt.edu

AMOUNT: Tuition + stipend paid in Egyptian pounds

DEADLINE(S): FEB 1

FIELD(S): Middle East Studies

For graduate students in the master of arts program at the American University in Cairo, Egypt, who do not hold Egyptian citizenship. Must have a GPA of at least 3.4. Financial need NOT a factor.

2 awards annually. Renewable. Contact Mary Davidson at above address for complete information.

839 — ARCHAEOLOGICAL INSTITUTE OF AMERICA (Anna C. & Oliver C. Colburn Fellowship)

Boston Univ
656 Beacon St.
Boston MA 02215-2006
617/353-9361
FAX 617/353-6550
E-Mail: aia@bu.edu
Internet: www.archeological.org

AMOUNT: $14,000

DEADLINE(S): JAN 31

FIELD(S): Classical Studies

Open to US or Canadian citizens/permanent residents who are at predoctoral stage or who have received Ph.D. within last 5 years. Award is contingent upon student's acceptance as an incoming Associate Member or Student Associate Member of the American School of Classical Studies at Athens, Greece. Candidates for fellowship must apply concurrently to the American School for Associate/ Student Membership. Maximum 1 year duration. Must submit report on use at end of tenure.

1 award annually. Contact AIA for an application. Awards announced by April 15th.

840 — ARCHAEOLOGICAL INSTITUTE OF AMERICA (Olivia James Traveling Fellowship)

Boston Univ
656 Beacon St.
Boston MA 02215-2006
617/353-9361
FAX: 617/353-6550
E-Mail: aia@bu.edu
Internet: www.archeological.org

AMOUNT: $22,000

DEADLINE(S): NOV 1

FIELD(S): Classics; Sculpture; Architecture; Archaeology; History

Fellowships for US citizens/permanent residents to be used for travel and study in Greece, the Aegean Islands, Sicily, Southern Italy, Asia Minor, or Mesopotamia. Preference given to individuals engaged in dissertation research or to recent recipients of the Ph.D. (within 5 years). Award is not intended to support field excavation projects, and recipients may not hold other major fellowships during tenure. At conclusion, recipient must submit report on use of stipend.

Contact AIA for an application. Awards announced by February 1st.

841 — ARCTIC INSTITUTE OF NORTH AMERICA (Lorraine Allison Scholarship)

University of Calgary
2500 University Dr. NW
Calgary Alberta T2N 1N4 CANADA
403/220-7515
FAX: 403/282-4609

AMOUNT: $2,000

DEADLINE(S): MAY 1

FIELD(S): Northern Canadian Studies

Open to any student enrolled in a Canadian university in a program of graduate study related to northern issues which best address academic excellence; a commitment to northern Canadian research and a desire for beneficial results.

Scholars from Yukon and the Northwest Territories are encouraged to apply. Write for complete information.

842 — ASIAN INSTITUTE OF TECHNOLOGY (AIT Scholarship Program)

Development Office
PO Box 4, Klongluang
Pathumthani 12120 THAILAND
(66)(2) 516-0110-44 or 524-5032
FAX: (66)(2) 516-2126
E-Mail: ascao@ait.ac.th
Internet: www.ait.ac.th

AMOUNT: US $12,600-$37,960

DEADLINE(S): FEB 15; JUN 15; OCT 15

FIELD(S): Advanced Technologies; Civil Engineering; Environment, Resources, & Development; Business Management

Scholarships and grants open to citizens of Asian countries who are accepted by the institute as a master's or doctotal candidate. Selection is based on academic criteria, practical experience, gender, and country of origin; priority to Mekong Region countries and Asian countries of the former USSR.

250 awards annually. Contact AIT for an application.

843 — ASSOCIATION FOR WOMEN IN PSYCHOLOGY/AMERICAN PSYCHOLOGICAL ASSOCIATION DIVISION 35 (Annual Student Research Prize)

Connecticut College
Box 548
270 Mohegan Ave.
New London CT 06320
860/439-2325
FAX: 860/439-5300

AMOUNT: $200

DEADLINE(S): APR 1

FIELD(S): Women's Issues

Undergraduate and graduate students may submit research papers relevant in some way to women's lives. Research can be either basic or applied. Entries should be of approximately journal length and written in APA style.

Send four copies of the paper and a self-addressed, stamped, postcard and business-sized envelope to Ingrid Johnston-Robledo, Ph.D., Department of Psychology, at the above address.

844 — ASSOCIATION FOR WOMEN IN SCIENCE EDUCATIONAL FOUNDATION (AWIS Predoctoral Awards)

1200 New York Ave. NW, Suite 650
Washington DC 20005
202/326-8940 or 800-886-AWIS
E-Mail: awis@awis.org
Internet: www.awis.org

AMOUNT: $1,000

DEADLINE(S): JAN 16

FIELD(S): Various Sciences and Social Sciences

Scholarships for female doctoral students. Summary page, description of research project, resume, references, transcripts, and biographical sketch required. US citizens may study at any graduate institution; non-citizens must study at US institutions.

5-10 awards annually. See website or write to above address for an application and complete information.

845 — ASSOCIATION FOR WOMEN IN SCIENCE EDUCATIONAL FOUNDATION (AWIS Pre-doctoral Awards)

1200 New York Ave. NW, Suite 650
Washington DC 20005
202/326-8940 or 800/886-AWIS
E-Mail: awis@awis.org
Internet: www.awis.org

AMOUNT: $1,000

DEADLINE(S): JAN 16

FIELD(S): Various Sciences and Social Sciences

Scholarships for female doctoral students. Summary page, description of research project, resume, references, transcripts, and biographical sketch required. US citizens may study at any graduate institution; non-citizens must be enrolled in US institutions.

5-10 awards annually. See website or write to above address for an application and more information.

846 — ASSOCIATION FOR WOMEN IN SCIENCE EDUCATIONAL FOUNDATION (Ruth Satter Memorial Award)

1200 New York Ave., NW, Suite 650
Washington DC 20005
202/326-8940 or 800/886-AWIS
E-Mail: awis@awis.org
Internet: www.awis.org

AMOUNT: $1,000

DEADLINE(S): JAN 16

FIELD(S): Various Sciences and Social Sciences

Scholarships for female doctoral students who have interrupted their education for at least three years to raise a family. Summary page, description of research project, resume, references, transcripts, biographical sketch, and letter from your department to confirm eligibility required. US citizens may study at any graduate institution; non-citizens must attend US institutions.

See website or write to above address for more information or an application.

847 — ASSOCIATION FOR WOMEN IN SCIENCE EDUCATIONAL FOUNDATION (Ruth Satter Memorial Award)

1200 New York Ave. NW, Suite 650
Washington DC 20005
202/326-8940 or 800/886-AWIS
E-Mail: awis@awis.org
Internet: www.awis.org

AMOUNT: $1,000

DEADLINE(S): JAN 16

FIELD(S): Various Sciences and Social Sciences

Scholarships for female doctoral students who have interupted their education three years or more to raise a family. Summary page, description of research project, resume, references, transcripts, biographical sketch, and proof of eligibility from department head required. US citizens may attend any graduate institution; non-citizens must be enrolled in US institutions.

See website or write to above address for more information or an application.

848 — AUSTRALIAN FEDERATION OF UNIVERSITY WOMEN - WESTERN AUSTRALIA (Joyce Riley Bursary)

Bursary Liaison Officer
PO Box 48
Nedlands WA 6909 AUSTRALIA
Written Inquiry

AMOUNT: Aus$1,700 - Aus$2,750

DEADLINE(S): JUL 31

FIELD(S): Humanities; Social Sciences

To support women graduates of a Western Australian university to complete a higher degree or post-doctoral research in Humanities or Social Sciences at a recognized university in any country.

Membership in AFUW or in IFUW is required. Contact above location for further information.

849 — AUSTRALIAN FEDERATION OF UNIVERSITY WOMEN - WESTERN AUSTRALIA (Joyce Riley Bursary)

Bursary Liaison Officer
PO Box 48
Nedlands WA 6009 AUSTRALIA
Written Inquiry

AMOUNT: Aus$1,700 - Aus$2,750

DEADLINE(S): JUL 31

FIELD(S): Humanities; Social Sciences

To support women graduates of a recognized university to complete a higher degree or post-doctoral research at a university in Western Australia.

Membership in AFUW or in IFUW is required. Write to above address for complete information.

850 — AUSTRIAN CULTURAL INSTITUTE (Franz Werfel Scholarship)

950 Third Ave.
20th Fl.
New York NY 10022
212/759-5165
FAX: 212/319-9636
E-Mail: desk@aci.org
Internet: www.austriaculture.net

AMOUNT: ATS 11,000/month (US $845) + ATS 7,500 (US $570)

DEADLINE(S): FEB 28

FIELD(S): Austrian Studies; Literature

Open to professors teaching Austrian literature at American universities/colleges to enable research at Austrian archives, libraries, & other research institutions. Must have an excellent knowledge of German & be no more than 35 years old. Scholars also receive yearly literary symposium invitation, yearly book donations, one-month research grant every three years, & Austrian newspaper subscription. Must submit letters of recommendation, curriculum vitae, & transcripts.

Renewable. See website or contact ACI for an application kit.

851 — BLAKEMORE FOUNDATION (Asian Language Fellowship Grants)

1201 Third Ave., 40th Fl.
Seattle WA 98101-3099
206/583-8778
FAX: 206/583-8500
E-Mail: blakemore@perkinscoie.com

AMOUNT: Tuition, transportation, basic living costs

DEADLINE(S): JAN 15

FIELD(S): Asian languages

Fellowships for advanced language study in Asia. For use at an instition selected by the applicant and approved by the Foundation. Applicant must be a graduate or professional school student, a teacher, a professional, or a business person; be working towards a specific career objective involving the regular use of an Asian language; be near an advanced level in that language; be a U.S. citizen or permanent resident. For full-time study during the term of the grant.

12-18 annual awards. For one year of study.

852 — BLUES HEAVEN FOUNDATION, INC. (Muddy Waters Scholarship)

2120 S. Michigan Ave.
Chicago IL 60616
312/808-1286

AMOUNT: $2,000

DEADLINE(S): APR 30

FIELD(S): Music; Music Education; African-American Studies; Folklore; Performing Arts; Arts Management; Journalism; Radio/TV/Film

Scholarship is made on a competitive basis with consideration given to scholastic achievement, concentration of studies, and financial need. Applicant must have full-time enrollment status in a Chicago area college/university in at least their first year of undergraduate studies or a graduate program. Scholastic aptitude, extracurricular involvement, grade point average, and financial need are all considered.

Contact Blues Heaven Foundation, Inc. to receive an application between February and April.

853 — BOLOGNA CENTER OF THE JOHNS HOPKINS UNIVERSITY - PAUL H. NITZE SCHOOL OF ADVANCED INTERNATIONAL STUDIES (Fellowships for Non-Americans)

Admissions Office
Via Belmeloro 11
40126 Bologna ITALY
+39/51/232-185
FAX: +39/51/228-505
E-Mail: admission@jhubc.it
Internet: www.jhubc.it

AMOUNT: Partial to full tuition

DEADLINE(S): FEB 1

FIELD(S): European Studies; International Relations; International Economics

One year at SAIS Bologna Center is open to graduate students with some background in political science, economics, history, or law and who are interested in problems confronting Europe and/or international relations. Possibility to continue for the second year toward an M.A. at SAIS in Washington, DC. Program is conducted in English; therefore, English fluency is required. This program is for non-US citizens.

Contact Bologna Center for an application.

854 — BOLOGNA CENTER OF THE JOHNS HOPKINS UNIVERSITY - PAUL H. NITZE SCHOOL OF ADVANCED INTERNATIONAL STUDIES (Fellowships for Americans)

SAIS
1740 Massachusetts Ave., NW
Washington DC 20036
E-mail: admission@jhubc.it
Internet: www.jhubc.it

AMOUNT: Partial to full tuition

DEADLINE(S): JAN 15

FIELD(S): European Studies; International Relations; International Economics

One year at SAIS Bologna Center in Italy is open to graduate students with some background in political science, economics, history, or law and who are interested in problems confronting Europe and/ or international relations. Must be US citizen/ permanent resident. Courses are conducted in English.

Contact SAIS for an application.

855 — BRITISH ACADEMY (Sir Ernest Cassel Educational Trust)

8 Malvern Terrace
Islington, London N1 1HR ENGLAND UK
0171 607 7879

AMOUNT: 100-500 pounds per annum

DEADLINE(S): SEP; DEC; FEB; APR (end of ea. month)

FIELD(S): Language, literature, or civilizaiton of any country

Research grants for the more junior teaching members of universities for research abroad and are for the study of any country or civilization, concentrating on the fields mentioned above.

Obtain application from the Secretary at the Trust.

856 — BRITISH ASSOCIATION FOR AMERICAN STUDIES (Short-Term Awards)

Dr. Jenel Virden
University of Hull
Hull HU6 7RX ENGLAND UK
01482 465303

AMOUNT: 400 pounds sterling

DEADLINE(S): DEC 1

FIELD(S): American Studies; American History

Open to graduate/postgraduate British scholars for brief visits to the US for research in American history, politics, geography, culture, and literature. Preference given to younger scholars.

Contact Dr. Jenel Virden for an application.

857 — BRITISH COLUMBIA HERITAGE TRUST (Scholarships)

PO Box 9818 Stn Prov Govt.
Victoria BC V8W 9W3 CANADA
250/356-1433

AMOUNT: $5,000

DEADLINE(S): FEB 15

FIELD(S): British Columbia History; Architecture; Archaeology; Archival Management

Open to graduate students who are Canadian citizens or permanent residents. Criteria are scholarly record and academic performance, educational and career objectives, and proposed program of study.

Write for complete information.

858 — BRITISH INSTITUTE OF PERSIAN STUDIES (Research Grants)

Institute of Archaeology
University College London
London WC1H 0PY ENGLAND UK
0171 490 4404
FAX: 0171 490 4404
Internet: www.lancs.ac.uk/users/research/
RESTRI~SELECT/15.HTM

AMOUNT: Cost of travel, field work, and some maintenance

DEADLINE(S): APR 1

FIELD(S): Persian Studies

Grants for research in any field of Persian studies concerned with the arts, archaeology, anthropology, history, literature, linguistics, religion, philosophy, and cognate subjects. Can be used for research and/or fieldwork in Iran, or for research visits to archives, museums, outside Iran but with Iran material, or similiar projects involving visits to such locations in Britain.

Applicants should hold British and/or Commonwealth passports and should normally be resident in the United Kingdom. Write to Ms. Juliet Dryden, Assistant Secretary at the University.

859 — CAMARGO FOUNDATION (Residential Fellowship)

c/o Jerome Foundation
125 Park Square Ct.
400 Sibley St.
St. Paul MN 55101-1928
651/290-2237

AMOUNT: Residency at Foundation in France

DEADLINE(S): FEB 1

FIELD(S): French & Francophone Stuides; Creative Arts

3-4 month residency at study center in Cassis, France, for graduate study, postgraduate study, or career support. May be professors, independent scholars, grad students, writers, visual artists, or composers with specific projects to complete. Each fellow will be asked to outline the accepted project during regularly scheduled sessions, and are asked to give copy of any completed work to the Camargo library. French language is recommended but not required.

22 awards annually. Not renewable. Contact Mr. William Reichard at the Camargo Foundation for an application. Awards are announced by April 1st.

860 — CANADIAN BUREAU FOR INTERNATIONAL EDUCATION (Canadian International Development Agency Awards Program for Canadians)

220 Laurier Ave., W., Ste. 1100
Ottawa Ontario K1P 5Z9 CANADA
613/237-4820

FAX: 613/237-1073
E-Mail: smelanson@cbie.ca
Internet: www.cbie.ca

AMOUNT: $10,000/yr. Canadian (max.)

DEADLINE(S): FEB 1

FIELD(S): International Relations/Development; Business

For Canadian citizens/permanent residents seeking to participate in international development through a volunteer project of their own initiative. The development activity may be the fieldwork component of a master's degree program or a professional work/ research project. Ph.D. candidates are NOT eligible. Also offers internships to master's students in business, administration, and management programs. Awards tenable up to twelve months and are taxable.

50 awards annually. Contact CBIE for an application.

861 — CANADIAN EMBASSY (Canadian Studies Graduate Student Fellowship Program)

501 Pennsylvania Ave., NW
Washington DC 20001
202/682-7717
FAX: 202/682-7791
E-Mail: dan.abele@dfait-maeci.gc.ca
Internet: www.canadianembassy.org

AMOUNT: US $850/month (up to 9 months)

DEADLINE(S): OCT 31

FIELD(S): Canadian Studies

Grants for full-time doctoral students at accredited US or Canadian colleges/universities whose dissertations are related in substantial part to the study of Canada, Canda/US, or Canada/North America. Must be US citizen or permanent resident.

Contact the Canadian Embassy for an application.

862 — CANADIAN FEDERATION OF UNIVERSITY WOMEN (Margaret Dale Philp Award)

251 Bank St., Ste. 600
Ottawa Ontario K2P 1X3 CANADA
613/234-2732
Internet: www.cfuw.ca

AMOUNT: $1,000

DEADLINE(S): NOV 15

FIELD(S): Humanities; Social Sciences

For women who reside in Canada and are pursuing graduate studies in the humanities or social sciences, with special consideration given to study in Canadian history. Must hold at least a bachelor's degree or equivalent from a recognized university and have been accepted into, or be currently enrolled in the proposed program and place of study.

$20 filing fee. Contact CFUW for an application after August 1st. Candidates will be notified by May 31st. Funded by CFUW/Kitchener-Waterloo.

863 — CANADIAN INSTITUTE OF UKRAINIAN STUDIES (Helen Darcovich Memorial Fellowship)

352 Athabasca Hall
Univ Alberta
Edmonton Alberta T6G 2E8 CANADA
Written Inquiry

AMOUNT: $8,000 (max.)

DEADLINE(S): MAY 1

FIELD(S): Ukrainian Studies

Awarded to student writing a dissertation on a Ukrainian or Ukrainian-Canadian topic in Education, History, Law, Humanities, Arts, Social Sciences, Women's Studies, or Library Sciences. Judged on proposal, academic grades, references, writing samples, and publishing record. Canadian citizens/permanent residents at any institution, and foreign students at the University of Alberta, will receive extra points. All degree requirements except dissertation must be completed.

1 award annually. Not renewable. Contact above address for an application.

864 — CANADIAN INSTITUTE OF UKRAINIAN STUDIES (Marusia & Michael Dorosh Master's Fellowship)

352 Athabasca Hall
Univ Alberta
Edmonton Alberta T6G 2E8 CANADA
Written Inquiry

AMOUNT: $4,500 (max.)

DEADLINE(S): MAY 1

FIELD(S): Ukrainian Studies

Awarded to student writing a thesis on a Ukrainian or Ukrainian-Canadian topic in Education, History, Law, Humanities, Arts, Social Sciences, Women's Studies, or Library Sciences. Judged on points system in which thesis proposal, academic grades, references and writing samples are weighed. Canadian citizens/permanent residents at any institution, and foreign students at the University of Alberta, will receive extra points. Students in non-thesis programs not eligible.

1 award annually. Not renewable. Contact above address for an application.

865 — CANADIAN INSTITUTE OF UKRAINIAN STUDIES (Research Grants)

352 Athabasca Hall
Univ Alberta
Edmonton Alberta T6G 2E8 CANADA
Written Inquiry

AMOUNT: Varies

DEADLINE(S): MAY 1

FIELD(S): Ukrainian Studies

Postgraduate research grants are available in Ukrainian and Ukrainian-Canadian Studies in History, Literature, Language, Education, Social Sciences, and Library Sciences.

Contact above address for an application and the "Guide to Research Applications."

866 — CENTER FOR 17TH- AND 18TH-CENTURY STUDIES (Fellowships)

UCLA
310 Reyce Hall
Los Angeles CA 90095-1404
310/206-8522
FAX: 310/206-8577
E-Mail: c1718cs@humnet.ucla.edu

AMOUNT: $1,000-$18,400

DEADLINE(S): MAR 15

FIELD(S): British Literature/History (17th & 18th Centuries)

Undergraduate stipends, graduate assistantships, and Ahmanson & Getty postdoctoral fellowships are for advanced study and research regarding British literature and history of the 17th and 18th centuries. Tenable at the William Andrews Clark Memorial Library at the University of California, Los Angeles.

Contact the Center for current year's theme and an application.

867 — CENTER FOR CHINESE STUDIES (Research Grant Program)

20 Chungshan S. Rd.
Taipei Taiwan 10001 R.O.C.
886-2-2314-7321
FAX: 886-2-2371-2126
E-Mail: ccsgrant@msg.ncl.edu.tw
Internet: cc.ncl.edu.tw

AMOUNT: NT$25,000-55,000

DEADLINE(S): APR 30

FIELD(S): Chinese Studies

Grants for professors' work in Sinology. Intended for research in the Republic of China. Can be used in Chinese studies-related departments of colleges, universities, or research institutions. Must be non-Chinese.

Contact Ms. Keng Li-chun at CCS for an application.

868 — CENTER FOR HELLENIC STUDIES (Resident Junior Fellowships)

3100 Whitehaven Street NW
Washington DC 20008
202/234-3738

AMOUNT: Up to $20,000

DEADLINE(S): OCT 15

FIELD(S): Literature, history, philosophy, language, or religion of Ancient Greece

Resident fellowships for post-doctoral scholars with professional competence and some publication in Ancient Greek areas shown above.

Twelve resident fellowships per year. Write for complete information.

869 — CENTRE FOR INDEPENDENT STUDIES (Liberty & Society Scholarship)

PO Box 92
St. Leonards NSW 2065
Sydney AUSTRALIA
02 9438 4377
FAX: 02 9439 7310
E-Mail: cis@cis.org.au
Internet: www.cis.org.au

AMOUNT: Varies

DEADLINE(S): Varies

FIELD(S): Classical Liberalism

For undergraduate and graduate students under the age of 30 who have good university results to attend weekend seminars in Sydney, Australia. Preference is given to people from the Oceania region. Must demonstrate financial need.

60 awards annually. Not renewable. Contact Jenny Lindsay at the Centre for an application.

870 — CHARLES A. AND ANNE MORROW LINDBERGH FOUNDATION (Grants for Research Projects)

2150 Third Ave., N, Ste. 310
Anoka MN 55303-2200
612/576-1596
FAX: 612/576-1664
E-Mail: lindbergh@isd.net
Internet: www.isd.net/lindbergh

AMOUNT: $10,580 (max.)

DEADLINE(S): JUN 15

FIELD(S): Aviation; Aerospace; Agriculture; Education; Arts; Humanities; Biomedical Research; Exploration; Health & Population Sciences; Intercultural Communication; Waste Disposal Minimization & Management.; Adaptive Technology; Conservation

Open to individuals whose proposed projects represent a significant contribution toward the achievement of balance between the advance of technology and preservation of the natural environment. Financial need NOT a factor. Funding is NOT for tuition.

10 awards annually. See website for application.

871 — CHRISTIAN A. JOHNSON ENDEAVOR FOUNDATION (Native American Fellows)

Harvard Univ., 79 John F. Kennedy St.
Cambridge MA 02138
617/495-1152
FAX: 617/496-3900
Internet: www.ksg.harvard.edu/hpaied/cjohn.htm

AMOUNT: Varies

DEADLINE(S): MAY 1

FIELD(S): Social sciences, government, or program related to Native American studies

Fellowships for students of Native American ancestry who attend a John F. Kennedy School of Government degree program. Applicant, parent, or grandparent must hold membership in a federally or state-recognized tribe, band, or other organized group of Native Americans. Must be commited to a career in American Indian affairs. Awards based on merit and need.

Renewable, based on renomination and availability of funds. To apply, contact John F. Kennedy School of Government at above address.

872 — CONCORDIA UNIVERSITY (Barry J. Schwartz Memorial Bursary)

Religion Dept.
1455 de Maisonneuve Blvd. West
Montreal Quebec H3G 1M8 CANADA
514/848-3809
FAX: 514/848-2812
E-Mail: awardsgs@vax2.concordia.ca

AMOUNT: $350

DEADLINE(S): SEP 20

FIELD(S): Judaic Studies

Open to a graduate student who has made a significant academic contribution in the field of Judaic Studies. The recipient is chosen by the Department of Religion.

1 award annually. Not renewable. Contact the Graduate Program Director of the Religion Department at Concordia University for an application.

873 — CONFERENCE ON LATIN AMERICAN HISTORY (James R. Scobie Memorial Award for Preliminary Ph.D Research)

Conference on Latin American History
508 College of Business
Auburn Univ
AL 36849-5236
205/844-4161
FAX 205/844-6673

AMOUNT: $1,000

DEADLINE(S): APR 1

FIELD(S): Latin American History

Travel Grant will be awarded each year for use during the following summer for preliminary Ph.D research (not dissertation research).

Write for complete information.

874 — COUNCIL FOR EUROPEAN STUDIES (Predissertation Fellowships)

Columbia Univ
807-807A International Affairs Bldg.
New York NY 10027
212/854-4172
FAX: 212/854-8808
E-Mail: ces@columbia.edu
Internet: www.europanet.org

AMOUNT: $4,000 stipend (max.)

DEADLINE(S): FEB 1

FIELD(S): Cultural Anthropology; History (post 1750); Political Science; Sociology; Geography; Urban & Regional Planning

Awards are for research in France to determine viability of projected doctoral dissertation in modern history and social sciences. Recipients test research design of dissertation, determine availability of archival materials, and contact French scholars. Must be US citizen or permanent resident at a US institution and have completed at least two but no more than three years of full-time doctoral study by end of year. Institutional membership in Council is required.

6 awards annually. See website or contact Council for an application.

875 — DOROT FOUNDATION (The Dorot Fellowships in Israel)

439 Benefit St.
Providence RI 02903
401/351-8866

AMOUNT: $13,500/yr.

DEADLINE(S): FEB 15

FIELD(S): Jewish studies (art, culture, politics, religion, economics, environment)

A fellowship for American Jews, ages 20-40, to study in Israel. Not for those in Jewish professional careers—program is to develop lay leaders. Must have already demonstrated commitment to public service to the general and/or Fewish community and be committed to learning about Jewish heritage and show leadership qualities. Must have a BS/BA degree.

Send written request for application. Include your telephone number.

876 — DR. M. AYLWIN COTTON FOUNDATION (Fellowships)

Albany Trustee Co. Ltd.
PO Box 232
Pollet House

St. Peter's Port
Guernsey GY1 4LA CHANNEL ISLANDS
(44) 1481 724136
FAX: (44) 1481 710478
E-Mail: albany@box232.co.gg

AMOUNT: up to 10,000 pounds sterling

DEADLINE(S): FEB 28

FIELD(S): Mediterranean Studies

One-year fellowships open to scholarly researchers who hold a Ph.D. or equivalent level of achievement. Award is for personal academic research and may not be used for doctoral research.

Contact above location for an application.

877 — DR. M. AYLWIN COTTON FOUNDATION (Publication Grants)

Albany Trustee Co. Ltd.
PO Box 232
Pollet House
St. Peter's Port
Guernsey GY1 4LA CHANNEL ISLANDS
(44) 1481 724136
FAX: (44) 1481 710478
E-Mail: albany@box232.co.gg

AMOUNT: Varies (individually negotiated)

DEADLINE(S): FEB 28

FIELD(S): Mediterranean Studies

Grant to pay expenses for publication of academic research already completed or imminently available for publication on the subject of Mediterranean Studies. Topics may be, but are not limited to, archaeology, architecture, history, language, and art of the Mediterranean.

Contact above location for an application.

878 — DUBLIN INSTITUTE FOR ADVANCED STUDIES (Research Scholarships)

10 Burlington Road
Dublin 4 IRELAND
614 0100
FAX: 668 0561

AMOUNT: 5,000-8,200

DEADLINE(S): MAR 31

FIELD(S): Theoretical Physics; Cosmic Physics; Astronomy; Celtic Studies

Open to candidates holding Ph.D degrees or equivalent and to those with M.A. degrees who can demonstrate their capacity for original research in the above fields. Scholars are required to be in full-time attendance in the schools. No nationality or citizenship requirements.

Awards are renewable and intended to enable holders to establish research careers. The Institute does not award degrees. 18 awards per year. Contact Registrar at above location for complete information.

879 — DUMBARTON OAKS (Awards in Byzantine Studies, Pre-Columbian Studies, & History of Landscape Architecture)

1703 32nd St., NW
Washington DC 20007
202/339-6410

AMOUNT: $37,700/yr. (max.)

DEADLINE(S): NOV 1

FIELD(S): Byzantine Studies; Pre-Columbian Studies; History of Landscape Architecture

Residential doctoral & postdoctoral fellowships, and junior & summer fellowships for undergraduates are to support study and/or research in the above areas. All fellows are expected to be able to communicate satisfactorily in English.

Contact Dumbarton Oaks for an application.

880 — DUMBARTON OAKS (Summer Fellowships for Byzantine Studies)

1703 32nd Street, NW
Washington DC 20007-2961
202/339-6410

AMOUNT: $185/wk.

DEADLINE(S): NOV 1

FIELD(S): Byzantine Studies

Six- to nine-week summer fellowships open to advanced graduate students. Qualified students of history, archaeology, history of art, philology, theology, and other disciplines are eligible to apply. Post-doctoral fellowships are also available.

Approximately 10 awards annually. Contact Dumbarton Oaks for an application.

881 — EMBASSY OF THE CZECH REPUBLIC (Scholarships for Czechs Living Abroad)

3900 Spring of Freedom St., NW
Washington DC 20008
202/274-9114
FAX: 202/966-8540
E-Mail: washington@embassy.mzv.cz
Internet: www.czech.cz/washington

AMOUNT: Varies

DEADLINE(S): APR 30

FIELD(S): Czech language & literature, history, theology, and/or ethnography

Scholarships for undergraduate and graduate citizens of the Czech Republic who are living in the U.S. The ideal applicant should use his/her knowledge for the benefit of the Czech community abroad.

20 annual awards. For a maximum of two semesters of study. See website or write/call for further information.

882 — EUROPEAN UNIVERSITY INSTITUTE (Jean Monnet Fellowship)

Via Dei Roccettini 9
I-50016 San Domenico Di Fiesole (FL) Italy
0039-055-46851
FAX: 0039-055-4685444
E-Mail: applyjmf@datacomm.iue.it
Internet: www.iue.it/JMF/Welcome.html

AMOUNT: 2,000,000-3,500,000 Italian lire per month (i.e. 1,025-1,750 ECU) + medical & family allowances (depends on whether fellow is in receipt of payment from another source and on extent of duties carried out at the Institute)

DEADLINE(S): NOV 1

FIELD(S): Europe: History, Society, Politics, Economics, Law

Post-doctoral fellowships. Fellows are required to make scholarly contribution to research on Europe within one of EUI's research projects or on topic, falling within general interests of the Institute. Publication of research is expected.

25 fellowships annually. Financial need NOT considered. See website or contact Dr. Andreas Frijdal at above address for complete information.

883 — FORD FOUNDATION/NATIONAL RESEARCH COUNCIL (Postdoctoral Fellowship for Minorities)

National Research Council
2101 Constitution Ave.
Washington DC 20418
202/334-2860
E-Mail: infofell@nas.edu
Internet: http//www.nas.edu/fo/index.html

AMOUNT: $25,000 + relocation and research allowance

DEADLINE(S): JAN 3

FIELD(S): Life and physical sciences, mathematics, engineering sciences, behavioral and social sciences, and the humanities

For U.S. citizens who received a Ph.D or Sc.D in the last 7 years and who are Native Amer. Indian or Alaskan, Black/African American, Mexican American, Native Pacific Islander, or Puerto Rican and who are or plan to be in a teaching or research career.

Contact above website or address for complete information.

884 — FORD FOUNDATION/NATIONAL RESEARCH COUNCIL (Predoctoral/ Dissertation Fellowships for Minorities)

2101 Constitution Ave.
Washington DC 20418
202/334-2872

E-Mail: infofell@nas.edu
Internet: http//www.nas.edu/fo/index.html

AMOUNT: $14,000 annual stipend + $6,000 grant to institution; $18,000 for dissertation fellowship

DEADLINE(S): NOV 3

FIELD(S): Most fields of study: sciences, humanities, engineering, behavioral science, social sciences, and computer science

Predoctoral and dissertation fellowships for students whose ethnicity is Alaskan Native, Black/African American, Mexican American/Chicano, Native American Indian, Native Pacific Islander, or Puerto Rican. For research-based programs leading to careers in college teaching and research.

Contact above address or website.

885 — FRIENDS OF THE UNIVERSITY OF WISCONSIN (Madison Libraries Humanities Grants-in-Aid)

728 State St.
Madison WI 53706
608/262-3243 or 608/265-2750 (ans. mach.)

AMOUNT: $1,000/mo.

DEADLINE(S): APR 1; OCT 1

FIELD(S): Research in the humanities appropriate to the collections

Two grants-in-aid annually for one-month's study in such areas as the history of science from the Middle Ages through the Enlightenment, a collection of avant-garde AMerican "little magazines," a American women writers to 1920, Scandinavian and Germanic literature, Dutch post-Reformation theology and church history, French political pamphlets of the 16th & 17th centuries, and many other fields.

Must be in Ph.D. program or be able to deomonstrate a recored of solid intellectual accomplishment. Must live outside a 75-mile radius of Madison, Wisconsin, U.S. Call/write for details.

886 — GERMAN ACADEMIC EXCHANGE SERVICE (DAAD Programs)

950 Third Ave. at 57th St.
New York NY 10022
212/758-3223
FAX: 212/755-5780
E-Mail: daadny@daad.org
Internet: www.daad.org

AMOUNT: Varies (with program)

DEADLINE(S): Varies (with program)

FIELD(S): Varies (with program)

Grants are available to faculty and full-time students who are citizens or permanent residents of the US or Canada. Programs are for study in Germany in a variety of fields.

See website or contact DAAD Programs Administrator for an application.

887 — GERMAN MARSHALL FUND OF THE UNITED STATES (Research Support Program)

11 Dupont Circle, NW, Ste. 750
Washington DC 20036
202/745-3950
FAX: 202/265-1662
E-Mail: info@gmfus.org
Internet: www.gmfus.org

AMOUNT: $3,000 (max. predissertation); $20,000 (max. dissertation); $40,000 (max. advanced research)

DEADLINE(S): NOV 15

FIELD(S): European Studies; US-European Issues

For US citizens/permanent residents who are graduate students or more senior scholars to improve understanding of economic, political, & social developments relating to Europe, European integration, & US-Europe relations. Criteria include achievements; quality, importance, & originality of proposed research; disciplinary and/or policy relevance of project & expanded results, need for support, & likelihood of completion. Funds may be used towards European travel costs.

See website or contact GMFUS for an application.

888 — GERMAN MARSHALL FUND OF THE UNITED STATES (Italian Marshall Fellowship Program)

11 Dupont Circle, NW, Ste. 750
Washington DC 20036
202/745-3950
FAX: 202/265-1662
E-Mail: info@gmfus.org
Internet: www.gmfus.org

AMOUNT: 18,000 Euro max./semester + 1,000 Euro max. for travel, etc.

DEADLINE(S): NOV 15

FIELD(S): Italian Studies; US-Italian Issues

For US citizens/permanent residents who are advanced scholars (postdoc.) seeking to improve the understanding of international role of Italy, particularly in field of US-European relations. Applicants are expected to reside at an Italian institution in order to carry out full-time research. Criteria include scholarly qualifications; acheivements & promise; quality, originality, & importance of proposed research; contemporary relevance; and likelihood of completion.

See website or contact GMFUS for an application.

889 — GIACOMO LEOPARDI CENTER (Scholarships for Italian Language Study in Italy)

Via del Castello
61020 Belforte all'Isauro
39 0722 726000
FAX: 39 0722 726010
E-Mail: centroleopardi@wnt.it
Internet: www.learningvacations.com/leop.htm

AMOUNT: Cost of tuition (about $750)

DEADLINE(S): Varies

FIELD(S): Italian language and literature

The Center is in a castle built in the late Middle Ages. The castle is the site of school for teaching the Italian language and culture. Students are lodged in rooms in the Castle. Scholarships are for the first 300 to apply, and they are for tuition only. Students still must pay for food and lodging.

New classes start every Monday of the year. Most details are found on the website.

890 — GLADYS KRIEBLE DELMAS FOUNDATION (Predoctoral & Postdoctoral Grants in Venice & the Veneto)

521 5th Avenue, Suite 1612
New York NY 10175-1699
212/687-0011
FAX: 212/687-8877
E-Mail: DelmasFdtn@aol.com
Internet: www.delmas.org

AMOUNT: $500-$12,500

DEADLINE(S): DEC 15

FIELD(S): Research of Venice and the former Venetian empire and study of contemporary Venetian society and culture.

Pre- and postdoctoral grants for historical research on Venice. Humanities and social sciences are eligible areas of study, including archaeology, architecture, art, bibliography, economics, history, history of science, law, literature, music, political science, religion, and theater.

Applicants must have experience in advanced research and be U.S. citizens/residents; grad students must have fulfilled all doctoral requirements except dissertation by Dec. 15.

891 — GRADUATE INSTITUTE OF INTERNATIONAL STUDIES (Scholarships)

P.O. Box 36
132 Rue do Lausanne
CH-1211 Geneva 21 SWITZERLAND
(+41 22) 731 17 30
FAX: (+41-22) 731 27 77
E-Mail: info@hei.unige.ch
Internet: http://heiwww.unige.ch

AMOUNT: Varies

DEADLINE(S): None

FIELD(S): International history and politics, political science, international economics, international law

Scholarships to support graduate diploma and Ph.D students already registered at the Institute. Open to applicants with excellent, active knowledge of one of the institute's two working languages, French & English, and sufficient passive knowledge of the other.

Contact above sources for complete information.

892 — HENRY A. MURRAY RESEARCH CENTER OF RADCLIFFE COLLEGE (Jeanne Humphrey Block Dissertation Award Program)

10 Garden Street
Cambridge MA 02138
617/495-8140
FAX: 617/496-3993
E-Mail: mrc@radcliffe.edu
Internet: www.radcliffe.edu/murray

AMOUNT: $2,500

DEADLINE(S): APR 1

FIELD(S): Women's Issues

For female doctoral students. Proposals should focus on sex and gender differences or some developmental issue of particular concern to American girls or women. Projects drawing on center data will be given priority, although this is not a requirement.

See website or write to above address for more information.

893 — HILLEL INTERNATIONAL CENTER (The Bittker Fellowship)

Eran Gasko
1640 Rhode Island Ave. NW
Washington DC 20036
202/857-6637, 202/857-6560
FAX: 202/857-6693
E-Mail: smusher@hillel.org
Internet: www.hillel.org/careermoves/bittker.htm

AMOUNT: Professional Experience

DEADLINE(S): None specified

FIELD(S): Student Leadership/Jewish Awareness

One-year professional experience for an oustanding recent graduate, who coordinates student leadership and Jewish awareness activities nationwide. The Fellow establishes the network of student leaders and enhances their communication through national publications, conference calls, and the Internet. Task forces include Jewish Awareness/Identity, Women's Issues, Graduate Student Life, and Education.

Contact Eran Gasko, Human Resources, for an application.

894 — HILLEL INTERNATIONAL CENTER (The Public Policy Fellowship)

Eran Gasko
1640 Rhode Island Ave. NW
Washington DC 20036
202/857-6543, 202/857-6560
FAX: 202/857-6693
E-Mail: smusher@hillel.org
Internet: www.hillel.org/careermoves/
publicpolicy.htm

AMOUNT: Professional Experience

DEADLINE(S): None specified

FIELD(S): Public Policy/Social Issues

One-year professional experience for an oustanding recent Jewish graduate, who coordinates public policy initiatives nationwide. The Fellow strives to increase student activism in political and social issues. S/he works with students and national organizations to create innovative initiatives in social action, campus community relations councils, environmental issues, Israel programming, and international relief efforts.

Contact Eran Gasko, Human Resources, for an application.

895 — INSTITUT D'ETUDES FRANCAISES D'AVIGNON/BRYN MAWR COLLEGE (Scholarships for Summer Study in Avignon, France)

Institut d'etudes francaises d'Avignon
Bryn Mfawr College
Bryn Mawr PA 1901000-2899
610/526-5083
FAX: 610/526-7479
Internet: www.brynmawr.edu/Adm/academic/
special/avignon/details.html

AMOUNT: Varies

DEADLINE(S): MAR 15

FIELD(S): French-related studies

Scholarships based on academic excellence and financial need for a six-week summer study program in Avignon, France. Program is offered to male and female students from other colleges as well as Bryn Mawr. For graduates and undergraduates who have completed three years of college-level French or equivalent.

Contact the Director of the Institute for application information.

896 — INSTITUTE FOR ADVANCED STUDIES IN THE HUMANITIES (Visiting Research Fellowships)

Univ Edinburgh
Hope Park Square
Edinburgh EH8 9NW SCOTLAND UK
0131 650 4671
FAX: 0131 668 2252

E-Mail: iash@ed.ac.uk
Internet: www.ed.ac.uk/iash/homepage.html

AMOUNT: Non-stipendiary*

DEADLINE(S): DEC 1

FIELD(S): Arts; Social Sciences; Law; Music; Divinity

Postdoctoral research fellowships of between two and six months are tenable at the Institute for Advanced Studies in the Humanities. Based on academic record and publications. *Most fellowships are honorary, but limited support towards expenses is available to a small number of candidates. Fellows are allocated a study room within the Institute and hold one or two seminars during their tenure. Must submit research report at end of fellowship. No teaching required.

15 awards annually. Not renewable. Contact Mrs. Anthea Taylor for an application.

897 — INSTITUTE FOR HUMANE STUDIES (Humane Studies Fellowship)

4084 University Dr., Ste. 101
Fairfax VA 22030-6812
703/934-6920 or 800/697-8799
FAX: 703/352-7535
E-Mail: ihs@gmu.edu
Internet: www.theihs.org

AMOUNT: up to $12,000

DEADLINE(S): DEC 31

FIELD(S): Social Sciences; Law; Humanities; Jurisprudence; Journalism

Awards are for graduate and advanced undergraduate students pursuing degrees at any accredited domestic or foreign school. Based on academic performance, demonstrated interest in classical liberal ideas, and potential to contribute to the advancement of a free society.

90 awards annually. Apply online or contact IHS for an application.

898 — INSTITUTE FOR THE STUDY OF WORLD POLITICS (Dissertation Fellowships)

1755 Massachusetts Ave. NW
Washington DC 20036
202/588-9797
Internet: fundforpeace.org/iswp.htm

AMOUNT: Varies

DEADLINE(S): FEB 16

FIELD(S): International Relations; Environmental Issues; Population Studies (Social Science aspects); Human Rights; Arms Control; Third World Development; Agricultural Development; Public Health, etc.

For doctoral candidates conducting dissertation research in above areas to promote scholarly examination of political, economic, and social issues

that affect the security, well-being, and dignity of the peoples of the world. Financial need is a consideration. For citizens of any country.

Write for complete information.

899 — INSTITUTE FOR THE STUDY OF WORLD POLITICS (Dorothy Danforth Compton Fellowships)

1755 Massachusetts Ave. NW
Washington DC 20036
202/588-9797
Internet: fundforpeace.org/iswp.htm

AMOUNT: Varies

DEADLINE(S): MAR 16

FIELD(S): International Relations; Environmental Issues; Population Studies (Social Science aspects); Human Rights; Arms Control; Third World Development; Agricultural Development; Public Health, etc.

For masters or doctoral candidates researching in the above areas to promote scholarly examination of political, economic, and social issues that affect the security, well-being, and dignity of the peoples of the world. Must be African American, Hispanic American, and Native American students who are U.S. citizens and studying in U.S. institutions. Financial need is a consideration.

Write for complete information.

900 — INTER-AMERICAN FOUNDATION (Field Research Fellowship Programs for U.S., Latin American, and Caribbean Citizens)

901 N. Stuart St., 10th Floor
Arlington VA 22203
703/841-3800
FAX: 703/527-3529
E-Mail: correo@aif.gov
Internet: www.iaf.gov

AMOUNT: Varies

DEADLINE(S): APR 28

FIELD(S): International Relations, Social Sciences, Humanities, Latin American Studies

Fellowships for Latin American, Carribean, and U.S. doctoral level students for field research in Latin America and the Caribbean. Must be enrolled in U.S. university.

Access website for deadline and application information. Organization does not mail information.

901 — INTER-AMERICAN FOUNDATION (Master's Research Fellowships)

901 N. Stuart St., 10th Floor
Arlington VA 22203
703/841-3800
FAX: 703/527-3529
E-Mail: correo@aif.gov;Internet: www.iaf.gov

AMOUNT: Varies

DEADLINE(S): APR

FIELD(S): Latin American & Caribbean Studies, Internations Relations, Social Sciences, Humanities, etc.

Open to masters students enrolled in U.S. universities for field research in Latin American or the Caribbean. For citizens of Caribbean and Latin American independent countries, and the U.S.

Access website for deadline and application information. Organization does not mail information.

902 — INTERNATIONAL INSTITUTE FOR APPLIED SYSTEMS ANALYSIS (Fellowships for Young Scientists' Summer Program at the IIASA in Vienna, Austria)

A-2361 Laxenburg
AUSTRIA
617/576-5019
FAX: 617/576-5050
E-Mail: mcollins@amacad.org
Internet: http://www.iiasa.ac.at

AMOUNT: Airfare and modest living expenses

DEADLINE(S): JAN 15

FIELD(S): Population, global change, economics, air pollution, transportation, forestry resorces, energy stratiegy, risk modeling, dynamic systems modeling

For advanced graduate and predoctoral candidates with research interests compatible with IIASA projects. Must have working level of written and spoken English and academic accomplishments and publications demonstrating superior qualifications.

4-7 annual awards. Contact Dr. Margaret Goud Collins (in U.S.) or Ms. Margaret Traber (in Austria).

903 — INTERNATIONAL INSTITUTE FOR POPULATION SCIENCES (Master & Ph.D. of Population Studies Fellowships)

Govandi Station Road
Deonar, Mumbai-400 088, Maharashtra
INDIA
(091) 22-5563254/5/6
FAX: (091) 22-5563257
E-Mail: iips@bom3.vsnl.net.in
Internet: www.unescap.org/pop/popin/
profiles/india/welcome.htm or
www.ncst.emet.in/other/iips

AMOUNT: Varies

DEADLINE(S): MAY

FIELD(S): Population Studies

Must have a master's degree of a recognized university in any of th e following: statistics, mathematics, economics, sociology, anthropology, psychology,

geography, social work, etc. For the Ph.D. fellowship, must have master's degree in Population Studies with at least 55% marks and National Educational Test (NET); master's degree in social sciences, statistics, mathematics with at least 55% marks also eligible, but must complete one year at Institute first.

Correspondance course also available. Not renewable. Contact the Director of IIPS for applications.

904 — INTERNATIONAL INSTITUTE FOR POPULATION SCIENCES (Diploma of Population Studies Grant)

Govandi Station Road
Deonar, Mumbai-400 088, Maharashtra
INDIA
(091) 22-5563254/5/6
FAX: (091) 22-5563257
E-Mail: iips@bom3.vsnl.net.in
Internet: www.unescap.org/pop/popin/
profiles/india/welcome.htm or
www.ncst.emet.in/other/iips

AMOUNT: Varies

DEADLINE(S): MAY

FIELD(S): Population Studies

Must have a bachelor's degree with some experience of handling population data. No restrictions as to citizenship.

Not renewable. Contact the Director of IIPS for an application.

905 — INTERNATIONAL INSTITUTE FOR POPULATION SCIENCES (Short-Term Training Programmes for Indian Officials & Foreign Nationals)

Govandi Station Road
Deonar, Mumbai-400 088, Maharashtra INDIA
(091) 22-5563254/5/6
FAX: (091) 22-5563257
E-Mail: iips@bom3.vsnl.net.in
Internet: www.unescap.org/pop/popin/
profiles/india/welcome.htm or
www.ncst.emet.in/other/iips

AMOUNT: Varies

DEADLINE(S): MAY

FIELD(S): Population Studies

These courses range from 2 weeks to 3 months. One program is for personnel working in the Population Research Centres, Medical Colleges, Health & Family Welfare Departments, Universities, etc. of India or for Senior Officials of the Planning Departments of various States of India. Another is for officials of foreign countries. The expenses of such training programs are borne by sponsoring agencies.

Not renewable. Contact the Director of IIPS for an application.

906 — INTERNATIONAL RESEARCH AND EXCHANGES BOARD (Mongolia Research Fellowship Program)

1616 H St., NW
Washington DC 20006
202/628-8188
FAX: 202/628-8189
E-Mail: edickson@irex.org
Internet: www.irex.org

AMOUNT: $7,000

DEADLINE(S): DEC 15

FIELD(S): Humanities; Social Sciences

Open to US and Mongolian citizens pursuing predoctoral or postdoctoral studies/research in the humanities and social sciences as related to Mongolia. Financial need NOT a factor.

4-5 awards annually. Not renewable. See website or contact Emilie Dickson for an application.

907 — INTERNATIONAL RESEARCH AND EXCHANGES BOARD (Consortium for the Humanities & Social Sciences)

1616 H St., NW
Washington DC 20006
202/628-8188
FAX: 202/628-8189
E-Mail: edickson@irex.org
Internet: www.irex.org

AMOUNT: $10,000 (max.)

DEADLINE(S): JAN 14

FIELD(S): Humanities; Social Sciences

Grant is open to students of any nationality who are pursuing a doctoral, postgraduate, or professional degree in the humanities or social sciences. Award must benefit a university in Armenia, Azerbaijan, Georgia, Russia, and/or Ukraine. Financial need NOT a factor.

20 awards annually. Not renewable. See website or contact Emilie Dickson for an application.

908 — INTERNATIONAL RESEARCH AND EXCHANGES BOARD (Russian-US Young Leadership Fellows for Public Service Program for US Citizens)

1616 H St., NW
Washington DC 20006
202/628-8188
FAX: 202/628-8189
E-Mail: irex@info.irex.org
Internet: www.irex.org

AMOUNT: Stipend + tuition, travel, living, & housing

DEADLINE(S): NOV 30

FIELD(S): Russian Studies

Grants of two weeks to two months are available to graduate students who are US citizens/permanent residents for brief visits to pursue scholarly projects on Central & Eastern Europe, Eurasia, or Mongolia. Must have received equivalent of a bachelor's degree, have a working knowledge of the Russian language, and be below the age of 30 at time of application. Postdoctoral humanities scholars may do research in Turkey or Iran. Financial need NOT a factor.

20 awards annually. Not renewable. Contact Jessica Jeffcoat, Senior Program Officer, for an application.

909 — JAMES MADISON MEMORIAL FELLOWSHIP (Fellowship for Teachers)

2000 K St. NW
Washington DC 20006
202/653-8700 or 1-800/525-6928
FAX: 202/653-6045
Internet: www.jamesmadison.com

AMOUNT: $24,000 prorated over study period

DEADLINE(S): MAR 1

FIELD(S): Teaching American History/ government, or social studies—concentration on the U.S. Constitution

Fellowships for teachers (senior fellows) in grades 7-12 in the above fields to pursue an MA degree. Also for full-time college seniors and grad students (junior fellows). U.S. citizens or U.S. nationals. Fellows are selected from each state and from D.C., Puerto Rico, Guam, Virgin Islands, American Samoa, Northern Mariana Islands, and Palau. Program designed to enhance teaching about the U.S. Constitution.

Application is on website or contact: American College Testing, P.O. Box 4030, Iowa City, IA 52243-4030; 800/525-6928, E-Mail: Recogprog@ACT-ACT4-PO.act.org

910 — JAPAN FOUNDATION (Doctoral and Research Fellowships)

152 W. 57th Street
39th Floor
New York NY 10019
212/489-0299
FAX: 212/489-0409

AMOUNT: Approx 310,000 yen per month stipend + 239,000 yen for housing

DEADLINE(S): NOV 1 (U.S. citizens/residents); DEC 1 (Non-U.S. citizens/residents)

FIELD(S): Japanese Studies/Language

Fellowships intended to provide Ph.D candidates, scholars, and researchers an opportunity to conduct studies in Japan.

Should be sufficiently proficient in Japanese language to pursue research in Japan.

911 — JAPAN-AMERICA SOCIETY OF WASHINGTON (H. William Tanaka Scholarship)

1020 19th St. NW LL#40
Washington DC 20036
202/833-2210
202/833-2456

AMOUNT: $15,000

DEADLINE(S): DEC 1

FIELD(S): Japanese

Open to graduate and postgraduate students for study in Japan who are enrolled in a school in the District of Columbia, Maryland, Virginia, or West Virginia. Selection based on scholastic achievement, motivation, and financial need.

For U.S. citizens. Write to organization for complete information and application.

912 — JAPANESE AMERICAN CITIZENS LEAGUE (Minoru Yasui Memorial Scholarship)

1765 Sutter St.
San Francisco CA 94115
415/921-5225
FAX: 415/931-4671
E-Mail: jacl@jacl.org
Internet: www.jacl.org

AMOUNT: Varies

DEADLINE(S): APR 1

FIELD(S): Human & Civil Rights; Sociology; Law; Education

Open to JACL members or their children only. For graduate students with a strong interest in human and civil rights. Student must be currently enrolled in, or planning to enroll in, an accredited graduate school. Financial need NOT a factor.

40 awards annually. For membership information or an application, send a self-addressed, stamped envelope to above address.

913 — JEWISH BRAILLE INSTITUTE OF AMERICA (Scholarships)

110 E. 30th St.
New York NY 10016
212/889-2525
FAX: 212/689-3692
E-Mail: admin@jewishbraille.org
Internet: www.jewishbraille.org

AMOUNT: Varies

DEADLINE(S): None specified

FIELD(S): Jewish Studies

Jewish faith. Open to legally blind graduate students who are pursuing studies leading to professional careers in Jewish service such as a rabbi, cantor, Jewish communal worker, etc. Must demonstrate financial need.

Write for complete information.

914 — JEWISH COMMUNITY CENTERS ASSOCIATION (JCCA Scholarship Program)

15 East 26th Street
New York NY 10010-1579
212/532-4958, ext. 246
FAX: 212/481-4174
E-Mail: Webmaster@jcca.org
Internet: www.jcca.org

AMOUNT: Up to $7,500

DEADLINE(S): FEB 15

FIELD(S): Social Work; Jewish Communal Studies; Physical Education; Early Childhood Education; Cultural Arts

Open to graduate students of the Jewish faith who are enrolled in a master's degree program and are committed to a career in the Jewish community center field in North America. Must have an undergraduate GPA of at least 3.0, leadership potential, and a strong Jewish background.

8 awards annually. Financial need NOT a factor. Contact Michelle Cohen at above address for an application.

915 — JOHN CARTER BROWN LIBRARY (Research Fellowships)

Box 1894
Providence RI 02912
401/863-2725
E-Mail: JCBL_Fellowships@Brown.edu
Internet: www.brown.edu/Facilities/
John_Carter_Brown_Library

AMOUNT: $1,000/month (short-term); $$2,800/ month and up (long-term)

DEADLINE(S): JAN 15

FIELD(S): History of the Western hemisphere during the colonial period and its relationships with Europe

Research fellowships for Americans or foreign nationals engaged in pre- or postdoctoral or independent research. Short-term fellowships are for 2 to 4 months; long-term fellowships are 5 to 9 months. The Library's holdings are concentrated on the above fields.

Fellows are expected to be in continuous residence at the Library for the fellowship's term. Graduate students are not eligible for long-term fellowships.

916 — KOSCIUSZKO FOUNDATION (Study/ Research Programs for Americans in Poland)

15 East 65th Street
New York NY 10021-6595
212/734-2130
FAX 212/628-4552
Internet: www.kosciuszkofoundation.org/
grants/poland.htm

AMOUNT: Varies

DEADLINE(S): JAN 15

FIELD(S): Polish Language, Literature, History, and/or Culture

Open to American students entering their junior or senior college year and graduate students enrolled in an M.A. or Ph.D program with the exception of Ph.D candidates at the dissertation level. For study at universities in Poland.

$50 non-refundable application fee. Application is at website. Contact organization or visit website for complete information.

917 — MEMORIAL FOUNDATION FOR JEWISH CULTURE (International Fellowships in Jewish Studies)

15 East 26th St.
Room 1903
New York NY 10010
212/679-4074

AMOUNT: $1,000-$4,000 per year

DEADLINE(S): OCT 31

FIELD(S): Jewish Studies

Program is to assist well qualified individuals in carrying out an independent scholarly literary or art project in a field of Jewish specialization. Applicants should possess knowledge & experience necessary to implement the project.

Grants are for one academic year but may be renewed. Write for complete information.

918 — MEMORIAL FOUNDATION FOR JEWISH CULTURE (International Doctoral Scholarship)

15 East 26th St.
Room 1903
New York NY 10010
212/679-4074

AMOUNT: $1,000-$5,000 per year

DEADLINE(S): OCT 31

FIELD(S): Jewish Studies

Scholarships open to graduate students enrolled in a doctoral program at a recognized university. Program is to help train qualified individuals for careers in Jewish scholarship. Priority is given to applicants at the dissertation level.

Scholarships are renewable up to 4 years. Write for complete information.

919 — MEMORIAL FOUNDATION FOR JEWISH CULTURE (Post-Rabbinic Scholarships)

15 East 26th St., Room 1703
New York NY 10010
212/679-4074

AMOUNT: Up to $3,000

DEADLINE(S): NOV 30

FIELD(S): Rabbinical Studies

Open to newly ordained rabbis for advanced training as judges on rabbinical courts, heads of institutions of higher learning, or other advanced religious leadership positions.

Applicants should be enrolled full-time in a rabbinical seminarym yeshivam or other institution of Jewish higher learning. Write for complete information.

920 — MEMORIAL FOUNDATION FOR JEWISH CULTURE (Soviet Jewry Community Service Scholarship Program)

15 East 26th St., Room 1703
New York NY 10010
212/679-4074

AMOUNT: Not specified

DEADLINE(S): NOV 30

FIELD(S): Jewish studies

Open to Jews from the former Soviet Union enrolled or planning to enroll in recognized institutions of higher Jewish learning. Must agree to serve a community of Soviet Jews anywhere in the world for a minimum of three years.

Grants are to help prepare well qualified Soviet Jews to serve in the FSU. Write for complete information.

921 — MINISTRY OF EDUCATION OF THE REPUBLIC OF CHINA (Scholarships for Foreign Students)

5 South Chung-Shan Road
Taipei
Taiwan REPUBLIC OF CHINA
(86) (02) 356-5696
FAX: (86) (02) 397-6778

AMOUNT: NT$10,000 (per month)

DEADLINE(S): Varies (inquire of school)

FIELD(S): Chinese studies or language

Undergraduate and graduate scholarships are available to foreign students wishing to study in Taiwan. Must have already studied in R.O.C. for at least one term. Must study full time.

Scholarships are renewable. 300 awards per year. Write for complete information or please contact colleges directly.

922 — MINISTRY OF EDUCATION, SCIENCE, AND CULTURE (Icelandic Studies Scholarships)

Solvholsgata 4
Reykjavik IS-150 ICELAND
354/560-9500
FAX: 354/562-3068

E-Mail: postur@mrn.stjr.is
Internet: www.mrn.stjr.is

AMOUNT: Tuition + 444,000 kronur

DEADLINE(S): Varies

FIELD(S): Icelandic Studies

Eight-month scholarship is open to students at any level of study to pursue studies in Icelandic language, literature, and history at the University of Iceland.

25 awards annually. Contact Ministry of Education for an application.

923 — NATIONAL ITALIAN AMERICAN FOUNDATION (Bolla Wines Scholarship)

1860 19th St. NW
Washington DC 20009-5599
202/530-5315

AMOUNT: $1,000

DEADLINE(S): MAY 31

FIELD(S): International studies—emphasis on Italian business or Italian-American history.

For undergraduate or graduate students of Italian heritage with a GPA of 3.0+ and a background in international studies. Must write an essay on "The Importance of Italy in Today's Business World." (3-pages, double spaced, typed.)

Community service and financial need considered. Write for appliacation and details.

924 — NATIONAL PARKS SERVICE (Science Scholars Program)

1849 C St., NW
Washington DC 20240
202/208-6843
E-Mail: aspiceland@goparks.org
Internet: www.nps.gov

AMOUNT: $25,000/yr.

DEADLINE(S): JUN 15

FIELD(S): Biological, Physical, Social, & Cultural Sciences

Three-year scholarships to Ph.D. candidates pursuing degrees in above fields. Objectives are to encourage young scientists to engage in park-related research, conduct innovative research on issues central to the National Parks, and encourage use of parks as laboratories for sciences. NPF will transfer the scholarship funds to each student's university, providing for tuition, field work, stipend, & other research expenses. Must submit research proposal.

4 awards annually. See website or contact Dr. Gary E. Machlis, Program Director, at NPS for an application. Winners announced shortly after August 15th.

925 — NEWBERRY LIBRARY (Long-Term Fellowships)

60 West Walton Street
Chicago IL 60610-3380
312/943-9090
E-Mail: research@newberry.org
Internet: www.newberry.org

AMOUNT: Up to $30,000

DEADLINE(S): JAN 20

FIELD(S): Humanities, History, & related fields

Six postdoctoral fellowship programs are available for scholars wishing to use the Library's collection for writing or research. Fellowships last six to eleven months, and each have slightly different requirements.

See website for details and an application or write to above address.

926 — NEWBERRY LIBRARY (Monticello College Foundation Fellowship For Women)

60 West Walton Street
Chicago IL 60610-3380
312/255-3660
E-Mail: research@newberry.org
Internet: www.newberry.org

AMOUNT: $12,500

DEADLINE(S): JAN 20

FIELD(S): Humanities, History, Study of Women

Six-month post-doctoral fellowships for women in the early stages of their academic careers. For research, writing, and participation in the intellectual life of the Library. Applicant's topic must be related to Newberry's collections; preference given to proposals concerned with the study of women.

See website for application or write to above address.

927 — NEWBERRY LIBRARY (Short-Term Fellowships)

60 West Walton Street
Chicago IL 60610-3380
312/943-9090
E-Mail: research@newberry.org
Internet: www.newberry.org

AMOUNT: $800-$1,500/month

DEADLINE(S): MAR 1

FIELD(S): Humanities, History, & related fields

Nine programs for postdoctoral scholars or doctoral students at the dissertation stage. Study varies from two weeks to three months and is for those making use of Newberry's collections. Each program has slightly different requirements.

See website for details and applications or write to above address.

928 — NEWBERRY LIBRARY (Special Fellowships)

60 West Walton Street
Chicago IL 60610-3380
312/255-3666
E-Mail: research@newberry.org
Internet: www.newberry.org

AMOUNT: Varies

DEADLINE(S): DEC 15

FIELD(S): Humanities, History, & related fields

Fellowships for three months to one year for doctoral or postdoctoral students to study in Germany, France, or Great Britain in fields related to Newberry's collections. Some deadlines JAN 20th. Specific locations are: Wolfenb, ttel, Germany; Ecole Nationale des Chartes, Paris, France; and the British Academy, Great Britain.

See website for more details and applications or write to above address.

929 — NEWBERRY LIBRARY (Weiss/Brown Publication Subvention Award)

60 West Walton Street
Chicago IL 60610-3380
312/255-3666
E-Mail: research@newberry.org
Internet: www.newberry.org

AMOUNT: up to $15,000

DEADLINE(S): JAN 20

FIELD(S): European Civilization/History/Culture

Awards for authors of scholarly books already accepted for publication. Subject matter must cover European civilization before 1700 in the areas of music, theatre, French or Italian literature or cultural studies. Applicants must provide detailed information regarding the publication and the subvention request.

See website for more details and application or write to above address.

930 — NORWEGIAN INFORMATION SERVICE (Norwegian Emigration Fund of 1975)

825 Third Ave, 38th Floor
New York NY 10022-7584
212/421-7333

AMOUNT: Varies (NOK 5,000 to NOK 70,000)

DEADLINE(S): FEB 1

FIELD(S): History of Norwegian emigration and relations betwwe the U.S. and Norway

Purpose of the fund is to award scholarships to Americans for advanced or specialized studies in Norway of subjects dealing with emigration history and relations between Norway and the U.S.

Must be U.S. citizen or resident. U.S.institutions may also be eligible. Write for complete information.

931 — OPEN SOCIETY INSTITUTE (Individual Project Fellowships)

400 West 59th St.
New York NY 10019
212/548-0600 or 212/757-2323
FAX: 212/548-4679 or 212/548-4600
Internet: www.soros.org/fellow/individual.html

AMOUNT: Varies

DEADLINE(S): Varies

FIELD(S): Any field of study related to creating an open society: reliance on the rule of law, the existence of a democratically elected government, a diverse and vigorous civil society, and respect for minorities and minority opinions.

Two-year fellowships for use in selected universities in the U.S. for international students. For students/professionals in fields related to environmental policy, legislation, and remediation techniques applicable to their home countries.

To apply, contact the Soros Foundation/Open Society Institute. Further details on website.

932 — PACIFIC CULTURAL FOUNDATION (Grants on Chinese Studies)

38 Chungking South Rd. Sec. 3 Taipei
Taipei Taiwan R.O.C.
3377155

AMOUNT: Varies

DEADLINE(S): MAR 1; SEP 1

FIELD(S): Chinese Studies

Various grants open to citizens residing in the free world outside of Taiwan for post-graduate research and publication Chinese studies (both Taiwan and Mainland). Must have at least a master's degree.

Write for complete information.

933 — PALESTINE EXPLORATION FUND RESEARCH GRANT

Hinde Mews Marylebone Lane
London W1M 5RR England
0171 935-5379

AMOUNT: Variable in pounds sterling

DEADLINE(S): JAN 31

FIELD(S): Palestine Studies

Grants are offered for specific research into any aspect of Palestine and/or Palestinian life down to the end of the period of Ottoman rule.

Contact Dr. Rupert Chapman; Executive Secretary (address above) for complete information.

934 — PHI BETA KAPPA (Mary Isabel Sibley Fellowship)

1785 Massachusetts Ave., NW, 4th Floor
Washington DC 20036

202/265-3808
FAX: 202/986-1601
E-Mail: lsurles@pbk.org
AMOUNT: $20,000
DEADLINE(S): JAN 15
FIELD(S): Greek Studies (odd-numbered years); French Studies (even-numbered years)

Candidates must be unmarried women between 25 and 35 years of age who have demonstrated their ability to carry on original research. Must hold doctorate or have fulfilled all requirements for doctorate except dissertation, and must be planning to devote full-time work to research of language and literature during the fellowship year that begins in September. Eligibility is NOT restricted to members of Phi Beta Kappa.

Contact the Fellowship Committee for an application.

935 — PITT RIVERS MUSEUM (James A. Swan Fund)

Unversity of Oxford South Parks Road
Oxford OX1 3PP England UK
+44-1865-270927
E-Mail: peter.mitchell@prm.ox.ac.uk
(please mark "Swan Fund")
AMOUNT: 1,000-2,000 pounds sterling
DEADLINE(S): MAR 1
FIELD(S): African Studies, Archaelogy, Anthropology

Research grants for graduate students and established researchers relating to the Later Stone Age prehistory of southern Africa, contemporary Bushman and Pygmy peoples, or relevant museum collections.

Approximately 10 awards per year. Renewable. Contact the Secretary at above address for complete information.

936 — POPULATION COUNCIL (Fellowships in Population Sciences)

One Dag Hammarskjold Plaza
New York NY 10017
212/339-0636
FAX: 212/755-6052
E-Mail: rmohanam@popcouncil.org
Internet: www.popcouncil.org
AMOUNT: $25,000/yr. for 2 years
DEADLINE(S): OCT 31
FIELD(S): Population Sciences

Postdoctoral fellowships for study in population sciences in Nairobi, Kenya, Africa. Open to citizens of any country.

Two awards per year. Selection criteria will stress academic excellence and prospective contribution to the population field. For information and applications contact Raji Mohanam at above address. In Kenya, contact: Carol Libamira, APPRC

Coordinator, Population Council, Mutichoice Towers, Upper Hill, P.O. Box 17643, Nairobi, Kenya. 254/2.713.480/1-3.

937 — POPULATION COUNCIL (Fellowships in Social Sciences)

Policy Research Division
One Dag Hammarskjold Plaza
New York NY 10017
212/339-0671
FAX: 212/755-6052
E-Mail: ssfellowship@popcouncil.org
Internet: www.popcouncil.org
AMOUNT: Monthly stipend, partial tuition/fees, transportation, book/supply allowance, & health insurance
DEADLINE(S): DEC 15
FIELD(S): Population Studies; Demography; Sociology; Anthropology; Economics; Public Health; Geography

Twelve-month award is open to doctoral & postdoctoral scholars for advanced training in above fields that deal with developing world. Doctoral students may request support for dissertation fieldwork/writing. Postdoctorates may pursue research, midcareer training, or resident training. Based on academic excellence, prospective contribution, & well-conceived research proposal. Preference given to those from developing countries.

See website or contact Fellowship Coordinator for an application.

938 — QUEEN'S UNIVERSITY OF BELFAST (Mary McNeill Scholarship in Irish Studies)

8 Fitzwilliam Street
Belfast BT9 6AW NORTHERN IRELAND
+44 1232 273386
FAX: +44 1232 439238
E-Mail: irish.studies@qub.ac.uk
Internet: www.qub.ac.uk/iis/
AMOUNT: 2,500 pounds sterling
DEADLINE(S): MAY 31
FIELD(S): Irish Studies

Scholarships at Queen's University in Belfast, Northern Ireland, for American and Canadian students pursuing an M.A. degree in Irish studies. Course is a one-year program. Subjects which can be studied within above field include archeology, English, modern history, economic/social history, sociology, and politics. Award is based on academic merit and reasons for taking the course.

Contact Professor Brian Walker, Institute of Irish Studies, at above address for an application.

939 — QUEEN'S UNIVERSITY OF BELFAST (Research Fellowships)

Institute of Irish Studies
Belfast BT7 1NN NORTHERN IRELAND
273386
AMOUNT: 12,500 pounds sterling + fees
DEADLINE(S): FEB 29
FIELD(S): Irish Studies

Fellowships awarded for one year at the Institute of Irish Studies. Candidates should normally hold a good honors degree and have completed their Ph.D.

Write for complete information.

940 — ROCKEFELLER FOUNDATION (African Dissertation Internship Awards)

420 Fifth Ave.
New York NY 10018-2702
212/869-8500
212/764-3468
Internet: www.rockfound.org
AMOUNT: Cost of project
DEADLINE(S): None given
FIELD(S): Agriculture, environment, health, life sciences, population, and schooling

For African graduate students in U.S. and Canadian universities (but not to permanent residents) to return to Africa to carry out dissertation research at a local university or research institution. Priority given to above topics.

Students are strongly urged to be in the field for at least 12 months. Contact above location for details.

941 — SCHOOL OF ORIENTAL AND AFRICAN STUDIES (Master's Scholarships)

Thornhaugh St.
Russell Square
London WC1H 0XG ENGLAND
0171-637-2388
FAX: 0171-436 3844
AMOUNT: 6,855 pounds sterling
DEADLINE(S): MAR 31
FIELD(S): Oriental Studies; African Studies

Scholarships are open to master's degree students in the above areas. Awards tenable at the University of London School of Oriental and African Studies.

8 awards annually. Contact T. Harvey, Registrar, for an application and/or enrollment information.

942 — SMITHSONIAN INSTITUTION (Fellowship Program)

Office of fellowships & Grants
955 L'Enfant Plaza, Suite 7000
Washington DC 20560
202/287-3271

E-Mail: http://www.si.edu/research+study
Internet: siofg@sivm.si.edu

AMOUNT: $3,000-$25,000 depending on level and length

DEADLINE(S): JAN 15

FIELD(S): Animal behavior, ecology, environmental science (including emphasis on the tropics, anthropology (& archaeology), astrophysics, astronomy, earth sciences, paleobiology, evolutionary/systematic biology, history of science and technology, history of art, esp. American, contemporary, African, and Asian, 20th century American crafts, decorative arts, social/cultural history of the US, or folklife.

For research in residence at the Smithsonian for graduate students, both pre- and postdoctoral.

Research to be in the fields listed above.

943 — SMITHSONIAN INSTITUTION (Minority Student Internship Program)

Fellowships & Grants
955 L'Enfant Plaza, Suite 7000
MRC 902
Washington DC 20560
202/287-3271
FAX: 202/287-3691
E-Mail: siofg@ofg.si.edu
Internet: www.si.edu/research+study

AMOUNT: $300/week + possible travel expenses

DEADLINE(S): FEB 15

FIELD(S): Humanities, Environmental Studies, Cultural Studies, Natural History, Earth Science, Art History, Biology, & related fields

Ten-week internships in residence at the Smithsonian for US minority students to participate in research or museum-related activities in above fields. For undergrads or grads with at least a 3.0 GPA. Essay, resume, transcripts, and references required with application. Internships are full-time and are offered for Summer, Fall, or Spring tenures.

Write for application.

944 — SOCIAL SCIENCE RESEARCH COUNCIL (Eurasia Fellowship Program)

810 Seventh Ave., 31st Fl.
New York NY 10019
212/377-2700
FAX: 212/377-2727
E-Mail: eurasia@ssrc.org
Internet: www.ssrc.org

AMOUNT: $10,000 (graduate); $15,000 (dissertation); $24,000 (postdoctoral)

DEADLINE(S): NOV 1

FIELD(S): Soviet Studies

Open to US citizens/permanent residents enrolled in accredited graduate, dissertation, or postdoctoral programs in any discipline of the social sciences or humanities. Purpose is to enhance their disciplinary, methodological, or language training in relation to research on the Soviet Union and its successor states. Grants for summer language institutes also available.

See website or contact SSRC for an application.

945 — SOCIAL SCIENCE RESEARCH COUNCIL (Near & Middle East Fellowship Program)

810 Seventh Ave., 31st Fl.
New York NY 10019
212/377-2700
FAX: 212/377-2727
E-Mail: szanton@ssrc.org
Internet: www.ssrc.org

AMOUNT: Varies

DEADLINE(S): NOV 1

FIELD(S): Near & Middle East Studies

Open to US citizens currently enrolled in Ph.D. program in social sciences or humanities and will have completed two academic years of work toward the doctorate by June of following year. Graduates spend four to nine months preparing for dissertation research through training and study in the Middle East. Also open to US citizens to pursue dissertation research requiring field work in the Middle East. Research must be concerned with period since beginning of Islam.

See website or contact SSRC for an application.

946 — SOCIAL SCIENCE RESEARCH COUNCIL (Religion & Immigration Fellowship Program)

810 Seventh Ave.
31st Fl.
New York NY 10019
212/377-2700
FAX: 212/377-2727
E-Mail: religion@ssrc.org
Internet: www.ssrc.org

AMOUNT: $15,000 (doctoral); $20,000 (postdoctoral)

DEADLINE(S): JAN 12

FIELD(S): Religion & Immigration

Six-month postdoctoral and twelve-month doctoral dissertation awards are open to US citizens, permanent residents, and international students matriculated in a US university. Purpose is to foster innovative research that will advance theoretical understandings of the relationship between religion and the incorporation of immigrants into American society.

See website or contact SSRC for an application.

947 — SOCIAL SCIENCE RESEARCH COUNCIL (Southeast Asia Fellowship Program)

810 Seventh Ave., 31st Fl.
New York NY 10019
212/377-2700
FAX: 212/377-2727
E-Mail: Lam@ssrc.org
Internet: www.ssrc.org

AMOUNT: $15,000 (dissertation); $30,000 (postdoctoral)

DEADLINE(S): DEC 15

FIELD(S): Vietnam Studies

Provides 12- to 24-month dissertation and postdoctoral support for research on Vietnam across the disciplines of the social sciences and humanities. Must be enrolled full-time in Ph.D. programs in any of the social sciences or humanities at accredited universities in the US or Canada and establish an affiliation with a Vietnamese institution. Postdoctoral fellows should already have sufficient command of the Vietnamese language to conduct research in Vietnam.

See website or contact SSRC for an application after September 30th. Awards announced by June.

948 — SOCIETY FOR THE PSYCHOLOGICAL STUDY OF SOCIAL ISSUES (Clara Mayo Grants in Support of Master's Thesis and Pre-Dissertation Research on Sexism, Racism, or Prejudice)

PO Box 1248
Ann Arbor MI 48106-1248
Phone/TTY: 313/662-9130
FAX: 313/662-5607
E-Mail: spssi@spssi.org
Internet: www.spssi.org

AMOUNT: up to $1,000

DEADLINE(S): MAR 31

FIELD(S): Sexism, Racism, & Prejudice

These grants support research from students working on a master's thesis (preference given to those in terminal master's program) or pre-dissertation research on sexism, racism, or prejudice. Studies of application of theory or design of interventions/treatments to address these problems are welcome. Proposals that include college/university agreement to match amount requested are favored, but those without matching funds also considered.

4 awards annually. Applications availble on website. NO SCHOLARSHIPS AVAILABLE—REQUESTS FOR FINANCIAL AID WILL NOT BE ANSWERED.

949 — SOCIETY FOR THE PSYCHOLOGICAL STUDY OF SOCIAL ISSUES (Otto Klineburg Intercultural and International Relations Award)

PO Box 1248
Ann Arbor MI 48106-1248
Phone/TTY: 313/662-9130
FAX: 313/662-5607
E-Mail: spssi@spssi.org
Internet: www.spssi.org

AMOUNT: $1,000

DEADLINE(S): FEB 1

FIELD(S): Intercultural & International Relations

Annual award for the best paper or article on intercultural or international relations. Originality of the contribution, whether theoretical or empirical, will be given special weight. Entries can be either papers published during the current year or unpublished manuscripts. Send five copies of entry.

Contact SPSSI for details. Applications available on website. SPSSI DOES NOT OFFER SCHOLARSHIPS—INQUIRIES FOR FINANCIAL AID WILL NOT BE ANSWERED.

950 — SOCIETY FOR THE PSYCHOLOGICAL STUDY OF SOCIAL ISSUES (Gordon Allport Intergroup Relations Prize)

PO Box 1248
Ann Arbor MI 48106-1248
Phone/TTY: 313/662-9130
FAX: 313/662-9130
E-Mail: spssi@spssi.org
Internet: www.spssi.org

AMOUNT: $1,000

DEADLINE(S): DEC 31

FIELD(S): Sociology/Intergroup Relations

Annual award for the best paper or article on intergroup relations. Originality of the contribution, whether theoretical or empirical, is given special consideration. The research area encompassing intergroup relations includes such dimensions as age, sex, socioeconomic status, and race. Entries can be either papers published during the current year or unpublished manuscripts. Send five copies of entry.

Contact SPSSI for details. Applications available on website. SPSSI DOES NOT OFFER SCHOLARSHIPS—REQUESTS FOR FINANCIAL AID WILL NOT BE ANSWERED.

951 — SOCIETY FOR THE PSYCHOLOGICAL STUDY OF SOCIAL ISSUES (Grants-in-Aid Program)

PO Box 1248
Ann Arbor MI 48106-1248
Phone/TTY: 313/662-9130
FAX: 313/662-5607

E-Mail: spssi@spssi.org
Internet: www.spssi.org

AMOUNT: up to $2,000

DEADLINE(S): APR 1; NOV 13

FIELD(S): Social Problem Areas

For scientific/graduate student research in social problem areas related to the basic interests and goals of SPSSI, particularly those that are not likely to receive support from traditional sources. Proposals especially encouraged in the fields of sexism and racism. SPSSI prefers unique/timely projects, underrepresented institutions/new investigators, volunteer research teams, and actual, not pilot, projects. Funds not normally provided for travel or living expenses.

Contact SPSSI for details. Applications available on website. NO SCHOLARSHIPS AVAILABLE—REQUESTS FOR FINANCIAL AID WILL NOT BE ANSWERED.

952 — SOCIETY FOR THE PSYCHOLOGICAL STUDY OF SOCIAL ISSUES (The Sages Program: Action Grants for Experienced Scholars)

PO Box 1248
Ann Arbor MI 48106-1248
Phone/TTY: 313/662-9130
FAX: 313/662-5607
E-Mail: spssi@spssi.org
Internet: www.spssi.org

AMOUNT: Up to $2,000

DEADLINE(S): MAY 1

FIELD(S): Social Issues

Encourages intervention projects, non-partisan advocacy projects, and projects implementing public policy by retired social scientists over the age of 60. Proposals are invited for research projects applying social science principles to social issues in cooperation with a community, city, state, or federal organization or other not-for-profit group. Projects may also be done in cooperation with universities or colleges throughout the world or with the United Nations.

Contact SPSSI for details. Applications available on website. SCHOLARSHIPS NOT AVAILABLE—REQUESTS FOR FINANCIAL AID WILL NOT BE ANSWERED.

953 — SOCIETY FOR THE PSYCHOLOGICAL STUDY OF SOCIAL ISSUES (Louise Kidder Early Career Award)

PO Box 1248
Ann Arbor MI 48106-1248
Phone/TTY: 313/662-9130
FAX: 313/662-5607

E-Mail: spssi@spssi.org
Internet: www.spssi.org

AMOUNT: $500 + plaque

DEADLINE(S): MAY 1

FIELD(S): Social Issues Research

Award recognizes social issues researchers who have made substantial contributions to the field early in their careers. Nominees should be investigators who have made substantial contributions to social issues research within five years of receiving a graduate degree and who have demonstrated the potential to continue such contributions. To enter, send 3 copies of cover letter (stating accomplishments/future contributions), curriculum vitae, & 3 letters of support.

Contact SPSSI for details. Applications available on website. NO SCHOLARSHIPS AVAILABLE—REQUESTS FOR FINANCIAL AID WILL NOT BE ANSWERED.

954 — SONOMA CHAMBOLLE-MUSIGNY SISTER CITIES, INC. (Henri Cardinaux Memorial Scholarship)

Chamson Scholarship Committee
PO Box 1633
Sonoma CA 95476-1633
707/939-1344
FAX: 707/939-1344
E-Mail: Baileysci@vom.com

AMOUNT: up to $1,500 (travel + expenses)

DEADLINE(S): JUL 15

FIELD(S): Culinary Arts; Wine Industry; Art; Architecture; Music; History; Fashion

Hands-on experience working in above or similiar fields & living with a family in small French village in Burgundy or other French city. Must be Sonoma County, CA, resident at least 18 years of age & be able to communicate in French. Transcripts, employer recommendation, photograph, & essay (stating why, where, & when) required.

1 award. Non-renewable. Also offers opportunity for candidate in Chambolle-Musigny to obtain work experience & cultural exposure in Sonoma, CA.

955 — SONS OF NORWAY FOUNDATION (King Olav V Norwegian-American Heritage Fund)

1455 West Lake Street
Minneapolis MN 55408
612/827-3611

AMOUNT: $250-$3,000

DEADLINE(S): MAR 1

FIELD(S): Norwegian Studies

For U.S. citizens 18 or older who have demonstrated a keen and sincere interest in the Norwegian heritage. Must be enrolled in a recognized educational institution and be studying such topics as arts, crafts, literature, history, music, folklore, etc. of Norway.

Financial need is a consideration but it is secondary to scholarship. 12 awards per year.

956 — SONS OF NORWAY FOUNDATION (King Olav V Norwegian-American Heritage Fund)

1455 West Lake Street
Minneapolis MN 55408
Written inquiry

AMOUNT: $250-$3,000

DEADLINE(S): MAR 1

FIELD(S): American Studies

For Norwegian citizens 18 or older who have demonstrated a keen and sincere interest in the heritage of the United States. Must be enrolled in a recognized educational institution and be studying such topics as arts, crafts, literature, history, music, folklore, etc. of the U.S.

Financial need is a consideration but it is secondary to scholarship. 12 awards per year.

957 — SWEDISH INFORMATION SERVICE (Bicentennial Swedish-American Exchange Fund)

Bicentennial Fund
One Dag Hammarskjold Plaza, 45th Floor
New York NY 10017-2201
212/483-2550
FAX: 212/752-4789
E-Mail: swedinfor@ix.netcom.com

AMOUNT: 20,000 Swedish crowns (for three- to six-week intensive study visits in Sweden)

DEADLINE(S): FEB (Friday of the first week)

FIELD(S): Politics, public administration, working life, human environment, mass media, business and industry, education and culture

Program is to provide opportunity for those in a positio to influence public opinion and contribute to the development of their society. Must be U.S. citizen or permanent resident. Must have necessary experience and education for fulfilling his/her project.

Send SASE to above address for details.

958 — THE AMERICAN CLASSICAL LEAGUE (Ed Phinney Commemorative Scholarship)

Miami University
Oxford OH 45056
513/529-7741
FAX: 513/529-7742
E-Mail: AmericanClassicalLeague@muohio.edu
or a.c.l@mich.edu
Internet: www.umich.edu/~acleague/
phinney.html

AMOUNT: Up to $500

DEADLINE(S): JAN 15

FIELD(S): Teachers or teacher candidates in the classics (Latin and/or Greek)

Scholarships of up to $500 to apply to first-time attendance at the League's institute OR up to $500 to cover cost of other activities that serve to enhance a teacher's skills in the classroom in the classics OR up to $150 for purchase of materials from the ACL Teaching and Materials Resource Center. Memberships required except for first-time attendance at institute.

Send request for information to above address.

959 — THE CENTER FOR CROSS-CULTURAL STUDY (Tuition Awards for Study in Sevill, Spain)

446 Main St.
Amherst MA 01002-2314
413/256-0011 or 1-800/377-2621
FAX: 413/256-1968
E-Mail: cccs@crocker.com
Internet: www.cccs.com

AMOUNT: $500

DEADLINE(S): Varies

FIELD(S): Study of Spanish and Spanish Culture

Partial tuition assistance is available at this facility in Spain. Applicants must submit an original essay in Spanish, between 2 or 3 double-spaced, typed pages. Also required as a short description in English of your experience with the Spanish language and culture and a faculty recommendation.

Awards are for one semester or academic year programs in Seville. Contact organization for specific details regarding the essays.

960 — THE FRENCH INSTITUTE FOR CULTURE AND TECHNOLOGY (The Chateaubriand Doctoral Research Scholarship Program)

972 Fifth Ave.
New York NY 10021
Internet: www.english.upenn.edu/~morgan/fi/
announce.chateau-hum.html

AMOUNT: 9,000 francs/mo. stipend + health insurance + travel to and from France

DEADLINE(S): JAN 20

FIELD(S): French studies: literature, humanities, the arts, history philosophy, political sciences

Scholarship for doctoral study in France in the above fields. For U.S. citizens.

Write to organization for details.

961 — THE KOSCIUSZKO FOUNDATION (The Metchie J.E. Budka Award)

15 East 65th St.
New York NY 10021-6595

212/734-2130
FAX: 212/628-4552
Internet: www.kosciuszkofoundation.org/new/
budka.htm

AMOUNT: $1,000

DEADLINE(S): JUL 15

FIELD(S): Polish studies: literature, history, Polish-U.S. relations

A competition for graduate students for work at U.S. colleges/universities in the fields of Polish literature from the 14th century to 1919 and/or Polish history from 962 to 1939.

See details at website or contact organization for further information.

962 — THE LEMMERMANN FOUNDATION (Fondazione Lemmermann Scholarship Awards)

c/o Studio Avvocati Romanelli, via Cosseria, 5
00192 Roma ITALIA
(+39-6) 324.30.23
FAX: (+39-6) 321.26.46
E-Mail: lemmerma@bbs.nexus.it
Internet: http://vivaldi.nexus.it/altri/
lemmermann/

AMOUNT: Italian lire 1.500.000

DEADLINE(S): MAR 15; SEP 30

FIELD(S): Italian/Roman studies in the subject areas of literature, archaeology, history of art

For university students who need to study in Rome to carry out research and prepare their theses concerning Rome and the Roman culture from the period Pre-Roman to present day time in the subject areas above.

Contact above organization for details. Access website for application form.

963 — TRENT UNIVERSITY (Graduate Teaching/Research Assistantships)

P.O. Box 4800
Graduate Studies Officer
Peterborough Ontario CANADA K9J 7B8
705/748-1245

AMOUNT: $3,500 per term

DEADLINE(S): FEB 15

FIELD(S): Anthropology, Geography, Archaeology, Biology, Canadian Studies, Philosophy, Cultural Studies, Computer Science, Mathematics, Physics, Chemistry, Environmental Science/Studies

Teaching/research assistantships at Trent University in the above fields. Open to masters and doctoral candidates. Tenable for up to 4 terms spanning 2-3 years of study.

80 awards per year. Write for complete information.

964 — U.S. DEPT. OF EDUCATION (Fulbright-Hays Doctoral Dissertation Research Abroad Fellowships)

International Education &
Graduate Programs Service
600 Independence Ave. SW
Washington DC 20202-5331
202/401-9774

AMOUNT: $10,000-$70,000

DEADLINE(S): OCT (late); NOV (early)

FIELD(S): Foreign language or area studies

Dissertation research abroad fellowships for Doctoral candidates in less common foreign languages/area studies (West European countries excluded) who are planning to teach in U.S. after graduation. U.S. citizen or permanent resident.

Approximateley 75 fellowships per year. Write for complete information.

965 — U.S. DEPT. OF EDUCATION (Fulbright-Hays Faculty Research Abroad Grants)

Center for International Education
ATRB Mail Stop 5331
Washington DC 20202-5331
202/401-9777
FAX: 202/205-9489
E-Mail: elizawashington@ed.gov

AMOUNT: $40,000 average award

DEADLINE(S): NOV 6

FIELD(S): Foreign Language & Area Studies (geography, history, culture, economy, & politics of a region or country)

Research abroad grants for college/university faculty. To contribute to the development of the study of modern foreign languages and area studies in the United States by providing opportunities for scholars to conduct research abroad.

Approx. 20 awards per year. Write for complete information.

966 — U.S. DEPT. OF EDUCATION, INTERNATIONAL EDUCATION AND GRADUATE PROGRAM SERVICE (Foreign Language and Area Studies (FLAS) Fellowships Program)

600 Independence Ave. SW
Washington DC 20202-5331
FAX: 202/205-5331

AMOUNT: $8,000 allowance + tuition ($1,500 for summer fellowships)

DEADLINE(S): Varies

FIELD(S): Foreign language or area studies

Fellowships for graduate students in foreign languages/area studies. U.S. citizen or permanent resident. Fellowships arranged through specified participating universities. Funding varies with school. Some programs are for study abroad.

Contact U.S. Dept. of Educ. at above program for list of participating schools and deadline dates.

967 — UNA ELLIS-FERMOR MEMORIAL RESEARCH FUND (Funds for Publication)

Academic Awards
Registry, Royal Holloway
Univ. of London, Egham Hill
Egham, Surrey TW20 0EX ENGLAND UK
01784 443352

AMOUNT: Up to 200 pounds

DEADLINE(S): APR (3rd Fri.)

FIELD(S): Drama: English, Irish, or Scandinavian

Grants for expenses connected with publication of materials in the field of English, Irish, or Scandinavian drama or a comparative study in which one of these fields is a component.

Contact organization for application instructions.

968 — UNIVERSITY OF ALBERTA (Grant Notley Memorial Postdoctoral Fellowship)

Faculty of Grad Studies & Research
105 Administration Bldg.
Edmonton Alberta T6G 2M7 CANADA
403/492-3499
FAX 403/492-0692

AMOUNT: Canadian $35,000/yr. + one-time C$3,000 research grant & airfare

DEADLINE(S): JAN 4

FIELD(S): Canadian Studies

Must have recently completed a doctoral program or will do so in the immediate future. University of Alberta doctoral graduates not normally eligible. Award is tenable for two years at the University of Alberta for research in politics, history, economy, or society of Western Canada or related fields. A Fellow may teach one half-course per year, but must be primarily a research scholar. Curriculum vitae, transcripts, and letters of appraisal required.

Available only in alternate years; next award is for 2001-2002. Contact the Scholarship Coordinator at the University of Alberta for an application.

969 — UNIVERSITY OF VIRGINIA (Albert Gallatin Fellowship in International Affairs)

International Studies Office
208 Minor Hall
Charlottesville VA 22903
804/982-3010
FAX: 804/982-3011
E-Mail: rgd@virginia.edu
Internet: www.virginia.edu/~intstu

AMOUNT: $11,250 and round trip travel from New York to Geneva

DEADLINE(S): MAR 2

FIELD(S): International studies

Nine-month fellowships for American doctoral candidates in international studies for study at the Graduate Institute for International Studies, Geneva; Switzerland. Must have a fairly functional ability in French as well as English proficiency.

Term is October through June. Write for complete information.

970 — UNIVERSITY OF WAIKATO, NEW ZEALAND (Rewi Alley Scholarship in Modern Chinese Studies)

Private Bag 3105
Hamilton NEW ZEALAND
07 856 2889 Ext. 8964 or 6732
FAX: 07 838 4370
E-Mail: rgty_dbc

AMOUNT: $400

DEADLINE(S): AUG 31

FIELD(S): Study of China

For study and research on China at a New Zealand university or other approved institutiion.

Contact Scholarships Administrator, University of Waikato, at above location.

971 — WELLESLEY COLLEGE (Mary McEwen Schimke Scholarship)

Center for Work & Service
106 Central St.
Wellesley MA 02481-8203
781/283-3525
FAX: 781/283-3674
E-Mail: fellowships@bulletin.wellesley.edu
Internet: www.wellesley.edu/CWS/step2/fellow.html

AMOUNT: $1,000 (max.)

DEADLINE(S): JAN 3

FIELD(S): Literature; History

This supplemental award is open to women graduates of any American institution to provide relief from household and childcare expenses while pursuing graduate study at institutions other than Wellesley College. Award is made on basis of scholarly expectation and identified need. Candidate must be over 30 years of age and currently engaged in graduate study in literature and/or history. Preference given to American Studies.

See website or send self-addressed, stamped envelope to Rose Crawford, Secretary to the Committee on Extramural Graduate Fellowships & Scholarships, for an application.

972 — WILLIAM ANDREWS CLARK MEMORIAL LIBRARY (Postdoctoral Fellowships)

UCLA
2520 Cimarron St.
Los Angeles CA 90018-2098
323/735-7605
FAX: 323/732-8744
E-Mail: clarkfel@humnet.ucla.edu
Internet: www.humnet.ucla.edu/humnet/clarklib

AMOUNT: $2,000+/month

DEADLINE(S): MAR 15

FIELD(S): British History, Literature, & Culture

Three-month to one-year fellowships are for postdoctoral scholars to pursue advanced study and research regarding British literature and history of the 17th and 18th centuries. Tenable at the William Andrews Clark Memorial Library at UCLA.

See website or contact UCLA for an application.

973 — WOODROW WILSON NATIONAL FELLOWSHIP FOUNDATION/JOHNSON & JOHNSON (Dissertation Grants in Women's & Children's Health)

CN 5281
Princeton NJ 08543-5281
609/452-7007
FAX: 609/452-0066
E-Mail: charoltte@woodrow.org
Internet: www.woodrow.org

AMOUNT: $2,000 (for travel, books, microfilming, taping, computer services, etc.)

DEADLINE(S): NOV 8

FIELD(S): Women's & Children's Health

Open to doctoral students in nursing, public health, anthropology, history, sociology, psychology, or social work, who have completed all predissertation requirements at US graduate schools. Must have at least six months left to complete dissertation, which should include significant research on issues related to women's & children's health. Must submit transcripts, proposal, bibliography, & interest. Based on originality & scholarly validity.

15 awards annually. See website or contact WWNFF for an application. Winners announced in February.

974 — WOODROW WILSON NATIONAL FELLOWSHIP FOUNDATION (Women's Studies Doctoral Dissertation Grants)

CN 5281
Princeton NJ 08543-5281
609/452-7007
FAX: 609/452-0066

E-Mail: charlotte@woodrow.org
Internet: www.woodrow.org

AMOUNT: $1,500 (for travel, books, microfilming, taping, computer services, etc.)

DEADLINE(S): NOV 8

FIELD(S): Women's Studies

To encourage original and significant research about women that crosses disciplinary, regional, or cultural boundaries. Must be in doctoral program in the US and have completed all predissertation requirements in any field of study. Must submit transcripts, reference letter, dissertation proposal, bibliography, statement of interest in women's studies, and timetable for completion. Awards based on originality & significance, scholarly validity, & academic ability.

15 awards annually. See website or contact WWNFF for application.

975 — YALE CENTER FOR BRITISH ART (Fellowships)

Box 208280
New Haven CT 06520-8280
203/432-2850

AMOUNT: Travel, accommodations, per diem

DEADLINE(S): JAN 15

FIELD(S): British Art; History; Literature

Fellowships to enable scholars engaged in postdoctoral or equivalent research in British art, history, or literature to study the Center's holdings of paintings, drawings, prints, and rare books and to make use of its research facilities.

12 awards annually. Grants normally run for a period of four weeks. Write for complete information.

ART

976 — AMERICA-ISRAEL CULTURAL FOUNDATION (Sharett Scholarship Program)

32 Allenby Road
Tel Aviv 63-325 ISRAEL
03 5174177
FAX: 03 5178991

AMOUNT: Varies

DEADLINE(S): MAR 15

FIELD(S): Art; Performing Arts

Scholarships are available ONLY to Israeli nationals for study in Israel. Scholarships are for one year of study and are renewable.

450 scholarships per year. Application forms available in February. Write for complete information.

977 — AMERICAN ACADEMY IN ROME (Rome Prize Fellowships in the School of Fine Arts)

7 East 60th Street
New York NY 10022-1001
212/751-7200
FAX: 212/751-7220
E-Mail: aainfo@aol.com
Internet: www.aarome.org

AMOUNT: $9,000-$15,000

DEADLINE(S): NOV 15

FIELD(S): Landscape Architecture; Architecture; Musical Composition; Visual Arts; Design Arts

For US citizens with a major and/or career interest in above fields for advanced study in Rome to pursue independent projects, which vary in content & scope. Applicants for six-month and one-year fellowships must hold a degree in the field of application. Six-month applicants must also have at least seven years professional experience and be practicing in the applied field. Interview, portfolio, recommendations, curriculum vitae, and research proposal required.

14 awards annually. Contact the Programs Department at the American Academy in Rome for an application.

978 — AMERICAN ACADEMY IN ROME (Rome Prize Predoctoral Fellowships)

7 East 60th Street
New York, NY 10022-1001
212/751-7200
FAX: 212/751-7220
Internet: www.aarome.org

AMOUNT: $15,000-$17,800

DEADLINE(S): NOV 15

FIELD(S): Archaeology; Art History; Modern Italian Studies; Post-Classical Humanistic Studies

For doctoral study in Rome, Italy. Applicant must be US citizen with a major and/or career interest in above fields. Recommendations, proof of eligibility, and research proposal required.

$40 application fee. Contact the Programs Department at the American Academy in Rome for an application.

979 — AMERICAN ACADEMY IN ROME (Rome Prize Postdoctoral Fellowships)

7 East 60th Street
New York NY 10022-1001
212/751-7200
FAX: 212/751-7220
Internet: www.aarome.org

AMOUNT: $15,000-$17,800

DEADLINE(S): NOV 15

FIELD(S): Archaeology; Art History; Modern Italian Studies; Post-classical Humanistic Studies

For postgraduate study in Rome, Italy. Applicant must be US citizen or permanent resident with a major and/or career interest in above fields. Recommendations, proof of eligibility, and research proposal required.

Contact the Programs Department at the American Academy in Rome for an application.

980 — AMERICAN COUNCIL OF LEARNED SOCIETIES (ACLS Fellowships)

Office of Fellowshops & Grants
228 E. 45th St.
New York NY 10017
Written Inquiry

AMOUNT: Up to $20,000

DEADLINE(S): SEP 30

FIELD(S): Humanities, Social Sciences, and other areas having predominately humanistic emphasis

Open to U.S. citizens or legal residents who hold the Ph.D or its equivalent. Fellowships are designed to help scholars devote 6 to 12 continuous months to full-time research.

Write for complete information.

981 — AMERICAN INSTITUTE OF ARCHITECTS, NEW YORK CHAPTER (Haskell Awards for Student Architectural Journalism)

200 Lexington Ave., 6th floor
New York NY 10016
212/683-0023 Ext. 14

AMOUNT: Varies

DEADLINE(S): FEB 13

FIELD(S): Architectural Writing

Awards to encourage fine writing on architecture and related design subjects and to foster regard for intelligent criticism among future professionals. For students enrolled in a professional architecture or related program, such as art history, interior design, urban studies, and landscape architecture. Submit a news story, an essay or feature article, book review, or journal accompanied by a 100-word statement describing the purpose of the piece.

Write to above location for complete information.

982 — AMERICAN MOTHERS, INC. (Gertrude Fogelson Cultural and Creative Arts Awards)

1296 E. 21st St.
Brooklyn NY 11201
718/253-5676

AMOUNT: Up to $1,000

DEADLINE(S): JAN 1 (annually)

FIELD(S): Visual arts, creative writing, and vocal music

An award to encourage and honor mothers in artistic pursuits.

Write to Alice Miller at above address for details.

983 — AMERICAN NUMISMATIC SOCIETY (Fellowships and Grants)

Broadway at 155th Street
New York NY 10032
212/234-3130
FAX: 212/234-3381
E-Mail: info@AmNumSoc.org
Internet: www.amnumsoc2.org

AMOUNT: $2,000 (grants-in-aid); $5,000 (fellowships)

DEADLINE(S): MAR 1

FIELD(S): Numismatics

Grants-in-aid for students who have completed at least one year of graduate study at a North American university. Fellowships of up to $5,000 are for graduate students whose dissertations will make significant use of numismatic evidence.

See website or contact the American Numismatic Society for an application.

984 — AMERICAN RESEARCH INSTITUTE IN TURKEY (ARIT Fellowship Program)

Univ Penn Museum
33rd & Spruce Streets
Philadelphia PA 19104-6324
215/898-3474
FAX: 215/898-0657
E-Mail: leinwand@sas.upenn.edu
Internet: mec.sas.upenn.edu/ARIT

AMOUNT: Varies

DEADLINE(S): NOV 15

FIELD(S): Humanities; Social Sciences; Turkish Studies

Two-month to one-year fellowships are for postdoctoral scholars & advanced graduate students engaged in research on ancient, medieval, or modern times in Turkey, in any field of the humanities & social sciences. Predoctoral students must have fulfilled all preliminary requirements for doctorate except dissertation. Applicants must maintain an affiliation with an educational institution in the US or Canada. Must submit curriculum vitae, research proposal, & referees.

Contact ARIT for an application.

985 — AMERICAN RESEARCH INSTITUTE IN TURKEY (KRESS/ARIT Predoctoral Fellowship in the History of Art & Archaeology)

Univ Penn Museum
33rd & Spruce Streets
Philadelphia PA 19104-6324
215/898-3474
FAX: 215/898-0657

E-Mail: leinwand@sas.upenn.edu
Internet: mec.sas.upenn.edu/ARIT

AMOUNT: $15,000 (max.)

DEADLINE(S): NOV 15

FIELD(S): Archaeology; Architectural History; Art History

Fellowships of up to one year are for students engaged in advanced dissertation research in above fields that necessitates a period of study in Turkey. Must be US citizen or matriculating at a US university. Must submit curriculum vitae, research proposal, and referees.

Contact ARIT for an application.

986 — AMERICAN RESEARCH INSTITUTE IN TURKEY (Mellon Research Fellowships for Central and Eastern European Scholars in Turkey)

Univ Penn Museum
33rd & Spruce Streets
Philadelphia PA 19104-6324
215/898-3474
FAX: 215/898-0657
E-Mail: leinwand@sas.upenn.edu
Internet: mec.sas.upenn.edu/ARIT

AMOUNT: Stipend up to $10,500 for 2-3 month project (includes travel, living expenses, work-related costs)

DEADLINE(S): MAR 5

FIELD(S): Humanities; Social Sciences

For Czech, Hungarian, Polish, Slovakian, Bulgarian, and Romanian scholars holding a Ph.D. or equivalent who are engaged in advanced research in any field of the social sciences or the humanities involving Turkey. Must be permanent residents of these countries and must obtain formal permission for any research to be carried out.

3 awards annually. Previous fellows not eligible. See website or write to above address for details.

987 — AMERICAN RESEARCH INSTITUTE IN TURKEY (National Endowment for the Humanities Fellowships for Research in Turkey)

Univ Penn Museum
33rd & Spruce Streets
Philadelphia PA 19104-6324
215/898-3474
FAX: 215/898-0657
E-Mail: leinwand@sas.upenn.edu
Internet: mec.sas.upenn.edu/ARIT

AMOUNT: $10,000-$30,000

DEADLINE(S): NOV 15

FIELD(S): Humanities

Postdoctoral fellowships are to conduct research in Turkey for four to twelve months. Fields of study cover all periods in the general range of the humanities, including humanistically oriented aspects of the social sciences, prehistory, history, art, archaeology, literature, linguistics, and cultural history. There are two institutes, one in Istanbul and one in Ankara. Both have residential facilities for fellows and provide general assistance.

2-3 awards annually. Contact ARIT for an application. Notification by January 25th.

988 — ARCHAEOLOGICAL INSTITUTE OF AMERICA (Olivia James Traveling Fellowship)

Boston Univ
656 Beacon St.
Boston MA 02215-2006
617/353-9361
FAX: 617/353-6550
E-Mail: aia@bu.edu
Internet: www.archeological.org

AMOUNT: $22,000

DEADLINE(S): NOV 1

FIELD(S): Classics; Sculpture; Architecture; Archaeology; History

Fellowships for US citizens/permanent residents to be used for travel and study in Greece, the Aegean Islands, Sicily, Southern Italy, Asia Minor, or Mesopotamia. Preference given to individuals engaged in dissertation research or to recent recipients of the Ph.D. (within 5 years). Award is not intended to support field excavation projects, and recipients may not hold other major fellowships during tenure. At conclusion, recipient must submit report on use of stipend.

Contact AIA for an application. Awards announced by February 1st.

989 — ARTS MANAGEMENT P/L (Marten Bequest Travelling Scholarships)

Station House, Rawson Place
790 George St.
Sydney NSW 2000 Australia
(612)9212 5066
FAX: (612)9211 7762
E-Mail: vbraden@ozemail.com.au

AMOUNT: Aus. $18,000

DEADLINE(S): OCT 30

FIELD(S): Art; Performing Arts; Creative Writing

Open to native-born Australians aged 21-35 (17-35 ballet) who are of outstanding ability and promise in one or more categories of the Arts. The scholarships are intended to augment a scholar's own resources towards a cultural education, and it may be used for study, maintenance, and travel either in Australia or overseas. Categories are: instrumental music, painting, singing, sculpture, architecture, ballet, prose, poetry, and acting.

1 scholarship granted in each of 9 categories which rotate in 2 groups on an annual basis. Contact

Claudia Crosariol, Projects Administrator, for more information/entry form.

990 — ARTS MANAGEMENT P/L (Portia Geach Memorial Award)

Station House, Rawson Place
790 George St.
Sydney NSW 2000 AUSTRALIA
(612)9212 5066
FAX: (612)9211 7762
E-Mail: vbraden@ozemail.com.au

AMOUNT: Aus. $18,000

DEADLINE(S): AUG 28

FIELD(S): Portrait Painting

Award for a female painter who is an Australia resident, either Australian-born or British-born. Portrait is to be of a person distinguished in arts, letters, or sciences; self-portraits are accepted.

$30 entry fee per painting. Contact Claudia Crosariol, Projects Administrator, for more information/entry form.

991 — ASIAN CULTURAL COUNCIL (Fellowship Grants for Asian Citizens)

1290 Ave. of the Americas
New York NY 10104
212/373-4300

AMOUNT: Varies

DEADLINE(S): FEB 1

FIELD(S): Visual Arts; Performing Arts

Fellowships open to Asian citizens. Grants may be used for graduate study, research, specialized training, or the pursuit of creative activity in the United States. Some grants also available to Americans pursuing research and study in Asia.

Send self-addressed, stamped envelope for complete information.

992 — ASIAN CULTURAL COUNCIL (Research Fellowships for U.S. Citizens to Study in Asia & Asians to Study in U.S.)

1290 Ave. of the Americas
New York NY 10104
212/373-4300

AMOUNT: Varies

DEADLINE(S): FEB 1; AUG 1

FIELD(S): Visual Arts; Performing Arts

Doctoral and postdoctoral fellowships open to U.S. citizens who wish to do research in Asia on Asian visual or performing arts. Funds also available for students from Asia for study and research in the U.S.

Send self-address, stamped envelope (SASE) for complete information.

993 — ASIFA (Helen Victoria Haynes World Peace Storyboard & Animation Contest)

3400 W. 111th St.
Box 324
Chicago IL 60655
E-mail: morgPk@aol.com
Internet: www.swcp.com/~asifa/whatsnew.htm

AMOUNT: $500 + software & ASIFA conference registration

DEADLINE(S): APR 30

FIELD(S): Animation; Cartooning

For high school and college students to design, draw, and mount a storyboard for an animated short for the Annual ASIFA/Central Conference & Retreat. The storyboard should depict your vision of how to acheive World Peace.

2 prize packages: 1 for high school students & 1 for college students. See website for official rules or contact Mary Lou Haynes at above address for more information.

994 — AUSTRALIAN FEDERATION OF UNIVERSITY WOMEN - WESTERN AUSTRALIA (Joyce Riley Bursary)

Bursary Liaison Officer
PO Box 48
Nedlands WA 6909 AUSTRALIA
Written Inquiry

AMOUNT: Aus$1,700 - Aus$2,750

DEADLINE(S): JUL 31

FIELD(S): Humanities; Social Sciences

To support women graduates of a Western Australian university to complete a higher degree or post-doctoral research in Humanities or Social Sciences at a recognized university in any country.

Membership in AFUW or in IFUW is required. Contact above location for further information.

995 — AUSTRALIAN FEDERATION OF UNIVERSITY WOMEN - WESTERN AUSTRALIA (Joyce Riley Bursary)

Bursary Liaison Officer
PO Box 48
Nedlands WA 6009 AUSTRALIA
Written Inquiry

AMOUNT: Aus$1,700 - Aus$2,750

DEADLINE(S): JUL 31

FIELD(S): Humanities; Social Sciences

To support women graduates of a recognized university to complete a higher degree or post-doctoral research at a university in Western Australia.

Membership in AFUW or in IFUW is required. Write to above address for complete information.

996 — AUSTRIAN CULTURAL INSTITUTE (Fine Arts & Music Grants)

950 Third Ave., 20th Fl.
New York NY 10022
212/759-5165
FAX: 212/319-9636
E-Mail: desk@aci.org
Internet: www.austriaculture.net

AMOUNT: ATS 7,800/month (US $600) + ATS 2,500 (US $190) start grant

DEADLINE(S): FEB 14

FIELD(S): Music; Drama; Art

Open to foreign students for studies at academies of music and dramatic art or at art academies in Austria. Must be advanced students between 20 and 35 years old and have a working knowledge of German. Very high level of qualification is required and final admission is subject to artistic entrance exam. Must submit letters of recommendation, curriculum vitae, and transcripts.

Not renewable. See website or contact ACI for an application kit.

997 — AUSTRIAN CULTURAL INSTITUTE (Grants from Federal Ministry of Science & Transport for Austrian Artists)

950 Third Ave., 20th Fl.
New York NY 10022
212/759-5165 or +43/1/53120-2321
FAX: 212/319-9636 or +43/1/53120-4499
E-Mail: desk@aci.org
Internet: www.austriaculture.net

AMOUNT: ATS 15,000/month + travel expenses & use of studio

DEADLINE(S): Varies

FIELD(S): Art

Grants of three to six months are for Austrian citizens/permanent residents who wish to pursue studies in the US, specifically New York City or Chicago. Awarded by a jury upon review of portfolios.

See website or contact ACI for an application kit, or write to Federal Ministry of Science & Transport, Bundesministerium fur Wissenschaft, Verkehr und Kunst, Abt. III/7, Minoritenplatz 5, Postfach 104, A-1014 Vienna, Austria.

998 — BLUES HEAVEN FOUNDATION, INC. (Muddy Waters Scholarship)

2120 S. Michigan Ave.
Chicago IL 60616
312/808-1286

AMOUNT: $2,000

DEADLINE(S): APR 30

FIELD(S): Music; Music Education; African-American Studies; Folklore; Performing Arts; Arts Management; Journalism; Radio/TV/Film

Scholarship is made on a competitive basis with consideration given to scholastic achievement, concentration of studies, and financial need. Applicant must have full-time enrollment status in a Chicago area college/university in at least their first year of undergraduate studies or a graduate program. Scholastic aptitude, extracurricular involvement, grade point average, and financial need are all considered.

Contact Blues Heaven Foundation, Inc. to receive an application between February and April.

999 — CANADIAN-SCANDINAVIAN FOUNDATION (Travel Grants)

McGill Univ Libraries
3459 McTavish St.
Montreal Quebec H3A 1Y1 CANADA
514/398-4740 or 514/398-4111
FAX: 514/398-7356 or 514/398-7437
E-Mail: lundgren@felix.geog.mcgill.ca

AMOUNT: $1,000

DEADLINE(S): JAN 31

FIELD(S): Scandinavian Studies

Travel grants for Canadian citizens to study in Scandinavian countries: Denmark, Finland, Iceland, Norway, & Sweden. For students at the graduate level and higher who do not have a salaried position. Financial need NOT a factor.

5 awards annually. Contact Dr. Moller, Vice President, at above address for an application. Or, contact Dr. J. Lundgren, CSF Secretary, Geography Dept., McGill University, 805 Sherbrooke St. W., Montreal, Quebec H3A 2K6 Canada.

1000 — CHARLES A. AND ANNE MORROW LINDBERGH FOUNDATION (Grants for Research Projects)

2150 Third Ave., N, Ste. 310
Anoka MN 55303-2200
612/576-1596
FAX: 612/576-1664
E-Mail: lindbergh@isd.net
Internet: www.isd.net/lindbergh

AMOUNT: $10,580 (max.)

DEADLINE(S): JUN 15

FIELD(S): Aviation; Aerospace; Agriculture; Education; Arts; Humanities; Biomedical Research; Exploration; Health & Population Sciences; Intercultural Communication; Waste Disposal Minimization & Management.; Adaptive Technology; Conservation

Open to individuals whose proposed projects represent a significant contribution toward the achievement of balance between the advance of technology and preservation of the natural environment. Financial need NOT a factor. Funding is NOT for tuition.

10 awards annually. See website for application.

1001 — CONCORDIA UNIVERSITY (Joyce Melville Memorial Scholarship)

Fine Arts Dept.
1455 de Maisonneuve Blvd. West
MF 103-1
Montreal Quebec H3G 1M8 CANADA
514/848-3809
FAX: 514/848-2812
E-Mail: awardsgs@vax2.concordia.ca

AMOUNT: $1,000

DEADLINE(S): SEP 20

FIELD(S): Printing; Drawing; Photography; Printmaking; Sculpture; Ceramics & Fibres; Cinema/Film Production; Open Media; Painting

Candidates must be full-time female students in the third year of their Master of Fine Arts program. Selection shall be based on the student's submissions (c.v., statement of involvement in social & women's issues, and slides) and faculty recommendation. Recipient is chosen by the Graduate Studio Arts Advisory Committee.

1 award annually. Not renewable. Contact the Graduate Program Director in the Fine Arts Department at Concordia University for an application.

1002 — COSTUME SOCIETY OF AMERICA (Stella Blum Research Grant)

55 Edgewater Dr.
PO Box 73
Earleville MD 21919
800/CSA-9447 or 410/275-1619
FAX: 410/275-8936
Internet: www.costumesocietyamerica.com

AMOUNT: $3,000 (to be used for research expenses: transportation/living at research site, photographic reproductions/film, postage, telephone, typing, computer searches, & graphics)

DEADLINE(S): FEB 1

FIELD(S): North American Costume

For graduate students at accredited institutions. Award is based on merit, NOT need. Judging criteria includes: creativity & innovation, specific awareness of & attention to costume matters, impact on the broad field of costume, awareness of interdisciplinarity of the field, ability to successfully implement the proposed project in a timely manner, and faculty advisor recommendation. Must be member of the Costume Society of America.

1 award annually. Not renewable. Contact CSA for an application or membership information. Winner announced in May.

1003 — COUNCIL FOR BASIC EDUCATION
(Arts Education Fellowships)

2506 Buckelew Drive
Falls Church VA 22046
703/876-5782

AMOUNT: $2,800 stipend + $200 grant to school

DEADLINE(S): JAN

FIELD(S): Teaching of the arts (visual arts, creative writing, dance, media, music, theatre)

Fellowships for K-12 teachers in the above fields, artist-teachers, or professional artists who teach at least 20 hours per week. Funding from the National Endowment for the Arts and the Getty Center for Education in the Arts, and others.

Contact organization for details.

1004 — DISTRICT OF COLUMBIA COMMISSION ON THE ARTS & HUMANITIES
(Grants)

410 Eighth St. NW, 5th Floor
Washington DC 20004
202/724-5613
TDD 202/727-3148
FAX: 202/727-4135

AMOUNT: $2,500

DEADLINE(S): MAR 1

FIELD(S): Performing Arts, Literature, Visual Arts

Applicants for grants must be professional artists and residents of Washington DC for at least one year prior to submitting application. Awards intended to generate art endeavors within the Washington DC community.

Open also to art organizations that train, exhibit, or perform within DC. 150 grants per year. Write for complete information.

1005 — ELIZABETH GREENSHIELDS FOUNDATION (Grants)

1814 Sherbrooke St., W., Ste. 1
Montreal Quebec H3H 1E4 CANADA
514/937-9225
FAX: 514/937-0141
E-Mail: egreen@total.net

AMOUNT: Canadian $10,000

DEADLINE(S): None

FIELD(S): Painting; Drawing; Printmaking; Sculpture

Grants are to aid artists in the early stages of their careers. Work must be representational or figurative. Applicants must have started or completed art school

training and/or must demonstrate, through past work and future plans, a commitment to making art a lifetime career. Funds may be used for any art-related purpose: study, travel, studio-rental, purchase of materials, etc.

45-55 awards annually. Contact Micheline Leduc, Administrator, for an application.

1006 — FASHION GROUP INTERNATIONAL OF GREATER WASHINGTON DC (Scholarships)

P.O. Box 71055
Chevy Chase MD 20813-1055
212/593-1715 (in New York)
Internet: fgi.org/washington.htm

AMOUNT: Up to $2,500

DEADLINE(S): APR 1

FIELD(S): Fashion-related areas

Scholarshps for students majoring in fashion-related fields. Must be permanent residents of the Greater Metropolitan Washington DC area. Must either graduate from high school in June and/or have been admitted to an accredited institution or be enrolled in a university or college as an undergraduate or graduate student.

Application form and details are available on website or contact organization for further information.

1007 — FLORIDA ARTS COUNCIL (Individual Artists' Fellowships)

FL Dept. of State
Div. of Cultural Affairs
State Capitol
Tallahassee FL 32399-0250
850/487-2980
TDD: 850/414-2214
FAX: 850/922-5259

AMOUNT: $5,000

DEADLINE(S): JAN 16

FIELD(S): Visual Arts; Dance; Folk Arts; Media; Music; Theater; Literary Arts; Interdisciplinary

Fellowships awarded to individual artists in the above areas. Must be Florida residents, U.S. citizens, and over 18 years old. May NOT be a degree-seeking student—funding is for support of artistic endeavors only.

38 awards per year. Write for complete information.

1008 — FONDATION DES ETATS-UNIS (Harriet Hale Woolley Scholarships

15, Boulevard Jourdan
755690 PARIS CEDEX 14, FRANCE
(1)45.89.35.79

AMOUNT: $8,500 payable in French francs

DEADLINE(S): JAN 31

FIELD(S): Art and music

For U.S. unmarried citizens between ages 21-29 with evidence of artistic or musical accomplishment,

good moral character, personality, etc. A serious project for graduate study in Paris must be approved by the Fondation director and should include enrollment in a recognized school or private instruction.

For academic year Oct. 1 through June 30. Contact the Director, Harriet Hale Woolley Scholarships, at above location.

1009 — GEORGE BIRD GRINNELL AMERICAN INDIAN CHILDREN'S FUND (Al Qoyawayma Award)

11602 Montague Ct.
Potomac MD 20854
301/424-2440
FAX: 301/424-8281
E-Mail: Grinnell_Fund@MSN.com

AMOUNT: $1,000

DEADLINE(S): JUN 1

FIELD(S): Science; Engineering

Open to Native American undergraduate and graduate students majoring in science or engineering and who have demonstrated an outstanding interest and skill in any one of the arts. Must be American Indian/Alaska Native (documented with Certified Degree of Indian Blood), be enrolled in college/university, be able to demonstrate commitment to serving community or other tribal nations, and document financial need.

Contact Dr. Paula M. Mintzies, President, for an application after January 1st.

1010 — GETTY RESEARCH INSTITUTE FOR THE HISTORY OF ART AND THE HUMANITIES (Fellowships)

1200 Getty Center Dr., Ste. 1100
Los Angeles CA 90049-1688
310/440-7392
FAX: 310/440-7782
E-Mail: residentialgrants@getty.edu
Internet: www.getty.edu/gri/scholars

AMOUNT: $18,000 (doctoral); $22,000 (postdoctoral)

DEADLINE(S): NOV 1

FIELD(S): Arts; Humanities; Social Sciences

Open to doctoral and postdoctoral scholars whose areas of research fall within the year's chosen theme. Predoctoral candidates should expect to complete dissertations during the fellowship year. Postdoctorates should have received doctorate in humanities or social sciences within the last three years and be rewriting dissertations for publication. Tenable at the Getty Research Institute in Los Angeles, CA.

Contact Getty Institute for an application and current theme.

1011 — GLADYS KRIEBLE DELMAS FOUNDATION (Predoctoral & Postdoctoral Grants in Venice & the Veneto)

521 5th Avenue, Suite 1612
New York NY 10175-1699
212/687-0011
FAX: 212/687-8877
E-Mail: DelmasFdtn@aol.com
Internet: www.delmas.org

AMOUNT: $500-$12,500

DEADLINE(S): DEC 15

FIELD(S): Research of Venice and the former Venetian empire and study of contemporary Venetian society and culture.

Pre- and postdoctoral grants for historical research on Venice. Humanities and social sciences are eligible areas of study, including archaeology, architecture, art, bibliography, economics, history, history of science, law, literature, music, political science, religion, and theater.

Applicants must have experience in advanced research and be U.S. citizens/residents; grad students must have fulfilled all doctoral requirements except dissertation by Dec. 15.

1012 — HAROLD HYAM WINGATE FOUNDATION (Wingate Scholarships)

38 Curzon St.
London W1Y 8EY ENLAND UK
0171 465 1521

AMOUNT: Up to 10,000 pounds/yr.

DEADLINE(S): FEB 1

FIELD(S): Creative works

Financial support for individuals of great potential or proven excellence to develop original work of intellectual, scientific, artistic, social, or environmental value, and to outstanding talented musicians. Not for taught courses or for leading to professional qualifications, or for electives or for completing courses already begun or for a higher degree. For citizens of the United Kingdom or other Commonwealth countries, Ireland, Israel, or of European countries.

Must be age 24 or older. May be held for up to three years.

1013 — HAYSTACK MOUNTAIN SCHOOL OF CRAFTS (Scholarship Program)

Admissions Office
PO Box 518
Deer Isle ME 04627
207/348-2306

AMOUNT: $500-$1,000

DEADLINE(S): MAR 25

FIELD(S): Crafts

Open to technical assistants and work-study students in graphics, ceramics, weaving, jewelry, glass, blacksmithing, fabric, or wood. Tenable for one of the six two- to three-week summer sessions at Haystack Mountain School. One year of graduate study or equivalent experience is required for TA applicants.

Contact Candy Haskell for an application.

1014 — HOME FASHION PRODUCTS ASSN. (Home Textile Surface Design Competition)

355 Lexington Ave.
New York NY 10017
212/661-4261

AMOUNT: $1,000

DEADLINE(S): OCT 30

FIELD(S): Home textile surface design

Annual home furnishings textile design competition open to undergraduate students enrolled in an accredited 2-year or 4-year school of art or design. Must have completed one year of college level study in this field. Not for interior design students.

Applications accepted from department chairman only—NOT individuals. Write for complete information.

1015 — HUNTINGTON LIBRARY (Research Fellowships)

1151 Oxford Rd.
San Marino CA 91108
626/405-2194

AMOUNT: $2,000/month

DEADLINE(S): DEC 15

FIELD(S): American History/Literature; British History/Literature; Art History; Science History

Open to doctoral and postdoctoral scholars for research at the Huntington Library. Fellows are expected to be in residence at the Library throughout their tenure.

100 awards annually. Contact the Committee on Fellowships for an application.

1016 — ILLINOIS ARTS COUNCIL (Artists Fellowship Awards)

100 W. Randolph, Suite 10-500
Chicago IL 60601-3298
312/814-6750

AMOUNT: $500; $5,000; $10,000

DEADLINE(S): SEP 1

FIELD(S): Choreography; Visual Arts; Poetry Prose; Film; Video; Playwriting; Music Composition; Crafts; Ethnic & Folk Arts; Performance Art; Photography; Audio Art.

Open to professional artists who are Illinois residents. Awards are in recognition of work in the above areas; they are not for continuing study. Students are NOT eligible.

Write to address above for application form.

1017 — INSTITUTE FOR ADVANCED STUDIES IN THE HUMANITIES (Visiting Research Fellowships)

Univ Edinburgh
Hope Park Square
Edinburgh EH8 9NW SCOTLAND UK
0131 650 4671
FAX: 0131 668 2252
E-Mail: iash@ed.ac.uk
Internet: www.ed.ac.uk/iash/homepage.html

AMOUNT: Non-stipendiary*

DEADLINE(S): DEC 1

FIELD(S): Arts; Social Sciences; Law; Music; Divinity

Postdoctoral research fellowships of between two and six months are tenable at the Institute for Advanced Studies in the Humanities. Based on academic record and publications. *Most fellowships are honorary, but limited support towards expenses is available to a small number of candidates. Fellows are allocated a study room within the Institute and hold one or two seminars during their tenure. Must submit research report at end of fellowship. No teaching required.

15 awards annually. Not renewable. Contact Mrs. Anthea Taylor for an application.

1018 — INSTITUTE FOR HUMANE STUDIES (IHS Film & Fiction Scholarships)

4084 University Drive, Suite 101
Fairfax VA 22030-6812
703/934-6920 or 800/697-8799
FAX: 703/352-7535
E-Mail: ihs@gmu.edu
Internet: www.theihs.org

AMOUNT: up to $10,000

DEADLINE(S): JAN 15

FIELD(S): Filmmaking; Fiction Writing; Playwriting

Open to graduate students pursuing a Master of Fine Arts (M.F.A.) degree in one of above fields. Should have a demonstrated interest in classical liberal ideas and their application in contemporary society, and demonstrate the desire, motivation, and creative ability to succeed in their chosen profession.

Apply online or contact IHS for an application.

1019 — IRISH ARTS COUNCIL (Awards and Opportunities)

70 Merrion Square
Dublin 2 Ireland
Tel+353 1 618 0200
FAX:+353 1 661 0349/676 1302
E-Mail: info@artscouncil.ie
Internet: www.artscouncil.ie

AMOUNT: 500-1,500 pounds sterling

DEADLINE(S): Varies (with program)

FIELD(S): Creative Arts; Visual Arts; Performing Arts

Numerous programs open to young & established artists who are Irish citizens or legal residents. Purpose is to assist in pursuit of talents & recognize achievements.

Contact above address for an application.

1020 — ISTITUTO ITALIANO PER GLI STUDI STORICI (Federico Chabod & Adolfo Omodeo Scholarships)

12 Via Benedetto Croce
80134 Naples ITALY
0039/81/551-7159
FAX: 0039/81/551-2390
E-Mail: iiss@iol.it

AMOUNT: 12 million lires

DEADLINE(S): SEP 30

FIELD(S): History; Philosophy; Literature; Arts; Economics

Open to non-Italian citizens who have completed a university degree in the humanities (history, philosophy, & arts) in a non-Italian university. Intended to allow young scholars to participate in the work of the Institute and to complete personal scholarly research with the help of teaching staff of the Institute. Must submit birth certificate, university diploma, scholarly work, program of studies with indication of language skills, research proposal, & reference.

Renewable. Contact Dott.ssa Marta Herling, Secretary, for an application.

1021 — ISTITUTO ITALIANO PER GLI STUDI STORICI - ITALIAN INSTITUTE FOR HISTORICAL STUDIES (Federico Chabod & Adolfo Omodeo Scholarships)

Via Benedetto Croce, 12
80134 Napoli ITALY
0039/81-5517159
FAX: 0039/81-5512390

AMOUNT: 12,000,000 Lira

DEADLINE(S): SEP 30

FIELD(S): Humanities; Social Sciences; History; Philosophy; Arts; Economics; Literature

For non-Italian citizens who have completed a university degree in Humanities dept. of a non-Italian university. Intended to allow young scholars to participate in the work of the Institute and to complete personal scholarly research with the help of teaching staff of the Institute. Must include birth certificate, proof of citizenship, university diploma, scholarly work, curriculum of studies w/ indication of language skills, research proposal, & reference letter.

2 awards annually. Contact Marta Herling, Secretary, at above address for an application.

1022 — JANSONS LEGAT (Scholarships)

Blommeseter, Norderhov
3512 Honefoss NORWAY
32 1354 65
FAX: 32 1356 26
E-Mail: janlegat@online.no

AMOUNT: NOK 75.000,-

DEADLINE(S): MAR 15

FIELD(S): Business; Industry; Handcraft

Scholarships for Norwegian citizens for career support and/or postgraduate study. Financial need is NOT a factor.

30 awards annually. Contact Reidun Haugen for an application.

1023 — JOHN K. & THIRZA F. DAVENPORT FOUNDATION (Scholarships in the Arts)

20 North Main Street
South Yarmouth MA 02664-3143
508/398-2293
FAX: 508/394-6765

AMOUNT: Varies

DEADLINE(S): JUL 15

FIELD(S): Theatre, Music, Art

For Barnstable County, Massachusetts residents in their last two years of undergraduate or graduate (preferred) study in visual or performing arts. Must demonstrate financial need.

6-8 awards annually. Renewable. Contact Mrs. Chris M. Walsh for more information.

1024 — LESLIE T. POSEY & FRANCES U. POSEY FOUNDATION (Scholarships)

1800 Second St., Suite 905
Sarasota FL 34236
813/957-0442

AMOUNT: $1,000-$4,000

DEADLINE(S): MAR 1

FIELD(S): Art (Painting or Sculpture)

Open to graduate Art students who majored in traditional painting or sculpture. The school or artist with whom the student wishes to study should be known for teaching traditional art. For full-time study.

Write to Robert E. Perkins, Exec. Dir., at address above for complete information.

1025 — LIBERACE FOUNDATION FOR THE PERFORMING AND CREATIVE ARTS (Scholarship Fund)

1775 East Tropicana Avenue
Las Vegas NV 89119-6529
Internet: www.liberace.org

AMOUNT: Varies

DEADLINE(S): MAR 15

FIELD(S): Music; Theatre; Dance; Visual Arts

Provides grants to accredited INSTITUTIONS that offer training in above fields. Grants are to be used exclusively for scholarship assistance to talented and deserving students. Recipients should be promising and deserving upperclassmen (Jr., Sr., Graduate) enrolled in a course of study leading up to a career in the arts.

NO DIRECT-TO STUDENT GRANTS ARE MADE. Student's school must apply on their behalf. See website or write to above address for details.

1026 — LIGHT WORK (Artist-in-Residence Program)

316 Waverly Avenue
Syracuse NY 13244
315/443-1300
FAX: 315/443-9516
E-Mail: cdlight@syr.edu

AMOUNT: $2,000 stipend

DEADLINE(S): None

FIELD(S): Photography

Career support for mid-career professional artists from around the world working with photography or digital imaging. Residency is for one month, and financial need is NOT considered.

12-15 awards annually. Not renewable. Contact Jeffrey Hoone, Director, at above address for an application.

1027 — MARYLAND INSTITUTE COLLEGE OF ART (Fellowship Grants)

1300 West Mt. Royal Ave.
Baltimore MD 21217
301/225-2255

AMOUNT: $16,950

DEADLINE(S): MAR 1

FIELD(S): Fine Arts

Fellowship grants open to master of fine arts candidates at Maryland Institute College of Art. Applicants must have BA or BFA degree with at least 40 studio credits & 6 art history credits.

Approximately 80 grants per year. Financial need is a consideration. Write for complete information.

1028 — METROPOLITAN MUSEUM OF ART (Bothmer, Dale, Mills, Whitney, & Forchheimer Art History Fellowships)

1000 Fifth Ave.
New York NY 10028-0198
212/879-5500
Internet: www.metmuseum.org

AMOUNT: $20,000 stipend + $3,000 for travel (pre-doctoral); $26,000 stipend + $3,000 for travel (postdoctoral)

DEADLINE(S): NOV 5

FIELD(S): Art History; Fine Arts

Fellowships are for graduate students and postgraduate scholars and are tenable at the Museum. Bothmer Fellowship is in Greek & Roman art; Dale Fellowship is in fine arts of the western world, preferably to Americans under age 40; Mills Scholarships are for any area of Museum's collections; and Whitney Fellowships give preference to students in the decorative arts who are under age 40. No application forms.

Renewable. Contact Marcie Karp for guidelines.

1029 — METROPOLITAN MUSEUM OF ART (Internships)

1000 Fifth Ave.
New York NY 10028-0198
212/570-3710
Internet: www.metmuseum.org

AMOUNT: $2,750 (grads); $2,500 (juniors & seniors); up to $12,000 for certain longer programs

DEADLINE(S): JAN; FEB

FIELD(S): Art History

Internships for undergraduates and graduates who intend to pursue careers in art museums. Programs vary in length and requirements. Interns work in curatorial, education, conservation, administration, or library department of museum. Some require demonstration of economic need. Duration ranges from nine weeks to ten months. Volunteer positions also available.

Contact Marcie Karp for details.

1030 — METROPOLITAN MUSEUM OF ART (Mellon, Weissman, & Frohlich Fellowships in Conservation)

1000 Fifth Ave.
New York NY 10028-0198
Internet: www.metmuseum.org

AMOUNT: $20,000 stipend + $2,500 for travel

DEADLINE(S): JAN 7

FIELD(S): Art Conservation

Fellowships for graduate students and senior scholars tenable at the Museum. Art Conservation topics include paintings, sculpture, metalwork, glass, ceramics, furniture, archaeological objects, musical instruments, arms & armor, paper/photographs, textile, and costume. Fellowships range in duration from nine months to two years, and are not granted every year in each department.

Contact Marcie Karp for guidelines. Applicants will be notified by March 31st.

1031 — METROPOLITAN MUSEUM OF ART (Theodore Rousseau Fellowships)

1000 Fifth Ave.
New York NY 10028-0198
212/570-3710
Internet: www.metmuseum.org

AMOUNT: $20,000 stipend + $3,000 for travel

DEADLINE(S): NOV 5

FIELD(S): Art History

Three- to twelve-month fellowships are for training students whose goal is to enter museums as curators of painting, by enabling them to undertake related study in Europe. Purpose is to develop the skills of connoisseurship by supporting first-hand examination of paintings in major European collections, rather than library research for degree. Should have been enrolled for at least one year in advanced degree program. No application form.

Contact Marcie Karp for guidelines. Announcements of awards will be made by February 25th.

1032 — MINISTRY OF THE FLEMISH COMMUNITY (Fellowships)

Embassy of Belgium
3330 Garfield St., NW
Washington DC 20008
202/625-5850/51
FAX: 202/342-8346
E-Mail: flemishcomdc@wizard.net

AMOUNT: Monthly stipend, tuition, & health care coverage

DEADLINE(S): JAN 31

FIELD(S): Art; Music; Humanities; Social Science; Political Science; Law; Economics; Science; Medicine

Open to US citizens under age 35 who wish to pursue graduate or postgraduate studies in Flanders, Belgium.

Contact Flemish Community for registration forms.

1033 — MONTANA ARTS COUNCIL (Individual Artists Fellowships)

City County Building,
316 North Park Ave., Rm. 252
Helena MT 59620-2201

406/444-6430
FAX: 406/444-6548
E-Mail: montana@artswire.org

AMOUNT: $2,000

DEADLINE(S): MAY 1

FIELD(S): Music and art

Fellowships for artists or musicians who have been Montana residents for at least a year.

Contact Julie SMith, director, at above location.

1034 — NATIONAL FEDERATION OF THE BLIND (Humanities Scholarship)

805 5th Avenue
Grinnell IA 50112
515/236-3366

AMOUNT: $3,000

DEADLINE(S): MAR 31

FIELD(S): Humanities (Art, English, Foreign Languages, History, Philosophy, Religion)

Open to legally blind students pursuing or planning to pursue a full-time postsecondary education in the US. Scholarships are awarded on basis of academic excellence, service to the community, and financial need. Must include transcripts and two letters of recommendation. Membership NOT required.

1 award annually. Renewable. Contact Mrs. Peggy Elliot, Scholarship Committee Chairman, for an application.

1035 — NATIONAL GALLERY OF ART (Predoctoral Fellowship Program)

Center for Advanced Study in the Visual Arts
Washington DC 20565
202/842-6482
FAX: 202/842-6733
E-Mail: advstudy@nga.gov
Internet: www.nga.gov/resources/casva.htm

AMOUNT: $16,000

DEADLINE(S): NOV 15

FIELD(S): Art History

Ten predoctoral fellowship programs (between 12-36 months each) for productive scholarly work in the history, theory, and criticism of art, architecture, and urbanism. Applicants must have completed their residence requirements and coursework for the Ph.D. as well as general or preliminary examinations before the date of application. Students must have certification of competence in two foreign languages. Must be either US citizen or enrolled in a US university.

Contact the National Gallery of Art for an application and list of specific fellowships.

1036 — NATIONAL HUMANITIES CENTER (Lilly Fellowships in Religion and the Humanities)

PO Box 12256
Research Triangle Park NC 27709-2256
919/549-0661
FAX: 919/990-8535
E-Mail: nhc@ga.unc.edu
Internet: www.nhc.rtp.nc.us:8080

AMOUNT: Stipend ($35,000-$50,000) + Travel Expenses (for fellow & dependents)

DEADLINE(S): OCT 15

FIELD(S): Religion & the Humanities

Postdoctoral fellowships for the study of religion by humanistic scholars from fields other than religion and theology. Fellows will form the core of a monthly seminar on religion and the humanities. Curriculum vitae, 1,000-word proposal, and three letters of recommendation are required.

3-4 awards annually. Contact NHC for application materials.

1037 — NATIONAL LEAGUE OF AMERICAN PEN WOMEN, INC. (Scholarships for Mature Women)

1300 Seventeenth St. NW
Washington DC 20036
717/225-3023

AMOUNT: $1,000

DEADLINE(S): JAN 15 (even-numbered years)

FIELD(S): Art; Music; Creative Writing

The National League of American Pen Women gives three $1,000 grants in even-numbered years to women aged 35 and over. Should submit three 4"x6" or bigger color prints, manuscripts, or musical compositions suited to the criteria for the year.

Send SASE for details at the above address.

1038 — NAVAL HISTORICAL CENTER (Internship Program)

Washington Navy Yard
901 M St., SE
Washington DC 20374-5060
202/433-6901
FAX: 202/433-8200
E-Mail: efurgol@nhc.navy.mil
Internet: www.history.navy.mil

AMOUNT: $400 possible honoraria; otherwise, unpaid

DEADLINE(S): None

FIELD(S): Education; History; Public Relations; Design

Registered students of colleges/universities and graduates thereof are eligible for this program, which must be a minimum of 3 weeks, full or part-time. Four specialities available: Curator, Education, Public Relations, and Design. Interns receive orientation & assist in their departments, and must complete individual project which contributes to Center. Must submit a letter of recommendation, unofficial transcript, and writing sample of not less than 1,000 words.

Contact Dr. Edward M. Furgol, Curator, for an application.

1039 — NEW YORK STATE THEATRE INSTITUTE (Internships in Theatrical Production)

155 River St.
Troy NY 12180
518/274-3573
nysti@crisny.org
Internet: www.crisny.org/not-for-profit/nysti/int.htm

AMOUNT: None

DEADLINE(S): None

FIELD(S): Fields of study related to theatrical production, including box office and PR

Internships for college students, high school seniors, and educators-in-residence interested in developing skills in above fields. Unpaid, but college credit is earned. Located at Russell Sage College in Troy, NY. Gain experience in box office, costumes, education, electrics, music, stage management, scenery, properties, performance, and public relations. Interns come from all over the world.

Must be associated with an accredited institution. See website for more information. Call Ms. Arlene Leff, Intern Director at above location. Include your postal mailing address.

1040 — NEWBERRY LIBRARY (Long-Term Fellowships)

60 West Walton Street
Chicago IL 60610-3380
312/943-9090
E-Mail: research@newberry.org
Internet: www.newberry.org

AMOUNT: Up to $30,000

DEADLINE(S): JAN 20

FIELD(S): Humanities, History, & related fields

Six postdoctoral fellowship programs are available for scholars wishing to use the Library's collection for writing or research. Fellowships last six to eleven months, and each have slightly different requirements.

See website for details and an application or write to above address.

1041 — NEWBERRY LIBRARY (Short-Term Fellowships)

60 West Walton Street
Chicago IL 60610-3380
312/943-9090
E-Mail: research@newberry.org
Internet: www.newberry.org

AMOUNT: $800-$1,500/month

DEADLINE(S): MAR 1

FIELD(S): Humanities, History, & related fields

Nine programs for postdoctoral scholars or doctoral students at the dissertation stage. Study varies from two weeks to three months and is for those making use of Newberry's collections. Each program has slightly different requirements.

See website for details and applications or write to above address.

1042 — NEWBERRY LIBRARY (Special Fellowships)

60 West Walton Street
Chicago IL 60610-3380
312/255-3666
E-Mail: research@newberry.org
Internet: www.newberry.org

AMOUNT: Varies

DEADLINE(S): DEC 15

FIELD(S): Humanities, History, & related fields

Fellowships for three months to one year for doctoral or postdoctoral students to study in Germany, France, or Great Britain in fields related to Newberry's collections. Some deadlines JAN 20th. Specific locations are: Wolfenb, ttel, Germany; Ecole Nationale des Chartes, Paris, France; and the British Academy, Great Britain.

See website for more details and applications or write to above address.

1043 — NOVA SCOTIA COLLEGE OF ART AND DESIGN (Scholarships)

5163 Duke Street
Halifax Nova Scotia B3J 3J6 Canada
902/494-8130
FAX: 902/425-2987
E-Mail: ann@nscad.ns.ca
Internet: www.nscad.ns.ca

AMOUNT: $100-$5,000

DEADLINE(S): Varies

FIELD(S): Art; Fine Arts

The Nova Scotia College of Art and Design administers a number of scholarships and bursary awards that acknowledge high achievement and special promise. Awards restricted to students accepted to or officially registered at the college.

Contact L. Ann Read, Student Services, at above address for school catalog & details on specific scholarships.

1044 — ORIENTAL CERAMIC SOCIETY (George De Manasce Memorial Trust Fund)

30B Torrington Square
London WC1E 7JL ENGLAND UK
071 636 7985
FAX: 071 580 6749

AMOUNT: Varies

DEADLINE(S): Varies (every 3 or 4 years only)

FIELD(S): Oriental Arts

Bursary is awarded for a particular research project, rather than for coursework or living expenses. After the research has been completed, the candidate is required to give a lecture to the Society on their subject, which is of a high enough standard to be published in the Transactions of the Oriental Ceramic Society. The Society supports knowledge & understanding of the arts of Asia and provides a valuable link between collectors, curators, scholars, and others.

Award is given only every three or four years. Membership is also available. Contact Mrs. Jean Martin, Secretary/Administrator.

1045 — PARAMOUNT PICTURES (Paramount Internships in Film & Television)

5555 Melrose Ave.
Hollywood, CA 90038
213/956-5145

AMOUNT: Approximately $25,000

DEADLINE(S): FEB 1

FIELD(S): Film & Video; Screenwriting

Post-graduate producing, directing, film, & TV writing internships at Paramount Pictures. Open to new graduates of the graduate film programs at New York University, Columbia University, UCLA, USC, & The American Film Institute.

Application is through the school. DO NOT apply directly to Paramount. Renewable. Write for complete information.

1046 — PIXAR ANIMATION STUDIOS (Summer Internships)

1001 W. Cutting Blvd.
Richmond CA 94804
510/412-6017
FAX: 510/236-0388
E-Mail: hr@pixar.com
Internet: www.pixar.com

AMOUNT: Varies

DEADLINE(S): MAR

FIELD(S): Animation

Summer internships offer "hands on" experience for currently enrolled college/university students, based on departmental needs. Send a resume with name/address/phone, position, work experience/education, internships, and hardware/software experience. Must also submit reels: VHS (NTSC or PAL) or 3/4" (NTSC), 5 minutes in length starting with most recent work, music optional—visual skills nicer, and credit list explaining your reel & software used.

Call the job hotline for details/available positions.

1047 — RHYTHM & HUES STUDIOS (Computer Graphics Scholarship)

5404 Jandy Place
Los Angeles CA 90066
310/448-7619
E-Mail: scholarship@rhythm.com
Internet: www.iwc.pair.com/scholarshipage/subjects/arts/companimat.html

AMOUNT: $1,000/category

DEADLINE(S): JUN 1

FIELD(S): Computer Modeling; Computer Character Animation; Digital Cinematography

Open to all students enrolled full-time in an accredited undergraduate or graduate degree program within six months of the deadline. Entries should include cover sheet stating name, address, phone, SSN, school, major, faculty advisor name/address/phone, and category under which entry is being submitted. Also include photocopy of current student ID and type-written description of entry, including hardware/software used.

1 award in modeling, 1 in animation, & 3 in cinematography; 1 $4,000 grant also goes to each winner's academic department. Contact Rhythm & Hues Studios for more information.

1048 — RIPON COLLEGE (Performance/Recognition Tuition Scholarships)

Admissions Office
300 Seward St., PO Box 248
Ripon WI 54971
920/748-8102 or 800/94-RIPON
E-Mail: adminfo@ripon.edu
Internet: www.ripon.edu

AMOUNT: $5,000-$10,000/yr.

DEADLINE(S): MAR 1

FIELD(S): Music; Forensics; Art; Theatre

Open to undergraduate and graduate students attending or planning to attend Ripon College. Purpose is to recognize and encourage academic potential and accomplishment in above fields. Interview, audition, or nomination may be required.

Renewable. Contact Office of Admission for an application.

1049 — SAMUEL H. KRESS FOUNDATION (Fellowship Program)

174 East 80th Street
New York NY 10021
212/861-4993
FAX: 212/628-3146
Internet: www.shkf.org

AMOUNT: $1,000-$25,000

DEADLINE(S): Varies

FIELD(S): Art History; Art Conservation

Conservation fellowships, curatorial fellowships, art history fellowships, and travel fellowships are open to US citizens or individuals matriculated at US institutions. Must be nominated by your department or museum.

Contact Lisa Ackerman at the Kress Foundation for an information sheet detailing each fellowship; see your department for an application and nomination information.

1050 — SIR ROBERT MENZIES CENTRE FOR AUSTRALIAN STUDIES (Visual Arts Fellowship)

28 Russell Square
London WC1B 5DS ENGLAND UK
+44 0171-862 8854
FAX: +44 0171-580 9627
E-Mail: mcintyre@sas.ac.uk

AMOUNT: 4,000 pounds sterling (max.)

DEADLINE(S): MAY 28

FIELD(S): Visual/Performing Arts

For British students to study at Western Australian Academy of Performing Arts. Must have a good degree/equivalent at approved tertiary institution and suitable evidence of postgraduate visual arts achievement & experience. Younger scholars preferred, but while there is no formal age limit, must be able to make contribution in field for at least ten years. Must spend at least three months studying in Australia. Must submit curriculum vitae, references, and proposal.

Contact Kirsten McIntyre for an application no later than May 28th; actual deadline to return application is June 4th.

1051 — SKIDMORE, OWINGS & MERRILL FOUNDATION (Interior Architecture Traveling Fellowship Program)

224 S. Michigan Ave., Suite 1000
Chicago IL 60604
312/554-9090
FAX 312/360-4545

AMOUNT: $7,500

DEADLINE(S): Varies (consult with school)

FIELD(S): Architecture or Interior Design

ART

For a student graduating with a B.A. or M.A. degree from and accredited U.S. architectural or FIDER school. It will allow the Fellow to visit buildings and settings that are central to his or her area of interest and study.

Must submit portfolio and a proposed travel itinerary, etc. Write for complete information.

1052 — SMITHSONIAN INSTITUTION (Cooper-Hewitt, National Design Museum-Mark Kaminski Summer Internship)

2 East 91st Street
New York NY 10128
212/860-6868
FAX: 212/860-6909

AMOUNT: $2,500 for 10-week period

DEADLINE(S): MAR 31

FIELD(S): Architecture, Architectural History, Design and Criticism, Museum Education, Museum Studies

These internships are open to college students considering a career in one of the above areas of study. Also open to graduate students who have not yet completed their M.A. degree. This ten-week program is designed to acquaint participants with the programs, policies, procedures, and operations of Cooper-Hewitt Museum and of museums in general.

One award each summer. Internship commences in June and ends in August. Housing is not provided. Write to Linda Herd at the above address for complete information.

1053 — SMITHSONIAN INSTITUTION (Cooper-Hewitt, National Design Museum-Peter Krueger Summer Internship Program)

Cooper-Hewitt National Design Museum
2 East 91st St.
New York NY 10128
212/860-6868
FAX: 212/860-6909

AMOUNT: $2,500

DEADLINE(S): MAR 31

FIELD(S): Art History, Design, Museum Studies, and Museum Education, or Architectural History

Ten-week summer internships open to graduate and undergraduate students considering a career in the museum profession. Interns will assist on special research or exhibition projects and participate in daily museum activities.

Six awards each summer. Internship commences in June and ends in August. Housing is not provided. Write for complete information.

1054 — SMITHSONIAN INSTITUTION (Cooper-Hewitt, National Design Museum-The Lippincott & Margulies Summer Internship)

Cooper-Hewitt National Design Museum
2 East 91st St.
New York NY 10128
212/860-6868
FAX 212/860-6909

AMOUNT: $2,500

DEADLINE(S): MAR 31

FIELD(S): Graphic, environmental, and industrial design

Ten-week summer internships open to graduate and undergraduate students considering a career in the fields listed above.

One award each summer. Internship commences in June and ends in August. Housing is not provided. Write for complete information.

1055 — SMITHSONIAN INSTITUTION (Cooper-Hewitt National Design Museum; Peter Krueger-Christie's Fellowship)

2 East 91st Street
New York NY 10128-9990
212/849-8372

AMOUNT: Stipend: $18,000 + $2,000 for research-related travel

DEADLINE(S): APR 30

FIELD(S): Design & Decorative Arts

Research fellowship open to a promising young scholar who submits a work plan for a research project in such fields as drawings & prints, textiles, wallcoverings, and western European and American decorative arts.

Award is not renewable and cannot be deferred. Write for complete information.

1056 — SMITHSONIAN INSTITUTION (Fellowship Program)

Office of fellowships & Grants
955 L'Enfant Plaza, Suite 7000
Washington DC 20560
202/287-3271
E-Mail: http://www.si.edu/research+study
Internet: siofg@sivm.si.edu

AMOUNT: $3,000-$25,000 depending on level and length

DEADLINE(S): JAN 15

FIELD(S): Animal behavior, ecology, environmental science (including emphasis on the tropics, anthropology (& archaeology), astrophysics, astronomy, earth sciences, paleobiology, evolutionary/systematic biology, history of science and technology, history of art, esp. American, contemporary, African,

and Asian, 20th century American crafts, decorative arts, social/cultural history of the US, or folklife.

For research in residence at the Smithsonian for graduate students, both pre- and postdoctoral.

Research to be in the fields listed above.

1057 — SMITHSONIAN INSTITUTION (Minority Student Internship Program)

Fellowships & Grants
955 L'Enfant Plaza, Suite 7000
MRC 902
Washington DC 20560
202/287-3271
FAX: 202/287-3691
E-Mail: siofg@ofg.si.edu
Internet: www.si.edu/research+study

AMOUNT: $300/week + possible travel expenses

DEADLINE(S): FEB 15

FIELD(S): Humanities, Environmental Studies, Cultural Studies, Natural History, Earth Science, Art History, Biology, & related fields

Ten-week internships in residence at the Smithsonian for US minority students to participate in research or museum-related activities in above fields. For undergrads or grads with at least a 3.0 GPA. Essay, resume, transcripts, and references required with application. Internships are full-time and are offered for Summer, Fall, or Spring tenures.

Write for application.

1058 — SOCIETY FOR TECHNICAL COMMUNICATION (Graduate Scholarships)

901 N. Stuart St., Suite 904
Arlington VA 22203-1854
703/522-4114
FAX: 703/522-2075
E-Mail: stc@stc-va.org
Internet: www.stc-va.org

AMOUNT: $2,500

DEADLINE(S): FEB 15

FIELD(S): Technical Communication

Open to full-time graduate students who are enrolled in an accredited master's or doctoral degree program for careers in any area of technical communication: technical writing, editing, graphic design, multimedia art, etc.

Awards tenable at recognized colleges & universities in U.S. and Canada. Seven awards per year. Visit website or write for further information.

1059 — SOLOMON R. GUGGENHEIM MUSEUM (Internship Programs)

1071 Fifth Ave.
New York NY 10128-0173
212/423-3526

FAX: 212/423-3650

E-Mail: aderusha@guggenheim.org

AMOUNT: Varies (some positions non-paid)

DEADLINE(S): FEB 15 (Summer); JUL 15 (Fall); NOV 15 (Spring)

FIELD(S): Art Administration; Art History

Various internships, which offer practical museum training experience, are available for undergraduates, recent graduates, and graduate students in art history, administration, conservation, education, and related fields. Location varies, including New York, Italy, and Spain. Housing NOT included. Cover letter, resume, transcripts, letters of recommendation, list of foreign languages/relevant coursework, and essay (less than 500 words, describing interest) required.

Contact the Internship Coordinator, Education Department, at the Museum for details of each internship and application procedures.

1060 — SONOMA CHAMBOLLE-MUSIGNY SISTER CITIES, INC. (Henri Cardinaux Memorial Scholarship)

Chamson Scholarship Committee

PO Box 1633

Sonoma CA 95476-1633

707/939-1344

FAX: 707/939-1344

E-Mail: Baileysci@vom.com

AMOUNT: up to $1,500 (travel + expenses)

DEADLINE(S): JUL 15

FIELD(S): Culinary Arts; Wine Industry; Art; Architecture; Music; History; Fashion

Hands-on experience working in above or similiar fields & living with a family in small French village in Burgundy or other French city. Must be Sonoma County, CA, resident at least 18 years of age & be able to communicate in French. Transcripts, employer recommendation, photograph, & essay (stating why, where, & when) required.

1 award. Non-renewable. Also offers opportunity for candidate in Chambolle-Musigny to obtain work experience & cultural exposure in Sonoma, CA.

1061 — STUDENT AWARDS AGENCY FOR SCOTLAND (Scottish Studentships for Advanced Postgraduate Study)

Gyleview House

3 Redheughs Rigg

South Gyle

Edinburgh EH12 9HH SCOTLAND UK

Written inquiry or 0131 244 5847

AMOUNT: Varies

DEADLINE(S): MAY 1

FIELD(S): Arts; Humanities

Studentships for full-time research for graduate and advanced post-graduate study. Candidates must have been ordinarily residents in the British Isles for at least three years immediately preceding the start of postgraduate study and ordinarily residents of Scotland at the time of application. They should not have been resident during the three years period wholly for the purpose of receiving full-time education.

Must apply through university. Citizenship restrictions for EU applicants may apply. Further particulars & application forms are available from the post-graduate section at the above address.

1062 — TELETOON (Animation Scholarship Award Competition)

BCE Place

181 Bay St.

PO Box 787

Toronto Ontario CANADA

416/956-2060

E-Mail: pascaleg@teletoon.com

Internet: www.teletoon.com

AMOUNT: $1,500-$5,000

DEADLINE(S): MAY 14

FIELD(S): Animation

For young Canadian talent to pursue studies & embark on career in animation. Based on whose work best embodies development & promotion of original animated content & those who become innovators in their field. Additional grand prize goes to student for overall commitment, creativity, accomplishment, & passion for animation. Entrance Scholarships for high schools students, Continuing Ed Scholarships for college, & Most Promising Student for graduating college students.

10 awards annually. See website or contact Teletoon for official rules.

1063 — TENNESSEE ARTS COMMISSION (Individual Artists' Fellowships)

401 Charlotte Ave.

Nashville TN 37243-0780

615/741-1701

AMOUNT: $2,000

DEADLINE(S): JAN 11

FIELD(S): Visual Arts; Performing Arts; Creative Arts

Open to artists who are residents of Tennessee. Duration of award is one year. Applicants must be professional artists. FULL-TIME STUDENTS ARE NOT ELIGIBLE.

Write for complete information.

1064 — THE ALICIA PATTERSON FOUNDATION (Fellowships for Journalists, Writers, Editors, and Photographers)

1730 Pennsylvania Ave. NW, Suite 180

Washington DC 20006

301/951-8512

E-Mail: apfengel@charm.net

Internet: www.aliciapatterson.org

AMOUNT: $30,000/year

DEADLINE(S): OCT 1

FIELD(S): Print Journalism/Writing, Editing, Photography

Full-time fellowships for persons working in one of the above fields for the purpose of completing a research project.

Five to seven fellows per year. Recipients may not be employed, but may do freelance work during the fellowship period. Send for details or check website for rules regarding submission of samples, recommendations, etc.

1065 — THE CHRISTOPHERS (Video Contest)

12 East 48th Street

New York NY 10017

212/759-4050

FAX: 212/838-5073

E-Mail: tci@idt.net

Internet: www.christophers.org

AMOUNT: $3,000 (1st prize); $2,000 (2nd); $1,000 (3rd); 5 honorable mentions + all winners aired nationwide on TV series "Christopher Closeup"

DEADLINE(S): JUN 18

FIELD(S): Film & Video

Contest for college students in good standing to use any style or format to create on film or video an image expressing the annual theme in five minutes or less. 1999's theme is "One person CAN make a difference." Entries must be submitted on 3/4" VHS cassette ONLY, labeled with entry title, length, name, & address of entrant. Official entry form must be included. Contest judged on ability to capture theme, artistic/technical proficiency, & adherence to rules.

Winners notified in September. See website or contact Father Thomas J. McSweeney, Director, for an official entry form and/or current year's theme.

1066 — THE LEMMERMANN FOUNDATION (Fondazione Lemmermann Scholarship Awards)

c/o Studio Avvocati Romanelli

via Cosseria, 5

00192 Roma ITALIA

(+39-6) 324.30.23

FAX: (+39-6) 321.26.46

E-Mail: lemmerma@bbs.nexus.it
Internet: http://vivaldi.nexus.it/altri/
lemmermann/

AMOUNT: Italian lire 1.500.000

DEADLINE(S): MAR 15; SEP 30

FIELD(S): Italian/Roman studies in the subject areas of literature, archaeology, history of art

For university students who need to study in Rome to carry out research and prepare their theses concerning Rome and the Roman culture from the period Pre-Roman to present day time in the subject areas above.

Contact above organization for details. Access website for application form.

1067 — THE REUTER FOUNDATION (The Peter Sullivan Memorial Fellowships for News Graphics Journalists)

The Director, 85 Fleet St.
London EC4P 4AJ ENGLAND
(+44) 171 542 2913
E-Mail: rtrfoundation@easynet.co.uk
Internet: www.foundation.reuters.com/
sullivan.html

AMOUNT: Travel, tuition, and living allowance

DEADLINE(S): SEP 30

FIELD(S): Journalism—news graphics

Fellowships for working, full-time news graphics journalists with at least five years experience. The three-month program offers an opportunity for talented news graphic journalists and designers to create a university study plan suited to their individual needs. Must be fluent in either Spanish or English.

Access website or write for application details. Application form is on website.

1068 — THE WALT DISNEY COMPANY (American Teacher Awards)

P.O. Box 9805
Calabasas CA 91372

AMOUNT: $2,500 (36 awards); $25,000 (Outstanding Teacher of the Year)

DEADLINE(S): FEB 15

FIELD(S): Teachers: athletic coach, early childhood, English, foreign language/ESL, general elementary, mathematics, performing arts, physical education/health, science, social studies, visual arts, voc/tech education

Awards for K-12 teachers in the above fields.

Teachers, or anyone who knows a great teacher, can write for applications at the above address.

1069 — UNIVERSITY FILM & VIDEO ASSOCIATION (Carole Fielding Student Grants)

University of Baltimore
School of Comm.
1420 N. Charles Street
Baltimore MD 21201
410/837-6061

AMOUNT: $1,000 to $4,000

DEADLINE(S): MAR 31

FIELD(S): Film, video, multi-media production

Open to undergraduate/graduate students. Categories are narrative, experimental, animation, documentary, multi-media/Installation and research. Applicant must be sponsored by a faculty member who is an active member of the Univesity Film and Video Association.

Write to the above address for application and complete details.

1070 — UNIVERSITY OF ILLINOIS COLLEGE OF FINE & APPLIED ARTS (Kate Neal Kinley Fellowship)

College of Fine and Applied Arts, 608 E.
Lorado Taft Dr., #117
Champaign IL 61820
217/333-1661

AMOUNT: $7,000 (3); $1,000 (3)

DEADLINE(S): FEB 1

FIELD(S): Art, Music, Architecture

Graduate fellowship for advanced study in the U.S. or abroad. Open to applicants with a bachelor's degree in the above areas. Preference given (but not limited) to applicants under 25 years of age and to graduates of the College of Fine and Applied Arts of the University of Illinois at Urbana-Champaign. Others are considered.

Write to Dr. Kathleen F. Conlin, Chair, Kinley Memorial Fellowship Committee, at above address. for complete information. Recipients may not participate in regular remunerative employment while engaged upon the Fellowship.

1071 — UNIVERSITY OF MANCHESTER (Awards for Research)

Secretary, Research and Graduate Support Unit
Manchester M13 9PL England
0161 275 2035
FAX: 0161 275 2445/7216

AMOUNT: Maintenance grant (approx) 5000 pounds p.a. plus payment of UK tuition fees.

DEADLINE(S): MAY 1

FIELD(S): Arts, Economics, Social Studies, Education, Science, Engineering, Biological Sciences, Law

The university offers research studentships for doctoral research in all disciplines. These awards are highly competitive. Applicants should hold at least a 2:1 degree or equivalent. Awards are renewable for up to 2 years.

Approx 50 awards per year. Please contact address above for complete information.

1072 — UNIVERSITY OF NEWCASTLE—DEPT. OF MUSIC (Runciman Arts Studentship)

Arts Faculty Secretary, Percy Bldg.
Univ. of Newcastle
Newcastle upon Tyne
NE1 7RU ENGLAND UK
E-mail: susan.lloyd@ncl.ac.uk

AMOUNT: 4,000 pounds

DEADLINE(S): Varies

FIELD(S): The arts

This studentship provides financial support for a limited number of high quality postgraduate students pursing studies in the arts. All home applicants are required to apply for British Academy funding as well as for this one; oeverseas coandidates may apply and are required to apply to the british Academy under the Overseas Research Students Award scheme.

Contact school for details and application.

1073 — WAVERLY COMMUNITY HOUSE INC. (F. Lammot Belin Arts Scholarships)

Scholarships Selection Committee
P.O. Box 142
Waverly PA 18471
717/586-8191

AMOUNT: $10,000

DEADLINE(S): DEC 15

FIELD(S): Painting; Sculpture; Music; Drama; Dance; Literature; Architecture; Photography

Applicants must have resided in the Abington or Pocono regions of Northeastern Pennsylvania. They must furnish proof of exceptional ability in their chosen field but no formal training in any academic or professional program.

U.S. citizenship required. Finalists must appear in person before the selection committee. Write for complete information.

1074 — WOLFSONIAN-FLORIDA INTERNATIONAL UNIVERSITY (Fellowship Program)

1001 Washington Ave.
Miami Beach FL 33139
305/535-2632
FAX: 305/531-2133
E-Mail: wharton@fiu.edu

AMOUNT: Stipend, housing, travel, & research allowance

DEADLINE(S): MAY 31

FIELD(S): Art History; Architectural History

Postgraduate fellowships at the Wolfsonian to do scholarly research in the decorative arts, design, and architecture of the late-nineteenth to the mid-twentieth centuries. Offers full-time, in-residence research for a period of three to six weeks within the academic term, which runs from January to July each year. Also hosts Visiting Scholars in conjunction with institutional appointments. Honorary Associate Appointments also available. Financial need NOT a factor.

Contact the Research & Programs Officer for an application. Awards announced October 31st.

1075 — YALE CENTER FOR BRITISH ART (Fellowships)

Box 208280
New Haven CT 06520-8280
203/432-2850

AMOUNT: Travel, accommodations, per diem

DEADLINE(S): JAN 15

FIELD(S): British Art; History; Literature

Fellowships to enable scholars engaged in postdoctoral or equivalent research in British art, history, or literature to study the Center's holdings of paintings, drawings, prints, and rare books and to make use of its research facilities.

12 awards annually. Grants normally run for a period of four weeks. Write for complete information.

ENGLISH LANGUAGE / LITERATURE

1076 — ACADEMY OF MOTION PICTURE ARTS AND SCIENCES (Nicholl Fellowships in Screenwriting)

8949 Wilshire Blvd.
Beverly Hills CA 90211-1972
310/247-3000
E-Mail: gbeal@oscars.org
Internet: www.oscars.org/nicholl

AMOUNT: $25,000

DEADLINE(S): MAY 1

FIELD(S): Screenwriting

Academy awards competition is open to any screenwriter who has not sold any form of a screenplay for more than $5,000. Screenplays must be originally written in English. Award may not be used for educational purposes.

Up to 5 awards annually. Send self-addressed, stamped, business-sized envelope after January 1st to AMPAS for an application.

1077 — AMERICAN ANTIQUARIAN SOCIETY (Visiting Academic Research Fellowships)

185 Salisbury St.
Worcester MA 01609-1634
508/752-5813
FAX: 508/754-9069
E-Mail: cfs@mwa.org

AMOUNT: Up to $35,000

DEADLINE(S): JAN 15

FIELD(S): American History; Bibliography; Printing & Publishing; American Literature (through 1876)

Fellowships of one to twelve months duration at the society library. For graduate and postgraduate research in the above fields.

Recipients are expected to be in regular and continuous residence at the society library during the period of the grant. Write for complete information.

1078 — AMERICAN ASSOCIATION OF LAW LIBRARIES (George A. Strait Minority Stipend Grant)

53 W Jackson Blvd., Ste. 940
Chicago IL 60604
312/939-4764
FAX: 312/431-1097
Internet: http://www.aalnet.org

AMOUNT: $3,500 stipend

DEADLINE(S): APR 1

FIELD(S): Law Librarianship

Open to a minority group member who is a college graduate with library experience and is working toward an advanced degree which would further his or her law library career. Must demonstrate financial need.

Write, E-mail, or visit website for complete information.

1079 — AMERICAN ASSOCIATION OF LAW LIBRARIES (Law Librarian Scholarships—Law School Graduates)

53 W. Jackson Blvd., Suite 940
Chicago IL 60604
312/939-4764
FAX: 312/431-1097
E-Mail: aalhq@aall.org
Internet: http://www.aallnet.org

AMOUNT: Varies

DEADLINE(S): APR 1

FIELD(S): Law Librarianship

Open to graduates of accredited law schools who are degree candidates in an accredited library school and plan to pursue a career in law librarianship.

Write for complete information.

1080 — AMERICAN COUNCIL OF LEARNED SOCIETIES (ACLS Fellowships)

Office of Fellowshops & Grants
228 E. 45th St.
New York NY 10017
Written Inquiry

AMOUNT: Up to $20,000

DEADLINE(S): SEP 30

FIELD(S): Humanities, Social Sciences, and other areas having predominately humanistic emphasis

Open to U.S. citizens or legal residents who hold the Ph.D or its equivalent. Fellowships are designed to help scholars devote 6 to 12 continuous months to full-time research.

Write for complete information.

1081 — AMERICAN LIBRARY ASSOCIATION/ LIBRARY & INFORMATION TECHNOLOGY ASSOCIATION (LITA/GEAC Scholarship)

50 E. Huron St.
Chicago IL 60611
312/280-4269
E-Mail: lita@ala.org
Internet: www.ala.org

AMOUNT: $2,500

DEADLINE(S): APR 1

FIELD(S): Library Automation and Information Technology

Recipient must enter ALA-accredited master's degree program with an emphasis on library automation and information technology. Academic excellence, leadership, and evidence of commitment to career in library automation and info tech (prior activity & experience).

Application from Library and Information Technology Association, ALA, at above location; or access fax-on-demand: 1-800/545-2433, press 8, document 415.

1082 — AMERICAN LIBRARY ASSOCIATION (EBSCO/NRMT Scholarship)

50 E. Huron St.
Chicago IL 60611
312/280-4281
E-Mail: pjackson@ala.org
Internet: www.ala.org/work/awards/ scholar.html

AMOUNT: $1,000

DEADLINE(S): APR 1

FIELD(S): Library Science

For U.S. or Canadian citizen entering an ALA-accredited program leading to an M.A. degree. Must be ALA/New Members Round Table member at time of award. Financial need considered.

Contact organization for application or access fax-on-demand: 1-800/545-2433, press 8, document 415.

1083 — AMERICAN LIBRARY ASSOCIATION (LITA/LSSI and LITA/OCLC Minority Scholarships)

50 E. Huron St.
Chicago IL 60611
213/280-4270
FAX: 312/280-3256
E-Mail: lita@ala.org
Internet: www.ala.org

AMOUNT: $2,500

DEADLINE(S): APR 1

FIELD(S): Library Automation and Information Technology

Recipient must enter ALA-accredited master's degree program with an emphasis on library automation. For ethnic minorities: African-American, American Indian or Alaskan Native, Asian or Pacific Islander, or Hispanic.

Write to organization for application or access fax-on-demand: 1-800/545-2433, press 8, document 415.

1084 — AMERICAN LIBRARY ASSOCIATION (Mary V. Gaver Scholarship)

50 E. Huron St.
Chicago IL 60611
312/280-4281
FAX: 312/280-3256
E-Mail: pjackson@ala.org
Internet: www.ala.org

AMOUNT: $3,000

DEADLINE(S): APR 1

FIELD(S): Library Science, specializing in youth services

For U.S. and Canadian citizens or permanent residents who have completed no more than 12 semester hours towards master's degrees in library science prior to June 1 following deadline date. Commitment to career as a youth services specialist in library work and academic excellence are considered.

Acceptance into master's program at time of application not necessary, but winners must enroll in ALA-accredited program. Contact organization for application or access fax-on-demand: 1-800/545-2433, press 8, document 415.

1085 — AMERICAN LIBRARY ASSOCIATION/ AMERICAN ASSOCIATION OF SCHOOL LIBRARIANS (School Librarian's Workshop Scholarship)

50 E. Huron St.
Chicago IL 60611
312/280-4384

AMOUNT: $2,500

DEADLINE(S): FEB 1

FIELD(S): School Library Media

Recipient must enter ALA-accredited master's degree program or school library media program (full-time) that meets ALA curriculum guidelines for NCATE-accredited unit.

Demonstrated interest in working with children or young adults in a school library media program in public or private educational setting; academic excellence and leadership potential are considerations. Write for complete information.

1086 — AMERICAN LIBRARY ASSOCIATION/ ASSOCIATION FOR LIBRARY SERVICE TO CHILDREN (Bound-to-Stay-Bound Books Scholarship)

50 E. Huron St.
Chicago IL 60611
312/280-1398 or 2167
FAX: 312/280-3256
E-Mail: alsc@ala.org
Internet: www.ala.org

AMOUNT: $6,000

DEADLINE(S): MAR 1

FIELD(S): Library Science, service to children

Open to U.S. and Canadian citizens pursuing master's or advanced degree in schools offering ALA-accredited programs. Recipients expected to work directly with children in any type of library for at least one year following educational program. Must not have begun coursework.

Academic excellence and leadership qualities are considerations. Apply to Association for Library Service to Children at above location.

1087 — AMERICAN LIBRARY ASSOCIATION/ ASSOCIATION FOR LIBRARY SERVICE TO CHILDREN (Frederic G. Melcher Scholarship)

50 East Huron St.
Chicago IL 60611
312/280-1398 or 2167
FAX: 312/280-3256
E-Mail: alsc@ala.org
Internet: www.ala.org

AMOUNT: $6,000

DEADLINE(S): MAR 1

FIELD(S): Library Science-service to children

Open to U.S. and Canadian citizens entering ALA-accredited master's degree programs. Recipients are expected to work in library service to children for at least one year following graduation. May not have begun coursework.

Academic excellence, leadership qualities, and desire to work with children in any type of library are considerations. Apply to Association for Library Service to Children, ALA, at above location.

1088 — AMERICAN MOTHERS, INC. (Gertrude Fogelson Cultural and Creative Arts Awards)

1296 E. 21st St.
Brooklyn NY 11201
718/253-5676

AMOUNT: Up to $1,000

DEADLINE(S): JAN 1 (annually)

FIELD(S): Visual arts, creative writing, and vocal music

An award to encourage and honor mothers in artistic pursuits.

Write to Alice Miller at above address for details.

1089 — AMERICAN PHILOLOGICAL ASSOCIATION (Thesaurus Linguae Latinae Fellowship in Latin Lexicography)

c/o Department of Classics
Holy Cross College
Worcester MA 01610
508/793-2203

AMOUNT: $31,500

DEADLINE(S): NOV 15

FIELD(S): Philology (Latin; German)

Open to U.S. citizens or permanent residents who hold the Ph.D degree and have a thorough familiarity with and a special interest in Latin plus a reading knowledge of German.

Fellowship enables American scholars to participate in the work of the Thesaurus Linguae Latinae in Munich (Germany). Write for complete information.

1090 — AMERICAN RESEARCH INSTITUTE IN TURKEY (National Endowment for the Humanities Fellowships for Research in Turkey)

Univ Penn Museum
33rd & Spruce Streets
Philadelphia PA 19104-6324
215/898-3474
FAX: 215/898-0657
E-Mail: leinwand@sas.upenn.edu
Internet: mec.sas.upenn.edu/ARIT

AMOUNT: $10,000-$30,000

DEADLINE(S): NOV 15

FIELD(S): Humanities

Postdoctoral fellowships are to conduct research in Turkey for four to twelve months. Fields of study cover all periods in the general range of the humanities, including humanistically oriented aspects of the social sciences, prehistory, history, art, archaeology, literature, linguistics, and cultural history. There are two institutes, one in Istanbul and one in Ankara. Both have residential facilities for fellows and provide general assistance.

2-3 awards annually. Contact ARIT for an application. Notification by January 25th.

1091 — AMERICAN SCHOOL OF CLASSICAL STUDIES AT ATHENS (Fellowships)

6-8 Charlton St.
Princeton NJ 08540-5232
609/683-0800
FAX: 609/924-0578
E-Mail: ascsa@axcsa.org
Internet: www.ats.edu/spons

AMOUNT: Up to $7,840 + room, partial board, and fee waiver

DEADLINE(S): JAN 5

FIELD(S): Classical Studies; Archaeology; Ancient Greece

Fellowships for study at ASCSA in Greece. Open to graduate students at American & Canadian colleges & universities. Recent graduates also are eligible. Residency in Greece required.

Access website for complete information and application or write for details.

1092 — AMERICAN SCHOOL OF CLASSICAL STUDIES AT ATHENS (Katherine Keene Summer Session Scholarship for Teachers)

993 Lenox Drive, Suite 101
Lawrence NJ 08648
609/844-7577
E-Mail: ascsa@ascsa.org
Internet: www.asca.org

AMOUNT: $2,500

DEADLINE(S): FEB 15

FIELD(S): Classical Studies; Ancient Greece

Scholarships for American public secondary school teachers to attend summer sessions in the above program in Greece. Must include these topics in his/her course material.

Access website for complete information and application or write to Committee on Summer Sessions at above address for details.

1093 — ARCHAEOLOGICAL INSTITUTE OF AMERICA (Olivia James Traveling Fellowship)

Boston Univ
656 Beacon St.
Boston MA 02215-2006
617/353-9361
FAX: 617/353-6550

E-Mail: aia@bu.edu
Internet: www.archeological.org

AMOUNT: $22,000

DEADLINE(S): NOV 1

FIELD(S): Classics; Sculpture; Architecture; Archaeology; History

Fellowships for US citizens/permanent residents to be used for travel and study in Greece, the Aegean Islands, Sicily, Southern Italy, Asia Minor, or Mesopotamia. Preference given to individuals engaged in dissertation research or to recent recipients of the Ph.D. (within 5 years). Award is not intended to support field excavation projects, and recipients may not hold other major fellowships during tenure. At conclusion, recipient must submit report on use of stipend.

Contact AIA for an application. Awards announced by February 1st.

1094 — ARTS MANAGEMENT P/L (Kathleen Mitchell Award)

Station House, Rawson Place
790 George St.
Sydney NSW 2000 AUSTRALIA
(612)9212 5066
FAX: (612)9211 7762
E-Mail: vbraden@ozemail.com.au

AMOUNT: Aus. $4,000

DEADLINE(S): JAN 31

FIELD(S): Novelwriting

Award for female Australian residents who were Australian-born or British-born. Novels must have been published while the author is under 30 years of age and during the two years prior to the deadline. "For the advancement, improvement, and betterment of Australian literature, to improve the educational style of such authors, and to provide them with additional amounts and thus enable them to improve their literary efforts."

Contact Claudia Crosariol, Projects Administrator, for more information/entry form.

1095 — ARTS MANAGEMENT P/L (Marten Bequest Travelling Scholarships)

Station House, Rawson Place
790 George St.
Sydney NSW 2000 Australia
(612)9212 5066
FAX: (612)9211 7762
E-Mail: vbraden@ozemail.com.au

AMOUNT: Aus. $18,000

DEADLINE(S): OCT 30

FIELD(S): Art; Performing Arts; Creative Writing

Open to native-born Australians aged 21-35 (17-35 ballet) who are of outstanding ability and promise in

one or more categories of the Arts. The scholarships are intended to augment a scholar's own resources towards a cultural education, and it may be used for study, maintenance, and travel either in Australia or overseas. Categories are: instrumental music, painting, singing, sculpture, architecture, ballet, prose, poetry, and acting.

1 scholarship granted in each of 9 categories which rotate in 2 groups on an annual basis. Contact Claudia Crosariol, Projects Administrator, for more information/entry form.

1096 — ARTS MANAGEMENT P/L (Miles Franklin Literary Award)

Station House, Rawson Place
790 George St.
Sydney NSW 2000 AUSTRALIA
(612)9212 5066
FAX: (612)9211 7762
E-Mail: vbraden@ozemail.com.au

AMOUNT: Aus. $27,000

DEADLINE(S): JAN 31

FIELD(S): Novel/Playwriting

Annual award for the best book on some aspect of Australian life published in the 12-month period prior to the award deadline each year. If no novel is worthy of the award, a play will be chosen. More than one entry may be submitted by each author; a novel/play written by two or more authors in collaboration is also eligible.

Winner announced in May or June. Contact Claudia Crosariol, Projects Administrator, for complete information/entry form.

1097 — ASSOCIATION FOR LIBRARY & INFORMATION SCIENCE EDUCATION (Alise Research Grants Program)

PO Box 7640
Arlington VA 22207
703/243-8040

AMOUNT: $5,000

DEADLINE(S): SEP 15

FIELD(S): Library Science

Grants are to help support research costs. Open to members of the Association for Library & Information Science.

For membership information or an application, write to above address.

1098 — ASSOCIATION FOR WOMEN IN SCIENCE EDUCATIONAL FOUNDATION (AWIS Predoctoral Awards)

1200 New York Ave. NW, Suite 650
Washington DC 20005
202/326-8940 or 800-886-AWIS

E-Mail: awis@awis.org
Internet: www.awis.org
AMOUNT: $1,000
DEADLINE(S): JAN 16
FIELD(S): Various Sciences and Social Sciences

Scholarships for female doctoral students. Summary page, description of research project, resume, references, transcripts, and biographical sketch required. US citizens may study at any graduate institution; non-citizens must study at US institutions.

5-10 awards annually. See website or write to above address for an application and complete information.

1099 — ASSOCIATION FOR WOMEN IN SCIENCE EDUCATIONAL FOUNDATION (AWIS Pre-doctoral Awards)

1200 New York Ave. NW, Suite 650
Washington DC 20005
202/326-8940 or 800/886-AWIS
E-Mail: awis@awis.org
Internet: www.awis.org
AMOUNT: $1,000
DEADLINE(S): JAN 16
FIELD(S): Various Sciences and Social Sciences

Scholarships for female doctoral students. Summary page, description of research project, resume, references, transcripts, and biographical sketch required. US citizens may study at any graduate institution; non-citizens must be enrolled in US institutions.

5-10 awards annually. See website or write to above address for an application and more information.

1100 — ASSOCIATION FOR WOMEN IN SCIENCE EDUCATIONAL FOUNDATION (Ruth Satter Memorial Award)

1200 New York Ave., NW, Suite 650
Washington DC 20005
202/326-8940 or 800/886-AWIS
E-Mail: awis@awis.org
Internet: www.awis.org
AMOUNT: $1,000
DEADLINE(S): JAN 16
FIELD(S): Various Sciences and Social Sciences

Scholarships for female doctoral students who have interrupted their education for at least three years to raise a family. Summary page, description of research project, resume, references, transcripts, biographical sketch, and letter from your department to confirm eligibility required. US citizens may study at any graduate institution; non-citizens must attend US institutions.

See website or write to above address for more information or an application.

1101 — ASSOCIATION FOR WOMEN IN SCIENCE EDUCATIONAL FOUNDATION (Ruth Satter Memorial Award)

1200 New York Ave. NW, Suite 650
Washington DC 20005
202/326-8940 or 800/886-AWIS
E-Mail: awis@awis.org
Internet: www.awis.org
AMOUNT: $1,000
DEADLINE(S): JAN 16
FIELD(S): Various Sciences and Social Sciences

Scholarships for female doctoral students who have interupted their education three years or more to raise a family. Summary page, description of research project, resume, references, transcripts, biographical sketch, and proof of eligibility from department head required. US citizens may attend any graduate institution; non-citizens must be enrolled in US institutions.

See website or write to above address for more information or an application.

1102 — AUSTRALIAN FEDERATION OF UNIVERSITY WOMEN - WESTERN AUSTRALIA (Joyce Riley Bursary)

Bursary Liaison Officer
PO Box 48
Nedlands WA 6909 AUSTRALIA
Written Inquiry
AMOUNT: Aus$1,700 - Aus$2,750
DEADLINE(S): JUL 31
FIELD(S): Humanities; Social Sciences

To support women graduates of a Western Australian university to complete a higher degree or post-doctoral research in Humanities or Social Sciences at a recognized university in any country.

Membership in AFUW or in IFUW is required. Contact above location for further information.

1103 — AUSTRALIAN FEDERATION OF UNIVERSITY WOMEN - WESTERN AUSTRALIA (Joyce Riley Bursary)

Bursary Liaison Officer
PO Box 48
Nedlands WA 6009 AUSTRALIA
Written Inquiry
AMOUNT: Aus$1,700 - Aus$2,750
DEADLINE(S): JUL 31
FIELD(S): Humanities; Social Sciences

To support women graduates of a recognized university to complete a higher degree or post-doctoral research at a university in Western Australia.

Membership in AFUW or in IFUW is required. Write to above address for complete information.

1104 — AUSTRIAN CULTURAL INSTITUTE (Franz Werfel Scholarship)

950 Third Ave., 20th Fl.
New York NY 10022
212/759-5165
FAX: 212/319-9636
E-Mail: desk@aci.org
Internet: www.austriaculture.net
AMOUNT: ATS 11,000/month (US $845) + ATS 7,500 (US $570)
DEADLINE(S): FEB 28
FIELD(S): Austrian Studies; Literature

Open to professors teaching Austrian literature at American universities/colleges to enable research at Austrian archives, libraries, & other research institutions. Must have an excellent knowledge of German & be no more than 35 years old. Scholars also receive yearly literary symposium invitation, yearly book donations, one-month research grant every three years, & Austrian newspaper subscription. Must submit letters of recommendation, curriculum vitae, & transcripts.

Renewable. See website or contact ACI for an application kit.

1105 — BETA PHI MU INTERNATIONAL LIBRARY SCIENCE HONOR SOCIETY (Sarah Rebecca Reed Scholarship; Harold Lancour Scholarship for Foreign Study)

Florida State University School of Studies
Tallahassee FL 32306-2048
904/644-8111
FAX 904/644-6253
AMOUNT: $1,500 (Reed); $1,000 (Lancour)
DEADLINE(S): MAR 15
FIELD(S): Librarianship

Open to students eligible for admittance to a graduate library school program accredited by the American Library Association.

Write to Executive Secretary Dr. F. William Summers at above address for complete information & application form.

1106 — BETA PHI MU INTERNATIONAL LIBRARY SCIENCE HONOR SOCIETY (Frank B. Sessa Scholarship for Continuing Education)

Florida State University School of Studies
Tallahassee FL 32306-2048
904/644-8111
FAX 904/644-6253
AMOUNT: $750
DEADLINE(S): MAR 15
FIELD(S): Librarianship

Continuing education program open to Beta Phi Mu members. Applicants should submit resume and an explanation of proposed study or research.

Write to Executive Secretary Dr. F. William Summers at above address for complete information & application.

1107 — BIBLIOGRAPHICAL SOCIETY OF AMERICA (Fellowships)

PO Box 1537
Lenox Hill Station
New York NY 10021
Phone/FAX: 212/452-2710
E-Mail: bsa@bibsocamer.org
Internet: www.bibsocamer.org

AMOUNT: up to $1,500/month

DEADLINE(S): DEC 1

FIELD(S): Bibliography & History of the Book Trades

Graduate research fellowships for one or two months. Topics may concentrate on books and documents in any field but focus should be on the physical book or manuscript as historical evidence, history of book production, publication, distribution, or establishing a text.

8 awards annually. Contact BSA for an application.

1108 — BLUES HEAVEN FOUNDATION, INC. (Muddy Waters Scholarship)

2120 S. Michigan Ave.
Chicago IL 60616
312/808-1286

AMOUNT: $2,000

DEADLINE(S): APR 30

FIELD(S): Music; Music Education; African-American Studies; Folklore; Performing Arts; Arts Management; Journalism; Radio/TV/Film

Scholarship is made on a competitive basis with consideration given to scholastic achievement, concentration of studies, and financial need. Applicant must have full-time enrollment status in a Chicago area college/university in at least their first year of undergraduate studies or a graduate program. Scholastic aptitude, extracurricular involvement, grade point average, and financial need are all considered.

Contact Blues Heaven Foundation, Inc. to receive an application between February and April.

1109 — BRITISH ACADEMY—HRB (Postgraduate Awards)

10 Carlton House Terrace
London SW1Y 5AH ENGLAND
0171-969-5200

AMOUNT: Varies

DEADLINE(S): MAY 1

FIELD(S): Humanities

Postgraduate research awards normally will be offered only to candidates who possess at least a good upper (or equivalent) second-class honours degree, but applicants are considered on their merits. Awards are also available in the professional and vocational areas of the humanities.

Open to residents of UK for at least 3 years. Fees-only awards for non-UK EEC nationals ages 18-35. Further information is available from the U.K. higher education institution at which the candidate intends to study..

1110 — BRITISH ACADEMY (Sir Ernest Cassel Educational Trust)

8 Malvern Terrace
Islington, London N1 1HR ENGLAND UK
0171 607 7879

AMOUNT: 100-500 pounds per annum

DEADLINE(S): SEP; DEC; FEB; APR (end of ea. month)

FIELD(S): Language, literature, or civilizaiton of any country

Research grants for the more junior teaching members of universities for research abroad and are for the study of any country or civilization, concentrating on the fields mentioned above.

Obtain application from the Secretary at the Trust.

1111 — BRITISH ASSOCIATION FOR AMERICAN STUDIES (Short-Term Awards)

Dr. Jenel Virden
University of Hull
Hull HU6 7RX ENGLAND UK
01482 465303

AMOUNT: 400 pounds sterling

DEADLINE(S): DEC 1

FIELD(S): American Studies; American History

Open to graduate/postgraduate British scholars for brief visits to the US for research in American history, politics, geography, culture, and literature. Preference given to younger scholars.

Contact Dr. Jenel Virden for an application.

1112 — BRITISH FEDERATION OF WOMEN GRADUATES (Theodora Bosanquet Bursary)

BFWG Charitable Fdn.
28 Great James St.
London WC1N 3ES ENGLAND UK
0171/404 6447
FAX: 0171/404 6505
E-Mail: bfwg.charity@btinternet.com
Internet: www.ifuw.org

AMOUNT: 4 weeks free accomodation

DEADLINE(S): OCT 31

FIELD(S): History; British Literature

Open to women scholars or women postgraduate students who are carrying out research in history or English literature requiring the use of libraries, archives, or other scholarly resources in London. Bursary offered up to four weeks during period from July 1st to October 1st, and covers only accomodation; holder is responsible for all travel & other expenses. After completing tenure, holder must submit short report to Trustees on work carried out. Referees required.

Contact the Grants Administrator-TBB for an application.

1113 — BRITISH INSTITUTE IN EASTERN AFRICA (Research Grants)

PO Box 30710
Nairobi Kenya E. AFRICA
+254-2-43721
FAX: +254-2-43365
E-Mail: pjlane@insightkenya.com
Internet: britac3.britac.ac.uk/institutes/eafrica

AMOUNT: 500-5,000 pounds sterling

DEADLINE(S): MAY 31; NOV 30

FIELD(S): Archaeology; History; Linguistics; Ethnography

Grants are for graduate or postgraduate fieldwork in Eastern Africa. Does NOT cover salaries, overheads, student fees, or stipends. Preference is given, but not limited, to UK and Commonwealth citizens. Financial need is NOT a factor.

15 awards annually. Not renewable. Contact Dr. Paul Lane at the British Institute in Nairobi for an application.

1114 — CATHOLIC LIBRARY ASSOCIATION (The Reverend Andrew L. Bouwhuis Memorial Scholarship)

Catholic Library Assn.
100 North St., Suite 224
Pittsfield MA 01201-5109
413/443-2CLA
FAX: 413/442-2CLA
E-Mail: cla@vgernet.net
Internet: www.cathla.org

AMOUNT: $1,500

DEADLINE(S): FEB 1

FIELD(S): Library science

Promise of success, based on collegiate record, evidence of need for financial help, and acceptance in a graduate school program, are the criteria for awarding the scholarship. The recipient may enter any graduate library school.

1 award annually. Applications available in November. See website or contact the Scholarship Committee at above address for complete information.

1115 — CENTER FOR 17TH- AND 18TH-CENTURY STUDIES (Fellowships)

UCLA
310 Reyce Hall
Los Angeles CA 90095-1404
310/206-8522
FAX: 310/206-8577
E-Mail: c1718cs@humnet.ucla.edu

AMOUNT: $1,000-$18,400

DEADLINE(S): MAR 15

FIELD(S): British Literature/History (17th & 18th Centuries)

Undergraduate stipends, graduate assistantships, and Ahmanson & Getty postdoctoral fellowships are for advanced study and research regarding British literature and history of the 17th and 18th centuries. Tenable at the William Andrews Clark Memorial Library at the University of California, Los Angeles.

Contact the Center for current year's theme and an application.

1116 — CENTER FOR HELLENIC STUDIES (Resident Junior Fellowships)

3100 Whitehaven Street NW
Washington DC 20008
202/234-3738

AMOUNT: Up to $20,000

DEADLINE(S): OCT 15

FIELD(S): Literature, history, philosophy, language, or religion of Ancient Greece

Resident fellowships for post-doctoral scholars with professional competence and some publication in Ancient Greek areas shown above.

Twelve resident fellowships per year. Write for complete information.

1117 — CONCORDIA UNIVERSITY (Wynne Francis Award and David McKeen Awards)

Dept. English
1455 de Maisonneuve Blvd. West
LB 501
Montreal Quebec H3G 1M8 CANADA
514/848-3809
FAX: 514/848-2812
E-Mail: awardsgs@vax2.concordia.ca

AMOUNT: $500; $350

DEADLINE(S): FEB 1

FIELD(S): English

Wynne Francis Award is for a graduate student's critical essay on Canadian poetry. May deal with any aspect of Canadian poetry, including biography, ethnic, regionalist, feminist, or comparative studies; textual analysis/literary theory; or other. Essays written for grad courses, as well as chapters/sections of M.A. thesis, are eligible. David Mckeen Awards are for academic & creative writing students who have received their M.A. degree during an academic year.

3 awards annually. Not renewable. Contact the Graduate Program Director in the Department of English at Concordia University for applications.

1118 — COUNCIL FOR BASIC EDUCATION (Arts Education Fellowships)

2506 Buckelew Drive
Falls Church VA 22046
703/876-5782

AMOUNT: $2,800 stipend + $200 grant to school

DEADLINE(S): JAN

FIELD(S): Teaching of the arts (visual arts, creative writing, dance, media, music, theatre)

Fellowships for K-12 teachers in the above fields, artist-teachers, or professional artists who teach at least 20 hours per week. Funding from the National Endowment for the Arts and the Getty Center for Education in the Arts, and others.

Contact organization for details.

1119 — DISTRICT OF COLUMBIA COMMISSION ON THE ARTS & HUMANITIES (Grants)

410 Eighth St. NW, 5th Floor
Washington DC 20004
202/724-5613
TDD 202/727-3148
FAX: 202/727-4135

AMOUNT: $2,500

DEADLINE(S): MAR 1

FIELD(S): Performing Arts, Literature, Visual Arts

Applicants for grants must be professional artists and residents of Washington DC for at least one year prior to submitting application. Awards intended to generate art endeavors within the Washington DC community.

Open also to art organizations that train, exhibit, or perform within DC. 150 grants per year. Write for complete information.

1120 — ETA SIGMA PHI (Summer Scholarships)

Prof. Caroline A. Perkins
Dept. Classical Studies
Marshall Univ
Huntington WV 25701
804/223-6244
FAX: 804/223-6045
E-Mail: perkins@marshall.edu

AMOUNT: $2,800 Rome; $3,400 Athens; $2,400 Cumae

DEADLINE(S): FEB 1

FIELD(S): Classics

Open to members of Eta Sigma Phi. Scholarships are for study at the American Academy in Rome, the American School of Classical Studies in Athens, and the Vergilian Society Program at Cumae. Attention will be given to work in Greek and Latin and intention to teach.

Contact Professor Caroline Perkins at Marshall University for an application.

1121 — FLORIDA ARTS COUNCIL (Individual Artists' Fellowships)

FL Dept. of State
Div. of Cultural Affairs
State Capitol
Tallahassee FL 32399-0250
850/487-2980
TDD: 850/414-2214
FAX: 850/922-5259

AMOUNT: $5,000

DEADLINE(S): JAN 16

FIELD(S): Visual Arts; Dance; Folk Arts; Media; Music; Theater; Literary Arts; Interdisciplinary

Fellowships awarded to individual artists in the above areas. Must be Florida residents, U.S. citizens, and over 18 years old. May NOT be a degree-seeking student—funding is for support of artistic endeavors only.

38 awards per year. Write for complete information.

1122 — FORD FOUNDATION/NATIONAL RESEARCH COUNCIL (Predoctoral/Dissertation Fellowships for Minorities)

2101 Constitution Ave.
Washington DC 20418
202/334-2872
E-Mail: infofell@nas.edu
Internet: http//www.nas.edu/fo/index.html

AMOUNT: $14,000 annual stipend + $6,000 grant to institution; $18,000 for dissertation fellowship

DEADLINE(S): NOV 3

FIELD(S): Most fields of study: sciences, humanities, engineering, behavioral science, social sciences, and computer science

Predoctoral and dissertation fellowships for students whose ethnicity is Alaskan Native, Black/African American, Mexican American/Chicano, Native American Indian, Native Pacific Islander, or Puerto Rican. For research-based programs leading to careers in college teaching and research.

Contact above address or website.

1123 — FOREST ROBERTS THEATRE (Mildred & Albert Panowski Playwriting Award)

Northern Michigan Univ
1401 Presque Isle Ave.
Marquette MI 49855-5364
906/227-2553
FAX: 906/227-2567
Internet: www.nmu.edu/theatre

AMOUNT: $2,000

DEADLINE(S): Varies

FIELD(S): Playwriting

This competition is open to any playwright, but only one play per playwright may be entered. Entries must be original, full-length plays not previously produced or published. May be co-authored, based upon factual material, or an adaptation. Scripts must be typewritten or word processed and securely bound within a cover or folder and clearly identified.

1 award annually. Not renewable. Contact James Panowski at above address for contest rules and entry blank.

1124 — FREEDOM FROM RELIGION FOUNDATION (Student Essay Contest)

PO Box 750
Madison WI 53701
608/256-5800
Internet: www.infidels.org/org/ffrf

AMOUNT: $1,000; $500; $250

DEADLINE(S): JUL 15

FIELD(S): Humanities; English; Education; Philosophy; Science

Essay contest on topics related to church-state entanglement in public schools or growing up a "freethinker" in religious-oriented society. Topics change yearly, but all are on general theme of maintaining separation of church and state. New topics available in February. For high school seniors & currently enrolled college/technical students. Must be US citizen.

Send SASE to address above for complete information. Please indicate whether wanting information for college competition or high school. Information will be sent when new topics are announced each February. See website for details.

1125 — FRIENDS OF THE UNIVERSITY OF WISCONSIN (Madison Libraries Humanities Grants-in-Aid)

728 State St.
Madison WI 53706
608/262-3243 or 608/265-2750 (ans. mach.)

AMOUNT: $1,000/mo.

DEADLINE(S): APR 1; OCT 1

FIELD(S): Research in the humanities appropriate to the collections

Two grants-in-aid annually for one-month's study in such areas as the history of science from the Middle Ages through the Enlightenment, a collection of avant-garde AMerican "little magazines," a American women writers to 1920, Scandinavian and Germanic literature, Dutch post-Reformation theology and church history, French political pamphlets of the 16th & 17th centuries, and many other fields.

Must be in Ph.D. program or be able to deomonstrate a recored of solid intellectual accomplishment. Must live outside a 75-mile radius of Madison, Wisconsin, U.S. Call/write for details.

1126 — GATES MILLENIUM SCHOLARS PROGRAM (Scholarships for Graduate Students)

8260 Willow Oaks Corporate Dr.
Fairfax VA 22031-4511
877/690-4677
Internet: www.gmsp.org

AMOUNT: Varies

DEADLINE(S): FEB 1

FIELD(S): Engineering; Mathematics; Science; Education; Library Science

College presidents, professors, & deans may nominate graduate students who are African-Americans, Native Americans, Hispanic Americans, or Asian Americans in above fields. Based on academic performance, commitment to academic study, involvement in community service & school activities, potential for leadership, career goals, and financial need. Must submit transcripts and letters of recommendation. Must be US citizen with a minimum 3.3 GPA

Application materials available November 1st; scholars will be notified in May. Funded by the Bill & Melinda Gates Foundation, and administered by the United Negro College Fund.

1127 — GENERAL SEMANTICS FOUNDATION (Project Grants)

Harry Maynard, President
14 Charcoal Hill
Westport CT 06880
203/226-1394

AMOUNT: $300-$4,500

DEADLINE(S): None

FIELD(S): General Semantics

Project grants to support research specifically in the field of general semantics or explicitly related to general semantics. Open to graduates or postgraduates who have knowledge in this field and present evidence to that effect.

Write for complete information. Inquiries should include documentation of ongoing work in general semantics (usually under university support).

1128 — GEORGE MASON UNIVERSITY (Associated Writing Programs Award Series; St. Martin's Press Award)

Tallwood House, Mail Stop 1E3
Fairfax VA 22030
703/934-6920
FAX: 703/352-7535
E-Mail: awp@gmu.edu
Internet: http://web.gmu.edu/departments/awp/

AMOUNT: $2,000 honorarium; (AWP); $10,000 advance against royalties (St. Martin's Press)

DEADLINE(S): JAN 1 (through FEB 28—postmark)

FIELD(S): Writing: poetry, short fiction, creative nonfiction and novels

AWP competition is for book-length manuscripts in poetry, short fiction, and creative nonfiction; St. Martin's Press Young Writers Award is for a novel whose author is 32 years of age or younger. Open to authors writing in English, regardless of their nationality or residence.

Novel manuscripts will be judged and published by St. Martin's Press. All genres require a handling fee of $10 for AWP members and $15 for nonmembers. Contact above address or website for details.

1129 — GEORGE MASON UNIVERSITY (Mary Roberts Rinehart Awards)

English Dept.
MSN 3E4
4400 University Dr.
Fairfax VA 22030-4444
703/993-1180
FAX: 703/993-1161

AMOUNT: $2,000-$2,500

DEADLINE(S): NOV 30

FIELD(S): Creative Writing

Grants are given to unpublished writers to complete previously unpublished works of fiction, poetry, biography, autobiography, or history with a strong narrative quality. Need not be US citizen, but works must be in English, and awards are in US dollars. Submitted samples of a nominee's writing may be up to 30 pages in length for all categories. Financial need NOT considered.

3 awards annually. Candidates must be nominated by writing program faculty member or a sponsoring writer, agent, or editor. Contact William Miller at address above for complete information.

1130 — GEORGE WASHINGTON UNIVERSITY (George McCandlish Fellowship in American Literature)

Graduate Studies—English Dept.
Washington DC 20052
202/994-6180
Internet: www.gwu.edu

AMOUNT: $6,000 (approx.)

DEADLINE(S): FEB 15

FIELD(S): American Literature

Fellowship at George Washington University for a promising student enrolling in a doctoral degree program in American literature. Grade point average of 3.50 or better required.

Fellowship is for one year. Contact the Director of Graduate Studies at the above address for complete information.

1131 — GEORGIA LIBRARY ASSOCIATION ADMINISTRATIVE SERVICES (Hubbard Scholarship Fund)

SOLINET
1438 W. Peachtree St., NW
Atlanta GA 30309-2955
Written Inquiry

AMOUNT: $3,000

DEADLINE(S): MAY 1

FIELD(S): Library Science

For graduating seniors and graduates of accredited colleges who have been accepted into an ALA-accredited degree program. Must be ready to begin study in fall term of award year and intend to complete degree requirements within two years. Recipients agree to work (following graduation) for one year in a library or library-related capacity in Georgia OR to pay back a prorated amount of the award within two years (with interest).

Contact GLA for an application.

1132 — GERMANISTIC SOCIETY OF AMERICA (Foreign Study Scholarships)

809 United Nations Plaza
New York NY 10017-3580
212/984-5330

AMOUNT: $11,000

DEADLINE(S): OCT 23

FIELD(S): History; Political Science; International Relations; Public Affairs; Language; Philosophy; Literature

Open to US citizens who hold a bachelor's degree. Must plan to pursue graduate study at a West German university. Selection based on proposed project, language fluency, academic achievement, and references.

Contact Germanistic Society for an application.

1133 — GLADYS KRIEBLE DELMAS FOUNDATION (Predoctoral & Postdoctoral Grants in Venice & the Veneto)

521 5th Avenue, Suite 1612
New York NY 10175-1699
212/687-0011
FAX: 212/687-8877
E-Mail: DelmasFdtn@aol.com
Internet: www.delmas.org

AMOUNT: $500-$12,500

DEADLINE(S): DEC 15

FIELD(S): Research of Venice and the former Venetian empire and study of contemporary Venetian society and culture.

Pre- and postdoctoral grants for historical research on Venice. Humanities and social sciences are eligible areas of study, including archaeology, architecture, art, bibliography, economics, history, history of science, law, literature, music, political science, religion, and theater.

Applicants must have experience in advanced research and be U.S. citizens/residents; grad students must have fulfilled all doctoral requirements except dissertation by Dec. 15.

1134 — HAROLD HYAM WINGATE FOUNDATION (Wingate Scholarships)

38 Curzon St.
London W1Y 8EY ENLAND UK
0171 465 1521

AMOUNT: Up to 10,000 pounds/yr.

DEADLINE(S): FEB 1

FIELD(S): Creative works

Financial support for individuals of great potential or proven excellence to develop original work of intellectual, scientific, artistic, social, or environmental value, and to outstanding talented musicians. Not for taught courses or for leading to professional qualifications, or for electives or for completing courses already begun or for a higher degree. For citizens of the United Kingdom or other Commonwealth countries, Ireland, Israel, or of European countries.

Must be age 24 or older. May be held for up to three years.

1135 — HUNTINGTON LIBRARY (Research Fellowships)

1151 Oxford Rd.
San Marino CA 91108
626/405-2194

AMOUNT: $2,000/month

DEADLINE(S): DEC 15

FIELD(S): American History/Literature; British History/Literature; Art History; Science History

Open to doctoral and postdoctoral scholars for research at the Huntington Library. Fellows are expected to be in residence at the Library throughout their tenure.

100 awards annually. Contact the Committee on Fellowships for an application.

1136 — ILLINOIS ARTS COUNCIL (Artists Fellowship Awards)

100 W. Randolph, Suite 10-500
Chicago IL 60601-3298
312/814-6750

AMOUNT: $500; $5,000; $10,000

DEADLINE(S): SEP 1

FIELD(S): Choreography; Visual Arts; Poetry Prose; Film; Video; Playwriting; Music Composition; Crafts; Ethnic & Folk Arts; Performance Art; Photography; Audio Art.

Open to professional artists who are Illinois residents. Awards are in recognition of work in the above areas; they are not for continuing study. Students are NOT eligible.

Write to address above for application form.

1137 — INSTITUTE FOR ADVANCED STUDIES IN THE HUMANITIES (Visiting Research Fellowships)

Univ Edinburgh
Hope Park Square
Edinburgh EH8 9NW SCOTLAND UK
0131 650 4671
FAX: 0131 668 2252
E-Mail: iash@ed.ac.uk
Internet: www.ed.ac.uk/iash/homepage.html

AMOUNT: Non-stipendiary*

DEADLINE(S): DEC 1

FIELD(S): Arts; Social Sciences; Law; Music; Divinity

Postdoctoral research fellowships of between two and six months are tenable at the Institute for Advanced Studies in the Humanities. Based on academic record and publications. *Most fellowships are honorary, but limited support towards expenses is available to a small number of candidates. Fellows are allocated a study room within the Institute and hold one or two seminars during their tenure. Must submit research report at end of fellowship. No teaching required.

15 awards annually. Not renewable. Contact Mrs. Anthea Taylor for an application.

1138 — INSTITUTE FOR HUMANE STUDIES (Humane Studies Fellowship)

4084 University Dr., Ste. 101
Fairfax VA 22030-6812
703/934-6920 or 800/697-8799

FAX: 703/352-7535
E-Mail: ihs@gmu.edu
Internet: www.theihs.org
AMOUNT: up to $12,000
DEADLINE(S): DEC 31
FIELD(S): Social Sciences; Law; Humanities;
Jurisprudence; Journalism

Awards are for graduate and advanced undergraduate students pursuing degrees at any accredited domestic or foreign school. Based on academic performance, demonstrated interest in classical liberal ideas, and potential to contribute to the advancement of a free society.

90 awards annually. Apply online or contact IHS for an application.

1139 — INSTITUTE FOR HUMANE STUDIES (IHS Film & Fiction Scholarships)

4084 University Drive, Suite 101
Fairfax VA 22030-6812
703/934-6920 or 800/697-8799
FAX: 703/352-7535
E-Mail: ihs@gmu.edu
Internet: www.theihs.org
AMOUNT: up to $10,000
DEADLINE(S): JAN 15
FIELD(S): Filmmaking; Fiction Writing;
Playwriting

Open to graduate students pursuing a Master of Fine Arts (M.F.A.) degree in one of above fields. Should have a demonstrated interest in classical liberal ideas and their application in contemporary society, and demonstrate the desire, motivation, and creative ability to succeed in their chosen profession.

Apply online or contact IHS for an application.

1140 — INSTITUTE FOR HUMANE STUDIES (Summer Residential Program)

4084 University Dr., Ste. 101
Fairfax VA 22030-6812
703/934-6920 or 800/697-8799
FAX: 703/352-7535
E-Mail: ihs@gmu.edu
Internet: www.theihs.org
AMOUNT: All seminar fees: program cost, room/board, materials, and books
DEADLINE(S): MAR 1
FIELD(S): Social Sciences; Humanities; Law;
Journalism; Public Policy; Education; Writing

For college students, recent graduates, and graduate students who share an interest in learning and exchanging ideas about the scope of individual rights. One-week and weekend seminars at various campus locations across the U.S.

Apply online or contact IHS for an application.

1141 — INTERNATIONAL FEDERATION FOR INFORMATION AND DOCUMENTATION (Dr. Shawky Salem Training Grant)

Attn/Executive Director
FID
P.O. Box 90402
2509 LK the Hague
NETHERLANDS
+31 70 3140671
FAX: +31 70 3140667
E-Mail: FID@PYTHON.KONBIB.NL
AMOUNT: Travel & per diem allowance
DEADLINE(S): FEB 1
FIELD(S): Library Science

Open to candidates of Arab nationality who have worked or taught in library & information science for at least 10 years in an Arab country. Must speak & write English, French, or German. For one to three weeks of study in a Western country.

Write for complete information.

1142 — IOWA SCHOOL OF LETTERS (The John Simmons Short Fiction Award)

Univ Iowa
102 Dey House
507 N. Clinton St.
Iowa City IA 52242-1000
319/335-0416
AMOUNT: Winners' manuscripts will be published by University of Iowa under standard press contract
DEADLINE(S): Varies (AUG 1-SEP 30)
FIELD(S): Creative Writing: Fiction

Any writer who has not previously published a volume of prose fiction is eligible to enter the competition. The manuscript must be a collection of short stories of at least 150 typewritten pages. Writers who have published a volume of poetry are eligible. Revised manuscripts which have been previously entered may be resubmitted.

Send a self-addressed, stamped envelope to Connie Brothers at above address for guidelines.

1143 — IRISH ARTS COUNCIL (Awards and Opportunities)

70 Merrion Square
Dublin 2 Ireland
Tel+353 1 618 0200
FAX:+353 1 661 0349/676 1302
E-Mail: info@artscouncil.ie
Internet: www.artscouncil.ie

AMOUNT: 500-1,500 pounds sterling
DEADLINE(S): Varies (with program)
FIELD(S): Creative Arts; Visual Arts; Performing Arts

Numerous programs open to young & established artists who are Irish citizens or legal residents. Purpose is to assist in pursuit of talents & recognize achievements.

Contact above address for an application.

1144 — ISTITUTO ITALIANO PER GLI STUDI STORICI (Federico Chabod & Adolfo Omodeo Scholarships)

12 Via Benedetto Croce
80134 Naples ITALY
0039/81/551-7159
FAX: 0039/81/551-2390
E-Mail: iiss@iol.it
AMOUNT: 12 million lires
DEADLINE(S): SEP 30
FIELD(S): History; Philosophy; Literature; Arts;
Economics

Open to non-Italian citizens who have completed a university degree in the humanities (history, philosophy, & arts) in a non-Italian university. Intended to allow young scholars to participate in the work of the Institute and to complete personal scholarly research with the help of teaching staff of the Institute. Must submit birth certificate, university diploma, scholarly work, program of studies with indication of language skills, research proposal, & reference.

Renewable. Contact Dott.ssa Marta Herling, Secretary, for an application.

1145 — ISTITUTO ITALIANO PER GLI STUDI STORICI - ITALIAN INSTITUTE FOR HISTORICAL STUDIES (Federico Chabod & Adolfo Omodeo Scholarships)

Via Benedetto Croce, 12
80134 Napoli ITALY
0039/81-5517159
FAX: 0039/81-5512390
AMOUNT: 12,000,000 Lira
DEADLINE(S): SEP 30
FIELD(S): Humanities; Social Sciences; History;
Philosophy; Arts; Economics; Literature

For non-Italian citizens who have completed a university degree in Humanities dept. of a non-Italian university. Intended to allow young scholars to participate in the work of the Institute and to complete personal scholarly research with the help of teaching staff of the Institute. Must include birth certificate, proof of citizenship, university diploma, scholarly work, curriculum of studies w/ indication of language skills, research proposal, & reference letter.

2 awards annually. Contact Marta Herling, Secretary, at above address for an application.

1146 — JOHN FITZGERALD KENNEDY LIBRARY FOUNDATION (Hemingway Research Grants)

JFK Library, Columbia Point
Boston MA 02125-3313
617/929-4540 or 617/929-4524
FAX: 617/929-4538

AMOUNT: $200 to $1,000

DEADLINE(S): MAR 15

FIELD(S): American Literature (Hemingway)

Grant is to defray the cost of research. Open to qualified researchers desiring to research in the Hemingway Collection. Preference given to Ph.D candidates doing research on newly opened or unused portions of collection. However, all proposals are welcome.

Library houses 90-95% of the Hemingway manuscripts. Candidates must demonstrate need to use collection.

1147 — MEDICAL LIBRARY ASSOCIATION (Continuing Education Award)

65 E. Wacker Pl., Ste. 1900
Chicago IL 60601-7298
312/419-9094, ext. 28

AMOUNT: $100-$500

DEADLINE(S): OCT 1

FIELD(S): Medical Librarianship

To support continuing education for those NOT working towards a degree or certificate. Applicants must hold a graduate degree in library science, be a practicing medical librarian with at least two years of experience, and be a regular member of the association. Must be US or Canadian citizen/legal resident.

Contact MLA for membership information and/or an application.

1148 — MEDICAL LIBRARY ASSOCIATION (Minority Scholarship)

65 E. Wacker Pl., Ste. 1900
Chicago IL 60601-7298
312/419-9094, ext. 28

AMOUNT: $2,000

DEADLINE(S): DEC 1

FIELD(S): Medical Librarianship

Graduate scholarship for minority students just entering field of medical librarianship or who have at least half of their academic requirements to complete at an ALA-accredited school. Must be US or Canadian citizen/legal resident.

Contact MLA for an application.

1149 — NATIONAL COUNCIL OF TEACHERS OF ENGLISH RESEARCH FOUNDATION (NCTE) (Teacher-Researcher Grants)

Project Assistant
1111 Kenyon Rd
Urbana IL 61801
217/328-3870

AMOUNT: $5,000

DEADLINE(S): FEB 15

FIELD(S): Teaching (Research-K-12)

Open to pre-K-12 teachers for classroom-based research on the teaching of English/Language Arts. Grants are intended to support investigation of research questions that grow out of teachers' classroom experiences and concerns.

Applicants must be NCTE members. Write for complete information.

1150 — NATIONAL FEDERATION OF THE BLIND (Humanities Scholarship)

805 5th Avenue
Grinnell IA 50112
515/236-3366

AMOUNT: $3,000

DEADLINE(S): MAR 31

FIELD(S): Humanities (Art, English, Foreign Languages, History, Philosophy, Religion)

Open to legally blind students pursuing or planning to pursue a full-time postsecondary education in the US. Scholarships are awarded on basis of academic excellence, service to the community, and financial need. Must include transcripts and two letters of recommendation. Membership NOT required.

1 award annually. Renewable. Contact Mrs. Peggy Elliot, Scholarship Committee Chairman, for an application.

1151 — NATIONAL HUMANITIES CENTER (Lilly Fellowships in Religion and the Humanities)

PO Box 12256
Research Triangle Park NC 27709-2256
919/549-0661
FAX: 919/990-8535
E-Mail: nhc@ga.unc.edu
Internet: www.nhc.rtp.nc.us:8080

AMOUNT: Stipend ($35,000-$50,000) + Travel Expenses (for fellow & dependents)

DEADLINE(S): OCT 15

FIELD(S): Religion & the Humanities

Postdoctoral fellowships for the study of religion by humanistic scholars from fields other than religion and theology. Fellows will form the core of a monthly seminar on religion and the humanities. Curriculum vitae, 1,000-word proposal, and three letters of recommendation are required.

3-4 awards annually. Contact NHC for application materials.

1152 — NATIONAL LEAGUE OF AMERICAN PEN WOMEN, INC. (Scholarships for Mature Women)

1300 Seventeenth St. NW
Washington DC 20036
717/225-3023

AMOUNT: $1,000

DEADLINE(S): JAN 15 (even-numbered years)

FIELD(S): Art; Music; Creative Writing

The National League of American Pen Women gives three $1,000 grants in even-numbered years to women aged 35 and over. Should submit three 4"x6" or bigger color prints, manuscripts, or musical compositions suited to the criteria for the year.

Send SASE for details at the above address.

1153 — NATIONAL SPEAKERS ASSOCIATION (NSA Scholarship)

1500 S. Priest Drive
Tempe AZ 85281
602/968-2552
FAX: 602/968-0911
E-Mail: INFORMATION@NSASPEAKER.ORG
Internet: www.nsaspeaker.org

AMOUNT: $3,000

DEADLINE(S): JUN 1

FIELD(S): Speech

For college juniors, seniors, and graduate students who are majoring or minoring in speech. Must be full-time student with above-average academic record. Applicant should be a well-rounded student, capable of leadership, with the potential to make an impact using oral communication skills. Must submit official transcript, 500-word essay on career objectives, and letter of recommendation from speech teacher/department head along with application (7 copies each).

4 awards annually. Financial need NOT a factor. See website or contact Melanie Stroud at above address for an application/more information.

1154 — NATIONAL WRITERS ASSOCIATION FOUNDATION (Scholarship)

3140 S. Peoria
PMB 295
Aurora CO 80014
303/841-0246
FAX: 303/751-8593

E-Mail: sandywrter@aol.com
Internet: www.nationalwriters.com

AMOUNT: $1,000

DEADLINE(S): DEC 31

FIELD(S): Writing

Scholarship for career support. Financial need must be demonstrated.

1 award annually. See website or contact Sandy Whelchel for an application.

1155 — NEW YORK STATE THEATRE INSTITUTE (Internships in Theatrical Production)

155 River St.
Troy NY 12180
518/274-3573
nysti@crisny.org
Internet: www.crisny.org/not-for-profit/nysti/int.htm

AMOUNT: None

DEADLINE(S): None

FIELD(S): Fields of study related to theatrical production, including box office and PR

Internships for college students, high school seniors, and educators-in-residence interested in developing skills in above fields. Unpaid, but college credit is earned. Located at Russell Sage College in Troy, NY. Gain experience in box office, costumes, education, electrics, music, stage management, scenery, properties, performance, and public relations. Interns come from all over the world.

Must be associated with an accredited institution. See website for more information. Call Ms. Arlene Leff, Intern Director at above location. Include your postal mailing address.

1156 — NEWBERRY LIBRARY (Long-Term Fellowships)

60 West Walton Street
Chicago IL 60610-3380
312/943-9090
E-Mail: research@newberry.org
Internet: www.newberry.org

AMOUNT: Up to $30,000

DEADLINE(S): JAN 20

FIELD(S): Humanities, History, & related fields

Six postdoctoral fellowship programs are available for scholars wishing to use the Library's collection for writing or research. Fellowships last six to eleven months, and each have slightly different requirements.

See website for details and an application or write to above address.

1157 — NEWBERRY LIBRARY (Monticello College Foundation Fellowship For Women)

60 West Walton Street
Chicago IL 60610-3380
312/255-3660
E-Mail: research@newberry.org
Internet: www.newberry.org

AMOUNT: $12,500

DEADLINE(S): JAN 20

FIELD(S): Humanities, History, Study of Women

Six-month post-doctoral fellowships for women in the early stages of their academic careers. For research, writing, and participation in the intellectual life of the Library. Applicant's topic must be related to Newberry's collections; preference given to proposals concerned with the study of women.

See website for application or write to above address.

1158 — NEWBERRY LIBRARY (Short-Term Fellowships)

60 West Walton Street
Chicago IL 60610-3380
312/943-9090
E-Mail: research@newberry.org
Internet: www.newberry.org

AMOUNT: $800-$1,500/month

DEADLINE(S): MAR 1

FIELD(S): Humanities, History, & related fields

Nine programs for postdoctoral scholars or doctoral students at the dissertation stage. Study varies from two weeks to three months and is for those making use of Newberry's collections. Each program has slightly different requirements.

See website for details and applications or write to above address.

1159 — NEWBERRY LIBRARY (Special Fellowships)

60 West Walton Street
Chicago IL 60610-3380
312/255-3666
E-Mail: research@newberry.org
Internet: www.newberry.org

AMOUNT: Varies

DEADLINE(S): DEC 15

FIELD(S): Humanities, History, & related fields

Fellowships for three months to one year for doctoral or postdoctoral students to study in Germany, France, or Great Britain in fields related to Newberry's collections. Some deadlines JAN 20th. Specific locations are: Wolfenb, ttel, Germany; Ecole Nationale des Chartes, Paris, France; and the British Academy, Great Britain.

See website for more details and applications or write to above address.

1160 — NEWBERRY LIBRARY (Weiss/Brown Publication Subvention Award)

60 West Walton Street
Chicago IL 60610-3380
312/255-3666
E-Mail: research@newberry.org
Internet: www.newberry.org

AMOUNT: up to $15,000

DEADLINE(S): JAN 20

FIELD(S): European Civilization/History/Culture

Awards for authors of scholarly books already accepted for publication. Subject matter must cover European civilization before 1700 in the areas of music, theatre, French or Italian literature or cultural studies. Applicants must provide detailed information regarding the publication and the subvention request.

See website for more details and application or write to above address.

1161 — NORTH CAROLINA DEPARTMENT OF PUBLIC INSTRUCTION (Scholarship Loan Program for Prospective Teachers)

301 N. Wilmington St.
Raleigh NC 27601-2825
919/715-1120

AMOUNT: Up to $2,500/yr.

DEADLINE(S): FEB

FIELD(S): Education: Teaching, school psychology and counseling, speech/language impaired, audiology, library/media services

For NC residents planning to teach in NC public schools. At least 3.0 high school GPA required; must maintain 2.5 GPA during freshman year and 3.0 cumulative thereafter. Recipients are obligated to teach one year in an NC public school for each year of assistance. Those who do not fulfill their teaching obligation are required to repay the loan plus interest.

200 awards per year. For full-time students. Applications available in Dec. from high school counselors and college and univerwity departments of education.

1162 — ONTARIO MINISTRY OF EDUCATION AND TRAINING (John Charles Polanyi Prizes)

189 Red River Rd., 4th Floor
Box 4500
Thunder Bay Ontario P7B 6G9 CANADA
800/465-3957
TDD: 800/465-3958
Internet: osap.gov.on.ca

AMOUNT: $15,000

DEADLINE(S): Varies

FIELD(S): Physics; Chemistry; Physiology; Medicine; Literature; Economics

Monetary prizes are awarded to Canadian citizens/permanent residents who are continuing postdoctoral studies at an Ontario university. Awards are designed to encourage and reward academic excellence.

5 awards annually. Contact your university or the Ontario Council of Graduate Studies for an application.

1163 — PARAMOUNT PICTURES (Paramount Internships in Film & Television)

5555 Melrose Ave.
Hollywood, CA 90038
213/956-5145

AMOUNT: Approximately $25,000

DEADLINE(S): FEB 1

FIELD(S): Film & Video; Screenwriting

Post-graduate producing, directing, film, & TV writing internships at Paramount Pictures. Open to new graduates of the graduate film programs at New York University, Columbia University, UCLA, USC, & The American Film Institute.

Application is through the school. DO NOT apply directly to Paramount. Renewable. Write for complete information.

1164 — PHI BETA KAPPA (Mary Isabel Sibley Fellowship)

1785 Massachusetts Ave., NW, 4th Floor
Washington DC 20036
202/265-3808
FAX: 202/986-1601
E-Mail: lsurles@pbk.org

AMOUNT: $20,000

DEADLINE(S): JAN 15

FIELD(S): Greek Studies (odd-numbered years); French Studies (even-numbered years)

Candidates must be unmarried women between 25 and 35 years of age who have demonstrated their ability to carry on original research. Must hold doctorate or have fulfilled all requirements for doctorate except dissertation, and must be planning to devote full-time work to research of language and literature during the fellowship year that begins in September. Eligibility is NOT restricted to members of Phi Beta Kappa.

Contact the Fellowship Committee for an application.

1165 — POETRY SOCIETY OF AMERICA (George Bogin Memorial Award)

15 Gramercy Park
New York NY 10003
212/254-9628
FAX: 212/673-2352
Internet: www.poetrysociety.org

AMOUNT: $500

DEADLINE(S): DEC 21

FIELD(S): Poetry

Prizes for the best selections of four or five poems that reflect the encounter of the ordinary and the extraordinary, use language in an original way, and take a stand against oppression in any of its forms.

$5 entry fee for non-members. Contact PSA for submission guidelines.

1166 — POETRY SOCIETY OF AMERICA (Robert H. Winner Memorial Award)

15 Gramercy Park
New York NY 10003
212/254-9628
FAX: 212/673-2352
Internet: www.poetrysociety.org

AMOUNT: $2,500

DEADLINE(S): DEC 21

FIELD(S): Poetry

For poets over 50 years of age who have not published or who have no more than one book. This award acknowledges original work done in midlife by someone who has not had substantial recognition. Send a brief but cohesive manuscript of up to 10 poems or 20 pages. Poems entered here may be submitted to other contests as well. Please include date of birth on cover page.

$5 entry fee for non-members. Contact PSA for submission guidelines.

1167 — POETRY SOCIETY OF AMERICA (Shelley Memorial Award)

15 Gramercy Park
New York NY 10003
212/254-9628
FAX: 212/673-2352
Internet: www.poetrysociety.org

AMOUNT: $250-$1,000

DEADLINE(S): DEC 21

FIELD(S): Poetry

This contest (NOT scholarship) is open to both PSA members and non-members. All submissions must be unpublished on the date of entry and not scheduled for publication by the date of the PSA awards ceremony held in the spring.

$5 entry fee for non-members. Contact PSA for submission guidelines.

1168 — PRINCESS GRACE FOUNDATION-USA (Grants for Young Playwrights)

150 East 58th Street, 21st Floor
New York NY 10155
212/317-1470
FAX: 212/317-1473
E-Mail: pgfusa@pgfusa.com
Internet: www.pgfusa.com

AMOUNT: $7,500 + 10-week residency at New Dramatists, Inc., New York City & other benefits

DEADLINE(S): MAR 31

FIELD(S): Playwriting

Grants for young playwrights up to age 30 who are US citizens or permanent residents. Awards based primarily on artistic quality of submitted play, appropriateness of activities to individual's artistic growth, and potential future excellence. Script will be included in New Dramatists' lending library, be distributed to catalogue subscribers for one year, and possibly be published through the Dramatists' Play Service.

1 award annually. See website or contact Ms. Toby E. Boshak, Executive Director, for an application.

1169 — RIPON COLLEGE (Performance/Recognition Tuition Scholarships)

Admissions Office
300 Seward St.
PO Box 248
Ripon WI 54971
920/748-8102 or 800/94-RIPON
E-Mail: adminfo@ripon.edu
Internet: www.ripon.edu

AMOUNT: $5,000-$10,000/yr.

DEADLINE(S): MAR 1

FIELD(S): Music; Forensics; Art; Theatre

Open to undergraduate and graduate students attending or planning to attend Ripon College. Purpose is to recognize and encourage academic potential and accomplishment in above fields. Interview, audition, or nomination may be required.

Renewable. Contact Office of Admission for an application.

1170 — SPECIAL LIBRARIES ASSOCIATION (Affirmative Action Scholarship Program)

1700 Eighteenth St., NW
Washington DC 20009-2508
202/234-4700
FAX: 202/265-9317
E-Mail: sla@sla.org
Internet: www.sla.org

AMOUNT: $6,000

DEADLINE(S): OCT 31

FIELD(S): Library Science

Open to minority students who are accepted to or enrolled in an accredited master's of library science program. Must submit evidence of financial need. For graduate study leading to a master's degree.

Extra consideration will be given to members of Special Libraries Assn and to persons who have worked in and for special libraries. Write for complete information.

1171 — SPECIAL LIBRARIES ASSOCIATION (ISI Scholarship Program)

1700 Eighteenth St., NW
Washington DC 20009-2508
202/234-4700
FAX: 202/265-9317
E-Mail: sla@sla.org
Internet: www.sla.org

AMOUNT: $1,000

DEADLINE(S): OCT 31

FIELD(S): Library Science

Open to members of the Special Library Association who are U.S. or Canadian citizens and are enrolled in a beginning graduate study program leading to a Ph.D in Library Science.

Applicants must submit evidence of high academic schievement and financial need. Write for complete information.

1172 — SPECIAL LIBRARIES ASSOCIATION (Plenum Scholarship Program)

1700 Eighteenth St., NW
Washington DC 20009-2508
202/234-4700
FAX: 202/265-9317
E-Mail: sla@sla.org
Internet: www.sla.org

AMOUNT: Varies

DEADLINE(S): OCT 31

FIELD(S): Library Science

Open to members of the Special Libraries Association who are enrolled in a Ph.D. program in Library Science. Must submit evidence of high academic achievement and financial need.

Applicants need special library work experience. Write for complete information.

1173 — SPECIAL LIBRARIES ASSOCIATION (SLA Scholarship Program)

1700 Eighteenth St., NW
Washington DC 20009-2508
202/234-4700
FAX: 202/265-9317
E-Mail: sla@sla.org
Internet: www.sla.org

AMOUNT: $6,000

DEADLINE(S): OCT 31

FIELD(S): Library Science

Open to college graduates or college seniors with an interest in special librarianship. Scholarship is for graduate study in librarianship leading to a master's degree at a recognized school of library or information science.

Applicants must submit evidence of financial need. Write for complete information.

1174 — STANLEY DRAMA AWARD (Playwriting/Musical Awards Competition)

Dept of Theatre, Wagner College
One Campus Rd.
Staten Island NY 10301
718/390-3325

AMOUNT: $2,000

DEADLINE(S): OCT 1

FIELD(S): Playwriting; Music Composition

Annual award for an original full-length play or musical which has not been professionally produced or received tradebook publication. Must submit musical works on cassette tape with book and lyrics. A series of 2-3 thematically related one-act plays will also be considered. When submitting scripts, send self-addressed, stamped envelope large enough to accomodate the script.

Contact the Department of Theatre at Wagner College for complete information.

1175 — TENNESSEE ARTS COMMISSION (Individual Artists' Fellowships)

401 Charlotte Ave.
Nashville TN 37243-0780
615/741-1701

AMOUNT: $2,000

DEADLINE(S): JAN 11

FIELD(S): Visual Arts; Performing Arts; Creative Arts

Open to artists who are residents of Tennessee. Duration of award is one year. Applicants must be professional artists. FULL-TIME STUDENTS ARE NOT ELIGIBLE.

Write for complete information.

1176 — THE ALICIA PATTERSON FOUNDATION (Fellowships for Journalists, Writers, Editors, and Photographers)

1730 Pennsylvania Ave. NW, Suite 180
Washington DC 20006
301/951-8512
E-Mail: apfengel@charm.net
Internet: www.aliciapatterson.org

AMOUNT: $30,000/year

DEADLINE(S): OCT 1

FIELD(S): Print Journalism/Writing, Editing, Photography

Full-time fellowships for persons working in one of the above fields for the purpose of completing a research project.

Five to seven fellows per year. Recipients may not be employed, but may do freelance work during the fellowship period. Send for details or check website for rules regarding submission of samples, recommendations, etc.

1177 — THE BRITISH ACADEMY, HUMANITIES RESEARCH BOARD (Postgraduate Professional Awards, Vocational Courses, and Librarianship and Information Science Program Awards)

10 Carlton House Terrace
London SW1Y 5AH ENGLAND
0181 951 4900
FAX: 0181 951 1358

AMOUNT: Tuition, fees, travel, and expenses

DEADLINE(S): JUN 1

FIELD(S): Humanities

Open to U.K. residents of at least 3 years who graduated from a U.K. university or hold a qualification regarded by the Department as equivalent to a university first degree. Fees-only awards for non-U.K. residents who are ECC nationals.

Applicants must be between the ages of 18 and 40. Write for complete information.

1178 — THE JOHN F. KENNEDY CENTER FOR THE PERFORMING ARTS (Awards, Fellowships, and Scholarships)

The Kennedy Center
Washington DC 20566-0001
202/416-8857
FAX: 202/416-8802
E-Mail: skshaffer@mail.kennedy-center.org
Internet: www.kennedy-center.org/education/actf

AMOUNT: Varies

DEADLINE(S): Varies

FIELD(S): Playwriting, stage design, and acting

Various scholarships and awards in the above fields.

Contact organization for a booklet: "The Kennedy Center American College Theater Festival" for details and/or visit website.

1179 — THE LEMMERMANN FOUNDATION (Fondazione Lemmermann Scholarship Awards)

c/o Studio Avvocati Romanelli
via Cosseria, 5
00192 Roma ITALIA
(+39-6) 324.30.23

FAX: (+39-6) 321.26.46

E-Mail: lemmerma@bbs.nexus.it

Internet: http://vivaldi.nexus.it/altri/lemmermann/

AMOUNT: Italian lire 1.500.000

DEADLINE(S): MAR 15; SEP 30

FIELD(S): Italian/Roman studies in the subject areas of literature, archaeology, history of art

For university students who need to study in Rome to carry out research and prepare their theses concerning Rome and the Roman culture from the period Pre-Roman to present day time in the subject areas above.

Contact above organization for details. Access website for application form.

1180 — THE WALT DISNEY COMPANY (American Teacher Awards)

P.O. Box 9805

Calabasas CA 91372

AMOUNT: $2,500 (36 awards); $25,000 (Outstanding Teacher of the Year)

DEADLINE(S): FEB 15

FIELD(S): Teachers: athletic coach, early childhood, English, foreign language/ESL, general elementary, mathematics, performing arts, physical education/health, science, social studies, visual arts, voc/tech education

Awards for K-12 teachers in the above fields.

Teachers, or anyone who knows a great teacher, can write for applications at the above address.

1181 — UNA ELLIS-FERMOR MEMORIAL RESEARCH FUND (Funds for Publication)

Academic Awards, Registry

Royal Holloway

Univ. of London

Egham Hill

Egham, Surrey TW20 0EX ENGLAND UK

01784 443352

AMOUNT: Up to 200 pounds

DEADLINE(S): APR (3rd Fri.)

FIELD(S): Drama: English, Irish, or Scandinavian

Grants for expenses connected with publication of materials in the field of English, Irish, or Scandinavian drama or a comparative study in which one of these fields is a component.

Contact organization for application instructions.

1182 — UNIVERSITY FILM & VIDEO ASSOCIATION (Carole Fielding Student Grants)

University of Baltimore

School of Comm.

1420 N. Charles Street

Baltimore MD 21201

410/837-6061

AMOUNT: $1,000 to $4,000

DEADLINE(S): MAR 31

FIELD(S): Film, video, multi-media production

Open to undergraduate/graduate students. Categories are narrative, experimental, animation, documentary, multi-media/Installation and research. Applicant must be sponsored by a faculty member who is an active member of the Univesity Film and Video Association.

Write to the above address for application and complete details.

1183 — UNIVERSITY OF MARYLAND INSTITUTE FOR ADVANCED COMPUTER STUDIES (Graduate Fellowships)

University of Maryland, UMIACS

College Park MD 20742

301/405-6722

E-Mail: fellows@umiacs.umd.edu

Internet: www.umiacs.umd.edu/fellow.html

AMOUNT: $18,000/yr. + tuition, health benefits, office space, etc.

DEADLINE(S): JAN 15

FIELD(S): Computer science, electrical engineering, geography, philosophy, linguistics, business, and management

Two-year graduate fellowships in the above fields for full-time students interested in interdisciplinary applications of computing at the Univ. of Maryland. After the first two years, external research funds may be provided to continue support for the fellow, depending upon satisfactory progress and the availability of funds.

Three new awards each year. Selection will be based on academic excellence and compatibility between students' research interest and those of UMIACS faculty.

1184 — UNIVERSITY OF NEWCASTLE—DEPT. OF MUSIC (Runciman Arts Studentship)

Arts Faculty Secretary

Percy Bldg.

Univ. of Newcastle

Newcastle upon Tyne

NE1 7RU ENGLAND UK

E-mail: susan.lloyd@ncl.ac.uk

AMOUNT: 4,000 pounds

DEADLINE(S): Varies

FIELD(S): The arts

This studentship provides financial support for a limited number of high quality postgraduate students pursing studies in the arts. All home applicants are required to apply for British Academy funding as well as for this one; oeverseas coandidates may apply and are required to apply to the british Academy under the Overseas Research Students Award scheme.

Contact school for details and application.

1185 — UNIVERSITY OF VIRGINIA (Hoyns Fellowship)

219 Bryan Hall

Dept. of English

Charlottesville VA 22903

804/924-6675

AMOUNT: Tuition costs; stipend

DEADLINE(S): JAN 15

FIELD(S): Creative Writing

Open to anyone who is accepted into the Creative Writing MFA program at the University of Virginia. An original 30- to 40-page fiction manuscript or 10 pages of poetry will be required.

Write to program administrator Lisa Russ Spaar for complete information.

1186 — WAVERLY COMMUNITY HOUSE INC. (F. Lammot Belin Arts Scholarships)

Scholarships Selection Committee

P.O. Box 142

Waverly PA 18471

717/586-8191

AMOUNT: $10,000

DEADLINE(S): DEC 15

FIELD(S): Painting; Sculpture; Music; Drama; Dance; Literature; Architecture; Photography

Applicants must have resided in the Abington or Pocono regions of Northeastern Pennyslvania. They must furnish proof of exceptional ability in their chosen field but no formal training in any academic or professional program.

U.S. citizenship required. Finalists must appear in person before the selection committee. Write for complete information.

1187 — WELLESLEY COLLEGE (Mary McEwen Schimke Scholarship)

Center for Work & Service

106 Central St.

Wellesley MA 02481-8203

781/283-3525

FAX: 781/283-3674

E-Mail: fellowships@bulletin.wellesley.edu

Internet: www.wellesley.edu/CWS/step2/fellow.html

AMOUNT: $1,000 (max.)

DEADLINE(S): JAN 3

FIELD(S): Literature; History

This supplemental award is open to women graduates of any American institution to provide relief from household and childcare expenses while pursuing graduate study at institutions other than Wellesley College. Award is made on basis of scholarly expectation and identified need. Candidate must be over 30 years of age and currently engaged in graduate study in literature and/or history. Preference given to American Studies.

See website or send self-addressed, stamped envelope to Rose Crawford, Secretary to the Committee on Extramural Graduate Fellowships & Scholarships, for an application.

1188 — WILLIAM ANDREWS CLARK MEMORIAL LIBRARY (Postdoctoral Fellowships)

UCLA
2520 Cimarron St.
Los Angeles CA 90018-2098
323/735-7605
FAX: 323/732-8744
E-Mail: clarkfel@humnet.ucla.edu
Internet: www.humnet.ucla.edu/humnet/clarklib

AMOUNT: $2,000+/month

DEADLINE(S): MAR 15

FIELD(S): British History, Literature, & Culture

Three-month to one-year fellowships are for postdoctoral scholars to pursue advanced study and research regarding British literature and history of the 17th and 18th centuries. Tenable at the William Andrews Clark Memorial Library at UCLA.

See website or contact UCLA for an application.

1189 — WOMEN ON BOOKS (Scholarships for African-American Women)

879 Rainier Ave. N., Suite A105
Renton WA 98055
206/626-2323

AMOUNT: $1,000

DEADLINE(S): JUN (Mid-month)

FIELD(S): English or journalism, with intention to pursue a writing career

Scholarships for African-American women pursuing careers in writing. Must major in English or journalism in a four-year university, have a min. GPA of 2.5, and demonstrate financial need.

Write for details.

1190 — YALE CENTER FOR BRITISH ART (Fellowships)

Box 208280
New Haven CT 06520-8280
203/432-2850

AMOUNT: Travel, accommodations, per diem

DEADLINE(S): JAN 15

FIELD(S): British Art; History; Literature

Fellowships to enable scholars engaged in postdoctoral or equivalent research in British art, history, or literature to study the Center's holdings of paintings, drawings, prints, and rare books and to make use of its research facilities.

12 awards annually. Grants normally run for a period of four weeks. Write for complete information.

FOREIGN LANGUAGE

1191 — AFRICAN STUDIES CENTER (African Language Scholarships—Title VI)

c/o UCLA
10244 Bunche Hall
Los Angeles CA 90002
213/825-3686/2877/2944

AMOUNT: $10,000 + tuition & fees

DEADLINE(S): JAN 8

FIELD(S): African Studies

For students in graduate programs studying an African Language at UCLA. U.S. citizen or permanent resident.

5-10 Awards per year. Awards can be renewed once. Write for complete information.

1192 — AMERICAN INSTITUTE OF INDIAN STUDIES (Language Program)

1130 E. 59th St.
Chicago IL 60637
773/702-8638
E-Mail: aiis@uchicago.edu
Internet: ccat.sas.upenn.edu/aiis/

AMOUNT: $3,000 + travel

DEADLINE(S): JAN 31

FIELD(S): Languages of India

Fellowships for classes held in India for US citizens who have a minimum of 2 years, or 240 hours, of classroom instruction in a language of India: Hindi, Bengali, Tamil, or Telugu.

10 awards annually. Contact AIIS for an application.

1193 — AMERICAN RESEARCH INSTITUTE IN TURKEY (Summer Fellowship for Turkish Language Study at Bosphorus University, Istanbul)

Campus Box 1230
One Brookings Dr.
St. Louis MO 63130-4899
314/935-5166
FAX: 314/935-7462
E-Mail: iwright@artsci.wustl.edu
Internet: www.boun.edu.tr/web.htm

AMOUNT: Travel, Tuition, & Stipend

DEADLINE(S): FEB 1

FIELD(S): Turkish Language Study: Elementary, Intermediate, & Advanced Levels

Eight-week summer program at Bosphorus University in Istanbul. Covers round-trip airfare, application & tuition fees, room & board, and maintenance stipend. For US citizens who are full-time graduate students enrolled in a degree program. Must have a minimum "B" average. Personal info, 500-word statement of academic purpose, contact info for three professors, and transcripts required to apply.

15 awards annually. Contact Iris Wright, Administrative Assistant, Center for the Study of Islamic Societies and Civilizations, Washington University, at above address.

1194 — AUSTRALIAN FEDERATION OF UNIVERSITY WOMEN - WESTERN AUSTRALIA (Joyce Riley Bursary)

Bursary Liaison Officer
PO Box 48
Nedlands WA 6909 AUSTRALIA
Written Inquiry

AMOUNT: Aus$1,700 - Aus$2,750

DEADLINE(S): JUL 31

FIELD(S): Humanities; Social Sciences

To support women graduates of a Western Australian university to complete a higher degree or post-doctoral research in Humanities or Social Sciences at a recognized university in any country.

Membership in AFUW or in IFUW is required. Contact above location for further information.

1195 — AUSTRALIAN FEDERATION OF UNIVERSITY WOMEN - WESTERN AUSTRALIA (Joyce Riley Bursary)

Bursary Liaison Officer
PO Box 48
Nedlands WA 6009 AUSTRALIA
Written Inquiry

AMOUNT: Aus$1,700 - Aus$2,750

DEADLINE(S): JUL 31

FIELD(S): Humanities; Social Sciences

To support women graduates of a recognized university to complete a higher degree or post-doctoral research at a university in Western Australia.

Membership in AFUW or in IFUW is required. Write to above address for complete information.

1196 — AUSTRIAN CULTURAL INSTITUTE (Grants for Foreign Students to Study German in Austria)

950 Third Ave., 20th Floor
New York NY 10022
212/759-5165
FAX: 212/319-9636
E-Mail: desk@aci.org
Internet: www.austriaculture.net

AMOUNT: ATS 10,000 (approx. US $900) for 4 weeks; ATS 8,000 (approx. US $750) for 3 weeks. Additionally, the costs for the language course are refunded up to ATS 7,000 (approx. US $650).

DEADLINE(S): JAN 31

FIELD(S): German Language

For students foreign to Austria between the ages of 20 and 35 who have completed at least 2 years of college and have a working knowledge of German. To be used during July and August at one of several language Institutes throughout Austria. This is a highly competitive scholarship program and is offered to applicants around the world.

Contact Austrian Cultural Institute for an application.

1197 — BAJA CALIFORNIA LANGUAGE COLLEGE (Spanish Language Immersion Contest)

Barcelona #191
Ensenada BC MEXICO
619/758-9711
E-Mail: college@bajacal.com
Internet: www.bajacal.com

AMOUNT: $1,000

DEADLINE(S): APR 30

FIELD(S): Spanish Language

For all levels of study. Must compete in contest offered weekly by bi-lingual newspaper La Presna de Minnesota (www.laprensa-mn.com). Contest runs from February to April.

2 awards annually. See website or contact Keith Rolle for more information. US address: PO Box 7556, San Diego, CA 92167.

1198 — BLAKEMORE FOUNDATION (Asian Language Fellowship Grants)

1201 Third Ave., 40th Fl.
Seattle WA 98101-3099
206/583-8778
FAX: 206/583-8500
E-Mail: blakemore@perkinscoie.com

AMOUNT: Tuition, transportation, basic living costs

DEADLINE(S): JAN 15

FIELD(S): Asian languages

Fellowships for advanced language study in Asia. For use at an instition selected by the applicant and approved by the Foundation. Applicant must be a graduate or professional school student, a teacher, a professional, or a business person; be working towards a specific career objective involving the regular use of an Asian language; be near an advanced level in that language; be a U.S. citizen or permanent resident. For full-time study during the term of the grant.

12-18 annual awards. For one year of study.

1199 — BRITISH ACADEMY (Sir Ernest Cassel Educational Trust)

8 Malvern Terrace
Islington, London N1 1HR ENGLAND UK
0171 607 7879

AMOUNT: 100-500 pounds per annum

DEADLINE(S): SEP; DEC; FEB; APR (end of ea. month)

FIELD(S): Language, literature, or civilizaiton of any country

Research grants for the more junior teaching members of universities for research abroad and are for the study of any country or civilization, concentrating on the fields mentioned above.

Obtain application from the Secretary at the Trust.

1200 — CAMARGO FOUNDATION (Residential Fellowship)

c/o Jerome Foundation
125 Park Square Ct.
400 Sibley St.
St. Paul MN 55101-1928
651/290-2237

AMOUNT: Residency at Foundation in France

DEADLINE(S): FEB 1

FIELD(S): French & Francophone Stuides; Creative Arts

3-4 month residency at study center in Cassis, France, for graduate study, postgraduate study, or career support. May be professors, independent scholars, grad students, writers, visual artists, or composers with specific projects to complete. Each fellow will be asked to outline the accepted project during regularly scheduled sessions, and are asked to give copy of any completed work to the Camargo library. French language is recommended but not required.

22 awards annually. Not renewable. Contact Mr. William Reichard at the Camargo Foundation for an application. Awards are announced by April 1st.

1201 — CEMANAHUAC EDUCATIONAL COMMUNITY (Scholarships for Teachers of Spanish)

Cemanahuac Educational Community,
Apartado 5-21
Cuernavace, Morelos MEXICO
(52-73) 18-6407
FAX: (52-73) 12-5418
E-Mail: 74052.2570@compuserve.com
www.cemanahuac.com/

AMOUNT: Varies

DEADLINE(S): Varies

FIELD(S): Spanish language

Scholarships for U.S. teachers of Spanish are available through the American Association of Teachers of Spanish and Portuguese (970/351-1095) and the American Council on the Teaching of Foreign Languages (914/963-8830) for use at Cemanahuac in Mexico. And, 50+ U.S. school systems have arranged with Cemanahuac for reduced rates for educators struggling to meet the needs of children and their families from a Hispanic background. Contact Cemanahuac for list of districts.

Contact organization for details, and contact AATSP and ACTFL for scholarship possibilities.

1202 — CENTER FOR ARABIC STUDY ABROAD (CASA Fellowships)

Johns-Hopkins Univ
1619 Massachusetts Ave., NW
Washington DC 20036-1983
202/663-5750
E-Mail: CASA@MAIL.JHUWASH.JHU.EDU
Internet: www.sais-jhu.edu/languages/CASA

AMOUNT: Tuition, allowance, & airfare

DEADLINE(S): DEC 31

FIELD(S): Advanced Arabic Language Training

Fellowships for summer and full-year intensive Arabic training at the American University in Cairo, Egypt. Open to graduate students and a limited number of undergraduates. A minimum two years of Arabic study is required. Must be US citizen/permanent resident.

20 awards annually. Contact D. Whaley, Program Administrator, for an application.

1203 — CENTER FOR HELLENIC STUDIES (Resident Junior Fellowships)

3100 Whitehaven Street NW
Washington DC 20008
202/234-3738

AMOUNT: Up to $20,000

DEADLINE(S): OCT 15

FIELD(S): Literature, history, philosophy, language, or religion of Ancient Greece

Resident fellowships for post-doctoral scholars with professional competence and some publication in Ancient Greek areas shown above.

Twelve resident fellowships per year. Write for complete information.

1204 — CENTRO DE IDIOMAS DEL SURESTE A.C. (Intensive Spanish Scholarship)

Calle 14 #106 X 25 Colonia Mexico
Merida Yucatan 97128 MEXICO
99-26-94-94
FAX: 99-26-90-20

AMOUNT: Varies

DEADLINE(S): Varies (45 days before enrollment)

FIELD(S): Spanish Language

Scholarships for Spanish language study at CIS, open to students currently enrolled in an undergraduate or graduate program. No citizenship requirements. Preference given to students with financial need.

Renewable. Contact Chloe C. Pacheco at CIS for an application.

1205 — FORD FOUNDATION/NATIONAL RESEARCH COUNCIL (Postdoctoral Fellowship for Minorities)

National Research Council
2101 Constitution Ave.
Washington DC 20418
202/334-2860
E-Mail: infofell@nas.edu
Internet: http//www.nas.edu/fo/index.html

AMOUNT: $25,000 + relocation and research allowance

DEADLINE(S): JAN 3

FIELD(S): Life and physical sciences, mathematics, engineering sciences, behavioral and social sciences, and the humanities

For U.S. citizens who received a Ph.D or Sc.D in the last 7 years and who are Native Amer. Indian or Alaskan, Black/African American, Mexican American, Native Pacific Islander, or Puerto Rican and who are or plan to be in a teaching or research career.

Contact above website or address for complete information.

1206 — FORD FOUNDATION/NATIONAL RESEARCH COUNCIL (Predoctoral/ Dissertation Fellowships for Minorities)

2101 Constitution Ave.
Washington DC 20418
202/334-2872
E-Mail: infofell@nas.edu
Internet: http//www.nas.edu/fo/index.html

AMOUNT: $14,000 annual stipend + $6,000 grant to institution; $18,000 for dissertation fellowship

DEADLINE(S): NOV 3

FIELD(S): Most fields of study: sciences, humanities, engineering, behavioral science, social sciences, and computer science

Predoctoral and dissertation fellowships for students whose ethnicity is Alaskan Native, Black/ African American, Mexican American/Chicano, Native American Indian, Native Pacific Islander, or Puerto Rican. For research-based programs leading to careers in college teaching and research.

Contact above address or website.

1207 — GERMAN ACADEMIC EXCHANGE SERVICE (DAAD Programs)

950 Third Ave. at 57th St.
New York NY 10022
212/758-3223
FAX: 212/755-5780
E-Mail: daadny@daad.org
Internet: www.daad.org

AMOUNT: Varies (with program)

DEADLINE(S): Varies (with program)

FIELD(S): Varies (with program)

Grants are available to faculty and full-time students who are citzens or permanent residents of the US or Canada. Programs are for study in Germany in a variety of fields.

See website or contact DAAD Programs Administrator for an application.

1208 — GERMANISTIC SOCIETY OF AMERICA (Foreign Study Scholarships)

809 United Nations Plaza
New York NY 10017-3580
212/984-5330

AMOUNT: $11,000

DEADLINE(S): OCT 23

FIELD(S): History; Political Science; International Relations; Public Affairs; Language; Philosophy; Literature

Open to US citizens who hold a bachelor's degree. Must plan to pursue graduate study at a West German university. Selection based on proposed project, language fluency, academic achievement, and references.

Contact Germanistic Society for an application.

1209 — GIACOMO LEOPARDI CENTER (Scholarships for Italian Language Study in Italy)

Via del Castello
61020 Belforte all'Isauro
39 0722 726000
FAX: 39 0722 726010
E-Mail: centroleopardi@wnt.it
Internet: www.learningvacations.com/ leop.htm

AMOUNT: Cost of tuition (about $750)

DEADLINE(S): Varies

FIELD(S): Italian language and literature

The Center is in a castle built in the late Middle Ages. The castle is the site of school for teaching the Italian language and culture. Students are lodged in rooms in the Castle. Scholarships are for the first 300 to apply, and they are for tuition only. Students still must pay for food and lodging.

New classes start every Monday of the year. Most details are found on the website.

1210 — INSTITUT D'ETUDES FRANCAISES D'AVIGNON/BRYN MAWR COLLEGE (Scholarships for Summer Study in Avignon, France)

Institut d'etudes francaises d'Avignon
Bryn Mfawr College
Bryn Mawr PA 1901000-2899
610/526-5083
FAX: 610/526-7479
Internet: www.brynmawr.edu/Adm/academic/ special/avignon/details.html

AMOUNT: Varies

DEADLINE(S): MAR 15

FIELD(S): French-related studies

Scholarships based on academic excellence and financial need for a six-week summer study program in Avignon, France. Program is offered to male and female students from other colleges as well as Bryn Mawr. For graduates and undergraduates who have completed three years of college-level French or equivalent.

Contact the Director of the Institute for application information.

1211 — JAPAN FOUNDATION (Doctoral and Research Fellowships)

152 W. 57th Street, 39th Floor
New York NY 10019
212/489-0299
FAX: 212/489-0409

AMOUNT: Approx 310,000 yen per month stipend + 239,000 yen for housing

DEADLINE(S): NOV 1 (U.S. citizens/residents); DEC 1 (Non-U.S. citizens/residents)

FIELD(S): Japanese Studies/Language

Fellowships intended to provide Ph.D candidates, scholars, and researchers an opportunity to conduct studies in Japan.

Should be sufficiently proficient in Japanese language to pursue research in Japan.

1212 — JAPAN-AMERICA SOCIETY OF WASHINGTON (H. William Tanaka Scholarship)

1020 19th St. NW LL#40
Washington DC 20036
202/833-2210
202/833-2456

AMOUNT: $15,000

DEADLINE(S): DEC 1

FIELD(S): Japanese

Open to graduate and postgraduate students for study in Japan who are enrolled in a school in the District of Columbia, Maryland, Virginia, or West Virginia. Selection based on scholastic achievement, motivation, and financial need.

For U.S. citizens. Write to organization for complete information and application.

1213 — LONDON CHAMBER OF COMMERCE AND INDUSTRY EXAMINATIONS BOARD (Charles R. E. Bell Fund Scholarships)

Thena House
112 Station Rd.
Sidcup Kent DA15 7BJ ENGLAND UK
081/302-0261

AMOUNT: 1,500 pounds sterling

DEADLINE(S): DEC 31

FIELD(S): Business Administration; Languages

Open to students who are engaged in commerce/business or are commercial education teachers. Scholarships support postgraduate study in the United Kingdom or abroad. Must be UK citizen or legal resident. Financial need is considered.

Contact London Chamber of Commerce for an application.

1214 — NATIONAL FEDERATION OF THE BLIND (Humanities Scholarship)

805 5th Avenue
Grinnell IA 50112
515/236-3366

AMOUNT: $3,000

DEADLINE(S): MAR 31

FIELD(S): Humanities (Art, English, Foreign Languages, History, Philosophy, Religion)

Open to legally blind students pursuing or planning to pursue a full-time postsecondary education in the US. Scholarships are awarded on basis of academic excellence, service to the community, and financial need. Must include transcripts and two letters of recommendation. Membership NOT required.

1 award annually. Renewable. Contact Mrs. Peggy Elliot, Scholarship Committee Chairman, for an application.

1215 — NATIONAL HUMANITIES CENTER (Lilly Fellowships in Religion and the Humanities)

PO Box 12256
Research Triangle Park NC 27709-2256
919/549-0661
FAX: 919/990-8535
E-Mail: nhc@ga.unc.edu
Internet: www.nhc.rtp.nc.us:8080

AMOUNT: Stipend ($35,000-$50,000) + Travel Expenses (for fellow & dependents)

DEADLINE(S): OCT 15

FIELD(S): Religion & the Humanities

Postdoctoral fellowships for the study of religion by humanistic scholars from fields other than religion and theology. Fellows will form the core of a monthly seminar on religion and the humanities. Curriculum vitae, 1,000-word proposal, and three letters of recommendation are required.

3-4 awards annually. Contact NHC for application materials.

1216 — NORWICH JUBILEE ESPERANTO FOUNDATION (Travel Grants)

37 Granville Court
Oxford OX3 0HS ENGLAND
01865-245509

AMOUNT: 1,000 pounds sterling (max.)

DEADLINE(S): None

FIELD(S): Esperanto

Travel grants open to those who speak Esperanto and wish to improve their use of the language through travel in the UK. Candidates must be under the age of 26 and be able to lecture in Esperanto.

Up to 25 awards annually. Renewable. Inquiries MUST include fluency and interest in Esperanto. Contact Kathleen M. Hall, Secretary to the Foundation, for an application.

1217 — PHI BETA KAPPA (Mary Isabel Sibley Fellowship)

1785 Massachusetts Ave., NW, 4th Floor
Washington DC 20036
202/265-3808
FAX: 202/986-1601
E-Mail: lsurles@pbk.org

AMOUNT: $20,000

DEADLINE(S): JAN 15

FIELD(S): Greek Studies (odd-numbered years); French Studies (even-numbered years)

Candidates must be unmarried women between 25 and 35 years of age who have demonstrated their ability to carry on original research. Must hold doctorate or have fulfilled all requirements for doctorate except dissertation, and must be planning to devote full-time work to research of language and literature during the fellowship year that begins in September. Eligibility is NOT restricted to members of Phi Beta Kappa.

Contact the Fellowship Committee for an application.

1218 — SOCIAL SCIENCE RESEARCH COUNCIL (Eurasia Fellowship Program)

810 Seventh Ave., 31st Fl.
New York NY 10019
212/377-2700
FAX: 212/377-2727
E-Mail: eurasia@ssrc.org
Internet: www.ssrc.org

AMOUNT: $10,000 (graduate); $15,000 (dissertation); $24,000 (postdoctoral)

DEADLINE(S): NOV 1

FIELD(S): Soviet Studies

Open to US citizens/permanent residents enrolled in accredited graduate, dissertation, or postdoctoral programs in any discipline of the social sciences or humanities. Purpose is to enhance their disciplinary, methodological, or language training in relation to research on the Soviet Union and its successor states. Grants for summer language institutes also available.

See website or contact SSRC for an application.

1219 — SONOMA CHAMBOLLE-MUSIGNY SISTER CITIES, INC. (Henri Cardinaux Memorial Scholarship)

Chamson Scholarship Committee
PO Box 1633
Sonoma CA 95476-1633
707/939-1344
FAX: 707/939-1344
E-Mail: Baileysci@vom.com

AMOUNT: up to $1,500 (travel + expenses)

DEADLINE(S): JUL 15

FIELD(S): Culinary Arts; Wine Industry; Art; Architecture; Music; History; Fashion

Hands-on experience working in above or similiar fields & living with a family in small French village in Burgundy or other French city. Must be Sonoma County, CA, resident at least 18 years of age & be able to communicate in French. Transcripts, employer recommendation, photograph, & essay (stating why, where, & when) required.

1 award. Non-renewable. Also offers opportunity for candidate in Chambolle-Musigny to obtain work experience & cultural exposure in Sonoma, CA.

1220 — SUOMI-SEURA/FINLAND SOCIETY

Mariankatu 8
00170 Helsinki Finland
358-9-6841210

AMOUNT: Fim 1000-2000

DEADLINE(S): MAR 1

FIELD(S): Seminar on Finnish Language and Culture

Grant & travel grant to students from outside Europe. Applicants must be of Finnish descent.

1221 — THE AMERICAN CLASSICAL LEAGUE (Ed Phinney Commemorative Scholarship)

Miami University
Oxford OH 45056
513/529-7741
FAX: 513/529-7742
E-Mail: mericanClassicalLeague@muohio.edu
or a.c.l@mich.edu
Internet: www.umich.edu/~acleague/
phinney.html

AMOUNT: Up to $500

DEADLINE(S): JAN 15

FIELD(S): Teachers or teacher candidates in the classics (Latin and/or Greek)

Scholarships of up to $500 to apply to first-time attendance at the League's institute OR up to $500 to cover cost of other activities that serve to enhance a teacher's skills in the classroom in the classics OR up to $150 for purchase of materials from the ACL Teaching and Materials Resource Center. Memberships required except for first-time attendance at institute.

Send request for information to above address.

1222 — THE BRITISH COUNCIL (Bursaries/ Scholarships for Residents of Myanmar (Burma) in English Language Classes)

78 Kanna Rd./P.O. Box 638
Yangon MYANMAR (BURMA)
(00 95 1) 254 658
FAX: (00 95 1)
E-Mail: admin@bc-burma.bcouncil.org
Internet: www.britcoun.org/burma/burnews.htm

AMOUNT: Varies

DEADLINE(S): Varies

FIELD(S): English Language

The British Council's Teaching Centre in Rangoon has an extensive program in teaching the English language. Interested persons can contact the Centre Manager at her E-mail address: sheilagh.neilson@bc-burma.bccouncil.org

The website listed here gives more details; the British council lists hundreds of educational programs world wide on its website. Enter "scholarship" as the search word.

1223 — THE CENTER FOR CROSS-CULTURAL STUDY (Tuition Awards for Study in Sevill, Spain)

446 Main St.
Amherst MA 01002-2314
413/256-0011 or 1-800/377-2621
FAX: 413/256-1968
E-Mail: cccs@crocker.com
Internet: www.cccs.com

AMOUNT: $500

DEADLINE(S): Varies

FIELD(S): Study of Spanish and Spanish Culture

Partial tuition assistance is available at this facility in Spain. Applicants must submit an original essay in Spanish, between 2 or 3 double-spaced, typed pages. Also required as a short description in English of your experience with the Spanish language and culture and a faculty recommendation.

Awards are for one semester or academic year programs in Seville. Contact organization for specific details regarding the essays.

1224 — THE WALT DISNEY COMPANY (American Teacher Awards)

P.O. Box 9805
Calabasas CA 91372

AMOUNT: $2,500 (36 awards); $25,000 (Outstanding Teacher of the Year)

DEADLINE(S): FEB 15

FIELD(S): Teachers: athletic coach, early childhood, English, foreign language/ESL, general elementary, mathematics, performing arts, physical education/health, science, social studies, visual arts, voc/tech education

Awards for K-12 teachers in the above fields.

Teachers, or anyone who knows a great teacher, can write for applications at the above address.

1225 — U.S. DEPT. OF EDUCATION (Fulbright-Hays Doctoral Dissertation Research Abroad Fellowships)

International Education &
Graduate Programs Service
600 Independence Ave. SW
Washington DC 20202-5331
202/401-9774

AMOUNT: $10,000-$70,000

DEADLINE(S): OCT (late); NOV (early)

FIELD(S): Foreign language or area studies

Dissertation research abroad fellowships for Doctoral candidates in less common foreign languages/area studies (West European countries excluded) who are planning to teach in U.S. after graduation. U.S. citizen or permanent resident.

Approximateley 75 fellowships per year. Write for complete information.

1226 — U.S. DEPT. OF EDUCATION (Fulbright-Hays Faculty Research Abroad Grants)

Center for International Education
ATRB Mail Stop 5331
Washington DC 20202-5331
202/401-9777

FAX: 202/205-9489
E-Mail: elizawashington@ed.gov

AMOUNT: $40,000 average award

DEADLINE(S): NOV 6

FIELD(S): Foreign Language & Area Studies (geography, history, culture, economy, & politics of a region or country)

Research abroad grants for college/university faculty. To contribute to the development of the study of modern foreign languages and area studies in the United States by providing opportunities for scholars to conduct research abroad.

Approx. 20 awards per year. Write for complete information.

1227 — U.S. DEPT. OF EDUCATION, INTERNATIONAL EDUCATION AND GRADUATE PROGRAM SERVICE (Foreign Language and Area Studies (FLAS) Fellowships Program)

600 Independence Ave. SW
Washington DC 20202-5331
FAX: 202/205-5331

AMOUNT: $8,000 allowance + tuition ($1,500 for summer fellowships)

DEADLINE(S): Varies

FIELD(S): Foreign language or area studies

Fellowships for graduate students in foreign languages/area studies. U.S. citizen or permanent resident. Fellowships arranged through specified participating universities. Funding varies with school. Some programs are for study abroad.

Contact U.S. Dept. of Educ. at above program for list of participating schools and deadline dates.

1228 — UNIVERSITY OF ROCHESTER (Mildred R. Burton Summer Study Grants/ Scholarships for Summer Language Study)

Box 270251
Rochester NY 14627-0251
716/275-3221 or 888/822-2256
Internet: www.rochester.edu/College/MLC/
burton.html

AMOUNT: Varies

DEADLINE(S): MAR 17

FIELD(S): Foreign language

Scholarships for undergraduate students to complete an approved course of summer language study in a country where that language is spoken. Preference will be given to Univ. of Rochester students who intend to study in a program run by the University if such a program is available in the language the student wishes to study. Must have completed at least one year of foreign language study at U.R. and graduate students in the Dept. of Modern Languages & Cultures.

Based on merit and need. Applications are available from the Dept. of Modern Languages & Cultures.

PERFORMING ARTS

1229 — ACADEMY OF VOCAL ARTS (Scholarships)

1920 Spruce Street
Philadelphia PA 19103-6685
215/735-1685

AMOUNT: Full Tuition

DEADLINE(S): Varies (2 weeks prior to auditions in Spring)

FIELD(S): Vocal Music; Operatic Acting

Tenable only at the Academy Of Vocal Arts. Open to unusually gifted singers with at least two years college vocal training or equivalent. College degree recommended. Award includes full tuition scholarships and complete training in voice, operatic acting, and repertoire. Winners are selected in Spring competitive auditions. Total student enrollment limited to 30.

Contact the Academy of Vocal Arts for an application.

1230 — AMERICA-ISRAEL CULTURAL FOUNDATION (Sharett Scholarship Program)

32 Allenby Road
Tel Aviv 63-325 ISRAEL
03 5174177
FAX: 03 5178991

AMOUNT: Varies

DEADLINE(S): MAR 15

FIELD(S): Art; Performing Arts

Scholarships are available ONLY to Israeli nationals for study in Israel. Scholarships are for one year of study and are renewable.

450 scholarships per year. Application forms available in February. Write for complete information.

1231 — AMERICAN ACADEMY IN ROME (Rome Prize Fellowships in the School of Fine Arts)

7 East 60th Street
New York NY 10022-1001
212/751-7200
FAX: 212/751-7220
E-Mail: aainfo@aol.com
Internet: www.aarome.org

AMOUNT: $9,000-$15,000

DEADLINE(S): NOV 15

FIELD(S): Landscape Architecture; Architecture; Musical Composition; Visual Arts; Design Arts

For US citizens with a major and/or career interest in above fields for advanced study in Rome to pursue independent projects, which vary in content & scope. Applicants for six-month and one-year fellowships must hold a degree in the field of application. Six-month applicants must also have at least seven years professional experience and be practicing in the applied field. Interview, portfolio, recommendations, curriculum vitae, and research proposal required.

14 awards annually. Contact the Programs Department at the American Academy in Rome for an application.

1232 — AMERICAN ACCORDION MUSICOLOGICAL SOCIETY (Contest)

334 South Broadway
Pitman NJ 08071
609/854-6628

AMOUNT: $100 - $250

DEADLINE(S): SEP 10

FIELD(S): Music Composition for Accordion

Annual competition open to amateur or professional music composers who write a serious piece music (of six minutes or more) for the accordion.

Write for complete information.

1233 — AMERICAN ALLIANCE FOR HEALTH, PHYSICAL EDUCATION, RECREATION & DANCE

1900 Association Drive
Reston VA 20191
703/476-3400 or 800/213-7193
E-Mail: webmaster@aahperd.org
Internet: www.aahperd.org

AMOUNT: Varies

DEADLINE(S): Varies

FIELD(S): Health education, leisure and recreation, girls and women in sports, sport and physical education, dance

This organization has six national sub-organizations specializing in the above fields. Some have grants and fellowships for both individuals and group projects. The website has the details for each group.

Visit website for details or write to above address for details.

1234 — AMERICAN MOTHERS, INC. (Gertrude Fogelson Cultural and Creative Arts Awards)

1296 E. 21st St.
Brooklyn NY 11201
718/253-5676

AMOUNT: Up to $1,000

DEADLINE(S): JAN 1 (annually)

FIELD(S): Visual arts, creative writing, and vocal music

An award to encourage and honor mothers in artistic pursuits.

Write to Alice Miller at above address for details.

1235 — ARTS MANAGEMENT P/L (Lady Mollie Askin Ballet Travelling Scholarship)

Station House
Rawson Place
790 George St.
Sydney NSW 2000 AUSTRALIA
(612)9212 5066
FAX: (612)9211 7762
E-Mail: vbraden@ozemail.com.au

AMOUNT: Aus. $15,000

DEADLINE(S): APR 18

FIELD(S): Ballet

"For the furtherance of culture & advancement of education in Australia & elsewhere to be awarded by the Trustees to Australian citizens who shall be adjudged of outstanding ability & promise in ballet." Must be between ages of 17 & 30 at deadline. Award may be used for study, maintenance, & travel either in Australia or overseas. Must submit proof of citizenship, curriculum vitae, references, summary of aims/activities, VHS w/ 2 pieces, & 5 photographs of positions.

Winner announced in June or July. Contact Claudia Crosariol, Projects Administrator, for more information/entry form.

1236 — ARTS MANAGEMENT P/L (Marten Bequest Travelling Scholarships)

Station House
Rawson Place
790 George St.
Sydney NSW 2000 Australia
(612)9212 5066
FAX: (612)9211 7762
E-Mail: vbraden@ozemail.com.au

AMOUNT: Aus. $18,000

DEADLINE(S): OCT 30

FIELD(S): Art; Performing Arts; Creative Writing

Open to native-born Australians aged 21-35 (17-35 ballet) who are of outstanding ability and promise in one or more categories of the Arts. The scholarships are intended to augment a scholar's own resources towards a cultural education, and it may be used for study, maintenance, and travel either in Australia or overseas. Categories are: instrumental music, painting, singing, sculpture, architecture, ballet, prose, poetry, and acting.

1 scholarship granted in each of 9 categories which rotate in 2 groups on an annual basis. Contact Claudia Crosariol, Projects Administrator, for more information/entry form.

1237 — ARTS MANAGEMENT P/L (Sir Robert Askin Operatic Travelling Scholarship)

Station House
Rawson Place
790 George St.
Sydney NSW 2000 AUSTRALIA
(612)9212 5066
FAX: (612)9211 7762
E-Mail: vbraden@ozemail.com.au

AMOUNT: Aus. $15,000

DEADLINE(S): SEP 25

FIELD(S): Opera Singing

For male Australian citizens between the ages of 18 and 30. Entrants should submit a photo, reviews, and an audio tape comprising three contrasting works (including period up to Mozart in original language & one work in English). Must include summary of proposed aims/activities, including names of teachers/institutions, travel plans, and dates. Must include proof of citizenship, curriculum vitae, and at least three references.

Contact Claudia Crosariol, Projects Administrator, for more information/entry form.

1238 — ASIAN CULTURAL COUNCIL (Fellowship Grants for Asian Citizens)

1290 Ave. of the Americas
New York NY 10104
212/373-4300

AMOUNT: Varies

DEADLINE(S): FEB 1

FIELD(S): Visual Arts; Performing Arts

Fellowships open to Asian citizens. Grants may be used for graduate study, research, specialized training, or the pursuit of creative activity in the United States. Some grants also available to Americans pursuing research and study in Asia.

Send self-addressed, stamped envelope for complete information.

1239 — ASIAN CULTURAL COUNCIL (Research Fellowships for U.S. Citizens to Study in Asia & Asians to Study in U.S.)

1290 Ave. of the Americas
New York NY 10104
212/373-4300

AMOUNT: Varies

DEADLINE(S): FEB 1; AUG 1

FIELD(S): Visual Arts; Performing Arts

Doctoral and postdoctoral fellowships open to U.S. citizens who wish to do research in Asia on Asian visual or performing arts. Funds also available for students from Asia for study and research in the U.S.

Send self-address, stamped envelope (SASE) for complete information.

1240 — AUSTRALIAN FEDERATION OF UNIVERSITY WOMEN - WESTERN AUSTRALIA (Joyce Riley Bursary)

Bursary Liaison Officer
PO Box 48
Nedlands WA 6909 AUSTRALIA
Written Inquiry

AMOUNT: Aus$1,700 - Aus$2,750

DEADLINE(S): JUL 31

FIELD(S): Humanities; Social Sciences

To support women graduates of a Western Australian university to complete a higher degree or post-doctoral research in Humanities or Social Sciences at a recognized university in any country.

Membership in AFUW or in IFUW is required. Contact above location for further information.

1241 — AUSTRALIAN FEDERATION OF UNIVERSITY WOMEN - WESTERN AUSTRALIA (Joyce Riley Bursary)

Bursary Liaison Officer
PO Box 48
Nedlands WA 6009 AUSTRALIA
Written Inquiry

AMOUNT: Aus$1,700 - Aus$2,750

DEADLINE(S): JUL 31

FIELD(S): Humanities; Social Sciences

To support women graduates of a recognized university to complete a higher degree or post-doctoral research at a university in Western Australia.

Membership in AFUW or in IFUW is required. Write to above address for complete information.

1242 — AUSTRIAN CULTURAL INSTITUTE (Fine Arts & Music Grants)

950 Third Ave., 20th Fl.
New York NY 10022
212/759-5165
FAX: 212/319-9636
E-Mail: desk@aci.org
Internet: www.austriaculture.net

AMOUNT: ATS 7,800/month (US $600) + ATS 2,500 (US $190) start grant

DEADLINE(S): FEB 14

FIELD(S): Music; Drama; Art

Open to foreign students for studies at academies of music and dramatic art or at art academies in Austria. Must be advanced students between 20 and 35 years old and have a working knowledge of German. Very high level of qualification is required and final admission is subject to artistic entrance exam. Must submit letters of recommendation, curriculum vitae, and transcripts.

Not renewable. See website or contact ACI for an application kit.

1243 — BLUES HEAVEN FOUNDATION, INC. (Muddy Waters Scholarship)

2120 S. Michigan Ave.
Chicago IL 60616
312/808-1286

AMOUNT: $2,000

DEADLINE(S): APR 30

FIELD(S): Music; Music Education; African-American Studies; Folklore; Performing Arts; Arts Management; Journalism; Radio/TV/Film

Scholarship is made on a competitive basis with consideration given to scholastic achievement, concentration of studies, and financial need. Applicant must have full-time enrollment status in a Chicago area college/university in at least their first year of undergraduate studies or a graduate program. Scholastic aptitude, extracurricular involvement, grade point average, and financial need are all considered.

Contact Blues Heaven Foundation, Inc. to receive an application between February and April.

1244 — CHAMBER MUSIC AMERICA (Gruber Foundation Award/Heidi Castleman Award for Excellence in Chamber Music Teaching)

305 Seventh Ave.
New York NY 10001
212/242-2022
E-Mail: info@chamber-music.org
Internet: www.chamber-music.org

AMOUNT: $1,000

DEADLINE(S): DEC

FIELD(S): Chamber Music

Awards to honor teachers' efforts to involved students ages 6 to 18 in performing chamber music. Must be a music educator responsible for a chamber music program in elementary or high school.

Contact CMA for an application after August 1st.

1245 — CONCORDIA UNIVERSITY (Philip Cohen Award)

Leonardo Project, L DS 201-1
1455 de Maisonneuve Blvd. West
Montreal Quebec H3G 1M8 CANADA
514/848-3809
FAX: 514/848-2812
E-Mail: awardsgs@vax2.concordia.ca

AMOUNT: $750

DEADLINE(S): SEP 20

FIELD(S): Music

This award goes to an outstanding performer registered as a full-time graduate student in an interdisciplinary master's or doctoral program. In addition to his or her musical accomplishments, the recipient will normally demonstrate high academic potential in one or more disciplines outside of music.

1 award annually. Not renewable. Contact Philip Cohen, Adjunct Professor Artistic Director, Leonardo Project, Concordia University for an application.

1246 — CONCORSO INTERNAZIONALE DI VIOLINO (Premio N. Paganini)

Comune di Genova
Gasella Postale 586
c/o Ufficio Postale
16100 Genova ITALY
0039-010-557111
FAX: 0039-010-2469272
E-Mail: torisimomail.comune.ge.it
Internet: www.comune.genova.it

AMOUNT: 3-20 million liras

DEADLINE(S): MAY 31

FIELD(S): Violin

Contest for violinists of any nationality who are between the ages of 16 and 33.

9 awards annually. See website or contact above address for official rules.

1247 — CONCORSO INTERNAZIONALE PER QUARTETTO D'ARCHI (Premio Paolo Borciani)

Teatro Municipale Valli
Piazza Martiri del 7 luglio
42100 Reggio Emilia ITALY
39/0522/458811-458908
FAX: 39/0522/458822

AMOUNT: 36,000,000 Italian Lira (1st prize); 26,000,000 IL (2nd prize); 12,000,000 IL (3rd prize) - All receive medal & diploma

DEADLINE(S): JAN 31

FIELD(S): String Quartets

This competition, which takes place in June at above address, is open to string quartets of all nationalities whose members are younger than 35 years of age; the total age of the ensemble shall not exceed 120 years in June of contest year. Biography, photos, reference letters, tape recordings, and birth certificates required. Participating quartets receive free room and board.

Entry fee. Contact above address for competition guidelines and application procedures.

1248 — CONCORSO PIANISTICO INTERNAZIONALE (International Piano Competition)

Via Paradiso 6
20038 Seregno (Milan) ITALY
hone/FAX: +39/0362/222.914
E-Mail: pozzoli@concorsopozzoli.it
Internet: www.concorsopozzoli.it

AMOUNT: Varies

DEADLINE(S): MAY 30

FIELD(S): Piano

International piano competition for persons age 32 and older held every two years. Open to persons of all nationalities.

For details access website and/or send for booklet which explains in detail the prizes and requirements.

1249 — CONCOURS CLARA HASKIL (International Piano Competition)

Rue de Conseil 31
Case postale 234
CH-1800 Vevey 1 SWITZERLAND
41-21-922 67 04
FAX: 41-21-922 67 34

AMOUNT: Sfr 20 000.-

DEADLINE(S): JUL 1

FIELD(S): Piano

Competition for pianists of all nationalities who are not more than 27 years of age. Travelling expenses are the responsibility of the candidate, as is accomodation; however, competition office can supply addresses of welcoming families (generally free of charge). Must submit three good-quality, black & white, 9x15cm photographs for brochure along with completed application form.

Sfr 250.- entry fee. Contact the Association Clara Haskil for brochure detailing timetable, programme, and regulations.

1250 — CONCOURS GEZA ANDA (International Piano Competition)

Bleicherweg 18
CH-8002 Zurich SWITZERLAND
0041/1/205 11 11
FAX: 0041/1/205 12 85
E-Mail: info@ihag-handelsbank.ch
Internet: www.ihag-handelsbank.ch

AMOUNT: CHF 30,000.-

DEADLINE(S): MAR 1

FIELD(S): Piano

Pianists under 31 years of age from any nation may participate in the June competition. Competition is divided into four rounds: Audition, Recital, Mozart Piano Concerto with orchestra, and Piano Concerto with orchestra. Applications must be accompanied by a curriculum vitae, certificate of birth (photocopy), and two photographs (suitable for publication). The Jury will select candidates for audition on the basis of written applications.

Application fee of CH 300.- required. Travel & accomodation expenses not included. Contact Concours Geza Anda for an application packet.

1251 — CONTEMPORARY RECORD SOCIETY (CRS Competitions)

724 Winchester Road
Broomall PA 19008
610/544-5920
FAX: 610/544-5921
E-Mail: crsnews@erols.com
Internet: www.erols.com/crsnews

AMOUNT: up to $2,500

DEADLINE(S): DEC 1

FIELD(S): Music

All musicians are accepted for consideration.

3 awards annually. Renewable. Contact Caroline Hunt at CRS for an application.

1252 — COSTUME SOCIETY OF AMERICA (Stella Blum Research Grant)

55 Edgewater Dr.
PO Box 73
Earleville MD 21919
800/CSA-9447 or 410/275-1619
FAX: 410/275-8936
Internet: www.costumesocietyamerica.com

AMOUNT: $3,000 (to be used for research expenses: transportation/living at research site, photographic reproductions/film, postage, telephone, typing, computer searches, & graphics)

DEADLINE(S): FEB 1

FIELD(S): North American Costume

For graduate students at accredited institutions. Award is based on merit, NOT need. Judging criteria includes: creativity & innovation, specific awareness of & attention to costume matters, impact on the broad field of costume, awareness of interdisciplinarity of the field, ability to successfully implement the proposed project in a timely manner, and faculty advisor recommendation. Must be member of the Costume Society of America.

1 award annually. Not renewable. Contact CSA for an application or membership information. Winner announced in May.

1253 — COUNCIL FOR BASIC EDUCATION (Arts Education Fellowships)

2506 Buckelew Drive
Falls Church VA 22046
703/876-5782

AMOUNT: $2,800 stipend + $200 grant to school

DEADLINE(S): JAN

FIELD(S): Teaching of the arts (visual arts, creative writing, dance, media, music, theatre)

Fellowships for K-12 teachers in the above fields, artist-teachers, or professional artists who teach at least 20 hours per week. Funding from the National

Endowment for the Arts and the Getty Center for Education in the Arts, and others.

Contact organization for details.

1254 — COUNTESS OF MUNSTER MUSICAL TRUST (Grants & Loans)

Wormley Hill
Godalming, Surrey
GU8 5SG ENGLAND
0044 1428 685427
FAX: 0044 1428 685064
E-Mail: munstertrust@compuserve.com

AMOUNT: 5,000 pounds sterling (max.)

DEADLINE(S): JAN 31

FIELD(S): Music Performance

British and British Commonwealth nationals who are postgraduate students may apply for grants (for study & maintenance) and loans (for instrument purchase). Lower age limit is 18. Upper age limits: 25 (instrumentalists), 27 (female singers), 28 (male singers), & 28 (for instrument loans). Must demonstrate financial need.

80-100 awards annually. Contact The Secretary at address above for complete information.

1255 — CURTIS INSTITUTE OF MUSIC (Tuition Scholarships)

Admissions Office
1726 Locust St.
Philadelphia PA 19103-6187
215/893-5262
FAX: 215/893-7900
Internet: www.curtis.edu

AMOUNT: Full tuition

DEADLINE(S): JAN 15

FIELD(S): Music, Voice, Opera

Full-tuition scholarships open to students in the above areas who are accepted for full-time study at the Curtis Institute of Music. (Opera is for master of music only.)

Scholarships are renewable. Write or see website for complete information.

1256 — DELTA OMICRON (Triennial Composition Competition for Solo Piano

12297 W. Tennessee Place
Lakewood CO 80228-3325
606-266-1215

AMOUNT: $500 + premiere performance at Conference

DEADLINE(S): MAR 18

FIELD(S): Music composition competition

Award for solo piano composition with a time length from seven to ten minutes. No music fraternity affiliation required.

Prior publication or performance not allowed. Entry fee of $10 is required. Contact Judith Eidson at above address for details.

1257 — DELTA OMICRON INTERNATIONAL MUSIC FRATERNITY (Triennial Composition Competition for Sacred Choral Anthem for Three- or Four-Part Voices)

12297 W. Tennessee Pl.
Lakewood CO 80228-3325
606/266-1215

AMOUNT: $500 and premiere

DEADLINE(S): MAR 20

FIELD(S): Music Composition

Sacred choral anthem for 3- or 4-part voices; SSA, SAB, or SATB with keyboard accompaniment or a capella with optional obligato. Competition open to composers of college age or over. No music fraternity affiliation required.

Prior publication or public performance of entry is NOT allowed. Entry fee of $10 is required. Contact Judith Eidson at above address for complete information.

1258 — DISTRICT OF COLUMBIA COMMISSION ON THE ARTS & HUMANITIES (Grants)

410 Eighth St. NW, 5th Floor
Washington DC 20004
202/724-5613
TDD 202/727-3148
FAX: 202/727-4135

AMOUNT: $2,500

DEADLINE(S): MAR 1

FIELD(S): Performing Arts, Literature, Visual Arts

Applicants for grants must be professional artists and residents of Washington DC for at least one year prior to submitting application. Awards intended to generate art endeavors within the Washington DC community.

Open also to art organizations that train, exhibit, or perform within DC. 150 grants per year. Write for complete information.

1259 — F.J. CONNELL MUSIC SCHOLARSHIP TRUST

1187 Simcoe St.
Moose Jaw Saskatchewan S6H 3J5 CANADA
306/694-2045

AMOUNT: $750 (Canadian)

DEADLINE(S): OCT 1

FIELD(S): Music

For students studying any aspect of music, such as education, performance, composition, history, etc. Must have completed the equivalent of one year of

full-time music studies and be planning a professional career in music. No citizenship or residency requirements, but recipients will usually be Canadians.

Contact above location for details.

1260 — FLORIDA ARTS COUNCIL (Individual Artists' Fellowships)

FL Dept. of State
Div. of Cultural Affairs
State Capitol
Tallahassee FL 32399-0250
850/487-2980
TDD: 850/414-2214
FAX: 850/922-5259

AMOUNT: $5,000

DEADLINE(S): JAN 16

FIELD(S): Visual Arts; Dance; Folk Arts; Media; Music; Theater; Literary Arts; Interdisciplinary

Fellowships awarded to individual artists in the above areas. Must be Florida residents, U.S. citizens, and over 18 years old. May NOT be a degree-seeking student—funding is for support of artistic endeavors only.

38 awards per year. Write for complete information.

1261 — FONDATION DES ETATS-UNIS (Harriet Hale Woolley Scholarships

15, Boulevard Jourdan
755690 PARIS CEDEX 14, FRANCE
(1)45.89.35.79

AMOUNT: $8,500 payable in French francs

DEADLINE(S): JAN 31

FIELD(S): Art and music

For U.S. unmarried citizens between ages 21-29 with evidence of artistic or musical accomplishment, good moral character, personality, etc. A serious project for graduate study in Paris must be approved by the Fondation director and should include enrollment in a recognized school or private instruction.

For academic year Oct. 1 through June 30. Contact the Director, Harriet Hale Woolley Scholarships, at above location.

1262 — FRANCIS CHAGRIN FUND (Grants)

Francis House
Francis Street
London SWIP 1DE ENGLAND
0044 171 828 9696
FAX: 0044 171 931 9928
E-Mail: spnm@spnm.org.uk
Internet: www.spnm.org.uk

AMOUNT: 250 pounds sterling (max.)

DEADLINE(S): None

FIELD(S): Music Composition

For British composers or composers resident in the UK. The fund considers applications for: 1) reproduction of scores & parts by photocopying or other reprographic means; 2) covering & binding of scores & parts; and 3) reproduction of tapes for use in performance. Financial need is NOT considered.

Not renewable. Contact Katy Bignold at above address for an application.

1263 — FRIBOURG FESTIVAL OF SACRED MUSIC (International Competition in Composition of Sacred Music)

PO Box 292
CH-1701 Fribourg SWITZERLAND
026 322 48 00
FAX 026 322 83 31
E-Mail: sacredmusicfr@pingnet.ch

AMOUNT: 1st prize: Sw. Fr. 8,000; 2nd prize: Sw. Fr. 2,000; 3rd prize: 1,000.

DEADLINE(S): JUL 28 (odd-numbered years)

FIELD(S): Composition of Sacred Music

Bi-annual competition to encourage creation of original musical works taking their inspiration from sacred texts in the Christian tradition. Open to musical composers of all ages and nationalities. Composition must be original and never have been performed, not even partially. A work usually is of 20 minutes in duration, according to given theme. Composer must send 6 copies of score & bio-data. Jury of composers selects winners.

Contact Nicole Renevey, Administrator, for technical restrictions of music piece. NOT A SCHOLARSHIP.

1264 — GEORGE BIRD GRINNELL AMERICAN INDIAN CHILDREN'S FUND (Al Qoyawayma Award)

11602 Montague Ct.
Potomac MD 20854
301/424-2440
FAX: 301/424-8281
E-Mail: Grinnell_Fund@MSN.com

AMOUNT: $1,000

DEADLINE(S): JUN 1

FIELD(S): Science; Engineering

Open to Native American undergraduate and graduate students majoring in science or engineering and who have demonstrated an outstanding interest and skill in any one of the arts. Must be American Indian/Alaska Native (documented with Certified Degree of Indian Blood), be enrolled in college/university, be able to demonstrate commitment to serving community or other tribal nations, and document financial need.

Contact Dr. Paula M. Mintzies, President, for an application after January 1st.

1265 — GLADYS KRIEBLE DELMAS FOUNDATION (Predoctoral & Postdoctoral Grants in Venice & the Veneto)

521 5th Avenue, Suite 1612
New York NY 10175-1699
212/687-0011
FAX: 212/687-8877
E-Mail: DelmasFdtn@aol.com
Internet: www.delmas.org

AMOUNT: $500-$12,500

DEADLINE(S): DEC 15

FIELD(S): Research of Venice and the former Venetian empire and study of contemporary Venetian society and culture.

Pre- and postdoctoral grants for historical research on Venice. Humanities and social sciences are eligible areas of study, including archaeology, architecture, art, bibliography, economics, history, history of science, law, literature, music, political science, religion, and theater.

Applicants must have experience in advanced research and be U.S. citizens/residents; grad students must have fulfilled all doctoral requirements except dissertation by Dec. 15.

1266 — HAROLD HYAM WINGATE FOUNDATION (Wingate Scholarships)

38 Curzon St.
London W1Y 8EY ENLAND UK
0171 465 1521

AMOUNT: Up to 10,000 pounds/yr.

DEADLINE(S): FEB 1

FIELD(S): Creative works

Financial support for individuals of great potential or proven excellence to develop original work of intellectual, scientific, artistic, social, or environmental value, and to outstanding talented musicians. Not for taught courses or for leading to professional qualifications, or for electives or for completing courses already begun or for a higher degree. For citizens of the United Kingdom or other Commonwealth countries, Ireland, Israel, or of European countries.

Must be age 24 or older. May be held for up to three years.

1267 — HATTORI FOUNDATION FOR YOUNG MUSICIANS (Awards for Young Soloists)

72 E. Leopold Rd.
London 8W19 7J2 ENGLAND UK
0181 944 5319
FAX: 0181 946 6970

AMOUNT: 1,000 pounds sterling (max.)

DEADLINE(S): None

FIELD(S): Music Performace (Instrumental)

Awards for British nationals or foreign nationals who are UK residents. Must be aged 15-20 and show promise of an international career as a soloist. Course fees and instrument purchase are not funded. Financial need is NOT a factor.

10 awards annually. Renewable. Contact Ms. Kim Gaynok for details.

1268 — HATTORI FOUNDATION FOR YOUNG MUSICIANS (Postgraduate Awards)

72 E. Leopold Rd.
London 8W19 7J2 ENGLAND UK
0181 944 5319
FAX: 0181 946 6970

AMOUNT: 6,000 pounds sterling (max.)

DEADLINE(S): APR 30

FIELD(S): Music Performace (Instrumental)

Postgraduate awards for British nationals or foreign nationals who are UK residents. Must be aged 21-27 and show promise of an international career as a soloist or ensemble. Course fees and instrument purchase are not funded. Financial need is NOT a factor.

20 awards annually. Renewable. Contact Ms. Kim Gaynok for details.

1269 — ILLINOIS ARTS COUNCIL (Artists Fellowship Awards)

100 W. Randolph, Suite 10-500
Chicago IL 60601-3298
312/814-6750

AMOUNT: $500; $5,000; $10,000

DEADLINE(S): SEP 1

FIELD(S): Choreography; Visual Arts; Poetry Prose; Film; Video; Playwriting; Music Composition; Crafts; Ethnic & Folk Arts; Performance Art; Photography; Audio Art.

Open to professional artists who are Illinois residents. Awards are in recognition of work in the above areas; they are not for continuing study. Students are NOT eligible.

Write to address above for application form.

1270 — INSTITUTE FOR ADVANCED STUDIES IN THE HUMANITIES (Visiting Research Fellowships)

Univ Edinburgh
Hope Park Square
Edinburgh EH8 9NW SCOTLAND UK
0131 650 4671
FAX: 0131 668 2252
E-Mail: iash@ed.ac.uk
Internet: www.ed.ac.uk/iash/homepage.html

AMOUNT: Non-stipendiary*

DEADLINE(S): DEC 1

FIELD(S): Arts; Social Sciences; Law; Music; Divinity

Postdoctoral research fellowships of between two and six months are tenable at the Institute for Advanced Studies in the Humanities. Based on academic record and publications. *Most fellowships are honorary, but limited support towards expenses is available to a small number of candidates. Fellows are allocated a study room within the Institute and hold one or two seminars during their tenure. Must submit research report at end of fellowship. No teaching required.

15 awards annually. Not renewable. Contact Mrs. Anthea Taylor for an application.

1271 — INSTITUTE OF INTERNATIONAL EDUCATION (Arts International Fund For Performing Arts)

809 United Nations Plaza
New York NY 10017
212/984-5370
Internet: www.iie.org/ai

AMOUNT: $500-$2,000

DEADLINE(S): SEP; JAN; MAY

FIELD(S): Performing Arts

Grants to support U.S. artists at international festivals and exhibitions. The festival must take place outside the U.S. and be international in scope with representation from at least two countries outside the host country or have a U.S. theme with representation from at least three U.S. performing artists or groups.

Must be open to the general public. Call for details.

1272 — INTERNATIONAL COMPETITION FOR SYMPHONIC COMPOSITION (Premio Citta Di Trieste)

Piazza Dell'unita D'Italia 4 - Palazzo municipale
34121 Trieste Italy
040-366030

AMOUNT: 10 mil. lira (1st)

DEADLINE(S): APR 30

FIELD(S): Music Composition

Open to anyone who submits an original composition for full orchestra (normal symphonic instrumentation). Composition must never have been performed and be unpublished.

Previous first-prize winners are excluded from competition. Write to secretariat of the music award at address above for complete information.

1273 — INTERNATIONALER MUSIKWETTBEWERB (International Music Competition of the Ard Munich)

Bayerischer Rundfunk
D-80300 Munchen GERMANY
0049(0)89 5900 2471

FAX: 0049(0)89 5900 3573
E-Mail: ard.conc@br-mail.de

AMOUNT: 20,000 DM (1st prize); 14,000 DM (2nd); 10,000 DM (3rd)

DEADLINE(S): APR 23

FIELD(S): Piano; Violin; Horn; Organ

For outstanding young musicians, aged 17-30, who are at concert standard. Performance is evaluated on technique, musical presentation, artistic personality, and voice & tonal quality.

Contact Gisela Mauss at above address for official rules and entry form.

1274 — INTERNATIONAL TRUMPET GUILD (Conference Scholarships)

241 East Main St., #247
Westfield MA 01086-1633
413/564-0337
FAX: 413/568-1913
E-Mail: treasurer@trumpetguild.org
Internet: www.dana.edu/~itg or www.trumpetguild.org

AMOUNT: $200 + waive Conference registration fee

DEADLINE(S): FEB 15

FIELD(S): Trumpet

Music competition for trumpet players under age 25 to enable them to attend ITG's annual conference. Must be a student member of the International Trumpet Guild by the deadline. Must submit the appropriate taped audition to the current scholarship competition chair. Generally, the student's trumpet playing must be at a relatively advanced level in order to play the repertoire.

See website for membership information and audition requirements.

1275 — IRISH ARTS COUNCIL (Awards and Opportunities)

70 Merrion Square
Dublin 2 Ireland
Tel+353 1 618 0200
FAX:+353 1 661 0349/676 1302
E-Mail: info@artscouncil.ie
Internet: www.artscouncil.ie

AMOUNT: 500-1,500 pounds sterling

DEADLINE(S): Varies (with program)

FIELD(S): Creative Arts; Visual Arts; Performing Arts

Numerous programs open to young & established artists who are Irish citizens or legal residents. Purpose is to assist in pursuit of talents & recognize achievements.

Contact above address for an application.

1276 — ISTITUTO ITALIANO PER GLI STUDI STORICI (Federico Chabod & Adolfo Omodeo Scholarships)

12 Via Benedetto Croce
80134 Naples ITALY
0039/81/551-7159
FAX: 0039/81/551-2390
E-Mail: iiss@iol.it

AMOUNT: 12 million lires

DEADLINE(S): SEP 30

FIELD(S): History; Philosophy; Literature; Arts; Economics

Open to non-Italian citizens who have completed a university degree in the humanities (history, philosophy, & arts) in a non-Italian university. Intended to allow young scholars to participate in the work of the Institute and to complete personal scholarly research with the help of teaching staff of the Institute. Must submit birth certificate, university diploma, scholarly work, program of studies with indication of language skills, research proposal, & reference.

Renewable. Contact Dott.ssa Marta Herling, Secretary, for an application.

1277 — JACOB'S PILLOW DANCE FESTIVAL (Scholarships)

PO Box 287
Lee MA 02138
413/637-1322
FAX: 413/243-4744
Internet: www.jacobspillow.org

AMOUNT: Varies

DEADLINE(S): APR 5

FIELD(S): Dance

Pre-professional dance training for 16-year-old dancers at the School at Jacob's Pillow. Must demonstrate financial need.

Not renewable. Contact J.R. Glover for an application.

1278 — JOHN K. & THIRZA F. DAVENPORT FOUNDATION (Scholarships in the Arts)

20 North Main Street
South Yarmouth MA 02664-3143
508/398-2293
FAX: 508/394-6765

AMOUNT: Varies

DEADLINE(S): JUL 15

FIELD(S): Theatre, Music, Art

For Barnstable County, Massachusetts residents in their last two years of undergraduate or graduate (preferred) study in visual or performing arts. Must demonstrate financial need.

6-8 awards annually. Renewable. Contact Mrs. Chris M. Walsh for more information.

1279 — JULIUS AND ESTHER STULBERG COMPETITION, INC. (International String Competition)

P.O. Box 50107
Kalamazoo MI 49005
616/372-6237
FAX: 616/372-7513

AMOUNT: $3,000 (1st prize); $2,000 (2nd); $1,000 (3rd)

DEADLINE(S): JAN 10

FIELD(S): Stringed Instruments (Violin, Viola, Cello, Double Bass)

Contest is open to talented musicians aged 19 or younger who perform on violin, viola, cello, or double bass.

Application fee of $30.00. Send self-addressed, stamped envelope to above location for complete information.

1280 — KATHLEEN FERRIER MEMORIAL SCHOLARSHIP FUND (Kathleen Ferrier Awards)

52 Rosebank Holyport Road
London SW6 6LY England
0171/381-0985 (telephone & FAX)

AMOUNT: 17,500 pounds sterling

DEADLINE(S): MAR 1 (applications available in JAN)

FIELD(S): Singing Competition

Competitive annual awards are open to British singers (and those from the Commonwealth and the Republic of Ireland) who are over 21 but not over the age of 28 on the day of the final auditions.

Write to Administrator at above address for complete information.

1281 — KURT WEILL FOUNDATION FOR MUSIC (Grants Program)

7 East 20th St.
New York NY 10003
212/505-5240
FAX: 212/353-9663
E-Mail: kwfinfo@kwf.org
Internet: www.kwf.org

AMOUNT: Varies

DEADLINE(S): NOV 1

FIELD(S): Music

Fellowships and travel grants open to doctoral candidates to support dissertation research on Kurt Weill and his music. Will also support travel anywhere in the world to study primary documents. Grants also available to fund productions and performances of Kurt Weill's music.

See website or contact Kurt Weill Foundation for an application.

1282 — LABAN/BARTENIEFF INSTITUTE OF MOVEMENT STUDIES (Work-Study Programs)

234 Fifth Ave., Rm. 203
New York NY 10001
212/477-4299
FAX: 212/477-3702
E-Mail: limsinfo@erols.com

AMOUNT: $500-$1,500

DEADLINE(S): MAY 1

FIELD(S): Human Movement Studies

Open to graduate students and professionals in dance, education, health fields, behavioral sciences, fitness, athletic training, etc. Tenable for work-study ONLY at the Laban/Bartenieff Institute in New York.

Contact LIMS for an application.

1283 — LIBERACE FOUNDATION FOR THE PERFORMING AND CREATIVE ARTS (Scholarship Fund)

1775 East Tropicana Avenue
Las Vegas NV 89119-6529
Internet: www.liberace.org

AMOUNT: Varies

DEADLINE(S): MAR 15

FIELD(S): Music; Theatre; Dance; Visual Arts

Provides grants to accredited INSTITUTIONS that offer training in above fields. Grants are to be used exclusively for scholarship assistance to talented and deserving students. Recipients should be promising and deserving upperclassmen (Jr., Sr., Graduate) enrolled in a course of study leading up to a career in the arts.

NO DIRECT-TO STUDENT GRANTS ARE MADE. Student's school must apply on their behalf. See website or write to above address for details.

1284 — LIEDERKRANZ FOUNDATION, INC. (Scholarship Awards)

6 East 87th Street
New York NY 10128
212/534-0880

AMOUNT: $1,000-$5,000

DEADLINE(S): DEC 1

FIELD(S): Vocal Music

Awards can be used anywhere. Age limit for General Voice 20-35 years old, and limit for Wagnerian Voice is 25-45 years. There is a $35 application fee.

14-18 scholarships annually. NOT renewable. Contact competition director John Balme at address above for application regulations, audition schedules, and other details.

1285 — LOREN L. ZACHARY SOCIETY FOR THE PERFORMING ARTS (National Vocal Competition for Young Opera Singers)

2250 Gloaming Way
Beverly Hills CA 90210
310/276-2731
FAX: 310/275-8245

AMOUNT: $10,000 (1st prize); $1,000 (finalists)

DEADLINE(S): JAN (NY); MAR (LA); MAY (final competition)

FIELD(S): Opera Singing

Annual vocal competition open to young (aged 21-33 females; 21-35 males) Opera singers. The competition is geared toward finding employment for them in European Opera houses. Financial assistance is only possible through participation in the audition program. Financial need NOT considered.

$35 application fee. 10 awards annually. Send self-addressed, stamped envelope to Mrs. Nedra Zachary at address above for an application.

1286 — MARTIN MUSICAL SCHOLARSHIP FUND (Scholarships)

Lawn Cottage, 23a Brackley Road
Beckenham, Kent BR3 1RB ENGLAND
PHONE/FAX: 0181-658-9432

AMOUNT: Up to 2,000 pounds sterling

DEADLINE(S): DEC 1

FIELD(S): Instrumental Music

Scholarships are administered by the London Philharmonic Orchestra. For applicants of exceptional talent under age 25. Awards are for study at any approved institution in England for non-U.K. citizens; citizens of the U.K. may study anywhere. Candidates must be studying for a career as either soloist, chamber musician, or orchestral player. Additional programs are for viola players, violinists, and wood wind performers.

Not open to organists, singers, composers, or for academic studies. Awards are valid for two years. Auditions are held in London the January following the December deadline date. Write for complete information.

1287 — MENDELSSOHN SCHOLARSHIP FOUNDATION (Composers Scholarships)

c/o Royal Academy of Music
Marylebone Road
London NW1 5HT England
(0)1-636-5400

AMOUNT: 6,000 pounds sterling

DEADLINE(S): None

FIELD(S): Musical Composition

Open to composers of any nationality under the age of 30 who are residents (for at least 3 years) in the UK or Ireland. For further studies in composition.

Contact Miss Jean Shannon at address above for complete information.

1288 — MERCYHURST COLLEGE D'ANGELO SCHOOL OF MUSIC (Young Artists Competition)

501 E. 38th Street
Erie PA 16546
814/824-2394
FAX: 814/824-2438
E-Mail: kwok@mercyhurst.edu

AMOUNT: $10,000 (1st prize); $5,000 (2nd); $3,000 (3rd)

DEADLINE(S): FEB 1

FIELD(S): Voice; Strings; Piano

For musicians aged 18-30 (voice-age 35). There is a rotating cycle of areas (strings 2000, piano 2001, voice 2002). As well as dollar awards, there are performance contracts.

Contact Glen Kwok at above address for an application and repertoire requirements in the Fall of the year preceding competition.

1289 — MERCYHURST COLLEGE D'ANGELO SCHOOL OF MUSIC (Scholarships)

501 E. 38th Street
Erie PA 16546
814/824-2394
FAX: 814/824-2438
E-Mail: kwok@mercyhurst.edu

AMOUNT: up to $10,000

DEADLINE(S): None

FIELD(S): Music

For music students who wish to attend the D'Angelo School of Music At Mercyhurst College in Erie, Pennsylvania. Audition required.

Renewable for four years. Contact Glen Kwok for an application.

1290 — MINISTRY OF THE FLEMISH COMMUNITY (Fellowships)

Embassy of Belgium
3330 Garfield St., NW
Washington DC 20008
202/625-5850/51
FAX: 202/342-8346
E-Mail: flemishcomdc@wizard.net

AMOUNT: Monthly stipend, tuition, & health care coverage

DEADLINE(S): JAN 31

FIELD(S): Art; Music; Humanities; Social Science; Political Science; Law; Economics; Science; Medicine

Open to US citizens under age 35 who wish to pursue graduate or postgraduate studies in Flanders, Belgium.

Contact Flemish Community for registration forms.

1291 — MONTANA ARTS COUNCIL (Individual Artists Fellowships)

City County Building
316 North Park Ave., Rm. 252
Helena MT 59620-2201
406/444-6430
FAX: 406/444-6548
E-Mail: montana@artswire.org

AMOUNT: $2,000

DEADLINE(S): MAY 1

FIELD(S): Music and art

Fellowships for artists or musicians who have been Montana residents for at least a year.

Contact Julie SMith, director, at above location.

1292 — MUSIC ACADEMY OF THE WEST (Scholarships)

1070 Fairway Road
Santa Barbara CA 93108-2899
805/969-4726
FAX: 805/969-0686
E-Mail: catalog@musicacademy.org
Internet: www.musicacademy.org

AMOUNT: Tuition, room & board

DEADLINE(S): Varies

FIELD(S): Music

Scholarships for this eight-week summer session for musicians age 16 and up. Maximum age for vocalists is 32. Student must pay transportation and limited fees. Deadlines run from January 9 through March 15, depending on instrument. Audition dates are set up throughout the U.S.

Access website for details and application, or write for information.

1293 — McCORD CAREER CENTER (Level II McCord Medical/Music Scholarship)

Healdsburg High School
1024 Prince St.
Healdsburg CA 95448
707/431-3473

AMOUNT: Varies

DEADLINE(S): APR 30

FIELD(S): Medicine; Music

For graduates of Healdsburg High School who are planning a career in music or medicine. Must be enrolled full-time at a college/university as an undergraduate junior or senior in the fall, or earning an advanced degree in graduate or medical school,

or entering into a vocational/certificate program. Transcripts, proof of attendance, and an essay are required.

Contact the McCord Career Center at Healdsburg High School for an application.

1294 — NATIONAL ASSOCIATION OF TEACHERS OF SINGING (Artist Awards Competition)

2800 University Blvd. North
Jacksonville FL 32211
904/744-9022
FAX: 904/744-9033
E-Mail: WmVessels@aol.com
Internet: www.nats.org

AMOUNT: Varies

DEADLINE(S): Varies

FIELD(S): Singing

Purpose of the program is to select young singers who are ready for professional careers and to encourage them to carry on the tradition of fine singing. Selection based on present accomplishments rather than future potential. Applicants should be between 21 and 35 years old and have studied with a NATS teacher or a member of NATS.

Contact NATS for an application.

1295 — NATIONAL GUILD OF COMMUNITY SCHOOLS OF THE ARTS (Young Composers Awards)

40 N. Van Brunt St., Ste. 32
Englewood NJ 07631
201/871-3337
FAX: 201/871-7639

AMOUNT: $1,000 (1st place); $500 (2nd)

DEADLINE(S): MAY 1

FIELD(S): Music Composition

Competition open to students aged 13-18 (as of June 30th of award year) who are enrolled in a public or private secondary school, recognized musical school, or engaged in private study of music with an established teacher in the US or Canada. Must be US or Canadian citizen/legal resident.

Contact Lolita Mayadas, Executive Director, for an application.

1296 — NATIONAL ITALIAN AMERICAN FOUNDATION (Nina Santavicca Scholarship)

1860 19th St. NW
Washington DC 20009-5599
202/530-5315

AMOUNT: $1,000

DEADLINE(S): MAY 31

FIELD(S): Music major-piano

Open to undergraduate or graduate music students, preferably piano, of Italian heritage.

Academic merit, financial need, and community service considered.

1297 — NATIONAL LEAGUE OF AMERICAN PEN WOMEN, INC. (Scholarships for Mature Women)

1300 Seventeenth St. NW
Washington DC 20036
717/225-3023

AMOUNT: $1,000

DEADLINE(S): JAN 15 (even-numbered years)

FIELD(S): Art; Music; Creative Writing

The National League of American Pen Women gives three $1,000 grants in even-numbered years to women aged 35 and over. Should submit three 4"x6" or bigger color prints, manuscripts, or musical compositions suited to the criteria for the year.

Send SASE for details at the above address.

1298 — NEW JERSEY STATE OPERA (Cash Awards)

50 Park PL Robert Treat Center
Newark NJ 07102
201/623-5757

AMOUNT: Awards total $10,000

DEADLINE(S): Varies

FIELD(S): Opera

Professional singers between the ages of 22 and 34 can apply for this competition. Singers competing should have been represented by an artist's management firm for no more than one year. Management representation not required for entry.

Contact address above for complete information.

1299 — NEW JERSEY STATE OPERA (International Vocal Competition)

Robert Treat Center-10th Floor
Newark NJ 07102
201/623-5757
FAX 201/623-5761

AMOUNT: $10,000 total

DEADLINE(S): Varies

FIELD(S): Opera singing

Professional opera singers between the ages of 22 and 34 can apply for this international competition.

Renewable yearly. Contact Mrs. Wanda Anderton at above address for information.

1300 — NEW SCHOOL FOR MUSIC STUDY (Graduate Fellowships in Piano Teaching)

P.O. Box 360
Kingston, NJ 08528-0360
609/921-2900

AMOUNT: $2,000 to $6,000

DEADLINE(S): MAR 15

FIELD(S): Piano Performance and Pedagogy

Graduate fellowships awarded on merit and teaching potential. Tenable at New School for Music Study. One- or 2-year certificate program in piano pedagogy. M.M. offered in conjunction with Westminster Choir College of Rider University.

2-6 Awards per year. Must speak fluent English. Renewable up to 2 years. Contact Ted Cooper (director) at the address above.

1301 — NEW YORK STATE THEATRE INSTITUTE (Internships in Theatrical Production)

155 River St.
Troy NY 12180
518/274-3573
nysti@crisny.org
Internet: www.crisny.org/not-for-profit/nysti/int.htm

AMOUNT: None

DEADLINE(S): None

FIELD(S): Fields of study related to theatrical production, including box office and PR

Internships for college students, high school seniors, and educators-in-residence interested in developing skills in above fields. Unpaid, but college credit is earned. Located at Russell Sage College in Troy, NY. Gain experience in box office, costumes, education, electrics, music, stage management, scenery, properties, performance, and public relations. Interns come from all over the world.

Must be associated with an accredited institution. See website for more information. Call Ms. Arlene Leff, Intern Director at above location. Include your postal mailing address.

1302 — NEWBERRY LIBRARY (Long-Term Fellowships)

60 West Walton Street
Chicago IL 60610-3380
312/943-9090
E-Mail: research@newberry.org
Internet: www.newberry.org

AMOUNT: Up to $30,000

DEADLINE(S): JAN 20

FIELD(S): Humanities, History, & related fields

Six postdoctoral fellowship programs are available for scholars wishing to use the Library's collection for writing or research. Fellowships last six to eleven months, and each have slightly different requirements.

See website for details and an application or write to above address.

1303 — NEWBERRY LIBRARY (Short-Term Fellowships)

60 West Walton Street
Chicago IL 60610-3380
312/943-9090
E-Mail: research@newberry.org
Internet: www.newberry.org

AMOUNT: $800-$1,500/month

DEADLINE(S): MAR 1

FIELD(S): Humanities, History, & related fields

Nine programs for postdoctoral scholars or doctoral students at the dissertation stage. Study varies from two weeks to three months and is for those making use of Newberry's collections. Each program has slightly different requirements.

See website for details and applications or write to above address.

1304 — NEWBERRY LIBRARY (Special Fellowships)

60 West Walton Street
Chicago IL 60610-3380
312/255-3666
E-Mail: research@newberry.org
Internet: www.newberry.org

AMOUNT: Varies

DEADLINE(S): DEC 15

FIELD(S): Humanities, History, & related fields

Fellowships for three months to one year for doctoral or postdoctoral students to study in Germany, France, or Great Britain in fields related to Newberry's collections. Some deadlines JAN 20th. Specific locations are: Wolfenb,ttel, Germany; Ecole Nationale des Chartes, Paris, France; and the British Academy, Great Britain.

See website for more details and applications or write to above address.

1305 — NEWBERRY LIBRARY (Weiss/Brown Publication Subvention Award)

60 West Walton Street
Chicago IL 60610-3380
312/255-3666
E-Mail: research@newberry.org
Internet: www.newberry.org

AMOUNT: up to $15,000

DEADLINE(S): JAN 20

FIELD(S): European Civilization/History/Culture

Awards for authors of scholarly books already accepted for publication. Subject matter must cover European civilization before 1700 in the areas of music, theatre, French or Italian literature or cultural studies. Applicants must provide detailed information regarding the publication and the subvention request.

See website for more details and application or write to above address.

1306 — OMAHA SYMPHONY GUILD (International New Music Competition)

1605 Howard St.
Omaha NE 68102
402/342-3836
FAX: 402/342-3819
E-Mail: bravo@omahasymphony.org
Internet: www.omahasymphony.org

AMOUNT: $3,000

DEADLINE(S): APR 15

FIELD(S): Musical Composition

For composers aged 25 or above to enter a composition of 20 minutes in length or less. Composition is scored for chamber orchestra or ensemble. Work must be previously unpublished and not performed by a professional orchestra.

$30 entry fee. 1 award annually. Not renewable. Contact Kimberly Mettenbrink for application procedures.

1307 — ONTARIO CHORAL FEDERATION (Leslie Bell Prize)

100 Richmond Street East, Suite 200
Toronto Ontario M5C 2P9 Canada
416/363-7488

AMOUNT: $5,000

DEADLINE(S): Varies (Early in even-numbered years)

FIELD(S): Choral Conducting

Scholarship open to Ontario residents pursuing graduate/post-graduate or specialized training. Awarded to emerging choral conductors (aged 18-35). Canadian citizenship required.

Awards are presented in even-numbered years. Write for complete information.

1308 — OPERA AMERICA (Fellowship Program)

1156 15th St. NW, Suite 810
Washington DC 20005
202/293-4466
FAX: 202/393-0735

AMOUNT: $1,200/month + transportation & housing

DEADLINE(S): MAY 7

FIELD(S): General or Artistic Administration, Technical Direction, or Production Management

Open to opera personnel, individuals entering opera administration from other disciplines, and graduates of arts administration or technical/production training programs who are committed to a career in opera in North America.

Must be U.S. or Canadian citizen or legal resident lawfully eligible to receive stipend.

1309 — ORGAN HISTORICAL SOCIETY (E. Power Biggs Fellowship)

PO Box 26811
Richmond VA 23261
804/353-9226

AMOUNT: Funding of attendance at Annual Convention

DEADLINE(S): DEC 31

FIELD(S): Historic Pipe Organs

Fellowships are to encourage students and others to become involved in the appreciation of historic pipe organs by funding their attendance at the OHS Annual Convention.

3-4 awards annually. Contact Robert Zanca, Biggs Committee Chair, for an application.

1310 — QUEEN ELISABETH INTERNATIONAL MUSIC COMPETITION OF BELGIUM

Rue Aux Lanes 20
1000 Brussels BELGIUM
32 2 513 00 99
FAX: 32 2 514 32 97
E-Mail: info@concours-reine-elisabeth.be
Internet: www.concours-reine-elisabeth.be

AMOUNT: 50,000-500,000 BF

DEADLINE(S): JAN 15

FIELD(S): Singing

Categories: opera, oratio, & lied—Open to singers of all nationalities who are under thirty-two years of age. Applications must include certified copy of birth certificate, proof of nationality, curriculum vitae, a list with main repertoire, and three photographs, including one b&w glossy. During actual participation in concert, host family may accomodate singers free of charge. Semi-finalists not from Belgium are entitled to 50% reimbursement of travelling expenses.

Contact Ms. Cecile Ferriere for an application.

1311 — QUEEN MARIE JOSE (International Musical Prize Contest)

Box 19
CH-1252 Meinier
Geneva SWITZERLAND
Internet: musnov1.unige.ch/prixrmj/

AMOUNT: 15,000 Swiss francs

DEADLINE(S): MAY 31

FIELD(S): Music Composition

This competition is open to composers of all nationalities without age limit. It is designed to award a new work never performed before and is given every other year.

Not renewable. See website or write for yearly subject and official rules.

1312 — QUEEN SONJA INTERNATIONAL MUSIC COMPETITION (Voice Competition)

PO Box 5190 Majorstua
N-0302 Oslo NORWAY
+47/23367067, ext. 430
FAX: +47/22463630

AMOUNT: $40,000 approximate total prize money

DEADLINE(S): MAY 15

FIELD(S): Voice

Applicants must be between the ages of 17 and 31. In addition to cash awards for the 4 finalists (places 1-4) the Board of Directors will endeavor to provide them with solo engagements in Norway.

Write to above address for complete information and conditions for applications. NO SCHOLARSHIPS ARE GIVEN.

1313 — RIPON COLLEGE (Performance/Recognition Tuition Scholarships)

Admissions Office
300 Seward St., PO Box 248
Ripon WI 54971
920/748-8102 or 800/94-RIPON
E-Mail: adminfo@ripon.edu
Internet: www.ripon.edu

AMOUNT: $5,000-$10,000/yr.

DEADLINE(S): MAR 1

FIELD(S): Music; Forensics; Art; Theatre

Open to undergraduate and graduate students attending or planning to attend Ripon College. Purpose is to recognize and encourage academic potential and accomplishment in above fields. Interview, audition, or nomination may be required.

Renewable. Contact Office of Admission for an application.

1314 — ROYAL & SUN ALLIANCE (Ronnie Scott Scholarships for the Study of Jazz)

Parkside, Horsham
West Sussex RH12 1XA ENGLAND
0171 580 3545
Internet: www.royal-and-sunalliance.com/jazz/scholar

AMOUNT: 2,000 pounds sterling

DEADLINE(S): Varies

FIELD(S): Music: Jazz

Scholarships for young musicians, aged between 18 and 25, who have secured places in approved jazz courses in the United Kingdom.

More information on website. Call or write above organization for details.

1315 — ROYAL PHILHARMONIC SOCIETY (Julius Isserlis Scholarship)

10 Stratford Place
London W1N 9AE England
71/491-8110
FAX 71/493-7463

AMOUNT: 10,000 pounds sterling per year for two years

DEADLINE(S): Varies

FIELD(S): Music, Performing Arts (various categories)

Scholarship awarded by competition to enable music students in varying performance categories & nationalities to study outside of Great Britain. Applicants MUST permanently reside in the United Kingdom and be between the ages of 15 & 25.

Competition is held every two years (1997— violin, viola). Write to General Administrator at the above address for complete information.

1316 — RYAN DAVIES MEMORIAL FUND (Grants)

1 Squire Court
The Marina
Swansea, Wales, UK SA1 3XB
011-44-1792-301500 (phone/fax)

AMOUNT: up to $2,500 each

DEADLINE(S): MAY 30

FIELD(S): Performing Arts

Grants to assist performing artists (up to age 30) in any level of study up through postgraduate. Must be of Welsh extraction and demonstrate financial need.

8 awards annually. Contact Mike Evans, Secretary, at address above for complete information.

1317 — SAN ANGELO SYMPHONY SOCIETY (Sorantin Young Artist Award)

PO Box 5922
San Angelo TX 76902
915/658-5877
FAX: 915/653-1045

AMOUNT: $3,000 (winner); $1,000 (3 others); $400 (runners-up)

DEADLINE(S): OCT 15

FIELD(S): Music: Voice, Instrumental, Piano

A competition open to instrumentalists who have not reached their 28th birthdays by November 22nd and to vocalists who have not reached their 31st birthdays by November 22nd. Provides opportunity for a cash award with the symphony orchestra.

Contact the San Angelo Symphony Society for an application. Please note: There will not be a competition in 1999.

1318 — SAN FRANCISCO CONSERVATORY OF MUSIC (Various Scholarships)

1201 Ortega St.
San Francisco CA 94122
415/564-8086
Internet: www.sfcm.edu

AMOUNT: Varies

DEADLINE(S): Varies

FIELD(S): Music

A variety of scholarships for music students attending the San Francisco Conservatory of Music. Graduate assistantships are available for full-time candidates for Master of Music degree.

See website or write for detailed information.

1319 — SONOMA CHAMBOLLE-MUSIGNY SISTER CITIES, INC. (Henri Cardinaux Memorial Scholarship)

Chamson Scholarship Committee
PO Box 1633
Sonoma CA 95476-1633
707/939-1344
FAX: 707/939-1344
E-Mail: Baileysci@vom.com

AMOUNT: up to $1,500 (travel + expenses)

DEADLINE(S): JUL 15

FIELD(S): Culinary Arts; Wine Industry; Art; Architecture; Music; History; Fashion

Hands-on experience working in above or similiar fields & living with a family in small French village in Burgundy or other French city. Must be Sonoma County, CA, resident at least 18 years of age & be able to communicate in French. Transcripts, employer recommendation, photograph, & essay (stating why, where, & when) required.

1 award. Non-renewable. Also offers opportunity for candidate in Chambolle-Musigny to obtain work experience & cultural exposure in Sonoma, CA.

1320 — STEPHEN ARLEN MEMORIAL FUND (Grant Award)

English Nat'l Opera
London Coliseum
St. Martin's Lane
London WC2N 4ES ENGLAND

0171 836 0111
FAX: 0171 845 9274

AMOUNT: 1,500-3,000 pounds sterling

DEADLINE(S): FEB 28

FIELD(S): Opera; Ballet; Drama; Music

Grant is made annually to an artist under 30 years of age who has completed formal training and now wishes to pursue a career in the arts. Awarded to artist proposing an independent project rather than to fund further training. Must be United Kingdom resident.

Contact The Secretary at above address for an application.

1321 — STUDENT AWARDS AGENCY FOR SCOTLAND (Scottish Studentships for Advanced Postgraduate Study)

Gyleview House
3 Redheughs Rigg
South Gyle
Edinburgh EH12 9HH SCOTLAND UK
Written inquiry or 0131 244 5847

AMOUNT: Varies

DEADLINE(S): MAY 1

FIELD(S): Arts; Humanities

Studentships for full-time research for graduate and advanced post-graduate study. Candidates must have been ordinarily residents in the British Isles for at least three years immediately preceding the start of postgraduate study and ordinarily residents of Scotland at the time of application. They should not have been resident during the three years period wholly for the purpose of receiving full-time education.

Must apply through university. Citizenship restrictions for EU applicants may apply. Further particulars & application forms are available from the post-graduate section at the above address.

1322 — SUZUKI ASSOCIATION OF THE AMERICAS (Music Teacher Scholarships)

P.O. Box 17310
Boulder CO 80308
303/444-0948
FAX: 303/444-0984
E-Mail: Suzuki@rmi.net
Internet: www.suzukiassociation.org/ scholar1.htm

AMOUNT: $150-$500

DEADLINE(S): FEB 15

FIELD(S): Teaching: Music

Scholarships for music teachers and prospective music teachers who are full-time college students. Membership in above organization for a minimum of six months prior to application required. Visit website for details.

Request membership information or application from above location.

1323 — TENNESSEE ARTS COMMISSION (Individual Artists' Fellowships)

401 Charlotte Ave.
Nashville TN 37243-0780
615/741-1701

AMOUNT: $2,000

DEADLINE(S): JAN 11

FIELD(S): Visual Arts; Performing Arts; Creative Arts

Open to artists who are residents of Tennessee. Duration of award is one year. Applicants must be professional artists. FULL-TIME STUDENTS ARE NOT ELIGIBLE.

Write for complete information.

1324 — THE JOHN F. KENNEDY CENTER FOR THE PERFORMING ARTS (Awards, Fellowships, and Scholarships)

The Kennedy Center
Washington DC 20566-0001
202/416-8857
FAX: 202/416-8802
E-Mail: skshaffer@mail.kennedy-center.org
Internet: www.kennedy-center.org/education/actf

AMOUNT: Varies

DEADLINE(S): Varies

FIELD(S): Playwriting, stage design, and acting

Various scholarships and awards in the above fields.

Contact organization for a booklet: "The Kennedy Center American College Theater Festival" for details and/or visit website.

1325 — THE KOSCIUSZKO FOUNDATION (Annual Chopin Piano Competition)

15 East 65th St.
New York NY 10021
212/734-2130
Internet: www.kosciuszkofoundation.org/grants/chopin.htm

AMOUNT: Up to $2,500

DEADLINE(S): Varies

FIELD(S): Music: Piano-works of Chopin

A piano competition open to citizens and permanent residents of the U.S. and international students with valid student visas. Must be between the ages of 16 and 22. Preliminaries are held in the spring in Chicago and New York City. Must have ready a program of 60 minutes, mostly Chopin. Winners will perform recitals both in the U.S. and Poland.

Contact organization for exact requirements.

1326 — THE KOSCIUSZKO FOUNDATION (Marcella Sembrich Voice Competition)

15 East 65th St.
New York NY 10021-6595
212/734-2130 or 1-800/287-9956
FAX: 212/628-4552
E-Mail: thekf@pagasusnet.com
Internet: www.kosciuszkofoundation.org/grants/sembrich.htm

AMOUNT: Up to $1,000 + travel to various domestic and international recitals

DEADLINE(S): DEC 15

FIELD(S): Music: Voice

A voice competition open to citizens and permanent residents of the U.S. and international students with valid student visas. Must be between at least age 18. An entry fee of $35 is required.

For details of required repertoire and exact dates, check website and/or contact organization.

1327 — THE KUN SHOULDER REST, INC. (Listing of Music Competitions)

200 MacLaren St.
Ottawa Ontario CANADA K2P 0L6
+1 (613) 232-1861
FAX: +1 (613) 232-9771
E-Mail: kun@kunrest.com
Internet: www.kunrest.com

AMOUNT: Varies

DEADLINE(S): Varies

FIELD(S): Music: Various instruments and voice

This manufacturer of shoulder rests for violinists offers a listing of international competitions in various types of music, primarily (but not limited to) for players of stringed instruments.

The listing is available on the website above, or a list can be requested of the company.

1328 — THE NATIONAL ASSOCIATION OF NEGRO MUSICIANS, INC. (Brantley Choral Arranging Competition)

237 East 115th St.
P.O. Box S-011
Chicago IL 60628
773/779-1325
Internet: www.edtech.morehouse.edu/cgrimes/brantley.htm

AMOUNT: $500

DEADLINE(S): APR 30

FIELD(S): Music: choral arrangement

An annual competition for African-Americans talented in music arrangement. The work must be a choral arrangement of a Negro spiritual. Should be between 3-5 minutes in length. Arranger's name must

not appear on the score—use a "nom de plume." See more information on website.

There is a $25 entrance fee. For specific details, contact organization.

1329 — THE SINFONIA FOUNDATION (Research Assistance Grant)

10600 Old State Road
Evansville IN 47711-1399
800/473-2649
FAX: 812/867-0633
E-Mail: SFDN@Sinfonia.org
Internet: www.Sinfonia.org

AMOUNT: Up to $1,000

DEADLINE(S): MAY 1

FIELD(S): American Music

Graduate grants for research related to American music or music in America. Show evidence of previous successful writing and research or show evidence of unusual knowledge or competence in the field to be researched.

3-4 awards annually. Financial need NOT considered. See website or contact Maria Russell at above address for further information.

1330 — THE WALT DISNEY COMPANY (American Teacher Awards)

P.O. Box 9805
Calabasas CA 91372

AMOUNT: $2,500 (36 awards); $25,000 (Outstanding Teacher of the Year)

DEADLINE(S): FEB 15

FIELD(S): Teachers: athletic coach, early childhood, English, foreign language/ESL, general elementary, mathematics, performing arts, physical education/health, science, social studies, visual arts, voc/tech education

Awards for K-12 teachers in the above fields.

Teachers, or anyone who knows a great teacher, can write for applications at the above address.

1331 — THELONIOUS MONK INSTITUTE OF JAZZ (International Jazz Trumpet Competition)

5225 Wisconsin Ave. NW
Washington DC 20001
202/364-7272; FAX: 202/364-0176; Internet: jazzcentralstation.com/jcs/station/musicexp/foundati/tmonk/ijtc.html

AMOUNT: $20,000 (1st); $10,000 (2nd); $5,000 (3rd); $1,000 (additional finalists)

DEADLINE(S): AUG 5

FIELD(S): Music: Jazz trumpet

Competition for the world's most promising young musicians to receive college-level training by America's jazz masters, world-wide recognition, and performance opportunities. Musicians under contract with a major label are not eligible. Decisions based on audiotape presentation and application.

Application is on website or contact above organization for current information regarding application. Instructions for audiotape selections are very specific.

1332 — THELONIOUS MONK INSTITUTE OF JAZZ (International Jazz Composers Competition)

5225 Wisconsin Ave. NW
Washington DC 20001
202/364-7272
FAX: 202/364-0176
Internet: jazzcentralstation.com/jcs/station/musicexp/foundati/tmonk/ijtc.html

AMOUNT: $10,000 grand prize

DEADLINE(S): AUG 5

FIELD(S): Music: Composition for jazz trumpet

Competition presented by the Thelonious Monk Institute of Jazz and BMI to reward excellence in jazz composition. Composition to be written for trumpet. Can be written for up to five instruments with trumpet being the featured instrument. Solos for trumpet okay. Composers must not have had their jazz compositions recorded on a major label or recorded by a major jazz artist.

Application is on website or contact above organization for current information regarding application. Instructions for audiotape selections are very specific.

1333 — UNIVERSITY FILM & VIDEO ASSOCIATION (Carole Fielding Student Grants)

University of Baltimore
School of Comm.
1420 N. Charles Street
Baltimore MD 21201
410/837-6061

AMOUNT: $1,000 to $4,000

DEADLINE(S): MAR 31

FIELD(S): Film, video, multi-media production

Open to undergraduate/graduate students. Categories are narrative, experimental, animation, documentary, multi-media/Installation and research. Applicant must be sponsored by a faculty member who is an active member of the Univesity Film and Video Association.

Write to the above address for application and complete details.

1334 — UNIVERSITY OF ILLINOIS COLLEGE OF FINE & APPLIED ARTS (Kate Neal Kinley Fellowship)

College of Fine and Applied Arts, 608 E. Lorado Taft Dr., #117
Champaign IL 61820
217/333-1661

AMOUNT: $7,000 (3); $1,000 (3)

DEADLINE(S): FEB 1

FIELD(S): Art, Music, Architecture

Graduate fellowship for advanced study in the U.S. or abroad. Open to applicants with a bachelor's degree in the above areas. Preference given (but not limited) to applicants under 25 years of age and to graduates of the College of Fine and Applied Arts of the University of Illinois at Urbana-Champaign. Others are considered.

Write to Dr. Kathleen F. Conlin, Chair, Kinley Memorial Fellowship Committee, at above address. for complete information. Recipients may not participate in regular remunerative employment while engaged upon the Fellowship.

1335 — UNIVERSITY OF NEWCASTLE—DEPT. OF MUSIC (Runciman Arts Studentship)

Arts Faculty Secretary, Percy Bldg.,
Univ. of Newcastle
Newcastle upon Tyne, NE1 7RU ENGLAND UK
E-mail: susan.lloyd@ncl.ac.uk

AMOUNT: 4,000 pounds

DEADLINE(S): Varies

FIELD(S): The arts

This studentship provides financial support for a limited number of high quality postgraduate students pursing studies in the arts. All home applicants are required to apply for British Academy funding as well as for this one; oeverseas coandidates may apply and are required to apply to the british Academy under the Overseas Research Students Award scheme.

Contact school for details and application.

1336 — UNIVERSITY OF NORTH TEXAS (Music Scholarships)

College of Music Auditions
P.O. Box 311367
Denton TX 76203-6887
817/565-2791
Internet: www.unt.edu/scholarships/Musicgen.htm

AMOUNT: Varies

DEADLINE(S): Varies

FIELD(S): Music

Several scholarships for music students are offered at the University of North Texas. Specialties and eligibility requirements vary.

See website for more information. Contact school for details.

1337 — UTA ALUMNI ASSOCIATION (Sue & Art Mosby Scholarship Endowment in Music)

University of Texas at Arlington
Box 19457
Arlington TX 76019
Internet: www.uta.edu/alumni/scholar.htm

AMOUNT: $500

DEADLINE(S): Varies

FIELD(S): Music

Must be a full-time student in good standing at the University of Texas at Arlington. Must demonstrate financial need and musical ability with potential to complete UTA degree. Audition required.

1 award annually. Contact UTA Alumni Association for an application.

1338 — WAMSO (Young Artist Competition)

1111 Nicollet Mall
Minneapolis MN 55403
612/371-5654

AMOUNT: $3,000 1st prize + $2,250 WAMSO Achievement Award & performance with MN Orchestra

DEADLINE(S): OCT 15

FIELD(S): Piano & Orchestral Instruments

Competition offers 4 prizes and possible scholarships to high school and college students in schools in IN, IA, MN, MO, NE, ND, SD, WI, & the Canadian provinces of Manitoba & Ontario. Entrants may not have passed their 26th birthday on date of competition (which is usually held in January).

For list of repertoires and complete information, specify your instrument & write to address above.

1339 — WAVERLY COMMUNITY HOUSE INC. (F. Lammot Belin Arts Scholarships)

Scholarships Selection Committee
P.O. Box 142
Waverly PA 18471
717/586-8191

AMOUNT: $10,000

DEADLINE(S): DEC 15

FIELD(S): Painting; Sculpture; Music; Drama; Dance; Literature; Architecture; Photography

Applicants must have resided in the Abington or Pocono regions of Northeastern Pennsylvania. They must furnish proof of exceptional ability in their chosen field but no formal training in any academic or professional program.

U.S. citizenship required. Finalists must appear in person before the selection committee. Write for complete information.

PHILOSOPHY

1340 — AMERICAN COUNCIL OF LEARNED SOCIETIES (ACLS Fellowships)

Office of Fellowshops & Grants
228 E. 45th St.
New York NY 10017
Written Inquiry

AMOUNT: Up to $20,000

DEADLINE(S): SEP 30

FIELD(S): Humanities, Social Sciences, and other areas having predominately humanistic emphasis

Open to U.S. citizens or legal residents who hold the Ph.D or its equivalent. Fellowships are designed to help scholars devote 6 to 12 continuous months to full-time research.

Write for complete information.

1341 — ASSOCIATION FOR WOMEN IN SCIENCE EDUCATIONAL FOUNDATION (AWIS Predoctoral Awards)

1200 New York Ave. NW, Suite 650
Washington DC 20005
202/326-8940 or 800-886-AWIS
E-Mail: awis@awis.org
Internet: www.awis.org

AMOUNT: $1,000

DEADLINE(S): JAN 16

FIELD(S): Various Sciences and Social Sciences

Scholarships for female doctoral students. Summary page, description of research project, resume, references, transcripts, and biographical sketch required. US citizens may study at any graduate institution; non-citizens must study at US institutions.

5-10 awards annually. See website or write to above address for an application and complete information.

1342 — ASSOCIATION FOR WOMEN IN SCIENCE EDUCATIONAL FOUNDATION (AWIS Pre-doctoral Awards)

1200 New York Ave. NW, Suite 650
Washington DC 20005
202/326-8940 or 800/886-AWIS
E-Mail: awis@awis.org
Internet: www.awis.org

AMOUNT: $1,000

DEADLINE(S): JAN 16

FIELD(S): Various Sciences and Social Sciences

Scholarships for female doctoral students. Summary page, description of research project, resume, references, transcripts, and biographical sketch required. US citizens may study at any graduate institution; non-citizens must be enrolled in US institutions.

5-10 awards annually. See website or write to above address for an application and more information.

1343 — ASSOCIATION FOR WOMEN IN SCIENCE EDUCATIONAL FOUNDATION (Ruth Satter Memorial Award)

1200 New York Ave., NW, Suite 650
Washington DC 20005
202/326-8940 or 800/886-AWIS
E-Mail: awis@awis.org
Internet: www.awis.org

AMOUNT: $1,000

DEADLINE(S): JAN 16

FIELD(S): Various Sciences and Social Sciences

Scholarships for female doctoral students who have interrupted their education for at least three years to raise a family. Summary page, description of research project, resume, references, transcripts, biographical sketch, and letter from your department to confirm eligibility required. US citizens may study at any graduate institution; non-citizens must attend US institutions.

See website or write to above address for more information or an application.

1344 — ASSOCIATION FOR WOMEN IN SCIENCE EDUCATIONAL FOUNDATION (Ruth Satter Memorial Award)

1200 New York Ave. NW, Suite 650
Washington DC 20005
202/326-8940 or 800/886-AWIS
E-Mail: awis@awis.org
Internet: www.awis.org

AMOUNT: $1,000

DEADLINE(S): JAN 16

FIELD(S): Various Sciences and Social Sciences

Scholarships for female doctoral students who have interrupted their education three years or more to raise a family. Summary page, description of research project, resume, references, transcripts, biographical sketch, and proof of eligibility from department head required. US citizens may attend any graduate institution; non-citizens must be enrolled in US institutions.

See website or write to above address for more information or an application.

1345 — AUSTRALIAN FEDERATION OF UNIVERSITY WOMEN - WESTERN AUSTRALIA (Joyce Riley Bursary)

Bursary Liaison Officer
PO Box 48
Nedlands WA 6909 AUSTRALIA
Written Inquiry

AMOUNT: Aus$1,700 - Aus$2,750

DEADLINE(S): JUL 31

FIELD(S): Humanities; Social Sciences

To support women graduates of a Western Australian university to complete a higher degree or post-doctoral research in Humanities or Social Sciences at a recognized university in any country.

Membership in AFUW or in IFUW is required. Contact above location for further information.

1346 — AUSTRALIAN FEDERATION OF UNIVERSITY WOMEN - WESTERN AUSTRALIA (Joyce Riley Bursary)

Bursary Liaison Officer
PO Box 48
Nedlands WA 6009 AUSTRALIA
Written Inquiry

AMOUNT: Aus$1,700 - Aus$2,750

DEADLINE(S): JUL 31

FIELD(S): Humanities; Social Sciences

To support women graduates of a recognized university to complete a higher degree or post-doctoral research at a university in Western Australia.

Membership in AFUW or in IFUW is required. Write to above address for complete information.

1347 — B.M. WOLTMAN FOUNDATION (Lutheran Scholarships for Students of the Ministry and Teaching)

7900 U.S. 290 E.
Austin TX 78724
512/926-4272

AMOUNT: $500-$2,500

DEADLINE(S): Varies

FIELD(S): Theology (Lutheran Ministry); Teacher Education (Lutheran Schools)

Scholarships for undergrads and graduate students studying for careers in the Lutheran ministry or for teaching in a Lutheran school. For Texas residents attending, or planning to attend, any college in Texas.

45 awards. Renewable. Send for details.

1348 — BAPTIST UNION OF GREAT BRITAIN (Grants)

129 Broadway
Didcot Oxon OX11 8RT ENGLAND

01235 512077
FAX: 01235 811537

AMOUNT: Varies

DEADLINE(S): MAY 30

FIELD(S): Theology; Church History

Open to UK citizens attending accredited Baptist universities in the UK for graduate study or research in theology and church history.

Write for complete information.

1349 — BROSS PRIZE FOUNDATION (Scholarly Award)

Lake Forest College
555 N. Sheridan Rd.
Lake Forest IL 60045
847/735-5169
FAX: 847/735-6192

AMOUNT: $15,000 (1st prize); $9,500 (2nd); $4,000 (3rd)

DEADLINE(S): SEP 1

FIELD(S): Any Discipline & the Christian Religion

No restrictions, though usually awarded to established scholars or advanced graduate students. Manuscript must be in English and be at least 50,000 words and unpublished. Three copies of each manuscript must be submitted, and author's name should NOT appear on title page or manuscript; name & return address should be submitted on separate page. Also enclose necessary return postage.

3 awards, once every 10 years. Not renewable. Contact Ron Miller at above address for details.

1350 — CHRISTIAN CHURCH-DISCIPLES OF CHRIST (Disciple Chaplains' Scholarship)

PO Box 1986
Indianapolis IN 46206-1986
317/635-3100
FAX: 317/635-4426
E-Mail: cwebb@dhm.disciples.org

AMOUNT: Varies

DEADLINE(S): MAR 15

FIELD(S): Theology

Open to members of the Christian Church (Disciples of Christ) who are first year seminarians preparing for the ordained ministry. Must have above average GPA (minimum C+), be enrolled as a full-time student in an accredited school or seminary, and demonstrate financial need. Must submit transcripts and references.

Renewable. Contact Division of Homeland Ministries at above address for an application.

1351 — CHRISTIAN CHURCH-DISCIPLES OF CHRIST (James M. Philputt Memorial Scholarship/Loan)

PO Box 1986
Indianapolis IN 46206-1986
317/635-3100
FAX 317/635-4426
cwebb@dhm.disciples.org

AMOUNT: Varies

DEADLINE(S): MAR 15

FIELD(S): Theology

Open to Christian Church (Disciples of Christ) members who are preparing for the ordained ministry in a graduate/seminary program at the University of Chicago, Union Theological Seminary, Vanderbilt University, or Yale University. Must be enrolled as a full-time student, have an above average GPA (minimum C+), and demonstrate financial need. Must submit transcripts and references. Three years of service in professional ministry will repay entire scholarship/loan.

Renewable. Contact Division of Homeland Ministries at above address for an application.

1352 — CHRISTIAN CHURCH-DISCIPLES OF CHRIST (Katherine J. Schutze Memorial and Edwin G. & Lauretta M. Michael Scholarship)

PO Box 1986
Indianapolis IN 46206-1986
317/635-3100
FAX: 317/635-4426
E-Mail: cwebb@dhm.disciples.org

AMOUNT: Varies

DEADLINE(S): MAR 15

FIELD(S): Theology

Open to Christian Church (Disciples of Christ) members who are female seminary students preparing for the ordained ministry. Must be enrolled as a full-time student in an accredited school or seminary, have an above average GPA (minimum C+), and demonstrate financial need. Must submit transcripts and references. Schutze scholarship is open to all women who meet above criteria; Michael Scholarship is for minister's wives only.

Renewable. Contact Division of Homeland Ministries at above address for an application.

1353 — CHRISTIAN CHURCH-DISCIPLES OF CHRIST (Rowley/Ministerial Education Scholarship)

PO Box 1986
Indianapolis IN 46206-1986
317/635-3100
FAX 317/635-4426
E-Mail: cwebb@dhm.disciples.org

AMOUNT: Varies

DEADLINE(S): MAR 15

FIELD(S): Theology

Open to Christian Church (Disciples of Christ) members who are seminary students preparing for the ordained ministry. Must be enrolled as a full-time student in an accredited school or seminary, have an above average GPA (minimum C+), and demonstrate financial need. Must submit transcripts and references.

Renewable. Contact Division of Homeland Ministries at above address for an application.

1354 — CHRISTIAN CHURCH-DISCIPLES OF CHRIST (Star Supporter Scholarship/Loan)

PO Box 1986
Indianapolis IN 46206-1986
317/635-3100
FAX: 317/635-4426
E-Mail: cwebb@dhm.disciples.org

AMOUNT: $2,000

DEADLINE(S): MAR 15

FIELD(S): Theology

Open to Christian Church (Disciples of Christ) members who are Black/Afro-American students preparing for the ordained ministry. Must be enrolled as a full-time student at an accredited school or seminary, have an above average GPA (minimum C+), and demonstrate financial need. Must submit transcripts and references. Three years of service in a full-time professional ministry will repay the scholarship/loan.

100 awards annually. Renewable. Contact Division of Homeland Ministries at above address for an application.

1355 — CONCORDIA UNIVERSITY (Rose & Norman Goldberg Award and Maria Teresa Hausmann Bursary)

Philosophy Dept.
1455 de Maisonneuve Blvd. West
PR 202
Montreal Quebec H3G 1M8 CANADA
514/848-3809
FAX: 514/848-2812
E-Mail: awardsgs@vax2.concordia.ca

AMOUNT: $250; $750

DEADLINE(S): SEP 20

FIELD(S): Philosophy

The award and the bursary are each tenable by a full-time Master's student in the Philosophy program. They are awarded on the basis of financial need and the student's performance in the program. Recipients are chosen by the Department of Philosophy.

2 awards annually. Not renewable. Contact the Graduate Program Director in the Philosophy Department at Concordia University for an application.

1356 — CYNTHIA E. AND CLARA H. HOLLIS FOUNDATION

100 Summer St.
Boston MA 02110
Written inquiry

AMOUNT: Varies

DEADLINE(S): APR 1

FIELD(S): Nursing, social work, dental or medical technology, and religion

Scholarships for Massachusetts with preference given to students in the above fields. For undergraduates, graduates, voc-tech, and adult education. Must demonstrate financial need.

Send SASE to Walter E. Palmer, Esq., 35 Harvard St., Brookline, MA 02146 for application details. Scholarship forms are also available from the rector of All Saints Church, Brookline High School, and St. Mary's High School, all in Brookline, Massachusetts.

1357 — EMBASSY OF THE CZECH REPUBLIC (Scholarships for Czechs Living Abroad)

3900 Spring of Freedom St., NW
Washington DC 20008
202/274-9114
FAX: 202/966-8540
E-Mail: washington@embassy.mzv.cz
Internet: www.czech.cz/washington

AMOUNT: Varies

DEADLINE(S): APR 30

FIELD(S): Czech language & literature, history, theology, and/or ethnography

Scholarships for undergraduate and graduate citizens of the Czech Republic who are living in the U.S. The ideal applicant should use his/her knowledge for the benefit of the Czech community abroad.

20 annual awards. For a maximum of two semesters of study. See website or write/call for further information.

1358 — ENGEN SEMINARY FUND (Scholarships)

Evangelical Lutheran Church in America
Box 400
Presho SD 57568
605/895-2670

AMOUNT: Varies (according to income)

DEADLINE(S): SEP 30

FIELD(S): Lutheran Ministry

Scholarships for students who are members of the Evangelical Lutheran Church in America and attend an accredited ELCA seminary in preparation for the parish ministry. Must be seeking a Master's of Divinity at Luther Seminary, Wartburg Seminary, or Trinity Seminary. Preference given to students from South Dakota. Must demonstrate financial need.

12-80 awards annually. Renewable. Contact Pastor Lori L. Hope for more information; applications can be obtained from the financial aid offices of the three mentioned seminaries.

1359 — EPISCOPAL CHURCH FOUNDATION (Graduate Fellowship Program)

815 Second Ave.
3rd Floor
New York NY 10017-4564
212/697-2858 or 800/697-2858
FAX: 212/297-0142

AMOUNT: up to $17,500

DEADLINE(S): NOV 1

FIELD(S): Theology

Fellowships to encourage doctoral study by recent seminary graduates who wish to qualify for the teaching ministry of the Episcopal church in the US. Must be recommended by the dean.

3 new awards annually. Contact Dean's office at any accredited Episcopal seminary for application materials.

1360 — FELLOWS MEMORIAL FUND (Scholarship Loans)

Pensacola Junior College
1000 College Blvd.
Pensacola FL 32504-8998
904/484-1700

AMOUNT: Varies

DEADLINE(S): Varies

FIELD(S): Theology; Health

Loans for ministerial students of the Episcopal faith and others whose religious beliefs are not in substantial conflict with the faith and doctrines of the Episcopal Church. Must be graduate students and residents of one of the following Florida counties: Escambia, Santa Rosa, Okaloosa, or Walton. Qualified health programs include medicine, nursing, medical technology, radiography, respiratory therapy, physical therapy, and physician's assistant.

Loans are interest-free until four months after graduation. Thereafter, favorable interest rates will apply with the total to be repaid by the end of eleven years.

1361 — FORD FOUNDATION/NATIONAL RESEARCH COUNCIL (Predoctoral/ Dissertation Fellowships for Minorities)

2101 Constitution Ave.
Washington DC 20418
202/334-2872
E-Mail: infofell@nas.edu
Internet: http//www.nas.edu/fo/index.html

AMOUNT: $14,000 annual stipend + $6,000 grant to institution; $18,000 for dissertation fellowship

DEADLINE(S): NOV 3

FIELD(S): Most fields of study: sciences, humanities, engineering, behavioral science, social sciences, and computer science

Predoctoral and dissertation fellowships for students whose ethnicity is Alaskan Native, Black/ African American, Mexican American/Chicano, Native American Indian, Native Pacific Islander, or Puerto Rican. For research-based programs leading to careers in college teaching and research.

Contact above address or website.

1362 — FREEDOM FROM RELIGION FOUNDATION (Student Essay Contest)

PO Box 750
Madison WI 53701
608/256-5800
Internet: www.infidels.org/org/ffrf

AMOUNT: $1,000; $500; $250

DEADLINE(S): JUL 15

FIELD(S): Humanities; English; Education; Philosophy; Science

Essay contest on topics related to church-state entanglement in public schools or growing up a "freethinker" in religious-oriented society. Topics change yearly, but all are on general theme of maintaining separation of church and state. New topics available in February. For high school seniors & currently enrolled college/technical students. Must be US citizen.

Send SASE to address above for complete information. Please indicate whether wanting information for college competition or high school. Information will be sent when new topics are announced each February. See website for details.

1363 — GERMANISTIC SOCIETY OF AMERICA (Foreign Study Scholarships)

809 United Nations Plaza
New York NY 10017-3580
212/984-5330

AMOUNT: $11,000

DEADLINE(S): OCT 23

FIELD(S): History; Political Science; International Relations; Public Affairs; Language; Philosophy; Literature

Open to US citizens who hold a bachelor's degree. Must plan to pursue graduate study at a West German university. Selection based on proposed project, language fluency, academic achievement, and references.

Contact Germanistic Society for an application.

1364 — GLADYS KRIEBLE DELMAS FOUNDATION (Predoctoral & Postdoctoral Grants in Venice & the Veneto)

521 5th Avenue, Suite 1612
New York NY 10175-1699
212/687-0011
FAX: 212/687-8877
E-Mail: DelmasFdtn@aol.com
Internet: www.delmas.org

AMOUNT: $500-$12,500

DEADLINE(S): DEC 15

FIELD(S): Research of Venice and the former Venetian empire and study of contemporary Venetian society and culture.

Pre- and postdoctoral grants for historical research on Venice. Humanities and social sciences are eligible areas of study, including archaeology, architecture, art, bibliography, economics, history, history of science, law, literature, music, political science, religion, and theater.

Applicants must have experience in advanced research and be U.S. citizens/residents; grad students must have fulfilled all doctoral requirements except dissertation by Dec. 15.

1365 — GRAND AVENUE PRESBYTERIAN CHURCH (Davis Foute Eagleton Memorial Student Loan Fund)

Secretary
1601 N. Travis St.
Sherman TX 75092-3761
903/893-7428
E-Mail: Snyder@texoma.net

AMOUNT: Varies

DEADLINE(S): AUG 15 (fall); DEC 15 (spring)

FIELD(S): Theology; Christian Service

Open to full-time students of any Christian denomination in an accredited seminary, college, or university who desire to prepare for career in parish ministry, chaplain ministry, or other Christian service. Loans made in following priority: Members of Grand Ave. Presbyterian Church, current Austin College students/alumni, Presbyterians in Pres. schools, Presbyterians in other schools, non-Presbyterians in Pres. schools, and Presbyterians in graduate religion studies.

Contact Susan G. Snyder, Secretary, DFE Board, for an application.

1366 — HARDING FOUNDATION (Grants)

Box 130
Raymondville TX 78580
956/689-2706
FAX: 956/689-5740

AMOUNT: $3,000

DEADLINE(S): JAN 20

FIELD(S): Theology

For ministerial students enrolled in a master's program in theology leading to ordination in the United Methodist Church. Must desire to serve in the South Texas Conference or Southern District of the Rio Grande Conference of the Methodist Church. Financial need NOT a factor.

5-6 awards annually. Renewable up to 3 years. Contact Mrs. Glenn Harding, Corresponding Secretary, at the Harding Foundation for an application.

1367 — HASTINGS CENTER (International Visiting Scholars Program)

Route 9-D
Garrison NY 10524-5555
914/424-4040
FAX: 914/424-4545
E-Mail: mail@thehastingscenter.org

AMOUNT: $500-$1,000 stipend

DEADLINE(S): None

FIELD(S): Biomedical Ethics

Open to advanced scholars from eastern Europe and developing countries who have made a significant contribution to International Biomedical Ethics in their own countries. Fellowship for four- to six-weeks stay at Hastings Center. Stipend limited to those requiring financial assistance.

Write for complete information.

1368 — HISPANIC THEOLOGICAL INITIATIVE (Scholarships & Grants)

12 Library Place
Princeton NJ 08540
609/252-1721
FAX: 609/252-1738
E-Mail: hti@emory.edu
Internet: www.ptsem.edu

AMOUNT: $15,000 (faculty semester grant); $8,000 (faculty summer grant); $14,000 (dissertation); $12,000 (Ph.D.); $4,000 (M.Div.)

DEADLINE(S): DEC 5 (Postdoc./faculty); JAN 11 (M.Div. & Dissertation)

FIELD(S): Theology

Scholarships for Hispanic students studying theology through the Hispanic Theological Initiative. Also postdoctoral grants for faculty appointments will be awarded to junior, non-tenured faculty. Recipients must be committed to serving Latino faith communities in the US, Canada, and Puerto Rico.

25 M.Div. grants, 7 Ph.D. grants, and 7 dissertation grants awarded annually. See website or contact Zaida Maldonado Perez at HTI for an application.

1369 — INSTITUTE FOR ADVANCED STUDIES IN THE HUMANITIES (Visiting Research Fellowships)

Univ Edinburgh
Hope Park Square
Edinburgh EH8 9NW SCOTLAND UK
0131 650 4671
FAX: 0131 668 2252
E-Mail: iash@ed.ac.uk
Internet: www.ed.ac.uk/iash/homepage.html

AMOUNT: Non-stipendiary*

DEADLINE(S): DEC 1

FIELD(S): Arts; Social Sciences; Law; Music; Divinity

Postdoctoral research fellowships of between two and six months are tenable at the Institute for Advanced Studies in the Humanities. Based on academic record and publications. *Most fellowships are honorary, but limited support towards expenses is available to a small number of candidates. Fellows are allocated a study room within the Institute and hold one or two seminars during their tenure. Must submit research report at end of fellowship. No teaching required.

15 awards annually. Not renewable. Contact Mrs. Anthea Taylor for an application.

1370 — INSTITUTE FOR HUMANE STUDIES (Humane Studies Fellowship)

4084 University Dr., Ste. 101
Fairfax VA 22030-6812
703/934-6920 or 800/697-8799
FAX: 703/352-7535
E-Mail: ihs@gmu.edu
Internet: www.theihs.org

AMOUNT: up to $12,000

DEADLINE(S): DEC 1

FIELD(S): Social Sciences; Law; Humanities; Jurisprudence; Journalism

Awards are for graduate and advanced undergraduate students pursuing degrees at any accredited domestic or foreign school. Based on academic performance, demonstrated interest in classical liberal ideas, and potential to contribute to the advancement of a free society.

90 awards annually. Apply online or contact IHS for an application.

1371 — ISTITUTO ITALIANO PER GLI STUDI STORICI (Federico Chabod & Adolfo Omodeo Scholarships)

12 Via Benedetto Croce
80134 Naples ITALY
0039/81/551-7159
FAX: 0039/81/551-2390
E-Mail: iiss@iol.it

AMOUNT: 12 million lires

DEADLINE(S): SEP 30

FIELD(S): History; Philosophy; Literature; Arts; Economics

Open to non-Italian citizens who have completed a university degree in the humanities (history, philosophy, & arts) in a non-Italian university. Intended to allow young scholars to participate in the work of the Institute and to complete personal scholarly research with the help of teaching staff of the Institute. Must submit birth certificate, university diploma, scholarly work, program of studies with indication of language skills, research proposal, & reference.

Renewable. Contact Dott.ssa Marta Herling, Secretary, for an application.

1372 — ISTITUTO ITALIANO PER GLI STUDI STORICI - ITALIAN INSTITUTE FOR HISTORICAL STUDIES (Federico Chabod & Adolfo Omodeo Scholarships)

Via Benedetto Croce, 12
80134 Napoli ITALY
0039/81-5517159
FAX: 0039/81-5512390

AMOUNT: 12,000,000 Lira

DEADLINE(S): SEP 30

FIELD(S): Humanities; Social Sciences; History; Philosophy; Arts; Economics; Literature

For non-Italian citizens who have completed a university degree in Humanities dept. of a non-Italian university. Intended to allow young scholars to participate in the work of the Institute and to complete personal scholarly research with the help of teaching staff of the Institute. Must include birth certificate, proof of citizenship, university diploma, scholarly work, curriculum of studies w/ indication of language skills, research proposal, & reference letter.

2 awards annually. Contact Marta Herling, Secretary, at above address for an application.

1373 — KING'S COLLEGE LONDON (Cleave Cockerill Postgraduate Studentship)

Office of the Dean
Strand London WC2R 2LS ENGLAND
0171/836-5454
FAX: 0171/873-2344
E-Mail: r.a.burridge@kcl.ac.uk
Internet: http://www.kcl.ac.uk/kis/college/dean/

AMOUNT: Up to 1,000 pounds sterling

DEADLINE(S): None

FIELD(S): Theology

The studentship may be awarded by the council to a candidate in holy orders in the Church of England who wishes to proceed to a higher degree in Theology. Preference will be given to graduates of King's College.

Write for complete information.

1374 — MARK B. HOLZMAN GRADUATE EDUCATION FOUNDATION

Nine South DuPont Hwy.
Georgetown DE 19947
302/855-2816

AMOUNT: Varies

DEADLINE(S): MAY 31

FIELD(S): Dentistry, law,, medicine, and the ministry

Scholarships to residents of Delaware for graduate study in the above fields.

Send SASE to Connie E. Mears, c/o Wilmington Trust Co., at above address for details.

1375 — NATIONAL FEDERATION OF THE BLIND (Humanities Scholarship)

805 5th Avenue
Grinnell IA 50112
515/236-3366

AMOUNT: $3,000

DEADLINE(S): MAR 31

FIELD(S): Humanities (Art, English, Foreign Languages, History, Philosophy, Religion)

Open to legally blind students pursuing or planning to pursue a full-time postsecondary education in the US. Scholarships are awarded on basis of academic excellence, service to the community, and financial need. Must include transcripts and two letters of recommendation. Membership NOT required.

1 award annually. Renewable. Contact Mrs. Peggy Elliot, Scholarship Committee Chairman, for an application.

1376 — NATIONAL HUMANITIES CENTER (Lilly Fellowships in Religion and the Humanities)

PO Box 12256
Research Triangle Park NC 27709-2256
919/549-0661
FAX: 919/990-8535
E-Mail: nhc@ga.unc.edu
Internet: www.nhc.rtp.nc.us:8080

AMOUNT: Stipend ($35,000-$50,000) + Travel Expenses (for fellow & dependents)

DEADLINE(S): OCT 15

FIELD(S): Religion & the Humanities

Postdoctoral fellowships for the study of religion by humanistic scholars from fields other than religion and theology. Fellows will form the core of a monthly seminar on religion and the humanities. Curriculum vitae, 1,000-word proposal, and three letters of recommendation are required.

3-4 awards annually. Contact NHC for application materials.

1377 — NEWBERRY LIBRARY (Long-Term Fellowships)

60 West Walton Street
Chicago IL 60610-3380
312/943-9090
E-Mail: research@newberry.org
Internet: www.newberry.org

AMOUNT: Up to $30,000

DEADLINE(S): JAN 20

FIELD(S): Humanities, History, & related fields

Six postdoctoral fellowship programs are available for scholars wishing to use the Library's collection for writing or research. Fellowships last six to eleven months, and each have slightly different requirements.

See website for details and an application or write to above address.

1378 — NEWBERRY LIBRARY (Monticello College Foundation Fellowship For Women)

60 West Walton Street
Chicago IL 60610-3380
312/255-3660
E-Mail: research@newberry.org
Internet: www.newberry.org

AMOUNT: $12,500

DEADLINE(S): JAN 20

FIELD(S): Humanities, History, Study of Women

Six-month post-doctoral fellowships for women in the early stages of their academic careers. For research, writing, and participation in the intellectual life of the Library. Applicant's topic must be related to Newberry's collections; preference given to proposals concerned with the study of women.

See website for application or write to above address.

1379 — NEWBERRY LIBRARY (Short-Term Fellowships)

60 West Walton Street
Chicago IL 60610-3380
312/943-9090
E-Mail: research@newberry.org
Internet: www.newberry.org

AMOUNT: $800-$1,500/month

DEADLINE(S): MAR 1

FIELD(S): Humanities, History, & related fields

Nine programs for postdoctoral scholars or doctoral students at the dissertation stage. Study varies from two weeks to three months and is for those making use of Newberry's collections. Each program has slightly different requirements.

See website for details and applications or write to above address.

1380 — NEWBERRY LIBRARY (Special Fellowships)

60 West Walton Street
Chicago IL 60610-3380
312/255-3666
E-Mail: research@newberry.org
Internet: www.newberry.org

AMOUNT: Varies

DEADLINE(S): DEC 15

FIELD(S): Humanities, History, & related fields

Fellowships for three months to one year for doctoral or postdoctoral students to study in Germany, France, or Great Britain in fields related to Newberry's collections. Some deadlines JAN 20th. Specific locations are: Wolfenb, ttel, Germany; Ecole Nationale des Chartes, Paris, France; and the British Academy, Great Britain.

See website for more details and applications or write to above address.

1381 — NORTH AMERICAN BAPTIST SEMINARY (Financial Aid Grants)

1525 S. Grange Ave.
Sioux Falls SD 57105
605/336-6588

AMOUNT: Up to $1,200

DEADLINE(S): AUG 1

FIELD(S): Theology

Financial aid grants are open to students who are enrolled full-time at North American Baptist Seminary. Financial need is a consideration.

Approx 70 awards per year. Write for complete information.

1382 — OMAHA PRESBYTERIAN SEMINARY FOUNDATION (Apollos Program)

2120 S. 72nd St., Ste. 427
Omaha NE 68124
402/397-5138
FAX: 402/397-4944
E-Mail: ompbysemfo@aol.com

AMOUNT: $2,000-$3,000/yr.

DEADLINE(S): MAY 1

FIELD(S): Theology

Scholarships and grants are open to members of the Presbyterian Church (USA) who are pursuing master's of divinity studies at one of ten Presbyterian seminaries in the US. Must be candidate/inquirer under care of Presbytery. Financial need NOT a factor.

36 awards annually. Renewable up to 2 years. Contact Richard H. Skelley for an application.

1383 — PEW YOUNGER SCHOLARS PROGRAM (Graduate Fellowships)

G-123 Hesburgh Library, University of Notre Dame
Notre Dame IN 46556
219/631-4531
FAX: 219/631-8721
E-Mail: Karen.M.Heinig.2@nd.edu
Internet: www.nd.edu/~pesp/pew/PYSPHistory.html

AMOUNT: $13,000

DEADLINE(S): NOV 30

FIELD(S): Social Sciences, Humanities, Theology

Program is for use at any Christian undergraduate school and most seminaries. Check with organization to see if your school qualifies. Apply during senior year. Recipients may enter a competition in which ten students will be awarded a $39,000 ($13,000/yr.) fellowship for three years of dissertation study. For use at top-ranked Ph.D. programs at outstanding universities.

NOT for study in medicine, law business, performing arts, fine arts, or the pastorate. Check website and/or organization for details.

1384 — ROBERT SCHRECK MEMORIAL FUND (Grants)

C/O Texas Commerce Bank-Trust Dept
PO Drawer 140
El Paso TX 79980
915/546-6515

AMOUNT: $500 - $1500

DEADLINE(S): JUL 15; NOV 15

FIELD(S): Medicine; Veterinary Medicine; Physics; Chemistry; Architecture; Engineering; Episcopal Clergy

Grants to undergraduate juniors or seniors or graduate students who have been residents of El Paso County for at least two years. Must be U.S. citizen or legal resident and have a high grade point average. Financial need is a consideration.

Write for complete information.

1385 — ROBSON MCLEAN WS (Brown Downie Church of Scotland Fellowship)

28 Abercromby Place
Edinburgh EH3 6QF Scotland UK
0131 556 0556
FAX: 0131 556 9939
E-Mail: info@robson-mclean.co.uk
Internet: www.robson-mclean.co.uk

AMOUNT: 7,000 pounds sterling

DEADLINE(S): MAY 1 (even years; next award in 2000)

FIELD(S): Theology

Fellowship is to encourage special study. Competition is open to postgraduates attending any of the theological colleges of the Church of Scotland who are graduates in arts of a Scottish university or have distinguished themselves in some area. Applicants must be preparing for the ministry with the Church of Scotland.

1-2 awards every two years. Renewable. Financial need NOT considered. See website or contact W.F. MacTaggart, Clerk, at above address for more information.

1386 — SOCIAL SCIENCE RESEARCH COUNCIL (Religion & Immigration Fellowship Program)

810 Seventh Ave, 31st Fl.
New York NY 10019
212/377-2700
FAX: 212/377-2727
E-Mail: religion@ssrc.org
Internet: www.ssrc.org

AMOUNT: $15,000 (doctoral); $20,000 (postdoctoral)

DEADLINE(S): JAN 12

FIELD(S): Religion & Immigration

Six-month postdoctoral and twelve-month doctoral dissertation awards are open to US citizens, permanent residents, and international students matriculated in a US university. Purpose is to foster innovative research that will advance theoretical understandings of the relationship between religion and the incorporation of immigrants into American society.

See website or contact SSRC for an application.

1387 — SOCIETY FOR THE PSYCHOLOGICAL STUDY OF SOCIAL ISSUES (Gordon Allport Intergroup Relations Prize)

PO Box 1248
Ann Arbor MI 48106-1248
Phone/TTY: 313/662-9130
FAX: 313/662-9130
E-Mail: spssi@spssi.org
Internet: www.spssi.org

AMOUNT: $1,000

DEADLINE(S): DEC 31

FIELD(S): Sociology/Intergroup Relations

Annual award for the best paper or article on intergroup relations. Originality of the contribution, whether theoretical or empirical, is given special consideration. The research area encompassing intergroup relations includes such dimensions as age, sex, socioeconomic status, and race. Entries can be either papers published during the current year or unpublished manuscripts. Send five copies of entry.

Contact SPSSI for details. Applications available on website. SPSSI DOES NOT OFFER SCHOLARSHIPS—REQUESTS FOR FINANCIAL AID WILL NOT BE ANSWERED.

1388 — THE AMERICAN SCHOOLS OF ORIENTAL RESEARCH (George A. Barton Fellowship)

Boston University
656 Beacon St.
Boston MA 02215-2010
617/353-6570
FAX: 617/353-6575
E-Mail: asor@bu.edu
Internet: www.asor.org/ASORint.html

AMOUNT: $2,000 + room and board

DEADLINE(S): SEP 30

FIELD(S): Theology

Fellowships for doctoral or postdoctoral students with recent Ph.D.s or seminarians in theology. For persons from any country. For study at the Albright Institute in Israel.

Contact above location for detailed informationl.

1389 — THE HEATH EDUCATION FUND (Scholarships for Ministers, Priests, and Missionaries)

Barnett Bank, N.A.
P.O. Box 40200
Jacksonville FL 32203-0200
904/464-2877

AMOUNT: $750-$1,000

DEADLINE(S): JUL 31

FIELD(S): Ministry, missionary work, or social work

Scholarships to high school graduates from the southeastern U.S. who wish to study in the above fields. Eligible states of residence: Alabama, Florida, Georgia, Kentucy, Louisiana, Maryland, Mississippi, North & couth Carolina, Tennessee, Virginia, and West Virginia.

Write to Barnett Bank's Trust Co., N.A., at above address for details and guidelines. Send SASE and letter with brief background of applicant, field of study, religious denomination and reason for request. Preference to Methodists or Episcopalians.

1390 — TRENT UNIVERSITY (Graduate Teaching/Research Assistantships)

P.O. Box 4800
Graduate Studies Officer
Peterborough Ontario CANADA K9J 7B8
705/748-1245

AMOUNT: $3,500 per term

DEADLINE(S): FEB 15

FIELD(S): Anthropology, Geography, Archaeology, Biology, Canadian Studies, Philosophy, Cultural Studies, Computer Science, Mathematics, Physics, Chemistry, Environmental Science/Studies

Teaching/research assistantships at Trent University in the above fields. Open to masters and doctoral candidates. Tenable for up to 4 terms spanning 2-3 years of study.

80 awards per year. Write for complete information.

1391 — UNITARIAN UNIVERSALIST ASSOCIATION (Graduate Theological Scholarships)

Attn: Ministerial Dept.
25 Beacon St.
Boston MA 02108
617/742-2100 Ext. 403
FAX: 617/725-4979
E-Mail: cmay@uua.org
Internet: www.uua.org

AMOUNT: $800-$2,000

DEADLINE(S): APR 15

FIELD(S): Theology

Financial aid to students who have completed first year of theological program at grad level. Must have registered their intentions with the Unitarian Universalist Association of Congregations to become Unitarian Universalist ministers.

Write for complete information.

1392 — UNIVERSITY OF MARYLAND INSTITUTE FOR ADVANCED COMPUTER STUDIES (Graduate Fellowships)

University of Maryland, UMIACS
College Park MD 20742
301/405-6722
E-Mail: fellows@umiacs.umd.edu
Internet: www.umiacs.umd.edu/fellow.html

AMOUNT: $18,000/yr. + tuition, health benefits, office space, etc.

DEADLINE(S): JAN 15

FIELD(S): Computer science, electrical engineering, geography, philosophy, linguistics, business, and management

Two-year graduate fellowships in the above fields for full-time students interested in interdisciplinary applications of computing at the Univ. of Maryland. After the first two years, external research funds may be provided to continue support for the fellow, depending upon satisfactory progress and the availability of funds.

Three new awards each year. Selection will be based on academic excellence and compatibility between students' research interest and those of UMIACS faculty.

1393 — UNIVERSITY OF OXFORD (Hall-Houghton Studentship)

University Offices
Wellington Square
Oxford OX1 2JD ENGLAND
01865-270001
FAX: 01865-270708

AMOUNT: 500 pounds sterling

DEADLINE(S): FEB 1

FIELD(S): Theology

For University of Oxford post-graduate study of the Greek New Testament or Septuagint version of the Hebrew Scriptures in relation to the Hebrew Bible and the Greek Testament or the Syriac versions of the Holy Scriptures.

Not normally awarded to those in their first year of graduate work. Awards renewable. Contact Secretary; Hall-Houghton Trustees; at address above for complete information.

1394 — UNIVERSITY OF OXFORD (Squire and Marriott Bursaries)

University Offices
Wellington Square
Oxford OX1 2JD England
0865-270117

AMOUNT: Varies

DEADLINE(S): MAR; SEP

FIELD(S): Theology

Applicants must have the intention of offering themselves for ordination in the Church of England or any church in communion therewith and be in need of financial assistance for their university education.

Approximately 6 bursaries per year. Renewable. For study at the University of Oxford. Contact Mrs. E.A. MacAllister, Assistant to the Secretary, Board of the Faculty of Theology (address above) for complete information.

1395 — WILLIAM HONYMAN GILLESPIE TRUST (Scholarships)

Tods Murray WS
66 Queen St.
Edinburgh EH2 4NE SCOTLAND UK
0131 226 4771
FAX: 0131 225 3676

AMOUNT: 1,000 pounds sterling

DEADLINE(S): MAY 15

FIELD(S): Theology

Must be a graduate student of theology at a Scottish university. Financial need NOT a factor.

1-2 awards annually. Renewable. Contact D. Mcletchie for an application.

1396 — WOMEN OF THE EVANGELICAL LUTHERAN CHURCH IN AMERICA (The Belmer-Flora Prince Scholarships)

8765 West Higgins Road
Chicago IL 60631-4189
800/638-3522, ext. 2747
FAX: 773/380-2419
E-Mail: womnelca@elca.org

AMOUNT: $2,000 max.

DEADLINE(S): MAR 1

FIELD(S): Christian Service

Assists women who are members of the ELCA studying for ELCA service abroad that does not lead to a church-certified profession. Must be a US citizen at least 21 years of age who has experienced an interruption of two or more years since completion of high school. Academic records of any coursework completed in last five years as well as written confirmation of admission from educational institution are required.

Renewable for an additional year. Contact Faith Fretheim, Program Director, for an application.

1397 — WOODROW WILSON NATIONAL FELLOWSHIP FOUNDATION (Charlotte W. Newcombe Dissertation Fellowships)

CN 5281
Princeton NJ 08543-5281
609/452-7007
FAX: 609/452-0066
E-Mail: charoltte@woodrow.org
Internet: www.woodrow.org

AMOUNT: $15,500

DEADLINE(S): DEC 6

FIELD(S): Theology; Social Sciences; Humanities; Education

Open to Ph.D. candidates writing on topics of religious and ethical values. Must be pursuing full-time dissertation writing at graduate schools in the US, having completed all pre-dissertation requirements.

35 awards annually. Not renewable. See website or contact WWNFF for an application. Notification made in April.

SCHOOL OF NATURAL RESOURCES

1398 — AMERICAN FOUNDATION FOR THE BLIND (Paul W. Ruckes Scholarship)

11 Penn Plaza, Ste. 300
New York NY 10001
212/502-7661 or TDD 212/502-7771
E-Mail: juliet@afb.org
Internet: www.afb.org

AMOUNT: $1,000

DEADLINE(S): APR 30

FIELD(S): Engineering, computer, physical, or life sciences

Open to blind or visually impaired undergraduate or graduate students pursuing degrees in the above fields. U.S. citizenship required.

Write to the above address or visit website for complete information.

1399 — AMERICAN INDIAN SCIENCE AND ENGINEERING SOCIETY (A.T. Anderson Memorial Scholarship)

PO Box 9828
Albuquerque NM 87119-9828
505/765-1052
FAX: 505/765-5608
E-Mail: scholarships@aises.org
Internet: www.aises.org/scholarships

AMOUNT: $1,000-$2,000

DEADLINE(S): JUN 15

FIELD(S): Medicine; Natural Resources; Science; Engineering

Open to undergraduate and graduate students who are at least 1/4 American Indian or recognized as member of a tribe. Must be member of AISES ($10 fee), enrolled full-time at an accredited institution, and demonstrate financial need.

Renewable. See website or contact Patricia Browne for an application and/or membership information.

1400 — ASIAN INSTITUTE OF TECHNOLOGY (AIT Scholarship Program)

Development Office
PO Box 4, Klongluang
Pathumthani 12120 THAILAND
(66)(2) 516-0110-44 or 524-5032
FAX: (66)(2) 516-2126
E-Mail: ascao@ait.ac.th
Internet: www.ait.ac.th

AMOUNT: US $12,600-$37,960

DEADLINE(S): FEB 15; JUN 15; OCT 15

FIELD(S): Advanced Technologies; Civil Engineering; Environment, Resources, & Development; Business Management

Scholarships and grants open to citizens of Asian countries who are accepted by the institute as a master's or doctotal candidate. Selection is based on academic criteria, practical experience, gender, and country of origin; priority to Mekong Region countries and Asian countries of the former USSR.

250 awards annually. Contact AIT for an application.

1401 — AUSTRIAN CULTURAL INSTITUTE (Max Kade Foundation Grants)

950 Third Ave., 20th Fl.
New York NY 10022
212/759-5165 or +43/1/51581-253
FAX: 212/319-9636
E-Mail: desk@aci.org
Internet: www.austriaculture.net

AMOUNT: Varies

DEADLINE(S): Varies

FIELD(S): Medicine; Natural Sciences; Engineering

Open to young Austrian scientists with several years of experience at universities or institutions. Must demonstrate capacity to pursue independent teaching or research activities in the US. Proficiency in English required.

See website or contact ACI for an application kit, or write to Osterreichische Akademie der Wissenschaften, Kommission fur Max Kade Stipendien, Dr. Ignaz Seipel-Platz 2, A-1010 Vienna, Austria.

1402 — BOEING (Polish Graduate Student Scholarship Program)

Phone for details
314/234-2149

AMOUNT: Tuition, books, and fees for three years

DEADLINE(S): Varies

FIELD(S): Scientific and technical fields

Scholarships for students from Poland to pursue graduate studies in scientific and technical areas at American colleges or universities.

Call Jim Schlueter at above telephone number.

1403 — CHARLES A. AND ANNE MORROW LINDBERGH FOUNDATION (Grants for Research Projects)

2150 Third Ave., N, Ste. 310
Anoka MN 55303-2200
612/576-1596
FAX: 612/576-1664
E-Mail: lindbergh@isd.net
Internet: www.isd.net/lindbergh

AMOUNT: $10,580 (max.)

DEADLINE(S): JUN 15

FIELD(S): Aviation; Aerospace; Agriculture; Education; Arts; Humanities; Biomedical Research; Exploration; Health & Population Sciences; Intercultural Communication; Waste Disposal Minimization & Management.; Adaptive Technology; Conservation

Open to individuals whose proposed projects represent a significant contribution toward the achievement of balance between the advance of technology and preservation of the natural environment. Financial need NOT a factor. Funding is NOT for tuition.

10 awards annually. See website for application.

1404 — COMMISSAO INVOTAN/ICCTI (NATO Science Fellowships Program)

Av. D. Carlos I
126-6 o
1200 Lisbon PORTUGAL
+351.1.396 0313 (dir)
FAX: +351.1.397 5144

SCHOOL OF NATURAL RESOURCES

AMOUNT: Varies
DEADLINE(S): JAN 1; MAR 1
FIELD(S): Sciences and engineering

Doctoral and postdoctoral fellowships in almost all scientific areas, including interdisciplinary areas. For citizens of NATO countries and NATO's Cooperation Partner countries who wish to study or do research in Portugal.

May be renewable under certain terms. Approximately 40 new fellowships each year. Write for complete information.

1405 — COMMISSAO INVOTAN/ICCTI (NATO Science Fellowships-Advanced and Senior Programs)

Av. D. Carlos I
126 o
1200 Lisbon PORTUGAL
+351.1.396 0313 (DIR)
FAX: +351.1.397 5144

AMOUNT: Varies
DEADLINE(S): APR 1; OCT 1
FIELD(S): Natural and social sciences and engineering

Doctoral and postdoctoral fellowships in almost all scientific areas, social sciences, and engineering. For citizens of Portugal who wish to study and/or do research in another NATO member country.

May be renewable under certain terms. Approximately 50 new fellowships each year. Write for complete information.

1406 — COMMISSAO INVOTAN/ICCTI (NATO Senior Guest Fellowship)

Av. D. Carlos I
126 o
1200 Lisbon PORTUGAL
+351.1.396 0313 (dir)
FAX: +351.1.397 5144

AMOUNT: Varies
DEADLINE(S): APR 1; OCT 1
FIELD(S): Sciences and engineering

Postdoctoral fellowships open to senior scientists from other NATO countries and from countries of central & eastern Europe, NATO's Cooperation Partners. Must have high professional standing and wish to spend three weeks to a year in Portugal.

20 annual awards. Write for complete information.

1407 — FORD FOUNDATION/NATIONAL RESEARCH COUNCIL (Predoctoral/Dissertation Fellowships for Minorities)

2101 Constitution Ave.
Washington DC 20418
202/334-2872

E-Mail: infofell@nas.edu
Internet: http//www.nas.edu/fo/index.html

AMOUNT: $14,000 annual stipend + $6,000 grant to institution; $18,000 for dissertation fellowship
DEADLINE(S): NOV 3
FIELD(S): Most fields of study: sciences, humanities, engineering, behavioral science, social sciences, and computer science

Predoctoral and dissertation fellowships for students whose ethnicity is Alaskan Native, Black/African American, Mexican American/Chicano, Native American Indian, Native Pacific Islander, or Puerto Rican. For research-based programs leading to careers in college teaching and research.

Contact above address or website.

1408 — FREEDOM FROM RELIGION FOUNDATION (Student Essay Contest)

PO Box 750
Madison WI 53701
608/256-5800
Internet: www.infidels.org/org/ffrf

AMOUNT: $1,000; $500; $250
DEADLINE(S): JUL 15
FIELD(S): Humanities; English; Education; Philosophy; Science

Essay contest on topics related to church-state entanglement in public schools or growing up a "freethinker" in religious-oriented society. Topics change yearly, but all are on general theme of maintaining separation of church and state. New topics available in February. For high school seniors & currently enrolled college/technical students. Must be US citizen.

Send SASE to address above for complete information. Please indicate whether wanting information for college competition or high school. Information will be sent when new topics are announced each February. See website for details.

1409 — INSTITUTE FOR ADVANCED STUDY (Post-doctoral Fellowship Awards)

Olden Lane
Princeton NJ 08540
609/734-8000

AMOUNT: Varies according to school
DEADLINE(S): Varies
FIELD(S): Historical Studies; Social Sciences; Natural Sciences; Mathematics

Post-doctoral fellowships at the institute for advanced study for those whose term can be expected to result in work of significance and individuality.

150-160 fellowships per academic year although some can be extended. Request application materials from school's administrative officer.

1410 — JAPAN SOCIETY FOR THE PROMOTION OF SCIENCE (Post-doctoral Fellowships for Foreign Researchers)

Jochi-Kioizaka Bldg., 6-26-3 Kioi-cho
Chiyoda-Ku
Tokyo 102 JAPAN
+81-3-3263-1721
Telex: J32281
FAX: +81-3-3263-1854

AMOUNT: 270,000 yen per month
DEADLINE(S): SEP 25; MAY 23
FIELD(S): Humanities; Social Sciences; Natural Sciences; Engineering; Medicine

Post-doctoral fellowships for advanced study & research in Japan.

Write for complete information

1411 — JEWISH FEDERATION OF METROPOLITAN CHICAGO (Academic Scholarship Program for Studies in the Sciences)

One South Franklin St.
Chicago IL 60606
Written inquiry

AMOUNT: Varies
DEADLINE(S): MAR 1
FIELD(S): Mathematics, engineering, or science

Scholarships for college juniors, seniors, and graduate students who are Jewish and are residents of Chicago, IL and Cook County.

Academic achievement and financial need are considered. Applications accepted after Dec. 1.

1412 — LAND AND WATER RESOURCES R&D CORPORATION (Postgraduate Scholarships)

GPO Box 2182
Canberra ACT 2601 AUSTRALIA
02/6257 3379
FAX: 02/6257 3420
E-Mail: public@lwrrdc.gov.au
Internet: www.lwrrdc.gov.au

AMOUNT: $25,000/yr.
DEADLINE(S): JUN
FIELD(S): Natural Resources

Postgraduate scholarships for Australian citizens in the area of land, water, and vegetation resources to study/research in Australia. Financial need NOT a factor.

4 awards annually. Renewable up to three years. Contact Dr. Phil Price at LWRDC for an application. Award is made in September.

1413 — LAND AND WATER RESOURCES R&D CORPORATION (Travelling Fellowships)

GPO Box 2182
Canberra ACT 2601 AUSTRALIA
02/6257 3379
FAX: 02/6257 3420
E-Mail: public@lwrrdc.gov.au
Internet: www.lwrrdc.gov.au

AMOUNT: $10,000 (max.)

DEADLINE(S): JUN

FIELD(S): Natural Resources

Postgraduate fellowships for Australian researchers in the area of land, water, and vegetation resources, with overseas agencies to visit; LWRDC assists with financial and other support. Financial need NOT a factor.

6 awards annually. Not renewable. Contact Dr. Phil Price at LWRDC for an application. Award is made in September.

1414 — LAND AND WATER RESOURCES R&D CORPORATION (Visiting Fellowships)

GPO Box 2182
Canberra ACT 2601 AUSTRALIA
02/6257 3379
FAX: 02/6257 3420
E-Mail: public@lwrrdc.gov.au
Internet: www.lwrrdc.gov.au

AMOUNT: $10,000 (max.)

DEADLINE(S): JUN

FIELD(S): Natural Resources

Postgraduate fellowships for travel to Australia by overseas scientists in the area of land, water, and vegetation resources. Usually, fellows come at invitation of an Australian researcher; LWRDC assists with financial and other support. Financial need NOT a factor.

6 awards annually. Not renewable. Contact Dr. Phil Price at LWRDC for an application. Award is made in September.

1415 — NATIONAL RESEARCH COUNCIL OF CANADA (Research Associateships)

Research Associates Office
Ottawa Ontario K1A 0R6 CANADA
613/993-9150
FAX: 613/990-7669
Internet: www.nrc.ca/careers

AMOUNT: $39,366 Canadian

DEADLINE(S): None

FIELD(S): Natural Sciences; Engineering

Two-year research associateships are tenable at NRCC labs throughout Canada. Open to recent Ph.D.s in natural sciences or recent master's or Ph.D.s in engineering. Degrees should have been received within the last five years. Preference given to Canadians.

Renewable. See website or contact NRCC for an application.

1416 — NATIONAL SCIENCES AND ENGINEERING RESEARCH COUNCIL OF CANADA (Graduate Scholarships)

Scholarships/Fellowships Division
350 Albert Street
Ottawa Ontario K1A 1H5 CANADA
613/996-3769
FAX: 613/996-2589
E-Mail: schol@nserc.ca
Internet: http://www.nserc.ca

AMOUNT: $15,700/year for 1st & 2nd years at masters or Ph.D level; $17,400/year (Ph.D level ONLY) 3rd & 4th years

DEADLINE(S): NOV 24

FIELD(S): Natural Sciences, Engineering, Biology, or Chemistry

Open to Canadian citizens or permanent residents who have earned or will soon earn a bachelors or masters degree in science or engineering. Academic excellence and research aptitude are considerations.

Write for complete information.

1417 — NATIONAL SCIENCES AND ENGINEERING RESEARCH COUNCIL OF CANADA (Postdoctoral Fellowships)

Scholarships/Fellowships Division
350 Albert Street
Ottawa Ontario K1A 1H5 CANADA
613/996-3762
FAX: 613/996-2589
E-Mail: schol@nserc.ca
Internet: http://www.nserc.ca

AMOUNT: Individually negotiated

DEADLINE(S): Varies—average: $43,000

FIELD(S): Natural Sciences, Engineering, Biology, or Chemistry

Open to Canadian citizens or permanent residents who hold doctoral degrees in science or engineering. Academic excellence and research aptitude are considerations.

Write for complete information.

1418 — NORTH ATLANTIC TREATY ORGANIZATION (NATO Science Fellowships for Non-U.S. Citizens)

Boulevard Leopold III
Brussels BELGIUM
2/707-4231
E-Mail: science.fell@hq.nato.int
Internet: www.nato.int/science

AMOUNT: Varies (with country)

DEADLINE(S): Varies (with country)

FIELD(S): Most fields of Scientific study

Graduate and postdoctoral fellowships are available in almost all scientific fields, including interdisciplinary areas. Open to citizens of NATO member countries and NATO partner countries who wish to study and/or do research in another NATO member country or NATO partner country.

Program administered in each NATO country by a National Administrator. Write address above for address of your country's administrator.

1419 — OPEN SOCIETY INSTITUTE (Environmental Management Fellowships)

400 West 59th St.
New York NY 10019
212/548-0600 or 212/757-2323
FAX: 212/548-4679 or 212/548-4600
Internet: www.soros.org/efp.html

AMOUNT: Fees, room, board, living stipend, textbooks, international transportation, health insurance

DEADLINE(S): NOV 15

FIELD(S): Earth sciences, natural sciences, humanities (exc. language), anthropology, sociology, mathematics, or engineering

Two-year fellowships for use in selected universities in the U.S. for international students. For students/professionals in fields related to environmental policy, legislation, and remediation techniques applicable to their home countries.

To apply, contact your local Soros Foundation or Open Society Institute. Further details on website.

1420 — RESOURCES FOR THE FUTURE (Gilbert F. White Fellowship Program)

1616 P Street NW
Washington DC 20036-1400
202/328-5067
Internet: www.rff.org

AMOUNT: Based upon current salary + research support, office, and up to $1,000 for moving or living expenses.

DEADLINE(S): FEB 26

FIELD(S): Social Sciences; Natural Resources; Energy; Environment

Postdoctoral resident fellowships for professionals in the above fields who wish to devote eleven months to scholarly work on a social or policy problem in these. Faculty members on sabbatical encouraged to apply.

All information is on website. Address inquiries and applications to Coordinator for Academic Programs. NO fax submissions.

1421 — RESOURCES FOR THE FUTURE (Joseph L. Fisher Dissertation Fellowships)

1616 P Street NW
Washington DC 20036-1400
202/328-5000
Internet: www.rff.org

AMOUNT: $12,000/yr

DEADLINE(S): FEB 26

FIELD(S): Economics and other Social Sciences related to environment, natural resources, or energy

Fellowship to graduate students in the final year of their dissertatio research in the above fields.

All information is on website. NO fax submissions.

1422 — RESOURCES FOR THE FUTURE (RFF Summer Internship Program)

1616 P Street NW
Washington DC 20036-1400
202/328-5000
E-Mail: lewis@rff.org or voigt@rff.org
Internet: www.rff.org

AMOUNT: $375/week

DEADLINE(S): MAR 12

FIELD(S): Social Sciences, Natural Resources, Energy, Environment

Resident paid summer internships for undergraduate and graduate students for research in the above fields. Divisions are Center for Risk Management, Energy and Natural Resources, and Quality of the Environment. Candidates should have outstanding policy analysis and writing skills. For both U.S. and non-U.S. citizens.

All information is on website. Address inquiries and applications to Sue Lewis (Energy & Natural Resources and Quality of the Environment) or Marilyn Voigt (Center for Risk Management). NO fax submissions.

1423 — RESOURCES FOR THE FUTURE (Walter O. Spofford, Jr., Memorial Internship)

1616 P Street NW
Washington DC 20036-1400
202/328-5000
E-Mail: moran@rff.org
Internet: www.rff.org

AMOUNT: Individually negotiated

DEADLINE(S): MAR 12

FIELD(S): Chinese environmental issues in the areas of Social Sciences, Natural Resources, Energy, Environment

Resident paid internships for graduate students for research in the above fields. Candidates should have outstanding policy analysis and writing skills.

All information is on website. Address inquiries and applications to Mary Moran, Coordinator for Academic Programs. NO fax submissions.

1424 — THE BRITISH COUNCIL (Postgraduate Scholarships to Mexico)

10 Spring Gardens
London SW1A 2BN ENGLAND UK
+44 (0) 171 930 8466
FAX: +44 (0) 161 957 7188
E-Mail: education.enquiries@britcoun.org
Internet: www.britcoun.org/mexico/mexschol.htm

AMOUNT: Varies

DEADLINE(S): Varies

FIELD(S): Science and technology

The British Council in Mexico offers the opportunity, funded by the Mexican Council for Science and Technology (CONACYT), to British citizens to study in Mexico. Another way to receive information is to contact: CONACYT, Av. Constituyentes No. 1046, Col. Lomas Altas, C.P. 11950, Mexico, D.F. or E-mail to informa@mailer.main.conacyt.mx.

Contact with the source of information in London or in Mexico for details. In Mexico, the British Council Information Centre E-mails are: carmina.ramon@bc-mexico.sprint.com (Mexico City) or teresa.riggen@bc-mexico.sprint.com (Guadalajara).

1425 — THE BRITISH COUNCIL (Scholarships for Citizens of Mexico)

10 Spring Gardens
London SW1A 2BN ENGLAND UK
+44 (0) 171 930 8466
FAX: +44 (0) 161 957 7188
E-Mail: education.enquiries@britcoun.org
Internet: www.britcoun.org/mexico/mexschol.htm

AMOUNT: Varies

DEADLINE(S): Varies

FIELD(S): Social sciences, applied sciences, technology

The British Council in Mexico offers approximately 100 scholarshps per year in the above fields for undergraduates and graduates to study in the United Kingdon. Good level of English language retired.

The website listed here gives more details. For more information, contact: leticia.magana@bc-mexico.sprint.com. or contact organization in London.

1426 — THE DAPHNE JACKSON MEMORIAL FELLOWSHIPS TRUST (Fellowships in Science/Engineering)

School of Physical Sciences
Dept. of Physics
University of Surrey
Guildford, Surrey
GU2 5XH ENGLAND UK

01483 259166
FAX: 01483 259501
E-Mail: J.Woolley@surrey.ac.uk
Internet: www.sst.ph.ic.ac.uk/trust/

AMOUNT: Varies

DEADLINE(S): Varies

FIELD(S): Science or engineering, including information sciences

Fellowships to enable well-qualified and highly motivated scientists and engineers to return to appropriate careers following a career break due to family comitments. May be used on a flexible, part-time basis. Tenable at various U.K. universities.

See website and/or contact organization for details.

1427 — THE NORWAY-AMERICA ASSOCIATION (The Norwegian Marshall Fund)

Drammensveien 20C
N-0255 Oslo 2 NORWAY
011 47-22-44-76-83

AMOUNT: Up to $5,000

DEADLINE(S): Varies

FIELD(S): All fields of study

The Marshall Fund was established in 1977 as a token of Norway's gratitude to the U.S. for support after WWII. Objective is to promote research in Norway by Americans in science and humanities. For U.S. citizens.

Contact above location for further information.

1428 — TROPICAL AGRICULTURAL RESEARCH AND HIGHER EDUCATION CENTER - CATIE (Education for Development and Conservation Program)

7170 Turrialba
COSTA RICA
506/556-1016
FAX: 506/556-0914
E-Mail: gpaez@catie.ac.cr
Internet: www.catie.ac.cr

AMOUNT: US$32,000 (scholarship); US$16,750 (tuition assistance)

DEADLINE(S): DEC

FIELD(S): Agriculture; Natural Resource Sciences

For postgraduate students from member countries of CATIE to attend CATIE. Countries are Mexico, Belize, Guatemala, El Salvador, Honduras, Nicaragua, Costa Rica, Panama, Venezuela, Dominican Republic, and Colombia. Must have a university degree, successful completion of the admission process, minimum of two years of experience, and must work for a relevant technical school or academic agricultural organization, public or private. Must demonstrate financial need.

25 awards annually. Not renewable. Contact Dr. Gilberto Paez at CATIE for an application.

1429 — US ARMS CONTROL AND DISARMAMENT AGENCY (William C. Foster Visiting Scholars Program)

320 21st St. NW
Room 5726
Washington DC 20451
703/647-8090

AMOUNT: Salary + per diem

DEADLINE(S): JAN 31

FIELD(S): Arms Control; Nonproliferation; Disarmament

Program open to faculty of recognized institutions of higher learning who wish to lend their expertise in areas relevant to the ACDA for a period of one year. U.S. citizenship or permanent residency required.

Write for complete information.

1430 — WOODS HOLE OCEANOGRAPHIC INSTITUTION (Research Fellowships in Marine Policy and Ocean Management)

360 Woods Hole Road
Woods Hole MA 02543-1541
508/289-2219
FAX: 508/457-2188
E-Mail: mgately@whoi.edu
Internet: www.whoi.edu

AMOUNT: Varies

DEADLINE(S): FEB 16

FIELD(S): Social Sciences, Law, Natural Sciences

For professionals in the above fields who wish to apply their training to investigations of problems involving the use of the oceans. WHOI's objective is to provide a year-long advanced learning experience in ocean policy problems involving the interdisciplinary application of social science and natural science to marine policy problems. Fields currently emphasized: economics, statistics, public policy, natural resource management, and international relations.

For an application/more information, contact the Education Office, Clark Laboratory 223, MS #31, at above address.

AGRICULTURE

1431 — ABBIE SARGENT MEMORIAL SCHOLARSHIP INC. (Scholarships)

295 Sheep Davis Road
Concord NH 03301
603/224-1934
FAX: 603/228-8432

AMOUNT: $400

DEADLINE(S): MAR 15

FIELD(S): Agriculture; Veterinary Medicine; Home Economics

Open to New Hampshire residents who are high school graduates with good grades and character. For undergraduate or graduate study. Must be legal resident of U.S. and demonstrate financial need.

Three annual awards. Renewable with reapplication. Write for complete information.

1432 — AMERICAN FOUNDATION FOR THE BLIND (Paul W. Ruckes Scholarship)

11 Penn Plaza, Ste. 300
New York NY 10001
212/502-7661 or TDD 212/502-7771
E-Mail: juliet@afb.org
Internet: www.afb.org

AMOUNT: $1,000

DEADLINE(S): APR 30

FIELD(S): Engineering, computer, physical, or life sciences

Open to blind or visually impaired undergraduate or graduate students pursuing degrees in the above fields. U.S. citizenship required.

Write to the above address or visit website for complete information.

1433 — AMERICAN ORCHID SOCIETY (Grants for Orchid Research)

6000 S. Olive Ave.
West Palm Beach FL 33405-4199
561/585-8666

AMOUNT: $500-$12,000/yr.

DEADLINE(S): JAN 1; AUG 1

FIELD(S): Orchids: Biological Research, Floriculture, & Horticulture

Grants are for experimental projects and fundamental and applied research on orchids. Qualified graduate students with appropriate interests may apply for grants in support of their research if it involves or applies to orchids. Postgraduates may apply ONLY on behalf of the accredited institution of higher learning or appropriate research institute they represent.

Renewable up to 3 years. Contact Orchid Society for an application.

1434 — ASIAN INSTITUTE OF TECHNOLOGY (AIT Scholarship Program)

Development Office
PO Box 4, Klongluang
Pathumthani 12120 THAILAND
(66)(2) 516-0110-44 or 524-5032
FAX: (66)(2) 516-2126
E-Mail: ascao@ait.ac.th
Internet: www.ait.ac.th

AMOUNT: US $12,600-$37,960

DEADLINE(S): FEB 15; JUN 15; OCT 15

FIELD(S): Advanced Technologies; Civil Engineering; Environment, Resources, & Development; Business Management

Scholarships and grants open to citizens of Asian countries who are accepted by the institute as a master's or doctotal candidate. Selection is based on academic criteria, practical experience, gender, and country of origin; priority to Mekong Region countries and Asian countries of the former USSR.

250 awards annually. Contact AIT for an application.

1435 — BEDDING PLANTS FOUNDATION, INC. (Barbara Carlson & Dosatron International, Inc. Scholarships)

PO Box 280
East Lansing MI 48826-0280
517/333-4617
FAX: 517/333-4494
E-Mail: BPFI@aol.com
Internet: www.bpfi.org

AMOUNT: $1,000

DEADLINE(S): MAY 15

FIELD(S): Horticulture

Open to graduate and undergraduate students already attending a four-year college/university who are majoring in horticulture or related field. For Carlson Scholarship, should intend to intern or work for public gardens. Cash award, with checks issued jointly in name of recipient and college/institution he or she will attend for current year. Must submit references & transcripts.

2 awards annually. See website or send printed self-addressed mailing label (or self-addressed, stamped envelope) to BPFI after January 1st for an application. Recipients will be notified.

1436 — BEDDING PLANTS FOUNDATION, INC. (Ed Markham International Scholarship)

PO Box 280
East Lansing MI 48826-0280
517/333-4617
FAX: 517/333-4494
E-Mail: BPFI@aol.com
Internet: www.bpfi.org

AMOUNT: $1,000

DEADLINE(S): MAY 15

FIELD(S): Horticulture AND International Business

Open to graduate and undergraduate students already attending a four-year college/university who are majoring in horticulture or related field. Should wish to further understanding of domestic & international marketing through international horticulturally related study, work, or travel. Cash award, with checks issued jointly in name of recipient and college/institution he or she will attend for current year. Must submit references & transcripts.

1 award annually. See website or send printed self-addressed mailing label (or self-addressed, stamped envelope) to BPFI after January 1st for an application. Recipient will be notified.

1437 — BEDDING PLANTS FOUNDATION, INC. (Fran Johnson Non-Traditional Scholarship)

PO Box 280
East Lansing MI 48826-0280
517/333-4617
FAX: 517/333-4494
E-Mail: BPFI@aol.com
Internet: www.bpfi.org

AMOUNT: $500-$1,000
DEADLINE(S): MAY 15
FIELD(S): Horticulture; Floriculture

Open to undergraduate & graduate students at 2- or 4-year college/university in US or Canada. Must be US or Canadian citizen with major in horticulture or related field, specifically bedding plants or other floral crops. Must be reentering an academic program after an absence of at least 5 years. Cash award, with checks issued jointly in name of recipient and college/institution he or she will attend for current year. Must submit references & transcripts.

1 award annually. See website or send printed self-addressed mailing label (or self-addressed, stamped envelope) to BPFI after January 1st for an application. Recipient will be notified.

1438 — BEDDING PLANTS FOUNDATION, INC. (Harold Bettinger Memorial Scholarship)

PO Box 280
East Lansing MI 48826-0280
517/333-4617
FAX: 517/333-4494
E-Mail: BPFI@aol.com
Internet: www.bpfi.org

AMOUNT: $1,000
DEADLINE(S): MAY 15
FIELD(S): Horticulture AND Business/Marketing

Open to graduate and undergraduate students already attending a four-year college/university who have either a horticulture major with business/marketing emphasis OR a business/marketing major with horticulture emphasis. Cash award, with checks issued jointly in name of recipient and college/institution he or she will attend for current year. Must submit references & transcripts.

1 award annually. See website or send printed self-addressed mailing label (or self-addressed, stamped envelope) to BPFI after January 1st for an application. Recipient will be notified.

1439 — BEDDING PLANTS FOUNDATION, INC. (James K. Rathmell, Jr. Memorial Scholarship)

PO Box 280
East Lansing MI 48826-0280
517/333-4617
FAX: 517/333-4494
E-Mail: BPFI@aol.com
Internet: www.bpfi.org

AMOUNT: $2,500 (max.)
DEADLINE(S): MAY 15
FIELD(S): Horticulture; Floriculture

Open to undergraduates entering junior or senior year at a four-year college/university, and graduate students. Must have plans to work/study outside of US in the field of floriculture or horticulture, with preference to those planning to work/study six months or longer. Cash award, with checks issued jointly in name of recipient and college/institution he or she will attend for current year. Must submit references & transcripts.

1 award annually. See website or send printed self-addressed mailing label (or self-addressed, stamped envelope) to BPFI after January 1st for an application. Recipient will be notified.

1440 — BEDDING PLANTS FOUNDATION, INC. (John Carew Memorial Scholarship)

PO Box 280
East Lansing MI 48826-0280
517/333-4617
FAX: 517/333-4494
E-Mail: BPFI@aol.com
Internet: www.bpfi.org

AMOUNT: $1,500
DEADLINE(S): MAY 15
FIELD(S): Horticulture

Open to graduate students at an accredited university in the US or Canada who are majoring in horticulture or related field. Should have specific interest in bedding or flowering potted plants. Cash award, with checks issued jointly in name of recipient and college/institution he or she will attend for current year. Must submit references & transcripts.

1 award annually. See website or send printed self-addressed mailing label (or self-addressed, stamped envelope) to BPFI after January 1st for an application. Recipient will be notified.

1441 — BEDDING PLANTS FOUNDATION, INC. (Research Grants)

PO Box 280
East Lansing MI 48826-0280
517/333-4617
FAX: 517/333-4494
E-Mail: BPFI@aol.com
Internet: www.bpfi.org

AMOUNT: Varies
DEADLINE(S): JAN 15
FIELD(S): Horticulture

Open to horticulturists and researchers in related sciences to pursue research projects in the US and Canada. Projects should be pertinent to the bedding and potted plant industry. Areas of interest include garden performance, greenhouse waste, water quality/alkalinity control, biocontrol methods, production techniques, pest control, and disease problems. Recipients must submit progress reports twice a year. Ten copies each of application and proposal required.

Renewable. See website or send printed self-addressed mailing label (or self-addressed, stamped envelope) to BPFI for an application.

1442 — BEDDING PLANTS FOUNDATION, INC. (Seed Companies Scholarship)

PO Box 280
East Lansing MI 48826-0280
517/333-4617
FAX: 517/333-4494
E-Mail: BPFI@aol.com
Internet: www.bpfi.org

AMOUNT: $1,000
DEADLINE(S): MAY 15
FIELD(S): Horticulture

Open to undergraduate students entering junior or senior year at a four-year college/university—and graduate students—who are majoring in horticulture or related field, with the intention of pursuing a career in the seed industry. Cash award, with checks issued jointly in name of recipient and college/institution he or she will attend for current year. Must submit references & transcripts.

1 award annually. See website or send printed self-addressed mailing label (or self-addressed, stamped envelope) to BPFI after January 1st for an application. Recipient will be notified.

1443 — BOEING (Polish Graduate Student Scholarship Program)

Phone
Phone for details
314/234-2149

AMOUNT: Tuition, books, and fees for three years
DEADLINE(S): Varies
FIELD(S): Scientific and technical fields

Scholarships for students from Poland to pursue graduate studies in scientific and technical areas at American colleges or universities.

Call Jim Schlueter at above telephone number.

1444 — CHARLES A. AND ANNE MORROW LINDBERGH FOUNDATION (Grants for Research Projects)

2150 Third Ave., N, Ste. 310
Anoka MN 55303-2200
612/576-1596
FAX: 612/576-1664
E-Mail: lindbergh@isd.net
Internet: www.isd.net/lindbergh

AMOUNT: $10,580 (max.)

DEADLINE(S): JUN 15

FIELD(S): Aviation; Aerospace; Agriculture; Education; Arts; Humanities; Biomedical Research; Exploration; Health & Population Sciences; Intercultural Communication; Waste Disposal Minimization & Management.; Adaptive Technology; Conservation

Open to individuals whose proposed projects represent a significant contribution toward the achievement of balance between the advance of technology and preservation of the natural environment. Financial need NOT a factor. Funding is NOT for tuition.

10 awards annually. See website for application.

1445 — FLORIDA FEDERATION OF GARDEN CLUBS, INC. (FFGC Scholarships for College Students)

6065 21st St., SW
Vero Beach FL 32968-9427
561/778-1023
Internet: www.ffgc.org

AMOUNT: $1,500-$3,500

DEADLINE(S): MAY 1

FIELD(S): Ecology; Environmental Issues; Land Management; City Planning; Environmental Control; Horticulture; Landscape Design; Conservation; Botany; Forestry; Marine Biology; Floriculture; Agriculture

Various scholarships for Florida residents with a "B" average or better enrolled full-time as a junior, senior, or graduate student at a Florida college or university.

See website or contact Melba Campbell at FFGC for an application.

1446 — FORD FOUNDATION/NATIONAL RESEARCH COUNCIL (Postdoctoral Fellowship for Minorities)

National Research Council
2101 Constitution Ave.
Washington DC 20418
202/334-2860
E-Mail: infofell@nas.edu
Internet: http//www.nas.edu/fo/index.html

AMOUNT: $25,000 + relocation and research allowance

DEADLINE(S): JAN 3

FIELD(S): Life and physical sciences, mathematics, engineering sciences, behavioral and social sciences, and the humanities

For U.S. citizens who received a Ph.D or Sc.D in the last 7 years and who are Native Amer. Indian or Alaskan, Black/African American, Mexican American, Native Pacific Islander, or Puerto Rican and who are or plan to be in a teaching or research career.

Contact above website or address for complete information.

1447 — FORD FOUNDATION/NATIONAL RESEARCH COUNCIL (Predoctoral/Dissertation Fellowships for Minorities)

2101 Constitution Ave.
Washington DC 20418
202/334-2872
E-Mail: infofell@nas.edu
Internet: http//www.nas.edu/fo/index.html

AMOUNT: $14,000 annual stipend + $6,000 grant to institution; $18,000 for dissertation fellowship

DEADLINE(S): NOV 3

FIELD(S): Most fields of study: sciences, humanities, engineering, behavioral science, social sciences, and computer science

Predoctoral and dissertation fellowships for students whose ethnicity is Alaskan Native, Black/African American, Mexican American/Chicano, Native American Indian, Native Pacific Islander, or Puerto Rican. For research-based programs leading to careers in college teaching and research.

Contact above address or website.

1448 — GARDEN CLUB OF AMERICA (GCA Interchange Fellowship)

14 East 60th Street
New York NY 10022-1046
212/753-8287
FAX: 212/753-0134
Internet: www.gcamerica.org

AMOUNT: Varies (tuition, housing + allowance)

DEADLINE(S): NOV 15

FIELD(S): Horticulture and Landscape Architecture

Funds one graduate academic year for a British student wishing to study in the US. The purpose of this program is to foster British-American relations through the interchange of scholars in horticulture, landscape architecture, and related fields.

1 award annually. Send a self-addressed, stamped envelope to Ms. Shelley Burch at above address for complete information/an application.

1449 — GARDEN CLUB OF AMERICA (Katharine M. Grosscup Scholarships)

Cleveland Botanical Garden
11030 East Blvd.
Cleveland OH 44106
FAX: 216/721-2056
Internet: www.gcamerica.org

AMOUNT: up to $3,000

DEADLINE(S): FEB 15

FIELD(S): Horticulture & related fields

Financial assistance to college juniors, seniors, or graduate students, preferably from (though not restricted to) Ohio, Pennsylvania, West Virginia, Michigan, and Indiana. Purpose is to encourage the study of horticulture and related fields.

Funds several students annually. See website or contact Mrs. Nancy Stevenson at above address for more information/an application.

1450 — GARDEN CLUB OF AMERICA (Martin McLaren Scholarship)

14 East 60th Street
New York NY 10022-1046
212/753-8287
FAX: 212/753-0134
Internet: www.gcamerica.org

AMOUNT: Varies (tuition, housing + allowance)

DEADLINE(S): NOV 15

FIELD(S): Horticulture and Landscape Architecture

A work-study program for an American graduate student to study at universities and botanical gardens in the UK. The purpose of this program is to foster British-American relations through the interchange of scholars in horticulture, landscape architecture, and related fields.

1 award annually. Send a self-addressed, stamped envelope to Ms. Shelley Burch at above address for complete information/an application.

1451 — GOLF COURSE SUPERINTENDENTS ASSOCIATION OF AMERICA (GCSAA Essay Contest)

1421 Research Park Dr.
Lawrence KS 66049-3859
785/832-3678
FAX: 785/832-3665
E-Mail: psmith@gcsaa.org
Internet: www.gcsaa.org

AMOUNT: $2,000 (total prizes)

DEADLINE(S): MAR 31

FIELD(S): Turfgrass Science; Agronomy; Golf Course Management

Contest open to undergraduate and graduate students pursuing degrees in one of the above fields.

Essays should be 7-12 pages long and should focus on the golf course management profession.

See website or contact Pam Smith at GCSAA for details.

1452 — GOLF COURSE SUPERINTENDENTS ASSOCIATION OF AMERICA (GCSAA Watson Fellowships)

1421 Research Park Dr.
Lawrence KS 66049-3859
785/832-3678
FAX: 785/832-3665
E-Mail: psmith@gcsaa.org
Internet: www.gcsaa.org

AMOUNT: $5,000+

DEADLINE(S): OCT 1

FIELD(S): Golf Course Management

Available to candidates for master's and doctoral degrees in fields related to golf course management. The goal of this program is to identify tomorrow's leading teachers and researchers.

See website or contact Pam Smith at GCSAA for an application.

1453 — GOLF COURSE SUPERINTENDENTS ASSOCIATION OF AMERICA (Valderrama Award)

1421 Research Park Dr.
Lawrence KS 66049-3859
785/832-3678
FAX: 785/832-3665
E-Mail: psmith@gcsaa.org
Internet: www.gcsaa.org

AMOUNT: $7,000

DEADLINE(S): MAR

FIELD(S): Golf/Turfgrass Management

Awarded to a citizen of Spain who wishes to study golf/turfgrass management in the United States. Selection is based on academic achievement, interest in the profession, and leadership potential.

See website or contact Pam Smith at GCSAA for an application.

1454 — HERB SOCIETY OF AMERICA, INC. (Research Grant Program)

9019 Kirtland Chardon Rd.
Kirtland OH 44094
440/256-0514
FAX: 440/256-0541
Internet: www.herbsociety.org

AMOUNT: $5,000 (max.)

DEADLINE(S): JAN 31

FIELD(S): Herbal Research

Open to graduate and postgraduate students with a proposed program of scientific, academic, or artistic investigation of herbal plants. This grant is for research only and can be terminated at any time. Financial need NOT a factor.

1-2 awards annually. Contact Herb Society for an application.

1455 — HUBBARD FARMS CHARITABLE FOUNDATION

P.O. Box 505
Walpole NH 03608-0505
603/756-3311

AMOUNT: Varies

DEADLINE(S): APR 1; OCT 1

FIELD(S): Poultry science, genetics, and other life sciences

Scholarships are for financially needy students at universities that the foundation trustees consider to be leaders in the field of progress in technology and efficiency of production of poultry products.

Send SASE to Jane F. Kelly, Clerk, at above address for current application guidelines.

1456 — INSTITUTE FOR THE STUDY OF WORLD POLITICS (Dissertation Fellowships)

1755 Massachusetts Ave. NW
Washington DC 20036
202/588-9797
Internet: fundforpeace.org/iswp.htm

AMOUNT: Varies

DEADLINE(S): FEB 16

FIELD(S): International Relations; Environmental Issues; Population Studies (Social Science aspects); Human Rights; Arms Control; Third World Development; Agricultural Development; Public Health, etc.

For doctoral candidates conducting dissertation research in above areas to promote scholarly examination of political, economic, and social issues that affect the security, well-being, and dignity of the peoples of the world. Financial need is a consideration. For citizens of any country.

Write for complete information.

1457 — INSTITUTE FOR THE STUDY OF WORLD POLITICS (Dorothy Danforth Compton Fellowships)

1755 Massachusetts Ave. NW
Washington DC 20036
202/588-9797
Internet: fundforpeace.org/iswp.htm

AMOUNT: Varies

DEADLINE(S): MAR 16

FIELD(S): International Relations; Environmental Issues; Population Studies (Social Science aspects); Human Rights; Arms Control; Third World Development; Agricultural Development; Public Health, etc.

For masters or doctoral candidates researching in the above areas to promote scholarly examination of political, economic, and social issues that affect the security, well-being, and dignity of the peoples of the world. Must be African American, Hispanic American, and Native American students who are U.S. citizens and studying in U.S. institutions. Financial need is a consideration.

Write for complete information.

1458 — INTERNATIONAL CROPS RESEARCH INSTITUTE FOR THE SEMI-ARID TROPICS (Training & Fellowships Program)

ICRISAT PO
Patancheru-502 324
Medak Dist., AP INDIA
91-40-3296161
FAX: 91-40-241239
E-Mail: icrisat@cgiar.org
Internet: www.icrisat.org

AMOUNT: Varies

DEADLINE(S): None

FIELD(S): Agricultural Sciences

Open to holders of BSC or MSC degrees in agriculture or related fields who are qualified for admission to a postgraduate degree program. For thesis research on agreed projects in fields related to agriculture in the semi-arid tropics. Must demonstrate financial need.

20-25 awards annually. Contact ICRISAT for an application.

1459 — INTERNATIONAL INSTITUTE OF TROPICAL AGRICULTURE (Graduate Research Fellowship Program)

OYO Road PMB 5320
Ibadan NIGERIA
234-22-241-2626
FAX: 234-22-241-2221

AMOUNT: Varies

DEADLINE(S): MAR; SEPT

FIELD(S): Agriculture

For graduate students from sub-Saharan Africa who are prepared to conduct agricultural research in a tropical African country. May be enrolled at any university in the world.

Write to Leader of Training Program; Iita; L.W. Lambourn & Co., Carolyn House, 26 Dingwall RD, Croydon CR9 3EE, England, or address above.

1460 — INTERNATIONAL SOCIETY OF ARBORICULTURE (Research Trust)

Dr. Bruce Roberts, Dept. Botany & Microbiolgy
Ohio Wesleyan University
Delaware OH 43015
740/386-3508

AMOUNT: $5,000 (max.)

DEADLINE(S): NOV 1

FIELD(S): Horticulture; Botany; Entomology; Phytopathology

For horticulturists, plant pathologists, plant physiologists, entomologists, soil specialists, and others engaging in the scientific study of shade trees. Grants can be used only for expenses associated with conducting approved research projects, e.g. equipment, supplies, etc. Funds are NOT to be used for expenses associated with attending school, e.g. tuition, books, lab fees, food, lodging, etc. Proposals must be received by November 1st.

Contact Dr. Bruce Roberts for an application.

1461 — LAND AND WATER RESOURCES R&D CORPORATION (Postgraduate Scholarships)

GPO Box 2182
Canberra ACT 2601 AUSTRALIA
02/6257 3379
FAX: 02/6257 3420
E-Mail: public@lwrrdc.gov.au
Internet: www.lwrrdc.gov.au

AMOUNT: $25,000/yr.

DEADLINE(S): JUN

FIELD(S): Natural Resources

Postgraduate scholarships for Australian citizens in the area of land, water, and vegetation resources to study/research in Australia. Financial need NOT a factor.

4 awards annually. Renewable up to three years. Contact Dr. Phil Price at LWRDC for an application. Award is made in September.

1462 — LAND AND WATER RESOURCES R&D CORPORATION (Travelling Fellowships)

GPO Box 2182
Canberra ACT 2601 AUSTRALIA
02/6257 3379
FAX: 02/6257 3420
E-Mail: public@lwrrdc.gov.au
Internet: www.lwrrdc.gov.au

AMOUNT: $10,000 (max.)

DEADLINE(S): JUN

FIELD(S): Natural Resources

Postgraduate fellowships for Australian researchers in the area of land, water, and vegetation resources, with overseas agencies to visit; LWRDC assists with financial and other support. Financial need NOT a factor.

6 awards annually. Not renewable. Contact Dr. Phil Price at LWRDC for an application. Award is made in September.

1463 — LAND AND WATER RESOURCES R&D CORPORATION (Visiting Fellowships)

GPO Box 2182
Canberra ACT 2601 AUSTRALIA
02/6257 3379
FAX: 02/6257 3420
E-Mail: public@lwrrdc.gov.au
Internet: www.lwrrdc.gov.au

AMOUNT: $10,000 (max.)

DEADLINE(S): JUN

FIELD(S): Natural Resources

Postgraduate fellowships for travel to Australia by overseas scientists in the area of land, water, and vegetation resources. Usually, fellows come at invitation of an Australian researcher; LWRDC assists with financial and other support. Financial need NOT a factor.

6 awards annually. Not renewable. Contact Dr. Phil Price at LWRDC for an application. Award is made in September.

1464 — LANDSCAPE ARCHITECTURE FOUNDATION (LAF/CLASS Fund Scholarships)

Use website below
Use website
202/216-2356
E-Mail: tpadian@asla.org
Internet: www.asla.org

AMOUNT: $500-$2,000

DEADLINE(S): MAR 31

FIELD(S): Landscape Architecture or Ornamental Horticulture

Scholarships and internships for students enrolled in certain California colleges: California Polytechnic Institute (Pomona or San Luis Obispo), UCLA, UC-Irvine, and UC-Davis who show promise and a commitment to landscape architecture as a profession.

Access website for complete information.

1465 — LINCOLN UNIVERSITY (MacMillan Brown Agricultural Scholarship)

PO Box 94
Canterbury NEW ZEALAND
(64) (3) 325 2811
FAX: (64) (3) 325 3850

AMOUNT: NZ$1,000

DEADLINE(S): MAR 31

FIELD(S): Agriculture; Horticulture

Open to students who are eligible to proceed to the degree of doctor of philosophy who wish to undertake research work in some problem bearing on agriculture or horticulture.

3 awards annually. Award is normally made for one year but recipients can reapply. Contact the Scholarships Officer at Lincoln University for an application and information on other scholarship programs.

1466 — NATIONAL COUNCIL OF FARMER COOPERATIVES (Graduate Awards)

50 F St., NW, Ste. 900
Washington DC 20001
202/626-8700
FAX: 202/626-8722

AMOUNT: $1,000 (1st prize); $800 (2nd); $600 (3rd)

DEADLINE(S): APR 1

FIELD(S): American Cooperatives

Open to graduate students working on theses or dissertations dealing with some aspect of economics, finance, operation, law, or structure of American cooperatives. May be in such fields as economics, business communications, sociology, etc.

3 awards annually. Not renewable. Contact NCFC Education Foundation for registration form.

1467 — NATIONAL COUNCIL OF STATE GARDEN CLUBS, INC. (Scholarships)

4401 Magnolia Ave.
St. Louis MO 63110-3492
314/776-7574
FAX: 314/776-5108
E-Mail: scsgc.franm@worldnet.att.net
Internet: www.gardenclub.org

AMOUNT: $3,500

DEADLINE(S): MAR 1

FIELD(S): Horticulture, Floriculture, Landscape Design, City Planning, Land Management, and allied subjects.

Open to junior, seniors and graduate students who are U.S. citizens and are studying any of the above or related subjects. Student must have the endorsement of the state in which he/she resides permanently. Applications will be forwarded to the National State Chairman and judged on a national level.

32 scholarships are awarded. Write to the above address for complete information.

1468 — NATIONAL JUNIOR HORTICULTURAL ASSOCIATION (Scottish Gardening Scholarship)

702 W. Elm
Durant OK 74701
580/924-0771

AMOUNT: Transportation, food & lodging, tuition, + $100/month stipend

DEADLINE(S): DEC 31

FIELD(S): Horticulture

Work/Study garden experience at Threave School of Gardening at Castle Douglas, Scotland. An American student (aged 18-21) is selected to study there with approximately 14 other students from Great Britain for a period of one year starting the second week of August. Applicants must have a high school diploma and good academic standing. Previous work in ornamental horticulture is essential (at least one full summer's employment).

Contact NJHA for application procedures.

1469 — NATIONAL RESEARCH FOUNDATION (NRF Honors & Postgraduate Bursaries)

PO Box 2600
Pretoria 0001 SOUTH AFRICA
+27 012/481-4000
FAX: +27 012/349-1179
E-Mail: info@nrf.ac.za
Internet: www.nrf.ac.za

AMOUNT: Varies

DEADLINE(S): Varies

FIELD(S): Agriculture; Chemistry; Earth Sciences; Engineering; Biology; Mathematics; Physics; Forestry; Veterinary Science; Pharmaceutics

Open to South African citizens pursuing graduate/postgraduate studies in above fields.

500 awards annually. Contact NRF for an application.

1470 — NORTHERN NEW JERSEY UNIT-HERB SOCIETY OF AMERICA (Scholarship)

2068 Dogwood Drive
Scotch Plains NJ 07076
908/233-2348

AMOUNT: $2,000

DEADLINE(S): FEB 15

FIELD(S): Horticulture; Botany

For New Jersey residents, undergraduate through postgraduate, who will attend colleges/universities east of the Mississippi River. Financial need is considered.

1 award annually. Renewable. Contact Mrs. Charlotte R. Baker at above address for an application.

1471 — OAK RIDGE INSTITUTE FOR SCIENCE AND EDUCATION (Applied Health Physics Fellowship Program)

P.O. Box 117
Oak Ridge TN 37831-0117
423/576-2194 or 423/576-9279
E-Mail: COXRE@ORAU.GOV or GRADFELL@ORAU.GOV

AMOUNT: $14,400 stipend + tuition and fees up to $9,000/yr paid to university + transportation costs up to $300/month

DEADLINE(S): JAN 26

FIELD(S): Engineering, mathematics, physical and life sciences

Fellowship in applied health physics to implement DOE's nuclear energy-related mission. Candidates must have B.A. degree in life or physical sciences, engineering, or mathematics. Recipients are subject to a service obligation of one year of full-time employment in a DOE facility for each academic year of fellowhip award.

For details and application, contact above location.

1472 — OAK RIDGE INSTITUTE FOR SCIENCE AND EDUCATION (Industrial Hygiene Graduate Fellowship Program)

P.O. Box 117
Oak Ridge TN 37831-0117
423-576-9655
FAX: 423/576-8293
E-Mail: kinneym@orau.gov

AMOUNT:

DEADLINE(S): JAN 26

FIELD(S): Industrial Hygiene

A fellowship for first-year master's candidates who have undergraduate degrees in physical, life, environmental, or health sciences or enginering and who wish to pursue studies in industrial hygiene.

For details and application, contact above location.

1473 — OAK RIDGE INSTITUTE FOR SCIENCE AND EDUCATION (Nuclear Engineering & Health Physics Fellowship Program)

105 Mitchell Rd. MS-16
Oak Ridge TN 37831-0117
423/576-2600 or 423/241-2890
E-Mail: johnsons@orau.gov or daltonj@arou.gov

AMOUNT: $14,400/yr.

DEADLINE(S): JAN 26

FIELD(S): Engineering, physical and life sciences

Fellowships in nuclear engineering or applied health physics to implement DOE's nuclear energy-related mission. Candidates must have B.A. degree in life or physical sciences or engineering.

For details and application, contact Sandra Johnson or Jennifer Dalton at above location.

1474 — OPEN SOCIETY INSTITUTE (Environmental Management Fellowships)

400 West 59th St.
New York NY 10019

212/548-0600 or 212/757-2323
FAX: 212/548-4679 or 212/548-4600
Internet: www.soros.org/efp.html

AMOUNT: Fees, room, board, living stipend, textbooks, international transportation, health insurance

DEADLINE(S): NOV 15

FIELD(S): Earth sciences, natural sciences, humanities (exc. language), anthropology, sociology, mathematics, or engineering

Two-year fellowships for use in selected universities in the U.S. for international students. For students/professionals in fields related to environmental policy, legislation, and remediation techniques applicable to their home countries.

To apply, contact your local Soros Foundation or Open Society Institute. Further details on website.

1475 — POTASH AND PHOSPHATE INSTITUTE (J. Fielding Reed PPI Fellowships)

655 Engineering Dr., Ste. 110
Norcross GA 30092
770/447-0335

AMOUNT: $2,000

DEADLINE(S): JAN 15

FIELD(S): Soil & Plant Sciences

Open to graduate students pursuing degrees at US or Canadian institutions. Awards are based on scholastic excellence.

Contact PPI for an application.

1476 — PROFESSIONAL GROUNDS MANAGEMENT SOCIETY (Anne Seaman Memorial Scholarships)

120 Cockeysville Rd., Ste. 104
Hunt Valley MD 21030
Written Inquiry

AMOUNT: $250-$1,000

DEADLINE(S): JUL 5

FIELD(S): Grounds Management

Scholarships in grounds management or closely related field to be used toward a 2- or 4-year degree or graduate study. Applicants must be US or Canadian citizens.

1-4 awards annually. Contact PGMS for an application.

1477 — PURINA MILLS, INC. (Research Fellowship)

c/o Susan Spiess-1W
PO Box 66812
St. Louis MO 63166-6812
314/768-4614
FAX: 314/768-4399

AMOUNT: $12,500

DEADLINE(S): FEB

FIELD(S): Animal Science; Dairy Science; Poultry Science

For outstanding graduate students in food and companion animal sciences. Awards are made primarily in the field of nutrition and interrelated disciplines as applied to animal, dairy, and poultry science. Students doing or expecting to do their graduate work in accredited graduate programs at US universities and institutions are eligible to apply. Must submit official transcripts, three letters of recommendation, description of research proposal, and resume.

3 awards annually (one in each subject). Not renewable. Contact Susan Spiess, Research Fellowship Coordinator, for an application. List of winners will be sent to all applicants.

1478 — QUEEN'S UNIVERSITY OF BELFAST (Thomas Henry Scholarship)

Newforge Lane
Belfast BT9 SPX N.IRELAND
Belfast 255450

AMOUNT: Fees & expenses—established annually by board of electors

DEADLINE(S): MAY 1

FIELD(S): Agriculture; Veterinary Medicine

Scholarships for encouragement of graduate research in agriculture or agricultural science in Northern Ireland. Must be United Kingdom citizen.

Renewable for 3 years. Contact Dean of Faculty (address above) for complete information.

1479 — RAYMOND J. HARRIS EDUCATION TRUST

P.O. Box 7899
Philadelphia PA 19101-7899
Written inquiry

AMOUNT: Varies

DEADLINE(S): FEB 1

FIELD(S): Medicine, law, engineering, dentistry, or agriculture

Scholarships for Christian men to obtain a professional education in medicine, law, engineering, dentistry, or agriculture at nine Philadelphia area colleges.

Contact Mellon Bank, N.A. at above location for details and the names of the nine colleges.

1480 — RESEARCH COUNCIL OF NORWAY (Senior Scientist Visiting Fellowship)

P.O. Box 2700 St. Hanshaugen
N-0131 Oslo NORWAY
+47 22 03 70 00
FAX: +47 22 03 70 01

E-Mail: intstip@nfr.no
Internet: www.forskningsradet.no

AMOUNT: NOK 25,000-1st 2 months; NOK 10,000-succeeding months

DEADLINE(S): Varies

FIELD(S): Bioproduction & Processing (including agriculture and veterinary science); Industry & Energy; Culture & Society (including social sciences and the humanities); Medicine & Health; Environment & Development; Science & Technology

Fellowships for scientists to work at Norwegian research institutes. Project funding does not include salary; expenses connected with the stay in Norway are covered.

For a list of institutions, contact the Research Council at above location. Then apply to institution, which then will submit fellowship application.

1481 — ROCKEFELLER FOUNDATION (African Dissertation Internship Awards)

420 Fifth Ave.
New York NY 10018-2702
212/869-8500
212/764-3468
Internet: www.rockfound.org

AMOUNT: Cost of project

DEADLINE(S): None given

FIELD(S): Agriculture, environment, health, life sciences, population, and schooling

For African graduate students in U.S. and Canadian universities (but not to permanent residents) to return to Africa to carry out dissertation research at a local university or research institution. Priority given to above topics.

Students are strongly urged to be in the field for at least 12 months. Contact above location for details.

1482 — SOIL AND WATER CONSERVATION SOCIETY (Kenneth E. Grant Research Scholarship)

7515 N.E. Ankeny Road
Ankeny IA 50021-9764
515/289-2331 or 1-800/THE-SOIL
FAX: 515/289-1227
E-Mail: charliep@swcs.org
Internet: www.swcs.org

AMOUNT: $1,300

DEADLINE(S): FEB 13

FIELD(S): Science and art of soil, water and related natural resources management

For SWCS members. Fellowship for graduate-level research on a specific SWCS topic. Must demonstrate integrity, ability, and competence, be eligible for grad work at an accredited institution, and show reasonable need for financial assistance.

Award is for an analytical study or report of a case example of an ecosystem-based approach to resource planning and decision-making. Write or visit websire for more information.

1483 — SOIL AND WATER CONSERVATION SOCIETY (Melville H. Cohee Student Leader Conservation Scholarship)

7515 N.E. Ankeny Road
Ankeny IA 50021-9764
515/289-2331 or 1-800-THE-SOIL
FAX 515/289-1227
E-Mail: charliep@swcs.org
Internet: www.swcs.org

AMOUNT: $900

DEADLINE(S): FEB 113

FIELD(S): Conservation or Natural Resource-Related Field

Open to 1+ year member of SWCS having served as an officer in a student chapter with 15+ members. GPA of 3.0 or better. Final year F/T undergrad or graduate.

2 awards. Course load must be 50% or more at accredited college or university. Financial need is not a factor. Write or visit website for complete information.

1484 — SOIL AND WATER CONSERVATION SOCIETY (SWCS Internships)

7515 N.E. Ankeny Road
Ankeny IA 50021-9764
515/289-2331 or 1-800/THE-SOIL
FAX: 515/289-1227
E-Mail: charliep@swcs.org
Internet: www.swcs.org

AMOUNT: Varies—most are uncompensated

DEADLINE(S): Varies

FIELD(S): Journalism, marketing, database management, meeting planning, public policy research, environmental education, landscape architecture

Internships for undergraduates and graduates to gain experience in the above fields as they relate to soil and water conservation issues. Intership openings vary through the year in duration, compensation, and objective. SWCS will coordinate particulars with your academic advisor.

Contact SWCS for internship availability at any timne during the year or see website for jobs page.

1485 — SONOMA CHAMBOLLE-MUSIGNY SISTER CITIES, INC. (Henri Cardinaux Memorial Scholarship)

Chamson Scholarship Committee
PO Box 1633
Sonoma CA 95476-1633
707/939-1344

FAX: 707/939-1344

E-Mail: Baileysci@vom.com

AMOUNT: up to $1,500 (travel + expenses)

DEADLINE(S): JUL 15

FIELD(S): Culinary Arts; Wine Industry; Art; Architecture; Music; History; Fashion

Hands-on experience working in above or similiar fields & living with a family in small French village in Burgundy or other French city. Must be Sonoma County, CA, resident at least 18 years of age & be able to communicate in French. Transcripts, employer recommendation, photograph, & essay (stating why, where, & when) required.

1 award. Non-renewable. Also offers opportunity for candidate in Chambolle-Musigny to obtain work experience & cultural exposure in Sonoma, CA.

1486 — THE DAPHNE JACKSON MEMORIAL FELLOWSHIPS TRUST (Fellowships in Science/ Engineering)

School of Physical Sciences
Dept. of Physics
University of Surrey
Guildford, Surrey
GU2 5XH ENGLAND UK
01483 259166
FAX: 01483 259501
E-Mail: J.Woolley@surrey.ac.uk
Internet: www.sst.ph.ic.ac.uk/trust/

AMOUNT: Varies

DEADLINE(S): Varies

FIELD(S): Science or engineering, including information sciences

Fellowships to enable well-qualified and highly motivated scientists and engineers to return to appropriate careers following a career break due to family comitments. May be used on a flexible, part-time basis. Tenable at various U.K. universities.

See website and/or contact organization for details.

1487 — TROPICAL AGRICULTURAL RESEARCH AND HIGHER EDUCATION CENTER - CATIE (Education for Development and Conservation Program)

7170 Turrialba
COSTA RICA
506/556-1016
FAX: 506/556-0914
E-Mail: gpaez@catie.ac.cr
Internet: www.catie.ac.cr

AMOUNT: US$32,000 (scholarship); US$16,750 (tuition assistance)

DEADLINE(S): DEC

FIELD(S): Agriculture; Natural Resource Sciences

For postgraduate students from member countries of CATIE to attend CATIE. Countries are Mexico, Belize, Guatemala, El Salvador, Honduras, Nicaragua, Costa Rica, Panama, Venezuela, Dominican Republic, and Colombia. Must have a university degree, successful completion of the admission process, minimum of two years of experience, and must work for a relevant technical school or academic agricultural organization, public or private. Must demonstrate financial need.

25 awards annually. Not renewable. Contact Dr. Gilberto Paez at CATIE for an application.

1488 — UNITED AGRIBUSINESS LEAGUE (UAL Scholarship Program)

54 Corporate Park
Irvine CA 92606-5105
800/223-4590 or 949/975-1424
FAX: 949/975-1671
E-Mail: ual@earthlink.net
Internet: www.ual.org

AMOUNT: Varies

DEADLINE(S): APR 16

FIELD(S): Agriculture; Agribusiness

Any ag student presently enrolled, or who will be enrolled any time during the year of application in any accredited college/university offering a degree in agriculture, may apply. Minimum GPA of 2.5 is required. With application, must submit essay on "My Future In Agribusiness," resume of education/ work/community activities/etc., and three letters of recommendation. Financial need will not be considered unless you specifically request it & provide documentation.

Over $10,000 available annually. Renewable with new application. Contact Christine M. Steele, Executive Secretary, for more information.

1489 — WOODROW WILSON NATIONAL FELLOWSHIP FOUNDATION/U.S. DEPARTMENTS OF COMMERCE AND AGRICULTURE (Fellowships)

CN 5329
Princeton NJ 08543-5329
609/452-7007
FAX: 609/452-0066
E-Mail: richard@woodrow.org
Internet: www.woodrow.org

AMOUNT: Varies

DEADLINE(S): Varies

FIELD(S): Commerce; Agriculture

Open to minority students in the US who are interested in careers in commerce or agriculture.

See website or contact WWNFF for an application.

EARTH SCIENCE

1490 — AFRICAN NETWORK OF SCIENTIFIC AND TECHNOLOGICAL INSTITUTIONS - ANSTI (Postgraduate Fellowships)

PO Box 30592
Nairobi Kenya AFRICA
254-2-621234 or 254-2-622619/20
FAX: 254-2-215991
E-Mail: j.massaquoi@unesco.org OR
ANSTI@Net2000ke.com

AMOUNT: Fees, subsistence, & international travel

DEADLINE(S): JUN

FIELD(S): Basic & Engineering Sciences

Scholarships for postgraduate studies outside of applicant's home country. Must be African nationals not older than 36 years of age and hold a good bachelor's degree (at least 2nd class upper division). Applicants should apply for admission to host university as soon as possible. Fellowships tenable only in African universities.

10 awards annually. Renewable up to 2 years. Contact Professor J.G.M. Massaquoi for an application.

1491 — AMERICAN ASSOCIATION OF PETROLEUM GEOLOGISTS (AAPG Foundation Grants-in-Aid)

PO Box 979
Tulsa OK 74101-2642
918/584-2555
FAX: 918/560-2642
E-Mail: rgriffin@aapg.org
Internet: www.aapg.org/fdn.html

AMOUNT: $2,000 (max.)

DEADLINE(S): JAN 31

FIELD(S): Petroleum Geology; Environmental Geology

Grants are to support research projects leading to a masters or doctoral degree. Preference given to projects related to the search for hydrocarbons, economic sedimentary minerals, or environmental geology. Must submit transcripts and endorsements and demonstrate financial need.

80-129 awards annually. Renewable. Contact Rebecca Griffin at AAPG for an application.

1492 — AMERICAN ASSOCIATION OF UNIVERSITY WOMEN EDUCATIONAL FOUNDATION/AMERICAN ASTRONOMICAL SOCIETY (Annie Jump Cannon Award in Astronomy)

Dept. RR.INT
1111 16th St., NW
Washington DC 20036-4873

202/728-7622
FAX: 202/463-7169
E-Mail: foundation@aauw.org
Internet: www.aauw.org

AMOUNT: $5,000

DEADLINE(S): FEB 10

FIELD(S): Astronomy

This award honors a woman postdoctoral scholar for significant research in astronomy. Nominees must be in the early stages of a career in astronomy. Preference is given to those who have held a doctorate in astronomy or a related field for at least one year. There are no restrictions regarding the nominee's nationality or the location of her research. Nominees from previous years are eligible to apply.

Contact AAUW for an application.

1493 — AMERICAN CONGRESS ON SURVEYING AND MAPPING (American Association for Geodetic Surveying Graduate Fellowship Award)

5410 Grosvenor Lane, Ste. 100
Bethesda MD 20814-2144
301/493-0200, ext. 102
FAX: 301/493-8245
E-Mail: lillym@mindspring.com
Internet: www.survmap.org

AMOUNT: $2,000

DEADLINE(S): DEC 1

FIELD(S): Geodesy; Geodetic Surveying

Open to students enrolled in or accepted to a graduate program in geodetic surveying or geodesy. Preference given to those having at least two years of employment experience in the surveying profession. Must submit personal statement (including goals & financial need), letters of recommendation, and transcripts. Must join ACSM.

1 award annually. Contact Lilly Matheson at ACSM for membership information and/or an application.

1494 — AMERICAN CONGRESS ON SURVEYING AND MAPPPING (Cartography and Geographic Information Society Scholarship)

5410 Grosvenor Lane, Ste. 100
Bethesda MD 20814-2144
301/493-0200, ext. 102
301/493-8245
E-Mail: lillym@mindspring.com
Internet: www.survmap.org

AMOUNT: $1,000

DEADLINE(S): DEC 1

FIELD(S): Cartography; Geographic Information Science

Open to outstanding students enrolled full-time in a four-year or graduate degree program. Preference given to undergraduates with junior or senior standing, the purpose being to encourage completion of undergrad program and/or pursuit of graduate education in above fields. Must submit personal statement (including goals & financial need), letters of recommendation, and transcripts. Must join ACSM.

1 award annually. Contact Lilly Matheson at ACSM for membership information and/or an application.

1495 — AMERICAN FOUNDATION FOR THE BLIND (Paul W. Ruckes Scholarship)

11 Penn Plaza, Ste. 300
New York NY 10001
212/502-7661 or TDD 212/502-7771
E-Mail: juliet@afb.org
Internet: www.afb.org

AMOUNT: $1,000

DEADLINE(S): APR 30

FIELD(S): Engineering, computer, physical, or life sciences

Open to blind or visually impaired undergraduate or graduate students pursuing degrees in the above fields. U.S. citizenship required.

Write to the above address or visit website for complete information.

1496 — AMERICAN GEOPHYSICAL UNION (Horton Research Grant)

2000 Florida Ave., NW
Washington DC 20009-1277
202/462-6900, ext. 515
FAX: 202/328-0566
E-Mail: wsinghateh@agu.org
Internet: www.agu.org/inside/honors.html

AMOUNT: $8,000-$10,000

DEADLINE(S): MAR 1

FIELD(S): Hydrology; Water Resources Policies

Grants are to support research in hydrology and/or water resources policy sciences by Ph.D. candidates. Proposals may be in physical, chemical, or biological aspects, economics, systems analysis, sociology, or law.

Contact Wynetta Singhateh at AGU for an application.

1497 — AMERICAN INDIAN SCIENCE AND ENGINEERING SOCIETY (A.T. Anderson Memorial Scholarship)

PO Box 9828
Albuquerque NM 87119-9828
505/765-1052
FAX: 505/765-5608
E-Mail: scholarships@aises.org
Internet: www.aises.org/scholarships

AMOUNT: $1,000-$2,000

DEADLINE(S): JUN 15

FIELD(S): Medicine; Natural Resources; Science; Engineering

Open to undergraduate and graduate students who are at least 1/4 American Indian or recognized as member of a tribe. Must be member of AISES ($10 fee), enrolled full-time at an accredited institution, and demonstrate financial need.

Renewable. See website or contact Patricia Browne for an application and/or membership information.

1498 — AMERICAN INDIAN SCIENCE AND ENGINEERING SOCIETY (EPA Tribal Lands Environmental Science Scholarship)

PO Box 9828
Albuquerque NM 87119-9828
505/765-1052
FAX: 505/765-5608
E-Mail: scholarships@aises.org
Internet: www.aises.org/scholarships

AMOUNT: $4,000

DEADLINE(S): JUN 15

FIELD(S): Biochemistry; Biology; Chemical Engineering; Chemistry; Entomology; Environmental Economics/Science; Hydrology; Environmental Studies

Open to American Indian college juniors, seniors, and graduate students enrolled full-time at an accredited institution. Must demonstrate financial need. Certificate of Indian blood NOT required.

Renewable. See website or contact Patricia Browne for an application.

1499 — AMERICAN MUSEUM OF NATURAL HISTORY (Graduate Student Fellowship Program)

Central Park West at 79th St.
New York NY 10024-5192
FAX: 212/769-5495
E-Mail: bynum@amnh.org
Internet: research.amnh.org

AMOUNT: Stipend & health insurance

DEADLINE(S): JAN 15

FIELD(S): Paleontology; Earth & Planetary Sciences; Entomology; Evolutionary & Molecular Biology

One-year fellowships through partnership w/ Columbia, Cornell, & Yale Universities & City University of New York to help advance training of Ph.D. candidates in scientific disciplines practiced at Museum. Must include resume/curriculum vitae, GRE scores, TOEFL score for foreign students, official transcripts, letters of recommendation, and statement of research interest/summary of thesis proposal/progress to date.

Renewable up to 4 years. Must apply to Museum AND cooperating university. See website or contact Office of Grants & Fellowships for application.

1500 — AMERICAN MUSEUM OF NATURAL HISTORY (International Graduate Student Fellowship Program)

Central Park West at 79th St.
New York NY 10024-5192
FAX: 212/769-5495
E-Mail: bynum@amnh.org
Internet: research.amnh.org

AMOUNT: Stipend, tuition, & travel

DEADLINE(S): JAN 15

FIELD(S): Biodiversity & Conservation; Public Policy; Entomology; Evolutionary & Molecular Biology

One-year joint program w/ Columbia, Cornell, & Yale Universities & City University of NY to help advance training of Ph.D. candidates who are non-US citizens. Purpose is to gain skills & experience to bear on environmental problems of their home countries. Must submit resume/curriculum vitae, GRE & TOEFL scores, official transcripts, letters of recommendation, & statement of purpose.

Renewable up to 4 years. Must apply to Museum AND cooperating university. See website or contact Office of Grants & Fellowships for application.

1501 — AMERICAN MUSEUM OF NATURAL HISTORY (Research Fellowships)

Central Park West at 79th St.
New York NY 10024-5192
FAX: 212/769-5495
E-Mail: bynum@amnh.org
Internet: research.amnh.org

AMOUNT: Varies

DEADLINE(S): JAN 15

FIELD(S): Zoology; Paleontology; Anthropology; Earth & Planetary Sciences

Support to recent postdoctoral investigators and established scientists to carry out a specific project within a limited time period. Appointments are usually for one year, and candidates are expected to be in residence at the Museum or one of its field stations. Fellows are judged on research abilities/ experience and merits/scope of proposed research. Application requires project description/ bibliography, budget, letters of recommendation, and curriculum vitae.

See website or contact the Office of Grants & Fellowships for an application.

1502 — AMERICAN SOCIETY FOR ENGINEERING EDUCATION (Army Research Laboratory Postdoctoral Fellowships)

1818 N St., NW, Ste. 600
Washington DC 20036
202/331-3525
FAX: 202/265-8504
E-Mail: projects@asee.org
Internet: www.asee.org/fellowship/

AMOUNT: $45,000-$55,000 + travel/relocation allowance

DEADLINE(S): Varies

FIELD(S): Engineering; Physical Sciences

Postdoctoral fellowships for US citizens/permanent residents to do research at Army Research Laboratories. Candidates must have completed their Ph.D. prior to appointment. Program is designed to increase involvement of creative and highly trained scientists and engineers from academia and industry in scientific and technical areas of interest and relevance to the Army. Research proposal should include clear objective and defined outcome. Financial need NOT a factor.

15 awards annually. Renewable. Contact Sandi Crawford at ASEE for an application packet.

1503 — AMERICAN SOCIETY OF CIVIL ENGINEERS (Trent R. Dames and William W. Moore Fellowship)

1801 Alexander Bell Drive
Reston VA 20191-4400
800/548-ASCE or 703/295-6000
FAX: 703/295-6333
E-Mail: student@asce.org
Internet: www.asce.org

AMOUNT: $5,000-$10,000

DEADLINE(S): FEB 20

FIELD(S): Geotechnical Engineering; Earth Sciences

For practicing engineers, earth scientists, professors, or graduate students to explore new applications of geotechnical engineering or the earth sciences to social, economic, environmental, and political issues. ASCE membership is not required.

Offered every two years (2000, 20002, etc.). See website or contact ASCE for an application between October and February.

1504 — AMERICAN WATER RESOURCES ASSOCIATION (Richard A. Herbert Memorial Scholarships)

AWRRI
101 Comer Hall
Auburn Univ AL 36849-5431
715/355-3684
FAX: 715/355-3648

E-Mail: stdi@ltus.com
Internet: www.uwin.siu.ed/~awra

AMOUNT: $1,000 + complimentary AWRA membership

DEADLINE(S): APR 30

FIELD(S): Water Resources & related fields

For full-time undergraduates working towards 1st degree and for graduates. Based on academic performance, including cumulative GPA, relevance of curriculum to water resources, & leadership in extracurricular activities related to water resources. Quality & relevance of research is also considered from graduate students. Transcripts, letters of reference, & summary of academic interests/achievements, extracurricular interests, & career goals required (2 page limit).

2 awards annually: 1 undergrad & 1 graduate. Recipients announced in the summer. Contact Stephen Dickman, AWRA Student Activities Committee, for an application.

1505 — AMERICAN WATER WORKS ASSOCIATION (Abel Wolman Fellowship)

6666 W. Quincy Ave.
Denver CO 80235
303/347-6206
FAX: 303/794-8915
E-Mail: vbaca@awwa.org
Internet: www.org/tande/eduframe.htm

AMOUNT: $15,000 stipend +$1,000 for supplies +up to $4,000 for tuition, etc.

DEADLINE(S): JAN 15

FIELD(S): Research in water supply and treatment

For students who show potential for leadership and anticipate completion of the requirments for a Ph.D. within two years of the award. Applicants will be evaluated on the quality of academic record, the significance of the proposed research to water supply and treatment, and the potential to do high quality research. Must be citizen or permanent resident of the U.S., Canada, or Mexico.

Renewable for a second year. Write for complete information.

1506 — AMERICAN WATER WORKS ASSOCIATION (Academic Achievement Award)

6666 West Quincy Ave.
Denver CO 80235
303/347-6206
FAX: 303/794-8915
E-Mail: vbaca@awwa.org
Internet: www.org/tande/eduframe.htm

AMOUNT: 1st place: $1,000; 2nd place: $500

DEADLINE(S): OCT 1

FIELD(S): Subject related to drinking water supply industry

Award for a master's thesis or doctoral dissertation that has potential value to the water supply industry. This is not a scholarship but a cash award for outstanding work that has been completed.

Write for complete information.

1507 — AMERICAN WATER WORKS ASSOCIATION (Holly A. Cornell Scholarship)

6666 W. Quincy Ave.
Denver CO 80235
303/347-6206
FAX: 303/794-8915
E-Mail: vbaca@awwa.org
Internet: www.org/tande/eduframe.htm

AMOUNT: $5,000

DEADLINE(S): JAN 15

FIELD(S): Engineering (Water Supply and Treatment)

Open to females and minorities (as defined by the U.S. Equal Opportunity Commission) who anticipate completion of a master's degree in engineering no sooner than December of the following year. Program was created by CH2M Hill, Inc. in honor of one of the firm's founders.

Contact organization for complete information.

1508 — AMERICAN WATER WORKS ASSOCIATION (Lars Scholarship)

6666 W. Quincy Ave.
Denver CO 80235
303/347-6206
FAX: 303/794-8915
E-Mail: vbaca@awwa.org
Internet: awwa.org/tande/eduframe.htm

AMOUNT: $5,000 (Masters); $7,000 (Ph.D.)

DEADLINE(S): JAN 15

FIELD(S): Science and Engineering in the field of Water Supply and/or Treatment

For M.A. and Ph.D. level students at an institution of higher learning in Canada, Guam, Puerto Rico, Mexico, or the United States. For research into water supply and/or treatment.

Write for complete information.

1509 — AMERICAN WATER WORKS ASSOCIATION (Thomas R. Camp Scholarship)

6666 W. Quincy Ave.
Denver CO 80235
303/347-6206
FAX: 303/794-8915
E-Mail: vbaca@awwa.org
Internet: www.org/tande/eduframe.htm

AMOUNT: $5,000

DEADLINE(S): JAN 15

FIELD(S): Research in the drinking water field

For students pursuing an M.A. or Ph.D. in the field of drinking water. This award is granted to Doctoral students in even years and Master's students in odd years. Can be used at an institution of higher education in Canada, Guam, Puerto rico, Mexico, or the U.S.

One award each year. Contact above location for details.

1510 — ASIAN INSTITUTE OF TECHNOLOGY (AIT Scholarship Program)

Development Office
PO Box 4, Klongluang
Pathumthani 12120 THAILAND
(66)(2) 516-0110-44 or 524-5032
FAX: (66)(2) 516-2126
E-Mail: ascao@ait.ac.th
Internet: www.ait.ac.th

AMOUNT: US $12,600-$37,960

DEADLINE(S): FEB 15; JUN 15; OCT 15

FIELD(S): Advanced Technologies; Civil Engineering; Environment, Resources, & Development; Business Management

Scholarships and grants open to citizens of Asian countries who are accepted by the institute as a master's or doctotal candidate. Selection is based on academic criteria, practical experience, gender, and country of origin; priority to Mekong Region countries and Asian countries of the former USSR.

250 awards annually. Contact AIT for an application.

1511 — ASSOCIATION FOR WOMEN IN SCIENCE EDUCATIONAL FOUNDATION (AWIS Predoctoral Awards)

1200 New York Ave. NW, Suite 650
Washington DC 20005
202/326-8940 or 800-886-AWIS
E-Mail: awis@awis.org
Internet: www.awis.org

AMOUNT: $1,000

DEADLINE(S): JAN 16

FIELD(S): Various Sciences and Social Sciences

Scholarships for female doctoral students. Summary page, description of research project, resume, references, transcripts, and biographical sketch required. US citizens may study at any graduate institution; non-citizens must study at US institutions.

5-10 awards annually. See website or write to above address for an application and complete information.

1512 — ASSOCIATION FOR WOMEN IN SCIENCE EDUCATIONAL FOUNDATION (AWIS Pre-doctoral Awards)

1200 New York Ave. NW, Suite 650
Washington DC 20005
202/326-8940 or 800/886-AWIS
E-Mail: awis@awis.org
Internet: www.awis.org

AMOUNT: $1,000

DEADLINE(S): JAN 16

FIELD(S): Various Sciences and Social Sciences

Scholarships for female doctoral students. Summary page, description of research project, resume, references, transcripts, and biographical sketch required. US citizens may study at any graduate institution; non-citizens must be enrolled in US institutions.

5-10 awards annually. See website or write to above address for an application and more information.

1513 — ASSOCIATION FOR WOMEN IN SCIENCE EDUCATIONAL FOUNDATION (Ruth Satter Memorial Award)

1200 New York Ave., NW, Suite 650
Washington DC 20005
202/326-8940 or 800/886-AWIS
E-Mail: awis@awis.org
Internet: www.awis.org

AMOUNT: $1,000

DEADLINE(S): JAN 16

FIELD(S): Various Sciences and Social Sciences

Scholarships for female doctoral students who have interrupted their education for at least three years to raise a family. Summary page, description of research project, resume, references, transcripts, biographical sketch, and letter from your department to confirm eligibility required. US citizens may study at any graduate institution; non-citizens must attend US institutions.

See website or write to above address for more information or an application.

1514 — ASSOCIATION FOR WOMEN IN SCIENCE EDUCATIONAL FOUNDATION (Ruth Satter Memorial Award)

1200 New York Ave. NW, Suite 650
Washington DC 20005
202/326-8940 or 800/886-AWIS
E-Mail: awis@awis.org
Internet: www.awis.org

AMOUNT: $1,000

DEADLINE(S): JAN 16

FIELD(S): Various Sciences and Social Sciences

Scholarships for female doctoral students who have interrupted their education three years or more to raise a family. Summary page, description of research project, resume, references, transcripts, biographical sketch, and proof of eligibility from department head required. US citizens may attend any graduate institution; non-citizens must be enrolled in US institutions.

See website or write to above address for more information or an application.

1515 — AUSTRALIAN FEDERATION OF UNIVERSITY WOMEN - WESTERN AUSTRALIA (Mary & Elsie Stevens Bursary)

Bursary Liaison Officer
PO Box 48
Nedlands WA 6009 AUSTRALIA
Written Inquiry

AMOUNT: Aus$1,750

DEADLINE(S): JUL 31

FIELD(S): Mathematics or Physical Sciences, such as Physics, Chemistry, Geology, Astronomy, or other innate sciences

Bursary is to support women graduates of a Western Australian University to complete a higher degree or post-doctoral research in Mathematics or one of the Physical Sciences at a recognized university in any country or women who have been accepted to work toward a higher degree at a university in Western Australia.

Membership in AFUW or in IFUW is required. Write for complete information.

1516 — AUSTRALIAN FEDERATION OF UNIVERSITY WOMEN - WESTERN AUSTRALIA (Mary & Ilsie Stevens Bursary)

Bursary Liaison Officer
PO Box 48
Nedlands WA 6009 AUSTRALIA
Written Inquiry

AMOUNT: Aus$1,750

DEADLINE(S): JUL 31

FIELD(S): Mathematics or Physical sciences, such as Physics, Chemistry, Geology, Astronomy, or other innate sciences

Bursary is to support women graduates of a recognized university to complete a higher degree or post-doctoral research in Mathematics or in one of the Physical Sciences at a university in Western Australia.

Membership in AFUW or in IFUW is required. Write for complete information.

1517 — AUSTRIAN CULTURAL INSTITUTE (Max Kade Foundation Grants)

950 Third Ave.
20th Fl.
New York NY 10022
212/759-5165 or +43/1/51581-253
FAX: 212/319-9636

E-Mail: desk@aci.org
Internet: www.austriaculture.net

AMOUNT: Varies

DEADLINE(S): Varies

FIELD(S): Medicine; Natural Sciences; Engineering

Open to young Austrian scientists with several years of experience at universities or institutions. Must demonstrate capacity to pursue independent teaching or research activities in the US. Proficiency in English required.

See website or contact ACI for an application kit, or write to Osterreichische Akademie der Wissenschaften, Kommission fur Max Kade Stipendien, Dr. Ignaz Seipel-Platz 2, A-1010 Vienna, Austria.

1518 — BOEING (Polish Graduate Student Scholarship Program)

Phone for details
314/234-2149

AMOUNT: Tuition, books, and fees for three years

DEADLINE(S): Varies

FIELD(S): Scientific and technical fields

Scholarships for students from Poland to pursue graduate studies in scientific and technical areas at American colleges or universities.

Call Jim Schlueter at above telephone number.

1519 — BRITISH ASSOCIATION FOR AMERICAN STUDIES (Short-Term Awards)

Dr. Jenel Virden
University of Hull
Hull HU6 7RX ENGLAND UK
01482 465303

AMOUNT: 400 pounds sterling

DEADLINE(S): DEC 1

FIELD(S): American Studies; American History

Open to graduate/postgraduate British scholars for brief visits to the US for research in American history, politics, geography, culture, and literature. Preference given to younger scholars.

Contact Dr. Jenel Virden for an application.

1520 — BRITISH FEDERATION OF WOMEN GRADUATES (Johnstone & Florence Stoney Studentship)

4 Mandeville Courtyard
142 Battersea Park Rd.
London SW11 4NB ENGLAND UK
PHONE/FAX: 0171/498-8037

AMOUNT: 1,000+ pounds sterling

DEADLINE(S): SEP 10

FIELD(S): Biology; Geology; Meteorology; Radiology

For female UK citizens planning to pursue graduate research, preferably undertaken in Australia, New Zealand, or South Africa. Must have completed at least four academic terms or three semesters; award is not given for first year of research. Chief criteria is academic excellence and proven ability to carry out independent research. Postdoctoral studies also eligible.

1 award annually. Application fee of 12 pounds sterling required. Send a self-addressed, stamped envelope (or self-addressed envelope with international reply coupons) for an application. Results announced by end of October.

1521 — BRITISH INSTITUTE OF ARCHAEOLOGY AT ANKARA (Travel Grants)

Assistant Secretary
10 Carlton House Terrace
London SW1Y 5AH ENGLAND UK
+44 0171 969 5204

AMOUNT: 500 pounds sterling (max.)

DEADLINE(S): FEB 1

FIELD(S): Archaeology & Geography of Turkey

Travel grants to enable undergraduate and graduate students to familiarize themselves with the archaeology and geography of Turkey, its museums, and ancient sites. For citizens of the British Commonwealth.

Contact British Institute for an application.

1522 — BRITISH LIBRARY (Helen Wallis Research Fellowship)

Map Library
96 Euston Rd.
London NW1 2DB ENGLAND UK
+44 0171 412 7525
FAX: +44 0171 412 7780
E-Mail: tony.campbell@bl.uk
Internet: www.ihrinfo.ac.uk/maps/wallis.html

AMOUNT: 300 pounds sterling

DEADLINE(S): MAY 1

FIELD(S): Cartography

Fellowships for those working towards a doctorate or pursuing postdoctoral work to do research in the book and map collections of the British Library. Award is for full- or part-time appointment, for a minimum of six months and a maximum of one year. Financial need NOT a factor.

1 award annually. Not renewable. To apply, submit a letter of application, indicating the period you intend to be in London and outlining your proposed research project, together with a full curriculum vitae and the names of three referees, to Tony Campbell, Map Librarian, at above address.

1523 — BRITISH LIBRARY (J.B. Harley Research Fellowships)

Map Library
96 Euston Rd.
London NW1 2DB ENGLAND UK
+44 0171 412 7525
FAX: +44 0171 412 7780
E-Mail: tony.campbell@bl.uk
Internet: www.ihrinfo.ac.uk/maps/harley.html

AMOUNT: 500-1,000 pounds sterling

DEADLINE(S): NOV 1

FIELD(S): History of Cartography

Two- to four-week fellowships for those working towards a doctorate or pursuing postdoctoral work to do research in London, UK on the history of cartography. Applicants are judged on scholarly criteria and should be working towards publication. Preference will be given to interpretive studies in map history, irrespective of area, theme, or period. Financial need NOT a factor.

2-3 awards annually. Not renewable. To apply, submit four copies each of research proposal (less than 1,000 words) and curriculum vitae (including relevant publications) to Tony Campbell, Map Librarian, at above address.

1524 — BROOKHAVEN WOMEN IN SCIENCE (Renate W. Chasman Scholarship)

PO Box 183
Upton NY 11973-5000
E-mail: pam@bnl.gov

AMOUNT: $2,000

DEADLINE(S): APR 1

FIELD(S): Natural Sciences; Engineering; Mathematics

Open ONLY to women who are residents of the boroughs of Brooklyn or Queens or the counties of Nassau or Suffolk in New York who are re-entering school after a period of study. For juniors, seniors, or first-year graduate students.

1 award annually. Not renewable. Contact Pam Mansfield at above location for an application. Phone calls are NOT accepted.

1525 — CANADIAN FEDERATION OF UNIVERSITY WOMEN (CFUW Memorial/ Professional Fellowship)

251 Bank St., Ste. 600
Ottawa Ontario K2P 1X3 CANADA
613/234-2732
Internet: www.cfuw.ca

AMOUNT: $5,000

DEADLINE(S): NOV 15

FIELD(S): Science & Technology

Open to women who are Canadian citizens/ permanent residents enrolled in a master's degree program in science and technology. Must hold at least a bachelor's degree or equivalent from a recognized university and have been accepted into, or be currently enrolled in the proposed program and place of study. May be studying abroad.

$25 filing fee. Contact CFUW for an application after August 1st. Candidates will be notified by May 31st.

1526 — CANADIAN SOCIETY OF EXPLORATION GEOPHYSICISTS (CSEG Trust Fund)

905, 510-5th St., SW
Calgary Alberta T2P 3S2 CANADA
403/262-0015
FAX: 403/262-7383
E-Mail: info@cseg.org
Internet: www.cseg.org

AMOUNT: $1,500 Canadian

DEADLINE(S): JUL 15

FIELD(S): Exploration Geophysics

For undergraduate students whose grades are above average or for graduate students. Must be pursuing a course of studies in Canada directed toward a career in exploration geophysics in industry, teaching, or research. Certain awards impose additional qualifications; completion of questionnaire will aid in determining if applicant meets those qualifications. Letters of recommendation required. Financial need is considered.

Contact Heather Payne at CSEG for an application.

1527 — CAVE RESEARCH FOUNDATION (KARST Research Fellowship Program)

c/o Dr. John C. Tinsley
US Geological Survey
345 Middlefield Rd.
M/S 977
Menlo Park, CA 94025
415/329-4928
FAX: 415/329-5163
E-Mail: jtinsley@usgs.gov

AMOUNT: $3,500

DEADLINE(S): JAN 31

FIELD(S): Cave Research (KARST)

Fellowships to support graduate study in any KARST-related discipline, anywhere in the world. Meritorious proposals that do not receive fellowships may receive smaller grants. All awards made directly to student.

2-3 awards per year. Write for complete information.

1528 — CHARLES A. AND ANNE MORROW LINDBERGH FOUNDATION (Grants for Research Projects)

2150 Third Ave., N, Ste. 310
Anoka MN 55303-2200
612/576-1596
FAX: 612/576-1664
E-Mail: lindbergh@isd.net
Internet: www.isd.net/lindbergh

AMOUNT: $10,580 (max.)

DEADLINE(S): JUN 15

FIELD(S): Aviation; Aerospace; Agriculture; Education; Arts; Humanities; Biomedical Research; Exploration; Health & Population Sciences; Intercultural Communication; Waste Disposal Minimization & Management.; Adaptive Technology; Conservation

Open to individuals whose proposed projects represent a significant contribution toward the achievement of balance between the advance of technology and preservation of the natural environment. Financial need NOT a factor. Funding is NOT for tuition.

10 awards annually. See website for application.

1529 — COMMONWEALTH DEPARTMENT OF PRIMARY INDUSTRIES & ENERGY (Post-graduate Forestry Research Awards)

Assistant Secretary
Forests Branch—DPIE
GPO Box 858
Canberra 2601 ACT AUSTRALIA
062/724371

AMOUNT: Approximately $18,400 (Australian) + allowances

DEADLINE(S): DEC 1

FIELD(S): Forest and wood products.

Applications invited for the above awards at any Australian university for full-time research leading to MS or Ph.D degree. Australian citizens or permanent residents who have lived in Australia continuously for the past year are eligible.

Application forms and additional information including priority research areas may be obtained from the address above.

1530 — CONSULTING ENGINEERS COUNCIL OF NEW JERSEY (Louis Goldberg Scholarship Fund)

66 Morris Ave.
Springfield NJ 07081
973/564-5848
FAX: 973/564-7480

AMOUNT: $1,000

DEADLINE(S): JAN 1

FIELD(S): Engineering or Land Surveying

Open to undergraduate students who have completed at least two years of study (or fifth year in a five-year program) at an ABET-accredited college or university in New Jersey, are in top half of their class, and are considering a career as a consulting engineer or land surveyor. Must be U.S. citizen.

Recipients will be eligible for American Consulting Engineers Council national scholarships of $2,000 to $5,000. Write for complete information.

1531 — COOPERATIVE INSTITUTE FOR RESEARCH IN ENVIRONMENTAL SCIENCES (CIRES Visiting Fellowships)

Univ Colorado
Campus Box 216
Boulder CO 80309-0216
303/492-1143
Internet: cires.colorado.edu/ciresvf.html

AMOUNT: Varies

DEADLINE(S): DEC 15

FIELD(S): Environmental & Earth Sciences

One-year visiting fellowships for recent Ph.D.s and senior scientists, including faculty on sabbatical. To be used towards research in the areas of physics, chemistry, & dynamics of Earth system; global & regional environmental change; climate system monitoring, diagnostics, & modeling; and remote sensing measurement techniques. Must submit curriculum vitae, publications list, 2-4 page description of proposed research, and letters of recommendation.

5 awards annually. Renewable. See website or contact CIRES for an application. CIRES receives sponsorship from the National Oceanic and Atmosphere Administration's Environmental Research Laboratories.

1532 — COUNCIL FOR EUROPEAN STUDIES (Predissertation Fellowships)

Columbia Univ
807-807A International Affairs Bldg.
New York NY 10027
212/854-4172
FAX: 212/854-8808
E-Mail: ces@columbia.edu
Internet: www.europanet.org

AMOUNT: $4,000 stipend (max.)

DEADLINE(S): FEB 1

FIELD(S): Cultural Anthropology; History (post 1750); Political Science; Sociology; Geography; Urban & Regional Planning

Awards are for research in France to determine viability of projected doctoral dissertation in modern history and social sciences. Recipients test research design of dissertation, determine availability of archival materials, and contact French scholars. Must be US citizen or permanent resident at a US institution and have completed at least two but no more than three years of full-time doctoral study by end of year. Institutional membership in Council is required.

6 awards annually. See website or contact Council for an application.

1533 — DUBLIN INSTITUTE FOR ADVANCED STUDIES (Research Scholarships)

10 Burlington Road
Dublin 4 IRELAND
614 0100
FAX: 668 0561

AMOUNT: 5,000-8,200

DEADLINE(S): MAR 31

FIELD(S): Theoretical Physics; Cosmic Physics; Astronomy; Celtic Studies

Open to candidates holding Ph.D degrees or equivalent and to those with M.A. degrees who can demonstrate their capacity for original research in the above fields. Scholars are required to be in full-time attendance in the schools. No nationality or citizenship requirements.

Awards are renewable and intended to enable holders to establish research careers. The Institute does not award degrees. 18 awards per year. Contact Registrar at above location for complete information.

1534 — ECOLOGICAL SOCIETY OF AMERICA (Murray F. Buell and E. Lucy Braun Awards)

Ariz. State Univ. West
P.O. Box 37100
Phoenix AZ 85069
602/543-6934
FAX: 602/543-6073
E-Mail: sam.scheiner@asu.edu
Internet: www.sdsc.edu./ESA/student.htm

AMOUNT: $400

DEADLINE(S): JAN 31

FIELD(S): Ecology

A contest for the outstanding oral paper and/or outstanding poster presentation at the ESA Annual Meeting. For grads, undergrads, or recent doctorate (not more than 9 months past graduation).

Request info. from Dr. Samuel Scheiner, Dept. of Life Sciences, at above location for details.

1535 — EDWARD AND ANNA RANGE SCHMIDT CHARITABLE TRUST (Grants & Emergency Financial Assistance)

PO Box 770982
Eagle River AK 99577
Written Inquiry

AMOUNT: Varies

DEADLINE(S): None

FIELD(S): Earth & Environmental Sciences

Open to Alaska residents or students in Alaska programs. Grants are awarded for a variety of expenses incurred by students, such as internship support, travel, expenses related to workshops and science fairs, support needed to secure employment in earth science-related fields, or emergency needs. Alaska Natives and other minorities are urged to apply.

Not renewable. Requests are given immediate consideration. Application should be made by letter from a sponsor (teacher, advisor, or other adult familiar with applicant's situation). Both sponsor and applicant should send letter describing applicant, nature of financial need, and amount requested.

1536 — ELECTROCHEMICAL SOCIETY (Summer Research Fellowships)

10 S. Main St.
Pennington NJ 08534
609/737-1902
FAX: 609/737-2745
E-Mail: ecs@electrtochem
Internet: www.electrochem.org

AMOUNT: $4,000 (ECS); $3,000 (DOE)

DEADLINE(S): JAN 1

FIELD(S): Energy; Chemical Engineering; Chemistry; Electrical Engineering

Summer fellowships are open to graduate students at accredited colleges and universities in any country. Purpose is to support research of interest to ECS, such as research aimed at reducing energy consumption.

8 awards annually (3 ECS, 5 Department of Energy). Contact ECS for an application.

1537 — ENGINEERING & PHYSICAL SCIENCES RESEARCH COUNCIL (Studentships)

North Star Ave
Polaris House
Swindon SN2 1ET England
01 793-444000

AMOUNT: Maintenance & approved fees

DEADLINE(S): JUL 31

FIELD(S): Engineering & Physical Science

Research studentships for up to 3 years for Ph.D students, 1 year advanced course studentships for master's students. Tenable at U.K. institutions. Must be UK resident with relevant connection to UK for full award or with European Union member state with relevant connection to UK for fees-only award. Must have appropriate academic qualifications.

Approx 3,800 awards per year. Applications must be made through heads of departments. EPSRC does not accept applications direct from students. Write for complete information.

1538 — ENGINEERING GEOLOGY FOUNDATION

c/o John W. Williams
Dept. of Geology
San Jose State Univ.
San Jose CA 95192-0102
408/924-5050

AMOUNT: Up to $1,000

DEADLINE(S): FEB 1

FIELD(S): Engineering Geology

Graduate scholarships for AEG members. Awards based on ability, scholarship, character, extracurricular activities, and potential for contributions to the profession.

Write for complete information.

1539 — EPPLEY FOUNDATION FOR RESEARCH (Postdoctoral Research Grants)

245 Park Avenue, 40th Floor
New York NY 10167
Written inquiry

AMOUNT: Up to $25,000

DEADLINE(S): FEB 1; MAY 1; AUG 1; NOV 1

FIELD(S): Physical Sciences; Biological Sciences

Postdoctoral grants for original advanced research in any of the physical or biological sciences. Open to established research scientists who are attached to a recognized institution.

Write for complete information.

1540 — FANNIE AND JOHN HERTZ FOUNDATION (Fellowship)

Box 5032
Livermore CA 94551-5032
925/373-1642
Internet: www.hertzfoundation.org

AMOUNT: $25,000 stipend/yr. + $15,000 (max.) tuition allowance/yr.

DEADLINE(S): NOV 5

FIELD(S): Applied Physical Sciences

Open to graduate students with a minimum 3.75 GPA for studies in applied physical sciences, including math, engineering, computer science, biology, oceanography, aeronautics, astronomy, physics, and earth science. Must be US citizen/permanent resident. Does not support study in pursuit of M.D. degree, although will support Ph.D. portion of a joint M.D./Ph.D. study program.

Renewable up to 5 years. Only 36 US schools are currently considered tenable. See website for an application and list of specific fields of study that are acceptable.

1541 — FLORIDA FEDERATION OF GARDEN CLUBS, INC. (FFGC Scholarships for College Students)

6065 21st St., SW
Vero Beach FL 32968-9427
561/778-1023
Internet: www.ffgc.org

AMOUNT: $1,500-$3,500

DEADLINE(S): MAY 1

FIELD(S): Ecology; Environmental Issues; Land Management; City Planning; Environmental Control; Horticulture; Landscape Design; Conservation; Botany; Forestry; Marine Biology; Floriculture; Agriculture

Various scholarships for Florida residents with a "B" average or better enrolled full-time as a junior, senior, or graduate student at a Florida college or university.

See website or contact Melba Campbell at FFGC for an application.

1542 — FORD FOUNDATION/NATIONAL RESEARCH COUNCIL (Postdoctoral Fellowship for Minorities)

National Research Council
2101 Constitution Ave.
Washington DC 20418
202/334-2860
E-Mail: infofell@nas.edu
Internet: http//www.nas.edu/fo/index.html

AMOUNT: $25,000 + relocation and research allowance

DEADLINE(S): JAN 3

FIELD(S): Life and physical sciences, mathematics, engineering sciences, behavioral and social sciences, and the humanities

For U.S. citizens who received a Ph.D or Sc.D in the last 7 years and who are Native Amer. Indian or Alaskan, Black/African American, Mexican American, Native Pacific Islander, or Puerto Rican and who are or plan to be in a teaching or research career.

Contact above website or address for complete information.

1543 — FORD FOUNDATION/NATIONAL RESEARCH COUNCIL (Predoctoral/Dissertation Fellowships for Minorities)

2101 Constitution Ave.
Washington DC 20418
202/334-2872
E-Mail: infofell@nas.edu
Internet: http//www.nas.edu/fo/index.html

AMOUNT: $14,000 annual stipend + $6,000 grant to institution; $18,000 for dissertation fellowship

DEADLINE(S): NOV 3

FIELD(S): Most fields of study: sciences, humanities, engineering, behavioral science, social sciences, and computer science

Predoctoral and dissertation fellowships for students whose ethnicity is Alaskan Native, Black/African American, Mexican American/Chicano, Native American Indian, Native Pacific Islander, or Puerto Rican. For research-based programs leading to careers in college teaching and research.

Contact above address or website.

1544 — FOREST HISTORY SOCIETY (Alfred D. Bell Jr. Travel Grants)

701 Wm. Vickers Ave.
Durham NC 27701-3162
919/682-9319
FAX: 919/682-2349
E-Mail: coakes@duke.edu
Internet: www.lib.duke.edu/forest/

AMOUNT: $850 (max.)

DEADLINE(S): None

FIELD(S): Forest & Conservation History

Open to graduates and postgraduates for research in the library and archives of the Forest History Society. Application packet includes a description of the main library and archival collections.

5-6 awards annually. Not renewable. Contact Cheryl Oakes for an application.

1545 — GAMMA THETA UPSILON INTERNATIONAL GEOGRAPHIC HONOR SOCIETY (Buzzard, Richason, & Maxfield Presidents Scholarships)

1725 State St.
La Crosse WI 54601
608/785-8355
FAX: 608/785-8332
E-Mail: holdevh@mail.uwlax.edu

AMOUNT: $500

DEADLINE(S): JUN 1

FIELD(S): Geography

Undergraduate and graduate scholarships are open to Gamma Theta Upsilon members who maintain at least a "B" grade point average in any accredited geography program.

Contact Dr. Virgil Holder, Dept. of Geography, University of Wisconsin, at above address for an application.

1546 — GEOLOGICAL SOCIETY OF AMERICA (Graduate Student Research Grants)

3300 Penrose Pl.
PO Box 9140
Boulder CO 80301-9140

303/447-2020, ext. 137
FAX: 303/447-1133
E-Mail: lcarter@geosociety.org
Internet: www.geosociety.org

AMOUNT: Varies

DEADLINE(S): FEB 1

FIELD(S): Geological Research

Provides partial support of master's and doctoral thesis research in geological sciences for graduate students at universities in the US, Canada, Mexico, and Central America. GSA Membership is NOT required.

187 awards in 1998; average amount was $1,654. Applications may be downloaded from website (available in December) but will not be accepted by e-mail or fax. Contact Leah J. Carter, Research Grants Administrator, for more information.

1547 — INSTITUTION OF MINING AND METALLURGY (Edgar Pam Fellowship)

Hallam Court
77 Hallam St.
London W1N 4BR ENGLAND
071 580 3802
FAX: 0171 436 5388

AMOUNT: 2,250 pounds sterling (max.)

DEADLINE(S): MAR 15

FIELD(S): Exploration Geology; Extractive Metallurgy

For postgraduate study in subjects related to above fields. Open to young graduates domiciled in Australia, Canada, New Zealand, South Africa, or the United Kingdom who wish to undertake advanced study or research in the U.K. Based on academic excellence and scholarship, NOT financial need. Preference will be given to IMM members.

Contact P.J. Martindale for an application.

1548 — INSTITUTION OF MINING AND METALLURGY (G. Vernon Hobson Bequest)

Hallam Court
77 Hallam St.
London W1N 6BR ENGLAND
0171 580 3802
FAX: 0171 436 5388

AMOUNT: 2,000 pounds sterling

DEADLINE(S): MAR 15

FIELD(S): Teaching of Geology as applied to Mining

Awards for the advancement of teaching and practice of geology as applied to mining. Awards may be used for travel, research, or other appropriate endeavor. Based on academic excellence and scholarship. Preference given to IMM members.

Contact P.J. Martindale at above address for an application.

1549 — INTERNATIONAL ASTRONOMICAL UNION (Exchange of Astronomers Travel Grant)

98BIS
Boulevard Arago
75014 Paris FRANCE
33.1/43 25 83 58

AMOUNT: Travel costs only

DEADLINE(S): None

FIELD(S): Astronomy

Travel grants for graduate students, postdoctoral fellows, or faculty-staff members at any recognized educational research institution or observatory. The program is designed to enable qualified persons to visit institutions abroad. Trip should be at least three months to allow ample time to interact with host institution and for benefits to astronomy on both sides.

Contact International Astronomical Union for an application.

1550 — INTERNATIONAL DESALINATION ASSOCIATION (Channabasappa Memorial Scholarship Fund)

P.O. Box 387
Topsfield MA 01983
978/887-0410
FAX: 978/887-0411
E-Mail: idalpab@ix.netcom.com
Internet: www.ida.bm

AMOUNT: Up to $6,000

DEADLINE(S): Varies

FIELD(S): Desalination or water technologies

Open to applicants who have their bachelor's degree from a recognized university & graduated in top 10% of their class. Scholarships support graduate study & research in desalination & water re-use.

For complete information write to Patricia Burke or Nancy Fitzgerald at above address.

1551 — INTERNATIONAL DEVELOPMENT RESEARCH CENTRE (John G. Bene Fellowship in Social Forestry)

PO Box 8500
250 Albert St.
Ottawa Ontario K1G 3H9 CANADA
613/236-6163, ext. 2098
Internet: www.idrc.ca/awards

AMOUNT: $15,000 (Canadian)

DEADLINE(S): FEB 1

FIELD(S): Social Forestry

Open to Canadian students pursuing a master's or doctoral degree at a Canadian university. Award is for research on the relationship of forest resources to the social, economic, and environmental welfare of people in developing countries.

See website or contact IDRC for an application and complete listing of available awards.

1552 — INTERNATIONAL INSTITUTE FOR APPLIED SYSTEMS ANALYSIS (Fellowships for Young Scientists' Summer Program at the IIASA in Vienna, Austria)

A-2361 Laxenburg
AUSTRIA
617/576-5019
FAX: 617/576-5050
E-Mail: mcollins@amacad.org
Internet: http://www.iiasa.ac.at

AMOUNT: Airfare and modest living expenses

DEADLINE(S): JAN 15

FIELD(S): Population, global change, economics, air pollution, transportation, forestry resorces, energy stratiegy, risk modeling, dynamic systems modeling

For advanced graduate and predoctoral candidates with research interests compatible with IIASA projects. Must have working level of written and spoken English and academic accomplishments and publications demonstrating superior qualifications.

4-7 annual awards. Contact Dr. Margaret Goud Collins (in U.S.) or Ms. Margaret Traber (in Austria).

1553 — KING FAISAL FOUNDATION (Graduate Scholarship Program)

PO Box 352
Riyadh 11411 SAUDI ARABIA
966/1 465-2255
FAX: 966/1 465-6524
E-Mail: info@kff.com OR mprd@kff.com
Internet: www.kff.com OR
www.kingfaisalfoundation.org

AMOUNT: $400/mo. US allowance + tuition/fees paid directly to university + health insurance & travel

DEADLINE(S): None

FIELD(S): Medicine; Engineering; Physics; Chemistry; Geology

Open to graduate students who are Muslims under the age of 40. Must have BS degree, GPA of 86% or higher, and be accepted unconditionally by a university either in Europe or North America. Must be fluent in the language of area providing the studies. Selection based on academic performance.

Contact King Faisal Foundation for an application.

1554 — LAND AND WATER RESOURCES R&D CORPORATION (Postgraduate Scholarships)

GPO Box 2182
Canberra ACT 2601 AUSTRALIA
02/6257 3379

FAX: 02/6257 3420

E-Mail: public@lwrrdc.gov.au

Internet: www.lwrrdc.gov.au

AMOUNT: $25,000/yr.

DEADLINE(S): JUN

FIELD(S): Natural Resources

Postgraduate scholarships for Australian citizens in the area of land, water, and vegetation resources to study/research in Australia. Financial need NOT a factor.

4 awards annually. Renewable up to three years. Contact Dr. Phil Price at LWRDC for an application. Award is made in September.

1555 — LAND AND WATER RESOURCES R&D CORPORATION (Travelling Fellowships)

GPO Box 2182

Canberra ACT 2601 AUSTRALIA

02/6257 3379

FAX: 02/6257 3420

E-Mail: public@lwrrdc.gov.au

Internet: www.lwrrdc.gov.au

AMOUNT: $10,000 (max.)

DEADLINE(S): JUN

FIELD(S): Natural Resources

Postgraduate fellowships for Australian researchers in the area of land, water, and vegetation resources, with overseas agencies to visit; LWRDC assists with financial and other support. Financial need NOT a factor.

6 awards annually. Not renewable. Contact Dr. Phil Price at LWRDC for an application. Award is made in September.

1556 — LAND AND WATER RESOURCES R&D CORPORATION (Visiting Fellowships)

GPO Box 2182

Canberra ACT 2601 AUSTRALIA

02/6257 3379

FAX: 02/6257 3420

E-Mail: public@lwrrdc.gov.au

Internet: www.lwrrdc.gov.au

AMOUNT: $10,000 (max.)

DEADLINE(S): JUN

FIELD(S): Natural Resources

Postgraduate fellowships for travel to Australia by overseas scientists in the area of land, water, and vegetation resources. Usually, fellows come at invitation of an Australian researcher; LWRDC assists with financial and other support. Financial need NOT a factor.

6 awards annually. Not renewable. Contact Dr. Phil Price at LWRDC for an application. Award is made in September.

1557 — LINK FOUNDATION (Energy Fellowship Program)

Center for Governmental Research

37 South Washington St.

Rochester NY 14608

Written inquiry

AMOUNT: $18,000

DEADLINE(S): DEC 1

FIELD(S): Energy Research

Awards will be made to doctoral students in academic or other non-profit institutions for energy research.

Write to address above for complete information.

1558 — LOUISIANA OFFICE OF STUDENT FINANCIAL ASSISTANCE (Rockefeller State Wildlife Scholarship)

PO Box 91202

Baton Rouge LA 70821-9202

800/259-5626, ext. 1012

FAX: 504/922-0790

Internet: www.osfa.state.la.us

AMOUNT: $1,000/yr.

DEADLINE(S): JUN 1

FIELD(S): Forestry; Wildlife; Marine Science

Open to Louisiana residents pursuing undergraduate or graduate study in a Louisiana college/university. Must have minimum 2.5 GPA. Recipients must attain a degree in one of the three eligible fields or repay the funds plus interest.

30 awards annually. Renewable up to 5 years undergraduate study & 2 years graduate study. Apply by completing the Free Application for Federal Student Aid (FAFSA). See your school's financial aid office or contact LOSFA for FAFSA form.

1559 — MATHESON GAS PRODUCTS FOUNDATION (Scholarships)

PO Box 624

959 Rte. 46 E.

Parsippany NJ 07054-0624

Internet: www.mathesongas.com

AMOUNT: $5,000

DEADLINE(S): None

FIELD(S): Chemistry; Physics; Chemical Engineering; Material Science; Semiconductor Engineering

Open to financially needy graduate students who are African American, Latino, Asian, Native American, or female. Must be US citizens/permanent residents studying in above fields or related area.

Send self-addressed, stamped envelope to Jerry Cantrella, Director of Personnel, for an application.

1560 — MINERALOGICAL SOCIETY OF AMERICA (MSA Grant for Research in Crystallography)

1015 18th St., NW, Ste. 601

Washington DC 20036-5274

202/775-4344

FAX: 202/775-0018

E-Mail: j_a_speer@minsocam.org

Internet: www.minsocam.org

AMOUNT: $3,500

DEADLINE(S): JUN 1

FIELD(S): Crystallography

Research grant based on qualifications of applicant; quality, innovativeness, & scientific significance of proposed research; and the likelihood of success of the project. Applicant must have reached his or her 25th birthday but not have reached his or her 36th birthday on the date the grant is awarded. There are no restrictions on how the grant funds may be spent, as long as they are used in support of research. MSA Counsellors may not apply.

See website or contact Dr. J. Alex Speer at the MSA Business Office for an application.

1561 — MINERALOGICAL SOCIETY OF AMERICA (MSA Grant for Student Research in Mineralogy and Petrology)

1015 18th St., NW, Ste. 601

Washington DC 20036-5274

202/775-4344

FAX: 202/775-0018

E-Mail: j_a_speer@minsocam.org

Internet: www.minsocam.org

AMOUNT: $3,500

DEADLINE(S): JUN 1

FIELD(S): Mineralogy; Petrology

Research grant for undergraduate or graduate students based on qualifications of applicant; the quality, innovativeness, & scientific significance of the proposed research; and the likelihood of success of the project. There are no restrictions on how the grant funds may be spent, as long as they are used in support of research.

See website or contact Dr. J. Alex Speer at the MSA Business Office for an application.

1562 — NATIONAL AERONAUTICS AND SPACE ADMINISTRATION (Graduate Student Researcher's Program-Underrepresented Minority Focus)

Mail Code FEH

NASA Headquarters

Washington, DC 20546

202/453-8344

AMOUNT: $22,000 1st year, renewable up to 3 years

DEADLINE(S): FEB 1

FIELD(S): Science, Engineering, Mathematics

For underrepresented minority groups in the fields of science and engineering (including African-Americans, American Indians, Hispanics, and Pacific Islanders), who may end up with a career in space science and/or aerospace technology. Must be US citizen and enrolled or accepted as a full-time graduate student at an accredited US college or university.

Write for complete information.

1563 — NATIONAL CENTER FOR ATMOSPHERIC RESEARCH (Graduate Student Research Fellowships)

PO Box 3000
Boulder CO 80307
303/497-1601
FAX: 303/497-1646
E-Mail: barbm@ucar.edu
Internet: www.asp.ucar.edu

AMOUNT: $16,810/yr. + travel

DEADLINE(S): Varies

FIELD(S): Atmospheric Sciences

Open to graduate students to support university Ph.D. thesis research conducted in collaboration with NCAR scientists.

Contact administrator Barbara Hansford for availability information.

1564 — NATIONAL COUNCIL FOR THE SOCIAL STUDIES (Grant for the Enhancement of Geographic Literacy)

3501 Newark St. NW
Washington DC 20016
202/966-7840
FAX: 202/966-2061
Internet: www.ncss.org/awards/grants.html

AMOUNT: $2,500

DEADLINE(S): JUL 3

FIELD(S): Social Studies

Grant is co-sponsored by the George F. Cram Company, map publishers. For teachers of any level who present a program to promote and enhance geography education in the schools. Must incorporate the National Georgraphy Standards in "Geography for Life," the "Fundamental Themes in Geography," and appropriate sections of "Expectations of Excellence: Curriculum Standards for Social Studies."

Check website or contact organization for details.

1565 — NATIONAL FEDERATION OF THE BLIND (Howard Brown Rickard Scholarship)

805 Fifth Avenue
Grinnell IA 50112
515/236-3366

AMOUNT: $3,000

DEADLINE(S): MAR 31

FIELD(S): Law; Medicine; Engineering; Architecture; Natural Sciences

For legally blind students pursuing or planning to pursue a full-time postsecondary course of study in the US. Based on academic excellence, service to the community, and financial need. Membership NOT required.

1 award annually. Renewable. Contact Mrs. Peggy Elliot, Scholarship Committee Chairman, for an application.

1566 — NATIONAL PARKS SERVICE (Science Scholars Program)

1849 C St., NW
Washington DC 20240
202/208-6843
E-Mail: aspiceland@goparks.org
Internet: www.nps.gov

AMOUNT: $25,000/yr.

DEADLINE(S): JUN 15

FIELD(S): Biological, Physical, Social, & Cultural Sciences

Three-year scholarships to Ph.D. candidates pursuing degrees in above fields. Objectives are to encourage young scientists to engage in park-related research, conduct innovative research on issues central to the National Parks, and encourage use of parks as laboritories for sciences. NPF will transfer the scholarship funds to each student's university, providing for tuition, field work, stipend, & other research expenses. Must submit research proposal.

4 awards annually. See website or contact Dr. Gary E. Machlis, Program Director, at NPS for an application. Winners announced shortly after August 15th.

1567 — NATIONAL PHYSICAL SCIENCE CONSORTIUM (Graduate Fellowships for Minorities & Women in the Physical Sciences)

MSC 3NPS
Box 30001
Las Cruces NM 88003-8001
800/952-4118 or 505/646-6038
FAX: 505/646-6097
E-Mail: npse@nmsu.edu
Internet: www.npsc.org

AMOUNT: $12,500 (years 1-4); $15,000 (years 5-6)

DEADLINE(S): NOV 5

FIELD(S): Astronomy; Chemistry; Computer Science; Geology; Materials Science; Mathematics; Physics

Open to "all US citizens" with an emphasis on Black, Hispanic, Native American, and female students. Must be pursuing graduate studies and have a minimum 3.0 GPA.

Renewable up to 6 years. See website or contact NPSC for an application.

1568 — NATIONAL RESEARCH COUNCIL OF CANADA (Research Associateships)

Research Associates Office
Ottawa Ontario K1A 0R6 CANADA
613/993-9150
FAX: 613/990-7669
Internet: www.nrc.ca/careers

AMOUNT: $39,366 Canadian

DEADLINE(S): None

FIELD(S): Natural Sciences; Engineering

Two-year research associateships are tenable at NRCC labs throughout Canada. Open to recent Ph.D.s in natural sciences or recent master's or Ph.D.s in engineering. Degrees should have been received within the last five years. Preference given to Canadians.

Renewable. See website or contact NRCC for an application.

1569 — NATIONAL RESEARCH FOUNDATION (NRF Honors & Postgraduate Bursaries)

PO Box 2600
Pretoria 0001 SOUTH AFRICA
+27 012/481-4000
FAX: +27 012/349-1179
E-Mail: info@nrf.ac.za
Internet: www.nrf.ac.za

AMOUNT: Varies

DEADLINE(S): Varies

FIELD(S): Agriculture; Chemistry; Earth Sciences; Engineering; Biology; Mathematics; Physics; Forestry; Veterinary Science; Pharmaceutics

Open to South African citizens pursuing graduate/postgraduate studies in above fields.

500 awards annually. Contact NRF for an application.

1570 — NATIONAL SCIENCES AND ENGINEERING RESEARCH COUNCIL OF CANADA (Graduate Scholarships)

Scholarships/Fellowships Division
350 Albert Street
Ottawa Ontario K1A 1H5 CANADA
613/996-3769
FAX: 613/996-2589
E-Mail: schol@nserc.ca
Internet: http://www.nserc.ca

AMOUNT: $15,700/year for 1st & 2nd years at masters or Ph.D level; $17,400/year (Ph.D level ONLY) 3rd & 4th years

DEADLINE(S): NOV 24

FIELD(S): Natural Sciences, Engineering, Biology, or Chemistry

Open to Canadian citizens or permanent residents who have earned or will soon earn a bachelors or masters degree in science or engineering. Academic excellence and research aptitude are considerations.

Write for complete information.

1571 — NATIONAL SCIENCES AND ENGINEERING RESEARCH COUNCIL OF CANADA (Postdoctoral Fellowships)

Scholarships/Fellowships Division
350 Albert Street
Ottawa Ontario K1A 1H5 CANADA
613/996-3762
FAX: 613/996-2589
E-Mail: schol@nserc.ca
Internet: http://www.nserc.ca

AMOUNT: Individually negotiated

DEADLINE(S): Varies—average: $43,000

FIELD(S): Natural Sciences, Engineering, Biology, or Chemistry

Open to Canadian citizens or permanent residents who hold doctoral degrees in science or engineering. Academic excellence and research aptitude are considerations.

Write for complete information.

1572 — NATIONAL SPELEOLOGICAL SOCIETY (Ralph W. Stone Research Grant)

2813 Cave Ave.
Huntsville AL 35810-4431
256/852-1300
FAX: 256/851-9241
E-Mail: nss@caves.org OR
geosccw@showme.missouri.edu

AMOUNT: $1,500

DEADLINE(S): Varies

FIELD(S): Speleology (Cave-Related Research)

Grant for members only of National Speleological Society for cave-related graduate thesis research in the biological, social, or earth sciences.

Contact NSS for an application, or write to Award Chairman Carol Wicks, University of Missouri, 101 Geology Building, Columbia, MO 65211.

1573 — NEWBERRY LIBRARY (Long-Term Fellowships)

60 West Walton Street
Chicago IL 60610-3380
312/943-9090
E-Mail: research@newberry.org
Internet: www.newberry.org

AMOUNT: Up to $30,000

DEADLINE(S): JAN 20

FIELD(S): Humanities, History, & related fields

Six postdoctoral fellowship programs are available for scholars wishing to use the Library's collection for writing or research. Fellowships last six to eleven months, and each have slightly different requirements.

See website for details and an application or write to above address.

1574 — NEWBERRY LIBRARY (Short-Term Fellowships)

60 West Walton Street
Chicago IL 60610-3380
312/943-9090
E-Mail: research@newberry.org
Internet: www.newberry.org

AMOUNT: $800-$1,500/month

DEADLINE(S): MAR 1

FIELD(S): Humanities, History, & related fields

Nine programs for postdoctoral scholars or doctoral students at the dissertation stage. Study varies from two weeks to three months and is for those making use of Newberry's collections. Each program has slightly different requirements.

See website for details and applications or write to above address.

1575 — NEWBERRY LIBRARY (Special Fellowships)

60 West Walton Street
Chicago IL 60610-3380
312/255-3666
E-Mail: research@newberry.org
Internet: www.newberry.org

AMOUNT: Varies

DEADLINE(S): DEC 15

FIELD(S): Humanities, History, & related fields

Fellowships for three months to one year for doctoral or postdoctoral students to study in Germany, France, or Great Britain in fields related to Newberry's collections. Some deadlines JAN 20th. Specific locations are: Wolfenb, ttel, Germany; Ecole Nationale des Chartes, Paris, France; and the British Academy, Great Britain.

See website for more details and applications or write to above address.

1576 — OAK RIDGE ASSOCIATED UNIVERSITIES (Laboratory Graduate Research Participation Program)

P.O. Box 117
Oak Ridge TN 37831-0117
423/576-4813

AMOUNT: $1,000-$1,200/mo. + allowance for dependents + tuition and fees reimbursement to a max. of $3,500/yr.

DEADLINE(S): Ongoing

FIELD(S): Life sciences, physical, and social sciences, mathematics, and engineering

For graduate students in one of the fields listed above who have completed all degree requirements except thesis or dissertation research. For full-time research under the joint direction of the major professor and a DOE staff member at one of various locations, primarily in the South. For six to twelve months.

Funded through U.S. Dept. of Energy, Office of Energy Reseach, and Office of Fossil Energy. Write for complete information.

1577 — OAK RIDGE ASSOCIATED UNIVERSITIES (National Science Foundation Graduate Research Fellowships)

PO Box 3010
Oak Ridge TN 37831-3010
423/241-4300
FAX: 423/241-4513
E-Mail: nsfgrfp@orau.gov
Internet: www.orau.gov/nsf/nsffel.htm

AMOUNT: $15,000 stipend + $10,500 tuition allowance

DEADLINE(S): NOV 4

FIELD(S): Science; Math; Engineering; Computer Science

Three-year fellowships for graduate study leading to research-based master's or doctoral degrees in the above fields. Must be US citizens, nationals, or permanent residents at the time of application. Fellowships are awarded on the basis of ability. Women, minorities, and those with disabilities are strongly encouraged to apply. One-time International Research Travel Allowance available.

1,000 awards annually. Contact Jeannette Bouchard for an application/more information.

1578 — OAK RIDGE INSTITUTE FOR SCIENCE AND EDUCATION (Alexander Hollaender Distinguished Post-doctoral Fellowships)

P.O. Box 117
Oak Ridge TN 37831-0117
423/576-3192 or 423/576-9975

AMOUNT: $37,500 + inbound travel, moving, and medical insurance

DEADLINE(S): JAN 15

FIELD(S): Biomedical, life, and environmental sciences and other related scientific disciplines, including global change and human genome

One-year post-doctoral fellowships for research and training in energy-related life, biomedical, and environmental sciences at one of participating laboratories in the U.S. Must have completed doctorate within last two years.

Must be U.S. citizen or legal resident.

1579 — OAK RIDGE INSTITUTE FOR SCIENCE AND EDUCATION (Applied Health Physics Fellowship Program)

P.O. Box 117
Oak Ridge TN 37831-0117
423/576-2194 or 423/576-9279
E-Mail: COXRE@ORAU.GOV or
GRADFELL@ORAU.GOV

AMOUNT: $14,400 stipend + tuition and fees up to $9,000/yr paid to university + transportation costs up to $300/month

DEADLINE(S): JAN 26

FIELD(S): Engineering, mathematics, physical and life sciences

Fellowship in applied health physics to implement DOE's nuclear energy-related mission. Candidates must have B.A. degree in life or physical sciences, engineering, or mathematics. Recipients are subject to a service obligation of one year of full-time employment in a DOE facility for each academic year of fellowhip award.

For details and application, contact above location.

1580 — OAK RIDGE INSTITUTE FOR SCIENCE AND EDUCATION (Industrial Hygiene Graduate Fellowship Program)

P.O. Box 117
Oak Ridge TN 37831-0117
423-576-9655
FAX: 423/576-8293
E-Mail: kinneym@orau.gov

AMOUNT:

DEADLINE(S): JAN 26

FIELD(S): Industrial Hygiene

A fellowship for first-year master's candidates who have undergraduate degrees in physical, life, environmental, or health sciences or enginering and who wish to pursue studies in industrial hygiene.

For details and application, contact above location.

1581 — OAK RIDGE INSTITUTE FOR SCIENCE AND EDUCATION (Professional Internship Program/Oak Ridge National Laboratory)

P.O. Box 117
Oak Ridge TN 37831-0117
423/576-3426
423/576-3427

AMOUNT: $210 to $300/week + travel, tuition, and fees

DEADLINE(S): FEB 5; JUN 1; OCT 1

FIELD(S): Chemistry, environmental science, geology, hydrogeology, hydrology, chemical engineering, civil engineering, environmental engineering, mechanical engineering, computer science (technical database development)

Opportunities for graduates and undergraduates to participate in energy-related research projects that correlate with their academic and career goals. For 3 to 12 consecutive months.

Funded through Oak Ridge National Laboratory.

1582 — OAK RIDGE INSTITUTE FOR SCIENCE AND EDUCATION (Professional Internship Program/Pittsburgh Energy Technology Center)

P.O. Box 117
Oak Ridge TN 37831-0117
423/576-3426
423/576-3427

AMOUNT: $235 to $325/week + travel, tuition, and fees

DEADLINE(S): FEB 5; JUN 1; OCT 1

FIELD(S): Chemistry, physics, environmental science, geology, chemical or environmental engineering, computer science, or statistics.

Opportunities for graduates and undergraduates to participate in fossil energy-related research projects that correlate with their academic and career goals. For 3 to 12 consecutive months.

Funded through U.S. Dept. of Energy, Office of Fossil Energy, and Pittsburgh Energy Technology Center.

1583 — OAK RIDGE INSTITUTE FOR SCIENCE AND EDUCATION (Professional Internship Program/Savannah River Site)

P.O. Box 117
Oak Ridge TN 37831-0117
423/576-3426
423/576-3427

AMOUNT: $260 to $340/week + travel

DEADLINE(S): FEB 5; JUN 1; SEP 1

FIELD(S): Chemistry, computer science, environmental science, geology, engineering, or physics

Opportunities for high school junior and seniors, undergraduates, and graduates to participate in research projects that correlate with their academic majors and career goals. For 3 to 12 consecutive months at the Savannah River Site, SC.

Funded through the Savannah River Site, SC.

1584 — OAK RIDGE INSTITUTE FOR SCIENCE AND EDUCATION (Science and Engineering Research Semester)

P.O. Box 117
Oak Ridge TN 37831-0117
423/576-2358
423/576-2310

AMOUNT: $225/week + travel + housing

DEADLINE(S): OCT; MAR

FIELD(S): Computer science, physical sciences, environmental and life sciences, and mathematics

Opportunities for high school junior and seniors and a few slots for graduates to participate in energy-related with laboratory scientists at Oak Ridge National Laboratory, TN. One semester with possibility of summer extension. Available two times a year.

Funded through the U.S. Dept. of Energy, Office of Energy Research.

1585 — OAK RIDGE INSTITUTE FOR SCIENCE AND EDUCATION (U.S. Geological Survey Earth Sciences Internship Program)

P.O. Box 117
Oak Ridge TN 37831-0117
423/576-2358
423/576-4813

AMOUNT: $19,000 to $38,000, dependent on level

DEADLINE(S): Ongoing

FIELD(S): Geology, geography, biology, chemistry, environmental sciences, hydrology, forestry, civil engineering, computer sciences

Internships for undergrads, grads, or recent grads (within one year) students studying in the above fields to conduct projects to prepare for careers in earth sciences for up to two years. Location: USGS sites across the U.S.

Funded through the U.S. Dept. of the Interior, U.S.G.S.

1586 — OAK RIDGE INSTITUTE FOR SCIENCE AND EDUCATION (Nuclear Engineering & Health Physics Fellowship Program)

105 Mitchell Rd. MS-16
Oak Ridge TN 37831-0117
423/576-2600 or 423/241-2890
E-Mail: johnsons@orau.gov or
daltonj@arou.gov

AMOUNT: $14,400/yr.

DEADLINE(S): JAN 26

FIELD(S): Engineering, physical and life sciences

Fellowships in nuclear engineering or applied health physics to implement DOE's nuclear energy-related mission. Candidates must have B.A. degree in life or physical sciences or engineering.

For details and application, contact Sandra Johnson or Jennifer Dalton at above location.

1587 — OPEN SOCIETY INSTITUTE (Environmental Management Fellowships)

400 West 59th St.
New York NY 10019
212/548-0600 or 212/757-2323
FAX: 212/548-4679 or 212/548-4600
Internet: www.soros.org/efp.html

AMOUNT: Fees, room, board, living stipend, textbooks, international transportation, health insurance

DEADLINE(S): NOV 15

FIELD(S): Earth sciences, natural sciences, humanities (exc. language), anthropology, sociology, mathematics, or engineering

Two-year fellowships for use in selected universities in the U.S. for international students. For students/professionals in fields related to environmental policy, legislation, and remediation techniques applicable to their home countries.

To apply, contact your local Soros Foundation or Open Society Institute. Further details on website.

1588 — OXFORD FORESTRY INSTITUTE (Master's Fellowship in Forestry)

South Parks Road
Oxford OX1 3RB ENGLAND UK
+44(0)1865 275055
FAX: +44(0)1865 275074
E-Mail: Peter.Savill@plants.ox.ac.uk
Internet: ifs.plants.ox.ac.uk

AMOUNT: Full funding (currently 17,798 pounds sterling)

DEADLINE(S): FEB

FIELD(S): Forestry & its Relation to Land Use

For students pursuing a master's degree in forestry. Preference will be given to those who have a first or second class honors degree in a biological subject. Must be a citizen of a developing Commonwealth country.

Contact Peter Savill at Oxford Forestry Institute for an application.

1589 — POPULATION COUNCIL (Fellowships in Social Sciences)

Policy Research Division
One Dag Hammarskjold Plaza
New York NY 10017
212/339-0671
FAX: 212/755-6052
E-Mail: ssfellowship@popcouncil.org
Internet: www.popcouncil.org

AMOUNT: Monthly stipend, partial tuition/fees, transportation, book/supply allowance, & health insurance

DEADLINE(S): DEC 15

FIELD(S): Population Studies; Demography; Sociology; Anthropology; Economics; Public Health; Geography

Twelve-month award is open to doctoral & postdoctoral scholars for advanced training in above fields that deal with developing world. Doctoral students may request support for dissertation fieldwork/writing. Postdoctorates may pursue research, midcareer training, or resident training. Based on academic excellence, prospective contribution, & well-conceived research proposal. Preference given to those from developing countries.

See website or contact Fellowship Coordinator for an application.

1590 — RESEARCH COUNCIL OF NORWAY (Senior Scientist Visiting Fellowship)

P.O. Box 2700 St. Hanshaugen
N-0131 Oslo NORWAY
+47 22 03 70 00
FAX: +47 22 03 70 01
E-Mail: intstip@nfr.no
Internet: www.forskningsradet.no

AMOUNT: NOK 25,000-1st 2 months; NOK 10,000-succeeding months

DEADLINE(S): Varies

FIELD(S): Bioproduction & Processing (including agriculture and veterinary science); Industry & Energy; Culture & Society (including social sciences and the humanities); Medicine & Health; Environment & Development; Science & Technology

Fellowships for scientists to work at Norwegian research institutes. Project funding does not include salary; expenses connected with the stay in Norway are covered.

For a list of institutions, contact the Research Council at above location. Then apply to institution, which then will submit fellowship application.

1591 — RESOURCES FOR THE FUTURE (Gilbert F. White Fellowship Program)

1616 P Street NW
Washington DC 20036-1400
202/328-5067
Internet: www.rff.org

AMOUNT: Based upon current salary + research support, office, and up to $1,000 for moving or living expenses.

DEADLINE(S): FEB 26

FIELD(S): Social Sciences; Natural Resources; Energy; Environment

Postdoctoral resident fellowships for professionals in the above fields who wish to devote eleven months to scholarly work on a social or policy problem in these. Faculty members on sabbatical encouraged to apply.

All information is on website. Address inquiries and applications to Coordinator for Academic Programs. NO fax submissions.

1592 — RESOURCES FOR THE FUTURE (Joseph L. Fisher Dissertation Fellowships)

1616 P Street NW
Washington DC 20036-1400
202/328-5000
Internet: www.rff.org

AMOUNT: $12,000/yr

DEADLINE(S): FEB 26

FIELD(S): Economics and other Social Sciences related to environment, natural resources, or energy

Fellowship to graduate students in the final year of their dissertatio research in the above fields.

All information is on website. NO fax submissions.

1593 — RESOURCES FOR THE FUTURE (RFF Summer Internship Program)

1616 P Street NW
Washington DC 20036-1400
202/328-5000
E-Mail: lewis@rff.org or voigt@rff.org
Internet: www.rff.org

AMOUNT: $375/week

DEADLINE(S): MAR 12

FIELD(S): Social Sciences, Natural Resources, Energy, Environment

Resident paid summer internships for undergraduate and graduate students for research in the above fields. Divisions are Center for Risk Management, Energy and Natural Resources, and Quality of the Environment. Candidates should have outstanding policy analysis and writing skills. For both U.S. and non-U.S. citizens.

All information is on website. Address inquiries and applications to Sue Lewis (Energy & Natural Resources and Quality of the Environment) or Marilyn Voigt (Center for Risk Management). NO fax submissions.

1594 — RESOURCES FOR THE FUTURE (Walter O. Spofford, Jr., Memorial Internship)

1616 P Street NW
Washington DC 20036-1400
202/328-5000
E-Mail: moran@rff.org
Internet: www.rff.org

AMOUNT: Individually negotiated

DEADLINE(S): MAR 12

FIELD(S): Chinese environmental issues in the areas of Social Sciences, Natural Resources, Energy, Environment

Resident paid internships for graduate students for research in the above fields. Candidates should have outstanding policy analysis and writing skills.

All information is on website. Address inquiries and applications to Mary Moran, Coordinator for Academic Programs. NO fax submissions.

1595 — ROCKEFELLER FOUNDATION (African Dissertation Internship Awards)

420 Fifth Ave.
New York NY 10018-2702
212/869-8500
212/764-3468
Internet: www.rockfound.org

AMOUNT: Cost of project

DEADLINE(S): None given

FIELD(S): Agriculture, environment, health, life sciences, population, and schooling

For African graduate students in U.S. and Canadian universities (but not to permanent residents) to return to Africa to carry out dissertation research at a local university or research institution. Priority given to above topics.

Students are strongly urged to be in the field for at least 12 months. Contact above location for details.

1596 — ROYAL SOCIETY (John Murray Fund)

6 Carlton House Terrace
REF REA
London SW1Y 5AG ENGLAND UK
071/839 5561

AMOUNT: Up to 3000 pounds sterling

DEADLINE(S): DEC 10

FIELD(S): Oceanography; Limnology; Zoology; Botany; Geology; Mathematics; Physics

Grants open to British post-doctoral applicants. Award is to be used for the encouragement of travel & work in oceanography or limnology.

The award may be held for 1 year. It is not renewable. Write for complete information—REF JELL.

1597 — ROYAL SOCIETY OF EDINBURGH (BP Research Fellowships)

22/24 George St.
Edinburgh EH2 2PQ SCOTLAND
0131 225 6057
FAX: 0131 220 6889
E-Mail: rse@rse.org.uk

AMOUNT: 17,606 to 26,508 pounds sterling

DEADLINE(S): MAR 10

FIELD(S): Mechanical, Chemical, or Control Engineering; Organic Chemistry; Solid State Physics; Information Technology; Geologic Sciences

Research fellowships to Scotland higher education institutions. For post-doctoral researchers age 35 or under on the date of appointment (usually Oct. 1). For research in above disciplines.

Write for complete information.

1598 — SCIENCE ADVANCEMENT PROGRAMS RESEARCH CORPORATION (Research Awards)

101 N. Wilmot Rd., Ste. 250
Tucson AZ 85711
520/571-1111
FAX: 520/571-1119
E-Mail: awards@rescorp.org
Internet: www.rescorp.org

AMOUNT: Varies

DEADLINE(S): Varies

FIELD(S): Astronomy; Chemistry; Physics

Several awards for research are available to faculty members and assistant professors who teach in university departments of astronomy, chemistry, and physics.

See website or contact above address for details.

1599 — SMITHSONIAN INSTITUTION (Fellowship Program)

Office of fellowships & Grants
955 L'Enfant Plaza, Suite 7000
Washington DC 20560
202/287-3271
E-Mail: http://www.si.edu/research+study
Internet: siofg@sivm.si.edu

AMOUNT: $3,000-$25,000 depending on level and length

DEADLINE(S): JAN 15

FIELD(S): Animal behavior, ecology, environmental science (including emphasis on the tropics, anthropology (& archaeology), astrophysics, astronomy, earth sciences, paleobiology, evolutionary/ systematic biology, history of science and technology, history of art, esp. American, contemporary, African, and Asian, 20th century American crafts, decorative arts, social/cultural history of the US, or folklife.

For research in residence at the Smithsonian for graduate students, both pre- and postdoctoral.

Research to be in the fields listed above.

1600 — SMITHSONIAN INSTITUTION (Minority Student Internship Program)

Fellowships & Grants
955 L'Enfant Plaza, Suite 7000
MRC 902
Washington DC 20560
202/287-3271
FAX: 202/287-3691
E-Mail: siofg@ofg.si.edu
Internet: www.si.edu/research+study

AMOUNT: $300/week + possible travel expenses

DEADLINE(S): FEB 15

FIELD(S): Humanities, Environmental Studies, Cultural Studies, Natural History, Earth Science, Art History, Biology, & related fields

Ten-week internships in residence at the Smithsonian for US minority students to participate in research or museum-related activities in above fields. For undergrads or grads with at least a 3.0 GPA. Essay, resume, transcripts, and references required with application. Internships are full-time and are offered for Summer, Fall, or Spring tenures.

Write for application.

1601 — SMITHSONIAN INSTITUTION (National Air & Space Museum Guggenheim Fellowship)

National Air and Space Museum, MRC 312
Washington DC 20560
Written inquiry

AMOUNT: $14,000 (predoctoral); $25,000 (postdoctoral)

DEADLINE(S): JAN 15

FIELD(S): Historical research related to aviation and space

Predoctoral applicants should have completed preliminary course work and exams and be engaged in dissertation research. Postdoctoral applicants should have received their Ph.D within the past seven years. Contact Fellowship Coordinator at above location.

Open to all nationalities. Fluency in English required. Duration is 6-12 months.

1602 — SMITHSONIAN INSTITUTION (National Air & Space Museum Verville Fellowship)

National Air and Space Museum, MRC 312
Washington DC 20560
Written inquiry

AMOUNT: $30,000 stipend for 12 months + travel and misc. expenses

DEADLINE(S): JAN 15

FIELD(S): Analysis of major trends, developments, and accomplishments in the history of aviation or space studies

A competitive nine- to twelve-month in-residence fellowship in the above field of study. Advanced degree is NOT a requirement. Contact Fellowship Coordinator at above location.

Open to all nationalities. Fluency in English required.

1603 — SOCIETY OF EXPLORATION GEOPHYSICISTS (SEG) FOUNDATION (Scholarships)

P.O. Box 702740
Tulsa OK 74170-2740
918/497-5530

AMOUNT: $500-$3,000

DEADLINE(S): MAR 1

FIELD(S): Geophysics

Open to a high school student with above average grades planning to enter college the next fall term or an undergraduate college student whose grades are above average, or a graduate college student whose studies are directed toward a career in exploration geophysics in operations, teaching, or research.

Write to the above address for complete information.

1604 — SOIL AND WATER CONSERVATION SOCIETY (Melville H. Cohee Student Leader Conservation Scholarship)

7515 N.E. Ankeny Road
Ankeny IA 50021-9764
515/289-2331 or 1-800-THE-SOIL
FAX 515/289-1227
E-Mail: charliep@swcs.org
Internet: www.swcs.org

AMOUNT: $900

DEADLINE(S): FEB 113

FIELD(S): Conservation or Natural Resource-Related Field

Open to 1+ year member of SWCS having served as an officer in a student chapter with 15+ members. GPA of 3.0 or better. Final year F/T undergrad or graduate.

2 awards. Course load must be 50% or more at accredited college or university. Financial need is not a factor. Write or visit website for complete information.

1605 — THE DAPHNE JACKSON MEMORIAL FELLOWSHIPS TRUST (Fellowships in Science/Engineering)

School of Physical Sciences, Dept. of Physics, University of Surrey
Guildford, Surrey GU2 5XH ENGLAND UK
01483 259166
FAX: 01483 259501
E-Mail: J.Woolley@surrey.ac.uk
Internet: www.sst.ph.ic.ac.uk/trust/

AMOUNT: Varies

DEADLINE(S): Varies

FIELD(S): Science or engineering, including information sciences

Fellowships to enable well-qualified and highly motivated scientists and engineers to return to appropriate careers following a career break due to family comitments. May be used on a flexible, part-time basis. Tenable at various U.K. universities.

See website and/or contact organization for details.

1606 — U.S. DEPARTMENT OF DEFENSE (GLSIP-General Laboratory Scientific Interchange Program: NRC-NRL Post-Doctoral Program)

Naval Research Laboratory
Office of Program Admin. &
Dev. Code 1006.17
Washington, D.C. 20375-5321
202/767-3865
DSN: 297-3865
FAX: 202/404-8110
Internet: www.acq.osd.mil/ddre/edugate/s-aindx.html

AMOUNT: Research Program

DEADLINE(S): None specified

FIELD(S): Computer science, artificial intelligence, plasma physics, acoustics, radar, fluid dynamics, chemistry, materials sci, optical sci, condensed matter and radiation, electronic sci, environmental sci, marine geosciences, remote sensing, oceanography, marine meteorology, space technology/sciences.

U.S. citizens who are recent postdoctoral graduates are selected on the basis of overall qualifications and techincal proposals.

Contact Jessica Hileman for more information.

1607 — U.S. ENVIRONMENTAL PROTECTION AGENCY—NATIONAL NETWORK FOR ENVIRONMENTAL MANAGEMENT STUDIES (Fellowships)

401 M St., SW
Mailcode 1704
Washington DC 20460
202/260-5283
FAX: 202/260-4095
E-Mail: jojokian.sheri@epa.gov
Internet: www.epa.gov/enviroed/students.html

AMOUNT: Varies

DEADLINE(S): DEC

FIELD(S): Environmental Policies, Regulations, & Law; Environmental Management & Administration; Environmental Science; Public Relations & Communications; Computer Programming & Development

Fellowships are open to undergraduate and graduate students working on research projects in the above fields, either full-time during the summer or part-time during the school year. Must be US citizen or legal resident. Financial need NOT a factor.

85-95 awards annually. Not renewable. See website or contact the Career Service Center of participating universities for an application.

1608 — UNIVERSITY OF MARYLAND INSTITUTE FOR ADVANCED COMPUTER STUDIES (Graduate Fellowships)

University of Maryland, UMIACS
College Park MD 20742
301/405-6722
E-Mail: fellows@umiacs.umd.edu
Internet: www.umiacs.umd.edu/fellow.html

AMOUNT: $18,000/yr. + tuition, health benefits, office space, etc.

DEADLINE(S): JAN 15

FIELD(S): Computer science, electrical engineering, geography, philosophy, linguistics, business, and management

Two-year graduate fellowships in the above fields for full-time students interested in interdisciplinary applications of computing at the Univ. of Maryland. After the first two years, external research funds may be provided to continue support for the fellow, depending upon satisfactory progress and the availability of funds.

Three new awards each year. Selection will be based on academic excellence and compatibility between students' research interest and those of UMIACS faculty.

1609 — UNIVERSITY OF WAIKATO (Hilary Jolly Memorial Scholarship)

Scholarships Office
Private Bag 3105
Hamilton NEW ZEALAND
07-856 2889, ext. 6320 or 6723
FAX: 07 838 4600
E-Mail: scholarships@waikato.ac.nz

AMOUNT: Varies

DEADLINE(S): None

FIELD(S): Fresh Water Ecology (Limnology)

Open to graduate students at the University of Waikato who are New Zealand citizens or permanent residents. Awarding of the scholarship will be based on academic merit, research ability, and the importance of the proposed research projects. Must commence research work within three months of being advised of award.

Contact Maureen Phillips, Assistant Manager-Scholarships, for an application.

1610 — US DEPARTMENT OF DEFENSE (National Defense Science & Engineering Graduate Fellowship Programs)

200 Park Drive, Suite 211, P.O. Box 13444
Research Triangle Park, NC 27709-3444
919/549-8505
Internet: www.acq.osd.mil/ddre/edugate/s-aindx.html

AMOUNT: Full tuition and fees (tenure of 36 months)

DEADLINE(S): JAN

FIELD(S): Mathematical, physical, biological, ocean, and engineering sciences

Must be US citizens or nationals at or near the beginning of their graduate study in science or engineering, leading to a doctoral degree. NDSEG Fellowships are awarded for study and research in these disciplines of military importance.

Approximately 90 new three-year graduate fellowships each April. Fellows may choose appropriate US institutions of higher education, offering degrees in science and engineering. Contact the Program Administrator for more information.

1611 — VANDERBILT UNIVERSITY (A. J. Dyer Observatory Research Assistantship)

c/o Dyer Observatory
1000 Oman Dr.
Brentwood TN 37027
615/373-4897

AMOUNT: Full-tuition + $11,750 stipend

DEADLINE(S): FEB 1

FIELD(S): Astronomy

Research assistantships in observational astronomy at Arthur J. Dyer Observatory. Includes stipend plus full tuition costs for graduate study at Vanderbilt University.

Write for complete information.

1612 — WATER ENVIRONMENT FEDERATION (Robert A. Canham Scholarship)

Access website
Internet: www.wef.org

AMOUNT: $2,500

DEADLINE(S): MAR 1

FIELD(S): Water environment areas

Open to post-baccalaureate students in the environmental engineering or sciences field who agree to work in the environmental field for at least two years after completion of the degree. Must be a member of the Water Environment Federation.

A detailed statement of career goals and aspirations and three letters of recommendation are required. Write for complete information. Access website for details and application—go to "Member Programs," then to "Canham Scholarship." Organization will not mail this information!

1613 — WATER ENVIRONMENT FEDERATION (Student Paper Competition)

Access website
Internet: www.wef.org

AMOUNT: $1,000 (1st prize); $500 (2nd); $250 (3rd)

DEADLINE(S): FEB 1

FIELD(S): Water pollution control and related fields

Awards for 500- 1,000-word abstracts dealing with water pollution control, water quality problems, water-related concerns, or hazardous wastes. Open to undergrad (A.A. and B.A.) and grad students.

Also open to recently graduated students (within 1 calendar year of Feb. 1 deadline). See website for details—go to "Member Programs" then to "Student Paper Competition." Organization will not mail this information.

1614 — WOMEN'S AUXILIARY TO THE AMERICAN INSTITUTE OF MINING METALLURGICAL & PETROLEUM ENGINEERS (WAAIME Scholarship Loan Fund)

345 E. 47th St., 14th Floor
New York NY 10017-2304
212/705-7692

AMOUNT: Varies

DEADLINE(S): MAR 15

FIELD(S): Earth Sciences, as related to the Minerals Industry

Open to undergraduate juniors and seniors and grad students, whose majors relate to an interest in the minerals industry. Eligible applicants receive a scholarship loan for all or part of their education. Recipients repay only 50%, with no interest charges.

Repayment to begin by 6 months after graduation and be completed within 6 years. Write to WAAIME Scholarship Loan Fund (address above) for complete information.

1615 — WOODROW WILSON NATIONAL FELLOWSHIP FOUNDATION (Leadership Program for Teachers)

CN 5281
Princeton NJ 08543-5281
609/452-7007
FAX: 609/452-0066
E-Mail: marchioni@woodrow.org OR
irish@woodrow.org
Internet: www.woodrow.org

AMOUNT: Varies

DEADLINE(S): Varies

FIELD(S): Science; Mathematics

WWLPT offers summer institutes for middle and high school teachers in science and mathematics. One- and two-week teacher outreach, TORCH Institutes, are held in the summer throughout the US.

See website or contact WWNFF for an application.

1616 — WOODS HOLE OCEANOGRAPHIC INSTITUTION (Fellowships for Summer Study in Geophysical Fluid Dynamics)

360 Woods Hole Road
Woods Hole MA 02543-1541

508/289-2219
FAX: 508/457-2188
E-Mail: mgately@whoi.edu
Internet: www.whoi.edu

AMOUNT: Varies

DEADLINE(S): FEB 16

FIELD(S): Geophysical Fluid Dynamics

A ten-week research and study program for graduate and postdoctoral students to explore specific topics in the general area of geophysical fluid dynamics. Fellows and invited staff members exchange ideas through lectures and seminars, and they work together on the formation and exploration of tractable research problems in a designated area of current interest in the field.

Up to ten competitive fellowships annually. For an application/more information, contact the Education Office, Clark Laboratory 223, MS #31, at above address.

1617 — WOODS HOLE OCEANOGRAPHIC INSTITUTION (Postdoctoral Awards in Ocean Science and Engineering)

360 Woods Hole Road
Woods Hole MA 02543-1541
508/289-2219
FAX: 508/457-2188
E-Mail: mgately@whoi.edu
Internet: www.whoi.edu

AMOUNT: Varies

DEADLINE(S): FEB 16

FIELD(S): Chemistry, Engineering, Geology, Geophysics, Mathematics, Meteorology, Physics, Biology, Oceanography

Eighteen-month postdoctoral scholar awards are offered to recipients of new or recent doctorates in the above fields. The awards are designed to further the education and training of the applicant with primary emphasis placed on the individual's research promise.

For an application/more information, contact the Education Office, Clark Laboratory 223, MS #31, at above address.

1618 — WOODS HOLE OCEANOGRAPHIC INSTITUTION (Research Fellowships in Marine Policy and Ocean Management)

360 Woods Hole Road
Woods Hole MA 02543-1541
508/289-2219
FAX: 508/457-2188
E-Mail: mgately@whoi.edu
Internet: www.whoi.edu

AMOUNT: Varies

DEADLINE(S): FEB 16

FIELD(S): Social Sciences, Law, Natural Sciences

For professionals in the above fields who wish to apply their training to investigations of problems involving the use of the oceans. WHOI's objective is to provide a year-long advanced learning experience in ocean policy problems involving the interdisciplinary application of social science and natural science to marine policy problems. Fields currently emphasized: economics, statistics, public policy, natural resource management, and international relations.

For an application/more information, contact the Education Office, Clark Laboratory 223, MS #31, at above address.

ENVIRONMENTAL STUDIES

1619 — ACADEMY OF NATURAL SCIENCES OF PHILADELPHIA (Jessup & McHenry Fund Grants)

The Academy of Natural Sciences, 1900 Benjamin Franklin Parkway
Philadelphia PA 19103-1195
215/299-1,000

AMOUNT: $250 (travel); Max $1,000

DEADLINE(S): MAR 1; OCT 1

FIELD(S): Botany/McHenry Award; Research in Natural Science/Jessup Award

Grants to support research are primarily intended to assist predoctoral and immediate postdoctoral students. The work must be done at the Academy of Natural Sciences in Philadelphia and must have the sponsorship of an Academy staff member.

In general grants are awarded for a minimum of 2 weeks and a maximum of 16-week periods. Students from the Philadelphia area are NOT eligible. Write for complete information.

1620 — AMERICAN FOUNDATION FOR THE BLIND (Paul W. Ruckes Scholarship)

11 Penn Plaza, Ste. 300
New York NY 10001
212/502-7661 or TDD 212/502-7771
E-Mail: juliet@afb.org
Internet: www.afb.org

AMOUNT: $1,000

DEADLINE(S): APR 30

FIELD(S): Engineering, computer, physical, or life sciences

Open to blind or visually impaired undergraduate or graduate students pursuing degrees in the above fields. U.S. citizenship required.

Write to the above address or visit website for complete information.

1621 — AMERICAN INDIAN SCIENCE AND ENGINEERING SOCIETY (A.T. Anderson Memorial Scholarship)

PO Box 9828
Albuquerque NM 87119-9828
505/765-1052
FAX: 505/765-5608
E-Mail: scholarships@aises.org
Internet: www.aises.org/scholarships

AMOUNT: $1,000-$2,000

DEADLINE(S): JUN 15

FIELD(S): Medicine; Natural Resources; Science; Engineering

Open to undergraduate and graduate students who are at least 1/4 American Indian or recognized as member of a tribe. Must be member of AISES ($10 fee), enrolled full-time at an accredited institution, and demonstrate financial need.

Renewable. See website or contact Patricia Browne for an application and/or membership information.

1622 — AMERICAN INDIAN SCIENCE AND ENGINEERING SOCIETY (EPA Tribal Lands Environmental Science Scholarship)

PO Box 9828
Albuquerque NM 87119-9828
505/765-1052
FAX: 505/765-5608
E-Mail: scholarships@aises.org
Internet: www.aises.org/scholarships

AMOUNT: $4,000

DEADLINE(S): JUN 15

FIELD(S): Biochemistry; Biology; Chemical Engineering; Chemistry; Entomology; Environmental Economics/Science; Hydrology; Environmental Studies

Open to American Indian college juniors, seniors, and graduate students enrolled full-time at an accredited institution. Must demonstrate financial need. Certificate of Indian blood NOT required.

Renewable. See website or contact Patricia Browne for an application.

1623 — AMERICAN MUSEUM OF NATURAL HISTORY (International Graduate Student Fellowship Program)

Central Park West at 79th St.
New York NY 10024-5192
FAX: 212/769-5495
E-Mail: bynum@amnh.org
Internet: research.amnh.org

AMOUNT: Stipend, tuition, & travel

DEADLINE(S): JAN 15

FIELD(S): Biodiversity & Conservation; Public Policy; Entomology; Evolutionary & Molecular Biology

One-year joint program w/ Columbia, Cornell, & Yale Universities & City University of NY to help advance training of Ph.D. candidates who are non-US citizens. Purpose is to gain skills & experience to bear on environmental problems of their home countries. Must submit resume/curriculum vitae, GRE & TOEFL scores, official transcripts, letters of recommendation, & statement of purpose.

Renewable up to 4 years. Must apply to Museum AND cooperating university. See website or contact Office of Grants & Fellowships for application.

1624 — AMERICAN PLANNING ASSOCIATION (Minority Scholarship and Fellowship Programs)

122 South Michigan Ave., Ste. 1600
Chicago IL 60605
312/431-9100
FAX: 312/431-9985

AMOUNT: $2,000-$5,000 (grads); $2,500 (undergrads)

DEADLINE(S): MAY 14

FIELD(S): Urban planning, community development, environmental sciences, public administration, transportation, or urban studies

Scholarships for African-Americans, Hispanics, or Native American students pursing undergraduate degrees in the U.S. in the above fields. Must have completed first year. Fellowships for graduate students. Programs must be approved by the Planning Accreditation Board. U.S. citizenship.

Call or write for complete information.

1625 — AMERICAN WATER WORKS ASSOCIATION (Abel Wolman Fellowship)

6666 W. Quincy Ave.
Denver CO 80235
303/347-6206
FAX: 303/794-8915
E-Mail: vbaca@awwa.org
Internet: www.org/tande/eduframe.htm

AMOUNT: $15,000 stipend +$1,000 for supplies +up to $4,000 for tuition, etc.

DEADLINE(S): JAN 15

FIELD(S): Research in water supply and treatment

For students who show potential for leadership and anticipate completion of the requirments for a Ph.D. within two years of the award. Applicants will be evaluated on the quality of academic record, the significance of the proposed research to water supply and treatment, and the potential to do high quality research. Must be citizen or permanent resident of the U.S., Canada, or Mexico.

Renewable for a second year. Write for complete information.

1626 — AMERICAN WATER WORKS ASSOCIATION (Academic Achievement Award)

> 6666 West Quincy Ave.
> Denver CO 80235
> 303/347-6206
> FAX: 303/794-8915
> E-Mail: vbaca@awwa.org
> Internet: www.org/tande/eduframe.htm

AMOUNT: 1st place: $1,000; 2nd place: $500

DEADLINE(S): OCT 1

FIELD(S): Subject related to drinking water supply industry

Award for a master's thesis or doctoral dissertation that has potential value to the water supply industry. This is not a scholarship but a cash award for outstanding work that has been completed.

Write for complete information.

1627 — AMERICAN WATER WORKS ASSOCIATION (Holly A. Cornell Scholarship)

> 6666 W. Quincy Ave.
> Denver CO 80235
> 303/347-6206
> FAX: 303/794-8915
> E-Mail: vbaca@awwa.org
> Internet: www.org/tande/eduframe.htm

AMOUNT: $5,000

DEADLINE(S): JAN 15

FIELD(S): Engineering (Water Supply and Treatment)

Open to females and minorities (as defined by the U.S. Equal Opportunity Commission) who anticipate completion of a master's degree in engineering no sooner than December of the following year. Program was created by CH2M Hill, Inc. in honor of one of the firm's founders.

Contact organization for complete information.

1628 — AMERICAN WATER WORKS ASSOCIATION (Lars Scholarship)

> 6666 W. Quincy Ave.
> Denver CO 80235
> 303/347-6206
> FAX: 303/794-8915
> E-Mail: vbaca@awwa.org
> Internet: awwa.org/tande/eduframe.htm

AMOUNT: $5,000 (Masters); $7,000 (Ph.D.)

DEADLINE(S): JAN 15

FIELD(S): Science and Engineering in the field of Water Supply and/or Treatment

For M.A. and Ph.D. level students at an institution of higher learning in Canada, Guam, Puerto Rico, Mexico, or the United States. For research into water supply and/or treatment.

Write for complete information.

1629 — AMERICAN WATER WORKS ASSOCIATION (Thomas R. Camp Scholarship)

> 6666 W. Quincy Ave.
> Denver CO 80235
> 303/347-6206
> FAX: 303/794-8915
> E-Mail: vbaca@awwa.org
> Internet: www.org/tande/eduframe.htm

AMOUNT: $5,000

DEADLINE(S): JAN 15

FIELD(S): Research in the drinking water field

For students pursuing an M.A. or Ph.D. in the field of drinking water. This award is granted to Doctoral students in even years and Master's students in odd years. Can be used at an institution of higher education in Canada, Guam, Puerto rico, Mexico, or the U.S.

One award each year. Contact above location for details.

1630 — ASIAN INSTITUTE OF TECHNOLOGY (AIT Scholarship Program)

> Development Office
> PO Box 4, Klongluang
> Pathumthani 12120 THAILAND
> (66)(2) 516-0110-44 or 524-5032
> FAX: (66)(2) 516-2126
> E-Mail: ascao@ait.ac.th
> Internet: www.ait.ac.th

AMOUNT: US $12,600-$37,960

DEADLINE(S): FEB 15; JUN 15; OCT 15

FIELD(S): Advanced Technologies; Civil Engineering; Environment, Resources, & Development; Business Management

Scholarships and grants open to citizens of Asian countries who are accepted by the institute as a master's or doctotal candidate. Selection is based on academic criteria, practical experience, gender, and country of origin; priority to Mekong Region countries and Asian countries of the former USSR.

250 awards annually. Contact AIT for an application.

1631 — BOEING (Polish Graduate Student Scholarship Program)

> Phone for details
> 314/234-2149

AMOUNT: Tuition, books, and fees for three years

DEADLINE(S): Varies

FIELD(S): Scientific and technical fields

Scholarships for students from Poland to pursue graduate studies in scientific and technical areas at American colleges or universities.

Call Jim Schlueter at above telephone number.

1632 — CHARLES A. AND ANNE MORROW LINDBERGH FOUNDATION (Grants for Research Projects)

> 2150 Third Ave., N, Ste. 310
> Anoka MN 55303-2200
> 612/576-1596
> FAX: 612/576-1664
> E-Mail: lindbergh@isd.net
> Internet: www.isd.net/lindbergh

AMOUNT: $10,580 (max.)

DEADLINE(S): JUN 15

FIELD(S): Aviation; Aerospace; Agriculture; Education; Arts; Humanities; Biomedical Research; Exploration; Health & Population Sciences; Intercultural Communication; Waste Disposal Minimization & Management.; Adaptive Technology; Conservation

Open to individuals whose proposed projects represent a significant contribution toward the achievement of balance between the advance of technology and preservation of the natural environment. Financial need NOT a factor. Funding is NOT for tuition.

10 awards annually. See website for application.

1633 — COOPERATIVE INSTITUTE FOR RESEARCH IN ENVIRONMENTAL SCIENCES (CIRES Visiting Fellowships)

> Univ Colorado
> Campus Box 216
> Boulder CO 80309-0216
> 303/492-1143
> Internet: cires.colorado.edu/ciresvf.html

AMOUNT: Varies

DEADLINE(S): DEC 15

FIELD(S): Environmental & Earth Sciences

One-year visiting fellowships for recent Ph.D.s and senior scientists, including faculty on sabbatical. To be used towards research in the areas of physics, chemistry, & dynamics of Earth system; global & regional environmental change; climate system monitoring, diagnostics, & modeling; and remote sensing measurement techniques. Must submit curriculum vitae, publications list, 2-4 page description of proposed research, and letters of recommendation.

5 awards annually. Renewable. See website or contact CIRES for an application. CIRES receives sponsorship from the National Oceanic and Atmosphere Administration's Environmental Research Laboratories.

1634 — ECOLOGICAL SOCIETY OF AMERICA (Murray F. Buell and E. Lucy Braun Awards)

Ariz. State Univ. West
P.O. Box 37100
Phoenix AZ 85069
602/543-6934
FAX: 602/543-6073
E-Mail: sam.scheiner@asu.edu
Internet: www.sdsc.edu./ESA/student.htm

AMOUNT: $400

DEADLINE(S): JAN 31

FIELD(S): Ecology

A contest for the outstanding oral paper and/or outstanding poster presentation at the ESA Annual Meeting. For grads, undergrads, or recent doctorate (not more than 9 months past graduation).

Request info. from Dr. Samuel Scheiner, Dept. of Life Sciences, at above location for details.

1635 — EDMUND NILES HUYCK PRESERVE (Research Grants)

Main St.
Rensselaerville NY 12147
518/797-3440

AMOUNT: $2,500 (max.)

DEADLINE(S): FEB 1

FIELD(S): Ecology; Behavior; Evolution; Natural History

Open to graduate and postgraduate scientists conducting research on the natural resources of the Huyck Preserve. Housing and lab space are provided at the preserve. Funds are NOT available to help students defray college expenses.

Contact Preserve for an application.

1636 — EDWARD AND ANNA RANGE SCHMIDT CHARITABLE TRUST (Grants & Emergency Financial Assistance)

PO Box 770982
Eagle River AK 99577
Written Inquiry

AMOUNT: Varies

DEADLINE(S): None

FIELD(S): Earth & Environmental Sciences

Open to Alaska residents or students in Alaska programs. Grants are awarded for a variety of expenses incurred by students, such as internship support, travel, expenses related to workshops and science fairs, support needed to secure employment in earth science-related fields, or emergency needs. Alaska Natives and other minorities are urged to apply.

Not renewable. Requests are given immediate consideration. Application should be made by letter from a sponsor (teacher, advisor, or other adult familiar with applicant's situation). Both sponsor and applicant should send letter describing applicant, nature of financial need, and amount requested.

1637 — FIRST UNITED METHODIST CHURCH (Robert Stevenson & Doreene E. Cater Scholarships)

302 5th Ave., S.
St. Cloud MN 56301
FAX: 320/251-0878
E-Mail: FUMCloud@aol.com

AMOUNT: $100-$300

DEADLINE(S): JUN 1

FIELD(S): Humanitarian & Christian Service: Teaching, Medicine, Social Work, Environmental Studies, etc.

Stevenson Scholarship is open to undergraduate members of the First United Methodist Church of St. Cloud. Cater Scholarship is open to members of the Minnesota United Methodist Conference who are entering the sophomore year or higher of college work. Both require two letters of reference, transcripts, and financial need.

5-6 awards annually. Contact Scholarship Committee for an application.

1638 — FLORIDA FEDERATION OF GARDEN CLUBS, INC. (FFGC Scholarships for College Students)

6065 21st St., SW
Vero Beach FL 32968-9427
561/778-1023
Internet: www.ffgc.org

AMOUNT: $1,500-$3,500

DEADLINE(S): MAY 1

FIELD(S): Ecology; Environmental Issues; Land Management; City Planning; Environmental Control; Horticulture; Landscape Design; Conservation; Botany; Forestry; Marine Biology; Floriculture; Agriculture

Various scholarships for Florida residents with a "B" average or better enrolled full-time as a junior, senior, or graduate student at a Florida college or university.

See website or contact Melba Campbell at FFGC for an application.

1639 — FORD FOUNDATION/NATIONAL RESEARCH COUNCIL (Predoctoral/Dissertation Fellowships for Minorities)

2101 Constitution Ave.
Washington DC 20418
202/334-2872
E-Mail: infofell@nas.edu
Internet: http://www.nas.edu/fo/index.html

AMOUNT: $14,000 annual stipend + $6,000 grant to institution; $18,000 for dissertation fellowship

DEADLINE(S): NOV 3

FIELD(S): Most fields of study: sciences, humanities, engineering, behavioral science, social sciences, and computer science

Predoctoral and dissertation fellowships for students whose ethnicity is Alaskan Native, Black/African American, Mexican American/Chicano, Native American Indian, Native Pacific Islander, or Puerto Rican. For research-based programs leading to careers in college teaching and research.

Contact above address or website.

1640 — FOREST HISTORY SOCIETY (Alfred D. Bell Jr. Travel Grants)

701 Wm. Vickers Ave.
Durham NC 27701-3162
919/682-9319
FAX: 919/682-2349
E-Mail: coakes@duke.edu
Internet: www.lib.duke.edu/forest/

AMOUNT: $850 (max.)

DEADLINE(S): None

FIELD(S): Forest & Conservation History

Open to graduates and postgraduates for research in the library and archives of the Forest History Society. Application packet includes a description of the main library and archival collections.

5-6 awards annually. Not renewable. Contact Cheryl Oakes for an application.

1641 — GARDEN CLUB OF AMERICA (Catherine H. Beattie Fellowship)

Ctr. Plant Conservation, MO Botanical Garden
PO Box 299
St. Louis MO 63166-0299
314/577-9452
FAX: 314/577-9465
E-Mail: sud@mobot.org
Internet: www.mobot.org/cpc/beattie.html

AMOUNT: up to $4,000

DEADLINE(S): DEC 31

FIELD(S): Flora Conservation

Research grant to a graduate student to promote conservation of rare and endangered flora in the US. Preference to students whose projects focus on the endangered flora of the Carolinas and southeastern US.

1 award annually. See website or contact Ms. Anukriti Sud at above address for more information/an application.

1642 — GARDEN CLUB OF AMERICA (Frances M. Peacock Scholarship)

Cornell Lab of Orinthology
159 Sapsucker Woods Rd.
Ithica, NY 14850
FAX: 607/254-2415
E-Mail: 1h17@cornell.edu
Internet: www.gcamerica.org

AMOUNT: $4,000

DEADLINE(S): JAN 15

FIELD(S): Habitats of Threatened/Endangered Native Birds

To provide financial aid to "an advanced student (college senior or graduate student) to study areas in the US that provide winter or summer habitat for our threatened and endangered native birds." Proposals will be judged upon the significance of the research project, prior accomplishments of awardee, and appropriateness of research topic.

1 award annually. Not renewable. Funds can be used at the discretion of the awardee: for fees, expenses, or even tuition provided they are directly related to the project at hand. Contact Scott Sutcliffe, Associate Director, for more information.

1643 — HILLEL INTERNATIONAL CENTER (The Public Policy Fellowship)

Eran Gasko
1640 Rhode Island Ave. NW
Washington DC 20036
202/857-6543
202/857-6560
FAX: 202/857-6693
E-Mail: smusher@hillel.org
Internet: www.hillel.org/careermoves/publicpolicy.htm

AMOUNT: Professional Experience

DEADLINE(S):·None specified

FIELD(S): Public Policy/Social Issues

One-year professional experience for an oustanding recent Jewish graduate, who coordinates public policy initiatives nationwide. The Fellow strives to increase student activism in political and social issues. S/he works with students and national organizations to create innovative initiatives in social action, campus community relations councils, environmental issues, Israel programming, and international relief efforts.

Contact Eran Gasko, Human Resources, for an application.

1644 — HUBBARD FARMS CHARITABLE FOUNDATION

P.O. Box 505
Walpole NH 03608-0505
603/756-3311

AMOUNT: Varies

DEADLINE(S): APR 1; OCT 1

FIELD(S): Poultry science, genetics, and other life sciences

Scholarships are for financially needy students at universities that the foundation trustees consider to be leaders in the field of progress in technology and efficiency of production of poultry products.

Send SASE to Jane F. Kelly, Clerk, at above address for current application guidelines.

1645 — INSTITUTE FOR THE STUDY OF WORLD POLITICS (Dissertation Fellowships)

1755 Massachusetts Ave. NW
Washington DC 20036
202/588-9797
Internet: fundforpeace.org/iswp.htm

AMOUNT: Varies

DEADLINE(S): FEB 16

FIELD(S): International Relations; Environmental Issues; Population Studies (Social Science aspects); Human Rights; Arms Control; Third World Development; Agricultural Development; Public Health, etc.

For doctoral candidates conducting dissertation research in above areas to promote scholarly examination of political, economic, and social issues that affect the security, well-being, and dignity of the peoples of the world. Financial need is a consideration. For citizens of any country.

Write for complete information.

1646 — INSTITUTE FOR THE STUDY OF WORLD POLITICS (Dorothy Danforth Compton Fellowships)

1755 Massachusetts Ave. NW
Washington DC 20036
202/588-9797
Internet: fundforpeace.org/iswp.htm

AMOUNT: Varies

DEADLINE(S): MAR 16

FIELD(S): International Relations; Environmental Issues; Population Studies (Social Science aspects); Human Rights; Arms Control; Third World Development; Agricultural Development; Public Health, etc.

For masters or doctoral candidates researching in the above areas to promote scholarly examination of political, economic, and social issues that affect the security, well-being, and dignity of the peoples of the world. Must be African American, Hispanic American, and Native American students who are U.S. citizens and studying in U.S. institutions. Financial need is a consideration.

Write for complete information.

1647 — INTERNATIONAL DESALINATION ASSOCIATION (Channabasappa Memorial Scholarship Fund)

P.O. Box 387
Topsfield MA 01983
978/887-0410
FAX: 978/887-0411
E-Mail: idalpab@ix.netcom.com
Internet: www.ida.bm

AMOUNT: Up to $6,000

DEADLINE(S): Varies

FIELD(S): Desalination or water technologies

Open to applicants who have their bachelor's degree from a recognized university & graduated in top 10% of their class. Scholarships support graduate study & research in desalination & water re-use.

For complete information write to Patricia Burke or Nancy Fitzgerald at above address.

1648 — INTERNATIONAL INSTITUTE FOR APPLIED SYSTEMS ANALYSIS (Fellowships for Young Scientists' Summer Program at the IIASA in Vienna, Austria)

A-2361 Laxenburg
AUSTRIA
617/576-5019
FAX: 617/576-5050
E-Mail: mcollins@amacad.org
Internet: http://www.iiasa.ac.at

AMOUNT: Airfare and modest living expenses

DEADLINE(S): JAN 15

FIELD(S): Population, global change, economics, air pollution, transportation, forestry resorces, energy stratiegy, risk modeling, dynamic systems modeling

For advanced graduate and predoctoral candidates with research interests compatible with IIASA projects. Must have working level of written and spoken English and academic accomplishments and publications demonstrating superior qualifications.

4-7 annual awards. Contact Dr. Margaret Goud Collins (in U.S.) or Ms. Margaret Traber (in Austria).

1649 — KUALA BELALONG FIELD STUDIES CENTRE, UNIVERSITI BRUNEI DERUSSALEM (Research Fellowship)

c/o Colin Maycock, Research Coordinator
Bander Seri Begawen 2028
Brunei Derussalem
673-2-249001, ext. 376
FAX: 673-2-249502
E-Mail: KBFSC@ubd.edu.bn
Internet: www.ubd.edu.bn/hmkbfsc.htm

AMOUNT: $B 3,000/month (12 months)

DEADLINE(S): OCT

FIELD(S): Biodiversity, Rain Forest Ecology & Dynamics

Applicants must hold a Ph.D. in a relevant subject, submit a detailed research proposal, and be planning to attend at the Kuala Belalong Field Studies Centre, Universiti Brunei Darussalem.

Write for complete information.

1650 — LAND AND WATER RESOURCES R&D CORPORATION (Postgraduate Scholarships)

GPO Box 2182
Canberra ACT 2601 AUSTRALIA
02/6257 3379
FAX: 02/6257 3420
E-Mail: public@lwrrdc.gov.au
Internet: www.lwrrdc.gov.au

AMOUNT: $25,000/yr.

DEADLINE(S): JUN

FIELD(S): Natural Resources

Postgraduate scholarships for Australian citizens in the area of land, water, and vegetation resources to study/research in Australia. Financial need NOT a factor.

4 awards annually. Renewable up to three years. Contact Dr. Phil Price at LWRDC for an application. Award is made in September.

1651 — LAND AND WATER RESOURCES R&D CORPORATION (Travelling Fellowships)

GPO Box 2182
Canberra ACT 2601 AUSTRALIA
02/6257 3379
FAX: 02/6257 3420
E-Mail: public@lwrrdc.gov.au
Internet: www.lwrrdc.gov.au

AMOUNT: $10,000 (max.)

DEADLINE(S): JUN

FIELD(S): Natural Resources

Postgraduate fellowships for Australian researchers in the area of land, water, and vegetation resources, with overseas agencies to visit; LWRDC assists with financial and other support. Financial need NOT a factor.

6 awards annually. Not renewable. Contact Dr. Phil Price at LWRDC for an application. Award is made in September.

1652 — LAND AND WATER RESOURCES R&D CORPORATION (Visiting Fellowships)

GPO Box 2182
Canberra ACT 2601 AUSTRALIA
02/6257 3379
FAX: 02/6257 3420
E-Mail: public@lwrrdc.gov.au
Internet: www.lwrrdc.gov.au

AMOUNT: $10,000 (max.)

DEADLINE(S): JUN

FIELD(S): Natural Resources

Postgraduate fellowships for travel to Australia by overseas scientists in the area of land, water, and vegetation resources. Usually, fellows come at invitation of an Australian researcher; LWRDC assists with financial and other support. Financial need NOT a factor.

6 awards annually. Not renewable. Contact Dr. Phil Price at LWRDC for an application. Award is made in September.

1653 — LOUISIANA OFFICE OF STUDENT FINANCIAL ASSISTANCE (Rockefeller State Wildlife Scholarship)

PO Box 91202
Baton Rouge LA 70821-9202
800/259-5626, ext. 1012
FAX: 504/922-0790
Internet: www.osfa.state.la.us

AMOUNT: $1,000/yr.

DEADLINE(S): JUN 1

FIELD(S): Forestry; Wildlife; Marine Science

Open to Louisiana residents pursuing undergraduate or graduate study in a Louisiana college/university. Must have minimum 2.5 GPA. Recipients must attain a degree in one of the three eligible fields or repay the funds plus interest.

30 awards annually. Renewable up to 5 years undergraduate study & 2 years graduate study. Apply by completing the Free Application for Federal Student Aid (FAFSA). See your school's financial aid office or contact LOSFA for FAFSA form.

1654 — NATIONAL ENVIRONMENTAL HEALTH ASSOCIATION (NEHA/AAS Scholarship)

720 S. Colorado Blvd., Ste. 970
South Tower
Denver CO 80246-1925
303/756-9090
E-Mail: veronica.white@juno.com
Internet: www.neha.org

AMOUNT: Varies

DEADLINE(S): FEB 1

FIELD(S): Environmental Health/Science; Public Health

Undergraduate scholarships to be used for tuition and fees during junior or senior year at an Environmental Health Accreditation Council accredited school or NEHA school. Graduate scholarships are for students or career professionals who are enrolled in a graduate program of studies in environmental health sciences and/or public health. Transcript, letters of recommendation, and financial need considered.

Renewable. Scholarships are paid directly to the college/university for the fall semester of the award. Contact Veronica White, NEHA Liason, for an application.

1655 — NATIONAL PARKS SERVICE (Science Scholars Program)

1849 C St., NW
Washington DC 20240
202/208-6843
E-Mail: aspiceland@goparks.org
Internet: www.nps.gov

AMOUNT: $25,000/yr.

DEADLINE(S): JUN 15

FIELD(S): Biological, Physical, Social, & Cultural Sciences

Three-year scholarships to Ph.D. candidates pursuing degrees in above fields. Objectives are to encourage young scientists to engage in park-related research, conduct innovative research on issues central to the National Parks, and encourage use of parks as laboratories for sciences. NPF will transfer the scholarship funds to each student's university, providing for tuition, field work, stipend, & other research expenses. Must submit research proposal.

4 awards annually. See website or contact Dr. Gary E. Machlis, Program Director, at NPS for an application. Winners announced shortly after August 15th.

1656 — OAK RIDGE ASSOCIATED UNIVERSITIES (Laboratory Graduate Research Participation Program)

P.O. Box 117
Oak Ridge TN 37831-0117
423/576-4813

AMOUNT: $1,000-$1,200/mo. + allowance for dependents + tuition and fees reimbursement to a max. of $3,500/yr.

DEADLINE(S): Ongoing

FIELD(S): Life sciences, physical, and social sciences, mathematics, and engineering

For graduate students in one of the fields listed above who have completed all degree requirements except thesis or dissertation research. For full-time research under the joint direction of the major professor and a DOE staff member at one of various locations, primarily in the South. For six to twelve months.

Funded through U.S. Dept. of Energy, Office of Energy Reseach, and Office of Fossil Energy. Write for complete information.

1657 — OAK RIDGE INSTITUTE FOR SCIENCE AND EDUCATION (Alexander Hollaender Distinguished Post-doctoral Fellowships)

P.O. Box 117
Oak Ridge TN 37831-0117

423/576-3192 or 423/576-9975

AMOUNT: $37,500 + inbound travel, moving, and medical insurance

DEADLINE(S): JAN 15

FIELD(S): Biomedical, life, and environmental sciences and other related scientific disciplines, including global change and human genome

One-year post-doctoral fellowships for research and training in energy-related life, biomedical, and environmental sciences at one of participating laboratories in the U.S. Must have completed doctorate within last two years.

Must be U.S. citizen or legal resident.

1658 — OAK RIDGE INSTITUTE FOR SCIENCE AND EDUCATION (Applied Health Physics Fellowship Program)

P.O. Box 117
Oak Ridge TN 37831-0117
423/576-2194 or 423/576-9279
E-Mail: COXRE@ORAU.GOV or
GRADFELL@ORAU.GOV

AMOUNT: $14,400 stipend + tuition and fees up to $9,000/yr paid to university + transportation costs up to $300/month

DEADLINE(S): JAN 26

FIELD(S): Engineering, mathematics, physical and life sciences

Fellowship in applied health physics to implement DOE's nuclear energy-related mission. Candidates must have B.A. degree in life or physical sciences, engineering, or mathematics. Recipients are subject to a service obligation of one year of full-time employment in a DOE facility for each academic year of fellowhip award.

For details and application, contact above location.

1659 — OAK RIDGE INSTITUTE FOR SCIENCE AND EDUCATION (Industrial Hygiene Graduate Fellowship Program)

P.O. Box 117
Oak Ridge TN 37831-0117
423-576-9655
FAX: 423/576-8293
E-Mail: kinneym@orau.gov

AMOUNT:

DEADLINE(S): JAN 26

FIELD(S): Industrial Hygiene

A fellowship for first-year master's candidates who have undergraduate degrees in physical, life, environmental, or health sciences or enginering and who wish to pursue studies in industrial hygiene.

For details and application, contact above location.

1660 — OAK RIDGE INSTITUTE FOR SCIENCE AND EDUCATION (Professional Internship Program/Oak Ridge National Laboratory)

P.O. Box 117
Oak Ridge TN 37831-0117
423/576-3426
423/576-3427

AMOUNT: $210 to $300/week + travel, tuition, and fees

DEADLINE(S): FEB 5; JUN 1; OCT 1

FIELD(S): Chemistry, environmental science, geology, hydrogeology, hydrology, chemical engineering, civil engineering, environmental engineering, mechanical engineering, computer science (technical database development)

Opportunities for graduates and undergraduates to participate in energy-related research projects that correlate with their academic and career goals. For 3 to 12 consecutive months.

Funded through Oak Ridge National Laboratory.

1661 — OAK RIDGE INSTITUTE FOR SCIENCE AND EDUCATION (Professional Internship Program/Pittsburgh Energy Technology Center)

P.O. Box 117
Oak Ridge TN 37831-0117
423/576-3426
423/576-3427

AMOUNT: $235 to $325/week + travel, tuition, and fees

DEADLINE(S): FEB 5; JUN 1; OCT 1

FIELD(S): Chemistry, physics, environmental science, geology, chemical or environmental engineering, computer science, or statistics.

Opportunities for graduates and undergraduates to participate in fossil energy-related research projects that correlate with their academic and career goals. For 3 to 12 consecutive months.

Funded through U.S. Dept. of Energy, Office of Fossil Energy, and Pittsburgh Energy Technology Center.

1662 — OAK RIDGE INSTITUTE FOR SCIENCE AND EDUCATION (Professional Internship Program/Savannah River Site)

P.O. Box 117
Oak Ridge TN 37831-0117
423/576-3426
423/576-3427

AMOUNT: $260 to $340/week + travel

DEADLINE(S): FEB 5; JUN 1; SEP 1

FIELD(S): Chemistry, computer science, environmental science, geology, engineering, or physics

Opportunities for high school junior and seniors, undergraduates, and graduates to participate in research projects that correlate with their academic majors and career goals. For 3 to 12 consecutive months at the Savannah River Site, SC.

Funded through the Savannah River Site, SC.

1663 — OAK RIDGE INSTITUTE FOR SCIENCE AND EDUCATION (Science and Engineering Research Semester)

P.O. Box 117
Oak Ridge TN 37831-0117
423/576-2358
423/576-2310

AMOUNT: $225/week + travel + housing

DEADLINE(S): OCT; MAR

FIELD(S): Computer science, physical sciences, environmental and life sciences, and mathematics

Opportunities for high school junior and seniors and a few slots for graduates to participate in energy-related with laboratory scientists at Oak Ridge National Laboratory, TN. One semester with possibility of summer extension. Available two times a year.

Funded through the U.S. Dept. of Energy, Office of Energy Research.

1664 — OAK RIDGE INSTITUTE FOR SCIENCE AND EDUCATION (U.S. Geological Survey Earth Sciences Internship Program)

P.O. Box 117
Oak Ridge TN 37831-0117
423/576-2358
423/576-4813

AMOUNT: $19,000 to $38,000, dependent on level

DEADLINE(S): Ongoing

FIELD(S): Geology, geography, biology, chemistry, environmental sciences, hydrology, forestry, civil engineering, computer sciences

Internships for undergrads, grads, or recent grads (within one year) students studying in the above fields to conduct projects to prepare for careers in earth sciences for up to two years. Location: USGS sites across the U.S.

Funded through the U.S. Dept. of the Interior, U.S.G.S.

1665 — OAK RIDGE INSTITUTE FOR SCIENCE AND EDUCATION (Nuclear Engineering & Health Physics Fellowship Program)

105 Mitchell Rd. MS-16
Oak Ridge TN 37831-0117
423/576-2600 or 423/241-2890
E-Mail: johnsons@orau.gov or
daltonj@arou.gov

AMOUNT: $14,400/yr.

DEADLINE(S): JAN 26

FIELD(S): Engineering, physical and life sciences

Fellowships in nuclear engineering or applied health physics to implement DOE's nuclear energy-related mission. Candidates must have B.A. degree in life or physical sciences or engineering.

For details and application, contact Sandra Johnson or Jennifer Dalton at above location.

1666 — OPEN SOCIETY INSTITUTE (Environmental Management Fellowships)

400 West 59th St.
New York NY 10019
212/548-0600 or 212/757-2323
FAX: 212/548-4679 or 212/548-4600
Internet: www.soros.org/efp.html

AMOUNT: Fees, room, board, living stipend, textbooks, international transportation, health insurance

DEADLINE(S): NOV 15

FIELD(S): Earth sciences, natural sciences, humanities (exc. language), anthropology, sociology, mathematics, or engineering

Two-year fellowships for use in selected universities in the U.S. for international students. For students/professionals in fields related to environmental policy, legislation, and remediation techniques applicable to their home countries.

To apply, contact your local Soros Foundation or Open Society Institute. Further details on website.

1667 — RESEARCH COUNCIL OF NORWAY (Senior Scientist Visiting Fellowship)

P.O. Box 2700 St. Hanshaugen
N-0131 Oslo NORWAY
+47 22 03 70 00
FAX: +47 22 03 70 01
E-Mail: intstip@nfr.no
Internet: www.forskningsradet.no

AMOUNT: NOK 25,000-1st 2 months; NOK 10,000-succeeding months

DEADLINE(S): Varies

FIELD(S): Bioproduction & Processing (including agriculture and veterinary science); Industry & Energy; Culture & Society (including social sciences and the humanities); Medicine & Health; Environment & Development; Science & Technology

Fellowships for scientists to work at Norwegian research institutes. Project funding does not include salary; expenses connected with the stay in Norway are covered.

For a list of institutions, contact the Research Council at above location. Then apply to institution, which then will submit fellowship application.

1668 — RESOURCES FOR THE FUTURE (Gilbert F. White Fellowship Program)

1616 P Street NW
Washington DC 20036-1400
202/328-5067
Internet: www.rff.org

AMOUNT: Based upon current salary + research support, office, and up to $1,000 for moving or living expenses.

DEADLINE(S): FEB 26

FIELD(S): Social Sciences; Natural Resources; Energy; Environment

Postdoctoral resident fellowships for professionals in the above fields who wish to devote eleven months to scholarly work on a social or policy problem in these. Faculty members on sabbatical encouraged to apply.

All information is on website. Address inquiries and applications to Coordinator for Academic Programs. NO fax submissions.

1669 — RESOURCES FOR THE FUTURE (Joseph L. Fisher Dissertation Fellowships)

1616 P Street NW
Washington DC 20036-1400
202/328-5000
Internet: www.rff.org

AMOUNT: $12,000/yr

DEADLINE(S): FEB 26

FIELD(S): Economics and other Social Sciences related to environment, natural resources, or energy

Fellowship to graduate students in the final year of their dissertatio research in the above fields.

All information is on website. NO fax submissions.

1670 — RESOURCES FOR THE FUTURE (RFF Summer Internship Program)

1616 P Street NW
Washington DC 20036-1400
202/328-5000
E-Mail: lewis@rff.org or voigt@rff.org
Internet: www.rff.org

AMOUNT: $375/week

DEADLINE(S): MAR 12

FIELD(S): Social Sciences, Natural Resources, Energy, Environment

Resident paid summer internships for undergraduate and graduate students for research in the above fields. Divisions are Center for Risk Management, Energy and Natural Resources, and Quality of the Environment. Candidates should have outstanding policy analysis and writing skills. For both U.S. and non-U.S. citizens.

All information is on website. Address inquiries and applications to Sue Lewis (Energy & Natural Resources and Quality of the Environment) or Marilyn Voigt (Center for Risk Management). NO fax submissions.

1671 — RESOURCES FOR THE FUTURE (Walter O. Spofford, Jr., Memorial Internship)

1616 P Street NW
Washington DC 20036-1400
202/328-5000
E-Mail: moran@rff.org
Internet: www.rff.org

AMOUNT: Individually negotiated

DEADLINE(S): MAR 12

FIELD(S): Chinese environmental issues in the areas of Social Sciences, Natural Resources, Energy, Environment

Resident paid internships for graduate students for research in the above fields. Candidates should have outstanding policy analysis and writing skills.

All information is on website. Address inquiries and applications to Mary Moran, Coordinator for Academic Programs. NO fax submissions.

1672 — ROB AND BESSIE WELDER WILDLIFE FOUNDATION (Scholarship Program)

PO Box 1400
Sinton TX 78387-1400
512/364-2650
E-Mail: welderWF@aol.com
Internet: hometown.aol.com/welderwf/welderweb.html

AMOUNT: $950/month (masters); $1,000/month (doctoral)

DEADLINE(S): OCT 15

FIELD(S): Wildlife Ecology & Management

Open to graduate students who are approved candidates for M.S. or Ph.D. degrees at accredited US institutions. Financial need NOT a factor.

15-20 awards annually. Renewable. See website or contact Foundation for an application.

1673 — ROCKEFELLER FOUNDATION (African Dissertation Internship Awards)

420 Fifth Ave.
New York NY 10018-2702
212/869-8500
212/764-3468
Internet: www.rockfound.org

AMOUNT: Cost of project

DEADLINE(S): None given

FIELD(S): Agriculture, environment, health, life sciences, population, and schooling

For African graduate students in U.S. and Canadian universities (but not to permanent residents) to return to Africa to carry out dissertation research at a local university or research institution. Priority given to above topics.

Students are strongly urged to be in the field for at least 12 months. Contact above location for details.

1674 — SIGURD OLSON ENVIRONMENTAL INSTITUTE—LOONWATCH (Sigurd T. Olson Research Fund)

Northland College
Ashland WI 54806
715/682-1223

AMOUNT: Up to $2,000

DEADLINE(S): JAN 15

FIELD(S): Research on the Common Loon (Gavia immer)

Open to graduate students and higher for study of Loon populations in the upper Great Lakes.

Renewable. Write for complete information.

1675 — SMITHSONIAN INSTITUTION (Fellowship Program)

Office of fellowships & Grants
955 L'Enfant Plaza, Suite 7000
Washington DC 20560
202/287-3271
E-Mail: http://www.si.edu/research+study
Internet: siofg@sivm.si.edu

AMOUNT: $3,000-$25,000 depending on level and length

DEADLINE(S): JAN 15

FIELD(S): Animal behavior, ecology, environmental science (including emphasis on the tropics, anthropology (& archaeology), astrophysics, astronomy, earth sciences, paleobiology, evolutionary/ systematic biology, history of science and technology, history of art, esp. American, contemporary, African, and Asian, 20th century American crafts, decorative arts, social/cultural history of the US, or folklife.

For research in residence at the Smithsonian for graduate students, both pre- and postdoctoral.

Research to be in the fields listed above.

1676 — SMITHSONIAN INSTITUTION (Minority Student Internship Program)

Fellowships & Grants
955 L'Enfant Plaza, Suite 7000
MRC 902
Washington DC 20560
202/287-3271

FAX: 202/287-3691
E-Mail: siofg@ofg.si.edu
Internet: www.si.edu/research+study

AMOUNT: $300/week + possible travel expenses

DEADLINE(S): FEB 15

FIELD(S): Humanities, Environmental Studies, Cultural Studies, Natural History, Earth Science, Art History, Biology, & related fields

Ten-week internships in residence at the Smithsonian for US minority students to participate in research or museum-related activities in above fields. For undergrads or grads with at least a 3.0 GPA. Essay, resume, transcripts, and references required with application. Internships are full-time and are offered for Summer, Fall, or Spring tenures.

Write for application.

1677 — SMITHSONIAN INSTITUTION ENVIRONMENTAL RESEARCH CENTER (Work/ Learn Program in Environmental Studies)

P.O. Box 28
Edgewater MD 21037
301/261-4084
E-Mail: education@serc.si.edu

AMOUNT: $190/week + dorm housing; minority graduate students receive $240/wk.

DEADLINE(S): MAR 1; NOV 1

FIELD(S): Environmental Studies; Ecology; Ornithology; Marine Life; Computer Science; Chemistry; Mathematics.

Work/learn internships at the center open to undergraduate & graduate students. Competitive program which offers unique opportunity to gain exposure to & experience in environmental research. Selected students paid $240 per week when they live at the center in Edgewater. No academic credit.

Projects generally coincide with academic semesters & summer sessions and are normally 12-15 weeks in duration. Write for complete information. Can E-mail for application.

1678 — SOIL AND WATER CONSERVATION SOCIETY (Kenneth E. Grant Research Scholarship)

7515 N.E. Ankeny Road
Ankeny IA 50021-9764
515/289-2331 or 1-800/THE-SOIL
FAX: 515/289-1227
E-Mail: charliep@swcs.org
Internet: www.swcs.org

AMOUNT: $1,300

DEADLINE(S): FEB 13

FIELD(S): Science and art of soil, water and related natural resources management

For SWCS members. Fellowship for graduate-level research on a specific SWCS topic. Must demonstrate integrity, ability, and competence, be eligible for grad work at an accredited institution, and show reasonable need for financial assistance.

Award is for an analytical study or report of a case example of an ecosystem-based approach to resource planning and decision-making. Write or visit websire for more information.

1679 — SOIL AND WATER CONSERVATION SOCIETY (Melville H. Cohee Student Leader Conservation Scholarship)

7515 N.E. Ankeny Road
Ankeny IA 50021-9764
515/289-2331 or 1-800-THE-SOIL
FAX 515/289-1227
E-Mail: charliep@swcs.org
Internet: www.swcs.org

AMOUNT: $900

DEADLINE(S): FEB 113

FIELD(S): Conservation or Natural Resource-Related Field

Open to 1+ year member of SWCS having served as an officer in a student chapter with 15+ members. GPA of 3.0 or better. Final year F/T undergrad or graduate.

2 awards. Course load must be 50% or more at accredited college or university. Financial need is not a factor. Write or visit website for complete information.

1680 — SOIL AND WATER CONSERVATION SOCIETY (SWCS Internships)

7515 N.E. Ankeny Road
Ankeny IA 50021-9764
515/289-2331 or 1-800/THE-SOIL
FAX: 515/289-1227
E-Mail: charliep@swcs.org
Internet: www.swcs.org

AMOUNT: Varies—most are uncompensated

DEADLINE(S): Varies

FIELD(S): Journalism, marketing, database management, meeting planning, public policy research, environmental education, landscape architecture

Internships for undergraduates and graduates to gain experience in the above fields as they relate to soil and water conservation issues. Intership openings vary through the year in duration, compensation, and objective. SWCS will coordinate particulars with your academic advisor.

Contact SWCS for internship availability at any timne during the year or see website for jobs page.

1681 — SWEDISH INFORMATION SERVICE (Bicentennial Swedish-American Exchange Fund)

Bicentennial Fund
One Dag Hammarskjold Plaza, 45th Floor
New York NY 10017-2201
212/483-2550
FAX: 212/752-4789
E-Mail: swedinfor@ix.netcom.com

AMOUNT: 20,000 Swedish crowns (for three- to six-week intensive study visits in Sweden)

DEADLINE(S): FEB (Friday of the first week)

FIELD(S): Politics, public administration, working life, human environment, mass media, business and industry, education and culture

Program is to provide opportunity for those in a positio to influence public opinion and contribute to the development of their society. Must be U.S. citizen or permanent resident. Must have necessary experience and education for fulfilling his/her project.

Send SASE to above address for details.

1682 — THE DAPHNE JACKSON MEMORIAL FELLOWSHIPS TRUST (Fellowships in Science/ Engineering)

School of Physical Sciences
Dept. of Physics
University of Surrey
Guildford, Surrey
GU2 5XH ENGLAND UK
01483 259166
FAX: 01483 259501
E-Mail: J.Woolley@surrey.ac.uk
Internet: www.sst.ph.ic.ac.uk/trust/

AMOUNT: Varies

DEADLINE(S): Varies

FIELD(S): Science or engineering, including information sciences

Fellowships to enable well-qualified and highly motivated scientists and engineers to return to appropriate careers following a career break due to family comitments. May be used on a flexible, part-time basis. Tenable at various U.K. universities.

See website and/or contact organization for details.

1683 — TRENT UNIVERSITY (Graduate Teaching/Research Assistantships)

P.O. Box 4800
Graduate Studies Officer
Peterborough Ontario CANADA K9J 7B8
705/748-1245

AMOUNT: $3,500 per term

DEADLINE(S): FEB 15

FIELD(S): Anthropology, Geography, Archaeology, Biology, Canadian Studies, Philosophy, Cultural Studies, Computer Science, Mathematics, Physics, Chemistry, Environmental Science/Studies

Teaching/research assistantships at Trent University in the above fields. Open to masters and doctoral candidates. Tenable for up to 4 terms spanning 2-3 years of study.

80 awards per year. Write for complete information.

1684 — TUSKEGEE UNIVERSITY (Graduate Research Fellowships and Assistantships)

Admissions Office
Tuskegee University
1506 Franklin Rd., AL 36088
334/727/8500

AMOUNT: Tuition

DEADLINE(S): MAR 15

FIELD(S): Chemistry; Engineering; Environmental Science; Life Sciences; Nutrition; Education

Graduate research fellowships and graduate assistantships are available to qualified individuals who wish to enter Tuskegee University's graduate program in pursuit of a master's degree.

Write for complete information.

1685 — U.S. DEPARTMENT OF DEFENSE (GLSIP-General Laboratory Scientific Interchange Program: NRC-NRL Post-Doctoral Program)

Naval Research Laboratory
Office of Program Admin. &
Dev. Code 1006.17
Washington, D.C. 20375-5321
202/767-3865
DSN: 297-3865
FAX: 202/404-8110
Internet: www.acq.osd.mil/ddre/edugate/s-aindx.html

AMOUNT: Research Program

DEADLINE(S): None specified

FIELD(S): Computer science, artificial intelligence, plasma physics, acoustics, radar, fluid dynamics, chemistry, materials sci, optical sci, condensed matter and radiation, electronic sci, environmental sci, marine geosciences, remote sensing, oceanography, marine meteorology, space technology/sciences.

U.S. citizens who are recent postdoctoral graduates are selected on the basis of overall qualifications and techinal proposals.

Contact Jessica Hileman for more information.

1686 — U.S. ENVIRONMENTAL PROTECTION AGENCY—NATIONAL NETWORK FOR ENVIRONMENTAL MANAGEMENT STUDIES (Fellowships)

401 M St., SW
Mailcode 1704
Washington DC 20460
202/260-5283
FAX: 202/260-4095
E-Mail: jojokian.sheri@epa.gov
Internet: www.epa.gov/enviroed/students.html

AMOUNT: Varies

DEADLINE(S): DEC

FIELD(S): Environmental Policies, Regulations, & Law; Environmental Management & Administration; Environmental Science; Public Relations & Communications; Computer Programming & Development

Fellowships are open to undergraduate and graduate students working on research projects in the above fields, either full-time during the summer or part-time during the school year. Must be US citizen or legal resident. Financial need NOT a factor.

85-95 awards annually. Not renewable. See website or contact the Career Service Center of participating universities for an application.

1687 — WATER ENVIRONMENT FEDERATION (Robert A. Canham Scholarship)

Access website
Internet: www.wef.org

AMOUNT: $2,500

DEADLINE(S): MAR 1

FIELD(S): Water environment areas

Open to post-baccalaureate students in the environmental engineering or sciences field who agree to work in the environmental field for at least two years after completion of the degree. Must be a member of the Water Environment Federation.

A detailed statement of career goals and aspirations and three letters of recommendation are required. Write for complete information. Access website for details and application—go to "Member Programs," then to "Canham Scholarship." Organization will not mail this information!

1688 — WATER ENVIRONMENT FEDERATION (Student Paper Competition)

Access website
Internet: www.wef.org

AMOUNT: $1,000 (1st prize); $500 (2nd); $250 (3rd)

DEADLINE(S): FEB 1

FIELD(S): Water pollution control and related fields

Awards for 500- 1,000-word abstracts dealing with water pollution control, water quality problems, water-related concerns, or hazardous wastes. Open to undergrad (A.A. and B.A.) and grad students.

Also open to recently graduated students (within 1 calendar year of Feb. 1 deadline). See website for details—go to "Member Programs" then to "Student Paper Competition." Organization will not mail this information.

1689 — WATER RESOURCES RESEARCH CENTRE - VITUKI (Hydrological Methods of Environmental Management Scholarship)

Kvassay J. ut l.
Budapest 1095 HUNGARY
+3612153043
FAX: +3612153043
E-Mail: training@vituki.hu
Internet: www.datanet.hu/hydroinfo/

AMOUNT: USD 10,000

DEADLINE(S): NOV 15

FIELD(S): Hydrology; Environmental Management

Must be a graduate student with a BSc. degree, have a command of the English language, and be aged 40 years or younger.

10 awards annually. Not renewable. Contact VITUKI for an application.

1690 — WYOMING TRUCKING ASSOCIATION (Scholarships)

PO Box 1909
Casper WY 82602
Written Inquiry

AMOUNT: $250-$300

DEADLINE(S): MAR 1

FIELD(S): Transportation Industry

For Wyoming high school graduates enrolled in a Wyoming college, approved trade school, or the University of Wyoming. Must be pursuing a course of study which will result in a career in the transportation industry in Wyoming, including but not limited to: safety, environmental science, diesel mechanics, truck driving, vocational trades, business management, sales management, computer skills, accounting, office procedures, and management.

1-10 awards annually. Write to WYTA for an application.

MARINE SCIENCE

1691 — ACADEMY OF NATURAL SCIENCES OF PHILADELPHIA (Jessup & McHenry Fund Grants)

The Academy of Natural Sciences, 1900 Benjamin Franklin Parkway
Philadelphia PA 19103-1195
215/299-1,000

AMOUNT: $250 (travel); Max $1,000

DEADLINE(S): MAR 1; OCT 1

FIELD(S): Botany/McHenry Award; Research in Natural Science/Jessup Award

Grants to support research are primarily intended to assist predoctoral and immediate postdoctoral students. The work must be done at the Academy of Natural Sciences in Philadelphia and must have the sponsorship of an Academy staff member.

In general grants are awarded for a minimum of 2 weeks and a maximum of 16-week periods. Students from the Philadelphia area are NOT eligible. Write for complete information.

1692 — AFRICAN NETWORK OF SCIENTIFIC AND TECHNOLOGICAL INSTITUTIONS - ANSTI (Postgraduate Fellowships)

PO Box 30592
Nairobi Kenya AFRICA
254-2-621234 or 254-2-622619/20
FAX: 254-2-215991
E-Mail: j.massaquoi@unesco.org OR
ANSTI@Net2000ke.com

AMOUNT: Fees, subsistence, & international travel

DEADLINE(S): JUN

FIELD(S): Basic & Engineering Sciences

Scholarships for postgraduate studies outside of applicant's home country. Must be African nationals not older than 36 years of age and hold a good bachelor's degree (at least 2nd class upper division). Applicants should apply for admission to host university as soon as possible. Fellowships tenable only in African universities.

10 awards annually. Renewable up to 2 years. Contact Professor J.G.M. Massaquoi for an application.

1693 — AMERICAN FISHERIES SOCIETY (J. Frances Allen Scholarship)

5410 Grosvenor Ln., Ste. 110
Bethesda MD 20814-2199
301/897-8616
FAX: 301/897-8096
E-Mail: main@fisheries.org
Internet: www.fisheries.org

AMOUNT: $2,500

DEADLINE(S): MAR 1

FIELD(S): Fisheries

Open to female Ph.D. students for study with a focus on fisheries.

Contact the Unit Services Coordinator for an application.

1694 — AMERICAN FOUNDATION FOR THE BLIND (Paul W. Ruckes Scholarship)

11 Penn Plaza, Ste. 300
New York NY 10001
212/502-7661 or TDD 212/502-7771
E-Mail: juliet@afb.org
Internet: www.afb.org

AMOUNT: $1,000

DEADLINE(S): APR 30

FIELD(S): Engineering, computer, physical, or life sciences

Open to blind or visually impaired undergraduate or graduate students pursuing degrees in the above fields. U.S. citizenship required.

Write to the above address or visit website for complete information.

1695 — AMERICAN INDIAN SCIENCE AND ENGINEERING SOCIETY (A.T. Anderson Memorial Scholarship)

PO Box 9828
Albuquerque NM 87119-9828
505/765-1052
FAX: 505/765-5608
E-Mail: scholarships@aises.org
Internet: www.aises.org/scholarships

AMOUNT: $1,000-$2,000

DEADLINE(S): JUN 15

FIELD(S): Medicine; Natural Resources; Science; Engineering

Open to undergraduate and graduate students who are at least 1/4 American Indian or recognized as member of a tribe. Must be member of AISES ($10 fee), enrolled full-time at an accredited institution, and demonstrate financial need.

Renewable. See website or contact Patricia Browne for an application and/or membership information.

1696 — AMERICAN MUSEUM OF NATURAL HISTORY (Grants)

Central Park West at 79th St.
New York NY 10024-5192
FAX: 212/769-5495
E-Mail: bynum@amnh.org
Internet: research.amnh.org

AMOUNT: $200-$2,000

DEADLINE(S): JAN 15

FIELD(S): Zoology; Paleontology; Anthropology

Modest short-term awards are offered to advanced graduate students and postdoctoral researchers who are commencing their careers in above fields. Two letters of recommendation and description (less than 2 pages) of proposed investigation are required. Budget must show clearly amounts and items for which award will be used. Grantees must submit progress report upon completion. Research projects need not be carried out at American Museum of Natural History.

200 awards annually. See website or contact Office of Grants & Fellowships for details on specific programs: Frank M. Chapman Memorial Fund for Ornithology, Lerner Gray Fund for Marine Research, Theodore Roosevelt Memorial Fund, & Collection Study Grant.

1697 — AMERICAN SOCIETY FOR ENGINEERING EDUCATION (Army Research Laboratory Postdoctoral Fellowships)

1818 N St., NW, Ste. 600
Washington DC 20036
202/331-3525
FAX: 202/265-8504
E-Mail: projects@asee.org
Internet: www.asee.org/fellowship/

AMOUNT: $45,000-$55,000 + travel/relocation allowance

DEADLINE(S): Varies

FIELD(S): Engineering; Physical Sciences

Postdoctoral fellowships for US citizens/permanent residents to do research at Army Research Laboratories. Candidates must have completed their Ph.D. prior to appointment. Program is designed to increase involvement of creative and highly trained scientists and engineers from academia and industry in scientific and technical areas of interest and relevance to the Army. Research proposal should include clear objective and defined outcome. Financial need NOT a factor.

15 awards annually. Renewable. Contact Sandi Crawford at ASEE for an application packet.

1698 — AMERICAN WATER RESOURCES ASSOCIATION (Richard A. Herbert Memorial Scholarships)

AWRRI
101 Comer Hall
Auburn Univ AL 36849-5431
715/355-3684
FAX: 715/355-3648
E-Mail: stdi@ltus.com
Internet: www.uwin.siu.ed/~awra

AMOUNT: $1,000 + complimentary AWRA membership

DEADLINE(S): APR 30

FIELD(S): Water Resources & related fields

For full-time undergraduates working towards 1st degree and for graduates. Based on academic performance, including cumulative GPA, relevance of curriculum to water resources, & leadership in extracurricular activities related to water resources. Quality & relevance of research is also considered from graduate students. Transcripts, letters of reference, & summary of academic interests/achievements, extracurricular interests, & career goals required (2 page limit).

2 awards annually: 1 undergrad & 1 graduate. Recipients announced in the summer. Contact Stephen Dickman, AWRA Student Activities Committee, for an application.

1699 — ASIAN INSTITUTE OF TECHNOLOGY (AIT Scholarship Program)

Development Office
PO Box 4, Klongluang
Pathumthani 12120 THAILAND
(66)(2) 516-0110-44 or 524-5032
FAX: (66)(2) 516-2126
E-Mail: ascao@ait.ac.th
Internet: www.ait.ac.th

AMOUNT: US $12,600-$37,960

DEADLINE(S): FEB 15; JUN 15; OCT 15

FIELD(S): Advanced Technologies; Civil Engineering; Environment, Resources, & Development; Business Management

Scholarships and grants open to citizens of Asian countries who are accepted by the institute as a master's or doctotal candidate. Selection is based on academic criteria, practical experience, gender, and country of origin; priority to Mekong Region countries and Asian countries of the former USSR.

250 awards annually. Contact AIT for an application.

1700 — ATLANTIC SALMON FEDERATION (Olin Fellowships)

Box 429
St Andrews NB E0G 2X0 CANADA
506/529-4581
FAX 506/529-4985
Internet: www.ASF.ca/awards/awards.html

AMOUNT: $1,000-$3,000

DEADLINE(S): MAR 15

FIELD(S): Fisheries; Marine Biology

ASF graduate fellowships are offered annually to individuals seeking to improve their knowledge or skills in advanced fields while looking for solutions to current problems in Atlantic salmon biology, management, or conservation. Must be legal resident of the US or Canada. Fellowships may be applied toward a wide range of endeavors, including graduate work, sabbatical research, and management experience.

See website or contact ASF for an application.

1701 — BOEING (Polish Graduate Student Scholarship Program)

Phone for details
314/234-2149

AMOUNT: Tuition, books, and fees for three years

DEADLINE(S): Varies

FIELD(S): Scientific and technical fields

Scholarships for students from Poland to pursue graduate studies in scientific and technical areas at American colleges or universities.

Call Jim Schlueter at above telephone number.

1702 — BROOKHAVEN NATIONAL LABORATORY (Post-doctoral Research Associateships)

Brookhaven National Laboratory
Upton L.I. NY 11973-5000
516/344-3336

AMOUNT: $29,000 minimum

DEADLINE(S): Varies

FIELD(S): Chemistry, Physics, Materials Science, Biology, Oceanography, and Biomedical Sciences.

Post-doctoral research associateships tenable at Brookhaven National Laboratory for research to promote fundamental and applied research in the above fields. A recent doctoral degree is required.

25 associateships per year. Renewable for two additional years.

1703 — BROOKHAVEN WOMEN IN SCIENCE (Renate W. Chasman Scholarship)

PO Box 183
Upton NY 11973-5000
E-mail: pam@bnl.gov

AMOUNT: $2,000

DEADLINE(S): APR 1

FIELD(S): Natural Sciences; Engineering; Mathematics

Open ONLY to women who are residents of the boroughs of Brooklyn or Queens or the counties of Nassau or Suffolk in New York who are re-entering school after a period of study. For juniors, seniors, or first-year graduate students.

1 award annually. Not renewable. Contact Pam Mansfield at above location for an application. Phone calls are NOT accepted.

1704 — CANADIAN FEDERATION OF UNIVERSITY WOMEN (CFUW Memorial/ Professional Fellowship)

251 Bank St., Ste. 600
Ottawa Ontario K2P 1X3 CANADA
613/234-2732
Internet: www.cfuw.ca

AMOUNT: $5,000

DEADLINE(S): NOV 15

FIELD(S): Science & Technology

Open to women who are Canadian citizens/ permanent residents enrolled in a master's degree program in science and technology. Must hold at least a bachelor's degree or equivalent from a recognized university and have been accepted into, or be currently enrolled in the proposed program and place of study. May be studying abroad.

$25 filing fee. Contact CFUW for an application after August 1st. Candidates will be notified by May 31st.

1705 — COOPERATIVE INSTITUTE FOR RESEARCH IN ENVIRONMENTAL SCIENCES (CIRES Visiting Fellowships)

Univ Colorado
Campus Box 216
Boulder CO 80309-0216
303/492-1143
Internet: cires.colorado.edu/ciresvf.html

AMOUNT: Varies

DEADLINE(S): DEC 15

FIELD(S): Environmental & Earth Sciences

One-year visiting fellowships for recent Ph.D.s and senior scientists, including faculty on sabbatical. To be used towards research in the areas of physics, chemistry, & dynamics of Earth system; global & regional environmental change; climate system monitoring, diagnostics, & modeling; and remote sensing measurement techniques. Must submit curriculum vitae, publications list, 2-4 page description of proposed research, and letters of recommendation.

5 awards annually. Renewable. See website or contact CIRES for an application. CIRES receives sponsorship from the National Oceanic and Atmosphere Administration's Environmental Research Laboratories.

1706 — ENGINEERING & PHYSICAL SCIENCES RESEARCH COUNCIL (Studentships)

North Star Ave
Polaris House
Swindon SN2 1ET England
01 793-444000

AMOUNT: Maintenance & approved fees

DEADLINE(S): JUL 31

FIELD(S): Engineering & Physical Science

Research studentships for up to 3 years for Ph.D students, 1 year advanced course studentships for master's students. Tenable at U.K. institutions. Must be UK resident with relevant connection to UK for full award or with European Union member state with relevant connection to UK for fees-only award. Must have appropriate academic qualifications.

Approx 3,800 awards per year. Applications must be made through heads of departments. EPSRC does not accept applications direct from students. Write for complete information.

1707 — EPPLEY FOUNDATION FOR RESEARCH (Postdoctoral Research Grants)

245 Park Avenue, 40th Floor
New York NY 10167
Written inquiry

AMOUNT: Up to $25,000

DEADLINE(S): FEB 1; MAY 1; AUG 1; NOV 1

FIELD(S): Physical Sciences; Biological Sciences

Postdoctoral grants for original advanced research in any of the physical or biological sciences. Open to established research scientists who are attached to a recognized institution.

Write for complete information.

1708 — FANNIE AND JOHN HERTZ FOUNDATION (Fellowship)

Box 5032
Livermore CA 94551-5032
925/373-1642
Internet: www.hertzfoundation.org

AMOUNT: $25,000 stipend/yr. + $15,000 (max.) tuition allowance/yr.

DEADLINE(S): NOV 5

FIELD(S): Applied Physical Sciences

Open to graduate students with a minimum 3.75 GPA for studies in applied physical sciences, including math, engineering, computer science, biology, oceanography, aeronautics, astronomy, physics, and earth science. Must be US citizen/permanent resident. Does not support study in pursuit of M.D. degree, although will support Ph.D. portion of a joint M.D./Ph.D. study program.

Renewable up to 5 years. Only 36 US schools are currently considered tenable. See website for an application and list of specific fields of study that are acceptable.

1709 — FLORIDA FEDERATION OF GARDEN CLUBS, INC. (FFGC Scholarships for College Students)

6065 21st St., SW
Vero Beach FL 32968-9427
561/778-1023
Internet: www.ffgc.org

AMOUNT: $1,500-$3,500

DEADLINE(S): MAY 1

FIELD(S): Ecology; Environmental Issues; Land Management; City Planning; Environmental Control; Horticulture; Landscape Design; Conservation; Botany; Forestry; Marine Biology; Floriculture; Agriculture

Various scholarships for Florida residents with a "B" average or better enrolled full-time as a junior, senior, or graduate student at a Florida college or university.

See website or contact Melba Campbell at FFGC for an application.

1710 — FORD FOUNDATION/NATIONAL RESEARCH COUNCIL (Postdoctoral Fellowship for Minorities)

National Research Council
2101 Constitution Ave.
Washington DC 20418
202/334-2860
E-Mail: infofell@nas.edu
Internet: http//www.nas.edu/fo/index.html

AMOUNT: $25,000 + relocation and research allowance

DEADLINE(S): JAN 3

FIELD(S): Life and physical sciences, mathematics, engineering sciences, behavioral and social sciences, and the humanities

For U.S. citizens who received a Ph.D or Sc.D in the last 7 years and who are Native Amer. Indian or Alaskan, Black/African American, Mexican American, Native Pacific Islander, or Puerto Rican and who are or plan to be in a teaching or research career.

Contact above website or address for complete information.

1711 — FORD FOUNDATION/NATIONAL RESEARCH COUNCIL (Predoctoral/Dissertation Fellowships for Minorities)

2101 Constitution Ave.
Washington DC 20418
202/334-2872
E-Mail: infofell@nas.edu
Internet: http//www.nas.edu/fo/index.html

AMOUNT: $14,000 annual stipend + $6,000 grant to institution; $18,000 for dissertation fellowship

DEADLINE(S): NOV 3

FIELD(S): Most fields of study: sciences, humanities, engineering, behavioral science, social sciences, and computer science

Predoctoral and dissertation fellowships for students whose ethnicity is Alaskan Native, Black/ African American, Mexican American/Chicano, Native American Indian, Native Pacific Islander, or Puerto Rican. For research-based programs leading to careers in college teaching and research.

Contact above address or website.

1712 — LAND AND WATER RESOURCES R&D CORPORATION (Postgraduate Scholarships)

GPO Box 2182
Canberra ACT 2601 AUSTRALIA
02/6257 3379
FAX: 02/6257 3420
E-Mail: public@lwrrdc.gov.au
Internet: www.lwrrdc.gov.au

AMOUNT: $25,000/yr.

DEADLINE(S): JUN

FIELD(S): Natural Resources

Postgraduate scholarships for Australian citizens in the area of land, water, and vegetation resources to study/research in Australia. Financial need NOT a factor.

4 awards annually. Renewable up to three years. Contact Dr. Phil Price at LWRDC for an application. Award is made in September.

1713 — LAND AND WATER RESOURCES R&D CORPORATION (Travelling Fellowships)

GPO Box 2182
Canberra ACT 2601 AUSTRALIA
02/6257 3379
FAX: 02/6257 3420
E-Mail: public@lwrrdc.gov.au
Internet: www.lwrrdc.gov.au

AMOUNT: $10,000 (max.)

DEADLINE(S): JUN

FIELD(S): Natural Resources

Postgraduate fellowships for Australian researchers in the area of land, water, and vegetation resources, with overseas agencies to visit; LWRDC assists with financial and other support. Financial need NOT a factor.

6 awards annually. Not renewable. Contact Dr. Phil Price at LWRDC for an application. Award is made in September.

1714 — LAND AND WATER RESOURCES R&D CORPORATION (Visiting Fellowships)

GPO Box 2182
Canberra ACT 2601 AUSTRALIA
02/6257 3379
FAX: 02/6257 3420
E-Mail: public@lwrrdc.gov.au
Internet: www.lwrrdc.gov.au

AMOUNT: $10,000 (max.)

DEADLINE(S): JUN

FIELD(S): Natural Resources

Postgraduate fellowships for travel to Australia by overseas scientists in the area of land, water, and vegetation resources. Usually, fellows come at invitation of an Australian researcher; LWRDC assists with financial and other support. Financial need NOT a factor.

6 awards annually. Not renewable. Contact Dr. Phil Price at LWRDC for an application. Award is made in September.

1715 — LOUISIANA OFFICE OF STUDENT FINANCIAL ASSISTANCE (Rockefeller State Wildlife Scholarship)

PO Box 91202
Baton Rouge LA 70821-9202
800/259-5626, ext. 1012
FAX: 504/922-0790
Internet: www.osfa.state.la.us

AMOUNT: $1,000/yr.

DEADLINE(S): JUN 1

FIELD(S): Forestry; Wildlife; Marine Science

Open to Louisiana residents pursuing undergraduate or graduate study in a Louisiana college/university. Must have minimum 2.5 GPA. Recipients must attain a degree in one of the three eligible fields or repay the funds plus interest.

30 awards annually. Renewable up to 5 years undergraduate study & 2 years graduate study. Apply by completing the Free Application for Federal Student Aid (FAFSA). See your school's financial aid office or contact LOSFA for FAFSA form.

1716 — NATIONAL CENTER FOR ATMOSPHERIC RESEARCH (Graduate Student Research Fellowships)

PO Box 3000
Boulder CO 80307
303/497-1601
FAX: 303/497-1646
E-Mail: barbm@ucar.edu
Internet: www.asp.ucar.edu

AMOUNT: $16,810/yr. + travel

DEADLINE(S): Varies

FIELD(S): Atmospheric Sciences

Open to graduate students to support university Ph.D. thesis research conducted in collaboration with NCAR scientists.

Contact administrator Barbara Hansford for availability information.

1717 — NATIONAL PARKS SERVICE (Science Scholars Program)

1849 C St., NW
Washington DC 20240
202/208-6843
E-Mail: aspiceland@goparks.org
Internet: www.nps.gov

AMOUNT: $25,000/yr.

DEADLINE(S): JUN 15

FIELD(S): Biological, Physical, Social, & Cultural Sciences

Three-year scholarships to Ph.D. candidates pursuing degrees in above fields. Objectives are to encourage young scientists to engage in park-related research, conduct innovative research on issues central to the National Parks, and encourage use of parks as laboratories for sciences. NPF will transfer the scholarship funds to each student's university, providing for tuition, field work, stipend, & other research expenses. Must submit research proposal.

4 awards annually. See website or contact Dr. Gary E. Machlis, Program Director, at NPS for an application. Winners announced shortly after August 15th.

1718 — NATIONAL RESEARCH COUNCIL OF CANADA (Research Associateships)

Research Associates Office
Ottawa Ontario K1A 0R6 CANADA
613/993-9150
FAX: 613/990-7669
Internet: www.nrc.ca/careers

AMOUNT: $39,366 Canadian

DEADLINE(S): None

FIELD(S): Natural Sciences; Engineering

Two-year research associateships are tenable at NRCC labs throughout Canada. Open to recent Ph.D.s in natural sciences or recent master's or Ph.D.s in engineering. Degrees should have been received within the last five years. Preference given to Canadians.

Renewable. See website or contact NRCC for an application.

1719 — NATIONAL SCIENCES AND ENGINEERING RESEARCH COUNCIL OF CANADA (Graduate Scholarships)

Scholarships/Fellowships Division
350 Albert Street
Ottawa Ontario K1A 1H5 CANADA
613/996-3769
FAX: 613/996-2589
E-Mail: schol@nserc.ca
Internet: http://www.nserc.ca

AMOUNT: $15,700/year for 1st & 2nd years at masters or Ph.D level; $17,400/year (Ph.D level ONLY) 3rd & 4th years

DEADLINE(S): NOV 24

FIELD(S): Natural Sciences, Engineering, Biology, or Chemistry

Open to Canadian citizens or permanent residents who have earned or will soon earn a bachelors or masters degree in science or engineering. Academic excellence and research aptitude are considerations.

Write for complete information.

1720 — NATIONAL SCIENCES AND ENGINEERING RESEARCH COUNCIL OF CANADA (Postdoctoral Fellowships)

Scholarships/Fellowships Division
350 Albert Street
Ottawa Ontario K1A 1H5 CANADA
613/996-3762
FAX: 613/996-2589
E-Mail: schol@nserc.ca
Internet: http://www.nserc.ca

AMOUNT: Individually negotiated

DEADLINE(S): Varies—average: $43,000

FIELD(S): Natural Sciences, Engineering, Biology, or Chemistry

Open to Canadian citizens or permanent residents who hold doctoral degrees in science or engineering. Academic excellence and research aptitude are considerations.

Write for complete information.

1721 — OAK RIDGE ASSOCIATED UNIVERSITIES (Laboratory Graduate Research Participation Program)

P.O. Box 117
Oak Ridge TN 37831-0117
423/576-4813

AMOUNT: $1,000-$1,200/mo. + allowance for dependents + tuition and fees reimbursement to a max. of $3,500/yr.

DEADLINE(S): Ongoing

FIELD(S): Life sciences, physical, and social sciences, mathematics, and engineering

For graduate students in one of the fields listed above who have completed all degree requirements except thesis or dissertation research. For full-time research under the joint direction of the major professor and a DOE staff member at one of various locations, primarily in the South. For six to twelve months.

Funded through U.S. Dept. of Energy, Office of Energy Research, and Office of Fossil Energy. Write for complete information.

1722 — OAK RIDGE ASSOCIATED UNIVERSITIES (National Science Foundation Graduate Research Fellowships)

PO Box 3010
Oak Ridge TN 37831-3010
423/241-4300
FAX: 423/241-4513
E-Mail: nsfgrfp@orau.gov
Internet: www.orau.gov/nsf/nsffel.htm

AMOUNT: $15,000 stipend + $10,500 tuition allowance

DEADLINE(S): NOV 4

FIELD(S): Science; Math; Engineering; Computer Science

Three-year fellowships for graduate study leading to research-based master's or doctoral degrees in the above fields. Must be US citizens, nationals, or permanent residents at the time of application. Fellowships are awarded on the basis of ability. Women, minorities, and those with disabilities are strongly encouraged to apply. One-time International Research Travel Allowance available.

1,000 awards annually. Contact Jeannette Bouchard for an application/more information.

1723 — OAK RIDGE INSTITUTE FOR SCIENCE AND EDUCATION (Alexander Hollaender Distinguished Post-doctoral Fellowships)

P.O. Box 117
Oak Ridge TN 37831-0117
423/576-3192 or 423/576-9975

AMOUNT: $37,500 + inbound travel, moving, and medical insurance

DEADLINE(S): JAN 15

FIELD(S): Biomedical, life, and environmental sciences and other related scientific disciplines, including global change and human genome

One-year post-doctoral fellowships for research and training in energy-related life, biomedical, and environmental sciences at one of participating laboratories in the U.S. Must have completed doctorate within last two years.

Must be U.S. citizen or legal resident.

1724 — OAK RIDGE INSTITUTE FOR SCIENCE AND EDUCATION (Applied Health Physics Fellowship Program)

P.O. Box 117
Oak Ridge TN 37831-0117
423/576-2194 or 423/576-9279
E-Mail: COXRE@ORAU.GOV or GRADFELL@ORAU.GOV

AMOUNT: $14,400 stipend + tuition and fees up to $9,000/yr paid to university + transportation costs up to $300/month

DEADLINE(S): JAN 26

FIELD(S): Engineering, mathematics, physical and life sciences

Fellowship in applied health physics to implement DOE's nuclear energy-related mission. Candidates must have B.A. degree in life or physical sciences, engineering, or mathematics. Recipients are subject to a service obligation of one year of full-time employment in a DOE facility for each academic year of fellowhip award.

For details and application, contact above location.

1725 — OAK RIDGE INSTITUTE FOR SCIENCE AND EDUCATION (Industrial Hygiene Graduate Fellowship Program)

P.O. Box 117
Oak Ridge TN 37831-0117
423-576-9655
FAX: 423/576-8293
E-Mail: kinneym@orau.gov

AMOUNT:

DEADLINE(S): JAN 26

FIELD(S): Industrial Hygiene

A fellowship for first-year master's candidates who have undergraduate degrees in physical, life, environmental, or health sciences or enginering and who wish to pursue studies in industrial hygiene.

For details and application, contact above location.

1726 — OAK RIDGE INSTITUTE FOR SCIENCE AND EDUCATION (Professional Internship Program/Oak Ridge National Laboratory)

P.O. Box 117
Oak Ridge TN 37831-0117
423/576-3426
423/576-3427

AMOUNT: $210 to $300/week + travel, tuition, and fees

DEADLINE(S): FEB 5; JUN 1; OCT 1

FIELD(S): Chemistry, environmental science, geology, hydrogeology, hydrology, chemical engineering, civil engineering, environmental engineering, mechanical engineering, computer science (technical database development)

Opportunities for graduates and undergraduates to participate in energy-related research projects that correlate with their academic and career goals. For 3 to 12 consecutive months.

Funded through Oak Ridge National Laboratory.

1727 — OAK RIDGE INSTITUTE FOR SCIENCE AND EDUCATION (Professional Internship Program/Pittsburgh Energy Technology Center)

P.O. Box 117
Oak Ridge TN 37831-0117
423/576-3426
423/576-3427

AMOUNT: $235 to $325/week + travel, tuition, and fees

DEADLINE(S): FEB 5; JUN 1; OCT 1

FIELD(S): Chemistry, physics, environmental science, geology, chemical or environmental engineering, computer science, or statistics.

Opportunities for graduates and undergraduates to participate in fossil energy-related research projects that correlate with their academic and career goals. For 3 to 12 consecutive months.

Funded through U.S. Dept. of Energy, Office of Fossil Energy, and Pittsburgh Energy Technology Center.

1728 — OAK RIDGE INSTITUTE FOR SCIENCE AND EDUCATION (Professional Internship Program/Savannah River Site)

P.O. Box 117
Oak Ridge TN 37831-0117
423/576-3426
423/576-3427

AMOUNT: $260 to $340/week + travel

DEADLINE(S): FEB 5; JUN 1; SEP 1

FIELD(S): Chemistry, computer science, environmental science, geology, engineering, or physics

Opportunities for high school junior and seniors, undergraduates, and graduates to participate in research projects that correlate with their academic majors and career goals. For 3 to 12 consecutive months at the Savannah River Site, SC.

Funded through the Savannah River Site, SC.

1729 — OAK RIDGE INSTITUTE FOR SCIENCE AND EDUCATION (Science and Engineering Research Semester)

P.O. Box 117
Oak Ridge TN 37831-0117
423/576-2358
423/576-2310

AMOUNT: $225/week + travel + housing

DEADLINE(S): OCT; MAR

FIELD(S): Computer science, physical sciences, environmental and life sciences, and mathematics

Opportunities for high school junior and seniors and a few slots for graduates to participate in energy-related with laboratory scientists at Oak Ridge National Laboratory, TN. One semester with possibility of summer extension. Available two times a year.

Funded through the U.S. Dept. of Energy, Office of Energy Research.

1730 — OAK RIDGE INSTITUTE FOR SCIENCE AND EDUCATION (Nuclear Engineering & Health Physics Fellowship Program)

105 Mitchell Rd. MS-16
Oak Ridge TN 37831-0117
423/576-2600 or 423/241-2890
E-Mail: johnsons@orau.gov or daltonj@arou.gov

AMOUNT: $14,400/yr.

DEADLINE(S): JAN 26

FIELD(S): Engineering, physical and life sciences

Fellowships in nuclear engineering or applied health physics to implement DOE's nuclear energy-related mission. Candidates must have B.A. degree in life or physical sciences or engineering.

For details and application, contact Sandra Johnson or Jennifer Dalton at above location.

1731 — OPEN SOCIETY INSTITUTE (Environmental Management Fellowships)

400 West 59th St.
New York NY 10019
212/548-0600 or 212/757-2323
FAX: 212/548-4679 or 212/548-4600
Internet: www.soros.org/efp.html

AMOUNT: Fees, room, board, living stipend, textbooks, international transportation, health insurance

DEADLINE(S): NOV 15

FIELD(S): Earth sciences, natural sciences, humanities (exc. language), anthropology, sociology, mathematics, or engineering

Two-year fellowships for use in selected universities in the U.S. for international students. For students/professionals in fields related to environmental policy, legislation, and remediation techniques applicable to their home countries.

To apply, contact your local Soros Foundation or Open Society Institute. Further details on website.

1732 — OUR WORLD-UNDERWATER SCHOLARSHIP SOCIETY (Scholarship & Internships)

PO Box 4428
Chicago IL 60680
312/666-6525
FAX: 312/666-6846
Internet: www.owuscholarship.org

AMOUNT: $20,000 (experience-based scholarship)

DEADLINE(S): NOV 30

FIELD(S): Marine & Aquatics related disciplines

Must be certified SCUBA divers no younger than 21 and no older than 24 on March 1st of the scholarship year. Cannot have yet received a postgraduate degree. Experiences include active participation in field studies, underwater research, scientific expeditions, laboratory assignments, equipment testing and design, and photographic instruction. Financial need NOT a factor. Funds are used for transportation and minimal living expenses, if necessary.

1 scholarship and several internships annually. Contact the Secretary for an application.

1733 — ROYAL SOCIETY (John Murray Fund)

6 Carlton House Terrace
REF REA
London SW1Y 5AG ENGLAND UK
071/839 5561

AMOUNT: Up to 3000 pounds sterling

DEADLINE(S): DEC 10

FIELD(S): Oceanography; Limnology; Zoology; Botany; Geology; Mathematics; Physics

Grants open to British post-doctoral applicants. Award is to be used for the encouragement of travel & work in oceanography or limnology.

The award may be held for 1 year. It is not renewable. Write for complete information—REF JELL.

1734 — SEASPACE (Scholarships)

PO Box 3753
Houston TX 77253-3753
E-mail: captx@iname.com
Internet: www.seaspace.ycg.org/schship.htm

AMOUNT: $1,000-$4,000

DEADLINE(S): FEB 1

FIELD(S): Marine/Aquatic Sciences

Open to college juniors, seniors, and graduate students attending school in the US. Must have a 3.3/4.0 GPA and demonstrate financial need.

15-25 awards annually. Not renewable. See website or contact Carolyn Peterson for an application.

1735 — THE DAPHNE JACKSON MEMORIAL FELLOWSHIPS TRUST (Fellowships in Science/Engineering)

School of Physical Sciences
Dept. of Physics
University of Surrey
Guildford, Surrey
GU2 5XH ENGLAND UK
01483 259166
FAX: 01483 259501
E-Mail: J.Woolley@surrey.ac.uk
Internet: www.sst.ph.ic.ac.uk/trust/

AMOUNT: Varies

DEADLINE(S): Varies

FIELD(S): Science or engineering, including information sciences

Fellowships to enable well-qualified and highly motivated scientists and engineers to return to appropriate careers following a career break due to family comitments. May be used on a flexible, part-time basis. Tenable at various U.K. universities.

See website and/or contact organization for details.

1736 — THE SWIRE INSTITUTE OF MARINE SCIENCE

The University of Hong Kong
Cape d'Aguilar
Shek O
Hong Kong
852/2809-2179
FAX: 852/2809-2197

AMOUNT: $1,000/month (approximately)

DEADLINE(S): JUL 1

FIELD(S): Marine Ecology

Studentships, scholarships, and short-term fellowships. Requires an honours degree in marine science.

Write for complete information.

1737 — U.S. DEPARTMENT OF DEFENSE (GLSIP-General Laboratory Scientific Interchange Program: NRC-NRL Post-Doctoral Program)

Naval Research Laboratory
Office of Program Admin. &
Dev. Code 1006.17
Washington, D.C. 20375-5321
202/767-3865
DSN: 297-3865
FAX: 202/404-8110
Internet: www.acq.osd.mil/ddre/edugate/s-aindx.html

AMOUNT: Research Program

DEADLINE(S): None specified

FIELD(S): Computer science, artificial intelligence, plasma physics, acoustics, radar, fluid dynamics, chemistry, materials sci, optical sci, condensed matter and radiation, electronic sci, environmental sci, marine geosciences, remote sensing, oceanography, marine meteorology, space technology/sciences.

U.S. citizens who are recent postdoctoral graduates are selected on the basis of overall qualifications and technical proposals.

Contact Jessica Hileman for more information.

1738 — UNIVERSITY OF GLASGOW (Scholarships in Naval Architecture and Ocean Engineering)

Glasgow G12 8QQ
Scotland UNITED KINGDOM
0141 330 4322
FAX: 0141 330 5917
E-Mail: naval@eng.gla.ac.uk
Internet: www.eng.gla.ac.uk/Naval/questions/scholar.htm

AMOUNT: 250 pounds per annum and more

DEADLINE(S): APR 30

FIELD(S): Naval Architecture; Ocean Engineering

Scholarships for undergraduate and graduate students in the above fields. Several awards are available, varying in amount and in year in school of recipients. First-year students can also apply to The Royal Institution of Naval Architects, 10 Upper Belgrave St., London, SW1X 8BQ, England (e-mail: hq@rina.org.uk).

See website for further information. Write for application forms.

1739 — US DEPARTMENT OF DEFENSE (National Defense Science & Engineering Graduate Fellowship Programs)

200 Park Drive, Suite 211
P.O. Box 13444
Research Triangle Park, NC 27709-3444
919/549-8505
Internet: www.acq.osd.mil/ddre/edugate/s-aindx.html

AMOUNT: Full tuition and fees (tenure of 36 months)

DEADLINE(S): JAN

FIELD(S): Mathematical, physical, biological, ocean, and engineering sciences

Must be US citizens or nationals at or near the beginning of their graduate study in science or engineering, leading to a doctoral degree. NDSEG Fellowships are awarded for study and research in these disciplines of military importance.

Approximately 90 new three-year graduate fellowships each April. Fellows may choose appropriate US institutions of higher education, offering degrees in science and engineering. Contact the Program Administrator for more information.

1740 — WATER ENVIRONMENT FEDERATION (Robert A. Canham Scholarship)

Access website
Internet: www.wef.org

AMOUNT: $2,500

DEADLINE(S): MAR 1

FIELD(S): Water environment areas

Open to post-baccalaureate students in the environmental engineering or sciences field who agree to work in the environmental field for at least two years after completion of the degree. Must be a member of the Water Environment Federation.

A detailed statement of career goals and aspirations and three letters of recommendation are required. Write for complete information. Access website for details and application—go to "Member Programs," then to "Canham Scholarship." Organization will not mail this information!

1741 — WATER ENVIRONMENT FEDERATION (Student Paper Competition)

Access website
Internet: www.wef.org

AMOUNT: $1,000 (1st prize); $500 (2nd); $250 (3rd)

DEADLINE(S): FEB 1

FIELD(S): Water pollution control and related fields

Awards for 500- 1,000-word abstracts dealing with water pollution control, water quality problems, water-related concerns, or hazardous wastes. Open to undergrad (A.A. and B.A.) and grad students.

Also open to recently graduated students (within 1 calendar year of Feb. 1 deadline). See website for details—go to "Member Programs" then to "Student Paper Competition." Organization will not mail this information.

1742 — WOMAN'S SEAMEN'S FRIEND SOCIETY OF CONNECTICUT, INC. (Scholarships)

74 Forbes Ave.
New Haven CT 06512
203/467-3887

AMOUNT: Varies

DEADLINE(S): APR 1 (summer); MAY 15 (fall/spring)

FIELD(S): Marine Sciences; Merchant Seafarers

Open to Connecticut residents who are merchant seafarers and their dependents attending any institution of higher learning; CT residents studying at state maritime academies; CT residents majoring in marine science in-state or out-of-state; and residents of other states majoring in marine science in CT. Based on financial need, academic achievement, letters of recommendation, and proposed programs of study. Awards also available for graduate work in marine science.

Renewable. Contact Woman's Seamen's Friend Society for applications.

1743 — WOODS HOLE OCEANOGRAPHIC INSTITUTION (Postdoctoral Awards in Ocean Science and Engineering)

360 Woods Hole Road
Woods Hole MA 02543-1541
508/289-2219
FAX: 508/457-2188
E-Mail: mgately@whoi.edu
Internet: www.whoi.edu

AMOUNT: Varies

DEADLINE(S): FEB 16

FIELD(S): Chemistry, Engineering, Geology, Geophysics, Mathematics, Meteorology, Physics, Biology, Oceanography

Eighteen-month postdoctoral scholar awards are offered to recipients of new or recent doctorates in the above fields. The awards are designed to further the education and training of the applicant with primary emphasis placed on the individual's research promise.

For an application/more information, contact the Education Office, Clark Laboratory 223, MS #31, at above address.

1744 — WOODS HOLE OCEANOGRAPHIC INSTITUTION (Research Fellowships in Marine Policy and Ocean Management)

> 360 Woods Hole Road
> Woods Hole MA 02543-1541
> 508/289-2219
> FAX: 508/457-2188
> E-Mail: mgately@whoi.edu
> Internet: www.whoi.edu

AMOUNT: Varies

DEADLINE(S): FEB 16

FIELD(S): Social Sciences, Law, Natural Sciences

For professionals in the above fields who wish to apply their training to investigations of problems involving the use of the oceans. WHOI's objective is to provide a year-long advanced learning experience in ocean policy problems involving the interdisciplinary application of social science and natural science to marine policy problems. Fields currently emphasized: economics, statistics, public policy, natural resource management, and international relations.

For an application/more information, contact the Education Office, Clark Laboratory 223, MS #31, at above address.

NATURAL HISTORY

1745 — AMERICAN ACADEMY IN ROME (Rome Prize Predoctoral Fellowships)

> 7 East 60th Street
> New York, NY 10022-1001
> 212/751-7200
> FAX: 212/751-7220
> Internet: www.aarome.org

AMOUNT: $15,000-$17,800

DEADLINE(S): NOV 15

FIELD(S): Archaeology; Art History; Modern Italian Studies; Post-Classical Humanistic Studies

For doctoral study in Rome, Italy. Applicant must be US citizen with a major and/or career interest in above fields. Recommendations, proof of eligibility, and research proposal required.

$40 application fee. Contact the Programs Department at the American Academy in Rome for an application.

1746 — AMERICAN ACADEMY IN ROME (Rome Prize Postdoctoral Fellowships)

> 7 East 60th Street
> New York NY 10022-1001
> 212/751-7200
> FAX: 212/751-7220
> Internet: www.aarome.org

AMOUNT: $15,000-$17,800

DEADLINE(S): NOV 15

FIELD(S): Archaeology; Art History; Modern Italian Studies; Post-classical Humanistic Studies

For postgraduate study in Rome, Italy. Applicant must be US citizen or permanent resident with a major and/or career interest in above fields. Recommendations, proof of eligibility, and research proposal required.

Contact the Programs Department at the American Academy in Rome for an application.

1747 — AMERICAN ASSOCIATION FOR THE ADVANCEMENT OF SCIENCE (Science & Engineering Fellowships)

> 1200 New York Ave., NW
> Washington DC 20005
> 202/326-6700
> FAX: 202/289-4950
> E-Mail: science_policy@aaas.org
> Internet: www.aas.org

AMOUNT: $40,000+

DEADLINE(S): JAN 15

FIELD(S): Science; Engineering

Post-doctoral fellowships open to AAAS members or applicants concurrently applying for membership. Prospective fellows must demonstrate exceptional competence in an area of science or have a broad scientific or technical background. Those with MA degrees and at least three years of poast-degree professional experience may also apply.

U.S. citizenship required. For complete information on these one-year fellowships write to Director, Science Fellows Program at address above.

1748 — AMERICAN COUNCIL OF LEARNED SOCIETIES (ACLS Fellowships)

> Office of Fellowshops & Grants
> 228 E. 45th St.
> New York NY 10017
> Written Inquiry

AMOUNT: Up to $20,000

DEADLINE(S): SEP 30

FIELD(S): Humanities, Social Sciences, and other areas having predominately humanistic emphasis

Open to U.S. citizens or legal residents who hold the Ph.D or its equivalent. Fellowships are designed to help scholars devote 6 to 12 continuous months to full-time research.

Write for complete information.

1749 — AMERICAN FOUNDATION FOR THE BLIND (Paul W. Ruckes Scholarship)

> 11 Penn Plaza, Ste. 300
> New York NY 10001
> 212/502-7661 or TDD 212/502-7771
> E-Mail: juliet@afb.org
> Internet: www.afb.org

AMOUNT: $1,000

DEADLINE(S): APR 30

FIELD(S): Engineering, computer, physical, or life sciences

Open to blind or visually impaired undergraduate or graduate students pursuing degrees in the above fields. U.S. citizenship required.

Write to the above address or visit website for complete information.

1750 — AMERICAN MUSEUM OF NATURAL HISTORY (Grants)

> Central Park West at 79th St.
> New York NY 10024-5192
> FAX: 212/769-5495
> E-Mail: bynum@amnh.org
> Internet: research.amnh.org

AMOUNT: $200-$2,000

DEADLINE(S): JAN 15

FIELD(S): Zoology; Paleontology; Anthropology

Modest short-term awards are offered to advanced graduate students and postdoctoral researchers who are commencing their careers in above fields. Two letters of recommendation and description (less than 2 pages) of proposed investigation are required. Budget must show clearly amounts and items for which award will be used. Grantees must submit progress report upon completion. Research projects need not be carried out at American Museum of Natural History.

200 awards annually. See website or contact Office of Grants & Fellowships for details on specific programs: Frank M. Chapman Memorial Fund for Ornithology, Lerner Gray Fund for Marine Research, Theodore Roosevelt Memorial Fund, & Collection Study Grant.

1751 — AMERICAN MUSEUM OF NATURAL HISTORY (Graduate Student Fellowship Program)

> Central Park West at 79th St.
> New York NY 10024-5192
> FAX: 212/769-5495
> E-Mail: bynum@amnh.org
> Internet: research.amnh.org

AMOUNT: Stipend & health insurance

DEADLINE(S): JAN 15

FIELD(S): Paleontology; Earth & Planetary Sciences; Entomology; Evolutionary & Molecular Biology

One-year fellowships through partnership w/ Columbia, Cornell, & Yale Universities & City University of New York to help advance training of Ph.D. candidates in scientific disciplines practiced at Museum. Must include resume/curriculum vitae, GRE scores, TOEFL score for foreign students, official transcripts, letters of recommendation, and statement of research interest/summary of thesis proposal/progress to date.

Renewable up to 4 years. Must apply to Museum AND cooperating university. See website or contact Office of Grants & Fellowships for application.

1752 — AMERICAN MUSEUM OF NATURAL HISTORY (Research Fellowships)

Central Park West at 79th St.
New York NY 10024-5192
FAX: 212/769-5495
E-Mail: bynum@amnh.org
Internet: research.amnh.org

AMOUNT: Varies

DEADLINE(S): JAN 15

FIELD(S): Zoology; Paleontology; Anthropology; Earth & Planetary Sciences

Support to recent postdoctoral investigators and established scientists to carry out a specific project within a limited time period. Appointments are usually for one year, and candidates are expected to be in residence at the Museum or one of its field stations. Fellows are judged on research abilities/experience and merits/scope of proposed research. Application requires project description/bibliography, budget, letters of recommendation, and curriculum vitae.

See website or contact the Office of Grants & Fellowships for an application.

1753 — AMERICAN RESEARCH INSTITUTE IN TURKEY (ARIT Fellowship Program)

Univ Penn Museum
33rd & Spruce Streets
Philadelphia PA 19104-6324
215/898-3474
FAX: 215/898-0657
E-Mail: leinwand@sas.upenn.edu
Internet: mec.sas.upenn.edu/ARIT

AMOUNT: Varies

DEADLINE(S): NOV 15

FIELD(S): Humanities; Social Sciences; Turkish Studies

Two-month to one-year fellowships are for postdoctoral scholars & advanced graduate students engaged in research on ancient, medieval, or modern times in Turkey, in any field of the humanities & social sciences. Predoctoral students must have fulfilled all preliminary requirements for doctorate except dissertation. Applicants must maintain an affiliation with an educational institution in the US or Canada. Must submit curriculum vitae, research proposal, & referees.

Contact ARIT for an application.

1754 — AMERICAN RESEARCH INSTITUTE IN TURKEY (KRESS/ARIT Predoctoral Fellowship in the History of Art & Archaeology)

Univ Penn Museum
33rd & Spruce Streets
Philadelphia PA 19104-6324
215/898-3474
FAX: 215/898-0657
E-Mail: leinwand@sas.upenn.edu
Internet: mec.sas.upenn.edu/ARIT

AMOUNT: $15,000 (max.)

DEADLINE(S): NOV 15

FIELD(S): Archaeology; Architectural History; Art History

Fellowships of up to one year are for students engaged in advanced dissertation research in above fields that necessitates a period of study in Turkey. Must be US citizen or matriculating at a US university. Must submit curriculum vitae, research proposal, and referees.

Contact ARIT for an application.

1755 — AMERICAN RESEARCH INSTITUTE IN TURKEY (Mellon Research Fellowships for Central and Eastern European Scholars in Turkey)

Univ Penn Museum
33rd & Spruce Streets
Philadelphia PA 19104-6324
215/898-3474
FAX: 215/898-0657
E-Mail: leinwand@sas.upenn.edu
Internet: mec.sas.upenn.edu/ARIT

AMOUNT: Stipend up to $10,500 for 2-3 month project (includes travel, living expenses, work-related costs)

DEADLINE(S): MAR 5

FIELD(S): Humanities; Social Sciences

For Czech, Hungarian, Polish, Slovakian, Bulgarian, and Romanian scholars holding a Ph.D. or equivalent who are engaged in advanced research in any field of the social sciences or the humanities involving Turkey. Must be permanent residents of these countries and must obtain formal permission for any research to be carried out.

3 awards annually. Previous fellows not eligible. See website or write to above address for details.

1756 — AMERICAN RESEARCH INSTITUTE IN TURKEY (National Endowment for the Humanities Fellowships for Research in Turkey)

Univ Penn Museum
33rd & Spruce Streets
Philadelphia PA 19104-6324
215/898-3474
FAX: 215/898-0657
E-Mail: leinwand@sas.upenn.edu
Internet: mec.sas.upenn.edu/ARIT

AMOUNT: $10,000-$30,000

DEADLINE(S): NOV 15

FIELD(S): Humanities

Postdoctoral fellowships are to conduct research in Turkey for four to twelve months. Fields of study cover all periods in the general range of the humanities, including humanistically oriented aspects of the social sciences, prehistory, history, art, archaeology, literature, linguistics, and cultural history. There are two institutes, one in Istanbul and one in Ankara. Both have residential facilities for fellows and provide general assistance.

2-3 awards annually. Contact ARIT for an application. Notification by January 25th.

1757 — AMERICAN SCHOOL OF CLASSICAL STUDIES AT ATHENS (Fellowships)

6-8 Charlton St.
Princeton NJ 08540-5232
609/683-0800
FAX: 609/924-0578
E-Mail: ascsa@axcsa.org
Internet: www.ats.edu/spons

AMOUNT: Up to $7,840 + room, partial board, and fee waiver

DEADLINE(S): JAN 5

FIELD(S): Classical Studies; Archaeology; Ancient Greece

Fellowships for study at ASCSA in Greece. Open to graduate students at American & Canadian colleges & universities. Recent graduates also are eligible. Residency in Greece required.

Access website for complete information and application or write for details.

1758 — AMERICAN UNIVERSITY IN CAIRO (International Graduate Fellowships in Sociology-Anthropology)

420 Fifth Ave.
3rd Floor
New York NY 10017-2729
212/730-8800
FAX: 212/730-1600
E-Mail: aucegypt@aucnyo.edu
Internet: www.aucegypt.edu

AMOUNT: Tuition + stipend paid in Egyptian pounds

DEADLINE(S): FEB 1

FIELD(S): Sociology; Anthropology

For graduate students in the master of arts program at the American University in Cairo, Egypt, who do not hold Egyptian citizenship. Must have a GPA of at least 3.4. Financial need NOT a factor.

2 awards annually. Renewable. Contact Mary Davidson at above address for complete information.

1759 — ARCHAEOLOGICAL INSTITUTE OF AMERICA (Harriet & Leon Pomerance Fellowship)

Boston Univ
656 Beacon St.
Boston MA 02215-2006
617/353-9361
FAX 617/353-6550
E-Mail: aia@bu.edu
Internet: www.archeological.org

AMOUNT: $4,000

DEADLINE(S): NOV 1

FIELD(S): Archaeology

Fellowship will enable a graduate or postgraduate student to work on an individual project of a scholarly nature related to Aegean Bronze Age Archaeology. Preference given to candidates whose projects require travel to the Mediterranean. Must be US or Canadian resident. At conclusion of tenure, recipient must submit report on use of stipend.

1 award annually. Contact AIA for an application. Awards announced by February 1st.

1760 — ARCHAEOLOGICAL INSTITUTE OF AMERICA (Olivia James Traveling Fellowship)

Boston Univ
656 Beacon St.
Boston MA 02215-2006
617/353-9361
FAX: 617/353-6550
E-Mail: aia@bu.edu
Internet: www.archeological.org

AMOUNT: $22,000

DEADLINE(S): NOV 1

FIELD(S): Classics; Sculpture; Architecture; Archaeology; History

Fellowships for US citizens/permanent residents to be used for travel and study in Greece, the Aegean Islands, Sicily, Southern Italy, Asia Minor, or Mesopotamia. Preference given to individuals engaged in dissertation research or to recent recipients of the Ph.D. (within 5 years). Award is not intended to support field excavation projects, and recipients may not hold other major fellowships during tenure. At

conclusion, recipient must submit report on use of stipend.

Contact AIA for an application. Awards announced by February 1st.

1761 — ARCHAEOLOGICAL INSTITUTE OF AMERICA (Woodruff Traveling Fellowship)

Boston Univ
656 Beacon St.
Boston MA 02215-2006
617/353-9361
FAX: 617/353-6550
E-Mail: aia@bu.edu
Internet: www.archeological.org

AMOUNT: $6,000

DEADLINE(S): NOV 1

FIELD(S): Archaeology

One-year fellowship is to support dissertation archaeological research in Italy and the western Mediterranean. Applicants must have completed all requirements for Ph.D. except dissertation. Preference given to field oriented projects. Ph.D. students working in any time period are eligible. Funds can be used for travel, room & board, and other legitimate research expenses, and can be combined with external funds. At conclusion of tenure, must submit report on use.

Contact AIA for an application. Awards announced by February 1st.

1762 — ASSOCIATION FOR WOMEN IN SCIENCE EDUCATIONAL FOUNDATION (AWIS Predoctoral Awards)

1200 New York Ave. NW, Suite 650
Washington DC 20005
202/326-8940 or 800-886-AWIS
E-Mail: awis@awis.org
Internet: www.awis.org

AMOUNT: $1,000

DEADLINE(S): JAN 16

FIELD(S): Various Sciences and Social Sciences

Scholarships for female doctoral students. Summary page, description of research project, resume, references, transcripts, and biographical sketch required. US citizens may study at any graduate institution; non-citizens must study at US institutions.

5-10 awards annually. See website or write to above address for an application and complete information.

1763 — ASSOCIATION FOR WOMEN IN SCIENCE EDUCATIONAL FOUNDATION (AWIS Pre-doctoral Awards)

1200 New York Ave. NW, Suite 650
Washington DC 20005
202/326-8940 or 800/886-AWIS

E-Mail: awis@awis.org
Internet: www.awis.org

AMOUNT: $1,000

DEADLINE(S): JAN 16

FIELD(S): Various Sciences and Social Sciences

Scholarships for female doctoral students. Summary page, description of research project, resume, references, transcripts, and biographical sketch required. US citizens may study at any graduate institution; non-citizens must be enrolled in US institutions.

5-10 awards annually. See website or write to above address for an application and more information.

1764 — ASSOCIATION FOR WOMEN IN SCIENCE EDUCATIONAL FOUNDATION (Ruth Satter Memorial Award)

1200 New York Ave., NW, Suite 650
Washington DC 20005
202/326-8940 or 800/886-AWIS
E-Mail: awis@awis.org
Internet: www.awis.org

AMOUNT: $1,000

DEADLINE(S): JAN 16

FIELD(S): Various Sciences and Social Sciences

Scholarships for female doctoral students who have interrupted their education for at least three years to raise a family. Summary page, description of research project, resume, references, transcripts, biographical sketch, and letter from your department to confirm eligibility required. US citizens may study at any graduate institution; non-citizens must attend US institutions.

See website or write to above address for more information or an application.

1765 — ASSOCIATION FOR WOMEN IN SCIENCE EDUCATIONAL FOUNDATION (Ruth Satter Memorial Award)

1200 New York Ave. NW, Suite 650
Washington DC 20005
202/326-8940 or 800/886-AWIS
E-Mail: awis@awis.org
Internet: www.awis.org

AMOUNT: $1,000

DEADLINE(S): JAN 16

FIELD(S): Various Sciences and Social Sciences

Scholarships for female doctoral students who have interrupted their education three years or more to raise a family. Summary page, description of research project, resume, references, transcripts, biographical sketch, and proof of eligibility from department head required. US citizens may attend any graduate institution; non-citizens must be enrolled in US institutions.

See website or write to above address for more information or an application.

1766 — BOEING (Polish Graduate Student Scholarship Program)

Phone for details
314/234-2149

AMOUNT: Tuition, books, and fees for three years

DEADLINE(S): Varies

FIELD(S): Scientific and technical fields

Scholarships for students from Poland to pursue graduate studies in scientific and technical areas at American colleges or universities.

Call Jim Schlueter at above telephone number.

1767 — BRITISH COLUMBIA HERITAGE TRUST (Scholarships)

PO Box 9818 Stn Prov Govt.
Victoria BC V8W 9W3 CANADA
250/356-1433

AMOUNT: $5,000

DEADLINE(S): FEB 15

FIELD(S): British Columbia History; Architecture; Archaeology; Archival Management

Open to graduate students who are Canadian citizens or permanent residents. Criteria are scholarly record and academic performance, educational and career objectives, and proposed program of study.

Write for complete information.

1768 — BRITISH INSTITUTE IN EASTERN AFRICA (Research Grants)

PO Box 30710
Nairobi Kenya E. AFRICA
+254-2-43721
FAX: +254-2-43365
E-Mail: pjlane@insightkenya.com
Internet: britac3.britac.ac.uk/institutes/eafrica

AMOUNT: 500-5,000 pounds sterling

DEADLINE(S): MAY 31; NOV 30

FIELD(S): Archaeology; History; Linguistics; Ethnography

Grants are for graduate or postgraduate fieldwork in Eastern Africa. Does NOT cover salaries, overheads, student fees, or stipends. Preference is given, but not limited, to UK and Commonwealth citizens. Financial need is NOT a factor.

15 awards annually. Not renewable. Contact Dr. Paul Lane at the British Institute in Nairobi for an application.

1769 — BRITISH INSTITUTE OF ARCHAEOLOGY AT ANKARA (Travel Grants)

Assistant Secretary
10 Carlton House Terrace
London SW1Y 5AH ENGLAND UK
+44 0171 969 5204

AMOUNT: 500 pounds sterling (max.)

DEADLINE(S): FEB 1

FIELD(S): Archaeology & Geography of Turkey

Travel grants to enable undergraduate and graduate students to familiarize themselves with the archaeology and geography of Turkey, its museums, and ancient sites. For citizens of the British Commonwealth.

Contact British Institute for an application.

1770 — BRITISH SCHOOL OF ARCHAEOLOGY IN IRAQ (Various Fellowships & Grants)

31-34 Gordon Square
London WCIH OPY ENGLAND UK
+44 0171 733 8912
FAX: +44 0171 274 9265

AMOUNT: 1,000 pounds sterling (approx.)

DEADLINE(S): MAR 31; SEP 30

FIELD(S): Archaeology

Grants for graduate research on history or languages of Iraq and neighboring countries from earliest times to 1700 A.D. Candidates must be residents of the United Kingdom or citizens of the British Commonwealth. Recipients normally must spend up to six months in Iraq, but this requirement has been dropped until the political situation improves.

Contact the Secretary for an application.

1771 — COUNCIL FOR EUROPEAN STUDIES (Predissertation Fellowships)

Columbia Univ
807-807A International Affairs Bldg.
New York NY 10027
212/854-4172
FAX: 212/854-8808
E-Mail: ces@columbia.edu
Internet: www.europanet.org

AMOUNT: $4,000 stipend (max.)

DEADLINE(S): FEB 1

FIELD(S): Cultural Anthropology; History (post 1750); Political Science; Sociology; Geography; Urban & Regional Planning

Awards are for research in France to determine viability of projected doctoral dissertation in modern history and social sciences. Recipients test research design of dissertation, determine availability of archival materials, and contact French scholars. Must be US citizen or permanent resident at a US institution and have completed at least two but no more than three years of full-time doctoral study by end of year. Institutional membership in Council is required.

6 awards annually. See website or contact Council for an application.

1772 — COUNCIL FOR EUROPEAN STUDIES (Predissertation Fellowships in Anthropology)

Columbia Univ
807-807A International Affairs Bldg.
New York NY 10027
212/854-4172
FAX: 212/854-8808
E-Mail: ces@columbia.edu
Internet: www.europanet.org OR www.h-net.msu/~sae/fellow1.html

AMOUNT: $4,000 stipend

DEADLINE(S): FEB 1

FIELD(S): Cultural Anthropology

Awards are for short-term (three months) research in Europe to determine viability of projected doctoral dissertation in anthropology. Must be attending a US or Canadian university and have completed at least two but no more than three years of full-time doctoral study by end of year. Should have, or be close to, finishing coursework and/or Ph.D. qualifying exams, but have not fully formulated nor defended a dissertation proposal.

See website or contact Council for an application.

1773 — EDMUND NILES HUYCK PRESERVE (Research Grants)

Main St.
Rensselaerville NY 12147
518/797-3440

AMOUNT: $2,500 (max.)

DEADLINE(S): FEB 1

FIELD(S): Ecology; Behavior; Evolution; Natural History

Open to graduate and postgraduate scientists conducting research on the natural resources of the Huyck Preserve. Housing and lab space are provided at the preserve. Funds are NOT available to help students defray college expenses.

Contact Preserve for an application.

1774 — EPILEPSY FOUNDATION OF AMERICA (Behavioral Sciences Research Training Fellowships)

4351 Garden City Drive
Landover MD 20785-2267
301/459-3700 or FAX: 301/577-2684
FDD: 800/332-2070
E-Mail: postmaster@efa.org
Internet: www.efa.org

AMOUNT: Up to $30,000

DEADLINE(S): FEB 1

FIELD(S): Epilepsy as related to Behavioral Sciences (includes sociology, social work, psychology, anthropology, nursing, political science, etc.)

A one-year training experience for postdoctoral scholars to develop expertise in the area of epilepsy research relative to the behavioral sciences. The project must be carried out at an approved facility. Amount depends on experience and qualifications of the applicant and the scope and duration of proposed project.

Contact EFA for an application.

1775 — FORD FOUNDATION/NATIONAL RESEARCH COUNCIL (Postdoctoral Fellowship for Minorities)

National Research Council
2101 Constitution Ave.
Washington DC 20418
202/334-2860
E-Mail: infofell@nas.edu
Internet: http//www.nas.edu/fo/index.html

AMOUNT: $25,000 + relocation and research allowance

DEADLINE(S): JAN 3

FIELD(S): Life and physical sciences, mathematics, engineering sciences, behavioral and social sciences, and the humanities

For U.S. citizens who received a Ph.D or Sc.D in the last 7 years and who are Native Amer. Indian or Alaskan, Black/African American, Mexican American, Native Pacific Islander, or Puerto Rican and who are or plan to be in a teaching or research career.

Contact above website or address for complete information.

1776 — FORD FOUNDATION/NATIONAL RESEARCH COUNCIL (Predoctoral/Dissertation Fellowships for Minorities)

2101 Constitution Ave.
Washington DC 20418
202/334-2872
E-Mail: infofell@nas.edu
Internet: http//www.nas.edu/fo/index.html

AMOUNT: $14,000 annual stipend + $6,000 grant to institution; $18,000 for dissertation fellowship

DEADLINE(S): NOV 3

FIELD(S): Most fields of study: sciences, humanities, engineering, behavioral science, social sciences, and computer science

Predoctoral and dissertation fellowships for students whose ethnicity is Alaskan Native, Black/African American, Mexican American/Chicano, Native American Indian, Native Pacific Islander, or Puerto Rican. For research-based programs leading to careers in college teaching and research.

Contact above address or website.

1777 — GLADYS KRIEBLE DELMAS FOUNDATION (Predoctoral & Postdoctoral Grants in Venice & the Veneto)

521 5th Avenue, Suite 1612
New York NY 10175-1699
212/687-0011
FAX: 212/687-8877
E-Mail: DelmasFdtn@aol.com
Internet: www.delmas.org

AMOUNT: $500-$12,500

DEADLINE(S): DEC 15

FIELD(S): Research of Venice and the former Venetian empire and study of contemporary Venetian society and culture.

Pre- and postdoctoral grants for historical research on Venice. Humanities and social sciences are eligible areas of study, including archaeology, architecture, art, bibliography, economics, history, history of science, law, literature, music, political science, religion, and theater.

Applicants must have experience in advanced research and be U.S. citizens/residents; grad students must have fulfilled all doctoral requirements except dissertation by Dec. 15.

1778 — INSTITUTE FOR ADVANCED STUDIES IN THE HUMANITIES (Visiting Research Fellowships)

Univ Edinburgh
Hope Park Square
Edinburgh EH8 9NW SCOTLAND UK
0131 650 4671
FAX: 0131 668 2252
E-Mail: iash@ed.ac.uk
Internet: www.ed.ac.uk/iash/homepage.html

AMOUNT: Non-stipendiary*

DEADLINE(S): DEC 1

FIELD(S): Arts; Social Sciences; Law; Music; Divinity

Postdoctoral research fellowships of between two and six months are tenable at the Institute for Advanced Studies in the Humanities. Based on academic record and publications. *Most fellowships are honorary, but limited support towards expenses is available to a small number of candidates. Fellows are allocated a study room within the Institute and hold one or two seminars during their tenure. Must submit research report at end of fellowship. No teaching required.

15 awards annually. Not renewable. Contact Mrs. Anthea Taylor for an application.

1779 — L.S.B. LEAKEY FOUNDATION (Franklin Mosher Baldwin Memorial Fellowships)

PO Box 29346
1002A O'Reilly Ave.
San Francisco CA 94129

415/561-4646
FAX: 415/561-4647
E-Mail: grants@leakeyfoundation.org
Internet: www.leakeyfoundation.org

AMOUNT: $12,000/yr. (max.)

DEADLINE(S): FEB 15

FIELD(S): Human Origins

For scholars and students with citizenship in an African country who seek to obtain an advanced degree or specialized training in an area of study related to human origins. Award is for a program of approved special training and/or advanced training towards an MA, PH.D., or equivalent. Sponsor letters required.

Renewable an additional year. Contact the Leakey Foundation for an application. Notification of award will be in mid-May.

1780 — L.S.B. LEAKEY FOUNDATION (General Grants)

PO Box 29346
1002A O'Reilly Ave.
San Francisco CA 94129
415/561-4646
FAX: 415/561-4647
E-Mail: grants@leakeyfoundation.org
Internet: www.leakeyfoundation.org

AMOUNT: $3,000-$12,000 (grad.); up to $20,000 (post-doc.)

DEADLINE(S): AUG 15; JAN 5

FIELD(S): Archaeology; Paleontology; Primatology; Anthropology

Advanced doctoral students as well as established scientists/postdoctorates are eligible. Priority is to exploratory phases of promising new research projects relating to human origins. Financial need NOT a factor.

30 awards annually. Contact the Leakey Foundation for an application. Notification of award will be in mid-December or mid-May.

1781 — L.S.B. LEAKEY FOUNDATION (Special Research Grants: Fellowships for Great Ape Research, Study of Foraging Peoples, & Paleoanthropology Award)

PO Box 29346
1002A O'Reilly Ave.
San Francisco CA 94129
415/561-4646
FAX: 415/561-4647
E-Mail: grants@leakeyfoundation.org
Internet: www.leakeyfoundation.org

AMOUNT: up to $40,000

DEADLINE(S): AUG 15; JAN 5

FIELD(S): Anthropology; Primatology; Paleontology

Available to postdoctoral and senior scientists for exceptional research projects studying great apes, hunters and gatherers, or multidisciplinary paleoanthropology. This is a highly competitive program; you may want to check with the Program & Grants Officer a month before the deadline to see if your research topic is competitive enough. Financial need NOT a factor.

30 awards annually. Renewable. Contact the Leakey Foundation for specific details and an application. Notification of award will be in mid-December or mid-May.

1782 — NATIONAL HUMANITIES CENTER (Burroughs Wellcome Fund Fellowships in the History of Modern Medicine)

PO Box 12256
Research Triangle Park NC 27709-2256
919/549-0661
FAX: 919/990-8535
E-Mail: nhc@ga.unc.edu
Internet: www.nhc.rtp.nc.us:8080

AMOUNT: Stipend ($35,000-$50,000) + Travel Expenses (fellow & dependents)

DEADLINE(S): OCT 15

FIELD(S): History of Medicine/Biomedical Science; Medical Anthropology

Postdoctoral fellowships for historians of medicine or biomedical science, medical anthropologists, and other scholars whose work concerns the history of twentieth-century medicine. Curriculum vitae, 1,000-word proposal, and three letters of recommendation are required.

1 award annually. Contact NHC for application materials.

1783 — NAVAL HISTORICAL CENTER (Internship Program)

Washington Navy Yard
901 M St., SE
Washington DC 20374-5060
202/433-6901
FAX: 202/433-8200
E-Mail: efurgol@nhc.navy.mil
Internet: www.history.navy.mil

AMOUNT: $400 possible honoraria; otherwise, unpaid

DEADLINE(S): None

FIELD(S): Education; History; Public Relations; Design

Registered students of colleges/universities and graduates thereof are eligible for this program, which must be a minimum of 3 weeks, full or part-time. Four specialities available: Curator, Education, Public Relations, and Design. Interns receive orientation & assist in their departments, and must complete individual project which contributes to Center. Must submit a letter of recommendation, unofficial transcript, and writing sample of not less than 1,000 words.

Contact Dr. Edward M. Furgol, Curator, for an application.

1784 — NEWBERRY LIBRARY (Long-Term Fellowships)

60 West Walton Street
Chicago IL 60610-3380
312/943-9090
E-Mail: research@newberry.org
Internet: www.newberry.org

AMOUNT: Up to $30,000

DEADLINE(S): JAN 20

FIELD(S): Humanities, History, & related fields

Six postdoctoral fellowship programs are available for scholars wishing to use the Library's collection for writing or research. Fellowships last six to eleven months, and each have slightly different requirements.

See website for details and an application or write to above address.

1785 — NEWBERRY LIBRARY (Short-Term Fellowships)

60 West Walton Street
Chicago IL 60610-3380
312/943-9090
E-Mail: research@newberry.org
Internet: www.newberry.org

AMOUNT: $800-$1,500/month

DEADLINE(S): MAR 1

FIELD(S): Humanities, History, & related fields

Nine programs for postdoctoral scholars or doctoral students at the dissertation stage. Study varies from two weeks to three months and is for those making use of Newberry's collections. Each program has slightly different requirements.

See website for details and applications or write to above address.

1786 — NEWBERRY LIBRARY (Special Fellowships)

60 West Walton Street
Chicago IL 60610-3380
312/255-3666
E-Mail: research@newberry.org
Internet: www.newberry.org

AMOUNT: Varies

DEADLINE(S): DEC 15

FIELD(S): Humanities, History, & related fields

Fellowships for three months to one year for doctoral or postdoctoral students to study in Germany, France, or Great Britain in fields related to Newberry's collections.

Some deadlines JAN 20th. Specific locations are: Wolfenb, ttel, Germany; Ecole Nationale des Chartes, Paris, France; and the British Academy, Great Britain.

See website for more details and applications or write to above address.

1787 — OAK RIDGE ASSOCIATED UNIVERSITIES (Laboratory Graduate Research Participation Program)

P.O. Box 117
Oak Ridge TN 37831-0117
423/576-4813

AMOUNT: $1,000-$1,200/mo. + allowance for dependents + tuition and fees reimbursement to a max. of $3,500/yr.

DEADLINE(S): Ongoing

FIELD(S): Life sciences, physical, and social sciences, mathematics, and engineering

For graduate students in one of the fields listed above who have completed all degree requirements except thesis or dissertation research. For full-time research under the joint direction of the major professor and a DOE staff member at one of various locations, primarily in the South. For six to twelve months.

Funded through U.S. Dept. of Energy, Office of Energy Reseach, and Office of Fossil Energy. Write for complete information.

1788 — OAK RIDGE INSTITUTE FOR SCIENCE AND EDUCATION (Alexander Hollaender Distinguished Post-doctoral Fellowships)

P.O. Box 117
Oak Ridge TN 37831-0117
423/576-3192 or 423/576-9975

AMOUNT: $37,500 + inbound travel, moving, and medical insurance

DEADLINE(S): JAN 15

FIELD(S): Biomedical, life, and environmental sciences and other related scientific disciplines, including global change and human genome

One-year post-doctoral fellowships for research and training in energy-related life, biomedical, and environmental sciences at one of participating laboratories in the U.S. Must have completed doctorate within last two years.

Must be U.S. citizen or legal resident.

1789 — POPULATION COUNCIL (Fellowships in Population Sciences)

One Dag Hammarskjold Plaza
New York NY 10017
212/339-0636
FAX: 212/755-6052
E-Mail: rmohanam@popcouncil.org
Internet: www.popcouncil.org

AMOUNT: $25,000/yr. for 2 years

DEADLINE(S): OCT 31

FIELD(S): Population Sciences

Postdoctoral fellowships for study in population sciences in Nairobi, Kenya, Africa. Open to citizens of any country.

Two awards per year. Selection criteria will stress academic excellence and prospective contribution to the population field. For information and applications contact Raji Mohanam at above address. In Kenya, contact: Carol Libamira, APPRC Coordinator, Population Council, Mutichoice Towers, Upper Hill, P.O. Box 17643, Nairobi, Kenya. 254/2.713.480/1-3.

1790 — POPULATION COUNCIL (Fellowships in Social Sciences)

Policy Research Division
One Dag Hammarskjold Plaza
New York NY 10017
212/339-0671
FAX: 212/755-6052
E-Mail: ssfellowship@popcouncil.org
Internet: www.popcouncil.org

AMOUNT: Monthly stipend, partial tuition/fees, transportation, book/supply allowance, & health insurance

DEADLINE(S): DEC 15

FIELD(S): Population Studies; Demography; Sociology; Anthropology; Economics; Public Health; Geography

Twelve-month award is open to doctoral & postdoctoral scholars for advanced training in above fields that deal with developing world. Doctoral students may request support for dissertation fieldwork/writing. Postdoctorates may pursue research, midcareer training, or resident training. Based on academic excellence, prospective contribution, & well-conceived research proposal. Preference given to those from developing countries.

See website or contact Fellowship Coordinator for an application.

1791 — SMITHSONIAN CENTER FOR MATERIALS RESEARCH AND EDUCATION (Archeological Conservation Fellowship and Internship)

MSC Rm D2002
4210 Silver Hill Rd.
Suitland MD 20746-2863
301/238-3700
FAX: 301/238-3709
E-Mail: cal.etp@cal.si.edu
Internet: www.si.edu/scmre/

AMOUNT: up to $14,000 (Internship); up to $24,000 (Fellowship)

DEADLINE(S): MAR 1

FIELD(S): Archaeological Conservation

One-year graduate internship is open to students entering the internship year in a graduate conservation training program/equivalent. One-year postgraduate fellowship is open to recent graduates of recognized conservation training programs/persons with comparable training & experience. Both include travel, living expenses, & health insurance. Send cover letter, expectations, curriculum vitae, & references. For fellowship, include transcripts & any written materials.

Contact Carol A. Grissom or Harriet F. (Rae) Beaubien for applications.

1792 — SMITHSONIAN INSTITUTION (Cooper-Hewitt, National Design Museum-Mark Kaminski Summer Internship)

2 East 91st Street
New York NY 10128
212/860-6868
FAX: 212/860-6909

AMOUNT: $2,500 for 10-week period

DEADLINE(S): MAR 31

FIELD(S): Architecture, Architectural History, Design and Criticism, Museum Education, Museum Studies

These internships are open to college students considering a career in one of the above areas of study. Also open to graduate students who have not yet completed their M.A. degree. This ten-week program is designed to acquaint participants with the programs, policies, procedures, and operations of Cooper-Hewitt Museum and of museums in general.

One award each summer. Internship commences in June and ends in August. Housing is not provided. Write to Linda Herd at the above address for complete information.

1793 — SMITHSONIAN INSTITUTION (Cooper-Hewitt, National Design Museum-Peter Krueger Summer Internship Program)

Cooper-Hewitt National Design Museum
2 East 91st St.
New York NY 10128
212/860-6868
FAX: 212/860-6909

AMOUNT: $2,500

DEADLINE(S): MAR 31

FIELD(S): Art History, Design, Museum Studies, and Museum Education, or Architectural History

Ten-week summer internships open to graduate and undergraduate students considering a career in the museum profession. Interns will assist on special research or exhibition projects and participate in daily museum activities.

Six awards each summer. Internship commences in June and ends in August. Housing is not provided. Write for complete information.

1794 — SMITHSONIAN INSTITUTION (Fellowship Program)

Office of fellowships & Grants
955 L'Enfant Plaza, Suite 7000
Washington DC 20560
202/287-3271
E-Mail: http://www.si.edu/research+study
Internet: siofg@sivm.si.edu

AMOUNT: $3,000-$25,000 depending on level and length

DEADLINE(S): JAN 15

FIELD(S): Animal behavior, ecology, environmental science (including emphasis on the tropics, anthropology (& archaeology), astrophysics, astronomy, earth sciences, paleobiology, evolutionary/systematic biology, history of science and technology, history of art, esp. American, contemporary, African, and Asian, 20th century American crafts, decorative arts, social/cultural history of the US, or folklife.

For research in residence at the Smithsonian for graduate students, both pre- and postdoctoral.

Research to be in the fields listed above.

1795 — SMITHSONIAN INSTITUTION (Minority Student Internship Program)

Fellowships & Grants
955 L'Enfant Plaza, Suite 7000
MRC 902
Washington DC 20560
202/287-3271
FAX: 202/287-3691
E-Mail: siofg@ofg.si.edu
Internet: www.si.edu/research+study

AMOUNT: $300/week + possible travel expenses

DEADLINE(S): FEB 15

FIELD(S): Humanities, Environmental Studies, Cultural Studies, Natural History, Earth Science, Art History, Biology, & related fields

Ten-week internships in residence at the Smithsonian for US minority students to participate in research or museum-related activities in above fields. For undergrads or grads with at least a 3.0 GPA. Essay, resume, transcripts, and references required with application. Internships are full-time and are offered for Summer, Fall, or Spring tenures.

Write for application.

1796 — SOCIETY OF VERTEBRATE PALEONTOLOGY (Bryan Patterson Award)

60 Revere Dr., Ste. 500
Northbrook IL 60062
Written Inquiry

AMOUNT: $600

DEADLINE(S): APR 15

FIELD(S): Paleontology

Research grant open to graduate students who are Society of Vertebrate Paleontology members. Proposals should be for field work on vertebrate paleontology that is imaginative—NOT pedestrian and venturesome—NOT run of the mill.

Applicant's sponsor must also be current member of SVP. Write for complete information.

1797 — STOCKHOLM UNIVERSITY - INTERNATIONAL GRADUATE PROGRAMME (Master's Programme in Swedish Social Studies)

Universitetsvagen 10F
Frescati
S-106 91 Stockholm SWEDEN
+46 8 163466
FAX: +46 8 155508
E-Mail: igp@statsvet.su.se
Internet: www.statsvet.su.se/IGP/home.html

AMOUNT: Tuition

DEADLINE(S): MAR 1

FIELD(S): Social Sciences; Economics; History; Anthropology; Sociology; Social Work; Political Science

Open to students who have completed a university degree in the social sciences with one of the above majors and who wish to study at Stockholm University in Sweden. Language of instruction is English.

Contact Stockholm University for an application.

1798 — THE DAPHNE JACKSON MEMORIAL FELLOWSHIPS TRUST (Fellowships in Science/Engineering)

School of Physical Sciences, Dept. of Physics, University of Surrey
Guildford, Surrey GU2 5XH ENGLAND UK
01483 259166
FAX: 01483 259501
E-Mail: J.Woolley@surrey.ac.uk
Internet: www.sst.ph.ic.ac.uk/trust/

AMOUNT: Varies

DEADLINE(S): Varies

FIELD(S): Science or engineering, including information sciences

Fellowships to enable well-qualified and highly motivated scientists and engineers to return to appropriate careers following a career break due to family comitments. May be used on a flexible, part-time basis. Tenable at various U.K. universities.

See website and/or contact organization for details.

1799 — THE LEMMERMANN FOUNDATION (Fondazione Lemmermann Scholarship Awards)

c/o Studio Avvocati Romanelli
via Cosseria, 5
00192 Roma ITALIA
(+39-6) 324.30.23
FAX: (+39-6) 321.26.46
E-Mail: lemmerma@bbs.nexus.it
Internet: http://vivaldi.nexus.it/altri/lemmermann/

AMOUNT: Italian lire 1.500.000

DEADLINE(S): MAR 15; SEP 30

FIELD(S): Italian/Roman studies in the subject areas of literature, archaeology, history of art

For university students who need to study in Rome to carry out research and prepare their theses concerning Rome and the Roman culture from the period Pre-Roman to present day time in the subject areas above.

Contact above organization for details. Access website for application form.

1800 — TRENT UNIVERSITY (Graduate Teaching/Research Assistantships)

P.O. Box 4800
Graduate Studies Officer
Peterborough Ontario CANADA K9J 7B8
705/748-1245

AMOUNT: $3,500 per term

DEADLINE(S): FEB 15

FIELD(S): Anthropology, Geography, Archaeology, Biology, Canadian Studies, Philosophy, Cultural Studies, Computer Science, Mathematics, Physics, Chemistry, Environmental Science/Studies

Teaching/research assistantships at Trent University in the above fields. Open to masters and doctoral candidates. Tenable for up to 4 terms spanning 2-3 years of study.

80 awards per year. Write for complete information.

1801 — UNIVERSITY OF CAMBRIDGE DEPT. OF SOCIAL ANTHROPOLOGY (Evans Fellowship)

Free School Lane
Cambridge CB2 3RF ENGLAND UK
(0223) 334599

AMOUNT: 6,000 pounds sterling

DEADLINE(S): MAR

FIELD(S): Anthropology; Archaeology

Fellowships and grants for postgraduate research in Southeast Asia (preferred areas are Borneo, Malay Peninsula, Singapore, and Thailand) for students attending the University of Cambridge. Must demonstrate financial need and disclose funding from other sources.

2-3 awards annually. Renewable up to 3 years. Contact Dr. L. Howe for an application.

1802 — WENNER-GREN FOUNDATION FOR ANTHROPOLOGICAL RESEARCH (Developing Countries Training Fellowships)

220 Fifth Ave.
New York NY 10001-7708
212/683-5000

AMOUNT: Up to $12,500 per year, for periods from 6 months to 3 years.

DEADLINE(S): Varies (nine months in advance of the anticipated starting date of training)

FIELD(S): Anthropology and closely related disciplines

For pre- or postdoctorate scholars and advanced students from developing countries seeking additional training in anthropology. Must demonstrate the unavailability of such training in their home country, their provisional acceptance by a host institution, and their intention to return and work in their home country.

Applicant must have a home sponsor who is a member of the institution with which he/she is affiliated in the home country and a host sponsor who is a member of the institution in which the candidate plans to pursue training.

1803 — WENNER-GREN FOUNDATION FOR ANTHROPOLOGY RESEARCH (International Collaborative Research Grants)

220 Fifth Ave.
New York NY 10001-7708
212/683-5000

AMOUNT: Up to $25,000

DEADLINE(S): Varies (by arrangement)

FIELD(S): Anthropology and closely related disciplines

For anthropological research projects undertaken jointly by two or more investigators from different countries.

Both investigators must hold the doctorate or equipvalent in anthropology or related discipline.

1804 — WENNER-GREN FOUNDATION FOR ANTHROPOLOGICAL RESEARCH (Predoctoral Grants)

220 Fifth Ave.
New York NY 10001-7708
212/683-5000
Internet: www.wennergren.org

AMOUNT: Up to $15,000

DEADLINE(S): MAY 1; NOV 1

FIELD(S): Anthropology & closely related disciplines

Pre-doctoral grants are awarded to eligible individuals to support Ph.D dissertation or thesis research. Application must be made jointly with a thesis advisor or other scholar responsible for supervising the project.

Write for complete information. Qualified students of all nationalities are eligible.

1805 — WENNER-GREN FOUNDATION FOR ANTHROPOLOGICAL RESEARCH (Regular Grants)

220 Fifth Ave.
New York NY 10001-7708
212/683-5000

AMOUNT: Up to $15,000

DEADLINE(S): MAY 1; NOV 1

FIELD(S): Anthropology, archaeology, and closely related disciplines

For scholars holding the doctorate or equivalent qualificaiton in anthropology or a related discipline. Applications can be made by the scholar either as an individual or on behalf of an organization.

Write for complete information. Qualified students of all nationalities are eligible.

1806 — WENNER-GREN FOUNDATION FOR ANTHROPOLOGICAL RESEARCH (Richard Carley Hunt Postdoctoral Fellowships)

220 Fifth Ave.
New York NY 10001-7708
212/683-5000

AMOUNT: Up to $15,000

DEADLINE(S): MAY 1; NOV 1

FIELD(S): Anthropology, archaeology, and closely related fields.

For scholars within 5 years of receipt of the doctorate to aid the writeup of research results for publication. Must hold doctorate at the time of application.

Qualified scholars are eligible without regard to nationality or institutional affiliation.

1807 — WOODROW WILSON NATIONAL FELLOWSHIP FOUNDATION/JOHNSON & JOHNSON (Dissertation Grants in Women's & Children's Health)

CN 5281
Princeton NJ 08543-5281
609/452-7007
FAX: 609/452-0066
E-Mail: charoltte@woodrow.org
Internet: www.woodrow.org

AMOUNT: $2,000 (for travel, books, microfilming, taping, computer services, etc.)

DEADLINE(S): NOV 8

FIELD(S): Women's & Children's Health

Open to doctoral students in nursing, public health, anthropology, history, sociology, psychology, or social work, who have completed all predissertation requirements at US graduate schools. Must have at least six months left to complete dissertation, which should include significant research on issues related to women's & children's health. Must submit transcripts, proposal, bibliography, & interest. Based on originality & scholarly validity.

15 awards annually. See website or contact WWNFF for an application. Winners announced in February.

SCHOOL OF SCIENCE

1808 — AEROSPACE EDUCATION FOUNDATION (Theodore Von Karman Graduate Scholarship Program)

1501 Lee Highway
Arlington VA 22209
703/247-5839

AMOUNT: $5,000

DEADLINE(S): JAN

FIELD(S): Science, Mathematics, Engineering

Open to Air Force ROTC graduate students who will pursue advanced degrees in the fields of science, mathematics, physics, or engineering. U.S. citizen or legal resident.

5 awards per year based on aptitude, attitude, and career plans. Write for complete information.

1809 — AFRICAN NETWORK OF SCIENTIFIC AND TECHNOLOGICAL INSTITUTIONS - ANSTI (Postgraduate Fellowships)

PO Box 30592
Nairobi Kenya AFRICA
254-2-621234 or 254-2-622619/20
FAX: 254-2-215991
E-Mail: j.massaquoi@unesco.org OR
ANSTI@Net2000ke.com

AMOUNT: Fees, subsistence, & international travel

DEADLINE(S): JUN

FIELD(S): Basic & Engineering Sciences

Scholarships for postgraduate studies outside of applicant's home country. Must be African nationals not older than 36 years of age and hold a good bachelor's degree (at least 2nd class upper division). Applicants should apply for admission to host university as soon as possible. Fellowships tenable only in African universities.

10 awards annually. Renewable up to 2 years. Contact Professor J.G.M. Massaquoi for an application.

1810 — AMERICAN ASSOCIATION FOR THE ADVANCEMENT OF SCIENCE (Science & Engineering Fellowships)

1200 New York Ave., NW
Washington DC 20005
202/326-6700
FAX: 202/289-4950
E-Mail: science_policy@aaas.org
Internet: www.aas.org

AMOUNT: $40,000+

DEADLINE(S): JAN 15

FIELD(S): Science; Engineering

Post-doctoral fellowships open to AAAS members or applicants concurrently applying for membership. Prospective fellows must demonstrate exceptional competence in an area of science or have a broad scientific or technical background. Those with MA degrees and at least three years of poast-degree professional experience may also apply.

U.S. citizenship required. For complete information on these one-year fellowships write to Director, Science Fellows Program at address above.

1811 — AMERICAN FOUNDATION FOR THE BLIND (Paul W. Ruckes Scholarship)

11 Penn Plaza, Ste. 300
New York NY 10001
212/502-7661 or TDD 212/502-7771
E-Mail: juliet@afb.org
Internet: www.afb.org

AMOUNT: $1,000

DEADLINE(S): APR 30

FIELD(S): Engineering, computer, physical, or life sciences

Open to blind or visually impaired undergraduate or graduate students pursuing degrees in the above fields. U.S. citizenship required.

Write to the above address or visit website for complete information.

1812 — AMERICAN INDIAN SCIENCE AND ENGINEERING SOCIETY (A.T. Anderson Memorial Scholarship)

PO Box 9828
Albuquerque NM 87119-9828
505/765-1052
FAX: 505/765-5608
E-Mail: scholarships@aises.org
Internet: www.aises.org/scholarships

AMOUNT: $1,000-$2,000

DEADLINE(S): JUN 15

FIELD(S): Medicine; Natural Resources; Science; Engineering

Open to undergraduate and graduate students who are at least 1/4 American Indian or recognized as member of a tribe. Must be member of AISES ($10 fee), enrolled full-time at an accredited institution, and demonstrate financial need.

Renewable. See website or contact Patricia Browne for an application and/or membership information.

1813 — AMERICAN SOCIETY FOR ENGINEERING EDUCATION (Army Research Laboritory Postdoctoral Fellowships)

1818 N St., NW, Ste. 600
Washington DC 20036
202/331-3525
FAX: 202/265-8504
E-Mail: projects@asee.org
Internet: www.asee.org/fellowship/

AMOUNT: $45,000-$55,000 + travel/relocation allowance

DEADLINE(S): Varies

FIELD(S): Engineering; Physical Sciences

Postdoctoral fellowships for US citizens/permanent residents to do research at Army Research Laboratories. Candidates must have completed their Ph.D. prior to appointment. Program is designed to increase involvement of creative and highly trained scientists and engineers from academia and industry in scientific and technical areas of interest and relevance to the Army. Research proposal should include clear objective and defined outcome. Financial need NOT a factor.

15 awards annually. Renewable. Contact Sandi Crawford at ASEE for an application packet.

1814 — ASSOCIATED WESTERN UNIVERSITIES, INC. (AWU Faculty Fellowships)

4190 South Highland Dr., Suite 211
Salt Lake City UT 84124-2600
801-273-8900

AMOUNT: Varies.

DEADLINE(S): FEB 15

FIELD(S): Engineering, Mathematics, Science, Technology

Research fellowships for qualified college and university faculty members to encourage participation and contribution to research at one of 62 cooperating facilities. It is not necessary to be enrolled at an AWU member institution. Collaborations that include graduate and/or undergraduate students are encouraged.

For detailed information and list of cooperating facilities, contact above location.

1815 — ASSOCIATED WESTERN UNIVERSITIES, INC. (AWU Graduate Fellowship Program)

4190 South Highland Dr. Suite 211
Salt Lake City, UT 84124-2600
801/273-8900

AMOUNT: Stipend ($1,300 per month & up) + tuition assistance and travel allowance

DEADLINE(S): FEB 15

FIELD(S): Engineering, Mathematics, Science, Technology

Open to master's and doctoral degree candidates to conduct research toward a thesis or dissertation at one of more than 62 cooperating facilities. Institutional affiliation and citizenship restrictions may apply for some awards or facilities. It is not necessary to be enrolled at an AWU member institution to apply for a fellowship.

Write to the above address for complete information.

1816 — ASSOCIATED WESTERN UNIVERSITIES, INC. (AWU Postgraduate Fellowship)

4190 South Highland Dr. Suite 211
Salt Lake City UT 84124-2600
801/273-8900

AMOUNT: Stipend established by the host facility and varies by experience and discipline.

DEADLINE(S): Varies (Two to three months before the starting date)

FIELD(S): Engineering, Mathematics, Science, Technology

For college and university graduates who have completed all institutional requirements for an advanced degree from an accredited college or university in the U.S. A commitment to a professional career in science or engineering research is expected. U.S. citizenship or permanent resident status is required. Research is to be done at one of the 62 cooperating universities.

For detailed information and a list of cooperating facilities contact above address.

1817 — ASSOCIATED WESTERN UNIVERSITIES, INC. (AWU Visiting Scientist Fellowships)

4190 South Highland Dr., Suite 211
Salt Lake City UT 84124-2600
801/273-8900

AMOUNT: Varies

DEADLINE(S): Varies (Two months prior to starting date)

FIELD(S): Engineering, Science, Mathematics, and Technology

Research fellowships for professionals with continued commitment to science and engineering. For use at one of 62 participating universities. US citizenship or permanent residency required.

For detailed information and list of cooperating facitilies contact above location.

1818 — AUSTRIAN CULTURAL INSTITUTE (Bertha Von Suttner Scholarship)

950 Third Ave.
20th Fl.
New York NY 10022
212/759-5165
FAX: 212/319-9636
E-Mail: desk@aci.org OR info@oead.ac.at
Internet: www.austriaculture.net

AMOUNT: ATS 8,500/month (US $650) + ATS 2,500 (US $200) book allowance + tuition & health insurance

DEADLINE(S): APR 15

FIELD(S): Sciences (EXCEPT Medicine)

Open to doctoral students in the field of sciences (medicine excluded) who intend to write their thesis in Austria. Must be 20 to 27 years old (in exceptional cases up to 29 years). Applications should be made by the Austrian doctoral father/mother.

Renewable. See website or contact ACI for an application kit, or write to Osterreichischer Akademischer Austauschdienst, Berggasse 21/7, A-1090 Wien, Austria.

1819 — BOEING (Polish Graduate Student Scholarship Program)

Phone
Phone for details
314/234-2149

AMOUNT: Tuition, books, and fees for three years

DEADLINE(S): Varies

FIELD(S): Scientific and technical fields

Scholarships for students from Poland to pursue graduate studies in scientific and technical areas at American colleges or universities.

Call Jim Schlueter at above telephone number.

1820 — BUSINESS & PROFESSIONAL WOMEN'S FOUNDATION (BPW Career Advancement Scholarship Program)

2012 Massachusetts Ave., NW
Washington DC 20036-1070
202/293-1200, ext. 169
FAX: 202/861-0298
Internet: www.bpwusa.org

AMOUNT: $500-$1,000

DEADLINE(S): APR 15

FIELD(S): Biology, Science, Education, Engineering, Social Science, Paralegal, Humanities, Business, Math, Computers, Law, MD, DD

For women (US citizens) aged 25+ accepted into accredited program at US institution (+Puerto Rico & Virgin Islands). Must graduate within 12 to 24 months from the date of grant and demonstrate critical finanacial need. Must have a plan to upgrade skills, train for a new career field, or to enter/re-enter the job market.

Full- or part-time study. For info see website or send business-sized, self-addressed, double-stamped envelope.

1821 — CANADIAN FEDERATION OF UNIVERSITY WOMEN (CFUW Memorial/ Professional Fellowship)

> 251 Bank St., Ste. 600
> Ottawa Ontario K2P 1X3 CANADA
> 613/234-2732
> Internet: www.cfuw.ca

AMOUNT: $5,000

DEADLINE(S): NOV 15

FIELD(S): Science & Technology

Open to women who are Canadian citizens/ permanent residents enrolled in a master's degree program in science and technology. Must hold at least a bachelor's degree or equivalent from a recognized university and have been accepted into, or be currently enrolled in the proposed program and place of study. May be studying abroad.

$25 filing fee. Contact CFUW for an application after August 1st. Candidates will be notified by May 31st.

1822 — COMMISSAO INVOTAN/ICCTI (NATO Science Fellowships Program)

> Av. D. Carlos I
> 126-6 o
> 1200 Lisbon PORTUGAL
> +351.1.396 0313 (dir)
> FAX: +351.1.397 5144

AMOUNT: Varies

DEADLINE(S): JAN 1; MAR 1

FIELD(S): Sciences and engineering

Doctoral and postdoctoral fellowships in almost all scientific areas, including interdisciplinary areas. For citizens of NATO countries and NATO's Cooperation Partner countries who wish to study or do research in Portugal.

May be renewable under certain terms. Approximately 40 new fellowships each year. Write for complete information.

1823 — COMMISSAO INVOTAN/ICCTI (NATO Science Fellowships-Advanced and Senior Programs)

> Av. D. Carlos I
> 126 o
> 1200 Lisbon PORTUGAL
> +351.1.396 0313 (DIR)
> FAX: +351.1.397 5144

AMOUNT: Varies

DEADLINE(S): APR 1; OCT 1

FIELD(S): Natural and social sciences and engineering

Doctoral and postdoctoral fellowships in almost all scientific areas, social sciences, and engineering. For citizens of Portugal who wish to study and/or do research in another NATO member country.

May be renewable under certain terms. Approximately 50 new fellowships each year. Write for complete information.

1824 — COMMISSAO INVOTAN/ICCTI (NATO Senior Guest Fellowship)

> Av. D. Carlos I
> 126 o
> 1200 Lisbon PORTUGAL
> +351.1.396 0313 (dir)
> FAX: +351.1.397 5144

AMOUNT: Varies

DEADLINE(S): APR 1; OCT 1

FIELD(S): Sciences and engineering

Postdoctoral fellowships open to senior scientists from other NATO countries and from countries of central & eastern Europe, NATO's Cooperation Partners. Must have high professional standing and wish to spend three weeks to a year in Portugal.

20 annual awards. Write for complete information.

1825 — EUROPEAN COMMISSION (Marie Curie Fellowships)

> Rue de la Loi, 200
> B-1049 Brussels BELGIUM
> (+32.2) 295.08.43
> FAX: (+32.2) 296.21.33
> E-Mail: improving@dg12.cec.be
> Internet: www.cordis.lu/improving

AMOUNT: Varies

DEADLINE(S): Varies

FIELD(S): All areas of Scientific Research

Must be citizens of Member and Associated States of the European Union. "Improving Human Potential" grants go mainly to postdoctoral researchers of under 35 years of age (the scheme will also finance predoctoral research and experienced scientists) who wish to execute research in a country other than that of their nationality or recent residence.

1,000 awards annually. See website or contact the European Commission for an application.

1826 — FORD FOUNDATION/NATIONAL RESEARCH COUNCIL (Predoctoral/Dissertation Fellowships for Minorities)

> 2101 Constitution Ave.
> Washington DC 20418
> 202/334-2872

E-Mail: infofell@nas.edu
Internet: http//www.nas.edu/fo/index.html

AMOUNT: $14,000 annual stipend + $6,000 grant to institution; $18,000 for dissertation fellowship

DEADLINE(S): NOV 3

FIELD(S): Most fields of study: sciences, humanities, engineering, behavioral science, social sciences, and computer science

Predoctoral and dissertation fellowships for students whose ethnicity is Alaskan Native, Black/ African American, Mexican American/Chicano, Native American Indian, Native Pacific Islander, or Puerto Rican. For research-based programs leading to careers in college teaching and research.

Contact above address or website.

1827 — FOUNDATION FOR SCIENCE AND DISABILITY, INC. (FSD Science Student Grant Fund)

> 503 NW 89th Street
> Gainesville FL 32607-1400
> 352/374-5774
> FAX: 352/374-5781
> E-Mail: rmankin@gainesville.usda.ufl.edu

AMOUNT: $1,000

DEADLINE(S): DEC 1

FIELD(S): Mathematics; Science; Medicine; Engineering; Computer Science

Open to graduate students with disabilities. May also apply as a fourth-year undergraduate accepted into a graduate or professional program. Awards are for some special purpose in connection with a science project or thesis in any of above fields. Student is required to write a 250-word essay which includes a description of professional goals/objectives, as well as purpose of grant. Transcripts and two letters of recommendation from faculty members are also required.

Contact Dr. Richard Mankin at above address for an application.

1828 — FREEDOM FROM RELIGION FOUNDATION (Student Essay Contest)

> PO Box 750
> Madison WI 53701
> 608/256-5800
> Internet: www.infidels.org/org/ffrf

AMOUNT: $1,000; $500; $250

DEADLINE(S): JUL 15

FIELD(S): Humanities; English; Education; Philosophy; Science

Essay contest on topics related to church-state entanglement in public schools or growing up a "freethinker" in religious-oriented society. Topics change yearly, but all are on general theme of maintaining separation of church and state. New topics available in February. For high school seniors & currently enrolled college/technical students. Must be US citizen.

Send SASE to address above for complete information. Please indicate whether wanting information for college competition or high school. Information will be sent when new topics are announced each February. See website for details.

1829 — GATES MILLENIUM SCHOLARS PROGRAM (Scholarships for Graduate Students)

8260 Willow Oaks Corporate Dr.
Fairfax VA 22031-4511
877/690-4677
Internet: www.gmsp.org

AMOUNT: Varies

DEADLINE(S): FEB 1

FIELD(S): Engineering; Mathematics; Science; Education; Library Science

College presidents, professors, & deans may nominate graduate students who are African-Americans, Native Americans, Hispanic Americans, or Asian Americans in above fields. Based on academic performance, commitment to academic study, involvement in community service & school activities, potential for leadership, career goals, and financial need. Must submit transcripts and letters of recommendation. Must be US citizen with a minimum 3.3 GPA

Application materials available November 1st; scholars will be notified in May. Funded by the Bill & Melinda Gates Foundation, and administered by the United Negro College Fund.

1830 — GEORGE BIRD GRINNELL AMERICAN INDIAN CHILDREN'S FUND (Al Qoyawayma Award)

11602 Montague Ct.
Potomac MD 20854
301/424-2440
FAX: 301/424-8281
E-Mail: Grinnell_Fund@MSN.com

AMOUNT: $1,000

DEADLINE(S): JUN 1

FIELD(S): Science; Engineering

Open to Native American undergraduate and graduate students majoring in science or engineering and who have demonstrated an outstanding interest and skill in any one of the arts. Must be American Indian/Alaska Native (documented with Certified Degree of Indian Blood), be enrolled in college/university, be able to demonstrate commitment to serving community or other tribal nations, and document financial need.

Contact Dr. Paula M. Mintzies, President, for an application after January 1st.

1831 — GIRTON COLLEGE (Fellowships)

Secretary to the Electors
Cambridge CB3 OJG ENGLAND UK
338 999

AMOUNT: 9,000 pounds sterling (pre-Ph.D.)
11,100-11,700 pounds sterling (post-Ph.D.)

DEADLINE(S): Varies (usually around Oct. 4)

FIELD(S): Humanities or Science

Applications are invited for research fellowships at Girton College, Cambridge, Great Britain. Tenable for three years beginning Oct 1. The fellowships are open to men and women graduates of any university.

A statement of 1,000 words maximum outlining the research to be undertaken must be submitted. Write for form and complete information.

1832 — INSTITUTE OF CANCER RESEARCH (Studentships)

123 Old Brompton Road
London SW7 3RP ENGLAND
+44 0181 643 8901
FAX: +44 0181 643 6940
E-Mail: renate@icr.ac.uk
Internet: www.icr.ac.uk

AMOUNT: Full fees + stipend

DEADLINE(S): JAN

FIELD(S): Science

For postgraduate students to study at ICR. Must have upper second class honour degree (UK) or above in a science degree (or equivalent overseas qualification). Financial need is NOT considered.

10-20 awards annually. Renewable for 3 years. Contact Renate Divers at above address for an application.

1833 — INTERNATIONAL COUNCIL FOR CANADIAN STUDIES (Government of France Graduate Awards)

325 Dalhousie, S-800
Ottawa Ontario CANADA K1N 7G2
613/789-7828
FAX: 613/789-7830
E-Mail: general@iccs-ciec.ca
Internet: www.iccs-ciec.ca

AMOUNT: Tuition, travel, and living allowance

DEADLINE(S): OCT 31

FIELD(S): Pure and Applied Sciences, Social Sciences, Engineering, Medicine

One-year graduate scholarships open to Canadian citizens for study and research at the doctoral level. Sound knowledge of the French language is required.

Must hold masters degree. Cannot be held concurrently with other scholarships or remuneration. Write or access website for complete information.

1834 — JEWISH FEDERATION OF METROPOLITAN CHICAGO (Academic Scholarship Program for Studies in the Sciences)

One South Franklin St.
Chicago IL 60606
Written inquiry

AMOUNT: Varies

DEADLINE(S): MAR 1

FIELD(S): Mathematics, engineering, or science

Scholarships for college juniors, seniors, and graduate students who are Jewish and are residents of Chicago, IL and Cook County.

Academic achievement and financial need are considered. Applications accepted after Dec. 1.

1835 — KNIGHT SCIENCE JOURNALISM FELLOWSHIPS

77 Massachusetts Ave.
MIT E32-300
Cambridge MA 02139
617/253-3442
FAX: 617/258-8100
E-Mail: boyce@mit.edu
Internet: web.mit.edu/knight-science

AMOUNT: $35,000

DEADLINE(S): MAR 1

FIELD(S): Science Journalism

Program at MIT open to science journalists (print, web, or broadcast) from the US with at least three years experience. Fellows attend seminars with leading scientists & engineers, visit laboratories, audit classes, and attend workshops on science journalism. Foreign journalists may apply if they can obtain funding in their own countries. Financial need NOT a factor.

Contact Boyce Rensberger for an application.

1836 — MINISTRY OF THE FLEMISH COMMUNITY (Fellowships)

Embassy of Belgium
3330 Garfield St., NW
Washington DC 20008
202/625-5850/51
FAX: 202/342-8346
E-Mail: flemishcomdc@wizard.net

AMOUNT: Monthly stipend, tuition, & health care coverage

DEADLINE(S): JAN 31

FIELD(S): Art; Music; Humanities; Social Science; Political Science; Law; Economics; Science; Medicine

Open to US citizens under age 35 who wish to pursue graduate or postgraduate studies in Flanders, Belgium.

Contact Flemish Community for registration forms.

1837 — NAT'L CONSORTIUM FOR GRADUATE DEGREES FOR MINORITIES IN ENGINEERING & SCIENCE, INC. (GEM Fellowship Programs)

P.O. Box 537
Notre Dame IN 46556
219/631-7771
FAX: 219/287-1486
E-Mail: gem.1@nd.edu
Internet: www.nd.edu/~gem

AMOUNT: Full tuition & fees + annual stipend $20,000-$40,000 (M.S.) & $60,000-$100,000 (Ph.D.)

DEADLINE(S): DEC 1

FIELD(S): Engineering, Science

Master's & doctoral fellowships for underrepresented minorities (African American, Native American, Mexican American, Puerto Rican, & other Hispanic Americans). Must be US citizen. University must be a member of the Consortium (over 80 are).

200 M.S. & 25 Ph.D. fellowships annually. Financial need is NOT a factor. Contact G. George Simms, Executive Director, for an application.

1838 — NATIONAL PARKS SERVICE (Science Scholars Program)

1849 C St., NW
Washington DC 20240
202/208-6843
E-Mail: aspiceland@goparks.org
Internet: www.nps.gov

AMOUNT: $25,000/yr.

DEADLINE(S): JUN 15

FIELD(S): Biological, Physical, Social, & Cultural Sciences

Three-year scholarships to Ph.D. candidates pursuing degrees in above fields. Objectives are to encourage young scientists to engage in park-related research, conduct innovative research on issues central to the National Parks, and encourage use of parks as laboratories for sciences. NPF will transfer the scholarship funds to each student's university, providing for tuition, field work, stipend, & other research expenses. Must submit research proposal.

4 awards annually. See website or contact Dr. Gary E. Machlis, Program Director, at NPS for an application. Winners announced shortly after August 15th.

1839 — NATIONAL SCIENCES AND ENGINEERING RESEARCH COUNCIL OF CANADA (Graduate Scholarships)

Scholarships/Fellowships Division
350 Albert Street
Ottawa Ontario K1A 1H5 CANADA
613/996-3769
FAX: 613/996-2589

E-Mail: schol@nserc.ca
Internet: http://www.nserc.ca

AMOUNT: $15,700/year for 1st & 2nd years at masters or Ph.D level; $17,400/year (Ph.D level ONLY) 3rd & 4th years

DEADLINE(S): NOV 24

FIELD(S): Natural Sciences, Engineering, Biology, or Chemistry

Open to Canadian citizens or permanent residents who have earned or will soon earn a bachelors or masters degree in science or engineering. Academic excellence and research aptitude are considerations.

Write for complete information.

1840 — NATIONAL SCIENCES AND ENGINEERING RESEARCH COUNCIL OF CANADA (Postdoctoral Fellowships)

Scholarships/Fellowships Division
350 Albert Street
Ottawa Ontario K1A 1H5 CANADA
613/996-3762
FAX: 613/996-2589
E-Mail: schol@nserc.ca
Internet: http://www.nserc.ca

AMOUNT: Individually negotiated

DEADLINE(S): Varies—average: $43,000

FIELD(S): Natural Sciences, Engineering, Biology, or Chemistry

Open to Canadian citizens or permanent residents who hold doctoral degrees in science or engineering. Academic excellence and research aptitude are considerations.

Write for complete information.

1841 — NATIONAL SCIENCE FOUNDATION (NATO Postdoctoral Science Fellowship Program)

4201 Wilson Blvd.
Rm. 907
Arlington VA 22230
703/306-1630
FAX: 703/306-0468
E-Mail: porter@nsf.gov
Internet: www.ehr.nsf.gov/

AMOUNT: $2,750/month stipend + travel allowance

DEADLINE(S): NOV 1

FIELD(S): Science & Engineering

Postdoctoral fellowships in almost all scientific areas, including interdisciplinary areas. For US citizens who wish to study and/or do research in another NATO member country.

35 awards annually. See website or contact the National Administrator at above address.

1842 — NATIONAL SPACE CLUB (Dr. Robert H. Goddard Scholarship)

2000 L Street, NW, Suite 710
Washington DC 20036-4907
202/973-8661

AMOUNT: $10,000

DEADLINE(S): JAN 8

FIELD(S): Science & Engineering

Open to undergraduate juniors and seniors and graduate students who have scholastic plans leading to future participation in the aerospace sciences and technology. Must be US citizen. Award based on transcript, letters of recommendation, accomplishments, scholastic plans, and proven past research and participation in space related science and engineering. Personal need is considered, but is not controlling.

Renewable. Send a self-addressed, stamped envelope for more information.

1843 — NATIONAL SPACE CLUB (Dr. Robert H. Goddard Historical Essay Award)

2000 L Street, NW, Suite 710
Washington DC 20036-4907
202/973-8661

AMOUNT: $1,000 + plaque

DEADLINE(S): DEC 4

FIELD(S): Aerospace History

Essay competition open to any US citizen on a topic dealing with any significant aspect of the historical development of rocketry and astronautics. Essays should not exceed 5,000 words and should be fully documented. Will be judged on originality and scholarship.

Previous winners not eligible. Send self-addressed, stamped envelope for complete information.

1844 — NATIONAL TECHNICAL ASSOCIATION, INC. (Scholarship Competitions for Minorities and Women in Science and Engineering)

6919 North 19th St.
Philadelphia PA 19126-1506
215/549-5743
FAX: 215/549-6509
E-Mail: ntamfj1@aol.com
Internet: www.huenet.com/nta

AMOUNT: $500-$5,000

DEADLINE(S): Varies

FIELD(S): Science, mathematics, engineering, and applied technology

Scholarships competitions for minorities and women pursuing degrees in the above fields. Additional scholarships are available through local chapters of NTA.

Check website or write to above address for details and for locations of local chapters.

1845 — NORTH ATLANTIC TREATY ORGANIZATION (NATO Science Fellowships for Non-U.S. Citizens)

Boulevard Leopold III
Brussels BELGIUM
2/707-4231
E-Mail: science.fell@hq.nato.int
Internet: www.nato.int/science

AMOUNT: Varies (with country)

DEADLINE(S): Varies (with country)

FIELD(S): Most fields of Scientific study

Graduate and postdoctoral fellowships are available in almost all scientific fields, including interdisciplinary areas. Open to citizens of NATO member countries and NATO partner countries who wish to study and/or do research in another NATO member country or NATO partner country.

Program administered in each NATO country by a National Administrator. Write address above for address of your country's administrator.

1846 — NORTHERN IRELAND DEPT. OF EDUCATION (Post-graduate Studentships)

Rathgael House
Balloo Road
Bangor Co. Down BT19 7PR N.IRELAND
01247-279279

AMOUNT: 5,295 pounds sterling + fees

DEADLINE(S): Varies (Check with Northern Ireland universities)

FIELD(S): Humanities; Science; Social Science

Research (Ph.D) and advanced courses (MA/MS) awards available for study in Northern Ireland. Must have been a resident of the United Kingdom for at least three years.

Research studentships renewable if work is satisfactory. Write for complete information.

1847 — NOVARTIS FOUNDATION (Bursary Scheme)

41 Portland Place
London W1N 4BN ENGLAND UK
+44 171 636 9456
FAX: +44 171 436 2840
E-Mail: abrown@novartisfound.org.uk
Internet: www.novartisfound.org.uk

AMOUNT: Travel & subsistence—up to $6,000/person

DEADLINE(S): Varies

FIELD(S): Science; Medicine

Travel fellowships to young scientists (postgrad/doc) to attend international meetings in connection with the Novartis Foundation Symposia. Must be between the ages of 23 and 35, and be active in the field of science in question. Symposia is normally in London, and a 4-week to 12-week host laboratory in the department of one of the symposium participants follows. Specific topics vary. Must submit qualifications, resume, career history/goals, and research interests.

8 awards annually. Not renewable. See website or contact Allyson Brown for application procedures.

1848 — OAK RIDGE ASSOCIATED UNIVERSITIES (National Science Foundation Graduate Research Fellowships)

PO Box 3010
Oak Ridge TN 37831-3010
423/241-4300
FAX: 423/241-4513
E-Mail: nsfgrfp@orau.gov
Internet: www.orau.gov/nsf/nsffel.htm

AMOUNT: $15,000 stipend + $10,500 tuition allowance

DEADLINE(S): NOV 4

FIELD(S): Science; Math; Engineering; Computer Science

Three-year fellowships for graduate study leading to research-based master's or doctoral degrees in the above fields. Must be US citizens, nationals, or permanent residents at the time of application. Fellowships are awarded on the basis of ability. Women, minorities, and those with disabilities are strongly encouraged to apply. One-time International Research Travel Allowance available.

1,000 awards annually. Contact Jeannette Bouchard for an application/more information.

1849 — OAK RIDGE INSTITUTE FOR SCIENCE AND EDUCATION (Applied Health Physics Fellowship Program)

P.O. Box 117
Oak Ridge TN 37831-0117
423/576-2194 or 423/576-9279
E-Mail: COXRE@ORAU.GOV or GRADFELL@ORAU.GOV

AMOUNT: $14,400 stipend + tuition and fees up to $9,000/yr paid to university + transportation costs up to $300/month

DEADLINE(S): JAN 26

FIELD(S): Engineering, mathematics, physical and life sciences

Fellowship in applied health physics to implement DOE's nuclear energy-related mission. Candidates must have B.A. degree in life or physical sciences, engineering, or mathematics. Recipients are subject to a service obligation of one year of full-time employment in a DOE facility for each academic year of fellowhip award.

For details and application, contact above location.

1850 — OAK RIDGE INSTITUTE FOR SCIENCE AND EDUCATION (Industrial Hygiene Graduate Fellowship Program)

P.O. Box 117
Oak Ridge TN 37831-0117
423-576-9655
FAX: 423/576-8293
E-Mail: kinneym@orau.gov

AMOUNT:

DEADLINE(S): JAN 26

FIELD(S): Industrial Hygiene

A fellowship for first-year master's candidates who have undergraduate degrees in physical, life, environmental, or health sciences or enginering and who wish to pursue studies in industrial hygiene.

For details and application, contact above location.

1851 — OAK RIDGE INSTITUTE FOR SCIENCE AND EDUCATION/U.S. DEPT. OF ENERGY (Office of Civilian Radioactive Waste Management Fellowship)

P.O. Box 117
Oak Ridge TN 37831-0117
423/576-0128
FAX: 423/576-8293
E-Mail: drostp@orau.gov

AMOUNT: $14,000/yr.

DEADLINE(S): JAN 16 (Received, not postmarked)

FIELD(S): Physical or life sciences, math, or engineering

Fellowships for graduate students at various participating universities to conduct research in the management of spent nuclear fuel and high-level raqdioactive waste. For M.A. and Ph.D. candidates. For up to 48 months. Must be U.S. citizen or permanent resident.

Funded through U.S. Department of Energy, Office of Civilian Radioactive Waste Management. Contact or call Ms. Portia Drost, MS-16, at above address for details.

1852 — OAK RIDGE INSTITUTE FOR SCIENCE AND EDUCATION (Nuclear Engineering & Health Physics Fellowship Program)

105 Mitchell Rd. MS-16
Oak Ridge TN 37831-0117
423/576-2600 or 423/241-2890

E-Mail: johnsons@orau.gov or
daltonj@arou.gov

AMOUNT: $14,400/yr.

DEADLINE(S): JAN 26

FIELD(S): Engineering, physical and life sciences

Fellowships in nuclear engineering or applied health physics to implement DOE's nuclear energy-related mission. Candidates must have B.A. degree in life or physical sciences or engineering.

For details and application, contact Sandra Johnson or Jennifer Dalton at above location.

1853 — RESEARCH COUNCIL OF NORWAY (Senior Scientist Visiting Fellowship)

P.O. Box 2700 St. Hanshaugen
N-0131 Oslo NORWAY
+47 22 03 70 00
FAX: +47 22 03 70 01
E-Mail: intstip@nfr.no
Internet: www.forskningsradet.no

AMOUNT: NOK 25,000-1st 2 months; NOK 10,000-succeeding months

DEADLINE(S): Varies

FIELD(S): Bioproduction & Processing (including agriculture and veterinary science); Industry & Energy; Culture & Society (including social sciences and the humanities); Medicine & Health; Environment & Development; Science & Technology

Fellowships for scientists to work at Norwegian research institutes. Project funding does not include salary; expenses connected with the stay in Norway are covered.

For a list of institutions, contact the Research Council at above location. Then apply to institution, which then will submit fellowship application.

1854 — SIGMA XI—THE SCIENTIFIC RESEARCH SOCIETY (Research Grants)

P.O. Box 13975
99 Alexander Dr.
Research Triangle Park NC 27709
919/549-4691

AMOUNT: Up to $2,500 in astronomy or eye/vision research; up to $1,000 in any other scientific field

DEADLINE(S): FEB 1; MAY 1; NOV 1

FIELD(S): Science research

Grants to support scientific investigation in any field. All funds must be expended directly in support of the proposed investigation. Priority is given to research scientists in the early stages of their careers.

Write for complete information.

1855 — SOCIETY OF HISPANIC PROFESSIONAL ENGINEERS FOUNDATION (SHPE Scholarships)

5400 E. Olympic Blvd., Ste. 210
Los Angeles CA 90022
323/888-2080

AMOUNT: $500-$3,000

DEADLINE(S): APR 15

FIELD(S): Engineering; Science

Open to deserving students of Hispanic descent who are seeking careers in engineering or science. For full-time undergraduate or graduate study at a college or university. Based on academic achievement and financial need.

Send self-addressed, stamped envelope to above address for an application.

1856 — THE BRITISH COUNCIL (Postgraduate Scholarships to Mexico)

10 Spring Gardens
London SW1A 2BN ENGLAND UK
+44 (0) 171 930 8466
FAX: +44 (0) 161 957 7188
E-Mail: education.enquiries@britcoun.org
Internet: www.britcoun.org/mexico/mexschol.htm

AMOUNT: Varies

DEADLINE(S): Varies

FIELD(S): Science and technology

The British Council in Mexico offers the opportunity, funded by the Mexican Council for Science and Technology (CONACYT), to British citizens to study in Mexico. Another way to receive information is to contact: CONACYT, Av. Constituyentes No. 1046, Col. Lomas Altas, C.P. 11950, Mexico, D.F. or E-mail to informa@mailer.main.conacyt.mx.

Contact with the source of information in London or in Mexico for details. In Mexico, the British Council Information Centre E-mails are: carmina.ramon@bc-mexico.sprint.com (Mexico City) or teresa.riggen@bc-mexico.sprint.com (Guadalajara).

1857 — THE BRITISH COUNCIL (Scholarships for Citizens of Mexico)

10 Spring Gardens
London SW1A 2BN ENGLAND UK
+44 (0) 171 930 8466
FAX: +44 (0) 161 957 7188
E-Mail: education.enquiries@britcoun.org
Internet: www.britcoun.org/mexico/mexschol.htm

AMOUNT: Varies

DEADLINE(S): Varies

FIELD(S): Social sciences, applied sciences, technology

The British Council in Mexico offers approximately 100 scholarshps per year in the above fields for undergraduates and graduates to study in the United Kingdon. Good level of English language retired.

The website listed here gives more details. For more information, contact: leticia.magana@bc-mexico.sprint.com. or contact organization in London.

1858 — THE DAPHNE JACKSON MEMORIAL FELLOWSHIPS TRUST (Fellowships in Science/Engineering)

School of Physical Sciences
Dept. of Physics
University of Surrey
Guildford, Surrey
GU2 5XH ENGLAND UK
01483 259166
FAX: 01483 259501
E-Mail: J.Woolley@surrey.ac.uk
Internet: www.sst.ph.ic.ac.uk/trust/

AMOUNT: Varies

DEADLINE(S): Varies

FIELD(S): Science or engineering, including information sciences

Fellowships to enable well-qualified and highly motivated scientists and engineers to return to appropriate careers following a career break due to family comitments. May be used on a flexible, part-time basis. Tenable at various U.K. universities.

See website and/or contact organization for details.

1859 — THE NORWAY-AMERICA ASSOCIATION (The Norwegian Marshall Fund)

Drammensveien 20C
N-0255 Oslo 2 NORWAY
011 47-22-44-76-83

AMOUNT: Up to $5,000

DEADLINE(S): Varies

FIELD(S): All fields of study

The Marshall Fund was established in 1977 as a token of Norway's gratitude to the U.S. for support after WWII. Objective is to promote research in Norway by Americans in science and humanities. For U.S. citizens.

Contact above location for further information.

1860 — THE NOVARTIS FOUNDATION (Scientific Research Fellowships/Bursaries)

41 Portland Place
London W1N 4BN ENGLAND UK
+44 171 636 9456
FAX: +44 171 436 2840
E-Mail: abrown@Novartisfound.org.uk
Internet: www.novartisfound.demon.co.uk/bursary.htm

AMOUNT: Travel expenses, meals, lodging

DEADLINE(S): Varies

FIELD(S): Sciences

Fellowships/bursaries for young scientists, ages 23-35, to attend aFoundation symposium and then spend from 4-12 weeks in the laboratory of one of the symposium participants. For subject matter, see "Nature" or other appropriate journals or check with the Foundation or an office of the British Council.

For application details, see website or contact organization.

1861 — THE WALT DISNEY COMPANY (American Teacher Awards)

P.O. Box 9805

Calabasas CA 91372

AMOUNT: $2,500 (36 awards); $25,000 (Outstanding Teacher of the Year)

DEADLINE(S): FEB 15

FIELD(S): Teachers: athletic coach, early childhood, English, foreign language/ESL, general elementary, mathematics, performing arts, physical education/health, science, social studies, visual arts, voc/tech education

Awards for K-12 teachers in the above fields.

Teachers, or anyone who knows a great teacher, can write for applications at the above address.

1862 — UNCF/MERCK SCIENCE INITIATIVE (Graduate Science Research Dissertation Fellowships)

8260 Willow Oaks Corporate Dr.

PO Box 10444

Fairfax VA 22031-4511

703/205-3503

FAX: 703/205-3574

E-Mail: uncfmerck@uncf.org

Internet: www.uncf.org/merck

AMOUNT: $40,000/yr. (max.)

DEADLINE(S): JAN 31

FIELD(S): Life & Physical Sciences

Open to African-Americans enrolled full-time in a Ph.D. degree program and within 1-3 years of completing dissertation. Awards are intended to help students complete coursework, conduct research, and prepare dissertation for degree in the biomedically relevant life or physical sciences. Must be US citizen/ permanent resident. Financial need NOT a factor.

12 awards annually. Not renewable. Contact Jerry Bryant, Ph.D., for an application.

1863 — UNCF/MERCK SCIENCE INITIATIVE (Postdoctoral Science Research Fellowships)

8260 Willow Oaks Corporate Dr.

PO Box 10444

Fairfax VA 22031-4511

703/205-3503

FAX: 703/205-3574

E-Mail: uncfmerck@uncf.org

Internet: www.uncf.org/merck

AMOUNT: $70,000/yr. (max.)

DEADLINE(S): JAN 31

FIELD(S): Life & Physical Sciences

Open to African-Americans who will receive a Ph.D. degree by the end of the current academic year and will be appointed as a postdoctoral fellow during the next calendar year. Awards are intended to support postgraduate students to obtain postdoctoral training and to prepare for a career in biomedical research. Must be US citizen/permanent resident. Financial need NOT a factor.

10 awards annually. Not renewable. Contact Jerry Bryant, Ph.D., for an application.

1864 — UNIVERSITY OF MANCHESTER (Awards for Research)

Secretary, Research and Graduate Support Unit

Manchester M13 9PL England

0161 275 2035

FAX: 0161 275 2445/7216

AMOUNT: Maintenance grant (approx) 5000 pounds p.a. plus payment of UK tuition fees.

DEADLINE(S): MAY 1

FIELD(S): Arts, Economics, Social Studies, Education, Science, Engineering, Biological Sciences, Law

The university offers research studentships for doctoral research in all disciplines. These awards are highly competitive. Applicants should hold at least a 2:1 degree or equivalent. Awards are renewable for up to 2 years.

Approx 50 awards per year. Please contact address above for complete information.

1865 — UNIVERSITY OF WESTERN AUSTRALIA (Gledden Post-graduate Studentship)

Nedlands 6009

WESTERN AUSTRALIA

08 9380 2490

FAX: 08 9380 1919

E-Mail: medwards@acs.uwa.edu.au

Internet: www.acs.uwa.edu.au/research/

AMOUNT: $A16,000 + allowances

DEADLINE(S): OCT 31

FIELD(S): Mining and engineering

Program open to UWA graduates for overseas research in applied science.

Contact Ms. Margaret Edwards, Senior Administrative Officer, at above address or visit website for complete information.

1866 — US ARMS CONTROL AND DISARMAMENT AGENCY (William C. Foster Visiting Scholars Program)

320 21st St. NW, Room 5726

Washington DC 20451

703/647-8090

AMOUNT: Salary + per diem

DEADLINE(S): JAN 31

FIELD(S): Arms Control; Nonproliferation; Disarmament

Program open to faculty of recognized institutions of higher learning who wish to lend their expertise in areas relevant to the ACDA for a period of one year. U.S. citizenship or permanent residency required.

Write for complete information.

1867 — US DEPARTMENT OF DEFENSE (National Defense Science & Engineering Graduate Fellowship Programs)

200 Park Drive, Suite 211

P.O. Box 13444

Research Triangle Park, NC 27709-3444

919/549-8505

Internet: www.acq.osd.mil/ddre/edugate/s-aindx.html

AMOUNT: Full tuition and fees (tenure of 36 months)

DEADLINE(S): JAN

FIELD(S): Mathematical, physical, biological, ocean, and engineering sciences

Must be US citizens or nationals at or near the beginning of their graduate study in science or engineering, leading to a doctoral degree. NDSEG Fellowships are awarded for study and research in these disciplines of military importance.

Approximately 90 new three-year graduate fellowships each April. Fellows may choose appropriate US institutions of higher education, offering degrees in science and engineering. Contact the Program Administrator for more information.

1868 — WINSTON CHURCHILL FOUNDATION (Scholarships)

PO Box 1240

Gracie Station

New York NY 10028-0048

212/879-3480

FAX: 212/897-3480

E-Mail: churchillf@aol.com

AMOUNT: $27,000 (includes tuition, fees, travel, & living/spousal allowances)

DEADLINE(S): NOV 15

FIELD(S): Engineering; Mathematics; Science

Open to US citizens enrolled in one of 55 participating US colleges and universities to pursue graduate study at Churchill College at Cambridge University in England. Must be between the ages of 19 and 26. Financial need NOT a factor.

11 awards annually. Not renewable. Must apply through home institution.

1869 — WOODROW WILSON NATIONAL FELLOWSHIP FOUNDATION (Leadership Program for Teachers)

CN 5281
Princeton NJ 08543-5281
609/452-7007
FAX: 609/452-0066
E-Mail: marchioni@woodrow.org OR irish@woodrow.org
Internet: www.woodrow.org

AMOUNT: Varies

DEADLINE(S): Varies

FIELD(S): Science; Mathematics

WWLPT offers summer institutes for middle and high school teachers in science and mathematics. One-and two-week teacher outreach, TORCH Institutes, are held in the summer throughout the US.

See website or contact WWNFF for an application.

BIOLOGY

1870 — ACADEMY OF NATURAL SCIENCES OF PHILADELPHIA (Jessup & McHenry Fund Grants)

The Academy of Natural Sciences, 1900 Benjamin Franklin Parkway
Philadelphia PA 19103-1195
215/299-1,000

AMOUNT: $250 (travel); Max $1,000

DEADLINE(S): MAR 1; OCT 1

FIELD(S): Botany/McHenry Award; Research in Natural Science/Jessup Award

Grants to support research are primarily intended to assist predoctoral and immediate postdoctoral students. The work must be done at the Academy of Natural Sciences in Philadelphia and must have the sponsorship of an Academy staff member.

In general grants are awarded for a minimum of 2 weeks and a maximum of 16-week periods. Students from the Philadelphia area are NOT eligible. Write for complete information.

1871 — AECI LIMITED (AECI Post Graduate Research Fellowship)

Private Bag X2
Modderfontein SOUTH AFRICA 1645
011/605-3100

AMOUNT: Varies (South African Rands 3600)

DEADLINE(S): SEP 30

FIELD(S): Chemistry, Physics, Metallurgy, Biochemistry, Microbiology, Chemical Engineering, Civil Engineering, Industrial Engineering, Electrical Engineering, Mechanical Engineering, Instrument Engineering

Open to South African citizens who are graduate students who want to do research in one of the above areas. This fellowship is offered to strengthen postgraduate study and research in South Africa, particularly in the fields above.

Write to the above address for complete information.

1872 — AFRICAN NETWORK OF SCIENTIFIC AND TECHNOLOGICAL INSTITUTIONS - ANSTI (Postgraduate Fellowships)

PO Box 30592
Nairobi Kenya AFRICA
254-2-621234 or 254-2-622619/20
FAX: 254-2-215991
E-Mail: j.massaquoi@unesco.org OR ANSTI@Net2000ke.com

AMOUNT: Fees, subsistence, & international travel

DEADLINE(S): JUN

FIELD(S): Basic & Engineering Sciences

Scholarships for postgraduate studies outside of applicant's home country. Must be African nationals not older than 36 years of age and hold a good bachelor's degree (at least 2nd class upper division). Applicants should apply for admission to host university as soon as possible. Fellowships tenable only in African universities.

10 awards annually. Renewable up to 2 years. Contact Professor J.G.M. Massaquoi for an application.

1873 — AMERICAN ASSOCIATION FOR THE ADVANCEMENT OF SCIENCE (Science & Engineering Fellowships)

1200 New York Ave., NW
Washington DC 20005
202/326-6700
FAX: 202/289-4950
E-Mail: science_policy@aaas.org
Internet: www.aas.org

AMOUNT: $40,000+

DEADLINE(S): JAN 15

FIELD(S): Science; Engineering

Post-doctoral fellowships open to AAAS members or applicants concurrently applying for membership. Prospective fellows must demonstrate exceptional competence in an area of science or have a broad scientific or technical background. Those with MA degrees and at least three years of poast-degree professional experience may also apply.

U.S. citizenship required. For complete information on these one-year fellowships write to Director, Science Fellows Program at address above.

1874 — AMERICAN FOUNDATION FOR PHARMACEUTICAL EDUCATION (Predoctoral Fellowships)

One Church St., Suite 202
Rockville MD 20850
301/738-2160
FAX: 301/738-2161

AMOUNT: $6,000 to $10,000/yr.

DEADLINE(S): MAR 1

FIELD(S): Pharmacology

Several predoctoral fellowships for pharmaceutical students with no more than three years remaining to earn the Ph.D.

Student accepts a teaching appointment in a Pharmacy college. U.S. citizen or legal resident. Write for complete information.

1875 — AMERICAN FOUNDATION FOR THE BLIND (Paul W. Ruckes Scholarship)

11 Penn Plaza, Ste. 300
New York NY 10001
212/502-7661 or TDD 212/502-7771
E-Mail: juliet@afb.org
Internet: www.afb.org

AMOUNT: $1,000

DEADLINE(S): APR 30

FIELD(S): Engineering, computer, physical, or life sciences

Open to blind or visually impaired undergraduate or graduate students pursuing degrees in the above fields. U.S. citizenship required.

Write to the above address or visit website for complete information.

1876 — AMERICAN INDIAN SCIENCE AND ENGINEERING SOCIETY (EPA Tribal Lands Environmental Science Scholarship)

PO Box 9828
Albuquerque NM 87119-9828
505/765-1052
FAX: 505/765-5608
E-Mail: scholarships@aises.org
Internet: www.aises.org/scholarships

AMOUNT: $4,000

DEADLINE(S): JUN 15

FIELD(S): Biochemistry; Biology; Chemical Engineering; Chemistry; Entomology; Environmental Economics/Science; Hydrology; Environmental Studies

Open to American Indian college juniors, seniors, and graduate students enrolled full-time at an accredited institution. Must demonstrate financial need. Certificate of Indian blood NOT required.

Renewable. See website or contact Patricia Browne for an application.

1877 — AMERICAN MUSEUM OF NATURAL HISTORY (Grants)

Central Park West at 79th St.
New York NY 10024-5192
FAX: 212/769-5495
E-Mail: bynum@amnh.org
Internet: research.amnh.org

AMOUNT: $200-$2,000

DEADLINE(S): JAN 15

FIELD(S): Zoology; Paleontology; Anthropology

Modest short-term awards are offered to advanced graduate students and postdoctoral researchers who are commencing their careers in above fields. Two letters of recommendation and description (less than 2 pages) of proposed investigation are required. Budget must show clearly amounts and items for which award will be used. Grantees must submit progress report upon completion. Research projects need not be carried out at American Museum of Natural History.

200 awards annually. See website or contact Office of Grants & Fellowships for details on specific programs: Frank M. Chapman Memorial Fund for Ornithology, Lerner Gray Fund for Marine Research, Theodore Roosevelt Memorial Fund, & Collection Study Grant.

1878 — AMERICAN MUSEUM OF NATURAL HISTORY (Graduate Student Fellowship Program)

Central Park West at 79th St.
New York NY 10024-5192
FAX: 212/769-5495
E-Mail: bynum@amnh.org
Internet: research.amnh.org

AMOUNT: Stipend & health insurance

DEADLINE(S): JAN 15

FIELD(S): Paleontology; Earth & Planetary Sciences; Entomology; Evolutionary & Molecular Biology

One-year fellowships through partnership w/ Columbia, Cornell, & Yale Universities & City University of New York to help advance training of Ph.D. candidates in scientific disciplines practiced at Museum. Must include resume/curriculum vitae, GRE scores, TOEFL score for foreign students, official transcripts, letters of recommendation, and statement of research interest/summary of thesis proposal/progress to date.

Renewable up to 4 years. Must apply to Museum AND cooperating university. See website or contact Office of Grants & Fellowships for application.

1879 — AMERICAN MUSEUM OF NATURAL HISTORY (International Graduate Student Fellowship Program)

Central Park West at 79th St.
New York NY 10024-5192
FAX: 212/769-5495
E-Mail: bynum@amnh.org
Internet: research.amnh.org

AMOUNT: Stipend, tuition, & travel

DEADLINE(S): JAN 15

FIELD(S): Biodiversity & Conservation; Public Policy; Entomology; Evolutionary & Molecular Biology

One-year joint program w/ Columbia, Cornell, & Yale Universities & City University of NY to help advance training of Ph.D. candidates who are non-US citizens. Purpose is to gain skills & experience to bear on environmental problems of their home countries. Must submit resume/curriculum vitae, GRE & TOEFL scores, official transcripts, letters of recommendation, & statement of purpose.

Renewable up to 4 years. Must apply to Museum AND cooperating university. See website or contact Office of Grants & Fellowships for application.

1880 — AMERICAN MUSEUM OF NATURAL HISTORY (Research Fellowships)

Central Park West at 79th St.
New York NY 10024-5192
FAX: 212/769-5495
E-Mail: bynum@amnh.org
Internet: research.amnh.org

AMOUNT: Varies

DEADLINE(S): JAN 15

FIELD(S): Zoology; Paleontology; Anthropology; Earth & Planetary Sciences

Support to recent postdoctoral investigators and established scientists to carry out a specific project within a limited time period. Appointments are usually for one year, and candidates are expected to be in residence at the Museum or one of its field stations. Fellows are judged on research abilities/experience and merits/scope of proposed research. Application requires project description/bibliography, budget, letters of recommendation, and curriculum vitae.

See website or contact the Office of Grants & Fellowships for an application.

1881 — AMERICAN ORCHID SOCIETY (Grants for Orchid Research)

6000 S. Olive Ave.
West Palm Beach FL 33405-4199
561/585-8666

AMOUNT: $500-$12,000/yr.

DEADLINE(S): JAN 1; AUG 1

FIELD(S): Orchids: Biological Research, Floriculture, & Horticulture

Grants are for experimental projects and fundamental and applied research on orchids. Qualified graduate students with appropriate interests may apply for grants in support of their research if it involves or applies to orchids. Postgraduates may apply ONLY on behalf of the accredited institution of higher learning or appropriate research institute they represent.

Renewable up to 3 years. Contact Orchid Society for an application.

1882 — AMERICAN ORNITHOLOGISTS' UNION (AOU Student Research Awards)

Nat'l Museum Natural History
MRC-116
Washington DC 20560-0116
202/357-2051
FAX: 202/633-8084
E-Mail: aou@nmnh.si.edu
Internet: pica.wru.umt.edu/aou/aou.html

AMOUNT: $500-$1,500

DEADLINE(S): FEB

FIELD(S): Ornithology

Student research grants for undergraduates, graduates, and postgraduates; must not have received Ph.D. Must be a member of the American Ornithologists' Union. Financial need NOT a factor.

5-15 awards annually. Not renewable. For membership information or an application, contact James Dean at AOU.

1883 — AMERICAN SOCIETY FOR ENGINEERING EDUCATION (Army Research Laboritory Postdoctoral Fellowships)

1818 N St., NW, Ste. 600
Washington DC 20036
202/331-3525
FAX: 202/265-8504
E-Mail: projects@asee.org
Internet: www.asee.org/fellowship/

AMOUNT: $45,000-$55,000 + travel/relocation allowance

DEADLINE(S): Varies

FIELD(S): Engineering; Physical Sciences

Postdoctoral fellowships for US citizens/permanent residents to do research at Army Research Laboratories. Candidates must have completed their Ph.D. prior to appointment. Program is designed to increase involvement of creative and highly trained scientists and engineers from academia and industry in scientific and technical areas of interest and relevance to the Army. Research proposal should include clear objective and defined outcome. Financial need NOT a factor.

15 awards annually. Renewable. Contact Sandi Crawford at ASEE for an application packet.

1884 — AMERICAN SOCIETY FOR ENOLOGY AND VITICULTURE (Scholarship)

PO Box 1855
Davis CA 95617
530/753-3142

AMOUNT: Varies (no predetermined amounts)

DEADLINE(S): MAR 1

FIELD(S): Enology (Wine Making); Viticulture (Grape Growing)

For college juniors, seniors, or graduate students enrolled in an accredited North American college or university in a science curriculum basic to the wine and grape industry. Must be resident of North America, have a minimum 3.0 GPA (undergrad) or 3.2 GPA (grad), and demonstrate financial need.

Renewable. Contact ASEV for an application.

1885 — AMERICAN WINE SOCIETY EDUCATIONAL FOUNDATION (Scholarships and Grants)

1134 West Market St.
Bethlehem PA 18018-4910
610/865-2401 or 610/758-3845
FAX: 610/758-4344
E-Mail: lhso@lehigh.edu

AMOUNT: $2,000

DEADLINE(S): MAR 31

FIELD(S): Wine industry professional study: enology, viticulture, health aspects of food and wine, and using and appreciating fine wines.

To provide academic scholarships and research grants to students based on academic excellence. Must show financial need and genuine interest in pursuing careers in wine-related fields. For North American citizens, defined as U.S., Canada, Mexico, the Bahamas, and the West Indies at all levels of education.

Contact L.H. Sperling at above location for application.

1886 — ANIMAL BEHAVIOR OFFICE (Research Grants)

2611 E. 10th St.
Office 170
Bloomington IN 47408
508/793-7204

AMOUNT: up to $1,000

DEADLINE(S): JAN

FIELD(S): Animal Behavior

Open to graduate students researching animal behavior. Students must be ABS members.

For membership information or an application, write to above address.

1887 — ARCTIC INSTITUTE OF NORTH AMERICA (Jennifer Robinson Memorial Scholarship)

Univ Calgary
2500 University Dr., NW
Calgary Alberta T2N 1N4 CANADA
403/220-7515
FAX: 403/282-4609

AMOUNT: $5,000

DEADLINE(S): JAN 7

FIELD(S): Biology

Open to a graduate student in Northern Biology who proposes a research project having Northern relevance and demonstrates a commitment to field-oriented research. Award will go to the student who best exemplifies the scholarship qualities of the late Jennifer Robinson.

Contact the Arctic Institute for an application. Award announced in February.

1888 — ASSOCIATED WESTERN UNIVERSITIES, INC. (AWU Faculty Fellowships)

4190 South Highland Dr., Suite 211
Salt Lake City UT 84124-2600
801-273-8900

AMOUNT: Varies.

DEADLINE(S): FEB 15

FIELD(S): Engineering, Mathematics, Science, Technology

Research fellowships for qualified college and university faculty members to encourage participation and contribution to research at one of 62 cooperating facilities. It is not necessary to be enrolled at an AWU member institution. Collaborations that include graduate and/or undergraduate students are encouraged.

For detailed information and list of cooperating facilities, contact above location.

1889 — ASSOCIATED WESTERN UNIVERSITIES, INC. (AWU Graduate Fellowship Program)

4190 South Highland Dr. Suite 211
Salt Lake City, UT 84124-2600
801/273-8900

AMOUNT: Stipend ($1,300 per month & up) + tuition assistance and travel allowance

DEADLINE(S): FEB 15

FIELD(S): Engineering, Mathematics, Science, Technology

Open to master's and doctoral degree candidates to conduct research toward a thesis or dissertation at

one of more than 62 cooperating facilities. Institutional affiliation and citizenship restrictions may apply for some awards or facilities. It is not necessary to be enrolled at an AWU member institution to apply for a fellowship.

Write to the above address for complete information.

1890 — ASSOCIATED WESTERN UNIVERSITIES, INC. (AWU Postgraduate Fellowship)

4190 South Highland Dr. Suite 211
Salt Lake City UT 84124-2600
801/273-8900

AMOUNT: Stipend established by the host facility and varies by experience and discipline.

DEADLINE(S): Varies (Two to three months before the starting date)

FIELD(S): Engineering, Mathematics, Science, Technology

For college and university graduates who have completed all institutional requirements for an advanced degree from an accredited college or university in the U.S. A commitment to a professional career in science or engineering research is expected. U.S. citizenship or permanent resident status is required. Research is to be done at one of the 62 cooperating universities.

For detailed information and a list of cooperating facilities contact above address.

1891 — ASSOCIATED WESTERN UNIVERSITIES, INC. (AWU Visiting Scientist Fellowships)

4190 South Highland Dr., Suite 211
Salt Lake City UT 84124-2600
801/273-8900

AMOUNT: Varies

DEADLINE(S): Varies (Two months prior to starting date)

FIELD(S): Engineering, Science, Mathematics, and Technology

Research fellowships for professionals with continued commitment to science and engineering. For use at one of 62 participating universities. US citizenship or permanent residency required.

For detailed information and list of cooperating facilities contact above location.

1892 — ASSOCIATION FOR WOMEN IN SCIENCE EDUCATIONAL FOUNDATION (AWIS Predoctoral Awards)

1200 New York Ave. NW, Suite 650
Washington DC 20005
202/326-8940 or 800-886-AWIS
E-Mail: awis@awis.org
Internet: www.awis.org

AMOUNT: $1,000

DEADLINE(S): JAN 16

FIELD(S): Various Sciences and Social Sciences

Scholarships for female doctoral students. Summary page, description of research project, resume, references, transcripts, and biographical sketch required. US citizens may study at any graduate institution; non-citizens must study at US institutions.

5-10 awards annually. See website or write to above address for an application and complete information.

1893 — ASSOCIATION FOR WOMEN IN SCIENCE EDUCATIONAL FOUNDATION (AWIS Pre-doctoral Awards)

1200 New York Ave. NW, Suite 650
Washington DC 20005
202/326-8940 or 800/886-AWIS
E-Mail: awis@awis.org
Internet: www.awis.org

AMOUNT: $1,000

DEADLINE(S): JAN 16

FIELD(S): Various Sciences and Social Sciences

Scholarships for female doctoral students. Summary page, description of research project, resume, references, transcripts, and biographical sketch required. US citizens may study at any graduate institution; non-citizens must be enrolled in US institutions.

5-10 awards annually. See website or write to above address for an application and more information.

1894 — ASSOCIATION FOR WOMEN IN SCIENCE EDUCATIONAL FOUNDATION (Ruth Satter Memorial Award)

1200 New York Ave., NW, Suite 650
Washington DC 20005
202/326-8940 or 800/886-AWIS
E-Mail: awis@awis.org
Internet: www.awis.org

AMOUNT: $1,000

DEADLINE(S): JAN 16

FIELD(S): Various Sciences and Social Sciences

Scholarships for female doctoral students who have interrupted their education for at least three years to raise a family. Summary page, description of research project, resume, references, transcripts, biographical sketch, and letter from your department to confirm eligibility required. US citizens may study at any graduate institution; non-citizens must attend US institutions.

See website or write to above address for more information or an application.

1895 — ASSOCIATION FOR WOMEN IN SCIENCE EDUCATIONAL FOUNDATION (Ruth Satter Memorial Award)

1200 New York Ave. NW, Suite 650
Washington DC 20005
202/326-8940 or 800/886-AWIS
E-Mail: awis@awis.org
Internet: www.awis.org

AMOUNT: $1,000

DEADLINE(S): JAN 16

FIELD(S): Various Sciences and Social Sciences

Scholarships for female doctoral students who have interupted their education three years or more to raise a family. Summary page, description of research project, resume, references, transcripts, biographical sketch, and proof of eligibility from department head required. US citizens may attend any graduate institution; non-citizens must be enrolled in US institutions.

See website or write to above address for more information or an application.

1896 — BODOSSAKI FOUNDATION (Academic Prizes)

20 Amalias Ave.
GR-105 57 Athens GREECE
3220 962
FAX: 3237 976

AMOUNT: Drs. 7,000,000

DEADLINE(S): DEC 31

FIELD(S): Pure mathematics, theoretical and applied computer science, operations research, cardiovascular diseases, developmental biology

Awards to support the creative work of young Greek academics and scientists and reward their endeavor in the advancement of learning and the creation of sound values. Must be of Greek nationality, parentage, or descent under age 40.

Contact above address for details.

1897 — BOEING (Polish Graduate Student Scholarship Program)

Phone for details
314/234-2149

AMOUNT: Tuition, books, and fees for three years

DEADLINE(S): Varies

FIELD(S): Scientific and technical fields

Scholarships for students from Poland to pursue graduate studies in scientific and technical areas at American colleges or universities.

Call Jim Schlueter at above telephone number.

1898 — BRITISH FEDERATION OF WOMEN GRADUATES (Johnstone & Florence Stoney Studentship)

4 Mandeville Courtyard
142 Battersea Park Rd.
London SW11 4NB ENGLAND UK
PHONE/FAX: 0171/498-8037

AMOUNT: 1,000+ pounds sterling

DEADLINE(S): SEP 10

FIELD(S): Biology; Geology; Meteorology; Radiology

For female UK citizens planning to pursue graduate research, preferably undertaken in Australia, New Zealand, or South Africa. Must have completed at least four academic terms or three semesters; award is not given for first year of research. Chief criteria is academic excellence and proven ability to carry out independent research. Postdoctoral studies also eligible.

1 award annually. Application fee of 12 pounds sterling required. Send a self-addressed, stamped envelope (or self-addressed envelope with international reply coupons) for an application. Results announced by end of October.

1899 — BROOKHAVEN NATIONAL LABORATORY (Post-doctoral Research Associateships)

Brookhaven National Laboratory
Upton L.I. NY 11973-5000
516/344-3336

AMOUNT: $29,000 minimum

DEADLINE(S): Varies

FIELD(S): Chemistry, Physics, Materials Science, Biology, Oceanography, and Biomedical Sciences.

Post-doctoral research associateships tenable at Brookhaven National Laboratory for research to promote fundamental and applied research in the above fields. A recent doctoral degree is required.

25 associateships per year. Renewable for two additional years.

1900 — BROOKHAVEN WOMEN IN SCIENCE (Renate W. Chasman Scholarship)

PO Box 183
Upton NY 11973-5000
E-mail: pam@bnl.gov

AMOUNT: $2,000

DEADLINE(S): APR 1

FIELD(S): Natural Sciences; Engineering; Mathematics

Open ONLY to women who are residents of the boroughs of Brooklyn or Queens or the counties of Nassau or Suffolk in New York who are re-entering school after a period of study. For juniors, seniors, or first-year graduate students.

1 award annually. Not renewable. Contact Pam Mansfield at above location for an application. Phone calls are NOT accepted.

1901 — BUSINESS & PROFESSIONAL WOMEN'S FOUNDATION (BPW Career Advancement Scholarship Program)

2012 Massachusetts Ave., NW
Washington DC 20036-1070
202/293-1200, ext. 169
FAX: 202/861-0298
Internet: www.bpwusa.org
AMOUNT: $500-$1,000
DEADLINE(S): APR 15
FIELD(S): Biology, Science, Education, Engineering, Social Science, Paralegal, Humanities, Business, Math, Computers, Law, MD, DD

For women (US citizens) aged 25+ accepted into accredited program at US institution (+Puerto Rico & Virgin Islands). Must graduate within 12 to 24 months from the date of grant and demonstrate critical finanacial need. Must have a plan to upgrade skills, train for a new career field, or to enter/re-enter the job market.

Full- or part-time study. For info see website or send business-sized, self-addressed, double-stamped envelope.

1902 — EDMUND NILES HUYCK PRESERVE (Research Grants)

Main St.
Rensselaerville NY 12147
518/797-3440
AMOUNT: $2,500 (max.)
DEADLINE(S): FEB 1
FIELD(S): Ecology; Behavior; Evolution; Natural History

Open to graduate and postgraduate scientists conducting research on the natural resources of the Huyck Preserve. Housing and lab space are provided at the preserve. Funds are NOT available to help students defray college expenses.

Contact Preserve for an application.

1903 — ENGINEERING & PHYSICAL SCIENCES RESEARCH COUNCIL (Studentships)

North Star Ave
Polaris House
Swindon SN2 1ET England
01 793-444000
AMOUNT: Maintenance & approved fees
DEADLINE(S): JUL 31
FIELD(S): Engineering & Physical Science

Research studentships for up to 3 years for Ph.D students, 1 year advanced course studentships for master's students. Tenable at U.K. institutions. Must be UK resident with relevant connection to UK for full award or with European Union member state with relevant connection to UK for fees-only award. Must have appropriate academic qualifications.

Approx 3,800 awards per year. Applications must be made through heads of departments. EPSRC does not accept applications direct from students. Write for complete information.

1904 — ENTOMOLOGICAL SOCIETY OF AMERICA (Jeffrey P. LaFage Graduate Student Research Award)

9301 Annapolis Road
Lanham MD 20706
301/731-4535
FAX: 301/731-4538
E-Mail: esa@entsoc.org
Internet: www.entsoc.org
AMOUNT: $2,000
DEADLINE(S): JUL 1
FIELD(S): Biology/Entomology, specializing in the area of termite control

For graduate students in master's or doctoral degree programs at accredited universities throughout the world. For innovative research proposals into control of termites or other insect pests of the urban environment.

Renewable. Contact above location for details.

1905 — ENTOMOLOGICAL SOCIETY OF AMERICA (Stan Beck Fellowship)

9301 Annapolis Road, Suite 300
Lanham MD 20706
301/731-4535
FAX: 301/731-4538
E-Mail: esa@entsoc.org
Internet: www.entsoc.org
AMOUNT: $4,000
DEADLINE(S): SEP 1
FIELD(S): Entomology

For undergraduate or graduate study in entomology. Must be enrolled in a recognized college or university in the US. To assist needy students whose need may be based on physical limitations or economic, minority, or environmental condition.

Secure a nomination from an ESA member. Send SASE for complete information.

1906 — EPILEPSY FOUNDATION OF AMERICA (Junior Investigator Research Grants)

4351 Garden City Drive
Landover MD 20785-2267
301/459-3700 or 800/EFA-1000
FAX: 301/577-2684
TDD: 800/332-2070
E-Mail: postmaster@efa.org
Internet: www.efa.org
AMOUNT: up to $40,000
DEADLINE(S): SEP 1
FIELD(S): Epilepsy as related to Biological, Behavioral, & Social Sciences

One-year research grants to support basic and clinical research in the biological, behavioral, and social sciences which will advance the understanding, treatment, and prevention of epilepsy. Priority given to beginning investigators just entering the field of epilepsy research, to new or innovative projects. Applications evaluated on basis of scientific merit.

Contact EFA for an application.

1907 — EPILEPSY FOUNDATION OF AMERICA (Pre-doctoral Research Training Fellowship)

4351 Garden City Drive
Landover MD 20785-2267
301/459-3700 or 800/EFA-1000
FAX: 301/577-2684
TDD: 800/332-2070
E-Mail: postmaster@efa.org
Internet: www.efa.org
AMOUNT: up to $15,000
DEADLINE(S): SEP 1
FIELD(S): Epilepsy as related to Neuroscience, Physiology, Pharmacology, Psychology, Biochemistry, Genetics, Nursing, or Pharmacy

One-year of support for qualified individuals who are pursuing dissertation research with an epilepsy-related theme, and who are working under the guidance of a mentor with expertise in the area of epilepsy investigation. Graduate students pursuing Ph.D. degree in above fields may apply.

Contact EFA for an application.

1908 — EPPLEY FOUNDATION FOR RESEARCH (Postdoctoral Research Grants)

245 Park Avenue
40th Floor
New York NY 10167
Written inquiry
AMOUNT: Up to $25,000
DEADLINE(S): FEB 1; MAY 1; AUG 1; NOV 1
FIELD(S): Physical Sciences; Biological Sciences

Postdoctoral grants for original advanced research in any of the physical or biological sciences. Open to established research scientists who are attached to a recognized institution.

Write for complete information.

1909 — EUROPEAN MOLECULAR BIOLOGY ORGANIZATION (EMBO Fellowships)

Meyerhofstrasse 1
D69117 Heidelberg GERMANY
49 6221 383031
FAX: 49 6221 384879
E-Mail: EMBO@EMBL-Heidelberg.de
Internet: www.EMBO.org

AMOUNT: Varies (by country)

DEADLINE(S): FEB 15; AUG 15

FIELD(S): Molecular Biology

Postdoctoral fellowships in molecular biology. Financial need is NOT considered.

160 awards annually. Renewable up to 2 years. Contact Frank Gannon at above address for an application.

1910 — FANNIE AND JOHN HERTZ FOUNDATION (Fellowship)

Box 5032
Livermore CA 94551-5032
925/373-1642
Internet: www.hertzfoundation.org

AMOUNT: $25,000 stipend/yr. + $15,000 (max.) tuition allowance/yr.

DEADLINE(S): NOV 5

FIELD(S): Applied Physical Sciences

Open to graduate students with a minimum 3.75 GPA for studies in applied physical sciences, including math, engineering, computer science, biology, oceanography, aeronautics, astronomy, physics, and earth science. Must be US citizen/permanent resident. Does not support study in pursuit of M.D. degree, although will support Ph.D. portion of a joint M.D./Ph.D. study program.

Renewable up to 5 years. Only 36 US schools are currently considered tenable. See website for an application and list of specific fields of study that are acceptable.

1911 — FLORIDA FEDERATION OF GARDEN CLUBS, INC. (FFGC Scholarships for College Students)

6065 21st St., SW
Vero Beach FL 32968-9427
561/778-1023
Internet: www.ffgc.org

AMOUNT: $1,500-$3,500

DEADLINE(S): MAY 1

FIELD(S): Ecology; Environmental Issues; Land Management; City Planning; Environmental Control; Horticulture; Landscape Design; Conservation; Botany; Forestry; Marine Biology; Floriculture; Agriculture

Various scholarships for Florida residents with a "B" average or better enrolled full-time as a junior, senior, or graduate student at a Florida college or university.

See website or contact Melba Campbell at FFGC for an application.

1912 — FORD FOUNDATION/NATIONAL RESEARCH COUNCIL (Postdoctoral Fellowship for Minorities)

National Research Council
2101 Constitution Ave.
Washington DC 20418
202/334-2860
E-Mail: infofell@nas.edu
Internet: http//www.nas.edu/fo/index.html

AMOUNT: $25,000 + relocation and research allowance

DEADLINE(S): JAN 3

FIELD(S): Life and physical sciences, mathematics, engineering sciences, behavioral and social sciences, and the humanities

For U.S. citizens who received a Ph.D or Sc.D in the last 7 years and who are Native Amer. Indian or Alaskan, Black/African American, Mexican American, Native Pacific Islander, or Puerto Rican and who are or plan to be in a teaching or research career.

Contact above website or address for complete information.

1913 — FORD FOUNDATION/NATIONAL RESEARCH COUNCIL (Predoctoral/Dissertation Fellowships for Minorities)

2101 Constitution Ave.
Washington DC 20418
202/334-2872
E-Mail: infofell@nas.edu
Internet: http//www.nas.edu/fo/index.html

AMOUNT: $14,000 annual stipend + $6,000 grant to institution; $18,000 for dissertation fellowship

DEADLINE(S): NOV 3

FIELD(S): Most fields of study: sciences, humanities, engineering, behavioral science, social sciences, and computer science

Predoctoral and dissertation fellowships for students whose ethnicity is Alaskan Native, Black/African American, Mexican American/Chicano, Native American Indian, Native Pacific Islander, or Puerto Rican. For research-based programs leading to careers in college teaching and research.

Contact above address or website.

1914 — FOUNDATION FOR SCIENCE AND DISABILITY, INC. (FSD Science Student Grant Fund)

503 NW 89th Street
Gainesville FL 32607-1400
352/374-5774
FAX: 352/374-5781
E-Mail: rmankin@gainesville.usda.ufl.edu

AMOUNT: $1,000

DEADLINE(S): DEC 1

FIELD(S): Mathematics; Science; Medicine; Engineering; Computer Science

Open to graduate students with disabilities. May also apply as a fourth-year undergraduate accepted into a graduate or professional program. Awards are for some special purpose in connection with a science project or thesis in any of above fields. Student is required to write a 250-word essay which includes a description of professional goals/objectives, as well as purpose of grant. Transcripts and two letters of recommendation from faculty members are also required.

Contact Dr. Richard Mankin at above address for an application.

1915 — GARDEN CLUB OF AMERICA (Anne S. Chatham Fellowship in Medicinal Botany)

MO Botanical Garden
PO Box 299
St. Louis MO 63166-0299
314/577-9503
FAX: 314/577-9596
E-Mail: miller@mobot.org
Internet: www.mobot.org/mobot/research/applied_research/chatham.html

AMOUNT: $4,000

DEADLINE(S): JAN 15

FIELD(S): Medicinal Botany

Open to Ph.D. candidates and Ph.D.s to protect and preserve knowledge about the medicinal use of plants by providing research support in the field of ethnobotany.

1 award annually. Contact Dr. James S. Miller at above address for more information/an application.

1916 — GARDEN CLUB OF AMERICA (GCA Awards in Tropical Botany)

WWF
1250 24th St., NW
Washington DC 20037-1175
202/778-9714
FAX: 202/293-9211
E-Mail: marlar.oo@wwfus.org
Internet: www.gcamerica.org

AMOUNT: $5,500

DEADLINE(S): DEC 31

FIELD(S): Tropical Botany

Grant open to Ph.D. candidates to enable field study in tropical botany. Purpose is to promote the preservation of tropical forests by enlarging the body of botanists with field experience.

2 awards annually. Contact Ms. Marlar Oo at above address for more information/an application.

1917 — HARRY FRANK GUGGENHEIM FOUNDATION (Dissertation Fellowships)

527 Madison Ave.
New York NY 10022-4304
212/644-4907

AMOUNT: $10,000

DEADLINE(S): FEB 1

FIELD(S): Behavioral Sciences; Social Sciences; Biology

Awards are intended for support during the writing of the Ph.D. thesis in disciplines addressing the causes, manifestations, and control of violence, aggression, and dominance. Applicants must have completed research and be ready to write.

Contact Guggenheim Foundation for an application.

1918 — HARRY FRANK GUGGENHEIM FOUNDATION (Postdoctoral Research Grants)

527 Madison Ave.
New York NY 10022-4304
212/644-4907

AMOUNT: $30,000 (max.)

DEADLINE(S): AUG 1

FIELD(S): Behavioral Sciences; Social Sciences; Biology

One- to two-year grants are open to postdoctoral researchers in the above fields whose work leads to a better understanding of the causes, manifestations, and control of violence, aggression, and dominance in the modern world.

25-35 awards annually. Contact Guggenheim Foundation for an application.

1919 — HUBBARD FARMS CHARITABLE FOUNDATION

P.O. Box 505
Walpole NH 03608-0505
603/756-3311

AMOUNT: Varies

DEADLINE(S): APR 1; OCT 1

FIELD(S): Poultry science, genetics, and other life sciences

Scholarships are for financially needy students at universities that the foundation trustees consider to be leaders in the field of progress in technology and efficiency of production of poultry products.

Send SASE to Jane F. Kelly, Clerk, at above address for current application guidelines.

1920 — INSTITUTE OF PAPER SCIENCE AND TECHNOLOGY (Fellowship Program)

500 10th St. NW
Atlanta GA 30318
404/853-9500

AMOUNT: Full tuition plus $11,250 stipend

DEADLINE(S): MAR 15

FIELD(S): Chemistry; Chemical Engineering; Physics; Biology; Mechanical Engineering; Pulp and Paper Technology

Open to graduate students who are U.S., Mexican, or Canadian citizens or legal residents who hold a BS degree in the above fields. For a pursuit of a master of Science or Ph.D degree at the institute.

35 fellowships annually. Address inquiries to director of admissions.

1921 — INTERNATIONAL SCHOOL OF CRYSTALLOGRAPHY (Postgraduate Courses)

Piazza di Porta San Donato 1
40126 Bologna ITALY
39 051 243556
FAX: 39 051 243336
E-Mail: riva@geomin.unibo.it
Internet: www.geomin.unibo.it/orgv/erice/erice.htm

AMOUNT: Half to full subsistence + fees

DEADLINE(S): NOV 30

FIELD(S): Solid State Chemistry; Physics; Molecular Biology; Molecular Biophysics; Pharmaceutics

Open to young postgraduates to pursue interdisciplinary studies in crystallography in Erice, Sicily, Italy. Must speak English and have some experience in the topic to be discussed (topics change every year). These 15-day courses are held at the International Foundation and Centre for Scientific Culture—Ettore Majorana.

See website or contact Lodovico Riva di Sanseverino for an application.

1922 — INTERNATIONAL SOCIETY OF ARBORICULTURE (Research Trust)

Dr. Bruce Roberts, Dept. Botany & Microbiolgy
Ohio Wesleyan University
Delaware OH 43015
740/386-3508

AMOUNT: $5,000 (max.)

DEADLINE(S): NOV 1

FIELD(S): Horticulture; Botany; Entomology; Phytopathology

For horticulturists, plant pathologists, plant physiologists, entomologists, soil specialists, and others engaging in the scientific study of shade trees. Grants can be used only for expenses associated with conducting approved research projects, e.g. equipment, supplies, etc. Funds are NOT to be used for expenses associated with attending school, e.g. tuition, books, lab fees, food, lodging, etc. Proposals must be received by November 1st.

Contact Dr. Bruce Roberts for an application.

1923 — KARL-ENIGK-STIFTUNG (Research Grant)

Buenteweg 2
D-30559
Hannover GERMANY
0049/511/953-8010
FAX: 0049/511/953-82-8010
E-Mail: bhuesch@vw.tiho-hannover.de
Internet: www.tiho-hannover.de

AMOUNT: 2,700 DM/month (for living expenses)

DEADLINE(S): None

FIELD(S): Experimental Parasitology

Grants for postgraduate research in German-speaking countries. Financial need NOT considered.

2 awards annually. Renewable up to 2 years. Contact Chancellor Linnemann at above address for an application.

1924 — LIFE SCIENCES RESEARCH FOUNDATION (LSRF Postdoctoral Fellowships)

Lewis Thomas Lab
Princeton Univ
Washington Rd.
Princeton NJ 08544
609/258-3551
E-Mail: sdirenzo@molbio.princeton.edu
Internet: lsrf.molbio.princeton.edu

AMOUNT: $40,000

DEADLINE(S): OCT 1

FIELD(S): Biological Sciences

Three-year fellowships for non-US citizens to do postdoctoral research at nonprofit institutions in the US. Based on quality of previous accomplishments and merit of the proposal. Applicant cannot be holding a faculty appointment, and there can be no more than one LSRF fellow per laboratory. Once each year, all current fellows will meet to present their research. Fellowship cannot support research with patent commitment or similar agreement.

Contact LSRF for an application.

1925 — LOUISIANA OFFICE OF STUDENT FINANCIAL ASSISTANCE (Rockefeller State Wildlife Scholarship)

PO Box 91202
Baton Rouge LA 70821-9202
800/259-5626, ext. 1012

FAX: 504/922-0790

Internet: www.osfa.state.la.us

AMOUNT: $1,000/yr.

DEADLINE(S): JUN 1

FIELD(S): Forestry; Wildlife; Marine Science

Open to Louisiana residents pursuing undergraduate or graduate study in a Louisiana college/university. Must have minimum 2.5 GPA. Recipients must attain a degree in one of the three eligible fields or repay the funds plus interest.

30 awards annually. Renewable up to 5 years undergraduate study & 2 years graduate study. Apply by completing the Free Application for Federal Student Aid (FAFSA). See your school's financial aid office or contact LOSFA for FAFSA form.

1926 — LOVELACE RESPIRATORY RESEARCH INSTITUTE/UNIVERSITY OF NEW MEXICO (Graduate Fellowships)

PO Box 5890

Albuquerque NM 87185

505/845-1159

FAX: 505/845-1198

E-Mail: jseagrav@lrri.org

Internet: www.lrri.org

AMOUNT: $16,000

DEADLINE(S): None

FIELD(S): Biomedical Sciences; Aerosol Science; Respiratory Toxicology; Physiology; Immunology; Lung Cancer

Open to graduate students admitted to the graduate program in Biomedical Sciences at the University of New Mexico. Experimental work for thesis may be performed with a staff scientist at LRRI, contingent on available funding. Must be US citizens or have J-1 visa.

1-3 awards annually. Contact JeanClare Seagrave for an application.

1927 — LOVELACE RESPIRATORY RESEARCH INSTITUTE/UNIVERSITY OF NEW MEXICO (Postdoctoral Fellowships)

PO Box 5890

Albuquerque NM 87185

505/845-1159

FAX: 505/845-1198

E-Mail: jpainter@lrri.org

Internet: www.lrri.org

AMOUNT: $26,000+ (depending on area & qualifications)

DEADLINE(S): None

FIELD(S): Biomedical Sciences; Aerosol Science; Respiratory Toxicology; Physiology; Immunology; Lung Cancer

Open to postdoctoral researchers who have completed a Ph.D., D.V.M., or M.D. from an accredited institution in one of the above fields. Must be US citizen or have J-1 visa.

1-3 awards annually. Contact Joann Painter for an application.

1928 — MANOMET CENTER FOR CONSERVATION SCIENCES (Kathleen S. Anderson Award)

PO Box 1770

Manomet MA 02345

508/224-6521 FAX: 508/224-9220

AMOUNT: $1,000

DEADLINE(S): DEC 1

FIELD(S): Ornithology

Research grant open to anyone beginning a career in biology for ecological and behavioral studies of birds, especially research for bird conservation. Research must be conducted in the western hemisphere.

Contact Manomet Center for an application. Please note: This is a RESEARCH GRANT ONLY, not a scholarship.

1929 — MYCOLOGICAL SOCIETY OF AMERICA (Graduate Fellowships)

c/o L. M. Kohn, Dept. of Botany, Univ. Toronto, Erindale Campus

Mississauga Ontario L5L 1C6 CANADA

905/828-3997

Internet: www.erin.utoronto.ca/soc/msa/

AMOUNT: $2,000 and $1,000

DEADLINE(S): Varies

FIELD(S): Mycology

Fellowships for the study of fungi by Ph.D candidates at accredited U.S. or Canadian universities. Only for student members of the Mycological Society of America. Previous recipients are not eligible.

Two $2,000 and one $1,000 awards per year. Contact above address for complete information.

1930 — NATIONAL ASSOCIATION OF WATER COMPANIES—NEW JERSEY CHAPTER (Scholarship)

Elizabethtown Water Co.

600 South Ave.

Westfield NJ 07090

908/654-1234

FAX: 908/232-2719

AMOUNT: $2,500

DEADLINE(S): APR 1

FIELD(S): Business Administration; Biology; Chemistry; Engineering; Communications

For U.S. citizens who have lived in NJ at least 5 years and plan a career in the investor-owned water utility industry in disciplines such as those above. Must be undergrad or graduate student in a 2- or 4-year NJ college or university.

GPA of 3.0 or better required. Contact Gail P. Brady for complete information.

1931 — NATIONAL PARKS SERVICE (Science Scholars Program)

1849 C St., NW

Washington DC 20240

202/208-6843

E-Mail: aspiceland@goparks.org

Internet: www.nps.gov

AMOUNT: $25,000/yr.

DEADLINE(S): JUN 15

FIELD(S): Biological, Physical, Social, & Cultural Sciences

Three-year scholarships to Ph.D. candidates pursuing degrees in above fields. Objectives are to encourage young scientists to engage in park-related research, conduct innovative research on issues central to the National Parks, and encourage use of parks as laboratories for sciences. NPF will transfer the scholarship funds to each student's university, providing for tuition, field work, stipend, & other research expenses. Must submit research proposal.

4 awards annually. See website or contact Dr. Gary E. Machlis, Program Director, at NPS for an application. Winners announced shortly after August 15th.

1932 — NATIONAL RESEARCH COUNCIL (Howard Hughes Medical Institute Predoctoral Fellowships in Biological Sciences)

2101 Constitution Ave.

Washington DC 20418

202/334-2872

FAX: 202/334-2872

E-Mail: infofell@nas.edu

Internet: national-academics.org/osep.fo

AMOUNT: $16,000 stipend + tuition at US institution

DEADLINE(S): NOV 9

FIELD(S): Biochemistry; Biophysics; Epidemiology; Genetics; Immunology; Microbiology; Neuroscience; Pharmacology; Physiology; Virology

Five-year award is open to college seniors and first-year graduate students pursuing a Ph.D. or Sc.D. degree. US citizens/nationals may choose any institution in the US or abroad; foreign students must choose US institution. Based on ability, academic records, proposed study/research, previous experience, reference reports, and GRE scores.

80 awards annually. See website or contact NRC for an application.

1933 — NATIONAL RESEARCH COUNCIL OF CANADA (Research Associateships)

Research Associates Office
Ottawa Ontario K1A 0R6 CANADA
613/993-9150
FAX: 613/990-7669
Internet: www.nrc.ca/careers

AMOUNT: $39,366 Canadian

DEADLINE(S): None

FIELD(S): Natural Sciences; Engineering

Two-year research associateships are tenable at NRCC labs throughout Canada. Open to recent Ph.D.s in natural sciences or recent master's or Ph.D.s in engineering. Degrees should have been received within the last five years. Preference given to Canadians.

Renewable. See website or contact NRCC for an application.

1934 — NATIONAL RESEARCH FOUNDATION (NRF Honors & Postgraduate Bursaries)

PO Box 2600
Pretoria 0001 SOUTH AFRICA
+27 012/481-4000
FAX: +27 012/349-1179
E-Mail: info@nrf.ac.za
Internet: www.nrf.ac.za

AMOUNT: Varies

DEADLINE(S): Varies

FIELD(S): Agriculture; Chemistry; Earth Sciences; Engineering; Biology; Mathematics; Physics; Forestry; Veterinary Science; Pharmaceutics

Open to South African citizens pursuing graduate/postgraduate studies in above fields.

500 awards annually. Contact NRF for an application.

1935 — NATIONAL SCIENCES AND ENGINEERING RESEARCH COUNCIL OF CANADA (Graduate Scholarships)

Scholarships/Fellowships Division
350 Albert Street
Ottawa Ontario K1A 1H5 CANADA
613/996-3769
FAX: 613/996-2589
E-Mail: schol@nserc.ca
Internet: http://www.nserc.ca

AMOUNT: $15,700/year for 1st & 2nd years at masters or Ph.D level; $17,400/year (Ph.D level ONLY) 3rd & 4th years

DEADLINE(S): NOV 24

FIELD(S): Natural Sciences, Engineering, Biology, or Chemistry

Open to Canadian citizens or permanent residents who have earned or will soon earn a bachelors or masters degree in science or engineering. Academic excellence and research aptitude are considerations.

Write for complete information.

1936 — NATIONAL SCIENCES AND ENGINEERING RESEARCH COUNCIL OF CANADA (Postdoctoral Fellowships)

Scholarships/Fellowships Division
350 Albert Street
Ottawa Ontario K1A 1H5 CANADA
613/996-3762
FAX: 613/996-2589
E-Mail: schol@nserc.ca
Internet: http://www.nserc.ca

AMOUNT: Individually negotiated

DEADLINE(S): Varies—average: $43,000

FIELD(S): Natural Sciences, Engineering, Biology, or Chemistry

Open to Canadian citizens or permanent residents who hold doctoral degrees in science or engineering. Academic excellence and research aptitude are considerations.

Write for complete information.

1937 — NORTHERN NEW JERSEY UNIT-HERB SOCIETY OF AMERICA (Scholarship)

2068 Dogwood Drive
Scotch Plains NJ 07076
908/233-2348

AMOUNT: $2,000

DEADLINE(S): FEB 15

FIELD(S): Horticulture; Botany

For New Jersey residents, undergraduate through postgraduate, who will attend colleges/universities east of the Mississippi River. Financial need is considered.

1 award annually. Renewable. Contact Mrs. Charlotte R. Baker at above address for an application.

1938 — NOVARTIS FOUNDATION (Bursary Scheme)

41 Portland Place
London W1N 4BN ENGLAND UK
+44 171 636 9456
FAX: +44 171 436 2840
E-Mail: abrown@novartisfound.org.uk
Internet: www.novartisfound.org.uk

AMOUNT: Travel & subsistence—up to $6,000/person

DEADLINE(S): Varies

FIELD(S): Science; Medicine

Travel fellowships to young scientists (postgrad/doc) to attend international meetings in connection with the Novartis Foundation Symposia. Must be between the ages of 23 and 35, and be active in the field of science in question. Symposia is normally in London, and a 4-week to 12-week host laboratory in the department of one of the symposium participants follows. Specific topics vary. Must submit qualifications, resume, career history/goals, and research interests.

8 awards annually. Not renewable. See website or contact Allyson Brown for application procedures.

1939 — OAK RIDGE ASSOCIATED UNIVERSITIES (Laboratory Graduate Research Participation Program)

P.O. Box 117
Oak Ridge TN 37831-0117
423/576-4813

AMOUNT: $1,000-$1,200/mo. + allowance for dependents + tuition and fees reimbursement to a max. of $3,500/yr.

DEADLINE(S): Ongoing

FIELD(S): Life sciences, physical, and social sciences, mathematics, and engineering

For graduate students in one of the fields listed above who have completed all degree requirements except thesis or dissertation research. For full-time research under the joint direction of the major professor and a DOE staff member at one of various locations, primarily in the South. For six to twelve months.

Funded through U.S. Dept. of Energy, Office of Energy Reseach, and Office of Fossil Energy. Write for complete information.

1940 — OAK RIDGE ASSOCIATED UNIVERSITIES (National Science Foundation Graduate Research Fellowships)

PO Box 3010
Oak Ridge TN 37831-3010
423/241-4300
FAX: 423/241-4513
E-Mail: nsfgrfp@orau.gov
Internet: www.orau.gov/nsf/nsffel.htm

AMOUNT: $15,000 stipend + $10,500 tuition allowance

DEADLINE(S): NOV 4

FIELD(S): Science; Math; Engineering; Computer Science

Three-year fellowships for graduate study leading to research-based master's or doctoral degrees in the above fields. Must be US citizens, nationals, or permanent residents at the time of application. Fellowships are awarded on the basis of ability. Women, minorities, and those with disabilities are strongly encouraged to apply. One-time International Research Travel Allowance available.

1,000 awards annually. Contact Jeannette Bouchard for an application/more information.

1941 — OAK RIDGE INSTITUTE FOR SCIENCE AND EDUCATION (Alexander Hollaender Distinguished Post-doctoral Fellowships)

P.O. Box 117
Oak Ridge TN 37831-0117
423/576-3192 or 423/576-9975

AMOUNT: $37,500 + inbound travel, moving, and medical insurance

DEADLINE(S): JAN 15

FIELD(S): Biomedical, life, and environmental sciences and other related scientific disciplines, including global change and human genome

One-year post-doctoral fellowships for research and training in energy-related life, biomedical, and environmental sciences at one of participating laboratories in the U.S. Must have completed doctorate within last two years.

Must be U.S. citizen or legal resident.

1942 — OAK RIDGE INSTITUTE FOR SCIENCE AND EDUCATION (Applied Health Physics Fellowship Program)

P.O. Box 117
Oak Ridge TN 37831-0117
423/576-2194 or 423/576-9279
E-Mail: COXRE@ORAU.GOV or
GRADFELL@ORAU.GOV

AMOUNT: $14,400 stipend + tuition and fees up to $9,000/yr paid to university + transportation costs up to $300/month

DEADLINE(S): JAN 26

FIELD(S): Engineering, mathematics, physical and life sciences

Fellowship in applied health physics to implement DOE's nuclear energy-related mission. Candidates must have B.A. degree in life or physical sciences, engineering, or mathematics. Recipients are subject to a service obligation of one year of full-time employment in a DOE facility for each academic year of fellowhip award.

For details and application, contact above location.

1943 — OAK RIDGE INSTITUTE FOR SCIENCE AND EDUCATION (Industrial Hygiene Graduate Fellowship Program)

P.O. Box 117
Oak Ridge TN 37831-0117
423-576-9655
FAX: 423/576-8293
E-Mail: kinneym@orau.gov

AMOUNT:
DEADLINE(S): JAN 26

FIELD(S): Industrial Hygiene

A fellowship for first-year master's candidates who have undergraduate degrees in physical, life, environmental, or health sciences or enginering and who wish to pursue studies in industrial hygiene.

For details and application, contact above location.

1944 — OAK RIDGE INSTITUTE FOR SCIENCE AND EDUCATION (U.S. Geological Survey Earth Sciences Internship Program)

P.O. Box 117
Oak Ridge TN 37831-0117
423/576-2358
423/576-4813

AMOUNT: $19,000 to $38,000, dependent on level

DEADLINE(S): Ongoing

FIELD(S): Geology, geography, biology, chemistry, environmental sciences, hydrology, forestry, civil engineering, computer sciences

Internships for undergrads, grads, or recent grads (within one year) students studying in the above fields to conduct projects to prepare for careers in earth sciences for up to two years. Location: USGS sites across the U.S.

Funded through the U.S. Dept. of the Interior, U.S.G.S.

1945 — OAK RIDGE INSTITUTE FOR SCIENCE AND EDUCATION/U.S. DEPT. OF ENERGY (Office of Civilian Radioactive Waste Management Fellowship)

P.O. Box 117
Oak Ridge TN 37831-0117
423/576-0128
FAX: 423/576-8293
E-Mail: drostp@orau.gov

AMOUNT: $14,000/yr.

DEADLINE(S): JAN 16 (Received, not postmarked)

FIELD(S): Physical or life sciences, math, or engineering

Fellowships for graduate students at various participating universities to conduct research in the management of spent nuclear fuel and high-level raqdioactive waste. For M.A. and Ph.D. candidates. For up to 48 months. Must be U.S. citizen or permanent resident.

Funded through U.S. Department of Energy, Office of Civilian Radioactive Waste Management. Contact or call Ms. Portia Drost, MS-16, at above address for details.

1946 — OAK RIDGE INSTITUTE FOR SCIENCE AND EDUCATION (Nuclear Engineering & Health Physics Fellowship Program)

105 Mitchell Rd. MS-16
Oak Ridge TN 37831-0117
423/576-2600 or 423/241-2890

E-Mail: johnsons@orau.gov or
daltonj@arou.gov

AMOUNT: $14,400/yr.

DEADLINE(S): JAN 26

FIELD(S): Engineering, physical and life sciences

Fellowships in nuclear engineering or applied health physics to implement DOE's nuclear energy-related mission. Candidates must have B.A. degree in life or physical sciences or engineering.

For details and application, contact Sandra Johnson or Jennifer Dalton at above location.

1947 — ONTARIO MINISTRY OF EDUCATION AND TRAINING (John Charles Polanyi Prizes)

189 Red River Rd.
4th Floor, Box 4500
Thunder Bay Ontario P7B 6G9 CANADA
800/465-3957
TDD: 800/465-3958
Internet: osap.gov.on.ca

AMOUNT: $15,000

DEADLINE(S): Varies

FIELD(S): Physics; Chemistry; Physiology; Medicine; Literature; Economics

Monetary prizes are awarded to Canadian citizens/permanent residents who are continuing postdoctoral studies at an Ontario university. Awards are designed to encourage and reward academic excellence.

5 awards annually. Contact your university or the Ontario Council of Graduate Studies for an application.

1948 — OPEN SOCIETY INSTITUTE (Environmental Management Fellowships)

400 West 59th St.
New York NY 10019
212/548-0600 or 212/757-2323
FAX: 212/548-4679 or 212/548-4600
Internet: www.soros.org/efp.html

AMOUNT: Fees, room, board, living stipend, textbooks, international transportation, health insurance

DEADLINE(S): NOV 15

FIELD(S): Earth sciences, natural sciences, humanities (exc. language), anthropology, sociology, mathematics, or engineering

Two-year fellowships for use in selected universities in the U.S. for international students. For students/professionals in fields related to environmental policy, legislation, and remediation techniques applicable to their home countries.

To apply, contact your local Soros Foundation or Open Society Institute. Further details on website.

1949 — PHARMACEUTICAL RESEARCH AND MANUFACTURERS OF AMERICA FOUNDATION (Fellowships in Pharmacology-Morphology)

1100 15th St. NW
Washington DC 20005
202/835-3470
FAX: 202/467-4823
E-Mail: CRobinson%phrma@mcimail.com
Internet: www.phrmaf.org

AMOUNT: Stipend support + $500 for travel

DEADLINE(S): JAN 15

FIELD(S): Pharmacology and a morphologic specialty, such as anatomy or pathology

For postdoctoral researchers who have specialized in either pharmacology or morphologic disciplines (i.e. anatomy or pathology) for training in the complementary discipline.

Contact above website or address for appliction and details. A two-year award.

1950 — POTASH AND PHOSPHATE INSTITUTE (J. Fielding Reed PPI Fellowships)

655 Engineering Dr., Ste. 110
Norcross GA 30092
770/447-0335

AMOUNT: $2,000

DEADLINE(S): JAN 15

FIELD(S): Soil & Plant Sciences

Open to graduate students pursuing degrees at US or Canadian institutions. Awards are based on scholastic excellence.

Contact PPI for an application.

1951 — ROCKEFELLER FOUNDATION (African Dissertation Internship Awards)

420 Fifth Ave.
New York NY 10018-2702
212/869-8500
212/764-3468
Internet: www.rockfound.org

AMOUNT: Cost of project

DEADLINE(S): None given

FIELD(S): Agriculture, environment, health, life sciences, population, and schooling

For African graduate students in U.S. and Canadian universities (but not to permanent residents) to return to Africa to carry out dissertation research at a local university or research institution. Priority given to above topics.

Students are strongly urged to be in the field for at least 12 months. Contact above location for details.

1952 — ROYAL SOCIETY (John Murray Fund)

6 Carlton House Terrace
REF REA

London SW1Y 5AG ENGLAND UK
071/839 5561

AMOUNT: Up to 3000 pounds sterling

DEADLINE(S): DEC 10

FIELD(S): Oceanography; Limnology; Zoology; Botany; Geology; Mathematics; Physics

Grants open to British post-doctoral applicants. Award is to be used for the encouragement of travel & work in oceanography or limnology.

The award may be held for 1 year. It is not renewable. Write for complete information—REF JELL.

1953 — SMITHSONIAN INSTITUTION (Fellowship Program)

Office of fellowships & Grants
955 L'Enfant Plaza, Suite 7000
Washington DC 20560
202/287-3271
E-Mail: http://www.si.edu/research+study
Internet: siofg@sivm.si.edu

AMOUNT: $3,000-$25,000 depending on level and length

DEADLINE(S): JAN 15

FIELD(S): Animal behavior, ecology, environmental science (including emphasis on the tropics, anthropology (& archaeology), astrophysics, astronomy, earth sciences, paleobiology, evolutionary/ systematic biology, history of science and technology, history of art, esp. American, contemporary, African, and Asian, 20th century American crafts, decorative arts, social/cultural history of the US, or folklife.

For research in residence at the Smithsonian for graduate students, both pre- and postdoctoral.

Research to be in the fields listed above.

1954 — SMITHSONIAN INSTITUTION (Minority Student Internship Program)

Fellowships & Grants
955 L'Enfant Plaza, Suite 7000
MRC 902
Washington DC 20560
202/287-3271
FAX: 202/287-3691
E-Mail: siofg@ofg.si.edu
Internet: www.si.edu/research+study

AMOUNT: $300/week + possible travel expenses

DEADLINE(S): FEB 15

FIELD(S): Humanities, Environmental Studies, Cultural Studies, Natural History, Earth Science, Art History, Biology, & related fields

Ten-week internships in residence at the Smithsonian for US minority students to participate in research or museum-related activities in above fields. For undergrads or grads with at least a 3.0 GPA.

Essay, resume, transcripts, and references required with application. Internships are full-time and are offered for Summer, Fall, or Spring tenures.

Write for application.

1955 — SOCIETY OF BIOLOGICAL PSYCHIATRY (A.E. Bennett Research Awards)

c/o Elliott Richelson MD
Mayo Clinic Jacksonville
4500 San Pablo Rd.
Jacksonville FL 32224
904/953-2842

AMOUNT: $1,500

DEADLINE(S): JAN 31

FIELD(S): Biological Psychiatry

Awards are given in basic science and clinical science for purpose of stimulating international research in biological psychiatry by young investigators under the age of 35.

All co-authors must also be under 35. Candidate must be actively involved in the area of research described in submission. Studies and data must not have been published elsewhere.

1956 — SOCIETY OF BIOLOGICAL PSYCHIATRY (DISTA Fellowship Award)

c/o Elliot Richelson, MD
Mayo Clinic Jacksonville
4500 San Pablo Rd.
Jacksonville FL 32224
904/953-2842

AMOUNT: $1,500

DEADLINE(S): DEC 15

FIELD(S): Biological Psychiatry

Open to medical graduates in their 3rd, 4th, or 5th year of residency or fellowship training. Selection will be based on past excellence and potential for professional growth in the area of biological psychiatry or clinical neuroscience.

Nominations are made by university department of psychiatry. Write for complete information.

1957 — SONOMA CHAMBOLLE-MUSIGNY SISTER CITIES, INC. (Henri Cardinaux Memorial Scholarship)

Chamson Scholarship Committee
PO Box 1633
Sonoma CA 95476-1633
707/939-1344
FAX: 707/939-1344
E-Mail: Baileysci@vom.com

AMOUNT: up to $1,500 (travel + expenses)

DEADLINE(S): JUL 15

FIELD(S): Culinary Arts; Wine Industry; Art; Architecture; Music; History; Fashion

Hands-on experience working in above or similiar fields & living with a family in small French village in Burgundy or other French city. Must be Sonoma County, CA, resident at least 18 years of age & be able to communicate in French. Transcripts, employer recommendation, photograph, & essay (stating why, where, & when) required.

1 award. Non-renewable. Also offers opportunity for candidate in Chambolle-Musigny to obtain work experience & cultural exposure in Sonoma, CA.

1958 — SOUTH AFRICAN ASSOCIATION OF WOMEN GRADUATES (Bertha Stoneman Award for Botany)

PO Box 2163
Grahamstown 6140 SOUTH AFRICA
0461-25284

AMOUNT: R500-00 p.a.

DEADLINE(S): OCT 31

FIELD(S): Botany

Open to female graduate botany students at the master's degree level or higher who have completed at least one year's post-graduate study. Award should be used in South Africa. Must be members of SAAWG. Financial need is a consideration but is not necessarily paramount.

Renewable if research is proceeding well. Write to Fellowships Secretary for complete information.

1959 — TERATOLOGY SOCIETY (Student Travel Grants)

9650 Rockville Pike
Bethesda MD 20814
301/571-1841

AMOUNT: $400

DEADLINE(S): MAY 1

FIELD(S): Teratology

Travel assistance grants open to graduates & post-grads for attendance at the Teratology Society's annual meeting for abstract presentation. Purpose is to promote interest in & advance study of Biological Abnormalities.

35-40 awards per year. Write for complete information.

1960 — THE DAPHNE JACKSON MEMORIAL FELLOWSHIPS TRUST (Fellowships in Science/ Engineering)

School of Physical Sciences, Dept. of Physics,
University of Surrey
Guildford, Surrey GU2 5XH ENGLAND UK
01483 259166
FAX: 01483 259501

E-Mail: J.Woolley@surrey.ac.uk
Internet: www.sst.ph.ic.ac.uk/trust/

AMOUNT: Varies

DEADLINE(S): Varies

FIELD(S): Science or engineering, including information sciences

Fellowships to enable well-qualified and highly motivated scientists and engineers to return to appropriate careers following a career break due to family comitments. May be used on a flexible, part-time basis. Tenable at various U.K. universities.

See website and/or contact organization for details.

1961 — THE NOVARTIS FOUNDATION (Scientific Research Fellowships/Bursaries)

41 Portland Place
London W1N 4BN ENGLAND UK
+44 171 636 9456
FAX: +44 171 436 2840
E-Mail: abrown@Novartisfound.org.uk
Internet: www.novartisfound.demon.co.uk/ bursary.htm

AMOUNT: Travel expenses, meals, lodging

DEADLINE(S): Varies

FIELD(S): Sciences

Fellowships/bursaries for young scientists, ages 23-35, to attend aFoundation symposium and then spend from 4-12 weeks in the laboratory of one of the symposium participants. For subject matter, see "Nature" or other appropriate journals or check with the Foundation or an office of the British Council.

For application details, see website or contact organization.

1962 — TRENT UNIVERSITY (Graduate Teaching/Research Assistantships)

P.O. Box 4800
Graduate Studies Officer
Peterborough Ontario CANADA K9J 7B8
705/748-1245

AMOUNT: $3,500 per term

DEADLINE(S): FEB 15

FIELD(S): Anthropology, Geography, Archaeology, Biology, Canadian Studies, Philosophy, Cultural Studies, Computer Science, Mathematics, Physics, Chemistry, Environmental Science/Studies

Teaching/research assistantships at Trent University in the above fields. Open to masters and doctoral candidates. Tenable for up to 4 terms spanning 2-3 years of study.

80 awards per year. Write for complete information.

1963 — TUSKEGEE UNIVERSITY (Graduate Research Fellowships and Assistantships)

Admissions Office
Tuskegee University
1506 Franklin Rd., AL 36088
334/727/8500

AMOUNT: Tuition

DEADLINE(S): MAR 15

FIELD(S): Chemistry; Engineering; Environmental Science; Life Sciences; Nutrition; Education

Graduate research fellowships and graduate assistantships are available to qualified individuals who wish to enter Tuskegee University's graduate program in pursuit of a master's degree.

Write for complete information.

1964 — U.S. DEPARTMENT OF DEFENSE (GLSIP-General Laboratory Scientific Interchange Program: NRC-NRL Post-Doctoral Program)

Naval Research Laboratory
Office of Program Admin. & Dev. Code 1006.17
Washington, D.C. 20375-5321
202/767-3865
DSN: 297-3865
FAX: 202/404-8110
Internet: www.acq.osd.mil/ddre/edugate/s-aindx.html

AMOUNT: Research Program

DEADLINE(S): None specified

FIELD(S): Computer science, artificial intelligence, plasma physics, acoustics, radar, fluid dynamics, chemistry, materials sci, optical sci, condensed matter and radiation, electronic sci, environmental sci, marine geosciences, remote sensing, oceanography, marine meteorology, space technology/sciences.

U.S. citizens who are recent postdoctoral graduates are selected on the basis of overall qualifications and techincal proposals.

Contact Jessica Hileman for more information.

1965 — UNCF/MERCK SCIENCE INITIATIVE (Graduate Science Research Dissertation Fellowships)

8260 Willow Oaks Corporate Dr.
PO Box 10444
Fairfax VA 22031-4511
703/205-3503
FAX: 703/205-3574
E-Mail: uncfmerck@uncf.org
Internet: www.uncf.org/merck

AMOUNT: $40,000/yr. (max.)

DEADLINE(S): JAN 31

FIELD(S): Life & Physical Sciences

Open to African-Americans enrolled full-time in a Ph.D. degree program and within 1-3 years of completing dissertation. Awards are intended to help students complete coursework, conduct research, and prepare dissertation for degree in the biomedically relevant life or physical sciences. Must be US citizen/permanent resident. Financial need NOT a factor.

12 awards annually. Not renewable. Contact Jerry Bryant, Ph.D., for an application.

1966 — UNCF/MERCK SCIENCE INITIATIVE (Postdoctoral Science Research Fellowships)

8260 Willow Oaks Corporate Dr.
PO Box 10444
Fairfax VA 22031-4511
703/205-3503
FAX: 703/205-3574
E-Mail: uncfmerck@uncf.org
Internet: www.uncf.org/merck

AMOUNT: $70,000/yr. (max.)

DEADLINE(S): JAN 31

FIELD(S): Life & Physical Sciences

Open to African-Americans who will receive a Ph.D. degree by the end of the current academic year and will be appointed as a postdoctoral fellow during the next calendar year. Awards are intended to support postgraduate students to obtain postdoctoral training and to prepare for a career in biomedical research. Must be US citizen/permanent resident. Financial need NOT a factor.

10 awards annually. Not renewable. Contact Jerry Bryant, Ph.D., for an application.

1967 — UNIVERSITY OF CALIFORNIA-DAVIS (Brad Webb Scholarship Fund)

Dept. Enology & Viticulture
Shield's Ave.
Davis CA 95616
530/752-2390 (undergrad) or 530/752-9246 (graduate)
Internet: faoman.ucdavis.edu

AMOUNT: Varies

DEADLINE(S): Varies

FIELD(S): Enology/Viticulture

Open to students attending or planning to attend UC Davis. Award is made in memory of Brad Webb, friend of NSRS President, Dan Cassidy.

Contact the Department of Enology & Viticulture for an application.

1968 — US DEPARTMENT OF DEFENSE (National Defense Science & Engineering Graduate Fellowship Programs)

200 Park Drive, Suite 211, P.O. Box 13444
Research Triangle Park, NC 27709-3444
919/549-8505

Internet: www.acq.osd.mil/ddre/edugate/s-aindx.html

AMOUNT: Full tuition and fees (tenure of 36 months)

DEADLINE(S): JAN

FIELD(S): Mathematical, physical, biological, ocean, and engineering sciences

Must be US citizens or nationals at or near the beginning of their graduate study in science or engineering, leading to a doctoral degree. NDSEG Fellowships are awarded for study and research in these disciplines of military importance.

Approximately 90 new three-year graduate fellowships each April. Fellows may choose appropriate US institutions of higher education, offering degrees in science and engineering. Contact the Program Administrator for more information.

1969 — WILSON ORNITHOLOGICAL SOCIETY (Fuertes, Nice, & Stewart Grants)

Museum of Zoology
Univ of Michigan
1109 Geddes Ave.
Ann Arbor MI 48109-1079
Internet: www.ummz.lsa.umich.edu/birds/wos.html

AMOUNT: $600 (Fuertes); $200 (Nice & Stewart)

DEADLINE(S): JAN 15

FIELD(S): Ornithology

Grants to support research on birds only—NOT for general college funding. Open to anyone presenting a suitable research problem in ornithology. Research proposal required.

5-6 awards annually. Not renewable. See website for an application.

1970 — WOODS HOLE OCEANOGRAPHIC INSTITUTION (Postdoctoral Awards in Ocean Science and Engineering)

360 Woods Hole Road
Woods Hole MA 02543-1541
508/289-2219
FAX: 508/457-2188
E-Mail: mgately@whoi.edu
Internet: www.whoi.edu

AMOUNT: Varies

DEADLINE(S): FEB 16

FIELD(S): Chemistry, Engineering, Geology, Geophysics, Mathematics, Meteorology, Physics, Biology, Oceanography

Eighteen-month postdoctoral scholar awards are offered to recipients of new or recent doctorates in the above fields. The awards are designed to further the education and training of the applicant with primary emphasis placed on the individual's research promise.

For an application/more information, contact the Education Office, Clark Laboratory 223, MS #31, at above address.

CHEMISTRY

1971 — AECI LIMITED (AECI Post Graduate Research Fellowship)

Private Bag X2
Modderfontein SOUTH AFRICA 1645
011/605-3100

AMOUNT: Varies (South African Rands 3600)

DEADLINE(S): SEP 30

FIELD(S): Chemistry, Physics, Metallurgy, Biochemistry, Microbiology, Chemical Engineering, Civil Engineering, Industrial Engineering, Electrical Engineering, Mechanical Engineering, Instrument Engineering

Open to South African citizens who are graduate students who want to do research in one of the above areas. This fellowship is offered to strengthen postgraduate study and research in South Africa, particularly in the fields above.

Write to the above address for complete information.

1972 — AFRICAN NETWORK OF SCIENTIFIC AND TECHNOLOGICAL INSTITUTIONS - ANSTI (Postgraduate Fellowships)

PO Box 30592
Nairobi Kenya AFRICA
254-2-621234 or 254-2-622619/20
FAX: 254-2-215991
E-Mail: j.massaquoi@unesco.org OR
ANSTI@Net2000ke.com

AMOUNT: Fees, subsistence, & international travel

DEADLINE(S): JUN

FIELD(S): Basic & Engineering Sciences

Scholarships for postgraduate studies outside of applicant's home country. Must be African nationals not older than 36 years of age and hold a good bachelor's degree (at least 2nd class upper division). Applicants should apply for admission to host university as soon as possible. Fellowships tenable only in African universities.

10 awards annually. Renewable up to 2 years. Contact Professor J.G.M. Massaquoi for an application.

1973 — AMERICAN ASSOCIATION FOR THE ADVANCEMENT OF SCIENCE (Science & Engineering Fellowships)

1200 New York Ave., NW
Washington DC 20005

202/326-6700
FAX: 202/289-4950
E-Mail: science_policy@aaas.org
Internet: www.aas.org

AMOUNT: $40,000+

DEADLINE(S): JAN 15

FIELD(S): Science; Engineering

Post-doctoral fellowships open to AAAS members or applicants concurrently applying for membership. Prospective fellows must demonstrate exceptional competence in an area of science or have a broad scientific or technical background. Those with MA degrees and at least three years of poast-degree professional experience may also apply.

U.S. citizenship required. For complete information on these one-year fellowships write to Director, Science Fellows Program at address above.

1974 — AMERICAN FOUNDATION FOR PHARMACEUTICAL EDUCATION (Predoctoral Fellowships)

One Church St., Suite 202
Rockville MD 20850
301/738-2160
FAX: 301/738-2161

AMOUNT: $6,000 to $10,000/yr.

DEADLINE(S): MAR 1

FIELD(S): Pharmacology

Several predoctoral fellowships for pharmaceutical students with no more than three years remaining to earn the Ph.D.

Student accepts a teaching appointment in a Pharmacy college. U.S. citizen or legal resident. Write for complete information.

1975 — AMERICAN FOUNDATION FOR THE BLIND (Paul W. Ruckes Scholarship)

11 Penn Plaza, Ste. 300
New York NY 10001
212/502-7661 or TDD 212/502-7771
E-Mail: juliet@afb.org
Internet: www.afb.org

AMOUNT: $1,000

DEADLINE(S): APR 30

FIELD(S): Engineering, computer, physical, or life sciences

Open to blind or visually impaired undergraduate or graduate students pursuing degrees in the above fields. U.S. citizenship required.

Write to the above address or visit website for complete information.

1976 — AMERICAN INDIAN SCIENCE AND ENGINEERING SOCIETY (EPA Tribal Lands Environmental Science Scholarship)

PO Box 9828
Albuquerque NM 87119-9828
505/765-1052
FAX: 505/765-5608
E-Mail: scholarships@aises.org
Internet: www.aises.org/scholarships

AMOUNT: $4,000

DEADLINE(S): JUN 15

FIELD(S): Biochemistry; Biology; Chemical Engineering; Chemistry; Entomology; Environmental Economics/Science; Hydrology; Environmental Studies

Open to American Indian college juniors, seniors, and graduate students enrolled full-time at an accredited institution. Must demonstrate financial need. Certificate of Indian blood NOT required.

Renewable. See website or contact Patricia Browne for an application.

1977 — AMERICAN SOCIETY FOR ENGINEERING EDUCATION (Army Research Laboratory Postdoctoral Fellowships)

1818 N St., NW, Ste. 600
Washington DC 20036
202/331-3525
FAX: 202/265-8504
E-Mail: projects@asee.org
Internet: www.asee.org/fellowship/

AMOUNT: $45,000-$55,000 + travel/relocation allowance

DEADLINE(S): Varies

FIELD(S): Engineering; Physical Sciences

Postdoctoral fellowships for US citizens/permanent residents to do research at Army Research Laboratories. Candidates must have completed their Ph.D. prior to appointment. Program is designed to increase involvement of creative and highly trained scientists and engineers from academia and industry in scientific and technical areas of interest and relevance to the Army. Research proposal should include clear objective and defined outcome. Financial need NOT a factor.

15 awards annually. Renewable. Contact Sandi Crawford at ASEE for an application packet.

1978 — AMERICAN WATER WORKS ASSOCIATION (Abel Wolman Fellowship)

6666 W. Quincy Ave.
Denver CO 80235
303/347-6206
FAX: 303/794-8915
E-Mail: vbaca@awwa.org
Internet: www.org/tande/eduframe.htm

AMOUNT: $15,000 stipend +$1,000 for supplies +up to $4,000 for tuition, etc.

DEADLINE(S): JAN 15

FIELD(S): Research in water supply and treatment

For students who show potential for leadership and anticipate completion of the requirments for a Ph.D. within two years of the award. Applicants will be evaluated on the quality of academic record, the significance of the proposed research to water supply and treatment, and the potential to do high quality research. Must be citizen or permanent resident of the U.S., Canada, or Mexico.

Renewable for a second year. Write for complete information.

1979 — AMERICAN WATER WORKS ASSOCIATION (Academic Achievement Award)

6666 West Quincy Ave.
Denver CO 80235
303/347-6206
FAX: 303/794-8915
E-Mail: vbaca@awwa.org
Internet: www.org/tande/eduframe.htm

AMOUNT: 1st place: $1,000; 2nd place: $500

DEADLINE(S): OCT 1

FIELD(S): Subject related to drinking water supply industry

Award for a master's thesis or doctoral dissertation that has potential value to the water supply industry. This is not a scholarship but a cash award for outstanding work that has been completed.

Write for complete information.

1980 — AMERICAN WATER WORKS ASSOCIATION (Holly A. Cornell Scholarship)

6666 W. Quincy Ave.
Denver CO 80235
303/347-6206
FAX: 303/794-8915
E-Mail: vbaca@awwa.org
Internet: www.org/tande/eduframe.htm

AMOUNT: $5,000

DEADLINE(S): JAN 15

FIELD(S): Engineering (Water Supply and Treatment)

Open to females and minorities (as defined by the U.S. Equal Opportunity Commission) who anticipate completion of a master's degree in engineering no sooner than December of the following year. Program was created by CH2M Hill, Inc. in honor of one of the firm's founders.

Contact organization for complete information.

1981 — AMERICAN WATER WORKS ASSOCIATION (Lars Scholarship)

6666 W. Quincy Ave.
Denver CO 80235
303/347-6206
FAX: 303/794-8915
E-Mail: vbaca@awwa.org
Internet: awwa.org/tande/eduframe.htm

AMOUNT: $5,000 (Masters); $7,000 (Ph.D.)

DEADLINE(S): JAN 15

FIELD(S): Science and Engineering in the field of Water Supply and/or Treatment

For M.A. and Ph.D. level students at an institution of higher learning in Canada, Guam, Puerto Rico, Mexico, or the United States. For research into water supply and/or treatment.

Write for complete information.

1982 — AMERICAN WATER WORKS ASSOCIATION (Thomas R. Camp Scholarship)

6666 W. Quincy Ave.
Denver CO 80235
303/347-6206
FAX: 303/794-8915
E-Mail: vbaca@awwa.org
Internet: www.org/tande/eduframe.htm

AMOUNT: $5,000

DEADLINE(S): JAN 15

FIELD(S): Research in the drinking water field

For students pursuing an M.A. or Ph.D. in the field of drinking water. This award is granted to Doctoral students in even years and Master's students in odd years. Can be used at an institution of higher education in Canada, Guam, Puerto rico, Mexico, or the U.S.

One award each year. Contact above location for details.

1983 — ASSOCIATED WESTERN UNIVERSITIES, INC. (AWU Faculty Fellowships)

4190 South Highland Dr., Suite 211
Salt Lake City UT 84124-2600
801-273-8900

AMOUNT: Varies.

DEADLINE(S): FEB 15

FIELD(S): Engineering, Mathematics, Science, Technology

Research fellowships for qualified college and university faculty members to encourage participation and contribution to research at one of 62 cooperating facilities. It is not necessary to be enrolled at an AWU member institution. Collaborations that include graduate and/or undergraduate students are encouraged.

For detailed information and list of cooperating facilities, contact above location.

1984 — ASSOCIATED WESTERN UNIVERSITIES, INC. (AWU Graduate Fellowship Program)

4190 South Highland Dr. Suite 211
Salt Lake City, UT 84124-2600
801/273-8900

AMOUNT: Stipend ($1,300 per month & up) + tuition assistance and travel allowance

DEADLINE(S): FEB 15

FIELD(S): Engineering, Mathematics, Science, Technology

Open to master's and doctoral degree candidates to conduct research toward a thesis or dissertation at one of more than 62 cooperating facilities. Institutional affiliation and citizenship restrictions may apply for some awards or facilities. It is not necessary to be enrolled at an AWU member institution to apply for a fellowship.

Write to the above address for complete information.

1985 — ASSOCIATED WESTERN UNIVERSITIES, INC. (AWU Postgraduate Fellowship)

4190 South Highland Dr. Suite 211
Salt Lake City UT 84124-2600
801/273-8900

AMOUNT: Stipend established by the host facility and varies by experience and discipline.

DEADLINE(S): Varies (Two to three months before the starting date)

FIELD(S): Engineering, Mathematics, Science, Technology

For college and university graduates who have completed all institutional requirements for an advanced degree from an accredited college or university in the U.S. A commitment to a professional career in science or engineering research is expected. U.S. citizenship or permanent resident status is required. Research is to be done at one of the 62 cooperating universities.

For detailed information and a list of cooperating facilities contact above address.

1986 — ASSOCIATED WESTERN UNIVERSITIES, INC. (AWU Visiting Scientist Fellowships)

4190 South Highland Dr., Suite 211
Salt Lake City UT 84124-2600
801/273-8900

AMOUNT: Varies

DEADLINE(S): Varies (Two months prior to starting date)

FIELD(S): Engineering, Science, Mathematics, and Technology

Research fellowships for professionals with continued commitment to science and engineering.

For use at one of 62 participating universities. US citizenship or permanent residency required.

For detailed information and list of cooperating facitilies contact above location.

1987 — ASSOCIATION FOR WOMEN IN SCIENCE EDUCATIONAL FOUNDATION (AWIS Predoctoral Awards)

1200 New York Ave. NW, Suite 650
Washington DC 20005
202/326-8940 or 800-886-AWIS
E-Mail: awis@awis.org
Internet: www.awis.org

AMOUNT: $1,000

DEADLINE(S): JAN 16

FIELD(S): Various Sciences and Social Sciences

Scholarships for female doctoral students. Summary page, description of research project, resume, references, transcripts, and biographical sketch required. US citizens may study at any graduate institution; non-citizens must study at US institutions.

5-10 awards annually. See website or write to above address for an application and complete information.

1988 — ASSOCIATION FOR WOMEN IN SCIENCE EDUCATIONAL FOUNDATION (AWIS Pre-doctoral Awards)

1200 New York Ave. NW, Suite 650
Washington DC 20005
202/326-8940 or 800/886-AWIS
E-Mail: awis@awis.org
Internet: www.awis.org

AMOUNT: $1,000

DEADLINE(S): JAN 16

FIELD(S): Various Sciences and Social Sciences

Scholarships for female doctoral students. Summary page, description of research project, resume, references, transcripts, and biographical sketch required. US citizens may study at any graduate institution; non-citizens must be enrolled in US institutions.

5-10 awards annually. See website or write to above address for an application and more information.

1989 — ASSOCIATION FOR WOMEN IN SCIENCE EDUCATIONAL FOUNDATION (Ruth Satter Memorial Award)

1200 New York Ave., NW, Suite 650
Washington DC 20005
202/326-8940 or 800/886-AWIS
E-Mail: awis@awis.org
Internet: www.awis.org

AMOUNT: $1,000

DEADLINE(S): JAN 16

FIELD(S): Various Sciences and Social Sciences

Scholarships for female doctoral students who have interrupted their education for at least three years to raise a family. Summary page, description of research project, resume, references, transcripts, biographical sketch, and letter from your department to confirm eligibility required. US citizens may study at any graduate institution; non-citizens must attend US institutions.

See website or write to above address for more information or an application.

1990 — ASSOCIATION FOR WOMEN IN SCIENCE EDUCATIONAL FOUNDATION (Ruth Satter Memorial Award)

1200 New York Ave. NW, Suite 650
Washington DC 20005
202/326-8940 or 800/886-AWIS
E-Mail: awis@awis.org
Internet: www.awis.org

AMOUNT: $1,000

DEADLINE(S): JAN 16

FIELD(S): Various Sciences and Social Sciences

Scholarships for female doctoral students who have interrupted their education three years or more to raise a family. Summary page, description of research project, resume, references, transcripts, biographical sketch, and proof of eligibility from department head required. US citizens may attend any graduate institution; non-citizens must be enrolled in US institutions.

See website or write to above address for more information or an application.

1991 — AT&T BELL LABORATORIES (Graduate Research Program For Women)

101 Crawfords Corner Road
Holmdel NJ 07733-3030
Written inquiry

AMOUNT: Full tuition & fees + $13,200 stipend per year

DEADLINE(S): JAN 15

FIELD(S): Engineering; Math; Sciences; Computer Science

For women students who have been accepted into an accredited doctoral program for the following fall. U.S. citizen or permanent resident.

Fellowships are renewable for up to 5 years of graduate study. Write to special programs manager-GRPW for complete information.

1992 — AUSTRALIAN FEDERATION OF UNIVERSITY WOMEN - WESTERN AUSTRALIA (Mary & Elsie Stevens Bursary)

Bursary Liaison Officer
PO Box 48
Nedlands WA 6009 AUSTRALIA
Written Inquiry

AMOUNT: Aus$1,750

DEADLINE(S): JUL 31

FIELD(S): Mathematics or Physical Sciences, such as Physics, Chemistry, Geology, Astronomy, or other innate sciences

Bursary is to support women graduates of a Western Australian University to complete a higher degree or post-doctoral research in Mathematics or one of the Physical Sciences at a recognized university in any country or women who have been accepted to work toward a higher degree at a university in Western Australia.

Membership in AFUW or in IFUW is required. Write for complete information.

1993 — AUSTRALIAN FEDERATION OF UNIVERSITY WOMEN - WESTERN AUSTRALIA (Mary & Ilsie Stevens Bursary)

Bursary Liaison Officer
PO Box 48
Nedlands WA 6009 AUSTRALIA
Written Inquiry

AMOUNT: Aus$1,750

DEADLINE(S): JUL 31

FIELD(S): Mathematics or Physical sciences, such as Physics, Chemistry, Geology, Astronomy, or other innate sciences

Bursary is to support women graduates of a recognized university to complete a higher degree or post-doctoral research in Mathematics or in one of the Physical Sciences at a university in Western Australia.

Membership in AFUW or in IFUW is required. Write for complete information.

1994 — BIOCHEMICAL SOCIETY (General Travel Fund)

59 Portland Place
London W1N 3AJ ENGLAND UK
0171 299 4439
FAX: 0171 637 3626
E-Mail: alisonm@biochemsoc.org.uk
Internet: www.biochemsoc.org.uk

AMOUNT: up to 500 pounds sterling

DEADLINE(S): JAN 1; MAR 1; MAY 1; SEP 1

FIELD(S): Biochemistry

Grants for 3rd+ year doctorate/postdoctorate members of the Biochemical Society in meeting the cost of attending scientific meetings or short visits to other laboratories. Meetings must have substantial biochemical content, and the applicant must give evidence of active participation in the meeting. Members resident in the UK and Irish Republic may go to a meeting anywhere in the world. Those resident elsewhere must go to meetings in the UK or Irish Republic.

Travel restrictions relaxed for FEBS and IUBMB meetings. New members may apply after they have been a member for two years. Contact the Assistant Director, Personnel and Administration, for an application.

1995 — BIOCHEMICAL SOCIETY (Krebs Memorial Scholarship)

59 Portland Place
London W1N 3AJ ENGLAND UK
0171 299 4439
FAX: 0171 637 3626
E-Mail: alisonm@biochemsoc.org.uk
Internet: www.biochemsoc.org.uk

AMOUNT: Varies (maintenance grant + necessary fees)

DEADLINE(S): APR 30

FIELD(S): Biochemistry

Biochemistry or allied biomedical science scholarships are tenable at any British university. For those studying for a Ph.D., especially for those whose careers have been interrupted for non-academic reasons beyond their own control and/or who are unlikely to qualify for an award from public funds. Application should be forwarded through head of department concerned who must be able to place applicant in top 5% Ph.D. candidates. Postdoctoral candidates may apply.

Renewable up to three years. Scholarship not available to new applicants until previous applicant's tenure has come to close. Contact the Assistant Director, Personnel and Administration, for an application.

1996 — BOEING (Polish Graduate Student Scholarship Program)

Phone for details
314/234-2149

AMOUNT: Tuition, books, and fees for three years

DEADLINE(S): Varies

FIELD(S): Scientific and technical fields

Scholarships for students from Poland to pursue graduate studies in scientific and technical areas at American colleges or universities.

Call Jim Schlueter at above telephone number.

1997 — BROOKHAVEN NATIONAL LABORATORY (Post-doctoral Research Associateships)

Brookhaven National Laboratory
Upton L.I. NY 11973-5000
516/344-3336

AMOUNT: $29,000 minimum

DEADLINE(S): Varies

FIELD(S): Chemistry, Physics, Materials Science, Biology, Oceanography, and Biomedical Sciences.

Post-doctoral research associateships tenable at Brookhaven National Laboratory for research to promote fundamental and applied research in the above fields. A recent doctoral degree is required.

25 associateships per year. Renewable for two additional years.

1998 — BROOKHAVEN WOMEN IN SCIENCE (Renate W. Chasman Scholarship)

PO Box 183
Upton NY 11973-5000
E-mail: pam@bnl.gov

AMOUNT: $2,000

DEADLINE(S): APR 1

FIELD(S): Natural Sciences; Engineering; Mathematics

Open ONLY to women who are residents of the boroughs of Brooklyn or Queens or the counties of Nassau or Suffolk in New York who are re-entering school after a period of study. For juniors, seniors, or first-year graduate students.

1 award annually. Not renewable. Contact Pam Mansfield at above location for an application. Phone calls are NOT accepted.

1999 — CANADIAN SOCIETY FOR CHEMISTRY (Ichikizaki Fund for Young Chemists)

130 Slater St., Ste. 550
Ottawa Ontario KIP 6E2 CANADA
613/232-6252
FAX: 613/232-5862
E-Mail: cic_prog@fox.nstn.ca
Internet: www.chem-inst-can.org

AMOUNT: $10,000 (max.)

DEADLINE(S): DEC 31

FIELD(S): Organic Chemistry

For young chemists who show unique achievements in basic research to aid in attending international conferences/symposia. Must be member of CSC or Chemical Society of Japan, not have passed 34th birthday, have research specialty in synthetic organic chemistry, & be scheduled to attend (within 1 year) an international conference/symposium directly related to this area. Must submit resume, copies of research papers, proposed budget, & title of paper to be presented.

10 awards annually. Renewable with reapplication. Contact the Program Manager, Awards, for an application. Award is primarily for established researchers, but postgraduates and graduates also considered.

2000 — CHEMICAL INSTITUTE OF CANADA (Pestcon Graduate Scholarship)

130 Slater St., Ste. 550
Ottawa Ontario KIP 6E2 CANADA
613/232-6252
FAX: 613/232-5862

E-Mail: cic_prog@fox.nstn.ca
Internet: www.chem-inst-can.org

AMOUNT: $3,000

DEADLINE(S): MAR 1

FIELD(S): Pesticide & Contaminant Research

Open to Canadian students (including landed immigrants) for graduate study in any area of pesticide and contaminant research, including alternative pest control strategies. Preference given to students already actively engaged in a research program. Along with application, candidate must submit curriculum vitae, project description, offical transcript, supervisor's name & address, and reference name & address.

1 award annually. Contact the Program Manager, Awards, for an application. Award is announced prior to June 1st, and payment is in two equal installments (October 1st & January 1st, depending on satisfactory academic progress).

2001 — CONCORDIA UNIVERSITY (Mrs. Tauba W. Landsberger Award)

Dept. Chemistry
1455 de Maisonneuve Blvd. West
H 1139
Montreal Quebec H3G 1M8 CANADA
514/848-3809
FAX: 514/848-2812
E-Mail: awardsgs@vax2.concordia.ca

AMOUNT: US $500

DEADLINE(S): SEP 20

FIELD(S): Chemistry; Biochemistry

This award is given to a master's or doctoral student doing research in analytical chemistry. The award will be granted on the basis of academic excellence and will be chosen by the Department of Chemistry & Biochemistry.

1 award annually. Not renewable. Contact the Chair at the Department of Chemistry & Biochemistry at Concordia University for an application.

2002 — COOPERATIVE INSTITUTE FOR RESEARCH IN ENVIRONMENTAL SCIENCES (CIRES Visiting Fellowships)

Univ Colorado
Campus Box 216
Boulder CO 80309-0216
303/492-1143
Internet: cires.colorado.edu/ciresvf.html

AMOUNT: Varies

DEADLINE(S): DEC 15

FIELD(S): Environmental & Earth Sciences

One-year visiting fellowships for recent Ph.D.s and senior scientists, including faculty on sabbatical. To be used towards research in the areas of physics, chemistry, & dynamics of Earth system; global &

regional environmental change; climate system monitoring, diagnostics, & modeling; and remote sensing measurement techniques. Must submit curriculum vitae, publications list, 2-4 page description of proposed research, and letters of recommendation.

5 awards annually. Renewable. See website or contact CIRES for an application. CIRES receives sponsorship from the National Oceanic and Atmosphere Administration's Environmental Research Laboritories.

2003 — ELECTROCHEMICAL SOCIETY (Summer Research Fellowships)

10 S. Main St.
Pennington NJ 08534
609/737-1902
FAX: 609/737-2745
E-Mail: ecs@electrtochem
Internet: www.electrochem.org

AMOUNT: $4,000 (ECS); $3,000 (DOE)

DEADLINE(S): JAN 1

FIELD(S): Energy; Chemical Engineering; Chemistry; Electrical Engineering

Summer fellowships are open to graduate students at accredited colleges and universities in any country. Purpose is to support research of interest to ECS, such as research aimed at reducing energy consumption.

8 awards annually (3 ECS, 5 Department of Energy). Contact ECS for an application.

2004 — ENGINEERING & PHYSICAL SCIENCES RESEARCH COUNCIL (Studentships)

North Star Ave
Polaris House
Swindon SN2 1ET England
01 793-444000

AMOUNT: Maintenance & approved fees

DEADLINE(S): JUL 31

FIELD(S): Engineering & Physical Science

Research studentships for up to 3 years for Ph.D students, 1 year advanced course studentships for master's students. Tenable at U.K. institutions. Must be UK resident with relevant connection to UK for full award or with European Union member state with relevant connection to UK for fees-only award. Must have appropriate academic qualifications.

Approx 3,800 awards per year. Applications must be made through heads of departments. EPSRC does not accept applications direct from students. Write for complete information.

2005 — EPILEPSY FOUNDATION OF AMERICA (Pre-doctoral Research Training Fellowship)

4351 Garden City Drive
Landover MD 20785-2267
301/459-3700 or 800/EFA-1000

FAX: 301/577-2684
TDD: 800/332-2070
E-Mail: postmaster@efa.org
Internet: www.efa.org

AMOUNT: up to $15,000

DEADLINE(S): SEP 1

FIELD(S): Epilepsy as related to Neuroscience, Physiology, Pharmacology, Psychology, Biochemistry, Genetics, Nursing, or Pharmacy

One-year of support for qualified individuals who are pursuing dissertation research with an epilepsy-related theme, and who are working under the guidance of a mentor with expertise in the area of epilepsy investigation. Graduate students pursuing Ph.D. degree in above fields may apply.

Contact EFA for an application.

2006 — EPPLEY FOUNDATION FOR RESEARCH (Postdoctoral Research Grants)

245 Park Avenue
40th Floor
New York NY 10167
Written inquiry

AMOUNT: Up to $25,000

DEADLINE(S): FEB 1; MAY 1; AUG 1; NOV 1

FIELD(S): Physical Sciences; Biological Sciences

Postdoctoral grants for original advanced research in any of the physical or biological sciences. Open to established research scientists who are attached to a recognized institution.

Write for complete information.

2007 — FORD FOUNDATION/NATIONAL RESEARCH COUNCIL (Postdoctoral Fellowship for Minorities)

National Research Council
2101 Constitution Ave.
Washington DC 20418
202/334-2860
E-Mail: infofell@nas.edu
Internet: http//www.nas.edu/fo/index.html

AMOUNT: $25,000 + relocation and research allowance

DEADLINE(S): JAN 3

FIELD(S): Life and physical sciences, mathematics, engineering sciences, behavioral and social sciences, and the humanities

For U.S. citizens who received a Ph.D or Sc.D in the last 7 years and who are Native Amer. Indian or Alaskan, Black/African American, Mexican American, Native Pacific Islander, or Puerto Rican and who are or plan to be in a teaching or research career.

Contact above website or address for complete information.

2008 — FORD FOUNDATION/NATIONAL RESEARCH COUNCIL (Predoctoral/Dissertation Fellowships for Minorities)

2101 Constitution Ave.
Washington DC 20418
202/334-2872
E-Mail: infofell@nas.edu
Internet: http//www.nas.edu/fo/index.html

AMOUNT: $14,000 annual stipend + $6,000 grant to institution; $18,000 for dissertation fellowship

DEADLINE(S): NOV 3

FIELD(S): Most fields of study: sciences, humanities, engineering, behavioral science, social sciences, and computer science

Predoctoral and dissertation fellowships for students whose ethnicity is Alaskan Native, Black/African American, Mexican American/Chicano, Native American Indian, Native Pacific Islander, or Puerto Rican. For research-based programs leading to careers in college teaching and research.

Contact above address or website.

2009 — FOUNDATION FOR SCIENCE AND DISABILITY, INC. (FSD Science Student Grant Fund)

503 NW 89th Street
Gainesville FL 32607-1400
352/374-5774
FAX: 352/374-5781
E-Mail: rmankin@gainesville.usda.ufl.edu

AMOUNT: $1,000

DEADLINE(S): DEC 1

FIELD(S): Mathematics; Science; Medicine; Engineering; Computer Science

Open to graduate students with disabilities. May also apply as a fourth-year undergraduate accepted into a graduate or professional program. Awards are for some special purpose in connection with a science project or thesis in any of above fields. Student is required to write a 250-word essay which includes a description of professional goals/objectives, as well as purpose of grant. Transcripts and two letters of recommendation from faculty members are also required.

Contact Dr. Richard Mankin at above address for an application.

2010 — GEORGETOWN UNIVERSITY (Doctoral Program in Chemistry)

Department of Chemistry
Washington DC 20057-1227
202/687-6073

AMOUNT: Tuition + $16,920 stipend/12 months

DEADLINE(S): None

FIELD(S): Chemistry

Doctoral fellowships at Georgetown University are open to students who have their BA/BS or equivalent degree and have been accepted by the university as Ph.D. candidates in chemistry.

45-55 awards annually. Renewable. Contact the Department of Chemistry for an application.

2011 — H. FLETCHER BROWN FUND (Scholarships)

c/o PNC Bank
Trust Dept.
P.O. Box 791
Wilmington DE 19899
302/429-1186

AMOUNT: Varies

DEADLINE(S): APR 15

FIELD(S): Medicine; Dentistry; Law; Engineering; Chemistry

Open to U.S. citizens born in Delaware and still residing in Delaware. For 4 years of study (undergrad or grad) leading to a degree that enables applicant to practice in chosen field.

Scholarships are based on need, scholastic achievement, and good moral character. Applications available in February. Write for complete information.

2012 — INSTITUTE OF PAPER SCIENCE AND TECHNOLOGY (Fellowship Program)

500 10th St. NW
Atlanta GA 30318
404/853-9500

AMOUNT: Full tuition plus $11,250 stipend

DEADLINE(S): MAR 15

FIELD(S): Chemistry; Chemical Engineering; Physics; Biology; Mechanical Engineering; Pulp and Paper Technology

Open to graduate students who are U.S., Mexican, or Canadian citizens or legal residents who hold a BS degree in the above fields. For a pursuit of a master of Science or Ph.D degree at the institute.

35 fellowships annually. Address inquiries to director of admissions.

2013 — INTERNATIONAL SCHOOL OF CRYSTALLOGRAPHY (Postgraduate Courses)

Piazza di Porta San Donato 1
40126 Bologna ITALY
39 051 243556
FAX: 39 051 243336
E-Mail: riva@geomin.unibo.it
Internet: www.geomin.unibo.it/orgv/erice/erice.htm

AMOUNT: Half to full subsistence + fees

DEADLINE(S): NOV 30

FIELD(S): Solid State Chemistry; Physics; Molecular Biology; Molecular Biophysics; Pharmaceutics

Open to young postgraduates to pursue interdisciplinary studies in crystallography in Erice, Sicily, Italy. Must speak English and have some experience in the topic to be discussed (topics change every year). These 15-day courses are held at the International Foundation and Centre for Scientific Culture—Ettore Majorana.

See website or contact Lodovico Riva di Sanseverino for an application.

2014 — KING FAISAL FOUNDATION (Graduate Scholarship Program)

PO Box 352
Riyadh 11411 SAUDI ARABIA
966/1 465-2255
FAX: 966/1 465-6524
E-Mail: info@kff.com OR mprd@kff.com
Internet: www.kff.com OR
www.kingfaisalfoundation.org

AMOUNT: $400/mo. US allowance + tuition/fees paid directly to university + health insurance & travel

DEADLINE(S): None

FIELD(S): Medicine; Engineering; Physics; Chemistry; Geology

Open to graduate students who are Muslims under the age of 40. Must have BS degree, GPA of 86% or higher, and be accepted unconditionally by a university either in Europe or North America. Must be fluent in the language of area providing the studies. Selection based on academic performance.

Contact King Faisal Foundation for an application.

2015 — LOUISIANA OFFICE OF STUDENT FINANCIAL ASSISTANCE (Tuition Opportunity Program for Students-Teachers Award)

PO Box 91202
Baton Rouge LA 70821-9202
800/259-5626, ext. 1012
FAX: 504/922-0790
Internet: www.osfa.state.la.us

AMOUNT: $4,000/yr. (education majors); $6,000/yr. (math/chemistry majors)

DEADLINE(S): JUN 1

FIELD(S): Education; Math; Chemistry

Open to Louisiana residents pursuing undergraduate or graduate study at Louisiana colleges/universities and majoring in one of the above fields leading to teacher certification. Loans are forgiven by working as a certified teacher in Louisiana one year for each year loan is received.

Apply by completing the Free Application for Federal Student Aid (FAFSA). See your school's financial aid office or contact LOSFA for FAFSA form.

2016 — MATHESON GAS PRODUCTS FOUNDATION (Scholarships)

PO Box 624
959 Rte. 46 E.
Parsippany NJ 07054-0624
Internet: www.mathesongas.com

AMOUNT: $5,000

DEADLINE(S): None

FIELD(S): Chemistry; Physics; Chemical Engineering; Material Science; Semiconductor Engineering

Open to financially needy graduate students who are African American, Latino, Asian, Native American, or female. Must be US citizens/permanent residents studying in above fields or related area.

Send self-addressed, stamped envelope to Jerry Cantrella, Director of Personnel, for an application.

2017 — NAACP NATIONAL OFFICE (NAACP Willems Scholarship)

4805 Mount Hope Drive
Baltimore MD 21215
401/358-8900

AMOUNT: $2,000 undergrads; $3,000 grads

DEADLINE(S): APR 30

FIELD(S): Engineering; Chemistry; Physics; Mathematics

Open to NAACP male members majoring in one of the above areas. Undergrads must have GPA of 2.5+; graduates' GPAs must be 3.0+. Renewable if the required GPA is maintained.

Financial need must be established. Two letters of recommendation typed on letterhead from teachers or professors in the major field of specialization. Write for complete information. Include a legal size, self-addressed, stamped envelope.

2018 — NATIONAL AERONAUTICS AND SPACE ADMINISTRATION (Graduate Student Researcher's Program-Underrepresented Minority Focus)

Mail Code FEH
NASA Headquarters
Washington, DC 20546
202/453-8344

AMOUNT: $22,000 1st year, renewable up to 3 years

DEADLINE(S): FEB 1

FIELD(S): Science, Engineering, Mathematics

For underrepresented minority groups in the fields of science and engineering (including African-Americans, American Indians, Hispanics, and Pacific Islanders), who may end up with a career in space science and/or aerospace technology. Must be US citizen and enrolled or accepted as a full-time graduate student at an accredited US college or university.

Write for complete information.

2019 — NATIONAL ASSOCIATION OF WATER COMPANIES—NEW JERSEY CHAPTER (Scholarship)

Elizabethtown Water Co.
600 South Ave.
Westfield NJ 07090
908/654-1234
FAX: 908/232-2719

AMOUNT: $2,500

DEADLINE(S): APR 1

FIELD(S): Business Administration; Biology; Chemistry; Engineering; Communications

For U.S. citizens who have lived in NJ at least 5 years and plan a career in the investor-owned water utility industry in disciplines such as those above. Must be undergrad or graduate student in a 2- or 4-year NJ college or university.

GPA of 3.0 or better required. Contact Gail P. Brady for complete information.

2020 — NATIONAL CENTER FOR ATMOSPHERIC RESEARCH (Graduate Student Research Fellowships)

PO Box 3000
Boulder CO 80307
303/497-1601
FAX: 303/497-1646
E-Mail: barbm@ucar.edu
Internet: www.asp.ucar.edu

AMOUNT: $16,810/yr. + travel

DEADLINE(S): Varies

FIELD(S): Atmospheric Sciences

Open to graduate students to support university Ph.D. thesis research conducted in collaboration with NCAR scientists.

Contact administrator Barbara Hansford for availability information.

2021 — NATIONAL PARKS SERVICE (Science Scholars Program)

1849 C St., NW
Washington DC 20240
202/208-6843
E-Mail: aspiceland@goparks.org
Internet: www.nps.gov

AMOUNT: $25,000/yr.

DEADLINE(S): JUN 15

FIELD(S): Biological, Physical, Social, & Cultural Sciences

Three-year scholarships to Ph.D. candidates pursuing degrees in above fields. Objectives are to encourage young scientists to engage in park-related research, conduct innovative research on issues central to the National Parks, and encourage use of parks as laboratories for sciences. NPF will transfer the scholarship funds to each student's university, providing for tuition, field work, stipend, & other research expenses. Must submit research proposal.

4 awards annually. See website or contact Dr. Gary E. Machlis, Program Director, at NPS for an application. Winners announced shortly after August 15th.

2022 — NATIONAL PHYSICAL SCIENCE CONSORTIUM (Graduate Fellowships for Minorities & Women in the Physical Sciences)

MSC 3NPS
Box 30001
Las Cruces NM 88003-8001
800/952-4118 or 505/646-6038
FAX: 505/646-6097
E-Mail: npse@nmsu.edu
Internet: www.npsc.org

AMOUNT: $12,500 (years 1-4); $15,000 (years 5-6)

DEADLINE(S): NOV 5

FIELD(S): Astronomy; Chemistry; Computer Science; Geology; Materials Science; Mathematics; Physics

Open to "all US citizens" with an emphasis on Black, Hispanic, Native American, and female students. Must be pursuing graduate studies and have a minimum 3.0 GPA.

Renewable up to 6 years. See website or contact NPSC for an application.

2023 — NATIONAL RESEARCH COUNCIL (Howard Hughes Medical Institute Predoctoral Fellowships in Biological Sciences)

2101 Constitution, Ave.
Washington DC 20418
202/334-2872
FAX: 202/334-2872
E-Mail: infofell@nas.edu
Internet: national-academics.org/osep.fo

AMOUNT: $16,000 stipend + tuition at US institution

DEADLINE(S): NOV 9

FIELD(S): Biochemistry; Biophysics; Epidemiology; Genetics; Immunology; Microbiology; Neuroscience; Pharmacology; Physiology; Virology

Five-year award is open to college seniors and first-year graduate students pursuing a Ph.D. or Sc.D. degree. US citizens/nationals may choose any institution in the US or abroad; foreign students must choose US institution. Based on ability, academic records, proposed study/research, previous experience, reference reports, and GRE scores.

80 awards annually. See website or contact NRC for an application.

2024 — NATIONAL RESEARCH COUNCIL OF CANADA (Research Associateships)

Research Associates Office
Ottawa Ontario K1A 0R6 CANADA
613/993-9150
FAX: 613/990-7669
Internet: www.nrc.ca/careers

AMOUNT: $39,366 Canadian

DEADLINE(S): None

FIELD(S): Natural Sciences; Engineering

Two-year research associateships are tenable at NRCC labs throughout Canada. Open to recent Ph.D.s in natural sciences or recent master's or Ph.D.s in engineering. Degrees should have been received within the last five years. Preference given to Canadians.

Renewable. See website or contact NRCC for an application.

2025 — NATIONAL RESEARCH FOUNDATION (NRF Honors & Postgraduate Bursaries)

PO Box 2600
Pretoria 0001 SOUTH AFRICA
+27 012/481-4000
FAX: +27 012/349-1179
E-Mail: info@nrf.ac.za
Internet: www.nrf.ac.za

AMOUNT: Varies

DEADLINE(S): Varies

FIELD(S): Agriculture; Chemistry; Earth Sciences; Engineering; Biology; Mathematics; Physics; Forestry; Veterinary Science; Pharmaceutics

Open to South African citizens pursuing graduate/postgraduate studies in above fields.

500 awards annually. Contact NRF for an application.

2026 — NATIONAL SCIENCES AND ENGINEERING RESEARCH COUNCIL OF CANADA (Graduate Scholarships)

Scholarships/Fellowships Division
350 Albert Street
Ottawa Ontario K1A 1H5 CANADA
613/996-3769
FAX: 613/996-2589
E-Mail: schol@nserc.ca
Internet: http://www.nserc.ca

AMOUNT: $15,700/year for 1st & 2nd years at masters or Ph.D level; $17,400/year (Ph.D level ONLY) 3rd & 4th years

DEADLINE(S): NOV 24

FIELD(S): Natural Sciences, Engineering, Biology, or Chemistry

Open to Canadian citizens or permanent residents who have earned or will soon earn a bachelors or masters degree in science or engineering. Academic excellence and research aptitude are considerations.

Write for complete information.

2027 — NATIONAL SCIENCES AND ENGINEERING RESEARCH COUNCIL OF CANADA (Postdoctoral Fellowships)

Scholarships/Fellowships Division
350 Albert Street
Ottawa Ontario K1A 1H5 CANADA
613/996-3762
FAX: 613/996-2589
E-Mail: schol@nserc.ca
Internet: http://www.nserc.ca

AMOUNT: Individually negotiated

DEADLINE(S): Varies—average: $43,000

FIELD(S): Natural Sciences, Engineering, Biology, or Chemistry

Open to Canadian citizens or permanent residents who hold doctoral degrees in science or engineering. Academic excellence and research aptitude are considerations.

Write for complete information.

2028 — NOVARTIS FOUNDATION (Bursary Scheme)

41 Portland Place
London W1N 4BN ENGLAND UK
+44 171 636 9456
FAX: +44 171 436 2840
E-Mail: abrown@novartisfound.org.uk
Internet: www.novartisfound.org.uk

AMOUNT: Travel & subsistence—up to $6,000/person

DEADLINE(S): Varies

FIELD(S): Science; Medicine

Travel fellowships to young scientists (postgrad/doc) to attend international meetings in connection with the Novartis Foundation Symposia. Must be between the ages of 23 and 35, and be active in the field of science in question. Symposia is normally in London, and a 4-week to 12-week host laboratory in the department of one of the symposium participants follows. Specific topics vary. Must submit qualifications, resume, career history/goals, and research interests.

8 awards annually. Not renewable. See website or contact Allyson Brown for application procedures.

2029 — OAK RIDGE ASSOCIATED UNIVERSITIES (National Science Foundation Graduate Research Fellowships)

PO Box 3010
Oak Ridge TN 37831-3010
423/241-4300

FAX: 423/241-4513
E-Mail: nsfgrfp@orau.gov
Internet: www.orau.gov/nsf/nsffel.htm
AMOUNT: $15,000 stipend + $10,500 tuition allowance
DEADLINE(S): NOV 4
FIELD(S): Science; Math; Engineering; Computer Science

Three-year fellowships for graduate study leading to research-based master's or doctoral degrees in the above fields. Must be US citizens, nationals, or permanent residents at the time of application. Fellowships are awarded on the basis of ability. Women, minorities, and those with disabilities are strongly encouraged to apply. One-time International Research Travel Allowance available.

1,000 awards annually. Contact Jeannette Bouchard for an application/more information.

2030 — OAK RIDGE INSTITUTE FOR SCIENCE AND EDUCATION (Applied Health Physics Fellowship Program)

P.O. Box 117
Oak Ridge TN 37831-0117
423/576-2194 or 423/576-9279
E-Mail: COXRE@ORAU.GOV or GRADFELL@ORAU.GOV
AMOUNT: $14,400 stipend + tuition and fees up to $9,000/yr paid to university + transportation costs up to $300/month
DEADLINE(S): JAN 26
FIELD(S): Engineering, mathematics, physical and life sciences

Fellowship in applied health physics to implement DOE's nuclear energy-related mission. Candidates must have B.A. degree in life or physical sciences, engineering, or mathematics. Recipients are subject to a service obligation of one year of full-time employment in a DOE facility for each academic year of fellowhip award.

For details and application, contact above location.

2031 — OAK RIDGE INSTITUTE FOR SCIENCE AND EDUCATION (Industrial Hygiene Graduate Fellowship Program)

P.O. Box 117
Oak Ridge TN 37831-0117
423-576-9655
FAX: 423/576-8293
E-Mail: kinneym@orau.gov
AMOUNT:
DEADLINE(S): JAN 26
FIELD(S): Industrial Hygiene

A fellowship for first-year master's candidates who have undergraduate degrees in physical, life, environmental, or health sciences or enginering and who wish to pursue studies in industrial hygiene.

For details and application, contact above location.

2032 — OAK RIDGE INSTITUTE FOR SCIENCE AND EDUCATION (Professional Internship Program/Oak Ridge National Laboratory)

P.O. Box 117
Oak Ridge TN 37831-0117
423/576-3426
423/576-3427
AMOUNT: $210 to $300/week + travel, tuition, and fees
DEADLINE(S): FEB 5; JUN 1; OCT 1
FIELD(S): Chemistry, environmental science, geology, hydrogeology, hydrology, chemical engineering, civil engineering, environmental engineering, mechanical engineering, computer science (technical database development)

Opportunities for graduates and undergraduates to participate in energy-related research projects that correlate with their academic and career goals. For 3 to 12 consecutive months.

Funded through Oak Ridge National Laboratory.

2033 — OAK RIDGE INSTITUTE FOR SCIENCE AND EDUCATION (Professional Internship Program/Pittsburgh Energy Technology Center)

P.O. Box 117
Oak Ridge TN 37831-0117
423/576-3426
423/576-3427
AMOUNT: $235 to $325/week + travel, tuition, and fees
DEADLINE(S): FEB 5; JUN 1; OCT 1
FIELD(S): Chemistry, physics, environmental science, geology, chemical or environmental engineering, computer science, or statistics.

Opportunities for graduates and undergraduates to participate in fossil energy-related research projects that correlate with their academic and career goals. For 3 to 12 consecutive months.

Funded through U.S. Dept. of Energy, Office of Fossil Energy, and Pittsburgh Energy Technology Center.

2034 — OAK RIDGE INSTITUTE FOR SCIENCE AND EDUCATION (Professional Internship Program/Savannah River Site)

P.O. Box 117
Oak Ridge TN 37831-0117
423/576-3426
423/576-3427
AMOUNT: $260 to $340/week + travel
DEADLINE(S): FEB 5; JUN 1; SEP 1
FIELD(S): Chemistry, computer science, environmental science, geology, engineering, or physics

Opportunities for high school junior and seniors, undergraduates, and graduates to participate in research projects that correlate with their academic majors and career goals. For 3 to 12 consecutive months at the Savannah River Site, SC.

Funded through the Savannah River Site, SC.

2035 — OAK RIDGE INSTITUTE FOR SCIENCE AND EDUCATION (U.S. Geological Survey Earth Sciences Internship Program)

P.O. Box 117
Oak Ridge TN 37831-0117
423/576-2358
423/576-4813
AMOUNT: $19,000 to $38,000, dependent on level
DEADLINE(S): Ongoing
FIELD(S): Geology, geography, biology, chemistry, environmental sciences, hydrology, forestry, civil engineering, computer sciences

Internships for undergrads, grads, or recent grads (within one year) students studying in the above fields to conduct projects to prepare for careers in earth sciences for up to two years. Location: USGS sites across the U.S.

Funded through the U.S. Dept. of the Interior, U.S.G.S.

2036 — OAK RIDGE INSTITUTE FOR SCIENCE AND EDUCATION, U.S. DEPARTMENT OF ENERGY (Fusion Energy Sciences Fellowship Program)

105 Mitchell Road, MS-16
Oak Ridge TN 37831
423/576-2600
FAX: 423/576-8293
E-Mail: johnsons@orau.giv
AMOUNT: $1,300/mo. + $200/mo.
DEADLINE(S): JAN 26 (Received, not postmarked)
FIELD(S): Fusion energy sciences

Fellowships for Ph.D. candidates to pursue a degree in the fusion energy sciences at one of several participating universities throughout the U.S. Must be U.S. citizens or permanent residents. For students entering first or second year of graduate study. Must have B.A. degree in related field, such as applied mathematics or physics; chemical, electrical, mechanical, metallurgical, or nuclear engineering; or materials science.

Contact Sandra Johnson at above location for details and list of participating institutions.

2037 — OAK RIDGE INSTITUTE FOR SCIENCE AND EDUCATION/U.S. DEPT. OF ENERGY (Office of Civilian Radioactive Waste Management Fellowship)

P.O. Box 117
Oak Ridge TN 37831-0117
423/576-0128
FAX: 423/576-8293
E-Mail: drostp@orau.gov

AMOUNT: $14,000/yr.

DEADLINE(S): JAN 16 (Received, not postmarked)

FIELD(S): Physical or life sciences, math, or engineering

Fellowships for graduate students at various participating universities to conduct research in the management of spent nuclear fuel and high-level raqdioactive waste. For M.A. and Ph.D. candidates. For up to 48 months. Must be U.S. citizen or permanent resident.

Funded through U.S. Department of Energy, Office of Civilian Radioactive Waste Management. Contact or call Ms. Portia Drost, MS-16, at above address for details.

2038 — OAK RIDGE INSTITUTE FOR SCIENCE AND EDUCATION (Nuclear Engineering & Health Physics Fellowship Program)

105 Mitchell Rd. MS-16
Oak Ridge TN 37831-0117
423/576-2600 or 423/241-2890
E-Mail: johnsons@orau.gov or
daltonj@arou.gov

AMOUNT: $14,400/yr.

DEADLINE(S): JAN 26

FIELD(S): Engineering, physical and life sciences

Fellowships in nuclear engineering or applied health physics to implement DOE's nuclear energy-related mission. Candidates must have B.A. degree in life or physical sciences or engineering.

For details and application, contact Sandra Johnson or Jennifer Dalton at above location.

2039 — ONTARIO MINISTRY OF EDUCATION AND TRAINING (John Charles Polanyi Prizes)

189 Red River Rd.
4th Floor, Box 4500
Thunder Bay Ontario P7B 6G9 CANADA
800/465-3957
TDD: 800/465-3958
Internet: osap.gov.on.ca

AMOUNT: $15,000

DEADLINE(S): Varies

FIELD(S): Physics; Chemistry; Physiology; Medicine; Literature; Economics

Monetary prizes are awarded to Canadian citizens/permanent residents who are continuing postdoctoral studies at an Ontario university. Awards are designed to encourage and reward academic excellence.

5 awards annually. Contact your university or the Ontario Council of Graduate Studies for an application.

2040 — OPEN SOCIETY INSTITUTE (Environmental Management Fellowships)

400 West 59th St.
New York NY 10019
212/548-0600 or 212/757-2323
FAX: 212/548-4679 or 212/548-4600
Internet: www.soros.org/efp.html

AMOUNT: Fees, room, board, living stipend, textbooks, international transportation, health insurance

DEADLINE(S): NOV 15

FIELD(S): Earth sciences, natural sciences, humanities (exc. language), anthropology, sociology, mathematics, or engineering

Two-year fellowships for use in selected universities in the U.S. for international students. For students/professionals in fields related to environmental policy, legislation, and remediation techniques applicable to their home countries.

To apply, contact your local Soros Foundation or Open Society Institute. Further details on website.

2041 — ROBERT SCHRECK MEMORIAL FUND (Grants)

C/O Texas Commerce Bank-Trust Dept
PO Drawer 140
El Paso TX 79980
915/546-6515

AMOUNT: $500 - $1500

DEADLINE(S): JUL 15; NOV 15

FIELD(S): Medicine; Veterinary Medicine; Physics; Chemistry; Architecture; Engineering; Episcopal Clergy

Grants to undergraduate juniors or seniors or graduate students who have been residents of El Paso County for at least two years. Must be U.S. citizen or legal resident and have a high grade point average. Financial need is a consideration.

Write for complete information.

2042 — ROYAL SOCIETY OF CHEMISTRY (Corday-Morgan Memorial Fund)

Burlington House
Piccadilly
London W1V 0BN ENGLAND UK
+44 71 437 8656
FAX: +44 71 734 1227

AMOUNT: 500 pounds sterling (max.)

DEADLINE(S): None

FIELD(S): Chemistry

Assists members of any established Chemical Society/Institute in the Commonwealth to visit chemical establishments in another Commonwealth country. The intention is to help applicants make stop-overs in or diversions to such countries while travelling elsewhere for other purposes. Visits must clearly benefit the country concerned, and the visitor would be expected to give lectures, etc. Must be citizens of, and domiciled in, any Commonwealth country.

Contact the International Awards Officer at RSC for an application. Applications will normally be considered within one month of receipt.

2043 — ROYAL SOCIETY OF CHEMISTRY (Grants to Visit Developing Countries)

Burlington House
Piccadilly
London W1V 0BN ENGLAND UK
+44 71 437 8656
FAX: +44 71 734 1227

AMOUNT: 500 pounds sterling (max.)

DEADLINE(S): None

FIELD(S): Chemistry

Grants for members of the Royal Society of Chemistry to visit chemical establishments in developing countries. The visits must be clearly of benefit to the country concerned, and the visitor would be expected to give lectures, etc. The intention is to help applicants make stop-overs in or diversions to a developing country while travelling elsewhere for other purposes. Support for travel within a developing country may be given where appropriate.

Contact the International Affairs Officer at RSC for an application. Applications will normally be considered within one month of receipt.

2044 — ROYAL SOCIETY OF CHEMISTRY (JWT Jones Travelling Fellowship)

Burlington House
Piccadilly
London W1V 0BN ENGLAND UK
+44 71 437 8656
FAX: +44 71 734 1227

AMOUNT: 5,000 pounds sterling (max. - for airfare/allowance)

DEADLINE(S): JAN 1; APR 1; JUL 1; OCT 1

FIELD(S): Chemistry

For chemists to carry out short-term studies in well-established scientific centres abroad & to learn & use techniques not accessible to them in their own country. Must be members of the Royal Society of Chemistry & be under 37 years of age. Should hold at least a Masters or Ph.D. degree in chemistry or related subject

& already be in post & actively engaged in research. Must show that being in foreign lab will be beneficial, & must return to home country when done.

Contact Stanley S. Langer at RSC for an application.

2045 — ROYAL SOCIETY OF CHEMISTRY (Research Fund)

Burlington House
Piccadilly
London W1V 0BN ENGLAND UK
+44 71 437 8656
FAX: +44 71 734 1227

AMOUNT: up to 1,000 pounds sterling

DEADLINE(S): OCT 31

FIELD(S): Chemistry

Assists members of the Royal Society of Chemistry in their research by the provision of grants for things such as the purchase of chemicals, equipment, or for running expenses of chemical education research. Consideration is on merit, but account will be taken of any other source of financial aid available. Preference will be given to those working in less-endowed institutions and to those supporting their own research.

Applications are limited to one per department and must be submitted through the head of the department. Contact Stanley S. Langer at RSC for an application.

2046 — ROYAL SOCIETY OF EDINBURGH (BP Research Fellowships)

22/24 George St.
Edinburgh EH2 2PQ SCOTLAND
0131 225 6057
FAX: 0131 220 6889
E-Mail: rse@rse.org.uk

AMOUNT: 17,606 to 26,508 pounds sterling

DEADLINE(S): MAR 10

FIELD(S): Mechanical, Chemical, or Control Engineering; Organic Chemistry; Solid State Physics; Information Technology; Geologic Sciences

Research fellowships to Scotland higher education institutions. For post-doctoral researchers age 35 or under on the date of appointment (usually Oct. 1). For research in above disciplines.

Write for complete information.

2047 — SCIENCE ADVANCEMENT PROGRAMS RESEARCH CORPORATION (Research Awards)

101 N. Wilmot Rd., Ste. 250
Tucson AZ 85711
520/571-1111
FAX: 520/571-1119
E-Mail: awards@rescorp.org
Internet: www.rescorp.org

AMOUNT: Varies

DEADLINE(S): Varies

FIELD(S): Astronomy; Chemistry; Physics

Several awards for research are available to faculty members and assistant professors who teach in university departments of astronomy, chemistry, and physics.

See website or contact above address for details.

2048 — SMITHSONIAN INSTITUTION (National Air & Space Museum Guggenheim Fellowship)

National Air and Space Museum, MRC 312
Washington DC 20560
Written inquiry

AMOUNT: $14,000 (predoctoral); $25,000 (postdoctoral)

DEADLINE(S): JAN 15

FIELD(S): Historical research related to aviation and space

Predoctoral applicants should have completed preliminary course work and exams and be engaged in dissertation research. Postdoctoral applicants should have received their Ph.D within the past seven years. Contact Fellowship Coordinator at above location.

Open to all nationalities. Fluency in English required. Duration is 6-12 months.

2049 — SMITHSONIAN INSTITUTION (National Air & Space Museum Verville Fellowship)

National Air and Space Museum, MRC 312
Washington DC 20560
Written inquiry

AMOUNT: $30,000 stipend for 12 months + travel and misc. expenses

DEADLINE(S): JAN 15

FIELD(S): Analysis of major trends, developments, and accomplishments in the history of aviation or space studies

A competitive nine- to twelve-month in-residence fellowship in the above field of study. Advanced degree is NOT a requirement. Contact Fellowship Coordinator at above location.

Open to all nationalities. Fluency in English required.

2050 — THE DAPHNE JACKSON MEMORIAL FELLOWSHIPS TRUST (Fellowships in Science/ Engineering)

School of Physical Sciences
Dept. of Physics
University of Surrey
Guildford, Surrey
GU2 5XH ENGLAND UK
01483 259166
FAX: 01483 259501

E-Mail: J.Woolley@surrey.ac.uk
Internet: www.sst.ph.ic.ac.uk/trust/

AMOUNT: Varies

DEADLINE(S): Varies

FIELD(S): Science or engineering, including information sciences

Fellowships to enable well-qualified and highly motivated scientists and engineers to return to appropriate careers following a career break due to family comitments. May be used on a flexible, part-time basis. Tenable at various U.K. universities.

See website and/or contact organization for details.

2051 — THE NOVARTIS FOUNDATION (Scientific Research Fellowships/Bursaries)

41 Portland Place
London W1N 4BN ENGLAND UK
+44 171 636 9456
FAX: +44 171 436 2840
E-Mail: abrown@Novartisfound.org.uk
Internet: www.novartisfound.demon.co.uk/ bursary.htm

AMOUNT: Travel expenses, meals, lodging

DEADLINE(S): Varies

FIELD(S): Sciences

Fellowships/bursaries for young scientists, ages 23-35, to attend a Foundation symposium and then spend from 4-12 weeks in the laboratory of one of the symposium participants. For subject matter, see "Nature" or other appropriate journals or check with the Foundation or an office of the British Council.

For application details, see website or contact organization.

2052 — TRENT UNIVERSITY (Graduate Teaching/Research Assistantships)

P.O. Box 4800
Graduate Studies Officer
Peterborough Ontario CANADA K9J 7B8
705/748-1245

AMOUNT: $3,500 per term

DEADLINE(S): FEB 15

FIELD(S): Anthropology, Geography, Archaeology, Biology, Canadian Studies, Philosophy, Cultural Studies, Computer Science, Mathematics, Physics, Chemistry, Environmental Science/Studies

Teaching/research assistantships at Trent University in the above fields. Open to masters and doctoral candidates. Tenable for up to 4 terms spanning 2-3 years of study.

80 awards per year. Write for complete information.

2053 — TUSKEGEE UNIVERSITY (Graduate Research Fellowships and Assistantships)

Admissions Office
Tuskegee University
1506 Franklin Rd., AL 36088
334/727/8500

AMOUNT: Tuition

DEADLINE(S): MAR 15

FIELD(S): Chemistry; Engineering; Environmental Science; Life Sciences; Nutrition; Education

Graduate research fellowships and graduate assistantships are available to qualified individuals who wish to enter Tuskegee University's graduate program in pursuit of a master's degree.

Write for complete information.

2054 — U.S. DEPARTMENT OF DEFENSE (GLSIP-General Laboratory Scientific Interchange Program: NRC-NRL Post-Doctoral Program)

Naval Research Laboratory
Office of Program Admin. & Dev. Code 1006.17
Washington, D.C. 20375-5321
202/767-3865
DSN: 297-3865
FAX: 202/404-8110
Internet: www.acq.osd.mil/ddre/edugate/s-aindx.html

AMOUNT: Research Program

DEADLINE(S): None specified

FIELD(S): Computer science, artificial intelligence, plasma physics, acoustics, radar, fluid dynamics, chemistry, materials sci, optical sci, condensed matter and radiation, electronic sci, environmental sci, marine geosciences, remote sensing, oceanography, marine meteorology, space technology/sciences.

U.S. citizens who are recent postdoctoral graduates are selected on the basis of overall qualifications and techincal proposals.

Contact Jessica Hileman for more information.

2055 — UNCF/MERCK SCIENCE INITIATIVE (Graduate Science Research Dissertation Fellowships)

8260 Willow Oaks Corporate Dr.
PO Box 10444
Fairfax VA 22031-4511
703/205-3503
FAX: 703/205-3574
E-Mail: uncfmerck@uncf.org
Internet: www.uncf.org/merck

AMOUNT: $40,000/yr. (max.)

DEADLINE(S): JAN 31

FIELD(S): Life & Physical Sciences

Open to African-Americans enrolled full-time in a Ph.D. degree program and within 1-3 years of completing dissertation. Awards are intended to help students complete coursework, conduct research, and prepare dissertation for degree in the biomedically relevant life or physical sciences. Must be US citizen/permanent resident. Financial need NOT a factor.

12 awards annually. Not renewable. Contact Jerry Bryant, Ph.D., for an application.

2056 — UNCF/MERCK SCIENCE INITIATIVE (Postdoctoral Science Research Fellowships)

8260 Willow Oaks Corporate Dr.
PO Box 10444
Fairfax VA 22031-4511
703/205-3503
FAX: 703/205-3574
E-Mail: uncfmerck@uncf.org
Internet: www.uncf.org/merck

AMOUNT: $70,000/yr. (max.)

DEADLINE(S): JAN 31

FIELD(S): Life & Physical Sciences

Open to African-Americans who will receive a Ph.D. degree by the end of the current academic year and will be appointed as a postdoctoral fellow during the next calendar year. Awards are intended to support postgraduate students to obtain postdoctoral training and to prepare for a career in biomedical research. Must be US citizen/permanent resident. Financial need NOT a factor.

10 awards annually. Not renewable. Contact Jerry Bryant, Ph.D., for an application.

2057 — UNIVERSITY COLLEGE LONDON (Ramsay Memorial Fellowships Trust)

Gower Street
London WC1E 6BT ENGLAND
Written inquiry

AMOUNT: 17,000 pounds sterling(approx.)

DEADLINE(S): NOV 15

FIELD(S): Chemistry

Post-doctoral fellowships for full-time research in the United Kingdom open to applicants born within the British Commonwealth who generally have graduated with distinction in chemistry at a university within the Commonwealth.

Fellowships normally tenable for a period of two years. Applicants must be under 35 years of age. Write for complete information.

2058 — UNIVERSITY OF ALBERTA (Alberta Research Council Graduate Scholarship in Carbohydrate Chemistry)

Scholarship Coordinator
Faculty of Grad Studies & Research
105 Administration Bldg.
Edmonton Alberta T6G 2M7 CANADA
780/492-3499
FAX: 780/492-0692

AMOUNT: $20,000

DEADLINE(S): MAR 1

FIELD(S): Carbohydrate Chemistry

For a Ph.D. student engaged in thesis research in carbohydrate chemistry in the Deptartment of Chemistry. Tenable at the University of Alberta only. Must be nominated by the Department.

Renewable twice subject to review of progress and performance. Contact the Faculty of Graduate Studies & Research for nomination procedures.

2059 — UNIVERSITY OF OXFORD (Graduate Unilever Scholarship)

St. Cross College
Oxford OX1 3LZ ENGLAND UK
+44 01865-278492

AMOUNT: 1,774 pounds sterling

DEADLINE(S): MAR 15

FIELD(S): Biochemistry; Engineering

Supplementary award is open to students undertaking graduate/postgraduate research at Oxford University.

Renewable up to 3 years. Contact Tutor for Admissions for an application.

2060 — US DEPARTMENT OF DEFENSE (National Defense Science & Engineering Graduate Fellowship Programs)

200 Park Drive, Suite 211, P.O. Box 13444
Research Triangle Park, NC 27709-3444
919/549-8505
Internet: www.acq.osd.mil/ddre/edugate/s-aindx.html

AMOUNT: Full tuition and fees (tenure of 36 months)

DEADLINE(S): JAN

FIELD(S): Mathematical, physical, biological, ocean, and engineering sciences

Must be US citizens or nationals at or near the beginning of their graduate study in science or engineering, leading to a doctoral degree. NDSEG Fellowships are awarded for study and research in these disciplines of military importance.

Approximately 90 new three-year graduate fellowships each April. Fellows may choose appropriate US institutions of higher education, offering degrees in science and engineering. Contact the Program Administrator for more information.

2061 — WOODS HOLE OCEANOGRAPHIC INSTITUTION (Postdoctoral Awards in Ocean Science and Engineering)

360 Woods Hole Road
Woods Hole MA 02543-1541
508/289-2219
FAX: 508/457-2188
E-Mail: mgately@whoi.edu
Internet: www.whoi.edu

AMOUNT: Varies

DEADLINE(S): FEB 16

FIELD(S): Chemistry, Engineering, Geology, Geophysics, Mathematics, Meteorology, Physics, Biology, Oceanography

Eighteen-month postdoctoral scholar awards are offered to recipients of new or recent doctorates in the above fields. The awards are designed to further the education and training of the applicant with primary emphasis placed on the individual's research promise.

For an application/more information, contact the Education Office, Clark Laboratory 223, MS #31, at above address.

MATHEMATICS

2062 — ABDUS SALAM INTERNATIONAL CENTRE FOR THEORETICAL PHYSICS - ICTP

Strada Costiera, 11
I-34014 Trieste ITALY
+39 040 2240 111
FAX: +39 040 224 163
E-Mail: sci_info@ictp.trieste.it
Internet: www.ictp.trieste.it

AMOUNT: Tuition, living expenses, & travel

DEADLINE(S): DEC 31

FIELD(S): Mathematics; Physics

ICTP helps "to foster the growth of advanced studies and research in physical and mathematical sciences, especially in developing countries." Applicants must have degree in mathematics or physics and a good knowledge of specialized English. Postgraduate researchers must have at least a M.Sc. plus at least two years research experience. Diploma Course requires only a B.Sc. degree. Admittance is granted on a competitive basis. Financial need NOT a factor.

See website or contact ICTP for an application.

2063 — AECI LIMITED (AECI Post Graduate Research Fellowship)

Private Bag X2
Modderfontein SOUTH AFRICA 1645
011/605-3100

AMOUNT: Varies (South African Rands 3600)

DEADLINE(S): SEP 30

FIELD(S): Chemistry, Physics, Metallurgy, Biochemistry, Microbiology, Chemical Engineering, Civil Engineering, Industrial Engineering, Electrical Engineering, Mechanical Engineering, Instrument Engineering

Open to South African citizens who are graduate students who want to do research in one of the above areas. This fellowship is offered to strengthen post-graduate study and research in South Africa, particularly in the fields above.

Write to the above address for complete information.

2064 — AEROSPACE EDUCATION FOUNDATION (Theodore Von Karman Graduate Scholarship Program)

1501 Lee Highway
Arlington VA 22209
703/247-5839

AMOUNT: $5,000

DEADLINE(S): JAN

FIELD(S): Science, Mathematics, Engineering

Open to Air Force ROTC graduate students who will pursue advanced degrees in the fields of science, mathematics, physics, or engineering. U.S. citizen or legal resident.

5 awards per year based on aptitude, attitude, and career plans. Write for complete information.

2065 — AMERICAN ASSOCIATION FOR THE ADVANCEMENT OF SCIENCE (Science & Engineering Fellowships)

1200 New York Ave., NW
Washington DC 20005
202/326-6700
FAX: 202/289-4950
E-Mail: science_policy@aaas.org
Internet: www.aas.org

AMOUNT: $40,000+

DEADLINE(S): JAN 15

FIELD(S): Science; Engineering

Post-doctoral fellowships open to AAAS members or applicants concurrently applying for membership. Prospective fellows must demonstrate exceptional competence in an area of science or have a broad scientific or technical background. Those with MA degrees and at least three years of poast-degree professional experience may also apply.

U.S. citizenship required. For complete information on these one-year fellowships write to Director, Science Fellows Program at address above.

2066 — AMERICAN ASSOCIATION OF UNIVERSITY WOMEN EDUCATIONAL FOUNDATION (Selected Professions Fellowships)

Dept. 60
2201 N. Dodge St.
Iowa City IA 52243-4030
319/337-1716, ext. 60
FAX 319/337-1204
Internet: www.aauw.org

AMOUNT: $5,000-$15,000

DEADLINE(S): JAN 2 (most); NOV 15 (engineering dissertation only)

FIELD(S): Architecture; Computer/Information Sciences; Engineering; Mathematics/Statistics

For women in final year of graduate study in fields where women's participation has been low. Must be US citizen or permanent resident. Special consideration given to applicants who show professional promise in innovative or neglected areas of research and/or practice in areas of public interest. Women in engineering master's programs are eligible to apply for either first or final year of study; special award for engineering doctoral students writing dissertation.

Applications available August-December.

2067 — AMERICAN FOUNDATION FOR THE BLIND (Paul W. Ruckes Scholarship)

11 Penn Plaza, Ste. 300
New York NY 10001
212/502-7661 or TDD 212/502-7771
E-Mail: juliet@afb.org
Internet: www.afb.org

AMOUNT: $1,000

DEADLINE(S): APR 30

FIELD(S): Engineering, computer, physical, or life sciences

Open to blind or visually impaired undergraduate or graduate students pursuing degrees in the above fields. U.S. citizenship required.

Write to the above address or visit website for complete information.

2068 — AMERICAN INSTITUTE OF AERONAUTICS AND ASTRONAUTICS (Graduate Student Awards)

1801 Alexander Bell Drive, Suite 500
Reston VA 20191-4344
800/639-AIAA or 703/264-7500
FAX: 703/264-7551
Internet: www.aiaa.org

AMOUNT: $5,000

DEADLINE(S): None specified

FIELD(S): Astronautics; Aeronautics; Aeronautical Engineering

For graduate student research in the aerospace field.

Eight awards. Contact above address for complete information.

2069 — AMERICAN MATHEMATICAL SOCIETY (Centennial Fellowships)

PO Box 6248
Providence RI 02940-6248
401/455-4106 or 401/455-4000
FAX: 401/331-3842
E-Mail: ams@ams.org
Internet: www.ams.org

AMOUNT: $38,000 stipend + $1,500 expense allowance

DEADLINE(S): DEC 1

FIELD(S): Mathematics

For citizens/permanent residents of a country in North America who have held their doctoral degree for at least two years at the time of award. May not have permanent tenure and must have less than two years of research support at time of award. May use stipend for full year or may combine with half-time teaching and use it as half support for two years. Selection based on research potential, track record, letters of recommendation, and quality/feasibility of plan.

4-5 awards annually. See website or contact the Executive Director of AMS for an application. Awards announced in February.

2070 — AMERICAN SOCIETY FOR ENGINEERING EDUCATION (Army Research Laboritory Postdoctoral Fellowships)

1818 N St., NW, Ste. 600
Washington DC 20036
202/331-3525
FAX: 202/265-8504
E-Mail: projects@asee.org
Internet: www.asee.org/fellowship/

AMOUNT: $45,000-$55,000 + travel/relocation allowance

DEADLINE(S): Varies

FIELD(S): Engineering; Physical Sciences

Postdoctoral fellowships for US citizens/permanent residents to do research at Army Research Laboratories. Candidates must have completed their Ph.D. prior to appointment. Program is designed to increase involvement of creative and highly trained scientists and engineers from academia and industry in scientific and technical areas of interest and relevance to the Army. Research proposal should include clear objective and defined outcome. Financial need NOT a factor.

15 awards annually. Renewable. Contact Sandi Crawford at ASEE for an application packet.

2071 — AMERICAN SOCIETY FOR QUALITY (Richard A. Freund International Scholarship)

P.O. Box 3005
Milwaukee WI 53201-3005
800/248-1946 or
814/272-8575 - ask for item B0499
FAX: 414/272-1734
E-Mail: cs@asq/org
Internet: www.asq.org

AMOUNT: $5,000

DEADLINE(S): APR 1

FIELD(S): Quality control in engineering, statistics, management, etc.

Scholarship for members and nonmembers worldwide enrolled in a Master's degree or higher level program with a concentration in any of the above fields of study. 3.25+ GPA required in undergraduate studies in engineering, sciences, or business.

Two letters of recommendation from persons qualified to assess the candidate's scholarly experience and a formal written statement (all in English) of approximately 250 words addressing the applicant's educational and career goals are required.

2072 — ARMED FORCES COMMUNICATIONS AND ELECTRONICS ASSOCIATION (AFCEA Fellowshps)

4400 Fair Lakes Court
Fairfax VA 22033-3899
800/336-4583 Ext. 6149 or 703/631-6149
Internet: www.afcea.org/awards/
scholarships.htm

AMOUNT: $25,000

DEADLINE(S): FEB 1

FIELD(S): Electrical engineering, electronics, computer science, computer engineering, physics, mathematics

Fellowships in the above fields for students working on doctoral degrees in accredited universities in the U.S.

Send a self-addressed, stamped envelope with information on the name of your school, field of study, GPA, and year in school to AFCEA Educational Foundation at above address. Applications available November through Jan 1.

2073 — ASSOCIATED WESTERN UNIVERSITIES, INC. (AWU Faculty Fellowships)

4190 South Highland Dr., Suite 211
Salt Lake City UT 84124-2600
801-273-8900

AMOUNT: Varies.

DEADLINE(S): FEB 15

FIELD(S): Engineering, Mathematics, Science, Technology

Research fellowships for qualified college and university faculty members to encourage participation and contribution to research at one of 62 cooperating facilities. It is not necessary to be enrolled at an AWU member institution. Collaborations that include graduate and/or undergraduate students are encouraged.

For detailed information and list of cooperating facilities, contact above location.

2074 — ASSOCIATED WESTERN UNIVERSITIES, INC. (AWU Graduate Fellowship Program)

4190 South Highland Dr. Suite 211
Salt Lake City, UT 84124-2600
801/273-8900

AMOUNT: Stipend ($1,300 per month & up) + tuition assistance and travel allowance

DEADLINE(S): FEB 15

FIELD(S): Engineering, Mathematics, Science, Technology

Open to master's and doctoral degree candidates to conduct research toward a thesis or dissertation at one of more than 62 cooperating facilities. Institutional affiliation and citizenship restrictions may apply for some awards or facilities. It is not necessary to be enrolled at an AWU member institution to apply for a fellowship.

Write to the above address for complete information.

2075 — ASSOCIATED WESTERN UNIVERSITIES, INC. (AWU Postgraduate Fellowship)

4190 South Highland Dr. Suite 211
Salt Lake City UT 84124-2600
801/273-8900

AMOUNT: Stipend established by the host facility and varies by experience and discipline.

DEADLINE(S): Varies (Two to three months before the starting date)

FIELD(S): Engineering, Mathematics, Science, Technology

For college and university graduates who have completed all institutional requirements for an advanced degree from an accredited college or university in the U.S. A commitment to a professional career in science or engineering research is expected. U.S. citizenship or permanent resident status is required. Research is to be done at one of the 62 cooperating universities.

For detailed information and a list of cooperating facilities contact above address.

2076 — ASSOCIATED WESTERN UNIVERSITIES, INC. (AWU Visiting Scientist Fellowships)

4190 South Highland Dr., Suite 211
Salt Lake City UT 84124-2600
801/273-8900

AMOUNT: Varies

DEADLINE(S): Varies (Two months prior to starting date)

FIELD(S): Engineering, Science, Mathematics, and Technology

Research fellowships for professionals with continued commitment to science and engineering. For use at one of 62 participating universities. US citizenship or permanent residency required.

For detailed information and list of cooperating facitilies contact above location.

2077 — ASSOCIATION FOR WOMEN IN SCIENCE EDUCATIONAL FOUNDATION (AWIS Predoctoral Awards)

1200 New York Ave. NW, Suite 650
Washington DC 20005
202/326-8940 or 800-886-AWIS
E-Mail: awis@awis.org
Internet: www.awis.org

AMOUNT: $1,000

DEADLINE(S): JAN 16

FIELD(S): Various Sciences and Social Sciences

Scholarships for female doctoral students. Summary page, description of research project, resume, references, transcripts, and biographical sketch required. US citizens may study at any graduate institution; non-citizens must study at US institutions.

5-10 awards annually. See website or write to above address for an application and complete information.

2078 — ASSOCIATION FOR WOMEN IN SCIENCE EDUCATIONAL FOUNDATION (AWIS Pre-doctoral Awards)

1200 New York Ave. NW, Suite 650
Washington DC 20005
202/326-8940 or 800/886-AWIS
E-Mail: awis@awis.org
Internet: www.awis.org

AMOUNT: $1,000

DEADLINE(S): JAN 16

FIELD(S): Various Sciences and Social Sciences

Scholarships for female doctoral students. Summary page, description of research project, resume, references, transcripts, and biographical sketch required. US citizens may study at any graduate institution; non-citizens must be enrolled in US institutions.

5-10 awards annually. See website or write to above address for an application and more information.

2079 — ASSOCIATION FOR WOMEN IN SCIENCE EDUCATIONAL FOUNDATION (Ruth Satter Memorial Award)

1200 New York Ave., NW, Suite 650
Washington DC 20005

202/326-8940 or 800/886-AWIS
E-Mail: awis@awis.org
Internet: www.awis.org

AMOUNT: $1,000

DEADLINE(S): JAN 16

FIELD(S): Various Sciences and Social Sciences

Scholarships for female doctoral students who have interrupted their education for at least three years to raise a family. Summary page, description of research project, resume, references, transcripts, biographical sketch, and letter from your department to confirm eligibility required. US citizens may study at any graduate institution; non-citizens must attend US institutions.

See website or write to above address for more information or an application.

2080 — ASSOCIATION FOR WOMEN IN SCIENCE EDUCATIONAL FOUNDATION (Ruth Satter Memorial Award)

1200 New York Ave. NW, Suite 650
Washington DC 20005
202/326-8940 or 800/886-AWIS
E-Mail: awis@awis.org
Internet: www.awis.org

AMOUNT: $1,000

DEADLINE(S): JAN 16

FIELD(S): Various Sciences and Social Sciences

Scholarships for female doctoral students who have interrupted their education three years or more to raise a family. Summary page, description of research project, resume, references, transcripts, biographical sketch, and proof of eligibility from department head required. US citizens may attend any graduate institution; non-citizens must be enrolled in US institutions.

See website or write to above address for more information or an application.

2081 — AT&T BELL LABORATORIES (Graduate Research Program For Women)

101 Crawfords Corner Road
Holmdel NJ 07733-3030
Written inquiry

AMOUNT: Full tuition & fees + $13,200 stipend per year

DEADLINE(S): JAN 15

FIELD(S): Engineering; Math; Sciences; Computer Science

For women students who have been accepted into an accredited doctoral program for the following fall. U.S. citizen or permanent resident.

Fellowships are renewable for up to 5 years of graduate study. Write to special programs manager-GRPW for complete information.

2082 — AUSTRALIAN FEDERATION OF UNIVERSITY WOMEN - WESTERN AUSTRALIA (Mary & Elsie Stevens Bursary)

Bursary Liaison Officer
PO Box 48
Nedlands WA 6009 AUSTRALIA
Written Inquiry

AMOUNT: Aus$1,750

DEADLINE(S): JUL 31

FIELD(S): Mathematics or Physical Sciences, such as Physics, Chemistry, Geology, Astronomy, or other innate sciences

Bursary is to support women graduates of a Western Australian University to complete a higher degree or post-doctoral research in Mathematics or one of the Physical Sciences at a recognized university in any country or women who have been accepted to work toward a higher degree at a university in Western Australia.

Membership in AFUW or in IFUW is required. Write for complete information.

2083 — AUSTRALIAN FEDERATION OF UNIVERSITY WOMEN - WESTERN AUSTRALIA (Mary & Ilsie Stevens Bursary)

Bursary Liaison Officer
PO Box 48
Nedlands WA 6009 AUSTRALIA
Written Inquiry

AMOUNT: Aus$1,750

DEADLINE(S): JUL 31

FIELD(S): Mathematics or Physical sciences, such as Physics, Chemistry, Geology, Astronomy, or other innate sciences

Bursary is to support women graduates of a recognized university to complete a higher degree or post-doctoral research in Mathematics or in one of the Physical Sciences at a university in Western Australia.

Membership in AFUW or in IFUW is required. Write for complete information.

2084 — BODOSSAKI FOUNDATION (Academic Prizes)

20 Amalias Ave.
GR-105 57 Athens GREECE
3220 962
FAX: 3237 976

AMOUNT: Drs. 7,000,000

DEADLINE(S): DEC 31

FIELD(S): Pure mathematics, theoretical and applied computer science, operations research, cardiovascular diseases, developmental biology

Awards to support the creative work of young Greek academics and scientists and reward their endeavor in the advancement of learning and the creation of sound values. Must be of Greek nationality, parentage, or descent under age 40.

Contact above address for details.

2085 — BOEING (Polish Graduate Student Scholarship Program)

Phone for details
314/234-2149

AMOUNT: Tuition, books, and fees for three years

DEADLINE(S): Varies

FIELD(S): Scientific and technical fields

Scholarships for students from Poland to pursue graduate studies in scientific and technical areas at American colleges or universities.

Call Jim Schlueter at above telephone number.

2086 — BROOKHAVEN NATIONAL LABORATORY (Post-doctoral Research Associateships)

Brookhaven National Laboratory
Upton L.I. NY 11973-5000
516/344-3336

AMOUNT: $29,000 minimum

DEADLINE(S): Varies

FIELD(S): Chemistry, Physics, Materials Science, Biology, Oceanography, and Biomedical Sciences.

Post-doctoral research associateships tenable at Brookhaven National Laboratory for research to promote fundamental and applied research in the above fields. A recent doctoral degree is required.

25 associateships per year. Renewable for two additional years.

2087 — BROOKHAVEN WOMEN IN SCIENCE (Renate W. Chasman Scholarship)

PO Box 183
Upton NY 11973-5000
E-mail: pam@bnl.gov

AMOUNT: $2,000

DEADLINE(S): APR 1

FIELD(S): Natural Sciences; Engineering; Mathematics

Open ONLY to women who are residents of the boroughs of Brooklyn or Queens or the counties of Nassau or Suffolk in New York who are re-entering school after a period of study. For juniors, seniors, or first-year graduate students.

1 award annually. Not renewable. Contact Pam Mansfield at above location for an application. Phone calls are NOT accepted.

2088 — BUSINESS & PROFESSIONAL WOMEN'S FOUNDATION (BPW Career Advancement Scholarship Program)

2012 Massachusetts Ave., NW
Washington DC 20036-1070
202/293-1200, ext. 169
FAX: 202/861-0298
Internet: www.bpwusa.org

AMOUNT: $500-$1,000

DEADLINE(S): APR 15

FIELD(S): Biology, Science, Education, Engineering, Social Science, Paralegal, Humanities, Business, Math, Computers, Law, MD, DD

For women (US citizens) aged 25+ accepted into accredited program at US institution (+Puerto Rico & Virgin Islands). Must graduate within 12 to 24 months from the date of grant and demonstrate critical finanacial need. Must have a plan to upgrade skills, train for a new career field, or to enter/re-enter the job market.

Full- or part-time study. For info see website or send business-sized, self-addressed, double-stamped envelope.

2089 — CONCORDIA UNIVERSITY (Nick Herscovis Memorial Scholarship)

Mathematics Dept.
1455 de Maisonneuve Blvd. West
L HB 242
Montreal Quebec H3G 1M8 CANADA
514/848-3809
FAX: 514/848-2812
E-Mail: awardsgs@vax2.concordia.ca

AMOUNT: $1,000

DEADLINE(S): SEP 20

FIELD(S): Teaching of Mathematics

This award is tenable by a full-time Master's student in the Teaching of Mathematics program. It is awarded on the basis of financial need and the student's performance in the program. Recipient is chosen by the Department of Mathematics.

1 award annually. Not renewable. Contact the Graduate Program Director in the Mathematics Department at Concordia University for an application.

2090 — DUBLIN INSTITUTE FOR ADVANCED STUDIES (Research Scholarships)

10 Burlington Road
Dublin 4 IRELAND
614 0100
FAX: 668 0561

AMOUNT: 5,000-8,200

DEADLINE(S): MAR 31

FIELD(S): Theoretical Physics; Cosmic Physics; Astronomy; Celtic Studies

Open to candidates holding Ph.D degrees or equivalent and to those with M.A. degrees who can demonstrate their capacity for original research in the above fields. Scholars are required to be in full-time attendance in the schools. No nationality or citizenship requirements.

Awards are renewable and intended to enable holders to establish research careers. The Institute does not award degrees. 18 awards per year. Contact Registrar at above location for complete information.

2091 — ENGINEERING & PHYSICAL SCIENCES RESEARCH COUNCIL (Studentships)

North Star Ave
Polaris House
Swindon SN2 1ET England
01 793-444000

AMOUNT: Maintenance & approved fees

DEADLINE(S): JUL 31

FIELD(S): Engineering & Physical Science

Research studentships for up to 3 years for Ph.D students, 1 year advanced course studentships for master's students. Tenable at U.K. institutions. Must be UK resident with relevant connection to UK for full award or with European Union member state with relevant connection to UK for fees-only award. Must have appropriate academic qualifications.

Approx 3,800 awards per year. Applications must be made through heads of departments. EPSRC does not accept applications direct from students. Write for complete information.

2092 — EPPLEY FOUNDATION FOR RESEARCH (Postdoctoral Research Grants)

245 Park Avenue
40th Floor
New York NY 10167
Written inquiry

AMOUNT: Up to $25,000

DEADLINE(S): FEB 1; MAY 1; AUG 1; NOV 1

FIELD(S): Physical Sciences; Biological Sciences

Postdoctoral grants for original advanced research in any of the physical or biological sciences. Open to established research scientists who are attached to a recognized institution.

Write for complete information.

2093 — FANNIE AND JOHN HERTZ FOUNDATION (Fellowship)

Box 5032
Livermore CA 94551-5032
925/373-1642
Internet: www.hertzfoundation.org

AMOUNT: $25,000 stipend/yr. + $15,000 (max.) tuition allowance/yr.

DEADLINE(S): NOV 5

FIELD(S): Applied Physical Sciences

Open to graduate students with a minimum 3.75 GPA for studies in applied physical sciences, including math, engineering, computer science, biology, oceanography, aeronautics, astronomy, physics, and earth science. Must be US citizen/permanent resident. Does not support study in pursuit of M.D. degree, although will support Ph.D. portion of a joint M.D./Ph.D. study program.

Renewable up to 5 years. Only 36 US schools are currently considered tenable. See website for an application and list of specific fields of study that are acceptable.

2094 — FORD FOUNDATION/NATIONAL RESEARCH COUNCIL (Postdoctoral Fellowship for Minorities)

National Research Council
2101 Constitution Ave.
Washington DC 20418
202/334-2860
E-Mail: infofell@nas.edu
Internet: http//www.nas.edu/fo/index.html

AMOUNT: $25,000 + relocation and research allowance

DEADLINE(S): JAN 3

FIELD(S): Life and physical sciences, mathematics, engineering sciences, behavioral and social sciences, and the humanities

For U.S. citizens who received a Ph.D or Sc.D in the last 7 years and who are Native Amer. Indian or Alaskan, Black/African American, Mexican American, Native Pacific Islander, or Puerto Rican and who are or plan to be in a teaching or research career.

Contact above website or address for complete information.

2095 — FORD FOUNDATION/NATIONAL RESEARCH COUNCIL (Predoctoral/Dissertation Fellowships for Minorities)

2101 Constitution Ave.
Washington DC 20418
202/334-2872
E-Mail: infofell@nas.edu
Internet: http//www.nas.edu/fo/index.html

AMOUNT: $14,000 annual stipend + $6,000 grant to institution; $18,000 for dissertation fellowship

DEADLINE(S): NOV 3

FIELD(S): Most fields of study: sciences, humanities, engineering, behavioral science, social sciences, and computer science

Predoctoral and dissertation fellowships for students whose ethnicity is Alaskan Native, Black/African American, Mexican American/Chicano, Native American Indian, Native Pacific Islander, or Puerto Rican. For research-based programs leading to careers in college teaching and research.

Contact above address or website.

2096 — FOUNDATION FOR SCIENCE AND DISABILITY, INC. (FSD Science Student Grant Fund)

503 NW 89th Street
Gainesville FL 32607-1400
352/374-5774
FAX: 352/374-5781
E-Mail: rmankin@gainesville.usda.ufl.edu

AMOUNT: $1,000

DEADLINE(S): DEC 1

FIELD(S): Mathematics; Science; Medicine; Engineering; Computer Science

Open to graduate students with disabilities. May also apply as a fourth-year undergraduate accepted into a graduate or professional program. Awards are for some special purpose in connection with a science project or thesis in any of above fields. Student is required to write a 250-word essay which includes a description of professional goals/objectives, as well as purpose of grant. Transcripts and two letters of recommendation from faculty members are also required.

Contact Dr. Richard Mankin at above address for an application.

2097 — GATES MILLENIUM SCHOLARS PROGRAM (Scholarships for Graduate Students)

8260 Willow Oaks Corporate Dr.
Fairfax VA 22031-4511
877/690-4677
Internet: www.gmsp.org

AMOUNT: Varies

DEADLINE(S): FEB 1

FIELD(S): Engineering; Mathematics; Science; Education; Library Science

College presidents, professors, & deans may nominate graduate students who are African-Americans, Native Americans, Hispanic Americans, or Asian Americans in above fields. Based on academic performance, commitment to academic study, involvement in community service & school activities, potential for leadership, career goals, and financial need. Must submit transcripts and letters of recommendation. Must be US citizen with a minimum 3.3 GPA

Application materials available November 1st; scholars will be notified in May. Funded by the Bill & Melinda Gates Foundation, and administered by the United Negro College Fund.

2098 — INSTITUTE FOR ADVANCED STUDY (Post-doctoral Fellowship Awards)

Olden Lane
Princeton NJ 08540
609/734-8000

AMOUNT: Varies according to school

DEADLINE(S): Varies

FIELD(S): Historical Studies; Social Sciences; Natural Sciences; Mathematics

Post-doctoral fellowships at the institute for advanced study for those whose term can be expected to result in work of significance and individuality.

150-160 fellowships per academic year although some can be extended. Request application materials from school's administrative officer.

2099 — INSTITUTE FOR OPERATIONS RESEARCH AND THE MANAGEMENT SCIENCES (INFORMS Summer Internship Directory)

P.O. Box 64794
Baltimore MD 21264-4794
800/4INFORMS
FAX: 410/684-2963
E-Mail: jps@informs.org
Internet: www.informs.org/INTERN/

AMOUNT: Varies

DEADLINE(S): Varies

FIELD(S): Fields related to information management: business management, engineering, mathematics

A website listing of summer internships in the field of operations research and management sciences. Both applicants and employers can register online.

Access website for list.

2100 — INSTITUTE OF PAPER SCIENCE AND TECHNOLOGY (Fellowship Program)

500 10th St. NW
Atlanta GA 30318
404/853-9500

AMOUNT: Full tuition plus $11,250 stipend

DEADLINE(S): MAR 15

FIELD(S): Chemistry; Chemical Engineering; Physics; Biology; Mechanical Engineering; Pulp and Paper Technology

Open to graduate students who are U.S., Mexican, or Canadian citizens or legal residents who hold a BS degree in the above fields. For a pursuit of a master of Science or Ph.D degree at the institute.

35 fellowships annually. Address inquiries to director of admissions.

2101 — INTERNATIONAL SCHOOL OF CRYSTALLOGRAPHY (Postgraduate Courses)

Piazza di Porta San Donato 1
40126 Bologna ITALY
39 051 243556
FAX: 39 051 243336
E-Mail: riva@geomin.unibo.it
Internet: www.geomin.unibo.it/orgv/erice/erice.htm

AMOUNT: Half to full subsistence + fees

DEADLINE(S): NOV 30

FIELD(S): Solid State Chemistry; Physics; Molecular Biology; Molecular Biophysics; Pharmaceutics

Open to young postgraduates to pursue interdisciplinary studies in crystallography in Erice, Sicily, Italy. Must speak English and have some experience in the topic to be discussed (topics change every year). These 15-day courses are held at the International Foundation and Centre for Scientific Culture—Ettore Majorana.

See website or contact Lodovico Riva di Sanseverino for an application.

2102 — JEWISH FEDERATION OF METROPOLITAN CHICAGO (Academic Scholarship Program for Studies in the Sciences)

One South Franklin St.
Chicago IL 60606
Written inquiry

AMOUNT: Varies

DEADLINE(S): MAR 1

FIELD(S): Mathematics, engineering, or science

Scholarships for college juniors, seniors, and graduate students who are Jewish and are residents of Chicago, IL and Cook County.

Academic achievement and financial need are considered. Applications accepted after Dec. 1.

2103 — KING FAISAL FOUNDATION (Graduate Scholarship Program)

PO Box 352
Riyadh 11411 SAUDI ARABIA
966/1 465-2255
FAX: 966/1 465-6524
E-Mail: info@kff.com OR mprd@kff.com
Internet: www.kff.com OR
www.kingfaisalfoundation.org

AMOUNT: $400/mo. US allowance + tuition/fees paid directly to university + health insurance & travel

DEADLINE(S): None

FIELD(S): Medicine; Engineering; Physics; Chemistry; Geology

Open to graduate students who are Muslims under the age of 40. Must have BS degree, GPA of 86% or higher, and be accepted unconditionally by a university either in Europe or North America. Must be fluent in the language of area providing the studies. Selection based on academic performance.

Contact King Faisal Foundation for an application.

2104 — LOUISIANA OFFICE OF STUDENT FINANCIAL ASSISTANCE (Tuition Opportunity Program for Students-Teachers Award)

PO Box 91202
Baton Rouge LA 70821-9202
800/259-5626, ext. 1012
FAX: 504/922-0790
Internet: www.osfa.state.la.us

AMOUNT: $4,000/yr. (education majors); $6,000/yr. (math/chemistry majors)

DEADLINE(S): JUN 1

FIELD(S): Education; Math; Chemistry

Open to Louisiana residents pursuing undergraduate or graduate study at Louisiana colleges/universities and majoring in one of the above fields leading to teacher certification. Loans are forgiven by working as a certified teacher in Louisiana one year for each year loan is received.

Apply by completing the Free Application for Federal Student Aid (FAFSA). See your school's financial aid office or contact LOSFA for FAFSA form.

2105 — MATHESON GAS PRODUCTS FOUNDATION (Scholarships)

PO Box 624
959 Rte. 46 E.
Parsippany NJ 07054-0624
Internet: www.mathesongas.com

AMOUNT: $5,000

DEADLINE(S): None

FIELD(S): Chemistry; Physics; Chemical Engineering; Material Science; Semiconductor Engineering

Open to financially needy graduate students who are African American, Latino, Asian, Native American, or female. Must be US citizens/permanent residents studying in above fields or related area.

Send self-addressed, stamped envelope to Jerry Cantrella, Director of Personnel, for an application.

2106 — NAACP NATIONAL OFFICE (NAACP Willems Scholarship)

4805 Mount Hope Drive
Baltimore MD 21215
401/358-8900

AMOUNT: $2,000 undergrads; $3,000 grads

DEADLINE(S): APR 30

FIELD(S): Engineering; Chemistry; Physics; Mathematics

Open to NAACP male members majoring in one of the above areas. Undergrads must have GPA of 2.5+; graduates' GPAs must be 3.0+. Renewable if the required GPA is maintained.

Financial need must be established. Two letters of recommendation typed on letterhead from teachers or professors in the major field of specialization. Write for complete information. Include a legal size, self-addressed, stamped envelope.

2107 — NATIONAL AERONAUTICS AND SPACE ADMINISTRATION (Graduate Student Researcher's Program-Underrepresented Minority Focus)

Mail Code FEH
NASA Headquarters
Washington, DC 20546
202/453-8344

AMOUNT: $22,000 1st year, renewable up to 3 years

DEADLINE(S): FEB 1

FIELD(S): Science, Engineering, Mathematics

For underrepresented minority groups in the fields of science and engineering (including African-Americans, American Indians, Hispanics, and Pacific Islanders), who may end up with a career in space science and/or aerospace technology. Must be US citizen and enrolled or accepted as a full-time graduate student at an accredited US college or university.

Write for complete information.

2108 — NATIONAL AERONAUTICS AND SPACE ADMINISTRATION (NASA Training Grants)

NASA Headquarters, Code FE
Washington DC 20548
202/358-1517

AMOUNT: $22,000

DEADLINE(S): Varies

FIELD(S): Space Science/Physics

Grants for research in various specified topics in the fields listed above.

Contact Ahmad Nurriddin at above location for details.

2109 — NATIONAL PHYSICAL SCIENCE CONSORTIUM (Graduate Fellowships for Minorities & Women in the Physical Sciences)

MSC 3NPS
Box 30001
Las Cruces NM 88003-8001
800/952-4118 or 505/646-6038
FAX: 505/646-6097
E-Mail: npse@nmsu.edu
Internet: www.npsc.org

AMOUNT: $12,500 (years 1-4); $15,000 (years 5-6)

DEADLINE(S): NOV 5

FIELD(S): Astronomy; Chemistry; Computer Science; Geology; Materials Science; Mathematics; Physics

Open to "all US citizens" with an emphasis on Black, Hispanic, Native American, and female students. Must be pursuing graduate studies and have a minimum 3.0 GPA.

Renewable up to 6 years. See website or contact NPSC for an application.

2110 — NATIONAL RESEARCH FOUNDATION (NRF Honors & Postgraduate Bursaries)

PO Box 2600
Pretoria 0001 SOUTH AFRICA
+27 012/481-4000
FAX: +27 012/349-1179
E-Mail: info@nrf.ac.za
Internet: www.nrf.ac.za

AMOUNT: Varies

DEADLINE(S): Varies

FIELD(S): Agriculture; Chemistry; Earth Sciences; Engineering; Biology; Mathematics; Physics; Forestry; Veterinary Science; Pharmaceutics

Open to South African citizens pursuing graduate/postgraduate studies in above fields.

500 awards annually. Contact NRF for an application.

2111 — NATIONAL TECHNICAL ASSOCIATION, INC. (Scholarship Competitions for Minorities and Women in Science and Engineering)

6919 North 19th St.
Philadelphia PA 19126-1506
215/549-5743
FAX: 215/549-6509
E-Mail: ntamfj1@aol.com
Internet: www.huenet.com/nta

AMOUNT: $500-$5,000

DEADLINE(S): Varies

FIELD(S): Science, mathematics, engineering, and applied technology

Scholarships competitions for minorities and women pursuing degrees in the above fields. Additional scholarships are available through local chapters of NTA.

Check website or write to above address for details and for locations of local chapters.

2112 — OAK RIDGE ASSOCIATED UNIVERSITIES (Laboratory Graduate Research Participation Program)

P.O. Box 117
Oak Ridge TN 37831-0117
423/576-4813

AMOUNT: $1,000-$1,200/mo. + allowance for dependents + tuition and fees reimbursement to a max. of $3,500/yr.

DEADLINE(S): Ongoing

FIELD(S): Life sciences, physical, and social sciences, mathematics, and engineering

For graduate students in one of the fields listed above who have completed all degree requirements except thesis or dissertation research. For full-time research under the joint direction of the major professor and a DOE staff member at one of various locations, primarily in the South. For six to twelve months.

Funded through U.S. Dept. of Energy, Office of Energy Reseach, and Office of Fossil Energy. Write for complete information.

2113 — OAK RIDGE ASSOCIATED UNIVERSITIES (National Science Foundation Graduate Research Fellowships)

PO Box 3010
Oak Ridge TN 37831-3010
423/241-4300
FAX: 423/241-4513
E-Mail: nsfgrfp@orau.gov
Internet: www.orau.gov/nsf/nsffel.htm

AMOUNT: $15,000 stipend + $10,500 tuition allowance

DEADLINE(S): NOV 4

FIELD(S): Science; Math; Engineering; Computer Science

Three-year fellowships for graduate study leading to research-based master's or doctoral degrees in the above fields. Must be US citizens, nationals, or permanent residents at the time of application. Fellowships are awarded on the basis of ability. Women, minorities, and those with disabilities are strongly encouraged to apply. One-time International Research Travel Allowance available.

1,000 awards annually. Contact Jeannette Bouchard for an application/more information.

2114 — OAK RIDGE INSTITUTE FOR SCIENCE AND EDUCATION (Applied Health Physics Fellowship Program)

P.O. Box 117
Oak Ridge TN 37831-0117
423/576-2194 or 423/576-9279
E-Mail: COXRE@ORAU.GOV or
GRADFELL@ORAU.GOV

AMOUNT: $14,400 stipend + tuition and fees up to $9,000/yr paid to university + transportation costs up to $300/month

DEADLINE(S): JAN 26

FIELD(S): Engineering, mathematics, physical and life sciences

Fellowship in applied health physics to implement DOE's nuclear energy-related mission. Candidates must have B.A. degree in life or physical sciences, engineering, or mathematics. Recipients are subject to a service obligation of one year of full-time employment in a DOE facility for each academic year of fellowhip award.

For details and application, contact above location.

2115 — OAK RIDGE INSTITUTE FOR SCIENCE AND EDUCATION (Industrial Hygiene Graduate Fellowship Program)

P.O. Box 117
Oak Ridge TN 37831-0117
423-576-9655
FAX: 423/576-8293
E-Mail: kinneym@orau.gov

AMOUNT:

DEADLINE(S): JAN 26

FIELD(S): Industrial Hygiene

A fellowship for first-year master's candidates who have undergraduate degrees in physical, life, environmental, or health sciences or enginering and who wish to pursue studies in industrial hygiene.

For details and application, contact above location.

2116 — OAK RIDGE INSTITUTE FOR SCIENCE AND EDUCATION (Professional Internship Program/Oak Ridge National Laboratory)

P.O. Box 117
Oak Ridge TN 37831-0117
423/576-3426
423/576-3427

AMOUNT: $210 to $300/week + travel, tuition, and fees

DEADLINE(S): FEB 5; JUN 1; OCT 1

FIELD(S): Chemistry, environmental science, geology, hydrogeology, hydrology, chemical engineering, civil engineering, environmental engineering, mechanical engineering, computer science (technical database development)

Opportunities for graduates and undergraduates to participate in energy-related research projects that correlate with their academic and career goals. For 3 to 12 consecutive months.

Funded through Oak Ridge National Laboratory.

2117 — OAK RIDGE INSTITUTE FOR SCIENCE AND EDUCATION (Professional Internship Program/Pittsburgh Energy Technology Center)

P.O. Box 117
Oak Ridge TN 37831-0117
423/576-3426
423/576-3427

AMOUNT: $235 to $325/week + travel, tuition, and fees

DEADLINE(S): FEB 5; JUN 1; OCT 1

FIELD(S): Chemistry, physics, environmental science, geology, chemical or environmental engineering, computer science, or statistics.

Opportunities for graduates and undergraduates to participate in fossil energy-related research projects that correlate with their academic and career goals. For 3 to 12 consecutive months.

Funded through U.S. Dept. of Energy, Office of Fossil Energy, and Pittsburgh Energy Technology Center.

2118 — OAK RIDGE INSTITUTE FOR SCIENCE AND EDUCATION (Professional Internship Program/Savannah River Site)

P.O. Box 117
Oak Ridge TN 37831-0117
423/576-3426
423/576-3427

AMOUNT: $260 to $340/week + travel

DEADLINE(S): FEB 5; JUN 1; SEP 1

FIELD(S): Chemistry, computer science, environmental science, geology, engineering, or physics

Opportunities for high school junior and seniors, undergraduates, and graduates to participate in research projects that correlate with their academic majors and career goals. For 3 to 12 consecutive months at the Savannah River Site, SC.

Funded through the Savannah River Site, SC.

2119 — OAK RIDGE INSTITUTE FOR SCIENCE AND EDUCATION (Science and Engineering Research Semester)

P.O. Box 117
Oak Ridge TN 37831-0117
423/576-2358
423/576-2310

AMOUNT: $225/week + travel + housing

DEADLINE(S): OCT; MAR

FIELD(S): Computer science, physical sciences, environmental and life sciences, and mathematics

Opportunities for high school junior and seniors and a few slots for graduates to participate in energy-related with laboratory scientists at Oak Ridge National Laboratory, TN. One semester with possibility of summer extension. Available two times a year.

Funded through the U.S. Dept. of Energy, Office of Energy Research.

2120 — OAK RIDGE INSTITUTE FOR SCIENCE AND EDUCATION, U.S. DEPARTMENT OF ENERGY (Fusion Energy Sciences Fellowship Program)

105 Mitchell Road, MS-16
Oak Ridge TN 37831
423/576-2600
FAX: 423/576-8293
E-Mail: johnsons@orau.giv

AMOUNT: $1,300/mo. + $200/mo.

DEADLINE(S): JAN 26 (Received, not postmarked)

FIELD(S): Fusion energy sciences

Fellowships for Ph.D. candidates to pursue a degree in the fusion energy sciences at one of several participating universities throughout the U.S. Must be U.S. citizens or permanent residents. For students entering first or second year of graduate study. Must have B.A. degree in related field, such as applied mathematics or physics; chemical, electrical, mechanical, metallurgical, or nuclear engineering; or materials science.

Contact Sandra Johnson at above location for details and list of participating institutions.

2121 — OAK RIDGE INSTITUTE FOR SCIENCE AND EDUCATION/U.S. DEPT. OF ENERGY (Office of Civilian Radioactive Waste Management Fellowship)

P.O. Box 117
Oak Ridge TN 37831-0117
423/576-0128
FAX: 423/576-8293
E-Mail: drostp@orau.gov

AMOUNT: $14,000/yr.

DEADLINE(S): JAN 16 (Received, not postmarked)

FIELD(S): Physical or life sciences, math, or engineering

Fellowships for graduate students at various participating universities to conduct research in the management of spent nuclear fuel and high-level raqdioactive waste. For M.A. and Ph.D. candidates. For up to 48 months. Must be U.S. citizen or permanent resident.

Funded through U.S. Department of Energy, Office of Civilian Radioactive Waste Management. Contact or call Ms. Portia Drost, MS-16, at above address for details.

2122 — OAK RIDGE INSTITUTE FOR SCIENCE AND EDUCATION (Nuclear Engineering & Health Physics Fellowship Program)

105 Mitchell Rd. MS-16
Oak Ridge TN 37831-0117
423/576-2600 or 423/241-2890
E-Mail: johnsons@orau.gov or
daltonj@arou.gov

AMOUNT: $14,400/yr.

DEADLINE(S): JAN 26

FIELD(S): Engineering, physical and life sciences

Fellowships in nuclear engineering or applied health physics to implement DOE's nuclear energy-related mission. Candidates must have B.A. degree in life or physical sciences or engineering.

For details and application, contact Sandra Johnson or Jennifer Dalton at above location.

2123 — ONTARIO MINISTRY OF EDUCATION AND TRAINING (John Charles Polanyi Prizes)

189 Red River Rd.
4th Floor, Box 4500
Thunder Bay Ontario P7B 6G9 CANADA
800/465-3957
TDD: 800/465-3958
Internet: osap.gov.on.ca

AMOUNT: $15,000

DEADLINE(S): Varies

FIELD(S): Physics; Chemistry; Physiology; Medicine; Literature; Economics

Monetary prizes are awarded to Canadian citizens/permanent residents who are continuing postdoctoral studies at an Ontario university. Awards are designed to encourage and reward academic excellence.

5 awards annually. Contact your university or the Ontario Council of Graduate Studies for an application.

2124 — OPEN SOCIETY INSTITUTE (Environmental Management Fellowships)

400 West 59th St.
New York NY 10019
212/548-0600 or 212/757-2323
FAX: 212/548-4679 or 212/548-4600
Internet: www.soros.org/efp.html

AMOUNT: Fees, room, board, living stipend, textbooks, international transportation, health insurance

DEADLINE(S): NOV 15

FIELD(S): Earth sciences, natural sciences, humanities (exc. language), anthropology, sociology, mathematics, or engineering

Two-year fellowships for use in selected universities in the U.S. for international students. For students/professionals in fields related to environmental policy, legislation, and remediation techniques applicable to their home countries.

To apply, contact your local Soros Foundation or Open Society Institute. Further details on website.

2125 — ROYAL SOCIETY (John Murray Fund)

6 Carlton House Terrace
REF REA

London SW1Y 5AG ENGLAND UK
071/839 5561

AMOUNT: Up to 3000 pounds sterling

DEADLINE(S): DEC 10

FIELD(S): Oceanography; Limnology; Zoology; Botany; Geology; Mathematics; Physics

Grants open to British post-doctoral applicants. Award is to be used for the encouragement of travel & work in oceanography or limnology.

The award may be held for 1 year. It is not renewable. Write for complete information—REF JELL.

2126 — ROYAL SOCIETY OF EDINBURGH (BP Research Fellowships)

22/24 George St.
Edinburgh EH2 2PQ SCOTLAND
0131 225 6057
FAX: 0131 220 6889
E-Mail: rse@rse.org.uk

AMOUNT: 17,606 to 26,508 pounds sterling

DEADLINE(S): MAR 10

FIELD(S): Mechanical, Chemical, or Control Engineering; Organic Chemistry; Solid State Physics; Information Technology; Geologic Sciences

Research fellowships to Scotland higher education institutions. For post-doctoral researchers age 35 or under on the date of appointment (usually Oct. 1). For research in above disciplines.

Write for complete information.

2127 — SCIENCE ADVANCEMENT PROGRAMS RESEARCH CORPORATION (Research Awards)

101 N. Wilmot Rd., Ste. 250
Tucson AZ 85711
520/571-1111
FAX: 520/571-1119
E-Mail: awards@rescorp.org
Internet: www.rescorp.org

AMOUNT: Varies

DEADLINE(S): Varies

FIELD(S): Astronomy; Chemistry; Physics

Several awards for research are available to faculty members and assistant professors who teach in university departments of astronomy, chemistry, and physics.

See website or contact above address for details.

2128 — SMITHSONIAN INSTITUTION (National Air & Space Museum Guggenheim Fellowship)

National Air and Space Museum, MRC 312
Washington DC 20560
Written inquiry

AMOUNT: $14,000 (predoctoral); $25,000 (postdoctoral)

DEADLINE(S): JAN 15

FIELD(S): Historical research related to aviation and space

Predoctoral applicants should have completed preliminary course work and exams and be engaged in dissertation research. Postdoctoral applicants should have received their Ph.D within the past seven years. Contact Fellowship Coordinator at above location.

Open to all nationalities. Fluency in English required. Duration is 6-12 months.

2129 — SMITHSONIAN INSTITUTION (National Air & Space Museum Verville Fellowship)

National Air and Space Museum, MRC 312
Washington DC 20560
Written inquiry

AMOUNT: $30,000 stipend for 12 months + travel and misc. expenses

DEADLINE(S): JAN 15

FIELD(S): Analysis of major trends, developments, and accomplishments in the history of aviation or space studies

A competitive nine- to twelve-month in-residence fellowship in the above field of study. Advanced degree is NOT a requirement. Contact Fellowship Coordinator at above location.

Open to all nationalities. Fluency in English required.

2130 — THE DAPHNE JACKSON MEMORIAL FELLOWSHIPS TRUST (Fellowships in Science/Engineering)

School of Physical Sciences
Dept. of Physics
University of Surrey
Guildford, Surrey
GU2 5XH ENGLAND UK
01483 259166
FAX: 01483 259501
E-Mail: J.Woolley@surrey.ac.uk
Internet: www.sst.ph.ic.ac.uk/trust/

AMOUNT: Varies

DEADLINE(S): Varies

FIELD(S): Science or engineering, including information sciences

Fellowships to enable well-qualified and highly motivated scientists and engineers to return to appropriate careers following a career break due to family comitments. May be used on a flexible, part-time basis. Tenable at various U.K. universities.

See website and/or contact organization for details.

2131 — THE NOVARTIS FOUNDATION (Scientific Research Fellowships/Bursaries)

41 Portland Place
London W1N 4BN ENGLAND UK
+44 171 636 9456
FAX: +44 171 436 2840
E-Mail: abrown@Novartisfound.org.uk
Internet: www.novartisfound.demon.co.uk/bursary.htm

AMOUNT: Travel expenses, meals, lodging

DEADLINE(S): Varies

FIELD(S): Sciences

Fellowships/bursaries for young scientists, ages 23-35, to attend aFoundation symposium and then spend from 4-12 weeks in the laboratory of one of the symposium participants. For subject matter, see "Nature" or other appropriate journals or check with the Foundation or an office of the British Council.

For application details, see website or contact organization.

2132 — THE UNIVERSITY OF WALES (Graduate/Postgraduate Scholarships in Physics)

University of Wales, Aberystwyth
Cerdigion SY23 WALES UK
(01970) 622805
FAX: (01970) 622803
E-Mail: A.Evans@aber.ac.uk
Internet: www.aber.ac.uk/~dphwww/pgrad/pgscholar.html

AMOUNT: Varies

DEADLINE(S): MAR 2

FIELD(S): Physics

Scholarships for graduate/postgraduate students in physics at this university in Wales. May include travel/conference funds. Tenable for three years and open to UK/EU stents with an upper second or first class honours degree or equivalent.

For more info., contact Dr. Andrews Evans. See website for more details.

2133 — THE UNIVERSITY OF WALES (Scholarships in Physics With Technical English)

University of Wales, Aberystwyth, Penglais
Cerdigion SY23 2BZ WALES UK
+44-(0)1970-62287
FAX: +44-(0)1970-622826
E-Mail: kpi@aber.ac.uk
Internet: www.aber.ac.uk/~dphwww/tech/tech.html

AMOUNT: Costs of courses

DEADLINE(S): None

FIELD(S): Physics and English

Scholarships for non-English-speaking students who wish to pursue studies in physics at this university in Wales. The scholarship provides an English language course, weekly tutorials in Technical English, and the course work in physics once English in learned to complete the technical work. Student needs IELTS 6.5 or TOFEL 580 or equivalent. Must qualify for British university entrance in physics and mathematics for an Honours Degree Course.

For more information, write, phone, fax, or E-mail Dr. Keith Birkinshaw, Dept. of Physics. Also, see website for more details.

2134 — THE WALT DISNEY COMPANY (American Teacher Awards)

P.O. Box 9805
Calabasas CA 91372

AMOUNT: $2,500 (36 awards); $25,000 (Outstanding Teacher of the Year)

DEADLINE(S): FEB 15

FIELD(S): Teachers: athletic coach, early childhood, English, foreign language/ESL, general elementary, mathematics, performing arts, physical education/health, science, social studies, visual arts, voc/tech education

Awards for K-12 teachers in the above fields.

Teachers, or anyone who knows a great teacher, can write for applications at the above address.

2135 — TRENT UNIVERSITY (Graduate Teaching/Research Assistantships)

P.O. Box 4800
Graduate Studies Officer
Peterborough Ontario CANADA K9J 7B8
705/748-1245

AMOUNT: $3,500 per term

DEADLINE(S): FEB 15

FIELD(S): Anthropology, Geography, Archaeology, Biology, Canadian Studies, Philosophy, Cultural Studies, Computer Science, Mathematics, Physics, Chemistry, Environmental Science/Studies

Teaching/research assistantships at Trent University in the above fields. Open to masters and doctoral candidates. Tenable for up to 4 terms spanning 2-3 years of study.

80 awards per year. Write for complete information.

2136 — UNCF/MERCK SCIENCE INITIATIVE (Graduate Science Research Dissertation Fellowships)

8260 Willow Oaks Corporate Dr.
PO Box 10444
Fairfax VA 22031-4511

703/205-3503
FAX: 703/205-3574
E-Mail: uncfmerck@uncf.org
Internet: www.uncf.org/merck

AMOUNT: $40,000/yr. (max.)

DEADLINE(S): JAN 31

FIELD(S): Life & Physical Sciences

Open to African-Americans enrolled full-time in a Ph.D. degree program and within 1-3 years of completing dissertation. Awards are intended to help students complete coursework, conduct research, and prepare dissertation for degree in the biomedically relevant life or physical sciences. Must be US citizen/permanent resident. Financial need NOT a factor.

12 awards annually. Not renewable. Contact Jerry Bryant, Ph.D., for an application.

2137 — US DEPARTMENT OF DEFENSE (National Defense Science & Engineering Graduate Fellowship Programs)

200 Park Drive, Suite 211, P.O. Box 13444
Research Triangle Park, NC 27709-3444
919/549-8505
Internet: www.acq.osd.mil/ddre/edugate/s-aindx.html

AMOUNT: Full tuition and fees (tenure of 36 months)

DEADLINE(S): JAN

FIELD(S): Mathematical, physical, biological, ocean, and engineering sciences

Must be US citizens or nationals at or near the beginning of their graduate study in science or engineering, leading to a doctoral degree. NDSEG Fellowships are awarded for study and research in these disciplines of military importance.

Approximately 90 new three-year graduate fellowships each April. Fellows may choose appropriate US institutions of higher education, offering degrees in science and engineering. Contact the Program Administrator for more information.

2138 — WINSTON CHURCHILL FOUNDATION (Scholarships)

PO Box 1240
Gracie Station
New York NY 10028-0048
212/879-3480
FAX: 212/897-3480
E-Mail: churchillf@aol.com

AMOUNT: $27,000 (includes tuition, fees, travel, & living/spousal allowances)

DEADLINE(S): NOV 15

FIELD(S): Engineering; Mathematics; Science

Open to US citizens enrolled in one of 55 participating US colleges and universities to pursue graduate study at Churchill College at Cambridge University in England. Must be between the ages of 19 and 26. Financial need NOT a factor.

11 awards annually. Not renewable. Must apply through home institution.

2139 — WOMEN IN DEFENSE (HORIZONS Scholarship Foundation)

NDIA
2111 Wilson Blvd., Ste. 400
Arlington VA 22201-3061
703/247-2552
FAX: 703/522-1885
E-Mail: dnwlee@moon.jic.com
Internet: www.adpa.org/wid/horizon/Scholar.htm

AMOUNT: $500+

DEADLINE(S): NOV 1; JUL 1

FIELD(S): Engineering, Computer Science, Physics, Mathematics, Business, Law, International Relations, Political Science, Operations Research, Economics, and fields relevant to a career in the areas of national security and defense.

For women who are U.S. citizens, have minimum GPA of 3.25, demonstrate financial need, are currently enrolled at an accredited university/college (full- or part-time—both grads and undergrad juniors/seniors are eligible), and demonstrate interest in pursuing a career related to national security.

Application is online or send SASE, #10 envelope, to Woody Lee, HORIZONS Scholarship Director.

2140 — WOODROW WILSON NATIONAL FELLOWSHIP FOUNDATION (Leadership Program for Teachers)

CN 5281
Princeton NJ 08543-5281
609/452-7007
FAX: 609/452-0066
E-Mail: marchioni@woodrow.org OR irish@woodrow.org
Internet: www.woodrow.org

AMOUNT: Varies

DEADLINE(S): Varies

FIELD(S): Science; Mathematics

WWLPT offers summer institutes for middle and high school teachers in science and mathematics. One- and two-week teacher outreach, TORCH Institutes, are held in the summer throughout the US.

See website or contact WWNFF for an application.

2141 — WOODS HOLE OCEANOGRAPHIC INSTITUTION (Postdoctoral Awards in Ocean Science and Engineering)

360 Woods Hole Road
Woods Hole MA 02543-1541
508/289-2219
FAX: 508/457-2188
E-Mail: mgately@whoi.edu
Internet: www.whoi.edu

AMOUNT: Varies

DEADLINE(S): FEB 16

FIELD(S): Chemistry, Engineering, Geology, Geophysics, Mathematics, Meteorology, Physics, Biology, Oceanography

Eighteen-month postdoctoral scholar awards are offered to recipients of new or recent doctorates in the above fields. The awards are designed to further the education and training of the applicant with primary emphasis placed on the individual's research promise.

For an application/more information, contact the Education Office, Clark Laboratory 223, MS #31, at above address.

2142 — WOODS HOLE OCEANOGRAPHIC INSTITUTION (Research Fellowships in Marine Policy and Ocean Management)

360 Woods Hole Road
Woods Hole MA 02543-1541
508/289-2219
FAX: 508/457-2188
E-Mail: mgately@whoi.edu
Internet: www.whoi.edu

AMOUNT: Varies

DEADLINE(S): FEB 16

FIELD(S): Social Sciences, Law, Natural Sciences

For professionals in the above fields who wish to apply their training to investigations of problems involving the use of the oceans. WHOI's objective is to provide a year-long advanced learning experience in ocean policy problems involving the interdisciplinary application of social science and natural science to marine policy problems. Fields currently emphasized: economics, statistics, public policy, natural resource management, and international relations.

For an application/more information, contact the Education Office, Clark Laboratory 223, MS #31, at above address.

MEDICAL DOCTOR

2143 — ACCESS GROUP (Loan Programs)

1411 Foulk Road
Box 7430
Wilmington DE 19803-0430
302/477-4190 or 800/282-1550
FAX: 302/477-4080
Internet: www.accessgroup.org

AMOUNT: Varies

DEADLINE(S): Varies (last day of current school term)

FIELD(S): Law, Business, Medical, Dental

Loans at competitive rates to graduate students attending law, business, medical, dental, and a variety of other graduate and professional schools.

Must be a US citizen or legal resident. No co-signer required for qualified applicants. No need to locate a lender, and no interview required. Visit website or contact Pat Curry at above address for complete information.

2144 — AMERICAN ACADEMY OF CHILD AND ADOLESCENT PSYCHIATRY (Minority Medical Student Fellowships)

3615 Wisconsin Ave., NW
Washington DC 20016-3007
800/333-7636, ext. 113 or 202/966-7300
FAX: 202/966-2891
E-Mail: kpope@aacap.org
Internet: www.aacap.org

AMOUNT: $2,500 stipend + attendance at AACAP annual meeting

DEADLINE(S): APR 1

FIELD(S): Child & Adolescent Psychiatry; Drug Abuse & Addiction

Three fellowship programs each include stipend to work with child and adolescent psychiatrist researcher or clinician during the summer, as well as expenses to AACAP Annual Meeting, where student will present poster, attend symposia & workshops, and meet with leaders in field. Must be an African American, Asian American, Alaskan Native, Mexican American, Hispanic, or Pacific Islander attending an accredited US medical school.

Contact Kayla Pope, Director of Research & Training, for program guidelines and an application.

2145 — AMERICAN ACADEMY OF CHILD AND ADOLESCENT PSYCHIATRY (Resident Awards)

3615 Wisconsin Ave., NW
Washington DC 20016-3007
800/333-7636, ext. 113 or 202/966-7300
FAX: 202/966-2891
E-Mail: kpope@aacap.org
Internet: www.aacap.org

AMOUNT: $100-$2,500 (for travel, lodging, etc. + attendace at Annual Meeting)

DEADLINE(S): MAR 15

FIELD(S): Child & Adolescent Psychiatry

Presidential Scholar Awards recognize specialized competence among child & adolescent psychiatry

residents in research, public policy, and innovative service systems. Award is for one week's tutorial & exchange in specified area of study with senior Academy leader. Must make formal presentation at Annual Meeting. Robinson-Cunningham Award recognizes a paper on some aspect of child & adolescent psychiatry. Must have been started during residency.

Must be nominated for Presidential Scholar Award. Manuscripts for Robinson-Cunningham Award due June 1st. Contact Kayla Pope at AACAP for more information.

2146 — AMERICAN ACADEMY OF CHILD AND ADOLESCENT PSYCHIATRY (Pilot Research Award)

3615 Wisconsin Ave., NW
Washington DC 20016-3007
800/333-7636, ext. 113 or 202/966-7300
FAX: 202/966-2891
E-Mail: kpope@aacap.org
Internet: www.aacap.org

AMOUNT: $9,000 + 5 days at AACAP annual meeting

DEADLINE(S): MAR 15

FIELD(S): Child & Adolescent Psychiatry

Must be board eligible, certified in child & adolescent psychiatry, or enrolled in child psychiatry residency/ fellowship program. Must have full-time faculty appointment in accredited medical school or be in fully accredited clinical/research training program. May not have had more than two years experience following graduation from residency/fellowship training nor have had any previous significant, non-salary, individual research funding. Matched with investigator.

Must complete work within one year. 5 awards annually. Contact Kayla Pope at AACAP for application guidelines.

2147 — AMERICAN ACADEMY OF PEDIATRICS (Residency Scholarship Program)

141 NW Point Blvd
PO Box 927
Elk Grove Village IL 60007
847/981-6759
FAX: 847/228-5097

AMOUNT: $1,000 - $5,000

DEADLINE(S): FEB

FIELD(S): Pediatrics

Funds for physicians who have completed their internship & have at least 1 year remaining in an accredited pediatric resident program or for a pediatric resident with a definite commitment for another year of residency in a program accredited by the Residency Review Committee for Pediatrics.

Renewable. AAP members automatically receive applications. Contact Jackie Bucko at above address/ phone.

2148 — AMERICAN ASSOCIATION OF UNIVERSITY WOMEN EDUCATIONAL FOUNDATION (Selected Professions Fellowships for Women of Color)

Dept. 60
2201 N. Dodge St.
Iowa City IA 52243-4030
319/337-1716, ext. 60
FAX: 319/337-1204
Internet: www.aauw.org

AMOUNT: $5,000-$12,000

DEADLINE(S): JAN 2

FIELD(S): Business Administration; Law; Medicine

For women of color in their final year of graduate study to increase their participation in historically underrepresented fields. Must be US citizen or permanent resident. Special consideration is given to applicants who show professional promise in innovative or neglected areas of research and/or practice in areas of public interest.

Contact AAUW for an application between August 1st & December 20th.

2149 — AMERICAN COLLEGE OF LEGAL MEDICINE (Student Writing Competition)

611 E. Wells St.
Milwaukee WI 53202
800/433-9137 or 414/276-1881
FAX: 414/276-3349
E-Mail: info@aclm.org
Internet: www.aclm.org

AMOUNT: $1,000

DEADLINE(S): FEB 1

FIELD(S): Legal Medicine

Award for the best paper on any aspect of legal medicine. Open to postgraduate students enrolled in an accredited school of law, medicine, dentistry, podiatry, nursing, pharmacy, health science, or health care administration in the US or Canada.

3 awards annually. Contact Laura Morrone at ACLM for entry rules.

2150 — AMERICAN HEART ASSOCIATION (Helen N. and Harold B. Shapira Scholarship)

4701 West 77th Street
Minneapolis MN 55435
612/835-3300

AMOUNT: $1,000

DEADLINE(S): APR 1

FIELD(S): Medicine

For pre-med undergraduate students & medical students who are accepted to or enrolled in an accredited Minnesota college or university. Medical students should be in a curriculum that is related to the heart and circulatory system.

May be renewed once. U.S. citizenship or legal residency required. Write for complete information.

2151 — AMERICAN INDIAN SCIENCE AND ENGINEERING SOCIETY (A.T. Anderson Memorial Scholarship)

PO Box 9828
Albuquerque NM 87119-9828
505/765-1052
FAX: 505/765-5608
E-Mail: scholarships@aises.org
Internet: www.aises.org/scholarships

AMOUNT: $1,000-$2,000

DEADLINE(S): JUN 15

FIELD(S): Medicine; Natural Resources; Science; Engineering

Open to undergraduate and graduate students who are at least 1/4 American Indian or recognized as member of a tribe. Must be member of AISES ($10 fee), enrolled full-time at an accredited institution, and demonstrate financial need.

Renewable. See website or contact Patricia Browne for an application and/or membership information.

2152 — AMERICAN MEDICAL ASSOCIATION FOUNDATION (Jerry L. Pettis Memorial Scholarship)

515 N. State St.
Chicago IL 60610
312/464-4543
FAX: 312/464-5678
E-Mail: rita_palulonis@ama-assn.org
Internet: www.ama-assn.org/med-sci/erf

AMOUNT: $2,500

DEADLINE(S): JAN 31

FIELD(S): Medicine: Communication of Science

Open to junior or senior medical students with a demonstrated interest and involvement in the communication of science. Recipient will be selected from among nominees proposed by the deans of AMA-approved medical schools. Each school may propose one student. Must submit letter of nomination from Office of Dean, letter of application, curriculum vitae, and reprints/other materials prepared by student to support nomination. Financial need NOT a factor.

Contact Rita M. Palulonis, Associate Director, at the AMA Foundation for nomination procedures. Recipient will be announced by May 1st.

2153 — AMERICAN MEDICAL ASSOCIATION FOUNDATION (Johnson F. Hammond, MD, Memorial Scholarship)

515 N. State St.
Chicago IL 60610

312/464-4543
FAX: 312/464-5678
E-Mail: rita_palulonis@ama-assn.org
Internet: www.ama-assn.org/med-sci/erf

AMOUNT: $3,000

DEADLINE(S): JAN 31

FIELD(S): Medicine: Medical Journalism

For medical students with demonstrated interest & involvement in medical journalism. Recipient selected from nominees proposed by deans of AMA-approved medical schools. Each school may propose one student. Must submit letters of nomination, recommendation, & application, as well as curriculum vitae & reprints of published articles prepared by student to support nomination. Must have high moral character & outstanding academic achievement. Financial need NOT a factor.

Contact Rita M. Palulonis, Associate Director, at the AMA Foundation for nomination procedures. Recipient will be announced by May 1st.

2154 — AMERICAN MEDICAL ASSOCIATION FOUNDATION (Rock Sleyster, MD, Memorial Scholarship)

515 N. State St.
Chicago IL 60610
312/464-4567
FAX: 312/464-5973
E-Mail: maria_ramos@ama-assn.org
Internet: www.ama-assn.org/amafoundation

AMOUNT: $2,500

DEADLINE(S): MAY 1

FIELD(S): Psychiatry

One-year awards for US citizens enrolled as students in US or Canadian medical schools, who aspire to specialize in psychiatry. Based on demonstrated interest in psychiatry, scholarship, & financial need. Each medical school in the US and Canada is invited to submit nominees, in accordance with the size of the 3rd year class. Must submit application form, three letters supporting the nomination, AMA Foundation Student Financial Statement, & medical school transcript.

20 awards annually. Contact Harry S. Jonas, MD, Director, at the AMA Foundation for nomination procedures. Recipients will be announced by September 1st.

2155 — AMERICAN PSYCHIATRIC ASSOCIATION (APA/GlaxoWellcome Fellowship Program)

1400 K St., NW
Washington DC 20005
202/682-6097
FAX: 202/682-6837

E-Mail: apa@psych.org

Internet: www.psych.org

AMOUNT: Varies

DEADLINE(S): MAR 31

FIELD(S): Psychiatry

A fellowship program to acquaint selected psychiatry residents with the work of APA and with national issues affecting psychiatry. Must have passed a national or state board exam and be nominated by an accredited psychiatric residency training program. Must be member of APA or have applied for membership. Based on clinical acumen, statements of effectiveness, leadership, curriculum vitae, educational performance, evaluation, honors/awards, teaching, and research.

Contact APA for membership information or an application. Notification is in June.

2156 — ARMENIAN GENERAL BENEVOLENT UNION (Educational Loan Program)

Education Dept., 31 W. 52nd St.

New York NY 10019-6118

212/765-8260

FAX: 212/765-8209/8209

E-Mail: agbuny@aol.com

AMOUNT: $5,000 to $7,500/yr.

DEADLINE(S): APR 1

FIELD(S): Law (J.D.) and Medicine (M.D.)

Loans for full-time students of Armenian heritage pursuing their first professional degrees in law or medicine. Must be attending highly competitive institutions in the U.S. GPA of 3.5 or more required.

Loan repayments begin within 12 months of completion of full-time study and extend 5 to ten years, depending on the size of the loan. Interest is 3% Write for complete information.

2157 — ARTHUR M. MILLER FUND

P.O. Box 1122

Wichita KS 67201-0004

316/261-4609

AMOUNT: Varies

DEADLINE(S): MAR 31

FIELD(S): Medicine or related fields

Scholarships for Kansas residents for the study of medicine or related fields at accredited instutitions.

Send SASE for formal application.

2158 — ASSOCIATION OF AMERICAN MEDICAL COLLEGES (AAMC MedLoans Program)

2450 N St., NW

Washington DC 20037-1126

800/858-5050 or 202/828-0400

FAX: 202/828-1125

AMOUNT: Varies

DEADLINE(S): None

FIELD(S): Medicine

This program provides medical students access to the Stafford Loan (GSL), Supplemental Loans for Students (SLS), Alternative Loan Program (ALP), and Health Education Assistance Loan (HEAL). No application fees, cosigners, state residency requirements, collateral prior business relationships, or in-school interest payments are required.

Contact your medical school's financial aid office or AAMC's MEDLOANS Program for an application.

2159 — ASSOCIATION OF SURGEONS OF GREAT BRITAIN AND IRELAND (Moynihan Travelling Fellowship)

RCS

35-43 Lincoln's Inn Fields

London WC2A 3PN ENGLAND UK

0171 973 0300

FAX: 0171 430 9235

E-Mail: admin@asgbi.org.uk

Internet: asgbi.org.uk

AMOUNT: 4,000 pounds sterling

DEADLINE(S): OCT 4

FIELD(S): General Surgery (or sub-specialty thereof)

For residents of the UK and the Republic of Ireland who are Specialist Registrars towards the end of higher surgical training or Consultants within three years of appointment. Purpose is to enable them to broaden their education and to present and discuss their contribution to British and Irish surgery overseas. Must submit curriculum vitae of publications & appointments and proposal of costs, travel, & objectives. Financial need NOT a factor.

1 award annually. Not renewable. Contact Mrs. N. Lewis at ASGBI for an application. Overseas Surgical Fellowship also available for surgeons who wish to work short-term in the Third World.

2160 — AUSTRIAN CULTURAL INSTITUTE (Max Kade Foundation Grants)

950 Third Ave.

20th Fl.

New York NY 10022

212/759-5165 or +43/1/51581-253

FAX: 212/319-9636

E-Mail: desk@aci.org

Internet: www.austriaculture.net

AMOUNT: Varies

DEADLINE(S): Varies

FIELD(S): Medicine; Natural Sciences; Engineering

Open to young Austrian scientists with several years of experience at universities or institutions. Must demonstrate capacity to pursue independent teaching or research activities in the US. Proficiency in English required.

See website or contact ACI for an application kit, or write to Osterreichische Akademie der Wissenschaften, Kommission fur Max Kade Stipendien, Dr. Ignaz Seipel-Platz 2, A-1010 Vienna, Austria.

2161 — BECA FOUNDATION (Alice Newell Joslyn Medical Fund)

310 Via Vera Cruz, Ste. 101

San Marcos CA 92069

760/471-5465

FAX: 760/471-9175

AMOUNT: $500-$2,000

DEADLINE(S): MAR 1

FIELD(S): Medicine; Health Care; Nursing; Dental/ Medical Assisting; Physical Therapy

Open to Latino students who live in or attend college in San Diego County, CA, at time of application. For high school seniors and those already in college pursuing undergraduate or graduate education. Based on financial need, scholastic determination, and community/cultural awareness. BECA also provides a mentor to each scholarship recipient.

Send self-addressed, stamped envelope to BECA for an application.

2162 — BODOSSAKI FOUNDATION (Academic Prizes)

20 Amalias Ave.

GR-105 57 Athens GREECE

3220 962

FAX: 3237 976

AMOUNT: Drs. 7,000,000

DEADLINE(S): DEC 31

FIELD(S): Pure mathematics, theoretical and applied computer science, operations research, cardiovascular diseases, developmental biology

Awards to support the creative work of young Greek academics and scientists and reward their endeavor in the advancement of learning and the creation of sound values. Must be of Greek nationality, parentage, or descent under age 40.

Contact above address for details.

2163 — BOEING (Polish Graduate Student Scholarship Program)

Phone for details

314/234-2149

AMOUNT: Tuition, books, and fees for three years

DEADLINE(S): Varies

FIELD(S): Scientific and technical fields

Scholarships for students from Poland to pursue graduate studies in scientific and technical areas at American colleges or universities.

Call Jim Schlueter at above telephone number.

2164 — BUSINESS & PROFESSIONAL WOMEN'S FOUNDATION (BPW Career Advancement Scholarship Program)

2012 Massachusetts Ave., NW
Washington DC 20036-1070
202/293-1200, ext. 169
FAX: 202/861-0298
Internet: www.bpwusa.org

AMOUNT: $500-$1,000

DEADLINE(S): APR 15

FIELD(S): Biology, Science, Education, Engineering, Social Science, Paralegal, Humanities, Business, Math, Computers, Law, MD, DD

For women (US citizens) aged 25+ accepted into accredited program at US institution (+Puerto Rico & Virgin Islands). Must graduate within 12 to 24 months from the date of grant and demonstrate critical finanacial need. Must have a plan to upgrade skills, train for a new career field, or to enter/re-enter the job market.

Full- or part-time study. For info see website or send business-sized, self-addressed, double-stamped envelope.

2165 — CHARLES A. LAUFFER SCHOLARSHIP FUND (Scholarship-Loans)

PO Box 15507
St. Petersburg FL 33733
727/827-6907
FAX: 727/827-6934

AMOUNT: $1,500-$4,000

DEADLINE(S): JUN 1

FIELD(S): Medicine

Special low-interest (2%) scholarship-loans open to 3rd and 4th year med students who will practice in the US. Academic standing and financial need are considerations.

25 awards annually. Contact Charles A. Lauffer Fund for an application.

2166 — CHEMICAL INDUSTRY INSTITUTE OF TOXICOLOGY (Postdoctoral Fellowships)

PO Box 12137
Research Triangle Park NC 27709
919/558-1200
FAX: 919/558-1430

AMOUNT: Varies

DEADLINE(S): None

FIELD(S): Toxicology; Pathology

CIIT provides stipends and support to postdoctoral research fellows who pursue original research related to chemical toxicity and/or pathology. Tenable only at CIIT's laboratory.

10-15 awards annually. Renewable up to 3 years. Contact CIIT for an application.

2167 — CHINESE AMERICAN MEDICAL SOCIETY (Scholarships)

281 Edgewood Ave.
Teaneck NJ 07666
201/833-1506
FAX: 201/833-8252
E-Mail: hws@columbia.edu
Internet: www.camsociety.org

AMOUNT: $1,000-$1,500

DEADLINE(S): MAR 31

FIELD(S): Medicine; Dentistry

Scholarships for graduate students of Chinese ancestry who reside in the US and will attend medical or dental school. Financial need NOT a factor.

4-6 awards annually. Not renewable. Contact Dr. H. H. Wang at CAMS for an application.

2168 — COLUMBIANA COUNTY PUBLIC HEALTH LEAGUE TRUST FUND (Grants)

PO Box 1428
Steubenville OH 43952
740/283-8433
FAX: 740/282-4530

AMOUNT: Varies

DEADLINE(S): FEB 28

FIELD(S): Respiratory Illness; Medicine; Medical Research; Pharmacy; Medical Technology; Physical Therapy; Nursing; Dental Hygiene; Occupational Therapy

Open to undergraduate and graduate Columbiana County, Ohio, residents who are pursuing medical education or research in one of the above fields. Preference given to respiratory illness. Students of veterinary medicine NOT eligible.

Contact Sherrill Schmied for an application.

2169 — COMMANDER, NAVAL RESERVE RECRUITING COMMAND (Health Professionals Loan Repayment Program - HPLRP)

Attn Code 132
4400 Dauphine St.
New Orleans LA 70146
Written Inquiry

AMOUNT: Loan repayment up to $3,000 per year ($20,000 total)

DEADLINE(S): None specified

FIELD(S): Physicians: surgery & anesthesia; Nurses: nurse anesthesia, operating room nursing, med-surg nursing.

Open to health professionals fully qualified in critically short wartime specialties who serve in a military reserve (Selected Reserve or Individual Mobilization Augmentee Program). May be repaid on an individual's outstanding educational loan balance.

Navy: above address; Army: Headquarters, Dept. of the Army, 5109 Leesburg Pike, Falls Church, VA 22041-3258; US Air Force Reserve Personnel Center, ATTN: ARPC/SGI, Denver, CO 80280-5000.

2170 — CONCORDIA UNIVERSITY (J.P. Zewig Scholarship)

1455 de Maisonneuve Blvd. West
Room M 201
Montreal Quebec H3G 1M8 CANADA
514/848-3809
FAX: 514/848-2812
E-Mail: awardsgs@vax2.concordia.ca

AMOUNT: Varies

DEADLINE(S): SEP 20

FIELD(S): Psychology; Exercise Science; Behaviourial Medicine

This one-year scholarship is awarded to a graduate student pursuing research in the above areas. Candidates are to be nominated by Faculty members from these areas of research.

1 award annually. Not renewable. Contact the Graduate Awards Office in the School of Graduate Studies at Concordia University for nomination procedures.

2171 — DEKALB COUNTY PRODUCERS SUPPLY & FARM BUREAU (Medical Scholarship)

1350 W. Prairie Drive
Sycamore, IL 60178
815/756-6361

AMOUNT: Varies

DEADLINE(S): JUNE

FIELD(S): Medical Doctor; Nursing

Applicants (or their parents) must have been voting or associate members of Dekalb County Farm Bureau for at least 2 years prior to application; agree to practice in rural Illinois for 3 years upon completion of training & be a US citizen.

Must have been accepted to or be attending medical school or a nursing program. Write to Virginia Fleetwood at above address for complete information.

2172 — DEPARTMENT OF THE ARMY (Armed Forces Health Professions Scholarships)

Attn: RC-HS
1307 Third Ave.
Fort Knox KY 40121

502/626-0367
FAX: 502/626-0923
AMOUNT: Tuition + monthly stipend
DEADLINE(S): None
FIELD(S): Medicine; Osteopathy; Nurse Anesthetist; Veterinary Medicine; Optometry; Psychology; Dentistry

Open to health professionals and students participating in a Reserve Service of the US Armed Forces, training in the specialties listed above. Varying lengths of service are required to pay back the stipend. Must be US citizen. Award is based on a competitive process, including GPA. Financial need NOT a factor.

400 awards annually. Contact Major Beecher at above address for an application.

2173 — DEPARTMENT OF THE ARMY (Health Professionals Loan Repayment Program)

Attn: RC-HS
1307 Third Ave.
Fort Knox KY 40121
502/626-0367
FAX: 502/626-0923
AMOUNT: $20,000/yr. (max.)
DEADLINE(S): None
FIELD(S): Medicine; Nursing

Loan repayment is open to health professionals fully qualified in critically short wartime specialties who serve in a military reserve. Specialties include physician assistants; general dentists; oral surgeons; critical care & nurse anesthetists; general, thoracic, & orthopedic surgeons; urologists; diagnostic radiologists; psychiatrists; preventative & critical care medicine; and primary care physicians.

Contact Major Beecher at above address for an application.

2174 — DUPAGE COUNTY MEDICAL SOCIETY FOUNDATION (Scholarship Program)

498 Hillside Ave., #1
Glen Ellyn IL 60137
630/858-9603
AMOUNT: $250-$1,000
DEADLINE(S): APR 30
FIELD(S): Medical/Health-Care Fields

Open to voting residents of Dupage County, Illinois, who are accepted to or enrolled in a professional training program at a qualified school. Based on financial need and scholastic ability. Program does not apply to undergraduate studies, such as pre-med; students would be eligible after completing four-year pre-med program and having been accepted into medical school.

Contact Medical Society for an application.

2175 — EDUCATIONAL COMMISSION FOR FOREIGN MEDICAL GRADUATES (International Fellowships in Medical Education)

2401 Pennsylvania Ave., NW, Ste. 475
Washington DC 20037
202/293-9320
FAX: 202/457-0751
AMOUNT: $2,200/month, roundtrip airfare, + health insurance for fellow & dependents
DEADLINE(S): AUG 15
FIELD(S): Medical Education

For faculty from schools of medicine outside the United States to study aspects of medical education that have the potential to improve medical education in their home country institutions and departments. Must reside and work in home country at time of application and plan to return there once fellowship ends. Must communicate effectively in English and have not less than three years of work experience following completion of formal & clinical training.

20 awards annually. Notification in February. NO AWARDS FOR DEGREE PROGRAMS, TUITION GRANTS, OR SPECIALTY TRAINING.

2176 — EDWARD BANGS KELLEY AND ELZA KELLEY FOUNDATION, INC. (Scholarship Program)

PO Drawer M
Hyannis MA 02601-1412
508/775-3117
AMOUNT: $4,000 (max.)
DEADLINE(S): APR 30
FIELD(S): Medicine; Nursing; Health Sciences

Open to residents of Barnstable County, Massachusetts. Scholarships are intended to benefit health and welfare of Barnstable County residents. Awards support study at recognized undergraduate, graduate, and professional institutions. Financial need is considered.

Contact Foundation for an application.

2177 — EPILEPSY FOUNDATION OF AMERICA (Behavioral Sciences Student Fellowships)

4351 Garden City Drive
Landover MD 20785-2267
301/459-3700 or 800/EFA-1000
FAX: 301/577-2684
TDD: 800/332-2070
E-Mail: postmaster@efa.org
Internet: www.efa.org
AMOUNT: $2,000
DEADLINE(S): FEB 1
FIELD(S): Epilepsy as related to Behavioral Sciences

Three-month fellowships awarded to students in the behavioral sciences for work on an epilepsy study project. For students of vocational rehabilitation counseling. Students propose an epilepsy-related study or training project to be carried out at a US institution of their choice. A preceptor must accept responsibility for supervision of the student and the project.

Contact EFA for an application.

2178 — EPILEPSY FOUNDATION OF AMERICA (Behavioral Sciences Research Training Fellowships)

4351 Garden City Drive
Landover MD 20785-2267
301/459-3700 or FAX: 301/577-2684
FDD: 800/332-2070
E-Mail: postmaster@efa.org
Internet: www.efa.org
AMOUNT: Up to $30,000
DEADLINE(S): FEB 1
FIELD(S): Epilepsy as related to Behavioral Sciences (includes sociology, social work, psychology, anthropology, nursing, political science, etc.)

A one-year training experience for postdoctoral scholars to develop expertise in the area of epilepsy research relative to the behavioral sciences. The project must be carried out at an approved facility. Amount depends on experience and qualifications of the applicant and the scope and duration of proposed project.

Contact EFA for an application.

2179 — EPILEPSY FOUNDATION OF AMERICA (Junior Investigator Research Grants)

4351 Garden City Drive
Landover MD 20785-2267
301/459-3700 or 800/EFA-1000
FAX: 301/577-2684
TDD: 800/332-2070
E-Mail: postmaster@efa.org
Internet: www.efa.org
AMOUNT: up to $40,000
DEADLINE(S): SEP 1
FIELD(S): Epilepsy as related to Biological, Behavioral, & Social Sciences

One-year research grants to support basic and clinical research in the biological, behavioral, and social sciences which will advance the understanding, treatment, and prevention of epilepsy. Priority given to beginning investigators just entering the field of epilepsy research, to new or innovative projects. Applications evaluated on basis of scientific merit.

Contact EFA for an application.

2180 — EPILEPSY FOUNDATION OF AMERICA (Pre-doctoral Research Training Fellowship)

4351 Garden City Drive
Landover MD 20785-2267
301/459-3700 or 800/EFA-1000
FAX: 301/577-2684
TDD: 800/332-2070
E-Mail: postmaster@efa.org
Internet: www.efa.org

AMOUNT: up to $15,000

DEADLINE(S): SEP 1

FIELD(S): Epilepsy as related to Neuroscience, Physiology, Pharmacology, Psychology, Biochemistry, Genetics, Nursing, or Pharmacy

One-year of support for qualified individuals who are pursuing dissertation research with an epilepsy-related theme, and who are working under the guidance of a mentor with expertise in the area of epilepsy investigation. Graduate students pursuing Ph.D. degree in above fields may apply.

Contact EFA for an application.

2181 — FELLOWS MEMORIAL FUND (Scholarship Loans)

Pensacola Junior College
1000 College Blvd.
Pensacola FL 32504-8998
904/484-1700

AMOUNT: Varies

DEADLINE(S): Varies

FIELD(S): Theology; Health

Loans for ministerial students of the Episcopal faith and others whose religious beliefs are not in substantial conflict with the faith and doctrines of the Episcopal Church. Must be graduate students and residents of one of the following Florida counties: Escambia, Santa Rosa, Okaloosa, or Walton. Qualified health programs include medicine, nursing, medical technology, radiography, respiratory therapy, physical therapy, and physician's assistant.

Loans are interest-free until four months after graduation. Thereafter, favorable interest rates will apply with the total to be repaid by the end of eleven years.

2182 — FINANCE AUTHORITY OF MAINE (Health Professions Loan Program)

119 State House Station
Augusta ME 04333
207/287-2183 (in state: 800/228-3734)
FAX: 207/626-8208
Internet: www.famemaine.com

AMOUNT: $5,000-$15,000

DEADLINE(S): None

FIELD(S): Medicine, dentistry, optometry, or veterinary medicine

For persons who have been Maine residents for at least one year. Must be enrolled in postgraduate health profession school within the U.S.

Contact organization or access website for details.

2183 — FIRST UNITED METHODIST CHURCH (Robert Stevenson & Doreene E. Cater Scholarships)

302 5th Ave., S.
St. Cloud MN 56301
FAX: 320/251-0878
E-Mail: FUMCloud@aol.com

AMOUNT: $100-$300

DEADLINE(S): JUN 1

FIELD(S): Humanitarian & Christian Service: Teaching, Medicine, Social Work, Environmental Studies, etc.

Stevenson Scholarship is open to undergraduate members of the First United Methodist Church of St. Cloud. Cater Scholarship is open to members of the Minnesota United Methodist Conference who are entering the sophomore year or higher of college work. Both require two letters of reference, transcripts, and financial need.

5-6 awards annually. Contact Scholarship Committee for an application.

2184 — FOUNDATION FOR SCIENCE AND DISABILITY, INC. (FSD Science Student Grant Fund)

503 NW 89th Street
Gainesville FL 32607-1400
352/374-5774
FAX: 352/374-5781
E-Mail: rmankin@gainesville.usda.ufl.edu

AMOUNT: $1,000

DEADLINE(S): DEC 1

FIELD(S): Mathematics; Science; Medicine; Engineering; Computer Science

Open to graduate students with disabilities. May also apply as a fourth-year undergraduate accepted into a graduate or professional program. Awards are for some special purpose in connection with a science project or thesis in any of above fields. Student is required to write a 250-word essay which includes a description of professional goals/objectives, as well as purpose of grant. Transcripts and two letters of recommendation from faculty members are also required.

Contact Dr. Richard Mankin at above address for an application.

2185 — FOUNDATION FOR SEACOAST HEALTH (Scholarship Program)

P.O. Box 4606
Portsmouth NH 03802-4606
603/433-3008
FAX: 603/433-2036
E-Mail: ffsh@nh.ultranet.com
Internet: www.nh.ultranet.com/~ffsh

AMOUNT: $1,000-10,000

DEADLINE(S): FEB 1

FIELD(S): Health-related fields

Open to undergraduate and graduate students pursuing health-related fields of study who are legal residents of the following cities in New Hampshire: Portsmouth, Newington, New Castle, Rye, Greenland, N. Hampton, or these cities in Maine: Kittery, Eliot, or York, Maine. Must have resided in the area for at least two years.

Write or check website for details. $150,000 awarded annually; 35 awards given

2186 — GRASS FOUNDATION (Robert S. Morison Fellowship)

77 Reservoir Road
Quincy MA 02170
617/843-0209
617/479-5726

AMOUNT: $40,000 stipend per year + additional $4,000 for research expenses & travel to one scientific meeting.

DEADLINE(S): NOV 1 (of even-numbered years)

FIELD(S): Neurology; Neurosurgery; Neuroscience

Open to MDs preparing for an academic career who have been accepted into or just completed a residency in above areas & wish to undertake a 2-year program of basic research training at a recognized institution in North America.

This is a 2-year program which starts in July of odd-numbered years. Write for complete information.

2187 — H. FLETCHER BROWN FUND (Scholarships)

c/o PNC Bank
Trust Dept.
P.O. Box 791
Wilmington DE 19899
302/429-1186

AMOUNT: Varies

DEADLINE(S): APR 15

FIELD(S): Medicine; Dentistry; Law; Engineering; Chemistry

Open to U.S. citizens born in Delaware and still residing in Delaware. For 4 years of study (undergrad or grad) leading to a degree that enables applicant to practice in chosen field.

Scholarships are based on need, scholastic achievement, and good moral character. Applications available in February. Write for complete information.

2188 — HEADQUARTERS, USAF RESERVE PERSONNEL CENTER (Health Professionals Loan Repayment Program - HPLRP)

6760 E. Irvington PL #7000
Denver CO 80280-7000
1-800-525-0102 ext 231 or 237
DSN 926-6490 or 6484
Commercial: 303/676-6484 or 6490
FAX: 303/676-6164
FAX: DSN: 926-6164
E-Mail: spresley@arpcmail.den.disa.mil

AMOUNT: Loan Repayment up to $3,000 per year ($20,000 total)

DEADLINE(S): None specified

FIELD(S): Physicians and nurses in critical wartime health-care specialties participating in the Selected Reserve.

Open to health professionals fully qualified in critically short wartime specialties who serve in a military reserve (Selected Reserve or Individual Mobilization Augmentee Program). To repay an individual's outstandihng educational loan balance.

Direct questions to: Medical Readiness & Incentives Division, SrA Sonja Presley at above location.

2189 — INSTITUTO NACIONAL DE CARDIOLOGIA (Residency Fellowships)

Juan Badiano #1
Tlalpan Mexico 14080 DF MEXICO
525/573-0502

AMOUNT: Stipend plus room and board (for Mexican citizens only)

DEADLINE(S): AUG 31

FIELD(S): Cardiology; Nephrology; Pathology; Anesthesiology; Surgery; Rheumatology

A rotating residency designed to acquaint the fellow with all aspects of his or her specialty during a 2- to 3-month stay in each department of the 270-bed institute.

Program conducted in accordance with the National University of Mexico. It is open to all medical school graduates who are Mexican citizens and who have two years of training in a hospital devoted to general medicine. Write for complete information.

2190 — INTERNATIONAL COUNCIL FOR CANADIAN STUDIES (Government of France Graduate Awards)

325 Dalhousie, S-800
Ottawa Ontario CANADA K1N 7G2
613/789-7828
FAX: 613/789-7830

E-Mail: general@iccs-ciec.ca
Internet: www.iccs-ciec.ca

AMOUNT: Tuition, travel, and living allowance

DEADLINE(S): OCT 31

FIELD(S): Pure and Applied Sciences, Social Sciences, Engineering, Medicine

One-year graduate scholarships open to Canadian citizens for study and research at the doctoral level. Sound knowledge of the French language is required.

Must hold masters degree. Cannot be held concurrently with other scholarships or remuneration. Write or access website for complete information.

2191 — INTERNATIONAL ORDER OF THE KING'S DAUGHTERS AND SONS (Health Careers Scholarships)

c/o Mrs. Fred Cannon
Box 1310
Brookhaven MS 39602
Written Inquiry

AMOUNT: $1,000 (max.)

DEADLINE(S): APR 1

FIELD(S): Medicine; Dentistry; Nursing; Physical Therapy; Occupational Therapy; Medical Technologies; Pharmacy

Open to students accepted to/enrolled in an accredited US or Canadian four-year or graduate school. RN candidates must have completed first year of program; MD or DDS candidates must be for at least the second year of medical or dental school; all others must be in at least third year of four-year program. Pre-med students NOT eligible. Must be US or Canadian citizen.

Send self-addressed, stamped envelope, along with a letter stating the field of study and present level, to the Director at above address for an application.

2192 — JAPAN SOCIETY FOR THE PROMOTION OF SCIENCE (Post-doctoral Fellowships for Foreign Researchers)

Jochi-Kioizaka Bldg., 6-26-3 Kioi-cho
Chiyoda-Ku
Tokyo 102 JAPAN
+81-3-3263-1721
Telex: J32281
FAX: +81-3-3263-1854

AMOUNT: 270,000 yen per month

DEADLINE(S): SEP 25; MAY 23

FIELD(S): Humanities; Social Sciences; Natural Sciences; Engineering; Medicine

Post-doctoral fellowships for advanced study & research in Japan.

Write for complete information

2193 — JAPANESE AMERICAN CITIZENS LEAGUE (Magoichi & Shizuko Kato Memorial Scholarship)

1765 Sutter St.
San Francisco CA 94115
415/921-5225
FAX: 415/931-4671
E-Mail: jacl@jacl.org
Internet: www.jacl.org

AMOUNT: Varies

DEADLINE(S): APR 1

FIELD(S): Medicine; Ministry

Open to JACL members or their children only. For graduate students planning a career in medicine or ministry, and who are enrolled in, or are planning to enroll in, an accredited graduate school. Financial need NOT a factor.

For membership information or an application, send a self-addressed, stamped envelope to above address.

2194 — JEWISH VOCATIONAL SERVICE (Marcus & Theresa Levie Educational Fund Scholarships)

1 S. Franklin St.
Chicago IL 60606
312/346-6700

AMOUNT: To $5,000

DEADLINE(S): MAR 1

FIELD(S): Social Work, Medicine, Dentistry, Nursing, & other related professions & vocations

Open to Cook County residents of the Jewish faith who plan careers in the above fields. For undergraduate juniors and seniors and graduate students. Applications available Dec. 1 from Scholarship Secretary.

Must show financial need. 85-100 awards per year. Renewal possible with reapplication. Write for complete information.

2195 — JOSEPH COLLINS FOUNDATION (Grants for Medical Students)

153 East 53rd St.
New York NY 10022
Written inquiry

AMOUNT: Up to $5,000

DEADLINE(S): MAR 1

FIELD(S): General Medicine, Psychiatry, or Neurology

Grants for needy medical students who have broad cultural interests, have completed at least one year of medical school, and are attending an accredited medical school in a state east of or contiguous to the Mississippi River.

Applications are NOT sent to or accepted from students. Obtain applications from the medical school and return it to them for forwarding to the Foundation. The school is to apply on the student's behalf.

2196 — KIDNEY FOUNDATION OF CANADA (Scholarships)

300-5165 Sherbrooke St. W.
Montreal Quebec H4A 1T6 CANADA
800/361-7494, ext. 223 or 514/369-4806
FAX: 514/369-2492
E-Mail: research@kidney.ca
Internet: www.kidney.ca

AMOUNT: $45,000/yr. (Canadian)

DEADLINE(S): OCT 15

FIELD(S): Nephrology; Urology

Provides salary for up to two years of an initial faculty appointment at the rank of Assistant Professor or its equivalent, at an approved medical school in Canada. Candidates should have an M.D. and have completed clinical training. Ph.D.s are also eligible, with at least two years of research training. Awarded based on the research program outlined in application. Applications should be made on behalf of candidates by the institutions offering faculty appointment.

5 awards annually. See website or contact the Manager, National Research Program, at the Kidney Foundation for an application.

2197 — KING FAISAL FOUNDATION (Graduate Scholarship Program)

PO Box 352
Riyadh 11411 SAUDI ARABIA
966/1 465-2255
FAX: 966/1 465-6524
E-Mail: info@kff.com OR mprd@kff.com
Internet: www.kff.com OR
www.kingfaisalfoundation.org

AMOUNT: $400/mo. US allowance + tuition/fees paid directly to university + health insurance & travel

DEADLINE(S): None

FIELD(S): Medicine; Engineering; Physics; Chemistry; Geology

Open to graduate students who are Muslims under the age of 40. Must have BS degree, GPA of 86% or higher, and be accepted unconditionally by a university either in Europe or North America. Must be fluent in the language of area providing the studies. Selection based on academic performance.

Contact King Faisal Foundation for an application.

2198 — LADY ALLEN OF HURTWOOD MEMORIAL TRUST (Travel Grants)

21 Aspull Common
Leigh Lancs WN7 3PB ENGLAND
01942-674895

AMOUNT: up to 1,000 pounds sterling

DEADLINE(S): JAN 15

FIELD(S): Welfare And Education Of Children

A travel grant to those whose proposed project will directly benefit their work with children. People working with children and young people may apply, particularly those working with disabled and disadvantaged children. Successful candidates must write up an account of the work which the scholarship has funded. GRANTS ARE NOT FOR ACADEMIC STUDY; ONLY QUALIFIED INDIVIDUALS MAY APPLY.

Contact Dorothy E. Whitaker, Trustee, for application forms—available between May and December each year.

2199 — MARK B. HOLZMAN GRADUATE EDUCATION FOUNDATION

Nine South DuPont Hwy.
Georgetown DE 19947
302/855-2816

AMOUNT: Varies

DEADLINE(S): MAY 31

FIELD(S): Dentistry, law,, medicine, and the ministry

Scholarships to residents of Delaware for graduate study in the above fields.

Send SASE to Connie E. Mears, c/o Wilmington Trust Co., at above address for details.

2200 — MARYLAND HIGHER EDUCATION COMMISSION (Professional School Scholarships)

State Scholarship Admin
16 Francis St.
Annapolis MD 21401-1781
800/974-1024 or 410/974-5370
TTY: 800/735-2258

AMOUNT: $200-$1,000

DEADLINE(S): MAR 1

FIELD(S): Dentistry; Pharmacy; Medicine; Law; Nursing; Social Work

Open to Maryland residents who have been admitted as full-time students at a participating graduate institution of higher learning in Maryland or an undergraduate/graduate nursing program. Must fill out government FAFSA form.

Renewable up to 4 years. Contact MHEC for an application and see your school's financial aid office for FAFSA.

2201 — MINISTRY OF THE FLEMISH COMMUNITY (Fellowships)

Embassy of Belgium
3330 Garfield St., NW
Washington DC 20008

202/625-5850/51
FAX: 202/342-8346
E-Mail: flemishcomdc@wizard.net

AMOUNT: Monthly stipend, tuition, & health care coverage

DEADLINE(S): JAN 31

FIELD(S): Art; Music; Humanities; Social Science; Political Science; Law; Economics; Science; Medicine

Open to US citizens under age 35 who wish to pursue graduate or postgraduate studies in Flanders, Belgium.

Contact Flemish Community for registration forms.

2202 — MINNESOTA HIGHER EDUCATION SERVICES OFFICE (Health Professions Loan Forgiveness)

Capitol Square Bldg., Ste. 400
550 Cedar St.
St. Paul MN 55101
612/296-3974
FAX: 612/297-8880
E-Mail: info@heso.state.mn.us
Internet: www.heso.state.mn.us/

AMOUNT: Varies

DEADLINE(S): None

FIELD(S): Health Professions

Five loan repayment programs for health professionals who agree to serve in federally designated Health Professional Shortage Areas, in designated, underserved urban or rural areas, in licensed nursing homes, or in intermediate care facilities for persons with mental retardation or related conditions.

For details contact Office of Rural Health and Primary Care at 612/282-3838 or 800/366-5424 (Minnesota only).

2203 — McCORD CAREER CENTER (Level II McCord Medical/Music Scholarship)

Healdsburg High School
1024 Prince St.
Healdsburg CA 95448
707/431-3473

AMOUNT: Varies

DEADLINE(S): APR 30

FIELD(S): Medicine; Music

For graduates of Healdsburg High School who are planning a career in music or medicine. Must be enrolled full-time at a college/university as an undergraduate junior or senior in the fall, or earning an advanced degree in graduate or medical school, or entering into a vocational/certificate program. Transcripts, proof of attendance, and an essay are required.

Contact the McCord Career Center at Healdsburg High School for an application.

2204 — NATIONAL FEDERATION OF THE BLIND (Howard Brown Rickard Scholarship)

805 Fifth Avenue
Grinnell IA 50112
515/236-3366

AMOUNT: $3,000

DEADLINE(S): MAR 31

FIELD(S): Law; Medicine; Engineering; Architecture; Natural Sciences

For legally blind students pursuing or planning to pursue a full-time postsecondary course of study in the US. Based on academic excellence, service to the community, and financial need. Membership NOT required.

1 award annually. Renewable. Contact Mrs. Peggy Elliot, Scholarship Committee Chairman, for an application.

2205 — NATIONAL HEALTH SERVICE CORPS (NHSC Scholarship Program)

2070 Chain Bridge Rd,, Ste. 450
Vienna VA 22182-2536
800/221-9393
Internet: www.bphc.hrsa.dhhs.gov/nhsc

AMOUNT: Full tuition/books/fees/supplies + monthly stipend

DEADLINE(S): MAR

FIELD(S): Family Medicine; General Internal Medicine; General Pediatrics; Obstetrics/Gynecology; Family Nurse Practitioners; Primary Care Physician Assistants; Certified Nurse-Midwives

Must be US citizen attending or enrolled in fully accredited US allopathic/osteopathic medical school, nursing program, or physician assistant program. For each year of support received, you must serve one year in federally designated health professional shortage area of greatest need. Minimum two years service commitment begins upon completion of your residency and/or training.

300 awards annually. Renewable up to 4 years. Contact NHSC for an application.

2206 — NATIONAL ITALIAN AMERICAN FOUNDATION (Carmela Gagliardi Fellowship)

1860 19th St. NW
Washington DC. 20009-5599
202/530-5315

AMOUNT: $5,000

DEADLINE(S): MAR 31

FIELD(S): Fellowship in medicine

Open to students of Italian descent enrolled in or accepted to an accredited medical school program and are in the top 25% of their class. Financial need must be demonstrated.

Five fellowships to be awarded. Write for application and details.

2207 — NATIONAL ITALIAN AMERICAN FOUNDATION (Giargiari Fellowship)

1860 Nineteenth St. NW
Washington DC 20009-5599
202/530-5315

AMOUNT: $5,000

DEADLINE(S): MAY 31

FIELD(S): Medicine

For to 2nd, 3rd, and 4th year Italian American students enrolled in an accredited U.S. medical school. Write a 5-page, double-spaced, typed essay on "Italian Americans in the Medical Field."

Academic merit, financial need, and community service are considered. Contact organization for application and details.

2208 — NATIONAL ITALIAN AMERICAN FOUNDATION (Zecchino Post-Graduate Orthopaedic Fellowship)

1860 19th St.
Washington DC 20009-5599
202/530-5315

AMOUNT: $2,000

DEADLINE(S): MAY 31

FIELD(S): Fellowship in orthopaedic medicine

Open to an Italian American graduate M.D. at the completion of his/her 4 years of orthopaedic residence at a hospital approved by the American Academy of Orthopaedic surgeons. The fellowship is to attend the Rizzoli Orthopaedic Institute at the University of Bologna.

Financial need, community service, and academic merit are considered.

2209 — NAVAL RESERVE RECRUITING COMMAND (Armed Forces Health Professions Scholarships)

Attn: Code 132
4400 Dauphine St.
New Orleans LA 70146
Written inquiry

AMOUNT: Varies

DEADLINE(S): None specified

FIELD(S): Physicians: Anesthesiology, surgical specialties; Nursing: Anesthesia, operating room, or medical surgical nursing.

For health professionals and students participating in a Reserve Service of the U.S. Armed Forces training in the specialties listed above and for undergraduate nursing students. A monthly stipend is paid, and varying lengths of service are required to pay back the stipend.

Navy: above address; OR Army: Headquarters, Dept. of the Army, 5109 Leesburg Pike, Falls Church, VA 22041-3258; OR US Air Force Reserve Personnel Center, ATTN: ARPC SGI, Denver, CO 80280-5000.

2210 — NAVY RECRUITING COMMAND (Armed Forces Health Professions Scholarships)

Commander
801 N. Randolph St.
Code 325
Arlington VA 22203-1991
800/USA-NAVY or 703/696-4926
E-Mail: omegahouse@erols.com
Internet: www.navyjobs.com

AMOUNT: $938/month stipend + tuition, fees, books, lab fees, etc.

DEADLINE(S): APR 28

FIELD(S): Medicine, Dentistry, Optometry, Physical Therapy, Pharmacology, Health Care Administration, Industrial Hygiene, etc.

Open to US citizens enrolled or accepted for enrollment in any of the above fields at an accredited institution in the US or Puerto Rico. Must qualify for appointment as a Navy officer and sign a contractual agreement. Must be between the ages of 18 & 36 and have a GPA of at least 3.0.

See website, contact local Navy Recruiting Office, or contact Lieutenant Roger A. House, MPA, CAAMA, Medical Service Corps at above address.

2211 — NEW JERSEY OFFICE OF STUDENT ASSISTANCE (King Scholarship)

CN 540
Trenton NJ 08625
609/984-2709
TDD: 609/588-2526

AMOUNT: Varies. Shall not exceed maximum of tuition charged at the university where student is enrolled.

DEADLINE(S): None specified

FIELD(S): Medical: M.D., D.O., or D.M.D.

For disadvanted or minority graduate students pursuing degrees in medicine (M.D. or D.O.) or dentistry. Must have been New Jersey residents 12 months prior to receiving the award and plan to enroll full-time at the University of Medicine and Dentistry of New Jersey.

Obtain application through Graduate Office and EOF Campus director at educational institution.

2212 — NEW YORK STATE HIGHER EDUCATION SERVICES CORPORATION (N.Y. State Regents Professional/Health Care Opportunity Scholarships)

Cultural Education Center, Rm. 5C64
Albany NY 12230
518/486-1319
Internet: www.hesc.com

AMOUNT: $1,000-$10,000/yr.

DEADLINE(S): Varies

FIELD(S): Medicine and dentistry and related fields, architecture, nursing, psychology, audiology, landscape architecture, social work, chiropractic, law, pharmacy, accounting, speech language pathology

For NY state residents who are economically disadvantaged and members of a minority group underrepresented in the chosen profession and attending school in NY state. Some programs carry a service obligation in New York for each year of support. For U.S. citizens or qualifying noncitizens.

Medical/dental scholarships require one year of professional work in NY.

2213 — NOVARTIS FOUNDATION (Bursary Scheme)

41 Portland Place
London W1N 4BN ENGLAND UK
+44 171 636 9456
FAX: +44 171 436 2840
E-Mail: abrown@novartisfound.org.uk
Internet: www.novartisfound.org.uk

AMOUNT: Travel & subsistence—up to $6,000/person

DEADLINE(S): Varies

FIELD(S): Science; Medicine

Travel fellowships to young scientists (postgrad/doc) to attend international meetings in connection with the Novartis Foundation Symposia. Must be between the ages of 23 and 35, and be active in the field of science in question. Symposia is normally in London, and a 4-week to 12-week host laboratory in the department of one of the symposium participants follows. Specific topics vary. Must submit qualifications, resume, career history/goals, and research interests.

8 awards annually. Not renewable. See website or contact Allyson Brown for application procedures.

2214 — OAK RIDGE INSTITUTE FOR SCIENCE AND EDUCATION (Industrial Hygiene Graduate Fellowship Program)

P.O. Box 117
Oak Ridge TN 37831-0117
423-576-9655
FAX: 423/576-8293
E-Mail: kinneym@orau.gov

AMOUNT:

DEADLINE(S): JAN 26

FIELD(S): Industrial Hygiene

A fellowship for first-year master's candidates who have undergraduate degrees in physical, life, environmental, or health sciences or enginering and who wish to pursue studies in industrial hygiene.

For details and application, contact above location.

2215 — ONTARIO MINISTRY OF EDUCATION AND TRAINING (John Charles Polanyi Prizes)

189 Red River Rd.
4th Floor, Box 4500
Thunder Bay Ontario P7B 6G9 CANADA
800/465-3957
TDD: 800/465-3958
Internet: osap.gov.on.ca

AMOUNT: $15,000

DEADLINE(S): Varies

FIELD(S): Physics; Chemistry; Physiology; Medicine; Literature; Economics

Monetary prizes are awarded to Canadian citizens/permanent residents who are continuing postdoctoral studies at an Ontario university. Awards are designed to encourage and reward academic excellence.

5 awards annually. Contact your university or the Ontario Council of Graduate Studies for an application.

2216 — PHARMACEUTICAL RESEARCH AND MANUFACTURERS OF AMERICA FOUNDATION (Fellowships for Careers in Clinical Pharmacology)

1100 Fifteenth St. NW
Washington DC 20005
202/835-3470
FAX: 202/467-4823
E-Mail: CRobinson%mcimail.com
Internet: www.phrmaf.org

AMOUNT: Not specified

DEADLINE(S): OCT 1

FIELD(S): Clinical Pharmacology

Postdoctoral fellowships for physicians, dentists, and veterinarians currently engaged in clinical training in clinical training in the general field of pharmacology.

See above website for details and downloading application or contact via mail or phone.

2217 — PHARMACEUTICAL RESEARCH AND MANUFACTURERS OF AMERICA FOUNDATION (Fellowships in Pharmacology-Morphology)

1100 15 th St. NW
Washington DC 20005
202/835-3470
FAX: 202/467-4823
E-Mail: CRobinson%phrma@mcimail.com
Internet: www.phrmaf.org

AMOUNT: Stipend support + $500 for travel

DEADLINE(S): JAN 15

FIELD(S): Pharmacology and a morphologic specialty, such as anatomy or pathology

For postdoctoral researchers who have specialized in either pharmacology or morphologic disciplines

(i.e. anatomy or pathology) for training in the complementary discipline.

Contact above website or address for appliction and details. A two-year award.

2218 — PILOT INTERNATIONAL FOUNDATION (Marie Newton Sepia Memorial Scholarship)

P.O. Box 5600
Macon GA 31208-5600
Written inquiries

AMOUNT: Varies

DEADLINE(S): MAR 1

FIELD(S): Disabilities/Brain-related Disorders in Children

This program assists graduate students preparing for careers working with children having disabilities/brain disorders. Must have GPA of 3.5 or greater.

Applicants must be sponsored by a Pilot Club in their home town or in the city in which their college or university is located. Send a self-addressed, stamped envelope for complete information.

2219 — PILOT INTERNATIONAL FOUNDATION (PIF/Lifeline Scholarship)

P.O. Box 5600
Macon GA 31208-5600
Written inquiries

AMOUNT: Varies

DEADLINE(S): MAR 1

FIELD(S): Disabilities/Brain-related Disorders

This program assists ADULT students re-entering the job market, preparing for a second career, or improving their professional skills for an established career. Applicants must be preparing for, or already involved in, careers working with people with disabilities/brain-related disorders. GPA of 3.5 or more is required.

Must be sponsored by a Pilot Club in your home town, or in the city in which your college or university is located. Send a self-addressed, stamped envelope for complete information.

2220 — PILOT INTERNATIONAL FOUNDATION (Ruby Newhall Memorial Scholarship)

P.O. Box 5600
Macon, GA 31208-5600
Written Inquiries

AMOUNT: Varies

DEADLINE(S): MAR 15

FIELD(S): Disabilities/Brain-related disorders

For international students who have studied in the US for at least one year, and who intend to return to their home country six months after graduation. Applicants must be full-time students majoring in a field related to human health and welfare, and have a GPA of 3.5 or more.

Applicants must be sponsored by a Pilot Club in their home town, or in the city in which their college or university is located. Send a self-addressed, stamped envelope for complete information.

2221 — RAYMOND J. HARRIS EDUCATION TRUST

P.O. Box 7899
Philadelphia PA 19101-7899
Written inquiry

AMOUNT: Varies

DEADLINE(S): FEB 1

FIELD(S): Medicine, law, engineering, dentistry, or agriculture

Scholarships for Christian men to obtain a professional education in medicine, law, engineering, dentistry, or agriculture at nine Philadelphia area colleges.

Contact Mellon Bank, N.A. at above location for details and the names of the nine colleges.

2222 — RESEARCH COUNCIL OF NORWAY (Senior Scientist Visiting Fellowship)

P.O. Box 2700 St. Hanshaugen
N-0131 Oslo NORWAY
+47 22 03 70 00
FAX: +47 22 03 70 01
E-Mail: intstip@nfr.no
Internet: www.forskningsradet.no

AMOUNT: NOK 25,000-1st 2 months; NOK 10,000-succeeding months

DEADLINE(S): Varies

FIELD(S): Bioproduction & Processing (including agriculture and veterinary science); Industry & Energy; Culture & Society (including social sciences and the humanities); Medicine & Health; Environment & Development; Science & Technology

Fellowships for scientists to work at Norwegian research institutes. Project funding does not include salary; expenses connected with the stay in Norway are covered.

For a list of institutions, contact the Research Council at above location. Then apply to institution, which then will submit fellowship application.

2223 — ROBERT SCHRECK MEMORIAL FUND (Grants)

C/O Texas Commerce Bank-Trust Dept
PO Drawer 140
El Paso TX 79980
915/546-6515

AMOUNT: $500 - $1500

DEADLINE(S): JUL 15; NOV 15

FIELD(S): Medicine; Veterinary Medicine; Physics; Chemistry; Architecture; Engineering; Episcopal Clergy

Grants to undergraduate juniors or seniors or graduate students who have been residents of El Paso County for at least two years. Must be U.S. citizen or legal resident and have a high grade point average. Financial need is a consideration.

Write for complete information.

2224 — ROYAL COLLEGE OF OBSTETRICIANS AND GYNECOLOGISTS (Eden Travelling Fellowship)

27 Sussex Place Regent's Park
London NW1 4RG ENGLAND UK
+44 (0) 171 772 6263
FAX: +44 (0) 171 723 0575

AMOUNT: 5,000 Pounds Sterling (maximum)

DEADLINE(S): JUL 31

FIELD(S): Obstetrics; Gynecology

Traveling fellowship open to medical graduates of any approved British or Commonwealth University (whether members of the college or not) and of not less than 2 years standing.

The successful candidate will be required to give an undertaking that he/she will complete program within a specified time. Write for complete information.

2225 — SOCIETY OF BIOLOGICAL PSYCHIATRY (A.E. Bennett Research Awards)

c/o Elliott Richelson MD
Mayo Clinic Jacksonville
4500 San Pablo Rd.
Jacksonville FL 32224
904/953-2842

AMOUNT: $1,500

DEADLINE(S): JAN 31

FIELD(S): Biological Psychiatry

Awards are given in basic science and clinical science for purpose of stimulating international research in biological psychiatry by young investigators under the age of 35.

All co-authors must also be under 35. Candidate must be actively involved in the area of research described in submission. Studies and data must not have been published elsewhere.

2226 — SOCIETY OF BIOLOGICAL PSYCHIATRY (DISTA Fellowship Award)

c/o Elliot Richelson, MD
Mayo Clinic Jacksonville
4500 San Pablo Rd.
Jacksonville FL 32224
904/953-2842

AMOUNT: $1,500

DEADLINE(S): DEC 15

FIELD(S): Biological Psychiatry

Open to medical graduates in their 3rd, 4th, or 5th year of residency or fellowship training. Selection will be based on past excellence and potential for professional growth in the area of biological psychiatry or clinical neuroscience.

Nominations are made by university department of psychiatry. Write for complete information.

2227 — SOCIETY OF BIOLOGICAL PSYCHIATRY (Ziskind-Somerfield Research Award)

Elliot Richelson
MD Mayo Clinic Jacksonville
Jacksonville
FL 32224
904/953-2842

AMOUNT: $2,500

DEADLINE(S): JAN 31

FIELD(S): Biological Psychiatry

Open to senior investigators who are members of the Society of Biological Psychiatry. Award is for basic or clinical research by senior investigators 35 or older.

Candidates must be members in good standing of the society of Biological Psychiatry. Write for complete information.

2228 — TY COBB EDUCATIONAL FOUNDATION (Graduate Scholarship Program)

PO Box 725
Forest Park GA 30298
Written Inquiry

AMOUNT: $3,000

DEADLINE(S): JUN 15

FIELD(S): Medicine; Dentistry

Open to graduate students who are residents of Georgia, have satisfactory grades, and are able to demonstrate financial need.

Write to Ms. Rosie Atkins, Secretary, for an application.

2229 — U.S. DEPT. OF HEALTH & HUMAN SERVICES (Indian Health Service Health Professions Scholarship Program)

Twinbrook Metro Plaza, Suite 100
12300 Twinbrook Pkwy.
Rockville MD 20852
301/443-0234
FAX: 301/443-4815
Internet: www.ihs.gov/Recruitment/DHPS/SP/SBTOC3.asp

AMOUNT: Tuition + fees & monthly stipend of $938.

DEADLINE(S): APR 1

FIELD(S): Health professions, accounting, social work

Open to Native Americans or Alaska natives who are graduate students or college juniors or seniors in a program leading to a career in a fields listed above. U.S. citizenship required. Renewable annually with reapplication.

Scholarship recipients must intend to serve the Indian people. They incur a one-year service obligation to the IHS for each year of support for a minimum of two years. Write for complete information.

2230 — UNIFORMED SERVICES UNIVERSITY OF THE HEALTH SCIENCES (Fellowships)

Schools of Medicine & Nursing
4301 Jones Bridge Rd.
Bethesda MD 20814-4799
301/295-3101 or 800/772-1743

AMOUNT: Tuition

DEADLINE(S): NOV 1

FIELD(S): Medicine; Nursing

Open to graduate students who wish to attend the F. Edward Hebert School of Medicine or the Graduate School of Nursing with the understanding that they will be trained for service to the nation, including assignments abroad or at sea. While enrolled, students serve as reserve commissioned officers. Must be US citizen.

Contact Uniformed Services University for an application.

2231 — UNIVERSITY OF EDINBURGH (Faculty of Medicine Bursaries & Scholarships)

7-11 Nicolson St.
Edinburgh SCOTLAND EH8 9BE UK
+44 (0) 131 650 1000
Internet: www.iprs.ed.ac.uk/progawards/medicine/

AMOUNT: Varies

DEADLINE(S): MAR 1; NOV 1

FIELD(S): Medicine

Various scholarships, bursaries, and travel awards for medical students at all levels of study. For use at the University of Edinburgh, Scotland. Some are for students from other companies; some are for women; some are for specific specialties.

Access website for more information and/or contact school for details and appropriate application forms.

2232 — US AIR FORCE OPPORTUNITY CENTER (Armed Forces Health Professions Scholarships)

P.O. Box 3505
Attn AFHPSP/FAP
Capitol Heights MD 20790-9605
Written inquiry

AMOUNT: $913 per month stipend + tuition, fees, books, lab fees, etc.

DEADLINE(S): None

FIELD(S): Medicine; Dentistry; and Clinical Psychology (Ph.D)

Open to U.S. citizens enrolled or accepted for enrollment in any of the above fields at an accredited institution in the U.S. or Puerto Rico. Must qualify for appointment as an Air Force officer and sign a contractual agreement.

Write for complete information or call local recruiter (use blue pages in local telephone directories for telephone number).

2233 — USAF READY RESERVE STIPEND PROGRAM

6760 East Irvington Place
Denver CO 80280-7000
1/800-525-01-2 ext 231 or 237
DSN 926-6490 or 6480
Commercial: 303/676-6484 or 6490
FAX: 303/676-6164
FAX: DSN: 926-6164
E-Mail: spresley@arpcmail.den.disa.mil

AMOUNT: Varies

DEADLINE(S): None

FIELD(S): Physicians and nurses

Designed to grow individuals with critical wartime health-care specialties for service in the Ready Reserve. Under AFRRSP a financial stipend will be paid to persons engaged in training in certain health-care specialties in return for a commitment to subseuently serve in the Ready Reserve.

Direct questions to: Medical Readiness & Incentives Division, SrA Sonja Presley, at above location.

2234 — USAF RESERVE PERSONNEL CENTER (Armed Forces Health Professionas Scholarships)

6760 E. Irvington Pl. #7000
Denver CO 80280-7000
Written inquiry

AMOUNT: Varies

DEADLINE(S): None specified

FIELD(S): Physicans: Anesthesiology, surgical specialties; Nursing: Anesthesia, operating room, or medical surgical nursing.

For health professionals and students participating in a Reserve Service of the U.S. Armed Forces training in the specialties listed above and for undergraduate nursing students. A monthly stipend is paid, and varying lengths of service are required to pay back the stipend.

Air Force: above address; Army: Headquarters, Dept. of the Army, 5109 Leesburg Pike, Falls Church, VA 22041-3258; Navy: Naval Reserve Recruiting Command, 4400 Dauphine St., New Orleans, LA 70146.

2235 — USAF RESERVE BONUS PROGRAM

6760 East Irvington Place #7000
Denver CO 80280-7000
1/800-525-0102 ext 231 or 237
DSN 926-6490 or 6484
Commercial: 303/676-6484 or 6490
FAX: 303/676-6164
FAX: DSN: 926-6164
E-Mail: spresley@arpcmail.den.disa.mil

AMOUNT: $10,000/yr. for physicians; $3,000/year for Operating Room Nurses

DEADLINE(S): None

FIELD(S): Physicians and nurses in critically needed specialties.

A bonus pay program to recruit critically needed medical specialties into the Selected Reserve of the U.S. Air Force.

Direct questions to: Medical Readiness & Incentives Division, SrA Sonja Presley at above location.

2236 — VIRGIN ISLANDS BOARD OF EDUCATION (Nursing & Other Health Scholarships)

P.O. Box 11900
St. Thomas VI 00801
809/774-4546

AMOUNT: Up to $1,800

DEADLINE(S): MAR 31

FIELD(S): Nursing; Medicine; Health-related Areas

Open to bona fide residents of the Virgin Islands who are accepted by an accredited school of nursing or an accredited institution offering courses in one of the health-related fields.

This scholarship is granted for one academic year. Recipients may reapply with at least a 'C' average. Write for complete information.

2237 — WASHINGTON STATE HIGHER EDUCATION COORDINATING BOARD (Health Professional Loan Repayment & Scholarship Program)

PO Box 43430
Olympia WA 98504-3430
360/753-7850
FAX: 360/753-7808
Internet: www.hecb.wa.gov

AMOUNT: Varies

DEADLINE(S): APR (scholarship); FEB (loan repayment); JUL (loan repayment)

FIELD(S): Health Care

Scholarships are open to students in accredited undergraduate or graduate health care programs leading to eligibility for licensure in Washington state. Must agree to work in designated shortage area for minimum of three years. Loan repayment recipients receive payment from program for purpose of repaying education loans secured while attending program of health care training leading to licensure in Washington state. Financial need NOT a factor.

Renewable up to 5 years. Contact Program Manager for a loan repayment application after November 15th and for scholarship application after January 15th.

2238 — WASHINGTON STATE HIGHER EDUCATION COORDINATING BOARD (WICHE Professional Student Exchange)

PO Box 43430
Olympia WA 98504-3430
360/753-7850
FAX: 360/753-7808

AMOUNT: $8,000-$12,000

DEADLINE(S): OCT 15

FIELD(S): Optometry; Osteopathy

Program provides state support to Washington residents pursuing undergraduate or graduate study out-of-state.

12 awards annually (10 renewals, two new). Contact Program Manager for an application.

2239 — WOMEN OF THE EVANGELICAL LUTHERAN CHURCH IN AMERICA (The Kahler-Vickers/Raup-Emma Wettstein Scholarships)

8765 West Higgins Road
Chicago IL 60631-4189
800/638-3522, ext. 2747
FAX: 773/380-2419
E-Mail: womnelca@elca.org

AMOUNT: $2,000 max.

DEADLINE(S): MAR 1

FIELD(S): Health Professions & Christian Service

Assists women who are members of the ELCA studying for service in health professions associated with ELCA projects abroad that do not lead to church-certified professions. Must be US citizen and have experienced an interruption of two or more years since completion of high school. Academic records of coursework completed in last five years as well as proof of admission from educational institution are required.

Renewable for an additional year. Contact Faith Fretheim, Program Director, for an application.

2240 — ZETA PHI BETA SORORITY EDUCATIONAL FOUNDATION (S. Evelyn Lewis Memorial Scholarship in Medical Health Sciences)

1734 New Hampshire Ave., NW
Washington DC 20009
Internet: www.zpb1920.org/nefforms.htm

AMOUNT: $500-$1,000

DEADLINE(S): FEB 1

FIELD(S): Medicine; Health Sciences

Open to graduate and undergraduate young women enrolled in a program leading to a degree in medicine or health sciences. Award is for full-time study for one academic year (Fall-Spring) and is paid directly to college/university. Must submit proof of enrollment.

Send self-addressed, stamped envelope to above address between September 1st and December 15th for an application.

MEDICAL RELATED DISCIPLINES

2241 — ABBIE SARGENT MEMORIAL SCHOLARSHIP INC. (Scholarships)

295 Sheep Davis Road
Concord NH 03301
603/224-1934
FAX: 603/228-8432

AMOUNT: $400

DEADLINE(S): MAR 15

FIELD(S): Agriculture; Veterinary Medicine; Home Economics

Open to New Hampshire residents who are high school graduates with good grades and character. For undergraduate or graduate study. Must be legal resident of U.S. and demonstrate financial need.

Three annual awards. Renewable with reapplication. Write for complete information.

2242 — ACCESS GROUP (Loan Programs)

1411 Foulk Road
Box 7430
Wilmington DE 19803-0430
302/477-4190 or 800/282-1550
FAX: 302/477-4080
Internet: www.accessgroup.org

AMOUNT: Varies

DEADLINE(S): Varies (last day of current school term)

FIELD(S): Law, Business, Medical, Dental

Loans at competitive rates to graduate students attending law, business, medical, dental, and a variety of other graduate and professional schools.

Must be a US citizen or legal resident. No co-signer required for qualified applicants. No need to locate a lender, and no interview required. Visit website or contact Pat Curry at above address for complete information.

2243 — AMERICAN ACADEMY OF FIXED PROSTHODONTICS (Tylman Research Grants)

Dept. Restorative Dentistry, Univ Illinois-Chicago
801 S. Paulina St.
Chicago IL 60612-7212
312/413-1181

AMOUNT: $2,000

DEADLINE(S): MAR 1

FIELD(S): Prosthodontics

Grants offered annually to support student research in the field of fixed prosthodontics. Students in accredited graduate and postgraduate programs may apply with the approval of their program director.

Up to 8 awards annually. Contact Dr. Kent Knoernschild at above address for an application.

2244 — AMERICAN ACADEMY OF OPTOMETRY (Julius F. Neumueller Award)

6110 Executive Blvd. Suite 506
Rockville, MD 20852
301/984-1441

AMOUNT: $500

DEADLINE(S): JUN 1

FIELD(S): Optometry

Cash award offered each year for paper selected by committee in field of geometric optics. Open to students who are enrolled in an accredited school or college of optometry and are nominated by the dean/president.

Write for complete information.

2245 — AMERICAN COLLEGE OF HEALTHCARE EXECUTIVES (Albert W. Dent Scholarship)

One North Franklin St., Ste. 1700
Chicago IL 60606-3491
312/424-2800
FAX: 312/424-0023
E-Mail: ache@ache.org
Internet: www.ache.org

AMOUNT: $3,500

DEADLINE(S): MAR 31

FIELD(S): Health Care Management

Open to minority US and Canadian citizens who are graduate students in their final year of a healthcare management program. Must be enrolled full-time in an accredited institution and be in good academic standing. Financial need will be considered. Must be Associate Member—may apply for membership with scholarship application.

Not renewable. For more information or an application, contact Steven M. Rauchenecker, CHE, Associate Director, Membership, at above address or see website.

2246 — AMERICAN COLLEGE OF HEALTHCARE EXECUTIVES (Foster G. McGaw Scholarship)

One North Franklin St., Ste. 1700
Chicago IL 60606-3491
312/424-2800
FAX: 312/424-0023
E-Mail: ache@ache.org
Internet: www.ache.org

AMOUNT: $3,500

DEADLINE(S): MAR 31

FIELD(S): Health Care Management

Open to US or Canadian citizens who are graduate students in their final year of a healthcare management program. Must be enrolled full-time in an accredited institution and be in good academic standing. Financial need will be considered. Must be Associate Member—may apply for membership with scholarship application.

Not renewable. For more information or an application, contact Steven M. Rauchenecker, CHE, Associate Director, Membership, at above address or see website.

2247 — AMERICAN COLLEGE OF LEGAL MEDICINE (Student Writing Competition)

611 E. Wells St.
Milwaukee WI 53202
800/433-9137 or 414/276-1881
FAX: 414/276-3349
E-Mail: info@aclm.org
Internet: www.aclm.org

AMOUNT: $1,000

DEADLINE(S): FEB 1,

FIELD(S): Legal Medicine

Award for the best paper on any aspect of legal medicine. Open to postgraduate students enrolled in an accredited school of law, medicine, dentistry, podiatry, nursing, pharmacy, health science, or health care administration in the US or Canada.

3 awards annually. Contact Laura Morrone at ACLM for entry rules.

2248 — AMERICAN COLLEGE OF MEDICAL PRACTICE EXECUTIVES (ACMPE Scholarships)

104 Inverness Terrace East
Englewood CO 80112-5306
303/643-9573 Ext. 206

AMOUNT: $500 to $2,000

DEADLINE(S): JUN 1

FIELD(S): Health Care Administration/Medical Practice Management

Open to undergraduate or graduate students who are pursuing a degree relevant to medical practice management at an accredited university or college.

Send #10 SASE to receive application.

2249 — AMERICAN FOUNDATION FOR PHARMACEUTICAL EDUCATION (Predoctoral Fellowships)

One Church St., Suite 202
Rockville MD 20850
301/738-2160
FAX: 301/738-2161

AMOUNT: $6,000 to $10,000/yr.

DEADLINE(S): MAR 1

FIELD(S): Pharmacology

Several predoctoral fellowships for pharmaceutical students with no more than three years remaining to earn the Ph.D.

Student accepts a teaching appointment in a Pharmacy college. U.S. citizen or legal resident. Write for complete information.

2250 — AMERICAN INDIAN SCIENCE AND ENGINEERING SOCIETY (A.T. Anderson Memorial Scholarship)

PO Box 9828
Albuquerque NM 87119-9828
505/765-1052
FAX: 505/765-5608
E-Mail: scholarships@aises.org
Internet: www.aises.org/scholarships

AMOUNT: $1,000-$2,000

DEADLINE(S): JUN 15

FIELD(S): Medicine; Natural Resources; Science; Engineering

Open to undergraduate and graduate students who are at least 1/4 American Indian or recognized as member of a tribe. Must be member of AISES ($10 fee), enrolled full-time at an accredited institution, and demonstrate financial need.

Renewable. See website or contact Patricia Browne for an application and/or membership information.

2251 — AMERICAN INSTITUTE OF THE HISTORY OF PHARMACY (Grant-in-Aid)

725 N. Charter St.
Madison WI 53706-1508
608/262-5378

AMOUNT: Varies

DEADLINE(S): FEB 1

FIELD(S): History of Pharmacy

Open to graduate students who are studying the history of pharmacy. Applicants must present a budget.

Contact Institute for an application.

2252 — AMERICAN OPTOMETRIC ASSOCIATION (Student Loan Program)

243 N. Lindbergh Blvd.
St Louis MO 63141
314/991-4100
FAX 314/991-4101
Internet: www.opted.org

AMOUNT: $8,500/yr. ($65,500 max.)

DEADLINE(S): None

FIELD(S): Optometry

Open to student members of AOA who are in good academic standing and pursuing a Doctor of Optometry degree in an accredited college of optometry.

Contact AOA for membership information or an application.

2253 — AMERICAN OPTOMETRIC FOUNDATION (William Ezell OD Fellowship)

6110 Executive Blvd., Ste. 506
Bethesda MD 20852
301/984-4734

AMOUNT: Maximum of $6000 annually

DEADLINE(S): MAY 15

FIELD(S): Optometry

Open to applicants with a degree in Optometry who are pursuing their Ph.D & plan to make Optometric teaching and/or research their career.

Write for complete information.

2254 — AMERICAN PHARMACEUTICAL ASSOCIATION AUXILIARY (Irene A. Parks Student Loan Fund)

c/o Mrs. Peggy Gawronski
305 W. Old Middle Creek
Prestonburg KY 41653
606/886-0249

AMOUNT: Up to $500

DEADLINE(S): OCT 15

FIELD(S): Pharmacy

Loans are available for pharmacy students in their last two years of pharmacy school. Repayment of loan plus interest to begin 60 days after graduation. Must show financial need.

Complete information is available from the address above or from pharmacy college deans.

2255 — AMERICAN SOCIETY FOR CLINICAL LABORATORY SCIENCE (Ruth M. French Graduate or Undergraduate Scholarship)

> 7910 Woodmont Ave., Suite 530
> Bethesda MD 20814
> 301/657-2768
> FAX: 301/657-2909

AMOUNT: $1,000

DEADLINE(S): MAR 1

FIELD(S): Clinical Laboratory Science or Medical Technology

Scholarships for students in the above field enrolled in an approved undergraduate or graduate program. Undergrads must be in last year of study. U.S. citizenship or permanent U.S. residency required.

Contact address above for complete information. Enclose self-addressed, stamped business size envelope. Applications available after Nov. 1.

2256 — AMERICAN SPEECH-LANGUAGE-HEARING FOUNDATION (Graduate Student Scholarships)

> 10801 Rockville Pike
> Rockville MD 20852
> 301/897-5700
> FAX 301/571-0457

AMOUNT: $4,000

DEADLINE(S): JUN 6

FIELD(S): Communication sciences/disorders; speech pathology;speech therapy

Open to full-time graduate students in communication sciences and disorders programs and demonstrating outstanding academic achievement.

Applications available in February.

2257 — AMERICAN SPEECH-LANGUAGE-HEARING FOUNDATION (Kala Singh Memorial Fund-International/Minority Student Scholarship)

> 10801 Rockville Pike
> Rockville Pike, Rockville, MD 20852
> 301/897-5700
> FAX: 301/571-0457

AMOUNT: $2,000

DEADLINE(S): JUN 6

FIELD(S): Communication sciences and disorders, speech/language pathology, audiology

Applicants must be international/ethnic minority graduate student studying communication sciences and disorders in the U.S. and demonstrating outstanding academic achievement.

Applications available in February.

2258 — AMERICAN SPEECH-LANGUAGE-HEARING FOUNDATION (Leslie Isenberg Fund for Student With Disability)

> 10801 Rockville Pike
> Rockville Pike, Rockville MD 20852
> 301/897-5700
> FAX: 301/571-0457

AMOUNT: $2,000

DEADLINE(S): JUN 6

FIELD(S): Communication sciences & disorders

Open to full-time graduate student with disability enrolled in a communication sciences and disorders program and demonstrating outstanding academic achievement.

Applications available in February.

2259 — AMERICAN SPEECH-LANGUAGE-HEARING FOUNDATION (New Investigator Research Grant)

> 10801 Rockville Pike
> Rockville MD 20852
> 301/897-5700
> FAX 301/571-0457

AMOUNT: $5,000

DEADLINE(S): JUL 20

FIELD(S): Speech/Language Pathology; Audiology

Research grant for new investigators to support clinical research in the above areas. Grants are designed to encourage research activities by new scientists who have earned their M.A. or Ph.D. within the last 5 years. Students enrolled in degree programs are ineligible.

Seven awards. Applications available in February.

2260 — AMERICAN SPEECH-LANGUAGE-HEARING FOUNDATION (Student Research Grant in Clinical or Rehabilitative Audiology)

> 10801 Rockville Pike
> Rockville MD 20852
> 301/897-5700
> FAX 301/571-0457

AMOUNT: $2,000

DEADLINE(S): JUN 13

FIELD(S): Audiology

Student research grants available to graduate or post-graduate students in communication sciences and disorders desiring to conduct research in audiology.

Applications available in February.

2261 — AMERICAN SPEECH-LANGUAGE-HEARING FOUNDATION (Young Scholars Award for Minority Student)

> 10801 Rockville Pike
> Rockville MD 20852

> 301/897-5700
> FAX 301/571-0457

AMOUNT: $2,000

DEADLINE(S): JUN 6

FIELD(S): Speech/Language Pathology; Audiology

Open to ethnic minorities who are full-time college seniors accepted for graduate study in speech-language pathology or audiology. Applicants must be US citizens.

Applications available in February.

2262 — ARCHBOLD MEDICAL CENTER (Archbold Scholarship/Loan)

> Dept. of Education
> P.O. Box 1018
> Thomasville GA 31799-1018
> 912/228-2795

AMOUNT: $4,000-$6,000; $500 for technical courses

DEADLINE(S): None specified

FIELD(S): Healthcare fields such as Registered Nurse, Medical Lab, Pharmacy, Physical Therapy, etc.

Open to undergrad and grad students accepted into an accredited healthcare school and within 2 years of completing course work. Student must agree to work at AMC for 3 years following graduation (1 year for tech school students).

Must be Georgia resident. Personal interview required. Repayment is required if recipient fails to work at Archbold for the designated period. Write for complete information.

2263 — ARTHUR M. MILLER FUND

> P.O. Box 1122
> Wichita KS 67201-0004
> 316/261-4609

AMOUNT: Varies

DEADLINE(S): MAR 31

FIELD(S): Medicine or related fields

Scholarships for Kansas residents for the study of medicine or related fields at accredited instutitions.

Send SASE for formal application.

2264 — ASSOCIATION FOR WOMEN IN SCIENCE EDUCATIONAL FOUNDATION (AWIS Predoctoral Awards)

> 1200 New York Ave. NW, Suite 650
> Washington DC 20005
> 202/326-8940 or 800-886-AWIS
> E-Mail: awis@awis.org
> Internet: www.awis.org

AMOUNT: $1,000

DEADLINE(S): JAN 16

FIELD(S): Various Sciences and Social Sciences

Scholarships for female doctoral students. Summary page, description of research project, resume, references, transcripts, and biographical sketch required. US citizens may study at any graduate institution; non-citizens must study at US institutions.

5-10 awards annually. See website or write to above address for an application and complete information.

2265 — ASSOCIATION FOR WOMEN IN SCIENCE EDUCATIONAL FOUNDATION (AWIS Pre-doctoral Awards)

1200 New York Ave. NW, Suite 650
Washington DC 20005
202/326-8940 or 800/886-AWIS
E-Mail: awis@awis.org
Internet: www.awis.org

AMOUNT: $1,000

DEADLINE(S): JAN 16

FIELD(S): Various Sciences and Social Sciences

Scholarships for female doctoral students. Summary page, description of research project, resume, references, transcripts, and biographical sketch required. US citizens may study at any graduate institution; non-citizens must be enrolled in US institutions.

5-10 awards annually. See website or write to above address for an application and more information.

2266 — ASSOCIATION FOR WOMEN IN SCIENCE EDUCATIONAL FOUNDATION (Ruth Satter Memorial Award)

1200 New York Ave., NW, Suite 650
Washington DC 20005
202/326-8940 or 800/886-AWIS
E-Mail: awis@awis.org
Internet: www.awis.org

AMOUNT: $1,000

DEADLINE(S): JAN 16

FIELD(S): Various Sciences and Social Sciences

Scholarships for female doctoral students who have interrupted their education for at least three years to raise a family. Summary page, description of research project, resume, references, transcripts, biographical sketch, and letter from your department to confirm eligibility required. US citizens may study at any graduate institution; non-citizens must attend US institutions.

See website or write to above address for more information or an application.

2267 — ASSOCIATION FOR WOMEN IN SCIENCE EDUCATIONAL FOUNDATION (Ruth Satter Memorial Award)

1200 New York Ave. NW, Suite 650
Washington DC 20005
202/326-8940 or 800/886-AWIS

E-Mail: awis@awis.org
Internet: www.awis.org

AMOUNT: $1,000

DEADLINE(S): JAN 16

FIELD(S): Various Sciences and Social Sciences

Scholarships for female doctoral students who have interupted their education three years or more to raise a family. Summary page, description of research project, resume, references, transcripts, biographical sketch, and proof of eligibility from department head required. US citizens may attend any graduate institution; non-citizens must be enrolled in US institutions.

See website or write to above address for more information or an application.

2268 — ASSOCIATION FOR WOMEN VETERINARIANS (Student Scholarship)

6200 Jefferson St., NE
#117
Albuquerque NM 87109-3434
Written Inquiry

AMOUNT: $1,500

DEADLINE(S): FEB 18

FIELD(S): Veterinary Medicine

Open to second or third year veterinary medicine students in the U.S. or Canada who are U.S. or Canadian citizens. Both women and men are eligible. Essay is required.

Write for complete information or contact the Dean of your veterinary school.

2269 — AUSTRALIAN FEDERATION OF UNIVERSITY WOMEN-SA INC. (Winifred E. Preedy Postgraduate Bursary)

GPO 634
Adelaide 5001 SOUTH AUSTRALIA
Written Inquiry

AMOUNT: $Aust 5,000

DEADLINE(S): MAR 1

FIELD(S): Dentistry

For women who are enrolled in a master's degree or Ph.D. in dentistry or a related field (either coursework or research). Must have completed at least one year of degree and be past or present students of Dentistry at the University of Adelaide. Must not be in full-time employment or on fully-paid study leave. Selection based primarily on academic merit; community activities and financial need also considered.

Not renewable. Write to Fellowships Trustee, AFUW-SA Inc. Trust Fund for an application.

2270 — AUSTRIAN CULTURAL INSTITUTE (Max Kade Foundation Grants)

950 Third Ave.
20th Fl.
New York NY 10022
212/759-5165 or +43/1/51581-253
FAX: 212/319-9636
E-Mail: desk@aci.org
Internet: www.austriaculture.net

AMOUNT: Varies

DEADLINE(S): Varies

FIELD(S): Medicine; Natural Sciences; Engineering

Open to young Austrian scientists with several years of experience at universities or institutions. Must demonstrate capacity to pursue independent teaching or research activities in the US. Proficiency in English required.

See website or contact ACI for an application kit, or write to Osterreichische Akademie der Wissenschaften, Kommission fur Max Kade Stipendien, Dr. Ignaz Seipel-Platz 2, A-1010 Vienna, Austria.

2271 — BECA FOUNDATION (Alice Newell Joslyn Medical Fund)

310 Via Vera Cruz, Ste. 101
San Marcos CA 92069
760/471-5465
FAX: 760/471-9175

AMOUNT: $500-$2,000

DEADLINE(S): MAR 1

FIELD(S): Medicine; Health Care; Nursing; Dental/Medical Assisting; Physical Therapy

Open to Latino students who live in or attend college in San Diego County, CA, at time of application. For high school seniors and those already in college pursuing undergraduate or graduate education. Based on financial need, scholastic determination, and community/cultural awareness. BECA also provides a mentor to each scholarship recipient.

Send self-addressed, stamped envelope to BECA for an application.

2272 — BOEING (Polish Graduate Student Scholarship Program)

Phone for details
314/234-2149

AMOUNT: Tuition, books, and fees for three years

DEADLINE(S): Varies

FIELD(S): Scientific and technical fields

Scholarships for students from Poland to pursue graduate studies in scientific and technical areas at American colleges or universities.

Call Jim Schlueter at above telephone number.

2273 — BRITISH DENTAL ASSOCIATION (The Dentsply Fund)

64 Wimpole Street
London W1M 8AL England
0171-935-0875

AMOUNT: 200 to 800 pounds

DEADLINE(S): MAY 31

FIELD(S): Dentistry

Loans and grants to provide financial assistance towards the special education and training for students suffering hardship during their studies. Not suitable for new students. UK citizens may study at any accredited institution in any country. Non-UK citizens must study at a UK institution.

Renewable. 15 awards per year. Write for complete information.

2274 — BUSINESS & PROFESSIONAL WOMEN'S FOUNDATION (BPW Career Advancement Scholarship Program)

2012 Massachusetts Ave., NW
Washington DC 20036-1070
202/293-1200, ext. 169
FAX: 202/861-0298
Internet: www.bpwusa.org

AMOUNT: $500-$1,000

DEADLINE(S): APR 15

FIELD(S): Biology, Science, Education, Engineering, Social Science, Paralegal, Humanities, Business, Math, Computers, Law, MD, DD

For women (US citizens) aged 25+ accepted into accredited program at US institution (+Puerto Rico & Virgin Islands). Must graduate within 12 to 24 months from the date of grant and demonstrate critical finanacial need. Must have a plan to upgrade skills, train for a new career field, or to enter/re-enter the job market.

Full- or part-time study. For info see website or send business-sized, self-addressed, double-stamped envelope.

2275 — CALIFORNIA GRANGE FOUNDATION (Deaf Activities Scholarships)

Pat Avila, 2101 Stockton Blvd.
Sacramento CA 95817
Written inquiry

AMOUNT: Varies

DEADLINE(S): APR 1

FIELD(S): Course work which will be of benefit to the deaf community

Scholarships students entering, continuing, or returning to college to pursue studies that will benefit the deaf community.

Write for information after Feb. 1 of each year.

2276 — CHINESE AMERICAN MEDICAL SOCIETY (Scholarships)

281 Edgewood Ave.
Teaneck NJ 07666
201/833-1506
FAX: 201/833-8252
E-Mail: hws@columbia.edu
Internet: www.camsociety.org

AMOUNT: $1,000-$1,500

DEADLINE(S): MAR 31

FIELD(S): Medicine; Dentistry

Scholarships for graduate students of Chinese ancestry who reside in the US and will attend medical or dental school. Financial need NOT a factor.

4-6 awards annually. Not renewable. Contact Dr. H. H. Wang at CAMS for an application.

2277 — COLUMBIANA COUNTY PUBLIC HEALTH LEAGUE TRUST FUND (Grants)

PO Box 1428
Steubenville OH 43952
740/283-8433
FAX: 740/282-4530

AMOUNT: Varies

DEADLINE(S): FEB 28

FIELD(S): Respiratory Illness; Medicine; Medical Research; Pharmacy; Medical Technology; Physical Therapy; Nursing; Dental Hygiene; Occupational Therapy

Open to undergraduate and graduate Columbiana County, Ohio, residents who are pursuing medical education or research in one of the above fields. Preference given to respiratory illness. Students of veterinary medicine NOT eligible.

Contact Sherrill Schmied for an application.

2278 — CONGRESSIONAL HISPANIC CAUCUS INSTITUTE, INC. (CHCI Fellowship Program)

504 C St., NE
Washington DC 20002
800/EXCEL-DC or 202/543-1771
E-Mail: comments@chci.org
Internet: www.chci.org

AMOUNT: Monthly stipend, round-trip transportation, & health insurance

DEADLINE(S): MAR 1

FIELD(S): Public Policy; Public Health; Telecommunications; Business

Paid work experience is open to Hispanics who have graduated from a college/university (with BA/BS/ graduate degree) within one year of application deadline, and to currently enrolled graduate students. Must have high academic achievement (minimum 3.0 GPA), superior analytical/communication skills, leadership potential, and consistent active participation in activities for the common good. Must be US citizen/ permanent resident or have student work visa.

16 awards annually. See website or contact CHCI for an application.

2279 — DELTA SOCIETY (James M. Harris/ Sarah W. Sweatt Student Travel Grant)

289 Perimeter Rd. East
Benton WA 98055-1329
425/226-7357
FAX: 425/235-1076
E-Mail: deltasociety@cis.compuserve.com
Internet: www.deltasociety.org

AMOUNT: Varies

DEADLINE(S): Varies

FIELD(S): Human-Animal Interactions; Animal Assisted Therapy; Service Animals; Pet Loss

Travel grants for graduate/postgraduate students to attend Delta Society's annual conference. Must be a full-time student in veterinary human health care. Student must provide detailed plan of how conference information will be shared. Must also attend the full conference and demonstrate ability to cover costs of registration, hotel, and meals. Financial need NOT a factor.

2-4 awards annually. Contact Michelle Cobey for an application.

2280 — DEPARTMENT OF THE ARMY (Armed Forces Health Professions Scholarships)

Attn: RC-HS
1307 Third Ave.
Fort Knox KY 40121
502/626-0367
FAX: 502/626-0923

AMOUNT: Tuition + monthly stipend

DEADLINE(S): None

FIELD(S): Medicine; Osteopathy; Nurse Anesthetist; Veterinary Medicine; Optometry; Psychology; Dentistry

Open to health professionals and students participating in a Reserve Service of the US Armed Forces, training in the specialties listed above. Varying lengths of service are required to pay back the stipend. Must be US citizen. Award is based on a competitive process, including GPA. Financial need NOT a factor.

400 awards annually. Contact Major Beecher at above address for an application.

2281 — DEPARTMENT OF THE ARMY (Health Professionals Loan Repayment Program)

Attn: RC-HS
1307 Third Ave.
Fort Knox KY 40121

502/626-0367

FAX: 502/626-0923

AMOUNT: $20,000/yr. (max.)

DEADLINE(S): None

FIELD(S): Medicine; Nursing

Loan repayment is open to health professionals fully qualified in critically short wartime specialties who serve in a military reserve. Specialties include physician assistants; general dentists; oral surgeons; critical care & nurse anesthetists; general, thoracic, & orthopedic surgeons; urologists; diagnostic radiologists; psychiatrists; preventative & critical care medicine; and primary care physicians.

Contact Major Beecher at above address for an application.

2282 — DUPAGE COUNTY MEDICAL SOCIETY FOUNDATION (Scholarship Program)

498 Hillside Ave.

#1

Glen Ellyn IL 60137

630/858-9603

AMOUNT: $250-$1,000

DEADLINE(S): APR 30

FIELD(S): Medical/Health-Care Fields

Open to voting residents of Dupage County, Illinois, who are accepted to or enrolled in a professional training program at a qualified school. Based on financial need and scholastic ability. Program does not apply to undergraduate studies, such as pre-med; students would be eligible after completing four-year pre-med program and having been accepted into medical school.

Contact Medical Society for an application.

2283 — E. A. BAKER FOUNDATION FOR PREVENTION OF BLINDNESS (Fellowships & Research Grants)

1929 Bayview Ave.

Toronto Ontario M4G 3E8 CANADA

416/480-7659

Internet: www.cnib.ca

AMOUNT: $40,000 (max.)

DEADLINE(S): DEC 1

FIELD(S): Ophthalmology

Fellowships and research grants are for Canadian citizens to pursue advanced graduate training in ophthalmic sub-specialties. Funds must be used primarily to further prevention of blindness in Canada.

See website for more information.

2284 — EDWARD BANGS KELLEY AND ELZA KELLEY FOUNDATION, INC. (Scholarship Program)

PO Drawer M

Hyannis MA 02601-1412

508/775-3117

AMOUNT: $4,000 (max.)

DEADLINE(S): APR 30

FIELD(S): Medicine; Nursing; Health Sciences

Open to residents of Barnstable County, Massachusetts. Scholarships are intended to benefit health and welfare of Barnstable County residents. Awards support study at recognized undergraduate, graduate, and professional institutions. Financial need is considered.

Contact Foundation for an application.

2285 — EPILEPSY FOUNDATION OF AMERICA (Pre-doctoral Research Training Fellowship)

4351 Garden City Drive

Landover MD 20785-2267

301/459-3700 or 800/EFA-1000

FAX: 301/577-2684

TDD: 800/332-2070

E-Mail: postmaster@efa.org

Internet: www.efa.org

AMOUNT: up to $15,000

DEADLINE(S): SEP 1

FIELD(S): Epilepsy as related to Neuroscience, Physiology, Pharmacology, Psychology, Biochemistry, Genetics, Nursing, or Pharmacy

One-year of support for qualified individuals who are pursuing dissertation research with an epilepsy-related theme, and who are working under the guidance of a mentor with expertise in the area of epilepsy investigation. Graduate students pursuing Ph.D. degree in above fields may apply.

Contact EFA for an application.

2286 — FINANCE AUTHORITY OF MAINE (Health Professions Loan Program)

119 State House Station

Augusta ME 04333

207/287-2183 (in state: 800/228-3734)

FAX: 207/626-8208

Internet: www.famemaine.com

AMOUNT: $5,000-$15,000

DEADLINE(S): None

FIELD(S): Medicine, dentistry, optometry, or veterinary medicine

For persons who have been Maine residents for at least one year. Must be enrolled in postgraduate health profession school within the U.S.

Contact organization or access website for details.

2287 — FIRST UNITED METHODIST CHURCH (Robert Stevenson & Doreene E. Cater Scholarships)

302 5th Ave., S.

St. Cloud MN 56301

FAX: 320/251-0878

E-Mail: FUMCloud@aol.com

AMOUNT: $100-$300

DEADLINE(S): JUN 1

FIELD(S): Humanitarian & Christian Service: Teaching, Medicine, Social Work, Environmental Studies, etc.

Stevenson Scholarship is open to undergraduate members of the First United Methodist Church of St. Cloud. Cater Scholarship is open to members of the Minnesota United Methodist Conference who are entering the sophomore year or higher of college work. Both require two letters of reference, transcripts, and financial need.

5-6 awards annually. Contact Scholarship Committee for an application.

2288 — FOUNDATION FOR SEACOAST HEALTH (Scholarship Program)

P.O. Box 4606

Portsmouth NH 03802-4606

603/433-3008

FAX: 603/433-2036

E-Mail: ffsh@nh.ultranet.com

Internet: www.nh.ultranet.com/~ffsh

AMOUNT: $1,000-10,000

DEADLINE(S): FEB 1

FIELD(S): Health-related fields

Open to undergraduate and graduate students pursuing health-related fields of study who are legal residents of the following cities in New Hampshire: Portsmouth, Newington, New Castle, Rye, Greenland, N. Hampton, or these cities in Maine: Kittery, Eliot, or York, Maine. Must have resided in the area for at least two years.

Write or check website for details. $150,000 awarded annually; 35 awards given

2289 — FUND FOR PODIATRIC MEDICAL EDUCATION (Scholarships)

9312 Old Georgetown Road

Bethesda MD 20814-1698

301/581-9200

FAX: 301/530-2752

AMOUNT: $1,000

DEADLINE(S): JUN 1

FIELD(S): Podiatry

Scholarships for 3rd and 4th year graduate podiatry students. GPA, financial need, and community service are considerations.

150 awards annually. Not renewable. Contact above address for an application.

2290 — H. FLETCHER BROWN FUND (Scholarships)

c/o PNC Bank
Trust Dept.
P.O. Box 791
Wilmington DE 19899
302/429-1186

AMOUNT: Varies

DEADLINE(S): APR 15

FIELD(S): Medicine; Dentistry; Law; Engineering; Chemistry

Open to U.S. citizens born in Delaware and still residing in Delaware. For 4 years of study (undergrad or grad) leading to a degree that enables applicant to practice in chosen field.

Scholarships are based on need, scholastic achievement, and good moral character. Applications available in February. Write for complete information.

2291 — HEALTH RESEARCH COUNCIL OF NEW ZEALAND (Post-doctoral Fellowships)

PO Box 5541
Wellesley St
Auckland 1036 NEW ZEALAND
09/3798-227
FAX: 09/3779-988

AMOUNT: NZ$40,500 + NZ$1,750 research expenses & air fare

DEADLINE(S): Varies (Biomedical APR 1; Public Health APR 1/SEP 1)

FIELD(S): Biomedical & Public Health Research

Awards are based on the academic standing and research capabilities of applicants who should have Ph.D. or equivalent degree.

Fellowships are tenable in New Zealand and are normally awarded for period of 24 months and may be extended for an additional 24 months. Write for complete information.

2292 — INSTITUTE FOR THE STUDY OF WORLD POLITICS (Dissertation Fellowships)

1755 Massachusetts Ave. NW
Washington DC 20036
202/588-9797
Internet: fundforpeace.org/iswp.htm

AMOUNT: Varies

DEADLINE(S): FEB 16

FIELD(S): International Relations; Environmental Issues; Population Studies (Social Science aspects); Human Rights; Arms Control; Third World

Development; Agricultural Development; Public Health, etc.

For doctoral candidates conducting dissertation research in above areas to promote scholarly examination of political, economic, and social issues that affect the security, well-being, and dignity of the peoples of the world. Financial need is a consideration. For citizens of any country.

Write for complete information.

2293 — INSTITUTE FOR THE STUDY OF WORLD POLITICS (Dorothy Danforth Compton Fellowships)

1755 Massachusetts Ave. NW
Washington DC 20036
202/588-9797
Internet: fundforpeace.org/iswp.htm

AMOUNT: Varies

DEADLINE(S): MAR 16

FIELD(S): International Relations; Environmental Issues; Population Studies (Social Science aspects); Human Rights; Arms Control; Third World Development; Agricultural Development; Public Health, etc.

For masters or doctoral candidates researching in the above areas to promote scholarly examination of political, economic, and social issues that affect the security, well-being, and dignity of the peoples of the world. Must be African American, Hispanic American, and Native American students who are U.S. citizens and studying in U.S. institutions. Financial need is a consideration.

Write for complete information.

2294 — INTERNATIONAL ORDER OF THE KING'S DAUGHTERS AND SONS (Health Careers Scholarships)

c/o Mrs. Fred Cannon
Box 1310
Brookhaven MS 39602
Written Inquiry

AMOUNT: $1,000 (max.)

DEADLINE(S): APR 1

FIELD(S): Medicine; Dentistry; Nursing; Physical Therapy; Occupational Therapy; Medical Technologies; Pharmacy

Open to students accepted to/enrolled in an accredited US or Canadian four-year or graduate school. RN candidates must have completed first year of program; MD or DDS candidates must be for at least the second year of medical or dental school; all others must be in at least third year of four-year program. Pre-med students NOT eligible. Must be US or Canadian citizen.

Send self-addressed, stamped envelope, along with a letter stating the field of study and present level, to the Director at above address for an application.

2295 — INTERNATIONAL SCHOOL OF CRYSTALLOGRAPHY (Postgraduate Courses)

Piazza di Porta San Donato 1
40126 Bologna ITALY
39 051 243556
FAX: 39 051 243336
E-Mail: riva@geomin.unibo.it
Internet: www.geomin.unibo.it/orgv/erice/erice.htm

AMOUNT: Half to full subsistence + fees

DEADLINE(S): NOV 30

FIELD(S): Solid State Chemistry; Physics; Molecular Biology; Molecular Biophysics; Pharmaceutics

Open to young postgraduates to pursue interdisciplinary studies in crystallography in Erice, Sicily, Italy. Must speak English and have some experience in the topic to be discussed (topics change every year). These 15-day courses are held at the International Foundation and Centre for Scientific Culture—Ettore Majorana.

See website or contact Lodovico Riva di Sanseverino for an application.

2296 — JEWISH VOCATIONAL SERVICE (Marcus & Theresa Levie Educational Fund Scholarships)

1 S. Franklin St.
Chicago IL 60606
312/346-6700

AMOUNT: To $5,000

DEADLINE(S): MAR 1

FIELD(S): Social Work, Medicine, Dentistry, Nursing, & other related professions & vocations

Open to Cook County residents of the Jewish faith who plan careers in the above fields. For undergraduate juniors and seniors and graduate students. Applications available Dec. 1 from Scholarship Secretary.

Must show financial need. 85-100 awards per year. Renewal possible with reapplication. Write for complete information.

2297 — KING FAISAL FOUNDATION (Graduate Scholarship Program)

PO Box 352
Riyadh 11411 SAUDI ARABIA
966/1 465-2255
FAX: 966/1 465-6524
E-Mail: info@kff.com OR mprd@kff.com
Internet: www.kff.com OR
www.kingfaisalfoundation.org

AMOUNT: $400/mo. US allowance + tuition/fees paid directly to university + health insurance & travel

DEADLINE(S): None

FIELD(S): Medicine; Engineering; Physics; Chemistry; Geology

Open to graduate students who are Muslims under the age of 40. Must have BS degree, GPA of 86% or higher, and be accepted unconditionally by a university either in Europe or North America. Must be fluent in the language of area providing the studies. Selection based on academic performance.

Contact King Faisal Foundation for an application.

2298 — LABAN/BARTENIEFF INSTITUTE OF MOVEMENT STUDIES (Work-Study Programs)

234 Fifth Ave., Rm. 203
New York NY 10001
212/477-4299
FAX: 212/477-3702
E-Mail: limsinfo@erols.com

AMOUNT: $500-$1,500

DEADLINE(S): MAY 1

FIELD(S): Human Movement Studies

Open to graduate students and professionals in dance, education, health fields, behavioral sciences, fitness, athletic training, etc. Tenable for work-study ONLY at the Laban/Bartenieff Institute in New York.

Contact LIMS for an application.

2299 — MARK B. HOLZMAN GRADUATE EDUCATION FOUNDATION

Nine South DuPont Hwy.
Georgetown DE 19947
302/855-2816

AMOUNT: Varies

DEADLINE(S): MAY 31

FIELD(S): Dentistry, law,, medicine, and the ministry

Scholarships to residents of Delaware for graduate study in the above fields.

Send SASE to Connie E. Mears, c/o Wilmington Trust Co., at above address for details.

2300 — MARYLAND HIGHER EDUCATION COMMISSION (Professional School Scholarships)

State Scholarship Admin
16 Francis St.
Annapolis MD 21401-1781
800/974-1024 or 410/974-5370
TTY: 800/735-2258

AMOUNT: $200-$1,000

DEADLINE(S): MAR 1

FIELD(S): Dentistry; Pharmacy; Medicine; Law; Nursing; Social Work

Open to Maryland residents who have been admitted as full-time students at a participating graduate institution of higher learning in Maryland or an undergraduate/graduate nursing program. Must fill out government FAFSA form.

Renewable up to 4 years. Contact MHEC for an application and see your school's financial aid office for FAFSA.

2301 — MINISTRY OF THE FLEMISH COMMUNITY (Fellowships)

Embassy of Belgium
3330 Garfield St., NW
Washington DC 20008
202/625-5850/51
FAX: 202/342-8346
E-Mail: flemishcomdc@wizard.net

AMOUNT: Monthly stipend, tuition, & health care coverage

DEADLINE(S): JAN 31

FIELD(S): Art; Music; Humanities; Social Science; Political Science; Law; Economics; Science; Medicine

Open to US citizens under age 35 who wish to pursue graduate or postgraduate studies in Flanders, Belgium.

Contact Flemish Community for registration forms.

2302 — McCORD CAREER CENTER (Level II McCord Medical/Music Scholarship)

Healdsburg High School
1024 Prince St.
Healdsburg CA 95448
707/431-3473

AMOUNT: Varies

DEADLINE(S): APR 30

FIELD(S): Medicine; Music

For graduates of Healdsburg High School who are planning a career in music or medicine. Must be enrolled full-time at a college/university as an undergraduate junior or senior in the fall, or earning an advanced degree in graduate or medical school, or entering into a vocational/certificate program. Transcripts, proof of attendance, and an essay are required.

Contact the McCord Career Center at Healdsburg High School for an application.

2303 — NATIONAL ASSOCIATION OF THE DEAF (Stokoe Scholarship)

814 Thayer Ave.
Silver Spring MD 20910-4500
301/587-1788
TTY: 301/587-1789
FAX: 301/587-1791
E-Mail: NADinfo@nad.org
Internet: www.nad.org

AMOUNT: $2,000

DEADLINE(S): MAR 15

FIELD(S): Sign Language; Deaf Community

Open to deaf students who have graduated from a four-year college program and are pursuing part-time or full-time graduate studies in a field related to sign language or the deaf community, or a deaf graduate student who is developing a special project on one of these topics.

Send a self-addressed, stamped, business-sized envelope to NAD for an application.

2304 — NATIONAL ENVIRONMENTAL HEALTH ASSOCIATION (NEHA/AAS Scholarship)

720 S. Colorado Blvd., Ste. 970
South Tower
Denver CO 80246-1925
303/756-9090
E-Mail: veronica.white@juno.com
Internet: www.neha.org

AMOUNT: Varies

DEADLINE(S): FEB 1

FIELD(S): Environmental Health/Science; Public Health

Undergraduate scholarships to be used for tuition and fees during junior or senior year at an Environmental Health Accreditation Council accredited school or NEHA school. Graduate scholarships are for students or career professionals who are enrolled in a graduate program of studies in environmental health sciences and/or public health. Transcript, letters of recommendation, and financial need considered.

Renewable. Scholarships are paid directly to the college/university for the fall semester of the award. Contact Veronica White, NEHA Liason, for an application.

2305 — NATIONAL FEDERATION OF THE BLIND (Howard Brown Rickard Scholarship)

805 Fifth Avenue
Grinnell IA 50112
515/236-3366

AMOUNT: $3,000

DEADLINE(S): MAR 31

FIELD(S): Law; Medicine; Engineering; Architecture; Natural Sciences

For legally blind students pursuing or planning to pursue a full-time postsecondary course of study in the US. Based on academic excellence, service to the community, and financial need. Membership NOT required.

1 award annually. Renewable. Contact Mrs. Peggy Elliot, Scholarship Committee Chairman, for an application.

2306 — NATIONAL HEALTH RESEARCH AND DEVELOPMENT PROGRAM (Training & Career Awards)

15th Floor, Jeanne Mance Bldg.
Ottawa Ontario K1A 1B4 CANADA
613/954-8549
FAX: 613/954-7363
E-Mail: nhrdpinfo@hc-sc.gc.ca
Internet: www.hc-sc.gc.ca/hppb/nhrdp/

AMOUNT: $18,000 (Master's & Ph.D.); $30,000 (Postdoctoral); $50,000 (Scholar)

DEADLINE(S): MAR 1

FIELD(S): Health; Health Policy

For Canadian citizens or legally landed immigrants who are graduates or postgraduates whose research has a broad health and public policy perspective. If applicants want to study outside of Canada, justification is required. Financial need is NOT a factor.

Contact the Information Officer at NHRDP for an application.

2307 — NATIONAL HUMANITIES CENTER (Burroughs Wellcome Fund Fellowships in the History of Modern Medicine)

PO Box 12256
Research Triangle Park NC 27709-2256
919/549-0661
FAX: 919/990-8535
E-Mail: nhc@ga.unc.edu
Internet: www.nhc.rtp.nc.us:8080

AMOUNT: Stipend ($35,000-$50,000) + Travel Expenses (fellow & dependents)

DEADLINE(S): OCT 15

FIELD(S): History of Medicine/Biomedical Science; Medical Anthropology

Postdoctoral fellowships for historians of medicine or biomedical science, medical anthropologists, and other scholars whose work concerns the history of twentieth-century medicine. Curriculum vitae, 1,000-word proposal, and three letters of recommendation are required.

1 award annually. Contact NHC for application materials.

2308 — NATIONAL ITALIAN AMERICAN FOUNDATION (Carmela Gagliardi Fellowship)

1860 19th St. NW
Washington DC. 20009-5599
202/530-5315

AMOUNT: $5,000

DEADLINE(S): MAR 31

FIELD(S): Fellowship in medicine

Open to students of Italian descent enrolled in or accepted to an accredited medical school program and are in the top 25% of their class. Financial need must be demonstrated.

Five fellowships to be awarded. Write for application and details.

2309 — NATIONAL ITALIAN AMERICAN FOUNDATION (Giargiari Fellowship)

1860 Nineteenth St. NW
Washington DC 20009-5599
202/530-5315

AMOUNT: $5,000

DEADLINE(S): MAY 31

FIELD(S): Medicine

For to 2nd, 3rd, and 4th year Italian American students enrolled in an accredited U.S. medical school. Write a 5-page, double-spaced, typed essay on "Italian Americans in the Medical Field."

Academic merit, financial need, and community service are considered. Contact organization for application and details.

2310 — NATIONAL RESEARCH COUNCIL (Howard Hughes Medical Institute Predoctoral Fellowships in Biological Sciences)

2101 Constitution Ave.
Washington DC 20418
202/334-2872
FAX: 202/334-2872
E-Mail: infofell@nas.edu
Internet: national-academics.org/osep.fo

AMOUNT: $16,000 stipend + tuition at US institution

DEADLINE(S): NOV 9

FIELD(S): Biochemistry; Biophysics; Epidemiology; Genetics; Immunology; Microbiology; Neuroscience; Pharmacology; Physiology; Virology

Five-year award is open to college seniors and first-year graduate students pursuing a Ph.D. or Sc.D. degree. US citizens/nationals may choose any institution in the US or abroad; foreign students must choose US institution. Based on ability, academic records, proposed study/research, previous experience, reference reports, and GRE scores.

80 awards annually. See website or contact NRC for an application.

2311 — NATIONAL RESEARCH FOUNDATION (NRF Honors & Postgraduate Bursaries)

PO Box 2600
Pretoria 0001 SOUTH AFRICA
+27 012/481-4000
FAX: +27 012/349-1179
E-Mail: info@nrf.ac.za
Internet: www.nrf.ac.za

AMOUNT: Varies

DEADLINE(S): Varies

FIELD(S): Agriculture; Chemistry; Earth Sciences; Engineering; Biology; Mathematics; Physics; Forestry; Veterinary Science; Pharmaceutics

Open to South African citizens pursuing graduate/postgraduate studies in above fields.

500 awards annually. Contact NRF for an application.

2312 — NATIONAL STRENGTH & CONDITIONING ASSN. (Challenge Scholarships)

P.O. Box 38909
Colorado Springs CO 80937-8909
719/632-6722
FAX: 719/632-6722
E-Mail: nsca@usa.net
Internet: www.colosoft.com/nsca

AMOUNT: $1,000

DEADLINE(S): MAR 1

FIELD(S): Fields related to body strength & conditioning

Open to National Strength & Conditioning Association members. Awards are for undergraduate or graduate study.

For membership information or an application, write to the above address.

2313 — NATIONAL STRENGTH & CONDITIONING ASSN. (Student Research Grant Program)

P.O. Box 38909
Colorado Springs CO 80937-8909
719/632-6722
FAX: 719/632-6367
E-Mail: nsca@usa.net
Internet: www.colosoft.com/nsca

AMOUNT: $1,500

DEADLINE(S): FEB 3 (letter of intent); MAR 17 (submission)

FIELD(S): Fields related to body strength & conditioning

Research grants for graduate students who are members of National Strength & Conditioning Association. A graduate faculty member is required to serve as a co-investigator in the study.

Two annual awards. For membership information or an application, write to the above address.

2314 — NAVY RECRUITING COMMAND (Armed Forces Health Professions Scholarships)

Commander
801 N. Randolph St.
Code 325

Arlington VA 22203-1991
800/USA-NAVY or 703/696-4926
E-Mail: omegahouse@erols.com
Internet: www.navyjobs.com

AMOUNT: $938/month stipend + tuition, fees, books, lab fees, etc.

DEADLINE(S): APR 28

FIELD(S): Medicine, Dentistry, Optometry, Physical Therapy, Pharmacology, Health Care Administration, Industrial Hygiene, etc.

Open to US citizens enrolled or accepted for enrollment in any of the above fields at an accredited institution in the US or Puerto Rico. Must qualify for appointment as a Navy officer and sign a contractual agreement. Must be between the ages of 18 & 36 and have a GPA of at least 3.0.

See website, contact local Navy Recruiting Office, or contact Lieutenant Roger A. House, MPA, CAAMA, Medical Service Corps at above address.

2315 — NEW JERSEY OFFICE OF STUDENT ASSISTANCE (King Scholarship)

CN 540
Trenton NJ 08625
609/984-2709
TDD: 609/588-2526

AMOUNT: Varies. Shall not exceed maximum of tuition charged at the university where student is enrolled.

DEADLINE(S): None specified

FIELD(S): Medical: M.D., D.O., or D.M.D.

For disadvanted or minority graduate students pursuing degrees in medicine (M.D. or D.O.) or dentistry. Must have been New Jersey residents 12 months prior to receiving the award and plan to enroll full-time at the University of Medicine and Dentistry of New Jersey.

Obtain application through Graduate Office and EOF Campus director at educational institution.

2316 — NEW YORK STATE HIGHER EDUCATION SERVICES CORPORATION (N.Y. State Regents Professional/Health Care Opportunity Scholarships)

Cultural Education Center, Rm. 5C64
Albany NY 12230
518/486-1319
Internet: www.hesc.com

AMOUNT: $1,000-$10,000/yr.

DEADLINE(S): Varies

FIELD(S): Medicine and dentistry and related fields, architecture, nursing, psychology, audiology, landscape architecture, social work, chiropractic, law, pharmacy, accounting, speech language pathology

For NY state residents who are economically disadvantaged and members of a minority group underrepresented in the chosen profession and attending school in NY state. Some programs carry a service obligation in New York for each year of support. For U.S. citizens or qualifying noncitizens.

Medical/dental scholarships require one year of professional work in NY.

2317 — NORTH CAROLINA DEPARTMENT OF PUBLIC INSTRUCTION (Scholarship Loan Program for Prospective Teachers)

301 N. Wilmington St.
Raleigh NC 27601-2825
919/715-1120

AMOUNT: Up to $2,500/yr.

DEADLINE(S): FEB

FIELD(S): Education: Teaching, school psychology and counseling, speech/language impaired, audiology, library/media services

For NC residents planning to teach in NC public schools. At least 3.0 high school GPA required; must maintain 2.5 GPA during freshman year and 3.0 cumulative thereafter. Recipients are obligated to teach one year in an NC public school for each year of assistance. Those who do not fulfill their teaching obligation are required to repay the loan plus interest.

200 awards per year. For full-time students. Applications available in Dec. from high school counselors and college and univerwity departments of education.

2318 — NOVARTIS FOUNDATION (Bursary Scheme)

41 Portland Place
London W1N 4BN ENGLAND UK
+44 171 636 9456
FAX: +44 171 436 2840
E-Mail: abrown@novartisfound.org.uk
Internet: www.novartisfound.org.uk

AMOUNT: Travel & subsistence—up to $6,000/person

DEADLINE(S): Varies

FIELD(S): Science; Medicine

Travel fellowships to young scientists (postgrad/doc) to attend international meetings in connection with the Novartis Foundation Symposia. Must be between the ages of 23 and 35, and be active in the field of science in question. Symposia is normally in London, and a 4-week to 12-week host laboratory in the department of one of the symposium participants follows. Specific topics vary. Must submit qualifications, resume, career history/goals, and research interests.

8 awards annually. Not renewable. See website or contact Allyson Brown for application procedures.

2319 — OAK RIDGE INSTITUTE FOR SCIENCE AND EDUCATION (Industrial Hygiene Graduate Fellowship Program)

P.O. Box 117
Oak Ridge TN 37831-0117
423-576-9655
FAX: 423/576-8293
E-Mail: kinneym@orau.gov

AMOUNT:

DEADLINE(S): JAN 26

FIELD(S): Industrial Hygiene

A fellowship for first-year master's candidates who have undergraduate degrees in physical, life, environmental, or health sciences or enginering and who wish to pursue studies in industrial hygiene.

For details and application, contact above location.

2320 — PHARMACEUTICAL RESEARCH AND MANUFACTURERS ASSOCIATION FOUNDATION (Fellowships for Advanced Predoctoral Training in Pharmacology or Toxicology)

1100 15th Street NW
Washington DC 20005
202/835-3400
FAX: 202/467-4823
E-Mail: CRobinson%phrma@mcimail.com
Internet: www.phrmaf.org

AMOUNT: $12,000 stipend + $500 expense money for thesis prep.

DEADLINE(S): SEP 15

FIELD(S): Pharmacology/Toxicology

Open to full-time students enrolled in schools of medicine, pharmacy, dentistry, or veterinary medicine for beginning thesis research.

Write for complete information or contact above website.

2321 — PHARMACEUTICAL RESEARCH AND MANUFACTURERS ASSOCIATION FOUNDATION (Fellowships for Advanced Predoctoral Training in Pharmaceutics)

1100 15th Street NW
Washington DC 20005
202/835-3470
FAX: 202/467-4823
E-Mail: CRobenson%phrma@mcimail.com
Internet: www.phrmaf.org

AMOUNT: $12,000 stipend + $500 for thesis preparation

DEADLINE(S): OCT 1

FIELD(S): Pharmaceutics

For predoctoral students engaged in thesis research in basic pharmaceutics, biopharmaceutics, and pharmaceutical technology. Should have degree in pharmacy, chemistry, or biology.

For application and details contact above website or address.

2322 — PHARMACEUTICAL RESEARCH AND MANUFACTURERS OF AMERICA FOUNDATION (Fellowships for Careers in Clinical Pharmacology)

1100 Fifteenth St. NW
Washington DC 20005
202/835-3470
FAX: 202/467-4823
E-Mail: CRobinson%mcimail.com
Internet: www.phrmaf.org

AMOUNT: Not specified

DEADLINE(S): OCT 1

FIELD(S): Clinical Pharmacology

Postdoctoral fellowships for physicians, dentists, and veterinarians currently engaged in clinical training in clinical training in the general field of pharmacology.

See above website for details and downloading application or contact via mail or phone.

2323 — PHARMACEUTICAL RESEARCH AND MANUFACTURERS OF AMERICA FOUNDATION (Faculty Awards in Basic Pharmacology/ Toxicology)

1100 15th Street NW
Washington DC 20005
202/835-3470
FAX: 202/467-4823
E-Mail: CRobinson%phrma@mcimail.com
Internet: www.phrmaf.org

AMOUNT: Unspecified amount paid to institution for salary and fringe benefits of apppointee

DEADLINE(S): SEP 15

FIELD(S): Pharmacology/Toxicology

Awards for post-doctoral faculty members or assistant professors who are beginning careers in academic pharmacology or toxicology or who are being considered for such an appointment in schools of medicine, pharmacy, dentistry, or veterinary medicine.

Contact above location or access the website for application and details.

2324 — PHARMACEUTICAL RESEARCH AND MANUFACTURERS OF AMERICA FOUNDATION (Fellowships in Pharmacology-Morphology)

1100 15 th St. NW
Washington DC 20005
202/835-3470
FAX: 202/467-4823

E-Mail: CRobinson%phrma@mcimail.com
Internet: www.phrmaf.org

AMOUNT: Stipend support + $500 for travel

DEADLINE(S): JAN 15

FIELD(S): Pharmacology and a morphologic specialty, such as anatomy or pathology

For postdoctoral researchers who have specialized in either pharmacology or morphologic disciplines (i.e. anatomy or pathology) for training in the complementary discipline.

Contact above website or address for appliction and details. A two-year award.

2325 — PHARMACEUTICAL RESEARCH AND MANUFACTURERS OF AMERICA FOUNDATION (Postdoctoral Fellowships in Pharmaceutics)

1100 15th Street NW
Washington DC 20005
202/835-3470
FAX: 202/467-4823
E-Mail: CRobinson%phrma@mcimail.com
Internet: www.phrmaf.org

AMOUNT: $25,000/year

DEADLINE(S): OCT 1

FIELD(S): Pharmaceutics

Fellowship for to postdoctoral researchers.

Fellowships for one or two years. Contact above website or address for application and details.

2326 — PHARMACEUTICAL RESEARCH AND MANUFACTURERS OF AMERICA FOUNDATION (Faculty Awards in Clinical Pharmacology)

1100 15th Street NW
Washington DC 20005
202/835-3470
FAX: 202/467-4823
E-Mail: CRobinson%phrma@mcimail.com
Internet: www.phrmaf.org

AMOUNT: Up to $40,000 per year for 3 years

DEADLINE(S): OCT 1

FIELD(S): Clinical Pharmacology

Awards for post-doctoral full-time, junior faculty members and assistant professors who have completed one year's training at the residency level and two years' clinical experience related to human clinical pharmacology.

Contact above website or address for application and details. A three-year award.

2327 — PHYSICIAN ASSISTANT FOUNDATION (Scholarships, Traineeships, & Grants)

950 N. Washington St.
Alexandria VA 22314-1552

703/519-5686
Internet: www.aapa.org

AMOUNT: Varies

DEADLINE(S): FEB 1

FIELD(S): Physician Assistant

Must be attending an accredited physician assistant program in order to qualify. Judging is based on financial need, academic standing, community involvement, and knowledge of physician assistant profession.

Contact Edna C. Scott, Administrative Manager, for an application.

2328 — POPULATION COUNCIL (Fellowships in Social Sciences)

Policy Research Division
One Dag Hammarskjold Plaza
New York NY 10017
212/339-0671
FAX: 212/755-6052
E-Mail: ssfellowship@popcouncil.org
Internet: www.popcouncil.org

AMOUNT: Monthly stipend, partial tuition/fees, transportation, book/supply allowance, & health insurance

DEADLINE(S): DEC 15

FIELD(S): Population Studies; Demography; Sociology; Anthropology; Economics; Public Health; Geography

Twelve-month award is open to doctoral & postdoctoral scholars for advanced training in above fields that deal with developing world. Doctoral students may request support for dissertation fieldwork/writing. Postdoctorates may pursue research, midcareer training, or resident training. Based on academic excellence, prospective contribution, & well-conceived research proposal. Preference given to those from developing countries.

See website or contact Fellowship Coordinator for an application.

2329 — QUEEN'S UNIVERSITY OF BELFAST (Thomas Henry Scholarship)

Newforge Lane
Belfast BT9 SPX N.IRELAND
Belfast 255450

AMOUNT: Fees & expenses—established annually by board of electors

DEADLINE(S): MAY 1

FIELD(S): Agriculture; Veterinary Medicine

Scholarships for encouragement of graduate research in agriculture or agricultural science in Northern Ireland. Must be United Kingdom citizen.

Renewable for 3 years. Contact Dean of Faculty (address above) for complete information.

2330 — RAYMOND J. HARRIS EDUCATION TRUST

P.O. Box 7899
Philadelphia PA 19101-7899
Written inquiry

AMOUNT: Varies

DEADLINE(S): FEB 1

FIELD(S): Medicine, law, engineering, dentistry, or agriculture

Scholarships for Christian men to obtain a professional education in medicine, law, engineering, dentistry, or agriculture at nine Philadelphia area colleges.

Contact Mellon Bank, N.A. at above location for details and the names of the nine colleges.

2331 — RESEARCH COUNCIL OF NORWAY (Senior Scientist Visiting Fellowship)

P.O. Box 2700 St. Hanshaugen
N-0131 Oslo NORWAY
+47 22 03 70 00
FAX: +47 22 03 70 01
E-Mail: intstip@nfr.no
Internet: www.forskningsradet.no

AMOUNT: NOK 25,000-1st 2 months; NOK 10,000-succeeding months

DEADLINE(S): Varies

FIELD(S): Bioproduction & Processing (including agriculture and veterinary science); Industry & Energy; Culture & Society (including social sciences and the humanities); Medicine & Health; Environment & Development; Science & Technology

Fellowships for scientists to work at Norwegian research institutes. Project funding does not include salary; expenses connected with the stay in Norway are covered.

For a list of institutions, contact the Research Council at above location. Then apply to institution, which then will submit fellowship application.

2332 — ROBERT SCHRECK MEMORIAL FUND (Grants)

C/O Texas Commerce Bank-Trust Dept
PO Drawer 140
El Paso TX 79980
915/546-6515

AMOUNT: $500 - $1500

DEADLINE(S): JUL 15; NOV 15

FIELD(S): Medicine; Veterinary Medicine; Physics; Chemistry; Architecture; Engineering; Episcopal Clergy

Grants to undergraduate juniors or seniors or graduate students who have been residents of El Paso County for at least two years. Must be U.S. citizen or legal resident and have a high grade point average. Financial need is a consideration.

Write for complete information.

2333 — ROCKEFELLER FOUNDATION (African Dissertation Internship Awards)

420 Fifth Ave.
New York NY 10018-2702
212/869-8500
212/764-3468
Internet: www.rockfound.org

AMOUNT: Cost of project

DEADLINE(S): None given

FIELD(S): Agriculture, environment, health, life sciences, population, and schooling

For African graduate students in U.S. and Canadian universities (but not to permanent residents) to return to Africa to carry out dissertation research at a local university or research institution. Priority given to above topics.

Students are strongly urged to be in the field for at least 12 months. Contact above location for details.

2334 — ROYAL COLLEGE OF VETERINARY SURGEONS (Sir Frederick Smith & Miss Aleen Cust Research Fellowships)

Belgravia House
62-64 Horseferry Rd.
London SW1P 2AF ENGLAND UK
0171 222 2001
FAX: 0171 222 2004
E-Mail: admin@rcvs.org.uk

AMOUNT: 1,000 pounds/yr. + 200 pounds

DEADLINE(S): Varies

FIELD(S): Veterinary Science

Postgraduate fellowships, tenable for up to three years, are for research at an approved institution in the UK. For the Miss Aleen Cust Fellowship, you must be a British citizen and a member of the RCVS. No citizenship/membership requirement for the Sir Frederick Smith Fellowship. Women applicants are given preference.

Notices are placed in the veterinary press when the awards are available. Applicants apply in open competition. Contact RCVS for an application and/or list of approved institutions.

2335 — ROYAL COLLEGE OF VETERINARY SURGEONS (Trust Fund)

Belgravia House
62-64 Horseferry Rd.
London SW1P 2AF ENGLAND UK
0171 222 2001
FAX: 0171 222 2004
E-Mail: admin@rcvs.org.uk

AMOUNT: Varies

DEADLINE(S): FEB 1

FIELD(S): Veterinary Science

Various postgraduate awards for members ONLY of RCVS. Open to veterinary surgeons in veterinary school and in practice in the UK. Some awards tenable for up to three years; others have varying requirements.

Notices are placed in the veterinary press when awards are available. Contact RCVS for application and details.

2336 — SIR ROBERT MENZIES MEMORIAL FOUNDATION LIMITED (Research Scholarship in Allied Health Sciences)

210 Clarendon Street
East Melbourne Vic 3002 AUSTRALIA
03 9419 5699
FAX: 03 9417 7049
E-Mail: menzies@vicnet.net.au
Internet: www.vincent.net.au/~menzies

AMOUNT: $AUD.24,000 p.a.

DEADLINE(S): JUN 30

FIELD(S): Allied Health

Postgraduate research scholarships for Australian citizens enrolled as full-time Ph.D. students at Australian institutions. Must be studying allied health fields, such as nursing, physiotherapy, psychology, occupational therapy, speech pathology, etc. Award is based on academic excellence. Financial need NOT a factor.

1 award annually. Contact Ms. Sandra Mackenzie for an application.

2337 — SOUTH AFRICAN DENTAL ASSOCIATION (Lever Ponds Fellowship; Julius Staz Scholarship)

Private Bag 1
Houghton 2041 South Africa
011-484-5288

AMOUNT: R20,000/R8,000

DEADLINE(S): JUL 30

FIELD(S): Dental Research

Post-doctoral fellowships & scholarships open to suitably qualified South African nationals. Purpose is to promote dental research & ensure its continuation in South Africa.

As a general rule awards will be made for projects which are to be carried out in South Africa. Write for complete information.

2338 — TY COBB EDUCATIONAL FOUNDATION (Graduate Scholarship Program)

PO Box 725
Forest Park GA 30298
Written Inquiry

AMOUNT: $3,000

DEADLINE(S): JUN 15

FIELD(S): Medicine; Dentistry

Open to graduate students who are residents of Georgia, have satisfactory grades, and are able to demonstrate financial need.

Write to Ms. Rosie Atkins, Secretary, for an application.

2339 — U.S. DEPARTMENT OF DEFENSE (GLSIP-General Laboratory Scientific Interchange Program: NRC-NRL Post-Doctoral Program)

Naval Research Laboratory
Office of Program Admin. & Dev. Code 1006.17
Washington, D.C. 20375-5321
202/767-3865
DSN: 297-3865
FAX: 202/404-8110
Internet: www.acq.osd.mil/ddre/edugate/s-aindx.html

AMOUNT: Research Program

DEADLINE(S): None specified

FIELD(S): Computer science, artificial intelligence, plasma physics, acoustics, radar, fluid dynamics, chemistry, materials sci, optical sci, condensed matter and radiation, electronic sci, environmental sci, marine geosciences, remote sensing, oceanography, marine meteorology, space technology/sciences.

U.S. citizens who are recent postdoctoral graduates are selected on the basis of overall qualifications and technical proposals.

Contact Jessica Hileman for more information.

2340 — U.S. DEPT. OF HEALTH & HUMAN SERVICES (Indian Health Service Health Professions Scholarship Program)

Twinbrook Metro Plaza, Suite 100
12300 Twinbrook Pkwy.
Rockville MD 20852
301/443-0234
FAX: 301/443-4815
Internet: www:ihs.gov/Recruitment/DHPS/SP/SBTOC3.asp

AMOUNT: Tuition + fees & monthly stipend of $938.

DEADLINE(S): APR 1

FIELD(S): Health professions, accounting, social work

Open to Native Americans or Alaska natives who are graduate students or college juniors or seniors in a program leading to a career in a fields listed above. U.S. citizenship required. Renewable annually with reapplication.

Scholarship recipients must intend to serve the Indian people. They incur a one-year service obligation to the IHS for each year of support for a minimum of two years. Write for complete information.

2341 — UNIFORMED SERVICES UNIVERSITY OF THE HEALTH SCIENCES (Fellowships)

Schools of Medicine & Nursing
4301 Jones Bridge Rd.
Bethesda MD 20814-4799
301/295-3101 or 800/772-1743

AMOUNT: Tuition

DEADLINE(S): NOV 1

FIELD(S): Medicine; Nursing

Open to graduate students who wish to attend the F. Edward Hebert School of Medicine or the Graduate School of Nursing with the understanding that they will be trained for service to the nation, including assignments abroad or at sea. While enrolled, students serve as reserve commissioned officers. Must be US citizen.

Contact Uniformed Services University for an application.

2342 — UNIVERSITY OF EDINBURGH (Faculty of Medicine Bursaries & Scholarships)

7-11 Nicolson St.
Edinburgh SCOTLAND EH8 9BE UK
+44 (0) 131 650 1000
Internet: www.iprs.ed.ac.uk/progawards/medicine/

AMOUNT: Varies

DEADLINE(S): MAR 1; NOV 1

FIELD(S): Medicine

Various scholarships, bursaries, and travel awards for medical students at all levels of study. For use at the University of Edinburgh, Scotland. Some are for students from other companies; some are for women; some are for specific specialties.

Access website for more information and/or contact school for details and appropriate application forms.

2343 — UNIVERSITY OF UTAH COLLEGE OF PHARMACY (Pharmacy Scholarships)

30 So. 2000 E.
Rm. 203
Salt Lake City UT 84112-5820
801/581-4960
FAX: 801/581-3716
E-Mail: ccoffman@deans.pharm.utah.edu

AMOUNT: $500-$2,500

DEADLINE(S): APR

FIELD(S): Pharmacy

Several scholarship programs for students enrolled in the professional pharmacy program at the University of Utah College of Pharmacy. For juniors through doctoral level. Some require financial need; others are merit-based.

60 awards annually. Contact Cathy Coffman for an application.

2344 — US AIR FORCE OPPORTUNITY CENTER (Armed Forces Health Professions Scholarships)

P.O. Box 3505
Attn AFHPSP/FAP
Capitol Heights MD 20790-9605
Written inquiry

AMOUNT: $913 per month stipend + tuition, fees, books, lab fees, etc.

DEADLINE(S): None

FIELD(S): Medicine; Dentistry; and Clinical Psychology (Ph.D)

Open to U.S. citizens enrolled or accepted for enrollment in any of the above fields at an accredited institution in the U.S. or Puerto Rico. Must qualify for appointment as an Air Force officer and sign a contractual agreement.

Write for complete information or call local recruiter (use blue pages in local telephone directories for telephone number).

2345 — WASHINGTON STATE HIGHER EDUCATION COORDINATING BOARD (Health Professional Loan Repayment & Scholarship Program)

PO Box 43430
Olympia WA 98504-3430
360/753-7850
FAX: 360/753-7808
Internet: www.hecb.wa.gov

AMOUNT: Varies

DEADLINE(S): APR (scholarship); FEB (loan repayment); JUL (loan repayment)

FIELD(S): Health Care

Scholarships are open to students in accredited undergraduate or graduate health care programs leading to eligibility for licensure in Washington state. Must agree to work in designated shortage area for minimum of three years. Loan repayment recipients receive payment from program for purpose of repaying education loans secured while attending program of health care training leading to licensure in Washington state. Financial need NOT a factor.

Renewable up to 5 years. Contact Program Manager for a loan repayment application after November 15th and for scholarship application after January 15th.

2346 — WASHINGTON STATE HIGHER EDUCATION COORDINATING BOARD (WICHE Professional Student Exchange)

PO Box 43430
Olympia WA 98504-3430

360/753-7850
FAX: 360/753-7808
AMOUNT: $8,000-$12,000
DEADLINE(S): OCT 15
FIELD(S): Optometry; Osteopathy

Program provides state support to Washington residents pursuing undergraduate or graduate study out-of-state.

12 awards annually (10 renewals, two new). Contact Program Manager for an application.

2347 — WOMEN OF THE EVANGELICAL LUTHERAN CHURCH IN AMERICA (The Kahler-Vickers/Raup-Emma Wettstein Scholarships)

8765 West Higgins Road
Chicago IL 60631-4189
800/638-3522, ext. 2747
FAX: 773/380-2419
E-Mail: womnelca@elca.org
AMOUNT: $2,000 max.
DEADLINE(S): MAR 1
FIELD(S): Health Professions & Christian Service

Assists women who are members of the ELCA studying for service in health professions associated with ELCA projects abroad that do not lead to church-certified professions. Must be US citizen and have experienced an interruption of two or more years since completion of high school. Academic records of coursework completed in last five years as well as proof of admission from educational institution are required.

Renewable for an additional year. Contact Faith Fretheim, Program Director, for an application.

2348 — WOMEN'S SPORTS FOUNDATION (Dorothy Harris Endowed Scholarship)

Eisenhower Park
East Meadow NY 11554
800/227-3988
FAX: 516/542-4716
E-Mail: WoSport@aol.com
Internet: www.lifetimetv.com/WoSport
AMOUNT: $1,500
DEADLINE(S): DEC 11
FIELD(S): Physical Education; Sports Management; Sports Psychology; Sports Sociology

For female graduate students who will pursue a full-time course of study in one of the above fields at an accredited graduate school in the Fall.

1-2 awards annually. Awarded in March. See website or write to above address for details.

2349 — WOODROW WILSON NATIONAL FELLOWSHIP FOUNDATION/JOHNSON & JOHNSON (Dissertation Grants in Women's & Children's Health)

CN 5281
Princeton NJ 08543-5281
609/452-7007
FAX: 609/452-0066
E-Mail: charoltte@woodrow.org
Internet: www.woodrow.org
AMOUNT: $2,000 (for travel, books, microfilming, taping, computer services, etc.)
DEADLINE(S): NOV 8
FIELD(S): Women's & Children's Health

Open to doctoral students in nursing, public health, anthropology, history, sociology, psychology, or social work, who have completed all predissertation requirements at US graduate schools. Must have at least six months left to complete dissertation, which should include significant research on issues related to women's & children's health. Must submit transcripts, proposal, bibliography, & interest. Based on originality & scholarly validity.

15 awards annually. See website or contact WWNFF for an application. Winners announced in February.

2350 — ZETA PHI BETA SORORITY EDUCATIONAL FOUNDATION (S. Evelyn Lewis Memorial Scholarship in Medical Health Sciences)

1734 New Hampshire Ave., NW
Washington DC 20009
Internet: www.zpb1920.org/nefforms.htm
AMOUNT: $500-$1,000
DEADLINE(S): FEB 1
FIELD(S): Medicine; Health Sciences

Open to graduate and undergraduate young women enrolled in a program leading to a degree in medicine or health sciences. Award is for full-time study for one academic year (Fall-Spring) and is paid directly to college/university. Must submit proof of enrollment.

Send self-addressed, stamped envelope to above address between September 1st and December 15th for an application.

MEDICAL RESEARCH

2351 — ACC/MERCK ADULT CARDIOLOGY RESEARCH FELLOWSHIP AWARDS

9111 Old Georgetown Road
Bethesda MD 20814-1699
800/253-4636 Ext. 672
FAX: 301/897-9745
AMOUNT: $35,000

DEADLINE(S): DEC 2
FIELD(S): Adult cardiology research

One-year fellowships to support research training in adult cardiology set up by The American College of Cardiology and The Merck Company Foundation. For students currently in adult cardiology fellowship training.

Six fellowships. Obtain applications from the ACC/Merck Fellowship awards Committee, American College of Cardiology, at above address.

2352 — AGENCY FOR HEALTH CARE POLICY AND RESEARCH (Doctoral Dissertation Research Grant)

PO Box 8547
Silver Spring MD 20907-8547
E-mail: info@ahcpr.gov
Internet: www.ahcpr.gov
AMOUNT: up to $20,000
DEADLINE(S): Varies
FIELD(S): Health Services Research

Doctoral dissertation grants for research on any aspect of health care services (organization, delivery, financing, quality, etc.). Open to social, management, medical, or health sciences doctoral candidates. Awards are made on a competitive basis.

Contact AHCPR for details.

2353 — ALBERTA HERITAGE FOUNDATION FOR MEDICAL RESEARCH (Studentships)

3125 Manulife Pl.
10180 101 St.
Edmonton Alberta T5J 3S4 CANADA
780/423-5727
E-Mail: Postmaster@ahfmr.ab.ca
Internet: www.ahfmr.ab.ca
AMOUNT: $19,000 + research allowance of $1,000
DEADLINE(S): MAR 1; OCT 1
FIELD(S): Medical & Health Research

Open to highly qualified full-time graduate students completing master's or doctoral degree at a university in Alberta. Students in health-related fields may go outside Alberta to study when expertise is not available in Alberta. Must be Canadian citizen or legal resident.

40-50 awards annually. Contact Alberta Heritage Foundation for an application.

2354 — ALCOHOLIC BEVERAGE MEDICAL RESEARCH FOUNDATION (Grants for Alcohol Research)

1122 Kenilworth, Ste. 407
Baltimore MD 21204-2189
410/821-7066
FAX: 410/821-7065
E-Mail: info@abmrf.org

AMOUNT: $40,000/yr. (max.)

DEADLINE(S): FEB 1; SEP 1

FIELD(S): Biomedical & Psychosocial Research on Alcohol Effects

Open to the staff or faculty ONLY of public or private non-profit organizations in the US and Canada for research into the biomedical and psychosocial effects of alcoholic beverages. Graduate/medical students and postdoctoral fellows are NOT eligible; NO funding for thesis/dissertation research.

40 awards annually. Contact Research Foundation for an application ONLY if you fit criteria.

2355 — AMERICAN ACADEMY OF ALLERGY, ASTHMA, & IMMUNOLOGY (Summer Fellowships)

611 East Wells Street
Milwaukee WI 53202-3889
414/272-6071
FAX: 414/272-6070
E-Mail: info@aaaai.org
Internet: www.aaaai.org

AMOUNT: $2,000

DEADLINE(S): APR 15

FIELD(S): Allergy, Asthma, AIDS, Immunology

Fellowship program open to medical students interested in pursuing research in allergy and immunology during their summer recess. Applicants must have completed at least 8 months of medical school and be a US or Canadian residents. Application should include a summary of the clincal/laboratory research project, biographical sketch, and curriculum vitae.

10-15 fellowships annually. Past Summer Fellowship Grant recipients are not eligible. Contact Undergraduate & Graduate Medical Education Committee, c/o Cynthia Schopf, for an application.

2356 — AMERICAN ACADEMY OF IMPLANT DENTISTRY RESEARCH FOUNDATION (Research Grants)

211 E. Chicago Ave., Suite 750
Chicago IL 60611-2616
312/335-1550

AMOUNT: $10,000 maximum

DEADLINE(S): OCT 31

FIELD(S): Dental Research: Implants

Postdoctoral grants open to applicants with DDS degrees. Awards support worthy dental research projects.

Write for complete information.

2357 — AMERICAN ACADEMY OF PERIODONTOLOGY (Balint Orban Prize)

737 N. Michigan Ave., Ste. 800
Chicago IL 60611-2690
312/787-5518

AMOUNT: $500

DEADLINE(S): MAR 10

FIELD(S): Dental Research

Open to students enrolled in graduate or postgraduate training in periodontology. Award is for the best research paper on periodontology. Academy also awards gold medal and cash payment of $4,000 to people who have made outstanding contributions to the understanding and treatment of periodontal disease.

Contact Academy for an application.

2358 — AMERICAN DIABETES ASSOCIATION (Career Development Awards)

1701 N. Beauregard St.
Alexandria VA 22311
703/549-1500, ext. 2376
E-Mail: research@diabetes.org
Internet: www.diabetes.org/research/

AMOUNT: up to $100,000/yr. for 4 years; includes up to $50,000/yr. for salary support & up to 15% for indirect costs

DEADLINE(S): FEB 1 (for JUL 1 funding); AUG 1 (for JAN 1 funding)

FIELD(S): Diabetes Research

This program supports investigators who are establishing their independence. At time of award, applicant must hold assistant professor or justified equivalent academic position within his/her institution. Must be US citizen/permanent resident and hold MD or Ph.D. degree or appropriate health or science degree. Must hold full-time or clinical faculty position or equivalent at university-affiliated institution within the US and US possessions.

See website or contact American Diabetes Association for an application.

2359 — AMERICAN DIABETES ASSOCIATION (Clinical Research Awards)

1701 N. Beauregard St.
Alexandria VA 22311
703/549-1500, ext. 2376
E-Mail: research@diabetes.org
Internet: www.diabetes.org/research/

AMOUNT: up to $100,000/yr. for 3 years; includes up to $20,000/yr. for salary support & up to 15% for indirect costs

DEADLINE(S): FEB 1 (for JUL 1 funding); AUG 1 (for JAN 1 funding)

FIELD(S): Diabetes Research

This program supports investigators whose studies directly involve humans. Studies must focus on intact human subjects in which the effect of a change in the individual's external or internal environment is evaluated. Must be US citizen/permanent resident and hold MD or Ph.D. degree or appropriate health or science degree. Must hold full-time or clinical faculty position or equivalent at university-affiliated institution within the US and US possessions.

See website or contact American Diabetes Association for an application.

2360 — AMERICAN DIABETES ASSOCIATION (Lions SightFirst Diabetic Retinopathy Research Awards)

1701 N. Beauregard St.
Alexandria VA 22311
703/549-1500, ext. 2376
E-Mail: research@diabetes.org
Internet: www.diabetes.org/research/

AMOUNT: up to $60,000/yr. for 2 years

DEADLINE(S): FEB 1

FIELD(S): Diabetes Research

Program supports clinical or applied research in diabetic retinopathy in the US and abroad. Awards given to support new treatment regimens, epidemiology, and translation research. Training and equipment grants also considered. Must hold MD or Ph.D. degree or appropriate health or science degree. Must also hold full-time or clinical faculty position or equivalent at university-affiliated institution in the US and US possessions. No citizenship/residency restrictions.

Funding for July 1st. See website or contact American Diabetes Association for an application.

2361 — AMERICAN DIABETES ASSOCIATION (Mentor-Based Postdoctoral Fellowships)

1701 N. Beauregard St.
Alexandria VA 22311
703/549-1500, ext. 2376
E-Mail: research@diabetes.org
Internet: www.diabetes.org/research/

AMOUNT: up to $30,000/yr. for 4 years

DEADLINE(S): OCT 1

FIELD(S): Diabetes Research

Supports postdoctoral fellows working with established diabetes investigators. Investigator must meet citizenship & employment eligibility requirements. Must be US citizen/permanent resident. Fellow must have MD or Ph.D. degree, no more than three years of postdoctoral research experience, and cannot serve internship or residency during award period. Must hold full-time or clinical faculty position/equivalent at university-affiliated institution in US or possessions.

For July 1st funding. See website or contact American Diabetes Association for an application.

2362 — AMERICAN DIABETES ASSOCIATION (Medical Scholars Program Awards & Physician-Scientist Training Awards)

1701 N. Beauregard St.
Alexandria VA 22311
703/549-1500, ext. 2376
E-Mail: research@diabetes.org
Internet: www.diabetes.org/research/

AMOUNT: Medical Scholars: $30,000 for 1 year + $20,000 stipend & up to $10,000 lab costs; Physician-Scientist: $30,000/yr. for 3 years + $20,000 stipend & $10,000 tuition or lab costs

DEADLINE(S): FEB 1

FIELD(S): Diabetes Research

The goal of these programs is to produce new leaders in diabetes research. The Medical Scholars Program provides one year of research support to students in medical school. The Physician-Scientist Award provides three years of support for the doctoral portion of an MD/Ph.D. degree. Must be US citizen/permanent resident.

For July 1st funding. See website or contact American Diabetes Association for an application.

2363 — AMERICAN FEDERATION FOR AGING RESEARCH (AFAR Research Grants)

1414 Avenue of the Americas, 18th Fl.
New York NY 10019
212/752-2327
FAX: 212/832-2298
Internet: www.afar.org

AMOUNT: $50,000

DEADLINE(S): DEC 15

FIELD(S): Medical Research

This one- to two-year award is open to junior faculty (M.D.s and Ph.D.s) to do research that will serve as the basis for longer term research efforts. AFAR-sponsored investigators study a broad range of biomedical and clinical topics.

Contact AFAR for an application.

2364 — AMERICAN FEDERATION FOR AGING RESEARCH (AFAR/Pfizer Research Grants in Age-Related Neurodegenerative Diseases)

1414 Avenue of the Americas, 18th Fl.
New York NY 10019
212/752-2327
FAX: 212/832-2298
Internet: www.afar.org

AMOUNT: $50,000 (max.)

DEADLINE(S): DEC 15

FIELD(S): Age-Related Research in Neurosciences

Postdoctoral research grants are for projects that involve basic, clinical, or epidemiological research in age-related neurodegenerative diseases. Candidates may propose to use award over the course of one or two years as justified by proposed research. Preference given to candidates in first or second year of a junior faculty appointment.

4 awards annually. Contact AFAR for an application.

2365 — AMERICAN FEDERATION FOR AGING RESEARCH (Glenn Foundation/AFAR Scholarships for Research in the Biology of Aging)

1414 Avenue of the Americas, 18th Fl.
New York NY 10019
212/752-2327
FAX: 212/832-2298
Internet: www.afar.org

AMOUNT: $4,000 (student); $1,500 (mentor)

DEADLINE(S): FEB 25

FIELD(S): Aging Research

Designed to attract potential scientists and clinicians to aging research, this program provides Ph.D. and M.D. students the opportunity to conduct a three-month research project. Students will work in an area of biomedical research in aging under the auspices of a mentor.

Contact AFAR for an application.

2366 — AMERICAN FEDERATION FOR AGING RESEARCH (ISOA/AFAR Program for Drug Discovery in Cognitive Decline & Dementia)

1414 Avenue of the Americas, 18th Fl.
New York NY 10019
212/752-2327
FAX: 212/832-2298
Internet: www.afar.org

AMOUNT: $50,000

DEADLINE(S): OCT 15

FIELD(S): Cognitive Decline & Dementia Research

Postdoctoral research grants for junior faculty (M.D.s & Ph.D.s) are to promote translational research and drug discovery for new agents in the treatment of cognitive decline and dementia.

2 awards annually. Contact AFAR for an application.

2367 — AMERICAN FEDERATION FOR AGING RESEARCH (John A. Hartford/AFAR Academic Geriatrics Fellowship Program)

1414 Avenue of the Americas, 18th Fl.
New York NY 10019
212/752-2327
FAX: 212/832-2298
Internet: www.afar.org

AMOUNT: $50,000

DEADLINE(S): FEB 18

FIELD(S): Geriatric Research

This program for postdoctorates was designed to foster the development of a new generation of academic physicians competent in and committed to geriatric medicine.

10 awards annually. Contact AFAR for an application.

2368 — AMERICAN FEDERATION FOR AGING RESEARCH (John A. Hartford/AFAR Medical Student Geriatric Scholars Program)

1414 Avenue of the Americas, 18th Fl.
New York NY 10019
212/752-2327
FAX: 212/832-2298
Internet: www.afar.org

AMOUNT: $3,000 stipend

DEADLINE(S): FEB 7

FIELD(S): Geriatric Research

This program is to encourage medical students, particularly budding researchers, to consider geriatrics as a career. Program awards short-term scholarships through a national competition and provides Ph.D. and M.D. students the opportunity to train at an acclaimed center of excellence in geriatrics.

Contact AFAR for an application.

2369 — AMERICAN FEDERATION FOR AGING RESEARCH (MERCK/AFAR Fellowships in Geriatric Clinical Pharmacology)

1414 Avenue of the Americas, 18th Fl.
New York NY 10019
212/752-2327
FAX: 212/832-2298
Internet: www.afar.org

AMOUNT: $60,000/yr.

DEADLINE(S): NOV 1

FIELD(S): Geriatric Pharmacology Research

Two-year's funding for full-time postdoctoral research and training in geriatric pharmacology.

2 awards annually. Contact AFAR for an application.

2370 — AMERICAN FEDERATION FOR AGING RESEARCH (MERCK/AFAR Research Scholarships in Geriatric Pharmacology for Medical & Pharmacy Students)

1414 Avenue of the Americas, 18th Fl.
New York NY 10019
212/752-2327
FAX: 212/832-2298
Internet: www.afar.org

AMOUNT: $4,000

DEADLINE(S): JAN 21

FIELD(S): Geriatric Pharmacology Research

Open to Medical and Pharm.D. students to undertake a two- to three-month full-time research project in geriatric pharmacology.

9 awards annually. Contact AFAR for an application.

2371 — AMERICAN FEDERATION FOR AGING RESEARCH (Paul Beeson Physician Faculty Scholars in Aging Research Program)

1414 Avenue of the Americas, 18th Fl.
New York NY 10019
212/752-2327
FAX: 212/832-2298
Internet: www.afar.org

AMOUNT: $450,000 (max.)

DEADLINE(S): NOV 15

FIELD(S): Geriatric Research

Three-year postdoctoral awards to allow junior faculty to devote their time to research and training activities related to aging and care of the elderly.

60 awards annually. Contact AFAR for an application.

2372 — AMERICAN FOUNDATION FOR AGING RESEARCH (Fellowship Program)

NC State Univ.
Biochem Dept.
Box 7622
Raleigh NC 27695-7622
919/515-5679

AMOUNT: $500-$1,000

DEADLINE(S): None

FIELD(S): Aging (as related to molecular/celluar biology, immunobiology, cancer, neurobiology, biochemistry, and/or molecular biophysics)

Applicants in degree programs must be undergraduate, graduate, or pre-doctoral students at colleges/universities in the US. Individuals most often chosen utilize modern and innovative approaches and technologies. Letters of reference from research advisor & two instructors are required, as well as official transcripts.

Number of awards varies. $3 processing fee for pre-application; no fee for submission of full application. All interested student researchers should write directly to AFAR Headquarters to receive application forms— specify year in school & type of proposed research.

2373 — AMERICAN FOUNDATION FOR PHARMACEUTICAL EDUCATION (Predoctoral Fellowships)

One Church St., Suite 202
Rockville MD 20850

301/738-2160
FAX: 301/738-2161

AMOUNT: $6,000 to $10,000/yr.

DEADLINE(S): MAR 1

FIELD(S): Pharmacology

Several predoctoral fellowships for pharmaceutical students with no more than three years remaining to earn the Ph.D.

Student accepts a teaching appointment in a Pharmacy college. U.S. citizen or legal resident. Write for complete information.

2374 — AMERICAN FOUNDATION FOR UROLOGIC DISEASE (Health Policy Research Program)

1128 North Charles St.
Baltimore MD 21201-5559
410/468-1800
FAX: 410/468-1808
E-Mail: admin@afud.org
Internet: www.afud.org

AMOUNT: $44,000/yr.

DEADLINE(S): SEP 3

FIELD(S): Health Care Services & Urology

A trained urologist (MD/DO) within five years of residency who aspires to conduct research in health care services as it relates to urology may apply for this two-year program. Must be willing to spend 80% of their time on research project and be dedicated to a career in academic urology. Should demonstrate interest/accomplishments in health-related areas. An accredited medical education research institution or department within such an institution must sponsor them.

Selection based on scientific merit of proposal, how well proposal prepares applicant for future urologic research, and track record of success. Contact AFUD for an application packet.

2375 — AMERICAN FOUNDATION FOR UROLOGIC DISEASE (M.D. Post-Resident Research Program)

1128 North Charles St.
Baltimore MD 21201-5559
410/468-1800
FAX: 410/468-1808
E-Mail: admin@afud.org
Internet: www.afud.org

AMOUNT: $44,000/yr.

DEADLINE(S): SEP 3

FIELD(S): Urologic Research

A trained urologist (MD/DO), within five years of post-residency, who aspires to learn scientific techniques, is committed to a career in research, and

who is able to provide evidence of current and/or prior interest/accomplishments in research may apply for this two-year program. Must be willing to spend 80% of their time on their research project. An accredited medical education research institution or department within such an institution must sponsor the candidate.

Selection based on scientific merit of proposal, how well proposal will prepare applicant for future urologic research, and track record of success. Contact AFUD for an application packet.

2376 — AMERICAN FOUNDATION FOR UROLOGIC DISEASE (M.D./Ph.D. One-Year Research Program)

1128 North Charles St.
Baltimore MD 21201-5559
410/468-1800
FAX: 410/468-1808
E-Mail: admin@afud.org
Internet: www.afud.org

AMOUNT: $25,000/yr.

DEADLINE(S): SEP 3

FIELD(S): Urology Research

A fellowship program for urologists who have completed their residency within five years of the date of application. An accredited medical education research institution or department within such an institution must sponsor the candidate. Selection based on scientific merit, how well proposal prepares applicant for future urologic research, and track record of success. Does NOT fund urology resident for lab research before or during residency training.

Contact AFUD for an application packet.

2377 — AMERICAN FOUNDATION FOR UROLOGIC DISEASE (Ph.D. Post-Doctoral Research Program)

1128 North Charles St.
Baltimore MD 21201-5559
410/468-1800
FAX: 410/468-1808
E-Mail: admin@afud.org
Internet: www.afud.org

AMOUNT: $46,000/yr.

DEADLINE(S): SEP 3

FIELD(S): Urology Research

Post-doctoral basic scientist with a research interest in urologic or related diseases and dysfunctions may apply to this two-year program. An accredited medical education research institution or department within such an institution must sponsor the candidate. Selection based on scientific merit, how well proposal prepares applicant for future urologic research, and track record of success.

Contact AFUD for an application packet.

2378 — AMERICAN FOUNDATION FOR UROLOGIC DISEASE (Summer Medical Student Fellowship)

1128 North Charles St.
Baltimore MD 21201-5559
410/468-1800
FAX: 410/468-1808
E-Mail: admin@afud.org
Internet: www.afud.org

AMOUNT: $2,000

DEADLINE(S): FEB 2

FIELD(S): Urology Research

Introductory Research Fellowships are offered to outstanding medical students to work in urology research laboratories during the summer for two months. An accredited medical research institution/department must sponsor the candidate.

Contact AFUD for an application packet.

2379 — AMERICAN FOUNDATION FOR UROLOGIC DISEASE/NATIONAL CANCER INSTITUTE (Intramural Urologic Oncology Ph.D./Postdoctoral Research Training Program)

1128 North Charles St.
Baltimore MD 21201-5559
410/468-1800
FAX: 410/468-1808
E-Mail: lesley@afud.org
Internet: www.afud.org

AMOUNT: $28,700-35,900

DEADLINE(S): None

FIELD(S): Urologic Oncology

2-3 year fellowship. Must have Ph.D. and less than five years of postdoctoral experience. Background in molecular biology, cell biology, or protein chemistry is optimal but not required. Fellows participate in lab data clubs/seminars/journal clubs, etc., as well as attend NIH-wide lectures & seminars, and short-term molecular biology & clinical research training courses on campus. Opportunity to participate in weekly clinical urology conferences.

Contact AFUD for an application packet, or write to the National Cancer Institute, Bldg. 10, Room 2B47, 10 Center Drive, MSC 1501, Bethesda, MD 20892-1501. May also be eligible for loan repayment.

2380 — AMERICAN FOUNDATION FOR UROLOGIC DISEASE/NATIONAL CANCER INSTITUTE (Intramural Urologic Oncology Research Training Program)

1128 North Charles St.
Baltimore MD 21201-5559
410/468-1800

FAX: 410/468-1808
E-Mail: lesley@afud.org
Internet: www.afud.org

AMOUNT: $52,000-58,000

DEADLINE(S): None

FIELD(S): Urologic Oncology

Physicians who have recently completed Urology Residency, who desire exposure to research experience utilizing basic molecular & cellular biologic techniques in projects relevant to urology may apply. Must have less than five years of post-doctoral research experience (clinical residency training NOT counted as post-doctoral research). Fellows rotate on Urologic Oncology Branch, NCI's service, are trained in clinical protocols, and do new studies.

Contact AFUD for an application packet, or write to the National Cancer Institute, Bldg. 10, Room 2B47, 10 Center Drive, MSC 1501, Bethesda, MD 20892-1501. Fellows also eligible for NIH Loan Repayment Program.

2381 — AMERICAN FOUNDATION FOR UROLOGIC DISEASE/NATIONAL INSTITUTE OF DIABETES AND DIGESTIVE AND KIDNEY DISEASES (Intramural Urology Research Training Program)

1128 North Charles St.
Baltimore MD 21201-5559
410/468-1800 or 301/594-7717
FAX: 410/468-1808
E-Mail: admin@afud.org OR
NybergL@ep.niddk.nih.gov
Internet: www.afud.org

AMOUNT: $45,000-$52,000

DEADLINE(S): None

FIELD(S): Urologic Research

2-3 year fellowship. Physicians who have recently completed Urology Residency, who desire exposure to research experience utilizing basic molecular & cellular biologic techniques in projects relevant to urology may apply. Must have less than five years of post-doctoral research experience (clinical residency training NOT counted as post-doctoral research). Particpate in lab data clubs/seminars/journal clubs, and attend NIH-wide lectures/seminars & training courses.

Contact AFUD for an application packet, or write to Dr. Leroy Nyberg, NIDDK, Natcher Building Room 6AS13D, Bethesda, MD 20892.

2382 — AMERICAN GERIATRICS SOCIETY (Edward Henderson Student Research Award)

770 Lexington Ave #300
New York NY 10021
212/308-1414

AMOUNT: $500 travel stipend to attend annual meeting

DEADLINE(S): DEC 8

FIELD(S): Gerontology; Aging; Geriatrics

Open to medical students. Special consideration given to students who have engaged in research or clinical investigation in geriatrics or are participating in an ongoing clinical project. Formal paper is not required but is welcome.

The award includes a travel stipend is presented at the Society's annual meeting. The recipient attends as an invited guest.

2383 — AMERICAN INDIAN SCIENCE AND ENGINEERING SOCIETY (A.T. Anderson Memorial Scholarship)

PO Box 9828
Albuquerque NM 87119-9828
505/765-1052
FAX: 505/765-5608
E-Mail: scholarships@aises.org
Internet: www.aises.org/scholarships

AMOUNT: $1,000-$2,000

DEADLINE(S): JUN 15

FIELD(S): Medicine; Natural Resources; Science; Engineering

Open to undergraduate and graduate students who are at least 1/4 American Indian or recognized as member of a tribe. Must be member of AISES ($10 fee), enrolled full-time at an accredited institution, and demonstrate financial need.

Renewable. See website or contact Patricia Browne for an application and/or membership information.

2384 — AMERICAN LIVER FOUNDATION (Postdoctoral Research Fellow Program)

Research Dept.
1425 Pompton Ave.
Cedar Grove NJ 07009
973/256-2550

AMOUNT: $10,000

DEADLINE(S): JAN 15

FIELD(S): Liver Research

Research training fellowships are open to recent MDs & Ph.D.s and are tenable at eligible institutions in the US or its possessions. Purpose is to encourage development of individuals with research potential who require additional research training and experience.

Contact ALF for an application.

2385 — AMERICAN LIVER FOUNDATION
(Student Research Fellowships)

Research Dept.
1425 Pompton Ave.
Cedar Grove NJ 07009
973/256-2550

AMOUNT: $2,500 stipend

DEADLINE(S): JAN 15

FIELD(S): Medical Research

Three-month fellowships open to medical students, veterinary students, & Ph.D. candidates. Purpose is to encourage them to gain exposure in the research laboratory and possibly consider liver research as a career option.

Contact ALF for an application.

2386 — AMERICAN LUNG ASSOCIATION
(Clinical Research Grant)

Medical Affairs Division
1740 Broadway
New York NY 10019-4374
212/315-8793
Internet: www.lungusa.org

AMOUNT: $25,000/yr.

DEADLINE(S): NOV 1

FIELD(S): Lung Disease

To provide starter or seed money to investigators working in clinical areas relevant to lung disease. Must be U.S. citizen or permanent resident training in a U.S. institution.

Must hold a doctorate degree, faculty apppointment with an academic institution, and have completed two years of postdoctoral research training.

2387 — AMERICAN LUNG ASSOCIATION
(Dalsemer Research Scholar Award)

Medical Affairs Division
1740 Broadway
New York NY 10019-4374
212/315-8793
Internet: www.lungusa.org

AMOUNT: Up to $25,000/year

DEADLINE(S): NOV 1

FIELD(S): Interstitial Lung Disease

Open to physicians who have completed grad training in pulmonary disease and are beginning a faculty track in a U.S. school of medicine. Must be a U.S. or permanent U.S. resident training in a U.S. institution.

Renewable for a second year. Write or visit website for application and details.

2388 — AMERICAN LUNG ASSOCIATION
(Johnie Murphy Career Investigator Award)

Medical Affairs Division
1740 Broadway
New York NY 10019-4374
212/315-8793
Internet: www.lungusa.org

AMOUNT: $35,000/year

DEADLINE(S): OCT 1

FIELD(S): Lung Disease

Awards provide stable salary and/or project support for investigators making transition from junior to mid-level faculty. Designed to support physician investigators, but applications from other scientists may be considered.

Must be U.S. citizen or permanent resident training in a U.S. institution. institution. Renewable for an additional two years. Write or visit website for application and complete information.

2389 — AMERICAN LUNG ASSOCIATION
(Lung Health Research Dissertation Grants)

Medical Affairs Division
1740 Broadway
New York NY 10019-4374
212/315-8793
Internet: www.lungusa.org

AMOUNT: Up to $21,000/yr.

DEADLINE(S): OCT 1

FIELD(S): Lung Health

Open to doctoral students matriculating in a full-time program with an academic career focus in the fields of science related to the social, behavioral, epidemiologic, psychological, and educational aspects of lung health. Nurses in any field who are interested in lung disease may apply.

Applicants must be U.S. citizens or permanent residents enrolled in a U.S. institution. May be renewed for a second year. Write for complete information. Write or visit website for application and/or details.

2390 — AMERICAN LUNG ASSOCIATION
(Nursing Research Training Award)

Medical Affairs Division
1740 Broadway
New York NY 10019-4374
Up to $11000/year

AMOUNT: 212/315-8793

DEADLINE(S): OCT 1

FIELD(S): Lung Disease Research

Open to professional nurses holding master's degrees who are matriculated in full-time doctoral programs with a focus relevant to lung disease. Priority given to those who will pursue an academic career.

Must be US or Canadian citizen or permanent resident of the US training in a US institution. Renewable for an additional year. Write for complete information.

2391 — AMERICAN LUNG ASSOCIATION
(Pediatric Pulmonary Research Training Fellowship)

Medical Affairs Division
1740 Broadway
New York NY 10019-4374
212/315-8793
www.lungusa.org/research

AMOUNT: $32,500

DEADLINE(S): OCT 1

FIELD(S): Pediatric Lung Disease

Open to U.S. or Canadian citizens or permanent residents of the U.S. who hold MD, DO, Ph.D, or Sc.D degrees (or comparable qualifications) & are committed to a career in investigative or academic medicine relative to pediatric lung disease.

For training at a U.S. institution. Renewable for 1 year. Write or visit website for application and complete information.

2392 — AMERICAN LUNG ASSOCIATION
(Research Grants)

Medical Affairs Division
1740 Broadway
New York NY 10019-4374
212/315-8793
Internet: www.lungusa.org

AMOUNT: $25,000/yr.

DEADLINE(S): NOV 1

FIELD(S): Lung Disease

Open to U.S. or permanent residents training in a U.S. institution. Research may be laboratory, clinical, epidemiological, social, environmental, or other areas of investigation relevant to lung biology.

Post-doctoral support for new—not already established—investigators. Targeted for instructors or assistant professors who have completed at least 2 years of research training. Write or visit website for applications and complete information.

2393 — AMERICAN LUNG ASSOCIATION
(Research Training Fellowships)

Medical Affairs Division
1740 Broadway
New York NY 10019-4374
212/315-8793
Internet: www.lungusa.org

AMOUNT: $32,500/yr.

DEADLINE(S): OCT 1

FIELD(S): Lung Biology & Disease

For U.S. citizens or permanent residents training in a U.S. institution. Must hold M.D., Ph.D., or have comparable qualifications and be seeking further training as a scientific investigator.

Awards are for one year and may be renewed for another year subject to availability of funds. Write or access website for complete information and application.

2394 — AMERICAN MEDICAL ASSOCIATION FOUNDATION (Grant Program)

515 N. State St.
Chicago IL 60610
312/464-4543
FAX: 312/464-5678
E-Mail: rita_palulonis@ama-assn.org
Internet: www.ama-assn.org/med-sci/erf

AMOUNT: Varies

DEADLINE(S): None

FIELD(S): Medical Research

Research grants fund either small research projects or provide interim funding to researchers who are anticipating grants for major initiatives from other sources. Only direct expenses associated with proposed research are funded. All grant applications are peer-reviewed and funding decisions are made during Board's five annual meetings. No official application form; those interested should submit letter of application, research proposal, budget, and curriculum vitae.

Contact Rita M. Palulonis, Associate Director, at the AMA Foundation for details.

2395 — AMERICAN RESPIRATORY CARE FOUNDATION (GlaxoWellcome Fellowship for Asthma Care Management Education)

11030 Ables Ln.
Dallas TX 75229-4593
972/243-2272
E-Mail: info@aarc.org
Internet: www.aarc.org/awards

AMOUNT: $3,500 cash + certificate & travel to convention

DEADLINE(S): JUN 30

FIELD(S): Asthma Education Research

Provides supplementary support for a one-year period to permit a postdoctoral fellow to complete a research project in asthma education. It is designed to foster projects that address issues of asthma education, asthma self-management, and asthma awareness. Abstract required.

See website or contact Norma Hernandez at ARCF for details. Selection by September 1st.

2396 — AMERICAN RESPIRATORY CARE FOUNDATION (Monaghan/Trudell Fellowship for Aerosol Technique Development & Respironics Fellowships in Non-Invasive Respiratory Care/Mechanical Ventilation)

11030 Ables Ln.
Dallas TX 75229-4593
972/243-2272
E-Mail: info@aarc.org
Internet: www.aarc.org/awards

AMOUNT: $1,000 cash + certificate & travel to convention

DEADLINE(S): JUN 30

FIELD(S): Respiratory Therapy Research

These three postdoctoral fellowship programs are designed to foster and support projects dealing with aerosol delivery issues, non-invasive techniques to provide ventilatory support, and mechanical ventilation issues. Projects may include modeling studies, in-vitro studies, or clinical studies, and may be device development, device evaluation, cost-effectiveness analysis, or education programs. Abstract required.

See website or contact Norma Hernandez at ARCF for details. Selection by September 1st.

2397 — AMERICAN RESPIRATORY CARE FOUNDATION (NBRC/AMP H. Frederic Helmholz, Jr., MD Educational Research Fund)

11030 Ables Ln.
Dallas TX 75229-4593
972/243-2272
E-Mail: info@aarc.org
Internet: www.aarc.org/awards

AMOUNT: $3,000 cash + certificate & travel to convention

DEADLINE(S): JUN 30

FIELD(S): Respiratory Care Research

Supports educational or credentialing research. A master's thesis or doctoral dissertation with practical value to the respiratory care profession are acceptable submissions by a candidate. Others may submit a complete research proposal for consideration.

See website or contact Norma Hernandez at ARCF for an application. Selection by September 1st.

2398 — AMERICAN RESPIRATORY CARE FOUNDATION (Parker B. Francis Respiratory Research Grant & Jerome M. Sullivan Research Fund)

11030 Ables Ln.
Dallas TX 75229-4593
972/243-2272
E-Mail: info@aarc.org
Internet: www.aarc.org/awards

AMOUNT: Varies

DEADLINE(S): JUN 30

FIELD(S): Respiratory Care Research;
Cardiopulmonary Research

Provides funds for clinical or basic research projects in respiratory care, cardiopulmonary medicine, and related topics. Principal investigator may be a physician or respiratory therapist; however, respiratory therapist must be either the principal investigator or co-principal investigator. Award amounts and frequency is at discretion of ARCF and dependent upon quality of proposals.

See website or contact Norma Hernandez at ARCF for an application. Selection by September 1st.

2399 — AMERICAN SPEECH-LANGUAGE-HEARING FOUNDATION (Graduate Student Scholarships)

10801 Rockville Pike
Rockville MD 20852
301/897-5700
FAX 301/571-0457

AMOUNT: $4,000

DEADLINE(S): JUN 6

FIELD(S): Communication sciences/disorders;
speech pathology;speech therapy

Open to full-time graduate students in communication sciences and disorders programs and demonstrating outstanding academic achievement.

Applications available in February.

2400 — AMERICAN SPEECH-LANGUAGE-HEARING FOUNDATION (Kala Singh Memorial Fund-International/Minority Student Scholarship)

10801 Rockville Pike
Rockville Pike, Rockville, MD 20852
301/897-5700
FAX: 301/571-0457

AMOUNT: $2,000

DEADLINE(S): JUN 6

FIELD(S): Communication sciences and disorders, speech/language pathology, audiology

Applicants must be international/ethnic minority graduate student studying communication sciences and disorders in the U.S. and demonstrating outstanding academic achievement.

Applications available in February.

2401 — AMERICAN SPEECH-LANGUAGE-HEARING FOUNDATION (Leslie Isenberg Fund for Student With Disability)

10801 Rockville Pike
Rockville Pike, Rockville MD 20852

301/897-5700
FAX: 301/571-0457
AMOUNT: $2,000
DEADLINE(S): JUN 6
FIELD(S): Communication sciences & disorders

Open to full-time graduate student with disability enrolled in a communication sciences and disorders program and demonstrating outstanding academic achievement.

Applications available in February.

2402 — AMERICAN SPEECH-LANGUAGE-HEARING FOUNDATION (New Investigator Research Grant)

10801 Rockville Pike
Rockville MD 20852
301/897-5700
FAX 301/571-0457
AMOUNT: $5,000
DEADLINE(S): JUL 20
FIELD(S): Speech/Language Pathology; Audiology

Research grant for new investigators to support clinical research in the above areas. Grants are designed to encourage research activities by new scientists who have earned their M.A. or Ph.D. within the last 5 years. Students enrolled in degree programs are ineligible.

Seven awards. Applications available in February.

2403 — AMERICAN SPEECH-LANGUAGE-HEARING FOUNDATION (Student Research Grant in Clinical or Rehabilitative Audiology)

10801 Rockville Pike
Rockville MD 20852
301/897-5700
FAX 301/571-0457
AMOUNT: $2,000
DEADLINE(S): JUN 13
FIELD(S): Audiology

Student research grants available to graduate or post-graduate students in communication sciences and disorders desiring to conduct research in audiology.

Applications available in February.

2404 — AMERICAN SPEECH-LANGUAGE-HEARING FOUNDATION (Young Scholars Award for Minority Student)

10801 Rockville Pike
Rockville MD 20852
301/897-5700
FAX 301/571-0457
AMOUNT: $2,000
DEADLINE(S): JUN 6

FIELD(S): Speech/Language Pathology; Audiology

Open to ethnic minorities who are full-time college seniors accepted for graduate study in speech-language pathology or audiology. Applicants must be US citizens.

Applications available in February.

2405 — AMYOTROPHIC LATERAL SCLEROSIS ASSOCIATION (Research Grant Program)

27001 Agoura Rd., Ste. 150
Calabasas Hills CA 91301-5104
818/880-9007
FAX: 818/880-9006
E-Mail: ruth@alsa-national.org
Internet: www.alsa.org
AMOUNT: $60,000 (max.-research grants); $35,000 (max.-starter grants)
DEADLINE(S): DEC 1
FIELD(S): Amyotrophic Lateral Sclerosis Research

Two- to three-year postdoctoral research grants & one-year starter awards are available to pursue basic or clinical research relevant to amyotrophic lateral sclerosis. Clinical research includes research conducted with human subjects & materials of human origin, but not clinical trials nor patient management studies. To apply, submit one-page abstract, describing proposed project, including contact info, title, nature of project, length of time, & funding required.

Contact Ruth Papadatos, Research Coordinator, for more information. Annoncement of awards made in June, with funding to commence in August.

2406 — ARTHRITIS FOUNDATION OF AUSTRALIA (Domestic & Overseas Fellowships)

GPO Box 121
Sydney NSW 2001 AUSTRALIA
02 9552 6085
FAX: 02 9552 6078
AMOUNT: $32,000/yr. (domestic); USD $21,000 + $1,000 for travel (overseas)
DEADLINE(S): JUN 18
FIELD(S): Arthritis Research

Fellowships for Australian citizens/permanent residents who have several years of postgraduate experience. Domestic fellowships are tenable in Australia for one year for postdoctorate clinical or scientifc research. Preference given to applicants aged 35 years or less. Overseas fellowships are tenable in any research centre for one year for clinical or scientific research. Must return to work in Australia at end of fellowship.

Renewable. Contact AFA for an application.

2407 — ARTHRITIS FOUNDATION OF AUSTRALIA (Domestic Scholarships)

GPO Box 121
Sydney NSW 2001 AUSTRALIA
02 9552 6085
FAX: 02 9552 6078
AMOUNT: $15,000-$23,700
DEADLINE(S): JUN 18
FIELD(S): Arthritis Research

One-year scholarships for Australian citizens/permanent residents who are enrolled in studies leading to a master's or doctoral degree in an Australian institution. Designed to develop the intellectual and technical expertise required for a career involving laboratory and clincial investigation.

Contact AFA for an application.

2408 — ARTHRITIS SOCIETY (Research Scholarships, Fellowships, & Grants)

393 University Ave., Ste. 1700
Toronto Ontario M5G 1E6 CANADA
416/979-7228
FAX: 416/979-8366
E-Mail: info@on.arthritis.ca
Internet: www.arthritis.ca.home.html
AMOUNT: Varies
DEADLINE(S): Varies (according to program)
FIELD(S): Arthritis Research

The society offers a variety of scholarships, fellowships, and grants for postdoctorate research related to arthritis.

Some awards are for Canadian citizens or permanent residents; others are not restricted. Write for complete information.

2409 — ARTHUR M. MILLER FUND

P.O. Box 1122
Wichita KS 67201-0004
316/261-4609
AMOUNT: Varies
DEADLINE(S): MAR 31
FIELD(S): Medicine or related fields

Scholarships for Kansas residents for the study of medicine or related fields at accredited instutitions.

Send SASE for formal application.

2410 — ASSOCIATION FOR SPINA BIFIDA AND HYDROCEPHALUS (Research Fellowships)

ASBAH House
42 Park Rd.
Peterborough PE1 2UQ ENGLAND UK
44 01733 555 988
FAX: 44 01733 555 985

E-Mail: postmaster@asbah.demon.co.uk

Internet: www.asbah.demon.co.uk

AMOUNT: Varies

DEADLINE(S): None

FIELD(S): Spina Bifida/Hydrocephalus Research

Graduate and postgraduate research fellowships in the United Kingdom for medical, social, or educational research in Spina Bifida/Hydrocephalus. Normally awarded to a UK resident.

Awarded only every 5 years or so of an agreed duration. Not renewable. Contact Andrew Russell at ASBAH for an application.

2411 — ASTHMA AND ALLERGY FOUNDATION OF AMERICA (Various Fellowships and Grants)

611 E. Wells St.

Milwaukee WI 53202-3889

414/272-6071

FAX: 414/272-6070

E-Mail: info@aaaai.org

Internet: www.aaaai.org

AMOUNT: $20,000+, depending on program

DEADLINE(S): JAN 6; JAN 12 (depending on program)

FIELD(S): Immunology; Allergy; Asthma

Postdoctoral research grants for study in the above areas.

Write or access website for more information.

2412 — AUSTRIAN CULTURAL INSTITUTE (Max Kade Foundation Grants)

950 Third Ave., 20th Fl.

New York NY 10022

212/759-5165 or +43/1/51581-253

FAX: 212/319-9636

E-Mail: desk@aci.org

Internet: www.austriaculture.net

AMOUNT: Varies

DEADLINE(S): Varies

FIELD(S): Medicine; Natural Sciences; Engineering

Open to young Austrian scientists with several years of experience at universities or institutions. Must demonstrate capacity to pursue independent teaching or research activities in the US. Proficiency in English required.

See website or contact ACI for an application kit, or write to Osterreichische Akademie der Wissenschaften, Kommission fur Max Kade Stipendien, Dr. Ignaz Seipel-Platz 2, A-1010 Vienna, Austria.

2413 — AUSTRIAN CULTURAL INSTITUTE (Thesis Scholarship)

950 Third Ave., 20th Fl.

New York NY 10022

212/759-5165

FAX: 212/319-9636

E-Mail: desk@aci.org

Internet: www.austriaculture.net

AMOUNT: ATS 260,000 three times/year (US $19,850)

DEADLINE(S): None

FIELD(S): Biochemistry; Genetics; Microbiology

Open to excellent doctoral students in above fields who intend to write their thesis on the subjects of cancer, cell cycle, cell biology, evolutionary biology, gene expression, gene therapy, or microbiological genetics.

See website or contact ACI for an application kit, or write to Forschungsinstitut fur Molekulare Pathologie GesmbH, Dr. Bohr-Gasse 7, A-1030 Wien, Austria, or write to Universitatsinstitute im Vienna Biocenter, Dr. Bohr-Gasse 9, A-1030 Wien, Austria.

2414 — BECA FOUNDATION (Alice Newell Joslyn Medical Fund)

310 Via Vera Cruz, Ste. 101

San Marcos CA 92069

760/471-5465

FAX: 760/471-9175

AMOUNT: $500-$2,000

DEADLINE(S): MAR 1

FIELD(S): Medicine; Health Care; Nursing; Dental/Medical Assisting; Physical Therapy

Open to Latino students who live in or attend college in San Diego County, CA, at time of application. For high school seniors and those already in college pursuing undergraduate or graduate education. Based on financial need, scholastic determination, and community/cultural awareness. BECA also provides a mentor to each scholarship recipient.

Send self-addressed, stamped envelope to BECA for an application.

2415 — BODOSSAKI FOUNDATION (Academic Prizes)

20 Amalias Ave.

GR-105 57 Athens GREECE

3220 962

FAX: 3237 976

AMOUNT: Drs. 7,000,000

DEADLINE(S): DEC 31

FIELD(S): Pure mathematics, theoretical and applied computer science, operations research, cardiovascular diseases, developmental biology

Awards to support the creative work of young Greek academics and scientists and reward their endeavor in the advancement of learning and the creation of sound values. Must be of Greek nationality, parentage, or descent under age 40.

Contact above address for details.

2416 — BOEING (Polish Graduate Student Scholarship Program)

Phone for details

314/234-2149

AMOUNT: Tuition, books, and fees for three years

DEADLINE(S): Varies

FIELD(S): Scientific and technical fields

Scholarships for students from Poland to pursue graduate studies in scientific and technical areas at American colleges or universities.

Call Jim Schlueter at above telephone number.

2417 — BROOKHAVEN NATIONAL LABORATORY (Post-doctoral Research Associateships)

Brookhaven National Laboratory

Upton L.I. NY 11973-5000

516/344-3336

AMOUNT: $29,000 minimum

DEADLINE(S): Varies

FIELD(S): Chemistry, Physics, Materials Science, Biology, Oceanography, and Biomedical Sciences.

Post-doctoral research associateships tenable at Brookhaven National Laboratory for research to promote fundamental and applied research in the above fields. A recent doctoral degree is required.

25 associateships per year. Renewable for two additional years.

2418 — CALEDONIAN RESEARCH FOUNDATION (Personal Research Fellowships)

39 Castle St.

Edinburgh EH2 3BH SCOTLAND UK

0131 225 1200

FAX: 0131 225 4412

E-Mail: crf@murraybeith.co.uk

AMOUNT: 17,570-27,515 pounds sterling & travel/subsistance grants

DEADLINE(S): MAR 10

FIELD(S): Biomedical Sciences Research

Three-year fellowships tenable in Scotland are for pursuing research in the biological, biochemical, physical, or clinical sciences related to medicine. Must possess doctorate or equivalent higher qualification, and on the date of appointment applicants should normally be either aged 32 or under, or have between 2 and 6 years postdoctoral experience. Referees required.

Contact CRF for an application.

2419 — CALEDONIAN RESEARCH FOUNDATION (Support Research Fellowships)

39 Castle St.
Edinburgh EH2 3BH SCOTLAND UK
0131 225 1200
FAX: 0131 225 4412
E-Mail: crf@murraybeith.co.uk

AMOUNT: 17,570 pounds sterling & travel/subsistance grants

DEADLINE(S): MAR 10

FIELD(S): Biomedical Sciences Research

Awards provide a 12-month period of study leave to carry out research on a full-time basis in the biological, biochemical, physical, or clinical sciences related to medicine. Must be existing members of staff, normally under age 40, who have held a teaching appointment for at least 5 years in any higher education institution in Scotland. Referees required.

Contact CRF for an application.

2420 — CANADIAN CANCER SOCIETY (McEachern Award)

10 Alcorn Ave., Suite 200
Toronto Ontario M4V 3B1 Canada
416/961-7223
FAX: 416/961-4189

AMOUNT: $38,550 (Canadian) + tuition and travel reimbursement ($1,000 max.)

DEADLINE(S): OCT (mid-month each year)

FIELD(S): Cancer Care/Clinical Research

Grants designed to provide an opportunity for physicians to undertake training for a career in clinical oncology in Canada. Must have completed not less than 3 years of post-grad training after receipt of MD degree.

Awards can be used anywhere in the world; if the fellowship program is taken outside of Canada the candidate must return to Canada to work upon its completion. Must be Canadian citizen or landed immigrant. Write for complete information.

2421 — CANADIAN LIVER FOUNDATION (Fellowships)

365 Bloor St. East, Ste. 200
Toronto Ontario M4W 3L4 CANADA
416/964-1953

AMOUNT: up to $40,000 Canadian

DEADLINE(S): NOV 1

FIELD(S): Liver Research

One-year fellowships open to fully qualified and trained hepatologists or basic scientists (M.D. or Ph.D.)

for specialized clinical or experimental training in Hepatic disease. Candidates should have completed the basic graduate program. Must be sponsored by an investigator with a record of productive medical research.

Renewable for an additional year. Contact CLF for an application.

2422 — CANADIAN LIVER FOUNDATION (Graduate Studentship Awards)

365 Bloor St. East, Ste. 200
Toronto Ontario M4W 3L4 CANADA
416/964-1953

AMOUNT: $16,000 Canadian per annum

DEADLINE(S): FEB 15

FIELD(S): Liver Research

Open to academically superior students for full-time graduate study in a Canadian university in a discipline relative to the objectives of the Canadian Liver Foundation.

Contact CLF for an application.

2423 — CANCER RESEARCH FUND OF THE DAMON RUNYON-WALTER WINCHELL FOUNDATION (Postdoctoral Research Fellowships)

675 Third Ave., 25th Fl.
New York NY 10017
800/445-2494
Internet: www.cancerresearchfund.org

AMOUNT: $37,000-$58,000 (depending on training)

DEADLINE(S): AUG 15; DEC 15; MAR 15

FIELD(S): Cancer Research

Three-year postdoctoral fellowships for basic and physician scientists to advance cancer research. Covers all areas of theoretical and experimental research relevant to the study of cancer and the search for its causes, therapies, and preventions. Candidates must have sponsor and hold a recent MD, Ph.D., DDS, DVM, or equivalent degree. Research is usually done in the US.

60 awards annually. See website for an application.

2424 — CHARLES A. AND ANNE MORROW LINDBERGH FOUNDATION (Grants for Research Projects)

2150 Third Ave., N, Ste. 310
Anoka MN 55303-2200
612/576-1596
FAX: 612/576-1664
E-Mail: lindbergh@isd.net
Internet: www.isd.net/lindbergh

AMOUNT: $10,580 (max.)

DEADLINE(S): JUN 15

FIELD(S): Aviation; Aerospace; Agriculture; Education; Arts; Humanities; Biomedical Research; Exploration; Health & Population Sciences; Intercultural Communication; Waste Disposal Minimization & Management.; Adaptive Technology; Conservation

Open to individuals whose proposed projects represent a significant contribution toward the achievement of balance between the advance of technology and preservation of the natural environment. Financial need NOT a factor. Funding is NOT for tuition.

10 awards annually. See website for application.

2425 — CHARLES H. HOOD FOUNDATION (Child Health Research Program)

95 Berkeley St., Rm. 201
Boston MA 02116
617/695-9439
FAX: 617/423-4619

AMOUNT: $50,000/yr.

DEADLINE(S): APR; OCT

FIELD(S): Child Health Research

Two-year grants to support postdoctorate clinical or basic science research which will help diminish health problems affecting significant numbers of children. Foundation is particularly interested in supporting junior faculty in departments that care for children, including but not limited to, pediatrics, pediatric surgery, pediatric medical & surgical subspecialities, and perinatal obstetrics. Research must be carried out at a New England biomedical institution.

Contact Charles H. Hood Foundation for application packet.

2426 — CHEMICAL INDUSTRY INSTITUTE OF TOXICOLOGY (Postdoctoral Fellowships)

PO Box 12137
Research Triangle Park NC 27709
919/558-1200
FAX: 919/558-1430

AMOUNT: Varies

DEADLINE(S): None

FIELD(S): Toxicology; Pathology

CIIT provides stipends and support to postdoctoral research fellows who pursue original research related to chemical toxicity and/or pathology. Tenable only at CIIT's laboratory.

10-15 awards annually. Renewable up to 3 years. Contact CIIT for an application.

2427 — COLUMBIANA COUNTY PUBLIC HEALTH LEAGUE TRUST FUND (Grants)

PO Box 1428
Steubenville OH 43952

740/283-8433
FAX: 740/282-4530
AMOUNT: Varies
DEADLINE(S): FEB 28
FIELD(S): Respiratory Illness; Medicine; Medical Research; Pharmacy; Medical Technology; Physical Therapy; Nursing; Dental Hygiene; Occupational Therapy

Open to undergraduate and graduate Columbiana County, Ohio, residents who are pursuing medical education or research in one of the above fields. Preference given to respiratory illness. Students of veterinary medicine NOT eligible.

Contact Sherrill Schmied for an application.

2428 — CROHN'S AND COLITIS FOUNDATION OF AMERICA (Career Development Award)

386 Park Ave., S.
17th Floor
New York NY 10016-8804
800/932-2423 or 212/685-3440
FAX 212/779-4098
AMOUNT: $40,000 salary for 2 years + $20,000/yr. for supplies
DEADLINE(S): JAN 1; JUL 1
FIELD(S): Inflammatory Bowel Disease

Open to holders of MD or Ph.D. degrees for research projects in the field of inflammatory bowel disease. MDs need five years of postdoctoral experience; Ph.D.s need two years. Must be employed by a public or private non-profit institution or a government agency engaged in healthcare or health related research in the US.

Contact Carol Cox at CCFA for an application.

2429 — CROHN'S AND COLITIS FOUNDATION OF AMERICA (Research Grants)

386 Park Ave., S.
17th Floor
New York NY 10016-8804
212/685-3440 or 800/932-2423
FAX 212/779-4098
AMOUNT: $80,000/yr.
DEADLINE(S): JAN 1; JUL 1
FIELD(S): Inflammatory Bowel Disease

Two-year postdoctoral research grants are open to MDs and Ph.D.s employed by a public or private non-profit institution or government agency. Peer review considerations will include scientific merit of the proposed research. Must disclose all other funding sources.

Contact Carol Cox at CCFA for an application.

2430 — CROHN'S AND COLITIS FOUNDATION OF AMERICA (Research Fellowship Award)

386 Park Ave., S.
17th Floor
New York NY 10016-8804
800/932-2423 or 212/685-3440
FAX 212/779-4098
AMOUNT: $30,000/yr.
DEADLINE(S): JAN 1; JUL 1
FIELD(S): Inflammatory Bowel Disease

Postdoctoral research fellowships are open to MDs and Ph.D.s with a demonstrated interest and capability in research. Awards are to encourage research and develop the potential of young basic and/or clinical scientists. Must be employed by a public or private non-profit institution or government agency.

Renewable up to 3 years. Contact Carol Cox at CCFA for an application.

2431 — CROHN'S AND COLITIS FOUNDATION OF AMERICA (Student Research Fellowship Awards)

386 Park Ave., S.
17th Floor
New York NY 10016-8804
212/685-3440 or 800/932-2423
FAX: 212/779-4098
AMOUNT: $2,500
DEADLINE(S): FEB 1
FIELD(S): Inflammatory Bowel Disease

For graduate students not yet engaged in thesis research in accredited North American Institutions to conduct full-time research with a mentor investigating a subject relevant to IBD. Project duration is a minimum of 10 weeks.

16 awards annually. Contact Carol Cox at CCFA for an application.

2432 — CYSTIC FIBROSIS FOUNDATION (Research & Training Programs)

6931 Arlington Rd.
Bethesda MD 20814
301/951-4422 or 800/FIGHT-CF
Internet: www.cff.org
AMOUNT: $55,000/yr. (max.)
DEADLINE(S): Varies
FIELD(S): Cystic Fibrosis Research

Several doctoral/postdoctoral grants for research and training related to cystic fibrosis are available. Senior level undergraduates planning to pursue graduate training may also apply. Summer programs available.

Contact CFF for an application and/or see website for listing of programs offered.

2433 — CYSTIC FIBROSIS FOUNDATION (Student Traineeship Research Grants)

6931 Arlington Rd.
Bethesda MD 20814
301/951-4422 or 800/FIGHT-CF
Internet: www.cff.org
AMOUNT: $1,500
DEADLINE(S): None
FIELD(S): Cystic Fibrosis Research

Doctoral research grants are to introduce students to research related to cystic fibrosis and to maintain an interest in this area of biomedicine. Must be in or about to enter a doctoral program. Senior level undergraduates planning to pursue graduate training may also apply. The project's duration should be 10 weeks or more.

Contact CFF for an application and/or see website for listing of programs offered.

2434 — DEBRA (Research Grant Programme)

DEBRA House
13 Wellington Business Park
Dukes Ride
Crowthorne, Berkshire RG45 6LS ENGLAND
+44 1344 771961
FAX: +44 1344 762661
E-Mail: John.Dart@btinternet.com
Internet: www.debra.org.uk
AMOUNT: $150,000 over 3 years (average)
DEADLINE(S): APR 1; OCT 1
FIELD(S): Medical Research: Epidermolysis Bullosa

For scientists or clinicians with Ph.D. or equivalent. Must work in an institution willing to host the project and administer the finance.

15 awards annually. Contact John Dart at DEBRA for an application.

2435 — DERMATOLOGY FOUNDATION (Postdoctoral Career Development Awards)

1560 Sherman Ave.
Evanston IL 60201
847/328-2256
FAX: 847/328-0509
AMOUNT: $40,000
DEADLINE(S): OCT 1
FIELD(S): Dermatology and Cutaneous Biology

Available to faculty members in departments of dermatology. For research to enhance academic careers and to support establishment and development of health policy careers for dermatologists.

Renewable for two years.

2436 — DIGESTIVE DISORDERS FOUNDATION (Fellowships & Grants)

3 St. Andrews Place
London NW1 4LB ENGLAND UK
+44 0171 486 0341
FAX: +44 0171 224 2012
E-Mail: ddf@digestivedisorders.org.uk
Internet: www.digestivedisorders.org.uk

AMOUNT: Varies

DEADLINE(S): Varies

FIELD(S): Digestive Disorders Research

One- to three-year fellowships are for UK residents, covering a full-time salary and providing a medical or science graduate with training in basic science research methods. Can be awarded for research training and work overseas, provided that fellows intend to return to the UK to utilise their new experience. Fellows must undertake element of basic science training during this period. Encouraged to research any aspect of digestive tract, including liver & pancreas.

Contact Julia Young at DDF for an application.

2437 — DUPAGE COUNTY MEDICAL SOCIETY FOUNDATION (Scholarship Program)

498 Hillside Ave.
#1
Glen Ellyn IL 60137
630/858-9603

AMOUNT: $250-$1,000

DEADLINE(S): APR 30

FIELD(S): Medical/Health-Care Fields

Open to voting residents of Dupage County, Illinois, who are accepted to or enrolled in a professional training program at a qualified school. Based on financial need and scholastic ability. Program does not apply to undergraduate studies, such as pre-med; students would be eligible after completing four-year pre-med program and having been accepted into medical school.

Contact Medical Society for an application.

2438 — EDUCATIONAL AND RESEARCH FOUNDATION FOR THE AAFPRS (Resident Research Grants)

310 S. Henry St.
Alexandria VA 22314
703/299-9291, ext. 229 or 800/332-FACE
FAX: 703/299-8898
E-Mail: info@aafprs.org
Internet: www.aafprs.org

AMOUNT: $5,000

DEADLINE(S): DEC 15

FIELD(S): Facial Plastic Surgery Research

Open to residents who are AAFPRS members. Residents at any level may apply even if the research work will be done during their fellowship year. Mentor(s), if any, should also be AAFPRS members. Awards will be made prior to July 1st of each year.

3 awards annually. See website or contact AAFPRS for an application.

2439 — EDUCATIONAL AND RESEARCH FOUNDATION OF THE AAFPRS (Investigative Development Grants)

310 S. Henry St.
Alexandria VA 22314
703/299-9291, ext. 229 or 800/332-FACE
FAX: 703/299-8898
E-Mail: info@aafprs.org
Internet: www.aafprs.org

AMOUNT: $15,000

DEADLINE(S): DEC 15

FIELD(S): Facial Plastic Surgery Research

Grant is to support the work of a young faculty member in facial plastic surgery conducting significant clinical or laboratory research and the training of resident surgeons in research. Applicants and their mentors must be AAFPRS members.

See website or contact AAFPRS for an application.

2440 — EDUCATIONAL AND RESEARCH FOUNDATION OF THE AAFPRS (Bernstein Grant)

310 S. Henry St.
Alexandria VA 22314
703/299-9291, ext. 229 or 800/332-FACE
FAX: 703/299-8898
E-Mail: info@aafprs.org
Internet: www.aafprs.org

AMOUNT: $25,000

DEADLINE(S): DEC 15

FIELD(S): Facial Plastic Surgery Research

Award is to encourage original research projects by AAFPRS Fellow members which will advance facial plastic and reconstructive surgery.

See website or contact AAFPRS for an application.

2441 — EDWARD BANGS KELLEY AND ELZA KELLEY FOUNDATION, INC. (Scholarship Program)

PO Drawer M
Hyannis MA 02601-1412
508/775-3117

AMOUNT: $4,000 (max.)

DEADLINE(S): APR 30

FIELD(S): Medicine; Nursing; Health Sciences

Open to residents of Barnstable County, Massachusetts. Scholarships are intended to benefit health and welfare of Barnstable County residents.

Awards support study at recognized undergraduate, graduate, and professional institutions. Financial need is considered.

Contact Foundation for an application.

2442 — EPILEPSY FOUNDATION OF AMERICA (Behavioral Sciences Student Fellowships)

4351 Garden City Drive
Landover MD 20785-2267
301/459-3700 or 800/EFA-1000
FAX: 301/577-2684
TDD: 800/332-2070
E-Mail: postmaster@efa.org
Internet: www.efa.org

AMOUNT: $2,000

DEADLINE(S): FEB 1

FIELD(S): Epilepsy as related to Behavioral Sciences

Three-month fellowships awarded to students in the behavioral sciences for work on an epilepsy study project. For students of vocational rehabilitation counseling. Students propose an epilepsy-related study or training project to be carried out at a US institution of their choice. A preceptor must accept responsibility for supervision of the student and the project.

Contact EFA for an application.

2443 — EPILEPSY FOUNDATION OF AMERICA (Behavioral Sciences Research Training Fellowships)

4351 Garden City Drive
Landover MD 20785-2267
301/459-3700 or FAX: 301/577-2684
FDD: 800/332-2070
E-Mail: postmaster@efa.org
Internet: www.efa.org

AMOUNT: Up to $30,000

DEADLINE(S): FEB 1

FIELD(S): Epilepsy as related to Behavioral Sciences (includes sociology, social work, psychology, anthropology, nursing, political science, etc.)

A one-year training experience for postdoctoral scholars to develop expertise in the area of epilepsy research relative to the behavioral sciences. The project must be carried out at an approved facility. Amount depends on experience and qualifications of the applicant and the scope and duration of proposed project.

Contact EFA for an application.

2444 — EPILEPSY FOUNDATION OF AMERICA (Fritz E. Dreifuss International Visiting Professorships)

4351 Garden City Drive
Landover MD 20785-2267
301/459-3700 or 800/EFA-1000

FAX: 301/577-2684
E-Mail: postmaster@efa.org
Internet: www.efa.org
AMOUNT: Varies
DEADLINE(S): None
FIELD(S): Epilepsy

To promote the exchange of medical and scientific information and expertise on epilepsy between the US and other countries. A visiting professor spends from 3 to 6 weeks at a host institution; at least one party in exchange must be from the US. Interested countries/institutions should submit specific needs and interests to EFA. EFA selects a professor and pays transportation & incidental expenses; host institution provides living/subsistence costs.

Contact EFA for an application.

2445 — EPILEPSY FOUNDATION OF AMERICA (Health Sciences Student Fellowships)

4351 Garden City Drive
Landover MD 20785-2267
301/459-3700 or 800/EFA-1000
FAX: 301/577-2684
TDD: 800/332-2070
E-Mail: postmaster@efa.org
Internet: www.efa.org
AMOUNT: $2,000
DEADLINE(S): FEB 1
FIELD(S): Epilepsy Research

Three-month fellowships awarded to medical and health sciences students for work on an epilepsy study project. The project is carried out at a US institution of the student's choice where there are ongoing programs of research, training, or service in epilepsy. A preceptor must accept responsibility for supervision of the student and the project.

Contact EFA for an application.

2446 — EPILEPSY FOUNDATION OF AMERICA (Junior Investigator Research Grants)

4351 Garden City Drive
Landover MD 20785-2267
301/459-3700 or 800/EFA-1000
FAX: 301/577-2684
TDD: 800/332-2070
E-Mail: postmaster@efa.org
Internet: www.efa.org
AMOUNT: up to $40,000
DEADLINE(S): SEP 1
FIELD(S): Epilepsy as related to Biological, Behavioral, & Social Sciences

One-year research grants to support basic and clinical research in the biological, behavioral, and social sciences which will advance the understanding,

treatment, and prevention of epilepsy. Priority given to beginning investigators just entering the field of epilepsy research, to new or innovative projects. Applications evaluated on basis of scientific merit.

Contact EFA for an application.

2447 — EPILEPSY FOUNDATION OF AMERICA (Pre-doctoral Research Training Fellowship)

4351 Garden City Drive
Landover MD 20785-2267
301/459-3700 or 800/EFA-1000
FAX: 301/577-2684
TDD: 800/332-2070
E-Mail: postmaster@efa.org
Internet: www.efa.org
AMOUNT: up to $15,000
DEADLINE(S): SEP 1
FIELD(S): Epilepsy as related to Neuroscience, Physiology, Pharmacology, Psychology, Biochemistry, Genetics, Nursing, or Pharmacy

One-year of support for qualified individuals who are pursuing dissertation research with an epilepsy-related theme, and who are working under the guidance of a mentor with expertise in the area of epilepsy investigation. Graduate students pursuing Ph.D. degree in above fields may apply.

Contact EFA for an application.

2448 — EPILEPSY FOUNDATION OF AMERICA (Research Training Fellowships)

4351 Garden City Drive
Landover MD 20785-2267
301/459-3700 or 800/EFA-1000
FAX: 301/577-2684
E-Mail: postmaster@efa.org
Internet: www.efa.org
AMOUNT: up to $40,000
DEADLINE(S): SEP 1
FIELD(S): Epilepsy Research

One-year training experience in an epilepsy-related research project, which may be either basic or clinical but must address a question of fundamental importance. Preference is given to applicants whose proposals have a pediatric or developmental emphasis. Application is open to physicians or Ph.D. neuroscientists who desire postdoctoral research experience. Must be carried out at a facility where there is an ongoing epilepsy research program.

Contact EFA for an application.

2449 — EPILEPSY FOUNDATION OF AMERICA (Research/Clinical Training Fellowships)

4351 Garden City Drive
Landover MD 20785-2267
301/459-3700 or 800/EFA-1000

FAX: 301/577-2684
E-Mail: postmaster@efa.org
Internet: www.efa.org
AMOUNT: up to $40,000
DEADLINE(S): SEP 1
FIELD(S): Epilepsy Research

One-year training experience in an epilepsy-related project which may be either basic or clinical, but there must be an equal emphasis on clinical training and clinical epileptology. Application open to individuals who have received their M.D. degree and completed residency training. Must be carried out at a facility where there is an ongoing epilepsy research program.

Contact EFA for an application.

2450 — EPILEPSY FOUNDATION OF AMERICA (William G. Lennox International Clinical Research Fellowships)

4351 Garden City Drive
Landover MD 20785-2267
301/459-3700 or 800/EFA-1000
FAX: 301/577-2684
E-Mail: postmaster@efa.org
Internet: www.efa.org
AMOUNT: Up to $40,000
DEADLINE(S): SEP 1
FIELD(S): Epilepsy

One-year training experience to promote the exchange of medical and scientific information and expertise on epilepsy between the US and other countries. Application is open to individuals who have received their M.D. degree (or foreign equivalent) and completed residency training. At least one party must be from US. Must be carried out at an approvable facility where there is an ongoing epilepsy research program, either in the US or abroad.

Contact EFA for an application.

2451 — FIGHT FOR SIGHT RESEARCH DIVISION OF PREVENT BLINDNESS AMERICA (Postdoctoral Research Fellowship)

500 E. Remington Rd.
Schaumburg IL 60173
847/843-2020
FAX: 847/843-8458
E-Mail: info@preventblindness.org
AMOUNT: $5,000-$14,000
DEADLINE(S): MAR 1
FIELD(S): Ophthalmology; Visual Sciences

Open to individuals who hold a doctorate degree and who are interested in an academic career involving basic or clinical research in opthalmology or visual sciences.

Contact Prevent Blindness America for an application.

2452 — FIGHT FOR SIGHT RESEARCH DIVISION OF PREVENT BLINDNESS AMERICA (Grants-in-Aid)

500 E. Remington Rd.
Schaumburg IL 60173
847/843-2020
FAX: 847/843-8458
E-Mail: info@preventblindness.org

AMOUNT: $1,000-$12,000

DEADLINE(S): MAR 1

FIELD(S): Ophthalmology; Visual Sciences

Grants for research that may lead to advances in preventing blindness, treatment and cures of visual disorders, restoring vision, and preserving sight. Support is used to help defray costs of personnel, equipment, and supplies.

Contact Prevent Blindness America for an application.

2453 — FIGHT FOR SIGHT RESEARCH DIVISION OF PREVENT BLINDNESS AMERICA (Student Research Fellowship)

500 E. Remington Rd.
Schaumburg IL 60173
847/843-2020
FAX: 847/843-8458
E-Mail: info@preventblindness.org

AMOUNT: $500/month ($1,500 max.)

DEADLINE(S): MAR 1

FIELD(S): Ophthalmology; Visual Sciences

Stipend open to undergraduates, medical students, or graduate students for full-time eye-related research, usually during the summer months.

Renewable. Contact Prevent Blindness America for an application.

2454 — FIRST UNITED METHODIST CHURCH (Robert Stevenson & Doreene E. Cater Scholarships)

302 5th Ave., S.
St. Cloud MN 56301
FAX: 320/251-0878
E-Mail: FUMCloud@aol.com

AMOUNT: $100-$300

DEADLINE(S): JUN 1

FIELD(S): Humanitarian & Christian Service: Teaching, Medicine, Social Work, Environmental Studies, etc.

Stevenson Scholarship is open to undergraduate members of the First United Methodist Church of St. Cloud. Cater Scholarship is open to members of the Minnesota United Methodist Conference who are entering the sophomore year or higher of college work. Both require two letters of reference, transcripts, and financial need.

5-6 awards annually. Contact Scholarship Committee for an application.

2455 — FOUNDATION FOR CHIROPRACTIC EDUCATION AND RESEARCH (Research Fellowships & Residencies)

1330 Beacon St., Ste. 315
Brookline MA 02446-3202
617/734-3397 or 888/690-1378
FAX: 617/734-0989
E-Mail: rosnerfcer@aol.com
Internet: www.fcer.org

AMOUNT: $3,000-$10,000/yr.

DEADLINE(S): MAR 1

FIELD(S): Chiropractic Research

Research fellowships and residencies are available to postgraduate students who have received their D.C. or equivalent. Research should be pertaining to the theory and practice of chiropractics. Must demonstrate financial need.

8 awards annually. Renewable 3-4 years. Contact Anthony Rosner, Ph.D., for an application.

2456 — FOUNDATION FOR SEACOAST HEALTH (Scholarship Program)

P.O. Box 4606
Portsmouth NH 03802-4606
603/433-3008
FAX: 603/433-2036
E-Mail: ffsh@nh.ultranet.com
Internet: www.nh.ultranet.com/~ffsh

AMOUNT: $1,000-10,000

DEADLINE(S): FEB 1

FIELD(S): Health-related fields

Open to undergraduate and graduate students pursuing health-related fields of study who are legal residents of the following cities in New Hampshire: Portsmouth, Newington, New Castle, Rye, Greenland, N. Hampton, or these cities in Maine: Kittery, Eliot, or York, Maine. Must have resided in the area for at least two years.

Write or check website for details. $150,000 awarded annually; 35 awards given

2457 — FRAXA RESEARCH FOUNDATION (Grants & Fellowships)

45 Pleasant St.
Newburyport MA 01950
978/462-1866
FAX: 978/463-9985
E-Mail: info@fraxa.org or kclapp@fraxa.org
Internet: www.fraxa.org

AMOUNT: $30,000/yr. (max.)

DEADLINE(S): MAY 1; NOV 1

FIELD(S): Fragile X Syndrome Research

Postdoctoral fellowships and investigator-initiated grants are available for medical research into Fragile X Syndrome, the #1 inherited cause of mental retardation. Some areas include: function of FMRP (RNA-building protein found in dendritic spines), neural tissue culture models, cognitive & behavioral tests, seizure disorders associated with fragile X syndrome, and investigations into neural gene therapy vectors. Financial need NOT a factor.

10-20 awards annually. Renewable for a second year. Contact Katherine Clapp for an application and guidelines.

2458 — GRASS FOUNDATION (Grass Fellowships in Neurophysiology)

77 Reservoir Road
Quincy MA 02170
617/843-0219, 617-479-5726

AMOUNT: Travel; research & living expenses

DEADLINE(S): DEC 1

FIELD(S): Neuroscience

Open to late pre-doctoral (MD or Ph.D) & early post-doctoral (usually no more than 3 years) researchers. Fellowships support neurophysiological research during the summer (10-14 weeks) at the Marine Biological Laboratory in Woods Hole, MA.

Number of fellowships each year varies. Eleven were granted in 1996. Write to the above address and ask for Bulletin FA-297 which contains detailed application instructions and appropriate forms.

2459 — GRASS FOUNDATION (Robert S. Morison Fellowship)

77 Reservoir Road
Quincy MA 02170
617/843-0209
617/479-5726

AMOUNT: $40,000 stipend per year + additional $4,000 for research expenses & travel to one scientific meeting.

DEADLINE(S): NOV 1 (of even-numbered years)

FIELD(S): Neurology; Neurosurgery; Neuroscience

Open to MDs preparing for an academic career who have been accepted into or just completed a residency in above areas & wish to undertake a 2-year program of basic research training at a recognized institution in North America.

This is a 2-year program which starts in July of odd-numbered years. Write for complete information.

2460 — HEALTH RESEARCH COUNCIL OF NEW ZEALAND (Post-doctoral Fellowships)

PO Box 5541
Wellesley St
Auckland 1036 NEW ZEALAND
09/3798-227
FAX: 09/3779-988

AMOUNT: NZ$40,500 + NZ$1,750 research expenses & air fare

DEADLINE(S): Varies (Biomedical APR 1; Public Health APR 1/SEP 1)

FIELD(S): Biomedical & Public Health Research

Awards are based on the academic standing and research capabilities of applicants who should have Ph.D. or equivalent degree.

Fellowships are tenable in New Zealand and are normally awarded for period of 24 months and may be extended for an additional 24 months. Write for complete information.

2461 — HEART AND STROKE FOUNDATION OF CANADA (Medical Scientist Traineeship)

160 George St., Suite 200
Ottawa K1N 9M2 Canada
613/241-4361 Ext. 327 or 331
FAX: 613/241-3278
E-Mail: mctaylor@hookup.net
Internet: www.hwc.ca:8080/hsfc/

AMOUNT: Varies

DEADLINE(S): NOV 1

FIELD(S): Cardiovascular/Cerebrovascular Research

Research traineeship for outstanding candidates through medical school training undertaking full-time, independent research in the cardiovascular/cerebrovascular fields.

For use at Canadian universities. Write for complete information.

2462 — HEART AND STROKE FOUNDATION OF CANADA (Nursing Research Fellowship)

160 George St., Suite 200
Ottawa K1n 9M2 Canada
613/241-4361 Ext. 327 or 331
FAX: 613/241-3278
E-Mail: mctaylor@hookup.net
Internet: www.hwc.ca:research

AMOUNT: Varies

DEADLINE(S): NOV 1

FIELD(S): Cardiovascular/Cerebrovascular Nursing Research

An "in-training" award for qualified nurses undertaking academic preparation in some are of cardiovascular or cerebrovascular nursing leading to a Master's or Ph.D. degree.

Renewable annually and may be held for a mzximum of two years.

2463 — HEART AND STROKE FOUNDATION OF CANADA (Research Traineeship)

160 George St., Suite 200
Ottawa K1N 9M2 Canada
613/241-4361 Ext. 327 or 331
FAX: 613/241-3278
E-Mail: mctaylor@hookup.net
Internet: www.hwc.ca:research

AMOUNT: Varies

DEADLINE(S): NOV 1

FIELD(S): Cardiovascular/Cerebrovascular Research

For highly qualified graduated students undertaking full-time research training in the fields listed above. My apply as either an M.Sc. or Ph.D. student. Applicants possessing medical degree, but not licensed to practice medicine in Canada, are eligible to apply.

For use at Canadian universities but exceptions may be made. Renewable annually and may be held for a maximum of four years.

2464 — HEART AND STROKE FOUNDATION OF ONTARIO (Scientific Fellowships in Prevention Research)

477 Mount Pleasant Rd., 4th Floor
Toronto, Ontario M4S 2L9
Not given

AMOUNT: Varies

DEADLINE(S): NOV 1

FIELD(S): Cardiovascular/Cerebrovascular Research

Post-doctoral fellowships for candidates who have completed all formal academic training and who wish to acquire two years of supervised research in an established research setting. Must have a Ph.D. or M.D. and be committed to a career in the prevention of cardiovascular disease. Awardee can apply for a special three-year Research Scholarship after the two-year research period.

Two awards. Contact: Miss Evelyn T. McGloin, Director, Research Administration at above address.

2465 — HEART FOUNDATION OF AUSTRALIA (Career Research Fellowship)

Research Manager
PO Box 2
Woden ACT 2606 AUSTRALIA
02 6269 2652
FAX: 02 6282 5147
E-Mail:
Christine.Sharrad@heartfoundation.com.au
Internet: www.heartfoundation.com.au

AMOUNT: Salary & allowance

DEADLINE(S): MAY 31

FIELD(S): Cardiovascular Health

Applicants should be established researchers whose usual place of residence is in Australia. This prestigious senior position will be considered for those of exceptional merit with a proven record of independent research. Level of appointment will be within the range of Research Fellow/Senior Research Fellow/Principal Research Fellow. Awarded for an initial period of five years.

See website or contact the Research Manager at the Heart Foundation for an application.

2466 — HEART FOUNDATION OF AUSTRALIA (Overseas & Clinical Research Fellowships)

Research Manager
PO Box 2
Woden ACT 2606 AUSTRALIA
02 6269 2652
FAX: 02 6282 5147
E-Mail:
Christine.Sharrad@heartfoundation.com.au
Internet: www.heartfoundation.com.au

AMOUNT: Salary, allowance, & airfare for Fellow & dependant family members

DEADLINE(S): MAY 31

FIELD(S): Cardiovascular Research

For graduates who have demonstrated expertise and significant achievement in cardiovascular research. Overseas fellowships are tenable for three years, of which the first two are spent at an overseas institution and the third in an Australian institution. Clinical fellowships can be taken in any recognized institution and are tenable for one to two years.

See website or contact the Research Manager at the Heart Foundation for an application.

2467 — HEART FOUNDATION OF AUSTRALIA (Postgraduate Medical & Non-Medical Research Scholarships)

Research Manager
PO Box 2
Woden ACT 2606 AUSTRALIA
02 6269 2652
FAX: 02 6282 5147
E-Mail:
Christine.Sharrad@heartfoundation.com.au
Internet: www.heartfoundation.com.au

AMOUNT: $23,997 (medical); $18,135 (non-medical)

DEADLINE(S): MAY 31 (medical); OCT 31 (non-medical)

FIELD(S): Cardiovascular Function, Disease, & related areas

For full-time postgraduate research studies leading to a Ph.D. at an Australian university or institution for both medical and non-medical graduates. Scholarships are normally awarded for three years. Maintenance/departmental allowance will be paid to the institution administering the award. A thesis allowance of up to $500 is payable, upon application, in the final year of the scholarship.

See website or contact the Research Manager at the Heart Foundation for an application.

2468 — HEART FOUNDATION OF AUSTRALIA (Postdoctoral Research Fellowship)

Research Manager
PO Box 2
Woden ACT 2606 AUSTRALIA
02 6269 2652
FAX: 02 6282 5147
E-Mail: Christine.Sharrad@heartfoundation.com.au
Internet: www.heartfoundation.com.au

AMOUNT: Salary & allowance

DEADLINE(S): MAY 31

FIELD(S): Cardiovascular Research

Available to medical and non-medical graduates who are usually six years post-MBBS or an MD or have been awarded a Ph.D. in the last four years. They are tenable in Australian institutions for two years in the first instance.

See website or contact the Research Manager at the Heart Foundation for an application.

2469 — HEART FOUNDATION OF AUSTRALIA (Senior Research Fellowship in Nutrition)

Research Manager
PO Box 2
Woden ACT 2606 AUSTRALIA
02 6269 2652
FAX: 02 6282 5147
E-Mail: Christine.Sharrad@heartfoundation.com.au
Internet: www.heartfoundation.com.au

AMOUNT: Salary & allowance

DEADLINE(S): MAY 31

FIELD(S): Cardiovascular Health

Applicants should be established researchers whose usual place of residence is in Australia. This prestigious senior position will be considered for those of exceptional merit with a proven record of independent research. Level of appointment will be within range of Research Fellow/Senior Research Fellow. Awarded for a period of five years.

See website or contact the Research Manager at the Heart Foundation for an application.

2470 — HEART FOUNDATION OF AUSTRALIA (Travel Grants)

Research Manager
PO Box 2
Woden ACT 2606 AUSTRALIA

02 6269 2652
FAX: 02 6282 5147
E-Mail: Christine.Sharrad@heartfoundation.com.au
Internet: www.heartfoundation.com.au

AMOUNT: Varies (minimum airfare necessary to travel)

DEADLINE(S): None

FIELD(S): Cardiovascular Function, Disease, & related areas

For junior investigators (postdoctoral to six years) to enable them to take up pre-arranged posts in overseas institutions of high standing if funds unavailable from other sources. Also for junior investigators going overseas to present their work at international meetings of high standing. And for HF Fellows to attend conference pursuant to current research. And for junior investigators in Western Australia & N. Territory to travel to eastern states for meetings.

See website or contact the Research Manager at the Heart Foundation for an application.

2471 — HEART FOUNDATION OF AUSTRALIA (Warren McDonald International Fellowship)

Research Manager
PO Box 2
Woden ACT 2606 AUSTRALIA
02 6269 2652
FAX: 02 6282 5147
E-Mail: Christine.Sharrad@heartfoundation.com.au
Internet: www.heartfoundation.com.au

AMOUNT: Stipend + travel grant for Fellow & immediate family dependants

DEADLINE(S): MAY 31

FIELD(S): Cardiovascular Research

To enable a senior overseas researcher of proven ability in the cardiovascular field to make a significant research contribution to an Australian research group. Tenable for up to one year in Australian universities, hospitals, or research institutions. Applicants must be nominated by the head of the institution; the nominating institution must undertake to provide laboratory and research facilities for the person nominated (grant covers departmental expenses).

See website or contact the Research Manager at the Heart Foundation for nomination procedures.

2472 — HEISER PROGRAM FOR RESEARCH IN LEPROSY AND/OR TUBERCULOSIS (Post-doctoral Fellowships and Research Grants)

450 E. 63rd St
New York NY 10021
212/751-6233

AMOUNT: Up to $28,000 per year plus travel allowance

DEADLINE(S): FEB 1

FIELD(S): Leprosy or Tuberculosis Research

Fellowships for researchers who hold M.D./Ph.D or equivalent degree. Candidates should be interested in obtaining research training directly related to the study of leprosy and/or tuberculosis.

Write for complete information.

2473 — HELEN HAY WHITNEY FOUNDATION (Postdoctoral Research Fellowships)

450 E. 63rd St.
New York NY 10021-7928
212/751-8228
FAX: 212/688-6794

AMOUNT: $25,000 stipend + $2,000 research allowance

DEADLINE(S): AUG 15 (Postmark. Application forms available MAR 15)

FIELD(S): Basic Biomedical Sciences

For candidates in the final stages of obtaining the M.D., Ph.D, or equivalent degree and are seeking beginning postdoctoral training in basic biomedical research. Resident non-U.S. citizens may train only in the U.S. U.S. citizens may train abroad.

Fellowship is for 3 years contingent on satisfactory performance. Stipend increases by $2,000 each year. Write for complete information.

2474 — HOWARD HUGHES MEDICAL INSTITUTE (Postdoctoral Research Fellowships for Physicians)

Office of Grants & Special Programs
4000 Jones Bridge Rd.
Chevy Chase MD 20815-6789
301/215-8884
FAX: 301/215-8888
E-Mail: grantpos@hhmi.org
Internet: www.hhmi.org/grants/graduate/postdoc/

AMOUNT: $40,000-$60,000 stipend (based on experience)

DEADLINE(S): DEC 6

FIELD(S): Medical Research

Open to interns, residents, & physicians who received 1st med degree within 10 years. Must have completed 2 years postgraduate study & may not hold faculty appointment. Must select research mentor & devise research plan suitable for 3-year full-time period. Project should ask question about basic biological processes or disease mechanisms. Based on ability & promise for research career as physician-scientist. US students may study anywhere; others must study in US.

See website for online application; must apply via the internet.

2475 — HOWARD HUGHES MEDICAL INSTITUTE (Research Training Fellowships for Medical Students)

Office of Grants & Special Programs
4000 Jones Bridge Rd.
Chevy Chase MD 20815-6789
301/215-8884
FAX: 301/215-8888
E-Mail: fellows@hhmi.org
Internet: www.hhmi.org/grants/graduate/medical/

AMOUNT: $16,000 stipend
DEADLINE(S): DEC 2
FIELD(S): Medical Research

Open to students currently enrolled in M.D. or D.O. programs at US medical schools. Applicant must select research mentor and devise research plan suitable for a one-year research training period. Project should ask question about basic biological processes or disease mechanisms. Fellows must engage in full-time research and cannot hold award concurrently with medical school coursework. Based on ability & promise for research career as physician-scientist.

See website for online application; must apply via the internet.

2476 — IMPERIAL CANCER RESEARCH FUND (Postdoctoral Fellowships)

PO Box 123
Lincoln's Inn Fields
London WC2A 3PX United Kingdom
+44 171 242 0200
FAX: +44 171 269 3585
E-Mail: jhiggins@icrf.icnet.uk
Internet: www.icnet.uk

AMOUNT: 20,000 to 25,500 pounds sterling
DEADLINE(S): Varies
FIELD(S): Cancer Research

For postgraduate students wishing to engage in cancer research at an Imperial Cancer Research Fund laboratory. Ph.D. is required.

See website or contact Johanna Higgins, Administration Manager, for complete information.

2477 — INTERNATIONAL AGENCY FOR RESEARCH ON CANCER (Cancer Research Fellowship Programme)

150 cours Albert Thomas
F-69372 Lyon cedex 08 FRANCE
+33 (4) 72 73 84 48
FAX: +33 (4) 72 73 83 22
E-Mail: elakroud@iarc.fr
Internet: www.iarc.fr/

AMOUNT: Varies

DEADLINE(S): DEC 31
FIELD(S): Cancer Research

Applicants should be junior scientists with some postdoctoral research experience related to cancer: epidemiology, biostatistics, environmental/viral carcinogenesis, cell biology, cell genetics, molecular biology, & mechanisms of carcinogenesis. Applicants can be from any country, and this one-year fellowship is tenable in any suitable institution in any country abroad. Must speak language of host country. Fellows expected to return to a post in their home country.

Preference is given to applicants who have not previously received postdoctoral training abroad in cancer research. Contact Dr. R. Montesano or Mrs. E. El Akroud at IARC for an application.

2478 — INTERNATIONAL AGENCY FOR RESEARCH ON CANCER (Postdoctoral Fellowships at IARC)

150 cours Albert Thomas
F-69372 Lyon cedex 08 FRANCE
+33 (4) 72 73 84 48
FAX: +33 (4) 72 73 83 22
E-Mail: elakroud@iarc.fr
Internet: www.iarc.fr/

AMOUNT: FRAFR138 240.-, tax free + travel, health insurance, & sometimes a dependent's allowance
DEADLINE(S): DEC 31
FIELD(S): Cancer Research

One-year fellowships for junior scientists with experience in a research area relevant to the work of the Agency who are under 35 years of age, with a Ph.D. or M.D. degree or equivalent and no more than 3 years' postdoctoral research experience. Awards tenable at the Agency. Official working languages at IARC are English and French. IARC encourages women to apply.

5 awards annually. Contact Mrs. E. El Akroud at IARC for an application. Candidates will be notified before the end of April.

2479 — INTERNATIONAL COUNCIL FOR CANADIAN STUDIES (Government of France Graduate Awards)

325 Dalhousie, S-800
Ottawa Ontario CANADA K1N 7G2
613/789-7828
FAX: 613/789-7830
E-Mail: general@iccs-ciec.ca
Internet: www.iccs-ciec.ca

AMOUNT: Tuition, travel, and living allowance
DEADLINE(S): OCT 31
FIELD(S): Pure and Applied Sciences, Social Sciences, Engineering, Medicine

One-year graduate scholarships open to Canadian citizens for study and research at the doctoral level. Sound knowledge of the French language is required.

Must hold masters degree. Cannot be held concurrently with other scholarships or remuneration. Write or access website for complete information.

2480 — INTERNATIONAL UNION AGAINST CANCER (Research Fellowships)

3, rue Conseil-General
1205 Geneva SWITZERLAND
4122/809 1840
FAX: 4122/809 1810
E-Mail: fellows@uicc.org
Internet: www.uicc.org/fellows

AMOUNT: Varies (with program)
DEADLINE(S): Varies (with program)
FIELD(S): Cancer Research

Long-, medium-, and short-term fellowships are available to qualified cancer professionals actively engaged in cancer research, clinical oncology, or oncology nursing.

See website or contact UICC for an application.

2481 — JANE COFFIN CHILDS MEMORIAL FUND FOR MEDICAL RESEARCH (Postdoctoral Fellowships)

333 Cedar St.
New Haven CT 06510
203/785-4612

AMOUNT: $33,500-$37,000
DEADLINE(S): FEB 1
FIELD(S): Cancer Research

Open to applicants with Ph.D., MD, or equal experience in field of proposed study. US citizens may hold fellowship in the US or a foreign country. Foreign citizens may hold fellowship in US only. No more than one year of postdoctoral training.

25 awards annually. Contact Memorial Fund for an application.

2482 — JAPAN SOCIETY FOR THE PROMOTION OF SCIENCE (Post-doctoral Fellowships for Foreign Researchers)

Jochi-Kioizaka Bldg., 6-26-3 Kioi-cho
Chiyoda-Ku
Tokyo 102 JAPAN
+81-3-3263-1721
Telex: J32281
FAX: +81-3-3263-1854

AMOUNT: 270,000 yen per month
DEADLINE(S): SEP 25; MAY 23
FIELD(S): Humanities; Social Sciences; Natural Sciences; Engineering; Medicine

Post-doctoral fellowships for advanced study & research in Japan.

Write for complete information

2483 — JUVENILE DIABETES FOUNDATION INTERNATIONAL (Research Grants; Career Development Awards; Post-doctoral Fellowships)

120 Wall Street
Grant Administration
New York NY 10005-4001
212/889-7575

AMOUNT: Varies

DEADLINE(S): FEB 15 (for grants); SEP 15 (for CDAs & fellowships)

FIELD(S): Diabetes Research

Research grants; CDAs & Postdoctoral fellowships to support research into the causes, treatment, prevention, and cure of diabetes and its complications.

Approximately 155 new awards per year. Write for complete information.

2484 — KIDNEY FOUNDATION OF CANADA (Biomedical Fellowship)

300-5165 Sherbrooke St. West
Montreal Quebec H4A 1T6 CANADA
800/361-7494, ext. 223 or 514/369-4806
FAX: 514/369-2472
E-Mail: research@kidney.ca
Internet: www.kidney.ca

AMOUNT: $33,000-$44,000 (Canadian)

DEADLINE(S): OCT 15

FIELD(S): Nephrology; Urology

One-year fellowships for postdoctorate Canadian citizens/landed immigrants for full-time research conducted within Canada or abroad that may further current knowledge of the kidney and urinary tract. Priority is given to those applicants at the beginning of their research training, and planning a career in Canada. Amount of funding depends on experience.

Renewable. See website or contact the Manager, National Research Program, at the Kidney Foundation for an application.

2485 — KIDNEY FOUNDATION OF CANADA (Biomedical Research Grant)

300-5165 Sherbrooke St. West
Montreal Quebec H4A 1T6 CANADA
800/361-7494, ext. 223 or 514/369-4806
FAX: 514/369-2472
E-Mail: research@kidney.ca
Internet: www.kidney.ca

AMOUNT: up to $50,000/yr. (Canadian)

DEADLINE(S): OCT 15

FIELD(S): Nephrology; Urology

Funds for kidney research to Canadian citizens/landed immigrants holding staff appointments at Canadian universities or other recognized Canadian institutions. Grants must be used for research conducted within Canada, and priority is given to young investigators in the field of research in the kidney and urinary tract.

Renewable. See website or contact the Manager, National Research Program, at the Kidney Foundation for an application.

2486 — KIDNEY FOUNDATION OF CANADA (Scholarships)

300-5165 Sherbrooke St. W.
Montreal Quebec H4A 1T6 CANADA
800/361-7494, ext. 223 or 514/369-4806
FAX: 514/369-2492
E-Mail: research@kidney.ca
Internet: www.kidney.ca

AMOUNT: $45,000/yr. (Canadian)

DEADLINE(S): OCT 15

FIELD(S): Nephrology; Urology

Provides salary for up to two years of an initial faculty appointment at the rank of Assistant Professor or its equivalent, at an approved medical school in Canada. Candidates should have an M.D. and have completed clinical training. Ph.D.s are also eligible, with at least two years of research training. Awarded based on the research program outlined in application. Applications should be made on behalf of candidates by the institutions offering faculty appointment.

5 awards annually. See website or contact the Manager, National Research Program, at the Kidney Foundation for an application.

2487 — KING FAISAL FOUNDATION (Graduate Scholarship Program)

PO Box 352
Riyadh 11411 SAUDI ARABIA
966/1 465-2255
FAX: 966/1 465-6524
E-Mail: info@kff.com OR mprd@kff.com
Internet: www.kff.com OR www.kingfaisalfoundation.org

AMOUNT: $400/mo. US allowance + tuition/fees paid directly to university + health insurance & travel

DEADLINE(S): None

FIELD(S): Medicine; Engineering; Physics; Chemistry; Geology

Open to graduate students who are Muslims under the age of 40. Must have BS degree, GPA of 86% or higher, and be accepted unconditionally by a university either in Europe or North America. Must be fluent in the language of area providing the studies. Selection based on academic performance.

Contact King Faisal Foundation for an application.

2488 — LADY ALLEN OF HURTWOOD MEMORIAL TRUST (Travel Grants)

21 Aspull Common
Leigh Lancs WN7 3PB ENGLAND
01942-674895

AMOUNT: up to 1,000 pounds sterling

DEADLINE(S): JAN 15

FIELD(S): Welfare And Education Of Children

A travel grant to those whose proposed project will directly benefit their work with children. People working with children and young people may apply, particularly those working with disabled and disadvantaged children. Successful candidates must write up an account of the work which the scholarship has funded. GRANTS ARE NOT FOR ACADEMIC STUDY; ONLY QUALIFIED INDIVIDUALS MAY APPLY.

Contact Dorothy E. Whitaker, Trustee, for application forms—available between May and December each year.

2489 — LALOR FOUNDATION (Fellowships)

PO Box 2493
Providence RI 02906-0493
401/272-1973
Internet: www.lalorfound.org

AMOUNT: $25,000 (to cover stipend, institutional overhead, laboratory, & misc. expenses)

DEADLINE(S): JAN 15

FIELD(S): Reproductive Biology

Postdoctoral grants to support research in reproductive physiology. Individual must be nominated by their institution and may be a citizen of any country. Should have training and experience of at least equal to the Ph.D. or M.D. level. People who have held the doctoral degree for less than five years are preferred. Applicant's institution must be exempt from federal income taxes; if not in US, must be same type of institution. Financial need NOT a factor.

25+ awards annually. Renewable for an additional year. See website or contact Cynthia B. Patterson, President, for an application.

2490 — LEPRA (Medical Elective Student Grant)

Fairfax House, Causton Road
Colchester Essex CO1 1PU ENGLAND UK
01206 562286
FAX: 01206 762151

E-Mail: irene_allen@lepra.org.uk

Internet: www.lepra.org.uk

AMOUNT: 1,500 pounds sterling

DEADLINE(S): None

FIELD(S): Leprosy Research

Grants for British and Commonwealth medical students who wish to undertake an overseas leprosy project during their two-month clinical studies elective period. Must be UK or Commonwealth citizen and demonstrate financial need.

10-20 awards annually. Contact Information Officer at LEPRA for an application.

2491 — LEUKEMIA SOCIETY OF AMERICA (Scholarships, Fellowships, and Grants)

600 Third Ave., 4th Floor

New York NY 10016

212/450-8843

FAX: 212/856-9686

E-Mail: lermandb@leukemia.org

Internet: www.leukemia.org

AMOUNT: $33,250-$70,000/year for up to 5 years

DEADLINE(S): SEP 15

FIELD(S): Leukemia and Allied Diseases Research

Post-doctoral awards for applicants with Ph.D., MD, or equivalent degrees. Amount, type, and length of award is based on experience and training.

Application forms and instructions are on website listed above.

2492 — LOVELACE RESPIRATORY RESEARCH INSTITUTE/UNIVERSITY OF NEW MEXICO (Graduate Fellowships)

PO Box 5890

Albuquerque NM 87185

505/845-1159

FAX: 505/845-1198

E-Mail: jseagrav@lrri.org

Internet: www.lrri.org

AMOUNT: $16,000

DEADLINE(S): None

FIELD(S): Biomedical Sciences; Aerosol Science; Respiratory Toxicology; Physiology; Immunology; Lung Cancer

Open to graduate students admitted to the graduate program in Biomedical Sciences at the University of New Mexico. Experimental work for thesis may be performed with a staff scientist at LRRI, contingent on available funding. Must be US citizens or have J-1 visa.

1-3 awards annually. Contact JeanClare Seagrave for an application.

2493 — LOVELACE RESPIRATORY RESEARCH INSTITUTE/UNIVERSITY OF NEW MEXICO (Postdoctoral Fellowships)

PO Box 5890

Albuquerque NM 87185

505/845-1159

FAX: 505/845-1198

E-Mail: jpainter@lrri.org

Internet: www.lrri.org

AMOUNT: $26,000+ (depending on area & qualifications)

DEADLINE(S): None

FIELD(S): Biomedical Sciences; Aerosol Science; Respiratory Toxicology; Physiology; Immunology; Lung Cancer

Open to postdoctoral researchers who have completed a Ph.D., D.V.M., or M.D. from an accredited institution in one of the above fields. Must be US citizen or have J-1 visa.

1-3 awards annually. Contact Joann Painter for an application.

2494 — LUPUS FOUNDATION OF AMERICA, INC. (Finzi Student Summer Fellowship)

1300 Piccard Drive, Suite 200

Rockville MD 20850-4303

800/558-0121 or 301/670-9292

FAX: 301/670-9486

E-Mail: LupusInfo@aol.com

Internet: www.lupus.org/lupus

AMOUNT: $2,000

DEADLINE(S): FEB 1

FIELD(S): Lupus Erythematosus Research

Summer fellowships open to undergrads, grads, and post-grads, but applicants already having college degree are preferred. Research is conducted under the supervision of an established investigator; student is responsible for locating supervisor and lab (must be in the US). Projects may be basic, clinical, or psychosocial research and must be related to the causes, treatments, prevention, or cure of lupus.

10 fellowships annually. Notification of award is in April. See website or write for complete information.

2495 — LUPUS FOUNDATION OF AMERICA, INC. (Research Grant)

1300 Piccard Drive, Suite 200

Rockville MD 20850-4303

301/670-9292 or 800/558-0121

FAX: 301/670-9486

E-Mail: LupusInfo@aol.com

Internet: www.lupus.org/lupus

AMOUNT: $15,000

DEADLINE(S): APR 1

FIELD(S): Lupus Erythematosus Research

Junior investigators, defined as assistant professor and below rank if in academic medicine are eligible. Research must be conducted in the US and involve clinical, basic, or psychological research related to the causes, treatments, prevention, or cure of Lupus Erythematosus. First year Fellows are not eligible.

5 awards annually. Renewable for a second year. Award notification is October 1st. See website or write to above address for further information.

2496 — MEDICAL RESEARCH COUNCIL (Doctoral and Postdoctoral Scholarships for Study Abroad)

PO Box 19070

Tygerberg 7505 SOUTH AFRICA

021/938-0227

FAX: 021/938-0368

E-Mail: mjenkins@mrc.ac.za

Internet: www.mrc.ac.za/

AMOUNT: Varies

DEADLINE(S): MAR 31

FIELD(S): Medicine/Dentistry

MRC offers doctoral and postdoctoral scholarships to South African citizens under the age of 50. Candidates in possession of at least a master's degree or equivalent or a bachelor's degree in medicine or dentistry may be considered for a doctoral scholarship. Candidates may be considered for the postdoctoral scholarship if they have a degree in medicine plus 2 years research experience, a bachelor's degree in dentistry plus 2 years research, or a doctorate in health.

See website or contact Mrs. Marina Jenkins, Research Grants Administration, at MRC for an application.

2497 — MEDICAL RESEARCH COUNCIL (Masters and Doctoral Scholarships)

PO Box 19070

Tygerberg 7505 SOUTH AFRICA

021/938-0227

FAX: 021/938-0368

E-Mail: mjenkins@mrc.ac.za

Internet: www.mrc.ac.za/

AMOUNT: Varies

DEADLINE(S): SEP 30

FIELD(S): Medical Sciences

MRC offers scholarships to South African citizens and permanent residents for study in the medical sciences. Students must have obtained at least an honours degree and should be seeking a master's or doctoral degree. Only applications by candidates who plan to undertake their research with MRC-funded researchers will be considered.

See website or contact Mrs. Marina Jenkins, Research Grants Administration, at MRC for an application.

2498 — MEDICAL RESEARCH COUNCIL (Postdoctoral Scholarships for Study in South Africa)

PO Box 19070
Tygerberg 7505 SOUTH AFRICA
021/938-0227
FAX: 021/938-0368
E-Mail: mjenkins@mrc.ac.za
Internet: www.mrc.ac.za/

AMOUNT: Varies

DEADLINE(S): AUG 31

FIELD(S): Health Sciences

MRC offers postdoctoral scholarships to South African citizens under the age of 50. Must be in possession of a doctorate degree in an approved field of health sciences.

See website or contact Mrs. Marina Jenkins, Research Grants Administration, at MRC for an application.

2499 — MEDICAL RESEARCH COUNCIL (Studentships, Fellowships, and Training Awards)

Research Careers Awards Group
20 Park Crescent
London W1N 4AL ENGLAND
0171/636-5422
FAX: 0171/670-5002
E-Mail: fellows@headoffice.mrc.ac.uk
Internet: www.mrc.ac.uk

AMOUNT: Varies

DEADLINE(S): Varies

FIELD(S): Biomedical/Dental Research

Various fellowships, studentships, and grants for graduate and postgraduate students in the above fields. For study in the UK.

Renewable up to three years, but subject to annual review. See website or write to above address for more information.

2500 — MEDICAL RESEARCH COUNCIL OF CANADA (Doctoral Research Award Program)

Holland Cross, Tower B, 5th Floor
1600 Scott St.
Ottawa Ontario K1A 0W9 CANADA
613/954-1963
FAX: 613/954-1800
E-Mail: llepage@mrc.gc.ca

AMOUNT: $19,030

DEADLINE(S): OCT 15

FIELD(S): Medical Research

A national competition for students engaged in doctoral-level full-time medical research in Canada.

Contact MRC for an application.

2501 — MILHEIM FOUNDATION FOR CANCER RESEARCH (Cancer Research Grants)

US Bank
200 University Blvd.
Denver CO 80206
303/316-5946
FAX: 303/388-9387

AMOUNT: $1,125-$23,485

DEADLINE(S): MAR 15

FIELD(S): Cancer Research

Graduate and postgraduate grants for research into the prevention, treatment, and cure of cancer. Funds must be expended in US. Grants may not be used to pay salaries of academic personnel, including MDs, Ph.Ds, and those studying for those degrees.

Contact Trust Administrator Barbara S. Cole for an application.

2502 — MONTREAL NEUROLOGICAL INSTITUTE (Izaak Walton Preston Robb Fellowship & Jeanne Timmins Costello Fellowships)

3801 rue University
Montreal Quebec H3A 2B4 CANADA
514/398-1903

AMOUNT: $25,000 Canadian

DEADLINE(S): OCT 15

FIELD(S): Neurosciences

Fellowships at the Institute for research and study in clinical and basic neurosciences. Open to neurologists, neurosurgeons, and Ph.D.s of all nationalities.

Contact the Director for an application.

2503 — MUSCULAR DYSTROPHY ASSOCIATION (Postdoctoral Research Grants)

3300 E. Sunrise Dr.
Tucson AZ 85718-3208
520/529-2000
FAX: 520/529-5300
Internet: www.mdausa.org

AMOUNT: Varies

DEADLINE(S): Varies

FIELD(S): Neuromuscular Disease Research

Open to professional and faculty members at appropriate educational, medical, or research institutions. Must be qualified to conduct and supervise a program of original research, have access to institutional resources necessary to conduct the proposed research project, and hold a Doctor of Medicine/Philosophy/Science or equivalent degree. NO scholarships available.

See website or call MDA for an application.

2504 — MYASTHENIA GRAVIS FOUNDATION OF AMERICA, INC. (Kermit E. Osserman Fellowships)

123 W. Madison St., Ste. 800
Chicago IL 60602-4503
312/853-0522 or 800/541-5454
FAX: 312/853-0523
E-Mail: myastheniagravis@msn.com
Internet: www.myasthenia.org

AMOUNT: $30,000 (max. for stipend, supplies, & travel)

DEADLINE(S): NOV 1

FIELD(S): Myasthenia Gravis

Twelve-month postdoctoral research fellowships are for clinical or basic research pertinent to myasthenia gravis (MG) or related neuromuscular disorders. Proposal must be less than ten pages and should include specific aims, experiemental design, research methods, and description of research environment. Must also submit budget, curriculum vitae, and letters of recommendation. Must be US resident doing research in US or abroad OR be foreign national researching in US.

Contact the Research & Grants Committee for an application. Awards decision usually made in February.

2505 — MYASTHENIA GRAVIS FOUNDATION OF AMERICA, INC. (Henry R. Viets Medical/ Graduate Student Research Fellowships)

123 W. Madison St., Ste.800
Chicago IL 60602-4503
312/853-0522 or 800/541-5454
FAX: 312/853-0523
E-Mail: myastheniagravis@msn.com
Internet: www.myasthenia.org

AMOUNT: $3,000

DEADLINE(S): MAR 15

FIELD(S): Myasthenia Gravis

Awarded to current medical students or medical graduate students interested in the scientific basis of Myasthenia Gravis (MG) or related neuromuscular conditions. Must describe question you propose to study, its association to MG, and how you will approach project. Must submit eight copies each of cover letter, curriculum vitae, and letter of recommendation from sponsoring preceptor.

4-8 awards annually. Renewable. Contact the Research & Grants Committee for an application.

2506 — NATIONAL ALLIANCE FOR RESEARCH ON SCHIZOPHRENIA AND DEPRESSION (Young, Independent, & Distinguished Investigator Awards)

60 Cutter Mill Rd., Ste. 404
Great Neck NY 11021-3196
516/829-0091

FAX: 516/487-6930
E-Mail: amoran@ix.netcom.com
Internet: www.narsad.org

AMOUNT: $30,000-$100,000/yr. (max.)

DEADLINE(S): OCT 25 (Young); FEB 5 (Ind.); JUN 15 (Dist.)

FIELD(S): Schizophrenia; Depression/Affective Disorders

One- to two-year grants are open to postdoctoral scholars, assistant/associate professors, and establisted scientists to pursue research on schizophrenia or depression (including all affective disorders). Financial need NOT a factor.

Over 200 awards annually. Not renewable. See website or contact Audra Moran, NARSAD Grants Administrator, for an application.

2507 — NATIONAL ASSOCIATION OF STATE MENTAL HEALTH PROGRAM DIRECTORS RESEARCH INSTITUTE (Postdoctoral Research Fellowships)

Exec. Director
66 Canal Center Plaza, Ste. 302
Alexandria VA 22314
703/739-9333
FAX: 703/548-9517

AMOUNT: Varies

DEADLINE(S): DEC 1

FIELD(S): Mental Health Services Research

Open to holders of Ph.Ds, M.D.s, or equivalent degrees who are interested in pursuing careers in mental health services research. Minorities and women are especially encouraged to apply. Fellows will improve their knowledge of public mental health systems and services and increase their theoretical, methodological, and analytic skills during the two-year program.

Contact Executive Director Noel A. Mazade, Ph.D, for an application.

2508 — NATIONAL FEDERATION OF THE BLIND (Howard Brown Rickard Scholarship)

805 Fifth Avenue
Grinnell IA 50112
515/236-3366

AMOUNT: $3,000

DEADLINE(S): MAR 31

FIELD(S): Law; Medicine; Engineering; Architecture; Natural Sciences

For legally blind students pursuing or planning to pursue a full-time postsecondary course of study in the US. Based on academic excellence, service to the community, and financial need. Membership NOT required.

1 award annually. Renewable. Contact Mrs. Peggy Elliot, Scholarship Committee Chairman, for an application.

2509 — NATIONAL HEADACHE FOUNDATION (Research Grant)

428 W. St. James Pl., 2nd Floor
Chicago IL 60614-2750
888-NHF-5552 or 773/388-6394
FAX: 773/525-7357
Internet: www.headaches.org

AMOUNT: Varies

DEADLINE(S): DEC 1

FIELD(S): Headache & Pain Research

Grant proposals are accepted for research in the field of headache and pain from individual investigators who have graduated from US medical schools. Grant may be used for data analysis, interpretation, reading of results, etc. NHF looks for research protocols that are objectively sound and whose results can, when published in the medical literature, contribute to the better understanding and treatment of headache and pain. Financial need NOT a factor.

To apply, send page listing title of research project, principal/co-investigator(s)/institution, abstract of research plan, total cost, and amount requested. Contact Suzanne E. Simons at NHF for an application.

2510 — NATIONAL HEADACHE FOUNDATION (Seymour Diamond Clinical Fellowship in Headache Education)

428 W. St. James Pl., 2nd Floor
Chicago IL 60614-2750
888-NHF-5552 or 773/388-6394
FAX: 773/525-7357
Internet: www.headaches.org

AMOUNT: $40,000

DEADLINE(S): FEB 1

FIELD(S): Headache & Pain Research

To encourage, provide for, & engage physicians towards the clinical management of headache patients. Program is hands-on approach at a headache clinic with objectives to develop ocmpetence in headache problems, to publish research paper, and to prepare applicant for career treating headache patients. Must be graduate of approved medical school in US and be at least postgraduate year four. Personal interview may be required. Financial need NOT a factor.

Must submit curriculum vitae, statement of experience/training, 3 letters of recommendation from department heads/supervisors, & outline of proposed clinical research project. Contact Suzanne E. Simons at NHF for an application.

2511 — NATIONAL HEMOPHILIA FOUNDATION (Career Development Award in Bleeding Disorders Research)

116 W. 32nd St., 11th Floor
New York NY 10001
800/42-HANDI or 212/328-3700
FAX: 212/328-3788
E-Mail: dkenny@hemophilia.org
Internet: www.hemophilia.org

AMOUNT: $70,000/yr.

DEADLINE(S): FEB 1

FIELD(S): Hemophilia/Bleeding Disorders Research

Candidates must hold an MD, Ph.D., or equivalent degree and be an assistant professor (or equivalent) with up to six years of experience since completion of training. May be affiliated with or be faculty members of domestic organizations, such as universities, colleges, hospitals, and laboritories. Must commit to spending 90% of their effort on research during award tenure. Proposals reviewed on significance/originality, appropriateness, experience, budget, & safety.

Renewable up to 3 years. Contact Denise Kenny at NHF for an application.

2512 — NATIONAL HEMOPHILIA FOUNDATION (Judith Graham Pool Postdoctoral Research Fellowships)

116 W. 32nd St., 11th Floor
New York NY 10001
800/42-HANDI or 212/328-3700
FAX: 212/328-3788
E-Mail: dkenny@hemophilia.org
Internet: www.hemophilia.org

AMOUNT: $35,000

DEADLINE(S): DEC 1

FIELD(S): Hemophilia Research

Two-year postdoctoral fellowships awarded through professional and graduate schools or research institutions in the US for hemophilia-related research. Applicant must have completed doctoral training and must enter the JGP Fellowship Program from a doctoral, postdoctoral, internship, or residency training program. Not open to established investigators or faculty members. Financial need NOT a factor.

5 awards annually. Renewable up to 2 years. Contact Denise Kenny at NHF for an application.

2513 — NATIONAL HUMANITIES CENTER (Burroughs Wellcome Fund Fellowships in the History of Modern Medicine)

PO Box 12256
Research Triangle Park NC 27709-2256
919/549-0661
FAX: 919/990-8535

E-Mail: nhc@ga.unc.edu

Internet: www.nhc.rtp.nc.us:8080

AMOUNT: Stipend ($35,000-$50,000) + Travel Expenses (fellow & dependents)

DEADLINE(S): OCT 15

FIELD(S): History of Medicine/Biomedical Science; Medical Anthropology

Postdoctoral fellowships for historians of medicine or biomedical science, medical anthropologists, and other scholars whose work concerns the history of twentieth-century medicine. Curriculum vitae, 1,000-word proposal, and three letters of recommendation are required.

1 award annually. Contact NHC for application materials.

2514 — NATIONAL ITALIAN AMERICAN FOUNDATION (Carmela Gagliardi Fellowship)

1860 19th St. NW

Washington DC. 20009-5599

202/530-5315

AMOUNT: $5,000

DEADLINE(S): MAR 31

FIELD(S): Fellowship in medicine

Open to students of Italian descent enrolled in or accepted to an accredited medical school program and are in the top 25% of their class. Financial need must be demonstrated.

Five fellowships to be awarded. Write for application and details.

2515 — NATIONAL ITALIAN AMERICAN FOUNDATION (Giargiari Fellowship)

1860 Nineteenth St. NW

Washington DC 20009-5599

202/530-5315

AMOUNT: $5,000

DEADLINE(S): MAY 31

FIELD(S): Medicine

For to 2nd, 3rd, and 4th year Italian American students enrolled in an accredited U.S. medical school. Write a 5-page, double-spaced, typed essay on "Italian Americans in the Medical Field."

Academic merit, financial need, and community service are considered. Contact organization for application and details.

2516 — NATIONAL MULTIPLE SCLEROSIS SOCIETY (Postdoctoral Fellowship Program)

733 Third Avenue

New York NY 10017

212/986-3240

AMOUNT: Varies with qualifications and experience

DEADLINE(S): FEB 1

FIELD(S): Multiple Sclerosis Research Training

Open to individuals who hold or are candidates for an M.D., Ph.D, or equivalent degree who have completed less than one year of prior postdoctoral training at the time of application.

U.S. citizenship NOT required for training in U.S. institutions. Applicants who plan to train in other countries MUST be U.S. citizens. Write for complete information.

2517 — NATIONAL MULTIPLE SCLEROSIS SOCIETY (Research Grants/Research Training)

733 Third Avenue, 6th Fl.

New York NY 10017-3288

212/986-3240

AMOUNT: Varies

DEADLINE(S): Varies (with program)

FIELD(S): Multiple Sclerosis

The society supports research in areas related to multiple sclerosis which may serve to advance the society's aims. It also offers postdoctoral fellowship grants to help promising new investigators prepare for independent research in MS.

Must have MD or Ph.D to apply; write for complete information.

2518 — NATIONAL RESEARCH COUNCIL (Howard Hughes Medical Institute Predoctoral Fellowships in Biological Sciences)

2101 Constitution Ave.

Washington DC 20418

202/334-2872

FAX: 202/334-2872

E-Mail: infofell@nas.edu

Internet: national-academics.org/osep.fo

AMOUNT: $16,000 stipend + tuition at US institution

DEADLINE(S): NOV 9

FIELD(S): Biochemistry; Biophysics; Epidemiology; Genetics; Immunology; Microbiology; Neuroscience; Pharmacology; Physiology; Virology

Five-year award is open to college seniors and first-year graduate students pursuing a Ph.D. or Sc.D. degree. US citizens/nationals may choose any institution in the US or abroad; foreign students must choose US institution. Based on ability, academic records, proposed study/research, previous experience, reference reports, and GRE scores.

80 awards annually. See website or contact NRC for an application.

2519 — NATIONAL UNIVERSITY OF SINGAPORE (Mobil-NUS Postgraduate Medical Research Scholarship)

3rd Level, MD5

Lower Kent Ridge Rd.

Singapore 119074 SINGAPORE

65/874 3300

FAX: 65/773 1462

E-Mail: pmdseowa@nus.edu.sg

Internet: www.med.nus.edu.sg/spms/spmsmain.html

AMOUNT: S$2,000 montly stipend, S$500 book allowance, roundtrip airfare, & course/registration fees

DEADLINE(S): MAR 1; JUL 15

FIELD(S): Medical Research

2-year scholarships for outstanding foreign candidates with medical degrees to pursue studies at NUS. Must undergo the MSc programme, which aims to provide training in clinical research methodology to those interested in pursuing careers as clinical research scientists or managers in health care institutes & the biomedical pharmaceutical industry. Must have at least 3 years post-medical registration clinical expereince. Must speak English.

Contact the Director of the Graduate School of Medical Studies at above address for an application.

2520 — NOVARTIS FOUNDATION (Bursary Scheme)

41 Portland Place

London W1N 4BN ENGLAND UK

+44 171 636 9456

FAX: +44 171 436 2840

E-Mail: abrown@novartisfound.org.uk

Internet: www.novartisfound.org.uk

AMOUNT: Travel & subsistence—up to $6,000/person

DEADLINE(S): Varies

FIELD(S): Science; Medicine

Travel fellowships to young scientists (postgrad/doc) to attend international meetings in connection with the Novartis Foundation Symposia. Must be between the ages of 23 and 35, and be active in the field of science in question. Symposia is normally in London, and a 4-week to 12-week host laboratory in the department of one of the symposium participants follows. Specific topics vary. Must submit qualifications, resume, career history/goals, and research interests.

8 awards annually. Not renewable. See website or contact Allyson Brown for application procedures.

2521 — OAK RIDGE INSTITUTE FOR SCIENCE AND EDUCATION (Alexander Hollaender Distinguished Post-doctoral Fellowships)

P.O. Box 117
Oak Ridge TN 37831-0117
423/576-3192 or 423/576-9975

AMOUNT: $37,500 + inbound travel, moving, and medical insurance

DEADLINE(S): JAN 15

FIELD(S): Biomedical, life, and environmental sciences and other related scientific disciplines, including global change and human genome

One-year post-doctoral fellowships for research and training in energy-related life, biomedical, and environmental sciences at one of participating laboratories in the U.S. Must have completed doctorate within last two years.

Must be U.S. citizen or legal resident.

2522 — OAK RIDGE INSTITUTE FOR SCIENCE AND EDUCATION (Industrial Hygiene Graduate Fellowship Program)

P.O. Box 117
Oak Ridge TN 37831-0117
423-576-9655
FAX: 423/576-8293
E-Mail: kinneym@orau.gov

AMOUNT:

DEADLINE(S): JAN 26

FIELD(S): Industrial Hygiene

A fellowship for first-year master's candidates who have undergraduate degrees in physical, life, environmental, or health sciences or enginering and who wish to pursue studies in industrial hygiene.

For details and application, contact above location.

2523 — ORENTREICH FOUNDATION FOR THE ADVANCEMENT OF SCIENCE (Research Grants)

Biomedical Research Stn.
RD 2, Box 375
Cold Spring-on-Hudson NY 10516-9802
914/265-4200
FAX: 914/265-4210
E-Mail: ofas1@juno.com

AMOUNT: Varies

DEADLINE(S): None

FIELD(S): Biomedical Research

Applicants must be at or above postgraduate level in science or medicine at accredited universities or research institutions in the US. Research is typically focused on aging, dermatology, endocrinology, and serum markers for human diseases. Must submit an outline of proposed joint or collaborative research, including brief overview of current research in field of interest, scientific objectives, protocol summary, curriculum vitae, needed funding, and budget.

Contact OFAS for details. Note: OFAS generally makes only occasional and limited grants and is usually the initiator of such projects.

2524 — PFIZER PHARMACEUTICALS (Pfizer/ AGS Postdoctoral Fellowship Program)

Pfizer Inc.
235 East 42nd St.
New York, NY 10017-5755
800/201-1214

AMOUNT: $40,000 per year for 2 years

DEADLINE(S): DEC 1

FIELD(S): Research in Health Outcomes in Geriatrics

Postdoctoral research fellowships in geriatric medicine open to recent MDs & DOs who will complete their residency training by July 1 of year following deadline date.

Call for complete information and application materials.

2525 — PHARMACEUTICAL RESEARCH AND MANUFACTURERS ASSOCIATION FOUNDATION (Fellowships for Advanced Predoctoral Training in Pharmacology or Toxicology)

1100 15th Street NW
Washington DC 20005
202/835-3400
FAX: 202/467-4823
E-Mail: CRobinson%phrma@mcimail.com
Internet: www.phrmaf.org

AMOUNT: $12,000 stipend + $500 expense money for thesis prep.

DEADLINE(S): SEP 15

FIELD(S): Pharmacology/Toxicology

Open to full-time students enrolled in schools of medicine, pharmacy, dentistry, or veterinary medicine for beginning thesis research.

Write for complete information or contact above website.

2526 — PHARMACEUTICAL RESEARCH AND MANUFACTURERS OF AMERICA FOUNDATION (Faculty Awards in Basic Pharmacology/ Toxicology)

1100 15th Street NW
Washington DC 20005
202/835-3470
FAX: 202/467-4823
E-Mail: CRobinson%phrma@mcimail.com
Internet: www.phrmaf.org

AMOUNT: Unspecified amount paid to institution for salary and fringe benefits of apppointee

DEADLINE(S): SEP 15

FIELD(S): Pharmacology/Toxicology

Awards for post-doctoral faculty members or assistant professors who are beginning careers in academic pharmacology or toxicology or who are being considered for such an appointment in schools of medicine, pharmacy, dentistry, or veterinary medicine.

Contact above location or access the website for application and details.

2527 — PILOT INTERNATIONAL FOUNDATION (Marie Newton Sepia Memorial Scholarship)

P.O. Box 5600
Macon GA 31208-5600
Written inquiries

AMOUNT: Varies

DEADLINE(S): MAR 1

FIELD(S): Disabilities/Brain-related Disorders in Children

This program assists graduate students preparing for careers working with children having disabilities/ brain disorders. Must have GPA of 3.5 or greater.

Applicants must be sponsored by a Pilot Club in their home town or in the city in which their college or university is located. Send a self-addressed, stamped envelope for complete information.

2528 — PILOT INTERNATIONAL FOUNDATION (PIF/Lifeline Scholarship)

P.O. Box 5600
Macon GA 31208-5600
Written inquiries

AMOUNT: Varies

DEADLINE(S): MAR 1

FIELD(S): Disabilities/Brain-related Disorders

This program assists ADULT students re-entering the job market, preparing for a second career, or improving their professional skills for an established career. Applicants must be preparing for, or already involved in, careers working with people with disabilities/brain-related disorders. GPA of 3.5 or more is required.

Must be sponsored by a Pilot Club in your home town, or in the city in which your college or university is located. Send a self-addressed, stamped envelope for complete information.

2529 — PILOT INTERNATIONAL FOUNDATION (Ruby Newhall Memorial Scholarship)

P.O. Box 5600
Macon, GA 31208-5600
Written Inquiries

AMOUNT: Varies

DEADLINE(S): MAR 15

FIELD(S): Disabilities/Brain-related disorders

For international students who have studied in the US for at least one year, and who intend to return to their home country six months after graduation. Applicants must be full-time students majoring in a field related to human health and welfare, and have a GPA of 3.5 or more.

Applicants must be sponsored by a Pilot Club in their home town, or in the city in which their college or university is located. Send a self-addressed, stamped envelope for complete information.

2530 — RESEARCH COUNCIL OF NORWAY (Senior Scientist Visiting Fellowship)

P.O. Box 2700 St. Hanshaugen
N-0131 Oslo NORWAY
+47 22 03 70 00
FAX: +47 22 03 70 01
E-Mail: intstip@nfr.no
Internet: www.forskningsradet.no

AMOUNT: NOK 25,000-1st 2 months; NOK 10,000-succeeding months

DEADLINE(S): Varies

FIELD(S): Bioproduction & Processing (including agriculture and veterinary science); Industry & Energy; Culture & Society (including social sciences and the humanities); Medicine & Health; Environment & Development; Science & Technology

Fellowships for scientists to work at Norwegian research institutes. Project funding does not include salary; expenses connected with the stay in Norway are covered.

For a list of institutions, contact the Research Council at above location. Then apply to institution, which then will submit fellowship application.

2531 — SCOTTISH RITE CHARITABLE FOUNDATION (Research Grants)

Roeher Institute
Kinsmen Bldg.
4700 Keele St.
North York Ontario M3J 1P3 CANADA
416/661-9611
TDD: 416/661-2023
FAX: 416/661-5701
E-Mail: mail@aacl.org
Internet: www.aacl.org

AMOUNT: $10,000 (max. grads); $35,000 (max. postdocs)

DEADLINE(S): APR 30

FIELD(S): Human Services; Intellectual Disability

Open to Canadian citizens/landed immigrants enrolled in masters or doctoral programs at Canadian universities. Must state intent to pursue career in Canada and have definite research projects supported by an academic advisor or a Roeher Institute associate/consultant. Also available to postdoctoral researchers.

Renewable. Contact the Secretary, Awards Adjudicating Committee, at the Scottish Rite for an application and details on preferred research topics.

2532 — SIGRID JUSELIUS FOUNDATION (Medical Research Grants)

Aleksanterinkatu 48 B
00100 Helsinki Finland
09-634 461
FAX: 09-634 452

AMOUNT: FIM 30.000-150 .000

DEADLINE(S): APR 15; SEP 15

FIELD(S): Medical Research

Grants for advanced post-doctoral research work in medical science. Non-Finnish scientists may apply for scholarship ONLY through a Finnish colleague in the scientist's particular field. Award must be used in Finland.

10 non-Finnish researchers received grants for 1-12 months in 1997. The total amount of these grants was USD $124,000. Write for complete information.

2533 — STROKE ASSOCIATION (Clinical Fellowships)

Stroke House
Whitecross St.
London EC1Y 8JJ ENGLAND UK
0171 566 0300
FAX: 0171 490 2686

AMOUNT: 25,000 pounds sterling

DEADLINE(S): JAN

FIELD(S): Stroke Research

Purpose is to equip a trainee for a career in the prevention, treatment, or rehabilitation of strokes. Applicable to universities and hospitals in the UK.

3 awards annually. Not renewable. Contact the Research Secretary for an application. Awards made in June.

2534 — STROKE ASSOCIATION (Programme Grants)

Stroke House
Whitecross St.
London EC1Y 8JJ ENGLAND UK
0171 566 0300
FAX: 0171 490 2686

AMOUNT: 250,000 pounds sterling, up to 5 years

DEADLINE(S): JAN

FIELD(S): Stroke Research

Open to medically qualified and other clinically active researchers in the UK in the relevant fields; specific topics within the field of stroke research change annually.

Applications judged by peer review on their merit. Applicable to universities and hospitals in the UK.

2 awards annually. Renewable, but subject to review after three years. Contact the Research Secretary for an application. Awards made in October.

2535 — STROKE ASSOCIATION (Stroke Research Awards)

Stroke House
Whitecross St.
London EC1Y 8JJ ENGLAND UK
0171 566 0300
FAX: 0171 490 2686

AMOUNT: 60,000 pounds sterling/yr.

DEADLINE(S): Varies

FIELD(S): Stroke Research

Open to medically qualified and other clinically active researchers in the UK in the relevant fields: applied research in epidemiology, prevention, acute treatment, assessment, and rehabilitation. Applications judged by peer review on their merit without limitations of age. Applicable to universities and hospitals in the UK. Awards cover salaries for researchers/support staff, some equipment, consumables, and essential travel.

20-30 awards annually. Renewable up to three years. Contact the Research Secretary for an application.

2536 — STROKE ASSOCIATION (Stroke Therapy Research Bursaries)

Stroke House
Whitecross St.
London EC1Y 8JJ ENGLAND UK
0171 566 0300
FAX: 0171 490 2686

AMOUNT: 20,000 pounds sterling/yr.

DEADLINE(S): JAN

FIELD(S): Stroke Research

Purpose is to provide a research training programme and appropriate supervision to equip a trainee for a career in stroke research. Primarily intended for nurses and therapists, but consideration will be given to other health professionals. Applicable to universities and hospitals in the UK.

3 awards annually. Renewable for an additional year. Contact the Research Secretary for an application. Awards made in June.

2537 — THE ALZHEIMER'S ASSOCIATION (Research Grants)

919 N. Michigan Ave., Suite 1000
Chicago IL 60611-1676
312/335-8700
FAX: 312/335-1110
www.alz.org

AMOUNT: Varies

DEADLINE(S): Varies

FIELD(S): Alzheimer's Disease Research

Doctorate and post-doctorate research grants for proposals in the field of Alzheimer's disease and related disorders, especially early detection.

Access website or write for further information.

2538 — THE ARC (Research Grants Program in Mental Retardation)

500 E. Border St., Suite 300
Arlington, TX 76010
817/261-6003
FAX: 817/277-3491
E-Mail: thearc@metronet.com
Internet: http://www.theArc.org/welcome.html

AMOUNT: Up to $25,000

DEADLINE(S): APR 1

FIELD(S): Prevention, amelioration, or cure of mental retardation

The Arc invites applications from researchers from diverse sources—individuals and universities, hospitals, and professional organizations with research interests.

Contact Dr. Michael Wehmeyer, Assistant Director, Department of Research and Program Services, The Arc, at above address, or Ann Balson.

2539 — THE HAN'T FOUNDATION (Quest Award in Micro-Meteorites)

P.O. Box 6694
Coddingtown, CA 95406-0694
Written Inquiries Only

AMOUNT: $2001

DEADLINE(S): June 5

FIELD(S): Medical Research in Geoscience

Open to full-time undergraduate or graduate students majoring in bio-physical effects of micro-meteorites in all geophysical environments.

Must be ethnic minority and a US citizen. Must have been born on June 5th and demonstrate financial need. Write to the above address for more information.

2540 — U.S. DEPT. OF HEALTH & HUMAN SERVICES (Indian Health Service Health Professions Scholarship Program)

Twinbrook Metro Plaza, Suite 100
12300 Twinbrook Pkwy.
Rockville MD 20852
301/443-0234
FAX: 301/443-4815
Internet: www.ihs.gov/Recruitment/DHPS/SP/SBTOC3.asp

AMOUNT: Tuition + fees & monthly stipend of $938.

DEADLINE(S): APR 1

FIELD(S): Health professions, accounting, social work

Open to Native Americans or Alaska natives who are graduate students or college juniors or seniors in a program leading to a career in a fields listed above. U.S. citizenship required. Renewable annually with reapplication.

Scholarship recipients must intend to serve the Indian people. They incur a one-year service obligation to the IHS for each year of support for a minimum of two years. Write for complete information.

2541 — U.S. PHARMACOPEIA (USP Fellowship Program)

12601 Twinbrook Parkway
Rockville MD 20852
301/816-8226
FAX: 301/998-6806
E-Mail: nbm@usp.org
Internet: www.usp.org

AMOUNT: $15,000

DEADLINE(S): JAN 31

FIELD(S): Drug Standards; Drug Information Studies

Doctoral & postdoctoral fellowships for students to do research at health professions schools where USP subcommittee perons are on faculty/affiliated. Applicants for Standards Fellowships must have completed second year in a Ph.D. program. Applicants for Information Fellowships must have been accepted for full-time study in a doctoral program, be accepted to a Fellowship Program, or have a postdoctoral research (non-faculty) appointment. Financial need NOT a factor.

12 awards annually. Renewable for an additional year. Contact Nancy Best Mabie at USP for an application.

2542 — UNCF/MERCK SCIENCE INITIATIVE (Graduate Science Research Dissertation Fellowships)

8260 Willow Oaks Corporate Dr.
PO Box 10444
Fairfax VA 22031-4511
703/205-3503
FAX: 703/205-3574
E-Mail: uncfmerck@uncf.org
Internet: www.uncf.org/merck

AMOUNT: $40,000/yr. (max.)

DEADLINE(S): JAN 31

FIELD(S): Life & Physical Sciences

Open to African-Americans enrolled full-time in a Ph.D. degree program and within 1-3 years of completing dissertation. Awards are intended to help students complete coursework, conduct research, and prepare dissertation for degree in the biomedically relevant life or physical sciences. Must be US citizen/permanent resident. Financial need NOT a factor.

12 awards annually. Not renewable. Contact Jerry Bryant, Ph.D., for an application.

2543 — UNCF/MERCK SCIENCE INITIATIVE (Postdoctoral Science Research Fellowships)

8260 Willow Oaks Corporate Dr.
PO Box 10444
Fairfax VA 22031-4511
703/205-3503
FAX: 703/205-3574
E-Mail: uncfmerck@uncf.org
Internet: www.uncf.org/merck

AMOUNT: $70,000/yr. (max.)

DEADLINE(S): JAN 31

FIELD(S): Life & Physical Sciences

Open to African-Americans who will receive a Ph.D. degree by the end of the current academic year and will be appointed as a postdoctoral fellow during the next calendar year. Awards are intended to support postgraduate students to obtain postdoctoral training and to prepare for a career in biomedical research. Must be US citizen/permanent resident. Financial need NOT a factor.

10 awards annually. Not renewable. Contact Jerry Bryant, Ph.D., for an application.

2544 — UNIFORMED SERVICES UNIVERSITY OF THE HEALTH SCIENCES (Fellowships)

Schools of Medicine & Nursing
4301 Jones Bridge Rd.
Bethesda MD 20814-4799
301/295-3101 or 800/772-1743

AMOUNT: Tuition

DEADLINE(S): NOV 1

FIELD(S): Medicine; Nursing

Open to graduate students who wish to attend the F. Edward Hebert School of Medicine or the Graduate School of Nursing with the understanding that they will be trained for service to the nation, including assignments abroad or at sea. While enrolled, students serve as reserve commissioned officers. Must be US citizen.

Contact Uniformed Services University for an application.

2545 — UNIVERSITY OF EDINBURGH (Faculty of Medicine Bursaries & Scholarships)

7-11 Nicolson St.
Edinburgh SCOTLAND EH8 9BE UK
+44 (0) 131 650 1000
Internet: www.iprs.ed.ac.uk/progawards/medicine/

AMOUNT: Varies

DEADLINE(S): MAR 1; NOV 1

FIELD(S): Medicine

Various scholarships, bursaries, and travel awards for medical students at all levels of study. For use at the University of Edinburgh, Scotland. Some are for students from other companies; some are for women; some are for specific specialties.

Access website for more information and/or contact school for details and appropriate application forms.

2546 — WASHINGTON STATE HIGHER EDUCATION COORDINATING BOARD (Health Professional Loan Repayment & Scholarship Program)

PO Box 43430
Olympia WA 98504-3430
360/753-7850
FAX: 360/753-7808
Internet: www.hecb.wa.gov

AMOUNT: Varies

DEADLINE(S): APR (scholarship); FEB (loan repayment); JUL (loan repayment)

FIELD(S): Health Care

Scholarships are open to students in accredited undergraduate or graduate health care programs leading to eligibility for licensure in Washington state. Must agree to work in designated shortage area for minimum of three years. Loan repayment recipients receive payment from program for purpose of repaying education loans secured while attending program of health care training leading to licensure in Washington state. Financial need NOT a factor.

Renewable up to 5 years. Contact Program Manager for a loan repayment application after November 15th and for scholarship application after January 15th.

2547 — WELLCOME TRUST (Post-doctoral Research Travel Grants to United States)

183 Euston Road
London NW1 2BE ENGLAND
0171 611 8888/Direct: 8401
FAX: 0171 611 8545/Direct 8700
E-Mail: larter@wellcome.ac.uk

AMOUNT: Varies with cost

DEADLINE(S): None

FIELD(S): Research in the Biomedical Sciences

Post-doctoral research travel grants to the U.S. for citizens or legal residents of Great Britain or Ireland. Maximum stay is 3 months. Full-time established research workers in health sciences may apply.

Write for complete information.

2548 — WHITEHALL FOUNDATION, INC. (Research Grants & Grants-in-Aid)

251 Royal Palm Way, Ste. 211

Palm Beach FL 33480
561/655-4474
FAX: 561/659-4978
E-Mail: WhitehallF@aol.com
Internet: www.whitehall.org

AMOUNT: $30,000-$75,000/yr.

DEADLINE(S): Varies

FIELD(S): Basic Neurobiology Research (Invertebrate & Vertebrate, excluding Clinical)

Research grants of up to 3 years are available to established scientists of all ages working at accredited US institutions; principal investigator must hold no less than position of assistant professor or equivalent. One-year grants-in-aid are for researchers at assistant professor level who experience difficulty in competing for research funds because they have not yet become firmly established; also made to senior scientists.

See website or contact Whitehall Foundation for applications and up-to-date information on deadlines and policies.

2549 — WOMEN OF THE EVANGELICAL LUTHERAN CHURCH IN AMERICA (The Kahler-Vickers/Raup-Emma Wettstein Scholarships)

8765 West Higgins Road
Chicago IL 60631-4189
800/638-3522, ext. 2747
FAX: 773/380-2419
E-Mail: womnelca@elca.org

AMOUNT: $2,000 max.

DEADLINE(S): MAR 1

FIELD(S): Health Professions & Christian Service

Assists women who are members of the ELCA studying for service in health professions associated with ELCA projects abroad that do not lead to church-certified professions. Must be US citizen and have experienced an interruption of two or more years since completion of high school. Academic records of coursework completed in last five years as well as proof of admission from educational institution are required.

Renewable for an additional year. Contact Faith Fretheim, Program Director, for an application.

2550 — WOMEN'S SPORTS FOUNDATION (Evian Rehydration, WSF Girls/Women In Sports, & Lilo Leeds Women's Sports/Fitness Participation Endowment Research Grants)

Eisenhower Park
East Meadow NY 11554
800/227-3988
FAX: 516/542-4716
E-Mail: WoSport@aol.com
Internet: www.lifetimetv.com/WoSport

AMOUNT: $1,000-$5,000

DEADLINE(S): SEP 15

FIELD(S): Female Sports & Fitness

Any bona fide researcher, including university affiliated, organizationally affiliated, or independent, may apply. The Evian grant is for research on rehydration in female sports and fitness; the Girls/Women In Sports grant is for research pertaining to girls' and women's sports; and the Lilo Leeds grant is for research that creates a greater understanding of the factors that influence the participation of girls and women in sports and fitness activities.

1 Evian grant, 2-3 Girls/Women In Sports grants, & 1-2 Lilo Leeds grants annually. See website or write to above address for details.

2551 — WOODROW WILSON NATIONAL FELLOWSHIP FOUNDATION/JOHNSON & JOHNSON (Dissertation Grants in Women's & Children's Health)

CN 5281
Princeton NJ 08543-5281
609/452-7007
FAX: 609/452-0066
E-Mail: charoltte@woodrow.org
Internet: www.woodrow.org

AMOUNT: $2,000 (for travel, books, microfilming, taping, computer services, etc.)

DEADLINE(S): NOV 8

FIELD(S): Women's & Children's Health

Open to doctoral students in nursing, public health, anthropology, history, sociology, psychology, or social work, who have completed all predissertation requirements at US graduate schools. Must have at least six months left to complete dissertation, which should include significant research on issues related to women's & children's health. Must submit transcripts, proposal, bibliography, & interest. Based on originality & scholarly validity.

15 awards annually. See website or contact WWNFF for an application. Winners announced in February.

2552 — ZETA PHI BETA SORORITY EDUCATIONAL FOUNDATION (S. Evelyn Lewis Memorial Scholarship in Medical Health Sciences)

1734 New Hampshire Ave., NW
Washington DC 20009
Internet: www.zpb1920.org/nefforms.htm

AMOUNT: $500-$1,000

DEADLINE(S): FEB 1

FIELD(S): Medicine; Health Sciences

Open to graduate and undergraduate young women enrolled in a program leading to a degree in medicine or health sciences. Award is for full-time study for one academic year (Fall-Spring) and is paid directly to college/university. Must submit proof of enrollment.

Send self-addressed, stamped envelope to above address between September 1st and December 15th for an application.

MEDICAL TECHNOLOGIES

2553 — AMERICAN ALLIANCE FOR HEALTH, PHYSICAL EDUCATION, RECREATION & DANCE

1900 Association Drive
Reston VA 20191
703/476-3400 or 800/213-7193
E-Mail: webmaster@aahperd.org
Internet: www.aahperd.org

AMOUNT: Varies

DEADLINE(S): Varies

FIELD(S): Health education, leisure and recreation, girls and women in sports, sport and physical education, dance

This organization has six national sub-organizations specializing in the above fields. Some have grants and fellowships for both individuals and group projects. The website has the details for each group.

Visit website for details or write to above address for details.

2554 — AMERICAN ART THERAPY ASSOCIATION (AATA Scholarship Fund)

1202 Allanson Rd.
Mundelein IL 60060
708/949-6064
FAX: 708/566-4580

AMOUNT: Varies

DEADLINE(S): JUN 15

FIELD(S): Art Therapy

For graduate students enrolled in an AATA-approved graduate art therapy program with a GPA of at least 3.25. Must demonstrate financial need.

Send a self-addressed, stamped envelope to AATA for an application.

2555 — AMERICAN ART THERAPY ASSOCIATION (Cay Drachnik Minorities Fund)

1202 Allanson Rd.
Mundelein IL 60060
708/949-6064
FAX: 708/566-4580

AMOUNT: Varies (for purchase of books only)

DEADLINE(S): JUN 15

FIELD(S): Art Therapy

For ethnic minority group members enrolled in an AATA-approved program. Fund is specifically for

the purchase of books. Must demonstrate financial need through letters of reference, copies of financial aid forms, etc.

Contact AATA for an application.

2556 — AMERICAN ART THERAPY ASSOCIATION (Gladys Agell Award for Excellence in Research)

1202 Allanson Rd.
Mundelein IL 60060
708/949-6064
FAX: 708/566-4580

AMOUNT: Varies

DEADLINE(S): JUN 15

FIELD(S): Art Therapy

For AATA student members. Award is designed to encourage student research and goes to the most outstanding project completed within the past year in the area of applied art therapy. Must verify student status in an AATA-approved program. Research project must follow APA guidelines.

Contact AATA for an application.

2557 — AMERICAN ART THERAPY ASSOCIATION (Myra Levick Scholarship Fund)

1202 Allanson Rd.
Mundelein IL 60060
708/949-6064
FAX: 708/566-4580

AMOUNT: Varies

DEADLINE(S): JUN 15

FIELD(S): Art Therapy

For graduate students accepted into an AATA-approved art therapy program. Must have an undergraduate GPA of at least 3.0 and demonstrate financial need.

Contact AATA for an application.

2558 — AMERICAN ART THERAPY ASSOCIATION (Rawley Silver Scholarship Fund)

1202 Allanson Rd.
Mundelein IL 60060
708/949-6064
FAX: 708/566-4580

AMOUNT: Varies

DEADLINE(S): JUN 15

FIELD(S): Art Therapy

For graduate students whose academic record or prior experience is deemed excellent by letters of reference. Applicants must be enrolled in or accepted by an AATA-approved art therapy program and demonstrate financial need.

Contact AATA for an application.

2559 — AMERICAN DENTAL HYGIENISTS ASSOCIATION INSTITUTE FOR ORAL HEALTH (Irene Woodall Graduate Scholarship)

444 N. Michigan Ave., Ste. 3400
Chicago IL 60611
800/735-4916 or 312/440-8900
FAX: 312/440-8929
Internet: www.adha.org

AMOUNT: $1,000

DEADLINE(S): JUN 1

FIELD(S): Dental Hygiene

For applicants enrolled in a full-time master's degree program in dental hygiene or related field in the US. Must have a minimum 3.0 GPA, demonstrate financial need, and have completed a minimum one year in a dental hygiene curriculum prior to receiving an award. Statement of research interests must be provided.

1 award annually. Not renewable. Contact Linda Caradine at ADHA for an application.

2560 — AMERICAN DENTAL HYGIENISTS ASSOCIATION INSTITUTE FOR ORAL HEALTH (John O. Butler Graduate Scholarships)

444 N. Michigan Ave., Ste. 3400
Chicago IL 60611
800/735-4916 or 312/440-8900
FAX: 312/440-8929
Internet: www.adha.org

AMOUNT: $2,000

DEADLINE(S): JUN 1

FIELD(S): Dental Hygiene; Dental Hygiene Education

For applicants enrolled in a full-time master's degree program in dental hygiene or dental hygiene education in the US. Must have a minimum 3.0 GPA, demonstrate financial need, and have completed a minimum one year in a dental hygiene curriculum prior to receiving an award. Statement of research interests must be provided.

7 awards annually. Not renewable. Contact Linda Caradine at ADHA for an application. Sponsored by the John O. Butler Company.

2561 — AMERICAN DENTAL HYGIENISTS ASSOCIATION INSTITUTE FOR ORAL HEALTH (Dr. Alfred C. Fones Scholarship)

444 N. Michigan Ave., Ste. 3400
Chicago IL 60611
800/735-4916 or 312/440-8900
FAX: 312/440-8929
Internet: www.adha.org

AMOUNT: $1,500

DEADLINE(S): JUN 1

FIELD(S): Dental Hygiene Education

Awarded to an applicant in the baccalaureate or graduate degree categories who intends to become a dental hygiene teacher/educator. Must have a minimum 3.0 GPA, demonstrate financial need, attend an accredited four-year US institution, and have completed a minimum one year in a dental hygiene curriculum prior to receiving an award.

1 award annually. Not renewable. Contact Linda Caradine at ADHA for an application.

2562 — AMERICAN DENTAL HYGIENISTS ASSOCIATION INSTITUTE FOR ORAL HEALTH (Irene E. Newman Scholarship)

444 N. Michigan Ave., Ste. 3400
Chicago IL 60611
800/735-4916 or 312/440-8900
FAX: 312/440-8929
Internet: www.adha.org

AMOUNT: $1,500

DEADLINE(S): JUN 1

FIELD(S): Dental Hygiene

Awarded to an applicant in the baccalaureate or graduate degree categories who demonstrates strong potential in public health or community dental health. Must have a minimum 3.0 GPA, demonstrate financial need, attend an accredited four-year US institution full-time, and have completed a minimum one year in a dental hygiene curriculum prior to receiving an award.

1 award annually. Not renewable. Contact Linda Caradine at ADHA for an application.

2563 — AMERICAN DENTAL HYGIENISTS ASSOCIATION INSTITUTE FOR ORAL HEALTH (ADHA Part-Time Scholarship)

444 N. Michigan Ave., Ste. 3400
Chicago IL 60611
800/735-4916 or 312/440-8900
FAX: 312/440-8929
Internet: www.adha.org

AMOUNT: $1,500

DEADLINE(S): JUN 1

FIELD(S): Dental Hygiene

For students enrolled part-time in a Certificate/ Associate, Baccalaureate, or Graduate Degree program in the US. Must have a minimum 3.0 GPA, demonstrate financial need, and have completed a minimum one year in a dental hygiene program. See application for specific requirements for each degree program.

1 award annually. Not renewable. Contact Linda Caradine at ADHA for an application.

2564 — AMERICAN DENTAL HYGIENISTS ASSOCIATION INSTITUTE FOR ORAL HEALTH (Sigma Phi Alpha Graduate Scholarship)

444 N. Michigan Ave., Ste. 3400
Chicago IL 60611
800/735-4916 or 312/440-8900
FAX: 312/440-8929
Internet: www.adha.org

AMOUNT: $1,000

DEADLINE(S): JUN 1

FIELD(S): Dental Hygiene

Applicants must be enrolled as full-time master's or doctoral students in the US. Must have a minimum 3.0 GPA, demonstrate financial need, and have completed a minimum one year in a dental hygiene curriculum prior to receiving an award. Applicants must include a statement of professional activities related to dental hygiene, and recipients will be encouraged to submit a manuscript to the ADHA for publication. Statement on research interests must be provdided.

1 award annually. Not renewable. Contact Linda Caradine at ADHA for an application.

2565 — AMERICAN INDIAN SCIENCE AND ENGINEERING SOCIETY (A.T. Anderson Memorial Scholarship)

PO Box 9828
Albuquerque NM 87119-9828
505/765-1052
FAX: 505/765-5608
E-Mail: scholarships@aises.org
Internet: www.aises.org/scholarships

AMOUNT: $1,000-$2,000

DEADLINE(S): JUN 15

FIELD(S): Medicine; Natural Resources; Science; Engineering

Open to undergraduate and graduate students who are at least 1/4 American Indian or recognized as member of a tribe. Must be member of AISES ($10 fee), enrolled full-time at an accredited institution, and demonstrate financial need.

Renewable. See website or contact Patricia Browne for an application and/or membership information.

2566 — AMERICAN RESPIRATORY CARE FOUNDATION (International Fellowships)

11030 Ables Ln.
Dallas TX 75229-4593
972/243-2272
E-Mail: info@aarc.org
Internet: www.aarc.org/awards

AMOUNT: Per diem allowance, lodging, & convention

DEADLINE(S): JUN 30

FIELD(S): Respiratory Therapy

Opportunity for influential healthcare professionals from other countries to observe respiratory care practice & education in the US. The three-week itinerary provides for visits to two US cities before traveling to attend the AARC International Respiratory Congress. Fellows observe respiratory care through tours of acute care hospitals, respiratory therapy schools, home care programs, nursing facilities, pulmonary rehab centers, & medical products companies.

See website or contact Norma Hernandez at ARCF for an application. Selection by September 1st.

2567 — AMERICAN SOCIETY FOR CLINICAL LABORATORY SCIENCE (Ruth M. French Graduate or Undergraduate Scholarship)

7910 Woodmont Ave., Suite 530
Bethesda MD 20814
301/657-2768
FAX: 301/657-2909

AMOUNT: $1,000

DEADLINE(S): MAR 1

FIELD(S): Clinical Laboratory Science or Medical Technology

Scholarships for students in the above field enrolled in an approved undergraduate or graduate program. Undergrads must be in last year of study. U.S. citizenship or permanent U.S. residency required.

Contact address above for complete information. Enclose self-addressed, stamped business size envelope. Applications available after Nov. 1.

2568 — AMERICAN SOCIETY OF RADIOLOGIC TECHNOLOGISTS (Isadore N. Stern Scholarship)

15000 Central Ave., SE
Albuquerque NM 87123-3917
505/298-4500
FAX: 505/298-5063
Internet: www.asrt.org

AMOUNT: $1,000

DEADLINE(S): JAN 31

FIELD(S): Radiologic Sciences

For undergraduate and graduate students with a minimum 3.0 GPA. Must have at least one-year membership with ASRT, ARRT registered/unrestricted state license, and must have worked in the radiologic sciences profession for at least one year in the past five years.

4 awards annually. Financial need is NOT a factor. For membership information or an application, contact Renee Lines at the above address.

2569 — AMERICAN SPEECH-LANGUAGE-HEARING FOUNDATION (Graduate Student Scholarships)

10801 Rockville Pike
Rockville MD 20852
301/897-5700
FAX 301/571-0457

AMOUNT: $4,000

DEADLINE(S): JUN 6

FIELD(S): Communication sciences/disorders; speech pathology;speech therapy

Open to full-time graduate students in communication sciences and disorders programs and demonstrating outstanding academic achievement.

Applications available in February.

2570 — AMERICAN SPEECH-LANGUAGE-HEARING FOUNDATION (Kala Singh Memorial Fund-International/Minority Student Scholarship)

10801 Rockville Pike
Rockville Pike, Rockville, MD 20852
301/897-5700
FAX: 301/571-0457

AMOUNT: $2,000

DEADLINE(S): JUN 6

FIELD(S): Communication sciences and disorders, speech/language pathology, audiology

Applicants must be international/ethnic minority graduate student studying communication sciences and disorders in the U.S. and demonstrating outstanding academic achievement.

Applications available in February.

2571 — AMERICAN SPEECH-LANGUAGE-HEARING FOUNDATION (Leslie Isenberg Fund for Student With Disability)

10801 Rockville Pike
Rockville Pike, Rockville MD 20852
301/897-5700
FAX: 301/571-0457

AMOUNT: $2,000

DEADLINE(S): JUN 6

FIELD(S): Communication sciences & disorders

Open to full-time graduate student with disability enrolled in a communication sciences and disorders program and demonstrating outstanding academic achievement.

Applications available in February.

2572 — AMERICAN SPEECH-LANGUAGE-HEARING FOUNDATION (New Investigator Research Grant)

10801 Rockville Pike
Rockville MD 20852
301/897-5700
FAX 301/571-0457

AMOUNT: $5,000

DEADLINE(S): JUL 20

FIELD(S): Speech/Language Pathology; Audiology

Research grant for new investigators to support clinical research in the above areas. Grants are designed to encourage research activities by new scientists who have earned their M.A. or Ph.D. within the last 5 years. Students enrolled in degree programs are ineligible.

Seven awards. Applications available in February.

2573 — AMERICAN SPEECH-LANGUAGE-HEARING FOUNDATION (Student Research Grant in Clinical or Rehabilitative Audiology)

10801 Rockville Pike
Rockville MD 20852
301/897-5700
FAX 301/571-0457

AMOUNT: $2,000

DEADLINE(S): JUN 13

FIELD(S): Audiology

Student research grants available to graduate or post-graduate students in communication sciences and disorders desiring to conduct research in audiology.

Applications available in February.

2574 — AMERICAN SPEECH-LANGUAGE-HEARING FOUNDATION (Student Research in Early Childhood Language Development)

10801 Rockville Pike
Rockville MD 20852
301/897-5700
FAX 301/571-0457

AMOUNT: $2,000

DEADLINE(S): JUN

FIELD(S): Research in early childhood language development

Research grant for graduate or post-graduate students in communication sciences and disorders desiring to conduct research in early childhood language development.

Applications available in February.

2575 — AMERICAN SPEECH-LANGUAGE-HEARING FOUNDATION (Young Scholars Award for Minority Student)

10801 Rockville Pike
Rockville MD 20852
301/897-5700
FAX 301/571-0457

AMOUNT: $2,000

DEADLINE(S): JUN 6

FIELD(S): Speech/Language Pathology; Audiology

Open to ethnic minorities who are full-time college seniors accepted for graduate study in speech-language pathology or audiology. Applicants must be US citizens.

Applications available in February.

2576 — ARCHBOLD MEDICAL CENTER (Archbold Scholarship/Loan)

Dept. of Education
P.O. Box 1018
Thomasville GA 31799-1018
912/228-2795

AMOUNT: $4,000-$6,000; $500 for technical courses

DEADLINE(S): None specified

FIELD(S): Healthcare fields such as Registered Nurse, Medical Lab, Pharmacy, Physical Therapy, etc.

Open to undergrad and grad students accepted into an accredited healthcare school and within 2 years of completing course work. Student must agree to work at AMC for 3 years following graduation (1 year for tech school students).

Must be Georgia resident. Personal interview required. Repayment is required if recipient fails to work at Archbold for the designated period. Write for complete information.

2577 — ARTHUR M. MILLER FUND

P.O. Box 1122
Wichita KS 67201-0004
316/261-4609

AMOUNT: Varies

DEADLINE(S): MAR 31

FIELD(S): Medicine or related fields

Scholarships for Kansas residents for the study of medicine or related fields at accredited instutitions.

Send SASE for formal application.

2578 — AUSTRIAN CULTURAL INSTITUTE (Max Kade Foundation Grants)

950 Third Ave.
20th Fl.
New York NY 10022
212/759-5165 or +43/1/51581-253

FAX: 212/319-9636

E-Mail: desk@aci.org

Internet: www.austriaculture.net

AMOUNT: Varies

DEADLINE(S): Varies

FIELD(S): Medicine; Natural Sciences; Engineering

Open to young Austrian scientists with several years of experience at universities or institutions. Must demonstrate capacity to pursue independent teaching or research activities in the US. Proficiency in English required.

See website or contact ACI for an application kit, or write to Osterreichische Akademie der Wissenschaften, Kommission fur Max Kade Stipendien, Dr. Ignaz Seipel-Platz 2, A-1010 Vienna, Austria.

2579 — BECA FOUNDATION (Alice Newell Joslyn Medical Fund)

310 Via Vera Cruz, Ste. 101

San Marcos CA 92069

760/471-5465

FAX: 760/471-9175

AMOUNT: $500-$2,000

DEADLINE(S): MAR 1

FIELD(S): Medicine; Health Care; Nursing; Dental/Medical Assisting; Physical Therapy

Open to Latino students who live in or attend college in San Diego County, CA, at time of application. For high school seniors and those already in college pursuing undergraduate or graduate education. Based on financial need, scholastic determination, and community/cultural awareness. BECA also provides a mentor to each scholarship recipient.

Send self-addressed, stamped envelope to BECA for an application.

2580 — BOEING (Polish Graduate Student Scholarship Program)

Phone

Phone for details

314/234-2149

AMOUNT: Tuition, books, and fees for three years

DEADLINE(S): Varies

FIELD(S): Scientific and technical fields

Scholarships for students from Poland to pursue graduate studies in scientific and technical areas at American colleges or universities.

Call Jim Schlueter at above telephone number.

2581 — CALIFORNIA GRANGE FOUNDATION (Deaf Activities Scholarships)

Pat Avila, 2101 Stockton Blvd.

Sacramento CA 95817

Written inquiry

AMOUNT: Varies

DEADLINE(S): APR 1

FIELD(S): Course work which will be of benefit to the deaf community

Scholarships students entering, continuing, or returning to college to pursue studies that will benefit the deaf community.

Write for information after Feb. 1 of each year.

2582 — CANADIAN FEDERATION OF UNIVERSITY WOMEN (CFUW Memorial/Professional Fellowship)

251 Bank St., Ste. 600

Ottawa Ontario K2P 1X3 CANADA

613/234-2732

Internet: www.cfuw.ca

AMOUNT: $5,000

DEADLINE(S): NOV 15

FIELD(S): Science & Technology

Open to women who are Canadian citizens/permanent residents enrolled in a master's degree program in science and technology. Must hold at least a bachelor's degree or equivalent from a recognized university and have been accepted into, or be currently enrolled in the proposed program and place of study. May be studying abroad.

$25 filing fee. Contact CFUW for an application after August 1st. Candidates will be notified by May 31st.

2583 — COLUMBIANA COUNTY PUBLIC HEALTH LEAGUE TRUST FUND (Grants)

PO Box 1428

Steubenville OH 43952

740/283-8433

FAX: 740/282-4530

AMOUNT: Varies

DEADLINE(S): FEB 28

FIELD(S): Respiratory Illness; Medicine; Medical Research; Pharmacy; Medical Technology; Physical Therapy; Nursing; Dental Hygiene; Occupational Therapy

Open to undergraduate and graduate Columbiana County, Ohio, residents who are pursuing medical education or research in one of the above fields. Preference given to respiratory illness. Students of veterinary medicine NOT eligible.

Contact Sherrill Schmied for an application.

2584 — CONCORDIA UNIVERSITY (J.P. Zewig Scholarship)

1455 de Maisonneuve Blvd. West

Room M 201

Montreal Quebec H3G 1M8 CANADA

514/848-3809

FAX: 514/848-2812

E-Mail: awardsgs@vax2.concordia.ca

AMOUNT: Varies

DEADLINE(S): SEP 20

FIELD(S): Psychology; Exercise Science; Behaviourial Medicine

This one-year scholarship is awarded to a graduate student pursuing research in the above areas. Candidates are to be nominated by Faculty members from these areas of research.

1 award annually. Not renewable. Contact the Graduate Awards Office in the School of Graduate Studies at Concordia University for nomination procedures.

2585 — CYNTHIA E. AND CLARA H. HOLLIS FOUNDATION

100 Summer St.

Boston MA 02110

Written inquiry

AMOUNT: Varies

DEADLINE(S): APR 1

FIELD(S): Nursing, social work, dental or medical technology, and religion

Scholarships for Massachusetts with preference given to students in the above fields. For undergraduates, graduates, voc-tech, and adult education. Must demonstrate financial need.

Send SASE to Walter E. Palmer, Esq., 35 Harvard St., Brookline, MA 02146 for application details. Scholarship forms are also available from the rector of All Saints Church, Brookline High School, and St. Mary's High School, all in Brookline, Massachusetts.

2586 — DELTA SOCIETY (James M. Harris/Sarah W. Sweatt Student Travel Grant)

289 Perimeter Rd. East

Benton WA 98055-1329

425/226-7357

FAX: 425/235-1076

E-Mail: deltasociety@cis.compuserve.com

Internet: www.deltasociety.org

AMOUNT: Varies

DEADLINE(S): Varies

FIELD(S): Human-Animal Interactions; Animal Assisted Therapy; Service Animals; Pet Loss

Travel grants for graduate/postgraduate students to attend Delta Society's annual conference. Must be a full-time student in veterinary human health care. Student must provide detailed plan of how conference information will be shared. Must also attend the full conference and demonstrate ability to cover costs of registration, hotel, and meals. Financial need NOT a factor.

2-4 awards annually. Contact Michelle Cobey for an application.

2587 — DEPARTMENT OF THE ARMY (Health Professionals Loan Repayment Program)

Attn: RC-HS
1307 Third Ave.
Fort Knox KY 40121
502/626-0367
FAX: 502/626-0923

AMOUNT: $20,000/yr. (max.)

DEADLINE(S): None

FIELD(S): Medicine; Nursing

Loan repayment is open to health professionals fully qualified in critically short wartime specialties who serve in a military reserve. Specialties include physician assistants; general dentists; oral surgeons; critical care & nurse anesthetists; general, thoracic, & orthopedic surgeons; urologists; diagnostic radiologists; psychiatrists; preventative & critical care medicine; and primary care physicians.

Contact Major Beecher at above address for an application.

2588 — DUPAGE COUNTY MEDICAL SOCIETY FOUNDATION (Scholarship Program)

498 Hillside Ave., #1
Glen Ellyn IL 60137
630/858-9603

AMOUNT: $250-$1,000

DEADLINE(S): APR 30

FIELD(S): Medical/Health-Care Fields

Open to voting residents of Dupage County, Illinois, who are accepted to or enrolled in a professional training program at a qualified school. Based on financial need and scholastic ability. Program does not apply to undergraduate studies, such as pre-med; students would be eligible after completing four-year pre-med program and having been accepted into medical school.

Contact Medical Society for an application.

2589 — EASTER SEAL SOCIETY OF IOWA, INC. (Scholarships & Awards)

P.O. Box 4002
Des Moines IA 50333-4002
515/289-1933

AMOUNT: $400-$600

DEADLINE(S): APR 15

FIELD(S): Physical Rehabilitation, Mental Rehabilitation, and related areas

Open ONLY to Iowa residents who are full-time undergraduate sophomores, juniors, seniors, or graduate students at accredited institutions planning a career in the broad field of rehabilitation. Must indicate financial need and be in top 40% of their class.

6 scholarships per year. Must re-apply each year.

2590 — EDUCATIONAL AND SCIENTIFIC TRUST OF THE PENNSYLVANIA MEDICAL SOCIETY (Loan Program for Allied Health/Nursing Students)

777 East Park Drive
PO Box 8820
Harrisburg PA 17105-8820
717/558-7750, Ext. 1257
FAX: 717/558-7818
E-Mail: studentloans-trust@pamedsoc.org
Internet: www.pitt.edu/HOME/GHNet/PA_Trust

AMOUNT: Up to $1,500 for bona fide Pennsylvania residents

DEADLINE(S): JUN 1

FIELD(S): Nursing and allied health fields

Open to Pennsylvania residents with demonstrated financial need who are seeking a career in nursing or an allied health field. Must be attending a Pennsylvania institution.

Approx. 200 loans per year. Must be U.S. citizen. Contact above location for complete information.

2591 — EDWARD BANGS KELLEY AND ELZA KELLEY FOUNDATION, INC. (Scholarship Program)

PO Drawer M
Hyannis MA 02601-1412
508/775-3117

AMOUNT: $4,000 (max.)

DEADLINE(S): APR 30

FIELD(S): Medicine; Nursing; Health Sciences

Open to residents of Barnstable County, Massachusetts. Scholarships are intended to benefit health and welfare of Barnstable County residents. Awards support study at recognized undergraduate, graduate, and professional institutions. Financial need is considered.

Contact Foundation for an application.

2592 — ESPN (Internship Programs)

Human Resources Dept.
ESPN, Inc.
ESPN Plaza
Bristol CT 06010
No phone calls. Internet:
espnet.sportszone.com/editors/studios/97faq.html

AMOUNT: Paid Internships

DEADLINE(S): OCT 1; MAR 1; JUN 1

FIELD(S): Television Industry, Public Relations, Sports

12-week internships in the spring, summer, and fall for undergraduate juniors/seniors and graduate students. Some areas require weekend/evening hours and a strong knowledge of sports. Interns receive hourly wages and take part in many company-sponsored activities. ESPN does not provide housing for students, but we do try to assist in finding suitable living arrangements once selected.

To apply for internship programs, please send cover letter and resume to the above address. If applying to the Communications Dept., please also enclose writing samples and send attention to Diane Lamb.

2593 — FELLOWS MEMORIAL FUND (Scholarship Loans)

Pensacola Junior College, 1000 College Blvd.
Pensacola FL 32504-8998
904/484-1706

AMOUNT: Individually determined

DEADLINE(S): Varies (Individually arranged)

FIELD(S): Nursing and Medical Technology

Loans for students accepted for training in nursing or in one of the several fields of medical technology at accredited schools or colleges. Appropriate for two- or four-year nursing programs, graduate nursing study, medical or surgical technology, anesthesiology, and radiological technology. Must be residents of one of the following Florida counties: Escambia, Santa Rosa, Okaloosa, or Walton

Loans are interest-free until four months after graduation. Thereafter, favorable interest rates will apply with the total to be paid by the end of eleven years.

2594 — FELLOWS MEMORIAL FUND (Scholarship Loans)

Pensacola Junior College
1000 College Blvd.
Pensacola FL 32504-8998
904/484-1700

AMOUNT: Varies

DEADLINE(S): Varies

FIELD(S): Theology; Health

Loans for ministerial students of the Episcopal faith and others whose religious beliefs are not in substantial conflict with the faith and doctrines of the Episcopal Church. Must be graduate students and residents of one of the following Florida counties: Escambia, Santa Rosa, Okaloosa, or Walton. Qualified health programs include medicine, nursing, medical technology, radiography, respiratory therapy, physical therapy, and physician's assistant.

Loans are interest-free until four months after graduation. Thereafter, favorable interest rates will apply with the total to be repaid by the end of eleven years.

2595 — FIRST UNITED METHODIST CHURCH (Robert Stevenson & Doreene E. Cater Scholarships)

302 5th Ave., S.
St. Cloud MN 56301
FAX: 320/251-0878
E-Mail: FUMCloud@aol.com

AMOUNT: $100-$300

DEADLINE(S): JUN 1

FIELD(S): Humanitarian & Christian Service: Teaching, Medicine, Social Work, Environmental Studies, etc.

Stevenson Scholarship is open to undergraduate members of the First United Methodist Church of St. Cloud. Cater Scholarship is open to members of the Minnesota United Methodist Conference who are entering the sophomore year or higher of college work. Both require two letters of reference, transcripts, and financial need.

5-6 awards annually. Contact Scholarship Committee for an application.

2596 — FOUNDATION FOR SEACOAST HEALTH (Scholarship Program)

P.O. Box 4606
Portsmouth NH 03802-4606
603/433-3008
FAX: 603/433-2036
E-Mail: ffsh@nh.ultranet.com
Internet: www.nh.ultranet.com/~ffsh

AMOUNT: $1,000-10,000

DEADLINE(S): FEB 1

FIELD(S): Health-related fields

Open to undergraduate and graduate students pursuing health-related fields of study who are legal residents of the following cities in New Hampshire: Portsmouth, Newington, New Castle, Rye, Greenland, N. Hampton, or these cities in Maine: Kittery, Eliot, or York, Maine. Must have resided in the area for at least two years.

Write or check website for details. $150,000 awarded annually; 35 awards given

2597 — GRACE FOUNDATION SCHOLARSHIP TRUST FUND

P.O. Box 924
Menlo Park CA 94026-0924
Written inquiry

AMOUNT: $1,000 to $4,000

DEADLINE(S): JAN 31

FIELD(S): Christian

One-year scholarships for full or partial tuition payment for full-time study at an accredited college or university. For training future Christian ministers and professional workers in developing countries in Asia/Southeast Asia. Candidates must have completed one or more years of college in or near their native country, be a strong Christian, have a 3.0 or higher GPA, and be pursuing a career in either the ministry, medicine, teaching, or social service.

Renewable up to graduation—four years maximum—pending maintenance of 3.0 GPA. Applications available between Sept. 1 and Oct. 31. Must demonstrate financial need.

2598 — INTERNATIONAL ORDER OF THE KING'S DAUGHTERS AND SONS (Health Careers Scholarships)

c/o Mrs. Fred Cannon
Box 1310
Brookhaven MS 39602
Written Inquiry

AMOUNT: $1,000 (max.)

DEADLINE(S): APR 1

FIELD(S): Medicine; Dentistry; Nursing; Physical Therapy; Occupational Therapy; Medical Technologies; Pharmacy

Open to students accepted to/enrolled in an accredited US or Canadian four-year or graduate school. RN candidates must have completed first year of program; MD or DDS candidates must be for at least the second year of medical or dental school; all others must be in at least third year of four-year program. Pre-med students NOT eligible. Must be US or Canadian citizen.

Send self-addressed, stamped envelope, along with a letter stating the field of study and present level, to the Director at above address for an application.

2599 — JEWISH VOCATIONAL SERVICE (Marcus & Theresa Levie Educational Fund Scholarships)

1 S. Franklin St.
Chicago IL 60606
312/346-6700

AMOUNT: To $5,000

DEADLINE(S): MAR 1

FIELD(S): Social Work, Medicine, Dentistry, Nursing, & other related professions & vocations

Open to Cook County residents of the Jewish faith who plan careers in the above fields. For undergraduate juniors and seniors and graduate students. Applications available Dec. 1 from Scholarship Secretary.

Must show financial need. 85-100 awards per year. Renewal possible with reapplication. Write for complete information.

2600 — KING FAISAL FOUNDATION (Graduate Scholarship Program)

PO Box 352
Riyadh 11411 SAUDI ARABIA
966/1 465-2255
FAX: 966/1 465-6524
E-Mail: info@kff.com OR mprd@kff.com
Internet: www.kff.com OR www.kingfaisalfoundation.org

AMOUNT: $400/mo. US allowance + tuition/fees paid directly to university + health insurance & travel

DEADLINE(S): None

FIELD(S): Medicine; Engineering; Physics; Chemistry; Geology

Open to graduate students who are Muslims under the age of 40. Must have BS degree, GPA of 86% or higher, and be accepted unconditionally by a university either in Europe or North America. Must be fluent in the language of area providing the studies. Selection based on academic performance.

Contact King Faisal Foundation for an application.

2601 — LABAN/BARTENIEFF INSTITUTE OF MOVEMENT STUDIES (Work-Study Programs)

234 Fifth Ave., Rm. 203
New York NY 10001
212/477-4299
FAX: 212/477-3702
E-Mail: limsinfo@erols.com

AMOUNT: $500-$1,500

DEADLINE(S): MAY 1

FIELD(S): Human Movement Studies

Open to graduate students and professionals in dance, education, health fields, behavioral sciences, fitness, athletic training, etc. Tenable for work-study ONLY at the Laban/Bartenieff Institute in New York.

Contact LIMS for an application.

2602 — MARYLAND HIGHER EDUCATION COMMISSION (Tuition Reimbursement of Firefighters & Rescue Squad Members)

State Scholarship Admin.
16 Francis St.
Annapolis MD 21401
410/974-5370
TTY: 800/735-2258
Internet: www.ubalt.edu/www.mhec

AMOUNT: Varies (current resident undergraduate tuition rate at Univ. MD-College Park)

DEADLINE(S): JUL 1

FIELD(S): Firefighting; Emergency Medical Technology

Open to firefighters and rescue squad members who successfully comple one year of coursework in a firefighting or EMT program and a two-year service obligation in Maryland.

Contact MHEC for an application.

2603 — MINNESOTA HIGHER EDUCATION SERVICES OFFICE (Health Professions Loan Forgiveness)

Capitol Square Bldg., Ste. 400
550 Cedar St.
St. Paul MN 55101
612/296-3974
FAX: 612/297-8880
E-Mail: info@heso.state.mn.us
Internet: www.heso.state.mn.us/

AMOUNT: Varies

DEADLINE(S): None

FIELD(S): Health Professions

Five loan repayment programs for health professionals who agree to serve in federally designated Health Professional Shortage Areas, in designated, underserved urban or rural areas, in licensed nursing homes, or in intermediate care facilities for persons with mental retardation or related conditions.

For details contact Office of Rural Health and Primary Care at 612/282-3838 or 800/366-5424 (Minnesota only).

2604 — McCORD CAREER CENTER (Level II McCord Medical/Music Scholarship)

Healdsburg High School
1024 Prince St.
Healdsburg CA 95448
707/431-3473

AMOUNT: Varies

DEADLINE(S): APR 30

FIELD(S): Medicine; Music

For graduates of Healdsburg High School who are planning a career in music or medicine. Must be enrolled full-time at a college/university as an undergraduate junior or senior in the fall, or earning an advanced degree in graduate or medical school, or entering into a vocational/certificate program. Transcripts, proof of attendance, and an essay are required.

Contact the McCord Career Center at Healdsburg High School for an application.

2605 — NATIONAL ASSOCIATION OF AMERICAN BUSINESS CLUBS (AMBUCS Scholarships for Therapists)

P.O. Box 5127
High Point NC 27262
910/869-2166
FAX: 910/887-8451
E-Mail: ambucs@ambucs.com
Internet: www.ambucs.com

AMOUNT: $500-$6,000

DEADLINE(S): APR 15

FIELD(S): Physical Therapy, Music Therapy, Occupational Therapy, Speech-Language Pathology, Audiology, Rehabilitation, Recreation Therapy, and related areas.

Open to undergraduate juniors and seniors or graduate students who have good scholastic standing and plan to enter the fields listed above. GPA of 3.0 or better (4.0 scale) and US citizenship required. Must demonstrate financial need.

Renewable. Please include a self-addressed stamped envelope (SASE); applications are mailed in December; incomplete applications will not be considered.

2606 — NATIONAL ASSOCIATION OF THE DEAF (Stokoe Scholarship)

814 Thayer Ave.
Silver Spring MD 20910-4500
301/587-1788
TTY: 301/587-1789
FAX: 301/587-1791
E-Mail: NADinfo@nad.org
Internet: www.nad.org

AMOUNT: $2,000

DEADLINE(S): MAR 15

FIELD(S): Sign Language; Deaf Community

Open to deaf students who have graduated from a four-year college program and are pursuing part-time or full-time graduate studies in a field related to sign language or the deaf community, or a deaf graduate student who is developing a special project on one of these topics.

Send a self-addressed, stamped, business-sized envelope to NAD for an application.

2607 — NATIONAL ATHLETIC TRAINERS' ASSOCIATION (NATA Scholarship Program)

2952 Stemmons Freeway
Dallas TX 75247
214/637-6282
FAX: 214/637-2206

AMOUNT: $2,000

DEADLINE(S): FEB 1

FIELD(S): Athletic Training

Open to student members of NATA who have excellent academic records and have excelled as student athletic trainers. Undergraduates may apply after completion of sophomore year, and graduates may apply after completion of fall semester of their undergraduate senior year. Must have a minimum 3.0 GPA.

Send self-addressed, stamped envelope to NATA for membership information or an application.

2608 — NATIONAL HEALTH SERVICE CORPS (NHSC Scholarship Program)

2070 Chain Bridge Rd,, Ste. 450
Vienna VA 22182-2536
800/221-9393
Internet: www.bphc.hrsa.dhhs.gov/nhsc

AMOUNT: Full tuition/books/fees/supplies + monthly stipend

DEADLINE(S): MAR

FIELD(S): Family Medicine; General Internal Medicine; General Pediatrics; Obstetrics/Gynecology; Family Nurse Practitioners; Primary Care Physician Assistants; Certified Nurse-Midwives

Must be US citizen attending or enrolled in fully accredited US allopathic/osteopathic medical school, nursing program, or physician assistant program. For each year of support received, you must serve one year in federally designated health professional shortage area of greatest need. Minimum two years service commitment begins upon completion of your residency and/or training.

300 awards annually. Renewable up to 4 years. Contact NHSC for an application.

2609 — NATIONAL STRENGTH & CONDITIONING ASSN. (Challenge Scholarships)

P.O. Box 38909
Colorado Springs CO 80937-8909
719/632-6722
FAX: 719/632-6722
E-Mail: nsca@usa.net
Internet: www.colosoft.com/nsca

AMOUNT: $1,000

DEADLINE(S): MAR 1

FIELD(S): Fields related to body strength & conditioning

Open to National Strength & Conditioning Association members. Awards are for undergraduate or graduate study.

For membership information or an application, write to the above address.

2610 — NATIONAL STRENGTH & CONDITIONING ASSN. (Student Research Grant Program)

P.O. Box 38909
Colorado Springs CO 80937-8909
719/632-6722
FAX: 719/632-6367
E-Mail: nsca@usa.net
Internet: www.colosoft.com/nsca

AMOUNT: $1,500

DEADLINE(S): FEB 3 (letter of intent); MAR 17 (submission)

FIELD(S): Fields related to body strength & conditioning

Research grants for graduate students who are members of National Strength & Conditioning Association. A graduate faculty member is required to serve as a co-investigator in the study.

Two annual awards. For membership information or an application, write to the above address.

2611 — NAVY RECRUITING COMMAND (Armed Forces Health Professions Scholarships)

Commander
801 N. Randolph St.
Code 325
Arlington VA 22203-1991
800/USA-NAVY or 703/696-4926
E-Mail: omegahouse@erols.com
Internet: www.navyjobs.com

AMOUNT: $938/month stipend + tuition, fees, books, lab fees, etc.

DEADLINE(S): APR 28

FIELD(S): Medicine, Dentistry, Optometry, Physical Therapy, Pharmacology, Health Care Administration, Industrial Hygiene, etc.

Open to US citizens enrolled or accepted for enrollment in any of the above fields at an accredited institution in the US or Puerto Rico. Must qualify for appointment as a Navy officer and sign a contractual agreement. Must be between the ages of 18 & 36 and have a GPA of at least 3.0.

See website, contact local Navy Recruiting Office, or contact Lieutenant Roger A. House, MPA, CAAMA, Medical Service Corps at above address.

2612 — NEW YORK STATE DEPARTMENT OF HEALTH - PRIMARY CARE SERVICE CORPS (Scholarships)

Corning Tower, Room 1084
Empire State Plaza
Albany NY 12237-0053
518/473-7019

AMOUNT: $15,000

DEADLINE(S): APR 3

FIELD(S): Certified Physician Assistant; Nurse Practitioner; Midwife

Open to New York State residents enrolled at, accepted to, or applied at an approved graduate, undergraduate, or certificate course of study. Must be within 24 months of completion of professional training full-time, or within 48 months of completion on a part-time basis.

Contact NY State Dept. of Health for an application.

2613 — NEW YORK STATE HIGHER EDUCATION SERVICES CORPORATION (N.Y. State Regents Professional/Health Care Opportunity Scholarships)

Cultural Education Center, Rm. 5C64
Albany NY 12230
518/486-1319
Internet: www.hesc.com

AMOUNT: $1,000-$10,000/yr.

DEADLINE(S): Varies

FIELD(S): Medicine and dentistry and related fields, architecture, nursing, psychology, audiology, landscape architecture, social work, chiropractic, law, pharmacy, accounting, speech language pathology

For NY state residents who are economically disadvantaged and members of a minority group underrepresented in the chosen profession and attending school in NY state. Some programs carry a service obligation in New York for each year of support. For U.S. citizens or qualifying noncitizens.

Medical/dental scholarships require one year of professional work in NY.

2614 — NORTH CAROLINA DEPARTMENT OF PUBLIC INSTRUCTION (Scholarship Loan Program for Prospective Teachers)

301 N. Wilmington St.
Raleigh NC 27601-2825
919/715-1120

AMOUNT: Up to $2,500/yr.

DEADLINE(S): FEB

FIELD(S): Education: Teaching, school psychology and counseling, speech/language impaired, audiology, library/media services

For NC residents planning to teach in NC public schools. At least 3.0 high school GPA required; must maintain 2.5 GPA during freshman year and 3.0 cumulative thereafter. Recipients are obligated to teach one year in an NC public school for each year of assistance. Those who do not fulfill their teaching obligation are required to repay the loan plus interest.

200 awards per year. For full-time students. Applications available in Dec. from high school counselors and college and univerwity departments of education.

2615 — NOVARTIS FOUNDATION (Bursary Scheme)

41 Portland Place
London W1N 4BN ENGLAND UK
+44 171 636 9456
FAX: +44 171 436 2840
E-Mail: abrown@novartisfound.org.uk
Internet: www.novartisfound.org.uk

AMOUNT: Travel & subsistence—up to $6,000/person

DEADLINE(S): Varies

FIELD(S): Science; Medicine

Travel fellowships to young scientists (postgrad/doc) to attend international meetings in connection with the Novartis Foundation Symposia. Must be between the ages of 23 and 35, and be active in the field of science in question. Symposia is normally in London, and a 4-week to 12-week host laboratory in the department of one of the symposium participants follows. Specific topics vary. Must submit qualifications, resume, career history/goals, and research interests.

8 awards annually. Not renewable. See website or contact Allyson Brown for application procedures.

2616 — OAK RIDGE INSTITUTE FOR SCIENCE AND EDUCATION (Industrial Hygiene Graduate Fellowship Program)

P.O. Box 117
Oak Ridge TN 37831-0117
423-576-9655
FAX: 423/576-8293
E-Mail: kinneym@orau.gov

AMOUNT:

DEADLINE(S): JAN 26

FIELD(S): Industrial Hygiene

A fellowship for first-year master's candidates who have undergraduate degrees in physical, life, environmental, or health sciences or enginering and who wish to pursue studies in industrial hygiene.

For details and application, contact above location.

2617 — PILOT INTERNATIONAL FOUNDATION (Marie Newton Sepia Memorial Scholarship)

P.O. Box 5600
Macon GA 31208-5600
Written inquiries

AMOUNT: Varies

DEADLINE(S): MAR 1

FIELD(S): Disabilities/Brain-related Disorders in Children

This program assists graduate students preparing for careers working with children having disabilities/brain disorders. Must have GPA of 3.5 or greater.

Applicants must be sponsored by a Pilot Club in their home town or in the city in which their college or university is located. Send a self-addressed, stamped envelope for complete information.

2618 — PILOT INTERNATIONAL FOUNDATION (PIF/Lifeline Scholarship)

P.O. Box 5600
Macon GA 31208-5600
Written inquiries

AMOUNT: Varies

DEADLINE(S): MAR 1

FIELD(S): Disabilities/Brain-related Disorders

This program assists ADULT students re-entering the job market, preparing for a second career, or improving their professional skills for an established career. Applicants must be preparing for, or already involved in, careers working with people with disabilities/brain-related disorders. GPA of 3.5 or more is required.

Must be sponsored by a Pilot Club in your home town, or in the city in which your college or university is located. Send a self-addressed, stamped envelope for complete information.

2619 — PILOT INTERNATIONAL FOUNDATION (Ruby Newhall Memorial Scholarship)

P.O. Box 5600
Macon, GA 31208-5600
Written Inquiries

AMOUNT: Varies

DEADLINE(S): MAR 15

FIELD(S): Disabilities/Brain-related disorders

For international students who have studied in the US for at least one year, and who intend to return to their home country six months after graduation. Applicants must be full-time students majoring in a field related to human health and welfare, and have a GPA of 3.5 or more.

Applicants must be sponsored by a Pilot Club in their home town, or in the city in which their college or university is located. Send a self-addressed, stamped envelope for complete information.

2620 — ROCKEFELLER FOUNDATION (African Dissertation Internship Awards)

420 Fifth Ave.
New York NY 10018-2702
212/869-8500
212/764-3468
Internet: www.rockfound.org

AMOUNT: Cost of project

DEADLINE(S): None given

FIELD(S): Agriculture, environment, health, life sciences, population, and schooling

For African graduate students in U.S. and Canadian universities (but not to permanent residents) to return to Africa to carry out dissertation research at a local university or research institution. Priority given to above topics.

Students are strongly urged to be in the field for at least 12 months. Contact above location for details.

2621 — SERTOMA FOUNDATION INTERNATIONAL (Communicative Disorders Scholarships)

1912 East Meyer Blvd.
Kansas City MO 64132
Phone & TTY: 816/333/8300
FAX: 816/333-4320

AMOUNT: $2,500

DEADLINE(S): None specified

FIELD(S): Audiology or Speech Pathology

For students pursuing master's degrees in the above fields from institutions in the U.S., Canada, or Mexico. Must be a citizen and permanent resident of one of those countries. The institution must be: 1. U.S.-accredited by ASHA's Council on Academic Accreditation; 2. Canada-a university which offers such a program; 3. Mexico-licenciatura program for Human Communication at the University of the Americas, Mexico City. Must have at least 3.2 GPA.

30 awards. Send for application beginning in October. Send #10 SASE to "$2,500 Scholarships" at above address.

2622 — SIR ROBERT MENZIES MEMORIAL FOUNDATION LIMITED (Research Scholarship in Allied Health Sciences)

210 Clarendon Street
East Melbourne Vic 3002 AUSTRALIA
03 9419 5699
FAX: 03 9417 7049
E-Mail: menzies@vicnet.net.au
Internet: www.vincent.net.au/~menzies

AMOUNT: $AUD.24,000 p.a.

DEADLINE(S): JUN 30

FIELD(S): Allied Health

Postgraduate research scholarships for Australian citizens enrolled as full-time Ph.D. students at Australian institutions. Must be studying allied health fields, such as nursing, physiotherapy, psychology, occupational therapy, speech pathology, etc. Award is based on academic excellence. Financial need NOT a factor.

1 award annually. Contact Ms. Sandra Mackenzie for an application.

2623 — STATE STUDENT ASSISTANCE COMMISSION OF INDIANA (Scholarships for Special Education Teachers & Physical/ Occupational Therapists)

150 W. Market St.
5th Fl.
Indianapolis IN 46204
317/232-2350
FAX: 317/232-3260
E-Mail: grants@ssaci.in.us
Internet: www.ai.org/ssaci/

AMOUNT: $1,000

DEADLINE(S): Varies (with college)

FIELD(S): Special Education; Physical & Occupational Therapy

Open to Indiana residents pursuing full-time undergraduate or graduate study in special education or physical or occupational therapy at an Indiana college/university. Must be US citizen, have a minimum 2.0 GPA, and demonstrate financial need.

See website or contact SSACI for an application.

2624 — THRASHER RESEARCH FUND (Research Fellowship)

50 East North Temple St.
Salt Lake City UT 84150
801/240-4753
FAX 801/240-1625

AMOUNT: Up to $50,000/yr.—up to 3 years.

DEADLINE(S): None

FIELD(S): Child Research

Supports child health research in the areas of nutrition and infectious diseases and practical field projects aimed at improving the health and well being of mothers and children.

Investigators should consult with fund personnel before submitting prospectus. Write for complete information.

2625 — U.S. DEPT. OF HEALTH & HUMAN SERVICES (Indian Health Service Health Professions Scholarship Program)

Twinbrook Metro Plaza, Suite 100
12300 Twinbrook Pkwy.
Rockville MD 20852
301/443-0234
FAX: 301/443-4815
Internet: www.ihs.gov/Recruitment/DHPS/SP/ SBTOC3.asp

AMOUNT: Tuition + fees & monthly stipend of $938.

DEADLINE(S): APR 1

FIELD(S): Health professions, accounting, social work

Open to Native Americans or Alaska natives who are graduate students or college juniors or seniors in a program leading to a career in a fields listed above. U.S. citizenship required. Renewable annually with reapplication.

Scholarship recipients must intend to serve the Indian people. They incur a one-year service obligation to the IHS for each year of support for a minimum of two years. Write for complete information.

2626 — UNIFORMED SERVICES UNIVERSITY OF THE HEALTH SCIENCES (Fellowships)

Schools of Medicine & Nursing
4301 Jones Bridge Rd.
Bethesda MD 20814-4799
301/295-3101 or 800/772-1743

AMOUNT: Tuition

DEADLINE(S): NOV 1

FIELD(S): Medicine; Nursing

Open to graduate students who wish to attend the F. Edward Hebert School of Medicine or the Graduate School of Nursing with the understanding that they will be trained for service to the nation, including assignments abroad or at sea. While enrolled, students serve as reserve commissioned officers. Must be US citizen.

Contact Uniformed Services University for an application.

2627 — UNIVERSITY OF EDINBURGH (Faculty of Medicine Bursaries & Scholarships)

7-11 Nicolson St.
Edinburgh SCOTLAND EH8 9BE UK
+44 (0) 131 650 1000
Internet: www.iprs.ed.ac.uk/progawards/medicine/

AMOUNT: Varies

DEADLINE(S): MAR 1; NOV 1

FIELD(S): Medicine

Various scholarships, bursaries, and travel awards for medical students at all levels of study. For use at the University of Edinburgh, Scotland. Some are for students from other companies; some are for women; some are for specific specialties.

Access website for more information and/or contact school for details and appropriate application forms.

2628 — WASHINGTON STATE HIGHER EDUCATION COORDINATING BOARD (Health Professional Loan Repayment & Scholarship Program)

PO Box 43430
Olympia WA 98504-3430
360/753-7850
FAX: 360/753-7808
Internet: www.hecb.wa.gov

AMOUNT: Varies

DEADLINE(S): APR (scholarship); FEB (loan repayment); JUL (loan repayment)

FIELD(S): Health Care

Scholarships are open to students in accredited undergraduate or graduate health care programs leading to eligibility for licensure in Washington state. Must agree to work in designated shortage area for minimum of three years. Loan repayment recipients

receive payment from program for purpose of repaying education loans secured while attending program of health care training leading to licensure in Washington state. Financial need NOT a factor.

Renewable up to 5 years. Contact Program Manager for a loan repayment application after November 15th and for scholarship application after January 15th.

2629 — WOMEN OF THE EVANGELICAL LUTHERAN CHURCH IN AMERICA (The Kahler-Vickers/Raup-Emma Wettstein Scholarships)

8765 West Higgins Road
Chicago IL 60631-4189
800/638-3522, ext. 2747
FAX: 773/380-2419
E-Mail: womnelca@elca.org

AMOUNT: $2,000 max.

DEADLINE(S): MAR 1

FIELD(S): Health Professions & Christian Service

Assists women who are members of the ELCA studying for service in health professions associated with ELCA projects abroad that do not lead to church-certified professions. Must be US citizen and have experienced an interruption of two or more years since completion of high school. Academic records of coursework completed in last five years as well as proof of admission from educational institution are required.

Renewable for an additional year. Contact Faith Fretheim, Program Director, for an application.

2630 — WOMEN'S SPORTS FOUNDATION (Dorothy Harris Endowed Scholarship)

Eisenhower Park
East Meadow NY 11554
800/227-3988
FAX: 516/542-4716
E-Mail: WoSport@aol.com
Internet: www.lifetimetv.com/WoSport

AMOUNT: $1,500

DEADLINE(S): DEC 11

FIELD(S): Physical Education; Sports Management; Sports Psychology; Sports Sociology

For female graduate students who will pursue a full-time course of study in one of the above fields at an accredited graduate school in the Fall.

1-2 awards annually. Awarded in March. See website or write to above address for details.

2631 — WOMEN'S SPORTS FOUNDATION (Jackie Joyner-Kersee & Zina Garrison Minority Internships)

Eisenhower Park
East Meadow NY 11554
800/227-3988

FAX: 516/542-4716
E-Mail: WoSport@aol.com
Internet: www.lifetimetv.com/WoSport

AMOUNT: $4,000-$5,000

DEADLINE(S): Ongoing

FIELD(S): Sports-related fields

Provides women of color an opportunity to gain experience in a sports-related career and interact in the sports community. May be undergraduates, college graduates, graduate students, or women in a career change. Internships are located at the Women's Sports Foundation in East Meadow, New York.

4-6 awards annually. See website or write to above address for details.

2632 — ZETA PHI BETA SORORITY EDUCATIONAL FOUNDATION (S. Evelyn Lewis Memorial Scholarship in Medical Health Sciences)

1734 New Hampshire Ave., NW
Washington DC 20009
Internet: www.zpb1920.org/nefforms.htm

AMOUNT: $500-$1,000

DEADLINE(S): FEB 1

FIELD(S): Medicine; Health Sciences

Open to graduate and undergraduate young women enrolled in a program leading to a degree in medicine or health sciences. Award is for full-time study for one academic year (Fall-Spring) and is paid directly to college/university. Must submit proof of enrollment.

Send self-addressed, stamped envelope to above address between September 1st and December 15th for an application.

NURSING

2633 — AMERICAN COLLEGE OF LEGAL MEDICINE (Student Writing Competition)

611 E. Wells St.
Milwaukee WI 53202
800/433-9137 or 414/276-1881
FAX: 414/276-3349
E-Mail: info@aclm.org
Internet: www.aclm.org

AMOUNT: $1,000

DEADLINE(S): FEB 1

FIELD(S): Legal Medicine

Award for the best paper on any aspect of legal medicine. Open to postgraduate students enrolled in an accredited school of law, medicine, dentistry, podiatry, nursing, pharmacy, health science, or health care administration in the US or Canada.

3 awards annually. Contact Laura Morrone at ACLM for entry rules.

2634 — AMERICAN COLLEGE OF NURSE-MIDWIVES FOUNDATION (Scholarship Program)

818 Connecticut Ave., NW, Ste. 900
Washington DC 20006
202/728-9865
FAX: 202/728-9897

AMOUNT: Varies

DEADLINE(S): FEB 15

FIELD(S): Nurse-Midwifery

Open to students currently enrolled in ACNM-accredited certificate or graduate nurse-midwifery programs in the US. Student membership in ACNM and completion of one clinical module or semester required.

Contact the directors of nurse-midwifery programs at accredited schools or contact ACNM for membership information and/or an application.

2635 — AMERICAN INDIAN SCIENCE AND ENGINEERING SOCIETY (A.T. Anderson Memorial Scholarship)

PO Box 9828
Albuquerque NM 87119-9828
505/765-1052
FAX: 505/765-5608
E-Mail: scholarships@aises.org
Internet: www.aises.org/scholarships

AMOUNT: $1,000-$2,000

DEADLINE(S): JUN 15

FIELD(S): Medicine; Natural Resources; Science; Engineering

Open to undergraduate and graduate students who are at least 1/4 American Indian or recognized as member of a tribe. Must be member of AISES ($10 fee), enrolled full-time at an accredited institution, and demonstrate financial need.

Renewable. See website or contact Patricia Browne for an application and/or membership information.

2636 — AMERICAN NURSES FOUNDATION (Nursing Research Grants Program)

600 Maryland Ave., SW, Ste. 100W
Washington DC 20024
202/651-7298
FAX: 202/651-7354
Internet: www.nursingworld.org/anf

AMOUNT: $3,500 (min.)

DEADLINE(S): MAY

FIELD(S): Nursing Research

Designed for registered nurses who are beginning researchers who hold at least a bachelor's degree in nursing. Priority based on scientific merit of proposal with consideration to investigator's ability to conduct the study. Separate application category for experienced researchers entering new field.

25 awards annually. Contact ANF for an application booklet beginning in January. Specific deadline is the first weekday in the first week of May.

2637 — ARCHBOLD MEDICAL CENTER (Archbold Scholarship/Loan)

Dept. of Education
P.O. Box 1018
Thomasville GA 31799-1018
912/228-2795

AMOUNT: $4,000-$6,000; $500 for technical courses

DEADLINE(S): None specified

FIELD(S): Healthcare fields such as Registered Nurse, Medical Lab, Pharmacy, Physical Therapy, etc.

Open to undergrad and grad students accepted into an accredited healthcare school and within 2 years of completing course work. Student must agree to work at AMC for 3 years following graduation (1 year for tech school students).

Must be Georgia resident. Personal interview required. Repayment is required if recipient fails to work at Archbold for the designated period. Write for complete information.

2638 — ARTHUR M. MILLER FUND

P.O. Box 1122
Wichita KS 67201-0004
316/261-4609

AMOUNT: Varies

DEADLINE(S): MAR 31

FIELD(S): Medicine or related fields

Scholarships for Kansas residents for the study of medicine or related fields at accredited instutitions.

Send SASE for formal application.

2639 — ASSOCIATION OF OPERATING ROOM NURSES (AORN Scholarship Program)

2170 S. Parker Rd., Ste. 300
Denver CO 80231-5711
303/755-6300 or 800/755-6304, ext. 8366
FAX: 303/755-4219
E-Mail: sstokes@aorn.org
Internet: www.aorn.org

AMOUNT: Tuition & fees

DEADLINE(S): APR 1; OCT 1

FIELD(S): Nursing

Open to students who have been AORN members for at least 12 consecutive months prior to deadline date. Awards support bachelor's, master's, and doctoral degree programs accredited by the NLN or other acceptable accrediting body. For full- or part-time study of nursing or complementary fields in the US. Must have a minimum 3.0 GPA.

Renewable. Contact AORN for an applicaton.

2640 — ASSOCIATION OF WOMEN'S HEALTH, OBSTETRIC, AND NEONATAL NURSES (Nursing Research Grants Program)

2000 L St., NW, Ste. 740
Washington DC 20036-4907
202/261-2900
FAX: 202/728-0575
E-Mail: lisas@awhonn.org
Internet: www.awhonn.org

AMOUNT: $5,000-$15,000

DEADLINE(S): NOV 1

FIELD(S): Nursing

Open to graduate and postgraduate members of AWHONN who wish to pursue research in neonatal and women's health. Membership application may accompany grant application. Financial need NOT a factor.

5-6 awards annually. Not renewable. Contact Lisa Smith at AWHONN for membership information or an application.

2641 — AUSTRIAN CULTURAL INSTITUTE (Max Kade Foundation Grants)

950 Third Ave.
20th Fl.
New York NY 10022
212/759-5165 or +43/1/51581-253
FAX: 212/319-9636
E-Mail: desk@aci.org
Internet: www.austriaculture.net

AMOUNT: Varies

DEADLINE(S): Varies

FIELD(S): Medicine; Natural Sciences; Engineering

Open to young Austrian scientists with several years of experience at universities or institutions. Must demonstrate capacity to pursue independent teaching or research activities in the US. Proficiency in English required.

See website or contact ACI for an application kit, or write to Osterreichische Akademie der Wissenschaften, Kommission fur Max Kade Stipendien, Dr. Ignaz Seipel-Platz 2, A-1010 Vienna, Austria.

2642 — BECA FOUNDATION (Alice Newell Joslyn Medical Fund)

310 Via Vera Cruz, Ste. 101
San Marcos CA 92069
760/471-5465
FAX: 760/471-9175

AMOUNT: $500-$2,000

DEADLINE(S): MAR 1

FIELD(S): Medicine; Health Care; Nursing; Dental/Medical Assisting; Physical Therapy

Open to Latino students who live in or attend college in San Diego County, CA, at time of application. For high school seniors and those already in college pursuing undergraduate or graduate education. Based on financial need, scholastic determination, and community/cultural awareness. BECA also provides a mentor to each scholarship recipient.

Send self-addressed, stamped envelope to BECA for an application.

2643 — BOEING (Polish Graduate Student Scholarship Program)

Phone
Phone for details
314/234-2149

AMOUNT: Tuition, books, and fees for three years

DEADLINE(S): Varies

FIELD(S): Scientific and technical fields

Scholarships for students from Poland to pursue graduate studies in scientific and technical areas at American colleges or universities.

Call Jim Schlueter at above telephone number.

2644 — CANADIAN CANCER SOCIETY (Clinical Cancer Nursing Fellowships/a.k.a. Maurice Legault Fellowships)

10 Alcorn Ave., Suite 200
Toronto Ontario M4V 3B1 Canada
416/961-7223
FAX 416/961-4189

AMOUNT: $18,500 (Canadian)

DEADLINE(S): OCT (Mid-month each year)

FIELD(S): Nursing

Open to graduates of approved diploma schools of nursing or of a university baccalaureate program in nursing who hold current registration as a nurse in a Canadian province or territory.

Must be Canadian citizen or landed immigrant and resident of Canada. Write for complete information.

2645 — CANADIAN LUNG ASSOCIATION (Canadian Nurses Respiratory Society Fellowships & Research Grants)

1900 City Park Dr., Ste. 508
Gloucester Ontario K1J 1A3 CANADA
613/747-6776
FAX: 613/747-7430

AMOUNT: $2,000-$30,000

DEADLINE(S): NOV 1

FIELD(S): Respiratory Nursing

Open to registered nurses studying respiratory nursing at the master's or Ph.D level at a Canadian institution. Purpose is to increase the number of nurses with expertise in clinical practice and research related to respiratory nursing. Must be Canadian citizen/permanent resident.

Contact CLA for an application.

2646 — CANADIAN NURSES FOUNDATION (Study Awards Program)

50 Driveway
Ottawa Ontario K2P 1E2 CANADA
613/237-2133

AMOUNT: $1,500-$2,000 (undergraduate); $3,000-$3,500 (master's); $4,500-$6,000 (doctoral)

DEADLINE(S): APR 15

FIELD(S): Nursing

For members of the Canadian Nurses Foundation who have been accepted into a university program and agree to work in Canada one year for each year funded. Must be Canadian citizen.

45-55 awards annually. Contact CNF for membership information or an application.

2647 — COLUMBIANA COUNTY PUBLIC HEALTH LEAGUE TRUST FUND (Grants)

PO Box 1428
Steubenville OH 43952
740/283-8433
FAX: 740/282-4530

AMOUNT: Varies

DEADLINE(S): FEB 28

FIELD(S): Respiratory Illness; Medicine; Medical Research; Pharmacy; Medical Technology; Physical Therapy; Nursing; Dental Hygiene; Occupational Therapy

Open to undergraduate and graduate Columbiana County, Ohio, residents who are pursuing medical education or research in one of the above fields. Preference given to respiratory illness. Students of veterinary medicine NOT eligible.

Contact Sherrill Schmied for an application.

2648 — COMMANDER, NAVAL RESERVE RECRUITING COMMAND (Health Professionals Loan Repayment Program - HPLRP)

Attn Code 132
4400 Dauphine St.
New Orleans LA 70146
Written Inquiry

AMOUNT: Loan repayment up to $3,000 per year ($20,000 total)

DEADLINE(S): None specified

FIELD(S): Physicians: surgery & anesthesia; Nurses: nurse anesthesia, operating room nursing, med-surg nursing.

Open to health professionals fully qualified in critically short wartime specialties who serve in a military reserve (Selected Reserve or Individual Mobilization Augmentee Program). May be repaid on an individual's outstanding educational loan balance.

Navy: above address; Army: Headquarters, Dept. of the Army, 5109 Leesburg Pike, Falls Church, VA 22041-3258; US Air Force Reserve Personnel Center, ATTN: ARPC/SGI, Denver, CO 80280-5000.

2649 — CONCORDIA UNIVERSITY (J.P. Zewig Scholarship)

1455 de Maisonneuve Blvd. West
Room M 201
Montreal Quebec H3G 1M8 CANADA
514/848-3809
FAX: 514/848-2812
E-Mail: awardsgs@vax2.concordia.ca

AMOUNT: Varies

DEADLINE(S): SEP 20

FIELD(S): Psychology; Exercise Science; Behaviourial Medicine

This one-year scholarship is awarded to a graduate student pursuing research in the above areas. Candidates are to be nominated by Faculty members from these areas of research.

1 award annually. Not renewable. Contact the Graduate Awards Office in the School of Graduate Studies at Concordia University for nomination procedures.

2650 — CYNTHIA E. AND CLARA H. HOLLIS FOUNDATION

100 Summer St.
Boston MA 02110
Written inquiry

AMOUNT: Varies

DEADLINE(S): APR 1

FIELD(S): Nursing, social work, dental or medical technology, and religion

Scholarships for Massachusetts with preference given to students in the above fields. For undergraduates, graduates, voc-tech, and adult education. Must demonstrate financial need.

Send SASE to Walter E. Palmer, Esq., 35 Harvard St., Brookline, MA 02146 for application details. Scholarship forms are also available from the rector of All Saints Church, Brookline High School, and St. Mary's High School, all in Brookline, Massachusetts.

2651 — DEKALB COUNTY PRODUCERS SUPPLY & FARM BUREAU (Medical Scholarship)

1350 W. Prairie Drive
Sycamore, IL 60178
815/756-6361

AMOUNT: Varies

DEADLINE(S): JUNE

FIELD(S): Medical Doctor; Nursing

Applicants (or their parents) must have been voting or associate members of Dekalb County Farm Bureau for at least 2 years prior to application; agree to practice in rural Illinois for 3 years upon completion of training & be a US citizen.

Must have been accepted to or be attending medical school or a nursing program. Write to Virginia Fleetwood at above address for complete information.

2652 — DEMOCRATIC NURSING ORGANISATION OF SOUTH AFRICA (DENOSA Study Fund)

PO Box 1280
Pretoria 0001 SOUTH AFRICA
+27-12-3432316
FAX: +27-12-3440750
E-Mail: denosahq@cis.co.za

AMOUNT: Varies

DEADLINE(S): JAN 31

FIELD(S): Nursing; Health

Bursaries for graduate and postgraduate students who have been members of DENOSA for at least three years. Must be a South African citizen enrolled at an approved education institution in South Africa. Financial need is NOT a factor.

110 awards annually. Not renewable. Contact Ms. T. Gwagwa for an application.

2653 — DEPARTMENT OF THE ARMY (Armed Forces Health Professions Scholarships)

Attn: RC-HS
1307 Third Ave.
Fort Knox KY 40121
502/626-0367
FAX: 502/626-0923

AMOUNT: Tuition + monthly stipend

DEADLINE(S): None

FIELD(S): Medicine; Osteopathy; Nurse Anesthetist; Veterinary Medicine; Optometry; Psychology; Dentistry

Open to health professionals and students participating in a Reserve Service of the US Armed Forces, training in the specialties listed above. Varying lengths of service are required to pay back the stipend. Must be US citizen. Award is based on a competitive process, including GPA. Financial need NOT a factor.

400 awards annually. Contact Major Beecher at above address for an application.

2654 — DEPARTMENT OF THE ARMY (Health Professionals Loan Repayment Program)

Attn: RC-HS
1307 Third Ave.
Fort Knox KY 40121
502/626-0367
FAX: 502/626-0923

AMOUNT: $20,000/yr. (max.)

DEADLINE(S): None

FIELD(S): Medicine; Nursing

Loan repayment is open to health professionals fully qualified in critically short wartime specialties who serve in a military reserve. Specialties include physician assistants; general dentists; oral surgeons; critical care & nurse anesthetists; general, thoracic, & orthopedic surgeons; urologists; diagnostic radiologists; psychiatrists; preventative & critical care medicine; and primary care physicians.

Contact Major Beecher at above address for an application.

2655 — DUPAGE COUNTY MEDICAL SOCIETY FOUNDATION (Scholarship Program)

498 Hillside Ave., #1
Glen Ellyn IL 60137
630/858-9603

AMOUNT: $250-$1,000

DEADLINE(S): APR 30

FIELD(S): Medical/Health-Care Fields

Open to voting residents of Dupage County, Illinois, who are accepted to or enrolled in a professional training program at a qualified school. Based on financial need and scholastic ability. Program does not apply to undergraduate studies, such as pre-med; students would be eligible after completing four-year pre-med program and having been accepted into medical school.

Contact Medical Society for an application.

2656 — EDUCATIONAL AND SCIENTIFIC TRUST OF THE PENNSYLVANIA MEDICAL SOCIETY (Loan Program for Allied Health/Nursing Students)

777 East Park Drive
PO Box 8820
Harrisburg PA 17105-8820
717/558-7750, Ext. 1257
FAX: 717/558-7818
E-Mail: studentloans-trust@pamedsoc.org
Internet: www.pitt.edu/HOME/GHNet/
PA_Trust

AMOUNT: Up to $1,500 for bona fide Pennsylvania residents

DEADLINE(S): JUN 1

FIELD(S): Nursing and allied health fields

Open to Pennsylvania residents with demonstrated financial need who are seeking a career in nursing or an allied health field. Must be attending a Pennsylvania institution.

Approx. 200 loans per year. Must be U.S. citizen. Contact above location for complete information.

2657 — EDWARD BANGS KELLEY AND ELZA KELLEY FOUNDATION, INC. (Scholarship Program)

PO Drawer M
Hyannis MA 02601-1412
508/775-3117

AMOUNT: $4,000 (max.)

DEADLINE(S): APR 30

FIELD(S): Medicine; Nursing; Health Sciences

Open to residents of Barnstable County, Massachusetts. Scholarships are intended to benefit health and welfare of Barnstable County residents. Awards support study at recognized undergraduate, graduate, and professional institutions. Financial need is considered.

Contact Foundation for an application.

2658 — ENGLISH NATIONAL BOARD FOR NURSING, MIDWIFERY AND HEALTH VISITING (Bursaries and Grants)

ENB Careers, P.O. Box 2EN
London W1A 2EN ENGLAND UK
0171 391 6200 or 0171 391 6205
FAX: 0171 391 6207
Internet: www.enb.org.uk/carsect.htm

AMOUNT: Varies

DEADLINE(S): Varies

FIELD(S): Nursing, Midwifery, Health Visiting

ENB is the statutory body for education in the above fields in England. Information on careers, bursaries, and grants can be obtained from the organization.

Phone, fax, or mail for information; see website.

2659 — EPILEPSY FOUNDATION OF AMERICA (Behavioral Sciences Student Fellowships)

4351 Garden City Drive
Landover MD 20785-2267
301/459-3700 or 800/EFA-1000
FAX: 301/577-2684
TDD: 800/332-2070
E-Mail: postmaster@efa.org
Internet: www.efa.org

AMOUNT: $2,000

DEADLINE(S): FEB 1

FIELD(S): Epilepsy as related to Behavioral Sciences

Three-month fellowships awarded to students in the behavioral sciences for work on an epilepsy study project. For students of vocational rehabilitation counseling. Students propose an epilepsy-related study or training project to be carried out at a US institution of their choice. A preceptor must accept responsibility for supervision of the student and the project.

Contact EFA for an application.

2660 — EPILEPSY FOUNDATION OF AMERICA (Behavioral Sciences Research Training Fellowships)

4351 Garden City Drive
Landover MD 20785-2267
301/459-3700 or FAX: 301/577-2684
FDD: 800/332-2070
E-Mail: postmaster@efa.org
Internet: www.efa.org

AMOUNT: Up to $30,000

DEADLINE(S): FEB 1

FIELD(S): Epilepsy as related to Behavioral Sciences (includes sociology, social work, psychology, anthropology, nursing, political science, etc.)

A one-year training experience for postdoctoral scholars to develop expertise in the area of epilepsy research relative to the behavioral sciences. The project must be carried out at an approved facility. Amount depends on experience and qualifications of the applicant and the scope and duration of proposed project.

Contact EFA for an application.

2661 — EPILEPSY FOUNDATION OF AMERICA (Junior Investigator Research Grants)

4351 Garden City Drive
Landover MD 20785-2267
301/459-3700 or 800/EFA-1000
FAX: 301/577-2684
TDD: 800/332-2070
E-Mail: postmaster@efa.org
Internet: www.efa.org

AMOUNT: up to $40,000

DEADLINE(S): SEP 1

FIELD(S): Epilepsy as related to Biological, Behavioral, & Social Sciences

One-year research grants to support basic and clinical research in the biological, behavioral, and social sciences which will advance the understanding, treatment, and prevention of epilepsy. Priority given to beginning investigators just entering the field of epilepsy research, to new or innovative projects. Applications evaluated on basis of scientific merit.

Contact EFA for an application.

2662 — EPILEPSY FOUNDATION OF AMERICA (Pre-doctoral Research Training Fellowship)

4351 Garden City Drive
Landover MD 20785-2267
301/459-3700 or 800/EFA-1000
FAX: 301/577-2684
TDD: 800/332-2070
E-Mail: postmaster@efa.org
Internet: www.efa.org

AMOUNT: up to $15,000

DEADLINE(S): SEP 1

FIELD(S): Epilepsy as related to Neuroscience, Physiology, Pharmacology, Psychology, Biochemistry, Genetics, Nursing, or Pharmacy

One-year of support for qualified individuals who are pursuing dissertation research with an epilepsy-related theme, and who are working under the guidance of a mentor with expertise in the area of epilepsy investigation. Graduate students pursuing Ph.D. degree in above fields may apply.

Contact EFA for an application.

2663 — FELLOWS MEMORIAL FUND (Scholarship Loans)

Pensacola Junior College, 1000 College Blvd.
Pensacola FL 32504-8998
904/484-1706

AMOUNT: Individually determined

DEADLINE(S): Varies (Individually arranged)

FIELD(S): Nursing and Medical Technology

Loans for students accepted for training in nursing or in one of the several fields of medical technology at accredited schools or colleges. Appropriate for two- or four-year nursing programs, graduate nursing study, medical or surgical technology, anesthesiology, and radiological technology. Must be residents of one of the following Florida counties: Escambia, Santa Rosa, Okaloosa, or Walton

Loans are interest-free until four months after graduation. Thereafter, favorable interest rates will apply with the total to be paid by the end of eleven years.

2664 — FELLOWS MEMORIAL FUND (Scholarship Loans)

Pensacola Junior College
1000 College Blvd.
Pensacola FL 32504-8998
904/484-1700

AMOUNT: Varies

DEADLINE(S): Varies

FIELD(S): Theology; Health

Loans for ministerial students of the Episcopal faith and others whose religious beliefs are not in substantial conflict with the faith and doctrines of the Episcopal Church. Must be graduate students and residents of one of the following Florida counties: Escambia, Santa Rosa, Okaloosa, or Walton. Qualified health programs include medicine, nursing, medical technology, radiography, respiratory therapy, physical therapy, and physician's assistant.

Loans are interest-free until four months after graduation. Thereafter, favorable interest rates will apply with the total to be repaid by the end of eleven years.

2665 — FIRST UNITED METHODIST CHURCH (Robert Stevenson & Doreene E. Cater Scholarships)

302 5th Ave., S.
St. Cloud MN 56301
FAX: 320/251-0878
E-Mail: FUMCloud@aol.com

AMOUNT: $100-$300

DEADLINE(S): JUN 1

FIELD(S): Humanitarian & Christian Service: Teaching, Medicine, Social Work, Environmental Studies, etc.

Stevenson Scholarship is open to undergraduate members of the First United Methodist Church of St. Cloud. Cater Scholarship is open to members of the Minnesota United Methodist Conference who are entering the sophomore year or higher of college work. Both require two letters of reference, transcripts, and financial need.

5-6 awards annually. Contact Scholarship Committee for an application.

2666 — FOUNDATION FOR NEONATAL RESEARCH AND EDUCATION (FNRE Scholarships & Grants)

701 Lee St., Ste. 450
Des Plaines IL 60016
847/299-6266
FAX: 847/297-6768
E-Mail: CKenner835@aol.com

AMOUNT: up to $1,500 (scholarship); $10,000 (research grant)

DEADLINE(S): Varies

FIELD(S): Nursing

Scholarships are for nurses who want to go back and get further education. Research grants are also available.

3 scholarships & 1 research grant annually. Contact Carole Kenner, President, for more information.

2667 — FOUNDATION FOR SEACOAST HEALTH (Scholarship Program)

P.O. Box 4606
Portsmouth NH 03802-4606
603/433-3008
FAX: 603/433-2036

E-Mail: ffsh@nh.ultranet.com

Internet: www.nh.ultranet.com/~ffsh

AMOUNT: $1,000-10,000

DEADLINE(S): FEB 1

FIELD(S): Health-related fields

Open to undergraduate and graduate students pursuing health-related fields of study who are legal residents of the following cities in New Hampshire: Portsmouth, Newington, New Castle, Rye, Greenland, N. Hampton, or these cities in Maine: Kittery, Eliot, or York, Maine. Must have resided in the area for at least two years.

Write or check website for details. $150,000 awarded annually; 35 awards given

2668 — GRACE FOUNDATION SCHOLARSHIP TRUST FUND

P.O. Box 924

Menlo Park CA 94026-0924

Written inquiry

AMOUNT: $1,000 to $4,000

DEADLINE(S): JAN 31

FIELD(S): Christian

One-year scholarships for full or partial tuition payment for full-time study at an accredited college or university. For training future Christian ministers and professional workers in developing countries in Asia/Southeast Asia. Candidates must have completed one or more years of college in or near their native country, be a strong Christian, have a 3.0 or higher GPA, and be pursuing a career in either the ministry, medicine, teaching, or social service.

Renewable up to graduation—four years maximum—pending maintenance of 3.0 GPA. Applications available between Sept. 1 and Oct. 31. Must demonstrate financial need.

2669 — HEADQUARTERS, USAF RESERVE PERSONNEL CENTER (Health Professionals Loan Repayment Program - HPLRP)

6760 E. Irvington PL #7000

Denver CO 80280-7000

1-800-525-0102 ext 231 or 237

DSN 926-6490 or 6484

Commercial: 303/676-6484 or 6490

FAX: 303/676-6164

FAX: DSN: 926-6164

E-Mail: spresley@arpcmail.den.disa.mil

AMOUNT: Loan Repayment up to $3,000 per year ($20,000 total)

DEADLINE(S): None specified

FIELD(S): Physicians and nurses in critical wartime health-care specialties participating in the Selected Reserve.

Open to health professionals fully qualified in critically short wartime specialties who serve in a military reserve (Selected Reserve or Individual Mobilization Augmentee Program). To repay an individual's outstandihng educational loan balance.

Direct questions to: Medical Readiness & Incentives Division, SrA Sonja Presley at above location.

2670 — INTERNATIONAL ORDER OF THE KING'S DAUGHTERS AND SONS (Health Careers Scholarships)

c/o Mrs. Fred Cannon

Box 1310

Brookhaven MS 39602

Written Inquiry

AMOUNT: $1,000 (max.)

DEADLINE(S): APR 1

FIELD(S): Medicine; Dentistry; Nursing; Physical Therapy; Occupational Therapy; Medical Technologies; Pharmacy

Open to students accepted to/enrolled in an accredited US or Canadian four-year or graduate school. RN candidates must have completed first year of program; MD or DDS candidates must be for at least the second year of medical or dental school; all others must be in at least third year of four-year program. Pre-med students NOT eligible. Must be US or Canadian citizen.

Send self-addressed, stamped envelope, along with a letter stating the field of study and present level, to the Director at above address for an application.

2671 — JEWISH VOCATIONAL SERVICE (Marcus & Theresa Levie Educational Fund Scholarships)

1 S. Franklin St.

Chicago IL 60606

312/346-6700

AMOUNT: To $5,000

DEADLINE(S): MAR 1

FIELD(S): Social Work, Medicine, Dentistry, Nursing, & other related professions & vocations

Open to Cook County residents of the Jewish faith who plan careers in the above fields. For undergraduate juniors and seniors and graduate students. Applications available Dec. 1 from Scholarship Secretary.

Must show financial need. 85-100 awards per year. Renewal possible with reapplication. Write for complete information.

2672 — KING FAISAL FOUNDATION (Graduate Scholarship Program)

PO Box 352

Riyadh 11411 SAUDI ARABIA

966/1 465-2255

FAX: 966/1 465-6524

E-Mail: info@kff.com OR mprd@kff.com

Internet: www.kff.com OR

www.kingfaisalfoundation.org

AMOUNT: $400/mo. US allowance + tuition/fees paid directly to university + health insurance & travel

DEADLINE(S): None

FIELD(S): Medicine; Engineering; Physics; Chemistry; Geology

Open to graduate students who are Muslims under the age of 40. Must have BS degree, GPA of 86% or higher, and be accepted unconditionally by a university either in Europe or North America. Must be fluent in the language of area providing the studies. Selection based on academic performance.

Contact King Faisal Foundation for an application.

2673 — LADY ALLEN OF HURTWOOD MEMORIAL TRUST (Travel Grants)

21 Aspull Common

Leigh Lancs WN7 3PB ENGLAND

01942-674895

AMOUNT: up to 1,000 pounds sterling

DEADLINE(S): JAN 15

FIELD(S): Welfare And Education Of Children

A travel grant to those whose proposed project will directly benefit their work with children. People working with children and young people may apply, particularly those working with disabled and disadvantaged children. Successful candidates must write up an account of the work which the scholarship has funded. GRANTS ARE NOT FOR ACADEMIC STUDY; ONLY QUALIFIED INDIVIDUALS MAY APPLY.

Contact Dorothy E. Whitaker, Trustee, for application forms—available between May and December each year.

2674 — MARCH OF DIMES BIRTH DEFECTS FOUNDATION (Nursing Scholarships)

1275 Mamaroneck Avenue

White Plains NY 10605

888-MODIMES or 914/997-4456

E-Mail: EducationServices@modimes.org

Internet: www.modimes.org

AMOUNT: $5,000

DEADLINE(S): JAN 30

FIELD(S): Maternal-Child Nursing

Scholarships recognize and promote excellence in the nursing care of mothers and infants. Nurses currently enrolled in a graduate program of nursing (master's or doctorate), with a concentration in maternal-child nursing may appply. Must be members of AWHONN, ACNM, or NANN.

See website for membership information in the above groups or contact March of Dimes for an application.

2675 — MARYLAND HIGHER EDUCATION COMMISSION (Professional School Scholarships)

State Scholarship Admin
16 Francis St.
Annapolis MD 21401-1781
800/974-1024 or 410/974-5370
TTY: 800/735-2258

AMOUNT: $200-$1,000

DEADLINE(S): MAR 1

FIELD(S): Dentistry; Pharmacy; Medicine; Law; Nursing; Social Work

Open to Maryland residents who have been admitted as full-time students at a participating graduate institution of higher learning in Maryland or an undergraduate/graduate nursing program. Must fill out government FAFSA form.

Renewable up to 4 years. Contact MHEC for an application and see your school's financial aid office for FAFSA.

2676 — MINNESOTA HIGHER EDUCATION SERVICES OFFICE (Health Professions Loan Forgiveness)

Capitol Square Bldg., Ste. 400
550 Cedar St.
St. Paul MN 55101
612/296-3974
FAX: 612/297-8880
E-Mail: info@heso.state.mn.us
Internet: www.heso.state.mn.us/

AMOUNT: Varies

DEADLINE(S): None

FIELD(S): Health Professions

Five loan repayment programs for health professionals who agree to serve in federally designated Health Professional Shortage Areas, in designated, underserved urban or rural areas, in licensed nursing homes, or in intermediate care facilities for persons with mental retardation or related conditions.

For details contact Office of Rural Health and Primary Care at 612/282-3838 or 800/366-5424 (Minnesota only).

2677 — MYASTHENIA GRAVIS FOUNDATION OF AMERICA, INC. (Nursing Research Fellowship)

123 W. Madison St., Ste. 800
Chicago IL 60602-4503
312/853-0522 or 800/541-5454
FAX: 312/853-0523
E-Mail: myastheniagravis@msn.com
Internet: www.myasthenia.org

AMOUNT: $1,500 (max.)

DEADLINE(S): None

FIELD(S): Myasthenia Gravis

Fellowships are for nurses or nursing students interested in studying problems encountered by patients with Myasthenia Gravis (MG) or related neuromuscular conditions. Must describe the question you propose to study, its association to MG, and how you will approach project. Must submit four copies each of cover letter, proposed budget, curriculum vitae, and letter of recommendation from sponsoring preceptor.

Contact Edward S. Trainer, Executive Director, for an application.

2678 — McCORD CAREER CENTER (Level II McCord Medical/Music Scholarship)

Healdsburg High School
1024 Prince St.
Healdsburg CA 95448
707/431-3473

AMOUNT: Varies

DEADLINE(S): APR 30

FIELD(S): Medicine; Music

For graduates of Healdsburg High School who are planning a career in music or medicine. Must be enrolled full-time at a college/university as an undergraduate junior or senior in the fall, or earning an advanced degree in graduate or medical school, or entering into a vocational/certificate program. Transcripts, proof of attendance, and an essay are required.

Contact the McCord Career Center at Healdsburg High School for an application.

2679 — NATIONAL FEDERATION OF THE BLIND (Howard Brown Rickard Scholarship)

805 Fifth Avenue
Grinnell IA 50112
515/236-3366

AMOUNT: $3,000

DEADLINE(S): MAR 31

FIELD(S): Law; Medicine; Engineering; Architecture; Natural Sciences

For legally blind students pursuing or planning to pursue a full-time postsecondary course of study in the US. Based on academic excellence, service to the community, and financial need. Membership NOT required.

1 award annually. Renewable. Contact Mrs. Peggy Elliot, Scholarship Committee Chairman, for an application.

2680 — NATIONAL FOUNDATION FOR LONG-TERM HEALTH CARE (James D. Durante Nurse Scholarship Program)

1201 L Street, NW
Washington DC 20005-4015

202/842-4444
Hotline Info: 202/898-9352
FAX: 202/842-3860
E-Mail: bbride@ahca.org
Internet: www.ahca.org

AMOUNT: $500

DEADLINE(S): MAY 30

FIELD(S): Nursing

Open to LPN and RN students who seek to continue or further their education and are interested in long-term care. Must work in an AHCA-member nursing facility.

20 awards annually. Send a self-addressed, stamped, legal-sized envelope in late winter for an application.

2681 — NATIONAL HEALTH SERVICE CORPS (NHSC Scholarship Program)

2070 Chain Bridge Rd,, Ste. 450
Vienna VA 22182-2536
800/221-9393
Internet: www.bphc.hrsa.dhhs.gov/nhsc

AMOUNT: Full tuition/books/fees/supplies + monthly stipend

DEADLINE(S): MAR

FIELD(S): Family Medicine; General Internal Medicine; General Pediatrics; Obstetrics/Gynecology; Family Nurse Practitioners; Primary Care Physician Assistants; Certified Nurse-Midwives

Must be US citizen attending or enrolled in fully accredited US allopathic/osteopathic medical school, nursing program, or physician assistant program. For each year of support received, you must serve one year in federally designated health professional shortage area of greatest need. Minimum two years service commitment begins upon completion of your residency and/or training.

300 awards annually. Renewable up to 4 years. Contact NHSC for an application.

2682 — NATIONAL HEMOPHILIA FOUNDATION (Nursing Excellence Fellowship)

116 W. 32nd St., 11th Floor
New York NY 10001
800/42-HANDI or 212/328-3700
FAX: 212/328-3788
E-Mail: dkenny@hemophilia.org
Internet: www.hemophilia.org

AMOUNT: $10,000

DEADLINE(S): APR 1

FIELD(S): Hemophilia Care; Nursing

Only registered nurses from an accredited nursing school enrolled in a graduate nursing program or currently employed or interested in hemophilia care to conduct nursing researrch or clinical projects may apply. Financial need NOT a factor.

1 award annually. Not renewable. Contact Denise Kenny at NHF for an application.

2683 — NATIONAL STUDENT NURSES' ASSOCIATION FOUNDATION (Scholarship Program)

555 W. 57th St., Ste. 1327
New York NY 10019
212/581-2211
FAX: 212/581-2368
E-Mail: nsna@nsna.org
Internet: www.nsna.org

AMOUNT: $1,000-$2,000

DEADLINE(S): FEB 1

FIELD(S): Nursing

Open to students currently enrolled in state-approved nursing schools or pre-nursing in associate degree, baccalaureate, diploma, generic doctorate, and generic master's programs. Funds available for graduate study ONLY if first degree in nursing. Based on academic achievement, financial need, and involvement in nursing student organizations and community activities related to health care. Transcripts required.

$10 application fee. See website, or, beginning in August, send self-addressed, business-sized envelope with 55 cents postage to NSNA for an application. Winners will be notified in March. GRADUATING HIGH SCHOOL SENIORS NOT ELIGIBLE.

2684 — NAVAL RESERVE RECRUITING COMMAND (Armed Forces Health Professions Scholarships)

Attn: Code 132
4400 Dauphine St.
New Orleans LA 70146
Written inquiry

AMOUNT: Varies

DEADLINE(S): None specified

FIELD(S): Physicians: Anesthesiology, surgical specialties; Nursing: Anesthesia, operating room, or medical surgical nursing.

For health professionals and students participating in a Reserve Service of the U.S. Armed Forces training in the specialties listed above and for undergraduate nursing students. A monthly stipend is paid, and varying lengths of service are required to pay back the stipend.

Navy: above address; OR Army: Headquarters, Dept. of the Army, 5109 Leesburg Pike, Falls Church, VA 22041-3258; OR US Air Force Reserve Personnel Center, ATTN: ARPC SGI, Denver, CO 80280-5000.

2685 — NEW YORK STATE DEPARTMENT OF HEALTH - PRIMARY CARE SERVICE CORPS (Scholarships)

Corning Tower, Room 1084
Empire State Plaza
Albany NY 12237-0053
518/473-7019

AMOUNT: $15,000

DEADLINE(S): APR 3

FIELD(S): Certified Physician Assistant; Nurse Practitioner; Midwife

Open to New York State residents enrolled at, accepted to, or applied at an approved graduate, undergraduate, or certificate course of study. Must be within 24 months of completion of professional training full-time, or within 48 months of completion on a part-time basis.

Contact NY State Dept. of Health for an application.

2686 — NEW YORK STATE HIGHER EDUCATION SERVICES CORPORATION (N.Y. State Regents Professional/Health Care Opportunity Scholarships)

Cultural Education Center, Rm. 5C64
Albany NY 12230
518/486-1319
Internet: www.hesc.com

AMOUNT: $1,000-$10,000/yr.

DEADLINE(S): Varies

FIELD(S): Medicine and dentistry and related fields, architecture, nursing, psychology, audiology, landscape architecture, social work, chiropractic, law, pharmacy, accounting, speech language pathology

For NY state residents who are economically disadvantaged and members of a minority group underrepresented in the chosen profession and attending school in NY state. Some programs carry a service obligation in New York for each year of support. For U.S. citizens or qualifying noncitizens.

Medical/dental scholarships require one year of professional work in NY.

2687 — OAK RIDGE INSTITUTE FOR SCIENCE AND EDUCATION (Industrial Hygiene Graduate Fellowship Program)

P.O. Box 117
Oak Ridge TN 37831-0117
423-576-9655
FAX: 423/576-8293
E-Mail: kinneym@orau.gov

AMOUNT:

DEADLINE(S): JAN 26

FIELD(S): Industrial Hygiene

A fellowship for first-year master's candidates who have undergraduate degrees in physical, life, environmental, or health sciences or enginering and who wish to pursue studies in industrial hygiene.

For details and application, contact above location.

2688 — ONCOLOGY NURSING FOUNDATION (Scholarships, Grants, Awards, & Honors)

501 Holiday Dr.
Pittsburgh PA 15220-2749
412/921-7373, ext. 242
FAX: 412/921-6565
E-Mail: celia@ons.org

AMOUNT: Varies (with program)

DEADLINE(S): Varies (with program)

FIELD(S): Oncology Nursing

For registered nurses seeking further training or to engage in research in the field of oncology. Various programs range from bachelor's degree level through postmasters and career development. Also honors and awards for oncology nurses who have contributed to professional literature and excellence in their field. Some require ONF membership.

Contact Celia A. Hindes, CFRE, for an application. Notification by early April. Awards are offered by Oncology Nursing Society, Oncology Nursing Foundation, Oncology Nursing Certification Corporation, and Oncology Nursing Press, Inc.

2689 — SIGMA THETA TAU INTERNATIONAL (Research Grants)

550 West North Street
Indianapolis IN 46202
888/634-7575 or 317/634-8171
FAX: 317/634-8188
E-Mail: research@stti.iupui.edu

AMOUNT: $2,500-$10,000

DEADLINE(S): Varies

FIELD(S): Nursing Research

Several research grant programs are available to support well-defined research projects in various fields of nursing. Open to registered nurses who have their masters degree in nursing. Some require membership in Sigma Theta Tau. Must submit research proposal.

Contact Sigma Theta Tau for an application packet which lists the grant programs and their specific criteria.

2690 — SIR ROBERT MENZIES MEMORIAL FOUNDATION LIMITED (Research Scholarship in Allied Health Sciences)

210 Clarendon Street
East Melbourne Vic 3002 AUSTRALIA
03 9419 5699
FAX: 03 9417 7049

E-Mail: menzies@vicnet.net.au

Internet: www.vincent.net.au/~menzies

AMOUNT: $AUD.24,000 p.a.

DEADLINE(S): JUN 30

FIELD(S): Allied Health

Postgraduate research scholarships for Australian citizens enrolled as full-time Ph.D. students at Australian institutions. Must be studying allied health fields, such as nursing, physiotherapy, psychology, occupational therapy, speech pathology, etc. Award is based on academic excellence. Financial need NOT a factor.

1 award annually. Contact Ms. Sandra Mackenzie for an application.

2691 — U.S. DEPT. OF HEALTH & HUMAN SERVICES (Indian Health Service Health Professions Scholarship Program)

Twinbrook Metro Plaza, Suite 100

12300 Twinbrook Pkwy.

Rockville MD 20852

301/443-0234

FAX: 301/443-4815

Internet: www.ihs.gov/Recruitment/DHPS/SP/SBTOC3.asp

AMOUNT: Tuition + fees & monthly stipend of $938.

DEADLINE(S): APR 1

FIELD(S): Health professions, accounting, social work

Open to Native Americans or Alaska natives who are graduate students or college juniors or seniors in a program leading to a career in a fields listed above. U.S. citizenship required. Renewable annually with reapplication.

Scholarship recipients must intend to serve the Indian people. They incur a one-year service obligation to the IHS for each year of support for a minimum of two years. Write for complete information.

2692 — UNIFORMED SERVICES UNIVERSITY OF THE HEALTH SCIENCES (Fellowships)

Schools of Medicine & Nursing

4301 Jones Bridge Rd.

Bethesda MD 20814-4799

301/295-3101 or 800/772-1743

AMOUNT: Tuition

DEADLINE(S): NOV 1

FIELD(S): Medicine; Nursing

Open to graduate students who wish to attend the F. Edward Hebert School of Medicine or the Graduate School of Nursing with the understanding that they will be trained for service to the nation, including assignments abroad or at sea. While enrolled, students serve as reserve commissioned officers. Must be US citizen.

Contact Uniformed Services University for an application.

2693 — USAF READY RESERVE STIPEND PROGRAM

6760 East Irvington Place

Denver CO 80280-7000

1/800-525-01-2 ext 231 or 237

DSN 926-6490 or 6480

Commercial: 303/676-6484 or 6490

FAX: 303/676-6164

FAX: DSN: 926-6164

E-Mail: spresley@arpcmail.den.disa.mil

AMOUNT: Varies

DEADLINE(S): None

FIELD(S): Physicians and nurses

Designed to grow individuals with critical wartime health-care specialties for service in the Ready Reserve. Under AFRRSP a financial stipend will be paid to persons engaged in training in certain health-care specialties in return for a commitment to subseuently serve in the Ready Reserve.

Direct questions to: Medical Readiness & Incentives Division, SrA Sonja Presley, at above location.

2694 — USAF RESERVE PERSONNEL CENTER (Armed Forces Health Professionas Scholarships)

6760 E. Irvington Pl. #7000

Denver CO 80280-7000

Written inquiry

AMOUNT: Varies

DEADLINE(S): None specified

FIELD(S): Physicians: Anesthesiology, surgical specialties; Nursing: Anesthesia, operating room, or medical surgical nursing.

For health professionals and students participating in a Reserve Service of the U.S. Armed Forces training in the specialties listed above and for undergraduate nursing students. A monthly stipend is paid, and varying lengths of service are required to pay back the stipend.

Air Force: above address; Army: Headquarters, Dept. of the Army, 5109 Leesburg Pike, Falls Church, VA 22041-3258; Navy: Naval Reserve Recruiting Command, 4400 Dauphine St., New Orleans, LA 70146.

2695 — USAF RESERVE BONUS PROGRAM

6760 East Irvington Place #7000

Denver CO 80280-7000

1/800-525-0102 ext 231 or 237

DSN 926-6490 or 6484

Commercial: 303/676-6484 or 6490

FAX: 303/676-6164

FAX: DSN: 926-6164

E-Mail: spresley@arpcmail.den.disa.mil

AMOUNT: $10,000/yr. for physicians; $3,000/year for Operating Room Nurses

DEADLINE(S): None

FIELD(S): Physicians and nurses in critically needed specialties.

A bonus pay program to recruit critically needed medical specialties into the Selected Reserve of the U.S. Air Force.

Direct questions to: Medical Readiness & Incentives Division, SrA Sonja Presley at above location.

2696 — VIRGIN ISLANDS BOARD OF EDUCATION (Nursing & Other Health Scholarships)

P.O. Box 11900

St. Thomas VI 00801

809/774-4546

AMOUNT: Up to $1,800

DEADLINE(S): MAR 31

FIELD(S): Nursing; Medicine; Health-related Areas

Open to bona fide residents of the Virgin Islands who are accepted by an accredited school of nursing or an accredited institution offering courses in one of the health-related fields.

This scholarship is granted for one academic year. Recipients may reapply with at least a 'C' average. Write for complete information.

2697 — WASHINGTON STATE HIGHER EDUCATION COORDINATING BOARD (Health Professional Loan Repayment & Scholarship Program)

PO Box 43430

Olympia WA 98504-3430

360/753-7850

FAX: 360/753-7808

Internet: www.hecb.wa.gov

AMOUNT: Varies

DEADLINE(S): APR (scholarship); FEB (loan repayment); JUL (loan repayment)

FIELD(S): Health Care

Scholarships are open to students in accredited undergraduate or graduate health care programs leading to eligibility for licensure in Washington state. Must agree to work in designated shortage area for minimum of three years. Loan repayment recipients receive payment from program for purpose of repaying education loans secured while attending program of health care training leading to licensure in Washington state. Financial need NOT a factor.

Renewable up to 5 years. Contact Program Manager for a loan repayment application after November 15th and for scholarship application after January 15th.

2698 — WOMEN OF THE EVANGELICAL LUTHERAN CHURCH IN AMERICA (The Kahler-Vickers/Raup-Emma Wettstein Scholarships)

8765 West Higgins Road
Chicago IL 60631-4189
800/638-3522, ext. 2747
FAX: 773/380-2419
E-Mail: womnelca@elca.org

AMOUNT: $2,000 max.

DEADLINE(S): MAR 1

FIELD(S): Health Professions & Christian Service

Assists women who are members of the ELCA studying for service in health professions associated with ELCA projects abroad that do not lead to church-certified professions. Must be US citizen and have experienced an interruption of two or more years since completion of high school. Academic records of coursework completed in last five years as well as proof of admission from educational institution are required.

Renewable for an additional year. Contact Faith Fretheim, Program Director, for an application.

2699 — WOODROW WILSON NATIONAL FELLOWSHIP FOUNDATION/JOHNSON & JOHNSON (Dissertation Grants in Women's & Children's Health)

CN 5281
Princeton NJ 08543-5281
609/452-7007
FAX: 609/452-0066
E-Mail: charoltte@woodrow.org
Internet: www.woodrow.org

AMOUNT: $2,000 (for travel, books, microfilming, taping, computer services, etc.)

DEADLINE(S): NOV 8

FIELD(S): Women's & Children's Health

Open to doctoral students in nursing, public health, anthropology, history, sociology, psychology, or social work, who have completed all predissertation requirements at US graduate schools. Must have at least six months left to complete dissertation, which should include significant research on issues related to women's & children's health. Must submit transcripts, proposal, bibliography, & interest. Based on originality & scholarly validity.

15 awards annually. See website or contact WWNFF for an application. Winners announced in February.

2700 — ZETA PHI BETA SORORITY EDUCATIONAL FOUNDATION (S. Evelyn Lewis Memorial Scholarship in Medical Health Sciences)

1734 New Hampshire Ave., NW
Washington DC 20009
Internet: www.zpb1920.org/nefforms.htm

AMOUNT: $500-$1,000

DEADLINE(S): FEB 1

FIELD(S): Medicine; Health Sciences

Open to graduate and undergraduate young women enrolled in a program leading to a degree in medicine or health sciences. Award is for full-time study for one academic year (Fall-Spring) and is paid directly to college/university. Must submit proof of enrollment.

Send self-addressed, stamped envelope to above address between September 1st and December 15th for an application.

NUTRITION

2701 — ABBIE SARGENT MEMORIAL SCHOLARSHIP INC. (Scholarships)

295 Sheep Davis Road
Concord NH 03301
603/224-1934
FAX: 603/228-8432

AMOUNT: $400

DEADLINE(S): MAR 15

FIELD(S): Agriculture; Veterinary Medicine; Home Economics

Open to New Hampshire residents who are high school graduates with good grades and character. For undergraduate or graduate study. Must be legal resident of U.S. and demonstrate financial need.

Three annual awards. Renewable with reapplication. Write for complete information.

2702 — AMERICAN ASSOCIATION OF CEREAL CHEMISTS (Undergraduate Scholarships and Graduate Fellowships)

3340 Pilot Knob Rd.
St. Paul MN 55121-2097
Written Inquiry

AMOUNT: $1,000-$2,000 (undergrad); $2,000-$3,000 (graduate)

DEADLINE(S): APR 1

FIELD(S): Cereal Science/Technology

Open to undergraduate and graduate students majoring or interested in a career in cereal science or technology (incl. baking or related areas) as evidenced by coursework or employment. Undergrads must have completed at least one quarter or semester of college/

university work. Strong academic record and career interest important; AACC membership helpful but not necessary. Department head endorsement required. Financial need NOT a factor.

Fields such as culinary arts or dietetics NOT eligible. 30 awards annually. Write for an application.

2703 — AMERICAN ASSOCIATION OF FAMILY AND CONSUMER SCIENCES (International Fellowships)

1555 King Street
Alexandria VA 22314-2752
703/706-4600
FAX: 703/706-4663
E-Mail: info@aafcs.org
Internet: www.aafcs.org

AMOUNT: $3,000-$5,000

DEADLINE(S): DEC 31

FIELD(S): Home Economics/Family and Consumer Sciences

Various fellowships for citizens of countries other than the US who wish to pursue undergraduate or graduate study at an accredited college or university in the US. $15 application fee per application request required of international students living in the US. No fee is required of students residing outside the US. All students must become members of AAFCS before applying for fellowships.

5 fellowships annually. See website for details.

2704 — AMERICAN CULINARY FEDERATION, INC. (Ray & Gertrude Marshall Scholarship Fund)

10 San Bartola Dr.
St. Augustine FL 32086
904/824-4468 or 800/624-9458
FAX: 904/825-4758
E-Mail: acf@aug.com
Internet: www.acfchefs.org/acf.html

AMOUNT: $500-$1,000

DEADLINE(S): FEB 15; JUN 15; OCT 15

FIELD(S): Culinary Arts

For junior members of the American Culinary Federation enrolled in a postsecondary culinary arts program. Must have been in program for one complete grading period. The fee for a junior/apprentice membership is $55/year.

Contact ACF for membership information and/or an application.

2705 — AMERICAN SOCIETY FOR NUTRITIONAL SCIENCES (Predoctoral Fellowships)

9650 Rockville Pike
Bethesda MD 20814-3990

301/530-7050
Internet: www.faseb.org/asns
AMOUNT: $5,000
DEADLINE(S): DEC 1
FIELD(S): Nutrition

One-year research fellowships are open to advanced Ph.D. candidates enrolled in a nutritional sciences program registered with the American Society for Nutritional Sciences' directory of graduate programs.

See website or contact ASNS for an application.

2706 — AMERICAN WINE SOCIETY EDUCATIONAL FOUNDATION (Scholarships and Grants)

1134 West Market St.
Bethlehem PA 18018-4910
610/865-2401 or 610/758-3845
FAX: 610/758-4344
E-Mail: lhso@lehigh.edu
AMOUNT: $2,000
DEADLINE(S): MAR 31
FIELD(S): Wine industry professional study: enology, viticulture, health aspects of food and wine, and using and appreciating fine wines.

To provide academic scholarships and research grants to students based on academic excellence. Must show financial need and genuine interest in pursuing careers in wine-related fields. For North American citizens, defined as U.S., Canada, Mexico, the Bahamas, and the West Indies at all levels of education.

Contact L.H. Sperling at above location for application.

2707 — CALIFORNIA DIETETIC ASSOCIATION (Zellmer Scholarship Trust Fund)

Ken Burke, Dept. Nutrition & Dietetics, School of Allied Health Professions
Loma Linda University
Loma Linda CA 92350
310/822-0177 or 909/558-4593
FAX: 909/558-4291
E-Mail: ken-burke@sahp.llu.edu
AMOUNT: Varies
DEADLINE(S): MAY 15
FIELD(S): Dietetics

Open to members of the American Dietetic Association who are either California residents or planning to attend school in California. Must have obtained master's or doctoral degree in nutrition or related fields from accredited institution, or shall have been advanced to candidacy for the doctoral degree from such institution. Based on personal commitment to profession of dietetics and proposed course of study/research and its benefit to dietetics.

Contact Ken Burke at Loma Linda University for an application after January 15th, or contact CDA.

2708 — CANADIAN HOME ECONOMICS ASSOCIATION (CHEA Graduate Study Scholarship Awards)

151 rue Slater St., Suite 307
Ottawa Ontario K1P 5H3 CANADA
613/238-8817
AMOUNT: $1,000 to $5,000
DEADLINE(S): Varies
FIELD(S): Home Economics; Food Management

Scholarships open to graduate students pursuing a course of study leading to a higher academic degree in home economics or food management. Canadian citizen or legal resident. Financial need is considered but not required.

10 awards per year. Write for complete information.

2709 — FOOD INDUSTRY SCHOLARSHIP FUND OF NEW HAMPSHIRE (Scholarships)

110 Stark St.
Manchester NH 03101-1977
Written Inquiry
AMOUNT: $1,000
DEADLINE(S): MAR
FIELD(S): Food Industry

Open to students who are residents of New Hampshire and planning to enter a career in the food industry.

Contact Fund for an application.

2710 — INSTITUTE FOR THE STUDY OF WORLD POLITICS (Dissertation Fellowships)

1755 Massachusetts Ave. NW
Washington DC 20036
202/588-9797
Internet: fundforpeace.org/iswp.htm
AMOUNT: Varies
DEADLINE(S): FEB 16
FIELD(S): International Relations; Environmental Issues; Population Studies (Social Science aspects); Human Rights; Arms Control; Third World Development; Agricultural Development; Public Health, etc.

For doctoral candidates conducting dissertation research in above areas to promote scholarly examination of political, economic, and social issues that affect the security, well-being, and dignity of the peoples of the world. Financial need is a consideration. For citizens of any country.

Write for complete information.

2711 — INSTITUTE FOR THE STUDY OF WORLD POLITICS (Dorothy Danforth Compton Fellowships)

1755 Massachusetts Ave. NW
Washington DC 20036
202/588-9797
Internet: fundforpeace.org/iswp.htm
AMOUNT: Varies
DEADLINE(S): MAR 16
FIELD(S): International Relations; Environmental Issues; Population Studies (Social Science aspects); Human Rights; Arms Control; Third World Development; Agricultural Development; Public Health, etc.

For masters or doctoral candidates researching in the above areas to promote scholarly examination of political, economic, and social issues that affect the security, well-being, and dignity of the peoples of the world. Must be African American, Hispanic American, and Native American students who are U.S. citizens and studying in U.S. institutions. Financial need is a consideration.

Write for complete information.

2712 — INSTITUTE OF FOOD TECHNOLOGISTS (Graduate Fellowships)

221 N. La Salle St. #300
Chicago IL 60601
312/782-8424
AMOUNT: $1,000-$10,000
DEADLINE(S): FEB 1
FIELD(S): Food Science & Technology

Open either to senior undergraduates who will be enrolled in graduate studies when the fellowship becomes effective or to a current graduate student continuing a course of study leading to a MS or Ph.D in food science/technology.

School may be in the U.S. or Canada. Write for complete information.

2713 — INTERNATIONAL ASSOCIATION OF CULINARY PROFESSIONALS FOUNDATION (Scholarships)

304 W. Liberty St., Ste. 201
Louisville KY 40202-3068
502/587-7953
FAX: 502/589-3602
E-Mail: emcknight@hdqtrs.com
Internet: www.iacp.com
AMOUNT: $500-$10,000
DEADLINE(S): DEC 1
FIELD(S): Culinary Arts

Culinary scholarships are for basic, continuing, and specialty education courses in the US or abroad. Must have a high school diploma or equivalent by June following deadline. Selection based on merit, foodservice work experience, and financial need. Awards cover partial tuition costs and, occasionally, course-related expenses, such as research, room and board, or travel.

$25 application fee. 60 awards annually. Contact Ellen McKnight, Director of Development, at IACP for an application between June 1st and December 1st.

2714 — KAPPA OMICRON NU (Adviser's Fellowships)

4990 Northwind Dr., Suite 140
East Lansing MI 48823
517/351-8335

AMOUNT: $2,000

DEADLINE(S): JAN 15

FIELD(S): Home economics

Fellowships open to members of Kappa Omicron Nu - National Home Economics Honor Society. Awards support full time study in home economics at the graduate or post-graduate level.

Write for complete information.

2715 — KAPPA OMICRON NU (Doctoral Fellowships)

4990 Northwind Dr. Suite 140
East Lansing MI 48823
517/351-8335

AMOUNT: $2,000

DEADLINE(S): JAN 15

FIELD(S): Home Economics and Related Fields

Fellowships for doctoral candidates open to Kappa Omicron Nu members with demonstrated scholarship; research and leadership potential. Study should be at a college or university having strong research programs and supporting disciplines.

Three awards per year. Write for complete information.

2716 — KAPPA OMICRON NU (Master's Fellowships)

4990 Northwind Dr. Suite 140
East Lansing MI 48823
517/351-8335

AMOUNT: $1,000 - $2,000

DEADLINE(S): APR 1

FIELD(S): Home Economics and Related Fields

Open to Kappa Omicron Nu members who have demonstrated scholarship, research, and leadership potential. For graduate study at institutions with strong research programs and supporting disciplines for the chosen major.

$2,000 Eileen C. Maddex Fellowship is awarded annually; $1,000 National Alumni Fellowship is

awarded biannually in uneven years. Write for complete information.

2717 — KAPPA OMICRON NU (Research/ Project Grants)

4990 Northwind Dr. Suite 140
East Lansing MI 48823
517/351-8335

AMOUNT: $500 and $3,500

DEADLINE(S): FEB 15

FIELD(S): Home Economics and Related Fields

Open to Kappa Omicron Nu members who have demonstrated scholarship; research; and leadership potential. Awards are for home economics research at institutions having strong research programs.

Two grants. Write for complete information

2718 — NATIONAL ITALIAN AMERICAN FOUNDATION (GRI/ICIF Culinary Scholarships)

1860 19th St. NW
Washington DC 20009-5599
202/530-5315

AMOUNT: $6,000

DEADLINE(S): MAY 31

FIELD(S): Culinary arts

For graduates of Italian ancestry who are culinary school graduates. Must meet criteria established by the Italian Culinary Institute for Foreigners and the Gruppo Ristoratori Italiani. For study in Italy.

Five scholarships to be awarded. Before applying, contact Enrico Bazzoni at 718/875-0547 or E-mail at EABChef@AOL.com.

2719 — NATIONAL RESTAURANT ASSOCIATION EDUCATIONAL FOUNDATION (Graduate Degree Scholarship)

250 S. Wacker Dr., Suite 1400
Chicago IL 60606-5834
800/765-2122, ext. 733 or 312/715-1010
FAX: 312/715-1362
E-Mail: bdejesus@foodtrain.org
Internet: www.edfound.org

AMOUNT: $2,000

DEADLINE(S): FEB 15

FIELD(S): Culinary/Restaurant/Hospitality Degree

For graduate students who are US citizens/ permanent residents or non-citizens attending US school. Must have taken a minimum of one food-service related course and/or have performed a minimum of 1,000 hours of restaurant and hospitality work experience. For full-time or substantial part-time study. Letter of recommendation on school/company letterhead must be submitted with the completed, typed application.

Applications available November 1st. See website or contact Bridgette de Jesus, Program Coordinator, for more information.

2720 — SONOMA CHAMBOLLE-MUSIGNY SISTER CITIES, INC. (Henri Cardinaux Memorial Scholarship)

Chamson Scholarship Committee
PO Box 1633
Sonoma CA 95476-1633
707/939-1344
FAX: 707/939-1344
E-Mail: Baileysci@vom.com

AMOUNT: up to $1,500 (travel + expenses)

DEADLINE(S): JUL 15

FIELD(S): Culinary Arts; Wine Industry; Art; Architecture; Music; History; Fashion

Hands-on experience working in above or similiar fields & living with a family in small French village in Burgundy or other French city. Must be Sonoma County, CA, resident at least 18 years of age & be able to communicate in French. Transcripts, employer recommendation, photograph, & essay (stating why, where, & when) required.

1 award. Non-renewable. Also offers opportunity for candidate in Chambolle-Musigny to obtain work experience & cultural exposure in Sonoma, CA.

2721 — TUSKEGEE UNIVERSITY (Graduate Research Fellowships and Assistantships)

Admissions Office
Tuskegee University, 1506 Franklin Rd., AL 36088
334/727/8500

AMOUNT: Tuition

DEADLINE(S): MAR 15

FIELD(S): Chemistry; Engineering; Environmental Science; Life Sciences; Nutrition; Education

Graduate research fellowships and graduate assistantships are available to qualified individuals who wish to enter Tuskegee University's graduate program in pursuit of a master's degree.

Write for complete information.

2722 — U.S. DEPT. OF HEALTH & HUMAN SERVICES (Indian Health Service Health Professions Scholarship Program)

Twinbrook Metro Plaza, Suite 100
12300 Twinbrook Pkwy.
Rockville MD 20852
301/443-0234
FAX: 301/443-4815
Internet: www.ihs.gov/Recruitment/DHPS/SP/ SBTOC3.asp

AMOUNT: Tuition + fees & monthly stipend of $938.

DEADLINE(S): APR 1

FIELD(S): Health professions, accounting, social work

Open to Native Americans or Alaska natives who are graduate students or college juniors or seniors in a program leading to a career in a fields listed above. U.S. citizenship required. Renewable annually with reapplication.

Scholarship recipients must intend to serve the Indian people. They incur a one-year service obligation to the IHS for each year of support for a minimum of two years. Write for complete information.

SCHOOL OF SOCIAL SCIENCE

2723 — AMERICAN COUNCIL OF LEARNED SOCIETIES (ACLS Fellowships)

Office of Fellowshops & Grants
228 E. 45th St.
New York NY 10017
Written Inquiry

AMOUNT: Up to $20,000

DEADLINE(S): SEP 30

FIELD(S): Humanities, Social Sciences, and other areas having predominately humanistic emphasis

Open to U.S. citizens or legal residents who hold the Ph.D or its equivalent. Fellowships are designed to help scholars devote 6 to 12 continuous months to full-time research.

Write for complete information.

2724 — AMERICAN PSYCHOLOGICAL FOUNDATION (Wayne F. Placek Awards for Scientific Research on Lesbian and Gay Issues)

750 First St., NE
Washington DC 20002-4242
202/336-5814
E-Mail: foundation@apa.org
Internet: psychology.ucdavis.edu/rainbow/html/apfawards.html

AMOUNT: up to $30,000

DEADLINE(S): MAR 15

FIELD(S): Behavioral/Social Science

To increase public's understanding of homosexuality & to alleviate stress that gays/lesbians experience in this & future civilizations. Proposals invited for empirical research from all fields of behavioral/social sciences. Proposals encouraged that deal with attitudes, prejudice, workplace issues, and subgroups historically underrepresented in scientific research. Must have doctoral degree/equivalent & be associated w/ college/university or research institute.

2 awards annually. Small grants (up to $5,000) also available for pilot studies/exploratory research in gay/lesbian issues. Contact above address for details.

2725 — AMERICAN RESEARCH INSTITUTE IN TURKEY (ARIT Fellowship Program)

Univ Penn Museum
33rd & Spruce Streets
Philadelphia PA 19104-6324
215/898-3474
FAX: 215/898-0657
E-Mail: leinwand@sas.upenn.edu
Internet: mec.sas.upenn.edu/ARIT

AMOUNT: Varies

DEADLINE(S): NOV 15

FIELD(S): Humanities; Social Sciences; Turkish Studies

Two-month to one-year fellowships are for postdoctoral scholars & advanced graduate students engaged in research on ancient, medieval, or modern times in Turkey, in any field of the humanities & social sciences. Predoctoral students must have fulfilled all preliminary requirements for doctorate except dissertation. Applicants must maintain an affiliation with an educational institution in the US or Canada. Must submit curriculum vitae, research proposal, & referees.

Contact ARIT for an application.

2726 — AMERICAN RESEARCH INSTITUTE IN TURKEY (Mellon Research Fellowships for Central and Eastern European Scholars in Turkey)

Univ Penn Museum
33rd & Spruce Streets
Philadelphia PA 19104-6324
215/898-3474
FAX: 215/898-0657
E-Mail: leinwand@sas.upenn.edu
Internet: mec.sas.upenn.edu/ARIT

AMOUNT: Stipend up to $10,500 for 2-3 month project (includes travel, living expenses, work-related costs)

DEADLINE(S): MAR 5

FIELD(S): Humanities; Social Sciences

For Czech, Hungarian, Polish, Slovakian, Bulgarian, and Romanian scholars holding a Ph.D. or equivalent who are engaged in advanced research in any field of the social sciences or the humanities involving Turkey. Must be permanent residents of these countries and must obtain formal permission for any research to be carried out.

3 awards annually. Previous fellows not eligible. See website or write to above address for details.

2727 — AMERICAN SCHOOL OF CLASSICAL STUDIES AT ATHENS (Katherine Keene Summer Session Scholarship for Teachers)

993 Lenox Drive, Suite 101
Lawrence NJ 08648
609/844-7577

E-Mail: ascsa@ascsa.org
Internet: www.asca.org

AMOUNT: $2,500

DEADLINE(S): FEB 15

FIELD(S): Classical Studies; Ancient Greece

Scholarships for American public secondary school teachers to attend summer sessions in the above program in Greece. Must include these topics in his/her course material.

Access website for complete information and application or write to Committee on Summer Sessions at above address for details.

2728 — ASIAN INSTITUTE OF TECHNOLOGY (AIT Scholarship Program)

Development Office
PO Box 4, Klongluang
Pathumthani 12120 THAILAND
(66)(2) 516-0110-44 or 524-5032
FAX: (66)(2) 516-2126
E-Mail: ascao@ait.ac.th
Internet: www.ait.ac.th

AMOUNT: US $12,600-$37,960

DEADLINE(S): FEB 15; JUN 15; OCT 15

FIELD(S): Advanced Technologies; Civil Engineering; Environment, Resources, & Development; Business Management

Scholarships and grants open to citizens of Asian countries who are accepted by the institute as a master's or doctotal candidate. Selection is based on academic criteria, practical experience, gender, and country of origin; priority to Mekong Region countries and Asian countries of the former USSR.

250 awards annually. Contact AIT for an application.

2729 — ASSOCIATION FOR INSTITUTIONAL RESEARCH (Fellowship to Summer Institute)

114 Stone Building, FSU
Tallahassee FL 32306-4462
850/644-4470
FAX: 850/644-8824
E-Mail: air@mailer.fsu.edu
Internet: http://airweb.org

AMOUNT: Varies

DEADLINE(S): JAN 15

FIELD(S): Social sciences, education

The Association provides fellowships to doctoral and postdoctoral researchers for its summer institute on "Improving Institutional Research in Postsecondary Educational Institutions."

Contact organization for details.

2730 — ASSOCIATION FOR INSTITUTIONAL RESEARCH (Research Grant)

114 Stone Building, FSU
Tallahassee FL 32306-4462
850/644-4470
FAX: 850/644-8824
E-Mail: air@mailer.fsu.edu
Internet: http://airweb.org

AMOUNT: $30,000/yr.

DEADLINE(S): JAN 15

FIELD(S): Social sciences, education, finance, economics

The Association provides one-year grants for doctoral or post-doctoral research appropriate for its program "Improving Institutional Research in Postsecondary Educational Institutions."

Must submit proposal, including budget. Contact organization for details.

2731 — ASSOCIATION FOR WOMEN IN SCIENCE EDUCATIONAL FOUNDATION (AWIS Predoctoral Awards)

1200 New York Ave. NW, Suite 650
Washington DC 20005
202/326-8940 or 800-886-AWIS
E-Mail: awis@awis.org
Internet: www.awis.org

AMOUNT: $1,000

DEADLINE(S): JAN 16

FIELD(S): Various Sciences and Social Sciences

Scholarships for female doctoral students. Summary page, description of research project, resume, references, transcripts, and biographical sketch required. US citizens may study at any graduate institution; non-citizens must study at US institutions.

5-10 awards annually. See website or write to above address for an application and complete information.

2732 — ASSOCIATION FOR WOMEN IN SCIENCE EDUCATIONAL FOUNDATION (AWIS Pre-doctoral Awards)

1200 New York Ave. NW, Suite 650
Washington DC 20005
202/326-8940 or 800/886-AWIS
E-Mail: awis@awis.org
Internet: www.awis.org

AMOUNT: $1,000

DEADLINE(S): JAN 16

FIELD(S): Various Sciences and Social Sciences

Scholarships for female doctoral students. Summary page, description of research project, resume, references, transcripts, and biographical sketch required. US citizens may study at any graduate institution; non-citizens must be enrolled in US institutions.

5-10 awards annually. See website or write to above address for an application and more information.

2733 — ASSOCIATION FOR WOMEN IN SCIENCE EDUCATIONAL FOUNDATION (Ruth Satter Memorial Award)

1200 New York Ave., NW, Suite 650
Washington DC 20005
202/326-8940 or 800/886-AWIS
E-Mail: awis@awis.org
Internet: www.awis.org

AMOUNT: $1,000

DEADLINE(S): JAN 16

FIELD(S): Various Sciences and Social Sciences

Scholarships for female doctoral students who have interrupted their education for at least three years to raise a family. Summary page, description of research project, resume, references, transcripts, biographical sketch, and letter from your department to confirm eligibility required. US citizens may study at any graduate institution; non-citizens must attend US institutions.

See website or write to above address for more information or an application.

2734 — ASSOCIATION FOR WOMEN IN SCIENCE EDUCATIONAL FOUNDATION (Ruth Satter Memorial Award)

1200 New York Ave. NW, Suite 650
Washington DC 20005
202/326-8940 or 800/886-AWIS
E-Mail: awis@awis.org
Internet: www.awis.org

AMOUNT: $1,000

DEADLINE(S): JAN 16

FIELD(S): Various Sciences and Social Sciences

Scholarships for female doctoral students who have interupted their education three years or more to raise a family. Summary page, description of research project, resume, references, transcripts, biographical sketch, and proof of eligibility from department head required. US citizens may attend any graduate institution; non-citizens must be enrolled in US institutions.

See website or write to above address for more information or an application.

2735 — AUSTRALIAN FEDERATION OF UNIVERSITY WOMEN - WESTERN AUSTRALIA (Joyce Riley Bursary)

Bursary Liaison Officer
PO Box 48
Nedlands WA 6909 AUSTRALIA
Written Inquiry

AMOUNT: Aus$1,700 - Aus$2,750

DEADLINE(S): JUL 31

FIELD(S): Humanities; Social Sciences

To support women graduates of a Western Australian university to complete a higher degree or post-doctoral research in Humanities or Social Sciences at a recognized university in any country.

Membership in AFUW or in IFUW is required. Contact above location for further information.

2736 — AUSTRALIAN FEDERATION OF UNIVERSITY WOMEN - WESTERN AUSTRALIA (Joyce Riley Bursary)

Bursary Liaison Officer
PO Box 48
Nedlands WA 6009 AUSTRALIA
Written Inquiry

AMOUNT: Aus$1,700 - Aus$2,750

DEADLINE(S): JUL 31

FIELD(S): Humanities; Social Sciences

To support women graduates of a recognized university to complete a higher degree or post-doctoral research at a university in Western Australia.

Membership in AFUW or in IFUW is required. Write to above address for complete information.

2737 — BUSINESS & PROFESSIONAL WOMEN'S FOUNDATION (BPW Career Advancement Scholarship Program)

2012 Massachusetts Ave., NW
Washington DC 20036-1070
202/293-1200, ext. 169
FAX: 202/861-0298
Internet: www.bpwusa.org

AMOUNT: $500-$1,000

DEADLINE(S): APR 15

FIELD(S): Biology, Science, Education, Engineering, Social Science, Paralegal, Humanities, Business, Math, Computers, Law, MD, DD

For women (US citizens) aged 25+ accepted into accredited program at US institution (+Puerto Rico & Virgin Islands). Must graduate within 12 to 24 months from the date of grant and demonstrate critical finanacial need. Must have a plan to upgrade skills, train for a new career field, or to enter/re-enter the job market.

Full- or part-time study. For info see website or send business-sized, self-addressed, double-stamped envelope.

2738 — CANADIAN FEDERATION OF UNIVERSITY WOMEN (Margaret Dale Philp Award)

251 Bank St., Ste. 600
Ottawa Ontario K2P 1X3 CANADA
613/234-2732
Internet: www.cfuw.ca

AMOUNT: $1,000

DEADLINE(S): NOV 15

FIELD(S): Humanities; Social Sciences

For women who reside in Canada and are pursuing graduate studies in the humanities or social sciences, with special consideration given to study in Canadian history. Must hold at least a bachelor's degree or equivalent from a recognized university and have been accepted into, or be currently enrolled in the proposed program and place of study.

$20 filing fee. Contact CFUW for an application after August 1st. Candidates will be notified by May 31st. Funded by CFUW/Kitchener-Waterloo.

2739 — CHRISTIAN A. JOHNSON ENDEAVOR FOUNDATION (Native American Fellows)

Harvard Univ., 79 John F. Kennedy St.
Cambridge MA 02138
617/495-1152
FAX: 617/496-3900
Internet: www.ksg.harvard.edu/hpaied/
cjohn.htm

AMOUNT: Varies

DEADLINE(S): MAY 1

FIELD(S): Social sciences, government, or program related to Native American studies

Fellowships for students of Native American ancestry who attend a John F. Kennedy School of Government degree program. Applicant, parent, or grandparent must hold membership in a federally or state-recognized tribe, band, or other organized group of Native Americans. Must be commited to a career in American Indian affairs. Awards based on merit and need.

Renewable, based on renomination and availability of funds. To apply, contact John F. Kennedy School of Government at above address.

2740 — EAST TEXAS HISTORICAL ASSOCIATION (Ottis Lock Endowment Awards)

PO Box 6223
SFA Station
Nacogdoches TX 75962
409/468-2407

AMOUNT: $500

DEADLINE(S): MAY 1

FIELD(S): History; Social Science

Open to residents of East Texas who will be pursuing undergraduate or graduate studies at an East Texas college or university.

Renewable with adequate progress towards degree. Contact East Texas Historical Association for an application.

2741 — EPILEPSY FOUNDATION OF AMERICA (Junior Investigator Research Grants)

4351 Garden City Drive
Landover MD 20785-2267
301/459-3700 or 800/EFA-1000
FAX: 301/577-2684
TDD: 800/332-2070
E-Mail: postmaster@efa.org
Internet: www.efa.org

AMOUNT: up to $40,000

DEADLINE(S): SEP 1

FIELD(S): Epilepsy as related to Biological, Behavioral, & Social Sciences

One-year research grants to support basic and clinical research in the biological, behavioral, and social sciences which will advance the understanding, treatment, and prevention of epilepsy. Priority given to beginning investigators just entering the field of epilepsy research, to new or innovative projects. Applications evaluated on basis of scientific merit.

Contact EFA for an application.

2742 — EUROPEAN CENTRE OF ANALYSIS IN THE SOCIAL SCIENCES [ECASS] (Bursaries for Essex Summer School)

Univ. of Essex, Wivenhoe Park
Colchester, Essex CO4 3SQ ENGLAND UK
+44 (0) 1206 873087
FAX: +44 (0) 1206 872403
E-Mail: ecass@essex.ac.uk
Internet: www.irc.essex.ac.uk/ecass/

AMOUNT: Accomodation, subsistence, and some travel aid

DEADLINE(S): FEB 28

FIELD(S): Social Sciences

Bursaries for scientific researchers carrying out non-proprietary research who are nationals of a member state of the European Community or of an Associated State (currently Iceland, Liechtenstein, Norway, and Israel) and who are working in these countries. U.K. researchers or those working inside the U.K. are not eligible for these bursaries. Emphasis is on Data Analysis and Collection in the Social Sciences. Must be computer literate and fluent in English.

Visits are usually 2 weeks to 3 months. Bursary recipients are required to spend at least an additional twelve working days at ECASS.

2743 — EUROPEAN UNIVERSITY INSTITUTE (Jean Monnet Fellowship)

Via Dei Roccettini 9
I-50016 San Domenico Di Fiesole (FL) Italy
0039-055-46851
FAX: 0039-055-4685444

E-Mail: applyjmf@datacomm.iue.it
Internet: www.iue.it/JMF/Welcome.html

AMOUNT: 2,000,000-3,500,000 Italian lire per month (i.e. 1,025-1,750 ECU) + medical & family allowances (depends on whether fellow is in receipt of payment from another source and on extent of duties carried out at the Institute)

DEADLINE(S): NOV 1

FIELD(S): Europe: History, Society, Politics, Economics, Law

Post-doctoral fellowships. Fellows are required to make scholarly contribution to research on Europe within one of EUI's research projects or on topic, falling within general interests of the Institute. Publication of research is expected.

25 fellowships annually. Financial need NOT considered. See website or contact Dr. Andreas Frijdal at above address for complete information.

2744 — EUROPEAN UNIVERSITY INSTITUTE (National Postgraduate Scholarships)

Via De Roccettini 9
San Domenico Di Fiesole (FI 50016) ITALY
0039/055-46851
FAX: 0039/055-4685444
E-Mail: applyres@datacomm.iue.it
Internet: www.iue.it

AMOUNT: $1,000/month + travel & medical/family allowances

DEADLINE(S): JAN 31

FIELD(S): Political Science; Social Sciences; Law; Economics; History

Open to graduate & postgraduate students at the Institute who have good honors and a research project having European dimension. Awards are available only to nationals of the Institute's member states. US citizens must have sufficient personal funds or another grant to cover maintenance & tuition; may apply to Fulbright Commission which may award up to two grants per academic year to US citizens with tuition-fee waivers.

130 awards annually. Renewable. Contact Dr. Andreas Frijdal for an application.

2745 — FORD FOUNDATION/NATIONAL RESEARCH COUNCIL (Postdoctoral Fellowship for Minorities)

National Research Council
2101 Constitution Ave.
Washington DC 20418
202/334-2860
E-Mail: infofell@nas.edu
Internet: http//www.nas.edu/fo/index.html

AMOUNT: $25,000 + relocation and research allowance

DEADLINE(S): JAN 3

FIELD(S): Life and physical sciences, mathematics, engineering sciences, behavioral and social sciences, and the humanities

For U.S. citizens who received a Ph.D or Sc.D in the last 7 years and who are Native Amer. Indian or Alaskan, Black/African American, Mexican American, Native Pacific Islander, or Puerto Rican and who are or plan to be in a teaching or research career.

Contact above website or address for complete information.

2746 — FORD FOUNDATION/NATIONAL RESEARCH COUNCIL (Predoctoral/ Dissertation Fellowships for Minorities)

2101 Constitution Ave.
Washington DC 20418
202/334-2872
E-Mail: infofell@nas.edu
Internet: http//www.nas.edu/fo/index.html

AMOUNT: $14,000 annual stipend + $6,000 grant to institution; $18,000 for dissertation fellowship

DEADLINE(S): NOV 3

FIELD(S): Most fields of study: sciences, humanities, engineering, behavioral science, social sciences, and computer science

Predoctoral and dissertation fellowships for students whose ethnicity is Alaskan Native, Black/ African American, Mexican American/Chicano, Native American Indian, Native Pacific Islander, or Puerto Rican. For research-based programs leading to careers in college teaching and research.

Contact above address or website.

2747 — FRENCH-AMERICAN FOUNDATION (Bicentennial Fellowships)

41 East 72nd St.
New York NY 10021
212/288-4000
FAX: 212/288-4765
E-Mail: French_AmerFdn@msn.com

AMOUNT: 10,000 French francs/mo.

DEADLINE(S): FEB 2

FIELD(S): Social sciences

For doctoral students in the social sciences to travel to France for one year to conduct research essential to the completion of their dissertations. Must have completed all other requirements for Ph.D. May not use the award until exams are passed.

Requires application with a statement of purpose, full academic records, plan of research, bibliography, abstract, and three academic recommendations.

2748 — GETTY RESEARCH INSTITUTE FOR THE HISTORY OF ART AND THE HUMANITIES (Fellowships)

1200 Getty Center Dr., Ste. 1100
Los Angeles CA 90049-1688
310/440-7392
FAX: 310/440-7782
E-Mail: residentialgrants@getty.edu
Internet: www.getty.edu/gri/scholars

AMOUNT: $18,000 (doctoral); $22,000 (postdoctoral)

DEADLINE(S): NOV 1

FIELD(S): Arts; Humanities; Social Sciences

Open to doctoral and postdoctoral scholars whose areas of research fall within the year's chosen theme. Predoctoral candidates should expect to complete dissertations during the fellowship year. Postdoctorates should have received doctorate in humanities or social sciences within the last three years and be rewriting dissertations for publication. Tenable at the Getty Research Institute in Los Angeles, CA.

Contact Getty Institute for an application and current theme.

2749 — GLADYS KRIEBLE DELMAS FOUNDATION (Predoctoral & Postdoctoral Grants in Venice & the Veneto)

521 5th Avenue, Suite 1612
New York NY 10175-1699
212/687-0011
FAX: 212/687-8877
E-Mail: DelmasFdtn@aol.com
Internet: www.delmas.org

AMOUNT: $500-$12,500

DEADLINE(S): DEC 15

FIELD(S): Research of Venice and the former Venetian empire and study of contemporary Venetian society and culture.

Pre- and postdoctoral grants for historical research on Venice. Humanities and social sciences are eligible areas of study, including archaeology, architecture, art, bibliography, economics, history, history of science, law, literature, music, political science, religion, and theater.

Applicants must have experience in advanced research and be U.S. citizens/residents; grad students must have fulfilled all doctoral requirements except dissertation by Dec. 15.

2750 — HARRY FRANK GUGGENHEIM FOUNDATION (Dissertation Fellowships)

527 Madison Ave.
New York NY 10022-4304
212/644-4907

AMOUNT: $10,000

DEADLINE(S): FEB 1

FIELD(S): Behavioral Sciences; Social Sciences; Biology

Awards are intended for support during the writing of the Ph.D. thesis in disciplines addressing the causes, manifestations, and control of violence, aggression, and dominance. Applicants must have completed research and be ready to write.

Contact Guggenheim Foundation for an application.

2751 — HARRY FRANK GUGGENHEIM FOUNDATION (Postdoctoral Research Grants)

527 Madison Ave.
New York NY 10022-4304
212/644-4907

AMOUNT: $30,000 (max.)

DEADLINE(S): AUG 1

FIELD(S): Behavioral Sciences; Social Sciences; Biology

One- to two-year grants are open to postdoctoral researchers in the above fields whose work leads to a better understanding of the causes, manifestations, and control of violence, aggression, and dominance in the modern world.

25-35 awards annually. Contact Guggenheim Foundation for an application.

2752 — INSTITUTE FOR ADVANCED STUDY (Post-doctoral Fellowship Awards)

Olden Lane
Princeton NJ 08540
609/734-8000

AMOUNT: Varies according to school

DEADLINE(S): Varies

FIELD(S): Historical Studies; Social Sciences; Natural Sciences; Mathematics

Post-doctoral fellowships at the institute for advanced study for those whose term can be expected to result in work of significance and individuality.

150-160 fellowships per academic year although some can be extended. Request application materials from school's administrative officer.

2753 — INSTITUTE FOR ADVANCED STUDIES IN THE HUMANITIES (Visiting Research Fellowships)

Univ Edinburgh
Hope Park Square
Edinburgh EH8 9NW SCOTLAND UK
0131 650 4671
FAX: 0131 668 2252
E-Mail: iash@ed.ac.uk
Internet: www.ed.ac.uk/iash/homepage.html

AMOUNT: Non-stipendiary*

DEADLINE(S): DEC 1

FIELD(S): Arts; Social Sciences; Law; Music; Divinity

Postdoctoral research fellowships of between two and six months are tenable at the Institute for Advanced Studies in the Humanities. Based on academic record and publications. *Most fellowships are honorary, but limited support towards expenses is available to a small number of candidates. Fellows are allocated a study room within the Institute and hold one or two seminars during their tenure. Must submit research report at end of fellowship. No teaching required.

15 awards annually. Not renewable. Contact Mrs. Anthea Taylor for an application.

2754 — INSTITUTE FOR HUMANE STUDIES (Humane Studies Fellowship)

4084 University Dr., Ste. 101
Fairfax VA 22030-6812
703/934-6920 or 800/697-8799
FAX: 703/352-7535
E-Mail: ihs@gmu.edu
Internet: www.theihs.org

AMOUNT: up to $12,000

DEADLINE(S): DEC 31

FIELD(S): Social Sciences; Law; Humanities; Jurisprudence; Journalism

Awards are for graduate and advanced undergraduate students pursuing degrees at any accredited domestic or foreign school. Based on academic performance, demonstrated interest in classical liberal ideas, and potential to contribute to the advancement of a free society.

90 awards annually. Apply online or contact IHS for an application.

2755 — INSTITUTE FOR HUMANE STUDIES (Summer Residential Program)

4084 University Dr., Ste. 101
Fairfax VA 22030-6812
703/934-6920 or 800/697-8799
FAX: 703/352-7535
E-Mail: ihs@gmu.edu
Internet: www.theihs.org

AMOUNT: All seminar fees: program cost, room/board, materials, and books

DEADLINE(S): MAR 1

FIELD(S): Social Sciences; Humanities; Law; Journalism; Public Policy; Education; Writing

For college students, recent graduates, and graduate students who share an interest in learning and exchanging ideas about the scope of individual rights. One-week and weekend seminars at various campus locations across the U.S.

Apply online or contact IHS for an application.

2756 — INTER-AMERICAN FOUNDATION (Field Research Fellowship Programs for U.S., Latin American, and Caribbean Citizens)

901 N. Stuart St., 10th Floor
Arlington VA 22203
703/841-3800
FAX: 703/527-3529
E-Mail: correo@aif.gov
Internet: www.iaf.gov

AMOUNT: Varies

DEADLINE(S): APR 28

FIELD(S): International Relations, Social Sciences, Humanities, Latin American Studies

Fellowships for Latin American, Carribean, and U.S. doctoral level students for field research in Latin America and the Caribbean. Must be enrolled in U.S. university.

Access website for deadline and application information. Organization does not mail information.

2757 — INTER-AMERICAN FOUNDATION (Master's Research Fellowships)

901 N. Stuart St., 10th Floor
Arlington VA 22203
703/841-3800
FAX: 703/527-3529
E-Mail: correo@aif.gov
Internet: www.iaf.gov

AMOUNT: Varies

DEADLINE(S): APR

FIELD(S): Latin American & Caribbean Studies, Internations Relations, Social Sciences, Humanities, etc.

Open to masters students enrolled in U.S. universities for field research in Latin American or the Caribbean. For citizens of Caribbean and Latin American independent countries, and the U.S.

Access website for deadline and application information. Organization does not mail information.

2758 — INTERNATIONAL COUNCIL FOR CANADIAN STUDIES (Government of France Graduate Awards)

325 Dalhousie, S-800
Ottawa Ontario CANADA K1N 7G2
613/789-7828
FAX: 613/789-7830
E-Mail: general@iccs-ciec.ca
Internet: www.iccs-ciec.ca

AMOUNT: Tuition, travel, and living allowance

DEADLINE(S): OCT 31

FIELD(S): Pure and Applied Sciences, Social Sciences, Engineering, Medicine

One-year graduate scholarships open to Canadian citizens for study and research at the doctoral level. Sound knowledge of the French language is required.

Must hold masters degree. Cannot be held concurrently with other scholarships or remuneration. Write or access website for complete information.

2759 — INTERNATIONAL RESEARCH AND EXCHANGES BOARD (Mongolia Research Fellowship Program)

1616 H St., NW
Washington DC 20006
202/628-8188
FAX: 202/628-8189
E-Mail: edickson@irex.org
Internet: www.irex.org

AMOUNT: $7,000

DEADLINE(S): DEC 15

FIELD(S): Humanities; Social Sciences

Open to US and Mongolian citizens pursuing predoctoral or postdoctoral studies/research in the humanities and social sciences as related to Mongolia. Financial need NOT a factor.

4-5 awards annually. Not renewable. See website or contact Emilie Dickson for an application.

2760 — INTERNATIONAL RESEARCH AND EXCHANGES BOARD (Consortium for the Humanities & Social Sciences)

1616 H St., NW
Washington DC 20006
202/628-8188
FAX: 202/628-8189
E-Mail: edickson@irex.org
Internet: www.irex.org

AMOUNT: $10,000 (max.)

DEADLINE(S): JAN 14

FIELD(S): Humanities; Social Sciences

Grant is open to students of any nationality who are pursuing a doctoral, postgraduate, or professional degree in the humanities or social sciences. Award must benefit a university in Armenia, Azerbaijan, Georgia, Russia, and/or Ukraine. Financial need NOT a factor.

20 awards annually. Not renewable. See website or contact Emilie Dickson for an application.

2761 — INTERNATIONAL RESEARCH AND EXCHANGES BOARD (Short-Term Travel Grants)

1616 H St., NW
Washington DC 20006
202/628-8188
FAX: 202/628-8189
E-Mail: irex@info.irex.org
Internet: www.irex.org

AMOUNT: $3,000 (max.)

DEADLINE(S): FEB 1; JUN 1

FIELD(S): Humanities; Social Sciences

Open to US citizens/permanent residents who wish to pursue postdoctoral research in Central/Eastern Europe or Mongolia. Must have Ph.D. or equivalent professional degree. Financial need NOT a factor.

Not renewable. See website or contact Denise Cormaney, Senior Program Officer, for an application.

2762 — ISTITUTO ITALIANO PER GLI STUDI STORICI - ITALIAN INSTITUTE FOR HISTORICAL STUDIES (Federico Chabod & Adolfo Omodeo Scholarships)

Via Benedetto Croce, 12
80134 Napoli ITALY
0039/81-5517159
FAX: 0039/81-5512390

AMOUNT: 12,000,000 Lira

DEADLINE(S): SEP 30

FIELD(S): Humanities; Social Sciences; History; Philosophy; Arts; Economics; Literature

For non-Italian citizens who have completed a university degree in Humanities dept. of a non-Italian university. Intended to allow young scholars to participate in the work of the Institute and to complete personal scholarly research with the help of teaching staff of the Institute. Must include birth certificate, proof of citizenship, university diploma, scholarly work, curriculum of studies w/ indication of language skills, research proposal, & reference letter.

2 awards annually. Contact Marta Herling, Secretary, at above address for an application.

2763 — JAPAN SOCIETY FOR THE PROMOTION OF SCIENCE (Post-doctoral Fellowships for Foreign Researchers)

Jochi-Kioizaka Bldg., 6-26-3 Kioi-cho
Chiyoda-Ku
Tokyo 102 JAPAN
+81-3-3263-1721
Telex: J32281
FAX: +81-3-3263-1854

AMOUNT: 270,000 yen per month

DEADLINE(S): SEP 25; MAY 23

FIELD(S): Humanities; Social Sciences; Natural Sciences; Engineering; Medicine

Post-doctoral fellowships for advanced study & research in Japan.

Write for complete information

2764 — LONDON SCHOOL OF ECONOMICS & POLITICAL SCIENCE (Roseberry Studentship)

Houghton St.
Scholarships Office
London WC2A 2AE ENGLAND
071-405 7686

AMOUNT: 1,000 pounds sterling (approx)

DEADLINE(S): MAY 1

FIELD(S): Social Sciences

A Roseberry studentship will be offered for graduate work at the school in the social sciences. Preference will be given to candidates who are studying some aspect of transport.

Studentship may be renewed. Write for complete information.

2765 — LONDON SCHOOL OF ECONOMICS AND POLITICAL SCIENCE (Jackson Lewis Scholarship)

Houghton St.
Scholarships Office
London WC2A 2AE ENGLAND
071/955 7163

AMOUNT: 850 pounds sterling

DEADLINE(S): MAY 1

FIELD(S): Social Sciences

Open to applicants who register as full-time students of the school & pursue graduate work in the social sciences. Scholarships normally tenable for two years. Financial need is a consideration.

Write for complete information.

2766 — MINISTRY OF THE FLEMISH COMMUNITY (Fellowships)

Embassy of Belgium
3330 Garfield St., NW
Washington DC 20008
202/625-5850/51
FAX: 202/342-8346
E-Mail: flemishcomdc@wizard.net

AMOUNT: Monthly stipend, tuition, & health care coverage

DEADLINE(S): JAN 31

FIELD(S): Art; Music; Humanities; Social Science; Political Science; Law; Economics; Science; Medicine

Open to US citizens under age 35 who wish to pursue graduate or postgraduate studies in Flanders, Belgium.

Contact Flemish Community for registration forms.

2767 — NATIONAL ACADEMY OF EDUCATION (Spencer Postdoctoral Fellowship Program)

NY Univ, School of Education
726 Broadway, Rm. 509
New York NY 10003-9580
212/998-9035
FAX: 212/995-4435
E-Mail: nae.info@nyu.edu
Internet: www.nae.nyu.edu

AMOUNT: $45,000

DEADLINE(S): DEC 1

FIELD(S): Education; Humanities; Social Sciences

Fellowships of one or two years are open to individual researchers in education, humanities, or social and behavioral sciences. Research must have apparent relevance to education. Doctoral degree must have been received within the last five years. Based on past research record and quality of proposed project. Must submit project description, career history, referee form, curriculum vitae/resume, and example of past research relevant to education.

30 awards annually. Not renewable. Contact NAE for an application. Recipients notified in May.

2768 — NATIONAL COUNCIL FOR THE SOCIAL STUDIES (Grant for the Enhancement of Geographic Literacy)

3501 Newark St. NW
Washington DC 20016
202/966-7840
FAX: 202/966-2061
Internet: www.ncss.org/awards/grants.html

AMOUNT: $2,500

DEADLINE(S): JUL 3

FIELD(S): Social Studies

Grant is co-sponsored by the George F. Cram Company, map publishers. For teachers of any level who present a program to promote and enhance geography education in the schools. Must incorporate the National Georgraphy Standards in "Geography for Life," the "Fundamental Themes in Geography," and appropriate sections of "Expectations of Excellence: Curriculum Standards for Social Studies."

Check website or contact organization for details.

2769 — NATIONAL HUMANITIES CENTER (Lilly Fellowships in Religion and the Humanities)

PO Box 12256
Research Triangle Park NC 27709-2256
919/549-0661
FAX: 919/990-8535
E-Mail: nhc@ga.unc.edu
Internet: www.nhc.rtp.nc.us:8080

AMOUNT: Stipend ($35,000-$50,000) + Travel Expenses (for fellow & dependents)

DEADLINE(S): OCT 15

FIELD(S): Religion & the Humanities

Postdoctoral fellowships for the study of religion by humanistic scholars from fields other than religion and theology. Fellows will form the core of a monthly seminar on religion and the humanities. Curriculum vitae, 1,000-word proposal, and three letters of recommendation are required.

3-4 awards annually. Contact NHC for application materials.

2770 — NATIONAL PARKS SERVICE (Science Scholars Program)

1849 C St., NW
Washington DC 20240
202/208-6843
E-Mail: aspiceland@goparks.org
Internet: www.nps.gov

AMOUNT: $25,000/yr.

DEADLINE(S): JUN 15

FIELD(S): Biological, Physical, Social, & Cultural Sciences

Three-year scholarships to Ph.D. candidates pursuing degrees in above fields. Objectives are to encourage young scientists to engage in park-related research, conduct innovative research on issues central to the National Parks, and encourage use of parks as laboratories for sciences. NPF will transfer the scholarship funds to each student's university, providing for tuition, field work, stipend, & other research expenses. Must submit research proposal.

4 awards annually. See website or contact Dr. Gary E. Machlis, Program Director, at NPS for an application. Winners announced shortly after August 15th.

2771 — NEWBERRY LIBRARY (Long-Term Fellowships)

60 West Walton Street
Chicago IL 60610-3380
312/943-9090
E-Mail: research@newberry.org
Internet: www.newberry.org

AMOUNT: Up to $30,000

DEADLINE(S): JAN 20

FIELD(S): Humanities, History, & related fields

Six postdoctoral fellowship programs are available for scholars wishing to use the Library's collection for writing or research. Fellowships last six to eleven months, and each have slightly different requirements.

See website for details and an application or write to above address.

2772 — NEWBERRY LIBRARY (Monticello College Foundation Fellowship For Women)

60 West Walton Street
Chicago IL 60610-3380
312/255-3660
E-Mail: research@newberry.org
Internet: www.newberry.org

AMOUNT: $12,500

DEADLINE(S): JAN 20

FIELD(S): Humanities, History, Study of Women

Six-month post-doctoral fellowships for women in the early stages of their academic careers. For research, writing, and participation in the intellectual life of the Library. Applicant's topic must be related to Newberry's collections; preference given to proposals concerned with the study of women.

See website for application or write to above address.

2773 — NEWBERRY LIBRARY (Short-Term Fellowships)

60 West Walton Street
Chicago IL 60610-3380
312/943-9090
E-Mail: research@newberry.org
Internet: www.newberry.org

AMOUNT: $800-$1,500/month

DEADLINE(S): MAR 1

FIELD(S): Humanities, History, & related fields

Nine programs for postdoctoral scholars or doctoral students at the dissertation stage. Study varies from two weeks to three months and is for those making use of Newberry's collections. Each program has slightly different requirements.

See website for details and applications or write to above address.

2774 — NEWBERRY LIBRARY (Special Fellowships)

60 West Walton Street
Chicago IL 60610-3380
312/255-3666
E-Mail: research@newberry.org
Internet: www.newberry.org

AMOUNT: Varies

DEADLINE(S): DEC 15

FIELD(S): Humanities, History, & related fields

Fellowships for three months to one year for doctoral or postdoctoral students to study in Germany, France, or Great Britain in fields related to Newberry's collections. Some deadlines JAN 20th. Specific locations are: Wolfenb, ttel, Germany; Ecole Nationale des Chartes, Paris, France; and the British Academy, Great Britain.

See website for more details and applications or write to above address.

2775 — NORTHERN IRELAND DEPT. OF EDUCATION (Post-graduate Studentships)

Rathgael House
Balloo Road
Bangor Co. Down BT19 7PR N.IRELAND
01247-279279

AMOUNT: 5,295 pounds sterling + fees

DEADLINE(S): Varies (Check with Northern Ireland universities)

FIELD(S): Humanities; Science; Social Science

Research (Ph.D) and advanced courses (MA/MS) awards available for study in Northern Ireland. Must have been a resident of the United Kingdom for at least three years.

Research studentships renewable if work is satisfactory. Write for complete information.

2776 — OAK RIDGE ASSOCIATED UNIVERSITIES (National Science Foundation Graduate Research Fellowships)

PO Box 3010
Oak Ridge TN 37831-3010
423/241-4300
FAX: 423/241-4513
E-Mail: nsfgrfp@orau.gov
Internet: www.orau.gov/nsf/nsffel.htm

AMOUNT: $15,000 stipend + $10,500 tuition allowance

DEADLINE(S): NOV 4

FIELD(S): Science; Math; Engineering; Computer Science

Three-year fellowships for graduate study leading to research-based master's or doctoral degrees in the above fields. Must be US citizens, nationals, or permanent residents at the time of application. Fellowships are awarded on the basis of ability. Women, minorities, and those with disabilities are strongly encouraged to apply. One-time International Research Travel Allowance available.

1,000 awards annually. Contact Jeannette Bouchard for an application/more information.

2777 — PEACE RESEARCH CENTRE (Peace Research Loan Scholarship)

c/o Gujarat Vidyapith
Ahmedabad-380014 INDIA
7450746

AMOUNT: 2,000/Rs (25% returnable)

DEADLINE(S): JUNE

FIELD(S): Peace Research, Peace Education, Nonviolence

Financial aid for students between the ages of 21 and 65 in a Master of Arts program concentrating on research regarding peace, peace education, and nonviolence.

Duration of one year only.

2778 — PEW YOUNGER SCHOLARS PROGRAM (Graduate Fellowships)

G-123 Hesburgh Library, University of Notre Dame
Notre Dame IN 46556
219/631-4531
FAX: 219/631-8721
E-Mail: Karen.M.Heinig.2@nd.edu
Internet: www.nd.edu/~pesp/pew/PYSPHistory.html

AMOUNT: $13,000

DEADLINE(S): NOV 30

FIELD(S): Social Sciences, Humanities, Theology

Program is for use at any Christian undergraduate school and most seminaries. Check with organization to see if your school qualifies. Apply during senior year. Recipients may enter a competition in which ten students will be awarded a $39,000 ($13,000/yr.) fellowship for three years of dissertation study. For use at top-ranked Ph.D. programs at outstanding universities.

NOT for study in medicine, law business, performing arts, fine arts, or the pastorate. Check website and/or organization for details.

2779 — PI GAMMA MU INTERNATIONAL HONOR SOCIETY IN SOCIAL SCIENCE (Scholarships)

1001 Millington, Ste. B
Winfield KS 67156
316/221-3128
FAX: 316/221-7124
E-Mail: pgm@sckans.edu
Internet: sckans.edu/~pgm

AMOUNT: $1,000-$2,000

DEADLINE(S): JAN 30

FIELD(S): Social Science

Applicants must be members of Pi Gamma Mu and pursuing graduate study in social science. Criteria for selection include GPA, letters of recommendation, extracurricular activities, and financial need.

10 awards annually. Not renewable. Contact Executive Director Sue Watters for an application.

2780 — RESEARCH COUNCIL OF NORWAY (Senior Scientist Visiting Fellowship)

P.O. Box 2700 St. Hanshaugen
N-0131 Oslo NORWAY
+47 22 03 70 00
FAX: +47 22 03 70 01
E-Mail: intstip@nfr.no
Internet: www.forskningsradet.no

AMOUNT: NOK 25,000-1st 2 months; NOK 10,000-succeeding months

DEADLINE(S): Varies

FIELD(S): Bioproduction & Processing (including agriculture and veterinary science); Industry & Energy; Culture & Society (including social sciences and the humanities); Medicine & Health; Environment & Development; Science & Technology

Fellowships for scientists to work at Norwegian research institutes. Project funding does not include salary; expenses connected with the stay in Norway are covered.

For a list of institutions, contact the Research Council at above location. Then apply to institution, which then will submit fellowship application.

2781 — RESOURCES FOR THE FUTURE (Gilbert F. White Fellowship Program)

1616 P Street NW
Washington DC 20036-1400
202/328-5067
Internet: www.rff.org

AMOUNT: Based upon current salary + research support, office, and up to $1,000 for moving or living expenses.

DEADLINE(S): FEB 26

FIELD(S): Social Sciences; Natural Resources; Energy; Environment

Postdoctoral resident fellowships for professionals in the above fields who wish to devote eleven months to scholarly work on a social or policy problem in these. Faculty members on sabbatical encouraged to apply.

All information is on website. Address inquiries and applications to Coordinator for Academic Programs. NO fax submissions.

2782 — RESOURCES FOR THE FUTURE (Joseph L. Fisher Dissertation Fellowships)

1616 P Street NW
Washington DC 20036-1400
202/328-5000
Internet: www.rff.org

AMOUNT: $12,000/yr

DEADLINE(S): FEB 26

FIELD(S): Economics and other Social Sciences related to environment, natural resources, or energy

Fellowship to graduate students in the final year of their dissertatio research in the above fields.

All information is on website. NO fax submissions.

2783 — RESOURCES FOR THE FUTURE (RFF Summer Internship Program)

1616 P Street NW
Washington DC 20036-1400
202/328-5000
E-Mail: lewis@rff.org or voigt@rff.org
Internet: www.rff.org

AMOUNT: $375/week

DEADLINE(S): MAR 12

FIELD(S): Social Sciences, Natural Resources, Energy, Environment

Resident paid summer internships for undergraduate and graduate students for research in the above fields. Divisions are Center for Risk Management, Energy and Natural Resources, and

Quality of the Environment. Candidates should have outstanding policy analysis and writing skills. For both U.S. and non-U.S. citizens.

All information is on website. Address inquiries and applications to Sue Lewis (Energy & Natural Resources and Quality of the Environment) or Marilyn Voigt (Center for Risk Management). NO fax submissions.

2784 — RESOURCES FOR THE FUTURE (Walter O. Spofford, Jr., Memorial Internship)

1616 P Street NW
Washington DC 20036-1400
202/328-5000
E-Mail: moran@rff.org
Internet: www.rff.org

AMOUNT: Individually negotiated

DEADLINE(S): MAR 12

FIELD(S): Chinese environmental issues in the areas of Social Sciences, Natural Resources, Energy, Environment

Resident paid internships for graduate students for research in the above fields. Candidates should have outstanding policy analysis and writing skills.

All information is on website. Address inquiries and applications to Mary Moran, Coordinator for Academic Programs. NO fax submissions.

2785 — SOCIAL SCIENCES AND HUMANITIES RESEARCH COUNCIL OF CANADA (Postdoctoral Fellowships)

350 Albert St.
PO Box 1610
Ottawa Ontario K1P 6G4 CANADA
613/992-0691
FAX: 613/992-2803
E-Mail: z-info@sshrc.ca
Internet: www.sshrc.ca

AMOUNT: $28,428 Canadian

DEADLINE(S): OCT

FIELD(S): Social Sciences; Humanities

For Canadian citizens to do postdoctoral research in the humanities and social sciences. Financial need NOT a factor.

Renewable for one year. Consult website for complete program information or contact Jayne Holowachuk at SSHRC for an application.

2786 — SOCIAL SCIENCES AND HUMANITIES RESEARCH COUNCIL OF CANADA (Doctoral Fellowships)

350 Alberta St.
PO Box 1610
Ottawa Ontario K1P 6G4 CANADA
613/992-0691
FAX: 613/992-2803

E-Mail: z-info@sshrc.ca
Internet: www.sshrc.ca
AMOUNT: $16,620 Canadian
DEADLINE(S): SEP
FIELD(S): Social Sciences; Humanities

Doctoral fellowships in the humanities and social sciences for Canadian citizens. Financial need NOT a factor.

Renewable for three years. Consult website for complete program information or contact Jayne Holowachuk at SSHRC for an application.

2787 — SOCIAL SCIENCE RESEARCH COUNCIL (Eurasia Fellowship Program)

810 Seventh Ave., 31st Fl.
New York NY 10019
212/377-2700
FAX: 212/377-2727
E-Mail: eurasia@ssrc.org
Internet: www.ssrc.org
AMOUNT: $10,000 (graduate); $15,000 (dissertation); $24,000 (postdoctoral)
DEADLINE(S): NOV 1
FIELD(S): Soviet Studies

Open to US citizens/permanent residents enrolled in accredited graduate, dissertation, or postdoctoral programs in any discipline of the social sciences or humanities. Purpose is to enhance their disciplinary, methodological, or language training in relation to research on the Soviet Union and its successor states. Grants for summer language institutes also available.

See website or contact SSRC for an application.

2788 — SOCIAL SCIENCE RESEARCH COUNCIL (International Predissertation Fellowship Program)

810 Seventh Ave.
New York NY 10019
212/277-2700
AMOUNT: Varies
DEADLINE(S): Varies (TBA by participating universities)
FIELD(S): Economics; Political Science; Psychology; Sociology; other Social Science disciplines

Open to Ph.D. candidates enrolled in social science programs at 23 select universities and interested in supplementing disciplinary skills with area and language studies or acquiring advanced disciplinary training. Study program is preparation for research on Africa, Central Asia & the Caucasus, China, Latin America, the Caribbean, Near & Middle East, and South or Southeast Asia.

Contact Ellen Perecman for an application.

2789 — SOCIAL SCIENCE RESEARCH COUNCIL (Near & Middle East Fellowship Program)

810 Seventh Ave., 31st Fl.
New York NY 10019
212/377-2700
FAX: 212/377-2727
E-Mail: szanton@ssrc.org
Internet: www.ssrc.org
AMOUNT: Varies
DEADLINE(S): NOV 1
FIELD(S): Near & Middle East Studies

Open to US citizens currently enrolled in Ph.D. program in social sciences or humanities and will have completed two academic years of work toward the doctorate by June of following year. Graduates spend four to nine months preparing for dissertation research through training and study in the Middle East. Also open to US citizens to pursue dissertation research requiring field work in the Middle East. Research must be concerned with period since beginning of Islam.

See website or contact SSRC for an application.

2790 — SOCIAL SCIENCE RESEARCH COUNCIL (Program on Philanthropy & the Non-Profit Sector)

810 Seventh Ave., 31st Fl.
New York NY 10019
212/377-2700
FAX: 212/377-2727
E-Mail: phil-np@ssrc.org
Internet: www.ssrc.org
AMOUNT: $18,000 research support + $5,000 write-up support
DEADLINE(S): DEC 8
FIELD(S): Humanities; Social Sciences

Open to full-time graduate students in the social sciences and humanities enrolled in doctoral programs in the US to support research on this country. Must have completed all requirements for Ph.D. except research component. Fellowship supports nine to twelve months of research and related expenses. Based on strong record of achievement. Research must contribute to knowledge in disciplines of philanthropy and nonprofit studies. Financial need NOT a factor.

7 awards annually. Contact Nazli Parvizi for an application.

2791 — SOCIAL SCIENCE RESEARCH COUNCIL (Southeast Asia Fellowship Program)

810 Seventh Ave., 31st Fl.
New York NY 10019
212/377-2700
FAX: 212/377-2727
E-Mail: Lam@ssrc.org
Internet: www.ssrc.org

AMOUNT: $15,000 (dissertation); $30,000 (postdoctoral)
DEADLINE(S): DEC 15
FIELD(S): Vietnam Studies

Provides 12- to 24-month dissertation and postdoctoral support for research on Vietnam across the disciplines of the social sciences and humanities. Must be enrolled full-time in Ph.D. programs in any of the social sciences or humanities at accredited universities in the US or Canada and establish an affiliation with a Vietnamese institution. Postdoctoral fellows should already have sufficient command of the Vietnamese language to conduct research in Vietnam.

See website or contact SSRC for an application after September 30th. Awards announced by June.

2792 — SOCIETY FOR THE PSYCHOLOGICAL STUDY OF SOCIAL ISSUES (Applied Social Issues Internship Program)

PO Box 1248
Ann Arbor MI 48106-1248
Phone/TTY: 313/662-9130
FAX: 313/662-5607
E-Mail: spssi@spssi.org
Internet: www.spssi.org
AMOUNT: $1,500-$2,500
DEADLINE(S): NOV 10
FIELD(S): Social Science & related fields

Internship awards cover research costs, community organizing, summer stipends, etc. Encourages intervention projects, non-partisan lobbying, applied research, & implementing public policy. Proposals are invited for applying social science principles to social issues, in cooperation with a community, city, or state government organization, public interest group, or other not-for-profit entity. College seniors, graduate students, and first-year postdoctorates may apply.

Contact SPSSI for details. Applications available on website. NO SCHOLARSHIPS AVAILABLE—REQUESTS FOR FINANCIAL AID WILL NOT BE ANSWERED.

2793 — SOCIETY FOR THE PSYCHOLOGICAL STUDY OF SOCIAL ISSUES (Clara Mayo Grants in Support of Master's Thesis and Pre-Dissertation Research on Sexism, Racism, or Prejudice)

PO Box 1248
Ann Arbor MI 48106-1248
Phone/TTY: 313/662-9130
FAX: 313/662-5607
E-Mail: spssi@spssi.org
Internet: www.spssi.org
AMOUNT: up to $1,000

DEADLINE(S): MAR 31

FIELD(S): Sexism, Racism, & Prejudice

These grants support research from students working on a master's thesis (preference given to those in terminal master's program) or pre-dissertation research on sexism, racism, or prejudice. Studies of application of theory or design of interventions/treatments to address these problems are welcome. Proposals that include college/university agreement to match amount requested are favored, but those without matching funds also considered.

4 awards annually. Applications availble on website. NO SCHOLARSHIPS AVAILABLE—REQUESTS FOR FINANCIAL AID WILL NOT BE ANSWERED.

2794 — SOCIETY FOR THE PSYCHOLOGICAL STUDY OF SOCIAL ISSUES (Otto Klineburg Intercultural and International Relations Award)

PO Box 1248
Ann Arbor MI 48106-1248
Phone/TTY: 313/662-9130
FAX: 313/662-5607
E-Mail: spssi@spssi.org
Internet: www.spssi.org

AMOUNT: $1,000

DEADLINE(S): FEB 1

FIELD(S): Intercultural & International Relations

Annual award for the best paper or article on intercultural or international relations. Originality of the contribution, whether theoretical or empirical, will be given special weight. Entries can be either papers published during the current year or unpublished manuscripts. Send five copies of entry.

Contact SPSSI for details. Applications available on website. SPSSI DOES NOT OFFER SCHOLARSHIPS—INQUIRIES FOR FINANCIAL AID WILL NOT BE ANSWERED.

2795 — SOCIETY FOR THE PSYCHOLOGICAL STUDY OF SOCIAL ISSUES (James Marshall Public Policy Fellowship)

PO Box 1248
Ann Arbor MI 48106-1248
313/662-9130
FAX: 313/662-5607
E-Mail: spssi@umich.edu
Internet: www.spssi.org

AMOUNT: $42,000 + health/vacation benefits

DEADLINE(S): JAN 10

FIELD(S): Public Policy, Social Science

Develops more effective interaction between those engaged in social research and the social policy arena. Working closely with the American Psychological Association's Public Policy Office in Washington, DC, the fellow provides SPSSI a link to legislation and national testimony. Activities range from legislative work, to developing/advocating for specific bills, to policy-relevant research/writing on issues such as international peace, abortion, and chlid poverty.

Contact SPSSI for details. NO SCHOLARSHIPS AVAILABLE—REQUESTS FOR FINANCIAL AID WILL NOT BE ANSWERED.

2796 — SOCIETY FOR THE PSYCHOLOGICAL STUDY OF SOCIAL ISSUES (Gordon Allport Intergroup Relations Prize)

PO Box 1248
Ann Arbor MI 48106-1248
Phone/TTY: 313/662-9130
FAX: 313/662-9130
E-Mail: spssi@spssi.org
Internet: www.spssi.org

AMOUNT: $1,000

DEADLINE(S): DEC 31

FIELD(S): Sociology/Intergroup Relations

Annual award for the best paper or article on intergroup relations. Originality of the contribution, whether theoretical or empirical, is given special consideration. The research area encompassing intergroup relations includes such dimensions as age, sex, socioeconomic status, and race. Entries can be either papers published during the current year or unpublished manuscripts. Send five copies of entry.

Contact SPSSI for details. Applications available on website. SPSSI DOES NOT OFFER SCHOLARSHIPS—REQUESTS FOR FINANCIAL AID WILL NOT BE ANSWERED.

2797 — SOCIETY FOR THE PSYCHOLOGICAL STUDY OF SOCIAL ISSUES (Grants-in-Aid Program)

PO Box 1248
Ann Arbor MI 48106-1248
Phone/TTY: 313/662-9130
FAX: 313/662-5607
E-Mail: spssi@spssi.org
Internet: www.spssi.org

AMOUNT: up to $2,000

DEADLINE(S): APR 1; NOV 13

FIELD(S): Social Problem Areas

For scientific/graduate student research in social problem areas related to the basic interests and goals of SPSSI, particularly those that are not likely to receive support from traditional sources. Proposals especially encouraged in the fields of sexism and racism. SPSSI prefers unique/timely projects, underrepresented institutions/new investigators, volunteer research teams, and actual, not pilot, projects. Funds not normally provided for travel or living expenses.

Contact SPSSI for details. Applications available on website. NO SCHOLARSHIPS AVAILABLE—REQUESTS FOR FINANCIAL AID WILL NOT BE ANSWERED.

2798 — SOCIETY FOR THE PSYCHOLOGICAL STUDY OF SOCIAL ISSUES (The Sages Program: Action Grants for Experienced Scholars)

PO Box 1248
Ann Arbor MI 48106-1248
Phone/TTY: 313/662-9130
FAX: 313/662-5607
E-Mail: spssi@spssi.org
Internet: www.spssi.org

AMOUNT: Up to $2,000

DEADLINE(S): MAY 1

FIELD(S): Social Issues

Encourages intervention projects, non-partisan advocacy projects, and projects implementing public policy by retired social scientists over the age of 60. Proposals are invited for research projects applying social science principles to social issues in cooperation with a community, city, state, or federal organization or other not-for-profit group. Projects may also be done in cooperation with universities or colleges throughout the world or with the United Nations.

Contact SPSSI for details. Applications available on website. SCHOLARSHIPS NOT AVAILABLE—REQUESTS FOR FINANCIAL AID WILL NOT BE ANSWERED.

2799 — SOCIETY FOR THE PSYCHOLOGICAL STUDY OF SOCIAL ISSUES (Louise Kidder Early Career Award)

PO Box 1248
Ann Arbor MI 48106-1248
Phone/TTY: 313/662-9130
FAX: 313/662-5607
E-Mail: spssi@spssi.org
Internet: www.spssi.org

AMOUNT: $500 + plaque

DEADLINE(S): MAY 1

FIELD(S): Social Issues Research

Award recognizes social issues researchers who have made substantial contributions to the field early in their careers. Nominees should be investigators who have made substantial contributions to social issues research within five years of receiving a graduate degree and who have demonstrated the potential to continue such contributions. To enter, send 3 copies of cover letter (stating accomplishments/future contributions), curriculum vitae, & 3 letters of support.

Contact SPSSI for details. Applications available on website. NO SCHOLARSHIPS AVAILABLE—REQUESTS FOR FINANCIAL AID WILL NOT BE ANSWERED.

2800 — SOCIETY FOR THE PSYCHOLOGICAL STUDY OF SOCIAL ISSUES (The Social Issues Dissertation Award)

PO Box 1248
Ann Arbor MI 48106-1248
Phone/TTY: 313/662-9130
FAX: 313/662-5607
E-Mail: spssi@spssi.org
Internet: www.spssi.org

AMOUNT: $600 (1st prize); $400 (2nd prize)
DEADLINE(S): APR 1
FIELD(S): Psychology, Social Science

Open to Ph.D. dissertations in psychology (or in a social science with psychological subject matter) based on social issues. Judged on scientific excellence and potential application to social problems. With application, include 500-word dissertation summary, identification (phone, address, school, etc.), and certification by your dissertation advisor of the acceptance date of dissertation.

Contact SPSSI for details. Applications available on website. NO SCHOLARSHIPS AVAILABLE—REQUESTS FOR FINANCIAL AID WILL NOT BE ANSWERED.

2801 — SOCIETY FOR THE PSYCHOLOGICAL STUDY OF SOCIAL ISSUES (SPSSI-Sponsored Research Workshop)

PO Box 1248
Ann Arbor MI 48106-1248
Phone/TTY: 313/662-9130
FAX: 313/662-5607
E-Mail: spssi@spssi.org
Internet: www.spssi.org

AMOUNT: up to $4,000
DEADLINE(S): OCT 5
FIELD(S): Social Science & related fields

A series of small research-oriented workshops to foster awareness of the state of social research in important areas of social policy. Formats vary from year to year. Proposals will be judged on description, site, timeline, organization, budget, and product(s).

No more than 30 participants. Contact SPSSI for details. Applications available on website. NO SCHOLARSHIPS AVAILABLE—REQUESTS FOR FINANCIAL AID WILL NOT BE ANSWERED.

2802 — STOCKHOLM UNIVERSITY - INTERNATIONAL GRADUATE PROGRAMME (Master's Programme in Swedish Social Studies)

Universitetsvagen 10F
Frescati
S-106 91 Stockholm SWEDEN
+46 8 163466
FAX: +46 8 155508
E-Mail: igp@statsvet.su.se
Internet: www.statsvet.su.se/IGP/home.html

AMOUNT: Tuition
DEADLINE(S): MAR 1
FIELD(S): Social Sciences; Economics; History; Anthropology; Sociology; Social Work; Political Science

Open to students who have completed a university degree in the social sciences with one of the above majors and who wish to study at Stockholm University in Sweden. Language of instruction is English.

Contact Stockholm University for an application.

2803 — STOCKHOLM UNIVERSITY - INTERNATIONAL GRADUATE PROGRAMME (Advanced Study Programme)

Universitetsvagen 10F
Frescati
S-106 91 Stockholm SWEDEN
+46 8 163466
FAX: +46 8 155508
E-Mail: igp@statsvet.su.se
Internet: www.statsvet.su.se/IGP/home.html

AMOUNT: Tuition
DEADLINE(S): MAR 31
FIELD(S): Social Sciences

Open to doctoral students from accredited institutions of higher learning who wish to pursue advanced study in the social sciences at Stockholm University in Sweden. Language of instruction is English. Financial need NOT a factor.

Contact Stockholm University for an application.

2804 — SVENSKA HANDELSBANKEN FOUNDATIONS FOR SOCIAL SCIENCE RESEARCH (Research Grants)

Secretary of the board
S-10670 Stockholm SWEDEN
Written Inquiry

AMOUNT: Stipend + expenses
DEADLINE(S): FEB 28
FIELD(S): Economics/Social Sciences

Graduate research grants in economics and social science. Area of interest must concern international payments and capital movement, the domestic payments, markets, and economic planning.

Grants are tenable in Sweden for up to one year. Renewable depending upon progress. Non-Swedish graduate students are requested to work in Sweden under supervision of a Swedish research institution. Write for complete information.

2805 — THE BRITISH COUNCIL (Scholarships for Citizens of Mexico)

10 Spring Gardens
London SW1A 2BN ENGLAND UK
+44 (0) 171 930 8466
FAX: +44 (0) 161 957 7188
E-Mail: education.enquiries@britcoun.org
Internet: www.britcoun.org/mexico/mexschol.htm

AMOUNT: Varies
DEADLINE(S): Varies
FIELD(S): Social sciences, applied sciences, technology

The British Council in Mexico offers approximately 100 scholarshps per year in the above fields for undergraduates and graduates to study in the United Kingdom. Good level of English language retired.

The website listed here gives more details. For more information, contact: leticia.magana@bc-mexico.sprint.com. or contact organization in London.

2806 — THE WALT DISNEY COMPANY (American Teacher Awards)

P.O. Box 9805
Calabasas CA 91372

AMOUNT: $2,500 (36 awards); $25,000 (Outstanding Teacher of the Year)
DEADLINE(S): FEB 15
FIELD(S): Teachers: athletic coach, early childhood, English, foreign language/ESL, general elementary, mathematics, performing arts, physical education/health, science, social studies, visual arts, voc/tech education

Awards for K-12 teachers in the above fields.

Teachers, or anyone who knows a great teacher, can write for applications at the above address.

2807 — UNIVERSITY OF MANCHESTER (Awards for Research)

Secretary, Research and Graduate Support Unit
Manchester M13 9PL England
0161 275 2035
FAX: 0161 275 2445/7216

AMOUNT: Maintenance grant (approx) 5000 pounds p.a. plus payment of UK tuition fees.
DEADLINE(S): MAY 1
FIELD(S): Arts, Economics, Social Studies, Education, Science, Engineering, Biological Sciences, Law

The university offers research studentships for doctoral research in all disciplines. These awards are highly competitive. Applicants should hold at least a 2:1 degree or equivalent. Awards are renewable for up to 2 years.

Approx 50 awards per year. Please contact address above for complete information.

2808 — US ARMS CONTROL AND DISARMAMENT AGENCY (William C. Foster Visiting Scholars Program)

320 21st St. NW
Room 5726
Washington DC 20451
703/647-8090

AMOUNT: Salary + per diem

DEADLINE(S): JAN 31

FIELD(S): Arms Control; Nonproliferation; Disarmament

Program open to faculty of recognized institutions of higher learning who wish to lend their expertise in areas relevant to the ACDA for a period of one year. U.S. citizenship or permanent residency required.

Write for complete information.

2809 — WEATHERHEAD CENTER FOR INTERNATIONAL AFFAIRS (Harvard Academy for International and Area Studies: Pre- and Postdoctoral Fellowships)

1737 Cambridge St.
Cambridge MA 02138
617/495-2137
E-Mail: bhastie@cfia.harvard.edu
Internet: http://hdc-www.harvard.edu/cfia/cfiaprog/1998-99.htm

AMOUNT: $20,000-35,000 + health insurance

DEADLINE(S): OCT 9

FIELD(S): Social science combined with a particular part of the world

Fellowships for research conducted while in residence at the CFIA (Harvard) to assist predoctoral and postdoctoral scholars preparing for an academic career involving both a social science discipline and a particular area of the world. Travel for research allowed.

Visit website or write to the above address for complete information.

2810 — WILLIAM T. GRANT FOUNDATION (Faculty Scholars Program—Research on Children, Adolescents, & Youth)

570 Lexington Ave.
New York NY 10022-6837
212/752-0071

AMOUNT: $50,000/yr. (max.)

DEADLINE(S): JUL 1

FIELD(S): Mental Health of Children, Adolescents, & Youth

For faculty members at universities and non-profit institutions, national and international. Award is for beginning investigators interested in the causes and consequences of factors which compromise the healthy mental development of children.

Renewable up to 5 years. Write for complete information.

2811 — WOODROW WILSON INTERNATIONAL CENTER FOR SCHOLARS (Fellowships in the Humanities and Social Sciences)

1000 Jefferson Dr. SW
SRI MRC 02
Washington DC 20560
202/357-2841
FAX: 202/633-9043
E-Mail: wcfellow@sivm.si.edu
Internet: www.wwics.si.ed

AMOUNT: Up to $62,000

DEADLINE(S): OCT 1

FIELD(S): Humanities; Social Sciences

Open to individuals from any country who have outstanding capabilities and experience from a wide variety of backgrounds. Academic participants limited to post-doctoral level and should have published a major work beyond Ph.D dissertation.

Approximately 35 fellowships annually to scholars with outstanding project proposals, especially those transcending narrow specialties. Write for complete information.

2812 — WOODROW WILSON NATIONAL FELLOWSHIP FOUNDATION (Charlotte W. Newcombe Dissertation Fellowships)

CN 5281
Princeton NJ 08543-5281
609/452-7007
FAX: 609/452-0066
E-Mail: charoltte@woodrow.org
Internet: www.woodrow.org

AMOUNT: $15,500

DEADLINE(S): DEC 6

FIELD(S): Theology; Social Sciences; Humanities; Education

Open to Ph.D. candidates writing on topics of religious and ethical values. Must be pursuing full-time dissertation writing at graduate schools in the US, having completed all pre-dissertation requirements.

35 awards annually. Not renewable. See website or contact WWNFF for an application. Notification made in April.

2813 — WOODS HOLE OCEANOGRAPHIC INSTITUTION (Research Fellowships in Marine Policy and Ocean Management)

360 Woods Hole Road
Woods Hole MA 02543-1541
508/289-2219
FAX: 508/457-2188
E-Mail: mgately@whoi.edu
Internet: www.whoi.edu

AMOUNT: Varies

DEADLINE(S): FEB 16

FIELD(S): Social Sciences, Law, Natural Sciences

For professionals in the above fields who wish to apply their training to investigations of problems involving the use of the oceans. WHOI's objective is to provide a year-long advanced learning experience in ocean policy problems involving the interdisciplinary application of social science and natural science to marine policy problems. Fields currently emphasized: economics, statistics, public policy, natural resource management, and international relations.

For an application/more information, contact the Education Office, Clark Laboratory 223, MS #31, at above address.

2814 — WORLD BANK (Graduate Scholarship Program)

1818 H St., NW, Rm. M-4035
Washington DC 20433
Written inquiry

AMOUNT: Tuition + fees, allowance, travel, etc.

DEADLINE(S): FEB 1

FIELD(S): Social sciences, law, business, public administration

For nationals of World Bank member countries under the age of 40. Must have a superior academic record, at least two years' experience in public service engaged in development-related activities, and have gained admittance to a university to pursue a post-graduate degree. Must return to hom country after degree.

For two years.

COMMUNICATIONS

2815 — AMERICA-ISRAEL CULTURAL FOUNDATION (Sharett Scholarship Program)

32 Allenby Road
Tel Aviv 63-325 ISRAEL
03 5174177
FAX: 03 5178991

AMOUNT: Varies

DEADLINE(S): MAR 15

FIELD(S): Art; Performing Arts

Scholarships are available ONLY to Israeli nationals for study in Israel. Scholarships are for one year of study and are renewable.

450 scholarships per year. Application forms available in February. Write for complete information.

2816 — AMERICAN INSTITUTE OF POLISH CULTURE (Scholarships)

1440 79th St. Causeway, Ste. 117
Miami FL 33141
305/864-2349
FAX: 305/865-5150
E-Mail: info@ampolinstitute.org
Internet: www.ampolinstitute.org

AMOUNT: $1,000

DEADLINE(S): FEB 15

FIELD(S): Journalism; Public Relations; Communications

Awards are to encourage young Americans of Polish descent to pursue the above professions. Can be used for full-time study at any accredited American college. Criteria for selection include achievement, talent, and involvement in public life.

$25 processing fee. Renewable. Send self-addressed, stamped envelope to Mrs. Harriet Irsay for an application.

2817 — AMERICAN POLITICAL SCIENCE ASSOCIATION (Congressional Fellowships for Print & Broadcast Journalists)

1527 New Hampshire Ave., NW
Washington DC 20036-1206
202/483-2512
FAX: 202/483-2657
E-Mail: biggs@apsanet.net
Internet: www.apsanet.org

AMOUNT: $35,000 stipend + travel allowance

DEADLINE(S): DEC 1

FIELD(S): Print/Broadcast Journalism

Program gives journalists an opportunity to work as congressional aides for nine months and to strengthen their understanding of Congress and national politics. Must have bachelor's degree and 2-10 years of full-time experience in print or broadcast journalism. Preference given to candidates with background in political reporting but without extensive Washington experience.

Contact the Director, Congressional Fellowship Program, at APSA for an application.

2818 — AMERICAN RADIO RELAY LEAGUE FOUNDATION (The PHD ARA Scholarship)

225 Main Street
Newington CT 06111
860/594-0200
FAX: 860/594-0259
Internet: www.arrl.org/

AMOUNT: $1,000

DEADLINE(S): FEB 1

FIELD(S): Journalism; Computer Science; Electronic Engineering

For undergraduate or graduate students who are residents of the ARRL Midwest Division (IA, KS, MO, NE) who hold any class of radio amateur license—or student may be the child of a deceased radio amateur.

1 award annually. Contact ARRL for an application.

2819 — ARMENIAN GENERAL BENEVOLENT UNION (Educational Loan Program)

Education Dept., 31 W. 52nd St.
New York NY 10019-6118
212/765-8260
FAX: 212/765-8209
E-Mail: agbuny@aol.com

AMOUNT: $5,000 to $7,500/yr.

DEADLINE(S): APR 1

FIELD(S): Education Administration, International Relations/Foreign Affairs, Communication, Journalism, or Public Administration

Loans for full-time students of Armenian heritage pursuing master's degrees in one of the above fields. Must be attending highly competitive institutions in the U.S. GPA of 3.5 or more required.

Loan repayment period begins within 12 months of completion of full-time study and extends five to ten years, depending on the size of the loan. Interest is 3% Write for complete information.

2820 — ASIAN INSTITUTE OF TECHNOLOGY (AIT Scholarship Program)

Development Office
PO Box 4, Klongluang
Pathumthani 12120 THAILAND
(66)(2) 516-0110-44 or 524-5032
FAX: (66)(2) 516-2126
E-Mail: ascao@ait.ac.th
Internet: www.ait.ac.th

AMOUNT: US $12,600-$37,960

DEADLINE(S): FEB 15; JUN 15; OCT 15

FIELD(S): Advanced Technologies; Civil Engineering; Environment, Resources, & Development; Business Management

Scholarships and grants open to citizens of Asian countries who are accepted by the institute as a master's or doctoral candidate. Selection is based on academic criteria, practical experience, gender, and country of origin; priority to Mekong Region countries and Asian countries of the former USSR.

250 awards annually. Contact AIT for an application.

2821 — ASSOCIATED PRESS TELEVISION-RADIO ASSOCIATION OF CALIFORNIA/NEVADA (APTRA-Clete Roberts & Kathryn Dettman Memorial Journalism Scholarship Awards)

Rachel Ambrose
221 S. Figueroa St., #300
Los Angeles CA 90012
213/626-1200
E-Mail: rambrose@ap.org

AMOUNT: $1,500

DEADLINE(S): DEC 10

FIELD(S): Broadcast Journalism

Recipients will be students with a broadcast journalism career objective who are enrolled in a California or Nevada college or university. Applicants must complete an entry form and may submit examples of broadcast-related work. Scholarships will be awarded at APTRA's annual awards banquet in March at the Disneyland Hotel in Anaheim, CA.

4 awards annually. Contact Rachel Ambrose at APTRA for an entry form.

2822 — AUSTRALIAN FEDERATION OF UNIVERSITY WOMEN - WESTERN AUSTRALIA (Joyce Riley Bursary)

Bursary Liaison Officer
PO Box 48
Nedlands WA 6909 AUSTRALIA
Written Inquiry

AMOUNT: Aus$1,700 - Aus$2,750

DEADLINE(S): JUL 31

FIELD(S): Humanities; Social Sciences

To support women graduates of a Western Australian university to complete a higher degree or post-doctoral research in Humanities or Social Sciences at a recognized university in any country.

Membership in AFUW or in IFUW is required. Contact above location for further information.

2823 — AUSTRALIAN FEDERATION OF UNIVERSITY WOMEN - WESTERN AUSTRALIA (Joyce Riley Bursary)

Bursary Liaison Officer
PO Box 48
Nedlands WA 6009 AUSTRALIA
Written Inquiry

AMOUNT: Aus$1,700 - Aus$2,750

DEADLINE(S): JUL 31

FIELD(S): Humanities; Social Sciences

To support women graduates of a recognized university to complete a higher degree or post-doctoral research at a university in Western Australia.

Membership in AFUW or in IFUW is required. Write to above address for complete information.

2824 — BLUES HEAVEN FOUNDATION, INC. (Muddy Waters Scholarship)

2120 S. Michigan Ave.
Chicago IL 60616
312/808-1286

AMOUNT: $2,000

DEADLINE(S): APR 30

FIELD(S): Music; Music Education; African-American Studies; Folklore; Performing Arts; Arts Management; Journalism; Radio/TV/Film

Scholarship is made on a competitive basis with consideration given to scholastic achievement, concentration of studies, and financial need. Applicant must have full-time enrollment status in a Chicago area college/university in at least their first year of undergraduate studies or a graduate program. Scholastic aptitude, extracurricular involvement, grade point average, and financial need are all considered.

Contact Blues Heaven Foundation, Inc. to receive an application between February and April.

2825 — BROADCAST EDUCATION ASSOCIATION (Scholarships in Broadcasting)

1771 N St., NW
Washington DC 20036-2891
202/429-5354
E-Mail: fweaver@nab.org
Internet: www.beaweb.org

AMOUNT: $1,250-$5,000

DEADLINE(S): JAN 14

FIELD(S): Broadcasting; Radio

For full-time juniors, seniors, and graduate students at BEA Member universities. Applicant should show evidence of superior academic performance and potential to become an outstanding electronic media professional. There should be compelling evidence that applicant possesses high integrity and a well-articulated sense of personal and professional responsibility. Awards exclusively for tuition, student fees, textbooks/supplies, and dorm room & board.

15 awards annually. Not renewable. Contact BEA or your campus faculty for an application no later than December 17th. See website for list of BEA member institutions.

2826 — BUCKS COUNTY COURIER TIMES (Summer Internship Program)

8400 Route 13
Levittown PA 19057
215/949-4185
215/949-4177
E-Mail: cper@calkinsnewspapers.com

AMOUNT: $4,380 ($365/wk.)

DEADLINE(S): FEB 1

FIELD(S): News; Business; Feature Reporting

12-week internship for minority students at the Bucks County Courier Times. Must be US resident and have car. Financial need NOT a factor.

5 awards annually. Renewable. Contact Carolyn Per at above address for an application.

2827 — CANADIAN ASSOCIATION OF BROADCASTERS (Raymond Crepault Scholarship)

P.O. Box 627, Stn. B
Ottawa Ontario K1P 5S2 CANADA
613/233-4035

AMOUNT: Up to $5,000

DEADLINE(S): JUN 30

FIELD(S): Communications

Open to French-speaking Canadian citizens enrolled full-time as undergrads or grad students at a Canadian university. Financial need and ability to complete studies must be demonstrated.

Write for complete information.

2828 — CENTER FOR ENVIRONMENTAL JOURNALISM/UNIVERSITY OF COLORADO AT BOULDER (Ted Scripps Fellowship)

Univ of Colorado
Macky 201, Campus Box 287
Boulder CO 80309-0287
303/492-0459
FAX: 303/492-0585
E-Mail: ackland@spot.colorado.edu
Internet: campuspress.colorado.edu/cej.html
OR www.scripps.com/foundation

AMOUNT: $27,000 for 9 months

DEADLINE(S): MAR 1

FIELD(S): Print or Broadcast Journalism

Five journalists will be selected to spend the academic year at the University of Colorado at Boulder studying environmental science and policy. For print or broadcast journalists with a minimum of five years professional experience. Can be general assignment reporters, editors, and freelancers.

5 awards annually. May also contact the Scripps Howard Foundation for details: PO Box 5380, Cincinnati, OH 45202.

2829 — CONCORDIA UNIVERSITY (Susan Carson Memorial Bursary and Gordon Fisher Bursaries)

Journalism Dept.
1455 de Maisonneuve Blvd. West
Loyola BR 305

Montreal Quebec H3G 1M8 CANADA
514/848-3809
FAX: 514/848-2812
E-Mail: awardsgs@vax2.concordia.ca

AMOUNT: $1,800; $2,000

DEADLINE(S): SEP 20

FIELD(S): Journalism

Based on academic achievement/performance and financial need. Recipient of Susan Carson award must also demonstrate the highest ideals, concern for humankind, and qualities of citizenship. Selection will be made by the Chair of the Journalism Department in consultation with colleagues and/or relatives of the late Ms. Susan Carson. Preference will be given to students who have custody of one or more dependent children. No preference considered for Gordon Fisher awards.

3 awards annually. Not renewable. Contact the Chair of the Journalism Department at Concordia University for applications.

2830 — CONGRESSIONAL HISPANIC CAUCUS INSTITUTE, INC. (CHCI Fellowship Program)

504 C St., NE
Washington DC 20002
800/EXCEL-DC or 202/543-1771
E-Mail: comments@chci.org
Internet: www.chci.org

AMOUNT: Monthly stipend, round-trip transportation, & health insurance

DEADLINE(S): MAR 1

FIELD(S): Public Policy; Public Health; Telecommunications; Business

Paid work experience is open to Hispanics who have graduated from a college/university (with BA/BS/graduate degree) within one year of application deadline, and to currently enrolled graduate students. Must have high academic achievement (minimum 3.0 GPA), superior analytical/communication skills, leadership potential, and consistent active participation in activities for the common good. Must be US citizen/permanent resident or have student work visa.

16 awards annually. See website or contact CHCI for an application.

2831 — CUBAN AMERICAN NATIONAL FOUNDATION (The Mas Family Scholarships)

7300 NW 35 Terrace
Miami FL 33122
305/592-7768
FAX: 305/592-7889
E-Mail canfnet.org
Internet: www.canfnet.org

AMOUNT: Individually negotiated

DEADLINE(S): MAR 15

FIELD(S): Engineering, Business, International Relations, Economics, Communications, Journalism

For Cuban-Americans students, graduates and undergraduates, born in Cuba or direct descendants of those who left Cuba. Must be in top 10% of high school class or maintain a 3.5 GPA in college.

10,000 awards/year. Recipients may re-apply for subsequent years. Financial need considered along with academic success, SAT and GRE scores, and leadership potential. Essays and proof of Cuban descent required.

2832 — DOW JONES NEWSPAPER FUND, INC. (Newspaper Editing Intern/Scholarship Program)

PO Box 300
Princeton NJ 08543-0300
609/452-2820 or 800/DOWFUND
E-Mail: dowfund@wsj.dowjones.com
Internet: www.dj.com/dowfund

AMOUNT: $1,000 + paid summer internship

DEADLINE(S): NOV 15

FIELD(S): Journalism; Editing

Summer internships for college juniors, seniors, and graduate students to work as copy editors at daily newspapers. Must demonstrate a commitment to a career in journalism, though journalism major not required. Interns are paid by the newspapers for which they work and attend a two-week training program paid for by the Newspaper Fund. Those returning to full-time studies will receive a $1,000 scholarship.

80 awards annually. Applications available from August 15th to November 1st. Contact Dow Jones for an application.

2833 — DOW JONES NEWSPAPER FUND, INC. (Online Newspaper Editing Intern/Scholarship Program)

PO Box 300
Princeton NJ 08543-0300
609/452-2820 or 800/DOWFUND
E-Mail: dowfund@wsj.dowjones.com
Internet: www.dj.com/dowfund

AMOUNT: $1,000 + paid summer internship

DEADLINE(S): NOV 15

FIELD(S): Journalism; Online Editing

Summer internships for college juniors, seniors, and graduate students to work as editors for online newspapers. Must demonstrate a commitment to a career in journalism, though journalism major not required. Interns are paid by the newspapers for which they work and attend a two-week training program paid for by the Newspaper Fund. Those returning to full-time studies will receive a $1,000 scholarship.

12 awards annually. Applications available from August 15th to November 1st. Contact Dow Jones for an application.

2834 — DOW JONES NEWSPAPER FUND, INC. (Real-Time Financial News Service Intern/ Scholarship Program)

PO Box 300
Princeton NJ 08543-0300
609/452-2820 or 800/DOWFUND
E-Mail: dowfund@wsj.dowjones.com
Internet: www.dj.com/dowfund

AMOUNT: $1,000 + paid summer internship

DEADLINE(S): NOV 15

FIELD(S): Journalism; Financial Journalism; Editing

Summer internship for college juniors, seniors, and graduate students to work as editors and reporters for real-time financial news services. Must demonstrate a commitment to a similar career, though journalism major not required. Interns are paid by the news serivice for which they work and will attend a two-week training program paid for by the Newspaper Fund. Students returning to full-time studies will receive a $1,000 scholarship.

12 awards annually. Applications available from August 15th to November 1st. Contact Dow Jones for an application.

2835 — ESPN (Internship Programs)

Human Resources Dept.
ESPN, Inc.
ESPN Plaza
Bristol CT 06010
No phone calls. Internet:
espnet.sportszone.com/editors/studios/
97faq.html

AMOUNT: Paid Internships

DEADLINE(S): OCT 1; MAR 1; JUN 1

FIELD(S): Television Industry, Public Relations, Sports

12-week internships in the spring, summer, and fall for undergraduate juniors/seniors and graduate students. Some areas require weekend/evening hours and a strong knowledge of sports. Interns receive hourly wages and take part in many company-sponsored activities. ESPN does not provide housing for students, but we do try to assist in finding suitable living arrangements once selected.

To apply for internship programs, please send cover letter and resume to the above address. If applying to the Communications Dept., please also enclose writing samples and send attention to Diane Lamb.

2836 — FRENCH-AMERICAN FOUNDATION (Bicentennial Fellowships)

41 East 72nd St.
New York NY 10021
212/288-4000
FAX: 212/288-4765
E-Mail: French_AmerFdn@msn.com

AMOUNT: 10,000 French francs/mo.

DEADLINE(S): FEB 2

FIELD(S): Social sciences

For doctoral students in the social sciences to travel to France for one year to conduct research essential to the completion of their dissertations. Must have completed all other requirements for Ph.D. May not use the award until exams are passed.

Requires application with a statement of purpose, full academic records, plan of research, bibliography, abstract, and three academic recommendations.

2837 — HERBERT HOOVER PRESIDENTIAL LIBRARY ASSOCIATION (Travel Grants)

PO Box 696
West Branch IA 52245
319/643-5327
FAX: 319/643-2391
E-Mail: info@hooverassoc.org
Internet: www.hooverassoc.org

AMOUNT: Varies

DEADLINE(S): MAR 1

FIELD(S): History; Journalism; Communications

Travel grants for graduates, postgraduates, and other qualified researchers to defray expenses of travel to West Branch, Iowa, to do research in the archives of the Herbert Hoover Presidential Library. Financial need is NOT a factor.

15-20 awards annually. Renewable with reapplication. Contact Patricia Hand at above address for an application.

2838 — HILLEL INTERNATIONAL CENTER (The Bittker Fellowship)

Eran Gasko
1640 Rhode Island Ave. NW
Washington DC 20036
202/857-6637
202/857-6560
FAX: 202/857-6693
E-Mail: smusher@hillel.org
Internet: www.hillel.org/careermoves/bittker.htm

AMOUNT: Professional Experience

DEADLINE(S): None specified

FIELD(S): Student Leadership/Jewish Awareness

One-year professional experience for an oustanding recent graduate, who coordinates student leadership and Jewish awareness activities nationwide. The Fellow establishes the network of student leaders and enhances their communication through national publications, conference calls, and the Internet. Task forces include Jewish Awareness/Identity, Women's Issues, Graduate Student Life, and Education.

Contact Eran Gasko, Human Resources, for an application.

COMMUNICATIONS

2839 — HILLEL INTERNATIONAL CENTER (The Public Policy Fellowship)

Eran Gasko
1640 Rhode Island Ave. NW
Washington DC 20036
202/857-6543
202/857-6560
FAX: 202/857-6693
E-Mail: smusher@hillel.org
Internet: www.hillel.org/careermoves/publicpolicy.htm

AMOUNT: Professional Experience
DEADLINE(S): None specified
FIELD(S): Public Policy/Social Issues

One-year professional experience for an oustanding recent Jewish graduate, who coordinates public policy initiatives nationwide. The Fellow strives to increase student activism in political and social issues. S/he works with students and national organizations to create innovative initiatives in social action, campus community relations councils, environmental issues, Israel programming, and international relief efforts.

Contact Eran Gasko, Human Resources, for an application.

2840 — INSTITUTE FOR HUMANE STUDIES (Felix Morley Journalism Competition)

4084 University Dr., Ste. 101
Fairfax VA 22030-6812
703/934-6920 or 800/697-8799
FAX: 703/352-7535
E-Mail: ihs@gmu.edu
Internet: www.theihs.org

AMOUNT: $2,500 (1st prize)
DEADLINE(S): DEC 1
FIELD(S): Journalism/Writing

This competition awards cash prizes to outstanding young writers whose work demonstrates an appreciation of classical liberal principles (i.e. individual rights; their protection through private property, contract, and laws; voluntarism in human relations; and the self-ordering market, free trade, free migration, and peace). Must be full-time students and aged 25 or younger.

Must submit 3-5 articles, editorials, opinion pieces, essays, and reviews published in student newspapers or other periodicals between July 1st and December 1st. See website for complete rules or contact IHS for an entry form.

2841 — INSTITUTE FOR HUMANE STUDIES (Humane Studies Fellowship)

4084 University Dr., Ste. 101
Fairfax VA 22030-6812

703/934-6920 or 800/697-8799
FAX: 703/352-7535
E-Mail: ihs@gmu.edu
Internet: www.theihs.org

AMOUNT: up to $12,000
DEADLINE(S): DEC 31
FIELD(S): Social Sciences; Law; Humanities; Jurisprudence; Journalism

Awards are for graduate and advanced undergraduate students pursuing degrees at any accredited domestic or foreign school. Based on academic performance, demonstrated interest in classical liberal ideas, and potential to contribute to the advancement of a free society.

90 awards annually. Apply online or contact IHS for an application.

2842 — INSTITUTE FOR HUMANE STUDIES (Summer Residential Program)

4084 University Dr., Ste. 101
Fairfax VA 22030-6812
703/934-6920 or 800/697-8799
FAX: 703/352-7535
E-Mail: ihs@gmu.edu
Internet: www.theihs.org

AMOUNT: All seminar fees: program cost, room/board, materials, and books
DEADLINE(S): MAR 1
FIELD(S): Social Sciences; Humanities; Law; Journalism; Public Policy; Education; Writing

For college students, recent graduates, and graduate students who share an interest in learning and exchanging ideas about the scope of individual rights. One-week and weekend seminars at various campus locations across the U.S.

Apply online or contact IHS for an application.

2843 — INTER AMERICAN PRESS ASSOCIATION (Scholarships for Young Journalists)

2911 NW 39th St.
MIAMI FL 33142
305/634-2465 or 305/376-3522
Internet: www.sipiapa.com

AMOUNT: Varies
DEADLINE(S): DEC 31
FIELD(S): Journalism

Program offers young professional journalists throughout the Western Hemisphere the opportunity to study or work abroad for nine months.

Send SASE for complete information. Access website for information on the organization.

2844 — INTERNATIONAL DEVELOPMENT RESEARCH CENTRE (Fellowship in Journalism - Internship with L'Agence Periscoop Multimedia)

PO Box 8500
Ottawa Ontario K1G 3H9 CANADA
613/236-6163, ext. 2098
FAX: 613/563-0815
Internet: www.idrc.ca/awards

AMOUNT: $30,000 Canadian
DEADLINE(S): MAY 1
FIELD(S): Journalism

Open to Canadian citizens or permanent residents employed by a Canadian newspaper, news agency, radio, or television station with at least three years experience. Guaranteed leave of absence and re-employment by employer is required. Recipient will be a member of the Agence Periscoop Multimedia team in France and must be fluent in spoken and written French.

Contact IDRC for an application.

2845 — INTERNATIONAL DEVELOPMENT RESEARCH CENTRE (Fellowship in Journalism - Internship with Gemini News Service)

PO Box 8500
Ottawa Ontario K1G 3H9 CANADA
613/236-6163, ext. 2098
FAX: 613/563-0815
Internet: www.idrc.ca/awards

AMOUNT: $30,000 Canadian
DEADLINE(S): MAY 1
FIELD(S): Journalism

Open to Canadian citizens or permanent residents employed by a Canadian newspaper, news agency, radio, or television station with at least three years of experience. Guaranteed leave of absence and re-employment by employer is required. Recipient will be a member of the Gemini News Service in London and will be assigned to a developing country for a few months.

Contact IDRC for an application.

2846 — INVESTIGATIVE REPORTERS AND EDITORS (Small News Organization Fellowships)

138 Neff Annex
Missouri School of Journalism
Columbia MO 65211
573/882-2042
FAX: 573/882-5431
E-Mail: jourire@muccmail.missouri.edu
Internet: www.ire.org/resources/scholarship/smallnews/

AMOUNT: Costs to attend various conferences
DEADLINE(S): NOV 1; DEC 15 (depending on which event)

FIELD(S): Journalism: Investigative

Fellowships for reporters producing solid investigative projects in small news organizations to receive financial assistance to attend any of the various conferences of the above organization.

See website and/or contact organization for further information.

2847 — JOHN F. KENNEDY LIBRARY FOUNDATION (Theodore C. Sorensen Research Fellowship)

Columbia Point
Boston MA 02125-3313
617/929-4534 or 617/929-4533
FAX: 617/929-4599

AMOUNT: $3,600

DEADLINE(S): MAR 15

FIELD(S): Domestic policy, political journalism, polling, or press relations

To support a scholar while he/she researches in the fields listed above.

Contact William Johnson, Chief Archivist, at above location for application information.

2848 — KNIGHT SCIENCE JOURNALISM FOUNDATION (Fellowships)

77 Massachusetts Ave.
MIT E32-300
Cambridge MA 02139-4307
617/253-3442
Internet: web.mit.edu/Knight-science/

AMOUNT: $35,000

DEADLINE(S): MAR 1

FIELD(S): Science Journalism

Program at MIT open to science journalists (print or broadcast) with at least 3 years experience. Fellows attend seminars with leading scientists & engineers, visit laboratories, audit classes, and attend workshops on science journalism. Open to science and technology journalists from the US; foreign journalists may apply if they can obtain funding in their own countries.

See website or contact above address for an application.

2849 — LOS ANGELES PROFESSIONAL CHAPTER OF SOCIETY OF PROFESSIONAL JOURNALISTS (Bill Farr Scholarship)

SPJ/LA Scholarships
9951 Barcelona Lane
Cypress CA 90630-3759
Written Inquiry

AMOUNT: up to $1,000

DEADLINE(S): MAR 1

FIELD(S): Journalism

Open to college juniors, seniors, or graduate students who attend school in Los Angeles, Orange, or Ventura counties in California and are preparing for a career in journalism.

Contact SPJ/LA at above address for an application. Applications available year-round.

2850 — LOS ANGELES PROFESSIONAL CHAPTER OF SOCIETY OF PROFESSIONAL JOURNALISTS (Helen Johnson Scholarship)

SPJ/LA Scholarships
9951 Barcelona Lane
Cypress CA 90630-3759
Written Inquiry

AMOUNT: up to $1,000

DEADLINE(S): MAR 1

FIELD(S): Broadcast Journalism

Open to college juniors, seniors, or graduate students who reside or attend school in Los Angeles, Ventura, or Orange counties in California and are preparing for a career in broadcast journalism.

Contact SPJ/LA at above address for an application. Applications available year-round.

2851 — LOS ANGELES PROFESSIONAL CHAPTER OF SOCIETY OF PROFESSIONAL JOURNALISTS (Ken Inouye Scholarship)

SPJ/LA Scholarships
9951 Barcelona Lane
Cypress CA 90630-3759
Written Inquiry

AMOUNT: up to $1,000

DEADLINE(S): MAR 1

FIELD(S): Journalism

Open to ethnic minority students who will be juniors, seniors, or graduate students the following year. Must reside or attend school in Los Angeles, Orange, or Ventura counties in California and be preparing for a career in journalism.

Contact SPJ/LA at above address for an application. Applications available year-round.

2852 — LOS ANGELES PROFESSIONAL CHAPTER OF SOCIETY OF PROFESSIONAL JOURNALISTS (Carl Greenberg Prize)

SPJ/LA Scholarships
9951 Barcelona Lane
Cypress CA 90630-3759
Written Inquiry

AMOUNT: up to $1,000

DEADLINE(S): MAR 1

FIELD(S): Journalism: Political or Investigative Reporting

Open to college juniors, seniors, or graduate students who reside or attend school in Lost Angeles, Orange, or Ventura counties in California and are preparing for a career in journalism. Award based on the best published political or investigative report.

Contact SPJ/LA at above address for an application. Applications available year-round.

2853 — NATION INSTITUTE (Nation Internship Program)

33 Irving Pl.
8th Fl.
New York NY 10003
212/209-5400
E-Mail: instinfo@nationinstitute.org
Internet: www.thenation.com/institute/masur.htm

AMOUNT: $150/week stipend

DEADLINE(S): NOV 12; MAR 17

FIELD(S): Journalism; Publishing

Full-time internships for college students and recent graduates interested in magazine journalism and publishing. Each applicant evaluated on basis of his/her resume, recommendations, and writing samples. All ages are welcome, though most interns have completed junior year of college. Possible housing and travel grants based on financial need. Internships take place in New York and Washington, DC. Must submit career goals, resume, recommendations, & writing samples.

16 awards annually. Contact Nation Institute for an application.

2854 — NATIONAL ASSOCIATION OF BLACK JOURNALISTS (NABJ Scholarship Program)

3100 Taliaferro Hall
University of Maryland
College Park MD 20742-7717
301/405-8500
FAX: 301/405-8555
E-Mail: nabj@jmail.umd.edu OR nabj@nabj.org
Internet: nabj.org

AMOUNT: $2,500

DEADLINE(S): MAR 20

FIELD(S): Journalism: print, photography, radio, television OR planning a career in one of those fields

Minimum of 10 scholarships for African-American undergraduate or graduate students who are accepted to or enrolled in an accredited, four-year journalism program majoring in print, photo, radio, or television journalism OR planning a career in one of those fields. GPA of 2.5 or better (4.0 scale) is required. Also, 2 four-year scholarships are for African-American high school seniors planning to pursue education for a journalism career.

Access website for application forms or contact above location. Write for complete information.

2855 — NATIONAL ASSOCIATION OF BLACK JOURNALISTS (NABJ Summer Internships)

3100 Taliaferro Hall
University of Maryland
College Park MD 20742-7717
301/405-8500
FAX: 301/405-8555
E-Mail: nabj@jmail.umd.edu OR
nabj@nabj.org
Internet: nabj.org

AMOUNT: Varies

DEADLINE(S): DEC 15

FIELD(S): Journalism: print, photography, radio, television OR planning a career in one of those fields

Internships for African-American sophomores, juniors, seniors, and graduate students committed to careers in journalism. Programs are throughout the U.S. Minimum 2.5 GPA required.

Access website for application forms or contact above location for further information. For foreign or U.S. students. Write for complete information.

2856 — NATIONAL ASSOCIATION OF HISPANIC JOURNALISTS (NAHJ Scholarship Program)

1193 National Press Bldg.
Washington DC 20045-2100
202/662-7483
FAX: 202/662-7144
Internet: www.nahj.org

AMOUNT: $1,000-$2,000

DEADLINE(S): FEB 25

FIELD(S): Print/Broadcast Journalism; Photojournalism

Open to high school seniors, undergraduates, and graduate students who are committed to a career in print or broadcast journalism or photojournalism. Tenable at two- or four-year schools in the US and its territories. Hispanic ancestry NOT required.

See website or send a self-addressed, stamped envelope to Ana Carrion at NAHJ for an application.

2857 — NATIONAL ASSOCIATION OF HISPANIC JOURNALISTS (Newhouse Scholarship Program)

1193 National Press Bldg.
Washington DC 20045-2100
202/662-7483
FAX: 202/662-7144
Internet: www.nahj.org

AMOUNT: $5,000

DEADLINE(S): FEB 25

FIELD(S): Print/Broadcast Journalism; Photojournalism

Open to undergraduate juniors and seniors and graduate students who are committed to pursuing a career in print or broadcast journalism or photojournalism. Awards tenable at accredited institutions in the US and its territories. It is not necessary to be a journalism or broadcast major, and Hispanic ancestry is NOT required.

See website or send a self-addressed, stamped envelope to Ana Carrion at NAHJ for an application.

2858 — NATIONAL ASSOCIATION OF WATER COMPANIES—NEW JERSEY CHAPTER (Scholarship)

Elizabethtown Water Co.
600 South Ave.
Westfield NJ 07090
908/654-1234
FAX: 908/232-2719

AMOUNT: $2,500

DEADLINE(S): APR 1

FIELD(S): Business Administration; Biology; Chemistry; Engineering; Communications

For U.S. citizens who have lived in NJ at least 5 years and plan a career in the investor-owned water utility industry in disciplines such as those above. Must be undergrad or graduate student in a 2- or 4-year NJ college or university.

GPA of 3.0 or better required. Contact Gail P. Brady for complete information.

2859 — NATIONAL BROADCASTING SOCIETY (Alpha Epsilon Rho Scholarships)

P.O. Box 1058
St. Charles MO 63302-1058
888/NBS-1-COM Ext. 2000

AMOUNT: $500 to $1,000

DEADLINE(S): JAN 1

FIELD(S): Broadcasting

Open ONLY to active student members of NBS-AERho as nominated by local chapters.

Awards are renewable. Contact local NBS-AERho chapter for complete information.

2860 — NATIONAL COUNCIL OF FARMER COOPERATIVES (Graduate Awards)

50 F St., NW, Ste. 900
Washington DC 20001
202/626-8700
FAX: 202/626-8722

AMOUNT: $1,000 (1st prize); $800 (2nd); $600 (3rd)

DEADLINE(S): APR 1

FIELD(S): American Cooperatives

Open to graduate students working on theses or dissertations dealing with some aspect of economics, finance, operation, law, or structure of American cooperatives. May be in such fields as economics, business communications, sociology, etc.

3 awards annually. Not renewable. Contact NCFC Education Foundation for registration form.

2861 — NATIONAL PRESS PHOTOGRAPHERS FOUNDATION (Kit C. King Graduate Scholarship Fund)

3200 Croasdaile Drive, Suite 306
Durham NC 27705
919/383-7246 or 800/289-6772
FAX: 919/383-7261
E-Mail: nppa@mindspring.com
Internet: sunsite.unc.edu/nppa/scholarships

AMOUNT: $500

DEADLINE(S): MAR 1

FIELD(S): Photojournalism

Open to anyone pursuing an advanced degree in journalism with an emphasis in photojournalism. Must prove acceptance in such program at a school in the US or Canada. Academic ability and financial need are considered, but primary consideration is a portfolio that demonstrates talent and initiative in documentary photojournalism. Portfolio should include 6+ photos (picture-story counts as one) or for video journalists, tape of 3 stories.

See website or contact NPPF for an application/specific details.

2862 — NATIONAL PRESS PHOTOGRAPHERS FOUNDATION, KAPPA ALPHA MU (College Photographer of the Year Competition)

Univ MO School of Journalism
105 Lee Hills Hall
Columbia MO 65211
573/882-4442
E-Mail: info@cpoy.org
Internet: www.cpoy.org

AMOUNT: $250-$1,000 + plaque/certificate & film

DEADLINE(S): MAR 31

FIELD(S): Photojournalism

Undergraduate or graduate students who have NOT worked two years or more as full-time professional photographers may enter. All entries must have been taken or published for the first time between March 1st & Feb 28th of the current year. First prize includes a 3-month paid internship at the Dallas Morning News and a camera as well as above-mentioned prizes. You may enter as many pictures as you like, and there is no entry fee.

See website or contact CPOY Coordinator Catherine Mohesky or CPOY Director David Rees for rules and entry form.

2863 — NATIONAL SCIENCES AND ENGINEERING RESEARCH COUNCIL OF CANADA (Graduate Scholarships)

Scholarships/Fellowships Division
350 Albert Street
Ottawa Ontario K1A 1H5 CANADA
613/996-3769
FAX: 613/996-2589
E-Mail: schol@nserc.ca
Internet: http://www.nserc.ca

AMOUNT: $15,700/year for 1st & 2nd years at masters or Ph.D level; $17,400/year (Ph.D level ONLY) 3rd & 4th years

DEADLINE(S): NOV 24

FIELD(S): Natural Sciences, Engineering, Biology, or Chemistry

Open to Canadian citizens or permanent residents who have earned or will soon earn a bachelors or masters degree in science or engineering. Academic excellence and research aptitude are considerations.

Write for complete information.

2864 — NATIONAL SCIENCES AND ENGINEERING RESEARCH COUNCIL OF CANADA (Postdoctoral Fellowships)

Scholarships/Fellowships Division
350 Albert Street
Ottawa Ontario K1A 1H5 CANADA
613/996-3762
FAX: 613/996-2589
E-Mail: schol@nserc.ca
Internet: http://www.nserc.ca

AMOUNT: Individually negotiated

DEADLINE(S): Varies—average: $43,000

FIELD(S): Natural Sciences, Engineering, Biology, or Chemistry

Open to Canadian citizens or permanent residents who hold doctoral degrees in science or engineering. Academic excellence and research aptitude are considerations.

Write for complete information.

2865 — NEW YORK FINANCIAL WRITERS' ASSOCIATION (Scholarship Program)

PO Box 20281
Greeley Square Station
New York NY 10001-0003
800/533-7551

AMOUNT: $3,000

DEADLINE(S): MAR

FIELD(S): Financial Journalism

Open to undergraduate and graduate students enrolled in an accredited college or university in metropolitan New York City and are pursuing a course of study leading to a financial or business journalism career.

Contact NYFWA for an application.

2866 — NEW YORK STATE SENATE (Legislative Fellows Program; R. J. Roth Journalism Fellowship; R. A. Wiebe Public Service Fellowship)

NYS Senate Student Programs Office, 90 South Swan St., Rm. 401
Albany NY 12247
518/455-2611
FAX: 518/432-5470
E-Mail: students@senate.state.ny.us

AMOUNT: $25,000 stipend (not a scholarship)

DEADLINE(S): MAY (first Friday)

FIELD(S): Political Science; Government; Public Service; Journalism; Public Relations

One year programs for U.S. citizens who are grad students and residents of New York state or enrolled in accredited programs in New York state. Fellows work as regular legislative staff members of the office to which they are assigned. The Roth Fellowship is for communications/journalism majors, and undergrads may be considered for this program.

14 fellowships per year. Fellowships take place at the New York State Legislative Office. Write for complete information.

2867 — NEW YORK STATE THEATRE INSTITUTE (Internships in Theatrical Production)

155 River St.
Troy NY 12180
518/274-3573
nysti@crisny.org
Internet: www.crisny.org/not-for-profit/nysti/int.htm

AMOUNT: None

DEADLINE(S): None

FIELD(S): Fields of study related to theatrical production, including box office and PR

Internships for college students, high school seniors, and educators-in-residence interested in developing skills in above fields. Unpaid, but college credit is earned. Located at Russell Sage College in Troy, NY. Gain experience in box office, costumes, education, electrics, music, stage management, scenery, properties, performance, and public relations. Interns come from all over the world.

Must be associated with an accredited institution. See website for more information. Call Ms. Arlene Leff,

Intern Director at above location. Include your postal mailing address.

2868 — OUTDOOR WRITERS ASSOCIATION OF AMERICA (Bodie McDowell Scholarship Program)

27 Fort Missoula Rd., Ste. 1
Missoula MT 59804
406/728-7434

AMOUNT: $2,000-$3,000

DEADLINE(S): FEB

FIELD(S): Outdoor Communications/Journalism

This scholarship is open to undergraduate and graduate students interested in writing about outdoor activities, not including organized sports. Acceptable topics include hiking, backpacking, climbing, etc. Availability varies with school participation.

Send self-addressed, stamped envelope to OWAA for an application.

2869 — PHILLIPS FOUNDATION (Journalism Fellowship Program)

7811 Montrose Rd., Ste. 100
Potomac MD 20854
301/340-2100
FAX: 301/424-0245
Internet: www.phillips.com

AMOUNT: $50,000 (full-time); $25,000 (part-time)

DEADLINE(S): MAR 1

FIELD(S): Journalism

For working print journalists with less than five years of professional experience to complete a one-year writing project supportive of American culture and a free society. Subject matter changes each year.

1 full-time & 2 part-time awards annually. Contact Phillips Foundation for an application.

2870 — PRESS CLUB OF DALLAS FOUNDATION (Scholarship)

400 N. Olive
Dallas TX 75201
214/740-9988

AMOUNT: $1,000-$3,000

DEADLINE(S): APR 15

FIELD(S): Journalism and Public Relations

Open to students who are at least sophmore level in undergraduate studies or working towards a masters degree in the above fields in a Texas college or university. This scholarship is renewable by re-application.

Write to Carol Wortham at the above address for complete information.

2871 — RADIO FREE EUROPE/RADIO LIBERTY (Intern Program for Journalists)

1201 Connecticut Ave.
Washington DC 20036
Written inquiry
FAX: 202/457-6992
E-Mail: goblep@rferl.org
Internet: www.rferl.org/welcome/intern.html

AMOUNT: Varies

DEADLINE(S): Varies

FIELD(S): Broadcast journalism, political science, international relations

For journalists early in their careers from Central and eastern Europe and the successor states to the Soviet Union. Also for western journalists. Interns will receive technical, academic, and on-the-job training. Up to 40 interns will participate in four-week programs offered in English and Russian at RFE/RL's broadcast center in Prague.

Visit website for details. Western journalists contact above location; European journalists contact RFE/RL, Vinohradska 1, 110 00 Prague 1, Czech Republic. Phone: (011 4202) 2112 3325.

2872 — SCRIPPS HOWARD FOUNDATION (Jack R. Howard Fellowships in International Journalism)

312 Walnut St.
PO Box 5380
Cincinnati OH 45201-5380
513/977-3847
FAX: 513/977-3800
E-Mail: cottingham@scripps.com
Internet: www.scripps.com/foundation

AMOUNT: Tuition & living expenses

DEADLINE(S): Varies

FIELD(S): Journalism

Fellowships provide tuition and living expenses for four experienced foreign journalists to participate in Columbia University's graduate journalism program. During the school year, the fellows attend biweekly seminars that examine trends in international journalism and address cross-cultural issues in the news media. Upon returning to their home countries, the journalists may improve the standards of journalism by setting an example and sharing training.

4 awards annually. Contact Patty Cottingham, Executive Director, for an application.

2873 — SCRIPPS HOWARD FOUNDATION (Robert P. Scripps Graphic Arts Scholarships)

312 Walnut St.
PO Box 5380
Cincinnati OH 45201-5380
513/977-3847

FAX: 513/977-3800
E-Mail: cottingham@scripps.com
Internet: www.scripps.com/foundation

AMOUNT: Varies

DEADLINE(S): Varies

FIELD(S): Newspaper Operations Management

Students must be attending the University of Rochester (NY) and majoring in newspaper operations management.

5 awards annually. Applications are available at the university.

2874 — SCRIPPS HOWARD FOUNDATION (Ted Scripps Scholarships & Lecture)

312 Walnut St.
PO Box 5380
Cincinnati OH 45201-5380
513/977-3847
FAX: 513/977-3800
E-Mail: cottingham@scripps.com
Internet: www.scripps.com/foundation

AMOUNT: $3,000 + medal

DEADLINE(S): Varies

FIELD(S): Journalism

Students must be attending the University of Nevada at Reno and majoring in journalism.

4 awards annually. Applications are available at the university.

2875 — SOCIETY FOR TECHNICAL COMMUNICATION (Graduate Scholarships)

901 N. Stuart St., Suite 904
Arlington VA 22203-1854
703/522-4114
FAX: 703/522-2075
E-Mail: stc@stc-va.org
Internet: www.stc-va.org

AMOUNT: $2,500

DEADLINE(S): FEB 15

FIELD(S): Technical Communication

Open to full-time graduate students who are enrolled in an accredited master's or doctoral degree program for careers in any area of technical communication: technical writing, editing, graphic design, multimedia art, etc.

Awards tenable at recognized colleges & universities in U.S. and Canada. Seven awards per year. Visit website or write for further information.

2876 — SOCIETY OF PROFESSIONAL JOURNALISTS (Mark of Excellence Awards Competition)

16 South Jackson St.
Greencastle IN 46135-1514

765/653-3333
FAX: 765/653-4631
E-Mail: spj@link2000.net
Internet: http://spj.org/prodevelopment/
MOE97/moe97/rules.htm

AMOUNT: Varies

DEADLINE(S): JAN 31

FIELD(S): All fields of study

A competition for professional journalists, though journalists may be studying in any field. Awards are for print or broadcast journalism.

See website for details.

2877 — SOIL AND WATER CONSERVATION SOCIETY (SWCS Internships)

7515 N.E. Ankeny Road
Ankeny IA 50021-9764
515/289-2331 or 1-800/THE-SOIL
FAX: 515/289-1227
E-Mail: charliep@swcs.org
Internet: www.swcs.org

AMOUNT: Varies—most are uncompensated

DEADLINE(S): Varies

FIELD(S): Journalism, marketing, database management, meeting planning, public policy research, environmental education, landscape architecture

Internships for undergraduates and graduates to gain experience in the above fields as they relate to soil and water conservation issues. Intership openings vary through the year in duration, compensation, and objective. SWCS will coordinate particulars with your academic advisor.

Contact SWCS for internship availability at any timne during the year or see website for jobs page.

2878 — SWEDISH INFORMATION SERVICE (Bicentennial Swedish-American Exchange Fund)

Bicentennial Fund, One Dag Hammarskjold Plaza, 45th Floor
New York NY 10017-2201
212/483-2550
FAX: 212/752-4789
E-Mail: swedinfor@ix.netcom.com

AMOUNT: 20,000 Swedish crowns (for three- to six-week intensive study visits in Sweden)

DEADLINE(S): FEB (Friday of the first week)

FIELD(S): Politics, public administration, working life, human environment, mass media, business and industry, education and culture

Program is to provide opportunity for those in a positio to influence public opinion and contribute to the development of their society. Must be U.S. citizen or permanent resident. Must have necessary experience and education for fulfilling his/her project.

Send SASE to above address for details.

2879 — THE ALICIA PATTERSON FOUNDATION (Fellowships for Journalists, Writers, Editors, and Photographers)

1730 Pennsylvania Ave. NW, Suite 180
Washington DC 20006
301/951-8512
E-Mail: apfengel@charm.net
Internet: www.aliciapatterson.org

AMOUNT: $30,000/year

DEADLINE(S): OCT 1

FIELD(S): Print Journalism/Writing, Editing, Photography

Full-time fellowships for persons working in one of the above fields for the purpose of completing a research project.

Five to seven fellows per year. Recipients may not be employed, but may do freelance work during the fellowship period. Send for details or check website for rules regarding submission of samples, recommendations, etc.

2880 — THE CARTER CENTER MENTAL HEALTH PROGRAM (Rosalynn Carter Fellowships for Mental Health Journalism)

One Copenhill, 453 Freedom Parkway
Atlanta GA 30307
404/420-5165
FAX: 404/420-5158
E-Mail: jgates@emory.edu
Internet: http://www.emory.edu/
CARTER_CENTER

AMOUNT: $10,000 + 2 trips to Center

DEADLINE(S): MAY 1

FIELD(S): Print or Broadcast Journalism

Five one-year fellowships for journalists to pursue an individual project related to mental health or mental illness. Must have at least two years of experience in print or broadcast journalism. Fellows are matched with a memember of the Advisory Board for mentoring during their fellowship year.

Call or write for application information.

2881 — THE CONCLAVE (Talent-Based Scholarships)

4517 Minnetonka Blvd.
#104
Minneapolis MN 55416
612/927-4487
FAX: 612/927-6427
E-Mail: info@theconclave.com
Internet: www.theconclave.com

AMOUNT: Tuition

DEADLINE(S): APR 14

FIELD(S): Broadcasting

Open to US citizens/permanent residents who have received a high school diploma and wish to attend a nine-month program at either the Brown Institute in Minneapolis or Specs-Howard in Detroit, Michigan. Financial need NOT a factor.

2 awards annually. Not renewable. Contact John Sweeney at the Conclave for an application.

2882 — THE FUND FOR INVESTIGATIVE JOURNALISM, INC. (Grants for Journalists)

5120 Kenwood Drive
Annandale VA 22003
703/750-3849
E-Mail:fundfij@aol.com
Internet: http://fij.org

AMOUNT: $500 and up

DEADLINE(S): JUN 1; NOV 1

FIELD(S): Journalism

Grants for journalists working outside the protection and backing of major news organizations. Limited to journalists seeking help for investigative pieces involving corruption, malfeasance, incompetence, and societal ills in general as well as for media criticism. No application form. Write a letter outlining the story, what he or she expects to prove, how this will be done, and the sources for the proof.

Include a letter of commitment from an editor or publisher to consider publishing or broadcasting the final product. Check website for details.

2883 — THE REUTER FOUNDATION (Fellowships at Oxford for Journalists)

The Director, 85 Fleet St.
London EC4P 4AJ ENGLAND
(+44) 171 542 2913
E-Mail: rtrfoundation@easynet.co.uk
Internet: www.foundation.reuters.com/
usjourn.html

AMOUNT: Travel, tuition, and living allowance

DEADLINE(S): OCT 31

FIELD(S): Journalism—print and broadcast

Fellowships for working journalists at Green College, Oxford University, in London for working journalists with at least five years experience. Program is for three months). Subjects include news writing, TV news production, and reporting on the environment, and medical, international, and business news.

Access website or write for application details. Application form is on website.

2884 — THE REUTER FOUNDATION (Fellowships for Journalists)

13 Norham Gardens
Oxford OX2 6PS ENGLAND
01865 513576
FAX: 01865 513576
Internet: www.green.ox.ac.uk/rfp

AMOUNT: Travel, tuition, and living allowance

DEADLINE(S): Varies

FIELD(S): Journalism—all areas

Fellowships for working journalists at Green College, Oxford University, in London. Programs vary in length (three to nine months), and deadline dates vary for application. Subjects include news writing, TV news production, and reporting on the environment, and medical, international, and business news.

Access website or write for application details.

2885 — THE REUTER FOUNDATION (Fellowships for Journalists: Oxford, Stanford, & Bordeaux)

The Director, 85 Fleet St.
London EC4P 4AJ ENGLAND
(+44) 171 542 2913
E-Mail: rtrfoundation@easynet.co.uk
Internet: www.foundation.reuters.com/
unijour.html

AMOUNT: Travel, tuition, and living allowance

DEADLINE(S): DEC 31

FIELD(S): Journalism

Fellowships at Green College (Oxford University), in London; Stanford University in Calif., U.S.; or L'Universite de Bordeaux III, France for journalists with at least five years experience. Must be fluent in the language of the school attended. Open to journalists of all media and to specialist writers in economic, environmental, medical and scientific subjects. Three, six, or nine months.

Fully funded fellowships are for journalists from the developing world and central/eastern Europe. English-speaking journalists from other parts of the world may apply for self-funded fellowships. Application form and details are on website.

2886 — THE REUTER FOUNDATION (Fellowships in Medical Journalism)

The Director, 85 Fleet St.
London EC4P 4AJ ENGLAND
(+44) 171 542 2913
E-Mail: rtrfoundation@easynet.co.uk
Internet: www.foundation.reuters.com/
medic.html

AMOUNT: Travel, tuition, and living allowance

DEADLINE(S): SEP 15 (Columbia); OCT 31 (Oxford)

FIELD(S): Medical Journalism

Fellowships for English-speaking journalists, world-wide, for research and study relating to medical issues. Tenable at the Universities of Oxford, England, and Columbia, New York, U.S. The Oxford award is for one term within the Reuter Foundation Programme for international journalists at Green College at Oxford. Terms start in October, January, and April. The Columbia award is for one semested starting in January. Must be between ages of 28 and 45.

Access application form and information are on website or write for application details.

2887 — THE REUTER FOUNDATION (The Alva Clarke Memorial Fellowship for Journalists From the Caribbean)

The Director, 85 Fleet St.
London EC4P 4AJ ENGLAND
(+44) 171 542 2913
E-Mail: rtrfoundation@easynet.co.uk
Internet: www.foundation.reuters.com/alva.html

AMOUNT: Travel, tuition, and living allowance

DEADLINE(S): DEC 31

FIELD(S): Journalism

Fellowships at Green College (Oxford University) in London for full-time journalists from a country in the Caribbean. Must be fluent in English. For three months, starting in October, January, or April.

Application form and details are on website.

2888 — THE REUTER FOUNDATION (The Mogadishu Fellowship for Photojournalists)

The Director, 85 Fleet St.
London EC4P 4AJ ENGLAND
(+44) 171 542 2913
E-Mail: rtrfoundation@easynet.co.uk
Internet: www.foundation.reuters.com/photo.html

AMOUNT: Travel, tuition, and living allowance

DEADLINE(S): DEC 31

FIELD(S): Photojournalism

A one-semester practical study opportunity for full-time photojournalists from Africa. Tenable at the School of Journalism at the University of Missouri-Columbia, U.S. from January to May. Fellows may also spend one or two weeks with the Reuters News Pictures Desk in Washington DC or London. Must be under age 35 and have at least three years professional experience.

Access website or write for application details.

2889 — THE REUTER FOUNDATION (The Peter Sullivan Memorial Fellowships for News Graphics Journalists)

The Director, 85 Fleet St.
London EC4P 4AJ ENGLAND
(+44) 171 542 2913
E-Mail: rtrfoundation@easynet.co.uk
Internet: www.foundation.reuters.com/sullivan.html

AMOUNT: Travel, tuition, and living allowance

DEADLINE(S): SEP 30

FIELD(S): Journalism—news graphics

Fellowships for working, full-time news graphics journalists with at least five years experience. The three-month program offers an opportunity for talented news graphic journalists and designers to create a university study plan suited to their individual needs. Must be fluent in either Spanish or English.

Access website or write for application details. Application form is on website.

2890 — THE REUTER FOUNDATION (The Willie Vicoy Fellowship for Photojournalists)

The Director, 85 Fleet St.
London EC4P 4AJ ENGLAND
(+44) 171 542 2913
E-Mail: rtrfoundation@easynet.co.uk
Internet: www.foundation.reuters.com/photo.html

AMOUNT: Travel, tuition, and living allowance

DEADLINE(S): DEC 31

FIELD(S): Photojournalism

A one-semester practical study opportunity for full-time photojournalists from the developing world and countries in transition. Tenable at the School of Journalism at the University of Missouri-Columbia, U.S. from August to December. Fellows may also spend one or two weeks with the Reuters News Pictures Desk in Washington DC or London. Must be under age 35 and have at least three years professional experience.

Access website or write for application details.

2891 — THE UNIVERSITY OF NEW MEXICO FOUNDATION (The Kelly Richmond Memorial Fund)

Univ. of New Mexico
Hodgin Hall, 2nd Fl.
Albuquerque NM 87131
Internet: www.ire.org/resources/scholarship

AMOUNT: Varies

DEADLINE(S): None

FIELD(S): Journalism: Investigative reporting

Scholarship for journalism students at the University of New Mexico to honor Kelly Richmond, an award-winning journalist who died of lung cancer at age 33.

Write for details.

2892 — U.S. ENVIRONMENTAL PROTECTION AGENCY—NATIONAL NETWORK FOR ENVIRONMENTAL MANAGEMENT STUDIES (Fellowships)

401 M St., SW
Mailcode 1704
Washington DC 20460
202/260-5283
FAX: 202/260-4095
E-Mail: jojokian.sheri@epa.gov
Internet: www.epa.gov/enviroed/students.html

AMOUNT: Varies

DEADLINE(S): DEC

FIELD(S): Environmental Policies, Regulations, & Law; Environmental Management & Administration; Environmental Science; Public Relations & Communications; Computer Programming & Development

Fellowships are open to undergraduate and graduate students working on research projects in the above fields, either full-time during the summer or part-time during the school year. Must be US citizen or legal resident. Financial need NOT a factor.

85-95 awards annually. Not renewable. See website or contact the Career Service Center of participating universities for an application.

2893 — UNITED METHODIST COMMUNICATIONS (Stoody-West Fellowship for Graduate Study in Journalism)

P.O. Box 320
Nashville TN 37202
615/742-5140
FAX: 615/742-5404
Internet: www.scholarships@umcom.umc.org

AMOUNT: $6,000

DEADLINE(S): FEB 15

FIELD(S): Religious Journalism

Christian faith. Fellowship open to students enrolled in accredited graduate schools of communication or journalism (print; electronic or audiovisual) and planning to engage in religious journalism.

Purpose of the fellowship is to enhance the recipient's potential professional competence, thereby helping to perpetuate the standards exemplified by Ralph Stoody and Arthur West. Write for complete information.

2894 — UTA ALUMNI ASSOCIATION (Lloyd Clark Scholarship Journalism)

University of Texas at Arlington
Box 19457
Arlington TX 76019
Internet: www.uta.edu/alumni/scholar.htm

AMOUNT: $250

DEADLINE(S): Varies

FIELD(S): Journalism

Must be a full-time junior or higher with at least 15 hours completed at the University of Texas at Arlington and have a commitment to a career in journalism. Must show noticeable academic achievement and evidence of success in journalism. Financial need may be considered. Writing sample required.

1 award annually. Contact UTA Alumni Association for an application.

2895 — W. EUGENE SMITH MEMORIAL FUND, INC. (Grants)

c/o ICP
1130 Fifth Ave.
New York NY 10128
212/860-1777
FAX: 212/860-1482

AMOUNT: $20,000; $5,000

DEADLINE(S): JUL 15

FIELD(S): Photojournalism

Career support for photojournalists of any nationality. Must submit a photographic project with a written proposal, illustrated in the humanistic manner of W. Eugene Smith. Financial need NOT a factor.

2 awards annually. Not renewable. Contact Ms. Anna Winand for an application.

2896 — WOMEN ON BOOKS (Scholarships for African-American Women)

879 Rainier Ave. N., Suite A105
Renton WA 98055
206/626-2323

AMOUNT: $1,000

DEADLINE(S): JUN (Mid-month)

FIELD(S): English or journalism, with intention to pursue a writing career

Scholarships for African-American women pursuing careers in writing. Must major in English or journalism in a four-year university, have a min. GPA of 2.5, and demonstrate financial need.

Write for details.

2897 — WOMEN'S SPORTS FOUNDATION (Jackie Joyner-Kersee & Zina Garrison Minority Internships)

Eisenhower Park
East Meadow NY 11554
800/227-3988
FAX: 516/542-4716
E-Mail: WoSport@aol.com
Internet: www.lifetimetv.com/WoSport

AMOUNT: $4,000-$5,000

DEADLINE(S): Ongoing

FIELD(S): Sports-related fields

Provides women of color an opportunity to gain experience in a sports-related career and interact in the sports community. May be undergraduates, college graduates, graduate students, or women in a career change. Internships are located at the Women's Sports Foundation in East Meadow, New York.

4-6 awards annually. See website or write to above address for details.

HISTORY

2898 — AMERICAN ANTIQUARIAN SOCIETY (Visiting Academic Research Fellowships)

185 Salisbury St.
Worcester MA 01609-1634
508/752-5813
FAX: 508/754-9069
E-Mail: cfs@mwa.org

AMOUNT: Up to $35,000

DEADLINE(S): JAN 15

FIELD(S): American History; Bibliography; Printing & Publishing; American Literature (through 1876)

Fellowships of one to twelve months duration at the society library. For graduate and postgraduate research in the above fields.

Recipients are expected to be in regular and continuous residence at the society library during the period of the grant. Write for complete information.

2899 — AMERICAN COUNCIL OF LEARNED SOCIETIES (ACLS Fellowships)

Office of Fellowshops & Grants
228 E. 45th St.
New York NY 10017
Written Inquiry

AMOUNT: Up to $20,000

DEADLINE(S): SEP 30

FIELD(S): Humanities, Social Sciences, and other areas having predominately humanistic emphasis

Open to U.S. citizens or legal residents who hold the Ph.D or its equivalent. Fellowships are designed to help scholars devote 6 to 12 continuous months to full-time research.

Write for complete information.

2900 — AMERICAN HISTORICAL ASSOCIATION (Albert J. Beveridge Grants for Research in the History of the Western Hemisphere)

400 A St., SE
Washington DC 20003
202/544-2422
FAX: 202/544-8307
E-Mail: aha@theaha.org
Internet: www.theaha.org

AMOUNT: $1,000 (max.)

DEADLINE(S): FEB 1

FIELD(S): Western Hemisphere History (Americas)

For graduate or postgraduate research projects on the history of the Western Hemisphere. Must be AHA member.

See website or contact AHA for membership information and grant details.

2901 — AMERICAN HISTORICAL ASSOCIATION (J. Franklin Jameson Fellowship)

400 A St., SE
Washington DC 20003
202/544-2422
FAX: 202/544-8307
E-Mail: aha@theaha.org
Internet: www.theaha.org

AMOUNT: $10,000

DEADLINE(S): JAN 15

FIELD(S): American History

To support significant scholarly research in the collections of the Library of Congress by young historians. Must have earned a Ph.D. or equivalent within the last five years.

See website or contact AHA for details.

2902 — AMERICAN HISTORICAL ASSOCIATION (Michael Kraus Research Award Grant)

400 A St., SE
Washington DC 20003
202/544-2422
FAX: 202/544-8307
E-Mail: aha@theaha.org
Internet: www.theaha.org

AMOUNT: $800

DEADLINE(S): FEB 1

FIELD(S): American Colonial History

For research in American colonial history with particular reference to intercultural aspects of American and European relations. Must be AHA member.

See website or contact AHA for details.

2903 — AMERICAN HISTORICAL ASSOCIATION (Published Book Awards)

400 A St., SE
Washington DC 20003
202/544-2422
FAX: 202/544-8307
E-Mail: aha@theaha.org
Internet: www.theaha.org

AMOUNT: Varies

DEADLINE(S): MAY 15

FIELD(S): Historical Writing (already-published books only)

Awards offered for already-published books on historical subjects, ranging from 17th Century European history to the history of the feminist movement.

Not a contest and NOT for high school. FOR ALREADY-PUBLISHED WORKS ONLY. See website or contact AHA for details.

2904 — AMERICAN RESEARCH INSTITUTE IN TURKEY (ARIT Fellowship Program)

Univ Penn Museum
33rd & Spruce Streets
Philadelphia PA 19104-6324
215/898-3474
FAX: 215/898-0657
E-Mail: leinwand@sas.upenn.edu
Internet: mec.sas.upenn.edu/ARIT

AMOUNT: Varies

DEADLINE(S): NOV 15

FIELD(S): Humanities; Social Sciences; Turkish Studies

Two-month to one-year fellowships are for postdoctoral scholars & advanced graduate students engaged in research on ancient, medieval, or modern times in Turkey, in any field of the humanities & social sciences. Predoctoral students must have fulfilled all preliminary requirements for doctorate except dissertation. Applicants must maintain an affiliation with an educational institution in the US or Canada. Must submit curriculum vitae, research proposal, & referees.

Contact ARIT for an application.

2905 — AMERICAN RESEARCH INSTITUTE IN TURKEY (Mellon Research Fellowships for Central and Eastern European Scholars in Turkey)

Univ Penn Museum
33rd & Spruce Streets
Philadelphia PA 19104-6324
215/898-3474
FAX: 215/898-0657

E-Mail: leinwand@sas.upenn.edu
Internet: mec.sas.upenn.edu/ARIT

AMOUNT: Stipend up to $10,500 for 2-3 month project (includes travel, living expenses, work-related costs)

DEADLINE(S): MAR 5

FIELD(S): Humanities; Social Sciences

For Czech, Hungarian, Polish, Slovakian, Bulgarian, and Romanian scholars holding a Ph.D. or equivalent who are engaged in advanced research in any field of the social sciences or the humanities involving Turkey. Must be permanent residents of these countries and must obtain formal permission for any research to be carried out.

3 awards annually. Previous fellows not eligible. See website or write to above address for details.

2906 — AMERICAN RESEARCH INSTITUTE IN TURKEY (National Endowment for the Humanities Fellowships for Research in Turkey)

Univ Penn Museum
33rd & Spruce Streets
Philadelphia PA 19104-6324
215/898-3474
FAX: 215/898-0657
E-Mail: leinwand@sas.upenn.edu
Internet: mec.sas.upenn.edu/ARIT

AMOUNT: $10,000-$30,000

DEADLINE(S): NOV 15

FIELD(S): Humanities

Postdoctoral fellowships are to conduct research in Turkey for four to twelve months. Fields of study cover all periods in the general range of the humanities, including humanistically oriented aspects of the social sciences, prehistory, history, art, archaeology, literature, linguistics, and cultural history. There are two institutes, one in Istanbul and one in Ankara. Both have residential facilities for fellows and provide general assistance.

2-3 awards annually. Contact ARIT for an application. Notification by January 25th.

2907 — AMERICAN SCHOOL OF CLASSICAL STUDIES AT ATHENS (Katherine Keene Summer Session Scholarship for Teachers)

993 Lenox Drive, Suite 101
Lawrence NJ 08648
609/844-7577
E-Mail: ascsa@ascsa.org
Internet: www.asca.org

AMOUNT: $2,500

DEADLINE(S): FEB 15

FIELD(S): Classical Studies; Ancient Greece

Scholarships for American public secondary school teachers to attend summer sessions in the above program in Greece. Must include these topics in his/her course material.

Access website for complete information and application or write to Committee on Summer Sessions at above address for details.

2908 — AMERICAN SOCIETY OF ARMS COLLECTORS (Antique Weapons Research Fellowship)

Robert Palmer
511 Spradley Dr.
Troy AL 36079
334/566-4526
E-Mail: Palmerhaus@mindspring.com

AMOUNT: $5,000

DEADLINE(S): MAR 15

FIELD(S): Antique Arms & Armor

Open to graduate students and other scholars for research into the origin, manufacture, use, and history of rare or historical weapons. Applicants should be seeking a master's or doctoral degree in an area consistent with the Society's aims and purposes. Research must eventually result in a scholarly report that can be published in the Society's bulletin. Financial need NOT a factor.

1-2 awards annually. Not renewable. Contact Robert Palmer for an application.

2909 — ARCHAEOLOGICAL INSTITUTE OF AMERICA (Olivia James Traveling Fellowship)

Boston Univ
656 Beacon St.
Boston MA 02215-2006
617/353-9361
FAX: 617/353-6550
E-Mail: aia@bu.edu
Internet: www.archeological.org

AMOUNT: $22,000

DEADLINE(S): NOV 1

FIELD(S): Classics; Sculpture; Architecture; Archaeology; History

Fellowships for US citizens/permanent residents to be used for travel and study in Greece, the Aegean Islands, Sicily, Southern Italy, Asia Minor, or Mesopotamia. Preference given to individuals engaged in dissertation research or to recent recipients of the Ph.D. (within 5 years). Award is not intended to support field excavation projects, and recipients may not hold other major fellowships during tenure. At conclusion, recipient must submit report on use of stipend.

Contact AIA for an application. Awards announced by February 1st.

2910 — ASSOCIATION FOR WOMEN IN SCIENCE EDUCATIONAL FOUNDATION (AWIS Predoctoral Awards)

1200 New York Ave. NW, Suite 650
Washington DC 20005
202/326-8940 or 800-886-AWIS
E-Mail: awis@awis.org
Internet: www.awis.org

AMOUNT: $1,000

DEADLINE(S): JAN 16

FIELD(S): Various Sciences and Social Sciences

Scholarships for female doctoral students. Summary page, description of research project, resume, references, transcripts, and biographical sketch required. US citizens may study at any graduate institution; non-citizens must study at US institutions.

5-10 awards annually. See website or write to above address for an application and complete information.

2911 — ASSOCIATION FOR WOMEN IN SCIENCE EDUCATIONAL FOUNDATION (AWIS Pre-doctoral Awards)

1200 New York Ave. NW, Suite 650
Washington DC 20005
202/326-8940 or 800/886-AWIS
E-Mail: awis@awis.org
Internet: www.awis.org

AMOUNT: $1,000

DEADLINE(S): JAN 16

FIELD(S): Various Sciences and Social Sciences

Scholarships for female doctoral students. Summary page, description of research project, resume, references, transcripts, and biographical sketch required. US citizens may study at any graduate institution; non-citizens must be enrolled in US institutions.

5-10 awards annually. See website or write to above address for an application and more information.

2912 — ASSOCIATION FOR WOMEN IN SCIENCE EDUCATIONAL FOUNDATION (Ruth Satter Memorial Award)

1200 New York Ave., NW, Suite 650
Washington DC 20005
202/326-8940 or 800/886-AWIS
E-Mail: awis@awis.org
Internet: www.awis.org

AMOUNT: $1,000

DEADLINE(S): JAN 16

FIELD(S): Various Sciences and Social Sciences

Scholarships for female doctoral students who have interrupted their education for at least three years to raise a family. Summary page, description of research project, resume, references, transcripts, biographical sketch, and letter from your department to confirm eligibility required. US citizens may study at any graduate institution; non-citizens must attend US institutions.

See website or write to above address for more information or an application.

2913 — ASSOCIATION FOR WOMEN IN SCIENCE EDUCATIONAL FOUNDATION (Ruth Satter Memorial Award)

1200 New York Ave. NW, Suite 650
Washington DC 20005
202/326-8940 or 800/886-AWIS
E-Mail: awis@awis.org
Internet: www.awis.org

AMOUNT: $1,000

DEADLINE(S): JAN 16

FIELD(S): Various Sciences and Social Sciences

Scholarships for female doctoral students who have interrupted their education three years or more to raise a family. Summary page, description of research project, resume, references, transcripts, biographical sketch, and proof of eligibility from department head required. US citizens may attend any graduate institution; non-citizens must be enrolled in US institutions.

See website or write to above address for more information or an application.

2914 — AUSTRALIAN FEDERATION OF UNIVERSITY WOMEN - WESTERN AUSTRALIA (Joyce Riley Bursary)

Bursary Liaison Officer
PO Box 48
Nedlands WA 6909 AUSTRALIA
Written Inquiry

AMOUNT: Aus$1,700 - Aus$2,750

DEADLINE(S): JUL 31

FIELD(S): Humanities; Social Sciences

To support women graduates of a Western Australian university to complete a higher degree or post-doctoral research in Humanities or Social Sciences at a recognized university in any country.

Membership in AFUW or in IFUW is required. Contact above location for further information.

2915 — AUSTRALIAN FEDERATION OF UNIVERSITY WOMEN - WESTERN AUSTRALIA (Joyce Riley Bursary)

Bursary Liaison Officer
PO Box 48
Nedlands WA 6009 AUSTRALIA
Written Inquiry

AMOUNT: Aus$1,700 - Aus$2,750

DEADLINE(S): JUL 31

FIELD(S): Humanities; Social Sciences

To support women graduates of a recognized university to complete a higher degree or post-doctoral research at a university in Western Australia.

Membership in AFUW or in IFUW is required. Write to above address for complete information.

2916 — AUSTRALIAN WAR MEMORIAL (John Treloar Grants-In-Aid & AWM Research Fellowship)

GPO Box 345
Canberra ACT 2601 AUSTRALIA
02/6243 4210
FAX: 02/6243 4325
E-Mail: ian.hodges@awm.gov.au
Internet: www.awm.gov.au

AMOUNT: $A6,000 (max. grant); $A12,000 (max. fellowship)

DEADLINE(S): Varies

FIELD(S): Australian Military History

Grants and fellowships for students at any level in any country to study Australian Military History. Financial need NOT a factor.

Not renewable. Contact Ian Hodges at AWM for an application.

2917 — BOLOGNA CENTER OF THE JOHNS HOPKINS UNIVERSITY - PAUL H. NITZE SCHOOL OF ADVANCED INTERNATIONAL STUDIES (Fellowships for Non-Americans)

Admissions Office
Via Belmeloro 11
40126 Bologna ITALY
+39/51/232-185
FAX: +39/51/228-505
E-Mail: admission@jhubc.it
Internet: www.jhubc.it

AMOUNT: Partial to full tuition

DEADLINE(S): FEB 1

FIELD(S): European Studies; International Relations; International Economics

One year at SAIS Bologna Center is open to graduate students with some background in political science, economics, history, or law and who are interested in problems confronting Europe and/or international relations. Possibility to continue for the second year toward an M.A. at SAIS in Washington, DC. Program is conducted in English; therefore, English fluency is required. This program is for non-US citizens.

Contact Bologna Center for an application.

2918 — BOLOGNA CENTER OF THE JOHNS HOPKINS UNIVERSITY - PAUL H. NITZE SCHOOL OF ADVANCED INTERNATIONAL STUDIES (Fellowships for Americans)

SAIS
1740 Massachusetts Ave., NW
Washington DC 20036
E-Mail: admission@jhubc.it
Internet: www.jhubc.it

AMOUNT: Partial to full tuition

DEADLINE(S): JAN 15

FIELD(S): European Studies; International Relations; International Economics

One year at SAIS Bologna Center in Italy is open to graduate students with some background in political science, economics, history, or law and who are interested in problems confronting Europe and/or international relations. Must be US citizen/permanent resident. Courses are conducted in English.

Contact SAIS for an application.

2919 — BRANDEIS UNIVERSITY (Irving & Rose Crown Ph.D. Fellowships & Tuition Scholarships)

Department of History
Mailstop 036
Waltham MA 02454-9110
736/736-2270

AMOUNT: $15,000

DEADLINE(S): FEB 15

FIELD(S): American History

All persons accepted to Ph.D. programs at Brandeis University receive fellowships and tuition scholarships. Both programs are based on merit.

Renewable. Contact the Department of History for an application.

2920 — BRITISH ASSOCIATION FOR AMERICAN STUDIES (Short-Term Awards)

Dr. Jenel Virden
University of Hull
Hull HU6 7RX ENGLAND UK
01482 465303

AMOUNT: 400 pounds sterling

DEADLINE(S): DEC 1

FIELD(S): American Studies; American History

Open to graduate/postgraduate British scholars for brief visits to the US for research in American history, politics, geography, culture, and literature. Preference given to younger scholars.

Contact Dr. Jenel Virden for an application.

2921 — BRITISH COLUMBIA HERITAGE TRUST (Scholarships)

PO Box 9818 Stn Prov Govt.
Victoria BC V8W 9W3 CANADA
250/356-1433

AMOUNT: $5,000

DEADLINE(S): FEB 15

FIELD(S): British Columbia History; Architecture; Archaeology; Archival Management

Open to graduate students who are Canadian citizens or permanent residents. Criteria are scholarly record and academic performance, educational and career objectives, and proposed program of study.

Write for complete information.

2922 — BRITISH FEDERATION OF WOMEN GRADUATES (Theodora Bosanquet Bursary)

BFWG Charitable Fdn.
28 Great James St.
London WC1N 3ES ENGLAND UK
0171/404 6447
FAX: 0171/404 6505
E-Mail: bfwg.charity@btinternet.com
Internet: www.ifuw.org

AMOUNT: 4 weeks free accomodation

DEADLINE(S): OCT 31

FIELD(S): History; British Literature

Open to women scholars or women postgraduate students who are carrying out research in history or English literature requiring the use of libraries, archives, or other scholarly resources in London. Bursary offered up to four weeks during period from July 1st to October 1st, and covers only accomodation; holder is responsible for all travel & other expenses. After completing tenure, holder must submit short report to Trustees on work carried out. Referees required.

Contact the Grants Administrator-TBB for an application.

2923 — BRITISH INSTITUTE IN EASTERN AFRICA (Research Grants)

PO Box 30710
Nairobi Kenya E. AFRICA
+254-2-43721
FAX: +254-2-43365
E-Mail: pjlane@insightkenya.com
Internet: britac3.britac.ac.uk/institutes/eafrica

AMOUNT: 500-5,000 pounds sterling

DEADLINE(S): MAY 31; NOV 30

FIELD(S): Archaeology; History; Linguistics; Ethnography

Grants are for graduate or postgraduate fieldwork in Eastern Africa. Does NOT cover salaries, overheads, student fees, or stipends. Preference is given, but not limited, to UK and Commonwealth citizens. Financial need is NOT a factor.

15 awards annually. Not renewable. Contact Dr. Paul Lane at the British Institute in Nairobi for an application.

2924 — CANADIAN FEDERATION OF UNIVERSITY WOMEN (Margaret Dale Philp Award)

251 Bank St., Ste. 600
Ottawa Ontario K2P 1X3 CANADA
613/234-2732
Internet: www.cfuw.ca

AMOUNT: $1,000

DEADLINE(S): NOV 15

FIELD(S): Humanities; Social Sciences

For women who reside in Canada and are pursuing graduate studies in the humanities or social sciences, with special consideration given to study in Canadian history. Must hold at least a bachelor's degree or equivalent from a recognized university and have been accepted into, or be currently enrolled in the proposed program and place of study.

$20 filing fee. Contact CFUW for an application after August 1st. Candidates will be notified by May 31st. Funded by CFUW/Kitchener-Waterloo.

2925 — CENTER FOR 17TH- AND 18TH-CENTURY STUDIES (Fellowships)

UCLA
310 Reyce Hall
Los Angeles CA 90095-1404
310/206-8522
FAX: 310/206-8577
E-Mail: c1718cs@humnet.ucla.edu

AMOUNT: $1,000-$18,400

DEADLINE(S): MAR 15

FIELD(S): British Literature/History (17th & 18th Centuries)

Undergraduate stipends, graduate assistantships, and Ahmanson & Getty postdoctoral fellowships are for advanced study and research regarding British literature and history of the 17th and 18th centuries. Tenable at the William Andrews Clark Memorial Library at the University of California, Los Angeles.

Contact the Center for current year's theme and an application.

2926 — CHRISTIAN A. JOHNSON ENDEAVOR FOUNDATION (Native American Fellows)

Harvard Univ., 79 John F. Kennedy St.
Cambridge MA 02138
617/495-1152
FAX: 617/496-3900
Internet: www.ksg.harvard.edu/hpaied/cjohn.htm

AMOUNT: Varies

DEADLINE(S): MAY 1

FIELD(S): Social sciences, government, or program related to Native American studies

Fellowships for students of Native American ancestry who attend a John F. Kennedy School of Government degree program. Applicant, parent, or grandparent must hold membership in a federally or state-recognized tribe, band, or other organized group of Native Americans. Must be commited to a career in American Indian affairs. Awards based on merit and need.

Renewable, based on renomination and availability of funds. To apply, contact John F. Kennedy School of Government at above address.

2927 — CONFERENCE ON LATIN AMERICAN HISTORY (James R. Scobie Memorial Award for Preliminary Ph.D Research)

Conference on Latin American History
508 College of Business
Auburn Univ
AL 36849-5236
205/844-4161
FAX 205/844-6673

AMOUNT: $1,000

DEADLINE(S): APR 1

FIELD(S): Latin American History

Travel Grant will be awarded each year for use during the following summer for preliminary Ph.D research (not dissertation research).

Write for complete information.

2928 — COUNCIL FOR EUROPEAN STUDIES (Predissertation Fellowships)

Columbia Univ
807-807A International Affairs Bldg.
New York NY 10027
212/854-4172
FAX: 212/854-8808
E-Mail: ces@columbia.edu
Internet: www.europanet.org

AMOUNT: $4,000 stipend (max.)

DEADLINE(S): FEB 1

FIELD(S): Cultural Anthropology; History (post 1750); Political Science; Sociology; Geography; Urban & Regional Planning

Awards are for research in France to determine viability of projected doctoral dissertation in modern history and social sciences. Recipients test research design of dissertation, determine availability of archival materials, and contact French scholars. Must be US citizen or permanent resident at a US institution and have completed at least two but no more than three years of full-time doctoral study by end of year. Institutional membership in Council is required.

6 awards annually. See website or contact Council for an application.

2929 — DIRKSEN CONGRESSIONAL CENTER (Congressional Research Grants Program)

301 S. 4th St., Suite A
Pekin IL 61554
309/347-7113
FAX 309/347-6432
E-Mail: fmackaman@pekin.net

AMOUNT: $3,000

DEADLINE(S): MAR 31 (postmark)

FIELD(S): Political Science, American History (with emphasis on U.S. Congress or Congressional Leadership)

For persons already holding a B.A. degree with a serious interest in studying the U.S. Congress. Research must be original culminating in new knowledge or new interpretation or both. Political scientists, historians, biographers, journalists, and others may apply.

Contact Frank H. Mackaman at above address for details.

2930 — EAST TEXAS HISTORICAL ASSOCIATION (Ottis Lock Endowment Awards)

PO Box 6223
SFA Station
Nacogdoches TX 75962
409/468-2407

AMOUNT: $500

DEADLINE(S): MAY 1

FIELD(S): History; Social Science

Open to residents of East Texas who will be pursuing undergraduate or graduate studies at an East Texas college or university.

Renewable with adequate progress towards degree. Contact East Texas Historical Association for an application.

2931 — ECONOMIC HISTORY ASSOCIATION (Arthur H. Cole Grants-in-Aid)

226A Summerfield Hall, University of Kansas,
Dept. of Economics
Lawrence KS 66045
913/864-3501
FAX: 913/864-5270
E-Mail: eha@falcon.cc.ukans.edu

AMOUNT: $1,500

DEADLINE(S): APR 1

FIELD(S): Economic History

Open to recent Ph.D.s wanting to do research in the area of economic history. Supports research in the field regardless of time period or geographic area. Must be members of the Economic History Association. For membership information, contact above address.

Contact above location for details of grant.

2932 — EUROPEAN UNIVERSITY INSTITUTE (Jean Monnet Fellowship)

Via Dei Roccettini 9
I-50016 San Domenico Di Fiesole (FL) Italy
0039-055-46851
FAX: 0039-055-4685444
E-Mail: applyjmf@datacomm.iue.it
Internet: www.iue.it/JMF/Welcome.html

AMOUNT: 2,000,000-3,500,000 Italian lire per month (i.e. 1,025-1,750 ECU) + medical & family allowances (depends on whether fellow is in receipt of payment from another source and on extent of duties carried out at the Institute)

DEADLINE(S): NOV 1

FIELD(S): Europe: History, Society, Politics, Economics, Law

Post-doctoral fellowships. Fellows are required to make scholarly contribution to research on Europe within one of EUI's research projects or on topic, falling within general interests of the Institute. Publication of research is expected.

25 fellowships annually. Financial need NOT considered. See website or contact Dr. Andreas Frijdal at above address for complete information.

2933 — EUROPEAN UNIVERSITY INSTITUTE (National Postgraduate Scholarships)

Via De Roccettini 9
San Domenico Di Fiesole (FI 50016) ITALY
0039/055-46851
FAX: 0039/055-4685444
E-Mail: applyres@datacomm.iue.it
Internet: www.iue.it

AMOUNT: $1,000/month + travel & medical/family allowances

DEADLINE(S): JAN 31

FIELD(S): Political Science; Social Sciences; Law; Economics; History

Open to graduate & postgraduate students at the Institute who have good honors and a research project having European dimension. Awards are available only to nationals of the Institute's member states. US citizens must have sufficient personal funds or another grant to cover maintenance & tuition; may apply to Fulbright Commission which may award up to two grants per academic year to US citizens with tuition-fee waivers.

130 awards annually. Renewable. Contact Dr. Andreas Frijdal for an application.

2934 — FOLGER SHAKESPEARE LIBRARY (Long-term Fellowships)

c/o Carol Brobeck
201 E. Capitol St., SE
Washington, DC 20003
202/675-0348
E-Mail: Brobeck@Folger.edu

AMOUNT: up to $45,000

DEADLINE(S): NOV 1

FIELD(S): Renaissance Studies

Two Mellon Postdoctoral Research Fellowships, three National Endowment for the Humanities Fellowships, and one or two Folger Library Long-term Fellowships available to senior scholars who have made substantial contributions in their fields of research and are pursuing projects appropriate to the Folger collections.

Fellowships are for 6-9 months. To apply, send seven copies each of an application form, a 500-word description of the research project, and a curriculum vitae. Three letters of reference should be sent to the Fellowship Committee.

2935 — FOLGER SHAKESPEARE LIBRARY (Short-term Research Fellowships)

c/o Carol Brobeck
201 E. Capital St., SE
Washington, DC 20003
202/675-0348

AMOUNT: $1,700/month stipend

DEADLINE(S): MAR 1

FIELD(S): Renaissance Studies

Short-term (1-3 months) post-doctoral fellowships for research at the Folger Library, which houses an extensive collection of renaissance books and manuscripts.

Submit four copies each of an application form, a 500-word description of the research project, and a curriculum vitae. Three letters of reference should be sent to the Fellowship Committee.

2936 — FORD FOUNDATION/NATIONAL RESEARCH COUNCIL (Postdoctoral Fellowship for Minorities)

National Research Council
2101 Constitution Ave.
Washington DC 20418
202/334-2860
E-Mail: infofell@nas.edu
Internet: http//www.nas.edu/fo/index.html

AMOUNT: $25,000 + relocation and research allowance

DEADLINE(S): JAN 3

FIELD(S): Life and physical sciences, mathematics, engineering sciences, behavioral and social sciences, and the humanities

For U.S. citizens who received a Ph.D or Sc.D in the last 7 years and who are Native Amer. Indian or Alaskan, Black/African American, Mexican American, Native Pacific Islander, or Puerto Rican and who are or plan to be in a teaching or research career.

Contact above website or address for complete information.

2937 — FORD FOUNDATION/NATIONAL RESEARCH COUNCIL (Predoctoral/Dissertation Fellowships for Minorities)

2101 Constitution Ave.
Washington DC 20418
202/334-2872
E-Mail: infofell@nas.edu
Internet: http//www.nas.edu/fo/index.html

AMOUNT: $14,000 annual stipend + $6,000 grant to institution; $18,000 for dissertation fellowship

DEADLINE(S): NOV 3

FIELD(S): Most fields of study: sciences, humanities, engineering, behavioral science, social sciences, and computer science

Predoctoral and dissertation fellowships for students whose ethnicity is Alaskan Native, Black/African American, Mexican American/Chicano, Native American Indian, Native Pacific Islander, or Puerto Rican. For research-based programs leading to careers in college teaching and research.

Contact above address or website.

2938 — FRENCH-AMERICAN FOUNDATION (Bicentennial Fellowships)

41 East 72nd St.
New York NY 10021
212/288-4000
FAX: 212/288-4765
E-Mail: French_AmerFdn@msn.com

AMOUNT: 10,000 French francs/mo.

DEADLINE(S): FEB 2

FIELD(S): Social sciences

For doctoral students in the social sciences to travel to France for one year to conduct research essential to the completion of their dissertations. Must have completed all other requirements for Ph.D. May not use the award until exams are passed.

Requires application with a statement of purpose, full academic records, plan of research, bibliography, abstract, and three academic recommendations.

2939 — FRIENDS OF THE UNIVERSITY OF WISCONSIN (Madison Libraries Humanities Grants-in-Aid)

728 State St.
Madison WI 53706
608/262-3243 or 608/265-2750 (ans. mach.)

AMOUNT: $1,000/mo.

DEADLINE(S): APR 1; OCT 1

FIELD(S): Research in the humanities appropriate to the collections

Two grants-in-aid annually for one-month's study in such areas as the history of science from the Middle Ages through the Enlightenment, a collection of avant-garde AMerican "little magazines," a American women writers to 1920, Scandinavian and Germanic literature, Dutch post-Reformation theology and church history, French political pamphlets of the 16th & 17th centuries, and many other fields.

Must be in Ph.D. program or be able to deomonstrate a recored of solid intellectual accomplishment. Must live outside a 75-mile radius of Madison, Wisconsin, U.S. Call/write for details.

2940 — GERMANISTIC SOCIETY OF AMERICA (Foreign Study Scholarships)

809 United Nations Plaza
New York NY 10017-3580
212/984-5330

AMOUNT: $11,000

DEADLINE(S): OCT 23

FIELD(S): History; Political Science; International Relations; Public Affairs; Language; Philosophy; Literature

Open to US citizens who hold a bachelor's degree. Must plan to pursue graduate study at a West German university. Selection based on proposed project, language fluency, academic achievement, and references.

Contact Germanistic Society for an application.

2941 — GLADYS KRIEBLE DELMAS FOUNDATION (Predoctoral & Postdoctoral Grants in Venice & the Veneto)

521 5th Avenue, Suite 1612
New York NY 10175-1699
212/687-0011
FAX: 212/687-8877
E-Mail: DelmasFdtn@aol.com
Internet: www.delmas.org

AMOUNT: $500-$12,500

DEADLINE(S): DEC 15

FIELD(S): Research of Venice and the former Venetian empire and study of contemporary Venetian society and culture.

Pre- and postdoctoral grants for historical research on Venice. Humanities and social sciences are eligible areas of study, including archaeology, architecture, art, bibliography, economics, history, history of science, law, literature, music, political science, religion, and theater.

Applicants must have experience in advanced research and be U.S. citizens/residents; grad students must have fulfilled all doctoral requirements except dissertation by Dec. 15.

2942 — GRADUATE INSTITUTE OF INTERNATIONAL STUDIES (Scholarships)

P.O. Box 36
132 Rue do Lausanne
CH-1211 Geneva 21 SWITZERLAND
(+41 22) 731 17 30
FAX: (+41-22) 731 27 77
E-Mail: info@hei.unige.ch
Internet: http://heiwww.unige.ch

AMOUNT: Varies

DEADLINE(S): None

FIELD(S): International history and politics, political science, international economics, international law

Scholarships to support graduate diploma and Ph.D students already registered at the Institute. Open to applicants with excellent, active knowledge of one of the institute's two working languages, French & English, and sufficient passive knowledge of the other.

Contact above sources for complete information.

2943 — HARRY S. TRUMAN LIBRARY INSTITUTE (Dissertation Year Fellowship)

500 W. U.S. Hwy. 24
Independence MO 64050-1798
816/833-0425
FAX: 816/833-2715
E-Mail: library@truman.nara.gov
Internet: www.trumanlibrary.org/institut/scholars.htm

AMOUNT: $16,000

DEADLINE(S): FEB 1

FIELD(S): American History: Harry S. Truman or His Era

Grants are given to support graduate students working on some aspect of the life and career of Harry S. Truman or the public and foreign policy issues which were prominent during the Truman years. Applicants should have substantially completed their research and be prepared to devote full time to writing their dissertation. Preference given to projects based on extensive research at Truman Library. No budget required. Financial need NOT a factor.

1-2 awards annually. See website or contact Grants Administrator for an application. Applicants notified of decision within four weeks of deadline.

2944 — HARRY S. TRUMAN LIBRARY INSTITUTE (Harry S. Truman Book Award)

500 W. U.S. Hwy. 24
Independence MO 64050-1798
816/833-0425
FAX: 816/833-2715

E-Mail: library@truman.nara.gov
Internet: www.trumanlibrary.org/institut/scholars.htm

AMOUNT: $1,000

DEADLINE(S): JAN 20

FIELD(S): American History: Harry S. Truman or His Era

Award is for the best book written within a two-year period dealing primarily and substantially with some aspect of US history between April 12, 1945 and January 20, 1953, or with the public career of Harry S. Truman. Three copies of each book entered must be submitted.

Awarded only in even-numbered years. See website or contact Book Awards Administrator for guidelines.

2945 — HARRY S. TRUMAN LIBRARY INSTITUTE (Research Grants)

500 W. U.S. Hwy. 24
Independence MO 64050-1798
816/833-0425
FAX: 816/833-2715
E-Mail: library@truman.nara.gov
Internet: www.trumanlibrary.org/institut/scholars.htm

AMOUNT: $2,500 (max.)

DEADLINE(S): APR 1; OCT 1

FIELD(S): American History: Harry S. Truman or His Era

Grants enable graduate students, postdoctoral scholars, and other researchers to come to the Harry S. Truman Library for one to three weeks to use its collections. Awards are to offset expenses incurred for this purpose only. Preference given to projects that have application to enduring public policy and foreign policy issues and that have high probability of being published or publicly disseminated in some other way. Potential contribution of scholar considered.

Awards given every two years. See website or contact Grants Administrator for an application. Applicants notified of results in writing six weeks after deadline.

2946 — HARRY S. TRUMAN LIBRARY INSTITUTE (Scholar's Award)

500 W. U.S. Hwy. 24
Independence MO 64050-1798
816/833-0425
FAX: 816/833-2715
E-Mail: library@truman.nara.gov
Internet: www.trumanlibrary.org/institut/scholars.htm

AMOUNT: $30,000 (max.)

DEADLINE(S): DEC 15

FIELD(S): American History: Harry S. Truman or His Era

For postdoctoral scholars working on some aspect of life and career of Harry S. Truman or public and foreign policy issues which were prominent during the Truman years. Award is to free a scholar from teaching or other employment for a substantial period. Contingent upon receipt of underwriting support and of strong proposals. Work should be based in part on extensive research at the Truman Library and be intended to result in book-lenth manuscript. No budget required.

Awarded only in even-numbered years. See website or contact Grants Administrator for an application. Applicants notified of decision by April 15th.

2947 — HARVARD BUSINESS SCHOOL (Newcomen Postdoctoral Fellowship in Business History)

Harvard Business School
Morgan 295, Soldiers Field
Boston MA 02163
617/495-6008
E-Mail: esampson@hbs.edu

AMOUNT: $46,000

DEADLINE(S): NOV 1

FIELD(S): Business & Economic History

Open to scholars who received the Ph.D in history, economics, or a related discipline within the past 10 years and wish to improve their skills as they relate to these fields and engage in research at the Harvard Business School.

For complete information write to Nancy F. Koehn, Associate, at the above address, or E-mail assistant, Elizabeth Sampson, at above address.

2948 — HERBERT HOOVER PRESIDENTIAL LIBRARY ASSOCIATION (Travel Grants)

PO Box 696
West Branch IA 52245
319/643-5327
FAX: 319/643-2391
E-Mail: info@hooverassoc.org
Internet: www.hooverassoc.org

AMOUNT: Varies

DEADLINE(S): MAR 1

FIELD(S): History; Journalism; Communications

Travel grants for graduates, postgraduates, and other qualified researchers to defray expenses of travel to West Branch, Iowa, to do research in the archives of the Herbert Hoover Presidential Library. Financial need is NOT a factor.

15-20 awards annually. Renewable with reapplication. Contact Patricia Hand at above address for an application.

2949 — HUNTINGTON LIBRARY (Research Fellowships)

1151 Oxford Rd.
San Marino CA 91108
626/405-2194

AMOUNT: $2,000/month

DEADLINE(S): DEC 15

FIELD(S): American History/Literature; British History/Literature; Art History; Science History

Open to doctoral and postdoctoral scholars for research at the Huntington Library. Fellows are expected to be in residence at the Library throughout their tenure.

100 awards annually. Contact the Committee on Fellowships for an application.

2950 — INSTITUT FUR EUROPAISCHE GESCHICHTE (Fellowship Program)

Alte Universitatsstrasse 19
D-55116 Mainz GERMANY
49/6131-399360
FAX: 49/6131-237988
E-Mail: ieg2@inst-euro-history.uni-mainz.de
Internet: www.inst-euro-history.uni-mainz.de

AMOUNT: Varies (stipend, family allowance, health insurance, travel, & rent)

DEADLINE(S): None

FIELD(S): European History (16th-20th Centuries)

Six- to twelve-month fellowships for those at the advanced stages of their dissertatiion or already in possession of their doctorate. Must have thorough command of German, and may be from Europe or overseas. Must submit curriculum vitae, description of proposed research topic, and copies of transcripts.

20 awards annually. Contact Dr. Heinz Duchardt for an application.

2951 — INSTITUTE FOR ADVANCED STUDY (Post-doctoral Fellowship Awards)

Olden Lane
Princeton NJ 08540
609/734-8000

AMOUNT: Varies according to school

DEADLINE(S): Varies

FIELD(S): Historical Studies; Social Sciences; Natural Sciences; Mathematics

Post-doctoral fellowships at the institute for advanced study for those whose term can be expected to result in work of significance and individuality.

150-160 fellowships per academic year although some can be extended. Request application materials from school's administrative officer.

2952 — INSTITUTE FOR ADVANCED STUDIES IN THE HUMANITIES (Visiting Research Fellowships)

Univ Edinburgh
Hope Park Square
Edinburgh EH8 9NW SCOTLAND UK
0131 650 4671
FAX: 0131 668 2252
E-Mail: iash@ed.ac.uk
Internet: www.ed.ac.uk/iash/homepage.html

AMOUNT: Non-stipendiary*

DEADLINE(S): DEC 1

FIELD(S): Arts; Social Sciences; Law; Music; Divinity

Postdoctoral research fellowships of between two and six months are tenable at the Institute for Advanced Studies in the Humanities. Based on academic record and publications. *Most fellowships are honorary, but limited support towards expenses is available to a small number of candidates. Fellows are allocated a study room within the Institute and hold one or two seminars during their tenure. Must submit research report at end of fellowship. No teaching required.

15 awards annually. Not renewable. Contact Mrs. Anthea Taylor for an application.

2953 — INTERNATIONAL MEDIEVAL INSTITUTE (K.H. Wick Bursary Fund for Attending Meetings)

University of Leeds, Parkinson Bldg., Rm. 1.03
Leeds LSs2 9JT ENGLAND UK
+44 (113) 233-3614
FAX: +44 (113) 233-3616
E-Mail: imc@leeds.ac.uk
Internet: www.leeds.ac.uk/imi/imc/khwick.htm

AMOUNT: Varies

DEADLINE(S): Varies

FIELD(S): Medieval history

This fund is to help pay for attendance at the International Medieval Congress held at Leeds University in England each July. Open to students and independednt and retired scholars. Preference is given to scholars from Central and Eastern Europe.

Contact listed office for details.

2954 — ISTITUTO ITALIANO PER GLI STUDI STORICI (Federico Chabod & Adolfo Omodeo Scholarships)

12 Via Benedetto Croce
80134 Naples ITALY
0039/81/551-7159
FAX: 0039/81/551-2390
E-Mail: iiss@iol.it

AMOUNT: 12 million lires

DEADLINE(S): SEP 30

FIELD(S): History; Philosophy; Literature; Arts; Economics

Open to non-Italian citizens who have completed a university degree in the humanities (history, philosophy, & arts) in a non-Italian university. Intended to allow young scholars to participate in the work of the Institute and to complete personal scholarly research with the help of teaching staff of the Institute. Must submit birth certificate, university diploma, scholarly work, program of studies with indication of language skills, research proposal, & reference.

Renewable. Contact Dott.ssa Marta Herling, Secretary, for an application.

2955 — ISTITUTO ITALIANO PER GLI STUDI STORICI - ITALIAN INSTITUTE FOR HISTORICAL STUDIES (Federico Chabod & Adolfo Omodeo Scholarships)

Via Benedetto Croce, 12
80134 Napoli ITALY
0039/81-5517159
FAX: 0039/81-5512390

AMOUNT: 12,000,000 Lira

DEADLINE(S): SEP 30

FIELD(S): Humanities; Social Sciences; History; Philosophy; Arts; Economics; Literature

For non-Italian citizens who have completed a university degree in Humanities dept. of a non-Italian university. Intended to allow young scholars to participate in the work of the Institute and to complete personal scholarly research with the help of teaching staff of the Institute. Must include birth certificate, proof of citizenship, university diploma, scholarly work, curriculum of studies w/ indication of language skills, research proposal, & reference letter.

2 awards annually. Contact Marta Herling, Secretary, at above address for an application.

2956 — JAMES MADISON MEMORIAL FELLOWSHIP (Fellowship for Teachers)

2000 K St. NW
Washington DC 20006
202/653-8700 or 1-800/525-6928
FAX: 202/653-6045
Internet: www.jamesmadison.com

AMOUNT: $24,000 prorated over study period

DEADLINE(S): MAR 1

FIELD(S): Teaching American History/government, or social studies—concentration on the U.S. Constitution

Fellowships for teachers (senior fellows) in grades 7-12 in the above fields to pursue an MA degree. Also for full-time college seniors and grad students (junior fellows). U.S. citizens or U.S. nationals. Fellows are selected from each state and from D.C., Puerto Rico, Guam, Virgin Islands, American Samoa, Northern Mariana Islands, and Palau. Program designed to enhance teaching about the U.S. Constitution.

Application is on website or contact: American College Testing, P.O. Box 4030, Iowa City, IA 52243-4030; 800/525-6928; E-mail: Recogprog@ACT-ACT4-PO.act.org

2957 — JOHN CARTER BROWN LIBRARY (Research Fellowships)

Box 1894
Providence RI 02912
401/863-2725
E-Mail: JCBL_Fellowships@Brown.edu
Internet: www.brown.edu/Facilities/
John_Carter_Brown_Library

AMOUNT: $1,000/month (short-term); $$2,800/month and up (long-term)

DEADLINE(S): JAN 15

FIELD(S): History of the Western hemisphere during the colonial period and its relationships with Europe

Research fellowships for Americans or foreign nationals engaged in pre- or postdoctoral or independent research. Short-term fellowships are for 2 to 4 months; long-term fellowships are 5 to 9 months. The Library's holdings are concentrated on the above fields.

Fellows are expected to be in continuous residence at the Library for the fellowship's term. Graduate students are not eligible for long-term fellowships.

2958 — JOHN F. KENNEDY LIBRARY FOUNDATION (Abba P. Schwartz Research Fellowship)

Columbia Point
Boston MA 02125-3313
617/929-4534 or 617/929-4533
FAX: 617/929-4599

AMOUNT: Up to $3,100

DEADLINE(S): MAR 15

FIELD(S): Immigration, naturalization, or refugee policies

To support a scholar while he/she researches in the fields listed above.

Contact William Johnson, Chief Archivist, at above location for application information.

2959 — JOHN F. KENNEDY LIBRARY FOUNDATION (Kennedy Research Grants)

Columbia Point
Boston MA 02125-3313
617/929-4534 or 617/929-4533
FAX: 617/929-4599

AMOUNT: $500-$1,000

DEADLINE(S): MAR 15

FIELD(S): History/Political Science: Kennedy presidential period

To support a scholar while he/she researches in the fields listed above.

Contact William Johnson, Chief Archivist, at above location for application information.

2960 — JOHN F. KENNEDY LIBRARY FOUNDATION (Marjorie Kovler Research Fellowship)

Columbia Point
Boston MA 02125-3313
617/929-4534 or 617/929-4533
FAX: 617/929-4599

AMOUNT: $2,500

DEADLINE(S): MAR 15

FIELD(S): History, Law Political Science-specializing in foreign intelligence and the presidency or a related topic.

To support a scholar while he/she researches in the fields listed above.

Contact William Johnson, Chief Archivist, at above location for application information.

2961 — NATIONAL FEDERATION OF THE BLIND (Humanities Scholarship)

805 5th Avenue
Grinnell IA 50112
515/236-3366

AMOUNT: $3,000

DEADLINE(S): MAR 31

FIELD(S): Humanities (Art, English, Foreign Languages, History, Philosophy, Religion)

Open to legally blind students pursuing or planning to pursue a full-time postsecondary education in the US. Scholarships are awarded on basis of academic excellence, service to the community, and financial need. Must include transcripts and two letters of recommendation. Membership NOT required.

1 award annually. Renewable. Contact Mrs. Peggy Elliot, Scholarship Committee Chairman, for an application.

2962 — NATIONAL HUMANITIES CENTER (Burroughs Wellcome Fund Fellowships in the History of Modern Medicine)

PO Box 12256
Research Triangle Park NC 27709-2256
919/549-0661
FAX: 919/990-8535
E-Mail: nhc@ga.unc.edu
Internet: www.nhc.rtp.nc.us:8080

AMOUNT: Stipend ($35,000-$50,000) + Travel Expenses (fellow & dependents)

DEADLINE(S): OCT 15

FIELD(S): History of Medicine/Biomedical Science; Medical Anthropology

Postdoctoral fellowships for historians of medicine or biomedical science, medical anthropologists, and other scholars whose work concerns the history of twentieth-century medicine. Curriculum vitae, 1,000-word proposal, and three letters of recommendation are required.

1 award annually. Contact NHC for application materials.

2963 — NATIONAL HUMANITIES CENTER (Lilly Fellowships in Religion and the Humanities)

PO Box 12256
Research Triangle Park NC 27709-2256
919/549-0661
FAX: 919/990-8535
E-Mail: nhc@ga.unc.edu
Internet: www.nhc.rtp.nc.us:8080

AMOUNT: Stipend ($35,000-$50,000) + Travel Expenses (for fellow & dependents)

DEADLINE(S): OCT 15

FIELD(S): Religion & the Humanities

Postdoctoral fellowships for the study of religion by humanistic scholars from fields other than religion and theology. Fellows will form the core of a monthly seminar on religion and the humanities. Curriculum vitae, 1,000-word proposal, and three letters of recommendation are required.

3-4 awards annually. Contact NHC for application materials.

2964 — NATIONAL SPACE CLUB (Dr. Robert H. Goddard Historical Essay Award)

2000 L Street, NW, Suite 710
Washington DC 20036-4907
202/973-8661

AMOUNT: $1,000 + plaque

DEADLINE(S): DEC 4

FIELD(S): Aerospace History

Essay competition open to any US citizen on a topic dealing with any significant aspect of the historical development of rocketry and astronautics. Essays should not exceed 5,000 words and should be fully documented. Will be judged on originality and scholarship.

Previous winners not eligible. Send self-addressed, stamped envelope for complete information.

2965 — NAVAL HISTORICAL CENTER (Internship Program)

Washington Navy Yard
901 M St., SE
Washington DC 20374-5060
202/433-6901
FAX: 202/433-8200
E-Mail: efurgol@nhc.navy.mil
Internet: www.history.navy.mil

AMOUNT: $400 possible honoraria; otherwise, unpaid

DEADLINE(S): None

FIELD(S): Education; History; Public Relations; Design

Registered students of colleges/universities and graduates thereof are eligible for this program, which must be a minimum of 3 weeks, full or part-time. Four specialities available: Curator, Education, Public Relations, and Design. Interns receive orientation & assist in their departments, and must complete individual project which contributes to Center. Must submit a letter of recommendation, unofficial transcript, and writing sample of not less than 1,000 words.

Contact Dr. Edward M. Furgol, Curator, for an application.

2966 — NEWBERRY LIBRARY (Long-Term Fellowships)

60 West Walton Street
Chicago IL 60610-3380
312/943-9090
E-Mail: research@newberry.org
Internet: www.newberry.org

AMOUNT: Up to $30,000

DEADLINE(S): JAN 20

FIELD(S): Humanities, History, & related fields

Six postdoctoral fellowship programs are available for scholars wishing to use the Library's collection for writing or research. Fellowships last six to eleven months, and each have slightly different requirements.

See website for details and an application or write to above address.

2967 — NEWBERRY LIBRARY (Monticello College Foundation Fellowship For Women)

60 West Walton Street
Chicago IL 60610-3380
312/255-3660
E-Mail: research@newberry.org
Internet: www.newberry.org

AMOUNT: $12,500

DEADLINE(S): JAN 20

FIELD(S): Humanities, History, Study of Women

Six-month post-doctoral fellowships for women in the early stages of their academic careers. For research, writing, and participation in the intellectual life of the Library. Applicant's topic must be related to Newberry's collections; preference given to proposals concerned with the study of women.

See website for application or write to above address.

2968 — NEWBERRY LIBRARY (Short-Term Fellowships)

60 West Walton Street
Chicago IL 60610-3380
312/943-9090
E-Mail: research@newberry.org
Internet: www.newberry.org

AMOUNT: $800-$1,500/month

DEADLINE(S): MAR 1

FIELD(S): Humanities, History, & related fields

Nine programs for postdoctoral scholars or doctoral students at the dissertation stage. Study varies from two weeks to three months and is for those making use of Newberry's collections. Each program has slightly different requirements.

See website for details and applications or write to above address.

2969 — NEWBERRY LIBRARY (Special Fellowships)

60 West Walton Street
Chicago IL 60610-3380
312/255-3666
E-Mail: research@newberry.org
Internet: www.newberry.org

AMOUNT: Varies

DEADLINE(S): DEC 15

FIELD(S): Humanities, History, & related fields

Fellowships for three months to one year for doctoral or postdoctoral students to study in Germany, France, or Great Britain in fields related to Newberry's collections. Some deadlines JAN 20th. Specific locations are: Wolfenb, ttel, Germany; Ecole Nationale des Chartes, Paris, France; and the British Academy, Great Britain.

See website for more details and applications or write to above address.

2970 — NEWBERRY LIBRARY (Weiss/Brown Publication Subvention Award)

60 West Walton Street
Chicago IL 60610-3380
312/255-3666
E-Mail: research@newberry.org
Internet: www.newberry.org

AMOUNT: up to $15,000

DEADLINE(S): JAN 20

FIELD(S): European Civilization/History/Culture

Awards for authors of scholarly books already accepted for publication. Subject matter must cover European civilization before 1700 in the areas of music, theatre, French or Italian literature or cultural studies. Applicants must provide detailed information regarding the publication and the subvention request.

See website for more details and application or write to above address.

2971 — OAK RIDGE ASSOCIATED UNIVERSITIES (National Science Foundation Graduate Research Fellowships)

PO Box 3010
Oak Ridge TN 37831-3010
423/241-4300
FAX: 423/241-4513
E-Mail: nsfgrfp@orau.gov
Internet: www.orau.gov/nsf/nsffel.htm

AMOUNT: $15,000 stipend + $10,500 tuition allowance

DEADLINE(S): NOV 4

FIELD(S): Science; Math; Engineering; Computer Science

Three-year fellowships for graduate study leading to research-based master's or doctoral degrees in the above fields. Must be US citizens, nationals, or permanent residents at the time of application. Fellowships are awarded on the basis of ability. Women, minorities, and those with disabilities are strongly encouraged to apply. One-time International Research Travel Allowance available.

1,000 awards annually. Contact Jeannette Bouchard for an application/more information.

2972 — OMOHUNDRO INSTITUTE OF EARLY AMERICAN HISTORY AND CULTURE (Andrew W. Mellon Postdoctoral Research Fellowship)

PO Box 8781
Williamsburg VA 23187-8781
804/221-1110
E-Mail: IEAHC1@facstaff.wm.edu

AMOUNT: $30,000 + benefits package, office/research/computer facilities, & travel

DEADLINE(S): NOV 1

FIELD(S): Early American Studies

1-year postdoctoral fellowship for research on North America's indigenous & immigrant peoples during colonial, Revolutionary, & early national periods of US & related histories of Canada, Caribbean, Latin America, British Isles, Europe, & Africa, 16th century to 1815. Manuscript must have significant potential for publication as distinguished, book-length contribution to scholarship. Must have received Ph.D. at least 12 months prior. No teaching responsibility.

Fellows devote most of time to research & writing, working closely with members of editorial staff, and participate in colloquia & other scholarly activities.

2973 — ONTARIO MINISTRY OF EDUCATION AND TRAINING (Sir John A. MacDonald Graduate Fellowship)

189 Red River Rd., 4th Floor
Box 4500
Thunder Bay Ontario P7B 6G9 CANADA
800/465-3957
TDD: 800/465-3958
Internet: osap.gov.on.ca

AMOUNT: $8,500

DEADLINE(S): Varies

FIELD(S): Canadian History

Fellowship is awarded to a Canadian citizen/permanent resident enrolling in a doctoral program at an Ontario university. Awards are designed to encourage and reward academic excellence.

1 award annually. Renewable up to 3 years. Contact Ministry of Education & Training for an application.

2974 — PHI ALPHA THETA HISTORY HONOR SOCIETY (Doctoral Scholarship Awards)

6201 Hamilton Blvd., Ste. 116
Allentown PA 18106-9691
800/394-8195
FAX: 610/336-4929
E-Mail: phialpha@ptd.net

AMOUNT: $750-$1,000

DEADLINE(S): MAR 1

FIELD(S): History

Grants are for advanced study by graduate student members of Phi Alpha Theta working on a Ph.D. in history. Must have passed general examinations no later than February of application year. Phi Alpha Theta and John Pine Memorial Scholarship Awards are included in this category.

4 awards annually. Contact PAT National Headquarters for an application.

2975 — PHI ALPHA THETA HISTORY HONOR SOCIETY (Graduate Scholarship Awards)

6201 Hamilton Blvd., Ste. 116
Allentown PA 18106-9691
800/394-8195
FAX: 610/336-4929
E-Mail: phialpha@ptd.net

AMOUNT: $750-$1,250

DEADLINE(S): MAR 1

FIELD(S): History

Grants are for student members of Phi Alpha Theta who are entering graduate school for the first time for work leading to a master's degree in history. A.F. Zimmerman, Thomas S. Morgan Memorial, and William E. Parrish Scholarship Awards are included in this category.

5 awards annually. Contact PAT National Headquarters for an application.

2976 — PHI ALPHA THETA HISTORY HONOR SOCIETY (Nels Andrew N. Cleven Founder's Paper Prize Awards)

6201 Hamilton Blvd., Ste. 116
Allentown PA 18106-9691
800/394-8195
FAX: 610/336-4929
E-Mail: phialpha@ptd.net

AMOUNT: $150-$250

DEADLINE(S): JUL 1

FIELD(S): History

Open to undergraduate and graduate Phi Alpha Theta members who submit essays on a historical topic. Should combine original historical research on a significant subject, based on source material and manuscripts, if possible, with good English composition and superior style. Must include bibliography. Papers should not exceed 25 typewritten pages in length. Dr. George P. Hammond Prize and Dr. Lynn W. Turner Prize included in this category.

3 awards annually. Contact PAT National Headquarters for guidelines.

2977 — PHI ALPHA THETA HISTORY HONOR SOCIETY/WORLD HISTORY ASSOCIATION (World History Paper Prize)

6201 Hamilton Blvd., Ste. 116
Allentown PA 18106-9691
800/394-8195
FAX: 610/336-4929
E-Mail: phialpha@ptd.net

AMOUNT: $200

DEADLINE(S): JUL 1

FIELD(S): World History

Open to undergraduate and graduate students who submit an essay on world history, which is one that examines any historical issue with global implications. Must be member of either Phi Alpha Theta or the World History Association, and must have composed the paper while enrolled at an accredited college/university during previous academic year (proven by letter from faculty). Bibliography must be included. Papers must be no longer than 25 typewritten pages.

2 awards annually. Contact PAT National Headquarters for guidelines.

2978 — PHI ALPHA THETA HISTORY HONOR SOCIETY/WESTERNERS INTERNATIONAL (Doctoral Dissertation Awards)

6201 Hamilton Blvd., Ste. 116
Allentown PA 18106-9691
800/394-8195
FAX: 610/336-4929
E-Mail: phialpha@ptd.net

AMOUNT: $500

DEADLINE(S): MAY 1

FIELD(S): Western U.S. History

Open to Phi Alpha Theta members who have completed a doctoral dissertation in Western US history during the previous year. Dissertation advisor must submit letter of endorsement. Award will be presented at Phi Alpha Theta Luncheon at the Western History Association Annual Meeting. Must submit three copies of dissertation and advisor endorsement to the committee chair.

1 award annually. Contact PAT National Headquarters for submission details.

2979 — PONTIFICAL INSTITUTE OF MEDIEVAL STUDIES (Fellowships)

59 Queen's Park Crescent
Toronto Ontario M55 2C4 CANADA
416/926-7290
FAX: 416/926-7292
E-Mail: sheila.campbell@utoronto.ca

AMOUNT: Varies

DEADLINE(S): Varies

FIELD(S): Medieval Studies

Postdoctoral fellowships for students to attend the Pontifical Institute of Medieval Studies. Financial need NOT a factor.

4 awards annually. Not renewable. Contact Professor Campbell for an application.

2980 — PRINCETON UNIVERSITY—SHELBY CULLOM DAVIS CENTER FOR HISTORICAL STUDIES (Post-doctoral Fellowships)

c/o 129 Dickinson Hall
History Dept.
Princeton NJ 08544
609/258-4997

AMOUNT: Up to $56,000 per year

DEADLINE(S): DEC 1

FIELD(S): History

Post-doctoral fellowships at Princeton University for highly recommended young scholars and senior scholars with established reputations. Theme for 1996-98 is "Animals and Human Society."

Candidates must have completed their dissertations.

2981 — SMITHSONIAN INSTITUTION (Fellowship Program)

Office of fellowships & Grants
955 L'Enfant Plaza, Suite 7000
Washington DC 20560
202/287-3271
E-Mail: http://www.si.edu/research+study
Internet: siofg@sivm.si.edu

AMOUNT: $3,000-$25,000 depending on level and length

DEADLINE(S): JAN 15

FIELD(S): Animal behavior, ecology, environmental science (including emphasis on the tropics, anthropology (& archaeology), astrophysics, astronomy, earth sciences, paleobiology, evolutionary/systematic biology, history of science and technology, history of art, esp. American, contemporary, African, and Asian, 20th century American crafts, decorative arts, social/cultural history of the US, or folklife.

For research in residence at the Smithsonian for graduate students, both pre- and postdoctoral.

Research to be in the fields listed above.

2982 — SMITHSONIAN INSTITUTION (Minority Student Internship Program)

Fellowships & Grants
955 L'Enfant Plaza, Suite 7000
MRC 902
Washington DC 20560
202/287-3271
FAX: 202/287-3691
E-Mail: siofg@ofg.si.edu
Internet: www.si.edu/research+study

AMOUNT: $300/week + possible travel expenses

DEADLINE(S): FEB 15

FIELD(S): Humanities, Environmental Studies, Cultural Studies, Natural History, Earth Science, Art History, Biology, & related fields

Ten-week internships in residence at the Smithsonian for US minority students to participate in research or museum-related activities in above fields. For undergrads or grads with at least a 3.0 GPA. Essay, resume, transcripts, and references required with application. Internships are full-time and are offered for Summer, Fall, or Spring tenures.

Write for application.

2983 — SMITHSONIAN INSTITUTION (National Air & Space Museum Guggenheim Fellowship)

National Air and Space Museum, MRC 312
Washington DC 20560
Written inquiry

AMOUNT: $14,000 (predoctoral); $25,000 (postdoctoral)

DEADLINE(S): JAN 15

FIELD(S): Historical research related to aviation and space

Predoctoral applicants should have completed preliminary course work and exams and be engaged in dissertation research. Postdoctoral applicants should have received their Ph.D within the past seven years. Contact Fellowship Coordinator at above location.

Open to all nationalities. Fluency in English required. Duration is 6-12 months.

2984 — SMITHSONIAN INSTITUTION (National Air & Space Museum Verville Fellowship)

National Air and Space Museum, MRC 312
Washington DC 20560
Written inquiry

AMOUNT: $30,000 stipend for 12 months + travel and misc. expenses

DEADLINE(S): JAN 15

FIELD(S): Analysis of major trends, developments, and accomplishments in the history of aviation or space studies

A competitive nine- to twelve-month in-residence fellowship in the above field of study. Advanced degree is NOT a requirement. Contact Fellowship Coordinator at above location.

Open to all nationalities. Fluency in English required.

2985 — SOCIAL SCIENCE RESEARCH COUNCIL (International Predissertation Fellowship Program)

810 Seventh Ave.
New York NY 10019
212/277-2700

AMOUNT: Varies

DEADLINE(S): Varies (TBA by participating universities)

FIELD(S): Economics; Political Science; Psychology; Sociology; other Social Science disciplines

Open to Ph.D. candidates enrolled in social science programs at 23 select universities and interested in supplementing disciplinary skills with area and language studies or acquiring advanced disciplinary training. Study program is preparation for research on Africa, Central Asia & the Caucasus, China, Latin America, the Caribbean, Near & Middle East, and South or Southeast Asia.

Contact Ellen Perecman for an application.

2986 — SOCIETY OF AMERICAN HISTORIANS (Allan Nevins Prize)

603 Fayerweather MC 2538
Columbia University
New York NY 10027
212/854-5943

AMOUNT: $1,000

DEADLINE(S): DEC 31

FIELD(S): American History

Award for best dissertation of the preceding year. Qualified individuals who have written appropriate doctoral dissertations may be recommended by their departments.

In addition to the award, the manuscript is submitted for publication which usually results in a publishing contract. Write for complete information.

2987 — SONOMA CHAMBOLLE-MUSIGNY SISTER CITIES, INC. (Henri Cardinaux Memorial Scholarship)

Chamson Scholarship Committee
PO Box 1633
Sonoma CA 95476-1633
707/939-1344
FAX: 707/939-1344
E-Mail: Baileysci@vom.com

AMOUNT: up to $1,500 (travel + expenses)

DEADLINE(S): JUL 15

FIELD(S): Culinary Arts; Wine Industry; Art; Architecture; Music; History; Fashion

Hands-on experience working in above or similiar fields & living with a family in small French village in Burgundy or other French city. Must be Sonoma County, CA, resident at least 18 years of age & be able to communicate in French. Transcripts, employer recommendation, photograph, & essay (stating why, where, & when) required.

1 award. Non-renewable. Also offers opportunity for candidate in Chambolle-Musigny to obtain work experience & cultural exposure in Sonoma, CA.

2988 — SONS OF THE REPUBLIC OF TEXAS (Presidio La Bahia Award)

1717 8th St.
Bay City TX 77414
409/245-6644
E-Mail: srttexas@srttexas.org
Internet: www.srttexas.org

AMOUNT: $1,200+

DEADLINE(S): SEP 30

FIELD(S): Texas History: Spanish Colonial Period

A competition on the best book, paper, or article which promotes suitable preservation of relics, appropriate dissemination of data, and research into Texas heritage with particular attention to the Spanish Colonial period. Research writings have proved in the past to be the most successful type of entry, however, careful consideration will be given to other literary forms, as well as art, architecture, and archaeological discovery. Entries accepted June-September.

Contact Melinda Williams, SRT Executive Secretary, for a brochure.

2989 — SOUTHERN BAPTIST HISTORICAL LIBRARY AND ARCHIVES (Study Grants)

901 Commerce St., Ste. 400
Nashville TN 37203-3630
615/244-0344
FAX: 615/782-4821
E-Mail: bsumners@edge.net
Internet: www.sbhla.org

AMOUNT: $500 (max.)

DEADLINE(S): APR 1

FIELD(S): History of Baptists

For graduate and postgraduate students or researchers conducting research in a major facet of Baptist history. Major sources of information for study are in the Southern Baptist Historical Library and Archives.

3-4 awards annually. See website for guidelines and an application.

2990 — STATE HISTORICAL SOCIETY OF WISCONSIN (Alice E. Smith Fellowship)

816 State St.
Madison WI 53706
608/264-6464
FAX: 608/264-6486
E-Mail: mestevens@mail.shsw.wisc.edu
Internet: www.shsw.wisc.edu/research/fellowships.html

AMOUNT: $2,000

DEADLINE(S): JUL 15

FIELD(S): American History

Grant open to any woman doing graduate research in American history. Preference will be given to graduate research on history of the Midwest or Wisconsin. Transcripts, work samples, and references are neither required nor sought. Four copies of a two-page letter of application should describe in detail the applicant's current research.

Send letter of application to State Historian at address above.

2991 — STATE LIBRARY OF NEW SOUTH WALES (C. H. Currey Memorial Fellowship)

Macquarie Street
Sydney NSW 2000 AUSTRALIA
02/9273 1414
FAX: 02/9273 1248

AMOUNT: A$20,000

DEADLINE(S): JUL 31

FIELD(S): Australian History

Open to historians for research into Australian history utilizing original sources.

Contact State Library for an application.

2992 — STATE LIBRARY OF NEW SOUTH WALES (Nancy Keesing Fellowship)

MacQuarie St.
Sydney NSW 2000 AUSTRALIA
(02) 9273 1466
FAX: (02) 9273 1245
E-Mail: aventres@slnsw.gov.au
Internet: www.slnsw.gov.au

AMOUNT: A$10,000

DEADLINE(S): MAR 31

FIELD(S): Australian History

Fellowships for graduate students and postgraduates to study the Mitchell Collection at the State Library of New South Wales.

Contact Alan Ventress, Mitchell Librarian, for an application.

2993 — STOCKHOLM UNIVERSITY - INTERNATIONAL GRADUATE PROGRAMME (Master's Programme in Swedish Social Studies)

Universitetsvagen 10F
Frescati
S-106 91 Stockholm SWEDEN
+46 8 163466
FAX: +46 8 155508
E-Mail: igp@statsvet.su.se
Internet: www.statsvet.su.se/IGP/home.html

AMOUNT: Tuition

DEADLINE(S): MAR 1

FIELD(S): Social Sciences; Economics; History; Anthropology; Sociology; Social Work; Political Science

Open to students who have completed a university degree in the social sciences with one of the above majors and who wish to study at Stockholm University in Sweden. Language of instruction is English.

Contact Stockholm University for an application.

2994 — THE J. EDGAR HOOVER FOUNDATION

50 Gull Point Rd.
Hilton Head Island SC 29928
803/671-5020

AMOUNT: $500

DEADLINE(S): Ongoing

FIELD(S): Government, law enforcement

Scholarships for the study of government, the promotion of good citizenship, and law enforcement. The foundation strives to safeguard the heritage and freedom of the U.S., to promote good citizenship through an appreciation of the American form of government, and to combat communism or any other ideology or doctrine opposed to the principles set forth in the U.S. Constitution.

Send letter to Cartha D. De Loach, Chair, at above address.

2995 — U.S. ARMY MILITARY HISTORY INSTITUTE (Advanced Research Grant Program)

22 Ashburn Dr.
Carlisle PA 17013-5008
717/245-3089 or 717/245-3092

AMOUNT: $750 (max.)

DEADLINE(S): JAN 1

FIELD(S): Military History; U.S. Army History

Applicants must hold graduate degree or have equivalent professional experience in pursuing research topics in the discipline of military history and the U.S. Army. Research is done at the Institute.

2 awards annually. Contact USAMHI for an application.

2996 — UNIVERSITY OF DELAWARE HAGLEY PROGRAM (Graduate Fellowship)

Dept of History
Univ of Delaware
Newark DE 19716-2547
302/831-8226

AMOUNT: Full tuition + stipend of $10,000 (including travel allowance)

DEADLINE(S): JAN 31

FIELD(S): History of Technology & Industrialization

Graduate fellowship for study of the history of industrialization in America. Applicants must have strong American history background and take aptitude portion of the GRE no later than December to assure full consideration of application. Financial need NOT a factor.

4-6 awards annually. Contact the Department of History for an application.

2997 — UNIVERSITY OF LONDON-WARBURG INSTITUTE (Albin Salton Fellowship)

Woburn Square
London WC1H 0AB ENGLAND UK
020 7862 8949
FAX: 020 7862 8955
Internet: www.sas.ac.uk/warburg

AMOUNT: 850-2,080 pounds sterling

DEADLINE(S): DEC 4

FIELD(S): Classical Studies (Intellectual & Cultural History, esp. Medieval & Renaissance)

Short-term fellowship (1-2 months) open to scholars who have completed at least two years' research toward the doctorate and are under 35 years of age. Focus should be on cultural contacts between Europe, the East, and the New World in the late medieval, Renaissance, and early modern periods. Preference to those who do not live within daily travelling distance of the Institute. Must submit curriculum vitae, outline of proposed research, references, and published work.

Contact Warburg Institute for an application.

2998 — UNIVERSITY OF LONDON-WARBURG INSTITUTE (Brian Hewson Crawford Fellowship)

Woburn Square
London WC1H OAB ENGLAND UK
020 7862 8949
FAX: 020 7862 8955
Internet: www.sas.ac.uk/warburg

AMOUNT: 850-1,400 pounds sterling

DEADLINE(S): DEC 4

FIELD(S): Classical Studies (Intellectual & Cultural History)

Short-term (1-2 months) research fellowship for scholars who have completed at least two years' research toward the doctorate and are under 35 years of age. Open to European scholars other than of British nationality. Preference given to those who do not live within daily travelling distance of the Institute. Must submit curriculum vitae, outline of proposed research, references, and published work.

Contact Warburg Institute for an application.

2999 — UNIVERSITY OF LONDON-WARBURG INSTITUTE (Frances A. Yates Fellowships)

Woburn Square
London WC1H 0AB ENGLAND UK
020 7862 8949
FAX: 020 7862 8955
Internet: www.sas.ac.uk/warburg

AMOUNT: 850-2,080 pounds sterling (short-term: 1-3 months); 14,000-15,500 pounds sterling (long-term: 1-3 years)

DEADLINE(S): DEC 4

FIELD(S): Classical Studies (Intellectual & Cultural History, esp. Medieval & Renaissance)

Short- and long-term research fellowships open to scholars who have completed at least two years' research toward the doctorate and are under 35 years of age. Preference to those who do not live within daily travelling distance of the Institute. Must submit curriculum vitae, outline of proposed research, references, and published work. Candidates domiciled in UK applying for short-term awards may apply for three-month fellowships only.

11 awards annually (10 short-term, 1 long-term). Contact Warburg Institute for an application.

3000 — UNIVERSITY OF LONDON-WARBURG INSTITUTE (Henri Frankfort Fellowship)

Woburn Square
London WC1H 0AB ENGLAND UK
020 7862 8949
FAX: 020 7862 8955
Internet: www.sas.ac.uk/warburg

AMOUNT: 850-2,000 pounds sterling

DEADLINE(S): DEC 4

FIELD(S): Classical Studies (Intellectual & Cultural History, esp. of the ancient Near East)

Short-term (1-3 months) research fellowship open to scholars who have completed at least two years' research toward the doctorate and are under 35 years of age. Preference to those who do not live within daily travelling distance of the Institute. Must submit curriculum vitae, outline of proposed research, references, and published work. Fellowship NOT intended to support archaeological excavation.

Contact Warburg Institute for an application.

3001 — UNIVERSITY OF LONDON-WARBURG INSTITUTE (NORD/LB Warburg-Wolfenbuttel Fellowship)

Woburn Square
London WC1H 0AB ENGLAND UK
020 7862 8949
FAX: 020 7862 8955
Internet: www.sas.ac.uk/warburg

AMOUNT: 850-2,000 pounds sterling

DEADLINE(S): DEC 4

FIELD(S): Classical Studies (Intellectual & Cultural History, esp. of Early & Modern Europe)

Tenable for two months at the Warburg Institute in London and two months at the Herzog August Bibliothek Wolfenbuttel, Germany, for research into the above topic. Must be under 35 years of age and have completed at least two years' research toward the doctorate. Preference to those who do not live within daily travelling distance to the Institute. Must submit curriculum vitae, outline of proposed research, references, and published work.

Contact Warburg Institute for an application and specific conditions for this fellowship.

3002 — UNIVERSITY OF LONDON INSTITUTE OF CLASSICAL STUDIES (Michael Ventris Memorial Award)

Senate House
Malet St.
London WC1E 7HM ENGLAND UK
Written Inquiry

AMOUNT: 1,500 pounds sterling

DEADLINE(S): JAN 31

FIELD(S): Mycenaean Civilization

Open to postgraduate students in the field of Mycenaean civilization or kindred subjects. Award is intended to support a specific project, which may be part of a continuing study program, at the University of London Institute of Classical Studies. Open to applicants from all countries.

Write for an application.

3003 — UNIVERSITY OF MANITOBA (J.W. Dafoe Graduate Fellowship)

Faculty of Grad Studies
500 University Ctr.
Winnipeg Manitoba R3T 2N2 CANADA
204/474-9836
Internet: www.umanitoba.ca/faculties/graduate_studies/forms

AMOUNT: $15,000/yr.

DEADLINE(S): FEB 15

FIELD(S): Political Studies; Economics; History; International Relations

Open to entering M.A. students at the University of Manitoba in one of the above departments; area of study must focus on international relations.

1 award award annually. Renewable an additional year. Contact Faculty of Graduate Studies for an application.

3004 — UNIVERSITY OF VIRGINIA (Albert Gallatin Fellowship in International Affairs)

International Studies Office
208 Minor Hall
Charlottesville VA 22903
804/982-3010
FAX: 804/982-3011
E-Mail: rgd@virginia.edu
Internet: www.virginia.edu/~intstu

AMOUNT: $11,250 and round trip travel from New York to Geneva

DEADLINE(S): MAR 2

FIELD(S): International studies

Nine-month fellowships for American doctoral candidates in international studies for study at the Graduate Institute for International Studies, Geneva; Switzerland. Must have a fairly functional ability in French as well as English proficiency.

Term is October through June. Write for complete information.

3005 — WELLESLEY COLLEGE (Mary McEwen Schimke Scholarship)

Center for Work & Service
106 Central St.

Wellesley MA 02481-8203
781/283-3525
FAX: 781/283-3674
E-Mail: fellowships@bulletin.wellesley.edu
Internet: www.wellesley.edu/CWS/step2/
fellow.html
AMOUNT: $1,000 (max.)
DEADLINE(S): JAN 3
FIELD(S): Literature; History

This supplemental award is open to women graduates of any American institution to provide relief from household and childcare expenses while pursuing graduate study at institutions other than Wellesley College. Award is made on basis of scholarly expectation and identified need. Candidate must be over 30 years of age and currently engaged in graduate study in literature and/or history. Preference given to American Studies.

See website or send self-addressed, stamped envelope to Rose Crawford, Secretary to the Committee on Extramural Graduate Fellowships & Scholarships, for an application.

3006 — WILLIAM ANDREWS CLARK MEMORIAL LIBRARY (Postdoctoral Fellowships)

UCLA
2520 Cimarron St.
Los Angeles CA 90018-2098
323/735-7605
FAX: 323/732-8744
E-Mail: clarkfel@humnet.ucla.edu
Internet: www.humnet.ucla.edu/humnet/
clarklib
AMOUNT: $2,000+/month
DEADLINE(S): MAR 15
FIELD(S): British History, Literature, & Culture

Three-month to one-year fellowships are for postdoctoral scholars to pursue advanced study and research regarding British literature and history of the 17th and 18th centuries. Tenable at the William Andrews Clark Memorial Library at UCLA.

See website or contact UCLA for an application.

3007 — WOODROW WILSON NATIONAL FELLOWSHIP FOUNDATION/JOHNSON & JOHNSON (Dissertation Grants in Women's & Children's Health)

CN 5281
Princeton NJ 08543-5281
609/452-7007
FAX: 609/452-0066
E-Mail: charoltte@woodrow.org
Internet: www.woodrow.org

AMOUNT: $2,000 (for travel, books, microfilming, taping, computer services, etc.)
DEADLINE(S): NOV 8
FIELD(S): Women's & Children's Health

Open to doctoral students in nursing, public health, anthropology, history, sociology, psychology, or social work, who have completed all predissertation requirements at US graduate schools. Must have at least six months left to complete dissertation, which should include significant research on issues related to women's & children's health. Must submit transcripts, proposal, bibliography, & interest. Based on originality & scholarly validity.

15 awards annually. See website or contact WWNFF for an application. Winners announced in February.

3008 — WORLD BANK (Graduate Scholarship Program)

1818 H St., NW, Rm. M-4035
Washington DC 20433
Written inquiry
AMOUNT: Tuition + fees, allowance, travel, etc.
DEADLINE(S): FEB 1
FIELD(S): Social sciences, law, business, public administration

For nationals of World Bank member countries under the age of 40. Must have a superior academic record, at least two years' experience in public service engaged in development-related activities, and have gained admittance to a university to pursue a post-graduate degree. Must return to hom country after degree.

For two years.

3009 — YALE CENTER FOR BRITISH ART (Fellowships)

Box 208280
New Haven CT 06520-8280
203/432-2850
AMOUNT: Travel, accommodations, per diem
DEADLINE(S): JAN 15
FIELD(S): British Art; History; Literature

Fellowships to enable scholars engaged in postdoctoral or equivalent research in British art, history, or literature to study the Center's holdings of paintings, drawings, prints, and rare books and to make use of its research facilities.

12 awards annually. Grants normally run for a period of four weeks. Write for complete information.

LAW

3010 — ACADEMY OF CRIMINAL JUSTICE SCIENCES (Affirmative Action Mini-Grant Program)

Bush Bldg., 2nd Floor
403 Wapping St.
Frankfort KY 40502
502/564-3251
E-Mail: AnnMarie.Kazyaka@mail.state.ky.us
AMOUNT: $550 (max.)
DEADLINE(S): OCT 1
FIELD(S): Criminology/Criminal Justice

For students to attend & present a research paper at ACJS annual meeting. Must be member of group that has experienced historical discrimination: African American, Asian American, Native American, Hispanics. Must also be a Ph.D. student enrolled in criminal justice, criminology, or related program. Submit completed manuscript that is theoretical or describes a qualitative/quantitative research project, no more than 30 pages in lengh. Or submit proposal.

Papers reviewed for organization, clarity of presentation, and quality of theoretical/methodological work. Contact AnnMarie Kazyaka, Chair, ACJS Affirmative Action Committee for more information. Notification is in December.

3011 — ACCESS GROUP (Loan Programs)

1411 Foulk Road
Box 7430
Wilmington DE 19803-0430
302/477-4190 or 800/282-1550
FAX: 302/477-4080
Internet: www.accessgroup.org
AMOUNT: Varies
DEADLINE(S): Varies (last day of current school term)
FIELD(S): Law, Business, Medical, Dental

Loans at competitive rates to graduate students attending law, business, medical, dental, and a variety of other graduate and professional schools.

Must be a US citizen or legal resident. No co-signer required for qualified applicants. No need to locate a lender, and no interview required. Visit website or contact Pat Curry at above address for complete information.

3012 — AMERICAN ASSOCIATION OF LAW LIBRARIES (Scholarships for Library School Graduates Attending Law School)

53 W. Jackson Blvd., Suite 940
Chicago IL 60604
312/939-4764

FAX: 312-431-1097
E-Mail: aallhq@aall.org
http://www.aallnet.org
AMOUNT: Varies
DEADLINE(S): MAR 1
FIELD(S): Law Librarianship

Open to a library school graduate who is working toward a law degree in an accredited law school and has no more than 36 semester (54 quarter) credit hours of study remaining before qualifying for a law degree.

Applicants should have meaningful law library experience. Write for complete information.

3013 — AMERICAN ASSOCIATION OF UNIVERSITY WOMEN EDUCATIONAL FOUNDATION (Selected Professions Fellowships for Women of Color)

Dept. 60
2201 N. Dodge St.
Iowa City IA 52243-4030
319/337-1716, ext. 60
FAX: 319/337-1204
Internet: www.aauw.org
AMOUNT: $5,000-$12,000
DEADLINE(S): JAN 2
FIELD(S): Business Administration; Law; Medicine

For women of color in their final year of graduate study to increase their participation in historically underrepresented fields. Must be US citizen or permanent resident. Special consideration is given to applicants who show professional promise in innovative or neglected areas of research and/or practice in areas of public interest.

Contact AAUW for an application between August 1st & December 20th.

3014 — AMERICAN COLLEGE OF LEGAL MEDICINE (Student Writing Competition)

611 E. Wells St.
Milwaukee WI 53202
800/433-9137 or 414/276-1881
FAX: 414/276-3349
E-Mail: info@aclm.org
Internet: www.aclm.org
AMOUNT: $1,000
DEADLINE(S): FEB 1
FIELD(S): Legal Medicine

Award for the best paper on any aspect of legal medicine. Open to postgraduate students enrolled in an accredited school of law, medicine, dentistry, podiatry, nursing, pharmacy, health science, or health care administration in the US or Canada.

3 awards annually. Contact Laura Morrone at ACLM for entry rules.

3015 — AMERICAN HISTORICAL ASSOCIATION (Littleton-Griswold Grants)

400 A St., SE
Washington DC 20003
202/544-2422
FAX: 202/544-8307
E-Mail: aha@theaha.org
Internet: www.theaha.org
AMOUNT: $1,000
DEADLINE(S): FEB 1
FIELD(S): American Legal History

Support for a research project on American legal history in the fields of law and society. Must be a graduate student and AHA member.

See website or contact AHA for membership information and grant details.

3016 — AMERICAN PHILOSOPHICAL SOCIETY (Henry Phillips Grants in Jurisprudence)

104 South 5th Street
Philadelphia PA 19106-3387
E-Mail: eroach@amphilsoc.org
Internet: www.amphilsoc.org
AMOUNT: $6,000 (max.)
DEADLINE(S): DEC 1
FIELD(S): Jurisprudence research: history and theory of the law

Grants for post-doctoral research in jurisprudence for scholars with a Ph.D. or J.D. degree. Grants are for research only, not for study, salary replacement, travel to conferences, or assistance with publication or translation.

See website for details. Written requests must include self-addressed mailing label, indication of eligibility, nature of research, and proposed use of grant funds. Foreign applicants must also state why study in US is necessary.

3017 — AMERICAN SOCIETY OF COMPOSERS, AUTHORS, AND PUBLISHERS (Nathan Burkan Memorial Competition)

One Lincoln Plaza
New York NY 10023
212/621-6280
FAX: 212/621-6481
Internet: www.ascap.com
AMOUNT: $500 (1st prize); $200 (2nd)
DEADLINE(S): JUN 30
FIELD(S): Copyright Law

Prizes for third-year students at accredited law schools in the US for best paper on copyright law.

Contact the Dean of your school or ASCAP for competition rules.

3018 — ARMENIAN GENERAL BENEVOLENT UNION (Educational Loan Program)

Education Dept., 31 W. 52nd St.
New York NY 10019-6118
212/765-8260
FAX: 212/765-8209/8209
E-Mail: agbuny@aol.com
AMOUNT: $5,000 to $7,500/yr.
DEADLINE(S): APR 1
FIELD(S): Law (J.D.) and Medicine (M.D.)

Loans for full-time students of Armenian heritage pursuing their first professional degrees in law or medicine. Must be attending highly competitive institutions in the U.S. GPA of 3.5 or more required.

Loan repayments begin within 12 months of completion of full-time study and extend 5 to ten years, depending on the size of the loan. Interest is 3% Write for complete information.

3019 — ASSOCIATION OF CERTIFIED FRAUD EXAMINERS (Scholarships)

The Gregor Building, 716 West Ave
Austin TX 78701
800/245-3321 or 512/478-9070
FAX: 512/478-9297
E-Mail: acfe@tpoint.net
Internet: www.cfenet.com
AMOUNT: $500
DEADLINE(S): MAY 15
FIELD(S): Accounting and/or criminal justice

Scholarships for full time graduate or undergraduate students majoring in accounting or criminal justice degree programs. Awards are based on overall academic achievement, three letters of recommendation, and an original 250-workd essay explaining why the applicant deserves the award and how fraud awareness will afect his or her professional career development. Also required is a letter of recommendation from a Certified Fraud Examiner or a local CFE Chapter.

Contact organization for applications and further details.

3020 — ASSOCIATION OF FORMER INTELLIGENCE OFFICERS/AFIO (Lt. Gen. Eugene F. Tighe, Jr., Memorial Scholarship)

1142 Miramonte Glen
Escondido CA 92026-1724
760/432-8844
AMOUNT: $1,000
DEADLINE(S): JAN 10
FIELD(S): Government, Political Science, Criminal Justice, and Law

Open to undergraduate and graduate students. Students must have a 3.0 GPA and be full-time students. For use at all four-year and grad schools in the U.S. and affiliated institutions overseas.

Send SASE to the above address for complete information. Note: LAST scholarship granted January 10, 2000.

3021 — AUSTRALIAN FEDERATION OF UNIVERSITY WOMEN - WESTERN AUSTRALIA (Joyce Riley Bursary)

Bursary Liaison Officer
PO Box 48
Nedlands WA 6909 AUSTRALIA
Written Inquiry

AMOUNT: Aus$1,700 - Aus$2,750

DEADLINE(S): JUL 31

FIELD(S): Humanities; Social Sciences

To support women graduates of a Western Australian university to complete a higher degree or post-doctoral research in Humanities or Social Sciences at a recognized university in any country.

Membership in AFUW or in IFUW is required. Contact above location for further information.

3022 — AUSTRALIAN FEDERATION OF UNIVERSITY WOMEN - WESTERN AUSTRALIA (Joyce Riley Bursary)

Bursary Liaison Officer
PO Box 48
Nedlands WA 6009 AUSTRALIA
Written Inquiry

AMOUNT: Aus$1,700 - Aus$2,750

DEADLINE(S): JUL 31

FIELD(S): Humanities; Social Sciences

To support women graduates of a recognized university to complete a higher degree or post-doctoral research at a university in Western Australia.

Membership in AFUW or in IFUW is required. Write to above address for complete information.

3023 — BOLOGNA CENTER OF THE JOHNS HOPKINS UNIVERSITY - PAUL H. NITZE SCHOOL OF ADVANCED INTERNATIONAL STUDIES (Fellowships for Non-Americans)

Admissions Office
Via Belmeloro 11
40126 Bologna ITALY
+39/51/232-185
FAX: +39/51/228-505
E-Mail: admission@jhubc.it
Internet: www.jhubc.it

AMOUNT: Partial to full tuition

DEADLINE(S): FEB 1

FIELD(S): European Studies; International Relations; International Economics

One year at SAIS Bologna Center is open to graduate students with some background in political science, economics, history, or law and who are interested in problems confronting Europe and/or international relations. Possibility to continue for the second year toward an M.A. at SAIS in Washington, DC. Program is conducted in English; therefore, English fluency is required. This program is for non-US citizens.

Contact Bologna Center for an application.

3024 — BOLOGNA CENTER OF THE JOHNS HOPKINS UNIVERSITY - PAUL H. NITZE SCHOOL OF ADVANCED INTERNATIONAL STUDIES (Fellowships for Americans)

SAIS
1740 Massachusetts Ave., NW
Washington DC 20036
E-Mail: admission@jhubc.it
Internet: www.jhubc.it

AMOUNT: Partial to full tuition

DEADLINE(S): JAN 15

FIELD(S): European Studies; International Relations; International Economics

One year at SAIS Bologna Center in Italy is open to graduate students with some background in political science, economics, history, or law and who are interested in problems confronting Europe and/or international relations. Must be US citizen/permanent resident. Courses are conducted in English.

Contact SAIS for an application.

3025 — BUSINESS & PROFESSIONAL WOMEN'S FOUNDATION (BPW Career Advancement Scholarship Program)

2012 Massachusetts Ave., NW
Washington DC 20036-1070
202/293-1200, ext. 169
FAX: 202/861-0298
Internet: www.bpwusa.org

AMOUNT: $500-$1,000

DEADLINE(S): APR 15

FIELD(S): Biology, Science, Education, Engineering, Social Science, Paralegal, Humanities, Business, Math, Computers, Law, MD, DD

For women (US citizens) aged 25+ accepted into accredited program at US institution (+Puerto Rico & Virgin Islands). Must graduate within 12 to 24 months from the date of grant and demonstrate critical finanacial need. Must have a plan to upgrade skills, train for a new career field, or to enter/re-enter the job market.

Full- or part-time study. For info see website or send business-sized, self-addressed, double-stamped envelope.

3026 — CANADIAN BAR ASSOCIATION (Viscount Bennett Fellowship)

902-50 O'Connor St.
Ottawa Ontario K1P 6L2 CANADA
613/237-2925
FAX: 613/237-0815

AMOUNT: $20,000

DEADLINE(S): NOV 15

FIELD(S): Law

Fellowship is open to Canadian citizens who have graduated from an approved law school in Canada or who, at the time of application, are pursuing final year studies at an approved law school.

Contact Canadian Bar Association for an application.

3027 — DEPARTMENT OF JUSTICE CANADA (Civil Law/Common Law Exchange Program Scholarships)

284 Wellington St.
EMB 6th Fl.
Ottawa Ontario K1A 0H8 CANADA
613/957-3706
FAX: 613/941-2269
Internet: canada.justice.gc.ca/Recrutement/bourse/bourse_en.html

AMOUNT: $2,500 + $500 (for long distance travel)

DEADLINE(S): Varies

FIELD(S): Canadian Law

Open to second and third year law students at Canadian universities. Objective is to increase understanding of Canada's civil law and common law systems of justice in a manner that promotes better understanding of the differences between Quebec and other provinces. Common law students will study one full university session in a civil law program; civil law students will study in a common law program. Must know both English and French.

Contact Mireille Provost, Program Analyst, or your home law faculty for an application.

3028 — DEPARTMENT OF JUSTICE CANADA (Legal Studies for Aboriginal People Program)

284 Wellington St.
EMB Ste. 6206
Ottawa Ontario K1A 0H8 CANADA
613/941-0388 or 888/606-5111
FAX: 613/941-2269
E-Mail: LSAP@justice.gc.ca
Internet: canada.justice.gc.ca/Recrutement/bourse/intermediaire_en.html

AMOUNT: Varies

DEADLINE(S): MAR 31 (pre-law); JUN 1 (law school)

FIELD(S): Law

Must be non-status Indian or Metis of Canadian citizenship, living in Canada, who has received acceptance to or is registered in pre-law orientation or law school. Purpose of program is to promote equitable representation of Aboriginal people in the legal profession.

See website or contact Mireille Provost, Program Administrator, for an application.

3029 — EUROPEAN UNIVERSITY INSTITUTE (Jean Monnet Fellowship)

Via Dei Roccettini 9
I-50016 San Domenico Di Fiesole (FL) Italy
0039-055-46851
FAX: 0039-055-4685444
E-Mail: applyjmf@datacomm.iue.it
Internet: www.iue.it/JMF/Welcome.html

AMOUNT: 2,000,000-3,500,000 Italian lire per month (i.e. 1,025-1,750 ECU) + medical & family allowances (depends on whether fellow is in receipt of payment from another source and on extent of duties carried out at the Institute)

DEADLINE(S): NOV 1

FIELD(S): Europe: History, Society, Politics, Economics, Law

Post-doctoral fellowships. Fellows are required to make scholarly contribution to research on Europe within one of EUI's research projects or on topic, falling within general interests of the Institute. Publication of research is expected.

25 fellowships annually. Financial need NOT considered. See website or contact Dr. Andreas Frijdal at above address for complete information.

3030 — EUROPEAN UNIVERSITY INSTITUTE (National Postgraduate Scholarships)

Via De Roccettini 9
San Domenico Di Fiesole (FI 50016) ITALY
0039/055-46851
FAX: 0039/055-4685444
E-Mail: applyres@datacomm.iue.it
Internet: www.iue.it

AMOUNT: $1,000/month + travel & medical/family allowances

DEADLINE(S): JAN 31

FIELD(S): Political Science; Social Sciences; Law; Economics; History

Open to graduate & postgraduate students at the Institute who have good honors and a research project having European dimension. Awards are available only to nationals of the Institute's member states. US citizens must have sufficient personal funds or another grant to cover maintenance & tuition; may apply to Fulbright Commission which may award up to two grants per academic year to US citizens with tuition-fee waivers.

130 awards annually. Renewable. Contact Dr. Andreas Frijdal for an application.

3031 — FRENCH-AMERICAN FOUNDATION (Bicentennial Fellowships)

41 East 72nd St.
New York NY 10021
212/288-4000
FAX: 212/288-4765
E-Mail: French_AmerFdn@msn.com

AMOUNT: 10,000 French francs/mo.

DEADLINE(S): FEB 2

FIELD(S): Social sciences

For doctoral students in the social sciences to travel to France for one year to conduct research essential to the completion of their dissertations. Must have completed all other requirements for Ph.D. May not use the award until exams are passed.

Requires application with a statement of purpose, full academic records, plan of research, bibliography, abstract, and three academic recommendations.

3032 — GLADYS KRIEBLE DELMAS FOUNDATION (Predoctoral & Postdoctoral Grants in Venice & the Veneto)

521 5th Avenue, Suite 1612
New York NY 10175-1699
212/687-0011
FAX: 212/687-8877
E-Mail: DelmasFdtn@aol.com
Internet: www.delmas.org

AMOUNT: $500-$12,500

DEADLINE(S): DEC 15

FIELD(S): Research of Venice and the former Venetian empire and study of contemporary Venetian society and culture.

Pre- and postdoctoral grants for historical research on Venice. Humanities and social sciences are eligible areas of study, including archaeology, architecture, art, bibliography, economics, history, history of science, law, literature, music, political science, religion, and theater.

Applicants must have experience in advanced research and be U.S. citizens/residents; grad students must have fulfilled all doctoral requirements except dissertation by Dec. 15.

3033 — GRADUATE INSTITUTE OF INTERNATIONAL STUDIES (Scholarships)

P.O. Box 36
132 Rue do Lausanne
CH-1211 Geneva 21 SWITZERLAND
(+41 22) 731 17 30
FAX: (+41-22) 731 27 77
E-Mail: info@hei.unige.ch
Internet: http://heiwww.unige.ch

AMOUNT: Varies

DEADLINE(S): None

FIELD(S): International history and politics, political science, international economics, international law

Scholarships to support graduate diploma and Ph.D students already registered at the Institute. Open to applicants with excellent, active knowledge of one of the institute's two working languages, French & English, and sufficient passive knowledge of the other.

Contact above sources for complete information.

3034 — H. FLETCHER BROWN FUND (Scholarships)

c/o PNC Bank
Trust Dept.
P.O. Box 791
Wilmington DE 19899
302/429-1186

AMOUNT: Varies

DEADLINE(S): APR 15

FIELD(S): Medicine; Dentistry; Law; Engineering; Chemistry

Open to U.S. citizens born in Delaware and still residing in Delaware. For 4 years of study (undergrad or grad) leading to a degree that enables applicant to practice in chosen field.

Scholarships are based on need, scholastic achievement, and good moral character. Applications available in February. Write for complete information.

3035 — INSTITUTE FOR ADVANCED STUDIES IN THE HUMANITIES (Visiting Research Fellowships)

Univ Edinburgh
Hope Park Square
Edinburgh EH8 9NW SCOTLAND UK
0131 650 4671
FAX: 0131 668 2252
E-Mail: iash@ed.ac.uk
Internet: www.ed.ac.uk/iash/homepage.html

AMOUNT: Non-stipendiary*

DEADLINE(S): DEC 1

FIELD(S): Arts; Social Sciences; Law; Music; Divinity

Postdoctoral research fellowships of between two and six months are tenable at the Institute for Advanced Studies in the Humanities. Based on academic record and publications. *Most fellowships are honorary, but limited support towards expenses is available to a small number of candidates. Fellows are allocated a study room within the Institute and hold one or two seminars during their tenure. Must submit research report at end of fellowship. No teaching required.

15 awards annually. Not renewable. Contact Mrs. Anthea Taylor for an application.

3036 — INSTITUTE FOR HUMANE STUDIES
(Humane Studies Fellowship)

4084 University Dr., Ste. 101
Fairfax VA 22030-6812
703/934-6920 or 800/697-8799
FAX: 703/352-7535
E-Mail: ihs@gmu.edu
Internet: www.theihs.org

AMOUNT: up to $12,000

DEADLINE(S): DEC 31

FIELD(S): Social Sciences; Law; Humanities; Jurisprudence; Journalism

Awards are for graduate and advanced undergraduate students pursuing degrees at any accredited domestic or foreign school. Based on academic performance, demonstrated interest in classical liberal ideas, and potential to contribute to the advancement of a free society.

90 awards annually. Apply online or contact IHS for an application.

3037 — INSTITUTE FOR HUMANE STUDIES
(Koch Summer Fellow Program)

4084 University Dr., Ste. 101
Fairfax VA 22030-6812
703/934-6920 or 800/697-8799
FAX: 703/352-7535
E-Mail: ihs@gmu.edu
Internet: www.theihs.org

AMOUNT: $1,500 + airfare & housing

DEADLINE(S): MAR 1

FIELD(S): Economics; Politics; Law; Government; Public Policy

For undergraduates and graduates to build skills and gain experience by participating in an 8-week summer internship program. Includes 2 week-long seminars, the internship, and research & writing projects with professionals. College transcripts, essays, and application required. Financial need NOT a factor.

32 awards annually. Not renewable. Apply online or contact IHS for an application.

3038 — INSTITUTE FOR HUMANE STUDIES
(Summer Residential Program)

4084 University Dr., Ste. 101
Fairfax VA 22030-6812
703/934-6920 or 800/697-8799
FAX: 703/352-7535
E-Mail: ihs@gmu.edu
Internet: www.theihs.org

AMOUNT: All seminar fees: program cost, room/board, materials, and books

DEADLINE(S): MAR 1

FIELD(S): Social Sciences; Humanities; Law; Journalism; Public Policy; Education; Writing

For college students, recent graduates, and graduate students who share an interest in learning and exchanging ideas about the scope of individual rights. One-week and weekend seminars at various campus locations across the U.S.

Apply online or contact IHS for an application.

3039 — INTER-AMERICAN BAR ASSOCIATION
(Writing Competition)

1211 Connecticut Ave., NW, Ste. 202
Washington DC 20036
202/393-1217
FAX: 202/393-1241
E-Mail: iaba@iaba.org
www.iaba.org

AMOUNT: $400-$800

DEADLINE(S): FEB 15

FIELD(S): Law

Writing competition for law students on one of the Association's themes. Papers may be prepared in English, Spanish, Portuguese, or French.

Contact organization for details.

3040 — INTER-AMERICAN FOUNDATION (Field Research Fellowship Programs for U.S., Latin American, and Caribbean Citizens)

901 N. Stuart St., 10th Floor
Arlington VA 22203
703/841-3800
FAX: 703/527-3529
E-Mail: correo@aif.gov
Internet: www.iaf.gov

AMOUNT: Varies

DEADLINE(S): APR 28

FIELD(S): International Relations, Social Sciences, Humanities, Latin American Studies

Fellowships for Latin American, Carribean, and U.S. doctoral level students for field research in Latin America and the Caribbean. Must be enrolled in U.S. university.

Access website for deadline and application information. Organization does not mail information.

3041 — INTER-AMERICAN FOUNDATION
(Master's Research Fellowships)

901 N. Stuart St., 10th Floor
Arlington VA 22203
703/841-3800
FAX: 703/527-3529
E-Mail: correo@aif.gov
Internet: www.iaf.gov

AMOUNT: Varies

DEADLINE(S): APR

FIELD(S): Latin American & Caribbean Studies, Internations Relations, Social Sciences, Humanities, etc.

Open to masters students enrolled in U.S. universities for field research in Latin American or the Caribbean. For citizens of Caribbean and Latin American independent countries, and the U.S.

Access website for deadline and application information. Organization does not mail information.

3042 — JAPANESE AMERICAN CITIZENS
LEAGUE (Minoru Yasui Memorial Scholarship)

1765 Sutter St.
San Francisco CA 94115
415/921-5225
FAX: 415/931-4671
E-Mail: jacl@jacl.org
Internet: www.jacl.org

AMOUNT: Varies

DEADLINE(S): APR 1

FIELD(S): Human & Civil Rights; Sociology; Law; Education

Open to JACL members or their children only. For graduate students with a strong interest in human and civil rights. Student must be currently enrolled in, or planning to enroll in, an accredited graduate school. Financial need NOT a factor.

40 awards annually. For membership information or an application, send a self-addressed, stamped envelope to above address.

3043 — JOHN F. KENNEDY LIBRARY
FOUNDATION (Abba P. Schwartz Research Fellowship)

Columbia Point
Boston MA 02125-3313
617/929-4534 or 617/929-4533
FAX: 617/929-4599

AMOUNT: Up to $3,100

DEADLINE(S): MAR 15

FIELD(S): Immigration, naturalization, or refugee policies

To support a scholar while he/she researches in the fields listed above.

Contact William Johnson, Chief Archivist, at above location for application information.

3044 — JOHN F. KENNEDY LIBRARY
FOUNDATION (Marjorie Kovler Research Fellowship)

Columbia Point
Boston MA 02125-3313
617/929-4534 or 617/929-4533
FAX: 617/929-4599

AMOUNT: $2,500
DEADLINE(S): MAR 15
FIELD(S): History, Law Political Science-specializing in foreign intelligence and the presidency or a related topic.

To support a scholar while he/she researches in the fields listed above.

Contact William Johnson, Chief Archivist, at above location for application information.

3045 — JOHN RANKIN FUND (Travel Scholarships in Accounting or Law)

Trustees of the John Rankin Fund, c/o Jonathan Stone Esq., The Hall
East Ilsley, Newbury RG20 7LW
Written inquiry

AMOUNT: 5,000 pounds
DEADLINE(S): MAR 31
FIELD(S): Accounting, Law

A bi-annual award for either a law or accounting student, barrister, solicitor, or qualified accountant to study abroad. Applicant must be under 26 on Oct. 1 of the year of application. Next award in 2000.

Write to organization for information.

3046 — LONDON SCHOOL OF ECONOMICS AND POLITICAL SCIENCE (Morris Finer Memorial Studentships)

Houghton St.
Scholarships Office
London WC2A 2AE ENGLAND
071-405 7686
FAX: 071-242 0392

AMOUNT: Varies
DEADLINE(S): MAY 1
FIELD(S): Law

Open to graduate students who wish to undertake either contemporary or historical research at the school in a socio-legal field connected with labor law, social services law, criminal law, family law, welfare law, or any other area in law.

Write for complete information.

3047 — MARK B. HOLZMAN GRADUATE EDUCATION FOUNDATION

Nine South DuPont Hwy.
Georgetown DE 19947
302/855-2816

AMOUNT: Varies
DEADLINE(S): MAY 31
FIELD(S): Dentistry, law,, medicine, and the ministry

Scholarships to residents of Delaware for graduate study in the above fields.

Send SASE to Connie E. Mears, c/o Wilmington Trust Co., at above address for details.

3048 — MARYLAND HIGHER EDUCATION COMMISSION (Professional School Scholarships)

State Scholarship Admin
16 Francis St.
Annapolis MD 21401-1781
800/974-1024 or 410/974-5370
TTY: 800/735-2258

AMOUNT: $200-$1,000
DEADLINE(S): MAR 1
FIELD(S): Dentistry; Pharmacy; Medicine; Law; Nursing; Social Work

Open to Maryland residents who have been admitted as full-time students at a participating graduate institution of higher learning in Maryland or an undergraduate/graduate nursing program. Must fill out government FAFSA form.

Renewable up to 4 years. Contact MHEC for an application and see your school's financial aid office for FAFSA.

3049 — MINISTRY OF THE FLEMISH COMMUNITY (Fellowships)

Embassy of Belgium
3330 Garfield St., NW
Washington DC 20008
202/625-5850/51
FAX: 202/342-8346
E-Mail: flemishcomdc@wizard.net

AMOUNT: Monthly stipend, tuition, & health care coverage
DEADLINE(S): JAN 31
FIELD(S): Art; Music; Humanities; Social Science; Political Science; Law; Economics; Science; Medicine

Open to US citizens under age 35 who wish to pursue graduate or postgraduate studies in Flanders, Belgium.

Contact Flemish Community for registration forms.

3050 — MISSISSIPPI OFFICE OF STATE STUDENT FINANCIAL AID (Public Management Graduate Internship Program)

3825 Ridgewood Road
Jackson MS 39211-6453
601/982-6663
1-800-327-2980

AMOUNT: $1,000/month (up to 8 months)
DEADLINE(S): Varies (Established by program coordinator)
FIELD(S): Criminal Justice; Public Administration; Public Policy

For students pursuing a graduate degree in criminal Justice, Public Administration, or Public Policy, this program provides the opportunity to have practical experience working for state or local agencies and offices, including the state legislature. The intern works a semester with the state or local agency. For U.S. residents or eligible non-citizens who possess an alien registration card and who are enrolled at certain universities in Mississippi.

Must have earned a "B" or higher grade in one Quantitative Research Methods course.

3051 — NATIONAL COUNCIL OF FARMER COOPERATIVES (Graduate Awards)

50 F St., NW, Ste. 900
Washington DC 20001
202/626-8700
FAX: 202/626-8722

AMOUNT: $1,000 (1st prize); $800 (2nd); $600 (3rd)
DEADLINE(S): APR 1
FIELD(S): American Cooperatives

Open to graduate students working on theses or dissertations dealing with some aspect of economics, finance, operation, law, or structure of American cooperatives. May be in such fields as economics, business communications, sociology, etc.

3 awards annually. Not renewable. Contact NCFC Education Foundation for registration form.

3052 — NATIONAL FEDERATION OF THE BLIND (Howard Brown Rickard Scholarship)

805 Fifth Avenue
Grinnell IA 50112
515/236-3366

AMOUNT: $3,000
DEADLINE(S): MAR 31
FIELD(S): Law; Medicine; Engineering; Architecture; Natural Sciences

For legally blind students pursuing or planning to pursue a full-time postsecondary course of study in the US. Based on academic excellence, service to the community, and financial need. Membership NOT required.

1 award annually. Renewable. Contact Mrs. Peggy Elliot, Scholarship Committee Chairman, for an application.

3053 — NEW YORK STATE HIGHER EDUCATION SERVICES CORPORATION (N.Y. State Regents Professional/Health Care Opportunity Scholarships)

Cultural Education Center, Rm. 5C64
Albany NY 12230
518/486-1319
Internet: www.hesc.com

AMOUNT: $1,000-$10,000/yr.

DEADLINE(S): Varies

FIELD(S): Medicine and dentistry and related fields, architecture, nursing, psychology, audiology, landscape architecture, social work, chiropractic, law, pharmacy, accounting, speech language pathology

For NY state residents who are economically disadvantaged and members of a minority group underrepresented in the chosen profession and attending school in NY state. Some programs carry a service obligation in New York for each year of support. For U.S. citizens or qualifying noncitizens.

Medical/dental scholarships require one year of professional work in NY.

3054 — OAK RIDGE ASSOCIATED UNIVERSITIES (Laboratory Graduate Research Participation Program)

P.O. Box 117
Oak Ridge TN 37831-0117
423/576-4813

AMOUNT: $1,000-$1,200/mo. + allowance for dependents + tuition and fees reimbursement to a max. of $3,500/yr.

DEADLINE(S): Ongoing

FIELD(S): Life sciences, physical, and social sciences, mathematics, and engineering

For graduate students in one of the fields listed above who have completed all degree requirements except thesis or dissertation research. For full-time research under the joint direction of the major professor and a DOE staff member at one of various locations, primarily in the South. For six to twelve months.

Funded through U.S. Dept. of Energy, Office of Energy Reseach, and Office of Fossil Energy. Write for complete information.

3055 — OPEN SOCIETY INSTITUTE (Individual Project Fellowships)

400 West 59th St.
New York NY 10019
212/548-0600 or 212/757-2323
FAX: 212/548-4679 or 212/548-4600
Internet: www.soros.org/fellow/individual.html

AMOUNT: Varies

DEADLINE(S): Varies

FIELD(S): Any field of study related to creating an open society: reliance on the rule of law, the existence of a democratically elected government, a diverse and vigorous civil society, and respect for minorities and minority opinions.

Two-year fellowships for use in selected universities in the U.S. for international students. For students/

professionals in fields related to environmental policy, legislation, and remediation techniques applicable to their home countries.

To apply, contact the Soros Foundation/Open Society Institute. Further details on website.

3056 — PRESIDENT'S COMMISSION ON WHITE HOUSE FELLOWSHIPS

712 Jackson Place NW
Washington DC 20503
202/395-4522
FAX: 202/395-6179
E-Mail: almanac@ace.esusda.gov

AMOUNT: Wage (up to GS-14 Step 3; approximately $65,000 in 1995)

DEADLINE(S): DEC 1

FIELD(S): Public Service; Government; Community Involvement; Leadership

Mid-career professionals spend one year as special assistants to senior executive branch officials in Washington. Highly competitive. Non-partisan; no age or educational requirements. Fellowship year runs September 1 through August 31.

1,200 candidates applying for 11 to 19 fellowships each year. Write for complete information.

3057 — RAYMOND J. HARRIS EDUCATION TRUST

P.O. Box 7899
Philadelphia PA 19101-7899
Written inquiry

AMOUNT: Varies

DEADLINE(S): FEB 1

FIELD(S): Medicine, law, engineering, dentistry, or agriculture

Scholarships for Christian men to obtain a professional education in medicine, law, engineering, dentistry, or agriculture at nine Philadelphia area colleges.

Contact Mellon Bank, N.A. at above location for details and the names of the nine colleges.

3058 — ROYAL THAI EMBASSY, OFFICE OF EDUCATIONAL AFFAIRS (Revenue Dept. Scholarships for Thai Students)

1906 23rd St. NW
Washington DC 20008
202/667-9111 or 202/667-8010
FAX: 202/265-7239

AMOUNT: Varies

DEADLINE(S): APR

FIELD(S): Computer science (telecommunications), law, economics, finanace, business administration

Scholarships for students under age 35 from Thailand who have been accepted to study in the U.S or U.K. for

the needs of the Revenue Dept., Ministry of Finance. Must pursue any level degree in one of the above fields.

Selections are based on academic records, employment history, and advisor recommendations.

3059 — SIR ROBERT MENZIES MEMORIAL FOUNDATION LIMITED (Scholarship in Law)

210 Clarendon Street
East Melbourne Vic 3002 AUSTRALIA
03 9419 5699
FAX: 03 9417 7049
E-Mail: menzies@vicnet.net.au
Internet: www.vincent.net.au/~menzies

AMOUNT: University fees, living, & travel expenses

DEADLINE(S): AUG 31

FIELD(S): Law

For Australian citizens with at least an Upper Second Class Honours Degree in Law from an Australian University to pursue postgraduate studies at universities in the United Kingdom. Qualities sought include academic excellence, leadership (proven & potential), extracurricular activities/interests, ability to contribute to the life of a British university, and interest in the service of others. Financial need NOT a factor.

1-2 awards annually. Contact Ms. Sandra Mackenzie for an application.

3060 — THE AMERICAN ASSOCIATION OF ATTORNEY-CERTIFIED PUBLIC ACCOUNTANTS FOUNDATION (Student Writing Competition)

24196 Alicia Parkway, Suite K
Mission Viejo CA 92691
800/CPA-ATTY
FAX: 714/768-7062

AMOUNT: $250-$1,500

DEADLINE(S): APR 1

FIELD(S): Accounting; Law

Essay contest for accounting and/or law students.

Contact organization for current topics and rules.

3061 — THE J. EDGAR HOOVER FOUNDATION

50 Gull Point Rd.
Hilton Head Island SC 29928
803/671-5020

AMOUNT: $500

DEADLINE(S): Ongoing

FIELD(S): Government, law enforcement

Scholarships for the study of government, the promotion of good citizenship, and law enforcement. The foundation strives to safeguard the heritage and freedom of the U.S., to promote good citizenship through an appreciation of the American form of government, and to combat communism or any other ideology or doctrine opposed to the principles set forth in the U.S. Constitution.

Send letter to Cartha D. De Loach, Chair, at above address.

3062 — U.S. ENVIRONMENTAL PROTECTION AGENCY—NATIONAL NETWORK FOR ENVIRONMENTAL MANAGEMENT STUDIES (Fellowships)

401 M St., SW
Mailcode 1704
Washington DC 20460
202/260-5283
FAX: 202/260-4095
E-Mail: jojokian.sheri@epa.gov
Internet: www.epa.gov/enviroed/students.html

AMOUNT: Varies

DEADLINE(S): DEC

FIELD(S): Environmental Policies, Regulations, & Law; Environmental Management & Administration; Environmental Science; Public Relations & Communications; Computer Programming & Development

Fellowships are open to undergraduate and graduate students working on research projects in the above fields, either full-time during the summer or part-time during the school year. Must be US citizen or legal resident. Financial need NOT a factor.

85-95 awards annually. Not renewable. See website or contact the Career Service Center of participating universities for an application.

3063 — UNITARIAN UNIVERSALIST ASSN. (Otto M. Stanfield Legal Scholarship)

25 Beacon Street
Boston MA 02144
617/742-2100

AMOUNT: Varies

DEADLINE(S): FEB 15

FIELD(S): Law

Scholarships for law students. Applicants must be Unitarian Universalists.

No phone calls please.

3064 — UNIVERSITY OF CAMBRIDGE - SIDNEY SUSSEX COLLEGE (Evan Lewis-Thomas Law Studentships)

Tutor for Graduate Students
Cambridge CB2 3HU ENGLAND UK
+44/01223-338800

AMOUNT: 1,000+ pounds sterling, up to full support

DEADLINE(S): FEB 1

FIELD(S): Law & Jurisprudence

Open to master's and doctoral students for research or advanced courses in law or cognate subjects in the University of Cambridge. Preference given to those who nominate Sidney Sussex as their College of first preference on CIGAS Form and those who are under 26 years of age. Financial need considered in determing award amount.

Renewable up to 3 years, subject to reviews of diligence and progress. Contact Sidney Sussex College for an application.

3065 — UNIVERSITY OF GLASGOW (Post-graduate Awards in Law & Financial Studies)

University of Glasgow
Glasgow G12 8QQ SCOTLAND UK
041/330-4551

AMOUNT: Research council maintenance equivalent

DEADLINE(S): FEB 28

FIELD(S): Financial Studies/Law

Research in topic specified by applicant approved by school of law. For study at the university of Glasgow. Must have good honours degree.

Awarded annually. Renewable. Contact Mrs. A.E. Wilson Clerk of the faculty for complete information.

3066 — UNIVERSITY OF MANCHESTER (Awards for Research)

Secretary, Research and Graduate Support Unit
Manchester M13 9PL England
0161 275 2035
FAX: 0161 275 2445/7216

AMOUNT: Maintenance grant (approx) 5000 pounds p.a. plus payment of UK tuition fees.

DEADLINE(S): MAY 1

FIELD(S): Arts, Economics, Social Studies, Education, Science, Engineering, Biological Sciences, Law

The university offers research studentships for doctoral research in all disciplines. These awards are highly competitive. Applicants should hold at least a 2:1 degree or equivalent. Awards are renewable for up to 2 years.

Approx 50 awards per year. Please contact address above for complete information.

3067 — UNIVERSITY OF SOUTH DAKOTA (Criminal Justice Dept. Scholarships)

414 East Clark St.
Vermillion SD 57069-2390
605/677-5446
E-Mail: admiss@usd.edu
Internet: www.usd.edu/cjus/
scholarships.htm#orderofpolice

AMOUNT: Varies

DEADLINE(S): Varies

FIELD(S): Criminal Justice; Political Science; Public Service

The University of South Dakota's Department of Crimal Justice administers 17 different award programs in the above fields. Some require a high GPA and/or financial need, others require an essay or research project.

See website or contact USD for specific details of each award. The Criminal Justice Department gives out an average of $77,000/year to USD students.

3068 — UNIVERSITY OF VIRGINIA (Albert Gallatin Fellowship in International Affairs)

International Studies Office
208 Minor Hall
Charlottesville VA 22903
804/982-3010
FAX: 804/982-3011
E-Mail: rgd@virginia.edu
Internet: www.virginia.edu/~intstu

AMOUNT: $11,250 and round trip travel from New York to Geneva

DEADLINE(S): MAR 2

FIELD(S): International studies

Nine-month fellowships for American doctoral candidates in international studies for study at the Graduate Institute for International Studies, Geneva; Switzerland. Must have a fairly functional ability in French as well as English proficiency.

Term is October through June. Write for complete information.

3069 — US ARMS CONTROL AND DISARMAMENT AGENCY (Hubert H. Humphrey Fellowship Program)

Office of Chief Science Advisor
320 21st St. NW
Room 5726
Washington DC 20451
202/647-8090

AMOUNT: $8,000 stipend + up to $6,000 tuition grant

DEADLINE(S): MAR 15

FIELD(S): Arms Control, Nonproliferation, and Disarmament

Doctoral dissertation research fellowships for applicants who have completed all Ph.D. course work except for the dissertation at an accredited U.S. institution. Must be U.S. citizen or permanent resident.

Third-year law students also may apply. Fellowships normally awarded for a period of 12 months. Write for complete information.

3070 — WESTERN SOCIETY OF CRIMINOLOGY (Student Paper Competition)

Criminal Justice Division
Cal State Univ
6000 J St.
Sacramento CA 95819-6085
Internet: www.sonoma.edu/CJA/WSC/WSCstu00.html

AMOUNT: $125 (1st prize); $75 (2nd) + certificates

DEADLINE(S): DEC 15

FIELD(S): Criminology

Any student currently enrolled full- or part-time in an academic program at either the undergraduate or graduate level may enter. All entries must be papers relating to criminology. Papers must be 10 to 20 pages, typewritten, double-spaced on 8 1/2 x 11 white paper, using a standard format for the organization of papers and citations. Two copies must be submitted.

Send your entries to the attention of Dr. Miki Vohryzek-Bolden in the Criminal Justice Division at California State University. Winners will be notified in writing by February 7th.

3071 — WOMEN IN DEFENSE (HORIZONS Scholarship Foundation)

NDIA
2111 Wilson Blvd., Ste. 400
Arlington VA 22201-3061
703/247-2552
FAX: 703/522-1885
E-Mail: dnwlee@moon.jic.com
Internet: www.adpa.org/wid/horizon/Scholar.htm

AMOUNT: $500+

DEADLINE(S): NOV 1; JUL 1

FIELD(S): Engineering, Computer Science, Physics, Mathematics, Business, Law, International Relations, Political Science, Operations Research, Economics, and fields relevant to a career in the areas of national security and defense.

For women who are U.S. citizens, have minimum GPA of 3.25, demonstrate financial need, are currently enrolled at an accredited university/college (full- or part-time—both grads and undergrad juniors/seniors are eligible), and demonstrate interest in pursuing a career related to national security.

Application is online or send SASE, #10 envelope, to Woody Lee, HORIZONS Scholarship Director.

3072 — WOODS HOLE OCEANOGRAPHIC INSTITUTION (Research Fellowships in Marine Policy and Ocean Management)

360 Woods Hole Road
Woods Hole MA 02543-1541
508/289-2219
FAX: 508/457-2188
E-Mail: mgately@whoi.edu
Internet: www.whoi.edu

AMOUNT: Varies

DEADLINE(S): FEB 16

FIELD(S): Social Sciences, Law, Natural Sciences

For professionals in the above fields who wish to apply their training to investigations of problems involving the use of the oceans. WHOI's objective is to provide a year-long advanced learning experience in ocean policy problems involving the interdisciplinary application of social science and natural science to marine policy problems. Fields currently emphasized: economics, statistics, public policy, natural resource management, and international relations.

For an application/more information, contact the Education Office, Clark Laboratory 223, MS #31, at above address.

3073 — WORLD BANK (Graduate Scholarship Program)

1818 H St., NW, Rm. M-4035
Washington DC 20433
Written inquiry

AMOUNT: Tuition + fees, allowance, travel, etc.

DEADLINE(S): FEB 1

FIELD(S): Social sciences, law, business, public administration

For nationals of World Bank member countries under the age of 40. Must have a superior academic record, at least two years' experience in public service engaged in development-related activities, and have gained admittance to a university to pursue a post-graduate degree. Must return to hom country after degree.

For two years.

3074 — WYOMING PEACE OFFICERS ASSOCIATION (WPOA Scholarships)

1556 Riverbend Dr.
Douglas WY 82633
307/358-3617
FAX: 307/358-9603

AMOUNT: $500/semester

DEADLINE(S): JUL 31

FIELD(S): All fields of study; Law Enforcement

Available to dependents of active (dues current), lifetime, or deceased WPOA members regardless of field of study or college attended, or students planning to enroll in a law enforcement program at a Wyoming college or university. Applicants must complete 12 semester credit hours and maintain at least a "C" average. Scholarship is awarded upon completion of each semester.

4 awards annually. Renewable up to four semesters. Contact Lucille Taylor at WPOA for an application.

POLITICAL SCIENCE

3075 — AMERICA ISRAEL PUBLIC AFFAIRS COMMITTEE (Internships)

440 First St., NW, Ste. 600
Washington DC 20001
202/639-5327
Internet: www.aipac.org

AMOUNT: Internship

DEADLINE(S): SEP 15; DEC 1; JAN 15; APR 1

FIELD(S): U.S.-Israel Issues

For highly qualified pro-Israel students for internships in national & regional offices working to strengthen the U.S.-Israel relationship. Interns are expected to return to campus to promote pro-Israel political activity. Cover letter stating interest, resume indicating political experience (student government, etc.) & involvement, one-page typewritten essay about involvement in pro-Israel work on campus, & letter of recommendation from AIPAC campus liaison required.

Contact Steve Bocknek at AIPAC for an application.

3076 — AMERICAN MUSEUM OF NATURAL HISTORY (International Graduate Student Fellowship Program)

Central Park West at 79th St.
New York NY 10024-5192
FAX: 212/769-5495
E-Mail: bynum@amnh.org
Internet: research.amnh.org

AMOUNT: Stipend, tuition, & travel

DEADLINE(S): JAN 15

FIELD(S): Biodiversity & Conservation; Public Policy; Entomology; Evolutionary & Molecular Biology

One-year joint program w/ Columbia, Cornell, & Yale Universities & City University of NY to help advance training of Ph.D. candidates who are non-US citizens. Purpose is to gain skills & experience to bear on environmental problems of their home countries. Must submit resume/curriculum vitae, GRE & TOEFL scores, official transcripts, letters of recommendation, & statement of purpose.

Renewable up to 4 years. Must apply to Museum AND cooperating university. See website or contact Office of Grants & Fellowships for application.

3077 — ARMENIAN GENERAL BENEVOLENT UNION (Educational Loan Program)

Education Dept., 31 W. 52nd St.
New York NY 10019-6118
212/765-8260
FAX: 212/765-8209
E-Mail: agbuny@aol.com

AMOUNT: $5,000 to $7,500/yr.

DEADLINE(S): APR 1

FIELD(S): Education Administration, International Relations/Foreign Affairs, Communication, Journalism, or Public Administration

Loans for full-time students of Armenian heritage pursuing master's degrees in one of the above fields. Must be attending highly competitive institutions in the U.S. GPA of 3.5 or more required.

Loan repayment period begins within 12 months of completion of full-time study and extends five to ten years, depending on the size of the loan. Interest is 3% Write for complete information.

3078 — ASSOCIATION FOR WOMEN IN SCIENCE EDUCATIONAL FOUNDATION (AWIS Predoctoral Awards)

1200 New York Ave. NW, Suite 650
Washington DC 20005
202/326-8940 or 800-886-AWIS
E-Mail: awis@awis.org
Internet: www.awis.org

AMOUNT: $1,000

DEADLINE(S): JAN 16

FIELD(S): Various Sciences and Social Sciences

Scholarships for female doctoral students. Summary page, description of research project, resume, references, transcripts, and biographical sketch required. US citizens may study at any graduate institution; non-citizens must study at US institutions.

5-10 awards annually. See website or write to above address for an application and complete information.

3079 — ASSOCIATION FOR WOMEN IN SCIENCE EDUCATIONAL FOUNDATION (AWIS Pre-doctoral Awards)

1200 New York Ave. NW, Suite 650
Washington DC 20005
202/326-8940 or 800-886-AWIS
E-Mail: awis@awis.org
Internet: www.awis.org

AMOUNT: $1,000

DEADLINE(S): JAN 16

FIELD(S): Various Sciences and Social Sciences

Scholarships for female doctoral students. Summary page, description of research project,
resume, references, transcripts, and biographical sketch required. US citizens may study at any graduate institution; non-citizens must be enrolled in US institutions.

5-10 awards annually. See website or write to above address for an application and more information.

3080 — ASSOCIATION FOR WOMEN IN SCIENCE EDUCATIONAL FOUNDATION (Ruth Satter Memorial Award)

1200 New York Ave., NW, Suite 650
Washington DC 20005
202/326-8940 or 800/886-AWIS
E-Mail: awis@awis.org
Internet: www.awis.org

AMOUNT: $1,000

DEADLINE(S): JAN 16

FIELD(S): Various Sciences and Social Sciences

Scholarships for female doctoral students who have interrupted their education for at least three years to raise a family. Summary page, description of research project, resume, references, transcripts, biographical sketch, and letter from your department to confirm eligibility required. US citizens may study at any graduate institution; non-citizens must attend US institutions.

See website or write to above address for more information or an application.

3081 — ASSOCIATION FOR WOMEN IN SCIENCE EDUCATIONAL FOUNDATION (Ruth Satter Memorial Award)

1200 New York Ave. NW, Suite 650
Washington DC 20005
202/326-8940 or 800/886-AWIS
E-Mail: awis@awis.org
Internet: www.awis.org

AMOUNT: $1,000

DEADLINE(S): JAN 16

FIELD(S): Various Sciences and Social Sciences

Scholarships for female doctoral students who have interupted their education three years or more to raise a family. Summary page, description of research project, resume, references, transcripts, biographical sketch, and proof of eligibility from department head required. US citizens may attend any graduate institution; non-citizens must be enrolled in US institutions.

See website or write to above address for more information or an application.

3082 — ASSOCIATION OF FORMER INTELLIGENCE OFFICERS/AFIO (Lt. Gen. Eugene F. Tighe, Jr., Memorial Scholarship)

1142 Miramonte Glen
Escondido CA 92026-1724
760/432-8844

AMOUNT: $1,000

DEADLINE(S): JAN 10

FIELD(S): Government, Political Science, Criminal Justice, and Law

Open to undergraduate and graduate students. Students must have a 3.0 GPA and be full-time students. For use at all four-year and grad schools in the U.S. and affiliated institutions overseas.

Send SASE to the above address for complete information. Note: LAST scholarship granted January 10, 2000.

3083 — ASSOCIATION TO UNITE THE DEMOCRATS (Mayme & Herb Frank Fund)

502 H Street, SW
Washington DC 20024-2726
202/544-5150
FAX: 202/544-3742
E-Mail: AtUnite@aol.com
Internet: www.iaud.org

AMOUNT: $500-$2,000

DEADLINE(S): APR 1; OCT 1

FIELD(S): Political Science

For graduate students with strong academic standing. Must have coursework that places major emphasis on international integration and federalism and write a thesis or dissertation or have independent project relating to international integration and federalism. Financial need is NOT considered.

10 awards annually. Renewable. Contact Capt. Tom Hudgens at above address for an application.

3084 — AUSTRALIAN FEDERATION OF UNIVERSITY WOMEN - WESTERN AUSTRALIA (Joyce Riley Bursary)

Bursary Liaison Officer
PO Box 48
Nedlands WA 6909 AUSTRALIA
Written Inquiry

AMOUNT: Aus$1,700 - Aus$2,750

DEADLINE(S): JUL 31

FIELD(S): Humanities; Social Sciences

To support women graduates of a Western Australian university to complete a higher degree or post-doctoral research in Humanities or Social Sciences at a recognized university in any country.

Membership in AFUW or in IFUW is required. Contact above location for further information.

3085 — AUSTRALIAN FEDERATION OF UNIVERSITY WOMEN - WESTERN AUSTRALIA (Joyce Riley Bursary)

Bursary Liaison Officer
PO Box 48
Nedlands WA 6009 AUSTRALIA
Written Inquiry

AMOUNT: Aus$1,700 - Aus$2,750

DEADLINE(S): JUL 31

FIELD(S): Humanities; Social Sciences

To support women graduates of a recognized university to complete a higher degree or post-doctoral research at a university in Western Australia.

Membership in AFUW or in IFUW is required. Write to above address for complete information.

3086 — BLAKEMORE FOUNDATION (Asian Language Fellowship Grants)

1201 Third Ave., 40th Fl.
Seattle WA 98101-3099
206/583-8778
FAX: 206/583-8500
E-Mail: blakemore@perkinscoie.com

AMOUNT: Tuition, transportation, basic living costs

DEADLINE(S): JAN 15

FIELD(S): Asian languages

Fellowships for advanced language study in Asia. For use at an instition selected by the applicant and approved by the Foundation. Applicant must be a graduate or professional school student, a teacher, a professional, or a business person; be working towards a specific career objective involving the regular use of an Asian language; be near an advanced level in that language; be a U.S. citizen or permanent resident. For full-time study during the term of the grant.

12-18 annual awards. For one year of study.

3087 — BOLOGNA CENTER OF THE JOHNS HOPKINS UNIVERSITY - PAUL H. NITZE SCHOOL OF ADVANCED INTERNATIONAL STUDIES (Fellowships for Non-Americans)

Admissions Office
Via Belmeloro 11
40126 Bologna ITALY
+39/51/232-185
FAX: +39/51/228-505
E-Mail: admission@jhubc.it
Internet: www.jhubc.it

AMOUNT: Partial to full tuition

DEADLINE(S): FEB 1

FIELD(S): European Studies; International Relations; International Economics

One year at SAIS Bologna Center is open to graduate students with some background in political science, economics, history, or law and who are interested in problems confronting Europe and/or international relations. Possibility to continue for the second year toward an M.A. at SAIS in Washington, DC. Program is conducted in English; therefore, English fluency is required. This program is for non-US citizens.

Contact Bologna Center for an application.

3088 — BOLOGNA CENTER OF THE JOHNS HOPKINS UNIVERSITY - PAUL H. NITZE SCHOOL OF ADVANCED INTERNATIONAL STUDIES (Fellowships for Americans)

SAIS
1740 Massachusetts Ave., NW
Washington DC 20036
E-Mail: admission@jhubc.it
Internet: www.jhubc.it

AMOUNT: Partial to full tuition

DEADLINE(S): JAN 15

FIELD(S): European Studies; International Relations; International Economics

One year at SAIS Bologna Center in Italy is open to graduate students with some background in political science, economics, history, or law and who are interested in problems confronting Europe and/or international relations. Must be US citizen/permanent resident. Courses are conducted in English.

Contact SAIS for an application.

3089 — BRITISH ASSOCIATION FOR AMERICAN STUDIES (Short-Term Awards)

Dr. Jenel Virden
University of Hull
Hull HU6 7RX ENGLAND UK
01482 465303

AMOUNT: 400 pounds sterling

DEADLINE(S): DEC 1

FIELD(S): American Studies; American History

Open to graduate/postgraduate British scholars for brief visits to the US for research in American history, politics, geography, culture, and literature. Preference given to younger scholars.

Contact Dr. Jenel Virden for an application.

3090 — BROOKING INSTITUTION (Research Fellowships)

1775 Massachusetts Ave., NW
Washington DC 20036-2188
202/797-6000

AMOUNT: $17,500 stipend

DEADLINE(S): DEC 15

FIELD(S): Foreign Policy; Government; Economics

Open to Ph.D candidates nominated by their graduate departments. Applications from individuals not nominated cannot be accepted. Awards support research by Ph.D candidates who have completed all coursework except for the dissertation.

9 awards annually. Nomination forms may be obtained by your department head or from the address above.

3091 — CANADIAN BUREAU FOR INTERNATIONAL EDUCATION (Canadian International Development Agency Awards Program for Canadians)

220 Laurier Ave., W., Ste. 1100
Ottawa Ontario K1P 5Z9 CANADA
613/237-4820
FAX: 613/237-1073
E-Mail: smelanson@cbie.ca
Internet: www.cbie.ca

AMOUNT: $10,000/yr. Canadian (max.)

DEADLINE(S): FEB 1

FIELD(S): International Relations/Development; Business

For Canadian citizens/permanent residents seeking to participate in international development through a volunteer project of their own initiative. The development activity may be the fieldwork component of a master's degree program or a professional work/research project. Ph.D. candidates are NOT eligible. Also offers internships to master's students in business, administration, and management programs. Awards tenable up to twelve months and are taxable.

50 awards annually. Contact CBIE for an application.

3092 — CANADIAN BUREAU FOR INTERNATIONAL EDUCATION (Celanese Canada Internationalist Council Fellowships)

220 Laurier Ave., W., Ste. 1100
Ottawa Ontario K1P 5Z9 CANADA
613/237-4820
FAX: 613/237-1073
E-Mail: smelanson@cbie.ca
Internet: www.cbie.ca

AMOUNT: $10,000 Canadian

DEADLINE(S): MAR 1

FIELD(S): International Relations

Open to university graduates from all disciplines of study. For Canadians who hold at least one university degree or are in the final year of a degree program. The latest degree must normally have been awarded no longer than five years from the date of application. For study, research, and/or work outside Canada. May include more than one location.

125-150 awards annually. Contact CBIE for an application.

3093 — CHRISTIAN A. JOHNSON ENDEAVOR FOUNDATION (Native American Fellows)

Harvard Univ., 79 John F. Kennedy St.
Cambridge MA 02138
617/495-1152
FAX: 617/496-3900
Internet: www.ksg.harvard.edu/hpaied/cjohn.htm

AMOUNT: Varies

DEADLINE(S): MAY 1

FIELD(S): Social sciences, government, or program related to Native American studies

Fellowships for students of Native American ancestry who attend a John F. Kennedy School of Government degree program. Applicant, parent, or grandparent must hold membership in a federally or state-recognized tribe, band, or other organized group of Native Americans. Must be commited to a career in American Indian affairs. Awards based on merit and need.

Renewable, based on renomination and availability of funds. To apply, contact John F. Kennedy School of Government at above address.

3094 — CONFERENCE OF MINORITY PUBLIC ADMINISTRATORS (Scholarships and Travel Grants)

P.O. Box 3010
Fort Worth TX 76113
817/871-8325
Internet: www.compa.org

AMOUNT: $400 (travel grants); up to $1,500 (academic year)

DEADLINE(S): Varies

FIELD(S): Public administration/public affairs

COMPA offers two academic scholarships, at least five travel grants, and a $1,000 gift to the college that has the largest number of stdent registrants at its annual conference. Travel grants are for attending the conference. For minorities and women pursuing full-time education in the above fields and committed to excellence in public service and administration in city, county, state, and federal governments.

Contact Edwin Cook at above location for details.

3095 — CONGRESSIONAL HISPANIC CAUCUS INSTITUTE, INC. (CHCI Fellowship Program)

504 C St., NE
Washington DC 20002
800/EXCEL-DC or 202/543-1771
E-Mail: comments@chci.org
Internet: www.chci.org

AMOUNT: Monthly stipend, round-trip transportation, & health insurance

DEADLINE(S): MAR 1

FIELD(S): Public Policy; Public Health; Telecommunications; Business

Paid work experience is open to Hispanics who have graduated from a college/university (with BA/BS/graduate degree) within one year of application deadline, and to currently enrolled graduate students. Must have high academic achievement (minimum 3.0 GPA), superior analytical/communication skills, leadership potential, and consistent active participation in activities for the common good. Must be US citizen/permanent resident or have student work visa.

16 awards annually. See website or contact CHCI for an application.

3096 — COUNCIL FOR EUROPEAN STUDIES (Predissertation Fellowships)

Columbia Univ
807-807A International Affairs Bldg.
New York NY 10027
212/854-4172
FAX: 212/854-8808
E-Mail: ces@columbia.edu
Internet: www.europanet.org

AMOUNT: $4,000 stipend (max.)

DEADLINE(S): FEB 1

FIELD(S): Cultural Anthropology; History (post 1750); Political Science; Sociology; Geography; Urban & Regional Planning

Awards are for research in France to determine viability of projected doctoral dissertation in modern history and social sciences. Recipients test research design of dissertation, determine availability of archival materials, and contact French scholars. Must be US citizen or permanent resident at a US institution and have completed at least two but no more than three years of full-time doctoral study by end of year. Institutional membership in Council is required.

6 awards annually. See website or contact Council for an application.

3097 — CUBAN AMERICAN NATIONAL FOUNDATION (The Mas Family Scholarships)

7300 NW 35 Terrace
Miami FL 33122
305/592-7768
FAX: 305/592-7889
E-Mail canfnet.org
Internet: www.canfnet.org

AMOUNT: Individually negotiated

DEADLINE(S): MAR 15

FIELD(S): Engineering, Business, International Relations, Economics, Communications, Journalism

For Cuban-Americans students, graduates and undergraduates, born in Cuba or direct descendants of those who left Cuba. Must be in top 10% of high school class or maintain a 3.5 GPA in college.

10,000 awards/year. Recipients may re-apply for subsequent years. Financial need considered along with academic success, SAT and GRE scores, and leadership potential. Essays and proof of Cuban descent required.

3098 — DIRKSEN CONGRESSIONAL CENTER (Congressional Research Grants Program)

301 S. 4th St., Suite A
Pekin IL 61554
309/347-7113
FAX 309/347-6432
E-Mail: fmackaman@pekin.net

AMOUNT: $3,000

DEADLINE(S): MAR 31 (postmark)

FIELD(S): Political Science, American History (with emphasis on U.S. Congress or Congressional Leadership)

For persons already holding a B.A. degree with a serious interest in studying the U.S. Congress. Research must be original culminating in new knowledge or new interpretation or both. Political scientists, historians, biographers, journalists, and others may apply.

Contact Frank H. Mackaman at above address for details.

3099 — EPILEPSY FOUNDATION OF AMERICA (Behavioral Sciences Research Training Fellowships)

4351 Garden City Drive
Landover MD 20785-2267
301/459-3700 or FAX: 301/577-2684
FDD: 800/332-2070
E-Mail: postmaster@efa.org
Internet: www.efa.org

AMOUNT: Up to $30,000

DEADLINE(S): FEB 1

FIELD(S): Epilepsy as related to Behavioral Sciences (includes sociology, social work, psychology, anthropology, nursing, political science, etc.)

A one-year training experience for postdoctoral scholars to develop expertise in the area of epilepsy research relative to the behavioral sciences. The project must be carried out at an approved facility. Amount depends on experience and qualifications of the applicant and the scope and duration of proposed project.

Contact EFA for an application.

3100 — EUROPEAN UNIVERSITY INSTITUTE (Jean Monnet Fellowship)

Via Dei Roccettini 9
I-50016 San Domenico Di Fiesole (FL) Italy
0039-055-46851
FAX: 0039-055-4685444
E-Mail: applyjmf@datacomm.iue.it
Internet: www.iue.it/JMF/Welcome.html

AMOUNT: 2,000,000-3,500,000 Italian lire per month (i.e. 1,025-1,750 ECU) + medical & family allowances (depends on whether fellow is in receipt of payment from another source and on extent of duties carried out at the Institute)

DEADLINE(S): NOV 1

FIELD(S): Europe: History, Society, Politics, Economics, Law

Post-doctoral fellowships. Fellows are required to make scholarly contribution to research on Europe within one of EUI's research projects or on topic, falling within general interests of the Institute. Publication of research is expected.

25 fellowships annually. Financial need NOT considered. See website or contact Dr. Andreas Frijdal at above address for complete information.

3101 — EUROPEAN UNIVERSITY INSTITUTE (National Postgraduate Scholarships)

Via De Roccettini 9
San Domenico Di Fiesole (FI 50016) ITALY
0039/055-46851
FAX: 0039/055-4685444
E-Mail: applyres@datacomm.iue.it
Internet: www.iue.it

AMOUNT: $1,000/month + travel & medical/family allowances

DEADLINE(S): JAN 31

FIELD(S): Political Science; Social Sciences; Law; Economics; History

Open to graduate & postgraduate students at the Institute who have good honors and a research project having European dimension. Awards are available only to nationals of the Institute's member states. US citizens must have sufficient personal funds or another grant to cover maintenance & tuition; may apply to Fulbright Commission which may award up to two grants per academic year to US citizens with tuition-fee waivers.

130 awards annually. Renewable. Contact Dr. Andreas Frijdal for an application.

3102 — FLETCHER SCHOOL OF LAW AND DIPLOMACY (Scholarships)

Tufts University
Medford MA 02155
617/627-3040

AMOUNT: $2,000-$30,000

DEADLINE(S): JAN 15

FIELD(S): International Relations

Scholarships open to applicants who are accepted/enrolled as full-time graduate students at the Fletcher School of Law and Diplomacy at Tufts University.

120 scholarships per year. Renewable. Write for complete information.

3103 — FORD FOUNDATION/NATIONAL RESEARCH COUNCIL (Predoctoral/ Dissertation Fellowships for Minorities)

2101 Constitution Ave.
Washington DC 20418
202/334-2872
E-Mail: infofell@nas.edu
Internet: http//www.nas.edu/fo/index.html

AMOUNT: $14,000 annual stipend + $6,000 grant to institution; $18,000 for dissertation fellowship

DEADLINE(S): NOV 3

FIELD(S): Most fields of study: sciences, humanities, engineering, behavioral science, social sciences, and computer science

Predoctoral and dissertation fellowships for students whose ethnicity is Alaskan Native, Black/African American, Mexican American/Chicano, Native American Indian, Native Pacific Islander, or Puerto Rican. For research-based programs leading to careers in college teaching and research.

Contact above address or website.

3104 — FRENCH-AMERICAN FOUNDATION (Bicentennial Fellowships)

41 East 72nd St.
New York NY 10021
212/288-4000
FAX: 212/288-4765
E-Mail: French_AmerFdn@msn.com

AMOUNT: 10,000 French francs/mo.

DEADLINE(S): FEB 2

FIELD(S): Social sciences

For doctoral students in the social sciences to travel to France for one year to conduct research essential to the completion of their dissertations. Must have completed all other requirements for Ph.D. May not use the award until exams are passed.

Requires application with a statement of purpose, full academic records, plan of research, bibliography, abstract, and three academic recommendations.

3105 — GENERAL FEDERATION OF WOMEN'S CLUBS OF MASSACHUSETTS (International Affairs Scholarships)

245 Dutton Road, Box 679
Sudbury MA 01776-0679
508/481-3354

AMOUNT: $500

DEADLINE(S): MAR 1

FIELD(S): International affairs; International relations

For undergraduate and/or graduate study abroad for legal residents of Massachusetts. Letter of endorsement from sponsoring GFWC of MA club, personal statement of "what I hope to gain from this experience", letter of reference from department head of your major, transcripts, and personal interview required with application.

For further information or an application, send self-addressed, stamped envelope to Sheila E. Shea, Counselor, International Affairs Department, at above address.

3106 — GERMAN MARSHALL FUND OF THE UNITED STATES (Research Support Program)

11 Dupont Circle, NW, Ste. 750
Washington DC 20036
202/745-3950
FAX: 202/265-1662
E-Mail: info@gmfus.org
Internet: www.gmfus.org

AMOUNT: $3,000 (max. predissertation); $20,000 (max. dissertation); $40,000 (max. advanced research)

DEADLINE(S): NOV 15

FIELD(S): European Studies; US-European Issues

For US citizens/permanent residents who are graduate students or more senior scholars to improve understanding of economic, political, & social developments relating to Europe, European integration, & US-Europe relations. Criteria include achievements; quality, importance, & originality of proposed research; disciplinary and/or policy relevance of project & expanded results, need for support, & likelihood of completion. Funds may be used towards European travel costs.

See website or contact GMFUS for an application.

3107 — GERMAN MARSHALL FUND OF THE UNITED STATES (Italian Marshall Fellowship Program)

11 Dupont Circle, NW, Ste. 750
Washington DC 20036
202/745-3950
FAX: 202/265-1662
E-Mail: info@gmfus.org
Internet: www.gmfus.org

AMOUNT: 18,000 Euro max./semester + 1,000 Euro max. for travel, etc.

DEADLINE(S): NOV 15

FIELD(S): Italian Studies; US-Italian Issues

For US citizens/permanent residents who are advanced scholars (postdoc.) seeking to improve the understanding of international role of Italy, particularly in field of US-European relations. Applicants are expected to reside at an Italian institution in order to carry out full-time research. Criteria include scholarly qualifications; acheivements & promise; quality, originality, & importance of proposed research; contemporary relevance; and likelihood of completion.

See website or contact GMFUS for an application.

3108 — GERMANISTIC SOCIETY OF AMERICA (Foreign Study Scholarships)

809 United Nations Plaza
New York NY 10017-3580
212/984-5330

AMOUNT: $11,000

DEADLINE(S): OCT 23

FIELD(S): History; Political Science; International Relations; Public Affairs; Language; Philosophy; Literature

Open to US citizens who hold a bachelor's degree. Must plan to pursue graduate study at a West German university. Selection based on proposed project, language fluency, academic achievement, and references.

Contact Germanistic Society for an application.

3109 — GLADYS KRIEBLE DELMAS FOUNDATION (Predoctoral & Postdoctoral Grants in Venice & the Veneto)

521 5th Avenue, Suite 1612
New York NY 10175-1699
212/687-0011
FAX: 212/687-8877
E-Mail: DelmasFdtn@aol.com
Internet: www.delmas.org

AMOUNT: $500-$12,500

DEADLINE(S): DEC 15

FIELD(S): Research of Venice and the former Venetian empire and study of contemporary Venetian society and culture.

Pre- and postdoctoral grants for historical research on Venice. Humanities and social sciences are eligible areas of study, including archaeology, architecture, art, bibliography, economics, history, history of science, law, literature, music, political science, religion, and theater.

Applicants must have experience in advanced research and be U.S. citizens/residents; grad students

must have fulfilled all doctoral requirements except dissertation by Dec. 15.

3110 — GRADUATE INSTITUTE OF INTERNATIONAL STUDIES (Scholarships)

P.O. Box 36
132 Rue do Lausanne
CH-1211 Geneva 21 SWITZERLAND
(+41 22) 731 17 30
FAX: (+41-22) 731 27 77
E-Mail: info@hei.unige.ch
Internet: http://heiwww.unige.ch

AMOUNT: Varies

DEADLINE(S): None

FIELD(S): International history and politics, political science, international economics, international law

Scholarships to support graduate diploma and Ph.D students already registered at the Institute. Open to applicants with excellent, active knowledge of one of the institute's two working languages, French & English, and sufficient passive knowledge of the other.

Contact above sources for complete information.

3111 — HILLEL INTERNATIONAL CENTER (The Bittker Fellowship)

Eran Gasko
1640 Rhode Island Ave. NW
Washington DC 20036
202/857-6637
202/857-6560
FAX: 202/857-6693
E-Mail: smusher@hillel.org
Internet: www.hillel.org/careermoves/bittker.htm

AMOUNT: Professional Experience

DEADLINE(S): None specified

FIELD(S): Student Leadership/Jewish Awareness

One-year professional experience for an oustanding recent graduate, who coordinates student leadership and Jewish awareness activities nationwide. The Fellow establishes the network of student leaders and enhances their communication through national publications, conference calls, and the Internet. Task forces include Jewish Awareness/Identity, Women's Issues, Graduate Student Life, and Education.

Contact Eran Gasko, Human Resources, for an application.

3112 — HILLEL INTERNATIONAL CENTER (The Public Policy Fellowship)

Eran Gasko
1640 Rhode Island Ave. NW
Washington DC 20036
202/857-6543

202/857-6560
FAX: 202/857-6693
E-Mail: smusher@hillel.org
Internet: www.hillel.org/careermoves/publicpolicy.htm

AMOUNT: Professional Experience

DEADLINE(S): None specified

FIELD(S): Public Policy/Social Issues

One-year professional experience for an oustanding recent Jewish graduate, who coordinates public policy initiatives nationwide. The Fellow strives to increase student activism in political and social issues. S/he works with students and national organizations to create innovative initiatives in social action, campus community relations councils, environmental issues, Israel programming, and international relief efforts.

Contact Eran Gasko, Human Resources, for an application.

3113 — INSTITUTE FOR HUMANE STUDIES (Humane Studies Fellowship)

4084 University Dr., Ste. 101
Fairfax VA 22030-6812
703/934-6920 or 800/697-8799
FAX: 703/352-7535
E-Mail: ihs@gmu.edu
Internet: www.theihs.org

AMOUNT: up to $12,000

DEADLINE(S): DEC 31

FIELD(S): Social Sciences; Law; Humanities; Jurisprudence; Journalism

Awards are for graduate and advanced undergraduate students pursuing degrees at any accredited domestic or foreign school. Based on academic performance, demonstrated interest in classical liberal ideas, and potential to contribute to the advancement of a free society.

90 awards annually. Apply online or contact IHS for an application.

3114 — INSTITUTE FOR HUMANE STUDIES (Koch Summer Fellow Program)

4084 University Dr., Ste. 101
Fairfax VA 22030-6812
703/934-6920 or 800/697-8799
FAX: 703/352-7535
E-Mail: ihs@gmu.edu
Internet: www.theihs.org

AMOUNT: $1,500 + airfare & housing

DEADLINE(S): MAR 1

FIELD(S): Economics; Politics; Law; Government; Public Policy

For undergraduates and graduates to build skills and gain experience by participating in an 8-week summer internship program. Includes 2 week-long seminars, the internship, and research & writing projects with professionals. College transcripts, essays, and application required. Financial need NOT a factor.

32 awards annually. Not renewable. Apply online or contact IHS for an application.

3115 — INSTITUTE FOR HUMANE STUDIES (Summer Residential Program)

4084 University Dr., Ste. 101
Fairfax VA 22030-6812
703/934-6920 or 800/697-8799
FAX: 703/352-7535
E-Mail: ihs@gmu.edu
Internet: www.theihs.org

AMOUNT: All seminar fees: program cost, room/board, materials, and books

DEADLINE(S): MAR 1

FIELD(S): Social Sciences; Humanities; Law; Journalism; Public Policy; Education; Writing

For college students, recent graduates, and graduate students who share an interest in learning and exchanging ideas about the scope of individual rights. One-week and weekend seminars at various campus locations across the U.S.

Apply online or contact IHS for an application.

3116 — INSTITUTE FOR THE STUDY OF WORLD POLITICS (Dissertation Fellowships)

1755 Massachusetts Ave. NW
Washington DC 20036
202/588-9797
Internet: fundforpeace.org/iswp.htm

AMOUNT: Varies

DEADLINE(S): FEB 16

FIELD(S): International Relations; Environmental Issues; Population Studies (Social Science aspects); Human Rights; Arms Control; Third World Development; Agricultural Development; Public Health, etc.

For doctoral candidates conducting dissertation research in above areas to promote scholarly examination of political, economic, and social issues that affect the security, well-being, and dignity of the peoples of the world. Financial need is a consideration. For citizens of any country.

Write for complete information.

3117 — INSTITUTE FOR THE STUDY OF WORLD POLITICS (Dorothy Danforth Compton Fellowships)

1755 Massachusetts Ave. NW
Washington DC 20036
202/588-9797
Internet: fundforpeace.org/iswp.htm

AMOUNT: Varies

DEADLINE(S): MAR 16

FIELD(S): International Relations; Environmental Issues; Population Studies (Social Science aspects); Human Rights; Arms Control; Third World Development; Agricultural Development; Public Health, etc.

For masters or doctoral candidates researching in the above areas to promote scholarly examination of political, economic, and social issues that affect the security, well-being, and dignity of the peoples of the world. Must be African American, Hispanic American, and Native American students who are U.S. citizens and studying in U.S. institutions. Financial need is a consideration.

Write for complete information.

3118 — INTER-AMERICAN FOUNDATION (Field Research Fellowship Programs for U.S. , Latin American, and Caribbean Citizens)

901 N. Stuart St., 10th Floor
Arlington VA 22203
703/841-3800
FAX: 703/527-3529
E-Mail: correo@aif.gov
Internet: www.iaf.gov

AMOUNT: Varies

DEADLINE(S): APR 28

FIELD(S): International Relations, Social Sciences, Humanities, Latin American Studies

Fellowships for Latin American, Carribean, and U.S. doctoral level students for field research in Latin America and the Caribbean. Must be enrolled in U.S. university.

Access website for deadline and application information. Organization does not mail information.

3119 — INTER-AMERICAN FOUNDATION (Master's Research Fellowships)

901 N. Stuart St., 10th Floor
Arlington VA 22203
703/841-3800
FAX: 703/527-3529
E-Mail: correo@aif.gov
Internet: www.iaf.gov

AMOUNT: Varies

DEADLINE(S): APR

FIELD(S): Latin American & Caribbean Studies, Internations Relations, Social Sciences, Humanities, etc.

Open to masters students enrolled in U.S. universities for field research in Latin American or the Caribbean. For citizens of Caribbean and Latin American independent countries, and the U.S.

Access website for deadline and application information. Organization does not mail information.

3120 — INTERNATIONAL RESEARCH AND EXCHANGES BOARD (Russian-US Young Leadership Fellows for Public Service Program for Russian Citizens)

1616 H St., NW
Washington DC 20006
202/628-8188
FAX: 202/628-8189
E-Mail: irex@info.irex.org
Internet: www.irex.org

AMOUNT: Stipend + tuition, travel, living & housing

DEADLINE(S): NOV 30

FIELD(S): Community, Governmental, & Corporate Affairs; Policy Research & Development; Humanities

Grants of two to twelve months are available to graduate students who are Russian citizens/permanent residents for brief visits to pursue scholarly projects on Central & Eastern Europe, Eurasia, or Mongolia. Must have equivalent of bachelor's degree and be below the age of 30 at time of application. Postdoctoral humanities scholars may pursue research in Turkey or Iran. Financial need NOT a factor.

45 awards annually. Not renewable. Contact Jessica Jeffcoat, Senior Program Officer, for an application.

3121 — JAMES MADISON MEMORIAL FELLOWSHIP (Fellowship for Teachers)

2000 K St. NW
Washington DC 20006
202/653-8700 or 1-800/525-6928
FAX: 202/653-6045
Internet: www.jamesmadison.com

AMOUNT: $24,000 prorated over study period

DEADLINE(S): MAR 1

FIELD(S): Teaching American History/government, or social studies—concentration on the U.S. Constitution

Fellowships for teachers (senior fellows) in grades 7-12 in the above fields to pursue an MA degree. Also for full-time college seniors and grad students (junior fellows). U.S. citizens or U.S. nationals. Fellows are selected from each state and from D.C., Puerto Rico, Guam, Virgin Islands, American Samoa, Northern Mariana Islands, and Palau. Program designed to enhance teaching about the U.S. Constitution.

Application is on website or contact: American College Testing, P.O. Box 4030, Iowa City, IA 52243-4030; 800/525-6928; E-mail: Recogprog@ACT-ACT4-PO.act.org

3122 — JOHN F. KENNEDY LIBRARY FOUNDATION (Abba P. Schwartz Research Fellowship)

Columbia Point
Boston MA 02125-3313
617/929-4534 or 617/929-4533
FAX: 617/929-4599

AMOUNT: Up to $3,100

DEADLINE(S): MAR 15

FIELD(S): Immigration, naturalization, or refugee policies

To support a scholar while he/she researches in the fields listed above.

Contact William Johnson, Chief Archivist, at above location for application information.

3123 — JOHN F. KENNEDY LIBRARY FOUNDATION (Kennedy Research Grants)

Columbia Point
Boston MA 02125-3313
617/929-4534 or 617/929-4533
FAX: 617/929-4599

AMOUNT: $500-$1,000

DEADLINE(S): MAR 15

FIELD(S): History/Political Science: Kennedy presidential period

To support a scholar while he/she researches in the fields listed above.

Contact William Johnson, Chief Archivist, at above location for application information.

3124 — JOHN F. KENNEDY LIBRARY FOUNDATION (Marjorie Kovler Research Fellowship)

Columbia Point
Boston MA 02125-3313
617/929-4534 or 617/929-4533
FAX: 617/929-4599

AMOUNT: $2,500

DEADLINE(S): MAR 15

FIELD(S): History, Law Political Science-specializing in foreign intelligence and the presidency or a related topic.

To support a scholar while he/she researches in the fields listed above.

Contact William Johnson, Chief Archivist, at above location for application information.

3125 — JOHN F. KENNEDY LIBRARY FOUNDATION (Theodore C. Sorensen Research Fellowship)

Columbia Point
Boston MA 02125-3313

617/929-4534 or 617/929-4533
FAX: 617/929-4599

AMOUNT: $3,600

DEADLINE(S): MAR 15

FIELD(S): Domestic policy, political journalism, polling, or press relations

To support a scholar while he/she researches in the fields listed above.

Contact William Johnson, Chief Archivist, at above location for application information.

3126 — KANSAS BOARD OF REGENTS (James B. Pearson Fellowship)

700 SW Harrison St., Ste. 1410
Topeka KS 66603-3760
785/296-3517

AMOUNT: $1,000-$8,000

DEADLINE(S): APR 1

FIELD(S): Foreign Affairs

Fellowships to encourage Kansas residents who are graduate students from Kansas public universities to experience the global perspective gained from study abroad. Preference is given to applicants whose studies are directly related to foreign affairs.

Contact Kansas Board of Regents or your graduate school office for an application.

3127 — LONDON SCHOOL OF ECONOMICS AND POLITICAL SCIENCE (Scholarships)

Scholarships Office
Houghton St.
London WC2A 2AE ENGLAND UK
+44 (0) 171 955 7162/7155
FAX: +44 (0) 171 831 1684
E-Mail: scholarships@lse.ac.uk
Internet: www.lse.ac.uk/index/EDUCATE/
CONTACTS.HTM or www.lse.ac.uk/index/
restore/GRADUATE/Financial/text/funding.htm
or www.britcoun.org/eis/profiles/lse/
lseschp.htm

AMOUNT: Varies with award

DEADLINE(S): Varies

FIELD(S): Economics; Accounting; Finance; Political Science; International Relations

Various scholarships, awards, and prizes are available to international students. Several are for students from specific countries, and some are limited to certain fields of study. Some include all expenses, and others pay partial expenses. For undergraduates and graduate students.

Accessing LSE's website and using their "search" option, write in "scholarships," and a vast array of programs will appear.

3128 — MINISTRY OF THE FLEMISH COMMUNITY (Fellowships)

Embassy of Belgium
3330 Garfield St., NW
Washington DC 20008
202/625-5850/51
FAX: 202/342-8346
E-Mail: flemishcomdc@wizard.net

AMOUNT: Monthly stipend, tuition, & health care coverage

DEADLINE(S): JAN 31

FIELD(S): Art; Music; Humanities; Social Science; Political Science; Law; Economics; Science; Medicine

Open to US citizens under age 35 who wish to pursue graduate or postgraduate studies in Flanders, Belgium.

Contact Flemish Community for registration forms.

3129 — MISSISSIPPI OFFICE OF STATE STUDENT FINANCIAL AID (Public Management Graduate Internship Program)

3825 Ridgewood Road
Jackson MS 39211-6453
601/982-6663
1-800-327-2980

AMOUNT: $1,000/month (up to 8 months)

DEADLINE(S): Varies (Established by program coordinator)

FIELD(S): Criminal Justice; Public Administration; Public Policy

For students pursuing a graduate degree in criminal Justice, Public Administration, or Public Policy, this program provides the opportunity to have practical experience working for state or local agencies and offices, including the state legislature. The intern works a semester with the state or local agency. For U.S. residents or eligible non-citizens who possess an alien registration card and who are enrolled at certain universities in Mississippi.

Must have earned a "B" or higher grade in one Quantitative Research Methods course.

3130 — NEW YORK CITY DEPT. CITYWIDE ADMINISTRATIVE SERVICES (Urban Fellows Program)

1 Centre St., 24th Fl.
New York NY 10007
212/487-5600
FAX: 212/487-5720

AMOUNT: $18,000 stipend

DEADLINE(S): JAN 20

FIELD(S): Public Administration; Urban Planning; Government; Public Service; Urban Affairs

Fellowship program provides one academic year (9 months) of full-time work experience in urban government. Open to graduating college seniors and recent college graduates. U.S. citizenship required.

Write for complete information.

3131 — NEW YORK STATE SENATE (Legislative Fellows Program; R. J. Roth Journalism Fellowship; R. A. Wiebe Public Service Fellowship)

NYS Senate Student Programs Office, 90 South Swan St., Rm. 401
Albany NY 12247
518/455-2611
FAX: 518/432-5470
E-Mail: students@senate.state.ny.us

AMOUNT: $25,000 stipend (not a scholarship)

DEADLINE(S): MAY (first Friday)

FIELD(S): Political Science; Government; Public Service; Journalism; Public Relations

One year programs for U.S. citizens who are grad students and residents of New York state or enrolled in accredited programs in New York state. Fellows work as regular legislative staff members of the office to which they are assigned. The Roth Fellowship is for communications/journalism majors, and undergrads may be considered for this program.

14 fellowships per year. Fellowships take place at the New York State Legislative Office. Write for complete information.

3132 — OAK RIDGE ASSOCIATED UNIVERSITIES (Laboratory Graduate Research Participation Program)

P.O. Box 117
Oak Ridge TN 37831-0117
423/576-4813

AMOUNT: $1,000-$1,200/mo. + allowance for dependents + tuition and fees reimbursement to a max. of $3,500/yr.

DEADLINE(S): Ongoing

FIELD(S): Life sciences, physical, and social sciences, mathematics, and engineering

For graduate students in one of the fields listed above who have completed all degree requirements except thesis or dissertation research. For full-time research under the joint direction of the major professor and a DOE staff member at one of various locations, primarily in the South. For six to twelve months.

Funded through U.S. Dept. of Energy, Office of Energy Reseach, and Office of Fossil Energy. Write for complete information.

3133 — OPEN SOCIETY INSTITUTE (Individual Project Fellowships)

400 West 59th St.
New York NY 10019
212/548-0600 or 212/757-2323
FAX: 212/548-4679 or 212/548-4600
Internet: www.soros.org/fellow/individual.html

AMOUNT: Varies

DEADLINE(S): Varies

FIELD(S): Any field of study related to creating an open society: reliance on the rule of law, the existence of a democratically elected government, a diverse and vigorous civil society, and respect for minorities and minority opinions.

Two-year fellowships for use in selected universities in the U.S. for international students. For students/professionals in fields related to environmental policy, legislation, and remediation techniques applicable to their home countries.

To apply, contact the Soros Foundation/Open Society Institute. Further details on website.

3134 — PARLIAMENT OF AUSTRALIA (Australian Parliamentary Fellowship in Association with Australasian Political Science Assn.)

Information and Research Service
Parliament House
Canberra ACT 2600 AUSTRALIA
61 02 6277 2772
FAX: 61 02 6277 2528
E-Mail: Kate.Matthews@aph.gov.au
Internet: www.aph.gov.au/library/

AMOUNT: Aus. $41,430

DEADLINE(S): SEP

FIELD(S): Australian Parliament/Austral-Asian Political Studies

Post-graduate fellowships to conduct research on the Parliament, its performance, and how its members deal with issues. Fellows are also expected to be available to members of the Parliament interested in their field of expertise.

Write for complete information.

3135 — PEACE RESEARCH CENTRE (Peace Research Loan Scholarship)

c/o Gujarat Vidyapith
Ahmedabad-380014 INDIA
7450746

AMOUNT: 2,000/Rs (25% returnable)

DEADLINE(S): JUNE

FIELD(S): Peace Research, Peace Education, Nonviolence

Financial aid for students between the ages of 21 and 65 in a Master of Arts program concentrating on research regarding peace, peace education, and nonviolence.

Duration of one year only.

3136 — PRESIDENT'S COMMISSION ON WHITE HOUSE FELLOWSHIPS

712 Jackson Place NW
Washington DC 20503
202/395-4522
FAX: 202/395-6179
E-Mail: almanac@ace.esusda.gov

AMOUNT: Wage (up to GS-14 Step 3; approximately $65,000 in 1995)

DEADLINE(S): DEC 1

FIELD(S): Public Service; Government; Community Involvement; Leadership

Mid-career professionals spend one year as special assistants to senior executive branch officials in Washington. Highly competitive. Non-partisan; no age or educational requirements. Fellowship year runs September 1 through August 31.

1,200 candidates applying for 11 to 19 fellowships each year. Write for complete information.

3137 — RADIO FREE EUROPE/RADIO LIBERTY (Intern Program for Journalists)

1201 Connecticut Ave.
Washington DC 20036
Written inquiry
FAX: 202/457-6992
E-Mail: goblep@rferl.org
Internet: www.rferl.org/welcome/intern.html

AMOUNT: Varies

DEADLINE(S): Varies

FIELD(S): Broadcast journalism, political science, international relations

For journalists early in their careers from Central and eastern Europe and the successor states to the Soviet Union. Also for western journalists. Interns will receive technical, academic, and on-the-job training. Up to 40 interns will participate in four-week programs offered in English and Russian at RFE/RL's broadcast center in Prague.

Visit website for details. Western journalists contact above location; European journalists contact RFE/RL, Vinohradska 1, 110 00 Prague 1, Czech Republic. Phone: (011 4202) 2112 3325.

3138 — SOCIAL SCIENCE RESEARCH COUNCIL (Abe Fellowship Program)

810 Seventh Ave., 31st Fl.
New York NY 10019
212/377-2700
FAX: 212/377-2727

E-Mail: ranis@ssrc.org

Internet: www.ssrc.org

AMOUNT: Varies

DEADLINE(S): SEP 1

FIELD(S): International Relations & Policy

Open to citizens of the US and Japan as well as other nationals who can demonstrate strong and serious long-term affiliations in the research communities of either US or Japan. Fellowships support postdoctoral research on contemporary policy-relevant issues and provides up to 12 months of full-time support. Candidates should spend at least one-third of tenure in residence abroad in Japan or the US. Previous language training not required unless project deems necessary.

See website or contact SSRC for an application.

3139 — SOCIAL SCIENCE RESEARCH COUNCIL (International Predissertation Fellowship Program)

810 Seventh Ave.

New York NY 10019

212/277-2700

AMOUNT: Varies

DEADLINE(S): Varies (TBA by participating universities)

FIELD(S): Economics; Political Science; Psychology; Sociology; other Social Science disciplines

Open to Ph.D. candidates enrolled in social science programs at 23 select universities and interested in supplementing disciplinary skills with area and language studies or acquiring advanced disciplinary training. Study program is preparation for research on Africa, Central Asia & the Caucasus, China, Latin America, the Caribbean, Near & Middle East, and South or Southeast Asia.

Contact Ellen Perecman for an application.

3140 — SOCIETY FOR THE PSYCHOLOGICAL STUDY OF SOCIAL ISSUES (Otto Klineburg Intercultural and International Relations Award)

PO Box 1248

Ann Arbor MI 48106-1248

Phone/TTY: 313/662-9130

FAX: 313/662-5607

E-Mail: spssi@spssi.org

Internet: www.spssi.org

AMOUNT: $1,000

DEADLINE(S): FEB 1

FIELD(S): Intercultural & International Relations

Annual award for the best paper or article on intercultural or international relations. Originality of the contribution, whether theoretical or empirical, will be given special weight. Entries can be either papers published during the current year or unpublished manuscripts. Send five copies of entry.

Contact SPSSI for details. Applications available on website. SPSSI DOES NOT OFFER SCHOLARSHIPS—INQUIRIES FOR FINANCIAL AID WILL NOT BE ANSWERED.

3141 — SOCIETY FOR THE PSYCHOLOGICAL STUDY OF SOCIAL ISSUES (James Marshall Public Policy Fellowship)

PO Box 1248

Ann Arbor MI 48106-1248

313/662-9130

FAX: 313/662-5607

E-Mail: spssi@umich.edu

Internet: www.spssi.org

AMOUNT: $42,000 + health/vacation benefits

DEADLINE(S): JAN 10

FIELD(S): Public Policy, Social Science

Develops more effective interaction between those engaged in social research and the social policy arena. Working closely with the American Psychological Association's Public Policy Office in Washington, DC, the fellow provides SPSSI a link to legislation and national testimony. Activities range from legislative work, to developing/advocating for specific bills, to policy-relevant research/writing on issues such as international peace, abortion, and chlid poverty.

Contact SPSSI for details. NO SCHOLARSHIPS AVAILABLE—REQUESTS FOR FINANCIAL AID WILL NOT BE ANSWERED.

3142 — SOIL AND WATER CONSERVATION SOCIETY (SWCS Internships)

7515 N.E. Ankeny Road

Ankeny IA 50021-9764

515/289-2331 or 1-800/THE-SOIL

FAX: 515/289-1227

E-Mail: charliep@swcs.org

Internet: www.swcs.org

AMOUNT: Varies—most are uncompensated

DEADLINE(S): Varies

FIELD(S): Journalism, marketing, database management, meeting planning, public policy research, environmental education, landscape architecture

Internships for undergraduates and graduates to gain experience in the above fields as they relate to soil and water conservation issues. Intership openings vary through the year in duration, compensation, and objective. SWCS will coordinate particulars with your academic advisor.

Contact SWCS for internship availability at any timne during the year or see website for jobs page.

3143 — STOCKHOLM UNIVERSITY - INTERNATIONAL GRADUATE PROGRAMME (Master's Programme in Swedish Social Studies)

Universitetsvagen 10F

Frescati

S-106 91 Stockholm SWEDEN

+46 8 163466

FAX: +46 8 155508

E-Mail: igp@statsvet.su.se

Internet: www.statsvet.su.se/IGP/home.html

AMOUNT: Tuition

DEADLINE(S): MAR 1

FIELD(S): Social Sciences; Economics; History; Anthropology; Sociology; Social Work; Political Science

Open to students who have completed a university degree in the social sciences with one of the above majors and who wish to study at Stockholm University in Sweden. Language of instruction is English.

Contact Stockholm University for an application.

3144 — SWEDISH INFORMATION SERVICE (Bicentennial Swedish-American Exchange Fund)

Bicentennial Fund, One Dag Hammarskjold Plaza, 45th Floor

New York NY 10017-2201

212/483-2550

FAX: 212/752-4789

E-Mail: swedinfor@ix.netcom.com

AMOUNT: 20,000 Swedish crowns (for three- to six-week intensive study visits in Sweden)

DEADLINE(S): FEB (Friday of the first week)

FIELD(S): Politics, public administration, working life, human environment, mass media, business and industry, education and culture

Program is to provide opportunity for those in a positio to influence public opinion and contribute to the development of their society. Must be U.S. citizen or permanent resident. Must have necessary experience and education for fulfilling his/her project.

Send SASE to above address for details.

3145 — THE J. EDGAR HOOVER FOUNDATION

50 Gull Point Rd.

Hilton Head Island SC 29928

803/671-5020

AMOUNT: $500

DEADLINE(S): Ongoing

FIELD(S): Government, law enforcement

Scholarships for the study of government, the promotion of good citizenship, and law enforcement. The foundation strives to safeguard the heritage and freedom of the U.S., to promote good citizenship through an appreciation of the American form of government, and to combat communism or any other ideology or doctrine opposed to the principles set forth in the U.S. Constitution.

Send letter to Cartha D. De Loach, Chair, at above address.

3146 — UNIVERSITY OF MANITOBA (J.W. Dafoe Graduate Fellowship)

Faculty of Grad Studies
500 University Ctr.
Winnipeg Manitoba R3T 2N2 CANADA
204/474-9836
Internet: www.umanitoba.ca/faculties/
graduate_studies/forms

AMOUNT: $15,000/yr.

DEADLINE(S): FEB 15

FIELD(S): Political Studies; Economics; History; International Relations

Open to entering M.A. students at the University of Manitoba in one of the above departments; area of study must focus on international relations.

1 award award annually. Renewable an additional year. Contact Faculty of Graduate Studies for an application.

3147 — UNIVERSITY OF SOUTH DAKOTA (Criminal Justice Dept. Scholarships)

414 East Clark St.
Vermillion SD 57069-2390
605/677-5446
E-Mail: admiss@usd.edu
Internet: www.usd.edu/cjus/
scholarships.htm#orderofpolice

AMOUNT: Varies

DEADLINE(S): Varies

FIELD(S): Criminal Justice; Political Science; Public Service

The University of South Dakota's Department of Crimal Justice administers 17 different award programs in the above fields. Some require a high GPA and/or financial need, others require an essay or research project.

See website or contact USD for specific details of each award. The Criminal Justice Department gives out an average of $77,000/year to USD students.

3148 — UNIVERSITY OF VIRGINIA (Albert Gallatin Fellowship in International Affairs)

International Studies Office
208 Minor Hall
Charlottesville VA 22903
804/982-3010
FAX: 804/982-3011

E-Mail: rgd@virginia.edu
Internet: www.virginia.edu/~intstu

AMOUNT: $11,250 and round trip travel from New York to Geneva

DEADLINE(S): MAR 2

FIELD(S): International studies

Nine-month fellowships for American doctoral candidates in international studies for study at the Graduate Institute for International Studies, Geneva; Switzerland. Must have a fairly functional ability in French as well as English proficiency.

Term is October through June. Write for complete information.

3149 — US ARMS CONTROL AND DISARMAMENT AGENCY (Hubert H. Humphrey Fellowship Program)

Office of Chief Science Advisor
320 21st St. NW
Room 5726
Washington DC 20451
202/647-8090

AMOUNT: $8,000 stipend + up to $6,000 tuition grant

DEADLINE(S): MAR 15

FIELD(S): Arms Control, Nonproliferation, and Disarmament

Doctoral dissertation research fellowships for applicants who have completed all Ph.D. course work except for the dissertation at an accredited U.S. institution. Must be U.S. citizen or permanent resident.

Third-year law students also may apply. Fellowships normally awarded for a period of 12 months. Write for complete information.

3150 — US ARMS CONTROL AND DISARMAMENT AGENCY (William C. Foster Visiting Scholars Program)

320 21st St. NW
Room 5726
Washington DC 20451
703/647-8090

AMOUNT: Salary + per diem

DEADLINE(S): JAN 31

FIELD(S): Arms Control; Nonproliferation; Disarmament

Program open to faculty of recognized institutions of higher learning who wish to lend their expertise in areas relevant to the ACDA for a period of one year. U.S. citizenship or permanent residency required.

Write for complete information.

3151 — WOLCOTT FOUNDATION (Fellowships)

402 Beasley St.
Monroe LA 71203-4006
318/343-1602

AMOUNT: Tuition, books, & fees + $1,800 relocation allowance loan

DEADLINE(S): JAN 15

FIELD(S): Business Administration; Public Service; International Relations; Government; Public Admnistration

Open to students enrolled in accredited programs leading to a master's degree. Must be US citizen and have a minimum 3.0 GPA. Preference given to applicants with Masonic background. Fellowships are for a maximum of 36 semester hours and are tenable at George Washington University in Washington, DC.

Contact Dr. Beryl C. Franklin for an application.

3152 — WOMEN IN DEFENSE (HORIZONS Scholarship Foundation)

NDIA
2111 Wilson Blvd., Ste. 400
Arlington VA 22201-3061
703/247-2552
FAX: 703/522-1885
E-Mail: dnwlee@moon.jic.com
Internet: www.adpa.org/wid/horizon/
Scholar.htm

AMOUNT: $500+

DEADLINE(S): NOV 1; JUL 1

FIELD(S): Engineering, Computer Science, Physics, Mathematics, Business, Law, International Relations, Political Science, Operations Research, Economics, and fields relevant to a career in the areas of national security and defense.

For women who are U.S. citizens, have minimum GPA of 3.25, demonstrate financial need, are currently enrolled at an accredited university/college (full- or part-time—both grads and undergrad juniors/seniors are eligible), and demonstrate interest in pursuing a career related to national security.

Application is online or send SASE, #10 envelope, to Woody Lee, HORIZONS Scholarship Director.

3153 — WOODS HOLE OCEANOGRAPHIC INSTITUTION (Research Fellowships in Marine Policy and Ocean Management)

360 Woods Hole Road
Woods Hole MA 02543-1541
508/289-2219
FAX: 508/457-2188
E-Mail: mgately@whoi.edu
Internet: www.whoi.edu

AMOUNT: Varies

DEADLINE(S): FEB 16

FIELD(S): Social Sciences, Law, Natural Sciences

For professionals in the above fields who wish to apply their training to investigations of problems involving the use of the oceans. WHOI's objective is to provide a year-long advanced learning experience in ocean policy problems involving the interdisciplinary application of social science and natural science to marine policy problems. Fields currently emphasized: economics, statistics, public policy, natural resource management, and international relations.

For an application/more information, contact the Education Office, Clark Laboratory 223, MS #31, at above address.

3154 — WORLD BANK (Graduate Scholarship Program)

1818 H St., NW, Rm. M-4035
Washington DC 20433
Written inquiry

AMOUNT: Tuition + fees, allowance, travel, etc.

DEADLINE(S): FEB 1

FIELD(S): Social sciences, law, business, public administration

For nationals of World Bank member countries under the age of 40. Must have a superior academic record, at least two years' experience in public service engaged in development-related activities, and have gained admittance to a university to pursue a post-graduate degree. Must return to hom country after degree.

For two years.

PSYCHOLOGY

3155 — ALBERT ELLIS INSTITUTE (Fellowship Training Program)

45 East 65th St.
New York NY 10021-6593
212/535-0822

AMOUNT: $6,000/yr.

DEADLINE(S): Varies

FIELD(S): Psychology

Two-year postdoctoral fellowships and one-year predoctoral internships in cognitive behavior therapy. Applicants must have a Ph.D. in psychology, an M.D., or an M.S.W. and be eligible for state certification, or be working on their dissertation.

9 awards annually. Contact Catharine MacLaren for an application.

3156 — AMERICAN ACADEMY OF CHILD AND ADOLESCENT PSYCHIATRY (Minority Medical Student Fellowships)

3615 Wisconsin Ave., NW
Washington DC 20016-3007
800/333-7636, ext. 113 or 202/966-7300
FAX: 202/966-2891
E-Mail: kpope@aacap.org
Internet: www.aacap.org

AMOUNT: $2,500 stipend + attendance at AACAP annual meeting

DEADLINE(S): APR 1

FIELD(S): Child & Adolescent Psychiatry; Drug Abuse & Addiction

Three fellowship programs each include stipend to work with child and adolescent psychiatrist researcher or clinician during the summer, as well as expenses to AACAP Annual Meeting, where student will present poster, attend symposia & workshops, and meet with leaders in field. Must be an African American, Asian American, Alaskan Native, Mexican American, Hispanic, or Pacific Islander attending an accredited US medical school.

Contact Kayla Pope, Director of Research & Training, for program guidelines and an application.

3157 — AMERICAN ASSOCIATION FOR MARRIAGE & FAMILY THERAPISTS (Graduate Student Research Awards)

1133 15th St., NW, Suite 300
Washington DC 20005-2710
202/452-0109
FAX: 202/223-2329
Internet: www.aamft.org

AMOUNT: $2,500 + up to $1,000 for travel to Annual Conference

DEADLINE(S): MAR 15

FIELD(S): Marriage & Family Therapy

Awards for graduate students to assist in completion of thesis or dissertation pertaining to couples and family therapy or family therapy training.

Write for complete information and application.

3158 — AMERICAN ASSOCIATION FOR MARRIAGE & FAMILY THERAPISTS (Minority Fellowships)

1133 15th St., NW, Suite 300
Washington DC 20005-2710
202/452-0109
FAX: 202/223-2329
Internet: www.aamft.org

AMOUNT: $2,500 + up to $1,000 for travel to Annual Conference

DEADLINE(S): JAN 31

FIELD(S): Marriage & Family Therapy

Fellowships for minority graduate students enrolled in a graduate degree program or post-degree training program in marriage and family therapy. Includes waiver of conference registration fee.

Write for complete information and application.

3159 — AMERICAN PSYCHOLOGICAL FOUNDATION (Wayne F. Placek Awards for Scientific Research on Lesbian and Gay Issues)

750 First St., NE
Washington DC 20002-4242
202/336-5814
E-Mail: foundation@apa.org
Internet: psychology.ucdavis.edu/rainbow/html/apfawards.html

AMOUNT: up to $30,000

DEADLINE(S): MAR 15

FIELD(S): Behavioral/Social Science

To increase public's understanding of homosexuality & to alleviate stress that gays/lesbians experience in this & future civilizations. Proposals invited for empirical research from all fields of behavioral/social sciences. Proposals encouraged that deal with attitudes, prejudice, workplace issues, and subgroups historically underrepresented in scientific research. Must have doctoral degree/equivalent & be associated w/ college/university or research institute.

2 awards annually. Small grants (up to $5,000) also available for pilot studies/exploratory research in gay/lesbian issues. Contact above address for details.

3160 — ASSOCIATION FOR WOMEN IN SCIENCE EDUCATIONAL FOUNDATION (AWIS Predoctoral Awards)

1200 New York Ave. NW, Suite 650
Washington DC 20005
202/326-8940 or 800-886-AWIS
E-Mail: awis@awis.org
Internet: www.awis.org

AMOUNT: $1,000

DEADLINE(S): JAN 16

FIELD(S): Various Sciences and Social Sciences

Scholarships for female doctoral students. Summary page, description of research project, resume, references, transcripts, and biographical sketch required. US citizens may study at any graduate institution; non-citizens must study at US institutions.

5-10 awards annually. See website or write to above address for an application and complete information.

3161 — ASSOCIATION FOR WOMEN IN SCIENCE EDUCATIONAL FOUNDATION (AWIS Pre-doctoral Awards)

1200 New York Ave. NW, Suite 650
Washington DC 20005
202/326-8940 or 800/886-AWIS
E-Mail: awis@awis.org
Internet: www.awis.org

AMOUNT: $1,000

DEADLINE(S): JAN 16

FIELD(S): Various Sciences and Social Sciences

Scholarships for female doctoral students. Summary page, description of research project, resume, references, transcripts, and biographical sketch required. US citizens may study at any graduate institution; non-citizens must be enrolled in US institutions.

5-10 awards annually. See website or write to above address for an application and more information.

3162 — ASSOCIATION FOR WOMEN IN SCIENCE EDUCATIONAL FOUNDATION (Ruth Satter Memorial Award)

1200 New York Ave., NW, Suite 650
Washington DC 20005
202/326-8940 or 800/886-AWIS
E-Mail: awis@awis.org
Internet: www.awis.org

AMOUNT: $1,000

DEADLINE(S): JAN 16

FIELD(S): Various Sciences and Social Sciences

Scholarships for female doctoral students who have interrupted their education for at least three years to raise a family. Summary page, description of research project, resume, references, transcripts, biographical sketch, and letter from your department to confirm eligibility required. US citizens may study at any graduate institution; non-citizens must attend US institutions.

See website or write to above address for more information or an application.

3163 — ASSOCIATION FOR WOMEN IN SCIENCE EDUCATIONAL FOUNDATION (Ruth Satter Memorial Award)

1200 New York Ave. NW, Suite 650
Washington DC 20005
202/326-8940 or 800/886-AWIS
E-Mail: awis@awis.org
Internet: www.awis.org

AMOUNT: $1,000

DEADLINE(S): JAN 16

FIELD(S): Various Sciences and Social Sciences

Scholarships for female doctoral students who have interrupted their education three years or more to raise a family. Summary page, description of research project, resume, references, transcripts, biographical sketch, and proof of eligibility from department head required. US citizens may attend any graduate institution; non-citizens must be enrolled in US institutions.

See website or write to above address for more information or an application.

3164 — AUSTRALIAN FEDERATION OF UNIVERSITY WOMEN - WESTERN AUSTRALIA (Joyce Riley Bursary)

Bursary Liaison Officer
PO Box 48
Nedlands WA 6909 AUSTRALIA
Written Inquiry

AMOUNT: Aus$1,700 - Aus$2,750

DEADLINE(S): JUL 31

FIELD(S): Humanities; Social Sciences

To support women graduates of a Western Australian university to complete a higher degree or post-doctoral research in Humanities or Social Sciences at a recognized university in any country.

Membership in AFUW or in IFUW is required. Contact above location for further information.

3165 — AUSTRALIAN FEDERATION OF UNIVERSITY WOMEN - WESTERN AUSTRALIA (Joyce Riley Bursary)

Bursary Liaison Officer
PO Box 48
Nedlands WA 6009 AUSTRALIA
Written Inquiry

AMOUNT: Aus$1,700 - Aus$2,750

DEADLINE(S): JUL 31

FIELD(S): Humanities; Social Sciences

To support women graduates of a recognized university to complete a higher degree or post-doctoral research at a university in Western Australia.

Membership in AFUW or in IFUW is required. Write to above address for complete information.

3166 — BRITISH COLUMBIA PARAPLEGIC FOUNDATION (Douglas John Wilson Scholarship)

780 SW Marine Dr.
Vancouver BC V6P 5Y7 Canada
604/324-3611
FAX: 604/324-3671

AMOUNT: Varies

DEADLINE(S): JUL 31

FIELD(S): Rehabilitation Counseling

For a person with a disability studying for a degree in rehabilitation counseling at a university in British Columbia. Must be a Canadian citizen or landed immigrant or a resident of British Columbia.

To assist with tuition, books, transportation, or other educational expenses.

3167 — CALIFORNIA ASSOCIATION OF MARRIAGE AND FAMILY THERAPISTS (CAMFT Education Foundation Scholarships)

7901 Raytheon Rd.
San Diego CA 92111
858/292-2638
FAX: 858/292-2666
E-Mail: brandi@camft.org
Internet: www.camft.org

AMOUNT: $1,000

DEADLINE(S): FEB 28

FIELD(S): Marriage & Family Therapy

Open to graduate students and licensed professionals. Awards support graduate research in marriage and family therapy and/or education. Preference (but not limited) to CAMFT members/California residents. Must demonstrate financial need.

6 awards annually. Contact Brandi Kaufman at CAMFT for an application.

3168 — COMMITTEE ON INTERNATIONAL RELATIONS IN PSYCHOLOGY (CIRP David International Travel Award)

Office Int'l Affairs, APA
750 First St., NE
Washington DC 20002
202/336-6025
FAX: 202/218-3599
E-Mail: international@apa.org

AMOUNT: Varies

DEADLINE(S): FEB 1

FIELD(S): Human Reproductive Behavior; Population Concerns

Provides support every two out of three years to a young psychologist with a demonstrated interest in above fields to participate in an international or regional congress. To qualify, you must be a graduate student or have received a Ph.D., Psy.D., or Ed.D. in psychology in the past five years.

Request information and application materials from above address.

3169 — CONCORDIA UNIVERSITY (J.P. Zewig Scholarship)

1455 de Maisonneuve Blvd. West
Room M 201
Montreal Quebec H3G 1M8 CANADA
514/848-3809
FAX: 514/848-2812
E-Mail: awardsgs@vax2.concordia.ca

AMOUNT: Varies

DEADLINE(S): SEP 20

FIELD(S): Psychology; Exercise Science; Behaviourial Medicine

This one-year scholarship is awarded to a graduate student pursuing research in the above areas. Candidates are to be nominated by Faculty members from these areas of research.

1 award annually. Not renewable. Contact the Graduate Awards Office in the School of Graduate Studies at Concordia University for nomination procedures.

3170 — DELTA SOCIETY (James M. Harris/ Sarah W. Sweatt Student Travel Grant)

289 Perimeter Rd. East
Benton WA 98055-1329
425/226-7357
FAX: 425/235-1076
E-Mail: deltasociety@cis.compuserve.com
Internet: www.deltasociety.org

AMOUNT: Varies

DEADLINE(S): Varies

FIELD(S): Human-Animal Interactions; Animal Assisted Therapy; Service Animals; Pet Loss

Travel grants for graduate/postgraduate students to attend Delta Society's annual conference. Must be a full-time student in veterinary human health care. Student must provide detailed plan of how conference information will be shared. Must also attend the full conference and demonstrate ability to cover costs of registration, hotel, and meals. Financial need NOT a factor.

2-4 awards annually. Contact Michelle Cobey for an application.

3171 — DEPARTMENT OF THE ARMY (Armed Forces Health Professions Scholarships)

Attn: RC-HS
1307 Third Ave.
Fort Knox KY 40121
502/626-0367
FAX: 502/626-0923

AMOUNT: Tuition + monthly stipend

DEADLINE(S): None

FIELD(S): Medicine; Osteopathy; Nurse Anesthetist; Veterinary Medicine; Optometry; Psychology; Dentistry

Open to health professionals and students participating in a Reserve Service of the US Armed Forces, training in the specialties listed above. Varying lengths of service are required to pay back the stipend. Must be US citizen. Award is based on a competitive process, including GPA. Financial need NOT a factor.

400 awards annually. Contact Major Beecher at above address for an application.

3172 — EASTER SEAL SOCIETY OF IOWA, INC. (Scholarships & Awards)

P.O. Box 4002
Des Moines IA 50333-4002
515/289-1933

AMOUNT: $400-$600

DEADLINE(S): APR 15

FIELD(S): Physical Rehabilitation, Mental Rehabilitation, and related areas

Open ONLY to Iowa residents who are full-time undergraduate sophomores, juniors, seniors, or graduate students at accredited institutions planning a career in the broad field of rehabilitation. Must indicate financial need and be in top 40% of their class.

6 scholarships per year. Must re-apply each year.

3173 — EPILEPSY FOUNDATION OF AMERICA (Behavioral Sciences Student Fellowships)

4351 Garden City Drive
Landover MD 20785-2267
301/459-3700 or 800/EFA-1000
FAX: 301/577-2684
TDD: 800/332-2070
E-Mail: postmaster@efa.org
Internet: www.efa.org

AMOUNT: $2,000

DEADLINE(S): FEB 1

FIELD(S): Epilepsy as related to Behavioral Sciences

Three-month fellowships awarded to students in the behavioral sciences for work on an epilepsy study project. For students of vocational rehabilitation counseling. Students propose an epilepsy-related study or training project to be carried out at a US institution of their choice. A preceptor must accept responsibility for supervision of the student and the project.

Contact EFA for an application.

3174 — EPILEPSY FOUNDATION OF AMERICA (Behavioral Sciences Research Training Fellowships)

4351 Garden City Drive
Landover MD 20785-2267
301/459-3700 or FAX: 301/577-2684
FDD: 800/332-2070
E-Mail: postmaster@efa.org
Internet: www.efa.org

AMOUNT: Up to $30,000

DEADLINE(S): FEB 1

FIELD(S): Epilepsy as related to Behavioral Sciences (includes sociology, social work, psychology, anthropology, nursing, political science, etc.)

A one-year training experience for postdoctoral scholars to develop expertise in the area of epilepsy research relative to the behavioral sciences. The project must be carried out at an approved facility. Amount depends on experience and qualifications of the applicant and the scope and duration of proposed project.

Contact EFA for an application.

3175 — EPILEPSY FOUNDATION OF AMERICA (Junior Investigator Research Grants)

4351 Garden City Drive
Landover MD 20785-2267
301/459-3700 or 800/EFA-1000
FAX: 301/577-2684
TDD: 800/332-2070
E-Mail: postmaster@efa.org
Internet: www.efa.org

AMOUNT: up to $40,000

DEADLINE(S): SEP 1

FIELD(S): Epilepsy as related to Biological, Behavioral, & Social Sciences

One-year research grants to support basic and clinical research in the biological, behavioral, and social sciences which will advance the understanding, treatment, and prevention of epilepsy. Priority given to beginning investigators just entering the field of epilepsy research, to new or innovative projects. Applications evaluated on basis of scientific merit.

Contact EFA for an application.

3176 — EPILEPSY FOUNDATION OF AMERICA (Pre-doctoral Research Training Fellowship)

4351 Garden City Drive
Landover MD 20785-2267
301/459-3700 or 800/EFA-1000
FAX: 301/577-2684
TDD: 800/332-2070
E-Mail: postmaster@efa.org
Internet: www.efa.org

AMOUNT: up to $15,000

DEADLINE(S): SEP 1

FIELD(S): Epilepsy as related to Neuroscience, Physiology, Pharmacology, Psychology, Biochemistry, Genetics, Nursing, or Pharmacy

One-year of support for qualified individuals who are pursuing dissertation research with an epilepsy-related theme, and who are working under the guidance of a mentor with expertise in the area of epilepsy investigation. Graduate students pursuing Ph.D. degree in above fields may apply.

Contact EFA for an application.

3177 — ESPN (Internship Programs)

Human Resources Dept.
ESPN, Inc.
ESPN Plaza
Bristol CT 06010

No phone calls. Internet: espnet.sportszone.com/editors/studios/97faq.html

AMOUNT: Paid Internships

DEADLINE(S): OCT 1; MAR 1; JUN 1

FIELD(S): Television Industry, Public Relations, Sports

12-week internships in the spring, summer, and fall for undergraduate juniors/seniors and graduate students. Some areas require weekend/evening hours and a strong knowledge of sports. Interns receive hourly wages and take part in many company-sponsored activities. ESPN does not provide housing for students, but we do try to assist in finding suitable living arrangements once selected.

To apply for internship programs, please send cover letter and resume to the above address. If applying to the Communications Dept., please also enclose writing samples and send attention to Diane Lamb.

3178 — FORD FOUNDATION/NATIONAL RESEARCH COUNCIL (Postdoctoral Fellowship for Minorities)

National Research Council
2101 Constitution Ave.
Washington DC 20418
202/334-2860
E-Mail: infofell@nas.edu
Internet: http//www.nas.edu/fo/index.html

AMOUNT: $25,000 + relocation and research allowance

DEADLINE(S): JAN 3

FIELD(S): Life and physical sciences, mathematics, engineering sciences, behavioral and social sciences, and the humanities

For U.S. citizens who received a Ph.D or Sc.D in the last 7 years and who are Native Amer. Indian or Alaskan, Black/African American, Mexican American, Native Pacific Islander, or Puerto Rican and who are or plan to be in a teaching or research career.

Contact above website or address for complete information.

3179 — FORD FOUNDATION/NATIONAL RESEARCH COUNCIL (Predoctoral/Dissertation Fellowships for Minorities)

2101 Constitution Ave.
Washington DC 20418
202/334-2872
E-Mail: infofell@nas.edu
Internet: http//www.nas.edu/fo/index.html

AMOUNT: $14,000 annual stipend + $6,000 grant to institution; $18,000 for dissertation fellowship

DEADLINE(S): NOV 3

FIELD(S): Most fields of study: sciences, humanities, engineering, behavioral science, social sciences, and computer science

Predoctoral and dissertation fellowships for students whose ethnicity is Alaskan Native, Black/African American, Mexican American/Chicano, Native American Indian, Native Pacific Islander, or Puerto Rican. For research-based programs leading to careers in college teaching and research.

Contact above address or website.

3180 — FRENCH-AMERICAN FOUNDATION (Bicentennial Fellowships)

41 East 72nd St.
New York NY 10021
212/288-4000
FAX: 212/288-4765
E-Mail: French_AmerFdn@msn.com

AMOUNT: 10,000 French francs/mo.

DEADLINE(S): FEB 2

FIELD(S): Social sciences

For doctoral students in the social sciences to travel to France for one year to conduct research essential to the completion of their dissertations. Must have completed all other requirements for Ph.D. May not use the award until exams are passed.

Requires application with a statement of purpose, full academic records, plan of research, bibliography, abstract, and three academic recommendations.

3181 — HARRY FRANK GUGGENHEIM FOUNDATION (Dissertation Fellowships)

527 Madison Ave.
New York NY 10022-4304
212/644-4907

AMOUNT: $10,000

DEADLINE(S): FEB 1

FIELD(S): Behavioral Sciences; Social Sciences; Biology

Awards are intended for support during the writing of the Ph.D. thesis in disciplines addressing the causes, manifestations, and control of violence, aggression, and dominance. Applicants must have completed research and be ready to write.

Contact Guggenheim Foundation for an application.

3182 — HARRY FRANK GUGGENHEIM FOUNDATION (Postdoctoral Research Grants)

527 Madison Ave.
New York NY 10022-4304
212/644-4907

AMOUNT: $30,000 (max.)

DEADLINE(S): AUG 1

FIELD(S): Behavioral Sciences; Social Sciences; Biology

One- to two-year grants are open to postdoctoral researchers in the above fields whose work leads to a better understanding of the causes, manifestations, and control of violence, aggression, and dominance in the modern world.

25-35 awards annually. Contact Guggenheim Foundation for an application.

3183 — INSTITUTE FOR ADVANCED STUDIES IN THE HUMANITIES (Visiting Research Fellowships)

Univ Edinburgh
Hope Park Square
Edinburgh EH8 9NW SCOTLAND UK
0131 650 4671
FAX: 0131 668 2252
E-Mail: iash@ed.ac.uk
Internet: www.ed.ac.uk/iash/homepage.html

AMOUNT: Non-stipendiary*

DEADLINE(S): DEC 1

FIELD(S): Arts; Social Sciences; Law; Music; Divinity

Postdoctoral research fellowships of between two and six months are tenable at the Institute for Advanced Studies in the Humanities. Based on academic record and publications. *Most fellowships are honorary, but limited support towards expenses is available to a small number of candidates. Fellows are allocated a study room within the Institute and hold one or two seminars during their tenure. Must submit research report at end of fellowship. No teaching required.

15 awards annually. Not renewable. Contact Mrs. Anthea Taylor for an application.

3184 — INSTITUTE FOR HUMANE STUDIES (Humane Studies Fellowship)

4084 University Dr., Ste. 101
Fairfax VA 22030-6812
703/934-6920 or 800/697-8799
FAX: 703/352-7535
E-Mail: ihs@gmu.edu
Internet: www.theihs.org

AMOUNT: up to $12,000

DEADLINE(S): DEC 31

FIELD(S): Social Sciences; Law; Humanities; Jurisprudence; Journalism

Awards are for graduate and advanced undergraduate students pursuing degrees at any accredited domestic or foreign school. Based on academic performance, demonstrated interest in classical liberal ideas, and potential to contribute to the advancement of a free society.

90 awards annually. Apply online or contact IHS for an application.

3185 — LABAN/BARTENIEFF INSTITUTE OF MOVEMENT STUDIES (Work-Study Programs)

234 Fifth Ave.
Rm. 203
New York NY 10001
212/477-4299
FAX: 212/477-3702
E-Mail: limsinfo@erols.com

AMOUNT: $500-$1,500

DEADLINE(S): MAY 1

FIELD(S): Human Movement Studies

Open to graduate students and professionals in dance, education, health fields, behavioral sciences, fitness, athletic training, etc. Tenable for work-study ONLY at the Laban/Bartenieff Institute in New York.

Contact LIMS for an application.

3186 — LADY ALLEN OF HURTWOOD MEMORIAL TRUST (Travel Grants)

21 Aspull Common
Leigh Lancs WN7 3PB ENGLAND
01942-674895

AMOUNT: up to 1,000 pounds sterling

DEADLINE(S): JAN 15

FIELD(S): Welfare And Education Of Children

A travel grant to those whose proposed project will directly benefit their work with children. People working with children and young people may apply, particularly those working with disabled and disadvantaged children. Successful candidates must write up an account of the work which the scholarship has funded. GRANTS ARE NOT FOR ACADEMIC STUDY; ONLY QUALIFIED INDIVIDUALS MAY APPLY.

Contact Dorothy E. Whitaker, Trustee, for application forms—available between May and December each year.

3187 — NATIONAL ACADEMY OF EDUCATION (Spencer Postdoctoral Fellowship Program)

NY Univ, School of Education
726 Broadway, Rm. 509
New York NY 10003-9580
212/998-9035
FAX: 212/995-4435
E-Mail: nae.info@nyu.edu
Internet: www.nae.nyu.edu

AMOUNT: $45,000

DEADLINE(S): DEC 1

FIELD(S): Education; Humanities; Social Sciences

Fellowships of one or two years are open to individual researchers in education, humanities, or social and behavioral sciences. Research must have apparent relevance to education. Doctoral degree must have been received within the last five years. Based on past research record and quality of proposed project. Must submit project description, career history, referee form, curriculum vitae/resume, and example of past research relevant to education.

30 awards annually. Not renewable. Contact NAE for an application. Recipients notified in May.

3188 — NATIONAL CHAMBER OF COMMERCE FOR WOMEN (Scholarships & Research Grants)

10 Waterside Plaza, Suite 6H
New York NY 10010
212/685-3454

AMOUNT: Varies

DEADLINE(S): None

FIELD(S): Behavioral Science

Scholarships and grants open to women who are post-graduates, graduate students, and professionals in the behavioral sciences. Awards support study and/ or research projects. Preference (but not limited) to organizational behavior and business ethics.

Write for complete information.

3189 — NEW YORK STATE HIGHER EDUCATION SERVICES CORPORATION (N.Y. State Regents Professional/Health Care Opportunity Scholarships)

Cultural Education Center, Rm. 5C64
Albany NY 12230
518/486-1319
Internet: www.hesc.com

AMOUNT: $1,000-$10,000/yr.

DEADLINE(S): Varies

FIELD(S): Medicine and dentistry and related fields, architecture, nursing, psychology, audiology, landscape architecture, social work, chiropractic, law, pharmacy, accounting, speech language pathology

For NY state residents who are economically disadvantaged and members of a minority group underrepresented in the chosen profession and attending school in NY state. Some programs carry a service obligation in New York for each year of support. For U.S. citizens or qualifying noncitizens.

Medical/dental scholarships require one year of professional work in NY.

3190 — OAK RIDGE ASSOCIATED UNIVERSITIES (National Science Foundation Graduate Research Fellowships)

PO Box 3010
Oak Ridge TN 37831-3010
423/241-4300
FAX: 423/241-4513

E-Mail: nsfgrfp@orau.gov
Internet: www.orau.gov/nsf/nsffel.htm

AMOUNT: $15,000 stipend + $10,500 tuition allowance

DEADLINE(S): NOV 4

FIELD(S): Science; Math; Engineering; Computer Science

Three-year fellowships for graduate study leading to research-based master's or doctoral degrees in the above fields. Must be US citizens, nationals, or permanent residents at the time of application. Fellowships are awarded on the basis of ability. Women, minorities, and those with disabilities are strongly encouraged to apply. One-time International Research Travel Allowance available.

1,000 awards annually. Contact Jeannette Bouchard for an application/more information.

3191 — OLFACTORY RESEARCH FUND (Tova Fellowship & Annual Grant Program)

145 E. 32nd St.
9th Floor
New York NY 10016-6002
212/725-2755
FAX: 212/779-9072
E-Mail: info@olfactory.org
Internet: www.olfactory.org

AMOUNT: $50,000 (max.)

DEADLINE(S): JAN 15

FIELD(S): Olfactory Research

For talented investigators with proven ability to conduct high quality research. Research should seek to integrate study of olfaction with current issues in developmental, perceptual, social/cognitive psychology, and related disciplines. Investigations of relationship of human odor perception to biology/ genetics of odor receptors also welcome. Applicant must possess professional post-baccalaureate degree. Brief summary, proposal, budget, & curriculum vitae required.

Contact Olfactory Research Fund for guidelines.

3192 — OPEN SOCIETY INSTITUTE (Individual Project Fellowships)

400 West 59th St.
New York NY 10019
212/548-0600 or 212/757-2323
FAX: 212/548-4679 or 212/548-4600
Internet: www.soros.org/fellow/individual.html

AMOUNT: Varies

DEADLINE(S): Varies

FIELD(S): Any field of study related to creating an open society: reliance on the rule of law, the existence of a democratically elected government, a diverse and vigorous civil society, and respect for minorities and minority opinions.

Two-year fellowships for use in selected universities in the U.S. for international students. For students/professionals in fields related to environmental policy, legislation, and remediation techniques applicable to their home countries.

To apply, contact the Soros Foundation/Open Society Institute. Further details on website.

3193 — PARAPSYCHOLOGY FOUNDATION (D. Scott Rogo Award for Parapsychological Award)

228 E. 71st St.
New York NY 10021
212/628-1550
FAX: 212/628-1559

AMOUNT: $3,000

DEADLINE(S): APR 15

FIELD(S): Parapsychology

Annual award given to an author working on a manuscript pertaining to the science of parapsychology. A brief synopsis of the proposed contents of the manuscript should be included in the initial application.

Contact Parapsychology Foundation for more information. Recipient notified around May 1st.

3194 — PARAPSYCHOLOGY FOUNDATION (Eileen J. Garrett Scholarship)

228 E. 71st St.
New York NY 10021
212/628-1550
FAX: 212/628-1559

AMOUNT: $3,000

DEADLINE(S): JUL 15

FIELD(S): Parapsychology

Open to any undergraduate or graduate student wishing to pursue the academic study of the science of parapsychology. Funding is for study, research, and experimentation only. Applicants must demonstrate previous academic interest in parapsycholgy. Letters of reference are required from three individuals who are familiar with the applicant's work and/or studies in parapsychology.

Contact Parapsychology Foundation for an application.

3195 — PARAPSYCHOLOGY FOUNDATION (Grant Program)

228 E. 71st St.
New York NY 10021
212/628-1550
FAX: 212/628-1559

AMOUNT: $3,000 (max.)

DEADLINE(S): None

FIELD(S): Parapsychology

Grants are open to scientists, universities, laboratories, and others conducting research in telepathy, precognition, psychokinesis, and related phenomena. Grants will NOT cover travel expenses or academic degree study.

Contact Parapsychology Foundation for an application.

3196 — PILOT INTERNATIONAL FOUNDATION (Marie Newton Sepia Memorial Scholarship)

P.O. Box 5600
Macon GA 31208-5600
Written inquiries

AMOUNT: Varies

DEADLINE(S): MAR 1

FIELD(S): Disabilities/Brain-related Disorders in Children

This program assists graduate students preparing for careers working with children having disabilities/brain disorders. Must have GPA of 3.5 or greater.

Applicants must be sponsored by a Pilot Club in their home town or in the city in which their college or university is located. Send a self-addressed, stamped envelope for complete information.

3197 — PILOT INTERNATIONAL FOUNDATION (PIF/Lifeline Scholarship)

P.O. Box 5600
Macon GA 31208-5600
Written inquiries

AMOUNT: Varies

DEADLINE(S): MAR 1

FIELD(S): Disabilities/Brain-related Disorders

This program assists ADULT students re-entering the job market, preparing for a second career, or improving their professional skills for an established career. Applicants must be preparing for, or already involved in, careers working with people with disabilities/brain-related disorders. GPA of 3.5 or more is required.

Must be sponsored by a Pilot Club in your home town, or in the city in which your college or university is located. Send a self-addressed, stamped envelope for complete information.

3198 — PILOT INTERNATIONAL FOUNDATION (Ruby Newhall Memorial Scholarship)

P.O. Box 5600
Macon, GA 31208-5600
Written Inquiries

AMOUNT: Varies

DEADLINE(S): MAR 15

FIELD(S): Disabilities/Brain-related disorders

For international students who have studied in the US for at least one year, and who intend to return to their home country six months after graduation. Applicants must be full-time students majoring in a field related to human health and welfare, and have a GPA of 3.5 or more.

Applicants must be sponsored by a Pilot Club in their home town, or in the city in which their college or university is located. Send a self-addressed, stamped envelope for complete information.

3199 — SCOTTISH RITE CHARITABLE FOUNDATION (Research Grants)

Roeher Institute, Kinsmen Bldg.
4700 Keele St.
North York Ontario M3J 1P3 CANADA
416/661-9611
TDD: 416/661-2023
FAX: 416/661-5701
E-Mail: mail@aacl.org
Internet: www.aacl.org

AMOUNT: $10,000 (max. grads); $35,000 (max. postdocs)

DEADLINE(S): APR 30

FIELD(S): Human Services; Intellectual Disability

Open to Canadian citizens/landed immigrants enrolled in masters or doctoral programs at Canadian universities. Must state intent to pursue career in Canada and have definite research projects supported by an academic advisor or a Roeher Institute associate/consultant. Also available to postdoctoral researchers.

Renewable. Contact the Secretary, Awards Adjudicating Committee, at the Scottish Rite for an application and details on preferred research topics.

3200 — SIR ROBERT MENZIES MEMORIAL FOUNDATION LIMITED (Research Scholarship in Allied Health Sciences)

210 Clarendon Street
East Melbourne Vic 3002 AUSTRALIA
03 9419 5699
FAX: 03 9417 7049
E-Mail: menzies@vicnet.net.au
Internet: www.vincent.net.au/~menzies

AMOUNT: $AUD.24,000 p.a.

DEADLINE(S): JUN 30

FIELD(S): Allied Health

Postgraduate research scholarships for Australian citizens enrolled as full-time Ph.D. students at Australian institutions. Must be studying allied health fields, such as nursing, physiotherapy, psychology, occupational therapy, speech pathology, etc. Award is based on academic excellence. Financial need NOT a factor.

1 award annually. Contact Ms. Sandra Mackenzie for an application.

3201 — SOCIAL SCIENCE RESEARCH COUNCIL (International Predissertation Fellowship Program)

810 Seventh Ave.
New York NY 10019
212/277-2700

AMOUNT: Varies

DEADLINE(S): Varies (TBA by participating universities)

FIELD(S): Economics; Political Science; Psychology; Sociology; other Social Science disciplines

Open to Ph.D. candidates enrolled in social science programs at 23 select universities and interested in supplementing disciplinary skills with area and language studies or acquiring advanced disciplinary training. Study program is preparation for research on Africa, Central Asia & the Caucasus, China, Latin America, the Caribbean, Near & Middle East, and South or Southeast Asia.

Contact Ellen Perecman for an application.

3202 — SOCIAL SCIENCE RESEARCH COUNCIL (Sexuality Research Fellowship Program)

810 Seventh Ave.
31st Fl.
New York NY 10019
212/377-2700
FAX: 212/377-2727
E-Mail: srfp@ssrc.org
Internet: www.ssrc.org

AMOUNT: $28,000 (dissertation); $38,000 (postdoctoral)

DEADLINE(S): DEC 15

FIELD(S): Human Sexuality

Provides 12-month dissertation and 24-month postdoctoral support for social and behavioral research on sexuality conducted in the US. Should address complexity and contextual nature of human sexuality by linking study of human sexuality to intellectual trajectory of their own disciplines and by exploring connections across disciplines, methods, and issues.

10 dissertation & 4 postdoctoral awards annually. See website or contact SSRC for an application. Announcement of awards in March.

3203 — SOCIETY FOR THE PSYCHOLOGICAL STUDY OF SOCIAL ISSUES (Applied Social Issues Internship Program)

PO Box 1248
Ann Arbor MI 48106-1248
Phone/TTY: 313/662-9130

FAX: 313/662-5607
E-Mail: spssi@spssi.org
Internet: www.spssi.org

AMOUNT: $1,500-$2,500

DEADLINE(S): NOV 10

FIELD(S): Social Science & related fields

Internship awards cover research costs, community organizing, summer stipends, etc. Encourages intervention projects, non-partisan lobbying, applied research, & implementing public policy. Proposals are invited for applying social science principles to social issues, in cooperation with a community, city, or state government organization, public interest group, or other not-for-profit entity. College seniors, graduate students, and first-year postdoctorates may apply.

Contact SPSSI for details. Applications available on website. NO SCHOLARSHIPS AVAILABLE—REQUESTS FOR FINANCIAL AID WILL NOT BE ANSWERED.

3204 — SOCIETY FOR THE PSYCHOLOGICAL STUDY OF SOCIAL ISSUES (Clara Mayo Grants in Support of Master's Thesis and Pre-Dissertation Research on Sexism, Racism, or Prejudice)

PO Box 1248
Ann Arbor MI 48106-1248
Phone/TTY: 313/662-9130
FAX: 313/662-5607
E-Mail: spssi@spssi.org
Internet: www.spssi.org

AMOUNT: up to $1,000

DEADLINE(S): MAR 31

FIELD(S): Sexism, Racism, & Prejudice

These grants support research from students working on a master's thesis (preference given to those in terminal master's program) or pre-dissertation research on sexism, racism, or prejudice. Studies of application of theory or design of interventions/treatments to address these problems are welcome. Proposals that include college/university agreement to match amount requested are favored, but those without matching funds also considered.

4 awards annually. Applications availble on website. NO SCHOLARSHIPS AVAILABLE—REQUESTS FOR FINANCIAL AID WILL NOT BE ANSWERED.

3205 — SOCIETY FOR THE PSYCHOLOGICAL STUDY OF SOCIAL ISSUES (James Marshall Public Policy Fellowship)

PO Box 1248
Ann Arbor MI 48106-1248
313/662-9130
FAX: 313/662-5607
E-Mail: spssi@umich.edu
Internet: www.spssi.org

AMOUNT: $42,000 + health/vacation benefits

DEADLINE(S): JAN 10

FIELD(S): Public Policy, Social Science

Develops more effective interaction between those engaged in social research and the social policy arena. Working closely with the American Psychological Association's Public Policy Office in Washington, DC, the fellow provides SPSSI a link to legislation and national testimony. Activities range from legislative work, to developing/advocating for specific bills, to policy-relevant research/writing on issues such as international peace, abortion, and chlid poverty.

Contact SPSSI for details. NO SCHOLARSHIPS AVAILABLE—REQUESTS FOR FINANCIAL AID WILL NOT BE ANSWERED.

3206 — SOCIETY FOR THE PSYCHOLOGICAL STUDY OF SOCIAL ISSUES (Gordon Allport Intergroup Relations Prize)

PO Box 1248
Ann Arbor MI 48106-1248
Phone/TTY: 313/662-9130
FAX: 313/662-9130
E-Mail: spssi@spssi.org
Internet: www.spssi.org

AMOUNT: $1,000

DEADLINE(S): DEC 31

FIELD(S): Sociology/Intergroup Relations

Annual award for the best paper or article on intergroup relations. Originality of the contribution, whether theoretical or empirical, is given special consideration. The research area encompassing intergroup relations includes such dimensions as age, sex, socioeconomic status, and race. Entries can be either papers published during the current year or unpublished manuscripts. Send five copies of entry.

Contact SPSSI for details. Applications available on website. SPSSI DOES NOT OFFER SCHOLARSHIPS—REQUESTS FOR FINANCIAL AID WILL NOT BE ANSWERED.

3207 — SOCIETY FOR THE PSYCHOLOGICAL STUDY OF SOCIAL ISSUES (Grants-in-Aid Program)

PO Box 1248
Ann Arbor MI 48106-1248
Phone/TTY: 313/662-9130
FAX: 313/662-5607
E-Mail: spssi@spssi.org
Internet: www.spssi.org

AMOUNT: up to $2,000

DEADLINE(S): APR 1; NOV 13

FIELD(S): Social Problem Areas

For scientific/graduate student research in social problem areas related to the basic interests and goals of SPSSI, particularly those that are not likely to receive support from traditional sources. Proposals especially encouraged in the fields of sexism and racism. SPSSI prefers unique/timely projects, underrepresented institutions/new investigators, volunteer research teams, and actual, not pilot, projects. Funds not normally provided for travel or living expenses.

Contact SPSSI for details. Applications available on website. NO SCHOLARSHIPS AVAILABLE—REQUESTS FOR FINANCIAL AID WILL NOT BE ANSWERED.

3208 — SOCIETY FOR THE PSYCHOLOGICAL STUDY OF SOCIAL ISSUES (The Sages Program: Action Grants for Experienced Scholars)

PO Box 1248
Ann Arbor MI 48106-1248
Phone/TTY: 313/662-9130
FAX: 313/662-5607
E-Mail: spssi@SPSSI.org
Internet: www.spssi.org

AMOUNT: Up to $2,000

DEADLINE(S): MAY 1

FIELD(S): Social Issues

Encourages intervention projects, non-partisan advocacy projects, and projects implementing public policy by retired social scientists over the age of 60. Proposals are invited for research projects applying social science principles to social issues in cooperation with a community, city, state, or federal organization or other not-for-profit group. Projects may also be done in cooperation with universities or colleges throughout the world or with the United Nations.

Contact SPSSI for details. Applications available on website. SCHOLARSHIPS NOT AVAILABLE—REQUESTS FOR FINANCIAL AID WILL NOT BE ANSWERED.

3209 — SOCIETY FOR THE PSYCHOLOGICAL STUDY OF SOCIAL ISSUES (Louise Kidder Early Career Award)

PO Box 1248
Ann Arbor MI 48106-1248
Phone/TTY: 313/662-9130
FAX: 313/662-5607
E-Mail: spssi@SPSSI.org
Internet: www.spssi.org

AMOUNT: $500 + plaque

DEADLINE(S): MAY 1

FIELD(S): Social Issues Research

Award recognizes social issues researchers who have made substantial contributions to the field early in their careers. Nominees should be investigators who

have made substantial contributions to social issues research within five years of receiving a graduate degree and who have demonstrated the potential to continue such contributions. To enter, send 3 copies of cover letter (stating accomplishments/future contributions), curriculum vitae, & 3 letters of support.

Contact SPSSI for details. Applications available on website. NO SCHOLARSHIPS AVAILABLE—REQUESTS FOR FINANCIAL AID WILL NOT BE ANSWERED.

3210 — SOCIETY FOR THE PSYCHOLOGICAL STUDY OF SOCIAL ISSUES (The Social Issues Dissertation Award)

PO Box 1248
Ann Arbor MI 48106-1248
Phone/TTY: 313/662-9130
FAX: 313/662-5607
E-Mail: spssi@spssi.org
Internet: www.spssi.org

AMOUNT: $600 (1st prize); $400 (2nd prize)

DEADLINE(S): APR 1

FIELD(S): Psychology, Social Science

Open to Ph.D. dissertations in psychology (or in a social science with psychological subject matter) based on social issues. Judged on scientific excellence and potential application to social problems. With application, include 500-word dissertation summary, identification (phone, address, school, etc.), and certification by your dissertation advisor of the acceptance date of dissertation.

Contact SPSSI for details. Applications available on website. NO SCHOLARSHIPS AVAILABLE—REQUESTS FOR FINANCIAL AID WILL NOT BE ANSWERED.

3211 — SOCIETY FOR THE PSYCHOLOGICAL STUDY OF SOCIAL ISSUES (SPSSI-Sponsored Research Workshop)

PO Box 1248
Ann Arbor MI 48106-1248
Phone/TTY: 313/662-9130
FAX: 313/662-5607
E-Mail: spssi@spssi.org
Internet: www.spssi.org

AMOUNT: up to $4,000

DEADLINE(S): OCT 5

FIELD(S): Social Science & related fields

A series of small research-oriented workshops to foster awareness of the state of social research in important areas of social policy. Formats vary from year to year. Proposals will be judged on description, site, timeline, organization, budget, and product(s).

No more than 30 participants. Contact SPSSI for details. Applications available on website. NO SCHOLARSHIPS AVAILABLE—REQUESTS FOR FINANCIAL AID WILL NOT BE ANSWERED.

3212 — SOCIETY FOR THE SCIENTIFIC STUDY OF SEXUALITY (Student Research Grant)

PO Box 208
Mount Vernon IA 52314-0208
319/895-8407
FAX: 319/895-6203
E-Mail: TheSociety@worldnet.att.net
Internet: www.ssc.wisc.edu/ssss

AMOUNT: $750

DEADLINE(S): FEB 1; SEP 1

FIELD(S): Human Sexuality

Open to students doing research in the area of human sexuality. Must be enrolled in a degree-granting program at an accredited institution; can be master's thesis or doctoral dissertation, but this is not a requirement. With application, must submit letter from Department Chairperson stating your status and educational purpose of research, 150-word abstract of proposed research, short biographical sketch, and proposed budget.

3 awards annually. Contact Ilsa Lottes, Ph.D., at SSSS for an application. Recipients announced in November at SSSS annual meeting.

3213 — SOCIETY FOR THE TEACHING OF PSYCHOLOGY (Teaching Awards Program)

Dept. Psychology
Ball State Univ.
Muncie IN 47306
765/747-6058
E-Mail: mkite@bsu.edu

AMOUNT: $500 + plaque

DEADLINE(S): JAN 4

FIELD(S): Psychology Education

For outstanding teachers of psychology in each of four environments: 1) 4-year colleges/universities, 2) 2-year colleges, 3) high school, and 4) graduate students.

For nomination procedures, contact Mary Kite, Ph.D., at above address.

3214 — THE ARC (Research Grants Program in Mental Retardation)

500 E. Border St., Suite 300
Arlington, TX 76010
817/261-6003
FAX: 817/277-3491
E-Mail: thearc@metronet.com
Internet: http://www.theArc.org/welcome.html

AMOUNT: Up to $25,000

DEADLINE(S): APR 1

FIELD(S): Prevention, amelioration, or cure of mental retardation

The Arc invites applications from researchers from diverse sources—individuals and universities, hospitals, and professional organizations with research interests.

Contact Dr. Michael Wehmeyer, Assistant Director, Department of Research and Program Services, The Arc, at above address, or Ann Balson.

3215 — U.S. DEPARTMENT OF TRANSPORTATION (Dwight D. Eisenhower Transportation Fellowships)

U.S. Dept. of Transportation
Fed. Hwy. Admin.
6300 Georgetown Pike, HHI-20
McLean VA 22101-2296
703/235-0538

AMOUNT: Varies

DEADLINE(S): FEB

FIELD(S): Transportation—such majors as chemistry; materials science; corrosion; civil, chemical, & electronics engineering; structures; human factors; computer science; psychology.

Research fellowships for undergrads and grad students at any Dept. of Transportation facility or selected IHE. For three to twelve months. Research must focus on transportation-related research and development in the above fields.

Contact Ilene Payne, Director, Universities and grants Programs at above location for details.

3216 — US AIR FORCE OPPORTUNITY CENTER (Armed Forces Health Professions Scholarships)

P.O. Box 3505
Attn AFHPSP/FAP
Capitol Heights MD 20790-9605
Written inquiry

AMOUNT: $913 per month stipend + tuition, fees, books, lab fees, etc.

DEADLINE(S): None

FIELD(S): Medicine; Dentistry; and Clinical Psychology (Ph.D)

Open to U.S. citizens enrolled or accepted for enrollment in any of the above fields at an accredited institution in the U.S. or Puerto Rico. Must qualify for appointment as an Air Force officer and sign a contractual agreement.

Write for complete information or call local recruiter (use blue pages in local telephone directories for telephone number).

3217 — WILLIAM T. GRANT FOUNDATION (Faculty Scholars Program—Research on Children, Adolescents, & Youth)

570 Lexington Ave.
New York NY 10022-6837
212/752-0071

AMOUNT: $50,000/yr. (max.)

DEADLINE(S): JUL 1

FIELD(S): Mental Health of Children, Adolescents, & Youth

For faculty members at universities and non-profit institutions, national and international. Award is for beginning investigators interested in the causes and consequences of factors which compromise the healthy mental development of children.

Renewable up to 5 years. Write for complete information.

3218 — WOMEN'S SPORTS FOUNDATION (Dorothy Harris Endowed Scholarship)

Eisenhower Park
East Meadow NY 11554
800/227-3988
FAX: 516/542-4716
E-Mail: WoSport@aol.com
Internet: www.lifetimetv.com/WoSport

AMOUNT: $1,500

DEADLINE(S): DEC 11

FIELD(S): Physical Education; Sports Management; Sports Psychology; Sports Sociology

For female graduate students who will pursue a full-time course of study in one of the above fields at an accredited graduate school in the Fall.

1-2 awards annually. Awarded in March. See website or write to above address for details.

3219 — WOMEN'S SPORTS FOUNDATION (Jackie Joyner-Kersee & Zina Garrison Minority Internships)

Eisenhower Park
East Meadow NY 11554
800/227-3988
FAX: 516/542-4716
E-Mail: WoSport@aol.com
Internet: www.lifetimetv.com/WoSport

AMOUNT: $4,000-$5,000

DEADLINE(S): Ongoing

FIELD(S): Sports-related fields

Provides women of color an opportunity to gain experience in a sports-related career and interact in the sports community. May be undergraduates, college graduates, graduate students, or women in a career change. Internships are located at the Women's Sports Foundation in East Meadow, New York.

4-6 awards annually. See website or write to above address for details.

3220 — WOODROW WILSON NATIONAL FELLOWSHIP FOUNDATION/JOHNSON & JOHNSON (Dissertation Grants in Women's & Children's Health)

CN 5281
Princeton NJ 08543-5281
609/452-7007
FAX: 609/452-0066
E-Mail: charoltte@woodrow.org
Internet: www.woodrow.org

AMOUNT: $2,000 (for travel, books, microfilming, taping, computer services, etc.)

DEADLINE(S): NOV 8

FIELD(S): Women's & Children's Health

Open to doctoral students in nursing, public health, anthropology, history, sociology, psychology, or social work, who have completed all predissertation requirements at US graduate schools. Must have at least six months left to complete dissertation, which should include significant research on issues related to women's & children's health. Must submit transcripts, proposal, bibliography, & interest. Based on originality & scholarly validity.

15 awards annually. See website or contact WWNFF for an application. Winners announced in February.

3221 — ZETA PHI BETA SORORITY EDUCATIONAL FOUNDATION (Lullelia W. Harrison Scholarship in Counseling)

1734 New Hampshire Ave., NW
Washington DC 20009
Internet: www.zpb1920.org/nefforms.htm

AMOUNT: $500-$1,000

DEADLINE(S): FEB 1

FIELD(S): Counseling

Open to graduate and undergraduate level students enrolled in a degree program in counseling. Award is for full-time study for one academic year (Fall-Spring). Must submit proof of enrollment.

Send self-addressed, stamped envelope to above address between September 1st and December 15th for an application.

SOCIOLOGY

3222 — AMERICAN UNIVERSITY IN CAIRO (International Graduate Fellowships in Sociology-Anthropology)

420 Fifth Ave.
3rd Floor
New York NY 10017-2729
212/730-8800
FAX: 212/730-1600

E-Mail: aucegypt@aucnyo.edu

Internet: www.aucegypt.edu

AMOUNT: Tuition + stipend paid in Egyptian pounds

DEADLINE(S): FEB 1

FIELD(S): Sociology; Anthropology

For graduate students in the master of arts program at the American University in Cairo, Egypt, who do not hold Egyptian citizenship. Must have a GPA of at least 3.4. Financial need NOT a factor.

2 awards annually. Renewable. Contact Mary Davidson at above address for complete information.

3223 — ASSOCIATION FOR WOMEN IN SCIENCE EDUCATIONAL FOUNDATION (AWIS Predoctoral Awards)

1200 New York Ave. NW, Suite 650

Washington DC 20005

202/326-8940 or 800-886-AWIS

E-Mail: awis@awis.org

Internet: www.awis.org

AMOUNT: $1,000

DEADLINE(S): JAN 16

FIELD(S): Various Sciences and Social Sciences

Scholarships for female doctoral students. Summary page, description of research project, resume, references, transcripts, and biographical sketch required. US citizens may study at any graduate institution; non-citizens must study at US institutions.

5-10 awards annually. See website or write to above address for an application and complete information.

3224 — ASSOCIATION FOR WOMEN IN SCIENCE EDUCATIONAL FOUNDATION (AWIS Pre-doctoral Awards)

1200 New York Ave. NW, Suite 650

Washington DC 20005

202/326-8940 or 800/886-AWIS

E-Mail: awis@awis.org

Internet: www.awis.org

AMOUNT: $1,000

DEADLINE(S): JAN 16

FIELD(S): Various Sciences and Social Sciences

Scholarships for female doctoral students. Summary page, description of research project, resume, references, transcripts, and biographical sketch required. US citizens may study at any graduate institution; non-citizens must be enrolled in US institutions.

5-10 awards annually. See website or write to above address for an application and more information.

3225 — ASSOCIATION FOR WOMEN IN SCIENCE EDUCATIONAL FOUNDATION (Ruth Satter Memorial Award)

1200 New York Ave., NW, Suite 650

Washington DC 20005

202/326-8940 or 800/886-AWIS

E-Mail: awis@awis.org

Internet: www.awis.org

AMOUNT: $1,000

DEADLINE(S): JAN 16

FIELD(S): Various Sciences and Social Sciences

Scholarships for female doctoral students who have interrupted their education for at least three years to raise a family. Summary page, description of research project, resume, references, transcripts, biographical sketch, and letter from your department to confirm eligibility required. US citizens may study at any graduate institution; non-citizens must attend US institutions.

See website or write to above address for more information or an application.

3226 — ASSOCIATION FOR WOMEN IN SCIENCE EDUCATIONAL FOUNDATION (Ruth Satter Memorial Award)

1200 New York Ave. NW, Suite 650

Washington DC 20005

202/326-8940 or 800/886-AWIS

E-Mail: awis@awis.org

Internet: www.awis.org

AMOUNT: $1,000

DEADLINE(S): JAN 16

FIELD(S): Various Sciences and Social Sciences

Scholarships for female doctoral students who have interupted their education three years or more to raise a family. Summary page, description of research project, resume, references, transcripts, biographical sketch, and proof of eligibility from department head required. US citizens may attend any graduate institution; non-citizens must be enrolled in US institutions.

See website or write to above address for more information or an application.

3227 — AUSTRALIAN FEDERATION OF UNIVERSITY WOMEN - WESTERN AUSTRALIA (Joyce Riley Bursary)

Bursary Liaison Officer

PO Box 48

Nedlands WA 6909 AUSTRALIA

Written Inquiry

AMOUNT: Aus$1,700 - Aus$2,750

DEADLINE(S): JUL 31

FIELD(S): Humanities; Social Sciences

To support women graduates of a Western Australian university to complete a higher degree or post-doctoral research in Humanities or Social Sciences at a recognized university in any country.

Membership in AFUW or in IFUW is required. Contact above location for further information.

3228 — AUSTRALIAN FEDERATION OF UNIVERSITY WOMEN - WESTERN AUSTRALIA (Joyce Riley Bursary)

Bursary Liaison Officer

PO Box 48

Nedlands WA 6009 AUSTRALIA

Written Inquiry

AMOUNT: Aus$1,700 - Aus$2,750

DEADLINE(S): JUL 31

FIELD(S): Humanities; Social Sciences

To support women graduates of a recognized university to complete a higher degree or post-doctoral research at a university in Western Australia.

Membership in AFUW or in IFUW is required. Write to above address for complete information.

3229 — B'NAI B'RITH YOUTH ORGANIZATION (Scholarship Program)

1640 Rhode Island Avenue NW

Washington DC 20036

202/857-6633

AMOUNT: $2,500 per year

DEADLINE(S): Varies (spring)

FIELD(S): Social Work

Open to U.S. citizens of Jewish faith who are first- or second-year grad students attending accredited graduate schools of social work or who are college seniors planning to attend a graduate school of social work.

Must show evidence of good scholarship, interest in working for Jewish agencies, and have knowledge of Jewish communal structure & institutions. Renewable. Write for complete information.

3230 — CHRISTIAN A. JOHNSON ENDEAVOR FOUNDATION (Native American Fellows)

Harvard Univ., 79 John F. Kennedy St.

Cambridge MA 02138

617/495-1152

FAX: 617/496-3900

Internet: www.ksg.harvard.edu/hpaied/cjohn.htm

AMOUNT: Varies

DEADLINE(S): MAY 1

FIELD(S): Social sciences, government, or program related to Native American studies

Fellowships for students of Native American ancestry who attend a John F. Kennedy School of Government degree program. Applicant, parent, or grandparent must hold membership in a federally or state-recognized tribe, band, or other organized group of Native Americans. Must be commited to a career in American Indian affairs. Awards based on merit and need.

Renewable, based on renomination and availability of funds. To apply, contact John F. Kennedy School of Government at above address.

3231 — COUNCIL FOR EUROPEAN STUDIES (Predissertation Fellowships)

Columbia Univ
807-807A International Affairs Bldg.
New York NY 10027
212/854-4172
FAX: 212/854-8808
E-Mail: ces@columbia.edu
Internet: www.europanet.org

AMOUNT: $4,000 stipend (max.)

DEADLINE(S): FEB 1

FIELD(S): Cultural Anthropology; History (post 1750); Political Science; Sociology; Geography; Urban & Regional Planning

Awards are for research in France to determine viability of projected doctoral dissertation in modern history and social sciences. Recipients test research design of dissertation, determine availability of archival materials, and contact French scholars. Must be US citizen or permanent resident at a US institution and have completed at least two but no more than three years of full-time doctoral study by end of year. Institutional membership in Council is required.

6 awards annually. See website or contact Council for an application.

3232 — COUNCIL OF JEWISH FEDERATIONS (Federation Executive Recruitment & Education Program Scholarships)

111 8th Ave.
New York NY 10011
212/598-3583
FAX: 212/475-6571
E-Mail: susan_sherr@cjfny.org

AMOUNT: $7,500 and $20,000

DEADLINE(S): FEB 1

FIELD(S): Social Work; Public Administration

Two-year course of study leading to a master's degree in social work and/or Jewish communal service and public administration. Applicants must demonstrate strong commitment to Jewish community service and have at least a 3.0 GPA.

Recipients must agree to work for a North America Jewish Federation for at least 3 years after graduation. Write for complete information.

3233 — CYNTHIA E. AND CLARA H. HOLLIS FOUNDATION

100 Summer St.
Boston MA 02110
Written inquiry

AMOUNT: Varies

DEADLINE(S): APR 1

FIELD(S): Nursing, social work, dental or medical technology, and religion

Scholarships for Massachusetts with preference given to students in the above fields. For undergraduates, graduates, voc-tech, and adult education. Must demonstrate financial need.

Send SASE to Walter E. Palmer, Esq., 35 Harvard St., Brookline, MA 02146 for application details. Scholarship forms are also available from the rector of All Saints Church, Brookline High School, and St. Mary's High School, all in Brookline, Massachusetts.

3234 — DELTA SOCIETY (James M. Harris/ Sarah W. Sweatt Student Travel Grant)

289 Perimeter Rd. East
Benton WA 98055-1329
425/226-7357
FAX: 425/235-1076
E-Mail: deltasociety@cis.compuserve.com
Internet: www.deltasociety.org

AMOUNT: Varies

DEADLINE(S): Varies

FIELD(S): Human-Animal Interactions; Animal Assisted Therapy; Service Animals; Pet Loss

Travel grants for graduate/postgraduate students to attend Delta Society's annual conference. Must be a full-time student in veterinary human health care. Student must provide detailed plan of how conference information will be shared. Must also attend the full conference and demonstrate ability to cover costs of registration, hotel, and meals. Financial need NOT a factor.

2-4 awards annually. Contact Michelle Cobey for an application.

3235 — EASTER SEAL SOCIETY OF IOWA, INC. (Scholarships & Awards)

P.O. Box 4002
Des Moines IA 50333-4002
515/289-1933

AMOUNT: $400-$600

DEADLINE(S): APR 15

FIELD(S): Physical Rehabilitation, Mental Rehabilitation, and related areas

Open ONLY to Iowa residents who are full-time undergraduate sophomores, juniors, seniors, or graduate students at accredited institutions planning a career in the broad field of rehabilitation. Must indicate financial need and be in top 40% of their class.

6 scholarships per year. Must re-apply each year.

3236 — EPILEPSY FOUNDATION OF AMERICA (Behavioral Sciences Research Training Fellowships)

4351 Garden City Drive
Landover MD 20785-2267
301/459-3700 or FAX: 301/577-2684
FDD: 800/332-2070
E-Mail: postmaster@efa.org
Internet: www.efa.org

AMOUNT: Up to $30,000

DEADLINE(S): FEB 1

FIELD(S): Epilepsy as related to Behavioral Sciences (includes sociology, social work, psychology, anthropology, nursing, political science, etc.)

A one-year training experience for postdoctoral scholars to develop expertise in the area of epilepsy research relative to the behavioral sciences. The project must be carried out at an approved facility. Amount depends on experience and qualifications of the applicant and the scope and duration of proposed project.

Contact EFA for an application.

3237 — ESPN (Internship Programs)

Human Resources Dept.
ESPN, Inc.
ESPN Plaza
Bristol CT 06010
No phone calls. Internet:
espnet.sportszone.com/editors/studios/
97faq.html

AMOUNT: Paid Internships

DEADLINE(S): OCT 1; MAR 1; JUN 1

FIELD(S): Television Industry, Public Relations, Sports

12-week internships in the spring, summer, and fall for undergraduate juniors/seniors and graduate students. Some areas require weekend/evening hours and a strong knowledge of sports. Interns receive hourly wages and take part in many company-sponsored activities. ESPN does not provide housing for students, but we do try to assist in finding suitable living arrangements once selected.

To apply for internship programs, please send cover letter and resume to the above address. If applying to the Communications Dept., please also enclose writing samples and send attention to Diane Lamb.

3238 — FIRST UNITED METHODIST CHURCH (Robert Stevenson & Doreene E. Cater Scholarships)

302 5th Ave., S.
St. Cloud MN 56301
FAX: 320/251-0878
E-Mail: FUMCloud@aol.com

AMOUNT: $100-$300

DEADLINE(S): JUN 1

FIELD(S): Humanitarian & Christian Service: Teaching, Medicine, Social Work, Environmental Studies, etc.

Stevenson Scholarship is open to undergraduate members of the First United Methodist Church of St. Cloud. Cater Scholarship is open to members of the Minnesota United Methodist Conference who are entering the sophomore year or higher of college work. Both require two letters of reference, transcripts, and financial need.

5-6 awards annually. Contact Scholarship Committee for an application.

3239 — FORD FOUNDATION/NATIONAL RESEARCH COUNCIL (Predoctoral/ Dissertation Fellowships for Minorities)

2101 Constitution Ave.
Washington DC 20418
202/334-2872
E-Mail: infofell@nas.edu
Internet: http//www.nas.edu/fo/index.html

AMOUNT: $14,000 annual stipend + $6,000 grant to institution; $18,000 for dissertation fellowship

DEADLINE(S): NOV 3

FIELD(S): Most fields of study: sciences, humanities, engineering, behavioral science, social sciences, and computer science

Predoctoral and dissertation fellowships for students whose ethnicity is Alaskan Native, Black/ African American, Mexican American/Chicano, Native American Indian, Native Pacific Islander, or Puerto Rican. For research-based programs leading to careers in college teaching and research.

Contact above address or website.

3240 — FOUNDATION FOR SEACOAST HEALTH (Scholarship Program)

P.O. Box 4606
Portsmouth NH 03802-4606
603/433-3008
FAX: 603/433-2036
E-Mail: ffsh@nh.ultranet.com
Internet: www.nh.ultranet.com/~ffsh

AMOUNT: $1,000-10,000

DEADLINE(S): FEB 1

FIELD(S): Health-related fields

Open to undergraduate and graduate students pursuing health-related fields of study who are legal residents of the following cities in New Hampshire: Portsmouth, Newington, New Castle, Rye, Greenland, N. Hampton, or these cities in Maine: Kittery, Eliot, or York, Maine. Must have resided in the area for at least two years.

Write or check website for details. $150,000 awarded annually; 35 awards given

3241 — FRENCH-AMERICAN FOUNDATION (Bicentennial Fellowships)

41 East 72nd St.
New York NY 10021
212/288-4000
FAX: 212/288-4765
E-Mail: French_AmerFdn@msn.com

AMOUNT: 10,000 French francs/mo.

DEADLINE(S): FEB 2

FIELD(S): Social sciences

For doctoral students in the social sciences to travel to France for one year to conduct research essential to the completion of their dissertations. Must have completed all other requirements for Ph.D. May not use the award until exams are passed.

Requires application with a statement of purpose, full academic records, plan of research, bibliography, abstract, and three academic recommendations.

3242 — GRACE FOUNDATION SCHOLARSHIP TRUST FUND

P.O. Box 924
Menlo Park CA 94026-0924
Written inquiry

AMOUNT: $1,000 to $4,000

DEADLINE(S): JAN 31

FIELD(S): Christian

One-year scholarships for full or partial tuition payment for full-time study at an accredited college or university. For training future Christian ministers and professional workers in developing countries in Asia/Southeast Asia. Candidates must have completed one or more years of college in or near their native country, be a strong Christian, have a 3.0 or higher GPA, and be pursuing a career in either the ministry, medicine, teaching, or social service.

Renewable up to graduation—four years maximum—pending maintenance of 3.0 GPA. Applications available between Sept. 1 and Oct. 31. Must demonstrate financial need.

3243 — HILLEL INTERNATIONAL CENTER (The Public Policy Fellowship)

Eran Gasko
1640 Rhode Island Ave. NW
Washington DC 20036
202/857-6543
202/857-6560
FAX: 202/857-6693
E-Mail: smusher@hillel.org
Internet: www.hillel.org/careermoves/ publicpolicy.htm

AMOUNT: Professional Experience

DEADLINE(S): None specified

FIELD(S): Public Policy/Social Issues

One-year professional experience for an oustanding recent Jewish graduate, who coordinates public policy initiatives nationwide. The Fellow strives to increase student activism in political and social issues. S/he works with students and national organizations to create innovative initiatives in social action, campus community relations councils, environmental issues, Israel programming, and international relief efforts.

Contact Eran Gasko, Human Resources, for an application.

3244 — INSTITUTE FOR ADVANCED STUDIES IN THE HUMANITIES (Visiting Research Fellowships)

Univ Edinburgh
Hope Park Square
Edinburgh EH8 9NW SCOTLAND UK
0131 650 4671
FAX: 0131 668 2252
E-Mail: iash@ed.ac.uk
Internet: www.ed.ac.uk/iash/homepage.html

AMOUNT: Non-stipendiary*

DEADLINE(S): DEC 1

FIELD(S): Arts; Social Sciences; Law; Music; Divinity

Postdoctoral research fellowships of between two and six months are tenable at the Institute for Advanced Studies in the Humanities. Based on academic record and publications. *Most fellowships are honorary, but limited support towards expenses is available to a small number of candidates. Fellows are allocated a study room within the Institute and hold one or two seminars during their tenure. Must submit research report at end of fellowship. No teaching required.

15 awards annually. Not renewable. Contact Mrs. Anthea Taylor for an application.

3245 — INSTITUTE FOR HUMANE STUDIES (Humane Studies Fellowship)

4084 University Dr., Ste. 101
Fairfax VA 22030-6812

703/934-6920 or 800/697-8799
FAX: 703/352-7535
E-Mail: ihs@gmu.edu
Internet: www.theihs.org

AMOUNT: up to $12,000

DEADLINE(S): DEC 31

FIELD(S): Social Sciences; Law; Humanities;
Jurisprudence; Journalism

Awards are for graduate and advanced undergraduate students pursuing degrees at any accredited domestic or foreign school. Based on academic performance, demonstrated interest in classical liberal ideas, and potential to contribute to the advancement of a free society.

90 awards annually. Apply online or contact IHS for an application.

3246 — INTERNATIONAL ASSOCIATION OF FIRE CHIEFS FOUNDATION (Scholarship Program)

1257 Wiltshire Rd.
York PA 17403
717/854-9083

AMOUNT: $250-$4,000

DEADLINE(S): AUG 15

FIELD(S): Business and Urban Administration, Fire Science

Open to members of a fire service of a state, county, provincial, municipal, community, industrial, or federal fire department.

Renewable. Write for complete information.

3247 — JAMES FORD BELL FOUNDATION (Summer Internship Program)

2925 Dean Pkwy., Ste. 811
Minneapolis MN 55416
612/285-5435
FAX: 612/285-5435
E-Mail: famphiladv@uswest.net

AMOUNT: $4,000 for 3 months

DEADLINE(S): APR 30

FIELD(S): Nonprofit Management; Community Service

Paid summer internships for graduate students pursuing careers in such areas as health and human services, conservation biology, education, and philanthropy. Must have an interest in non-profit management and community service. Preference given to individuals planning to remain in Twin Cities after graduation.

Contact Foundation for a list of internship opportunities after January 1st; students must apply for specific positions at organizations, not through the program itself.

3248 — JAPANESE AMERICAN CITIZENS LEAGUE (Minoru Yasui Memorial Scholarship)

1765 Sutter St.
San Francisco CA 94115
415/921-5225
FAX: 415/931-4671
E-Mail: jacl@jacl.org
Internet: www.jacl.org

AMOUNT: Varies

DEADLINE(S): APR 1

FIELD(S): Human & Civil Rights; Sociology; Law; Education

Open to JACL members or their children only. For graduate students with a strong interest in human and civil rights. Student must be currently enrolled in, or planning to enroll in, an accredited graduate school. Financial need NOT a factor.

40 awards annually. For membership information or an application, send a self-addressed, stamped envelope to above address.

3249 — JEWISH COMMUNITY CENTERS ASSOCIATION (JCCA Scholarship Program)

15 East 26th Street
New York NY 10010-1579
212/532-4958, ext. 246
FAX: 212/481-4174
E-Mail: Webmaster@jcca.org
Internet: www.jcca.org

AMOUNT: Up to $7,500

DEADLINE(S): FEB 15

FIELD(S): Social Work; Jewish Communal Studies; Physical Education; Early Childhood Education; Cultural Arts

Open to graduate students of the Jewish faith who are enrolled in a master's degree program and are committed to a career in the Jewish community center field in North America. Must have an undergraduate GPA of at least 3.0, leadership potential, and a strong Jewish background.

8 awards annually. Financial need NOT a factor. Contact Michelle Cohen at above address for an application.

3250 — JEWISH VOCATIONAL SERVICE (Marcus & Theresa Levie Educational Fund Scholarships)

1 S. Franklin St.
Chicago IL 60606
312/346-6700

AMOUNT: To $5,000

DEADLINE(S): MAR 1

FIELD(S): Social Work, Medicine, Dentistry, Nursing, & other related professions & vocations

Open to Cook County residents of the Jewish faith who plan careers in the above fields. For undergraduate juniors and seniors and graduate students. Applications available Dec. 1 from Scholarship Secretary.

Must show financial need. 85-100 awards per year. Renewal possible with reapplication. Write for complete information.

3251 — LADY ALLEN OF HURTWOOD MEMORIAL TRUST (Travel Grants)

21 Aspull Common
Leigh Lancs WN7 3PB ENGLAND
01942-674895

AMOUNT: up to 1,000 pounds sterling

DEADLINE(S): JAN 15

FIELD(S): Welfare And Education Of Children

A travel grant to those whose proposed project will directly benefit their work with children. People working with children and young people may apply, particularly those working with disabled and disadvantaged children. Successful candidates must write up an account of the work which the scholarship has funded. GRANTS ARE NOT FOR ACADEMIC STUDY; ONLY QUALIFIED INDIVIDUALS MAY APPLY.

Contact Dorothy E. Whitaker, Trustee, for application forms—available between May and December each year.

3252 — MARYLAND HIGHER EDUCATION COMMISSION (Professional School Scholarships)

State Scholarship Admin
16 Francis St.
Annapolis MD 21401-1781
800/974-1024 or 410/974-5370
TTY: 800/735-2258

AMOUNT: $200-$1,000

DEADLINE(S): MAR 1

FIELD(S): Dentistry; Pharmacy; Medicine; Law; Nursing; Social Work

Open to Maryland residents who have been admitted as full-time students at a participating graduate institution of higher learning in Maryland or an undergraduate/graduate nursing program. Must fill out government FAFSA form.

Renewable up to 4 years. Contact MHEC for an application and see your school's financial aid office for FAFSA.

3253 — NATIONAL COUNCIL OF FARMER COOPERATIVES (Graduate Awards)

50 F St., NW, Ste. 900
Washington DC 20001
202/626-8700
FAX: 202/626-8722

AMOUNT: $1,000 (1st prize); $800 (2nd); $600 (3rd)

DEADLINE(S): APR 1

FIELD(S): American Cooperatives

Open to graduate students working on theses or dissertations dealing with some aspect of economics, finance, operation, law, or structure of American cooperatives. May be in such fields as economics, business communications, sociology, etc.

3 awards annually. Not renewable. Contact NCFC Education Foundation for registration form.

3254 — NATIONAL HEMOPHILIA FOUNDATION (Social Work Excellence Fellowship)

116 W. 32nd St.
11th Floor
New York NY 10001
800/42-HANDI or 212/328-3700
FAX: 212/328-3788
E-Mail: dkenny@hemophilia.org
Internet: www.hemophilia.org

AMOUNT: $5,000

DEADLINE(S): APR 1

FIELD(S): Hemophilia Care; Social Work

Award is for a social worker interested in bleeding disorders care for conducting psychosocial research or a clinical project of relevance and benefit to providers and consumers in the bleeding disorders community. Must hold an MSW from an accredited school of social work, be enrolled in a DSW program, or be licensed by the state to practice as a master's level clinical social worker and work in a bleeding disorders program. Financial need NOT a factor.

1 award annually. Not renewable. Contact Denise Kenny at NHF for an application.

3255 — NATIONAL PARKS SERVICE (Science Scholars Program)

1849 C St., NW
Washington DC 20240
202/208-6843
E-Mail: aspiceland@goparks.org
Internet: www.nps.gov

AMOUNT: $25,000/yr.

DEADLINE(S): JUN 15

FIELD(S): Biological, Physical, Social, & Cultural Sciences

Three-year scholarships to Ph.D. candidates pursuing degrees in above fields. Objectives are to encourage young scientists to engage in park-related research, conduct innovative research on issues central to the National Parks, and encourage use of parks as laboratories for sciences. NPF will transfer the scholarship funds to each student's university, providing for tuition, field work, stipend, & other research expenses. Must submit research proposal.

4 awards annually. See website or contact Dr. Gary E. Machlis, Program Director, at NPS for an application. Winners announced shortly after August 15th.

3256 — NEW YORK CITY DEPT. CITYWIDE ADMINISTRATIVE SERVICES (Urban Fellows Program)

1 Centre St., 24th Fl.
New York NY 10007
212/487-5600
FAX: 212/487-5720

AMOUNT: $18,000 stipend

DEADLINE(S): JAN 20

FIELD(S): Public Administration; Urban Planning; Government; Public Service; Urban Affairs

Fellowship program provides one academic year (9 months) of full-time work experience in urban government. Open to graduating college seniors and recent college graduates. U.S. citizenship required.

Write for complete information.

3257 — NEW YORK STATE HIGHER EDUCATION SERVICES CORPORATION (N.Y. State Regents Professional/Health Care Opportunity Scholarships)

Cultural Education Center, Rm. 5C64
Albany NY 12230
518/486-1319
Internet: www.hesc.com

AMOUNT: $1,000-$10,000/yr.

DEADLINE(S): Varies

FIELD(S): Medicine and dentistry and related fields, architecture, nursing, psychology, audiology, landscape architecture, social work, chiropractic, law, pharmacy, accounting, speech language pathology

For NY state residents who are economically disadvantaged and members of a minority group underrepresented in the chosen profession and attending school in NY state. Some programs carry a service obligation in New York for each year of support. For U.S. citizens or qualifying noncitizens.

Medical/dental scholarships require one year of professional work in NY.

3258 — OPEN SOCIETY INSTITUTE (Environmental Management Fellowships)

400 West 59th St.
New York NY 10019
212/548-0600 or 212/757-2323
FAX: 212/548-4679 or 212/548-4600
Internet: www.soros.org/efp.html

AMOUNT: Fees, room, board, living stipend, textbooks, international transportation, health insurance

DEADLINE(S): NOV 15

FIELD(S): Earth sciences, natural sciences, humanities (exc. language), anthropology, sociology, mathematics, or engineering

Two-year fellowships for use in selected universities in the U.S. for international students. For students/professionals in fields related to environmental policy, legislation, and remediation techniques applicable to their home countries.

To apply, contact your local Soros Foundation or Open Society Institute. Further details on website.

3259 — OPEN SOCIETY INSTITUTE (Individual Project Fellowships)

400 West 59th St.
New York NY 10019
212/548-0600 or 212/757-2323
FAX: 212/548-4679 or 212/548-4600
Internet: www.soros.org/fellow/
individual.html

AMOUNT: Varies

DEADLINE(S): Varies

FIELD(S): Any field of study related to creating an open society: reliance on the rule of law, the existence of a democratically elected government, a diverse and vigorous civil society, and respect for minorities and minority opinions.

Two-year fellowships for use in selected universities in the U.S. for international students. For students/professionals in fields related to environmental policy, legislation, and remediation techniques applicable to their home countries.

To apply, contact the Soros Foundation/Open Society Institute. Further details on website.

3260 — PEACE RESEARCH CENTRE (Peace Research Loan Scholarship)

c/o Gujarat Vidyapith
Ahmedabad-380014 INDIA
7450746

AMOUNT: 2,000/Rs (25% returnable)

DEADLINE(S): JUNE

FIELD(S): Peace Research, Peace Education, Nonviolence

Financial aid for students between the ages of 21 and 65 in a Master of Arts program concentrating on research regarding peace, peace education, and nonviolence.

Duration of one year only.

3261 — POPULATION COUNCIL (Fellowships in Population Sciences)

One Dag Hammarskjold Plaza
New York NY 10017
212/339-0636
FAX: 212/755-6052
E-Mail: rmohanam@popcouncil.org
Internet: www.popcouncil.org

AMOUNT: $25,000/yr. for 2 years

DEADLINE(S): OCT 31

FIELD(S): Population Sciences

Postdoctoral fellowships for study in population sciences in Nairobi, Kenya, Africa. Open to citizens of any country.

Two awards per year. Selection criteria will stress academic excellence and prospective contribution to the population field. For information and applications contact Raji Mohanam at above address. In Kenya, contact: Carol Libamira, APPRC Coordinator, Population Council, Mutichoice Towers, Upper Hill, P.O. Box 17643, Nairobi, Kenya. 254/2.713.480/1-3.

3262 — POPULATION COUNCIL (Fellowships in Social Sciences)

Policy Research Division
One Dag Hammarskjold Plaza
New York NY 10017
212/339-0671
FAX: 212/755-6052
E-Mail: ssfellowship@popcouncil.org
Internet: www.popcouncil.org

AMOUNT: Monthly stipend, partial tuition/fees, transportation, book/supply allowance, & health insurance

DEADLINE(S): DEC 15

FIELD(S): Population Studies; Demography; Sociology; Anthropology; Economics; Public Health; Geography

Twelve-month award is open to doctoral & postdoctoral scholars for advanced training in above fields that deal with developing world. Doctoral students may request support for dissertation fieldwork/writing. Postdoctorates may pursue research, midcareer training, or resident training. Based on academic excellence, prospective contribution, & well-conceived research proposal. Preference given to those from developing countries.

See website or contact Fellowship Coordinator for an application.

3263 — PRESIDENT'S COMMISSION ON WHITE HOUSE FELLOWSHIPS

712 Jackson Place NW
Washington DC 20503
202/395-4522

FAX: 202/395-6179
E-Mail: almanac@ace.esusda.gov

AMOUNT: Wage (up to GS-14 Step 3; approximately $65,000 in 1995)

DEADLINE(S): DEC 1

FIELD(S): Public Service; Government; Community Involvement; Leadership

Mid-career professionals spend one year as special assistants to senior executive branch officials in Washington. Highly competitive. Non-partisan; no age or educational requirements. Fellowship year runs September 1 through August 31.

1,200 candidates applying for 11 to 19 fellowships each year. Write for complete information.

3264 — SCOTTISH RITE CHARITABLE FOUNDATION (Research Grants)

Roeher Institute, Kinsmen Bldg.
4700 Keele St.
North York Ontario M3J 1P3 CANADA
416/661-9611
TDD: 416/661-2023
FAX: 416/661-5701
E-Mail: mail@aacl.org
Internet: www.aacl.org

AMOUNT: $10,000 (max. grads); $35,000 (max. postdocs)

DEADLINE(S): APR 30

FIELD(S): Human Services; Intellectual Disability

Open to Canadian citizens/landed immigrants enrolled in masters or doctoral programs at Canadian universities. Must state intent to pursue career in Canada and have definite research projects supported by an academic advisor or a Roeher Institute associate/consultant. Also available to postdoctoral researchers.

Renewable. Contact the Secretary, Awards Adjudicating Committee, at the Scottish Rite for an application and details on preferred research topics.

3265 — SOCIAL SCIENCE RESEARCH COUNCIL (International Predissertation Fellowship Program)

810 Seventh Ave.
New York NY 10019
212/277-2700

AMOUNT: Varies

DEADLINE(S): Varies (TBA by participating universities)

FIELD(S): Economics; Political Science; Psychology; Sociology; other Social Science disciplines

Open to Ph.D. candidates enrolled in social science programs at 23 select universities and interested in supplementing disciplinary skills with area and language studies or acquiring advanced disciplinary training. Study

program is preparation for research on Africa, Central Asia & the Caucasus, China, Latin America, the Caribbean, Near & Middle East, and South or Southeast Asia.

Contact Ellen Perecman for an application.

3266 — SOCIETY FOR THE PSYCHOLOGICAL STUDY OF SOCIAL ISSUES (Applied Social Issues Internship Program)

PO Box 1248
Ann Arbor MI 48106-1248
Phone/TTY: 313/662-9130
FAX: 313/662-5607
E-Mail: spssi@spssi.org
Internet: www.spssi.org

AMOUNT: $1,500-$2,500

DEADLINE(S): NOV 10

FIELD(S): Social Science & related fields

Internship awards cover research costs, community organizing, summer stipends, etc. Encourages intervention projects, non-partisan lobbying, applied research, & implementing public policy. Proposals are invited for applying social science principles to social issues, in cooperation with a community, city, or state government organization, public interest group, or other not-for-profit entity. College seniors, graduate students, and first-year postdoctorates may apply.

Contact SPSSI for details. Applications available on website. NO SCHOLARSHIPS AVAILABLE—REQUESTS FOR FINANCIAL AID WILL NOT BE ANSWERED.

3267 — SOCIETY FOR THE PSYCHOLOGICAL STUDY OF SOCIAL ISSUES (Clara Mayo Grants in Support of Master's Thesis and Pre-Dissertation Research on Sexism, Racism, or Prejudice)

PO Box 1248
Ann Arbor MI 48106-1248
Phone/TTY: 313/662-9130
FAX: 313/662-5607
E-Mail: spssi@spssi.org
Internet: www.spssi.org

AMOUNT: up to $1,000

DEADLINE(S): MAR 31

FIELD(S): Sexism, Racism, & Prejudice

These grants support research from students working on a master's thesis (preference given to those in terminal master's program) or pre-dissertation research on sexism, racism, or prejudice. Studies of application of theory or design of interventions/treatments to address these problems are welcome. Proposals that include college/university agreement to match amount requested are favored, but those without matching funds also considered.

4 awards annually. Applications availble on website. NO SCHOLARSHIPS AVAILABLE—REQUESTS FOR FINANCIAL AID WILL NOT BE ANSWERED.

3268 — SOCIETY FOR THE PSYCHOLOGICAL STUDY OF SOCIAL ISSUES (Otto Klineburg Intercultural and International Relations Award)

PO Box 1248
Ann Arbor MI 48106-1248
Phone/TTY: 313/662-9130
FAX: 313/662-5607
E-Mail: spssi@spssi.org
Internet: www.spssi.org

AMOUNT: $1,000

DEADLINE(S): FEB 1

FIELD(S): Intercultural & International Relations

Annual award for the best paper or article on intercultural or international relations. Originality of the contribution, whether theoretical or empirical, will be given special weight. Entries can be either papers published during the current year or unpublished manuscripts. Send five copies of entry.

Contact SPSSI for details. Applications available on website. SPSSI DOES NOT OFFER SCHOLARSHIPS— INQUIRIES FOR FINANCIAL AID WILL NOT BE ANSWERED.

3269 — SOCIETY FOR THE PSYCHOLOGICAL STUDY OF SOCIAL ISSUES (James Marshall Public Policy Fellowship)

PO Box 1248
Ann Arbor MI 48106-1248
313/662-9130
FAX: 313/662-5607
E-Mail: spssi@umich.edu
Internet: www.spssi.org

AMOUNT: $42,000 + health/vacation benefits

DEADLINE(S): JAN 10

FIELD(S): Public Policy, Social Science

Develops more effective interaction between those engaged in social research and the social policy arena. Working closely with the American Psychological Association's Public Policy Office in Washington, DC, the fellow provides SPSSI a link to legislation and national testimony. Activities range from legislative work, to developing/advocating for specific bills, to policy-relevant research/writing on issues such as international peace, abortion, and chlid poverty.

Contact SPSSI for details. NO SCHOLARSHIPS AVAILABLE—REQUESTS FOR FINANCIAL AID WILL NOT BE ANSWERED.

3270 — SOCIETY FOR THE PSYCHOLOGICAL STUDY OF SOCIAL ISSUES (Gordon Allport Intergroup Relations Prize)

PO Box 1248
Ann Arbor MI 48106-1248
Phone/TTY: 313/662-9130

FAX: 313/662-9130
E-Mail: spssi@spssi.org
Internet: www.spssi.org

AMOUNT: $1,000

DEADLINE(S): DEC 31

FIELD(S): Sociology/Intergroup Relations

Annual award for the best paper or article on intergroup relations. Originality of the contribution, whether theoretical or empirical, is given special consideration. The research area encompassing intergroup relations includes such dimensions as age, sex, socioeconomic status, and race. Entries can be either papers published during the current year or unpublished manuscripts. Send five copies of entry.

Contact SPSSI for details. Applications available on website. SPSSI DOES NOT OFFER SCHOLARSHIPS— REQUESTS FOR FINANCIAL AID WILL NOT BE ANSWERED.

3271 — SOCIETY FOR THE PSYCHOLOGICAL STUDY OF SOCIAL ISSUES (Grants-in-Aid Program)

PO Box 1248
Ann Arbor MI 48106-1248
Phone/TTY: 313/662-9130
FAX: 313/662-5607
E-Mail: spssi@spssi.org
Internet: www.spssi.org

AMOUNT: up to $2,000

DEADLINE(S): APR 1; NOV 13

FIELD(S): Social Problem Areas

For scientific/graduate student research in social problem areas related to the basic interests and goals of SPSSI, particularly those that are not likely to receive support from traditional sources. Proposals especially encouraged in the fields of sexism and racism. SPSSI prefers unique/timely projects, underrepresented institutions/new investigators, volunteer research teams, and actual, not pilot, projects. Funds not normally provided for travel or living expenses.

Contact SPSSI for details. Applications available on website. NO SCHOLARSHIPS AVAILABLE— REQUESTS FOR FINANCIAL AID WILL NOT BE ANSWERED.

3272 — SOCIETY FOR THE PSYCHOLOGICAL STUDY OF SOCIAL ISSUES (The Sages Program: Action Grants for Experienced Scholars)

PO Box 1248
Ann Arbor MI 48106-1248
Phone/TTY: 313/662-9130
FAX: 313/662-5607
E-Mail: spssi@spssi.org
Internet: www.spssi.org

AMOUNT: Up to $2,000

DEADLINE(S): MAY 1

FIELD(S): Social Issues

Encourages intervention projects, non-partisan advocacy projects, and projects implementing public policy by retired social scientists over the age of 60. Proposals are invited for research projects applying social science principles to social issues in cooperation with a community, city, state, or federal organization or other not-for-profit group. Projects may also be done in cooperation with universities or colleges throughout the world or with the United Nations.

Contact SPSSI for details. Applications available on website. SCHOLARSHIPS NOT AVAILABLE— REQUESTS FOR FINANCIAL AID WILL NOT BE ANSWERED.

3273 — SOCIETY FOR THE PSYCHOLOGICAL STUDY OF SOCIAL ISSUES (Louise Kidder Early Career Award)

PO Box 1248
Ann Arbor MI 48106-1248
Phone/TTY: 313/662-9130
FAX: 313/662-5607
E-Mail: spssi@spssi.org
Internet: www.spssi.org

AMOUNT: $500 + plaque

DEADLINE(S): MAY 1

FIELD(S): Social Issues Research

Award recognizes social issues researchers who have made substantial contributions to the field early in their careers. Nominees should be investigators who have made substantial contributions to social issues research within five years of receiving a graduate degree and who have demonstrated the potential to continue such contributions. To enter, send 3 copies of cover letter (stating accomplishments/future contributions), curriculum vitae, & 3 letters of support.

Contact SPSSI for details. Applications available on website. NO SCHOLARSHIPS AVAILABLE— REQUESTS FOR FINANCIAL AID WILL NOT BE ANSWERED.

3274 — SOCIETY FOR THE PSYCHOLOGICAL STUDY OF SOCIAL ISSUES (The Social Issues Dissertation Award)

PO Box 1248
Ann Arbor MI 48106-1248
Phone/TTY: 313/662-9130
FAX: 313/662-5607
E-Mail: spssi@spssi.org
Internet: www.spssi.org

AMOUNT: $600 (1st prize); $400 (2nd prize)

DEADLINE(S): APR 1

FIELD(S): Psychology, Social Science

Open to Ph.D. dissertations in psychology (or in a social science with psychological subject matter) based on social issues. Judged on scientific excellence and potential application to social problems. With application, include 500-word dissertation summary, identification (phone, address, school, etc.), and certification by your dissertation advisor of the acceptance date of dissertation.

Contact SPSSI for details. Applications available on website. NO SCHOLARSHIPS AVAILABLE— REQUESTS FOR FINANCIAL AID WILL NOT BE ANSWERED.

3275 — SOCIETY FOR THE PSYCHOLOGICAL STUDY OF SOCIAL ISSUES (SPSSI-Sponsored Research Workshop)

PO Box 1248
Ann Arbor MI 48106-1248
Phone/TTY: 313/662-9130
FAX: 313/662-5607
E-Mail: spssi@spssi.org
Internet: www.spssi.org

AMOUNT: up to $4,000

DEADLINE(S): OCT 5

FIELD(S): Social Science & related fields

A series of small research-oriented workshops to foster awareness of the state of social research in important areas of social policy. Formats vary from year to year. Proposals will be judged on description, site, timeline, organization, budget, and product(s).

No more than 30 participants. Contact SPSSI for details. Applications available on website. NO SCHOLARSHIPS AVAILABLE—REQUESTS FOR FINANCIAL AID WILL NOT BE ANSWERED.

3276 — STOCKHOLM UNIVERSITY - INTERNATIONAL GRADUATE PROGRAMME (Master's Programme in Swedish Social Studies)

Universitetsvagen 10F
Frescati
S-106 91 Stockholm SWEDEN
+46 8 163466
FAX: +46 8 155508
E-Mail: igp@statsvet.su.se
Internet: www.statsvet.su.se/IGP/home.html

AMOUNT: Tuition

DEADLINE(S): MAR 1

FIELD(S): Social Sciences; Economics; History; Anthropology; Sociology; Social Work; Political Science

Open to students who have completed a university degree in the social sciences with one of the above majors and who wish to study at Stockholm University in Sweden. Language of instruction is English.

Contact Stockholm University for an application.

3277 — THE HEATH EDUCATION FUND (Scholarships for Ministers, Priests, and Missionaries)

Barnett Bank, N.A., P.O. Box 40200
Jacksonville FL 32203-0200
904/464-2877

AMOUNT: $750-$1,000

DEADLINE(S): JUL 31

FIELD(S): Ministry, missionary work, or social work

Scholarships to high school graduates from the southeastern U.S. who wish to study in the above fields. Eligible states of residence: Alabama, Florida, Georgia, Kentucy, Louisiana, Maryland, Mississippi, North & couth Carolina, Tennessee, Virginia, and West Virginia.

Write to Barnett Bank's Trust Co., N.A., at above address for details and guidelines. Send SASE and letter with brief background of applicant, field of study, religious denomination and reason for request. Preference to Methodists or Episcopalians.

3278 — U.S. DEPARTMENT OF TRANSPORTATION (Dwight D. Eisenhower Transportation Fellowships)

U.S. Dept. of Transportation, Fed. Hwy. Admin., 6300 Georgetown Pike, HHI-20
McLean VA 22101-2296
703/235-0538

AMOUNT: Varies

DEADLINE(S): FEB

FIELD(S): Transportation—such majors as chemistry; materials science; corrosion; civil, chemical, & electronics engineering; structures; human factors; computer science; psychology.

Research fellowships for undergrads and grad students at any Dept. of Transportation facility or selected IHE. For three to twelve months. Research must focus on transportation-related research and development in the above fields.

Contact Ilene Payne, Director, Universities and grants Programs at above location for details.

3279 — U.S. DEPT. OF HEALTH & HUMAN SERVICES (Indian Health Service Health Professions Scholarship Program)

Twinbrook Metro Plaza, Suite 100
12300 Twinbrook Pkwy.
Rockville MD 20852
301/443-0234
FAX: 301/443-4815
Internet: www.ihs.gov/Recruitment/DHPS/SP/SBTOC3.asp

AMOUNT: Tuition + fees & monthly stipend of $938.

DEADLINE(S): APR 1

FIELD(S): Health professions, accounting, social work

Open to Native Americans or Alaska natives who are graduate students or college juniors or seniors in a program leading to a career in a fields listed above. U.S. citizenship required. Renewable annually with reapplication.

Scholarship recipients must intend to serve the Indian people. They incur a one-year service obligation to the IHS for each year of support for a minimum of two years. Write for complete information.

3280 — WILLIAM T. GRANT FOUNDATION (Faculty Scholars Program—Research on Children, Adolescents, & Youth)

570 Lexington Ave.
New York NY 10022-6837
212/752-0071

AMOUNT: $50,000/yr. (max.)

DEADLINE(S): JUL 1

FIELD(S): Mental Health of Children, Adolescents, & Youth

For faculty members at universities and non-profit institutions, national and international. Award is for beginning investigators interested in the causes and consequences of factors which compromise the healthy mental development of children.

Renewable up to 5 years. Write for complete information.

3281 — WOMEN'S SPORTS FOUNDATION (Dorothy Harris Endowed Scholarship)

Eisenhower Park
East Meadow NY 11554
800/227-3988
FAX: 516/542-4716
E-Mail: WoSport@aol.com
Internet: www.lifetimetv.com/WoSport

AMOUNT: $1,500

DEADLINE(S): DEC 11

FIELD(S): Physical Education; Sports Management; Sports Psychology; Sports Sociology

For female graduate students who will pursue a full-time course of study in one of the above fields at an accredited graduate school in the Fall.

1-2 awards annually. Awarded in March. See website or write to above address for details.

3282 — WOMEN'S SPORTS FOUNDATION (Jackie Joyner-Kersee & Zina Garrison Minority Internships)

Eisenhower Park
East Meadow NY 11554
800/227-3988
FAX: 516/542-4716

E-Mail: WoSport@aol.com

Internet: www.lifetimetv.com/WoSport

AMOUNT: $4,000-$5,000

DEADLINE(S): Ongoing

FIELD(S): Sports-related fields

Provides women of color an opportunity to gain experience in a sports-related career and interact in the sports community. May be undergraduates, college graduates, graduate students, or women in a career change. Internships are located at the Women's Sports Foundation in East Meadow, New York.

4-6 awards annually. See website or write to above address for details.

3283 — WOODROW WILSON NATIONAL FELLOWSHIP FOUNDATION/JOHNSON & JOHNSON (Dissertation Grants in Women's & Children's Health)

CN 5281

Princeton NJ 08543-5281

609/452-7007

FAX: 609/452-0066

E-Mail: charoltte@woodrow.org

Internet: www.woodrow.org

AMOUNT: $2,000 (for travel, books, microfilming, taping, computer services, etc.)

DEADLINE(S): NOV 8

FIELD(S): Women's & Children's Health

Open to doctoral students in nursing, public health, anthropology, history, sociology, psychology, or social work, who have completed all predissertation requirements at US graduate schools. Must have at least six months left to complete dissertation, which should include significant research on issues related to women's & children's health. Must submit transcripts, proposal, bibliography, & interest. Based on originality & scholarly validity.

15 awards annually. See website or contact WWNFF for an application. Winners announced in February.

3284 — ZETA PHI BETA SORORITY EDUCATIONAL FOUNDATION (Mildred Cater Bradham Social Work Fellowship)

1734 New Hampshire Ave., NW

Washington DC 20009

Internet: www.zpb1920.org/nefforms.htm

AMOUNT: $500-$1,000

DEADLINE(S): FEB 1

FIELD(S): All fields of study

Open to members of Zeta Phi Beta Sorority, Inc. who are pursuing a graduate or professional degree in social work at an accredited college/university. Award is for full-time study for one academic year (Fall-Spring) and is payable to the college/university of awardee's choice. University must submit documentation of academic study to the Scholarship Chairperson.

Renewable. Send self-addressed, stamped envelope to above address between September 1st and December 15th for an application.

SCHOOL OF VOCATIONAL ED

3285 — AERO CLUB OF NEW ENGLAND (Aviation Scholarships)

4 Emerson Drive

Acton MA 01720

978/263-7793

E-Mail: pattis22@aol.com

Internet: www.acone.org

AMOUNT: $500-$2,000

DEADLINE(S): MAR 31

FIELD(S): Aviation and related fields

Several scholarships with varying specifications for eligibility for New England residents to be used at FAA-approved flight schools in New England states.

Information and applications are on website above.

3286 — AIRCRAFT ELECTRONICS ASSOCIATION EDUCATIONAL FOUNDATION (Scholarships)

PO Box 1963

Independence MO 64055

816/373-6565

FAX: 816/478-3100

Internet: aeaavnews.org

AMOUNT: $1,000-$16,000

DEADLINE(S): Varies

FIELD(S): Avionics; Aircraft Repair

Various scholarships for high school and college students attending post-secondary institutions, including technical schools. Some are for study in Canada or Europe as well as the US.

25 programs. See website or contact AEA for specific details and applications.

3287 — AMERICAN ASSOCIATION OF COSMETOLOGY SCHOOLS (ACE Grants)

11811 N. Tatum Blvd., Ste. 1085

Phoenix AZ 85028

602/788-1170

FAX: 602/404-8900

E-Mail: jim@beautyschools.org

Internet: www.beautyschools.org

AMOUNT: $1,000 (average)

DEADLINE(S): None

FIELD(S): Cosmetology

Grants for US citizens/permanent residents who are accepted to a participating ACE grant school. Must be high school graduate or equivalent. Financial need is NOT a factor.

500+ awards annually. Not renewable. Contact Jim Cox at the American Association of Cosmetology Schools for an application.

3288 — AMERICAN INSTITUTE OF AERONAUTICS AND ASTRONAUTICS (Technical Committee Graduate Awards)

1801 Alexander Bell Drive, Suite 500

Reston VA 20191-4344

800/NEW-AIAA or 703/264-7500

FAX: 703/264-7551

E-Mail: custserv@aiaa.org

Internet: www.aiaa.org

AMOUNT: $1,000

DEADLINE(S): JAN 31

FIELD(S): Science, Engineering, Astronautics, Aeronautics

Open to graduate students who have completed at least one year of full-time graduate study. Must have in place or underway a university approved thesis or research project specializing in one of the listed technical areas. GPA of 3.0 or higher. Graduate study program must be in support of field of science and engineering encompassed by a specialized area. Must be endorsed by graduate advisor and appropriate university department head.

Write to the above address for complete information.

3289 — AMERICAN INSTITUTE OF AERONAUTICS AND ASTRONAUTICS (Graduate Student Awards)

1801 Alexander Bell Drive, Suite 500

Reston VA 20191-4344

800/639-AIAA or 703/264-7500

FAX: 703/264-7551

Internet: www.aiaa.org

AMOUNT: $5,000

DEADLINE(S): None specified

FIELD(S): Astronautics; Aeronautics; Aeronautical Engineering

For graduate student research in the aerospace field.

Eight awards. Contact above address for complete information.

3290 — AMERICAN INSTITUTE OF BAKING (Scholarships)

1213 Bakers Way

Manhattan KS 66502

800/633-5737

FAX: 785/537-1493

SCHOOL OF VOCATIONAL ED

E-Mail: kembers@aibonline.org
Internet: www.aibonline.org

AMOUNT: $500-$4,000

DEADLINE(S): None

FIELD(S): Baking Industry; Electrical/Electronic Maintenance

Award is to be used towards tuition for a 16- or 10-week course in baking science and technology or maintenance engineering at the Institute. Experience in baking, mechanics, or an approved alternative is required. Awards are intended for people who plan to seek new positions in the baking and maintenance engineering fields.

45 awards annually. Contact AIB for an application.

3291 — AMERICAN WINE SOCIETY EDUCATIONAL FOUNDATION (Scholarships and Grants)

1134 West Market St.
Bethlehem PA 18018-4910
610/865-2401 or 610/758-3845
FAX: 610/758-4344
E-Mail: lhso@lehigh.edu

AMOUNT: $2,000

DEADLINE(S): MAR 31

FIELD(S): Wine industry professional study: enology, viticulture, health aspects of food and wine, and using and appreciating fine wines.

To provide academic scholarships and research grants to students based on academic excellence. Must show financial need and genuine interest in pursuing careers in wine-related fields. For North American citizens, defined as U.S., Canada, Mexico, the Bahamas, and the West Indies at all levels of education.

Contact L.H. Sperling at above location for application.

3292 — ARTS MANAGEMENT P/L (Marten Bequest Travelling Scholarships)

Station House, Rawson Place
790 George St.
Sydney NSW 2000 Australia
(612)9212 5066
FAX: (612)9211 7762
E-Mail: vbraden@ozemail.com.au

AMOUNT: Aus. $18,000

DEADLINE(S): OCT 30

FIELD(S): Art; Performing Arts; Creative Writing

Open to native-born Australians aged 21-35 (17-35 ballet) who are of outstanding ability and promise in one or more categories of the Arts. The scholarships are intended to augment a scholar's own resources towards a cultural education, and it may be used for study, maintenance, and travel either in Australia or

overseas. Categories are: instrumental music, painting, singing, sculpture, architecture, ballet, prose, poetry, and acting.

1 scholarship granted in each of 9 categories which rotate in 2 groups on an annual basis. Contact Claudia Crosariol, Projects Administrator, for more information/entry form.

3293 — AVIATION COUNCIL OF PENNSYLVANIA (Scholarships)

3111 Arcadia Ave.
Allentown PA 18103
215/797-1133

AMOUNT: $1,000

DEADLINE(S): JUL 31

FIELD(S): Aviation maintenance, aviaiton management, or pilot training

Scholarships for individuals in the above fields who are residents of Pennsylvania but can attend school outside Pennsylvania.

Three awards yearly.

3294 — AVIATION INSURANCE ASSOCIATION (Scholarship)

Aviation Technology Department
1 Purdue Airport
West Lafayette, IN 47906-3398
954/986-8080

AMOUNT: $1,000

DEADLINE(S): FEB

FIELD(S): Aviation

Scholarships for aviation students who have completed at least 30 college credits, 15 of which are in aviation. Must have GPA of at least 2.5 and be a U.S. citizen.

Write to Professor Bernard Wuile at Purdue University at above address for application and details.

3295 — AVIATION MAINTENANCE EDUCATION FUND (AMEF Scholarship Program)

P.O. Box 2826
Redmond WA 98073
206/827-2295

AMOUNT: $250 - $1000

DEADLINE(S): None

FIELD(S): Aviation Maintenance Technology

AMEF scholarship program open to any worthy applicant who is enrolled in a federal aviation administration (FAA) certified aviation maintenance technology program.

Write for complete information.

3296 — BUSINESS & PROFESSIONAL WOMEN'S FOUNDATION (BPW Career Advancement Scholarship Program)

2012 Massachusetts Ave., NW
Washington DC 20036-1070
202/293-1200, ext. 169
FAX: 202/861-0298
Internet: www.bpwusa.org

AMOUNT: $500-$1,000

DEADLINE(S): APR 15

FIELD(S): Biology, Science, Education, Engineering, Social Science, Paralegal, Humanities, Business, Math, Computers, Law, MD, DD

For women (US citizens) aged 25+ accepted into accredited program at US institution (+Puerto Rico & Virgin Islands). Must graduate within 12 to 24 months from the date of grant and demonstrate critical finanacial need. Must have a plan to upgrade skills, train for a new career field, or to enter/re-enter the job market.

Full- or part-time study. For info see website or send business-sized, self-addressed, double-stamped envelope.

3297 — COOPERATIVE ASSOCIATION OF STATES FOR SCHOLARSHIPS (CASS) (Scholarships)

c/o Commonwealth Liaison
Unit 310 The Garrison
St. Michael BARBADOS
809/436-8754

AMOUNT: Varies

DEADLINE(S): None

FIELD(S): Business application/computer science

Scholarships for economically disadvanted deaf youth, ages 17-25, with strong leadership potential and an interest in computer science/business applications. Must be from Barbados, St. Kitts/Nevis, Grenada, St. Vincent, Antigua/Barbuda, St. Lucia, Dominica, or Jamaica.

Write to E. Caribbean Reg. Coordinator (CASS) at above address.

3298 — DELTA SOCIETY (James M. Harris/ Sarah W. Sweatt Student Travel Grant)

289 Perimeter Rd. East
Benton WA 98055-1329
425/226-7357
FAX: 425/235-1076
E-Mail: deltasociety@cis.compuserve.com
Internet: www.deltasociety.org

AMOUNT: Varies

DEADLINE(S): Varies

FIELD(S): Human-Animal Interactions; Animal Assisted Therapy; Service Animals; Pet Loss

460

Travel grants for graduate/postgraduate students to attend Delta Society's annual conference. Must be a full-time student in veterinary human health care. Student must provide detailed plan of how conference information will be shared. Must also attend the full conference and demonstrate ability to cover costs of registration, hotel, and meals. Financial need NOT a factor.

2-4 awards annually. Contact Michelle Cobey for an application.

3299 — FOOD INDUSTRY SCHOLARSHIP FUND OF NEW HAMPSHIRE (Scholarships)

110 Stark St.
Manchester NH 03101-1977
Written Inquiry

AMOUNT: $1,000

DEADLINE(S): MAR

FIELD(S): Food Industry

Open to students who are residents of New Hampshire and planning to enter a career in the food industry.

Contact Fund for an application.

3300 — HAYSTACK MOUNTAIN SCHOOL OF CRAFTS (Scholarship Program)

Admissions Office
PO Box 518
Deer Isle ME 04627
207/348-2306

AMOUNT: $500-$1,000

DEADLINE(S): MAR 25

FIELD(S): Crafts

Open to technical assistants and work-study students in graphics, ceramics, weaving, jewelry, glass, blacksmithing, fabric, or wood. Tenable for one of the six two- to three-week summer sessions at Haystack Mountain School. One year of graduate study or equivalent experience is required for TA applicants.

Contact Candy Haskell for an application.

3301 — HILGENFELD FOUNDATION FOR MORTUARY EDUCATION (Scholarships)

P.O. Box 4311
Fullerton CA 92831
Written inquiry

AMOUNT: Varies

DEADLINE(S): None

FIELD(S): Funeral Service/Mortuary Science Education

Scholarships for graduate students enrolled in a college offering a program in Funeral Service or Mortuary Science or for those who plan to teach in this field.

Write for application information.

3302 — ILLINOIS PILOTS ASSOCIATION (Scholarships)

46 Apache Lane
Huntley IL 60142
Written request

AMOUNT: $500

DEADLINE(S): APR 1

FIELD(S): Aviation

Scholarships for individuals in aviation who are residents of Illinois and attending a college or university in Illinois.

Write for details.

3303 — INTERNATIONAL ASSOCIATION OF FIRE CHIEFS FOUNDATION (Scholarship Program)

1257 Wiltshire Rd.
York PA 17403
717/854-9083

AMOUNT: $250-$4,000

DEADLINE(S): AUG 15

FIELD(S): Business and Urban Administration, Fire Science

Open to members of a fire service of a state, county, provincial, municipal, community, industrial, or federal fire department.

Renewable. Write for complete information.

3304 — JAMES F. LINCOLN ARC WELDING FOUNDATION (Scholarships)

22801 Clair Ave.
Cleveland OH 44117-1199
216/481-4300

AMOUNT: Varies

DEADLINE(S): MAY 1 (through JUN 15, depending on program)

FIELD(S): Arc welding and engineering design

Open to high school students, college undergraduates, and graduate students, and to professionals working in the fields of arc welding and engineering design. Various programs are available.

Send self-addressed, stamped envelope to Richard S. Sabo, Executive Director, at above address.

3305 — JOHN K. & THIRZA F. DAVENPORT FOUNDATION (Scholarships in the Arts)

20 North Main Street
South Yarmouth MA 02664-3143
508/398-2293
FAX: 508/394-6765

AMOUNT: Varies

DEADLINE(S): JUL 15

FIELD(S): Theatre, Music, Art

For Barnstable County, Massachusetts residents in their last two years of undergraduate or graduate (preferred) study in visual or performing arts. Must demonstrate financial need.

6-8 awards annually. Renewable. Contact Mrs. Chris M. Walsh for more information.

3306 — MARYLAND HIGHER EDUCATION COMMISSION (Tuition Reimbursement of Firefighters & Rescue Squad Members)

State Scholarship Admin.
16 Francis St.
Annapolis MD 21401
410/974-5370
TTY: 800/735-2258
Internet: www.ubalt.edu/www.mhec

AMOUNT: Varies (current resident undergraduate tuition rate at Univ. MD-College Park)

DEADLINE(S): JUL 1

FIELD(S): Firefighting; Emergency Medical Technology

Open to firefighters and rescue squad members who successfully comple one year of coursework in a firefighting or EMT program and a two-year service obligation in Maryland.

Contact MHEC for an application.

3307 — MINNESOTA AUTOMOBILE DEALERS ASSOCIATION (MADA Scholarships)

277 University Ave. W.
St. Paul MN 55103-2085
612/291-2400
Internet: www.mada.org

AMOUNT: Tuition for one quarter at an accredited Minnesota technical institution

DEADLINE(S): Varies

FIELD(S): Automotive mechanics, automotive body repair, parts and service management, automotive machinist, automotive diagnostic technician

Tuition reimbursement in the above fields of study for students currently enrolled in a Minnesota technical school. Must have completed two quarters of study in the field, be planning to enroll in further study, have maintained an above average GPA, and be nominated by an instructor or class advisor at a Minnesota technical institution.

Contact instructor, guidance counselor, or check website above for more information.

3308 — McCORD CAREER CENTER (Level II McCord Medical/Music Scholarship)

Healdsburg High School
1024 Prince St.
Healdsburg CA 95448
707/431-3473

AMOUNT: Varies

DEADLINE(S): APR 30

FIELD(S): Medicine; Music

For graduates of Healdsburg High School who are planning a career in music or medicine. Must be enrolled full-time at a college/university as an undergraduate junior or senior in the fall, or earning an advanced degree in graduate or medical school, or entering into a vocational/certificate program. Transcripts, proof of attendance, and an essay are required.

Contact the McCord Career Center at Healdsburg High School for an application.

3309 — NATIONAL AIR TRANSPORTATION ASSOCIATION FOUNDATION (John W. Godwin, Jr., Memorial Scholarship Fund)

4226 King Street
Alexandria VA 22302
808/808-NATA or 703/845-9000
FAX: 703/845-8176

AMOUNT: $2,500

DEADLINE(S): None

FIELD(S): Flight training

Scholarship for flight training for any certificate and/or flight rating issued by the FAA, at any NATA-Member company offering flight training. Must accumulate a minimum of 15 dual or solo flight hours each calendar month.

Contact organization for details.

3310 — NATIONAL ASSN OF EXECUTIVE SECRETARIES AND ADMINISTRATIVE ASSISTANTS (Scholarship Award Program)

900 S. Washington St., Suite G-13
Falls Church VA 22046
Written inquiry

AMOUNT: $250

DEADLINE(S): MAY 31

FIELD(S): Secretarial

Open to post secondary students working toward a college degree (Associates; Bachelors; Masters) who are NAESAA members or the spouse, child, or grandchild of a member.

Scholarship may be used for Certified Professional Secretary Exam or to buy required books. Write for complete information.

3311 — NATIONAL GAY PILOTS ASSOCIATION (Pilot Scholarships)

NGPA-EF, P.O. Box 2010-324
South Burlington VT 05407-2010
703/660-3852 or
24-hr. voice mail: 703/660-3852
Internet: www.ngpa.org

AMOUNT: $1,500

DEADLINE(S): JUL 31

FIELD(S): Pilot training and related fields in aerospace, aerodynamics, engineering, airport management, etc.

Scholarships for tuition or flight training costs for student pilots enrolled at a college or university offering an accredited aviation curriculum in the above fields. Also for flight training costs in a professional pilot training program at any training facility certified by the FAA. Not for training for a Private Pilot license. Send SASE for application or visit website for further instructions.

For gay/lesbian applicants or others who can provide evidence of volunteering in an AIDS organization or in any group that supports the gay/lesbian community and their rights.

3312 — NATIONAL SPACE CLUB (Dr. Robert H. Goddard Historical Essay Award)

2000 L Street, NW, Suite 710
Washington DC 20036-4907
202/973-8661

AMOUNT: $1,000 + plaque

DEADLINE(S): DEC 4

FIELD(S): Aerospace History

Essay competition open to any US citizen on a topic dealing with any significant aspect of the historical development of rocketry and astronautics. Essays should not exceed 5,000 words and should be fully documented. Will be judged on originality and scholarship.

Previous winners not eligible. Send self-addressed, stamped envelope for complete information.

3313 — NINETY-NINES, INC. (Amelia Earhart Memorial Scholarships)

Box 965, 7100 Terminal Drive
Oklahoma City OK 73159-0965
800/994-1929 or 405/685-7969
FAX: 405/685-7985
E-Mail: 10476.406@compuserve.com
Internet: ninety-nines.org

AMOUNT: Varies

DEADLINE(S): Varies

FIELD(S): Advanced Aviation Ratings

Scholarships for female licensed pilots who are members of the 99s, Inc.

15-20 awards annually. Financial need considered. Contact Lu Hollander at above address for application and/or membership information.

3314 — NINETY-NINES, SAN FERNANDO VALLEY CHAPTER/VAN NUYS AIRPORT (Aviation Career Scholarships)

PO Box 8160
Van Nuys CA 91409
818/989-0081

AMOUNT: $3,000

DEADLINE(S): MAY 1

FIELD(S): Aviation Careers

For men and women of the greater Los Angeles area pursuing careers as professional pilots, flight instructors, mechanics, or other aviation career specialists. Applicants must be at least 21 years of age and US citizens.

3 awards annually. Send self-addressed, stamped, business-sized envelope to above address for application.

3315 — OAK RIDGE ASSOCIATED UNIVERSITIES (National Science Foundation Graduate Research Fellowships)

PO Box 3010
Oak Ridge TN 37831-3010
423/241-4300
FAX: 423/241-4513
E-Mail: nsfgrfp@orau.gov
Internet: www.orau.gov/nsf/nsffel.htm

AMOUNT: $15,000 stipend + $10,500 tuition allowance

DEADLINE(S): NOV 4

FIELD(S): Science; Math; Engineering; Computer Science

Three-year fellowships for graduate study leading to research-based master's or doctoral degrees in the above fields. Must be US citizens, nationals, or permanent residents at the time of application. Fellowships are awarded on the basis of ability. Women, minorities, and those with disabilities are strongly encouraged to apply. One-time International Research Travel Allowance available.

1,000 awards annually. Contact Jeannette Bouchard for an application/more information.

3316 — SOCIETY FOR TECHNICAL COMMUNICATION (Graduate Scholarships)

901 N. Stuart St., Suite 904
Arlington VA 22203-1854
703/522-4114
FAX: 703/522-2075
E-Mail: stc@stc-va.org
Internet: www.stc-va.org

AMOUNT: $2,500

DEADLINE(S): FEB 15

FIELD(S): Technical Communication

Open to full-time graduate students who are enrolled in an accredited master's or doctoral degree program for careers in any area of technical communication: technical writing, editing, graphic design, multimedia art, etc.

Awards tenable at recognized colleges & universities in U.S. and Canada. Seven awards per year. Visit website or write for further information.

3317 — THE BRITISH ACADEMY, HUMANITIES RESEARCH BOARD (Postgraduate Professional Awards, Vocational Courses, and Librarianship and Information Science Program Awards)

10 Carlton House Terrace
London SW1Y 5AH ENGLAND
0181 951 4900
FAX: 0181 951 1358

AMOUNT: Tuition, fees, travel, and expenses

DEADLINE(S): JUN 1

FIELD(S): Humanities

Open to U.K. residents of at least 3 years who graduated from a U.K. university or hold a qualification regarded by the Department as equivalent to a university first degree. Fees-only awards for non-U.K. residents who are ECC nationals.

Applicants must be between the ages of 18 and 40. Write for complete information.

3318 — THE WALT DISNEY COMPANY (American Teacher Awards)

P.O. Box 9805
Calabasas CA 91372

AMOUNT: $2,500 (36 awards); $25,000 (Outstanding Teacher of the Year)

DEADLINE(S): FEB 15

FIELD(S): Teachers: athletic coach, early childhood, English, foreign language/ESL, general elementary, mathematics, performing arts, physical education/health, science, social studies, visual arts, voc/tech education

Awards for K-12 teachers in the above fields.

Teachers, or anyone who knows a great teacher, can write for applications at the above address.

3319 — WHIRLY-GIRLS INC. (International Women Helicopter Pilots Scholarships)

Executive Towers 10-D
207 West Clarendon Ave.
Phoenix AZ 85013
602/263-0190
FAX 602/264-5812

AMOUNT: $4500

DEADLINE(S): NOV 15

FIELD(S): Helicopter Flight Training

Three scholarships available to licensed women pilots for flight training. Two are awarded to Whirly-Girls who are helicopter pilots; one is awarded to a licensed woman pilot holding a private license (airplane, balloon, or glider).

Applications are available April 15. Write, call, or fax for complete information.

3320 — WYOMING TRUCKING ASSOCIATION (Scholarships)

PO Box 1909
Casper WY 82602
Written Inquiry

AMOUNT: $250-$300

DEADLINE(S): MAR 1

FIELD(S): Transportation Industry

For Wyoming high school graduates enrolled in a Wyoming college, approved trade school, or the University of Wyoming. Must be pursuing a course of study which will result in a career in the transportation industry in Wyoming, including but not limited to: safety, environmental science, diesel mechanics, truck driving, vocational trades, business management, sales management, computer skills, accounting, office procedures, and management.

1-10 awards annually. Write to WYTA for an application.

GENERAL

3321 — A.H. BEAN FOUNDATION

c/o First Alabama Bank, 2222 Ninth St.
Tuscaloosa AL 35401
Written inquiry

AMOUNT: $200-$600

DEADLINE(S): None given

FIELD(S): All fields of study

Schlarships for Alabama residents who are Christian individuals who are active members of a church, enrolled in a postsecondary educational institution, and recommended for aid by a minister.

Write to Trust Dept. at above location for details. Transcript and minister's recommendation required.

3322 — ABRAHAM BURTMAN CHARITY TRUST

Burns Bldg., P.O. Box 608
Dover NH 03820-0608
603/742-2332

AMOUNT: $1,000

DEADLINE(S): MAY 1

FIELD(S): All areas of study

Scholarships for financially needy residents of New Hampshire.

Send SASE to David A. Goodwin at above address for application guidelines.

3323 — ACADEMIC STUDY GROUP (Travel Bursaries to Israel)

John D. A. Levy, ASG, 25 Lyndale Ave.
London NW2 2QB ENGLAND UK
0171 435 6803

AMOUNT: Varies

DEADLINE(S): MAR; NOV

FIELD(S): All fields of study

Travel opportunities to Israel are offered by this charitable foundation, which promotes collaboration between British scholars and their Israeli counterparts.

To apply, send a detailed curriculum vitae, summary of the reason to visit Israel, plus names of academic counterparts in Israel.

3324 — ACADEMY OF FINLAND (Research Fellowships)

P.O. Box 99
00551 Helsinki Finland
+358 774881

AMOUNT: 15.5 (Finnish)

DEADLINE(S): JAN 31; SEP 30

FIELD(S): All areas of study

Postgraduate and postdoctoral fellowships to fund researchers and research projects in all fields of science and letters. Research must be done in Finland and application must be through the university or institute of interest.

Write for complete information.

3325 — ACADIA UNIVERSITY (Graduate Teaching Assistantships)

Director of Research and Graduate Studies
Wolfville NS BOP 1XO Canada
902/585-1498

AMOUNT: $8,000 (Canadian)

DEADLINE(S): FEB 1

FIELD(S): All fields of study

Fellowships open to full-time graduate students at Acadia University.

Approximately 15 awards per year. Write for complete information.

3326 — AFRO-ASIATIC INSTITUTE IN WIEN (Scholarships)

Turkenstrasse 3
Study Advisory Dept.
V-1090 Vienna, AUSTRIA
310/5145-211
E-Mail: aai.wien.stuvef@magnet.at

AMOUNT: 5,000-7,000 Austrian schillings per month

DEADLINE(S): APR 30

FIELD(S): All fields of study

Open to needy applicants from developing countries in Africa, Asia, and Latin America for study in Austria. Applicants must have good study results, have already begun studies in Austria, and be regular or preliminary course students.

Awards are renewable; write for complete information.

3327 — AIR TRAFFIC CONTROL ASSOCIATION INC (Scholarships for Children of Air Traffic Specialists)

2300 Clarendon Blvd. #711
Arlington VA 22201
703/522-5717
FAX: 703/527-7251
E-Mail: atca@worldnit.att.net
Internet: www.atca.org

AMOUNT: Varies

DEADLINE(S): MAY 1

FIELD(S): All fields of study

For children of persons serving or having served as air traffic control specialists (either natural or adopted) with either government, U.S. military, or in a private facility in the U.S. Must be enrolled in an accredited college or university and planning to continue the following year in bachelor's program or higher. Attendance must be equal to at least half-time (6 hours).

Write for complete information.

3328 — ALABAMA COMMISSION ON HIGHER EDUCATION (Scholarships; Grants; Loans; Work Study Programs)

P.O. Box 302000
Montgomery AL 36130-2000
Written inquiry

AMOUNT: Varies

DEADLINE(S): Varies

FIELD(S): All fields of study

The commission administers a number of financial aid programs tenable at post secondary institutions in Alabama. Some awards are need-based.

Write for the "Financial Aid Sources in Alabama" brochure or contact high school guidance counselor or college financial aid officer.

3329 — ALBERT BAKER FUND (Student Loans)

5 Third St. #717
San Francisco CA 94103
415/543-7028

AMOUNT: Up to $3,500

DEADLINE(S): SEP 1

FIELD(S): All fields of study

Open to students who are members of the First Church of Christ Scientist in Boston, MA. Students' residency can be anywhere in the world. For study in the U.S. Student must have other primary lender and be enrolled in an accredited college or university. Interest rate is 3% below prime.

All students must have cosigner who is a U.S. citizen. Average of 160 awards per year. Write or call for complete information. Applicant must be the one who calls.

3330 — ALBERTA HERITAGE SCHOLARSHIP FUND (Ralph Steinhauer Awards of Distinction)

6th Floor, 9940 - 106 St.
Edmonton Alberta T5K 2V1 Canada
403/427-8640

AMOUNT: $10,000-Masters; $15,000-Doctoral

DEADLINE(S): FEB 1

FIELD(S): All fields of study

For Canadian residents to pursue graduate studies at an institution in Alberta. Awards are for academic excellence and to provide a means by which Alberta graduate faculties may attract or retain top scholars in order to assist in making Alberta a center of academic excellence.

15 awards. Write for complete information.

3331 — ALBERTA HERITAGE SCHOLARSHIP FUND (Sir James Lougheed Award of Distinction)

6th Floor, 9940 106 St.
Edmonton Alberta T5K 2V1
403/427-8640

AMOUNT: $10,000 Master's/$15,000 Doctorates

DEADLINE(S): FEB 1

FIELD(S): All fields of study

In recognition of academic excellence and to provide students in graduate programs with opportunities for advanced study anywhere in the world.

For individuals who qualify as Alberta residents and who are enrolled or plan to enroll as full-time students outside the province of Alberta.

3332 — ALEXANDER FAMILY EDUCATIONAL FOUNDATION WELFARE TRUST

c/o Nicolas Alexander, 802 N.E. 199th
Portland OR 97233
503/666-9491

AMOUNT: $3,000-$5,000

DEADLINE(S): MAR 1

FIELD(S): All fields of study

Scholarships for residents of Oregon.

Send SASE to above address for formal application.

3333 — ALEXANDER GRAHAM BELL ASSOCIATION FOR THE DEAF (College Scholarship Awards)

3417 Volta Place, NW
Washington DC 20007-2778
202/337-5220 (voice/TTY)
E-Mail: agbell2@aol.com
Internet: www.agbell.org

AMOUNT: Varies

DEADLINE(S): DEC 1 (Request application by then. Deadline is MAR 15 postmark)

FIELD(S): All fields of study

For prelingually deaf or hard-of-hearing students who use speech and speechreading to communicate and who are attending or have been admitted to a college or university that primarily enrolls students with normal hearing.

Must have a 60dB or greater hearing loss in the better ear in the speech frequencies of 500, 1000, and 2000 Hz. Application requests must be made IN WRITING to the Bell Association's Financial Aid Coordinator; make sure you indicate which program you would like to apply for, and include your name and address on your letter.

3334 — ALEXANDER GRAHAM BELL ASSOCIATION FOR THE DEAF (Parent Infant Preschool Awards)

3417 Volta Place, NW
Washington DC 20007-2778
202/337-5220 (voice/TTY)
E-Mail: agbell2@aol.com
Internet: www.agbell.org

AMOUNT: Varies

DEADLINE(S): SEP 1 (Request application by then. Deadline is OCT 1 postmark)

FIELD(S): All fields of study

Stipends are awarded to parents of infants (younger than 6 years old) who have been diagnosed with moderate to profound hearing losses. May be used to cover expenses associated with early intervention educational and rehabilitative services. The parent or guardian must be committed to an auditory-oral philosophy of education. Family must demonstrate financial need.

Must request application IN WRITING to the Bell Association's Financial Aid Coordinator; make sure you indicate which program you would like to apply for, and include your name and address on the letter.

3335 — ALEXANDER VON HUMBOLDT FOUNDATION (Feodor Lynen Research Fellowships)

Jean-Paul-Strasse 12
53173 Bonn
Germany

0228/833 101
FAX: 0228/833 212
E-Mail: ma@alex.avh.uni-bonn.de
Internet: www.avh.de

AMOUNT: DM 4,200/month (approx.)

DEADLINE(S): None

FIELD(S): All fields of study

Open to highly qualified German scholars (under 38 years of age) who wish to do postdoctoral research abroad in cooperation with a former Humboldt guest scientist in any field. Duration is one to four years.

Approx 150 fellowships per year. Write for complete information.

3336 — ALEXANDER VON HUMBOLDT FOUNDATION (Japan Society for the Promotion of Science Research Fellowships)

Jean-Paul-Strasse 12
D-53173 Bonn Federal Republic of Germany
0228/833-0

AMOUNT: 270000 yen per month + expenses & allowances

DEADLINE(S): None

FIELD(S): All fields of study

Open to highly qualified German scholars who have received their doctoral degree within the last five years and wish to do postdoctoral research at Japanese universities in any field. Duration is 12-24 months.

Approx 15 fellowships per year. Write for complete information.

3337 — ALEXANDER VON HUMBOLDT FOUNDATION (Research Fellowships for Foreign Scholars)

Jean-Paul-Strasse 12
D-53173
Germany
0228-833-0 fax 0228-833272

AMOUNT: Varies

DEADLINE(S): None specified

FIELD(S): All fields of study

Open to any qualified scholar (up to age 40) for postdoctoral research in Germany in any field. Humanities and Social Sciences scholars must prove (by a language certificate) that they have a good command of the German language.

Approx 500 fellowships per year. Duration is 6-12 months. Write to the attention of the selection dept. for complete information.

3338 — AMERICAN ASSOCIATION OF BIOANALYSTS (David Birenbaum Scholarship Fund of AAB)

917 Locust St., Suite 1100
Saint Louis MO 63101-1413
314/241-1445
FAX: 314/241-1449
E-Mail: aab1445@primary.net

AMOUNT: Varies

DEADLINE(S): Varies

FIELD(S): All fields of study

Open to AAB members, their spouses, and children. Financial need is one of several considerations, including but not limited to, goals, history of acheivements, community involvment, etc.

Write to the above address for complete information.

3339 — AMERICAN ASSOCIATION OF UNIVERSITY WOMEN EDUCATIONAL FOUNDATION (Community Action Grants)

Dept. 60
2201 N. Dodge St.
Iowa City IA 52243-4030
319/337-1716, ext. 60
FAX: 319/337-1204
Internet: www.aauw.org

AMOUNT: $2,000-$7,000 (1-yr project); $5,000-$10,000 (2-yr project)

DEADLINE(S): FEB 1

FIELD(S): Education/Equity of Women & Girls

Seed money support to individual women (US citizens/permanent residents), AAUW branches, and states for innovative programs or non-degree research projects that promote education & equity for women and girls. Project must have direct public impact, be nonpartisan, & take place w/i US or its territories. One-year grants are for short-term projects; should have clearly defined educational activity. Two-year grants restricted to K-12 girls in math, science, & technology.

40 1-yr grants & 5 2-yr grants annually. Contact AAUW for details.

3340 — AMERICAN ASSOCIATION OF UNIVERSITY WOMEN EDUCATIONAL FOUNDATION (Postdoctoral Research Leave Fellowships)

Dept. 60
2201 N. Dodge St.
Iowa City IA 52243-4030
319/337-1716, ext. 60
FAX: 319/337-1204
Internet: www.aauw.org

AMOUNT: $27,000

DEADLINE(S): NOV 15

FIELD(S): All fields of study

These postdoctoral fellowships offer one-year of support for women who will have earned a doctoral degree by November 15th. Limited additional funds beyond $27,000 stipend may be available for postdoctoral support; AAUW will match institutional support, dollar for dollar, up to $5,000, for a limited number of the selected fellows.

14 awards annually: 4 each in the arts & humanities, social sciences, & natural sciences; 1 unrestricted; & 1 designated for a woman from an underrepresented group in any field. Contact AAUW for an application between August 1st & November 1st.

3341 — AMERICAN ASSOCIATION OF UNIVERSITY WOMEN EDUCATIONAL FOUNDATION (Career Development Grants)

Dept. 60
2201 N. Dodge St.
Iowa City IA 52243-4030
319/337-1716, ext. 60
FAX: 319/337-1204
Internet: www.aauw.org

AMOUNT: $2,000-$8,000

DEADLINE(S): JAN 2

FIELD(S): All fields of study

Grants support women currently holding a bachelor's degree who are preparing for career advancement, career change, or re-entry into the workforce. Special consideration given to AAUW members, women of color, & women pursuing their first advanced degree or credentials in nontraditional fields. Must be US citizen or permanent resident whose last degree was received at least 5 years ago.

75 awards annually. Academic Grants are for master's degrees or specialized training; Professional Development Institute Grants support participation in professional institutes. Contact AAUW for details. Applications available from August 1st to December 20th.

3342 — AMERICAN ASSOCIATION OF UNIVERSITY WOMEN EDUCATIONAL FOUNDATION (International Fellowships)

Dept. 60
2201 N. Dodge St.
Iowa City IA 52243-4030
319/337-1716, ext. 60
FAX: 319/337-1204
Internet: www.aauw.org

AMOUNT: $16,000 (fellowship); $5,000-$7,000 (grant)

DEADLINE(S): NOV 15

FIELD(S): All fields of study

For full-time study or research in the US to women who are not US citizens or permanent residents. Both graduate & postgraduate study is supported. Criteria for selection include outstanding academic ability, professional potential, & the importance of the field of study to changing the lives of women & girls in the country of origin. Post-fellowship Supplemental Community Action Grants also available.

45 awards annually; 6 are reserved for members of the International Federation of University Women, who may study in any country other than their own. Request application between August 1st & November 15th; deadline for completed application is January 15th.

3343 — AMERICAN ASSOCIATION OF UNIVERSITY WOMEN EDUCATIONAL FOUNDATION (American Dissertation Fellowships)

Dept. 60
2201 N. Dodge St.
Iowa City IA 52243-4030
319/337-1716, ext. 60
FAX: 319/337-1204
Internet: www.aauw.org

AMOUNT: $15,000

DEADLINE(S): NOV 15

FIELD(S): All fields of study (except engineering)

Dissertation fellowships are available to women who are in the final year of a doctoral degree program, & are completing the writing of dissertations between July 1st of the year following award & June 30th of the next year. Applicants must have completed all coursework, passed all required preliminary exams, & received approval for research proposals/plan by November of current year. Scholars engaged in research on gender issues are encouraged to apply.

51 awards annually. Renewable once on same topic. Students holding fellowship for writing dissertation in year prior are not eligible. Contact AAUW between August 1st & November 1st for an application.

3344 — AMERICAN COUNCIL OF THE BLIND (ACB Scholarship Program)

Attn: Holly Fults
1155 15th St. NW, Suite 720
Washington DC 20005
202/467-5081 or 800/424-8666

AMOUNT: $500-$4,000

DEADLINE(S): MAR 1

FIELD(S): All fields of study

Scholarships open to legally blind applicants who have been accepted to or are enrolled in an accredited institution for vocational, technical, undergraduate, graduate, or professional studies. U.S. citizen or legal resident.

25 scholarships awarded. Write for complete information.

3345 — AMERICAN FEDERATION OF TEACHERS (Robert G. Porter Scholars Program)

555 New Jersey Ave. NW
Washington DC 20001
202/393-7486
FAX: 202/879-4406
Internet: poconnor@aft.org

AMOUNT: $1,000

DEADLINE(S): MAR 31

FIELD(S): All fields of study

For members of the American Federation of Teachers seeking continuing education in their fields of study.

Three awards per year. Contact above location for details.

3346 — AMERICAN FOUNDATION FOR THE BLIND (Ferdinand Torres Scholarship)

11 Penn Plaza, Ste. 300
New York NY 10001
212/502-7661 or TDD: 212/502-7662
FAX: 212/502-7771
E-Mail: julit@afb.org
Internet: www.afb.org

AMOUNT: $1,000

DEADLINE(S): APR 30

FIELD(S): All fields of study

Open to legally blind, full-time students who present evidence of economic need. U.S. citizenship is not required. Students residing in the New York City area are given preference.

Write to the above address for complete information.

3347 — AMERICAN FOUNDATION FOR THE BLIND (Karen D. Carsel Memorial Scholarship)

11 Penn Plaza, Ste. 300
New York NY 10001
212/502-7661 or TDD 212/502-7662
FAX: 212/502-7771
E-Mail: juliet@afb.org
Internet: www.afb.org

AMOUNT: $500

DEADLINE(S): APR 30

FIELD(S): All areas of study

Open to legally blind, full-time graduate students in an accredited institution who present evidence of economic need. U.S. citizen.

Write or visit website for more information. E-mail and fax inquiries must include a complete U.S. postal service mailing address.

3348 — AMERICAN FRIENDS OF THE LONDON SCHOOL OF ECONOMICS (Scholarship Office)

733 15th St NW, Suite 700
Washington DC 20005
202/347-3232
E-Mail: plakias@aol.com

AMOUNT: Full tuition-approx. 8,300 pounds sterling

DEADLINE(S): FEB 15

FIELD(S): Social Sciences

Scholarships awarded annually to U.S. citizens or legal residents for one year of graduate study at the London School of Economics. For newly enrolled students only, but those who attended summer school are eligible.

Approx. Four scholarships per year. Write for complete information. Awards are based on financial need and academic merit.

3349 — AMERICAN GEOPHYSICAL UNION (Congressional Science Fellowship Program)

2000 Florida Ave. NW
Washington DC 20009
202/462-6900
FAX: 202/328-0566

AMOUNT: $40,000 stipend + expenses

DEADLINE(S): FEB 15

FIELD(S): All fields of study

One-year fellowship to work on the staff of one of the members of the United States Congress or Congressional Committee. Must be a member or applying for membership in the American Geophysical Union. U.S. citizen or permanent resident.

Write for complete information.

3350 — AMERICAN HEALTH AND BEAUTY AIDS INSTITUTE (Entrepreneurial Leadership Conference)

401 North Michigan ave.
Chicago IL 60611-4267
312/644-6610

AMOUNT: $100 travel allowance plus conference registration.

DEADLINE(S): None specified

FIELD(S): All fields of study.

The American Health and Beauty Aids Institute Entrepreneurial Leadership Conference is held each November. Two winners are chosen from each of the 117 Historically Black Colleges and Universities. Winners receive registration plus a $100 travel allowance. Program includes leadership workshops with presidents and key executives from multi-million dollar African-American-owned hair care corporations.

Eleven students will be selected for additional scholarships totaling over $30,000 in scholarship prizes. Submit an essay on entrepreneurship in the Black community.

3351 — AMERICAN INDIAN GRADUATE CENTER (Graduate Fellowships)

4520 Montgomery Blvd. NE #1B
Albuquerque NM 87109-1291
505/881-4584
FAX: 505/884-0427
E-Mail: AIGC@unm.edu

AMOUNT: Up to $3,000 per year

DEADLINE(S): JUNE 1

FIELD(S): All areas of study

Fellowships open to American Indians who are enrolled members of federally recognized tribes or Alaska native groups are accepted to or enrolled in an accredited master's or doctoral program in the U.S. U.S citizenship required.

Approximately 400 awards per year. Renewable. Write for complete information.

3352 — AMERICAN INDIAN HERITAGE FOUNDATION

6051 Arlington Blvd.
Falls Church VA 220044-2788
202-INDIANS
703/237-7500
FAX 703/532-1921

AMOUNT: Various, up to $26,000

DEADLINE(S): MAY 20

FIELD(S): All fields of study

9th Miss Indian USA Scholarship Program in Washington DC. Pageant: May 27-May 31, 1997. Crowning Ceremony May 30. Prizes for academic achievement, Miss Walk in Beauty, Miss Photogenic, Miss Congeniality, talent traditional dress, and evening gown sections..Must be of American Indian descent.

Must be a high school graduate between 18-26. Can never have co-habitated, been pregnant, or married.

3353 — AMERICAN INSTITUTE OF INDIAN STUDIES (AIIS Junior Fellowships)

1130 E. 59th St.
Chicago IL 60637
773/702-8638
E-Mail: aiis@midway.uchicago.edu
Internet: http://kaladarshan.arts.ohio-state.edu/aiis/aiishomepage.htm

AMOUNT: Up to $7,000

DEADLINE(S): JUL 1

FIELD(S): All fields of study

Open to doctoral candidates from all academic disciplines to perform dissertation research in India in all fields of study. Junior fellows will have formal affiliation with Indian universities and Indian research supervisors.

Awards are available for up to 11 months. Write for complete information.

3354 — AMERICAN JEWISH LEAGUE FOR ISRAEL (University Scholarship Fund)

130 E. 59th St., 14th Floor
New York NY 10022
212/371-1452

AMOUNT: $1,500

DEADLINE(S): MAY 1

FIELD(S): All fields of study

Open to U.S. citizens of Jewish faith who have been accepted for a year of undergrad or grad study in Israel at Bar Ilan Univ., Ben Gurion Univ., Haifa Univ., Hebrew Univ.-Jerusalem, Technion, Tel Aviv Univ., or Weizmann Institute of Science.

5-6 awards per year. Write for complete information.

3355 — AMERICAN MENSA EDUCATION & RESEARCH FOUNDATION (Scholarships)

3437 West 7th Street, Suite 264
Fort Worth TX 76107
817/332-2600
800/666-3672

AMOUNT: $200 to $1,000

DEADLINE(S): JAN 31

FIELD(S): All fields of study

Open to students enrolled for the academic year following the award in a degree program in an accredited American institution of postsecondary education. Applicants must submit an essay describing career, vocational, and academic goals.

Essay should be fewer than 550 words and must be specific rather than general. It MUST be on an official application. Send self-addressed, stamped envelope no later than January 1 for application.

3356 — AMERICAN MORGAN HORSE INSTITUTE (Scholarship Program)

P.O. Box 837
Shelburne VT 05482-0519
Written inquiry

AMOUNT: $3,000

DEADLINE(S): MAR 1

FIELD(S): All fields of study

Scholarships for students 21 years or younger who are or will be high school graduates or who hold a GED. Selection based on need, community service, and achievement with horses. Requests for applicaitons MUST include a stamped, self-addressed envelope (SASE).

Five scholarships yearly.

3357 — AMERICAN POLITICAL SCIENCE ASSN. (Congressional Fellowships for Scholars)

1527 New Hampshire Ave. NW
Washington DC 20036
202/483-2512
FAX: 202/483-2657
E-Mail: biggs@apsanet.net
Internet: apsanet.org

AMOUNT: $30,000 + travel

DEADLINE(S): DEC 1

FIELD(S): Background in any field of study

For scholars from all disciplines with an interest in communicaitons and public policy and show promise of making a significant contribution to the public's understanding of the political process. Must have earned a Ph.D. within the last 15 years. Program provides the opportunity to work for 9 months as a legislative aide.

Write to APSA-MCI Communications Fellowships at above location for details.

3358 — AMERICAN RADIO RELAY LEAGUE FOUNDATION ("You've Got A Friend in Pennsylvania" Scholarship)

225 Main Street
Newington CT 06111
860/594-0200
FAX: 860/594-0259
Internet: www.arrl.org/

AMOUNT: $1,000

DEADLINE(S): FEB 1

FIELD(S): All fields of study

For AARL members who hold a general radio license and are residents of Pennsylvania.

1 award annually. Contact ARRL for an application.

3359 — AMERICAN RADIO RELAY LEAGUE FOUNDATION (ARRL Scholarship Honoring Senator Barry Goldwater, K7UGA)

225 Main Street
Newington Ct 06111
860/594-0200
FAX: 860/594-0259
Internet: www.arrl.org/

AMOUNT: $5,000

DEADLINE(S): FEB 1

FIELD(S): All fields of study

Open to students who are licensed radio amateurs (at least novice level) & enrolled full-time as a bachelor's or graduate student at a regionally accredited institution.

1 award annually. Contact ARRL for an application.

3360 — AMERICAN RADIO RELAY LEAGUE FOUNDATION (Charles Clarke Cordle Memorial Scholarship)

225 Main Street
Newington CT 06111
860/594-0200
FAX: 860/594-0259
Internet: www.arrl.org/

AMOUNT: $1,000

DEADLINE(S): FEB 1

FIELD(S): All fields of study

For undergraduate or graduate residents of Georgia or Alabama who hold any class of amateur radio license. Must attend school in Georgia or Alabama and have a minimum 2.5 GPA.

1 award annually. Contact ARRL for an application.

3361 — AMERICAN RADIO RELAY LEAGUE FOUNDATION (Mary Lou Brown Scholarship)

225 Main Street
Newington CT 06111
860/594-0200
FAX: 860/594-0259
Internet: www.arrl.org/

AMOUNT: $2,500

DEADLINE(S): FEB 1

FIELD(S): All fields of study

Open to residents of the ARRL Northwest Division (AK, ID, MT, OR, WA) who are radio amateurs holding at least a general license. For study leading to a bachelor's degree or higher course of study. Must have GPA of at least 3.0 and a demonstrated interest in promoting the Amateur Radio Service.

Multiple scholarships annually, as income allows. Contact ARRL for an application.

3362 — AMERICAN RADIO RELAY LEAGUE FOUNDATION (The New England FEMARA Scholarships)

225 Main Street
Newington CT 06111
860/594-0200
FAX: 860/594-0259
Internet: www.arrl.org/

AMOUNT: $600

DEADLINE(S): FEB 1

FIELD(S): All fields of study

Open to residents of the New England states (ME, NH, VT, MA, CT, RI) who are radio amateurs with a technician license.

Multiple awards annually. Contact ARRL for an application.

3363 — AMERICAN RADIO RELAY LEAGUE FOUNDATION (The General Fund Scholarships)

225 Main Street
Newington CT 06111
860/594-0200
FAX: 860/594-0259
Internet: www.arrl.org/

AMOUNT: $1,000

DEADLINE(S): FEB 1

FIELD(S): All fields of study

Open to undergraduate or graduate students holding any level amateur radio license.

Multiple awards annually. Contact ARRL for an application.

3364 — AMERICAN RADIO RELAY LEAGUE FOUNDATION (The K2TEO Martin J. Green, Sr. Memorial Scholarship)

225 Main Street
Newington CT 06111
860/594-0200
FAX: 860/594-0259
Internet: www.arrl.org/

AMOUNT: $1,000

DEADLINE(S): FEB 1

FIELD(S): All fields of study

Open to undergraduate or graduate students holding any level amateur radio license. Preference is given to a student ham from a ham family.

1 award annually. Contact ARRL for an application.

3365 — AMERICAN RADIO RELAY LEAGUE FOUNDATION (The North Texas Section- Bob Nelson KB5BNU Memorial Scholarship)

225 Main Street
Newington CT 06111
860/594-0200
FAX: 860/594-0259
Internet: www.arrl.org/

AMOUNT: $750

DEADLINE(S): FEB 1

FIELD(S): All fields of study

For radio amateurs with any class of license who are residents of Texas or Oklahoma. Must be enrolled in a full-time degree program, with a minimum 12 credit hours per semester. Character, humanitarianism, and active amateur radio participation are highly important.

Multiple awards annually, when funds support it. Contact ARRL for an application.

3366 — AMERICAN RADIO RELAY LEAGUE FOUNDATION (The Chicago FM Club Scholarships)

225 Main Street
Newington CT 06111
860/594-0200
FAX: 860/594-0259
Internet: www.arrl.org/

AMOUNT: $500

DEADLINE(S): FEB 1

FIELD(S): All fields of study

Open to radio amateurs holding a technician license and who are residents of the FCC Ninth Call District (IN, IL, WI). Students must be in a postsecondary course of study at an accredited 2- or 4-year college or trade school. Must be US citizen or within three months of citizenship.

Multiple awards annually. Contact ARRL for an application.

3367 — AMERICAN RADIO RELAY LEAGUE FOUNDATION (The Michael J. Flosi Memorial Scholarship)

225 Main Street
Newington CT 06111
860/594-0200
FAX: 860/594-0259
Internet: www.arrl.org/

AMOUNT: $500

DEADLINE(S): FEB 1

FIELD(S): All fields of study

Open to radio amateurs holding a technician license and who are residents of the FCC Ninth Call District (IN, IL, WI). Must be a high school senior or graduate and be a US citizen or within three months of citizenship.

Multiple awards annually. Contact ARRL for an application.

3368 — AMERICAN RADIO RELAY LEAGUE FOUNDATION (The Eugene "Gene" Sallee, W4YFR Memorial Scholarship)

225 Main Street
Newington CT 06111
860/594-0200
FAX: 860/594-0259
Internet: www.arrl.org/

AMOUNT: $500

DEADLINE(S): FEB 1

FIELD(S): All fields of study

Open to radio amateurs holding a technician plus license and who are residents of Georgia. Must have a minimum 3.0 GPA.

1 award annually. Contact ARRL for an application.

3369 — AMERICAN SAMOA GOVERNMENT (Financial Aid Program)

Dept. of Education
Office of Student Financial Program
Pago Pago AMERICAN SAMOA 96799
684/633-5237

AMOUNT: $5,000

DEADLINE(S): APR 30

FIELD(S): All fields of study

Scholarships open to residents of American Samoa. Awards support undergraduate & graduate study at all accredited colleges & universities. Applicants from off islands may be eligible if their parents are citizens of American Samoa.

Approximately 50 awards per year. Renewable. Write for complete information.

3370 — AMERICAN SCANDINAVIAN FOUNDATION OF LOS ANGELES (Scholarship Program)

3445 Winslow Drive
Los Angeles CA 90026
213/661-4273

AMOUNT: $1,000

DEADLINE(S): MAR

FIELD(S): All fields of study

Open to full-time upper level and graduate students at Los Angeles area colleges/universities who exhibit a connection to Scandinavia via life experience, field of study, or heritage.

5 to be awarded. Not renewable.

3371 — AMERICAN-SCANDINAVIAN FOUNDATION (Awards for Scandinavians)

15 E. 65th St.
New York NY 10021
212/879-9779
FAX 212/249-3444
E-Mail: grants@amscan.org
Internet: www.amscan.org

AMOUNT: Varies

DEADLINE(S): Varies

FIELD(S): All fields of study

Fellowships and grants, usually at the graduate level, for Scandinavians to undertake study or research in the US. For citizens of Denmark, Finland, Iceland, Norway, and Sweden. Number and size of awards granted annually varies widely between countries.

Contact ASF for information sheet, which includes list of cooperating organizations that have specific details regarding eligibility, award size, and deadlines.

3372 — AMERICAN-SCANDINAVIAN FOUNDATION (Awards for Study in Scandinavia)

15 E. 65th St.
New York NY 10021
212/879-9779
FAX: 212/249-3444
E-Mail: grants@amscan.org
Internet: www.amscan.org

AMOUNT: $3,000-$18,000 (for travel, tuition/fees, materials, etc.)

DEADLINE(S): NOV 1

FIELD(S): All fields of study

Fellowships and grants for advanced study or research in Denmark, Finland, Iceland, Norway, or Sweden. Open to US citizens/permanent residents who will have completed their undergraduate education by time overseas program begins. Must have well-defined research or study project that makes stay in Scandinavia essential. ASF requires confirmation of invitation/affiliation from institutions/individuals detailed in proposal. Knowledge of host country's language desirable.

Contact ASF for an application.

3373 — AMITY INSTITUTE (Internships in the US for Teaching Languages)

10671 Roselle St., Suite 101
San Diego CA 92121
619/455-6364
FAX: 619/455-6597
E-Mail: mail@amity.org
Internet: www.amity.org

AMOUNT: Room & board + small spending allowance

DEADLINE(S): None

FIELD(S): All fields of study

Internships for unmarried native-speakers of Spanish, French, German, Russian, Japanese, & Swahili, aged 20-30, who can teach their languages & customs to students at schools in the US. Teaching is 15 hours/week for either a full academic year (Sept.-June), a semester (5 months), or a quarter (9 weeks). Most assignments are at US high schools in the Midwest region, and some are in elementary schools and colleges.

Must be able to communicate effectively in English. The program is NOT paid employment. Participants must provide their own transportation and $70-$100/month for personal expenses.

3374 — AMVETS (Coors/AMVETS Memorial Scholarship)

4647 Forbes Blvd.
Lanham, MD 20706-4380
301/459-9600 FAX: 301/459-7924

AMOUNT: $1,000 graduate scholarship

DEADLINE(S): APR 15

FIELD(S): All fields of study

Open to graduate students who are former members of the U.S. Armed Forces who have exhausted all financial aid and to graduate students who are dependents of American veterans. Applicants must show financial need and demonstrate academic achievement.

Write for more information.

3375 — AN UNCOMMON LEGACY FOUNDATION, INC. (Scholarships)

150 West 26th St., Suite 602
New York NY 10001
212/366-6507
FAX: 212/366-4425
Internet: www.uncommonlegacy.org/scholguidelines.html

AMOUNT: $1,000

DEADLINE(S): MAY 1

FIELD(S): All fields of study

Scholarships for outstanding lesbian undergraduate and graduate full-time students enrolled at accredited colleges or universities in the U.S. Min. GPA 3.0. Must demonstrate commitment or contribution to the lesbian community, demonstrate financial need, and follow required application procedures.

Application is available on website and at the organization. Notification dates occur at different times, according to state of residence.

3376 — APPALOOSA YOUTH FOUNDATION (Scholarships)

5070 Highway 8 West
Moscow ID 83843
208/882-5578

AMOUNT: $1,000-$2,000

DEADLINE(S): JUN 10

FIELD(S): All fields of study

Open to members of the Appaloosa Youth Association or the Appaloosa Horse Club, children of Appaloosa Horse Club members, and individuals sponsored by a regional club or racing association.

Nine scholarships per year—1 equine related, 8 all areas of study. Renewable. Must demonstrate financial need, number of children, and number of children in college. Contact the Youth Coordinator at address above for complete information.

3377 — ARCTIC EDUCATION FOUNDATION (Shareholder Scholarships)

Box 129
Barrow AK 99723
907/852-8633

AMOUNT: Varies according to need

DEADLINE(S): None specified

FIELD(S): All areas of study

Open to Arctic Slope Regional Corporation shareholders and their children. For full time undergraduate or graduate study at any accredited institution of higher education. Must maintain 2.0 or better GPA and demonstrate financial need.

Available for studies leading to certificates in any type of vocational training. Write for complete information.

3378 — ARKANSAS DEPARTMENT OF HIGHER EDUCATION (MIA/KIA Dependents' Scholarship)

114 East Capitol
Little Rock AR 72201-3818
501/371-2050 or 800/54-STUDY
FAX: 501/371-2001
E-Mail: finaid@adhe.arknet.edu
Internet: www.arscholarships.com

AMOUNT: Waiver of in-state tuition/on-campus room/fees

DEADLINE(S): AUG 1; DEC 1; MAY 1; JUL 1

FIELD(S): All fields of study

For full-time undergrad/graduate students who are dependent children/spouses of persons who were declared Killed in Action/Missing in Action/Prisoners of War 1960 or after. Must attend approved Arkansas public college/university or technical school. Arkansas residency not required, but parent/spouse must have been resident. Aid to receive bachelor's degree or certification of completion; student may pursue professional degree if undergrad education was not in Arkansas.

See website or contact ADHE for an application.

3379 — ARKANSAS SINGLE PARENT SCHOLARSHIP FUND (Scholarships)

614 E. Emma, Ste. 119
Springdale AR 72764
501/927-1402
FAX: 501/751-1110
E-Mail: jwobser@jtlshop.jonesnet.org
Internet: scholarships-ar-us.org

AMOUNT: up to $600/semester

DEADLINE(S): Varies

FIELD(S): All fields of study

Scholarships are for Arkansas single parents to assist with expenses that would, otherwise, keep them from attending school—childcare, transportation, books, tuition, etc.

Each of the 51 county affiliates has its own set of guidelines; please contact your county's office for details and/or an application. Contact information can be found on the ASPSF website.

3380 — ARMENIAN RELIEF SOCIETY OF EASTERN USA, INC. (Grants)

80 Bigelow Ave.
Watertown MA 02172
617/926-3801
FAX: 617/924-7328
E-Mail: ARSER@COMPUSERVE.COM

AMOUNT: $400-$1,000

DEADLINE(S): APR 1

FIELD(S): All fields of study

Open to undergrad and grad students of Armenian ancestry who are attending an accredited 4-year college or university in the U.S. and have completed at least one semester. Awards based on need, merit, and involvement in Armenian community.

Write to scholarship committee at address above for complete information. Enclose self-addressed stamped envelope and indicate whether undergrad or grad student.

3381 — ARMENIAN STUDENTS' ASSOCIATION OF AMERICA, INC. (Scholarships)

395 Concord Avenue
Belmont MA 02178
617/484-9548

AMOUNT: $500-$2,500

DEADLINE(S): JAN 15

FIELD(S): All fields of study

Applicants must be of Armenian ancestry and be full-time students who plan to attend a four-year, accredited college/university in the US full-time during the next academic year (must have completed or be in the process of completing first year of college or higher). Must demonstrate financial need, have good academic performance, show self help, and participate in extracurricular activities.

30 awards annually. $15 application fee. Contact ASA Scholarship Committee in the fall to request application forms. Deadline for requests is January 15th; completed application package must be returned by March 15th.

3382 — ARROW, INC. (American Indian Graduate Center Scholarship)

4520 Montgomery Blvd., NE Ste. 1-B
Albuquerque NM 87109-1291
505/881-4584

AMOUNT: Varies

DEADLINE(S): May 1

FIELD(S): All fields of study

Open to enrolled members from a federally-recognized American Indian tribe or Alaska Native group. Students must be pursuing a masters or doctorate degree as full-time student.

Write to the above address for complete information.

3383 — ARTHUR C. & FLORENCE S. BOEHMER FUND (Scholarships)

c/o Rinn & Elliot
P.O. Box 1827
Lodi CA 95241
209/369-2781

AMOUNT: Depends on yearly income

DEADLINE(S): JUN 15 (Applications available MAR 1 to JUN 15)

FIELD(S): Medical

Open to students who are graduates of a high school within the Lodi (San Joaquin County, CA) Unified School District. For undergraduate, graduate, or post-graduate study in the field of medicine at an accredited California institution.

Grade point average of 2.9 or better required. Scholarships are renewable. Write for complete information.

3384 — ARTS & ENTERTAINMENT NETWORK (A&E Teacher Grant Competition)

235 East 45th St.
New York NY 10017
212/661-4500

AMOUNT: $1,000 Savings Bond (12); $2,500 Savings Bond (Grand Prize + prizes for the school

DEADLINE(S): MAR 1

FIELD(S): All fields of study

Awards for teachers of grades 6-12 who have demonstrated how imaginative use of A&E programming results in innovative approaches to classroom instruction. Applicants are to write above a unique classroom project based on an A&E program. Also, a teacher's project can be submitted by a principal, school librarian, or peer teacher.

Three winners in each of four regions: Eastern, Central, Western, and Southern. Contact organization for details.

3385 — ASIAN PACIFIC AMERICAN SUPPORT GROUP (Scholarship)

USC, Student Union 410
Los Angeles CA 90089-4851
213/740-4999
FAX: 213/740-5284
E-Mail: apass@usc.edu
Internet: www.usc.edu/dept/APASS/

AMOUNT: $1,000-$2,500

DEADLINE(S): MAR 20

FIELD(S): All fields of study.

Scholarships for full-time students who have close ties with the Asian Pacific Community. GPA of 3.0 or above required.

15-20 awards per year. Recipients may re-apply for second year. Applications available Dec. 2.

3386 — ASSOCIATION FOR COMPUTING MACHINERY-WASHINGTON, DC CHAPTER (Samuel N. Alexander Fellowship Award)

1820 Dolley Madison Blvd.
McLean VA 22102
E-Mail: charwing@mitre.org
Internet: www.acm.org/chapters/dcacm/scholarships/

AMOUNT: $3,000

DEADLINE(S): MAY 1

FIELD(S): Any field of study involving computer applications

Fellowship for a doctoral candidate enrolled in a college or university in Maryland, Virginia, or the District of Columbia in a field involving computers. Applications from students in any academic dept. will be considered.

Access website for details and application or send to Charlotte W. Wales, the MITRE Corp., at above address.

3387 — ASSOCIATION FOR COMPUTING MACHINERY-WASHINGTON, DC CHAPTER (Master's Degree Grant)

1820 Dolley Madison Blvd.
McLean VA 22102
E-Mail: charwing@mitre.org
Internet: www.acm.org/chapters/dcacm/scholarships/

AMOUNT: $1,500

DEADLINE(S): MAY 1

FIELD(S): Any field of study involving computer applications

Grant for a candidate enrolled in a master's program at a college or university in Maryland, Virginia, or the District of Columbia in a field involving computers. Applications from students in any academic dept. will be considered.

Access website for details and application or send to Charlotte W. Wales, the MITRE Corp., at above address.

3388 — ASSOCIATION ON AMERICAN INDIAN AFFAIRS, INC. (Sequoyah Graduate Fellowships)

P.O. Box 268
Sisseton SD 57262
605/698-3998 or 605/698-3787
FAX: 605/698-3316

AMOUNT: Varies

DEADLINE(S): OCT 1

FIELD(S): All fields of study

Graduate fellowships for U.S. citizens with 1/4 or more American Indian or Alaskan Native blood who are members of a federally recognized tribe. For full-time study.

Ten awards each year. Send SASE to above address for application and details.

3389 — ASSOCIATION ON AMERICAN INDIAN AFFAIRS, INC. (Displaced Homemakers Scholarships)

Box 268
Sisseton SD 57262
605/698-3998 or 605/698-3787
FAX: 605/698-3316

AMOUNT: Varies

DEADLINE(S): SEP 1

FIELD(S): Any field of study

For mid-life homemakers (female or male) who are unable to fill their educational goals. Scholarship will augment the usual and expected financial sources of educational money to assist those students with child care, transportation, and some living expenses. Must demonstrate special financial needs as heads of households, single parents, or as displaced homemakers.

Must be at least 1/4 Indian blood from a federally recognized tribe and submit a one- or two-page essay outlining your life experience. Send SASE to above address for complete information.

3390 — ASSOCIATION OF COMMONWEALTH UNIVERSITIES (British Marshall Scholarships)

36 Gordon Square
London WC1H OPF UNITED KINGDOM
+44 (0) 171/387-8572
FAX: +44 (0) 171-387 2655

AMOUNT: Approximately 16,000 pounds sterling per year

DEADLINE(S): OCT 14

FIELD(S): All areas of study

Open to U.S. citizens (under 26 years of age) who are graduates of a U.S. college or university. Minimum GPA 3.7 (after freshman year) required. For undergraduate or graduate degree study of two years at a university in the UK.

Approx 40 awards per year. Contact British consulates at embassies in Washington DC, Chicago, Boston, San Francisco, Atlanta, or Houston or write to address above for complete information.

3391 — ASSOCIATION OF COMMONWEALTH UNIVERSITIES (Marshall Sherfield Fellowships)

British Embassy, Cultural Dept., 3100 Massachusetts Ave NW
Washington DC 20008-3600
202/588-588-6500

AMOUNT: Write/call for details

DEADLINE(S): None

FIELD(S): All areas of study

Post-doctoral fellowships for U.S. citizens who wish to conduct studies at a university in the UK.

2 awards. Contact British Embassy at address above for complete information.

3392 — ASSOCIATION OF INTERNATIONAL EDUCATION, JAPAN (Honors Scholarships for Private International Students)

4-5-29 Komaba
Meguro-KU
Tokyo 153 Japan
03-5454-5213
FAX: 03-4343-5233

AMOUNT: 49,000-70,000 yen per month

DEADLINE(S): Varies (Closing date is designated by the university.)

FIELD(S): All fields of study

Scholarships for study in Japan. For undergraduate and graduate students of all nationalities enrolled at junior colleges, technological or vocational schools, colleges, or universities. Grantees are selected on the basis of recommendations from the scholarship committee at their college or university in Japan.

4,540 awards per year. Apply through the school attended. Write for complete information.

3393 — ASSOCIATION OF INTERNATIONAL EDUCATION, JAPAN (Peace and Friendship Scholarship for Private International Students)

4-5-29 Komaba, Meguro-KU
Tokyo 153 JAPAN
03-5454-5213
FAX: 03-4343-5233

AMOUNT: 61,000 - 81,000 yen per month

DEADLINE(S): Varies (Closing date is designated by the university.)

FIELD(S): All fields of study

For privately financed international students from Asian countries and areas who play a central role in friendship and exchange activities between Japan and their countries. Must be enrolled at a junior college, technological or vocational school, college, or university.

Must demonstrate financial need. Apply through the school attended.

3394 — ASSOCIATION OF INTERNATIONAL EDUCATION, JAPAN (Short-term Student Exchange Scholarships for International Students)

4-5-29 Komaba, Meguro-ku
Tokyo 153-8503 JAPAN
03-5454-5214

FAX: 03-4343-5234

Internet: www.aiej.or.jp/information/tan98.htm

AMOUNT: 80,000 yen/month + travel, etc.

DEADLINE(S): JAN 20; MAY 15; SEP 11

FIELD(S): All fields of study

For international students planning to study in Japan. Must be enrolled or university in an undergraduate or graduate program and plan to continue with that program after the stay in Japan. Can be any nationality except Japanese. Must demonstrate financial need. Programs are from six months to one year.

1,700 scholarships. Must demonstrate financial need. Write to above address or check with your university for details. Information also at above website.

3395 — ASSOCIATION OF UNIVERSITIES & COLLEGES OF CANADA (International & Canadian Programs Branch—Scholarships; Research & Institutional Programs)

350 Albert St., Suite 600

Ottawa Ontario K1R 1B1 Canada

613/563-1236

FAX 613/563-9745

AMOUNT: Varies with program

DEADLINE(S): Varies

FIELD(S): All fields of study

AUCC administers numerous awards covering all academic disciplines that are available to Canadian citizens or permanent residents for study at eligible Canadian postsecondary institutions.

Write for complete information.

3396 — ATSUMI INTERNATIONAL SCHOLARSHIP FOUNDATION (Doctoral Scholarships)

3-5-8 Sekiguchi Bunkyoku

Tokyo 112 JAPAN

03-3943-7612

FAX: 03-3943-1512

E-Mail: aisf@sh0.po.iijnet.or.jp

Internet: www.kajima.co.jp/culture/atsumi/program

AMOUNT: Monthly stipend April through March

DEADLINE(S): SEP 30

FIELD(S): All fields of study

Scholarships for Ph.D. candidates from all over the world with non-Japanese nationality in their last year of study.

Contact organization for details.

3397 — AURORA FOUNDATION (Scholarships)

111 W. Downer Place

Aurora IL 60506-6112

630/896-7800

AMOUNT: Varies

DEADLINE(S): Varies

FIELD(S): All fields of study

Scholarships are administered by this Foundation for residents of the Greater Aurora Area, including the Tri-Cities and Kendall County, Illinois.

Write or call for details.

3398 — AUSTIN CHILDREN'S EDUCATIONAL OPPORTUNITY FOUNDATION

111 Congress, Ste. 3000

Austin TX 78701

512/472-0153

FAX: 512/310-1688

E-Mail/Internet: austinceo@aol.com

AMOUNT: Up to half of tuition-up to $1,000/yr.

DEADLINE(S): None

FIELD(S): All fields of study

Scholarships for children who are residents of Travis County, Texas, ages 6-14 (as of Sept. 1 of the school year) attending any school. Family must qualify for the federal school lunch program guidelines.

Contact Jane Kilgore at above location. First come, first served. Renewable for 3 years.

3399 — AUSTRALIAN FEDERATION OF UNIVERSITY WOMEN (Capital Territory Bursary)

GPO Box 520

Canberra ACT 2601 AUSTRALIA

Written Inquiry

AMOUNT: Aus$1,000

DEADLINE(S): JUL 31

FIELD(S): All fields of study

Bursary is for members of the International, British, Australian, or other national Federation of University Women for up to four weeks accomodation and board at Hall of Residence at the Australian National University. Must be a graduate from a university or tertiary institution in Australia, New Zealand, Papua New Guinea, or South Pacific. Travel costs will NOT be paid.

Contact AFUW for an application. Decision is reached by November.

3400 — AUSTRALIAN FEDERATION OF UNIVERSITY WOMEN - WESTERN AUSTRALIA (Bursaries)

Bursary Liaison Officer

PO Box 48

Nedlands WA 6009 AUSTRALIA

Written Inquiry

AMOUNT: Aus$1,700 - Aus$2,750

DEADLINE(S): JUL 31

FIELD(S): All fields of study

Bursaries to support women graduates of a Western Australian University to complete a higher degree or postdoctoral research at a recognized university in any country or women who have been accepted to work toward a higher degree at a university in Western Australia.

Membership in AFUW or in IFUW is required. Write for complete information.

3401 — AUSTRALIAN FEDERATION OF UNIVERSITY WOMEN - WESTERN AUSTRALIA (Georgina Sweet Fellowship)

PO Box 14

Bullcreek WA 6149 AUSTRALIA

Written Inquiry

AMOUNT: Aus$4,500

DEADLINE(S): JUL 31

FIELD(S): All fields of study

Members of the British Federation of Women Graduates may be recommended for this fellowship for advanced post-first degree study or research at an Australian University. Duration must be of not less than four months and not more than twelve.

Biennial award. Contact the Fellowships Convener at AFUW for an application. Decision is reached by November.

3402 — AUSTRALIAN FEDERATION OF UNIVERSITY WOMEN - WESTERN AUSTRALIA (Bursaries)

Bursary Liaison Officer

PO Box 48

Nedlands WA 6009 AUSTRALIA

Written Inquiry

AMOUNT: Aus$1,700 - Aus$2,750

DEADLINE(S): JUL 31

FIELD(S): All fields of study

Bursaries to support women graduates of a recognized university to complete a higher degree or post-doctoral research at a university in Western Australia.

Membership in AFUW or in IFUW is required. Write for complete information.

3403 — AUSTRALIAN FEDERATION OF UNIVERSITY WOMEN—QUEENSLAND FELLOWSHIP FUND (Freda Bage Fellowship)

Private Box 8/217 Hawken Drive

St. Lucia, QLD, 4067, Australia

(07) 3870 7516

AMOUNT: $A48 000 for three years.

DEADLINE(S): JULY 31

FIELD(S): All fields of study

For women conducting post-graduate research for a maximum of three years who are graduates of a university from any country. Not restricted to a formal university study and are tenable at any university or approved institution in Australia. Not tenable at the institution from which the applicant obtained her first degree. Can be used overseas by an Australian citizen.

Women on full-time salaries or on fully-paid study leave during the Fellowship year are not eligible.

3404 — AUSTRALIAN FEDERATION OF UNIVERSITY WOMEN—QUEENSLAND FELLOWSHIP FUND (Commemorative Fellowships)

Private Box 8/217 Hawken Drive
St. Jucia, QLD, 4067, Australia
(07) 3870 7516

AMOUNT: $A14 000 for one year.

DEADLINE(S): JUL 31

FIELD(S): All fields of study

For women conducting post-graduate research for a maximum of one year who are graduates of a university from any country. Not restricted to a formal university study and are tenable at any university or approved institution in Australia. Can be used overseas by an Australian citizen

Women on full-time salaries or on full-paid study leave during the Fellowship year are not eligible.

3405 — AUSTRALIAN FEDERATION OF UNIVERSITY WOMEN—SA INC. (Trust Fund Bursary)

GPO Box 634
Adelaide 5001 SOUTH AUSTRALIA
Written Inquiry

AMOUNT: $Aust 3,000

DEADLINE(S): MAR 1

FIELD(S): All fields of study

Fellowship/bursary open to women who are enrolled in a master's degree by coursework at an Australian university and have a good undergraduate academic record. May not be employed full-time or on a fully-paid study leave. Selection based primarily on academic merit; community activities and financial need also considered.

Write to Fellowship Trustee, AFUW-SA Inc. for an application.

3406 — AUSTRALIAN FEDERATION OF UNIVERSITY WOMEN—SA INC. (Jean Gilmore & Thenie Baddams Bursaries)

GPO Box 634
Adelaide 5001 SOUTH AUSTRALIA
Written Inquiry

AMOUNT: up to $Aust 6,000/each

DEADLINE(S): MAR 1

FIELD(S): All fields of study

For women enrolled in a master's degree by research or Ph.D. program at an Australian university and who have completed at least 1 year of research (not including an honors year). Cannot be in full-time paid employment or on fully-paid study leave. Research may be undertaken outside Australia as long as it is leading towards the degree for which the applicant is enrolled in Australia. Selection based primarily on academic merit; financial need is considered.

Lodgement fee of $Aust 12 must accompany each application. Contact Fellowships Trustee, AFUW-SA Inc. Trust Fund, for an application.

3407 — AUSTRALIAN FEDERATION OF UNIVERSITY WOMEN—VICTORIA INC (Lady Leitch Scholarships)

PO Box 816
MT. Eliza
Victoria 3199
Australia
9-787-3262

AMOUNT: AUS$5,000

DEADLINE(S): MAR 1

FIELD(S): All fields of study

Open to women who are members of the Australian of University Women. Scholarships support graduate study in any country. Financial need is a consideration.

Write for complete information.

3408 — AUSTRALIAN FEDERATION OF UNIVERSITY WOMEN-SA INC. (Doreen McCarthy, Barbara Crase, Cathy Candler, & Diamond Jubilee Bursaries)

GPO Box 634
Adelaide 5001 SOUTH AUSTRALIA
Written Inquiry

AMOUNT: $Aust 2,000-2,500

DEADLINE(S): MAR 1

FIELD(S): All fields of study

Three of the bursaries are for men or women undertaking graduate/postgraduate research degrees at a university in South Australia. Diamond Jubilee can be used for any coursework.

Write to Fellowships Trustee, AFUW-SA Inc. Trust Fund for applications.

3409 — AUSTRALIAN FEDERATION OF UNIVERSITY WOMEN-SA INC. (Padnendadlu Bursary)

GPO Box 634
Adelaide 5001 SOUTH AUSTRALIA
Written Inquiry

AMOUNT: $Aust 2,500

DEADLINE(S): MAR 1

FIELD(S): Any field of study

For indigenous Australian women undertaking graduate/postgraduate studies (coursework or research) at a university in South Australia.

Write to Fellowships Trustee, AFUW-SA Inc. Trust Fund for an application.

3410 — AUSTRALIAN FEDERATION OF UNIVERSITY WOMEN-VICTORIA INC (Victorian Beatrice Fincher Scholarship)

PO Box 816
Mount Eliza VIC 3930 AUSTRALIA
9-787-3262

AMOUNT: AUS$5,000

DEADLINE(S): MAR 1

FIELD(S): All fields of study

For women graduate students who are members of the Australian Federation of University Women or any international association affiliated with the International Federation of University Women. Must be seeking a higher degree from any Australian or overseas university and be conducting independent research which will benefit mankind. Travel costs will NOT be paid.

Contact Honorary Scholarship Secretary, AFUW-Vic. Inc. at above address.

3411 — AUSTRALIAN GOVERNMENT OVERSEAS POSTGRADUATE RESEARCH SCHOLARSHIP PROGRAM (For Study at Flinders University of South Australia)

GPO Box 2100
Adelaide SA 5002 South Australia
INT + 618/201-2759

AMOUNT: A$15,637 (tax-free) per year stipend + tuition + fees

DEADLINE(S): AUG 31

FIELD(S): All fields of study

Open to commencing Ph.D or masters level overseas students who will engage in quality research in areas of priority at Flinders University of South Australia. Scholarships are to support high quality research.

Write for a complete scholarship application kit.

3412 — AUSTRALIAN NATIONAL UNIVERSITY (ANU Scholarship Program)

Graduate Students Section
Canberra Act 0200 Australia
616/249-5949

AMOUNT: Aus.$14961 per annum + allowance

DEADLINE(S): SEP 30

FIELD(S): All areas of study

Open to graduate students at the Ph.D or master level who hold an honors degree with first class honors (or an equivalent qualification). No citizenship or financial requirements.

Over 100 awards per year. Write for complete information.

3413 — AUSTRALIAN RESEARCH COUNCIL (Australian Postdoctoral Fellowship)

GPO Box 9880
Canberra ACT 2601 AUSTRALIA
61 6 240 9694
FAX: 61 6 240 7324
E-Mail: rbfellow@deety
Internet: www.deetyz.gov.au/divisions/hed/research/research.htm

AMOUNT: $37,981-$40,770/year

DEADLINE(S): MAR 1

FIELD(S): All areas of study except clinical medicine and dentistry

Three-year fellowship for postgraduate students pursuing studies in Australia. Must be Australian citizen or resident at the time of commencing the fellowship. For researchers who have not yet submitted their Ph.D. but who will do so before the end of the year of submitting their application. Must have been awarded Ph.D. in the last three years.

55 annual awards. Renewable for three years. Contact Dept. of Employment, Education, and Training at above location.

3414 — AUSTRALIAN RESEARCH COUNCIL (Australian Research Fellowships/Queen Elizabeth II Fellowships)

GPO Box 9880
Canberra ACT 2601 AUSTRALIA
616 240 9694
FAX: 616 240 7324
E-Mail: rbfellow@deetya.gov.au
Internet: www.deetya.gov.au/divisions/hed/research/research.htm

AMOUNT: ARF: $42,917-$50,965/yr.; QEII: $46,135-50,965/yr.

DEADLINE(S): MAR 1

FIELD(S): All fields of study except clinical medicine and dentistry

Postdoctorate research fellowship; must have received Ph.D. at time of application. Prefer 3-8 years professional experience since Ph.D. Must be Australian citizen or resident at time of commencing fellowship.

15 awards in each catergory yearly. Contact David Murphy at Dept. of Employment, Education, and Training, and Youth Affairs at above location.

3415 — AUSTRALIAN RESEARCH COUNCIL (Overseas Postgraduate Research Scholarship)

GPO Box 9880
Canberra ACT 2601 AUSTRALIA
+61 6 240 9694
FAX: +61 6 240 7324
E-Mail: rbfellow@deetya.gov.au
www.deetya.govau/divisions/hed/research/research.htm

AMOUNT: Tuition fees

DEADLINE(S): Not given

FIELD(S): Area of university's strength

Scholarships for overseas students to conduct research for M.A. or doctorate degrees in Australia. Applicants may not be citizens of Australia or New Zealand.

300 awards yearly. Renewable for duration of course. Contact Dept. of

3416 — AUSTRALIAN RESEARCH COUNCIL (Senior Research Fellowships)

GPO Box 9880
Canberra ACT 2601 AUSTRALIA
616 240 9694
FAX: 616 240 7324
E-Mail: rbfellow@detya.gov.au
Internet: www.deetya.gov.au/divisions/hed/research/research.htm

AMOUNT: $52,573-$81,542

DEADLINE(S): MAR 1

FIELD(S): All areas of study except clinical medicine and dentistry

Five-year postdoctoral research fellowships for use at an Australian institution or organization. Must be Australian citizen or resident at time of fellowship. Prefer researchers who have more than eight years' professional experience since the award of their Ph.Ds.

15 annual awards. Renewable for five years. Contact David Murphy at Dept. of Employment, Education, Training, and Youth Affairs at above location.

3417 — AUSTRIAN CULTURAL INSTITUTE (APART - Austrian Program for Advanced Research & Technology)

950 Third Ave., 20th Fl.
New York NY 10022
212/759-5165 or +43/1/51581-207
FAX: 212/319-9636
E-Mail: desk@aci.org
Internet: www.austriaculture.net

AMOUNT: Varies

DEADLINE(S): Varies

FIELD(S): All fields of study

Three-year grant is open to Austrian graduates and qualified university lecturers for research in Austria or other countries. Must have a doctorate, proof of scientific achievement (publication), and present a research proposal.

See website or contact ACI for an application kit, or write to Osterreichische Akademie der Wissenschaften, Stipendienreferat, Dr. Ignaz Seipel-Platz 2, A-1010 Vienna, Austria.

3418 — AUSTRIAN CULTURAL INSTITUTE (Lise Meitner Scholarship)

950 Third Ave., 20th Fl.
New York NY 10022
212/759-5165
FAX: 212/319-9636
E-Mail: desk@aci.org
Internet: www.austriaculture.net

AMOUNT: ATS 310,000 (US $23,800)

DEADLINE(S): Varies

FIELD(S): All fields of study

Open to highly qualified postdoctoral students, scholars, and researchers to pursue study or research in Austria. Must be 20 to 35 years old.

Renewable. See website or contact ACI for information kit, or write to Fonds zur Forderung der wissenschaftlichen Forschung, Weyringergasse 35, A-1040 Wien, Austria.

3419 — AUSTRIAN CULTURAL INSTITUTE (Scholars From Around the World)

950 Third Ave., 20th Fl.
New York NY 10022
212/759-5165
FAX: 212/319-9636
E-Mail: desk@aci.org
Internet: www.austriaculture.net

AMOUNT: ATS 7,800-10,000/month (US $600-$770) + ATS 2,500 (US $190) start grant for tuition & health insurance

DEADLINE(S): FEB 28

FIELD(S): All fields of study

Open to applicants from around the world to enable doctoral or advanced graduate study projects at Austrian universities. Must have a working knowledge of German (especially in the field of research) and be 20 to 35 years old. Must submit letters of recommendation, curriculum vitae, and transcripts. Preference given to studies on Austria-related subjects.

Not renewable. See website or contact ACI for an application kit.

3420 — AUSTRIAN FEDERAL MINISTRY OF SCIENCE AND TRANSPORT (Exchange Scholarships)

Minoritenplatz 5
1014 Wien 1 AUSTRIA
+43/1/531 20-5219
FAX: +43/1/531 20-6205
E-Mail: eva.philipp@bmwf.gv.at
Internet: www.bmwf.gv.at AND
www.oead.ca.at

AMOUNT: Varies

DEADLINE(S): Varies

FIELD(S): All areas of study

Awards open to undergraduate and graduate students who wish to study in Austria.

Write or visit website for details.

3421 — AVON LATINA MODEL OF THE YEAR (Competition)

Rules Requests
1251 Sixth Ave.
New York NY 10020-1196
1-800/FOR-AVON

AMOUNT: Up to $15,000 in educational awards and modeling fees and gifts

DEADLINE(S): FEB 15

FIELD(S): All fields of study

For Hispanic females between the ages of 17 and 25 who are "intelligent, poised, and beautiful."

Send self-addressed, stamped envelope for application and official rules.

3422 — B & L EDUCATIONAL FOUNDATION

2111 Northridge Dr. NE
Grand Rapids MI 49505
616/364-8499

AMOUNT: $200-$2,000

DEADLINE(S): JUL 1; DEC 24

FIELD(S): All fields of study

Scholarships for indivduals who are residents of, or attending schools in, Michigan or Arizona.

Send SASE to above address for formal application and details.

3423 — BARNABAS MINISTRIES OF SHREVEPORT

4451 Charter Point Blvd.
Jacksonville FL 32211-1027
318/227-1313

AMOUNT: Varies

DEADLINE(S): Ongoing

FIELD(S): All fields of study

Scholarships and assistance to financially needy residents of the state of Louisiana.

Send letter to Dr. John Sullivan, Trustee, at above address.

3424 — BASIN ELECTRIC POWER COOPERATIVE (Scholarship Program)

Human Resources
1717 E. Interstate Ave.
Bismark ND 58501
800/242-2372

AMOUNT: $1,000

DEADLINE(S): MAR 14

FIELD(S): All fields of study

Available to children of full-time employees of Basin Electric Power Cooperative and its subsidiaries, and the children of member-system employees and consumers. Must be a student who is enrolled or planning to enroll in a full-time graduate or undergraduate course of study at an accredited two-year or four-year college, university, or vocational/technical school.

20 awards annually. Contact Basin Electric's Human Resources Division for an application.

3425 — BEDDING PLANTS FOUNDATION, INC. (BPI Family Member Scholarship)

PO Box 280
East Lansing MI 48826-0280
517/333-4617
FAX: 517/333-4494
E-Mail: BPFI@aol.com
Internet: www.bpfi.org

AMOUNT: $1,000

DEADLINE(S): MAY 15

FIELD(S): All fields of study

Open to graduate and undergraduate students at an accredited university in the US or Canada who are majoring in any field. Must be a child, parent, or spouse of a current member of Bedding Plants International. Cash award, with checks issued jointly in name of recipient and college/institution he or she will attend for current year. Must submit references & transcripts.

1 award annually. See website or send printed self-addressed mailing label (or self-addressed, stamped envelope) to BPFI after January 1st for an application. Recipient will be notified.

3426 — BEIT TRUST (Post-graduate Fellowships)

P.O. Box CH 76
Chisipite Harare Zimbabwe
Harare 496132

AMOUNT: Tuition and living expences

DEADLINE(S): SEP 30

FIELD(S): All fields of study

Applicants must be citizens of Zimbabwe and ordinarily reside in Zimbabwe. Fellowships for postgraduate study can be used at any recognized university in Great Britain, Ireland, or Southern Africa.

Fellowships renewable for 1-2 years. Applicants must hold a first degree of first class or upper second standard. Write for complete information.

3427 — BELGIAN AMERICAN EDUCATIONAL FOUNDATION (Graduate Fellowships)

195 Church St.
New Haven CT 06510
203/777-5765

AMOUNT: Tuition, fees, lodging, living expenses, roundtrip travel + $12,000 stipend

DEADLINE(S): JAN 31

FIELD(S): All fields of study

Fellowships for graduate study in Belgium. Should have speaking and reading knowledge of French, German, or Dutch and have master's degree or be working toward a Ph.D. Preference to applicants under 30 years old. US citizenship required.

10 awards per year. Write for complete information.

3428 — BIA HIGHER EDUCATION/HOPI SUPPLEMENTAL GRANT

P.O. Box 123
Kykotsmovi AZ 86039
520/734-2441, Ext. 520
800/762-9630
FAX: 520/734-2435

AMOUNT: Varies

DEADLINE(S): JUL 31 (fall); NOV 30 (spring); APR 30 (summer)

FIELD(S): All fields of study

For enrolled members of the Hopi Tribe pursuing associate, baccalaureate, graduate, or post-graduate degrees. Minimum 2.0 GPA required. Grant is a supplemental source of financial aid the eligible students.

Financial need is primary consideration.

3429 — BLINDED VETERANS ASSOCIATION (Kathern F. Gruber Scholarship Program)

477 H Street NW
Washington DC 20001-2694
800/669-7079 or 202/371-8880
FAX: 202/371-8258

AMOUNT: $1,000-$2,000

DEADLINE(S): APR 17

FIELD(S): All areas of study

Open to children and spouses of blinded veterans. The vet must be legally blind, either service or non-service connected. Must be accepted or already enrolled full-time in a college or vocational school and be a U.S. citizen.

8 scholarships of $2,000 and 2 of $1,000. Write for complete information.

3430 — BOB JONES UNIVERSITY (Rebate Program)

1700 Wade Hampton Blvd.
Greenville SC 29614
1-864-242-5100
FAX: 1-800-232-9258 Ext 2085

AMOUNT: $2,000-1st year; $1,000-2nd year.

DEADLINE(S): Varies (Beginning of semester)

FIELD(S): All areas of study

Bob Jones University is a private, Christian-oriented college which offers vocational, technical, and academic programs. The financial aid program requires that the student participate in a work program for at least 7 hours/week.

Renewable at $1,000. U.S. citizenship required.

3431 — BREWER FOUNDATION, INC.

3819 Woodlawn Road
Rocky Mount NC 27804
919/443-1333

AMOUNT: Varies

DEADLINE(S): None specified

FIELD(S): All fields of study

Scholarships for higher education to residents of North Carolina.

Contact Joseph B. Brewer, Jr., President, at foundation listed above for current application deadline and procedures.

3432 — BRITISH COLUMBIA MINISTRY OF SKILLS, EDUCATION, AND TRAINING (British Columbia Student Assistance Program)

2nd Floor
1106 Cook St.
Victoria BC V8V 3Z9 CANADA
604/387-6100

AMOUNT: Varies

DEADLINE(S): Varies (6 weeks before end of study period)

FIELD(S): All areas of study

Program open to residents of British Columbia who are enrolled full time for credit at a designated college, institute, or university. Canadian citizen or legal resident of British Columbia.

Program is comprised of federal and provincial student loans and provincial grant. Write for complete information.

3433 — BRITISH EMBASSY (Marshall Scholarship Program)

Education Services
3100 Massachusetts Ave. NW
Washington DC 20008-3600
202/588-7830
FAX: 202/588-7918
E-Mail: Study.UK@BC-WashingtonDC.Sprint.Com
Internet: http:www.britcoun.org/usa/usastud.html

AMOUNT: Tuition, fees, stipend, book allowance, transportation

DEADLINE(S): OCT 15

FIELD(S): All fields of study

Open to U.S. citizens who are under 26 years old and hold a bachelors degree from a U.S. university. Awards are for at least 2 years at a United Kingdom university. Grade point average of 3.7 or better is required.

40 new awards per year. Contact nearest British Consulate or contact website or address above for complete information.

3434 — BRITISH FEDERATION OF WOMEN GRADUATES (BFWG Scholarships for UK Citizens)

4 Mandeville Courtyard
142 Battersea Park Rd.
London SW11 4NB ENGLAND UK
PHONE/FAX: 0171/498-8037

AMOUNT: 750-1,000+ pounds sterling

DEADLINE(S): SEP 10

FIELD(S): All fields of study

For female UK citizens who plan to pursue graduate studies overseas. Must have completed at least four academic terms or three semesters; award is not made for first year of research. Chief criteria is academic excellence and proven ability to carry out independent research. Postdoctoral studies also eligible.

Application fee of 12 pounds sterling required. Send a self-addressed, stamped envelope (or self-addressed envelope with international reply coupons) for an application. Results announced by end of October.

3435 — BRITISH FEDERATION OF WOMEN GRADUATES (BFWG Scholarships for Non-UK Citizens)

4 Mandeville Courtyard
142 Battersea Park Rd.
London SW11 4NB ENGLAND UK
PHONE/FAX: 0171/498-8037

AMOUNT: 750-1,000+ pounds sterling

DEADLINE(S): SEP 10

FIELD(S): All fields of study

For females from any country who will pursue graduate studies in Great Britain. Must have completed at least four academic terms or three semesters; award is not made for first year of research. Chief criteria is academic excellence and proven ability to carry out independent research. Postdoctoral studies also eligible.

Application fee of 12 pounds sterling required. Send a self-addressed, stamped envelope (or self-addressed envelope with international reply coupons) for an application. Results announced by end of October.

3436 — BRITISH FEDERATION OF WOMEN GRADUATES (Foundation Grants)

BFWG Charitable Fdn.
28 Great James St.
London WC1N 3ES ENGLAND UK
0171/404 6447
FAX: 0171/404 6505
E-Mail: bfwg.charity@btinternet.com
Internet: www.ifuw.org

AMOUNT: 500-1,000 pounds sterling

DEADLINE(S): Varies

FIELD(S): All fields of study

For women studying at the postgraduate or postdoctoral level at approved institutions of higher education in Great Britain. Must demonstrate financial need.

160 awards annually. Not renewable. Contact the Grants Administrator-TBB for an application.

3437 — BRITISH FEDERATION OF WOMEN GRADUATES (Kathleen Hall Memorial Fellowships)

4 Mandeville Courtyard
142 Battersea Park Rd.
London SW11 4NB ENGLAND UK
PHONE/FAX: 0171/498-8037

AMOUNT: 1,000+ pounds sterling

DEADLINE(S): SEP 10

FIELD(S): All fields of study

For female graduate students whose studies will take place in Great Britain. Preference goes to students from countries of low per capita income. Chief criteria is academic excellence and proven ability to carry out independent research. Award is not made for the first year of research; must have completed a least four academic terms or three semesters. Postdoctoral studies also eligible.

Application fee of 12 pounds sterling required. Send a self-addressed, stamped envelope (or self-addressed envelope with international reply coupons) for an application. Results announced by end of October.

3438 — BRITISH FEDERATION OF WOMEN GRADUATES (Margaret K.B. Day Memorial & Beryl Mavis Green Scholarships for UK Citizens)

4 Mandeville Courtyard
142 Battersea Park Rd.
London SW11 4NB ENGLAND UK
PHONE/FAX: 0171/498 8037

AMOUNT: 1,000+ pounds sterling
DEADLINE(S): SEP 10
FIELD(S): All fields of study

For female UK citizens who will pursue graduate studies overseas. Must have completed at least four academic terms or three semesters; award is not made for first year of research. Chief criteria is academic excellence and proven ability to carry out research. Postdoctoral studies also eligible.

2 awards annually. Application fee of 12 pounds sterling required. Send a self-addressed, stamped envelope (or self-addressed envelope with international reply coupons) for an application. Results announced by end of October.

3439 — BRITISH FEDERATION OF WOMEN GRADUATES (Margaret K.B. Day Memorial & Beryl Mavis Green Scholarships for Non-UK Citizens)

4 Mandeville Courtyard
142 Battersea Park Rd.
London SW11 4NB ENGLAND UK
PHONE/FAX: 0171/498 8037

AMOUNT: 1,000+ pounds sterling
DEADLINE(S): SEP 10
FIELD(S): All fields of study

For female students of any nationality (except UK) who will pursue graduate studies in Great Britain. Must have completed at least four academic terms or three semesters; award is not given for first year of research. Chief criteria is academic excellence and proven ability to carry out independent research. Postdoctoral studies also eligible.

2 awards annually. Application fee of 12 pounds sterling required. Send a self-addressed, stamped envelope (or self-addressed envelope with international reply coupons) for an application. Results announced by end of October.

3440 — BRITISH FEDERATION OF WOMEN GRADUATES (Rose Sidgwick Memorial Fellowship)

4 Mandeville Courtyard
142 Battersea Park Rd.
London SW11 4NB ENGLAND UK
PHONE/FAX: 0171/498-8037

AMOUNT: US$16,500
DEADLINE(S): DEC 15
FIELD(S): All fields of study

Open only to British graduates below 30 years of age who are members of BFWG. To be used for 12 months of research in the US after recommendation by BFWG. Applicants are judged on their professional potential and the importance of their studies to women and girls in their country of origin. Preference will be given to women with prior commitment to this area. Must show outstanding academic ability. Travel costs will NOT be paid.

1 award annually. Send a self-addressed, stamped envelope (or self-addressed envelope with international reply coupons) to BFWG for an application. Notification is on April 30th.

3441 — BRITISH INFORMATION SERVICES (British Marshall Scholarships)

845 Third Ave.
New York NY 10022
212/758-0200
FAX: 212/758-5395

AMOUNT: Tuition, residence, travel, & related costs
DEADLINE(S): OCT 18
FIELD(S): All fields of study

Open to US citizens holding a bachelor's degree from an accredited US college or university. For study leading to a degree at a British university. Must be under 26 years old and have a grade point average of 3.5 or better (4.0 scale).

Tenable for 2 academic years and may be extended for a third year. Applications available after June 1 each year. Write for complete information.

3442 — BRITISH SCHOOLS AND UNIVERSITIES FOUNDATION, INC. (May & Ward Scholarships)

575 Madison Ave., Ste. 1006
New York NY 10022-2511
212/662-5576 or UK 0171-435-4648
FAX: 212/308-9834

AMOUNT: up to $12,500
DEADLINE(S): MAR 1
FIELD(S): All fields of study

For UK citizens to study in the US. Must have strong academic record, well-rounded interests, and demonstrate financial need. Must also show why you cannot study in your own country.

4-6 awards annually. Renewable for 2 years. For more information, contact above address or write to: 6 Windmill Hill, London NW3 6RU, England.

3443 — BRITISH SCHOOLS AND UNIVERSITIES FOUNDATION, INC. (May & Ward Scholarships)

575 Madison Ave., Ste. 1006
New York NY 10022-2511
212/662-5576 or UK 0171-435-4648
FAX: 212/308-9834

AMOUNT: up to $12,500
DEADLINE(S): MAR 1
FIELD(S): All fields of study

For US citizens to study in the UK. Must have strong academic record, well-rounded interests, and demonstrate financial need. Must also show why you cannot study in your own country.

4-6 awards annually. Renewable for 2 years. For more information, contact above address or write to: 6 Windmill Hill, London NW3 6RU, England.

3444 — BUCK INSTITUTE FOR EDUCATION (American Revolution Bicentennial Scholarships)

Marie Kanarr
18 Commercial Blvd.
Novato CA 94949
415/883-0122

AMOUNT: $500 to $2,000
DEADLINE(S): MAR 31
FIELD(S): All fields of study

For Marin County students who have been county residents since Sept. 1 of the year prior to submitting an application. Scholarships tenable at accredited colleges, universities, and vocational or trade programs.

Contact high school or college counselor or send self-addressed, stamped envelope with inquiry to organization for complete information.

3445 — BUDDHIST COMPASSION RELIEF TZU-CHI FOUNDATION, U.S.A. (Scholarships)

206 East Palm Ave.
Monrovia CA 91016
626/305-1188
FAX: 626/305-1185
Internet: www.tzuchi.org/usa/english

AMOUNT: $1,000
DEADLINE(S): MAY 31
FIELD(S): All fields of study

Scholarships for college-bound high school seniors (at least 3.8 GPA) and college students (at least 3.5 GPA). Must demonstrate financial need. Application process includes submitting a 500-word essay on why you think you should receive this scholarship and a description of your family background.

For more details on application requirements, contact organization or access website.

3446 — BUSINESS AND PROFESSIONAL WOMEN'S CLUBS—NEW YORK STATE (Grace LeGendre Fellowships and Endowment Fund, Inc.)

7509 State Route 5
Clinton NY 13323-3632
315/735-3114

AMOUNT: $1,000

DEADLINE(S): FEB 28

FIELD(S): All fields of study

For women who are permanent residents of NY state. Fellowships for graduate study (master or doctorate) at an accredited NY state college or university. U.S. citizenship required.

Applications available Oct. 1 through Jan. 31. Send a business-size, stamped, self-addressed envelope (SASE) for complete information.

3447 — BUTTE CREEK FOUNDATION

1350 E. Lassen Ave., No. 2
Chico CA 95926
530/895-1512

AMOUNT: Varies

DEADLINE(S): Ongoing

FIELD(S): All fields of study

Scholarships for residents of California.

Apply by letter to John Burghardt, President and Secretary, at above address.

3448 — CALEDONIAN RESEARCH FOUNDATION (Postgraduate Scholarships)

39 Castle St.
Edinburgh EH2 3BH SCOTLAND UK
0131 225 1200
FAX: 0131 225 4412
E-Mail: crf@murraybeith.co.uk

AMOUNT: Varies

DEADLINE(S): MAR 10

FIELD(S): All fields of study

Awards of up to three years duration are to fund research leading to Ph.D. degree from a Scottish university. There is no preference for subject, and at least one award annually is made in a non-scientific discipline. Applicants must have a first-class honours degree from a Scottish university.

Contact CRF for an application.

3449 — CALIFORNIA CHICANO NEWS MEDIA ASSOCIATION (Joel Garcia Memorial Scholarship)

c/o USC School of Journalism
3716 S. Hope St., Rm. 301
Los Angeles CA 90007-4344
213/743-2440

FAX: 213/744-1809
E-Mail: info@ccnma.org
Internet: www.ccnma.org

AMOUNT: $250-$2,000

DEADLINE(S): APR 2

FIELD(S): Journalism; News Media

For full-time high school senior, undergraduate, or graduate Latino students who are either California residents or plan to attend an accredited college/university in California. Awards based on commitment to above fields, scholastic achievement, community awareness, and financial need. Autobiographical essay explaining goals, two reference letters, official transcripts, and samples of work must be submitted with completed application. No faxed materials accepted.

See website or contact Julio Moran, Executive Director, for an application/more information.

3450 — CALIFORNIA COLLEGE DEMOCRATS (Internships)

See website
Internet: wwww.collegedems.org

AMOUNT: Varies

DEADLINE(S): None

FIELD(S): All fields of study

Internships available for various California Democratic office holders, candidates for office, and for several organizations, especially those working on environmental issues.

See website for list of statewide openings, which constantly changes. Some offer pay. Possible credit through your university.

3451 — CALIFORNIA STUDENT AID COMMISSION (Law Enforcement Dependents Scholarships - LEPD)

PO Box 419026
Rancho Cordova CA 95741-9026
916/526-7590 or TDD 916/526-7542
FAX: 916/526-8002
E-Mail: custsvcs@csac.ca.gov
Internet: www.csac.ca.gov

AMOUNT: $100-$9,036/year

DEADLINE(S): None given

FIELD(S): All fields of study

Need-based grant to dependents/spouses of California peace officers (Hwy Patrol/marshalls/sheriffs/police), specified CA Dept of Corrections and CA Youth Authority employees, and firefighters employed by public entities who have been killed or totally disabled in the line of duty. If you receive a Cal Grant, your LEPD will match your Cal Grant award. Receiving LEPD will not prevent you from receiving Cal Grant or any other grant/fee waiver.

Renewable up to four years. For more information, contact the California Student Aid Commission.

3452 — CALLEJO-BOTELLO FOUNDATION CHARITABLE TRUST

4314 North Central Expressway
Dallas TX 75206
214/741-6710

AMOUNT: Varies

DEADLINE(S): APR 23

FIELD(S): All areas of study

Scholarships for students planning to attend educational institutions in Texas.

Send SASE to William F. Callejo, Trustee, at above address

3453 — CANADA HUMAN RESOURCES DEVELOPMENT (Canada Student Loans Program)

P.O. Box 2090
Postal Station D
Ottawa Ontario K1P 6C6 CANADA
819/994-1844

AMOUNT: Maximum of $165 per week of study

DEADLINE(S): None

FIELD(S): All fields of study

Program provides loan assistance toward meeting the costs of full-time postsecondary study as a supplement to other resources available to the student. Canadian citizen or permanent resident.

Write for complete information.

3454 — CANADIAN ASSOCIATION OF UNIVERSITY TEACHERS (J. H. Stewart Reid Memorial Fellowship)

2675 Queensview Drive
Ottawa Ontario K2B 8K2
613/820-2270

AMOUNT: $5,000

DEADLINE(S): APR 30

FIELD(S): All fields of study

Open to Canadian citizens or permanent residents who have completed their comprehensive examinations (or equivalent) & have had their doctoral thesis proposal accepted by April 30. Must have a 1st class academic record in a grad program.

Write to awards officer at above address for complete information.

3455 — CANADIAN FEDERATION OF UNIVERSITY WOMEN (1989 Polytechnique Commemorative Award)

251 Bank St., Ste. 600
Ottawa Ontario K2P 1X3 CANADA

613/234-2732
Internet: www.cfuw.ca
AMOUNT: $1,400
DEADLINE(S): NOV 15
FIELD(S): All fields of study

For women who are Canadian citizens/permanent residents pursuing graduate studies in any field, with special consideration given to study of issues related particularly to women. The onus is on the candidate to justify the relevance of her work to women. Must hold at least a bachelor's degree or equivalent from a recognized university and have been accepted into, or be currently enrolled in the proposed program and place of study.

$20 filing fee. Contact CFUW for an application after August 1st. Candidates will be notified by May 31st.

3456 — CANADIAN FEDERATION OF UNIVERSITY WOMEN (Alice E. Wilson Awards)

251 Banks St., Ste. 600
Ottawa Ontario K2P 1X3 CANADA
613/234-2732
Internet: www.cfuw.ca
AMOUNT: $1,500
DEADLINE(S): NOV 15
FIELD(S): All fields of study

For women who are Canadian citizens/permanent residents pursuing graduate studies in any field, with special consideration given to candidates returning to study after at least three years. Must hold at least a bachelor's degree or equivalent from a recognized university and have been accepted into, or be currently enrolled in the proposed program and place of study.

$20 filing fee. 2 awards annually. Contact CFUW for an application after August 1st. Candidates will be notified by May 31st.

3457 — CANADIAN FEDERATION OF UNIVERSITY WOMEN (Bourse Georgette Lemoyne)

251 Bank St., Ste. 600
Ottawa Ontario K2P 1X3 CANADA
613/234-2732
Internet: www.cfuw.ca
AMOUNT: $2,000
DEADLINE(S): NOV 15
FIELD(S): All fields of study

For women who are Canadian citizens/permanent residents pursuing graduate studies at a Canadian university where one of the languages of administration and instruction is French. Must hold at least a bachelor's degree or equivalent from a recognized university and have been accepted into,

or be currently enrolled in the proposed program and place of study.

$20 filing fee. Contact CFUW for an application after August 1st. Candidates will be notified by May 31st.

3458 — CANADIAN FEDERATION OF UNIVERSITY WOMEN (Beverley Jackson Fellowship)

251 Bank St., Ste. 600
Ottawa Ontario K2P 1X3 CANADA
613/234-2732
Internet: www.cfuw.ca
AMOUNT: $3,000
DEADLINE(S): NOV 15
FIELD(S): All fields of study

For women who are Canadian citizens/permanent residents over the age of 35 and enrolled in graduate work at an Ontario university. Must hold at least a bachelor's degree or equivalent from a recognized university and have been accepted into, or be currently enrolled in the proposed program and place of study.

$25 filing fee. Contact CFUW for an application after August 1st. Candidates will be notified by May 31st. Funded by UWC North York.

3459 — CANADIAN FEDERATION OF UNIVERSITY WOMEN (Dr. Marion Elder Grant Fellowship)

251 Bank St., Ste. 600
Ottawa Ontario K2P 1X3 CANADA
613/234-2732
Internet: www.cfuw.ca
AMOUNT: $9,000
DEADLINE(S): NOV 15
FIELD(S): All fields of study

Open to women who are Canadian citizens/permanent residents studying full-time at the master's or doctoral level in Canada or abroad. Must hold at least a bachelor's degree or equivalent from a recognized university and have been accepted into, or be currently enrolled in the proposed program and place of study. Preference given to holder of a degree from Acadia University.

$25 filing fee. Contact CFUW for an application after August 1st. Candidates will be notified by May 31st. Funded by CFUW/Wolfville.

3460 — CANADIAN FEDERATION OF UNIVERSITY WOMEN (Margaret McWilliams Predoctoral Fellowship)

251 Bank St., Ste. 600
Ottawa Ontario K2P 1X3 CANADA
613/234-2732
Internet: www.cfuw.ca

AMOUNT: $10,000
DEADLINE(S): NOV 15
FIELD(S): All fields of study

For female graduate students who are Canadian citizens/permanent residents. Must have completed at least one full calendar year as a full-time student in doctoral level studies, and be a full-time student at time of application. Must hold at least a bachelor's degree or equivalent from a recognized university and have been accepted into, or be currently enrolled in the proposed program and place of study. May be studying abroad.

$35 filing fee. Contact CFUW for an application after August 1st. Candidates will be notified by May 31st.

3461 — CANADIAN NATIONAL INSTITUTE FOR THE BLIND (Various Scholarships and Grants)

100-5055 Joyce St.
Vancouver BC V5R 6B2 CANADA
604/431-2121
FAX: 604/431-2099
AMOUNT: Varies
DEADLINE(S): Varies
FIELD(S): All fields of study

Scholarships open to legally blind residents of British Columbia & the Yukon who are college or university students registered with CNIB. Awards tenable at recognized 2-year & 4-year undergraduate institutions. Canadian citizen.

Write for complete information.

3462 — CARL AND VIRGINIA JOHNSON DAY TRUST

108 West Madison
Yazoo City MS 39194-1018
601/746-4901
AMOUNT: Varies
DEADLINE(S): JUL 4 (for Fall loans); NOV (Thanksgiving day for Spring loans)
FIELD(S): All fields of study

Interest-free student loans for residents of Mississippi who are under 25 years old and attend Mississippi schools.

Approximately 100 loans per year. Write to Carolyn Johnson at above location for details.

3463 — CARNEGIE TRUST FOR THE UNIVERSITIES OF SCOTLAND (Carnegie Postgraduate Scholarships)

Cameron House
Abbey Park Place
Dunfermline Fife KY12 7PZ Scotland
0383/622148
AMOUNT: 6104 pounds sterling + allowed expenses
DEADLINE(S): MAR 15

FIELD(S): All areas

Scholarships for graduates of Scottish universities awarded by the Carnegie Trust for the universities of Scotland. Requires a first class honors degree. Scholarships are competitive and only tenable in the United Kingdom.

Candidates must be nominated by staff member of a Scottish university. Preference to recent graduates. Write for complete information.

3464 — CENTRAL SCHOLARSHIP BUREAU (Interest-free Loans)

1700 Reisterstown Road #220
Baltimore MD 21208
410-415-5558

AMOUNT: $500 - $8,000 (max thru grad school)

DEADLINE(S): JUN 1; DEC 1

FIELD(S): All fields of study

Interest-free loans for residents of metropolitan Baltimore area who have exhausted all other available avenues of funding. Aid is offered for study at any accredited undergrad or graduate institution.

Awards are made on a non-competitive basis to anyone with a sound educational plan. 125 loans per year. Must apply first through government and school. Write for complete information.

3465 — CENTRE FOR INTERNATIONAL MOBILITY - CIMO (Fulbright Student Grants)

IIE - US Student Programs
809 United Nations Plaza
New York NY 10017-3580
212/984-5330
E-Mail: scholars@cies.iie.org
Internet: www.iie.org

AMOUNT: Monthly allowance: FIM 5,900 (M.A. degree); FIM 4,100 (seniors)

DEADLINE(S): OCT 23

FIELD(S): Most fields of study

CIMO & the Fulbright Center offer scholarships to US citizens under 35 years of age to study and carry out research in Finland in various fields. Must hold an M.A. degree or be a graduating senior. Scholarships are for postgraduate academic studies and research for 4-9 months in a Finnish university. Applicants must establish contact with the receiving institute prior to application. Candidates currently residing in Finland are not eligible. Contact CIMO for an application.

3466 — CHARLES COOPER INDUSTRIAL SCHOOL

Chittenden Trust Co., 401 Main St.
Bennington VT 05201
Written inquiry

AMOUNT: Not specified

DEADLINE(S): None specified

FIELD(S): All areas of study

Student loans for higher education for Vermont residents.

Write to Loraine B. Smith at above address for application information.

3467 — CHARLES I. AND EMMA J. CLAPP SCHOLARSHIP FUND

c/o First of America Bank, 110 East Allegan St.
Otsego MI 49078
Written inquiry

AMOUNT: Varies

DEADLINE(S): Ongoing

FIELD(S): All fields of study

Interest-free student loans to nondrinkers. Female applicants must, in addition, be nonsmokers.

Contact Jim Yankoviak, Trust Officer, at above address for details.

3468 — CHARLES J. HUGHES FOUNDATION

P.O. Box 1498
Pagosa Springs CO 81147
970/264-2228

AMOUNT: Varies

DEADLINE(S): Ongoing

FIELD(S): All fields of study

Scholarships to students with learning disabilities who live in Colorado.

Apply by letter outlining financial need. Contact Terrence P. Allie, President, at above location.

3469 — CHARLESTON SCIENTIFIC AND CULTURAL EDUCATIONAL FUND

P.O. Box 190011
Charleston SC 29419-9011
803/723-2000

AMOUNT: Varies

DEADLINE(S): JUN 1

FIELD(S): All areas of study

Grants to natives of South Carolina for scientific, cultural, or educational pursuits in Charleston, SC.

Apply to: Wade H. Logan, III, P.O. Box 848, Charleston, SC 29402 for detailed information.

3470 — CHAUTAUQUA REGION COMMUNITY FOUNDATION INC. (Scholarships)

21 E. Third St., Suite 301
Jamestown NY 14701
716/661-3390

AMOUNT: $100-$2,000

DEADLINE(S): JUN 1 (college freshmen); JUL 15 (college students)

FIELD(S): All fields of study

Numerous scholarships with varying requirements open ONLY to students living in the vicinity of Jamestown, NY. Preference to students in 12 school districts in Southern Chautauqua County. For full-time study.

Write for complete information.

3471 — CHEYENNE AND ARAPAHO TRIBES OF OKLAHOMA (Scholarships)

P.O. Box 38
Concho OK 73022
405/262-0345 or 1-800/247-4612
FAX: 405/262-0745

AMOUNT: Based on unmet need and availability of funds

DEADLINE(S): JUN 1 (1st semester); NOV 1 (2nd semester); APR 1 (summer semester)

FIELD(S): All fields of study

For enrolled members of the Cheyenne-Arapaho Tribes of Oklahoma enrolled at the Concho agency. Must be certified to be at least 1/4 or more degree Cheyenne-Arapaho Indian, be a high school graduate or GED recipient, and in need of financial aid. For grads and undergrads. Summer and part-time students may be considered.

Write to Cheyenne-Arapaho Education Department at above address for details.

3472 — CHINESE CHRISTIAN HERALD CRUSADES (Chinese Collegiate Merit Scholarship for New York Schools)

Dr. Timothy Kok C. Tam
48 Allen St.
New York NY 10002
212/334-2033

AMOUNT: Up to $1,500

DEADLINE(S): JUL 31

FIELD(S): All fields of study

Open to Chinese students who are NOT U.S. citizens and who are attending a school within a 100-mile radius of New York City.

Two undergraduate and two graduate awards each year. Write for complete information.

3473 — CHINESE UNIVERSITY OF HONG KONG (Various Scholarships, Bursary, and Loan Programs)

Shatin NT
Office of Student Affairs
Hong Kong
852/2609-7209
FAX: 852/2603-7705
E-Mail: dorothy@sao.msmail.cuhk.edu.hk

AMOUNT: Varies with awards

DEADLINE(S): None specified

FIELD(S): All areas of study

Chinese University of Hong Kong awards are administered by the office of student affairs and are offered to admitted students of the Chinese University only.

Write for complete information.

3474 — CHOCTAW NATION OF OKLAHOMA HIGHER EDUCATION PROGRAM (Grants)

Drawer 1210
Durant OK 74702-1210
405/924-8280 or 1-800/522-6170
FAX: 405/924-1267

AMOUNT: Up to $1,600/yr.

DEADLINE(S): MAR 15

FIELD(S): All fields of study leading to a degree

For enrolled members of the Choctaw Nation of Oklahoma who are undergraduates or graduates. Must be seeking at least an Associate of Arts degree. Priority is given undergrads depending on availability of funds. For use at accredited colleges or universities.

Must submit copies of Certificate of Degree of Indian Blood and Tribal Membership cards showing Choctaw descent, photo, and transcripts. Apply between Jan. 1 and March 15. For renewal must re-apply each year.

3475 — CHUNG KUN AI FOUNDATION

P.O. Box 1559
Honolulu HI 96805
Written inquiry

AMOUNT: $2,000

DEADLINE(S): Ongoing

FIELD(S): All areas of study

Scholarships to financially needy residents of Hawaii with a GPA of at least 2.8.

Contact Samuel S. Chung, Trustee, at above address for application procedures.

3476 — CITIZENS' SCHOLARSHIP FOUNDATION OF WAKEFIELD, INC. (Scholarships)

467 Main St.
PO Box 321
Wakefield MA 01880
781/245-4890
FAX: 781/245-6761

AMOUNT: $300-$2,000

DEADLINE(S): MAR 15

FIELD(S): All fields of study

For full-time students (undergrads, graduates, voc-tech, continuing ed, etc.) who are residents of Wakefield, Massachusetts. Must demonstrate financial need.

300+ awards annually. Renewable with reapplication. Contact Lynne P. Zervas at above address or visit Wakefield High School's Guidance Office for an application.

3477 — CITY UNIVERSITY (Kitchin Scholarships)

International Office
City University
Northampton Square
London EC1V 0HB ENGLAND UK
+44 (0) 171 477 8019
FAX: +44 (0) 171 477 8562
E-Mail: international@city.ac.uk
Internet: www.britcoun.org/eis/profiles/cityuniversity/cituschp.htm

AMOUNT: Varies

DEADLINE(S): Varies

FIELD(S): All fields of study

Research scholarships for postgraduate students from non-European Union countries who are pursuing studies in engineering. For use at City University in London.

Selection based on academic merit. Renewable for term of course. Program is through the British Council. Contact Karen Jones at University for details.

3478 — CITY UNIVERSITY (Robert Kitchin (Saddlers) Scholarships for International Students)

International Office, City University,
Northampton Square
London EC1V 0HB ENGLAND UK
+44 (0) 171 477 8019
FAX: +44 (0) 171 477 8562
E-Mail: international@city.ac.uk
Internet: www.britcoun.org/eis/profiles/cityuniversity/cituschp.htm

AMOUNT: 3,900 pounds/yr.

DEADLINE(S): Varies

FIELD(S): All fields of study

Scholarships for postgraduate students from Brunei, Cyprus, Hong Kong, India, Indonesia, Japan, Malaysia, Pakistan, Singapore, Taiwan, Thailand, Turkey, Vietnam for use at City University in London.

Renewable for two additional years. Program is through the British Council. Contact Karen Jones at University for details.

3479 — COLLEGE FOUNDATION INC. (North Carolina's Federal Family Education Loan Program)

2100 Yonkers Rd.
P.O. Box 12100
Raleigh, NC 27605

919/821-4771 or 888/234-6400
E-Mail: info@cfi-nc.org
Internet: www.cfi-nc.org

AMOUNT: Varies

DEADLINE(S): Varies

FIELD(S): All fields of study

For North Carolina students attending eligible institutions of higher education and vocational schools in state or out of state, and for out-of-state students attending eligible institutions of higher education and vocational schools in North Carolina.

Write for complete information and application.

3480 — COLLEGE MISERICORDIA (Honor Scholarships)

301 Lake St.
Dallas PA 18612-1098
1-800/852-7675
Internet: http://miseri.edu/scholar.htm

AMOUNT: Full or part tuition

DEADLINE(S): MAR 1

FIELD(S): All fields of study

Scholarships for incoming freshmen and transfer students to this co-educational Catholic college in Pennsylvania. Must have attained outstanding academic records. For undergraduates and graduate students.

Renewable until graduation provided minimum GPAs are maintained. GPA requirements are outlined in the scholarship notification letter. Obtain applications from the Admissions Office.

3481 — COLLEGE OF SAINT ELIZABETH (Scholarships)

2 Convent Road
Morristown NJ 07960
973/290-4000
Internet: www.st-elizabeth/edu

AMOUNT: Varies

DEADLINE(S): Varies

FIELD(S): All fields of study

Various scholarships available for use at this private Catholic college for females in New Jersey.

Check website and/or write for details.

3482 — COLLEGE OF ST. FRANCIS (Various Scholarship/Grant Programs)

500 Wilcox St.
Joliet IL 60435
815/740-3360
Internet: www.stfrancis.edu

AMOUNT: Varies

DEADLINE(S): Varies

FIELD(S): All fields of study

Scholarships and grants for students at St. Francis College at all levels—incoming freshmen and transfers, undergraduates and graduates. Some are tied to certain requirements, such as athletics, biology, academic achievement, financial need, minority group, leadership, choir participation, and community activities.

See website and/or contact college for details on financial aid.

3483 — COMMISSION FRANCO-AMERICAINE D'ECHANGES UNIVERSITAIRES ET CULTURELS (Graduate Fellowship)

9 Rue Chardin
75016 Paris France
33 1 44 14 53 60
FAX 33 1 42 88 04 79

AMOUNT: Varies (according to category)

DEADLINE(S): Varies

FIELD(S): All fields of study

Fellowships for French citizens for study in the U.S. under Fulbright scholarship program.

20 posts for post exchanges for French secondary school teachers of English and U.S. secondary school teachers of French. Write for complete information.

3484 — COMMISSION FRANCO-AMERICAINE D'ECHANGES UNIVERSITAIRES ET CULTURELS (Graduate Fellowships)

9 Rue Chardin
75016 Paris FRANCE
33 (1) 44 14 53 60
FAX: 33 (1) 42 88 04 79

AMOUNT: Varies (according to category)

DEADLINE(S): AUG 1 (U.S. research scholars and students); OCT 23 (same); DEC 1 (French research scholars and students); DEC 15 (same); OCT 15 (U.S. exchange teachers); JAN 15 (French exchange teachers)

FIELD(S): All fields of study

Fellowships for U.S. citizens for study and research in France and for French citizens for study and research in the U.S. under Fulbright scholarship program.

20 posts for post exchanges for French secondary school teachers of English and U.S. secondary school teachers of French. Write for complete information.

3485 — COMMITTEE OF VICE-CHANCELLORS & PRINCIPALS OF THE UNIVERSITIES OF THE UNITED KINGDOM (Overseas Research Students Awards Scheme)

Attn: Nathalie Bonvalot
CVCP
Woburn House, 20 Tavistock Sq.
London WC1H 9HQ England
0171/419 4111
FAX: 0171/383 4573

E-Mail: info@cvcp.ac.uk
Internet: www.cvcp.ac.uk

AMOUNT: Pays the difference between the overseas and home fees

DEADLINE(S): APR (end of month)

FIELD(S): All fields of study

Program supports foreign students who want to do post-graduate research in the United Kingdom. Awards are tenable at UK universities and other institutions of higher educations and are made on a competitive basis.

900 awards. Write for complete information to the Secretary, ORS Awards Scheme.

3486 — COMMITTEE ON INSTITUTIONAL COOPERATION (CIC FreeApp Program)

302 E. John St., Ste. 1705
Champaign IL 61820-5698
800/457-4420 or 217/265-8005
FAX: 217/244-7127
E-Mail: aeprice@uiuc.edu
Internet: www.cic.uiuc.edu

AMOUNT: Application fee waived for 3 CIC graduate schools

DEADLINE(S): NOV 1

FIELD(S): All fields of study

For African Americans, Mexican Americans, Native Americans, and Puerto Ricans who will apply for admission to a Ph.D. program or Master of Fine Arts program at a CIC University (U Chicago, U Illinois, U Michigan, U Iowa, Indiana U, Michigan State, U Minnesota, Northwestern U, Ohio State U, Penn State U, Purdue U, & U Wisconsin). Must have a minimum undergraduate GPA of 3.0 and have serious intent to pursue career in teaching and academic research.

See website or contact Anne Price, CIC Secretary, for an application.

3487 — COMMONWEALTH SECRETARIAT (Commonwealth Fund for Technical Cooperation Awards)

Management & Training Svcs. Division,
Marlborough House, Pall Mall
London SW1Y 5HX UK
44 (0)171/839-3411
FAX: 44 (0)171/747-6570

AMOUNT: Varies

DEADLINE(S): Varies

FIELD(S): All fields of study

CFTC awards are for short-term courses from one week to six months and post-graduate diplomas and masters degree courses; no awards for secondary school or first-degree courses. Open to citizens of developing Commonwealth countries. For study in developing Commonwealth countries only, but not

in applicant's home country. Nominations must be endorsed by the official Point of Contact of the nominee's country of citizenship.

Contact government in home country for complete information.

3488 — COMMONWEALTH SCHOLARSHIP COMMISSION IN THE UK (Scholarship & Fellowship Plan)

36 Gordon Square
London WC1H OPF ENGLAND
171/387 8572
FAX: 171/387 2655

AMOUNT: Full cost of study + living allowance

DEADLINE(S): DEC 31

FIELD(S): All fields of study

Scholarships for graduate and post-graduate study and fellowships for academic staff; open to Commonwealth citizens living permanently in a Commonwealth country. Good academic record.

Write for complete information.

3489 — COMMONWEALTH OF VIRGINIA DEPARTMENT OF VETERANS' AFFAIRS (War Orphans Education Program)

270 Franklin Rd. SW
Room 1012
Poff Federal Building
Roanoke VA 24011-2215
703/857-7104

AMOUNT: Tuition + required fees

DEADLINE(S): None

FIELD(S): All fields of study

Open to surviving/dependent children (aged 16-25) of U.S. military personnel who were/are Virginia residents and as a result of war/armed conflict are deceased, disabled, prisoners of war, or missing in action.

Must attend a state-supported secondary or postsecondary educational institution to pursue any vocational, technical, undergraduate, or graduate program. Write for complete information.

3490 — COMMUNITY FOUNDATION OF GREATER LORAIN COUNTY (Various Scholarship Programs)

1865 N. Ridge Road E. - Suite A
Lorain OH 44055
216/277-0142
FAX: 216/277-6955

AMOUNT: Varies

DEADLINE(S): Varies

FIELD(S): All fields of study

For residents of Lorain County, Ohio. Various programs, ranging from opportunities for high school seniors through doctoral programs. Dollar amounts vary as do deadlines.

Contact the organization above for details.

3491 — COMMUNITY FOUNDATION OF WESTERN MASSACHUSETTS (Charles F. Warner Loan Fund)

P.O. Box 15769, 1500 Main Street
Springfield, MA 01115
413/732-2858

AMOUNT: $250

DEADLINE(S): MAR 15

FIELD(S): All fields of study

Open to residents of Springfield, MA to obtain an education. Four-five interest free loans are given annually.

Write to the above address for complete information.

3492 — COMMUNITY FOUNDATION OF WESTERN MASSACHUSETTS (Deerfield Plastics/Barker Family Fund)

P.O. Box 15769, 1500 Main Street
Springfield, MA 01115
413/732-2858

AMOUNT: $1,500

DEADLINE(S): MAR 15

FIELD(S): All fields of study

Open to dependents of Deerfield Plastic employees. Students must apply directly to Deerfield Plastics in Deerfield, Massachussetts.

Write to the above address for complete information.

3493 — COMMUNITY FOUNDATION OF WESTERN MASSACHUSETTS (Jane A. Korzeniowski Memorial Scholarship)

P.O. Box 15769, 1500 Main Street
Springfield, MA 01115
413/732-2858

AMOUNT: $200

DEADLINE(S): MAR 15

FIELD(S): All fields of study

Open to Chicopee residents who attend or plan to attend college. One award is given.

Write to the above address for complete information.

3494 — COMMUNITY FOUNDATION OF WESTERN MASSACHUSETTS (James Z. Naurison Scholarship)

P.O. Box 15769, 1500 Main Street
Springfield, MA 01115
413/732-2858

AMOUNT: $400-$2,000

DEADLINE(S): MAR 15

FIELD(S): All fields of study

Open to residents of Hampden, Hampshire, Franklin, and Berkshire counties, MA and Enfield and Suffield, CT. For graduates and undergraduates. Scholarships are renewable for up to four years.

Write to the above address for complete information.

3495 — COMMUNITY FOUNDATION OF WESTERN MASSACHUSETTS (Louis W. and Mary S. Doherty Scholarship)

P.O.Box 15769, 1500 Main St.
Springfield, MA 01115
413/732-2858

AMOUNT: $4,000-$5,000

DEADLINE(S): MAR

FIELD(S): All fields of study

Open to students from Hampden, Hampshire, or Franklin, Mass., counties who attend or plan to attend the University of Massachusetts at Amherst.

Write to the above address for complete information.

3496 — COMMUNITY FOUNDATION OF WESTERN MASSACHUSETTS (Maury Ferriter Memorial Scholarship)

P.O. Box 15769, 1500 Main St.
Springfield, MA 01115
413/732-2858

AMOUNT: $400

DEADLINE(S): MAR 15

FIELD(S): All fields of study

Open to students from Holyoke Catholic H.S., Amherst College, or Georgetown Law School. One scholarship is awarded annually.

Write to the above address for complete information.

3497 — CONCORDIA UNIVERSITY (David J. Azrieli Graduate Fellowship)

1455 de Maisonneuve Blvd. West, Room M 201
Montreal Quebec H3G 1M8 CANADA
514/848-3809
FAX: 514/848-2812
E-Mail: awardsgs@vax2.concordia.ca

AMOUNT: $15,000

DEADLINE(S): FEB 1

FIELD(S): All fields of study

This one-year fellowship is open to all full-time master's or doctoral students including visa students. Awarded to the highest ranking candidate in the Concordia Graduate Fellowship Competition.

1 award annually. Not renewable. Contact the Graduate Awards Office in the School of Graduate Studies at Concordia University for an application.

3498 — CONCORDIA UNIVERSITY (Graduate Fellowships)

1455 de Maisonneuve Blvd. West, Room M 201
Montreal Quebec H3G 1M8 CANADA
514/848-3809
FAX: 514/848-2812
E-Mail: awardsgs@vax2.concordia.ca

AMOUNT: $2,900/term (masters); $3,600/term (doctorate)

DEADLINE(S): FEB 1

FIELD(S): All fields of study

Open to any candidate intending to study full-time in a Master's or Doctoral program at Concordia University. Open to visa students. Awarded based on academic excellence. Duration of the award is maximum four terms at the master's level and a maximum of nine terms at the doctoral level. Eligibility is calculated from the applicant's date of entry into the program.

25 new awards annually. Renewable. Contact the Graduate Awards Office in the School of Graduate Studies at Concordia University for an application.

3499 — CONCORDIA UNIVERSITY (J W. McConnell Memorial Graduate Fellowships)

1455 de Maisonneuve Blvd. West, Room M 201
Montreal Quebec H3G 1M8 CANADA
514/848-3809
FAX: 514/848-2812
E-Mail: awardsgs@vax2.concordia.ca

AMOUNT: $2,900/term (masters); $3,600/term (doctorate)

DEADLINE(S): FEB 1

FIELD(S): All fields of study

Candidates must be Canadian citizens/permanent residents intending to study full-time in a Master's or Doctoral program at Concordia University. Financial need is taken into consideration when granting these awards. Awarded based on academic excellence. Duration of award is maximum four terms at master's level and maximum nine terms at doctoral level. Eligibility is calculated from the applicant's date of entry into the program.

20 new awards annually. Renewable. Contact the Graduate Awards Office in the School of Graduate Studies at Concordia University for an application.

3500 — CONCORDIA UNIVERSITY (John O'Brien & Stanley French Graduate Fellowships)

1455 de Maisonneuve Blvd. West, Room M 201
Montreal Quebec H3G 1M8 CANADA
514/848-3809
FAX: 514/848-2812
E-Mail: awardsgs@vax2.concordia.ca

AMOUNT: $3,300/term (masters); $4,000/term (doctoral)

DEADLINE(S): FEB 1

FIELD(S): All fields of study

Open to Canadian, permanent residents, and international/visa Master's or Doctoral students at Concordia University. Eligibility is calculated from the date of entry into the program. Tenable at the master's level within the first four terms and at the doctoral level within the first nine terms. These fellowships are awarded to the second and third highest ranking students in the Concordia Graduate Fellowship Competition.

2 awards annually. Renewable. Contact the Graduate Awards Office in the School of Graduate Studies at Concordia University for an application.

3501 — CONCORDIA UNIVERSITY (Loyola Alumni Association Inc. Educational Grant)

1455 de Maisonneuve Blvd. West, Room M 201
Montreal Quebec H3G 1M8 CANADA
514/848-3809
FAX: 514/848-2812
E-Mail: awardsgs@vax2.concordia.ca

AMOUNT: $1,500

DEADLINE(S): APR 1

FIELD(S): All fields of study

Full-time Concordia students at any level may apply for this entrance or in-course award. Any Concordia applicant is eligible, however, preference will be given to children and grandchildren of active Loyola Alumni Association members. Grant is awarded on the basis of scholastic achievement, the applicant's statement, and letters of reference.

5 awards annually. Contact the Graduate Awards Office in the School of Graduate Studies at Concordia University for an application.

3502 — CONCORDIA UNIVERSITY (Senior Scholarships)

Financial Aid Office
1455 de Maisonneuve Blvd. West
LB 085
Montreal Quebec H3G 1M8 CANADA
514/848-3809
FAX: 514/848-2812
E-Mail: awardsgs@vax2.concordia.ca

AMOUNT: $500

DEADLINE(S): AUG 31

FIELD(S): All fields of study

Candidates must be Canadian citizens/permanent residents, intending to study full-time and aged 60 years or more in the year of application. Awards are made on the basis of the academic record and an interview.

1 award annually. Renewable up to four years. Contact the Financial Aid and Awards Office at Concordia University for an application.

3503 — CONVERSE COUNTY 4-H FOUNDATION (Scholarships)

Extension Office
107 N. 5th
Douglas WY 82633
Written Inquiry

AMOUNT: Varies

DEADLINE(S): JAN

FIELD(S): All fields of study

Available to former Converse County 4-H program members who have completed at least three years of active 4-H club work and are currently enrolled in an institution of higher education. Eligible students may apply as often as they wish. Priority consideration is given to first-time applicants. Scholarships are for use during the Spring semester.

Write to the Converse County Extension Office for an application.

3504 — COOPER WOOD PRODUCTS FOUNDATION, INC.

P.O. Box 489
Rocky Mount VA 24151
Written inquiry

AMOUNT: Varies

DEADLINE(S): MAY 1

FIELD(S): All areas of study

Scholarships and loans for Virginia residents who intend to remain in Virginia after completion of education.

Write to Joyce Aldridge, Executive Secretary, at above address for application requirements.

3505 — CORPUS CHRISTI COLLEGE (Research Scholarships)

Tutor for Advanced Students
Cambridge CB21RH ENGLAND
01223-339391

AMOUNT: Tuition + 5892 pounds sterling (maintenance allowance)

DEADLINE(S): MAR 30

FIELD(S): All fields of study (except MBA or clinical medicine)

For post-graduate study. Open to students who apply to the Board of Graduate Studies and who name Corpus Christi College as their college of preference. Awards made in conjunction with awards from Cambridge Commonwealth or Overseas Trusts.

Awards are renewable for up to 3 years. Write for complete information.

3506 — COUNCIL FOR INTERNATIONAL EXCHANGE OF SCHOLARS (Fulbright Scholar Grant Program)

3007 Tilden St. NW, Suite 5M
Washington DC 20008-30009
202/686-7877
Internet: www.iie.org/fulbright

AMOUNT: Varies with country

DEADLINE(S): AUG 1

FIELD(S): All fields of study

Grant program designed to increase mutual understanding between people of US and people of other countries. For US citizens to lecture and/or conduct research abroad. Open to Ph.Ds or equivalent, faculty, scholars/researchers, and professionals.

Annually over 700 awards of 2-12 months in more than 130 countries. Write for complete information.

3507 — COUNCIL OF CITIZENS WITH LOW VISION INTERNATIONAL (CCLVI Telesensory Scholarship)

1400 N. Drake Road
Kalamazoo MI 49006
616/381-9566

AMOUNT: $1,000

DEADLINE(S): APR 15

FIELD(S): All fields of study

Open to an undergraduate or graduate students who are vision impaired but NOT legally blind and who have a GPA of 3.0 or better.

Four awards per year. Write for complete information.

3508 — CRESTAR BANK (Trivia Contest)

Student Lending Division
P.O. Box 27172
Richmond, VA 23261-7172
E-Mail: crestar@student-loans.com
Internet: www.student-loans.com

AMOUNT: up to $1,000

DEADLINE(S): Varies

FIELD(S): All fields of study

Annual scholarship contest to promote student loan web page. Open to students enrolled at accredited U.S. colleges and universities. Prizes awarded to students with the highest number of correctly answered questions.

Three $1,000 awards, three $500 awards, ten $100 book awards, ten $50 book awards, and 100 merchandise awards. Contest must be done online.

3509 — D'ARCY McNICKLE CENTER FOR AMERICAN INDIAN HISTORY (Francis C. Allen Fellowship)

Research & Education
60 W. Walton St.
Chicago IL 60610-3380
312/255-3666

AMOUNT: Varies

DEADLINE(S): FEB 1

FIELD(S): All fields of study

Open to women of Native American heritage who are pursuing academic programs at any stage beyond the undergraduate level.

Contact Research & Education Dept. for an application.

3510 — DALHOUSIE UNIVERSITY (Izaak Walton Killam Postdoctoral Fellowships)

Office of The Dean
Faculty of Graduate Studies
Halifax Nova Scotia B3H 4H6 Canada
902/494-2485

AMOUNT: $33,000 + travel allowances

DEADLINE(S): DEC 15

FIELD(S): All areas of study

Fellowships valued at $33,000 plus travel allowances are tenable for two years at Dalhousie University. Applicants should have received a Ph.D degree at a recognized university within the last 2 years.

Fellows may engage in teaching or other similar duties at the university. Write for complete information.

3511 — DANISH RECTORS' CONFERENCE (Government Scholarships for Foreign Nationals)

H.C. Andersens Boulevard 45
DK-1553 Copenhagen V Denmark
3392 5300l
Internet: www.rks.dk

AMOUNT: Free tuition; monthly allowance of 4,450-5,000 DKK

DEADLINE(S): MAR 1

FIELD(S): All fields of study

Open to nationals of 25 foreign countries (NOT the United States). Awards are to enable advanced students, graduates, and specialists to carry out research at a Danish university. Not for elementary study of Danish language and not for an academic degree.

Awards tenable for up to 9 months. Write for complete information.

3512 — DANISH SISTERHOOD OF AMERICA (Scholarship Program)

8004 Jasmine Blvd.
Port Richey, FL 34668-3224
Written inquiry only

AMOUNT: Varies

DEADLINE(S): Varies

FIELD(S): Continuing Education

Open to Danish Sisterhood of America members in good standing (and their children) who are attending approved schools. One-year or longer membership required. Awards are based on high academic achievement.

Write to National Vice President & Scholarship Chair Elizabeth K. Hunter at above address for complete information.

3513 — DATATEL SCHOLARS FOUNDATION (Angelfire Scholarships)

4375 Fair Lakes Court
Fairfax VA 22033
703/968-9000
E-Mail: scholars@datatel.com
Internet: www.datatel.com/scholars.htm

AMOUNT: $700-$2,000—based on tuition costs

DEADLINE(S): FEB 15

FIELD(S): All fields of study

Scholarships for part- or full-time students, both undergraduates and graduates. Must be: a military veteran of the Vietnam War; or a child or spouse of a military veteran of the Vietnam War; or a Vietnamese, Cambodian, or Laotian refugee who entered the United States between 1964 and 1975. Nationalization is not a requirement. For use at a higher learning institution selected from one of Datatel's more than 400 client sites.

Apply through the institution's Financial Aid or Scholarship office, which may nominate up to 2 students. Or contact organization for details.

3514 — DATATEL SCHOLARS FOUNDATION (Datatel Scholarships)

4375 Fair Lakes Court
Fairfax VA 22033
703/968-9000
E-Mail: scholars@datatel.com
Internet: www.datatel.com/scholars.htm

AMOUNT: $700-$2,000—based on tuition costs

DEADLINE(S): FEB 15

FIELD(S): All fields of study

Scholarships for part- or full-time students, both undergraduates and graduates. For use at a higher learning institution selected from one of Datatel's more than 400 client sites.

Apply through the institution's Financial Aid or Scholarship office, which may nominate up to 2 students. Or contact organization for details.

3515 — DAUGHTERS OF PENELOPE (Graduate Scholarships)

1909 Q St. NW, Suite 500
Washington, D.C. 20009
202/234-9741
FAX: 202/483-6983

AMOUNT: $1,000-$1,500

DEADLINE(S): JUN 20

FIELD(S): All fields of study

Open to female graduate or post-graduate students of Greek descent who are members of Daughters of Penelope or Maids of Athena or the daughter of a member of Daughters of Penelope or Order of AHEPA. Academic performance and need are main considerations.

5 annual awards. Renewable. For membership information or an application, write to the above address.

3516 — DAUGHTERS OF THE AMERICAN REVOLUTION (American Indians Scholarship)

Mrs. Lyle A. Ross
3738 South Mission Dr.
Lake Havasu City AZ 86406-4250
Written inquiry

AMOUNT: $500

DEADLINE(S): JUL 1; NOV 1

FIELD(S): All fields of study

Open to American Indians, both youth and adults, striving to get an education. Funds help students of any tribe in any state based on need, academic achievement, and ambition.

Send SASE to above address for complete information.

3517 — DEAKIN UNIVERSITY (Scholarships for International Students)

Deakin University
336 Glenferrie Road
Malvern Victoria 3144 Australia
(61-3)9244 5095
FAX: (61-3)9244 5094
E-Mail: du.info@deakin.edu.au

AMOUNT: Varies

DEADLINE(S): Varies

FIELD(S): All fields of study

Awards for international students include: Faculty of Business and Law Undergraduate Scholarships for Best International Students; Deakin University Research Scholarships for International Students

(DURSIS); Deakin University Faculty of Science and Technology's Doctoral Scholarships; OPRS at Deakin University

Contact university for specifics on above scholarships. Some include full tuition and living stipend.

3518 — DELLA M. BAILEY INDIAN SCHOLARSHIP TRUST

c/o First National Bank
P.O. Box 1007
Fairfield IA 52556
515/472-4121

AMOUNT: Varies

DEADLINE(S): Ongoing

FIELD(S): All fields of study

Scholarships for students of Native-American parentage.

Write to Melva Dahl at above address for application.

3519 — DELTA GAMMA FOUNDATION

3250 Riverside Dr.
P.O. Box 21397
Columbus OH 43221-0397
614/481-8169

AMOUNT: $1,000-$2,500

DEADLINE(S): MAR 1; APR 1

FIELD(S): All fields of study

Scholarships, fellowships, & loans open to Delta Gamma members & their dependents. Awards may be used for undergraduate or graduate study.

Approx 60 awards per year. Contact the Grants & Loans chairman, address above, for complete information.

3520 — DELTA PHI EPSILON EDUCATIONAL FOUNDATION

734 West Port Plaza, Suite 271
St. Louis MO 63146
314/275-2626
FAX: 314/275-2655
E-Mail: ealper@conentric.net
Internet: www.dphie.org

AMOUNT: Varies

DEADLINE(S): APR 1 (undergrads); APR 15 (grads)

FIELD(S): All fields of study

Scholarships for women students who are members or daughters or granddaughters of members of Delta Phi Epsilon sorority.

Applications available in January. Write or E-mail Ellen Alper, Executive Director, at above address.

3521 — DESCENDANTS OF THE SIGNERS OF THE DECLARATION OF INDEPENDENCE (Scholarship Grant)

609 Irving Ave.
Deale MD 20751
Written inquiry only

AMOUNT: Average $1,100

DEADLINE(S): MAR 15

FIELD(S): All areas of study

Undergrad and grad awards for students who are DSDI members (proof of direct descent of signer of Declaration of Independence necessary, STUDENT MUST BE A MEMBER OF D.S.D.I before he/she can apply). Write to Scholarhip Chairmanat the above address for membership. Must be full-time student accepted or enrolled in a recognized U.S. four-year college or university.

Applicants for membership must provide proof of direct, lineal descendancy from a Signer. Enclose stamped, self-addressed envelope.

3522 — DEXTER G. JOHNSON EDUCATIONAL AND BENEVOLENT TRUST (Student Loans)

P.O. Box 26663
Oklahoma City OK 73125
Written inquiry

AMOUNT: Varies

DEADLINE(S): Ongoing

FIELD(S): All fields of study

Educational loans for financially needy residents of Oklahoma for study at Oklahoma high schools, vocational schools, and Oklahoma State University, Oklahoma City University, or the University of Oklahoma. Preference given to physically disabled students.

Write to Betty Crews at above address for application details.

3523 — DIXIE YARNS FOUNDATION, INC. (George West Scholarship Fund)

P.O. Box 751
Chattanooga, TN 37401
423/493-7267

AMOUNT: Varies

DEADLINE(S): FEB 1

FIELD(S): All fields of study

Open only to children of employees of Dixie Yarns, Inc. for undergraduate study.

Write to the above address for complete information.

3524 — DODD & DOROTHY L. BRYAN FOUNDATION (Interest-Free Loans)

P.O. Box 6287, 4 N. Main, Suite 407
Sheridan WY 82801
307/672-9102

AMOUNT: $4,000

DEADLINE(S): JUL 15

FIELD(S): All fields of study

These "interest free" loans are available to undergraduate, graduate, and post-graduate students who live in one of these six counties: Sheridan WY, Johnson WY, Campbell WY, Rosebud MT, Big Horn MT, or Powder River MT. Applicants must demonstrate financial need.

Write to the above address for complete information.

3525 — DOG WRITERS' EDUCATIONAL TRUST (Scholarships)

Mary Ellen Tarman
P.O. Box E
Hummelstown PA 17036-0199
Written inquiries only

AMOUNT: Varies

DEADLINE(S): DEC 31

FIELD(S): All fields of study

For college students who have participaed in organized activities with dogs or whose parents or other close relatives have done so.

Scholarships support undergraduate or graduate study. Send SASE to above location for complete information.

3526 — EARTHWATCH (Center for Field Research Grants)

680 Mt. Auburn St., P.O. 9104
Watertown MA 02272
617/926-8200
FAX: 617/926-8532
E-Mail: cfr@earthwatch.org
Internet: www.earthwatch.org/cfr/cfr.html

AMOUNT: $7,000-$130,000/yr.—average $25,000

DEADLINE(S): Varies

FIELD(S): All fields of study

Research funds are available for postdoctoral scholars of any nationality based at recognized institutions or organizations in the areas of the earth, life and human science, and humanities. The mission of Earthwatch is to improve human understanding of the planet, the diversity of its inhabitants, and the processes which affect the quality of life on earth. Proposals are welcomed.

See website for more information and/or contact organization.

3527 — EARTHWATCH EUROPE (Research Grants)

57 Woodstock Road
Oxford OX2 6HJ ENGLAND UK
01865 311600
FAX: 01865 311383
E-Mail: cfr@uk.earthwatch.org
Internet: www.lancs.ac.uk/us

AMOUNT: 7,000-100,000 pounds sterling

DEADLINE(S): Varies

FIELD(S): All fields of study

Research funds are available for postdoctoral scholars of any nationality based at recognized institutions or organizations in the areas of the earth, life and human science, and humanities. The mission of Earthwatch is to improve human understanding of the planet, the diversity of its inhabitants, and the processes which affect the quality of life on earth. Proposals are welcomed.

See website for more information. Also, send for a detailed booklet. Contact by E-mail: J.Chadwick@lancaster.ac.uk.

3528 — EAST-WEST CENTER (Graduate Degree Fellowships)

1601 East-West Rd.
Honolulu HI 96848-1601
808/944-7735
FAX: 808/944-7730
E-Mail: EWCUHM@ewc.hawaii.edu
Internet: www.ewc.hawaii.edu

AMOUNT: Varies

DEADLINE(S): OCT 15

FIELD(S): All fields of study

Available to individuals interested in participating in the educational and research programs at the East-West Center while pursuing graduate degree study at the University of Hawaii. Must be citizen/permanent resident of the US, or be citizens of countries within Center's mandated geographical region, which encompasses most countries in Asia and the Pacific, including Russia. Must meet admission requirements of the University of Hawaii if not currently enrolled.

Contact EWC for an application. Funds provided by the US Government.

3529 — EBERHARDT I. FOR SCHOLARSHIP FOUNDATION

One Mellon Bank Center
Pittsburgh PA 15230-9897
Written inquiries

AMOUNT: Varies

DEADLINE(S): MAY 15

FIELD(S): All fields of study

Scholarships for residents of Pennsylvania who attend colleges and universities in Pennsylvania.

Contact college financial aid officer for current application guidelines.

3530 — ECKMANN FOUNDATION

12730 Carmel Country Road, Suite 120
San Diego CA 92130
Written inquiry

AMOUNT: Varies

DEADLINE(S): MAY 1

FIELD(S): All fields of study

Scholarships for individuals pursuing a Christian education and are residents of California.

Write to Helen L. Eckmann, Director, at above address.

3531 — EDUCATION ASSISTANCE CORPORATION (Federal Family Education Loan Program)

115 First Ave., SW
Aberdeen SD 57401
605/225-6423

AMOUNT: Varies

DEADLINE(S): None

FIELD(S): All fields of study

Loans for South Dakota residents enrolled in eligible schools on at least a half-time basis. Must be a US citizen or national or eligible non-resident (see federal guidelines).

Renewable. Write for an application and complete information.

3532 — EDUCATIONAL CREDIT MANAGEMENT CORPORATION (Loan Programs for Virginia Students)

411 E. Franklin St., Suite 300
Richmond VA 23219-2243
804/644-6400 or 888/775-ECMC
FAX: 804/344-6743
E-Mail: mellyson@ecmc.org

AMOUNT: Varies

DEADLINE(S): None

FIELD(S): All fields of study

Various loan programs open to students enrolled in approved institutions. Eligibility governed by ECMC and federal regulations.

Contact college financial aid office or write to address above for complete information.

3533 — EDUCATIONAL COMMUNICATIONS SCHOLARSHIP FOUNDATION (College Scholarship Award)

721 McKinley Rd., P.O. Box 5002
Lake Forest, IL 60045-5002
847/295-6650
847/295-3072
E-Mail: scholars@ecsf.org

AMOUNT: $1,000

DEADLINE(S): MAY 31

FIELD(S): All fields of study

The Foundation will award 50 scholarships of $1,000 each. College students with a grade point average of B+ or better who are US citizens may compete.

Requests for applications must be made by March 15. Write to the above address for complete information.

3534 — EDWARDS SCHOLARSHIP FUND (Undergraduate and Graduate Scholarships)

10 Post Office Square So., Suite 1230
Boston MA 02109
617/426-4434

AMOUNT: $250 to $5,000

DEADLINE(S): MAR 1

FIELD(S): All fields of study

Open ONLY to Boston residents under age 25 who can demonstrate financial need, scholastic ability, and good character. For undergraduate or graduate study but undergrads receive preference. Family home must be within Boston city limits.

Applicants must have lived in Boston from at least the beginning of their junior year in high school. Metropolitan Boston is NOT included.

3535 — EL PASO COMMUNITY FOUNDATION (Scholarships)

201 East Main, Suite 1616
El Paso TX 79901
915/533-4020
FAX: 915/532-0716

AMOUNT: Varies

DEADLINE(S): Varies

FIELD(S): All fields of study

Various scholarships for residents of El Paso County, Texas.

Contact organization for details.

3536 — ELMER O. AND IDA PRESTON EDUCATIONAL TRUST (Scholarships)

801 Grand Ave., Suite 3700
Des Moines IA 50309
515/243-4191

AMOUNT: $500-$700

DEADLINE(S): Varies

FIELD(S): All fields of study

Scholarships for male students, undergraduates and graduates, who are members of a Protestant church, are residents of Iowa, and attending any college in the state of Iowa.

Renewable. 35 awards. Contact organization for details.

3537 — EMANUEL STERNBERGER EDUCATIONAL FUND (Interest-Free Loan Program)

PO Box 1735
Greensboro NC 27402
910/275-6316

AMOUNT: $1,000 (1st year) & $2,000 (subsequent years if funds are available); maximum $5,000

DEADLINE(S): MAR 31

FIELD(S): All fields of study

Open to North Carolina residents who are entering their junior or senior year of college or are graduate students. Considerations include grades, economic situation, references, and credit rating.

Personal interview is required. Can be used at any college or university. Write for complete information.

3538 — EMBASSY OF JAPAN (Monbusho Scholarship Program for Research Studies)

255 Sussex Dr.
Ottawa Ontario CANADA K1N 9E6
613/241-8541
FAX: 613/241-4261
E-Mail: infocul@embjapan.can.org
Internet: www.embjapan.can.org

AMOUNT: 185,000 yen per month

DEADLINE(S): JUN 30

FIELD(S): All areas of study

Open to Canadian citizens for graduate study at Japanese universities as research students. Must be under 35, willing to learn Japanese, and be in good health.

Fifteen annual awards. Six months of Japanese language training provided. Apply through the most convenient Japanese diplomatic mission in Canada or write for complete information.

3539 — ETHEL AND EMERY FAST SCHOLARSHIP FOUNDATION, INC.

12620 Rolling Rd.
Potomac MD 20854
301/762-1102

AMOUNT: Varies

DEADLINE(S): Ongoing

FIELD(S): All fields of study

Scholarships for graduate and undergraduate Native Americans who have successfully completed one year of postsecondary studies and are full-time students.

Write or phone above location for application procedures.

3540 — ETHEL N. BOWEN FOUNDATION (Scholarships)

P.O. Box 1559
Bluefield WV 24701-1559
304/325-8181

AMOUNT: Varies

DEADLINE(S): APR 30

FIELD(S): All fields of study

Undergraduate and occasional graduate scholarships open to residents of southern West Virginia and southwest Virginia.

20-25 awards per year. Send self-addressed, stamped envelope for complete information.

3541 — EVEREG-FENESSE MESROBIAN-ROUPINIAN EDUCATIONAL SOCIETY, INC.

4140 Tanglewood Court
Bloomfield Hills MI 48301
Written inquiry

AMOUNT: Varies

DEADLINE(S): DEC 15

FIELD(S): All fields of study

Scholarships for students attending Armenian day schools, and for full-time undergraduate or graduate students of Armenian descent attending colleges and universities. Participating chapters of the society are New York/New Jersey, California, and Detroit, Michigan.

Applications available from designated local chapter representatives.

3542 — FEDERAL EMPLOYEE EDUCATION AND ASSISTANCE FUND (OK Scholarship Fund)

8441 W. Bowles Ave., Ste. 200
Littleton CO 80123-9501
303/933-7580
FAX: 303/933-7587
E-Mail: feeahq@aol.com
Internet: www.feea.org

AMOUNT: Full tuition

DEADLINE(S): None

FIELD(S): All fields of study

FEEA will provide a full college education to all the children who lost a parent in the Oklahoma City Bombing. By the time the program ends in 2018, over 200 children will have received a complete college education, including the six pre-schoolers from the daycare center who survived the bombing.

Contact FEEA for details.

3543 — FEDERAL EMPLOYEE EDUCATION AND ASSISTANCE FUND (FEEA Scholarship Program)

8441 W. Bowles Ave. Ste. 200
Littleton CO 80123-9501
303/933-7580
FAX 303/933-7587
E-Mail: feeahq@aol.com
Internet: www.feea.org

AMOUNT: $300-$1,500

DEADLINE(S): MAY 8

FIELD(S): All fields of study

Open to current civilian federal and postal employees (w/ at least 3 yrs. service) and dependent family members enrolled or planning to enroll in a 2-year, 4-year, or graduate degree program. Must have minimum 3.0 GPA, and an essay is required. Involvement in extracurricular/community activities is considered.

See website or send a business-sized, self-addressed, stamped envelope for an application between January and May. Notification mailed by August 31st.

3544 — FEDERAL EMPLOYEE EDUCATION AND ASSISTANCE FUND (NARFE Scholarship Program)

8441 W. Bowles Ave., Ste. 200
Littleton CO 80123-9501
800/627-3394 or 303/933-7580
FAX: 303/933-7587
E-Mail: feeahq@aol.com
Internet: www.feea.org

AMOUNT: Varies

DEADLINE(S): Varies

FIELD(S): All fields of study

FEEA, along with the National Association of the Retired Federal Employees (NARFE), offers scholarships to the children and grandchildren of federal retirees who are NARFE members.

Send a self-addressed, stamped envelope to FEEA for an application, or contact NARFE at above 800 number.

3545 — FEDERATION OF JEWISH AGENCIES OF GREATER PHILADELPHIA (Foreman Fleisher Fund)

226 S. 16th St.
13th Floor
Philadelphia PA 19102
215/585-5491

AMOUNT: Varies

DEADLINE(S): Ongoing

FIELD(S): All fields of study

Scholarships for Jewish women who seek professional education.

Contact Frances W. Freedman at above address for more information.

3546 — FELLOWSHIP FUND BRANCH OF AFUW-Q, INC. (Graduate Fellowships)

Private Box 8, 217 Hawken Drive, St. Lucia
Queensland 4067 AUSTRALIA
Internet: www.biosci.uq.edu.au/afuwffi

AMOUNT: Australian $14,000; $48,500

DEADLINE(S): JUL 31

FIELD(S): All fields of study

Awarded to women for advanced study or research in Australias. Open to graduates of a university or recognized tertiary institution from any country (not restricted to formal university study).

Tenable at any university or approved institute in Australia. If awarded to an Australian citizen, it is also tenable overseas. Send SASE or visit website for further information.

3547 — FERN BROWN MEMORIAL FUND

P.O. Box 1
Tulsa OK 74193
918/586-5594

AMOUNT: Varies

DEADLINE(S): Ongoing

FIELD(S): All fields of study

Scholarships for residents of Oklahoma.

Send SASE to Mike Bartel, V.P., Liberty Bank & Trust Co. of Tulsa, N.A., at above address.

3548 — FIRST CATHOLIC SLOVAK LADIES ASSOCIATION (College Scholarships)

24950 Chagrin Blvd.
Beachwood OH 44122-5634
800/464-4642 or 216/464-8015
FAX: 216/464-8717

AMOUNT: $1,000

DEADLINE(S): MAR 1

FIELD(S): All fields of study

For full-time undergraduate or graduate students who have been members of FCSLA for at least three years and who will attend an accredited institution in the US or Canada. Must submit transcripts, autobiographical statement, & wallet-size photo with application. Award must be used for tuition. Financial need is NOT a factor.

80 awards annually. Not renewable, though undergraduate recipients may reapply as graduate students. Contact the Receptionist at above address for an application.

3549 — FIRST CAVALRY DIVISION ASSOCIATION (Scholarships)

302 N. Main
Copperas Cove TX 76522
Written inquiry

AMOUNT: $600 per year up to 4 years max

DEADLINE(S): None specified

FIELD(S): All fields of study

Awards to children of soldiers who died or were declared 100% disabled from injuries while serving with the 1st Calvary Division during and since the Vietnam War or during Desert Storm.

If death occurred after 3/1/80 deceased parent must have been an Association member and serving with the division at the time of death. Send self-addressed stamped envelope for complete information.

3550 — FIRST CITIZENS FOUNDATION, INC.

P.O. Box 1377
Smithfield NC 27577-1377
Written inquiry

AMOUNT: Varies

DEADLINE(S): Varies

FIELD(S): All fields of study

Scholarships to students in North Carolina in financial distress for educational purposes in accredited trade schools, colleges, and universities.

Contact above location for deadline informaiton and application.

3551 — FLORIDA AIR ACADEMY SCHOLARSHIP FUND, INC.

1950 South Academy Dr.
Melbourne FL 32901
Written inquiry

AMOUNT: Varies

DEADLINE(S): Ongoing

FIELD(S): All fields of study

Scholarships for residents of Florida.

Write to above location for details.

3552 — FLORIDA DEPT. OF EDUCATION (Jose Marti Scholarship Challenge Grant Fund)

Student Financial Assist.
255 Collins
Tallahasee FL 32399-0400
850/487-0049 or 888/827-2004
E-Mail: OSFABF@mail.doe.state.fl.us
Internet: www.firn.edu/doe

AMOUNT: $2,000

DEADLINE(S): APR 1

FIELD(S): All fields of study

A need-based scholarship for students of Hispanic culture who were born in, or who have a natural parent who was born in Mexico, Spain, South America, Central America, or the Caribbean. Must apply as a high school senior or as a graduate student and have a minimum unweighted GPA of 3.0. Must enroll full-time, be a US citizen or eligible non-citizen, and be a Florida resident. Must also submit the FAFSA (available online at www.fafsa.ed.gov).

98 awards annually. Renewable. Forms (including FAFSA) available from your school's financial aid office or contact Florida Department of Education.

3553 — FLORIDA DEPT. OF EDUCATION (Scholarships for Children of Deceased or Disabled Veterans)

Student Financial Assist.
255 Collins
Tallahassee FL 32399-0400
850/487-0049 or 888/827-2004
E-Mail: OSFABF@mail.doe.state.fl.us
Internet: www.firn.edu/doe

AMOUNT: Tuition + fees for the academic year

DEADLINE(S): APR 1

FIELD(S): All fields of study

For dependent children of deceased or 100% disabled veterans, or for children of servicemen classified as POW or MIA for attendance at eligible public or private institutions. Residency requirements vary.

215 awards annually. Applications are available from Florida Department of Education or from Florida Department of Veterans' Affairs, PO Box 31003, St. Petersburg, FL 33731-8903.

3554 — FLORIDA STATE DEPT. OF EDUCATION (Seminole/Miccosukee Indian Scholarships)

Student Financial Assist.
255 Collins
Tallahassee FL 32399-0400
850/487-0049 or 888/827-2004
E-Mail: OSFABF@mail.doe.state.fl.us
Internet: www.firn.edu/doe

AMOUNT: Varies (determined by respective tribe)

DEADLINE(S): Varies (established by tribe)

FIELD(S): All fields of study

For Seminole and Miccosukee Indians of Florida who are enrolled as full-time or part-time undergraduate or graduate students at eligible Florida institutions.

23 awards annually. Applications available from each tribe's Higher Education Committee or contact Florida Department of Education.

3555 — FOND DU LAC RESERVATION (Scholarhip/Grants Program)

105 University Road
Cloquet MN 55720
218/879-4691

AMOUNT: Up to $3,000/year

DEADLINE(S): Varies

FIELD(S): All fields of study

For tribally enrolled members of the Fond du Lac Reservation who plan to pursue postsecondary education, including vocational schools in accredited higher education institutions. Must apply for all financial aid available and submit an education plan. Will assist out-of-state education for those attending colleges but not vocational schools.

Contact Bonnie Wallace, Career Education Specialist, at above address.

3556 — FOND REV. EDMOND GELINAS, INC. (Scholarships)

603 Stark Lane
Manchester NH 03102-8515
Written inquiry

AMOUNT: Varies

DEADLINE(S): JUL 1

FIELD(S): All fields of study

Scholarships to students in New Hampshire who are Catholic and of French or Canadian ancestry.

Write for application details.

3557 — FONDATION DES ETATS-UNIS (Scholarships)

15, boulevard Jourdan
75690 Paris Cedex 14 FRANCE
0153 8068 80
FAX: 0153 8068 99
E-Mail: fondusa@iway.fr

AMOUNT: Varies

DEADLINE(S): Varies

FIELD(S): All fields of study

For graduate students who are US citizens aged 21-29 to study in the US. Must demonstrate financial need.

4-5 awards annually. Contact Mike Sihapanya for an application.

3558 — FONDS F C A R (Fellowship Program)

140 Grande Allee Est., #450, 4th Floor
Quebec, Quebec G1R 5M8 Canada
418/643-8560 Ext. 1

AMOUNT: Canadian $11,000 (masters); Canadian $13,000 (doctorate); Canadian $22,000 (postdoctorate)

DEADLINE(S): OCT 7

FIELD(S): All fields of study

Master's, doctorate, or postdoctorate fellowship for full-time study. Students are eligible within 1st 2 years at master's level and 1st 3 years at doctorate level. Post-doctorate training within 2 years of receiving Ph.D.

Must be Canadian citizen and resident of Quebec. 700 awards per year. Contact Jacque Crochetiere at address above for complete information.

3559 — FOURTH TUESDAY (Pat Hoban Memorial Scholarship)

1387 Oxford Road NE, Suite 801
Atlanta GA 30307
770/662-4353
E-Mail: 4thtues@lambda.net
Internet: www.lambda.net/~4thtues/Schol.html

AMOUNT: $1,000

DEADLINE(S): Varies

FIELD(S): All fields of study

Scholarship for an Atlanta area lesbian attending an institution of higher education. Fourth Tuesday is a nonprofit professional social networking organization for lesbians.

Contact organization for details.

3560 — FRANK KNOX MEMORIAL FOUNDATION (Knox Fellowships at Harvard)

48 Westminster Palace Gardens
Artillery Row
London SW1P 1RR ENGLAND UK
44/171-222-1151
FAX: 44/171-222-5355

AMOUNT: Tuition & fees + $16,000 stipend

DEADLINE(S): OCT

FIELD(S): All fields of study

For UK citizens who are resident in the UK to pursue graduate study at Harvard University in Massachusetts. Must have graduated from a UK university and must apply within two years of graduation. Financial need NOT a factor.

4-6 awards annually. Renewable. Contact Anna Mason for an application.

3561 — FRANKLIN LINDSAY STUDENT AID FUND

P.O. Box 550
Austin TX 78789-0001
512/479-2645

AMOUNT: Up to $3,000 per year

DEADLINE(S): Varies

FIELD(S): All fields of study

Loans for undergraduate and grduate students who have completed at least one year of college attending Texas colleges or universities.

Send SASE for brochure to Texas Commerce Bank-Austin, Trust Div., at above address. May re-apply in subsequent years for up to $9,000 per student proved the recipient maintains at least a C average.

3562 — FRIEDRICH NAUMANN STIFTUNG FOUNDATION (Educational Scholarships)

Wisseuschaftliche Dienste +
Begabtenforderuug, Uouigsuriuterer Str. 407
53639 Uouigsuriuter
Written Inquiry

AMOUNT: Approx DM 1,100

DEADLINE(S): MAY 31; NOV 30

FIELD(S): All fields of study

Scholarship program is open to foreign applicants who reside in Germany, are fluent in German, are registered with a German university, or have been accepted as a Ph.D. student by a German university.

Write for complete information.

3563 — FUND FOR EDUCATION AND TRAINING (FEAT Loans)

1930 Connecticut Ave., NW
Washington DC 20009
202/483-2220
FAX: 202/483-1246

AMOUNT: $2,500

DEADLINE(S): None

FIELD(S): All fields of study

For male non-registrants of the Selective Service for undergraduate or graduate study, as well as career support. Financial need is NOT a factor.

Renewable. Contact Fran Donelan at above address for an application.

3564 — GABRIEL J. BROWN TRUST (Loan Program)

112 Avenue E West
Bismarck ND 58501-3662
701/223-5916

AMOUNT: Varies

DEADLINE(S): JUN 15

FIELD(S): All fields of study

Student loans for needy residents of North Dakota. Must have attended college four four semesters or six quarters or have acquired 48 credits. Students at Bismarck State College, Medcenter One College of Nursing, or the University of Mary may have attended only two semesters or three quarter or have acquired 24 credits. Must demonstrate financial need.

Interest rate is 6% per year. Send SASE for application guidelines.

3565 — GABRIEL J. BROWN TRUST (Trust Loan Fund)

112 Avenue E. West
Bismarck ND 58501
701/223-5916

AMOUNT: $1,000-4,000

DEADLINE(S): JUN 15

FIELD(S): All fields of study

Special low-interest loans (6%) open to residents of North Dakota who have completed at least 2 years of undergraduate study at a recognized college or university and have a 2.5 or better GPA. U.S. citizen.

Approximately 75 loans per year. Renewable. Write for complete information.

3566 — GENERAL FEDERATION OF WOMEN'S CLUBS OF MASSACHUSETTS (Memorial Education Fellowship)

245 Dutton Road, Box 679
Sudbury MA 01776-0679
508/583-4557

AMOUNT: $2,000

DEADLINE(S): MAR 1

FIELD(S): Varies (fields change yearly)

For female graduate students maintaining legal residence in Massachusetts for at least five years. Letter of endorsement from sponsoring GFWC of MA club, personal letter with goal/expected tuition, transcripts, personal interview, and letter of reference are all required with application.

For further information and an application, send self-addressed, stamped envelope to Tina Macrina, Chairman of Trustees, at above address.

3567 — GEORGE ABRAHAMIAN FOUNDATION (Scholarships for Rhode Island Armenians)

945 Admiral Street
Providence RI 02904
401/831-2887

AMOUNT: $600-$900

DEADLINE(S): SEP 1

FIELD(S): All areas of study

Open to undergraduate and graduate students who are US citizens of Armenian ancestry and live in Rhode Island, are of good character, have the ability to learn, and can demonstrate financial need. Must be affiliated with an Armenian Church and attend or plan to attend college in Rhode Island. Min. GPA of 3.0 required.

Renewable. Write for complete information.

3568 — GEORGE BIRD GRINNELL AMERICAN INDIAN CHILDREN'S FUND (Schulyer M. Meyer, Jr. Scholarship Award)

11602 Montague Ct.
Potomac MD 20854
301/424-2440
FAX: 301/424-8281
E-Mail: Grinnell_Fund@MSN.com

AMOUNT: $1,000/yr. (max.)

DEADLINE(S): JUN 1

FIELD(S): All fields of study

Opent to Native American students enrolled in undergraduate or graduate programs at two- or four-year institutions. Must be American Indian/Alaska Native (documented with Certified Degree of Indian Blood), be enrolled in college/university, be able to demonstrate commitment to serving community or other tribal nations, and document financial need.

Renewable. Contact Dr. Paula M. Mintzies, President, for an application after January 1st.

3569 — GEORGE GROTEFEND SCHOLARSHIP FUND (Grotefend Scholarship)

1644 Magnolia Ave.
Redding CA 96001
916/225-0227

AMOUNT: $150-$400

DEADLINE(S): APR 20

FIELD(S): All fields of study

Scholarships open to applicants who completed all 4 years of high school in Shasta County California. Awards support all levels of study at recognized colleges & universities.

300 awards per year. Write for complete information.

3570 — GEORGE W. AND ANNE A. HOOVER SCHOLARSHIP FUND (Student Loans)

2-16 South Market St., P.O. Box 57
Selinsgrave PA 17870
717/374-4252

AMOUNT: $2,500/yr. for two-yr. schools; $5,000/yr. for four-year schools

DEADLINE(S): None specified

FIELD(S): All fields of study

Student loans to individuals to attend colleges or universities.

Send self-addressed, stamped envelope to above address for details.

3571 — GEORGIA BOARD OF REGENTS (Scholarships)

244 Washington Street SW
Atlanta GA 30334
404/656-2272

AMOUNT: $500 for junior college; $750 for 4-year college; $1000 for grad school students

DEADLINE(S): Varies

FIELD(S): All areas of study

Must be legal Georgia resident enrolled or accepted in an institution of the university system of GA. Must be in upper 25% of class (based on high school & SAT scores) and demonstrate financial need.

DO NOT contact the GA Board of Regents above; contact the appropriate school for complete information.

3572 — GEORGIA STUDENT FINANCE COMMISSION (HOPE Scholarships)

2082 East Exchange Place
Tucker GA 30084
770/414-3085 (metro Atlanta) or 1-800/546-HOPE (toll-free in Georgia)
Internet: www.gsfc.org/gsfc/apphope.htm

AMOUNT: Varies

DEADLINE(S): Varies (end of spring term)

FIELD(S): All fields of study

The HOPE Scholarship Program (Helping Outstanding Pupils Educationally) is funded by the Georgia Lottery for Education. Program details are subject to change. For use at all Georgia colleges, universities, and technical institutes.

Applicants must complete the Free Applicaiton for Federal Student Aid (FAFSA) form. Contact the financial aid office at the public or private institution you plan to attend. High school students should check with counselor for eligibility requirements.

3573 — GERBER REWARDS (Scholarship Drawings)

P.O. Box 651
St. Petersburg FL 33731-0651
1-800/376-BABY
Internet: www.gerber.com

AMOUNT: Up to $250,000

DEADLINE(S): JUL; DEC

FIELD(S): All fields of study

Drawing for parents of a child up to 24 months. Purchase at least 16 Gerber food products, remove and save the UPC labels, and receive a game piece with a toll-free number.

Check the website or 800 number above for details.

3574 — GERONIMO CORPORATION, INC. (William B. Klusty Memorial Scholarship Fund for Native Americans)

206 Zion Road
Salisbury MD 21804
Internet: www.geronimo.org/scholarship

AMOUNT: $1,000

DEADLINE(S): Varies (2nd Friday of the fall quarter)

FIELD(S): All fields of study

Scholarships for Native American students, both undergraduate and graduate. Criteria are previous academic work, community involvement, career goals, leadership ability, finanancial need, and an explanation as to why the students should receive a scholarship (as explained in a 250-word, typed essay). Submit proof of Native American heritage. Must have 3.5 GPA.

Access website or contact organization for application.

3575 — GLENDALE COMMUNITY FOUNDATION (Scholarships)

P.O. Box 313
Glendale CA 91209-0313
818/241-8040
Internet: www.cwore.com/gcf/

AMOUNT: Varies

DEADLINE(S): Varies

FIELD(S): All fields of study

Scholarships through this Foundation for needy students who are residents of Glendale, La Canada Flintridge, La Crescenta, Montrose, or Verdugo City, California.

Contact organization for details.

3576 — GLORIA FECHT MEMORIAL SCHOLARSHIP FUND

402 W. Arrow Hwy. #10
San Dimas, CA 91773
619/562-0304
FAX: 619/562-4116
E-Mail: rlmtswingle@msn.com

AMOUNT: $2,000 - $3,000

DEADLINE(S): MAR 1

FIELD(S): All areas of study

For undergraduate and graduate females, who are residents of Southern California, have a 3.0 GPA, and an interest in golf. Must demonstrate financial need.

Renewable. 30 awards per year. For an application, write to the above address.

3577 — GOLDIE GIBSON SCHOLARSHIP FUND (Student Loans)

1601 S.E. Harned Drive
Bartlesville OK 74006
918/333-5268

AMOUNT: Varies

DEADLINE(S): Ongoing

FIELD(S): All fields of study

Student loans for residents of Oklahoma.

Renewable. Write to Ruth Andrews, Secretary-Treasurer, for application information.

3578 — GOLF COURSE SUPERINTENDENTS ASSOCIATION OF AMERICA (Legacy Awards)

1421 Research Park Dr.
Lawrence KS 66049-3859
785/832-3678

FAX: 785/832-3665
E-Mail: psmith@gcsaa.org
Internet: www.gcsaa.org

AMOUNT: $1,500

DEADLINE(S): APR 15

FIELD(S): All fields of study (except golf course management)

Available to the children and grandchildren of GCSAA members who have been an active member for five or more consecutive years. The student must be studying a field UNRELATED to golf course management. Must be enrolled full-time at an accredited institution of higher learning, or in the case of high school seniors, must be accepted at such institution for the next academic year.

See website or contact Pam Smith at GCSAA for an application.

3579 — GRACE EDWARDS SCHOLARSHIP FUND (Scholarships)

10 Post Office Square, Suite 1230
Boston MA 02109
Written inquiry

AMOUNT: Varies

DEADLINE(S): MAR 1

FIELD(S): All fields of study

Scholarhships for legal residents of Boston, Massachusetts. Must be under age 25 and demonstrate academic excellence and need.

Renewable for up to six years.

3580 — GRADUATE INSTITUTE OF PEACE STUDIES (Peace Education Scholarship)

Kyung Hee University, Jinjobup, Namyangju City
KyonggI, 473-860 KOREA
82-0346-556-7621 (~9)
FAX: 82-0346-556-7630

AMOUNT: Varies

DEADLINE(S): NOV; FEB

FIELD(S): Peace Studies

Open to graduate students with specialized field of Northeast Asia, peace and security, international and public policy, and social welfare.

2 awards annually. Financial need not a requirement. Contact Dean of academic Affairs at above address for complete information.

3581 — GRIFFITH UNIVERSITY (Post-graduate Research Scholarship)

Postgraduate Scholarships Officer
Office for Research
Nathan QLD 4111 Australia
07/3875-6596

AMOUNT: A$15,367 + travel and thesis allowance; dependent child allowance of A$1,500 p/a for some overseas students

DEADLINE(S): OCT 30

FIELD(S): All fields of study

Open to research masters or Ph.D. candidates accepted at Griffith University. Masters awards are renewable for up to 2 years; Ph.D. student awards are renewable for 3-1/2 years subject to satisfactory assessment.

Must demonstrate English proficiency. Scholarship does not cover full tuition cost which can range from Australian $12,000 to $14,000 per year. Write for complete information.

3582 — H.G. AND A.G. KEASBEY MEMORIAL FOUNDATION

One Logan Square, Suite 2000
Philadelphia PA 19103-6993
Written inquiry

AMOUNT: Varies

DEADLINE(S): Varies

FIELD(S): All areas of study

Scholarships to individuals primarily for study in the United Kingdom.

Contact Geraldine J. O'Neill, Executive Secretary, at above address for application guidelines.

3583 — HAGGAR CLOTHING COMPANY (Haggar Foundation Scholarship Program)

P.O. Box 311370
Denton TX 76203-1370
940/565-2302
FAX: 940/565-2738
E-Mail: bonner@unt.edu

AMOUNT: $4,000/yr.

DEADLINE(S): APR 30

FIELD(S): All fields of study

Open to an immediate relative of an employee of the Haggar Clothing Co. Applicants must be studying in the U.S.

Renewable for up to four years. Write to the above address for complete information.

3584 — HARNESS TRACKS OF AMERICA (Scholarship)

4640 East Sunrise, Suite 200
Tucson AZ 85718
520/529-2525
FAX 520/529-3235

AMOUNT: $3,000

DEADLINE(S): JUN 15

FIELD(S): All fields of study

Applicants MUST be children of licensed harness racing drivers, trainers, breeders, or caretakers (including retired or deceased) or young people actively engaged in harness racing. For study beyond the high school level.

Five scholarships per year for 1 year each awarded on the basis of merit & financial need. No student may be awarded more than 2 separate yearly scholarships. Write for complete information.

3585 — HARRY E. & FLORENCE W. SNAYBERGER MEMORIAL FOUNDATION (Grant Award)

c/o Pennsylvania National Bank & Trust Company
Trust Dept.
Center & Norwegian
Pottsville PA 17901-7150
717/622-4200

AMOUNT: Varies

DEADLINE(S): FEB

FIELD(S): All fields of study

Applicants must be residents of Schuylkill County, PA. Scholarships given based on college expense need.

Contact trust clerk Carolyn Bernatonis for complete information.

3586 — HARVARD UNIVERSITY—NIEMAN FOUNDATION (Fellowships for Journalists)

Walter Lippmann House
One Francis Ave.
Cambridge MA 02138
617/495-2237
FAX 617/495-8976
E-Mail: nieman@harvard.edu
Internet: www.Nieman.harvard.edu/nieman.html

AMOUNT: $25,000 stipend + tuition

DEADLINE(S): JAN 31 (American journalists); MAR 1 (foreign journalists)

FIELD(S): All fields of study

Must be full-time staff or freelance journalist working for the news or editorial dept. of newspaper, news service, radio, TV, or magazine of broad public interest and must have at least 3 years of professional experience in the media and must be fluent in English.

Consists of an academic year of non-credit study. Approximately 24 fellowships awarded annually. Fellows design their own course of study. Write for complete information.

3587 — HARVARD/RADCLIFFE OFFICE OF ADMISSIONS AND FINANCIAL AID (Scholarships; Grants; Loans & Work Study Programs)

3rd floor - Byerly Hall
8 Garden St.
Cambridge MA 02138
617/495-1581

AMOUNT: Varies

DEADLINE(S): None

FIELD(S): All fields of study

Needs-based funds available to all who are admitted and can show proof of need.

Applicants must be accepted for admission to Harvard/Radcliffe before they will be considered for funding. Many factors other than family income are considered. Write for complete information.

3588 — HATTIE M. STRONG FOUNDATION (No-interest Loans)

1620 Eye St. NW, Room 700
Washington DC 20006
202/331-1619
FAX: 202/466-2894

AMOUNT: Up to $3,000

DEADLINE(S): MAR 31 (Applications available JAN 1)

FIELD(S): All fields of study

Open to U.S. undergraduate and graduate students in their last year of study in the U.S. or abroad. Loans are made solely on the basis of individual merit. There is no interest and no collateral requirement. U.S. citizen or permanent resident. Repayment terms are based upon monthly income after graduation and arranged individually.

Financial need is a consideration. Approximately 240 awards per year. For complete information send SASE and include personal history, school attended, subject studied, date expected to complete studies, and amount of funds needed.

3589 — HAWAII COMMUNITY FOUNDATION

900 Fort St. Mall, Suite 1300
Honolulu HI 96813
808/556-5570
FAX: 808/521-6286

AMOUNT: Varies

DEADLINE(S): Varies

FIELD(S): All areas of study

Several different scholarship programs, each having its own criteria. Some are for specific college majors, others for specific ethnic groups, and others for specific high schools and colleges or geographic areas.

Send to the organization above for a listing of the programs.

3590 — HEBREW IMMIGRANT SOCIETY (HIAS Scholarship Program)

333 Seventh Ave.
New York NY 10001-5004
212/613-1358
FAX: 212/629-0921
Internet: www.hias.org

AMOUNT: $1,500

DEADLINE(S): MAR 15

FIELD(S): All fields of study

Open to refugees and asylees who were assisted by HIAS and who arrived in the US during or after 1985. For high school seniors planning to pursue postsecondary education or students already enrolled in undergraduate or graduate study who will continue the following year. Must have completed one year of study at a US school, be a US resident, and demonstrate financial need.

100+ awards annually. Not renewable. See website or send a self-addressed, stamped, business-sized envelope to Phoebe Lewis for an application.

3591 — HISPANIC SCHOLARSHIP FUND (Scholarships)

One Sansome St., Ste. 1000
San Francisco CA 94104
415/445-9930 or 877-HSF-INFO, ext. 33
FAX: 415/445-9942
E-Mail: info@hsf.net
Internet: www.hsf.net

AMOUNT: $500-$2,500

DEADLINE(S): OCT 15

FIELD(S): All fields of study

HSF scholarships are available to students who are of Hispanic background (at least half), are US citizens/permanent residents, have earned at least 15 undergraduate credits from an accredited college, have a minimum GPA of 2.5, and are enrolled in and attending college full-time (undergraduates min. 12 credits/term; graduate students min. 6 credits/term).

See website or send business-sized, self-addressed stamped envelope to HSF for an application.

3592 — HOME AFFAIRS BUREAU (Li Po Chun Overseas Postgraduate Scholarships)

Trust Funds, Temple, & Cemeteries Section
Room 2202, 22nd Fl.
Wu Chung House, 213 Queen's Road East
Wanchai HONG KONG
2519 9123
FAX: 2586 1948

AMOUNT: Varies

DEADLINE(S): JAN

FIELD(S): All fields of overseas post-graduate study.

Open to Hong Kong residents who have lived in Hong Kong at least 7 years. For postgraduate study at any accredited graduate institution outside of Hong Kong.

Renewable subject to satisfactory progress report from the university or institution. Contact Mr. Chow Ping Chong at above location for complete information.

3593 — HOME AFFAIRS BUREAU (Sir Robert Black Post-graduate Scholarships)

Trust Funds, Temples, & Cemeteries Section
Room 2202, 22nd Fl.
Wu Chung House, 213 Queen's Road East
Wanchai HONG KONG
2519 9123
FAX: 2586 1945

AMOUNT: Varies

DEADLINE(S): FEB

FIELD(S): All fields of post-graduate study

Open to Hong Kong residents who have lived in Hong Kong for at least five years. For postgraduate study at any accredited graduate institution.

Renewable subject to satisfactory progress report from the university or institution. Write for complete information.

3594 — HOMI BHABHA FELLOWSHIPS COUNCIL (Homi Bhabha Fellowship)

c/o National Centre for the Performing Arts
Nariman Point
Bombay 400 021 India
2833838 / 2834678

AMOUNT: Rs.10,000 - Rs.12,000 per month, plus essential travel and books

DEADLINE(S): None specified

FIELD(S): All fields of research

Open to Indian citizens between the ages of 30 and 45 to carry out postdoctoral research work (or its equivalent) in their area of specialization after completion of academic training.

For research projects carried out in India. Work abroad for a limited period is allowed if essential to the project. Recommendation and support of a recognized institution or of a person of eminence in the field concerned is normally required. Write for complete information.

3595 — HONOR SOCIETY OF PHI KAPPA PHI (First-Year Graduate Fellowship)

c/o LSU
Box 16000
Baton Rouge LA 70893-6000
504/388-4917

AMOUNT: $7,000; $1,000; Life memberships to all applicants

DEADLINE(S): FEB 1

FIELD(S): All fields of study/P.K.P. Members

Fellowships for the first year of graduate or professional study require maintaining a high scholastic standing and nomination by a PKP chapter. Student must be or about to become a member of the nominating chapter.

50 fellowships of up to $7,000 and 30 $1,000 awards per year. Students should obtain application from their local chapter officers.

3596 — HOPI SCHOLARSHIP

P.O. Box 123
Kykotsmovi AZ 86039
520/734-2441, Ext. 520
800/762-9630
FAX: 520/734-2435

AMOUNT: Varies

DEADLINE(S): JUL 31

FIELD(S): All fields of study

For enrolled members of the Hopi Tribe pursuing associate, baccalaureate, graduate, or post-graduate degrees. Minimum 3.0 GPA (3.2 for graduates). Entering freshmen must be in the top 10% of graduating class or score min. of 21 on ACT or 930 on SAT; undergrads must have and maintain 3.0 GPA.

Academic merit is primary consideration.

3597 — HORACE SMITH FUND (Loans)

P.O. Box 3034
1441 Main St.
Springfield MA 01101
413/739-4222

AMOUNT: Varies

DEADLINE(S): JUN 15 (college students); JUL 1 (high school)

FIELD(S): All areas of study

Open to graduates of Hampden County MA secondary schools for undergraduate or graduate study. Financial need is of primary importance. Applications available after April 1. No interest if paid back within a year after the student completes his/her education.

Renewable. Write for complete information.

3598 — HORACE SMITH FUND (Walter S. Barr Fellowships)

P.O. Box 3034
1441 Main St.
Springfield MA 01101
413/739-4222

AMOUNT: Varies

DEADLINE(S): FEB 1

FIELD(S): Any field of study

For residents of Hampden County, Massachusetts, who have received Bachelor Degrees. For full-time study. Applications are avaiolable after Sept. 1 at the above address.

Awards are made on the basis of shcolastic record, available resources, need, and other pertinent information.

3599 — HOWARD AND MAMIE NICHOLS SCHOLARSHIP TRUST (Scholarships)

Wells Fargo Bank Trust Dept.
5262 N. Blackstone
Fresno CA 93710
Written inquiries only

AMOUNT: Varies

DEADLINE(S): FEB 28

FIELD(S): All fields of study

Open to graduates of Kern County, California high schools for full-time undergraduate or graduate study at a postsecondary institution. Must demonstrate financial need and have a 2.0 or better GPA.

Approximately 100 awards per year. Renewable with reapplication. Write for complete information.

3600 — HUALAPAI TRIBAL COUNCIL (Scholarship Program)

P.O. Box 179
Peach Springs AZ 86434
520/769-2216

AMOUNT: Up to $2,500/semester

DEADLINE(S): Varies

FIELD(S): All areas of study

Scholarships are offered to American Indians only with priority given to members of the Hualapai Tribe. Must be enrolled as a student full-time and maintain passing grades. U.S. citizenship required.

Apply four weeks before each semester. Write to Sheri K. Yellowhawk at above address for complete information.

3601 — HUMANITARIAN TRUST (Grants)

36-38 Westbourne Grove
London W2 5SH ENGLAND UK
Written Inquiry

AMOUNT: 200 pounds sterling

DEADLINE(S): None

FIELD(S): All fields of study (except arts)

Grants for undergraduate, graduate, and postgraduate students to take courses in the UK.

15 awards annually. Not renewable. Contact Mrs. M. Meyers, Secretary, for an application.

3602 — HUMBOLDT AREA FOUNDATION (Scholarships)

P.O. Box 99
Bayside CA 95524
707/442-2993
FAX: 707/442/3811
E-Mail: hafound@northcoast.com
Internet: www.northcoast.com/~hafound

AMOUNT: Varies

DEADLINE(S): Varies

FIELD(S): All fields of study

Scholarships through this Foundation for needy students who are residents of Humboldt County, California.

Contact organization for details.

3603 — IAN KARTEN CHARITABLE TRUST (Karten Scholarships)

The Mill House, Newark Lane
Ripley, Surrey GU23 6DP ENGLAND
01483 225020
FAX: 01483 222420

AMOUNT: Varies

DEADLINE(S): MAY

FIELD(S): All fields of study

British and Israeli students may apply to help with the costs of research-based postgraduate courses leading to Ph.D. degrees at universities in the UK. May also apply for postgraduate training of musicians of outstanding merit at British conservatories. Must be under 30 years of age. Applicants must be able to demonstrate that they have a viable plan for funding most of their needs from other sources.

Renewable. Requests for applications should be submitted in March or April and should state the student's citizenship, date of birth, name of the course, date it finishes, qualification to which it leads, and the academic year for which scholarship is being sought. Must also include a stamped, addressed envelope.

3604 — IDP EDUCATION AUSTRALIA (Australian-European Awards Program)

GPO Box 2006
Canberra AUSTRALIA 2601
61 6 285 8222

AMOUNT: $20,180 AUD

DEADLINE(S): JUL 31

FIELD(S): All fields of study

Open to students from various countries in Europe for post-graduate study or research in Australia for one academic year. Program does not lead to a degree.

Candidates must seek placement in institutions of their choice. Contact Australian Embassy in your country or address above for complete information.

3605 — ILLINOIS STUDENT ASSISTANCE COMMISSION (Grants for Descendents of Police, Fire, or Correctional Officers)

1755 Lake Cook Rd.
Deerfield IL 60015-5209
800/899-ISAC
Internet: www.isac1.org

AMOUNT: Tuition and fees

DEADLINE(S): None

FIELD(S): All fields of study

Grants Illinois post-secondary students who are descendants of police, fire, and correctional personnel killed or disabled in the line of duty.

Thirty annual awards. Apply at end of academic year. Illinois residency and U.S. citizenship required. Access website or write for complete information.

3606 — ILLINOIS STUDENT ASSISTANCE COMMISSION (Illinois National Guard Grant)

1755 Lake Cook Rd.
Deerfield IL 60015-5209
800/899-ISAC
Internet: www.isac1.org

AMOUNT: Tuition and fees-average $1,350

DEADLINE(S): SEP 15

FIELD(S): All fields of study

Grants for qualified personnel of the Illinois National Guard attending public universities and community colleges.

2,500 annual awards. Illinois residency and U.S. citizenship required. Access website or write for complete information.

3607 — ILLINOIS STUDENT ASSISTANCE COMMISSION (Illinois Veterans' Grant)

1755 Lake Cook Rd.
Deerfield IL 60015-5209
800/899-ISAC
Internet: www.isac1.org

AMOUNT: Tuition and fees-average $1,350

DEADLINE(S): Varies

FIELD(S): All fields of study

Grants for veterans of the U.S. Armed Forces attending public universities and community colleges.

150,000 annual awards. Illinois residency and U.S. citizenship required. Apply three months after end of term. Write for complete information.

3608 — INDEPENDENCE FEDERAL SAVINGS BANK (Federal Family Education Loans)

1900 L St. NW, Ste. 700
Washington DC 20036-5001
800/733-0473 or 202/626-0473
FAX: 202/775-4533

E-Mail: ifsb@aol.com
Internet: www.ifsb.com

AMOUNT: up to $8,500

DEADLINE(S): None

FIELD(S): All fields of study

Loans are open to US citizens or legal residents who are undergraduate or graduate students accepted to or enrolled in a school approved by the US Department of Education. Includes Federal Subsidized/Unsubsidized Stafford Loans and Federal Parent Loans (Plus). Financial need considered for some loans. Repayment begins six months after graduation or when student withdraws/ stops attending school at least half time.

Contact IFSB for an application.

3609 — INSTITUTE FOR THE INTERNATIONAL EDUCATION OF STUDENTS (Scholarships)

223 West Ohio Street
Chicago IL 60610-4196
1-800/995-2300 or 312/944-1750
FAX: 312/944-1448
E-Mail: info@iesa.broad.org
Internet: iesabroad.org

AMOUNT: Varies

DEADLINE(S): APR 1 (fall semester & full-year students); OCT 1 (spring semester students)

FIELD(S): All fields of study

IES offers many scholarships for studying abroad in various countries; some are based on academic merit, and some are based on financial need. The organization wants to encourage students with a variety of interests and abilities and who represent a wide range of social and economic backgrounds to study abroad.

The website is quite comprehensive and includes application forms, scholarship lists, and descriptions of what is available country-by-country. If you do not have Web access, contact IES for the necessary materials.

3610 — INSTITUTE OF INTERNATIONAL EDUCATION (Fulbright Grants for Foreign Nations)

809 United Nations Plaza
New York NY 10017
212/984-5400

AMOUNT: Varies with country

DEADLINE(S): MAY 1; OCT 1

FIELD(S): All fields of study

Graduate fellowships for study and/or research in a country other than student's own. Proficiency in language of country of study is required. Fellowships must be applied for in the home country.

Institute is an administrative agency for a variety of sponsors. Write for complete information.

3611 — INSTITUTE OF INTERNATIONAL EDUCATION (Fulbright and International Fellowships for U.S. Citizens)

809 United Nations Plaza
New York NY 10017-3580
212/984-5330
FAX: 212/984-5325
Internet: www.iie.org/fulbright/

AMOUNT: Varies with country

DEADLINE(S): OCT 31

FIELD(S): All fields of study

Graduate fellowships for U.S. residents to study/ do research in a foreign country. Criteria include academic record and proficiency in the language of country student is visiting.

Contact your graduate institution or write to U.S. Student Programs Division at address above for complete information.

3612 — INSTITUTE OF INTERNATIONAL EDUCATION (Scholarships for Study in Switzerland)

809 United Nations Plaza
New York, NY 10017
212/883-8200
212/984-5330 (U.S. citizens)

AMOUNT: Between 1,350 and 1,650 Swiss francs per month

DEADLINE(S): OCT 23

FIELD(S): All fields of study

The Swiss government offers scholarships to foreign students for post-graduate study at a Swiss university. Awards are intended to enable holders to further their studies and begin research.

U.S. citizens should inquire of their graduate institution or write to address above: Attn: U.S. Student Programs Div.

3613 — INSTITUTO COLOMBIANO DE CREDITO EDUCATIVO Y ESTUDIOS TECNICOS EN EL EXTERIOR (ICETEX/Fulbright Commission Scholarships)

Carrera 3A No. 18-24
Bogota Colombia
91-2865566

AMOUNT: Varies

DEADLINE(S): None specified

FIELD(S): All areas of study

Open to professionals from countries with which Columbia has reciprocal agreements. For graduate study in Columbia. Fulbright Commission covers transportation to Columbia & tuition; ICETEX covers other costs and return transportation.

5 scholarships per year. Write for complete information.

3614 — INTERNATIONAL ASSOCIATION OF FIRE FIGHTERS (W.H. "Howie" McClennan Scholarship)

1750 New York Avenue NW
Washington DC 20006-5395
202/737-8484

AMOUNT: $2,500

DEADLINE(S): FEB 1

FIELD(S): All fields of study

Scholarship for sons, daughters, and legally adopted children of fire fighters who were members in good standing of the International Association of Fire Fighters and died in the line of duty.

Write to the above address for complete information.

3615 — INTERNATIONAL BILL ONEXIOCA II (Founders Memorial Award)

911 Bartlett Place
Windsor CA 95492
Written inquiry only

AMOUNT: $2,500

DEADLINE(S): JAN 31

FIELD(S): All fields of study

Annual award in memory of Hernesto K. Onexioca/ founder. Anyone with the legal surname of Onexioca who is not a relative of Onexioca by blood or marriage and was born on Jan. 1 is eligible to apply.

All inquiries MUST include proof of name and birth date. Those without such proof will NOT be acknowledged.

3616 — INTERNATIONAL COUNCIL FOR CANADIAN STUDIES (Government of Finland Scholarships)

325 Dalhousie, S-800
Ottawa Ontario K1N 7G2 CANADA
613/789-7828
FAX: 613/789-7830
E-Mail: general@iccs-ciec.ca
Internet: www.iccs-ciec.ca

AMOUNT: 1,000FM for tuition/registration; 4,000FM/mo. living allowance at master's or doctoral level, travel

DEADLINE(S): OCT 31

FIELD(S): All fields of study

Graduate scholarship open to Canadian citizen who has obtained a first degree from a Canadian university or college. Must have a working knowledge of English, German, Finnish, or Swedish and must NOT have reached 35th birthday by Jan. 1 of year of award.

Award tenable in Finland. Write or access website for further information.

3617 — INTERNATIONAL COUNCIL FOR CANADIAN STUDIES (Foreign Government Awards for Canadians)

325 Dalhousie St., S-800
Ottawa CANADA KIN 7G2
613/789-7828
FAX: 613/789-7830
E-Mail: general@iccs-ciec.ca
Internet: www.iccs-ciec.ca

AMOUNT: Varies (by country)

DEADLINE(S): Varies (by country)

FIELD(S): Most fields of study

For Canadian citizens who are at the masters, doctoral, or postdoctoral levels for study in Columbia, Finland, France, Germany, Italy Japan, Mexico, Netherlands, or Spain. Candidates are required to have sound working knowledge of the relevant language of instruction.

Write to the above address for complete information.

3618 — INTERNATIONAL COUNCIL FOR CANADIAN STUDIES (German Government Graduate Awards)

325 Dalhousie, S-800
Ottawa Ontario CANADA K1N 7G2
613/789-7828
FAX: 613/789-7830
E-Mail: general@iccs-ciec.ca
Internet: www.iccs-ciec.ca

AMOUNT: Tuition travel, and living allowance

DEADLINE(S): OCT 31

FIELD(S): All fields of study

Ten-month fellowships for research or graduate study at public universities, technical universities, and academies of art and music in Germany. Applicants must be Canadian citizens.

Graduating seniors, graduate students, and Ph.D candidates who are proficient in German are invited to apply. Write for complete information.

3619 — INTERNATIONAL COUNCIL FOR CANADIAN STUDIES (Government of Colombia Graduate Scholarships)

325 Dalhousie, S-800
Ottawa Ontario CANADA K1N 7G2
613/789-7828
FAX 613/789-7830
E-Mail: general@ices-ciec.ca
Internet: www.iccs-ciec.ca

AMOUNT: Tuition, travel, and living expenses

DEADLINE(S): JAN 29

FIELD(S): All fields of study available at a university in Colombia

One-year graduate scholarships for study at the master's and doctoral levels for Canadian citizens who will hold an undergraduate degree or its equivalent by the time the award takes effect. Knowledge of Spanish is essential. Tenable in Colombia.

Write or access website for further information.

3620 — INTERNATIONAL COUNCIL FOR CANADIAN STUDIES (Government of Mexico Graduate Scholarships)

325 Dalhousie, S-800
Ottawa Ontario CANADA K1N 7G2
613/789-7828
FAX: 613/789-7830
E-Mail: general@iccs-ciec.ca
Internet: www.iccs-ciec.ca

AMOUNT: Tuition, travel, and living allowance
DEADLINE(S): JAN 30
FIELD(S): All fields of study

One-year scholarhips for Canadian citizens who hold the equivalent of a Canadian undergraduate degree and have a good knowledge of Spanish. For study or research at a public university in Mexico at the master's, doctoral, or postdoctoral level.

Applications will be considered for residence specialities in the field of medicine. Preference to those under 35. Write for complete information.

3621 — INTERNATIONAL COUNCIL FOR CANADIAN STUDIES/ORGANIZATION OF AMERICAN STATES (OAS Fellowships for Canadians)

325 Dalhousie, S-800
Ottawa Ontario CANADA K1N 7G2
613/789-7828
FAX: 613/789-7830
E-Mail: general@iccs-ciec.ca
Internet: www.iccs-ciec.ca

AMOUNT: Tuition, travel, health insurance and subsistence allowance, study material
DEADLINE(S): JAN 30
FIELD(S): All fields of study

Graduate fellowships for Canadian citizens or permanent residents to study in member countries of the Organization of American States. Must know the language of host country. Preference to graduate studies or research projects conducted in Latin America and in the Caribbean.

For 3 months to 2 years. Write or access website for complete details.

3622 — INTERNATIONAL COUNCIL FOR CANADIAN STUDIES (Commonwealth Scholarship Plan for Canadians)

325 Dalhousie, S-800
Ottawa Ontario CANADA K1N 7G2
613/789-7828

FAX: 613/789-7830
E-Mail: general@iccs-ciec.ca
Internet: www.iccs-ciec.ca

AMOUNT: Varies by country
DEADLINE(S): OCT 31 (India, Sri Lanka, Uganda, and U.K.); DEC 31 (New Zealand)
FIELD(S): All fields of study

Graduate fellowships for Canadian citizens or permanent residents to study in countries listed above.

Write or access website for complete details.

3623 — INTERNATIONAL FEDERATION OF UNIVERSITY WOMEN (IFUW International Fellowships & Grants)

c/o AAUW
1111 16th St., NW
Washington DC 20036-4873
022/731-23-80
FAX 022/738-04-40

AMOUNT: Varies with program
DEADLINE(S): SEP 1
FIELD(S): All fields of study

Various fellowship and grant programs open to IFUW members for graduate study and research. Awards are presented every two years (in even-numbered years).

Contact American Association of University Women at above address for complete information, or contact the IFUW in your home country.

3624 — INTERNATIONAL SOCIETY FOR CLINICAL LABORATORY TECHNOLOGY (David Birenbaum Scholarship Fund)

917 Locust St., Suite 1100
St. Louis MO 63101-1413
314/241-1445

AMOUNT: Varies
DEADLINE(S): JUL 15
FIELD(S): All fields of study

Open to ISCLT members, and their spouses and dependent children. Requires graduation from an accredited high school or equivalent.

Write for complete information.

3625 — IOWA COLLEGE STUDENT AID COMMISSION (Federal Stafford Loan Program; Federal PLUS Loans)

200 Tenth St.
4th Floor
Des Moines IA 50309-3609
515/281-3501

AMOUNT: $2,625 - $4,000 undergraduate; $7,500 graduate
DEADLINE(S): None

FIELD(S): All fields of study

Loans open to Iowa residents enrolled in or attending approved institutions. Must be U.S. citizens or legal residents and demonstrate need.

Write for complete information.

3626 — ISRAEL AMATEUR RADIO CLUB (Holyland Award)

Mark Stern, 4Z4KX
PO Box 3033
Rishon 75130 ISRAEL
Internet: hamradio.iarc.org/contests/contests.html

AMOUNT: Trophies, plaques, & certificates
DEADLINE(S): MAY 31
FIELD(S): All fields of study

Worldwide contest to promote contacts between Radio Amateurs around the globe and Israelli Hams. For all licensed amateurs and SWL's worldwide. Object is to contact as many different Israelli amateur radio stations on as many bands, and from as many Areas, as possible in both modes, CW and SSB.

Contact the Contest Manager at IARC for details.

3627 — ITALIAN INSTITUTE (Scholarships and Grants)

39 Belgrave Square
London SW1X 8NX England
071/235-1461
FAX 071/235-4618
E-Mail: Italcultur@martex.cuk

AMOUNT: 1.000.000-1.200.000 lire monthly
DEADLINE(S): JAN 31
FIELD(S): Italian art, music, humanities, social studies, language, scientific studies, and/or Italian culture.

Open to British citizens with a master's degree or better for grad study at Italian universities. Awards for summer bursaries/short-term research grants & long-term scholarships/research grants. Must be fluent in Italian & under 36.

Preference to scholars researching Italian history literature and art, to scientists, and to those who plan to teach Italian in the UK. Write for complete information.

3628 — JACKQUELINE ELVIRA HODGES JOHNSON FUND, INC (Scholarship)

P.O. Box 1442
Walterboro, SC 29488
803/538-8640

AMOUNT: Varies
DEADLINE(S): APR 1
FIELD(S): All fields of study

This scholarship is for cancer survivors and residents of South Carolina who are college-bound high school seniors or students enrolled in postsecondary study. Must demonstrate financial need and have at least a 3.0 GPA

Write to the above address for complete information.

3629 — JACKSONVILLE UNIVERSITY (Scholarships & Grants Programs)

Director of Student Financial Assistance
Jacksonville FL 32211
904/745-7060

AMOUNT: Varies

DEADLINE(S): JAN 1

FIELD(S): All areas of study

Jacksonville University offers numerous scholarships, grants-in-aid, service awards, and campus employment. Financial need is not necessarily a consideration. Early applications are advised.

Candidates must apply for admission and for financial aid. 100 awards per year for study at Jacksonville University. Write for complete information.

3630 — JACKSONVILLE STATE UNIVERSITY

Financial Aid Office
Jacksonville AL 36265
Written inquiry

AMOUNT: Varies

DEADLINE(S): MAR 15

FIELD(S): All fields of study

Numerous scholarship programs tenable at Jacksonville State University, Alabama, in all subject areas and with various restrictions concerning residency, year in school, major, etc.

Write to above address for complete listing and application.

3631 — JAMES Z. NAURISON SCHOLARSHIP FUND

PO Box 15769
1500 Main St.
Springfield, MA 01115
413/732-2858

AMOUNT: $400 - $2,000

DEADLINE(S): MAR 15

FIELD(S): All fields of study

Open to undergraduate and graduate students who are residents of the Massachusetts counties of Berkshire, Franklin, Hampden, or Hampshire or of the cities of Suffield or Enfield, CT. Awards based on financial need and academic record. Must fill out FAFSA and send a copy with your application, along with transcript(s).

Renewable up to four years. Approximately 300 awards per year. Self-addressed stamped envelope must accompany request for application.

3632 — JAPANESE AMERICAN CITIZENS LEAGUE (Abe & Esther Hagiwara Student Aid Award)

1765 Sutter St.
San Francisco CA 94115
415/921-5225
E-Mail: jacl@jacl.org
Internet: www.jacl.org

AMOUNT: Varies

DEADLINE(S): APR 1

FIELD(S): All fields of study

Open to JACL members or their children only. MUST demonstrate severe financial need. The purpose of this award is to provide financial assistance to a student who otherwise would have to delay or terminate his/her education due to a lack of financing.

For membership information or an application, send a self-addressed, stamped envelope to above address.

3633 — JAPANESE AMERICAN CITIZENS LEAGUE (Graduate Awards)

1765 Sutter Street
San Francisco CA 94115
415/921-5225
E-Mail: jacl@jacl.org
Internet: www.jacl.org

AMOUNT: Varies

DEADLINE(S): APR 1

FIELD(S): All fields of study

Open to JACL members or their children only. For graduate students currently enrolled, or planning to enroll, in an accredited graduate school.

Various scholarships. For membership information or an application, send a self-addressed, stamped envelope to the above address, stating your level of study.

3634 — JAPANESE AMERICAN CITIZENS LEAGUE (Mike M. Masaoka Fellowships)

1765 Sutter St.
San Francisco CA 94115
415/921-5225
FAX: 415/931-4671
E-Mail: jacl@jacl.org
Internet: www.jacl.org

AMOUNT: $7,500 stipend

DEADLINE(S): MAY 1

FIELD(S): All fields of study

Congressional fellowships for students of Japanese ancestry who are American citizens. Successful candidates will serve fellowships in the office of U.S. Senators or Representatives for approximately three and one-half months. Terms are Sept.-Dec. and Feb.-May. Must be in 3rd or 4th year of college or in a graduate or professional program.

For membership information or an application, send self-addressed, stamped envelope to above address.

3635 — JAPANESE ASSOCIATION OF UNIVERSITY WOMEN (International Fellowships)

11-6-101 Samon-cho Shinjuku-ku
Tokyo 160-0017 JAPAN
+813/3358-2882
FAX: +813/3358-2289

AMOUNT: 600,000 Yen

DEADLINE(S): APR 30

FIELD(S): All fields of study

Scholarships for graduate study, postgraduate study, or career support. Must have affiliation with the International Federation of University Women. A plan of study or research which will advance the applicant's professional competence and which requires to be undertaken in Japan must be available.

Not renewable. Contact Fumiko Inoue at JAUW for an application.

3636 — JAPANESE GOVERNMENT (Monbusho Research Student Scholarships)

350 S. Grand Ave., Suite 1700
Los Angeles CA 90071
213/617-6700, ext. 338
FAX: 213/617-6728
Internet: embjapan.org/la

AMOUNT: Tuition + $1,400-$1,800/month

DEADLINE(S): AUG

FIELD(S): All fields of study

Scholarships for one-and-a-half or two years of graduate study in Japan. Must be under 35 years of age. Awards also include Japanese language training, round-trip airfare, partly subsidized housing expenses, one-time arrival allowance, and partly subsidized medical expenses.

For more information or an application, contact Mr. Cory Crocker, Consulate General of Japan, Information and Culture Center at above address.

3637 — JESSE MARVIN UNRUH ASSEMBLY FELLOWSHIP PROGRAM

6000 J St.
Sacramento CA 95819-6081
916/324-1761

AMOUNT: $1,707 monthly stipend + health, vision, and dental benefits

DEADLINE(S): FEB 1

FIELD(S): All fields of study

Graduate fellowships with California Assembly. Must have completed a BA or BS degree by the time the fellowship year begins in October. Fellowships are full-time employment with the California Assembly for 11 months.

Fellows earn a maximum of 12 units of graduate course credit. NO SCHOLARSHIPS are awarded. Write for complete information.

3638 — JEWISH FAMILY AND CHILDREN'S SERVICES (College Loan Fund)
1600 Scott St.
San Francisco CA 94115
415/561-1226

AMOUNT: $5,000 maximum (student loan)

DEADLINE(S): None

FIELD(S): All fields of study

Open to worthy college students of the Jewish faith with limited resources but with a demonstrated ability to repay. Must be U.S. permanent resident and living in San Francisco, San Mateo, Santa Clara, Marin, or Sonoma County, California.

Guarantors or co-makers are required but not collateral. Repayment terms flexible; interest usually set at 80% of current prime rate. Contact local JFCS office for forms and complete information.

3639 — JEWISH FAMILY AND CHILDREN'S SERVICES (Fogel Loan Fund)
1600 Scott St.
San Francisco CA 94115
415/561-1226

AMOUNT: Varies

DEADLINE(S): None

FIELD(S): All fields of study

Loans to help individuals of all ages for college or vocational studies and for personal, business, or professional purposes. Applicant must be a U.S. permanent resident of Jewish faith and have a sound plan for repayment.

Must be a resident of San Francisco, San Mateo, Santa Clara, Marin, or Sonoma counties, California. Guarantor or co-makers required but no collateral is needed. Contact JFCS office for complete information.

3640 — JEWISH FAMILY AND CHILDREN'S SERVICES (Jacob Rassen Memorial Scholarship Fund)
1600 Scott St.
San Francisco CA 94115
415/561-1226

AMOUNT: Up to $2,000

DEADLINE(S): None

FIELD(S): Study trip to Israel

Open to Jewish students under age 22 who demonstrate academic achievement and financial need and the desire to enhance Jewish identity and increase knowledge of & connection to Israel. Must be U.S. permanent resident.

The opportunity to travel and study in Israel. Must reside in San Francisco, San Mateo, Santa Clara, Marin, or Sonoma counties in California. Contact local JFCS office for forms and complete information.

3641 — JEWISH FAMILY AND CHILDREN'S SERVICES (Stanley Olson Youth Scholarship Fund)
1600 Scott St.
San Francisco CA 94115
415/561-1226

AMOUNT: Up to $2,500

DEADLINE(S): None

FIELD(S): All fields of study (preference to liberal arts majors)

Open to undergrad or grad students of Jewish faith who are 25 or younger; have demonstrated academic achievement and financial need and have been accepted for enrollment in a college or university. Must be U.S. permanent resident.

Must reside in San Francisco, San Mateo, Santa Clara, Marin, or Sonoma County CA. Contact local JFCS office for applications and complete information.

3642 — JEWISH SOCIAL SERVICE AGENCY OF METROPOLITAN WASHINGTON (Loan Fund)
6123 Montrose Road
Rockville MD 20852
301/881-3700

AMOUNT: Up to $2,000

DEADLINE(S): Ongoing

FIELD(S): All fields of study

Open to Jewish applicants 18 or older who are within eighteen months of completing an undergraduate or graduate degree or a vocational training program and are residents of the Washington metropolitan area. No-interest loan based on financial need.

A one-time award. U.S. citizen or permanent resident who will seek citizenship. Recipient must agree to a stipulation to pay $50 per month within three months after graduation. Write for complete information.

3643 — JEWISH VOCATIONAL SERVICE (JVS) (Community Scholarship Fund)
5700 Wilshire Blvd., Suite 2303
Los Angeles CA 90036
213/761-8888 Ext. 122
FAX: 213/761-8850

AMOUNT: Up to $2,000

DEADLINE(S): APR 15 (March 1 for application requests)

FIELD(S): All fields of study

For undergraduate students who are sophomores or higher, graduate or professional students, or students pursuing vocational training. Must be Jewish permanent residents of Los Angeles County, California with financial need, U.S. citizens or permanent residents, and are in a full-time course of study in an accredited institution.

Renewable annually. Preference given to students in California schools. Call or write for application.

3644 — JOHN D. AND CATHERINE T. MACARTHUR FOUNDATION (Fellows Program)
140 S. Dearborn St.
Chicago IL 60603
312/726-8000
TDD: 312/920-6285
FAX: 312/920-6258
Internet: www.macfdn.org

AMOUNT: $30,000-$75,000/yr. + health insurance

DEADLINE(S): None

FIELD(S): All fields of study

Provides unrestricted fellowships to exceptionally talented and promising individuals who have shown evidence of originality, dedication to creative pursuits, and capacity for self-direction. Awards income over five years so that fellows devote themselves to endeavors at their own pace. Applicants may be writers, scientists, artists, social scientists, humanists, activists, or workers in any other field, with or without institutional affiliations.

No proposals or applications required; award is to support individuals, not projects. Must be nominated by one of over 100 designated nominators across the US. See website or contact MacArthur Foundation for details.

3645 — JOHN GYLES EDUCATION FUND (Scholarships)
PO Box 4808
712 Riverside Dr.
Fredericton, New Brunswick E3B 5G4
CANADA
506/459-7460

AMOUNT: $3,000 (max.)

DEADLINE(S): APR 1; JUN 1; NOV 15

FIELD(S): All fields of study

Financial assistance for full-time postsecondary students who are citizens of either the US or Canada. Minimum GPA of 2.7 required. Criteria other than strictly academic ability and financial need are considered.

To receive application, please send ONLY a stamped (US 33cents)*, business-sized (#10), self-addressed envelope to The Secretary at above address. *US postage acceptable due to use of international mail services.

3646 — JOHN SIMON GUGGENHEIM MEMORIAL FOUNDATION (Fellowships)

90 Park Ave.
New York NY 10016
212/687-4470
FAX: 212/697-3248
E-Mail: fellowships@gf.org
Internet: www.gf.org

AMOUNT: $32,000 (average)

DEADLINE(S): OCT 1 (US & Canada); DEC 1 (Latin America & Caribbean)

FIELD(S): All fields of study

For postdoctoral/mid-career citizens and permanent residents of the US, Canada, Latin America, and the Caribbean. Fellowships are awarded to men and women who have already demonstrated exceptional capacity for productive scholarship or exceptional creative ability in the arts, irrespective of race, color, or creed.

200 awards annually. Not renewable. Contact the Guggenheim Foundation for an application.

3647 — JOHN T. HALL TRUST

P.O. Box 4655
Atlanta GA 30302-4655
Written inquiry

AMOUNT: Varies

DEADLINE(S): Ongoing

FIELD(S): All areas of study

Student loans to residents of Georgia for undergraduate and graduate education.

Write to Miss Dale Welch, c/o SunTrust Bank, Atlanta, at above address for application details.

3648 — JULIA HENRY FUND (Fellowships at Harvard and Yale Universities)

The Old Schools
Cambridge CB2 ENGLAND UK
Written request

AMOUNT: $15,535 + travel grant, tuition, health insurance

DEADLINE(S): DEC 5

FIELD(S): All fields of study

Scholarships for unmarried citizens under age 26 of the U.K./British Commonwealth to study at Harvard or Yale in the U.S. (One at each.) Undergraduates must have completed at least six terms in a U.K. university; graduates must be in their first year of study in a U.K. university. Recipients are expected to return to the British Isles or some part of the Commonwealth at the expiration of their term of tenure.

Request details and application forms from Dr. A. Clark, Secretary of the Trustees, University Registry, at above address.

3649 — KANSAS BOARD OF REGENTS (Ethnic Minority Graduate Fellowship)

700 SW Harrison St., Ste. 1410
Topeka KS 66603-3760
785/296-3517

AMOUNT: $8,000/yr. minimum

DEADLINE(S): Varies

FIELD(S): All fields of study

Created to encourage full-time enrollment in Kansas graduate programs by students who are Kansas residents and identified as ethnic minorities (American Indian/Alaskan Native, Asian/Pacific Islander, Black, or Hispanic). Students must secure employment in a Kansas educational institution upon graduation, working one year for each year of support, or repay the fellowship at 15% interest.

Contact your graduate school for an application.

3650 — KANSAS BOARD OF REGENTS (Kansas Comprehensive Grants)

700 SW Harrison St., Ste. 1410
Topeka KS 66603-3760
785/296-3518
FAFSA: 800/433-3243
Internet: www.fafsa.ed.gov

AMOUNT: $200-$2,500 (private); $100-$1,100 (public)

DEADLINE(S): APR 1

FIELD(S): All fields of study

Available to needy Kansas residents enrolled full-time at the seventeen private colleges/universities located in Kansas, the six public universities, and Washburn University. The Kansas Legislature provides limited assistance to financially needy students. To be considered, you must complete and submit the FAFSA, listing one or more eligible colleges in Step 5.

1 in 5 eligible students are funded annually. See website or contact your financial aid office for a copy of the FAFSA.

3651 — KANSAS BOARD OF REGENTS (Kansas Distinguished Scholarship Program)

700 SW Harrison St., Ste. 1410
Topeka KS 66603-3760
785/296-3517

AMOUNT: Varies

DEADLINE(S): Varies

FIELD(S): All fields of study

Created to encourage Kansas Brasenose, Chevening, Fulbright, Madison, Marshall, Mellon, Rhodes, and Truman scholars to continue graduate studies at Kansas public universities. Kansas reimburses tuition and fees to recipients subject to funding constraints.

Contact Kansas Board of Regents for an application.

3652 — KANSAS COMMISSION ON VETERANS' AFFAIRS (Scholarships)

700 SW Jackson St. #701
Topeka KS 66603
913/296-3976

AMOUNT: Free tuition and fees in state supported institutions

DEADLINE(S): Varies

FIELD(S): All areas of study

Open to dependent child of person who entered U.S. military service as a resident of Kansas & was prisoner of war, missing, or killed in action or died as a result of service-connected disabilities incurred during service in Vietnam.

Application must be made prior to enrollment. Renewable to maximum of 12 semesters. Write for complete information.

3653 — KANSAS STATE UNIVERSITY FOUNDATION (Various Scholarships)

Office of Student Financial Assistance, 104 Fairchild Hall
Manhattan KS 66506-1104
785/532-6420
FAX: 785/532-7628
E-Mail: ksusfa@ksu.edu
Internet: www.found.ksu.edu/Schshps/Sch-txt.htm

AMOUNT: Varies

DEADLINE(S): Varies

FIELD(S): All fields of study

More than 1,300 scholarships are administered by the KSU Foundation for students attending KSU at either the Manhattan or Salina campus.

Salina campus address: Office of Student Financial Assistance, 223 College Center, Salina, KS 67401; Phone: 785/826-2638; FAX: 785/826-2936; E-mail: Hheter@mail.sal.ksu.edu. Website above is the same for Salina.

3654 — KENNEDY FOUNDATION (Scholarships)

P.O. Box 27296
Denver CO 80227
303/933-2435

AMOUNT: Approx. $1,000

DEADLINE(S): JUN 30

FIELD(S): All fields of study

Scholarships for Colorado residents attending colleges or universities.

Send SASE to Jacqueline Kennedy, Vice President, at above location for application information.

3655 — KENNEDY MEMORIAL TRUST (Kennedy Scholarships)

16 Great College Street
London SW1P 3RX ENGLAND
171-222-1151

AMOUNT: Tuition; travel expenses; health insurance; stipend

DEADLINE(S): NOV 1

FIELD(S): Political Science; Public Service; Government; Arts & Sciences

Scholarships tenable in U.S. at Harvard or MIT. Open to United Kingdom citizens who are recent graduates or are currently studying for a 1st or higher degree & have spent 2 of the last five years at their university in Britain.

In awarding scholarships the trustees will take into consideration qualities of personal character as well as intellectual attainment and promise. Write for complete information.

3656 — KENNEDY MEMORIAL TRUST (Scholarships at Harvard and the Massachusetts Institute of Technology)

16 Great College Street
London SW1P ENGLAND UK
0171 222 1151
Internet: www.admin.cam.ac.uk/reporter/1997-8/special/07/94.html

AMOUNT: $15,000 stipend + travel and tuition

DEADLINE(S): OCT 24

FIELD(S): All fields of study

Scholarships in honor of John F. Kennedy for U.K. citizens, normally residents of the U.K., tenable in the U.S. at Harvard or MIT. The disciplines of humane studies, economics, and modern technology are favored. Business administration students must have completed two years' full-time employment in business or public service. Those studying for a first degree must be in final year during appliacation year.

Up to 12 annual awards. A one-year program; however, M.A. and Ph.D. candidates may apply for various positions, such as research or teaching assistants. See website for details.

3657 — KENTUCKY CENTER FOR VETERANS AFFAIRS (Benefits for Veterans' Dependents, Spouses, & Widows)

545 S. 3rd St., Room 123
Louisville KY 40202

502/595-4447
FAX: 502/595-4448

AMOUNT: Varies

DEADLINE(S): None

FIELD(S): All fields of study

Kentucky residents. Open to dependent children, spouses, and non-remarried widows of permanently and totally disabled war veterans who served during periods of federally recognized hostilities or who were MIA or a POW.

Veteran must be a resident of KY or, if deceased, a resident at time of death.

3658 — KENTUCKY HIGHER EDUCATION ASSISTANCE AUTHORITY (Student Loan Program)

1050 US-127 South, Suite 102
Frankfort KY 40601-4323
502/564-7990 or 800/928-8926

AMOUNT: $2625 to $18,500 (amount varies according to academic standing and whether student is dependent or independent)

DEADLINE(S): Varies

FIELD(S): All fields of study

Open to U.S. citizens or legal residents enrolled or accepted for enrollment (on at least a half-time basis) at an eligible postsecondary educational institution.

Write for complete information.

3659 — KEY BANK OF CENTRAL MAINE FOUNDATION

P.O. Box 1054
Augusta ME 04330
Written inquiry

AMOUNT: Varies

DEADLINE(S): Ongoing

FIELD(S): All fields of study

Scholarships for individuals to attend Main colleges and universities.

Send SASE to Key Bank of Maine at above address.

3660 — KNIGHTS OF COLUMBUS (Graduate Fellowships)

Catholic University of America
Room 110 McMahon Hall NE
Washington DC 20064
202/319-5185

AMOUNT: $5,000 stipend + full tuition

DEADLINE(S): FEB 1

FIELD(S): All fields of study

MUST qualify for admission to Catholic University of America graduate school and become a graduate degree candidate there. Must satisfy all university regulations.

Unspecified number of fellowships. Renewable. Write for complete information.

3661 — KNIGHTS TEMPLAR EDUCATIONAL FOUNDATION (Special Low-Interest Loans)

5097 N. Elston, Suite 101
Chicago IL 60630-2460
312/777-3300

AMOUNT: $6,000 maximum per student

DEADLINE(S): Varies

FIELD(S): All fields of study

Special low-interest loans (5% fixed rate). No payments while in school. Interest and repayments start after graduation or when you leave school. Open to voc-tech students or junior/senior undergraduate students or graduate students.

US citizen or legal resident. Request information from Charles R. Neumann (Grand Recorder-Secretary). Call or write to your state's grand commandery for proper application.

3662 — KOOMRUIAN EDUCATION FUND

3333 South Beaudry Ave., Box 16
Los Angeles, CA 90017-1466
Written inquiry

AMOUNT: Varies

DEADLINE(S): None specified

FIELD(S): All fields of study

Scholarships to students of Armenian descent residing in California.

Send SASE to Bank of America at above location.

3663 — KOSCIUSZKO FOUNDATION (Grants/ Fellowships to Polish Citizens for Study/ Teaching in the U.S.)

15 East 65th Street
New York NY 10021-6595
212/734-2130
FAX: 212/628-4552
E-Mail: thekf@pegasusnet.com
Internet: www.kosciuszkofoundaiton.org/grants/polish.htm

AMOUNT: $6,000-$25,000

DEADLINE(S): OCT 15

FIELD(S): All fields of study

Fellowships for postgraduate scholars, professionals, or artists with doctoral degrees. Grants are for those without doctoral degrees; M.A. is required. For Polish citizens living in Poland who wish to study in the U.S. Must have excellent command of English. Stipend covers housing, living costs, health and accident insurance, and travel.

Grants are for three to ten months, are not renewable, and don't cover tuition. Write for complete information to New York or Warsaw office or visit website. Warsaw address is Ul. Nowy Swiat 4, Room 118; 00-497 Warsxaws, Poland. Phone/fax: (48) (22) 621-7067.

3664 — KOSCIUSZKO FOUNDATION (Tuition Scholarships)

15 East 65th Street
New York NY 10021-6595
212/734-2130
FAX: 212/628-4552
Internet: www.kosciuszkofoundation.org/grants/tuitapp.htm

AMOUNT: $1,000-$5,000

DEADLINE(S): JAN 16

FIELD(S): All fields of study

Open to full-time graduate students of Polish descent who are U.S. citizens or permanent U.S. residents. Some scholarships are available for juniors and seniors.

There is a non-refundable $25 application fee. Candidates who are at least associate members of the Foundation are exempt from the application fee. Application is on website. Write or access website for complete information.

3665 — LADY DAVIS FELLOWSHIP TRUST (Graduate Fellowships)

Hebrew University, Givat Ram
Jerusalem 91904 ISRAEL
972-2-651-2306 (voice mail) or 972-2-658-4723
FAX: 972-2-566-3848
E-Mail: ldft@vms.huji.ac.il
Internet: http://sites.snunit.k12/ldft

AMOUNT: Travel, tuition, and reasonable living expenses

DEADLINE(S): NOV 30

FIELD(S): All areas of study

Fellowships for visiting professors, postdoctoral researchers, and doctoral students at the Hebrew University of Jerusalem and at the Technion, Israel Institute of Technology, Haifa. For scholars from any field of study, of any age, and from any region.

An opportunity to enjoy a young, world-class academic environment in a fascinating country.

3666 — LARAMIE COUNTY FARM BUREAU (Scholarships)

206 Main St.
Box 858
Pine Bluffs WY 82082-0858
Written Inquiry

AMOUNT: $300

DEADLINE(S): MAY 1

FIELD(S): All fields of study

Available to needy high school seniors and college students whose parents have been members of Laramie County Farm Bureau for more than one year and who are current members. Award may be used at any institution of postsecondary education. Interviews will be done by appointment.

3 awards annually. Write to above address for an application.

3667 — LEGACY SOCCER FOUNDATION, INC./ LEVER BROTHERS (Endowed Scholarships)

P.O. Box 3481
Winter Park FL 32790
407/263-8285
FAX: 407/740-8406
Internet: www.legacysoc.org

AMOUNT: Varies

DEADLINE(S): Varies

FIELD(S): All fields of study

Scholarships for Florida residents of either Brevard, Orange, Osceola, Seminole, or Volusa counties. Must be a U.S. citizen with a high school GPA of at least 2.5. Must graduate in top 1/3 of class and have played organized soccer for two out of past five years. Must meet financial aid requirements of the institution. Tenable at institutions in those same five counties.

Contact financial aid office at either Brevard Community College Foundation, Florida Tech, Seminole Community College, Valencia Community College Foundation, or Univ. of Central Florida for more information.

3668 — LEON M. JORDAN SCHOLARSHIP AND MONUMENT FUND

Box 15544
Kansas City MO 64106
Written inquiry

AMOUNT: Varies

DEADLINE(S): Varies

FIELD(S): All fields of study

Scholarships to residents of Missouri.

Write to Alexander Ellison, Treasurer, Advisory Committee, at above address for application details.

3669 — LEOPOLD SCHEPP FOUNDATION (Graduate Awards)

551 Fifth Ave., Suite 3000
New York NY 10176-2597
212/986-3078

AMOUNT: Up to $7,500

DEADLINE(S): None given

FIELD(S): All fields of study

Open to graduate students aged 40 or younger for full-time study at accredited colleges or universities.

Write detailing education to date, year in school, length of course of study, vocational goal, financial need, age, citizenship, and availability for interview in New York City.

200 awards per year. Applicant will not be considered who has only the dissertation to complete. Renewable with reapplication. Send SASE with above information for application.

3670 — LEOPOLD SCHEPP FOUNDATION (Post-doctoral Awards)

551 Fifth Ave., Suite 3000
New York NY 10176-2597
212/986-3078

AMOUNT: Up to $7,500

DEADLINE(S): None given

FIELD(S): All fields of study

Post-doctoral awards. For independent study and research in fields which will improve the general welfare of mankind. US citizenship or legal residency required.

Interested persons should inquire as to the availability of grants in their chosen field of study.

3671 — LINCOLN UNIVERSITY (Scholarships & Prizes)

PO Box 94
Canterbury NEW ZEALAND
(64) (3) 325 2811
FAX: (64) (3) 325 3850

AMOUNT: Varies

DEADLINE(S): Varies

FIELD(S): All fields of study

Hundreds of scholarships, bursaries, and prizes listed in the handbook published by Lincoln University, New Zealand. All fields of study, many for exchange students and travel, as well as for studying abroad.

Write to The Registrar, Lincoln University, at above address for booklet, "Scholarships and Prizes."

3672 — LLOYD D. SWEET SCHOLARSHIP FOUNDATION (Scholarships)

Box 638 (Attn: Academic year)
Chinook MT 59523
406/357-2236

AMOUNT: Varies

DEADLINE(S): MAR 2

FIELD(S): All fields of study

Scholarships open to graduates of Chinook (MT) High School. Awards are for full-time undergraduate or graduate study at accredited colleges and universities in the US.

Approximately 75 awards per year. Write for complete information.

3673 — LUBBOCK AREA FOUNDATION, INC. (Scholarships)

1655 Main St., #209
Lubbock TX 79401
806/762-8061
FAX: 806/762-8551
E-Mail: lubaf@worldnet.att.net

AMOUNT: Varies

DEADLINE(S): Varies

FIELD(S): All fields of study

Several scholarships are administered by this Foundation for residents of the Lubbock, Texas, area. Some are for graduates of specific high schools, some are for use at specific institutions, and one is for women age 50+.

Contact organization for specifics.

3674 — LUCY E. MEILLER EDUCATIONAL TRUST

P.O. Box 13888
Roanoke VA 24038
Written inquiry

AMOUNT: $3,000

DEADLINE(S): Ongoing

FIELD(S): All fields of study

Scholarships for financially needy residents of Virginia to attend colleges and universities.

Apply through the financial aid office the the Virginia college or university or contact Perry Gorham, Crestar Bank, at above address for details.

3675 — LULAC (LEAGUE OF UNITED LATIN AMERICAN CITIZENS) (National Scholarship Fund)

1133 20th St., NW, Ste. 750
Washington DC 20036
202/408-0060
FAX: 202/408-0064
Internet: www.lulac.org/

AMOUNT: Varies

DEADLINE(S): Varies

FIELD(S): All fields of study

Open to high school seniors, undergraduate, and graduate college students of Hispanic origin. Some are for specific fields of study such as business or engineering, and some have certain GPA requirments.

See high school counselor or send self-addressed stamped envelope for complete information. Application and E-mail info. is also on website.

3676 — LUTHERAN BROTHERHOOD (Stafford Student Loans)

625 Fourth Ave. South
Minneapolis MN 55415
800/328-7168

AMOUNT: $2,625-$8,500

DEADLINE(S): None

FIELD(S): All fields of study

Loans open to Lutheran students on a first-come, first-served basis who have been accepted for admission by an eligible higher education institution and are making satisfactory progress. Must meet federal requirements.

Contact address above for complete information.

3677 — LaFETRA OPERATING FOUNDATION (Fellowships for Training of Volunteers Abroad)

1221 Preservation Park Way
#100
Oakland CA 94612-1216
510/763-9206
FAX: 510/763-9290
E-Mail: fellowship@lafetra.org
Internet: www.lafetra.org

AMOUNT: Stipend for internship + travel & program costs

DEADLINE(S): DEC 18

FIELD(S): All fields of study

An internship in SF Bay Area, CA, to learn skills in volunteering, and a fellowship for living and working in another country. Open to persons of color, individuals who demonstrate financial need, and adult professionals in various fields. Applicants from the Bay Area are preferred because housing/transportation for SF training cannot be provided for persons outside that area, but those who can provide their own housing/transportation in SF are welcome to apply.

See website or contact above address for an application/more information.

3678 — MAINE COMMUNITY FOUNDATION (Scholarship Program)

P.O. Box 148
Ellsworth ME 04605
207/667-9735

AMOUNT: Varies

DEADLINE(S): Varies

FIELD(S): Varied fields of study

All scholarships are available to Maine residents only. The Maine Community Foundation offers over 80 scholarships, covering a wide range of fields of study. Interested applicants should contact the MCF for a complete listing of its scholarships and an application.

Write to the Nancy Eveld, Scholarship Coordinator, at the above address for complete information.

3679 — MAKARIOS SCHOLARSHIP FUND, INC. (Scholarships)

13 East 40th Street
New York NY 10016
212/696-4590 or 800/775-7217

AMOUNT: Varies

DEADLINE(S): MAY 5

FIELD(S): All fields of study

For students from Cyprus with valid student visas who are pursuing studies in an accredited United States college or university on a full-time basis. Includes Theodore & Wally Lappas Award and Thomas & Elaine Kyrus Endowment.

Financial need determines award. Applications must be typewritten and include various documents—please write or call for complete information.

3680 — MANITOBA STUDENT FINANCIAL ASSISTANCE PROGRAM

409 - 1181 Portage Avenue
Winnipeg Manitoba R3G OT3 CANADA
800/204-1685

AMOUNT: Varies

DEADLINE(S): Varies

FIELD(S): All fields of study

For Manitoba residents taking 60% + of full-course load (college/university) or 100% for private vocational schools. Must be Canadian citizen/permanent resident. May apply for assistance to attend out-of-country provided meet eligibility criteria. Funds include loans & other federal/provincial assistance, some of which is non-repayable. Assistance is also provided for Canadian aboriginal students, students w/ dependents, part-time stuents, & students w/ disabilities.

12,500 awards annually. Write for an application.

3681 — MARIN EDUCATIONAL FUND (Undergraduate Scholarship Program)

1010 'B' St., Suite 300
San Rafael CA 94901
415/459-4240

AMOUNT: $800 - $2,000

DEADLINE(S): MAR 2

FIELD(S): All fields of study

Open to Marin County (CA) residents only for undergraduate study in 2- or 4-year colleges and for fifth-year teaching credentials. Must be enrolled at least half-time and demonstrate financial need.

Write for complete information.

3682 — MARINE CORPS TANKERS ASSOCIATION (John Cornelius Memorial Scholarship)

1112 Alpine Heights Road
Alpine CA 91901-2814
619/445-8423

AMOUNT: $1,500+

DEADLINE(S): MAR 15

FIELD(S): All fields of study

Must be a survivor, a dependent, or under legal guardianship of a Marine Tanker—active duty, reserve, retired, or honorably discharged—who served in a Marine Tank unit OR be a Marine or Navy Corpsman who *personally* qualifies in the foregoing. Must be a member of MCTA, or will join. May apply as a high school senior, undergraduate, or graduate student. Letters of recommendation, transcripts, and personal narrative required with application.

12 awards annually. Renewable with reapplication. Notification by the end of April. Contact Phil Morell, Scholarship Chairman, for an application.

3683 — MARK R. FUSCO FOUNDATION

P.O. Box 9618
New Haven CT 06535
203/777-7451

AMOUNT: Varies

DEADLINE(S): Ongoing

FIELD(S): All fields of study

Scholarships for students who are residents of Connecticut for all academic fields. Acceptance based on academic record, SAT/ACT scores, financial need, and recommendations from instructors.

Write to Paul Morris, Secretary-Treasurer, at above address.

3684 — MARY E. HODGES FUND

222 Tauton Ave.
East Providence RI 02914-4556
401/435-4650

AMOUNT: Varies

DEADLINE(S): MAY 1

FIELD(S): All fields of study

Scholarships for sutdents who have a Rhode Island Masonic affiliation or who have been residents of Rhode Island for at least five years.

Send SASE to John M. Faulhaber, Secretary, at above address for details.

3685 — MARYLAND HIGHER EDUCATION COMMISSION (Delegate Scholarships)

State Scholarship Admin.
16 Francis St.
Annapolis MD 21401-1781

410/974-5370
TTY: 800/735-2258

AMOUNT: Varies: $200 minimum

DEADLINE(S): Varies

FIELD(S): All fields of study

For Maryland residents who are undergraduate or graduate students in Maryland (or out-of-state with a unique major). Must be U.S. citizen.

Duration is up to 4 years; 2-4 scholarships per district. Also for full- or part-time study at certain private career schools and diploma schools of nursing. Write to your delegate for complete information.

3686 — MARYLAND HIGHER EDUCATION COMMISSION (Edward T. Conroy Memorial Scholarships)

State Scholarship Admin.
16 Francis St.
Annapolis MD 21401-1781
410/974-5370
TTY: 800/735-2258

AMOUNT: Up to $3,800 for tuition and mandatory fees

DEADLINE(S): JUL 15

FIELD(S): All fields of study

For sons and daughters of persons 100% disabled or killed in the line of military duty who were Maryland residents at the time of disability or death, to sons and daughters of MIAs or POWs, and to sons, daughters, and un-remarried spouses of public safety employees disabled or killed in the line of duty. Also for 100%-disabled public safety employees.

For undergraduate or graduate study, full- or part-time, in an MD institution. Write for complete information.

3687 — MARYLAND HIGHER EDUCATION COMMISSION (Loan Assistance Repayment Program)

State Scholarship Admin.
16 Francis St.
Annapolis MD 21401-1781
410/974-5370
TTY: 800/735-2258

AMOUNT: Up to $7,500

DEADLINE(S): SEP 30

FIELD(S): Student loan repayment assistance

Open to employees of Maryland state or local government or non-profit organizations who have completed a degree at a Maryland institution. Priority given to those working in critical shortage employment fields.

Write for complete information.

3688 — MARYLAND HIGHER EDUCATION COMMISSION (Senatorial Scholarship Program)

State Scholarship Admin.
16 Francis St.
Annapolis MD 21401-1781
410/974-5370
TTY: 800/735-2258

AMOUNT: $400-$2,000

DEADLINE(S): MAR 1 (via FAFSA)

FIELD(S): All fields of study

Open to Maryland residents for undergrad or grad study at MD degree-granting institutions, certain private career schools, nursing diploma schools in Maryland. For full- or part-time study. SAT or ACT required for some applicants.

Students with unique majors or with impaired hearing may attend out of state. Duration is 1-4 years with automatic renewal until degree is granted. Senator selects recipients. Write for complete information.

3689 — MASSEY UNIVERSITY (Postdoctoral Fellowships)

Human Resources Section
Private Bag 11222
Palmerston North NEW ZEALAND
06/3569-099

AMOUNT: NZ$42,500-$44,000

DEADLINE(S): OCT 30

FIELD(S): All fields of study

Postdoctoral research fellowships open to applicants who hold a Ph.D degree. Awards are tenable at Massey University, New Zealand.

Up to 6 fellowships per year. Write for complete information.

3690 — MATSUMAE INTERNATIONAL FOUNDATION (Fellowships)

Rm.#6-002, New Marunouchi Bldg.
1-5-1, Marunouchi, Chiyoda-ku
Tokyo 100-0005 JAPAN
03-3214-7611
FAX: 03-3214-7613

AMOUNT: Airfare, insurance, lodging subsidy, & Y300,00 yen upon arrival + Y150,000 yen monthly stipend for tuition, expenses, research, meals & transportation

DEADLINE(S): JUL 31

FIELD(S): All fields of study

Must be of non-Japanese nationality, not over 40 years of age, & be able to communicate in either English or Japanese. Must either hold doctorate degree, or have minimum two years of research experience after receipt of Master's. Must not have been in Japan previously or be there at time of application. Must obtain acceptance from host institution before applying. Preference goes to fields of study such as natural science, engineering, and medicine.

20 awards annually. Contact Matsumae Foundation for an application packet.

3691 — MAY THOMPSON HENRY TRUST

P.O. Box 3448
Enid OK 73702
405/233-3535

AMOUNT: Varies

DEADLINE(S): Ongoing

FIELD(S): All fields of study

Scholarships for students attending state-supported Oklahoma colleges and universities.

Contact to Stella Knowles, Trust Officer, at Central National Bank & Trust Co. at above location for details.

3692 — MCDONALD'S (UNCF New York Tri-State Scholarships)

See your local McDonald's Tri-State restaurant

Internet: www.archingintoeducation.com/

AMOUNT: $1,000; $10,000

DEADLINE(S): MAR 31

FIELD(S): All fields of study

New York Tri-State residents (NYC, Long Island & specific counties in CT & NJ) who are planning to attend a United Negro College Fund institution are eligible.

50 $1,000 awards annually; 1 $10,000 award for a student demonstrating outstanding academic merit. Pick up an application in your local New York, New Jersey, or Connecticut McDonald's.

3693 — MERVYN'S (Kilmartin Educational Scholarship Program)

Mervyn's store
Apply in person

AMOUNT: Ask store manager

DEADLINE(S): Varies

FIELD(S): All fields of study

Scholarships for employees of Mervyn's stores who have accumulated at least 1,000 hours of employment with Mervyn's and have graduated from high school or an equivalent. Available nationwide.

Recipients are eligible to reapply.

3694 — MICHIGAN COMMISSION ON INDIAN AFFAIRS; MICHIGAN DEPT OF CIVIL RIGHTS (Tuition Waiver Program)

201 N. Washington Sq., Ste. 700
Lansing MI 48933
517/373-0654

AMOUNT: Tuition (only) waiver

DEADLINE(S): Varies (8 weeks prior to class registration)

FIELD(S): All areas

Open to any Michigan resident who is at least 1/4 North American Indian (certified by their tribal nation) & willing to attend any public Michigan community college, college, or university.

Award is for all levels of study and is renewable. Must be Michigan resident for at least 12 months before class registration. Write for complete information.

3695 — MICHIGAN GUARANTY AGENCY (Stafford and PLUS Loans)

P.O. Box 30047
Lansing MI 48909
1-800/642-5626
FAX: 517/335-6703

AMOUNT: Varies

DEADLINE(S): None

FIELD(S): All fields of study

Guaranteed student loans available to students or parents of students who are Michigan residents enrolled in an eligible institution.

Write for complete information.

3696 — MICHIGAN HIGHER EDUCATION ASSISTANCE AUTHORITY (Michigan Tuition Grants)

Office of Scholarships and Grants
P.O. Box 30462
Lansing MI 48909
517/373-3394

AMOUNT: $100 - $2,450

DEADLINE(S): Varies

FIELD(S): All fields of study (except BRE degree)

Open to Michigan residents enrolled at least half time at independent non-profit Michigan institutions (List available from above address). Both undergraduate and graduate students who can demonstrate financial need are eligible.

Grants renewable. Applicants must file the FAFSA form. Write for complete information.

3697 — MICHIGAN SOCIETY OF FELLOWS (Postdoctoral Fellowships in the Humanities & Arts, Sciences, and Professions)

Univ Michigan
3030 Rackham Bldg.
915 E. Washington St.
Ann Arbor MI 48109-1070
734/763-1259
E-Mail: society.of.fellows@umich.edu
Internet: www.rackham.umich.edu/Faculty/society.htm

AMOUNT: $36,000 annual stipend

DEADLINE(S): OCT 9

FIELD(S): Humanities; Arts; Social/Physical/Life Sciences; Professions

3-year fellowships at University of Michigan for postdoctorates near beginning of their careers selected for outstanding achievement, professional promise, & interdisciplinary interests. Fellows appointed as Assistant Professors/Research Scientists & as Postdoctoral Scholars in the Society. Should be in residence in Ann Arbor during fellowship, teach equivalent of one academic year, participate in Society, and devote time to research/artistic projects.

4 awards annually. Contact the Michigan Society of Fellows for an application. Final selections made in January.

3698 — MIDWEST STUDENT EXCHANGE PROGRAM (Tuition Reduction)

Minnesota Higher Education Office
550 Cedar St., Ste. 400
St. Paul MN 55101
612/626-8288
FAX: 612/626-8290

AMOUNT: Up to $2,500 tuition reduction

DEADLINE(S): FEB 1

FIELD(S): All fields of study

At least 10% reduction in out-of-state tuition for residents of Kansas, Michigan, Minnesota, Missouri, and Nebraska who attend participating institutions in those same states.

Contact your high school counselor or the Office of Admissions at the college you plan to attend for a list of participating institutions. When applying to a college, mark prominently on the form that you seek admission as a MSEP student.

3699 — MILITARY ORDER OF THE PURPLE HEART (Sons, Daughters, and Grandchildren Scholarship Program)

National Headquarters
5413-B Backlick Rd.
Springfield VA 22151
703/642-5360
FAX: 703/642-2054

AMOUNT: $1,000 per year (4 years maximum)

DEADLINE(S): MAR 15

FIELD(S): All fields of study

Open to children and grandchildren of Military Order of Purple Heart Members or Purple Heart Recipients. For full-time study at any level by US citizen or legal resident. Must demonstrate academic achievement and financial need.

Renewable for up to 4 years provided a 3.5 GPA is maintained. $5. processing fee. Write for complete information.

3700 — MINISTERIO DE ASUNTOS EXTERIORES (Scholarships)

US Student Programs Div., Inst. of Int. Ed., 809 United Nations Plaza
New York, NY 10017
212-984-5465

AMOUNT: Varies

DEADLINE(S): None

FIELD(S): All fields of study

Scholarships are available to graduate students at centers of higher education that are under the ministry of education and science. Applicants need good knowledge of Spanish. Award includes free tuition; medical and life insurance.

Administered by the Fulbright Commission. Applicants should contact Fulbright Commission on campus or write to the above address for complete information.

3701 — MINISTRY OF EDUCATION AND TRAINING; ONTARIO STUDENT ASSISTANCE PROGRAM (OSAP)

P.O. Box 4500
189 Red River Rd.
4th Floor
Thunder Bay, Ontario P7B 6G9 CANADA
807/343-7260
TDD 800/465-3958

AMOUNT: Varies

DEADLINE(S): Varies

FIELD(S): All areas of study

OSAP offers Federal and provincial loans to Canadian citizens or residents who live in Ontario and are enrolled in an approved Ontario college, university, or private postsecondary institution.

Bursaries are available to students with disabilities/ children. Write for information.

3702 — MINNESOTA HIGHER EDUCATION SERVICES OFFICE (Minnesota Indian Scholarship Program)

Indian Education, 1819 Bemidji Ave.
Bemidji MN 56601
218/755-2926

AMOUNT: Average $1,450/year

DEADLINE(S): None

FIELD(S): All fields of study

For Minnesota residents who are one-fourth or more Indian ancestry and members of or eligible for membership in a tribe. Must be high school graduates or GED recipients and be accepted by an approved college, university, or vocational school in Minnesota, and approved by the Minnesota Indian Scholarship Committee. Apply as early as possible before starting your post-high school program.

Indian students also must apply to federally funded grant programs, including the Pell Grant Program, their respective tribal anency, and the Minnesota Grant Program. Contact Joe Aitken at the above location.

3703 — MINNESOTA HIGHER EDUCATION SERVICES OFFICE (Scholarships, Grants, Loans, and Work-Study Programs)

Capitol Square Bldg., Suite 400
550 Cedar St.
St. Paul MN 55101
612/296-3974
FAX: 612/297-8880
E-Mail: info@heso.state.mn.us
Internet: www.heso.state.mn.us/

AMOUNT: Varies

DEADLINE(S): None specified

FIELD(S): All fields of study

Grants, scholarships, and loans for Minnesota residents to attend colleges and universities. Includes summer programs at college campuses for grades 7-12. Most programs require attendance at Minnesota institutions. High school juniors and seniors should begin planning ahead. Special programs for minorities, health fields, veterans and their dependents, and reciprocity for out-of-state tuition in certain other states.

Send for booklet "Focus on Financial Aid" at above address and/or check website.

3704 — MINNESOTA STATE DEPARTMENT OF VETERANS AFFAIRS (Veterans Grants)

Veterans Service Bldg.
20 W. 12th
2nd Floor
St. Paul MN 55155-2079
612/296-2562

AMOUNT: $350

DEADLINE(S): None

FIELD(S): All fields of study

Open to veterans who were residents of Minnesota at the time of their entry into the armed forces of the US and were honorably discharged after having served on active duty for at least 181 consecutive days. Must be US citizen/legal resident and planning to attend an accredited institution in Minnesota. Must also have time remaining on federal education period and have exhausted through use any federal educational entitlement. Must demonstrate financial need.

Contact the Minnesota State Department of Veterans Affairs for an application.

3705 — MONGOLIA SOCIETY (Dr. Gombojab Hangin Memorial Scholarship)

322 Goodbody Hall
Indiana Univ.
Bloomington IN 47405
812/855-4078
FAX: 812/855-7500
E-Mail: MONSOC@Indiana.edu

AMOUNT: $2,500

DEADLINE(S): JAN 1

FIELD(S): All fields of study

Open to students of Mongolian heritage (defined as an individual of Mongolian ethnic orgins who is a citizen of Mongolia, the People's Republic of China, or the former Soviet Union) to pursue studies in the U.S. Award does not include transportation from recipient's country to U.S. nor does it include room and board at university. Upon conclusion of the award year, recipient must write a report of his/her activities which resulted from receipt of the scholarship.

Recipient will receive scholarship monies in one lump sum after enrollment in the scholarship holder's institution in the U.S. Write for complete information.

3706 — MONGOLIA SOCIETY (Dr. Gombojab Hangin Memorial Scholarship)

322 Goodbody Hall
Indiana University
Bloomington IN 47405-7005
E-Mail: monsoc@indiana.edu

AMOUNT: up to $2,500

DEADLINE(S): JAN 1

FIELD(S): All fields of study

The scholarship is given to a student of Mongolian heritage (defined as an individual of Mongolian ethnic origins who has permanent residency in Mongolia, China, or the Former Soviet Union) to pursue studies in the US. Award will be made in competitive application. Does NOT include transportation, board, or lodging. Recipient will receive scholarship in one lump sum after enrollment, & must write report of activities which resulted from scholarship.

1 award annually. Each applicant must individually request the application in English, and the application must be returned written in English. Write to the Scholarship Committee at above address.

3707 — MORRIS SCHOLARSHIP FUND (Scholarships for Minorities in Iowa)

206 6th Ave., Suite 900
Des Moines IA 50309-4018
515/282-8192
FAX: 515/282-9117
E-Mail: morris@assoc-mgmt.com

Internet: www.assoc-mgmt.com/users/morris/ morris.html

AMOUNT: Varies

DEADLINE(S): FEB 1

FIELD(S): All fields of study

Program to provide fiancial assistance, motivation, and counseling for minority students pursuing higher education. Awards are based on academic achievement, community service, and financial need. Preference is given to Iowa residents attending an Iowa-based college or university.

Contact organization or check website for details.

3708 — MORTAR BOARD NATIONAL FOUNDATION (Fellowships)

1250 Chambers Road #170
Columbus OH 43212
614/488-4094

AMOUNT: $1,500

DEADLINE(S): JAN 31

FIELD(S): All fields of study

Fellowships are awarded only to Mortar Board members in good standing pursuing graduate or professional study.

At least 12 awards per year. Write for complete information.

3709 — MOTHER JOSEPH ROGAN MARYMOUNT FOUNDATION (Grant and Loan Programs)

c/o NationsBank
P.O. Box 14737
St. Louis MO 63101
314/391-6248

AMOUNT: $400 to $750

DEADLINE(S): MAY 1

FIELD(S): All fields of study

Grants and loans for students who are US citizens, live in the metropolitan St. Louis area, and are entering or enrolled in a high school, vocational/technical school, college, or university.

Applications are NOT accepted. Grants and loans are awarded by the administration and faculty of various St. Louis schools. Please do not send inquiries to this address. Contact your school for more information.

3710 — NAACP NATIONAL OFFICE (Agnes Jones Jackson Scholarship)

4805 Mt. Hope Dr.
Baltimore MD 21215
401/358-8900

AMOUNT: $1,500 undergrads; $2,500 grads

DEADLINE(S): APR 30

FIELD(S): All areas of study

Undergraduates must have GPA of 2.5+; graduates must possess 3.0 GPApplicants must be NAACP members and must be under the age of 25 by Apr. 30.

Send legal-size, self-addressed, stamped envelope to address above for application and complete information.

3711 — NATIONAL ALLIANCE FOR EXCELLENCE, INC. (National Scholarship Competition)

20 Thomas Avenue
Shrewsbury NJ 07702
732/747-0028
E-Mail: info@excellence.org
Internet: www.excellence.org

AMOUNT: $1,000-$5,000

DEADLINE(S): None

FIELD(S): All fields of study

National competition for merit-based scholarships, based entirely on talent & ability, NOT financial need. Students receive awards in presentation ceremonies with governors, senators, & other leaders. Must be US citizen attending or planning to attend college full-time. Four categories: Academic (must have minimum 3.7 GPA), Technological Innovations, Visual Arts (send 20 examples), & Performing Arts (send VHS of performance). Some require letters of recommendation.

$5 application fee required. See website for application form & complete eligibility, or write to above address.

3712 — NATIONAL ART MATERIALS TRADE ASSOCIATION (NAMTA Scholarships)

10115 Kincey Ave., Ste. 260
Huntersville NC 28078
704/948-5554
E-Mail: scholarships@namta.org

AMOUNT: $1,000

DEADLINE(S): MAR 1

FIELD(S): All fields of study

Open to undergraduate and graduate students who are employees or relatives of employees of a NAMTA member firm. Based on financial need, grades, activities, interests, and career goals.

Contact NAMTA for an application.

3713 — NATIONAL ASSOCIATION OF UNIVERSITY WOMEN (Fellowship Award)

1001 E. St. SE
Washington DC 20003-2847
Written inquiry

AMOUNT: $2,500

DEADLINE(S): APR 30

FIELD(S): All fields of study

Fellowship is offered by association in support of a woman who holds a master's degree and is enrolled in a program leading to a doctoral degree.

Priority is given to African-American women. Write for complete information.

3714 — NATIONAL CHAPTER OF CANADA IODE (War Memorial Doctoral Scholarship)

40 Orchard View Blvd., Suite 254
Toronto Ontario M4R 1B9 CANADA
416/487-4416
FAX: 416/487-4417

AMOUNT: $12,000 (study in Canada); $15,000 (study overseas within the Commonwealth)

DEADLINE(S): DEC 1

FIELD(S): All fields of study

Open to Canadian citizens who hold a first degree from a recognized Canadian institution. Candidates must be enrolled in a doctoral program or equivalent.

Write for complete information.

3715 — NATIONAL COLLEGIATE ATHLETIC ASSOCIATION (Graduate Scholarship Program)

6201 College Blvd.
Overland Park KS 66211-2422
913/339-1906

AMOUNT: $5,000 one-time grant

DEADLINE(S): Varies (according to sport)

FIELD(S): All fields of study

Grants to support graduate study by student-athletes attending NCAA-member institutions, are in their last year of intercollegiate athletics competition, and are nominated by their faculty athletic representative or Director of Athletics. GPA of 3.0 or better is required.

Contact your Athletic Director or address above for complete information.

3716 — NATIONAL COLLEGIATE ATHLETIC ASSOCIATION (Walter Byers Postgraduate Scholarship)

6201 College Blvd
Overland Park KS 66211
913\339-1906

AMOUNT: $12,500

DEADLINE(S): JAN (Mid)

FIELD(S): All fields of study

Open to NCAA student-athletes who are graduating seniors or graduates with a GPA of 3.5 or better and have been accepted into a graduate degree program at an accredited non-profit educational institution. Must be in final year of athletics eligibility at the institution from which they received their degree. For full time study.

Award goes to one male and one female student athlete. Must be nominated by faculty athletics representative.

3717 — NATIONAL DO SOMETHING LEAGUE (Community Project Awards)

423 West 55th St. 8th Fl.
New York NY 10019
212/523-1175
FAX: 212/582-1307
E-Mail: grants@dosomething.org
www.dosomething.org

AMOUNT: Up to $500; $10,000; $100,000

DEADLINE(S): MAR 1; JUL 1; NOV 1

FIELD(S): All fields of study, plus community activities

Grants and awards program funds young leaders up to age 30 to transform their ideas into community building action programs. Three sections: Elem. K-6, Secondary, 7-12, and Campus. Grants are up to $500. "Brick" awards are $100,000 (1) and $10,000 (9). Individuals and groups may apply.

Call or visit website above for details and online applications for either grant or award.

3718 — NATIONAL FALLEN FIREFIGHTERS FOUNDATION (Scholarship Program)

PO Drawer 498
Emmitsburg MD 21727
301/447-1365
FAX: 301/447-1645
E-Mail: firehero@erols.com
Internet: www.firehero.org/scholars.htm

AMOUNT: Varies

DEADLINE(S): APR 1

FIELD(S): All fields of study

For spouse or child of fallen firefighter who met criteria for inclusion on National Fallen Firefighters Memorial in MD. Children must be under age 30. Applicant must have high school diploma/equivalency and be pursuing undergraduate, graduate, or job skills training at an accredited university, college, or community college, either full- or part-time. Minimum 2.0 GPA & 2 letters of recommendation required; extracurricular activities & special circumstances considered.

Contact NFFF for an application.

3719 — NATIONAL FEDERATION OF THE BLIND (E.U. Parker Scholarship)

805 Fifth Avenue
Grinnell IA 50112
515/236-3366

AMOUNT: $3,000

DEADLINE(S): MAR 31

FIELD(S): All fields of study

For legally blind students pursuing or planning to pursue a full-time postsecondary course of study in the US. Based on academic excellence, service to the community, and financial need. Membership NOT required.

1 award annually. Renewable. Contact Mrs. Peggy Elliot, Scholarship Committee Chairman, for an application.

3720 — NATIONAL FEDERATION OF THE BLIND (Hermione Grant Calhoun Scholarship)

805 Fifth Avenue
Grinnell IA 50112
515/236-3366

AMOUNT: $3,000

DEADLINE(S): MAR 31

FIELD(S): All fields of study

Open to legally blind female undergraduate or graduate students pursuing or planning to pursue a full-time postsecondary course of study in the US. Based on academic excellence, service to the community, and financial need. Membership NOT required.

1 award annually. Renewable. Contact Mrs. Peggy Elliot, Scholarship Committee Chairman, for an application.

3721 — NATIONAL FEDERATION OF THE BLIND (Kuchler-Killian Memorial Scholarship)

805 Fifth Avenue
Grinnell IA 50112
515/236-3366

AMOUNT: $3,000

DEADLINE(S): MAR 31

FIELD(S): All fields of study

Open to legally blind students pursuing or planning to pursue a full-time postsecondary course of study in the US. Based on academic excellence, service to the community, and financial need. Membership NOT required.

1 award annually. Renewable. Contact Mrs. Peggy Elliot, Scholarship Committee Chairman, for an application.

3722 — NATIONAL FEDERATION OF THE BLIND (Melva T. Owen Memorial Scholarship)

805 Fifth Avenue
Grinnell IA 50112
515/236-3366

AMOUNT: $4,000

DEADLINE(S): MAR 31

FIELD(S): All fields of study

Open to legally blind students for all postsecondary areas of study directed towards attaining financial independence. Excludes religion and those seeking only to further their general and cultural education. For full-time study in the US. Based on academic excellence, service to the community, and financial need. Membership NOT required.

1 awards annually. Renewable. Contact Mrs. Peggy Elliot, Scholarship Committee Chairman, for an application.

3723 — NATIONAL FEDERATION OF THE BLIND (Mozelle and Willard Gold Memorial Scholarship)

805 Fifth Avenue
Grinnell IA 50112
515/236-3366

AMOUNT: $3,000

DEADLINE(S): MAR 31

FIELD(S): All fields of study

Open to legally blind students pursuing or planning to pursue a full-time postsecondary course of study in the US. Based on academic excellence, service to the community, and financial need. Membership NOT required.

1 award annually. Renewable. Contact Mrs. Peggy Elliot, Scholarship Committee Chairman, for an application.

3724 — NATIONAL FEDERATION OF THE BLIND (NFB General Scholarships)

805 Fifth Avenue
Grinnell IA 50112
515/236-3366

AMOUNT: $3,000-$4,000

DEADLINE(S): MAR 31

FIELD(S): All fields of study

Open to legally blind students pursuing or planning to pursue a full-time postsecondary course of study in the US. Based on academic excellence, service to the community, and financial need. Membership NOT required. One of the awards will be given to a person working full-time who is attending or planning to attend a part-time course of study which will result in a new degree and broader opportunities in present or future work.

15 awards annually (2 for $4,000, 13 for $3,000). Renewable. Contact Mrs. Peggy Elliot, Scholarship Committee Chairman, for an application.

3725 — NATIONAL FOREST FOUNDATION (Firefighters' Scholarship Fund)

1099 14th St., NW, Ste. 5600W
Washington DC 20005
202/501-2473
FAX: 202/219-6585
Internet: www.nffweb.org/

AMOUNT: $500-$3,000

DEADLINE(S): MAY 15

FIELD(S): All fields of study

This fund provides for the continued education of firefighters or the dependants of firefighters who have been significantly disabled or killed in the line of duty fighting forest fires after January 1, 1980. These individuals must be employed by the Forest Service, Department of Interior, or state firefighting agencies. The scholarships go to those seeking admission to a college, university, or trade/technical school.

Contact NFF for an application. Award announcements made by June 30th.

3726 — NATIONAL ITALIAN AMERICAN FOUNDATION (Daniel Stella Scholarship)

1860 19th St. NW
Washington DC 20009
202/530-5315

AMOUNT: $1,000

DEADLINE(S): MAY 31

FIELD(S): All fields of study

For graduate or undergraduate students of Italian ancestry who have Cooley's Anemia disease.

Financial need, scholastic merit, and community service are considered.

3727 — NATIONAL ITALIAN AMERICAN FOUNDATION (Guido-Zerilli-Marimo Scholarships)

1860 Nineteenth St. NW
Washington DC 20009-5599
202/530-5315

AMOUNT: $1,000

DEADLINE(S): MAY 31

FIELD(S): All fields of study

Open to undergraduate or graduate students at New York University who are of Italian heritage.

Three awards. Evidence of financial need, academic merit, and community service to be submitted with application.

3728 — NATIONAL ITALIAN AMERICAN FOUNDATION (NIAF/NOIAW Cornaro Scholarship)

1860 19th St.
Washington DC 20009-5599
202/530-5315

AMOUNT: $1,000

DEADLINE(S): MAY 31

FIELD(S): All areas of study

For female undergraduate and graduate students with Italian ancestry. Prepare a 3-page, double-spaced paper on a current issue of concern for Italian American women or a famous Italian American woman.

Three awards. Financial need, academic merit, and community service are considered.

3729 — NATIONAL ITALIAN AMERICAN FOUNDATION (Robert J. Di Pietro Scholarship)

1860 19th St. NW
Washington DC 20009-5599
202/530-5315

AMOUNT: $1,000

DEADLINE(S): MAY 31

FIELD(S): Any field of study.

For undergraduate and graduate students of Italian ancestry age 25 or under. Include essay of 400-600 words on how applicant intends to use his/her ethnicity throughout his/her chosen field of education to preserve and support this ethnicity throughout life. Submit 4 copies with name and title of essay on each.

Two awards given. Academic merit, financial need, and community service also considered.

3730 — NATIONAL ITALIAN AMERICAN FOUNDATION (Silvio Conte Internship)

1860 19th St. NW
Washington DC 20009-5599
202/530-5315

AMOUNT: $1,000

DEADLINE(S): MAY 31

FIELD(S): All fields of study

For undergraduate and graduate students of Italian descent interested in interning for one semester on Capitol Hill in Washington DC. Applicant must provide a letter of acceptance from a congressional office. Student is expected to write a 2-3 page double-spaced, typed paper on the importance of this experience to his/her career.

Academic merit, community service, and financial need considered.

3731 — NATIONAL ITALIAN AMERICAN FOUNDATION (Study Abroad Scholarships)

1860 19th St.
Washington DC 20009-5599
202/530-5315

AMOUNT: $2,000

DEADLINE(S): MAY 31

FIELD(S): Any field of study

For undergraduate or graduate students of Italian ancestry wishing to study in Italy. Programs are available at the American University of Rome and John Cabot University. Must show letter of acceptance.

Academic merit, community service, and financial need are considered. 5 awards given.

3732 — NATIONAL ITALIAN AMERICAN FOUNDATION (West Virginia Italian Heritage Festival Scholarships)

1860 19th St. NW
Washington DC 20009-5599
202/530-5315

AMOUNT: $3,500 total

DEADLINE(S): MAY 31

FIELD(S): Any field of study

For students entering college or already enrolled who are of Italian ancestry and reside in West Virginia.

Financial need, community service, and academic merit are considered.

3733 — NATIONAL TWENTY AND FOUR (Memorial Scholarships)

6000 Lucerne Ct. #2
Mequon WI 53092
Written Inquiry

AMOUNT: Up to $500/yr.

DEADLINE(S): MAY 1

FIELD(S): All areas of study

Open to members & children, grandchildren, or great-grandchildren of women who are members of the Twenty and Four, Honor Society of Women Legionnaires. Also for descendents of deceased former members. Must be between the ages of 16 and 25. For use at a school, college, university, or vocational institution beyond high school. Selection is based on financial need, scholastic standing, and school activities.

Write To "National Aide" for complete information ONLY if above qualifications are met.

3734 — NATIONAL UNIVERSITY OF SINGAPORE (Research Scholarships)

Lower Kent Ridge Road
Singapore 119074 SINGAPORE
65/775 6666

AMOUNT: S$1,200-$1,500

DEADLINE(S): MAY 15; DEC 15

FIELD(S): All fields of study

Scholarships awarded to outstanding university graduates for research leading to a master's or doctoral degree in various disciplines at the university.

Renewable for one year for master's and two years for Ph.D. students, subject to satisfactory academic progress. Write for complete information.

3735 — NATIONAL WELSH-AMERICAN FOUNDATION (Exchange Scholarship Program)

NWAF 24 Carverton Rd.
Trucksville PA 18708
717/696-6923

AMOUNT: Up to $5,000

DEADLINE(S): MAR 1

FIELD(S): All fields of study

Open to U.S. citizens of Welsh descent who are enrolled in undergraduate or graduate degree programs at recognized U.S. institutions. For study of Welsh-oriented subjects at a college in Wales.

Welsh family ties are required. Write for complete information.

3736 — NAVY-MARINE CORPS RELIEF SOCIETY (Spouse Tuition Aid Program)

801 North Randolph St., Suite 1228
Arlington VA 22203-1978
703/696-4960

AMOUNT: Up to 50% of tuition for on-base education programs, up to a maximum of $300 per undergraduate term, or $350 per graduate term, and $1,500 per academic year.

DEADLINE(S): None specified

FIELD(S): Any field of study

For spouses of active US Navy or Marine personnel and who reside overseas with the active dutry servicemember. Applicant need not be a full-time student.

Administered locally by an NMCRS Auxiliary.

3737 — NELLIE MAE (Student Loans)

50 Braintree Hill Park, Suite 300
Braintree MA 02184-1763
617/849-1325 or 800/634-9308

AMOUNT: Up to cost of education less financial aid

DEADLINE(S): None specified

FIELD(S): All fields of study

Variety of loans available for undergraduate and graduate study at accredited degree-granting colleges or universities. Varied repayment and interest rate options. Savings programs for on-time repayments.

Write for complete information.

3738 — NETHERLANDS ORGANIZATION FOR INTERNATIONAL COOPERATION IN HIGHER EDUCATION (Grants from Dutch Government & European Union)

Kortenaerkade 11
Postbus 29777
2502 LT Den Haag THE NETHERLANDS
+31 070 426 02 00
FAX: +31 070 426 03 99
E-Mail: nuffic@nuffic.nl
Internet: www.nuffic.nl

AMOUNT: Varies

DEADLINE(S): Varies

FIELD(S): All fields of study

The Dutch Government and European Union offer grants under several programmes for students who wish to study in The Netherlands. To be eligible, student must be from one of the following countries: Austria, Belgium, Denmark, Finland, France, Germany, Greece, Iceland, Ireland, Italy, Luxembourg, Norway, Portugal, Spain, Sweden, or the United Kingdom.

Contact the Netherlands Embassy in your country or NUFFIC at above address for details. Also ask about Cultural Agreements.

3739 — NETHERLANDS ORGANIZATION FOR INTERNATIONAL COOPERATION IN HIGHER EDUCATION (Cultural Agreements)

Kortenaerkade 11
Postbus 29777
2502 LT Den Haag THE NETHERLANDS
+31 070 426 02 00
FAX: +31 070 426 03 99
E-Mail: nuffic@nuffic.nl
Internet: www.nuffic.nl

AMOUNT: Varies

DEADLINE(S): Varies

FIELD(S): All fields of study

The Dutch government offers grants for periods of study/research in the Netherlands. Must be from Europe, China, India, Indonesia, Japan, Australia, Belarus, Egypt, Estonia, Georgia, Israel, Jordan, Latvia, Lithuania, Mexico, Morocco, Russia, Turkey, or Ukraine.

Contact the Netherlands Embassy in your country or NUFFIC at above address for details.

3740 — NETHERLANDS ORGANIZATION FOR INTERNATIONAL COOPERATION IN HIGHER EDUCATION (NFP - Netherlands Fellowships Programme)

Kortenaerkade 11
Postbus 29777
2502 LT Den Haag THE NETHERLANDS
+31 070 426 02 00
FAX: +31 070 426 03 99
E-Mail: nuffic@nuffic.nl
Internet: www.nuffic.nl

AMOUNT: Varies

DEADLINE(S): Varies

FIELD(S): All fields of study

The Dutch government offers grants for students & staff from developing countries who have already started a career in specialized field. Offers possibilities for taking part in certain international courses & training programmes given in the Netherlands.

Candidates must be nominated by their employers. The NFP also provides funds for training & courses that are tailor-made to meet specific needs. University Fellowships Programme also available for bachelor's students.

Contact the Netherlands Embassy in your country or NUFFIC at above address for details.

3741 — NETTIE MILLHOLLON EDUCATIONAL TRUST ESTATE (Student Loans)

309 West Saint Anna St.
P.O. Box 79782
Stanton TX 79782
915/756-2261

AMOUNT: Varies

DEADLINE(S): JUL 1 (for Fall); JAN 2 (for Spring)

FIELD(S): All fields of study

Students loans for financially needy Texas residents under 25 years of age. Rinancial need, character, evidence of ability, and desire to learn and further one's education, and unavailability of other financial resources are all considered. At least 2.5 GPA required.

Send SASE to above address for details.

3742 — NEVADA DEPT. OF EDUCATION (Student Incentive Grant Program)

700 E. Fifth St.
Carson City NV 89701
702/687-9228

AMOUNT: Varies

DEADLINE(S): Varies

FIELD(S): All fields of study

Student incentive grants available to Nevada residents enrolled in eligible Nevada institutions. For both graduate and undergraduate study.

Application must be made through the financial aid office of eligible participating institutions.

3743 — NEW BEDFORD PORT SOCIETY-LADIES BRANCH (Limited Scholarship Grant)

15 Johnny Cake Hill
New Bedford MA 02740
Written inquiry only

AMOUNT: $300-$400

DEADLINE(S): MAY 1

FIELD(S): All areas of study

Open to residents of greater New Bedford, MA, who are descended from seafarers such as whaling masters and other fishermen. For undergrad and marine biology studies.

Renewable. Write for complete information.

3744 — NEW ENGLAND BOARD OF HIGHER EDUCATION (New England Regional Student Program)

45 Temple Pl.
Boston MA 02111
617/357-9620

AMOUNT: Tuition reduction (varies)

DEADLINE(S): Varies

FIELD(S): All fields of study

Under this program New England residents may attend public colleges and universities in other New England states at a reduced tuition rate for certain majors which are not available in their own state's public istitutions.

Write to the above address for complete information.

3745 — NEW HAMPSHIRE HIGHER EDUCATION ASSISTANCE FOUNDATION (Federal Family Education Loan Program)

4 Barrell Court
P.O. Box 877
Concord NH 03302-0877
800/525-2577, ext. 119 or 603/225-6612

AMOUNT: Varies

DEADLINE(S): None

FIELD(S): All fields of study

Open to New Hampshire residents pursuing a college education in or out of state and to non-residents who attend a New Hampshire college or university. US citizenship required.

Also provides scholarship searches, career searches, college searches, and individual counseling to parents and prospective college students (all free of charge). Interested students/parents may call or write to above address.

3746 — NEW JERSEY DEPT. OF HIGHER EDUCATION (Educational Opportunity Fund Grants)

Office of Student Assistance
CN 540
Trenton NJ 08625
609/588-3230
800/792-8670 IN NJ
TDD: 609/588-2526

AMOUNT: $200-$2,100 undergrads; $200-$4,150 graduate students

DEADLINE(S): Varies

FIELD(S): All areas of study

Must be New Jersey resident for at least 12 months prior to application. Grants for economically and educationally disadvantaged students. For undergraduate or graduate study in New Jersey. Must demonstrate need and be U.S. citizen or legal resident.

Grants renewable. Write for complete information.

3747 — NEW JERSEY DEPT. OF MILITARY & VETERANS AFFAIRS (Veterans Tuition Credit Program)

Eggert Crossing Rd. CN340
Attn DVL6S
Trenton NJ 08625
609/530-6961
800/624-0508 in NJ

AMOUNT: $400 (full-time); $200 (half-time)

DEADLINE(S): OCT 1; MAR 1

FIELD(S): All fields of study

Open to US military veterans who served between Dec. 31 1960 & May 7 1975 and were residents of New Jersey for one year prior to application or were NJ residents at time of induction or discharge. Proof of residency is required.

Applies to all levels of study. Write for complete information.

3748 — NEW JERSEY OFFICE OF STUDENT ASSISTANCE (Educational Opportunity Fund Grant)

CN 540
Trenton NJ 08625
800/792-8670
TDD: 609/588-2526

AMOUNT: Up to $4,150/yr.

DEADLINE(S): None specified

FIELD(S): All fields of study

Grants for economically disacvantaged graduate students who have been N.J. residents for at least 12 months. Must indicate financial need. For use only at N.J. institutions participating in the EOF graduate program.

Obtain applications through the Graduate Office and EOF Campus Director at the educational institution. Call the Commission on Higher Education, EOF Office, at 609/984-2709 for further details.

3749 — NEW MEXICO FARM AND LIVESTOCK BUREAU (Memorial Scholarships)

PO Box 20004
Las Cruces NM 88004-9004
505/532-4702
FAX: 505/532-4710
E-Mail: nmflb@zianet.com

AMOUNT: Varies

DEADLINE(S): MAY 1

FIELD(S): All fields of study

Available to members of New Mexico Farm & Livestock Bureau families for one year of continuing education at an institution of their choice. Must be a resident of New Mexico and have a minimum 2.5 GPA. Transcripts, two letters of recommendation, and a recent photograph for publicity purposes are required. Financial need NOT a factor.

5 awards annually. Renewable through re-application. Contact Missy Aguayo at NMFLB for an application.

3750 — NEW YORK STATE EDUCATION DEPT. (Awards, Scholarships, and Fellowships)

Bureau of NEOP/UATEA/Scholarships, Rm. 1076 EB
Albany NY 12234
518/486-1319
FAX: 518/486-5346

AMOUNT: Varies

DEADLINE(S): Varies

FIELD(S): All fields of study

Various state and federal programs administered by the NY State Education Department open to residents of New York state. One year's NY residency immediately preceding effective date of award is required.

Write for complete information.

3751 — NEW YORK STATE HIGHER EDUCATION SERVICES CORPORATION (Vietnam Veterans and Persian Gulf Veterans Tuition Awards)

HESC, Student Information
Albany NY 12255
518/486-1319
Internet: www.hesc.com

AMOUNT: $500 (part-time); $1,000 (full-time). Total awards cannot exceed $10,000.

DEADLINE(S): MAY 1

FIELD(S): All fields of study

Scholarships for NY residents who are veterans of either the Vietnam War or the Persian Gulf War (Desert Storm/Desert Shield). For vocational/tech. training, undergraduate, and graduate study. Contact a local County Veterans' Service Agency or the N.Y. State Division of Veterans' Affairs for details.

Complete a Free Application for Federal Student Aid (FAFSA) and the New York State Tuition Assistance Program (TAP) application to apply.

3752 — NEW YORK STATE HIGHER EDUCATION SERVICES CORPORATION (Tuition Assistance Program (TAP) and Aid for Part-Time Study (APTS))

HESC, Student Information
Albany NY 12255
518/486-1319
Internet: www.hesc.com

AMOUNT: Varies

DEADLINE(S): MAY 1 (TAP)

FIELD(S): All fields of study

Grants for students at all levels, including some for part-time study.

Contact above location for details of these and other New York state programs.

3753 — NEW ZEALAND FEDERATION OF UNIVERSITY WOMEN (Waikato Merit Award)

P.O. Box 7065
Hamilton NEW ZEALAND
07-855 3776

AMOUNT: $2,000/year

DEADLINE(S): APR (1st Friday)

FIELD(S): All fields of study

For a woman student enrolled in a Ph.D. degree program at the University of Waikato.

Contact The Convenor, NZFUW, at above address for details.

3754 — NEW ZEALAND VICE-CHANCELLORS' COMMITTEE (Commonwealth Scholarship)

11th Floor
94 Dixon St.
Wellington NEW ZEALAND
64-4-381 8500
FAX: 64-4-381 8501
E-Mail: schols@nzvcc.ac.nz
Internet: www.nzvcc.ac.nz

AMOUNT: NZ $16,000/yr.

DEADLINE(S): JUL 31

FIELD(S): All fields of study

For citizens of Commonwealth countries to pursue graduate study in New Zealand. Must have an undergraduate degree of at least 2nd class honors level and be working for a master's or doctoral degree. Financial need NOT a factor.

10 awards annually. Renewable up to 3 years. Must apply first to Commonwealth Scholarship Agency in own country of citizenship. For a list of Commonwealth countries & agencies, see website or contact the Scholarships Officer at NZVCC.

3755 — NEWBERRY LIBRARY (Francis C. Allen Fellowships)

60 West Walton Street
Chicago IL 60610-3380
312/943-9090 or 312/255-3564
E-Mail: research@newberry.org
Internet: www.newberry.org

AMOUNT: Varies

DEADLINE(S): MAR 1

FIELD(S): All fields of study

One-month to one-year fellowships are available for women of American Indian heritage who are studying at any stage beyond the undergraduate level. Though candidates may be working in any graduate or pre-professional field, purpose of the fellowship is to encourage study in the humanities and social sciences. Financial support varies according to need and may include travel expenses.

Fellows are expected to spend a significant part of their residence at Newberry's Center for American Indian History. See website for application or write to above address.

3756 — NICHOLL SCHOLARSHIPS (Undergraduate and Graduate Scholarships)

P.O. Box HM 1179
Hamilton HM EX Bermuda
441/295-2244

AMOUNT: BD$15,000

DEADLINE(S): JUN 15

FIELD(S): All fields of study

Open to Bermuda residents with at least 5 years of schooling in Bermuda who are at least 18 and not more than 24 years old as of September 1 of year of application. For undergrad or graduate study at accredited universities in British Commonwealth countries or the US.

4 awards per year; renewable up to 4 years. Write for complete information.

3757 — NORTH CAROLINA DIVISION OF SERVICES FOR THE BLIND (Rehabilitation Assistance for Visually Impaired)

309 Ashe Ave.
Raleigh NC 27606
919/733-9700

AMOUNT: Tuition + fees; books & supplies

DEADLINE(S): None

FIELD(S): All areas of study

Open to North Carolina residents who are legally blind or have a progressive eye condition which may result in blindness (thereby creating an impediment for the individual) and who are undergrad or grad students at a NC school.

Write for complete information.

3758 — NORTH CAROLINA STATE EDUCATION ASSISTANCE AUTHORITY (Student Financial Aid for North Carolinians)

PO Box 2688
Chapel Hill NC 27515
919/549-8614

AMOUNT: Varies

DEADLINE(S): Varies

FIELD(S): All fields of study

The state of NC; private NC organizations & the federal government fund numerous scholarships, grants, work-study, and loan programs for North Carolina residents at all levels of study.

The NC State Education Assistance Authority annually publishes a financial aid booklet describing in detail various programs for North Carolina residents. A copy is available free to undergrads who plan to attend a school in NC.

3759 — NORTHWEST DANISH FOUNDATION (Scholarships)

Scandinavian Dept., Univ. of Washington-318
Raitt Hall
Box 353420
Seattle WA 98195-3420
206/543-0645 or 206/543-6084

AMOUNT: $250

DEADLINE(S): MAR 15

FIELD(S): All fields of study

Scholarship for students of Danish descent or married to someone of danish descent. Must be residents of Washington or Oregon. May be used for study in the U.S. or in Denmark.

Contact Professor Marianne Stecher-Hanson at above address or phone numbers or the Foundation at 206/523-3263.

3760 — NUCLEAR AGE PEACE FOUNDATION (Lena Chang Scholarship Awards)

1187 Coast Village Road, Suite 123
Santa Barbara CA 93108-2794
805/965-3443
FAX: 805/568-0466
E-Mail: wagingpeace@napf.org
Internet: www.wagingpeace.org

AMOUNT: $2,500

DEADLINE(S): JUL 1

FIELD(S): All fields of study

For ethnic minority students enrolled in an accredited college or university in undergraduate or graduate studies who can demonstrate financial need and academic excellence.

Write a typed, double-spaced essay (not to exceed three pages) on ways to achieve peace in the Nuclear Age and how you hope to contribute to that end. Also send separately two letters of recommendation (at least one from a college instructor and not from relatives) and a college transcript copy. Send SASE for official application form.

3761 — O'BRIEN FOUNDATION (Fellowship)

P.O. Box 7174—Station A
Saint John
New Brunswick E2L 4S6 Canada
506/634-3600

AMOUNT: Up to $15,000 (Canadian) per annum

DEADLINE(S): NOV 1

FIELD(S): All fields of study

Open primarily to residents of the Province of New Brunswick who have graduated from a university and intend to return to and remain in the province upon completion of their project. Must have degree or equivalent training.

For post-graduate study or research at any recognized university or research establishment in the world. Write for complete information.

3762 — OHIO BOARD OF REGENTS (Regents Graduate/Professional Fellowship Program)

State Grants & Scholarships Dept.
P.O. Box 182452
Columbus OH 43218-2452
888/833-1133
614/644-7420
FAX: 614/752-5903

AMOUNT: $3,500/yr. for up to 2 years

DEADLINE(S): None specified

FIELD(S): All fields of study

For holders of B.A. degrees who enroll for graduate school or professional study at participating Ohio colleges and universities.

Contact a college financial aid administrator, the university's graduate school, or the above location for details.

3763 — ONEIDA HIGHER EDUCATION (Various Fellowships, Internships, and Scholarships)

P.O. Box 365
Oneida WI 54155
920/869-4333 or 1-800/236-2214 Ext. 4333
FAX: 910/869-4039

AMOUNT: Varies with program

DEADLINE(S): APR 15 (fall term); OCT 1 (spring term); MAY 1 (summer term)

FIELD(S): All fields of study

For enrolled members of the Oneida Tribe of Indians of Wisconsin. Several programs are offered for all levels of study in various fields, including internships, emergency funding, and special scholarships for economics and business majors and those in the hotel/restaurant management field.

Some programs list deadlines dates different from those above. Send for descriptive brochure.

3764 — ONTARIO MINISTRY OF EDUCATION AND TRAINING (Ontario-Quebec Exchange Fellowships)

189 Red River Rd.
4th Floor, Box 4500
Thunder Bay Ontario P7B 6G9 CANADA
800/465-3957
TDD: 800/465-3958
Internet: osap.gov.on.ca

AMOUNT: $10,000 (master's); $12,000 (doctoral)

DEADLINE(S): Varies

FIELD(S): All fields of study

Fellowships are awarded to Ontario students enrolled in the first year of a full-time master's or doctoral degree program at a university in Quebec. Also for Quebec students studying in Ontario. Awards are designed to encourage and reward academic excellence.

16 awards annually (8 from each province). Contact the Ministry of Education & Training for an application.

3765 — ONTARIO MINISTRY OF EDUCATION AND TRAINING (Ontario Graduate Scholarship Program)

189 Red River Rd., 4th Floor
Box 4500
Thunder Bay Ontario P7B 6G9 CANADA
800/465-3957
TDD: 800/465-3958
Internet: osap.gov.on.ca

AMOUNT: $3,953/term

DEADLINE(S): Varies

FIELD(S): All fields of study

Scholarships are awarded to Canadian citizens/ permanent residents who are at the graduate level of study at an Ontario university. Awards are designed to encourage and reward academic excellence.

1,300 awards annually. Contact your university or the Ministry of Education & Training for an application.

3766 — OPEN SOCIETY INSTITUTE (Network Scholarship Programs)

400 West 59th St.
New York NY 10019
212/548-0600 or 212/757-2323
FAX: 212/548-4679 or 212/548-4600
Internet: www.soros.org

AMOUNT: Varies

DEADLINE(S): Varies

FIELD(S): All fields of study

Various financial aid programs for students, faculty, and professionals from Eastern and Central Europe, the former Soviet Union, Mongolia, Burma, and the former Yugoslavia.

See website for details of requirements for each program. To apply, contact your local Soros Foundation/Open Society Institute.

3767 — OREGON DEPARTMENT OF VETERANS' AFFAIRS (Educational Aid for Oregon Veterans)

700 Summer St. NE, Suite 150
Salem OR 97310-1270
800/692-9666 or 503/373-2085

AMOUNT: $35 to $50 per month

DEADLINE(S): None

FIELD(S): All fields of study

For veterans on active duty during the Korean War June 25, 1950 to Jan. 31, 1955 or who received a campaign or expeditionary medal or ribbon awarded by the Armed Forces of the United States for services after June 30, 1958. Must be resident of Oregon and U.S. citizen with a qualifying military service record at time of application. For study in an accredited Oregon school.

Write for complete information.

3768 — OREGON STATE SCHOLARSHIP COMMISSION (Federal Family Education Loan Program)

1500 Valley River Dr., #100
Eugene OR 97401
800/452-8807
503/687-7400
Internet: www.teleport.com~ossc

AMOUNT: $2,625-$6,635 undergrad; $8,500-$18,500 graduate (annual maximum)

DEADLINE(S): None specified

FIELD(S): All fields of study

Open to U.S. citizens or permanent residents who are attending an eligible Oregon institution and to Oregon residents attending any eligible institution outside of Oregon at least half-time.

Write or visit website for complete information.

3769 — OREGON STATE SCHOLARSHIP COMMISSION (Private Scholarship Programs Administered by the Commission)

1500 Valley River Drive, Suite 100
Eugene OR 97401
503/687-7395

AMOUNT: $250-$3,000

DEADLINE(S): MAR 1

FIELD(S): All fields of study

100 different private scholarship programs are administered by the Commission and are for Oregon

residents only. Some are tied to a specific field and/or level of study but in general they are available to all levels and fields of study.

Dependent students must have parents residing in Oregon. Independent students must live in Oregon for 12 months prior to Sept. 1 of the academic year for which the application is made. For complete information send a 55-cent, stamped, self-addressed #10 business-sized envelope to the above address.

3770 — ORGANIZATION OF AMERICAN STATES (Leo S. Rowe Pan American Fund)

1889 F Street, N.W., Second Floor
Washington DC 20006
202/458-6208

AMOUNT: Up to US $5,000/yr.

DEADLINE(S): None

FIELD(S): All fields of study

No-interest loans for undergrad and grad students from member countries of the Organization of American States who are studying or wish to study in the U.S.

Must be within two years of completing degree or research. Loan repayable within five years of completion of studies. Write for complete details.

3771 — P.E.O. SISTERHOOD (International Peace Scholarship Fund)

3700 Grand Ave.
Des Moines IA 50312
Written Inquiry

AMOUNT: $5,000 (max.)

DEADLINE(S): JAN 15

FIELD(S): All fields of study

For women who have been admitted to full-time graduate status, working toward a degree in a college or university in the US or Canada.

Write to the Chairman of P.E.O. for an application.

3772 — PARENTS AND FRIENDS OF LESBIANS AND GAYS—PFLAG CINCINNATI (Scholarships)

P.O. Box 19634
Cincinnati OH 45219
513/721-7900

AMOUNT: $500

DEADLINE(S): APR 15

FIELD(S): All fields of study

Scholarships for students who are gay, lesbian, bisexual, and transgender. Can be high school senior, undergraduate, or graduate student. Applications from students in the Cincinnati area will have preference.

Contact organization for details.

3773 — PARENTS, FAMILIES, AND FRIENDS OF LESBIANS AND GAYS-NEW ORLEANS CHAPTER (Scholarships)

P.O. Box 15515
New Orleans LA 70175
504/895-3936
E-Mail: lhpeebles@aol.com
Internet: www.gayneworleans.org/pflag/

AMOUNT: Varies

DEADLINE(S): FEB 17

FIELD(S): All fields of study

Scholarships for self-identified gay and lesbian students pursuing college degrees. For residents of Louisiana.

Application materials are at website (which also features great music!). Contact organization for details.

3774 — PARENTS, FAMILIES, AND FRIENDS OF LESBIANS AND GAYS-ATLANTA (Scholarships)

P.O. Box 8482
Atlanta GA 31106
770/662-6475
FAX: 404/864-3639
E-Mail: mcjcatl@mindspring.com

AMOUNT: Varies

DEADLINE(S): APR 1

FIELD(S): All fields of study

Scholarships for college-bound gay, lesbian, or bisexual high school seniors, undergraduates, graduates, or postgraduates who are either George residents or attend or will attend a college or university in Georgia. Part-time students considered for reduced awards.

Renewable. Contact organization for details.

3775 — PAUL O. AND MARY BOGHOSSIAN FOUNDATION

One Hospital Trust Plaza
Providence RI 02903
401/278-8752

AMOUNT: $500-$2,500

DEADLINE(S): MAY 1

FIELD(S): All fields of study

Scholarships for residents of Rhode Island.

Write c/o The Rhode Island Hospital Trust National Bank at above address for details and application.

3776 — PENINSULA COMMUNITY FOUNDATION (Crain Educational Grants Program)

1700 S. El Camino Real #300
San Mateo CA 94402
650/358-9369
FAX: 650/358-9817

AMOUNT: Up to $5,000

DEADLINE(S): MAR 27 (5 p.m.)

FIELD(S): All fields of study

Scholarships for students who have graduated from or are current high school seniors of a public or private high school in San Mateo County or Santa Clara County, California. Must be U.S. citizen have financial need, have demonstrated community involvement over a period of years, and maintain a GPA of at least 3.0. For full-time enrollment in an accredited two- or four-year college, university, or vocational school in the U.S.

Program was established to enable worthy high school graduates to pursue courses of study that they would otherwise by unable to follow due to limited financial means.

3777 — PENNSYLVANIA DEPARTMENT OF MILITARY AFFAIRS—BUREAU OF VETERANS AFFAIRS (Scholarships)

Fort Indiantown Gap
Annville PA 17003-5002
717/861-8904 or 717/861-8910
FAX: 717/861-8589

AMOUNT: Up to $500/term ($4,000 for 4 years)

DEADLINE(S): None

FIELD(S): All areas of study

Open to children of military veterans who died or were totally disabled as a result of war, armed conflict, or terrorist attack. Must have lived in Pennsylvania for 5 years prior to application, be age 16-23, & demonstrate financial need.

70 awards per year. Renewable. For study at Pennsylvania schools. Must be U.S. citizen. Write for complete information.

3778 — PETER BLOSSER STUDENT LOAN FUND

P.O. Box 6160
Chillicothe OH 45601-6160
614/773-0043

AMOUNT: $2,000 max/yr.

DEADLINE(S): None

FIELD(S): All areas of study

A student loan for students who have been residents of Ross County, Ohio, for at least three years, have a minimum GPA of 2.0, graduated from a Ross County high school, or received a GED in the state of Ohio. To be used at an institution in Ross County.

Renewable up to $8,000. 15-40 annual loans. Contact Marie Rosebrook at above address for details.

3779 — PHI ETA SIGMA (Scholarship Program)

228 Foy Union Bldg.
Auburn University AL 36849
205/826-5856

AMOUNT: $2,000 (10-each); $1,000 (22-each)

DEADLINE(S): MAR 1

FIELD(S): All areas of study

Must be member of Phi Eta Sigma. Contact local chapter advisor for application and requirements. DO NOT call or write address above—all information MUST be obtained from local chapter.

32 scholarships per year. Not renewable.

3780 — PINE BLUFFS AREA CHAMBER OF COMMERCE (Scholarship)

PO Box 486
Pine Bluffs WY 82082-0486
Written Inquiry

AMOUNT: $300

DEADLINE(S): Varies

FIELD(S): All fields of study

Available to a graduate of Pine Bluffs High School to attend any accredited college, trade, or technical school in the US. Award is based on need, aptitude, academic, and overall performance. Must submit an essay on plans to help community in which student will live.

1 award annually. Not renewable. Write to above address for an application.

3781 — POLISH UNIVERSITY CLUB OF NEW JERSEY (Scholarships)

177-179 Broadway
Clark NJ 07066
732/382-7197
Internet: www.njcommunity.org/puc/

AMOUNT: Varies

DEADLINE(S): Varies

FIELD(S): All fields of study

Scholarships for students holding bachelor's degrees who are of Polish ancestry and are U.S. citizens or who intend to apply for U.S. citizenship. Must reside in New Jersey.

Contact organization for details.

3782 — PORTUGUESE CONTINENTAL UNION (Scholarships)

899 Boylston Street
Boston MA 02115
617/536-2916

AMOUNT: Varies

DEADLINE(S): MAR 31

FIELD(S): All areas of study

Open to members of the Portuguese Continental Union of the U.S. with at least one year membership in good standing and who plan to enroll or are enrolled in any accredited college or university.

Financial need is a consideration. Write for complete information.

3783 — PRESBYTERIAN CHURCH (U.S.A.) (Native American Education Grant)

100 Witherspoon Street
Louisville KY 40202-1396
502/569-5760
E-Mail: MariaA@ctr.pcusa.org
Internet: www.pcusa.org/highered

AMOUNT: $200-$2,500

DEADLINE(S): JUN 1

FIELD(S): All fields of study

For Native Americans and Alaska Natives pursuing full-time post-secondary education. Must be members of the Presbyterian Church (U.S.A.), be US citizens or permanent residents, and demonstrate financial need.

Renewable. Contact Maria Alvarez at above address for more information.

3784 — PRESBYTERIAN CHURCH (U.S.A.) (Undergraduate/Graduate Loan Programs)

100 Witherspoon Street
Louisville KY 40202-1396
502/569-5735
E-Mail: FrancesC@ctr.pcusa.org
Internet: www.pcusa.org/highered

AMOUNT: $200-$7,000/year

DEADLINE(S): None

FIELD(S): All fields of study

Loans open to members of the Presbyterian Church (U.S.A.) who are US citizens or permanent residents. For full-time undergraduate or graduate study at an accredited college/university. No interest while in school; repayment begins six months after graduation or discontinuation of studies. Must demonstrate financial need, be in good academic standing, and give evidence of financial reliability.

Renewable. May apply for maximum amount in final year of study if have not previously borrowed. Contact Frances Cook at above address for more information.

3785 — PRIDE FOUNDATION & GREATER SEATTLE BUSINESS ASSOCIATION (Scholarships for Gays & Lesbians)

1122 E. Pike St., Ste. 1001
Seattle WA 98122-3934
206/323-3318 OR 1-800/735-7287-outside Seattle area
FAX: 206/323-1017
E-Mail: giving@pridefoundation.org
Internet: www.pridefoundation.org

AMOUNT: Up to $3,500

DEADLINE(S): MAR 1

FIELD(S): All fields of study

A variety of scholarships for gay, lesbian, bisexual, and transgender youth and adults who reside in Washington, Oregon, Idaho, Montana, or Alaska. For all levels of postsecondary education—community college, four-year college, or vocational training. Some require financial need.

Check website and/or write to organization for details. Applications available Nov. 1.

3786 — PROCTER FELLOWSHIPS (Fellowships at Princeton University)

The Old Schools
Cambridge CB2 ENGLAND UK
Written request

AMOUNT: $11,200 + tuition, health insurance

DEADLINE(S): DEC 5

FIELD(S): All fields of study

Scholarships for citizens of the U.K. or British Commonwealth to study at Princeton University in the U.S. Must have completed a B.A. degree at a U.K. university and be in second or third year of graduate research in a U.K. university when they take up the fellowship.

Request details and application forms from Dr. A. Clark, Secretary of the Trustees, University Registry, at above address.

3787 — PROFESSIONAL HORSEMEN'S SCHOLARSHIP FUND, INC.

c/o Mrs. Ann Grenci
204 Old Sleepy Hollow Road
Pleasantville NY 10570
561/694-6893 (Nov.-Apr.)
914/769-1493 (May-Oct. 15)

AMOUNT: Up to $1,000

DEADLINE(S): MAY 1

FIELD(S): All areas of study

For members or dependents of members of the Professional Horsemen's Association. Awards can be used for college or trade school.

Up to 10 awards annually. Write to Mrs. Ann Grenci at above address for complete information.

3788 — PUBLIC EMPLOYEES ROUNDTABLE (Public Service Scholarships)

P.O. Box 44801
Washington DC 20026-4801
202/401-4344
Internet: http://www.patriot.net/users/permail

AMOUNT: $500 (part-time); $1,000 (full-time)

DEADLINE(S): MAY 15

FIELD(S): All fields of study

Open to graduate students and undergraduate sophomores, juniors, and seniors who are planning a career in government service at the local, state, or federal level. Minimum of 3.5 cumulative GPA. Preference to applicants with some public service work experience (paid or unpaid).

10 to 15 awards per year. Applications available as of February 1. Send self-addressed, STAMPED envelope (SASE) for application and details. OR print out application on website and mail it to organization. NOTE: Above address may change, so check website for current address!

3789 — QUEEN'S UNIVERSITY OF BELFAST (Guiness Sports Bursary Awards)

Guiness Sports Bursary Awards, The Physical Education Centre
Botanic Park, Belfast BT9 5EX Northern Ireland
UK
+44 (0) 1232 245133
Internet: www.icbl.qub.ac.uk/prospectus/funding/sports.htm

AMOUNT: Varies

DEADLINE(S): Varies

FIELD(S): All fields of study

Sport has played an integral role in university life at Queen's. Thus, financial assistance is available for current and potential students who have participated in sports and are gifted athletes of good academic standing. Bursaries are open to full-time students.

Approximately 15 annual awards. Contact the University at the address above for complete information.

3790 — QUEEN'S UNIVERSITY OF BELFAST (Visiting Fellowships)

University Road
Academic Council
Belfast BT7 1NN NORTHERN IRELAND
01232 273002
FAX: 01232 313537
E-Mail: Academic.Council@QUB.AC.UK
Internet: www.QUB.AC.UK

AMOUNT: 16,655-20,107 pounds sterling

DEADLINE(S): DEC 1

FIELD(S): All fields of study

For postgraduate students to attend Queen's University of Belfast in Northern Ireland. Must have a doctorate degree or equivalent experience. Financial need is NOT a factor.

2 awards annually. Not renewable. Contact Mr. Colm Crean at QUB for an application.

3791 — QUEEN'S UNIVERSITY OF BELFAST (Visiting Studentships)

University Road
Academic Council
Belfast BT7 1NN NORTHERN IRELAND
01232 273002
FAX: 01232 313537
E-Mail: Academic.Council@QUB.AC.UK
Internet: www.QUB.AC.UK

AMOUNT: 5,455 pounds sterling per annum

DEADLINE(S): DEC 1

FIELD(S): All fields of study

For graduate students with at least a good honours degree, who wish to do research leading to a doctorate at Queen's University of Belfast in Northern Ireland. Financial need is NOT a factor.

3 awards annually. Renewable up to 3 years. Contact Mr. Colm Crean at QUB for an application.

3792 — RADIO AND TELEVISION NEWS DIRECTORS FOUNDATION (Jane Pauley Internship)

1000 Connecticut Ave., NW, Ste. 615
Washington DC 20036-5302
202/467-5218
FAX: 202/223-4007
E-Mail: danib@rtndf.org
Internet: www.rtndf.org

AMOUNT: $1,120/month

DEADLINE(S): MAR 1

FIELD(S): All fields of study (except journalism majors), w/ career goal of Electronic Journalism

Fully-paid, 6-month internship (JUL-DEC) at WISH-TV in Indianapolis for graduate student or recent college graduate not majoring in journalism, but whose career objective is in the electronic journalism industry. Intern will learn the nuts & bolts of developing local newscasts with an emphasis on producing, writing, & reporting skills. Must be US citizen. Travel, housing, & living expenses not included. Essay, resume, references, & letters of recommendation required.

1 internship annually. See website or contact Dani Browne at RTNDF for an application. Jane Pauley of NBC will make the final selection.

3793 — REALTY FOUNDATION OF NEW YORK (Scholarship Program)

551 Fifth Avenue, Ste. 1105
New York NY 10176-0166
212/697-3943

AMOUNT: Varies

DEADLINE(S): Varies

FIELD(S): All fields of study

Open to Realtors and their children or employees of real estate firms and their children. The student or his parent are required to be employed in the real estate industry in Metropoitan New York.

Write to the above address for complete information.

3794 — RED RIVER VALLEY FIGHTER PILOTS ASSOCIATION (River Rats Scholarship Grant Programs)

PO Box 1551
North Fork CA 93643
559/877-5000
FAX: 559/877-5001
E-Mail: AFBridger@aol.com
Internet: www.eos.net/rrva

AMOUNT: $500-$3,500

DEADLINE(S): MAY 15

FIELD(S): All fields of study

For a) immediate dependents (spouse/children) of any member of US Armed Forces who is listed in KIA/MIA status from any combat situation involving our military since 8/64; b) immediate dependents of military aircrew members killed as result of performing aircrew duties during non-combat mission; c) immediate dependents of current/deceased RRVA-members in good standing; and d) grandchildren of qualifying military relative. Must be US citizen/permanent resident.

15-40 awards annually. Renewable. Based on need, achievement, and activities. See website or contact Al Bache, Executive Director, for an application.

3795 — RESERVE OFFICERS ASSOCIATION OF THE UNITED STATES (Henry J. Reilly Memorial Scholarships for Graduates)

One Constitution Ave., NE
Washington DC 20002-5655
202/479-2200 or 800/809-9448
FAX: 202/479-0416
E-Mail: 71154.1267@compserve.com

AMOUNT: $500

DEADLINE(S): Varies (applications available in FEB)

FIELD(S): All fields of study

Must be active or associate members of ROA who are graduate students at a regionally accredited US college/university. Must be enrolled in at least two courses (if you are employed full-time, you may be eligible if enrolled in only one course) and have a minimum 3.2 GPA. Must demonstrate leadership qualities—letter of recommendation from military or civilian "reporting senior" is required, as well as two letters in regards to academic ability and curriculum vitae.

35 awards annually. Contact Ms. Mickey Hagen for an application—please specify your grade level. Undergrad program for ROA/ROAL members also available.

3796 — RHODE ISLAND HIGHER EDUCATION ASSISTANCE AUTHORITY (Loan Program; Plus Loans)

560 Jefferson Blvd.
Warwick RI 02886
401/736-1160

AMOUNT: Up to $5,500 for undergrads & up to $8,500 for graduates (subsidized); up to $5,000 for undergrads & up to $10,000 for graduates (unsubsidized)

DEADLINE(S): None specified

FIELD(S): All fields of study

Open to Rhode Island residents or non-residents attending an eligible school. Must be U.S. citizen or legal resident and be enrolled at least half-time. Rhode Island residents may attend schools outside the state.

Must demonstrate financial need. Write for current interest rates and complete information.

3797 — RICHARD E. MERWIN INTERNATIONAL AWARD

P.O. Box 6694
Coddingtown, CA 95406-0694
Written inquiry only

AMOUNT: $1000

DEADLINE(S): AUG 18

FIELD(S): All fields of Study

Must reside in the USA, and attend a school in Europe. Scholarships based on a 400 word essay on how to expand inter-cultural activity for study. Must have been born in Europe and desire to study there after living in the US.

For undergraduate or graduate study. Write for complete information.

3798 — RISING STAR INTERNSHIPS (Internships and Part-Time Employment for Students)

1904 Hidden Point Road
Annapolis MD 21401
410/974-4783
E-Mail: webmaster@rsinternships.com
Internet: www.rsinternships.com

AMOUNT: Varies

DEADLINE(S): None

FIELD(S): All fields

A website containing opportunities for internships and part-time student employment nationwide. The search is free, but there is a charge for students to post a resume. Organizations offering opportunities can do so for free for one month, but must pay $10 per month thereafter. Many vocational areas are available.

Most internships are unpaid.

3799 — ROCKEFELLER ARCHIVE CENTER (Grants-in-aid)

15 Dayton Ave.
Sleepy Hollow NY 10591
914/631-4505
FAX: 914/631-6017
E-Mail: archive@rockvax.rockefeller.edu
Internet: www.rockefeller.edu/archive.ctr

AMOUNT: $2,500 (US & Canada); $3,000 (all others)

DEADLINE(S): NOV 30

FIELD(S): All fields of study

Grants for graduate and postgraduate students of any nationality to support travel to the Rockefeller Archive Center. Must complete application specifying appropriate research topic. Financial need NOT a factor.

40 awards annually. Renewable. Contact the Rockefeller Center for an application.

3800 — RONALD E. McNAIR POST-BACCALAUREATE ACHIEVEMENT PROGRAM

U.S. Dept. of Educ., Student Financial
Assistance Programs
Washington DC 20202-5464
1-800/4-FED-AID

AMOUNT: Varies

DEADLINE(S): None

FIELD(S): All fields of graduate study

Program to prepare low-income, first-generation college students and students from groups under-represented in graduate education for higher level education. Assistance can be for summer internships, seminars, tutoring, counseling, etc.

Elegible students should contact the graduate school he or she plans to attend and/or call above number for other forms of federal financial assistance.

3801 — ROTARY FOUNDATION OF ROTARY INTERNATIONAL (Grants for University Teachers)

1 Rotary Center
1560 Sherman Ave.
Evanston IL 60201-3698
847/866-3000
FAX: 847/328-8554
E-Mail: sheynina@riorc.mhs.compuserve.com
Internet: www.rotary.org

AMOUNT: Varies - Up to $20,000

DEADLINE(S): Varies (with local Rotary Club)

FIELD(S): All fields of study

An opportunity for university teachers to teach at a university in a low-income country. Grants are for either three to five months (US$10,000) or six to ten months (US$20,000). Must be as a citizen of a country where there is a Rotary club.

Rotarians and their relatives are eligible as well as non-Rotarians. Contact local Rotary club for deadlines and application submissions. Check website for further information.

3802 — ROYAL NEIGHBORS OF AMERICA (Non-traditional Scholarship)

230 16th St.
Rock Island IL 61201
309/788-4561
FAX: 309/788-9234

AMOUNT: $1,000

DEADLINE(S): DEC 1

FIELD(S): All areas of study

For those who have been RNA members for at least two years and are 25 years of age or older.

10 awards per year. Contact Betty Walsh at above address/number.

3803 — ROYAL NORWEGIAN EMBASSY (May 8th Memorial Fund)

2720 34th St. NW
Washington DC 20008
202/333-6000

AMOUNT: Food & lodging; tuition is free

DEADLINE(S): MAR 15

FIELD(S): None specified

Scholarship commemorating 25th anniversary of Liberation of Norway for one year's residence at a Norwegian Folk High School. No formal credits, not college; objective is to prepare young people for everyday life in the community.

Must be between 18 and 22 years of age; your country must be among those selected for this year's bursaries. Other restrictions apply. Write for complete information.

3804 — ROYAL SOCIETY OF EDINBURGH (SOEID Research Fellowships)

22/24 George St.
Edinburgh EH2 2PQ SCOTLAND
0131 225 6057
FAX: 0131 220 6889
E-Mail: res@rse.org.uk

AMOUNT: 16,045 to 24,600 pounds sterling

DEADLINE(S): MAR 15

FIELD(S): All disciplines

Research fellowships for study at higher education institutions in Scotland. For postdoctoral researchers age 32 or under on the date of appointment (usually Oct. 1).

Write for complete information.

3805 — RURITAN NATIONAL FOUNDATION (Grant and Loan Program)

P.O. Box 487
Dublin VA 24084
703/674-9441

AMOUNT: Varies—minimum grant $200; minimum loan $500

DEADLINE(S): APR 1

FIELD(S): All fields of study

Grants and loans for postsecondary education. Applicant must be recommended by two active Ruritans. Clubs are located in 25 states.

Financial need, character, scholarship, and academic promise, and desire for further education are considered.

3806 — SACHS FOUNDATION (Scholarship Program)

90 S. Cascade Ave., Suite 1410
Colorado Springs CO 80903
719/633-2353

AMOUNT: $3,000 (undergrad); $4,000 (graduate)

DEADLINE(S): FEB 15

FIELD(S): All fields of study

Open to African-American residents of Colorado who are high school graduates, U.S. citizens, have a 3.4 or better GPA, & can demonstrate financial need. For undergrad study at any accredited college or university. Very few graduate grants are awarded.

Approximately 50 scholarships per year. Renewable if 2.5 or better GPA is maintained. Grants are for up to 4 years in duration. Write for complete information.

3807 — SAMUEL LEMBERG SCHOLARSHIP LOAN FUND INC. (Scholarships-Loans)

60 East 42nd St., Suite 1814
New York NY 10165
Written inquiry

AMOUNT: Up to $5,000 per academic year

DEADLINE(S): APR 1

FIELD(S): All fields of study

Special no-interest scholarship-loans open to Jewish men and women pursuing any undergraduate; graduate or professional degree. Recipients assume an obligation to repay their loans within 10 years after the completion of their studies.

Write for complete information.

3808 — SAN JOSE STATE UNIVERSITY (Scholarships)

Financial Aid Office SJSU
One Washington Square
San Jose CA 95192-0036
408/924-6095

FAX: 408/924-6089
E-Mail: ellioja@sjsuvm1.sjsu.edu

AMOUNT: $100 to $2,000 (based on GPA)

DEADLINE(S): MAR 15

FIELD(S): All fields of study

Students must have established a GPA at SJSU based on the successful completion of at least 8 graduate or 12 undergraduate units prior to filing an application. Incoming freshmen/transfer students not eligible. Must attend full-time and have filled out the FAFSA (however, foreign nationals are eligible to apply). Financial need considered.

300-500 awards annually. Contact Janet M. Elliot, Counselor, for an application. Note: Students should contact their department majors for information on any departmental scholarships that may be available.

3809 — SARA'S WISH FOUNDATION (Scholarships)

23 Ash Lane
Amherst MA 01002
413/256-0914
FAX: 413/253-3338
E-Mail: info@saraswish.org
Internet: saraswish.org

AMOUNT: Varies

DEADLINE(S): None

FIELD(S): All fields of study

Scholarships for individuals who share Sara Schewe's zest for life, love of adventure, and zeal to excel. Sara was killed in a bus accident in India while on a student tour. The scholarship is for students dedicated to community service, who actively participate in creative pursuits, and who will be advocates for safe travel conditions.

3810 — SCHOOL FOR INTERNATIONAL TRAINING (College Semester Abroad and Other Scholarships Related to International Education)

Kipling Road, P.O. Box 676
Brattleboro VT 05302-0676
1-800/336-1616
FAX: 802/258-3500
E-Mail: info@sit.edu
Internet: www.worldlearning.org/sit/financial.html

AMOUNT: $500-$2,500

DEADLINE(S): Varies

FIELD(S): All fields of study

Several scholarships are available through this organization for studying abroad or for training others in international relations areas. Some are for teachers,

some are for undergraduates, some are for former Peace Corps volunteers and other similar organizations, and some are for majors in fields such as international business management, foreign language and ESL teachers, etc.

Contact organization for detailed information concerning all of their programs.

3811 — SCREAMING POLITICIANS (Scholarship Essay Contest)

4720 Vineland Ave., Ste. 300
North Hollywood CA 91602
Internet: www.ScreamingPoliticians.com/scholar.htm

AMOUNT: $1,000

DEADLINE(S): JUL 4

FIELD(S): All fields of study

For high school/college student who most clearly writes a one-page interpretation of what they think Screaming Politicians' feelings, emotions, and thoughts are in a pre-selected song—1999's topic is "Shame." Must be US resident. High school students must plan on attending college/university following high school. Essay must be typed, double-spaced on legal size paper & in English. Must be stapled to entry form. LAST name & last 4 digits of SSN must be on each page.

1 award annually. 2 copies of essay must be mailed in flat, 9x12 envelope. See website to hear "Shame" and apply online. Or send self-addressed, stamped envelope for entry form.

3812 — SCREEN ACTORS GUILD FOUNDATION (John L. Dales Scholarship Fund)

5757 Wilshire Blvd.
Los Angeles CA 90036-3600
213/549-6610

AMOUNT: Varies - Determined annually

DEADLINE(S): APR 30

FIELD(S): All areas of study

Scholarships open to SAG members with at least five years membership or dependent children of members with at least eight years membership. Awards are for any level of undergraduate, graduate, or post-graduate study at an accredited institution.

Financial need is a consideration. Renewable yearly with reapplication. Write for complete information.

3813 — SEMINOLE TRIBE OF FLORIDA (Higher Education Awards)

6073 Stirling Road
Hollywood FL 33024
305/584-0400 ext. 154

AMOUNT: None specified

DEADLINE(S): APR 15; JUL 15; NOV 15

FIELD(S): All areas of study

Open to enrolled members of the Seminole Tribe of Florida or to those eligible to become a member. For undergraduate or graduate study at an accredited college or university.

Awards renewable. Write for complete information.

3814 — SERB NATIONAL FOUNDATION (Scholarships)

One Fifth Ave.
Pittsburgh PA 152222
1-800/538-SERB or 412/642-SERB
FAX: 642-1372
E-Mail: snf@serbnatlfed.org
Internet: serbnatlfed.org/benefits.htm

AMOUNT: Varies

DEADLINE(S): Varies (spring)

FIELD(S): All fields of study

Scholarships for students of Serbian ancestry attending postsecondary institutions in the U.S. Must have been members of the organization for at least two years.

Contact above organization for details.

3815 — SHOSHONE HIGHER EDUCATION PROGRAM (Shoshone Tribal Scholarship)

PO Box 628
Fort Washakie WY 82514
Written Inquiry

AMOUNT: Varies

DEADLINE(S): Varies

FIELD(S): All fields of study

Available to high school graduates who are enrolled members of the Wind River Shoshone Tribe and may be used at any public institution in Wyoming. Applicants must have a financial need analysis completed by the college financial aid office. New applicants should forward to the agency a letter of acceptance from a postsecondary institution, a transcript or GED certificate, and a letter stating a proposed course of full-time study and plans upon receiving a degree.

Renewable. Write to above address for an application at least six weeks prior to beginning of school year.

3816 — SIR ROBERT MENZIES CENTRE FOR AUSTRALIAN STUDIES (Australian Bicentennial Scholarships & Fellowships)

28 Russell Square
London WC1B 5DS ENGLAND UK
+44 0171-862 8854
FAX: +44 0171-580 9627
E-Mail: mcintyre@sas.ac.uk

AMOUNT: 4,000 pounds sterling (max.)

DEADLINE(S): MAY 28

FIELD(S): All fields of study

Purpose is to enable United Kingdom graduates to study in approved courses or undertake approved research in Australia. Must be a postgraduate student with at least an upper second class honours degree. Must demonstrate scholarly advantage of studying in Australia. Younger scholars preferred, but no formal age limit, but must be able to make contribution in field for ten years. Must spend at least three months studying in Australia. Must submit c.v. & proposal.

Contact Kirsten McIntyre for an application no later than May 28th; actual deadline to return application is June 4th.

3817 — SIR ROBERT MENZIES CENTRE FOR AUSTRALIAN STUDIES (Northcote Graduate Scholarships)

28 Russell Square
London WC1B 5DS ENGLAND UK
+44 0171-862 8854
FAX: +44 0171-580 9627
E-Mail: mcintyre@sas.ac.uk

AMOUNT: Travel, fees + allowance of A$17,427/yr.

DEADLINE(S): AUG 21

FIELD(S): All fields of study

Scholarships are to enable students resident in the UK to undertake a higher degree at an Australian university for a period of up to three years. Must be under the age of 30. Must submit statement on proposed course/research project, two references, statement from host institution indicating appropriateness of research & applicant's eligibility for admission, statement of why study must be in Australia, and a curriculum vitae. Yearly report required.

2 awards annually. Renewable. Contact Kirsten McIntyre for an application no later than August 21st; actual deadline to return application is August 28th. Awardees will be notified two months later.

3818 — SKY PEOPLE HIGHER EDUCATION (Northern Arapaho Tribal Scholarship)

PO Box 8480
Ethete WY 82520
Written Inquiry

AMOUNT: Varies

DEADLINE(S): Varies

FIELD(S): All fields of study

Scholarships are available to high school graduates who are enrolled members of the Northern Arapaho Tribe and may be used at any public institution in Wyoming. New applicants should forward to the agency a letter of acceptance from a postsecondary institution, a high school transcript or GED certificate,

and a letter stating a proposed course of full-time study and plans upon receiving a degree. Applications should be made a least six weeks prior to school year.

Renewable. Contact above address for an application.

3819 — SONOMA STATE UNIVERSITY (Scholarship Program)

Scholarship Office, 1801 East Cotati Avenue
Rohnert Park CA 94928
707/664-2261

AMOUNT: $250-$2,500

DEADLINE(S): MAR 1

FIELD(S): All fields of study

Student must be an applicant or full-time student of Sonoma State University and have a 3.0 GPA or higher. Some financial need must be demonstrated. Average of 300 awards given annually.

Contact Kay Ashbrook at above address for details.

3820 — SONS OF ITALY FOUNDATION (National Leadership Grants)

219 'E' Street NE
Washington DC 20002
202/547-2900 or 202/547-5106

AMOUNT: $2,000 to $5,000

DEADLINE(S): FEB 28

FIELD(S): All fields of study

National leadership grant competition is open to any full-time student of Italian heritage studying at an accredited college or university. For undergraduate or graduate study.

Write for complete information. Also contact local and state lodges for information regarding scholarships offered to members and their children.

3821 — SOROPTIMIST INTERNATIONAL OF GREAT BRITAIN & IRELAND (Golden Jubilee Fellowship)

127 Wellington Road S
Stockport SK1 3TS UK
0161/480 7686
FAX: 0161/477 6152

AMOUNT: 200 to 500 pounds sterling per annum

DEADLINE(S): APR 30

FIELD(S): All fields of study

Open to women residing within the boundaries of Soroptimist International of Great Britain & Ireland who NEED NOT be Soroptimists. Preference to mature women seeking to train or retrain for a business or profession.

Approximately 30 to 40 awards per year. Write for complete information, sending self-addressed envelope and international reply coupon. US residents NOT eligible.

3822 — SOUTH AFRICAN ASSOCIATION OF WOMEN GRADUATES (Isie Smuts Award)

P.O. Box 2163
Grahamstown 6140 South Africa
0461-25284

AMOUNT: R500-00 P.A.

DEADLINE(S): OCT 31

FIELD(S): All fields of study

Open to female graduate students (at the master's degree level or higher) who are working on their thesis. Must be members in good standing (2 years) of SAAWG and have completed at least one year's post-graduate study. Financial need is a consideration but not paramount.

Write to fellowships secretary for complete information.

3823 — SOUTH AFRICAN DEPARTMENT OF ARTS, CULTURE, SCIENCE, AND TECHNOLOGY (Scholarships)

Private Bag X894
Pretoria 0001 SOUTH AFRICA
012/337-8313
FAX: 012/323-0165
E-Mail: koz@dacsts.pwv.gov.za

AMOUNT: Stipend & expenses

DEADLINE(S): APR 30

FIELD(S): All fields of study

Scholarships to spend one academic year (10 months) in South Africa. Open to graduate students (under 31 years of age) who wish to gather information for a thesis or study project which they are working on for their home university.

22 awards annually. Contact Ms. F. Bassan for an application.

3824 — SOUTH CAROLINA STUDENT LOAN CORPORATION

P.O. Box 21487
Columbia SC 29221
803/798-0916
Internet: www.slc.sc.edu

AMOUNT: Varies

DEADLINE(S): Varies

FIELD(S): All areas of study

Open to South Carolina residents who are U.S. citizens or eligible non-citizens. Must be enrolled or accepted for enrollment at an eligible postsecondary school. Amount of loan determined by cost of school and financial need.

Interest is variable not to exceed at 8.25%. Loan must be renewed annually. Write or visit website for complete information.

3825 — SOUTH DAKOTA DIVISION OF VETERANS AFFAIRS (Aid to Veterans)

500 E. Capitol Ave.
Pierre SD 57501-5070
605/773-3269
FAX: 605/773-5380

AMOUNT: Free tuition in state-supported schools

DEADLINE(S): None specified

FIELD(S): All fields of study

Open to veterans (as defined by SDCL) who are residents of SD, were honorably discharged (as defined by SDCL), have exhausted their GI Bill, & have no other federal educational benefits available.

One-month free tuition for every month of qualified service. Benefit must be used within 20 years of cessation of hostilities or 6 years from discharge (whichever is later). Write for complete stipulations & information.

3826 — SOUTH DAKOTA DIVISION OF VETERANS AFFAIRS (Aid to Dependents of Deceased Veterans)

500 E. Capitol Ave.
Pierre SD 57501-5070
605/773-3269
FAX: 605/773-5380

AMOUNT: Free tuition in state-supported schools

DEADLINE(S): None specified

FIELD(S): All fields of study

Open to residents of SD under 25 years of age who are children of veterans who were residents of SD at least 6 months immediately prior to entry into active service & who died from any cause while in the service of the U.S. armed forces.

Must attend a state-supported college or university in SD. Write for complete information.

3827 — SOUTH DAKOTA DIVISION OF VETERANS AFFAIRS (Aid to Dependents of Prisoners of War or Missing in Action)

500 E. Capitol Ave.
Pierre SD 57501-5070
605/773-3269 FAX 605/773-5380

AMOUNT: 8 semesters or 12 quarters of free tuition and mandatory fees, other than subsistence expenses, in a state-supported institution.

DEADLINE(S): None specified

FIELD(S): All fields of study, including technical or vocational.

Open to children born before or during the period of time a parent served as a prisoner of war or was declared missing in action OR legally adopted OR in the legal custody of the parent prior to and during the time the parent served as a POW or was MIA OR the spouse of a POW or MIA. Once qualified, the return of the qualifying veteran will not remove any provisions or benefits.

No state benefits are available if equal or greater federal benefits are available; state benefits can supplement any lesser benefits from federal sources.

3828 — SPANISH EMBASSY (Canada-Spain Exchange Scholarships)

122-74 Stanley Avenue
Ottawa Ontario K1M 1P4 CANADA
613/747-2252
FAX: 613/744-1224
E-Mail: barrio@DocuWeb.ca
Internet: www.docuweb.ca/SpainInCanada/

AMOUNT: Tuition, travel, and living allowance

DEADLINE(S): MAR 31

FIELD(S): All fields of study except medicine

Open to Canadian citizens for studies or research at the doctoral level. Candidates must have an excellent knowledge of Spanish. Studies or research in medicine or related fields CANNOT be accommodated.

Write for complete information.

3829 — ST. ANDREW'S SOCIETY OF THE STATE OF NEW YORK (Scholarships)

3 West 51st St.
New York NY 10019
212/397-4849
FAX: 212/397-4846
E-Mail: standrewsny@msn.com

AMOUNT: $10,000

DEADLINE(S): DEC 15

FIELD(S): All fields of study

Scholarships for graduate students who will attend school within a 250-mile radius of New York. Must demonstrate financial need and be recommended by the president of your school—one recommendation allowed per school.

2 awards annually. Not renewable. Contact Jane Stephens for nomination procedures.

3830 — ST. DAVID'S SOCIETY (Scholarship)

3 West 51 St.
New York NY 10019
212/422-5480

AMOUNT: $500-$2,500

DEADLINE(S): JUN 1

FIELD(S): All fields of study

Scholarships for college students who are either of Welsh heritage, attending a Welsh school, or studying Welsh culture and/or language. For graduates or undergraduates.

Approximately 12 awards per year. Renewable.

3831 — STATE OF NEW JERSEY OFFICE OF STUDENT ASSISTANCE (NJClass Loan Program)

CN 540
Trenton NJ 08625
609/588-3200
800/35-NJ-LOAN
TDD: 609/588-2526

AMOUNT: May not exceed cost of attendance minus other financial assistance.

DEADLINE(S): None specified

FIELD(S): All areas of study

For U.S. citizens or legal residents who are N.J. residents. Must be enrolled at least half-time at an approved school making satisfactory academic progress towards a degree. Repayment is 15 years from date of first disbursement. Various options available.

Apply at least two months prior to need. Write for complete information.

3832 — STEVEN KNEZEVICH TRUST (Grants)

100 E. Wisconsin Ave., Suite 1020
Milwaukee WI 53202
414/271-6364

AMOUNT: $100 to $800

DEADLINE(S): NOV 1

FIELD(S): All areas of study

Undergraduate & graduate grants for students of Serbian descent. Must establish evidence of ancestral heritage. It is common practice for students to be interviewed in Milwaukee prior to granting the award.

Address inquiries to Stanley Hack. Include self-addressed stamped envelope.

3833 — STUDENT AID FOUNDATION, INC. (Loans)

2520 E. Piedmont Rd., Suite F-180
Marietta GA 30062
770/973-7077
FAX: 770/973-2220

AMOUNT: $2,500/yr. (undergrad); $3,000/yr. (graduate)

DEADLINE(S): APR 15

FIELD(S): All fields of study

Low-interest loans for women who are residents of Georgia or out-of-state women attending a Georgia school. Grades, financial need, personal integrity, and sense of responsibility are considerations.

70 loans annually. Renewable with re-application. Send a self-addressed, stamped envelope for an application.

3834 — SUNSHINE COAST BURSARY & LOAN SOCIETY (Scholarships & Loans)

c/o Mrs. M. Mackenzie
Box 44
Sechelt BC VON 3AO Canada
604/885-9436

AMOUNT: $500 loan; bursary amounts vary

DEADLINE(S): JUN 15

FIELD(S): All areas of study

Student must be graduate of one of the high schools of the Sunshine Coast School District #46 in Gibsons, Sechelt, or Pender Harbour, BC, Canada. Bursary and loans can be used at any postsecondary institution.

Application forms may be obtained from the address above or from a counselor at the high school previously attended by the student.

3835 — SWEDISH INSTITUTE/SVENSKA INSTITUTET (Fellowships for Study/Research in Sweden)

Dept. for Educational and Research Exchange,
Box 7434
SE-103 91 Stockholm SWEDEN
Written inquirty

AMOUNT: SEK 7,060/mo.

DEADLINE(S): DEC 1

FIELD(S): All fields of study

Program to encourage study or research in Sweden. For persons from any country except Nordic countries (Finland, Sweden, Norway, Denmark, or Iceland).

Contact above organization for details.

3836 — TAILHOOK FOUNDATION (Scholarship Fund)

9696 Business Park Ave.
San Diego CA 92131
619/689-9223
FAX: 619/578-8839
E-Mail: thookassn@aol.com

AMOUNT: $1,000

DEADLINE(S): JUL 1

FIELD(S): All fields of study

Scholarships for students at all levels whose parent was or is serving in any branch of military service on an aircraft carrier. Must be U.S. citizen and enrolled in or attending a four-year college or university.

5 awards per year. May re-apply for renewal.

3837 — TARAKNATH DAS FOUNDATION

Columbia University
1131 International Affairs
420 W. 118th St.
New York NY 10027
Not given

AMOUNT: $1,000-$3,500

DEADLINE(S): AUG 1

FIELD(S): All areas of study

For graduate students who are citizens of India and who have completed one year of graduate study in the U.S.

3-4 awards per year. Must demonstrate financial need. For details contact Dr. Leonard Gordon at above location.

3838 — TARGET STORES (Target Teachers Scholarships)

Citizen's Scholarship Fdn
1505 Riverview Rd.
St. Peter MN 56082-0480
800/316-6142
Internet: www.target.com

AMOUNT: $500-$1,500

DEADLINE(S): NOV 1

FIELD(S): All fields of study

Open to teachers and school administrators to further their education through classes, seminars, and other staff development opportunites.

1,800 awards annually (2 per store) + 96 District Teacher Scholarships annually. See website or contact your local Target store for an application.

3839 — TERESA F. HUGHES TRUST

Hawaiian Community Foundation
900 Fort St. Mall, Suite 1300
Honolulu HI 96813
808/566-5570

AMOUNT: Varies

DEADLINE(S): Ongoing

FIELD(S): All fields of study

Scholarships to financially needy Hawaiian residents who are orphans, half-orphans, social orphans (neglected or abused), and children born out-of-wedlock, for preschool, summer programs, private school, and college.

Write to Hawaiian Community Foundation at above address for details.

3840 — TEXAS A&M UNIVERSITY (Academic Excellence Awards)

Student Financial Aid Dept.
College Station TX 77843-1252
409/845-3236/3987

AMOUNT: $500-$1,500

DEADLINE(S): MAR 1

FIELD(S): All fields of study

Open to full-time undergraduate and graduate students at Texas A&M University. Awards are intended to recognize and assist students who are making excellent scholastic progress, campus and community activities, leadership positions, and work experience.

Approximately 600 awards per year. Awards granted for one year. Applications are available at the student financial aid office during January & February.

3841 — TEXAS A&M UNIVERSITY (Scholarships, Grants, and Loans)

Division of Student Affairs
College Station TX 77843-1252
409/845-3236/3987

AMOUNT: Varies

DEADLINE(S): Varies

FIELD(S): All fields of study

Texas A&M University offers several scholarship and loan programs. They awarded on the basis of academic criteria and/or combinations of financial need, campus/community activities, leadership positions, and work experience. klSome are for minorities, teacher candidates, cadets, and Texas high school class valedictorians. Applicants do not have to be prior Texas residents and should begin inquiries as high school seniors.

Send to above location for comprehensive information.

3842 — TEXAS HIGHER EDUCATION COORDINATING BOARD (Scholarships, Grants, and Loans)

P.O. Box 12788
Capitol Station
Austin TX 78711-2788
512/427-6340 or 800/242-3062 or TDD: 800/735-2988

AMOUNT: Varies

DEADLINE(S): Varies (with program)

FIELD(S): All fields of study

Open to students attending Texas institutions. Numerous state-administered student financial aid programs (including scholarships, grants, and loans) are offered.

Contact your school's financial aid office or write to the address above for the booklet "Financial Aid for Texas Students" which describes all programs in detail.

3843 — THE ALBERTA HERITAGE SCHOLARSHIP FUND

9940 106 St., 6th Fl.
Edmonton Alberta T5K 2V1 CANADA
403/427-8640

AMOUNT: Varies

DEADLINE(S): Varies

FIELD(S): All fields of study

Several scholarships and fellowships for all fields of study. For high school seniors, undergraduates, and graduates. Some are for specialized fields of study, and some are general. Includes opportunities to study abroad.

Send for pamphlet at above address for complete listing.

3844 — THE ALBERTA HERITAGE SCHOLARSHIP FUND (Alberta Ukrainian Centennial Commemorative Scholarship)

9440 106th St., 9th Fl.
Edmonton Alberta T5K 2V1 CANADA
403/427-8640

AMOUNT: Not specified

DEADLINE(S): FEB 1

FIELD(S): All fields of study

For a graduate student from Alberta to study in Ukraine.

A similar program is available for Ukrainian students to study in Alberta.

3845 — THE ALBERTA HERITAGE SCHOLARSHIP FUND (Alberta Ukrainian Centennial Commemorative Scholarship)

9440 106th St., 9th Fl.
Edmonton Alberta T5K 2V1 CANADA
403/427-8640

AMOUNT: Not specified

DEADLINE(S): FEB 1

FIELD(S): All fields of study

AN academic opportunities for a graduate student from Ukraine to study in Alberta, Canada.

Awarded every other year.

3846 — THE ANGLO-DANISH SOCIETY (The Denmark Liberation Scholarships)

Secretary, Danewood, 4 Daleside
Gerrards Cross, Bucks SL9 7JF ENGLAND UK
01753 884846

AMOUNT: 6,000-9,000 pounds

DEADLINE(S): JAN 12

FIELD(S): All fields of study

Scholarships for U.K. graduates students to study in Denmark. Can be used at an approved Danish university. Scholarships run for up to six months.

Applications available between October 1 and December 31. Write to Secretary of the Anglo-Danish Society; please enclose a stamped, self-addressed envelope or International Reply Coupon.

3847 — THE ANGLO-DANISH SOCIETY (The Hambros Bank Scholarships for U.K. Citizens to Study in Denmark)

Secretary, Danewood, 4 Daleside
Gerrards Cross, Bucks SL9 7JF ENGLAND UK
01753 884846

AMOUNT: 175 pounds/month

DEADLINE(S): JAN 12

FIELD(S): All fields of study

Scholarships for U.K. citizens to study in Denmark. Can be used at a Danish university. Scholarships run for up to six months.

Applications available between October 1 and December 31. Write to Secretary of the Anglo-Danish Society; please enclose a stamped, self-addressed envelope or International Reply Coupon.

3848 — THE ANGLO-DANISH SOCIETY (The Hambros Bank Scholarships for Danish Citizens to Study in the U.K.)

Secretary, Danewood, 4 Daleside
Gerrards Cross, Bucks SL9 7JF ENGLAND UK
01753 884846

AMOUNT: 175 pounds/month

DEADLINE(S): JAN 12

FIELD(S): All fields of study

Scholarships for Danish citizens to study in the United Kingdom. Scholarships run for up to six months.

Applications available between October 1 and December 31. Write to Secretary of the Anglo-Danish Society; please enclose a stamped, self-addressed envelope or International Reply Coupon.

3849 — THE ANGLO-ISRAEL ASSOCIATION (Wyndham Deedes Memorial Trust Fund)

9 Bentinck St.
London W1M 5RP ENGLAND UK
+44 (0) 171 486 2300 or +44 (0) 171 935 9505
FAX: +44 (0) 171 935 4690
Internet: www.shamash.org/ejin/brijnet/aia/

AMOUNT: 2,000 pounds

DEADLINE(S): MAR 1

FIELD(S): All fields of study (some aspect of life in Israel)

Travel scholarships for study in Israel for British citizens normally resident in the United Kingdom. Must have graduated from a British University or Institute of Higher Education. For intensive study of some aspect (sociological, scientific, cultural, economic, etc.) of life in Israel. The study, which must be up to six weeks, is to be in an area in which the applicant is specially qualified or interested.

See website for specific details and online application and/or contact organization.

3850 — THE AUGUSTUS SOCIETY (Scholarships)

PO Box 28255
Las Vegas NV 89126
Written inquiry

AMOUNT: $1,500

DEADLINE(S): None

FIELD(S): All fields of study

College scholarships for students of Italian-American ancestry who are residents of Clark County, Nevada. Considerations are need and ability.

Contact organization for details.

3851 — THE BRITISH COUNCIL (Scholarships for English Language Assistants to Mexico)

10 Spring Gardens
London SW1A 2BN ENGLAND UK
+44 (0) 171 930 8466
FAX: +44 (0) 161 957 7188
E-Mail: education.enquiries@britcoun.org
Internet: www.britcoun.org/mexico/mexschol.htm

AMOUNT: Varies

DEADLINE(S): Varies

FIELD(S): Teaching English

The British Council in Mexico offers the opportunity, funded by the Mexican Ministries of Education and Foreign Affairs, to British citizens to teach English in Mexico. Another way to receive information is by sending E-mail to: carmina.ramon@bc-mexico.sprint.com (in Mexico City) or teresa riggen@bc-mexico.sprint.com (in Guadalajara).

Another source of information is: leticia.magana@bc-mexico.sprint.com

3852 — THE BRITISH COUNCIL (Scholarships for Residents of Myanmar [Burma])

78 Kanna Rd./P.O. Box 638
Yangon MYANMAR (BURMA)
(00 95 1) 254 658
FAX: (00 95 1)
E-Mail: admin@bc-burma.bcouncil.org
Internet: www.britcoun.org/burma/burnews.htm

AMOUNT: Varies

DEADLINE(S): Varies

FIELD(S): All fields of study

The British Council lists several scholarship programs for residents of Myanmar (Burma). Some are for specific fields of study: computing, management, science), and some are general.

The website listed here gives more details; the British council lists hundreds of educational programs world wide on its website. Enter "scholarship" as the search word. Another contact is the Education Advisory Service. The E-mail is: Wendy@bc-burma.bcouncil.org. The Education Officer can provide further advice for anyone hoping to study in Britain.

3853 — THE BRITISH WOMEN PILOT'S ASSOCIATION (The Diana Britten Aerobatic Scholarship)

Brooklands Museum, Brooklands Road
Weybridge KT13 0QN Surrey ENGLAND UK
Written inquiry
Internet: www.aerobatics.org.uk/News/BWPAscholarship.htm

AMOUNT: Cost of training

DEADLINE(S): Varies

FIELD(S): Aviation

A scholarship for a licensed female British pilot to receive 10 hours of comprehensive instruction in aerobatics. Must hold a current PPL and medical clearance and have no previous aerobatic experience or training.

Visit website for more information. Write to organization for detailed application information and next deadline date.

3854 — THE BUFFETT FOUNDATION

222 Keiwit Plaza
Omaha NE 68131
402/451-6011

AMOUNT: Tuition and fees for Nebraska state colleges and universities; $500 per semester at other institutions

DEADLINE(S): APR 15; OCT 15

FIELD(S): All areas of study

Scholarships for financially needy residents of Nebraska.

Must demonstrate financial need. Send SASE to Allen Greenberg, c/o Devon Buffett, P.O. Box 4508, Decatur, IL 62525; 402/451-6011.

3855 — THE CULTURAL SOCIETY, INC.

200 West 19th St.
Panama City FL 32045
Written inquiry

AMOUNT: Varies

DEADLINE(S): Ongoing

FIELD(S): All areas of study

Scholarship for Muslim students.

Write to Dr. Yahya Abdul Rahim, President, at above address for application requirements.

3856 — THE CYPRUS CHILDREN'S FUND, INC. (Scholarship Endowment)

13 East 40th Street
New York NY 10016
212/696-4590 or 800/775-7217

AMOUNT: Varies

DEADLINE(S): MAY 5

FIELD(S): All fields of study

To students of Greek or Greek Cypriot origin. Applicants can be US residents, US citizens, or citizens of Greece or Cyprus. May be pursuing studies in accredited college or university in the US, Greece, or Cyprus.

1 scholarship annually. Financial need determines award. Applications must be typewritten and include various documents—please write or call for complete information.

3857 — THE E. PERRY AND GRACE BEATTY MEMORIAL FOUNDATION

P.O. Box 450
Youngstown OH 44501
Written inquiry

AMOUNT: $1,000

DEADLINE(S): Ongoing

FIELD(S): All fields of study

Scholarships for residents of Ohio.

Write to National City Bank, Northeast, at above address for current guidelines.

3858 — THE FRANK H. & EVA BUCK FOUNDATION (Frank H. Buck Scholarships)

P.O. Box 5610
Vacaville CA 95696
707/446-7700

AMOUNT: Tuition, books, room and board

DEADLINE(S): DEC 1

FIELD(S): All fields of study

Open to unique students (from the 9th grade forward) who have an overwhelming motivation to succeed in all endeavors. Preference is given to residents of Solano, Napa, Yolo, Sacramento, San Joaquin, and Contra Costa Counties. Renewable.

For students in private secondary schools and specialized trade schools as well as universities and college. Applications available in mid-Sept; apply by Dec. 1.

3859 — THE GRAND RAPIDS FOUNDATION (Alice Bridges Scholarships)

209-C Waters Building
161 Ottawa NW
Grand Rapids MI 49503
616/454-1751
FAX: 616/454-6455

AMOUNT: Varies

DEADLINE(S): APR 3

FIELD(S): All fields of study

Scholarships for part- or full-time students pursuing gradute-level study (M.A., M.D., Ph.D.) at an accredited Michigan university. Must have been a resident of Kent County, Michigan, for a minimum of two years at time of application OR prior to the beginning of their undergraduate education.

Renewable if 3.0 GPA is maintained and financial need continues. Send SASE to above address for details.

3860 — THE GRAND RAPIDS FOUNDATION (Guy D. & Mary Edith Halladay Graduate Scholarship)

209-C Waters Bldg.
161 Ottawa Ave. NW
Grand Rapids MI 49503-2703
616/454-1751
FAX: 616/454-6455

AMOUNT: Varies

DEADLINE(S): APR 3

FIELD(S): All fields of study

Open to students undertaking post-graduate courses at colleges in West Michigan. Must have been a resident of Kent County for at least 5 years, have 3.0 or better GPA, and demonstrate financial need.

Send SASE to above address for complete information.

3861 — THE HELLENIC FOUNDATION

P.O. Box 7224
York PA 17405
Written inquiry

AMOUNT: Tuition, books, and living expenses

DEADLINE(S): Ongoing

FIELD(S): All fields of study

Scholarships to financially needy residents of Pennsylvania for attendance at colleges and universities.

Write to John F. Grove, Jr., Trustee, at above location for details. Include information regarding academic records, recommendaitons, and statement of financial need.

3862 — THE HORIZONS FOUNDATION (Joseph Towner Fund for Gay and Lesbian Families)

870 Market St., #1155
San Francisco CA 94102
415/398-2333

AMOUNT: $500/term

DEADLINE(S): JUN 15

FIELD(S): All fields of study

Scholarships for postsecondary students who have at least one lesbian or gay parent residing in one of the following Bay Area counties: Alameda, Contra Costa, Marin, San Francisco, San Mateo, Santa Clara, Napa, Sonoma, and Solano.

Must have 2.5 GPA or better.

3863 — THE JERUSALEM FELLOWSHIPS (Internships in Israel for Leaders)

2124 Broadway, Suite 244
New York NY 10023
1-800/ FELLOWS
E-Mail: jf@aish.edu
Internet: www.jerusalemfellowships.org

AMOUNT: $3,500 and up

DEADLINE(S): Varies

FIELD(S): All fields of study

Program for young Jewish student leaders to deepen their understanding of the people of and explore the land of Israel. Open to all Jewish students; however, additional and more valuable scholarships are available in Alabama and the Southeastern United States through the Ruttenberg Foundation of Birmingham, AL. Additional programs available at Rutgers, Cornell, Penn State, U. of Georgia, emory, Tulane, and U of Alabama.

Check website for details. Applications available online or at above location; $25 application fee.

3864 — THE KOREAN AMERICAN SCHOLARSHIP FOUNDATION (Scholarships)

P.O. Box 486
Pacific Palisades CA 90272
310/459-4080
Internet: www.kasf.org

AMOUNT: Up to $1,000

DEADLINE(S): JAN 31

FIELD(S): All fields of study

Scholarships for students of Korean descent who are U.S. citizens or permanent residents.

Send SASE to Scholarship Committee at above addressor visit website.

3865 — THE LEVERHULME TRUST (Leverhulme Study Abroad Studentships)

1 Pemberton Row
London EC4A 3BA ENGLAND
0171/822-6964
FAX: 0171/822-5084
E-Mail: hcuhl@admin.sussex.ac.uk
Internet: infa.central.susx.ac.uk/Units/research/leverhulme.html

AMOUNT: 11,410 pounds sterling

DEADLINE(S): JAN 6

FIELD(S): All fields of study

For UK residents. For advanced study or research at a center of learning in any part of world except US & UK. Open to 1st degree grads of a UK university who are under 30. If older, must have completed undergraduate work in last five years.

Studentships are tenable for one or two years. Write for complete information after Sept. of each year.

3866 — THE NANSEN FUND, INC. (John Dana Archbold Fellowship)

77 Saddlebrook Lane
Houston TX 77024
713/680-8255
FAX: 713/686-3963

AMOUNT: Tuition + up to $10,000 for supplies, maintenance, and travel

DEADLINE(S): FEB 28

FIELD(S): All fields of study

Opportunity for Norwegian graduate students, including post-doctorates, wishing to study in the U.S. in odd-numbered years.

Contact organization above for further information.

3867 — THE NANSEN FUND, INC. (John Dana Archbold Fellowship)

77 Saddlebrook Lane
Houston TX 77024
713/680-8255
FAX: 713/686-3963

AMOUNT: Tuition + up to $10,000 for supplies, maintenance, and travel

DEADLINE(S): FEB 28

FIELD(S): All fields of study

Opportunity for graduate students, including post-doctorates, to study at the University of Oslo, Norway. For U.S. citizens in even-numbered years.

For details, contact organization above.

3868 — THE NATIONAL HEMOPHILIA FOUNDATION (Kevin Child Scholarship)

116 W. 32nd St.
11th Floor
New York NY 10001
212/328-3700 or 800/42-HANDI
FAX: 212/328-3799
E-Mail: info@hemophilia.org
Internet: www.hemophilia.org

AMOUNT: $1,000

DEADLINE(S): JUL 3

FIELD(S): All fields of study

Scholarships for college students with a bleeding disorder—hemophilia, etc. through HANDI (Hemophilia and AIDS/HIV Network for the Dissemination of Information).

Contact HANDI at above location for applications.

3869 — THE NUFFIELD FOUNDATION (Education for Women)

28 Bedford Square
London WC1 3EG ENGLAND UK
0171 631 0566

FAX: 0171 323 4877

Internet: www.nuffield.org

AMOUNT: 250-1,000 pounds

DEADLINE(S): None

FIELD(S): All fields of study

Scholarships for women ages 25-50 to help them in their employment prospects.

Contact Louise Morris or Pat Muduroglu at above location for details.

3870 — THE PARKERSBURG AREA COMMUNITY FOUNDATION (Scholarships)

501 Avery St.

Parkersburg WV 26102

304/428-4438

FAX: 304/428-1200

E-Mail: pkbgcomfdn@alpha.wvup.wvnet.edu

AMOUNT: Varies

DEADLINE(S): Varies

FIELD(S): All fields of study

This Foundation administers more than 40 different scholarship funds. Many are for high school seniors at specific area high schools; others are for dependents of employees of certain companies or are for specific subject areas.

Contact organization for details.

3871 — THE PAUL & DAISY SOROS FELLOWSHIPS FOR NEW AMERICANS (Graduate Fellowships)

400 West 59th St.

New York NY 10019

212/547-6926

FAX: 212/548-4623

E-Mail: pdsoros_fellows@sorosny.org

Internet: www.pdsoros.org

AMOUNT: $20,000/yr. + 1/2 tuition

DEADLINE(S): NOV 30

FIELD(S): All fields of study leading to a graduate degree

Two-year graduate level fellowships for "New Americans"—1)holds a Green Card, or 2)is a naturalized U.S. citizen, or 3)is the child of two naturalized citizens. Must hold a B.A. degree or be in final year of undergraduate study and be at least 20 but not older than 30 years of age. Must be pursuing a graduate degree in any professional or scholarly discipline, including the Fine and Performing Arts. For use only in the U.S.

Thirty awards per year. Applications and details are available from college academic advisors, the Internet, or the organization (see location/website).

3872 — THE RENTOKIL FOUNDATION (Scholarships for U.K. Citizens to Study in Denmark)

Sophus Berendsen A/S, 1 Klausdalbrovej

DK-2860 Soborg DENMARK

Written inquiry

AMOUNT: Varies

DEADLINE(S): DEC 31

FIELD(S): All fields of study

Scholarships for U.K. citizens to study in Denmark. For use anywhere in Denmark. Scholarships run for up to twelve months.

Applications available after October 1. Send a stamped, self-addressed envelope or International Reply Coupon for detailed information.

3873 — THE THAI NATIONAL COMMISSION FOR UNESCO (Sponsored Fellowships Programme)

Ext Rel Div, Ministry of Ed.

Rajdamneonnok Ave.

Dusit District Bangkek 10300 THAILAND

662/281-6370

FAX: 662/281-0953

E-Mail: duangtip@winning.com

AMOUNT: Varies

DEADLINE(S): MAR 15

FIELD(S): All fields of study

Fellowships, scholarships, & junior scholarships open to students who wish to study in Thailand. Must be a citizen of UNESCO member country. Postgraduates must be no more than than 45 years of age, undergrads no more than 30, and junior undergrads no more than 25.

12 grants annually, 10 grants are renewable. Of US $20, 145 available annually, $2,500 goes unclaimed. Contact the Director, External Relations Division, at above address.

3874 — THE UNIVERSITY OF HULL (70th Anniversary Scholarships)

Cecilia Yates, International Services Division, Univ. of Hull

Hull HU6 7RX ENGLAND UK

0044 1482 466553

FAX: 0044 1482 466554

E-Mail: C.Yates@admin.hull.ac.uk

Internet: www.hull.ac.uk/prospectus/schol-70ann.html

AMOUNT: 3100 to 4100 pounds (depending on discipline of study)

DEADLINE(S): Varies

FIELD(S): All fields of study

The University of Hull offers up to 50 Anniversary scholarships to students from Southeast and East Asia

regions. The programs are a partial tuition fee waiver. Not for MBA candidates.

Application form and more data are on website. Please write clearly in block capitals. Awards are based on academic achievement and potential.

3875 — THE UNIVERSITY OF HULL (70th Anniversary Scholarships—China Initiative)

Dr. Xiao Fang, Ass't. Registrar, International Services Division, Univ. of Hull

Hull HU6 7RX ENGLAND UK

0044 1482 466553 or 0044 1482 465359

FAX: 0044 1482 466554

E-Mail: x.fang@admin.hull.ac.uk

Internet: www.hull.ac.uk/prospectus/schol-70annchina.html

AMOUNT: Up to 1,000 pounds

DEADLINE(S): Varies

FIELD(S): All fields of study

The University of Hull offers scholarships to students from mainland China. The programs are a partial tuition fee waiver. For undergraduates and graduates.

Application forms and more data are on website. Please write clearly in block capitals. Awards are based on academic achievement and potential.

3876 — THE UNIVERSITY OF HULL (British Scholarships)

Cecilia Pereira-Yates, International Services Division, Univ. of Hull

Hull HU6 7RX ENGLAND UK

00 44 1482 466854

FAX: 00 44 1482 466854

E-Mail: c.pereira-yates@admin.hull.ac.uk

Internet: www.hull.ac.uk/prospectus/schol-british.html

AMOUNT: 3,100-4,100 pounds (undergrads); 2,000-4,000 (grads)

DEADLINE(S): Varies

FIELD(S): All fields of study

The British government, in collaboration with several universities, offers scholarships to students from Indonesia, Korea, Malaysia, and Thailand. The University of Hull is one of these universities. For undergraduates and graduates.

Inquire at above address/phone/E-mail.

3877 — THE UNIVERSITY OF HULL (Undergraduate and Postgraduate Scholarships)

Joanne Clarke, Secretary to the Scholarships Committe, Univ. of Hull

Hull HU6 7RX ENGLAND UK

01482 465319
FAX: 01482 465936
E-Mail: J.Clark@admin.humm.ac.uk
Internet: www.hull.ac.uk/prospectus/scholar-intro-scheme.html

AMOUNT: Varies

DEADLINE(S): Varies

FIELD(S): All fields of study

The University of Hull claims to operate on the the most extensive scholarhip plans in the United Kingdom—almost 1 million pounds per year. The is a large assortment of programs for many different ypes of students. Some are shared arrangements with private sources.

Check website and contact the university for application forms and details of available funding programs.

3878 — THE UNIVERSITY OF KANSAS (Self Graduate Fellowship)

222 Strong Hall
Lawrence KS 66045
785/864-7249
E-Mail: self@ukans.edu
Internet: www.ukans.edu/~selfpro

AMOUNT: $100,000 over four years

DEADLINE(S): JAN 31

FIELD(S): All fields of study

A program of graduate study which includes faculty mentors, retreats, access to the nation's top innovators and business leaders, a lifetime networking. A rare opportunity for exceptional learners to earn a Ph.D. at the University of Kansas at Lawrence. Must be *beginning* doctoral study at time of application. Must demonstrate strong leadership potential, exceptional undergraduate academic record, and be a U.S. citizen.

Contact the above address or visit the website.

3879 — THE WASIE FOUNDATION (Scholarship Program)

U.S. Bank Place, Suite 4700
601 2nd Ave So.
Minneapolis MN 55402
612/332-3883
FAX: 612/332-2440

AMOUNT: $1,000-$14,000

DEADLINE(S): MAR 1

FIELD(S): All fields of study

Scholarships for high school students, college undergraduates, and graduate students of Polish descent who are enrolled in specified private high schools and colleges in Minnesota. Approx. 70 awards per year.

Applicants must be full-time students who can demonstrate financial need. Applications available Sept. 1 in financial aid offices of the institutions. Contact organization for list of schools.

3880 — THOMAS J. WATSON FOUNDATION (The Thomas J. Watson Fellowship Program)

217 Angell St.
Providence RI 02906-2120
401/274-1952

AMOUNT: $18,000 single; $25,000 with accompanying financial & legal dependent

DEADLINE(S): NOV 1

FIELD(S): All fields of study

Open to graduating seniors at the 48 U.S. colleges on the foundation's roster. Fellowship provides for one year of independent study and travel abroad immediately following graduation.

Candidates must be nominated by their college. Up to 60 awards per year. Write for list of participating institutions and complete information.

3881 — TOKYU FOUNDATION FOR INBOUND STUDENTS (Scholarships for Inbound Students)

1-21-2 Dogenzaka
Shibuya-ku
Tokyo 150 Japan
03-3461-0844
FAX: 03-5458-1696

AMOUNT: Monthly award of 160,000 yen plus expenses for specified academic meetings

DEADLINE(S): NOV 15

FIELD(S): All fields of study

Post-graduate scholarships open to non-Japanese Asian-Pacific region citizens to promote international exchange. Must be under 30 years old for master's program and under 35 years old for Ph.D program.

24 awards per year. Scholarships are awarded for up to 24 months. Write for complete information.

3882 — TOWSON STATE UNIVERSITY (Scholarship & Award Programs)

Scholarship Office
Towson MD 21252
410-830-2654

AMOUNT: Varies

DEADLINE(S): Varies

FIELD(S): All fields of study

Numerous scholarship and award programs available to entering freshmen and to graduate and transfer students attending Towson State University.

Write for scholarships and awards booklet which describes each program in detai. Awards are for Towson State University students only.

3883 — TRI-STATE GENERATION AND TRANSMISSION ASSOCIATION (Scholarships)

12076 Grant St.
PO Box 33695
Denver CO 80233
303/452-6111

AMOUNT: $500

DEADLINE(S): Varies

FIELD(S): All fields of study

Available to children of Tri-State Generation and Transmission member-system employees or consumers.

2 awards annually. Write to above address for an application.

3884 — TULANE UNIVERSITY (Scholarships & Fellowships)

Admissions Office
New Orleans LA 70118
504/865-5731
Internet: www.tulane.edu

AMOUNT: Varies

DEADLINE(S): Varies

FIELD(S): All areas of study

Numerous need-based and merit-based scholarship & fellowship programs for undergraduate and graduate study at Tulane University. There is also an honors program for outstanding students accepted for enrollment at Tulane.

Write for complete information.

3885 — U.S. DEPARTMENT OF STATE (Internships)

Recruitment Division, P.O. Box 9317
Arlington VA 22219
Written inquiry

AMOUNT: Varies—unpaid and paid internships

DEADLINE(S): NOV 1; MAR 1; JUL 1

FIELD(S): All fields of study

Internships during summer, fall, or spring through the U.S. Department of State. Some assignments are in the U.S.; some are abroad. Most are unpaid.

Write to organization for application and other details.

3886 — U.S. DEPT OF INTERIOR; BUREAU OF INDIAN AFFAIRS (Higher Education Grant Programs)

1849 C St. NW/MS-3512 MIB
Washington DC 20240-0001
202/208-4871
Internet: www.doi.giv/bia

AMOUNT: Varies depending on need

DEADLINE(S): Varies

FIELD(S): All areas of study

Open to enrolled members of Indian tribes or Alaskan native descendants eligible to receive services from the Secretary of the Interior. For study leading to associate's, bachelor's, or graduate degree.

Must demonstrate financial need. Contact home agency, area office, tribe, BIA office, or financial aid office at chosen college. Check website for details, including address and phone numbers of area offices nationwide.

3887 — U.S. DEPT OF INTERIOR; BUREAU OF INDIAN AFFAIRS (Higher Education Grant Programs-Northern Calif. & Nevada)

Western Nevada Agency
1677 Hot Springs Rd.
Carson City NV 89707
702/887-3515
FAX: 702/887-0496
Internet: www.doi.giv/bia

AMOUNT: Varies depending on need

DEADLINE(S): JUL 15; DEC 15

FIELD(S): All areas of study

Open to enrolled members of Indian tribes or Alaskan native descendants eligible to receive services from the Secretary of the Interior who reside in Northern California or Nevada. For study leading to associate's, bachelor's, graduate degrees, or adult education.

Must demonstrate financial need. Contact home agency, area office, tribe, or BIA office. Check website for details, including address and phone numbers of area offices nationwide.

3888 — UNICO NATIONAL, INC. (Various Scholarships)

72 Burroughs Place
Bloomfield NJ 07003
973/748-9144
FAX: 973/748-9576
E-Mail: unico@uniconat.com
Internet: www.uniconat.com

AMOUNT: Varies

DEADLINE(S): Varies

FIELD(S): All fields of study

Scholarship program for Americans of Italian ancestry. Programs are administered through various state chapters.

Contact national organization above to locate state chapters; then contact state chapter for application details.

3889 — UNITED DAUGHTERS OF THE CONFEDERACY (Scholarships)

Business Office
Memorial Bldg.
328 North Blvd.
Richmond VA 23220-4057
804/355-1636
FAX: 804/353-1396
Internet: www.hsv.tis.nit/~maxs/UDC/index.html

AMOUNT: $800 to $1,000

DEADLINE(S): FEB 15

FIELD(S): All fields of study

Various programs for descendants of worthy Confederate veterans. Applicants who are collateral descendants must be active members of the United Daughters of the Confederacy or of the Children of the Confederacy & MUST be sponsored by a UDC chapter.

Most awards for undergraduate study. For complete information send self-addressed, stamped #10 envelope (SASE) to address above or contact the education director in the division where you reside. Division addresses are on Internet site.

3890 — UNITED FOOD & COMMERCIAL WORKERS UNION—UFCW LOCAL 555 (L. Walter Derry Scholarship Fund)

PO Box 23555
Tigard OR 97223
503/684-2822
FAX: 503/620-3816

AMOUNT: $1,900 (any field) + up to $2,500 (labor relations)

DEADLINE(S): MAY 14

FIELD(S): All fields of study

Members of Local 555 in good standing for at least 1 year prior to application deadline are eligible to apply, or sponsor their child or spouse. Confidential questionnaire, high school & college transcripts, & 3 personal references required. May be used at any accredited college/university, technical/vocational, or junior/community college for any course of study. Additional award in field of labor relations available; submit 500-word essay on plans, with application.

6 awards annually (5 in any field; 1 in labor relations). Contact Larry A. Weirich, Chairman, Scholarship Committee, for an application.

3891 — UNITED METHODIST CHURCH (Scholarship and Loan Program)

P.O. Box 871
Nashville TN 37202-0871
615/340-7346
FAX: 615/340-7367

E-Mail: jimnose@umhighered.org
Internet: www.gbhem.org

AMOUNT: Varies

DEADLINE(S): JUN 1

FIELD(S): All fields of study

Scholarships and loans for undergraduates and graduate students. Most graduate scholarships are limited to theology, higher education administraiton, or older adults changing careers. Must have been a full and active member of a United Methodist church for at least one year. U.S. citizenship/permanent residency required. Minimum GPA of 2.5 required.

Check with financial aid dept. at your United Methodist college, the chairperson of your annual conference board of Higher Education and campus Ministry, or the address above for application details.

3892 — UNITED NEGRO COLLEGE FUND (Scholarships)

8260 Willow Oaks Corporate Dr.
Fairfax VA 22031
703/205-3400 or 800/331-2244
Internet: www.uncf.org

AMOUNT: Varies

DEADLINE(S): Varies

FIELD(S): All areas of study

Scholarships available to students who enroll in one of the 39 United Negro College Fund member institutions. Financial need must be established through the financial aid office at a UNCF college.

For information and a list of the UNCF campuses write to the address above.

3893 — UNITED STUDENT AID FUNDS INC. (Guaranteed Student Loan Program; Plus Loans)

1912 Capital Ave. #320
Cheyenne WY 82001
307/635-3259

AMOUNT: $2,625 to $5,500 (undergrads); $8,500 (grads)

DEADLINE(S): None

FIELD(S): All fields of study

Low-interest loans are available to Wyoming residents who are citizens or permanent residents of the U.S. and enrolled at least 1/2-time in school. Must demonstrate financial need.

Write for complete information.

3894 — UNIVERSITY COLLEGE LONDON (International Scholarships)

International Office, University College London, Gower St.
London WC1E 6BT ENGLAND UK

+44 (0) 171 380 7708
FAX: +44 (0) 171 380 7380
E-Mail: international@ucl.ac.uk
Internet: www.britcoun.org/eis/profiles/
ucl.uclschp.htm OR ucl.ac.uk

AMOUNT: Varies

DEADLINE(S): Varies

FIELD(S): All fields of study

Scholarships for undergraduate, graduate, and postgraduate international students pursuing degrees in most fields of study. For use at University College London.

At website, specific details are listed. Contact Mark Pickerill for details.

3895 — UNIVERSITY OF ALBERTA (Izaak Walton Killam Memorial Postdoctoral Fellowship)

Faculty of Grad Studies & Research
105 Administration Bldg.
Edmonton Alberta T6G 2M7 CANADA
403/492-3499
FAX: 403/492-0692

AMOUNT: Canadian $35,000/yr. + one-time C$3,000 research grant & airfare

DEADLINE(S): JAN 4

FIELD(S): All fields of study

Applicants must have recently completed a doctoral program or will do so in the immediate future. Appointments are for two years, and there is no restriction as to citizenship. Awards tenable only at the University of Alberta, and students who have received their doctoral degree from the University of Alberta are NOT eligible. Curriculum vitae, transcripts, research proposal, and letters of appraisal are required with application.

Contact the Scholarship Coordinator at the University of Alberta for an application.

3896 — UNIVERSITY OF ALBERTA (Izaak Walton Killam Memorial Scholarship)

Scholarship Coordinator
Faculty of Grad Studies & Research
2-8 University Hall
Edmonton Alberta T6G 2J9 Canada
403/492-3499
FAX 403/492-0692

AMOUNT: Canadian $16,200 + one-time C$1,500 research grant + tuition & specific fees

DEADLINE(S): FEB 1 (for nomination by department—check w/ dept. head for internal deadline)

FIELD(S): All fields of study

Open to students registered in or admissible to a doctoral program who have at least 1 year of graduate work before start of tenure. Killam scholars should

not be one-sided & their intellect should be complemented by a sound character.

Approximately 10 awards per year granted for 2 years. Write for complete information.

3897 — UNIVERSITY OF ALBERTA (Ph.D Scholarship)

Scholarship Coordinator
Faculty of Grad Studies & Research
2-8 University Hall
Edmonton Alberta T6G 2J9 Canada
403/492-3499
FAX 403/492-0692

AMOUNT: Canadian $13,000 + tuition & specified fees

DEADLINE(S): Varies

FIELD(S): All fields of study

For superior Canadian scholars who are being newly admitted into a Ph.D program or are transferring into a Ph.D program from a master's program (within 1st 12 months of master's program). Recipients have a teaching obligation.

Department nomination at time of admission. Offered for 1 year with possible 2nd year renewal. Write for complete information.

3898 — UNIVERSITY OF ALBERTA (Ph.D. Scholarship)

Scholarship Coordinator
Faculty of Grad Studies and Research
2-8 University Hall
Edmonton Alberta T6G 2J9 Canada
403/492-3499
FAX: 403/492-0692

AMOUNT: $13,000 + tuition and fees.

DEADLINE(S): Varies

FIELD(S): All fields of study

For superior foreign scholars who are being newly admitted into a Ph.D. program or are transferring into a Ph.D. program from a master's program (within the first 12 months of master's program). Recipients have a teaching obligation.

Not for Canadian students. Department nomination at time of admission. Offered for 1 year with possible 2nd year renewal.

3899 — UNIVERSITY OF BIRMINGHAM (A.E. Hills Postgraduate Scholarship)

Admissions & Student Records
Academic Office
Edgebaston Birmingham B15 2TT ENGLAND
UK
0121/414-3091

AMOUNT: Tuition, Fees, & Maintainance

DEADLINE(S): JUL

FIELD(S): All fields of study

Scholarship for which enrolled students in all schools at the university may be nominated by their school. Tenable at the university for postgraduate study.

Write for complete information.

3900 — UNIVERSITY OF BIRMINGHAM (International Scholarships)

International Office, Univ. of Birminham
Edgebaston, Birmingham B15 2TT ENGLAND
UK
+44 (0) 121 414 3886
FAX: +44 (0) 121 414 3850
E-Mail: international@bham.ac.uk
Internet: www.britcoun.org/eis/profiles/
birmuniv.birmschp.htm OR bham.ac.uk

AMOUNT: Varies

DEADLINE(S): Varies

FIELD(S): All fields of study

Scholarships for undergraduate, graduate, and postgraduate international students pursuing degrees in most fields of study. For use at Birmingham University in Central England.

At "bham.ac.uk" website, go to homepage, then search, write scholarships, and list appears. At the first listed website, specific details are listed. Contact Ms. Suzanne Alexander for details.

3901 — UNIVERSITY OF CALGARY (Izaak Walton Killam Memorial Scholarships)

2500 University Dr. NW
Faculty of Graduate Studies
Calgary Alberta T2N 1N4 CANADA
403/220-5690

AMOUNT: Canadian $18,000 + $2,100 for research

DEADLINE(S): FEB 1

FIELD(S): All areas of study

Open to qualified graduates of any recognized university who are registered in or admissable to a doctoral program at the University of Calgary. Applicants must have completed at least one year of graduate study before accepting the award.

Eight to ten awards per year. Awards renewable upon presentation of evidence of satisfactory progress. Write for complete information.

3902 — UNIVERSITY OF CALGARY (Province of Alberta Graduate Scholarships and Fellowships)

2500 University Dr. NW
Faculty of Graduate Studies
Calgary Alberta T2N 1N4 CANADA
403/220-5690

AMOUNT: $9,300 Scholarship; $10,500 Fellowship (Canadian)

DEADLINE(S): FEB 1

FIELD(S): All areas of study

Candidates for the scholarships or fellowships must be registered in or admissible to a program leading to a master's or doctoral degree respectively. Canadian citizen or permanent resident.

60 to 70 awards per year. Write for complete information.

3903 — UNIVERSITY OF CAMBRIDGE (Hughes Hall Studentship)

Senior Tutor
Hughes Hall
Cambridge CB12 EW England
0223-334893

AMOUNT: Varies

DEADLINE(S): JUL

FIELD(S): All fields of study

Studentships are open to students who are accepted for graduate study at Cambridge University.

15-20 studentships per year. Write for complete information.

3904 — UNIVERSITY OF CAMBRIDGE (Newnham College Research Fellowships)

Newnham College
Cambridge CB3 9DF England
1223/33-5700 01223/335700

AMOUNT: 10,015 pounds sterling pre-Ph.D.; 12,218 pounds post-Ph.D.- 800 pounds deducted for residence

DEADLINE(S): FEB 1

FIELD(S): All areas of study

Research fellowships open only to women. Evidence of the ability to conduct independent research of at least Ph.D standard is required (usually a dissertation or published work). Tenable for up to three years.

Write for complete information.

3905 — UNIVERSITY OF CAMBRIDGE (Peterhouse Research Studentship)

Peterhouse
Senior Tutor
Cambridge CB2 1RD England
01223-338200

AMOUNT: 5,190 pounds sterling + university & college fees

DEADLINE(S): APR 1

FIELD(S): All fields of study

Open to Ph.D. candidates at the University of Cambridge. Awards tenable at Peterhouse.

Renewable for up to three years. Write for complete information.

3906 — UNIVERSITY OF CAMBRIDGE - SIDNEY SUSSEX COLLEGE (Research Studentship)

Tutor for Graduate Students
Cambridge CB2 3HU ENGLAND UK
+44/01223-338800

AMOUNT: 1,000+ pounds sterling, up to full support + 350 pounds sterling research expenses

DEADLINE(S): MAR 1

FIELD(S): All fields of study

Candidates may be from any country and must be Ph.D. students enrolled at or planning to attend the University of Cambridge. Must have been awarded (or likely to graduate with) First Class Honours degree or equivalent. Preference given to those who nominate Sidney Sussex College as first choice on CIGAS Form and those who are under 26 years of age. Financial need considered in determining award amount.

Renewable up to 3 years, subject to reviews of diligence and progress. Contact Sidney Sussex College for an application.

3907 — UNIVERSITY OF CAMBRIDGE— WOLFSON COLLEGE (Bursaries)

Barton Road
Cambridge Cams CB3 9BB England
01223/335900

AMOUNT: Varies approx 300 pounds sterling

DEADLINE(S): APR 30

FIELD(S): All fields of study

Bursaries awarded to post-graduate students admitted to Wolfson College.

Renewable. Write Dr. M.E. Shepherd at address above for complete information.

3908 — UNIVERSITY OF CAMBRIDGE—KINGS COLLEGE (External Studentships)

Kings College Head Tutor for Graduate Studies
Cambridge CB2 1ST GREAT BRITAIN
01223 331255
FAX: 01223 331193

AMOUNT: Partial awards

DEADLINE(S): APR 1

FIELD(S): All areas of study

Studentships for graduate research and study at Kings College. Open to students of all nationalities. Applicants should be under 30 years of age.

Renewable for up to three years. Write for complete information.

3909 — UNIVERSITY OF CAMBRIDGE-CHURCHILL COLLEGE (Research Studentships)

Tutor for Advanced Students
Cambridge CB3 ODS England
Written inquiry

AMOUNT: 5890 pounds sterling + fees

DEADLINE(S): FEB 15

FIELD(S): All fields of study

Studentships for research in any subject are available to students who intend to register for the Ph.D degree at the University of Cambridge. Must hold a first-class degree.

Write for complete information.

3910 — UNIVERSITY OF EXETER (Postgraduate Scholarships)

Northcote House
The Queen's Drive
Exeter EX4 4QJ Devon England
Written inquiry

AMOUNT: "Home" fees and maintenance allowance

DEADLINE(S): None specified

FIELD(S): All fields of study

Open to applicants who have been offered a place to study for a higher degree by research at Exeter University. Nominations are made by academic schools.

Available for study at the University of Exeter ONLY. Renewable for a maximum of 3 years. Contact the academic school in which you wish to study to see if funding is available.

3911 — UNIVERSITY OF GLASGOW (Postgraduate Scholarships)

Clerk to the Senate Office, University of Glasgow
Glasgow G12 8QQ Scotland
0141/330-6474
FAX: 0141/330-4021

AMOUNT: 5,304 pounds sterling + fees at the home student rate

DEADLINE(S): JAN 31 (medicine, science); FEB 28 (divinity, vet medicine); MAR 31 (English, law, finance, social sciences)

FIELD(S): All fields of study

Open to full-time graduate research students at the university. Awards will be based on merit. Particular attention will be paid to past academic achievements & to suitability for graduate work as may be indicated in the referees' reports.

Contact the address above for complete information.

3912 — UNIVERSITY OF GLASGOW (Thouron Award-Fellowship)

Registrar
University of Glasgow
Glasgow G12 8QQ
Written inquiry

AMOUNT: $1,247 per month plus fees

DEADLINE(S): OCT 20

FIELD(S): All fields of study

Up to ten awards are offered annually to British citizens for graduate study at the University of Pennsylvania in the US. Must be unmarried.

This is an exchange scholarship between UK universities and the University of Pennsylvania. Write for complete information.

3913 — UNIVERSITY OF HULL (Bursaries for Overseas Postgraduates)

Postgraduate Office
Hull HU6 7RX England
01482 346311

AMOUNT: 50% of current tuition

DEADLINE(S): APR 30

FIELD(S): All areas of study

Bursaries offered on a competitive basis to applicants who are considered most able academically & have research proposals which can be adequately catered at Hull. Should possess first or upper second class honours or higher degree.

Approximately 10 awards per year. Bursaries are renewable if satisfactory progress is made. A number of scholarships which include maintenance awards are also available to overseas students. The University of Hull also participates in the Overseas Research Students Awards Scheme, which covers payment of all tuition fees but no maintenance). Details on request. Write for complete information.

3914 — UNIVERSITY OF IOWA FOUNDATION (David Braverman Scholarship)

Univ of Iowa
3100 Burge Hall
Student Disability Services
Iowa City IA 52242
319/335-1462

AMOUNT: $1,500

DEADLINE(S): APR 1

FIELD(S): All fields of study

Scholarships available to disabled students who have been accepted in a University of Iowa graduate or professional program. Applicants must be able to demonstrate academic ability and service to the community.

Write for complete information.

3915 — UNIVERSITY OF LEEDS (Scholarships for International Students)

Research Degrees & Scholarships Office, Univ. of Leeds
Leeds LS2 9JT ENGLAND UK
+44 (0) 113 233 4007
FAX: +44 (0) 113 233 4023
E-Mail: scholarships@leeds.ac.uk
Internet: www.britcoun.org/eis/profiles/leeds/leedschp.htm

AMOUNT: Varies

DEADLINE(S): Varies

FIELD(S): All fields of study

Various scholarships for international students. Several of them are for students from specific countries, and some or limited to certain areas of study. All levels of study—undergraduate through doctoral.

Contact university or access website for complete information.

3916 — UNIVERSITY OF LEEDS (Tetley and Lipton Scholarships for Overseas Students)

Research Degrees & Scholarships Office
Leeds LS2 9JT ENGLAND UK
+44 (0) 113 233 4007
FAX: +44 (0) 113 233 4023
E-Mail: c.edwards@leeds.ac.uk
Internet: www.britcoun.org/eis/profiles/leeds/leedschp.htm

AMOUNT: 1,800 pounds sterling (undergrads, postgrads in taught courses; $2,490 (postgrad research)

DEADLINE(S): MAR 1 (undergraduates & taught postgraduates); APR 30 (research postgraduates)

FIELD(S): All fields of study

Scholarships open to overseas students of high academic standards who are accepted for admission by the university as a full-time undergraduate or graduate student.

70 awards per year. Awards renewable. Contact address above for complete information.

3917 — UNIVERSITY OF MANITOBA (Graduate Fellowship)

500 University Centre
Winnipeg Manitoba R3T 2N2 Canada
204/474-9836

AMOUNT: $10,000 Ph.D; $8,000 Master's thesis; $6,000 Master's course

DEADLINE(S): FEB 15

FIELD(S): All areas of study

Awards for graduate study at the Univ. of Manitoba only. All applicants must have GPA minum of B+ in the last two completed years of study.

Awards are renewable. Approx 115 new awards per year. Contact address above for complete information.

3918 — UNIVERSITY OF MELBOURNE (Postgraduate Scholarships)

Postgraduate Scholarships Office, Graduate Centre
Parkville Victoria 3052 Australia
Written inquiry

AMOUNT: A$15,000

DEADLINE(S): OCT 31

FIELD(S): All fields of study

Scholarships open to students enrolled in a master's degree by research program or a doctor of philosophy degree program at the University of Melbourne.

Write for complete information.

3919 — UNIVERSITY OF MISSOURI ROLLA (The Distinguished Scholars Program for Non-Missouri Residents)

G-1 Parker Hall
1870 Miner Circle
Rolla MO 65409-1060
573/341-4282 or 800/522-0938
FAX: 573/341-4274
E-Mail: umroll@umr.edu
Internet: www.umr.edu/~enrol/scholarnonmo.html

AMOUNT: $1,000-$5,000 reduced non-resident fees

DEADLINE(S): FEB 1

FIELD(S): All fields of study

Tuition reduction for out-of-state students at the University of Missouri, Rolla. Top students are automaticall considered when the submit the Undergraduate Application for Admission, Financial Aid & Scholarships.

Renewable provided students completes 24 credit hours/year and maintains a 2.5 cumulative GPA.

3920 — UNIVERSITY OF NEWCASTLE (Postgraduate Research Scholarships)

Research Scholarships & Finance Officer,
University of Newcastle
Newcastle NSW 2308 AUSTRALIA
(02) 49216829

AMOUNT: AUS. $15,888 per annum + travel/living allowance, establishment, & thesis allowances

DEADLINE(S): OCT 31 (Austr. residents); SEP 30 (international candidates)

FIELD(S): All areas of study

Scholarships available to support research for higher degree studies (2 years Masters; 3 years Ph.D) at the University of Newcastle. Awards are competitive.

Approximately 50 awards per year. Write for complete information.

3921 — UNIVERSITY OF NEWCASTLE (Research Higher Degrees Scholarships)

The Chancellery, University Drive
Newcastle Callaghan NSW 2308 AUSTRALIA
61+2+49217261
FAX: 61+2+49216908
E-Mail: grad.schol@newcastle.edu.au
Internet: www.newcastle.edu.au

AMOUNT: AUS. $15,888 per annum + travel/living allowance, establishment, & thesis allowances

DEADLINE(S): OCT 31 (Austr. residents); SEP 30 (international candidates)

FIELD(S): All areas of study

Scholarships available to support research for higher degree studies at the University of Newcastle. Awards are competitive.

All nationalities may apply. Write or access website for complete information.

3922 — UNIVERSITY OF NEW BRUNSWICK (Financial Aid for Graduate Students—Fellowships, Assistantships, and Scholarships)

School of Graduate Studies
P.O. Box 4400
Fredericton N.B. E3B 5A3 CANADA
506/453-4673
FAX: 506/453-4817

AMOUNT: Varies with award

DEADLINE(S): None

FIELD(S): All areas of study

Assistantships, fellowships, scholarships, and other awards are awarded on a competitive basis to graduate students who wish to study at the University of New Brunswick.

400-500 awards per year. Prospective students should write to the appropriate department at the school of graduate study for further information.

3923 — UNIVERSITY OF NEWCASTLE/ CATHEDRAL CHURCH OF ST. NICHOLAS (Organ and Choral Scholarships)

Master of the Music, Cathedral Church of St. Nicholas
Newcastle upon Tyne NE1 1PF ENGLAND UK
(0191) 232 1939

AMOUNT: 687 pounds/yr. (organ); 379 pounds/yr. (choral-for males)

DEADLINE(S): Varies

FIELD(S): All fields of study

Although these programs were originally intended for music students, they are open to all students who have been offered a place by the University if no qualified music students have received the awards.

Contact Dr. Eric Cross in the Music Department (+44 191 222 6736) or Mr. Tim Hone at the Cathedral Church.

3924 — UNIVERSITY OF NEW ENGLAND RESEARCH SCHOLARSHIPS

Research Services
Armidale NSW 2351 Australia
61+67 733571
FAX 61+67 733543

AMOUNT: $15,637 living allowance PA + dependent child allowance for overseas students

DEADLINE(S): OCT 31

FIELD(S): All fields of study

Scholarships for Ph.D or master's degree research for applicants who hold a bachelor's degree of at least upper second class honours level. Applicants must show evidence of personal financial support in addition to scholarship.

Tuition fees may apply. Write for complete information. Applications should be forwarded to the International Programs Office at the above address.

3925 — UNIVERSITY OF OXFORD (Paula Soans O'Brian Scholarship)

St. Cross College
Oxford OX1 3LZ ENGLAND UK
+44 01865-278492

AMOUNT: 1,774 pounds sterling

DEADLINE(S): MAR 15

FIELD(S): All fields of study

Supplementary award is open to students undertaking graduate/postgraduate research at Oxford University.

Renewable up to 3 years. Contact Tutor for Admissions for an application.

3926 — UNIVERSITY OF OXFORD-ST. CATHERINE'S COLLEGE (Overseas Graduate Scholarships)

Manor Road
Attn: Tutor for graduates
Oxford OX1 3UJ England
01865 271732

AMOUNT: 1,500 pounds sterling

DEADLINE(S): JUL 1

FIELD(S): All fields of study

A competitive scholarship is available each year to non-British citizens for graduate study at St. Catherine's College at Oxford University.

Awards are renewable. Write for complete information.

3927 — UNIVERSITY OF OXFORD-WOLFSON COLLEGE (Graduate Awards)

Academic Secretary-Wolfson College
Oxford OX2 6UD England
01865/274106

AMOUNT: 400 Pounds Sterling

DEADLINE(S): OCT 18

FIELD(S): All areas of study

Open to Wolfson College students after one year of post-grad study at Wolfson. At least 3 of 9 awards will be given to students in the Arts and Social Studies.

Contact academic secretary at Wolfson for complete information.

3928 — UNIVERSITY OF OXFORD— SOMERVILLE COLLEGE (Janet Watson Bursary)

College Secretary
Somerville College
Oxford OX2 6HD UNITED KINGDOM
1865-270629/19
FAX: 1865-270620

AMOUNT: 3,500 pounds sterling for each of 2 years

DEADLINE(S): MAR 2

FIELD(S): All fields of study

Bursary is offered for U.S. citizens who are graduate students wishing to read for a further degree at the University of Oxford in England. Renewable for a second year.

Write for complete information.

3929 — UNIVERSITY OF OXFORD-WOLFSON COLLEGE (Junior Research Fellowships)

Wolfson College
Oxford OX2 6UD England
01865/274102

AMOUNT: Varies

DEADLINE(S): MAR

FIELD(S): All areas of study

The college elects about 12 non-stipendiary junior research fellowships if candidates of sufficient merit present themselves without limitation of subject. Fellowships are for two years and are renewable for one additional two year term.

Write to president's secretary for complete information.

3930 — UNIVERSITY OF OXFORD—ST. CROSS COLLEGE (Major College Scholarships)

St. Cross College
Oxford OX1 3LZ England
01865-278490

AMOUNT: 1,675 pounds sterling

DEADLINE(S): FEB 15 (for Arts and Social Sciences); MAR 15 (for Sciences)

FIELD(S): All areas of study

Supplementary awards for students undertaking graduate study or research at Oxford University.

Write to admissions office at address above for complete information.

3931 — UNIVERSITY OF OXFORD—ST. HILDA'S COLLEGE (Graduate Scholarships)

The College Office
St. Hilda's College
Oxford OX4 1DY ENGLAND
01865/276815

AMOUNT: Up to 1,000 pounds sterling

DEADLINE(S): AUG 1

FIELD(S): All areas of study

Open to women graduates from any country accepted to read for a research degree by the University of Oxford and subsequently at St. Hilda's College.

Bursaries renewable for a 2nd year subject to satisfactory progress. Write for complete information and application form.

3932 — UNIVERSITY OF OXFORD—ST. HILDA'S COLLEGE (New Zealand Bursaries)

College Secretary, St. Hilda's College
Oxford OX4 1DY England
0865/276884

AMOUNT: Up to 1,700 pounds sterling

DEADLINE(S): AUG 1

FIELD(S): All fields of study

Open to women from New Zealand for undergraduate or graduate study at St. Hilda's college. Preference to descendents of the late Francis Bateman Raymond of Timaru New Zealand.

Bursaries renewable for a 2nd & 3rd year subject to satisfactory progress. Write for complete information and application form.

3933 — UNIVERSITY OF PORTSMOUTH (Partnership Programme-Learning at Work)

Nuffield Centre, St. Michael's Road
Portsmouth PO1 2ED ENGLAND UK
01705 84 3467
FAX: 01705 84 3503
E-Mail: partner@port.ac.uk
Internet: www.port.ac.uk/~partner/contact.htm

AMOUNT: Varies

DEADLINE(S): Varies

FIELD(S): All fields of study

A "Learning at Work" degree program tailored to individual needs. Available at various university locations.

Employers develop staff skills and employees enhance career development prospects learning through projects at work coordinated through the university.

See website for details and/or contact university.

3934 — UNIVERSITY OF QUEENSLAND (Post-graduate Research Scholarship)

Manager, International Education Office
Univ. of Queensland QLD 4072 Australia
617/365-1960

AMOUNT: A$14,740 per year

DEADLINE(S): SEP 30

FIELD(S): All fields of study

Scholarships for full-time post-graduate study at the University of Queensland.

Awards renewable if satisfactory progress is made during first year. Contact address above for complete information.

3935 — UNIVERSITY OF SOUTHAMPTON (University Research Studentships)

Highfield
Southampton SO17 1BJ England
070/359-5000

AMOUNT: Approx 5250 pounds sterling + tuition fees

DEADLINE(S): MAR 1

FIELD(S): All areas of study

Awards for research at the master's or Ph.D level in any department of the university.

Awards renewable for up to three years. Forty awards per year. Write to academic department concerned for complete information.

3936 — UNIVERSITY OF SYDNEY (Postgraduate Research Scholarships and International Postgraduate Awards)

International Office, University of Sydney
NSW 2006 AUSTRALIA
+61 2 9351 5838
FAX: +61 2 9351 4013
E-Mail: info@io.usyd.edu.au
Internet: www.usyd.edu.au/homepage/exterel/intgeninfo.html

AMOUNT: A$15,888/yr.

DEADLINE(S): AUG 30

FIELD(S): All fields of study

OPRS are funded by the Australian government. Awards are based on academic merit and research capacity for graduates from any country eligible to commence a higher degree by research. IPAs are awarded by The University of Sydney to OPRS holders who have been nominated as top-ranked candidates. Not for Australian or New Zealand citizens.

OPRS covers tuition for 2 years for MA research and 3 years for a Ph.D. Check website and/or write for complete information.

3937 — UNIVERSITY OF TASMANIA (Tasmania Research Scholarship)

Office for Research
GPO Box 252-01
Hobart Tasmania 7001 Australia
26 61-362-2766
FAX: 61-362-262744

AMOUNT: AUS. $15637 + ALLOWANCES

DEADLINE(S): OCT 31

FIELD(S): All fields of study

For Australian citizens for residents of Australia. Variety of post-graduate level school awards offered by various sections of the University.

Write to 'Research Scholarships Officer' at address above for complete information.

3938 — UNIVERSITY OF TENNESSEE (Hilton A. Smith Graduate Fellowship)

218 Student Services Bldg.
Knoxville TN 37996-0220
615/974-3251

AMOUNT: Tuition & fees + $5,000 stipend

DEADLINE(S): FEB 15

FIELD(S): All areas of study

Open to full-time graduate students admitted to or already attending the University of TN (Knoxville). GPA of 3.7 or better on all previous graduate and undergraduate work is required, and applicants should have superior rankings on rating forms.

15-25 awards per year. Write to the Office of Graduate Admissions & Records for complete information. Applications available November 1 to February 1 each year.

3939 — UNIVERSITY OF TENNESSEE KNOXVILLE

Graduate School
404 Andy Holt Tower
Knoxville TN 37996
615/974-2475

AMOUNT: Tuition & fees + $10,000 stipend (maximum)

DEADLINE(S): MAR 1

FIELD(S): All fields of study

Graduate fellowships open to Black Americans who are residents of the state of Tennessee and entering an approved program at the University of Tennessee Knoxville. U.S. citizenship required.

Write for complete information.

3940 — UNIVERSITY OF TORONTO (Graduate Fellowships)

c/o Registrar, Trinity College
Toronto Canada M5S 1H8
Written inquiry

AMOUNT: Varies

DEADLINE(S): FEB 1

FIELD(S): All areas of study

Graduate fellowships awarded annually by the College to men or women pursuing studies in the Graduate School of the University of Toronto. The fellowships provide residence and board in either Trinity College or St. Hilda's College and membership in the Senior Common Room. Includes James C. Cumming Fellowship, College Fellowships, and Provost Seeley Fellowships (for non-Canadian students).

5 fellowships awarded annually. May be held in conjunction with cash awards or teaching assistantships from other sources. Write to above address for an application/more information.

3941 — UNIVERSITY OF WAIKATO, NEW ZEALAND (Masters Award)

Private Bag 3105
Hamilton NEW ZEALAND
07 856 2889 Ext. 8964 or 6732
FAX: 07 838 4370
E-Mail: rgty_dbc

AMOUNT: $5,000/year

DEADLINE(S): NOV 30

FIELD(S): All fields of study

To help students study for a Master's degree at Waikato University, New Zealand. Must have a Bachelor's degree.

Contact Waikato University Scholarships Officer at above location.

3942 — UNIVERSITY OF WAIKATO, NEW ZEALAND (Postgraduate Award)

Private Bag 3105
Hamilton NEW ZEALAND
07 8562889 Ext. 8964 or 6732
FAX: 07 8384372
E-Mail: rgty_dbc

AMOUNT: $12,000/year + up to $550 for thesis preparation

DEADLINE(S): None given

FIELD(S): All fields of study

For students beginning a Master's Degree or Doctor of Philosophy program at the University of Waikato. Must be New Zealand citizen or permanent resident.

Contact Scholarships Administrator, University of Waikato, at above address.

3943 — UNIVERSITY OF WESTERN AUSTRALIA (University Postgraduate Awards for International Students)

Mounts Bay Rd.
Crawley Perth 6907 WESTERN AUSTRALIA
08/9380-2490
FAX: 08/9380-1919
E-Mail: medwards@aes.uwa.edu.au
Internet: www.aes.uwa.edu.au

AMOUNT: 14,800 Australian dollars per annum + other allowances

DEADLINE(S): AUG 31

FIELD(S): All fields of study

Awards for non-Australian, non-New Zealand, citizens or residents to study at the master's or Ph.D level. Master's awards tenable for two years. Ph.D awards tenable for three years. Must be held in conjunction with Overseas Postgraduate Research Scholarship, which covers payment of the full fee.

Approximately 12 awards to overseas students per year. Write for complete information.

3944 — UNIVERSITY OF WINDSOR (Graduate Studies & Research Scholarships)

Dean of Graduate Studies & Research
401 Sunset Ave. Rm. 325
Windsor Ontario N9B 3P4 Canada
519/253-4232, ext. 2109

AMOUNT: Tuition + $4,000 - $5,000 stipend

DEADLINE(S): FEB 1

FIELD(S): All areas of study

Scholarships are open to any student who is accepted as a master's or doctoral candidate at the University of Windsor. Graduate assistantships and research assistantships also are available.

Approximately 100 scholarships per year. Renewable. Write for complete information.

3945 — US COAST GUARD MUTUAL ASSISTANCE (Adm. Roland Student Loan Program)

2100 2nd Street, S.W.
Washington DC 20593-0001
202/267-1683

AMOUNT: Up to $2,700 per year (undergrads); $7,500 (grads)

DEADLINE(S): None specified

FIELD(S): All areas of study

For members and dependents of Coast Guard Mutual Assistance members who are enrolled at least half-time in an approved postsecondary school.

Loans renewable for up to four years. Must reapply annually. Write for complete information.

3946 — US DEPARTMENT OF DEFENSE (Student Educational Employment Program)

Alicia Pfenniger
US Army TARDEC
Armament RD&E Center (ARDEC)
ATTN: AMSTA-AR-TDD
Picatinny Arsenal, NJ 07908-5000
201/724-3437
Internet: www.acq.osd.mil/ddre/edugate/s-aindx.html

AMOUNT: Paid employment while in school

DEADLINE(S): None specified

FIELD(S): All fields of study

US citizens. Student Career Experience assigns work to students that relates to their career goals or interests. Includes benefits and can't interfere with academic studies. Non-competitive conversion to permanent position if requirements met. Student Temporary Employment is yearly, and the nature of the student's duties doesn't have to be related to academic/career goals. No opportunity for conversion.

Salary from $13,113 to $25,025. Appointment to Career Experience may not extend beyond 120 days after completion of education and work-study requirements. Students who discontinue their education are disqualified.

3947 — US DEPT OF EDUCATION (Patricia Roberts Harris Fellowship Program)

Office of Student Financial Assistance
Washington DC 20202
800/4FED-AID

AMOUNT: Varies

DEADLINE(S): Varies (with institution)

FIELD(S): All fields of study

Graduate fellowships. Open to minorities, women, and other groups that are under-represented in colleges, universities, academic, and professional fields. US citizen or legal resident.

Students must apply through the institution they plan to attend. Contact your financial aid office or call the above phone number for more information.

3948 — US DEPT OF VETERANS AFFAIRS (Vocational Rehabilitation)

810 Vermont Ave. NW (28)
Washington DC 20420
VA regional office in each state or 1-800-827-1000

AMOUNT: Tuition; books; fees; equipment; subsistence allowance

DEADLINE(S): Varies (Within 12 years from date of notification of entitlement to VA comp)

FIELD(S): All fields of study

Open to US military veterans disabled during active duty, honorably discharged & in need of rehab services to overcome an employment handicap. At least a 20% disability comp rating (or 10% with a serious employment handicap) required.

Program will provide college, trade, technical, on-job or on-farm training (at home or in a special rehab facility if vet's disability requires). Contact nearest VA office for complete information.

3949 — US EDUCATIONAL FOUNDATION IN INDIA (AT&T Leadership Award)

Fulbright House
12 Hailey Rd.
New Delhi 110 001 INDIA
91-11-3328944
FAX: 91-11-3329718
E-Mail: vijaya@usefid.emet.in

AMOUNT: $5,000

DEADLINE(S): SEP 15

FIELD(S): All fields of study

For first year undergraduate and graduate students who are citizens/permanent residents of Asian Pacific countries (Australia, China, Hong Kong, India, Indonesia, Japan, Korea, Malaysia, Philippines, Singapore, Taiwan, & Tailand). Must plan to attend accredited US college/university.

36 awards annually. Contact Vijaya Rao, Educational Advisor & AT&T Chair, at above address for an application.

3950 — UTA ALUMNI ASSOCIATION (African-American Endowed Scholarship)

University of Texas at Arlington
Box 19457
Arlington TX 76019
Internet: www.uta.edu/alumni/scholar.htm

AMOUNT: $350

DEADLINE(S): Varies

FIELD(S): All fields of study

Must be a full-time sophomore or higher in good standing at the University of Texas at Arlington. Must have demonstrated financial need and success and be of African-American descent.

1 award annually. Contact UTA Alumni Association for an application.

3951 — UTA ALUMNI ASSOCIATION (Frankie S. Hansell Endowed Scholarship)

University of Texas at Arlington
Box 19457
Arlington TX 76019
Internet: www.uta.edu/alumni/scholar.htm

AMOUNT: $1,000

DEADLINE(S): Varies

FIELD(S): All fields of study

For undergraduate or graduate students at the University of Texas at Arlington. Must be US citizen and demonstrate financial need. Preference is given to females.

3 awards annually. Contact UTA Alumni Association for an application.

3952 — UTA ALUMNI ASSOCIATION (Hispanic Scholarship)

University of Texas at Arlington
Box 19457
Arlington TX 76019
Internet: www.uta.edu/alumni/scholar.htm

AMOUNT: $250

DEADLINE(S): Varies

FIELD(S): All fields of study

For students of Hispanic origin who attend full-time with at least 15 hours completed at the University of Texas at Arlington. Must have a minimum 2.5 GPA, be in good standing, and demonstrate financial need, leadership ability, and potential for success. Transcripts and letter stating financial need are required.

1 award annually. Contact UTA Alumni Association for an application.

3953 — UTAH STATE BOARD OF REGENTS (State Student Incentive Grants)

355 W. North Temple #3 Triad, Suite 550
Salt Lake City UT 84180-1205
801/321-7188 or 800/418-2551
Internet: www.utah-student-assist.org

AMOUNT: $2,500

DEADLINE(S): Varies (Contact school's financial aid office.)

FIELD(S): All fields of study

Open to Utah residents attending eligible Utah schools who have substantial financial need. Grants are intended to enable such students to continue their studies. U.S. citizen or legal resident.

Awards are made through the financial aid office at each eligible institution.

3954 — VENTURE CLUBS OF THE AMERICAS (Student Aid Awards)

Two Penn Center Plaza, Suite 1000
Philadelphia PA 19102-1883
215/557-9300
FAX: 215/568-5200
E-Mail: siahq@voicenet.com

AMOUNT: $2,500 and $5,000

DEADLINE(S): DEC 31

FIELD(S): All fields of study

Awards for young, physically disabled individuals in need of further education who are between 15 and 40 years old. A Venture Club is an organization for young business and professional women sponsored by Soroptimist International of the Americas. The major selection criteria are financial need and the capacity to profit from further education.

Applicants should contact the nearest Venture Club or Soroptimist Club for application or send self-addressed, stamped envelope (SASE) to above address. Allow plenty of time before deadline date for application to be returned to the nearest local club.

3955 — VERMONT STUDENT ASSISTANCE CORPORATION (Non-Degree Grant)

PO Box 2000
Winooski VT 05404-2601
802/655-9602 or 800/642-3177
TDD: 800/281-3341
FAX: 802/654-3765
Internet: www.vsac.org

AMOUNT: $400 (max.) for one course/semester

DEADLINE(S): None

FIELD(S): All fields of study

Open to Vermont residents enrolled in a non-degree course that will improve employability or encourage further study. Must meet need test.

1,000+ awards annually. Contact VSAC for an application.

3956 — VINCENT L. HAWKINSON FOUNDATION FOR PEACE AND JUSTICE (Scholarship Award)

Grace University Lutheran Church, 324
Harvard St. SE
Minneapolis MN 55414
612/331-8125

AMOUNT: Approx. $1,500 (varies)

DEADLINE(S): APR 30

FIELD(S): All fields of study

Scholarships for students who either reside in or attend college in one of the following states: Minnesota, Iowa, Wisconsin, North Dakota or South Dakota. Must have demonstrated a commitment to peace and justice through study, internships, or projects that illustrate their commitment. For undergraduates, graduates, or M.A. candidates.

Two awards. Contact organization for details.

3957 — VIRGINIA STATE COUNCIL OF HIGHER EDUCATION (Tuition Assistance Grant Program)

101 N. 14th St
James Monroe Bldg.
Richmond VA 23219

804/786-1690
E-Mail: fainfo@schev.edu
AMOUNT: Up to $2,000
DEADLINE(S): JUL 31
FIELD(S): All fields of study except theology

Open to Virginia residents who are full-time undergraduate, graduate, or professional students at eligible private colleges and universities in Virginia. Must working in first degree. Late applications may be considered if funds are available.

Contact the financial aid office at the college you plan to attend.

3958 — W. ROSS MACDONALD SCHOOL (Rixon Rafter Scholarships)

Brant Ave
Brantford Ontario N3T 3J9 Canada
519/759-0730
AMOUNT: Varies
DEADLINE(S): SEP 30
FIELD(S): All fields of study

Scholarship awards for legally blind Canadians pursuing postsecondary studies at accredited Canadian institutions. Must have strong career aspirations.

Approx 20 awards per year. Write for complete information.

3959 — WARNBOROUGH UNIVERSITY (Scholarships)

International Office
Friars House
London SE1 8HB ENGLAND
+44 171 922 1200
FAX: +44 171 922 1201
E-Mail: admin@warnborough.edu
Internet: www.warnborough.edu
AMOUNT: US$500-$3,000
DEADLINE(S): None
FIELD(S): All areas of study

Scholarships for graduates and postgraduates who wish to study at Warnborough University in London. Eligibility based on financial status, merit, and statement on career goals.

60 awards per year. Write or visit website for further information.

3960 — WASHINGTON HIGHER EDUCATION COORDINATING BOARD (American Indian Endowed Scholarship)

P.O. Box 43430
Olympia, WA 98504-3430
360/753-7850
AMOUNT: $1,000

DEADLINE(S): MAY 15
FIELD(S): All fields of study

For undergraduate and graduate American Indian students who are residents of Washington state. The purpose is to create an educational opportunity for American Indians to attend and graduate from higher education institutions in the state of Washington. Interest earned from the endowment is used each year to award scholarships to financially needy, resident, American Indian students.

Awards are renewable. Amounts dependent upon endowment earnings. Applications are available in the spring from above address.

3961 — WASHINGTON HIGHER EDUCATION COORDINATING BOARD (Washington State Need Grant)

P.O. Box 43430
Olympia WA 98504-3430
360/753-7850
AMOUNT: Varies
DEADLINE(S): None specified
FIELD(S): All fields of study

Open to financially needy residents of Washington state who attend participating institutions.

For details, write to above address.

3962 — WASHINGTON STATE HIGHER EDUCATION COORDINATING BOARD (Aid to Blind Students)

PO Box 43430
Olympia WA 98504-3430
360/753-7845
FAX: 360/753-7808
AMOUNT: $200
DEADLINE(S): Varies
FIELD(S): All fields of study

Small grant is available to needy blind students who are Washington state residents. Recipients are reimbursed for special equipment, services, and books and supplies required because of their visual impairment.

Contact Program Manager for an application.

3963 — WASHINGTON STATE HIGHER EDUCATION COORDINATING BOARD (WICHE Regional Graduate Exchange)

PO Box 43430
Olympia WA 98504-3430
360/753-7850
FAX: 360/753-7808
AMOUNT: Reduced tuition rates at out-of-state schools
DEADLINE(S): Varies

FIELD(S): All fields of study

For distinctive master's and doctoral programs in which qualified residents may enroll at reduced tuition in certain out-of-state programs not offered in Washington State. The 14 participating states offer 128 programs at 38 graduate schools.

Graduate students apply to the school they wish to attend and request admission as "WICHE" students. Write to the above address for complete information.

3964 — WASHINGTON TRUST BANK (Herman Oscar Schumacher College Fund Trust)

Trust Dept., P.O. Box 2127
Spokane WA 99210-2127
509/353-4150
AMOUNT: $500
DEADLINE(S): OCT 1
FIELD(S): All fields of study

Scholarships for male residents of Spokane County, Washington. Preference given to orphans. Must have completed at least one full year at an accredited school of higher education as a full-time student.

25 annual awards. Must re-apply for renewal.

3965 — WASHINGTON UNIVERSITY IN ST. LOUIS (Olin Fellowships for Women in Graduate Study)

Graduate School of Arts/Sciences
Box 1187
St. Louis MO 63130
314/935-6818
E-Mail: mmwatkin@artsci.wustl.edu
AMOUNT: $21,000 - $34,000
DEADLINE(S): FEB 1
FIELD(S): All graduate and professional fields of study at Washington University

Open to any female graduate of a baccalaureate institution in the U.S. who plans to prepare for a career in higher education or professional fields at Washington University.

Awards are renewable for a period of four years or until the completion of the program (whichever is first).

3966 — WELLESLEY COLLEGE (Fellowships for Wellesley Graduates & Graduating Seniors)

Center for Work & Service
106 Central St.
Wellesley MA 02481-8203
781/283-3525
FAX: 781/283-3674
E-Mail: fellowships@bulletin.wellesley.edu
Internet: www. wellesley.edu/CWS/step2/fellow.html

AMOUNT: $1,200-$50,000

DEADLINE(S): JAN 3

FIELD(S): All fields of study

Numerous fellowship programs open to Wellesley College graduating seniors and Wellesley College graduates. For graduate study or research at institutions in the US or abroad. Awards are based on merit and need.

See website or send self-addressed, stamped envelope to Rose Crawford, Secretary to the Committee on Extramural Graduate Fellowships & Scholarships, for an application and information on specific fellowships.

3967 — WEST VIRGINIA UNIVERSITY (Arlen G. and Louise Stone Swiger Doctoral Fellowships)

Office of Academic Affairs & Research
P.O. Box 6203
Morgantown WV 26506-6203
304/293-7173
FAX: 304/293-7554
E-Mail: dmorela2@wvu.edu

AMOUNT: $12,000 + tuition & mandatory fees

DEADLINE(S): FEB 15

FIELD(S): All fields of study

Doctoral fellowships at West Virginia University for full-time students who are U.S. citizens.

Fellowships are renewable. Write for complete information.

3968 — WEST VIRGINIA UNIVERSITY (W.E.B. DuBois Fellowship)

Office of Academic Affairs & Research
P.O. Box 6203
Morgantown WV 26506-6203
304/293-7173

AMOUNT: $10,000 + tuition & mandatory fees

DEADLINE(S): MAR 1

FIELD(S): All fields of study

Graduate fellowships at West Virginia University for African-American applicants who have a bachelor's degree from an accredited college or university & are admitted to a graduate or professional program at West Virginia University. For full-time students.

Fellowships are renewable. Write for complete information.

3969 — WESTERN SUNBATHING ASSOCIATION (Scholarships)

PO Box 1168-107
Studio City CA 91604
E-Mail: WSANUDE@delphi.com
Internet: www.wsanude.com

AMOUNT: $1,000

DEADLINE(S): APR 1

FIELD(S): All fields of study

Open to students who have been, or whose parents have been, members of WSA for at least three years. Must be high school seniors or currently enrolled full- or part-time in an accredited postsecondary school. Must be less than 27 years of age and have a minimum 2.5 GPA. Based on academic records, leadership, and potential for growth. Financial need NOT a factor.

2 awards annually. Renewable. Contact Oliver Ellsworth at WSA for an application. Applicants notified by June 1st, and funds are forwarded directly to student's school. WSA is a region of the American Association for Nude Recreation.

3970 — WHEATLAND COMMUNITY SCHOLASTIC FUND, INC. (Scholarships)

1250 Oak St.
Wheatland WY 82001
Written Inquiry

AMOUNT: Varies

DEADLINE(S): Varies

FIELD(S): All fields of study

Available to graduates of Wheatland High School in Wyoming.

Write to Mr. Marvin L. Dunham at above address for an application.

3971 — WILLIAM B. RICE AID FUND INC. (Scholarship & Loan Program)

c/o Hudson Savings Bank
P.O. Box 868
Hudson MA 01749
508/562-2664

AMOUNT: $1,500

DEADLINE(S): APR; JUL; DEC

FIELD(S): All areas of study

Applicants must be residents of Hudson MA and demonstrate financial need. Scholarships are availably only to graduate students.

6 scholarships and 20 loans are available. Contact Alexander Harasku (treasurer) at address above for complete information.

3972 — WILLIAM F. COOPER SCHOLARSHIP

c/o First union National Bank-CMG, P.O. Box 9947
Savannah GA 31412
912/944-2154

AMOUNT: $1,000-$1,500 annually

DEADLINE(S): MAY 15

FIELD(S): All fields of study EXCEPT law, theology, or medicine (nursing acceptable)

Undergraduate scholarships for women based on financial need and GPA. Must be Georgia resident; first preference is for women who live in Chatham County.

15-20 yearly. Renewable.

3973 — WINSTON CHURCHILL MEMORIAL TRUST (Churchill Fellowships)

218 Northbourne Ave.
Braddon ACT 2612 Australia
06/247-8333

AMOUNT: A$15,000 (average)

DEADLINE(S): FEB 28

FIELD(S): All fields of study

Open to Australian residents over 18 who can demonstrate merit in a particular field and show the benefit to Australian society that would result from the proposed overseas study.

About 80 awards per year. Write for complete information.

3974 — WISCONSIN DEPARTMENT OF VETERANS AFFAIRS (Deceased Veterans' Survivors Economic Assistance Loan/ Education Grants)

P.O. Box 7843
Madison WI 53703-7843
608/266-1311 or 1-800/947-8387
Internet: badger.state.wi.us/agencies/dva

AMOUNT: Varies

DEADLINE(S): None specified

FIELD(S): All areas of study

Open to surviving spouses (who have not remarried) of deceased eligible veterans and to the minor dependent children of the deceased veterans. Must be residents of Wisconsin at the time of application.

Approximately 5,700 grants & loans per year. Contact a Wisconsin veterans' service officer in your county of residence for complete information.

3975 — WISCONSIN DEPARTMENT OF VETERANS AFFAIRS (Veterans Personal Loan/ Education Grants)

P.O. Box 7843
Madison WI 53703-7843
608/266-1311 or 1-800/947-8387
Internet: badger.state.wi.us/agencies/dva

AMOUNT: $10,000 maximum

DEADLINE(S): None specified

FIELD(S): All areas of study

For veterans (as defined in Wisconsin Statute 45.35.5) who are living in Wisconsin at the time of application. There are limitations on income.

Approximately 5,700 grants & loans per year. Write for complete information.

3976 — WISCONSIN HIGHER EDUCATION AIDS BOARD (Student Financial Aid Program)

P.O. Box 7885
Madison WI 53707
608/267-2206
FAX: 608/267-2808

AMOUNT: Varies

DEADLINE(S): VAries

FIELD(S): All fields of study

Board administers a variety of state and federal programs available to Wisconsin residents enrolled at least half-time and who maintain satisfactory academic record. Most require demonstration of financial need.

Write for complete information.

3977 — WOMEN OF THE EVANGELICAL LUTHERAN CHURCH IN AMERICA (The Amelia Kemp Scholarship)

8765 West Higgins Road
Chicago IL 60631-4189
800/638-3522, ext. 2747
FAX: 773/380-2419
E-Mail: womnelca@elca.org

AMOUNT: $2,000 max.

DEADLINE(S): MAR 1

FIELD(S): All fields of study

Assists women of color who are members of the ELCA studying in undergraduate, graduate, professional, or vocational courses of study leading to a career other than a church-certified profession. Must be US citizen and have experienced an interruption of two or more years since completion of high school. Academic records of coursework completed in last five years as well as proof of admission from educational institution are required.

Renewable for an additional year. Contact Faith Fretheim, Program Director, for an application.

3978 — WOMEN OF THE EVANGELICAL LUTHERAN CHURCH IN AMERICA (The Cronk Memorial-First Triennium Board-General-Mehring-Paepke-Piero/Wade/Wade-Edwin/Edna Robeck Scholarships)

8765 West Higgins Road
Chicago IL 60631-4189
800/638-3522, ext. 2747
FAX: 773/380-2419
E-Mail: womnelca@elca.org

AMOUNT: $2,000 max.

DEADLINE(S): MAR 1

FIELD(S): All fields of study

Assists women who are members of ELCA in undergraduate, graduate, professional, and vocational courses of study not leading to a church-certified profession. Must be US citizen and have experienced an interruption of two or more years since completion of high school. Academic records of coursework completed in last five years as well as proof of admission to educational institution are required.

Renewable an additional year. Contact Faith Fretheim, Program Director, for an application.

3979 — WOMEN'S RESEARCH AND EDUCATION INSTITUTE (Congressional Fellowships for Women and Public Policy)

1750 New York AVe., NW, Suite 350
Washington DC 20006
202/628-0444

AMOUNT: $9,500 stipend for academic year + $1,500 for tuition + $500 health care assistance

DEADLINE(S): FEB 14

FIELD(S): Government; Public Service; Women's Issues; Social Sciences

Annual fellowship program that places women graduate students in Congressional offices; Washington DC and on strategic committee Staffs; encouraging more effective participation by women in policy formation at all levels.

US citizen or legal resident. Fellows also receive 6 credit-hours. 8 fellows per year. Send self-addressed, stamped business-sized envelope for information.

3980 — WOMEN'S SPORTS FOUNDATION (AQHA Female Equestrian Award)

Eisenhower Park
East Meadow NY 11554
800/227-3988
FAX: 516/542-4716
E-Mail: WoSport@aol.com
Internet: www.lifetimetv.com/WoSport

AMOUNT: $2,000

DEADLINE(S): FEB 1

FIELD(S): All fields of study

Honors an outstanding female equestrian and rewards her for her accomplishments as a horsewoman and as an athlete. For female equestrians with national ranking and competition who exhibit leadership, sportsmanship, and commitment to the sport and its athletes.

1 award annually. Awarded in March. See website or write to above address for details.

3981 — WOMEN'S SPORTS FOUNDATION (Ocean Spray Travel & Training Grants)

Eisenhower Park
East Meadow NY 11554
800/227-3988

FAX: 516/542-4716
E-Mail: WoSport@aol.com
Internet: www.lifetimetv.com/WoSport

AMOUNT: Up to $1,500 (individual); up to $3,000 (team)

DEADLINE(S): NOV 15

FIELD(S): All fields of study

Provides financial assistance to aspiring female athletes and teams for coaching, specialized training, equipment, and/or travel. Must have regional and/or national ranking or successful competitive records, and have the potential to achieve higher performance levels and rankings. High school and college/university varsity and/or rec. teams are NOT eligible.

20 individual grants & 8 team grants annually. Awards made in February. See website or write to above address for details.

3982 — WORLD BANK VOLUNTEER SERVICES (Margaret McNamara Memorial Fund)

1818 H St., NW, Rm. G-1000
Washington DC 20433
202/473-8751
202/676-0419

AMOUNT: $6,000

DEADLINE(S): FEB 2

FIELD(S): All fields of study

For women from developing countries that are members of the World Bank (updated each year). Must NOT be a U.S. citizen or legal U.S. resident. Must have a record of service women and/or children in her country and plan to return to her country in about two years. For study at an accredited institution in the United States. Must be at least 25 years old by Jan. 1.

Five awards given. Not renewable. Applications available from Sept. to Jan. 15.

3983 — WORLD OF KNOWLEDGE (Today & Tomorrow Scholarship Program for International Graduate Students)

Princeton Forrestal Village
125-250 Village Blvd.
Princeton NJ 08540
1-888/953-7737
Internet: www.today-tomorrow.org

AMOUNT: $5,000

DEADLINE(S): MAY 31

FIELD(S): All fields of study

Scholarships for international graduate students who will be attending college in the United States. To apply, submit Entry Form (available on line or at above phone number) and write an 800- 1,100-word essay titled "Letter to a Friend." The letter should be to a friend in your native country who is planning to come to America. Describe what you found most difficult to get used to when you arrived in the U.S.

Ten awards. Check website and/or above location for details. Funded by the ICM/AT&T Association Loyalty Program.

3984 — WYOMING DEPARTMENT OF CORRECTIONS (Wayne Martinez Memorial Scholarships)

PO Box 393
Rawlins WY 82301
307/324-2622

AMOUNT: Varies

DEADLINE(S): Varies

FIELD(S): All fields of study

Available to employees and children of employees of the Wyoming Department of Corrections.

Write to above address, attention: application request, or call Amee Medina at above number for an application.

3985 — WYOMING DEPARTMENT OF VETERANS AFFAIRS (War Orphans Scholarships)

2360 E. Pershing Blvd.
Cheyenne WY 82001
Written Inquiry

AMOUNT: Tuition & mandatory fees

DEADLINE(S): Varies

FIELD(S): All fields of study

Available to a limited number of orphans of Wyoming war veterans and children of Wyoming service people who are listed officially in the military records of the US as being a prisoner of war or missing in action as a result of the Korean or Vietnam conflicts. Eligibility will be verified by the Department of Veterans Affairs.

Write to above address for an application.

3986 — WYOMING FARM BUREAU FEDERATION (Dodge Merit Award)

Box 1348
Laramie WY 82073
Written Inquiry

AMOUNT: $500

DEADLINE(S): MAR 1

FIELD(S): All fields of study

Available to a student from a Wyoming Farm Bureau family. May be used at any public institution of postsecondary education in Wyoming.

2 awards annually. Applications are available from each county Farm Bureau or from the above address.

3987 — WYOMING FEDERATION OF WOMEN'S CLUBS (Mary N. Brooks Education Fund-Daughters & Granddaughters)

316 Hwy. 14A East
Lovell WY 82431
307/548-2860

AMOUNT: $500

DEADLINE(S): MAR 1

FIELD(S): All fields of study

Available to a daughter or granddaughter of WFWC member in good standing attending any Wyoming institution of higher education.

Contact Mrs. Delsa H. Asay at above address for an application.

3988 — WYOMING REPUBLICAN FOUNDATION (Scholarships)

PO Box 416
Laramie WY 82020
Written Inquiry

AMOUNT: Varies

DEADLINE(S): MAR 1

FIELD(S): All fields of study

Available to any student at the University of Wyoming or a Wyoming community college. Full-time enrollment required.

Write to above address for an application. Award is provided by Republican donors statewide.

3989 — ZETA PHI BETA SORORITY EDUCATIONAL FOUNDATION (Deborah Partridge Wolfe International Fellowship for U.S. Students)

1734 New Hampshire Ave., NW
Washington DC 20009
Internet: www.zpb1920.org/nefforms.htm

AMOUNT: $500-$1,000

DEADLINE(S): FEB 1

FIELD(S): All fields of study

Open to graduate and undergraduate US students planning to study abroad. Award is for full-time study for one academic year (Fall-Spring) and is paid directly to recipient. Must submit documented proof of academic study and plan of program with signature of school administrator or Program Director.

Send self-addressed, stamped envelope to above address between September 1st and December 15th for an application.

3990 — ZETA PHI BETA SORORITY EDUCATIONAL FOUNDATION (Deborah Partridge Wolfe International Fellowship for Non-U.S. Students)

1734 New Hampshire Ave., NW
Washington DC 20009
Internet: www.zpb1920.org/nefforms.htm

AMOUNT: $500-$1,000

DEADLINE(S): FEB 1

FIELD(S): All fields of study

Open to graduate and undergraduate foreign students planning to study in the US. Award is for full-time study for one academic year (Fall-Spring) and is paid directly to recipient. Must submit documented proof of academic study and plan of program with signature of school administrator or Program Director.

Send self-addressed, stamped envelope (or self-addressed envelope with international reply coupons) to above address between September 1st and December 15th for an application.

3991 — ZETA PHI BETA SORORITY EDUCATIONAL FOUNDATION (General Graduate Scholarships)

1734 New Hampshire Ave., NW
Washington DC 20009
Internet: www.zpb1920.org/nefforms.htm

AMOUNT: $2,500/yr. (max.)

DEADLINE(S): FEB 1

FIELD(S): All fields of study

Open to graduate women working on a professional degree, masters, doctoral, or enrolled in postdoctoral study. Award is for full-time study for one academic year (Fall-Spring) and is paid directly to recipient.

Send self-addressed, stamped envelope to above address between September 1st and December 15th for an application.

3992 — ZETA PHI BETA SORORITY EDUCATIONAL FOUNDATION (Nancy B. Woolridge McGee Graduate Fellowship)

1734 New Hampshire Ave., NW
Washington DC 20009
Internet: www.zpb1920.org/nefforms.htm

AMOUNT: $500-$1,000

DEADLINE(S): FEB 1

FIELD(S): All fields of study

Open to members of Zeta Phi Beta Sorority, Inc. who are pursuing a graduate or professional degree in an accredited college/university program. Must have demonstrated scholarly distinction or unusual ability in chosen field. Award is for full-time study for one academic year (Fall-Spring) and is payable to the college/university. Must submit proof of enrollment.

Renewable. Send self-addressed, stamped envelope to above address between September 1st and December 15th for an application.

Helpful Publications

3993 — "EDUTRAX" QUARTERLY NEWSLETTER

AUTHOR:

National Scholarship Research Service
2280 Airport Blvd.
Santa Rosa, CA 95403
707/546-6777
FAX: 707/546-6785
E-mail: nsrs@metro.net

COST: $35 (annual subscription)

Provides incisive and comprehensive guidance on what to be, where to go to school, how to get in, and how to pay for it—plus timely articles on important developments in the education arena.

3994 — *** Personal Counseling Service *** By Dan Cassidy and his professional staff.

AUTHOR: Daniel J. Cassidy and various professionals

National Scholarship Research Service (NSRS)
& International (ISRS)
5577 Skylane Blvd., Suite 6A
Santa Rosa CA 95403
707/546-6777
FAX: 707/546-6785
E-mail: nsrs@aol.com

COST: Averages $250.00 to $500.00 depending on services chosen. Phone or personal counseling is available at $65 per hour.

NSRS & ISRS personal counseling service helping you decide 1. What to be, 2. Where to go, 3. How to get in, and 4. How to pay for it.

3995 — 270 WAYS TO PUT YOUR TALENT TO WORK IN THE HEALTH FIELD

AUTHOR:

National Health Council
1730 M St., NW, Suite 500
Washington DC 20036
202/785-3910
E-mail: info@nhcouncil.org
Internet: www.nhcouncil.org

COST: $15.00

A resource book containing career information on various health fields.

3996 — A CAREER GUIDE TO MUSIC EDUCATION

AUTHOR: Written by Barbara Payne
Music Educators National Conference
1806 Robert Fulton Dr.
Reston VA 20191
703/860-4000
Internet: http://www.menc.org

COST: Free (available only on Internet at above website)

A comprehensive guide to careers in music, how to find a job, prepare a resume, etc.

3997 — A GUIDE TO AVIATION EDUCATION RESOURCES

AUTHOR: Booklet #EP-1996-11-354-HQ
National Coalition for Aviation Education
P.O. Box 28086
Washington DC 20038
Internet: www2.db.erau.edu/~ncae/

COST: Free

A comprehensive directory of organizations related to aviation training: governmental, industrial, labor, etc. Lists sources of training and scholarships in various allied fields and includes addresses, phone numbers, E-mail addresses, and website locations. A great resource for education and funding for this field!

3998 — A TEACHER'S GUIDE TO FELLOWSHIPS AND AWARDS

AUTHOR: Lists financial aid sources for teachers in many fields.

Massachusetts Dept. of Education
350 Main St.
Malden MA 02148-5123
781/388-3300
Internet: www.doe.mass.edu/doedocs/tgfatoc.html

COST: Free

Available on website: www.doe.mass.edu/doedocs/tgfatoc.html

3999 — ABCs OF FINANCIAL AID (Montana Financial Aid Handbook)

AUTHOR: Montana Guaranteed Student Loan Program

MONTANA GUARANTEED STUDENT LOAN PROGRAM
2500 Broadway
Helena MT 59620-3101
406/444-6594 or 1-800/537-7508

COST: FREE

Describes educational costs and financial aid available in Montana for Montana residents or those attending school in Montana only. It covers application and award procedures and financial aid programs.

4000

— ACADEMIC YEAR ABROAD
AUTHOR: Sara J. Steen; Editor
Institute of International Education

IIE Books
809 United Nations Plaza
New York NY 10017-3580

COST: $44.95 + $5 handling

Provides information on more than 2,350 postsecondary study programs outside the U.S.

4001 — AFL-CIO GUIDE TO UNION-SPONSORED SCHOLARSHIPS

AUTHOR: AFL-CIO Department of Education
AFL-CIO
815 16th St. NW
Washington DC 20006

COST: Free to union members; $3.00 non-union

Comprehensive guide for union members and their dependent children. Describes local, national, and international union-sponsored scholarship programs. Includes a bibliography of other financial aid sources.

4002 — AMERICAN INSTITUTE OF ARCHITECTS INFORMATION POSTER AND BOOKLET

AUTHOR: AIA
American Institute of Architects
1735 New York Ave. NW
Washington DC 20006

COST: Free

Provides list of accredited professional programs and scholarship information.

4003 — ANIMATION SCHOOL DIRECTORY

AUTHOR: AWN
Animation World Network
6525 Sunset Blvd.
Garden Ste. 10
Hollywood CA 90028
323/468-2554
FAX: 323/464-5914
E-mail: sales@awn.com
Internet: www.awn.com

COST: $24.99 (+$3 shipping US; $5 Canada/Mexico; $8 other)

Reference guide to over 400 animation-related schools and educational institutions from 34 different countries. Free version is available online, however the deluxe edition contains special information, such as interviews, articles, links, and recommendations. May order online.

4004 — ANNUAL REGISTER OF GRANT SUPPORT

AUTHOR: Reed Reference Publishing
Reed Reference Publishing Company

121 Chanlon Rd.
New Providence NJ 07974
908-464-6800

COST: $199.95 + 7% shipping/handling + state sales tax

Annual reference book found in most major libraries. Details thousands of grants for research that are available to individuals and organizations.

4005 — ART CALENDAR

AUTHOR: Barbara L. Dougherty, Publisher
Art Calendar
P.O. Box 199
Upper Fairmount MD 21867-0199
410/651-9150
FAX: 410/651-5313
E-mail: barbdoug@dmv.com
Internet: www.artcalendar.com

COST: $32.00/one year

Monthly publication contains articles of interest to artists including listings of grants, fellowships, exhibits, etc. Annual edition lists opportunities without deadlines. Access website for more information. Sample copy of monthly is available for $5.

4006 — ASSISTANTSHIPS AND GRADUATE FELLOWSHIPS IN THE MATHEMATICAL SCIENCES

AUTHOR: AMS
American Mathematical Society
PO Box 6248
Providence RI 02940-6248
401/455-4000
FAX: 401/331-3842
Internet: www.ams.org

COST: $20.00 ($12.00 for individual AMS members)

Annual publication describing assistantships and fellowships in the mathematical sciences that are open to graduate students at accredited institutions. Updated edition is published every October.

4007 — AWARDS FOR POSTGRADUATE STUDY AT COMMONWEALTH UNIVERSITIES (Twelfh Edition 1997-99)

AUTHOR: ACU; ISBN #0-85143-158-5
Association of Commonwealth Universities
John Foster House
36 Gordon Square
London WC1H OPF England
01-387-8572

COST: 24 pounds sterling (30 by airmail)

Contains some 1,090 entries describing scholarships; grants; bursaries; loans; etc. for Commonwealth grads wishing to undertake post-grad study or research at a Commonwealth university outside their own country. 428 pages.

4008 — BARRON'S GUIDE TO LAW SCHOOLS (12th Edition)

AUTHOR: Barron's College Division; ISBN 0-8120-9558-8
Barron's Educational Series Inc.
250 Wireless Blvd.
Hauppauge NY 11788
800/645-3476 or 516/434-3311
Internet: www.barronseduc.com

COST: $14.95

Comprehensive guide covering more than 200 ABA-approved American law schools. Advice on attending law school.

4009 — BASIC FACTS ON STUDY ABROAD

AUTHOR: IIE
Institute of International Education
IIE Books
809 United Nations Plaza
New York NY 10017

COST: Free

Brochure offering essential information on planning for undergraduate and graduate study outside the U.S.

4010 — BIG BOOK OF MINORITY OPPORTUNITIES

AUTHOR: ISBN 0-89434-204-5
Garrett Park Press
PO Box 190
Garrett Park MD 20896
301/946-2553

COST: $39.00; $35.00 prepaid

Hundreds of attractive financial aid, career guidance, internship, and occupation information programs have been developed by colleges & universities, foundations, federal & state agencies, professional & trade associations, and others to help minorities meet their educational & career goals. Over 3,500 sources are listed with information provided on scholarships, fellowships, & other financial aid in various fields of study. 636 pages.

4011 — BIG BOOK OF OPPORTUNITIES FOR WOMEN

AUTHOR: ISBN 0-89434-183-9
Garrett Park Press
PO Box 190
Garrett Park MD 20896
301/946-2553

COST: $39.00; $35.00 prepaid

Hundreds of attractive financial aid, career guidance, internship, and occupation information programs have been developed by colleges & universities, foundations, federal & state agencies, professional & trade organizations, and others to help women meet their educational and career goals. Over 3,500 sources are listed with information on scholarships, fellowships, and other financial aid in various areas of study. 455 pages.

4012 — Bartending

AUTHOR: Call or e-mail for shipping quote and/or information on the Book version.
COMPLETE WORLD BARTENDING GUIDE (CD-Rom
Book also available)
c/o Bar Biz
2245 E. Colorado Blvd., Suite 104
Pasadena, CA 91107-6921
800/615-6888
International 888/303-5145
Internet: www.barbiz.com/bartend.htm

COST: $29.95 + shipping via UPS

Over 2,400 drink recipes, glassware database for each recipe, pop-up video tips from professional bartenders, powerful search engine allows you to look up recipes by key words or ingredients, wine database and tips for which wines go well with meals, over one hour of video instruction, and 200+ non-alcohol recipes.

4013 — CAREER GUIDE FOR SINGERS

AUTHOR: Mary McDonald, Author
OPERA America
1156 15th St. NW, Suite 810
Washington DC 20005-1704
202/293-4466
FAX 202/393-0735
E-mail: Frontdesk@operaam.org

COST: $45.00 non-members; $25.00 members

Directory of producing organizations, institutes, and workshops for advanced training, degree-granting educational institutions with opera/performance degrees, and major opera workshops, competitions, and grants. A resource for aspiring artists seeking opportunities in the opera field. Entries include casting policies, repertoire, and auditiion/application procedures, along with other pertinent information.

4014 — CFKR CAREER MATERIALS CATALOG

AUTHOR: CFKR
CFKR Career Materials
11860 Kemper Rd.c # 7
Auburn CA 95603
800/525-5626 or 530/889-2357
FAX 916/889-0433

E-mail: cfkr@cfkr.com
Internet: www.cfkr.com

COST: Free

A catalog of printed materials, software, and videotapes covering career planning, college financing, and college test preparation. Includes materials applicable to all ages—from the primary grades through graduate school.

4015 — CHALLENGE IN AGRICULTURE

AUTHOR:

American Farm Bureau Federation
225 Touhy Ave.
Park Ridge IL 60068
312/399-5700

COST: Free

Scholarship listings, career opportunities, and web page directory regarding careers and research in various agricultural fields.

4016 — CHRONICLE CAREER INDEX

AUTHOR: CGP; ISBN #1-55631-243-1
Chronicle Guidance Publications
66 Aurora St.
P.O. Box 1190
Moravia NY 13118-1190
1-800/622-7284 or 315/497-0330
FAX: 315/497-3359
Internet: www.chronicleguidance.com

COST: $14.25 + $1.43 shipping/handling (Order No. 502CI)

Listings of career and vocational materials for students and counselors. Describes over 500 sources of publications and audio-visual materials. 90 pages.

4017 — CHRONICLE FINANCIAL AID GUIDE (1998-1999 Edition)

AUTHOR: CGP; ISBN #1-55631-288-1
Chronicle Guidance Publications
66 Aurora St. P.O. Box 1190
Moravia NY 13118-1190
1-800/622-7284 or 315/497-0330
FAX: 315/497-3359;Internet:
www.chronicleguidance.com

COST: $22.47 + $2.25 shipping; Order #502A

Annual guide containing information on financial aid programs offered nationally and regionally by public and private organizations. Programs support study for high school seniors, college undergraduates, graduates, and adult learners. 330 pages.

4018 — CHRONICLE FOUR-YEAR COLLEGE DATABOOK (1998-1999 Edition)

AUTHOR: CGP; ISBN #1-55631-287-3

Chronicle Guidance Publications
66 Aurora St.
P.O. Box 1190
Moravia NY 13118-1190
1-800/622-7284 or 315/497-0330
FAX: 315/497-3359
Internet: www.chronicleguidance.com

COST: $22.49 + $2.25 shipping/handling (Order No. 502CM4)

Reference book in two sections. "Majors" section lists 2,160 institutions offering 760 majors classified by CIP. "Charts" section contains information and statistics on each of the schools. 372 pages.

4019 — CHRONICLE VOCATIONAL SCHOOL MANUAL (1998 Edition)

AUTHOR: CGP; ISBN #1-55631-285-7
Chronicle Guidance Publications
66 Aurora St.
P.O. Box 1190
Moravia NY 13118-1190
1-800/622-7284 or 315/497-0330
FAX: 315/497-3359
Internet: www.chronicleguidance.com

COST: $22.48 + 10% shipping/handling (Order No. 502VS)

More than 3,400 accredited vocational and technical schools and over 920 programs of study. Charts format gives statistical data on institutions listed alphabetically by state. Extensive cross-references.

4020 — COLLEGE ATHLETIC SCHOLARSHIP GUIDE

AUTHOR: Women's Sports Foundation
Women's Sports Foundation
Eisenhower Park
East Meadow NY 11554
800/227-3988
FAX: 516/542-4716
E-mail: WoSport@aol.com
Internet: www.lifetimetv.com/WoSport

COST: Free (1st copy; 2-100 copies .10 ea, 100+ .05 ea)

A listing of over 10,000 college athletic scholarships for women as well as a "game plan for success" with suggestions on how to go about a scholarship search. Updated annually. 32 pages.

4021 — COLLEGE BOUND FAMILY LIBRARY & SUPPORT PACKAGE

AUTHOR: Various professional authors
National Scholarship Research Service (NSRS) & International (ISRS)
5577 Skylane Blvd., Suite 6A
Santa Rosa CA 95403

707/546-6781
FAX: 707/546-6785
E-mail: nsrs@aol.com

COST: $199.95 (plus shipping & handling)

Includes Occupational Outlook Handbook, Guide to 4-Year Colleges, Complete Preparation for the SAT, Dan Cassidy's Worldwide College & Graduate Scholarship Directories, How to Win A Sports Scholarship, and much more (11 items in all).

4022 — COLLEGE DEGREES BY MAIL & MODEM

AUTHOR: John Bear, Ph.D. & Mariah Bear, M.A.;
ISBN: 1-58008-109-6
Ten Speed Press
PO Box 7123
Berkeley CA 94707
800/841-BOOK or 510/559-1600
FAX: 510/559-1629
E-mail: order@tenspeed.com
Internet: www.tenspeed.com

COST: $12.95 + $4.50 shipping

With the rise of Internet-based education, distance learning has never been hotter. You really can earn a fully accredited degree (undergraduate or graduate) in a wide range of fields without ever leaving your home. This guide is updated every year and provides full information on the top 100 distance-learning schools worldwide, including chapters on getting credit from life experience and how to tell the good schools from the bad. 216 pages.

4023 — COLLEGE FINANCIAL AID EMERGENCY KIT

AUTHOR: Joyce Lain Kennedy and Dr. Herm Davis
Sun Features Inc.
Box 368 (Kit)
Cardiff CA 92007
760/431-1660

COST: $6.95 (includes postage and handling)

40-page booklet filled with tips on how to meet tuition and room and board costs. It tells what is available, whom to ask, and how to ask.

4024 — COLLEGE FINANCIAL AID FOR DUMMIES

AUTHOR: Joyce Lain Kennedy and Dr. Herm Davis. ISBN: 0-7645-5049-7. Also in bookstores.
COLLEGE FINANCIAL AID FOR DUMMIES
IDG Books Worldwide, Inc.
919 E. Hillsdale Blvd., Suite 400
Foster City, Ca 94404
800/762-2974
Internet: www.dummies.com

COST: $19.99

This book is a major new guide to understanding the financial aid maze. Useful for high school and college students and also for adults returning to school.

4025 — COLLEGE IS POSSIBLE

AUTHOR:
Coalition of America's Colleges and Universities
Internet: www.collegeispossible.org

COST: Free (online)

An online resource guide for parents, students, and education professionals, containing information on preparing for college, choosing the right college, and paying for college.

4026 — COLLEGE READY REPORT: THE FIRST STEP TO COLLEGE

AUTHOR: Student Resources, Inc.
Student Resources, Inc.
260 Maple Avenue
Barrington RI 02806
800/676-2900

COST: $100

Students and parents fill out a questionnaire to receive an individualized report with valuable college information. This includes a quick reference to the twelve colleges which most closely match the student's profile, along with admissions selections guides, detailed summaries of the schools, and estimated costs and financial aid planning.

4027 — COLLEGES AND UNIVERSITIES IN THE USA—THE COMPLETE GUIDE FOR INTERNATONAL STUDENTS

AUTHOR: ISBN: 0-7689-0139-1
Peterson's, Inc.
PO Box 2123
Princeton NJ 08543-2123
800/225-0261
FAX: 609/924-5338
Internet: www.petersons.com

COST: $19.96

Includes details on more than 1,500 accredited institutions, information on financial aid, and helpful worksheets to speed your process. 1,514 pages.

4028 — DAN CASSIDY'S GUIDE TO PRIVATE SECTOR KINDERGARTEN-12TH GRADE (K-12) SCHOLARSHIPS

AUTHOR: Daniel J. Cassidy
National Scholarship Research Service (NSRS)
& International (ISRS)
5577 Skylane Blvd., Suite 6A
Santa Rosa CA 95403
707/546-6777

FAX: 707/546-6785
E-mail: nsrs@aol.com

COST: $20 (includes shipping)

A fifty-page booklet of scholarships for elementary and secondary private schools with introduction on how to apply. Note: Due to the fairly new nature of this subject, many awards are based for particular cities, states, and schools.

4029 — DAN CASSIDY'S GUIDE TO TRAVEL GRANTS

AUTHOR: Daniel J. Cassidy
National Scholarship Research Service (NSRS)
& International (ISRS)
5577 Skylane Blvd., Suite 6A
Santa Rosa CA 95403
707/546-6777
FAX: 707/546-6785
E-mail: nsrs@aol.com

COST: $20 (includes shipping)

A guide to finding funds for traveling for research, sabbaticals, and/or personal enrichment.

4030 — DAN CASSIDY'S GUIDE TO WINNING SCHOLARSHIPS

AUTHOR: Kit may also be purchased for $35. It includes this booklet, along with video "Kids, College, and Cash" and audio cassette "How to Win a Scholarship." Tapes may be purchased separately—$15 for the video and $10 for the audio cassette.
National Scholarship Research Service (NSRS)
& International (ISRS)
5577 Skylane Blvd., Suite 6A
Santa Rosa CA 95403
707/546-6777
FAX: 707/546-6785
E-mail: nsrs@aol.com

COST: $20 (includes shipping)

A fifty-page booklet covering such topics as early preparation for education financing and development of a plan for seeking scholarships from all sources, including government, schools, and the private sector.

4031 — DIRECTORY OF FINANCIAL AIDS FOR MINORITIES (1995-1997)

AUTHOR: Gail A. Schlachter & R. David Weber
Reference Service Press
5000 Windplay Dr., Suite 4
El Dorado Hills, CA 95762
916-939-9620

COST: $47.50 + $4.00 shipping

Describes over 2000 scholarships; fellowships; grants; loans; awards and internships set aside for

American minorities and minority organizations. Covers all levels of study. 666 pages. Cloth. ISBN 0-918276-28-4.

4032 — DIRECTORY OF FINANCIAL AID FOR STUDENTS OF ARMENIAN DESCENT

AUTHOR: Armenian Assembly of America
Armenian Assembly of America
122 'C' Street NW, Suite 350
Washington DC 20001
201/393-3434
Internet: www.geocities.org/CollegePark/4042/finaid.html

COST: Free

The Armenian Assembly prepares this annual booklet that describes numerous scholarship, loan, and grant programs available from sources in the Armenian community. Available online.

4033 — DIRECTORY OF FINANCIAL AIDS FOR WOMEN (1995-1997)

AUTHOR: Gail A. Schlachter
Reference Service Press
5000 Windplay Dr., Suite 4
El Dorado Hills, CA 95762
916/939-9620

COST: $45.00 + $4.00 shipping

Contains over 1500 descriptions of scholarships; fellowships; grants; loans; awards and internships set aside for women and women's organizations. Covers all levels of study. 498 pages. Cloth. ISBN 0-918276-27-6.

4034 — DIRECTORY OF POSTSECONDARY EDUCATIONAL RESOURCES IN ALASKA

AUTHOR: ACPE
Alaska Commission on Postsecondary Education
3030 Vintage Blvd.
Juneau AK 99801
907/465-2962 or 800/441-2962

COST: Free

Comprehensive directory of postsecondary institutions and programs in Alaska plus information on state and federal grants, loans, and scholarships for Alaska residents (those who have lived in Alaska for two years).

4035 — DIRECTORY OF RESEARCH GRANTS

AUTHOR: Oryx. ISBN: 1-57356-095-2. Pages: 1,232. Published 1999.
Oryx Press
PO Box 33889
Phoenix AZ 85067-3889
Internet: www.oryxpress.com

COST: $135.00

Annual reference book found in most major libraries. Provides current data on funds available from foundations, corporations, and state/local organizations, as well as from federal sources, for research projects in medicine, physical/social sciences, arts, humanities, and education. More than 5,900 sources.

4036 — DIRECTORY OF NATIONAL INFORMATION SOURCES ON DISABILITIES (7th Edition)

AUTHOR: NARIC

National Rehabilitation Information Center
1010 Wayne Ave., Suite 800
Silver Spring MD 20910-5633
800/346-2742 or 301/562-2400
TTY: 301/495-5626
FAX: 301/562-2401
E-mail: naricinfo@kra.com
Internet: www.naric.com/naric

COST: $5.00

Two-volume directory inventories public/federal/private resources at the national level that offer information and/or direct services to people with disabilities & people involved in educating, training, or helping people with disabilities.

4037 — DIRECTORY OF ACCREDITED INSTITUTIONS

AUTHOR: ACICS

Accrediting Council for Independent Colleges and Schools
750 1st St. NE, Suite 980
Washington DC 20002
202/336-6780
Internet: www.acics.org

COST: Free (and is also on website)

Annual directory containing information on more than 650 institutions offering business or business-related career programs and accredited by ACICS.

4038 — DIRECTORY OF MEMBER SCHOOLS

AUTHOR:

Association of Independent Schools in New England
100 Grossman Drive, Suite 301
Braintree MA 02184
1-800/886-2323
Internet: www.aisne.org

COST: Free

A directory of independent schools in five New England states; includes pre-school through postgraduate schools and both day and boarding programs. Some are coed, and others are for a single sex. Some are religious, and some are for students with learning disabilities. Access Internet for a list and/or call for more information.

4039 — DIRECTORY OF TECHNICAL SCHOOLS, COLLEGES, AND UNIVERSITIES OFFERING COURSES IN GRAPHIC COMMUNICATIONS

AUTHOR: NSTF

National Scholarship Trust Fund of the Graphic Arts
200 Deer Run Road
Sewickley PA 15153-2600
412/741-6860
FAX: 412/741-2311
E-mail: nstf@gatf.org
Internet: www.gatf.org

COST: Free

A listing of accredited institutions which offer degrees in graphic arts and related fields.

4040 — DOLLARS FOR COLLEGE: THE QUICK GUIDE TO SCHOLARSHIPS, FELLOWSHIPS, LOANS, AND OTHER FINANCIAL AID PROGRAMS FOR...

AUTHOR:

Garrett Park Press
PO Box 190
Garrett Park MD 20896
301/946-2553

COST: $7.95 each or $60 for set of all twelve booklets (+ $1.50 for shipping no matter how many are ordered)

User-friendly series of 12 booklets pinpoints awards in areas of particular concern to students: Art, Music, Drama; Business & Related Fields; The Disabled; Education; Engineering; Journalism & Mass Communications; Law; Liberal Arts—Humanities & Social Science; Medicine, Dentistry, & Related Fields; Nursing & Other Health Fields; Science; and Women In All Fields. Booklets are revised every 18 months, and each cites from 300 to 400 programs. 70-90 pages each.

4041 — EDUCATION AND TRAINING PROGRAMS IN OCEANOGRAPHY AND RELATED FIELDS

AUTHOR: Marine Technology Society

Marine Technology Society
1828 L St. NW, Suite 906
Washington DC 20036

COST: $6 shipping/handling

A guide to current marine degree programs and vocational instruction available in the marine field. Consolidates and highlights data needed by high school students as well as college students seeking advanced degrees.

4042 — EDUCATIONAL LEADERSHIP, EDUCATION UPDATE, & CURRICULUM UPDATE

AUTHOR: ASCD

Association for Supervision and Curriculum Development
1703 N. Beauregard St.
Alexandria VA 22311-1714
800/933-ASCD or 703/578-9600, ext. 2

COST: $49 for membership

Membership includes eight issues of Educational Leadership, giving you case studies of successful programs, interviews with experts, and features by educators & administrators in the field. Also included are eight issues of Education Update, advising you of significant trends affecting education, networking opportunities, and the newest resources & ASCD services. The quarterly newsletter, Curriculum Update, also included, examines current, major issues in education.

4043 — EEO BIMONTHLY

AUTHOR: Timothy M. Clancy; executive editor

CASS Recruitment Publications Inc.
1800 Sherman Place, Suite 300
Evanston IL 60201
708/475-8800
FAX 708/475-8807

COST: $42.00/Year

Bimonthly publication containing detailed career opportunity profiles on American companies; geographic employer listings and occupational index.

4044 — ENCYCLOPEDIA OF ASSOCIATIONS— Vol. 1

AUTHOR: ISBN #0-8103-7945-7

Gale Research Inc.
835 Penobscot Bldg.
Detroit MI 48226
800/223-GALE
313/961-2242

COST: $415.00

An outstanding research tool. 3-part set of reference books found in most major libraries. Contains detailed information on over 22000 associations; organizations; unions; etc. Includes name and key word index.

4045 — FELLOWSHIP GUIDE TO WESTERN EUROPE

AUTHOR: Gina Bria Vescori, Editor

Council for European Studies
Columbia Univ
807-807A International Affairs Bldg.
New York NY 10027

212/854-4172
FAX: 212/854-8808
E-mail: ces@columbia.edu
Internet: www.europanet.org

COST: $8.00 (prepaid—check to Columbia Univ.)

This booklet is intended to assist U.S. students in finding funds for European travel and study in the social sciences and humanities.

4046 — FINANCIAL AID FOR MINORITIES

AUTHOR:

Garrett Park Press
PO Box 190
Garrett Park MD 20896
301/946-2553

COST: $5.95 each or $30 for set of all six booklets

Several booklets with hundreds of sources of financial aid for minorities. When ordering, please specify which of the following you are interested in: Students Of Any Major; Business & Law; Education; Journalism & Mass Communications; Health Fields; or Engineering & Science. Booklets average 80 pages in length, and each lists between 300 and 400 different sources of aid.

4047 — FINANCIAL AID FOR THE DISABLED AND THEIR FAMILIES

AUTHOR: Gail Ann Schlachter and R. David Weber
Reference Service Press
5000 Windplay Dr., Suite 4
El Dorado Hills, CA 95762
916/939-9620

COST: $38.50 + $4.00 shipping

Contains descriptions of 900 scholarships; fellowships; grants; loans; awards and internships set aside for the disabled and their families. Covers all levels of study. 310 pages.

4048 — FINANCIAL AID FOR VETERANS; MILITARY PERSONNEL & THEIR FAMILIES

AUTHOR: Gail Ann Schlachter and R. David Weber
Reference Service Press
5000 Windplay Dr., Suite 4
El Dorado Hills, CA 95762
916/939-9620

COST: $38,50 + $4 shipping

Contains over 950 descriptions of scholarships; fellowships; grants; loans; awards and internships set aside for veterans; military personnel and their families. Covers all levels of study. 300 pages.

4049 — FINANCIAL AID INFORMATION FOR PHYSICIAN ASSISTANT STUDENTS

AUTHOR:

American Academy of Physician Assistants
950 North Washington St.
Alexandria VA 22314
708/836-2272

COST: Free

A comprehensive listing of scholarships, traineeships, grants, loans, and related publications relation to the physician assistant field of study.

4050 — FINANCIAL AID RESOURCE GUIDE- #17.97

AUTHOR:

NATIONAL CLEARINGHOUSE FOR PROFESSIONS IN SPECIAL EDUCATION
The Council for Exceptional Children
1920 Association Dr.
Reston VA 20191-1589
1/800-641-7824 or 703/264-9476 or TTY 703/264-9480
FAX: 703/264-1637
E-mail: ncpse@cec.sped.org
Internet: www.cec.sped.org/ncpse.htm

COST: Free

General information on finding financial assistance for students preparing for careers in special education and related services.

4051 — FINANCIAL ASSISTANCE FOR LIBRARY & INFORMATION STUDIES

AUTHOR: ALA

American Library Association
Office for Library Personnel Resources
50 E. Huron St.
Chicago IL 60611-2795
312/280-4282
FAX: 312/280-3256
Internet: www.ala.org

COST: $4.00 for postage/handling

An excellent summary of fellowships, scholarships, grants-in-aid, loan funds, and other financial assistance for library education. Published each fall for the following year.

4052 — FINDING MONEY FOR COLLEGE

AUTHOR: John Bear, Ph.D. & Mariah Bear, M.A.;
ISBN: 1-58008-117-7

Ten Speed Press
PO Box 7123
Berkeley CA 94707
800/841-BOOK or 510/559-1600
FAX: 510/559-1629
E-mail: order@tenspeed.com
Internet: www.tenspeed.com

COST: $8.95 + $4.50 shipping

Contains hundreds of listings with complete information, including names & addresses, as well as bonus chapters covering unconventional techniques of lowering tuition. Special sections cover grants based on gender, race or ethnic background, religion, and physical or learning disabilities. 168 pages.

4053 — FISKE GUIDE TO COLLEGES—1996 Edition

AUTHOR: New York Times Books; ISBN 812-92534-1
Times Books
400 Hahn Rd.
Westminster MD 21157

COST: $18.00

Describes the top-rated 265 out of 2,000 possible four-year schools in the U.S. They are rated for academics, social life, and quality of life.

4054 — FLORIDA STUDENT FINANCIAL AID— FACT SHEETS

AUTHOR: Florida Department of Education
Florida Department of Education
Office of Financial Assistance
State Programs
255 Collins
Tallahassee FL 32399-0400
850/487-0049 or 888/827-2004
E-mail: OSFABF@mail.doe.state.fl.us
Internet: www.firn.edu/doe

COST: Free

Booklet containing information on Florida grants, scholarships, and teacher programs.

4055 — FLY BUCKS

AUTHOR:

FLY BUCKS
2280 Airport Blvd.
Santa Rosa, CA 95403
707/546-6777
FAX: 707/546-6785

COST: $20 (includes shipping)

A thirty-page booklet containing over eighty sources of funding for education in aeronautics, aviation, aviation electronics, aviation writing, space science, aviation maintenance technology, and vertical flight.

4056 — GET SMART FAST

AUTHOR: Sondra Geoffrion
Access Success Associates
PO Box 1686
Goleta CA 93116

COST: $6.95 each + $2.50 postage U.S.; $4.00 foreign. California residents add sales tax

Your grades will improve dramatically with this 61-page handbook for academic success which explains how to master the art of studying, discovering what will be tested, preparing for and taking tests strategically, etc.

4057 — GETTING STARTED IN THE MUSIC BUSINESS

AUTHOR:

Texas Music Office
PO Box 13246
Austin TX 78711
512/463-6666
FAX: 512/463-4114
E-mail: music@governor.state.tx.us
Internet: www.governor.state.tx.us/music/tmlp_intro.htm

COST: Free Online Information

This online guide for musicians in Texas provides short-answer reference to the basic legal and business practices associated with the music industry. Links to many informative sites.

4058 — GRADUATE FACULTY AND PROGRAMS IN POLITICAL SCIENCE

AUTHOR: Patricia Spellman
American Political Science Association
1527 New Hampshire Ave., NW
Washington DC 20036-1206
202/483-2512
FAX: 202/483-2657
E-mail: apsa@apsanet.org
Internet: www.apsanet.org

COST: $35 (APSA members) + $4 shipping; $60 (non-members) + $6 shipping; $24 (APSA student members) + $4 shipping

This book summarizes US and Canadian graduate programs in political science at the masters and doctoral levels. Includes deadlines for applications and a section on financial aid for each campus.

4059 — GRANTS AND AWARDS AVAILABLE TO AMERICAN WRITERS

AUTHOR: ISBN: 0-934638-15-2
Pen American Center
568 Broadway
New York NY 10012-3225
212/334-1660
FAX 212/334-2181
E-mail: pen@echonyc.com

COST: $15 (+ tax if NY resident); + shipping charges for international airmail

More than 1,000 awards listed for poets, journalists, playwrights, etc., including American as well as international grants (including residencies at writers' colonies). Order by mail or fax only. 267 pages.

4060 — GRANTS IN THE HUMANITIES

AUTHOR: W.E. Coleman; ISBN #0-918212-80-4
Neal Schuman Publishers Inc.
100 Varick St.
New York NY 10013
212/925-8650

COST: $29.95

This book is intended primarily for scholars who are looking for funding sources that support research in the humanities. 175 pages.

4061 — GRANTS REGISTER (THE) 1997-1999

AUTHOR: Reference
St. Martin's Press Inc.
175 Fifth Ave
(Cash Sales)
New York NY 10010
800-321-9299

COST: $110.00 (call for shipping quote)

This reference book can be found in most major libraries. It is intended primarily for students and researchers at or above the graduate level. More than 700 funding sources.

4062 — GRANTS, FELLOWSHIPS, AND PRIZES OF INTEREST TO HISTORIANS

AUTHOR: AHA
American Historical Association
400 A St., SE
Washington DC 20003
202/544-2422
FAX: 202/544-8307
E-mail: aha@theaha.org
Internet: www.theaha.org

COST: $8.00 AHA members; $10.00 non-members

Offering information on more than 450 funding sources—from undergraduate scholarships to postdoctoral fellowships and awards for written work and publications—the AHA's annual guide can help individuals find funding to begin or continue a research project or degree program. Includes suggestions for writing successful grant proposals and a bibliography of other sources for grant, fellowship, and prize information. 226 pages.

4063 — GUIDE TO GRADUATE EDUCATION IN PUBLIC AFFAIRS AND PUBLIC ADMINISTRATION

AUTHOR: NASPAA
National Association of Schools of Public Affairs and Administration
1120 G St., NW, Suite 730
Washington DC 20005-3801

E-mail: info@naspaa.org
Internet: www.naspaa.org

COST: $15 (includes postage)

A directory that describes 200 programs in public affairs.

4064 — GUIDE TO GRADUATE PUBLIC POLICY EDUCATION AND ORGANIZATIONS

AUTHOR: APPAM
Association of Public Policy Analysis and Management
PO Box 18766
Washington DC 20037
E-mail: appam@ui.urban.org
Internet: qsilver.queensu.ca/appam/

COST: $15

Contains information on over 50 public policy graduate programs and public policy research institutions.

4065 — GUIDE TO PROGRAMS (NSF 97-150)

AUTHOR:
National Science Foundation
NSF Clearinghouse
PO Box 218
Jessup MD 20794-0218
301/947-2722
E-mail: pubs@nsf.gov
Internet: www.nsf.gov/

COST: Free

NSF graduate and postgraduate funding opportunities for US citizens/residents to travel/do research in the fields of Science, Mathematics, and Engineering. Available online or contact above address.

4066 — GUIDE TO SOURCES OF INFORMATION ON PARAPSYCHOLOGY

AUTHOR: Eileen J. Garrett Library
Parapsychology Foundation
228 E. 71st St.
New York NY 10021
212/628-1550
FAX 212/628-1559

COST: $3.00

An annual listing of sources of information on major parapsychology organizations, journals, books, and research.

4067 — HIGHER EDUCATION PROGRAMS

AUTHOR: Catalog available in hard copy, also. Check with organization for ordering information and price.
Presbyterian Church (U.S.A.)
100 Witherspoon Street

Louisville KY 40202-1396
www.theology.org/highed/catalog.html

COST: Free (on Internet)

An extensive online list of financial aid sources from undergraduate through postgraduate study for theology students in most, not all, religious groups. NOT limited to Presbyterians. Includes Protestant, Catholic, and Jewish sources. Many are not designated for specific groups. Some are for women and ethnic minorities. E-mail can be sent from the website.

4068 — HOW TO FIND OUT ABOUT FINANCIAL AID

AUTHOR: Gail Ann Schlachter
Reference Service Press
5000 Windplay Dr., Suite 4
El Dorado Hills, CA 95762
916/939-9620

COST: $37.50 + $4.00 shipping

A comprehensive guide to more than 700 print and online directories that identify over $21 billion in financial aid available to undergraduates; graduate students and researchers.

4069 — HOW TO PREPARE A RESEARCH PROPOSAL

AUTHOR: David R. Krathwohl; IBSN 0-8156-8112-7
Syracuse University Press
1600 Jamesville Ave.
New York NY 13244-5160
800/365-8929

COST: $14.95 + $4.00 Shipping

305 page book offering guidelines for funding and dissertations in the social and behavorial sciences.

4070 — INDEX OF MAJORS & GRADUATE DEGREES

AUTHOR: CBP; ISBN #0-87447-592-9
The College Board Publications
Two College Way
Forrester Center WV 25438
800/323-7155
FAX: 800/525-5562
Internet: www.collegeboard.org

COST: $18.95 + $4. + applicable tax

Describes over 600 major programs of study at 3,200 undergraduate and graduate schools. Also lists schools that have religious affiliations, special academic programs, and special admissions procedures. 695 pages.

4071 — INSIDER'S GUIDE TO MEDICAL SCHOOLS

AUTHOR: ISBN: 0-7689-0203-7
Peterson's, Inc.
PO Box 2123

Princeton NJ 08543-2123
800/225-0261
FAX: 609/924-5338
Internet: www.petersons.com

COST: $17.56

Get the inside scoop on admissions, the curriculum, the student body, and campus life from students at 138 medical schools. Plus valuable tips on getting into and preparing for medical school. 480 pages.

4072 — INTERNATIONAL FUNDING GUIDE

AUTHOR: AASCU; ISBN #0-88044-109-7
American Association of State Colleges & Universities c/o University Press of America
4720 Boston Way, Suite A
Lanham MD 20706
301/459-3366

COST: $22.50

Primarily intended to assist colleges and universities in finding support for their international activities. However it does contain detailed information on over 100 programs open to graduate and postgraduate researchers. 167 pages.

4073 — INTERNATIONAL JOBS

AUTHOR: Eric Kocher
Perseus Books
1 Jacob Way
Reading MA 01867

COST: $16.00

The 5th edition provides everything you need to navigate complex international job market (including websites).

4074 — INTERNATIONAL SCHOOL DIRECTORY

AUTHOR: ECIS; ISBN #0-9524052-2-9
European Council of International Schools
21 Lavant St.
Petersfield Hampshire GU32 3EL England
44-730-68244-63131

COST: $41.25 from Specialist Publishing Services; 23 Leckhampstead Road; Wicken; Milton Keynes; MK19 6B4; UK

Compendium of international schools at all levels of study. Provides detailed information on over 800 elementary; secondary and postsecondary schools. Organized by country. 580 pages.

4075 — Information on the Physician Assistant Profession

AUTHOR: Write to above address for information.
AMERICAN ACADEMY OF PHYSICIAN ASSISTANTS
950 North Washington St.

Alexandria VA 22314-1552
703/836-2272
FAX: 703/684-1924
E-mail: aapa@aapa.org
Internet: www.aapa.org

COST: Free

A pamphlet describing the profession of physican assistant—what to study and where to go to school, the salaries, and the specialties.

4076 — International Forestry and Natural Resources

AUTHOR: Hard copies no longer available; please feel free to download and print your own copy.
UNITED STATES DEPARTMENT OF AGRICULTURE (A Guide to Grants, Fellowships, and Scholarships in International Forestry and Natural Resources)
P.O. Box 96090
Washington DC 20090-6090
http://www.fs.fed.us/people/gf/gf00.htm

COST:

An online guide to grants, fellowships, and scholarships in international forestry and natural resources.

4077 — JOB OPPORTUNITIES FOR THE BLIND (JOB)

AUTHOR: JOB offers the only recorded (audio cassette) job magazine in the U.S., along with over 40 other publications (most on cassette; some in print for employer education).
National Federation of the Blind
1800 Johnson St.
Baltimore MD 21230
800-638-7518
301-659-9314

COST: Free

JOB is operated by the NFB in partnership with the U.S. Dept. of Labor. It offers a free recorded job magazine, other publications, and a national reference service to blind job seekers on all aspects of looking for work, to employers, and to those assisting blind persons.

4078 — JOURNALISM AND MASS COMMUNICATIONS ACCREDITATION

AUTHOR: Also—see website.
Accrediting Council on Education in Journalism and Mass Communications
Stauffer-Flint Hall
University of Kansas School of Journalism
Lawrence KS 66045
785/864-5225
FAX: 785/864-5225

E-mail: sshaw@kuhub.cc.ukans.edu

Internet: www.ukans.edu/~acejmc

COST: $1.00

Comprehensive listing of colleges and universities with accredited journalism and mass communications programs. Also listed are numerous related professional organizations, many of which offer scholarships, internships, etc.

4079 — JOURNALISM AND MASS COMMUNICATION DIRECTORY

AUTHOR: AEJMC

Association for Education in Journalism & Mass Communications

Univ. of SC

LeConte College, Rm. 121

Columbia SC 29208-0251

COST: $25.00 U.S.; $35.00 foreign

Annual directory listing more than 350 schools and departments of journalism and mass communication, information on national funds, fellowships, foundations, and collegiate and scholastic services. More than 3,000 individual members.

4080 — JOURNALIST'S ROAD TO SUCCESS: A Career and Scholarship Guide

AUTHOR: DJNF

Dow Jones Newspaper Fund

PO Box 300

Princeton NJ 08543-0300

800/DOW-FUND

E-mail: newsfund@wsj.dowjones.com

Internet: www.dj.com/newsfund

COST: $3.00 (prepaid check/money order)

Comprehensive source book for high school & college students who are interested in journalism careers. Intended to help students choose colleges that offer the best combination of academic programs, practical experience, & scholarships. Updated yearly, the Guide tells students how to prepare for a newspaper career, lists more than 400 colleges that offer news-editorial journalism majors, and lists hundreds of scholarships for the study of news-editorial journalism.

4081 — LANGUAGE LIAISON PROGRAM DIRECTORY

AUTHOR:

Language Liaison

1610 Woodstead Ct., Suite 130

The Woodlands TX 77380

281/367-7302 or 800/284-4448

FAX: 281/367-4498

E-mail: learn@launguageliaison.com

Internet: www.languageliaison.com

COST: Free

Want to learn another language? Learn it like a native in the country where it is spoken. New programs start every week year-round from two weeks to a year long. Programs are open to students, teachers, executives, teens, seniors, families, and leisure travelers. Includes activities, excursions, and homestays. See website for details on this program as well as various language tools.

4082 — LESKO'S SELF-HELP BOOKS

AUTHOR: Matthew Lesko

Information USA, Inc.

PO Box E

Kensington MD 20895

800/955-7693 or 301/924-0556

FAX: 301/929-8907

Internet: www.lesko.com

COST: Varies

A variety of self-help books on "free stuff." Author gives information on free government information, expert advice, and money. See website or contact publisher for a list of titles.

4083 — LIST OF SCHOLARSHIPS AND AWARDS IN ELECTRICAL, ELECTRONICS, AND COMPUTER ENGINEERING

AUTHOR:

IEEE-USA Computer Society

1828 L St. NW, Suite 1202

Washington DC 20036-5104

202/371-1013

FAX: 202/778-0884

Internet: www.ieeeusa.org

COST: Free

A source of information containing a multitude of scholarships in the above fields, including application information.

4084 — MAKING A DIFFERENCE—CAREER OPPORTUNITIES IN DISABILITY-RELATED FIELDS

AUTHOR: The Arc

The Arc, National Headquarters

P.O. Box 1047

Arlington TX 76004

817/261-6003

817/277-0553 (TDD)

COST: $10.00 (includes S/H)

A handbook of over 50 professions that serve people with disabilities. Includes career overview, employment settings, populations served, and salary/educational/certification requirements.

4085 — MAKING IT THROUGH COLLEGE

AUTHOR: PSC

Professional Staff Congress

25 W. 43rd St. 5th Floor

New York NY 10036

COST: $1.00

Handy booklet containing information on coping with competition, getting organized, study techniques, solving work overloads, and more. 14 pages.

4086 — MAKING THE MOST OF YOUR COLLEGE EDUCATION

AUTHOR: Marianne Ragins; Order Code: MMC-999dsc

The Scholarship Workshop

PO Box 176

Centreville VA 20122

912/755-8428

Internet: www.scholarshipworkshop.com

COST: $10.95 + $3 shipping & handling

This book shows you how to pack your college years with career-building experiences that can lead to graduate and professional schools clamoring to admit you; how to write an impressive professional resume; and how to gain keen entrepreneurial skills, an investment portfolio, and multiple job offers. Offers information on securing internships, travel opportunities, managing your money, using the Internet to your advantage, and other helpful advice.

4087 — MEDICAL SCHOOL ADMISSION REQUIREMENTS

AUTHOR: Cynthia T. Bennett

Association of American Medical Colleges

2450 N St., NW

Washington DC 20037-1126

202/828-0400

FAX: 202/828-1125

COST: $25 + $5 shipping

Contains admission requirements of accredited medical schools in the U.S. and Canada.

4088 — MEDICINE—A CHANCE TO MAKE A DIFFERENCE

AUTHOR: AMA

American Medical Association

Order Processing:515 N. State Street

Chicago IL 60610

COST: $5.00 + $4.95 shipping/handling (pkg. of 10 brochures)

For college students considering a career in medicine. Answers questions about the profession and medical education, including prerequisites, admission requirements, and choosing a medical school.

4089 — MUSIC SCHOLARSHIP GUIDE (3rd Edition)

AUTHOR: Sandra V. Fridy; ISBN 1-56545-050-7
Music Educators National Conference
1806 Robert Fulton Dr.
Reston VA 20191

COST: $33.00 ($26.40 MENC members)

Lists over 2,000 undergraduate music scholarships in more than 600 public and private edcuational institutions (colleges & universities) in the United States and Canada, including eligibility requirements, application deadlines, and contact information.

4090 — NATIONAL DIRECTORY OF CORPORATE GIVING

AUTHOR: TFC; ISBN 0-87954-400-7
Foundation Center (The)
79 Fifth Ave./16th Street
New York NY 10003
212/620-4230

COST: $199.50 (Including shipping/handling)

Book profiles 2000 programs making contributions to nonprofit organizations. A valuable tool to assist grant seekers in finding potential support.

4091 — NEED A LIFT? (48th edition-1999 Issue)

AUTHOR: Pre-paid only. Send check or money order to address above.
The American Legion
Attn: National Emblem Sales
PO Box 1055
Indianapolis IN 46206
317/630-1200
FAX: 317/630-1223
Internet: www.legion.org

COST: $3.00

Outstanding guide to federal and state government-related financial aid as well as private sector programs. Contains information on the financial aid process (how, when, and where to start) and addresses for scholarship, loan, and career information. 150 pages.

4092 — NEWSPAPERS, DIVERSITY & YOU

AUTHOR: DJNF
Dow Jones Newspaper Fund
PO Box 300
Princeton NJ 08543-0300
800/DOW-FUND
E-mail: newsfund@wsj.dowjones.com
Internet: www.dj.com/newsfund

COST: Free

Information on grants, scholarships, and internships specifically for minority high school and college students, along with articles written by professional journalists of color.

4093 — OCCUPATIONAL OUTLOOK HANDBOOK

AUTHOR: U.S. Dept. of Labor Bureau of Statistics; 1996-97 ISBN: 0-934783-72-1 (soft cover) and 0-934783-73-X (hard cover)
CFKR Career Materials
11860 Kemper Road, #7
Auburn CA 95603
800/525-5626 or 916/889-2357
FAX: 800/770-0433 or 916/889-0433
E-mail: cfkr@cfkr.com
Internet: www.cfkr.com

COST: $16.95 (soft cover); $21.95 (hard cover)

Annual publication designed to assist individuals in selecting appropriate careers. Describes approximately 250 occupations in great detail and includes current and projected job prospects for each. A great resource for teachers and counselors. Versions for Grades 5-12 and related activity books also available. 508 pages.

4094 — Order form for book list on theatre\writing careers

AUTHOR:
Theatre Directories
P.O. Box 510
Dorset VT 05251-0510
802/867-2223
FAX: 802/867-2223
Internet: http://genghis.com/theatre.htm

COST: Free pamphlet/directory of books

A pamphlet listing books on training programs for careers in theatre and playwriting.

4095 — PERSPECTIVES: AUDITION ADVICE FOR SINGERS

AUTHOR: Various leaders in the opera field.
OPERA America
1156 15th St., NW, Suite 810
Washington DC 20005-1704
202/293-4466
FAX 393-0735
E-mail: Frontdesk@operaam.org

COST: $15/non-members; $10/members

A collection of personal observations from professionals who want to help singers perpare for and perform winning auditions. Features 27 valuable essays from general directors, artistic administrators, training program directors, artist managers, stage directors, teachers, established singers, and university and conservatory directors.

4096 — PERSPECTIVES: THE SINGER/ MANAGER RELATIONSHIP

AUTHOR: Various leaders in the opera field.
OPERA America
1156 15th St., NW, Suite 810
Washington DC 20005-1704
202/293-4466
FAX 393-0735
E-mail: Frontdesk@operaam.org

COST: $15./nonmembers; $12./members

Features essays by leaders in the field about artist managers and their roles and responsibilities in identifying and advancing the careers of aspiring singers. Opera professionals, including artist managers, singers, and opera company casting representatives share experiences and give insights to the most frequently asked questions.

4097 — PHARMACY SCHOOL ADMISSION REQUIREMENTS

AUTHOR: AACP
American Association of Colleges of Pharmacy
Office of Student Affairs
1426 Prince St.
Alexandria VA 22314
703/739-2330

COST: $25.00 prepaid plus $3.00 shipping and handling.

100-page booklet containing comparative information charts along with the general history of accredited pharmacy programs and current admission requirements.

4098 — PING AMERICAN COLLEGE GOLF GUIDE

AUTHOR: Dean W. Frischknecht
Dean Frischknecht Publishing
PO Box 1179
Hillsboro OR 97123
503/648-1333
Internet: www.collegegolf.com

COST: $11.95

Alphabetical listing by state of two and four year colleges with intercollegiate golf programs. Includes scholarship and financial aid information, resumes, ratings, and scores. 304 pages. Updated annually.

4099 — PLANNING FOR A DENTAL EDUCATION

AUTHOR: AADS
American Association of Dental Schools
1625 Massachusetts Ave. NW
Washington DC 20036-2212

COST: Free

Brochure discusses dentistry as a career and offers advice on planning for a dental education.

4100 — POWER STUDY TO UP YOUR GRADES IN MATH

AUTHOR: Sondra Geoffrion
   Access Success Associates
   P.O. Box 1686
   Goleta CA 93116

COST: $4.95 + $2.50 U.S. postage ($4.00 foreign postage). California residents add sales tax.

One of five excellent booklets explaining correct procedures to solve problems with speed, accuracy, and correctness. Also how to prepare for and take tests.

4101 — POWER STUDY TO UP YOUR GRADES IN ENGLISH

AUTHOR: Sondra Geoffrion
   Access Success Associates
   P.O. Box 1686
   Goleta CA 93116

COST: $4.95 + $2.50 U.S. postage ($4.00 foreign postage). California residents add sales tax.

One of five excellent booklets explaining techniques to discover what will be tested, cut study time in half, prepare thoroughly, write essays, and take tests. Other titles cover math, social studies, science, and improving grade point average.

4102 — POWER STUDY TO UP YOUR GRADES IN SOCIAL STUDIES

AUTHOR: Sondra Geoffrion
   Access Success Associates
   P.O. Box 1686
   Goleta CA 93116

COST: $4.95 + $2.50 U.S. postage ($4.00 foreign postage)—California residents add sales tax

One of 5 excellent booklets explaining techniques to discover what will be tested; cut study time in half; prepare thoroughly; write essays; take tests. Other titles cover math; English; science and improving grade point average.

4103 — POWER STUDY TO UP YOUR GRADES IN SCIENCE

AUTHOR: Sondra Geoffrion
   Access Success Associates
   P.O. Box 1686
   Goleta CA 93116

COST: $4.95 + $2.50 U.S. postage ($4.00 foreign postage)—California residents add sales tax

One of 5 excellent booklets explaining how to discover what will be tested, cut study time in half, prepare thoroughly, write essays, and take tests. Other titles cover math, English, social studies, and improving grade point average.

4104 — PROCEEDINGS AND ADDRESSES OF THE AMERICAN PHILOSOPHICAL ASSN.

AUTHOR: APA
   The American Philosophical Association
   University of Delaware
   Newark DE 19716
   302/831-1112
   FAX: 302/831-8690
   E-mail: johnlong@udel.edu
   Internet: www.udel.edu/apa

COST: $15 per issue

November and May issues include lists of grants and fellowships of interest to philosophers. These, as well as travel stipends and other resources, are listed on the website.

4105 — Physician Assistant Programs Directory

AUTHOR: Order from above location.
   SpecWorks
   810 South Bond St.
   Baltimore MD 21231
   800/708-7581
   FAX: 410/558-1410

COST: $35.00

A catalog of of physician assistant educational programs, including addresses, admissions procedures and requirements, course outlines, length of program, university and institutional affiliations, tuition, and sources of financial assistance.

4106 — Pour Man's Friend: A Guide and Reference for Bar Personnel

AUTHOR: John C. Burton; ISBN: 0-9624625-0-0
   POUR MAN'S FRIEND (A Guide and Reference for Bar Personnel)
   Aperitifs Publishing
   1731 King Street
   Santa Rosa, CA 95404
   707/523-1611

COST: $14.95 + shipping

Includes comprehensive bartending techniques, ways to achieve top industry standards with current regulations and guidelines.

4107 — SCHOLARSHIPS & LOANS FOR NURSING EDUCATION

AUTHOR: National League for Nursing; ISBN #0-88737-730-0
   Jones and Bartlett Publishers
   40 Tall Pine Drive

Sudbury MA 01776
   800/832-0034
   FAX: 978/443-8000
   E-mail: info@jbpub.com
   Internet: www.jbpub.com

COST: $18.75 + $4.50 postage/handling

Information on all types of scholarships, awards, grants, fellowships, and loans for launching or continuing your career in nursing. 125 pages. Other books available: NLN STATE-APPROVED SCHOOLS OF NURSING ($39.95) and NURSING: THE CAREER OF A LIFETIME ($22.50).

4108 — SELECTED FINANCIAL AID REFERENCES FOR STUDENTS WITH DISABILITIES-#107.96

AUTHOR:
   NATIONAL CLEARINGHOUSE FOR PROFESSIONS IN SPECIAL EDUCATION
   The Council for Exceptional Children
   1920 Association Dr.
   Reston VA 20191-1589
   1/800-641-7824 or 703/264-9476 or TTY 703/264-9480
   FAX: 703/264-1637
   E-mail: ncpse@cec.sped.org
   Internet: www.cec.sped.org/ncpse.htm

COST: Free

A list of specific sources of financial assistance for students with disabilities preparing for careers in special education and related services, such as physical therapy, occupational therapy, speech-language pathology, and others.

4109 — SELECTED FINANCIAL AID RESOURCES FOR INDIVIDUALS FROM CULTURALLY/ETHNICALLY DIVERSE BACKGROUNDS-#104.96

AUTHOR:
   NATIONAL CLEARINGHOUSE FOR PROFESSIONS IN SPECIAL EDUCATION
   The Council for Exceptional Children
   1920 Association Dr.
   Reston VA 20191-1589
   1/800-641-7824 or 703/264-9476 or TTY 703/264-9480
   FAX: 703/264-1637
   E-mail: ncpse@cec.sped.org
   Internet: www.cec.sped.org/ncpse.htm

COST: Free

A list of specific sources of financial assistance for minority students preparing for careers in special education and related services, such as physical therapy, occupational therapy, speech-language pathology, and others.

4110 — SELECTED FINANCIAL AID RESOURCES FOR RELATED SERVICES-#103.97

AUTHOR:

NATIONAL CLEARINGHOUSE FOR
PROFESSIONS IN SPECIAL EDUCATION
The Council for Exceptional Children
1920 Association Dr.
Reston VA 20191-1589
1/800-641-7824 or 703/264-9476 or TTY 703/264-9480
FAX: 703/264-1637
E-mail: ncpse@cec.sped.org
Internet: www.cec.sped.org/ncpse.htm

COST: Free

A list of specific sources of financial assistance for students preparing for careers in services related to special education, such as physical therapy, occupational therapy, speech-language pathology, and others.

4111 — SELECTED FINANCIAL AID RESOURCES FOR SPECIAL EDUCATION-#102.97

AUTHOR:

NATIONAL CLEARINGHOUSE FOR
PROFESSIONS IN SPECIAL EDUCATION
The Council for Exceptional Children
1920 Association Dr.
Reston VA 20191-1589
1/800-641-7824 or 703/264-9476 or TTY 703/264-9480
FAX: 703/264-1637
E-mail: ncpse@cec.sped.org
Internet: www.cec.sped.org/ncpse.htm

COST: Free

A list of specific sources of financial assistance for students preparing for careers in special education and related services.

4112 — SPANISH ABROAD

AUTHOR: See website for details.
Spanish Abroad, Inc.
6520 N. 41st St.
Paradise Valley AZ 852253
1-888/722-7623 (toll-free U.S. & Canada) or 602/947-4652
FAX: 602/840-1545
E-mail: info@spanishabroad.com
Internet: www.spanishabroad.com

COST: Varies

This website is a vast source of opportunities for Spanish immersion programs in many countries around the world. Included is a page that has a list of financial aid and scholarships for this purpose.

4113 — STATE RESOURCE SHEETS

AUTHOR:

NATIONAL CLEARINGHOUSE FOR
PROFESSIONS IN SPECIAL EDUCATION
The Council for Exceptional Children
1920 Association Dr.
Reston VA 20191-1589
1/800-641-7824 or 703/264-9476 or TTY 703/264-9480
FAX: 703/264-1637
E-mail: ncpse@cec.sped.org
Internet: www.cec.sped.org/ncpse.htm

COST: Free

A list of sources of financial assistance in specific states for students preparing for careers in special education and related services, such as physical therapy, occupational therapy, speech-language pathology, and others. When ordering, specify the state or states in which you attend or may attend college.

4114 — STUDENT FINANCIAL AID AND SCHOLARSHIPS AT WYOMING COLLEGES

AUTHOR: UW
University of Wyoming Office of Student Financial Aid
PO Box 3335
Laramie WY 82071-3335
307/766-2116
FAX: 307/766-3800

COST: Free

Describes postsecondary student aid and scholarship programs that are available to Wyoming students. Booklets can be obtained at all Wyoming high schools and colleges.

4115 — STUDY ABROAD (Volume 30; 1998-1999)

AUTHOR: UNESCO
United Nations Educational, Scientific and Cultural Organization
Bernan Associates
UNESCO Agent
4611-F Assembly Drive
Lanham MD 20706

COST: $29.95 + postage/handling

Printed in English, French, & Spanish, this volume lists 3,700 international study programs in all academic and professional fields in more than 124 countries. Also available on CD-ROM.

4116 — STUDY IN THE NETHERLANDS: YOUR GATEWAY TO EUROPE

AUTHOR: NUFFIC Netherlands Organization for International Cooperation in Higher Education

Kortenaerkade 11
Postbus 29777
2502 LT Den Haag THE NETHERLANDS
+31 070 426 02 00
FAX: +31 070 426 03 99
E-mail: nuffic@nuffic.nl
Internet: www.nuffic.nl

COST: Free

Helpful booklet for students from foreign countries planning to study in The Netherlands. Includes details on applying for admission; practical matters such as money, housing, & scholarships; and courses & study programmes conducted in English and Dutch.

4117 — Studying in the UK: Sources of Funding for International Students

AUTHOR: Published by The British Council 1997
THE BRITISH COUNCIL, INTERNATIONAL STUDENT SERVICES
Regional Services Dept., Medlock St.
Manchester M15 5AA ENGLAND

COST:

A free booklet describing various forms of student financial aid for study in the United Kingdom.

4118 — TAFT CORPORATE GIVING DIRECTORY (1996 Edition)

AUTHOR: ISBN #0-914756-79-6
Taft Group
12300 Twinbrook Pkwy., Suite 520
Rockville MD 20852-1607
800/877-8238

COST: $375.00

This reference book is found in most major libraries. It contains comprehensive information on over 500 foundations sponsored by top corporations. 859 pages.

4119 — TEN STEPS IN WRITING THE RESEARCH PAPER

AUTHOR: Roberta Markman, Peter Markman, and Marie Waddell
Barron's Educational Series Inc.
250 Wireless Blvd.
Hauppauge NY 11788
800/645-3476
Internet: www.barronseduc.com

COST: $9.95, ISBN# 08120-1868-10

Arranged to lead the student step-by-step through the writing of a research paper—from finding a suitable subject to checking the final copy. Easy enough for the beginner, complete enough for the graduate student. 177 pages.

4120 — TEXAS MUSIC INDUSTRY DIRECTORY

AUTHOR:

State of Texas, Music Office
P.O. Box 13246
Austin TX 78711
512/463-4114
FAX: 512/463-4114
E-mail: music@governor.state.tx.us
Internet: www.governor.state.tx.us/music

COST: $18.00

A publication of the Texas Governor's Office which lists more than 8,000 Texas music business contacts, including events, classical music, books, and texas colleges offering music and music business courses. Could be a valuable resource to anyone considering a career in the business of music. 424 pages.

4121 — THE CARE BOOK (College Aid Resources for Education)

AUTHOR: Dr. Herm Davis; ISBN: #0-9656724-0-9
National College Scholarship Foundation, Inc. (NCSF)
16728 Frontenac Terrace
Rockville MD 20855
301/548-9423
FAX: 301/548-9453
E-mail: ncsfdn@aol.com

COST: $29.95

This publication was developed to be a hands-on daily reference for counselors as well as for families. It assists counselors and students to have a quick reference to find stats on a college and to compare college costs, enrollments, form requirements, etc. Includes a CD-ROM money planner.

4122 — THE FOUNDATION DIRECTORY

AUTHOR: ISBN #0-87954-449-6 (soft cover); 0-87954-484-8 (hard cover)
The Foundation Center
79 Fifth Ave.
New York NY 10003
800/424-9836

COST: $160.00 soft cover; $185.00 hard cover; + $4.50 shipping by UPS

Authoritative annual reference book found in most major libraries. Contains detailed information on over 6300 of America's largest foundations. Indexes allow grantseekers; researchers; etc. to quickly locate foundations of interest.

4123 — THE GUERRILLA GUIDE TO MASTERING STUDENT LOAN DEBT

AUTHOR: Anne Stockwell; ISBN: 0-06-273435-0
Harper Collins Publishers

THE GUERRILLA GUIDE TO MASTERING STUDENT LOAN DEBT
2275 Hidalgo Ave.
Los Angeles, CA 90039
323/664-4323

COST: US $14; CANADA $20 (plus tax/shipping)

Identifies which loans are best for you and explains how to repay them once you're in debt. Includes advice from loan officers, legislators, collection agents, and students.

4124 — THE NATIONAL DIRECTORY OF INTERNSHIPS

AUTHOR: ISBN 0-536-01123-0
National Society for Experiential Education
Simon & Schuster
5550 W. 74th St.
Indianapolis IN 46268
877/587-4666 (Simon & Schuster)
919/787-3263 (NSEE)
FAX: 919/787-3381
E-mail: info@nsee.org
Internet: www.nsee.org/

COST: $29.95 ($24.95 NSEE members) + $5.59 shipping

Lists thousands of internships in over 85 fields in government, nonprofit, and corporate settings. Includes work and service opportunities for college, graduate, and high school students, as well as those not in school, mid-career professionals, and retired people. Indexed by name of organization, geographic locations, and field of interest. 722 pages. Order from toll-free Simon & Schuster Custom Publishing number or access website for order form.

4125 — THEIR WORLD

AUTHOR: NCLD
National Center for Learning Disabilities
381 Park Ave. S., Suite 1401
New York NY 10016
212/545-7510
FAX: 212/545-9665
Internet: www.ncld.org

COST: $6.00

This annual magazine offers a wide range of practical material to benefit the millions of children and adults with learning disabilities, and their families as well as educators and other helping professionals.

4126 — UAA-102 COLLEGIATE AVIATION GUIDE

AUTHOR: Gary W. Kiteley, Executive Director
University Aviation Association
3410 Skyway Drive
Auburn AL 36830-6444

334/844-2434
FAX: 334/844-2432
E-mail: uaa@auburn.edu

COST: $30 non-members (+$4 S&H); $20 members (+$4 S&H)

Guide to college level aviation study. Detailed state-by-state listings of aviation programs offered by US colleges and universities.

4127 — UAA-116 COLLEGIATE AVIATION SCHOLARSHIP LISTING

AUTHOR: Gary W. Kiteley, Executive Director
University Aviation Association
3410 Skyway Drive
Auburn AL 36830-6444
334/844-2434
FAX: 334/844-2432
E-mail: uaa@auburn.edu

COST: $8 members (+$4 S&H); $15 non-members (+$4 S&H)

This guide includes a listing of financial aid sources, methods of applying for general purpose aid, and a listing of aviation scholarships arranged by broad classification.

4128 — VACATION STUDY ABROAD

AUTHOR: Sara J.Steen, Editor
Institute of International Education
IIE Books
809 United Nations Plaza
New York NY 10017-3580

COST: $39.95 + $5 shipping and handling

Guide to some 1,800 summer or short-term study-abroad programs sponsored by U.S. colleges, universities, private institutions, and foreign institutions. 400 pages.

4129 — WHAT COLOR IS YOUR PARACHUTE?

AUTHOR: Richard N. Bolles; ISBN #1-58008-123-1
Ten Speed Press
PO Box 7123
Berkeley CA 94707
800/841-BOOK or 510/559-1600
FAX: 510/559-1629
E-mail: order@tenspeed.com
Internet: www.tenspeed.com

COST: $16.95 + $4.50 shipping

Step-by-step career planning guide now in its 30th Anniversary Edition. Highly recommended for anyone who is job hunting or changing careers. Contains valuable tips on assessing your skills, writing resumes, and handling job interviews. 368 pages.

4130 — WINNING SCHOLARSHIPS FOR COLLEGE—AN INSIDER'S GUIDE

AUTHOR: Marianne Ragins; Order Code: DSC999
    The Scholarship Workshop
    PO Box 176
    Centreville VA 20122
    912/755-8428
    Internet: www.scholarshipworkshop.com

COST: $12.95 + $3 shipping & handling

Author Marianne Ragins, winner of more than $400,000 in scholarship funds, proves that it's not always those with the best grades or highest SAT scores who win scholarships. You'll see that rigorous research efforts, involvement in extracurricular activities, leadership potential, and special talents all combine to determine your chances of securing aid for college. Tips on using the Internet, scholarly resumes, selling yourself, test-taking tips, & writing essays.

4131 — WORLD DIRECTORY OF MEDICAL SCHOOLS

AUTHOR: WHO
    World Health Organization (1211 Geneva 27 Switzerland)
    WHO Publication Center
    49 Sheridan Ave.
    Albany NY 12210

COST: $35 (shipping/handling included)

Comprehensive book that describes the medical education programs and schools in each country. Arranged in order by country or area.

4132 — WORLD DIRECTORY OF SCHOOLS OF PUBLIC HEALTH

AUTHOR: WHO
    World Health Organization
    (1211 Geneva 27, Switzerland)
    WHO Publications Center
    49 Sheridan Ave.
    Albany NY 12210

COST: $29.10 (shipping/handling included)

Directory lists by country the institutions that offer postgraduate training in public health. Describes the basic postgraduate courses offered in each country.

4133 — WORLD FEDERATION OF INTERNATIONAL MUSIC COMPETITIONS BOOKLET

AUTHOR: WFIMC
    World Federation of International Music Competitions
    104, Rue de Carouge
    CH-1205 Geneva SWITZERLAND

41/22 321 36 20
FAX: 41/22 781 14 18
E-mail: fmcim@iprolink.ch

COST: Free

Annual directory describing international music performance and composition competitions for artists all over the world. Prizes consist of cash awards and performance engagements for top finalists.

4134 — WRITE YOUR WAY TO A HIGHER GPA

AUTHOR: Randall S. Hansen, Ph.D. & Katherine Hansen; ISBN: 0-89815-903-2
    Ten Speed Press
    PO Box 7123
    Berkeley CA 94707
    800/841-BOOK or 510/559-1600
    FAX: 510/559-1629
    E-mail: order@tenspeed.com
    Internet: www.tenspeed.com

COST: $11.95 + $4.50 shipping

This book tells how any student can use writing skills to get the highest grade possible in any class. Special focus on the Internet and other new resources. 240 pages.

4135 — WRITING CONTESTS FOR LAW STUDENTS

AUTHOR: Compiled at the Cecil C. Humphreys School of Law at the University of Memphis.
    University of Memphis
    See website
    See website
    www.people.memphis.edu/~law/contests.html

COST: Free

Comprehensive list of writing contests on various topics for law students.

4136 — Where There's a Will There's an "A" to Get Better Grades in College (or High School)

AUTHOR:
    WHERE THERE'S A WILL THERE'S AN A
    Olney "A" Seminars
    P.O. Box 686
    Scottsdale, AZ 85252-0686
    800/546-3883
    Internet: www.wheretheresawill.com

COST: $44.95

Video tape seminars on how to get better grades.

4137 — YOUR CAREER IN THE COMICS

AUTHOR: Author: Lee Nordling; Publisher: Andrews McMeel Publishing
    NEWSPAPER FEATURES COUNCIL, INC.

22 Byfield Lane
Greenwich CT 06830

COST: $9.95 + $3. postage + $1 packaging/handling

Detailed information on the business of being a professional cartoonist for newspapers. Learn from the artists and professionals themselves how cartoon syndication works.

Career Information

4138

ACCOUNTING/NET

600 Stewart St.

Ste. 1101

Seattle WA 98101

206/441-8285

FAX: 206/441-8385

E-mail: counselor@accountingstudents.com

Internet: www.accountingstudents.com/toolbox/index.html

4139 Accounting (Career Information)

AMERICAN INSTITUTE OF CERTIFIED PUBLIC ACCOUNTANTS

1211 Avenue of the Americas

New York NY 10036-8775

212/596-6200

FAX: 212/596-6213

Internet: www.aicpa.org

4140 Accounting (Career Information)

NATIONAL SOCIETY OF PUBLIC ACCOUNTANTS

1010 North Fairfax Street

Alexandria VA 22314-1574

703/549-6400

FAX: 703/549-2984

Internet: www.nsacct.org

4141 Accounting (Career Information)

INSTITUTE OF MANAGEMENT ACCOUNTANTS

10 Paragon Dr.

Montvale NJ 07645

201/573-9000

4142 Actuarial Science (Career Information)

SOCIETY OF ACTUARIES

475 N. Martingale Rd., Suite 800

Schaumburg IL 60173-2226

847/706-3509

FAX: 847/706-3599

4143 Acupuncture/Oriental Medicine & Drug/Alcoholism Recovery (Career Information)

NATIONAL ACUPUNCTURE DETOXIFICATION ASSOCIATION

3220 N Street NW, Ste. 275

Washington, DC 20007

503/222-1362

FAX: 503/228-4618

E-mail: AcuDetox@aol.com

Internet: www.healthy.net/pan/pa/acupuncture/nada/nadamain.htm

4144 Acupuncture/Oriental Medicine (Career Information)

CALIFORNIA SOCIETY FOR ORIENTAL MEDICINE (CSOM)

12926 Riverside Drive, #B

Sherman Oaks, CA 91423

FAX: 818/981-2766

Internet: www.quickcom.net/csom/

4145 Advertising (Career Information)

AMERICAN ADVERTISING FEDERATION

Education Services

1101 Vermont Ave., NW, Suite 500

Washington DC 20005-6306

4146 Aeronautics (Career Information)

AMERICAN INSTITUTE OF AERONAUTICS AND ASTRONAUTICS (Student Programs Department)

1801 Alexander Bell Drive, Suite 500

Reston VA 20191-4344

800/NEW-AIAA or 703/264-7500

FAX: 703/264-7551

Internet: www.aiaa.org

4147 Aerospace Education (Career Information)

AEROSPACE EDUCATION FOUNDATION

1501 Lee Highway

Arlington VA 22209-1198

800/727-3337, ext. 4880

FAX: 703/247-5853

E-mail: aefstaff@aef.org

4148 Agricultural & Biological Engineering (Career Information)

ASAE SOCIETY FOR ENGINEERING IN AGRICULTURAL FOOD AND BIOLOGICAL SYSTEMS

2950 Niles Rd.

St. Joseph MI 49085

4149 Agriculture (Career Information)

AMERICAN FARM BUREAU FEDERATION ("There's A New Challenge In Agriculture")

225 Touhy Ave.

Public Policy Division

Park Ridge IL 60068

847/685-8848

FAX: 847/685-8969

E-mail: susan@fb.com

4150 Agronomny; Crops; Soils; Environment (Career Information)

AMERICAN SOCIETY OF AGRONOMY

677 S. Segoe Rd.

Madison WI 53711

608/273-8080

FAX: 608/273-2021

4151 Airline (Career Information)

AIR TRANSPORT ASSOCIATION OF AMERICA

1301 Pennsylvania Ave. NW, Suite 1100

Washington DC 20004-1707

4152 Animal Science (Career Information)

NATIONAL ASSOCIATION OF ANIMAL BREEDERS (NAAB)

401 Bernadette Dr.

PO Box 1033

Columbia MO 65205

573/445-4406 or 573/445-9541

FAX: 573/446-2279

E-mail: naab-css.org

4153 Animation (Career Information)

WOMEN IN ANIMATION (WIA)

PO Box 17706

Encino CA 91416

E-mail: info@women.in.animation.org

Internet: women.in.animation.org

4154 Anthropology (Career Information)

AMERICAN ANTHROPOLOGICAL ASSOCIATION

4350 N. Fairfax Dr., Suite 640

Arlington VA 22203-1620

703/528-1902

FAX: 703/528-3546

Internet: www.ameranthassn.org

4155 Appraising (Career Information)

AMERICAN SOCIETY OF APPRAISERS

PO Box 17265

Washington DC 20041

4156 Apprenticeship (Career Information)

US DEPT OF LABOR; BUREAU OF APPRENTICESHIP AND TRAINING

200 Constitution Ave. NW

Room N-4649

Washington DC 20210

4157 Archaeology (Career Information)

ARCHAEOLOGICAL INSTITUTE OF AMERICA

Boston Univ

656 Beacon St.

Boston MA 02215-2006

617/353-9361

FAX: 617/353-6550

E-mail: aia@bu.edu

Internet: www.archaeological.org

4158 Architecture (Career Information)

AMERICAN ARCHITECTURAL FOUNDATION (AIA/ AAF Scholarship Program)

1735 New York Ave., NW

Washington DC 20006-5292

202/626-7511

FAX: 202/626-7420

E-mail: felberm@aiamail.aia.org

4159 Astronomy & Astrophysics (Career Information for Women)

HARVARD-SMITHSONIAN CENTER FOR ASTROPHYSICS

Publication Dept., MS-28

60 Garden St.

Cambridge MA 02138

617/495-7461

4160 Astronomy (Career Information)

AMERICAN ASTRONOMICAL SOCIETY

2000 Florida Ave. NW, Suite 400

Washington DC 20009

202/328-2010

FAX: 202/324-2560

E-mail: aas@aas.org

Internet: www.aas.org

4161 Audiology; Speech Pathology (Career Information)

AMERICAN SPEECH-LANGUAGE-HEARING ASSOCIATION

10801 Rockville Pike

Rockville MD 20852

4162 Automotive Engineering (Career Information)

SOCIETY OF AUTOMOTIVE ENGINEERS (SAE)

400 Commonwealth Drive

Warrendale PA 15096-0001

724/772-4047

E-mail: connie@sae.org

Internet: www.sae.org

4163 Aviation Maintenance (Career Information)

Professional Aviation Maintenance Association

636 Eye St., NW, Suite 300

Washington DC 20001-3736

202/216-9220

FAX: 202/216-9224

E-mail: hq@pama.org

Internet: www.pama.org

4164 Bartending (Career Information)

BARTENDERS' SCHOOL OF SANTA ROSA

1731 King St.

Santa Rosa CA 95404

707/523-1611

4165 Biologist (Career Information)

AMERICAN INSTITUTE OF BIOLOGICAL SCIENCES

1444 Eye St. NW, Suite 200

Washington DC 20005

202/628-1500, ext. 281

4166 Biotechnology (Career Information)

BIOTECHNOLOGY INDUSTRY ORGANIZATION

1625 'K' St. NW, Suite 1100

Washington DC 20006

202/857-0244

4167 Broadcast News (Career Information)

RADIO AND TELEVISION NEWS DIRECTORS ASSOCIATION

1000 Connecticut Ave., NW, Suite 615

Washington DC 20036-5302

202/659-6510

FAX: 202/223-4007

E-mail: michellet@rtndf.org

Internet: www.rtndf.org

4168 Broadcasting (Career Information)

AMERICAN WOMEN IN RADIO & TELEVISION

c/o Lauren Kravetz

1001 Pennsylvania Ave.

6th Floor

Washington DC 20004

202/624-7283

FAX: 202/624-7222

Internet: www.awrt.org

4169 Careers in the Public Life (Information)

NATIONAL ASSOCIATION OF SCHOOLS OF PUBLIC AFFAIRS AND ADMINISTRATION

1120 G St., NW, Suite 730

Washington DC 20005-3801

E-mail: info@naspaa.org

Internet: www.naspaa.org/publicservicecareers

4170 Cartooning (Career Information)

NEWSPAPER FEATURES COUNCIL

22 Byfield Lane

Greenwich CT 06830-3446

4171 Cartooning (Career Information)

NATIONAL CARTOONISTS SOCIETY

10 Columbus Circle, Suite 1620

New York NY 10019

Internet: www.reuben.org

4172 Chemical Engineering (Career Information)

AMERICAN INSTITUTE OF CHEMICAL ENGINEERS

Communications Dept.

345 E. 47th St.

New York NY 10017-2395

Internet: www.aiche.org/careers/

4173 Chiropractics (Career/College Information)

AMERICAN CHIROPRACTIC ASSOCIATION

1701 Clarendon Blvd.

Arlington VA 22209

800/377-8397 or 703/276-8800

FAX: 703/243-2593

4174 Chiropractics (Career/School Information)

INTERNATIONAL CHIROPRACTORS ASSOCIATION

1110 N. Glebe Rd., Suite 1000

Arlington VA 22201

4175 Civil Engineering (Career Information)

AMERICAN SOCIETY OF CIVIL ENGINEERS

1801 Alexander Bell Drive

Reston VA 20191-4400

800-548-ASCE or 703/295-6000

FAX: 703/295-6333

E-mail: student@asce.org

Internet: www.asce.org

4176 Clinical Chemist (Career Information)

AMERICAN ASSOCIATION FOR CLINICAL CHEMISTRY

2101 L St. NW, Suite 202

Washington DC 20037-1526

800/892-1400

FAX: 202/892-1400

E-mail: educatn@aacc.org

Internet: www.aacc.org

4177 College Information

UNIVERSITY OF CALIFORNIA SYSTEM
300 Lakeside Drive
17th Floor
Oakland CA 94612-3550

4178 College Information

CALIFORNIA STATE UNIVERSITY SYSTEM
400 Golden Shore
#318
Long Beach CA 90802-4275

4179 College Information

ASSOCIATION OF INDEPENDENT COLLEGES AND
UNIVERSITIES
1100 11th St., Suite 205
Sacramento CA 95814

4180 Computer Science (Career Information)

IEEE COMPUTER SOCIETY
1828 L St., NW, Suite 1202
Washington DC 20036-5104
202/371-1013
FAX: 202/778-0884
Internet: www.ieeeusa.org.usab

4181 Computer Science (Career Information)

ASSOCIATION FOR COMPUTING MACHINERY
1515 Broadway
17th Fl.
New York NY 10036
800/342-6626 or 212/626-0500
FAX: 212/944-1318
Internet: www.acm.org/membership/career/

4182 Construction (Career Information)

ASSOCIATED GENERAL CONTRACTORS OF
AMERICA
1957 'E' St., NW
Washington DC 20006

4183 Consulting Engineer (Career Information)

AMERICAN CONSULTING ENGINEERS COUNCIL
1015 15th St. NW #802
Washington DC 20005

4184 Cosmetology (Career Information)

AMERICAN ASSOCIATION OF COSMETOLOGY
SCHOOLS
11811 N. Tatum Blvd., Suite 1085
Phoenix AZ 85028
602/788-1170
FAX: 602/404-8900
E-mail: jim@beautyschools.org
Internet: www.beautyschools.org

4185 Crafts (Career Information)

AMERICAN CRAFT COUNCIL LIBRARY
72 Spring St.
New York NY 10012
212/274-0630
FAX: 212/274-0650

4186 Creative Writing (Career Information)

NATIONAL WRITERS ASSOCIATION
3140 S. Peoria
PMB 295
Aurora CO 80014
303/751-7844
FAX: 303/751-8593
E-mail: sandywrter@aol.com
Internet: www.nationalwriters.com

4187 Data Processing Management (Career Information)

ASSOCIATION OF INFORMATION TECHNOLOGY
PROFESSIONALS
315 S. Northwest Highway, Suite 200
Park Ridge IL 60068-4278

4188 Dental Assistant (Career Information)

AMERICAN DENTAL ASSISTANTS ASSOCIATION
203 N. LaSalle St., Suite 1320
Chicago IL 60601
312/541-1550 or 800/733-2322

4189 Dental Laboratory Technology (Career Information)

NATIONAL ASSOCIATION OF DENTAL
LABORATORIES
8201 Greensboro Dr., Suite 300
Mc Lean VA 22102
703/610-9035

4190 Dental Profession (Career Information)

ADA ENDOWMENT AND ASSISTANCE FUND INC.
211 E. Chicago Ave.
Chicago IL 60611

4191 Dietitian (Career Information)

AMERICAN DIETETIC ASSOCIATION (ADA)
Attn: Networks Team
216 W. Jackson Blvd.
Chicago IL 60606-6995
800/877-1600, ext. 4897
FAX: 312/899-0008
E-mail: network@eatright.org
Internet: www.eatright.org

4192 Disabled (Career Information)

THE ARC
PO Box 1047
Arlington TX 76004

4193 Drama/Acting (Career Information)

SCREEN ACTORS GUILD
5757 Wilshire Blvd.
Los Angeles CA 90036-3600
213/954-1600

4194 Education (Career Information)

AMERICAN FEDERATION OF TEACHERS
Public Affairs Department
555 New Jersey Ave. NW
Washington DC 20001
202/879-4400

4195 Electrical Engineering (Career Information)

INSTITUTE OF ELECTRICAL AND ELECTRONICS
ENGINEERS - US ACTIVITIES
1828 L St., NW, Suite 1202
Washington DC 20036-5104

4196 Engineering (Program/Career Information)

JUNIOR ENGINEERING TECHNICAL SOCIETY INC
(JETS)
1420 King St., Suite 405
Alexandria VA 22314
Internet: www.ASEE.org/JETS

4197 Engineering (Career Information)

NATIONAL SOCIETY OF PROFESSIONAL
ENGINEERS
1420 King St.
Alexandria VA 22314
703/684-2830

4198 Entomology (Career Information)
ENTOMOLOGICAL SOCIETY OF AMERICA
9301 Annapolis Rd.
Lanham MD 20706-3115
301/731-4535
FAX: 301/731-4538
E-mail: esa@entsoc.org
Internet: www.entsoc.org

4199 Environmental (Career/Studies Information)
US ENVIRONMENTAL PROTECTION AGENCY
401 M St. SW
Office of Communications, Education, and Public Affairs Environmental Education Division
Washington DC 20460

4200 FBI (Career Information)
FEDERAL BUREAU OF INVESTIGATION
Office of Public & Congressional Affairs
Washington DC 20535
Internet: www.fbi.gov

4201 Family & Consumer Science (Career Information)
AMERICAN ASSOCIATION OF FAMILY AND CONSUMER SCIENCES
1555 King Street
Alexandria VA 22314-2752
703/706-4600
FAX: 703/706-4663
E-mail: info@aafcs.org
Internet: www.aafcs.org

4202 Fashion Design (Educational Information)
FASHION INSTITUTE OF TECHNOLOGY
Seventh Ave. @ 27th St.
New York NY 10001-5992
800/GO-TO-FIT or 212/217-7684
E-mail: FITinfo@sfitva.cc.fitsuny.edu
Internet: www.fitnyc.suny.edu

4203 Film & Television (Career Information)
ACADEMY OF CANADIAN CINEMA AND TELEVISION
158 Pearl St.
Toronto Ontario M5H 1T3 CANADA
416/591-2040
FAX: 416/591-2157
Internet: www.academy.ca

4204 Fire Service (Career Information)
NATIONAL FIRE PROTECTION ASSN. (Public Fire Protection)
1 Batterymarch Park
PO Box 9101
Quincy MA 02269-9101

4205 Fisheries (Career/University Information)
AMERICAN FISHERIES SOCIETY
5410 Grovesnor Ln., Suite 110
Bethesda MD 20814-2199

4206 Floristry (Career Information)
SOCIETY OF AMERICAN FLORISTS
1601 Duke St.
Alexandria VA 22314

4207 Food & Nutrition Service (Career Information)
US DEPT OF AGRICULTURE; FOOD AND NUTRITION SERVICE
Personnel Division
Rm. 620
1301 Park Center Dr.
Alexandria VA 22302

4208 Food Service (Career Information)
NATIONAL RESTAURANT ASSOCIATION EDUCATIONAL FOUNDATION
250 S. Wacker Dr., Suite 1400
Chicago IL 60606-5834
800/765-2122, ext. 733 or 312/715-1010
FAX: 312/715-1362
E-mail: bdejesus@foodtrain.org
Internet: www.edfound.org

4209 Food Technology/Science (Career Information)
INSTITUTE OF FOOD TECHNOLOGISTS
221 N. LaSalle St.
Chicago IL 60601

4210 Forest Service (Career Information)
US DEPT. OF AGRICULTURE
14th & Independence Ave. Room 801 RPE
Washington DC 20250

4211 Forestry (Career Information ONLY)
SOCIETY OF AMERICAN FORESTERS
5400 Grosvenor Lane
Bethesda MD 20814-2198

4212 Funeral Director (Career Information)
NATIONAL FUNERAL DIRECTORS ASSOCIATION
11121 W. Oklahoma Ave.
Milwaukee WI 53227-0641
800/228-6332 or 414/541-2500
FAX: 541-2500
E-mail: nfda@nfda.org
Internet: www.nfda.org

4213 Gemology (Career Information)
GEMLINES.COM
1524 NW 52nd Street
Seattle WA 98107
FAX: 978/477-8361
E-mail: gemlines@yahoo.com
Internet: www.gemlines.com

4214 Geography (Career Information)
ASSOCIATION OF AMERICAN GEOGRAPHERS
1710 16th St. NW
Washington DC 20009-3198
202/234-1450
FAX: 202/234-2744
E-mail: gaia@aag.org
Internet: www.aag.org

4215 Geological Sciences (Career Information)
GEOLOGICAL SOCIETY OF AMERICA
3300 Penrose Pl.
PO Box 9140
Boulder CO 80301-9140
303/447-2020
FAX: 303/447-1133
E-mail: educate@geosociety.org
Internet: www.geosociety.org/educate/career.htm

4216 Geological Sciences (Career Information)
AMERICAN GEOLOGICAL INSTITUTE
4220 King St.
Alexandria VA 22302
703/379-2480
FAX: 703/379-7563
E-mail: ehr@agiweb.org
Internet: www.agiweb.org

4217 Geophysics (Career Information)
AMERICAN GEOPHYSICAL UNION
2000 Florida Ave., NW
Washington DC 20009
202/462-6900 or 800/966-2481
FAX: 202/328-0566
Internet: www.agu.org

4218 Graphic Arts (Career Information)
AMERICAN INSTITUTE OF GRAPHIC ARTS
164 Fifth Ave
New York NY 10010

4219 Graphic Communications (Career/ Education Information)
EDUCATION COUNCIL OF THE GRAPHIC ARTS INDUSTRY
1899 Preston White Dr.
Reston VA 20191
703/648-1768
FAX: 703/620-0994

4220 Heating & Air Conditioning Engineer (Career Information)
REFRIGERATION SERVICE ENGINEERS SOCIETY
1666 Rand Rd.
Des Plaines IL 60016-3552
708/297-6464
FAX: 847/297-5038
E-mail: rses@starnetinc.com
Internet: www.rses.org

4221 Homeopathic Medicine (Career Information)
NATIONAL CENTER FOR HOMEOPATHY
801 North Fairfax St., Suite 306
Alexandria, VA 22314
703/548-7790
FAX: 703/548-7792
E-mail: nchinfo@igc.apc.org
Internet: www.healthy.net/nch/

4222 Homeopathic Medicine (Career Information)
HOMEOPATHIC EDUCATIONAL SERVICES
2124B Kittredge St.
Berkeley, CA 94704
510/649-0294
FAX: 510/649-1955
Internet: www.homeopathic.com/ailments/ hesdent.htm

4223 Horticulture (Career Information)
AMERICAN ASSOCIATION OF NURSERYMEN
1250 'I' St. NW
Washington DC 20005

4224 Hospital Administration (Career Information)
AMERICAN COLLEGE OF HEALTH CARE EXECUTIVES
One N. Franklin St., Suite 1700
Chicago IL 60606-3491

4225 Hotel Management (Career Information)
AMERICAN HOTEL FOUNDATION
1201 New York Ave., NW, Suite 600
Washington DC 20005

4226 Illuminating Engineering (Career Information)
ILLUMINATING ENGINEERING SOCIETY OF NORTH AMERICA
120 Wall St. 17th Floor
New York NY 10005

4227 Insurance (Career Information)
COLLEGE OF INSURANCE
101 Murray Street
New York NY 10007
212/962-4111
FAX: 212/964-3381
Internet: www.tci.edu

4228 Journalism (Career Information)
AMERICAN SOCIETY OF NEWSPAPER EDITORS
11690B Sunrise Valley Dr.
Reston VA 20191-1409
703/453-1122
FAX: 703/453-1133
E-mail: asne@asne.org
Internet: www.asne.org

4229 Law (Career Information Booklet)
AMERICAN BAR ASSOCIATION
750 N. Lake Shore Dr.
Chicago IL 60611

4230 Law Librarianship (Career Information)
AMERICAN ASSOCIATION OF LAW LIBRARIES
53 W. Jackson Blvd., Suite 940
Chicago IL 60604
312/939-4764
FAX: 312/431-1097
E-mail: aallhq@aall.org
www.aallnet.org

4231 Learning Disabled (Education/Career Information)
LEARNING DISABILITIES ASSN OF AMERICA
4156 Library Rd.
Pittsburgh PA 15234
412/341-1515

4232 Management (Career Information)
AMERICAN MANAGEMENT ASSOCIATION
1601 Broadway
New York NY 10019-7420
212/903-8161
FAX: 212/903-8171
E-mail: cust_serv@amanet.org
Internet: www.amanet.org

4233 Massage Therapy (Career Information)
CANADIAN MASSAGE THERAPIST ALLIANCE - CMTA
365 Bloor St. East, Suite 1807
Toronto Ontario CANADA M4W 3L4
416/968-2149
FAX: 416/968-6818
Internet: www.collinscan.com/~collins/ clientspgs/cmtai.html

4234 Massage Therapy (Career Information)
AMERICAN MASSAGE THERAPY ASSOCIATION - AMTA
820 Davis St., Suite 100
Evanston IL 60201-4444
847/864-0123
FAX: 847/864-1178
Internet: www.amtamassage.org

4235 Massage Therapy (Career Information)
ASSOCIATION OF MASSAGE THERAPISTS- AUSTRALIA INCORPORATED
PO Box 627
South Yarra Victoria 341 AUSTRALIA
613 9510 3930
FAX: 613 9521 3209
E-mail: amta@amta.asn.au
Internet: www.amta.asn.au/AmtaStart.html

4236 Mathematical Sciences (Career Information)

MATHEMATICAL ASSOCIATION OF AMERICA
PO Box 90973
Washington DC 20090
800/331-1622

4237 Mathematics Teacher (Career Information)

NATIONAL COUNCIL OF TEACHERS OF MATHEMATICS
1906 Association Dr.
Reston VA 22091-1593
703/620-9840
FAX: 703/476-2970
E-mail: vwilliams@nctm.org
Internet
www.nctm.org

4238 Mechanical Engineering (Career Information)

AMERICAN SOCIETY OF MECHANICAL ENGINEERS
Three Park Avenue
New York NY 10016-5990
212/591-8131
FAX: 212/591-7143
E-mail: malaven@asme.org
Internet: www.asme.org

4239 Medical Laboratory Technology (Career Information)

AMERICAN SOCIETY OF CLINICAL PATHOLOGISTS
Careers
2100 W. Harrison
Chicago IL 60612

4240 Medical Records (Career Information)

AMERICAN HEALTH INFORMATION MANAGEMENT ASSOCIATION
919 N. Michigan Ave. Suite 1400
Chicago IL 60611

4241 Medicine (Career Information)

ROYAL SOCIETY OF MEDICINE
1 Wimpole Street
London W1M 8AE ENGLAND UK
0171 290 2900
FAX: 0171 290 2992
E-mail: Membership@Roysocmed.ac.uk
Internet: www.Roysocmed.ac.uk

4242 Medicine (Career Information)

AMERICAN MEDICAL ASSOCIATION
515 N. State St.
Chicago IL 60610

4243 Metallurgy & Materials Science (Career Information)

ASM FOUNDATION FOR EDUCATION & RESEARCH
Student Outreach Program
Materials Park OH 44073

4244 Microbiology (Career Information)

AMERICAN SOCIETY FOR MICROBIOLOGY (Office of Education & Training)
1325 Massachusetts Ave., NW
Washington DC 20005
202/942-9283

4245 Motion Picture (Career Information)

SOCIETY OF MOTION PICTURE AND TELEVISION ENGINEERS
595 W. Hartsdale Ave.
White Plains NY 10607
914/761-1100

4246 Music Therapy (Career Information)

NATIONAL ASSN FOR MUSIC THERAPY
8455 Colesville Rd., Suite 1000
Silver Spring MD 20910
301/589-3300
FAX 301/589-5175

4247 Naturopathic Medicine (Career Information)

AMERICAN ASSOCIATION OF NATUROPATHIC PHYSICIANS
601 Valley St., Suite 105
Seattle WA 98109
206/298-0126
FAX: 206/298-0129
E-mail: 74602.3715@compuserve.com
Internet: healer.infinite.org/
Naturopathic.Physician/Welcome.html

4248 Naval Architecture (Career Information)

SOCIETY OF NAVAL ARCHITECTS AND MARINE ENGINEERS
601 Pavonia Ave.
Jersey City NJ 07306

4249 Naval/Marine Engineering (Career Information)

SOCIETY OF NAVAL ARCHITECTS AND MARINE ENGINEERS
601 Pavonia Ave.
Jersey City NJ 07306

4250 Newspaper Industry (Career Information)

NEWSPAPER ASSN OF AMERICA
1921 Gallows Rd. #4
Vienna VA 22182-3900

4251 Nurse Anesthetist (Career Information)

AMERICAN ASSOCIATION OF NURSE ANESTHETISTS
222 S. Prospect Ave.
Park Ridge IL 60068-4001
708/692-7050

4252 Nursing (Career Information)

NATIONAL LEAGUE FOR NURSING
61 Broadway, 33rd Floor
New York NY 10006
800/669-1656 or 212/363-5555
FAX: 212/812-0393
E-mail: custhelp@nln.org
Internet: www.nln.org

4253 Oceanography & Marine Science (Career Information)

MARINE TECHNOLOGY SOCIETY
1828 L St. NW, Suite 906
Washington DC 20036
202/775-5966

4254 Operations Research & Management Science (Career Information)

INSTITUTE FOR OPERATIONS RESEARCH AND THE MANAGEMENT SCIENCES (INFORMS)
P.O. Box 64794
Baltimore MD 21264-4794
800/4INFORMS
FAX: 410/684-2963
E-mail: informs@informs.org
Internet: www.informs.org/Edu/Career/
booklet.html

4255 Optometry (Career Information)

NATIONAL OPTOMETRIC ASSOCIATION
PO Box F
E. Chicago IN 46312
219/398-1832
FAX: 219/398-1077

4256 Optometry (Career Information)

AMERICAN OPTOMETRIC ASSOCIATION
243 N. Lindbergh Blvd.
St. Louis MO 63141-7881
314/991-4100
FAX: 314/991-4101
Internet: www.opted.org

4257 Osteopathic Medicine (Career Information)

AMERICAN OSTEOPATHIC ASSOCIATION
Dept. of Predoctoral Education
142 East Ontario
Chicago IL 60611
1-800/621-1773 Ext. 7401

4258 Paleontology (Career Information)

PALEONTOLOGICAL SOCIETY
PO Box 1897
Lawrence, KS 66044-8897
Internet: www.uic.edu/orgs/paleo/homepage.html

4259 Pathology as Career in Medicine (Career Information Brochure)

INTERSOCIETY COMMITTEE ON PATHOLOGY INFORMATION
9650 Rockville Pike
Bethesda MD 20814-3993
301/571-1880
FAX: 301/571-1879

4260 Pediatrics (Career Information)

AMERICAN ACADEMY OF PEDIATRICS
141 NW Point Blvd.
PO Box 927
Elk Grove Village IL 60009

4261 Petroleum Engineering (Career Information)

SOCIETY OF PETROLEUM ENGINEERS
PO Box 833836
Richardson TX 75083-3836
972/952-9315
FAX: 972/952-9435
E-mail: twhipple@spelink.spe.org
Internet: www.spe.org

4262 Pharmacology (Career Information)

AMERICAN SOCIETY FOR PHARMACOLOGY & EXPERIMENTAL THERAPEUTICS INC.
9650 Rockville Pike
Bethesda MD 20814-3995

4263 Pharmacy (Career Information)

AMERICAN ASSOCIATION OF COLLEGES OF PHARMACY
Office of Student Affairs
1426 Prince St.
Alexandria VA 22314
703/739-2330

4264 Pharmacy (Career Information)

AMERICAN FOUNDATION FOR PHARMACEUTICAL EDUCATION
One Church St., Suite 202
Rockville MD 20850

4265 Pharmacy (School Information Booklet)

AMERICAN COUNCIL ON PHARMACEUTICAL EDUCATION
311 W. Superior #512
Chicago IL 60610
312/664-3575
FAX: 312/664-4652

4266 Physical Therapy (Career Information)

AMERICAN PHYSICAL THERAPY ASS'N.
1111 N. Fairfax St.
Alexandria VA 22314-1488
703/684-2782
FAX: 703/684-7343
Internet: www.apta.org

4267 Physics (Career Information)

AMERICAN INSTITUTE OF PHYSICS STUDENTS
One Physics Ellipse
College Park MD 20740-3843
212/661-9404

4268 Podiatry (Career Information)

FUND FOR PODIATRIC MEDICAL EDUCATION
9312 Old Georgetown Rd.
Bethesda MD 20814-1698
301/581-9200
FAX: 301/530-2752

4269 Precision Machining Technology (Career Information)

NATIONAL TOOLING AND MACHINING ASSN
9300 Livingston Rd.
Ft. Washington MD 20744

4270 Psychiatry (Career Information)

AMERICAN PSYCHIATRIC ASSN., DIVISION OF PUBLIC AFFAIRS
1400 K St. NW
Washington DC 20005

4271 Psychology (Career Information)

AMERICAN PSYCHOLOGICAL ASSOCIATION
750 First Street, NE
Washington DC 20002-4242
202/336-6027
FAX: 202/336-6012
E-mail: mfp@apa.org
Internet: www.apa.org

4272 Public Administration (Career Information)

AMERICAN SOCIETY FOR PUBLIC ADMINISTRATION
1120 G St., NW, Suite 700
Washington DC 20005-3801
E-mail: info@aspanet.org
Internet: www.aspanet.org

4273 Radiologic Technology (Career Information)

AMERICAN SOCIETY OF RADIOLOGIC TECHNOLOGISTS (ASRT)
15000 Central Ave., SE
Albuquerque NM 87123-3917
505/298-4500
FAX 505/298-5063
Internet: www.asrt.org

4274 Range Management (Career Information)

SOCIETY FOR RANGE MANAGEMENT
1839 York Street
Denver CO 80206
303/355-7070
FAX: 303/355-5059
E-mail: srmden@ix.netcom.com
Internet: srm.org

4275 Rehabilitation Counseling (Career Information)

NATIONAL REHABILITATION COUNSELING ASSN.
8807 Sudley Road #102
Manassas VA 22110-4719

4276 Respiratory Therapy (Career Information)

AMERICAN RESPIRATORY CARE FOUNDATION
11030 Ables Ln.
Dallas TX 75229-4593
972/243-2272
E-mail: info@aarc.org
Internet: www.aarc.org

4277 Safety Engineering (Career Information)

AMERICAN SOCIETY OF SAFETY ENGINEERS

1800 E. Oakton St.
Des Plaines IL 60018-2187
847/699-2929

4278 School Administration (Career Information)

AMERICAN ASSOCIATION OF SCHOOL ADMINISTRATORS

1801 North Moore Street
Arlington VA 22209-1813
Internet: www.aasa.org

4279 Science Teacher (Career Information)

NATIONAL SCIENCE TEACHERS ASSN

Attn Office of Public Information
1840 Wilson Blvd.
Arlington VA 22201
703/243-7100

4280 Secretary/Office Professional (Career Information)

PROFESSIONAL SECRETARIES INTERNATIONAL-THE ASSOCIATION FOR OFFICE PROFESSIONALS

10502 NW Ambassador Dr.
Kansas City MO 64195-0404
816/891-6600: FAX: 816-891-9118
E-mail: service@psi.org
Internet: www.gvi.net/psi

4281 Social Work (Career Information)

NATIONAL ASSN OF SOCIAL WORKERS

750 First St. NE, Suite 700
Washington DC 20002
202/408-8600
FAX: 202/336-8310

4282 Sociology (Career Information)

AMERICAN SOCIOLOGICAL ASSOCIATION

1722 N St. NW
Washington DC 20036
202/833-3410
FAX: 202/785-0146
E-mail: apap@asanet.org
Internet: www.asanet.org

4283 Soil Conservation (Career Information)

SOIL & WATER CONSERVATION SOCIETY

7515 NE Ankeny Rd.
Ankeny IA 50021-9764
515/289-2331 or 1-800/THE-SOIL
FAX: 515/289-1227
E-mail: charliep@secs.org
Internet: www.swcs.org

4284 Special Education Teaching (Career Information)

NATIONAL CLEARINGHOUSE FOR PROFESSIONS IN SPECIAL EDUCATION

The Council for Exceptional Children
1920 Association Dr.
Reston VA 20191-1589
800/641-7824 or 703/264-9476 or TTY 703/264-9480
FAX: 703/264-1637
E-mail: ncpse@cec.sped.org
Internet: www.cec.sped.org/ncpse.htm

4285 Speech & Hearing Therapy (Career Information-send SASE)

ALEXANDER GRAHAM BELL ASSOCIATION FOR THE DEAF

3417 Volta Place, NW
Washington DC 20007-2778
202/337-5220 (voice/TTY)
E-mail: Agbell2@aol.com
Internet: www.agbell.org

4286 United States Coast Guard (Career Information)

US COAST GUARD ACADEMY

Director of Admissions
31 Mohegan Ave.
New London CT 06320
FAX: 860/701-6700

4287 Urban Planning (Career Information)

AMERICAN PLANNING ASSOCIATION

122 South Michigan Ave., Suite 1600
Chicago IL 60605
312/431-9100
FAX: 312/431-9985

4288 Veterinarian (Career Information)

AMERICAN VETERINARY MEDICAL ASSOCIATION

1931 N. Meacham Rd., Suite 100
Schaumburg IL 60173

4289 Water Management (Career Information)

WATER ENVIRONMENT FEDERATION
See website.

Internet: www.wef.org

4290 Welding Technology (Career Information)

HOBART INSTITUTE OF WELDING TECHONOLOGY

Trade Square East
Troy OH 45373
513/332-5215
FAX 513/332-5200
E-mail: hiwt@welding.org
Internet: www.welding.org

4291 Women Pilots (Career Information)

THE NINETY-NINES, INC.

Box 965, 7100 Terminal Drive
Oklahoma City OK 73159
405/685-7969
FAX: 405/685-7985

4292 Writing (Career Information)

KIDZWRITE

To subscribe, send message: subscribe KidzWrite

E-mail Subscription:
majordomo@userhome.com

4293 Youth Leadership (Career Information)

BOYS & GIRLS CLUBS OF AMERICA

1230 W. Peachtree St., NW
Atlanta GA 30309

4294 Youth Leadership (Career Information)

BOY SCOUTS OF AMERICA

National Eagle Scout Association
S220
1325 W. Walnut Hill Lane
P.O. Box 152079
Irving TX 75015
972/580-2431

Alphabetical Index

"EDUTRAX" QUARTERLY NEWSLETTER 3993

*** Personal Counseling Service *** By Dan Cassidy and his professional staff. 3994

270 WAYS TO PUT YOUR TALENT TO WORK IN THE HEALTH FIELD 3995

A CAREER GUIDE TO MUSIC EDUCATION 3996

A GUIDE TO AVIATION EDUCATION RESOURCES 3997

A TEACHER'S GUIDE TO FELLOWSHIPS AND AWARDS 3998

A.H. BEAN FOUNDATION 3321

ABBIE SARGENT MEMORIAL SCHOLARSHIP INC. (Scholarships) 1431, 2241, 2701

ABCs OF FINANCIAL AID (Montana Financial Aid Handbook) 3999

ABDUS SALAM INTERNATIONAL CENTRE FOR THEORETICAL PHYSICS - ICTP 2062

ABRAHAM BURTMAN CHARITY TRUST 3322

ACADEMIC STUDY GROUP (Travel Bursaries to Israel) 3323

ACADEMIC YEAR ABROAD 4000

ACADEMY OF CANADIAN CINEMA AND TELEVISION 4203

ACADEMY OF CRIMINAL JUSTICE SCIENCES (Affirmative Action Mini-Grant Program) 3010

ACADEMY OF FINLAND (Research Fellowships) 3324

ACADEMY OF MOTION PICTURE ARTS AND SCIENCES (Nicholl Fellowships in Screenwriting) 1076

ACADEMY OF NATURAL SCIENCES OF PHILADELPHIA (Jessup & McHenry Fund Grants) 1619, 1691, 1870

ACADEMY OF VOCAL ARTS (Scholarships) 1229

ACADIA UNIVERSITY (Graduate Teaching Assistantships) 3325

ACC/MERCK ADULT CARDIOLOGY RESEARCH FELLOWSHIP AWARDS 2351

ACCESS GROUP (Loan Programs) 1, 2143, 2242, 3011

ACCOUNTING/NET 4138

ACCOUNTING/NET (Account For Your Future Scholarship Program) 18

ADA ENDOWMENT AND ASSISTANCE FUND INC. 4190

AECI LIMITED (AECI Post Graduate Research Fellowship) 475, 576, 628, 709, 1871, 1971, 2063

AERO CLUB OF NEW ENGLAND (Aviation Scholarships) 370, 3285

AEROSPACE EDUCATION FOUNDATION 4147

AEROSPACE EDUCATION FOUNDATION (Theodore Von Karman Graduate Scholarship Program) 274, 1808, 2064

AFL-CIO GUIDE TO UNION-SPONSORED SCHOLARSHIPS 4001

AFRICAN NETWORK OF SCIENTIFIC AND TECHNOLOGICAL INSTITUTIONS - ANSTI (Postgraduate Fellowships) 275, 476, 514, 577, 629, 710, 765,
.... 1490, 1692, 1809, 1872, 1972

AFRICAN STUDIES CENTER (African Language Scholarships—Title VI) 825, 1191

AFRO-ASIATIC INSTITUTE IN WIEN (Scholarships) 3326

AGENCY FOR HEALTH CARE POLICY AND RESEARCH (Doctoral Dissertation Research Grant) 2352

AIR TRAFFIC CONTROL ASSOCIATION INC (Scholarships for Children of Air Traffic Specialists) 3327

AIR TRANSPORT ASSOCIATION OF AMERICA 4151

AIRCRAFT ELECTRONICS ASSOCIATION EDUCATIONAL FOUNDATION (Scholarships) 19, 371, 3286

ALABAMA COMMISSION ON HIGHER EDUCATION (Scholarships; Grants; Loans; Work Study Programs) 3328

ALBERT BAKER FUND (Student Loans) 3329

ALBERT ELLIS INSTITUTE (Fellowship Training Program) 3155

ALBERTA HERITAGE FOUNDATION FOR MEDICAL RESEARCH (Studentships) 2353

ALBERTA HERITAGE SCHOLARSHIP FUND (Ralph Steinhauer Awards of Distinction) 3330, 3331

ALCOHOLIC BEVERAGE MEDICAL RESEARCH FOUNDATION (Grants for Alcohol Research) 2354

ALEXANDER FAMILY EDUCATIONAL FOUNDATION WELFARE TRUST 3332

ALEXANDER GRAHAM BELL ASSOCIATION FOR THE DEAF (College Scholarship Awards) 3333, 3334, 4285

ALEXANDER VON HUMBOLDT FOUNDATION (Feodor Lynen Research Fellowships) 3335, 3336, 3337

AMERICA ISRAEL PUBLIC AFFAIRS COMMITTEE (Internships) 3075

AMERICA-ISRAEL CULTURAL FOUNDATION (Sharett Scholarship Program) 976, 1230, 2815

AMERICAN ACADEMY IN ROME (Rome Prize Fellowships in the School of Fine Arts) 414, 826, 827, 977, 978, 979, 1231, 1745, 1746

AMERICAN ACADEMY OF ALLERGY, ASTHMA, & IMMUNOLOGY (Summer Fellowships) 2355

AMERICAN ACADEMY OF CHILD AND ADOLESCENT PSYCHIATRY (Minority Medical Student Fellowships) 2144, 2145, 2146, 3156

AMERICAN ACADEMY OF FIXED PROSTHODONTICS (Tylman Research Grants) 2243

AMERICAN ACADEMY OF IMPLANT DENTISTRY RESEARCH FOUNDATION (Research Grants) 2356

AMERICAN ACADEMY OF OPTOMETRY (Julius F. Neumueller Award) 2244

AMERICAN ACADEMY OF PEDIATRICS 4260

AMERICAN ACADEMY OF PEDIATRICS (Residency Scholarship Program) 2147

AMERICAN ACADEMY OF PERIODONTOLOGY (Balint Orban Prize) 2357

AMERICAN ACCOUNTING ASSOCIATION (Fellowships) 20

AMERICAN ACCORDION MUSICOLOGICAL SOCIETY (Contest) 1232

AMERICAN ADVERTISING FEDERATION 4145

AMERICAN ALLIANCE FOR HEALTH, PHYSICAL EDUCATION, RECREATION & DANCE 21, 182, 1233, 2553

AMERICAN ANTHROPOLOGICAL ASSOCIATION 4154

AMERICAN ANTIQUARIAN SOCIETY (Visiting Academic Research Fellowships) 1077, 2898

AMERICAN ARCHITECTURAL FOUNDATION (AIA/AAF Scholarship Program) 4158

AMERICAN ART THERAPY ASSOCIATION (AATA Scholarship Fund) 2554

AMERICAN ART THERAPY ASSOCIATION (Cay Drachnik Minorities Fund) 2555

AMERICAN ART THERAPY ASSOCIATION (Gladys Agell Award for Excellence in Research) 2556

AMERICAN ART THERAPY ASSOCIATION (Myra Levick Scholarship Fund) 2557

AMERICAN ART THERAPY ASSOCIATION (Rawley Silver Scholarship Fund) 2558

AMERICAN ASSOCIATION FOR CLINICAL CHEMISTRY 4176

AMERICAN ASSOCIATION FOR MARRIAGE & FAMILY THERAPISTS (Graduate Student Research Awards) 3157, 3158

AMERICAN ASSOCIATION FOR THE ADVANCEMENT OF SCIENCE (Science & Engineering Fellowships) 276, 1747, 1810, 1873, 1973, 2065

AMERICAN ASSOCIATION OF ADVERTISING AGENCIES, INC. (Multicultural Advertising Internship Program) 22, 23

AMERICAN ASSOCIATION OF BIOANALYSTS (David Birenbaum Scholarship Fund of AAB) 3338

AMERICAN ASSOCIATION OF CEREAL CHEMISTS (Undergraduate Scholarships and Graduate Fellowships) 2702

AMERICAN ASSOCIATION OF COLLEGES OF PHARMACY 4263

AMERICAN ASSOCIATION OF COSMETOLOGY SCHOOLS (ACE Grants) 3287, 4184

AMERICAN ASSOCIATION OF FAMILY AND CONSUMER SCIENCES (International Fellowships) 2703, 4201

AMERICAN ASSOCIATION OF HISPANIC CERTIFIED PUBLIC ACCOUNTANTS (Scholarships) 24

AMERICAN ASSOCIATION OF LAW LIBRARIES (George A. Strait Minority Stipend Grant) 1078, 1079, 3012, 4230

AMERICAN ASSOCIATION OF NATUROPATHIC PHYSICIANS 4247

AMERICAN ASSOCIATION OF NURSERYMEN 4223

AMERICAN ASSOCIATION OF NURSE ANESTHETISTS 4251

AMERICAN ASSOCIATION OF PETROLEUM GEOLOGISTS (AAPG Foundation Grants-in-Aid) 1491

AMERICAN ASSOCIATION OF SCHOOL ADMINISTRATORS (Educational Administration Scholarships) 183, 4278

AMERICAN ASSOCIATION OF UNIVERSITY WOMEN EDUCATIONAL FOUNDATION
(Selected Professions Fellowships for Women of Color) 25, 277, 415, 515, 578, 630, 711, 828, 1492,
.... 2066, 2148, 3013, 3339, 3340, 3341, 3342, 3343

AMERICAN ASTRONOMICAL SOCIETY 4160

AMERICAN BAR ASSOCIATION 4229

AMERICAN CHIROPRACTIC ASSOCIATION 4173

AMERICAN COLLEGE OF HEALTH CARE EXECUTIVES 4224

AMERICAN COLLEGE OF HEALTHCARE EXECUTIVES (Albert W. Dent Scholarship) 2245, 2246

AMERICAN COLLEGE OF LEGAL MEDICINE (Student Writing Competition) 2149, 2247, 2633, 3014

AMERICAN COLLEGE OF MEDICAL PRACTICE EXECUTIVES (ACMPE Scholarships) 2248

AMERICAN COLLEGE OF NURSE-MIDWIVES FOUNDATION (Scholarship Program) 2634

AMERICAN CONGRESS ON SURVEYING AND MAPPING
(American Association for Geodetic Surveying Graduate Fellowship Award) 1493, 1494

AMERICAN CONSULTING ENGINEERS COUNCIL 4183

AMERICAN COUNCIL OF LEARNED SOCIETIES (ACLS Fellowships) 766, 829, 980, 1080, 1340, 1748, 2723, 2899

AMERICAN COUNCIL OF THE BLIND (ACB Scholarship Program) 3344

AMERICAN COUNCIL ON PHARMACEUTICAL EDUCATION 4265

AMERICAN CRAFT COUNCIL LIBRARY 4185

AMERICAN CULINARY FEDERATION, INC. (Ray & Gertrude Marshall Scholarship Fund) 2704

AMERICAN DENTAL ASSISTANTS ASSOCIATION 4188

AMERICAN DENTAL HYGIENISTS ASSOCIATION INSTITUTE FOR ORAL HEALTH
(Irene Woodall Graduate Scholarship) 2559, 2560, 2561, 2562, 2563, 2564

AMERICAN DIABETES ASSOCIATION (Career Development Awards) 2358

AMERICAN DIABETES ASSOCIATION (Clinical Research Awards) 2359

AMERICAN DIABETES ASSOCIATION (Lions SightFirst Diabetic Retinopathy Research Awards) 2360

AMERICAN DIABETES ASSOCIATION (Mentor-Based Postdoctoral Fellowships) 2361

AMERICAN DIABETES ASSOCIATION (Medical Scholars Program Awards & Physician-Scientist Training Awards) 2362

AMERICAN DIETETIC ASSOCIATION (ADA) 4191

AMERICAN FARM BUREAU FEDERATION ("There's A New Challenge In Agriculture") 4149

AMERICAN FEDERATION FOR AGING RESEARCH (AFAR Research Grants) 2363, 2364, 2365, 2366, 2367, 2368, 2369, 2370, 2371

AMERICAN FEDERATION OF TEACHERS 4194

AMERICAN FEDERATION OF TEACHERS (Robert G. Porter Scholars Program) 3345

AMERICAN FISHERIES SOCIETY 4205

AMERICAN FISHERIES SOCIETY (J. Frances Allen Scholarship) 1693

AMERICAN FOUNDATION FOR AGING RESEARCH (Fellowship Program) 2372

AMERICAN FOUNDATION FOR PHARMACEUTICAL EDUCATION (Predoctoral Fellowships) 1874, 1974, 2249, 2373, 4264

AMERICAN FOUNDATION FOR THE BLIND (Delta Gamma Foundation Memorial Scholarship) 184, 278, 372, 416, 477, 516, 579, 631, 712,
.... 767, 1398, 1432, 1495, 1620, 1694, 1749,
.... 1811, 1875, 1975, 2067, 3346, 3347

AMERICAN FOUNDATION FOR UROLOGIC DISEASE (Health Policy Research Program) 2374, 2375, 2376, 2377, 2378, 2379, 2380, 2381

AMERICAN FRIENDS OF THE LONDON SCHOOL OF ECONOMICS (Scholarship Office) 3348

AMERICAN GEOLOGICAL INSTITUTE 4216

AMERICAN GEOPHYSICAL UNION 4217

AMERICAN GEOPHYSICAL UNION (Congressional Science Fellowship Program) 3349

AMERICAN GEOPHYSICAL UNION (Horton Research Grant) 1496

AMERICAN GERIATRICS SOCIETY (Edward Henderson Student Research Award) 2382

AMERICAN HEALTH AND BEAUTY AIDS INSTITUTE (Entrepreneurial Leadership Conference) 3350

AMERICAN HEALTH INFORMATION MANAGEMENT ASSOCIATION 4240

AMERICAN HEART ASSOCIATION (Helen N. and Harold B. Shapira Scholarship) 2150

AMERICAN HISTORICAL ASSOCIATION (Albert J. Beveridge Grants for Research in the History of the Western Hemisphere) 2900

AMERICAN HISTORICAL ASSOCIATION (J. Franklin Jameson Fellowship) 2901

AMERICAN HISTORICAL ASSOCIATION (Littleton-Griswold Grants) 3015

AMERICAN HISTORICAL ASSOCIATION (Michael Kraus Research Award Grant) 2902

AMERICAN HISTORICAL ASSOCIATION (Published Book Awards) 2903

AMERICAN HOTEL FOUNDATION 4225

AMERICAN INDIAN GRADUATE CENTER (Graduate Fellowships) 3351

AMERICAN INDIAN HERITAGE FOUNDATION 3352

AMERICAN INDIAN SCIENCE AND ENGINEERING SOCIETY (A.T. Anderson Memorial Scholarship) 279, 632, 1399, 1497, 1498, 1621,
.... 1622, 1695, 1812, 1876, 1976, 2151,
.... 2250, 2383, 2565, 2635

AMERICAN INSTITUTE FOR ECONOMIC RESEARCH (Visiting Research Fellowships at AIER) 26

AMERICAN INSTITUTE OF AERONAUTICS AND ASTRONAUTICS (Technical Committee Graduate Awards) 373, 374, 2068, 3288, 3289, 4146

AMERICAN INSTITUTE OF ARCHITECTS/AMERICAN ARCHITECTURAL FOUNDATION (Scholarship Program) 417

AMERICAN INSTITUTE OF ARCHITECTS/AMERICAN HOSPITAL ASSOCIATION
(AIA/AHA Fellowships in Health Facilities Planning and Design) 418

AMERICAN INSTITUTE OF ARCHITECTS INFORMATION POSTER AND BOOKLET 4002

AMERICAN INSTITUTE OF ARCHITECTS, NEW YORK CHAPTER (Haskell Awards for Student Architectural Journalism) 419, 981

AMERICAN INSTITUTE OF BAKING (Scholarships) 3290

AMERICAN INSTITUTE OF BIOLOGICAL SCIENCES 4165

AMERICAN INSTITUTE OF CERTIFIED PUBLIC ACCOUNTANTS 4139

AMERICAN INSTITUTE OF CHEMICAL ENGINEERS 4172

AMERICAN INSTITUTE OF GRAPHIC ARTS 4218

AMERICAN INSTITUTE OF INDIAN STUDIES (Senior Research Fellowships) 768, 830, 1192, 3353

AMERICAN INSTITUTE OF PHYSICS STUDENTS 4267

AMERICAN INSTITUTE OF POLISH CULTURE (Scholarships) 27, 2816

AMERICAN INSTITUTE OF THE HISTORY OF PHARMACY (Grant-in-Aid) 2251

AMERICAN JEWISH LEAGUE FOR ISRAEL (University Scholarship Fund) 3354

AMERICAN LIBRARY ASSOCIATION/LIBRARY & INFORMATION TECHNOLOGY ASSOCIATION (LITA/GEAC Scholarship) 1081

AMERICAN LIBRARY ASSOCIATION (EBSCO/NRMT Scholarship) 1082

AMERICAN LIBRARY ASSOCIATION (LITA/LSSI and LITA/OCLC Minority Scholarships) 1083

AMERICAN LIBRARY ASSOCIATION (Mary V. Gaver Scholarship) 1084

AMERICAN LIBRARY ASSOCIATION/AMERICAN ASSOCIATION OF SCHOOL LIBRARIANS (School Librarian's Workshop Scholarship) 1085

AMERICAN LIBRARY ASSOCIATION/ASSOCIATION FOR LIBRARY SERVICE TO CHILDREN
(Bound-to-Stay-Bound Books Scholarship) 1086, 1087

AMERICAN LIVER FOUNDATION (Postdoctoral Research Fellow Program) 2384

AMERICAN LIVER FOUNDATION (Student Research Fellowships) 2385

AMERICAN LUNG ASSOCIATION (Clinical Research Grant) 2386

AMERICAN LUNG ASSOCIATION (Dalsemer Research Scholar Award) 2387

AMERICAN LUNG ASSOCIATION (Johnie Murphy Career Investigator Award) 2388

AMERICAN LUNG ASSOCIATION (Lung Health Research Dissertation Grants) 2389

AMERICAN LUNG ASSOCIATION (Nursing Research Training Award) 2390

AMERICAN LUNG ASSOCIATION (Pediatric Pulmonary Research Training Fellowship) 2391

AMERICAN LUNG ASSOCIATION (Research Grants) 2392

AMERICAN LUNG ASSOCIATION (Research Training Fellowships) 2393

AMERICAN MANAGEMENT ASSOCIATION 4232

AMERICAN MASSAGE THERAPY ASSOCIATION - AMTA 4234

AMERICAN MATHEMATICAL SOCIETY (Centennial Fellowships) 2069

AMERICAN MEDICAL ASSOCIATION 4242

AMERICAN MEDICAL ASSOCIATION FOUNDATION (Jerry L. Pettis Memorial Scholarship) 2152, 2153, 2154, 2394

AMERICAN MENSA EDUCATION & RESEARCH FOUNDATION (Scholarships) 3355

AMERICAN MORGAN HORSE INSTITUTE (Scholarship Program) 3356

AMERICAN MOTHERS, INC. (Gertrude Fogelson Cultural and Creative Arts Awards) 982, 1088, 1234

AMERICAN MUSEUM OF NATURAL HISTORY (Graduate Student Fellowship Program) 1499, 1500, 1501, 1623, 1696, 1750, 1751, 1752, 1877, 1878, 1879, 1880, 3076

AMERICAN NUMISMATIC SOCIETY (Fellowships and Grants) 983

AMERICAN NURSES FOUNDATION (Nursing Research Grants Program) 2636

AMERICAN OPTOMETRIC ASSOCIATION 4256

AMERICAN OPTOMETRIC ASSOCIATION (Student Loan Program) 2252

AMERICAN OPTOMETRIC FOUNDATION (William Ezell OD Fellowship) 2253

AMERICAN ORCHID SOCIETY (Grants for Orchid Research) 1433, 1881

AMERICAN ORNITHOLOGISTS' UNION (AOU Student Research Awards) 1882

AMERICAN OSTEOPATHIC ASSOCIATION 4257

AMERICAN PHARMACEUTICAL ASSOCIATION AUXILIARY (Irene A. Parks Student Loan Fund) 2254

AMERICAN PHILOLOGICAL ASSOCIATION (Thesaurus Linguae Latinae Fellowship in Latin Lexicography) 1089

AMERICAN PHILOSOPHICAL SOCIETY (Henry Phillips Grants in Jurisprudence) 3016

AMERICAN PHILOSOPHICAL SOCIETY (Phillips Fund Grants for North Native American Research) 831

AMERICAN PHYSICAL THERAPY ASS'N. 4266

AMERICAN PLANNING ASSOCIATION 4287

AMERICAN PLANNING ASSOCIATION (Minority Scholarship and Fellowship Programs) 28, 420, 1624
AMERICAN POLITICAL SCIENCE ASSOCIATION (Congressional Fellowships for Print & Broadcast Journalists) 2817, 3357
AMERICAN PSYCHOLOGICAL ASSOCIATION 4271
AMERICAN PSYCHIATRIC ASSOCIATION (APA/GlaxoWellcome Fellowship Program) 2155
AMERICAN PSYCHIATRIC ASSN., DIVISION OF PUBLIC AFFAIRS 4270
AMERICAN PSYCHOLOGICAL FOUNDATION (Wayne F. Placek Awards for Scientific Research on Lesbian and Gay Issues) 832, 2724, 3159
AMERICAN PUBLIC TRANSIT ASSOCIATION (Transit Hall of Fame Scholarships) 29
AMERICAN RADIO RELAY LEAGUE FOUNDATION (The PHD ARA Scholarship) 517, 580, 581, 2818, 3358, 3359, 3360,
.... 3361, 3362, 3363, 3364, 3365, 3366, 3367, 3368
AMERICAN RESEARCH INSTITUTE IN TURKEY (ARIT Fellowship Program) 421, 422, 769, 770, 771, 833, 834, 835,
.... 984, 985, 986, 987, 1090, 1193, 1753, 1754,
.... 1755, 1756, 2725, 2726, 2904, 2905, 2906
AMERICAN RESPIRATORY CARE FOUNDATION 4276
AMERICAN RESPIRATORY CARE FOUNDATION (GlaxoWellcome Fellowship for Asthma Care Management Education) 2395, 2396, 2397, 2398, 2566
AMERICAN SAMOA GOVERNMENT (Financial Aid Program) 3369
AMERICAN SCANDINAVIAN FOUNDATION OF LOS ANGELES (Scholarship Program) 3370
AMERICAN SCHOOL OF CLASSICAL STUDIES AT ATHENS (Fellowships) 836, 837, 1091, 1092, 1757, 2727, 2907
AMERICAN SOCIOLOGICAL ASSOCIATION 4282
AMERICAN SOCIETY FOR CLINICAL LABORATORY SCIENCE (Ruth M. French Graduate or Undergraduate Scholarship) 2255, 2567
AMERICAN SOCIETY FOR ENGINEERING EDUCATION (Army Research Laboratory Postdoctoral Fellowships) 280, 281, 478, 518, 582, 633, 713,
.... 1502, 1697, 1813, 1883, 1977, 2070
AMERICAN SOCIETY FOR ENOLOGY AND VITICULTURE (Scholarship) 1884
AMERICAN SOCIETY FOR MICROBIOLOGY (Office of Education & Training) 4244
AMERICAN SOCIETY FOR NUTRITIONAL SCIENCES (Predoctoral Fellowships) 2705
AMERICAN SOCIETY FOR PHARMACOLOGY & EXPERIMENTAL THERAPEUTICS INC. 4262
AMERICAN SOCIETY FOR PUBLIC ADMINISTRATION 4272
AMERICAN SOCIETY FOR QUALITY (Richard A. Freund International Scholarship) 30, 634, 2071
AMERICAN SOCIETY OF AGRONOMY 4150
AMERICAN SOCIETY OF APPRAISERS 4155
AMERICAN SOCIETY OF ARMS COLLECTORS (Antique Weapons Research Fellowship) 2908
AMERICAN SOCIETY OF CIVIL ENGINEERS (Jack E. Leisch Memorial Scholarship) 31, 479, 480, 481, 482, 483, 484, 635, 714, 1503, 4175
AMERICAN SOCIETY OF CLINICAL PATHOLOGISTS 4239
AMERICAN SOCIETY OF COMPOSERS, AUTHORS, AND PUBLISHERS (Nathan Burkan Memorial Competition) 3017
AMERICAN SOCIETY OF MECHANICAL ENGINEERS (ASME Student Loans) 715, 4238
AMERICAN SOCIETY OF NEWSPAPER EDITORS 4228
AMERICAN SOCIETY OF RADIOLOGIC TECHNOLOGISTS (Isadore N. Stern Scholarship) 2568, 4273
AMERICAN SOCIETY OF SAFETY ENGINEERS 4277
AMERICAN SOCIETY OF TRAVEL AGENTS (ASTA) FOUNDATION (Scholarships, Grants, & Internships) 32, 33
AMERICAN SOCIETY OF WOMEN ACCOUNTANTS (Scholarships) 34
AMERICAN SPEECH-LANGUAGE-HEARING ASSOCIATION 4161
AMERICAN SPEECH-LANGUAGE-HEARING FOUNDATION (Graduate Student Scholarships) 185, 2256, 2399, 2569
AMERICAN SPEECH-LANGUAGE-HEARING FOUNDATION
(Kala Singh Memorial Fund-International/Minority Student Scholarship) 186, 2257, 2400, 2570
AMERICAN SPEECH-LANGUAGE-HEARING FOUNDATION (Leslie Isenberg Fund for Student With Disability) 187, 2258, 2401, 2571
AMERICAN SPEECH-LANGUAGE-HEARING FOUNDATION (New Investigator Research Grant) 188, 2259, 2402, 2572
AMERICAN SPEECH-LANGUAGE-HEARING FOUNDATION
(Student Research Grant in Clinical or Rehabilitative Audiology) 189, 190, 2260, 2403, 2573, 2574
AMERICAN SPEECH-LANGUAGE-HEARING FOUNDATION (Young Scholars Award for Minority Student) 191, 2261, 2404, 2575
AMERICAN UNIVERSITY IN CAIRO (Teaching English as a Foreign Language Fellowship) 192, 838, 1758, 3222
AMERICAN VACUUM SOCIETY (Graduate Research Award) 583
AMERICAN VACUUM SOCIETY (Russell and Sigurd Varian Fellow Award) 584
AMERICAN VETERINARY MEDICAL ASSOCIATION 4288

AMERICAN WATER RESOURCES ASSOCIATION (Richard A. Herbert Memorial Scholarships) 636, 1504, 1698

AMERICAN WATER WORKS ASSOCIATION (Abel Wolman Fellowship) 637, 638, 639, 640, 641, 1505, 1506, 1507,
.... 1508, 1509, 1625, 1626, 1627, 1628,
.... 1629, 1978, 1979, 1980, 1981, 1982

AMERICAN WINE SOCIETY EDUCATIONAL FOUNDATION (Scholarships and Grants) 1885, 2706, 3291

AMERICAN WOMEN IN RADIO & TELEVISION 4168

AMERICAN-SCANDINAVIAN FOUNDATION (Awards for Scandinavians) 3371, 3372

AMITY INSTITUTE (Internships in the US for Teaching Languages) 3373

AMVETS (Coors/AMVETS Memorial Scholarship) 3374

AMYOTROPHIC LATERAL SCLEROSIS ASSOCIATION (Research Grant Program) 2405

AN UNCOMMON LEGACY FOUNDATION, INC. (Scholarships) 3375

ANIMAL BEHAVIOR OFFICE (Research Grants) 1886

ANIMATION SCHOOL DIRECTORY 4003

ANNUAL REGISTER OF GRANT SUPPORT 4004

APICS EDUCATION AND RESEARCH FOUNDATION (Donald W. Fogarty International Student Paper Competition) 35

APPALOOSA YOUTH FOUNDATION (Scholarships) 3376

ARCHAEOLOGICAL INSTITUTE OF AMERICA (Olivia James Traveling Fellowship) 423, 839, 840, 988, 1093, 1759,
.... 1760, 1761, 2909, 4157

ARCHBOLD MEDICAL CENTER (Archbold Scholarship/Loan) 2262, 2576, 2637

ARCTIC EDUCATION FOUNDATION (Shareholder Scholarships) 3377

ARCTIC INSTITUTE OF NORTH AMERICA (Lorraine Allison Scholarship) 841, 1887

ARKANSAS DEPARTMENT OF HIGHER EDUCATION (MIA/KIA Dependents' Scholarship) 3378

ARKANSAS SINGLE PARENT SCHOLARSHIP FUND (Scholarships) 3379

ARMED FORCES COMMUNICATIONS AND ELECTRONICS ASSOCIATION (AFCEA Fellowshps) 519, 585, 2072

ARMENIAN GENERAL BENEVOLENT UNION (Educational Loan Program) 36, 193, 2156, 2819, 3018, 3077

ARMENIAN RELIEF SOCIETY OF EASTERN USA, INC. (Grants) 3380

ARMENIAN STUDENTS' ASSOCIATION OF AMERICA, INC. (Scholarships) 3381

ARROW, INC. (American Indian Graduate Center Scholarship) 3382

ART CALENDAR 4005

ARTHRITIS FOUNDATION OF AUSTRALIA (Domestic & Overseas Fellowships) 2406, 2407

ARTHRITIS SOCIETY (Research Scholarships, Fellowships, & Grants) 2408

ARTHUR ANDERSEN & CO. SCHOLARSHIP FOUNDATION (Fellowships for Doctoral Candidates at the Dissertation Stage) 37

ARTHUR C. & FLORENCE S. BOEHMER FUND (Scholarships) 3383

ARTHUR M. MILLER FUND 2157, 2263, 2409, 2577, 2638

ARTS & ENTERTAINMENT NETWORK (A&E Teacher Grant Competition) 3384

ARTS MANAGEMENT P/L (Kathleen Mitchell Award) 1094

ARTS MANAGEMENT P/L (Lady Mollie Askin Ballet Travelling Scholarship) 1235

ARTS MANAGEMENT P/L (Marten Bequest Travelling Scholarships) 424, 989, 1095, 1236, 3292

ARTS MANAGEMENT P/L (Miles Franklin Literary Award) 1096

ARTS MANAGEMENT P/L (Portia Geach Memorial Award) 990

ARTS MANAGEMENT P/L (Sir Robert Askin Operatic Travelling Scholarship) 1237

ASAE SOCIETY FOR ENGINEERING IN AGRICULTURAL FOOD AND BIOLOGICAL SYSTEMS 4148

ASIAN CULTURAL COUNCIL (Fellowship Grants for Asian Citizens) 991, 1238

ASIAN CULTURAL COUNCIL (Research Fellowships for U.S. Citizens to Study in Asia & Asians to Study in U.S.) 992, 1239

ASIAN INSTITUTE OF TECHNOLOGY (AIT Scholarship Program) 2, 38, 282, 375, 425, 485, 520, 586, 642,
.... 842, 1400, 1434, 1510, 1630, 1699, 2728, 2820

ASIAN PACIFIC AMERICAN SUPPORT GROUP (Scholarship) 3385

ASIAN PRODUCTIVITY ORGANIZATION (Productivity Fellowships) 39

ASIFA (Helen Victoria Haynes World Peace Storyboard & Animation Contest) 993

ASM FOUNDATION FOR EDUCATION & RESEARCH 4243

ASSISTANTSHIPS AND GRADUATE FELLOWSHIPS IN THE MATHEMATICAL SCIENCES 4006

ASSOCIATED GENERAL CONTRACTORS OF AMERICA 4182

ASSOCIATED PRESS TELEVISION-RADIO ASSOCIATION OF CALIFORNIA/NEVADA
(APTRA-Clete Roberts & Kathryn Dettman Memorial Journalism Scholarship Awards) 2821
ASSOCIATED WESTERN UNIVERSITIES, INC. (AWU Faculty Fellowships) 283, 284, 285, 286, 376, 377, 378, 379,
.... 426, 427, 428, 429, 486, 487, 488, 489,
.... 521, 522, 523, 524, 587, 588, 589, 590,
.... 643, 644, 645, 646, 716, 717, 718, 719,
.... 1814, 1815, 1816, 1817, 1888, 1889,
.... 1890, 1891, 1983, 1984, 1985, 1986,
.... 2073, 2074, 2075, 2076
ASSOCIATION FOR COMPUTING MACHINERY 4181
ASSOCIATION FOR COMPUTING MACHINERY (Listing of Internships & Summer Jobs) 525, 591
ASSOCIATION FOR COMPUTING MACHINERY-WASHINGTON, DC CHAPTER (Samuel N. Alexander Fellowship Award) 3386, 3387
ASSOCIATION FOR EDUCATION AND REHABILITATION OF THE BLIND AND VISUALLY IMPAIRED
(William and Dorothy Ferrell Scholarship) 194, 195
ASSOCIATION FOR INSTITUTIONAL RESEARCH (Research Grant) 40, 196, 197, 526, 2729, 2730
ASSOCIATION FOR LIBRARY & INFORMATION SCIENCE EDUCATION (Alise Research Grants Program) 1097
ASSOCIATION FOR SPINA BIFIDA AND HYDROCEPHALUS (Research Fellowships) 2410
ASSOCIATION FOR WOMEN IN PSYCHOLOGY/AMERICAN PSYCHOLOGICAL ASSOCIATION DIVISION 35
(Annual Student Research Prize) 843
ASSOCIATION FOR WOMEN IN SCIENCE EDUCATIONAL FOUNDATION (AWIS Predoctoral Awards) 41, 42, 43, 44, 287, 288, 289, 290, 527,
.... 528, 529, 530, 844, 845, 846, 847, 1098,
.... 1099, 1100, 1101, 1341, 1342, 1343, 1344,
.... 1511, 1512, 1513, 1514, 1762, 1763, 1764,
.... 1765, 1892, 1893, 1894, 1895, 1987, 1988,
.... 1989, 1990, 2077, 2078, 2079, 2080, 2264,
.... 2265, 2266, 2267, 2731, 2732, 2733, 2734,
.... 2910, 2911, 2912, 2913, 3078, 3079, 3080, 3081,
.... 3160, 3161, 3162, 3163, 3223, 3224, 3225, 3226
ASSOCIATION FOR WOMEN VETERINARIANS (Student Scholarship) 2268
ASSOCIATION OF AMERICAN GEOGRAPHERS 4214
ASSOCIATION ON AMERICAN INDIAN AFFAIRS, INC. (Sequoyah Graduate Fellowships) 3388, 3389
ASSOCIATION OF AMERICAN MEDICAL COLLEGES (AAMC MedLoans Program) 2158
ASSOCIATION OF CERTIFIED FRAUD EXAMINERS (Scholarships) 45, 3019
ASSOCIATION OF COMMONWEALTH UNIVERSITIES (British Marshall Scholarships) 3390, 3391
ASSOCIATION OF FORMER INTELLIGENCE OFFICERS/AFIO (Lt. Gen. Eugene F. Tighe, Jr., Memorial Scholarship) 3020, 3082
ASSOCIATION OF INDEPENDENT COLLEGES AND UNIVERSITIES 4179
ASSOCIATION OF INFORMATION TECHNOLOGY PROFESSIONALS 4187
ASSOCIATION OF INTERNATIONAL EDUCATION, JAPAN (Honors Scholarships for Private International Students) 3392, 3393, 3394
ASSOCIATION OF MASSAGE THERAPISTS-AUSTRALIA INCORPORATED 4235
ASSOCIATION OF MBAS (Business School Loan Scheme) 46
ASSOCIATION OF OPERATING ROOM NURSES (AORN Scholarship Program) 2639
ASSOCIATION OF SURGEONS OF GREAT BRITAIN AND IRELAND (Moynihan Travelling Fellowship) 2159
ASSOCIATION OF UNIVERSITIES & COLLEGES OF CANADA
(International & Canadian Programs Branch—Scholarships; Research & Institutional Programs) 3395
ASSOCIATION OF WOMEN'S HEALTH, OBSTETRIC, AND NEONATAL NURSES (Nursing Research Grants Program) 2640
ASSOCIATION TO UNITE THE DEMOCRATS (Mayme & Herb Frank Fund) 3083
ASTHMA AND ALLERGY FOUNDATION OF AMERICA (Various Fellowships and Grants) 2411
AT&T BELL LABORATORIES (Graduate Research Program For Women) 531, 592, 647, 720, 1991, 2081
ATLANTIC SALMON FEDERATION (Olin Fellowships) 1700
ATSUMI INTERNATIONAL SCHOLARSHIP FOUNDATION (Doctoral Scholarships) 3396
AURORA FOUNDATION (Scholarships) 3397
AUSTIN CHILDREN'S EDUCATIONAL OPPORTUNITY FOUNDATION 3398
AUSTRALIAN FEDERATION OF UNIVERSITY WOMEN - WESTERN AUSTRALIA (Joyce Riley Bursary) 772, 773, 848, 849, 994, 995, 1102, 1103,

.... 1194, 1195, 1240, 1241, 1345, 1346, 1515,
.... 1516, 1992, 1993, 2082, 2083, 2269, 2735,
.... 2736, 2822, 2823, 2914, 2915, 3021, 3022,
.... 3084, 3085, 3164, 3165, 3227, 3228, 3399,
.... 3400, 3401, 3402, 3403, 3404, 3405, 3406,
.... 3407, 3408, 3409, 3410

AUSTRALIAN GOVERNMENT OVERSEAS POSTGRADUATE RESEARCH SCHOLARSHIP PROGRAM
(For Study at Flinders University of South Australia) 3411
AUSTRALIAN NATIONAL UNIVERSITY (ANU Scholarship Program) 3412
AUSTRALIAN RESEARCH COUNCIL (Australian Postdoctoral Fellowship) 3413
AUSTRALIAN RESEARCH COUNCIL (Australian Research Fellowships/Queen Elizabeth II Fellowships) 3414
AUSTRALIAN RESEARCH COUNCIL (Overseas Postgraduate Research Scholarship) 3415
AUSTRALIAN RESEARCH COUNCIL (Senior Research Fellowships) 3416
AUSTRALIAN WAR MEMORIAL (John Treloar Grants-In-Aid & AWM Research Fellowship) 2916
AUSTRIAN CULTURAL INSTITUTE (APART - Austrian Program for Advanced Research & Technology) 3417
AUSTRIAN CULTURAL INSTITUTE (Bertha Von Suttner Scholarship) 1818
AUSTRIAN CULTURAL INSTITUTE (Fine Arts & Music Grants) 996, 1242
AUSTRIAN CULTURAL INSTITUTE (Franz Werfel Scholarship) 850, 1104
AUSTRIAN CULTURAL INSTITUTE (Grants from Federal Ministry of Science & Transport for Austrian Artists) 997, 1196
AUSTRIAN CULTURAL INSTITUTE (Lise Meitner Scholarship) 3418
AUSTRIAN CULTURAL INSTITUTE (Max Kade Foundation Grants) 291, 1401, 1517, 2160, 2270, 2412, 2578, 2641
AUSTRIAN CULTURAL INSTITUTE (Scholars From Around the World) 3419
AUSTRIAN CULTURAL INSTITUTE (Thesis Scholarship) 2413
AUSTRIAN FEDERAL MINISTRY OF SCIENCE AND TRANSPORT (Exchange Scholarships) 3420
AVIATION COUNCIL OF PENNSYLVANIA (Scholarships) 380, 3293
AVIATION INSURANCE ASSOCIATION (Scholarship) 381, 3294
AVIATION MAINTENANCE EDUCATION FUND (AMEF Scholarship Program) 3295
AVON LATINA MODEL OF THE YEAR (Competition) 3421
AWARDS FOR POSTGRADUATE STUDY AT COMMONWEALTH UNIVERSITIES (Twelfth Edition 1997-99) 4007
AYN RAND INSTITUTE (Atlas Shrugged Essay Contest for Graduate Business Students) 47
B & L EDUCATIONAL FOUNDATION 3422
B'NAI B'RITH YOUTH ORGANIZATION (Scholarship Program) 3229
B.M. WOLTMAN FOUNDATION (Lutheran Scholarships for Students of the Ministry and Teaching) 198, 1347
BAJA CALIFORNIA LANGUAGE COLLEGE (Spanish Language Immersion Contest) 1197
BAPTIST UNION OF GREAT BRITAIN (Grants) 1348
BARNABAS MINISTRIES OF SHREVEPORT 3423
BARRON'S GUIDE TO LAW SCHOOLS (12th Edition) 4008
BARTENDERS' SCHOOL OF SANTA ROSA 4164
BASIC FACTS ON STUDY ABROAD 4009
BASIN ELECTRIC POWER COOPERATIVE (Scholarship Program) 3424
BECA FOUNDATION (Alice Newell Joslyn Medical Fund) 2161, 2271, 2414, 2579, 2642
BEDDING PLANTS FOUNDATION, INC. (Harold Bettinger Memorial Scholarship) 3, 48, 49, 1435, 1436, 1437, 1438, 1439,
.... 1440, 1441, 1442, 3425
BEIT TRUST (Post-graduate Fellowships) 3426
BELGIAN AMERICAN EDUCATIONAL FOUNDATION (Graduate Fellowships) 3427
BETA PHI MU INTERNATIONAL LIBRARY SCIENCE HONOR SOCIETY
(Sarah Rebecca Reed Scholarship; Harold Lancour Scholarship for Foreign Study) 1105, 1106
BIA HIGHER EDUCATION/HOPI SUPPLEMENTAL GRANT 3428
BIBLIOGRAPHICAL SOCIETY OF AMERICA (Fellowships) 1107
BIG BOOK OF MINORITY OPPORTUNITIES 4010
BIG BOOK OF OPPORTUNITIES FOR WOMEN 4011
BIOCHEMICAL SOCIETY (General Travel Fund) 1994

BIOCHEMICAL SOCIETY (Krebs Memorial Scholarship) 1995
BIOTECHNOLOGY INDUSTRY ORGANIZATION 4166
BLAKEMORE FOUNDATION (Asian Language Fellowship Grants) 50, 199, 851, 1198, 3086
BLINDED VETERANS ASSOCIATION (Kathern F. Gruber Scholarship Program) 3429
BLUES HEAVEN FOUNDATION, INC. (Muddy Waters Scholarship) 51, 200, 852, 998, 1108, 1243, 2824
BOB JONES UNIVERSITY (Rebate Program) 3430
BODOSSAKI FOUNDATION (Academic Prizes) 532, 1896, 2084, 2162, 2415
BOEING (Polish Graduate Student Scholarship Program) 292, 382, 430, 490, 533, 593, 648, 721,
.... 1402, 1443, 1518, 1631, 1701, 1766, 1819,
.... 1897, 1996, 2085, 2163, 2272, 2416, 2580, 2643
BOLOGNA CENTER OF THE JOHNS HOPKINS UNIVERSITY -
PAUL H. NITZE SCHOOL OF ADVANCED INTERNATIONAL STUDIES (Fellowships for Non-Americans) 52, 53, 853, 854, 2917, 2918, 3023,
.... 3024, 3087, 3088
BOSTON SOCIETY OF ARCHITECTS (Rotch Travelling Scholarship) 431
BOY SCOUTS OF AMERICA 4294
BOYS & GIRLS CLUBS OF AMERICA 4293
BOYS & GIRLS CLUBS OF AMERICA (Robert W. Woodruff Fellowships) 54, 201
BRANDEIS UNIVERSITY (Irving & Rose Crown Ph.D. Fellowships & Tuition Scholarships) 2919
BREWER FOUNDATION, INC. 3431
BRITISH ACADEMY—HRB (Postgraduate Awards) 1109
BRITISH ACADEMY (Sir Ernest Cassel Educational Trust) 855, 1110, 1199
BRITISH ASSOCIATION FOR AMERICAN STUDIES (Short-Term Awards) 856, 1111, 1519, 2920, 3089
BRITISH COLUMBIA HERITAGE TRUST (Scholarships) 432, 857, 1767, 2921
BRITISH COLUMBIA MINISTRY OF SKILLS, EDUCATION, AND TRAINING (British Columbia Student Assistance Program) 3432
BRITISH COLUMBIA PARAPLEGIC FOUNDATION (Douglas John Wilson Scholarship) 3166
BRITISH DENTAL ASSOCIATION (The Dentsply Fund) 2273
BRITISH EMBASSY (Marshall Scholarship Program) 3433
BRITISH FEDERATION OF WOMEN GRADUATES (M.H. Joseph Prize for Non-UK Citizens) 293, 294, 433, 434, 491, 492, 594, 595,
.... 649, 650, 722, 723, 1112, 1520, 1898, 2922,
.... 3434, 3435, 3436, 3437, 3438, 3439, 3440
BRITISH INFORMATION SERVICES (British Marshall Scholarships) 3441
BRITISH INSTITUTE IN EASTERN AFRICA (Research Grants) 1113, 1768, 2923
BRITISH INSTITUTE OF ARCHAEOLOGY AT ANKARA (Travel Grants) 1521, 1769
BRITISH INSTITUTE OF PERSIAN STUDIES (Research Grants) 858
BRITISH LIBRARY (Helen Wallis Research Fellowship) 1522
BRITISH LIBRARY (J.B. Harley Research Fellowships) 1523
BRITISH SCHOOLS AND UNIVERSITIES FOUNDATION, INC. (May & Ward Scholarships) 3442, 3443
BRITISH SCHOOL OF ARCHAEOLOGY IN IRAQ (Various Fellowships & Grants) 1770
BROADCAST EDUCATION ASSOCIATION (Scholarships in Broadcasting) 2825
BROOKHAVEN NATIONAL LABORATORY (Post-doctoral Research Associateships) 724, 1702, 1899, 1997, 2086, 2417
BROOKHAVEN WOMEN IN SCIENCE (Renate W. Chasman Scholarship) 295, 493, 534, 596, 651, 725, 1524, 1703, 1900, 1998, 2087
BROOKING INSTITUTION (Research Fellowships) 55, 3090
BROSS PRIZE FOUNDATION (Scholarly Award) 1349
BUCK INSTITUTE FOR EDUCATION (American Revolution Bicentennial Scholarships) 3444
BUCKS COUNTY COURIER TIMES (Summer Internship Program) 2826
BUDDHIST COMPASSION RELIEF TZU-CHI FOUNDATION, U.S.A. (Scholarships) 3445
BUSINESS & PROFESSIONAL WOMEN'S FOUNDATION (BPW Career Advancement Scholarship Program) 4, 56, 172, 202, 296, 535, 774, 1820,
.... 1901, 2088, 2164, 2274, 2737, 3025, 3296
BUSINESS AND PROFESSIONAL WOMEN'S CLUBS—NEW YORK STATE
(Grace LeGendre Fellowships and Endowment Fund, Inc.) 3446
BUTTE CREEK FOUNDATION 3447
Bartending 4012

CALEDONIAN RESEARCH FOUNDATION (European Visiting Fellowships in the Humanities) 775
CALEDONIAN RESEARCH FOUNDATION (Personal Research Fellowships) 2418
CALEDONIAN RESEARCH FOUNDATION (Postgraduate Scholarships) 3448
CALEDONIAN RESEARCH FOUNDATION (Support Research Fellowships) 2419
CALIFORNIA ASSOCIATION OF MARRIAGE AND FAMILY THERAPISTS (CAMFT Education Foundation Scholarships) 3167
CALIFORNIA CHICANO NEWS MEDIA ASSOCIATION (Joel Garcia Memorial Scholarship) 3449
CALIFORNIA COLLEGE DEMOCRATS (Internships) 3450
CALIFORNIA DIETETIC ASSOCIATION (Zellmer Scholarship Trust Fund) 2707
CALIFORNIA GRANGE FOUNDATION (Deaf Activities Scholarships) 203, 2275, 2581
CALIFORNIA SOCIETY FOR ORIENTAL MEDICINE (CSOM) 4144
CALIFORNIA STUDENT AID COMMISSION (Law Enforcement Dependents Scholarships - LEPD) 3451
CALIFORNIA STATE UNIVERSITY SYSTEM 4178
CALLEJO-BOTELLO FOUNDATION CHARITABLE TRUST 3452
CAMARGO FOUNDATION (Residential Fellowship) 859, 1200
CANADA HUMAN RESOURCES DEVELOPMENT (Canada Student Loans Program) 3453
CANADIAN ASSOCIATION OF BROADCASTERS (Raymond Crepault Scholarship) 2827
CANADIAN ASSOCIATION OF UNIVERSITY TEACHERS (J. H. Stewart Reid Memorial Fellowship) 3454
CANADIAN BAR ASSOCIATION (Viscount Bennett Fellowship) 3026
CANADIAN BUREAU FOR INTERNATIONAL EDUCATION
(Canadian International Development Agency Awards Program for Canadians) 5, 57, 860, 3091, 3092
CANADIAN CANCER SOCIETY (Clinical Cancer Nursing Fellowships/a.k.a. Maurice Legault Fellowships) 2644
CANADIAN CANCER SOCIETY (McEachern Award) 2420
CANADIAN EMBASSY (Canadian Studies Graduate Student Fellowship Program) 861
CANADIAN FEDERATION OF UNIVERSITY WOMEN (CFUW Memorial/Professional Fellowship) 297, 652, 776, 862, 1525, 1704, 1821, 2582,
.... 2738, 2924, 3455, 3456, 3457, 3458, 3459, 3460
CANADIAN HOME ECONOMICS ASSOCIATION (CHEA Graduate Study Scholarship Awards) 2708
CANADIAN INSTITUTE OF UKRAINIAN STUDIES (Helen Darcovich Memorial Fellowship) 863, 864, 865
CANADIAN LIVER FOUNDATION (Fellowships) 2421
CANADIAN LIVER FOUNDATION (Graduate Studentship Awards) 2422
CANADIAN LUNG ASSOCIATION (Canadian Nurses Respiratory Society Fellowships & Research Grants) 2645
CANADIAN MASSAGE THERAPIST ALLIANCE - CMTA 4233
CANADIAN NATIONAL INSTITUTE FOR THE BLIND (Various Scholarships and Grants) 3461
CANADIAN NURSES FOUNDATION (Study Awards Program) 2646
CANADIAN SOCIETY FOR CHEMISTRY (Ichikizaki Fund for Young Chemists) 1999
CANADIAN SOCIETY FOR CHEMICAL ENGINEERING (J.E. Zajic Postgraduate Scholarship in Biochemical Engineering) 653
CANADIAN SOCIETY OF EXPLORATION GEOPHYSICISTS (CSEG Trust Fund) 1526
CANADIAN-SCANDINAVIAN FOUNDATION (Travel Grants) 999
CANCER RESEARCH FUND OF THE DAMON RUNYON-WALTER WINCHELL FOUNDATION (Postdoctoral Research Fellowships) 2423
CAREER GUIDE FOR SINGERS 4013
CARL AND VIRGINIA JOHNSON DAY TRUST 3462
CARNEGIE TRUST FOR THE UNIVERSITIES OF SCOTLAND (Carnegie Post-graduate Scholarships) 3463
CATHOLIC LIBRARY ASSOCIATION (The Reverend Andrew L. Bouwhuis Memorial Scholarship) 1114
CAVE RESEARCH FOUNDATION (KARST Research Fellowship Program) 1527
CEMANAHUAC EDUCATIONAL COMMUNITY (Scholarships for Teachers of Spanish) 1201
CENTER FOR 17TH- AND 18TH-CENTURY STUDIES (Fellowships) 866, 1115, 2925
CENTER FOR ARABIC STUDY ABROAD (CASA Fellowships) 1202
CENTER FOR CHINESE STUDIES (Research Grant Program) 867
CENTER FOR ENVIRONMENTAL JOURNALISM/UNIVERSITY OF COLORADO AT BOULDER (Ted Scripps Fellowship) 2828
CENTER FOR HELLENIC STUDIES (Resident Junior Fellowships) 868, 1116, 1203
CENTRAL SCHOLARSHIP BUREAU (Interest-free Loans) 3464
CENTRE FOR INTERNATIONAL MOBILITY - CIMO (Fulbright Student Grants) 3465

CENTRE FOR INDEPENDENT STUDIES (Liberty & Society Scholarship) 869

CENTRO DE IDIOMAS DEL SURESTE A.C. (Intensive Spanish Scholarship) 1204

CFKR CAREER MATERIALS CATALOG 4014

CHALLENGE IN AGRICULTURE 4015

CHAMBER MUSIC AMERICA
(Gruber Foundation Award/Heidi Castleman Award for Excellence in Chamber Music Teaching) 1244

CHARLES A. AND ANNE MORROW LINDBERGH FOUNDATION (Grants for Research Projects) 173, 204, 383, 654, 777, 870, 1000, 1403,
.... 1444, 1528, 1632, 2424

CHARLES A. LAUFFER SCHOLARSHIP FUND (Scholarship-Loans) 2165

CHARLES BABBAGE INSTITUTE (Adelle & Erwin Tomash Fellowship) 536

CHARLES COOPER INDUSTRIAL SCHOOL 3466

CHARLES H. HOOD FOUNDATION (Child Health Research Program) 2425

CHARLES I. AND EMMA J. CLAPP SCHOLARSHIP FUND 3467

CHARLES J. HUGHES FOUNDATION 3468

CHARLESTON SCIENTIFIC AND CULTURAL EDUCATIONAL FUND 3469

CHAUTAUQUA REGION COMMUNITY FOUNDATION INC. (Scholarships) 3470

CHEMICAL INDUSTRY INSTITUTE OF TOXICOLOGY (Postdoctoral Fellowships) 2166, 2426

CHEMICAL INSTITUTE OF CANADA (Pestcon Graduate Scholarship) 2000

CHEYENNE AND ARAPAHO TRIBES OF OKLAHOMA (Scholarships) 3471

CHINESE AMERICAN MEDICAL SOCIETY (Scholarships) 2167, 2276

CHINESE CHRISTIAN HERALD CRUSADES (Chinese Collegiate Merit Scholarship for New York Schools) 3472

CHINESE UNIVERSITY OF HONG KONG (Various Scholarships, Bursary, and Loan Programs) 3473

CHOCTAW NATION OF OKLAHOMA HIGHER EDUCATION PROGRAM (Grants) 3474

CHRISTIAN A. JOHNSON ENDEAVOR FOUNDATION (Native American Fellows) 871, 2739, 2926, 3093, 3230

CHRISTIAN CHURCH-DISCIPLES OF CHRIST (Disciple Chaplains' Scholarship) 1350, 1351, 1352, 1353, 1354

CHRONICLE CAREER INDEX 4016

CHRONICLE FINANCIAL AID GUIDE (1998-1999 Edition) 4017

CHRONICLE FOUR-YEAR COLLEGE DATABOOK (1998-1999 Edition) 4018

CHRONICLE VOCATIONAL SCHOOL MANUAL (1998 Edition) 4019

CHUNG KUN AI FOUNDATION 3475

CITIZENS' SCHOLARSHIP FOUNDATION OF WAKEFIELD, INC. (Scholarships) 3476

CITY UNIVERSITY (Kitchin Scholarships) 3477

CITY UNIVERSITY (Robert Kitchin (Saddlers) Scholarships for International Students) 3478

COLLEGE ATHLETIC SCHOLARSHIP GUIDE 4020

COLLEGE BOUND FAMILY LIBRARY & SUPPORT PACKAGE 4021

COLLEGE DEGREES BY MAIL & MODEM 4022

COLLEGE FINANCIAL AID EMERGENCY KIT 4023

COLLEGE FINANCIAL AID FOR DUMMIES 4024

COLLEGE FOUNDATION INC. (North Carolina's Federal Family Education Loan Program) 3479

COLLEGE IS POSSIBLE 4025

COLLEGE MISERICORDIA (Honor Scholarships) 3480

COLLEGE OF INSURANCE 4227

COLLEGE OF SAINT ELIZABETH (Scholarships) 3481

COLLEGE OF ST. FRANCIS (Various Scholarship/Grant Programs) 3482

COLLEGE READY REPORT: THE FIRST STEP TO COLLEGE 4026

COLLEGES AND UNIVERSITIES IN THE USA—THE COMPLETE GUIDE FOR INTERNATONAL STUDENTS 4027

COLORADO SOCIETY OF CPAs EDUCATIONAL FOUNDATION (Scholarships for Undergraduates and Graduates) 58, 59

COLUMBIA UNIVERSITY (Knight-Bagehot Fellowship Program in Economics and Business Journalism) 60

COLUMBIANA COUNTY PUBLIC HEALTH LEAGUE TRUST FUND (Grants) 2168, 2277, 2427, 2583, 2647

COMMANDER, NAVAL RESERVE RECRUITING COMMAND
(Health Professionals Loan Repayment Program - HPLRP) 2169, 2648

COMMISSAO INVOTAN/ICCTI (NATO Science Fellowships Program) 298, 299, 1404, 1405, 1822, 1823

COMMISSAO INVOTAN/ICCTI (NATO Senior Guest Fellowship) 300, 1406, 1824

COMMISSION FRANCO-AMERICAINE D'ECHANGES UNIVERSITAIRES ET CULTURELS (Graduate Fellowship) 3483, 3484

COMMITTEE OF VICE-CHANCELLORS & PRINCIPALS OF THE UNIVERSITIES OF THE UNITED KINGDOM
(Overseas Research Students Awards Scheme) 3485

COMMITTEE ON INSTITUTIONAL COOPERATION (CIC FreeApp Program) 3486

COMMITTEE ON INTERNATIONAL RELATIONS IN PSYCHOLOGY (CIRP David International Travel Award) 3168

COMMONWEALTH SECRETARIAT (Commonwealth Fund for Technical Cooperation Awards) 3487

COMMONWEALTH SCHOLARSHIP COMMISSION IN THE UK (Scholarship & Fellowship Plan) 3488

COMMONWEALTH DEPARTMENT OF PRIMARY INDUSTRIES & ENERGY (Post-graduate Forestry Research Awards) 1529

COMMONWEALTH OF VIRGINIA DEPARTMENT OF VETERANS' AFFAIRS (War Orphans Education Program) 3489

COMMUNITY FOUNDATION OF GREATER LORAIN COUNTY (Various Scholarship Programs) 3490

COMMUNITY FOUNDATION OF WESTERN MASSACHUSETTS (Charles F. Warner Loan Fund) 3491, 3492, 3493, 3494, 3495, 3496

CONCORDIA UNIVERSITY (Administration Management Society John Crawford Award) 205

CONCORDIA UNIVERSITY (Barry J. Schwartz Memorial Bursary) 872

CONCORDIA UNIVERSITY (Bank of Montreal Pauline Vanier MBA Fellowship) 61

CONCORDIA UNIVERSITY (Bessie Schulich Fellowship for Entrepreneurship) 62

CONCORDIA UNIVERSITY (David J. Azrieli Graduate Fellowship) 3497

CONCORDIA UNIVERSITY (Graduate Fellowships) 3498

CONCORDIA UNIVERSITY (J W. McConnell Memorial Graduate Fellowships) 3499

CONCORDIA UNIVERSITY (J.P. Zewig Scholarship) 2170, 2584, 2649, 3169

CONCORDIA UNIVERSITY (Joyce Melville Memorial Scholarship) 1001

CONCORDIA UNIVERSITY (John O'Brien & Stanley French Graduate Fellowships) 3500

CONCORDIA UNIVERSITY (Loyola Alumni Association Inc. Educational Grant) 3501

CONCORDIA UNIVERSITY (Mrs. Tauba W. Landsberger Award) 2001

CONCORDIA UNIVERSITY (Nick Herscovis Memorial Scholarship) 2089

CONCORDIA UNIVERSITY (Philip Cohen Award) 1245

CONCORDIA UNIVERSITY (Rose & Norman Goldberg Award and Maria Teresa Hausmann Bursary) 1355

CONCORDIA UNIVERSITY (Senior Scholarships) 3502

CONCORDIA UNIVERSITY (Susan Carson Memorial Bursary and Gordon Fisher Bursaries) 2829

CONCORDIA UNIVERSITY (Wynne Francis Award and David McKeen Awards) 1117

CONCORSO INTERNAZIONALE DI VIOLINO (Premio N. Paganini) 1246

CONCORSO INTERNAZIONALE PER QUARTETTO D'ARCHI (Premio Paolo Borciani) 1247

CONCORSO PIANISTICO INTERNAZIONALE (International Piano Competition) 1248

CONCOURS CLARA HASKIL (International Piano Competition) 1249

CONCOURS GEZA ANDA (International Piano Competition) 1250

CONFERENCE OF MINORITY PUBLIC ADMINISTRATORS (Scholarships and Travel Grants) 63, 3094

CONFERENCE ON LATIN AMERICAN HISTORY (James R. Scobie Memorial Award for Preliminary Ph.D Research) 873, 2927

CONGRESSIONAL HISPANIC CAUCUS INSTITUTE, INC. (CHCI Fellowship Program) 6, 2278, 2830, 3095

CONSULTING ENGINEERS COUNCIL OF NEW JERSEY (Louis Goldberg Scholarship Fund) 301, 1530

CONTEMPORARY RECORD SOCIETY (CRS Competitions) 1251

CONTRACT MANAGEMENT INSTITUTE (Scholarships) 64

CONVERSE COUNTY 4-H FOUNDATION (Scholarships) 3503

COOPER WOOD PRODUCTS FOUNDATION, INC. 3504

COOPERATIVE ASSOCIATION OF STATES FOR SCHOLARSHIPS (CASS) (Scholarships) 65, 537, 3297

COOPERATIVE INSTITUTE FOR RESEARCH IN ENVIRONMENTAL SCIENCES (CIRES Visiting Fellowships) 1531, 1633, 1705, 2002

CORNELL UNIVERSITY (Postdoctoral Fellowships) 778

CORNELL UNIVERSITY, JOHNSON GRADUATE SCHOOL OF MANAGEMENT (Thomas Angear Scholarships) 66

CORPUS CHRISTI COLLEGE (Research Scholarships) 3505

COSTUME SOCIETY OF AMERICA (Stella Blum Research Grant) 1002, 1252

COUNCIL FOR BASIC EDUCATION (Arts Education Fellowships) 1003, 1118, 1253

COUNCIL FOR EUROPEAN STUDIES (Predissertation Fellowships) 435, 874, 1532, 1771, 1772, 2928, 3096, 3231

COUNCIL FOR INTERNATIONAL EXCHANGE OF SCHOLARS (Fulbright Scholar Grant Program) 3506

COUNCIL OF CITIZENS WITH LOW VISION INTERNATIONAL (CCLVI Telesensory Scholarship) 3507

COUNCIL OF JEWISH FEDERATIONS (Federation Executive Recruitment & Education Program Scholarships) 67, 3232

COUNTESS OF MUNSTER MUSICAL TRUST (Grants & Loans) 1254

CRESTAR BANK (Trivia Contest) 3508

CROHN'S AND COLITIS FOUNDATION OF AMERICA (Career Development Award) 2428, 2429, 2430, 2431

CUBAN AMERICAN NATIONAL FOUNDATION (The Mas Family Scholarships) 7, 68, 302, 2831, 3097

CURTIS INSTITUTE OF MUSIC (Tuition Scholarships) 1255

CYNTHIA E. AND CLARA H. HOLLIS FOUNDATION 1356, 2585, 2650, 3233

CYSTIC FIBROSIS FOUNDATION (Research & Training Programs) 2432

CYSTIC FIBROSIS FOUNDATION (Student Traineeship Research Grants) 2433

D'ARCY McNICKLE CENTER FOR AMERICAN INDIAN HISTORY (Francis C. Allen Fellowship) 3509

DALHOUSIE UNIVERSITY (Izaak Walton Killam Postdoctoral Fellowships) 3510

DAN CASSIDY'S GUIDE TO PRIVATE SECTOR KINDERGARTEN-12TH GRADE (K-12) SCHOLARSHIPS 4028

DAN CASSIDY'S GUIDE TO TRAVEL GRANTS 4029

DAN CASSIDY'S GUIDE TO WINNING SCHOLARSHIPS 4030

DANISH RECTORS' CONFERENCE (Government Scholarships for Foreign Nationals) 3511

DANISH SISTERHOOD OF AMERICA (Scholarship Program) 3512

DATATEL SCHOLARS FOUNDATION (Angelfire Scholarships) 3513

DATATEL SCHOLARS FOUNDATION (Datatel Scholarships) 3514

DAUGHTERS OF PENELOPE (Graduate Scholarships) 3515

DAUGHTERS OF THE AMERICAN REVOLUTION (American Indians Scholarship) 3516

DEAKIN UNIVERSITY (Scholarships for International Students) 3517

DEBRA (Research Grant Programme) 2434

DEKALB COUNTY PRODUCERS SUPPLY & FARM BUREAU (Medical Scholarship) 2171, 2651

DELLA M. BAILEY INDIAN SCHOLARSHIP TRUST 3518

DELOITTE & TOUCHE FOUNDATION (Doctoral Fellowship Program) 69

DELTA GAMMA FOUNDATION 3519

DELTA OMICRON (Triennial Composition Competition for Solo Piano 1256

DELTA OMICRON INTERNATIONAL MUSIC FRATERNITY
(Triennial Composition Competition for Sacred Choral Anthem for Three- or Four-Part Voices) 1257

DELTA PHI EPSILON EDUCATIONAL FOUNDATION 3520

DELTA SOCIETY (James M. Harris/Sarah W. Sweatt Student Travel Grant) 2279, 2586, 3170, 3234, 3298

DEMOCRATIC NURSING ORGANISATION OF SOUTH AFRICA (DENOSA Study Fund) 2652

DEPARTMENT OF JUSTICE CANADA (Civil Law/Common Law Exchange Program Scholarships) 3027, 3028

DEPARTMENT OF THE ARMY (Armed Forces Health Professions Scholarships) 2172, 2173, 2280, 2281, 2587, 2653, 2654, 3171

DERMATOLOGY FOUNDATION (Post-doctoral Career Development Awards) 2435

DESCENDANTS OF THE SIGNERS OF THE DECLARATION OF INDEPENDENCE (Scholarship Grant) 3521

DEXTER G. JOHNSON EDUCATIONAL AND BENEVOLENT TRUST (Student Loans) 3522

DIGESTIVE DISORDERS FOUNDATION (Fellowships & Grants) 2436

DIRECTORY OF FINANCIAL AIDS FOR MINORITIES (1995-1997) 4031

DIRECTORY OF FINANCIAL AID FOR STUDENTS OF ARMENIAN DESCENT 4032

DIRECTORY OF FINANCIAL AIDS FOR WOMEN (1995-1997) 4033

DIRECTORY OF POSTSECONDARY EDUCATIONAL RESOURCES IN ALASKA 4034

DIRECTORY OF RESEARCH GRANTS 4035

DIRECTORY OF NATIONAL INFORMATION SOURCES ON DISABILITIES (7th Edition) 4036

DIRECTORY OF ACCREDITED INSTITUTIONS 4037

DIRECTORY OF MEMBER SCHOOLS 4038

DIRECTORY OF TECHNICAL SCHOOLS, COLLEGES, AND UNIVERSITIES
OFFERING COURSES IN GRAPHIC COMMUNICATIONS 4039

DIRKSEN CONGRESSIONAL CENTER (Congressional Research Grants Program) 2929, 3098

DISTRICT OF COLUMBIA COMMISSION ON THE ARTS & HUMANITIES (Grants) 1004, 1119, 1258

DIXIE YARNS FOUNDATION, INC. (George West Scholarship Fund) 3523

DODD & DOROTHY L. BRYAN FOUNDATION (Interest-Free Loans) 3524

DOG WRITERS' EDUCATIONAL TRUST (Scholarships) 3525

DOLLARS FOR COLLEGE: THE QUICK GUIDE TO SCHOLARSHIPS, FELLOWSHIPS, LOANS, AND
OTHER FINANCIAL AID PROGRAMS FOR... 4040

DOROT FOUNDATION (The Dorot Fellowships in Israel) 875

DOW JONES NEWSPAPER FUND (High School Journalism Teacher Fellowship Program) 206

DOW JONES NEWSPAPER FUND, INC. (Newspaper Editing Intern/Scholarship Program) 2832, 2833, 2834

DR. M. AYLWIN COTTON FOUNDATION (Fellowships) 876, 877

DRAPER LABORATORY (Research Assistantships) 70, 384, 538, 597, 726

DUBLIN INSTITUTE FOR ADVANCED STUDIES (Research Scholarships) 878, 1533, 2090

DUMBARTON OAKS (Awards in Byzantine Studies, Pre-Columbian Studies, & History of Landscape Architecture) 436, 879

DUMBARTON OAKS (Summer Fellowships for Byzantine Studies) 880

DUPAGE COUNTY MEDICAL SOCIETY FOUNDATION (Scholarship Program) 2174, 2282, 2437, 2588, 2655

E. A. BAKER FOUNDATION FOR PREVENTION OF BLINDNESS (Fellowships & Research Grants) 2283

EARTHWATCH (Center for Field Research Grants) 3526

EARTHWATCH EUROPE (Research Grants) 3527

EAST TEXAS HISTORICAL ASSOCIATION (Ottis Lock Endowment Awards) 2740, 2930

EAST-WEST CENTER (Graduate Degree Fellowships) 3528

EASTER SEAL SOCIETY OF IOWA, INC. (Scholarships & Awards) 207, 2589, 3172, 3235

EBERHARDT I. FOR SCHOLARSHIP FOUNDATION 3529

ECKMANN FOUNDATION 3530

ECOLOGICAL SOCIETY OF AMERICA (Murray F. Buell and E. Lucy Braun Awards) 655, 1534, 1634

ECONOMIC HISTORY ASSOCIATION (Arthur H. Cole Grants-in-Aid) 71, 2931

EDMUND NILES HUYCK PRESERVE (Research Grants) 1635, 1773, 1902

EDUCATION AND TRAINING PROGRAMS IN OCEANOGRAPHY AND RELATED FIELDS 4041

EDUCATION ASSISTANCE CORPORATION (Federal Family Education Loan Program) 3531

EDUCATION COUNCIL OF THE GRAPHIC ARTS INDUSTRY 4219

EDUCATIONAL AND RESEARCH FOUNDATION FOR THE AAFPRS (Resident Research Grants) 2438

EDUCATIONAL AND RESEARCH FOUNDATION OF THE AAFPRS (Investigative Development Grants) 2439, 2440

EDUCATIONAL AND SCIENTIFIC TRUST OF THE PENNSYLVANIA MEDICAL SOCIETY
(Loan Program for Allied Health/Nursing Students) 2590, 2656

EDUCATIONAL COMMISSION FOR FOREIGN MEDICAL GRADUATES (International Fellowships in Medical Education) 2175

EDUCATIONAL CREDIT MANAGEMENT CORPORATION (Loan Programs for Virginia Students) 3532

EDUCATIONAL COMMUNICATIONS SCHOLARSHIP FOUNDATION (College Scholarship Award) 3533

EDUCATIONAL LEADERSHIP, EDUCATION UPDATE, & CURRICULUM UPDATE 4042

EDWARD AND ANNA RANGE SCHMIDT CHARITABLE TRUST (Grants & Emergency Financial Assistance) 1535, 1636

EDWARD BANGS KELLEY AND ELZA KELLEY FOUNDATION, INC. (Scholarship Program) 2176, 2284, 2441, 2591, 2657

EDWARDS SCHOLARSHIP FUND (Undergraduate and Graduate Scholarships) 3534

EEO BIMONTHLY 4043

EL PASO COMMUNITY FOUNDATION (Scholarships) 3535

ELECTROCHEMICAL SOCIETY (Summer Research Fellowships) 598, 656, 1536, 2003

ELIZABETH GREENSHIELDS FOUNDATION (Grants) 1005

ELMER O. AND IDA PRESTON EDUCATIONAL TRUST (Scholarships) 3536

EMANUEL STERNBERGER EDUCATIONAL FUND (Interest-Free Loan Program) 3537

EMBASSY OF JAPAN (Monbusho Scholarship Program for Research Studies) 3538

EMBASSY OF THE CZECH REPUBLIC (Scholarships for Czechs Living Abroad) 881, 1357

EMORY COLLEGE (Andrew W. Mellon Post-doctoral Fellowships in the Humanities) 779

ENCYCLOPEDIA OF ASSOCIATIONS—Vol. 1 4044

ENGEN SEMINARY FUND (Scholarships) 1358
ENGINEERING & PHYSICAL SCIENCES RESEARCH COUNCIL (Studentships) 303, 1537, 1706, 1903, 2004, 2091
ENGINEERING FOUNDATION (Grants for Exploratory Research) 304
ENGINEERING GEOLOGY FOUNDATION 727, 1538
ENGLISH NATIONAL BOARD FOR NURSING, MIDWIFERY AND HEALTH VISITING (Bursaries and Grants) 2658
ENTOMOLOGICAL SOCIETY OF AMERICA (Jeffrey P. LaFage Graduate Student Research Award) 1904, 1905, 4198
EPILEPSY FOUNDATION OF AMERICA (Behavioral Sciences Research Training Fellowships) 1774, 1906, 1907, 2005, 2177, 2178, 2179, 2180,
.... 2285, 2442, 2443, 2444, 2445, 2446, 2447, 2448,
.... 2449, 2450, 2659, 2660, 2661, 2662, 2741, 3099,
.... 3173, 3174, 3175, 3176, 3236
EPISCOPAL CHURCH FOUNDATION (Graduate Fellowship Program) 1359
EPPLEY FOUNDATION FOR RESEARCH (Postdoctoral Research Grants) 494, 599, 657, 728, 1539, 1707, 1908, 2006, 2092
ESPN (Internship Programs) 72, 2592, 2835, 3177, 3237
ETA SIGMA PHI (Summer Scholarships) 1120
ETHEL AND EMERY FAST SCHOLARSHIP FOUNDATION, INC. 3539
ETHEL N. BOWEN FOUNDATION (Scholarships) 3540
EUROPEAN CENTRE OF ANALYSIS IN THE SOCIAL SCIENCES [ECASS] (Bursaries for Essex Summer School) 2742
EUROPEAN COMMISSION (Marie Curie Fellowships) 1825
EUROPEAN MOLECULAR BIOLOGY ORGANIZATION (EMBO Fellowships) 1909
EUROPEAN UNIVERSITY INSTITUTE (Jean Monnet Fellowship) 73, 882, 2743, 2932, 3029, 3100
EUROPEAN UNIVERSITY INSTITUTE (National Postgraduate Scholarships) 74, 2744, 2933, 3030, 3101
EVEREG-FENESSE MESROBIAN-ROUPINIAN EDUCATIONAL SOCIETY, INC. 3541
F.J. CONNELL MUSIC SCHOLARSHIP TRUST 208, 1259
FANNIE AND JOHN HERTZ FOUNDATION (Fellowship) 305, 385, 495, 539, 600, 658, 729, 1540, 1708, 1910, 2093
FASHION GROUP INTERNATIONAL OF GREATER WASHINGTON DC (Scholarships) 75, 1006
FASHION INSTITUTE OF TECHNOLOGY 4202
FEDERAL BUREAU OF INVESTIGATION 4200
FEDERAL EMPLOYEE EDUCATION AND ASSISTANCE FUND (OK Scholarship Fund) 3542, 3543, 3544
FEDERATION OF JEWISH AGENCIES OF GREATER PHILADELPHIA (Foreman Fleisher Fund) 3545
FELLOWS MEMORIAL FUND (Scholarship Loans) 1360, 2181, 2593, 2594, 2663, 2664
FELLOWSHIP FUND BRANCH OF AFUW-Q, INC. (Graduate Fellowships) 3546
FELLOWSHIP GUIDE TO WESTERN EUROPE 4045
FERN BROWN MEMORIAL FUND 3547
FIGHT FOR SIGHT RESEARCH DIVISION OF PREVENT BLINDNESS AMERICA (Postdoctoral Research Fellowship) 2451, 2452, 2453
FINANCE AUTHORITY OF MAINE (Health Professions Loan Program) 2182, 2286
FINANCIAL AID FOR MINORITIES 4046
FINANCIAL AID FOR THE DISABLED AND THEIR FAMILIES 4047
FINANCIAL AID FOR VETERANS; MILITARY PERSONNEL & THEIR FAMILIES 4048
FINANCIAL AID INFORMATION FOR PHYSICIAN ASSISTANT STUDENTS 4049
FINANCIAL AID RESOURCE GUIDE-#17.97 4050
FINANCIAL ASSISTANCE FOR LIBRARY & INFORMATION STUDIES 4051
FINDING MONEY FOR COLLEGE 4052
FIRST CATHOLIC SLOVAK LADIES ASSOCIATION (College Scholarships) 3548
FIRST CAVALRY DIVISION ASSOCIATION (Scholarships) 3549
FIRST CITIZENS FOUNDATION, INC. 3550
FIRST UNITED METHODIST CHURCH (Robert Stevenson & Doreene E. Cater Scholarships) 1637, 2183, 2287, 2454, 2595, 2665, 3238
FISKE GUIDE TO COLLEGES—1996 Edition 4053
FLETCHER SCHOOL OF LAW AND DIPLOMACY (Scholarships) 3102
FLORIDA AIR ACADEMY SCHOLARSHIP FUND, INC. 3551
FLORIDA ARTS COUNCIL (Individual Artists' Fellowships) 1007, 1121, 1260
FLORIDA DEPT. OF EDUCATION (Jose Marti Scholarship Challenge Grant Fund) 3552, 3553

FLORIDA FEDERATION OF GARDEN CLUBS, INC. (FFGC Scholarships for College Students) 437, 1445, 1541, 1638, 1709, 1911

FLORIDA STATE DEPT. OF EDUCATION (Seminole/Miccosukee Indian Scholarships) 3554

FLORIDA STUDENT FINANCIAL AID—FACT SHEETS 4054

FLY BUCKS 4055

FOLGER SHAKESPEARE LIBRARY (Long-term Fellowships) 2934

FOLGER SHAKESPEARE LIBRARY (Short-term Research Fellowships) 2935

FOND DU LAC RESERVATION (Scholarhip/Grants Program) 3555

FOND REV. EDMOND GELINAS, INC. (Scholarships) 3556

FONDATION DES ETATS-UNIS (Harriet Hale Woolley Scholarships 1008, 1261

FONDATION DES ETATS-UNIS (Scholarships) 3557

FONDATION MARCEL HICTER - COUNCIL OF EUROPE (Travel Bursary System) 76

FONDS F C A R (Fellowship Program) 3558

FOOD INDUSTRY SCHOLARSHIP FUND OF NEW HAMPSHIRE (Scholarships) 2709, 3299

FORD FOUNDATION/NATIONAL RESEARCH COUNCIL (Postdoctoral Fellowship for Minorities) 306, 307, 386, 496, 540, 601, 659, 730, 780,
.... 781, 883, 884, 1122, 1205, 1206, 1361, 1407,
.... 1446, 1447, 1542, 1543, 1639, 1710, 1711, 1775,
.... 1776, 1826, 1912, 1913, 2007, 2008, 2094, 2095,
.... 2745, 2746, 2936, 2937, 3103, 3178, 3179, 3239

FOREST HISTORY SOCIETY (Alfred D. Bell Jr. Travel Grants) 1544, 1640

FOREST ROBERTS THEATRE (Mildred & Albert Panowski Playwriting Award) 1123

FOUNDATION FOR CHIROPRACTIC EDUCATION AND RESEARCH (Research Fellowships & Residencies) 2455

FOUNDATION FOR NEONATAL RESEARCH AND EDUCATION (FNRE Scholarships & Grants) 2666

FOUNDATION FOR SCIENCE AND DISABILITY, INC. (FSD Science Student Grant Fund) 308, 541, 1827, 1914, 2009, 2096, 2184

FOUNDATION FOR SEACOAST HEALTH (Scholarship Program) 2185, 2288, 2456, 2596, 2667, 3240

FOURTH TUESDAY (Pat Hoban Memorial Scholarship) 3559

FRANCIS CHAGRIN FUND (Grants) 1262

FRANK KNOX MEMORIAL FOUNDATION (Knox Fellowships at Harvard) 3560

FRANKLIN LINDSAY STUDENT AID FUND 3561

FRAUNHOFER CENTER FOR RESEARCH IN COMPUTER GRAPHICS (Student & Scholar Exchange Programs) 542, 543, 602, 603

FRAXA RESEARCH FOUNDATION (Grants & Fellowships) 2457

FREEDOM FROM RELIGION FOUNDATION (Student Essay Contest) 209, 782, 1124, 1362, 1408, 1828

FRENCH-AMERICAN FOUNDATION (Bicentennial Fellowships) 2747, 2836, 2938, 3031, 3104, 3180, 3241

FRIBOURG FESTIVAL OF SACRED MUSIC (International Competition in Composition of Sacred Music) 1263

FRIEDRICH NAUMANN STIFTUNG FOUNDATION (Educational Scholarships) 3562

FRIENDS OF THE UNIVERSITY OF WISCONSIN (Madison Libraries Humanities Grants-in-Aid) 783, 885, 1125, 2939

FUND FOR EDUCATION AND TRAINING (FEAT Loans) 3563

FUND FOR PODIATRIC MEDICAL EDUCATION 4268

FUND FOR PODIATRIC MEDICAL EDUCATION (Scholarships) 2289

GABRIEL J. BROWN TRUST (Loan Program) 3564

GABRIEL J. BROWN TRUST (Trust Loan Fund) 3565

GALILLEE COLLEGE (Tuition Scholarships in Israel for Koreans) 77

GAMMA THETA UPSILON INTERNATIONAL GEOGRAPHIC HONOR SOCIETY (Buzzard, Richason, & Maxfield Presidents Scholarships) 1545

GARDEN CLUB OF AMERICA (Anne S. Chatham Fellowship in Medicinal Botany) 1915

GARDEN CLUB OF AMERICA (Catherine H. Beattie Fellowship) 1641

GARDEN CLUB OF AMERICA (Frances M. Peacock Scholarship) 1642

GARDEN CLUB OF AMERICA (GCA Awards in Tropical Botany) 1916

GARDEN CLUB OF AMERICA (GCA Interchange Fellowship) 438, 1448

GARDEN CLUB OF AMERICA (Katharine M. Grosscup Scholarships) 1449

GARDEN CLUB OF AMERICA (Martin McLaren Scholarship) 439, 1450

GATES MILLENIUM SCHOLARS PROGRAM (Scholarships for Graduate Students) 174, 210, 309, 1126, 1829, 2097

GEMLINES.COM 4213

GENERAL FEDERATION OF WOMEN'S CLUBS OF MASSACHUSETTS (International Affairs Scholarships) 3105, 3566
GENERAL SEMANTICS FOUNDATION (Project Grants) 1127
GENEVA ASSOCIATION (Ernst Meyer Prize & Research Grants) 78
GEOLOGICAL SOCIETY OF AMERICA 4215
GEOLOGICAL SOCIETY OF AMERICA (Graduate Student Research Grants) 1546
GEORGE ABRAHAMIAN FOUNDATION (Scholarships for Rhode Island Armenians) 3567
GEORGE BIRD GRINNELL AMERICAN INDIAN CHILDREN'S FUND (Al Qoyawayma Award) 310, 1009, 1264, 1830, 3568
GEORGE GROTEFEND SCHOLARSHIP FUND (Grotefend Scholarship) 3569
GEORGE MASON UNIVERSITY (Associated Writing Programs Award Series; St. Martin's Press Award) 1128
GEORGE MASON UNIVERSITY (Mary Roberts Rinehart Awards) 1129
GEORGE W. AND ANNE A. HOOVER SCHOLARSHIP FUND (Student Loans) 3570
GEORGE WASHINGTON UNIVERSITY (George McCandlish Fellowship in American Literature) 1130
GEORGETOWN UNIVERSITY (Doctoral Program in Chemistry) 2010
GEORGIA BOARD OF REGENTS (Scholarships) 3571
GEORGIA LIBRARY ASSOCIATION ADMINISTRATIVE SERVICES (Hubbard Scholarship Fund) 1131
GEORGIA STUDENT FINANCE COMMISSION (HOPE Scholarships) 3572
GERBER REWARDS (Scholarship Drawings) 3573
GERMAN ACADEMIC EXCHANGE SERVICE (DAAD Programs) 886, 1207
GERMAN MARSHALL FUND OF THE UNITED STATES (Research Support Program) 887, 888, 3106, 3107
GERMANISTIC SOCIETY OF AMERICA (Foreign Study Scholarships) 1132, 1208, 1363, 2940, 3108
GERONIMO CORPORATION, INC. (William B. Klusty Memorial Scholarship Fund for Native Americans) 3574
GET SMART FAST 4056
GETTING STARTED IN THE MUSIC BUSINESS 4057
GETTY RESEARCH INSTITUTE FOR THE HISTORY OF ART AND THE HUMANITIES (Fellowships) 784, 1010, 2748
GIACOMO LEOPARDI CENTER (Scholarships for Italian Language Study in Italy) 889, 1209
GIRTON COLLEGE (Fellowships) 785, 1831
GLADYS KRIEBLE DELMAS FOUNDATION (Predoctoral & Postdoctoral Grants in Venice & the Veneto) 79, 440, 786, 890, 1011, 1133, 1265, 1364, 1777, 2749, 2941, 3032, 3109
GLENDALE COMMUNITY FOUNDATION (Scholarships) 3575
GLORIA FECHT MEMORIAL SCHOLARSHIP FUND 3576
GOLDIE GIBSON SCHOLARSHIP FUND (Student Loans) 3577
GOLF COURSE SUPERINTENDENTS ASSOCIATION OF AMERICA (GCSAA Essay Contest) 1451, 1452, 1453, 3578
GRACE EDWARDS SCHOLARSHIP FUND (Scholarships) 3579
GRACE FOUNDATION SCHOLARSHIP TRUST FUND 211, 2597, 2668, 3242
GRADUATE FACULTY AND PROGRAMS IN POLITICAL SCIENCE 4058
GRADUATE INSTITUTE OF INTERNATIONAL STUDIES (Scholarships) 80, 891, 2942, 3033, 3110
GRADUATE INSTITUTE OF PEACE STUDIES (Peace Education Scholarship) 3580
GRAHAM FOUNDATION FOR ADVANCED STUDIES IN THE FINE ARTS (Research Grants) 441
GRAND AVENUE PRESBYTERIAN CHURCH (Davis Foute Eagleton Memorial Student Loan Fund) 1365
GRANTS AND AWARDS AVAILABLE TO AMERICAN WRITERS 4059
GRANTS IN THE HUMANITIES 4060
GRANTS REGISTER (THE) 1997-1999 4061
GRANTS, FELLOWSHIPS, AND PRIZES OF INTEREST TO HISTORIANS 4062
GRASS FOUNDATION (Grass Fellowships in Neurophysiology) 2458
GRASS FOUNDATION (Robert S. Morison Fellowship) 2186, 2459
GRIFFITH UNIVERSITY (Post-graduate Research Scholarship) 3581
GUIDE TO GRADUATE EDUCATION IN PUBLIC AFFAIRS AND PUBLIC ADMINISTRATION 4063
GUIDE TO GRADUATE PUBLIC POLICY EDUCATION AND ORGANIZATIONS 4064
GUIDE TO PROGRAMS (NSF 97-150) 4065
GUIDE TO SOURCES OF INFORMATION ON PARAPSYCHOLOGY 4066
H. FLETCHER BROWN FUND (Scholarships) 311, 2011, 2187, 2290, 3034

H.G. AND A.G. KEASBEY MEMORIAL FOUNDATION 3582

HAGGAR CLOTHING COMPANY (Haggar Foundation Scholarship Program) 3583

HARDING FOUNDATION (Grants) 1366

HARNESS TRACKS OF AMERICA (Scholarship) 3584

HAROLD HYAM WINGATE FOUNDATION (Wingate Scholarships) 1012, 1134, 1266

HARRY E. & FLORENCE W. SNAYBERGER MEMORIAL FOUNDATION (Grant Award) 3585

HARRY FRANK GUGGENHEIM FOUNDATION (Dissertation Fellowships) 1917, 2750, 3181

HARRY FRANK GUGGENHEIM FOUNDATION (Postdoctoral Research Grants) 1918, 2751, 3182

HARRY S. TRUMAN LIBRARY INSTITUTE (Dissertation Year Fellowship) 2943, 2944, 2945, 2946

HARVARD BUSINESS SCHOOL (Newcomen Postdoctoral Fellowship in Business History) 81, 2947

HARVARD UNIVERSITY—NIEMAN FOUNDATION (Fellowships for Journalists) 3586

HARVARD-SMITHSONIAN CENTER FOR ASTROPHYSICS 4159

HARVARD/RADCLIFFE OFFICE OF ADMISSIONS AND FINANCIAL AID (Scholarships; Grants; Loans & Work Study Programs) 3587

HASTINGS CENTER (International Visiting Scholars Program) 1367

HATTIE M. STRONG FOUNDATION (No-interest Loans) 3588

HATTORI FOUNDATION FOR YOUNG MUSICIANS (Awards for Young Soloists) 1267, 1268

HAWAII COMMUNITY FOUNDATION 3589

HAYSTACK MOUNTAIN SCHOOL OF CRAFTS (Scholarship Program) 1013, 3300

HEADQUARTERS, USAF RESERVE PERSONNEL CENTER (Health Professionals Loan Repayment Program - HPLRP) 2188, 2669

HEALTH RESEARCH COUNCIL OF NEW ZEALAND (Post-doctoral Fellowships) 2291, 2460

HEART AND STROKE FOUNDATION OF CANADA (Medical Scientist Traineeship) 2461, 2462, 2463

HEART AND STROKE FOUNDATION OF ONTARIO (Scientific Fellowships in Prevention Research) 2464

HEART FOUNDATION OF AUSTRALIA (Career Research Fellowship) 2465, 2466, 2467, 2468, 2469, 2470, 2471

HEBREW IMMIGRANT SOCIETY (HIAS Scholarship Program) 3590

HEISER PROGRAM FOR RESEARCH IN LEPROSY AND/OR TUBERCULOSIS (Post-doctoral Fellowships and Research Grants) 2472

HELEN HAY WHITNEY FOUNDATION (Postdoctoral Research Fellowships) 2473

HENRY A. MURRAY RESEARCH CENTER OF RADCLIFFE COLLEGE (Jeanne Humphrey Block Dissertation Award Program) 892

HERB SOCIETY OF AMERICA, INC. (Research Grant Program) 1454

HERBERT HOOVER PRESIDENTIAL LIBRARY ASSOCIATION (Travel Grants) 2837, 2948

HIGHER EDUCATION PROGRAMS 4067

HILGENFELD FOUNDATION FOR MORTUARY EDUCATION (Scholarships) 3301

HILLEL INTERNATIONAL CENTER (The Bittker Fellowship) 82, 212, 893, 2838, 3111

HILLEL INTERNATIONAL CENTER (The Public Policy Fellowship) 894, 1643, 2839, 3112, 3243

HISPANIC SCHOLARSHIP FUND (Scholarships) 3591

HISPANIC THEOLOGICAL INITIATIVE (Scholarships & Grants) 1368

HOBART INSTITUTE OF WELDING TECHONOLOGY 4290

HOBSONS PUBLISHING (Scholarship) 83

HOME AFFAIRS BUREAU (Li Po Chun Overseas Postgraduate Scholarships) 3592

HOME AFFAIRS BUREAU (Sir Robert Black Post-graduate Scholarships) 3593

HOME FASHION PRODUCTS ASSN. (Home Textile Surface Design Competition) 1014

HOMEOPATHIC EDUCATIONAL SERVICES 4222

HOMI BHABHA FELLOWSHIPS COUNCIL (Homi Bhabha Fellowship) 3594

HONOR SOCIETY OF PHI KAPPA PHI (First-Year Graduate Fellowship) 3595

HOPI SCHOLARSHIP 3596

HORACE SMITH FUND (Loans) 3597

HORACE SMITH FUND (Walter S. Barr Fellowships) 3598

HOUBLON-NORMAN FUND (Fellowships) 84

HOW TO FIND OUT ABOUT FINANCIAL AID 4068

HOW TO PREPARE A RESEARCH PROPOSAL 4069

HOWARD AND MAMIE NICHOLS SCHOLARSHIP TRUST (Scholarships) 3599

HOWARD HUGHES MEDICAL INSTITUTE (Postdoctoral Research Fellowships for Physicians) 2474, 2475

HUALAPAI TRIBAL COUNCIL (Scholarship Program) 3600
HUBBARD FARMS CHARITABLE FOUNDATION 1455, 1644, 1919
HUMANITARIAN TRUST (Grants) 3601
HUMBOLDT AREA FOUNDATION (Scholarships) 3602
HUNTINGTON LIBRARY (Research Fellowships) 1015, 1135, 2949
IAN KARTEN CHARITABLE TRUST (Karten Scholarships) 3603
IBM TJ WATSON RESEARCH CENTER (IBM Cooperative Fellowship Award) 544, 604
IDP EDUCATION AUSTRALIA (Australian-European Awards Program) 3604
IEEE (Fellowship in Electrical History) 545, 605
IEEE COMPUTER SOCIETY 4180
IEEE COMPUTER SOCIETY (Richard Merwin Student Scholarship) 546, 606
ILLINOIS ARTS COUNCIL (Artists Fellowship Awards) 1016, 1136, 1269
ILLINOIS PILOTS ASSOCIATION (Scholarships) 387, 3302
ILLINOIS STUDENT ASSISTANCE COMMISSION (David A. DeBolt Teacher Shortage Scholarship Program) 213, 214, 3605, 3606, 3607
ILLUMINATING ENGINEERING SOCIETY OF NORTH AMERICA 4226
IMPERIAL CANCER RESEARCH FUND (Postdoctoral Fellowships) 2476
INDEPENDENCE FEDERAL SAVINGS BANK (Federal Family Education Loans) 3608
INDEPENDENT ACCOUNTANTS INTERNATIONAL EDUCATIONAL FOUNDATION, INC.
(Robert Kaufman Memorial Scholarship Award) 85
INDEX OF MAJORS & GRADUATE DEGREES 4070
INSIDER'S GUIDE TO MEDICAL SCHOOLS 4071
INSTITUT D'ETUDES FRANCAISES D'AVIGNON/BRYN MAWR COLLEGE
(Scholarships for Summer Study in Avignon, France) 895, 1210
INSTITUT FUR EUROPAISCHE GESCHICHTE (Fellowship Program) 2950
INSTITUTE FOR ADVANCED STUDY (Post-doctoral Fellowship Awards) 1409, 2098, 2752, 2951
INSTITUTE FOR ADVANCED STUDIES IN THE HUMANITIES (Visiting Research Fellowships) 787, 896, 1017, 1137, 1270, 1369, 1778, 2753,
.... 2952, 3035, 3183, 3244
INSTITUTE FOR HUMANE STUDIES (Koch Summer Fellow Program) 86, 87, 215, 788, 789, 897, 1018, 1138, 1139,
.... 1140, 1370, 2754, 2755, 2840, 2841, 2842, 3036,
.... 3037, 3038, 3113, 3114, 3115, 3184, 3245
INSTITUTE FOR OPERATIONS RESEARCH AND THE MANAGEMENT SCIENCES
(INFORMS Summer Internship Directory) 88, 547, 607, 660, 2099, 4254
INSTITUTE FOR THE INTERNATIONAL EDUCATION OF STUDENTS (Scholarships) 3609
INSTITUTE FOR THE STUDY OF WORLD POLITICS (Dissertation Fellowships) 89, 90, 898, 899, 1456, 1457, 1645, 1646,
.... 2292, 2293, 2710, 2711, 3116, 3117
INSTITUTE OF ELECTRICAL & ELECTRONICS ENGINEERS (Charles Le Geyt Fortescue Fellowship) 608
INSTITUTE OF MANAGEMENT ACCOUNTANTS 4141
INSTITUTE OF CHARTERED ACCOUNTANTS OF NEW ZEALAND (Coopers & Lybrand Peter Barr Research Fellowship) 91
INSTITUTE OF ELECTRICAL AND ELECTRONICS ENGINEERS - US ACTIVITIES 4195
INSTITUTE OF INTERNAL AUDITORS RESEARCH FOUNDATION (Michael J. Barrett Doctoral Dissertation Award) 92
INSTITUTE OF INTERNATIONAL EDUCATION (Arts International Fund For Performing Arts) 1271
INSTITUTE OF INTERNATIONAL EDUCATION (Fulbright Grants for Foreign Nations) 3610
INSTITUTE OF INTERNATIONAL EDUCATION (Fulbright and International Fellowships for U.S. Citizens) 3611
INSTITUTE OF INTERNATIONAL EDUCATION (Scholarships for Study in Switzerland) 3612
INSTITUTE OF INDUSTRIAL ENGINEERS (Gilbreth Memorial Fellowship and E.J. Sierleja Memorial Fellowship) 661
INSTITUTE OF INDUSTRIAL ENGINEERS (United Parcel Service Scholarships for Female and Minority Students.) 662
INSTITUTE OF CANCER RESEARCH (Studentships) 1832
INSTITUTE OF PAPER SCIENCE AND TECHNOLOGY (Fellowship Program) 663, 731, 1920, 2012, 2100
INSTITUTE OF FOOD TECHNOLOGISTS 4209
INSTITUTE OF FOOD TECHNOLOGISTS (Graduate Fellowships) 2712
INSTITUTION OF ELECTRICAL ENGINEERS (Postgraduate Awards) 312, 388, 442, 497, 548, 609, 664, 732
INSTITUTION OF MECHANICAL ENGINEERS (Various Grants and Scholarships) 733

INSTITUTION OF MINING AND METALLURGY (Bosworth Smith Trust Fund) 734, 735, 736, 737, 738, 1547, 1548

INSTITUTO COLOMBIANO DE CREDITO EDUCATIVO Y ESTUDIOS TECNICOS EN EL EXTERIOR
(ICETEX/Fulbright Commission Scholarships) 3613

INSTITUTO NACIONAL DE CARDIOLOGIA (Residency Fellowships) 2189

INTER AMERICAN PRESS ASSOCIATION (Scholarships for Young Journalists) 2843

INTER-AMERICAN BAR ASSOCIATION (Writing Competition) 3039

INTER-AMERICAN FOUNDATION (Field Research Fellowship Programs for U.S. , Latin American, and Caribbean Citizens) 8, 93, 790, 900, 2756, 3040, 3118

INTER-AMERICAN FOUNDATION (Master's Research Fellowships) 9, 94, 791, 901, 2757, 3041, 3119

INTERNATIONAL AGENCY FOR RESEARCH ON CANCER (Cancer Research Fellowship Programme) 2477, 2478

INTERNATIONAL ASSOCIATION OF CULINARY PROFESSIONALS FOUNDATION (Scholarships) 2713

INTERNATIONAL ASSOCIATION OF FIRE CHIEFS FOUNDATION (Scholarship Program) 95, 3246, 3303, 3614

INTERNATIONAL ASTRONOMICAL UNION (Exchange of Astronomers Travel Grant) 1549

INTERNATIONAL BILL ONEXIOCA II (Founders Memorial Award) 3615

INTERNATIONAL CHIROPRACTORS ASSOCIATION 4174

INTERNATIONAL COMPETITION FOR SYMPHONIC COMPOSITION (Premio Citta Di Trieste) 1272

INTERNATIONAL COUNCIL FOR CANADIAN STUDIES (Government of France Graduate Awards) 313, 1833, 2190, 2479, 2758, 3616, 3617,
.... 3618, 3619, 3620, 3621, 3622

INTERNATIONAL COUNCIL OF SHOPPING CENTERS EDUCATIONAL FOUNDATION (Graduate Student Scholarships) 96

INTERNATIONAL CROPS RESEARCH INSTITUTE FOR THE SEMI-ARID TROPICS (Training & Fellowships Program) 1458

INTERNATIONAL DESALINATION ASSOCIATION (Channabasappa Memorial Scholarship Fund) 665, 1550, 1647

INTERNATIONAL DEVELOPMENT RESEARCH CENTRE (John G. Bene Fellowship in Social Forestry) 1551, 2844, 2845

INTERNATIONAL FEDERATION FOR INFORMATION AND DOCUMENTATION (Dr. Shawky Salem Training Grant) 1141

INTERNATIONAL FEDERATION OF UNIVERSITY WOMEN (IFUW International Fellowships & Grants) 3623

INTERNATIONAL FOUNDATION OF EMPLOYEE BENEFIT PLANS (Grants for Research Program) 97

INTERNATIONAL FUNDING GUIDE 4072

INTERNATIONAL INSTITUTE FOR APPLIED SYSTEMS ANALYSIS
(Fellowships for Young Scientists' Summer Program at the IIASA in Vienna, Austria) 98, 666, 902, 1552, 1648

INTERNATIONAL INSTITUTE FOR POPULATION SCIENCES (Master & Ph.D. of Population Studies Fellowships) 903, 904, 905

INTERNATIONAL INSTITUTE OF TROPICAL AGRICULTURE (Graduate Research Fellowship Program) 1459

INTERNATIONAL JOBS 4073

INTERNATIONAL MEDIEVAL INSTITUTE (K.H. Wick Bursary Fund for Attending Meetings) 2953

INTERNATIONALER MUSIKWETTBEWERB (International Music Competition of the Ard Munich) 1273

INTERNATIONAL ORDER OF THE ALHAMBRA (Graduate/Postgraduate Scholarship Grants) 216, 2191, 2294, 2598, 2670

INTERNATIONAL READING ASSOCIATION (Albert J. Harris Award) 217, 218, 219, 220, 221, 222, 223, 224, 225

INTERNATIONAL RESEARCH AND EXCHANGES BOARD
(Russian-US Young Leadership Fellows for Public Service Program for Russian Citizens) 10, 792, 793, 794, 795, 906, 907, 908,
.... 2759, 2760, 2761, 3120

INTERNATIONAL SCHOOL DIRECTORY 4074

INTERNATIONAL SCHOOL OF CRYSTALLOGRAPHY (Postgraduate Courses) 1921, 2013, 2101, 2295

INTERNATIONAL SOCIETY FOR CLINICAL LABORATORY TECHNOLOGY (David Birenbaum Scholarship Fund) 3624

INTERNATIONAL SOCIETY OF ARBORICULTURE (Research Trust) 1460, 1922

INTERNATIONAL SOCIETY OF WOMEN AIRLINE PILOTS (ISA International Career Scholarship) 389, 390, 391, 392, 393

INTERNATIONAL TRUMPET GUILD (Conference Scholarships) 1274

INTERNATIONAL UNION AGAINST CANCER (Research Fellowships) 2480

INTERNATIONAL UNION FOR VACUUM SCIENCE (Welch Foundation Scholarships) 610

INTERSOCIETY COMMITTEE ON PATHOLOGY INFORMATION 4259

INTERTEL FOUNDATION, INC. (Hollingworth Award Competition) 226

INVESTIGATIVE REPORTERS AND EDITORS (Small News Organization Fellowships) 2846

IOWA COLLEGE STUDENT AID COMMISSION (Federal Stafford Loan Program; Federal PLUS Loans) 3625

IOWA SCHOOL OF LETTERS (The John Simmons Short Fiction Award) 1142

IRISH ARTS COUNCIL (Awards and Opportunities) 443, 1019, 1143, 1275

ISRAEL AMATEUR RADIO CLUB (Holyland Award) 3626

ISTITUTO ITALIANO PER GLI STUDI STORICI (Federico Chabod & Adolfo Omodeo Scholarships) 99, 100, 796, 1020, 1021, 1144, 1145, 1276,
.... 1371, 1372, 2762, 2954, 2955

ITALIAN INSTITUTE (Scholarships and Grants) 3627

Information on the Physician Assistant Profession 4075

International Forestry and Natural Resources 4076

JACKQUELINE ELVIRA HODGES JOHNSON FUND, INC (Scholarship) 3628

JACKSONVILLE UNIVERSITY (Scholarships & Grants Programs) 3629

JACKSONVILLE STATE UNIVERSITY 3630

JACOB'S PILLOW DANCE FESTIVAL (Scholarships) 1277

JAMES F. LINCOLN ARC WELDING FOUNDATION (Scholarships) 667, 3304

JAMES FORD BELL FOUNDATION (Summer Internship Program) 101, 3247

JAMES MADISON MEMORIAL FELLOWSHIP (Fellowship for Teachers) 175, 227, 909, 2956, 3121

JAMES Z. NAURISON SCHOLARSHIP FUND 3631

JANE COFFIN CHILDS MEMORIAL FUND FOR MEDICAL RESEARCH (Postdoctoral Fellowships) 2481

JANSONS LEGAT (Scholarships) 11, 102, 668, 1022

JAPAN FOUNDATION (Doctoral and Research Fellowships) 910, 1211

JAPAN SOCIETY FOR THE PROMOTION OF SCIENCE (Post-doctoral Fellowships for Foreign Researchers) 314, 797, 1410, 2192, 2482, 2763

JAPAN-AMERICA SOCIETY OF WASHINGTON (H. William Tanaka Scholarship) 911, 1212

JAPANESE AMERICAN CITIZENS LEAGUE
(Sumitomo Bank of California Scholarship and Union Bank Scholarship) 103, 176, 228, 912, 2193, 3042, 3248, 3632, 3633, 3634

JAPANESE ASSOCIATION OF UNIVERSITY WOMEN (International Fellowships) 3635

JAPANESE GOVERNMENT (Monbusho In-Service Training For Teachers Scholarships) 229

JAPANESE GOVERNMENT (Monbusho Research Student Scholarships) 3636

JESSE MARVIN UNRUH ASSEMBLY FELLOWSHIP PROGRAM 3637

JEWISH BRAILLE INSTITUTE OF AMERICA (Scholarships) 913

JEWISH COMMUNITY CENTERS ASSOCIATION (JCCA Scholarship Program) 104, 230, 914, 3249

JEWISH FAMILY AND CHILDREN'S SERVICES (College Loan Fund) 3638, 3639, 3640, 3641

JEWISH FEDERATION OF METROPOLITAN CHICAGO (Academic Scholarship Program for Studies in the Sciences) 315, 1411, 1834, 2102

JEWISH SOCIAL SERVICE AGENCY OF METROPOLITAN WASHINGTON (Loan Fund) 3642

JEWISH VOCATIONAL SERVICE (JVS) (Community Scholarship Fund) 3643

JEWISH VOCATIONAL SERVICE (Marcus & Theresa Levie Educational Fund Scholarships) 2194, 2296, 2599, 2671, 3250

JOB OPPORTUNITIES FOR THE BLIND (JOB) 4077

JOHN CARTER BROWN LIBRARY (Research Fellowships) 915, 2957

JOHN D. AND CATHERINE T. MACARTHUR FOUNDATION (Fellows Program) 3644

JOHN F. KENNEDY LIBRARY FOUNDATION (Theodore C. Sorensen Research Fellowship) 2847, 2958, 2959, 2960, 3043, 3044,
.... 3122, 3123, 3124, 3125

JOHN FITZGERALD KENNEDY LIBRARY FOUNDATION (Hemingway Research Grants) 1146

JOHN GYLES EDUCATION FUND (Scholarships) 3645

JOHN K. & THIRZA F. DAVENPORT FOUNDATION (Scholarships in the Arts) 1023, 1278, 3305

JOHN RANKIN FUND (Travel Scholarships in Accounting or Law) 105, 3045

JOHN SIMON GUGGENHEIM MEMORIAL FOUNDATION (Fellowships) 3646

JOHN T. HALL TRUST 3647

JOSEPH COLLINS FOUNDATION (Grants for Medical Students) 2195

JOURNALISM AND MASS COMMUNICATIONS ACCREDITATION 4078

JOURNALISM AND MASS COMMUNICATION DIRECTORY 4079

JOURNALIST'S ROAD TO SUCCESS: A Career and Scholarship Guide 4080

JULIA HENRY FUND (Fellowships at Harvard and Yale Universities) 3648

JULIUS AND ESTHER STULBERG COMPETITION, INC. (International String Competition) 1279

JUNIOR ENGINEERING TECHNICAL SOCIETY INC (JETS) 4196

JUVENILE DIABETES FOUNDATION INTERNATIONAL (Research Grants; Career Development Awards; Post-doctoral Fellowships) 2483

KANSAS BOARD OF REGENTS (Ethnic Minority Graduate Fellowship) 3649

KANSAS BOARD OF REGENTS (James B. Pearson Fellowship) 3126
KANSAS BOARD OF REGENTS (Kansas Comprehensive Grants) 3650
KANSAS BOARD OF REGENTS (Kansas Distinguished Scholarship Program) 3651
KANSAS COMMISSION ON VETERANS' AFFAIRS (Scholarships) 3652
KANSAS STATE UNIVERSITY FOUNDATION (Various Scholarships) 3653
KAPPA OMICRON NU (Adviser's Fellowships) 2714
KAPPA OMICRON NU (Doctoral Fellowships) 2715
KAPPA OMICRON NU (Master's Fellowships) 2716
KAPPA OMICRON NU (Research/Project Grants) 2717
KARL-ENIGK-STIFTUNG (Research Grant) 1923
KARLA SCHERER FOUNDATION (Scholarships) 106
KATHLEEN FERRIER MEMORIAL SCHOLARSHIP FUND (Kathleen Ferrier Awards) 1280
KENNEDY FOUNDATION (Scholarships) 3654
KENNEDY MEMORIAL TRUST (Kennedy Scholarships) 3655
KENNEDY MEMORIAL TRUST (Scholarships at Harvard and the Massachusetts Institute of Technology) 3656
KENTUCKY CENTER FOR VETERANS AFFAIRS (Benefits for Veterans' Dependents, Spouses, & Widows) 3657
KENTUCKY HIGHER EDUCATION ASSISTANCE AUTHORITY (Student Loan Program) 3658
KEY BANK OF CENTRAL MAINE FOUNDATION 3659
KIDNEY FOUNDATION OF CANADA (Scholarships) 2196, 2484, 2485, 2486
KIDZWRITE 4292
KING FAISAL FOUNDATION (Graduate Scholarship Program) 316, 1553, 2014, 2103, 2197, 2297, 2487, 2600, 2672
KING'S COLLEGE LONDON (Cleave Cockerill Postgraduate Studentship) 1373
KNIGHT SCIENCE JOURNALISM FELLOWSHIPS 1835
KNIGHT SCIENCE JOURNALISM FOUNDATION (Fellowships) 2848
KNIGHTS OF COLUMBUS (Bishop Greco Graduate Fellowship Program) 231
KNIGHTS OF COLUMBUS (Graduate Fellowships) 3660
KNIGHTS TEMPLAR EDUCATIONAL FOUNDATION (Special Low-Interest Loans) 3661
KOOMRUIAN EDUCATION FUND 3662
KOSCIUSZKO FOUNDATION (Grants/Fellowships to Polish Citizens for Study/Teaching in the U.S.) 3663
KOSCIUSZKO FOUNDATION (Study/Research Programs for Americans in Poland) 916
KOSCIUSZKO FOUNDATION (Tuition Scholarships) 3664
KUALA BELALONG FIELD STUDIES CENTRE, UNIVERSITI BRUNEI DERUSSALEM (Research Fellowship) 1649
KURT WEILL FOUNDATION FOR MUSIC (Grants Program) 1281
L.S.B. LEAKEY FOUNDATION (Franklin Mosher Baldwin Memorial Fellowships) 1779
L.S.B. LEAKEY FOUNDATION (General Grants) 1780
L.S.B. LEAKEY FOUNDATION (Special Research Grants:
Fellowships for Great Ape Research, Study of Foraging Peoples, & Paleoanthropology Award) 1781
LABAN/BARTENIEFF INSTITUTE OF MOVEMENT STUDIES (Work-Study Programs) 232, 1282, 2298, 2601, 3185
LADIES OF NORTHANTS (Scholarship) 669
LADY ALLEN OF HURTWOOD MEMORIAL TRUST (Travel Grants) 107, 233, 2198, 2488, 2673, 3186, 3251
LADY DAVIS FELLOWSHIP TRUST (Graduate Fellowships) 3665
LALOR FOUNDATION (Fellowships) 2489
LAND AND WATER RESOURCES R&D CORPORATION (Postgraduate Scholarships) 1412, 1413, 1414, 1461, 1462, 1463, 1554, 1555,
.... 1556, 1650, 1651, 1652, 1712, 1713, 1714
LANDSCAPE ARCHITECTURE FOUNDATION (Edith H. Henderson Scholarship) 444
LANDSCAPE ARCHITECTURE FOUNDATION (LAF/CLASS Fund Scholarships) 445, 1464
LANGUAGE LIAISON PROGRAM DIRECTORY 4081
LARAMIE COUNTY FARM BUREAU (Scholarships) 3666
LEARNING DISABILITIES ASSN OF AMERICA 4231
LEGACY SOCCER FOUNDATION, INC./LEVER BROTHERS (Endowed Scholarships) 3667
LEON M. JORDAN SCHOLARSHIP AND MONUMENT FUND 3668

LEOPOLD SCHEPP FOUNDATION (Graduate Awards) 3669
LEOPOLD SCHEPP FOUNDATION (Post-doctoral Awards) 3670
LEPRA (Medical Elective Student Grant) 2490
LESKO'S SELF-HELP BOOKS 4082
LESLIE T. POSEY & FRANCES U. POSEY FOUNDATION (Scholarships) 1024
LEUKEMIA SOCIETY OF AMERICA (Scholarships, Fellowships, and Grants) 2491
LIBERACE FOUNDATION FOR THE PERFORMING AND CREATIVE ARTS (Scholarship Fund) 1025, 1283
LIEDERKRANZ FOUNDATION, INC. (Scholarship Awards) 1284
LIFE SCIENCES RESEARCH FOUNDATION (LSRF Postdoctoral Fellowships) 1924
LIGHT WORK (Artist-in-Residence Program) 1026
LINCOLN UNIVERSITY (MacMillan Brown Agricultural Scholarship) 1465
LINCOLN UNIVERSITY (Scholarships & Prizes) 3671
LINCOLN UNIVERSITY (Sir John Ormond Scholarships) 108
LINK FOUNDATION (Energy Fellowship Program) 1557
LIST OF SCHOLARSHIPS AND AWARDS IN ELECTRICAL, ELECTRONICS, AND COMPUTER ENGINEERING 4083
LLOYD D. SWEET SCHOLARSHIP FOUNDATION (Scholarships) 3672
LONDON CHAMBER OF COMMERCE AND INDUSTRY EXAMINATIONS BOARD (Charles R. E. Bell Fund Scholarships) 12, 109, 1213
LONDON SCHOOL OF ECONOMICS & POLITICAL SCIENCE (Roseberry Studentship) 2764
LONDON SCHOOL OF ECONOMICS AND POLITICAL SCIENCE (Scholarships) 110, 2765, 3046, 3127
LOREN L. ZACHARY SOCIETY FOR THE PERFORMING ARTS (National Vocal Competition for Young Opera Singers) 1285
LOS ANGELES PROFESSIONAL CHAPTER OF SOCIETY OF PROFESSIONAL JOURNALISTS (Bill Farr Scholarship) 2849, 2850, 2851, 2852
LOUISIANA OFFICE OF STUDENT FINANCIAL ASSISTANCE
(Tuition Opportunity Program for Students-Teachers Award) 177, 234, 1558, 1653, 1715, 1925, 2015, 2104
LOVELACE RESPIRATORY RESEARCH INSTITUTE/UNIVERSITY OF NEW MEXICO (Graduate Fellowships) 1926, 1927, 2492, 2493
LUBBOCK AREA FOUNDATION, INC. (Scholarships) 3673
LUCY E. MEILLER EDUCATIONAL TRUST 3674
LULAC (LEAGUE OF UNITED LATIN AMERICAN CITIZENS) (National Scholarship Fund) 3675
LUPUS FOUNDATION OF AMERICA, INC. (Finzi Student Summer Fellowship) 2494, 2495
LUTHERAN BROTHERHOOD (Stafford Student Loans) 3676
LaFETRA OPERATING FOUNDATION (Fellowships for Training of Volunteers Abroad) 3677
MACQUARIE BANK (Graduate Management Scholarship) 111
MAINE COMMUNITY FOUNDATION (Scholarship Program) 3678
MAKARIOS SCHOLARSHIP FUND, INC. (Scholarships) 3679
MAKING A DIFFERENCE—CAREER OPPORTUNITIES IN DISABILITY-RELATED FIELDS 4084
MAKING IT THROUGH COLLEGE 4085
MAKING THE MOST OF YOUR COLLEGE EDUCATION 4086
MANITOBA STUDENT FINANCIAL ASSISTANCE PROGRAM 3680
MANOMET CENTER FOR CONSERVATION SCIENCES (Kathleen S. Anderson Award) 1928
MARCH OF DIMES BIRTH DEFECTS FOUNDATION (Nursing Scholarships) 2674
MARIN EDUCATIONAL FUND (Undergraduate Scholarship Program) 3681
MARINE CORPS TANKERS ASSOCIATION (John Cornelius Memorial Scholarship) 3682
MARINE TECHNOLOGY SOCIETY 4253
MARK B. HOLZMAN GRADUATE EDUCATION FOUNDATION 1374, 2199, 2299, 3047
MARK R. FUSCO FOUNDATION 3683
MARTIN MUSICAL SCHOLARSHIP FUND (Scholarships) 1286
MARY E. HODGES FUND 3684
MARYLAND HIGHER EDUCATION COMMISSION (Professional School Scholarships) 2200, 2300, 2602, 2675, 3048, 3252, 3306,
.... 3685, 3686, 3687, 3688
MARYLAND INSTITUTE COLLEGE OF ART (Fellowship Grants) 1027
MASSEY UNIVERSITY (Postdoctoral Fellowships) 3689
MATHEMATICAL ASSOCIATION OF AMERICA 4236

MATHESON GAS PRODUCTS FOUNDATION (Scholarships) 317, 670, 739, 1559, 2016, 2105

MATSUMAE INTERNATIONAL FOUNDATION (Fellowships) 3690

MAY THOMPSON HENRY TRUST 3691

MCDONALD'S (UNCF New York Tri-State Scholarships) 3692

MEDICAL LIBRARY ASSOCIATION (Continuing Education Award) 1147

MEDICAL LIBRARY ASSOCIATION (Minority Scholarship) 1148

MEDICAL RESEARCH COUNCIL (Doctoral and Postdoctoral Scholarships for Study Abroad) 2496

MEDICAL RESEARCH COUNCIL (Masters and Doctoral Scholarships) 2497

MEDICAL RESEARCH COUNCIL (Postdoctoral Scholarships for Study in South Africa) 2498

MEDICAL RESEARCH COUNCIL (Studentships, Fellowships, and Training Awards) 2499

MEDICAL RESEARCH COUNCIL OF CANADA (Doctoral Research Award Program) 2500

MEDICAL SCHOOL ADMISSION REQUIREMENTS 4087

MEDICINE—A CHANCE TO MAKE A DIFFERENCE 4088

MEMORIAL FOUNDATION FOR JEWISH CULTURE (International Fellowships in Jewish Studies) 917, 918, 919, 920

MENDELSSOHN SCHOLARSHIP FOUNDATION (Composers Scholarships) 1287

MERCYHURST COLLEGE D'ANGELO SCHOOL OF MUSIC (Young Artists Competition) 1288, 1289

MERVYN'S (Kilmartin Educational Scholarship Program) 3693

METROPOLITAN MUSEUM OF ART (Bothmer, Dale, Mills, Whitney, & Forchheimer Art History Fellowships) 1028, 1029, 1030, 1031

MICHIGAN COMMISSION ON INDIAN AFFAIRS; MICHIGAN DEPT OF CIVIL RIGHTS (Tuition Waiver Program) 3694

MICHIGAN GUARANTY AGENCY (Stafford and PLUS Loans) 3695

MICHIGAN HIGHER EDUCATION ASSISTANCE AUTHORITY (Michigan Tuition Grants) 3696

MICHIGAN SOCIETY OF FELLOWS (Postdoctoral Fellowships in the Humanities & Arts, Sciences, and Professions) 3697

MIDWEST ROOFING CONTRACTORS ASSOCIATION (Construction Industry Scholarships) 498

MIDWEST STUDENT EXCHANGE PROGRAM (Tuition Reduction) 3698

MILHEIM FOUNDATION FOR CANCER RESEARCH (Cancer Research Grants) 2501

MILITARY ORDER OF THE PURPLE HEART (Sons, Daughters, and Grandchildren Scholarship Program) 3699

MINERALOGICAL SOCIETY OF AMERICA (MSA Grant for Research in Crystallography) 1560, 1561

MINISTERIO DE ASUNTOS EXTERIORES (Scholarships) 3700

MINISTRY OF EDUCATION AND TRAINING; ONTARIO STUDENT ASSISTANCE PROGRAM (OSAP) 3701

MINISTRY OF EDUCATION OF THE REPUBLIC OF CHINA (Scholarships for Foreign Students) 921

MINISTRY OF EDUCATION, SCIENCE, AND CULTURE (Icelandic Studies Scholarships) 922

MINISTRY OF THE FLEMISH COMMUNITY (Fellowships) 112, 798, 1032, 1290, 1836, 2201, 2301, 2766, 3049, 3128

MINNESOTA AUTOMOBILE DEALERS ASSOCIATION (MADA Scholarships) 671, 3307

MINNESOTA HIGHER EDUCATION SERVICES OFFICE (Health Professions Loan Forgiveness) 2202, 2603, 2676, 3702, 3703

MINNESOTA STATE DEPARTMENT OF VETERANS AFFAIRS (Veterans Grants) 3704

MISSISSIPPI OFFICE OF STATE STUDENT FINANCIAL AID (Public Management Graduate Internship Program) 113, 3050, 3129

MONGOLIA SOCIETY (Dr. Gombojab Hangin Memorial Scholarship) 3705, 3706

MONTANA ARTS COUNCIL (Individual Artists Fellowships) 1033, 1291

MONTREAL NEUROLOGICAL INSTITUTE (Izaak Walton Preston Robb Fellowship & Jeanne Timmins Costello Fellowships) 2502

MORRIS SCHOLARSHIP FUND (Scholarships for Minorities in Iowa) 3707

MORTAR BOARD NATIONAL FOUNDATION (Fellowships) 3708

MOTHER JOSEPH ROGAN MARYMOUNT FOUNDATION (Grant and Loan Programs) 3709

MUSCULAR DYSTROPHY ASSOCIATION (Postdoctoral Research Grants) 2503

MUSIC ACADEMY OF THE WEST (Scholarships) 1292

MUSIC SCHOLARSHIP GUIDE (3rd Edition) 4089

MYASTHENIA GRAVIS FOUNDATION OF AMERICA, INC. (Kermit E. Osserman Fellowships) 2504, 2505, 2677

MYCOLOGICAL SOCIETY OF AMERICA (Graduate Fellowships) 1929

McCORD CAREER CENTER (Level II McCord Medical/Music Scholarship) 1293, 2203, 2302, 2604, 2678, 3308

NAACP NATIONAL OFFICE (Agnes Jones Jackson Scholarship) 3710

NAACP NATIONAL OFFICE (NAACP Willems Scholarship) 318, 2017, 2106

NAT'L CONSORTIUM FOR GRADUATE DEGREES FOR MINORITIES IN ENGINEERING & SCIENCE, INC.
(GEM Fellowship Programs) 319, 1837

NATION INSTITUTE (Nation Internship Program) 2853

NATIONAL ACADEMY OF EDUCATION (Spencer Postdoctoral Fellowship Program) 178, 235, 799, 2767, 3187

NATIONAL ACUPUNCTURE DETOXIFICATION ASSOCIATION 4143

NATIONAL AERONAUTICS AND SPACE ADMINISTRATION
(Graduate Student Researcher's Program-Underrepresented Minority Focus) 394, 395, 672, 740, 1562, 2018, 2107, 2108

NATIONAL AIR TRANSPORTATION ASSOCIATION FOUNDATION
(John W. Godwin, Jr., Memorial Scholarship Fund) 114, 396, 3309

NATIONAL ALLIANCE FOR EXCELLENCE, INC. (National Scholarship Competition) 3711

NATIONAL ALLIANCE FOR RESEARCH ON SCHIZOPHRENIA AND DEPRESSION
(Young, Independent, & Distinguished Investigator Awards) 2506

NATIONAL ART MATERIALS TRADE ASSOCIATION (NAMTA Scholarships) 3712

NATIONAL ASSN FOR MUSIC THERAPY 4246

NATIONAL ASSN OF EXECUTIVE SECRETARIES AND ADMINISTRATIVE ASSISTANTS (Scholarship Award Program) 3310

NATIONAL ASSN OF SOCIAL WORKERS 4281

NATIONAL ASSOCIATION OF AMERICAN BUSINESS CLUBS (AMBUCS Scholarships for Therapists) 236, 2605

NATIONAL ASSOCIATION OF ANIMAL BREEDERS (NAAB) 4152

NATIONAL ASSOCIATION OF BLACK JOURNALISTS (NABJ Scholarship Program) 2854, 2855

NATIONAL ASSOCIATION OF DENTAL LABORATORIES 4189

NATIONAL ASSOCIATION OF HISPANIC JOURNALISTS (NAHJ Scholarship Program) 2856, 2857

NATIONAL ASSOCIATION OF PURCHASING MANAGEMENT (Doctoral Dissertation Grant Program) 115, 673

NATIONAL ASSOCIATION OF SCHOOLS OF PUBLIC AFFAIRS AND ADMINISTRATION 4169

NATIONAL ASSOCIATION OF STATE MENTAL HEALTH PROGRAM DIRECTORS RESEARCH INSTITUTE
(Postdoctoral Research Fellowships) 2507

NATIONAL ASSOCIATION OF TEACHERS OF SINGING (Artist Awards Competition) 1294

NATIONAL ASSOCIATION OF THE DEAF (Stokoe Scholarship) 237, 2303, 2606

NATIONAL ASSOCIATION OF UNIVERSITY WOMEN (Fellowship Award) 3713

NATIONAL ASSOCIATION OF WATER COMPANIES—NEW JERSEY CHAPTER (Scholarship) 116, 499, 674, 741, 1930, 2019, 2858

NATIONAL ATHLETIC TRAINERS' ASSOCIATION (NATA Scholarship Program) 2607

NATIONAL BLACK MBA ASSOCIATION INC. (Annual Scholarship Program) 117

NATIONAL BROADCASTING SOCIETY (Alpha Epsilon Rho Scholarships) 2859

NATIONAL CARTOONISTS SOCIETY 4171

NATIONAL CENTER FOR ATMOSPHERIC RESEARCH (Graduate Student Research Fellowships) 1563, 1716, 2020

NATIONAL CENTER FOR HOMEOPATHY 4221

NATIONAL CHAMBER OF COMMERCE FOR WOMEN (Scholarships & Research Grants) 118, 3188

NATIONAL CHAPTER OF CANADA IODE (War Memorial Doctoral Scholarship) 3714

NATIONAL CLEARINGHOUSE FOR PROFESSIONS IN SPECIAL EDUCATION 4284

NATIONAL COLLEGIATE ATHLETIC ASSOCIATION (Graduate Scholarship Program) 3715, 3716

NATIONAL COUNCIL FOR THE SOCIAL STUDIES (Grant for the Enhancement of Geographic Literacy) 1564, 2768

NATIONAL COUNCIL OF FARMER COOPERATIVES (Graduate Awards) 119, 1466, 2860, 3051, 3253

NATIONAL COUNCIL OF STATE GARDEN CLUBS, INC. (Scholarships) 446, 1467

NATIONAL COUNCIL OF TEACHERS OF ENGLISH RESEARCH FOUNDATION (NCTE) (Teacher-Researcher Grants) 1149, 4237

NATIONAL CUSTOMS BROKERS & FORWARDERS ASSN OF AMERICA INC (NCBFAA Scholarship) 120

NATIONAL DIRECTORY OF CORPORATE GIVING 4090

NATIONAL DO SOMETHING LEAGUE (Community Project Awards) 3717

NATIONAL ENVIRONMENTAL HEALTH ASSOCIATION (NEHA/AAS Scholarship) 1654, 2304

NATIONAL FALLEN FIREFIGHTERS FOUNDATION (Scholarship Program) 3718

NATIONAL FEDERATION OF THE BLIND (Educator of Tomorrow Award) 238, 320, 321, 447, 448, 549, 800, 1034, 1150,
.... 1214, 1375, 1565, 2204, 2305, 2508, 2679, 2961,
.... 3052, 3719, 3720, 3721, 3722, 3723, 3724

NATIONAL FIRE PROTECTION ASSN. (Public Fire Protection) 4204

NATIONAL FOREST FOUNDATION (Firefighters' Scholarship Fund) 3725

NATIONAL FOUNDATION FOR LONG-TERM HEALTH CARE (James D. Durante Nurse Scholarship Program) 2680

NATIONAL FUNERAL DIRECTORS ASSOCIATION 4212

NATIONAL GALLERY OF ART (Predoctoral Fellowship Program) 1035

NATIONAL GAY PILOTS ASSOCIATION (Pilot Scholarships) 397, 3311

NATIONAL GUILD OF COMMUNITY SCHOOLS OF THE ARTS (Young Composers Awards) 1295

NATIONAL HEADACHE FOUNDATION (Research Grant) 2509

NATIONAL HEADACHE FOUNDATION (Seymour Diamond Clinical Fellowship in Headache Education) 2510

NATIONAL HEALTH RESEARCH AND DEVELOPMENT PROGRAM (Training & Career Awards) 2306

NATIONAL HEALTH SERVICE CORPS (NHSC Scholarship Program) 2205, 2608, 2681

NATIONAL HEMOPHILIA FOUNDATION (Career Development Award in Bleeding Disorders Research) 2511

NATIONAL HEMOPHILIA FOUNDATION (Judith Graham Pool Postdoctoral Research Fellowships) 2512

NATIONAL HEMOPHILIA FOUNDATION (Nursing Excellence Fellowship) 2682

NATIONAL HEMOPHILIA FOUNDATION (Social Work Excellence Fellowship) 3254

NATIONAL HUMANITIES CENTER (Burroughs Wellcome Fund Fellowships in the History of Modern Medicine) 1782, 2307, 2513, 2962

NATIONAL HUMANITIES CENTER (Lilly Fellowships in Religion and the Humanities) 801, 1036, 1151, 1215, 1376, 2769, 2963

NATIONAL ITALIAN AMERICAN FOUNDATION (Norman R. Peterson Scholarship) 13, 121, 923, 1296, 2206, 2207, 2208, 2308,
.... 2309, 2514, 2515, 2718, 3726, 3727, 3728,
.... 3729, 3730, 3731, 3732

NATIONAL JUNIOR HORTICULTURAL ASSOCIATION (Scottish Gardening Scholarship) 1468

NATIONAL LEAGUE FOR NURSING 4252

NATIONAL LEAGUE OF AMERICAN PEN WOMEN, INC. (Scholarships for Mature Women) 1037, 1152, 1297

NATIONAL MULTIPLE SCLEROSIS SOCIETY (Postdoctoral Fellowship Program) 2516, 2517

NATIONAL OPTOMETRIC ASSOCIATION 4255

NATIONAL PARKS SERVICE (Science Scholars Program) 924, 1566, 1655, 1717, 1838,
.... 1931, 2021, 2770, 3255

NATIONAL PHYSICAL SCIENCE CONSORTIUM (Graduate Fellowships for Minorities & Women in the Physical Sciences) 550, 742, 1567, 2022, 2109

NATIONAL PRESS PHOTOGRAPHERS FOUNDATION (Kit C. King Graduate Scholarship Fund) 2861

NATIONAL PRESS PHOTOGRAPHERS FOUNDATION, KAPPA ALPHA MU
(College Photographer of the Year Competition) 2862

NATIONAL REHABILITATION COUNSELING ASSN. 4275

NATIONAL RESEARCH COUNCIL (Howard Hughes Medical Institute Predoctoral Fellowships in Biological Sciences) 1932, 2023, 2310, 2518

NATIONAL RESEARCH COUNCIL (Integrated Manufacturing Predoctoral Fellowships) 122, 675

NATIONAL RESEARCH COUNCIL OF CANADA (Research Associateships) 322, 1415, 1568, 1718, 1933, 2024

NATIONAL RESEARCH FOUNDATION (NRF Honors & Postgraduate Bursaries) 323, 1469, 1569, 1934, 2025, 2110, 2311

NATIONAL RESTAURANT ASSOCIATION EDUCATIONAL FOUNDATION (Graduate Degree Scholarship) 2719, 4208

NATIONAL SCIENCES AND ENGINEERING RESEARCH COUNCIL OF CANADA (Graduate Scholarships) 324, 325, 398, 399, 551, 552, 611, 612, 676,
.... 677, 1416, 1417, 1570, 1571, 1719, 1720, 1839,
.... 1840, 1935, 1936, 2026, 2027, 2863, 2864

NATIONAL SCIENCE FOUNDATION (NATO Postdoctoral Science Fellowship Program) 326, 1841

NATIONAL SCIENCE TEACHERS ASSN 4279

NATIONAL SOCIETY OF ACCOUNTANTS SCHOLARSHIP FOUNDATION (Stanley H. Stearman Scholarship Award) 123

NATIONAL SOCIETY OF BLACK ENGINEERS (Scholarships) 327, 400, 449, 500, 553, 613, 678, 743

NATIONAL SOCIETY OF PROFESSIONAL ENGINEERS 4197

NATIONAL SOCIETY OF PUBLIC ACCOUNTANTS 4140

NATIONAL SPACE CLUB (Dr. Robert H. Goddard Scholarship) 328, 329, 401, 402, 1842, 1843, 2964, 3312

NATIONAL SPEAKERS ASSOCIATION (NSA Scholarship) 1153

NATIONAL SPELEOLOGICAL SOCIETY (Ralph W. Stone Research Grant) 1572

NATIONAL STRENGTH & CONDITIONING ASSN. (Challenge Scholarships) 239, 240, 2312, 2313, 2609, 2610

NATIONAL STUDENT NURSES' ASSOCIATION FOUNDATION (Scholarship Program) 2683

NATIONAL TECHNICAL ASSOCIATION, INC.
(Scholarship Competitions for Minorities and Women in Science and Engineering) 330, 1844, 2111

NATIONAL TOOLING AND MACHINING ASSN 4269

NATIONAL TWENTY AND FOUR (Memorial Scholarships) 3733

NATIONAL UNIVERSITY OF SINGAPORE (Mobil-NUS Postgraduate Medical Research Scholarship) 2519, 3734

NATIONAL WELSH-AMERICAN FOUNDATION (Exchange Scholarship Program) 3735

NATIONAL WRITERS ASSOCIATION 4186

NATIONAL WRITERS ASSOCIATION FOUNDATION (Scholarship) 1154

NAVAL HISTORICAL CENTER (Internship Program) 124, 179, 241, 1038, 1783, 2965

NAVAL RESERVE RECRUITING COMMAND (Armed Forces Health Professions Scholarships) 2209, 2684

NAVY RECRUITING COMMAND (Armed Forces Health Professions Scholarships) 679, 2210, 2314, 2611

NAVY-MARINE CORPS RELIEF SOCIETY (Spouse Tuition Aid Program) 3736

NEED A LIFT? (48th edition-1999 Issue) 4091

NELLIE MAE (Student Loans) 3737

NETHERLANDS ORGANIZATION FOR INTERNATIONAL COOPERATION IN HIGHER EDUCATION
(Grants from Dutch Government & European Union) 3738, 3739, 3740

NETTIE MILLHOLLON EDUCATIONAL TRUST ESTATE (Student Loans) 3741

NEVADA DEPT. OF EDUCATION (Student Incentive Grant Program) 3742

NEW BEDFORD PORT SOCIETY- LADIES BRANCH (Limited Scholarship Grant) 3743

NEW ENGLAND BOARD OF HIGHER EDUCATION (New England Regional Student Program) 3744

NEW HAMPSHIRE HIGHER EDUCATION ASSISTANCE FOUNDATION (Federal Family Education Loan Program) 3745

NEW JERSEY DEPT. OF HIGHER EDUCATION (Educational Opportunity Fund Grants) 3746

NEW JERSEY DEPT. OF MILITARY & VETERANS AFFAIRS (Veterans Tuition Credit Program) 3747

NEW JERSEY OFFICE OF STUDENT ASSISTANCE (King Scholarship) 2211, 2315, 3748

NEW JERSEY STATE OPERA (Cash Awards) 1298

NEW JERSEY STATE OPERA (International Vocal Competition) 1299

NEW MEXICO FARM AND LIVESTOCK BUREAU (Memorial Scholarships) 3749

NEW SCHOOL FOR MUSIC STUDY (Graduate Fellowships in Piano Teaching) 1300

NEW YORK CITY DEPT. CITYWIDE ADMINISTRATIVE SERVICES (Urban Fellows Program) 125, 450, 3130, 3256

NEW YORK FINANCIAL WRITERS' ASSOCIATION (Scholarship Program) 2865

NEW YORK STATE DEPARTMENT OF HEALTH - PRIMARY CARE SERVICE CORPS (Scholarships) 2612, 2685

NEW YORK STATE EDUCATION DEPT. (Awards, Scholarships, and Fellowships) 3750

NEW YORK STATE HIGHER EDUCATION SERVICES CORPORATION
(N.Y. State Regents Professional/Health Care Opportunity Scholarships) 126, 331, 451, 2212, 2316, 2613, 2686,
.... 3053, 3189, 3257, 3751, 3752

NEW YORK STATE SENATE (Legislative Fellows Program;
R. J. Roth Journalism Fellowship; R. A. Wiebe Public Service Fellowship) 127, 2866, 3131

NEW YORK STATE THEATRE INSTITUTE (Internships in Theatrical Production) 128, 242, 1039, 1155, 1301, 2867

NEW ZEALAND FEDERATION OF UNIVERSITY WOMEN (Waikato Merit Award) 3753

NEW ZEALAND VICE-CHANCELLORS' COMMITTEE (Commonwealth Scholarship) 3754

NEWBERRY LIBRARY (Francis C. Allen Fellowships) 3755

NEWBERRY LIBRARY (Long-Term Fellowships) 802, 925, 1040, 1156, 1302, 1377, 1573, 1784, 2771, 2966

NEWBERRY LIBRARY (Monticello College Foundation Fellowship For Women) 803, 926, 1157, 1378, 2772, 2967

NEWBERRY LIBRARY (Short-Term Fellowships) 804, 927, 1041, 1158, 1303, 1379, 1574, 1785, 2773, 2968

NEWBERRY LIBRARY (Special Fellowships) 805, 928, 1042, 1159, 1304, 1380, 1575, 1786, 2774, 2969

NEWBERRY LIBRARY (Weiss/Brown Publication Subvention Award) 929, 1160, 1305, 2970

NEWSPAPER ASSN OF AMERICA 4250

NEWSPAPER FEATURES COUNCIL 4170

NEWSPAPERS, DIVERSITY & YOU 4092

NICHOLL SCHOLARSHIPS (Undergraduate and Graduate Scholarships) 3756

NINETY-NINES, INC. (Amelia Earhart Memorial Scholarships) 403, 3313

NINETY-NINES, SAN FERNANDO VALLEY CHAPTER/VAN NUYS AIRPORT (Aviation Career Scholarships) 129, 404, 3314

NORTH AMERICAN BAPTIST SEMINARY (Financial Aid Grants) 1381

NORTH ATLANTIC TREATY ORGANIZATION (NATO Science Fellowships for Non-U.S. Citizens) 332, 1418, 1845

NORTH CAROLINA DEPARTMENT OF PUBLIC INSTRUCTION (Scholarship Loan Program for Prospective Teachers) 243, 1161, 2317, 2614

NORTH CAROLINA DIVISION OF SERVICES FOR THE BLIND (Rehabilitation Assistance for Visually Impaired) 3757

NORTH CAROLINA STATE EDUCATION ASSISTANCE AUTHORITY (Student Financial Aid for North Carolinians) 3758

NORTHERN IRELAND DEPT. OF EDUCATION (Post-graduate Studentships) 806, 1846, 2775

NORTHERN NEW JERSEY UNIT-HERB SOCIETY OF AMERICA (Scholarship) 1470, 1937

NORTHWEST DANISH FOUNDATION (Scholarships) 3759

NORWEGIAN INFORMATION SERVICE (Norwegian Emigration Fund of 1975) 930

NORWICH JUBILEE ESPERANTO FOUNDATION (Travel Grants) 1216

NOVA SCOTIA COLLEGE OF ART AND DESIGN (Scholarships) 1043

NOVARTIS FOUNDATION (Bursary Scheme) 1847, 1938, 2028, 2213, 2318, 2520, 2615

NUCLEAR AGE PEACE FOUNDATION (Lena Chang Scholarship Awards) 3760

O'BRIEN FOUNDATION (Fellowship) 3761

OAK RIDGE ASSOCIATED UNIVERSITIES (Laboratory Graduate Research Participation Program) 333, 554, 680, 744, 1576, 1656, 1721, 1787, 1939, 2112, 3054, 3132

OAK RIDGE ASSOCIATED UNIVERSITIES (National Science Foundation Graduate Research Fellowships) 334, 405, 452, 501, 555, 614, 681, 745, 1577, 1722, 1848, 1940, 2029, 2113, 2776, 2971, 3190, 3315

OAK RIDGE INSTITUTE FOR SCIENCE AND EDUCATION
(Minority Student Administrative Summer Internship Program) 14, 130, 244, 335, 336, 337, 338, 339, 340, 341, 342, 502, 503, 504, 505, 506, 507, 556, 557, 558, 559, 560, 561, 615, 616, 682, 683, 684, 685, 686, 687, 688, 689, 690, 746, 747, 748, 749, 750, 751, 752, 753, 754, 1471, 1472, 1473, 1578, 1579, 1580, 1581, 1582, 1583, 1584, 1585, 1586, 1657, 1658, 1659, 1660, 1661, 1662, 1663, 1664, 1665, 1723, 1724, 1725, 1726, 1727, 1728, 1729, 1730, 1788, 1849, 1850, 1851, 1852, 1941, 1942, 1943, 1944, 1945, 1946, 2030, 2031, 2032, 2033, 2034, 2035, 2036, 2037, 2038, 2114, 2115, 2116, 2117, 2118, 2119, 2120, 2121, 2122, 2214, 2319, 2521, 2522, 2616, 2687

OCCUPATIONAL OUTLOOK HANDBOOK 4093

OHIO BOARD OF REGENTS (Regents Graduate/Professional Fellowship Program) 3762

OLFACTORY RESEARCH FUND (Tova Fellowship & Annual Grant Program) 3191

OMAHA PRESBYTERIAN SEMINARY FOUNDATION (Apollos Program) 1382

OMAHA SYMPHONY GUILD (International New Music Competition) 1306

OMOHUNDRO INSTITUTE OF EARLY AMERICAN HISTORY AND CULTURE
(Andrew W. Mellon Postdoctoral Research Fellowship) 2972

ONCOLOGY NURSING FOUNDATION (Scholarships, Grants, Awards, & Honors) 2688

ONEIDA HIGHER EDUCATION (Various Fellowships, Internships, and Scholarships) 3763

ONTARIO CHORAL FEDERATION (Leslie Bell Prize) 1307

ONTARIO MINISTRY OF EDUCATION AND TRAINING (John Charles Polanyi Prizes) 131, 1162, 1947, 2039, 2123, 2215, 2973, 3764, 3765

OPEN SOCIETY INSTITUTE (Environmental Management Fellowships) 508, 691, 755, 807, 1419, 1474, 1587, 1666, 1731, 1948, 2040, 2124, 3258

OPEN SOCIETY INSTITUTE (Individual Project Fellowships) 931, 3055, 3133, 3192, 3259

OPEN SOCIETY INSTITUTE (Network Scholarship Programs) 3766

OPERA AMERICA (Fellowship Program) 132, 1308

OREGON DEPARTMENT OF VETERANS' AFFAIRS (Educational Aid for Oregon Veterans) 3767

OREGON STATE SCHOLARSHIP COMMISSION (Federal Family Education Loan Program) 3768

OREGON STATE SCHOLARSHIP COMMISSION (Private Scholarship Programs Administered by the Commission) 3769

ORENTREICH FOUNDATION FOR THE ADVANCEMENT OF SCIENCE (Research Grants) 2523

ORGAN HISTORICAL SOCIETY (E. Power Biggs Fellowship) 1309

ORGANIZATION OF AMERICAN STATES (Leo S. Rowe Pan American Fund) 3770

ORIENTAL CERAMIC SOCIETY (George De Manasce Memorial Trust Fund) 1044

OUR WORLD-UNDERWATER SCHOLARSHIP SOCIETY (Scholarship & Internships) 1732

OUTDOOR WRITERS ASSOCIATION OF AMERICA (Bodie McDowell Scholarship Program) 2868

OXFORD FORESTRY INSTITUTE (Master's Fellowship in Forestry) 1588

Order form for book list on theatre\writing careers 4094

P.E.O. SISTERHOOD (International Peace Scholarship Fund) 3771

PACIFIC CULTURAL FOUNDATION (Grants on Chinese Studies) 932

PALEONTOLOGICAL SOCIETY 4258

PALESTINE EXPLORATION FUND RESEARCH GRANT 933

PARAMOUNT PICTURES (Paramount Internships in Film & Television) 1045, 1163

PARAPSYCHOLOGY FOUNDATION (D. Scott Rogo Award for Parapsychological Award) 3193

PARAPSYCHOLOGY FOUNDATION (Eileen J. Garrett Scholarship) 3194

PARAPSYCHOLOGY FOUNDATION (Grant Program) 3195

PARENTS AND FRIENDS OF LESBIANS AND GAYS—PFLAG CINCINNATI (Scholarships) 3772

PARENTS, FAMILIES, AND FRIENDS OF LESBIANS AND GAYS-NEW ORLEANS CHAPTER (Scholarships) 3773, 3774

PARLIAMENT OF AUSTRALIA (Australian Parliamentary Fellowship in Association with Australasian Political Science Assn.) 3134

PAUL O. AND MARY BOGHOSSIAN FOUNDATION 3775

PEACE RESEARCH CENTRE (Peace Research Loan Scholarship) 2777, 3135, 3260

PENINSULA COMMUNITY FOUNDATION (Crain Educational Grants Program) 3776

PENNSYLVANIA DEPARTMENT OF MILITARY AFFAIRS—BUREAU OF VETERANS AFFAIRS (Scholarships) 3777

PERSPECTIVES: AUDITION ADVICE FOR SINGERS 4095

PERSPECTIVES: THE SINGER/MANAGER RELATIONSHIP 4096

PETER BLOSSER STUDENT LOAN FUND 3778

PEW YOUNGER SCHOLARS PROGRAM (Graduate Fellowships) 808, 1383, 2778

PFIZER PHARMACEUTICALS (Pfizer/AGS Postdoctoral Fellowship Program) 2524

PHARMACEUTICAL RESEARCH AND MANUFACTURERS OF AMERICA FOUNDATION
(Fellowships in Pharmacology-Morphology) 1949, 2216, 2217, 2320, 2321, 2322, 2323,
.... 2324, 2325, 2326, 2525, 2526

PHARMACY SCHOOL ADMISSION REQUIREMENTS 4097

PHI ALPHA THETA HISTORY HONOR SOCIETY (Doctoral Scholarship Awards) 2974, 2975, 2976, 2977, 2978

PHI BETA KAPPA (Mary Isabel Sibley Fellowship) 934, 1164, 1217

PHI DELTA KAPPA, INC. (Graduate Fellowships in Educational Leadership) 245

PHI ETA SIGMA (Scholarship Program) 3779

PHILLIPS FOUNDATION (Journalism Fellowship Program) 2869

PHYSICIAN ASSISTANT FOUNDATION (Scholarships, Traineeships, & Grants) 2327

PI GAMMA MU INTERNATIONAL HONOR SOCIETY IN SOCIAL SCIENCE (Scholarships) 2779

PILOT INTERNATIONAL FOUNDATION (Marie Newton Sepia Memorial Scholarship) 246, 2218, 2527, 2617, 3196

PILOT INTERNATIONAL FOUNDATION (PIF/Lifeline Scholarship) 247, 2219, 2528, 2618, 3197

PILOT INTERNATIONAL FOUNDATION (Ruby Newhall Memorial Scholarship) 248, 2220, 2529, 2619, 3198

PINE BLUFFS AREA CHAMBER OF COMMERCE (Scholarship) 3780

PING AMERICAN COLLEGE GOLF GUIDE 4098

PITT RIVERS MUSEUM (James A. Swan Fund) 935

PIXAR ANIMATION STUDIOS (Summer Internships) 1046

PLANNING FOR A DENTAL EDUCATION 4099

POETRY SOCIETY OF AMERICA (George Bogin Memorial Award) 1165, 1166, 1167

POLISH UNIVERSITY CLUB OF NEW JERSEY (Scholarships) 3781

PONTIFICAL INSTITUTE OF MEDIEVAL STUDIES (Fellowships) 2979

POPULATION COUNCIL (Fellowships in Population Sciences) 133, 936, 1789, 3261

POPULATION COUNCIL (Fellowships in Social Sciences) 134, 937, 1589, 1790, 2328, 3262

PORTUGUESE CONTINENTAL UNION (Scholarships) 3782

POTASH AND PHOSPHATE INSTITUTE (J. Fielding Reed PPI Fellowships) 1475, 1950

POWER STUDY TO UP YOUR GRADES IN MATH 4100, 4101, 4102, 4103

PRESBYTERIAN CHURCH (U.S.A.) (Fund For Graduate Education) 249

PRESBYTERIAN CHURCH (U.S.A.) (Native American Education Grant) 3783

PRESBYTERIAN CHURCH (U.S.A.) (Undergraduate/Graduate Loan Programs) 3784

PRESIDENT'S COMMISSION ON WHITE HOUSE FELLOWSHIPS 135, 3056, 3136, 3263

PRESS CLUB OF DALLAS FOUNDATION (Scholarship) 136, 2870

PRIDE FOUNDATION & GREATER SEATTLE BUSINESS ASSOCIATION (Scholarships for Gays & Lesbians) 3785

PRINCESS GRACE FOUNDATION-USA (Grants for Young Playwrights) 1168

PRINCETON UNIVERSITY—SHELBY CULLOM DAVIS CENTER FOR HISTORICAL STUDIES (Post-doctoral Fellowships) 2980

PROCEEDINGS AND ADDRESSES OF THE AMERICAN PHILOSOPHICAL ASSN. 4104

PROCTER FELLOWSHIPS (Fellowships at Princeton University) 3786

PROFESSIONAL SECRETARIES INTERNATIONAL-THE ASSOCIATION FOR OFFICE PROFESSIONALS 4280

PROFESSIONAL GROUNDS MANAGEMENT SOCIETY (Anne Seaman Memorial Scholarships) 1476

PROFESSIONAL HORSEMEN'S SCHOLARSHIP FUND, INC. 3787

PUBLIC EMPLOYEES ROUNDTABLE (Public Service Scholarships) 3788

PURINA MILLS, INC. (Research Fellowship) 1477

Physician Assistant Programs Directory 4105

Pour Man's Friend: A Guide and Reference for Bar Personnel 4106

Professional Aviation Maintenance Association 4163

QUEEN ELISABETH INTERNATIONAL MUSIC COMPETITION OF BELGIUM 1310

QUEEN MARIE JOSE (International Musical Prize Contest) 1311

QUEEN SONJA INTERNATIONAL MUSIC COMPETITION (Voice Competition) 1312

QUEEN'S UNIVERSITY OF BELFAST (Mary McNeill Scholarship in Irish Studies) 938, 939, 1478, 2329, 3789, 3790, 3791

RADIO AND TELEVISION NEWS DIRECTORS ASSOCIATION 4167

RADIO AND TELEVISION NEWS DIRECTORS FOUNDATION (Jane Pauley Internship) 3792

RADIO FREE EUROPE/RADIO LIBERTY (Intern Program for Journalists) 2871, 3137

RAYMOND J. HARRIS EDUCATION TRUST 343, 1479, 2221, 2330, 3057

REALTY FOUNDATION OF NEW YORK (Scholarship Program) 3793

RED RIVER VALLEY FIGHTER PILOTS ASSOCIATION (River Rats Scholarship Grant Programs) 3794

REFRIGERATION SERVICE ENGINEERS SOCIETY 4220

RESEARCH COUNCIL OF NORWAY (Senior Scientist Visiting Fellowship) 137, 809, 1480, 1590, 1667, 1853,
....2222, 2331, 2530, 2780

RESERVE OFFICERS ASSOCIATION OF THE UNITED STATES
(Henry J. Reilly Memorial Scholarships for Graduates) 3795

RESOURCES FOR THE FUTURE (Joseph L. Fisher Dissertation Fellowships) 138, 1420, 1421, 1422, 1423, 1591, 1592, 1593, 1594,
....1668, 1669, 1670, 1671, 2781, 2782, 2783, 2784

RHODE ISLAND HIGHER EDUCATION ASSISTANCE AUTHORITY (Loan Program; Plus Loans) 3796

RHYTHM & HUES STUDIOS (Computer Graphics Scholarship) 1047

RICHARD E. MERWIN INTERNATIONAL AWARD 3797

RIPON COLLEGE (Performance/Recognition Tuition Scholarships) 1048, 1169, 1313

RISING STAR INTERNSHIPS (Internships and Part-Time Employment for Students) 3798

ROB AND BESSIE WELDER WILDLIFE FOUNDATION (Scholarship Program) 1672

ROBERT SCHRECK MEMORIAL FUND (Grants) 344, 453, 1384, 2041, 2223, 2332

ROBSON MCLEAN WS (Brown Downie Church of Scotland Fellowship) 1385

ROCKEFELLER ARCHIVE CENTER (Grants-in-aid) 3799

ROCKEFELLER FOUNDATION (African Dissertation Internship Awards) 250, 692, 940, 1481, 1595, 1673, 1951, 2333, 2620

ROCKEFELLER FOUNDATION (Postdoctoral Residency Program in the Humanities) 810

ROEHER INSTITUTE (Graduate Research Grants) 251

RONALD E. McNAIR POST-BACCALAUREATE ACHIEVEMENT PROGRAM 3800

ROTARY FOUNDATION OF ROTARY INTERNATIONAL (Grants for University Teachers) 3801

ROYAL & SUN ALLIANCE (Ronnie Scott Scholarships for the Study of Jazz) 1314

ROYAL COLLEGE OF OBSTETRICIANS AND GYNECOLOGISTS (Eden Travelling Fellowship) 2224

ROYAL COLLEGE OF VETERINARY SURGEONS (Sir Frederick Smith & Miss Aleen Cust Research Fellowships) 2334, 2335

ROYAL INSTITUTE OF BRITISH ARCHITECTS (RIBA Research Awards) 454

ROYAL NEIGHBORS OF AMERICA (Non-traditional Scholarship) 3802

ROYAL NORWEGIAN EMBASSY (May 8th Memorial Fund) 3803

ROYAL PHILHARMONIC SOCIETY (Julius Isserlis Scholarship) 1315

ROYAL SOCIETY (John Murray Fund) 1596, 1733, 1952, 2125

ROYAL SOCIETY OF CHEMISTRY (Corday-Morgan Memorial Fund) 2042, 2043, 2044, 2045

ROYAL SOCIETY OF EDINBURGH (BP Research Fellowships) 562, 693, 756, 1597, 2046, 2126, 3804

ROYAL SOCIETY OF MEDICINE 4241

ROYAL THAI EMBASSY, OFFICE OF EDUCATIONAL AFFAIRS (Revenue Dept. Scholarships for Thai Students) 139, 563, 617, 3058

RTCA, INC. (William E. Jackson Award) 406, 618

RURITAN NATIONAL FOUNDATION (Grant and Loan Program) 3805

RYAN DAVIES MEMORIAL FUND (Grants) 1316

S.S. HUEBNER FOUNDATION FOR INSURANCE EDUCATION (Fellowships) 140

SACHS FOUNDATION (Scholarship Program) 3806

SAMUEL H. KRESS FOUNDATION (Fellowship Program) 1049

SAMUEL LEMBERG SCHOLARSHIP LOAN FUND INC. (Scholarships-Loans) 3807

SAN ANGELO SYMPHONY SOCIETY (Sorantin Young Artist Award) 1317

SAN FRANCISCO CONSERVATORY OF MUSIC (Various Scholarships) 1318

SAN JOSE STATE UNIVERSITY (Scholarships) 3808

SARA'S WISH FOUNDATION (Scholarships) 3809

SCHOLARSHIPS & LOANS FOR NURSING EDUCATION 4107

SCHOOL FOR INTERNATIONAL TRAINING (College Semester Abroad and Other Scholarships Related to International Education) 3810

SCHOOL OF ORIENTAL AND AFRICAN STUDIES (Master's Scholarships) 941

SCIENCE ADVANCEMENT PROGRAMS RESEARCH CORPORATION (Research Awards) 1598, 2047, 2127

SCOTTISH RITE CHARITABLE FOUNDATION (Research Grants) 141, 252, 2531, 3199, 3264

SCREAMING POLITICIANS (Scholarship Essay Contest) 3811

SCREEN ACTORS GUILD 4193

SCREEN ACTORS GUILD FOUNDATION (John L. Dales Scholarship Fund) 3812

SCRIPPS HOWARD FOUNDATION (Jack R. Howard Fellowships in International Journalism) 2872

SCRIPPS HOWARD FOUNDATION (Robert P. Scripps Graphic Arts Scholarships) 2873

SCRIPPS HOWARD FOUNDATION (Ted Scripps Scholarships & Lecture) 2874

SEASPACE (Scholarships) 1734

SELECTED FINANCIAL AID REFERENCES FOR STUDENTS WITH DISABILITIES-#107.96 4108

SELECTED FINANCIAL AID RESOURCES FOR INDIVIDUALS FROM CULTURALLY/ETHNICALLY DIVERSE BACKGROUNDS-#104.96 .... 4109, 4110, 4111

SEMINOLE TRIBE OF FLORIDA (Higher Education Awards) 3813

SERB NATIONAL FOUNDATION (Scholarships) 3814

SERTOMA FOUNDATION INTERNATIONAL (Communicative Disorders Scholarships) 2621

SHOSHONE HIGHER EDUCATION PROGRAM (Shoshone Tribal Scholarship) 3815

SIGMA THETA TAU INTERNATIONAL (Research Grants) 2689

SIGMA XI—THE SCIENTIFIC RESEARCH SOCIETY (Research Grants) 1854

SIGRID JUSELIUS FOUNDATION (Medical Research Grants) 2532

SIGURD OLSON ENVIRONMENTAL INSTITUTE—LOONWATCH (Sigurd T. Olson Research Fund) 1674

SIGUROUR NORDAL INSTITUTE (Snorri Sturluson Icelandic Fellowships) 811

SIR ROBERT MENZIES CENTRE FOR AUSTRALIAN STUDIES (Visual Arts Fellowship) 1050, 3816, 3817

SIR ROBERT MENZIES MEMORIAL FOUNDATION LIMITED (Research Scholarship in Allied Health Sciences) 2336, 2622, 2690, 3059, 3200

SKIDMORE, OWINGS & MERRILL FOUNDATION (Interior Architecture Traveling Fellowship Program) 455, 456, 457, 509, 619, 694, 757, 1051

SKY PEOPLE HIGHER EDUCATION (Northern Arapaho Tribal Scholarship) 3818

SMITHSONIAN CENTER FOR MATERIALS RESEARCH AND EDUCATION
(Archeological Conservation Fellowship and Internship) 1791

SMITHSONIAN INSTITUTION (Cooper-Hewitt, National Design Museum-Mark Kaminski Summer Internship) 458, 459, 460, 1052, 1053, 1054,

.... 1055, 1792, 1793

SMITHSONIAN INSTITUTION (Fellowship Program) 942, 1056, 1599, 1675, 1794, 1953, 2981

SMITHSONIAN INSTITUTION (Minority Student Internship Program) 943, 1057, 1600, 1676, 1795, 1954, 2982

SMITHSONIAN INSTITUTION (National Air & Space Museum Guggenheim Fellowship) 407, 408, 1601, 1602, 2048, 2049, 2128,
.... 2129, 2983, 2984

SMITHSONIAN INSTITUTION ENVIRONMENTAL RESEARCH CENTER (Work/Learn Program in Environmental Studies) 1677

SOCIAL SCIENCES AND HUMANITIES RESEARCH COUNCIL OF CANADA (Postdoctoral Fellowships) 812, 813, 2785, 2786

SOCIAL SCIENCE RESEARCH COUNCIL (International Predissertation Fellowship Program) 142, 143, 814, 815, 816, 817, 944, 945, 946,
.... 947, 1218, 1386, 2787, 2788, 2789, 2790, 2791,
.... 2985, 3138, 3139, 3201, 3202, 3265

SOCIETY FOR IMAGING SCIENCE AND TECHNOLOGY (Raymond Davis Scholarship) 695

SOCIETY FOR RANGE MANAGEMENT 4274

SOCIETY FOR TECHNICAL COMMUNICATION (Graduate Scholarships) 1058, 2875, 3316

SOCIETY FOR THE PSYCHOLOGICAL STUDY OF SOCIAL ISSUES (Teaching Materials Development Program) 253, 948, 949, 950, 951, 952, 953, 1387,
.... 2792, 2793, 2794, 2795, 2796, 2797, 2798,
.... 2799, 2800, 2801, 3140, 3141, 3203, 3204,
.... 3205, 3206, 3207, 3208, 3209, 3210, 3211,
.... 3266, 3267, 3268, 3269, 3270, 3271, 3272,
.... 3273, 3274, 3275

SOCIETY FOR THE SCIENTIFIC STUDY OF SEXUALITY (Student Research Grant) 3212

SOCIETY FOR THE TEACHING OF PSYCHOLOGY (Teaching Awards Program) 3213

SOCIETY OF ACTUARIES 4142

SOCIETY OF AMERICAN FLORISTS 4206

SOCIETY OF AMERICAN FORESTERS 4211

SOCIETY OF AMERICAN HISTORIANS (Allan Nevins Prize) 2986

SOCIETY OF ARCHITECTURAL HISTORIANS (Rosann S. Berry Annual Meeting Fellowship;
Keepers Preservation Education Fund Fellowship; Architectural Study Tour Scholarship) 461

SOCIETY OF AUTOMOTIVE ENGINEERS (SAE) 4162

SOCIETY OF AUTOMOTIVE ENGINEERS (SAE Doctoral Scholars Program) 345

SOCIETY OF AUTOMOTIVE ENGINEERS (Yanmar/SAE Scholarship) 346

SOCIETY OF BIOLOGICAL PSYCHIATRY (A.E. Bennett Research Awards) 1955, 2225

SOCIETY OF BIOLOGICAL PSYCHIATRY (DISTA Fellowship Award) 1956, 2226

SOCIETY OF BIOLOGICAL PSYCHIATRY (Ziskind-Somerfield Research Award) 2227

SOCIETY OF EXPLORATION GEOPHYSICISTS (SEG) FOUNDATION (Scholarships) 1603

SOCIETY OF HISPANIC PROFESSIONAL ENGINEERS FOUNDATION (SHPE Scholarships) 347, 1855

SOCIETY OF MANUFACTURING ENGINEERING EDUCATION FOUNDATION (Scholarships& Fellowship) 696

SOCIETY OF MOTION PICTURE AND TELEVISION ENGINEERS 4245

SOCIETY OF NAVAL ARCHITECTS AND MARINE ENGINEERS (SNAME Graduate Scholarships) 462, 758, 4248, 4249

SOCIETY OF PETROLEUM ENGINEERS 4261

SOCIETY OF PROFESSIONAL JOURNALISTS (Mark of Excellence Awards Competition) 2876

SOCIETY OF VERTEBRATE PALEONTOLOGY (Bryan Patterson Award) 1796

SOCIETY OF WOMEN ENGINEERS (B.K. Krenzer Memorial Re-entry Scholarship) 348

SOCIETY OF WOMEN ENGINEERS (Chrysler Corporation Re-entry Scholarship) 349

SOCIETY OF WOMEN ENGINEERS (General Motors Foundation Graduate Scholarship) 350

SOCIETY OF WOMEN ENGINEERS (Microsoft Corporation Graduate Scholarships) 564

SOCIETY OF WOMEN ENGINEERS (Olive Lynn Salembier Scholarship) 351

SOIL & WATER CONSERVATION SOCIETY 4283

SOIL AND WATER CONSERVATION SOCIETY (SWCS Internships) 144, 463, 1482, 1483, 1484, 1604, 1678,
.... 1679, 1680, 2877, 3142

SOLOMON R. GUGGENHEIM MUSEUM (Internship Programs) 1059

SONOMA CHAMBOLLE-MUSIGNY SISTER CITIES, INC. (Henri Cardinaux Memorial Scholarship) 145, 464, 954, 1060, 1219, 1319, 1485, 1957,
.... 2720, 2987

SONOMA STATE UNIVERSITY (Scholarship Program) 3819
SONS OF ITALY FOUNDATION (National Leadership Grants) 3820
SONS OF NORWAY FOUNDATION (King Olav V Norwegian-American Heritage Fund) 955, 956
SONS OF THE REPUBLIC OF TEXAS (Presidio La Bahia Award) 2988
SOROPTIMIST INTERNATIONAL OF GREAT BRITAIN & IRELAND (Golden Jubilee Fellowship) 3821
SOUTH AFRICAN ASSOCIATION OF WOMEN GRADUATES (Bertha Stoneman Award for Botany) 1958, 3822
SOUTH AFRICAN DENTAL ASSOCIATION (Lever Ponds Fellowship; Julius Staz Scholarship) 2337
SOUTH AFRICAN DEPARTMENT OF ARTS, CULTURE, SCIENCE, AND TECHNOLOGY (Scholarships) 3823
SOUTH CAROLINA STUDENT LOAN CORPORATION 3824
SOUTH DAKOTA DIVISION OF VETERANS AFFAIRS (Aid to Veterans) 3825, 3826, 3827
SOUTHERN BAPTIST HISTORICAL LIBRARY AND ARCHIVES (Study Grants) 2989
SPANISH ABROAD 4112
SPANISH EMBASSY (Canada-Spain Exchange Scholarships) 3828
SPECIAL LIBRARIES ASSOCIATION (Affirmative Action Scholarship Program) 1170
SPECIAL LIBRARIES ASSOCIATION (ISI Scholarship Program) 1171
SPECIAL LIBRARIES ASSOCIATION (Plenum Scholarship Program) 1172
SPECIAL LIBRARIES ASSOCIATION (SLA Scholarship Program) 1173
SPENCER FOUNDATION (Dissertation Fellowships for Research Related to Education) 254
ST. ANDREW'S SOCIETY OF THE STATE OF NEW YORK (Scholarships) 3829
ST. DAVID'S SOCIETY (Scholarship) 3830
STANLEY DRAMA AWARD (Playwriting/Musical Awards Competition) 1174
STATE HISTORICAL SOCIETY OF WISCONSIN (Alice E. Smith Fellowship) 2990
STATE LIBRARY OF NEW SOUTH WALES (C. H. Currey Memorial Fellowship) 2991, 2992
STATE OF NEW JERSEY OFFICE OF STUDENT ASSISTANCE (NJClass Loan Program) 3831
STATE RESOURCE SHEETS 4113
STATE STUDENT ASSISTANCE COMMISSION OF INDIANA
(Scholarships for Special Education Teachers & Physical/Occupational Therapists) 255, 2623
STEPHEN ARLEN MEMORIAL FUND (Grant Award) 1320
STEVEN KNEZEVICH TRUST (Grants) 3832
STOCKHOLM UNIVERSITY - INTERNATIONAL GRADUATE PROGRAMME
(Master's Programme in Swedish Social Studies) 146, 1797, 2802, 2803, 2993, 3143, 3276
STROKE ASSOCIATION (Clinical Fellowships) 2533
STROKE ASSOCIATION (Programme Grants) 2534
STROKE ASSOCIATION (Stroke Research Awards) 2535
STROKE ASSOCIATION (Stroke Therapy Research Bursaries) 2536
STUDENT AID FOUNDATION, INC. (Loans) 3833
STUDENT AWARDS AGENCY FOR SCOTLAND (Scottish Studentships for Advanced Postgraduate Study) ... 818, 1061, 1321
STUDENT FINANCIAL AID AND SCHOLARSHIPS AT WYOMING COLLEGES 4114
STUDY ABROAD (Volume 30; 1998-1999) 4115
STUDY IN THE NETHERLANDS: YOUR GATEWAY TO EUROPE 4116
SUNSHINE COAST BURSARY & LOAN SOCIETY (Scholarships & Loans) 3834
SUOMI-SEURA/FINLAND SOCIETY 1220
SUZUKI ASSOCIATION OF THE AMERICAS (Music Teacher Scholarships) 1322
SVENSKA HANDELSBANKEN FOUNDATIONS FOR SOCIAL SCIENCE RESEARCH (Research Grants) 147, 2804
SWEDISH INFORMATION SERVICE (Bicentennial Swedish-American Exchange Fund) 148, 256, 957, 1681, 2878, 3144
SWEDISH INSTITUTE/SVENSKA INSTITUTET (Fellowships for Study/Research in Sweden) 3835
Studying in the UK: Sources of Funding for International Students 4117
TAFT CORPORATE GIVING DIRECTORY (1996 Edition) 4118
TAILHOOK FOUNDATION (Scholarship Fund) 3836
TARAKNATH DAS FOUNDATION 3837
TARGET STORES (Target Teachers Scholarships) 3838

TAU BETA PI ASSOCIATION, INC. (Graduate Fellowships) 352

TEACHERS COLLEGE AT COLUMBIA UNIVERSITY (Joseph Klingenstein Fellows Program & The Summer Institute) 257

TELETOON (Animation Scholarship Award Competition) 1062

TEN STEPS IN WRITING THE RESEARCH PAPER 4119

TENNESSEE ARTS COMMISSION (Individual Artists' Fellowships) 1063, 1175, 1323

TERATOLOGY SOCIETY (Student Travel Grants) 1959

TERESA F. HUGHES TRUST 3839

TEXAS A&M UNIVERSITY (Academic Excellence Awards) 3840

TEXAS A&M UNIVERSITY (Scholarships, Grants, and Loans) 3841

TEXAS HIGHER EDUCATION COORDINATING BOARD (Scholarships, Grants, and Loans) 3842

TEXAS MUSIC INDUSTRY DIRECTORY 4120

THE ALBERTA HERITAGE SCHOLARSHIP FUND 3843

THE ALBERTA HERITAGE SCHOLARSHIP FUND (Alberta Ukrainian Centennial Commemorative Scholarship) 3844, 3845

THE ALICIA PATTERSON FOUNDATION (Fellowships for Journalists, Writers, Editors, and Photographers) 1064, 1176, 2879

THE ALZHEIMER'S ASSOCIATION (Research Grants) 2537

THE AMERICAN CLASSICAL LEAGUE (Ed Phinney Commemorative Scholarship) 258, 958, 1221

THE AMERICAN ASSOCIATION OF ATTORNEY-CERTIFIED PUBLIC ACCOUNTANTS FOUNDATION
(Student Writing Competition) 149, 3060

THE AMERICAN SCHOOLS OF ORIENTAL RESEARCH (George A. Barton Fellowship) 1388

THE ANGLO-DANISH SOCIETY (The Denmark Liberation Scholarships) 3846

THE ANGLO-DANISH SOCIETY (The Hambros Bank Scholarships for U.K. Citizens to Study in Denmark) 3847, 3848

THE ANGLO-ISRAEL ASSOCIATION (Wyndham Deedes Memorial Trust Fund) 3849

THE ARC 4192

THE ARC (Research Grants Program in Mental Retardation) 259, 2538, 3214

THE AUGUSTUS SOCIETY (Scholarships) 3850

THE BRITISH ACADEMY, HUMANITIES RESEARCH BOARD
(Postgraduate Professional Awards, Vocational Courses, and Librarianship and Information Science Program Awards) 1177, 3317

THE BRITISH COUNCIL (Bursaries/Scholarships for Residents of Myanmar (Burma) in English Language Classes) 1222

THE BRITISH COUNCIL (Postgraduate Scholarships to Mexico) 353, 565, 620, 1424, 1856

THE BRITISH COUNCIL (Scholarships for Citizens of Mexico) 354, 1425, 1857, 2805

THE BRITISH COUNCIL (Scholarships for English Language Assistants to Mexico) 3851

THE BRITISH COUNCIL (Scholarships for Residents of Myanmar [Burma]) 3852

THE BRITISH WOMEN PILOT'S ASSOCIATION (The Diana Britten Aerobatic Scholarship) 3853

THE BUFFETT FOUNDATION 3854

THE CARE BOOK (College Aid Resources for Education) 4121

THE CARTER CENTER MENTAL HEALTH PROGRAM (Rosalynn Carter Fellowships for Mental Health Journalism) 2880

THE CENTER FOR CROSS-CULTURAL STUDY (Tuition Awards for Study in Sevill, Spain) 959, 1223

THE CHRISTOPHERS (Video Contest) 1065

THE CONCLAVE (Talent-Based Scholarships) 2881

THE COUNCIL FOR EXCEPTIONAL CHILDREN (Black Caucus Scholarship) 260

THE CULTURAL SOCIETY, INC. 3855

THE CYPRUS CHILDREN'S FUND, INC. (Scholarship Endowment) 3856

THE DAPHNE JACKSON MEMORIAL FELLOWSHIPS TRUST (Fellowships in Science/Engineering) 355, 409, 465, 510, 566, 621, 697, 759, 1426,
.... 1486, 1605, 1682, 1735, 1798, 1858,
.... 1960, 2050, 2130

THE E. PERRY AND GRACE BEATTY MEMORIAL FOUNDATION 3857

THE ELECTRICAL WOMEN'S ROUND TABLE INC. (Julia Kiene & Lyle Mamer Fellowships) 622

THE FOUNDATION DIRECTORY 4122

THE FRANK H. & EVA BUCK FOUNDATION (Frank H. Buck Scholarships) 3858

THE FRENCH INSTITUTE FOR CULTURE AND TECHNOLOGY (The Chateaubriand Doctoral Research Scholarship Program) 960

THE FUND FOR INVESTIGATIVE JOURNALISM, INC. (Grants for Journalists) 2882

THE GRAND RAPIDS FOUNDATION (Alice Bridges Scholarships) 3859

THE GRAND RAPIDS FOUNDATION (Guy D. & Mary Edith Halladay Graduate Scholarship) 3860

THE GUERRILLA GUIDE TO MASTERING STUDENT LOAN DEBT 4123

THE HAN'T FOUNDATION (Quest Award in Micro-Meteorites) 2539

THE HEATH EDUCATION FUND (Scholarships for Ministers, Priests, and Missionaries) 1389, 3277

THE HELLENIC FOUNDATION 3861

THE HORIZONS FOUNDATION (Joseph Towner Fund for Gay and Lesbian Families) 3862

THE INTERNATIONAL SOCIETY FOR OPTICAL ENGINEERING (Scholarships and Grants) 698

THE J. EDGAR HOOVER FOUNDATION 2994, 3061, 3145

THE JERUSALEM FELLOWSHIPS (Internships in Israel for Leaders) 3863

THE JOHN F. KENNEDY CENTER FOR THE PERFORMING ARTS (Awards, Fellowships, and Scholarships) 1178, 1324

THE KOREAN AMERICAN SCHOLARSHIP FOUNDATION (Scholarships) 3864

THE KOSCIUSZKO FOUNDATION (Annual Chopin Piano Competition) 1325

THE KOSCIUSZKO FOUNDATION (Marcella Sembrich Voice Competition) 1326

THE KOSCIUSZKO FOUNDATION (The Metchie J.E. Budka Award) 961

THE KUN SHOULDER REST, INC. (Listing of Music Competitions) 1327

THE LEMMERMANN FOUNDATION (Fondazione Lemmermann Scholarship Awards) 962, 1066, 1179, 1799

THE LEVERHULME TRUST (Leverhulme Study Abroad Studentships) 3865

THE NANSEN FUND, INC. (John Dana Archbold Fellowship) 3866, 3867

THE NATIONAL HEMOPHILIA FOUNDATION (Kevin Child Scholarship) 3868

THE NATIONAL DIRECTORY OF INTERNSHIPS 4124

THE NATIONAL ASSOCIATION OF NEGRO MUSICIANS, INC. (Brantley Choral Arranging Competition) 1328

THE NINETY-NINES, INC. 4291

THE NORWAY-AMERICA ASSOCIATION (The Norwegian Marshall Fund) 356, 819, 1427, 1859

THE NOVARTIS FOUNDATION (Scientific Research Fellowships/Bursaries) 1860, 1961, 2051, 2131

THE NUFFIELD FOUNDATION (Education for Women) 3869

THE PARKERSBURG AREA COMMUNITY FOUNDATION (Scholarships) 3870

THE PAUL & DAISY SOROS FELLOWSHIPS FOR NEW AMERICANS (Graduate Fellowships) 3871

THE RENTOKIL FOUNDATION (Scholarships for U.K. Citizens to Study in Denmark) 3872

THE REUTER FOUNDATION (Fellowships at Oxford for Journalists) 2883

THE REUTER FOUNDATION (Fellowships for Journalists) 2884, 2885

THE REUTER FOUNDATION (Fellowships in Medical Journalism) 2886

THE REUTER FOUNDATION (The Alva Clarke Memorial Fellowship for Journalists From the Caribbean) 2887

THE REUTER FOUNDATION (The Mogadishu Fellowship for Photojournalists) 2888

THE REUTER FOUNDATION (The Peter Sullivan Memorial Fellowships for News Graphics Journalists) 1067, 2889

THE REUTER FOUNDATION (The Willie Vicoy Fellowship for Photojournalists) 2890

THE SINFONIA FOUNDATION (Research Assistance Grant) 1329

THE SWIRE INSTITUTE OF MARINE SCIENCE 1736

THE THAI NATIONAL COMMISSION FOR UNESCO (Sponsored Fellowships Programme) 3873

THE UNIVERSITY OF HULL (70th Anniversary Scholarships) 3874, 3875, 3876, 3877

THE UNIVERSITY OF KANSAS (Self Graduate Fellowship) 3878

THE UNIVERSITY OF NEW MEXICO FOUNDATION (The Kelly Richmond Memorial Fund) 2891

THE UNIVERSITY OF WALES (Graduate/Postgraduate Scholarships in Physics) 2132, 2133

THE WALT DISNEY COMPANY (American Teacher Awards) 261, 1068, 1180, 1224, 1330, 1861, 2134, 2806, 3318

THE WASIE FOUNDATION (Scholarship Program) 3879

THEIR WORLD 4125

THELONIOUS MONK INSTITUTE OF JAZZ (International Jazz Trumpet Competition) 1331, 1332

THOMAS J. WATSON FOUNDATION (The Thomas J. Watson Fellowship Program) 3880

THRASHER RESEARCH FUND (Research Fellowship) 2624

TOKYU FOUNDATION FOR INBOUND STUDENTS (Scholarships for Inbound Students) 3881

TOWSON STATE UNIVERSITY (Scholarship & Award Programs) 3882

TRANSPORTATION ASSOCIATION OF CANADA (TAC Scholarships) 150

TRANSPORTATION CLUBS INTERNATIONAL (Ginger & Fred Deines Canada Scholarships) 151, 152

TRENT UNIVERSITY (Graduate Teaching/Research Assistantships) 567, 963, 1390, 1683, 1800, 1962, 2052, 2135

TRI-STATE GENERATION AND TRANSMISSION ASSOCIATION (Scholarships) 3883

TROPICAL AGRICULTURAL RESEARCH AND HIGHER EDUCATION CENTER - CATIE
(Education for Development and Conservation Program) 1428, 1487

TULANE UNIVERSITY (Scholarships & Fellowships) 3884

TUSKEGEE UNIVERSITY (Graduate Research Fellowships and Assistantships) 262, 357, 1684, 1963, 2053, 2721

TY COBB EDUCATIONAL FOUNDATION (Graduate Scholarship Program) 2228, 2338

U.S. ARMY MILITARY HISTORY INSTITUTE (Advanced Research Grant Program) 2995

U.S. DEPARTMENT OF DEFENSE
(G!SIP-General Laboratory Scientific Interchange Program: NRC-NRL Post-Doctoral Program) 410, 568, 623, 699, 1606, 1685,
.... 1737, 1964, 2054, 2339

U.S. DEPARTMENT OF STATE (Internships) 3885

U.S. DEPARTMENT OF TRANSPORTATION (Dwight D. Eisenhower Transportation Fellowships) 153, 358, 466, 511, 624, 700, 760, 3215, 3278

U.S. DEPT OF INTERIOR; BUREAU OF INDIAN AFFAIRS (Higher Education Grant Programs) 3886, 3887

U.S. DEPT. OF EDUCATION (Fulbright-Hays Doctoral Dissertation Research Abroad Fellowships) 964, 1225

U.S. DEPT. OF EDUCATION (Fulbright-Hays Faculty Research Abroad Grants) 965, 1226

U.S. DEPT. OF EDUCATION, INTERNATIONAL EDUCATION AND GRADUATE PROGRAM SERVICE
(Foreign Language and Area Studies (FLAS) Fellowships Program) 966, 1227

U.S. DEPT. OF HEALTH & HUMAN SERVICES (Indian Health Service Health Professions Scholarship Program) 154, 569, 2229, 2340, 2540, 2625,
.... 2691, 2722, 3279

U.S. ENVIRONMENTAL PROTECTION AGENCY—
NATIONAL NETWORK FOR ENVIRONMENTAL MANAGEMENT STUDIES (Fellowships) 570, 701, 1607, 1686, 2892, 3062

U.S. PHARMACOPEIA (USP Fellowship Program) 2541

UAA-102 COLLEGIATE AVIATION GUIDE 4126

UAA-116 COLLEGIATE AVIATION SCHOLARSHIP LISTING 4127

UNA ELLIS-FERMOR MEMORIAL RESEARCH FUND (Funds for Publication) 967, 1181

UNCF/MERCK SCIENCE INITIATIVE (Graduate Science Research Dissertation Fellowships) 1862, 1965, 2055, 2136, 2542

UNCF/MERCK SCIENCE INITIATIVE (Postdoctoral Science Research Fellowships) 1863, 1966, 2056, 2543

UNICO NATIONAL, INC. (Various Scholarships) 3888

UNIFORMED SERVICES UNIVERSITY OF THE HEALTH SCIENCES (Fellowships) 2230, 2341, 2544, 2626, 2692

UNITARIAN UNIVERSALIST ASSOCIATION (Graduate Theological Scholarships) 1391

UNITARIAN UNIVERSALIST ASSN. (Otto M. Stanfield Legal Scholarship) 3063

UNITED AGRIBUSINESS LEAGUE (UAL Scholarship Program) 1488

UNITED DAUGHTERS OF THE CONFEDERACY (Scholarships) 3889

UNITED FOOD & COMMERCIAL WORKERS UNION—UFCW LOCAL 555 (L. Walter Derry Scholarship Fund) 3890

UNITED METHODIST CHURCH (Scholarship and Loan Program) 3891

UNITED METHODIST COMMUNICATIONS (Stoody-West Fellowship for Graduate Study in Journalism) 2893

UNITED NEGRO COLLEGE FUND (Scholarships) 3892

UNITED STUDENT AID FUNDS INC. (Guaranteed Student Loan Program; Plus Loans) 3893

UNIVERSITY COLLEGE LONDON (International Scholarships) 3894

UNIVERSITY COLLEGE LONDON (Ramsay Memorial Fellowships Trust) 2057

UNIVERSITY FILM & VIDEO ASSOCIATION (Carole Fielding Student Grants) 1069, 1182, 1333

UNIVERSITY OF ALBERTA (Alberta Research Council Karl A. Clark Memorial Scholarship) 359, 2058

UNIVERSITY OF ALBERTA (Grant Notley Memorial Postdoctoral Fellowship) 968

UNIVERSITY OF ALBERTA (Izaak Walton Killam Memorial Postdoctoral Fellowship) 3895, 3896

UNIVERSITY OF ALBERTA (Ph.D Scholarship) 3897, 3898

UNIVERSITY OF BIRMINGHAM (A.E. Hills Postgraduate Scholarship) 3899

UNIVERSITY OF BIRMINGHAM (International Scholarships) 3900

UNIVERSITY OF CALIFORNIA-DAVIS (Brad Webb Scholarship Fund) 1967

UNIVERSITY OF CALGARY (Environmental Design Scholarships; Graduate Research Scholarships) 467

UNIVERSITY OF CALGARY (Izaak Walton Killam Memorial Scholarships) 3901
UNIVERSITY OF CALGARY (Province of Alberta Graduate Scholarships and Fellowships) 3902
UNIVERSITY OF CALIFORNIA SYSTEM 4177
UNIVERSITY OF CAMBRIDGE (Hughes Hall Studentship) 3903
UNIVERSITY OF CAMBRIDGE (ICL Research Studentship in Automatic Computing) 571
UNIVERSITY OF CAMBRIDGE (Newnham College Research Fellowships) 3904
UNIVERSITY OF CAMBRIDGE (Peterhouse Research Studentship) 3905
UNIVERSITY OF CAMBRIDGE - SIDNEY SUSSEX COLLEGE (Evan Lewis-Thomas Law Studentships) 3064, 3906
UNIVERSITY OF CAMBRIDGE—WOLFSON COLLEGE (Bursaries) 3907, 3908, 3909
UNIVERSITY OF CAMBRIDGE DEPT. OF SOCIAL ANTHROPOLOGY (Evans Fellowship) 1801
UNIVERSITY OF DELAWARE HAGLEY PROGRAM (Graduate Fellowship) 2996
UNIVERSITY OF EDINBURGH (Faculty of Medicine Bursaries & Scholarships) 2231, 2342, 2545, 2627
UNIVERSITY OF EXETER (Postgraduate Scholarships) 3910
UNIVERSITY OF GLASGOW (Post-graduate Awards in Law & Financial Studies) 155, 3065
UNIVERSITY OF GLASGOW (Post-graduate Scholarships) 3911
UNIVERSITY OF GLASGOW (Scholarships in Naval Architecture and Ocean Engineering) 468, 1738
UNIVERSITY OF GLASGOW (Thouron Award-Fellowship) 3912
UNIVERSITY OF HULL (Bursaries for Overseas Postgraduates) 3913
UNIVERSITY OF ILLINOIS COLLEGE OF FINE & APPLIED ARTS (Kate Neal Kinley Fellowship) 469, 1070, 1334
UNIVERSITY OF IOWA FOUNDATION (David Braverman Scholarship) 3914
UNIVERSITY OF LEEDS (Scholarships for International Students) 3915
UNIVERSITY OF LEEDS (Tetley and Lipton Scholarships for Overseas Students) 3916
UNIVERSITY OF LONDON-WARBURG INSTITUTE (Albin Salton Fellowship) 2997, 2998, 2999, 3000, 3001
UNIVERSITY OF LONDON INSTITUTE OF CLASSICAL STUDIES (Michael Ventris Memorial Award) 3002
UNIVERSITY OF MANCHESTER (Awards for Research) 156, 180, 263, 360, 1071, 1864, 2807, 3066
UNIVERSITY OF MANITOBA (Graduate Fellowship) 3917
UNIVERSITY OF MANITOBA (J.W. Dafoe Graduate Fellowship) 157, 3003, 3146
UNIVERSITY OF MANCHESTER INSTITUTE OF SCIENCE & TECHNOLOGY (Mohn Research Fellowship) 702, 761
UNIVERSITY OF MARYLAND INSTITUTE FOR ADVANCED COMPUTER STUDIES (Graduate Fellowships) 158, 572, 625, 1183, 1392, 1608
UNIVERSITY OF MELBOURNE (Postgraduate Scholarships) 3918
UNIVERSITY OF MISSOURI ROLLA (The Distinguished Scholars Program for Non-Missouri Residents) 3919
UNIVERSITY OF NEWCASTLE (Postgraduate Research Scholarships) 3920
UNIVERSITY OF NEWCASTLE (Research Higher Degrees Scholarships) 3921
UNIVERSITY OF NEW BRUNSWICK (Financial Aid for Graduate Students—Fellowships, Assistantships, and Scholarships) 3922
UNIVERSITY OF NEWCASTLE/CATHEDRAL CHURCH OF ST. NICHOLAS (Organ and Choral Scholarships) 3923
UNIVERSITY OF NEW ENGLAND RESEARCH SCHOLARSHIPS 3924
UNIVERSITY OF NEWCASTLE—DEPT. OF MUSIC (Runciman Arts Studentship) 1072, 1184, 1335
UNIVERSITY OF NORTH TEXAS (Merchandising and Hospitality Scholarships) 159, 264, 1336
UNIVERSITY OF OXFORD (Graduate Unilever Scholarship) 361, 2059
UNIVERSITY OF OXFORD (Hall-Houghton Studentship) 1393
UNIVERSITY OF OXFORD (Paula Soans O'Brian Scholarship) 3925
UNIVERSITY OF OXFORD (Squire and Marriott Bursaries) 1394
UNIVERSITY OF OXFORD-ST. CATHERINE'S COLLEGE (Overseas Graduate Scholarships) 3926
UNIVERSITY OF OXFORD-WOLFSON COLLEGE (Graduate Awards) 3927, 3928, 3929
UNIVERSITY OF OXFORD—ST. CROSS COLLEGE (Major College Scholarships) 3930
UNIVERSITY OF OXFORD—ST. HILDA'S COLLEGE (Graduate Scholarships) 3931, 3932
UNIVERSITY OF PORTSMOUTH (Partnership Programme-Learning at Work) 3933
UNIVERSITY OF QUEENSLAND (Post-graduate Research Scholarship) 3934
UNIVERSITY OF ROCHESTER (Mildred R. Burton Summer Study Grants/Scholarships for Summer Language Study) 1228
UNIVERSITY OF SOUTHAMPTON (University Research Studentships) 3935
UNIVERSITY OF SOUTHERN CALIFORNIA (Mellon Postdoctoral Fellowship) 820

UNIVERSITY OF SOUTH DAKOTA (Criminal Justice Dept. Scholarships) 3067, 3147

UNIVERSITY OF SYDNEY (Postgraduate Research Scholarships and International Postgraduate Awards) 3936

UNIVERSITY OF TASMANIA (Tasmania Research Scholarship) 3937

UNIVERSITY OF TENNESSEE (Hilton A. Smith Graduate Fellowship) 3938

UNIVERSITY OF TENNESSEE KNOXVILLE 3939

UNIVERSITY OF TORONTO (Graduate Fellowships) 3940

UNIVERSITY OF UTAH COLLEGE OF PHARMACY (Pharmacy Scholarships) 2343

UNIVERSITY OF VIRGINIA (Albert Gallatin Fellowship in International Affairs) 160, 969, 3004, 3068, 3148

UNIVERSITY OF VIRGINIA (Hoyns Fellowship) 1185

UNIVERSITY OF WAIKATO (Hilary Jolly Memorial Scholarship) 1609

UNIVERSITY OF WAIKATO, NEW ZEALAND (Rewi Alley Scholarship in Modern Chinese Studies) 970, 3941, 3942

UNIVERSITY OF WESTERN AUSTRALIA (Gledden Post-graduate Studentship) 1865, 3943

UNIVERSITY OF WINDSOR (Graduate Studies & Research Scholarships) 3944

UNIVERSITY OF WYOMING (Superior Students in Education Scholarship) 265

US AIR FORCE OPPORTUNITY CENTER (Armed Forces Health Professions Scholarships) 2232, 2344, 3216

US ARMS CONTROL AND DISARMAMENT AGENCY (William C. Foster Visiting Scholars Program) 362, 1429, 1866, 2808, 3069, 3149, 3150

US COAST GUARD ACADEMY 4286

US COAST GUARD MUTUAL ASSISTANCE (Adm. Roland Student Loan Program) 3945

US DEPARTMENT OF DEFENSE (National Defense Science & Engineering Graduate Fellowship Programs) 363, 1610, 1739, 1867, 1968, 2060, 2137, 3946

US DEPT OF AGRICULTURE; FOOD AND NUTRITION SERVICE 4207

US DEPT OF EDUCATION (Patricia Roberts Harris Fellowship Program) 3947

US DEPT OF LABOR; BUREAU OF APPRENTICESHIP AND TRAINING 4156

US DEPT OF VETERANS AFFAIRS (Vocational Rehabilitation) 3948

US DEPT. OF AGRICULTURE 4210

US EDUCATIONAL FOUNDATION IN INDIA (AT&T Leadership Award) 3949

US ENVIRONMENTAL PROTECTION AGENCY 4199

USAF READY RESERVE STIPEND PROGRAM 2233, 2693

USAF RESERVE PERSONNEL CENTER (Armed Forces Health Professionas Scholarships) 2234, 2694

USAF RESERVE BONUS PROGRAM 2235, 2695

UTA ALUMNI ASSOCIATION (African-American Endowed Scholarship) 3950

UTA ALUMNI ASSOCIATION (Frankie S. Hansell Endowed Scholarship) 3951

UTA ALUMNI ASSOCIATION (Hispanic Scholarship) 3952

UTA ALUMNI ASSOCIATION (Lloyd Clark Scholarship Journalism) 2894

UTA ALUMNI ASSOCIATION (Sue & Art Mosby Scholarship Endowment in Music) 1337

UTAH STATE BOARD OF REGENTS (State Student Incentive Grants) 3953

VACATION STUDY ABROAD 4128

VANDERBILT UNIVERSITY (A. J. Dyer Observatory Research Assistantship) 1611

VENTURE CLUBS OF THE AMERICAS (Student Aid Awards) 3954

VERMONT STUDENT ASSISTANCE CORPORATION (Non-Degree Grant) 3955

VERTICAL FLIGHT FOUNDATION (Scholarships) 411

VINCENT L. HAWKINSON FOUNDATION FOR PEACE AND JUSTICE (Scholarship Award) 3956

VIRGIN ISLANDS BOARD OF EDUCATION (Nursing & Other Health Scholarships) 2236, 2696

VIRGINIA STATE COUNCIL OF HIGHER EDUCATION (Tuition Assistance Grant Program) 3957

VON KARMAN INSTITUTE FOR FLUID DYNAMICS (Diploma Course Scholarship) 412

W. EUGENE SMITH MEMORIAL FUND, INC. (Grants) 2895

W. ROSS MACDONALD SCHOOL (Rixon Rafter Scholarships) 3958

W.E. UPJOHN INSTITUTE FOR EMPLOYMENT RESEARCH (Dissertation Award) 161, 162

WAMSO (Young Artist Competition) 1338

WARNBOROUGH UNIVERSITY (Scholarships) 3959

WASHINGTON HIGHER EDUCATION COORDINATING BOARD (American Indian Endowed Scholarship) 3960, 3961

WASHINGTON STATE HIGHER EDUCATION COORDINATING BOARD

(Health Professional Loan Repayment & Scholarship Program) 2237, 2238, 2345, 2346, 2546,
.... 2628, 2697, 3962, 3963
WASHINGTON TRUST BANK (Herman Oscar Schumacher College Fund Trust) 3964
WASHINGTON UNIVERSITY IN ST. LOUIS
(James Harrison Steedman Memorial Traveling Fellowship in Architecture—Design Competition) 470, 3965
WATER ENVIRONMENT FEDERATION 4289
WATER ENVIRONMENT FEDERATION (Robert A. Canham Scholarship) 703, 1612, 1687, 1740
WATER ENVIRONMENT FEDERATION (Student Paper Competition) 704, 1613, 1688, 1741
WATER RESOURCES RESEARCH CENTRE - VITUKI (Hydrological Methods of Environmental Management Scholarship) 1689
WAVERLY COMMUNITY HOUSE INC. (F. Lammot Belin Arts Scholarships) 471, 1073, 1186, 1339
WEATHERHEAD CENTER FOR INTERNATIONAL AFFAIRS
(Harvard Academy for International and Area Studies: Pre- and Postdoctoral Fellowships) 2809
WELLCOME TRUST (Post-doctoral Research Travel Grants to United States) 2547
WELLESLEY COLLEGE (Fellowships for Wellesley Graduates & Graduating Seniors) 3966
WELLESLEY COLLEGE (Mary McEwen Schimke Scholarship) 971, 1187, 3005
WENNER-GREN FOUNDATION FOR ANTHROPOLOGICAL RESEARCH (Developing Countries Training Fellowships) 1802, 1803, 1804, 1805, 1806
WEST VIRGINIA UNIVERSITY (Arlen G. and Louise Stone Swiger Doctoral Fellowships) 3967
WEST VIRGINIA UNIVERSITY (W.E.B. DuBois Fellowship) 3968
WESTERN SOCIETY OF CRIMINOLOGY (Student Paper Competition) 3070
WESTERN SUNBATHING ASSOCIATION (Scholarships) 3969
WHAT COLOR IS YOUR PARACHUTE? 4129
WHEATLAND COMMUNITY SCHOLASTIC FUND, INC. (Scholarships) 3970
WHIRLY-GIRLS INC. (International Women Helicopter Pilots Scholarships) 3319
WHITEHALL FOUNDATION, INC. (Research Grants & Grants-in-Aid) 2548
WILLIAM ANDREWS CLARK MEMORIAL LIBRARY (Postdoctoral Fellowships) 972, 1188, 3006
WILLIAM B. RICE AID FUND INC. (Scholarship & Loan Program) 3971
WILLIAM F. COOPER SCHOLARSHIP 3972
WILLIAM HONYMAN GILLESPIE TRUST (Scholarships) 1395
WILLIAM T. GRANT FOUNDATION (Faculty Scholars Program—Research on Children, Adolescents, & Youth) 2810, 3217, 3280
WILSON ORNITHOLOGICAL SOCIETY (Fuertes, Nice, & Stewart Grants) 1969
WINNING SCHOLARSHIPS FOR COLLEGE—AN INSIDER'S GUIDE 4130
WINSTON CHURCHILL FOUNDATION (Scholarships) 364, 1868, 2138
WINSTON CHURCHILL MEMORIAL TRUST (Churchill Fellowships) 3973
WISCONSIN DEPARTMENT OF VETERANS AFFAIRS (Deceased Veterans' Survivors Economic Assistance Loan/Education Grants) 3974, 3975
WISCONSIN HIGHER EDUCATION AIDS BOARD (Student Financial Aid Program) 3976
WOLCOTT FOUNDATION (Fellowships) 163, 3151
WOLFSONIAN-FLORIDA INTERNATIONAL UNIVERSITY (Fellowship Program) 472, 1074
WOMAN'S SEAMEN'S FRIEND SOCIETY OF CONNECTICUT, INC. (Scholarships) 1742
WOMEN GROCERS OF AMERICA (Mary Macey Scholarships) 15
WOMEN IN ANIMATION (WIA) 4153
WOMEN IN DEFENSE (HORIZONS Scholarship Foundation) 16, 164, 365, 573, 2139, 3071, 3152
WOMEN OF THE EVANGELICAL LUTHERAN CHURCH IN AMERICA (The Belmer-Flora Prince Scholarships) 1396, 2239, 2347, 2549, 2629, 2698, 3977, 3978
WOMEN ON BOOKS (Scholarships for African-American Women) 1189, 2896
WOMEN'S AUXILIARY TO THE AMERICAN INSTITUTE OF MINING METALLURGICAL & PETROLEUM ENGINEERS (WAAIME Scholarship Loan Fund) 705, 762, 1614
WOMEN'S RESEARCH AND EDUCATION INSTITUTE (Congressional Fellowships for Women and Public Policy) 3979
WOMEN'S SPORTS FOUNDATION (AQHA Female Equestrian Award) 3980
WOMEN'S SPORTS FOUNDATION (Dorothy Harris Endowed Scholarship) 165, 266, 2348, 2630, 3218, 3281
WOMEN'S SPORTS FOUNDATION (Evian Rehydration, WSF Girls/Women In Sports, & Lilo Leeds Women's Sports/Fitness Participation Endowment Research Grants) 2550
WOMEN'S SPORTS FOUNDATION (Jackie Joyner-Kersee & Zina Garrison Minority Internships) 166, 267, 2631, 2897, 3219, 3282
WOMEN'S SPORTS FOUNDATION (Ocean Spray Travel & Training Grants) 3981

WOODROW WILSON INTERNATIONAL CENTER FOR SCHOLARS (Fellowships in the Humanities and Social Sciences) 821, 2811

WOODROW WILSON NATIONAL FELLOWSHIP FOUNDATION/U.S. DEPARTMENTS OF COMMERCE AND AGRICULTURE (Fellowships) ... 17, 181, 268, 269, 270, 366, 822, 823, 824, 973, 974, 1397, 1489, 1615, 1807, 1869, 2140, 2349, 2551, 2699, 2812, 3007, 3220, 3283

WOODS HOLE OCEANOGRAPHIC INSTITUTION (Fellowships for Summer Study in Geophysical Fluid Dynamics) 1616

WOODS HOLE OCEANOGRAPHIC INSTITUTION (Postdoctoral Awards in Ocean Science and Engineering) 367, 1617, 1743, 1970, 2061, 2141

WOODS HOLE OCEANOGRAPHIC INSTITUTION (Research Fellowships in Marine Policy and Ocean Management) .. 167, 1430, 1618, 1744, 2142, 2813, 3072, 3153

WORLD BANK (Graduate Scholarship Program) 168, 2814, 3008, 3073, 3154

WORLD BANK VOLUNTEER SERVICES (Margaret McNamara Memorial Fund) 3982

WORLD DIRECTORY OF MEDICAL SCHOOLS 4131

WORLD DIRECTORY OF SCHOOLS OF PUBLIC HEALTH 4132

WORLD FEDERATION OF INTERNATIONAL MUSIC COMPETITIONS BOOKLET 4133

WORLD LEISURE AND RECREATION ASSOCIATION (Scholarships) 169, 271

WORLD OF KNOWLEDGE (Today & Tomorrow Scholarship Program for International Graduate Students) 3983

WRITE YOUR WAY TO A HIGHER GPA 4134

WRITING CONTESTS FOR LAW STUDENTS 4135

WYOMING DEPARTMENT OF CORRECTIONS (Wayne Martinez Memorial Scholarships) 3984

WYOMING DEPARTMENT OF VETERANS AFFAIRS (War Orphans Scholarships) 3985

WYOMING FARM BUREAU FEDERATION (Dodge Merit Award) 3986

WYOMING FEDERATION OF WOMEN'S CLUBS (Mary N. Brooks Education Fund-Daughters & Granddaughters) 3987

WYOMING PEACE OFFICERS ASSOCIATION (WPOA Scholarships) 3074

WYOMING REPUBLICAN FOUNDATION (Scholarships) 3988

WYOMING TRUCKING ASSOCIATION (Scholarships) 170, 706, 1690, 3320

Where There's a Will There's an "A" to Get Better Grades in College (or High School) 4136

XEROX TECHNICAL MINORITY SCHOLARSHIP (School-Year Tuition) 368, 369, 473, 474, 512, 513, 574, 575, 626, 627, 707, 708, 763, 764

Y'S MEN INTERNATIONAL - US AREA (Alexander Scholarship Loan Fund) 171, 272

YALE CENTER FOR BRITISH ART (Fellowships) 975, 1075, 1190, 3009

YOUR CAREER IN THE COMICS 4137

ZETA PHI BETA SORORITY EDUCATIONAL FOUNDATION (Isabel M. Herson Scholarship in Education) 273, 2240, 2350, 2552, 2632, 2700, 3221, 3284, 3989, 3990, 3991, 3992

ZONTA INTERNATIONAL FOUNDATION (Amelia Earhart Fellowship Awards) 413